THE COMPLETE SHORT STORIES OF

GUY DE MAUPASSANT

THE COMPLETE
SHORT STORIES
OF GUY DE
MAUPASSANT

INTRODUCTION BY

PROFESSOR ARTINE ARTINIAN

HANOVER HOUSE

GARDEN CITY, NEW YORK

Library of Congress Catalog Card Number 55-9990

CONTENTS

Introduction ix

Ball of Fat 1

The Secret 25

The Shepherd's Leap 28

Mouche—

    A Boating Man's Reminiscence 31

On a Spring Evening 37

The Legacy 40

Madame Tellier's Establishment 43

A Crisis 58

An Idyl 62

The Prisoners 65

Châli 72

The Story of a Farm Girl 78

At the Spa—Diary of

    the Marquis de Roseveyre 89

Madame Hermet 95

For Sale 100

Yvette 104

The Piece of String 148

The Funeral Pile 153

An Old Man 156

A Surprise 159

In the Moonlight 162

Love—Three Pages

    from a Sportsman's Book 165

On the River 169

The Necklace 172

Father Judas 178

The Inn 180

A Humble Drama 188

A Vagabond 191

A Little Walk 198

The Sisters Rondoli 202

The Dancers 219

Checkmate 222

The Accursed Bread 227

Mademoiselle Fifi 230

A Sale 237

An Affair of State 241

The Mask 247

A Cock Crowed 252

The Drowned Man 255

Mad? 260

The Revenge 263

The Father 269

A Normandy Joke 274

Monsieur Parent 277

Fear 299

The Hole—Cuts and

    Wounds Which Caused Death 304

Caresses 308

Bellflower 310

Simon's Papa 313

That Pig of a Morin 319

The Christening 325

Miss Harriet 328

Misti—Recollections of a Bachelor 341

In the Wood 344

Our Friends the English 347

A Family 352

Roger's Method 355

v

The Marquis de Fumerol 357

The Castaway 362

Saved 367

The Confession 371

The Devil 374

The Mother of Monsters 378

The Rabbit 382

The Keeper 387

The Madwoman 392

A Bad Error 394

Coco 397

Epiphany 400

Happiness 407

The Unknown 411

The Double Pins 415

The Signal 418

Graveyard Sirens 422

A Madman 426

Growing Old 431

M. Belhomme's Beast 434

A French Enoch Arden 439

The Little One 443

Julie Romain 447

A Memory 452

Confessing 456

Rosalie Prudent 459

A Parricide 462

The Olive Orchard 466

Hippolyte's Claim 482

Guillemot Rock 485

Benoist 487

A True Story 491

Fecundity 494

Alexander 500

A Way to Wealth 503

The Putter-to-Sleep 507

Am I Insane? 513

A Wife's Confession 515

A Divorce Case 518

Madame Parisse 522

Douchox 526

The Mother Superior's
   Twenty-five Francs 530

Forbidden Fruit 534

The Peddler 538

Old Objects 542

The Old Man 544

The Coconut-drink Vendor 549

The Charm Dispelled 551

Making a Convert 554

The Cake 558

A Dead Woman's Secret 561

Love's Awakening 564

Dreams 567

Bed No. 29 570

Marroca 577

Old Milon 582

A Philosopher 586

A Mistake 590

Florentine 593

The Orphan 597

Consideration 601

Woman's Wiles 604

A Cry of Alarm 608

Moonlight 612

Doubtful Happiness 615

In a Railway Carriage 618

Humiliation 623

The Wedding Night 626

The Noncommissioned Officer 631

In the Courtroom 635

A Peculiar Case 637

A Practical Joke 641

The Wreck 644

A Strange Fancy 651

After Death 655

On Cats 659

Old Amable 662

One Phase of Love 675

Good Reasons 680

A Fair Exchange 682

A Traveler's Notes 687

The Tobacco Shop 690

A Poor Girl 695

The Substitute 699

The Hermit 701

A Passion 706

The Orderly 711

Feminine Men 713

Joseph 716

Regret 720

The Deaf-mute 724

At the Church Door 729

Magnetism 732

The False Gems 735

The Colonel's Ideas 739

Was it a Dream? 742

Mademoiselle Pearl 745

Two Little Soldiers 755

The Will 759

A Country Excursion 762

Bertha 768

Walter Schnaffs' Adventure 774

The Log 779

Bric-a-brac 782

The Tomb 785

The Artist's Wife 787

In the Spring 791

Night: a Nightmare 795

The Rendezvous 798

An Artifice 802

Solitude 805

A Norman 808

The Specter 812

The Relic 816

In the Country 819

The Bed 822

The Awakening 825

Words of Love 828

The Legend of
    Mont-Saint-Michel 830

Christmas Eve 833

Madame Baptiste 835

Revenge 839

Queen Hortense 843

Complication 848

Forgiveness 851

The White Wolf 855

The Father 858

Toine 861

An Enthusiast 866

The Traveler's Story 876

A Jolly Fellow 880

Room No. 11 885

A Lively Friend 889

The Patron 893

The Impolite Sex 896

The Blind Man 900

The Corsican Bandit 902

The Duel 905

Mother Savage 910

The Love of Long Ago 915

The Farmer's Wife 917

Beside a Dead Man 922

The Lock 925

A Queer Night in Paris 928

A Duel 934

The Kiss 938

Old Mongilet 940

The Umbrella 944

Denis 949

The Donkey 953

The Question of Latin 958

Mother and Son!!! 964

He? 968

Monsieur Jocaste 972

The Avenger 975

The Conservatory 979

My Wife 982

Letter Found on a Corpse 986

The Little Cask 990

Rust 994

Poor Andrew 998

A Fishing Excursion 1001

After 1004

An Adventure in Paris 1008

The Spasm 1012

A Meeting 1016

A New Year's Gift 1021

A Family Affair 1025

My Uncle Sosthenes 1042

All Over 1047

My Landlady 1051

Paul's Mistress 1054

The Horrible 1066

The First Snowfall 1070

The Legacy 1075

The Wooden Shoes 1117

Boitelle 1121

Selfishness 1126

Of Doctor Heraclius Gloss 1129

The Watchdog 1157

Christening 1160

A Costly Outing 1162

A King's Son 1165

Waiter, a Bock! 1170

Mohammed Fripouli 1174

"Bell" 1179

Hautot and His Son 1182

The Victim 1190

The Englishman 1194

One Evening 1197

Sentiment 1207

Traveling 1210

Francis 1213

The Assassin 1216

Our Letters 1219

The Cripple 1222

Semillante 1226

In Port 1229

Suicides 1235

A Portrait 1238

A Miracle 1240

My Twenty-five Days 1244

Allouma 1249

A Lucky Burglar 1263

An Odd Feast 1265

Who Knows? 1268

A Traveler's Tale 1276

Little Louise Roque 1280

The Orient 1302

How He Got the
   Legion of Honor 1304

My Uncle Jules 1308

The Horla 1313

Useless Beauty 1328

INTRODUCTION

Guy de Maupassant was born on the 5th of August, 1850. Whether it was at the stately Château de Miromesnil, as it is probable, or at Fécamp, as it is possible, or at Sotteville, as the death certificate erroneously declares, or even at Yvetot, as one biographer claims, is of little consequence. We need only remember that he was born in Normandy and that he spent his entire youth there. Does he indeed ever permit us to forget that fact?

The elder son of Laure and Gustave de Maupassant, he was neither the nephew nor the godson of Gustave Flaubert; his mother and maternal uncle were intimate friends of the author of *Madame Bovary*, and that factor was to be of utmost importance in his early literary development. Until the age of thirteen he studied under the direction of his mother, who was a highly lettered person and who transmitted to him, among other things, a strong enthusiasm for Shakespeare. There followed a brief period of study at the seminary of Yvetot, culminating in his expulsion as an insubordinate pupil. He was subsequently sent to the *lycée* at Rouen, where he had as teacher Louis Bouilhet, who, with Flaubert, was to give direction to an increasing interest in literary expression.

The Prussian invasion of 1870 gave him an opportunity to serve his country and to add to his experience a vast field of observation which he frequently utilized later. Soon after the war he settled in Paris as a clerk in the Ministry of Marine to do routine work, which he detested and which he also depicted in his stories. This was likewise the happy period of intensive boat excursions on the Seine with carefree companions, a period of physical excesses; but above all it may be characterized as a period of severe apprenticeship under Flaubert, an apprenticeship perhaps unparalleled in the history of literature. A transfer to the more congenial atmosphere of the Ministry of Education was finally effected, and a little later, in 1880, abandoning the pseudonyms under which he had contributed a few poems, tales, and studies to various periodicals, he suddenly burst into full glory with the publication of *Boule de Suif* ("Ball of Fat").

That story first appeared in a collective volume, *Les Soirées de Médan*, which brought together five obscure writers with the most controversial name in French letters of the day, Emile Zola. The five were young and impatient for recognition on the literary scene, determined even to obtain it at any price. What brought them together was as much, if not more, the desire for notoriety as a certain admiration for the established author, the creator of *Nana*. As for Zola, rarely unwilling to lend his name to a cause, it was an opportunity to do something for these boisterous young men who called themselves his disciples. His "Attaque du Moulin" was naturally given first place in the volume. The other contributors drew lots for the order of their tales, Maupassant coming first, followed by Huysmans, Céard, Hennique, Alexis; and though luck alone had determined the position accorded "Ball of Fat," there was not the slightest doubt in anyone's mind as to where it rightfully belonged.

The columns of the most popular newspapers were immediately opened to

Maupassant, and practically overnight he became, with Zola, the highest-paid writer of the day. Ten years of poverty had come to an end. With royalties from his first volume of short stories, *La Maison Tellier* (Madame Tellier's Establishment), he could build a villa in his home town of Etretat on the Normandy coast. Part of the proceeds from his novel *Bel-Ami* were spent for a yacht which was to take him on frequent explorations of the Mediterranean coast. Each best-seller marked a move in living quarters culminating in the fashionable Avenue Victor Hugo. It also permitted him to contribute substantially to the support of his mother and younger brother particularly, as well as to come to the aid of indigent writers such as Villiers de l'Isle-Adam. But most gratifying for the once impecunious Guy was that every success helped to assure what he prized above all else—independence, material as well as literary. That was unquestionably his chief trait of character, perhaps largely instilled by his master Flaubert, whose death a few weeks after the appearance of "Ball of Fat" released Maupassant from any vestiges even of artistic tutelage.

Immediately after the appearance of "Ball of Fat," he devoted himself exclusively to literary activities of herculean proportions. The frequent excursions, for rest or escape from the society whose encroachments he resented, did not interrupt the steady flow of volumes which he seemed to produce with the ease and regularity of a Norman apple tree shedding its fruit. Within a decade he had produced the incredible total of nearly three hundred short stories, a half-dozen novels, and several other volumes, not to mention over two hundred miscellaneous articles, most of which have not yet appeared in book form.

This incessant labor aggravated the malady from which he had suffered even as a government employee, when he had contracted syphilis. His eyes hurt intensely, obliging him to reduce both reading and writing. Splitting migraines sent him in search of relief to every specialist in France, made him a victim of every remotely possible remedy, gradually transformed the robust Norman into a shadow of his former self, and intensified the acute pessimism which he shared with Flaubert. The crushing blow came in 1889, however, when his thirty-four-year-old brother Hervé had to be interned in an insane asylum. Maupassant could now see his own end unmistakably indicated, and was determined to avoid it, even if it meant taking his own life. But he counted without his servant François, who had been in his service since 1883 and whose love for his master was boundless.

In December 1891, when it was clear that his mind was disintegrating, Maupassant tried to cut his throat with a razor, only to be thwarted by François. Another attempt in January was also unsuccessful. François saved him again, but he could not save him from a worse fate, internment in a mental institution, where he remained until his death eighteen months later at the age of forty-three.

It cannot be too strongly recalled that virtually his entire literary career covered but a period of ten years. This reminder should help to dispel the persistent legend of Maupassant the rake, the male with the one-track mind. He did have his own notions of the role of women in the social order (too loudly proclaimed, actually, to be taken at face value), and between the ages of twenty and thirty he did sow his oats indiscriminately. But once he discovered his true vocation with "Ball of Fat" in 1880, to his internment ten years later, few writers in the history of letters have worked at their art more industriously or more conscientiously than he did.

It is a grave error, and a greater injustice, to associate Maupassant with the naturalists, that all too easy label of the manuals of literature. He shared Flaubert's burning aversion to "schools," and he deplored Zola's noisy proclamation of esthetic theories. His was the craftsman's cult of art in practice rather than in theorizing.

The association with Zola and his group was severed immediately with the success of "Ball of Fat." Thereafter he insisted on going his own way, scrupulously avoiding any affiliation—literary or ideological—which might in any way encroach upon his full development as an artist. It was this rare merit which inspired comparison of Maupassant with another *artiste pur*, Van Gogh, or, in an earlier period, with that isolated phenomenon in French letters, La Fontaine. For Maupassant did to the short story what his seventeenth-century predecessor had done to the fable—he killed it, by forging his own forms to such perfection that it was well-nigh impossible to go beyond it. And with the same results: precluding in his own country any possibility of disciples, though the imitators were legion.

For Maupassant's art is deceptively simple, like La Fontaine's, whose technique in the fable he frequently employed. To begin with, the disarmingly simple anecdotal exposition, followed by the most concentrated form of dramatic action, in which even significant details are rigorously subordinated to the whole. Description and dialogue are utilized with the same economy in creating the desired setting and climate for the psychological drama which is the core of a Maupassant story. And all in a style that defies analysis, for his French is free of any peculiarities likely to identify it with a particular period or fashion—it is, rather, in the classic tradition of such supreme artists of basic French as Racine and Voltaire. Like them, Maupassant achieves the highest tonal effects with words of the utmost simplicity. That explains his hold on such diametrically opposed craftsmen as Marcel Proust, Anatole France, Pierre Loti, Villiers de l'Isle-Adam, and Stéphane Mallarmé.

Outside of France, on the other hand—in England and in the United States, in the Scandinavian and Slavic countries particularly—the response was striking, for writers in those countries could learn from him lessons in clarity, in precision, and in polish which were lacking in their own literary traditions.

Another major error lies in associating Maupassant exclusively with such characteristics of the naturalists as objectivity and impersonality, with the "documentary" approach to his materials. Far from being the objective, detached, impassive observer only, Maupassant actually shows even in his earliest efforts a humanity, a tenderness and a sense of poetry which will increase with his own physical and spiritual problems, though he consistently made a brave effort in his work, in his correspondence, as well as in his conduct, to conceal his sensitivity. One needs but to read "Simon's Papa," and to remember that it was written long before "Ball of Fat."

Were further proof necessary, one would find it in the many brilliant stories dealing with the fantastic and the supernatural. A reading of "The Horla," "Who Knows?," "A Madman," "The Inn," "The Wolf"—to list but a sampling only—would place Maupassant high among the conjurers of the marvelous, a worthy successor of Poe and Hoffman.

Probably no foreign author of merit has had worse luck in the United States than Maupassant. During his lifetime some of his tales were appropriated by unscrupulous publishers and presented in modified, extended form. But the worst was to come after his death, when in the first American edition of his complete works, in 1903, no fewer than sixty-five stories not written by him were somehow published under his name. Undetected at the time, the error was perpetuated by many subsequent publishers for nearly fifty years. It was only in 1949 that a painstaking American biographer, scrupulous to the point of reading Maupassant in English translation in order to assess the impact of his work on Anglo-Saxon readers, discovered the colossal error.

The publishers of the present edition deserve thanks for setting the record straight on two counts. Every story in this volume was written by that master of the short story form. And all the stories he ever wrote are at long last brought together, including several which do not figure even in the most complete French edition. Maupassant can now be judged on his own merits, on his total production.

In presenting all these tales, we are not unmindful of the fact that our list would probably not enjoy Maupassant's full approval, for it includes a number of stories which he himself did not deem worthy of publication in book form. We do include them, however, since they were published by his family after his death and have since taken their place in his complete works. Moreover, is an author himself always the most discriminating judge as to what is best in his total production?

The only pieces of fiction—other than the novels—which rightfully have been omitted are either unfinished fragments or an early, sometimes crude, version of a story which he subsequently reworked and only the final version of which he himself included in book form, such as the "Letter from a Madman" which later became the celebrated "Horla." Such fragments and preliminary versions of tales would interest only the professional historian of his works.

Any writer producing some three hundred stories within ten years, along with other serious literary activities, may be expected to write a few poor ones. Maupassant did. But the sixty-five stories attributed to him for nearly fifty years are worse than poor—most of them are indescribably mediocre. We shall never know to what extent some of the adverse reactions to Maupassant in this country may be ascribed to those apocryphal tales.

And yet was ever a foreign writer more favored in the way he was first brought to the attention of the American public? He had the extraordinary good fortune to attract as godfathers two outstanding interpreters, Lafcadio Hearn and Henry James. The first translated some fifty of his tales between 1881 and 1887; whereas Henry James devoted to him an important chapter of his Partial Portraits, published in 1888, and the following year recommended him warmly to American readers in his introduction to the first volume of Maupassant stories to appear in the United States, The Odd Number. That collection of thirteen tales, carefully selected in order not to offend sensitive souls, was enthusiastically received by the critics, who compared the French writer to such luminaries on the American literary scene as Bret Harte, Sarah Orne Jewett, and Walt Whitman. One of them even went so far as to say that some of those stories could serve as texts for sermons.

The popularity of Maupassant continued undiminished for some years, resulting in no fewer than thirty translations of various works before the turn of the century, followed soon after by the first more or less "complete" edition. Moreover, Maupassant had become, even before his premature death in 1893, a "classic" in the true sense of the word—a selection of his stories was prepared for use in the classroom. A score of others have appeared since, making of him probably the most widely read of French authors in this country.

In 1891 George Moore was to make one of those rash predictions which critics occasionally indulge in and regret immediately after. Writing in the Illustrated

London News, he expressed doubt that any of the popular writer's works would be read fifty years later. The record shows how completely he was mistaken.

Impressive refutation of that prophecy came in the columns of the *New York Times*, which reported on May 6, 1940, that in the Soviet Union Maupassant was leading all foreign authors in the sales of their works since the revolution of 1917. Another refutation came from a poll completed in 1939 by the scholarly journal *Books Abroad*, in which seventy-four leading writers were asked the following question: "Would you be willing to tell *Books Abroad* what books have had the most influence in making a writer of you and in determining the character of your writing?" Here is the list of the authors mentioned most frequently:

> Shakespeare: 19 mentions
> Tolstoy: 13 mentions
> Dostoevsky, Flaubert, Goethe: 12 mentions
> Bible, Cervantes, Poe: 10 mentions
> Balzac, Dickens, Hugo, Zola: 9 mentions
> Heine, Homer, Maupassant, Whitman: 7 mentions
> Ibsen, Stendhal: 6 mentions

Granting the limitations inherent in any inquiry such as the above, admirers of Maupassant must have found it extremely gratifying to discover their favorite author surpassed among French authors only by Flaubert, Balzac, Hugo, and Zola, and to find him in the company of Heine, Homer, and Whitman.

A more recent refutation came from Japan, where in an informal poll (reported by the *Saturday Review* of February 20, 1954) Maupassant was one of five French writers to be accorded high rating among literary figures of world stature, the other four being Stendhal, Balzac, Molière, and Zola.

What about his status in English-speaking countries? There was no question of his wide popularity with the reading public. The present writer undertook to assess the esteem in which he is held by the most discriminating critics of all—fellow practitioners of the art of fiction as well as a few outstanding historians of that craft. Their frank replies are quite revealing.

One thing is immediately apparent. Virtually no mention is made of the chief criticism of Maupassant during his own lifetime. Practically no one (Seán O'Faoláin is an exception) protests against his "immorality"; only one or two merely express disapproval of his "outlook on life." Indeed, several voices rise to his defense on that score—Philip Gibbs, F. L. Lucas, William Saroyan, and a number of others. Another interesting fact is that the name Maupassant seems to be, for the English and Americans, synonymous with the short story. Few are those who mention his novels, not to speak of his other works; and those who do refer to his novels do so usually to compare them unfavorably with the shorter pieces.

Those who seem to know him best are his most fervent admirers. Llewelyn Powys has "always regarded him as a very great writer . . . his simplicity, lucidity, restraint and remorseless insight defie emulation." In the history of world letters Ellen Glasgow would gladly accord him the "small niche that is reserved for artistic perfection." John Erskine affirms that Maupassant is one of his great admirations. Theodore Dreiser considers him "one of the world's great writers." George Ade is "most enthusiastic about his work" and was "greatly influenced by him." According to Zona Gale, "he taught condensation as no one before him had done and as no one has since his time." Philip Gibbs has "a profound admiration for the genius of Maupassant, who was in my opinion the supreme master of the short story." Frank Swinnerton, immediately after reading a volume of stories with which he was not yet familiar, judges him "at his best, so magnificent as to surpass anything in that kind of writing except the best of Anton Chekhov. Chekhov had, I think, a loftier irony; Maupassant greater power, greater adroitness, greater pungency."

And what of Maupassant's influence on English and American writers of fiction? There is, to begin with, no doubt of his influence on individual authors. Ellen Glasgow, as a young writer, "read in the original, everything that he had written, and, however unaware of this I may have been, I must have been influenced by his method. The influence passed quickly, but it was good while it lasted." Whereas William Saroyan contributed the following striking testimonial:

I feel very strongly about Maupassant. I must tell you sincerely that to me he is truly one of the giants not only of literature but of living. I feel personally related to him; that is, to the kind of writer and human being he was. To me even his inferior stories are more important than the works of writers who worked harder but weren't his equal.

"In my own literary career and in my philosophic attitude to life I owe him an enormous debt," acknowledges Llewelyn Powys. George Ade was, as we have indicated, greatly influenced by his work. John Buchan was "much under his influence" as a young man; whereas Zona Gale considers him an invaluable guide, and concludes that "everyone who reads or who writes is indebted to Maupassant."

In spite of the impressive testimonies quoted above, a number voice the belief that on the whole the influence of Maupassant on the American short story was not a wholesome one. Sherwood Anderson expressed that conviction in his letter:

I came to feel that Maupassant had exerted a tremendous influence on the American short story, that for example, our Mr. O. Henry had stemmed directly from him but that on the whole the influence was not good. I have felt that what I think of as the plot short story—I almost said the trick short story—came from this influence.

Theodore Dreiser is also of that opinion, believing that "these newer writers have tried to imitate Maupassant's tone, and have missed his peculiar insight and emotional sincerity." "Maupassant had a most extraordinary influence upon young Americans who like myself were trying to write short stories in the early nineteen hundreds," testifies Henry Seidel Canby. Few people are consciously aware of that influence today, however; for, as maintained by Joseph Wood Krutch, Stephen Leacock, and others, "that influence has been so completely absorbed." Harry Hansen suggests that his influence on contemporary writers is negligible, but recognized the stamp he left on "the generation that was dominant around 1900." Some of the contributors, on the other hand, challenge the thesis that his influence was on the whole harmful. Their view is perhaps best formulated by Vincent Sheean:

Maupassant's influence may, at times, have led to mechanical trickery, as it did with, say, O. Henry and other American writers who manufactured short stories in large numbers; but this result is on the whole, it seems to me, less nefarious than the Chekhov one, because it has less to do with literature. Writers of commercial short stories for magazines may be descended, in a sense, from Maupassant, but most of them could never do anything better than what they do, and it is at least something that they have acquired a form to do it in. And upon serious writers of stories (who are few and far between, but do exist) Maupassant's influence has been good, because they have learned from him economy and a kind of lapidary industry.

Comparisons with Chekhov were of course inevitable, and it is again interesting to record the views expressed. Frank Swinnerton's opinion has already been indicated; for F. L. Lucas, Maupassant is not "as subtle and delicate at catching the shades of the soul as his great rival Chekhov; his is the clear French sunlight, with no mists. But one cannot have everything." Others, too, while preferring certain phases of the Russian artist's work, readily profess a greater predilection for the Frenchman. Somerset Maugham, who had stated his preference for Maupassant so persuasively in his prefaces to East and West and Tellers of Tales, reiterated it in his answer to our inquiry; and James Hilton concurred in the following terms:

I agree with Somerset Maugham that the Maupassant stories are much better models for modern writers than Chekhov's, though the Chekhov style is more fashionable nowadays. It is easy to write stories like Chekhov's, yet without Chekhov's genius; whereas even to write imitations of the Maupassant model is not so easy, on account of the more exact form and greater discipline of narration.

Llewelyn Powys considers Maupassant "far superior to Chekhov"; while Vincent Sheean concludes with the following telling judgment:

I believe Maupassant's place as the master of the short story is secure and permanent. The only other writer of stories who could challenge it is Chekhov, but Chekhov is such a different pair of sleeves—he was uneven; his very slight stories are far from masterly; his best stories were magnificent, but his worst ones were very nearly nothing; and the Chekhov influence has been on the whole rather bad than good. A great deal of pretentious and silly nonsense has been written under the spell of Chekhov's individual genius.

The reaction of the northern Europeans is fairly divergent. The two Norwegian winners of the Nobel Prize in literature, Sigrid Undset and Knut Hamsun, were not very enthusiastic in their laconic replies. Gunnar Gunnarsson and F. E. Sillanpää, on the other hand, readily acknowledge their debt to Maupassant, a direct one on the first and an indirect one on the second. It was the testimony of Johan Bojer, however, which was striking: "As far as I am concerned, he is the greatest writer France has produced . . . if as an old hand at the writing game I know anything at all, I learned it from Maupassant."

The German replies, on the contrary, present an impressively unanimous point of view. From the brief communication of Thomas Mann to the extended appraisal of Felix Salten come eulogies enough to gratify the most intransigent supporter of Maupassant. "I believe that the work of this Frenchman is immortal in the true sense of the word," writes Thomas Mann; and his brother Heinrich only concurs when he states, "Life and letters have seldom, if ever, attained such complete harmony as they have in his works." Franz Werfel considers him "one of the most original writers of all time." Bruno Frank does not care a great deal for his novels, but confesses that

he always seemed to me the unsurpassed and unsurpassable master of the short story. His incredibly abundant imagination, his deep and acute knowledge of the human soul, his miraculous technique in starting and building up a plot, the vigor and limpidness of his style, make him the lasting model for every short story writer.

"He is as imperishable as mankind," affirms Felix Salten, and adds that he remains "peerless" in the short story; while Stefan Zweig readily acknowledges:

I can state sincerely that I have remained faithful to few novelists of modern times as much as I have to him. . . . Maupassant had a mysterious sense of the right measure. He portrays a figure in ten strokes, describes a fate in twenty pages.

Finally, Arnold Zweig writes that he read him avidly as a high school student and has continued to frequent him since, judging him to be "second to none in vigor, artistic ability and insight . . . who portrayed an epoch in his short stories like Rembrandt or Goya in their drawings and etchings."*

In his own country, Maupassant's literary fortune has been an extremely interesting one, fluctuating with changing literary tastes, always rising strongly after a momentary dip. An unknown at the age of thirty, he achieved in 1880 a spectacular overnight success with his *Boule de Suif* ("Ball of Fat"), a success which continued uninterrupted throughout his life. The first three years following his initial triumph he devoted exclusively to short stories, producing them at seemingly breakneck speed to satisfy an insatiable public demand. There was soon a reaction on the part of many critics, however, who, while continuing to praise the unmistakably high qualities of his prose, deplored his insistent depiction of a very special segment of mankind; there was irritation at the disparity between the outstanding talent of the author and the limited scope of his medium, a growing impatience to see him undertake substantial projects rather than what the critics considered mere sketches. The first novel, *Une Vie* (A Woman's Life), was in part an answer to this challenge, and little by little even the conservatives were won over, including Brunetière, arch enemy of anything suggestive of Zola and naturalism. Maupassant was, moreover, generally regarded not as a naturalist, but rather as an independent, a "classicist," and such independents as Jules Lemaître and Anatole France spoke enthusiastically of him. With *Mont-Oriol* (1887) the author's horizon was perceptibly transformed, his pessimism and misanthropy became less narrow. Thereafter his novels assume increased importance both in his own preoccupations and in the interest of his public, now considerably enlarged by readers of the upper classes. But the evolution in his manner was suddenly broken by the disintegration of his mind. After his death editors disputed the privilege of publishing his posthumous works; at the close of the century began the appearance of the first edition of his complete works, to be followed by the first biographies and full-length studies. Somewhat later, even as a "definitive" edition of his work was issued (1908–1910), it was unmistakable that reactionary forces were at work on the prestige of our author; the "young" of the eighties and nineties who had protested against objectivity in literature were now attaining their period of full activity and influence, and the inevitable jealousies and antagonisms of embittered contemporaries were beginning to have their effect. Moreover, the vogue for the short-story form started by Maupassant had attracted hordes of imitators, largely incompetent imitators deluded by the apparent simplicity of the tales that had made Maupassant's fortune. Their abuses brought about a general reaction that was

*Readers who may be interested in the full contents of the contributions referred to above, as well as many others not cited, may consult them in the appendix of Artine Artinian's *Maupassant Criticism in France* (New York, King's Crown Press).

unavoidable; so through the war years and immediately after, his reputation seemed at a low ebb indeed, and naturally so, since those were the days of Dadaism and Surrealism.

The celebration in 1925 of the seventy-fifth anniversary of Maupassant's birth may be considered to inaugurate the period of "rehabilitation." Numerous monographs have been devoted to him in spite of the fact that his works lend themselves so little to literary dissection, the usual materials available to historians—sources, influences, literary relationships, etc.—being in his case relatively restricted. The crucial factor, however, is that in his own country he continues to attract readers both at the popular and critical levels. Just before the last war his first novel, *Une Vie*, was designated one of the ten masterpieces of French fiction by a jury made up of such opposed temperaments and literary tendencies as André Gide, Jean Giraudoux, Edmond Jaloux, André Maurois, François Mauriac, and Jean Cocteau. And more recently his second novel, *Bel-Ami*, was one of twenty novels voted the most popular in the French language.

Legends die hard; but I hope the present edition will help to kill several Maupassant legends in this country.

Some years ago we were examining in a leading New York book store a whole shelf of those delightful reprints issued by Thomas Mosher of Portland, Maine. As the manager walked by, we asked him if he knew whether Mosher had published anything by Maupassant. "De Maupassant!" came the startled answer, "Mosher published only *literature!*" It is true that he was a gentleman of the old school; perhaps his own reading had consisted only of "literature," guaranteed as such by his masters. And his faith in their judgment had no doubt been fortified by the way most publishers in the United States advertised Maupassant's works. Copy-writers have had a veritable field-day inciting the American reader with such epithets as *frank, unexpurgated, daring, shocking,* and have succeeded, apparently, in persuading even book-store managers that Maupassant is not "literature." It is true that much of Maupassant is for the adult readers for whom it was written (though some forty of his stories have been collected into an *édition pour la jeunesse*). Sex does have an important role in his world (as it does in anybody's), but he is completely free of pornography, taking sex in his stride like a healthy male, never dwelling on the matter needlessly or morbidly. So on that score he deserves to be saved from the fate that American copy-writers have contrived for him.

Another legend which I trust this volume will dispel concerns the recurring association of Maupassant with the "trick ending." I suppose that one can be traced to the nauseating frequency with which "The Necklace" is anthologized, as if it represented Maupassant at his best. Let any one who still believes that old chestnut keep count of stories in the present volume that have any resemblance to a trick ending.

Still another chestnut enjoying wide currency is that the Maupassant story is necessarily one of *action*. Nothing could be farther from the truth. The reader will discover many stories in which nothing "happens," many tales where mood and atmosphere are brilliantly created, yet with not the slightest loss of the magic pulse of life.

All of which adds up to the miracle of Maupassant's art at its best, which captures and holds the interest of the most casual reader and at the same time inspires the utmost respect and admiration of the sophisticated.

THE COMPLETE SHORT STORIES OF

GUY DE MAUPASSANT

BALL OF FAT

For many days now the fag end of the army had been straggling through the town.
They were not troops but a disbanded horde. The beards of the men were long and
filthy, their uniforms in tatters, and they advanced at an easy pace without flag or
regiment. All seemed worn-out and back-broken, incapable of a thought or a resolution, marching by habit solely and falling from fatigue as soon as they stopped.
In short, they were a mobilized, pacific people, bending under the weight of the
gun; some little squads on the alert, easy to take alarm and prompt in enthusiasm,
ready to attack or to flee; and in the midst of them some red breeches, the remains
of a division broken up in a great battle; some somber artillerymen in line with
these varied kinds of foot soldiers, and sometimes the brilliant helmet of a dragoon
on foot who followed with difficulty the shortest march of the lines.

Some legions of free shooters, under the heroic names of Avengers of the Defeat,
Citizens of the Tomb, Partakers of Death, passed in their turn with the air of
bandits.

Their leaders were former cloth or grain merchants, ex-merchants in tallow or
soap, warriors of circumstance, elected officers on account of their escutcheons and
the length of their mustaches, covered with arms and with braid, speaking in constrained voices, discussing plans of campaign and pretending to carry agonized
France alone on their swaggering shoulders but sometimes fearing their own soldiers, prison birds, that were often brave at first and later proved to be plunderers
and debauchees.

It was said that the Prussians were going to enter Rouen.

The National Guard who for two months had been carefully reconnoitering in
the neighboring woods, shooting sometimes their own sentinels and ready for a

combat whenever a little wolf stirred in the thicket, had now returned to their fire-sides. Their arms, their uniforms, all the murderous accouterments with which they had lately struck fear into the national heart for three leagues in every direction, had suddenly disappeared.

The last French soldiers finally came across the Seine to reach the Audemer bridge through Saint-Sever and Bourg-Achard; and marching behind, on foot, between two officers of ordnance, the general, in despair, unable to do anything with these incongruous tatters, himself lost in the breaking up of a people accustomed to conquer, and disastrously beaten in spite of his legendary bravery.

A profound calm, a frightful, silent expectancy had spread over the city. Many of the heavy citizens, emasculated by commerce, anxiously awaited the conquerors, trembling lest their roasting spits or kitchen knives be considered arms.

All life seemed stopped; shops were closed, the streets dumb. Sometimes an inhabitant, intimidated by this silence, moved rapidly along next the walls. The agony of waiting made them wish the enemy would come.

In the afternoon of the day which followed the departure of the French troops some uhlans, coming from one knows not where, crossed the town with celerity. Then a little later a black mass descended the side of St. Catherine, while two other invading bands appeared by the way of Darnetal and Bois-Guillaume. The advance guard of the three bodies joined one another at the same moment in Hôtel de Ville square, and by all the neighboring streets the German army continued to arrive, spreading out its battalions, making the pavement resound under their hard, rhythmic step.

Some orders of the commander, in a foreign, guttural voice, reached the houses which seemed dead and deserted, while behind closed shutters eyes were watching these victorious men, masters of the city, of fortunes, of lives, through the "rights of war." The inhabitants, shut up in their rooms, were visited with the kind of excitement that a cataclysm or some fatal upheaval of the earth brings to us, against which all force is useless. For the same sensation is produced each time that the established order of things is overturned, when security no longer exists and all that protect the laws of man and of nature find themselves at the mercy of unreasoning, ferocious brutality. The trembling of the earth crushing the houses and burying an entire people; a river overflowing its banks and carrying in its course the drowned peasants, carcasses of beeves and girders snatched from roofs, or a glorious army massacring those trying to defend themselves, leading other prisoners, pillaging in the name of the sword and thanking God to the sound of the cannon; all are alike frightful scourges which disconnect all belief in eternal justice, all the confidence that we have in the protection of Heaven and the reason of man.

Some detachments rapped at each door, then disappeared into the houses. It was occupation after invasion. Then the duty commences for the conquered to show themselves gracious toward the conquerors.

After some time, as soon as the first terror disappears, a new calm is established. In many families the Prussian officer eats at the table. He is sometimes well bred and, through politeness, pities France and speaks of his repugnance in taking part in this affair. One is grateful to him for this sentiment; then, one may be, someday or other, in need of his protection. By treating him well one has, perhaps, a less number of men to feed. And why should we wound anyone on whom we are entirely dependent? To act thus would be less bravery than temerity. And temerity is no longer a fault of the commoner of Rouen as it was at the time of the heroic defense when their city became famous. Finally each told himself that the highest judgment of French urbanity required that they be allowed to be polite to the strange soldier in the house, provided they did not show themselves familiar with him in public. Outside they would not make themselves known to each other, but at home they could chat freely, and the German might remain longer each evening warming his feet at their hearthstones.

The town even took on, little by little, its ordinary aspect. The French scarcely went out, but the Prussian soldiers grumbled in the streets. In short, the officers of the Blue Hussars, who dragged with arrogance their great weapons of death up and down the pavement, seemed to have no more grievous scorn for the simple citizens than the officers or the sportsmen who, the year before, drank in the same cafés.

There was, nevertheless, something in the air, something subtle and unknown, a strange, intolerable atmosphere like a penetrating odor, the odor of invasion. It filled the dwellings and the public places, changed the taste of the food, gave the impression of being on a journey, far away among barbarous and dangerous tribes.

The conquerors exacted money, much money. The inhabitants always paid and they were rich enough to do it. But the richer a trading Norman becomes the more he suffers at every outlay, at each part of his fortune that he sees pass from his hands into those of another.

Therefore, two or three leagues below the town, following the course of the river toward Croisset, Dieppedalle or Biessard, mariners and fishermen often picked up the swollen corpse of a German in uniform from the bottom of the river, killed by the blow of a knife, the head crushed with a stone, or perhaps thrown into the water by a push from the high bridge. The slime of the river bed buried these obscure vengeances, savage but legitimate, unknown heroisms, mute attacks more perilous than the battles of broad day and without the echoing sound of glory.

For hatred of the foreigner always arouses some intrepid ones who are ready to die for an idea.

Finally, as soon as the invaders had brought the town quite under subjection with their inflexible discipline, without having been guilty of any of the horrors for which they were famous along their triumphal line of march, people began to take courage, and the need of trade put new heart into the commerce of the country. Some had large interests at Havre, which the French army occupied, and they wished to try and reach this port by going to Dieppe by land and there embarking.

They used their influence with the German soldiers with whom they had an acquaintance, and finally an authorization of departure was obtained from the general in chief.

Then, a large diligence with four horses having been engaged for this journey, and ten persons having engaged seats in it, it was resolved to set out on Tuesday morning before daylight, in order to escape observation.

For some time before, the frost had been hardening the earth, and on Monday, toward three o'clock, great black clouds coming from the north brought the snow which fell without interruption during the evening and all night.

At half-past four in the morning the travelers met in the courtyard of Hôtel Normandie, where they were to take the carriage.

They were still full of sleep and shivering with cold under their wraps. They could only see each other dimly in the obscure light, and the accumulation of heavy winter garments made them all resemble fat curates in long cassocks. Only two of the men were acquainted; a third accosted them and they chatted: "I'm going to take my wife," said one. "I too," said another. "And I," said the third. The first added: "We shall not return to Rouen, and if the Prussians approach Havre, we shall go over to England." All had the same projects, being of the same mind.

As yet the horses were not harnessed. A little lantern, carried by a stableboy, went out one door from time to time, to immediately appear at another. The feet of the horses striking the floor could be heard, although deadened by the straw and litter, and the voice of a man talking to the beasts, sometimes swearing, came from the end of the building. A light tinkling of bells announced that they were taking down the harness; this murmur soon became a clear and continuous rhythm by the movement of the animal, stopping sometimes, then breaking into a brusque shake which was accompanied by the dull stamp of a sabot upon the hard earth.

The door suddenly closed. All noise ceased. The frozen citizens were silent; they remained immovable and stiff.

A curtain of uninterrupted white flakes constantly sparkled in its descent to the ground. It effaced forms and powdered everything with a downy moss. And nothing could be heard in the great silence. The town was calm and buried under the wintry frost as this fall of snow, unnamable and floating, a sensation rather than a sound (trembling atoms which only seem to fill all space), came to cover the earth.

The man reappeared with his lantern, pulling at the end of a rope a sad horse which would not come willingly. He placed him against the pole, fastened the traces, walked about a long time adjusting the harness, for he had the use of but one hand, the other carrying the lantern. As he went for the second horse he noticed the travelers, motionless, already white with snow, and said to them: "Why not get into the carriage? You will be under cover at least."

They had evidently not thought of it, and they hastened to do so. The three men installed their wives at the back and then followed them. Then the other forms, undecided and veiled, took in their turn the last places without exchanging a word.

The floor was covered with straw, in which the feet ensconced themselves. The ladies at the back having brought little copper foot stoves, with a carbon fire, lighted them and for some time, in low voices, enumerated the advantages of the appliances, repeating things that they had known for a long time.

Finally the carriage was harnessed with six horses instead of four, because the traveling was very bad, and a voice called out:

"Is everybody aboard?"

And a voice within answered: "Yes."

They were off. The carriage moved slowly, slowly for a little way. The wheels were imbedded in the snow; the whole body groaned with heavy cracking sounds; the horses glistened, puffed and smoked; and the great whip of the driver snapped without ceasing, hovering about on all sides, knotting and unrolling itself like a thin serpent, lashing brusquely some horse on the rebound, which then put forth its most violent effort.

Now the day was imperceptibly dawning. The light flakes, which one of the travelers, a Rouenese by birth, said looked like a shower of cotton, no longer fell. A faint light filtered through the great dull clouds, which rendered more brilliant the white of the fields, where appeared a line of great trees clothed in whiteness or a chimney with a cap of snow.

In the carriage each looked at the others curiously in the sad light of this dawn.

At the back, in the best places, M. Loiseau, wholesale merchant of wine, of Grand-Pont Street, and Mme. Loiseau were sleeping opposite each other. Loiseau had bought out his former patron, who failed in business, and made his fortune. He sold bad wine at a good price to small retailers in the country and passed among his friends and acquaintances as a knavish wag, a true Norman full of deceit and joviality.

His reputation as a sharper was so well established that one evening at the residence of the prefect, M. Tournel, author of some fables and songs, of keen, satirical mind, a local celebrity, having proposed to some ladies, who seemed to be getting a little sleepy, that they make up a game of "Loiseau tricks," the joke traversed the rooms of the prefect, reached those of the town and then, in the months to come, made many a face in the province expand with laughter.

Loiseau was especially known for his love of farce of every kind, for his jokes, good and bad; and no one could ever talk with him without thinking: "He is invaluable, this Loiseau." Of tall figure, his balloon-shaped front was surmounted by a ruddy face surrounded by gray whiskers.

His wife, large, strong and resolute, with a quick, decisive manner, was the order and arithmetic of this house of commerce, while he was the life of it through his joyous activity.

Beside them M. Carré-Lamadon held himself with great dignity, as if belonging to a superior caste; a considerable man in cottons, proprietor of three mills, officer of the Legion of Honor and member of the General Council. He had remained, during the Empire, chief of the friendly opposition, famous for making the emperor pay more dear for rallying to the cause than if he had combated it with blunted arms, according to his own story. Mme. Carré-Lamadon, much younger than her husband, was the consolation of officers of good family sent to Rouen in garrison. She sat opposite her husband, very dainty, petite and pretty, wrapped closely in furs and looking with sad eyes at the interior of the carriage.

Her neighbors, the Count and Countess Hubert de Breville, bore the name of one of the most ancient and noble families of Normandy. The count, an old gentleman of good figure, accentuated by the artifices of his toilette his resemblance to King Henry IV, who, following a glorious legend of the family, had impregnated one of the De Breville ladies, whose husband, for this reason, was made a count and governor of the province.

A colleague of M. Carré-Lamadon in the General Council, Count Hubert represented the Orléans party in the department.

The story of his marriage with the daughter of a little captain of a privateer had always remained a mystery. But as the countess had a grand air, received better than anyone and passed for having been loved by the son of Louis Philippe, all the nobility did her honor, and her salon remained the first in the country, the only one which preserved the old gallantry and to which the entree was difficult. The fortune of the Brevilles amounted, it was said, to five hundred thousand francs in income, all in good securities.

These six persons formed the foundation of the carriage company, the society side, serene and strong, honest, established people, who had both religion and principles.

By a strange chance all the women were upon the same seat, and the countess had for neighbors two sisters who picked at long strings of beads and muttered some "Paters" and "Aves." One was old and as pitted with smallpox as if she had received a broadside of grapeshot full in the face. The other, very sad, had a pretty face and a disease of the lungs, which, added to their devoted faith, illumined them and made them appear like martyrs.

Opposite these two devotees were a man and a woman who attracted the notice of all. The man, well known, was Cornudet the democrat, the terror of respectable people. For twenty years he had soaked his great red beard in the bocks of all the democratic cafés. He had consumed with his friends and confreres a rather pretty fortune left him by his father, an old confectioner, and he awaited the establishing of the Republic with impatience, that he might have the position he merited by his great expenditures. On the fourth of September, by some joke perhaps, he believed himself elected prefect, but when he went to assume the duties the clerks of the office were masters of the place and refused to recognize him, obliging him to retreat. Rather a good bachelor on the whole, inoffensive and serviceable, he had busied himself, with incomparable ardor, in organizing the defense against the Prussians. He had dug holes in all the plains, cut down young trees from the neighboring forests, sown snares over all routes and, at the approach of the enemy, took himself quickly back to the town. He now thought he could be of more use in Havre, where more entrenchments would be necessary.

The woman, one of those called a coquette, was celebrated for her embonpoint, which had given her the nick-name of "Ball of Fat." Small, round and fat as lard, with puffy fingers choked at the phalanges like chaplets of short sausages, with a stretched and shining skin, an enormous bosom which shook under her dress, she was, nevertheless, pleasing and sought after on account of a certain freshness and breeziness of disposition. Her face was a round apple, a peony bud ready to pop into bloom, and inside that opened two great black eyes shaded with thick brows that cast a shadow within; and below, a charming mouth, humid for kissing, furnished with shining, microscopic baby teeth. She was, it was said, full of admirable qualities.

As soon as she was recognized a whisper went around among the honest women, and the words "prostitute" and "public shame" were whispered so loud that she raised her head. Then she threw at her neighbors such a provoking, courageous look that a great silence reigned, and everybody looked down except Loiseau, who watched her with an exhilarated air.

And immediately conversation began among the three ladies, whom the presence of this girl had suddenly rendered friendly, almost intimate. It seemed to them they should bring their married dignity into union in opposition to that sold without shame; for legal love always takes on a tone of contempt for its free confrere.

The three men, also drawn together by an instinct of preservation at the sight of Cornudet, talked money with a certain high tone of disdain for the poor. Count Hubert talked of the havoc which the Prussians had caused, the losses which resulted from being robbed of cattle and from destroyed crops, with the assurance of a great lord, ten times millionaire, whom these ravages would scarcely cramp for a year. M. Carré-Lamadon, largely experienced in the cotton industry, had had need of sending six hundred thousand francs to England, as a trifle in reserve if it should be needed. As for Loiseau, he had arranged with the French administration to sell them all the wines that remained in his cellars, on account of which the State owed him a formidable sum which he counted on collecting at Havre.

And all three threw toward each other swift and amicable glances.

Although in different conditions, they felt themselves to be brothers through money, that grand freemasonry of those who possess it and make the gold rattle by putting their hands in their trousers' pockets.

The carriage went so slowly that at ten o'clock in the morning they had not gone four leagues. The men had got down three times to climb hills on foot. They began to be disturbed because they should be now taking breakfast at Tôtes, and they despaired now of reaching there before night. Each one had begun to watch for an inn along the route, when the carriage foundered in a snowdrift and it took two hours to extricate it.

Growing appetites troubled their minds; and no eating house, no wine-shop showed itself, the approach of the Prussians and the passage of the troops having frightened away all these industries.

The gentlemen ran to the farms along the way for provisions, but they did not even find bread, for the defiant peasant had concealed his stores for fear of being pillaged by the soldiers who, having nothing to put between their teeth, took by force whatever they discovered.

Toward one o'clock in the afternoon Loiseau announced that there was a decided hollow in his stomach. Everybody suffered with him, and the violent need of eating, ever increasing, had killed conversation.

From time to time someone yawned; another immediately imitated him; and each, in his turn, in accordance with his character, his knowledge of life and his social position, opened his mouth with carelessness or modesty, placing his hand quickly before the yawning hole from whence issued a vapor.

Ball of Fat, after many attempts, bent down as if seeking something under her skirts. She hesitated a second, looked at her neighbors, then sat up again tranquilly. The faces were pale and drawn. Loiseau affirmed that he would give a thousand francs for a small ham. His wife made a gesture as if in protest, but she kept quiet. She was always troubled when anyone spoke of squandering money and could not comprehend any pleasantry on the subject. "The fact is," said the count, "I cannot understand why I did not think to bring some provisions with me." Each reproached himself in the same way.

However, Cornudet had a flask of rum. He offered it; it was refused coldly. Loiseau alone accepted two swallows and then passed back the flask saying, by way of thanks: "It is good all the same; it is warming and checks the appetite." The alcohol put him in good humor, and he proposed that they do as they did on the little ship in the song, eat the fattest of the passengers. This indirect allusion to Ball of Fat choked the well-bred people. They said nothing. Cornudet alone laughed. The two good sisters had ceased to mumble their rosaries and, with their hands enfolded in their great sleeves, held themselves immovable, obstinately lowering their eyes, without doubt offering to Heaven the suffering it had brought upon them.

Finally at three o'clock, when they found themselves in the midst of an interminable plain, without a single village in sight, Ball of Fat, bending down quickly, drew from under the seat a large basket covered with a white napkin.

At first she brought out a little china plate and a silver cup, then a large dish in which there were two whole chickens, cut up and imbedded in their own jelly. And one could still see in the basket other good things, some pâtés, fruits and sweetmeats, provisions for three days if they should not see the kitchen of an inn. Four necks of bottles were seen among the packages of food. She took a wing of a chicken and began to eat it delicately with one of those biscuits called "Regence" in Normandy.

All looks were turned in her direction. Then the odor spread, enlarging the nostrils and making the mouth water, besides causing a painful contraction of the jaw behind the ears. The scorn of the women for this girl became ferocious, as if they had a desire to kill her and throw her out of the carriage into the snow, her silver cup, her basket, provisions and all.

But Loiseau with his eyes devoured the dish of chicken. He said: "Fortunately Madame had more precaution than we. There are some people who know how to think ahead always."

She turned toward him, saying: "If you would like some of it, sir? It is hard to go without breakfast so long."

He saluted her and replied: "Faith, I frankly cannot refuse; I can stand it no longer. Everything goes in time of war, does it not, madame?" And then, casting a comprehensive glance around, he added: "In moments like this, one can but be pleased to find people who are obliging."

He had a newspaper which he spread out on his knees that no spot might come to his pantaloons, and upon the point of a knife that he always carried in his pocket he took up a leg all glistening with jelly, put it between his teeth and masticated it with a satisfaction so evident that there ran through the carriage a great sigh of distress.

Then Ball of Fat, in a sweet and humble voice, proposed that the two sisters partake of her collation. They both accepted instantly and, without raising their eyes, began to eat very quickly, after stammering their thanks. Cornudet no longer refused the offers of his neighbor, and they formed with the sisters a sort of table, by spreading out some newspapers upon their knees.

The mouths opened and shut without ceasing; they masticated, swallowed, gulping ferociously. Loiseau in his corner was working hard and, in a low voice, was trying to induce his wife to follow his example. She resisted for a long time; then, when a drawn sensation ran through her body, she yielded. Her husband, rounding his phrase, asked their "charming companion" if he might be allowed to offer a little piece to Mme. Loiseau.

She replied: "Why, yes, certainly, sir," with an amiable smile as she passed the dish.

An embarrassing thing confronted them when they opened the first bottle of Bordeaux: they had but one cup. Each passed it after having tasted. Cornudet alone, for politeness without doubt, placed his lips at the spot left humid by his fair neighbor.

Then, surrounded by people eating, suffocated by the odors of the food, the Count and Countess de Breville, as well as Mme. and M. Carré-Lamadon, were suffering that odious torment which has preserved the name of Tantalus. Suddenly the young wife of the manufacturer gave forth such a sigh that all heads were turned in her direction; she was as white as the snow without; her eyes closed, her head drooped; she had lost consciousness. Her husband, much excited, implored the help of everybody. Each lost his head completely, until the elder of the two sisters, holding the head of the sufferer, slipped Ball of Fat's cup between her lips and forced her to swallow a few drops of wine. The pretty little lady revived, opened her eyes, smiled and declared in a dying voice that she felt very well now. But, in order that the attack might not return, the sister urged her to drink a full glass of Bordeaux and added: "It is just hunger, nothing more."

Then Ball of Fat, blushing and embarrassed, looked at the four travelers who had fasted and stammered: "Goodness knows! if I dared to offer anything to these gentlemen and ladies, I would——" Then she was silent, as if fearing an insult. Loiseau took up the word: "Ah! certainly in times like these all the world are brothers and ought to aid each other. Come, ladies, without ceremony; why the devil not accept? We do not know whether we shall even find a house where we can pass the night. At the pace we are going now we shall not reach Tôtes before noon tomorrow."

They still hesitated, no one daring to assume the responsibility of a "Yes." The count decided the question. He turned toward the fat, intimidated girl and, taking on a grand air of condescension, he said to her:

"We accept with gratitude, madame."

It is the first step that counts. The Rubicon passed, one lends himself to the occasion squarely. The basket was stripped. It still contained a *pâté de foie gras*, a *pâté* of larks, a piece of smoked tongue, some preserved pears, a loaf of hard bread, some wafers and a full cup of pickled gherkins and onions, of which crudities Ball of Fat, like all women, was extremely fond.

They could not eat this girl's provisions without speaking to her. And so they chatted, with reserve at first; then, as she carried herself well, with more abandon. The ladies De Breville and Carré-Lamadon, who were acquainted with all the ins and outs of good breeding, were gracious with a certain delicacy. The countess, especially, showed that amiable condescension of very noble ladies who do not fear being spoiled by contact with anyone and was charming. But the great Mme. Loiseau, who had the soul of a plebeian, remained crabbed, saying little and eating much.

The conversation was about the war, naturally. They related the horrible deeds of the Prussians, the brave acts of the French; and all of them, although running away, did homage to those who stayed behind. Then personal stories began to be told, and Ball of Fat related, with sincere emotion and in the heated words that such girls sometimes use in expressing their natural feelings, how she had left Rouen:

"I believed at first that I could remain," she said. "I had my house full of provisions, and I preferred to feed a few soldiers rather than expatriate myself, to go I knew not where. But as soon as I saw them, those Prussians, that was too much for me! They made my blood boil with anger, and I wept for very shame all day long. Oh! if I were only a man! I watched them from my windows, the great porkers with their pointed helmets, and my maid held my hands to keep me from throwing the furniture down upon them. Then one of them came to lodge at my house; I sprang at his throat the first thing; they are no more difficult to strangle than other people. And I should have put an end to that one then and there had they not pulled me away by the hair. After that it was necessary to keep out of sight. And finally, when I found an opportunity, I left town and—here I am!"

They congratulated her. She grew in the estimation of her companions, who had not shown themselves so hot-brained, and Cornudet, while listening to her, took on the approving, benevolent smile of an apostle, as a priest would if he heard a devotee praise God, for the long-bearded democrats have a monopoly of patriotism, as the men in cassocks have of religion. In his turn he spoke in a doctrinal tone, with the emphasis of a proclamation such as we see pasted on the walls about

town, and finished by a bit of eloquence whereby he gave that "scamp of a Badin-
guet" a good lashing.

Then Ball of Fat was angry, for she was a Bonapartist. She grew redder than a
cherry and, stammering with indignation, said:

"I would like to have seen you in his place, you other people. Then everything
would have been quite right; oh yes! It is you who have betrayed this man! One
would never have had to leave France if it had been governed by blackguards like
you!"

Cornudet, undisturbed, preserved a disdainful, superior smile, but all felt that
the high note had been struck, until the count, not without some difficulty, calmed
the exasperated girl and proclaimed with a manner of authority that all sincere
opinions should be respected. But the countess and the manufacturer's wife, who
had in their souls an unreasonable hatred for the people that favor a republic and
the same instinctive tenderness that all women have for a decorative, despotic government, felt themselves drawn, in spite of themselves, toward this prostitute so
full of dignity, whose sentiments so strongly resembled their own.

The basket was empty. By ten o'clock they had easily exhausted the contents
and regretted that there was not more. Conversation continued for some time, but
a little more coldly since they had finished eating.

The night fell; the darkness little by little became profound, and the cold, felt
more during digestion, made Ball of Fat shiver in spite of her plumpness. Then
Mme. de Breville offered her the little foot stove, in which the fuel had been renewed many times since morning; she accepted it immediately, for her feet were
becoming numb with cold. The ladies Carré-Lamadon and Loiseau gave theirs to
the two religious sisters.

The driver had lighted his lanterns. They shone out with a lively glimmer,
showing a cloud of foam beyond, the sweat of the horses; and, on both sides of the
way, the snow seemed to roll itself along under the moving reflection of the lights.

Inside the carriage one could distinguish nothing. But a sudden movement
seemed to be made between Ball of Fat and Cornudet; and Loiseau, whose eye
penetrated the shadow, believed that he saw the big-bearded man start back quickly
as if he had received a swift, noiseless blow.

Then some twinkling points of fire appeared in the distance along the road. It
was Tôtes. They had traveled eleven hours, which, with the two hours given to
resting and feeding the horses, made thirteen. They entered the town and stopped
before the Hotel of Commerce.

The carriage door opened! A well-known sound gave the travelers a start; it was
the scabbard of a sword hitting the ground. Immediately a German voice was heard
in the darkness.

Although the diligence was not moving, no one offered to alight, fearing someone might be waiting to murder them as they stepped out. Then the conductor
appeared, holding in his hand one of the lanterns which lighted the carriage to its
depth and showed the two rows of frightened faces whose mouths were open and
whose eyes were wide with surprise and fear.

Outside, beside the driver, in plain sight stood a German officer, an excessively
tall young man, thin and blond, squeezed into his uniform like a girl in a corset
and wearing on his head a flat oilcloth cap which made him resemble the porter of
an English hotel. His enormous mustache, of long straight hairs, growing gradually
thin at each side and terminating in a single blond thread so fine that one could

not perceive where it ended, seemed to weigh heavily on the corners of his mouth and, drawing down the cheeks, left a decided wrinkle about the lips.

In Alsatian French he invited the travelers to come in, saying in a suave tone: "Will you descend, gentlemen and ladies?"

The two good sisters were the first to obey, with the docility of saints accustomed ever to submission. The count and countess then appeared, followed by the manufacturer and his wife; then Loiseau, pushing ahead of him his larger half. The last named, as he set foot on the earth, said to the officer: "Good evening, sir," more as a measure of prudence than politeness. The officer, insolent as all powerful people usually are, looked at him without a word.

Ball of Fat and Cornudet, although nearest the door, were the last to descend, grave and haughty before the enemy. The fat girl tried to control herself and be calm. The democrat waved a tragic hand, and his long beard seemed to tremble a little and grow redder. They wished to preserve their dignity, comprehending that in such meetings as these they represented in some degree their great country; and somewhat disgusted with the docility of her companions, the fat girl tried to show more pride than her neighbors, the honest women, and as she felt that someone should set an example she continued her attitude of resistance assumed at the beginning of the journey.

They entered the vast kitchen of the inn, and the German, having demanded their traveling papers signed by the general in chief (in which the name, the description and profession of each traveler was mentioned) and having examined them all critically, comparing the people and their signatures, said: "It is quite right," and went out.

Then they breathed. They were still hungry and supper was ordered. A half-hour was necessary to prepare it, and while two servants were attending to this they went to their rooms. They found them along a corridor which terminated in a large glazed door.

Finally they sat down at table, when the proprietor of the inn himself appeared. He was a former horse merchant, a large, asthmatic man with a constant wheezing and rattling in his throat. His father had left him the name of Follenvie. He asked:

"Is Miss Elizabeth Rousset here?"

Ball of Fat started as she answered: "It is I."

"The Prussian officer wishes to speak with you immediately."

"With me?"

"Yes, that is, if you are Miss Elizabeth Rousset."

She was disturbed and, reflecting for an instant, declared flatly:

"That is my name, but I shall not go."

A stir was felt around her; each discussed and tried to think of the cause of this order. The count approached her, saying:

"You are wrong, madame, for your refusal may lead to considerable difficulty, not only for yourself but for all your companions. It is never worth while to resist those in power. This request cannot assuredly bring any danger; it is, without doubt, about some forgotten formality."

Everybody agreed with him, asking, begging, beseeching her to go, and at last they convinced her that it was best; they all feared the complications that might result from disobedience. She finally said:

"It is for you that I do this, you understand."

The countess took her by the hand, saying: "And we are grateful to you for it."

She went out. They waited before sitting down at table.

Each one regretted not having been sent for in the place of this violent, irascible girl and mentally prepared some platitudes in case they should be called in their turn.

But at the end of ten minutes she reappeared, out of breath, red to suffocation and exasperated. She stammered: "Oh! the rascal; the rascal!"

All gathered around to learn something, but she said nothing; and when the count insisted she responded with great dignity: "No, it does not concern you; I can say nothing."

Then they all seated themselves around a high soup tureen whence came the odor of cabbage. In spite of alarm the supper was gay. The cider was good; the beverage Loiseau and the good sisters took as a means of economy. The others called for wine; Cornudet demanded beer. He had a special fashion of uncorking the bottle, making froth on the liquid, carefully filling the glass and then holding it before the light to better appreciate the color. When he drank, his great beard, which still kept some of the foam of his beloved beverage, seemed to tremble with tenderness; his eyes were squinted, in order not to lose sight of his tipple, and he had the unique air of fulfilling the function for which he was born. One would say that there was in his mind a meeting, like that of affinities, between the two great passions that occupied his life—Pale Ale and Revolutions; and assuredly he could not taste the one without thinking of the other.

M. and Mme. Follenvie dined at the end of the table. The man, rattling like a cracked locomotive, had too much trouble in breathing to talk while eating, but his wife was never silent. She told all her impressions at the arrival of the Prussians, what they did, what they said, reviling them because they cost her some money and because she had two sons in the army. She addressed herself especially to the countess, flattered by being able to talk with a lady of quality.

When she lowered her voice to say some delicate thing her husband would interrupt, from time to time, with: "You had better keep silent, Madame Follenvie." But she paid no attention, continuing in this fashion:

"Yes, madame, those people there not only eat our potatoes and pork but our pork and potatoes. And it must not be believed that they are at all proper—oh no! Such filthy things they do, saving the respect I owe to you! And if you could see them exercise for hours in the day! They are all there in the field, marching ahead, then marching back, turning here and turning there. They might be cultivating the land or at least working on the roads of their own country! But no, madame, these military men are profitable to no one. Poor people have to feed them or perhaps be murdered! I am only an old woman without education, it is true, but when I see some endangering their constitutions by raging from morning to night I say: 'When there are so many people found to be useless, how unnecessary it is for others to take so much trouble to be nuisances!' Truly, is it not an abomination to kill people, whether they be Prussian or English or Polish or French? If one man revenges himself upon another who has done him some injury, it is wicked and he is punished; but when they exterminate our boys as if they were game, with guns, they give decorations, indeed, to the one who destroys the most! Now, you see, I can never understand that, never!"

Cornudet raised his voice: "War is a barbarity when one attacks a peaceable neighbor but a sacred duty when one defends his country."

The old woman lowered her head.

"Yes, when one defends himself it is another thing; but why not make it a duty to kill all the kings who make these wars for their pleasure?"

Cornudet's eyes flashed. "Bravo, my countrywoman!" said he.

M. Carré-Lamadon reflected profoundly. Although he was prejudiced as a captain of industry, the good sense of this peasant woman made him think of the opulence that would be brought into the country were the idle and consequently mischievous hands, and the troops which were now maintained in unproductiveness, employed in some great industrial work that it would require centuries to achieve.

Loiseau, leaving his place, went to speak with the innkeeper in a low tone of voice. The great man laughed, shook and squeaked, his corpulence quivered with joy at the jokes of his neighbor, and he bought of him six cases of wine for spring, after the Prussians had gone.

As soon as supper was finished, as they were worn out with fatigue, they retired.

However, Loiseau, who had observed things, after getting his wife to bed glued his eye and then his ear to a hole in the wall to try and discover what are known as "the mysteries of the corridor."

At the end of about an hour he heard a groping and, looking quickly, he perceived Ball of Fat, who appeared still more plump in a blue cashmere negligee trimmed with white lace. She had a candle in her hand and was directing her steps toward the great door at the end of the corridor. But a door at the side opened, and when she returned at the end of some minutes Cornudet, in his suspenders, followed her. They spoke low, then they stopped. Ball of Fat seemed to be defending the entrance to her room with energy. Loiseau, unfortunately, could not hear all their words, but finally, as they raised their voices, he was able to catch a few. Cornudet insisted with vivacity. He said:

"Come, now, you are a silly woman; what harm can be done?"

She had an indignant air in responding: "No, my dear, there are moments when such things are out of place. Here it would be a shame."

He doubtless did not comprehend and asked why. Then she cried out, raising her voice still more:

"Why? You do not see why? When there are Prussians in the house, in the very next room, perhaps?"

He was silent. This patriotic shame of the harlot, who would not suffer his caress so near the enemy, must have awakened the latent dignity in his heart, for after simply kissing her he went back to his own door with a bound.

Loiseau, much excited, left the aperture, cut a caper in his room, put on his pajamas, turned back the clothes that covered the bony carcass of his companion, whom he awakened with a kiss, murmuring: "Do you love me, dearie?"

Then all the house was still. And immediately there arose somewhere, from an uncertain quarter which might be the cellar but was quite as likely to be the garret, a powerful snoring, monotonous and regular, a heavy, prolonged sound, like a great kettle under pressure. M. Follenvie was asleep.

As they had decided that they would set out at eight o'clock the next morning, they all collected in the kitchen. But the carriage, the roof of which was covered with snow, stood undisturbed in the courtyard, without horses and without a conductor. They sought him in vain in the stables, in the hay and in the coach house. Then they resolved to scour the town and started out. They found themselves in a square, with a church at one end and some low houses on either side, where they perceived some Prussian soldiers. The first one they saw was paring potatoes. The second, further off, was cleaning the hairdresser's shop. Another, bearded to the eyes, was tending a troublesome brat, cradling it and trying to appease it; and the great peasant women, whose husbands were "away in the army," indicated by signs to their obedient conquerors the work they wished to have done: cutting wood, cooking the soup, grinding the coffee or what not. One of them even washed the linen of his hostess, an impotent old grandmother.

The count, astonished, asked questions of the beadle who came out of the rectory. The old man responded:

"Oh! those men are not wicked; they are not the Prussians we hear about. They are from far off, I know not where; and they have left wives and children in their country; it is not amusing to them, this war, I can tell you! I am sure they also weep for their homes and that it makes as much sorrow among them as it does among us. Here, now, there is not so much unhappiness for the moment, because the soldiers do no harm and they work as if they were in their own homes. You see, sir, among poor people it is necessary that they aid one another. These are the great traits which war develops."

Cornudet, indignant at the cordial relations between the conquerors and the conquered, preferred to shut himself up in the inn. Loiseau had a joke for the occasion: "They will repeople the land."

M. Carré-Lamadon had a serious word: "They try to make amends."

But they did not find the driver. Finally they discovered him in a café of the village, sitting at table fraternally with the officer of ordnance. The count called out to him:

"Were you not ordered to be ready at eight o'clock?"

"Well, yes; but another order has been given me since."

"By whom?"

"Faith! the Prussian commander."

"What was it?"

"Not to harness at all."

"Why?"

"I know nothing about it. Go and ask him. They tell me not to harness, and I don't harness. That's all."

"Did he give you the order himself?"

"No sir, the innkeeper gave the order for him."

"When was that?"

"Last evening, as I was going to bed."

The three men returned, much disturbed. They asked for M. Follenvie, but the servant answered that that gentleman, because of his asthma, never rose before ten o'clock. And he had given strict orders not to be wakened before that, except in case of fire.

They wished to see the officer, but that was absolutely impossible since, while he lodged at the inn, M. Follenvie alone was authorized to speak to him upon civil affairs. So they waited. The women went up to their rooms again and occupied themselves with futile tasks.

Cornudet installed himself near the great chimney in the kitchen, where there was a good fire burning. He ordered one of the little tables to be brought from the café, then a can of beer; he then drew out his pipe, which plays among democrats a part almost equal to his own, because in serving Cornudet it was serving its country. It was a superb pipe, an admirably colored meerschaum, as black as the teeth of its master, but perfumed, curved, glistening, easy to the hand, completing his physiognomy. And he remained motionless, his eyes as much fixed upon the flame of the fire as upon his favorite tipple and its frothy crown; and each time that he drank he passed his long thin fingers through his scanty gray hair with an air of satisfaction, after which he sucked in his mustache fringed with foam.

Loiseau, under the pretext of stretching his legs, went to place some wine among the retailers of the country. The count and the manufacturer began to talk politics. They could foresee the future of France. One of them believed in an Orléans, the other in some unknown savior for the country, a hero who would reveal himself when all were in despair: a Guesclin or a Joan of Arc, perhaps, or would it be another Napoleon First? Ah! if the Prince Imperial were not so young!

Cornudet listened to them and smiled like one who holds the word of destiny. His pipe perfumed the kitchen.

As ten o'clock struck M. Follenvie appeared. They asked him hurried questions, but he could only repeat two or three times, without variation, these words:

"The officer said to me: 'Monsieur Follenvie, you see to it that the carriage is not harnessed for those travelers tomorrow. I do not wish them to leave without my order. That is sufficient.' "

Then they wished to see the officer. The count sent him his card, on which M. Carré-Lamadon wrote his name and all his titles. The Prussian sent back word that he would meet the two gentlemen after he had breakfasted, that is to say, about one o'clock.

The ladies reappeared and ate a little something, despite their disquiet. Ball of Fat seemed ill and prodigiously troubled.

They were finishing their coffee when the word came that the officer was ready to meet the gentlemen. Loiseau joined them; but when they tried to enlist Cornudet, to give more solemnity to their proceedings, he declared proudly that he would have nothing to do with the Germans, and he betook himself to his chimney corner and ordered another liter of beer.

The three men mounted the staircase and were introduced to the best room of the inn, where the officer received them, stretched out in an armchair, his feet on the mantelpiece, smoking a long porcelain pipe and enveloped in a flamboyant dressing gown, appropriated, without doubt, from some dwelling belonging to a common citizen of bad taste. He did not rise nor greet them in any way, not even looking at them. It was a magnificent display of natural blackguardism transformed into the military victor.

At the expiration of some moments he asked: "What is it you wish?"

The count became spokesman: "We desire to go on our way, sir."

"No."

"May I ask the cause of this refusal?"

"Because I do not wish it."

"But I would respectfully observe to you, sir, that your general in chief gave us permission to go to Dieppe, and I know of nothing we have done to merit your severity."

"I do not wish it—that is all; you can go."

All three, having bowed, retired.

The afternoon was lamentable. They could not understand this caprice of the German, and the most singular ideas would come into their heads to trouble them.

Everybody stayed in the kitchen and discussed the situation endlessly, imagining all sorts of unlikely things. Perhaps they would be retained as hostages—but to what end?—or taken prisoners—or rather a considerable ransom might be demanded. At this thought a panic prevailed. The richest were the most frightened, already seeing themselves constrained to pay for their lives with sacks of gold poured into the hands of this insolent soldier. They racked their brains to think of some acceptable falsehoods to conceal their riches and make them pass themselves off for poor people, very poor people. Loiseau took off the chain to his watch and hid it away in his pocket. The falling night increased their apprehensions. The lamp was lighted and as there was still two hours before dinner, Mme. Loiseau proposed a game of thirty-one. It would be a diversion. They accepted. Cornudet himself having smoked out his pipe, took part for politeness.

The count shuffled the cards, dealt, and Ball of Fat had thirty-one at the outset; and immediately the interest was great enough to appease the fear that haunted their minds. Then Cornudet perceived that the house of Loiseau was given to tricks.

As they were going to the dinner table, M. Follenvie again appeared and in wheezing, rattling voice announced:

"The Prussian officer orders me to ask Miss Elizabeth Rousset if she has yet changed her mind."

Ball of Fat remained standing and was pale; then, suddenly becoming crimson, such a stifling anger took possession of her that she could not speak. But finally she flashed out: "You may say to the dirty beast, that idiot, that carrion of a Prussian, that I shall never change it; you understand, never, never, never!"

The great innkeeper went out. Then Ball of Fat was immediately surrounded, questioned and solicited by all to disclose the mystery of his visit. She resisted at first, but soon, becoming exasperated, she said: "What does he want? You really want to know what he wants? He wants to sleep with me."

Everybody was choked for words, and indignation was rife. Cornudet broke his glass, so violently did he bring his fist down upon the table. There was a clamor of censure against this ignoble soldier, a blast of anger, a union of all for resistance, as if a demand had been made on each one of the party for the sacrifice exacted of her. The count declared with disgust that those people conducted themselves after the fashion of the ancient barbarians. The women, especially, showed to Ball of Fat a most energetic and tender commiseration. The good sisters, who only showed themselves at mealtime, lowered their heads and said nothing.

They all dined, nevertheless, when the first furore had abated. But there was little conversation; they were thinking.

The ladies retired early, and the men, all smoking, organized a game at cards to which M. Follenvie was invited, as they intended to put a few casual questions to him on the subject of conquering the resistance of this officer. But he thought of nothing but the cards and, without listening or answering, would keep repeating: "To the game, sirs, to the game." His attention was so taken that he even forgot to expectorate, which must have put him some points to the good with the organ in his breast. His whistling lungs ran the whole asthmatic scale, from deep, profound tones to the sharp rustiness of a young cock essaying to crow.

He even refused to retire when his wife, who had fallen asleep previously, came to look for him. She went away alone, for she was an "early bird," always up with the sun, while her husband was a "night owl," always ready to pass the night with his friends. He cried out to her: "Leave my creamed chicken before the fire!" and then went on with his game. When they saw that they could get nothing from him they declared that it was time to stop, and each sought his bed.

They all rose rather early the next day, with an undefined hope of getting away, which desire the terror of passing another day in that horrible inn greatly increased.

Alas! the horses remained in the stable and the driver was invisible. For want of better employment they went out and walked around the carriage.

The breakfast was very doleful, and it became apparent that a coldness had arisen toward Ball of Fat and that the night, which brings counsel, had slightly modified their judgments. They almost wished now that the Prussian had secretly found this girl, in order to give her companions a pleasant surprise in the morning. What could be more simple? Besides, who would know anything about it? She could save appearances by telling the officer that she took pity on their distress. To her it would make so little difference!

No one had avowed these thoughts yet.

In the afternoon, as they were almost perishing from ennui, the count proposed that they take a walk around the village. Each wrapped up warmly and the little party set out, with the exception of Cornudet who preferred to remain near the fire, and the good sisters, who passed their time in the church or at the curate's.

The cold, growing more intense every day, cruelly pinched their noses and ears; their feet became so numb that each step was torture; and when they came to a field it seemed to them frightfully sad under this limitless white, so that everybody returned immediately, with hearts hard pressed and souls congealed.

The four women walked ahead, the three gentlemen followed just behind. Loiseau, who understood the situation, asked suddenly if they thought that girl there was going to keep them long in such a place as this. The count, always courteous, said that they could not exact from a woman a sacrifice so hard, unless it should come of her own will. M. Carré-Lamadon remarked that if the French made their return through Dieppe, as they were likely to, a battle would surely take place at Tôtes. This reflection made the two others anxious.

"If we could only get away on foot," said Loiseau.

The count shrugged his shoulders. "How can we think of it in this snow and with our wives?" he said. "And then we should be pursued and caught in ten minutes and led back prisoners at the mercy of these soldiers."

It was true, and they were silent.

The ladies talked of their clothes, but a certain constraint seemed to disunite them. Suddenly at the end of the street the officer appeared. His tall wasplike figure in uniform was outlined upon the horizon formed by the snow, and he was marching with knees apart, a gait particularly military, which is affected that they may not spot their carefully blackened boots.

He bowed in passing near the ladies and looked disdainfully at the men, who preserved their dignity by not seeing him, except Loiseau, who made a motion toward raising his hat.

Ball of Fat reddened to the ears, and the three married women resented the great humiliation of being thus met by this soldier in the company of this girl whom he had treated so cavalierly.

But they spoke of him, of his figure and his face. Mme. Carré-Lamadon, who had known many officers and considered herself a connoisseur of them, found this one not at all bad; she regretted even that he was not French, because he would make such a pretty hussar, one all the women would rave over.

Again in the house, no one knew what to do. Some sharp words, even, were said about things very insignificant. The dinner was silent, and almost immediately after it each one went to his room to kill time in sleep.

They descended the next morning with weary faces and exasperated hearts. The women scarcely spoke to Ball of Fat.

A bell began to ring. It was for a baptism. The fat girl had a child being brought up among the peasants of Yvetot. She had not seen it for a year or thought of it; but now the idea of a child being baptized threw into her heart a sudden and violent tenderness for her own, and she strongly wished to be present at the ceremony.

As soon as she was gone everybody looked at each other, then pulled their chairs together, for they thought that finally something should be decided upon. Loiseau had an inspiration: it was to hold Ball of Fat alone and let the others go.

M. Follenvie was charged with the commission but he returned almost immediately, for the German, who understood human nature, had put him out. He pretended that he would retain everybody so long as his desire was not satisfied.

Then the commonplace nature of Mme. Loiseau burst out with:

"Well, we are not going to stay here to die of old age. Since it is the trade of this creature to accommodate herself to all kinds, I fail to see how she has the right to refuse one more than another. I can tell you she has received all she could find in Rouen, even the coachmen! Yes, madame, the prefect's coachman! I know him very well, for he bought his wine at our house. And to think that today we should be drawn into this embarrassment by this affected woman, this minx! For my part, I find that this officer conducts himself very well. He has perhaps suffered privations for a long time, and doubtless he would have preferred us three; but no, he is contented with common property. He respects married women. And we must remember too that he is master. He has only to say 'I wish,' and he could take us by force with his soldiers."

The two women had a cold shiver. Pretty Mme. Carré-Lamadon's eyes grew brilliant and she became a little pale, as if she saw herself already taken by force by the officer.

The men met and discussed the situation. Loiseau, furious, was for delivering "the wretch" bound hand and foot to the enemy. But the count, descended through three generations of ambassadors and endowed with the temperament of a diplomatist, was the advocate of ingenuity.

"It is best to decide upon something," said he. Then they conspired.

The women kept together, the tone of their voices was lowered, each gave advice and the discussion was general. Everything was very harmonious. The ladies, especially, found delicate shades and charming subtleties of expression for saying the most unusual things. A stranger would have understood nothing, so great was the precaution of language observed. But the light edge of modesty with which every woman of the world is barbed only covers the surface; they blossom out in a scandalous adventure of this kind, being deeply amused and feeling themselves in their element, mixing love with sensuality as a greedy cook prepares supper for his master.

Even gaiety returned, so funny did the whole story seem to them at last. The count found some of the jokes a little off color, but they were so well told that he was forced to smile. In his turn Loiseau came out with some still bolder tales, and yet nobody was wounded. The brutal thought expressed by his wife dominated all minds: "Since it is her trade, why should she refuse this one more than another?"

The genteel Mme. Carré-Lamadon seemed to think that in her place she would refuse this one less than some others.

They prepared the blockade at length, as if they were about to surround a fortress. Each took some role to play, some arguments he would bring to bear, some maneuvers that he would endeavor to put into execution. They decided on the plan of attack, the ruse to employ, the surprise of assault that should force this living citadel to receive the enemy in her room.

Cornudet remained apart from the rest and was a stranger to the whole affair.

So entirely were their minds distracted that they did not hear Ball of Fat enter. The count uttered a light "Ssh!" which turned all eyes in her direction. There she was. The abrupt silence and a certain embarrassment hindered them from speaking to her at first. The countess, more accustomed to the duplicity of society than the others, finally inquired:

"Was it very amusing, that baptism?"

The fat girl, filled with emotion, told them all about it: the faces, the attitudes and even the appearance of the church. She added: "It is good to pray sometimes."

And up to the time for luncheon these ladies continued to be amiable toward her in order to increase her docility and her confidence in their counsel. At the table they commenced the approach. This was in the shape of a vague conversation upon devotion. They cited ancient examples: Judith and Holophernes, then, without reason, Lucrece and Sextus, and Cleopatra obliging all the generals of the enemy to pass by her couch and reducing them in servility to slaves. Then they brought out a fantastic story, hatched in the imagination of these ignorant millionaires, where the women of Rome went to Capua for the purpose of lulling Hannibal to sleep in their arms and his lieutenants and phalanxes of mercenaries as well. They cited all the women who have been taken by conquering armies, making a battlefield of their bodies, making them also a weapon and a means of success: and all those hideous and detestable beings who have conquered by their heroic caresses and sacrificed their chastity to vengeance or a beloved cause. They even spoke in veiled terms of that great English family which allowed one of its women to be inoculated with a horrible and contagious disease in order to transmit it to Bonaparte, who was miraculously saved by a sudden illness at the hour of the fatal rendezvous.

And all this was related in an agreeable, temperate fashion, except as it was enlivened by the enthusiasm deemed proper to excite emulation.

One might finally have believed that the sole duty of woman here below was a sacrifice of her person and a continual abandonment to soldierly caprices.

The two good sisters seemed not to hear, lost as they were in profound thought. Ball of Fat said nothing.

During the whole afternoon they let her reflect. But in the place of calling her "Madame," as they had up to this time, they simply called her "Mademoiselle" without knowing exactly why, as if they had a desire to put her down a degree in their esteem, which she had taken by storm, and make her feel her shameful situation.

The moment supper was served M. Follenvie appeared with his old phrase: "The Prussian officer orders me to ask if Miss Elizabeth Rousset has yet changed her mind."

Ball of Fat responded dryly: "No, sir."

But at dinner the coalition weakened. Loiseau made three unhappy remarks.

Each one beat his wits for new examples but found nothing; then the countess, without premeditation, perhaps feeling some vague need of rendering homage to religion, asked the elder of the good sisters to tell them some great deeds in the lives of the saints. It appeared that many of their acts would have been considered crimes in our eyes, but the Church gave absolution of them readily, since they were done for the glory of God or for the good of all. It was a powerful argument; the countess made the most of it.

Thus it may be by one of those tacit understandings, or the veiled complacency in which anyone who wears the ecclesiastical garb excels, it may be simply from the effect of a happy unintelligence, a helpful stupidity, but in fact the religious sister lent a formidable support to the conspiracy. They had thought her timid, but she showed herself courageous, verbose, even violent. She was not troubled by the chatter of the casuist; her doctrine seemed a bar of iron; her faith never hesitated; her conscience had no scruples. She found the sacrifice of Abraham perfectly simple, for she would immediately kill father or mother on an order from on high. And nothing, in her opinion, could displease the Lord if the intention was laudable. The countess put to use the authority of her unwitting accomplice and added to it the edifying paraphrase and axiom of Jesuit morals: "The need justifies the means."

Then she asked her: "Then, my sister, do you think that God accepts intentions and pardons the deed when the motive is pure?"

"Who could doubt it, madame? An action blamable in itself often becomes meritorious by the thought it springs from."

And they continued thus, unraveling the will of God, foreseeing his decisions, making themselves interested in things that, in truth, they would never think of noticing. All this was guarded, skillful, discreet. But each word of the saintly sister in a cap helped to break down the resistance of the unworthy courtesan. Then the conversation changed a little, the woman of the chaplet speaking of the houses of her order, of her Superior, of herself, of her dainty neighbor, the dear sister Saint Nicephore. They had been called to the hospitals of Havre to care for the hundreds of soldiers stricken with smallpox. They depicted these miserable creatures, giving details of the malady. And while they were stopped, en route, by the caprice of this Prussian officer, a great number of Frenchmen might die whom perhaps they could have saved! It was a specialty with her, caring for soldiers. She had been in Crimea, in Italy, in Austria, and in telling of her campaigns she revealed herself as one of those religious aids to drums and trumpets who seem made to follow camps, pick up the wonded in the thick of battle and, better than an officer, subdue with a word great bands of undisciplined recruits. A true good sister of the rataplan, whose ravaged face, marked with innumerable scars, appeared the image of the devastation of war.

No one could speak after her, so excellent seemed the effect of her words.

As soon as the repast was ended they quickly went up to their rooms, with the purpose of not coming down the next day until late in the morning.

The luncheon was quiet. They had given the grain of seed time to germinate and bear fruit. The countess proposed that they take a walk in the afternoon. The count, being agreeably inclined, gave an arm to Ball of Fat and walked behind the others with her. He talked to her in a familiar, paternal tone, a little disdainful, after the manner of men having girls in their employ, calling her "my dear child," from the height of his social position, of his undisputed honor. He reached the vital part of the question at once:

"Then you prefer to leave us here, exposed to the violences which follow a defeat, rather than consent to a favor which you have so often given in your life?"

Ball of Fat answered nothing.

Then he tried to reach her through gentleness, reason, and then the sentiments. He knew how to remain "the count," even while showing himself gallant or complimentary or very amiable if it became necessary. He exalted the service that she would render them and spoke of his appreciation, then suddenly became gaily familiar and said:

"And you know, my dear, it would be something for him to boast of that he had known a pretty girl; something it is difficult to find in his country."

Ball of Fat did not answer but joined the rest of the party. As soon as they entered the house she went to her room and did not appear again. The disquiet was extreme. What were they to do? If she continued to resist, what an embarrassment!

The dinner hour struck. They waited in vain. M. Follenvie finally entered and said that Miss Rousset was indisposed and would not be at the table. Everybody pricked up his ears. The count went to the innkeeper and said in a low voice:

"Is he in there?"

"Yes."

For convenience he said nothing to his companions but made a slight sign with his head. Immediately a great sigh of relief went up from every breast and a light appeared in their faces. Loiseau cried out:

"Holy Christopher! *I* pay for the champagne, if there is any to be found in the establishment." And Mme. Loiseau was pained to see the proprietor return with four quart bottles in his hands.

Each one had suddenly become communicative and buoyant. A wanton joy filled their hearts. The count suddenly perceived that Mme. Carré-Lamadon was charming, the manufacturer paid compliments to the countess. The conversation was lively, gay, full of touches.

Suddenly Loiseau, with anxious face and hand upraised, called out: "Silence!" Everybody was silent, surprised, already frightened. Then he listened intently and said: "S-s-sh!" his two eyes and his hands raised toward the ceiling, listening, and then continuing in his natural voice: "All right! All goes well!"

They failed to comprehend at first, but soon all laughed. At the end of a quarter of an hour he began the same farce again, renewing it occasionally during the whole afternoon. And he pretended to call to someone in the story above, giving him advice in a double meaning, drawn from the fountainhead—the mind of a commercial traveler. For some moments he would assume a sad air, breathing in a whisper: "Poor girl!" Then he would murmur between his teeth, with an appearance of rage: "Ugh! That scamp of a Prussian." Sometimes, at a moment when no more was thought about it, he would say in an affected voice, many times over: "Enough! enough!" and add, as if speaking to himself: "If we could only see her again; it isn't necessary that he should kill her, the wretch!"

Although these jokes were in deplorable taste they amused all and wounded no one, for indignation, like other things, depends upon its surroundings, and the atmosphere which had been gradually created around them was charged with sensual thoughts.

At the dessert the women themselves made some delicate and discreet allusions. Their eyes glistened; they had drunk much. The count, who preserved even in his flights his grand appearance of gravity, made a comparison, much relished, upon the subject of those wintering at the Pole, and the joy of shipwrecked sailors who saw an opening toward the south.

Loiseau suddenly arose, a glass of champagne in his hand, and said: "I drink to our deliverance." Everybody was on his feet; they shouted in agreement. Even the two good sisters consented to touch their lips to the froth of the wine which they had never before tasted. They declared that it tasted like charged lemonade, only much nicer.

Loiseau resumed: "It is unfortunate that we have no piano, for we might make up a quadrille."

Cornudet had not said a word nor made a gesture; he appeared plunged in very grave thoughts and made sometimes a furious motion, so that his great beard seemed to wish to free itself. Finally, toward midnight, as they were separating, Loiseau, who was staggering, touched him suddenly on the stomach and said to him in a stammer: "You are not very funny this evening; you have said nothing, citizen!" Then Cornudet raised his head brusquely and, casting a brilliant, terrible glance around the company, said: "I tell you all that you have been guilty of infamy!" He rose, went to the door and again repeated: "Infamy, I say!" and disappeared.

This made a coldness at first. Loiseau, interlocutor, was stupefied; but he recovered immediately and laughed heartily as he said: "He is very green, my friends. He is very green." And then, as they did not comprehend, he told them about the "mysteries of the corridor." Then there was a return of gaiety. The women behaved like lunatics. The count and M. Carré-Lamadon wept from the force of their laughter. They could not believe it.

"How is that? Are you sure?"

"I tell you I saw it."

"And she refused——"

"Yes, because the Prussian officer was in the next room."

"Impossible!"

"I swear it!"

The count was stifled with laughter. The industrial gentleman held his sides with both hands. Loiseau continued:

"And now you understand why he saw nothing funny this evening! No, nothing at all!" And the three started out half ill, suffocated.

They separated. But Mme. Loiseau, who was of a spiteful nature, remarked to her husband as they were getting into bed that "that grisette" of a little Carré-Lamadon was yellow with envy all the evening. "You know," she continued, "how some women will take to a uniform, whether it be French or Prussian. It is all the same to them. Oh, what a pity!"

And all night, in the darkness of the corridor, there were to be heard light noises like whisperings and walking in bare feet and imperceptible creakings. They did not go to sleep until late, that is sure, for there were threads of light shining under the doors for a long time. The champagne had its effect; they say it troubles sleep.

The next day a clear winter's sun made the snow very brilliant. The diligence, already harnessed, waited before the door while an army of white pigeons, in their thick plumage, with rose-colored eyes with a black spot in the center, walked up and down gravely among the legs of the six horses, seeking their livelihood in the manure there scattered.

The driver, enveloped in his sheepskin, had a lighted pipe under the seat, and all the travelers, radiant, were rapidly packing some provisions for the rest of the journey. They were only waiting for Ball of Fat. Finally she appeared.

She seemed a little troubled, ashamed. And she advanced timidly toward her companions, who all, with one motion, turned as if they had not seen her. The count, with dignity, took the arm of his wife and removed her from this impure contact.

The fat girl stopped, half stupefied; then, plucking up courage, she approached the manufacturer's wife with "Good morning, madame," humbly murmured. The lady made a slight bow of the head which she accompanied with a look of outraged virtue. Everybody seemed busy and kept themselves as far from her as if she had had some infectious disease in her skirts. Then they hurried into the carriage, where she came last, alone, and where she took the place she had occupied during the first part of the journey.

They seemed not to see her or know her; although Mme. Loiseau, looking at her from afar, said to her husband in a half tone: "Happily, I don't have to sit beside her."

The heavy carriage began to move, and the remainder of the journey commenced. No one spoke at first. Ball of Fat dared not raise her eyes. She felt indignant toward all her neighbors and at the same time humiliated at having yielded to the foul kisses of this Prussian into whose arms they had hypocritically thrown her.

Then the countess, turning toward Mme. Carré-Lamadon, broke the difficult silence:

"I believe you know Madame d'Etrelles?"

"Yes, she is one of my friends."

"What a charming woman!"

"Delightful! A very gentle nature and well educated besides; then she is an artist to the tips of her fingers, sings beautifully and draws to perfection."

The manufacturer chatted with the count, and in the midst of the rattling of the glass an occasional word escaped such as "coupon—premium—limit—expiration."

Loiseau, who had pilfered the old pack of cards from the inn, greasy through five years of contact with tables badly cleaned, began a game of bezique with his wife.

The good sisters took from their belt the long rosary which hung there, made together the sign of the cross and suddenly began to move their lips in a lively murmur, as if they were going through the whole of the "Oremus." And from time to time they kissed a medal, made the sign anew, then recommenced their muttering, which was rapid and continued.

Cornudet sat motionless, thinking.

At the end of three hours on the way, Loiseau put up the cards and said: "I am hungry."

His wife drew out a package from whence she brought a piece of cold veal. She cut it evenly in thin pieces and they both began to eat.

"Suppose we do the same," said the countess.

They consented to it and she undid the provisions prepared for the two couples. It was in one of those dishes whose lid is decorated with a china hare to signify that a *pâté* of hare is inside, a succulent dish of pork, where white rivers of lard cross the brown flesh of the game, mixed with some other viands hashed fine. A beautiful square of Gruyère cheese, wrapped in a piece of newspaper, preserved the imprint "divers things" upon the unctuous plate.

The two good sisters unrolled a big sausage which smelled of garlic, and Cornudet plunged his two hands into the vast pockets of his overcoat at the same time and drew out four hard eggs and a piece of bread. He removed the shells and threw them in the straw under his feet; then he began to eat the eggs, letting fall on his vast beard some bits of clear yellow which looked like stars caught there.

Ball of Fat, in the haste and distraction of her rising, had not thought of anything; and she looked at them exasperated, suffocating with rage at all of them eating so placidly. A tumultuous anger swept over her at first, and she opened her mouth to cry out at them, to hurl at them a flood of injury which mounted to her lips; but she could not speak, her exasperation strangled her.

No one looked at her or thought of her. She felt herself drowned in the scorn of these honest scoundrels who had first sacrificed her and then rejected her, like some improper or useless article. She thought of her great basketful of good things they had greedily devoured, of her two chickens shining with jelly, of her *pâtés*, her pears and the four bottles of Bordeaux; and her fury suddenly falling, as a cord drawn too tightly breaks, she felt ready to weep. She made terrible efforts to prevent it, making ugly faces, swallowing her sobs as children do; but the tears came and glistened in the corners of her eyes, and then two great drops, detaching themselves from the rest, rolled slowly down like little streams of water that filter through rock and, falling regularly, rebounded upon her breast. She sits erect, her eyes fixed, her face rigid and pale, hoping that no one will notice her.

But the countess perceives her and tells her husband by a sign. He shrugs his shoulders, as much as to say:

"What would you have me do? It is not my fault."

Mme. Loiseau indulged in a mute laugh of triumph and murmured:

"She weeps for shame."

The two good sisters began to pray again, after having wrapped in a paper the remainder of their sausage.

Then Cornudet, who was digesting his eggs, extended his legs to the seat opposite, crossed them, folded his arms, smiled like a man who is watching a good farce and began to whistle the "Marseillaise."

All faces grew dark. The popular song assuredly did not please his neighbors. They became nervous and agitated, having an appearance of wishing to howl, like dogs when they hear a barbarous organ. He perceived this but did not stop. Sometimes he would hum the words:

> "Sacred love of country
> Help, sustain th' avenging arm;
> Liberty, sweet Liberty,
> Ever fight, with no alarm."

They traveled fast, the snow being harder. But as far as Dieppe, during the long sad hours of the journey, across the jolts in the road, through the falling night, in the profound darkness of the carriage, he continued his vengeful, monotonous whistling with a ferocious obstinacy, constraining his neighbors to follow the song from one end to the other and to recall the words that belonged to each measure.

And Ball of Fat wept continually, and sometimes a sob, which she was not able to restrain, echoed between the two rows of people in the shadows.

THE SECRET

The little Baroness de Grangerie was drowsing on her couch, when the little Marquise of Rennedon entered abruptly, looking very disturbed, her bodice a little rumpled, her hat a little on one side, and dropped into a chair, exclaiming:

"Ouf, I've done it!"

Her friend, who had never seen her anything but placid and gentle, sat bolt upright in amazement. She demanded:

"What is it? What have you done?"

The marchioness, who did not seem able to remain in one place, got to her feet, and began to walk about the room; then she flung herself on the foot of the couch where her friend was resting and, taking her hands, said:

"Listen, darling, promise me never to repeat what I am going to tell you."

"I promise."

"On your immortal soul."

"On my immortal soul."

"Well, I have just revenged myself on Simon."

The other woman exclaimed:

"Oh, you've done right!"

"Yes, haven't I? Just think, during the past six months he has become more intolerable than ever, beyond words intolerable. When I married him, I knew well enough how ugly he was, but I thought that he was a kindly man. What a mistake I made! He must certainly have thought that I loved him for himself, with his fat paunch and his red nose, for he began to coo like a turtledove. You can imagine that it made me laugh, I nicknamed him 'Pigeon' for it. Men really do have the oddest notions about themselves. When he realized that I felt no more than friendship for him, he became suspicious, he began to speak bitterly to me, to treat me as if I were a coquette or a fast woman, or I don't know what. And then it became more serious because of . . . of . . . it's not very easy to put it into words. . . . In short, he was very much in love with me, very much in love . . . and he proved it to me often, far too often. Oh, my dearest, what torture it is to be . . . made love to by a clown of a man! . . . No, really, I couldn't bear it any longer . . . not any longer at all . . . it is just like having a tooth pulled every evening . . . much worse than that, much worse. Well, imagine among your acquaintances someone very ugly, very ridiculous, very repellent, with a fat paunch—that's the frightful part—and great hairy calves. You can just imagine him, can't you? Now imagine that this someone is your husband . . . and that . . . every evening . . . you understand. No, its loathsome! . . . loathsome! It made me sick, positively sick . . . sick in my basin. Really, I can't bear it any longer. There ought to be a law to protect wives in such cases. Just imagine it yourself, every evening! . . . Pah, it's beastly!

"It's not that I have been dreaming of romantic love affairs—not ever. There aren't any nowadays. All the men in our world are like stableboys or bankers; they care for nothing but horses or money; and if they love women, they love them only as they love horses, just to display them in their drawing rooms as they show off a pair of chestnuts in the Bois. Nothing else. Life today is such that romantic feelings can play no part.

"We should show ourselves merely as matter-of-fact and unemotional women. Intercourse is now no more than meetings at stated times, at which the same thing is always repeated. Besides, for whom could one feel any affection or tenderness? Men, our men, are generally speaking only correct tailor's dummies altogether wanting in intelligence and sensibility. If we look for any intellectual graces, like a person looking for water in a desert, we call the artists to our side; and we behold the arrival of intolerable *poseurs* or underbred Bohemians. As for me, like Diogenes I have been looking for a man, one real man in the whole of Parisian society; but I am already quite convinced that I shall not find him, and it will not be long before I blow out my lantern. To return to my husband, since it fairly turned my stomach to see him coming into my room in his shirt and drawers, I used all means, all, you understand me, to alienate him and to . . . disgust him with me. At first he was furious, and then he became jealous, he imagined that I was deceiving him. In the early days he contented himself with watching me. He glared like a tiger at all the men who came to the house, and then the persecution began. He followed me everywhere. He used abominable means to take me off guard. Then he never left me alone to talk with anyone. At all the balls, he remained planted behind me, poking out his clumsy hound's head as soon as I said a word. He followed me to the buffet, forbidding me to dance with this man and that man, taking me away in the very middle of the cotillion, making me look foolish and ridiculous and appear I don't know what sort of a person. It was after this that I ceased to go anywhere.

"In this intimacy, he became worse still. Would you believe that the wretch treated me as . . . as . . . I daren't say it . . . as a harlot.

"My dear! . . . he said to me one evening: 'Whose bed have you been sharing today?' I wept, and he was delighted.

"And then he became worse still. The other week he took me to dine in the Champs Elysées. Fate ordained that Baubiguac should be at the neighboring table. Then, if you please, Simon began to tread furiously on my feet and growl at me over the melon: 'You have given him a rendezvous, you slut! Just you wait!' Then—you could never guess what he did, my dear—he had the audacity to pull my hatpin gently out and he drove it into my arm. I uttered a loud cry. Everybody came running up. Then he staged a detestable comedy of mortification. You can imagine it.

"At that very moment I said to myself: 'I'll have my revenge, and before very long, too.' What would you have done?"

"Oh, I would have revenged myself!"

"Very well, that's what I've done to him."

"How?"

"What! Don't you understand?"

"But, my dear . . . still . . . well, yes."

"Yes, what? Gracious, just think of his head! Can't you just see him, with his fat face, his red nose, and his side whiskers hanging down like dog's ears."

"Yes."

"Well, I said to myself: 'I shall revenge myself for my own pleasure and Marie's,' for I always intended to tell you, but never anyone but you, mind. Just think of his face and then remember that he . . . that he . . . he is . . ."

"What . . . you've . . ."

"Oh, darling, never, never tell a soul, promise me again! But think how funny it is . . . think. . . . He has looked quite different to me since that very moment . . . and I burst out laughing all alone . . . all alone. . . . Just think of his head."

The baroness looked at her friend, and the wild laughter that welled up in her breast burst between her lips; she began to laugh, but she laughed as if she were hysterical, and with both hands pressed to her breast, her face puckered up, her breath strangled in her throat, she leaned forward as if she would fall over on her face.

Then the little marquise herself gave way to a stifling outburst of mirth. Between two cascades of little cries she repeated:

"Think . . . do think . . . isn't it funny? Tell me . . . think of his head . . . think of his side whiskers! . . . of his nose . . . just think . . . isn't it funny? but whatever you do, don't tell anyone . . . don't . . . tell . . . about it . . . ever!"

They continued for some minutes very nearly suffocated, unable to speak, weeping real tears in their ecstasy of amusement.

The baroness was the first to recover her self-control, and still shaking:

"Oh! . . . tell me how you did it . . . tell me . . . it's so funny . . . so funny!"

But the other woman could not speak . . . she stammered:

"When I had made up my mind . . . I said to myself: . . . 'Now . . . hurry up . . . you must make it happen at once.' . . . And I . . . did it . . . today . . ."

"Today!"

"Yes . . . right at once . . . and I told Simon to come and look for me at your house for our especial amusement . . . He's coming . . . at once . . . he's coming. . . . Just think . . . think . . . think of his head when you see him. . . ."

The baroness, a little sobered, panted as if she had just finished running a race. She answered:

"Oh, tell me how you did it . . . tell me."

"It was quite easy. I said to myself: 'He is jealous of Baubiguac; very well, Baubiguac it shall be. He is as clumsy as his feet, but quite honorable; incapable of gossiping.' Then I went to his house, after breakfast."

"You went to his house. On what excuse?"

"A collection . . . for orphans . . ."

"Tell me the whole tale . . . quickly . . . tell me the whole tale. . . ."

"He was so astounded to see me that he could not speak. And then he gave me two louis for my collection, and then as I got up to go away, he asked news of my husband; then I pretended to be unable to contain my feelings any longer, and I told him everything that was on my mind. I painted him even blacker than he is, look you. . . . Then Baubiguac was very touched, he began to think of ways in which he might help me . . . and as for me, I began to cry . . . but I cried as a woman cries . . . when she is crying on purpose. . . . He comforted me . . . he made me sit down . . . and then, as I didn't stop, he put his arm round me. . . . I said: 'Oh, my poor friend . . . my poor friend!' He repeated: 'My poor friend, my poor friend!' and he went on embracing me . . . all the time . . . until we reached the closest embrace of all. . . . There.

"When it was over, I made a terrible display of despair and reproaches. Oh, I treated him, I treated him as if he were the lowest of the low. . . . But I wanted to burst out laughing madly. I thought of Simon, of his head, of his side whiskers. Imagine it . . . just imagine it! I've done it to him. Even if he comes in this minute, I've done it to him. And he was so afraid of it happening. Come wars, earthquakes, epidemics, even if we all die . . . I've done it to him. Nothing can ever prevent it now! Think of his head . . . and say to yourself that I've done it to him!"

The baroness, who was almost choking to death, demanded:

"Shall you see Baubiguac again?"

"No, never. Certainly not. . . . I've had enough of him . . . he's no more desirable than my husband."

And they both began to laugh again so violently that they reeled like epileptics.

The ringing of a bell silenced their mirth.

The baroness murmured:

"It's he . . . look closely at him."

The door opened, and a stout man appeared, a ruddy-faced man with thick lips and drooping side whiskers; he rolled incensed eyes.

The two young women regarded him for a moment; then they flung themselves wildly down on the couch, in such a delirium of laughter that they groaned as if they were in the most dreadful agony.

And he repeated in a stupefied voice:

"Upon my word, are you mad? . . . are you mad? . . . are you mad?"

THE SHEPHERD'S LEAP

From Dieppe to Le Havre the coast seems like a single unbroken cliff some three hundred feet high and straight as a wall. From spot to spot this enormous mass of white rock suddenly dips and forms a tiny narrow valley of precipitous slopes covered with stubby grass and furze. This valley starts at the cultivated plateau and goes down to a pebbly beach where it resembles a shallow river bed. Nature created these valleys, torrential rains transformed them into river beds whittling away at the cliffs, boring to the very sea these ravines which serve men as passageways.

And sometimes a village is nestled in these valleys into which sweep the sea winds.

I spent the summer in one of these indentations of the coast. The peasant house where I stayed, oriented as it was towards the sea, permitted me to see from my window a great triangle of blue water framed by the green slopes of the valley and occasionally flecked by the white sails passing in the distance, spotlighted by the sun.

The road leading to the shore followed the bed of the ravine and, suddenly plunging down between two walls of marl, became a kind of deep rut before reaching a fine bed of pebbles, rolled, pounded, and polished by the waves through the ages.

This embanked passage is called "The Shepherd's Leap."

Here is the tragedy which gave it its name.

It is related that this village was once governed by an austere young priest. He had completed his seminary studies full of hatred for those who live according to natural laws rather than those of his God. Inflexibly severe toward himself, he was altogether intransigent toward others. One thing in particular roused his anger and disgust—love. Had he lived in the city in the midst of civilized and refined beings who conceal behind tenuous veils of sentiment and tenderness the brutal acts which nature inspires, had he heard in confession in the shadows of beautiful naves the perfumed sinners whose failings seem attenuated by the elegance of their fall and by the apparent idealism of an earthly kiss, he might not have been seized by the violent reactions, the excessive rages he felt at the sight of love-making in country ditches or on straw-covered floors of stables.

He considered them no better than animals, these people who had no notion whatever of love and who copulated like beasts. So he detested them for the vulgarity of their souls, for the revolting servitude of their instincts, for the disgusting gaiety of the older ones whenever they mentioned these filthy pleasures.

He was also no doubt tortured, in spite of himself, by the anguish of his own unappeased appetites, and unconsciously exhausted by the struggle between his rebellious flesh and his despotic and chaste spirit.

But everything relating to the flesh revolted him, put him beside himself; and his violent sermons, full of angry threats and allusions, brought sly smiles to the girls and boys who glanced at each other meaningfully across the width of the church; while the farmers in blue blouses, and their wives in black wraps, said to each other as they left church on their way toward their hovels, "He certainly doesn't joke about it, does he?"

Once, over practically nothing, he flew into a temper to the point of losing his senses. He had gone to make a sick call. No sooner had he entered the courtyard of the farm than he noticed a group of youngsters of the family and the neighborhood huddled around the doghouse. They were looking at something with great curiosity, breathless, with concentrated and silent attention. The priest joined them. It was the bitch in labor. In front of its house five puppies snuggled around their mother, who was licking them tenderly. And at the very moment when the priest looked over the children's heads, a sixth tiny whelp was born. Whereupon all the children, overcome with joy, began to shout and clap, "Another! Another!" It was a game for them, a natural game in which there was nothing impure. They looked upon this birth as if they were looking at apples falling from a tree. But the man in the black robe was convulsed with disgust. He lost his head, and with his enormous umbrella he began to strike the children, who ran off as fast as their small legs would carry them. Then, left alone in front of the bitch in labor, he struck her again and again. She could not run away, being attached, and as she squirmed and yelped pitifully, he jumped on her, crushing her under his boots, forcing the birth of a last puppy, and finishing her off with vicious kicks. He left the bloody body in the midst of the newborn, whimpering and clumsily seeking their mother's nipples.

He would take long walks, striding savagely, alone.

One May evening, as he was returning from a long walk along the cliff top, he was caught in a heavy downpour. Not a house in sight, everywhere the bare coast, tattooed by the heavy rainfall.

The rough sea tossed its foam high, and the enormous dark clouds rushed over the horizon, intensifying the downpour. The wind whistled, roared, flattened the new crops and shook the dripping priest, moulded the cassock to his legs, filling his ears with din and his excitable spirit with frenzy.

He removed his hat, lifting his forehead to the storm, and little by little he was approaching the declivity leading to the village. But at that moment such a blast struck him that he was stopped short, and suddenly he noticed near a sheep-fold the portable, wheeled cabin of a shepherd.

It was a shelter, and he rushed to it.

The dogs, lashed by the storm, did not stir; and he reached the wooden cabin, a sort of doghouse perched on wheels, which shepherds move from pasture to pasture in the summer.

Above a stool the door was ajar, revealing the straw inside.

The priest was about to go in when he noticed in the obscurity a couple of lovers embracing. He slammed the door and fastened the latch; then, hitching himself to the shafts, bending his spare frame, pulling like a horse, and heaving under his soaked robes, he ran toward the steep slope, the perilous slope, dragging the young couple startled in their embrace, who beat the door with their fists, thinking it was only someone's idea of a practical joke.

When he had reached the crest of the hill, he let go of the fragile cabin, which began to roll down the slope.

It went down, gaining momentum furiously, bouncing, staggering wildly, its shafts tilting the ground on its mad course.

An old tramp from his refuge in a ditch saw it go by in a flash over his head. Frightful screams came from the wooden box.

Suddenly one of its wheels broke loose, the cabin turned over on its side and began to roll down like a ball, the way a house loosened from its foundations would careen from a mountaintop. Then, reaching the edge of the last gully, it hurtled out in an arc, and, striking the bottom, it smashed into bits like an eggshell.

The lovers were picked up, both of them crushed—ground, rather—but still clinging to each other, in terror as in pleasure.

The priest would not allow the bodies inside his church, nor would he conduct services for them.

And on the following Sunday, from the pulpit, he spoke vehemently on the Seventh Commandment, threatening lovers with a mysterious vengeance and citing the frightful example of the poor couple struck down in their sin.

As he was leaving the church, two constables placed him under arrest.

A customs guard had witnessed the whole drama from a hide-out. He was sentenced to forced labor.

The peasant who told me this tale added gravely, "I knew him, monsieur. He was quite a man, but there certainly was no fooling with him."

MOUCHE

A BOATING MAN'S REMINISCENCE

He said to us:

"What queer things and queer women I have seen in those long-ago days when I used to go on the river! Many a time I have longed to write a little book, called *On the Seine*, describing the athletic carefree life, gay and penniless, a vigorous, roistering holiday life, that I led between twenty and thirty.

"I was a penniless clerk: now I am a successful man who can throw away vast sums of money to gratify a moment's whim. I had a thousand modest unattainable desires in my heart, which gilded my whole existence with all the imaginary hopes in the world. Today, I don't really know what fancy could make me rise from the armchair where I sit nodding. How simple and pleasant, and difficult, it is to live so, between an office in Paris and the river at Argenteuil! For ten years, my great, my only, my absorbing passion was the Seine. Oh, the lovely, calm, varied, and stinking river, filled with mirage and all uncleanliness! I think I loved it so much because it did, it seems to me, give me a sense of life. Oh, the strolls along the flowery banks, my friends the frogs dreaming on a water-lily leaf, their stomachs in the cool, and the frail coquettish water lilies in the middle of tall tinegrasses that all at once, behind a willow, opened to my eyes a leaf from a Japanese album as a kingfisher darted past me like a blue flame. I loved it all, with an instinctive sight-born love that spread through my body in a deep natural joy.

"As others cherish the memories of tender nights, I cherish memories of sunrises on misty mornings, floating wandering vapors, white as the dead before dawn; then, a first ray gliding over the meadows, lit with a rosy light that took the heart with gladness; and I cherish memories of a moon that silvered the quivering running water, of a glimmering radiance where all dreams came to life.

"And all that, symbol of the eternal illusion, was born, for me, from the foul water that drifted all the sewage of Paris down to the sea.

"And what a gay life I and the other boys led! There were five of us, a little circle of friends, serious-minded men today; and as we were all poor, we had founded in a frightful pothouse at Argenteuil an indescribable colony that possessed nothing but a dormitory bedroom where I have spent what were certainly the maddest evenings of my life. We cared for nothing but amusing ourselves and rowing, for we all, with no exception, looked upon rowing as a religion. I remember such singular adventures, such incredible jests invented by those five vagabonds, that no one could believe them today. You never get anything like it now, even on the Seine, for the whimsical madness that kept us brimful of life has died out of the modern spirit.

"We five owned one boat between us, bought with immense effort, and over which we have laughed as we shall never laugh again. It was a big yawl, rather heavy, but solid, roomy, and comfortable. I won't describe my comrades to you. There was one small, very mischievous fellow, nicknamed Petit Bleu; a tall fellow, of uncivilized appearance, with gray eyes and black hair, nicknamed Tomahawk; another, an indolent witty fellow nicknamed La Toque, the only one who never touched an oar, on the excuse that he would capsize the boat; a thin, elegant, very well-groomed young man nicknamed N'a-qu'un-Œil, in memory of a just-published novel by Claudel, and because he wore a monocle; and myself, Joseph Prunier by name. We lived in perfect harmony, our sole regret being that we had not a helmswoman. One woman is indispensable in a river boat. Indispensable because she keeps wits and hearts awake, because she livens, amuses, distracts, sets an edge to life, and produces a decorative effect, with a red sunshade gliding past the green banks. But we did not want an ordinary woman coxswain, we five who were like no one else in the world. We had to have something unexpected, uncommon, ready for anything, almost unfindable, in fact. We had tried several without success—girls at the helm, not helmswomen, idiotic river girls who always preferred the thin wine that went to their heads to the running water that bore the yawls. You kept them one Sunday then dismissed them in disgust.

"But one Saturday evening, N'a-qu'un-Œil brought us a little slender creature, lively, quick on her feet, loose-tongued and full of japes, the japes that pass for wit among the jackanapes, male and female, hatched on the sidewalks of Paris. She was pleasant-looking, not pretty; a mere sketch of a woman that had got no farther, one of those silhouettes that draughtsmen pencil in three strokes on a napkin in a restaurant after dinner, between a glass of brandy and a cigarette. Nature makes them like that sometimes.

"The first evening, she astonished and amused us, and was so unexpected in her ways that we could come to no conclusion about her. Dropped into this nest of men, who were ready for any mad prank, she quickly made herself mistress of the situation, and with the next day she had made a complete conquest of us.

"She was, moreover, quite crazy, born with a glass of absinthe in her stomach that her mother had drunk when she was brought to bed, and she had never been overcome by drink since, for her nurse, she said, enriched her blood with draughts of rum; and she herself never called all the bottles ranged behind the wine merchant's counter by any other name than 'my holy family.'

"I don't know which of us christened her 'Mouche,' nor why this name was given her, but it suited her very well, and stuck to her. And our yawl, which was called *Feuille-à-l'Envers*, bore on the Seine every week, between Asnières and Maisons-Lafitte, five youngsters, happy and healthy, ruled from under a painted paper parasol by a lively madcap young person who treated us as if we were slaves whose duty was to take her on the river, and whom we adored.

"We adored her, to begin with, for a thousand reasons, and afterwards for only one. She was a sort of little mill of talk in the stern of our craft, chattering to the wind that slipped over the water. She babbled endlessly, with the light continuous sound of those mechanical wings that turn in the breeze; and she said heedlessly the most unexpected, the most ridiculous, and the most amazing things. In her mind, all the parts of which seemed disparate like rags of all kinds and colors, not sewn together but only tacked, you got the whimsical imagination of a fairy tale, spiced wit, wantonness, impudence, things unexpected and things comical, and air—air and scenery like traveling in a balloon.

"We used to ask her questions to provoke answers found goodness knows where. The one with which we most often worried her was this:

" 'Why are you called Mouche?'

"She produced such fantastic reasons that we stopped rowing to laugh at it.

"She pleased us as a woman, too; and La Toque, who never rowed, and spent the whole day seated at her side in the helmsman's seat, one day answered the usual question: 'Why are you called Mouche?' by saying:

" 'Because she's a little blister fly.'

"Yes, a little buzzing fever-bearing cantharis, not the classic poisoned cantharis, gleaming and sheathed, but a little red-winged cantharis who was beginning to trouble the entire crew of the *Feuille-à-l'Envers* strangely.

"What senseless jests were perpetrated, though, on the leaf where this Mouche had alighted!

"Since the arrival of Mouche in the boat, N'a-qu'un-Œil had assumed a superior and preponderant role among us, the role of a gentleman who had a woman among four others who have not. He abused this privilege sometimes to the point of exasperating us by embracing Mouche under our eyes, seating her on his knees at the end of a meal, and by various other prerogatives as humiliating as irritating.

"We had made a separate place for them in the dormitory by a curtain.

"But I soon realized that my companions and I must be turning over the same arguments in our bachelor heads: 'Why, by virtue of what law of exceptions, on what inadmissible principle, would Mouche, who appeared unembarrassed by any sort of prejudice, be faithful to her lover when women of better classes were not faithful to their husbands?'

"Our reflection was justified. We were soon convinced of it. We only ought to have done it earlier, to save us from regret for lost time. Mouche deceived N'a-qu'un-Œil with all the other sailors of the *Feuille-à-l'Envers*.

"She deceived him without difficulty and without making any resistance, at the first word of request from each of us.

"Prudish folk are profoundly shocked, my God! Why? What fashionable courtesan has not a dozen lovers, and which of those lovers is stupid enough to be in ignorance of it? Is it not the fashion to spend an evening with a celebrated and sought-after woman, as one spends an evening at the Opéra, at the Français or the Odéon, because they are playing the minor classics there? Ten men combine together to keep a cocotte who finds it difficult to share out her time, as they club together to own a race-horse whom no one rides but a jockey, the equivalent of the *amant de cœur*.

"From motives of delicacy, we left Mouche to N'a-qu'un-Œil from Saturday evening to Monday morning. The days on the river were his. We only betrayed him during the week, in Paris, far from the Seine, which, for rowing men like us, was almost no betrayal at all.

"The situation was peculiar in this one way, that the four robbers of Mouche's favors were fully aware of the way they were shared out, and talked about it among themselves, and even to her, in veiled allusions that made her laugh heartily. Only N'a-qu'un-Œil seemed to know nothing about it; and this special position produced a certain awkwardness between him and us; it seemed to set him apart, isolate him, raise a barrier across our old confidence and our old intimacy. It gave him in our eyes a difficult and rather ridiculous part to play, the part of deceived lover, almost the part of husband.

"As he was very intelligent, and possessed of a peculiarly malicious wit, we sometimes wondered, not without a certain uneasiness, whether he had not his suspicions.

"He took care to enlighten us, in a fashion that was very painful for us. We were going to dine at Bougival, and we were rowing vigorously, when La Toque, who wore that morning the triumphant aspect of a satisfied man and, sitting side by side with the helmswoman, seemed to be pressing himself against her a little too freely in our opinion, halted the rowing, crying: 'Stop.'

"Eight oars were lifted out of the water.

"Then, turning to his neighbor, he demanded:

" 'Why are you called Mouche?'

"Before she could reply, the voice of N'a-qu'un-Œil, seated in the bows, observed dryly:

" 'Because she settles on every sort of carrion.'

"There was profound silence at first, and a sense of embarrassment followed by an attempt at laughter. Mouche herself remained quite unmoved.

"Then La Toque ordered:

" 'All together.'

"The boat shot forward again.

"The incident was closed, the air cleared.

"This little adventure occasioned no change in our habits. Its only effect was to re-establish the cordiality between N'a-qu'un-Œil and ourselves. He became once more the honored proprietor of Mouche, from Saturday evening to Monday morning, his superiority over us having been firmly established by this definition, which closed, moreover, the period allotted to questions about the word 'Mouche.' We contented ourselves for the future with the secondary role of grateful and attentive friends who profited discreetly on weekdays without any sort of competition among us.

"Everything went very well for about three months. But all at once Mouche adopted, towards all of us, strange attitudes. She was less gay, nervy, ill at ease, almost irritable. We were continually asking her:

" 'What's the matter with you?'

"She answered:

" 'Nothing. Leave me alone.'

"The truth was revealed to us by N'a-qu'un-Œil one Saturday evening. We had just sat down to table in the little dining room that the proprietor of our pothouse reserved for us in his wayside inn, and, soup over, we were waiting for the fried fish, when our friend, who was also apparently anxious, first took Mouche's hand and then spoke:

" 'My dear comrades,' said he, 'I have a very grave communication to make to you, which will perhaps occasion lengthy discussions. We shall have time, however, to argue between the courses. Our poor Mouche has announced a disastrous piece of news to me, bidding me at the same time to pass it on to you.

" 'She is *enceinte*.

" 'I add only two words.

" 'This is no time to desert her, and any attempt to settle the paternity is forbidden.'

"The first effect of this news was blank amazement, a sense of disaster; and we looked at one another, feeling a desire to accuse someone. But whom? Oh, whom? I have never felt, as sharply as in that moment, how treacherous is this cruel jest of nature that never allows a man to know beyond shadow of doubt whether he is the father of his child.

"Then, gradually, we experienced a certain sense of comfort and consolation, born contrariwise from a vague feeling of solidarity.

"Tomahawk, who hardly ever spoke, expressed this dawning serenity by these words:

" 'Faith, so much the worse, union is strength.'

"The gudgeon came in, borne by a scullion. We did not fling ourselves on it, as was our custom, because we were still disturbed in mind.

"N'a-qu'un-Œil went on:

" 'In these circumstances, she has had the delicacy to make full confession to me. My friends, we are all equally guilty. Give me your hands and let us adopt the child.'

"The decision was carried unanimously. We lifted our arms towards the dish of fried fish and took the oath.

" 'We will adopt it.'

"At that, in that moment, saved, delivered from the dreadful weight of anxiety which for a month had been torturing this dear, wanton little waif of love, Mouche cried:

" 'Oh, my friends, my friends! You are so kind . . . so kind . . . so kind. . . . Thank you all!'

"And she wept, for the first time, in our sight.

"Henceforth we talked in the boat about the child as if it were already born, and each of us showed an interest, with an exaggerated air of anxious concern, in the slow, regular change in our helmswoman's figure.

"We stopped rowing to ask:

" 'Mouche?'

"She replied:

" 'What now?'

" 'Is it a boy or a girl?'

" 'Boy.'

" 'What will he be?'

"Then she let her imagination take flight in the most fantastic fashion. She gave us the most interminable narratives, amazing inventions, stretching from the day of his birth to his final triumph. He was everything, this child, to the artless, passionate, loving dreams of this extraordinary little creature who now lived chaste among us five men, whom she called her 'five papas.' She saw him and described him as a sailor, discovering a new world greater than America, a general, regaining Alsace-Lorraine for France, then an emperor, founding a dynasty of wise and generous sovereigns who bestowed on our country lasting happiness, then a scientist, just discovering the secret of making gold, then that of eternal life, then an aeronaut, inventing means to visit the stars and making of infinite space a vast playground for men, the realization of all the most unforeseen and most magnificent dreams.

"God, how gay and amusing she was, poor little thing, until the end of the summer!

"It was the twentieth day of September that destroyed her dream. We had been lunching at Maisons-Lafitte, and we were passing Saint-Germain, when she felt thirsty and asked us to stop at Le Pecq.

"For some time now, she had been growing heavy, and this annoyed her very much. She could no longer leap about as before, nor jump from the boat to the bank, as she was used to doing. She still tried, in spite of our cries and our efforts; and twenty times, but for our arms outstretched to catch her, she would have fallen.

"This particular day, filled with just such bravado, as sometimes proves fatal to ill or tired athletes, she was rash enough to try to get on shore before the boat stopped.

"Just as we were coming alongside, without anyone being able to foresee or prevent her movement, she stood up, made a spring, and tried to jump onto the quay.

"She was too weak, and only the top of her foot touched the edge of the stone quay; she slipped, hit her stomach full on the sharp corner, gave a loud cry, and disappeared in the water.

"The whole five of us plunged in together, and brought out a poor swooning creature, pale as death and already suffering frightful pains.

"We had to carry her without delay to the nearest inn, where a doctor was summoned.

"Throughout the ten hours during which her premature labor lasted, she bore her abominable torture with heroic courage. We were standing miserably round her, on fever with grief and fear.

"Then she was delivered of a dead child; and for some days more we had the gravest fears for her life.

"At last one morning the doctor said to us: 'I think she is safe. She's made of steel, that girl.' And we entered her room together with glad hearts.

"N'a-qu'un-Œil, speaking for all of us, said to her:

" 'You're out of danger, little Mouche, and we're very happy.'

"Then she cried in front of us for the second time, and, her eyes swimming in tears, she stammered:

" 'Oh, if you knew, if you knew . . . how unhappy . . . how unhappy I am! . . . I shall never be comforted.'

" 'But why, little Mouche?'

" 'Because I killed him, I killed him! Oh, I never meant to! How unhappy I am!'

"She was sobbing. We stood round her, very upset, not knowing what to say to her.

"She went on:

" 'Did you men see him?'

"With one voice we answered:

" 'Yes.'

" 'It was a boy, wasn't it?'

" 'Yes.'

" 'He was beautiful, wasn't he?'

"We hesitated in some doubt. Petit-Bleu, the least scrupulous of us, decided to affirm:

" 'Very beautiful.'

"He was ill-advised, for she began moaning, almost howling with despair.

"Then N'a-qu'un-Œil, who perhaps loved her more than any of us, thought of a happy conceit to quiet her, and kissing her eyes, which her tears had dulled, said:

" 'Be comforted, little Mouche, be comforted, we'll make you another one.'

"The sense of humor that was bred in her bones woke suddenly, and, half convinced, half joking, still all tears and her heart contracted with pain, she asked, looking at all of us:

" 'Promise?'

"And we answered together:

" 'Promise.' "

ON A SPRING EVENING

Jeanne was going to marry her cousin Jacques. They had known each other since childhood, and love with them did not stand on ceremony as it usually does in the social world. They had been brought up together, so that the idea had never occurred to them that they might be in love with each other. The girl, a bit of a coquette, would flirt ingenuously with the young man, for she thought him decent and nice, and every time she saw him she kissed him affectionately, but without passion, without the thrill that seems to pucker the flesh, from the tips of the fingers to the tips of the toes.

As for him, he merely thought, "My little cousin is really sweet," and he thought of her with the kind of instinctive tenderness a man always feels for a pretty girl. His thoughts went no further.

Then one day Jeanne happened to overhear her mother say to her aunt (Aunt Alberte, since Aunt Lison had remained unmarried), "I assure you those two are on the point of falling in love. Anyone can see that. As far as I am concerned, Jacques is exactly the kind of son-in-law I want."

Whereupon Jeanne began at once to adore her cousin Jacques. So she would blush every time she saw him, her hand would tremble in his, she would lower her eyes when their glances met, and she would resort to all sorts of little tricks to encite a kiss; to such an extent that he could not fail to see through her stratagems. So on an impulse in which there was as much satisfied vanity as real affection, he pressed his cousin into his arms, whispering into her ear, "I love you, I love you!"

From that day on there had been only cooings, gallantries, etc., a display of all the amorous ways that their former intimacy made the more natural and entirely without embarrassment. In the living room Jacques would kiss his fiancée in front of the three old ladies, the three sisters—his mother, Jeanne's mother, and Aunt Lison. He would walk with her alone all day in the woods, by the stream, across the dewy fields where the grass was studded with wild flowers. And they awaited the wedding day without too much impatience, but wrapped in each other, bathed in an exquisite tenderness, tasting the delightful charm of gentle caresses, of holding hands, of loving glances—such long ones that their souls seemed to mingle— and vaguely disturbed by the still unrealized desire of passionate embraces, feeling somewhat upset by lips that drew them toward each other, which seemed to watch and wait and promise.

Sometimes, when they had spent the entire day in this kind of passionate warmth, in these platonic tendernesses, they felt in the evening a strange depression, and they both would sigh deeply, without knowing why, without understanding. . . .

The two mothers and their sister, Aunt Lison, watched this young love with smiling indulgence. Aunt Lison especially seemed very much moved by the sight of the young couple.

She was a small woman who said little, effaced herself at all times, made no noise, appeared only at mealtime, retired afterwards to her room where she spent all her time. She seemed like the classic sweet old lady, with gentle and sad eyes, and hardly seemed to count in the family.

The two widowed sisters, having once been socially prominent, considered her insignificant. They treated her with a complete familiarity tinged with a condescending kindness for the old maid. Her name was Lisa, for she was born in the days when Béranger ruled France. When she did not marry, when it became clear that she would probably never marry, they changed Lisa to Lison.

Today she was Aunt Lison, a humble neat little old maid, terribly timid even with her own family, whose affection for her bordered on habit, compassion, and kindly indifference.

The young people never went to her room to visit her. Only the maid entered her room. They had her come down when they wanted to speak with her. They hardly knew where her room was, where the whole of this poor solitary life was lived out. She did not occupy any space at all, practically. When she was not around, no one ever mentioned her, no one ever thought of her.

She was one of those completely subdued persons who remain unknown even to their relatives, as though unexplored, and whose death causes no emptiness in a house, one of those who do not know how to enter into the life, nor the habits nor the love of those who live beside them.

She always walked silently with short, hurried steps, never made the slightest noise, never bumped into anything, seemed to communicate to objects the property of absorbing rather than of deflecting sound; her hands seemed to be made of cotton, so lightly and delicately did they handle things.

When one said, "Aunt Lison," those two words seemed not to evoke a single thought in anyone's mind. It was as if one had said, "the coffeepot," or "the sugar bowl."

The dog Loute assuredly possessed a much more marked personality. People patted her all the time, calling her "Dear Loute, pretty Loute, my little Loute." They would mourn for her infinitely more than for Aunt Lison.

The cousins' marriage was to take place at the end of May. The young people lived, their eyes deep in each other's, their hands, their thoughts, their hearts in each other's. Spring, late that year, hesitant, shivering until then under the clear night frosts and the foggy coolness of the mornings, had just burst all of a sudden.

A few warm days, slightly hazy, had stirred up all the sap, opening leaves as by a miracle, spreading everywhere that sweet languorous odor of the buds and the first flowers.

Then one afternoon the sun had come out, victorious, drying at last the floating vapors, shining over the entire plain. Its bright gaiety had filled the countryside, had spread everywhere—to plants, animals, and men. Birds in love flitted about, beating their wings, calling each other.

Jeanne and Jacques, constrained with an exquisite happiness, but more timid than usual, uneasy with the new sensations which came into them with the ferment of the woods, had remained all day side by side on a bench before the gate of the château, no longer daring to go out alone, idly watching the big swans chase each other on the pond.

Then in the evening they had felt more relaxed and calm, and after dinner they had stayed by the open window talking quietly, while their mothers played piquet in the circle of the lamplight, and Aunt Lison knitted socks for the poor.

A full-grown forest stretched into the distance behind the pond, and above the new foliage of the great trees the moon had suddenly appeared. It had risen little by little across the branches which etched themselves upon its orbit; and, climbing the sky, in the midst of the stars which it blotted out, it had begun to pour onto the world that melancholy light of dreams so dear to the sentimental, to poets and lovers.

The young couple had watched it at first. Then, filled with the tender sweetness of the night, with the ethereal brightness of the fields and woods, they had gone out and walked slowly on the enormous lawn as far as the glistening pond.

When they had finished their four evening games of piquet, the two mothers, feeling sleepy, wished to go to bed.

"We must call the children," said one of them.

The other, glancing over the pale horizon where two shadows could be seen moving, replied, "Let's not disturb them. It's so beautiful out! Lison will wait for them, won't you, Lison?"

The old maid raised her troubled eyes and answered timidly, "Certainly. I shall be glad to." And the two sisters went to bed.

Then Aunt Lison arose, and leaving her work on the arm of the chair, came to look out of the window, to contemplate the glorious night.

The two lovers kept walking across the lawn from the pond to the doorstep, and back again. They clasped each other's hands and did not speak, as if no longer themselves but a part of the visible poetry which emanated from the earth. All of a sudden Jeanne saw in the window frame the silhouette of the old maid clearly outlined by the lamplight.

"Look," she said, "Aunt Lison is watching us."

Jacques raised his head. "Yes, Aunt Lison is watching us," he said. And they continued to dream, to walk slowly, to love each other.

But the dew was spreading on the grass. They began to feel the chill of the evening. "Let us go in now," she said. And they went inside.

When they went into the living room, Aunt Lison had resumed her knitting; her forehead was bent over her work, and her little thin fingers trembled a bit as if they were very tired.

Jeanne went over to her. "Auntie, we are going to bed now."

The old maid turned toward them. Her eyes were red as if she had been weeping. Jacques and his fiancée did not notice. But the young man did notice the girl's delicate shoes all covered with dew. He was genuinely concerned, and asked tenderly, "Aren't your dear little feet cold?"

And all at once the aunt's fingers were shaken with such a trembling that her work slipped from them, the ball of yarn rolling to the floor. The old maid, hiding her face in her hands, began to weep with great convulsive sobs.

The two children rushed up to her. Jeanne, on her knees, clasped her in her arms, and said over and over again, very much upset, "What is the matter, Aunt Lison? What is the matter? Aren't you well?"

Then the poor old lady, her voice still choked with tears and her body doubled up with sorrow, stammered, "It's . . . it's just when he asked you, 'Aren't your dear little feet cold?' . . . No one has ever, ever . . . said such things to me. . . ."

THE LEGACY

M. and Mme. Serbois were lunching, sitting opposite each other. Both looked gloomy.

She, a little blonde with rosy skin and blue eyes and a gentle manner, was eating slowly without raising her head, as though she were haunted by some sad and persistent thought. He, tall, broad, with side whiskers and the air of a statesman or businessman, seemed nervous and preoccupied. Finally he said, as though speaking to himself, "Really, it's astonishing."

"What is?" his wife asked.

"That Vaudrec shouldn't have left us anything."

Mme. Serbois blushed; she blushed instantly, as though a rosy veil had suddenly been drawn over the skin of her throat and face. "Perhaps there is a will at the notary's," she said. "It is too early for us to know."

She said it with assurance, and Serbois answered reflectively: "Yes, that is possible. After all, he was the best friend of both of us, always here, staying for dinner every other day. I know he gave you many presents—that was perhaps his way of repaying our hospitality—but really, one does think of friends like us in a will. I know that if it had been I who had not felt well, I would have made some provision for him, even though you are my natural heir."

Mme. Serbois lowered her eyes. And as her husband carved a chicken she touched her handkerchief to her nose the way one does in weeping.

He continued. "Yes, it is possible that there is a will at the notary's, and a little legacy for us. I wouldn't expect anything much, just a remembrance, nothing but a remembrance, a thought, to prove to me that he had an affection for us."

Then his wife said, in a hesitant voice: "If you like, after lunch we might call on Maître[1] Lemaneur, and we would know where we stand."

"An excellent idea," said M. Serbois. "That is what we shall do." He had tied a napkin around his neck to keep from spotting his clothes with gravy, and he had the look of a decapitated man continuing to talk; his fine black whiskers stood out against the white of the linen, and his face was that of a very superior butler.

When they entered the notary's office there was a slight stir among the clerks, and when M. Serbois announced himself—even though he was perfectly well known—the chief clerk jumped to his feet with noticeable alacrity and his assistant smiled. Then they were shown into Lemaneur's private office.

He was a round little man, his head looked like a ball fastened to another ball to which in turn were fastened a pair of legs so very short and round that they too almost seemed like balls. He greeted them, pointed to chairs, and said, with a slightly significant glance at Mme. Serbois: "I was just going to write you to ask

[1]"Master"—the title given a lawyer or notary.

you to come in. I wanted to acquaint you with M. Vaudrec's will. It concerns you."

M. Serbois could not refrain from saying "Ah! I was sure of it."

The notary said, "I will read you the document. It is very short." And taking up a paper he read:

"I, Paul-Emile-Cyprien Vaudrec, the undersigned, being of sound body and mind, do hereby express my last wishes.

"Since death can come at any moment, unexpectedly, I wish to take the precaution of writing my last will and testament, which will be deposited with my notary, Maître Lemaneur.

"Being without direct heirs, I bequeath my entire estate, consisting of securities amounting to 400,000 francs, and real property amounting to about 600,000 francs, to Mme. Clair-Hortense Serbois, unconditionally. I beg her to accept this gift from a friend who has died, as proof of his devoted, profound and respectful affection.

"Signed in Paris, June 15, 1883.
"Vaudrec."

Mme. Serbois had lowered her head and sat motionless, whereas her husband was glancing with stupefaction at her and at the notary. Maître Lemaneur continued, after a moment: "Madame cannot, of course, accept this legacy without your consent, Monsieur."

M. Serbois rose. "I must have time to think," he said.

The notary, who was smiling with a certain air of malice, agreed, "I understand the scruples that make you hesitate; society sometimes judges unkindly. Will you come back tomorrow at the same time and give me your answer?"

M. Serbois bowed. "Until tomorrow."

He took a ceremonious leave of the notary, offered his arm to his wife, who was redder than a peony and kept her eyes obstinately lowered, and he left the office with so imposing an air that the clerks were positively frightened.

Once inside their own house, behind closed doors, M. Serbois curtly declared: "You were Vaudrec's mistress."

His wife, taking off her hat, turned toward him with a spasmodic movement. "I?" she cried. "Oh!"

"Yes, you. No one leaves his entire estate to a woman unless . . ."

She had gone utterly pale, and her hands trembled a little as she tried to tie the long ribbons together to keep them from trailing on the floor. After a moment she said, "But . . . you're crazy, crazy. . . . An hour ago weren't you yourself hoping that he would—would leave you something?"

"Yes—he could have left me something. Me—not you."

She looked at him deeply, as though trying to capture that unknown something in another human being which can scarcely be sensed even during those rare moments when guards are down, and which are like half-open gateways to the mysterious recesses of the soul. Then she said, slowly, "But it seems to me that if— that a legacy of such a size would have looked just as strange coming from him to you, as to me."

"Why?"

"Because . . ." She turned her head in embarrassment, and did not go on.

He began to pace the room, and said: "Surely you cannot accept?"

She answered with indifference: "Very well. But in that case there is no need to wait until tomorrow. We can write Maître Lemaneur now."

Serbois stopped his pacing, and for several moments they stared at each other, trying to see, to know, to understand, to uncover and fathom the depths of each other's thoughts, in one of those ardent, mute questionings between two people who live together, who never get to know each other, but who constantly suspect and watch.

Then he suddenly murmured, close to her ear: "Admit that you were Vaudrec's mistress."

She shrugged. "Don't be stupid. Vaudrec loved me, I think, but he was never my lover."

He stamped his foot. "You lie. What you say is impossible."

She said calmly, "Nevertheless, it is true."

He resumed his pacing, then, stopping again, said, "Then explain to me why he left you everything."

She answered nonchalantly. "It is very simple. As you yourself said earlier, we were his only friends, he lived as much with us as in his own home, and when the time came to make his will he thought of us. Then, out of gallantry, he wrote my name because my name came to him naturally, just as it was always to me that he gave presents—not to you. He had the habit of bringing me flowers, of giving me a little gift on the fifth of every month, because it was the fifth of a month that we met. You know that. He almost never gave you anything—he didn't think of it. Men give remembrances to the wives of their friends—not to the husbands—so he left his last remembrance to me rather than to you. It is as simple as that."

She was so calm, so natural, that Serbois hesitated. Then: "Still, it would make a very bad impression. Everyone would believe the other thing. We cannot accept."

"Then we won't accept. It will be a million less in our pockets, that's all."

He began to talk the way one thinks aloud, without addressing his wife directly. "Yes, a million—impossible—our reputations would be ruined—too bad—he should have left half to me . . . that would have taken care of everything." And he sat down, crossed his legs and played with his whiskers—always his behavior at moments of deep meditation.

Mme. Serbois opened her work basket, took out a bit of embroidery and began to sew. "I don't in the least insist on accepting. It is up to you to think about it."

For a long time he did not answer; then, hesitantly: "Look—there would be one way, perhaps. You could sign half over to me, by deed of gift. We have no children: it would be perfectly legal. In that way nobody could talk."

She said, seriously: "I don't quite see how that would keep them from talking."

He lost his temper: "You must be stupid. We'll tell everyone that he left each of us half: and it will be true. No need to explain that the will was in your name."

Once again she gave him a piercing look. "As you like. I am willing."

Then he rose and resumed his pacing. He appeared to hesitate again, although by now his face was radiant. "No—perhaps it would be better to renounce it altogether—more dignified—still—in this way nothing could be said. . . . Even the most scrupulous could find nothing to object to. . . . Yes—that solves everything. . . ."

He stood close to his wife. "So, if you like, my darling, I'll go back alone to Maître Lemaneur and consult him and explain. I will tell him that you prefer this arrangement, that it is more fitting, that it will stop gossip. My accepting half shows that I am on sure ground, perfectly acquainted with the whole situation, that I know everything to be honorable and clear. It is as though I said to you, 'Accept, my dear: why shouldn't you, since I do?' Otherwise it would really be undignified.''

"As you wish," said Mme. Serbois, simply.

He went on, speaking fluently now: "Yes, by dividing the legacy everything is made crystal-clear. We inherit from a friend who wanted to make no difference between us, who didn't want to seem to be saying, 'I prefer one of you to the other after my death, just as I did during my life.' And you may be sure that if he had reflected a little, that is what he would have done. He didn't think, he didn't foresee the consequences. As you rightly said, it was to you that he always gave presents. It was to you that he wanted to offer a last resemblance."

She stopped him, a shade impatiently. "All right, I understand. You don't have to do so much explaining. Now go to the notary."

He stammered, blushing, suddenly confused. "You're right. I'm going."

He took his hat, and approaching her he held out his lips for a kiss, murmuring, "I'll be back soon, my darling."

She held up her forehead and he gave her a big kiss, his thick whiskers tickling her cheeks.

Then he went out, beaming happily.

And Mme. Serbois let her embroidery fall and began to weep.

MADAME TELLIER'S ESTABLISHMENT

Men went there every evening at about eleven o'clock, just as they went to the café. Six or eight of them used to meet there, always the same set—not fast men, but respectable tradesmen and young men in government or some other employ —and they used to drink their chartreuse and tease the girls, or else they would talk seriously with Madame, whom everybody respected, and then would go home at twelve o'clock. The younger men would sometimes stay the night.

It was a small, comfortable house at the corner of a street behind St. Etienne's Church. From the windows one could see the docks, full of ships which were being unloaded, and on the hill the old gray chapel, dedicated to the Virgin.

Madame, who came of a respectable family of peasant proprietors in the department of the Eure, had taken up her profession, just as she would have become a milliner or dressmaker. The prejudice against prostitution, which is so violent and deeply rooted in large towns, does not exist in the country places in Normandy. The peasant simply says: "It is a paying business," and sends his daughter to keep a harem of fast girls, just as he would send her to keep a girls' school.

She had inherited the house from an old uncle to whom it had belonged. Monsieur and Madame, who had formerly been innkeepers near Yvetot, had immediately sold their house, as they thought that the business at Fécamp was more profitable. They arrived one fine morning to assume the direction of the enterprise, which was declining on account of the absence of a head. They were good enough people in their way and soon made themselves liked by their staff and their neighbors.

Monsieur died of apoplexy two years later, for as his new profession kept him in idleness and without exercise, he had grown excessively stout, and his health had suffered. Since Madame had been a widow, all the frequenters of the establishment had wanted her, but people said that personally she was quite virtuous, and even the girls in the house could not discover anything against her. She was tall, stout and affable, and her complexion, which had become pale in the dimness of her house, the shutters of which were scarcely ever opened, shone as if it had been varnished. She had a fringe of curly false hair, which gave her a juvenile look, which in turn contrasted strongly with her matronly figure. She was always smiling and cheerful and was fond of a joke, but there was a shade of reserve about her which her new occupation had not quite made her lose. Coarse words always shocked her, and when any young fellow who had been badly brought up called her establishment by its right name, she was angry and disgusted.

In a word, she had a refined mind, and although she treated her women as friends, yet she very frequently used to say that she and they were not made of the same stuff.

Sometimes during the week she would hire a carriage and take some of her girls into the country, where they used to enjoy themselves on the grass by the side of the little river. They behaved like a lot of girls let out from a school and used to run races and play childish games. They would have a cold dinner on the grass and drink cider and go home at night with a delicious feeling of fatigue and in the carriage kiss Madame as a kind mother who was full of goodness and complaisance.

The house had two entrances. At the corner there was a sort of low café, which sailors and the lower orders frequented at night, and she had two girls whose special duty it was to attend to that part of the business. With the assistance of the waiter, whose name was Frederic and who was a short, light-haired, beardless fellow, as strong as a horse, they set the half bottles of wine and the jugs of beer on the shaky marble tables and then, sitting astride on the customers' knees, would urge them to drink.

The three other girls (there were only five in all) formed a kind of aristocracy and were reserved for the company on the first floor, unless they were wanted downstairs and there was nobody on the first floor. The salon of Jupiter, where the tradesmen used to meet, was papered in blue and embellished with a large drawing representing Leda stretched out under the swan. That room was reached by a winding staircase which ended at a narrow door opening on to the street, and above it all night long a little lamp burned behind wire bars, such as one still sees in some towns at the foot of the shrine of some saint.

The house, which was old and damp, rather smelled of mildew. At times there was an odor of eau de cologne in the passages, or a half-open door downstairs allowed the noise of the common men sitting and drinking downstairs to reach the first floor, much to the disgust of the gentlemen who were there. Madame, who was quite familiar with those of her customers with whom she was on friendly terms, did not leave the salon. She took much interest in what was going on in the town, and they regularly told her all the news. Her serious conversation was a change from the ceaseless chatter of the three women; it was a rest from the doubtful jokes of those stout individuals who every evening indulged in the commonplace amusement of drinking a glass of liquor in company with girls of easy virtue.

The names of the girls on the first floor were Fernande, Raphaelle and Rosa the Jade. As the staff was limited, Madame had endeavored that each member of it should be a pattern, an epitome of each feminine type, so that every customer might find as nearly as possible the realization of his ideal. Fernande represented the handsome blonde; she was very tall, rather fat and lazy, a country girl who could not get rid of her freckles and whose short, light, almost colorless, towlike hair, which was like combed-out flax, barely covered her head.

Raphaelle, who came from Marseilles, played the indispensable part of the handsome Jewess. She was thin, with high cheekbones covered with rouge, and her black hair, which was always covered with pomatum, curled onto her forehead. Her eyes would have been handsome if the right one had not had a speck in it. Her Roman nose came down over a square jaw, where two false upper teeth contrasted strangely with the bad color of the rest.

Rosa the Jade was a little roll of fat, nearly all stomach, with very short legs. From morning till night she sang songs which were alternately indecent or sentimental in a harsh voice, told silly, interminable tales and only stopped talking in order to eat, or left off eating in order to talk. She was never still, was as active as a squirrel, in spite of her fat and her short legs, and her laugh, which was a torrent of shrill cries, resounded here and there, ceaselessly, in a bedroom, in the loft, in the café, everywhere, and always about nothing.

The two women on the ground floor were Louise, who was nicknamed "la Cocotte," and Flora, whom they called "Balançière,"[1] because she limped a little. The former always dressed as Liberty with a tricolored sash, and the other as a Spanish woman with a string of copper coins, which jingled at every step she took, in her carroty hair. Both looked like cooks dressed up for the carnival and were like all other women of the lower orders, neither uglier nor better looking than they usually are. In fact, they looked just like servants at an inn and were generally called the "Two Pumps."

A jealous peace, very rarely disturbed, reigned among these five women, thanks to Madame's conciliatory wisdom and to her constant good humor; and the establishment, which was the only one of the kind in the little town, was very much frequented. Madame had succeeded in giving it such a respectable appearance; she was so amiable and obliging to everybody; her good heart was so well known, that she was treated with a certain amount of consideration. The regular customers spent money on her and were delighted when she was especially friendly toward them. When they met during the day they would say: "This evening, you know where," just as men say: "At the café after dinner." In a word, Madame Tellier's house was somewhere to go to, and her customers very rarely missed their daily meetings there.

One evening toward the end of May the first arrival, M. Poulin, who was a timber merchant and had been mayor, found the door shut. The little lantern behind the grating was not alight; there was not a sound in the house; everything seemed dead. He knocked gently at first, and then more loudly, but nobody answered the door. Then he went slowly up the street, and when he got to the market place he met M. Duvert, the gunmaker, who was going to the same place, so they went back together but did not meet with any better success. But suddenly they heard a loud noise close to them, and on going round the corner of the house they saw a number of English and French sailors who were hammering at the closed shutters of the café with their fists.

The two tradesmen immediately made their escape, for fear of being compro-
[1]Swing, or seesaw.

mised, but a low *pst* stopped them; it was M. Tournevau, the fish curer, who had recognized them and was trying to attract their attention. They told him what had happened, and he was all the more vexed at it, as he, a married man and father of a family, only went there on Saturdays—*securitatis causa*, as he said, alluding to a measure of sanitary policy which his friend Dr. Borde had advised him to observe. That was his regular evening, and now he would be deprived of it for the whole week.

The three men went as far as the quay together, and on the way they met young M. Phillippe, the banker's son, who frequented the place regularly, and M. Pinipesse, the collector. They all returned to the Rue aux Juifs together to make a last attempt. But the exasperated sailors were besieging the house, throwing stones at the shutters and shouting, and the five first-floor customers went away as quickly as possible and walked aimlessly about the streets.

Presently they met M. Dupuis, the insurance agent, and then M. Vassi, the judge of the tribunal of commerce, and they all took a long walk, going to the pier first of all. There they sat down in a row on the granite parapet and watched the rising tide, and when the promenaders had sat there for some time, M. Tournevau said: "This is not very amusing!"

"Decidedly not," M. Pinipesse replied, and they started off to walk again.

After going through the street on the top of the hill they returned over the wooden bridge which crosses the Retenue, passed close to the railway and came out again onto the market place, when suddenly a quarrel arose between M. Pinipesse and M. Tournevau about an edible fungus which one of them declared he had found in the neighborhood.

As they were out of temper already from annoyance, they would very probably have come to blows if the others had not interfered. M. Pinipesse went off furious, and soon another altercation arose between the ex-mayor, M. Poulin and M. Dupuis, the insurance agent, on the subject of the tax collector's salary and the profits which he might make. Insulting remarks were freely passing between them when a torrent of formidable cries were heard, and the body of sailors, who were tired of waiting so long outside a closed house, came into the square. They were walking arm in arm, two and two, and formed a long procession and were shouting furiously. The landsmen went and hid themselves under a gateway, and the yelling crew disappeared in the direction of the abbey. For a long time they still heard the noise which diminished like a storm in the distance, and then silence was restored. M. Poulin and M. Dupuis, who were enraged with each other, went in different directions without wishing each other good-by.

The other four set off again and instinctively went in the direction of Mme. Tellier's establishment which was still closed, silent, impenetrable. A quiet, but obstinate drunken man was knocking at the door of the café; then he stopped and called Frederic, the waiter, in a low voice, but finding that he got no answer, he sat down on the doorstep and awaited the course of events.

The others were just going to retire when the noisy band of sailors reappeared at the end of the street. The French sailors were shouting the "Marseillaise," and the Englishmen, "Rule Britannia." There was a general lurching against the wall, and then the drunken brutes went on their way toward the quay, where a fight broke out between the two nations in the course of which an Englishman had his arm broken and a Frenchman his nose split.

The drunken man who had stopped outside the door was crying by this time, as drunken men and children cry when they are vexed, and the others went away. By degrees calm was restored in the noisy town; here and there at moments the distant sound of voices could be heard, only to die away in the distance.

One man was still wandering about, M. Tournevau, the fish curer, who was vexed at having to wait until the next Saturday. He hoped for something to turn up; he did not know what, but he was exasperated at the police for thus allowing an establishment of such public utility, which they had under their control, to be thus closed.

He went back to it, examined the walls and tried to find out the reason. On the shutter he saw a notice stuck up, so he struck a wax vesta and read the following in a large, uneven hand: "Closed on account of the confirmation."

Then he went away, as he saw it was useless to remain, and left the drunken man lying on the pavement, fast asleep, outside the inhospitable door.

The next day all the regular customers, one after the other, found some reason for going through the Rue aux Juifs with a bundle of papers under their arm, to keep them in countenance, and with a furtive glance they all read that mysterious notice:

CLOSED ON ACCOUNT OF THE
CONFIRMATION

II

Madame had a brother who was a carpenter in their native place, Virville, in the department of Eure. When Madame had still kept the inn at Yvetot she had stood godmother to that brother's daughter, who had received the name of Constance, Constance Rivet, she herself being a Rivet on her father's side. The carpenter, who knew that his sister was in a good position, did not lose sight of her, although they did not meet often, as they were both kept at home by their occupations and lived a long way from each other. But when the girl was twelve years old and about to be confirmed, he seized the opportunity to write to his sister and ask her to come and be present at the ceremony. Their old parents were dead, and as Madame could not well refuse, she accepted the invitation. Her brother, whose name was Joseph, hoped that by dint of showing his sister attentions she might be induced to make her will in the girl's favor, as she had no children of her own.

His sister's occupation did not trouble his scruples in the least, and, besides, nobody knew anything about it at Virville. When they spoke of her they only said: "Madame Tellier is living at Fécamp," which might mean that she was living on her own private income. It was quite twenty leagues from Fécamp to Virville, and for a peasant twenty leagues on land are more than is crossing the ocean to an educated person. The people at Virville had never been farther than Rouen, and nothing attracted the people from Fécamp to a village of five hundred houses in the middle of a plain and situated in another department. At any rate, nothing was known about her business.

But the confirmation was coming on, and Madame was in great embarrassment. She had no undermistress and did not at all dare to leave her house, even for a day. She feared the rivalries between the girls upstairs and those downstairs would certainly break out; that Frederic would get drunk, for when he was in that state he would knock anybody down for a mere word. At last, however, she made up her mind to take them all with her with the exception of the man, to whom she gave a holiday until the next day but one.

When she asked her brother he made no objection but undertook to put them all up for a night. So on Saturday morning the eight o'clock express carried off Madame and her companions in a second-class carriage. As far as Beuzeille they were alone and chattered like magpies, but at that station a couple got in. The man, an aged peasant dressed in a blue blouse with a folding collar, wide sleeves, tight at the wrist and ornamented with white embroidery, wore an old high hat with long nap. He held an enormous green umbrella in one hand and a large basket in the other, from which the heads of three frightened ducks protruded. The woman, who sat stiffly in her rustic finery, had a face like a fowl and a nose that was as pointed as a bill. She sat down opposite her husband and did not stir as she was startled at finding herself in such smart company.

There was certainly an array of striking colors in the carriage. Madame was dressed in blue silk from head to foot and had over her dress a dazzling red shawl of imitation French cashmere. Fernande was panting in a Scottish-plaid dress whose bodice, which her companions had laced as tight as they could, had forced up her falling bosom into a double dome that was continually heaving up and down and which seemed liquid beneath the material. Raphaelle, with a bonnet covered with feathers so that it looked like a nestful of birds, had on a lilac dress with gold spots on it; there was something oriental about it that suited her Jewish face. Rosa the Jade had on a pink petticoat with large flounces and looked like a very fat child, an obese dwarf, while the Two Pumps looked as if they had cut their dresses out of old flowered curtains, dating from the Restoration.

Perceiving that they were no longer alone in the compartment, the ladies put on staid looks and began to talk of subjects which might give the others a high opinion of them. But at Bolbec a gentleman with light whiskers, with a gold chain and wearing two or three rings, got in and put several parcels wrapped in oilcloth into the net over his head. He looked inclined for a joke and a good-natured fellow.

"Are you ladies changing your quarters?" he asked. The question embarrassed them all considerably. Madame, however, quickly recovered her composure and said sharply, to avenge the honor of her corps:

"I think you might try and be polite!"

He excused himself and said: "I beg your pardon; I ought to have said your nunnery."

As Madame could not think of a retort, or perhaps as she thought herself justi-fied sufficiently, she gave him a dignified bow and pinched in her lips.

Then the gentleman, who was sitting between Rosa the Jade and the old peasant, began to wink knowingly at the ducks, whose heads were sticking out of the basket. When he felt that he had fixed the attention of his public he began to tickle them under their bills and spoke funnily to them, to make the company smile.

"We have left our little pond, qu-ack! qu-ack! to make the acquaintance of the little spit, qu-ack! qu-ack!"

The unfortunate creatures turned their necks away to avoid his caresses and made desperate efforts to get out of their wicker prison and then suddenly, all at once, uttered the most lamentable quacks of distress. The women exploded with laugh-ter. They leaned forward and pushed each other so as to see better; they were very much interested in the ducks, and the gentleman redoubled his airs, his wit and his teasing.

Rosa joined in and, leaning over her neighbor's legs, she kissed the three animals on the head. Immediately all the girls wanted to kiss them in turn, and the gentleman took them onto his knees, made them jump up and down and pinched them. The two peasants, who were even in greater consternation than their poultry, rolled their eyes as if they were possessed, without venturing to move, and their old wrinkled faces had not a smile or a movement.

Then the gentleman, who was a commercial traveler, offered the ladies braces by way of a joke and, taking up one of his packages, he opened it. It was a trick, for the parcel contained garters. There were blue silk, pink silk, red silk, violet silk, mauve silk garters, and the buckles were made of two gilt metal Cupids embracing each other. The girls uttered exclamations of delight and looked at them with that gravity which is natural to a woman when she is hankering after a bargain. They consulted one another by their looks or in a whisper and replied in the same manner, and Madame was longingly handling a pair of orange garters that were broader and more imposing than the rest, really fit for the mistress of such an establishment.

"Come, my kittens," he said, "you must try them on."

There was a torrent of exclamations, and they squeezed their petticoats between their legs, as if they thought he was going to ravish them, but he quietly waited his time and said: "Well, if you will not I shall pack them up again."

And he added cunningly: "I offer any pair they like to those who will try them on."

But they would not and sat up very straight and looked dignified.

But the Two Pumps looked so distressed that he renewed the offer to them. Flora especially hesitated, and he pressed her:

"Come, my dear, a little courage! Just look at that lilac pair; it will suit your dress admirably."

That decided her and, pulling up her dress, she showed a thick leg, fit for a milkmaid, in a badly fitting coarse stocking. The commercial traveler stooped down and fastened the garter below the knee first of all and then above it, and he tickled the girl gently, which made her scream and jump. When he had done he gave her the lilac pair and asked: "Who next?"

"I! I!" they all shouted at once, and he began on Rosa the Jade, who uncovered a shapeless, round thing without any ankle, a regular "sausage of a leg," as Raphaelle used to say.

The commercial traveler complimented Fernande and grew quite enthusiastic over her powerful columns.

The thin tibias of the handsome Jewess met with less flattery, and Louise Cocotte, by way of a joke, put her petticoats over the man's head, so that Madame was obliged to interfere to check such unseemly behavior.

Lastly Madame herself put out her leg, a handsome, muscular Norman leg, and in his surprise and pleasure the commercial traveler gallantly took off his hat to salute that master calf, like a true French cavalier.

The two peasants, who were speechless from surprise, looked askance out of the corners of their eyes. They looked so exactly like fowls that the man with the light whiskers, when he sat up, said, "Co—co—ri—co" under their very noses, and that gave rise to another storm of amusement.

The old people got out at Motteville with their basket, their ducks and their umbrella, and they heard the woman say to her husband as they went away:

"They are sluts who are off to that cursed place, Paris."

The funny commercial traveler himself got out at Rouen, after behaving so coarsely that Madame was obliged sharply to put him into his right place. She added as a moral: "This will teach us not to talk to the firstcomer."

At Oissel they changed trains, and at a little station farther on M. Joseph Rivet was waiting for them with a large cart and a number of chairs in it, which was drawn by a white horse.

The carpenter politely kissed all the ladies and then helped them into his conveyance.

Three of them sat on three chairs at the back, Raphaelle, Madame and her brother on the three chairs in front, and Rosa, who had no seat, settled herself as comfortably as she could on tall Fernande's knees, and then they set off.

But the horse's jerky trot shook the cart so terribly that the chairs began to dance, throwing the travelers into the air, to the right and to the left, as if they had been dancing puppets. This made them make horrible grimaces and screams, which, however, were cut short by another jolt of the cart.

They clung to the sides of the vehicle; their bonnets fell onto their backs, their noses on their shoulders, and the white horse trotted on, stretching out his head and holding out his tail quite straight, a little hairless rat's tail, with which he whisked his buttocks from time to time.

Joseph Rivet, with one leg on the shafts and the other bent under him, held the reins with elbows high and kept uttering a kind of chuckling sound which made the horse prick up its ears and go faster.

The green country extended on either side of the road, and here and there the colza in flower presented a waving expanse of yellow, from which there arose a strong, wholesome, sweet and penetrating smell which the wind carried to some distance.

The cornflowers showed their little blue heads among the rye, and the women wanted to pick them, but M. Rivet refused to stop.

Then sometimes a whole field appeared to be covered with blood, so thickly were the poppies growing, and the cart, which looked as if it were filled with flowers of more brilliant hue, drove on through the fields colored with wild flowers, to disappear behind the trees of a farm, then to reappear and go on again through the yellow or green standing crops studded with red or blue.

One o'clock struck as they drove up to the carpenter's door. They were tired out and very hungry, as they had eaten nothing since they left home. Madame Rivet ran out and made them alight, one after another, kissing them as soon as they were on the ground. She seemed as if she would never tire of kissing her sister-in-law, whom she apparently wanted to monopolize. They had lunch in the workshop, which had been cleared out for the next day's dinner.

A capital omelet, followed by boiled chitterlings and washed down by good sharp cider, made them all feel comfortable.

Rivet had taken a glass so that he might hobnob with them, and his wife cooked, waited on them, brought in the dishes, took them out and asked all of them in a whisper whether they had everything they wanted. A number of boards standing against the walls and heaps of shavings that had been swept into the corners gave out the smell of planed wood, of carpentering, that resinous odor which penetrates the lungs.

They wanted to see the little girl, but she had gone to church and would not be back until evening, so they all went out for a stroll in the country.

It was a small village through which the high road passed. Ten or a dozen houses on either side of the single street had for tenants the butcher, the grocer, the carpenter, the innkeeper, the shoemaker and the baker and others.

The church was at the end of the street. It was surrounded by a small churchyard, and four enormous lime trees which stood just outside the porch shaded it completely. It was built of flint, in no particular style, and had a slated steeple. When you got past it you were in the open country again, which was broken here and there by clumps of trees which hid some homestead.

Rivet had given his arm to his sister out of politeness, although he was in his working clothes, and was walking with her majestically. His wife, who was overwhelmed by Raphaelle's gold-striped dress, was walking between her and Fernande, and rotund Rosa was trotting behind with Louise Cocotte and Flora, the seesaw, who was limping along, quite tired out.

The inhabitants came to their doors; the children left off playing, and a window curtain would be raised so as to show a muslin cap, while an old woman with a crutch, who was almost blind, crossed herself as if it were a religious procession. They all looked for a long time after those handsome ladies from the town who had come so far to be present at the confirmation of Joseph Rivet's little girl, and the carpenter rose very much in the public estimation.

As they passed the church they heard some children singing; little shrill voices were singing a hymn, but Madame would not let them go in for fear of disturbing the little cherubs.

After a walk, during which Joseph Rivet enumerated the principal landed proprietors, spoke about the yield of the land and the productiveness of the cows and sheep, he took his flock of women home and installed them in his house, and as it was very small, he had put them into the rooms two and two.

Just for once Rivet would sleep in the workshop on the shavings; his wife was going to share her bed with her sister-in-law, and Fernande and Raphaelle were to sleep together in the next room. Louise and Flora were put into the kitchen, where they had a mattress on the floor, and Rosa had a little dark cupboard at the top of the stairs to herself, close to the loft, where the candidate for confirmation was to sleep.

When the girl came in she was overwhelmed with kisses; all the women wished to caress her with that need of tender expansion, that habit of professional wheedling which had made them kiss the ducks in the railway carriage.

They took her onto their laps, stroked her soft, light hair and pressed her in their arms with vehement and spontaneous outburts of affection, and the child, who was very good-natured and docile, bore it all patiently.

As the day had been a fatiguing one for everybody, they all went to bed soon after dinner. The whole village was wrapped in that perfect stillness of the country, which is almost like a religious silence, and the girls, who were accustomed to the noisy evenings of their establishment, felt rather impressed by the perfect repose of the sleeping village. They shivered, not with cold, but with those little shivers of solitude which come over uneasy and troubled hearts.

As soon as they were in bed, two and two together, they clasped each other in their arms, as if to protect themselves against this feeling of the calm and profound slumber of the earth. But Rosa the Jade, who was alone in her little dark cupboard, felt a vague and painful emotion come over her.

She was tossing about in bed, unable to get to sleep, when she heard the faint sobs of a crying child close to her head through the partition. She was frightened and called out and was answered by a weak voice, broken by sobs. It was the little girl who, being used to sleeping in her mother's room, was frightened in her small attic.

Rosa was delighted, got up softly so as not to awaken anyone and went and fetched the child. She took her into her warm bed, kissed her and pressed her to her bosom, caressed her, lavished exaggerated manifestations of tenderness on her and at last grew calmer herself and went to sleep. And till morning the candidate for confirmation slept with her head on Rosa's naked bosom.

At five o'clock the little church bell ringing the Angelus woke these women up, who as a rule slept the whole morning long.

The peasants were up already, and the women went busily from house to house, carefully bringing short, starched muslin dresses in bandboxes, or very long wax tapers with a bow of silk fringed with gold in the middle and with dents in the wax for the fingers.

The sun was already high in the blue sky which still had a rosy tint toward the horizon, like a faint trace of dawn, remaining. Families of fowls were walking about the hen houses, and here and there a black cock with a glistening breast raised his head, crowned by his red comb, flapped his wings and uttered his shrill crow, which the other cocks repeated.

Vehicles of all sorts came from neighboring parishes and discharged tall Norman women in dark dresses, with neck handkerchiefs crossed over the bosom and fastened with silver brooches, a hundred years old.

The men had put on blouses over their new frock coats or over their old dress coats of green cloth, the tails of which hung down below their blouses. When the horses were in the stable there was a double line of rustic conveyances along the road: carts, cabriolets, tilburies, charabancs, traps of every shape and age, resting on their shafts or pointing them in the air.

The carpenter's house was as busy as a beehive. The ladies, in dressing jackets and petticoats, with their long, thin, light hair which looked as if it were faded and worn by dyeing, were busy dressing the child, who was standing motionless on a table while Madame Tellier was directing the movements of her battalion. They washed her, did her hair, dressed her, and with the help of a number of pins they arranged the folds of her dress and took in the waist, which was too large.

Then when she was ready she was told to sit down and not to move, and the women hurried off to get ready themselves.

The church bell began to ring again, and its tinkle was lost in the air, like a feeble voice which is soon drowned in space. The candidates came out of the houses and went toward the parochial building which contained the school and the mansion house. This stood quite at one end of the village, while the church was situated at the other.

The parents, in their very best clothes, followed their children with awkward looks and with the clumsy movements of bodies that are always bent at work.

The little girls disappeared in a cloud of muslin which looked like whipped cream, while the lads, who looked like embryo waiters in a café and whose heads shone with pomatum, walked with their legs apart, so as not to get any dust or dirt onto their black trousers.

It was something for the family to be proud of; a large number of relatives from distant parts surrounded the child, and consequently the carpenter's triumph was complete.

Mme. Tellier's regiment, with its mistress as its head, followed Constance; her father gave his arm to his sister; her mother walked by the side of Raphaelle, Fernande with Rosa, and the Two Pumps together. Thus they walked majestically through the village, like a general's staff in full uniform, while the effect on the village was startling.

At the school the girls arranged themselves under the Sister of Mercy and the boys under the schoolmaster, and they started off, singing a hymn as they went. The boys led the way in two files between the two rows of vehicles, from which the horses had been taken out, and the girls followed in the same order. As all the people in the village had given the town ladies the precedence out of politeness, they came immediately behind the girls and lengthened the double line of the procession still more, three on the right and three on the left, while their dresses were as striking as a bouquet of fireworks.

When they went into the church the congregation grew quite excited. They pressed against each other; they turned round; they jostled one another in order to see. Some of the devout ones almost spoke aloud, so astonished were they at the sight of these ladies, whose dresses were trimmed more elaborately than the priest's chasuble.

The mayor offered them his pew, the first one on the right, close to the choir, and Mme. Tellier sat there with her sister-in-law; Fernande and Raphaelle, Rosa the Jade and the Two Pumps occupied the second seat, in company with the carpenter.

The choir was full of kneeling children, the girls on one side and the boys on the other, and the long wax tapers which they held looked like lances, pointing in all directions. Three men were standing in front of the lectern, singing as loud as they could.

They prolonged the syllables of the sonorous Latin indefinitely, holding onto the amens with interminable a—as, which the serpent of the organ kept up in the monotonous, long-drawn-out notes, emitted by the deep-throated pipes.

A child's shrill voice took up the reply, and from time to time a priest sitting in a stall and wearing a biretta got up, muttered something and sat down again. The three singers continued, with their eyes fixed on the big book of plain song lying open before them on the outstretched wings of an eagle mounted on a pivot.

Then silence ensued. The service went on, and toward the end of it Rosa, with her head in both her hands, suddenly thought of her mother and her village church on a similar occasion. She almost fancied that that day had returned when she was so small and almost hidden in her white dress, and she began to cry.

First of all she wept silently; the tears dropped slowly from her eyes, but her emotion increased with her recollections, and she began to sob. She took out her pocket handkerchief, wiped her eyes and held it to her mouth so as not to scream, but it was useless.

A sort of rattle escaped her throat, and she was answered by two other profound, heartbreaking sobs; for her two neighbors, Louise and Flora, who were kneeling near her, overcome by similar recollections, were sobbing by her side. There was a flood of tears, and as weeping is contagious, Madame soon found that her eyes were wet and on turning to her sister-in-law she saw that all the occupants of the pew were crying.

Soon throughout the church here and there a wife, a mother, a sister, seized by the strange sympathy of poignant emotion and agitated by the grief of those handsome ladies on their knees who were shaken by their sobs, was moistening her cambric pocket handkerchief and pressing her beating heart with her left hand.

Just as the sparks from an engine will set fire to dry grass, so the tears of Rosa and of her companions infected the whole congregation in a moment. Men, women, old men and lads in new blouses were soon sobbing; something super-human seemed to be hovering over their heads—a spirit, the powerful breath of an invisible and all-powerful being.

Suddenly a species of madness seemed to pervade the church, the noise of a crowd in a state of frenzy, a tempest of sobs and of stifled cries. It passed over the people like gusts of wind which bow the trees in a forest, and the priest, overcome by emotion, stammered out incoherent prayers, those inarticulate prayers of the soul when it soars toward heaven.

The people behind him gradually grew calmer. The cantors, in all the dignity of their white surplices, went on in somewhat uncertain voices, and the organ itself seemed hoarse, as if the instrument had been weeping. The priest, however, raised his hand as a sign for them to be still and went to the chancel steps. All were silent immediately.

After a few remarks on what had just taken place, which he attributed to a miracle, he continued, turning to the seats where the carpenter's guests were sitting:

"I especially thank you, my dear sisters, who have come from such a distance and whose presence among us, whose evident faith and ardent piety have set such a salutary example to all. You have edified my parish; your emotion has warmed all hearts; without you this day would not, perhaps, have had this really divine character. It is sufficient at times that there should be one chosen to keep in the flock, to make the whole flock blessed."

His voice failed him again from emotion, and he said no more but concluded the service.

They all left the church as quickly as possible; the children themselves were restless, tired with such a prolonged tension of the mind. Besides, the elders were hungry, and one after another left the churchyard to see about dinner.

There was a crowd outside, a noisy crowd, a babel of loud voices in which the shrill Norman accent was discernible. The villagers formed two ranks, and when the children appeared each family seized their own.

The whole houseful of women caught hold of Constance, surrounded her and kissed her, and Rosa was especially demonstrative. At last she took hold of one hand, while Mme. Tellier held the other, and Raphaelle and Fernande held up her long muslin petticoat so that it might not drag in the dust. Louise and Flora brought up the rear with Mme. Rivet, and the child, who was very silent and thoughtful, set off home in the midst of this guard of honor.

The dinner was served in the workshop on long boards supported by trestles, and through the open door they could see all the enjoyment that was going on. Everywhere people were feasting; through every window could be seen tables surrounded by people in their Sunday clothes. There was merriment in every house—men sitting in their shirt sleeves, drinking cider, glass after glass.

In the carpenter's house the gaiety took on somewhat of an air of reserve, the consequence of the emotion of the girls in the morning. Rivet was the only one who was in good cue, and he was drinking to excess. Mme. Tellier was looking at the clock every moment, for in order not to lose two days following they ought to take the 3:55 train, which would bring them to Fécamp by dark.

The carpenter tried very hard to distract her attention so as to keep his guests until the next day. But he did not succeed, for she never joked when there was business to be done, and as soon as they had had their coffee she ordered her girls to make haste and get ready. Then, turning to her brother, she said:

"You must have the horse put in immediately," and she herself went to complete her preparations.

When she came down again her sister-in-law was waiting to speak to her about the child, and a long conversation took place in which, however, nothing was settled. The carpenter's wife finessed and pretended to be very much moved, and Mme. Tellier, who was holding the girl on her knees, would not pledge herself to anything definite but merely gave vague promises: she would not forget her; there was plenty of time, and then, they were sure to meet again.

But the conveyance did not come to the door, and the women did not come downstairs. Upstairs they even heard loud laughter, falls, little screams and much clapping of hands, and so while the carpenter's wife went to the stable to see whether the cart was ready Madame went upstairs.

Rivet, who was very drunk and half undressed, was vainly trying to kiss Rosa, who was choking with laughter. The Two Pumps were holding him by the arms and trying to calm him, as they were shocked at such a scene after that morning's ceremony, but Raphaelle and Fernande were urging him on, writhing and holding their sides with laughter, and they uttered shrill cries at every useless attempt that the drunken fellow made.

The man was furious; his face was red; his dress disordered, and he was trying to shake off the two women who were clinging to him while he was pulling Rosa's bodice with all his might and ejaculating: "Won't you, you slut?"

But Madame, who was very indignant, went up to her brother, seized him by the shoulders and threw him out of the room with such violence that he fell against a wall in the passage, and a minute afterward they heard him pumping water onto his head in the yard. When he came back with the cart he was already quite calmed down.

They seated themselves in the same way as they had done the day before, and the little white horse started off with his quick, dancing trot. Under the hot sun their fun, which had been checked during dinner, broke out again. The girls now were amused at the jolts which the wagon gave, pushed their neighbors' chairs and burst out laughing every moment, for they were in the vein for it after Rivet's vain attempt.

There was a haze over the country; the roads were glaring and dazzled their eyes. The wheels raised up two trails of dust which followed the cart for a long time along the highroad, and presently Fernande, who was fond of music, asked Rosa to sing something. She boldly struck up the "Gros Curé de Meudon," but Madame made her stop immediately, as she thought it a song which was very unsuitable for such a day, and added:

"Sing us something of Béranger's."

After a moment's hesitation Rosa began Béranger's song, "The Grandmother," in her worn-out voice, and all the girls, and even Madame herself, joined in the chorus:

> "How I regret
>   My dimpled arms,
>   My well-made legs,
>   And my vanished charms!"

"That is first-rate," Rivet declared, carried away by the rhythm. They shouted the refrain to every verse, while Rivet beat time on the shafts with his foot and on the horse's back with the reins. The animal himself, carried away by the rhythm, broke into a wild gallop and threw all the women in a heap, one on top of the other, in the bottom of the conveyance.

They got up, laughing as if they were crazy, and the song went on, shouted at the top of their voices, beneath the burning sky and among the ripening grain, to the rapid gallop of the little horse who set off every time the refrain was sung and galloped a hundred yards, to their great delight. Occasionally a stone breaker by the roadside sat up and looked at the wild and shouting female load through his wire spectacles.

When they got out at the station the carpenter said:

"I am sorry you are going; we might have had some fun together."

But Madame replied very sensibly: "Everything has its right time, and we cannot always be enjoying ourselves."

And then he had a sudden inspiration: "Look here, I will come and see you at Fécamp next month." And he gave a knowing look with his bright and roguish eyes.

"Come," Madame said, "you must be sensible; you may come if you like, but you are not to be up to any of your tricks."

He did not reply, and as they heard the whistle of the train he immediately began to kiss them all. When it came to Rosa's turn he tried to get to her mouth which she, however, smiling with lips closed, turned away from him each time by a rapid movement of her head to one side. He held her in his arms, but he could not attain his object as his large whip, which he was holding in his hand and waving behind the girl's back in desperation, interfered with his efforts.

"Passengers for Rouen, take your seats, please!" a guard cried, and they got in. There was a slight whistle, followed by a loud one from the engine, which noisily puffed out its first jet of steam while the wheels began to turn a little with visible effort. Rivet left the station and went to the gate by the side of the line to get another look at Rosa, and as the carriage full of human merchandise passed him he began to crack his whip and to jump, singing at the top of his voice:

> "How I regret
>   My dimpled arms,
>   My well-made legs,
>   And my vanished charms!"

And then he watched a white pocket handkerchief which somebody was waving as it disappeared in the distance.

III

They slept the peaceful sleep of quiet consciences until they got to Rouen. When they returned to the house, refreshed and rested, Madame could not help saying:

"It was all very well, but I was already longing to get home."

They hurried over their supper, and then, when they had put on their usual light evening costumes, waited for their usual customers. The little colored lamp outside the door told the passers-by that the flock had returned to the fold, and in a moment the news spread; nobody knew how or by whom.

M. Philippe, the banker's son, even carried his audacity so far as to send a special messenger to M. Tournevau, who was in the bosom of his family.

The fish curer used every Sunday to have several cousins to dinner, and they were having coffee, when a man came in with a letter in his hand. M. Tournevau was much excited; he opened the envelope and grew pale; it only contained these words in pencil:

The cargo of fish has been found; the ship has come into port; good business for you. Come immediately.

He felt in his pockets, gave the messenger twopence and, suddenly blushing to his ears, he said: "I must go out." He handed his wife the laconic and mysterious note, rang the bell, and when the servant came in he asked her to bring him his hat and overcoat immediately. As soon as he was in the street he began to run, and the way seemed to him to be twice as long as usual, in consequence of his impatience.

Mme. Tellier's establishment had put on quite a holiday look. On the ground floor a number of sailors were making a deafening noise, and Louise and Flora drank with one and the other so as to merit their name of the Two Pumps more than ever. They were being called for everywhere at once; already they were not quite sober enough for their business, and the night bid fair to be a very jolly one.

The upstairs room was full by nine o'clock. M. Vassi, the judge of the tribunal of commerce, Madame's usual platonic wooer, was talking to her in a corner in a low voice, and they were both smiling, as if they were about to come to an understanding.

M. Poulin, the ex-mayor, was holding Rosa on his knees, and she, with her nose close to his, was running her hands through the old gentleman's white whiskers.

Tall Fernande, who was lying on the sofa, had both her feet on M. Pinipesse the tax collector's stomach and her back on young M. Philippe's waistcoat; her right arm was round his neck, and she held a cigarette in her left.

Raphaelle appeared to be discussing matters with M. Dupuis, the insurance agent, and she finished by saying: "Yes, my dear, I will."

Just then the door opened suddenly, and M. Tournevau came in. He was greeted with enthusiastic cries of: "Long live Tournevau!" And Raphaelle, who was twirling around, went and threw herself into his arms. He seized her in a vigorous embrace, and without saying a word, lifting her up as if she had been a feather, he carried her through the room.

Rosa was chatting to the ex-mayor, kissing him every moment and pulling both his whiskers at the same time in order to keep his head straight.

Fernande and Madame remained with the four men, and M. Philippe exclaimed: "I will pay for some champagne; get three bottles, Madame Tellier." And Fernande gave him a hug and whispered to him: "Play us a waltz, will you?" So he rose and sat down at the old piano in the corner and managed to get a hoarse waltz out of the entrails of the instrument.

The tall girl put her arms round the tax collector, Madame asked M. Vassi to take her in his arms, and the two couples turned round, kissing as they danced. M. Vassi, who had formerly danced in good society, waltzed with such elegance that Madame was quite captivated.

Frederic brought the champagne; the first cork popped, and M. Philippe played the introduction to a quadrille, through which the four dancers walked in society fashion, decorously, with propriety of deportment, with bows and curtsies, and then they began to drink.

M. Philippe next struck up a lively polka, and M. Tournevau started off with the handsome Jewess, whom he held up in the air without letting her feet touch the ground. M. Pinipesse and M. Vassi had started off with renewed vigor, and from time to time one or other couple would stop to toss off a long glass of sparkling wine. The dance was threatening to become never ending, when Rosa opened the door.

"I want to dance," she exclaimed. And she caught hold of M. Dupuis, who was sitting idle on the couch, and the dance began again.

But the bottles were empty. "I will pay for one," M. Tournevau said.

"So will I," M. Vassi declared.

"And I will do the same," M. Dupuis remarked.

Then all began to clap their hands, and it soon became a regular ball. From time to time Louise and Flora ran upstairs quickly, had a few turns while their customers downstairs grew impatient, and then they returned regretfully to the café. At midnight they were still dancing.

Madame shut her eyes to what was going on, and she had long private talks in corners with M. Vassi, as if to settle the last details of something that had already been agreed upon.

At last at one o'clock the two married men, M. Tournevau and M. Pinipesse, declared that they were going home and wanted to pay. Nothing was charged for except the champagne, and that only cost six francs a bottle instead of ten, which was the usual price, and when they expressed their surprise at such generosity Madame, who was beaming, said to them:

"We don't have a holiday every day."

A CRISIS

A big fire was burning, and the tea table was set for two. The Count de Sallure threw his hat, gloves and fur coat on a chair, while the countess, who had removed her opera cloak, was smiling amiably at herself in the glass and arranging a few stray curls with her jeweled fingers. Her husband had been looking at her for the past few minutes, as if on the point of saying something, but hesitating; finally he said:

"You have flirted outrageously tonight!" She looked him straight in the eyes with an expression of triumph and defiance on her face.

"Why, certainly," she answered. She sat down, poured out the tea, and her husband took his seat opposite her.

"It made me look quite—ridiculous!"

"Is this a scene?" she asked, arching her brows. "Do you mean to criticize my conduct?"

"Oh no, I only meant to say that Monsieur Burel's attentions to you were positively improper, and if I had the right—I—would not tolerate it."

"Why, my dear boy, what has come over you? You must have changed your views since last year. You did not seem to mind who courted me and who did not a year ago. When I found out that you had a mistress, a mistress whom you loved passionately, I pointed out to you then, as you did me tonight (but I had good reasons), that you were compromising yourself and Madame de Servy, that your conduct grieved me and made me look ridiculous; what did you answer me? That I was perfectly free, that marriage between two intelligent people was simply a partnership, a sort of social bond, but not a moral bond. Is it not true? You gave me to understand that your mistress was far more captivating than I, that she was more womanly; that is what you said: 'more womanly.' Of course you said all this in a very nice way, and I acknowledge that you did your very best to spare my feelings, for which I am very grateful to you, I assure you, but I understand perfectly what you meant.

"We then decided to live practically separated; that is, under the same roof but apart from each other. We had a child, and it was necessary to keep up appearances before the world, but you intimated that if I chose to take a lover you would not object in the least, providing it was kept secret. You even made a long and very interesting discourse on the cleverness of women in such cases; how well they could manage such things, etc., etc. I understood perfectly, my dear boy. You loved Madame de Servy very much at that time, and my conjugal— legal—affection was an impediment to your happiness, but since then we have lived on the very best of terms. We go out in society together, it is true, but here in our own house we are complete strangers. Now for the past month or two you act as if you were jealous, and I do not understand it."

"I am not jealous, my dear, but you are so young, so impulsive, that I am afraid you will expose yourself to the world's criticisms."

"You make me laugh! Your conduct would not bear a very close scrutiny. You had better not preach what you do not practice."

"Do not laugh, I pray. This is no laughing matter. I am speaking as a friend, a true friend. As to your remarks, they are very much exaggerated."

"Not at all. When you confessed to me your infatuation for Madame de Servy, I took it for granted that you authorized me to imitate you. I have not done so."

"Allow me to——"

"Do not interrupt me. I have not done so. I have no lover—as yet. I am looking for one, but I have not found one to suit me. He must be very nice—nicer than you are—that is a compliment, but you do not seem to appreciate it."

"This joking is entirely uncalled for."

"I am not joking at all; I am in dead earnest. I have not forgotten a single word of what you said to me a year ago, and when it pleases me to do so, no matter what you may say or do, I shall take a lover. I shall do it without your even suspecting it—you will be none the wiser—like a great many others."

"How can you say such things?"

"How can I say such things? But, my dear boy, you were the first one to laugh when Madame de Gers joked about poor, unsuspecting Monsieur de Servy."

"That might be, but it is not becoming language for you."

"Indeed! You thought it a good joke when it concerned Monsieur de Servy, but you do not find it so appropriate when it concerns you. What a queer lot men are! However, I am not fond of talking about such things; I simply mentioned it to see if you were ready."

"Ready—for what?"

"Ready to be deceived. When a man gets angry on hearing such things he is not quite ready. I wager that in two months you will be the first one to laugh if I mention a deceived husband to you. It is generally the case when you are the deceived one."

"Upon my word, you are positively rude tonight; I have never seen you that way."

"Yes—I have changed—for the worse, but it is your fault."

"Come, my dear, let us talk seriously. I beg of you, I implore you not to let Monsieur Burel court you as he did tonight."

"You are jealous; I knew it."

"No, no, but I do not wish to be looked upon with ridicule, and if I catch that man devouring you with his eyes like he did tonight—I—I will thrash him!"

"Could it be possible that you are in love with me?"

"Why not? I am sure I could do much worse."

"Thanks. I am sorry for you—because I do not love you any more."

The count got up, walked around the tea table and, going behind his wife, he kissed her quickly on the neck. She sprang up and with flashing eyes said: "How dare you do that? Remember, we are absolutely nothing to each other; we are complete strangers."

"Please do not get angry; I could not help it; you look so lovely tonight."

"Then I must have improved wonderfully."

"You look positively charming; your arms and shoulders are beautiful, and your skin——"

"Would captivate Monsieur Burel."

"How mean you are! But really, I do not recall ever having seen a woman as captivating as you are."

"You must have been fasting lately."

"What's that?"

"I say, you must have been fasting lately."

"Why—what do you mean?"

"I mean just what I say. You must have fasted for some time, and now you are famished. A hungry man will eat things which he will not eat at any other time. I am the neglected—dish, which you would not mind eating tonight."

"Marguerite! Whoever taught you to say those things?"

"You did. To my knowledge you have had four mistresses. Actresses, society women, gay women, etc., so how can I explain your sudden fancy for me, except by your long fast?"

"You will think me rude, brutal, but I have fallen in love with you for the second time. I love you madly!"

"Well, well! Then you—wish to——"

"Exactly."

"Tonight?"

"Oh, Marguerite!"

"There, you are scandalized again. My dear boy, let us talk quietly. We are strangers, are we not? I am your wife, it is true, but I am—free. I intended to engage my affection elsewhere, but I will give you the preference, providing—I receive the same compensation."

"I do not understand you; what do you mean?"

"I will speak more clearly. Am I as good looking as your mistresses?"

"A thousand times better."

"Better than the nicest one?"

"Yes, a thousand times."

"How much did she cost you in three months?"

"Really—what on earth do you mean?"

"I mean, how much did you spend on the costliest of your mistresses, in jewelry, carriages, suppers, etc., in three months?"

"How do I know?"

"You ought to know. Let us say, for instance, five thousand francs a month—is that about right?"

"Yes—about that."

"Well, my dear boy, give me five thousand francs and I will be yours for a month, beginning from tonight."

"Marguerite! Are you crazy?"

"No, I am not, but just as you say. Good night!"

The countess entered her boudoir. A vague perfume permeated the whole room. The count appeared in the doorway.

"How lovely it smells in here!"

"Do you think so? I always use Peau d'Espagne; I never use any other perfume."

"Really? I did not notice—it is lovely."

"Possibly, but be kind enough to go; I want to go to bed."

"Marguerite!"

"Will you please go?"

The count came in and sat on a chair.

Said the countess: "You will not go? Very well."

She slowly took off her waist, revealing her white arms and neck, then she lifted her arms above her head to loosen her hair.

The count took a step toward her.

The countess: "Do not come near me or I shall get really angry, do you hear?"

He caught her in his arms and tried to kiss her. She quickly took a tumbler of perfumed water standing on the toilet table and dashed it into his face.

He was terribly angry. He stepped back a few paces and murmured:

"How stupid of you!"

"Perhaps—but you know my conditions—five thousand francs!"

"Preposterous!"

"Why, pray?"

"Why? Because—whoever heard of a man paying his wife?"

"Oh! How horribly rude you are!"

"I suppose I am rude, but I repeat, the idea of paying one's wife is preposterous! Positively stupid!"

"Is it not much worse to pay a gay woman? It certainly would be stupid when you have a wife at home."

"That may be, but I do not wish to be ridiculous."

The countess sat down on the bed and took off her stockings, revealing her bare, pink feet.

The count approached a little nearer and said tenderly:

"What an odd idea of yours, Marguerite!"

"What idea?"

"To ask me for five thousand francs!"

"Odd? Why should it be odd? Are we not strangers? You say you are in love with me; all well and good. You cannot marry me, as I am already your wife, so you buy me. Mon Dieu! Have you not bought other women? Is it not much better to give me that money than to a strange woman who would squander it? Come, you will acknowledge that it is a novel idea to actually pay your own wife! An intelligent man like you ought to see how amusing it is; besides, a man never really loves anything unless it costs him a lot of money. It would add new zest to our—conjugal love, by comparing it with your—illegitimate love. Am I not right?"

She went toward the bell.

"Now then, sir, if you do not go I will ring for my maid!"

The count stood perplexed, displeased, and suddenly taking a handful of bank notes out of his pocket, he threw them at his wife, saying:

"Here are six thousand, you witch, but remember——"

The countess picked up the money, counted it and said:

"What?"

"You must not get used to it."

She burst out laughing and said to him:

"Five thousand francs each month, or else I shall send you back to your actresses, and if you are pleased with me—I shall ask for more."

AN IDYL

The train had just left Genoa, in the direction of Marseille, and was following the rocky and sinuous coast, gliding like an iron serpent between the sea and the mountains, creeping over the yellow sand edged with silver waves and entering into the black-mouthed tunnels like a beast into its lair.

In the last carriage, a stout woman and a young man sat opposite each other. They did not speak, but occasionally they would glance at each other. She was about twenty-five years old. Seated by the window, she silently gazed at the passing landscape. She was from Piedmont, a peasant, with large black eyes, a full bust and fat cheeks. She had deposited several parcels on the wooden seat and she held a basket on her knees.

The man might have been twenty years old. He was thin and sunburned, with the dark complexion that denotes work in the open. Tied up in a handkerchief was his whole fortune; a pair of heavy boots, a pair of trousers, a shirt and a coat. Hidden under the seat were a shovel and a pickax tied together with a rope.

He was going to France to seek work.

The sun, rising in the sky, spread a fiery light over the coast; it was toward the end of May and delightful odors entered into the railway carriage. The blooming orange and lemon trees exhaled a heavy, sweet perfume that mingled with the breath of the roses which grew in profusion along the railroad track, as well as in the gardens of the wealthy and the humble homes of the peasants.

Roses are so completely at home along this coast! They fill the whole region with their dainty and powerful fragrance and make the atmosphere taste like a delicacy, something better than wine, and as intoxicating.

The train was going at slow speed as if loath to leave behind this wonderful garden! It stopped every few minutes at small stations, at clusters of white houses, then went on again leisurely, emitting long whistles. Nobody got in. One would have thought that all the world had gone to sleep and made up its mind not to travel on that sultry spring morning. The plump peasant woman from time to time closed her eyes, but she would open them suddenly whenever her basket slid from her lap. She would catch it, replace it, look out of the window a little while and then doze off again. Tiny beads of perspiration covered her brow and she breathed with difficulty, as if suffering from a painful oppression.

The young man had let his head fall on his breast and was sleeping the sound sleep of the laboring man.

All of a sudden, just as the train left a small station, the peasant woman woke up and opening her basket, drew forth a piece of bread, some hard-boiled eggs, and a flask of wine and some fine, red plums. She began to munch contentedly.

The man also wakened, and he watched the woman, watched every morsel that traveled from her knees to her lips. He sat with his arms folded, his eyes set, and his lips tightly compressed.

The woman ate like a glutton, with relish. Every little while she would take a swallow of wine to wash down the eggs and then she would stop for breath.

Everything vanished, the bread, the eggs, the plums and the wine. As soon as she was finished her meal, the man closed his eyes. Then, feeling ill at ease, she loosened her blouse, and the man suddenly looked at her again.

She did not seem to mind and continued to unbutton her dress.

The pressure of her flesh causing the opening to gape, she revealed a portion of white linen chemise and a portion of her skin.

As soon as she felt more comfortable, she turned to her fellow traveler and remarked in Italian: "It's fine weather for traveling."

"Are you from Piedmont?" he asked. "I'm from Asti."

"And I'm from Casale."

They were neighbors, and they began to talk.

They exchanged the commonplace remarks that working people repeat over and over and which are all-sufficient for their slow-working and narrow minds. They spoke of their homes and found out that they had a number of mutual acquaintances.

They quoted names and became more and more friendly as they discovered more and more people they knew. Short, rapid words, with sonorous endings and the Italian cadence, gushed from their lips.

After that, they talked about themselves. She was married and had three children whom she had left with her sister, for she had found a situation as nurse, a good situation with a French lady at Marseille.

He was going to look for work.

He had been told that he would be able to find it in France, for they were building a great deal, he had heard.

They found nothing to talk about after that.

The heat was becoming terrible; it beat down like fire on the roof of the railway carriage. A cloud of dust flew behind the train and entered through the window, and the fragrance of the roses and orange blossoms had become stronger, heavier, and more penetrating.

The two travelers went to sleep again.

They awakened almost at the same time. The sun was nearing the edge of the horizon and shed its glorious light on the blue sea. The atmosphere was lighter and cooler.

The nurse was gasping. Her dress was open and her cheeks looked flabby and moist, and in an oppressed voice, she breathed:

"I have not nursed since yesterday; I feel as if I were going to faint."

The man did not reply; he hardly knew what to say.

She continued: "When a woman has as much milk as I, she must nurse three times a day or she'll feel uncomfortable. It feels like a weight on my heart, a weight that prevents my breathing and just exhausts me. It's terrible to have so much milk."

He replied: "Yes, it must be very annoying."

She really seemed ill and almost ready to faint. She murmured: "I only have to press and the milk flows out like a fountain. It is really interesting to see. You wouldn't believe it. In Casale, all the neighbours came to see it."

He replied: "Ah! really."

"Yes, really. I would show you, only it wouldn't help me. You can't make enough come out that way."

And she paused.

The train stopped at a station. Leaning on a fence was a woman holding a crying infant in her arms. She was thin and in rags.

The nurse watched her. Then she said in a compassionate tone: "There's a woman I could help. And the baby could help me, too. I'm not rich; am I not leaving my home, my people and my baby to take a place, but still, I'd give five francs to have that child and be able to nurse it for ten minutes. It would quiet him, and me too, I can tell you. I think I would feel as if I were being born again."

She paused again. Then she passed her hot hand several times across her wet brow and moaned: "Oh! I can't stand it any longer. I believe I shall die." And with an unconscious motion, she completely opened her waist.

Her right breast appeared all swollen and stiff, with its brown teat, and the poor woman gasped: "Ah! my God! my God! What shall I do?"

The train had left the station and was continuing its route amid the flowers that gave forth their penetrating fragrance.

Once in a while a fishing smack glided over the blue sea with its motionless sail, which was reflected in the clear water as if another boat were turned upside down.

The young man, embarrassed, stammered: "But—madame—I—might perhaps be—be able to help you."

In an exhausted whisper, she replied: "Yes, if you will be so kind, you'll do me a great favor. I can't stand it any longer, really I can't."

He got on his knees before her; and she leaned over to him with a motherly gesture as if he were a child. In the movement she made to draw near to the man, a drop of milk appeared on her breast. He absorbed it quickly, and, taking this heavy breast in his mouth like a fruit, he began to drink regularly and greedily.

He had passed his arms around the woman's waist and pressed her close to him in order not to lose a drop of the nourishment. And he drank with slow gulps, like a baby.

All of a sudden she said: "That's enough, now the other side!" And he obeyed her with alacrity.

She had placed both hands on his back and now was breathing happily, freely, enjoying the perfume of the flowers carried on the breeze that entered the open windows.

"It smells mighty good," she said.

He made no reply and continued to drink at the living fountain of her breast, closing his eyes to better taste the mild fluid.

But she gently pushed him from her.

"That's enough. I feel much better now. It has put life into me again."

He rose and wiped his mouth with the back of his hand.

While she replaced her breasts inside her dress, she said:

"You did me a great favor. I thank you very much!"

And he replied in a grateful tone:

"It is I who thank you, for I hadn't eaten a thing for two days!"

THE PRISONERS

No noise in the forest, save for the light tremor of snow falling upon the trees. It had been coming down since noon, a fine snow which powdered the branches with a frozen froth, which threw over the dead leaves of the thickets a silvery roof, spread out on the roads an immense soft white rug, and increased the boundless silence of that ocean of trees.

In front of the ranger's house a bare-armed young woman was chopping wood on a rock. She was tall, slender, and strong, a daughter of the woods, daughter and wife of rangers.

A voice called from within the house. "We are alone tonight, Berthine. You've got to come in. It's almost dark—Prussians and wolves may be about."

The woodchopper answered as she split a stump with vigorous blows, each of which lifted her chest with the upward thrust of her arms.

"I've finished, Mamma. I'm coming, I'm coming. Don't worry, it's still light."

She brought in kindling and logs, stacked them by the fireplace, went out again to close the enormous oak shutters, and, inside at last, closed the heavy bolts on the door.

Her mother, a wrinkled old woman whom age had made timorous, was spinning near the fire. "I don't like it when Papa is out. Two women aren't strong."

The young woman answered, "Oh! I guess I could kill a wolf or a Prussian." And she glanced at a large revolver hanging over the hearth.

Her husband had been taken into the army at the beginning of the Prussian invasion, and the two women had remained alone with the father, the old ranger Nicolas Pichon, called "High Horse," because he had obstinately refused to leave his home to go to the greater security of the city.

The nearest city was Rethel, ancient fortress perched on a rock. The Rethelois were patriots. They had decided to resist the invaders, to shut themselves in and withstand a siege according to the tradition of their city. Twice already, under Henry IV and under Louis XIV, the people of Rethel had distinguished themselves by their heroic stands. They would do it again this time, by God, or else they would burn within their walls!

So they had bought cannon and guns, equipped a militia, formed battalions and companies, and practiced every day on the central square. Everyone—bakers, grocers, butchers, notaries, lawyers, carpenters, bookdealers, even druggists—drilled in turn, at regular times, under the command of M. Lavigne, former noncommissioned officer of dragoons, now a dry-goods merchant, having married the daughter and inherited the shop of M. Revaudon, Sr.

He had taken the rank of major, commanding officer of the square, and, with all the young men away in the regular army, he had enlisted all the others and was training them for the resistance. Fat men no longer idled in the streets but walked briskly to reduce their fat and to improve their wind. Weak men carried loads to strengthen their muscles.

The Prussians were expected but did not arrive. And yet they were not far away; for twice already their scouts had come through the woods as far as the house of the ranger Nicolas Pichon, known as High Horse.

The old ranger, who could still run like a fox, had come to warn the city. They had set the cannon, but the enemy had not appeared.

The home of High Horse served as advance post in the forest of Aveline. Twice a week he would go to the city for provisions and would bring news of the country to the city dwellers.

He had left that very day to report that a small detachment of German infantry had stopped at his house the day before about two o'clock in the afternoon, and had left almost immediately. The noncommissioned officer in charge spoke French.

When the old man left home, he took along his two dogs, two lion-jawed watchdogs, for fear of the wolves, which were becoming savage, and he left his two women with the admonition to barricade themselves in the house as soon as it became dark.

His daughter feared nothing, but the old woman always shuddered and kept saying and over, "All this will turn out bad. You'll see it will turn out bad."

That evening she was even more anxious than usual. "Do you know what time Papa'll get home?" she asked.

"Oh! Not before eleven o'clock, for sure. When he has dinner with the major, he always gets back late." And she hooked the kettle over the fire to make soup. A moment later she stopped stirring to listen to a vague noise which came to her through the chimney. She murmured, "I hear footsteps in the woods—seven or eight men, at least."

The terrified mother stopped her spinning wheel, stammering, "Oh! Good Lord! And Papa not here."

She had not finished speaking when violent blows shook the door. As the women did not reply, a strong guttural voice shouted, "Open!"

Then, after a silence, the same voice continued, "Open! Or I break the door!"

Berthine slipped the big revolver into the pocket of her skirt, then pressing her ear to the door, she asked, "Who's there?"

The voice answered, "The detachment that came by the other day."

"What do you want?"

"I have been lost in the woods since this morning with my detachment. Open or I break the door."

She had no choice. Quickly she slipped the large bolt, then pulling the heavy door, she saw six men in the pale darkness of the snow, six Prussian soldiers, the same who had gone by the day before. She said firmly, "What have you come for at this hour?"

The noncommissioned officer repeated, "I am lost, completely lost. I recognized the house. Not eaten since this morning; my men either."

Berthine declared, "But Mamma and me are all alone tonight."

The soldier, who seemed like a good sort, replied, "It doesn't matter. I will not harm you, but you will give us something to eat. We are dead tired and starved."

The young woman stepped back. "Come in," she said.

They came in, covered with snow, their helmets topped by a kind of frothy cream which made them look like meringues, and they appeared worn out, exhausted.

She showed them the wooden benches along the two sides of the large table. "Sit down," she said. "I'll make you some soup. It's true you look all in." Then she closed the bolts of the door.

She added water to her kettle, put in more butter and potatoes, then unhooking a piece of bacon hanging in the fireplace, she cut half of it and dropped it in the soup.

The six men's eyes followed her every movement with aroused hunger. They had stacked their guns and helmets in a corner, and they were waiting, well-behaved like children on school benches.

The mother had begun to spin again, casting frequent apprehensive glances at the invaders. Nothing more was heard but the light whir of the spinning wheel and the crackling of the fire and the murmur of the simmering water.

But of a sudden a strange noise made them all start, something like labored breathing at the door, an animal's breathing, strong and loud.

The German officer had darted toward the guns. The ranger's daughter stopped him with a gesture, and said smiling, "It's the wolves. They are like you, they prowl and are hungry."

The man, incredulous, wished to have a look, and as soon as he opened the upper panel of the door, he saw two big gray beasts streaking away. He muttered as he resumed his place, "I wouldn't have believed it." And he waited for his stew to be ready.

They ate it voraciously, with mouths stretched back to the ears to swallow the more, eyes opening wide at the same time as jaws, and throat noises like the gurgling in a drainpipe.

The two women silently watched the rapid movements of the big red beards; and the potatoes disappeared into the moving fleeces.

As they were thirsty, Berthine went to the cellar to draw cider. She was gone for some time; it was a small vaulted wine cellar which, it was said, had served as prison and hiding place during the Revolution. One had access to it by means of a narrow spiral stairway closed by a trap door in the rear of the kitchen.

When Berthine reappeared, she was laughing, she was laughing to herself in a sly way. And she gave the Germans her full pitcher.

Then she ate too, with her mother, at the other end of the kitchen.

The soldiers had finished eating, and all six of them fell asleep around the table. From time to time a forehead would fall onto the table with a thud, whereupon the man, rudely awakened, would straighten.

Berthine said to the officer, "Lie down before the fire, why don't you? There's room enough for six. I'm going up to my room with Mamma."

The two women went up to the second floor. The men heard them lock their door, walk about a bit; then they made no more noise.

The Prussians stretched out on the tile floor, their feet toward the fire, their heads on their rolled up coats, and all six were soon snoring, on six different keys, sharp or sonorous, but steady and powerful.

They had been sleeping for some time when a shot rang out, so loud that one would have thought it directed against the walls of the house. The soldiers were on their feet at once. But two more detonations burst out, followed by three others.

The upstairs door opened suddenly, and Berthine appeared, barefoot, in her nightgown, a candle in her hand, looking scared to death. She stammered, "That's the French, there are at least two hundred of them. If they find you here, they'll burn the house down. Go down to the cellar, quick, and don't make any noise. If you make any noise, we're lost."

"All right, we will. How do we go down?"

The young woman hurriedly lifted the narrow square trap door, and the six men disappeared by the little spiral staircase, disappearing into the ground one after another, descending backwards for surer footing.

But when the point of the last helmet had gone out of sight, Berthine slammed the heavy oak board, thick as a wall, hard as steel, held by hinges and a lock worthy of a prison cell, and turned the key twice in the lock. Then she began to laugh silently and ecstatically, with a mad desire to dance over the heads of her prisoners.

They made no noise whatever, enclosed as if in a box, a box of stone, with air entering only through a barred vent.

Berthine immediately relit her fire, put her kettle on again, and made more soup, saying to herself, "Papa will be tired tonight."

Then she sat down and waited. The only sound to break the silence was the regular ticktock of the grandfather clock. From time to time she glanced impatiently at the clock, as if to say, "It sure is slow tonight."

But soon she thought she could hear murmuring below. Indistinct voices reached her through the stone vault of the cellar. The Prussians were beginning to suspect her ruse, and soon the officer climbed the little staircase and struck the trap door with his fists. Again he shouted, "Open!"

She rose, came close and, imitating his accent, said, "What do you want?"

"Open!"

"I won't."

The man was getting angry. "Open, or else I break the door!"

She began to laugh. "Break away, my good man, break away!"

So he began to strike the butt of his gun against the oaken trap door closed over his head. But it would have resisted blows from a catapult.

The ranger's daughter heard him go down again. Then, one after another, the soldiers came to try their strength and to inspect the trap door. But, doubtless judging their attempts futile, they all descended once more into the cellar and began to talk among themselves as before.

Berthine listened to them, then went to open the outside door and listened to the night.

A distant bark reached her. She began to whistle like a hunter, and almost instantly, two enormous dogs rose up in the dark and jumped playfully upon her. She grasped them by the neck and held them to keep them from running. Then she shouted with all her strength, "Hi, Papa!"

A voice replied, still far off, "Hi, Berthine."

She waited for a few seconds, then called again, "Hi, Papa!"

The voice, nearer now, answered, "Hi, Berthine!"

"Don't go past the vent," she said. "There are some Prussians in the cellar."

And suddenly the man's tall silhouette was outlined to the left, standing between two tree trunks. "Prussians in the cellar? What are they up to?"

His daughter began to laugh. "It's them that were here yesterday. Lost in the forest. I put them in the cellar to cool their heels." And she related the adventure, how she had scared them with revolver shots and locked them up in the cellar.

The old man, still serious, asked, "What do you expect me to do with them at this hour?"

She answered, "Go and get M. Lavigne and his men. He'll make them prisoners. Will he be glad!"

Old man Pichon smiled. "That's so. He will be glad!"

His daughter continued, "There's some soup for you. Eat it quick, then go."

The old ranger sat down and began to eat the soup after placing two full dishes on the floor for his dogs.

The Prussians, hearing the voices above, were now silent.

High Horse left a quarter of an hour later. And Berthine, head in hands, waited.

The prisoners began to move about again. They shouted now and beat incessantly with furious blows of their gun butts the solid trap door of the cellar.

Then they began to shoot through the vent, doubtless hoping to be heard should some German detachment be passing in the neighborhood.

The ranger's daughter did not stir; but all this noise annoyed her, made her nervous. A devilish anger was beginning to get hold of her. She had a mind to murder them, the scoundrels, just to make them quiet.

Then, her impatience increasing, she started to look at the clock, counting the minutes.

The father had left an hour and a half ago. He had reached the city by now. She could picture him telling M. Lavigne about it, and the major was turning pale with emotion, and ringing for his maid to bring his uniform and his arms. She could hear the drummer running through the streets. Frightened heads appeared at the windows. The citizen-soldiers left their houses, half-dressed, out of breath, buckling their belts, and rushing towards their commander's house.

Then the troops, with High Horse leading, began to march in the night, in the snow, towards the forest.

She looked at the clock. "They can get here in an hour."

A nervous impatience consumed her. The minutes seemed interminable. How long it was!

At last the time she had set for their arrival was indicated on the dial.

And she opened the door again to listen to their coming. She saw a shadow walking warily. She was frightened and cried out. It was her father. He said. "They sent me to see if there was anything new."

"No, nothing."

Whereupon he gave a prolonged, strident blast on his whistle into the night. And soon they saw something brown coming slowly under the trees: the vanguard of ten men.

High Horse repeated over and over, "Don't go in front of the cellar vent." And the firstcomers showed the others the dreaded vent.

The main body of the troop finally appeared, two hundred men in all, each one with two hundred rounds of ammunition.

M. Lavigne, on edge, excited, placed them in such a way as to completely surround the house, while leaving a large open space in front of the little black hole level with the ground, through which the cellar received air.

Then he entered the house and inquired about the strength and disposition of the enemy, now so quiet that one would have thought them vanished, passed out or escaped through the vent.

M. Lavigne kicked the trap door with his foot and called out, "Mr. Prussian officer?"

The German did not reply.

The major continued, "Mr. Prussian officer?" But his efforts were vain. For twenty minutes he summoned the silent officer to surrender with arms and effects, promising him and his soldiers safety and military honors. But he obtained no sign either of consent or hostility. The situation was becoming difficult.

The militiamen stamped their feet in the snow, clapped their shoulders vigorously, the way coachmen do to keep warm, and they watched the vent with an increasing and childish urge to go near it.

Finally one of them, named Potdevin, who was very agile, decided to risk it. He leaped forward like a deer. His attempt succeeded. The prisoners seemed to be dead.

A voice shouted, "Nobody's there!"

And another soldier crossed the open space before the dangerous hole. Now it became a game. Every second a man would dash from one group to the other, as children do at prisoner's base, and he would churn the snow in his wild sprint. They had made several fires to warm themselves, and this running profile of the national guard appeared illuminated in its swift trip from the right camp to the left.

Someone shouted, "Your turn, Maloison!"

Maloison was a fat baker whose girth caused merriment among his pals.

He hesitated. They made fun of him. When he finally made up his mind, he set out on the double, in a regular rhythm which nevertheless made him pant and which shook his heavy paunch.

The entire detachment laughed till the tears came. They cried out in encouragement, "Bravo, bravo, Maloison!"

He had covered about two thirds of his distance when a sudden long red flame burst from the vent. A detonation thundered, and the corpulent baker fell on his face with a dreadful cry.

No one rushed up to help him. And they watched him drag himself painfully on all fours in the snow, groaning the while, until, the fateful passage behind him, he fainted.

He had a bullet in the fat of his thigh, high up.

After the first surprise and the first terror, laughter broke out again.

But Major Lavigne appeared on the threshold of the ranger's house. He had just drawn up his plan of attack. He commanded in a vibrant voice, "Tinsmith Planchut and his men!"

Three men stepped forward. "Take down the gutters of the house."

And in a quarter of an hour they had brought the major twenty meters of gutter. Whereupon, with a thousand measures of precaution, he had them bore a small round hole in the edge of the trap door, and starting a flow of water from the pump to this opening, he declared in high glee, "We shall treat the Germans to a drink."

A frenzied hurrah of admiration burst forth, followed by joyous shouts and laughs. And the major organized work platoons which would relieve each other every five minutes. Then he commanded, "Pump!"

And the iron handle having been put into motion, a slight noise glided along the length of the gutters and soon fell into the cellar, from step to step, with the cadence of a waterfall.

They waited.

An hour went by, then two, then three. The French officer walked back and forth feverishly in the kitchen, putting his ear to the floor from time to time, trying to guess what the enemy was doing, wondering if he would soon capitulate.

He was stirring now, the enemy. They could hear him moving barrels, speaking, splashing.

Toward eight o'clock in the morning a voice came from the vent. "I wish to speak to the French officer."

Lavigne replied from the window, without thrusting his head out too far, "Do you surrender?"

"I surrender."

"In that case, hand over the guns."

They saw a gun fall from the hole into the snow, then too, then three, all of them. And the same voice declared, "I haven't any more. Hurry. I'm drowning."

The major comanded, "Cease pumping." The pump handle fell motionless. And having filled the kitchen with soldiers fully armed, he slowly lifted the oaken trap door.

Four soaked heads appeared, four blond heads with long light hair, and soon the other two—six shaking, dripping, frightened Germans came out of the trap door.

They were seized and tied. Then, as the French feared a surprise, they left at once, in two companies, one carrying Maloison on a mattress with poles.

They marched triumphantly into Rethel.

M. Lavigne was decorated for having captured a Prussian vanguard, and the fat baker was awarded the military medal for wounds received at the hands of the enemy.

CHÂLI

Admiral de la Vallée, who seemed to be half asleep in his armchair, said in a voice which sounded like an old woman's:

"I had a very singular little love adventure once; would you like to hear it?"

He spoke from the depths of his great armchair with that everlasting dry, wrinkled smile on his lips, that smile à la Voltaire, which made people take him for a terrible skeptic.

I

"I was thirty years of age and a first lieutenant in the navy, when I was intrusted with an astronomical expedition to Central India. The English government provided me with all the necessary means for carrying out my enterprise, and I was soon busied with a few followers in that vast, strange, surprising country.

"It would take me ten volumes to relate that journey. I went through wonderfully magnificent regions, was received by strangely handsome princes and was entertained with incredible magnificence. For two months it seemed to me as if I were walking in a fairy kingdom on the back of imaginary elephants. In the midst of wild forests I discovered extraordinary ruins, delicate and chiseled like jewels, fine as lace and enormous as mountains, those fabulous, divine monuments which are so graceful that one falls in love with their form as with a woman, feeling a physical and sensual pleasure in looking at them. As Victor Hugo says, 'Whilst wide awake I was walking in a dream.'

"Toward the end of my journey I reached Ganhard, which was formerly one of the most prosperous towns in Central India but is now much decayed. It is governed by a wealthy, arbitrary, violent, generous and cruel prince. His name is Rajah Maddan, a true oriental potentate, delicate and barbarous, affable and sanguinary, combining feminine grace with pitiless ferocity.

"The city lies at the bottom of a valley, on the banks of a little lake surrounded by pagodas which bathe their walls in the water. At a distance the city looks like a white spot which grows larger as one approaches it, and by degrees you discover the domes and spires, the slender and graceful summits of Indian monuments.

"At about an hour's distance from the gates I met a superbly caparisoned elephant surrounded by a guard of honor which the sovereign had sent me, and I was conducted to the palace with great ceremony.

"I should have liked to take the time to put on my gala uniform, but royal impatience would not admit of it. He was anxious to make my acquaintance, to know what he might expect from me.

"I was ushered into a great hall surrounded by galleries, in the midst of bronze-colored soldiers in splendid uniforms, while all about were standing men dressed in striking robes, studded with precious stones.

"I saw a shining mass, a kind of setting sun reposing on a bench like our garden benches without a back; it was the rajah who was waiting for me, motionless, in a robe of the purest canary color. He had some ten or fifteen mllion francs' worth of diamonds on him, and by itself, on his forehead, glistened the famous star of Delhi, which has always belonged to the illustrious dynasty of the Pariharas of Mundore, from whom my host was descended.

"He was a man of about five and twenty, who seemed to have some Negro blood in his veins, although he belonged to the purest Hindu race. He had large, almost motionless, rather vague eyes, fat lips, a curly beard, low forehead and dazzling sharp white teeth, which he frequently showed with a mechanical smile. He got up and gave me his hand in the English fashion and then made me sit down beside him on a bench which was so high that my feet hardly touched the ground and on which I was very uncomfortable.

"He immediately proposed a tiger hunt for the next day; war and hunting were his chief occupations, and he could hardly understand how one could care for anything else. He was evidently fully persuaded that I had only come all that distance to amuse him a little and to be the companion of his pleasures.

"As I stood greatly in need of his assistance, I tried to flatter his tastes, and he was so pleased with me that he immediately wished to show me how his trained boxers fought and led the way into a kind of arena situated within the palace.

"At his command two naked men appeared, their hands covered with steel claws. They immediately began to attack each other, trying to strike one another with these sharp weapons which left long cuts from which the blood flowed freely down their dark skins.

"It lasted for a long time, till their bodies were a mass of wounds, and the combatants were tearing each other's flesh with these pointed blades. One of them had his jaw smashed, while the ear of the other was split into three pieces.

"The prince looked on with ferocious pleasure, uttered grunts of delight and imitated all their movements with careless gestures, crying out constantly:

" 'Strike, strike hard!'

"One fell down unconscious and had to be carried out of the arena, covered with blood, while the rajah uttered a sigh of regret because it was over so soon.

"He turned to me to know my opinion; I was disgusted, but I congratulated him loudly. He then gave orders that I was to be conducted to Kuch-Mahal (the palace of pleasure), where I was to be lodged.

"This bijou palace was situated at the extremity of the royal park, and one of its walls was built into the sacred lake of Vihara. It was square, with three rows of galleries with colonnades of most beautiful workmanship. At each angle there were light, lofty or low towers, standing either singly or in pairs; no two were alike, and they looked like flowers growing out of that graceful plant of oriental architecture. All were surmounted by fantastic roofs, like coquettish ladies' caps.

"In the middle of the edifice a large dome raised its round cupola, like a woman's bosom, beside a beautiful clock tower.

"The whole building was covered with sculpture from top to bottom, with exquisite arabesques which delighted the eye, motionless processions of delicate figures whose attitudes and gestures in stone told the story of Indian manners and customs.

"The rooms were lighted by windows with dentelated arches, looking on to the gardens. On the marble floor were designs of graceful bouquets in onyx, lapis lazuli and agate.

"I had scarcely had time to finish my toilet when Haribada, a court dignitary who was specially charged to communicate between the prince and me, announced his sovereign's visit.

"The saffron-colored rajah appeared, again shook hands with me and began to tell me a thousand different things, constantly asking me for my opinion, which I had great difficulty in giving him. Then he wished to show me the ruins of the former palace at the other extremity of the gardens.

"It was a real forest of stones inhabited by a large tribe of apes. On our approach the males began to run along the walls, making the most hideous faces at us, while the females ran away, carrying off their young in their arms. The rajah shouted with laughter and pinched my arm to draw my attention and to testify his own delight and sat down in the midst of the ruins, while around us, squatting on the top of the walls, perching on every eminence, a number of animals with white whiskers put out their tongues and shook their fists at us.

"When he had seen enough of this the yellow rajah rose and began to walk sedately on, keeping me always at his side, happy at having shown me such things on the very day of my arrival and reminding me that a grand tiger hunt was to take place the next day in my honor.

"I was present at it, at a second, a third, at ten, twenty in succession. We hunted all the animals which the country produces in turn: the panther, the bear, elephant, antelope and the crocodile—half the beasts in creation, I should say. I was disgusted at seeing so much blood flow and tired of this monotonous pleasure.

"At length the prince's ardor abated and, at my urgent request, he left me a little leisure for work, contenting himself by loading me with costly presents. He sent me jewels, magnificent stuffs, and well-broken animals of all sorts, which Haribada presented to me with apparently as grave respect as if I had been the sun himself, although he heartily despised me at the bottom of his heart.

"Every day a procession of servants brought me, in covered dishes, a portion of each course that was served at the royal table. Every day he seemed to take an extreme pleasure in getting up some new entertainment for me—dances by the bayaderes, jugglers, reviews of the troops—and I was obliged to pretend to be most delighted with it so as not to hurt his feelings when he wished to show me his wonderful country in all its charm and all its splendor.

"As soon as I was left alone for a few moments I either worked or went to see the monkeys, whose company pleased me a great deal better than that of their royal master.

"One evening, however, on coming back from a walk, I found Haribada outside the gate of my palace. He told me in mysterious tones that a gift from the king was waiting for me in my abode, and he said that his master begged me to excuse him for not having sooner thought of offering me that of which I had been deprived for such a long time.

"After these obscure remarks the ambassador bowed and withdrew.

"When I went in I saw six little girls standing against the wall, motionless, side by side, like smelts on a skewer. The eldest was perhaps ten and the youngest eight years old. For the first moment I could not understand why this girls' school had taken up its abode in my rooms; then, however, I divined the prince's delicate attention: he had made me a present of a harem and had chosen it very young from an excess of generosity. There the more unripe the fruit is, in the higher estimation it is held.

"For some time I remained confused, embarrassed and ashamed in the presence of these children who looked at me with great grave eyes which seemed already to divine what I might want of them.

"I did not know what to say to them; I felt inclined to send them back, but I could not return the presents of a prince; it would have been a mortal insult. I was obliged, therefore, to install this troop of children in my palace.

"They stood motionless, looking at me, waiting for my orders, trying to read my thoughts in my eyes. Confound such a present! How absurdly it was in my way. At last, thinking that I must be looking rather ridiculous, I asked the eldest her name.

"'Châli,' she replied.

"This little creature, with her beautiful skin which was slightly yellow, like old ivory, was a marvel, a perfect statue, with her face and its long and severe lines.

"I then asked, in order to see what she would reply and also, perhaps, to embarrass her:

"'What have you come here for?'

"She replied in her soft, harmonious voice: 'I have come to be altogether at my lord's disposal and to do whatever he wishes.' She was evidently quite resigned.

"I put the same question to the youngest, who answered immediately in her shrill voice:

"'I am here to do whatever you ask me, my master.'

"This one was like a little mouse and was very taking, just as they all were, so I took her in my arms and kissed her. The others made a movement to go away, thinking, no doubt, that I had made my choice, but I ordered them to stay and, sitting down in the Indian fashion, I made them all sit round me and began to tell them fairy tales, for I spoke their language tolerably well.

"They listened very attentively and trembled, wringing their hands in agony. Poor little things, they were not thinking any longer of the reason why they were sent to me.

"When I had finished my story I called Latchmân, my confidential servant, and made him bring sweetmeats and cakes, of which they ate enough to make themselves ill. Then, as I began to find the adventure rather funny, I organized games to amuse my wives.

"One of these diversions had an enormous success. I made a bridge of my legs, and the six children ran underneath, the smallest beginning and the tallest always knocking against them a little, because she did not stoop enough. It made them shout with laughter, and these young voices sounding through the low vaults of my sumptuous palace seemed to wake it up and to people it with childlike gaiety and life.

"Next I took great interest in seeing to the sleeping apartments of my innocent concubines, and in the end I saw them safely locked up under the surveillance of four female servants whom the prince had sent me at the same time, in order to take care of my sultanas.

"For a week I took the greatest pleasure in acting the part of a father toward these living dolls. We had capital games of hide-and-seek and puss in the corner, which gave them the greatest pleasure. Every day I taught them a new game to their intense delight.

"My house now seemed to be one large nursery, and my little friends, dressed in beautiful silk stuffs and in materials embroidered with gold and silver, ran up and down the long galleries and the quiet rooms like little human animals.

"Châli was an adorable little creature, timid and gentle, who soon got to love me ardently, with some degree of shame, with hesitation, as if afraid of European morality, with reserve and scruples and yet with passionate tenderness. I cherished her as if I had been her father.

"The others continued to play in the palace like a lot of happy kittens, but Châli never left me except when I went to the prince.

"We passed delicious hours together in the ruins of the old castle, among the monkeys, who had become our friends.

"She used to lie on my knees and remain there, turning all sorts of things over in her little sphinx's head, or perhaps not thinking of anything, retaining that beautiful, charming, hereditary pose of that noble and dreamy people, the hieratic pose of the sacred statues.

"In a large brass dish I had one day brought provisions, cakes, fruits. The apes came nearer and nearer, followed by their young ones, who were more timid; at last they sat down round us in a circle without daring to come any nearer, waiting for me to distribute my delicacies. Then almost invariably a male more daring than the rest would come to me with outstretched hand, like a beggar, and I would give him something which he would take to his wife. All the others immediately began to utter furious cries, cries of rage and jealousy, and I could not make the terrible racket cease except by throwing each one his share.

"As I was very comfortable in the ruins, I had my instruments brought there so that I might be able to work. As soon, however, as they saw the copper fittings on my scientific instruments, the monkeys, no doubt taking them for some deadly engines, fled on all sides, uttering the most piercing cries.

"I often spent my evenings with Châli on one of the external galleries that looked on to the lake of Vihara. One night in silence we looked at the bright moon gliding over the sky, throwing a mantle of trembling silver over the water and, on the further shore, upon the row of small pagodas like carved mushrooms with their stalks in the water. Taking the thoughtful head of my little mistress between my hands, I printed a long, soft kiss on her polished brow, on her great eyes which were full of the secret of that ancient and fabulous land and on her calm lips which opened to my caress. I felt a confused, powerful, above all a poetical, sensation, the sensation that I possessed a whole race in this little girl, that mysterious race from which all the others seem to have taken their origin.

"The prince, however, continued to load me with presents. One day he sent me a very unexpected object which excited a passionate admiration in Châli. It was merely one of those cardboard boxes, covered with shells stuck on outside, which can be bought at any European seaside resort for a penny or two. But there it was a jewel beyond price, and, no doubt, was the first that had found its way into the kingdom. I put it on a table and left it there, wondering at the value which was set upon this trumpery article out of a bazaar.

"But Châli never got tired of looking at it, of admiring it ecstatically. From time to time she would say to me, 'May I touch it?' And when I had given her permission she raised the lid, closed it again with the greatest precaution, touched the shells very gently, and the contact seemed to give her real physical pleasure.

"However, I had finished my scientific work, and it was time for me to return.

I was a long time in making up my mind, kept back by my tenderness for my little friend, but at last I was obliged to fix the day of my departure.

"The prince got up fresh hunting excursions and fresh wrestling matches, and after a fortnight of these pleasures I declared that I could stay no longer, and he gave me my liberty.

"My farewell from Châli was heart-rending. She wept, lying beside me with her head on my breast, shaken with sobs. I did not know how to console her; my kisses were no good.

"All at once an idea struck me and, getting up, I went and got the shell box and, putting it into her hands, I said, 'That is for you; it is yours.'

"Then I saw her smile at first. Her whole face was lighted up with internal joy, with that profound joy which comes when impossible dreams are suddenly realized, and she embraced me ardently.

"All the same she wept bitterly when I bade her a last farewell.

"I gave paternal kisses and cakes to all the rest of my wives, and then I left for home."

II

"Two years had passed when my duties again called me to Bombay, and because I knew the country and the language well, I was left there to undertake another mission.

"I finished what I had to do as quickly as possible, and as I had a considerable amount of spare time on my hands, I determined to go and see my friend Rajah Maddan and my dear little Châli once more, though I expected to find her much changed.

"The rajah received me with every demonstration of pleasure and hardly left me for a moment during the first day of my visit. At night, however, when I was alone I sent for Haribada, and after several misleading questions I said to him:

"'Do you know what has become of little Châli whom the rajah gave me?'

"He immediately assumed a sad and troubled look and said, in evident embarrassment:

"'We had better not speak of her.'

"'Why? She was a dear little woman.'

"'She turned out badly, sir.'

"'What—Châli? What has become of her? Where is she?'

"'I mean to say that she came to a bad end.'

"'A bad end! Is she dead?'

"'Yes. She committed a very dreadful action.'

"I was very much distressed. I felt my heart beat; my breast was oppressed with grief, and I insisted on knowing what she had done and what had happened to her.

"The man became more and more embarrassed and murmured: 'You had better not ask about it.'

"'But I want to know.'

"'She stole——'

"'Who—Châli? What did she steal?'

"'Something that belonged to you.'

"'To me? What do you mean?'

" 'The day you left she stole that little box which the prince had given you; it was found in her hands.'

" 'What box are you talking about?'

" 'The box covered with shells.'

" 'But I gave it to her.'

"The Hindu looked at me with stupefaction and then replied: 'Well, she declared with the most sacred oaths that you had given it to her, but nobody could believe that you could have given a king's present to a slave, and so the rajah had her punished.'

" 'How was she punished? What was done to her?'

" 'She was tied up in a sack and thrown into the lake from this window, from the window of the room in which we are, where she had committed the theft.'

"I felt the most terrible grief that I ever experienced and made a sign to Haribada to go away so that he might not see my tears. I spent the night on the gallery which looked on to the lake, on the gallery where I had so often held the poor child on my knees, and pictured to myself her pretty little body lying decomposed in a sack in the dark waters beneath me.

"The next day I left again, in spite of the rajah's entreaties and evident vexation, and I now still feel as if I had never loved any woman but Châli."

THE STORY OF A FARM GIRL

As the weather was very fine the people on the farm had dined more quickly than usual and had returned to the fields.

The female servant, Rose, remained alone in the large kitchen, where the fire on the hearth was dying out under the large boiler of hot water. From time to time she took some water out of it and slowly washed her plates and dishes, stopping occasionally to look at the two streaks of light which the sun threw onto the long table through the window and which showed the defects in the glass.

Three venturesome hens were picking up the crumbs under the chairs, while the smell of the poultry yard and the warmth from the cow stall came in through the half-open door, and a cock was heard crowing in the distance.

When she had finished her work, wiped down the table, dusted the mantelpiece and put the plates onto the high dresser, close to the wooden clock with its enormous pendulum, she drew a long breath, as she felt rather oppressed without knowing exactly why. She looked at the black clay walls, the rafters that were blackened with smoke, from which spiders' webs were hanging amid pickled herrings and strings of onions, and then she sat down, rather overcome by the stale emanations from the floor, on which so many things had been spilled. With these was mingled the smell of the pans of milk, which were set out to raise the cream in the adjoining dairy.

She wanted to sew, as usual, but she did not feel strong enough for it, and so she went to get a mouthful of fresh air at the door, which seemed to do her good.

The fowls were lying on the smoking dunghill; some of them were scratching with one claw in search of worms, while the cock stood up proudly among them. Now and then he selected one of them and walked round her with a slight cluck of amorous invitation. The hen got up in a careless way as she received his attentions, supported herself on her legs and spread out her wings; then she shook her feathers to shake out the dust and stretched herself out on the dunghill again, while he crowed in sign of triumph, and the cocks in all the neighboring farmyards replied to him, as if they were uttering amorous challenges from farm to farm.

The girl looked at them without thinking; then she raised her eyes and was almost dazzled at the sight of the apple trees in blossom, which looked almost like powdered heads. Just then a colt, full of life and friskiness, galloped past her. Twice he jumped over the ditches and then stopped suddenly, as if surprised at being alone.

She also felt inclined to run; she felt inclined to move and to stretch her limbs and to repose in the warm, breathless air. She took a few undecided steps and closed her eyes, for she was seized with a feeling of animal comfort; then she went to look for the eggs in the hen loft. There were thirteen of them, which she took in and put into the storeroom, but the smell from the kitchen disgusted her again, and she went out to sit on the grass for a time.

The farmyard, which was surrounded by trees, seemed to be asleep. The tall grass, among which the tall yellow dandelions rose up like streaks of yellow light, was of a vivid green, the fresh spring green. The apple trees threw their shade all round them, and the thatched houses, on which the blue and yellow iris flowers with their swordlike leaves grew, smoked as if the moisture of the stables and barns was coming through the straw.

The girl went to the shed where the carts and traps were kept. Close to it, in a ditch, there was a large patch of violets whose scent was perceptible all round, while beyond it could be seen the open country, where the corn was growing, with clumps of trees in the distance and groups of laborers here and there, who looked as small as dolls, and white horses like toys, who were pulling a child's cart, driven by a man as tall as one's finger.

She took up a bundle of straw, threw it into the ditch and sat down upon it; then, not feeling comfortable, she undid it, spread it out and lay down upon it at full length on her back, with both arms under her head and her limbs stretched out.

Gradually her eyes closed, and she was falling into a state of delightful languor. She was, in fact, almost asleep, when she felt two hands on her bosom, and then she sprang up at a bound. It was Jacques, one of the farm laborers, a tall fellow from Picardy, who had been making love to her for a long time. He had been looking after the sheep and, seeing her lying down in the shade, he had come stealthily, holding his breath, with glistening eyes and bits of straw in his hair.

He tried to kiss her, but she gave him a smack in the face, for she was as strong as he, and he was shrewd enough to beg her pardon, so they sat down side by side and talked amicably. They spoke about the favorable weather, of their master, who was a good fellow, then of their neighbors, of all the people in the country round, of themselves, of their village, of their youthful days, of their recollections, of their relatives whom they had not seen for a long time and might not see again. She grew sad, as she thought of it, while he, with one fixed idea in his head, rubbed against her with a kind of shiver, overcome by desire.

"I have not seen my mother for a long time," she said. "It is very hard to be separated like that." And she directed her looks into the distance, toward the village in the north, which she had left.

Suddenly, however, he seized her by the neck and kissed her again, but she struck him so violently in the face with her clenched fist that his nose began to bleed, and he got up and laid his head against the stem of a tree. When she saw that she was sorry and, going up to him, she said:

"Have I hurt you?"

He, however, only laughed. "No, it was a mere nothing," though she had hit him right on the middle of the nose. "What a devil!" he said, and he looked at her with admiration, for she had inspired him with a feeling of respect and of a very different kind of admiration, which was the beginning of a real love for that tall, strong wench.

When the bleeding had stopped he proposed a walk, as he was afraid of his neighbor's heavy hand, if they remained side by side like that much longer, but she took his arm of her own accord in the avenue, as if they had been out for an evening walk, and said: "It is not nice of you to despise me like that, Jacques."

He protested, however. No, he did not despise her. He was in love with her; that was all.

"So you really want to marry me?" she asked.

He hesitated and then looked at her aside, while she looked straight ahead of her. She had fat red cheeks, a full, protuberant bust under her muslin dress, thick red lips, and her neck, which was almost bare, was covered with small beads of perspiration. He felt a fresh access of desire and, putting his lips to her ear, he murmured: "Yes, of course I do."

Then she threw her arms round his neck and kissed for such a long time that they both of them lost their breath. From that moment the eternal story of love began between them. They plagued one another in corners; they met in the moonlight under a haystack and gave each other bruises on the legs with their heavy nailed boots. By degrees, however, Jacques seemed to grow tired of her: he avoided her, scarcely spoke to her and did not try any longer to meet her alone, which made her sad and anxious, especially when she found that she was pregnant.

At first she was in a state of consternation; then she got angry, and her rage increased every day, because she could not meet him, as he avoided her most carefully. At last, one night when everyone in the farmhouse was asleep, she went out noiselessly in her petticoat, with bare feet, crossed the yard and opened the door of the stable where Jacques was lying in a large box of straw over his horses. He pretended to snore when he heard her coming, but she knelt down by his side and shook him until he sat up.

"What do you want?" he then asked of her. And she, with clenched teeth and trembling with anger, replied:

"I want—I want you to marry me, as you promised."

But he only laughed and replied: "Oh, if a man were to marry all the girls with whom he has made a slip, he would have more than enough to do."

Then she seized him by the throat, threw him on to his back, so that he could not disengage himself from her, and, half strangling him, she shouted into his face: "I am *enceinte*, do you hear? I am *enceinte!*"

He gasped for breath, as he was nearly choked, and so they remained, both of them, motionless and without speaking, in the dark silence which was only broken by the noise that a horse made as he pulled the hay out of the manger and then slowly chewed it.

When Jacques found that she was the stronger he stammered out: "Very well, I will marry you, as that is the case."

But she did not believe his promises. "It must be at once," she said. "You must have the banns put up."

"At once," he replied.

"Swear solemnly that you will."

He hesitated for a few moments and then said: "I swear it, by heaven."

Then she released her grasp and went away without another word.

She had no chance of speaking to him for several days, and as the stable was now always locked at night, she was afraid to make any noise, for fear of creating a scandal. One day, however, she saw another man come in at dinner time, and so she said: "Has Jacques left?"

"Yes," the man replied; "I have got his place."

This made her tremble so violently that she could not take the saucepan off the fire, and later, when they were all at work, she went up into her room and cried, burying her head in her bolster so that she might not be heard. During the day, however, she tried to obtain some information without exciting any suspicions, but she was so overwhelmed by the thoughts of her misfortune that she fancied that all the people whom she asked laughed maliciously. All she learned, however, was that he had left the neighborhood altogether.

II

Then a cloud of constant misery began for her. She worked mechanically, without thinking of what she was doing, with one fixed idea in her head: "Suppose people were to know."

This continual feeling made her so incapable of reasoning that she did not even try to think of any means of avoiding the disgrace that she knew must ensue, which was irreparable and drawing nearer every day and which was as sure as death itself. She got up every morning long before the others and persistently tried to look at her figure in a piece of broken looking glass at which she did her hair, as she was very anxious to know whether anybody would notice a change in her, and during the day she stopped working every few minutes to look at herself from top to toe, to see whether the size of her abdomen did not make her apron look too short.

The months went on. She scarcely spoke now, and when she was asked a question she did not appear to understand. She had a frightened look, with haggard eyes and trembling hands, which made her master say to her occasionally: "My poor girl, how stupid you have grown lately."

In church she hid behind a pillar and no longer ventured to go to confession. She feared to face the priest, to whom she attributed a superhuman power which enabled him to read people's consciences, and at mealtimes the looks of her fellow servants almost made her faint with mental agony. She was always fancying that she had been found out by the cowherd, a precocious and cunning little lad, whose bright eyes seemed always to be watching her.

One morning the postman brought her a letter, and as she had never received one in her life before, she was so upset by it that she was obliged to sit down. Perhaps it was from him? But as she could not read, she sat anxious and trembling with that piece of paper covered with ink in her hand; after a time, however, she put it into her pocket, as she did not venture to confide her secret to anyone. She often stopped in her work to look at the lines, written at regular intervals and terminating in a signature, imagining vaguely that she would suddenly discover their meaning. At last, as she felt half mad with impatience and anxiety, she went to the schoolmaster, who told her to sit down and read the letter to her, as follows:

"MY DEAR DAUGHTER: *I write to tell you that I am very ill. Our neighbor, Monsieur Dentu, begs you to come, if you can,*

"For your affectionate mother,
"CESAIRE DENTU,
"Deputy Mayor."

She did not say a word and went away, but as soon as she was alone her legs gave way, and she fell down by the roadside and remained there till night.

When she got back she told the farmer her trouble. He allowed her to go home for as long as she wanted, promised to have her work done by a charwoman and to take her back when she returned.

Her mother died soon after she got there, and the next day Rose gave birth to a seven months' child, a miserable little skeleton, thin enough to make anybody shudder. It seemed to be suffering continually, to judge from the painful manner in which it moved its poor little limbs, which were as thin as a crab's legs, but it lived, for all that. She said that she was married but that she could not saddle herself with the child, so she left it with some neighbors who promised to take great care of it, and she went back to the farm.

But then in her heart, which had been wounded so long, there arose something like brightness, an unknown love for that frail little creature which she had left behind her, but there was fresh suffering in that very love, suffering which she felt every hour and every minute, because she was parted from the child. What pained her most, however, was a mad longing to kiss it, to press it in her arms, to feel the warmth of its little body against her skin. She could not sleep at night; she thought of it the whole day long, and in the evening, when her work was done, she used to sit in front of the fire and look at it intently, like people do whose thoughts are far away.

They began to talk about her and to tease her about her lover. They asked her whether he was tall, handsome and rich. When was the wedding to be, and the christening? And often she ran away to cry by herself, for these questions seemed to hurt her, like the prick of a pin, and in order to forget their jokes she began to work still more energetically and, still thinking of her child, she sought for the means of saving up money for it and determined to work so that her master would be obliged to raise her wages.

Then by degrees she almost monopolized the work and persuaded him to get rid of one servant girl who had become useless since she had taken to working like two; she economized in the bread, oil and candles, in the corn which they gave to the fowls too extravagantly and in the fodder for the horses and cattle, which was rather wasted. She was as miserly about her master's money as if it had been her own, and by dint of making good bargains, of getting high prices for all their produce and by baffling the peasants' tricks when they offered anything for sale, he at last intrusted her with buying and selling everything, with the direction of all the laborers and with the quantity of provisions necessary for the household, so that in a short time she became indispensable to him. She kept such a strict eye on everything about her, that under her direction the farm prospered wonderfully, and for five miles round people talked of "Master Vallin's servant," and the farmer himself said everywhere: "That girl is worth more than her weight in gold."

But time passed by, and her wages remained the same. Her hard work was accepted as something that was due from every good servant and as a mere token of her good will, and she began to think rather bitterly that if the farmer could put fifty or a hundred crowns extra into the bank every month, thanks to her, she was still earning only her two hundred francs a year, neither more nor less, and so she made up her mind to ask for an increase of wages. She went to see the schoolmaster three times about it, but when she got there she spoke about something else. She felt a kind of modesty in asking for money, as if it were something disgraceful, but at last one day, when the farmer was having breakfast by himself in the kitchen, she said to him with some embarrassment that she wished to speak to him particularly. He raised his head in surprise, with both his hands on the table, holding his knife, with its point in the air, in one, and a piece of bread in the other. He looked fixedly at the girl, who felt uncomfortable under his gaze but asked for a week's holiday, so that she might get away, as she was not very well. He acceded to her request immediately and then added in some embarrassment himself:

"When you come back I shall have something to say to you myself."

III

The child was nearly eight months old, and she did not know it again. It had grown rosy and chubby all over, like a little bundle of living fat. She threw herself onto it as if it had been some prey and kissed it so violently that it began to scream with terror, and then she began to cry herself, because it did not know her and stretched out its arms to its nurse as soon as it saw her. But the next day it began to get used to her and laughed when it saw her, and she took it into the fields and ran about excitedly with it and sat down under the shade of the trees, and then, for the first time in her life, she opened her heart to somebody and told the infant her troubles, how hard her work was, her anxieties and her hopes, and she quite tired the child with the violence of her caresses.

She took the greatest pleasure in handling it, in washing and dressing it, for it seemed to her that all this was the confirmation of her maternity, and she would look at it, almost feeling surprised that it was hers, and she used to say to herself in a low voice as she danced it in her arms: "It is my baby; it is my baby."

She cried all the way home as she returned to the farm and had scarcely got in, before her master called her into his room. She went in, feeling astonished and nervous, without knowing why.

"Sit down there," he said.

She sat down, and for some moments they remained side by side in some embarrassment, with their arms hanging at their sides, as if they did not know what to do with them and looking each other in the face, after the manner of peasants.

The farmer, a stout, jovial, obstinate man of forty-five, who had lost two wives, evidently felt embarrassed, which was very unusual with him. But at last he made up his mind and began to speak vaguely, hesitating a little and looking out of the window as he talked.

"How is it, Rose," he said, "that you have never thought of settling in life?"

She grew as pale as death and, seeing that she gave him no answer, he went on:

"You are a good, steady, active and economical girl, and a wife like you would make a man's fortune."

She did not move but looked frightened; she did not even try to comprehend his meaning, for her thoughts were in a whirl, as if at the approach of some great danger; so after waiting for a few seconds he went on:

"You see, a farm without a mistress can never succeed, even with a servant like you are."

Then he stopped, for he did not know what else to say, and Rose looked at him with the air of a person who thinks that he is face to face with a murderer and ready to flee at the slightest movement he may make, but after waiting for about five minutes he asked her:

"Well, will it suit you?"

"Will what suit me, master?"

And he said quickly: "Why, to marry me, by Jove!"

She jumped up but fell back onto her chair as if she had been struck, and there she remained, motionless, like a person who is overwhelmed by some great misfortune. But at last the farmer grew impatient and said: "Come, what more do you want?"

She looked at him almost in terror; then suddenly the tears came into her eyes, and she said twice in a choking voice: "I cannot; I cannot!"

"Why not?" he asked. "Come, don't be silly; I will give you until tomorrow to think it over."

And he hurried out of the room, very glad to have finished a matter which had troubled him a good deal. He had no doubt that she would the next morning accept a proposal which she could never have expected and which would be a capital bargain for him, as he thus bound a woman to himself who would certainly bring him more than if she had the best dowry in the district.

Neither could there be any scruples about an unequal match between them, for in the country everyone is very nearly equal. The farmer works just like his laborers do; the latter frequently become masters in their turn, and the female servants constantly become the mistresses of the establishment, without making any change in their life or habits.

Rose did not go to bed that night. She threw herself, dressed as she was, onto her bed, and she had not even strength to cry left in her; she was so thoroughly astonished. She remained quite inert, scarcely knowing that she had a body and without being at all able to collect her thoughts, though at moments she remembered a part of that which had happened, and then she was frightened at the idea of what might happen. Her terror increased, and every time the great kitchen clock struck the hour she broke into a perspiration from grief. She lost her head and had a nightmare; her candle went out, and then she began to imagine that someone had thrown a spell over her, as country people so often fancy, and she felt a mad inclination to run away, to escape and flee before her misfortune, as a ship scuds before the wind.

An owl hooted, and she shivered, sat up, put her hands to her face, into her hair and all over her body, and then she went downstairs, as if she were walking in her sleep. When she got into the yard she stooped down so as not to be seen by any prowling scamp, for the moon which was setting shed a bright light over the fields. Instead of opening the gate she scrambled over the fence, and as soon as she was outside she started off. She went on straight before her with a quick, elastic trot, and from time to time she unconsciously uttered a piercing cry. Her long shadow accompanied her, and now and then some night bird flew over her head, while the dogs in the farmyards barked as they heard her pass. One even jumped over the ditch, followed her and tried to bite her, but she turned round at it and gave such a terrible yell that the frightened animal ran back and cowered in silence in its kennel.

The stars grew dim, and the birds began to twitter; day was breaking. The girl was worn out and panting, and when the sun rose in the purple sky she stopped, for her swollen feet refused to go any farther. But she saw a pond in the distance, a large pond whose stagnant water looked like blood under the reflection of this new day, and she limped on with short steps and with her hand on her heart, in order to dip both her feet in it.

She sat down on a tuft of grass, took off her sabots which were full of dust, pulled off her stockings and plunged her legs into the still water, from which bubbles were rising here and there.

A feeling of delicious coolness pervaded her from head to foot, and suddenly, while she was looking fixedly at the deep pool, she was seized with giddiness and with a mad longing to throw herself into it. All her sufferings would be over in there; over forever. She no longer thought of her child; she only wanted peace, complete rest, and to sleep forever, and she got up with raised arms and took two steps forward. She was in the water up to her thighs and she was just about to throw herself in, when sharp, pricking pains in her ankles made her jump back. She uttered a cry of despair, for from her knees to the tips of her feet long black leeches were sucking in her lifeblood and were swelling as they adhered to her flesh. She did not dare to touch them and screamed with horror, so that her cries of despair attracted a peasant who was driving along at some distance to the spot. He pulled off the leeches one by one, applied herbs to the wounds and drove the girl to her master's farm in his gig.

She was in bed for a fortnight, and as she was sitting outside the door on the first morning that she got up the farmer suddenly came and planted himself before her.

"Well," he said, "I suppose the affair is settled, isn't it?"

She did not reply at first, and then, as he remained standing and looking at her intently with his piercing eyes, she said with difficulty: "No, master, I cannot."

But he immediately flew into a rage. "You cannot, girl; you cannot? I should just like to know the reason why?"

She began to cry and repeated: "I cannot."

He looked at her and then exclaimed angrily: "Then I suppose you have a lover?"

"Perhaps that is it," she replied, trembling with shame.

The man got as red as a poppy and stammered out in a rage: "Ah! So you confess it, you slut! And pray, who is the fellow? Some penniless, half-starved ragamuffin, without a roof to his head, I suppose? Who is it, I say?"

And as she gave him no answer he continued: "Ah! So you will not tell me. Then I will tell you; it is Jean Bauda!"

"No, not he," she exclaimed.

"Then it is Pierre Martin?"

"Oh no, master."

And he angrily mentioned all the young fellows in the neighborhood, while she denied that he had hit upon the right one and every moment wiped her eyes with the corner of her blue apron. But he still tried to find it out with his brutish obstinacy and, as it were, scratched her heart to discover her secret as a terrier scratches at a hole to try and get at the animal which he scents in it. Suddenly, however, the man shouted: "By George! It is Jacques, the man who was here last year. They used to say that you were always talking together and that you thought about getting married."

Rose was choking and she grew scarlet, while her tears suddenly stopped and dried upon her cheeks, like drops of water on hot iron, and she exclaimed: "No, it is not he; it is not he!"

"Is that really a fact?" asked the cunning farmer who partly guessed the truth, and she replied hastily:

"I will swear it; I will swear it to you." She tried to think of something by which to swear, as she did not dare to invoke sacred things.

But he interrupted her: "At any rate, he used to follow you into every corner and devoured you with his eyes at mealtimes. Did you ever give him your promise, eh?"

This time she looked her master straight in the face. "No, never, never; I will solemnly swear to you that if he were to come today and ask me to marry him I would have nothing to do with him."

She spoke with such an air of sincerity that the farmer hesitated, and then he continued, as if speaking to himself: "What then? You have not had a misfortune, as they call it, or it would have been known, and as it has no consequences, no girl would refuse her master on that account. There must be something at the bottom of it, however."

She could say nothing; she had not the strength to speak, and he asked her again: "You will not?"

"I cannot, master," she said with a sigh, and he turned on his heel.

She thought she had got rid of him altogether and spent the rest of the day almost tranquilly, but as worn out as if she, instead of the old white horse, had been turning the threshing machine all day. She went to bed as soon as she could and fell asleep immediately. In the middle of the night, however, two hands touching the bed woke her. She trembled with fear, but she immediately recognized the farmer's voice when he said to her: "Don't be frightened, Rose, I have come to speak to you."

She was surprised at first, but when he tried to take liberties with her she understood what he wanted and began to tremble violently. She felt quite alone in the darkness, still heavy from sleep and quite unprotected, by the side of the man who stood near her. She certainly did not consent but resisted carelessly, herself struggling against that instinct which is always strong in simple natures and very imperfectly protected by the undecided will of an exhausted body. She turned her head now toward the wall and now toward the room, in order to avoid the attentions which the farmer tried to press on her, and her body writhed under the coverlet, weakened as she was by the fatigue of the struggle, while he became brutal, intoxicated by desire.

They lived together as man and wife, and one morning he said to her: "I have put up our banns, and we will get married next month."

She did not reply, for what could she say? She did not resist, for what could she do?

IV

She married him. She felt as if she were in a pit with inaccessible edges, from which she could never get out, and all kinds of misfortunes remained hanging over her head, like huge rocks, which would fall on the first occasion. Her husband gave her the impression of a man from whom she had stolen and who would find it out someday or other. And then she thought of her child who was the cause of her misfortunes but was also the cause of all her happiness on earth. She went to see him twice a year and she came back more unhappy each time.

But she gradually grew accustomed to her life; her fears were allayed; her heart was at rest, and she lived with an easier mind, although still with some vague fear floating in her mind. So years went on, and the child was six. She was almost happy now, when suddenly the farmer's temper grew very bad.

For two or three years he seemed to have been nursing some secret anxiety, to be troubled by some care, some mental disturbance, which was gradually increasing. He remained at table a long time after dinner, with his head in his hands, sad and devoured by sorrow. He always spoke hastily, sometimes even brutally, and it even seemed as if he bore a grudge against his wife, for at times he answered her roughly, almost angrily.

One day, when a neighbor's boy came for some eggs and she spoke rather crossly to him, for she was very busy, her husband suddenly came in and said to her in his unpleasant voice: "If that were your own child you would not treat him so."

She was hurt and did not reply, and then she went back into the house with all her grief awakened afresh. At dinner the farmer neither spoke to her nor looked at her and seemed to hate her, to despise her, to know something about the affair at last. In consequence she lost her head and did not venture to remain alone with him after the meal was over but left the room and hastened to the church.

It was getting dusk; the narrow nave was in total darkness, but she heard footsteps in the choir, for the sacristan was preparing the tabernacle lamp for the night. That spot of trembling light which was lost in the darkness of the arches looked to Rose like her last hope, and with her eyes fixed on it she fell on her knees. The chain rattled as the little lamps swung up into the air, and almost immediately the small bell rang out the Angelus through the increasing mist. She went up to him as he was going out.

"Is Monsieur le Curé at home?" she asked.

"Of course he is; this is his dinnertime."

She trembled as she rang the bell of the parsonage. The priest was just sitting down to dinner, and he made her sit down also. "Yes, yes, I know all about it; your husband has mentioned the matter to me that brings you here."

The poor woman nearly fainted, and the priest continued: "What do you want, my child?" And he hastily swallowed several spoonfuls of soup, some of which dropped on to his greasy cassock. But Rose did not venture to say anything more but got up to go, while the priest said: "Courage."

So she went out and returned to the farm, without knowing what she was doing. The farmer was waiting for her, as the laborers had gone away during her absence, and she fell heavily at his feet and, shedding a flood of tears, she said to him: "What have you got against me?"

He began to shout and to swear: "What have I got against you? That I have no children, by God! When a man takes a wife he does not want to be left alone with her until the end of his days. That is what I have against you. When a cow has no calves she is not worth anything, and when a woman has no children she is also not worth anything."

She began to cry and said: "It is not my fault! It is not my fault!"

He grew rather more gentle when he heard that and added: "I do not say that it is, but it is very annoying, all the same."

V

From that day forward she had only one thought—to have a child, another child. She confided her wish to everybody, and in consequence of this, a neighbor told her of an infallible method. This was to make her husband a glass of water with a pinch of ashes in it every evening. The farmer consented to try it but without success, so they said to each other: "Perhaps there are some secret ways?" And they tried to find out. They were told of a shepherd who lived ten leagues off, and so Vallin one day drove off to consult him. The shepherd gave him a loaf on which he had made some marks; it was kneaded up with herbs, and both of them were to eat a piece of it before and after their mutual caresses, but they ate the whole loaf without obtaining any results from it.

Next a schoolmaster unveiled mysteries and processes of love which were unknown in the country but infallible, so he declared, but none of them had the desired effect. Then the priest advised them to make a pilgrimage to the shrine at Fécamp. Rose went with the crowd and prostrated herself in the abbey and, mingling her prayers with the coarse wishes of the peasants around her, she prayed that she might be fruitful a second time, but it was in vain, and then she thought that she was being punished for her first fault and she was seized by terrible grief. She was wasting away with sorrow; her husband was growing old prematurely, and was wearing himself out in useless hopes.

Then war broke out between them; he called her names and beat her. They quarreled all day long, and when they were in bed together at night he flung insults and obscenities at her, panting with rage, until one night, not being able to think of any means of making her suffer more, he ordered her to get up and go and stand out of doors in the rain until daylight. As she did not obey him he seized her by the neck and began to strike her in the face with his fists, but she said nothing and did not move. In his exasperation he knelt on her, and with clenched teeth and mad with rage began to beat her. Then in her despair she rebelled and, flinging him against the wall with a furious gesture, she sat up and in an altered voice she hissed: "I have had a child; I have had one! I had it by Jacques; you know Jacques well. He promised to marry me, but he left this neighborhood without keeping his word."

The man was thunderstruck and could hardly speak, but at last he stammered out: "What are you saying? What are you saying?"

Then she began to sob, and amid her tears she said: "That was the reason why I did not want to marry you. I could not tell you, for you would have left me without any bread for my child. You have never had any children, so you cannot understand; you cannot understand!"

He said again, mechanically, with increasing surprise: "You have a child? You have a child?"

"You won me by force, as I suppose you know. I did not want to marry you," she said, still sobbing.

Then he got up, lighted the candle and began to walk up and down, with his arms behind him. She was cowering on the bed and crying, and suddenly he stopped in front of her and said: "Then it is my fault that you have no children?"

She gave him no answer, and he began to walk up and down again, and then, stopping again, he continued: "How old is your child?"

"Just six," she whispered.

"Why did you not tell me about it?" he asked.

"How could I?" she replied with a sigh.

He remained standing, motionless. "Come, get up," he said.

She got up with some difficulty, and then when she was standing on the floor he suddenly began to laugh with his hearty laugh of his good days, and, seeing how surprised she was, he added: "Very well, we will go and fetch the child, as you and I can have none together."

She was so scared that if she had the strength she would assuredly have run away, but the farmer rubbed his hands and said: "I wanted to adopt one, and now we have found one. I asked the curé about an orphan some time ago."

Then, still laughing, he kissed his weeping and agitated wife on both cheeks and shouted out, as if she could not hear him: "Come along, Mother, we will go and see whether there is any soup left; I should not mind a plateful."

She put on her petticoat, and they went downstairs; and while she was kneeling in front of the fireplace and lighting the fire under the saucepan, he continued to walk up and down the kitchen with long strides and said: "Well, I am really glad at this; I am not saying it for form's sake, but I am glad; I am really very glad."

AT THE SPA

DIARY OF THE MARQUIS DE ROSEVEYRE

June 12, 1880.—Loèche! I have to spend a month at Loèche! Good Lord! A month in the city which is considered the deadest, the dullest of spas! Did I say a city? It's a hole, barely a village! What it amounts to is a month in jail!

June 13.—All night long I thought about the trip which disgusts me. I can see only one solution, to take a woman along! Who knows? It might prove amusing. Moreover, it might be a good experiment to see whether I am ready for marriage.

A month of tête à têtes, a month of life in common with someone, uninterrupted, with scintillating conversations at all hours of the day and night. Damn!

Taking a woman along for a month is not, after all, so serious as taking her for life. Still, it's much more serious than taking her for a night. I know I could get rid of her with a few thousand francs; but then I would be alone at Loèche, which isn't so hot either!

The choice will be difficult. I want neither a coquette nor a fool. I must not seem ridiculous nor ashamed of her. I don't mind people's saying, "The Marquis de Roseveyre seems to be in luck," but I don't want them to whisper either, "That poor Marquis de Roseveyre!" What it amounts to actually is that I must seek in my temporary companion all the qualities that I would insist upon in my permanent one. The only difference in the two is the difference between a new object and a secondhand one. By Jove! It's not impossible; I'll think it over.

June 14.—Berthe! . . . That's the girl. Twenty, pretty, just out of the Conservatoire, waiting around for a part, a future star. Excellent manners, poise, intelligence, and—love. Secondhand, but might get by for new.

June 15.—She is free. No commitments—business or sentimental—she accepts. I ordered her trousseau myself to make sure she doesn't look like a strumpet.

June 20.—Basel. She is asleep. I'm going to start my travel journal.

She is altogether charming. When she met me at the station, I did not recognize her—she looked right out of the society page. The child certainly has a future . . . on the stage.

I was struck by the transformation in manners, looks, bearing, gestures, smile, voice, everything—absolutely impeccable. And what a hat! Quite divine, charming yet simple. She was the picture of a woman who needs no longer to attract, who needs no longer to please anyone, whose role is no longer to captivate those who look at her, but rather who wants to please one man only, discreetly, exclusively. And it was strikingly so in her entire appearance. The change was so complete, the metamorphosis so absolute and so clever that I offered her my arm as I would have done to my wife. She took it as naturally as if she were my wife.

Alone in the compartment, we were quiet for a time. Then she lifted her veil and smiled—nothing more. A smile in the best taste. Oh! I had feared the kiss, the pretense of affection, the eternal and banal stock in trade of hussies. Not at all; she behaved perfectly. She is really good.

Then we chatted, sometimes like a young couple, sometimes like strangers. It was pleasant. Frequently she would smile when she looked at me. Then it was I who wanted to kiss her, but I restrained myself.

At the frontier a uniformed official suddenly opened the door of our compartment and demanded, "Your name, sir?"

I was surprised. I answered, "The Marquis de Roseveyre."

"Your destination?"

"The spa at Loèche, in the canton of Valais."

He wrote in a record book, then went on, "Madame is your wife?"

What was I to do? What was I to say? I glanced at her, hesitating. She was pale and was looking away. I felt that I was about to insult her needlessly. Moreover, I had decided to make her my companion, for a month.

I said, "Yes, monsieur."

I could see her blush. It delighted me.

But upon our arrival here at the hotel, the proprietor handed her the registration book. She immediately gave it to me, and I noticed that she was watching me as I wrote. It was our first evening of intimacy! . . . Once the page was turned over, who would ever look at that page again? I wrote "The Marquis and Marquise de Roseveyre, destination Loèche."

June 21.—6 a.m. Basel. We are going to Berne. I certainly struck it lucky.

June 21.—10 p.m. Curious day. I am stirred, no doubt about it. It's inane and funny.

During the journey we spoke little. She had gotten up a bit early, so she was tired and drowsy. Immediately upon arrival at Berne, we wanted to contemplate the panorama of the Alps, which I did not know, and there we were going across the city like two honeymooners. Suddenly we saw an immense plain, and beyond, 'way beyond, the glaciers. From that distance they did not appear to be immense, and yet the view gave me a thrill. A radiant setting sun was beating down on us; the heat was frightful, but the snowy summits remained cold and white. The Jungfrau, the virgin, dominated her brothers, exposed her broad snowy side, and the others rose all around her endlessly, giants with pale heads, eternally frozen peaks which the setting sun made even brighter, like silver, against the deep blue of the evening.

Their inert and colossal numbers gave the impression of the frontier of an astonishing new universe, of a rugged, dead region, but fascinating like the sea, full of a mysterious seductive power. The air which had caressed those eternally frozen peaks seemed to come down to us over the narrow and flowered landscape unlike the fecundating air of the plains. It had a bitter, powerful, and sterile quality like the flavor of inaccessible spaces.

Berthe looked on, awe-struck, unable to say a word.

Suddenly she took my hand and squeezed it. My own heart was full of that kind of fever, the exaltation which grips us before certain unexpected sights. I took her trembling little hand and lifted it to my lips; and I kissed it, believe it or not, lovingly.

I was left somewhat shaken. But by whom? By her or by the glaciers?

June 24.—Loèche, 10 p.m. The entire trip has been delightful. We spent a half day at Thun looking at the rugged mountain frontier which we were to cross the next day.

At sunrise we crossed what is probably the most beautiful lake in Switzerland. Mules were waiting for us. We mounted them and started off. After lunch in a small city we began to climb, going up slowly into the wooded ravine, still dominated by the high peaks. Now and then on slopes which seemed to emerge from the skies we could distinguish white spots—chalets—set there heaven knows how. We crossed torrents, and sometimes, between two slender peaks covered with firs, we saw an immense pyramid of snow which seemed so near that one would swear that it could be reached in twenty minutes but which one could hardly reach in twenty-four hours.

Sometimes we crossed a chaos of stones, narrow plateaus strewn with fallen rocks as if two mountains had tilted against each other on that plain, leaving on the battlefield the remains of their granite bodies.

Berthe, exhausted, was sleeping on her mount, opening her eyes occasionally in order not to miss too much of the landscape. But she finally dozed off, and I held her up with one hand, delighted by this contact, to feel through her dress the sweet warmth of her body. We were still climbing when night came. We stopped in front of a tiny inn which seemed lost in the mountains.

We slept! Yes, slept!

At daybreak I ran to the window and could not restrain a shout. Berthe joined me and stood overwhelmed, ecstatic. It had been snowing while we slept.

All around us were huge, bare peaks whose gray bones protruded from beneath their white cloaks, peaks without pines, somber and frozen. They rose so high as to seem inaccessible.

An hour after we had set off again we noticed at the end of this funnel of granite and snow a black lake, without a ripple, and we followed it for a long time. A guide brought us some edelweiss, those pale flowers of the glaciers. Berthe made a corsage of them.

Suddenly the ravine widened before us, revealing a startling horizon—the entire chain of Piedmontese Alps beyond the valley of the Rhône.

The big peaks here and there dominated the galaxy of smaller ones. There was Mount Rose, serious and imposing; Mount Cervin, pyramid-like, where many men have lost their lives; Mount Dent du Sud, and a hundred other white heads glistening under the sun like diamonds.

But the path which we had been following came to a sudden stop on the edge of an abyss, and in the depths at the very bottom of the black hole two thousand meters deep we saw on a patch of grass surrounded by forbidding, precipitous cliffs, a few white specks resembling sheep in a field. It was the houses of Loèche.

The path was now so dangerous that we were obliged to dismount from our mules. It goes down along the cliff, zigzags, but continues to dominate the precipice as well as the village, which becomes larger and larger as you approach it. It is called the Gemmi Pass, one of the most beautiful in the Alps, if not actually the most beautiful.

Berthe was hanging on to me, exclaiming with joy and fright, happy and fearful like a child. Once, as we were a few steps from the guides and hidden by a protruding rock, she kissed me. I hugged her. . . .

I had said to myself, "At Loèche I shall make it clear that I am not with my wife."

But everywhere I had treated her as such, everywhere I had passed her off as the Marquise de Roseveyre. I could hardly register her now under another name. Moreover, I would have hurt her deeply, and really she was charming.

So I said to her, "You are bearing my name, my dear; I am considered your husband. I hope that your conduct with everyone will be extremely prudent and discreet. I don't want you to make any friends nor contacts of any sort. Act aloof, but in such a way that I shall not reproach myself for what I've done."

She replied, "Don't be afraid, René dear."

June 26.—Loèche is not a sad place. No. It is wild, but very beautiful. The wall of rocks two thousand meters high, down which cascade a hundred waterfalls looking like silver strands; the eternal voice of flowing water; the village buried in the Alps from which you can see, as from the bottom of a well, the sun crossing the sky in the distance; the neighboring glacier, dazzlingly white in the mountain notch, and the little valley—full of brooks, full of trees, full of life and freshness—which slopes toward the Rhône and permits one to see the snowy peaks of Piedmont on the horizon—all this delights and thrills me. But . . . what if Berthe were not here? . . .

The child is really perfect. Reserved and distinguished as none other. I hear people say, "How pretty the Marquise is!"

June 27.—First bath. From your own room you go down directly into the pools, where a score of bathers in long woolen suits are soaking already, men and women together. Some are eating, others reading, still others chatting. You are provided with small floating tables. Sometimes you play "Find the ring," which is not always decorous. Seen from the balconies around the pools, we look like giant toads in tubs.

Berthe sat down on the balcony to chat with me. All eyes were turned on her.

June 28.—Second bath. Four hours bathing. I will have had eight hours in eight days. Among my fellow bathers are the Prince of Vanoris (Italy), Count Lovenberg (Austria), Baron Samuel Vernhe (Hungary or elsewhere), plus fifteen or so of lesser importance, but all of the nobility. Everyone is a nobleman at spas.

Every one of them wants to be introduced to Berthe. I say, "Yes," and I beat it. . . . It's really too silly!

June 29.—Damnation! The Princess of Vanoris came after me, wishing to meet my wife, as we were returning to the hotel. I introduced Berthe, but begged her to scrupulously avoid any further contact with the lady.

July 2.—The Prince collared us and took us to his apartment, where the most distinguished guests were having tea. Berthe was certainly the loveliest of all the ladies present. But what am I to do?

July 3.—Well, who cares! Of these thirty noblemen, aren't at least ten counterfeit? Among these seventeen or eighteen women, are there more than a dozen actually married? And of those twelve, are there more than six without reproach? Who cares! They asked for it!

July 10.—Berthe is the queen of Loèche! Everyone is mad about her. She is feted, she is spoiled, she is worshipped! It is true that she is absolutely unique in grace and distinction. Everyone envies me.

The Princess of V. asked me, "Look here, Marquis, where in heaven did you find such a treasure?"

I felt like answering, "First prize in comedy at the Conservatory, contract at the Odéon, will be free on August 5, 1880!"

I wager her surprise would have been something worth seeing!

July 20.—Berthe is really astonishing. Not a single slip of tact nor of good taste. A jewel!

August 10.—Paris. It's all over. The day before we left I thought everyone was going to weep.

It was decided to see the sunrise on the Torrenthorn, then to come down again in time for our departure.

We started out about midnight on mules. The guides carried torches, and the long caravan started out in the winding paths of the pine forest. We crossed pastures where herds of cows wander around unattended. Then we reached the rocky level where even grass cannot grow.

Occasionally one could distinguish in the darkness to the left or to the right a white mass, a snowdrift, in a crevasse.

The cold was becoming intense, stinging one's eyes and flesh. The desiccating wind of the summits was blowing, burning our throats, bringing the frozen breaths of peaks of ice from a hundred leagues around.

It was still dark when we reached the crest. We unpacked our supplies in order to drink a toast of champagne to the rising sun.

The sky was becoming pale over our heads. We could already see a chasm directly under us; then another peak a few hundred yards away.

The entire horizon seemed livid, yet you still could not distinguish anything in the distance.

Soon, however, we saw to our left a giant peak, the Jungfrau, then another, then still another. They appeared little by little as if they had gotten up with the breaking day. And we remained speechless to find ourselves thus in the midst of these giants, in this desolate country of eternal snows. All at once in front of us appeared the endless Piedmontese chain. Other peaks appeared in the north. It was really the vast region of mountains with frozen tops, from the Rhindenhorn, as heavy as its name, to the barely visible phantom of the patriarch of the Alps, Mont Blanc. Some were erect and proud, others crouching, still others misshapen, but all equally white, as if some god had thrown on the hunchbacked earth a spotless tablecloth.

Some seemed so close that we could have jumped on them; others were so far that they were barely visible.

The sky turned red, and all of them became red too. The clouds seemed to be bleeding on them. It was superb, almost frightening.

Soon the burning sky paled, and the host of peaks became imperceptibly pink, a soft and delicate pink, like little girls' dresses.

And the sun rose above the tablecloth of snow. Whereupon the entire galaxy of glaciers immediately turned white, a glistening white, as if the horizon were replete with silvery domes.

The women were looking upon all this in ecstasy. At that very moment they were startled as a champagne cork was popped, and the Prince of V., handing a glass to Berthe, exclaimed, "I drink to the Marquise de Roseveyre!" Everyone joined in, "I drink to the Marquise de Roseveyre!"

She stood up on her mule and responded, "I drink to all my friends!"

Three hours later we took the train to Geneva, in the valley of the Rhône.

We were barely alone when Berthe, so happy and gay a moment before, began to sob, her head in her hands.

I threw myself at her feet. "What's the matter? Tell me!"

She stammered through her tears, "So . . . so . . . it's all over . . . being a respectable woman!"

No question about it. I was at that moment on the point of committing a folly, a colossal folly! . . . But I did not.

As soon as we reached Paris I left Berthe. I might not have had the strength to do it later.

(*The diary of the Marquis de Roseveyre presents no interest whatever in the next three years. But we do find the following entry under date of July 20, 1883:*)

July 20, 1883.—Florence. Sad reminder a moment ago. I was walking along the Caccine when a woman had her carriage stopped and called me. It was the Princess of V. As soon as she saw that I was within hearing distance, she shouted, "Oh! Marquis, my dear Marquis, how glad I am to meet you! I am dying to have news of the Marquise. She is quite the most charming woman I have ever encountered."

I stood startled, not knowing what to say, my heart pounding wildly. I finally stammered, "I beg you never to speak of her again, Princess; I lost her three years ago."

She took my hand. "Oh, how I do pity you!"

She left me, while I returned to the hotel, sad, irritated at myself, thinking of Berthe as if we had just left each other.

How frequently fate can be wrong!

How many respectable women were meant to be trollops, and act so.

Poor Berthe! How many others were meant to be respectable women. . . . And she . . . above all . . . perhaps . . . Well . . . better forget it.

MADAME HERMET

Madmen fascinate me. These beings live in a mysterious land of fantastic dreams, in that impenetrable cloud of insanity where all that they have seen on earth, all that they have loved, all that they have done, lives again for them in an imaginary existence outside all the laws that govern the world and order human thought.

For them the impossible does not exist, the unlikely disappears, the fairy world becomes the natural world, and the supernatural familiar. Logic, that ancient barrier, reason, that ancient wall, good sense, that ancient balustrade of the mind, is broken, shattered, demolished by their imagination, which has been loosed into freedom, has escaped into the realms of fantasy to which no bounds are set, and rushes forward in fabulous leaps without let or hindrance. For them everything happens and everything can happen. They make no efforts to conquer events, overcome resistances, surmount obstacles. A mere whim of their fantasy-creating will allows them to become princes, emperors or gods, to possess all the riches of the world, all the good things of life, allows them to enjoy all pleasures, allows them to be always strong, always beautiful, always young, always loved. Of all creatures on this earth, they alone are happy, since for them reality no longer exists. I like to hang over their vagabond minds, as one hangs over an abyss in whose depths boils an unknown torrent, come one knows not whence and going one knows not whither.

But it avails us nothing to hang over these ravines, since we could never know whence comes that stream or whither it goes. After all, it is only a stream, like the streams that run in broad daylight, and a sight of it would teach us very little.

It avails us as little to hang over the minds of madmen, for their most fantastic ideas are, in effect, no more than ideas already known to us, made strange only because they are no longer shackled by Reason. That capricious spring confounds and amazes us because we do not see the place of its rising. Doubtless a little stone dropped in its course is enough to produce these whirlpools. Nevertheless, madmen fascinate me, and I keep going back to them, attracted in spite of myself by this commonplace mystery of insanity.

But one day, as I was visiting one of their asylums, the doctor who was escorting me said:

"Come, I'll show you an interesting case."

And he opened a cell in which a woman of about forty years of age, still beautiful, was seated in a big armchair, gazing fixedly at her face in a small hand glass.

As soon as she saw us, she stood up, ran to the farther side of the room to get a veil thrown down on a chair, very carefully swathed her face in it, then returned, replying to our greetings by a sign of her head.

"Well," said the doctor, "how are you this morning?"

She uttered a deep sigh.

"Oh, ill, very ill, doctor, the marks get worse every day."

He replied with an air of conviction:

"No, certainly not, I assure you that you're mistaken."

She drew close to him to murmur:

"No. I'm sure of it. I've counted ten more marks this morning, three on the right cheek, four on the left cheek, and three on my forehead. It's frightful, frightful. I daren't let anyone see me now, not even my son, no, not even he! I'm ruined, I'm disfigured for life."

She sank back into her armchair and began to sob.

The doctor took a chair, seated himself near her, and in a gentle, comforting voice said:

"Come now, let me look, I assure you it's nothing. By a slight cauterizing, I can make them all disappear."

She shook her head, without saying a word. He tried to touch her veil, but she grasped it in both hands with such violence that her fingers went through it.

He began afresh to exhort and reassure her.

"Come, now, you know quite well that I remove the ugly pockmarks from your skin every time and that you can't see them at all when I have attended to them. If you don't show them to me, I can't cure you."

She murmured:

"I'm quite willing to let you look again but I don't know this gentleman who is with you."

"He is a doctor too, who can attend to you even better than I can."

Then she uncovered her face, but her fear and her emotion, her shame at being seen, made her blush even over her throat, to the point where her gown covered it. She lowered her eyes, turned her face now to the right and now to the left, to escape our gaze, and stammered:

"Oh, it makes me suffer agonies to let you see me like this. It's horrible, isn't it? Isn't it horrible?"

I looked at her in the utmost amazement, for she had nothing on her face, not a mark, not a stain, not a sign nor a scar.

She turned towards me, keeping her eyes lowered, and said to me:

"It was through nursing my son that I contracted this frightful disease. I saved him, but I am disfigured. I gave my beauty to my poor child. Well, I did my duty, and my conscience is at rest. If I suffer, only God knows it."

The doctor had taken from his pocket a slender water-color brush.

"Allow me," said he, "I'll put it all right for you."

She turned to him her right cheek, and he began to lay light touches on it, as if he were putting small dabs of paint on it. He did the same to the left cheek, then to the chin, then the forehead; then he cried:

"Look, it's all gone, all gone."

She took up her glass, gazed at herself for a long time with a searching intensity, a harrowing intensity, a savagely concentrated mental effort to discover something, then she sighed:

"No. There's very little to see now. Thank you very much indeed."

The doctor rose. He took leave of her, ushered me out and followed me; and as soon as the door was closed, said:

"I'll tell you that poor woman's dreadful story."

Her name is Mme. Hermet. She was very beautiful, a real coquette, loved of many, and full of the joy of life.

She was one of those women whose sole consolation in life is derived from, and their conduct dictated by, their beauty and their desire to please.

The unremitting anxiety to preserve her freshness, the care of her face, her hands, teeth, of every part of her body that she could display, absorbed all her time and all her attention.

She became a widow, with one son. The child was brought up in the same way as are all children of much-admired women. She loved him, however.

He grew up, and she grew old. Whether or not she saw the fatal moment coming, I don't know. Did she, like so many others, gaze every morning for hours and hours at the skin that used to be so delicate, so clear and fresh, and now is wrinkling a little under the eyes, creasing itself in a thousand lines that are imperceptible now but will deepen and deepen, day by day, month by month? And did she see, more and more strongly marked, advancing with slow relentless certainty, the long lines graven on the forehead, those thin serpents whose progress nothing halts? Did she endure the torture, the abominable torture, of the looking glass, of the small silver hand glass that she could not resolve to leave on the table, then threw down in anger, and a moment later picked up again, to see once more, ever nearer and nearer, the hateful silent ravages of approaching age? Did she shut herself up ten, twenty times a day, leaving, for no reason, the drawing room where her friends were chatting, to go up to her bedroom and, safeguarded by bolts and locks, gaze again on the destruction at work in the ripened fading flesh, to examine despairingly the hardly perceptible advance that so far no one else seems to notice but of which she herself is bitterly aware? She knows where the most serious ravages are, where the tooth of age bites deepest. And the glass, the small, quite round glass in its frame of chased silver, says dreadful things to her, for it speaks, it seems to laugh, it rails on her and predicts all that is coming to pass, all the miseries of her body, and the atrocious torture of her mind that will endure to the day of her death, which will be that of her deliverance.

Did she weep, distracted, on her knees, her forehead on the ground, and pray, pray, pray to Him who kills His creatures thus, giving them youth only to make age the more bitter, and lending them beauty only to take it back almost at once; did she pray Him, implore Him, to grant to her what He had never granted to anyone, to allow her to keep until her last day, charm and freshness and grace? Then, realizing that in vain does she implore the implacable Unknown who adds year to year in endless number, did she roll with writhing arms on the carpet of her room, did she beat her forehead on its furniture and stifle in her throat her frightful despairing cries?

She must have endured these tortures. For this is what happened:

One day (she was then thirty-five years old) her son, aged fifteen, fell ill.

He took to his bed before the doctors had been able to diagnose the cause of his illness or its nature. An abbé, his tutor, watched over him, hardly leaving his side, while Mme. Hermet came morning and evening to hear his report.

She entered in the morning in a rest gown, smiling, already scented, and asked, from the door:

"Well, George, are you getting better?"

The tall youngster, crimson, his face swollen, and wasted by the fever, would answer:

"Yes, Mummie, a little better."

She lingered a few moments in the bedroom, examining the bottles of medicine and making little grimaces of disgust, then suddenly cried: "Oh, I was forgetting something very important," and she took herself off, running, leaving behind her the delicate fragrance of her morning toilet.

At night she appeared in her evening gown, in a still greater hurry, for she was always late, and had just time to ask:

"Well, what did the doctor say?"

The abbé replied:

"He's not sure yet, madame."

But, one evening, the abbé replied:

"Madame, your son has taken smallpox."

She uttered a loud cry of fear and rushed away.

When her maid came to her room next morning the first thing she noticed in the room was a strong smell of burnt sugar, and she found her mistress, wideawake, her face pale for lack of sleep, and shaking with anguish in her bed.

As soon as the shutters were open Mme. Hermet asked, "How is George?"

"Oh, not at all well today, madame."

She did not get up until midday, ate two eggs with a cup of tea, as if she herself were ill, then she went out and consulted a chemist as to the best methods of keeping off the infection of smallpox.

She did not return until dinnertime, laden with phials, and shut herself at once in her room, where she soaked herself in disinfectants.

The *abbé* was waiting for her in the dining room. As soon as she caught sight of him she cried, in a voice full of emotion:

"Well?"

"Oh, no better. The doctor is very anxious."

She began to cry, and could eat nothing, so wretched was she.

The next day, at dawn, she sent for news: the report was no better, and she spent the whole day in her room, where small braziers were smoking and filling the room with powerful odors. Moreover, her maid declared that she heard her moaning all the evening.

A whole week passed in this way: she did nothing at all but go out for an hour or two to take the air, towards the middle of the afternoon.

She asked for news every hour now, and sobbed when each report was worse.

On the morning of the eleventh day, the *abbé* was announced, entered her room, his face grave and pale, and declining the chair that she offered him, said:

"Madame, your son is very ill, and he wants to see you."

She flung herself on her knees, crying:

"Oh, my God, oh, my God, I daren't! My God, my God! help me!"

The priest answered:

"The doctor holds out very little hope, madame, and George is waiting for you."

Then he went out.

Two hours later, as the boy, feeling himself near death, asked again for his mother, the *abbé* went back to her room and found her still on her knees, still weeping and repeating:

"I won't. . . . I won't. . . . I am too frightened. . . . I won't. . . ."

He tried to persuade her, to stiffen her resolution, to lead her out. He succeeded only in giving her a fit of hysteria which lasted for a long time and made her scream.

The doctor came again towards evening, was told of her cowardice, and declared that he himself would fetch her, by persuasion or force. But when, after having exhausted all his arguments, he put his arm around her to carry her off to her son, she seized the door and clung to it so desperately that no one could tear her away. Then, released, she prostrated herself at the doctor's feet, begging for pardon, and accusing herself of wickedness. She kept crying: "Oh, he's not going to die, tell me he's not going to die, I implore you, tell him that I love him, that I adore him. . . ."

The boy lay at the point of death. Realizing that he only had a few moments left, he begged them to persuade his mother to say good-by to him. With strange insight that the dying sometimes possess, he had realized the truth, divined it, and said: "If she is afraid to come in, just beg her to come along the balcony as far as my window so that at least I can see her and say good-by to her by a look, since I may not kiss her."

The doctor and the *abbé* went back once more to this woman. "You will run no risk at all," they declared, "since there will be glass between you and him."

She consented to come, covered her head, took a bottle of smelling salts, made three steps along the balcony, then suddenly, hiding her face in her hands, she moaned: "No . . . no . . . I shall never dare to look at him . . . never. . . . I'm too ashamed. . . . I'm too afraid. . . . No . . . I can't."

They tried to drag her along, but she held with both hands to the bars and uttered such wails that the people passing by in the street lifted their heads.

And the dying boy waited, his eyes turned towards this window, he waited, putting off death until he should have looked one last time on that gentle beloved face, his mother's blessed face.

He waited for a long time, and night fell. Then he turned his face to the wall and never spoke again.

When day broke, he was dead. The next day, she was a madwoman.

FOR SALE

To set out on foot, when the sun is just rising, and walk through the dew, by the side of the fields, at the verge of the quiet sea, what ecstasy!

What ecstasy! It enters in through the eyes with the radiant light, through the nostrils with the sharp air, through the skin with the caressing wind.

Why do we retain, so clear, so precious, so sharp a memory of a few moments of passionate union with the earth, the memory of a swift divine emotion, of the almost caressing greeting of a countryside revealed by a twist of the road, at the mouth of a valley, at the edge of a river, just as if we had come upon a charming and complaisant young girl?

I remember one day, among many. I was walking along the coast of Brittany towards the outthrust headland of Finistère. I walked quickly, thinking of nothing at all, along the edge of the water. This was in the neighborhood of Quimperlé, in the loveliest and most adorable part of Brittany.

It was a morning in spring, one of those mornings in which one is again just twenty, a morning to revive dead hopes and give back the dreams of first youth. I walked between the cornfields and the sea, along a road no better than a path. The corn was quite motionless, and the waves lifted very gently. The air was filled with the fragrance of ripening fields and the salt scent of the seaweed. I walked without a thought in my head, straight forward, continuing a journey begun fifteen days before, a tramp round the coast of Brittany. I felt gloriously fit, content, light of feet and light of heart. I just walked.

I thought of nothing. Why think of anything in hours filled by an instinctive happiness, a profound physical happiness, the happiness of the beasts of the fields and the birds soaring in the blue spaces beneath the sun? I heard the far-off sound of hymn singing. A procession perhaps, since this was Sunday. Then I rounded a little headland, stood still, amazed with delight. Five large fishing boats came into sight, filled with people, men, women, and children, on their way to the Indulgence at Plouneven.

They hugged the coast, moving slowly, helped scarcely at all by the soft, hardly breathing wind which swelled the brown sails faintly and then, as if wearied out, let them fall, all slack, round the masts.

The clumsy boats moved slowly, filled with such a crowd of folk. And the whole crowd was singing. The men standing against the sides of the boats, their heads covered with wide hats, sang their deep notes lustily, the women shrilled the treble air, and the thin voices of the children pierced that devout and monstrous uproar like the tuneless squeak of fifes.

The voyagers in all five boats shouted the same hymn, whose monotonous rhythm rose to the quiet sky, and the five boats sailed one behind the other, close together.

They passed close by in front of me, and I saw them draw away, I heard their song sink and die upon the air.

And I fell dreaming delightful dreams, as youth will dream, absurd divine dreams.

How swiftly it is gone, the age of dreams, the only happy age in a whole lifetime. No one is ever lonely, ever sad, ever gloomy or cast down, who bears within himself that most wonderful power of wandering, as soon as he is left to himself, into a world of happy dreams. What a fairy world, where anything may happen in the audacious imagination of the dreamer who roams therein! How adorable life appears covered in the gold dust of dreams.

Alas, those days are done!

I fell dreaming. Of what? Of all that a man never ceases to hope for, all that he desires, riches, honor, women.

And I walked on, taking great strides, my hand caressing the yellow locks of the corn which bowed itself under my fingers and thrilled my skin as if I had touched living hair.

I made my way round a little promontory and saw, at the end of a narrow open beach, a white-walled house built above three terraces that came down to the shore.

Why does this house send through me a shiver of delight? Do I know it? Sometimes, in such wanderings, we come upon corners of the country that we seem to have known for a very long time, so familiar are they to us, so do they wake a response in our hearts. Is it possible that we have never seen them before, that we have not lived in them in some former life? Everything about them stirs us, fills us with the most profound delight, the gentle swell of the horizon, the ordered trees, the color of the soil.

A charming house, rising from its high steps. Large fruit trees had established themselves along the terraces which came down to the water, like giant stairs. And on the rim of each terrace, like a crown of gold, ran a border of Spanish broom in full flower.

I halted in my tracks, possessed with a sudden love for this dwelling place. How I would have liked to own it, to live there, for ever!

I drew near the door, my heart beating quickly with envious desire, and saw, on one of the pillars of the gate, a big placard: "For Sale."

I felt a sharp thrill of delight, as if this dwelling had been offered to me, as if I had been given it. Why, yes, why? I do not know.

"For Sale." Then it no longer belonged to any special person, could belong to anyone on earth, to me, to me! Why this joy, this sense of utter delight, deep incomprehensible delight? I knew well enough, however, that I could not buy it. How could I pay for it? No matter, it was for sale. The caged bird belongs to its owner, the bird in the air is mine, not being man's.

I went into the garden. Oh, what a delightful garden, with its terraces lifted one above the other, its espaliers with arms stretched out like crucified martyrs, its clumps of golden broom, and two old fig trees at the end of each terrace!

When I stood on the last, I looked all round me. The shore of the little bay stretched at my feet, curved and sandy, separated from the open sea by three massive brown rocks, which closed the entry to the bay and must have acted as a breakwater on rough days.

On the headland, right opposite, two great stones, one upright, the other lying in the grass, a menhir and a dolmen, like two strange beings, husband and wife, turned to stone by an evil spell, seemed to watch unwinkingly the small house that they had seen built—they who for centuries had known this one-time solitary cove—the small house that they would see fall, crumple, vanish little by little and altogether disappear, the little house that was for sale.

Oh, old dolmen and old menhir, how I love you!

I knocked at the door as if I had been knocking at my own door. A woman came to open it, a servant, a little old servant, black-gowned, white-bonneted, looking like a working nun. It seemed to me as if I knew her too, this woman.

I said to her:

"You are not a Breton woman, are you?"

She answered:

"No, sir, I come from Lorraine."

She added:

"You have come to look over the house?"

"Oh, yes, certainly."

And I went in.

It seemed to me that I knew it all, the walls, the furniture. I was almost surprised not to find my own walking sticks in the hall.

I made my way into the drawing room, a charming drawing room carpeted with rush mats, which looked out over the sea through its three large windows. On the mantel shelf, Chinese vases and a large photograph of a woman. I went to it at once, convinced that I recognized her too. And I did recognize her, although I was certain that I had never met her. It was she, the inexpressible she, she for whom I was waiting, whom I desired, she whom I summoned, whose face haunted my dreams. She, she whom one seeks always, in every place, she whom one is every moment just going to see in the street, just going to discover on a country road the instant one's glance falls on a red sunshade over the cornfield, she who must surely already be in the hotel when I enter it on my travels, in the railway carriage I am just getting into, in the drawing room whose door is just opening to me.

It was she, assuredly, past all manner of doubt, it was she. I recognized her by her eyes which were looking at me, by her hair arranged English fashion, but above all by her mouth, by that smile which long ago I had surmised.

I asked at once:

"Who is this lady?"

The nunlike servant answered dryly:

"That is Madame."

I continued:

"She is your mistress?"

In her austere conventional fashion, she replied:

"Oh, no, sir."

I sat down and said firmly:

"Tell me about her."

She stood amazed, motionless, obstinately silent.

I persisted:

"She is the owner of the house, then?"

"Oh, no, sir."

"Then whose is this house?"

"It belongs to my master, Monsieur Tournelle."

I pointed a finger towards the photograph.

"And this lady, who is she?"

"That is Madame."

"Your master's wife?"

"Oh, no, sir."

"His mistress, then?"

The nun had nothing to say. I went on, pricked by a vague jealousy, by a confused anger against this man who found this woman first.

"Where are they now?"

The servant murmured:

"Monsieur the gentleman is in Paris, but about Madame I know nothing."

I shivered.

"Ah. They are no longer together?"

"No, sir."

I became wily, and said solemnly:

"Tell me what happened, probably I could be of service to your master. I know this woman, she's a bad lot."

The old servant looked at me, and seeing my honest expression, she trusted me.

"Oh, sir, she did my master a bad turn. He made her acquaintance in Italy, and he brought her away with him as if he had married her. She sang beautifully. He loved her so much, sir, that it was pitiful to see him. They were traveling in this district last year. And they discovered this house which had been built by a fool, an old fool who wanted to settle five miles from the village. Madame wanted to buy it outright, so that she could stay here with my master. And he bought the house to please her.

"They lived here all last summer, sir, and almost all the winter.

"And then, one morning at breakfast time, Monsieur called me.

" 'Césaire, has Madame come in?'

" 'No, sir.'

"We waited for her the whole day. My master was like a madman. We sought everywhere; we did not find her. She had gone, sir, we never knew where or how."

Oh, what a tide of joy surged in me! I would have liked to embrace the nun, to seize her round the waist and make her dance in the drawing room.

Oh, she had gone, she had escaped, she had left him, utterly wearied, disgusted with him! How happy I was!

The old woman went on:

"Monsieur almost died of grief, and he has gone back to Paris, leaving me here with my husband to sell the house. He is asking twenty thousand francs for it."

But I was no longer listening. I was thinking of her. And all at once it struck me that I had only to set out again to come upon her, that this very springtime she would have been driven to come back to the place, to see the house, this charming house that she must have loved so dearly, to see it emptied of him.

I flung ten francs into the old woman's hand. I snatched the photograph and rushed off at a run, pressing desperate kisses on the adorable face that looked up from the cardboard.

I regained the road and began to walk on, looking at her, her very self. How glorious that she was free, that she had got away! Without doubt I should meet her today or tomorrow, this week or next, now that she had left him. She had left him because my hour had come.

She was free, somewhere, in the world. I had only to find her now that I knew her.

And all the while I touched caressingly the bowed locks of ripe corn, I drank in the sea air that filled out my lungs, I felt the sun kissing my face. I had walked on, I walked on wild with joy, drunk with hope. I walked on, certain that I was going to meet her soon and lead her back to enjoy our turn in that charming home "For Sale." How she would revel in it, this time!

YVETTE

I

As they left the Café Riche, Jean de Servigny said to Léon Saval:

"We'll walk, if you don't mind walking. It's too fine to take a cab."

"It will suit me perfectly," answered his friend.

"It's barely eleven," continued Jean. "We shall be there long before midnight, so let us go slowly."

A restless crowd swarmed on the boulevard, the crowd which on summer nights is always to be seen there, contented and merry, walking, drinking, and talking, streaming past like a river. Here and there a café flung a brilliant splash of light on to the group which sat outside, drinking at round little tables loaded with bottles and glasses, and obstructing the hurrying crowd of passers-by. And in the road the cabs, with their red, blue, and green eyes, passed swiftly across the harsh glare of the lighted front, and for an instant revealed the silhouette of the thin, trotting horse, the profile of the driver on the box, and the dark, square body of the vehicle. The urbaine cabs gleamed as the light caught their yellow panels.

The two friends walked slowly along, smoking their cigars. They were in evening dress, their overcoats on their arms, flowers in their buttonholes and their hats a little on one side, with the careless tilt affected by men who have dined well and find the breeze warm.

Ever since their school days the two had been close friends, profoundly and loyally devoted to each other.

Jean de Servigny, small, slim, slightly bald, and frail, very elegant, with a curled mustache, bright eyes, and thin lips, was one of those night birds who seem to have been born and bred on the boulevards; inexhaustible, though he wore a perpetual air of fatigue, vigorous despite his pallor—one of those slender Parisians to whom gymnastics, fencing, the cold plunge, and the Turkish bath have given an artificial nervous strength. He was as well known for his conviviality as for his wit, his wealth, and his love affairs, and for that geniality, popularity, and fashionable gallantry which are the hallmark of a certain type of man.

In other ways too he was a true Parisian, quick-witted, sceptical, changeable, impulsive, energetic yet irresolute, capable of anything and of nothing, an egoist on principle and a philanthropist on impulse. He kept his expenditure within his income, and amused himself without ruining his health. Cold and passionate by turns, he was continually letting himself go and pulling himself up, a prey to conflicting impulses and yielding to all of them, following his instinct like any hardened pleasure seeker whose weathercock logic bids him follow every wind and profit from any train of events, without taking the trouble to set a single one of them in motion.

His companion, Léon Saval, rich also, was one of those superb giants who compel women to turn round and stare after them in the street. He had the air of a statue come to life, of a racial type: he was like one of those models which are sent to exhibitions. Too handsome, too tall, too broad, too strong, all his faults were those of excess. He had broken innumerable hearts.

As they reached the Vaudeville, he inquired:

"Have you let this lady know that you're bringing me?"

Servigny laughed.

"Let the Marquise Obardi know! Do you let a bus driver know in advance that you're going to get on to his bus at the corner of the boulevard?"

"Well, then, exactly who is she?" asked Saval, slightly perplexed.

"A parvenue," replied his friend, "a colossal fraud, a charming jade, sprung from Lord knows where, who appeared one day, Lord knows how, in the world of adventurers, in which she is well able to make herself prominent. Anyhow, what does it matter? They say her real name, her maiden name—for she has remained a maiden in every sense but the true one—is Octavie Bardin, whence Obardi, retaining the first letter of the Christian name and dropping the last letter of the surname. She's an attractive woman, too, and with your physique you're certain to become her lover. You can't introduce Hercules to Messalina without something coming of it. I ought to add, by the way, that though admission to the place is as free as to a shop, you are not obliged to buy what is on sale. Love and cards are the stock in trade, but no one will force you to purchase either. The way out is as accessible as the way in.

"It is three years now since she took a house in the Quartier de l'Etoile, a rather shady district, and opened it to all the scum of the Continent, which comes to Paris to display its most diverse, dangerous, and vicious accomplishments.

"I went to the house. How? I don't remember. I went, as we all go, because there's gambling, because the women are approachable and the men scoundrels. I like this crowd of decorated buccaneers, all foreign, all noble, all titled, all, except the spies, unknown to their ambassadors. They all talk of their honor on the slightest provocation, trot out their ancestors on no provocation at all, and present you with their life histories on any provocation. They are braggarts, liars, thieves, as dangerous as their cards, as false as their names, brave because they must be, like footpads who cannot rob their victims without risking their necks. In a word, the aristocracy of the galleys.

"I adore them. They're interesting to study, interesting to meet, amusing to listen to, often witty, never commonplace like the dregs of French officialdom. Their wives too are always pretty, with a little flavor of foreign rascality, and the mystery of their past lives, half of which were probably spent in a penitentiary. Most often they have glorious eyes and wonderful hair, the real professional physique, a grace which intoxicates, a seductive charm that drives men mad, a vicious but wholly irresistible fascination! They're the real old highway robbers, female birds of prey. And I adore them too.

"The Marquise Obardi is a perfect type of these elegant jades. A little overripe, but still beautiful, seductive, and feline, she's vicious to the marrow. There's plenty of fun in her house—gambling, dancing, supper . . . all the distractions of the world, the flesh, and the devil, in fact."

"Have you been, or are you, her lover?" asked Léon Saval.

Servigny answered:

"I haven't been, am not, and never shall be. It's the daughter I go there for."

"Oh, there's a daughter, then, is there?"

"There is indeed! She's a marvel. At present she's the principal attraction. A tall, glorious creature, just the right age, eighteen, as fair as her mother is dark, always merry, always ready for fun, always laughing at the top of her voice, and dancing like a thing possessed. Who's to have her? Who has had her? No one knows. There are ten of us waiting and hoping.

"A girl like that in the hands of a woman like the marquise is a fortune. And they don't show their hands, the rogues. No one can make it out. Perhaps they're waiting for a catch, a better one than I am. Well, I can assure you that if the chance comes my way I'll take it.

"This girl, Yvette, absolutely nonplusses me. She's a mystery. If she isn't the most finished monster of perverse ingenuity that I've ever seen, she's certainly the most extraordinary scrap of innocent girlhood to be found anywhere. She lives there among that disgraceful crew with easy and triumphant serenity, exquisitely wicked or exquisitely simple.

"She's an extraordinary girl to be the daughter of an adventuress, sprung up in that hotbed, like a beautiful plant nourished on manure, or she may be the daughter of some man of high rank, a great artist or a great nobleman, a prince or a king who found himself one night in her mother's bed. No one can understand just what she is, or what she thinks about. But you will see her."

Saval shouted with laughter.

"You're in love with her," he said.

"No, I am one of the competitors, which is not the same thing. By the way, I'll introduce you to my most serious rivals. But I have a real chance. I have a good start, and she regards me with favor."

"You're in love," repeated Saval.

"No, I'm not. She disturbs me, allures me, and makes me uneasy, at once attracts me and frightens me. I distrust her as I would a trap, yet I long for her with the longing of a thirsty man for a cool drink. I feel her charm and draw near it as nervously as if I were in the same room with a man suspected of being a clever thief. In her presence I feel an almost absurd inclination to believe in the possibility of her innocence, and a very reasonable distrust of her equally possible cunning. I feel that I am in contact with an abnormal being, a creature outside the laws of nature, delicious or detestable, I don't know."

For the third time Saval declared:

"You're in love, I tell you. You speak of her with the fervor of a poet and the lyricism of a troubadour. Come now, have it out with yourself, search your heart and admit it."

"Well, it may be so, after all. At least she's always in my mind. Yes, perhaps I am in love. I think of her too much. I think of her when I'm falling asleep and when I wake up; that's fairly serious. Her image haunts me, pursues me, is with me the whole time, in front of me, round me, in me. Is it love, this physical obsession? Her face is so sharply graven in my mind that I see it the moment I shut my eyes. I don't deny that my pulses race whenever I see her. I love her, then, but in an odd fashion. I long for her passionately, yet the idea of making her my wife would seem to me a monstrous absurd folly. I am also a little afraid of her, like a bird swooped upon by a hawk. And I'm jealous of her too, jealous of all that is hidden from me in her incomprehensible heart. I'm always asking myself: 'Is she a delightful little guttersnipe or a thoroughly bad lot?' She says things that would make a trooper blush, but so do parrots. Sometimes she's so brazenly indecent that I'm inclined to believe in her absolute purity, and sometimes her artlessness is so much too good to be true that I wonder if she ever was chaste. She provokes me and excites me like a harlot, and guards herself at the same time as though she were a virgin. She appears to love me, and laughs at me; in public she almost proclaims herself my mistress, and when we're alone together she treats me as though I were her brother or her footman.

"Sometimes I imagine that she has as many lovers as her mother. Sometimes I think that she knows nothing about life, absolutely nothing.

"And she has a passion for reading novels. At present, while waiting for a more amusing position, I am her bookseller. She calls me her librarian.

"Every week the Librairie Nouvelle sends her, from me, everything that has appeared; I believe she reads through the whole lot.

"It must make a strange salad in her head.

"This literary taste may account for some of her queer ways. When you see life through a maze of fifteen thousand novels, you must get a queer impression of things and see them from an odd angle.

"As for me, I wait. It is certainly true that I have never felt towards any woman as I feel towards her.

"It's equally certain that I shall never marry her.

"If she has had lovers, I shall make one more. If she has not, I shall be the first to take my seat in the train.

"It's all very simple. She can't possibly marry, ever. Who would marry the daughter of the Marquise Obardi, Octavie Bardin? Clearly no one, for any number of reasons.

"Where could she find a husband? In society? Never; the mother's house is a public resort, and the daughter attracts the clients. One can't marry into a family like that. In the middle classes, then? Even less. Besides, the marquise has a good head on her shoulders; she'd never give Yvette to anyone but a man of rank, and she'll never find him.

"In the lower classes, perhaps? Still less possible. There's no way out of it, then. The girl belongs neither to society nor to the middle class, nor to the lower classes, nor would marriage jockey her into any one of them. She belongs, by her parentage, her birth, her upbringing, heredity, manners, habits, to the world of gilded prostitution.

"She can't escape unless she becomes a nun, which is very unlikely, seeing that her manners and tastes are already what they are. So she has only one possible profession—love. That's where she'll go, if she has not already gone. She can't escape her destiny. From being a young girl, she'll become just a—'woman.' And I should very much like to be the man who brings about the transformation.

"I am waiting. There are any number of lovers. You'll come across a Frenchman, M. de Beloigne, a Russian who calls himself Prince Kravalow, and an Italian, Chevalier Valréali. These have all definitely entered themselves for the race, and are already training. There are also a number of camp followers of less account.

"The marquise is on the lookout. But I fancy she has her eye on me. She knows I'm very rich and she knows less about the others.

"Her house is the most extraordinary place of the kind that I have ever seen. You meet some very decent fellows there; we're going ourselves and we shall not be the only ones. As for the women, she has come across, or rather picked out, the choicest fruit on the professional stall. Lord knows where she found them. And she was magnificently inspired to make a point of taking those who had children of their own, daughters for choice. The result is that a greenhorn might think the house was full of honest women!"

They had reached the Avenue des Champs Elysées. A faint breeze whispered among the leaves, and was now and again wafted against their faces, like the soft breath of a giant fan swinging somewhere in the sky. Mute shadows drifted under the trees, others were visible as dark blots on the benches. And all these shadows spoke in very low tones, as though confiding important or shameful secrets.

"You cannot imagine," went on Servigny, "what a collection of fancy titles you come across in this rabbit warren. By the way, I hope you know I'm going to introduce you as Count Saval. Saval by itself would not be at all popular, I assure you."

"No, damn it, certainly not!" cried his friend. "I'm hanged if anyone is going to think me fool enough to scrape up a comic-opera title even for 'one night only,' and for that crowd. With your leave, we'll cut that out."

Servigny laughed.

"You old idiot! Why, I've been christened the Duc de Servigny. I don't know how or why it was done. I have just always been the Duc de Servigny; I never made trouble about it. It's no discomfort. Why without it I should be utterly looked down on!"

But Saval was not to be persuaded.

"You're a nobleman, you can carry it off. As for me, I shall remain, for better or worse, the only commoner in the place. That will be my mark of distinctive superiority."

But Servigny was obstinate.

"I tell you it can't be done, absolutely cannot be done. It would be positively indecent. You would be like a rag-and-bone man at an assemblage of emperors. Leave it to me; I'll introduce you as the Viceroy of Upper Mississippi, and no one will be surprised. If you're going to go in for titles, you might as well do it with an air."

"No; once more, I tell you I won't have it."

"Very well, then. I was a fool really to try persuading you, for I defy you to get in without someone decorating you with a title; it's like those shops a lady can't pass without being given a bunch of violets at the doorstep."

They turned to the right down the Rue de Berri, climbed to the first floor of a fine modern mansion, and left their coats and sticks in the hands of four flunkeys in knee breeches. The air was heavy with the warm festive odor of flowers, scent, and women; and a ceaseless murmur of voices, loud and confused, came from the crowded rooms beyond.

A tall, upright, solemn, potbellied man, in some sort master of the ceremonies, his face framed in white whiskers, approached the newcomers and, making a short, stiff bow, asked:

"What name, please?"

"Monsieur Saval," replied Servigny.

Whereupon the man flung open the door and in a loud voice announced to the crowd of guests:

"Monsieur le Duc de Servigny. Monsieur le Baron Saval!"

The first room was full of women. The eye was filled at once by a vast vision of bare bosoms lifting from billows of white lace.

The lady of the house stood talking to three friends; she turned and came forward with stately steps, grace in her bearing and a smile upon her lips.

Her low, narrow forehead was entirely hidden by masses of black, gleaming hair, thick and fleecy, encroaching even on her temples. She was tall, a little too massive, a little too fat, a little overripe, but very handsome, with a warm, heady, and powerful beauty. Her crown of hair, with the large black eyes beneath it, provoked entrancing dreams and made her subtly desirable. Her nose was rather thin, her mouth large and infinitely alluring, made for speech and conquest.

But her liveliest charm lay in her voice. It sprang from her mouth like water from a spring, so easily, so lightly, so well pitched, so clear, that listening to it was sheer physical joy. It thrilled the ear to hear the smooth words pour forth with the sparkling grace of a brook bubbling from the ground, and fascinated the eye to watch the lovely, too-red lips part to give them passage.

She held out her hand to Servigny, who kissed it, and, dropping the fan that hung from a thin chain of wrought gold, she gave her other hand to Saval, saying:

"You are welcome, Baron. My house is always open to any friend of the Duke's."

Then she fixed her brilliant eyes on the giant to whom she was being introduced. On her upper lip was a faint smudge of black down, the merest shadow of a mustache, more plainly visible when she spoke. Her scent was delicious, strong and intoxicating, some American or Indian perfume.

But other guests were arriving, marquis, counts, or princes. She turned to Servigny and said, with the graciousness of a mother:

"You will find my daughter in the other room. Enjoy yourselves, gentlemen. The house is yours."

She left them in order to greet the new arrivals, giving Saval that fugitive smiling glance with which women let men know that they have found favor.

Servigny took his friend's arm.

"I'll be your pilot," he said. "Here, where we are at present, are the women; this is the temple of the flesh, fresh or otherwise. Bargains as good as new, or better; very superior articles at greatly reduced rates. On the left is the gambling. That is the temple of money. You know all about that.

"At the far end, dancing; that is the temple of innocence. There are displayed the offspring, if we may believe it, of the ladies in here. Even lawful unions would be smiled on! There is the future, the hope . . . of our nights. And there, too, are the strangest exhibits in this museum of diseased morals, the young girls whose souls are double-jointed, like the limbs of little clowns who had acrobats for parents. Let us go and see them."

He bowed to right and left, a debonair figure, scattering pretty speeches and running his rapid, expert glance over every pair of bare shoulders whose possessor he recognized.

At the far end of the second room an orchestra was playing a waltz; they stopped at the door and watched. Some fifteen couples were dancing, the men gravely, their partners with fixed smiles on their lips. Like their mothers, they showed a great deal of bare skin; since the bodices of some were supported only by a narrow ribbon round the upper part of the arm, there were occasional glimpses of a dark shadow under the armpits.

Suddenly a tall girl started up and crossed the room, pushing the dancers aside, her absurdly long train gathered in her left hand. She ran with the short quick steps affected by women in a crowd, and cried out:

"Ah, there's Muscade. How are you, Muscade!"

Her face was glowing with life, and radiant with happiness. She had the white, golden-gleaming skin which goes with auburn hair. Her forehead was loaded with the sheaf of flaming, gleaming tresses that burdened her still slender neck.

She seemed made for motion as her mother was for speech, so natural, gracious, and simple were her movements. A sense of spiritual delight and physical contentment sprang from the mere sight of her as she walked, moved, bent her head or raised her arm.

"Ah, Muscade," she repeated. "How are you, Muscade?"

Servigny shook her hand vigorously, as though she were a man, and said:

"This is my friend, Baron Saval, Mam'selle Yvette."

She greeted the newcomer, then stared at him.

"How do you do? Are you always as tall as this?"

"Oh, no, mam'selle," answered Servigny, in the mocking tone he used to conceal his uneasiness in her presence. "He has put on his largest size today to please your mother, who likes quantity."

"Oh, very well, then," replied the girl in a seriocomic voice. "But when you come for my sake, please be a little smaller; I like the happy medium. Muscade here is about my size," and she offered him her little hand.

"Are you going to dance, Muscade?" she asked. "Let's dance this waltz."

Servigny made no answer, but with a sudden swift movement put his arm round her waist and away they went like a whirlwind.

They danced faster than any, turning and twirling with wild abandon, so tightly clasped that they looked like one. Their bodies held upright and their legs almost motionless, it was as though they were spun round by an invisible machine hidden under their feet. They seemed unwearying. One by one the other couples dropped out till they were left alone, waltzing on and on. They looked as though they no longer knew where they were or what they were doing, as though they were far away from the ballroom, in ecstasy. The band played steadily on, their eyes fixed on this bewitched pair; everyone was watching, and there was a burst of applause when at last they stopped.

She was rather flushed; her eyes were no longer frank, but strangely troubled, burning yet timid, unnaturally blue, with pupils unnaturally black.

Servigny was drunk with giddiness, and leaned against a door to recover his balance.

"You have a poor head, Muscade," she said. "You don't stand it as well as I do."

He smiled his nervous smile and looked at her with hungry eyes, a savage lust in his eyes and the curve of his lips.

She continued to stand in front of the young man, her throat heaving as she regained her breath.

"Sometimes," she continued, "you look just like a cat about to make a spring. Give me your arm, and let us go and find your friend."

Without speaking he offered her his arm, and they crossed the large room.

Saval was alone no longer; the Marquise Obardi had joined him, and was talking of trivial things, bewitching him with her maddening voice. Gazing intently at him, she seemed to utter words very different from those on her lips, words that came from the secret places of her heart. At sight of Servigny she smiled and, turning to him, said:

"Have you heard, my dear Duke, that I've just taken a villa at Bougival for a couple of months? Of course you'll come and see me; you'll bring your friend, won't you? I'm going down there on Monday, so will you both come and dine there next Saturday, and stay over the weekend?"

Servigny turned sharply to Yvette. She was smiling a serene, tranquil smile, and with an air of bland assurance said:

"Of course Muscade will come to dinner on Saturday; there's no need to ask him. We shall have all kinds of fun in the country."

He fancied that he saw a vague promise in her smile, and an unwonted decision in her voice.

The marquise thereupon raised her great black eyes to Saval's face, and said: "And you also, Baron?"

There was nothing equivocal about her smile.

He bowed.

"I shall be only too pleased."

"We'll scandalize the neighborhood—won't we, Muscade—and drive my admirers wild with rage," murmured Yvette, glancing, with a malice that was either candid or assured, towards the group of men who watched them from the other side of the room.

"To your heart's content, mam'selle," replied Servigny; by way of emphasizing the intimate nature of his friendship with her, he never called her "mademoiselle."

"Why does Mlle. Yvette always call my friend Servigny 'Muscade'?" asked Saval.

The girl assumed an air of innocence.

"He's like the little pea that the conjurers call 'Muscade.' You think you have your finger on it, but you never have."

"Quaint children, aren't they?" the marquise said carelessly, obviously thinking of far other things, and not for an instant lowering her eyes from Saval's face.

"I'm not quaint, I'm frank," said Yvette angrily. "I like Muscade, and he's always leaving me; it's so annoying."

Servigny made her a low bow.

"I'll never leave you again, mam'selle, day or night."

She made a gesture of alarm.

"Oh, no, that would never do! In the daytime, by all means, but at night you'd be in the way."

"Why?" he asked imprudently.

With calm audacity she replied:

"Because you couldn't possibly look so nice with your clothes off."

"What a dreadful thing to say!" exclaimed the marquise, without appearing in the least excited. "You can't possibly be so innocent as all that."

"I entirely agree with you," added Servigny in a jesting tone.

Yvette looked rather hurt, and said haughtily:

"You have just been guilty of blatant vulgarity; you have permitted yourself far too much of that sort of thing lately."

She turned her back on him, and shouted:

"Chevalier, come and defend me; I have just been insulted."

A thin, dark man came slowly towards them.

"Which is the culprit?" he asked, forcing a smile.

She nodded towards Servigny.

"That's the man; but all the same I like him better than all of you put together; he's not so boring."

The Chevalier Valréali bowed.

"We do what we can. Perhaps we are not so brilliant, but we are at least as devoted."

A tall, stout man with gray whiskers and a deep voice was just leaving.

"Your servant, Mlle. Yvette," he said as he passed.

"Ah, it's M. de Belvigne," she exclaimed, and turning to Saval she introduced him.

"Another candidate for my favor, tall, fat, rich, and stupid. That's how I like them. He's a real field marshal—one of those who hold the door open at restaurants. But you're taller than he is. Now what am I going to christen you? I know! I shall call you Rhodes Junior, after the Colossus who must have been your father. But you two must have really interesting things to discuss, far above our heads, so good night to you."

She ran across to the orchestra and asked them to play a quadrille.

Mme. Obardi's attention seemed to be wandering.

"You're always teasing her," she said softly. "You're spoiling the child's disposition and teaching her a number of bad habits."

"Then you haven't finished her education?" he replied.

She seemed not to understand, and continued to smile benevolently.

But observing the approach of a solemn gentleman whose breast was covered with orders, she ran up to him.

"Ah, Prince, how delightful!"

Servigny took Saval's arm once more and led him away, saying:

"There's my last serious rival, Prince Kravalow. Isn't she a glorious creature?"

"They're both glorious," replied Saval. "The mother's quite good enough for me."

Servigny bowed.

"She's yours for the asking, my dear."

The dancers elbowed them as they took their places for the quadrille, couple by couple, in two lines facing one another.

"Now let's go and watch the Greeks for a bit," said Servigny.

They entered the gambling room.

Round each table a circle of men stood watching. There was very little conversation; sometimes a little chink of gold, thrown down on the cloth or hastily mixed up, mingled its faint metallic murmur with the murmur of the players, as though the voice of gold were making itself heard amid the human voices.

The men were decorated with various orders and strange ribbons; and their diverse features all wore the same severe expression. They were more easily distinguished by their beards.

The stiff American with his horseshoe beard, the haughty Englishman with a hairy fan spread over his chest, the Spaniard with a black fleece reaching right up to his eyes, the Roman with the immense mustache bequeathed to Italy by Victor Emmanuel, the Austrian with his whiskers and clean-shaven chin, a Russian general whose lip was armed with two spears of twisted hair, Frenchmen with gay mustaches—they displayed the imaginative genius of every barber in the world.

"Aren't you going to play?" asked Servigny.

"No; what about you?"

"I never play here. Would you like to go now? We'll come back one day when it's quieter. There are too many people here today; there's nothing to be done."

"Yes, let us go."

They disappeared through a doorway which led into the hall.

As soon as they were out in the street, Servigny asked:

"Well, what do you think of it all?"

"It's certainly interesting. But I like the women better than the men."

"Good Lord, yes! Those women are the best hunting in the country. Don't you agree with me that love exhales from them like the perfumes from a barbershop? These are positively the only houses where one can really get one's money's worth. And what expert lovers they are! What artists! Have you ever eaten cakes made by a baker? They look so good, and they have no flavor at all. Well, the love of an ordinary woman always reminds me of baker's pastry, whereas the love you get from women like the Marquise Obardi—that really is love! Oh, they can make cakes all right, can these confectioners. You have to pay them twopence halfpenny for what you would get anywhere else for a penny, that's the only thing."

"Who is the man running the place at present?" asked Saval.

Servigny shrugged his shoulders to express utter ignorance.

"I have no idea," he said. "The last I knew certainly was an English peer, but he left three months ago. At the moment she must be living on the community, on the gambling and the gamblers, very likely, for she has her whims. But it's an understood thing, isn't it, that we are dining with her at Bougival on Saturday? There's more freedom in the country, and I shall end by finding out what notions Yvette has in her head!"

"I ask for nothing better," replied Saval. "I'm not doing anything that day."

As they returned down the Champs Elysées, under the embattled stars, they passed a couple lying on a bench, and Servigny murmured:

"How ridiculous, yet how utterly indispensable, is this business of love! A commonplace, and an ecstasy, always the same and always different! And the clown who is paying that girl a franc is only seeking the very thing I buy for ten thousand from some Obardi who is perhaps no younger, or more fascinating than that drab! What folly!"

He was silent for some minutes, then said:

"All the same, it wouldn't be a poor thing to be Yvette's first lover. For that I'd give . . . I'd give . . ."

He did not make up his mind what he would give. And Saval bade him good night at the corner of the Rue Royale.

II

The table had been laid on the veranda that overlooked the river. Villa Printemps, the house that the Marquise Obardi had taken, stood halfway up the hillside, at the very point where just below the garden wall the Seine made a turn towards Marly. Opposite the house the island of Croissy formed a background of tall trees, a mass of leafage. A long reach of the broad river was clearly visible as far as the floating café, La Grenouillère, half-hidden in the branches.

Night was coming down, calm and still, after a flaming riverside sunset; one of those tranquil evenings that bring with them a vague sense of happiness. Not a breath of air stirred the branches, no gust of wind disturbed the smooth translucent surface of the Seine. The air was warm, but not too hot; it was good to be alive. The grateful coolness of the riverbanks rose to the quiet sky.

The sun was disappearing behind the trees, wheeling towards other lands. The serene calm of the sleeping earth soothed their senses; under the vast quiet dome of the sky they felt the effortless surge of the universal life.

The scene enchanted them when they came out of the drawing room and sat down at the dinner table. A tender gaiety filled their hearts; they all felt it very good to be dining out there in the country with that broad river and glorious sunset for scenery and breathing that sweet pure air.

The marquise had taken Saval's arm, Yvette Servigny's.

These four made up the little party.

The two women were not in the least like their Parisian selves. Yvette was the more altered of the two; she spoke very little, and seemed tired and grave.

Saval hardly recognized her, and asked:

"What's the matter with you, mademoiselle? I find you very changed since last week. You have become quite a reasonable being."

"It's the effect of the country," she answered. "I am not the same there; I feel quite strange. And besides, I never am the same two days together. Today I behave like a lunatic, tomorrow I'll be like a funeral oration; I change like the weather, I don't know why. I'm capable of absolutely anything—at the right time. There are days when I could kill people; not animals—I could never kill animals—but people, certainly; and then there are days when I cry for just nothing. A hundred different ideas rush through my head. It depends, too, on my feeling when I get up in the morning. Every morning when I wake up I know just what I shall be like all day. Perhaps our dreams decide that sort of thing. Partly it depends on the book I have just been reading."

She was dressed in white flannel; the soft delicate folds of material covered her from head to foot. The bodice was loose, with big pleats, and suggested, without too rigidly defining, the firm sweeping contour of her already well-formed bosom. Her slender neck rose from fold upon fold of frothy lace, drooping languidly, its warm gleaming flesh even whiter than her dress and weighed down with its heavy burden of golden hair.

For a long minute Servigny gazed at her, then said:

"You are adorable tonight, mam'selle—I wish I could always see you like that."

"Don't propose to me, Muscade," she said, with a touch of her wonted archness. "On a day like this I should take you at your word, and that might cost you dear."

The marquise looked happy, very happy. She was dressed severely in black; the fine folds of the gown set off the superb, massive lines of her figure. There was a touch of red in the bodice, a spray of red carnations fell from her waist and was caught up at her side, a red rose was fastened in her dark hair. There was a flame in her tonight, in her whole being, in the simple dress with the blood-red blossoms, in the glance that lingered on her neighbor, in her slow voice, in her rare movements.

Saval too was grave and preoccupied. From time to time, with a gesture familiar to him, he stroked his brown Vandyke beard, and seemed sunk in thought.

For some moments no one spoke.

"There is sometimes a saving grace in silence," said Servigny at last, as the trout was being handed. "Neighbors are often closer to one another when silent than when speaking; isn't that so, Marquise?"

She turned slightly towards him and replied:

"Yes, it's true. It is so sweet for both of us to think of the same delightful thing."

She turned her burning gaze on Saval; for some moments they remained looking into one another's eyes. There was a slight, an almost imperceptible movement under the table.

"Mam'selle Yvette," continued Servigny, "you'll make me think you're in love if you continue to behave so beautifully. Now with whom can you be in love? Let's think it out together. I leave the vulgar herd of sighing swains on one side, and go straight for the principals. How about Prince Kravalow?"

At this name Yvette was roused.

"My poor dear Muscade, what are you thinking about? The prince looks like a Russian in the waxworks who would win medals at a hairdressing competition."

"Very well. The prince is out of it. Perhaps you have chosen the Vicomte Pierre de Belvigne?"

This time she broke into a fit of laughter and asked:

"Can you see me hanging round Raisiné's neck"—she called him Raisiné, Malvoisie, or Argenteuil according to the day of the week, for she nicknamed everyone—"and whispering in his ear: 'My dear little Pierre,' or 'My divine Pedro, my adored Pietri, my darling Pierrot, give your dear fat poodle-head to your darling little wifie because she wants to kiss it'?"

"Away with number two, then," said Servigny. "We are left with the Chevalier Valréali, whom the marquise seems to favor."

Yvette was as much amused as before.

"What, Old Lachrymose? Why, he's a professional mourner at the Madeleine; he follows all the high-class funerals. Whenever he looks at me I feel as though I were already dead."

"That's three. Then you've fallen hopelessly in love with Baron Saval, here present."

"With Rhodes Junior? No, he's too strong. It would feel like being in love with the Arc de Triomphe de l'Etoile."

"Well, then, mam'selle, it is plain that you're in love with me, for I'm the only one of your worshipers that we haven't already dealt with. I had kept myself to the end, out of modesty and prudence. It only remains for me to thank you."

"You, Muscade!" she replied with charming gaiety. "Oh, no, I like you very much . . . but I don't love you. . . . Wait, I don't want to discourage you. I don't love you yet. . . . You have a chance . . . perhaps. . . . Persevere, Muscade, be devoted, ardent, obedient, take plenty of trouble and all possible precautions, obey my lightest whims, be prepared to do anything I may choose . . . and we'll see . . . later."

"But, mam'selle, I'd rather do all this for you after than before, if you don't mind."

"After what . . . Muscade?" she asked him with the ingenuous air of a soubrette.

"Why, deuce take it, after you've shown me that you love me."

"Well, behave as though I did, and believe it if you want to."

"But, I must say . . ."

"Be quiet, Muscade. That's enough about it for this time."

He made her a military salute and held his tongue.

The sun had gone down behind the island, but the sky still glowed like a brazier, and the quiet water of the river was as though changed to blood. The sunset spilled a burning light over houses, people, everything; the scarlet rose in the marquise's hair was like a drop of crimson fallen upon her head from the clouds.

Yvette was looking the other way; her mother laid her hand on Saval's, as though by accident. But the young girl turned, and the marquise quickly snatched away her hand and fumbled at the folds of her bodice.

Servigny, who was watching them, said:

"If you like, mam'selle, we'll go for a walk on the island after dinner."

She was delighted with the idea.

"Oh, yes; that will be lovely; we'll go by ourselves, won't we, Muscade?"

"Yes, all by ourselves, mam'selle."

Once more they were silent.

The calm of the wide landscape, the restful slumber of eventide weighed on their hearts, their bodies, their voices. There are rare, quiet hours wherein speech is almost impossible. The servants made no noise. The flaming sky burnt low; slowly night folded the earth in shadow.

"Do you propose to stay here long?" asked Saval.

"Yes," replied the marquise, dwelling upon each word, "for just as long as I'm happy here."

As it was now too dark to see, lamps were brought. They flung across the table a strange pale light in the hollow darkness. A rain of little flies began falling upon the cloth. They were tiny midges, burnt as they flew over the glass chimneys of the lamps; their wings and legs singed, they powdered the table linen, the plates, and the glasses with a gray, creeping dust. The diners swallowed them in their wine, ate them in the saucers, watched them crawling over the bread. Their faces and hands were perpetually tickled by a flying swarm of innumerable tiny insects.

The wine had constantly to be thrown away, the plates covered; they took infinite precautions to protect the food they were eating. Yvette was amused at the game; Servigny carefully sheltered whatever she was raising to her lips, guarded the wineglass and held his napkin spread out over her head like a roof. But it was too much for the fastidious nerves of the marquise, and the meal was hastily brought to an end.

"Now let's go to the island," said Yvette, who had not forgotten Servigny's suggestion.

"Don't stay long, will you?" advised her mother languidly. "We'll come with you as far as the ferry."

They went off along the towpath, still two and two, the young girl in front with her friend. They could hear the marquise and Saval behind them talking very fast in very low voices. All round them was black, with a thick, inky blackness. But the sky, swarming with seeds of fire, seemed to spill them out on the river, for the dark water was richly patined with stars.

By this time the frogs were croaking; all along the banks their rolling, monotonous notes creaked out.

The soft voices of innumerable nightingales rose in the still air.

Yvette remarked abruptly:

"Hallo! They are no longer following us. Where are they?"

And she called: "Mother!"

There was no answer. "They can't be far away," continued the young girl. "I heard them a moment ago."

"They must have gone back," murmured Servigny. "Perhaps your mother was cold." He led her on.

A light shone in front of them; it was the inn of Martinet, a fisherman who also ran a tavern. At their call a man came out of the house, and they boarded a large boat moored in the grasses on the bank. The ferryman took up his oars, and the heavy boat advanced, waking the stars slumbering on the water and rousing them to a frenzied dancing that died slowly down in their wake. They touched the other bank and stepped off under the tall trees. The coolness of the moist earth floated up under the high thick branches that seemed to bear as many nightingales as leaves. A distant piano began to play a popular waltz.

Servigny had taken Yvette's arm; very softly he slipped his hand behind her waist and pressed it gently.

"What are you thinking of?" he asked.

"I? . . . Nothing, I'm so happy."

"Then you don't care for me?"

"Yes, I do, Muscade. I care for you, I care for you a great deal; only don't talk about it now. It's too beautiful here to listen to your nonsense."

He clasped her to him, though she strove, with little struggles, to free herself; through the flannel, so soft and fleecy to the touch, he could feel the warmth of her body.

"Yvette," he stammered.

"Yes; what is it?"

"It's . . . I who care for you."

"You . . . don't mean that, Muscade."

"Yes, I do; I've cared for you for a very long time."

She was still struggling to get away, striving to free her arm caught between their two bodies. They walked with difficulty, hampered by this link and by her struggles, zigzagging like a couple of drunkards.

He did not know what to say to her now, well aware that it is impossible to use to a young girl the words one would use to a grown woman; he was worried, wondering what he could do, wondering if she consented or did not understand, at his wit's end for words that would be at once tender, discreet, and unmistakable.

Every second he repeated:

"Yvette! Speak to me, Yvette!"

Suddenly he pressed an audacious kiss on her cheek. She made a little movement of withdrawal, and said in a vexed tone:

"Oh! How absurd you are. Will you leave me alone?"

Her voice revealed nothing of her thoughts and wishes; he saw that she was not too angry, and he stooped his lips to the nape of her neck, on the first few downy golden hairs, the adorable spot he had coveted so long.

Then she struggled with all her might to get free. But he held her firmly, and placing his other hand on her shoulder, forced her head round towards him, and took from her mouth a long, maddening kiss. She slipped between his arms with a quick twist of her whole body, stooped swiftly, and having thus dexterously escaped from his embrace, vanished in the darkness with a sharp rustling of petticoats like the whirring noise of a pheasant rising.

At first he remained motionless, stunned by her quickness and by her disappearance; then, hearing no further sound, he called in a low voice:

"Yvette!"

There was no answer; he began to walk on, ransacking the darkness with his eyes, searching in the bushes for the white patch that must be made by her dress. All was dark. He called again more loudly:

"Mam'selle Yvette!"

The nightingales were silent.

He hurried on, vaguely uneasy, calling ever louder and louder:

"Mam'selle Yvette! Mam'selle Yvette!"

Nothing! He stopped, listened. The whole island was silent; there was barely a rustle in the leaves overhead. The frogs alone kept up their sonorous croaking on the banks.

He wandered from copse to copse, descending first to the steep wooded slope of the swift main stream, then returning to the bare flat bank of the backwater. He went right up until he was opposite Bougival, then came back to the café La Grenouillère, hunting through all the thickets, constantly crying:

"Mam'selle Yvette, where are you? Answer! It is only a joke. Answer me, answer me! Don't make me hunt like this."

A distant clock began to strike. He counted the strokes; it was midnight. For two hours he had been running round the island. He thought that she had probably gone home, and, very uneasy, went back, going round by the bridge.

A servant, asleep in an armchair, was waiting in the hall. Servigny woke him and asked:

"Is it long since Mlle. Yvette came in? I left her out in the country, as I had to pay a call."

"Oh, yes, Your Grace," the fellow replied, "Mademoiselle came in before ten."

He walked up to his room and went to bed. But he lay with his eyes open, unable to sleep. That snatched kiss had disturbed her. What did she want? he wondered. What did she think? What did she know? How pretty she was, and how she had maddened him! His desire, dulled by the life he had led, by all the women he had known, was reawakened by this strange child, so fresh, provoking, and inexplicable.

He heard one o'clock strike, then two. He realized that he would get no sleep that night. He was hot and wet with sweat; he felt in his temples the quick thudding of his heart. He got up to open the window.

A cool breeze came in, and he drew long deep breaths of it. The night was utterly dark, silent, and still. But suddenly in the darkness of the garden he caught sight of a speck of light, like a little piece of glowing coal. "Ah, a cigar," he thought. "It can't be anyone but Saval. Léon," he called softly.

"Is that you, Jean?" a voice answered.

"Yes. Wait, I'm coming down."

He dressed, went out, and joined his friend, who was smoking astride an iron chair.

"What are you doing at this time of night?"

"Having a rest," replied Saval, and laughed.

Servigny shook his head.

"I congratulate you, my dear chap. As for me, I've run my head into a wall."

"You are telling me . . . ?"

"I am telling you . . . that Yvette is not like her mother."

"What happened? Tell me all about it."

Servigny recounted his unsuccessful efforts, then continued:

"Yes, the child really worries me. Do you realize that I haven't been able to get to sleep? What a queer thing a girl is. This one looks as simple as possible, and yet she's a complete mystery. One can understand at once a woman who has lived and loved, who knows what life is like. But with a young girl, on the other hand, one can't be sure of anything at all. I'm really beginning to think she's playing the fool with me."

Saval rocked gently on his chair.

"Be careful, my dear chap," he said very slowly; "she'll get you to marry her. Remember the illustrious examples in history. That was how Mlle. de Montijo became empress, and she was at least of decent family. Don't play the Napoleon."

"Have no fears about that," said Servigny. "I'm not a fool, nor an emperor. One has to be one or the other to lose one's head so completely. But, I say, are you sleepy?"

"Not a bit."

"Come for a walk along the riverside, then."

"Very well."

They opened the gate and started off down the river towards Marly.

It was the cool hour just before dawn, the hour of deepest sleep, deepest rest, utter quiet. Even the faint noises of the night were silent now. The nightingales sang no longer, the frogs had finished their croaking; some unknown animal, a bird perhaps, alone broke the stillness, making a feeble sawing noise, monotonous and regular, like the working of a machine. Servigny, who had at times a touch of the poet and of the philosopher too, said abruptly:

"Look here. This girl absolutely maddens me. In arithmetic, one and one make two. In love, one and one ought to make one, but they make two all the same. Do you know the feeling? The savage need of absorbing a women into oneself, or of being absorbed into her? I don't mean the mere physical desire to embrace her, but the mental and spiritual torment to be at one with another human being, to open one's whole soul to her, one's whole heart, and to penetrate to the uttermost depths of her mind. And never, never do you really know her or discover all the fluctuations of her will, her desires, and her thoughts. Never can you make even the slightest guess at the whole of the secret, the whole mystery of the spirit come so close to you, a spirit hidden behind two eyes as clear as water, as transparent as though there were no secret behind them. A spirit speaks to you through a beloved mouth, a mouth that seems yours because you desire it so passionately; one by one this spirit sends you its thoughts in the guise of words, and yet it remains farther from you than the stars are from one another, farther out of reach than the stars. Strange, isn't it!"

"I do not demand so much," replied Saval. "I do not bother to look behind the eyes. I don't care much for the inside; it's the outside I care for."

"Whatever you say, Yvette's a queer creature," murmured Servigny. "I wonder how she'll treat me in the morning."

As they reached the weir at Marly, they saw that the sky was paling. Cocks began to crow in the farmyards; the sound reached them slightly muffled by thick walls. A bird cried in a park on the left, continually repeating a simple and ridiculous little cadenza.

"Time to go back," said Saval, and they turned round.

When Servigny reached his room, the horizon gleamed rosily through the still open window. He pulled down the Venetian blinds and drew the heavy curtains across, got into bed, and at last fell asleep. And all the time he dreamt of Yvette.

A curious sound awoke him. He sat up and listened, but did not hear it again. Then suddenly there came against his shutters a rattling like hail. He jumped out of bed and ran to the window; throwing it open, he saw Yvette standing on the garden path, throwing great handfuls of gravel in his face.

She was dressed in pink and wore a broadbrimmed straw hat surmounted with a military plume; she was laughing with malicious mischief.

"Well, Muscade, still asleep? What can you have been doing last night to wake up so late? Did you have any adventures, my poor Muscade?"

"Coming, coming, mam'selle! Just a moment, while I stick my nose into the water jug, and I'll be down."

"Hurry up," she cried; "it's ten o'clock. And I've got a scheme to talk over with you, a plot we are going to carry out. Breakfast at eleven, you know."

He found her seated on a bench with a book on her knees, a novel. She took his arm with friendly familiarity, as frankly and gaily as though nothing had happened the night before, and leading him to the far end of the garden, said:

"This is my plan. We're going to disobey Mamma, and you are going to take me presently to the Grenouillère. I want to see it. Mamma says that decent women can't go there, but I don't care whether I can or I can't. You'll take me, Muscade, won't you? We'll have such sport with the people on the river."

The fragrance of her was delightful, but he could not discover what vague, faint scent it was that hung round her. It was not one of her mother's heavy perfumes, but a delicate fragrance in which he thought he recognized a faint whiff of iris powder and perhaps a touch of verbena.

Whence came this elusive scent—from her dress, her hair, or her skin? He was wondering about this when, as she spoke with her face very close to his, he felt her fresh breath full in his face, and found it quite as delightful. He fancied that the fleeting fragrance he had failed to recognize was the figment of his own bewitched senses, nothing but a delusive emanation from her youth and alluring grace.

"You will, won't you, Muscade?" she said. "It will be so hot after breakfast that Mother won't want to go out. She's very lazy when it's hot. We'll leave her with your friend, and you shall be my escort. We'll pretend we are going up to the woods. You don't know how I shall enjoy seeing the Grenouillère."

They reached the gate facing the Seine. A flood of sunlight fell on the quiet, gleaming river. A light heat mist was lifting, the steam of evaporated water, leaving a little glittering vapor on the surface of the stream. From time to time a boat went by, a light skiff or a heavy barge, and distant whistles could be heard, the short notes of the whistles on the Sunday trains that flooded the country with Parisians, and the long warning notes of the steamboats passing the weir at Marly.

But a small bell rang for breakfast, and they went in.

The meal was eaten in silence. A heavy July noon pressed on the earth and oppressed the dwelling thereon. The heat was almost tangible, paralyzing both mind and body. The sluggish words would not leave their lips; every movement was an effort, as though the air had acquired power of resistance and was more difficult to thrust through.

Yvette alone, though silent, was animated and possessed by impatience. As soon as dessert was finished she said:

"Supposing we went for a walk in the woods. It would be perfectly delightful under the trees."

"Are you mad?" murmured the marquise, who looked utterly exhausted. "How can one go out in weather like this?"

"Very well," replied the young girl slyly, "we'll leave you here with the baron to keep you company. Muscade and I will scramble up the hill and sit down and read on the grass."

She turned to Servigny, saying: "That's all right, isn't it?"

"At your service, mam'selle," he replied.

She ran off to fetch her hat. The marquise shrugged her shoulders and sighed: "Really, she's quite mad." Indolently she held out her beautiful white hand in a gesture of profound and seductive lassitude; the baron pressed a lingering kiss upon it.

Yvette and Servigny departed. At first they followed the river, then they crossed the bridge and went on to the island, and sat down under the willows on the bank of the main stream, for it was still too early to go to La Grenouillère.

The young girl at once took a book from her pocket and, laughing, said:

"Muscade, you're going to read to me." And she held out the volume for him to take. He made a deprecatory gesture. "I, mam'selle? But I can't read."

"Come, now, no excuses, no arguments," she replied severely. "You're a nice lover, you are. 'Everything for nothing'—that's your creed, isn't it?"

He took the book and opened it, and was surprised to find that it was a treatise on entomology, a history of ants by an English author. He remained silent, thinking that she was making fun of him.

"Go on, read," she said.

"Is this a bet," he asked, "or just a joke?"

"Neither. I saw the book in a shop; they told me it was the best book about ants, and I thought it would be nice to hear about the lives of the little creatures and watch them running about in the grass at the same time. So read away."

She lay down face downwards at full length, her elbows resting on the ground and her head between her hands, her eyes fixed on the grass.

" 'Without doubt,' " he read, " 'the anthropoid apes are of all animals those which approach most closely to man in their anatomical structure; but if we consider the habits of ants, their organization into societies, their vast communities, the houses and roads which they construct, their custom of domesticating animals and even at times of having slaves, we shall be forced to admit that they have the right to claim the place next to man on the ladder of intelligence.' "

He continued in a monotonous voice, stopping from time to time to ask: "Isn't that enough?"

She signed no with a shake of her head, and, having picked up a wandering ant on the point of a blade of grass she had plucked, she amused herself by making it run from one end of the stem to the other, turning it upside down as soon as the insect reached either end. She listened in silence and with concentrated attention to all the surprising details of the life of these frail creatures, their subterranean establishments, the way in which they bring up, keep, and feed little grubs in order to drink the secret liquor they secrete, just as we keep cows in our byres, their custom of domesticating little blind insects which clean their dwellings, and of going to war in order to bring back slaves to serve the victors, which the slaves do with such solicitude that the latter even lose the habit of feeding themselves.

And little by little, as though a maternal tenderness had awakened in her head for this creature at once so tiny and so intelligent, Yvette let it climb about her finger, watching it with loving eyes, longing to kiss it. And as Servigny was reading how they live in a community, how they play together in a friendly rivalry of strength and skill, the young girl, in her enthusiasm, tried to kiss the insect, which escaped from her finger and began to run over her face. She shrieked as violently as though a deadly peril threatened her, and with wild gestures she slapped at her cheek to get rid of the creature. Servigny, roaring with laughter, caught it near her hair and, at the spot where he had caught it, pressed a long kiss, from which Yvette did not recoil.

She got up, declaring: "I like that better than a novel. Now let's go to La Grenouillère."

They reached a part of the island which was laid out like a park, shaded with huge trees. Couples wandered under the lofty foliage beside the Seine, over which the boats were gliding. There were girls with young men, working girls with their sweethearts, who were walking in shirt sleeves, coats on their arms and tall hats on the back of their heads, looking weary and dissipated; citizens with their families, the wives in their Sunday best, the children running round their parents like a brood of chickens. A continuous distant buzz of human voices, a dull rumbling clamor, announced the nearness of the establishment beloved of boating parties. Suddenly it came into view, an enormous roofed barge moored to the bank, filled with a crowd of men and women who sat drinking at tables or stood up, shouting, singing, laughing, dancing, capering to the noise of a jingling piano, out of tune and as vibrant as a tin can. Tall, red-haired girls, displaying before and behind them the swelling, provocative curves of breasts and hips, walked up and down with eager, inviting glances, all three parts drunk, talking obscenities. Others were dancing wildly in front of young men who were half-naked, dressed only in rowing shorts and zephyrs and wearing colored jockey caps on their heads. There was a pervading odor of sweat and face powder, the combined exhalations of perfumeries and armpits. Those who were drinking at the tables were swallowing white and red and yellow and green liquids, screaming and yelling for no reason, yielding to a violent need to make a din, an animal instinct to fill ears and brain with noise. From time to time a swimmer dived from the roof, splashing those sitting near, who yelled at him like savages.

On the river a fleet of boats passed and repassed; long narrow skiffs went by, urged on by the powerful strokes of oarsmen whose bare arms showed rolls of muscle under the sunburned skin. The women in the boats, dressed in blue or red flannel, holding open umbrellas also blue or red over their heads, wore brilliant splashes of color under the burning sun; they lolled on their seat in the stern and seemed to glide along the water, motionless or drowsy. Heavier boats moved slowly past, loaded with people. A lighthearted student, bent on making himself conspicuous, rowed with a windmill stroke, bumping into all the boats, whose occupants swore at him. He eventually disappeared, crestfallen after nearly drowning two swimmers, followed by the jeers of the crowd jammed together on the floating café.

Yvette, radiant, passed through the middle of this noisy, struggling crowd on Servigny's arm. She seemed quite happy to be jostled by all and sundry, and stared at the girls with calm and friendly eyes.

"Look at that one, Muscade, what lovely hair she's got! They *do* seem to be enjoying themselves."

The pianist, an oarsman dressed in red, whose hat was very like a colossal straw parasol, began a waltz. Yvette promptly seized her companion by the waist and carried him off with the fury she always put into her dancing. They went on so long and with such frenzy that the whole crowd watched them. Those who were sitting drinking stood upon their tables and beat time with their feet, others smashed glasses. The pianist seemed to go mad; he banged at the ivory keys with galloping hands, gesticulating wildly with his whole body, swaying his head and its enormous covering with frantic movements.

Abruptly he stopped, slid down, and lay full length on the ground, buried under his hat, as though he were dead of exhaustion. There was a burst of laughter in the café, and everyone applauded. Four friends rushed up as though there had been an accident and, picking up their comrade, bore him off by all four limbs, placing on his stomach the roof under which he sheltered his head. Another jester followed, intoning the *De Profundis*, and a procession formed up behind the mock corpse. It went round all the paths in the island, gathering up drinkers, strollers, indeed everyone it met.

Yvette ran along enraptured, laughing heartily and talking to everyone, wild with the din and the bustle. Young men pushed against her and stared at her excitedly with eyes whose burning glances seemed to strip her naked. Servigny began to be afraid that the adventure might end unfortunately. The procession went on its way, getting faster and faster, for the four bearers had begun to race, followed by the yelling crowd. But suddenly they turned towards the bank, stopped dead at the edge, for an instant swung their comrade to and fro, and then, all letting go of him at once, they heaved him into the water. A great shout of merriment burst from every mouth, while the bewildered pianist splashed about, swearing, coughing, and spitting out the water; stuck fast in the mud, he struggled to climb up the bank. His hat, which was floating down the stream, was brought back by a boat.

Yvette danced with joy and clapped her hands, saying:

"Oh, Muscade, what fun, what fun!"

Servigny, now serious, watched her, a little embarrassed and a little dismayed to see her so much at ease in this vulgar mob. He felt a faint disgust born of the instinct that an aristocrat rarely loses, even in moments of utter abandon, the instinct that protects him from unpardonable familiarities and contacts that would be too degrading. "No one will credit you with too much breeding, my child," he said to himself, astounded. He had an impulse to speak to her aloud as familiarly as he always did in his thoughts, with as little ceremony as he would have used on meeting any woman who was common property. He no longer saw her as any different from the red-haired creatures who brushed against them, bawling obscene words in their harsh voices. Coarse, brief, and expressive, these words were the current speech of the crowd; they seemed to flit overhead, born there in the mob like flies in the dunghill over which they hover. No one seemed shocked or surprised; Yvette did not seem to notice them at all.

"Muscade, I want to bathe," she said. "Let's go out into deep water."

"At your service, ma'am," he replied.

They went to the bathing cabin to get costumes. She was ready first and waited for him on the bank, smiling at all who looked at her. Then they went off side by side in the warm water. She swam with a luxurious abandon, caressed by the stream, quivering with a sensual pleasure; at every stroke she raised herself as though she were ready to leap out of the river. He found difficulty in keeping up with her; he was out of breath and angry at his inferiority. But she slowed down and then turned quickly and floated, her arms crossed, her eyes staring towards the blue sky. He gazed at the soft, supple line of her body as she lay there on the surface of the river, at the rounded form and small firm tips of the shapely breasts revealed by her thin, clinging garment, the curving sweetness of her belly, the half-submerged thighs, the bare knees gleaming through the water, and the small foot thrust out. He saw every line of her, as though she were deliberately displaying herself to tempt him, offering herself to him or trying to make a fool of him again. He began to desire her with a passionate ardor, every nerve on edge. Abruptly she turned round and looked at him.

"What a nice head you have," she said with a laugh.

He was hurt, irritated by her teasing, filled with the savage fury of the derided lover. He yielded to a vague desire to punish her, to avenge himself; he wanted to hurt her.

"You'd like that sort of life, would you?" he said.

"What sort?" she asked, with her most innocent air.

"Come now, no more nonsense. You know perfectly well what I mean."

"No, honestly, I don't."

"We've had enough of this comedy. Will you or won't you?"

"I don't understand you in the least."

"You're not so stupid as all that. Besides, I told you last night."

"What? I've forgotten."

"That I love you."

"You!"

"Yes, I!"

"What a lie!"

"I swear it's true."

"Prove it, then."

"I ask for nothing better."

"Well, do, then."

"You didn't say that last night."

"You didn't propose anything."

"Oh, this is absurd!"

"Besides, I am not the one to be asked."

"That's very kind of you! Who is, then?"

"Mamma, of course."

He gave way to a fit of laughter.

"Your mother? No, really, that's too much!"

She had suddenly become very serious, and, looking into his eyes, said:

"Listen, Muscade, if you really love me enough to marry me, speak to Mamma first, and I'll give you my answer afterwards."

At that he lost his temper altogether, thinking that she was still playing the fool with him.

"What do you take me for, mam'selle? An idiot like the rest of your admirers?"

She continued to gaze at him with calm, clear eyes. After a moment's hesitation she said:

"I still don't understand."

"Now look here, Yvette," he said brusquely, with a touch of rudeness and ill nature in his voice. "Let's have done with this ridiculous comedy, which has already gone on too long. You keep on playing the innocent maiden, and, believe me, the part doesn't suit you at all. You know perfectly well that there can be no question of marriage between us—but only of love. I told you I loved you—it's quite true—I repeat, I do love you. Now don't pretend not to understand, and don't treat me as though I were a fool."

They were upright in the water, face to face, supporting themselves by little movements of the hands. For some seconds more she continued motionless, as though she could not make up her mind to understand his words, then suddenly she blushed to the roots of her hair. The blood rushed in a swift tide from her neck to her ears, which turned almost purple, and without a word she fled landwards, swimming with all her strength, with hurried, powerful strokes. He could not overtake her, and the pursuit left him breathless. He saw her leave the water, pick up her wrap, and enter her cabin, without turning her head.

He took a long time to dress, very puzzled what to do, planning what to say to her, and wondering whether to apologize or persevere.

When he was ready, she had gone, alone. He returned slowly, worried and anxious. The marquise, on Saval's arm, was strolling along the circular path round the lawn. At sight of Servigny she spoke with the careless air she had assumed on the previous evening:

"Didn't I tell you not to go out in such heat? Now Yvette has a sunstroke; she's gone to lie down. She was as scarlet as a poppy, poor child, and has a frightful headache. You must have been walking full in the sun, and up to some mischief or other, heaven knows what. You have no more sense than she has."

The young girl did not come down to dinner. When she was asked if she would like something brought up to her room, she replied through the closed door that she was not hungry—she had locked herself in and wished to be left alone. The two young men left by the ten o'clock train, promising to come again the following Thursday, and the marquise sat down by the open window and, musing, listened to the far-off sound of dance music jerked out at La Grenouillère, vibrating in the profoundly solemn silence of night.

Inured and hardened to love by love, as a man is to riding or rowing, she nevertheless had sudden moments of tenderness which attacked her like a disease. These passions seized roughly upon her, swept through her whole being, driving her mad, exhausting her or depressing her according to their nature, lofty, violent, dramatic, or sentimental.

She was one of those women who were created to love and be loved. From a very humble beginning she had climbed high through love, of which she had made a profession almost without being aware of it: acting by instinct, by inborn skill, she accepted money as she accepted kisses, naturally, without distinguishing between them, employing her amazing intuition in an unreasoning and utterly simple fashion, as animals, made cunning by the struggle for life, employ theirs. She had had many lovers for whom she felt no tenderness, yet at whose embraces she had not felt disgust. She endured all caresses with calm indifference, just as a traveler eats anything because he must live. But from time to time her heart or her flesh caught fire, and she fell into a passion which lasted weeks or months, according to the physical and moral qualities of her lover. These were the delicious moments of her life. She loved with her whole soul, her whole body, with ecstatic abandon. She threw herself into love like a suicide into a river, and let herself be carried away, ready to die if necessary, intoxicated, maddened, infinitely happy. Each time she thought she had never before felt anything like it, and she would have been entirely amazed if she had been reminded of the many different men of whom she had dreamed passionately all night long, gazing at the stars.

Saval had fascinated her, captured her body and soul. She dreamed of him now, soothed by his image and her remembrance of him, in the calm exaltation of a joy fulfilled, of a happiness present and certain.

A noise behind her made her turn round. Yvette had just come in, still in the same dress she had worn all day, but pale now, and with the burning eyes that are the mark of great weariness. She leaned on the ledge of the open window opposite her mother.

"I've something to tell you," she said.

The marquise, surprised, looked at her. Her love for her daughter was selfish; she was proud of her beauty, as one is proud of wealth; she was herself still too beautiful to be jealous, too careless to make the plans she was commonly supposed to entertain, yet too cunning to be unconscious of her daughter's value.

"Yes, child," she replied, "I'm listening; what is it?"

Yvette gave her a burning look, as though to read the depths of her soul, as though to detect every emotion which her words would rouse.

"This is it. Something extraordinary happened just now."

"What?"

"M. de Servigny told me he loved me."

The marquise waited, uneasy. But as Yvette said nothing more, she asked:

"How did he tell you? Explain!"

The young girl sat down by her mother's feet in a familiar coaxing attitude and, pressing her hand, said:

"He asked me to marry him."

Mme. Obardi made a sudden gesture of amazement, and cried:

"Servigny? You must be mad!"

Yvette's eyes had never left her mother's face, watching sharply for her thoughts and her surprise.

"Why must I be mad?" she asked gravely. "Why should M. de Servigny never marry me?"

"You must be wrong," stammered the marquise, embarrassed; "it can't be true. You can't have heard properly—or you misunderstood him. M. de Servigny is too rich to marry you, and too . . . too . . . Parisian to marry at all."

Yvette slowly rose to her feet.

"But if he loves me as he says he does?" she added.

Her mother replied somewhat impatiently:

"I thought you were old enough and knew enough of the world not to have such ideas in your head. Servigny is a man of the world and an egoist; he will only marry a woman of his own rank and wealth. If he asked you to marry him . . . it means he wants . . . he wants . . ."

The marquise, unable to voice her suspicions, was silent for a moment, then added:

"Now leave me alone, and go to bed."

And the young girl, as though she now knew all she wanted, replied obediently: "Yes, Mother."

She kissed her mother's forehead and departed with a calm step. Just as she was going out of the door, the marquise called her back:

"And your sunstroke?" she asked.

"I never had one. It was this affair which had upset me."

"We'll have another talk about it," added the marquise. "But, above all, don't be alone with him again after this occurrence for some time. And you may be quite sure that he won't marry you, do you understand, and that he only wants to . . . to compromise you."

This was the best she could do by way of expressing her thoughts. And Yvette returned to her room.

Mme. Obardi began to reflect.

Having lived for years in an amorous and opulent tranquillity, she had carefully guarded her mind from every thought that might preoccupy, trouble, or sadden her. She had always refused to ask herself what would become of Yvette; there was always time enough to think of that when difficulties arose. She knew, with her courtesan's instinct, that her daughter could not marry a rich and highborn man save by an extremely improbable piece of good fortune, one of those surprises of love which set adventuresses upon thrones. She did not really contemplate this possibility, too much preoccupied to form plans by which she herself would not be directly affected.

Yvette would doubtless follow in her mother's footsteps. She would become a light-o'-love; why not? But the marquise had never had the courage to ask herself when, or how, this would come about.

And now here was her daughter suddenly, without any preparation, asking her one of those questions which cannot be answered and forcing her to take up a definite position in an affair so difficult, so delicate, so dangerous in every sense, and which so profoundly troubled her conscience, the conscience any mother must display when her daughter is involved in an affair such as this.

She had too much natural wit, a wit which might nod but was never quite asleep, to be deceived for one moment in Servigny's intentions, for she knew men, by personal experience, especially men of that tribe. And so, at the first words uttered by Yvette, she had cried out, almost involuntarily:

"Servigny marry you? You must be mad!"

What had led him to use the old, old trick—he, the shrewd rake, the jaded man about town? What would he do now? And the child, how was she to be more explicitly warned or even forbidden? She was capable of any folly. Who would imagine that a great girl like that could be so innocent, so ignorant, and so unwary?

And the marquise, thoroughly perplexed and already exhausted by her mental efforts, was utterly at a loss, finding the situation really awkward.

Weary of the whole business, she thought:

"Oh, well, I'll keep a close watch on them and act according to events. If necessary, I'll even talk to Servigny; he's sensitive and can take a hint."

She did not ask herself what she should say to him, nor what he would reply, nor what sort of an agreement could be made between them, but, happy at being relieved of one anxiety without having had to make any decision, she began again to dream of her adored Saval. Her glance, wandering in the night, turned to the right towards the misty radiance that hovered over Paris; with both hands she threw kisses towards the great city, swift unnumbered kisses that flew into the darkness one after another; and very softly, as though she were still speaking to him, she murmured:

"I love you! I love you!"

III

Nor could Yvette sleep. Like her mother, she sat at the open window, resting her elbows on the sill, and tears, her first bitter tears, filled her eyes.

Till now she had lived and grown up in the heedless and serene self-confidence of happy youth. Why should she have analyzed, wondered, reflected? Why should she not have been like all young girls of her age? Why should doubt, fear, painful suspicions have troubled her? Because she seemed to talk about every subject, because she had taken the tone, the manner, the bold speech of those around her, she had seemed to know all about everything. But she knew hardly more than a girl brought up in a convent; her risky phrases came from her memory, from the faculty women possess of imitation and assimilation, not from a mind already sophisticated and debauched.

She talked of love in the same way that an artist's or musician's son talks of painting and music at ten or twelve years of age. She knew, or rather suspected, the sort of mystery hidden behind this word—too many jests had been whispered in her presence for her innocence to remain completely unenlightened—but how was she to tell from this that every household was not like the one she lived in? Her mother's hand was kissed with apparent respect; all their friends were titled; all were rich, or appeared to be; all spoke familiarly of princes of the blood royal. Two king's sons had actually come several times, in the evening, to the marquise's house. How was she to know?

And, besides, she was by nature innocent. She did not probe into things, she had not her mother's intuitive judgment of other people. She lived tranquilly, too full of the joy of life to worry about circumstances which might have roused suspicions in people of more quiet, more thoughtful, more secluded ways, who were less impulsive and less radiantly joyous. And now, in a single instant, by a few words whose brutality she had felt without understanding, Servigny had roused in her a sudden uneasiness, an uneasiness at first unreasoning, and now growing into a torturing fear.

She had gone home, had fled from him like a wounded animal; deeply wounded, indeed, by the words she repeated to herself again, trying to penetrate their farthest meaning, trying to guess their whole implication: "You know perfectly well that there can be no question of marriage between us—but of love!"

What had he meant? And why the harshness? There was something, then, some shameful secret, of which she was in ignorance? Doubtless she was the only one in ignorance of it. What was it? She was terrified, crushed, as at the discovery of a hidden infamy, the treachery of a friend, one of those calamities of the heart which strike at one's very reason.

She had thought, wondered, pored over it, wept, consumed with fears and suspicions. Then her young and buoyant nature calmed her, and she began to imagine an adventure, to build up an unusual and dramatic situation drawn from her remembrance of all the fanciful romances she had read. She recalled exciting changes of fortune, gloomy and heart-rending plots, and mingled them with her own story, to fling a romantic glory round the half-seen mystery which surrounded her.

She was no longer miserable, she was wholly wrapped up in her dreams. She lifted mysterious veils, imagined improbable complications, a thousand curious and terrible ideas, attractive through their very strangeness. Was she, by any chance, the natural daughter of a prince? Had her unfortunate mother been seduced and deserted, created a marquise by a king, King Victor Emmanuel perhaps, and had she even been forced to flee from the wrath of her family?

Or was she not more probably a child abandoned by her parents, very noble and famous parents, as the fruit of a guilty love, and found by the marquise, who had adopted her and brought her up? A hundred other notions raced through her head; she accepted or rejected them at the dictates of her fancy. She grew profoundly sorry for herself, at once very happy and very sad; above all, she was delighted at becoming the heroine of a romance with emotions to reveal, a part to act, a dignity and nobility to be upheld. And she thought of the part she would have to play in each plot she imagined. She saw it vaguely, as if she were a character in a novel by Scribe or George Sand. It would be compounded of equal parts of devotion, pride, self-sacrifice, greatness of soul, tenderness, and fine words. Her volatile little heart almost reveled in her new position.

She had continued till nightfall to ponder over her future course of action, wondering how to set to work to drag the truth from the marquise.

And at the coming of night, so suitable to a tragic situation, she had thought of a trick, a quite simple yet subtle trick, for getting what she wanted; it was to tell her mother very abruptly that Servigny had asked her to marry him. At this news Mme. Obardi, in her surprise, would surely let fall a word, an exclamation, that would illumine her daughter's mind.

So Yvette had promptly put her plan into execution. She expected a burst of astonishment, protests of affection, disclosures, accompanied by tears and every sign of emotion.

And lo and behold! her mother had not apparently been either surprised or heartbroken, merely annoyed; from the worried and peevish tone of her reply the young girl, in whose mind every latent power of feminine cunning, wit, and knowledge was suddenly aroused, realized that it was no good insisting, that the mystery was quite other and more painful than she had imagined, and that she must discover it for herself. So she had returned to her room with a sad heart, her spirit distressed, depressed now in the apprehension of a real misfortune, without knowing how or why she was suffering such an emotion. She rested her elbows on the window sill and wept.

She cried for a long time, now with no idle dreams: she made no attempt at further discovery. Little by little she was overcome with weariness, and closed her eyes. She dozed, for a few minutes, in the unrefreshing slumber of a person too exhausted to undress and get into bed; her sleep was long and fitful, roughly broken whenever her head slipped from between her hands.

She did not go to bed until the earliest gleam of daylight, when the chill of dawn drove her from the window.

During the next day and the day after she kept an air of melancholy and reserve. A ceaseless and urgent travail of thought was moving within her; she was learning to watch, to guess, to reason. A gleam, still vague, seemed to throw a new light upon the men and events passing around her; distrust invaded her soul, distrust of everyone that she had believed in, distrust of her mother. During those two days she conjectured every conceivable supposition. She envisaged every possibility, making the most extravagant resolutions, in the impulsiveness of her volatile and unrestrained nature. On the Wednesday she fixed on a plan, a whole scheme of conduct and an elaborate plan of espionage. On the Thursday morning she rose with the determination to be more cunning than the most experienced detective, to be armed against all the world.

She even decided to take as her motto the two words "Myself alone," and for more than an hour she wondered how they could with best effect be engraved round her monogram and stamped on her note paper.

Saval and Servigny arrived at ten o'clock. The young girl held out her hand with reserve, but without embarrassment, and said in a familiar though serious tone:

"Good morning, Muscade. How are you?"

"Pretty well, thank you, mam'selle. And you?"

He watched her narrowly. "What game is she playing now," he said to himself.

The marquise having taken Saval's arm, he took Yvette's, and they began to walk round the lawn, disappearing and reappearing behind the clumps of trees.

Yvette walked with a thoughtful air, her eyes on the gravel path, and she seemed scarcely to hear her companion's remarks, to which she made no reply.

Suddenly she asked:

"Are you really my friend, Muscade?"

"Of course, mam'selle."

"But really, really and truly?"

"Absolutely your friend, mam'selle, body and soul."

"Enough not to tell a lie for once, just for once?"

"Enough not even to tell one for twice, if necessary."

"Enough to tell me the whole truth, even if it's unpleasant?"

"Yes, mam'selle."

"Well, what do you really think, really, really think, of Prince Kravalow?"

"Oh, Lord!"

"There you are, already getting ready to tell a fib."

"No, I'm searching for the words, the right words. Well, dash it, the prince is a Russian—a real Russian, who speaks Russian, was born in Russia, and perhaps had a passport to get into France. There's nothing false about him except his name and his title."

She looked into his eyes.

"You mean he's a . . . a . . ."

He hesitated; then, making up his mind, said:

"An adventurer, mam'selle."

"Thank you. And the Chevalier Valréali is no better, is he?"

"It's as you say."

"And M. de Belvigne?"

"Ah, he's rather different. He's a gentleman, provincial of course; he's honorable . . . up to a point . . . but he's singed his wings through flying too near the candle."

"And you?"

Without hesitation he replied:

"I? Oh, I'm what's generally called a gay dog, a bachelor of good family who once had brains and frittered them away on making puns; who had health, and ruined it by playing the fool; moderate wealth, and wasted it doing nothing. All I have left is a certain experience of life, a pretty complete freedom from prejudice, a vast contempt for men, women included, a profound sense of the uselessness of my actions, and a wide tolerance of scoundrels in general. I still have momentary flashes of honesty, as you see, and I'm even capable of affection, as you could see if you would. With these qualities and defects I place myself at your orders, mam'-selle, body and soul, for you to dispose of at your pleasure. There!"

She did not laugh; she listened attentively, carefully scrutinizing his words and intentions.

"What do you think of the Comtesse de Lammy?" she continued.

"You must allow me not to give you my opinions on women," he said gaily.

"Not on any?"

"No, not on any."

"Then that means you must have a very low opinion of them, all of them. Now think, aren't there any exceptions?"

He laughed with the insolent air he almost always wore, and the brutal audacity that was his strength, his armor against life.

"Present company always excepted, of course," he said.

She flushed slightly, but coolly asked:

"Well, what do you think of me?"

"You want to know? Very well, then. I think you're a person of excellent sense, of considerable experience, or, if you prefer it, of great common sense; that you know very well how to mask your battery, amuse yourself at others' expense, hide your purpose, pull the strings and wait, without impatience, for the result."

"Is that all?" she asked.

"That's all," he replied.

"I'll make you alter your opinion, Muscade," she said very gravely. Then she went over to her mother, who was walking with bent head and tiny steps, with the languid gait one falls into when murmuring of things sweet and intimate. As she walked she drew designs, letters perhaps, with the tip of her sunshade, and talked to Saval without looking at him, talked long and slowly, resting on his arm, held close against his side. Yvette looked sharply at her, and a suspicion, so vague that she could not put it into words, as if it were a physical sensation only half-realized, flitted across her mind as the shadow of a wind-blown cloud flits across the earth.

The bell rang for lunch.

It was silent, almost gloomy.

There was storm in the air, as the saying goes. Vast motionless clouds lay in wait on the horizon, silent and heavy, but loaded with tempest.

When they had taken their coffee on the veranda, the marquise asked:

"Well, darling, are you going for a walk today with your friend Servigny? This is really the weather to enjoy the coolness of the woods."

Yvette threw her a rapid glance, and swiftly looked away again.

"No, Mother, I'm not going out today."

The marquise seemed disappointed.

"Do go for a little walk, child," she persisted. "It's so good for you."

"No, Mother," said Yvette sharply, "I'm going to stay in the house, and you know quite well why, because I told you the other night."

Mme. Obardi had quite forgotten, consumed with her need to be alone with Saval. She blushed, fidgeted, and, distracted by her own desire, uncertain how to secure a free hour or two, stammered:

"Of course; I never thought of it. You're quite right; I don't know where my wits are wandering."

Yvette took up a piece of embroidery which she called the "public welfare," busying herself with it five or six times a year, on days of utter boredom, and seated herself on a low chair beside her mother. The young men sat in deck chairs and smoked their cigars.

The hours went by in idle conversation that flagged continually. The marquise threw impatient glances at Saval, seeking for an excuse, any way of getting rid of her daughter. Realizing at last that she would not succeed, and not knowing what plan to adopt, she said to Servigny:

"You know, my dear Duke, that you're both going to stay the night here. To-morrow we are going to lunch at the restaurant Fournaise, at Chatou."

He understood, smiled, and said with a bow:

"I am at your service, Marquise."

Slowly the day wore on, slowly and uncomfortably, under the menace of the storm. Gradually the hour of dinner approached. The lowering sky was heavy with dull, sluggish clouds. They could not feel the least movement in the air.

The evening meal was eaten in silence. A sense of embarrassment and restraint, a sort of vague fear, silenced the two men and the two women.

When the table had been cleared, they remained on the veranda, speaking only at long intervals. Night was falling, a stifling night. Suddenly the horizon was torn by a great jagged flame that lit with its dazzling and pallid glare the four faces sunk in the shadows. Followed a distant noise, dull and faint, like the noise made by a cart crossing a bridge; the heat of the atmosphere increased, the air grew still more oppressive, the evening shadows more profound.

Yvette rose.

"I'm going to bed," she said. "The storm makes me feel ill."

She bent her forehead for the marquise to kiss, offered her hand to the two young men, and departed.

As her room was directly above the veranda, the leaves of a large chestnut tree planted in front of the door were soon gleaming with a green light. Servigny fixed his eyes on this pale gleam in the foliage, thinking now and then that he saw a shadow pass across it. But suddenly the light went out. Mme. Obardi sighed.

"My daughter is in bed," she said.

Servigny rose.

"I will follow your daughter's example, Marquise, if you will allow me."

He kissed her hand and disappeared in his turn.

She remained alone with Saval, in the darkness. At once she was in his arms, clasping him, embracing him. Then, though he tried to prevent it, she knelt down in front of him, murmuring: "I want to look at you in the lightning flashes."

But Yvette, her candle blown out, had come out on to her balcony, gliding barefooted like a shadow, and was listening, tortured by a painful and confused suspicion. She could not see, being exactly over their heads on the roof of the veranda. She heard nothing but a murmur of voices, and her heart beat so violently that the thudding of it filled her ears. A window shut overhead. So Servigny had just gone up to bed. Her mother was alone with the other.

A second flash split the sky, and for a second the whole familiar landscape was revealed in a vivid and sinister glare. She saw the great river, the color of molten lead, like a river in some fantastic dream country. At the same instant a voice below her said: "I love you." She heard no more; a strange shudder passed over her, her spirit was drowned in a fearful sea of trouble.

Silence, pressing, infinite, a silence that seemed the eternal silence of the grave, brooded over the world. She could not breathe, her lungs choked by some unknown and horrible weight. Another flash kindled the heavens and for an instant lit up the horizon; another followed on its heels, then another and another.

The voice she had already heard repeated more loudly: "Oh! How I love you! How I love you!" And Yvette knew the voice well; it was her mother's.

A large drop of warm water fell upon her forehead, and a slight, almost imperceptible quiver ran through the leaves, the shiver of the coming rain.

Then a tumult came hurrying from far off, a confused tumult like the noise of the wind in trees; it was the heavy shower pouring in a torrent upon the earth, the river, and the trees. In a few moments the water was streaming all round her, covering her, splashing her, soaking her like a bath. She did not move, thinking only of what was happening on the veranda. She heard them rise and go up to their rooms. Doors slammed inside the house. And obeying an irresistible longing for certitude, a maddening, torturing desire, the young girl ran down the stairs, softly opened the outer door, ran across the lawn under the furious downpour of rain, and hid in a clump of bushes to watch the windows.

One alone, her mother's, showed a light. And suddenly two shadows appeared on the luminous square, two shadows side by side. Then they drew closer and made only one; another flash of lightning flung a swift and dazzling jet of light upon the house-front, and she saw them embracing, their arms about one another's necks.

At that she was stunned; without thinking, without knowing what she did, she cried out with all her strength, in a piercing voice: "Mother!" as one cries to warn another creature of deadly peril.

Her desperate cry was lost in the clatter of the rain, but the engrossed pair started uneasily apart. One of the shadows disappeared, while the other tried to distinguish something in the darkness of the garden.

Fearing to be taken unawares and found by her mother, Yvette ran to the house, hurried upstairs, leaving a trail of water dripping from step to step, and locked herself in her room, determined to open to no one. Without taking off the soaking clothes which clung to her body, she fell upon her knees with clasped hands, imploring in her distress some superhuman protection, the mysterious help of Heaven, that unknown aid we pray for in our hours of weeping and despair. Every instant the great flashes threw their livid light into the room, and she saw herself fitfully reflected in her wardrobe mirror, with her wet hair streaming down her back, so strange a figure that she could not recognize herself.

She remained in this strait for a long time, so long that the storm passed without her noticing its departure. The rain ceased to fall, light flowed into the sky, though it was still dark with clouds, and a warm, fragrant, delicious freshness, the freshness of wet leaves and grass, drifted in at the open window. Yvette rose from her knees, took off her cold, sodden clothes without thinking at all of what she did, and got into bed. She fixed her eyes on the growing daylight, then wept again, then tried to think.

Her mother! With a lover! The shame of it! But she had read so many books in which women, even mothers, abandoned themselves in like fashion, only to rise once more to honor in the last few pages, that she was not utterly dumbfounded to find herself involved in a drama like all the dramas in the stories she read. The violence of her first misery, her first cruel bewilderment. was already slightly lessened by her confused recollections of similar situations. Her thoughts had roamed among so many tragic adventures, gracefully woven into their stories by the authors of romances, that gradually her horrible discovery began to seem the natural continuation of a novelette begun the night before.

"I will save my mother," she said to herself.

Almost calmed by this heroic resolution, she felt herself strong, great, ready upon the instant for sacrifice and combat. She thought over the means she must employ. Only one seemed good to her, and accorded with her romantic nature. And she rehearsed, like an actress before the performance, the interview she would have with her mother.

The sun had risen and the servants were up and about. The maid came with her chocolate. Yvette had the tray set down on the table, and said:

"Tell my mother that I'm not well, that I shall stay in bed till the gentlemen leave; tell her I did not sleep last night and that I wish not to be disturbed because I must try to sleep."

The astonished maid caught sight the soaked dress, thrown like a rag on the carpet.

"Mademoiselle has been out, then?" she said.

"Yes, I went for a walk in the rain to clear my head."

The servant picked up the petticoats, stockings, and muddy shoes and went out carrying them gingerly on her arm with an expression of disgust; they were dripping like the clothes of a drowned woman.

Yvette waited, knowing well that her mother would come.

The marquise entered, having leapt out of bed at the first words of the maid, for she had endured a vague uneasiness ever since that cry of "Mother!" pierced the darkness.

"What's the matter?" she said.

Yvette looked at her and faltered.

"I've . . . I've . . ."

Then, overcome by violent and sudden emotion, she began to sob.

The astonished marquise asked again:

"What's the matter with you?"

Then, forgetting all her schemes and the phrases so carefully prepared, the young girl hid her face in her hands and sobbed:

"Oh, Mother! Oh, Mother!"

Mme. Obardi remained standing by the bed, too excited to understand fully, but guessing, with that subtle instinct wherein her strength lay, almost everything there was to know.

Yvette, choked with sobs, could not speak, and her mother, exasperated at last and feeling the approach of a formidable revelation, asked sharply:

"Come, what's the matter with you? Tell me."

With difficulty Yvette stammered:

"Oh! Last night . . . I saw . . . your window."

"Well, what then?" asked the marquise, very pale.

Her daughter repeated, still sobbing:

"Oh, Mother! Oh, Mother!"

Mme. Obardi, whose fear and embarrassment were changing to anger, shrugged her shoulders and turned to go.

"I really think you must be mad. When it's all over, let me know."

But suddenly the young girl parted her hands and disclosed her tear-stained face.

"No . . . listen . . . I must speak to you. . . . Listen. Promise me . . . we'll both go away, far away, into the country, and we'll live like peasants and no one will know what's become of us. Will you, Mother? Please, please, I beg you, Mother, I implore you!"

The marquise, abashed, remained in the middle of the room. She had the hot blood of the people in her veins. Then shame, the shame of a mother, mingled with her vague sensation of fear and the exasperation of a passionate woman whose love is menaced. She shivered, equally ready to implore forgiveness or to fly into a rage.

"I don't understand you," she said.

"I saw you, Mother," continued Yvette, "last night. . . . You must never again . . . Oh, if you knew . . . we'll both go away . . . I'll love you so much that you'll forget . . ."

"Listen, my child," said Mme. Obardi in a trembling voice, "there are some things you don't yet understand. Well, never forget . . . never forget . . . that I forbid you . . . ever to speak to me . . . of . . . of . . . of those matters."

But the young girl caught desperately at her rôle of saviour and went on:

"No, Mother, I'm no longer a child, and I have the right to know. I know all sorts of disreputable people, adventurers, come to our house, and that that's why we are not respected; and I know more than that. Well, it mustn't be, I won't endure it. We'll go away; you can sell your jewels; we'll work if necessary, and we'll live like honest women somewhere far away. And if I manage to get married, so much the better."

Her mother looked at her out of angry black eyes, and answered:

"You're mad. Be good enough to get up and come out to lunch with the rest of us."

"No, Mother. There's someone here, you know whom, whom I won't see again. He must go out of this house, or I will. You must choose between us."

She was sitting up in bed, and raised her voice, speaking like a character on the stage; at last she had entered upon the drama so long dreamed of, and her grief was almost forgotten in absorption in her mission.

"You must be mad," repeated the astonished marquise again, finding nothing else to say.

"No, Mother," the young girl added, with dramatic verve, "that man will leave this house or I shall go; I shall not weaken."

"And where will you go? . . . What will you do?"

"I don't know; it doesn't matter much . . . I want us to be honest women."

The repetition of that phrase "honest women" aroused in the marquise the fury of a drab.

"Silence!" she shouted. "I won't be spoken to like that. I'm as good as any other woman, do you hear? I'm a harlot, it's true, and I'm proud of it; I'm worth a dozen of your honest women."

Yvette, overwhelmed, looked at her and stammered:

"Oh, Mother!"

But the marquise became frenzied with excitement.

"Yes, I am a harlot. What then? If I weren't a harlot, you'd be a kitchenmaid today, as I was once, and you'd work for twenty sous a day, and you'd wash the dishes, and your mistress would send you out on errands to the butcher's, d'you hear, and kick you out if you were idle; whereas here you are, idling all day long, just because I am a harlot. There! When you're only a poor servant girl with fifty francs of savings, you must get away from it somehow if you don't want to rot in the workhouse; and there's only one way for women, only one way, d'you hear, when you're a servant! We can't make fortunes on the stock exchange or at high finance. We've nothing but our bodies, nothing but our bodies."

She beat her breast like a penitent at confession, and advanced towards the bed, flushed and excited:

"So much the worse for a pretty girl; she must live on her looks or grind along in poverty all her life long . . . all her life. . . . There's no alternative."

Then, returning hastily to her old idea: "And your honest women, do they go without? It's they who are sluts, because they're not forced. They've money to live on and amuse themselves with; they have their lovers out of pure wantonness. It's they who are sluts!"

She stood beside Yvette's bed; Yvette, utterly overcome, wanted to scream for help and run away; she was crying noisily, like a beaten child.

The marquise was silent, and looked at her daughter; seeing the girl's utter despair, she was herself overcome by sorrow, remorse, tenderness, and pity; and falling upon the bed with outstretched arms, she too began to sob, murmuring:

"My poor darling, my poor darling, if you only knew how you hurt me."

And for a long time they both wept.

Then the marquise, whose grief never lasted very long, rose gently, and said very softly:

"Well, darling, that's how it is; it can't be helped. It can't be altered now. Life must be taken as it comes."

But Yvette continued to cry; the shock had been too severe and too unexpected for her to be able to reflect upon it calmly and recover herself.

"Come, get up, and come down to breakfast, so that nothing will be noticed," said her mother.

The young girl shook her head, unable to speak; at last she said very slowly, her voice choked with sobs:

"No, Mother, you know what I said; I won't change my mind. I will not leave my room till they have gone. I won't see any of those people again, never, never. If they come back, I . . . I . . . you won't see me again."

The marquise had dried her eyes and, worn out with her emotion, murmured:

"Come now, think it over, be sensible about it." Then again, after a minute's silence: "Yes, you had better rest this morning. I'll come and see you in the afternoon."

She kissed her daughter on the forehead and went away to get dressed, quite calm again.

As soon as her mother had disappeared, Yvette ran to the door and bolted it, so as to be alone, quite alone; then she began to reflect.

About eleven o'clock the maid knocked at the door and asked:

"Madame la Marquise wishes to know if you want anything, mademoiselle, and what will you have for lunch?"

"I'm not hungry," replied Yvette; "I only want to be left alone."

She stayed in bed as though she were really ill. About three o'clock there was another knock.

"Who's there?" she asked.

"It's I, darling," answered her mother's voice; "I've come to see how you are."

She hesitated. What should she do? She opened the door and got back into bed. The marquise came close, speaking softly as though to an invalid.

"Well, are you feeling better? Won't you eat an egg?"

"No, thank you, nothing."

Mme. Obardi had sat down beside the bed. Neither spoke for some time; then, at last, as her daughter remained immobile, her hands resting inertly on the sheets, the marquise added:

"Aren't you going to get up?"

"Yes, presently," answered Yvette. "I've thought a great deal, Mother," she continued slowly and seriously, "and this . . . this is my decision. The past is past; let us say no more about it. But the future will be different . . . or else . . . or else I know what I shall have to do. And now let us have done with this subject."

The marquise, who had thought that the explanation was all over, felt somewhat irritated. She had had more than enough. This great goose of a girl ought to have understood long ago. But she made no answer, only repeating:

"Are you going to get up?"

"Yes, I'm ready now."

The mother acted as maid to her daughter, bringing her her stockings, her corset, and her petticoats. Then she kissed her.

"Shall we go for a walk before dinner?"

"Yes, Mamma."

And they walked along the bank of the river, talking almost entirely of the most trivial affairs.

IV

Next morning Yvette went off alone to sit in the place where Servigny had read over the history of the ants.

"I will not leave it," she said to herself, "until I have come to a decision."

The river ran at her feet, the swift water of the main stream; it was full of eddies and great bubbles which swirled silently past her.

She had already envisaged every aspect of the situation and every means of escape from it. What was she to do if her mother failed to hold scrupulously to the condition she had laid down, if she did not give up her life, her friends, everything, to take refuge with her in some distant region?

She might go alone . . . away. But whither? How? What could she live on? By working? At what? Whom should she ask for work? And the melancholy and humble life of the working girl, of the daughters of the common folk, seemed to be a little shameful, and unworthy of her. She thought of becoming a governess, like the young ladies in novels, and of being loved and married by the son of the house. But for that rôle she should have been of noble descent, so that when an irate parent reproached her for stealing his son's heart, she could have answered proudly:

"My name is Yvette Obardi."

She could not. And besides, it was a rather commonplace, threadbare method.

A convent was scarcely any better. Besides, she felt no call towards a religious life, having nothing but an intermittent and fleeting piety. No one—since she was the thing she was—could save her by marrying her, she could not take help from a man, there was no possible way out and no certain resource at all.

She wanted something violent, something really great, really brave, something that would be held up for all to see: and she decided to die.

She came to this resolution quite suddenly, quite calmly, as though it were a question of a journey, without reflecting, without seeing what death means, without realizing that it is an end without a new beginning, a departure without a return, an eternal farewell to earth, to life.

She was attracted immediately by this desperate decision, with all the impulsiveness of a young and ardent spirit. And she pondered over the means she should employ. They all appeared to be painful and dangerous to carry out, and to demand, too, a violence which was repulsive to her.

She soon gave up the idea of dagger or pistol, which might only wound, maim, or disfigure her, and which required a steady and practiced hand—rejected hanging as vulgar, a pauper's sort of suicide, ridiculous and ugly—and drowning because she could swim. Poison was all that remained, but which poison? Almost all would hurt her or make her sick. She did not want to suffer, or to be sick. Then she thought of chloroform, having read in a newspaper of a young woman who suffocated herself by this means.

At once she felt something like pleasure in her resolve, a secret self-praise, a prick of vainglory. They should see the manner of woman she was!

She returned to Bougival and went to the chemist's, where she asked for a little chloroform for an aching tooth. The man, who knew her, gave her a very small phial of the drug. Then she walked over to Croissy, where she procured another little phial of poison. She got a third at Chatou, and a fourth at Rueil, and returned home late for lunch. As she was very hungry after her walk, she ate a hearty meal, with the sharp enjoyment of a hungry athlete.

Her mother, glad to see her excellent appetite, felt now quite confident, and said to her as they rose from the table:

"All our friends are coming to spend Sunday here. I've invited the prince, the chevalier, and M. de Belvigne."

Yvette turned slightly pale, but made no answer. She left the house almost at once, went to the railway station, and took a ticket to Paris.

Throughout the afternoon she went from chemist to chemist, buying a few drops of chloroform from each.

She returned in the evening, her pockets full of little bottles. Next day she continued her campaign, and, happening to go into a druggist's, she was able to buy half a pint all at once. She did not go out on Saturday—it was stuffy and overcast; she spent the whole of it on the veranda, lying in a long cane chair. She thought about nothing, filled with a placid resolution.

The next day, wishing to look her best, she put on a blue frock which became her marvelously well. And as she viewed herself in the mirror she thought suddenly: "Tomorrow I shall be dead." A strange shiver ran through her body. "Dead! I shall not speak, I shall not think, no one will see me any more. And I shall never see all this again." She scrutinized her face carefully, as though she had never seen it before, examining, above all, her eyes, discovering a thousand aspects of herself, a secret character in her face that she did not know, astonished to see herself, as though she were face to face with a stranger, a new friend.

"It is I," she said to herself, "it is I, in that glass. How strange it is to see oneself. We should never recognize ourselves, if we had no mirrors. Everyone else would know what we looked like, but we should have no idea of it."

She took the thick plaits of her hair and laid them across her breast, gazing at her own gestures, her poses and movements.

"How pretty I am!" she thought. "Tomorrow I shall be dead, there, lying on my bed."

She looked at her bed and imagined that she saw herself lying on it, white as the sheets.

Dead! In a week that face, those eyes, those cheeks, would be nothing but black rottenness, shut up in a box underground.

A frightful spasm of anguish constricted her heart.

The clear sunlight flooded the landscape, and the sweet morning air came in at the window.

She sat down and thought. Dead—it was as though the world was disappearing for her sake; and yet it was not like that, for nothing in the world would change, not even her room. Yes, her room would stay just the same, with the same bed, the same chairs, the same dressing table, but she would be gone for ever, and no one would be sorry, except perhaps her mother.

People would say: "How pretty she was, little Yvette!" and that was all. And when she looked at her hand resting on the arm of her chair, she thought again of the rottenness, the black and evil-smelling corruption that her flesh would become. And again a long shudder of horror ran through her whole body, and she could not understand how she could disappear without the whole world coming to an end, so strong was her feeling that she herself was part of everything, of the country, of the air, of the sun, of life.

A burst of laughter came from the garden, a clamor of voices, shouts, the noisy merriment of a country-house party just beginning, and she recognized the sonorous voice of M. de Belvigne, singing:

> "Je suis sous ta fenêtre,
> Ah! daigne enfin paraître."

She rose without thinking and went to look out. Everyone clapped. They were all there, all five of them, with two other gentlemen she did not know.

She drew back swiftly, torn by the thought that these men had come to enjoy themselves in her mother's house, in the house of a courtesan.

The bell rang for lunch.

"I will show them how to die," she told herself.

She walked downstairs with a firm step, with something of the resolution of a Christian martyr entering the arena where the lions awaited her.

She shook hands with them, smiling pleasantly but a little haughtily. Servigny asked her:

"Are you less grumpy today, mam'selle?"

"Today," she replied in a strange, grave voice, "I am for the wildest pleasures. I'm in my Paris mood. Take care." Then, turning to M. de Belvigne: "You shall be my pet today, my little Malvoisie. After lunch I'm taking you all to the fair at Marly."

Marly fair was indeed in full swing. The two newcomers were presented to her, the Comte Tamine and the Marquis de Boiquetot.

During the meal she hardly spoke, bending every effort of will to her resolve to make merry all that afternoon, so that none might guess, so that there should be all the more surprise; they would say: "Who would have thought it? She seemed so gay, so happy! One can never tell what is going on in their heads!"

She forced herself not to think of the evening, the hour she had chosen, when they would all be on the veranda.

She drank as much wine as she could get down, to sharpen her courage, and took two small glasses of brandy; when she left the table she was flushed and a little giddy; she felt herself warmed in body and spirit, her courage high, ready for adventure.

"Off we go!" she cried.

She took M. de Belvigne's arm, and arranged the order of the rest.

"Come along, you shall be my regiment. Servigny, I appoint you sergeant; you must march on the right, outside the ranks. You must make the Foreign Legion march in front, our two aliens, the prince and the chevalier, and behind them the two recruits who have joined the colors today. Quick march!"

They went off, Servigny playing an imaginary bugle, and the two new arrivals pretending to play the drum. M. de Belvigne, somewhat embarrassed, said to Yvette:

"Do be a little reasonable, Mlle. Yvette. You'll get yourself talked about."

"It's you I'm compromising, Raisiné," she replied. "As for myself, I don't care a rap. It will be all the same tomorrow. So much the worse for you; you shouldn't go about with girls like me."

They went through Bougival, to the amazement of the people in the streets. Everyone turned round and stared; the local inhabitants came to their doors; the travelers on the little railway which runs from Rueil to Marly yelled at them; the men standing on the platforms shouted:

"To the river! . . . To the river! . . ."

Yvette marched with a military step, holding Servigny by the arm, as if she were leading a prisoner. She was far from laughter; she wore an air of pale gravity, a sort of sinister immobility. Servigny interrupted his bugle solo in order to shout orders. The prince and the chevalier were enjoying themselves hugely, judging it all vastly diverting and very witty. The two recruits steadily played the drum.

On their arrival at the fairground they caused quite a sensation. The girls clapped, all the young folk giggled; a fat man arm in arm with his wife said to her enviously:

"They're enjoying life, they are."

Yvette caught sight of a merry-go-round and made Belvigne mount a wooden horse on her right, while the rest of the squad clambered on to horses behind them. When their turn was over she refused to get off, making her escort remain upon the back of her childish steed for five turns running. The delighted crowd flung witticisms at them. M. de Belvigne was very white when he got off, and felt sick.

Then she began careering through the stalls. She made each of the men get weighed before the eyes of a large crowd. She made them buy absurd toys, which they had to carry in their arms. The prince and the chevalier very soon had more than enough of the jest; Servigny and the two drummers alone kept up their spirits.

At last they reached the far end, and she looked at her followers with a curious expression, a glint of malice and perversity in her eyes. A strange fancy came into her head; she made them all stand in a row on the right bank overlooking the river, and said:

"Let him who loves me most throw himself into the water."

No one jumped. A crowd had formed behind them; women in white aprons gaped at them, and two soldiers in red breeches laughed stupidly.

"Then not one of you is ready to throw himself into the water at my request?" she repeated.

"So much the worse, damn it," murmured Servigny, and leapt, upright, into the river.

His fall flung drops of water right up to Yvette's feet. A murmur of surprise and amusement ran through the crowd. Then the young girl bent down, picked up a little piece of wood, and threw it into the river, crying: "Fetch it."

The young man began to swim, and seizing the floating stick in his mouth, like a dog, he brought it to land, clambered up the bank, dropped on one knee, and offered it to her.

"Good dog," she said, taking it, and patting his head.

"How can they do it?" cried a stout lady, vastly indignant.

"Nice goings on," said another.

"Damned if I'd take a ducking for any wench," said a man.

She took Belvigne's arm again, with the cutting remark: "You're a noodle; you don't know what you've missed."

As they went home she threw resentful glances at the passers-by.

"How stupid they all look," she observed; then, raising her eyes to her companion's face, added: "And you too, for the matter of that."

M. de Belvigne bowed. Turning round, she saw the the prince and the chevalier had disappeared. Servigny, wretched and soaked to the skin, was no longer playing the bugle, but walked with a melancholy air beside the two tired young men, who were not playing the drum now.

She began to laugh dryly.

"You seem to have had enough. That's what you call fun, isn't it? That's what you've come here for. I've given you your money's worth."

She walked on without another word, and suddenly Belvigne saw that she was crying.

"What's the matter?" he asked in alarm.

"Leave me alone," she murmured. "It's nothing to do with you."

But he insisted foolishly: "Now, now, mademoiselle, what is the matter with you? Has anybody hurt you?"

"Be quiet," she said irritably.

Abruptly, unable to withstand the terrible sorrow flooding her heart, she broke into such a violent fit of sobbing that she could not walk any further. She covered her face with her hands and gasped for breath, choking, strangled, stifled by the violence of her despair.

Belvigne stood helplessly beside her, repeating:

"I don't understand at all."

But Servigny rushed towards her. "Come along home, mam'selle, or they'll see you crying in the street. Why do you do these silly things, if they make you so unhappy?"

He led her forward, holding her arm. But as soon as they reached the gate of the villa she ran across the garden and up to her room, and locked herself in.

She did not reappear until dinnertime; she was pale and very grave. All the rest were gay enough, however. Servigny had bought a suit of workman's clothes in the neighborhood, corduroy trousers, a flowered shirt, a jersey, and a smock, and was talking like a peasant.

Yvette was in a fever for the ending of the meal, feeling her courage ebbing. As soon as coffee was over she went again to her room. She heard laughing voices under her window. The chevalier was telling jokes, foreign witticisms and puns, crude and not very savory. She listened in despair. Servigny, slightly drunk, was imitating a tipsy workman and was addressing the marquise as "Mrs. Obardi." Suddenly he said to Saval: "Hullo, Mr. Obardi." Everyone laughed.

Then Yvette made up her mind. First she took a sheet of her note paper and wrote:

Bougival, Sunday, 9 p.m.

I die so that I may not become a kept woman.

Yvette.

Then a postscript:

Good-by, Mother dear. Forgive me.

She sealed up the envelope, and addressed it to Mme. la Marquise Obardi.

Then she moved her armchair up to the window, set a little table within reach of her hand, and placed upon it the large bottle of chloroform, with a handful of cotton wool beside it.

An immense rose tree in full bloom, planted near the veranda and reaching right up to her window, filled the night with little gusts of faint, sweet fragrance; for some moments she sat breathing in the perfumed air. The crescent moon swung in the dark sky, its left side gnawed away, and veiled now and again with small clouds.

"I'm going to die," thought Yvette. "I'm going to die!" Her heart, swollen with sobs, bursting with grief, choked her. She longed to cry for mercy, to be reprieved, to be loved.

Servigny's voice came up to her; he was telling a shady story, constantly interrupted by bursts of laughter. The marquise seemed more amused than any of them; she repeated gaily: "No one can tell a story like that as well as he can."

Yvette took the bottle, uncorked it, and poured a little of the liquid on to the cotton wool. It had a queer, pungent, sweet smell, and as she lifted the pad of cotton wool to her lips, she swallowed the strong, irritating flavor of it, and it made her cough.

Then, closing her mouth, she began to breathe it in. She took long draughts of the deadly vapor, shutting her eyes and compelling herself to deaden every impulse of her mind so that she would no longer think nor realize what she was doing.

At first she felt as though her heart were swelling and growing, as though her spirit, just now heavy and burdened with sorrow, were growing light, as light as if the weight oppressing it had been raised, lessened, removed.

A lively and pleasant sensation filled her whole body, penetrating to the tips of her fingers and toes, entering into her flesh, a hazy drunkenness, a happy delirium.

She saw that the cotton wool was dry, and was surprised that she was not yet dead. Her senses were sharpened, intensified, and more alert. She heard every word uttered on the veranda. Prince Kravalow was relating how he had killed an Austrian general in a duel.

Far away, in the heart of the country, she heard the noises of the night; the intermittent barking of a dog, the short croak of toads, the faint shiver of the leaves.

She took up the bottle, soaked the little piece of cotton wool, and began again to breathe it in. For some moments she felt nothing; then the languid, delightful, secure contentment that she had felt at first took hold of her once more.

Twice she poured out more chloroform, greedy now of the physical and mental sensation, the drowsy languor in which her senses were drowning. She felt as though she no longer had bones or flesh or arms or legs. All had been gently taken from her, and she felt nothing. The chloroform had drained away her body, leaving nothing but her brain, wider, freer, more lively, more alert than she had ever felt it before.

She remembered a thousand things she had forgotten, little details of her childhood, trifles which gave her pleasure. Her mind, suddenly endowed with an agility hitherto unknown to it, leapt from one strange idea to another, ran through a thousand adventures, wandered at random in the past, and rambled through hopes of the future. This rapid, careless process of thought filled her with a sensual delight; she enjoyed a divine happiness in her dreams.

She still heard the voices, but could no longer distinguish the words, which seemed to her to take on another sense. She sank down and down, wandering in a strange and shifting fairyland.

She was on a large boat which glided beside a very pleasant country filled with flowers. She saw people on the banks, and these people were talking very loudly, and then she found herself on land again, without wondering how she got there, and Servigny, dressed like a prince, came to take her to a bullfight. The streets were full of people talking, and she listened to their conversations, which did not in the least surprise her, but were as though she had always known them; for through her dreamy intoxication she still heard her mother's friends laughing and chatting on the veranda.

Then all grew dim.

Then she awoke, deliciously sleepy, and had some difficulty in recalling herself to consciousness.

So she was not dead yet.

But she felt so rested, and in such comfort and in such peace of mind, that she was in no hurry to finish the affair. She would have liked this glorious languor to last for ever.

She breathed slowly and looked at the moon facing her above the trees. Something in her soul was changed. Her thoughts were no longer those of a short while ago. The chloroform, soothing her body and mind, had assuaged her grief, and put to sleep her will to die.

Why not live? Why should she not be loved? Why should she not live happily? Everything now seemed possible, easy, sure. Everything in life was sweet, was good, and charming. But because she wished to go on dreaming for ever, she poured more of this dream water on to the cotton wool and again began to breathe it in, occasionally removing the poison from her nostrils so that she would not take too much, so that she would not die.

She looked at the moon and saw a face in it, a woman's face. She began once more to roam about the country, adrift in the hazy visions of an opium dream. The face hung in the center of the sky; then it began to sing; in a well-known voice it sang the "Alléluia d'Amour." It was the marquise, who had just gone indoors to play the piano.

Yvette had wings now. She was flying through the night, a beautiful clear night, over woods and rivers. She flew with vast delight, opening and beating her wings, wafted by the wind as by a caressing touch. She whirled through the air, which kissed her skin, and glided along so fast, so fast, that she had no time to see anything below her, and she found herself sitting beside a pond, with a line in her hand—she was fishing.

Something tugged at the line; she pulled it in and brought up the magnificent pearl necklace she had once desired. She was not in the least astonished at the catch, and looked at Servigny, who had appeared beside her, though she did not know how, and was fishing too; he was just landing a wooden roundabout horse.

Then once again she felt that she was waking, and heard them calling to her from below.

Her mother had said: "Blow out the candle."

Then Servigny's voice, clear and humorous: "Mam'selle Yvette, blow out your candle."

They all took up the cry in chorus.

"Mam'selle Yvette, blow out your candle."

Again she poured chloroform on to the cotton wool, but, as she did not want to die, she kept it at some distance from her face, so that she could breathe the fresh air while filling her room with the asphyxiating odor of the narcotic, for she knew that someone would come upstairs. So she arranged herself in a charming attitude of abandonment, a mimicking of the abandon of death, and waited.

"I'm a little uneasy," said the marquise. "The foolish child has gone to sleep leaving the candle alight on the table. I'll send Clémence up to blow it out and to shut her balcony window, which she has left wide open."

In a few moments the maid knocked at the door and called:

"Mademoiselle, mademoiselle!"

After an interval of silence she began again: "Mademoiselle, Mme. la Marquise says please will you blow out your candle and shut the window."

Again she waited, then knocked more loudly and called:

"Mademoiselle, mademoiselle!"

As Yvette did not answer, the servant departed and told the marquise:

"Mademoiselle has certainly gone to sleep; her door is bolted and I can't wake her."

"But surely she won't go on sleeping like that?" murmured Mme. Obardi.

On Servigny's advice they all assembled under the young girl's window and shouted in chorus:

"Hip-Hip-Hurrah—Mam'selle Yvette!"

The cry rang out in the still night, piercing the clear moonlit air, and died away in the sleeping countryside; they heard it fade away like the noise of a train that has gone by.

As Yvette did not reply, the marquise said:

"I hope nothing's the matter with her; I'm beginning to be alarmed."

Then Servigny snatched the red roses and the still unopened buds from the big rose tree that grew up the wall, and began to hurl them through the window into her room. At the first which struck her, Yvette started and nearly cried out. Some fell on her dress, some in her hair, others flew over her head and landed on the bed, covering it with a rain of flowers.

Once more the marquise cried in a choking voice:

"Come, Yvette, answer!"

"Really, it's not normal," declared Servigny. "I'll climb up by the balcony."

But the Chevalier was indignant.

"Pardon me, pardon me, but that's too much of a favor, I protest; it's too good a way—and too good a time—for making a rendezvous!"

And all the others, thinking that the young girl was playing a trick on them, cried out:

"We protest. It's a put-up affair. He sha'n't go up, he sha'n't go up."

But the marquise repeated in her agitation:

"Someone must go and see."

"She favors the duke; we are betrayed," declared the prince, with a dramatic gesture.

"Let's toss for the honor," suggested the chevalier, and took a gold hundred-franc piece from his pocket.

He began with the prince. "Tails," he called. It was heads. The prince in his turn threw the coin, saying to Saval:

"Call, please."

"Heads," called Saval.

It was tails.

The prince proceeded to put the same question to all the others. All lost. Servigny, who alone remained facing him, drawled insolently:

"Damn it, he's cheating!"

The Russian placed his hand on his heart and offered the gold coin to his rival, saying:

"Spin it yourself, my dear Duke."

Servigny took it and tossed it, calling: "Heads!"

It was tails. He bowed, and pointed to the pillar of the balcony.

"Up you go, prince," he said.

But the prince was looking about him with a troubled air.

"What are you looking for?" asked the Chevalier.

"I . . . I should like a . . . a ladder."

There was a general roar of laughter, and Saval came forward, saying: "We'll help you."

He lifted the man in his herculean arms, with the advice: "Hold on to the balcony."

The prince promptly caught hold of it and, Saval letting go, he remained suspended, waving his legs. Servigny caught hold of the wildly struggling limbs that were groping for a foothold, and tugged at them with all his strength; the hands loosed their grip and the prince fell like a log on to the stomach of M. de Belvigne, who was hurrying forward to help support him.

"Whose turn now?" asked Servigny, but no one offered.

"Come on, Belvigne, a little courage."

"No, thank you, my boy. I'd sooner keep my bones whole."

"Well, you, then, chevalier? You should be used to scaling fortresses."

"I leave it to you, my dear Duke."

"Well . . . well . . . I don't know that I'm so keen on it as all that." And Servigny walked round the pillar with a scrutinizing eye. Then he leapt, caught hold of the balcony, hauled himself up like a gymnast on the horizontal bar, and clambered over the rail.

All the spectators applauded, with uplifted faces. But he reappeared directly, crying: "Come at once! Quickly! Yvette's unconscious!"

The marquise screamed loudly and dashed up the stairs.

The young girl, her eyes closed, lay like one dead. Her mother rushed wildly into the room and threw herself upon her.

"What is it? Tell me, what is it?" she asked.

Servigny picked up the bottle of chloroform which had fallen on the floor. "She's suffocated herself," he said. He set his ear to her heart, then added: "But she's not dead; we'll soon bring her round. Have you any ammonia here?"

"Any what . . . any what . . . sir?" said the distracted maid.

"Any sal volatile?"

"Yes, sir."

"Fetch it at once, and leave the door open, to make a draught."

The marquise had fallen upon her knees and was sobbing: "Yvette! Yvette! My child, my little girl, my child, listen, answer me, Yvette! My child! Oh! my God, my God, what is the matter with her?"

The frightened men wandered aimlessly about the room, bringing water, towels, glasses, and vinegar.

Someone said: "She ought to be undressed."

The marquise, who was almost out of her wits, tried to undress her daughter, but she no longer knew what she was doing. Her trembling hands fumbled uselessly at the clothing, and she moaned: "I . . . I . . . I can't, I can't."

The maid had returned with a medicine bottle; Servigny uncorked it and poured out half of its contents on to a handkerchief. He thrust it under Yvette's nose, and she began to choke.

"Good; she's breathing," he said. "It's nothing."

He bathed her temples, her cheeks, and her neck with the strong-smelling liquid. Then he signed to the maid to unlace the young girl, and when nothing but a petticoat was left over her chemise, he took her in his arms and carried her to the bed; he was shaken, his senses maddened by the fragrance of her half-naked body, by the touch of her flesh, and the softness of the half-seen breasts on which he pressed his lips.

When she was in bed he rose to his feet, very pale.

"She's coming to," he said; "it's nothing," for he had heard her breathing was continuous and regular. But seeing the men's eyes fixed upon Yvette stretched across the bed, a spasm of jealous fury seized him. He went up to them, saying:

"Gentlemen, there are too many of us in this room. Be good enough to leave M. Saval and myself alone with the marquise."

His voice was sharp and authoritative. The other men left at once.

Mme. Obardi had seized her lover in her arms and, with her face raised to his, was crying:

"Save her! . . . Oh, save her!"

But Servigny, who had turned around, saw a letter on the table. With a swift movement he picked it up and read the address. He guessed the whole affair at once and thought: "Perhaps the marquise had better not know about this." And tearing open the envelope, he read at a glance the two lines which it contained:

I die so that I may not become a kept woman.

Yvette.

Good-by, Mother dear. Forgive me.

"Deuce take it," he said to himself. "This needs thinking over"; and he hid the letter in his pocket. He returned to the bedside, and at once the thought came to him that the young girl had regained consciousness, but dared not show it, out of shame, humiliation, and a dread of being questioned.

The marquise had fallen on her knees and was weeping, her head resting on the foot of the bed. Suddenly she exclaimed:

"A doctor! We must have a doctor!"

But Servigny, who had been whispering to Saval, said to her:

"No, it's all right now. Just go out for a minute and I promise you that she'll be ready to kiss you when you come back."

The baron took Mme. Obardi's arm and led her away. Servigny sat down beside the bed and took Yvette's hand.

"Listen to me, mam'selle," he said.

She did not answer. She felt so happy, so comfortable, so cozy and warm that she would have liked never to move or speak again, but to live on in this state. A sense of infinite well-being possessed her, like no sensation she had ever known. The warm night air drifted into the room in a gentle, caressing breeze, and from time to time its faint breath blew sweetly across her face. It was a caress, the wind's kiss, the soft refreshing breath of a fan made of all the leaves in the wood, all the shadows of the night, all the mists of the river, and all the flowers, for the roses strewn upon the floor and the bed, and the rose tree that clung to the balcony mingled their languid fragrance with the healthy tang of the night breeze.

She drank in the good air, her eyes closed, her senses still half adrift in the intoxication of the drug; she no longer felt a wish to die, but a strong, imperious desire to live, to be happy, no matter how, to be loved, yes, loved.

"Mam'selle Yvette, listen to me," repeated Servigny.

She decided to open her eyes. Seeing her thus revived, he went on:

"Come now, what's all this foolishness?"

"I was so unhappy, Muscade," she murmured.

He gave her hand a benevolent squeeze.

"Well, this has been a deuce of a lot of use to you, now, hasn't it? Now promise me not to try again."

She did not answer, but made a little movement of her head, and emphasized it with a smile that he felt rather than saw.

He took from his pocket the letter he had found on the table.

"Am I to show this to your mother?" he asked.

"No," she signed with a movement of her head.

He did not know what more to say, for there seemed no way out of the situation.

"My dear little girl," he murmured, "we must all accept our share of things, however sad. I understand your grief, and I promise . . ."

"You're so kind. . . ." she stammered.

They were silent. He looked at her. There was tenderness and surrender in her glance, and suddenly she raised her arms, as if she wished to draw him to her. He bent over her, feeling that she was calling him, and their lips met.

For a long time they stayed thus with closed eyes. But he, realizing that he was on the point of losing control, raised his head and stood up. She was smiling at him now with real tenderness, and, gripping his shoulders with both hands, she tried to hold him back.

"I'm going to fetch your mother," he said.

"One more second," she murmured. "I'm so happy."

Then, after a brief interval of silence, she said very softly, so softly that he hardly heard her:

"You will love me very much, won't you?"

He knelt down by the bedside and kissed her wrist, which she held out to him.

"I adore you."

But there were footsteps at the door. He sprang up and cried in his ordinary voice, with its faint note of irony:

"You can come in. It's all over now."

The marquise flung herself upon her daughter with open arms, and embraced her frantically, covering her face with tears. Servigny, his heart full of joy and his body on fire with love, stepped out on to the balcony to breathe deeply of the cool night air, humming:

> *"Souvent femme varie;*
> *Bien fol est qui s'y fie."*

THE PIECE OF STRING

Along all the roads around Goderville the peasants and their wives were coming toward the burgh because it was market day. The men were proceeding with slow steps, the whole body bent forward at each movement of their long twisted legs; deformed by their hard work, by the weight on the plow which, at the same time, raised the left shoulder and swerved the figure, by the reaping of the wheat which made the knees spread to make a firm "purchase," by all the slow and painful labors of the country. Their blouses, blue, "stiff-starched," shining as if varnished, ornamented with a little design in white at the neck and wrists, puffed about their bony bodies, seemed like balloons ready to carry them off. From each of them a head, two arms and two feet protruded.

Some led a cow or a calf by a cord, and their wives, walking behind the animal, whipped its haunches with a leafy branch to hasten its progress. They carried large baskets on their arms from which, in some cases, chickens and, in others, ducks thrust out their heads. And they walked with a quicker, livelier step than their husbands. Their spare straight figures were wrapped in a scanty little shawl pinned over their flat bosoms, and their heads were enveloped in a white cloth glued to the hair and surmounted by a cap.

Then a wagon passed at the jerky trot of a nag, shaking strangely, two men seated side by side and a woman in the bottom of the vehicle, the latter holding onto the sides to lessen the hard jolts.

In the public square of Goderville there was a crowd, a throng of human beings and animals mixed together. The horns of the cattle, the tall hats, with long nap, of the rich peasant and the headgear of the peasant women rose above the surface of the assembly. And the clamorous, shrill, screaming voices made a continuous and savage din which sometimes was dominated by the robust lungs of some countryman's laugh or the long lowing of a cow tied to the wall of a house.

All that smacked of the stable, the dairy and the dirt heap, hay and sweat, giving forth that unpleasant odor, human and animal, peculiar to the people of the field.

Maître Hauchecome of Breaute had just arrived at Goderville, and he was directing his steps toward the public square when he perceived upon the ground a little piece of string. Maître Hauchecome, economical like a true Norman, thought that everything useful ought to be picked up, and he bent painfully, for he suffered from rheumatism. He took the bit of thin cord from the ground and began to roll it carefully when he noticed Maître Malandain, the harness maker, on the threshold of his door, looking at him. They had heretofore had business together on the subject of a halter, and they were on bad terms, both being good haters. Maître Hauchecome was seized with a sort of shame to be seen thus by his enemy, picking a bit of string out of the dirt. He concealed his "find" quickly under his blouse, then in his trousers' pocket; then he pretended to be still looking on the ground for something which he did not find, and he went toward the market, his head forward, bent double by his pains.

He was soon lost in the noisy and slowly moving crowd which was busy with interminable bargainings. The peasants milked, went and came, perplexed, always in fear of being cheated, not daring to decide, watching the vender's eye, ever trying to find the trick in the man and the flaw in the beast.

The women, having placed their great baskets at their feet, had taken out the poultry which lay upon the ground, tied together by the feet, with terrified eyes and scarlet crests.

They heard offers, stated their prices with a dry air and impassive face, or perhaps, suddenly deciding on some proposed reduction, shouted to the customer who was slowly going away: "All right, Maître Authirne, I'll give it to you for that."

Then little by little the square was deserted, and the Angelus ringing at noon, those who had stayed too long scattered to their shops.

At Jourdain's the great room was full of people eating, as the big court was full of vehicles of all kinds, carts, gigs, wagons, dumpcarts, yellow with dirt, mended and patched, raising their shafts to the sky like two arms or perhaps with their shafts in the ground and their backs in the air.

Just opposite the diners seated at the table the immense fireplace, filled with bright flames, cast a lively heat on the backs of the row on the right. Three spits were turning on which were chickens, pigeons and legs of mutton, and an appetizing odor of roast beef and gravy dripping over the nicely browned skin rose from the hearth, increased the jovialness and made everybody's mouth water.

All the aristocracy of the plow ate there at Maître Jourdain's, tavern keeper and horse dealer, a rascal who had money.

The dishes were passed and emptied, as were the jugs of yellow cider. Everyone told his affairs, his purchases and sales. They discussed the crops. The weather was favorable for the green things but not for the wheat.

Suddenly the drum beat in the court before the house. Everybody rose, except a few indifferent persons, and ran to the door or to the windows, their mouths still full and napkins in their hands.

After the public crier had ceased his drumbeating he called out in a jerky voice, speaking his phrases irregularly:

"It is hereby made known to the inhabitants of Goderville, and in general to all persons present at the market, that there was lost this morning on the road to Benzeville, between nine and ten o'clock, a black leather pocketbook containing five hundred francs and some business papers. The finder is requested to return same with all haste to the mayor's office or to Maître Fortune Houlbreque of Manneville; there will be twenty francs' reward."

Then the man went away. The heavy roll of the drum and the crier's voice were again heard at a distance.

Then they began to talk of this event, discussing the chances that Maître Houlbreque had of finding or not finding his pocketbook.

And the meal concluded. They were finishing their coffee when a chief of the gendarmes appeared upon the threshold.

He inquired:

"Is Maître Hauchecome of Breaute here?"

Maître Hauchecome, seated at the other end of the table, replied:

"Here I am."

And the officer resumed:

"Maître Hauchecome, will you have the goodness to accompany me to the mayor's office? The mayor would like to talk to you."

The peasant, surprised and disturbed, swallowed at a draught his tiny glass of brandy, rose and, even more bent than in the morning, for the first steps after each rest were specially difficult, set out, repeating: "Here I am, here I am."

The mayor was awaiting him, seated on an armchair. He was the notary of the vicinity, a stout, serious man with pompous phrases.

"Maître Hauchecome," said he, "you were seen this morning to pick up, on the road to Benzeville, the pocketbook lost by Maître Houlbreque of Manneville."

The countryman, astounded, looked at the mayor, already terrified by this suspicion resting on him without his knowing why.

"Me? Me? Me pick up the pocketbook?"

"Yes, you yourself."

"Word of honor, I never heard of it."

"But you were seen."

"I was seen, me? Who says he saw me?"

"Monsieur Malandain, the harness maker."

The old man remembered, understood and flushed with anger.

"Ah, he saw me, the clodhopper, he saw me pick up this string here, M'sieu the Mayor." And rummaging in his pocket, he drew out the little piece of string.

But the mayor, incredulous, shook his head.

"You will not make me believe, Maître Hauchecome, that Monsieur Malandain, who is a man worthy of credence, mistook this cord for a pocketbook."

The peasant, furious, lifted his hand, spat at one side to attest his honor, repeating:

"It is nevertheless the truth of the good God, the sacred truth, M'sieu the Mayor. I repeat it on my soul and my salvation."

The mayor resumed:

"After picking up the object you stood like a stilt, looking a long while in the mud to see if any piece of money had fallen out."

The good old man choked with indignation and fear.

"How anyone can tell—how anyone can tell—such lies to take away an honest man's reputation! How can anyone——"

There was no use in his protesting; nobody believed him. He was confronted with Monsieur Malandain, who repeated and maintained his affirmation. They abused each other for an hour. At his own request Maître Hauchecome was searched; nothing was found on him.

Finally the mayor, very much perplexed, discharged him with the warning that he would consult the public prosecutor and ask for further orders.

The news had spread. As he left the mayor's office the old man was surrounded and questioned with a serious or bantering curiosity in which there was no indignation. He began to tell the story of the string. No one believed him. They laughed at him.

He went along, stopping his friends, beginning endlessly his statement and his protestations, showing his pockets turned inside out to prove that he had nothing.

They said:

"Old rascal, get out!"

And he grew angry, becoming exasperated, hot and distressed at not being believed, not knowing what to do and always repeating himself.

Night came. He must depart. He started on his way with three neighbors to whom he pointed out the place where he had picked up the bit of string, and all along the road he spoke of his adventure.

In the evening he took a turn in the village of Breaute in order to tell it to everybody. He only met with incredulity.

It made him ill at night.

The next day about one o'clock in the afternoon Marius Paumelle, a hired man in the employ of Maître Breton, husbandman at Ymanville, returned the pocketbook and its contents to Maître Houlbreque of Manneville.

This man claimed to have found the object in the road, but not knowing how to read, he had carried it to the house and given it to his employer.

The news spread through the neighborhood. Maître Hauchecome was informed of it. He immediately went the circuit and began to recount his story completed by the happy climax. He was in triumph.

"What grieved me so much was not the thing itself as the lying. There is nothing so shameful as to be placed under a cloud on account of a lie."

He talked of his adventure all day long; he told it on the highway to people who were passing by, in the wineshop to people who were drinking there and to persons coming out of church the following Sunday. He stopped strangers to tell them about it. He was calm now, and yet something disturbed him without his knowing exactly what it was. People had the air of joking while they listened.

They did not seem convinced. He seemed to feel that remarks were being made behind his back.

On Tuesday of the next week he went to the market at Goderville, urged solely by the necessity he felt of discussing the case.

Malandain, standing at his door, began to laugh on seeing him pass. Why?

He approached a farmer from Crequetot who did not let him finish and, giving him a thump in the stomach, said to his face:

"You big rascal."

Then he turned his back on him.

Maître Hauchecome was confused; why was he called a big rascal?

When he was seated at the table in Jourdain's tavern he commenced to explain "the affair."

A horse dealer from Monvilliers called to him:

"Come, come, old sharper, that's an old trick; I know all about your piece of string!"

Hauchecome stammered:

"But since the pocketbook was found."

But the other man replied:

"Shut up, papa, there is one that finds and there is one that reports. At any rate you are mixed with it."

The peasant stood choking. He understood. They accused him of having had the pocketbook returned by a confederate, by an accomplice.

He tried to protest. All the table began to laugh.

He could not finish his dinner and went away in the midst of jeers.

He went home ashamed and indignant, choking with anger and confusion, the more dejected that he was capable, with his Norman cunning, of doing what they had accused him of and ever boasting of it as of a good turn. His innocence to him, in a confused way, was impossible to prove, as his sharpness was known. And he was stricken to the heart by the injustice of the suspicion.

Then he began to recount the adventures again, prolonging his history every day, adding each time new reasons, more energetic protestations, more solemn oaths which he imagined and prepared in his hours of solitude, his whole mind given up to the story of the string. He was believed so much the less as his defense was more complicated and his arguing more subtle.

"Those are lying excuses," they said behind his back.

He felt it, consumed his heart over it and wore himself out with useless efforts. He wasted away before their very eyes.

The wags now made him tell about the string to amuse them, as they make a soldier who has been on a campaign tell about his battles. His mind, touched to the depth, began to weaken.

Toward the end of December he took to his bed.

He died in the first days of January, and in the delirium of his death struggles he kept claiming his innocence, reiterating:

"A piece of string, a piece of string—look—here it is, M'sieu the Mayor."

THE FUNERAL PILE

Last Monday at Etretat the death occurred of an Indian prince, Bapu Sahib Khanderao Ghatgay, a relative of His Highness the Maharajah Gaikwar, Prince of Baroda, in the Province of Gujarat, Bombay Presidency.

For about three weeks previously a group of about ten young Indians had been noticed in the streets, small, lithe young fellows, completely black, and dressed in gray suits, with broad-peaked cloth caps. They were distinguished potentates who had come to Europe to study the military institutions of the principal Western nations. The group consisted of three princes, a friend of high caste, an interpreter, and three servants.

It was the head of this mission who had died, an old man of forty-two, the father-in-law of Sampatrao Kashivao Gaikwar, brother of His Highness the Gaikwar of Baroda. His son-in-law was with him. The others were Ganpatrao Shavanrao Gaikwar, cousin of His Highness Khasherao Gadhav; Vasudev Madhav Samarth, secretary and interpreter, and the servants, Ramchandra Bajaji, Ganu bin Pukaram Kokate, Rhambhaji bin Favji.

When the deceased gentleman was leaving his country he was overcome by sorrow, convinced that he would never return, and he wanted to abandon the trip, but he had to submit to the will of his noble relative, the Prince of Baroda, so he set out.

They came to spend the last weeks of summer at Etretat, and the curious used to watch them bathing every morning at the Roches Blanches baths.

Five or six days ago Bapu Sahib Khanderao Ghatgay began to suffer from pains in his gums, then the inflammation spread to his throat, which became ulcerated. Gangrene set in, and on Monday the doctors informed his young friend that he would not recover. He sank almost immediately after that, and when the unfortunate man seemed on the point of breathing his last, his friends caught him in their arms, lifted him out of bed, and placed him on the tiled floor, so that he might die in contact with Mother Earth, according to the laws of Brahma.

On the same day they requested the permission of the Mayor, M. Boissaye, to burn the corpse, also in accordance with the rites of their religion. The Mayor hesitated, then telegraphed to the Prefecture for instructions, stating, however, that, in the absence of any reply to the contrary, he would give his consent. As no reply had been received by nine o'clock in the evening, it was decided that, in view of the infectious character of the disease of which the Indian had died, his body would be cremated that very night on the shore beneath the cliffs, as the tide receded.

At present no objection has been raised against this decision of the Mayor's, who acted as a man of intelligence and resolution, with broad-minded ideas, and who was supported, moreover, by the advice of the three doctors who had followed the case and issued the certificate of death.

There was a dance that night at the Casino. It was a premature autumn evening, and rather cold. A strong wind was blowing in from the ocean, though the sea was not rough, and ragged, torn clouds scudded across the sky. They came up from the distant horizon, and as they approached the moon they became white, covered it rapidly, and obscured it for a second or two without actually hiding it. The tall cliffs which enclose the rounded seashore of Etretat, terminating in the two celebrated arcades known as "The Gates," remained hidden in the shadows, forming two huge black spots on the landscape under the tender light of the moon.

It had been raining all day.

The Casino orchestra was playing waltzes, polkas, and quadrilles. Suddenly a rumor spread through the crowd. People were saying that an Indian prince had just died at the Hôtel des Bains, and that the authorities had been approached for permission to burn the body. Nobody believed the story; or at least nobody thought it was likely to happen soon, it seemed so contrary to our customs, and as the night advanced everybody went home.

At midnight the lamplighter went from street to street extinguishing one after the other the yellow gas jets which lit up the sleeping houses, the mud and the puddles of water. He waited, watching for the moment when the little town would be empty and still.

Ever since midday a carpenter had been cutting wood, wondering in his amazement what was going to be done with all these boards sawn into little pieces, and why so much good material was being wasted. This wood was loaded on to a cart and taken off by side streets to the shore without arousing the suspicions of the few late pedestrians who met it. The cart went along the shingle to the very foot of the cliffs, and when its load had been emptied, the three Indian servants began to build up a funeral pile, which was longer than it was broad. They did all the work alone, for no profane hand could help them in this solemn task. It was one o'clock in the morning when the relatives of the dead man were informed that they could carry out their wishes.

The door of the little house which they occupied was opened, and in the narrow hall, dimly lighted, we saw the corpse lying on trestles, and wrapped in white silk. The form could be seen distinctly beneath its white covering, lying on its back. The Indians stood, motionless and very solemn, at his feet while one of them went through the prescribed ritual, murmuring in a monotonous whisper words we could not understand. He moved around the corpse, sometimes touching it, then, taking an urn which hung from three chains, he sprinkled it for a long time with the holy water of the Ganges, which Indians must always carry with them, wherever they may go.

Then the trestles were raised by four of them, who set out slowly. The moon had disappeared, leaving the muddy, empty streets in darkness, but the corpse on the trestles seemed luminous, the silk was so dazzling. It was an impressive sight to see the bright form of this body passing through the night, carried by men whose skin was so dark that one could not distinguish between their faces and hands and their clothes, in the shadows. Three Indians followed behind the corpse, then came the tall figure of an Englishman in a light gray overcoat, who stood head and shoulders above them, a charming and distinguished man, their guide, counselor, and friend in Europe.

Beneath the cold, foggy skies of this little Northern watering place I felt as if I were witnessing a symbolical spectacle. It seemed to me as though the conquered genius of India were being borne in front of me, while in its wake, as in a funeral procession, followed the victorious genius of England, dressed in a gray ulster.

The four bearers stopped a moment on the rolling shingle to get their breath, then they went on, walking very slowly now, and staggering beneath their burden. At last they reached the funeral pile, which had been built in a cave at the very foot of the cliffs, which rose to a height of some three hundred feet, all white, but looking sombre in the night. The pile was about three feet high. The corpse was laid upon it, and one of the Indians asked in what direction lay the North Star. It was pointed out to him, and the dead rajah was stretched out with his feet turned towards his native land. Twelve bottles of petroleum were then poured over him, and he was completely covered with fir planks. For another hour the relatives and servants kept adding to the pile, which looked like those heaps of wood which carpenters keep in their lofts. Then twenty bottles of oil were emptied on to the edifice, and right on the top a sack of shavings. A few feet away a light flickered in a little bronze spirit lamp, which had been burning since the corpse arrived.

The moment had come. The relatives went to set a flame to the pile. As the lamp was not burning well they poured some oil into it, and suddenly the flame shot up, lighting the great wall of rocks from top to bottom. An Indian who was stooping over the lamp stood up, with his two hands raised and his elbows folded, and a colossal black shadow was suddenly thrown upon the immense white cliffs, the shadow of Buddha, in his traditional pose. The little pointed cap which the man was wearing suggested the god's headdress. The effect was so striking and unexpected that I felt my heart beating as if some supernatural apparition had loomed up in front of me. It was indeed the ancient and sacred image, come from the heart of the Orient to this other end of Europe to watch over its child who was being burnt there.

The shadow disappeared. They approached with the lamp. The shavings at the top caught fire, then the flames spread to the wood, and a powerful light illuminated the shore, the shingle, and the foaming waves that broke on the sand. It grew larger every moment, till it lit up the dancing crests of the waves on the distant sea. The wind from the ocean blew in gusts, increasing the flames, which died down, twisted and shot up again, throwing out thousands of sparks. They ran along the cliffs with lightning speed, and were lost in the sky, where they mingled with the stars and added to the number. Some sea birds were aroused and uttered their plaintive cries, as they flew in wide curves, passing with outstretched wings through the brilliant light, and disappearing again into the darkness.

Very soon the funeral pile was one mass of burning wood, not red, but yellow, a dazzling yellow, a furnace lashed by the wind. Suddenly it shook beneath a gust stronger than the others, collapsed in part, falling towards the sea. The corpse was uncovered and was quite visible, a dark patch on a bed of fire, burning with long blue flames. When the pile collapsed on the right hand side the corpse turned like a man in his bed. It was at once covered up with fresh wood, and the flames roared more furiously than before.

Seated in a semicircle on the shingle, the Indians looked on with sad and serious faces. The rest of us, as it was cold, came close enough to the fire to feel the sparks and the smoke on our faces. There was no smell but that of pine and petroleum.

Hours passed and dawn appeared. Towards five o'clock nothing remained but a heap of ashes. The relatives picked them up, threw some into the air, some into the sea, and kept a little in a brass jar to be taken back to India. Then they withdrew to weep for the dead at home. In this fashion these young princes and their servants, with only the most elementary material, succeeded in cremating their relative with singular skill and remarkable dignity. Everything was accomplished in accordance with the rites and laws of their religion. The dead man rests in peace.

The following day there was great excitement in Etretat. Some pretended that a man had been burnt alive, others that it was an attempt to conceal a crime. It was said that the Mayor would be imprisoned; while certain people asserted that the Indian prince had succumbed to an attack of cholera. The men were amazed and the women indignant. All day a crowd lingered at the site of the funeral pile, looking for pieces of bone amongst the still warm shingle. Enough bones were picked up to make ten whole skeletons, for the farmers of the neighborhood often throw their dead sheep into the sea. The gamblers carefully placed these different fragments in their purses. But not one of them has a genuine piece of the Indian prince.

That evening a representative of the government came to hold an inquiry. He seemed, however, to view this strange case like a man of reason and intelligence. But what will he say in his report? The Indians declared that if they had been prevented from cremating their dead in France, they would have taken the corpse to a freer country, where they could conform to their own customs.

So I have seen a man burned on a funeral pile, and it has given me a desire to end in the same fashion. Everything is over at once. The slow work of nature is thus hastened by man, rather than retarded by a hideous coffin in which decomposition goes on for months. The body is dead and the spirit has departed. The purifying fire scatters in a few hours what was a human being, casting it to the winds, turning to air and ashes, instead of unspeakable putrefaction.

That is a clean and healthy method. Under the clay, in that closed box in which the body becomes pulp, a black stinking pulp, the process of putrefaction becomes something repugnant and atrocious. The coffin which descends into a muddy hole makes the heart ache, but the funeral pile flaming up to heaven has an element of greatness, beauty and solemnity.

AN OLD MAN

All the newspapers had carried the advertisement:

"The new watering place of Rondelis offers all desired advantages for a long stay and even for permanent residence. Its ferruginous waters, recognized as the best in the world for counteracting all impurities of the blood, seem also to possess particular qualities calculated to prolong human life. This singular circumstance is perhaps due in part to the exceptional situation of the town, which lies surrounded by mountains and in the very center of a pine forest. For several centuries it has been celebrated for numerous cases of extraordinary longevity."

And the public came in droves.

One morning the doctor in charge of the springs was asked to call on a new arrival, M. Daron, who had come to Rondelis only a few days before and had rented a charming villa on the edge of the forest. He was a little old man of eighty-six, still sprightly, wiry, healthy, active, who went to infinite pains to conceal his age.

He asked the doctor to be seated and immediately questioned him: "Doctor, if I am well, it is thanks to hygienic living. I am not very old, but have reached a certain age, and I keep free of all illness, all indisposition, even the slightest discomfort, by means of hygiene. I am told that the climate of this place is very favorable for the health. I am very willing to believe it, but before establishing myself here I want proof. I am therefore going to ask you to call on me once a week, to give me, very exactly, the following information:

"I wish first of all to have a complete, utterly complete, list of all the inhabitants of the town and surroundings who are more than eighty years old. I also need a few physical and psychological details concerning each. I wish to know their professions, their kinds of life, their habits. Each time one of these people dies, you will inform me, indicating the precise cause of death, as well as the circumstances."

Then he graciously added: "I hope, Doctor, that we may become good friends," and he stretched out his wrinkled little hand. The doctor took it, promising his devoted co-operation.

M. Daron had always had a strange fear of death. He had deprived himself of almost all the pleasures because they are dangerous, and whenever anyone expressed surprise that he did not drink wine—wine, that bringer of fancy and gaiety—he replied in a voice containing a note of fear: "I value my life." And he pronounced my, as if that life, his life, possessed some generally unknown value. He put into that my such a difference between his life and the life of others that no answer was possible.

Indeed, he had a very particular way of accentuating the possessive pronouns designating all the parts of his person or even things belonging to him. When he said "My eyes, my legs, my arms, my hands," it was clear that no mistake must be made: those organs did not belong to everyone. But this distinction was particularly noticeable when he spoke of his physician: "My doctor." One would have said that this doctor was his, only his, destined for him alone, to take care of his illnesses and nobody else's, and that he was superior to all the doctors in the universe, all, without exception.

He had never considered other men except as kinds of puppets, created as furniture for the natural world. He divided them into two classes: those whom he greeted because some chance had put him in contact with them, and those whom he did not greet. Both categories of individuals were to him equally insignificant.

But beginning with the day when the doctor of Rondelis brought him the list of the seventeen inhabitants of the town who were over eighty, he felt awaken in his heart a new interest, an unfamiliar solicitude for these old people whom he was going to see fall by the wayside one after the other.

He had no desire to make their acquaintance, but he had a very clear idea of their persons, and with the doctor, who dined with him every Thursday, he spoke only of them. "Well, Doctor, how is Joseph Poinçot today? We left him a little ill last week." And when the doctor had given him the patient's bill of health M. Daron proposed modifications in diet, experiments, methods of treatment which he might later apply to himself if they succeeded with the others. The seventeen old people were an experimental field from which much was to be learned.

One evening the doctor came in and announced: "Rosalie Tournel is dead." M. Daron shuddered and immediately demanded, "What of?" "Of an angina." The little old man uttered an "ah" of relief. Then he declared: "She was too fat, too big; she must have eaten too much. When I get to be her age, I'll be more careful." (He was two years older than Rosalie, but never admitted to being over seventy.)

A few months later, it was the turn of Henri Brissot. M. Daron was very moved. This time it was a man—thin, within three months of his own age, and very prudent. He dared ask for no details, but waited anxiously for the doctor to tell him. "Ah, he died suddenly, just like that? He was very well last week. He must have done something unwise, Doctor." The doctor, who was enjoying himself, replied, "I believe not. His children tell me he was very careful."

Then, no longer able to contain himself, M. Daron demanded, with anguish, "But . . . but . . . What did he die of, then?"

"Of pleurisy."

That was joyful news, really joyful. The little old man clapped his dry hands. "I knew it! I told you he had done something unwise. Pleurisy doesn't come just by itself. He took a breath of fresh air after his dinner, and the cold lodged on his chest. Pleurisy! That is an accident, not an illness. Only crazy men die of pleurisy."

And he ate his dinner gaily, talking of those who remained. "There are only fifteen now, but they are all strong, aren't they? All of life is like that, the weakest fall first; people who go beyond thirty have a good chance to reach sixty, those who pass sixty often get to eighty; and those who pass eighty almost always reach the century mark, because they are the most robust, the most careful, the most hardened."

Still two others disappeared during the year, one of dysentery and the other of a choking fit. M. Daron derived a great deal of amusement from the death of the former, and concluded that he must have eaten something exciting the day before. "Dysentery is the disease of the imprudent; you should have watched over his hygiene, Doctor." As for the choking fit, it could only have come from a heart condition, hitherto unrecognized.

But one evening the doctor announced the passing of Paul Timonet, a kind of mummy, of whom it had been hoped to make a centenarian, a living advertisement for the watering place. When M. Daron asked, as usual, "What did he die of?" the doctor replied, "Really, I don't know."

"What do you mean, you don't know? One always knows. Wasn't there some organic lesion?"

The doctor shook his head. "No, none."

"Perhaps some infection of the liver or kidneys?"

"No—they were perfectly sound."

"Did you observe whether the stomach functioned regularly? A stroke is often caused by bad digestion."

"There was no stroke."

M. Daron, very perplexed, became excited. "But he certainly died of something! What is your opinion?"

The doctor raised his arms. "I absolutely do not know. He died because he died, that's all."

Then M. Daron, in a voice full of emotion, demanded: "Exactly how old was that one? I can't remember."

"Eighty-nine."

And the little old man, with an air at once incredulous and reassured, cried, "Eighty-nine! So it wasn't old age! . . ."

A SURPRISE

My brother and I were brought up by our uncle, the Abbé Loisel—the Curé Loisel, as we called him. Our parents died when we were small, and he had taken us into his rectory and raised us.

For eighteen years he had had the parish of Join-le-Sault, not far from Yvetot. It was a small village, set in the very middle of the Norman plateau known as the pays de Caux, dotted with farms whose orchards rose up here and there amidst the fields.

The village, apart from the farm cottages scattered over the plain, consisted of a mere six houses fronting on both sides of the main road, with the church at one end and the new town hall at the other.

My brother and I passed our childhood playing in the cemetery. The place was sheltered from the wind, and there my uncle gave us our lessons, the three of us sitting side by side on the one stone tomb, that of my uncle's predecessor, whose wealthy family had seen to it that he was buried sumptuously.

To train our memories, my uncle made us learn by heart the names of the deceased that were painted on the black wooden crosses; and to train us in observation as well he made us begin our odd recitation now from one end of the graveyard, now from the other, or sometimes from the middle. He would point abruptly to a grave, and say, "The one in the third row, with the cross leaning to the left: whose is that?" When a burial took place, we made haste to learn what was to be painted on the wooden symbol, and we often went to the carpenter's shop, to see the epitaph before it was placed on the tomb. My uncle would ask, "Do you know the new one?" And we would reply in unison, "Yes, uncle," and immediately begin to recite: "Here lies Josephine Rosalie Gertrude Malandain, widow of Théodore Magloire Césaire, deceased at the age of seventy-two years, mourned by her family: a faithful daughter, faithful wife, and faithful mother. Her soul is in heaven."

My uncle was a tall, big-boned priest, square-built in his ideas as in his frame. His soul itself seemed hard and definite, like an answer in a catechism. He often spoke to us of God in a thundering voice, always uttering the word as violently as though he were firing a pistol. His God was not God the good and just, but simply God. He seemed to think of him as a burglar thinks of a policeman, or a prisoner of the judge.

He brought us up harshly, teaching us to tremble rather than to love.

When one of us was fourteen and the other fifteen, he sent us to board, at a special reduced rate, at the seminary in Yvetot. This was a large, dreary building, full of curés, whose pupils were almost without exception destined for the priesthood. I can never think of the place even now without a shudder. It smelled of prayers the way a fish market smells of fish. Oh! That dreary school, with its eternal religious ceremonies, its freezing Mass every morning, its periods of meditation, its gospel recitations, and the reading from pious books during meals! Oh! Those dreary days passed within those cloistering walls, where nothing was spoken of but God—the explosive God of my uncle.

We lived there in narrow, contemplative, unnatural piety—and also in a truly meritorious state of filth, for I well remember that the boys were made to wash their feet but three times a year, the night before each vacation. As for baths, they were as unknown as the name of Victor Hugo. Our masters apparently held them in the greatest contempt.

My brother and I graduated the same year, and with a few sous in our pockets we woke up one morning to find ourselves in Paris, working at eighteen hundred francs a year in a government office, thanks to the influence, exercised on our behalf, of the Archbishop of Rouen.

For a while we continued to be very good boys, my brother and I, living together in the little lodging we had rented, like two night birds torn from their nest and cast out into the dazzling sunlight, blinded and bewildered.

But little by little the Paris air, new comrades, and the theaters took away a little of our numbness. Certain new desires, different from heavenly joys, began to awaken within us, and, on a certain evening—the same evening—after long hesitation and uneasiness and the fears of a soldier before his first battle, we allowed ourselves to——how shall I put it?——allowed ourselves to be seduced by two little neighbors, two shopgirls, who worked and lived together.

Soon an exchange took place between our two establishments, a division. My brother took the girls' flat and kept one of them to live with him. The other came to live with me. Mine was named Louise. She was twenty-two, perhaps. A good girl, fresh, gay, and round—especially round in a certain place. She moved in with me like a little wife taking possession of a man and of everything connected with that man. She organized the household, made everything neat, cooked, kept careful account of expenses, and in addition introduced me to many pleasant things with which I was unfamiliar.

My brother was also very happy. The four of us always had dinner together, one day in his rooms, the next day in mine, and there was never a cloud or a care.

From time to time I received a letter from my uncle, who continued to think that I was living with my brother, and who gave me news of the village, of his maid, of recent deaths, of the crops and harvests—all mixed in with bits of advice on the dangers of life and the turpitudes of the world.

These letters arrived in the morning, by the eight o'clock mail. The concierge slipped them under the door, giving a knock with her broom handle to attract our attention. Louise would get out of bed, pick up the blue envelope, and sit down beside me and read me the letter from the "curé Loisel," as she also came to call him.

For six months we were happy.

Then, one night, about one o'clock in the morning, a violent peal of the doorbell made us jump. We hadn't been asleep—far from it—at that particular moment. Louise said, "What can that be?" And I answered, "I haven't any idea. Probably a mistake." And we stopped what we were doing and lay there pressed closely one against the other, our ears strained to catch any sound, very much on edge.

And then there was a second peal of the bell, and then a third, and then a fourth long peal filled our room with so much noise that we both sat up. This was no mistake: whoever it was, wanted us. I quickly pulled on my drawers and slippers and ran to the vestibule door, fearing some disaster. But before opening, I called, "Who is there? What do you want?"

A voice, a loud voice, the voice of my uncle, replied: "It's me, Jean. Open your door, I don't want to sleep on the stairs!"

I thought I would go crazy. But what was there to do? I rushed back into the bedroom and in a trembling voice said to Louise: "It's my uncle. Hide!" Then I opened the outer door and the curé Loisel almost knocked me down with his carpetbag.

"What were you up to, you scamp? Why didn't you open?"

I stammered that I had been asleep.

"Asleep at first, perhaps, but just now after you spoke to me—what were you up to then?"

I stammered that I had left my key in my trousers, and to prevent further discussion I threw my arms around his neck and kissed him violently on both cheeks.

That calmed him, and he explained his presence. "I'm here for four days, scapegrace," he announced. "I wanted to take a look at the hellhole of Paris, to give myself an idea of what the real hell is like." He gave a laugh like a roaring storm, then continued: "Put me up any way you can. We can lay one of your mattresses on the floor. But where's your brother? Asleep? Wake him up! Wake him up!"

I felt that I was rapidly losing my wits, but managed to say, "Jacques isn't home yet. He had a lot of extra work, night work, at the office."

My uncle accepted that, rubbed his hands, and asked me how my work was going. Then he made for the door of my bedroom. I almost seized him by his collar. "No, no, this way, uncle." An idea came to me. "You must be hungry after your trip. Come and have a bite of something."

He smiled. "You're right. I am hungry. I wouldn't mind a snack." And I pushed him into the dining room.

Dinner had been at our house that night, and the cupboard was full. I took out a piece of cold beef, and the curé lit into it heartily. I kept urging him to eat, kept filling his glass and reminding him of wonderful meals we had had in Normandy, to stimulate his appetite. When he had finished he pushed away his plate and said, "That's that: I've had all I can manage." But I had other things in reserve—I knew the good man's weakness—and I brought out a chicken pâté, a potato salad, a pot of cream, and some excellent wine that was left over from dinner. He almost fell over backwards in astonishment at my scale of living, pulled his plate toward him, and began all over again. It was getting late, and as he kept eating I kept trying to think of a way out, but nothing practical occurred to me.

Finally he got up from the table, and I felt my knees weaken. I tried to keep him where we were. "Here, uncle—some brandy. It's old, it's good." But he declared, "No, this time I'm really through. Let's see the rest of your quarters."

I well knew that there was no holding him back, and shivers ran up and down my spine. What would happen? What kind of a scene and scandal? What violence, perhaps?

I followed him, filled with a wild desire to open the window and throw myself into the street. I followed him stupidly, not daring to say a word to restrain him, knowing myself lost, almost fainting with anguish, yet nevertheless hoping that some chance would come to my aid.

He entered the bedroom. One last hope lifted my heart: Louise, sweet thing, had drawn the bed curtains, and not a thing in the room betrayed the presence of a woman. Her dresses, her collars and cuffs, her stockings, her shoes, her gloves, her pins and rings—everything had disappeared. I stammered: "Let's not go to bed now, uncle. The sun is almost up."

"You're a good boy to be willing to sit talking with an old man," he answered. "But I could do with an hour or two of sleep."

And he approached the bed, candle in hand. I waited, breathless, frantic. With one gesture he pulled the curtains open! It was a warm June night, and Louise and I had taken off the blankets, and on the bed was only a sheet, which Louise, in her desperation, had pulled over her head. Doubtless to make herself feel more securely hidden, she had rolled herself into a ball, and pressed tight against the sheet her—her contours were clearly visible.

I could hardly stand up.

My uncle turned to me, grinning so widely that I almost collapsed with astonishment. "So!" he cried, merrily. "Joking, were you! You didn't want to wake your brother. Well—*I'll* wake him, and you'll see how." And I saw his hand, his big peasant's hand, upraised; and as he choked with laughter it fell, with a terrific sound, on the—contours before him.

There was a terrible cry in the bed; and then a furious tempest under the sheet. It heaved, billowed and shook: the poor girl couldn't get out, so tightly had she rolled herself in.

Finally a leg appeared at one end, an arm at the other, then the head, then the bosom, naked and panting; and Louise, furious, sat up and looked at us with eyes shining like lanterns.

My uncle, speechless, started back, his mouth open, as though he had seen the devil himself. He was breathing like an ox.

I considered the situation too serious to cope with, and rushed madly out.

I didn't return for two days. Louise had gone, leaving the key with the concierge. I never saw her again.

My uncle? He disinherited me in favor of my brother, who, warned by Louise, swore that he had refused to continue living with me because of my dissolute behavior, which he was unwilling to countenance.

I will never marry. Women are too dangerous.

IN THE MOONLIGHT

Well merited was the name "soldier of God" by the Abbé Marignan. He was a tall, thin priest, fanatical to a degree, but just and of an exalted soul. All his beliefs were fixed, with never a waver. He thought that he understood God thoroughly, that he penetrated His designs, His wishes, His intentions.

Striding up and down the garden walk of his little country parsonage, sometimes a question arose in his mind: "Why did God make that?" Then in his thoughts, putting himself in God's place, he searched obstinately and nearly always was satisfied that he found the reason. He was not the man to murmur in transports of pious humility, "O Lord, thy ways are past finding out!" What he said was: "I am the servant of God; I ought to know the reason of what he does or to divine it if I do not."

Everything in nature seemed to him created with an absolute and admirable logic. The "wherefore" and the "because" were always balanced. The dawns were made to rejoice you on waking, the days to ripen the harvests, the rains to water them, the evenings to prepare for sleeping and the nights dark for sleep.

The four seasons corresponded perfectly to all the needs of agriculture, and to him the suspicion could never have come that nature has no intention and that all which lives has accustomed itself, on the contrary, to the hard conditions of different periods, of climates and of matter.

But he hated women; he hated them unconsciously and despised them by instinct. He often repeated the words of Christ, "Woman, what have I to do with thee?" and he would add, "One would almost say that God himself was ill pleased with that particular work of his hands." Woman for him was indeed the "child twelve times unclean" of whom the poet speaks. She was the temptress who had ensnared the first man and who still continued her damnable work; she was the being who is feeble, dangerous, mysteriously troublous. And even more than her poisonous beauty he hated her loving soul.

He had often felt women's tenderness attack him, and though he knew himself to be unassailable he grew exasperated at this need of loving which quivers continually in their hearts.

To his mind God had only created woman to tempt man and to test him. Man should not approach her without those precautions for defense which he would take, and the fears he would cherish, near an ambush. Woman, indeed, was just like a trap, with her arms extended and her lips open toward a man.

He had toleration only for nuns, rendered harmless by their vow; but he treated them harshly notwithstanding, because, ever at the bottom of their chained-up hearts, their chastened hearts, he perceived the eternal tenderness that constantly went out even to him although he was a priest.

He had a niece who lived with her mother in a little house near by. He was bent on making her a sister of charity. She was pretty and harebrained and a great tease. When the abbé sermonized she laughed; when he was angry at her she kissed him vehemently, pressing him to her heart while he would seek involuntarily to free himself from her embrace. Notwithstanding, it made him taste a certain sweet joy, awakening deep within him that sensation of fatherhood which slumbers in every man.

Often he talked to her of God, of his God, walking beside her along the footpaths through the fields. She hardly listened but looked at the sky, the grass, the flowers, with a joy of living which could be seen in her eyes. Sometimes she rushed forward to catch some flying creature and, bringing it back, would cry: "Look, my uncle, how pretty it is; I should like to kiss it." And this necessity to "kiss flies" or sweet flowers worried, irritated and revolted the priest who saw, even in that, the ineradicable tenderness which ever springs in the hearts of women.

One day the sacristan's wife, who kept house for the Abbé Marignan, told him very cautiously that his niece had a lover!

He experienced a dreadful emotion, and he stood choking, with the soap all over his face, in the act of shaving.

When he found himself able to think and speak once more he cried: "It is not true; you are lying, Melanie!"

But the peasant woman put her hand on her heart. "May our Lord judge me if I am lying, Monsieur le Curé. I tell you she goes to him every evening as soon as your sister is in bed. They meet each other beside the river. You have only to go there between ten o'clock and midnight and see for yourself."

He ceased scratching his chin and commenced to pace the room quickly, as he always did in his hours of gravest thought. When he tried to begin his shaving again he cut himself three times from nose to ear.

All day long he remained silent, swollen with anger and with rage. To his priestly zeal against the mighty power of love was added the moral indignation of a father, of a teacher, of a keeper of souls, who has been deceived, robbed, played with by a child. He felt the egotistical sorrow that parents feel when their daughter announces that she has chosen a husband without them and in spite of their advice.

After his dinner he tried to read a little, but he could not attune himself to it and he grew angrier and angrier. When it struck ten he took his cane, a formidable oaken club which he always carried when he had to go out at night to visit the sick. Smilingly he regarded the enormous cudgel, holding it in his solid, countryman's fist and cutting threatening circles with it in the air. Then suddenly he raised it and, grinding his teeth, he brought it down upon a chair, the back of which, split in two, fell heavily to the ground.

He opened his door to go out, but he stopped upon the threshold, surprised by such a splendor of moonlight as you seldom see.

Endowed as he was with an exalted spirit, such a spirit as must have belonged to those dreamer-poets, the Fathers of the Church, he felt himself suddenly softened and moved by the grand and serene beauty of the pale-faced night.

In his little garden, bathed in the soft brilliance, his fruit trees, all arow, were outlining in shadow upon the walk their slender limbs of wood scarce clothed with green; while the giant honeysuckle climbing on the house wall exhaled delicious sugared breaths which hovered through the warm clear night like a perfumed soul.

He began to breathe deep, drinking the air as drunkards drink their wine and walking slowly, ravished, surprised and almost oblivious of his niece.

As he stepped into the open country he stopped to contemplate the whole plain, inundated by this caressing radiance and drowned in the tender and languishing charm of the serene night. In chorus the frogs threw into space their short metallic notes, and with the seduction of the moonlight distant nightingales mingled that fitful music of theirs which brings no thoughts but dreams, a light and vibrant melody which seems attuned to kisses.

The abbé continued his walk, his courage failing, he knew not why. He felt, as it were, enfeebled and suddenly exhausted; he had a great desire to sit down, to pause right there and praise God in all His works.

Below him, following the bends of the little river, wound a great line of poplars. On and about the banks, wrapping all the tortuous watercourse in a kind of light, transparent wadding, hung suspended a fine mist, a white vapor, which the moon rays crossed and silvered and caused to gleam.

The priest paused yet again, penetrated to the depths of his soul by a strong and growing emotion. And a doubt, a vague uneasiness, seized on him; he felt that one of those questions he sometimes put to himself was now being born.

Why had God done this? Since the night is destined for sleep, for unconsciousness, for repose, for forgetfulness of everything, why, then, make it more charming than the day, sweeter than dawns and sunsets? And this slow, seductive star, more poetical than the sun and so discreet that it seems designed to light up things too delicate, too mysterious for the great luminary—why had it come to brighten all the shades? Why did not the sweetest of all songsters go to rest like the others? Why set himself to singing in the vaguely troubling dark? Why this half veil over the world? Why these quiverings of the heart, this emotion of the soul, this languor of the body? Why this display of seductions which mankind never sees, since night brings sleep? For whom was this sublime spectacle intended, this flood of poetry poured from heaven to earth? The abbé did not understand it at all.

But then, down there along the edge of the pasture, appeared two shadows walking side by side under the arched roof of the trees all soaked in glittering mist.

The man was the taller and had his arm about his mistress's neck; from time to time he kissed her on the forehead. They animated the lifeless landscape which enveloped them, a divine frame made, as it were, expressly for them. They seemed, these two, a single being, the being for whom this calm and silent night was destined; and they approached the priest like a living answer, the answer vouchsafed by his Master to his question.

He stood stock-still, overwhelmed and with a beating heart. He likened it to some Bible story such as the loves of Ruth and Boaz, the accomplishment of the will of the Lord in one of those great scenes talked of in Holy Writ. Through his head ran the versicles of the *Song of Songs*, the ardent cries, the calls of the body, all the passionate poetry of that poem which burns with tenderness and love. And he said to himself, "God perhaps has made such nights as this to clothe with his ideals the loves of men."

He withdrew before the couple, who went on arm in arm. It was really his niece, and now he asked himself if he had not been about to disobey God. For does not God indeed permit love, since He surrounds it visibly with splendor such as this?

And he fled in amaze, almost ashamed, as if he had penetrated into a temple where he had no right to enter.

LOVE

THREE PAGES FROM A SPORTSMAN'S BOOK

I have just read among the general news in one of the papers a drama of passion. He killed her and then he killed himself, so he must have loved her. What matters He or She? Their love alone matters to me, and it does not interest me because it moves me or astonishes me or because it softens me or makes me think, but because it recalls to my mind a remembrance of my youth, a strange recollection of a hunting adventure where Love appeared to me, as the Cross appeared to the early Christians, in the midst of the heavens.

I was born with all the instincts and the senses of primitive man, tempered by the arguments and the restraints of a civilized being. I am passionately fond of shooting, yet the sight of the wounded animal, of the blood on its feathers and on my hands, affects my heart so as almost to make it stop

That year the cold weather set in suddenly toward the end of autumn, and I was invited by one of my cousins, Karl de Rauville, to go with him and shoot ducks on the marshes at daybreak.

My cousin was a jolly fellow of forty with red hair, very stout and bearded, a country gentleman, an amiable semibrute of a happy disposition and endowed with that Gallic wit which makes even mediocrity agreeable. He lived in a house, half farmhouse, half château, situated in a broad valley through which a river ran. The hills right and left were covered with woods, old manorial woods where magnificent trees still remained and where the rarest feathered game in that part of France was to be found. Eagles were shot there occasionally, and birds of passage, such as rarely venture into our overpopulated part of the country, invariably lighted amid these giant oaks as if they knew or recognized some little corner of a primeval forest which had remained there to serve them as a shelter during their short nocturnal halt.

In the valley there were large meadows watered by trenches and separated by hedges; then, further on, the river, which up to that point had been kept between banks, expanded into a vast marsh. That marsh was the best shooting ground I ever saw. It was my cousin's chief care, and he kept it as a preserve. Through the rushes that covered it, and made it rustling and rough, narrow passages had been cut, through which flat-bottomed boats, impelled and steered by poles, passed along silently over dead water, brushing up against the reeds and making the swift fish take refuge in the weeds and the wild fowl, with their pointed black heads, dive suddenly.

I am passionately fond of the water: of the sea, though it is too vast, too full of movement, impossible to hold; of the rivers which are so beautiful but which pass on and flee away; and above all of the marshes, where the whole unknown existence of aquatic animals palpitates. The marsh is an entire world in itself on the world of earth—a different world which has its own life, its settled inhabitants and its passing travelers, its voices, its noises and above all its mystery. Nothing is more impressive, nothing more disquieting, more terrifying occasionally, than a fen. Why should a vague terror hang over these low plains covered with water? Is it the low rustling of the rushes, the strange will-o'-the-wisp lights, the silence which prevails on calm nights, the still mists which hang over the surface like a shroud; or is it the almost inaudible splashing, so slight and so gentle, yet sometimes more terrifying than the cannons of men or the thunders of the skies, which make these marshes resemble countries one has dreamed of, terrible countries holding an unknown and dangerous secret?

No, something else belongs to it—another mystery, perhaps the mystery of the creation itself! For was it not in stagnant and muddy water, amid the heavy humidity of moist land under the heat of the sun, that the first germ of life pulsated and expanded to the day?

I arrived at my cousin's in the evening. It was freezing hard enough to split the stones.

During dinner, in the large room whose sideboards, walls and ceiling were covered with stuffed birds with wings extended or perched on branches to which they were nailed—hawks, herons, owls, nightjars, buzzards, tercels, vultures, falcons— my cousin, who, dressed in a sealskin jacket, himself resembled some strange animal from a cold country, told me what preparations he had made for that same night.

We were to start at half-past three in the morning so as to arrive at the place which he had chosen for our watching place at about half-past four. On that spot a hut had been built of lumps of ice so as to shelter us somewhat from the trying wind which precedes daybreak, a wind so cold as to tear the flesh like a saw, cut it like the blade of a knife, prick it like a poisoned sting, twist it like a pair of pincers and burn it like fire.

My cousin rubbed his hands. "I have never known such a frost," he said; "it is already twelve degrees below zero at six o'clock in the evening."

I threw myself onto my bed immediately after we had finished our meal and went to sleep by the light of a bright fire burning in the grate.

At three o'clock he woke me. In my turn I put on a sheepskin and found my cousin Karl covered with a bearskin. After having each swallowed two cups of scalding coffee, followed by glasses of liqueur brandy, we started, accompanied by a gamekeeper and our dogs, Plongeon and Pierrot.

From the first moment that I got outside I felt chilled to the very marrow. It was one of those nights on which the earth seems dead with cold. The frozen air becomes resisting and palpable, such pain does it cause; no breath of wind moves it, it is fixed and motionless; it bites you, pierces through you, dries you, kills the trees, the plants, the insects, the small birds themselves, who fall from the branches onto the hard ground and become stiff themselves under the grip of the cold.

The moon, which was in her last quarter and was inclining all to one side, seemed fainting in the midst of space, so weak that she was unable to wane, forced to stay up yonder, seized and paralyzed by the severity of the weather. She shed a cold mournful light over the world, that dying and wan light which she gives us every month at the end of her period.

Karl and I walked side by side, our backs bent, our hands in our pockets and our guns under our arms. Our boots, which were wrapped in wool so that we might be able to walk without slipping on the frozen river, made no sound, and I looked at the white vapor which our dogs' breath made.

We were soon on the edge of the marsh and entered one of the lanes of dry rushes which ran through the low forest.

Our elbows, which touched the long ribbonlike leaves, left a slight noise behind us, and I was seized, as I had never been before, by the powerful and singular emotion which marshes cause in me. This one was dead, dead from cold, since we were walking on it in the middle of its population of dried rushes.

Suddenly, at the turn of one of the lanes, I perceived the ice hut which had been constructed to shelter us. I went in, and as we had nearly an hour to wait before the wandering birds would awake I rolled myself up in my rug in order to try and get warm. Then, lying on my back, I began to look at the misshapen moon, which had four horns through the vaguely transparent walls of this polar house. But the frost of the frozen marshes, the cold of these walls, the cold from the firmament penetrated me so terribly that I began to cough. My cousin Karl became uneasy.

"No matter if we do not kill much today," he said. "I do not want you to catch cold; we will light a fire." And he told the gamekeeper to cut some rushes.

We made a pile in the middle of our hut, which had a hole in the middle of the roof to let out the smoke, and when the red flames rose up to the clear crystal blocks they began to melt, gently, imperceptibly, as if they were sweating. Karl, who had remained outside, called out to me: "Come and look here!" I went out of the hut and remained struck with astonishment. Our hut, in the shape of a cone, looked like an enormous diamond with a heart of fire which had been suddenly planted there in the midst of the frozen water of the marsh. And inside we saw two fantastic forms, those of our dogs, who were warming themselves at the fire.

But a peculiar cry, a lost, a wandering cry, passed over our heads, and the light from our hearth showed us the wild birds. Nothing moves one so much as the first clamor of a life which one does not see, which passes through the somber air so quickly and so far off, just before the first streak of a winter's day appears on the horizon. It seems to me, at this glacial hour of dawn, as if that passing cry which is carried away by the wings of a bird is the sigh of a soul from the world!

"Put out the fire," said Karl; "it is getting daylight."

The sky was, in fact, beginning to grow pale, and the flights of ducks made long rapid streaks which were soon obliterated on the sky.

A stream of light burst out into the night; Karl had fired, and the two dogs ran forward.

And then nearly every minute now he, now I, aimed rapidly as soon as the shadow of a flying flock appeared above the rushes. And Pierrot and Plongeon, out of breath but happy, retrieved the bleeding birds whose eyes still, occasionally, looked at us.

The sun had risen, and it was a bright day with a blue sky, and we were thinking of taking our departure, when two birds with extended necks and outstretched wings glided rapidly over our heads. I fired, and one of them fell almost at my feet. It was a teal with a silver breast, and then, in the blue space above me, I heard a voice, the voice of a bird. It was a short, repeated, heart-rending lament; and the bird, the little animal that had been spared, began to turn round in the blue sky over our heads, looking at its dead companion which I was holding in my hand.

Karl was on his knees, his gun to his shoulder, watching it eagerly until it should be within shot. "You have killed the duck," he said, "and the drake will not fly away."

He certainly did not fly away; he circled over our heads continually and continued his cries. Never have any groans of suffering pained me so much as that desolate appeal, as that lamentable reproach of this poor bird which was lost in space.

Occasionally he took flight under the menace of the gun which followed his movements and seemed ready to continue his flight alone, but as he could not make up his mind to this he returned to find his mate.

"Leave her on the ground," Karl said to me; "he will come within shot by and by." And he did indeed come near us, careless of danger, infatuated by his animal love, by his affection for his mate which I had just killed.

Karl fired, and it was as if somebody had cut the string which held the bird suspended. I saw something black descend, and I heard the noise of a fall among the rushes. And Pierrot brought it to me.

I put them—they were already cold—into the same gamebag, and I returned to Paris the same evening.

ON THE RIVER

Last summer I rented a cottage on the banks of the Seine, several miles from Paris, and I used to go out to it every evening. After a while I formed the acquaintance of one of my neighbors, a man between thirty and forty years of age, who really was one of the queerest characters I ever have met. He was an old boating-man, crazy on the subject of boats, and was always either in, or on, or by the water. Surely he must have been born in a boat, and probably he will die in one someday, while taking a last outing.

One evening, as we were walking along the edge of the river, I asked him to tell me about some of his nautical experiences. Immediately his face lighted up, and he became eloquent, almost poetical, for his heart was full of an all-absorbing, irresistible, devouring passion—a love for the river.

"Ah," he said, "how many recollections I have of the river that flows at our feet! You street dwellers have no idea what the river really is. But let a fisherman pronounce the word. To him it means mystery, the unknown, a land of mirage and phantasmagoria, where odd things that have no real existence are seen at night and strange noises are heard; where one trembles without knowing the reason why, as when passing through a cemetery—and indeed the river is a cemetery without graves.

"Land, for a fisherman, has boundaries, but the river, on moonless nights, appears to him unlimited. A sailor doesn't feel the same way about the sea. The sea is often cruel, but it roars and foams; it gives us fair warning; the river is silent and treacherous. It flows stealthily, without a murmur, and the eternal, gentle motion of the water is more awful to me than the big ocean waves.

"Dreamers believe that the deep hides immense lands of blue, where the drowned roll around among the big fish in strange forests or in crystal caves. The river has only black depths, where the dead decay in the slime. But it's beautiful when the sun shines on it and the waters splash softly on the banks covered with whispering reeds.

"In speaking of the ocean the poet says:

> "Oh! what tragic tales of the vast, blue deep—
> The vast blue deep prayerful mothers fear—
> The sad waves tell, when at night, we hear,
> Their ceaseless moanings in our sleep!

Well, I believe that the stories the slender reeds tell one another in their wee, silvery voices are even more appalling than the ghastly tragedies related by the roaring waves.

"But as you have asked me to relate some of my recollections, I will tell you a strange adventure that happened to me here about ten years ago.

"Then, as now, I lived in old Mother Lafon's house, and a chum of mine, Louis Bernet, who since has given up boating, as well as his happy-go-lucky ways, to become a state councilor, was camping out in the village of C——, two miles away. We used to take dinner together every day, either at his place or at mine.

"One evening, as I was returning home alone, feeling rather tired and with difficulty rowing the twelve-foot boat that I always took out at night, I stopped to rest a little while near that point over there formed by reeds, about two hundred yards in front of the railway bridge. The weather was gorgeous; the moon shed a silvery light on the shining river, and the air was soft and still. The calmness of the surroundings tempted me, and I thought how pleasant it would be to fill my pipe here and smoke. The thought was immediately executed, and, laying hold of the anchor, I dropped it overboard. The boat, which was following the stream, slid to the end of the chain and came to a stop; I settled myself aft on a rug, as comfortably as I could. There was not a sound to be heard or a movement to be seen, though sometimes I noticed the almost imperceptible rippling of the water on the banks and watched the highest clumps of reeds, which at times assumed strange shapes that appeared to move.

"The river was perfectly calm, but I was affected by the extraordinary stillness that enveloped me. The frogs and toads, the nocturnal musicians of the swamps, were voiceless. Suddenly at my right a frog croaked. I started; it stopped, and all was silent. I resolved to light my pipe for distraction. But, strange to say, though I was an inveterate smoker I failed to enjoy it, and after a few puffs I grew sick and stopped smoking. Then I began to hum an air, but the sound of my voice depressed me.

"At last I lay down in the boat and watched the sky. For a while I remained quiet, but presently the slight pitching of the boat disturbed me. I felt as if it were swaying to and fro from one side of the river to the other and that an invisible force or being was drawing it slowly to the bottom and then raising it to let it drop again. I was knocked about as if in a storm; I heard strange noises; I jumped up; the water was shining and all was still. Then I knew that my nerves were slightly shaken and decided to leave the river. I pulled on the chain. The boat moved along, but presently I felt some resistance and pulled harder. The anchor refused to come up; it had caught in something at the bottom and remained stuck. I pulled and tugged but to no avail. With the oars I turned the boat around and forced her upstream, in order to alter the position of the anchor. This was all in vain, however, for the anchor did not yield; so in a rage I began to shake at the chain, which wouldn't budge.

"I sat down, discouraged, to ponder over my mishap. It was impossible to break the chain or to separate it from the boat, as it was enormous and was riveted to a piece of wood as big as my arm, but as the weather continued fine, I did not doubt but that some fisherman would come along and rescue me. The accident calmed me so much that I managed to remain quiet and smoke my pipe. I had a bottle of rum with me so I drank two or three glasses of it and began to laugh at my situation. It was so warm that it would not have mattered much had I been obliged to spend all night out of doors.

"Suddenly something jarred slightly against the side of the boat. I started, and a cold sweat broke over me from head to foot. The noise was due to a piece of wood drifting along with the current, but it proved sufficient to disturb my mind, and once more I felt the same strange nervousness creep over me. The anchor remained firm. Exhausted, I seated myself again.

"Meanwhile the river was covering itself with a white mist that lay close to the water, so that when I stood up neither the stream, nor my feet nor the boat were visible to me; I could distinguish only the ends of the reeds and, a little further away, the meadow, ashen in the moonlight, with large black patches formed by groups of Italian poplars reaching toward the sky. I was buried up to my waist in something that looked like a blanket of down of a peculiar whiteness, and all kinds of fantastic visions arose before me. I imagined that someone was trying to crawl into the boat, which I could no longer see, and that the river hidden under the thick fog was full of strange creatures that were swimming all around me. I felt a horrible depression steal over me; my temples throbbed; my heart beat wildly, and, losing all control over myself, I was ready to plunge overboard and swim to safety. But this idea suddenly filled me with horror. I imagined myself lost in the dense mist, floundering about aimlessly among the reeds and water plants, unable to find the banks of the river or the boat, and I felt as if I should certainly be drawn by my feet to the bottom of the dark waters. As I really should have had to swim against the current for at least five hundred yards before reaching a spot where I could safely land, it was nine chances to ten that, being unable to see in the fog, I should drown, although I was a fine swimmer.

"I tried to overcome my dread. I determined not to be afraid, but there was something in me besides my will, and that something was fainthearted. I asked myself what there was to fear; my courageous self railed at the other, the timid one; never before had I so fully realized the opposition that exists between the two beings we have in us, the one willing, the other resisting and each one triumphing in turn. But this foolish and unaccountable fear was growing worse and worse and was becoming positive terror. I remained motionless, with open eyes and straining ears, waiting. For what? I scarcely knew, but it must have been for something terrible. I believe that had a fish suddenly taken it into its head to jump out of the water, as frequently happens, I should have fallen in a dead faint. However, I managed to keep my senses after a violent effort to control myself. I took my bottle of brandy and again raised it to my lips.

"Suddenly I began to shout at the top of my voice, turning successively toward the four points of the horizon. After my throat had become completely paralyzed with shouting I listened. A dog was barking in the distance.

"I drank some more rum and lay down in the bottom of the boat. I remained thus at least one hour, perhaps two, without shutting my eyes, visited by nightmares. I did not dare to sit up, though I had an insane desire to do so; I put it off from second to second, saying: 'Now then, I'll get up,' but I was afraid to move. At last I raised myself with infinite care, as if my life depended on the slightest sound I might make, and peered over the edge of the boat. I was greeted by the most marvelous, stupendous sight that it is possible to imagine. It was a vision of fairyland, one of those phenomena that travelers in distant countries tell us about but that we are unable to believe.

"The mist, which two hours ago hung over the water, had lifted and settled on the banks of the stream. It formed on each side an unbroken hill, six or seven yards in height, that shone in the moonlight with the dazzling whiteness of snow. Nothing could be seen but the flashing river, moving between the two white mountains, and overhead a full moon that illuminated the milky-blue sky.

"All the hosts of the water had awakened; the frogs were croaking dismally, while from time to time a toad sent its short, monotonous and gloomy note to the stars. Strange to say, I was no longer frightened; I was surrounded by a land-scape so utterly unreal that the strangest freaks of nature would not have surprised me at all.

"How long this situation lasted I am unable to tell, for I finally dozed off to sleep. When I awoke the moon was gone and the sky was covered with clouds. The water splashed dismally; the wind was blowing; it was cold and completely dark. I finished the brandy and lay listening to the rustling of the reeds and the murmur of the river. I tried to see but failed to distinguish the boat or even my hands, although I held them close to my eyes. The darkness, however, was slowly decreasing. Suddenly I thought I saw a shadow glide past me. I shouted to it and a voice responded: it was a fisherman. I called to him and told him of my plight. He brought his boat alongside mine, and both began tugging at the chain. The anchor still would not yield. A cold, rainy day was setting in, one of those days that bring disaster and sadness. I perceived another boat, which we hailed. The owner added his strength to ours, and little by little the anchor gave way. It came up very slowly, laden with considerable weight. Finally a black heap appeared and we dragged it into my boat. It was the body of an old woman, with a big stone tied around her neck!"

THE NECKLACE

She was one of those pretty, charming young ladies, born, as if through an error of destiny, into a family of clerks. She had no dowry, no hopes, no means of be-coming known, appreciated, loved and married by a man either rich or distin-guished; and she allowed herself to marry a petty clerk in the office of the Board of Education.

She was simple, not being able to adorn herself, but she was unhappy, as one out of her class; for women belong to no caste, no race, their grace, their beauty and their charm serving them in the place of birth and family. Their inborn finesse, their instinctive elegance, their suppleness of wit, are their only aristocracy, making some daughters of the people the equal of great ladies.

She suffered incessantly, feeling herself born for all delicacies and luxuries. She suffered from the poverty of her apartment, the shabby walls, the worn chairs and the faded stuffs. All these things, which another woman of her station would not have noticed, tortured and angered her. The sight of the little Breton, who made this humble home, awoke in her sad regrets and desperate dreams. She thought of quiet antechambers with their oriental hangings lighted by high bronze torches and of the two great footmen in short trousers who sleep in the large armchairs, made sleepy by the heavy air from the heating apparatus. She thought of large drawing rooms hung in old silks, of graceful pieces of furniture carrying bric-a-brac of inestimable value and of the little perfumed coquettish apartments made for five o'clock chats with most intimate friends, men known and sought after, whose attention all women envied and desired.

When she seated herself for dinner before the round table, where the table-cloth had been used three days, opposite her husband who uncovered the tureen with a delighted air, saying: "Oh! the good potpie! I know nothing better than that," she would think of the elegant dinners, of the shining silver, of the tapestries peopling the walls with ancient personages and rare birds in the midst of fairy forests; she thought of the exquisite food served on marvelous dishes, of the whispered gallantries, listened to with the smile of the Sphinx while eating the rose-colored flesh of the trout or a chicken's wing.

She had neither frocks nor jewels, nothing. And she loved only those things. She felt that she was made for them. She had such a desire to please, to be sought after, to be clever and courted.

She had a rich friend, a schoolmate at the convent, whom she did not like to visit; she suffered so much when she returned. And she wept for whole days from chagrin, from regret, from despair and disappointment.

One evening her husband returned, elated, bearing in his hand a large envelope.

"Here," he said, "here is something for you."

She quickly tore open the wrapper and drew out a printed card on which were inscribed these words:

The Minister of Public Instruction and Madame George Ramponneau ask the honor of M. and Mme Loisel's company Monday evening, January 18, at the Minister's residence.

Instead of being delighted, as her husband had hoped, she threw the invitation spitefully upon the table, murmuring:

"What do you suppose I want with that?"

"But, my dearie, I thought it would make you happy. You never go out, and this is an occasion, and a fine one! I had a great deal of trouble to get it. Everybody wishes one, and it is very select; not many are given to employees. You will see the whole official world there."

She looked at him with an irritated eye and declared impatiently:

"What do you suppose I have to wear to such a thing as that?"

He had not thought of that; he stammered:

"Why, the dress you wear when we go to the theater. It seems very pretty to me."

He was silent, stupefied, in dismay, at the sight of his wife weeping. Two great tears fell slowly from the corners of her eyes toward the corners of her mouth; he stammered:

"What is the matter? What is the matter?"

By a violent effort she had controlled her vexation and responded in a calm voice, wiping her moist cheeks:

"Nothing. Only I have no dress and consequently I cannot go to this affair. Give your card to some colleague whose wife is better fitted out than I."

He was grieved but answered:

"Let us see, Matilda. How much would a suitable costume cost, something that would serve for other occasions, something very simple?"

She reflected for some seconds, making estimates and thinking of a sum that she could ask for without bringing with it an immediate refusal and a frightened exclamation from the economical clerk.

Finally she said in a hesitating voice:

"I cannot tell exactly, but it seems to me that four hundred francs ought to cover it."

He turned a little pale, for he had saved just this sum to buy a gun that he might be able to join some hunting parties the next summer, on the plains at Nanterre, with some friends who went to shoot larks up there on Sunday. Nevertheless, he answered:

"Very well. I will give you four hundred francs. But try to have a pretty dress."

The day of the ball approached, and Mme Loisel seemed sad, disturbed, anxious. Nevertheless, her dress was nearly ready. Her husband said to her one evening:

"What is the matter with you? You have acted strangely for two or three days."

And she responded: "I am vexed not to have a jewel, not one stone, nothing to adorn myself with. I shall have such a poverty-laden look. I would prefer not to go to this party."

He replied: "You can wear some natural flowers. At this season they look very chic. For ten francs you can have two or three magnificent roses."

She was not convinced. "No," she replied, "there is nothing more humiliating than to have a shabby air in the midst of rich women."

Then her husband cried out: "How stupid we are! Go and find your friend Madame Forestier and ask her to lend you her jewels. You are well enough acquainted with her to do this."

She uttered a cry of joy. "It is true!" she said. "I had not thought of that."

The next day she took herself to her friend's house and related her story of distress. Mme Forestier went to her closet with the glass doors, took out a large jewel case, brought it, opened it and said: "Choose, my dear."

She saw at first some bracelets, then a collar of pearls, then a Venetian cross of gold and jewels and of admirable workmanship. She tried the jewels before the glass, hesitated, but could neither decide to take them nor leave them. Then she asked:

"Have you nothing more?"

"Why, yes. Look for yourself. I do not know what will please you."

Suddenly she discovered in a black satin box a superb necklace of diamonds, and her heart beat fast with an immoderate desire. Her hands trembled as she took them up. She placed them about her throat, against her dress, and remained in ecstasy before them. Then she asked in a hesitating voice full of anxiety:

"Could you lend me this? Only this?"

"Why, yes, certainly."

She fell upon the neck of her friend, embraced her with passion, then went away with her treasure.

The day of the ball arrived. Mme Loisel was a great success. She was the prettiest of all, elegant, gracious, smiling and full of joy. All the men noticed her, asked her name and wanted to be presented. All the members of the Cabinet wished to waltz with her. The minister of education paid her some attention.

She danced with enthusiasm, with passion, intoxicated with pleasure, thinking of nothing, in the triumph of her beauty, in the glory of her success, in a kind of cloud of happiness that came of all this homage and all this admiration, of all these awakened desires and this victory so complete and sweet to the heart of woman.

She went home toward four o'clock in the morning. Her husband had been half asleep in one of the little salons since midnight with three other gentlemen whose wives were enjoying themselves very much.

He threw around her shoulders the wraps they had carried for the coming home, modest garments of everyday wear, whose poverty clashed with the elegance of the ball costume. She felt this and wished to hurry away in order not to be noticed by the other women who were wrapping themselves in rich furs.

Loisel detained her. "Wait," said he. "You will catch cold out there. I am going to call a cab."

But she would not listen and descended the steps rapidly. When they were in the street they found no carriage, and they began to seek for one, hailing the coachmen whom they saw at a distance.

They walked along toward the Seine, hopeless and shivering. Finally they found on the dock one of those old nocturnal coupés that one sees in Paris after nightfall, as if they were ashamed of their misery by day.

It took them as far as their door in Martyr Street, and they went wearily up to their apartment. It was all over for her. And on his part he remembered that he would have to be at the office by ten o'clock.

She removed the wraps from her shoulders before the glass for a final view of herself in her glory. Suddenly she uttered a cry. Her necklace was not around her neck.

Her husband, already half undressed, asked: "What is the matter?"

She turned toward him excitedly:

"I have—I have—I no longer have Madame Forestier's necklace."

He arose in dismay: "What! How is that? It is not possible."

And they looked in the folds of the dress, in the folds of the mantle, in the pockets, everywhere. They could not find it.

He asked: "You are sure you still had it when we left the house?"

"Yes, I felt it in the vestibule as we came out."

"But if you had lost it in the street we should have heard it fall. It must be in the cab."

"Yes. It is probable. Did you take the number?"

"No. And you, did you notice what it was?"

"No."

They looked at each other, utterly cast down. Finally Loisel dressed himself again.

"I am going," said he, "over the track where we went on foot, to see if I can find it."

And he went. She remained in her evening gown, not having the force to go to bed, stretched upon a chair, without ambition or thoughts.

Toward seven o'clock her husband returned. He had found nothing.

He went to the police and to the cab offices and put an advertisement in the newspapers, offering a reward; he did everything that afforded them a suspicion of hope.

She waited all day in a state of bewilderment before this frightful disaster. Loisel returned at evening, with his face harrowed and pale, and had discovered nothing.

"It will be necessary," said he, "to write to your friend that you have broken the clasp of the necklace and that you will have it repaired. That will give us time to turn around."

She wrote as he dictated.

At the end of a week they had lost all hope. And Loisel, older by five years, declared:

"We must take measures to replace this jewel."

The next day they took the box which had inclosed it to the jeweler whose name was on the inside. He consulted his books.

"It is not I, madame," said he, "who sold this necklace; I only furnished the casket."

Then they went from jeweler to jeweler, seeking a necklace like the other one, consulting their memories, and ill, both of them, with chagrin and anxiety.

In a shop of the Palais-Royal they found a chaplet of diamonds which seemed to them exactly like the one they had lost. It was valued at forty thousand francs. They could get it for thirty-six thousand.

They begged the jeweler not to sell it for three days. And they made an arrangement by which they might return it for thirty-four thousand francs if they found the other one before the end of February.

Loisel possessed eighteen thousand francs which his father had left him. He borrowed the rest.

He borrowed it, asking for a thousand francs of one, five hundred of another, five louis of this one and three louis of that one. He gave notes, made ruinous promises, took money of usurers and the whole race of lenders. He compromised his whole existence, in fact, risked his signature without even knowing whether he could make it good or not, and, harrassed by anxiety for the future, by the black misery which surrounded him and by the prospect of all physical privations and moral torture, he went to get the new necklace, depositing on the merchant's counter thirty-six thousand francs.

When Mme Loisel took back the jewels to Mme Forestier the latter said to her in a frigid tone:

"You should have returned them to me sooner, for I might have needed them."

She did open the jewel box as her friend feared she would. If she should perceive the substitution what would she think? What should she say? Would she take her for a robber?

Mme Loisel now knew the horrible life of necessity. She did her part, however, completely, heroically. It was necessary to pay this frightful debt. She would pay it. They sent away the maid; they changed their lodgings; they rented some rooms under a mansard roof.

She learned the heavy cares of a household, the odious work of a kitchen. She washed the dishes, using her rosy nails upon the greasy pots and the bottoms of the stewpans. She washed the soiled linen, the chemises and dishcloths, which she hung on the line to dry; she took down the refuse to the street each morning and brought up the water, stopping at each landing to breathe. And, clothed like a woman of the people, she went to the grocer's, the butcher's and the fruiterer's with her basket on her arm, shopping, haggling to the last sou her miserable money."

Every month it was necessary to renew some notes, thus obtaining time, and to pay others.

The husband worked evenings, putting the books of some merchants in order, and nights he often did copying at five sous a page.

And this life lasted for ten years.

At the end of ten years they had restored all, all, with interest of the usurer, and accumulated interest, besides.

Mme Loisel seemed old now. She had become a strong, hard woman, the crude woman of the poor household. Her hair badly dressed, her skirts awry, her hands red, she spoke in a loud tone and washed the floors in large pails of water. But sometimes, when her husband was at the office, she would seat herself before the window and think of that evening party of former times, of that ball where she was so beautiful and so flattered.

How would it have been if she had not lost that necklace? Who knows? Who knows? How singular is life and how full of changes! How small a thing will ruin or save one!

One Sunday, as she was taking a walk in the Champs Elysées to rid herself of the cares of the week, she suddenly perceived a woman walking with a child. It was Mme Forestier, still young, still pretty, still attractive. Mme Loisel was affected. Should she speak to her? Yes, certainly. And now that she had paid, she would tell her all. Why not?

She approached her. "Good morning, Jeanne."

Her friend did not recognize her and was astonished to be so familiarly addressed by this common personage. She stammered:

"But, madame—I do not know—— You must be mistaken."

"No, I am Matilda Loisel."

Her friend uttered a cry of astonishment: "Oh! my poor Matilda! How you have changed."

"Yes, I have had some hard days since I saw you, and some miserable ones— and all because of you."

"Because of me? How is that?"

"You recall the diamond necklace that you loaned me to wear to the minister's ball?"

"Yes, very well."

"Well, I lost it."

"How is that, since you returned it to me?"

"I returned another to you exactly like it. And it has taken us ten years to pay for it. You can understand that it was not easy for us who have nothing. But it is finished, and I am decently content."

Mme Forestier stopped short. She said:

"You say that you bought a diamond necklace to replace mine?"

"Yes. You did not perceive it then? They were just alike."

And she smiled with a proud and simple joy. Mme Forestier was touched and took both her hands as she replied:

"Oh, my poor Matilda! Mine were false. They were not worth over five hundred francs!"

FATHER JUDAS

The whole of this district was amazing, marked with a character of almost religious grandeur and sinister desolation.

In the center of a quiet ring of bare hills, where nothing grew but whins and a rare, freakish oak twisted by the wind, there lay a vast wild tarn, in whose black and stagnant waters shivered thousands of reeds.

A solitary house stood on the banks of this gloomy lake, a small low house inhabited by an old boatman, Father Joseph, who lived on the proceeds of his fishing. Every week he carried his fish down to the neighboring villages and returned with the simple provisions necessary to his existence.

I had the whim to visit this hermit, and he offered to go and raise his nets for me.

I accepted.

His boat was a worm-eaten old tub. Thin and bony, he rowed with a quiet monotonous movement which soothed my spirit, already caught up in the melancholy of the enclosing sky.

Amid this ancient landscape, sitting in this primitive boat, steered by this man from another age, I imagined myself transported to one of the early epochs of the world.

He raised his nets and threw the fish down at his feet with the gestures of a Biblical fisherman. Then he consented to take me to the end of the marsh, and suddenly I saw, on the other bank, a ruin, a gutted hovel, on the wall of which was a cross, a huge red cross: under the last gleams of the setting sun it looked as if it were traced in blood.

"What is that?" I asked.

Instantly the man crossed himself, and answered:

"That is where Judas died."

I was not surprised; I felt as though I might have expected this strange reply.

But I persisted:

"Judas? What Judas?"

He added: "The Wandering Jew, sir."

I begged him to tell me this legend.

But it was better than a legend, it was a piece of history, of almost contemporary history, for Father Joseph had known the man.

Once upon a time the hut was occupied by a tall woman, a beggar of sorts, who lived on public charity.

From whom she had got this hovel, Father Joseph no longer remembered. One night an old man with a white beard, so old that he looked a centenarian twice over and could hardly drag one foot after the other, passed by and asked this poor old woman for alms.

She answered:

"Sit down, Father, all here is for all the world, for it comes from all the world."

(Copyright, 1924, by Alfred A. Knopf, Inc.)

He sat down on a stone in front of the house. He shared the woman's bread, her bed of leaves, and her house.

He never left her. He had finished his travels.

Father Joseph added:

"It was Our Lady the Virgin who permitted that, sir, seeing that a woman had opened her door to Judas."

For this old vagabond was the Wandering Jew.

The countryside did not know this at once, but soon suspected it from the fact that he was always walking, the habit was so strong in him.

Another thing had roused their suspicions. The woman who sheltered the unknown man in her house passed for a Jewess, since she had never been seen at church.

For ten leagues around no one called her anything but "the Jewess."

When the little children of the district saw her coming to beg, they cried out: "Mother, mother, it's the Jewess!"

She and the old man began to wander round the neighborhood, holding their hands out at every door, babbling entreaties after every passer-by. They were seen at all hours of the day, on lonely paths, in village streets, or eating a piece of bread in the shade of a solitary tree, in the fierce heat of noon.

And they began to call the beggar "Father Judas."

One day he brought back in his sack two little live pigs which had been given him at a farm because he had cured the farmer of a sickness.

And soon he stopped begging, wholly occupied in leading his pigs about in search of food, guiding them along the tarn, under the solitary oak trees, and in the little valleys near by. The woman, on the contrary, wandered ceaselessly in quest of alms, but joined him again every evening.

No more than she he went to church, and had never been seen to make the sign of the cross at the wayside shrines. All this caused a deal of gossip.

One night his companion was taken ill with a fever and began to shake like a rag in the wind. He went to the town to get medicine, then shut himself up with her, and for six days no one saw him.

But the curé, having heard that "the Jewess" was about to pass away, came to bring the dying woman the consolations of his religion, and to offer her the last sacrament. Was she a Jewess? He did not know. In any event, he wished to try and save her soul.

He had scarcely knocked at the door when Father Judas appeared on the threshold, panting, his eyes blazing, all his long white beard quivering like running water: he screamed words of blasphemy in an unknown tongue, stretching out his thin arms to hinder the priest's entry.

The curé tried to speak, offered him money and assistance, but the old man continued to revile him, making the gesture of stoning him.

And the priest retreated, pursued by the beggar's curses.

Next day, Father Judas's companion died. He buried her himself in front of the doorway. They were so poor that no one interfered with them.

Once more the man was seen leading his pigs along the tarn and on the hillsides. And several times he began begging for food again. But now he got next to nothing, so many stories were going round about him. And everyone knew in what a fashion he had welcomed the curé.

He disappeared. It was during Holy Week. No uneasiness was felt.

But on Easter Monday some boys and girls who had gone for a walk up to the tarn heard a great noise in the hut. The door was shut; the boys broke it open and the two pigs escaped, leaping like deer. They were never seen again.

They all entered, and saw on the ground a few old rags, the beggar's hat, some bones, some dried blood and remains of flesh in the hollow of a skull.

His pigs had eaten him.

And Father Joseph added:

"It happened on Good Friday, at three in the afternoon."

I asked him: "How do you know?"

He replied: "It cannot be doubted."

I did not try to make him understand how natural it was for the famished beasts to eat their suffering master if he had died suddenly in his hut.

As for the cross on the wall, it appeared one morning, and no one knew what hand had painted it that strange colour.

After that, none doubted that the Wandering Jew had died in that place.

I believed it myself for an hour.

THE INN

Like all the little wooden inns in the higher Alps, tiny auberges situated in the bare and rocky gorges which intersect the white summits of the mountains, the inn of Schwarenbach is a refuge for travelers who are crossing the Gemmi.

It is open six months in the year and is inhabited by the family of Jean Hauser. As soon as the snow begins to fall and fills the valley so as to make the road down to Loèche impassable, the father, with mother, daughter, and the three sons, depart, leaving the house in charge of the old guide, Gaspard Hari, with the young guide, Ulrich Kunsi, and Sam, the great mountain dog.

The two men and the dog remain till spring in their snowy prison, with nothing before their eyes except immense, white slopes of the Balmhorn, surrounded by light, glistening summits and shut up, blocked up and buried by the snow which rises around them, enveloping and almost burying the little house up to the eaves.

It was the day on which the Hauser family were going to return to Loèche, as winter was approaching and the descent was becoming dangerous. Three mules started first, laden with baggage and led by the three sons. Then the mother, Jeanne Hauser, and her daughter Louise mounted a fourth mule and set off in their turn. The father followed them, accompanied by the two men in charge, who were to escort the family as far as the brow of the descent. First of all they skirted the small lake, now frozen over, at the foot of the mass of rocks which stretched in front of the inn; then they followed the valley which was dominated on all sides by snow-covered peaks.

A ray of sunlight glinted into that little white, glistening, frozen desert, illuminating it with a cold and dazzling flame. No living thing appeared among this ocean of hills; there was no stir in that immeasurable solitude, no noise disturbed the profound silence.

By degrees the young guide, Ulrich Kunsi, a tall, long-legged Swiss, left Daddy Hauser and old Gaspard behind in order to catch up with the mule which carried the two women. The younger one looked at him as he approached, as if she would call him with her sad eyes. She was a young, light-haired peasant girl, whose milk-white cheeks and pale hair seemed to have lost their color by long dwelling amid the ice. When Ulrich had caught up with the animal which carried the women he put his hand on the crupper and relaxed his speed. Mother Hauser began to talk to him and enumerated with minutest detail all that he would have to attend to during the winter. It was the first winter he would spend up there, while old Hari had already spent fourteen winters amid the snow at the inn of Schwarenbach.

Ulrich Kunsi listened without appearing to understand and looked incessantly at the girl. From time to time he replied: "Yes, Madame Hauser," but his thoughts seemed far away, and his calm features remained unmoved.

They reached Lake Daube, whose broad, frozen surface reached to the bottom of the valley. On the right the Daubenhorn showed its black mass, rising up in a peak above the enormous moraines of the Lömmeon glacier which soared above the Wildstrubel. As they approached the neck of the Gemmi, where the descent to Loèche begins, the immense horizon of the Alps of the Valais, from which the broad, deep valley of the Rhône separated them, came in view.

In the distance there was a group of white, unequal, flat, or pointed mountain summits which glistened in the sun: the Mischabel with its twin peaks, the huge group of the Weisshorn, the heavy Brünighorn, the lofty and formidable pyramid of Mont Cervin, slayer of men, and the Dent Blanche, that terrible coquette.

Then beneath them, as at the bottom of a terrible abyss, they saw Loèche, its houses looking like grains of sand which had been thrown into that enormous crevice which finishes and closes the Gemmi and which opens down below on to the Rhône.

The mule stopped at the edge of the path which turns and twists continually, zigzagging fantastically and strangely along the steep side of the mountain as far as the almost invisible little village at its feet. The women jumped into the snow, and the two old men joined them.

"Well," Father Hauser said, "good-by and keep up your spirits till next year, my friends," and old Hari replied: "Till next year."

They embraced each other, and then Mme. Hauser in her turn offered her cheek, and the girl did the same. When Ulrich Kunsi's turn came he whispered in Louise's ear:

"Do not forget those up yonder," and she replied: "No," in such a low voice that he guessed what she had said without hearing it.

"Well, adieu," Jean Hauser repeated, "and don't fall in." Then, going before the two women, he commenced the descent, and soon all three disappeared at the first turn in the road, while the two men returned to the inn at Schwarenbach.

They walked slowly side by side without speaking. The parting was over, and they would be alone together for four or five months. Then Gaspard Hari began to relate his life last winter. He had remained with Michael Canol, who was too old now to stand it, for an accident might happen during that long solitude. They had not been dull, however; the only thing was to be resigned to it from the first, and in the end one would find plenty of distraction, games and other means of whiling away the time.

Ulrich Kunsi listened to him with his eyes on the ground, for in thought he was with those who were descending to the village. They soon came in sight of the inn which was scarcely visible, so small did it look, a mere black speck at the foot of that enormous billow of snow. When they opened the door Sam, the great curly dog, began to romp round them.

"Come, my boy," old Gaspard said, "we have no women now, so we must get our own dinner ready. Go and peel the potatoes." And they both sat down on wooden stools and began to put the bread into the soup.

The next morning seemed very long to Kunsi. Old Hari smoked and smoked beside the hearth, while the young man looked out of the window at the snow-covered mountain opposite the house. In the afternoon he went out and, going over the previous day's ground again, he looked for the traces of the mule that had carried the two women; then when he had reached the neck of the Gemmi he laid himself down on his stomach and looked at Loèche.

The village, in its rocky pit, was not yet buried under the snow, although the white masses came quite close to it, balked, however, of their prey by the pine woods which protected the hamlet. From his vantage point the low houses looked like paving stones in a large meadow. Hauser's little daughter was there now in one of those gray-colored houses. In which? Ulrich Kunsi was too far away to be able to make them out separately. How he would have liked to go down while he was yet able!

But the sun had disappeared behind the lofty crest of the Wildstrubel, and the young man returned to the chalet. Daddy Hari was smoking and, when he saw his mate come in, proposed a game of cards to him. They sat down opposite each other for a long time and played the simple game called brisque; then they had supper and went to bed.

The following days were like the first, bright and cold, without any more snow. Old Gaspard spent his afternoons in watching the eagles and other rare birds which ventured on to those frozen heights, while Ulrich journeyed regularly to the neck of the Gemmi to look at the village. In the evening they played at cards, dice or dominoes and lost and won trifling sums, just to create an interest in the game.

One morning Hari, who was up first, called his companion. A moving cloud of white spray, deep and light, was falling on them noiselessly and burying them by degrees under a dark, thick coverlet of foam. This lasted four days and four nights. It was necessary to free the door and the windows, to dig out a passage and to cut steps to get over this frozen powder which a twelve-hour frost had made as hard as the granite of the moraines.

They lived like prisoners, not venturing outside their abode. They had divided their duties and performed them regularly. Ulrich Kunsi undertook the scouring, washing and everything that belonged to cleanliness. He also chopped up the wood, while Gaspard Hari did the cooking and attended to the fire. Their regular and monotonous work was relieved by long games at cards or dice, but they never quarreled and were always calm and placid. They were never even impatient or ill-humored, nor did they ever use hard words, for they had laid in a stock of patience for this wintering on the top of the mountain.

Sometimes old Gaspard took his rifle and went after chamois and occasionally killed one. Then there was a feast in the inn at Schwarenbach, and they reveled in fresh meat. One morning he went out as usual. The thermometer outside marked eighteen degrees of frost, and as the sun had not yet risen, the hunter hoped to surprise the animals at the approaches to the Wildstrubel. Ulrich, being alone, remained in bed until ten o'clock. He was of a sleepy nature but would not have dared to give way like that to his inclination in the presence of the old guide, who was ever an early riser. He breakfasted leisurely with Sam, who also spent his days and nights in sleeping in front of the fire; then he felt low-spirited and even frightened at the solitude and was seized by a longing for his daily game of cards, as one is by the domination of an invincible habit. So he went out to meet his companion who was to return at four o'clock.

The snow had leveled the whole deep valley, filled up the crevasses, obliterated all signs of the two lakes and covered the rocks, so that between the high summits there was nothing but an immense white, regular, dazzling and frozen surface. For three weeks Ulrich had not been to the edge of the precipice from which he had looked down onto the village, and he wanted to go there before climbing the slopes which led to the Wildstrubel. Loèche was now covered by the snow, and the houses could scarcely be distinguished, hidden as they were by that white cloak.

Turning to the right, Ulrich reached the Lömmeon glacier. He strode along with a mountaineer's long swinging pace, striking the snow, which was as hard as a rock, with his iron-shod stick and with piercing eyes looking for the little black, moving speck in the distance on that enormous white expanse.

When he reached the end of the glacier he stopped, and asked himself whether the old man had taken that road, and then he began to walk along the moraines with rapid and uneasy steps. The day was declining; the snow was assuming a rosy tint, and a dry, frozen wind blew in rough gusts over its crystal surface. Ulrich uttered a long, shrill, vibrating call. His voice sped through the deathlike silence in which the mountains were sleeping; it reached into the distance over the profound and motionless waves of glacial foam, like the cry of a bird over the waves of the sea; then it died away, and nothing answered him.

He started off again. The sun had sunk behind the mountaintops, which still were purpled with the reflection from the heavens, but the depths of the valley were becoming gray, and suddenly the young man felt frightened. It seemed to him as if the silence, the cold, the solitude, the wintry death of these mountains, were taking possession of him, were stopping and freezing his blood, making his limbs grow stiff and turning him into a motionless and frozen object, and he began to run rapidly toward the dwelling. The old man, he thought, would have returned during his absence. He had probably taken another road and would, no doubt, be sitting before the fire with a dead chamois at his feet.

He soon came in sight of the inn, but no smoke rose from it. Ulrich ran faster. Opening the door, he met Sam who ran up to him to greet him, but Gaspard Hari had not returned. Kunsi, in his alarm, turned round suddenly, as if he had expected to find his comrade hidden in a corner. Then he relighted the fire and made the soup, hoping every moment to see the old man come in. From time to time he went out to see if Gaspard were not in sight. It was night now, that wan night of the mountain, a livid night, with the crescent moon, yellow and dim, just disappearing behind the mountaintops and shining faintly on the edge of the horizon.

Then the young man went in and sat down to warm his hands and feet, while he pictured to himself every possible sort of accident. Gaspard might have broken a leg, have fallen into a crevasse, have taken a false step and dislocated his ankle. Perhaps he was lying on the snow, overcome and stiff with the cold, in agony of mind, lost and perhaps shouting for help, calling with all his might in the silence of the night.

But where? The mountain was so vast, so rugged, so dangerous in places, especially at that time of the year, that it would have required ten or twenty guides walking for a week in all directions to find a man in that immense space. Ulrich Kunsi, however, made up his mind to set out with Sam if Gaspard did not return by one in the morning, and he made his preparations.

He put provisions for two days into a bag, took his steel climbing irons, tied a long, thin, strong rope round his waist and looked to see that his iron-shod stick and his ax, which served to cut steps in the ice, were in order. Then he waited. The fire was burning on the hearth; the great dog was snoring in front of it, and the clock was ticking in its case of resounding wood, as regularly as a heart beating.

He waited, his ears on the alert for distant sounds, and shivered when the wind blew against the roof and the walls. It struck twelve, and he trembled. Then as he felt frightened and shivery, he put some water on the fire so that he might have hot coffee before starting. When the clock struck one he got up, woke Sam, opened the door and went off in the direction of the Wildstrubel. For five hours he ascended, scaling the rocks by means of his climbing irons, cutting into the ice, advancing continually and occasionally hauling up the dog, who remained below at the foot of some slope that was too steep for him, by means of the rope. About six o'clock he reached one of the summits to which old Gaspard often came after chamois, and he waited till it should be daylight.

The sky was growing pale overhead, and suddenly a strange light, springing, nobody could tell whence, suddenly illuminated the immense ocean of pale mountain peaks which stretched for many leagues around him. It seemed as if this vague brightness arose from the snow itself in order to spread itself into space. By degrees the highest and most distant summits assumed a delicate, fleshlike rose color, and the red sun appeared behind the ponderous giants of the Bernese Alps.

Ulrich Kunsi set off again, walking like a hunter, stooping and looking for any traces and saying to his dog: "Seek old fellow, seek!"

He was descending the mountain now, scanning the depths closely and from time to time shouting, uttering a loud, prolonged, familiar cry which soon died away in that silent vastness. Then he put his ear to the ground to listen. He thought he could distinguish a voice, and so he began to run and shout again. But he heard nothing more and sat down, worn out and in despair. Toward midday he breakfasted and gave Sam, who was as tired as himself, something to eat also; then he recommenced his search.

When evening came he was still walking, having traveled more than thirty miles over the mountains. As he was too far away to return home and too tired to drag himself along any farther, he dug a hole in the snow and crouched in it with his dog under a blanket which he had brought with him. The man and the dog lay side by side, warming themselves one against the other, but frozen to the marrow nevertheless. Ulrich scarcely slept, his mind haunted by visions and his limbs shaking with cold.

Day was breaking when he got up. His legs were as stiff as iron bars, and his spirits so low that he was ready to weep, while his heart was beating so that he almost fell with excitement whenever he thought he heard a noise.

Suddenly he imagined that he also was going to die of cold in the midst of this vast solitude. The terror of such a death roused his energies and gave him renewed vigor. He was descending toward the inn, falling down and getting up again, and followed at a distance by Sam, who was limping on three legs. They did not reach Schwarenbach until four o'clock in the afternoon. The house was empty, and the young man made a fire, had something to eat and went to sleep, so worn out that he did not think of anything more.

He slept for a long time, for a very long time, the unconquerable sleep of exhaustion. But suddenly a voice, a cry, a name: "Ulrich," aroused him from his profound slumber and made him sit up in bed. Had he been dreaming? Was it one of those strange appeals which cross the dreams of disquieted minds? No, he heard it still, that reverberating cry which had entered at his ears and remained in his brain, thrilling him to the tips of his sinewy fingers. Certainly somebody had cried out and called: "Ulrich!" There was somebody there near the house, there could be no doubt of that, and he opened the door and shouted: "Is it you, Gaspard?" with all the strength of his lungs. But there was no reply, no murmur, no groan, nothing. It was quite dark, and the snow looked wan.

The wind had risen, that icy wind which cracks the rocks and leaves nothing alive on those deserted heights. It came in sudden gusts, more parching and more deadly than the burning wind of the desert, and again Ulrich shouted: "Gaspard! Gaspard! Gaspard!" Then he waited again. Everything was silent on the mountain! Then he shook with terror, and with a bound he was inside the inn. He shut and bolted the door and then fell into a chair, trembling all over, for he felt certain that his comrade had called him at the moment of dissolution.

He was certain of that, as certain as one is of conscious life or of taste when eating. Old Gaspard Hari had been dying for two days and three nights somewhere, in some hole in one of those deep, untrodden ravines whose whiteness is more sinister than subterranean darkness. He had been dying for two days and three nights and he had just then died, thinking of his comrade. His soul, almost before it was released, had taken its flight to the inn where Ulrich was sleeping, and it had called him by that terrible and mysterious power which the spirits of the dead possess. That voiceless soul had cried to the worn-out soul of the sleeper; it had uttered its last farewell, or its reproach, or its curse on the man who had not searched carefully enough.

And Ulrich felt that it was there, quite close to him, behind the wall, behind the door which he had just fastened. It was wandering about like a night bird which skims a lighted window with his wings, and the terrified young man was ready to scream with horror. He wanted to run away but did not dare go out; he did not dare and would never dare in the future, for that phantom would remain there day and night round the inn, as long as the old man's body was not recovered and deposited in the consecrated earth of a churchyard.

Daylight came, and Kunsi recovered some of his courage with the return of the bright sun. He prepared his meal, gave his dog some food and then remained motionless on a chair, tortured at heart as he thought of the old man lying on the snow. Then as soon as night once more covered the mountains, new terrors assailed him. He now walked up and down the dark kitchen which was scarcely lighted by the flame of one candle. He walked from one end of it to the other with great strides, listening, listening to hear the terrible cry of the preceding night again break the dreary silence outside. He felt himself a lone, unhappy man, as no man had ever been alone before! Alone in this immense desert of snow, alone five thousand feet above the inhabited earth, above human habitations, above that stirring, noisy, palpitating life, alone under an icy sky! A mad longing impelled him to run away, no matter where, to get down to Loèche by flinging himself over the precipice, but he did not even dare to open the door, as he felt sure that the other, the *dead*, man would bar his road, so that he might not be obliged to remain up there alone.

Toward midnight, tired with walking, worn out by grief and fear, he fell into a doze in his chair, for he was afraid of his bed, as one is of a haunted spot. But suddenly the strident cry of the preceding evening pierced his ears, so shrill that Ulrich stretched out his arms to repulse the ghost, and he fell onto his back with his chair.

Sam, who was awakened by the noise, began to howl as frightened dogs do and trotted all about the house, trying to find out where the danger came from. When he got to the door he sniffed beneath it, smelling vigorously, with his coat bristling and his tail stiff while he growled angrily. Kunsi, who was terrified, jumped up and, holding his chair by one leg, cried: "Don't come in; don't come in, or I shall kill you." And the dog, excited by this threat, barked angrily at that invisible enemy who defied his master's voice. By degrees, however, he quieted down, came back and stretched himself in front of the fire. But he was uneasy and kept his head up and growled between his teeth.

Ulrich, in turn, recovered his senses, but as he felt faint with terror, he went and got a bottle of brandy out of the sideboard and drank off several glasses, one after another, at a gulp. His ideas became vague, his courage revived, and a feverish glow ran through his veins.

He ate scarcely anything the next day and limited himself to alcohol; so he lived for several days, like a drunken brute. As soon as he thought of Gaspard Hari he began to drink again and went on drinking until he fell onto the floor, overcome by intoxication. And there he remained on his face, dead drunk, his limbs benumbed, and snoring with his face to the ground. But scarcely had he digested the maddening and burning liquor than the same cry, "Ulrich," woke him like a bullet piercing his brain, and he got up, still staggering, stretching out his hands to save himself from falling and calling to Sam to help him. And the dog, who appeared to be going mad like his master, rushed to the door, scratched it with his claws and gnawed it with his long white teeth, while the young man, his neck thrown back and his head in the air, drank the brandy in gulps, as if it were cold water, so that it might by and by send his thoughts, his frantic terror and his memory to sleep again.

In three weeks he had consumed all his stock of ardent spirits. But his continual drunkenness only lulled his terror, which awoke more furiously than ever as soon as it was impossible for him to calm it by drinking. His fixed idea which had been intensified by a month of drunkenness and which was continually increasing in his absolute solitude penetrated him like a gimlet. He now walked about his house like a wild beast in its cage, putting his ear to the door to listen if the other were there and defying him through the wall. Then as soon as he dozed, overcome by fatigue, he heard the voice which made him leap to his feet.

At last one night, as cowards do when driven to extremity, he sprang to the door and opened it to see who was calling him and to force him to keep quiet. But such a gust of cold wind blew into his face that it chilled him to the bone. He closed and bolted the door again immediately without noticing that Sam had rushed out. Then as he was shivering with cold, he threw some wood on the fire and sat down in front of it to warm himself. But suddenly he started, for somebody was scratching at the wall and crying. In desperation he called out: "Go away!" but was answered by another long, sorrowful wail.

Then all his remaining senses forsook him from sheer fright. He repeated: "Go away!" and turned round to find some corner in which to hide, while the other person went round the house still crying and rubbing against the wall. Ulrich went to the oak sideboard which was full of plates and dishes and of provisions and, lifting it up with superhuman strength, he dragged it to the door so as to form a barricade. Then piling up all the rest of the furniture, the mattresses, paillasses and chairs, he stopped up the windows as men do when assailed by an enemy.

But the person outside now uttered long, plaintive, mournful groans, to which the young man replied by similar groans, and thus days and nights passed without their ceasing to howl at each other. The one was continually walking round the house and scraped the walls with his nails so vigorously that it seemed as if he wished to destroy them, while the other, inside, followed all his movements, stooping down and holding his ear to the walls and replying to all his appeals with terrible cries. One evening, however, Ulrich heard nothing more, and he sat down, so overcome by fatigue that he went to sleep immediately and awoke in the morning without a thought, without any recollection of what had happened, just as if his head had been emptied during his heavy sleep. But he felt hungry, and he ate.

The winter was over, and the Gemmi pass was practicable again, so the Hauser family started off to return to their inn. As soon as they had reached the top of the ascent the women mounted their mule and spoke about the two men whom they would meet again shortly. They were, indeed, rather surprised that neither of them had come down a few days before, as soon as the road became passable, in order to tell them all about their long winter sojourn. At last, however, they saw the inn, still covered with snow, like a quilt. The door and the windows were closed, but a little smoke was coming out of the chimney, which reassured old Hauser; on going up to the door, however, he saw the skeleton of an animal which had been torn to pieces by the eagles, a large skeleton lying on its side.

They all looked closely at it, and the mother said: "That must be Sam." Then she shouted: "Hi! Gaspard!" A cry from the interior of the house answered her, so sharp a cry that one might have thought some animal uttered it. Old Hauser repeated: "Hi! Gaspard!" and they heard another cry, similar to the first.

Then the three men, the father and the two sons, tried to open the door, but it resisted their efforts. From the empty cow stall they took a beam to serve as a battering-ram and hurled it against the door with all their might. The wood gave way, and the boards flew into splinters; then the house was shaken by a loud voice, and inside, behind the sideboard which was overturned, they saw a man standing upright, his hair falling onto his shoulders and a beard descending to his breast, with shining eyes and nothing but rags to cover him. They did not recognize him, but Louise Hauser exclaimed: "It is Ulrich, Mother." And her mother declared that it was Ulrich, although his hair was white.

He allowed them to go up to him and to touch him, but he did not reply to any of their questions, and they were obliged to take him to Loèche, where the doctors found that he was mad. Nobody ever knew what had become of his companion.

Little Louise Hauser nearly died that summer of decline, which the medical men attributed to the cold air of the mountains.

A HUMBLE DRAMA

Meetings constitute the charm of traveling. Who does not know the joy of coming, five hundred leagues from one's native land, upon a man from Paris, a college friend, or a neighbor in the country? Who has not spent a night, unable to sleep, in the little jingling stagecoach of countries where steam is still unknown, beside a strange young woman, half seen by the gleam of the lantern when she clambered into the carriage at the door of a white house in a little town?

And, when morning comes, and brain and ears are still numbed by the perpetual ringing of the bells and the noisy clatter of the windows, how charming to see your pretty tousled neighbor open her eyes, look about her, arrange her rebellious tresses with the tips of her slim fingers, adjust her hat, feel with her skillful hand whether her corsets have not slipped, whether her person is as it should be, and her skirt not too crushed!

She gives you, too, a single cold, inquisitive glance. Then she settles herself into her corner and seems to have no eyes for anything but the landscape.

In spite of yourself, you stare at her all the time: you think of her the whole time in spite of yourself. What is she? Where has she come from? Where is she going to? In spite of yourself, you sketch a little romance in your mind. She is pretty; she seems charming! Happy man! . . . Life might be exquisite by her side. Who knows? Perhaps she is the woman necessary to our emotions, our dreams, our desires.

And how delicious, too, is the regret with which you see her get off at the gate of a country house. A man is waiting there with two children and two servants. He takes her in his arms and kisses her as he helps her down. She stoops and takes up the little ones who are stretching out their hands, and caresses them lovingly; they go off down a path while the maids take the boxes which the conductor is handing down from the roof.

Good-by! It is finished. You will never see her again. Good-by to the woman who has spent the night at your side. You never knew her, never spoke to her; still you are a little sad when she goes. Good-by!

I have many of these memories of travel, grave and gay.

I was in Auvergne, wandering on foot among those delightful French mountains, not too high, not too wild, but friendly and homely. I had climbed the Sancy, and was just going into a little inn, near a pilgrims' chapel named Notre Dame de Vassivière, when I noticed an old woman, a strange, absurd figure, lunching by herself at the table inside.

She was at least seventy, tall, withered, and angular, with white hair arranged in old-fashioned sausage curls on her temples. She was dressed in the quaint and clumsy style of the wandering Englishwoman, like a person to whom clothes were a matter of complete indifference; she was eating an omelet and drinking water.

She had an odd expression, with restless eyes, the face of one whom life has treated harshly. I stared at her in spite of myself, wondering: "Who is she? What

sort of thing is this woman's life? Why is she wandering all alone in these mountains?"

She paid, then rose to go, readjusting upon her shoulders an extraordinary little
shawl whose two ends hung down over her arms. She took from a corner a long
alpenstock covered with names engraved in the rusty iron, then walked out, straight
and stiff, with the long strides of a postman setting off on his round.

A guide was waiting for her at the door. They moved off. I watched them
descend the valley, along the road indicated by a line of high wooden crosses. She
was taller than her companion and seemed to walk faster than he.

Two hours later I was climbing up the brim of that deep funnel in the heart
of which, in a vast and wonderful green cavity filled with trees, bushes, rocks, and
flowers, lies Lake Pavin, so round that it looks as though it had been made with
a compass, so clear and blue that one might suppose it a flood of azure poured
down from the sky, so charming that one would like to live in a hut on the slope
of the wood overlooking this crater where, quiet and cool, the water sleeps.

She was standing there motionless, gazing at the transparent water lying at the
bottom of the dead volcano. She was standing as though she would peer beneath
it, into its unknown depths, peopled, it is said, by trout of monstrous size who
have devoured all the other fish. As I passed close to her, I fancied that two tears
welled in her eyes. But she walked away with long strides to rejoin her guide, who
had stopped in a tavern at the foot of the rise leading to the lake.

I did not see her again that day.

Next day, as night was falling, I arrived at the castle of Murols. The old fortress,
a giant tower standing upon a peak in the center of a large valley, at the crossing
of three dales, rises towards the sky, brown, crannied, and battered, but round
from its broad circular base to the crumbling turrets of its summit.

It is more impressive than any other ruin in its simple bulk, its majesty, its
ancient air of power and austerity. It stands there solitary, high as a mountain, a
dead queen, but still a queen of the valleys crouching under it. The visitor approaches by a pine-clad slope, enters by a narrow door, and stops at the foot of the
walls, in the first enclosure, high above the whole countryside.

Within are fallen rooms, skeleton staircases, unknown pits, subterranean chambers, oubliettes, walls cleft through the middle, vaults still standing, none knows
how, a maze of stones and crannies where grass grows and animals creep.

I was alone, roaming about this ruin.

Suddenly, behind a piece of wall, I caught sight of a human being, almost a
phantom, as if it were the spirit of the ancient ruined building.

I started in amazement, almost in terror. Then I recognized the old woman I
had already met twice.

She was weeping. She was weeping big tears, and holding her handkerchief in
her hand.

I turned to go. She spoke to me, ashamed at having been discovered unawares.

"Yes, monsieur, I am crying. . . . It does not happen often."

"Excuse me, madame, for having disturbed you," I stammered in confusion, not
knowing what to answer. "Doubtless you are the victim of some misfortune."

"Yes—no," she murmured, "I am like a lost dog."

And putting her handkerchief over her eyes, she burst into sobs.

I took her hands and tried to console her, touched by her very moving grief.

And abruptly she began to tell me her history, as if she did not want to be left alone any longer to bear her grief.

"Oh! . . . Oh! . . . Monsieur. . . . If you knew . . . in what distress I live . . . in what distress. . . .

"I was happy. . . . I have a home . . . away in my own country. I cannot go back again, I shall never go back again, it is too cruel.

"I have a son. . . . It is he! It is he! Children do not know. . . . One has so short a time to live! If I saw him now, I might not know him! How I loved him! How I loved him! Even before he was born, when I felt him stir in my body. And then afterwards. How I embraced him, caressed him, cherished him. If you only knew how many nights I have spent watching him sleep, thinking of him. I was mad about him. He was eight years old when his father sent him away to boarding school. It was all over. He was no longer mine. Oh, my God! He used to come every Sunday, that was all.

"Then he went to college, in Paris. He only came four times a year; and each time I marveled at the changes in him, at finding him grown bigger without having seen him grow. I was robbed of his childhood, his trust, the love he would never have withdrawn from me, all my joy in feeling him grow and become a little man.

"I saw him four times a year! Think of it! At each of his visits his body, his eyes, his movements, his voice, his laugh, were no longer the same, were no longer mine. A child alters so swiftly, and, when you are not there to watch him alter, it is so sad; you will never find him again!

"One year he arrived with down upon his cheeks! He! My son! I was amazed . . . and—would you believe it?—sad. I scarcely dared to kiss him. Was this my baby, my small wee thing with fair curls, my baby of long ago, the darling child I had laid in long clothes upon my knee, who had drunk my milk with his little greedy lips, this tall brown boy who no longer knew how to caress me, who seemed to love me chiefly as a duty, who called me 'Mother' for convention's sake, and who kissed me on the forehead when I longed to crush him in my arms?

"My husband died. Then it was the turn of my parents. Then I lost my two sisters. When Death enters a house, it is as though he hastened to finish as much work as possible so that he need not return for a long time. He leaves but one or two alive to mourn the rest.

"I lived alone. In those days my big son was dutiful enough. I hoped to live and die near him.

"I went to join him, so that we might live together. He had acquired a young man's ways; he made me realize that I worried him. I went away; I was wrong; but I suffered so to feel that I, his mother, was intruding. I went back home.

"I hardly saw him again.

"He married. What joy! At last we were to be united again forever. I should have grandchildren! He had married an English girl who took a dislike to me. Why? Perhaps she felt that I loved him too much?

"I was again forced to go away. I found myself alone. Yes, monsieur.

"Then he went to England. He was going to live with them, his wife's parents. Do you understand? They have him, they have my son for their own! They have stolen him from me! He writes to me every month. At first he used to come and see me. Now he comes no more.

"It is four years since I have seen him. His face was wrinkled and his hair was turning white. Was it possible? This man, this almost old man, my son? My little pink baby of long ago? Doubtless I shall not see him again.

"And I travel all the year. I go to the right and to the left, as you see, all by myself.

"I am like a lost dog. Good-by, monsieur. Do not stay near me, it hurts me to have told you all this."

And, as I walked down the hill again, I turned round, and saw the old woman standing on a cracked wall, gazing at the mountains, the long valley, and Lake Chambon in the distance.

The skirts of her dress and the queer little shawl on her thin shoulders fluttered in the wind like a flag.

A VAGABOND

For more than a month Randel had been walking, seeking for work everywhere. He had left his native place, Ville-Avary, in the department of La Manche because there was no work to be had. He was a journeyman carpenter, twenty-seven years old, a steady fellow and good workman, but for two months he, the eldest son, had been obliged to live on his family, with nothing to do but loaf in the general stoppage of work. Bread was getting scarce with them; the two sisters went out as charwomen but earned little, and he, Jacques Randel, the strongest of them all, did nothing because he had nothing to do and ate the others' bread.

Then he went and inquired at the town hall, and the mayor's secretary told him that he would find work at the labor center. So he started, well provided with papers and certificates and carrying another pair of shoes, a pair of trousers and a shirt in a blue handkerchief at the end of his stick.

He had walked almost without stopping, day and night, along interminable roads, in the sun and rain, without ever reaching that mysterious country where workmen find work. At first he had the fixed idea that he must only work at his own trade, but at every carpenter's shop where he applied he was told that they had just dismissed men on account of work being so slack, and finding himself at the end of his resources, he made up his mind to undertake any job that he might come across on the road. And so by turns he was a navvy, stableman, stone sawyer; he split wood, lopped the branches of trees, dug wells, mixed mortar, tied up fagots, tended goats on a mountain, and all for a few pence, for he only obtained two or three days' work occasionally, by offering himself at a shamefully low price in order to tempt the avarice of employers and peasants.

And now for a week he had found nothing, and he had no money left. He was eating a piece of bread, thanks to the charity of some women from whom he had begged at house doors on the road. It was getting dark, and Jacques Randel, jaded, his legs failing him, his stomach empty and with despair in his heart, was walking barefoot on the grass by the side of the road, for he was taking care of his last pair of shoes, the other pair having already ceased to exist for a long time. It was a Saturday toward the end of autumn. The heavy gray clouds were being driven rapidly among the trees, and one felt that it would rain soon. The country was deserted at that time of the evening and on the eve of Sunday. Here and there in the fields there rose up stacks of thrashed-out corn like huge yellow mush-rooms, and the fields looked bare, as they had already been sown for the next year.

Randel was hungry with the hunger of some wild animal, such a hunger as drives wolves to attack men. Worn-out and weakened with fatigue, he took longer strides so as not to take so many steps, and with heavy head, the blood throbbing in his temples, with red eyes and dry mouth he grasped his stick tightly in his hand with a longing to strike the first passer-by whom he should meet, and who might be going home to supper, with all his force.

He looked at the sides of the road with the image of potatoes dug up and lying on the ground before his eyes; if he had found any he would have gathered some dead wood, made a fire in the ditch and have had a capital supper off the warm, round tubers, which he would first of all have held burning hot in his cold hands. But it was too late in the year, and he would have to gnaw a raw beetroot as he had done the day before, having picked one up in a field.

For the last two days he had spoken aloud as he quickened his steps, under the influence of his thoughts. He had never done much thinking hitherto, as he had given all his mind, all his simple faculties, to his industrial requirements. But now fatigue and this desperate search for work which he could not get, refusals and rebuffs, nights spent in the open air lying on the grass, long fasting, the con-tempt which he knew people with a settled abode felt for a vagabond, the question which he was continually asked: "Why did you not remain at home?" distress at not being able to use his strong arms which he felt so full of vigor, the recollection of his relations who had remained at home and who also had not a halfpenny, filled him by degrees with a rage which was accumulating every day, every hour, every minute, and which now escaped his lips in spite of himself in short growl-ing sentences.

As he stumbled over the stones which rolled beneath his bare feet he grumbled: "How wretched! how miserable! A set of hogs, to let a man die of hunger, a car-penter. A set of hogs—not twopence—not twopence. And now it is raining—a set of hogs!"

He was indignant at the injustice of fate and cast the blame on men, on all men, because Nature, that great, blind mother, is unjust, cruel and perfidious, and he repeated through his clenched teeth, "A set of hogs," as he looked at the thin gray smoke which rose from the roofs, for it was the dinner hour. And without thinking about that other injustice, which is human and which is called robbery and violence, he felt inclined to go into one of those houses to murder the in-habitants and to sit down to table in their stead.

He said to himself: "I have a right to live, and they are letting me die of hunger —and yet I only ask for work—a set of hogs!" And the pain in his limbs, the gnawing in his heart, rose to his head like terrible intoxication and gave rise to this simple thought in his brain: "I have the right to live because I breathe and be-cause the air is the common property of everybody, and so nobody has the right to leave me without bread!"

A thick, fine, icy-cold rain was coming down, and he stopped and murmured: "How miserable! Another month of walking before I get home." He was indeed returning home then, for he saw that he should more easily find work in his native town where he was known—and he did not mind what he did—than on the high-roads where everybody suspected him. As the carpentering business was not going well he would turn day laborer, be a mason's hodman, ditcher, break stones on the road. If he only earned tenpence a day, that would at any rate find him something to eat.

He tied the remains of his last pocket handkerchief round his neck to prevent the cold water from running down his back and chest, but he soon found that it was penetrating the thin material of which his clothes were made, and he glanced round him with the agonized look of a man who does not know where to hide his body and to rest his head and has no place of shelter in the whole world.

Night came on and wrapped the country in obscurity, and in the distance, in a meadow, he saw a dark spot on the grass; it was a cow, and so he got over the ditch by the roadside and went up to her without exactly knowing what he was doing. When he got close to her she raised her great head to him, and he thought: "If I only had a jug I could get a little milk." He looked at the cow, and the cow looked at him, and then suddenly, giving her a violent kick in the side, he said: "Get up!"

The animal got up slowly, letting her heavy udder hang down below her; then the man lay down on his back between the animal's legs and drank for a long time, squeezing the warm swollen teats which tasted of the cow stall with both hands, and drank as long as any milk remained in that living well. But the icy rain began to fall more heavily, and he saw no place of shelter on the whole of that bare plain. He was cold, and he looked at a light which was shining among the trees in the window of a house.

The cow had lain down again, heavily, and he sat down by her side and stroked her head, grateful for the nourishment she had given him. The animal's strong thick breath, which came out of her nostrils like two jets of steam in the evening air, blew onto the workman's face, who said: "You are not cold inside there!" He put his hands onto her chest and under her legs to find some warmth there, and then the idea struck him that he might pass the night against that large, warm stomach. So he found a comfortable place and laid his forehead against the great udder from which he had quenched his thirst just previously, and then, as he was worn out with fatigue, he fell asleep immediately.

He woke up, however, several times, with his back or his stomach half frozen, according as he put one or the other to the animal's flank. Then he turned over to warm and dry that part of his body which had remained exposed to the night air, and he soon went soundly to sleep again.

The crowing of a cock woke him; the day was breaking, it was no longer raining and the sky was bright. The cow was resting with her muzzle on the ground, and he stooped down, resting on his hands, to kiss those wide nostrils of moist flesh and said: "Good-by, my beauty, until next time. You are a nice animal! Good-by." Then he put on his shoes and went off, and for two hours he walked straight on before him, always following the same road, and then he felt so tired that he sat down on the grass. It was broad daylight by that time, and the church bells were ringing; men in blue blouses, women in white caps, some on foot, some in carts, began to pass along the road, going to the neighboring villages to spend Sunday with friends or relations.

A stout peasant came in sight, driving a score of frightened, bleating sheep in front of him whom an active dog kept together, so Randel got up and, raising his cap, he said: "You do not happen to have any work for a man who is dying of hunger?" But the other, giving an angry look at the vagabond, replied: "I have no work for fellows whom I meet on the road."

And the carpenter went back and sat down by the side of the ditch again. He waited there for a long time, watching the country people pass and looking for a kind, compassionate face before he renewed his request, and finally selected a man in an overcoat, whose stomach was adorned with a gold chain. "I have been looking for work," he said, "for the last two months and cannot find any, and I have not a halfpenny in my pocket."

But the semigentleman replied: "You should have read the notice which is stuck up at the beginning of the village: 'Begging is prohibited within the boundaries of this parish.' Let me tell you that I am the mayor, and if you do not get out of here pretty quickly, I shall have you arrested."

Randel, who was getting angry, replied: "Have me arrested if you like; I should prefer it, for at any rate I should not die of hunger." And he went back and sat down by the side of his ditch again, and in about a quarter of an hour two gendarmes appeared on the road. They were walking slowly, side by side, well in sight, glittering in the sun with their shining hats, their yellow accouterments and their metal buttons, as if to frighten evildoers and to put them to flight at a distance. He knew that they were coming after him, but he did not move, for he was seized with a sudden desire to defy them, to be arrested by them and to have his revenge later.

They came on without appearing to have seen him, walking with military steps, heavily, and balancing themselves as if they were doing the goose step; and then suddenly, as they passed him, they noticed him and stopped, looking at him angrily and threateningly. The brigadier came up to him and asked: "What are you doing here?"

"I am resting," the man replied calmly.

"Where do you come from?"

"If I had to tell you all the places I have been to, it would take me more than an hour."

"Where are you going to?"

"To Ville-Avary."

"Where is that?"

"In La Manche."

"Is that where you belong to?"

"It is."

"Why did you leave it?"

"To try for work."

The brigadier turned to his gendarme and said, in the angry voice of a man who is exasperated at last by the same trick: "They all say that, these scamps. I know all about it." And then he continued: "Have you any papers?"

"Yes, I have some."

"Give them to me."

Randel took his papers out of his pocket, his certificates, those poor worn-out dirty papers which were falling to pieces, and gave them to the soldier, who spelled them through, hemming and hawing, and then, having seen that they were all in order, he gave them back to Randel with the dissatisfied look of a man whom someone cleverer than himself has tricked.

After a few moments' further reflection he asked him: "Have you any money on you?"

"No."

"None whatever?"

"None."

"Not even a sou?"

"Not even a soul!"

"How do you live then?"

"On what people give me."

"Then you beg?"

And Randel answered resolutely: "Yes, when I can."

Then the gendarme said: "I have caught you on the highroad in the act of vagabondage and begging, without any resources or trade, and so I command you to come with me."

The carpenter got up and said: "Wherever you please." And placing himself between the two soldiers, even before he had received the order to do so, he added: "Come, lock me up; that will at any rate put a roof over my head when it rains."

And they set off toward the village, whose red tiles could be seen through the leafless trees, a quarter of a league off. Service was just going to begin when they went through the village. The square was full of people who immediately formed two hedges to see the criminal, who was being followed by a crowd of excited children, pass. Male and female peasants looked at the prisoner between the two gendarmes with hatred in their eyes and a longing to throw stones at him, to tear his skin with their nails, to trample him under their feet. They asked each other whether he had committed murder or robbery. The butcher, who was an ex-spahi, declared that he was a deserter. The tobacconist thought that he recognized him as the man who had that very morning passed a bad half-franc off on him, and the ironmonger declared that he was the murderer of Widow Malet, for whom the police had been looking for six months.

In the hall of the municipal council, into which his custodians took him, Randel saw the mayor again, sitting on the magisterial bench with the schoolmaster by his side.

"Ah! ah!" the magistrate exclaimed, "so here you are again, my fellow. I told you I should have you locked up. Well, Brigadier, what is he charged with?"

"He is a vagabond without house or home, Monsieur le Maire, without any resources or money, so he says, who was arrested in the act of begging, but he is provided with good testimonials, and his papers are all in order."

"Show me his papers," the mayor said. He took them, read them, reread, returned them and then said: "Search him"; they searched him but found nothing, and the mayor seemed perplexed and asked the workman:

"What were you doing on the road this morning?"

"I was looking for work."

"Work? On the highroad?"

"How do you expect me to find any if I hide in the woods?"

They looked at each other with the hatred of two wild beasts which belong to different hostile species, and the magistrate continued: "I am going to have you set at liberty, but do not be brought up before me again."

To which the carpenter replied: "I would rather you locked me up; I have had enough running about the country."

But the magistrate replied severely: "Be silent." And then he said to the two gendarmes: "You will conduct this man two hundred yards from the village and let him continue his journey."

"At any rate give me something to eat," the workman said, but the other grew indignant. "It only remains for us to feed you! Ah! ah! ah! that is rather strong!"

But Randel went on firmly: "If you let me nearly die of hunger again, you will force me to commit a crime, and then so much the worse for you other fat fellows."

The mayor had risen, and he repeated: "Take him away immediately, or I shall end by getting angry."

The two gendarmes thereupon seized the carpenter by the arms and dragged him out. He allowed them to do it without resistance, passed through the village again and found himself on the highroad once more; and when the men had accompanied him two hundred yards beyond the village the brigadier said: "Now off with you, and do not let me catch you about here again, for if I do, you will know it."

Randel went off without replying or knowing where he was going. He walked on for a quarter of an hour or twenty minutes, so stupefied that he no longer thought of anything. But suddenly, as he was passing a small house where the window was half open, the smell of the soup and boiled meat stopped him suddenly in front of it, and hunger, fierce, devouring, maddening hunger, seized him and almost drove him against the walls of the house like a wild beast.

He said aloud, in a grumbling voice: "In heaven's name, they must give me some this time." And he began to knock at the door vigorously with his stick, and as nobody came he knocked louder and called out: "Hallo! you people in there, open the door!" And then, as nothing moved, he went up to the window and pushed it open with his hand, and the close warm air of the kitchen, full of the smell of hot soup, meat and cabbage, escaped into the cold outer air, and with a bound the carpenter was in the house. Two covers were laid on the table; no doubt the proprietors of the house, on going to church, had left their dinner on the fire, their nice Sunday boiled beef and vegetable soup, while there was a loaf of new bread on the chimney piece between two bottles which seemed full.

Randel seized the bread first of all and broke it with as much violence as if he were strangling a man, and then he began to eat it voraciously, swallowing great mouthfuls quickly. But almost immediately the smell of the meat attracted him to the fireplace, and having taken off the lid of the saucepan, he plunged a fork into it and brought out a large piece of beef tied with a string. Then he took more cabbage, carrots and onions until his plate was full, and having put it on the table, he sat down before it, cut the meat into four pieces and dined as if he had been at home. When he had eaten nearly all the meat, besides a quantity of vegetables, he felt thirsty and took one of the bottles off the mantelpiece.

Scarcely had he poured the liquor into his glass than he saw it was brandy. So much the better; it was warming, it would instill some fire into his veins, and that would be all right, after being so cold; and he drank some. He found it very good, certainly, for he had grown unaccustomed to it, and he poured himself out another glassful which he drank at two gulps. And then almost immediately he felt quite merry and lighthearted from the effect of the alcohol, just as if some great happiness were flowing through his system.

He continued to eat, but more slowly, dipping his bread into the soup. His skin had become burning, and especially his forehead, where the veins were throbbing. But suddenly the church bells began to ring. Mass was over, and instinct rather than fear, the instinct of prudence which guides all beings and makes them clear-sighted in danger, made the carpenter get up. He put the remains of the loaf into one pocket and the brandy bottle into the other, and he furtively went to the window and looked out into the road. It was still deserted, so he jumped out and set off walking again, but instead of following the highroad he ran across the fields toward a wood which he saw a little way off.

He felt alert, strong, lighthearted, glad of what he had done and so nimble that he sprang over the inclosures of the fields at a single bound, and as soon as he was under the trees he took the bottle out of his pocket again and began to drink once more, swallowing it down as he walked, and then his ideas began to get confused, his eyes grew dim and his legs elastic as springs, and he started singing the old popular song:

> "Oh! how nice, how nice it is,
> To pick the sweet, wild strawberries."

He was now walking on thick, damp, cool moss, and the soft carpet under his feet made him feel absolutely inclined to turn head over heels, as he used to do as a child; so he took a run, turned a somersault, got up and began over again. And between each time he began to sing again:

> "Oh! how nice, how nice it is,
> To pick the sweet, wild strawberries."

Suddenly he found himself on the edge of a sunken road, and in the road he saw a tall girl, a servant who was returning to the village with two pails of milk. He watched, stooping down and with his eyes as bright as those of a dog who scents a quail, but she saw him, raised her head and said: "Was that you singing like that?" He did not reply, however, but jumped down into the road, although it was at least six feet down, and when she saw him suddenly standing in front of her she exclaimed: "Oh dear, how you frightened me!"

But he did not hear her, for he was drunk, he was mad, excited by another requirement which was more imperative than hunger, more feverish than alcohol; by the irresistible fury of the man who has been in want of everything for two months and who is drunk, who is young, ardent and inflamed by all the appetites which nature has implanted in the flesh of vigorous men.

The girl started back from him, frightened at his face, his eyes, his half-open mouth, his outstretched hands, but he seized her by the shoulders and without a word threw her down in the road.

She let her two pails fall, and they rolled over noisily and all the milk was spilt, and then she screamed, but comprehending that it would be of no use to call for help in that lonely spot and seeing that he was not going to make an attempt on her life, she yielded without much difficulty and not very angrily either, for he was a strong, handsome young fellow and really not rough.

When she got up the thought of her overturned pails suddenly filled her with fury, and taking off one of her wooden clogs, she threw it, in her turn, at the man to break his head since he did not pay her for her milk.

But he, mistaking the reason for this sudden violent attack, somewhat sobered and frightened at what he had done, ran off as fast as he could while she threw stones at him, some of which hit him in the back.

He ran for a long time, very long, until he felt more tired than he had ever been before. His legs were so weak that they could scarcely carry him; all his ideas were confused; he lost the recollection of everything and could no longer think about anything, and so he sat down at the foot of a tree and in five minutes was fast asleep. He was soon awakened, however, by a rough shake, and on opening his eyes he saw two cocked hats of polished leather bending over him and the two gendarmes of the morning, who were holding him and binding his arms.

"I knew I should catch you again," said the brigadier jeeringly. But Randel got up without replying. The two men shook him, quite ready to ill-treat him if he made a movement, for he was their prey now; he had become a jailbird, caught by hunters of criminals who would not let him go again.

"Now, start!" the brigadier said, and they set off. It was getting evening, and the autumn twilight was settling, heavy and dark, over the land, and in half an hour they reached the village, where every door was open, for the people had heard what had happened. Peasants and peasant women and girls, excited with anger, as if every man had been robbed and every woman violated, wished to see the wretch brought back, so that they might overwhelm him with abuse. They hooted him from the first house in the village until they reached the mansion house, where the mayor was waiting for him. Eager to avenge himself on this vagabond as soon as he saw him, he cried:

"Ah! my fine fellow! Here we are!" And he rubbed his hands, more pleased than he usually was, and continued: "I said so. I said so the moment I saw him in the road." And then with increased satisfaction:

"Oh! you blackguard! Oh! you dirty blackguard! You will get your twenty years, my fine fellow!"

A LITTLE WALK

When Father Leras, bookkeeper with Messrs Labuze and Company, went out of the store, he stood for some minutes, dazzled by the brilliancy of the setting sun.

He had toiled all day under the yellow light of the gas jet at the end of the rear shop, on the court which was as narrow and deep as a well. The little room in which for forty years he had spent his days was so dark that even in the middle of summer they could hardly dispense with the gas from eleven to three o'clock.

It was always cold and damp there, and the emanations from that sort of hole on which the window looked came into the gloomy room, filling it with an odor moldy and sewerlike.

M. Leras for forty years arrived at eight o'clock in the morning at this prison, and he remained till seven at night, bent over his books, writing with the faithfulness of a good employee.

He now earned three thousand francs per year, having begun with fifteen hundred francs. He had remained unmarried, his means not permitting him to take a wife. And never having enjoyed anything, he did not desire much. From time to time, nevertheless, weary of his monotonous and continuous work, he made a platonic vow:

"Cristi, if I had five thousand livres' income I would enjoy life!"

He had never enjoyed life, never having had more than his monthly salary.

His existence passed without events, without emotion and almost without hopes.

The faculty of dreaming, which everyone has in him, had never developed in the mediocrity of his ambitions.

He had entered the employ of Messrs Labuze and Company at twenty-one years of age. And he had never left it.

In 1856 he had lost his father, then his mother in 1859. And since then he had experienced nothing but a removal, his landlord having wanted to raise his rent.

Every day his morning alarm, exactly at six o'clock, made him jump out of bed by its fearful racket.

Twice, however, this machine had run down, in 1866 and in 1874, without his ever knowing why.

He dressed, made his bed, swept his room, dusted his armchair and the top of his commode. All these duties required an hour and a half.

Then he went out, bought a roll at the Lahure bakery, which had had a dozen different proprietors without losing its name, and he set out for the office, eating the bread on the way.

His whole existence was thus accomplished in the narrow dark office which was adorned with the same wallpaper. He had entered the employ young, an assistant to M. Burment and with the desire of taking his place.

He had taken his place and expected nothing further.

All that harvest of memories which other men make during their lives, the unforeseen events, the sweet or tragic love affairs, the adventurous journeys, all the hazards of a free existence, had been strange to him.

The days, the weeks, the months, the seasons, the years, were all alike. At the same hour every day he rose, left the house, arrived at the office, took his luncheon, went away, dined and retired without ever having interrupted the monotony of the same acts, the same deeds and the same thoughts.

Formerly he looked at his blond mustache and curly hair in the little round glass left by his predecessor. He now looked every morning, before going out, at his white mustache and his bald head in the same glass. Forty years had flown, long and rapid, empty as a day of sorrow and like the long hours of a bad night— forty years, of which nothing remained, not even a memory, not even a misfortune, since the death of his parents, nothing.

That day M. Leras stood dazzled at the street door by the brilliancy of the setting sun, and instead of returning to his house he had the idea of taking a little walk before dinner, something which he did four or five times a year.

He reached the boulevard, where many people were passing under the budding trees. It was an evening in springtime, one of those first soft, warm evenings which stir the heart with the intoxication of life.

M. Leras walked along with his mincing old man's step, with a gaiety in his eye, happy with the unusual joy and the mildness of the air.

He reached the Champs Elysées and proceeded, reanimated by the odors of youth which filled the breeze.

The whole sky glowed, and the Triumphal Arch stood with its dark mass against the shining horizon, like a giant struggling in a conflagration. When he had nearly reached the stupendous monument the old bookkeeper felt hungry and went into a wineshop to dine.

They served him in front of the shop, on the sidewalk, a sheep's-foot stew, a salad and some asparagus, and M. Leras made the best dinner he had made in a long while. He washed down his Brie cheese with a small bottle of good Bordeaux; he drank a cup of coffee, which seldom occurred to him, and finally a tiny glass of brandy.

When he had paid he felt quite lively and brisk, even a little perturbed. He said: "I will continue my walk as far as the entrance to the Bois de Boulogne. It will do me good."

He started. An old air which one of his neighbors used to sing long ago came to his mind:

> When the park grows green and gay
> Then doth my brave lover say,
> "Come with me, my sweet and fair,
> To get a breath of air."

He hummed it continually, beginning it over again and again. Night had fallen upon Paris, a night without wind, a night of sweet calm. M. Leras followed the Avenue du Bois de Boulogne and watched the cabs pass. They came with their bright lamps, one after another, giving a fleeting glimpse of a couple embracing, the woman in light-colored dress and the man clad in black.

It was a long procession of lovers, driving under the starry and sultry sky. They kept arriving continually. They passed, reclining in the carriages, silent, pressed to one another, lost in the hallucination, the emotion of desire, in the excitement of the approaching culmination. The warm darkness seemed full of floating kisses. A sensation of tenderness made the air languishing and stifling. All these embracing people, all these persons intoxicated with the same intention, the same thought, caused a fever around them. All these carriages full of caresses diffused as they passed, as it were, a subtile and disturbing emanation.

M. Leras, a little wearied finally by walking, took a seat on a bench to watch these carriages loaded with love. And almost immediately a woman came near to him and took her place at his side.

"Good evening, my little man," she said.

He did not reply. She continued:

"Don't you want a sweetheart?"

"You are mistaken, madame."

And she took his arm.

"Come, don't be a fool; listen——"

He had risen and gone away, his heart oppressed.

A hundred steps farther on another woman approached him.

"Won't you sit down a moment with me, my fine boy?"

He said to her:

"Why do you lead such a life?"

"Name of God, it isn't always for my pleasure."

He continued in a soft voice:

"Then what compels you?"

She: "Must live, you know." And she went away, singing.

M. Leras stood, astonished. Other women passed near him, similarly accosting him. It seemed to him that something dark was setting upon his head, something heartbreaking. And he seated himself again upon a bench. The carriages kept hurrying by.

"Better not to have come here," he thought. "I am all unsettled."

He began to think on all this love, venal or passionate, on all these kisses, bought or free, which streamed before him.

Love, he hardly knew what it meant. He never had had more than two or three sweethearts in all his life, his means not permitting. And he thought of that life which he had led, so different from the life of all, his life so dark, so dull, so flat, so empty.

There are beings who truly never have any luck. And all at once, as if a thick veil had been lifted, he perceived the misery, the infinite, monotonous misery of his existence: the past misery, the present misery, the future misery, the last days like the first, with nothing before him, nothing behind him, nothing around him, nothing in his heart, nothing anywhere.

The carriages kept passing. He saw appearing and disappearing in the rapid flight of the open fiacre the two beings, silent and embracing. It seemed to him that the whole of humanity was filing before him, intoxicated with joy, with pleasure, with happiness. And he was alone looking on at it, all alone. He would be still alone tomorrow, alone always, alone as no one else is alone.

He rose, took a few steps, and suddenly fatigued, as if he had walked for many miles, he sat down on the next bench.

What was awaiting him? What did he hope for? Nothing. He thought how good it must be when a man is old to find, on getting home, little prattling children there. To grow old is sweet when a person is surrounded by those beings who owe him their life, who love him, who caress him, saying those charming, foolish words which warm the heart and console him for everything.

And thinking of his empty room, neat and sad, where never a person entered but himself, a feeling of distress overwhelmed his soul. It seemed to him that room was more lamentable even than his little office.

No one came to it; no one spoke in it. It was dead, silent, without the echo of a human voice. One would say that the walls had something of the people who lived within, something of their look, their face, their words.

The houses inhabited by happy families are more gay than the habitations of the wretched. His room was empty of memories, like his life, and the thought of going back into that room all alone, of sleeping in his bed, of doing over again all his actions and all his duties of evening terrified him. And as if to put himself farther away from this gloomy lodging and from the moment when he would have to return to it, he rose and, finding all at once the first pathway of the park, he entered a clump of woods to sit upon the grass.

He heard round about him, above him, everywhere, a confused sound, immense and continuous, made of innumerable different voices, near and far, a vague and enormous palpitation of life—the breath of Paris respiring like some colossal being.

The sun already high cast a flood of light upon the Bois de Boulogne. Some carriages began to circulate, and the horseback riders gaily arrived.

A couple were going at a walk through a lonely bridle path.

Suddenly the young woman, raising her eyes, perceived something brown among the branches; she raised her hand, astonished and disturbed.

"Look—what is that?"

Then uttering a scream, she let herself fall into the arms of her companion, who placed her on the ground.

The guards, quickly summoned, unfastened an old man hanging to a branch by his braces.

It was agreed that the deceased had hanged himself the evening before.

The papers found upon him disclosed the fact that he was the bookkeeper for Messrs Labuze and Company and that his name was Leras.

They attributed his death to suicide, for which the cause could not be determined. Perhaps a sudden atack of madness.

THE SISTERS RONDOLI

"No," said Pierre Jouvent, "I do not know Italy. I started to go there twice, but each time I was stopped at the frontier and could not manage to get any further. And yet my two attempts gave me charming ideas of the manners of that beautiful country. Some time or other I must visit its cities, as well as the museums and works of art with which it abounds. I shall make another attempt as soon as possible to cross that impregnable border.

"You don't understand me, so I will explain myself. In 1874 I was seized with desire to see Venice, Florence, Rome, and Naples. I got this whim about the middle of June; then the powerful fever of spring stirs the desire for love and adventure. I am not, as you know, a great traveler; it appears to me a useless and tiresome business. Nights spent in a train, the disturbed slumbers of the railway carriage, with the attendant headaches and stiffness in every limb, the sudden waking in that rolling box, the unwashed feeling, the flying dust and smuts that fill your eyes and hair, the taste of coal in your mouth, and the bad dinners in draughty refreshment rooms, are, in my opinion, a horrible way of beginning a pleasure trip.

"After this introduction by the express, we have the miseries of the hotel; of some great hotel full of people, and yet so empty; the strange room, and the dubious bed! I am most particular about my bed; it is the sanctuary of life. We intrust our nude and fatigued bodies to it that they may be refreshed and rested between soft sheets and feathers.

"There we spend the most delightful hours of our existence, and the hours of love and of sleep. The bed is sacred, and should be respected, venerated, and loved by us as the best and most delightful of our earthly possessions.

"I cannot lift up the sheets of a hotel bed without a shiver of disgust. What took place there the night before? What dirty, odious people have slept in it! I begin, then, to think of all the horrible people with whom one rubs shoulders every day, hideous hunchbacks, people with flabby bodies, with dirty hands that make you wonder what their feet and the rest of their bodies are like. I think of those who exhale a smell of garlic and dirt that is loathsome. I think of the deformed and purulent, of the perspiration emanating from the sick, and of everything that is ugly in man. And all this, perhaps, in the bed in which I am going to sleep! The mere idea of it makes me feel ill as I get in.

"And then the hotel dinners—those dreary table d'hôte dinners in the midst of all sorts of extraordinary people, or else those terrible solitary dinners at a small table in a restaurant, feebly lighted up by a small, cheap candle under a shade.

"Again, those terribly dull evenings in some unknown town! Do you know anything more wretched than when it is getting dark on such an occasion? You go about as if in a dream, looking at faces which you have never seen before and will never see again; listening to people talking about matters which are quite indifferent to you or in a language that perhaps you do not understand. You have a terrible feeling, almost as if you were lost, and you continue to walk on, so as to avoid returning to the hotel, where you would feel still more lost because you are at home, in a home which belongs to anyone who can pay for it. At last you fall into a chair at some well-lit café, whose gilding and lights overwhelm you a thousand times more than the shadows in the streets. Then you feel so abominably lonely sitting in front of the foaming bock which a hurrying waiter has brought, that a kind of madness seizes you, the longing to go somewhere or other, no matter where, as long as you need not remain in front of that marble table and in the dazzling brightness.

"And then, suddenly, you perceive that you are really alone in the world, always and everywhere; and that in places which we know the familiar jostlings give us the illusion only of human brotherhood. At such moments of self-abandonment and somber isolation in distant cities you think broadly, clearly, and profoundly. Then one suddenly sees the whole of life outside the vision of eternal hope, outside the daily deceptions of daily habits and of the expectations of happiness, of which we always dream.

"It is only by going a long distance that we can fully understand how near, short-lived, and empty everything is; only by searching for the unknown do we perceive how commonplace and evanescent everything is; only by wandering over the face of the earth can we understand how small the world is, and how very much alike everywhere.

"How well I know, and how I hate and fear more than anything else those hap-hazard walks through unknown streets. This was the reason why, as nothing would induce me to undertake a tour in Italy by myself, I induced my friend Paul Pavilly to accompany me.

"You know Paul, and how woman is everything, the world, life itself, to him. There are many men like him, to whom existence becomes poetical and idealized by the presence of women. The earth is habitable only because they are there; the sun shines and is warm because it lights them; the air is soft and balmy because it blows upon their skin and ruffles the short hair on their temples, and the moon is charming because it makes them dream, and imparts a languorous charm to love. Every act and action of Paul has woman for its motive; all his thoughts, all his efforts, and hopes are centered on them.

"A poet has branded that type of man:
Je déteste surtout le barde à l'œil humide
Qui regarde une étoile en murmurant un nom,
Et pour qui la nature immense serait vide
S'il ne portrait en croupe ou Lisette ou Ninon.

Ces gens-là sont charmants qui se donnent la peine,
Afin qu'on s'intéresse à ce pauvre univers,
D'attacher des jupons aux arbres de la plaine
Et la cornette blanche au front des coteaux verts.

Certes ils n'ont pas compris tes musiques divines
Eternelle Nature aux frémissantes voix,
Ceux qui ne vont pas seuls par les creuses ravines
Et rêvent d'une femme au bruit que font les bois!

"When I mentioned Italy to Paul he at first absolutely refused to leave Paris. I, however, began to tell him of the adventures I had on my travels. I told him that Italian women are supposed to be charming, and I made him hope for the most refined society at Naples, thanks to certain letters of introduction which I had for a Signore Michael Amoroso whose acquaintances are very useful to travelers. So at last he allowed himself to be persuaded."

II

"We took the express one Thursday evening on the twenty-sixth of June. Hardly anyone goes south at that time of the year, so that we had the carriage to ourselves. Both of us were in a bad temper on leaving Paris, sorry for having yielded to the temptation of this journey, and regretting cool Marly, the beautiful Seine, and our lazy boating excursions, our delightful evenings spent on the banks of the river waiting for nightfall.

"As soon as the train started Paul settled himself comfortably into a corner, and said: 'It is most idiotic to go to this place.' As it was too late for him to change his mind then, I answered: 'Well, you should not have come.'

"He did not answer, and I felt very much inclined to laugh when I saw how furious he looked. He certainly looks like a squirrel, but then every one of us has retained the type of some animal or other as the mark of primal race. How many people have jaws like a bulldog, or heads like goats, rabbits, foxes, horses, or oxen. Paul was a squirrel turned into a man. He had its bright, quick eyes, its hair, its pointed nose, its small, fine, supple, active body, and a certain mysterious resemblance in his general bearing: in fact, a similarity of movements, of gestures, and of bearing which might almost be taken for an atavism.

"At last we both went to sleep—the noisy slumber of the railway carriage, which is broken by horrible cramps in the arms and neck, and by the sudden stopping of the train.

"We woke up as we were going along the Rhône. Soon the continuous noise of the grasshoppers came in through the window, a cry which seems to be the voice of the warm earth, the song of Provence. It seemed to instill into our looks, our breasts, and our souls the light and happy feeling of the South, the smell of the parched earth, of the stony and light soil of the olive tree with its gray-green foliage.

"When the train stopped again a porter ran along the train calling out 'Valence' in a sonorous voice, with an accent that again gave us that taste of Provence which the shrill note of the grasshoppers had already imparted to us.

"Nothing happened till we got to Marseille, where we breakfasted, but when we returned to our carriage we found a woman installed there. Paul, with a delighted look at me, unconsciously gave his short mustache a twirl, and passed his fingers like a comb through his hair, which had become slightly disordered with the night's journey. Then he sat down opposite the newcomer.

"Whenever I happen to see a new face, either while traveling or in society, I become obsessed with the desire to find out what character, mind, and intellectual capacities are hidden beneath those features.

"She was a young and pretty woman, a native of the South of France certainly, with splendid eyes, beautiful, wavy black hair, which was so thick, long, and strong that it seemed almost too heavy for her head. She was dressed with a certain southern bad taste which made her look a little vulgar. Her regular features had none of the grace and finish of the refined races, of that slight delicacy which members of the aristocracy inherit from their birth and which is the hereditary mark of blue blood.

"Her bracelets were too big to be of gold; she wore earrings with white stones too big to be diamonds, and she belonged unmistakably to the people. One would guess that she would talk too loud, and use exaggerated gestures.

"When the train started she remained motionless in her place, in the attitude of a woman who was in a rage. She had not even looked at us.

"Paul began to talk to me, evidently with an eye to effect, trying to attract her attention, as shopkeepers expose their choice wares to catch the notice of passers-by. She did not seem to hear.

"'Toulon! Ten minutes' wait! Refreshment room!' The porter shouted.

"Paul motioned to me to get out, and, as soon as we were on the platform, he said:

"'I wonder who on earth she can be?'

"I began to laugh. 'I am sure I don't know, and I don't in the least care.'

"He was quite excited.

"'She is an uncommonly fresh and pretty girl. What eyes she has, and how cross she looks. She must be dreadfully worried, for she takes no notice of anything.'

"'You will have all your trouble for nothing,' I ventured.

"He began to lose his temper.

"'I am not taking any trouble, my dear fellow. I think her an extremely pretty woman, that is all. If one could only speak to her! But I don't know how to begin. Can't you give me an idea? Can't you guess who she is?'

"'Upon my word, I cannot. I rather think she is some actress who is going to rejoin her company after some love adventure.'

"He seemed quite upset, as if I had said something insulting.

"'What makes you think that? On the contrary, I think she looks most respectable.'

"'Just look at her bracelets,' I said, 'her earrings, and her whole dress. I should not be the least surprised if she were a dancer or a circus rider, but most likely a dancer. Her whole style smacks very much of the theater.'

"He evidently did not like the idea.

"'She is much too young, I am sure; why, she is hardly twenty.'

"'Well,' I replied, 'there are many things which one can do before one is twenty; dancing and reciting are among them, without counting another business which is, perhaps, her sole occupation.'

"'Take your seats for Nice, Ventimiglia,' the guards and porters called out.

"We got in; our fellow passenger was eating an orange. She certainly was not refined. She had spread her handkerchief on her knees, and the way in which she tore off the peel and opened her mouth to put in the pieces, and then spat the pips out of the window, showed that her education had been decidedly vulgar. She seemed more unapproachable than ever, and she swallowed the fruit with an exceedingly comic air of rage.

"Paul devoured her with his eyes and tried to attract her attention and excite her curiosity, but in spite of his talk and of the manner in which he brought in well-known names, she did not pay the least attention to him.

"After passing Fréjus and St. Raphael, the train passes through a veritable garden, a paradise of roses, of groves of oranges and lemons covered with fruit and flowers at the same time. That delightful coast from Marseille to Genoa is a kingdom of perfumes in a land of flowers.

"June is the time to see it, when in every narrow valley and on every slope the most exquisite flowers are growing luxuriantly. And the roses! fields, hedges, groves of roses! They climb up the walls, blossom on the roofs, hang from the trees, peep out from among the bushes; they are white, red, yellow, large and small, ordinary and quiet, with a simple dress, or full in brilliant and heavy toilettes. Their powerful perfume makes the air heavy and relaxing, while the still more penetrating, lasting odor of the orange blossoms sweetens the atmosphere, till it might almost be called a sugarplum for the olfactory nerve.

"The shore, with its brown rocks, was bathed by the motionless Mediterranean. The hot summer sun stretched like a fiery cloth over the mountains, over the long expanses of sand, and over the hard, set blue sea. The train went on, through the tunnels, along the slopes, above the water, on straight, wall-like viaducts, and a soft, vague, saltish smell came up, a smell of drying seaweed, mingled at times with the strong, heavy perfume of the flowers.

"But Paul neither saw, nor looked at, nor smelled anything, for our fellow traveler engrossed all his attention.

"When we got to Cannes, as he wished to speak to me, he signed to me to get out again, and as soon as I had done so he took me by the arm.

" 'Do you know she is really charming. Just look at her eyes; and I never saw anything like her hair.'

" 'Don't excite yourself,' I replied. 'Tackle her, if you have any intentions that way. She does not look impregnable, I fancy, although she appears to be a little bit grumpy.'

" 'Why don't you speak to her?' he said. 'I don't know what to say, for I am always terribly stupid at first; I can never make advances to a woman in the street. I follow them, go round and round them, quite close to them, but I never know what to say at first. I only once tried to enter into conversation with a woman in that way. As I clearly saw that she was waiting for me to make overtures, and as I felt bound to say something, I stammered out, "I hope you are quite well, madame?" She laughed in my face, and I made my escape.'

"I promised Paul to do all I could to bring about a conversation, and when we had taken our places again, I politely asked our neighbor:

" 'Have you any objection to the smell of tobacco, madame?'

"She merely replied: 'Non capisco.'

"So she was an Italian! I felt an absurd inclination to laugh. As Paul did not understand a word of that language, I was obliged to act as his interpreter, so I said in Italian:

" 'I asked you, madame, whether you had any objection to tobacco smoke?'

"With an angry look, she replied, 'Che mi fa?'

"She had neither turned her head nor looked at me, and I really did not know whether to take this. What does it matter to me, for an authorization, a refusal, a real sign of indifference, or for a mere 'Leave me alone.'

" 'Madame,' I replied, 'if you mind the smell of tobacco in the least——'

"She again said, '*Mica,*' in a tone of voice which seemed to mean, 'I wish to goodness you would leave me alone!' It was, however, a kind of permission, so I said to Paul:

" 'You can smoke.'

"He looked at me in that curious sort of way that people have when they try to understand others who are talking in a strange language before them, and asked me:

" 'What did you say to her?'

" 'I asked if we might smoke, and she said we might do whatever we liked.'

"Whereupon I lighted my cigar.

" 'Did not she say anything more?'

" 'If you had counted her words you would have noticed that she used exactly six, two of which gave me to understand that she knew no French, so four remained, and a lot cannot be said in four words.'

"Paul seemed quite unhappy, disappointed, and at sea.

"But suddenly the Italian asked me, in that tone of discontent which seemed habitual to her, 'Do you know at what time we shall get to Genoa?'

" 'At eleven o'clock,' I replied. Then after a moment I went on:

" 'My friend and I are also going to Genoa, and if we can be of any service to you, we shall be very happy.' As she did not answer, I insisted: 'You are alone and if we can be of service . . .' But she interrupted with such a '*mica,*' that I did not venture on another word.

" 'What did she say?' Paul asked.

" 'She said that she thought you were charming.'

"But he was in no humor for joking, and begged me, dryly, not to make fun of him, so I translated her question and my polite offer, which had been so pertly rejected.

"Then he became as agitated as a squirrel in a cage.

" 'If we only knew,' he said, 'what hotel she was going to, we would go to the same. Try and find out, so as to have another opportunity for making her speak.'

"It was not particularly easy, and I did not know what pretext to invent, anxious as I was to make the acquaintance of this unapproachable person.

"We passed Nice, Monaco, Mentone, and the train stopped at the frontier for the examination of luggage.

"Although I hate those badly brought-up people who breakfast and dine in railway carriages, I went and bought a quantity of good things to make one last attack on her by their means. I felt sure that this girl must, ordinarily, be by no means inaccessible. Something had put her out and made her irritable, but very little would suffice, a mere word or some agreeable offer, make her unbend, to decide her and overcome her.

"We started again, and we three were still alone. I spread my eatables out on the seat. I cut up the fowl, put the slices of ham neatly on a piece of paper, and then carefully laid out our dessert, the strawberries, plums, cherries, and cakes, close to the girl.

"When she saw that we were going to eat she took a piece of chocolate and two small rolls out of her pocket and began to eat them with her beautiful sharp teeth.

" 'Ask her to have some of ours,' Paul said in a whisper.

" 'That is exactly what I want to do, but it is rather a difficult matter.'

"As she, however, glanced from time to time at our provisions, I felt sure that she would still be hungry when she had finished what she had. So as soon as her frugal meal was over, I said to her:

" 'It would be very kind of you if you would take some of this fruit.'

"Again she said 'Mica,' but less crossly than before.

" 'Well, then,' I said, 'may I offer you a little wine? I see you have not drunk anything. It is Italian wine, and as we are now in your own country, we should be very pleased to see such a pretty Italian mouth accept the offer of its French neighbors.'

"She shook her head slightly, evidently wishing to refuse, but very desirous of accepting, and her 'mica' this time was almost polite. I took the bottle, which was covered with straw in the Italian fashion, and filling the glass I offered it to her.

" 'Please drink it,' I said, 'to bid us welcome to your country.'

"She took the glass with her usual look, and emptied it at a draught, like a woman tormented with thirst, and then gave it back to me without even saying 'Thank you.'

"Then I offered her the cherries. 'Please take some,' I said; 'we shall be so pleased if you will.'

"Out of her corner she looked at all the fruit spread out beside her, and said so rapidly that I could scarcely follow her: 'A me non piacciono nè le ciliegie nè le susine; amo soltanto le fragole.'

" 'What does she say?' Paul asked.

" 'That she does not care for cherries or plums, but only for strawberries.'

"I put a newspaper full of wild strawberries on her lap, and she ate them quickly, throwing them into her mouth from some distance in a coquettish and charming manner.

"When she had finished the little red heap which we had seen rapidly diminishing, melting and disappearing under the rapid action of her hands, I asked her:

" 'What may I offer you now?'

" 'I will take a little chicken,' she replied.

"She certainly devoured half of it, tearing it to pieces with the rapid movements of her jaws like some carnivorous animal. Then she made up her mind to have some cherries, which she 'did not like,' then some plums, then some little cakes. Then she said, 'I have had enough,' and sat back in her corner.

"I was much amused, and tried to make her eat more, pressing her, in fact, till she suddenly got in a rage again, and flung such a furious 'mica' at me, that I would no longer run the risk of spoiling her digestion.

"I turned to my friend. 'My poor Paul,' I said, 'I am afraid we have had our trouble for nothing.'

"Night was coming on, one of those hot summer nights which extend their warm shade over the burning and exhausted earth. Here and there, in the distance by the sea, over capes and promontories bright stars began to shine on the dark horizon, which I was, at times, almost inclined to confound with lighthouses.

"The scent of the orange trees became more penetrating, and we breathed with delight, distending our lungs to inhale it more deeply. The balmy air was soft, delicious, almost divine.

"Suddenly I noticed something like a shower of stars under the dense shade of the trees along the line where it was quite dark. It might have been taken for drops of light, leaping, flying, playing and running among the leaves, or for small stars fallen from the skies in order to have an excursion on the earth; but they were only fireflies dancing a strange fiery ballet in the perfumed air.

"One of them happened to come into our carriage and shed its intermittent light, which seemed to be extinguished one moment and to be burning the next. I covered the carriage lamp with its blue shade and watched the strange fly careering about in its fiery flight. Suddenly it settled on the dark hair of our neighbor, who was dozing after dinner. Paul seemed delighted, his eyes fixed on the bright, sparkling spot which looked like a living jewel on the forehead of the sleeping woman.

"The Italian awoke about eleven o'clock, with the bright insect still in her hair. When I saw her move, I said: 'We are just getting to Genoa, madame,' and she murmured, without answering me, as if possessed by some obstinate and embarrassing thought:

" 'What am I going to do, I wonder?'

"And then she suddenly asked:

" 'Would you like me to come with you?'

"I was so taken aback that I really did not understand her.

" 'With us? What do you mean?'

"She repeated, looking more and more furious:

" 'Would you like me to go with you now, as soon as we get out of the train?'

" 'I am quite willing; but where do you want to go to? Where shall I take you to?'

"She shrugged her shoulders with an air of supreme indifference.

" 'Wherever you like; what does it matter to me?' She repeated her 'Che mi fa?' twice.

" 'But we are going to the hotel.'

" 'Very well, let us all go to the hotel,' she said, in a contemptuous voice.

"I turned to Paul, and said:

" 'She wants to know if we should like her to come with us.'

"My friend's utter surprise restored my self-possession. He stammered:

" 'With us? Where to? What for? How?'

" 'I don't know, but she made this strange proposal to me in a most irritable voice. I told her that we were going to the hotel, and she said: "Very well, let us all go there!" I suppose she is without a halfpenny. She certainly has a very strange way of making acquaintances.'

"Paul, who was very much excited, exclaimed:

" 'I am quite agreeable. Tell her that we will take her wherever she likes.' Then, after a moment's hesitation, he said uneasily:

" 'We must know, however, with whom she wants to go—with you or with me?'

"I turned to the Italian, who did not even seem to be listening to us, and said:

" 'We shall be very happy to take you with us, but my friend wants to know whether you will take my arm or his?'

"She opened her black eyes wide with vague surprise, and said, 'Che mi fa?'

"I was obliged to explain myself. 'In Italy, I believe when a man looks after a woman, fulfills all her wishes, and satisfies all her caprices, he is called a patito. Which of us two will you take for your patito?'

"Without the slightest hesitation she replied:

" 'You!'

"I turned to Paul. 'You see, my friend, she chooses me; you have no luck.'

" 'All the better for you,' he replied, in a rage. Then, after thinking for a few moments, he went on:

" 'Do you really care about taking this creature with you? She will spoil our journey. What are we to do with this woman, who looks like I don't know what? They will not take us in at any decent hotel.'

"I, however, was just beginning to find the Italian much nicer than I had thought her at first, and I was now very anxious to take her with us. The idea delighted me. I already felt those little shivers which the expectation of a night of love sends through the veins.

"I replied, 'My dear fellow, we have accepted, and it is too late to recede. You were the first to advise me to say yes.'

" 'It is very stupid,' he growled, 'but do as you please.'

"The train whistled, slackened speed, and we ran into the station.

"I got out of the carriage, and offered my new companion my hand. She jumped out lightly, and I gave her my arm, which she took with an air of seeming repugnance. As soon as we had claimed our luggage we started off into the town, Paul walking in complete silence, with a nervous step.

" 'To what hotel shall we go?' I asked him. 'It may be difficult to get into the City of Paris Hotel with a woman, especially with this Italian.'

"Paul interrupted me: 'Yes, with an Italian who looks more like a strumpet than a duchess. However, that is no business of mine. Do just as you please.'

"I was in a state of perplexity. I had written to the City of Paris to reserve our rooms, and now I did not know what to do.

"Two commissionnaires followed us with our luggage. I continued: 'You might as well go first, and say that we are coming; and give the landlord to understand that I have a——a friend with me, so that we should like rooms quite by themselves for us three, so as not to be brought in contact with other travelers. He will understand, and we will decide according to his answer.'

"But Paul growled, 'Thank you; such commissions and such a role do not suit me by any means. I did not come here to get ready your apartments or to minister to your pleasures.'

"But I was insistent: 'Look here, don't be angry. It is surely far better to go to a good hotel than to a bad one, and it is not difficult to ask the landlord for three separate bedrooms and a dining room.'

"I put a stress on three, and that decided him.

"He went on first, and I saw him enter the great doorway of a fine hotel, while I remained on the other side of the street dragging along my Italian, who did not say a word, and followed by the porters with the luggage.

"Paul came back at last, looking as dissatisfied as my companion.

" 'That is settled,' he said, 'and they will take us in; but there are only two bedrooms. You must settle it as you can.'

"I followed him, rather ashamed of going in with such a strange companion.

"There were two bedrooms separated by a small sitting room. I ordered a cold supper, and then I turned to the Italian with a perplexed look.

" 'We have only been able to get two rooms, so you must choose which you like.'

"She replied with her eternal 'Che mi fa?' I thereupon took up her little black wooden box, just like those which servants use, and took it into the room on the right, which I had chosen for her—for us. A bit of paper was fastened on to the box, on which was written, 'Mademoiselle Francesca Rondoli, Genoa.'

" 'Your name is Francesca?' I asked, and she nodded her head, without replying.

" 'We shall have supper directly,' I continued. 'Meanwhile, I daresay you would like to freshen yourself up a bit!'

"She answered with a 'mica,' a phrase which she employed just as frequently as 'Che mi fa?' but I went on: 'It is always pleasant after a journey.'

"Then I suddenly remembered that she had not, perhaps, the necessary objects, for she appeared to me in a very singular position, as if she had just escaped from some disagreeable adventure, and I brought her my dressing case.

"I put out all the little instruments for cleanliness and comfort which it contained: a nailbrush, a new toothbrush—for I always carry a selection of them about with me—my nail scissors, a nail file, and sponges. I uncorked a bottle of Eau de Cologne, one of lavender water, and a little bottle of new-mown hay, so that she might have a choice. Then I opened my powder box, and put out the powder puff, put my fine towels over the water jug, and placed a piece of new soap near the basin.

"She watched my movements with a vexed look in her wide-open eyes, without appearing either surprised or pleased by my forethought.

" 'Here is all that you require,' I then said: 'I will tell you when supper is ready.'

"When I returned to the sitting room I found that Paul had taken possession of the other room and had shut himself in, so I sat down to wait.

"A waiter went back and forth, bringing plates and glasses. He laid the table slowly, then put a cold fowl on it, and told me that all was ready.

"I knocked gently at Mademoiselle Rondoli's door. 'Come in,' she said, and when I did so I was struck by a strong, heavy smell of perfumes, as if I were in a hairdresser's shop.

"The Italian was sitting on her box in an attitude either of thoughtful discontent or absent-mindedness. The towel was still folded over the water jug, which was quite full, and the soap, untouched and dry, was lying beside the empty basin; but one would have thought that the young woman had drunk half of the bottles of scent. The Eau de Cologne, however, had been spared, as only about a third of it had gone; but to make up for that she had used a surprising amount of lavender water and new-mown hay. A cloud of violet powder, a vague white mist, seemed still to be floating in the air, from the effects of her over-powdering her face and neck. It seemed to cover her eyelashes, eyebrows, and the hair on her temples like snow, while her cheeks were plastered with it, and layers of it covered her nostrils, the corners of her eyes, and her chin.

"When she got up she exhaled such a strong odor of scent that it almost made me feel faint.

"When we sat down to supper I found that Paul was in a most execrable temper, and I could get nothing out of him but words of blame and irritation and disagreeable compliments.

"Mademoiselle Francesca ate like an ogre, and as soon as she had finished her meal she threw herself upon the sofa. As for me, I saw the decisive moment approaching for settling how we were to apportion the rooms. I determined to take the bull by the horns, and sitting down by the Italian I gallantly kissed her hand.

"She half opened her tired eyes and looked at me, sleepy and discontented.

" 'As we have only two bedrooms, will you allow me to share yours with you?'

" 'Do just as you like,' she said. 'It is all the same to me. *Che mi fa?*'

"Her indifference vexed me.

" 'But you are sure you do not mind my being in your room with you?' I said.

" 'It is all the same to me; do just as you like.'

" 'Should you like to go to bed at once?'

" 'Yes; I am very sleepy.'

"She got up, yawned, gave Paul her hand, who took it with a furious look, and I lighted her into our room. A disquieting feeling haunted me. 'Here is all you want,' I said again.

"This time I took care to pour half the water into the basin, and to put a towel near the soap.

"Then I went back to Paul. As soon as I got into the room, he said, 'You have got a nice sort of a creature there!' and I answered, laughing, 'My dear friend, don't speak ill of sour grapes,' and he replied, ill-temperedly:

" 'Just take care how this ends, my good fellow.'

"I almost trembled with that feeling of fear which assails us after some suspicious love escapade—that fear which spoils our pleasant meetings, our unexpected caresses, our chance kisses. However, I put a bold face on the matter. 'At any rate, the girl is no adventuress.'

"But the fellow had me in his power; he had seen the shadow of my anxiety on my face.

" 'What do you know about her? You really astonish me. You pick up an Italian woman traveling alone in the train, and she volunteers, with most singular cynicism, to go and be your mistress in any old hotel. You take her with you, and then you declare that she is not a tart! And you persuade yourself that you are not running more risk than if you were to go and spend the night with a woman who had smallpox.'

"He laughed with an unpleasant and angry laugh. I sat down, a prey to uneasiness. What was I to do, for he was right after all? And a struggle began within me, between desire and fear.

"He went on: 'Do as you like, I have warned you, so do not complain of the consequences.'

"But I saw such ironical gaiety in his eyes, such a delight in his revenge; he made fun of me so good-naturedly, that I did not hesitate any longer. I gave him my hand, and said, 'Good night. You know the old saying: "A victory without peril is a triumph without glory,' and upon my word, the victory is worth the danger.'

"And with a firm step I went into Francesca's room.

"I stopped short at the door in surprise and astonishment. She was already asleep, quite naked on the bed. Sleep had overcome her when she had finished undressing, and she was reposing in the charming attitude of one of Titian's women.

"It seemed as if she had lain down from sheer fatigue in order to take off her stockings, for they were lying on the bed. Then she had thought of something pleasant, no doubt, for she had waited to finish her reverie before moving, and then, closing her eyes, she had lost consciousness. A nightgown, embroidered about the neck such as one buys in cheap, ready-made shops, a beginner's luxury was lying on a chair.

"She was charming, young, firm, and fresh.

"What is prettier than a woman asleep? The body with its soft contours, whose every curve is a temptation, whose plump softness stirs the senses, seems to have been created for the repose of the bed. Only when it is lying upon the sheets does one get the full value of that undulating line which curves in at the waist, curves out at the hips, and then runs down the charming outline of the leg, ending at the point of the foot. I was on the point of forgetting my friend's prudent counsels, but suddenly turning to the washstand I saw everything as I had left it, and I sat down, anxious, and a prey to irresolution.

"I remained thus for a long time, not able to make up my mind what to do. Retreat was impossible, and I must either pass the night on a chair, or go to bed myself at my own risk and peril.

"I had no thoughts of sleeping either here or there, for my head was too excited and my eyes too occupied.

"I stirred incessantly, feverish, uncomfortable, enervated. Then I began to reason with myself, certainly with a view to capitulation: 'If I lie down that does not bind me to anything, and I shall certainly be more comfortable on a mattress than on a chair.'

"I undressed slowly, and then, stepping over the sleeping girl, I stretched myself out against the wall, turning my back on temptation.

"In this position I remained for a long time without going to sleep, when suddenly my neighbor awoke. She opened her eyes, looked astonished, and still discontented; then seeing that she had nothing on, she got up and calmly put on her nightgown with as much indifference as if I had not been present.

"Then . . . I seized the opportunity, but this did not appear to disturb her at all. She immediately went quietly to sleep again, with her head resting on her right arm. And I began to meditate on the weakness and folly of human nature. Then I went to sleep also.

"She got up early, like a woman who is used to work in the morning. She woke me up by doing so, and I watched her through my half-closed eyelids.

"She came and went without hurrying herself, as if she were astonished at having nothing to do. At last she went to the washstand, and in a moment she emptied all the scent that remained in my bottles. She certainly also used some water, but very little.

"When she was quite dressed she sat down on her box again, and holding one knee between her hands, seemed to be thinking.

"Then I pretended to notice her, and said:

" 'Good morning, Francesca.'

"Without seeming in at all a better temper than the previous night, she murmured, 'Good morning.'

"When I asked her whether she had slept well, she nodded 'Yes,' and jumping out of bed, I went and kissed her.

"She turned her face toward me like a child who is being kissed against its will; but I took her tenderly in my arms (the wine being poured out, I would have been very stupid not to drink any more of it). Gently I put my lips on her large eyes, which she closed with evident distaste under my kisses, on her fresh cheeks and full lips, which she turned away.

" 'You don't seem to like being kissed,' I said to her.

" 'Mica' was her only answer.

"I sat down on the trunk by her side, and, passing my arm through hers, I said: 'Mica! mica! mica! in reply to everything. I shall call you Mademoiselle Mica, I think.'

"For the first time I fancied I saw the shadow of a smile on her lips, but it passed by so quickly that I may have been mistaken.

" 'But if you never say anything but "mica" I shall not know what to do to try and please you. Let us see; what shall we do today?'

"She hesitated a moment as if some fancy had flitted through her head, and then she said carelessly: 'It is all the same to me; whatever you like.'

" 'Very well, Mademoiselle Mica, we will get a carriage and go for a drive.'

" 'As you please,' she said.

"Paul was waiting for us in the dining room, looking as bored as third parties generally do in love affairs. I assumed a delighted air, and shook hands with him with triumphant energy.

" 'What are you thinking of doing?' he asked.

" 'First of all we will go and see a little of the town, and then we might take a carriage, for a drive in the neighborhood.'

"We breakfasted in silence and then started on foot to visit the museums. We went through the Spinola Palace, the Doria Palace, the Marcello Durazzo, the Red and White Palaces. Francesca either looked at nothing or merely just glanced carelessly at all the various masterpieces. Paul followed us, growling all sorts of disagreeable things. Then we all three took a silent drive into the country and returned to dinner.

"The next day it was the same thing and the next day again; so on the third Paul said to me: 'Look here, I am going to leave you; I am not going to stop here for three weeks watching you make love to this creature.'

"I was perplexed and annoyed, for to my great surprise I had become singularly attached to Francesca. A man is but weak and foolish, carried away by the merest trifle, and a coward every time that his senses are excited or mastered. I clung to this unknown girl, silent and dissatisfied as she always was. I liked her somewhat ill-tempered face, the dissatisfied droop of her mouth, the weariness of her look; I liked her fatigued movements, the contemptuous way in which she yielded to my wishes, the very indifference of her caresses. A secret bond, that mysterious bond of animal love, the secret attachment to a possession which does not satiate, bound me to her. I told Paul so, quite frankly. He treated me as if I had been a fool, and then said:

" 'Very well, take her with you.'

"But she obstinately refused to leave Genoa, without giving any reason. I besought, I reasoned, I promised, but all was of no avail, and so I stayed on.

"Paul declared that he would go by himself, and went so far as to pack up his portmanteau; but he remained all the same.

"Thus a fortnight passed. Francesca was always silent and irritable, lived beside me rather than with me, responded to all desires, all my demands, and all my propositions with her perpetual 'Che mi fa?' or with her no less perpetual 'mica.'

"My friend got more and more furious, but my only answer was, 'You can go if you are tired of staying. I am not detaining you.'

"Then he called me names, overwhelmed me with reproaches, and exclaimed: 'Where do you think I can go to now? We had three weeks at our disposal, and here is a fortnight gone! I cannot continue my journey now; and, in any case, I am not going to Venice, Florence, and Rome all by myself. But you will pay for it, and more dearly than you think, most likely. You are not going to bring a man all the way from Paris in order to shut him up at a hotel in Genoa with an Italian adventuress.'

"When I told him, very calmly, to return to Paris, he exclaimed that he was going to do so the very next day; but the next day he was still there, still in a rage and swearing.

"By this time we began to be known in the streets, through which we wandered from morning till night, those narrow streets without footpaths which are like an immense stone labyrinth with tomblike passages. We went through those windy gorges, narrowed between such high walls that the sky is hardly visible. Sometimes French people would turn round astonished at meeting their fellow countrymen with this bored girl in her loud clothes, who looked singularly out of place, not to say compromising, beside us.

"She used to walk along, leaning on my arm, without looking at anything. Why did she remain with me, with us, who seemed to give her so little pleasure? Who was she? Where did she come from? What was she doing? Had she any plan or idea? How did she live? As an adventuress, or by chance meetings? I tried in vain to find out and to explain it. The better I knew her the more enigmatical she became. She was not one of those who make a living by, and a profession of, venal love. She rather seemed to me to be a girl of poor family who had been seduced and taken away, and then cast aside and lost. What did she think was going to become of her, or for whom was she waiting? She certainly did not appear to be trying to make a conquest of me, or to get any profit out of me.

"I tried to question her, to speak to her of her childhood and family; but she never gave me an answer. I stayed with her, my heart unfettered and my senses enchained, never wearied of holding this proud and quarrelsome woman in my arms, captivated by my senses, or rather seduced, overcome, by the youthful, healthy, powerful charm which emanated from her sweet-smelling person and from the robust lines of her body.

"Another week passed, and the term of my holiday was drawing to a close, for I had to be back in Paris by July 11. By this time Paul had come to take his part in the adventure, though still grumbling at me, while I invented pleasures, distractions, and excursions to amuse my mistress and my friend; and in order to do this I gave myself a large amount of trouble.

"One day I proposed an excursion to Santa Margherita, a charming little town in the midst of gardens, hidden at the foot of a slope which stretches far into the sea. We all three were following the excellent road which goes along the foot of the mountain. Suddenly Francesca said to me: 'I shall not be able to go with you tomorrow; I must go and see some of my relatives.'

"That was all; I did not ask her any questions, as I was quite sure she would not answer me.

"The next morning she got up very early; then, as I remained in bed, she sat down at the foot of it, and said in a constrained and hesitating voice:

" 'If I do not come back tonight, will you come and fetch me?'

" 'Most certainly I shall,' was my reply. 'Where must I come to?'

"Then she explained: 'You must go into Victor Emmanuel Street, down the Passage Falcone and Saint Raphael Street, and go into the furniture shop at the bottom, in a court, and there you must ask for Mme. Rondoli. That's where it is.'

"And so she went away, leaving me rather astonished.

"When Paul saw that I was alone he stammered out: 'Where is Francesca?' And when I told him what had happened he exclaimed:

" 'My dear fellow, we are in luck, let us bolt; as it is, our time is up. Two days, more or less, make no difference. Let us start at once; go and pack up your things. Off we go!'

"But I refused. I could not, as I told him, leave the girl in such a manner, after having lived with her for nearly three weeks. At any rate I ought to say good-by to her and make her accept a present; I certainly had no intention of behaving badly to her.

"But he would not listen; he pressed and worried me, but I would not give way.

"I remained indoors for several hours, expecting Francesca's return, but she did not come. At last, at dinner, Paul said with a triumphant air: 'She has thrown you over, my dear fellow; it is certainly very funny, very funny.'

"I must acknowledge that I was surprised and rather vexed. He laughed in my face, and made fun of me.

" 'It is not exactly a bad way of getting rid of you, though rather primitive. "Just wait for me, I shall be back in a moment." How long are you going to wait? I should not wonder if you were foolish enough to go and look for her at the address she gave you. "Does Mme. Rondoli live here, please?" I'll bet that you are longing to go there.'

" 'Not in the least,' I protested, 'and I assure you that if she does not come back tomorrow I shall start by the express at eight o'clock. I shall have waited twenty-four hours, and that is enough; my conscience will be quite clear.'

"I spent an uneasy and unpleasant evening, for I really had at heart a very tender feeling for her. I went to bed at twelve o'clock, and hardly slept at all. I got up at six, called Paul, packed up my things, and two hours later we started for France together."

III

"The next year, at just about the same period, I was seized, just as one is with a periodical fever, with a new desire to go to Italy, and I immediately made up my mind to carry it into effect. There is no doubt that every really well-educated man ought to see Florence, Venice, and Rome. There is the additional advantage of providing many subjects of conversation in society, and of giving one an opportunity for bringing forward artistic generalites which appear profound. This time I went alone, and I arrived at Genoa at the same time as the year before, but without any adventure on the road. I went to the same hotel, and actually happened to have the same room.

"I was scarcely in bed when the recollection of Francesca which, since the evening before, had been floating vaguely through my mind, haunted me with strange persistency.

"Have you ever been obsessed by the thought of a woman, long afterwards, on returning to the place where you loved her and she gave herself to you? It is one of the most powerful and painful sensations I know. It seems as if one could see her enter, smiling and holding out her arms. Her features, elusive yet clear, are before your eyes. She passes, returns and disappears. She tortures you like a nightmare, holds you, fills your heart, and stirs your senses by her unreal presence.

She is visible to the eye, her perfume haunts you, the taste of her kisses is on your lips, and the touch of her body caresses your skin. Yet, one knows one is alone, and one is strangely tortured by the phantom one has evoked. A heavy, heartbreaking melancholy invades you, as if you were abandoned forever. Everything looks depressing, filling the heart with a horrible sense of isolation and abandonment. Never return to the house, the room, the woods, the garden, the seat, the town, where you have held in your arms a woman you loved.

"I thought of her nearly the whole night, and by degrees the wish to see her again seized me, a confused desire at first, which gradually grew stronger and more intense. At last I made up my mind to spend the next day in Genoa, to try and find her, and if I should not succeed to take the evening train.

"Early in the morning I set out on my search. I remembered the directions she had given me when she left me, perfectly—Victor Emmanuel Street, the Passage Falcone, St. Raphael Street, house of the furniture dealer, at the bottom of the yard in a court.

"I found it without the least difficulty, and I knocked at the door of a somewhat dilapidated-looking dwelling. A fat woman opened it, who must once have been very handsome, but who actually was only very dirty. Although she was too fat, she still bore the lines of majestic beauty; her untidy hair fell over her forehead and shoulders, and one fancied one could see her fat body floating about in an enormous dressing gown covered with spots of dirt and grease. Round her neck she wore a great gilt necklace, and on her wrists were splendid bracelets of Genoa filigree work.

"In rather a hostile manner she asked me what I wanted, and I replied by requesting her to tell me whether Francesca Rondoli lived there.

" 'What do you want with her?' she asked.

" 'I had the pleasure of meeting her last year, and I should like to see her again.'

"The old woman looked at me suspiciously.

" 'Where did you meet her?' she asked.

" 'Why, here, in Genoa itself.'

" 'What is your name?'

"I hesitated a moment, and then I told her. I had scarcely done so when the Italian raised her arms as if to embrace me. 'Oh! you are the Frenchman; how glad I am to see you! But what grief you caused the poor child. She waited for you a month; yes, a whole month. At first she thought you would come to fetch her. She wanted to see whether you loved her. If you only knew how she cried when she saw that you were not coming! She cried till she seemed to have no tears left. Then she went to the hotel, but you had gone. She thought that most likely you were traveling in Italy, and that you would return by Genoa to fetch her, as she would not go with you. And she waited more than a month, monsieur; and she was so unhappy; so unhappy. I am her mother.'

"I really felt a little disconcerted, but I regained my self-possession, and asked: 'Is she here now?'

" 'No, she has gone to Paris with a painter, a delightful man, who loves her very much, and who gives her everything that she wants. Just look at what she sent me; they are very pretty, are they not?'

"And she showed me, with quite southern animation, her heavy bracelets and necklace. 'I have also,' she continued, 'earrings with stones in them, a silk dress, and some rings; but I only wear them on grand occasions. Oh! she is very happy, sir, very happy. She will be so pleased when I tell her you have been here. But pray come in and sit down. You will take something or other, surely?'

"But I refused, as I now wished to get away by the first train; but she took me by the arm and pulled me in, saying:

" 'Please, come in; I must tell her that you have been here.'

"I found myself in a small, rather dark room, furnished with only a table and a few chairs.

"She continued: 'Oh! She is very happy now, very happy. When you met her in the train she was very miserable, for her lover had just left her at Marseille, and she was coming back, poor child. But she liked you at once, though she was still rather sad, you understand. Now she has all she wants, and she writes and tells me everything that she does. His name is Bellemin, and they say he is a great painter in your country. He met her in the street here and fell in love with her immediately. But you will take a glass of syrup?—it is very good. Are you quite alone, this year?'

" 'Yes,' I said, 'quite alone.'

"I felt an increasing inclination to laugh, as my first disappointment was dispelled by what Mother Rondoli said. I was obliged, however, to drink a glass of her syrup.

" 'So you are quite alone?' she continued. 'How sorry I am that Francesca is not here now; she would have been company for you all the time you stayed. It is not very amusing to go about all by oneself, and she will be very sorry also.'

"Then, as I was getting up to go, she exclaimed:

" 'But would you not like Carlotta to go with you? She knows all the walks very well. She is my second daughter, sir.'

"No doubt she took my look of surprise for consent, for she opened the inner door and called out up the dark stairs which I could not see:

" 'Carlotta! Carlotta! come down, quickly, my dear child.'

"I tried to protest, but she would not listen.

" 'No; she will be very glad to go with you; she is very nice, and much more cheerful than her sister, and she is a good girl, a very good girl, whom I love very much.'

"I heard the clatter of slippers on the stairs, and a tall, slender, dark girl appeared, also with her hair hanging down, and whose youthful figure showed unmistakably beneath an old dress of her mother's.

"The latter at once told her how matters stood.

" 'This is Francesca's Frenchman, you know, the one whom she knew last year. He is quite alone, and has come to look for her, poor fellow; so I told him that you would go with him to keep him company.'

"The girl looked at me with her handsome dark eyes, and said, smiling:

" 'I have no objection, if he wishes it.'

"I could not possibly refuse and merely said:

" 'Of course I shall be very glad of your company.'

"Her mother pushed her out. 'Go and get dressed directly; put on your blue dress and your hat with the flowers, and make haste.'

"As soon as she had left the room the old woman explained herself: 'I have two others, but they are much younger. It costs a lot of money to bring up four children. Luckily the eldest is off my hands at present.'

"Then she told all about herself, about her husband, who had been an employee on the railway, but who was dead, and she expatiated on the good qualities of Carlotta, her second girl, who soon returned, dressed, as her sister had been, in a striking, peculiar manner.

"Her mother examined her from head to foot, and, after finding everything right, she said:

" 'Now, my children, you can go.' Then, turning to the girl, she said: 'Be sure you are back by ten o'clock tonight; you know the door is locked then.'

" 'All right, Mamma; don't alarm yourself,' Carlotta replied.

"She took my arm, and we went wandering about the streets, just as I had done the previous year with her sister.

"We returned to the hotel for lunch, and then I took my new friend to Santa Margherita, just as I had done with her sister the year previously.

"During the whole fortnight which I had at my disposal I took Carlotta to all the places of interest in and about Genoa. She gave me no cause to regret the other.

"She cried when I left her, and the morning of my departure I gave her four bracelets for her mother, besides a substantial token of my affection for herself.

"One of these days I intend to return to Italy, and I cannot help remembering, with a certain amount of uneasiness, mingled with hope, that Mme. Rondoli has two more daughters."

THE DANCERS

"Great misfortunes grieve me little," said John Bridelle, an old bachelor who passed for a skeptic. "I have seen war at close range; I could stride over dead bodies pitilessly. The strong brutalities of nature, where we can utter cries of horror or indignation, do not wring our hearts or send the shiver down the back as do the little wondering sights of life.

"Certainly the most violent grief that one can experience is for a mother the loss of a child, and for a son the loss of a mother. It is violent and terrible; it overturns and lacerates, but one is healed of such catastrophes, as of large, bleeding wounds. But certain accidents, certain things hinted at, suspected, certain secret griefs, certain perfidy, of the sort that stirs up in us a world of grievous thoughts, which opens before us suddenly the mysterious door of moral suffering, complicated, incurable, so much the more profound because it seems worthy, so much the more stinging because unseizable, the more tenacious because artificial, these leave upon the soul a train of sadness, a feeling of sorrow, a sensation of disenchantment that we are long in ridding ourselves of.

"I have ever before my eyes two or three things that possibly had not been noticed by others but which entered into my sympathies like deep, unhealable stings.

"You will not comprehend, perhaps, the emotion that has relieved me from these rapid impressions. I will tell you only one. It is old but lives with me as if it occurred yesterday. It may be imagination alone that keeps it fresh in my memory.

"I am fifty years old. I was young then and studious by nature. A little sad, a little dreamy, impregnated with a melancholy philosophy, I never cared much for the brilliant cafés, noisy comrades or stupid girls. I rose early, and one of my sweetest indulgences was to take a walk alone, about eight o'clock in the morning, in the nursery of the Luxembourg.

"Perhaps you do not know this nursery? It was like a forgotten garden of another century, a pretty garden, like the smile of an old person. Trimmed hedges separated the straight, regular walks, calm walks between two walls of foliage neatly pruned. The great scissors of the gardener clipped without mercy the offshoots of the branches. While here and there were walks bordered with flowers and clumps of little trees, arranged like collegians promenading, masses of magnificent roses and regiments of fruit trees.

"The whole of one corner of this delightful copse was inhabited by bees. Their straw houses, skillfully spaced upon the planks, opened to the sun their great odors, like the opening of a sewing thimble. And all along the path golden flies were buzzing, true mistresses of this peaceful place, ideal inhabitants of these walks and corridors.

"I went there nearly every morning. I would seat myself upon a bench and read. Sometimes I would allow my book to fall upon my knees, while I dreamed and listened to the living Paris all about me and enjoyed the infinite repose of these rows of ancient oaks.

"All at once I perceived that I was not alone a frequenter of this spot, reached through an opening in the fence. From time to time I encountered, face to face, an old man in the corner of the thicket. He wore shoes with silver buckles, trousers with a flap, a tobacco-colored coat, lace in place of a cravat, and an unheard-of hat with nap and edges worn, which made one think of the deluge.

"He was thin, very thin, angular, smiling, grimacing. His bright eyes sparkled, agitated by a continual movement of the pupils, and he always carried a superb cane with a gold head, which must have been a souvenir and a magnificent one.

"This good man astonished me at first, then interested me beyond measure. And I watched him behind a wall of foliage and followed him from afar, stopping behind shrubbery, so as not to be seen.

"It happened one morning as he believed himself entirely alone that he began some singular movements, some little bounds at first, then a bow; then he struck up some capers with his lank legs, then turned cleverly, as if on a pivot, bending and swaying in a droll fashion, smiling as if before the public, making gestures with outstretched arms, twisting his poor body like a jumping jack, throwing tender, ridiculous salutations to the open air. He was dancing!

"I remained petrified with amazement, asking myself which of the two was mad, he or I. But he stopped suddenly, advanced as actors do upon the stage, bowed and took a few steps backward, with the gracious smiles and kisses of the comedian, which he threw with trembling hand to the two rows of shapely trees.

"After that he resumed his walk with gravity.

"From this day I never lost sight of him. And each morning he recommenced his peculiar exercise.

"A foolish desire led me to speak to him. I ventured and, having bowed, I said:
" 'It is a fine day today, sir.'

"He bowed. 'Yes sir, it is like the weather of long ago.'

"A week after this we were friends, and I knew his history. He had been dancing master at the opera from the time of Louis XV. His beautiful cane was a gift from

Count de Clermont. And when he began to speak of dancing he never knew when to stop.

"One day he confided in me:

" 'I married La Castris, sir. I will present her to you if you wish, but she never comes here so early. This garden, you see, is our pleasure and our life. It is all that remains to us of former times. It seems to us that we could not exist if we did not have it. It is old and distinguished, is it not? Here I can seem to breathe air that has not changed since my youth. My wife and I pass every afternoon here. But I, I come again in the morning, because I rise so early.'

"After luncheon I returned to the Luxembourg, and soon I perceived my friend, who was giving his arm with great ceremony to a little old woman clothed in black, to whom I was presented. It was La Castris, the great dancer, loved of princes, loved of the king, loved of all that gallant century which seems to have left in the world an odor of love.

"We seated ourselves upon a bench. It was in the month of May. A perfume of flowers flitted through all the tidy walks; a pleasant sun glistened between the leaves and spread over us large spots of light. The black robe of La Castris seemed all permeated with brightness.

"The garden was empty. The roll of carriages could be heard in the distance.

" 'Will you explain to me,' I said to the old dancing master, 'what the minuet was?'

"He started. 'The minuet, sir, is the queen of dances and the dance of queens; do you understand? Since there are no more kings there are no more minuets.'

"And he commenced in pompous style a long, dithyrambic eulogy of which I comprehended nothing. I wanted him to describe the step to me, all the movements, the poses. He perplexed and exasperated himself with his lack of strength and then became nervous and spent. Then suddenly, turning toward his old companion, always silent and grave, he said:

" 'Elise, will you, I say—will you be so kind as to show this gentleman what the minuet really was?'

"She turned her unquiet eyes in every direction then, rising without a word, placed herself opposite him.

"Then I saw something never to be forgotten.

"They went forward and back with a childlike apishness, smiling to each other and balancing, bowing and hopping like two old puppets made to dance by some ancient mechanism a little out of repair and constructed long ago by some skillful workman, following the custom of his day.

"And I looked at them, my heart troubled with extraordinary sensations, my soul moved by an indescribable melancholy. I seemed to see a lamentable, comic apparition, the shadow of a century past and gone. I had a desire to laugh when I felt more like weeping.

"Then they stopped; they had ended the figure of the dance. For some seconds they remained standing before each other, smirking in a most surprising manner; then they embraced each other with a sob.

"I left town three days later for the provinces. I have never seen them again. When I returned to Paris two years later they had destroyed the nursery garden. What have the old couple done without the dear garden of other days, with its labyrinths, its odor of long ago and its walks shaded by graceful elms? Are they dead? Are they wandering through modern streets, like exiles without hope? Are they dancing somewhere, grotesque specters, a fantastic minuet among the cypresses in the cemetery, along the paths beside the tombs in the moonlight?

"The remembrance haunts me, oppresses and tortures me; it remains with me like a wound. Why? I cannot tell.

"You will find this very ridiculous, without doubt."

CHECKMATE

I was going to Turin by way of Corsica. At Nice I took ship for Bastia, and as soon as we were out at sea I saw a charming, quietly dressed young woman sitting on the bridge: she was looking out to sea. "Ah," I said to myself, "there's my friend for the voyage."

I took a seat opposite her and looked at her, my mind filled with the questions that leap into any man's mind when he sees an unknown and interesting woman: what was her class, her age, what sort of a woman was she? Then, from what he can see, he speculates on what he can't see. Eye and mind peer through the bodice and under the gown. He observes the line of the bust when she is seated: he tries to catch a glimpse of her ankle: he notes the texture of her hand, which reveals the fineness of the rest of her limbs, and the shape and size of her ear, which is a truer indication of birth than a birth certificate, that must always be open to dispute. He tries to hear her speak, to get at the character of her mind and the tenderness of her heart through the tones of her voice. For, to the experienced observer, the pitch and all the subtle gradations of the spoken word reveal the mysterious structure of the soul: difficult though it may be to grasp it, there is always perfect accord between thought itself and the organ of its expression.

So I observed my neighbor with grave attention, watching the signs, analyzing her movements, keeping my eyes open for the revelations her every attitude would make.

She opened a small black bag and took out a newspaper. I rubbed my hands: "Tell me what you read, and I will tell you what you are."

She began at the leading article with the air of a person savoring a delicate pleasure. The name of her paper leaped to my eyes: *Echo de Paris*. I was puzzled. She was reading one of Scholl's scandalous commentaries. Devil take her, she read Scholl. . . . Scholl. She began to smile: a pointed jest. So she was not a prude, or an innocent. So much the better. A reader of Scholl—yes, a lover of our native wit, its fine shades, and its salt, even its pepper. A good sign. I thought: let us try her on another tack.

I went and sat near her, and began to read, no less attentively, a volume of poetry that I had bought for the journey: the *Chanson d'amour* by Félix Frank.

I observed that she had snatched up the name on the binding with one rapid glance, like a bird on the wing snatching up a fly. Several passengers, men, walked past us to look at her. But she seemed to think of nothing but her column of town scandal. When she had finished it, she laid her paper down between us.

I bowed and said:

"May I glance through your paper?"

"Certainly."

"Do you care to look at this volume of verse in the meantime?"

"Yes, certainly. Is it amusing?"

The question puzzled me slightly. It is not usual to ask if a collection of verse is amusing. I answered:

"It's better than that; it's charming, delicate, and the work of an artist."

"Give it to me, then."

She took the book, opened it, and began to glance through it with a vaguely surprised air that made it clear she rarely read verse.

Some of it seemed to move her, some made her smile, but a different smile from the one she had worn when reading her paper.

I asked her suddenly:

"Do you like it?"

"Yes, but I like amusing things myself, very amusing things: I'm not senti-mental."

We began to talk. I learned that she was the wife of a captain of dragoons, stationed at Ajaccio, and that she was going to join her husband.

I very soon guessed that she had little love for this husband of hers. She did love him, but with the mild affection a woman retains for a husband who has not fulfilled the hopes roused in courting days. He had drifted from garrison to gar-rison, through a number of small, dull towns, such very dull towns. Now he was stationed in this island, which must be very gloomy indeed. No, everyone's life was not amusing. She would rather have gone on living at Lyons with her parents, for she knew everyone in Lyons. But now she had to go to Corsica. The minister was not inclined to favor her husband, who had, nevertheless, an excellent service record.

And we discussed the places where she would have liked to live.

"Do you like Paris?" I asked.

"Oh," she cried, "do I like Paris? How can you ask such a question?"

And she began talking about Paris with such ardent enthusiasm, such wild envy, that I thought: "This is the right string to touch."

She adored Paris from afar, with a passion of repressed gluttony, with the exag-gerated longing of a provincial and the maddened impatience of a caged bird who all day looks at a wood from the window where he hangs.

She began to question me, stammering in an agony of impatience: she wanted to be told everything, everything, in five minutes. She knew the names of all the famous people, and many others whom I had never heard mentioned.

"How is M. Gounod? And M. Sardou? Oh, how I love M. Sardou's plays! How amusing and witty they are! Every time I see one, I dream of it for a week. I've read a book of M. Daudet's, too, which I enjoyed enormously. Sapho—do you know it? Is M. Daudet nice-looking? Have you seen him? And M. Zola, what is he like? If you only knew how Germinal made me cry! Do you remember the little child who dies in the dark? How terrible that is! It nearly made me ill. There's nothing to laugh at in that, my word. I've read a book of M. Bourget's, too, Cruelle Enigme. I have a cousin who was so excited about this novel that she wrote to M. Bourget. I thought the book too romantic. I like something humorous better. Do you know M. Grévin? And M. Coquelin? And M. Damala?

And M. Rochefort? They say he's a great wit. And M. de Cassagnac? Is it true that he fights a duel every day? . . ."

Somewhere about the end of an hour, her stock of questions began to run low, and having satisfied her curiosity by the wildest flights of imagination, I was able to talk myself.

I told her stories about the doings of society, Parisian society, real society. She listened with all her ears and all her heart. She must indeed have gathered a pretty picture of the fair and famous ladies of Paris. There was nothing but love affairs, assignations, speedy conquests and impassioned defeats. She kept asking me:

"Oh, is real society like that?"

I smiled as one who knows:

"Of course. It's only the middle-class women who lead a dull, monotonous life for the sake of their virtue, a virtue for which no one thanks them."

And I set myself to undermine virtue with tremendous strokes of irony, philosophy and nonsense. I made magnificent and graceful fun of the poor wretches who let themselves grow old without ever having known the good things of life, the sweet, tender, gallant things that life offers, without ever having savoured the delicious pleasure of long, burning, stolen kisses, and all just because they have married a worthy dolt of a husband, the reserve of whose marital embraces allows them to go to their graves in ignorance of all the refinements of sensual pleasure and all the delicate ecstasies of love.

Then I cited further anecdotes, anecdotes of *cabinets particuliers*, intrigues which I swore were common knowledge. And the refrain of all my tales was a discreet, veiled eulogy of swift, secret love, of sensations snatched in passing, like fruit, and forgotten as soon as enjoyed.

Night fell, a calm, warm night. The big ship, shaken from stem to stern by its engines, glided over the sea, under the vast roof of the wine-dark sky, starred with fire.

The little provincial was not talking now. She drew slow breaths and sometimes sighed. Suddenly she rose.

"I'm going to bed," said she. "Good night, monsieur."

She shook hands with me.

I knew that on the following evening she would have to take the coach that runs from Bastia to Ajaccio across the mountains, making the journey by night.

I answered:

"Good night, madame."

And I too betook myself to the bunk in my cabin.

First thing next day, I took three places inside the coach, all three places, for myself.

As I was climbing into the old carriage that was going to leave Bastia at nightfall, the conductor asked me if I would not agree to give up one corner to a lady.

I asked brusquely:

"To what lady?"

"To the wife of an officer going to Ajaccio."

"Tell the lady that I shall be glad if she will occupy one of the seats."

She arrived, having, she said, been asleep all day. She apologized, thanked me, and got in.

The coach was a sort of hermetically sealed box, into which light entered only through the two doors. So there we were shut up together inside. The carriage proceeded at a trot, a quick trot; then began to follow the mountain road. A fresh, powerful scent of aromatic herbs drifted in through the lowered panes, the heady scent that Corsica so pours out into the surrounding air that sailors passing out at sea smell it, a pungent scent like the smell of bodies, like the sweat of the green earth impregnated with perfumes drawn out by the ardent sun and given to the passing wind.

I began to talk of Paris again, and again she listened to me with feverish attention. My stories grew daring, subtly décolleté: I used allusive, two-edged words, words that set the blood on fire.

The night was on us. I could see nothing now, not even the white patch that had been the girl's face. Only the coachman's lantern flung a ray of light over the four horses that were climbing the road at a walking pace.

Sometimes for a little while, until it died away in the distance behind us, we heard the sound of a torrent dashing over the rocks, and mingling with the sound of little bells. Gently I stretched out my foot and met hers, which was not withdrawn. Then I sat still, waiting, and suddenly, changing my tune, I talked tenderly, affectionately. I had reached out my hand and touched hers. She did not withdraw that either. I went on talking, nearer her ear, very near her mouth. Already I felt her heart beating against my breast. It was beating quickly and loudly —a good sign—then, slowly, I pressed my lips on her neck, sure that I had her, so sure that I would have wagered any money on it.

But all at once she started as if she had awakened, started so violently that I reeled to the other end of the coach. Then, before I was able to understand, to reflect, to think at all, I first of all received five or six staggering slaps, then a shower of blows rained on me, sharp, savage blows that struck me all over, unable as I was to parry them in the profound darkness that covered the struggle.

I put out my hands, trying vainly to seize her arms. Then, not knowing what else to do, I turned sharply round and presented my back to her furious attack, hiding my head in the corner of the panels.

She seemed to guess, perhaps from the sound of her blows, this despairing maneuver, and abruptly ceased to beat me.

A few seconds later she was back in her corner and had begun to cry, and she sobbed wildly for an hour at least.

I had seated myself again, very distressed and very much ashamed. I would have liked to speak to her, but what should I say? I could think of nothing! Apologize? That would be absurd. What would you have said! No more than I did, I'll take my oath.

She was crying softly now, and sometimes uttering deep sighs that filled me with grief and compassion. I would have liked to comfort her, to caress her as if she had been an unhappy child, to ask her pardon, kneel to her. But I did not dare.

These situations are too stupid.

She grew quiet at last, and we remained each in our own corner, still and silent, while the carriage rolled on, stopping now and then for fresh horses. We both shut our eyes very quickly at these halts, to avoid seeing one another when the bright light of a stable lantern shone into the coach. Then the coach set out again; and all the time the pungent, scented air of the Corsican mountains caressed our cheeks and our lips, and went to my head like wine.

Christ, what a glorious journey it would have been if . . . if my companion had not been such a little fool.

But gradually light filtered into the carriage, the pale light of early dawn. I looked at my neighbor. She was pretending to be asleep. The sun, risen behind the mountains, filled with its radiance a vast blue gulf set around with great granite-crested peaks. On the edge of the bay a white town came into sight, still lying in shadow.

Then my neighbor pretended to wake, she opened her eyes (they were red), she opened her mouth as if she were yawning and had been asleep a long time. She hesitated, blushed and stammered:

"Shall we be there soon?"

"Yes, madame, in an hour or so."

She added, gazing into space:

"It is very tiring to spend the night in a carriage."

"Yes, it breaks one's back."

"Especially after a crossing."

"Yes."

"Is not that Ajaccio in front of us?"

"Yes, madame."

"I wish we were there."

"I am sure you do."

Her voice sounded a little troubled; her manner was rather awkward, her glance did not meet mine very readily. But she seemed to have forgotten the whole episode.

I admired her. What instinctive intriguers these bitches are! What diplomatists!

We did indeed arrive in another hour; and a tall dragoon, with the figure of a Hercules, was standing in front of the office; he waved a handkerchief as the coach came in sight.

My neighbor flung herself wildly into his arms, and kissed him at least twenty times, repeating:

"Are you all right? How I have been aching to see you again!"

My trunk was handed down from the roof and I was discreetly withdrawing when she cried:

"Oh, you are going away without saying good-by to me."

I stammered:

"Madame, I did not wish to intrude on your happiness."

Then she said to her husband:

"Thank this gentleman, darling: he has been most kind to me on the journey. He even offered me a place in the coach which he had reserved for himself. It is nice to meet with such friendly companions."

The husband shook my hand and thanked me warmly.

The young wife watched us with a smile. I must have looked a rare fool.

THE ACCURSED BREAD

Daddy Taille had three daughters: Anna, the eldest, who was scarcely ever mentioned in the family; Rose, the second girl, who was eighteen, and Clara, the youngest, who was a girl of fifteen.

Old Taille was a widower and a foreman in M. Lebrument's button manufactory. He was a very upright man, very well thought of, abstemious, in fact, a sort of model workman. He lived at Havre in the Rue d'Angoulême.

When Anna ran away the old man flew into a fearful rage. He threatened to kill the seducer, who was head clerk in a large draper's establishment in that town. Then when he was told by various people that she was keeping very steady and investing money in government securities, that she was no gadabout but was maintained by a M. Dubois, who was a judge of the Tribunal of Commerce, the father was appeased.

He even showed some anxiety as to how she was faring, asked some of her old friends who had been to see her how she was getting on, and when told that she had her own furniture and that her mantelpiece was covered with vases and the walls with pictures, that there were clocks and carpets everywhere, he gave a broad, contented smile. He had been working for thirty years to get together a wretched five or six thousand francs. This girl was evidently no fool.

One fine morning the son of Touchard, the cooper at the other end of the street, came and asked him for the hand of Rose, the second girl. The old man's heart began to beat, for the Touchards were rich and in a good position. He was decidedly lucky with his girls.

The marriage was agreed upon. It was settled that it should be a grand affair, and the wedding dinner was to be held at Sainte-Addresse, at Mother Lusa's restaurant. It would cost a lot certainly, but never mind, it did not matter just for once in a way.

But one morning, just as the old man was going home to breakfast with his two daughters, the door opened suddenly and Anna appeared. She was elegantly dressed, wore rings and an expensive bonnet and looked undeniably pretty and nice. She threw her arms round her father's neck before he could say a word, then fell into her sisters' arms with many tears and then asked for a plate, so that she might share the family soup. Taille was moved to tears in his turn and said several times:

"That is right, dear; that is right."

Then she told them about herself. She did not wish Rose's wedding to take place at Sainte-Addresse—certainly not. It should take place at her house and would cost her father nothing. She had settled everything, so it was "no good to say any more about it—there!"

"Very well, my dear! Very well!" the old man said. "We will leave it so." But then he felt some doubt. Would the Touchards consent? But Rose, the bride-elect, was surprised and asked, "Why should they object, I should like to know? Just leave that to me; I will talk to Philip about it."

She mentioned it to her lover the very same day, and he declared that it would suit him exactly. Father and Mother Touchard were naturally delighted at the idea of a good dinner which would cost them nothing and said:

"You may be quite sure that everything will be in first-rate style, as Monsieur Dubois is made of money."

They asked to be allowed to bring a friend, Mme. Florence, the cook on the first floor, and Anna agreed to everything. The wedding was fixed for the last Tuesday of the month.

II

After the civil formalities and the religious ceremony the wedding party went to Anna's house. Among those whom the Tailles had brought was a cousin of a certain age, a M. Sauvetanin, a man given to philosophical reflections, serious and always very self-possessed, and Mme. Lamonoois, an old aunt.

M. Sauvetanin had been told off to give Anna his arm, as they were looked upon as the two most important persons in the company.

As soon as they had arrived at the door of Anna's house she let go her companion's arm and ran on ahead, saying, "I will show you the way," while the invited guests followed more slowly. When they got upstairs she stood on one side to let them pass, and they rolled their eyes and turned their heads in all directions to admire this mysterious and luxurious dwelling.

The table was laid in the drawing room as the dining room had been thought too small. Extra knives, forks and spoons had been hired from a neighboring restaurant, and decanters full of wine glittered under the rays of the sun, which shone in through the window.

The ladies went into the bedroom to take off their shawls and bonnets, and Father Touchard, who was standing at the door, squinted at the low, wide bed and made funny signs to the men, with many a wink and nod. Daddy Taille, who thought a great deal of himself, looked with fatherly pride at his child's well-furnished rooms and went from one to the other, holding his hat in his hand, making a mental inventory of everything and walking like a verger in a church.

Anna went backward and forward and ran about giving orders and hurrying on the wedding feast. Soon she appeared at the door of the drawing room and cried: "Come here, all of you, for a moment," and when the twelve guests did as they were asked they saw twelve glasses of Madeira on a small table.

Rose and her husband had their arms round each other's waists and were kissing each other in every corner. M. Sauvetanin never took his eyes off Anna; he no doubt felt that ardor, that sort of expectation, which all men, even if they are old and ugly, feel for women of a certain stamp.

They sat down, and the wedding breakfast began, the relatives sitting at one end of the table and the young people at the other. Mme. Touchard, the mother, presided on the right and the bride on the left. Anna looked after everybody, saw that the glasses were kept filled and the plates well supplied. The guests evidently felt a certain respectful embarrassment at the sight of the sumptuousness of the rooms and at the lavish manner in which they were treated. They all ate heartily of the good things provided, but there were no jokes such as are prevalent at weddings of that sort; it was all too grand, and it made them feel uncomfortable. Old Mme. Touchard, who was fond of a bit of fun, tried to enliven matters a little, and at the beginning of the dessert she exclaimed: "I say, Philip, do sing us something." The neighbors in their street considered that he had the finest voice in all Havre.

The bridegroom got up, smiled and, turning to his sister-in-law from politeness and gallantry, tried to think of something suitable for the occasion, something serious and correct, to harmonize with the seriousness of the repast.

Anna had a satisfied look on her face and leaned back in her chair to listen, and all assumed looks of attention, though prepared to smile should smiles be called for.

The singer announced, *The Accursed Bread* and, extending his right arm, which made his coat ruck up into his neck, he began.

It was decidedly long, three verses of eight lines each, with the last line and the last line but one repeated twice.

All went well for the first two verses; they were the usual commonplaces about bread gained by honest labor and by dishonesty. The aunt and the bride wept outright. The cook, who was present, at the end of the first verse looked at a roll which she held in her hand with moist eyes, as if they applied to her, while all applauded vigorously. At the end of the second verse the two servants, who were standing with their backs to the wall, joined loudly in the chorus, and the aunt and the bride wept outright. Daddy Taille blew his nose with a noise of a trombone; old Touchard brandished a whole loaf half over the table, and the cook shed silent tears onto the crust which she was still holding.

Amid the general emotion M. Sauvetanin said:

"That is the right sort of song, very different to the pointed things one generally hears at weddings."

Anna, who was visibly affected, kissed her hand to her sister and pointed to her husband with an affectionate nod, as if to congratulate her.

Intoxicated by his success, the young man continued, and unfortunately the last verse contained words about the bread of dishonor gained by young girls who had been led astray from the paths of virtue. No one took up the refrain about this bread, supposed to be eaten with tears, except old Touchard and the two servants. Anna had grown deadly pale and cast down her eyes, while the bridegroom looked from one to the other without understanding the reason for this sudden coldness, and the cook hastily dropped the crust as if it were poisoned.

M. Sauvetanin said solemnly, in order to save the situation: "That last couplet is not at all necessary," and Daddy Taille, who had got red up to his ears, looked round the table fiercely.

Then Anna, with her eyes swimming in tears, told the servants in the faltering voice of a woman trying to stifle her sobs to bring the champagne.

All the guests were suddenly seized with exuberant joy, and their faces became radiant again. And when old Touchard, who had seen, felt and understood nothing of what was going on, and, pointing to the guests so as to emphasize his words, sang the last words of the refrain: "Children, I warn you all to eat not of that bread," the whole company, when they saw the champagne bottles with their necks covered with gold foil appear, burst out singing, as if electrified by the sight:

"Children, I warn you all to eat not of that bread."

MADEMOISELLE FIFI

The Major Graf von Farlsberg, the Prussian commandant, was reading his newspaper, lying back in a great armchair, with his booted feet on the beautiful marble fireplace, where his spurs had made two holes which grew deeper every day during the three months that he had been in the château of Urville.

A cup of coffee was smoking on a small inlaid table which was stained with liquors, burnt by cigars, notched by the penknife of the victorious officer who occasionally would stop while sharpening a pencil to jot down figures or to make a drawing on it, just as it took his fancy.

When he had read his letters and the German newspapers which his baggage-master had brought him he got up, and after throwing three or four enormous pieces of green wood onto the fire—for these gentlemen were gradually cutting down the park in order to keep themselves warm—he went to the window. The rain was descending in torrents, a regular Normandy rain, which looked as if it were being poured out by some furious hand, a slanting rain, which was as thick as a curtain and which formed a kind of wall with oblique stripes and which deluged everything, a regular rain, such as one frequently experiences in the neighborhood of Rouen, which is the watering pot of France.

For a long time the officer looked at the sodden turf and at the swollen Andelle beyond it, which was overflowing its banks, and he was drumming a waltz from the Rhine on the windowpanes with his fingers, when a noise made him turn round; it was his second in command, Captain Baron von Kelweinstein.

The major was a giant with broad shoulders and a long, fair beard, which hung like a cloth onto his chest. His whole solemn person suggested the idea of a military peacock, a peacock who was carrying his tail spread out onto his breast. He had cold, gentle blue eyes and the scar from a sword cut which he had received in the war with Austria; he was said to be an honorable man as well as a brave officer.

The captain, a short, red-faced man who was tightly girthed in at the waist, had his red hair cropped quite close to his head and in certain lights almost looked as if he had been rubbed over with phosphorus. He had lost two front teeth one night, though he could not quite remember how. This defect made him speak so that he could not always be understood, and he had a bald patch on the top of his head, which made him look rather like a monk with a fringe of curly, bright golden hair round the circle of bare skin.

The commandant shook hands with him and drank his cup of coffee (the sixth that morning) at a draught, while he listened to his subordinate's report of what had occurred; and then they both went to the window and declared that it was a very unpleasant outlook. The major, who was a quiet man with a wife at home, could accommodate himself to everything, but the captain, who was rather fast, being in the habit of frequenting low resorts and much given to women, was mad at having been shut up for three months in the compulsory chastity of that wretched hole.

There was a knock at the door, and when the commandant said, "Come in," one of their automatic soldiers appeared and by his mere presence announced that breakfast was ready. In the dining room they met three other officers of lower rank: a lieutenant, Otto von Grossling, and two sublieutenants, Fritz Scheunebarg and Count von Eyrick, a very short, fair-haired man, who was proud and brutal toward men, harsh toward prisoners, and very violent.

Since he had been in France his comrades had called him nothing but "Mademoiselle Fifi." They had given him that nickname on account of his dandified style and small waist, which looked as if he wore stays, from his pale face, on which his budding mustache scarcely showed, and on account of the habit he had acquired of employing the French expression, fi, fi donc, which he pronounced with a slight whistle when he wished to express his sovereign contempt for persons or things.

The dining room of the château was a magnificent long room whose fine old mirrors, now cracked by pistol bullets, and Flemish tapestry, now cut to ribbons and hanging in rags in places from sword cuts, told too well what Mademoiselle Fifi's occupation was during his spare time.

There were three family portraits on the walls: a steel-clad knight, a cardinal and a judge, who were all smoking long porcelain pipes which had been inserted into holes in the canvas, while a lady in a long pointed waist proudly exhibited an enormous pair of mustaches drawn with a piece of charcoal.

The officers ate their breakfast almost in silence in that mutilated room which looked dull in the rain and melancholy under its vanquished appearance, although its old oak floor had become as solid as the stone floor of a public house.

When they had finished eating and were smoking and drinking, they began, as usual, to talk about the dull life they were leading. The bottle of brandy and of liquors passed from hand to hand, and all sat back in their chairs, taking repeated sips from their glasses and scarcely removing the long bent stems, which terminated in china bowls painted in a manner to delight a Hottentot, from their mouths.

As soon as their glasses were empty they filled them again with a gesture of resigned weariness, but Mademoiselle Fifi emptied his every minute, and a soldier immediately gave him another. They were enveloped in a cloud of strong tobacco smoke; they seemed to be sunk in a state of drowsy, stupid intoxication, in that dull state of drunkenness of men who have nothing to do, when suddenly the baron sat up and said: "By heavens! This cannot go on; we must think of something to do." And on hearing this, Lieutenant Otto and Sublieutenant Fritz, who pre-eminently possessed the grave, heavy German countenance, said: "What, Captain?"

He thought for a few moments and then replied: "What? Well, we must get up some entertainment if the commandant will allow us."

"What sort of an entertainment, Captain?" the major asked, taking his pipe out of his mouth.

"I will arrange all that, Commandant," the baron said. "I will send Le Devoir to Rouen, who will bring us some ladies. I know where they can be found. We will have supper here, as all the materials are at hand, and at least we shall have a jolly evening."

Graf von Farlsberg shrugged his shoulders with a smile: "You must surely be mad, my friend."

But all the other officers got up, surrounded their chief and said: "Let Captain have his own way, Commandant; it is terribly dull here."

And the major ended by yielding. "Very well," he replied, and the baron immediately sent for Le Devoir.

The latter was an old corporal who had never been seen to smile, but who carried out all orders of his superiors to the letter, no matter what they might be. He stood there with an impassive face while he received the baron's instructions and then went out; five minutes later a large wagon belonging to the military train, covered with a miller's tilt, galloped off as fast as four horses could take it under the pouring rain, and the officers all seemed to awaken from their lethargy; their looks brightened, and they began to talk.

Although it was raining as hard as ever, the major declared that it was not so dull, and Lieutenant von Grossling said with conviction that the sky was clearing up, while Mademoiselle Fifi did not seem to be able to keep in his place. He got up and sat down again, and his bright eyes seemed to be looking for something to destroy. Suddenly, looking at the lady with the mustaches, the young fellow pulled out his revolver and said: "You shall not see it." And without leaving his seat he aimed and with two successive bullets cut out both the eyes of the portrait.

"Let us make a mine!" he then exclaimed, and the conversation was suddenly interrupted, as if they had found some fresh and powerful subject of interest. The mine was his invention, his method of destruction and his favorite amusement.

When he left the château the lawful owner, Count Fernand d'Amoys d'Urville, had not had time to carry away or to hide anything except the plate, which had been stowed away in a hole made in one of the walls so that, as he was very rich and had good taste, the large drawing room, which opened into the dining room, had looked like the gallery in a museum before his precipitate flight.

Expensive oil paintings, water colors and drawings hung upon the walls, while on the tables, on the hanging shelves and in elegant glass cupboards there were a thousand knickknacks: small vases, statuettes, groups in Dresden china, grotesque Chinese figures, old ivory and Venetian glass, which filled the large room with their precious and fantastical array.

Scarcely anything was left now; not that the things had been stolen, for the major would not have allowed that, but Mademoiselle Fifi would have a mine, and on that occasion all the officers thoroughly enjoyed themselves for five minutes. The little marquis went into the drawing room to get what he wanted, and he brought back a small, delicate china teapot, which he filled with gunpowder, and carefully introduced a piece of German tinder into it, through the spout. Then he lighted it and took this infernal machine into the next room, but he came back immediately and shut the door. The Germans all stood expectantly, their faces full of childish, smiling curiosity, and as soon as the explosion had shaken the château they all rushed in at once.

Mademoiselle Fifi, who got in first, clapped his hands in delight at the sight of a terra-cotta Venus, whose head had been blown off, and each picked up pieces of porcelain and wondered at the strange shape of the fragments, while the major was looking with a paternal eye at the large drawing room which had been wrecked in such a Neronic fashion and which was strewn with the fragments of works of art. He went out first and said, with a smile: "He managed that very well!"

But there was such a cloud of smoke in the dining room mingled with the to bacco smoke that they could not breathe, so the commandant opened the window, and all the officers, who had gone into the room for a glass of cognac, went up to it.

The moist air blew into the room and brought a sort of spray with it which powdered their beards. They looked at the tall trees which were dripping with the rain, at the broad valley which was covered with mist and at the church spire in the distance which rose up like a gray point in the beating rain.

The bells had not rung since their arrival. That was the only resistance which the invaders had met with in the neighborhood. The parish priest had not refused to take in and to feed the Prussian soldiers; he had several times even drunk a bottle of beer or claret with the hostile commandant, who often employed him as a benevolent intermediary, but it was no use to ask him for a single stroke of the bells; he would sooner have allowed himself to be shot. That was his way of protesting against the invasion, a peaceful and silent protest, the only one, he said, which was suitable to a priest who was a man of mildness and not of blood; and everyone for twenty-five miles round praised Abbé Chantavoine's firmness and heroism in venturing to proclaim the public mourning by the obstinate silence of his church bells.

The whole village grew enthusiastic over his resistance and was ready to back up their pastor and to risk anything, as they looked upon that silent protest as the safeguard of the national honor. It seemed to the peasants that thus they had deserved better of their country than Belfort and Strassburg, that they had set an equally valuable example and that the name of their little village would become immortalized by that, but with that exception, they refused their Prussian conquerors nothing.

The commandant and his officers laughed among themselves at that inoffensive courage, and as the people in the whole country round showed themselves obliging and compliant toward them, they willingly tolerated their silent patriotism. Only little Count Wilhelm would have liked to force them to ring the bells. He was very angry at his superior's politic compliance with the priest's scruples, and every day he begged the commandant to allow him to sound "dingdong, dingdong" just once, only just once, just by way of a joke. And he asked it like a wheedling woman, in the tender voice of some mistress who wishes to obtain something, but the commandant would not yield, and to console *herself* Mademoiselle Fifi made a *mine* in the château.

The five men stood there together for some minutes, inhaling the moist air, and at last Sublieutenant Fritz said with a laugh: "The ladies will certainly not have fine weather for their drive." Then they separated, each to his own duties, while the captain had plenty to do in seeing about the dinner.

When they met again as it was growing dark, they began to laugh at seeing each other as dandified and smart as on the day of a grand review. The commandant's hair did not look as gray as it did in the morning, and the captain had shaved—had only kept his mustache on, which made him look as if he had a streak of fire under his nose.

In spite of the rain they left the window open, and one of them went to listen from time to time. At a quarter past six the baron said he heard a rumbling in the distance. They all rushed down, and soon the wagon drove up at a gallop with its four horses, splashed up to their backs, steaming and panting. Five women got out at the bottom of the steps, five handsome girls whom a comrade of the captain, to whom *Le Devoir* had taken his card, had selected with care.

They had not required much pressing, as they were sure of being well treated, for they had got to know the Prussians in the three months during which they had had to do with them. So they resigned themselves to the men as they did to the state of affairs. "It is part of our business, so it must be done," they said as they drove along, no doubt to allay some slight, secret scruples of conscience.

They went into the dining room immediately, which looked still more dismal in its dilapidated state when it was lighted up, while the table, covered with choice dishes, the beautiful china and glass and the plate, which had been found in the hole in the wall, where its owner had hidden it, gave to the place the look of a bandits' resort, where they were supping after committing a robbery. The captain was radiant; he took hold of the women as if he were familiar with them, appraising them, kissing them, valuing them for what they were worth as *ladies of pleasure*, and when the three young men wanted to appropriate one each he opposed them authoritatively, reserving to himself the right to apportion them justly, according to their several ranks, so as not to wound the hierarchy. Therefore, so as to avoid all discussion, jarring and suspicion of partiality, he placed them all in a line according to height and addressing the tallest, he said in a voice of command:

"What is your name?"

"Pamela," she replied, raising her voice.

Then he said: "Number one, called Pamela, is adjudged to the commandant."

Then, having kissed Blondina, the second, as a sign of proprietorship, he proffered stout Amanda to Lieutenant Otto, Eva, "the Tomato," to Sublieutenant Fritz, and Rachel, the shortest of them all, a very young, dark girl, with eyes as black as ink, a Jewess, whose snub nose confirmed by exception the rule which allots hooked noses to all her race, to the youngest officer, frail Count Wilhelm von Eyrick.

They were all pretty and plump, without any distinctive features, and all were very much alike in look and person from their daily dissipation and the life common to houses of public accommodation.

The three younger men wished to carry off their women immediately, under the pretext of finding them brushes and soap, but the captain wisely opposed this, for he said they were quite fit to sit down to dinner and that those who went up would wish for a change when they came down, and so would disturb the other couples, and his experience in such matters carried the day. There were only many kisses, expectant kisses.

Suddenly Rachel choked and began to cough until the tears came into her eyes, while smoke came through her nostrils. Under pretense of kissing her the count had blown a whiff of tobacco into her mouth. She did not fly into a rage and did not say a word, but she looked at her possessor with latent hatred in her dark eyes.

They sat down to dinner. The commandant seemed delighted; he made Pamela sit on his right and Blondina on his left and said as he unfolded his table napkin: "That was a delightful idea of yours, Captain."

Lieutenants Otto and Fritz, who were as polite as if they had been with fashionable ladies, rather intimidated their neighbors, but Baron von Kelweinstein gave the reins to all his vicious propensities, beamed, made doubtful remarks and seemed on fire with his crown of red hair. He paid them compliments in French from the other side of the Rhine and sputtered out gallant remarks, only fit for a low pothouse, from between his two broken teeth.

They did not understand him, however, and their intelligence did not seem to be awakened until he uttered nasty words and broad expressions which were mangled by his accent. Then all began to laugh at once, like mad women, and fell against each other, repeating the words which the baron then began to say all wrong, in order that he might have the pleasure of hearing them say doubtful things. They gave him as much of that stuff as he wanted, for they were drunk after the first bottle of wine and, becoming themselves once more and opening the door to their usual habits, they kissed the mustaches on the right and left of them, pinched their arms, uttered furious cries, drank out of every glass and sang French couplets and bits of German songs which they had picked up in their daily intercourse with the enemy.

Soon the men themselves, intoxicated by that which was displayed to their sight and touch, grew very amorous, shouted and broke the plates and dishes, while the soldiers behind them waited on them stolidly. The commandant was the only one who put any restraint upon himself.

Mademoiselle Fifi had taken Rachel onto his knees and, getting excited, at one moment kissed the little black curls on her neck, inhaling the pleasant warmth of her body and all the savor of her person through the slight space there was between her dress and her skin, and at another pinched her furiously through the material and made her scream, for he was seized with a species of ferocity and tormented by his desire to hurt her. He often held her close to him, as if to make her part of himself, and put his lips in a long kiss on the Jewess's rosy mouth until she lost her breath, and at last he bit her until a stream of blood ran down her chin and onto her bodice.

For the second time she looked him full in the face, and as she bathed the wound she said: "You will have to pay for that!"

But he merely laughed a hard laugh and said: "I will pay."

At dessert champagne was served, and the commandant rose, and in the same voice in which he would have drunk to the health of the Empress Augusta he drank: "To our ladies!" Then a series of toasts began, toasts worthy of the lowest soldiers and of drunkards, mingled with filthy jokes which were made still more brutal by their ignorance of the language. They got up, one after the other, trying to say something witty, forcing themselves to be funny, and the women, who were so drunk that they almost fell off their chairs, with vacant looks and clammy tongues applauded madly each time.

The captain, who no doubt wished to impart an appearance of gallantry to the orgy, raised his glass again and said: "To our victories over hearts!" Thereupon Lieutenant Otto, who was a species of bear from the Black Forest, jumped up, inflamed and saturated with drink and seized by an access of alcoholic patriotism, cried: "To our victories over France!"

Drunk as they were, the women were silent, and Rachel turned round with a shudder and said: "Look here, I know some Frenchmen in whose presence you would not dare to say that." But the little count, still holding her on his knees, began to laugh, for the wine had made him very merry, and said: "Ha! ha! ha! I have never met any of them myself. As soon as we show ourselves they run away!"

The girl, who was in a terrible rage, shouted into his face: "You are lying, you dirty scoundrel!"

For a moment he looked at her steadily, with his bright eyes upon her, as he had looked at the portrait before he destroyed it with revolver bullets, and then he began to laugh: "Ah yes, talk about them, my dear! Should we be here now if they were brave?" Then, getting excited, he exclaimed: "We are the masters! France belongs to us!" She jumped off his knees with a bound and threw herself into her chair, while he rose, held out his glass over the table and repeated: "France and the French, the woods, the fields and the houses of France belong to us!"

The others, who were quite drunk and who were suddenly seized by military enthusiasm, the enthusiasm of brutes, seized their glasses and, shouting, "Long live Prussia!" emptied them at a draught.

The girls did not protest, for they were reduced to silence and were afraid. Even Rachel did not say a word, as she had no reply to make, and then the little count put his champagne glass, which had just been refilled, onto the head of the Jewess and exclaimed: "All the women in France belong to us also!"

At that she got up so quickly that the glass upset, spilling the amber-colored wine onto her black hair, as if to baptize her, and broke into a hundred fragments as it fell onto the floor. With trembling lips she defied the looks of the officer, who was still laughing, and she stammered out in a voice choked with rage: "That —that—that—is not true—for you shall certainly not have any French women."

He sat down again, so as to laugh at his ease and, trying effectually to speak in the Parisian accent, he said: "That is good, very good! Then what did you come here for, my dear?"

She was thunderstruck and made no reply for a moment, for in her agitation she did not understand him at first, but as soon as she grasped his meaning she said to him indignantly and vehemently: "I! I am not a woman; I am only a strumpet, and that is all that Prussians want."

Almost before she had finished he slapped her full in her face, but as he was raising his hand again, as if he would strike her, she, almost mad with passion, took up a small dessert knife from the table and stabbed him right in the neck, just above the breastbone. Something that he was going to say was cut short in his throat, and he sat there with his mouth half open and a terrible look in his eyes.

All the officers shouted in horror and leaped up tumultuously, but, throwing her chair between Lieutenant Otto's legs, who fell down at full length, she ran to the window, opened it before they could seize her and jumped out into the night and pouring rain.

In two minutes Mademoiselle Fifi was dead. Fritz and Otto drew their swords and wanted to kill the women, who threw themselves at their feet and clung to their knees. With some difficulty the major stopped the slaughter and had the four terrified girls locked up in a room under the care of two soldiers. Then he organized the pursuit of the fugitive as carefully as if he were about to engage in a skirmish, feeling quite sure that she would be caught.

The table, which had been cleared immediately, now served as a bed on which to lay Fifi out, and the four officers made for the window, rigid and sobered, with the stern faces of soldiers on duty, and tried to pierce through the darkness of the night, amid the steady torrent of rain. Suddenly a shot was heard and then another a long way off, and for four hours they heard from time to time near or distant reports and rallying cries, strange words uttered as a call in guttural voices.

In the morning they all returned. Two soldiers had been killed and three others wounded by their comrades in the ardor of that chase and in the confusion of such a nocturnal pursuit, but they had not caught Rachel.

Then the inhabitants of the district were terrorized; the houses were turned topsy-turvy; the country was scoured and beaten up over and over again, but the Jewess did not seem to have left a single trace of her passage behind her.

When the general was told of it he gave orders to hush up the affair so as not to set a bad example to the army, but he severely censured the commandant, who in turn punished his inferiors. The general had said: "One does not go to war in order to amuse oneself and to caress prostitutes." And Graf von Farlsberg, in his exasperation, made up his mind to have his revenge on the district, but as he required a pretext for showing severity, he sent for the priest and ordered him to have the bell tolled at the funeral of Count von Eyrick.

Contrary to all expectation, the priest showed himself humble and most respectful, and when Mademoiselle Fifi's body left the Château d'Urville on its way to the cemetery, carried by soldiers, preceded, surrounded and followed by soldiers, who marched with loaded rifles, for the first time the bell sounded its funereal knell in a lively manner, as if a friendly hand were caressing it. At night it sounded again, and the next day and every day; it rang as much as anyone could desire. Sometimes even it would start at night and sound gently through the darkness, seized by strange joy, awakened; one could not tell why. All the peasants in the neighborhood declared that it was bewitched, and nobody except the priest and the sacristan would now go near the church tower, and they went because a poor girl was living there in grief and solitude, secretly nourished by those two men.

She remained there until the German troops departed, and then one evening the priest borrowed the baker's cart and himself drove his prisoner to Rouen. When they got there he embraced her, and she quickly went back on foot to the establishment from which she had come, where the proprietress, who thought that she was dead, was very glad to see her.

A short time afterward a patriot who had no prejudices, who liked her because of her bold deed and who afterward loved her for herself, married her and made a lady of her.

A SALE

The defendants, Brument (Césaire-Isidore) and Cornu (Prosper-Napoléon), appeared at the Seine-Inférieure assizes, charged with attempting the murder, by drowning, of the woman Brument, lawful wife of the first of the said defendants.

The two accused are seated side by side in the dock. They are two peasants. The first is little and stout, with short arms, short legs and a round head; his red face, all bursting with pimples, squats without the least sign of a neck on top of a body equally round and equally short. He breeds pigs and lives at Cacheville-la-Goupil, in the district of Criquetot.

Cornu (Prosper-Napoléon) is thin, of medium height, with arms of disproportionate length. He has a crooked jaw and he squints. A blue blouse as long as a shirt falls to his knees, and his scant yellow hair, plastered down on his skull, gives his face a worn, dirty, and hideously raddled air. He has been nicknamed "the priest" because he can give a perfect imitation of church hymns and even the sound of the church serpent. He keeps a public house at Criquetot, and this talent of his attracts to the place a great many customers who prefer "Cornu's mass" to the good God's.

Mme. Brument, seated on the witness stand, is a skinny peasant woman whose drowsy placidity is never shaken. She sits unmoving, hands crossed on knees, with an unwinking stare and an air of stupidity.

The president proceeds with the examination.

"Well, then, Mme. Brument, they entered your house and threw you into a barrel full of water. Tell us the facts in detail. Stand up."

She stands up. She seems as tall as a mast, under the bonnet that covers her head with a white dome. She tells her tale in a drawling voice:

"I was shelling haricots. And then they came in. I thought to myself: 'What's up with them? They're not themselves; they're up to mischief.' They kept looking at me out of the corners of their eyes, like this, especially Cornu, owing to his squint. I didn't like to see them together, because they're never up to much good when they're together. I says to them: 'What d'you want with me?' They didn't answer. I had, as you might say, a suspicion . . ."

The prisoner Brument interrupted her statement vehemently; he declared:

"I was tipsy."

Whereupon Cornu, turning towards his fellow criminal, pronounced in a voice as deep as the note of an organ:

"Say that I was tipsy as well and you'll be telling no lies."

The president, severely: "You wish us to understand that you were drunk?"

Brument: "Yes, I was tipsy all right."

Cornu: "It might happen to anyone."

The president, to the victim: "Proceed with your statement, Mme. Brument."

"Well, then Brument said to me: 'D'you want to earn five francs?' 'Yes,' said I, seeing you don't pick five francs up in every gutter. Then he says to me: 'Keep your eyes open and do as I do,' and then he goes and fetches the big empty barrel that stands under the spout at the corner; and then he turns it up, and then he carries it into my kitchen, and then he sets it down in the middle of the floor, and then he says to me: 'Go and fetch enough water to fill it.'

"So then I go to the pond with two buckets and I fetch water, and still more water for nigh on an hour, seeing that barrel's as big as a vat, saving your honor, Mr. President.

"While I was doing it, Brument and Cornu were having a drink, and then another drink, and then another drink. They were filling themselves up together, and I said: 'It's you that's full, fuller than the barrel.' And then that Brument answers: 'Don't you worry, get on with your job, your turn's coming, everyone gets what's coming to them.' I takes no notice of his talk, seeing he was tipsy.

"When the barrel was full to the brim, I says: 'There, I've done it.'

"And then Cornu gives me five francs. Not Brument—Cornu; it was Cornu gave me them. And Brument says to me: 'Do you want to earn another five francs?'

" 'Yes,' says I, seeing I'm not used to such present.

"Then he says to me:

" 'Strip.'

" 'You want me to strip?'

" 'Yes,' he says.

" 'How far do you want me to strip?'

"He says to me:

" 'If you don't like it, keep your chemise on, we've no objection to that.'

"Five francs is five francs, so I strips, but I didn't like stripping in front of those two good-for-nothings. I takes off my bonnet, and then my bodice, and then my petticoat, and then my sabots. Brument says to me: 'Keep your stockings on, we're decent fellows, we are.'

"And that Cornu repeats: 'We're decent fellows, we are.'

"And there I am, like our Mother Eve, as you might say. And they stands up, but they couldn't stand straight, they was so drunk, saving your honor, Mr. President.

"I says to them: 'What mischief are you up to?'

"And Brument says: 'Are we ready?'

"Cornu says: 'Ready it is.'

"And then they takes me, Brument by the head and Cornu by the feet, as you might say taking up a bundle of dirty clothes. I bawls, I does. And Brument says: 'Shut up, you willy wretch.'

"And then they lifts me up in their arms, and sticks me in the barrel full of water, and they put the heart across me, and I was chilled to my very innards.

"And Brument says:

" 'Anything else?'

Cornu says:

" 'No, that's all.'

"Brument says:

" 'The head's not in, and it counts.'

Cornu says:

" 'Put her head in.'

"And then Brument pushes in my head as it might be to drown me, until the water ran up my nose and I thought I was seeing Paradise. And he gives me a push. And I went under.

"And then he must have had a fright. He pulled me out and says to me: 'Go quick and dry yourself, you skinny wretch.'

"I rushes off and I runs to the priest's, and he lends me a petticoat of his servant's, seeing I'm in my skin, and he goes to fetch Mr. Chicot, the village policeman, who goes to Cliquetot to fetch the gendarmes, and they come with me to the house.

"And there we find Brument and Cornu going for each other like two rams.

"Brument was bawling: 'It's not true, I tell you, it's at least a cubic meter. It's the measure that's wrong.'

"Cornu was bawling: 'Four buckets, that doesn't make as much as you could call half a cubic meter. You needn't say anything more, that's what it is.'

"The sergeant puts his hands on their heads. That's all I have to say."

She sat down. There was laughter in the court. The astonished jurymen stared at each other. The president said solemnly:

"Prisoner Cornu, you appear to be the instigator of this infamous plot. Have you anything to say?"

And Cornu stood up in his turn.

"Your Worship, I was tipsy."

The president replied gravely:

"I know you were. Go on."

"I am going on. Well, Brument came to my place about nine o'clock, and he orders two brandies and says: 'Have one with me, Cornu.' And I sits down with him and drinks and I offers him another, out of politeness. Then he called for two more and I did the same, and we went on, drinking brandy after brandy, until about twelve we were blind.

"Then Brument begins to cry. I feels very sorry for him. I asks him what's the matter. He says: 'I must have a thousand francs by Thursday.' When I heard that, it turns me cold, you understand. And all of a sudden he comes out with the proposal: 'I'll sell you my wife.'

"I was tipsy and I'm a widower. It fairly got me, you understand. I didn't know his wife, but a wife's a wife, isn't she? I asks him: 'How much will you sell her for?'

"He thinks it over, or rather he pretends to think it over. When a man's tipsy, he's not in his right wits, and he answers: 'I'll sell her by the cubic meter.'

"That doesn't surprise me, seeing I was as tipsy as he was, and I'm used to cubic meters in my business. That's a thousand liters, and I was agreeable to that. Only the price was still to be settled. Everything depends on quality. I says to him: 'How much the cubic meter?'

"He answers:

"'Two thousand francs.'

"I gives a jump like a rabbit, and then I think to myself that a woman can't weigh more than three hundred liters. All the same, I says: 'That's too dear.'

"He answers:

"'I can't take less. I should lose on it.'

"A man isn't a pig dealer for nothing, you understand. He knows his job. But set a thief to catch a thief, and I'm a sharp man, too. Ah! ah! ah! So I say to him: 'If she was new, I wouldn't say it was too dear, but as you've used her—haven't you?—she's second-hand. I give you fifteen hundred francs the cubic meter, not a ha'penny more. Is it a bargain?'

"He answers:

"'It's a bargain. Shake on it.'

"I shakes and we sets off, arm in arm. Folks ought to help each other along in this life.

"But I had a sudden fear: 'How are you going to measure her in liters unless you melt her down?'

"Then he explains his idea, none too easily, seeing he was tipsy. He says: 'I take a barrel, I fill it with water to the brim. I put her inside. All the water that pours over I'll measure out, and that'll be the total.'

"I says:

"'Right, it's agreed. But the water that pours over will run away: what are you going to do to gather it up again?'

"Then he thinks I'm a booby, and he explains that he'll only have to pour back what's run out of the barrel as soon as his wife has got out of it. The amount of water we had to add, would be the total. I reckon ten buckets: that's a cubic meter. He's not so stupid when he's tipsy, the rascal, all the same!

"To cut it short, we go off to his house, and I examine the goods specified. As pretty women go, she's not a pretty woman. Everyone can see that for themselves, seeing she's sitting there. I says to myself: I've been done; never mind, it's all one: pretty or ugly, a woman's just as much use, isn't she now, Mr. President? And then I see for certain that she's as thin as a match. I says to myself: 'There's not four hundred liters there!' I know what I'm talking about, being used to dealing in liquids.

"She's told you the way we arranged it. I even let her keep her chemise and her stockings on, a clear loss to me.

"When it was over, what d'you think? She runs off. I says: 'Here! Brument, she's getting away.'

"He replies: 'Don't you be afraid, I'll always get her back again. She'll have to come home to go to bed. I'm going to reckon the deficit.'

"We measured it. Not four buckets. Ah, ah, ah, ah!"

The prisoner began to laugh, and continued to laugh until a gendarme was obliged to thump him on the back. Quiet again, he adds:

"To cut it short, Brument declares: 'Nothing doing, it's not enough.' I bawl, he bawls. I bawl louder, he stamps, I thump. That would have gone on till doomsday, seeing I was tipsy.

"Then in come the gendarmes. They curse me, and they play us a dirty trick. Sent to prison. I demand damages."

He sits down.

Brument swears that his fellow criminal's confession is true in every respect. The jury, overwhelmed, retired to consider their verdict.

They returned an hour later and acquitted the accused with severe strictures bearing on the sanctity of marriage and setting forth in precise terms the limits set to commercial transactions.

Brument, accompanied by his spouse, made his way towards the conjugal hearth.

Cornu returned to his business.

AN AFFAIR OF STATE

Paris had just heard of the disaster of Sedan. The Republic was proclaimed. All France was panting from a madness that lasted until the time of the commonwealth. Everybody was playing at soldier from one end of the country to the other.

Capmakers became colonels, assuming the duties of generals; revolvers and daggers were displayed on large rotund bodies enveloped in red sashes; common citizens turned warriors, commanding battalions of noisy volunteers and swearing like troopers to emphasize their importance.

The very fact of bearing arms and handling guns with a system excited a people who hitherto had only handled scales and measures and made them formidable to the first comer, without reason. They even executed a few innocent people to prove that they knew how to kill, and in roaming through virgin fields still belonging to the Prussians they shot stray dogs, cows chewing the cud in peace or sick horses put out to pasture. Each believed himself called upon to play a great role in military affairs. The cafés of the smallest villages, full of tradesmen in uniform, resembled barracks or field hospitals.

Now the town of Canneville did not yet know the exciting news of the army and the capital. It had, however, been greatly agitated for a month over an encounter between the rival political parties. The mayor, Viscount de Varnetot, a small thin man, already old, remained true to the Empire, especially since he saw rising up against him a powerful adversary in the great, sanguine form of Dr. Massarel, head of the Republican party in the district, venerable chief of the Masonic lodge, president of the Society of Agriculture and the Fire Department and organizer of the rural militia designed to save the country.

In two weeks he had induced sixty-three men to volunteer in defense of their country—married men, fathers of families, prudent farmers, and merchants of the town. These he drilled every morning in front of the mayor's window.

Whenever the mayor happened to appear Commander Massarel, covered with pistols, passing proudly up and down in front of his troops, would make them shout, "Long live our country!" And this, they noticed, disturbed the little viscount, who no doubt heard in it menace and defiance and perhaps some odious recollection of the great Revolution.

On the morning of the fifth of September, in uniform, his revolver on the table, the doctor gave consultation to an old peasant couple. The husband had suffered with a varicose vein for seven years but had waited until his wife had one too, so that they might go and hunt up a physician together, guided by the postman when he should come with the newspaper.

Dr. Massarel opened the door, grew pale, straightened himself abruptly and, raising his arms to heaven in a gesture of exaltation, cried out with all his might, in the face of the amazed rustics:

"Long live the Republic! Long live the Republic! Long live the Republic!"

Then he dropped into his armchair weak with emotion.

When the peasant explained that this sickness commenced with a feeling as if ants were running up and down his legs the doctor exclaimed: "Hold your peace. I have spent too much time with you stupid people. The Republic is proclaimed! The Emperor is a prisoner! France is saved! Long live the Republic!" And, running to the door, he bellowed: "Celeste! Quick! Celeste!"

The frightened maid hastened in. He stuttered, so rapidly did he try to speak. "My boots, my saber—my cartridge box—and—the Spanish dagger which is on my night table. Hurry now!"

The obstinate peasant, taking advantage of the moment's silence, began again: "This seemed like some cysts that hurt me when I walked."

The exasperated physician shouted: "Hold your peace! For heaven's sake! If you had washed your feet oftener, it would not have happened." Then, seizing him by the neck, he hissed in his face: "Can you not comprehend that we are living in a republic, stupid?"

But the professional sentiment calmed him suddenly, and he let the astonished old couple out of the house, repeating all the time:

"Return tomorrow, return tomorrow, my friends; I have no more time today."

While equipping himself from head to foot he gave another series of urgent orders to the maid:

"Run to Lieutenant Picard's and to Sublieutenant Pommel's and say to them that I want them here immediately. Send Torchebœuf to me too, with his drum. Quick now! Quick!" And when Celeste was gone he collected his thoughts and prepared to surmount the difficulties of the situation.

The three men arrived together. They were in their working clothes. The commander, who had expected to see them in uniform, had a fit of surprise.

"You know nothing, then? The Emperor has been taken prisoner. A republic is proclaimed. My position is delicate, not to say perilous."

He reflected for some minutes before the astonished faces of his subordinates and then continued:

"It is necessary to act, not to hesitate. Minutes now are worth hours at other times. Everything depends upon promptness of decision. You, Picard, go and find

the curate and get him to ring the bell to bring the people together, while I get
ahead of them. You, Torchebœuf, beat the call to assemble the militia in arms,
in the square, from even as far as the hamlets of Gerisaie and Salmare. You, Pommel, put on your uniform at once, that is, the jacket and cap. We, together, are
going to take possession of the *mairie* and summon Me. de Varnetot to transfer his
authority to me. Do you understand?"

"Yes."

"Act, then, and promptly. I will accompany you to your house, Pommel, since
we are to work together."

Five minutes later the commander and his subaltern, armed to the teeth, appeared in the square just at the moment when the little Viscount de Varnetot,
with hunting gaiters on and his rifle on his shoulder, appeared by another street,
walking rapidly and followed by three guards in green jackets, each carrying a
knife at his side and a gun over his shoulder.

While the doctor stopped, half stupefied, the four men entered the mayor's
house and the door closed behind them.

"We are forestalled," murmured the doctor; "it will be necessary now to wait for
reinforcements; nothing can be done for a quarter of an hour."

Here Lieutenant Picard appeared. "The curate refuses to obey," said he; "he has
even shut himself up in the church with the beadle and the porter."

On the other side of the square, opposite the white closed front of the *mairie*,
the church, mute and black, showed its great oak door with the wrought-iron trimmings.

Then, as the puzzled inhabitants put their noses out of the windows or came
out upon the steps of their houses, the rolling of a drum was heard, and Torchebœuf suddenly appeared, beating with fury the three quick strokes of the call to
arms. He crossed the square with disciplined step and then disappeared on a road
leading to the country.

The commander drew his sword, advanced alone to the middle distance between
the two buildings where the enemy was barricaded and, waving his weapon, above
his head, roared at the top of his lungs: "Long live the Republic! Death to trai-
tors!" Then he fell back where his officers were. The butcher, the baker and the
apothecary, feeling a little uncertain, put up their shutters and closed their shops.
The grocery alone remained open.

Meanwhile the men of the militia were arriving little by little, variously clothed
but all wearing caps, the cap constituting the whole uniform of the corps. They
were armed with their old rusty guns, guns that had hung on chimney pieces in
kitchens for thirty years, and looked quite like a detachment of country soldiers.

When there were about thirty around him the commander explained in a
few words the state of affairs. Then, turning toward his major, he said: "Now we
must act."

While the inhabitants collected, talked over, and discussed the matter the doctor
quickly formed his plan of campaign.

"Lieutenant Picard, you advance to the windows of the mayor's house and
order M. de Varnetot to turn over the town hall to me in the name of the Republic."

But the lieutenant was a master mason and refused.

"You are a scamp, you are. Trying to make a target of me! Those fellows in there are good shots, you know that. No, thanks! Execute your commissions yourself!"

The commander turned red. "I order you to go in the name of discipline," said he.

"I am not spoiling my features without knowing why," the lieutenant returned.

Men of influence, in a group near by, were heard laughing. One of them called out: "You are right, Picard, it is not the proper time." The doctor, under his breath, muttered: "Cowards!" And placing his sword and his revolver in the hands of a soldier, he advanced with measured step, his eye fixed on the windows as if he expected to see a gun or a cannon pointed at him.

When he was within a few steps of the building the doors at the two extremities, affording an entrance to two schools, opened, and a flood of little creatures, boys on one side, girls on the other, poured out and began playing in the open space, chattering around the doctor like a flock of birds. He scarcely knew what to make of it.

As soon as the last were out the doors closed. The greater part of the little monkeys finally scattered, and then the commander called out in a loud voice:

"Monsieur de Varnetot?" A window in the first story opened and M. de Varnetot appeared.

The commander began: "Monsieur, you are aware of the great events which have changed the system of government. The party you represent no longer exists. The side I represent now comes into power. Under these sad but decisive circumstances I come to demand you, in the name of the Republic, to put in my hand the authority vested in you by the outgoing power."

M. de Varnetot replied: "Doctor Massarel, I am mayor of Canneville, so placed by the proper authorities, and mayor of Canneville I shall remain until the title is revoked and replaced by an order from my superiors. As mayor, I am at home in the mairie, and there I shall stay. Furthermore, just try to put me out." And he closed the window.

The commander returned to his troops. But before explaining anything, measuring Lieutenant Picard from head to foot, he said:

"You are a numskull, you are—a goose, the disgrace of the army. I shall degrade you."

The lieutenant replied: "I'll attend to that myself." And he went over to a group of muttering civilians.

Then the doctor hesitated. What should he do? Make an assault? Would his men obey him? And then was he surely in the right? An idea burst upon him. He ran to the telegraph office on the other side of the square and hurriedly sent three dispatches: "To the Members of the Republican Government at Paris"; "To the New Republican Prefect of the Lower Seine at Rouen"; "To the New Republican Subprefect of Dieppe."

He exposed the situation fully; told of the danger run by the commonwealth from remaining in the hands of the monarchistic mayor, offered his devout services, asked for orders and signed his name, following it up with all his titles. Then he returned to his army corps and, drawing ten francs out of his pocket, said:

"Now, my friends, go and eat and drink a little something. Only leave here a detachment of ten men, so that no one leaves the mayor's house."

Ex-Lieutenant Picard, chatting with the watchmaker, overheard this. With a sneer he remarked: "Pardon me, but if they go out, there will be an opportunity for you to go in. Otherwise I can't see how you are to get in there!"

The doctor made no reply but went away to luncheon. In the afternoon he disposed of offices all about town, having the air of knowing of an impending surprise. Many times he passed before the doors of the mairie and of the church without noticing anything suspicious; one could have believed the two buildings empty.

The butcher, the baker and the apothecary reopened their shops and stood gossiping on the steps. If the Emperor had been taken prisoner, there must be a traitor somewhere. They did not feel sure of the revenue of a new republic.

Night came on. Toward nine o'clock the doctor returned quietly and alone to the mayor's residence, persuaded that his adversary had retired. And as he was trying to force an entrance with a few blows of a pickax the loud voice of a guard demanded suddenly: "Who goes there?" M. Massarel beat a retreat at the top of his speed.

Another day dawned without any change in the situation. The militia in arms occupied the square. The inhabitants stood around awaiting the solution. People from neighboring villages came to look on. Finally the doctor, realizing that his reputation was at stake, resolved to settle the thing in one way or another. He had just decided that it must be something energetic when the door of the telegraph office opened and the little servant of the directress appeared, holding in her hand two papers.

She went directly to the commander and gave him one of the dispatches; then, crossing the square, intimidated by so many eyes fixed upon her, with lowered head and mincing steps, she rapped gently at the door of the barricaded house as if ignorant that a part of the army was concealed there.

The door opened slightly; the hand of a man received the message, and the girl returned, blushing and ready to weep from being stared at.

The doctor demanded with stirring voice: "A little silence, if you please." And after the populace became quiet he continued proudly:

"Here is a communication which I have received from the government." And, raising the dispatch, he read:

"Old mayor deposed. Advise us what is most necessary. Instructions later.
                                            "For the Subprefect,
                                                    "SAPIN, Counselor."

He had triumphed. His heart was beating with joy. His hand trembled, when Picard, his old subaltern, cried out to him from the neighboring group:

"That's all right; but if the others in there won't go out, your paper hasn't a leg to stand on." The doctor grew a little pale. If they would not go out—in fact, he must go ahead now. It was not only his right but his duty. And he looked anxiously at the house of the mayoralty, hoping that he might see the door open and his adversary show himself. But the door remained closed. What was to be done? The crowd was increasing, surrounding the militia. Some laughed.

One thought, especially, tortured the doctor. If he should make an assault, he must march at the head of his men; and as with him dead all contest would cease, it would be at him and at him alone that M. de Varnetot and the three guards would aim. And their aim was good, very good! Picard had reminded him of that.

But an idea shone in upon him, and turning to Pommel, he said: "Go, quickly, and ask the apothecary to send me a napkin and a pole."

The lieutenant hurried off. The doctor was going to make a political banner, a white one, that would, perhaps, rejoice the heart of that old legitimist, the mayor.

Pommel returned with the required linen and a broom handle. With some pieces of string they improvised a standard, which Massarel seized in both hands. Again he advanced toward the house of mayoralty, bearing the standard before him. When in front of the door, he called out: "Monsieur de Varnetot!"

The door opened suddenly, and M. de Varnetot and the three guards appeared on the threshold. The doctor recoiled instinctively. Then he saluted his enemy courteously and announced, almost strangled by emotion: "I have come, sir, to communicate to you the instructions I have just received."

That gentleman, without any salutation whatever, replied: "I am going to withdraw, sir, but you must understand that it is not because of fear or in obedience to an odious government that has usurped the power." And, biting off each word, he declared: "I do not wish to have the appearance of serving the Republic for a single day. That is all."

Massarel, amazed, made no reply; and M. de Varnetot, walking off at a rapid pace, disappeared around the corner, followed closely by his escort. Then the doctor, slightly dismayed, returned to the crowd. When he was near enough to be heard he cried: "Hurrah! Hurrah! The Republic triumphs all along the line!"

But no emotion was manifested. The doctor tried again. "The people are free! You are free and independent! Do you understand? Be proud of it!"

The listless villagers looked at him with eyes unlit by glory. In his turn he looked at them, indignant at their indifference, seeking for some word that could make a grand impression, electrify this placid country and make good his mission. The inspiration came, and turning to Pommel, he said: "Lieutenant, go and get the bust of the ex-emperor, which is in the Council Hall, and bring it to me with a chair."

And soon the man reappears, carrying on his right shoulder Napoleon III in plaster and holding in his left hand a straw-bottomed chair.

Massarel met him, took the chair, placed it on the ground, put the white image upon it, fell back a few steps and called out in a sonorous voice:

"Tyrant! Tyrant! Here do you fall! Fall in the dust and in the mire. An expiring country groans under your feet. Destiny has called you the Avenger. Defeat and shame cling to you. You fall conquered, a prisoner to the Prussians, and upon the ruins of the crumbling Empire the young and radiant Republic arises, picking up your broken sword."

He awaited applause. But there was no voice, no sound. The bewildered peasants remained silent. And the bust, with its pointed mustaches extending beyond the cheeks on each side, the bust, so motionless and well groomed as to be fit for a hairdresser's sign, seemed to be looking at M. Massarel with a plaster smile, a smile ineffaceable and mocking.

They remained thus face to face, Napoleon on the chair, the doctor in front of him about three steps away. Suddenly the commander grew angry. What was to be done? What was there that would move this people and bring about a definite victory in opinion? His hand happened to rest on his hip and to come in contact there with the butt end of his revolver under his red sash. No inspiration, no further word would come. But he drew his pistol, advanced two steps and, taking aim, fired at the late monarch. The ball entered the forehead, leaving a little black hole like a spot, nothing more. There was no effect. Then he fired a second shot, which made a second hole, then a third; and then, without stopping, he emptied his revolver. The brow of Napoleon disappeared in white powder, but the eyes, the nose and the fine points of the mustaches remained intact. Then, exasperated, the doctor overturned the chair with a blow of his fist and, resting a foot on the remainder of the bust in a position of triumph, he shouted: "So let all tyrants perish!"

Still no enthusiasm was manifest, and as the spectators seemed to be in a kind of stupor from astonishment the commander called to the militiamen: "You may now go to your homes." And he went toward his own house with great strides, as if he were pursued.

His maid, when he appeared, told him that some patients had been waiting in his office for three hours. He hastened in. There were the two varicose-vein patients, who had returned at daybreak, obstinate but patient.

The old man immediately began his explanation: "This began by a feeling like ants running up and down the legs."

THE MASK

There was a fancy-dress ball that evening at the Elysée-Montmartre. It was to celebrate Mid-Lent, and the crowd was pouring, like the water rushing over a weir, down the illuminated corridor that led to the dance room. The overpowering clamor of the orchestra, crashing like a storm of music, split walls and roof, spread abroad through the neighborhood, and roused in the streets, and even in the near-by houses, the irresistible desire to leap, to be warm and amused, that slumbers in the depths of the human animal.

The regular frequenters of the place were arriving from all the four corners of Paris, people of all classes, who were fond of vulgar, roistering amusements that were a little vicious and not a little debauched. There were shop assistants, pimps, prostitutes—prostitutes in every sort of dress, from the common cotton to the finest batiste; wealthy prostitutes, the old wealthy ones, old and covered with diamonds; and the penniless sixteen-year-olds longing to enjoy themselves, to find men, to spend money. Elegants in tailed coats, in search of youthful flesh, deflowered of its primal innocence but still desirable, roved through the overheated crowd, peering, seemingly scenting it out, while the masks appeared absorbed in their desire for amusement. The famous quadrilles had already gathered round their caperings a crowded circle of people. The swaying hedge, the quivering mass of women and men who encircled the four dancers, knotted itself round like a serpent, advancing and withdrawing in time to the swerving movements of the dancers. The two women, whose thighs seemed fastened to their bodies by India-rubber springs, executed the most amazing movements with their legs. They flung them up in the air with such vigor that the limbs seemed to be flying towards the sky, then suddenly, parting them as if they were open to the navel, sliding one in front and the other behind, they touched the ground with the center of their bodies in a quick wide split, revolting and comical to watch.

Their partners leaped, pirouetted on their feet, whirled round, their arms flapping and raised like stumps of featherless wings, and one guessed that under their masks their breath was coming in gasps.

One of them, who had taken a part in the most famous of the quadrilles to replace a celebrated dancer who was absent, the magnificent Songe-au-gosse, and was doing his best to keep pace with the indefatigable Arête-de-veau, was executing fantastic solo steps that provoked the joy and ironic mirth of the public.

He was lean, attired like a dandy, with a handsome varnished mask on his face, a mask with a fair curling mustache and topped by a curled wig.

He had the appearance of a model from the Grévin museum, of a strange and fantastic caricature of a charming young man in a fashion plate, and he danced with an earnest but awkward effort and with a droll ecstasy. He seemed rusty beside the others as he tried to imitate their gambols: he seemed crippled, as clumsy as a pug dog playing with greyhounds. Mocking bravos encouraged him, and he, drunk with enthusiasm, leaped about with such frenzy that all at once, carried away by a wild rush, he ran full tilt into the wall of bystanders, which parted before him to let him pass, then closed up again round the inert body of the motionless dancer, lying face downwards.

Men picked him up and carried him away. There were shouts for a doctor. A gentleman came forward, young, very elegant, in a black coat with enormous pearls in his dress shirt. "I am a professor in the medical school," he said, modestly. They made way for him, and in a little room full of cartons, like a business man's office, he found the still unconscious dancer stretched across the chairs. The doctor tried first to remove the mask and discovered that it was fastened on in a complicated fashion, by a multitude of fine metal threads, which attached it cleverly to the edges of his wig and enclosed his entire head, in a solid ligature, of which one would have to know the secret. The neck itself was imprisoned in a false skin which formed a continuation of the chin, and this glovelike skin, painted flesh color, reached to the neck of his shirt.

They had to cut it all away with strong scissors, and when the doctor had made a gash from shoulder to temple in this amazing apparatus, he opened out this carapace and found therein an old face, the face of a pale, worn-out, thin, wrinkled man. The shock to those who carried in the young curled mask was so great that no one laughed, no one said a word.

They stared, where it lay on the rush chairs, at this sad face with its closed eyes, besprinkled with white hairs, some of them long, falling from the forehead over his face, others short, sprouting from cheeks and chin, and there beside this poor head—the small, charming, polished mask, the fresh, still smiling mask.

The man came to himself after remaining unconscious for a long time, but he seemed still so feeble, so ill, that the doctor feared some dangerous complications.

"Where do you live?" said he.

The old dancer seemed to search in his memory and then to remember, and he gave the name of a street which no one knew. So they had to ask him again for details of the neighborhood. He furnished them with infinite pain, with a slowness and indecision that betrayed the disturbance of his mind.

The doctor continued:

"I'll take you back there myself."

He had been seized with curiosity to know who this strange mummer was, to see where this amazing mountebank lived.

A cab soon carried them both to the other side of the slope of Montmartre.

It was in a tall house of poverty-stricken aspect, ascended by a shiny staircase, one of those forever unfinished houses, riddled with windows, standing between two amorphous stretches of ground, squalid dens where live a horde of ragged miserable wretches.

The doctor, clinging to the handrail, a winding wooden rod to which his hand stuck fast, supported the dazed old man, who was now regaining his strength, up to the fourth floor.

The door at which they had knocked opened, and a woman appeared, old too, and clean, with a white nightcap framing a bony face with strongly marked features, the characteristic, broad, good, roughhewn face of an industrious and faithful woman of the working class. She cried:

"My God, what's happened to him?"

When the affair had been explained to her in twenty words, she was reassured, and reassured the doctor himself by telling him that this was by no means the first of such adventures that had happened.

"He must go to bed, sir, that's all, he'll sleep, and next day there'll be nothing to show for it."

The doctor answered:

"But he can hardly speak."

"Oh, it's nothing, he's a little drunk, nothing else. He ate no dinner so that he should be supple, and then he drank two absinths to liven himself up. The absinth, you know, revives his legs, but it takes away his wits and his words. He's not of an age now to dance as he does. No, indeed, I've lost all hope of him ever getting any sense."

The doctor, surprised, insisted:

"But why does he dance like that, old as he is?"

She shrugged her shoulders; she was flushed with the anger that was slowly rousing in her.

"Oh, yes, why! To tell the truth, it's so that people will think he's young under his mask, so that the women will still take him for a gay dog and whisper nasty things in his ear, so that he can rub himself against their skin, all their dirty skins with their scents and their powder and their pomades. Oh, it's a nasty business! Well, I've had a life of it, I have, sir, for the forty years it's been going on. . . . But he must be got to bed first so he doesn't take any harm. Would it be too much trouble to you to give me a hand? When he's like that, I can't manage by myself."

The old man was sitting on the bed, with a drunken look, his long white hair fallen over his face.

His companion regarded him with pitying, angry eyes. She went on:

"Look what a fine face he has for his age, and he must go and disguise himself like a worthless scamp so that people will think he's young. If it's not a pity! He really has a fine face, sir! Wait, I'll show it to you before we put him to bed."

She went towards a table on which was the hand basin, the water jug, soap, comb and brush. She took the brush, then returned to the bed and, lifting the old drunkard's tangled head of hair, in the twinkling of an eye she gave him the face of a painter's model, with long curls falling on his neck. Then, stepping back to contemplate him:

"He really is handsome for his age, isn't he?"

"Very handsome," declared the doctor, who was beginning to find it very amusing.

She added:

"And if you had known him when he was twenty-five years old! But we must put him to bed, or else his absinths will upset him in his stomach. Now, sir, will you draw off his sleeve? . . . higher . . . that's it . . . good . . . the breeches now . . . wait, I'll take off his shoes . . . that's better. . . . Now, hold him up while I turn down the bed . . . there . . . lay him down. . . . If you think he'll disturb himself shortly to make room for me, you're mistaken. I must find my corner, anywhere, anyhow. He doesn't worry about it. There, you gay spark, you!"

As soon as he felt himself between his bedclothes, the good man shut his eyes, reopened them, shut them again, and his whole contented face expressed an energetic determination to sleep.

The doctor, examining him with an ever growing interest, asked:

"So he plays the young man at fancy-dress balls, does he?"

"At all of them, sir, and he comes back to me in the morning in such a condition you can't imagine. You know, it's regret that drives him there, and makes him put a cardboard face over his own. Yes, regret that he's no longer what he was, and so has no triumphs any more."

He was sleeping now, and beginning to snore. She contemplated him with a compassionate air, and added:

"Oh, he has had his triumphs, that man has! More than you'd think, sir, more than the fine society gentleman and more than any tenor or any general."

"Really? What was he then?"

"Oh, it surprises you at first, seeing that you didn't know him in his best days. When I met him, it was at a ball, too, for he was always attending them. I was taken as soon as I saw him—yes, taken like a fish on a line. He was charming, sir, so charming he'd bring tears to your eyes to look at him, dark as a crow, and curly-haired, with black eyes as large as windows. Oh, yes, he was a beautiful young man. He carried me off that evening, and I never left him again, sir, no, not for a day, in spite of everything. Oh, he has given me some bad times!"

The doctor asked:

"You are married?"

She answered simply:

"Yes, sir . . . or else he would have left me like the others. I have been his wife and his nurse, everything, everything he wanted . . . and he has made me weep for it . . . tears that I did not let him see. For he used to tell his adventures to me, to me . . . to me . . . sir—never realizing how it hurt me to listen to them. . . ."

"But what was his profession?"

"Oh, yes . . . I forgot to tell you. He was head assistant at Martel's, such an assistant as you never saw . . . an artist at ten francs the hour, on an average. . . ."

"Martel? . . . who was Martel?"

"The hairdresser, sir, the famous hairdresser of the Opera, who had all the actresses as his customers. Yes, all the smartest actresses came to have their hair done by Ambroise, and gave him rewards that made his fortune. Oh, sir, all women are alike, yes, all of them. When a man pleases them, they offer themselves to him. It's so easy . . . and that's a hard lesson to learn. For he used to tell me all . . .

he couldn't keep silent . . . no, he couldn't. These things give so much pleasure to men! and more pleasure still to tell about than to do, perhaps.

"When I saw him come home in the evening a little pale, with an air of contentment, and shining eyes, I used to say to myself: 'Another one. I am sure he's caught another one.' Then I used to long to question him, a longing that scorched my heart, and I longed not to know, too, to prevent him from talking if he began. And we used to look at each other.

"I knew well that he would not hold his tongue, that he was going to come to the point. I felt it in his manner, in the laughing manner he assumed to make me understand. 'I have had a good day today, Madeleine.' I pretended not to see, not to guess: I set the table; I brought the soup; I sat down opposite him.

"In those moments, sir, it was just as if my liking for him was being crushed out of my body with a stone. That's a bad thing, that is, a dreadful thing. But he didn't guess it, not he, he didn't know: he felt the need to tell someone about it, to boast, to show how much he was loved . . . and he had only me to tell it to . . . you understand . . . only me . . . so . . . I had to listen and take it like poison.

"He began to eat his soup and then he used to say:

" 'Another one, Madeleine.'

"I used to think: 'Now it's coming. My God, what a man! That I should have taken up with him!'

"Then he started: 'Another one, and a beauty. . . .' And it would be a little girl from the Vaudeville or maybe a little girl from the Variétés, and maybe one of the great ones too, the most famous of these theatrical ladies. He told me their names, described their rooms, and all, all, yes, all, sir. . . . Details that tore my heart. And he would keep on about it, he would tell his story again from beginning to end, so pleased that I used to pretend to laugh so that he would not be angry with me.

"Perhaps it wasn't all true. He was so fond of glorifying himself that he was quite capable of inventing such things! And perhaps, too, it was true. On those evenings, he made a show of being tired, of wanting to go to bed after supper. We had supper at eleven, sir, because he never came in earlier, on account of the evening hairdressing.

"When he had finished relating his adventures, he used to smoke cigarettes and walk up and down the room, and he was such a handsome fellow, with his mustache and his curly hair, that I thought: 'It's true, all the same, what he tells me. Since I'm mad about that man myself, why shouldn't other women be infatuated with him too?' Oh, I wanted to cry about it, to scream, to run away, to throw myself out of the window, as I was clearing the table while he went on smoking. He yawned when he opened his mouth, to show me how tired he was, and he used to say two or three times before getting into bed: 'God, how I shall sleep tonight!'

"I bear him no grudge for it, because he did not know he hurt me. No, he could not know it! He loved to boast about women like a peacock spreading his tail. He came to imagine that they all looked at him and wanted him. It made it hard when he began to grow old.

"Oh, sir, when I saw his first white hair, it gave me a shock that took my breath away, and then joy . . . a cruel joy—but so deep, so deep. I said to myself: 'It's the end.' I felt that I was going to be let out of prison. I should have him all to myself, when the others didn't want him any more.

"It was one morning, in our bed. He was still sleeping, and I was bending over him to waken him with a caress, when I saw in the curls on his temple a little thread that shone like silver. What a surprise! I would not have believed it possible. For a moment I thought of pulling it out, so that he shouldn't see it himself! but looking closely, I caught sight of another one higher up. White hairs! He was going to have white hairs! It made my heart beat and my skin wet; but all the same, in the bottom of my heart, I was very glad about it.

"It's not pleasant to think of it, but I went about my work in rare spirits that morning, and I didn't wake him just then; and when he had opened his eyes without being roused, I said to him:

" 'Do you know what I discovered when you were asleep?'

" 'No.'

" 'I discovered that you have some white hairs.'

"He gave a start of vexation that made him sit down as if I had tickled him, and he said in an annoyed way:

" 'It's not true.'

" 'Yes, on the left temple. There are four of them.'

"He jumped from the bed to run to the mirror.

"He did not find them. Then I showed him the first, the lowest down, the little curly one, and I said to him:

" 'It's not surprising considering the life you lead. Two years from now you'll be finished.'

"Well, sir, I spoke truly; two years later, you wouldn't have known him. How quickly a man changes! He was still handsome but he was losing his freshness, and women no longer ran after him. Oh, I had a hard life of it, I did, in those days: he made me suffer cruelly for it! Nothing pleased him, not the least thing. He left his profession for the hat trade, in which he got rid of a lot of money. And then he tried to be an actor, without any success, and then he began to frequent public dances. Well, he has had the good sense to keep a little of his money, on which we're living. It's enough, but it's not much. To think that at one time he had almost a fortune!

"Now you see what he does. It's like a frenzy that takes hold on him. He must be young, he must dance with women who smell of scent and pomade. Poor old darling that he is!"

Moved, ready to weep, she looked at her old husband, who was snoring. Then, drawing near him with light steps, she dropped a kiss on his hair. The doctor had risen and was preparing to leave; he could find nothing to say in the presence of this fantastic pair.

Then, as he was going, she asked:

"Will you just give me your address? If he gets worse I will come and fetch you."

A COCK CROWED

Mme. Bertha d'Avancelles had up till that time resisted all the prayers of her despairing adorer, Baron Joseph de Croissard. He had pursued her ardently in Paris during the winter, and now he was giving fetes and shooting parties in her honor at his château at Carville, in Normandy.

M. d'Avancelles, her husband, saw nothing and knew nothing, as usual. It was said that he lived apart from his wife on account of a physical weakness for which Mme. d'Avancelles would not pardon him. He was a short, stout, bald man, with short arms, legs, neck, nose, and very ugly; while Mme. d'Avancelles, on the contrary, was a tall, dark and determined young woman who laughed in her husband's face with sonorous peals while he called her openly "Mrs. Housewife." She looked at the broad shoulders, strong build and fair mustaches of her titled admirer, Baron Joseph de Croissard, with a certain amount of tenderness.

She had not, however, granted him anything as yet. The baron was ruining himself for her, and there was a constant round of feting, hunting parties and new pleasures to which he invited the neighboring nobility. All day long the hounds gave tongue in the woods as they followed the fox or the wild boar, and every night dazzling fireworks mingled their burning plumes with the stars while the illuminated windows of the drawing room cast long rays of light onto the wide lawns where shadows were moving to and fro.

It was autumn, the russet-colored season of the year, and the leaves were whirling about on the grass like flights of birds. One noticed the smell of damp earth in the air, of the naked earth, like one scents the odor of the bare skin when a woman's dress falls off her after a ball.

One evening in the previous spring, during an entertainment, Mme. d'Avancelles had said to M. de Croissard, who was worrying her by his importunities: "If I do succumb to you, my friend, it will not be before the fall of the leaf. I have too many things to do this summer to have any time for it." He had not forgotten that bold and amusing speech, and every day he became more pressing, every day he pushed his approaches nearer—to use a military phrase—and gained a hold on the heart of the fair, audacious woman who seemed only to be resisting for form's sake.

It was the day before a large wild-boar hunt, and in the evening Mme. Bertha said to the baron with a laugh: "Baron, if you kill the brute, I shall have something to say to you." And so at dawn he was up and out, to try and discover where the solitary animal had its lair. He accompanied his huntsmen, settled the places for the relays and organized everything personally to insure his triumph. When the horns gave the signal for setting out he appeared in a closely fitting coat of scarlet and gold, with his waist drawn in tight, his chest expanded, his eyes radiant and as fresh and strong as if he had just got out of bed. They set off; the wild boar bolted through the underwood as soon as he was dislodged, followed by the hounds in full cry, while the horses set off at a gallop through the narrow side-cuts in the forest. The carriages which followed the chase at a distance drove noiselessly along the soft roads.

From mischief Mme. d'Avancelles kept the baron by her side, lagging behind at a walk in an interminably long and straight drive, over which four rows of oaks hung so as to form almost an arch, while he, trembling with love and anxiety, listened with one ear to the young woman's bantering chatter and with the other to the blast of the horns and to the cry of the hounds as they receded in the distance.

"So you do not love me any longer?" she observed.

"How can you say such things?" he replied.

And she continued: "But you seem to be paying more attention to the sport than to me."

He groaned and said: "Did you not order me to kill the animal myself?"

And she replied gravely: "Of course I reckon upon it. You must kill it under my eyes."

Then he trembled in his saddle, spurred his horse until it reared and, losing all patience, exclaimed: "But, by Jove, madame, that is impossible if we remain here."

Then she spoke tenderly to him, laying her hand on his arm or stroking his horse's mane, as if from abstraction, and said with a laugh: "But you must do it —or else so much the worse for you."

Just then they turned to the right into a narrow path which was overhung by trees, and suddenly, to avoid a branch which barred their way, she leaned toward him so closely that he felt her hair tickling his neck. Suddenly he threw his arms brutally round her, and putting his heavily mustached mouth to her forehead, he gave her a furious kiss.

At first she did not move and remained motionless under that mad caress; then she turned her head with a jerk, and either by accident or design her little lips met his, under their wealth of light hair, and a moment afterward, either from confusion or remorse, she struck her horse with her riding whip and went off at full gallop, and they rode on like that for some time, without exchanging a look.

The noise of the hunt came nearer; the thickets seemed to tremble, and suddenly the wild boar broke through the bushes, covered with blood and trying to shake off the hounds who had fastened onto him, and the baron, uttering a shout of triumph, exclaimed: "Let him who loves me follow me!" And he disappeared in the copse as if the wood had swallowed him up.

When she reached an open glade a few minutes later he was just getting up, covered with mud, his coat torn and his hands bloody, while the brute was lying stretched out at full length with the baron's hunting knife driven into its shoulder up to the hilt.

The quarry was cut at night by torchlight. It was a warm and dull evening, and the wan moon threw a yellow light onto the torches which made the night misty with their resinous smoke. The hounds devoured the wild boar's entrails and snarled and fought for them, while the prickers and the gentlemen, standing in a circle round the spoil, blew their horns as loud as they could. The flourish of the hunting horns resounded beyond the woods on that still night and was repeated by the echoes of the distant valleys, awakening the timid stags, rousing the yelping foxes and disturbing the little rabbits in their gambols at the edge of the rides.

The frightened night birds flew over the eager pack of hounds, while the women, who were moved by all these strangely picturesque things, leaned rather heavily on the men's arms and turned aside into the forest rides before the hounds had finished their meal. Mme. d'Avancelles, feeling languid after that day of fatigue and tenderness, said to the baron: "Will you take a turn in the park, my friend?" And without replying, but trembling and nervous, he went with her, and immediately they kissed each other. They walked slowly under the almost leafless trees through which the moonbeams filtered, and their love, their desires, their longing for a closer embrace became so vehement that they nearly yielded to it at the foot of a tree.

The horns were not sounding any longer, and the tired hounds were sleeping in the kennels. "Let us return," the young woman said, and they went back.

When they got to the château and before they went in she said in a weak voice: "I am so tired that I shall go to bed, my friend." And as he opened his arms for a last kiss she ran away, saying as a last good-by: "No—I am going to sleep. Let him who loves me follow me!"

An hour later, when the whole silent château seemed dead, the baron crept stealthily out of his room and went and scratched at her door. As she did not reply he tried to open it and found that it was not locked.

She was in a reverie, resting her arms against the window ledge. He threw himself at her knees, which he kissed madly through her dress. She said nothing but buried her delicate fingers caressingly in his hair, and suddenly, as if she had formed some great resolution, whispered with a daring look: "I shall come back; wait for me." And, stretching out her hand, she pointed with her finger to an indistinct white spot at the end of the room; it was her bed.

Then with trembling hands, and scarcely knowing what he was doing, he quickly undressed, got into the cool sheets and, stretching himself out comfortably, almost forgot his love in the pleasure he found, tired out as he was, in the contact of the linen. She did not return, however, no doubt finding amusement in making him languish. He closed his eyes with a feeling of exquisite comfort and reflected peaceably while waiting for what he so ardently longed for. But by degrees his limbs grew languid and his thoughts became indistinct and fleeting, until his fatigue gained the upper hand and he fell asleep.

He slept that unconquerable heavy sleep of the worn-out hunter, slept through until daylight. Then, as the window had remained half open, the crowing of a cock suddenly woke him. The baron opened his eyes, and feeling a woman's body against his—finding himself, much to his surprise, in a strange bed, and remembering nothing for the moment—he stammered:

"What? Where am I? What is the matter?"

Then she, who had not been asleep at all, looking at this unkempt man with red eyes and swollen lips, replied in the haughty tone of voice in which she occasionally spoke to her husband:

"It is nothing; it is only a cock crowing. Go to sleep again, monsieur, it has nothing to do with you."

THE DROWNED MAN

I

Everyone in Fécamp knew the story of old Mother Patin. She had undoubtedly been unhappy with her man, had old Mother Patin; or her man had beaten her during his lifetime, as a man threshes wheat in his barns.

He was owner of a fishing smack, and he had married her a long time ago, because she was pleasing, although she was poor.

Patin, a good seaman but a brute, frequented old Auban's tavern, where, on ordinary days, he drank four or five brandies, and on days when he had made a good catch, eight or ten and even more, just for the fun of it, as he said.

The brandy was served to customers by old Auban's daughter, a pleasant-faced dark-haired girl, who drew custom to the house merely by her good looks, for no one had ever wagged a tongue against her.

When Patin entered the tavern, he was content to look at her and hold her in civil conversation, the easy conversation of a decent fellow. When he had drunk the first brandy, he was already finding her pleasant to look on; at the second, he was winking at her; at the third, he was saying: "Miss Désirée, if you would only . . ." without ever finishing the sentence; at the fourth, he was trying to hold her by her petticoat to embrace her; and when he had reached the tenth, it was old Auban who served him with the rest.

The old wine seller, who knew every trick of the trade, used to send Désirée round between the tables to liven up the orders for drinks; and Désirée, who was not old Auban's daughter for nothing, paraded her petticoat among the drinkers and bandied jests, with a smile on her lips, and a sly twinkle in her eye.

By dint of drinking brandies, Patin grew so familiar with Désirée's face that he thought of it even at sea, when he was throwing his nets into the water, out on the open sea, on windy nights and calm nights, on moonlit nights and black nights. He thought of it when he was standing at the helm in the after part of his boat, while his four companions slept with their hands on their arms. He saw her always smiling at him, pouring out the tawny brandy with a lift of her shoulders, and then coming towards him, saying:

"There! Is this what you want?"

And by dint of treasuring her so in eye and mind, he reached such a pitch of longing to marry her that, unable to restrain himself from it any longer, he asked her in marriage.

He was rich, owner of his boat, his nets and a house at the foot of the cliff, on the Retenue; while old Auban had nothing. The affair was arranged with much enthusiasm, and the wedding took place as quickly as possible, both parties being, for different reasons, anxious to make it an accomplished fact.

But three days after the marriage was over, Patin was no longer able to imagine in the least how he had come to think Désirée different from other women. He must have been a rare fool to hamper himself with a penniless girl who had wheedled him with her cognac, so she had, with the cognac into which she had put some filthy drug for him.

And he went cursing along the shore, breaking his pipe between his teeth, swearing at his tackle; and having cursed heartily, using every known term of abuse and applying them to everyone he could think of, he spat out such anger as remained in his spleen on the fish and crabs drawn in one of his nets, throwing them all in the baskets to an accompaniment of oaths and foul words.

Then, returning to his house, where he had his wife, old Auban's daughter, within reach of his tongue and his hand, he was very soon treating her as the lowest of the low. Then, as she listened resignedly, being used to the paternal violence, he became exasperated by her calm, and one evening he knocked her about. After this, his home became a place of terror.

For ten years, nothing was talked of on the Retenue but the beatings Patin inflicted on his wife, and his habit of cursing when he spoke to her, whatever the occasion. He cursed, in fact, in a unique way, with a wealth of vocabulary and a forceful vigor of delivery, possessed by no other man in Fécamp. As soon as his boat, returning from fishing, appeared at the mouth of the harbor, they waited expectantly for the first broadside he would discharge on the pier, from his deck, the moment he saw the white bonnet of his other half.

Standing in the stern, he tacked, his glance fixed ahead and on the sheets when the sea was running high, and in spite of the close attention required by the narrow difficult passage, in spite of the great waves running mountain-high in the narrow gully, he endeavored to pick out—from the midst of the women waiting in the spray of the breakers for the sailors—his woman, old Auban's daughter, the pauper wench.

Then, as soon as he had caught sight of her, in spite of the clamor of waves and wind, he poured on her a volley of abuse with such vocal energy that everyone laughed at it, although they pitied her deeply. Then, when his boat reached the quay, he had a habit of discharging his ballast of civilities, as he said, while he unloaded his fish, which attracted round him all the rascals and idlers of the harbor.

It issued from his mouth, now like cannon shots, terrible and short, now like thunderclaps that rolled for five minutes, such a tempest of oaths that he seemed to have in his lungs all the storms of the Eternal Father.

Then, when he had left his boat, and was face to face with her in the middle of a crowd of curious spectators and fishwives, he fished up again from the bottom of the hold a fresh cargo of insults and hard words, and escorted her in such fashion to their home, she in front, he behind, she weeping, he shouting.

Then, alone with her, doors shut, he came to blows on the least pretext. Anything was enough to make him lift his hand, and once he had begun, he never stopped, spitting in her face, all the time, the real causes of his hate. At each blow, at each thump, he yelled: "Oh, you penniless slut, oh, you guttersnipe, oh, you miserable starveling, I did a fine thing the day I washed my mouth out with the firewater of your scoundrel of a father."

She passed her days now, poor woman, in a state of incessant terror, in a continuous trembling of soul and of body, in stunned expectation of insults and thrashings.

And this lasted for ten years. She was so broken that she turned pale when she was talking to anyone, no matter who, and no longer thought of anything but the beatings that threatened her, and she had grown as skinny, yellow, and dried up as a smoked fish.

II

One night when her man was at sea she was awakened by the noise like the growling of a beast which the wind makes when it gets up, like an unleashed hound. She sat up in bed, uneasy, then, hearing nothing more, lay down again; but almost at once, there was a moaning in the chimney that shook the whole house and ran across the whole sky as if a pack of furious animals had crossed the empty spaces, panting and bellowing.

Then she got up and ran to the harbor. Other women were running from all sides with lanterns. Men came running and everyone was watching the foam flashing white in the darkness on the crest of the waves out at sea.

The storm lasted fifteen hours. Eleven sailors returned no more, and Patin was among them.

The wreckage of his boat, the *Jeune-Amélie*, was recovered off Dieppe. Near St.-Valéry, they picked up the bodies of his sailors, but his body was never found. As the hull of the small craft had been cut in two, his wife for a long time expected and dreaded his return; for if there had been a collision, it might have happened that the colliding vessel had taken him on board, and carried him to a distant country.

Then, slowly, she grew used to the thought that she was a widow, even though she trembled every time that a neighbor or a beggar or a tramping peddler entered her house abruptly.

Then, one afternoon, almost four years after the disappearance of her man, she stopped, on her way along the Rue aux Juifs, before the house of an old captain who had died recently and whose belongings were being sold.

Just at this moment, they were auctioning a parrot, a green parrot with a blue head, which was regarding the crowd with a discontented and uneasy air.

"Three francs," cried the seller, "a bird that talks like a lawyer, three francs."

A friend of widow Patin jogged her elbow.

"You ought to buy that, you being rich," she said. "It would be company for you; he is worth more than thirty francs, that bird. You can always sell him again for twenty to twenty-five easy."

"Four francs, ladies, four francs," the man repeated. "He sings vespers and preaches like the priest. He's a phenomenon . . . a miracle!"

Widow Patin raised the bid by fifty centimes, and they handed her the hook-nosed creature in a little cage and she carried him off.

Then she installed him in her house, and as she was opening the iron-wire door to give the creature a drink, she got a bite on the finger that broke the skin and drew blood.

"Oh, the wicked bird," said she.

However, she presented him with hemp seed and maize, then left him smoothing his feathers while he peered with a malicious air at his new home and his new mistress.

Next morning day was beginning to break, when widow Patin heard, with great distinctness, a loud, resonant, rolling voice, the voice of Patin, which shouted:

"Get up, slut."

Her terror was such that she hid her head under the bedclothes, for every morning, in the old days, as soon as he had opened his eyes, her dead husband shouted in her ears those three words that she knew well.

Trembling, huddled into a ball, her back turned to the thrashing that she was momentarily expecting, she murmured, her face hidden in the bed:

"God almighty, he's here! God almighty, he's here! He's come back, God almighty!"

Minutes passed; no other sound broke the silence of her room. Then, shuddering, she lifted her head from the bed, sure that he was there, spying on her, ready to strike.

She saw nothing, nothing but a ray of sun falling across the windowpane, and she thought:

"He's hiding, for sure."

She waited a long time, then, a little reassured, thought:

"I must have been dreaming, seeing he doesn't show himself."

She was shutting her eyes again, a little reassured, when right in her ears the furious voice burst out, the thunderous voice of her drowned man, shouting:

"Damn and blast it, get up, bitch."

She leaped out of bed, jerked out by her instinctive obedience, the passive obedience of a woman broken in by blows, who still remembers, after four years, and who will always remember, and always obey that voice. And she said:

"Here I am, Patin. What do you want?"

But Patin did not answer.

Then, bewildered, she looked round her, and she searched everywhere, in the cupboards, in the chimney, under the bed, without finding anyone, and at last let herself fall into a chair, distracted with misery, convinced that the spirit of Patin itself was there, near her, come back to torture her.

Suddenly, she remembered the loft, which could be reached from outside by a ladder. He had certainly hidden himself there to take her by surprise. He must have been kept by savages on some shore, unable to escape sooner, and he had come back, wickeder than ever. She could not doubt it, on the mere sound of his voice.

She asked, her head turned towards the ceiling:

"Are you up there, Patin?"

Patin did not answer.

Then she went out, and in an unutterable terror that set her heart beating madly, she climbed the ladder, opened the garret window, looked in, saw nothing, entered, searched, and found nothing.

Seated on a truss of hay, she began to cry; but while she was sobbing, shaken by an acute and supernatural terror, she heard, in the room below her, Patin telling his story. He seemed less angry, calmer, and he was saying:

"Filthy weather . . . high wind . . . filthy weather. I've had no breakfast, damn it."

She called through the ceiling:

"I'm here, Patin; I'll make you some soup. Don't be angry. I'm coming."

She climbed down at a run.

There was no one in her house.

She felt her body giving way as if Death had his hand on her, and she was going to run out to ask help from the neighbors, when just in her ear the voice cried:

"I've had no breakfast, damn it."

The parrot, in his cage, was regarding her with his round, malicious, wicked eye.

She stared back at him, in amazement, murmuring:

"Oh, it's you."

He answered, shaking his head:

"Wait, wait, wait, I'll teach you to faint."

What were her thoughts? She felt, she realized that this was none other than the dead man, who had returned and hidden himself in the feathers of this creature, to begin tormenting her again, that he was going to swear, as he did before, all day, and find fault with her, and shout insults to attract their neighbors' attention and make them laugh. Then she flung herself across the room, opened the cage, seized the bird, who defended himself and tore her skin with his beak and his claws. But she held him with all her might, in both hands, and throwing herself on the ground, rolled on top of him with the frenzy of a madman, crushed him to death and made a mere rag of flesh of him, a little soft green thing that no longer moved or spoke, and hung limp. Then, wrapping him in a dishcloth as a shroud, she went out, in her shift, and barefooted, crossed the quay, against which the sea was breaking in small waves, and, shaking the cloth, let fall this small green thing that looked like a handful of grass. Then she returned, threw herself on her knees before the empty cage, and utterly overcome by what she had done she asked pardon of the good God, sobbing as if she had just committed a horrible crime.

MAD?

When I was told: "You know that Jacques Parent has died mad in the asylum," a painful shiver, a shiver of fear and anguish, ran through my frame; and suddenly I saw him again, the tall, queer fellow, mad for many years perhaps, a disturbing, even a frightening, maniac.

He was a man of forty, tall, thin, slightly stooping, with the eyes of one suffering from hallucinations, black eyes so black that the pupils were imperceptible, expressive, wandering, morbid, haunted eyes. A strange, disturbing creature, bringing with him and spreading round him a vague uneasiness of soul and body, one of those incomprehensible nervous disorders that make supernatural influences seem credible.

He had an irritating mannerism: a mania for hiding his hands. He scarcely ever let them wander, as we all do, over objects or on tables. He never handled things lying about with that familiar gesture possessed by almost all men. He never left them naked, his long, bony, delicate, slightly feverish hands.

He thrust them into his pockets or folded his arms and tucked them under his armpits. You would have said he was afraid they would fall against his will to some forbidden task, perform some shameful or absurd action if he left them free and masters of their own movements.

When obliged to use them for the ordinary purposes of existence, he moved them in abrupt jerks, with swift movements of his arm, as though he was not going to let them have time to act by themselves, defy his will, and do some other thing. At table, he would snatch his glass, his fork, or his knife so swiftly that one never had time to foresee what he meant to do before it was done.

Now one evening I got the explanation of this amazing malady that preyed on his soul.

From time to time he would come and spend a few days with me in the country, and that evening he seemed unusually agitated!

A storm was rising in the sky, stifling and black, after a day of appalling heat. No breath of air stirred the leaves. A hot, furnacelike vapor blew in our faces: it made us breathe in gasps. I felt ill at ease, agitated, and was anxious to go to bed.

When he saw me rise to go, Jacques Parent seized my arm with a frightened gesture.

"Oh! no; stay a little longer," he said.

I stared at him in surprise, murmuring:

"This storm is affecting my nerves."

"Mine too!" he moaned, or rather shrieked. "I beg you to stay; I do not want to be alone."

He seemed to be quite out of his wits.

"What is the matter with you?" said I; "are you off your head?"

(Copyright, 1925, by Alfred A. Knopf, Inc.)

"Yes, sometimes," he stammered, "in evenings like this, electric evenings . . . . I . . . I . . . I am afraid . . . afraid of myself. . . . Don't you understand? I am endowed with a faculty . . . no . . . a power . . . no . . . a force. . . . Well, I don't know what to call it, but I have inside me such an extraordinary magnetic action that I am afraid, yes, afraid of myself, as I said just now!"

And with frantic shudders he hid his quivering hands under the lapels of his coat. I suddenly realized that I too was trembling with a vague, overmastering, horrible fear. I wanted to get away, escape, fly from the sight of him: I did not want to see his wandering eye pass over me, then avert itself, gaze round the ceiling, and seek some dark corner of the room to stare at, as though he wanted to hide his fatal glance too.

"You never told me that before," I stammered.

"Do I ever tell a soul?" he answered. "But tonight I cannot keep silent, and I would rather you knew all; besides, you might be able to help me.

"Magnetism! Do you know what it is? No. No one knows. But it is known that there is such a thing. It is recognised, doctors practice it, and one of the most famous, M. Charcot, teaches it; so there can be no doubt that it exists.

"A man, a human being, has the power, terrifying and incomprehensible, of putting another human being to sleep by the strength of his will, and, while he is asleep, of stealing his mind as one would steal a purse. He steals his mind, that is to say, his soul, the soul, the sanctuary, the secret of the ego, the soul, that deepest part of man, once thought impenetrable, the soul, the asylum of thoughts that cannot be confessed, of everything a man hides, everything he loves, everything he would conceal from all human creatures. That sanctuary he opens, violates, displays and flings to the public! Is it not frightful, criminal, infamous?

"Why, and how, is this done? Does anyone know? But what is known?

"It is all a mystery. We only communicate with things by means of our wretched, incomplete, infirm senses, so weak that they scarcely have the power to discover the world around us. It is all a mystery. Think of music, the divine art, the art that stirs the soul to its depths, ravishes, intoxicates it, maddens it. What is it? Nothing.

"You don't understand? Listen. Two bodies meet. The air vibrates. These vibrations are more or less numerous, more or less rapid, more or less violent, according to the nature of the shock. Now we have in our ears a little membrane that receives these vibrations of the air and transmits them to the brain in the form of sound. Imagine a glass of water turning to wine in your mouth. The drum of the ear accomplishes that incredible metamorphosis, the astounding miracle of turning movement into sound. That's all.

"Music, that complex and mysterious act, precise as algebra and vague as a dream, an art made of mathematics and the wind, only happens, then, as the result of the properties of a little membrane. If that membrane did not exist, sound would not exist either, since in itself it is merely vibration. Can one imagine music without the ear? No. Well, we are surrounded with things whose existence we never suspect, because we lack the organs that would reveal them to us.

"Magnetism is perhaps one of these. We can but have presentiments of that power, try fearfully to get in touch with these spirits who neighbor us, and catch glimpses of this new secret of nature, because we do not ourselves possess the revealing instrument.

"As for myself . . . As for myself, I am endowed with a horrible power. You might think there was another creature imprisoned within me, always longing to escape, to act in defiance of me; it moves, and gnaws at me, and wears me out. What sort of thing is it? I do not know, but there are two of us in my poor body, and it is often the other thing that is the stronger, as it is tonight.

"I need only look at people to send them to sleep as though I had given them a draught of opium. I need only stretch out my hands to produce . . . terrible . . . terrible things. If you knew? Yes. If you knew? And my power extends not merely over men, but over animals and even over . . . over objects. . . .

"It tortures me and terrifies me. Often I have longed to tear out my eyes and cut off my hands.

"But I will . . . I want you to know everything. Look, I'll show it you . . . not on human beings, that is done everywhere, but on . . . on . . . animals. Call Mirza."

He was walking in long strides, with the air of a man suffering from hallucinations, and he exposed his hands hidden in his breast. They seemed to me terrifying, as though he had bared two swords.

And I obeyed him mechanically, subjugated, quivering with terror and consumed by a kind of impetuous desire to see. I opened the door and whistled to my dog, who was lying in the hall. At once I heard the hurried sound of her claws on the stairs, and she appeared, wagging her tail with pleasure.

Then I signed to her to lie down in a chair; she jumped on it, and Jacques began to caress her, gazing at her.

At first she seemed restless; she shivered, turning her head to avoid the man's fixed stare, and seemed agitated by a growing fear. Suddenly she began to tremble, as dogs tremble. Her whole body palpitated, shaken by long-drawn shudders, and she tried to escape. But he laid his hand on the animal's head, and, at his touch, she uttered a long howl such as is heard at night in the country.

I myself felt drowsy, giddy, as one is on board ship. I saw the furniture sway and the walls move. "Enough, Jacques, enough," I stammered. But he was no longer listening to me, and stared at Mirza in a steady, frightening way. She closed her eyes now and let her head fall as though going to sleep. He turned to me.

"It is done," he said; "now look."

And, throwing his handkerchief to the other side of the room, he cried: "Fetch it!"

At that the animal rose, and, tottering along as though blind, moving her legs like a cripple, she went towards the piece of linen that was a white blotch by the wall. Several times she tried to take it in her mouth, but her jaws closed on one side of it, as though she had not seen it. At last she seized it, and returned with the same swaying somnambulistic gait.

It was a terrifying sight. "Lie down," he ordered. She lay down. Then, touching her forehead, he said: "A hare: seize him, seize him!" And the beast, still lying on her side, tried to run, stirring like a dog in the middle of a dream and uttering strange little ventriloquial barks without opening her mouth.

Jacques seemed to have gone mad. The sweat poured from his brow. "Bite him, bite your master," he cried. She gave two or three frightened twitches. One would have sworn she was resisting, struggling. "Bite him," he repeated. Then, rising, my dog came towards me, and I retreated towards the wall, shaking with terror, with my foot raised to kick her, to keep her off.

But Jacques commanded: "To me, at once." She turned back towards him.

Then, with his two great hands, he began to rub her head, as though he were freeing her from invisible bonds.

Mirza opened her eyes again. "It is finished," he said.

I dared not touch her, and pushed the door for her to go out. She went out slowly, trembling, exhausted, and again I heard her claws on the stairs.

But Jacques returned to me: "That is not all. It is this which frightens me most; look. Things obey me."

On my table was a sort of dagger that I used as a paper cutter. He stretched out his hand towards it, and the hand seemed to crawl slowly towards it; and suddenly I saw, yes, I saw the knife itself quiver, then move, then slide gently, of itself, over the wood towards the hand that lay still, waiting for it; it placed itself between his fingers.

I screamed with terror. I thought I was going mad myself, but the shrill sound of my own voice calmed me at once.

"All things come to me like that," continued Jacques. "That is why I hide my hands. What is it? Magnetism, electricity, the loadstone principle? I do not know, but it is horrible.

"And do you realize why it is horrible? When I am alone, as soon as I am alone, I cannot restrain myself from attracting everything that surrounds me.

"And I spend whole days changing the positions of things, never wearying of testing my abominable power, as if to see whether it has not left me."

He had buried his great hands in his pockets, and stared into the night. A slight sound, a faint quivering, seemed to pass through the trees.

It was the rain beginning to fall.

"It is frightening," I murmured.

"It is horrible," he repeated.

A murmur ran through the leaves, like a gust of wind. It was the storm, a heavy, torrential downpour.

Jacques began to breathe in great gasps that made his breast heave.

"Leave me," he said; "the rain will calm me. I want to be alone now."

THE REVENGE

SCENE 1

M. DE GARELLE, *alone, lying back in an armchair.*

Here I am at Cannes, a gay bachelor, which is humorous enough. I'm a bachelor. At Paris I hardly realized it. Away from home, it's another thing. Upon my word, I'm not complaining about it.

And my wife is married again!

I wonder if my successor is happy, happier than I am. What sort of a fool must he be to have married her after me! For the matter of that, I was no less a fool for marrying her first. She had her points, however, certain good points . . . physical ones . . . quite remarkably good, but she had serious moral blemishes too.

What a sly wench, what a liar, what a flirt she was, and how attractive to men who were not her husband! Was I a cuckold? God, it's sheer torture to be wondering that from morning to evening, and never to know for sure.

What plots and counterplots I laid to watch her, without learning anything! In any case, if I was a cuckold, I'm no longer, thanks to Naquet. How easy divorce is after all! It cost me ten francs for a riding whip, and a stiffness in my right arm, not counting the pleasure it gave me to lay on to my heart's content on a woman whom I strongly suspect of deceiving me.

What a thrashing, what a thrashing I gave her! . . .

He stands up, laughing, takes a few steps, and sits down again.

True, the verdict was given in her favor and against me . . . but what a thrashing!

Now I am spending the winter in the South, a gay bachelor. What luck! It's delightful to travel when you can always hope to meet a new love round every corner. Whom shall I meet, in this hotel, now, or on the Croisette, or perhaps in the street? Where is she, the woman who will love me tomorrow and whose lover I shall be? What will her eyes be like, her lips, her hair, her smile? What will she be like, the first woman who will give me her mouth and be folded in my arms? Dark or fair? Tall or short? Gay or grave? Plump or . . . ? She will be plump!

Oh! how I pity people who don't know, people who no longer know the exquisite pleasure of anticipation! The woman I really love is the unknown, the hoped-for, the desired, she who haunts my heart, whom my eyes have never seen in the flesh, she whose charms are augmented by every ideal perfection. Where is she? In this hotel, behind this door? In one of the rooms of this house, quite near, or still far away? What matter, so long as I desire her, so long as I am certain of meeting her! And I shall assuredly meet her, today or tomorrow, this week or the next, sooner or later; it is absolutely inevitable that I shall find her.

And I shall have, in all their charm, the divine joy of the first kiss, the first caresses, all the maddening ecstasy of lovers' discoveries, all the mystery of the unexplored, as desirable the first day as a conquered maidenhood. Oh! the fools who do not understand the adorable sensation of veils raised for the first time! Oh, the fools who marry . . . since . . . the said veils . . . ought not to be raised too often . . . on the same sight! . . .

Here comes a woman.

A woman crosses the far end of the corridor, elegant, slender, with a tapering waist.

Damn her, she has a figure, and an air. Let's try to catch sight of . . . her face. *She passes near him without seeing him, buried in the depths of the armchair.*

He murmurs:

Hell, it's my wife! My wife, or rather not my wife, Chantever's wife. What a charming hussy she is, after all!

Am I going to want to marry her again now? . . . Good, she's sitting down and she's reading *Gil Blas*. I'll lie low.

My wife! What a queer feeling it gives me! My wife! As a matter of fact, it's a year, more than a year, since she ceased to be my wife. . . . Yes, she had her points, physically speaking . . . very fine ones; what a leg! It makes me tremble only to think of it. And what a bosom, oh, perfect! Ouf! In the old days we used to play at drill, left—right—left—right—what a bosom! Left or right, it was superb.

But what a holy terror . . . where her morals were concerned!

Has she had lovers? What I suffered from that suspicion! Now, pouf! It doesn't worry me in the least.

I have never seen a more seductive creature when she was getting into bed.
She had a way of jumping up and slipping between the sheets . . .

Good, I am going to fall in love with her again . . .

Suppose I spoke to her? . . . But what shall I say to her?

And then she would shout for help, because of the thrashing she got. What a
thrashing! Perhaps I was a little brutal after all.

Suppose I speak to her? That would be amusing and rather an achievement after
all. Damn it, yes, I'll speak to her, and perhaps if I do it very well. . . . We shall
soon see. . . .

SCENE 2

He approaches the young woman, who is deep in the study of Gil Blas, *and in a
sweet voice:*

Will you allow me, madame, to recall myself to your memory?

MME. DE CHANTEVER *lifts her head sharply, cries out, and starts to run away.*

He bars her way, and says humbly:

You have nothing to fear, madame. I am not your husband now.

MME. DE CHANTEVER: Oh, you dare! After . . . after what has happened!

M. DE GARELLE: I dare . . . and I daren't. . . . You see. . . . Explain it to please
yourself. When I caught sight of you, I found it impossible not to come and speak
to you.

MME. DE CHANTEVER: I hope this joke may now be considered at an end?

M. DE GARELLE: It is not a joke.

MME. DE CHANTEVER: A bet, then, unless it's merely a piece of insolence.
Besides, a man who strikes a woman is capable of anything.

M. DE GARELLE: You are hard, madame. It seems to me, however, that you
ought not to reproach me today for an outburst that—moreover—I regret. On the
contrary, I was, I confess, expecting to be thanked by you.

MME. DE CHANTEVER (*astonished*): What? You must be mad! Or else you're
making fun of me as if I were a little girl from the country.

M. DE GARELLE: Not at all, madame, and if you don't understand me, you
must be very unhappy.

MME. DE CHANTEVER: What do you mean?

M. DE GARELLE: That if you were happy with the man who has taken my place,
you would be grateful to me for the violence that allowed you to make this new
union.

MME. DE CHANTEVER: You are pushing the joke too far, sir. Please leave me
alone.

M. DE GARELLE: But, madame, think of it! If I had not committed the infamous
crime of striking you, we should still be dragging our chains today.

MME. DE CHANTEVER (*wounded*): The fact is that you did me a service by
your cruelty.

M. DE GARELLE: I did, didn't I? A service that deserves better than your recent
greeting.

MME. DE CHANTEVER: Possibly. But your face is so disagreeable to me . . .

M. DE GARELLE: I will not say the same of yours.

MME. DE CHANTEVER: Your compliments are as distasteful to me as your
brutalities.

M. DE GARELLE: Well, what am I to do, madame? I have lost the right to beat you: I am compelled to make myself agreeable.

MME. DE CHANTEVER: Well, that's at least frank. But if you want to be really agreeable, you will go away.

M. DE GARELLE: I'm not carrying my wish to please you to those lengths yet.

MME. DE CHANTEVER: Then what it is you expect of me?

M. DE GARELLE: To redress my wrongs by admitting that I had wrongs.

MME. DE CHANTEVER (indignant): What? By admitting that you have had them? You must be losing your wits. You thrashed me cruelly and perhaps you consider that you behaved towards me in the most suitable manner possible.

M. DE GARELLE: Perhaps I did!

MME. DE CHANTEVER: What? Perhaps you did?

M. DE GARELLE: Yes, madame. You know the comedy called the Mari Cocu, Battu, et Content. Very well, was I or was I not a cuckold?—that's the whole question! In any case, it is you who were beaten, and not happy. . . .

MME. DE CHANTEVER (getting up): Sir, you insult me.

M. DE GARELLE (eagerly): I implore you to listen to me a moment. I was jealous, very jealous, which proves that I loved you. I beat you, which is a still stronger proof of it, and beat you severely, which proves it up to the hilt. Very well, if you were faithful, and beaten, you have real grounds for complaint, indisputably real, I confess, and . . .

MME. DE CHANTEVER: Don't pity me.

M. DE GARELLE: What do you mean by that? It can be taken in two ways. Either you mean that you scorn my pity or that it is undeserved. Very well, if the pity of which I acknowledge you to be worthy is undeserved, then the blows . . . the violent blows you have had from me were more than deserved.

MME. DE CHANTEVER: Take it as you please.

M. DE GARELLE: Good, I understand. So, when I was your husband, madame, I was a cuckold.

MME. DE CHANTEVER: I'm not saying that.

M. DE GARELLE: You leave it to be understood.

MME. DE CHANTEVER: I am leaving it to be understood that I don't want your pity.

M. DE GARELLE: Don't quibble, confess honestly that I was . . .

MME. DE CHANTEVER: Don't say that shameful word, which revolts and disgusts me.

M. DE GARELLE: I'll let you off the word, but you must acknowledge the thing itself.

MME. DE CHANTEVER: Never, it's not true.

M. DE GARELLE: Then, I pity you with all my heart, and the suggestion I was going to make to you has now no possible justification.

MME. DE CHANTEVER: What suggestion?

M. DE GARELLE: It's no use telling you about it, since it's only feasible if you did deceive me.

MME. DE CHANTEVER: Well, suppose for a moment that I did deceive you.

M. DE GARELLE: That's not sufficient. You must confess it.

MME. DE CHANTEVER: I confess it.

M. DE GARELLE: That's not sufficient. I must have proof.

MME. DE CHANTEVER (smiling): You're asking too much now.

M. DE GARELLE: No, madame. As I have said, I was going to make a very serious suggestion to you, very serious; if I hadn't intended to do so, I should not have come in search of you like this after what we have done to each other, what you did to me in the first place, and I to you afterwards. This suggestion, which can have the most serious consequences, for us both, is worthless if you did not deceive me.

MME. DE CHANTEVER: You are an amazing man. But what more do you want? I have deceived you—there.

M. DE GARELLE: I must have proof.

MME. DE CHANTEVER: But what proofs do you want me to give you? I haven't them on me, or rather I no longer have them.

M. DE GARELLE: It doesn't matter where they are. I must have them.

MME. DE CHANTEVER: But one can't keep proof of things of that kind . . . and . . . or, at any rate, of a flagrant délit. (After a pause) I think my word ought to be enough for you.

M. DE GARELLE (bowing): Then, you are ready to swear to it.

MME. DE CHANTEVER (lifting her hand): I swear it.

M. DE GARELLE (gravely): I believe you, madame. And with whom did you deceive me?

MME. DE CHANTEVER: Oh, but now you're asking too much.

M. DE GARELLE: It is absolutely necessary that I know his name.

MME. DE CHANTEVER: It is impossible to give it to you.

M. DE GARELLE: Why?

MME. DE CHANTEVER: Because I am a married woman.

M. DE GARELLE: Well?

MME. DE CHANTEVER: And in the case of a professional secret?

M. DE GARELLE: You're quite right.

MME. DE CHANTEVER: Besides, it was with M. de Chantever that I deceived you.

M. DE GARELLE: That's not true.

MME. DE CHANTEVER: Why not?

M. DE GARELLE: Because he would not have married you.

MME. DE CHANTEVER: Insolent creature! And this suggestion? . . .

M. DE GARELLE: It's this. You have just confessed that, thanks to you, I was one of those ridiculous creatures, always regarded as laughingstocks whatever they do—comic if they keep their mouths shut, and more grotesque still if they show their resentment—that people call deceived husbands. Well, madame, it is beyond question that the number of cuts with a riding whip you received are far from being an adequate compensation for the outrage and the conjugal injury I have experienced by your act, and it is no less beyond question that you owe me a more substantial compensation and a compensation of a different nature, now that I am no longer your husband.

MME. DE CHANTEVER: You're losing your senses. What do you mean?

M. DE GARELLE: I mean, madame, that you ought to restore to me today the delightful hours you stole from me when I was your husband to offer them to I don't know whom.

MME. DE CHANTEVER: You're mad.

M. DE GARELLE: Not at all. Your love belonged to me, didn't it? Your kisses were owing to me, all your kisses, without exception. Isn't that so? You diverted a part of them for the benefit of another man. Well, it's a matter of the utmost importance to me now that restitution should be made, made without any scandal, secret restitution, as free from scandal and as secret as were the shameless thefts.

MME. DE CHANTEVER: What do you take me for?

M. DE GARELLE: For the wife of M. de Chantever.

MME. DE CHANTEVER: Upon my word, this is too bad.

M. DE GARELLE: Pardon me, the man with whom you deceived me must have taken you for the wife of M. de Garelle. It's only just that my turn should come. What is too bad is to refuse to restore what is legitimately due.

MME. DE CHANTEVER: And if I said yes . . . you would . . .

M. DE GARELLE: Certainly.

MME. DE CHANTEVER: Then, what purpose would the device have served?

M. DE GARELLE: The revival of our love.

MME. DE CHANTEVER: You never loved me.

M. DE GARELLE: I am giving you the strongest possible proof of it, however.

MME. DE CHANTEVER: In what way?

M. DE GARELLE: You ask me in what way. When a man is fool enough to offer himself to a woman first as her husband and then as her lover, it proves that he loves her, or I don't know anything about love.

MME. DE CHANTEVER: Oh, don't let us confuse two different things. To marry a woman is a proof either of love or desire, but to make her your mistress is a proof of nothing but . . . scorn. In the first case, a man undertakes all the expense, all the tediums, all the responsibilities of love; in the second case, he leaves those burdens to the legitimate owner and keeps only the pleasure, with the privilege of disappearing the moment the woman ceases to please. The two cases are hardly on a par.

M. DE GARELLE: My dear girl, your logic is very weak. When a man loves a woman, he ought not to marry her, because if he marries her he can be sure she will deceive him, as you did, in my case. There's the proof. While it's incontestable that a mistress remains faithful to the lover with the same desperate intensity of purpose she adopts to deceive her husband. Isn't it so? If you want to create an indissoluble bond between a woman and yourself, arrange for another man to marry her, marriage is only a slender thread to be cut at will, and become that woman's lover: free love is a chain that is never broken—we have cut the thread, I offer you the chain.

MME. DE CHANTEVER: You're very amusing. But I refuse.

M. DE GARELLE: Then, I shall warn M. de Chantever.

MME. DE CHANTEVER: You will warn him of what?

M. DE GARELLE: I shall tell him that you deceived me.

MME. DE CHANTEVER: That I deceived you. . . . You . . .

M. DE GARELLE: Yes, when you were my wife.

MME. DE CHANTEVER: Well?

M. DE GARELLE: Well, he'll never forgive you for it.

MME. DE CHANTEVER: He?

M. DE GARELLE: Well, dammit, it's not the sort of thing to reassure him.

MME. DE CHANTEVER (laughing): Don't do that, Henry.

A VOICE ON THE STAIRCASE CALLING: Mathilde!

MME. DE CHANTEVER (softly): My husband! Good-by.

M. DE GARELLE (getting up): I am going to escort you to him and introduce myself.

MME. DE CHANTEVER: Don't do that.

M. DE GARELLE: You watch me.

MME. DE CHANTEVER: Please don't.

M. DE GARELLE: You accept the chain?

THE VOICE: Mathilde!

MME. DE CHANTEVER: Please go.

M. DE GARELLE: When shall I see you again?

MME. DE CHANTEVER: Here—this evening—after dinner.

M. DE GARELLE (kissing her hand): I love you. . . .

She runs away.

M. de Garelle returns calmly to his armchair and sinks into it.

Well, it's true. I like this rôle better than the previous one. She's charming, quite charming, and far more charming still since I have heard M. de Chantever's voice calling her "Mathilde" like that, in the proprietary tone that husbands have.

THE FATHER

As he lived at Batignolles and was a clerk in the Public Education Office, he took the omnibus every morning to the center of Paris, sitting opposite a girl with whom he fell in love.

She went to the shop where she was employed at the same time every day. She was a little brunette, one of those dark girls whose eyes are so dark that they look like spots and whose complexion has a look like ivory. He always saw her coming at the corner of the same street. She generally ran to catch the heavy vehicle and would spring upon the steps before the horses had quite stopped. Then getting inside rather out of breath and sitting down, she would look round her.

The first time that he saw her François Tessier felt that her face pleased him extremely. One sometimes meets a woman whom one longs to clasp madly in one's arms immediately without even knowing her. That girl answered to his inward desires, to his secret hopes, to that sort of ideal of love which one cherishes in the depths of the heart without knowing it.

He looked at her intently, in spite of himself, and she grew embarrassed at his looks and blushed. He saw it and tried to turn away his eyes, but he involuntarily fixed them upon her again every moment, although he tried to look in another direction, and in a few days they knew each other without having spoken. He gave up his place to her when the omnibus was full and got outside, though he was very sorry to do it. By this time she had gone so far as to greet him with a little smile, and although she always dropped her eyes under his looks, which she felt were too ardent, yet she did not appear offended at being looked at in such a manner.

They ended by speaking. A kind of rapid intimacy had become established between them, a daily intimacy of half an hour, which was certainly one of the most charming half-hours in his life to him. He thought of her all the rest of the time, saw her continually during the long office hours, for he was haunted and bewitched by that floating and yet tenacious recollection which the image of a beloved woman leaves in us, and it seemed to him that the entire possession of that little person would be maddening happiness to him, almost above human realization.

Every morning now she shook hands with him, and he preserved the feeling of that touch and the recollection of the gentle pressure of her little fingers until the next day. He almost fancied that he preserved the imprint of it on his skin, and he anxiously waited for this short omnibus ride all the rest of the time, while Sundays seemed to him heartbreaking days. However, there was no doubt that she loved him, for one Sunday in spring she promised to go and lunch with him at Maisons-Laffitte the next day.

II

She was at the railway station first, which surprised him, but she said: "Before going I want to speak to you. We have twenty minutes, and that is more than I shall take for what I have to say."

She trembled as she hung on his arm and looked down, while her cheeks were pale, but she continued: "I do not want you to be deceived in me, and I shall not go there with you unless you promise, unless you swear—not to do—not to do anything that is at all improper."

She had suddenly become as red as a poppy and said no more. He did not know what to reply, for he was happy and disappointed at the same time. At the bottom of his heart he perhaps preferred that it should be so, and yet during the night he had indulged in anticipations that sent the hot blood flowing through his veins. He should love her less, certainly, if he knew that her conduct was light, but then it would be so charming, so delicious for him! And he made all a man's usual selfish calculations in love affairs.

As he did not say anything she began to speak again in an agitated voice and with tears in her eyes: "If you do not promise to respect me altogether I shall return home."

And so he squeezed her arm tenderly and replied: "I promise you shall only do what you like." She appeared relieved in mind and asked with a smile: "Do you really mean it?"

And he looked into her eyes and replied, "I swear it."

"Now you may take the tickets," she said.

During the journey they could hardly speak, as the carriage was full, and when they got to Maisons-Laffitte they went toward the Seine. The sun, which shone full upon the river, upon the leaves and upon the turf, seemed to reflect in them his brightness, and they went hand in hand along the bank, looking at the shoals of little fish swimming near the bank, brimming over with happiness, as if they were raised from earth in their lightness of heart.

At last she said: "How foolish you must think me!"

"Why?" he asked.

"To come out like this all alone with you."

"Certainly not; it is quite natural."

"No, no, it is not natural for me—because I do not wish to commit a fault, and yet this is how girls fall. But if you only knew how wretched it is, every day the same thing, every day in the month and every month in the year. I live quite alone with Mamma, and as she has had a great deal of trouble, she is not very cheerful. I do the best I can and try to laugh in spite of everything, but I do not always succeed. But all the same it was wrong in me to come, though you, at any rate, will not be sorry."

By the way of an answer he kissed her ardently on the ear that was nearest him, but she started away from him with an abrupt movement and, getting suddenly angry, exclaimed: "Oh! Monsieur François, after what you swore to me!" And they went back to Maisons-Laffitte.

They had lunch at the Petit-Havre, a low house buried under four enormous poplar trees by the side of the river. The air, the heat, the small bottle of white wine and the sensation of being so close together made them red and silent with a feeling of oppression, but after the coffee they regained their high spirits and, having crossed the Seine, started off along the bank toward the village of La Frette. Suddenly he asked: "What is your name?"

"Louise."

"Louise," he repeated and said nothing more.

The river, which described a long curve, bathed a row of white houses in the distance which were reflected in the water. The girl picked the daisies and made them into a great bunch, while he sang vigorously, as intoxicated as a colt that has been turned into a meadow. On their left a vine-covered slope followed the river. Suddenly François stopped motionless with astonishment: "Oh! Look there!" he said.

The vines had come to an end, and the whole slope was covered with lilac bushes in flower. It was a violet-colored wood! A kind of great carpet stretched over the earth, reaching as far as the village, more than two miles off. She also stood surprised and delighted and murmured: "Oh! How pretty!" And, crossing a meadow, they walked toward that curious low hill which every year furnishes all the lilac which is sold through Paris on the carts of the flower peddlers.

A narrow path went beneath the trees, so they took it, and when they came to a small clearing they sat down.

Swarms of flies were buzzing around them and making a continuous, gentle sound, and the sun, the bright sun of a perfectly still day, shone over the bright slopes, and from that wood of flowers a powerful aroma was borne toward them, a wave of perfume, the breath of the flowers.

A church clock struck in the distance. They embraced gently, then clasped each other close, lying on the grass without the knowledge of anything except of that kiss. She had closed her eyes and held him in her arms, pressing him to her closely without a thought, with her reason bewildered and from head to foot in passionate expectation. And she surrendered herself altogether without knowing that she had given herself to him. But she soon came to herself with the feeling of a great misfortune, and she began to cry and sob with grief, with her face buried in her hands.

He tried to console her, but she wanted to start, to return and go home immediately, and she kept saying as she walked along quickly: "Good heavens! Good heavens!"

He said to her: "Louise! Louise! Please let us stop here." But now her cheeks were red and her eyes hollow, and as soon as they got to the railway station in Paris she left him without even saying good-by.

III

When he met her in the omnibus next day she appeared to him to be changed and thinner, and she said to him: "I want to speak to you; we will get down at the boulevard."

As soon as they were on the pavement she said: "We must bid each other good-by; I cannot meet you again after what has happened."

"But why?" he asked.

"Because I cannot; I have been culpable and I will not be so again."

Then he implored her, tortured by desire, maddened by the wish of having her entirely in the absolute freedom of nights of love, but she replied firmly: "No, I cannot; I cannot."

He, however, only grew all the more excited and promised to marry her, but she said: "No," and left him.

For over a week he did not see her. He could not manage to meet her, and as he did not know her address he thought he had lost her altogether. On the ninth day, however, there was a ring at his bell, and when he opened it she was there. She threw herself into his arms and did not resist any longer, and for three months she was his mistress. He was beginning to grow tired of her, when she told him a woman's most precious secret, and then he had one idea and wish—to break with her at any price. As, however, he could not do that, not knowing how to begin or what to say, full of anxiety, he took a decisive step. One night he changed his lodgings and disappeared.

The blow was so heavy that she did not look for the man who had abandoned her but threw herself at her mother's knees, confessed her misfortune and some months after gave birth to a boy.

IV

Years passed, and François Tessier grew old without there having been any alteration in his life. He led the dull, monotonous life of bureaucrats, without hopes and without expectations. Every day he got up at the same time, went through the same streets, went through the same door, past the same porter, went into the same office, sat in the same chair and did the same work. He was alone in the world, alone during the day in the midst of his different colleagues, and alone at night in his bachelor's lodgings, and he laid by a hundred francs a month against old age.

Every Sunday he went to the Champs Elysées to watch the elegant people, the carriages and the pretty women, and the next day he used to say to one of his colleagues: "The return of the carriages from the Bois de Boulogne was very brilliant yesterday." One fine Sunday morning, however, he went into the Parc Monceau where the mothers and nurses, sitting on the sides of the walks, watched the children playing, and suddenly François Tessier started. A woman passed by holding two children by the hand: a little boy of about ten and a little girl of four. It was she.

He walked another hundred yards and then fell into a chair, choking with emotion. She had not recognized him, and so he came back, wishing to see her again. She was sitting down now, and the boy was standing by her side very quietly, while the little girl was making sand castles. It was she; it was certainly she, but she had the serious looks of a lady, was dressed simply and looked self-possessed and dignified. He looked at her from a distance, for he did not venture to go near, but the little boy raised his head, and François Tessier felt himself tremble. It was his own son; there could be no doubt of that. And as he looked at him he thought he could recognize himself as he appeared in an old photograph taken years ago. He remained hidden behind a tree, waiting for her to go, that he might follow her.

He did not sleep that night. The idea of the child especially harassed him. His son! Oh! If he could only have known, have been sure. But what could he have done? However, he went to the house where she had once lived and asked about her. He was told that a neighbor, an honorable man of strict morals, had been touched by her distress and had married her; he knew the fault she had committed and had married her and had even recognized the child, his, François Tessier's child, as his own.

He returned to the Parc Monceau every Sunday, for then he always saw her, and each time he was seized with a mad, an irresistible longing to take his son into his arms, cover him with kisses and to steal him, to carry him off.

He suffered horribly in his wretched isolation as an old bachelor with nobody to care for him, and he also suffered atrocious mental torture, torn by paternal tenderness springing from remorse, longing and jealousy and from that need of loving one's own children which nature has implanted in all. And so at last he determined to make a despairing attempt and, going up to her as she entered the park, he said, standing in the middle of the path, pale and with trembling lips: "You do not recognize me?" She raised her eyes, looked at him, uttered an exclamation of horror, of terror and, taking the two children by the hand, she rushed away, dragging them after her, while he went home and wept inconsolably.

Months passed without his seeing her again. He suffered day and night, for he was a prey to his paternal love. He would gladly have died if he could only have kissed his son; he would have committed murder, performed any task, braved any danger, ventured anything. He wrote to her, but she did not reply, and after writing her some twenty letters he saw that there was no hope of altering her determination. Then he formed the desperate resolution of writing to her husband, being quite prepared to receive a bullet from a revolver if need be. His letter only consisted of a few lines, as follows:

MONSIEUR:

You must have a perfect horror of my name, but I am so miserable, so overcome by misery, that my only hope is in you, and therefore I venture to request you to grant me an interview of only five minutes.

I have the honor, etc.

The next day he received the reply:

MONSIEUR:

I shall expect you tomorrow, Tuesday, at five o'clock.

V

As he went up the staircase François Tessier's heart beat so violently that he had to stop several times. There was a dull and violent noise in his breast, the noise as of some animal galloping; he could only breathe with difficulty and had to hold onto the banisters in order not to fall.

He rang the bell on the third floor, and when a maidservant had opened the door he asked: "Does Monsieur Flamel live here?"

"Yes, monsieur. Kindly come in."

He was shown into the drawing-room; he was alone and waited, feeling bewildered, as in the midst of a catastrophe, until a door opened and a man came in. He was tall, serious and rather stout; he wore a black frock coat and pointed to a chair with his hand. François Tessier sat down and said, panting: "Monsieur— monsieur—I do not know whether you know my name—whether you know——"

M. Flamel interrupted him: "You need not tell it me, monsieur; I know it. My wife has spoken to me about you."

He spoke it in the dignified tone of voice of a good man who wishes to be severe, with the commonplace stateliness of an honorable man, and François Tessier continued: "Well, monsieur, I want to say this. I am dying of grief, of remorse, of shame, and I would like once, only once, to kiss the child."

M. Flamel rose and rang the bell, and when the servant came in he said: "Will you bring Louis here?" When she had gone out they remained face to face without speaking, having nothing more to say to one another, and waited. Then suddenly a little boy of ten rushed into the room and ran up to the man whom he believed to be his father, but he stopped when he saw a stranger, and M. Flamel kissed him and said: "Now go and kiss that gentleman, my dear." And the child went up to Tessier nicely and looked at him.

François Tessier had risen; he let his hat fall and was ready to fall himself as he looked at his son, while M. Flamel had turned away, from a feeling of delicacy, and was looking out of the window.

The child waited in surprise, but he picked up the hat and gave it to the stranger. Then François, taking the child up in his arms, began to kiss him wildly all over his face, on his eyes, his cheeks, on his mouth, on his hair, and the youngster, frightened at the shower of kisses, tried to avoid them, turned away his head and pushed away the man's face with his little hands. But suddenly François Tessier put him down, cried: "Good-by! Good-by!" and rushed out of the room as if he had been a thief.

A NORMANDY JOKE

The procession came in sight in the hollow road which was shaded by the tall trees which grew on the slopes of the farm. The newly married couple came first, then the relations, then the invited guests and lastly the poor of the neighborhood, while the village urchins, who hovered about the narrow road like flies, ran in and out of the ranks or climbed up the trees to see it better.

The bridegroom was a good-looking young fellow, Jean Patu, the richest farmer in the neighborhood. Above all things he was an ardent sportsman who seemed to lose all common sense in order to satisfy that passion, who spent large sums on his dogs, his keepers, his ferrets and his guns. The bride, Rosalie Roussel, had been courted by all the likely young fellows in the district, for they all thought her prepossessing and they knew that she would have a good dowry, but she had chosen Patu—partly, perhaps, because she liked him better than she did the others, but still more, like a careful Normandy girl, because he had more crown pieces.

When they went in at the white gateway of the husband's farm forty shots resounded without anyone seeing those who fired. The shooters were hidden in the ditches, and the noise seemed to please the men, who were sprawling about heavily in their best clothes, very much. Patu left his wife, and running up to a farm servant whom he perceived behind a tree, he seized his gun and fired a shot himself, kicking his heels about like a colt. Then they went on, beneath the apple trees heavy with fruit, through the high grass and through the herd of calves, who looked at them with their great eyes, got up slowly and remained standing with their muzzles turned toward the wedding party.

The men became serious when they came within measurable distance of the wedding dinner. Some of them, the rich ones, had on tall, shining silk hats, which seemed altogether out of place there; others had old head coverings with a long nap, which might have been taken for moleskin, while the humbler among them wore caps. All the women had on shawls, which they wore as loose wraps, holding the ends daintily under their arms. They were red, parti-colored, flaming shawls, and their brightness seemed to astonish the black fowls on the dung heap, the ducks on the side of the pond and the pigeons on the thatched roofs.

The extensive farm buildings awaited the party at the end of that archway of apple trees, and a sort of vapor came out of open door and windows, an almost overwhelming smell of eatables, which permeated the vast building, issuing from its openings and even from its very walls. The string of guests extended through the yard; when the foremost of them reached the house they broke the chain and dispersed, while behind they were still coming in at the open gate. The ditches were now lined with urchins and poor curious people. The shots did not cease but came from every side at once, injecting a cloud of smoke, and that powdery smell which has the same intoxicating effects as absinthe, into the atmosphere.

The women were shaking their dresses outside the door to get rid of the dust, were undoing their cap strings and folding their shawls over their arms. Then they went into the house to lay them aside altogether for the time. The table was laid in the great kitchen, which could hold a hundred persons; they sat down to dinner at two o'clock and at eight o'clock they were still eating; the men, in their shirt sleeves, with their waistcoats unbuttoned and with red faces, were swallowing the food and drink as if they were insatiable. The cider sparkled merrily, clear and golden in the large glasses, by the side of the dark, blood-colored wine; and between every dish they made the *trou*, the Normandy *trou*, with a glass of brandy which inflamed the body and put foolish notions into the head.

From time to time one of the guests, being as full as a barrel, would go out for a few moments to get a mouthful of fresh air, as they said, and then returned with redoubled appetite. The farmers' wives, with scarlet faces and their corsets nearly bursting, did not like to follow their example, until one of them, feeling more uncomfortable than the others, went out. Then all the rest followed her example and came back quite ready for any fun, and the rough jokes began afresh. Broadsides of doubtful jokes were exchanged across the table, all about the wedding night, until the whole arsenal of peasant wit was exhausted. For the last hundred years the same broad jokes had served for similar occasions, and although everyone knew them, they still hit the mark and made both rows of guests roar with laughter.

At the bottom of the table four young fellows, who were neighbors, were preparing some practical jokes for the newly married couple, and they seemed to have got hold of a good one by the way they whispered and laughed. Suddenly one of them, profiting by a moment of silence, exclaimed: "The poachers will have a good time tonight with this moon! I say, Jean, you will not be looking at the moon, will you?" The bridegroom turned to him quickly and replied: "Only let them come, that's all!" But the other young fellow began to laugh and said: "I do not think you will neglect your duty for them!"

The whole table was convulsed with laughter, so that the glasses shook, but the bridegroom became furious at the thought that anybody should profit by his wedding to come and poach on his land and repeated: "I only say: just let them come!"

Then there was a flood of talk with a double meaning which made the bride blush somewhat, although she was trembling with expectation, and when they had emptied the kegs of brandy they all went to bed. The young couple went into their own room, which was on the ground floor as most rooms in farmhouses are. As it was very warm they opened the windows and closed the shutters. A small lamp in bad taste, a present from the bride's father, was burning on the chest of drawers, and the bed stood ready to receive the young people, who did not stand upon all the ceremony which is usual among refined people.

The young woman had already taken off her wreath and her dress and was in her petticoat, unlacing her boots, while Jean was finishing his cigar and looking at her out of the corners of his eyes. It was an ardent look, more sensual than tender, for he felt more desire than love for her. Suddenly, with a brusque movement, like a man who is going to set to work, he took off his coat. She had already taken off her boots and was now pulling off her stockings; then she said to him: "Go and hide yourself behind the curtains while I get into bed."

He seemed as if he were going to refuse but with a cunning look went and hid himself with the exception of his head. She laughed and tried to cover up his eyes, and they romped in an amorous and happy manner, without shame or embarrassment. At last he did as she asked him, and in a moment she unfastened her petticoat, which slipped down her legs, fell at her feet and lay on the floor in a circle. She left it there, stepped over it, naked with the exception of her floating chemise, and slipped into the bed, whose springs creaked beneath her weight. He immediately went up to her, without his shoes and in his trousers, and, stooping over his wife, sought her lips, which she hid beneath the pillow, when a shot was heard in the distance, in the direction of the forest of Râpées, as he thought.

He raised himself anxiously, and running to the window, with his heart beating, he opened the shutters. The full moon flooded the yard with yellow light, and the silhouettes of the apple trees made black shadows at his feet, while in the distance the fields gleamed, covered with the ripe corn. But as he was leaning out, listening to every sound in the still night, two bare arms were put around his neck, and his wife whispered, trying to pull him back: "Do leave them alone; it has nothing to do with you. Come to bed."

He turned round, put his arms round her and drew her toward him, feeling her warm skin through the thin material, and lifting her up in his vigorous arms, he carried her toward their couch; but just as he was laying her on the bed, which yielded beneath her weight, they heard another report, considerably nearer this time. Jean, giving way to his tumultuous rage, swore aloud: "Good God! Do you think I shall not go out and see what it is because of you? Wait, wait a few minutes!" He put on his shoes again, took down his gun, which was always hanging within reach upon the wall, and, as his wife threw herself on her knees in her terror to implore him not to go, he hastily freed himself, ran to the window and jumped into the yard.

She waited one hour, two hours, until daybreak, but her husband did not return. Then she lost her head, aroused the house, related how angry Jean was and said that he had gone after the poachers, and immediately all the male farm servants, even the boys, went in search of their master. They found him two leagues from the farm, tied hand and foot, half dead with rage, his gun broken, his trousers turned inside out, three dead hares hanging round his neck and a placard on his chest with these words:

Who goes on the chase loses his place.

And later on when he used to tell this story of his wedding night he generally added: "Ah! As far as a joke went, it was a good joke. They caught me in a snare, as if I had been a rabbit, the dirty brutes, and they shoved my head into a bag. But if I can only catch them someday, they had better look out for themselves!"

That is how they amuse themselves in Normandy on a wedding day.

MONSIEUR PARENT

Little George was piling hills of sand in one of the walks. He scooped the sand up with both his hands, made it into a pyramid and then put a chestnut leaf on the top, and his father, sitting on an iron chair, was looking at him with concentrated and affectionate attention, seeing nobody else in the small public garden, which was full of people. All along the circular road other children were busy in the same manner or were indulging in other childish games, while nursemaids were strolling two and two with their bright cap ribbons floating behind them and carrying something wrapped up in lace in their arms. Here and there little girls in short petticoats and bare legs were talking seriously together while resting from trundling their hoops.

The sun was just disappearing behind the roofs of the Rue Saint-Lazare but still shed its rays obliquely on that little overdressed crowd. The chestnut trees were lighted up with its yellow rays, and the three fountains before the lofty porch of the church shone like molten silver.

M. Parent looked at his boy sitting there in the dusk; he followed his slightest movements with affection in his glance; but accidentally looking up at the church clock, he saw that he was five minutes late, so he got up, took the child by the arm and shook his sand-covered dress, wiped his hands and led him in the direction of the Rue Blanche. He walked quickly, so as not to get in after his wife, but as the child could not keep up the pace he took him up and carried him, though it made him pant when he had to walk up the steep street. Parent was a man of forty, turning gray already, rather stout. He had married, a few years previously, a young woman whom he dearly loved but who now treated him with the severity and authority of an all-powerful despot. She found fault with him continually for everything that he did or did not do, reproached him bitterly for his slightest acts, his habits, his simple pleasures, his tastes, his movements and walk and for having a round stomach and a placid voice.

He still loved her, however, but above all he loved the boy she had borne him, and George, who was now three, had become the greatest joy, in fact the preoccupation, of his heart. He himself had a modest private fortune and lived without doing anything on his twenty thousand francs a year, and his wife, who had been quite portionless, was constantly angry at her husband's inactivity.

At last he reached his house, put down the child, wiped his forehead and walked upstairs. When he got to the second floor he rang. An old servant who had brought him up, one of those mistress-servants who are the tyrants of families, opened the door to him, and he asked her anxiously: "Has Madame come in yet?"

The servant shrugged her shoulders. "When have you ever known Madame to come home at half-past six, monsieur?"

And he replied with some embarrassment: "Very well; all the better; it will give me time to change my things, for I am very hot."

The servant looked at him with angry and contemptuous pity and grumbled: "Oh! I can see that well enough, you are covered with perspiration, monsieur. I suppose you walked quickly and carried the child, and only to have to wait until half-past seven, perhaps, for Madame. I have made up my mind not to have it ready at that time but shall get it for eight o'clock, and if you have to wait, I cannot help it; roast meat ought not to be burnt!"

M. Parent, however, pretended not to hear and only said: "All right! all right. You must wash George's hands, for he has been making sand pits. I will go and change my clothes, tell the maid to give the child a good washing."

And he went into his own room, and as soon as he got in he locked the door, so as to be alone, quite alone. He was so used now to being abused and badly treated that he never thought himself safe except when he was locked in. He no longer ventured even to think, reflect and reason with himself unless he had secured himself against her looks and insinuations by locking himself in. Having thrown himself into a chair, in order to rest for a few minutes before he put on clean linen, he remembered that Julie was beginning to be a fresh danger in the house. She hated his wife—that was quite plain; but she hated still more his friend Paul Limousin, who had continued to be the familiar and intimate friend of the house after having been the inseparable companion of his bachelor days, which is very rare. It was Limousin who acted as a buffer between his wife and himself and who defended him ardently and even severely against her undeserved reproaches, against crying scenes and against all the daily miseries of his existence.

But now for six months Julie had constantly been saying things against her mistress. She would repeat twenty times a day: "If I were you, monsieur, I should not allow myself to be led by the nose like that. Well, well! But there—everyone according to his nature." And one day she had even ventured to be insolent to Henriette, who, however, merely said to her husband at night: "You know, the next time she speaks to me like that I shall turn her out of doors." But she, who feared nothing, seemed to be afraid of the old servant, and Parent attributed her mildness to her consideration for the old domestic who had brought him up and who had closed his mother's eyes. Now, however, Henriette's patience was exhausted; matters could not go on like that much longer, and he was frightened at the idea of what was going to happen. What could he do? To get rid of Julie seemed to him to be such a formidable undertaking that he hardly ventured to think of it; but it was just as impossible to uphold her against his wife, and before another month could pass the situation between the two would become unbearable. He remained sitting there with his arms hanging down, vaguely trying to discover some means to set matters straight, but without success, and he said to himself: "It is lucky that I have George; without him I should be very miserable."

Then he thought he would consult Limousin, but the recollection of the hatred that existed between his friend and the servant made him fear lest the former should advise him to turn her away, and again he was lost in doubt and sad uncertainty. Just then the clock struck seven, and he started up. Seven o'clock, and he had not even changed his clothes! Then, nervous and breathless, he undressed, put on a clean shirt and hastily finished his toilette as if he had been expected in the next room for some event of extreme importance; then he went into the drawing room, happy at having nothing to fear. He glanced at the newspaper, went and looked out of the window and then sat down on a sofa again. The door opened and the boy came in, washed, brushed and smiling, and Parent took him up in his arms and kissed him passionately; then he tossed him into the air and held him up to the ceiling but soon sat down again, as he was tired with all his efforts, and taking George onto his knee, he made him "ride a cockhorse." The child laughed and clapped his hands and shouted with pleasure, as his father did, laughing until his big stomach shook, for it amused him almost more than it did the child.

Parent loved the boy with all the heart of a weak, resigned, ill-used man. He loved with mad bursts of affection, with caresses and with all the bashful tenderness which was hidden in him and which had never found an outlet, even at the early period of his married life, for his wife had always shown herself cold and reserved. Just then, however, Julie came to the door, with a pale face and glistening eyes, and said in a voice which trembled with exasperation: "It is half-past seven, monsieur." Parent gave an uneasy and resigned look at the clock and replied: "Yes, it certainly is half-past seven."

"Well, my dinner is quite ready now."

Seeing the storm which was coming, he tried to turn it aside. "But did you not tell me when I came in that it would not be ready before eight?"

"Eight! What are you thinking about? You surely do not mean to let the child dine at eight o'clock? It would ruin his stomach. Just suppose that he only had his mother to look after him! She cares a great deal about her child. Oh yes, we will speak about her; she is a mother. What a pity it is that there should be any mothers like her!"

Parent thought it was time to cut short a threatened scene, and so he said: "Julie, I will not allow you to speak like that of your mistress. You understand me, do you not? Do not forget it for the future."

The old servant, who was nearly choked with surprise, turned round and went out, slamming the door so violently after her that the lusters on the chandelier rattled and for some seconds it sounded as if a number of little invisible bells were ringing in the drawing room.

George, who was surprised at first, began to clap his hands merrily, and blowing out his cheeks, he gave a great *boom* with all the strength of his lungs, to imitate the noise of the door banging. Then his father began telling him stories, but his mind was so preoccupied that he continually lost the thread of his story, and the child, who could not understand him, opened his eyes wide in astonishment.

Parent never took his eyes off the clock; he thought he could see the hands move, and he would have liked to stop them until his wife's return. He was not vexed with her for being late, but he was frightened, frightened of her and Julie, frightened at the thought of all that might happen. Ten minutes more would suffice to bring about an irreparable catastrophe, words and acts of violence that he did not dare to picture to himself. The mere idea of a quarrel, of loud voices, of insults flying through the air like bullets, of two women standing face to face, looking at each other and flinging abuse at each other, made his heart beat and his tongue feel as parched as if he had been walking in the sun. He felt as limp as a rag, so limp that he no longer had the strength to lift up the child and dance him on his knee.

Eight o'clock struck; the door opened once more and Julie came in again. She had lost her look of exasperation, but now she put on an air of cold and determined resolution which was still more formidable.

"Monsieur," she said, "I served your mother until the day of her death, and I have attended to you from your birth until now, and I think it may be said that I am devoted to the family."

She waited for a reply, and Parent stammered:

"Why, yes, certainly, my good Julie."

She continued: "You know quite well that I have never done anything for the sake of money but always for your sake, that I have never deceived you nor lied to you, that you have never had to find fault with me."

"Certainly, my good Julie."

"Very well then, monsieur, it cannot go on any longer like this. I have said nothing and left you in your ignorance, out of respect and liking for you, but it is too much, and everyone in the neighborhood is laughing at you. Everybody knows about it, and so I must tell you also, although I do not like to repeat it. The reason why Madame comes in at any time she chooses is that she is doing abominable things."

He seemed stupefied, unable to understand, and could only stammer out: "Hold your tongue, you know I have forbidden you——" But she interrupted him with irresistible resolution.

"No, monsieur, I must tell you everything now. For a long time Madame has been doing wrong with Monsieur Limousin; I have seen them kiss scores of times behind the doors. Ah! you may be sure that if Monsieur Limousin had been rich, Madame would never have married Monsieur Parent. If you remember how the marriage was brought about, you would understand the matter from beginning to end."

Parent had risen and stammered out, deadly pale: "Hold your tongue—hold your tongue or——"

She went on, however: "No, I mean to tell you everything. She married you from interest, and she deceived you from the very first day. It was all settled between them beforehand. You need only reflect for a few moments to understand it; and then she was not satisfied with having married you, as she did not love you, she has made your life miserable, so miserable that it has almost broken my heart when I have seen it."

He walked up and down the room with his hands clenched, repeating: "Hold your tongue—hold your tongue," for he could find nothing else to say; the old servant, however, would not yield; she seemed resolved on everything, but George, who had been at first astonished and then frightened at those angry voices, began to utter shrill screams. He hid behind his father and roared, with his face puckered up and his mouth open.

His son's screams exasperated Parent and filled him with rage and courage. He rushed at Julie with both arms raised, ready to strike her, and exclaiming: "Ah! you wretch! you will send the child out of his senses." He was almost touching her when she said:

"Monsieur, you may beat me if you like, me who reared you, but that will not prevent your wife from deceiving you or alter the fact that your child is not yours!"

He stopped suddenly and let his arms fall, and he remained standing opposite to her, so overwhelmed that he could understand nothing more, and she added: "You need only look at the child to know who is its father! He is the very image of Monsieur Limousin; you need only look at his eyes and forehead; why, a blind man could not be mistaken in him!"

But he had taken her by the shoulders and was now shaking her with all his might while he ejaculated: "Viper! viper! Go out the room, viper! Go out, or I shall kill you! Go out! Go out!"

And with a desperate effort he threw her into the next room. She fell on the table which was laid for dinner, breaking the glasses. Then, getting up, she put it between her master and herself, and while he was pursuing her, in order to take hold of her again, she flung terrible words at him: "You need only go out this evening after dinner and come in again immediately and you will see—you will see whether I have been lying! Just try it—and you will see." She had reached the kitchen door and escaped, but he ran after her, up the backstairs to her bedroom into which she had locked herself, and knocking at the door, he said: "You will leave my house this very instant."

"You may be certain of that, monsieur," was her reply. "In an hour's time I shall not be here any longer."

He then went slowly downstairs again, holding onto the banister so as not to fall, and went back to the drawing room where little George was sitting on the floor crying; he fell into a chair and looked at the child with dull eyes. He understood nothing, he knew nothing more; he felt dazed, stupefied, mad, as if he had just fallen on his head, and he scarcely even remembered the dreadful things the servant had told him. Then by degrees his reason grew clearer, like muddy water settling, and the abominable revelation began to work in his heart.

Julie had spoken so clearly, with so much force, assurance and sincerity, that he did not doubt her good faith, but he persisted in not believing her penetration. She might have been deceived, blinded by her devotion to him, carried away by unconscious hatred for Henriette. However, in measure as he tried to reassure and to convince himself, a thousand small facts recurred to his recollection: his wife's words, Limousin's looks, a number of unobserved, almost unseen trifles, her going out late, their simultaneous absence; and even some almost insignificant but strange gestures, which he could not understand, now assumed an extreme importance for him and established a connivance between them. Everything that had happened since his engagement surged through his overexcited brain in his misery, and he doggedly went through his five years of married life, trying to recollect every detail month by month, day by day, and every disquieting circumstance that he remembered stung him to the quick like a wasp's sting.

He was not thinking of George any more, who was quiet now and on the carpet, but seeing that no notice was being taken of him, the boy began to cry. Then his father ran up to him, took him into his arms and covered him with kisses. His child remained to him at any rate! What did the rest matter? He held him in his arms and pressed his lips onto his light hair and, relieved and composed, he whispered: "George—my little George—my dear little George!" But he suddenly remembered what Julie had said. Yes! she had said that he was Limousin's child. Oh, it could not be possible, surely! He could not believe it, could not doubt, even for a moment, that George was his own child. It was one of those low scandals which spring from servants' brains! And he repeated: "George—my dear little George." The youngster was quiet again now that his father was fondling him.

Parent felt the warmth of the little chest penetrate to his through their clothes, and it filled him with love, courage and happiness; that gentle heat soothed him, fortified him and saved him. Then he put the small curly head away from him a little and looked at it affectionately, still repeating: "George! Oh, my little George!" But suddenly he thought: "Suppose he were to resemble Limousin after all!"

There was something strange working within him, a fierce feeling, a poignant and violent sensation of cold in his whole body, in all his limbs, as if his bones had suddenly been turned to ice. Oh! if the child were to resemble Limousin—and he continued to look at George, who was laughing now. He looked at him with haggard, troubled eyes and tried to discover whether there was any likeness in his forehead, in his nose, mouth or cheeks. His thoughts wandered like they do when a person is going mad, and his child's face changed in his eyes and assumed a strange look and unlikely resemblances.

Julie had said: "A blind man could not be mistaken in him." There must, therefore, be something striking, an undeniable likeness. But what? The forehead? Yes, perhaps; Limousin's forehead, however, was narrower. The mouth, then? But Limousin wore a beard, and how could anyone verify the likeness between the plump chin of the child and the hairy chin of that man?

Parent thought: "I cannot see anything now, I am too much upset; I could not recognize anything at present. I must wait; I must look at him well tomorrow morning, when I am getting up." And immediately afterward he said to himself: "But if he is like me, I shall be saved! saved!" And he crossed the drawing room in two strides to examine the child's face by the side of his own in the looking glass. He had George on his arm so that their faces might be close together, and he spoke out loud almost without knowing. "Yes—we have the same nose—the same nose perhaps, but that is not sure—and the same look. But no, he has blue eyes. Then —good heavens! I shall go mad. I cannot see anything more—I am going mad!"

He went away from the glass to the other end of the drawing room and, putting the child into an easy chair, he fell into another and began to cry. He sobbed so violently that George, who was frightened at hearing him, immediately began to scream. The hall bell rang, and Parent gave a bound as if a bullet had gone through him.

"There she is," he said. "What shall I do?" And he ran and locked himself up in his room, so at any rate to have time to bathe his eyes. But in a few moments another ring at the bell made him jump again, and then he remembered that Julie had left without the housemaid knowing it, and so nobody would go to open the door. What was he to do? He went himself, and suddenly he felt brave, resolute, ready for dissimulation and the struggle. The terrible blow had matured him in a few moments, and then he wished to know the truth, he wished it with the rage of a timid man, with the tenacity of an easygoing man who has been exasperated.

But nevertheless he trembled! Was it fear? Yes. Perhaps he was still frightened of her? Does one know how much excited cowardice there often is in boldness? He went to the door with furtive steps and stopped to listen; his heart beat furiously, and he heard nothing but the noise of that dull throbbing in his chest and of George's shrill voice, who was still crying in the drawing room. Suddenly, however, the noise of the bell over his head startled him like an explosion; then he seized the lock, turned the key and, opening the door, saw his wife and Limousin standing before him on the steps.

With an air of astonishment which also betrayed a little irritation she said: "So you open the door now? Where is Julie?" His throat felt tight and his breathing was labored, and he tried to reply without being able to utter a word, so she continued:

"Are you dumb? I asked you where Julie is."

And then he managed to say: "She—she—has—gone."

Whereupon his wife began to get angry. "What do you mean by gone? Where has she gone? Why?"

By degrees he regained his coolness, and he felt rising in him an immense hatred for that insolent woman who was standing before him. "Yes, she has gone altogether. I sent her away."

"You have sent away Julie? Why, you must be mad."

"Yes, I sent her away because she was insolent—and because, because she was ill-using the child."

"Julie?"

"Yes, Julie."

"What was she insolent about?"

"About you."

"About me?"

"Yes, because the dinner was burnt and you did not come in."

"And she said?"

"She said offensive things about you which I ought not—which I could not listen to."

"What did she say?"

"It is no good repeating them."

"I want to hear them."

"She said it was unfortunate for a man like me to be married to a woman like you, unpunctual, careless, disorderly, a bad mother and a bad wife."

The young woman had gone into the anteroom followed by Limousin, who did not say a word at this unexpected position of things. She shut the door quickly, threw her cloak onto a chair and, going straight up to her husband, she stammered out:

"You say—you say—that I am——"

He was very pale and calm and replied:

"I say nothing, my dear. I am simply repeating what Julie said to me, as you wanted to know what it was, and I wish you to remark that I turned her off just on account of what she said."

She trembled with a violent longing to tear out his beard and scratch his face. In his voice and manner she felt that he was asserting his position as master, although she had nothing to say by way of reply, and she tried to assume the offensive by saying something unpleasant.

"I suppose you have had dinner?" she asked.

"No, I waited for you."

She shrugged her shoulders impatiently. "It is very stupid of you to wait after half-past seven," she said. "You might have guessed that I was detained, that I had a good many things to do, visits and shopping."

And then suddenly she felt that she wanted to explain how she had spent her time, and she told him in abrupt, haughty words that, having to buy some furniture in a shop a long distance off, very far off, in the Rue de Rennes, she had met Limousin at past seven o'clock on the Boulevard Saint-Germain and that then she had gone with him to have something to eat in a restaurant, as she did not like to go to one by herself although she was faint with hunger. That was how she had dinner, with Limousin, if it could be called dining, for they had only had some soup and half a fowl, as they were in a great hurry to get back, and Parent replied simply:

"Well, you were quite right. I am not finding fault with you."

Then Limousin, who had not spoken till then and who had been half hidden behind Henriette, came forward and put out his hand, saying: "Are you very well?"

Parent took his hand and, shaking it gently, replied: "Yes, I am very well."

But the young woman had felt a reproach in her husband's last words: "Finding fault! Why do you speak of finding fault? One might think that you meant to imply something."

"Not at all," he replied by way of excuse. "I simply meant that I was not at all anxious although you were late and that I did not find fault with you for it." She, however, took the high hand and tried to find a pretext for a quarrel.

"Although I was late? One might really think that it was one o'clock in the morning and that I spent my nights away from home."

"Certainly not, my dear. I said *late* because I could find no other word. You said you would be back at half-past six, and you returned at half-past eight. That was surely being late! I understand it perfectly well. I am not at all surprised even. But—but—I can hardly use any other word."

"But you pronounce them as if I had been out all night."

"Oh no; oh no!"

She saw that he would yield on every point, and she was going into her own room when at last she noticed that George was screaming, and then she asked with some feeling: "Whatever is the matter with the child?"

"I told you that Julie had been rather unkind to him."

"What has the wretch been doing to him?"

"Oh! Nothing much. She gave him a push, and he fell down."

She wanted to see her child and ran into the dining room but stopped short at the sight of the table covered with spilt wine, with broken decanters and glasses and overturned saltcellars. "Who did all that mischief?" she asked.

"It was Julie who——"

But she interrupted him furiously: "That is too much, really; Julie speaks of me as if I were a shameless woman, beats my child, breaks my plates and dishes, turns my house upside down, and it appears that you think it all quite natural."

"Certainly not, as I have got rid of her."

"Really!—you have got rid of her! But you ought to have given her in charge. In such cases one ought to call in the commissary of police!"

"But, my dear—I really could not—there was no reason. It would have been very difficult."

She shrugged her shoulders disdainfully. "There, you will never be anything but a poor wretched fellow, a man without a will, without any firmness or energy. Ah! she must have said some nice things to you, your Julie, to make you turn her off like that. I should like to have been here for a minute, only for a minute." Then she opened the drawing-room door and ran to George, took him into her arms and kissed him and said: "Georgie, what is it, my darling, my pretty one, my treasure?" But as she was fondling him he did not speak, and she repeated: "What is the matter with you?" And he, having seen with his child's eyes that something was wrong, replied, "Julie beat Papa."

Henriette turned toward her husband in stupefaction at first, but then an irresistible desire to laugh shone in her eyes, passed like a slight shiver over her delicate cheeks, made her upper lip curl and her nostrils dilate, and at last a clear, bright burst of mirth came from her lips, a torrent of gaiety which was lively and sonorous as the song of a bird. With little mischievous exclamations which issued from between her white teeth and hurt Parent as much as a bite would have done, she laughed: "Ha!—ha!—ha!—ha! she beat—she beat—my husband—ha!—ha!—ha! How funny! Do you hear, Limousin? Julie has beaten—has beaten—my—husband. Oh dear—oh dear—how very funny!"

But Parent protested: "No—no—it is not true, it is not true. It was I, on the contrary, who threw her into the dining room so violently that she knocked the table over. The child did not see clearly; I beat her!"

"Here, my darling," Henriette said to her boy; "did Julie beat Papa?"

"Yes, it was Julie," he replied. But then, suddenly turning to another idea, she said: "But the child has had no dinner? You have had nothing to eat, my pet?"

"No, Mamma."

Then she again turned furiously on her husband. "Why, you must be mad, utterly mad! It is half-past eight, and George has had no dinner!"

He excused himself as best he could, for he had nearly lost his wits by the overwhelming scene and the explanation and felt crushed by this ruin of his life.

"But, my dear, we were waiting for you, as I did not wish to dine without you. As you come home late every day, I expected you every moment."

She threw her bonnet, which she had kept on till then, into an easy chair, and in an angry voice she said: "It is really intolerable to have to do with people who can understand nothing, who can divine nothing and do nothing by themselves. So I suppose if I were to come in at twelve o'clock at night, the child would have had nothing to eat? Just as if you could not have understood that, as it was after half-past seven, I was prevented from coming home, that I had met with some hindrance!"

Parent trembled, for he felt that his anger was getting the upper hand, but Limousin interposed and, turning toward the young woman, he said: "My dear friend, you are altogether unjust. Parent could not guess that you would come here so late, as you never do so, and then how could you expect him to get over the difficulty all by himself after having sent away Julie?"

But Henriette was very angry and replied: "Well, at any rate, he must get over the difficulty himself, for I will not help him. Let him settle it!" And she went into her own room, quite forgetting that her child had not had anything to eat.

Then Limousin immediately set to work to help his friend. He picked up the broken glasses which strewed the table and took them out; he replaced the plates and knives and forks and put the child into his high chair while Parent went to look for the lady's maid to wait at table. She came in in great astonishment, as she had heard nothing in George's room, where she had been working. She soon, however, brought in the soup, a burnt leg of mutton and mashed potatoes.

Parent sat by the side of the child, very much upset and distressed at all that had happened. He gave the boy his dinner and endeavored to eat something himself, but he could only swallow with an effort, as if his throat had been paralyzed. By degrees he was seized by an insane desire to look at Limousin, who was sitting opposite to him and making bread pellets, to see whether George was like him. He did not venture to raise his eyes for some time; at last, however, he made up his mind to do so and gave a quick, sharp look at the face which he knew so well. He almost fancied that he had never looked at it carefully, since it looked so different to what he had anticipated. From time to time he scanned him, trying to find a likeness in the smallest lines of his face, in the slightest features, and then he looked at his son, under the pretext of feeding him.

Two words were sounding in his ears: "His father! his father! his father!" They buzzed in his temples at every beat of his heart. Yes, that man, that tranquil man who was sitting on the other side of the table, was, perhaps, the father of his son, of George, of his little George. Parent left off eating; he could not manage any more; a terrible pain, one of those attacks of pain which make men scream, roll on the ground and bite the furniture, was tearing at his entrails, and he felt inclined to take a knife and plunge it into his stomach. It would ease him and save him, and all would be over.

For how could he live now? Could he get up in the morning, join in the meals, go out into the streets, go to bed at night and sleep with that idea dominating him: "Limousin is little George's father!" No, he would not have the strength to walk a step, to dress himself, to think of anything, to speak to anybody! Every day, every hour, every moment, he would be trying to know, to guess, to discover this terrible secret. And the little boy—his dear little boy—he could not look at him any more without enduring the terrible pains of that doubt, of being tortured by it to the very marrow of his bones. He would be obliged to live there, to remain in that house, near a child whom he might love and yet hate! Yes, he should certainly end by hating him. What torture! Oh! If he were sure that Limousin was George's father, he might, perhaps, grow calm, become accustomed to his misfortune and his pain; but ignorance was intolerable.

Not to know—to be always trying to find out, to be continually suffering, to kiss the child every moment, another man's child, to take him out for walks, to carry him, to caress him, to love him and to think continually: "Perhaps he is not my child?" Wouldn't it be better not to see him, to abandon him—to lose him in the streets or to go away, far away, himself, so far away that he should never hear anything more spoken about, never!

He started when he heard the door open. His wife came. "I am hungry," she said; "are not you also, Limousin?"

He hesitated a little and then said: "Yes, I am, upon my word." And she had the leg of mutton brought in again, while Parent asked himself: "Have they had dinner? Or are they late because they have had a lovers' meeting?"

They both ate with a very good appetite. Henriette was very calm but laughed and joked, and her husband watched her furtively. She had on a pink dressing gown trimmed with white lace, and her fair head, her white neck and her plump hands stood out from that coquettish and perfumed dress as from a sea shell edged with foam. What had she been doing all day with that man? Parent could see them kissing and stammering out words of ardent love! How was it that he could not manage to know everything, to guess the whole truth by looking at them, sitting side by side, opposite to him?

What fun they must be making of him if he had been their dupe since the first day. Was it possible to make a fool of a man, of a worthy man, because his father had left him a little money? Why could one not see these things in people's souls? How was it that nothing revealed to upright souls the deceit of infamous hearts? How was it that voices had the same sound for adoring as for lying—why was a false, deceptive look the same as a sincere one? And he watched them, waiting to catch a gesture, a word, an intonation. Then suddenly he thought: "I will surprise them this evening," and he said: "My dear, as I have dismissed Julie I will see about getting another this very day, and I shall go out immediately to procure one by tomorrow morning, so I may not be in until late."

"Very well," she replied, "go; I shall not stir from here. Limousin will keep me company. We will wait for you." And then, turning to the maid, she said: "You had better put George to bed, and then you can clear away and go up to your own room."

Parent had got up; he was unsteady on his legs, dazed and giddy, and saying: "I shall see you again later on," he went out, holding onto the wall, for the floor seemed to roll like a ship. George had been carried out by his nurse, while Henriette and Limousin went into the drawing room.

As soon as the door was shut he said: "You must be mad, surely, to torment your husband as you do." She immediately turned on him. "Ah! Do you know that I think the habit you have got into lately of looking upon Parent as a martyr is very unpleasant."

Limousin threw himself into an easy chair and crossed his legs. "I am not setting him up as a martyr in the least, but I think that, situated as we are, it is ridiculous to defy this man as you do from morning till night."

She took a cigarette from the mantelpiece, lighted it and replied: "But I do not defy him, quite the contrary; only he irritates me by his stupidity, and I treat him as he deserves."

Limousin continued impatiently: "What you are doing is very foolish! However, all women are alike. Look here: Parent is an excellent, kind fellow, stupidly confiding and good, who never interferes with us, who does not suspect us for a moment, who leaves us quite free and undisturbed whenever we like, and you do all you can to put him into a rage and to spoil our life."

She turned to him. "I say, you worry me. You are a coward like all other men are! You are frightened of that poor creature!"

He immediately jumped up and said furiously: "I should like to know what he does and why you are so set against him? Does he make you unhappy? Does he beat you? Does he deceive you and go with another woman? No, it is really too bad to make him suffer merely because he is too kind and to hate him merely because you are unfaithful to him."

She went up to Limousin and, looking him full in the face, she said: "And you reproach me with deceiving him? You? You? What a filthy heart you must have."

He felt rather ashamed and tried to defend himself. "I am not reproaching you, my dear; I am only asking you to treat your husband gently, because we both of us require him to trust us. I think that you ought to see that."

They were close together—he, tall, dark, with long whiskers and the rather vulgar manner of a good-looking man who is very well satisfied with himself; she, small, fair and pink, a little Parisian, half shopkeeper, half one of those girls of easy virtue, born in a shop, brought up at its door to entice customers by her looks and married accidentally, in consequence, to a simple, unsophisticated man who saw her outside the door every morning when he went out and every evening when he came home.

"But do you not understand, you great booby," she said, "that I hate him just because he married me, because he bought me, in fact, because everything that he says and does, everything that he thinks, reacts on my nerves? He exasperates me every moment by his stupidity, which you call kindness—by his dullness, which you call his confidence, and then, above all, because he is my husband, instead of you! I feel him between us although he does not interfere with us much. And then? And then? No, after all, it is too idiotic of him not to guess anything! I wish he would at any rate be a little jealous. There are moments when I feel inclined to say to him, 'Don't you see, you stupid fool, that Paul is my lover?'"

Limousin began to laugh. "Meanwhile it would be a good thing if you were to keep quiet and not disturb our life."

"Oh! I shall not disturb it, you may be sure! There is nothing to fear with such a fool. But it is quite incomprehensible that you cannot understand how hateful he is to me, how he irritates me. You always seem to like him, and you shake hands with him cordially. Men are very surprising at times."

"One must know how to dissimulate, my dear."

"It is no question of dissimulation but of feeling. One might think that when you men deceive another you like him all the more on that account, while we women hate a man from the moment that we have betrayed him."

"I do not see why I should hate an excellent fellow because I love his wife."

"You do not see it? You do not see it? You, all of you, are wanting in that fineness of feeling! However, that is one of those things which one feels and which one cannot express. And then, moreover, one ought not. No, you would not understand, it is quite useless! You men have no delicacy of feeling."

And smiling with the gentle contempt of a debauched woman, she put both her hands onto his shoulders and held up her lips to him, and he stooped down and clasped her closely in his arms, and their lips met. And as they stood in front of the mirror another couple exactly like them embraced behind the clock.

They had heard nothing—neither the noise of the key nor the creaking of the door, but suddenly Henriette, with a loud cry, pushed Limousin away with both her arms, and they saw Parent, who was looking at them, livid with rage, without his shoes on and his hat over his forehead. He looked at them, one after the other, with a quick glance of his eyes without moving his head. He seemed possessed, and then, without saying a word, he threw himself on Limousin, seized him as if he were going to strangle him and flung him into the opposite corner of the room so violently that the lover lost his balance and, clutching at the air with his hands, banged his head against the wall.

But when Henriette saw that her husband was going to murder her lover she threw herself onto Parent, seized him by the neck and, digging her ten delicate and rosy fingers into his neck, she squeezed him so tightly, with all the vigor of a desperate woman, that the blood spurted out under her nails, and she bit his shoulder as if she wished to tear it with her teeth. Parent, half strangled and choked, loosened his hold on Limousin in order to shake off his wife, who was hanging onto his neck, and putting his arms around her waist, he flung her also to the other end of the drawing room.

Then, as his passion was short lived, like that of most good-tempered men, and as his strength was soon exhausted, he remained standing between the two, panting, worn out, not knowing what to do next. His brute fury had expended itself in that effort like the froth of a bottle of champagne, and his unwonted energy ended in a want of breath. As soon as he could speak, however, he said: "Go away —both of you—immediately—go away!"

Limousin remained motionless in his corner against the wall, too startled to understand anything as yet, too frightened to move a finger; while Henriette, with her hands resting on a small round table, her head bent forward with her hair hanging down, the bodice of her dress unfastened and bosom bare, waited like a wild animal which is about to spring. Parent went on in a stronger voice: "Go away immediately. Get out of the house!"

His wife, however, seeing that he had got over his first exasperation, grew bolder, drew herself up, took two steps toward him and, grown almost insolent already, she said: "Have you lost your head? What is the matter with you? What is the meaning of this unjustifiable violence?" But he turned toward her, and raising his fist to strike her, he stammered out: "Oh! Oh! this is too much—too much! I heard everything! Everything! Do you understand? Everything! you wretch—you wretch; you are two wretches! Get out of the house—both of you! Immediately— or I shall kill you! Leave the house!"

She saw that it was all over and that he knew everything, that she could not prove her innocence and that she must comply; but all her impudence had returned to her, and her hatred for the man, which was aroused now, drove her to audacity, making her feel the need of bravado and of defying him. So she said in a clear voice: "Come, Limousin, as he is going to turn me out of doors, I will go to your lodgings with you."

But Limousin did not move, and Parent, in a fresh access of rage, cried out: "Go, will you!—go, you wretches!—or else!—or else!" And he seized a chair and whirled it over his head.

Then Henriette walked quickly across the room, took her lover by the arm, dragged him from the wall, to which he appeared fixed, and led him toward the door, saying: "Do come, my friend. You see that the man is mad. Do come!"

As she went out she turned round to her husband, trying to think of something that she could do, something that she could invent to wound him to the heart as she left the house. An idea struck her, one of those venomous, deadly ideas in which all a woman's perfidy shows itself, and she said resolutely: "I am going to take my child with me."

Parent was stupefied and stammered: "Your—your child? You dare to talk of your child? You venture—you venture to ask for your child—after—after—— Oh! oh! that is too much! Go, you horrid wretch! Go!" She went up to him again, almost smiling, avenged already, and defying him, standing close to him and face to face, she said: "I want my child, and you have no right to keep him, because he is not yours. Do you understand? He is not yours—he is Limousin's."

And Parent cried out in bewilderment: "You lie—you lie—you wretch!"

But she continued: "You fool! Everybody knows it except you. I tell you, this is his father. You need only look at him to see it."

Parent staggered back from her, and then he suddenly turned round, took a candle and rushed into the next room. Almost immediately, however, he returned, carrying little George wrapped up in his bedclothes, and the child, who had been suddenly awakened, was crying from fright. Parent threw him into his wife's arms and then, without saying anything more, he pushed her roughly out toward the stairs, where Limousin was waiting from motives of prudence.

Then he shut the door again, double-locked it and bolted it, and he had scarcely got into the drawing room when he fell full length on the floor.

II

Parent lived alone, quite alone. During the five weeks that followed their separation the feeling of surprise at his new life prevented him from thinking much. He had resumed his bachelor life, his habits of lounging about, and he took his meals at a restaurant as he had done formerly. As he had wished to avoid any scandal he made his wife an allowance, which was settled by their lawyers. By degrees, however, the thoughts of the child began to haunt him. Often when he was at home alone at night he suddenly thought he heard George calling out "Papa," and his heart would begin to beat. One night he got up quickly and opened the door to see whether, by chance, the child might have returned, like dogs or pigeons do. Why should a child have less instinct than an animal?

After finding that he was mistaken he went and sat down in his armchair again and thought of the boy. Finally he thought of him for hours and whole days. It was not only a moral but still more a physical obsession, a nervous longing to kiss him, to hold and fondle him, to take him onto his knees and dance him. He felt the child's little arms around his neck, the little mouth pressing a kiss on his beard, the soft hair tickling his cheeks, and the remembrance of all those childish ways made him suffer like the desire for some loved woman who has run away. Twenty or a hundred times a day he asked himself the question whether he was or was not George's father, and at night, especially, he indulged in interminable speculations on the point and almost before he was in bed. Every night he recommenced the same series of despairing arguments.

After his wife's departure he had at first not felt the slightest doubt; certainly the child was Limousin's; but by degrees he began to waver. Henriette's words could not be of any value. She had merely braved him and tried to drive him to desperation, and calmly weighing the pros and cons, there seemed to be every chance that she had lied, though perhaps only Limousin could tell the truth. But how was he to find it out, how could he question him or persuade him to confess the real facts?

Sometimes Parent would get up in the middle of the night fully determined to go and see Limousin and to beg him, to offer him anything he wanted, to put an end to this intolerable misery. Then he would go back to bed in despair, reflecting that her lover would, no doubt, also lie. He would, in fact, be sure to lie, in order to avoid losing the child, if he were really his father. What could he, Parent, do then? Absolutely nothing!

And he began to feel sorry that he had thus suddenly brought about the crisis, that he had not taken time for reflection, that he had not waited and dissimulated for a month or two, so as to find out for himself. He ought to have pretended to suspect nothing and have allowed them to betray themselves at their leisure. It would have been enough for him to see the other kiss the child, to guess and to understand. A friend does not kiss a child as a father does. He should have watched them behind the doors. Why had he not thought of that? If Limousin, when left alone with George, had not at once taken him up, clasped him in his arms and kissed him passionately, if he had looked on indifferently while he was playing, without taking any notice of him, no doubt or hesitation could have been possible; in that case he would not have been the father, he would not have thought that he was, would not have felt that he was. Thus Parent would have kept the child while he got rid of the mother, and he would have been happy, perfectly happy.

He tossed about in bed, hot and unhappy, trying to recollect Limousin's ways with the child. But he could not remember anything suspicious, not a gesture, not a look, neither word nor caress. And then the child's mother took very little notice of him; if she had him by her lover she would, no doubt, have loved him more.

They had, therefore, separated him from his son out of vengeance, from cruelty, to punish him for having surprised them, and he made up his mind to go the next morning and obtain the magistrate's assistance to gain possession of George, but almost as soon as he had formed that resolution he felt assured of the contrary. From the moment that Limousin had been Henriette's lover, her adored lover, she would certainly have given herself up to him from the very first with that ardor of self-abandonment which belongs to women who love. The cold reserve which she had always shown in her intimate relations with him, Parent, was surely also an obstacle to her bearing him a son.

In that case he would be claiming, he would take with him, constantly keep and look after the child of another man. He would not be able to look at him, kiss him, hear him say "Papa" without being struck and tortured by the thought, "He is not my child." He was going to condemn himself to that torture and that wretched life every moment! No, it would be better to live alone, to grow old alone and to die alone.

And every day and every night these dreadful doubts and sufferings, which nothing could calm or end, would recommence. Especially did he dread the darkness of the evening, the melancholy feeling of the twilight. A flood of sorrow would invade his heart, a torrent of despair, which threatened to overwhelm him and drive him mad. He was as frightened of his own thoughts as men are of criminals, and he fled before them as one does from wild beasts. Above all things he feared his empty, dark, horrible dwelling and the deserted streets in which, here and there, a gas lamp flickers, where the isolated foot passenger whom one hears in the distance seems to be a night prowler and makes one walk faster or slower, according to whether he is coming toward you or following you.

And in spite of himself and by instinct Parent went in the direction of the broad, well-lighted, populous streets. The light and the crowd attracted him, occupied his mind and distracted his thoughts, and when he was tired walking aimlessly about among the moving crowd, when he saw the foot passengers becoming more scarce and the pavements less crowded, the fear of solitude and silence drove him into some large café full of drinkers and of light. He went there as a moth comes to a candle; he used to sit down at one of the little round tables and ask for a bock, which he used to drink slowly, feeling uneasy every time that a customer got up to go. He would have liked to take him by the arm, hold him back and beg him to stay a little longer, so much did he dread the time when the waiter would come up to him and say angrily: "Come, monsieur, it is closing time!"

Every evening he would stop till the very last. He saw them carry in the tables, turn out the gas jets one by one, except his and that at the counter. He looked unhappily at the cashier counting the money and locking it up in the drawer, and then he went, being usually pushed out by the waiters, who murmured: "Another one who has too much! One would think he had no place to sleep in."

And each night as soon as he was alone in the dark street he began to think of George again and to rack his brains in trying to discover whether or not he was this child's father.

He thus got into the habit of going to the beerhouses, where the continual elbowing of the drinkers brings you in contact with a familiar and silent public, where the clouds of tobacco smoke lull disquietude while the heavy beer dulls the mind and calms the heart. He almost lived there. He was scarcely up before he went there to find people to occupy his looks and his thoughts, and soon, as he became too listless to move, he took his meals there. About twelve o'clock he used to rap on the marble table, and the waiter would quickly bring a plate, a glass, a table napkin and his lunch, when he had ordered it. When he had finished he would slowly drink his cup of black coffee with his eyes fixed on the decanter of brandy, which would soon procure him an hour or two of forgetfulness. First of all he would dip his lips into the cognac, as if to get the flavor of it with the tip of his tongue. Then he would throw his head back and pour it into his mouth, drop by drop, and turn the strong liquor over on his palate, his gums and the mucous membrane of his cheeks; then he would swallow it slowly, to feel it going down his throat and into his stomach.

Thus after every meal he, during more than an hour, sipped three or four small glasses of brandy which stupefied him by degrees; then, having drunk it, he used to raise himself up on the seat covered with red velvet, pull his trousers up and his waistcoat down, so as to cover the linen which appeared between the two, draw down his shirt cuffs and take up the newspapers again, which he had already read in the morning, and read them all through again from beginning to end. Between four and five o'clock he would go for a walk on the boulevards, to get a little fresh air, as he used to say, and then come back to the seat which had been reserved for him and ask for his absinth. He used to talk to the regular customers whose acquaintance he had made. They discussed the news of the day and political events, and that carried him on till dinnertime, and he spent the evening as he had the afternoon, until it was time to close.

It was a terrible moment for him when he was obliged to go out into the dark and into the empty room full of dreadful recollections, of horrible thoughts and of mental agony. He no longer saw any of his old friends, none of his relations, nobody who might remind him of his past life. But as his apartments were a hell to him he took a room in a large hotel, a good room on the ground floor, so as to see the passers-by. He was no longer alone in that great building; he felt people swarming round him, he heard voices in the adjoining rooms, and when his former sufferings revived at the sight of his bed, which was turned back, and of his solitary fireplace he went out into the wide passages and walked up and down them like a sentinel, before all the closed doors, and looked sadly at the shoes standing in couples outside each, women's little boots by the side of men's thick ones, and he thought that no doubt all these people were happy and were sleeping sweetly side by side or in each other's arms in their warm beds.

Five years passed thus; five miserable years with no other events except from time to time a passing love affair. But one day when he was taking his usual walk between the Madeleine and the Rue Drouot he suddenly saw a lady whose bearing struck him. A tall gentleman and a child were with her, and all three were walking in front of him. He asked himself where he had seen them before, when suddenly he recognized a movement of her hand; it was his wife, his wife with Limousin and his child, his little George.

His heart beat as if it would suffocate him, but he did not stop, for he wished to see them, and he followed them. They looked like a family of the better middle class. Henriette was leaning on Paul's arm and speaking to him in a low voice and looking at him sideways occasionally. Parent saw her side face and recognized its graceful outlines, the movements of her lips, her smile and her caressing looks, but the child chiefly took up his attention. How tall and strong he was! Parent could not see his face but only his long fair curls. That tall boy with bare legs, who was walking by his mother's side like a little man, was George.

He saw them suddenly, all three, as they stopped in front of a shop. Limousin had grown very gray, had aged and was thinner; his wife, on the contrary, was as young-looking as ever and had grown stouter; George he would not have recognized, he was so different to what he had been formerly.

They went on again, and Parent followed them, then walked on quickly, passed them and then turned round so as to meet them face to face. As he passed the child he felt a mad longing to take him into his arms and run off with him, and he knocked against him, accidentally as it were. The boy turned round and looked at the clumsy man angrily, and Parent went off hastily, struck and hurt by the look. He slunk off like a thief, seized by a horrible fear lest he should have been seen and recognized by his wife and her lover, and he went to his café without stopping, fell breathless into his chair, and that evening he drank three absinths.

For four months he felt the pain of that meeting in his heart. Every night he saw the three again, happy and tranquil, father, mother and child walking on the boulevard before going in to dinner, and that new vision effaced the old one. It was another matter, another hallucination now, and also a fresh pain. Little George, his little George, the child he had so much loved and so often kissed formerly, disappeared in the far distance and he saw a new one, like a brother of the first, a little boy with bare legs who did not know him! He suffered terribly at that thought. The child's love was dead; there was no bond between them; the child would not have held out his arms when he saw him. He had even looked at him angrily.

Then by degrees he grew calmer, his mental torture diminished, the image that had appeared to his eyes and which haunted his nights became more indistinct and less frequent. He began once more to live like everybody else, like all those idle people who drink beer off marble-topped tables and wear out the seats of their trousers on the threadbare velvet of the couches.

He grew old amid the smoke from pipes, lost his hair under the gas lights, looked upon his weekly bath, on his fortnightly visit to the barber's to have his hair cut and on the purchase of a new coat or hat as an event. When he got to his café after buying a new hat he used to look at himself in the glass for a long time before sitting down and would take it off and put it on again several times following and at last ask his friend, the lady at the bar, who watched him with interest, whether she thought it suited him.

Two or three times a year he went to the theater, and in the summer he sometimes spent his evenings at one of the open-air concerts in the Champs Elysées. He brought back from them some airs which ran in his head for several weeks and which he even hummed, beating time with his foot, while he was drinking his beer; and so the years followed each other, slow, monotonous and long because they were quite uneventful.

He did not feel them glide past him. He went on toward death without fear or agitation, sitting at a table in a café, and only the great glass against which he rested his head, which was every day becoming balder, reflected the ravages of time which flies and devours men, poor men.

He only very rarely now thought of the terrible drama which had wrecked his life, for twenty years had passed since that terrible evening; but the life he had led since then had worn him out, and the landlord of his café would often say to him: "You ought to pull yourself together a little, Monsieur Parent; you should get some fresh air and go into the country! I assure you that you have changed very much within the last few months." And when his customer had gone out he used to say to the barmaid: "That poor Monsieur Parent is booked for another world; it is no good never to go out of Paris. Advise him to go out of town for a day occasionally, he has confidence in you. It is nice weather and will do him good." And she, full of pity and good will for such a regular customer, said to Parent every day: "Come, monsieur, make up your mind to get a little fresh air; it is so charming in the country when the weather is fine. Oh! if I could, I would spend my life there."

And she told him her dreams, the simple and poetical dreams of all the poor girls who are shut up from one year's end to the other in a shop and who see the noisy life of the streets go by while they think of the calm and pleasant life in the country, under the bright sun shining on the meadows, of deep woods and clear rivers, of cows lying in the grass and of all the different flowers, blue, red, yellow, purple, lilac, pink and white, which are so pretty, so fresh, so sweet, all the wild flowers which one picks as one walks.

She liked to speak to him frequently of her continual, unrealized and unrealizable longing, and he, an old man without hope, was fond of listening to her and used to go and sit near the counter to talk to Mademoiselle Zoé and to discuss the country with her. Then by degrees he was seized by a vague desire to go just once and see whether it was really so pleasant there, as she said, outside the walls of the great city, and so one morning he said to her: "Do you know where one can get a good lunch in the neighborhood of Paris?"

"Go to the Terrace at Saint-Germain."

He had been there formerly, just after he had got engaged, and so he made up his mind to go there again, and he chose a Sunday, without any special reason but merely because people generally do go out on Sundays even when they have nothing to do all the week. So one Sunday morning he went to Saint-Germain. It was at the beginning of July, on a very bright and hot day. Sitting by the door of the railway carriage, he watched the trees and the strangely built little houses in the outskirts of Paris fly past. He felt low spirited and vexed at having yielded to that new longing and at having broken through his usual habits. The view, which was continually changing and always the same, wearied him. He was thirsty; he would have liked to get out at every station and sit down in the café which he saw outside and drink a bock or two and then take the first train back to Paris. And then the journey seemed very long to him. He used to remain sitting for whole days as long as he had the same motionless objects before his eyes, but he found it very trying and fatiguing to remain sitting while he was being whirled along and to see the whole country fly by while he himself was motionless.

However, he found the Seine interesting every time he crossed it. Under the bridge at Chatou he saw some skiffs going at great pace under the vigorous strokes of the bare-armed oarsmen, and he thought: "There are some fellows who are certainly enjoying themselves!" And then the train entered the tunnel just before you get to the station at Saint-Germain and soon stopped at the arrival platform, where Parent got out and walked slowly, for he already felt tired, toward the Terrace with his hands behind his back, and when he got to the iron balustrade he stopped to look at the distant horizon.

The vast plain spread out before him like the sea, green and studded with large villages, almost as populous as towns. White roads crossed it, and it was well wooded in places; the ponds at Vésinet glistened like plates of silver, and the distant ridges of Sannois and Argenteuil were covered with light bluish mist so that they could scarcely be distinguished. The sun bathed the whole landscape in its full warm light, and the Seine, which twined like an endless serpent through the plain, flowed round the villages and along the slopes. Parent inhaled the warm breeze which seemed to make his heart young again, to enliven his spirits and to vivify his blood, and said to himself: "It is very nice here."

Then he went on a few steps and stopped again to look about him, and the utter misery of his existence seemed to be brought out into full relief by the intense light which inundated the country. He saw his twenty years of café life, dull, monotonous, heartbreaking. He might have traveled like others did, have gone among foreigners, to unknown countries beyond the sea, have interested himself somewhat in everything which other men are passionately devoted to, in arts and sciences; he might have enjoyed life in a thousand forms, that mysterious life which is either charming or painful, constantly changing, always inexplicable and strange.

Now, however, it was too late. He would go on drinking bock after bock until he died, without any family, without friends, without hope, without any curiosity about anything, and he was seized with a feeling of misery and a wish to run away, to hide himself in Paris, in his café and his befuddlement! All the thoughts, all the dreams, all the desires which are dormant in the sloth of the stagnating hearts had reawakened, brought to life by those rays of sunlight on the plain.

He felt that if he were to remain there any longer he should lose his head, and so he made haste to get to the Pavilion Henri IV for lunch, to try and forget his troubles under the influence of wine and alcohol and at any rate to have someone to speak to.

He took a small table in one of the arbors, from which one can see all the surrounding country, ordered his lunch and asked to be served at once. Then some more people arrived and sat down at tables near him, and he felt more comfortable; he was no longer alone. Three persons were lunching near him, and he looked at them two or three times without seeing them clearly, as one looks at total strangers. But suddenly a woman's voice sent a shiver through him which seemed to penetrate to his very marrow. "George," it had said, "will you carve the chicken?" Another voice replied: "Yes, mamma."

Parent looked up, and he understood, he guessed immediately who those people were! He should certainly not have known them again. His wife had grown quite white and very stout, an old, serious, respectable lady, and she held her head forward as she ate, for fear of spotting her dress, although she had a table napkin tucked under her chin. George had become a man; he had a slight beard, that unequal and almost colorless beard which fringes the cheeks of youths. He wore a high hat, a white waistcoat and a monocle—because it looked dandified, no doubt. Parent looked at him in astonishment! Was that George, his son? No, he did not know that young man; there could be nothing in common between them. Limousin had his back to him and was eating with his shoulders rather bent.

Well, all three of them seemed happy and satisfied; they came and dined in the country at well-known restaurants. They had had a calm and pleasant existence, a family existence in a warm and comfortable house, filled with all those trifles which make life agreeable, with affection, with all those tender words which people exchange continually when they love each other. They had lived thus, thanks to him, Parent, on his money, after having deceived him, robbed him, ruined him! They had condemned him, the innocent, the simple-minded, the jovial man, to all the miseries of solitude, to that abominable life which he had led between the pavement and the counter, to every moral torture and every physical misery! They had made him a useless being who was lost and wretched among other people, a poor old man without any pleasures or anything to look forward to and who hoped for nothing from anyone. For him the world was empty because he loved nothing in the world. He might go among other nations or go about the streets, go into all the houses in Paris, open every room, but he would not find the beloved face, the face of wife or child, that he was in search of, which smiles when it sees you, behind any door. And that idea worked upon him more than any other, the idea of a door which one opens to see and to embrace somebody behind it.

And that was the fault of those three wretches! The fault of that worthless woman, of that infamous friend and of that tall light-haired lad who put on insolent airs. Now he felt as angry with the child as he did with the other two. Was he not Limousin's son? Would Limousin have kept him and loved him otherwise? Would not Limousin very quickly have got rid of the mother and of the child if he had not felt sure that it was his, certainly his? Does anybody bring up other people's children? And now they were there, quite close to him, those three who had made him suffer so much.

Parent looked at them, irritated and excited at the recollection of all his sufferings and of his despair, and was especially exasperated at their placid and satisfied looks. He felt inclined to kill them, to throw his siphon of seltzer water at them, to split open Limousin's head which he every moment bent over his plate and raised up again immediately. And they continued to live like that, without cares or anxiety of any kind. No! no! That was really too much, after all! He would avenge himself; he would have his revenge now, on the spot, as he had them under his hand. But how? He tried to think of some means; he pictured such dreadful things as one reads of in the newspapers occasionally but could not hit on anything practical. And he went on drinking to excite himself, to give himself courage not to allow such an occasion to escape him, as he should certainly not meet with it again.

Suddenly an idea struck him, a terrible idea, and he left off drinking to mature it. A smile rose to his lips, and he murmured: "I have got them, I have got them. We will see, we will see."

A waiter asked him: "What would you like now, monsieur?"

"Nothing. Coffee and cognac. The best." And he looked at them as he sipped his brandy. There were too many people in the restaurant for what he wanted to do, so he would wait and follow them, for they would be sure to walk on the terrace or in the forest. When they had got a little distance off he would join them, and then he would have his revenge, yes, he would have his revenge! It was certainly not too soon, after twenty-three years of suffering. Ah! They little guessed what was to happen to them.

They finished their luncheon slowly, and they talked in perfect security. Parent could not hear what they were saying, but he saw their calm movements, and his wife's face, especially, exasperated him. She had assumed a haughty air, the air of a stout, devout woman, of an irreproachably devout woman, sheathed in principles, iron clad in virtue. Then they paid the bill and got up, and then he saw Limousin. He might have been taken for a retired diplomatist, for he looked a man of great importance with his soft white whiskers, the tips of which fell onto the facings of his coat.

They went out. George was smoking a cigar and had his hat on one side, and Parent followed them. First of all they went up and down the terrace and calmly admired the landscape, like people who have well satisfied their hunger, and then they went into the forest, and Parent rubbed his hands and followed them at a distance, hiding himself so as not to excite their suspicion too soon. They walked slowly, enjoying the fresh green foliage and the warm air. Henriette was holding Limousin's arm and walked upright at his side like a wife who is contented and proud of herself. George was cutting off the leaves with his stick and occasionally jumped over the ditches by the roadside like a fiery young horse ready to gallop off through the trees.

Parent came up to them by degrees, panting rather from excitement and fatigue, for he never walked now. He soon came up to them, but he was seized by fear, an inexplicable fear, and he passed them so as to turn round and meet them face to face. He walked on, his heart beating, for he knew that they were just behind him now, and he said to himself: "Come, now is the time. Courage! courage! Now is the moment!"

He turned around. They were all three sitting on the grass, at the foot of a huge tree, and were still talking. He made up his mind and came back rapidly, and then, stopping in front of them in the middle of the road, he said abruptly, in a voice broken by emotion: "It is I! Here I am! I suppose you did not expect me?" They all three looked at him carefully, for they thought that he was mad, and he continued: "One might think that you did not know me again. Just look at me! I am Parent, Henri Parent. You did not expect me, eh? You thought it was all over and that you would never see me again. Ah! But here I am once more, you see, and now we will have an explanation."

Henriette was terrified and hid her face in her hands, murmuring: "Oh! Good heavens!" And seeing this stranger who seemed to be threatening his mother, George sprang up, ready to seize him by the collar, while Limousin, who was thunderstruck, looked at this specter in horror, who, after panting for a few moments, continued: "So now we will have an explanation; the proper moment for it has come! Ah! you deceived me, you condemned me to the life of a convict, and you thought that I should never catch you!"

But the young man took him by the shoulders and pushed him back: "Are you mad?" he asked. "What do you want? Go on your way immediately, or I shall give you a thrashing!" But Parent replied: "What do I want? I want to tell you who these people are." George, however, was in a rage and shook him, was even going to strike him, but the other said: "Just let me go. I am your father. There, look whether they recognize me now, the wretches!" And the alarmed young man removed his hands and turned to his mother, while Parent, as soon as he was released, went toward her.

"Well," he said, "tell him who I am, you! Tell him that my name is Henri Parent, that I am his father because his name is George Parent, because you are my wife, because you are all three living on my money, on the allowance of ten thousand francs which I have made you since I drove you out of my house. Will you tell him also why I drove you out? Because I surprised you with this beggar, this wretch, your lover! Tell him what I was, an honorable man whom you married for my money and whom you deceived from the very first day. Tell him who you are and who I am."

He stammered and panted for breath in his rage, and the woman exclaimed in a heartrending voice: "Paul, Paul, stop him; make him be quiet; do not let him say this before my son!"

Limousin had also got up, and he said in a quite low voice: "Hold your tongue! Do you understand what you are doing?"

But Parent continued furiously: "I quite know what I am doing, and that is not all. There is one thing that I will know, something that has tormented me for twenty years."

And then turning to George, who was leaning against a tree in consternation, he said: "Listen to me. When she left my house she thought it was not enough to have deceived me but she also wanted to drive me to despair. You were my only consolation, and she took you with her, swearing that I was not your father but that he was your father! Was she lying? I do not know, and I have been asking myself the question for the last twenty years."

He went close up to her, tragic and terrible, and pulling away her hands with which she had covered her face, he continued: "Well, I call upon you now to tell me which of us two is the father of this young man; he or I, your husband or your lover. Come! Come! tell us." Limousin rushed at him, but Parent pushed him back, and sneering in his fury, he said: "Ah! you are brave now! You are braver than you were the day you ran out of doors because I was going to half murder you. Very well! If she will not reply, tell me yourself. You ought to know as well as she. Tell me, are you this young fellow's father? Come! Come! Tell me!"

Then he turned to his wife again. "If you will not tell me, at any rate tell your son. He is a man now, and he has the right to know who is his father. I do not know, and I never did know, never, never! I cannot tell you, my boy." He seemed to be losing his senses; his voice grew shrill, and he worked his arms about as if he had an epileptic attack. "Come! Give me an answer. She does not know. I will make a bet that she does not know. No—she does not know, by Jove! She used to go to bed with both of us! Ha! ha! ha! Nobody knows—nobody. How can one know such things? You will not know either, my boy; you will not know any more than I do—never. Look here. Ask her—you will find that she does not know. I do not know either. You can choose—yes, you can choose—him or me. Good evening. It is all over. If she makes up her mind to tell you, come and let me know, will you? I am living at the Hôtel des Continents. I should be glad to know. Good evening; I hope you will enjoy yourselves very much."

And he went away, gesticulating and talking to himself under the tall trees, into the empty cool air which was full of the smell of the sap. He did not turn round to look at them but went straight on, walking under the stimulus of his rage, under a storm of passion, with that one fixed idea in his mind, and presently he found himself outside the station. A train was about to start, and he got in. During the journey his anger calmed down; he regained his senses and returned to Paris, astonished at his own boldness and feeling as full of aches and fatigues as if he had broken some bones, but nevertheless he went to have a bock at his café.

When she saw him come in Mademoiselle Zoé was surprised and said: "What! Back already? Are you tired?"

"I am tired—very tired. You know, when one is not used to going out—but I have done with it. I shall not go into the country again. I had better have stopped here. For the future I shall not stir out again."

But she could not persuade him to tell her about his little excursion although she wanted very much to hear all about it, and for the first time in his life he got thoroughly drunk that night and had to be carried home.

FEAR

The train rushed through the shadows.

I was alone, facing an old gentleman who was looking out of the window. There was a strong smell of disinfectant in this P.L.M carriage, which must have come from Marseilles.

It was a moonless, airless, burning night. There were no stars to be seen, and the wind of the leaping train blew in our faces, warm, soft, oppressive and stifling.

We had left Paris three hours before, and we were approaching the heart of France without catching a glimpse of the country we were crossing.

All at once a fantastic apparition rushed into sight. There was a wood, and a big fire lit there, and two men standing round it.

We saw it for an instant: they looked like two tramps, in rags, reddened by the glare from the fire, with their bearded faces turned towards us, and all round them, like the setting of a play, rose the green trees; they were a bright and shining green, the vivid light reflected from the flames struck across the trunks, and the thick leafage was barred and stabbed and splashed by the light spreading through it.

Then the darkness swept back again.

It certainly was the strangest of visions. What were those two wanderers doing in that forest? Why a fire on this suffocating night?

My neighbor took out his watch and said:

"It is exactly midnight, sir: we have just seen a strange thing."

I agreed; we fell into conversation and tried to imagine what these persons could be: criminals burning evidence or sorcerers preparing a philtre? You don't light a fire in a forest at midnight, and in the height of summer, to boil soup. So what were they doing? We could not reach any likely explanation.

And my neighbor began to talk. He was an old man whose profession I found it impossible to guess. He was certainly an eccentric, highly cultured, and he seemed perhaps a little mad.

But is it always possible to say who are the wise and who are the fools in this life where reason is often called stupidity and folly genius?

He said:

"I am glad to have seen that. For a brief space of time I experienced a forgotten sensation.

"How disturbing the world must have been in the old days when it was full of mystery!

"With each veil lifted from the unknown world, the human imagination is laid waste a little farther. You, sir, don't feel that the night is very empty and filled with a tiresomely commonplace darkness, since it was robbed of its apparitions.

"'No more fantasy,' they say, 'no more strange beliefs, all the inexplicable is explicable. The supernatural sinks like a lake emptied by a canal; day by day science narrows the boundaries of the marvelous.'

"I, sir, I belong to the old race, to those who love to believe. I belong to the old simple race that is used to being baffled, used to not investigating and to not knowing. That delights in being surrounded by mysteries and shrinks from the simple and brutal truth.

"Yes, sir, we have laid waste the imagination by suppressing the invisible. I see our earth today as a forsaken world, empty and bare. The beliefs that flung a veil of poetry over it are gone.

"How I should like—when I go out at night—to shiver with the mortal terror that makes old women cross themselves when they pass the graveyard wall and the last few superstitious folk run before the weird wandering lights and the strange mists from the marshes! How I should like to believe in some vague terrifying thing that I thought I felt slipping past me in the darkness!

"How somber and terrible the shadows of evening must have been in the old days, when they were full of unknown fabulous beings, evil wandering spirits who took unforeseen shapes and froze the heart with dread! Their occult power was quite beyond the grasp of our minds, and they drew near with inevitable feet.

"When the supernatural disappeared, true fear disappeared from the earth too, for we are truly afraid only of what we do not understand. Visible dangers can move, disturb, terrify. But what is that compared with the overwhelming terror that fills your mind when you expect to meet a wandering ghost, or suffer the clinging arms of a dead man, or see running on you one of those frightful beasts invented by man's fear? The dark seems light to me, now that it is no longer haunted.

"And the proof of all this is that if we suddenly found ourselves alone in that wood, we should be pursued by the vision of the two strange beings who have just appeared to us in the glare of their fire rather than by dread of any real danger at all.

"We are truly afraid," he repeated, "only of what we do not understand."

A sudden memory woke in my mind, the memory of a story told us one Sunday by Turgenev, in Gustave Flaubert's house.

I don't know whether he had written it in any of his books.

No one was more subtly able to thrill us with a suggestion of the veiled unknown world than the great Russian storyteller, or to reveal—in the half-light of a strange tale—uncertain, disturbing, threatening things.

In his books we are sharply aware of that vague fear of the Invisible, the fear of the unknown thing behind the wall, behind the door, behind the external world. Perilous gleams of light break on us, as we read, revealing just enough to add to our mortal fear.

He seems sometimes to be showing us the inner meaning of strange coincidences, the unexpected connection between circumstances that were apparently fortuitous and really guided by a hidden malicious will. In his books we can imagine we feel an imperceptible hand guiding us through life in a mysterious way, as through a shifting dream whose meaning we never grasp.

He does not rush boldly into the supernatural world like Edgar Poe or Hoffmann; he tells simple stories, and a sense of something a little uncertain and a little uneasy creeps somehow into them.

That day he used those very words: "We are truly afraid only of what we do not understand."

Arms hanging down, legs stretched out and relaxed, hair quite white, he was sitting or rather lounging in a large armchair, drowned in that flowing tide of beard and silvery hair that gave him the air of an Eternal Father or a river god from Ovid.

He spoke slowly, with a certain indolence which lent a charm to his phrases, and a rather hesitating and awkward manner of speaking which emphasized the vivid rightness of his words. His wide pale eyes, like the eyes of a child, reflected all the changing fancies of his mind. This is what he told us:

He was hunting, as a young man, in a Russian forest. He had tramped all day, and towards the end of the afternoon he reached the edge of a quiet river.

It ran under the trees and among the trees, filled with floating grasses, deep, cold, and clear.

An overmastering desire seized the hunter to fling himself into this transparent water. He stripped and dived into the stream. He was a very tall and a very strong youth, active, and a splendid swimmer.

He let himself float gently in great content of mind, grasses and roots brushed past him, and tendrils of creeping plants trailed lightly over his skin, thrilling him.

Suddenly a hand touched his shoulder.

He turned round in startled wonder and saw a frightful creature staring hungrily at him.

It was like a woman or a monkey. Its vast wrinkled grimacing face smiled at him. Two nameless things, which must have been two breasts, floated in front of it, and its mass of tangled hair, burned by the sun, hung round its face and fell down its back.

Turgenev felt a piercing and appalling fear, the icy fear of the supernatural.

Without pausing to reflect, without thinking or understanding, he began to swim frantically towards the bank. But the monster swam quicker still, and touched his neck, his back, and his legs with little cacklings of delight. Mad with terror, the young man reached the bank at last and tore at full speed through the wood, with never a thought of recovering his clothes and his gun.

The frightful creature followed him, running as quickly as he did and growling all the time.

Spent and sick with fear, the fugitive was ready to drop to the ground when a boy who was watching his goats ran up, armed with a whip; he laid it about the fearsome human beast, who ran away howling with grief. And Turgenev saw her disappear among the leaves of the trees, like a female gorilla.

It was a madwoman, who had lived in this wood for thirty years, on the charity of the shepherds, and who spent half her days swimming in the river.

The great Russian writer added: "I have never felt such fear in my life, because I could not imagine what this monster could be."

I related this adventure to my companion, and he replied:

"Yes, we are afraid only of what we do not understand. We only truly experience that frightful spiritual convulsion which we call dread when our fear is touched with the superstitious terror of past ages. I myself have suffered this dread in all its horror, and that over something so simple and so stupid that I hardly dare tell you about it.

"I was traveling in Brittany, alone and on foot. I had walked across Finistère: desolate moors, bare earth where nothing will grow but the gorse that grows beside great sacred stone pillars. The evening before, I had seen the menacing headland of Raz, the end of the Old World, where two oceans, the Atlantic and the Channel, for ever surge and break; my mind was full of legends, stories read or told in this country of credulous and superstitious folk.

"I was walking at night from Penmarch to Pont-l'Abbé. Do you know Penmarch? A flat shore, utterly flat, very low-lying, seeming lower than the sea. Wherever you look you see the gray threatening sea, full of rocks slavered with foam, like raging beasts.

"I had dined in a fisherman's inn, and I had taken the road to the right, between two moors. It was growing very dark.

"Now and then a Druid stone, standing like a phantom, seemed to look at me as I passed, and a vague fear slowly took hold of me: fear of what? I had not the least idea. It was one of the evenings when the wind of passing spirits blows on your face, and your soul shudders and knows not why, and your heart beats in bewildered terror of some invisible thing, that terror whose passing I regret.

"The road seemed very long to me, interminably long and empty.

"There was no sound but the thunder of the waves down below, at my back; and sometimes the monotonous sinister sound seemed quite close, so close that I imagined the waves were at my heels, racing over the plain and foaming as they came, and I felt a wild impulse to save myself from them, to run for my life before their onrush.

"The wind, a little wind that blew in gusts, whistled through the gorse all round me. And quickly as I went, my arms and legs were cold with the horrid cold of mortal fear.

"Oh, how I longed to meet someone!

"It was so black that now I could hardly make out the road.

"And suddenly I heard a rolling sound, a long way in front of me. 'That's a carriage,' I thought. Then I heard nothing more.

"A moment later I distinctly heard the same noise again, nearer now.

"I saw no light, however, and I said to myself: 'They have no lantern. There's nothing to be surprised at in that, in this wild district.'

"The noise stopped once more, then began again. It was too shrill to be made by a wagon; and besides I did not hear the sound of a horse trotting, which surprised me, for the night was very still.

"'What can it be?' I wondered.

"It was approaching swiftly, very swiftly! I was sure now that I could hear only one wheel—no clatter of hoofs or feet—nothing. What could it be?

"It was close now, quite close; prompted by a quite instinctive fear, I flung myself down in a ditch and I saw pass right by me a wheelbarrow running all by itself —no one was pushing it—yes, a wheelbarrow—all by itself.

"My heart began such a violent leaping that I lay helpless on the grass, listening to the rolling of the wheel, which drew farther and farther away, going down to the sea. And I dared neither get up nor walk nor stir hand or foot; for if it had come back, if it had followed me, I should have died of terror.

"I was a long time before I recovered myself, a very long time. And I covered the rest of the road in such agony of mind that the least noise stopped the breath in my throat.

"You think it idiotic? But how terrifying! Thinking it over afterwards, I understood what it was; a barefooted child must have been pushing the wheelbarrow, and I had been expecting to see the head of a man of ordinary height.

"You can understand it . . . fear of some supernatural happening has crept into one's mind—a wheelbarrow running—all by itself. How terrifying!"

He was silent for a moment, then added:

"Believe me, sir, we are watching a strange and terrible spectacle—this invasion of cholera.

"You can smell the disinfectant poisoning the whole air in these carriages; it means that somewhere it is lurking.

"You should see Toulouse now. Go there, and you can feel that *he* is there. And it is no mere fear of disease that distracts the townspeople. The cholera is something more than that, it is the Unseen, it is one of the ancient plagues, a sort of malevolent spirit that has come back to the world, and astounds us as much as it terrifies us because it seems to belong to a lost age.

"The doctors make me laugh with their microbe. It is no insect that drives men to such a pitch of terror that they will jump out of the windows; it is cholera, the inexplicable and terrible being come from the recesses of the East.

"Walk through Toulouse and see them dancing in the streets.

"Why do men dance in days when death is abroad? They let off fireworks in the fields round the town; they light bonfires, orchestras play gay music on all the public promenades.

"Why this madness?

"It is because *he* is present: they are defying now, not the Microbe, but Cholera; they want to swagger past *him*, as they might swagger past an ambushed enemy spy. It is for *him* that they dance, and laugh and shout and light fires and play waltzes, for *him*, the angel of destruction, lurking in every place, unseen, threatening, like one of those old evil jinns conjured up by barbaric priests. . . ."

THE HOLE

CUTS AND WOUNDS WHICH CAUSED DEATH

That was the heading of the charge which brought Leopold Renard, upholsterer, before the Assize Court.

Round him were the principal witnesses, Mme. Flamèche, widow of the victim, Louis Ladureau, cabinetmaker, and Jean Durdent, plumber.

Near the criminal was his wife, dressed in black, a little ugly woman who looked like a monkey dressed as a lady.

This is how Renard described the drama:

"Good heavens, it is a misfortune of which I am the first and last victim and with which my will has nothing to do. The facts are their own commentary, Monsieur le Président. I am an honest man, a hard-working man, an upholsterer in the same street for the last sixteen years, known, liked, respected and esteemed by all, as my neighbors have testified, even the porter, who is not *folâtre* every day. I am fond of work, I am fond of saving, I like honest men and respectable pleasures. That is what has ruined me, so much the worse for me; but as my will had nothing to do with it, I continue to respect myself.

"Every Sunday for the last five years my wife and I have spent the day at Passy. We get fresh air, not to say that we are fond of fishing—as fond of it as we are of small onions. Mélie inspired me with that passion, the jade; she is more enthusiastic than I am, the scold, and all the mischief in this business is her fault, as you will see immediately.

"I am strong and mild-tempered, without a pennyworth of malice in me. But she, oh la la! She looks insignificant, she is short and thin, but she does more mischief than a weasel. I do not deny that she has some good qualities; she has some, and those very important to a man in business. But her character! Just ask about it in the neighborhood; even the porter's wife, who has just sent me about my business—she will tell you something about it.

"Every day she used to find fault with my mild temper: 'I would not put up with this! I would not put up with that.' If I had listened to her, Monsieur le Président, I should have had at least three bouts of fisticuffs a month."

Mme. Renard interrupted him: "And for good reasons too; they laugh best who laugh last."

He turned toward her frankly. "Oh! very well, I can blame you, since you were the cause of it."

Then, facing the president again, he said:

"I will continue. We used to go to Passy every Saturday evening, so as to be able to begin fishing at daybreak the next morning. It is a habit which has become second nature with us, as the saying is. Three years ago this summer I discovered a place, oh! such a spot! There, in the shade, were eight feet of water at least and perhaps ten, a hole with a *retour* under the bank, a regular retreat for fish and a paradise for any fisherman. I might look upon that hole as my property, Monsieur le Président, as I was its Christopher Columbus. Everybody in the neighborhood knew it, without making any opposition. They used to say: 'That is Renard's place'; and nobody would have gone to it, not even Monsieur Plumsay, who is renowned, be it said without any offense, for appropriating other people's places.

"Well, I went as usual to that place, of which I felt as certain as if I had owned it. I had scarcely got there on Saturday when I got into Delila, with my wife. Delila is my Norwegian boat which I had built by Fourmaise and which is light and safe. Well, as I said, we got into the boat and we were going to bait, and for baiting there is nobody to be compared with me, and they all know it. You want to know with what I bait? I cannot answer that question; it has nothing to do with the accident; I cannot answer, that is my secret. There are more than three hundred people who have asked me; I have been offered glasses of brandy and liquors, fried fish, matelote, to make me tell! But just go and try whether the chub will come. Ah! they have patted my stomach to get at my secret, my recipe. Only my wife knows, and she will not tell it any more than I shall! Is not that so, Mélie?"

The president of the court interrupted him:

"Just get to the facts as soon as you can."

The accused continued: "I am getting to them; I am getting to them. Well, on Saturday, July eighth, we left by the five-twenty-five train, and before dinner we went to ground bait as usual. The weather promised to keep fine, and I said to Mélie: 'All right for tomorrow!' And she replied: 'It looks like it.' We never talk more than that together.

"And then we returned to dinner. I was happy and thirsty, and that was the cause of everything. I said to Mélie: 'Look here, Mélie, it is fine weather, so suppose I drink a bottle of *Casque à mèche*.' That is a little white wine which we have christened so because if you drink too much of it it prevents you from sleeping and is the opposite of a nightcap. Do you understand me?

"She replied: 'You can do as you please, but you will be ill again and will not be able to get up tomorrow.' That was true, sensible, prudent and clear-sighted, I must confess. Nevertheless, I could not withstand it, and I drank my bottle. It all comes from that.

"Well, I could not sleep. By Jove! It kept me awake till two o'clock in the morning, and then I went to sleep so soundly that I should not have heard the angel shouting at the Last Judgment.

"In short, my wife woke me at six o'clock and I jumped out of bed, hastily put on my trousers and jersey, washed my face and jumped on board Delila. But it was too late, for when I arrived at my hole it was already taken! Such a thing had never happened to me in three years, and it made me feel as if I were being robbed under my own eyes. I said to myself, 'Confound it all! Confound it!' And then my wife began to nag me. 'Eh! What about your *Casque à mèche!* Get along, you drunkard! Are you satisfied, you great fool?' I could say nothing, because it was all quite true, and so I landed all the same near the spot and tried to profit by what was left. Perhaps, after all, the fellow might catch nothing and go away.

"He was a little thin man in white linen coat and waistcoat and with a large straw hat, and his wife, a fat woman who was doing embroidery, was behind him.

"When she saw us take up our position close to their place she murmured: 'I suppose there are no other places on the river!' And my wife, who was furious, replied: 'People who know how to behave make inquiries about the habits of the neighborhood before occupying reserved spots.'

"As I did not want a fuss I said to her: 'Hold your tongue, Mélie. Let them go on, let them go on; we shall see.'

"Well, we had fastened Delila under the willow trees and had landed and were fishing side by side, Mélie and I, close to the two others; but here, monsieur, I must enter into details.

"We had only been there about five minutes when our male neighbor's float began to go down two or three times, and then he pulled out a chub as thick as my thigh, rather less, perhaps, but nearly as big! My heart beat and the perspiration stood on my forehead, and Mélie said to me: 'Well, you sot, did you see that?'

"Just then Monsieur Bru, the grocer of Poissy, who was fond of gudgeon fishing, passed in a boat and called out to me: 'So somebody has taken your usual place, Monsieur Renard?' And I replied: 'Yes, Monsieur Bru, there are some people in this world who do not know the usages of common politeness.'

"The little man in linen pretended not to hear, nor his fat lump of a wife, either."

Here the president interrupted him a second time: "Take care, you are insulting the widow, Madame Flamèche, who is present."

Renard made his excuses: "I beg your pardon, I beg your pardon; my anger carried me away. . . . Well, not a quarter of an hour had passed when the little man caught another chub and another almost immediately and another five minutes later.

"The tears were in my eyes, and then I knew that Madame Renard was boiling with rage, for she kept on nagging at me: 'Oh, how horrid! Don't you see that he is robbing you of your fish? Do you think that you will catch anything? Not even a frog, nothing whatever. Why, my hands are burning just to think of it.'

"But I said to myself: 'Let us wait until twelve o'clock. Then this poaching fellow will go to lunch, and I shall get my place again.' As for me, Monsieur le Président, I lunch on the spot every Sunday; we bring our provisions in Delila. But there! At twelve o'clock the wretch produced a fowl out of a newspaper, and while he was eating, actually he caught another chub!

"Mélie and I had a morsel also, just a mouthful, a mere nothing, for our heart was not in it.

"Then I took up my newspaper, to aid my digestion. Every Sunday I read the Gil Blas in the shade like that, by the side of the water. It is Columbine's day, you know, Columbine who writes the articles in the Gil Blas. I generally put Madame Renard into a passion by pretending to know this Columbine. It is not true, for I do not know her and have never seen her, but that does not matter; she writes very well, and then she says things straight out for a woman. She suits me, and there are not many of her sort.

"Well, I began to tease my wife, but she got angry immediately and very angry, and so I held my tongue. At that moment our two witnesses, who are present here, Monsieur Ladureau and Monsieur Durdent, appeared on the other side of the river. We knew each other by sight. The little man began to fish again, and he caught so many that I trembled with vexation, and his wife said: 'It is an uncommonly good spot, and we will come here always, Desiré.' As for me, a cold shiver ran down my back, and Madame Renard kept repeating: 'You are not a man; you have the blood of a chicken in your veins'; and suddenly I said to her: 'Look here, I would rather go away, or I shall only be doing something foolish.'

"And she whispered to me as if she had put a red-hot iron under my nose: 'You are not a man. Now you are going to run away and surrender your place! Off you go, Bazaine!'

"Well, I felt that, but yet I did not move while the other fellow pulled out a bream. Oh! I never saw such a large one before, never! And then my wife began to talk aloud, as if she were thinking, and you can see her trickery. She said: 'That is what one might call stolen fish, seeing that we baited the place ourselves. At any rate they ought to give us back the money we have spent on bait.'

"Then the fat woman in the cotton dress said in turn: 'Do you mean to call us thieves, madame?' And they began to explain, and then they came to words. Oh Lord! those creatures know some good ones. They shouted so loud that our two witnesses, who were on the other bank, began to call out by way of a joke: 'Less noise over there; you will prevent your husbands from fishing.'

"The fact is that neither of us moved any more than if we had been two tree stumps. We remained there, with our noses over the water, as if we had heard nothing; but, by Jove, we heard all the same. 'You are a mere liar.'

" 'You are nothing better than a streetwalker.'

" 'You are only a trollop.'

" 'You are a regular strumpet.'

"And so on and so on; a sailor could not have said more.

"Suddenly I heard a noise behind me and turned round. It was the other one, the fat woman, who had fallen on to my wife with her parasol. *Whack! whack!* Mélie got two of them, but she was furious, and she hits hard when she is in a rage, so she caught the fat woman by the hair and then, *thump, thump.* Slaps in the face rained down like ripe plums. I should have let them go on—women among themselves, men among themselves—it does not do to mix the blows, but the little man in the linen jacket jumped up like a devil and was going to rush at my wife. Ah! no, no, not that, my friend! I caught the gentleman with the end of my fist, *crash, crash,* one on the nose, the other in the stomach. He threw up his arms and legs and fell on his back into the river, just into the hole.

"I should have fished him out most certainly, Monsieur le Président, if I had had the time. But unfortunately the fat woman got the better of it, and she was drubbing Mélie terribly. I know that I ought not to have assisted her while the man was drinking his fill, but I never thought that he would drown and said to myself: 'Bah, it will cool him.'

"I therefore ran up to the women to separate them, and all I received was scratches and bites. Good lord, what creatures! Well, it took me five minutes, and perhaps ten, to separate those two viragoes. When I turned around there was nothing to be seen, and the water was as smooth as a lake. The others yonder kept shouting: 'Fish him out!' It was all very well to say that, but I cannot swim and still less dive!

"At last the man from the dam came and two gentlemen with boat hooks, but it had taken over a quarter of an hour. He was found at the bottom of the hole in eight feet of water, as I have said, but he was dead, the poor little man in his linen suit! There are the facts, such as I have sworn to. I am innocent, on my honor."

The witnesses having deposed to the same effect, the accused was acquitted.

CARESSES

No, my friend, do not think any more of it. What you ask of me revolts and disgusts me. It is as if God—for I believe in God—had wanted to spoil every good thing that he made by attaching some horrible thing to it. He had given us love, the divinest thing the world ever knew, but, finding it too lovely and too fine for us, he imagined our senses, shameful, vile, revolting, brutal senses, senses that he seems to have fashioned in malicious jest and linked with the excretions of our bodies; he has conceived them in such a way that we cannot think of it without blushing, can only speak of it in hushed voices. The dreadful thing they do is wrapped in shame. It hides away, disgusts our souls, offends our eyes; despised by morality, hounded down by law, it consummates itself in darkness, as if it were a criminal.

Never speak to me of it, never!

I do not know whether I love you, but I know that your nearness pleases me, that your glance is sweet to me and your voice caresses my heart. From the day you had of me the frailness you desire, you would become hateful to me. The delicate bond that holds us to each other would be broken. An infamous abyss would lie between us.

Let us stay as we are. And . . . love me if you will, I will let you.

Your friend,
Geneviève

Madame, will you allow me also to speak to you with brutal frankness, without polite euphemisms, as I would speak to a friend who was anxious to take on himself a lifelong vow?

Neither do I know whether I love you. I should be sure of it only after the thing that so revolts you.

Have you forgotten Musset's poem:

> Je me souviens encor de ces spasmes terribles,
> De ces baisers muets, de ces muscles ardents,
> De cet être absorbé, blême et serrant les dents.
> S'ils ne sont pas divins, ces moments sont horribles.

We experience that sense of horror and overwhelming disgust only when the madness of our blood has led us into casual adventures. But when a woman is the being we have chosen, entirely charming and infinitely desirable, as you are for me, the caress of love becomes the sharpest, most complete, and supremest pleasure.

This caress, madame, is the proof of love. If our passion dies after that fierce embrace, we have been deceiving ourselves. If it grows, we love.

A philosopher, who did not practice his doctrines, has put us on our guard against this snare of nature's. Nature desires new life, he says, and, to compel us to create it, has set the double bait of love and pleasure round the snare. And he adds: "As soon as we have let ourselves be taken, as soon as the momentary madness has left us, we are filled with a profound sadness, understanding the trick that has deceived us, seeing, feeling, touching the secret hidden cause that has driven us in spite of ourselves."

That is often true, very often. Then we go away, in utter revulsion. Nature has conquered us, has thrown us against our will into arms that were opened for us because she willed them to open.

Yes, I know the cold savage kisses pressed on strange lips, the fixed burning gaze into eyes that one has never seen before and will never see again, and all that I can't tell, all that sears our mind with a bitter grief.

But if this hazy cloud of affection that we call love has closed round two human beings, if they never cease to think long of each other, and, when they are separated, to remember one another, all the time, day and night, hiding in their hearts the beloved's features and his smile and the sound of his voice; if they have been obsessed, possessed by the absent form whose image never leaves them, is it not natural that arms open at last, that lips meet and bodies touch?

Have you never wanted to kiss anyone? Tell me whether lips do not call to lips, whether the bright glance that seems to pierce our veins does not rouse fierce and irresistible desires.

True, you say, that is the snare, the shameful snare. What matter?—— I know it, I fall in it and I love it. Nature gives us the caress of love to hide her cunning, to force us—against our will—to perpetuate the human race. Let us therefore will the caress, make it ours, refine it, change it, idealize it, if you like. Let us too deceive Nature, the arch deceiver. Let us do more than she has willed, more than she could or dared teach us. Think that the caress of love is a precious thing taken from the earth in its rough state, and let us take it and work over it and perfect it, careless of the original design, the hidden will of the being you call God. And since it is thought that idealizes everything, let us idealize this thing, madame, even in all its terrible brutality, all its most impure forms, its most monstrous imaginings.

Let us love the caress that thrills as we love the heady vine, ripe fruit fragrant on the palate, and all the sharp pleasures of the body. Let us love flesh because it is beautiful, because it is white and firm, and round and sweet, delicious to lips and hands.

When artists seek the rarest and purest form for the chalice where art must drink to ecstasy they choose the curve of the breasts, whose bud is like a rose.

And in a learned book, called the *Dictionnaire des Sciences Médicales*, I read this definition of a woman's bosom, which might have been imagined by M. Joseph Prudhomme turned medical man:

"The breast in woman may be considered as at one and the same time an object of use and of pleasure."

Let us suppress, if you like it so, the usefulness and keep only the pleasure. Would it have been given this adorable form that calls aloud to be caressed, if it . had been designed only to nourish babies?

Yes, madame, leave the moralists to preach modesty, and the doctors caution; leave poets, deceivers that are themselves always deceived, to sing the chaste union of souls and bodiless happiness; leave ugly women to their duty and rational men to their futile needs; leave doctrinaires to their doctrines, priests to their commandments, and as for us, let us prize more than anything in the world the caress of love, which intoxicates and maddens us, makes us faint and exhausted, and gives us new life, which is sweeter than perfume, lighter than the light wind, sharper than

wounds, swift and devouring, which makes men pray and weep and groan and
shout and commit any crime and any heroic deed.

Let us love it, with no placid, normal, legal love; but violently, furiously, beyond
all bounds of reason. Let us seek it as men seek gold and diamonds, for it is more
precious than they, being beyond price and fleeting. Let us pursue it without faltering, let us die for it and through it.

And let me tell you, madame, a truth that you will not find, I think, in any book;
the only happy women on this earth are those to whom no caresses are lacking.
These live without anxiety, without torturing thoughts, desiring nothing save the
next kiss, which shall be as delightful and satisfying as the last one was.

The other women, in whose lives caresses are few or unsatisfying or raw, live
tormented by a thousand wretched anxieties, by the friction of greed or vanity,
and by all the things of life that turn to sorrow.

But women whose lives are filled with caresses need nothing, desire nothing,
regret nothing. They live in a dream, content and smiling, hardly ruffled by what
for others would be irreparable disasters, since the caress of love pays all, cures all
things, comforts for all.

I could say much more than this. . . .

HENRI.

These two letters, written on Japanese rice paper, were found in a little Russian
leather pocket book under a *prie-dieu* at the Madeleine, on Sunday, yesterday, after
one o'clock Mass, by

MAUFRIGNEUSE.

BELLFLOWER[1]

How strange are those old recollections which haunt us without our being able to
get rid of them!

This one is so very old that I cannot understand how it has clung so vividly and
tenaciously to my memory. Since then I have seen so many sinister things, either
affecting or terrible, that I am astonished at not being able to pass a single day
without the face of Mother Bellflower recurring to my mind's eye, just as I knew
her formerly long, long ago, when I was ten or twelve years old.

She was an old seamstress who came to my parents' house once a week, every
Thursday, to mend the linen. My parents lived in one of those country houses
called châteaux, which are merely old houses with pointed roofs, to which are
attached three or four adjacent farms.

The village, a large village, almost a small market town, was a few hundred yards
off and nestled round the church, a red brick church, which had become black with
age.

Well, every Thursday Mother Bellflower came between half-past six and seven
in the morning and went immediately into the linen room and began to work. She
was a tall, thin, bearded or rather hairy woman, for she had a beard all over her
face, a surprising, an unexpected beard, growing in improbable tufts, in curly
bunches which looked as if they had been sown by a madman over that great face,
[1]Clochette.

the face of a gendarme in petticoats. She had them on her nose, under her nose, round her nose, on her chin, on her cheeks, and her eyebrows, which were extraordinarily thick and long and quite gray, bushy and bristling, looked exactly like a pair of mustaches stuck on there by mistake.

She limped, not like lame people generally do, but like a ship pitching. When she planted her great bony, vibrant body on her sound leg, she seemed to be preparing to mount some enormous wave, and then suddenly she dipped as if to disappear in an abyss and buried herself in the ground. Her walk reminded one of a ship in a storm, and her head, which was always covered with an enormous white cap, whose ribbons fluttered down her back, seemed to traverse the horizon from north to south and from south to north at each limp.

I adored Mother Bellflower. As soon as I was up I used to go into the linen room, where I found her installed at work with a foot warmer under her feet. As soon as I arrived she made me take the foot warmer and sit upon it, so that I might not catch cold in that large chilly room under the roof.

"That draws the blood from your head," she would say to me.

She told me stories while mending the linen with her long, crooked, nimble fingers; behind her magnifying spectacles, for age had impaired her sight, her eyes appeared enormous to me, strangely profound, double.

As far as I can remember from the things which she told me and by which my childish heart was moved, she had the large heart of a poor woman. She told me what had happened in the village, how a cow had escaped from the cow house and had been found the next morning in front of Prosper Malet's mill looking at the sails turning, or about a hen's egg which had been found in the church belfry without anyone being able to understand what creature had been there to lay it, or the queer story of Jean Pila's dog who had gone ten leagues to bring back his master's breeches which a tramp had stolen while they were hanging up to dry out of doors after he had been caught in the rain. She told me these simple adventures in such a manner that in my mind they assumed the proportions of never-to-be-forgotten dramas, of grand and mysterious poems; and the ingenious stories invented by the poets, which my mother told me in the evening, had none of the flavor, none of the fullness or of the vigor of the peasant woman's narratives.

Well, one Thursday when I had spent all the morning in listening to Mother Clochette, I wanted to go upstairs to her again during the day after picking hazelnuts with the manservant in the wood behind the farm. I remember it all as clearly as what happened only yesterday.

On opening the door of the linen room I saw the old seamstress lying on the floor by the side of her chair, her face turned down and her arms stretched out, but still holding her needle in one hand and one of my shirts in the other. One of her legs in a blue stocking, the longer one no doubt, was extended under her chair, and her spectacles glistened by the wall, where they had rolled away from her.

I ran away uttering shrill cries. They all came running, and in a few minutes I was told that Mother Clochette was dead.

I cannot describe the profound, poignant, terrible emotion which stirred my childish heart. I went slowly down into the drawing room and hid myself in a dark corner in the depths of a great old armchair, where I knelt and wept. I remained there for a long time, no doubt, for night came on. Suddenly someone came in with a lamp—without seeing me, however—and I heard my father and mother talking with the medical man, whose voice I recognized.

He had been sent for immediately, and he was explaining the cause of the accident, of which I understood nothing, however. Then he sat down and had a glass of liqueur and a biscuit.

He went on talking, and what he then said will remain engraved on my mind until I die! I think that I can give the exact words which he used.

"Ah!" he said. "The poor woman! she broke her leg the day of my arrival here. I had not even had time to wash my hands after getting off the diligence before I was sent for in all haste, for it was a bad case, very bad.

"She was seventeen and a pretty girl, very pretty! Would anyone believe it? I have never told her story before; in fact, no one but myself and one other person, who is no longer living in this part of the country, ever knew it. Now that she is dead I may be less discreet.

"A young assistant teacher had just come to live in the village; he was good looking and had the bearing of a soldier. All the girls ran after him, but he was disdainful. Besides that, he was very much afraid of his superior, the schoolmaster, old Grabu, who occasionally got out of bed the wrong foot first.

"Old Grabu already employed pretty Hortense, who has just died here and who was afterward nicknamed Clochette. The assistant master singled out the pretty young girl who was no doubt flattered at being chosen by this disdainful conqueror; at any rate, she fell in love with him, and he succeeded in persuading her to give him a first meeting in the hayloft behind the school at night after she had done her day's sewing.

"She pretended to go home, but instead of going downstairs when she left the Grabus', she went upstairs and hid among the hay to wait for her lover. He soon joined her, and he was beginning to say pretty things to her, when the door of the hayloft opened and the schoolmaster appeared and asked: 'What are you doing up there, Sigisbert?' Feeling sure that he would be caught, the young schoolmaster lost his presence of mind and replied stupidly: 'I came up here to rest a little among the bundles of hay, Monsieur Grabu.'

"The loft was very large and absolutely dark. Sigisbert pushed the frightened girl to the farther end and said: 'Go there and hide yourself. I shall lose my situation, so get away and hide yourself.'

"When the schoolmaster heard the whispering he continued: 'Why, you are not by yourself.'

" 'Yes, I am, Monsieur Grabu!'

" 'But you are not, for you are talking.'

" 'I swear I am, Monsieur Grabu.'

" 'I will soon find out,' the old man replied and, double-locking the door, he went down to get a light.

"Then the young man, who was a coward such as one sometimes meets, lost his head, and he repeated, having grown furious all of a sudden: 'Hide yourself, so that he may not find you. You will deprive me of my bread for my whole life; you will ruin my whole career! Do hide yourself!'

"They could hear the key turning in the lock again, and Hortense ran to the window which looked out onto the street, opened it quickly and then in a low and determined voice said: 'You will come and pick me up when he is gone,' and she jumped out.

"Old Grabu found nobody and went down again in great surprise! A quarter of an hour later Monsieur Sigisbert came to me and related his adventure. The girl had remained at the foot of the wall, unable to get up, as she had fallen from the second story, and I went with him to fetch her. It was raining in torrents, and I brought the unfortunate girl home with me, for the right leg was broken in three places, and the bones had come out through the flesh. She did not complain and merely said with admirable resignation: 'I am punished, well punished!'

"I sent for assistance and for the workgirl's friends and told them a made-up story of a runaway carriage which had knocked her down and lamed her outside my door. They believed me, and the gendarmes for a whole month tried in vain to find the author of this accident.

"That is all! Now I say that this woman was a heroine and had the fiber of those who accomplish the grandest deeds in history.

"That was her only love affair, and she died a virgin. She was a martyr, a noble soul, a sublimely devoted woman! And if I did not absolutely admire her I should not have told you this story, which I would never tell anyone during her life; you understand why."

The doctor ceased; Mamma cried, and Papa said some words which I did not catch; then they left the room, and I remained on my knees in the armchair and sobbed, while I heard a strange noise of heavy footsteps and something knocking against the side of the staircase.

They were carrying away Clochette's body.

SIMON'S PAPA

Noon had just struck. The school door opened and the youngsters streamed out, tumbling over one another in their haste to get out quickly. But instead of promptly dispersing and going home to dinner as was their daily wont, they stopped a few paces off, broke up into knots and set to whispering.

The fact was that that morning Simon, the son of La Blanchotte, had, for the first time, attended school.

They had all of them in their families heard of La Blanchotte, and although in public she was welcome enough, the mothers among themselves treated her with compassion of a somewhat disdainful kind, which the children had caught without in the least knowing why.

As for Simon himself, they did not know him, for he never went abroad and did not play around with them through the streets of the village or along the banks of the river. So they loved him but little, and it was with a certain delight, mingled with astonishment, that they gathered in groups this morning, repeating to each other this sentence, concocted by a lad of fourteen or fifteen who appeared to know all about it, so sagaciously did he wink: "You know Simon—well, he has no papa."

La Blanchotte's son appeared in his turn upon the threshold of the school.

He was seven or eight years old, rather pale, very neat, with a timid and almost awkward manner.

He was making his way back to his mother's house when the various groups of his schoolfellows, perpetually whispering and watching him with the mischievous and heartless eyes of children bent upon playing a nasty trick, gradually surrounded

him and ended by enclosing him altogether. There he stood amid them, surprised
and embarrassed, not understanding what they were going to do with him. But
the lad who had brought the news, puffed up with the success he had met with,
demanded:

"What do you call yourself?"

He answered: "Simon."

"Simon what?" retorted the other.

The child, altogether bewildered, repeated: "Simon."

The lad shouted at him: "You must be named Simon something! That is not a
name—Simon indeed."

And he, on the brink of tears, replied for the third time:

"I am named Simon."

The urchins began laughing. The lad triumphantly lifted up his voice: "You
can see plainly that he has no papa."

A deep silence ensued. The children were dumfounded by this extraordinary,
impossibly monstrous thing—a boy who had not a papa; they looked upon him as
a phenomenon, an unnatural being, and they felt rising in them the hitherto
inexplicable pity of their mothers for La Blanchotte. As for Simon, he had propped
himself against a tree to avoid falling, and he stood there as if paralyzed by an
irreparable disaster. He sought to explain, but he could think of no answer for
them, no way to deny this horrible charge that he had no papa. At last he shouted
at them quite recklessly: "Yes, I have one."

"Where is he?" demanded the boy.

Simon was silent; he did not know. The children shrieked, tremendously excited. These sons of toil, nearly related to animals, experienced the cruel craving
which makes the fowls of a farmyard destroy one of their own kind as soon as it
is wounded. Simon suddenly spied a little neighbor, the son of a widow, whom
he had always seen, as he himself was to be seen, quite alone with his mother.

"And no more have you," he said, "no more have you a papa."

"Yes," replied the other, "I have one."

"Where is he?" rejoined Simon.

"He is dead," declared the brat with superb dignity; "he is in the cemetery, is
my papa."

A murmur of approval rose amid the scapegraces, as if the fact of possessing a
papa dead in a cemetery made their comrade big enough to crush the other one
who had no papa at all. And these rogues, whose fathers were for the most part
evildoers, drunkards, thieves, and ill-treaters of their wives, hustled each other as
they pressed closer and closer to Simon as though they, the legitimate ones, would
stifle in their presence one who was beyond the law.

The lad next Simon suddenly put his tongue out at him with a waggish air and
shouted at him:

"No papa! No papa!"

Simon seized him by the hair with both hands and set to work to demolish his
legs with kicks, while he bit his cheek ferociously. A tremendous struggle ensued
between the two boys, and Simon found himself beaten, torn, bruised, rolled on
the ground in the middle of the ring of applauding little vagabonds. As he arose,
mechanically brushing his little blouse all covered with dust with his hand, someone shouted at him:

"Go and tell your papa."

He then felt a great sinking in his heart. They were stronger than he; they had beaten him, and he had no answer to give them for he knew it was true that he had no papa. Full of pride, he tried for some moments to struggle against the tears which were suffocating him. He had a choking fit, and then without cries he began to weep with great sobs which shook him incessantly. Then a ferocious joy broke out among his enemies, and, just like savages in fearful festivals, they took one another by the hand and danced in a circle about him as they repeated in refrain:

"No papa! No papa!"

But suddenly Simon ceased sobbing. Frenzy overtook him. There were stones under his feet; he picked them up and with all his strength hurled them at his tormentors. Two or three were struck and ran away yelling, and so formidable did he appear that the rest became panic-stricken. Cowards, like a jeering crowd in the presence of an exasperated man, they broke up and fled. Left alone, the little thing without a father set off running toward the fields, for a recollection had been awakened which nerved his soul to a great determination. He made up his mind to drown himself in the river.

He remembered, in fact, that eight days ago a poor devil who begged for his livelihood had thrown himself into the water because he had no more money. Simon had been there when they fished him out again, and the sight of the fellow who had seemed to him so miserable and ugly had then impressed him—his pale cheeks, his long drenched beard and his open eyes being full of calm. The bystanders had said:

"He is dead."

And someone had added:

"He is quite happy now."

So Simon wished to drown himself also because he had no father, just as the wretched being did who had no money.

He reached the water and watched it flowing. Some fishes were rising briskly in the clear stream and occasionally made little leaps and caught the flies on the surface. He stopped crying in order to watch them, for their feeding interested him vastly. But at intervals, as in the lulls of a tempest, when tremendous gusts of wind snap off trees and then die away, this thought would return to him with intense pain:

"I am about to drown myself because I have no papa."

It was very warm and fine weather. The pleasant sunshine warmed the grass; the water shone like a mirror, and Simon enjoyed for some minutes the happiness of that languor which follows weeping, desirous even of falling asleep there upon the grass in the warmth of noon.

A little green frog leaped from under his feet. He endeavored to catch it. It escaped him. He pursued it and lost it three times following. At last he caught it by one of its hind legs and began to laugh as he saw the efforts the creature made to escape. It gathered itself up on its large legs and then with a violent spring suddenly stretched them out as stiff as two bars.

Its eyes stared wide open in their round, golden circle, and it beat the air with its front limbs, using them as though they were hands. It reminded him of a toy made with straight slips of wood nailed zigzag, one on the other, which by a similar movement regulated the exercise of the little soldiers fastened thereon. Then he thought of his home and of his mother and, overcome by great sorrow,

he again began to weep. His lips trembled, and he placed himself on his knees
and said his prayers as before going to bed. But he was unable to finish them, for
such hurried and violent sobs overtook him that he was completely overwhelmed.
He thought no more; he no longer heeded anything around him but was wholly
given up to tears.

Suddenly a heavy hand was placed upon his shoulder, and a rough voice asked
him:

"What is it that causes you so much grief, my fine fellow?"

Simon turned round. A tall workman with a black beard and hair all curled was
staring at him good-naturedly. He answered with his eyes and throat full of tears:

"They have beaten me because—I—I have no papa—no papa."

"What?" said the man, smiling. "Why, everybody has one."

The child answered painfully amid his spasms of grief:

"But I—I—I have none."

Then the workman became serious. He had recognized La Blanchotte's son
and, although a recent arrival to the neighborhood, he had a vague idea of her
history.

"Well," he said, "console yourself, my boy, and come with me home to your
mother. She will give you a papa."

And so they started on the way, the big one holding the little one by the hand.
The man smiled afresh, for he was not sorry to see this Blanchotte, who by popular
report was one of the prettiest girls in the countryside, and, perhaps, he said to
himself at the bottom of his heart, that a lass who had erred once might very well
err again.

They arrived in front of a very neat little white house.

"There it is," exclaimed the child, and he cried: "Mamma."

A woman appeared, and the workman instantly left off smiling, for he at once
perceived that there was no more fooling to be done with the tall pale girl who
stood austerely at her door as though to defend from one man the threshold of
that house where she had already been betrayed by another. Intimidated, his cap
in his hand, he stammered out:

"See, madame, I have brought you back your little boy who had lost himself
near the river."

But Simon flung his arms about his mother's neck and told her, as he again
began to cry:

"No, Mamma, I wished to drown myself because the others had beaten me—
had beaten me—because I have no papa."

A burning redness covered the young woman's cheeks, and, hurt to the quick,
she embraced her child passionately, while the tears coursed down her face. The
man, much moved, stood there, not knowing how to get away. But Simon suddenly ran to him and said:

"Will you be my papa?"

A deep silence ensued. La Blanchotte, dumb and tortured with shame, leaned
against the wall, her hands upon her heart. The child, seeing that no answer was
made him, replied:

"If you do not wish it I shall return to drown myself."

The workman took the matter as a jest and answered, laughing:

"Why, yes, I wish it certainly."

"What is your name then," went on the child, "so that I may tell the others when they wish to know your name?"

"Philip," answered the man.

Simon was silent a moment so that he might get the name well into his memory; then he stretched out his arms, quite consoled, and said:

"Well then, Philip, you are my papa."

The workman, lifting him from the ground, kissed him hastily on both cheeks and then strode away quickly.

When the child returned to school next day he was received with a spiteful laugh, and at the end of school, when the lads were on the point of recommencing, Simon threw these words at their heads as he would have done a stone: "He is named Philip, my papa."

Yells of delight burst out from all sides.

"Philip who? Philip what? What on earth is Philip? Where did you pick up your Philip?"

Simon answered nothing and, immovable in faith, he defied them with his eye, ready to be martyred rather than fly before them. The schoolmaster came to his rescue, and he returned home to his mother.

For a space of three months the tall workman, Philip, frequently passed by La Blanchotte's house and sometimes made bold to speak to her when he saw her sewing near the window. She answered him civilly, always sedately, never joking with him or permitting him to enter her house. Notwithstanding this, being, like all men, a bit of a coxcomb, he imagined that she was often rosier than usual when she chatted with him.

But a fallen reputation is so difficult to recover and always remains so fragile that, in spite of the shy reserve La Blanchotte maintained, they already gossiped in the neighborhood.

As for Simon, he loved his new papa much and walked with him nearly every evening when the day's work was done. He went regularly to school and mixed in a dignified way with his schoolfellows without ever answering them back.

One day, however, the lad who had first attacked him said to him:

"You have lied. You have not a papa named Philip."

"Why do you said that?" demanded Simon, much disturbed.

The youth rubbed his hands. He replied:

"Because if you had one he would be your mamma's husband."

Simon was confused by the truth of this reasoning; nevertheless, he retorted:

"He is my papa all the same."

"That can very well be," exclaimed the urchin with a sneer, "but that is not being your papa altogether."

La Blanchotte's little one bowed his head and went off dreaming in the direction of the forge belonging to old Loizon, where Philip worked.

This forge was entombed in trees. It was very dark there; the red glare of a formidable furnace alone lit up with great flashes five blacksmiths who hammered upon their anvils with a terrible din. Standing enveloped in flame, they worked like demons, their eyes fixed on the red-hot iron they were pounding and their dull ideas rising and falling with their hammers.

Simon entered without being noticed and quietly plucked his friend by the sleeve. Philip turned round. All at once the work came to a standstill, and the men looked on very attentively. Then in the midst of this unaccustomed silence rose the little slender pipe of Simon:

"Philip, explain to me what the lad at La Michande has just told me, that you are not altogether my papa."

"And why that?" asked the smith.

The child replied in all innocence:

"Because you are not my mamma's husband."

No one laughed. Philip remained standing, leaning his forehead upon the back of his great hands which held the handle of his hammer upright upon the anvil. He mused. His four companions watched him, and, like a tiny mite among these giants, Simon anxiously waited. Suddenly one of the smiths, voicing the sentiment of all, said to Philip:

"All the same La Blanchotte is a good and honest girl, stalwart and steady in spite of her misfortune, and one who would make a worthy wife for an honest man."

"That is true," remarked the three others.

The smith continued:

"Is it the girl's fault if she has fallen? She had been promised marriage, and I know more than one who is much respected today and has sinned every bit as much."

"That is true," responded the three men in chorus.

He resumed:

"How hard she has toiled, poor thing, to educate her lad all alone, and how much she has wept since she no longer goes out, save to church, God only knows."

"That also is true," said the others.

Then no more was heard save the roar of the bellows which fanned the fire of the furnace. Philip hastily bent himself down to Simon.

"Go and tell your mamma that I shall come to speak to her."

Then he pushed the child out by the shoulders. He returned to his work, and in unison the five hammers again fell upon their anvils. Thus they wrought the iron until nightfall, strong, powerful, happy, like Vulcans, satisfied. But as the great bell of a cathedral resounds upon feast days above the jingling of the other bells, so Philip's hammer, dominating the noise of the others, clanged second after second with a deafening uproar. His eye on the fire, he plied his trade vigorously, erect amid the sparks.

The sky was full of stars as he knocked at La Blanchotte's door. He had his Sunday blouse on, a fresh shirt, and his beard was trimmed. The young woman showed herself upon the threshold and said in a grieved tone:

"It is ill to come thus when night has fallen, M. Philip."

He wished to answer but stammered and stood confused before her.

She resumed:

"And you understand quite well that it will not do that I should be talked about any more."

Then he said all at once:

"What does that matter to me, if you will be my wife!"

No voice replied to him, but he believed that he heard in the shadow of the room the sound of a body falling. He entered very quickly, and Simon, who had gone to his bed, distinguished the sound of a kiss and some words that his mother said very softly. Then he suddenly found himself lifted up by the hands of his friend who, holding him at the length of his herculean arms, exclaimed to him:

"You will tell your schoolfellows that your papa is Philip Rémy, the blacksmith, and that he will pull the ears of all who do you any harm."

On the morrow, when the school was full and lessons about to begin, little Simon stood up quite pale, with trembling lips.

"My papa," he said in a clear voice, "is Philip Rémy, the blacksmith, and he has promised to box the ears of all who do me any harm."

This time no one laughed any longer, for he was very well known, was Philip Rémy the blacksmith, and he was a papa of whom anyone in the world would be proud.

THAT PIG OF A MORIN

"There, my friend," I said to Labarbe, "you have just repeated those five words, 'That pig of a Morin.' Why on earth do I never hear Morin's name mentioned without his being called a *pig?*"

Labarbe, who is a deputy, looked at me with eyes like an owl's and said: "Do you mean to say that you do not know Morin's story and yet come from La Rochelle?" I was obliged to declare that I did not know Morin's story, and then Labarbe rubbed his hands and began his recital.

"You knew Morin, did you not, and you remember his large linen draper's shop on the Quai de la Rochelle?"

"Yes, perfectly."

"All right, then. You must know that in 1862 or '63 Morin went to spend a fortnight in Paris for pleasure, or for his pleasures, but under the pretext of renewing his stock, and you also know what a fortnight in Paris means for a country shopkeeper; it makes his blood grow hot. The theater every evening, women's dresses rustling up against you and continual excitement; one goes almost mad with it. One sees nothing but dancers in tights, actresses in very low dresses, round legs, fat shoulders, all nearly within reach of one's hands, without daring or being able to touch, and one scarcely ever tastes an inferior dish. And one leaves it with heart still all in a flutter and a mind still exhilarated by a sort of longing for kisses which tickle one's lips.

"Morin was in that state when he took his ticket for La Rochelle by the eight-forty night express. And he was walking up and down the waiting room at the station when he stopped suddenly in front of a young lady who was kissing an old one. She had her veil up, and Morin murmured with delight: 'By Jove, what a pretty woman!'

"When she had said good-by to the old lady she went into the waiting room, and Morin followed her; then she went on to the platform, and Morin still followed her; then she got into an empty carriage, and he again followed her. There were very few travelers by the express; the engine whistled, and the train started. They were alone. Morin devoured her with his eyes. She appeared to be about nineteen or twenty and was fair, tall and with demure looks. She wrapped a railway rug round her legs and stretched herself on the seat to sleep.

"Morin asked himself: 'I wonder who she is?' And a thousand conjectures, a thousand projects went through his head. He said to himself: 'So many adventures are told as happening on railway journeys that this may be one that is going to present itself to me. Who knows? A piece of good luck like that happens very quickly, and perhaps I need only be a little venturesome. Was it not Danton who said: "Audacity, more audacity, and always audacity." If it was not Danton it was Mirabeau, but that does not matter. But then I have no audacity, and that is the difficulty. Oh! If one only knew, if one could only read people's minds! I will bet that every day one passes by magnificent opportunities without knowing it, though a gesture would be enough to let me know that she did not ask for anything better.'

"Then he imagined to himself combinations which led him to triumph. He pictured some chivalrous deed or merely some slight service which he rendered her, a lively, gallant conversation which ended in a declaration, which ended in—in what you think.

"But he could find no opening, had no pretext, and he waited for some fortunate circumstance with his heart ravaged and his mind topsy-turvy. The night passed, and the pretty girl still slept while Morin was meditating his own fall. The day broke and soon the first rays of sunlight appeared in the sky, a long, clear ray which shone on the face of the sleeping girl and woke her so she sat up, looked at the country, then at Morin and smiled. She smiled like a happy woman, with an engaging and bright look, and Morin trembled. Certainly that smile was intended for him; it was a discreet invitation, the signal which he was waiting for. That smile meant to say: 'How stupid, what a ninny, what a dolt, what a donkey you are to have sat there on your seat like a post all night. Just look at me, am I not charming? And you have sat like that for the whole night when you have been alone with a pretty woman, you great simpleton!'

"She was still smiling as she looked at him; she even began to laugh, and he lost his head trying to find something suitable to say, no matter what. But he could think of nothing, nothing, and then, seized with a coward's courage, he said to himself: 'So much the worse; I will risk everything,' and suddenly, without the slightest warning, he went toward her, his arms extended, his lips protruding, and, seizing her in his arms, kissed her.

"She sprang up with a bound, crying out: 'Help! help!' and screaming with terror; then she opened the carriage door and waved her arm outside; then, mad with terror, she was trying to jump out while Morin, who was almost distracted and feeling sure that she would throw herself out, held her by her skirt and stammered: 'Oh, madame! Oh, madame!'

"The train slackened speed and then stopped. Two guards rushed up at the young woman's frantic signals, and she threw herself into their arms, stammering: 'That man wanted—wanted—to—to——' And then she fainted.

"They were at Mauzé station, and the gendarme on duty arrested Morin. When the victim of his brutality had regained her consciousness she made her charge against him, and the police drew it up. The poor linen draper did not reach home till night, with a prosecution hanging over him for an outrage on morals in a public place."

II

"At that time I was editor of the *Fanal des Charentes*, and I used to meet Morin every day at the Café du Commerce. The day after his adventure he came to see me, as he did not know what to do. I did not hide my opinion from him but said to him: 'You are no better than a pig. No decent man behaves like that.'

"He cried. His wife had given him a beating, and he foresaw his trade ruined, his name dragged through the mire and dishonored, his friends outraged and taking no more notice of him. In the end he excited my pity, and I sent for my colleague Rivet, a bantering but very sensible little man, to give us his advice.

"He advised me to see the public prosecutor, who was a friend of mine, and so I sent Morin home and went to call on the magistrate. He told me that the woman who had been insulted was a young lady, Mademoiselle Henriette Bonnel, who had just received her certificate as governess in Paris and spent her holidays with her uncle and aunt, who were very respectable tradespeople in Mauzé, and what made Morin's case all the more serious was that the uncle had lodged a complaint. But the public official had consented to let the matter drop if this complaint were withdrawn, so that we must try and get him to do this.

"I went back to Morin's and found him in bed, ill with excitement and distress. His wife, a tall, rawboned woman with a beard, was abusing him continually, and she showed me into the room, shouting at me: 'So you have come to see that pig of a Morin. Well, there he is, the darling!' And she planted herself in front of the bed with her hands on her hips. I told him how matters stood, and he begged me to go and see her uncle and aunt. It was a delicate mission, but I undertook it, and the poor devil never ceased repeating: 'I assure you I did not even kiss her, no, not even that. I will take my oath to it!'

"I replied: 'It is all the same; you are nothing but a pig.' And I took a thousand francs which he gave me to employ them as I thought best, but as I did not care venturing to her uncle's house alone I begged Rivet to go with me, which he agreed to do on the condition that we went immediately, for he had some urgent business at La Rochelle that afternoon. So two hours later we rang at the door of a nice country house. A pretty girl came and opened the door to us, who was assuredly the young lady in question, and I said to Rivet in a low voice: 'Confound it! I begin to understand Morin!'

"The uncle, Monsieur Tonnelet, subscribed to the *Fanal* and was a fervent political co-religionist of ours. He received us with open arms and congratulated us and wished us joy; he was delighted at having the two editors in his house, and Rivet whispered to me: 'I think we shall be able to arrange the matter of that pig of a Morin for him.'

"The niece had left the room, and I introduced the delicate subject. I waved the specter of scandal before his eyes; I accentuated the inevitable depreciation which the young lady would suffer if such an affair got known, for nobody would believe in a simple kiss. The good man seemed undecided but could not make up his mind about anything without his wife, who would not be in until late that evening. But suddenly he uttered an exclamation of triumph: 'Look here, I have an excellent idea. I will keep you here to dine and sleep, and when my wife comes home I hope we shall be able to arrange matters.'

"Rivet resisted at first, but the wish to extricate that pig of a Morin decided him, and we accepted the invitation. So the uncle got up radiant, called his niece and proposed that we should take a stroll in his grounds, saying: 'We will leave serious matters until the morning.' Rivet and he began to talk politics, while I soon found myself lagging a little behind with the girl, who was really charming! charming! and with the greatest precaution I began to speak to her about her adventure and try to make her my ally. She did not, however, appear the least confused and listened to me like a person who was enjoying the whole thing very much.

"I said to her: 'Just think, mademoiselle, how unpleasant it will be for you. You will have to appear in court, to encounter malicious looks, to speak before everybody and to recount that unfortunate occurrence in the railway carriage in public. Do you not think, between ourselves, that it would have been much better for you to have put that dirty scoundrel back into his place without calling for assistance and merely to have changed your carriage?' She began to laugh and replied: 'What you say is quite true! But what could I do? I was frightened, and when one is frightened one does not stop to reason with oneself. As soon as I realized the situation I was very sorry that I had called out, but then it was too late. You must also remember that the idiot threw himself upon me like a madman, without saying a word and looking like a lunatic. I did not even know what he wanted of me.'

"She looked me full in the face, without being nervous or intimidated, and I said to myself: 'She is a funny sort of girl, that; I can quite see how that pig Morin came to make a mistake,' and I went on jokingly: 'Come, mademoiselle, confess that he was excusable; for, after all, a man cannot find himself opposite such a pretty girl as you are without feeling a legitimate desire to kiss her.'

"She laughed more than ever and showed her teeth and said: 'Between the desire and the act, monsieur, there is room for respect.' It was a funny expression to use, although it was not very clear, and I asked abruptly: 'Well, now, supposing I were to kiss you now, what would you do?' She stopped to look at me from head to foot and then said calmly: 'Oh! you? That is quite another matter.'

"I knew perfectly well, by Jove, that it was not the same thing at all, as everybody in the neighborhood called me 'Handsome Labarbe.' I was thirty years old in those days, but I asked her: 'And why, pray?'

"She shrugged her shoulders and replied: 'Well, because you are not so stupid as he is.' And then she added, looking at me slyly: 'Nor so ugly, either.'

"Before she could make a movement to avoid me I had implanted a hearty kiss on her cheek. She sprang aside, but it was too late, and then she said: 'Well, you are not very bashful, either! But don't do that sort of thing again.'

"I put on a humble look and said in a low voice: 'Oh! mademoiselle, as for me, if I long for one thing more than another, it is to be summoned before a magistrate on the same charge as Morin.'

" 'Why?' she asked.

"Looking steadily at her, I replied: 'Because you are one of the most beautiful creatures living, because it would be an honor and a glory for me to have offered you violence and because people would have said, after seeing you: "Well, Labarbe has richly deserved what he has got, but he is a lucky fellow all the same." '

"She began to laugh heartily again and said: 'How funny you are!' And she had not finished the word *funny* before I had her in my arms and was kissing her ardently wherever I could find a place, on her forehead, on her eyes, on her lips occasionally, on her cheeks, in fact all over her head, some part of which she was obliged to leave exposed, in spite of herself, in order to defend the others. At last she managed to release herself, blushing and angry. 'You are very unmannerly, monsieur,' she said, 'and I am sorry I listened to you.'

"I took her hand in some confusion and stammered out: 'I beg your pardon, mademoiselle. I have offended you; I have acted like a brute! Do not be angry with me for what I have done. If you knew——'

"I vainly sought for some excuse, and in a few moments she said: 'There is nothing for me to know, monsieur.' But I had found something to say, and I cried: 'Mademoiselle, I love you!'

"She was really surprised and raised her eyes to look at me, and I went on: 'Yes, mademoiselle, and pray listen to me. I do not know Morin, and I do not care anything about him. It does not matter to me the least if he is committed for trial and locked up meanwhile. I saw you here last year, and I was so taken with you that the thought of you has never left me since, and it does not matter to me whether you believe me or not. I thought you adorable, and the remembrance of you took such a hold on me that I longed to see you again, and so I made use of that fool Morin as a pretext, and here I am. Circumstances have made me exceed the due limits of respect, and I can only beg you to pardon me.'

"She read the truth in my looks and was ready to smile again; then she murmured: 'You humbug!' But I raised my hand and said in a sincere voice (and I really believe that I was sincere): 'I swear to you that I am speaking the truth.' She replied quite simply: 'Really?'

"We were alone, quite alone, as Rivet and her uncle had disappeared in a side walk, and I made her a real declaration of love while I squeezed and kissed her hands, and she listened to it as to something new and agreeable, without exactly knowing how much of it she was to believe, while in the end I felt agitated and at last really myself believed what I said. I was pale, anxious and trembling, and I gently put my arm round her waist and spoke to her softly, whispering into the little curls over her ears. She seemed dead, so absorbed in thought was she.

"Then her hand touched mine, and she pressed it, and I gently circled her waist with a trembling, and gradually a firmer, grasp. She did not move now, and I touched her cheeks with my lips, and suddenly, without seeking them, mine met hers. It was a long, long kiss, and it would have lasted longer still if I had not heard a *Hum! Hum!* just behind me. She made her escape through the bushes, and I, turning round, saw Rivet coming toward me and walking in the middle of the path. He said without even smiling: 'So that is the way in which you settle the affair of that pig Morin.'

"I replied conceitedly: 'One does what one can, my dear fellow. But what about the uncle? How have you got on with him? I will answer for the niece.'

" 'I have not been so fortunate with him,' he replied. Whereupon I took his arm and we went indoors."

III

"Dinner made me lose my head altogether. I sat beside her, and my hand continually met hers under the tablecloth, my foot touched hers and our looks encountered each other.

"After dinner we took a walk by moonlight, and I whispered all the tender things I could think of to her. I held her close to me, kissed her every moment, moistening my lips against hers, while her uncle and Rivet were disputing as they walked in front of us. We went in, and soon a messenger brought a telegram from her aunt, saying that she would return by the first train the next morning at seven o'clock.

" 'Very well, Henriette,' her uncle said, 'go and show the gentlemen their rooms.'
She showed Rivet his first, and he whispered to me: 'There was no danger of her
taking us into yours first.' Then she took me to my room, and as soon as she was
alone with me I took her in my arms again and tried to excite her senses and overcome her resistance, but when she felt that she was near succumbing she escaped
out of the room, and I got between the sheets, very much put out and excited
and feeling rather foolish, for I knew that I should not sleep much. I was wondering how I could have committed such a mistake when there was a gentle knock at
my door, and on my asking who was there a low voice replied: 'I.'

"I dressed myself quickly and opened the door, and she came in. 'I forgot to
ask you what you take in the morning,' she said, 'chocolate, tea or coffee?' I put
my arms around her impetuously and said, devouring her with kisses: 'I will take—
I will take——' But she freed herself from my arms, blew out my candle and disappeared and left me alone in the dark, furious, trying to find some matches and
not able to do so. At last I got some and I went into the passage, feeling half mad,
with my candlestick in my hand.

"What was I going to do? I did not stop to reason; I only wanted to find her,
and I would. I went a few steps without reflecting, but then I suddenly thought to
myself: 'Suppose I should go into the uncle's room, what should I say?' And I
stood still, with my head a void and my heart beating.

"But in a few moments I thought of an answer: 'Of course I shall say that I
was looking for Rivet's room, to speak to him about an important matter,' and I
began to inspect all the doors, trying to find hers, and at last I took hold of a
handle at a venture, turned it and went in. There was Henriette, sitting on her
bed and looking at me in tears. So I gently turned the key, and going up to her
on tiptoe, I said: 'I forgot to ask you for something to read, mademoiselle.' I will
not tell you the book I read, but it is the most wonderful of romances, the most
divine of poems. And when once I had turned the first page she let me turn over
as many leaves as I liked, and I got through so many chapters that our candles were
quite burned out.

"Then, after thanking her, I was stealthily returning to my room when a rough
hand seized me and a voice—it was Rivet's—whispered in my ear: 'So you have not
yet quite settled that affair of Morin's?'

"At seven o'clock the next morning she herself brought me a cup of chocolate.
I have never drunk anything like it, soft, velvety, perfumed, delicious. I could
scarcely take away my lips from the cup, and she had hardly left the room when
Rivet came in. He seemed nervous and irritable like a man who had not slept, and
he said to me crossly: 'If you go on like this, you will end by spoiling the affair of
that pig of a Morin!'

"At eight o'clock the aunt arrived. Our discussion was very short, for they withdrew their complaint, and I left five hundred francs for the poor of the town. They
wanted to keep us for the day, and they arranged an excursion to go and see some
ruins. Henriette made signs to me to stay, behind her uncle's back, and I accepted,
but Rivet was determined to go, and though I took him aside and begged and
prayed him to do this for me, he appeared quite exasperated and kept saying to
me: 'I have had enough of that pig of a Morin's affair, do you hear?'

"Of course I was obliged to go also, and it was one of the hardest moments of
my life. I could have gone on arranging that business as long as I lived, and when
we were in the railway carriage, after shaking hands with her in silence, I said to

Rivet: 'You are a mere brute!' And he replied: 'My dear fellow, you were beginning to excite me confoundedly.'

"On getting to the *Fanal* office, I saw a crowd waiting for us, and as soon as they saw us they all exclaimed: 'Well, have you settled the affair of that pig of a Morin?' All La Rochelle was excited about it, and Rivet, who had got over his ill-humor on the journey, had great difficulty in keeping himself from laughing as he said: 'Yes, we have managed it, thanks to Labarbe.' And we went to Morin's.

"He was sitting in an easy chair with mustard plasters on his legs and cold bandages on his head, nearly dead with misery. He was coughing with the short cough of a dying man, without anyone knowing how he had caught it, and his wife seemed like a tigress ready to eat him. As soon as he saw us he trembled violently as to make his hands and knees shake, so I said to him immediately: 'It is all settled, you dirty scamp, but don't do such a thing again.'

"He got up choking, took my hands and kissed them as if they had belonged to a prince, cried, nearly fainted, embraced Rivet and even kissed Madame Morin who gave him such a push as to send him staggering back into his chair. But he never got over the blow; his mind had been too much upset. In all the country round, moreover, he was called nothing but that pig of a Morin, and the epithet went through him like a sword thrust every time he heard it. When a street boy called after him: 'Pig!' he turned his head instinctively. His friends also overwhelmed him with horrible jokes and used to chaff him, whenever they were eating ham, by saying: 'It's a bit of you!' He died two years later.

"As for myself, when I was a candidate for the Chamber of Deputies in 1875 I called on the new notary at Foncerre, Monsieur Belloncle, to solicit his vote, and a tall, handsome and evidently wealthy lady received me. 'You do not know me again?' she said.

"I stammered out: 'But—no, madame.'

"'Henriette Bonnel?'

"'Ah!' And I felt myself turning pale, while she seemed perfectly at her ease and looked at me with a smile.

"As soon as she had left me alone with her husband he took both my hands, and squeezing them as if he meant to crush them, he said: 'I have been intending to go and see you for a long time, my dear sir, for my wife has very often talked to me about you. I know under what painful circumstances you made her acquaintance, and I know also how perfectly you behaved, how full of delicacy, tact and devotion you showed yourself in the affair . . .' He hesitated and then said in a lower tone, as if he had been saying something low and coarse: 'In the affair of that pig of a Morin.'"

THE CHRISTENING

In front of the farm gates the men were waiting in their Sunday clothes. The May sun shed its burning light on the flowering apple trees which roofed the whole farmyard with blossom in great round fragrant bunches of pink and white. Petals fell round them in a ceaseless shower, fluttering and eddying into the tall grass, where the dandelions glittered like flames and the poppies were splashed in drops of blood.

A sow slumbered on the side of the manure heap, and a band of little pigs with twisted, cordlike tails ran round her huge belly and swollen dugs.

Far away, through the trees behind the farmhouse, the church bell suddenly rang out. Its iron voice sent up a faint and distant cry to the radiant heavens. Swallows darted arrowlike across the blue spaces bounded by the still shafts of tall beeches. A faint smell of stables mingled with the soft sweet fragrance of the apple trees.

One of the men standing by the gate turned towards the house and cried:

"Coom, quick, Mélina; t'bell's ringin'."

He was about thirty years of age, a tall young peasant, as yet not bowed or deformed by long labor in the fields. His old father, gnarled like the trunk of an oak, with scarred wrists and crooked legs, announced: "Women, they bean't never ready first."

The two other sons laughed, and one, turning to the eldest brother, who had shouted first, said: "Go fetch 'em, Polyte. They'll not be here before noon, I'm thinkin'."

The young man entered the house.

A flock of ducks near at hand began to quack and flap their wings and waddled off down to the pond.

Then at the open door appeared a stout woman carrying a two-month-old child. The white strings of her high bonnet hung down her back, streaming over a shawl as violently scarlet as a house on fire. The child, wrapped in white garments, rested against the nurse's protruding stomach.

Next came the mother, a tall, strong girl barely eighteen, fair and smiling, holding her husband's arm. The two grandmothers followed, wrinkled like old apples, weariness apparent in their bowed backs, long since bent by rough and patient toil. One was a widow; she took the arm of the grandfather waiting at the gate, and they left at the head of the procession, just behind the child and the midwife. The rest of the family followed, the younger ones carrying paper bags full of sweets.

The little bell rang ceaselessly, calling with all its strength to the tiny mite it awaited. Children clambered on the dikes; heads appeared at gateways; milkmaids set down their pails and stood between them to watch the christening go by.

And the nurse moved on triumphantly with her living burden, stepping between puddles on the road which ran between the tree-crowned banks. And the old people advanced with ceremonious steps, walking a little crookedly, because of their age and infirmity. And the young folk were eager to dance and looked at the girls who came to see them go by; and the father and mother walked with graver mien, following the child who would take their place and carry on their name in the country, the honored name of Dentu.

They emerged on the plain and struck across the fields, avoiding the long roundabout road. Now the church came into view, with its pointed steeple. Just below the slate roof was an aperture, within which something swung swiftly backwards and forwards, passing and repassing behind the narrow window. It was the bell, still ringing, calling the newborn child to come for the first time to the house of God.

A dog had begun to follow the procession; they threw sweets to it, and it frisked round their feet.

The church door was open. By the altar stood the priest, a tall fellow, slim and strong, with red hair. He too was a Dentu, the child's uncle, another brother of the father. And he duly bestowed the name of Prosper-César upon his nephew, who began to cry when he tasted the symbolic salt.

When the ceremony was over, the family waited on the steps while the priest took off his surplice; then they started off once more. They went fast now, for there was the prospect of dinner before them. A crowd of urchins followed, and whenever a handful of sweets was thrown to them they struggled furiously; they fought hand to hand and pulled one another's hair; even the dog dashed into the fight for the sweets, more stubborn than the children, who tugged at his tail and ears and paws.

The nurse was tired; she turned to the priest walking beside her, and said: "How'd it be, sir, if you was to carry your nephew for a stretch? Ah'm that cramped in the belly, ah'd like a bit of a rest, like."

The priest took the child in his arms, the white clothes making a broad white stripe over the black cassock. He was embarrassed by the little burden, not knowing how to carry it or set it down. Everyone laughed, and one of the grandmothers shouted: "Aren't ye ever sorry, passon, that ye'll never have one of your own?"

The priest made no answer. He went forward with long strides, gazing intently at the blue-eyed baby, longing to kiss the rounded cheeks. He could no longer restrain the impulse; raising the child to his face, he gave it a long kiss.

The father shouted: "Hey there, passon, if ye'd like one, ye've only to say so."

They began to jest, after the fashion of peasants.

As soon as they were seated at table, the rough peasant merriment broke out like a tempest. The two other sons were also to marry soon; their sweethearts were present, invited just for the meal; the guests perpetually alluded to the future generations foreshadowed by these unions.

Their words were coarse and pungent; the blushing girls giggled, the men guffawed. They shouted and beat upon the table with their fists. The father and grandfather were not behindhand with scandalous suggestions. The mother smiled; the old women took their share in the fun and thrust in obscene remarks.

The priest, inured to these rustic orgies, sat quietly beside the nurse, tickling his nephew's little mouth. He seemed surprised at the child's appearance, as though he had never noticed it. He contemplated it with deliberate intentness, with dreamy gravity, and a tenderness arose in his heart, a strange, unknown tenderness, sharp and a little melancholy, for the frail little creature that was his brother's son.

He heard nothing, saw nothing, but stared at the child. He wanted to take him once more upon his knees, for still in his breast and in his heart he retained the soft pressure of the infant's body, as when he carried him back from the church.

He was touched by that scrap of humanity as by an ineffable mystery of which he had never before thought, a mystery sacred and august, a new spirit made flesh, the great mystery of newborn life, of wakening love, of the undying race of humanity going on for ever and ever.

The nurse was eating; her eyes shone in her red face. She was worried by the child, who prevented her from getting comfortably near the table.

"Give him to me," said the priest; "I'm not hungry." And he took the child. Then everything around him faded and disappeared; his eyes were fixed on the chubby pink face. Little by little the warmth of the tiny body penetrated through the shawls and the cassock to his legs, like a caress, so light, so good, so pure, so sweet, that his eyes filled with tears.

The noise of the revelers became terrific. The child, disturbed by the uproar, began to cry.

A voice sang out: "Hey there, passon, feed your baby."

And a burst of laughter shook the room. But the mother had risen; she took her son and carried him into the next room. She came back a few minutes later, announcing that he was fast asleep in his cradle.

The meal went on. From time to time men and women went out into the yard, then returned and sat down again. The meat, the vegetables, the cider, and the wine coursed down their throats, swelled their bellies, excited their spirits.

Night was falling when the coffee came in.

Long before then the priest had vanished, his absence arousing no surprise.

At last the young mother rose to see if the child were still asleep. It was dark now. She entered the room on tiptoe and advanced with arms outstretched, so as not to knock against the furniture. But a strange noise made her stop, and she hurried out again in a fright, sure that she had heard someone move. Pale and trembling, she regained the dining room and told her story. The men rose noisily, drunk and angry, and the father, a lamp in his hand, rushed out.

The priest was on his knees beside the cradle, sobbing. His forehead rested on the pillow, beside the child's head.

MISS HARRIET

There were seven of us in a four-in-hand, four women and three men, one of whom was on the box seat beside the coachman. We were following at a footpace the broad highway which serpentines along the coast.

Setting out from Etretat at break of day in order to visit the ruins of Tancarville, we were still asleep, chilled by the fresh air of the morning. The women especially, who were but little accustomed to these early excursions, let their eyelids fall and rise every moment, nodding their heads or yawning, quite insensible to the glory of the dawn.

It was autumn. On both sides of the road the bare fields stretched out, yellowed by the corn and wheat stubble which covered the soil like a bristling growth of beard. The spongy earth seemed to smoke. Larks were singing high up in the air, while other birds piped in the bushes.

At length the sun rose in front of us, a bright red on the plane of the horizon, and as it ascended, growing clearer from minute to minute, the country seemed to awake, to smile, to shake and stretch itself, like a young girl who is leaving her bed in her white, airy chemise. The Count d'Etraille, who was seated on the box, cried:

"Look! Look! A hare!" And he pointed toward the left, indicating a piece of hedge. The leveret threaded its way along, almost concealed by the field, only its large ears visible. Then it swerved across a deep rut, stopped, again pursued its easy course, changed its direction, stopped anew, disturbed, spying out every danger and undecided as to the route it should take. Suddenly it began to run with great bounds from its hind legs, disappearing finally in a large patch of beetroot. All the men woke up to watch the course of the beast.

René Lemanoir then exclaimed: "We are not at all gallant this morning," and, looking at his neighbor, the little Baroness of Stérennes, who was struggling with drowsiness, he said to her in a subdued voice: "You are thinking of your husband, Baroness. Reassure yourself; he will not return before Saturday, so you have still four days."

She responded to him with a sleepy smile.

"How rude you are." Then, shaking off her torpor, she added: "Now let somebody say something that will make us all laugh. You, Monsieur Chenal, who have the reputation of possessing a larger fortune than the Duke of Richelieu, tell us a love story in which you have been mixed up, anything you like."

Léon Chenal, an old painter who had once been very handsome, very strong, who was very proud of his physique and very amiable, took his long white beard in his hand and smiled; then after a few moments' reflection he became suddenly grave.

"Ladies, it will not be an amusing tale, for I am going to relate to you the most lamentable love affair of my life, and I sincerely hope that none of my friends has ever passed through a similar experience."

I

"At that time I was twenty-five years old and was making daubs along the coast of Normandy. I call 'making daubs' that wandering about with a bag on one's back from mountain to mountain under the pretext of studying and of sketching nature. I know nothing more enjoyable than that happy-go-lucky wandering life in which you are perfectly free, without shackles of any kind, without care, without preoccupation, without thought even of tomorrow. You go in any direction you please without any guide save your fancy, without any counselor save your eyes. You pull up because a running brook seduces you or because you are attracted in front of an inn by the smell of potatoes frying. Sometimes it is the perfume of clematis which decides you in your choice, or the naïve glance of the servant at an inn. Do not despise me for my affection for these rustics. These girls have soul as well as feeling, not to mention firm cheeks and fresh lips, while their hearty and willing kisses have the flavor of wild fruit. Love always has its price, come whence it may. A heart that beats when you make your appearance, an eye that weeps when you go away, these are things so rare, so sweet, so precious, that they must never be despised.

"I have had rendezvous in ditches in which cattle repose and in barns among the straw still steaming from the heat of the day. I have recollections of canvas spread on rude and creaky benches and of hearty, fresh, free kisses, more delicate, free from affectation and sincere than the subtle attractions of charming and distinguished women.

"But what you love most amid all these varied adventures are the country, the woods, the risings of the sun, the twilight, the light of the moon. For the painter these are honeymoon trips with Nature. You are alone with her in that long and tranquil rendezvous. You go to bed in the fields amid marguerites and wild poppies and, with eyes wide open, you watch the going down of the sun and descry in the distance the little village with its pointed clock tower which sounds the hour of midnight.

"You sit down by the side of a spring which gushes out from the foot of an oak, amid a covering of fragile herbs, growing and redolent of life. You go down on your knees, bend forward and drink the cold and pellucid water, wetting your mustache and nose; you drink it with a physical pleasure, as though you were kissing the spring, lip to lip. Sometimes, when you encounter a deep hole along the course of these tiny brooks, you plunge into it, quite naked, and on your skin, from head to foot, like an icy and delicious caress, you feel the lovely and gentle quivering of the current.

"You are gay on the hills, melancholy on the verge of pools, exalted when the sun is crowned in an ocean of blood-red shadows and when it casts on the rivers its red reflection. And at night under the moon, as it passes the vault of heaven, you think of things, singular things, which would never have occurred to your mind under the brilliant light of day.

"So in wandering through the same country we are in this year I came to the little village of Bénouville, on the Falaise, between Yport and Etretat. I came from Fécamp, following the coast, a high coast, perpendicular as a wall, with projecting and rugged rocks falling sheer down into the sea. I had walked since the morning on the close-clipped grass as smooth and as yielding as a carpet. Singing lustily, I walked with long strides, looking sometimes at the slow and lazy flight of a gull, with its short white wings, sailing in the blue heavens, sometimes at the green sea or at the brown sails of a fishing bark. In short, I had passed a happy day, a day of listlessness and of liberty.

"I was shown a little farmhouse where travelers were put up, a kind of inn, kept by a peasant, which stood in the center of a Norman court, surrounded by a double row of beeches.

"Quitting the Falaise, I gained the hamlet, which was hemmed in by trees, and I presented myself at the house of Mother Lecacheur.

"She was an old, wrinkled and austere rustic, who always seemed to yield to the pleasure of new customs with a kind of contempt.

"It was the month of May: the spreading apple trees covered the court with a whirling shower of blossoms which rained unceasingly both upon people and upon the grass.

"I said:

" 'Well, Madame Lecacheur, have you a room for me?'

"Astonished to find that I knew her name, she answered:

" 'That depends; everything is let, but, all the same, there will be no harm in looking.'

"In five minutes we were in perfect accord, and I deposited my bag upon the bare floor of a rustic room furnished with a bed, two chairs, a table and a washstand. The room opened into the large and smoky kitchen, where the lodgers took their meals with the people of the farm and with the farmer himself, who was a widower.

"I washed my hands, after which I went out. The old woman was fricasseeing a chicken for dinner in a large fireplace in which hung the stewpot, black with smoke.

" 'You have travelers then at the present time?' I said to her.

"She answered in an offended tone of voice:

" 'I have a lady, an English lady, who has attained to years of maturity. She is occupying my other room.'

"By means of an extra five sous a day I obtained the privilege of dining out in the court when the weather was fine.

"My cover was then placed in front of the door, and I commenced to gnaw with hunger the lean members of the Normandy chicken, to drink the clear cider and to munch the hunk of white bread which, though four days old, was excellent.

"Suddenly the wooden barrier which opened on to the highway was opened, and a strange person directed her steps toward the house. She was very slender, very tall, enveloped in a Scotch shawl with red borders. You would have believed that she had no arms, if you had not seen a long hand appear just above the hips holding a white tourist umbrella. The face of a mummy, surrounded with sausage rolls of plaited gray hair, which bounded at every step she took, made me think, I know not why, of a sour herring adorned with curling papers. Lowering her eyes, she passed quickly in front of me and entered the house.

"This singular apparition made me curious. She undoubtedly was my neighbor, the aged English lady of whom our hostess had spoken.

"I did not see her again that day. The next day, when I had begun to paint at the end of that beautiful valley which, you know, extends as far as Etretat, lifting my eyes suddenly, I perceived something singularly attired standing on the crest of the declivity; it looked like a pole decked out with flags. It was she. On seeing me she suddenly disappeared. I re-entered the house at midday for lunch and took my seat at the common table so as to make the acquaintance of this old and original creature. But she did not respond to my polite advances, was insensible even to my little attentions. I poured water out for her with great alacrity; I passed her the dishes with great eagerness. A slight, almost imperceptible movement of the head and an English word, murmured so low that I did not understand it, were her only acknowledgments.

"I ceased occupying myself with her, although she had disturbed my thoughts. At the end of three days I knew as much about her as did Madame Lecacheur herself.

"She was called Miss Harriet. Seeking out a secluded village in which to pass the summer, she had been attracted to Bénouville some six months before and did not seem disposed to quit it. She never spoke at table, ate rapidly, reading all the while a small book treating of some Protestant propaganda. She gave a copy of it to everybody. The curé himself had received no less than four copies at the hands of an urchin to whom she had paid two sous' commission. She said sometimes to our hostess abruptly, without preparing her in the least for the declaration:

" 'I love the Saviour more than all; I worship him in all creation; I adore him in all nature; I carry him always in my heart.'

"And she would immediately present the old woman with one of her brochures which were destined to convert the universe.

"In the village she was not liked. In fact, the schoolmaster had declared that she was an atheist and that a sort of reproach attached to her. The curé, who had been consulted by Madame Lecacheur, responded:

" 'She is a heretic, but God does not wish the death of the sinner, and I believe her to be a person of pure morals.'

"These words 'atheist,' 'heretic,' words which no one can precisely define, threw doubts into some minds. It was asserted, however, that this Englishwoman was rich and that she had passed her life in traveling through every country in the world, because her family had thrown her off. Why had her family thrown her off? Because of her natural impiety?

"She was, in fact, one of those people of exalted principles, one of those opinionated puritans of whom England produces so many, one of those good and insupportable old women who haunt the tables d'hôte of every hotel in Europe, who spoil Italy, poison Switzerland, render the charming cities of the Mediterranean uninhabitable, carry everywhere their fantastic manias, their petrified vestal manners, their indescribable toilets and a certain odor of India rubber, which makes one believe that at night they slip themselves into a case of that material. When I meet one of these people in a hotel I act like birds which see a manikin in a field.

"This woman, however, appeared so singular that she did not displease me.

"Madame Lecacheur, hostile by instinct to everything that was not rustic, felt in her narrow soul a kind of hatred for the ecstatic extravagances of the old girl. She had found a phrase by which to describe her, I know not how, but a phrase assuredly contemptuous, which had sprung to her lips, invented, probably, by some confused and mysterious travail of soul. She said: 'That woman is a demoniac.' This phrase, as uttered by that austere and sentimental creature, seemed to me irresistibly comic. I myself never called her now anything else but 'the demoniac,' feeling a singular pleasure in pronouncing this word on seeing her.

"I would ask Mother Lecacheur: 'Well, what is our demoniac about today?' To which my rustic friend would respond with an air of having been scandalized:

" 'What do you think, sir? She has picked up a toad which has had its leg battered and carried it to her room and has put it in her washstand and dressed it up like a man. If that is not profanation I should like to know what is!'

"On another occasion, when walking along the Falaise, she had bought a large fish which had just been caught, simply to throw it back into the sea again. The sailor from whom she had bought it, though paid handsomely, was greatly provoked at this act—more exasperated, indeed, than if she had put her hand into his pocket and taken his money. For a whole month he could not speak of the circumstance without getting into a fury and denouncing it as an outrage. Oh yes! She was indeed a demoniac, this Miss Harriet, and Mother Lecacheur must have had an inspiration of genius in thus christening her.

"The stableboy, who was called Sapeur because he had served in Africa in his youth, entertained other aversions. He said with a roguish air: 'She is an old hag who has lived her days.' If the poor woman had but known!

"Little kindhearted Céleste did not wait upon her willingly, but I was never able to understand why. Probably her only reason was that she was a stranger, of another race, of a different tongue and of another religion. She was in good truth a demoniac!

"She passed her time wandering about the country, adoring and searching for God in nature. I found her one evening on her knees in a cluster of bushes. Having discovered something red through the leaves, I brushed aside the branches, and Miss Harriet at once rose to her feet, confused at having been found thus, looking at me with eyes as terrible as those of a wild cat surprised in open day.

"Sometimes when I was working among the rocks I would suddenly descry her on the banks of the Falaise, standing like a semaphore signal. She gazed passionately at the vast sea glittering in the sunlight and the boundless sky empurpled with fire. Sometimes I would distinguish her at the bottom of an alley, walking quickly with her elastic English step, and I would go toward her, attracted by I know not what, simply to see her illuminated visage, her dried-up features, which seemed to glow with an ineffable, inward and profound happiness.

"Often I would encounter her in the corner of a field, sitting on the grass under the shadow of an apple tree with her little Bible lying open on her knee, while she looked meditatively into the distance.

"I could no longer tear myself away from that quiet country neighborhood, bound to it as I was by a thousand links of love for its soft and sweeping landscapes. At this farm I was out of the world, far removed from everything, but in close proximity to the soil the good, healthy, beautiful green soil. And, must I avow it, there was something besides curiosity which retained me at the residence of Mother Lecacheur. I wished to become acquainted a little with this strange Miss Harriet and to learn what passes in the solitary souls of those wandering old English dames."

II

"We became acquainted in a rather singular manner. I had just finished a study which appeared to me to display genius and power, as it must have, since it was sold for ten thousand francs fifteen years later. It was as simple, however, as that two and two make four, and had nothing to do with academic rules. The whole of the right side of my canvas represented a rock, an enormous rock covered with sea wrack, brown, yellow and red, across which the sun poured like a stream of oil. The light, without which one could see the stars concealed in the background, fell upon the stone and gilded it as if with fire. That was all. A first stupid attempt at dealing with light, with burning rays, with the sublime.

"On the left was the sea, not the blue sea, the slate-colored sea, but a sea of jade, as greenish, milky and thick as the overcast sky.

"I was so pleased with my work that I danced from sheer delight as I carried it back to the inn. I wished that the whole world could have seen it at one and the same moment. I can remember that I showed it to a cow which was browsing by the wayside, exclaiming at the same time: 'Look at that, my old beauty; you will not often see its like again.'

"When I had reached the front of the house I immediately called out to Mother Lecacheur, shouting with all my might:

" 'Ohé! Ohé! My mistress, come here and look at this.'

"The rustic advanced and looked at my work with stupid eyes which distinguished nothing and did not even recognize whether the picture was the representation of an ox or a house.

"Miss Harriet came into the house and passed in rear of me just at the moment when, holding out my canvas at arm's length, I was exhibiting it to the female innkeeper. The 'demoniac' could not help but see it, for I took care to exhibit the thing in such a way that it could not escape her notice. She stopped abruptly and stood motionless, stupefied. It was her rock which was depicted, the one which she usually climbed to dream away her time, undisturbed.

"She uttered a British 'Oh,' which was at once so accentuated and so flattering that I turned round to her, smiling, and said:

" 'This is my last work, mademoiselle.'

"She murmured ecstatically, comically and tenderly:

" 'Oh, monsieur, you must understand what it is to have a palpitation.'

"I colored up of course and was more excited by that compliment than if it had come from a queen. I was seduced, conquered, vanquished. I could have embraced her—upon my honor.

"I took my seat at the table beside her, as I had always done. For the first time she spoke, drawling out in a loud voice:

" 'Oh! I love nature so much.'

"I offered her some bread, some water, some wine. She now accepted these with the vacant smile of a mummy. I began to converse with her about the scenery.

"After the meal we rose from the table together and walked leisurely across the court; then, attracted by the fiery glow which the setting sun cast over the surface of the sea, I opened the outside gate which faced in the direction of the Falaise, and we walked on side by side, as satisfied as any two persons could be who have just learned to understand and penetrate each other's motives and feelings.

"It was a misty, relaxing evening, one of those enjoyable evenings which impart happiness to mind and body alike. All is joy; all is charm. The luscious and balmy air, loaded with the perfumes of herbs, with the perfumes of grass wrack, with the odor of the wild flowers, caresses the soul with a penetrating sweetness. We were going to the brink of the abyss which overlooked the vast sea and rolled past us at the distance of less than a hundred meters.

"We drank with open mouth and expanded chest that fresh breeze from the ocean which glides slowly over the skin, salted as it is by long contact with the waves.

"Wrapped up in her square shawl, inspired by the balmy air and with teeth firmly set, the Englishwoman gazed fixedly at the great sun ball as it descended toward the sea. Soon its rim touched the waters, just in rear of a ship which had appeared on the horizon, until by degrees it was swallowed up by the ocean. We watched it plunge, diminish and finally disappear.

"Miss Harriet contemplated with passionate regard the last glimmer of the flaming orb of day.

"She muttered: 'Oh! Love—I love——' I saw a tear start in her eye. She continued: 'I wish I were a little bird so that I could mount up into the firmament.'

"She remained standing as I had often before seen her, perched on the riverbank, her face as red as her flaming shawl. I should have liked to sketch her in my album. It would have been an ecstatic caricature. I turned my face away from her so as to be able to laugh.

"I then spoke to her of painting, as I would have done to a fellow artist, using the technical terms common among the devotees of the profession. She listened attentively to me, eagerly seeking to divine the sense of the obscure words, so as to penetrate my thoughts. From time to time she would exclaim: 'Oh! I understand; I understand. This is very interesting.' We returned home.

"The next day on seeing me she approached me eagerly, holding out her hand, and we became firm friends immediately.

"She was a brave creature with an elastic sort of a soul which became enthusiastic at a bound. She lacked equilibrium, like all women who are spinsters at the age of fifty. She seemed to be pickled in vinegary innocence, though her heart still retained something of youth and of girlish effervescence. She loved both nature and animals with a fervent ardor, a love like old wine, mellow through age, with a sensual love that she had never bestowed on men.

"One thing is certain: a mare roaming in a meadow with a foal at its side, a bird's nest full of young ones squeaking, with their open mouths and enormous heads, made her quiver with the most violent emotion.

"Poor solitary beings! Sad wanderers from table d'hôte to table d'hôte, poor beings, ridiculous and lamentable, I love you ever since I became acquainted with Miss Harriet!

"I soon discovered that she had something she would like to tell me but dared not, and I was amused at her timidity. When I started out in the morning with my box on my back she would accompany me as far as the end of the village, silent, but evidently struggling inwardly to find words with which to begin a conversation. Then she would leave me abruptly and, with jaunty step, walk away quickly.

"One day, however, she plucked up courage:

"'I would like to see how you paint pictures. Will you show me? I have been very curious.'

"And she colored up as though she had given utterance to words extremely audacious.

"I conducted her to the bottom of the Petit-Val, where I had commenced a large picture.

"She remained standing near me, following all my gestures with concentrated attention. Then suddenly, fearing, perhaps, that she was disturbing me, she said to me: 'Thank you,' and walked away.

"But in a short time she became more familiar and accompanied me every day, her countenance exhibiting visible pleasure. She carried her folding stool under her arm, would not consent to my carrying it, and she sat always by my side. She would remain there for hours, immovable and mute, following with her eye the point of my brush in its every movement. When I would obtain by a large splotch of color spread on with a knife a striking and unexpected effect she would, in spite of herself, give vent to a half-suppressed 'Oh!' of astonishment, of joy, of admiration. She had the most tender respect for my canvases, an almost religious respect for that human reproduction of a part of nature's work divine. My studies appeared to her to be pictures of sanctity, and sometimes she spoke to me of God with the idea of converting me.

"Oh! He was a queer good-natured being, this God of hers. He was a sort of village philosopher without any great resources and without great power, for she always figured him to herself as a being quivering over injustices committed under his eyes and helpless to prevent them.

"She was, however, on excellent terms with him, affecting even to be the confidante of his secrets and of his whims. She said:

"'God wills,' or, 'God does not will,' just like a sergeant announcing to a recruit: 'The colonel has commanded.'

"At the bottom of her heart she deplored my ignorance of the intention of the Eternal, which she strove, nay, felt herself compelled, to impart to me.

"Almost every day I found in my pockets, in my hat when I lifted it from the ground, in my box of colors, in my polished shoes standing in the mornings in front of my door those little pious brochures which she, no doubt, received directly from Paradise.

"I treated her as one would an old friend, with unaffected cordiality. But I soon perceived that she had changed somewhat in her manner, but for a while I paid little attention to it.

"When I walked about, whether to the bottom of the valley or through some country lanes, I would see her suddenly appear, as though she were returning from a rapid walk. She would then sit down abruptly, out of breath, as though she had been running or overcome by some profound emotion. Her face would be red, that

English red which is denied to the people of all other countries; then without any reason she would grow pale, become the color of the ground and seem ready to faint away. Gradually, however, I would see her regain her ordinary color, whereupon she would begin to speak.

"Then without warning she would break off in the middle of a sentence, spring up from her seat and march off so rapidly and so strongly that it would sometimes put me to my wit's end to try and discover whether I had done or said anything to displease or offend her.

"I finally came to the conclusion that this arose from her early habits and training, somewhat modified, no doubt, in honor of me, since the first days of our acquaintanceship.

"When she returned to the farm after walking for hours on the wind-beaten coast her long curled hair would be shaken out and hanging loose, as though it had broken away from its bearings. It was seldom that this gave her any concern, though sometimes she looked as though she had been dining sans cérémonie, her locks having become disheveled by the breezes.

"She would then go up to her room in order to adjust what I called her glass lamps. When I would say to her in familiar gallantry which, however, always offended her:

" 'You are as beautiful as a planet today, Miss Harriet,' a little blood would immediately mount into her cheeks, the blood of a young maiden, the blood of sweet fifteen.

"Then she would become abruptly savage and cease coming to watch me paint. But I always thought:

" 'This is only a fit of temper she is passing through.'

"But it did not always pass away. When I spoke to her sometimes she would answer me, either with an air of affected indifference or in sullen anger, and she became by turns rude, impatient and nervous. For a time I never saw her except at meals, and we spoke but little. I concluded at length that I must have offended her in something, and accordingly I said to her one evening:

" 'Miss Harriet, why is it that you do not act toward me as formerly? What have I done to displease you? You are causing me much pain!'

"She responded in an angry tone, in a manner altogether sui generis:

" 'I am always with you the same as formerly. It is not true, not true,' and she ran upstairs and shut herself up in her room.

"At times she would look upon me with strange eyes. Since that time I have often said to myself that those condemned to death must look thus when informed that their last day has come. In her eye there lurked a species of folly, a folly at once mysterious and violent—even more, a fever, an exasperated desire, impatient, at once incapable of being realized and unrealizable!

"Nay, it seemed to me that there was also going on within her a combat in which her heart struggled against an unknown force that she wished to overcome —perhaps, even something else. But what could I know? What could I know?"

III

"This was indeed a singular revelation.

"For some time I had commenced to work as soon as daylight appeared on a picture, the subject of which was as follows:

"A deep ravine, steep banks dominated by two declivities, lined with brambles and long rows of trees, hidden, drowned in milky vapor, clad in that misty robe which sometimes floats over valleys at break of day. At the extreme end of that thick and transparent fog you see coming, or rather already come, a human couple, a stripling and a maiden embraced, interlaced, she with head leaning on him, he inclined toward her, and lip to lip.

"A ray of the sun glistening through the branches has traversed the fog of dawn and illuminated it with a rosy reflection just behind the rustic lovers, whose vague shadows are reflected on it in clear silver. It was well done; yes indeed, well done.

"I was working on the declivity which led to the Val d'Etretat. This particular morning I had, by chance, the sort of floating vapor which was necessary for my purpose. Suddenly an object appeared in front of me, a kind of phantom; it was Miss Harriet. On seeing me she took to flight. But I called after her, saying: 'Come here; come here, mademoiselle, I have a nice little picture for you.'

"She came forward, though with seeming reluctance. I handed her my sketch. She said nothing but stood for a long time motionless, looking at it. Suddenly she burst into tears. She wept spasmodically, like men who have been struggling hard against shedding tears but who can do so no longer and abandon themselves to grief, though unwillingly. I got up, trembling, moved myself by the sight of a sorrow I did not comprehend, and I took her by the hand with a gesture of brusque affection, a true French impulse which impels one quicker than one thinks.

"She let her hands rest in mine for a few seconds, and I felt them quiver, as if her whole nervous system was twisting and turning. Then she withdrew her hands abruptly or, rather, tore them out of mine.

"I recognized that shiver as soon as I had felt it; I was deceived in nothing. Ah! The love shudder of a woman, whether she is fifteen or fifty years of age, whether she is one of the people or one of the *monde*, goes so straight to my heart that I never had any difficulty in understanding it!

"Her whole frail being trembled, vibrated, yielded. I knew it. She walked away before I had time to say a word, leaving me as surprised as if I had witnessed a miracle and as troubled as if I had committed a crime.

"I did not go in to breakfast. I took a walk on the banks of the Falaise, feeling that I could just as soon weep as laugh, looking on the adventure as both comic and deplorable and my position as ridiculous, fain to believe that I had lost my head.

"I asked myself what I ought to do. I debated whether I ought not to take my leave of the place, and almost immediately my resolution was formed.

"Somewhat sad and perplexed, I wandered about until dinnertime and entered the farmhouse just when the soup had been served up.

"I sat down at the table, as usual. Miss Harriet was there, munching away solemnly without speaking to anyone, without even lifting her eyes. She wore, however, her usual expression, both of countenance and manner.

"I waited patiently till the meal had been finished. Then, turning toward the landlady, I said: 'Madame Lecacheur, it will not be long now before I shall have to take my leave of you.'

"The good woman, at once surprised and troubled, replied in a quivering voice: 'My dear sir, what is it I have just heard you say? Are you going to leave us after I have become so much accustomed to you?'

"I looked at Miss Harriet from the corner of my eye. Her countenance did not change in the least, but the underservant came toward me with eyes wide open.

She was a fat girl of about eighteen years of age, rosy, fresh, strong as a horse, yet possessing a rare attribute in one in her position—she was very neat and clean. I had kissed her at odd times in out-of-the-way corners in the manner of a mountain guide, nothing more.

"The dinner being over, I went to smoke my pipe under the apple trees, walking up and down at my ease from one end of the court to the other. All the reflections which I had made during the day, the strange discovery of the morning, that grotesque and passionate attachment for me, the recollections which that revelation had suddenly called up, recollections at once charming and perplexing, perhaps, also, that look which the servant had cast on me at the announcement of my departure—all these things, mixed up and combined, put me now in an excited bodily state with the tickling sensation of kisses on my lips, and in my veins something which urged me on to commit some folly.

"Night having come on, casting its dark shadows under the trees, I descried Céleste, who had gone to shut the hen coops at the other end of the inclosure. I darted toward her, running so noiselessly that she heard nothing, and as she got up from closing the small traps by which the chickens went in and out, I clasped her in my arms and rained on her coarse, fat face a shower of kisses. She made a struggle, laughing all the same, as she was accustomed to do in such circumstances. What made me suddenly loose my grip of her? Why did I at once experience a shock? What was it that I heard behind me?

"It was Miss Harriet who had come upon us, who had seen us and who stood in front of us, as motionless as a specter. Then she disappeared in the darkness.

"I was ashamed, embarrassed, more annoyed at having been surprised by her than if she had caught me committing some criminal act.

"I slept badly that night; I was worried and haunted by sad thoughts. I seemed to hear loud weeping, but in this I was no doubt deceived. Moreover, I thought several times that I heard someone walking up and down in the house and that someone opened my door from the outside.

"Toward morning I was overcome by fatigue, and sleep seized on me. I got up late and did not go downstairs until breakfast time, being still in a bewildered state, not knowing what kind of face to put on.

"No one had seen Miss Harriet. We waited for her at table, but she did not appear. At length Mother Lecacheur went to her room. The Englishwoman had gone out. She must have set out at break of day, as she was wont to do, in order to see the sunrise.

"Nobody seemed astonished at this, and we began to eat in silence.

"The weather was hot, very hot, one of those still, sultry days when not a leaf stirs. The table had been placed out of doors under an apple tree, and from time to time Sapeur had gone to the cellar to draw a jug of cider, everybody was so thirsty. Céleste brought the dishes from the kitchen, a ragout of mutton with potatoes, a cold rabbit and a salad. Afterward she placed before us a dish of strawberries, the first of the season.

"As I wanted to wash and freshen these, I begged the servant to go and bring a pitcher of cold water.

"In about five minutes she returned, declaring that the well was dry. She had lowered the pitcher to the full extent of the cord and had touched the bottom, but on drawing the pitcher up again it was empty. Mother Lecacheur, anxious to examine the thing for herself, went and looked down the hole. She returned announcing that one could see clearly something in the well, something altogether unusual. But this, no doubt, was pottles of straw which, out of spite, had been cast down it by a neighbor.

"I wished also to look down the well, hoping to clear up the mystery, and perched myself close to its brink. I perceived indistinctly a white object. What could it be? I then conceived the idea of lowering a lantern at the end of a cord. When I did so the yellow flame danced on the layers of stone and gradually became clearer. All four of us were leaning over the opening, Sapeur and Céleste having now joined us. The lantern rested on a black-and-white, indistinct mass, singular, incomprehensible. Sapeur exclaimed:

"'It is a horse. I see the hoofs. It must have escaped from the meadow during the night and fallen in headlong.'

"But suddenly a cold shiver attacked my spine; I first recognized a foot, then a clothed limb; the body was entire, but the other limb had disappeared under the water.

"I groaned and trembled so violently that the light of the lamp danced hither and thither over the object, discovering a slipper.

"'It is a woman! Who—who—can it be? It is Miss Harriet.'

"Sapeur alone did not manifest horror. He had witnessed many such scenes in Africa.

"Mother Lecacheur and Céleste began to scream and to shriek and ran away.

"But it was necessary to recover the corpse of the dead. I attached the boy securely by the loins to the end of the pulley rope; then I lowered him slowly and watched him disappear in the darkness. In the one hand he had a lantern and held onto the rope with the other. Soon I recognized his voice, which seemed to come from the center of the earth, crying:

"'Stop.'

"I then saw him fish something out of the water. It was the other limb. He bound the two feet together and shouted anew:

"'Haul up.'

"I commenced to wind him up, but I felt my arms strain, my muscles twitch, and was in terror lest I should let the boy fall to the bottom. When his head appeared over the brink I asked:

"'What is it?' as though I only expected that he would tell me what he had discovered at the bottom.

"We both got onto the stone slab at the edge of the well and, face to face, hoisted the body.

"Mother Lecacheur and Céleste watched us from a distance, concealed behind the wall of the house. When they saw issuing from the well the black slippers and white stockings of the drowned person they disappeared.

"Sapeur seized the ankles of the poor, chaste woman, and we drew it up, inclined, as it was, in the most immodest posture. The head was in a shocking state, bruised and black, and the long gray hair, hanging down, was tangled and disordered.

"'In the name of all that is holy, how lean she is!' exclaimed Sapeur in a contemptuous tone.

"We carried her into the room, and as the women did not put in an appearance, I, with the assistance of the lad, dressed the corpse for burial.

"I washed her disfigured face. By the touch of my hand an eye was slightly opened; it seemed to scan me with that pale stare, with that cold, that terrible look which corpses have, a look which seems to come from the beyond. I plaited up, as well as I could, her disheveled hair, and I adjusted on her forehead a novel and singularly formed lock. Then I took off her dripping wet garments, baring, not without a feeling of shame, as though I had been guilty of some profanation, her shoulders and her chest and her long arms, slim as the twigs of branches.

"I next went to fetch some flowers, corn poppies, blue beetles, marguerites and fresh and perfumed herbs, with which to strew her funeral couch.

"Being the only person near her, it was necessary for me to perform the usual ceremonies. In a letter found in her pocket, written at the last moment, she asked that her body be buried in the village in which she had passed the last days of her life. A frightful thought then oppressed my heart. Was it not on my account that she wished to be laid at rest in this place?

"Toward the evening all the female gossips of the locality came to view the remains of the defunct, but I would not allow a single person to enter; I wanted to be alone, and I watched by the corpse the whole night.

"By the flickering light of the candles I looked at the body of this miserable woman, wholly unknown, who had died so lamentably and so far away from home. Had she left no friends, no relatives behind her? What had her infancy been? What had been her life? When had she come thither all alone, a wanderer, like a dog driven from home? What secrets of suffering and of despair were sealed up in that disagreeable body, in that spent and withered body, that impenetrable hiding place of a mystery which had driven her far away from affection and from love?

"How many unhappy beings there are! I felt that upon that human creature weighed the eternal injustice of implacable nature! Life was over with her without her ever having experienced, perhaps, that which sustains the most miserable of us all—to wit, the hope of being once loved! Otherwise why should she thus have concealed herself, have fled from the face of others? Why did she love everything so tenderly and so passionately, everything living that was not a man?

"I recognized also that she believed in a God and that she hoped for compensation from him for the miseries she had endured. She had now begun to decompose and to become, in turn, a plant. She who had blossomed in the sun was now to be eaten up by the cattle, carried away in herbs and in the flesh of beasts, again to become human flesh. But that which is called the soul had been extinguished at the bottom of the dark well. She suffered no longer. She had changed her life for that of others yet to be born.

"Hours passed away in this silent and sinister communion with the dead. A pale light at length announced the dawn of a new day, and a bright ray glistened on the bed, shedding a dash of fire on the bedclothes and on her hands. This was the hour she had so much loved, when the waking birds began to sing in the trees.

"I opened the window to its fullest extent; I drew back the curtains so that the whole heavens might look in upon us. Then, bending toward the glassy corpse, I took in my hands the mutilated head and slowly, without terror or disgust, imprinted a long, long kiss upon those lips which had never before received the salute of love."

Léon Chenal remained silent. The women wept. We heard on the box seat Count d'Etraille blow his nose from time to time. The coachman alone had gone to sleep. The horses, which felt no longer the sting of the whip, had slackened their pace and dragged softly along. And the four-in-hand, hardly moving at all, became suddenly torpid, as if laden with sorrow.

MISTI

RECOLLECTIONS OF A BACHELOR

My mistress at that time was a funny little woman. She was married, of course, for I've a perfect horror of unmarried women. After all, what pleasure can one have in possessing a woman who has the double disadvantage of belonging to no one and belonging to everyone? And honestly, quite apart from the moral side of the question, I can't understand love as a profession. It rather disgusts me. It's a weakness, I know, and I confess it.

The chiefest pleasure enjoyed by a bachelor who has a married woman for his mistress is that she provides him with a home, a comfortable, pleasant home in which everyone looks after him and spoils him, from the husband to the servants. Every pleasure is there united, love, friendship, even paternity, the bed and the table, which constitute the final happiness of life, together with the incalculable advantage of being able to change your household from time to time, of installing yourself by turns in every different class of family, in the country, during the summer, in the home of the workman who lets you a room in his house; in the middle-class home of the provincial, during the winter, even in the homes of the aristocracy, if you are ambitious.

I have another weakness: I like my mistresses' husbands. I admit that there are husbands, vulgar or coarse, who fill me with disgust for their wives, however charming these may be. But when the husband has wit or charm, I fall inevitably desperately in love. I am careful, if I break with the woman, not to break with the husband. In this way I have made my best friends, and in this manner I have ofttimes verified the incontestable superiority of the male over the female of the human species. The latter causes you every possible worry, makes scenes, reproaches you, and so forth; the former, who has quite as much right to complain, treats you, on the contrary, as though you were Providence fallen at his fireside.

Well, my mistress was a funny little woman, dark, fantastic, capricious, religious, superstitious, credulous as a monk, but charming. Above all, she had a way of kissing which I have never found in another woman . . . but this is not the place. . . . And such a soft skin! I derived infinite pleasure merely from holding her hand! And her eyes. . . . Her gaze passed over you like a slow caress, delicious and endless. Often I laid my head on her knees, and we remained motionless, she bending over me with that faint, enigmatic, disturbing little smile that women have, I lifting my eyes towards her, receiving like wine poured gently and deliciously into my heart, the shining gaze of her blue eyes, bright as though filled with thoughts of love, blue like a heaven of delights.

Her husband, a civil servant, was often away, leaving our evenings free. Often I spent them at her house, lying on the divan, my forehead pressed against one of her legs, while upon the other slept a huge black cat named Misti, which she adored. Our fingers met on the animal's muscular back and caressed one another amid its silky hair. I felt against my cheek its warm flank, throbbing with a perpetual "purr-purr." Sometimes it would stretch out a paw to my mouth, or set five unsheathed claws upon my eyelids, whose points pricked my eyes and made me close them in a flash.

Sometimes we went out to enjoy what we called our escapades. As a matter of fact they were very innocent. They consisted in supping at an outlying inn, or else, after we had dined at her house or mine, of visiting low taverns, like students on the spree.

We went to the lowest drinking places and sat down at the far end of smoky dens, on rickety chairs, at an old wooden table. A cloud of acrid smoke, which smelled still of the fried fish eaten at dinner, filled the room; men in blouses talked noisily and drank brandy; and the astonished waiter served us with cherries in brandy.

Trembling with delicious terror, she would raise her little black veil, folded double, to the tip of her nose, where it rested, and begin to drink with the pleasure of committing a delightful crime. Each cherry she swallowed gave her the sense of a sin committed, each sip of the coarse liquor ran down her throat like a delicate, forbidden pleasure.

Then she would say to me in a low voice: "Let us go." And we left. She went out quickly, her head lowered, with short steps, between the drinkers, who watched her pass with resentful glances; and when we found ourselves out in the street again, she would utter a deep sigh as though we had just escaped from dreadful peril.

Sometimes she asked me with a shudder: "If I were insulted in one of these places, what would you do?" And I would reply in a swaggering tone: "Why, defend you, damn it." And she would squeeze my arm in her happiness, with a vague wish, perhaps, to be insulted and defended, to see those men, even those ruffians, fight me for her.

One evening, as we were seated at a table in a Montmartre den, we saw a ragged old woman come in, holding in her hand a greasy pack of cards. Observing a lady, the old woman promptly came up to us, offering to tell my companion's fortune. Emma, whose mind believed anything and everything, shivered with pleasure and uneasiness, and made room beside her for the hag.

The ancient, wrinkled woman, with rings of raw flesh round her eyes and an empty, toothless mouth, set out her dirty cards on the table. She made them into heaps, picked them up, and set them out again, muttering inaudible words. Emma listened, pale, breathing quickly, panting with distress and curiosity.

The sorceress began to speak; she made vague predictions: happiness and children, a fair young man, a journey, money, a lawsuit, a dark gentleman, the return of a friend, a success, a death. The announcement of this death struck the young woman. Whose death? When? How?

"As to that," replied the old woman, "the cards are not strong enough; you must come and see me tomorrow. I'll tell you with the coffee mark, which never fails."

Emma turned anxiously to me.

"We may go tomorrow, mayn't we? Oh, please say yes! If not, you don't know how it will torment me."

I began to laugh.

"We'll go if you want to, darling."

The old woman gave us her address.

She lived on the sixth floor of an awful house behind the Buttes-Chaumont. We went there the next day.

Her room, a garret with two chairs and a bed, was full of strange things—bunches of herbs hanging from nails, dried animals, bottles and phials containing various colored liquids. On the table a stuffed black cat stared with glass eyes. He looked like the familiar spirit of this sinister dwelling.

Emma, faint with excitement, sat down, and said at once:

"Oh, darling, look at the cat! Isn't he just like Misti?"

And she explained to the old woman that she herself had a cat just like that one; oh, exactly like it.

"If you love a man," replied the sorceress solemnly, "you must not keep it."

"Why not?" asked Emma, struck with terror.

The old woman sat down beside her in a familiar way, and took her hand.

"It's the sorrow of my life," she said.

My friend was eager to hear. She pressed the old woman to tell her, questioned her, urged her: the superstitious credulity they shared made them sisters in mind and heart. At last the fortuneteller made up her mind.

"I loved that cat," she said, "like a brother. I was young in those days, and all alone; I did sewing at home. Monton was all I had. A lodger gave him to me. He was as clever as a child, and gentle too; he idolized me, dear lady, he idolized me more than a fetish. All day long he purred in my lap, all night on my pillow; I felt his heart beat, I did.

"Well, I made friends with a man, a nice boy who worked at a linen draper's. It went on for three months without my granting him anything. But you know how it is, one weakens—it happens to everybody; and besides, I had begun to love him, that I had. He was so nice, so nice and kind. He wanted us to live together all the time, for economy. At last I let him come and see me one evening. I hadn't made up my mind, oh, dear, no! but I liked the idea of being together for an hour.

"At the beginning he was very well behaved. He said pretty things to me which stirred my heart. Then he kissed me, madame, gave me a lover's kiss. I had shut my eyes and remained in a sort of paralysis of happiness. Suddenly I felt that he'd made a violent movement, and he screamed, a scream I shall never forget. I opened my eyes and saw that Monton had flown at his face and was tearing his skin with his claws, like a rag of linen. And the blood was streaming down, madame.

"I tried to pull the cat off, but he held tight, and went on scratching, and even bit me, he was so far out of his senses. At last I got hold of him and threw him out of the window, which was open, since it was summer.

"When I began to wash my poor friend's face, I saw that he had lost his eyes, both eyes.

"He had to go to the hospital. He died of misery a year after. I wanted to have him with me and feed him, but he would not. He seemed to hate me after it had happened.

"As for Monton, he broke his back in the fall. The porter had picked up the body. I had him stuffed, since I still felt attached to him. If he had done that, it was because he loved me, wasn't it?"

The old woman was silent, and stroked the dead beast with her hand; the carcass shook on its wire skeleton.

Emma, her heart wrung, had forgotten the predicted death. At any rate, she said nothing more about it, and went away after giving the woman five francs.

Her husband came back the next day, and so several days passed before I saw her. When I visited her again, I was surprised not to see Misti. I asked where he was. She blushed, and replied:

"I gave him away. I wasn't happy about him."

I was surprised.

"Not happy? Not happy? What about?"

She gave me a long kiss, and murmured in a low voice:

"I was afraid for your eyes, darling."

IN THE WOOD

The mayor was just going to sit down to breakfast, when he was told that the rural policeman was waiting for him at the mairie with two prisoners. He went there immediately and found old Hochedur standing up and watching a middle-class couple of mature years with stern looks.

The man, a fat old fellow with a red nose and white hair, seemed utterly dejected, while the woman, a little roundabout, stout creature with shining cheeks, looked at the agent who had arrested them with defiant eyes.

"What is it? What is it, Hochedur?"

The rural policeman made his deposition. He had gone out that morning at his usual time in order to patrol his beat from the forest of Champioux as far as the boundaries of Argenteuil. He had not noticed anything unusual in the country except that it was a fine day and that the wheat was doing well, when the son of old Bredel, who was going over his vines a second time, called out to him: "Here, Daddy Hochedur, go and have a look into the skirts of the wood, in the first thicket, and you will catch a pair of pigeons there who must be a hundred and thirty years old between them!"

He went in the direction that had been indicated to him and had gone into the thicket. There he heard words and gasps which made him suspect a flagrant breach of morality. Advancing, therefore, on his hands and knees as if to surprise a poacher, he had arrested this couple at the very moment when they were going to abandon themselves to their natural instincts.

The mayor looked at the culprits in astonishment, for the man was certainly sixty and the woman fifty-five at least. So he began to question them, beginning with the man, who replied in such a weak voice that he could scarcely be heard.

"What is your name?"

"Nicolas Beaurain."

"Your occupation?"

"Haberdasher in the Rue des Martyrs, in Paris."

"What were you doing in the wood?"

The haberdasher remained silent, with his eyes on his fat stomach and his hands resting on his thighs, and the mayor continued:

"Do you deny what the officer of the municipal authorities states?"

"No, monsieur."

"So you confess it?"

"Yes, monsieur."

"What have you to say in your defense?"

"Nothing, monsieur."

"Where did you meet the partner in your misdemeanor?"

"She is my wife, monsieur."

"Your wife?"

"Yes, monsieur."

"Then—then—you do not live together in Paris?"

"I beg your pardon, monsieur, but we are living together!"

"But in that case you must be mad, altogether mad, my dear sir, to get caught like that in the country at ten o'clock in the morning."

The haberdasher seemed ready to cry with shame, and he murmured: "It was she who enticed me! I told her it was stupid, but when a woman has got a thing into her head, you know, you cannot get it out."

The mayor, who liked open speaking, smiled and replied:

"In your case the contrary ought to have happened. You would not be here if she had had the idea only in her head."

Then M. Beaurain was seized with rage and, turning to his wife, he said: "Do you see to what you have brought us with your poetry? And now we shall have to go before the courts at our age for a breach of morals! And we shall have to shut up the shop, sell our good will and go to some other neighborhood! That's what it has come to!"

Mme. Beaurain got up and, without looking at her husband, explained herself without any embarrassment, without useless modesty and almost without hesitation.

"Of course, monsieur, I know that we have made ourselves ridiculous. Will you allow me to plead my case like an advocate, or rather like a poor woman? And I hope that you will be kind enough to send us home and to spare us the disgrace of a prosecution.

"Years ago, when I was young, I made Monsieur Beaurain's acquaintance on Sunday in this neighborhood. He was employed in a draper's shop, and I was a saleswoman in a ready-made clothing establishment. I remember it as if it were yesterday. I used to come and spend Sundays here occasionally with a friend of mine, Rose Levèque, with whom I lived in the Rue Pigalle, and Rose had a sweetheart, while I had not. He used to bring us here, and one Saturday he told me, laughing, that he should bring a friend with him the next day. I quite understood what he meant, but I replied that it would be no good, for I was virtuous, monsieur.

"The next day we met Monsieur Beaurain at the railway station. In those days he was good looking, but I had made up my mind not to yield to him, and I did not yield. Well, we arrived at Bezons. It was a lovely day, the sort of day that tickles your heart. When it is fine even now, just as it used to be formerly, I grow quite foolish, and when I am in the country I utterly lose my head. The verdure, the swallows flying so swiftly, the smell of the grass, the scarlet poppies, the daisies, all that makes me quite excited! It is like champagne when one is not used to it!

"Well, it was lovely weather, warm and bright, and it seemed to penetrate into your body by your eyes when you looked and by your mouth when you breathed. Rose and Simon hugged and kissed each other every minute, and that gave me something to look at! Monsieur Beaurain and I walked behind them without speaking much, for when people do not know each other well they cannot find much to talk about. He looked timid, and I liked to see his embarrassment. At last we got to the little wood; it was as cool as in a bath there, and we all four sat down. Rose and her lover joked me because I looked rather stern, but you will understand that I could not be otherwise. And then they began to kiss and hug again without putting any more restraint upon themselves than if we had not been there. Then they whispered together and got up and went off among the trees without saying a word. You may fancy how I felt, alone with this young fellow whom I saw for the first time. I felt so confused at seeing them go that it gave me courage and I began to talk. I asked him what his business was, and he said he was a linen draper's assistant, as I told you just now. We talked for a few minutes, and that made him bold, and he wanted to take liberties with me, but I told him sharply to keep his own place. Is not that true, Monsieur Beaurain?"

M. Beaurain, who was looking at his feet in confusion, did not reply, and she continued: "Then he saw that I was virtuous and he began to make love to me nicely, like an honorable man, and from that time he came every Sunday, for he was very much in love with me. I was very fond of him also, very fond of him! He was a good-looking fellow formerly, and in short he married me the next September, and we started business in the Rue des Martyrs.

"It was a hard struggle for some years, monsieur. Business did not prosper, and we could not afford many country excursions, and then we became unaccustomed to them. One has other things in one's head and thinks more of the cashbox than of pretty speeches when one is in business. We were growing old by degrees without perceiving it, like quiet people who do not think much about love. But one does not regret anything as long as one does not notice what one has lost.

"And after that, monsieur, business went better, and we became tranquil as to the future! Then, you see, I do not exactly know what passed within me—no, I really do not know—but I began to dream like a little boarding-school girl. The sight of the little carts full of flowers which are peddled about the streets made me cry; the smell of violets sought me out in my easy chair, behind my cashbox, and made my heart beat! Then I used to get up and go onto the doorstep to look at the blue sky between the roofs. When one looks at the sky from a street it seems like a river flowing over Paris, winding as it goes, and the swallows pass to and fro in it like fish. These sort of things are very stupid at my age! But what can one do, monsieur, when one has worked all one's life? A moment comes in which one perceives that one could have done something else, and then one regrets. Oh yes! One feels great regret! Just think that for twenty years I might have gone and had kisses in the wood, like other women. I used to think how delightful it would be to lie under the trees loving someone! And I thought of it every day and every night! I dreamed of the moonlight on the water, until I felt inclined to drown myself.

"I did not venture to speak to Monsieur Beaurain about this at first. I knew that he would make fun of me and send me back to sell my needles and cotton! And then, to speak the truth, Monsieur Beaurain never said much to me, but when I looked in the glass I also understood quite well that I also no longer appealed to anyone!

"Well, I made up my mind, and I proposed an excursion into the country to him to the place where we had first become acquainted. He agreed without any distrust, and we arrived here this morning about nine o'clock.

"I felt quite young again when I got among the corn, for a woman's heart never grows old! And really I no longer saw my husband as he is at present, but just like he was formerly! That I will swear to you, monsieur. As true as I am standing here, I was intoxicated. I began to kiss him, and he was more surprised than if I had tried to murder him. He kept saying to me: 'Why, you must be mad this morning! What is the matter with you?' I did not listen to him; I only listened to my own heart, and I made him come into the wood with me. There is the story. I have spoken the truth, Monsieur le Maire, the whole truth."

The mayor was a sensible man. He rose from his chair, smiled and said: "Go in peace, madame, and sin no more—under the trees."

OUR FRIENDS THE ENGLISH

A small leather-bound notebook lay on the upholstered seat of the railway carriage. I took it up and opened it. It was a traveler's diary, dropped by its owner.

Here are the last three pages of it copied out.

February 1. Mentone, capital of the consumptives, noted for its pulmonary tubercles. Quite different from the potato tubercle, which lives and grows in the earth for the purpose of nourishing and fattening men, this variety lives and grows in man for the purpose of nourishing and fattening the earth.

I got this scientific definition from a friendly doctor here, a very learned man.

Am looking for a hotel. Am directed to the Grrrrand Hotel of Russia, England, Germany, and the Netherlands. Pay homage to the landlord's cosmopolitan intellect and book a room in this caravanserai—which looks empty, it is so big.

Walk round the town, which is pretty and admirably situated at the foot of an imposing mountain peak (see guidebook). Meet various people who look ill, being taken for a walk by others who look bored. Have observed several people wearing comforters (note this, all naturalists who may be becoming anxious at the disappearance of these garments!).

Six P.M. Return for dinner. The tables are laid in an enormous room which could shelter three hundred guests; as a matter of fact, it holds just twenty-two. They come in one after another. The first is a tall, thin, clean-shaven Englishman. He is wearing a frock coat with a long skirt, fitting closely at the waist. His thin arms are enveloped in its sleeves like an umbrella sheathed in its cover. This garment reminds me at the same time of an ecclesiastical cassock and the civilian uniforms worn by ex-army captains and army pensioners. Down the front elevation runs a row of buttons clad in black serge like their master, and sewn very close to one another; they look like an army of wood lice. The buttonholes stand in a row opposite and have the air of making unseemly advances to the modest little buttons.

The waistcoat fastens on the same system. The owner of the garment does not look precisely a sporty boy.

He bows to me; I return the compliment.

Next item—three ladies, all English, a mother and two daughters. Each wears a helping of whipped white of egg on the top of her head; rather remarkable. The daughters are old, like the mother. The mother is old, like the daughters. All three are thin, flat-chested, tall, stiff, and tired-looking; their front teeth are designed to intimidate plates and men.

Other residents arrive, all English. A solitary one is fat and red-faced, with white whiskers. Every woman (there are fourteen) has a helping of white of egg on her head. I observe that this crowning delicacy is made of white lace (or is it tulle? I don't know). It appears to be unsweetened. All the ladies look as though they were pickled in vinegar, although there are several young girls, not bad-looking, but with no figures and with no apparent promise of them. I am reminded of Bouilhet's lines:

> Qu'importe ton sein maigre, ô mon objet aimé!
> On est plus près du cœur quand la poitrine est plate;
> Et je vois comme un merle en sa cage enfermé,
> L'amour entre les os, rêvant sur une patte.

Two young men, younger than the first, are likewise imprisoned in sacerdotal frock coats. They are lay priests, with wives and children; they are called parsons. They look more serious, less unbending, less kindly than our own priests. I would not take a hogshead of them for a pint of ours. But that's a matter of taste.

As soon as all the residents are present, the head parson begins to speak, and recites, in English, a sort of long benedicite; the whole table listens to it with that pickled look in their faces.

My dinner being thus dedicated, despite me, to the God of Israel and Albion, all started their soup.

Solemn silence reigned in the huge room—a silence which was surely not normal. I suppose the chaste sheep were annoyed at the invasion of a goat.

The women especially retain a stiff, starched look, as though they were afraid of dropping their headdress of whipped cream into the soup.

The head parson, however, addresses a few words to his neighbor, the under parson. As I have the misfortune to understand English, I observe with amazement that they are continuing a conversation, interrupted before dinner, on the texts of the prophets. Everyone listens attentively.

I am fed, always against my will, upon unbelievable quotations.

"I will pour water upon him that is thirsty," said Isaiah.

I did not know it. I knew none of the truths uttered by Jeremiah, Malachi, Ezekiel, and Elijah. These simple truths crawled down my ears and buzzed in my head like flies.

"Let him that is hungry ask for food!"

"The air belongeth to the birds, as the sea belongeth to the fish."

"The fig tree produceth figs, and the date palm dates."

"He who will not hear, to him knowledge is denied."

How much greater and more profound is our great Henry Monnier, who through the lips of one man, the immortal Prudhomme, has uttered more thrilling truths than have been compiled by all the goodly fellowship of the prophets.

Confronted by the sea, he exclaims: "How beautiful is the ocean, but what a lot of good land spoiled!"

He formulates the everlasting policy of the world: "This sword is the light of my life. I can use it to defend the Power that gave it to me, and, if need be, to attack it also."

Had I had the honor to be introduced to the English people surrounding me, I would certainly have edified them with quotations from our French prophet.

Dinner over, we went into the lounge.

I sat alone, in a corner. The British nation appeared to be hatching a plot on the other side of the room.

Suddenly a lady went to the piano.

"Ah," thought I, "a little mee-usic. So much the better."

She opened the instrument and sat down; the entire colony ranked itself round her like an army, the women in front, the men in the rear rank.

Were they going to sing an opera?

The head parson, now turned choirmaster, raised his hand, then lowered it; a frightful din rose up from every throat. They were singing a hymn.

The women squalled, the men barked, the windows shook. The hotel dog howled in the yard. Another answered him from a room.

I went off in a furious temper. I went for a walk round the town. No theater. No casino. No place of amusement. I had to go back to the hotel.

The English were still singing.

I went to bed. They went on singing. Till midnight they sang the praises of the Lord in the harshest, most hateful, most out-of-tune voices I ever heard. Maddened by the horrible spirit of imitation which drives a whole nation to such orgies, I buried my head beneath the sheets and sang:

> "Je plains le Seigneur, le Seigneur dieu d'Albion,
>   Dont on chante la gloire au salon.
>   Si le Seigneur a plus d'oreille
>   Que son peuple fidèle,
>   S'il aime le talent, la beauté,
>   La grâce, l'esprit, la gaieté,
>   L'excellente mimique
>   Et la bonne musique,
>   Je plains le Seigneur
>   De tout mon cœur."

When I finally dropped off to sleep, I had fearful nightmares. I saw prophets riding upon parsons, eating white of egg off the heads of corpses.

Horrible! Horrible!

February 2. As soon as I was up, I asked the landlord if these barbarian invaders of his hotel made a daily practice of this frightful diversion.

"Oh, no, sir," he answered with a smile. "Yesterday was Sunday, and Sunday is a holy day to them, you know."

I answered:

> "Rien n'est sacré pour un pasteur,
>   Ni le sommeil du voyageur,
>   Ni son dîner, ni son oreille;
>   Mais veillez que chose pareille
>   Ne recommence pas, ou bien
>   Sans hésiter, je prends le train."

Somewhat surprised, the landlord promised to look into the matter.

During the day I made a delightful excursion in the hills. At night, the same benedicite. Then the drawing room. What will they do? Nothing, for an hour.

Suddenly the same lady who accompanied the hymns the day before goes to the piano and opens it. I shiver with fright.

She plays . . . a waltz.

The girls begin to dance.

The head parson beats time on his knee from force of habit. The Englishmen one after another invite the ladies; the white of egg whirls round and round and round; will it turn into sauce?

This is much better. After the waltz comes a quadrille, then a polka.

Not having been introduced, I remain alone in a corner.

February 3. Another charming walk to the old castle, a picturesque ruin in the hills, on every peak of which remain the remnants of ancient buildings. Nothing could be more beautiful than the ruined castles among the chaos of rocks dominated by Alpine snow peaks (see guidebook). Wonderful country.

During dinner I introduced myself, after the French fashion, to the lady next to me. She does not answer—English politeness.

In the evening, another English ball.

February 4. Excursion to Monaco (see guidebooks).

In the evening, English ball. I am present, in the rôle of plague spot.

February 5. Excursion to San Remo (see guidebooks).

In the evening, English ball. Still in quarantine.

February 6. Excursion to Nice (see guidebooks).

In the evening, English ball. Bed.

February 7. Excursion to Cannes (see guidebooks).

In the evening, English ball. Have tea in my corner.

February 8. Sunday; my revenge. Am waiting for them.

They have resumed their pickled Sunday faces, and are preparing their throats for hymns.

So before dinner I slip into the drawing room, pocket the key of the piano, and say to the porter: "If the parsons want the key, tell them I have it, and ask them to see me."

During dinner various doubtful points in the Scriptures are discussed, texts elucidated, genealogies of Biblical personages evolved.

Then they go to the drawing room. The piano is approached. Sensation. Discussion; they seem thunderstruck. The white of egg nearly flies off. The head parson goes out, then returns. More discussion. Angry eyes are turned on me; here are the three parsons, bearing down on me in line. They are ambassadorial, really rather impressive. They bow. I get up. The eldest speaks:

"Monsieur, on me avé dit que vô avé pris la clef de la piano. Les dames vôdraient le avoir, pour chanté le cantique."

I answer: "Sir, I can perfectly well understand the request these ladies make, but I cannot concede to it. You are a religious man, sir; so am I, and my principles, stricter, no doubt, than yours, have determined me to oppose this profanation of the divine in which you are accustomed to indulge.

"I cannot, gentlemen, permit you to employ in the service of God an instrument used on weekdays for girls to dance to. We do not give public balls in our churches, sir, nor do we play quadrilles upon the organ. The use you make of this piano offends and disgusts me. You may take back my answer to the ladies."

The three parsons retired abashed. The ladies appeared bewildered. They sing their hymns without the piano.

February 9. Noon. The landlord has just given me notice; I am being expelled at the general request of the English people.

I meet the three parsons, who seem to be supervising my departure. I go straight up to them and bow.

"Gentlemen," I say, "you seem to have a deep knowledge of the Scriptures. I myself have more than a little scholarship. I even know a little Hebrew. Well, I should like to submit to you a case which profoundly troubles my Catholic conscience.

"You consider incest an abominable crime, do you not? Very well, the Bible gives us an instance of it which is very disturbing. Lot, fleeing from Sodom, was seduced, as you know, by his two daughters and yielded to their desires, being deprived of his wife, who had been turned into a pillar of salt. Of this appalling and double incestuous connection were born Ammon and Moab, from whom sprang two great peoples, the Ammonites and the Moabites. Well, Ruth, the reaper who disturbed the sleep of Boaz in order to make him a father, was a Moabite.

"Do you not know Victor Hugo's lines?—

> ". . . Ruth, une moabite,
> S'était couchée aux pieds de Booz, le sein nu,
> Espérant on ne sait quel rayon inconnu,
> Quand viendrait du réveil la lumière subite.

"The 'hidden ray' produced Obed, who was David's ancestor.

"Now then, was not Our Lord Jesus Christ descended from David?"

The three parsons looked at one another in consternation, and did not answer.

"You will say," I went on, "that I speak of the genealogy of Joseph, the lawful but ineffectual husband of Mary, mother of Christ. Joseph, as we all know, had nothing to do with his son's birth. So it was Joseph who was descended from a case of incest, and not the Divine Man. Granted. But I will add two further observations. The first is that Joseph and Mary, being cousins, must have had the same ancestry; the second, that it is a disgrace that we should have to read ten pages of genealogical tree for nothing.

"We ruin our eyes learning that A begat B, who begat C, who begat D, who begat E, who begat F, and when we are almost driven off our heads by this interminable rigmarole, we come to the last one, who begat nothing. That, gentlemen, may well be called the kernel of the mystery."

The three parsons, as one man, abruptly turned their backs on me, and fled.

Two P.M. I catch the train for Nice.

There the diary ended. Although these remarks reveal the author's very bad taste, uninspired wit, and uncommon coarseness, yet I think they might put certain travelers on their guard against the peril of the Englishman abroad.

I should add that there are undoubtedly charming Englishmen; I have often met them. But they are rarely our fellow guests at hotels.

A FAMILY

I was going to see my friend Simon Radevin once more, for I had not seen him for fifteen years. Formerly he was my most intimate friend, and I used to spend long, quiet and happy evenings with him. He was one of those men to whom one tells the most intimate affairs of the heart and in whom one finds, when quietly talking, rare, clever, ingenious and refined thoughts—thoughts which stimulate and capture the mind.

For years we had scarcely been separated: we had lived, traveled, thought and dreamed together, had liked the same things with the same liking, admired the same books, comprehended the same works, shivered with the same sensations and very often laughed at the same individuals, whom we understood completely by merely exchanging a glance.

Then he married—quite unexpectedly married a little girl from the provinces, who had come to Paris in search of a husband. How ever could that little, thin, insipidly fair girl, with her weak hands, her light, vacant eyes and her clear, silly voice, who was exactly like a hundred thousand marriageable dolls, have picked up that intelligent, clever young fellow? Can anyone understand these things? No doubt he had hoped for happiness, simple, quiet and long-enduring happiness, in the arms of a good, tender and faithful woman; he had seen all that in the transparent looks of that schoolgirl with light hair.

He had not dreamed of the fact that an active, living and vibrating man grows tired as soon as he has comprehended the stupid reality of a commonplace life, unless, indeed, he becomes so brutalized as to be callous to externals.

What would he be like when I met him again? Still lively, witty, lighthearted and enthusiastic, or in a state of mental torpor through provincial life? A man can change a great deal in the course of fifteen years!

The train stopped at a small station, and as I got out of the carriage a stout, a very stout man with red cheeks and a big stomach rushed up to me with open arms, exclaiming: "George!"

I embraced him, but I had not recognized him, and then I said in astonishment: "By Jove! You have not grown thin!"

And he replied with a laugh: "What did you expect? Good living, a good table and good nights! Eating and sleeping, that is my existence!"

I looked at him closely, trying to find the features I held so dear in that broad face. His eyes alone had not altered, but I no longer saw the same look in them, and I said to myself: "If looks be the reflection of the mind, the thoughts in that head are not what they used to be—those thoughts which I knew so well."

Yet his eyes were bright, full of pleasure and friendship, but they had not that clear, intelligent expression which tells better than do words the value of the mind. Suddenly he said to me:

"Here are my two eldest children." A girl of fourteen, who was almost a woman, and a boy of thirteen, in the dress of a pupil from a lycée, came forward in a hesitating and awkward manner, and I said in a low voice: "Are they yours?"

"Of course they are," he replied, laughing.

"How many have you?"

"Five! There are three more indoors."

He said that in a proud, self-satisfied, almost triumphant manner, and I felt profound pity, mingled with a feeling of vague contempt, for this vainglorious and simple reproducer of his species who spent his nights in his country house in uxorious pleasures.

I got into a carriage, which he drove himself, and we set off through the town, a dull, sleepy, gloomy town where nothing was moving in the streets save a few dogs and two or three maidservants. Here and there a shopkeeper standing at his door took off his hat, and Simon returned the salute and told me the man's name— no doubt to show me that he knew all the inhabitants personally. The thought struck me that he was thinking of becoming a candidate for the Chamber of Deputies, that dream of all who have buried themselves in the provinces.

We were soon out of the town; the carriage turned into a garden which had some pretensions to a park and stopped in front of a turreted house which tried to pass for a château.

"That is my den," Simon said, so that he might be complimented on it, and I replied that it was delightful.

A lady appeared on the steps, dressed up for a visitor, her hair done for a visitor and with phrases ready prepared for a visitor. She was no longer the light-haired insipid girl I had seen in church fifteen years previously, but a stout lady in curls and flounces, one of those ladies of uncertain age, without intellect, without any of those things which constitute a woman. In short she was a mother, a stout, commonplace mother, a human layer and brood mare, a machine of flesh which procreates, without mental care save for her children and her housekeeping book.

She welcomed me, and I went into the hall where three children, ranged according to their height, were ranked for review like firemen before a mayor. "Ah! ah! so there are the others?" said I. And Simon, who was radiant with pleasure, named them: "Jean, Sophie and Gontran."

The door of the drawing room was open. I went in, and in the depths of an easy chair I saw something trembling, a man, an old, paralyzed man. Mme. Radevin came forward and said: "This is my grandfather, monsieur; he is eighty-seven." And then she shouted into the shaking old man's ears: "This is a friend of Simon's, grandpapa."

The old gentleman tried to say "Good day" to me, and he muttered: "Oua, oua, oua," and waved his hand.

I took a seat, saying: "You are very kind, monsieur."

Simon had just come in, and he said with a laugh: "So! You have made Grandpapa's acquaintance. He is priceless, is that old man. He is the delight of the children, and he is so greedy that he almost kills himself at every meal. You have no idea what he would eat if he were allowed to do as he pleased. But you will see, you will see. He looks all the sweets over as if they were so many girls. You have never seen anything funnier; you will see it presently."

I was then shown to my room to change my dress for dinner, and hearing a great clatter behind me on the stairs, I turned round and saw that all the children were following me behind their father—to do me honor, no doubt.

My windows looked out onto a plain, a bare, interminable plain, an ocean of grass, of wheat and of oats without a clump of trees or any rising ground, a striking and melancholy picture of the life which they must be leading in that house.

A bell rang; it was for dinner, and so I went downstairs. Mme. Radevin took my arm in a ceremonious manner, and we went into the dining room. A footman wheeled in the old man's armchair, who gave a greedy and curious look at the dessert as with difficulty he turned his shaking head from one dish to the other.

Simon rubbed his hands, saying: "You will be amused." All the children understood that I was going to be indulged with the sight of their greedy grandfather and they began to laugh accordingly, while their mother merely smiled and shrugged her shoulders. Simon, making a speaking trumpet of his hands, shouted at the old man: "This evening there is sweet rice cream," and the wrinkled face of the grandfather brightened; he trembled violently all over, showing that he had understood and was very pleased. The dinner began.

"Just look!" Simon whispered. The grandfather did not like the soup and refused to eat it, but he was made to, on account of his health. The footman forced the spoon into his mouth, while the old man blew energetically, so as not to swallow the soup, which was thus scattered like a stream of water onto the table and over his neighbors. The children shook with delight at the spectacle, while their father, who was also amused, said: "Isn't the old man funny?"

During the whole meal they were all taken up solely with him. With his eyes he devoured the dishes which were put on the table and with trembling hands tried to seize them and pull them to him. They put them almost within his reach to see his useless efforts, his trembling clutches at them, the piteous appeal of his whole nature, of his eyes, of his mouth and of his nose as he smelled them. He slobbered onto his table napkin with eagerness while uttering inarticulate grunts, and the whole family was highly amused at this horrible and grotesque scene.

Then they put a tiny morsel onto his plate, which he ate with feverish gluttony in order to get something more as soon as possible. When the rice cream was brought in he nearly had a fit and groaned with greediness. Gontran called out to him: "You have eaten too much already; you will have no more." And they pretended not to give him any. Then he began to cry—cry and tremble more violently than ever, while all the children laughed. At last, however, they gave him his helping, a very small piece. As he ate the first mouthful of the pudding he made a comical and greedy noise in his throat and a movement with his neck like ducks do when they swallow too large a morsel, and then, when he had done, he began to stamp his feet so as to get more.

I was seized with pity for this pitiable and ridiculous Tantalus and interposed on his behalf. "Please, will you not give him a little more rice?"

But Simon replied: "Oh no, my dear fellow; if he were to eat too much, it might harm him at his age."

I held my tongue and thought over these words. Oh, ethics! Oh, logic! Oh, wisdom! At his age! So they deprived him of his only remaining pleasure out of

regard for his health! His health! What would he do with it, inert and trembling
wreck that he was? They were taking care of his life, so they said. His life? How
many days? Ten, twenty, fifty or a hundred? Why? For his own sake? Or to preserve, for some time longer, the spectacle of his impotent greediness in the family?

There was nothing left for him to do in this life, nothing whatever. He had one
single wish left, one sole pleasure; why not grant him that last solace constantly,
until he died?

After playing cards for a long time I went up to my room and to bed; I was
low-spirited and sad, sad, sad! I sat at my window, but I heard nothing but the
beautiful warbling of a bird in a tree, somewhere in the distance. No doubt the bird
was singing thus in a low voice during the night to lull his mate, who was sleeping
on her eggs.

And I thought of my poor friend's five children and to myself pictured him
snoring by the side of his ugly wife.

ROGER'S METHOD

I was walking with Roger one day when a street hawker bawled in our ears:

"New method of getting rid of mothers-in-law! Buy, oh buy!"

I stopped and said to my companion:

"Now that reminds me of a question I've long wanted to ask you. What is this
'Roger's method' your wife talks about so often? She jokes about it in such a gay,
confidential way that I take it to be some magic potion of which you hold the
secret. Whenever she's told of some young man who is exhausted and has lost
his nervous strength, she turns to you and says with a smile: 'Ah, you ought to
show him Roger's method.' And the funniest thing of all is that you always blush."

"Well, there's a reason for it," answered Roger. "If my wife really knew what
she was talking about, she'd stop it mighty quick. I'll tell you the story in strict
confidence. You know I married a widow with whom I was very much in love.
Now my wife has always been very free of speech, and before she became my
wife, we often had rather spicy little talks. After all, that's possible with widows;
they have the taste of it in their mouths, you see. She has a perfectly honest liking
for good smoking-room stories. The sins of the tongue do very little harm; she's
bold and I'm bashful; and before our wedding she liked to embarrass me with
jokes and questions which were not easy for me to answer. Perhaps it was her
forwardness which made me fall in love with her. And, talking of love, I was
absolutely devoted to her from head to toe, and she knew it too, the little baggage.

"We decided on a quiet wedding and no honeymoon. After the religious ceremony the witnesses were to lunch with us, and then we were to go for a drive,
returning to my house in the Rue du Helder for dinner. Well, the witnesses left,
and off we went in the carriage; I told the coachman to take us to the park. It
was the end of June, and gorgeous weather.

"As soon as we were alone, she began to laugh.

"'My dear Roger,' she said, 'now's the time to show yourself gallant. See what
you can do.'

"This invitation absolutely paralyzed me. I kissed her hand; I told her I loved her. I even had the pluck to kiss the nape of her neck twice, but the passers-by embarrassed me. And she kept on saying with a funny, provoking little air: 'What next? . . . What next? . . .'

"This 'what next?' drained all my strength away. After all, in a carriage, in the park, in broad daylight, one could hardly . . . well, you know what I mean.

"She was amused by my obvious embarrassment. From time to time she remarked: 'I'm very much afraid I've drawn a blank. You make me very uneasy.'

"I too began to be uneasy—about myself. As soon as I'm scared, I become perfectly useless.

"At dinner she was charming. In order to regain my courage, I'd sent away my servant, who embarrassed me. Oh, we were perfectly well behaved, but you know how foolish lovers are. We drank from the same glass, we ate off the same plate, with the same fork. We amused ourselves by beginning one biscuit from both ends, so that our lips met in the middle.

" 'I should like a little champagne,' she said.

"I had forgotten the bottle on the sideboard. I took it, untwisted the wires, and pressed the cork to make it fly off. It wouldn't go. Gabrielle smiled and murmured: 'An evil omen.'

"I pushed the swollen end of the cork with my thumb, I twisted it to the right, I twisted it to the left, but in vain, and suddenly I broke it right at the lip of the bottle.

" 'Poor Roger,' sighed Gabrielle.

"I took a corkscrew and screwed it into the piece left in the neck. I couldn't pull it out; I had to call Prosper back. My wife was now shrieking with laughter and saying: 'Well, well; I see I can depend on you.' She was a little tipsy.

"By the time we came to the coffee, she was half-seas over.

"A widow does not need to be put to bed with the maternal solicitude accorded to young girls, and Gabrielle calmly went to her room, saying: 'Smoke your cigar for a quarter of an hour.'

"When I rejoined her, I had lost confidence in myself, I admit. I felt unnerved, worried, ill at ease.

"I took my lawful place. She said nothing. She looked at me with a smile upon her lips, obviously desiring to chaff me. Irony, at such a moment, was the last straw. I must confess that it made me helpless—hand and foot.

"When Gabrielle observed my embarrassment, she did nothing to reassure me. On the contrary, she asked me with an air of detachment: 'Are you always as full of beans as this?'

"I could not help answering: 'Shut up; you're unbearable.'

"She went on laughing, but in an unrestrained, maudlin, exasperating way.

"True, I cut a sorry figure, and must have looked a proper fool.

"From time to time, between new fits of merriment, she would say, choking with laughter: 'Come on—be brave—buck up, you poor boy.'

"Then she continued to laugh so immoderately that she positively screamed.

"Finally I was so exhausted, so furious with myself and her, that I realized I should smack her unless I went away.

"I jumped out of bed and dressed myself quickly in a fiendish temper, without a word to her.

"She became grave at once and, seeing that I was angry, asked: 'What are you doing? Where are you going?'

"I did not answer, and went down into the street. I wanted to kill someone, to have my revenge, to do some quite insane thing. I strode straight ahead at a great rate, and suddenly the idea came to me to go off with a woman. Who knows?—it would be a trial, an experience, practice, perhaps. At all events it would be revenge. And if I were ever deceived by my wife, I should at least have deceived her first.

"I did not hesitate. I knew of a house not far from my own house; I ran there and went in like a man who throws himself into deep water to see if he can still swim.

"Well, I could swim; I swam very well. I stayed there a long time, enjoying my secret and subtle revenge. Then I found myself in the street once more, at the cool hour before dawn. I now felt calm and sure of myself, contented, tranquil, and still ready, I thought, for deeds of valor.

"I went slowly home, and quietly opened the door of my room.

"Gabrielle was reading, her elbow propped up on the pillow. She raised her head and asked in a frightened voice: 'Ah, there you are; where have you been?'

"I made no answer. I undressed with an air of assurance. I returned like a victorious lord to the place whence I had abjectedly fled.

"She was amazed, and was convinced that I had made use of some mysterious secret.

"And now on every occasion she speaks of 'Roger's method' as though she were referring to some infallible scientific device.

"Well, well, it's ten years ago now, and I'm afraid the same attempt would not have much chance of success today, for me, at any rate.

"But if any friend of yours is nervous about his wedding night, tell him of my stratagem, and tell him, too, that from twenty to thirty-five there's nothing like it for loosening the shoulders, as the squire of Brantôme would have said."

THE MARQUIS DE FUMEROL

Roger de Tourneville was sitting astride a chair in the midst of his friends and talking; he held a cigar in his hand and from time to time took a whiff and blew out a small cloud of smoke.

"We were at dinner when a letter was brought in, and my father opened it. You know my father, who thinks that he is king of France ad interim. I call him Don Quixote, because for twelve years he has been running a tilt against the windmill of the Republic without quite knowing whether it was in the name of Bourbon or of Orléans. At present he is holding the lance in the name of Orléans alone, because there is nobody else left. In any case, he thinks himself the first gentleman in France, the best known, the most influential, the head of the party, and as he is an irremovable senator, he thinks that the neighboring kings' thrones are very insecure.

"As for my mother, she is my father's inspiration, the soul of the kingdom and of religion, the right arm of God on earth and the scourge of evil thinkers.

"Well, this letter was brought in while we were at dinner. My father opened and read it, and then he said to my mother: 'Your brother is dying.' She grew very pale. My uncle was scarcely ever mentioned in the house, and I did not know him at all; all I knew from public talk was that he had led and was still leading the life of a buffoon. After having spent his fortune with an incalculable number of women, he had only retained two mistresses, with whom he was living in small apartments in the Rue des Martyrs.

"An ex-peer of France and ex-colonel of cavalry, it was said that he believed in neither God nor devil. Having no faith, therefore, in a future life, he had abused this present life in every way and had become a living wound to my mother's heart.

" 'Give me that letter, Paul,' she said, and when she had read it I asked for it in my turn. Here it is:

"MONSIEUR LE COMTE: *I think I ought to let you know that your brother-in-law, Count Fumerol, is going to die. Perhaps you would make preparations and not forget that I told you.*

"Your servant, MÉLANI.

" 'We must think,' my father murmured. 'In my position I ought to watch over your brother's last moments.'

"My mother continued: 'I will send for Abbé Poivron and ask his advice, and then I will go to my brother's with him and Roger. Stop here, Paul, for you must not compromise yourself, but a woman can and ought to do these things. For a politician in your position, it is another matter. It would be a fine thing for one of your opponents to be able to bring one of your most laudable actions up against you '

" 'You are right!' my father said. 'Do as you think best, my dear wife.'

"A quarter of an hour later the Abbé Poivron came into the drawing room, and the situation was explained to him, analyzed and discussed in all its bearings. If the Marquis de Fumerol, one of the greatest names in France, were to die without the succor of religion it would assuredly be a terrible blow to the nobility in general, to the Count de Tourneville in particular, and the freethinkers would be triumphant. The evilly disposed newspapers would sing songs of victory for six months; my mother's name would be dragged through the mire and brought into the slander of socialistic journals and my father's would be bespattered. It was impossible that such a thing should occur.

"A crusade was therefore immediately decided upon, which was to be led by the Abbé Poivron, a little fat, clean, slightly scented priest, the faithful vicar of a large church in a rich and noble quarter.

"The landau was ordered, and we three started, my mother, the curé and I, to administer the last sacraments to my uncle.

"It had been decided that first of all we should see Madame Mélani, who had written the letter and who was most likely the porter's wife or my uncle's servant, and I got down as a scout in front of a seven-storied house and went into a dark passage, where I had great difficulty in finding the porter's den. He looked at me distrustfully, and I said:

" 'Madame Mélani, if you please.'

" 'Don't know her!'

" 'But I have received a letter from her.'

" 'That may be, but I don't know her. Are you asking for some kept woman?'

" 'No, a servant probably. She wrote me about a place.'

" 'A servant—a servant? Perhaps it is the marquis's. Go and see, the fifth story on the left.'

"As soon as he found I was not asking for a kept woman he became more friendly and came as far as the passage with me. He was a tall thin man with white whiskers, the manners of a beadle, and majestic in movement.

"I climbed up a long spiral staircase whose balusters I did not venture to touch, and I gave three discreet knocks at the left-hand door on the fifth story. It opened immediately, and an enormous dirty woman appeared before me, who barred the entrance with her open arms which she placed upon the two doorposts and grumbled out:

" 'What do you want?'

" 'Are you Madame Mélani?'

" 'Yes.'

" 'I am the Viscount de Tourneville.'

" 'Ah! All right! Come in.'

" 'Well, the fact is, my mother is downstairs with a priest.'

" 'Oh! All right; go and bring them up, but take care of the porter.'

"I went downstairs and came up again with my mother who was followed by the abbé, and I fancied that I heard other footsteps behind us. As soon as we were in the kitchen, Mélani offered us chairs, and we all four sat down to deliberate.

" 'Is he very ill?' my mother asked.

" 'Oh yes, madame; he will not be here long.'

" 'Does he seem disposed to receive a visit from a priest?'

" 'Oh! I do not think so.'

" 'Can I see him?'

" 'Well—yes—madame—only—only—those young ladies are with him.'

" 'What young ladies?'

" 'Why—why—his lady friends, of course.'

" 'Oh!' Mamma had grown scarlet, and the Abbé Poivron had lowered his eyes.

"The affair began to amuse me, and I said: 'Suppose I go in first? I shall see how he receives me, and perhaps I shall be able to prepare his heart for you.'

"My mother, who did not suspect any trick, replied: 'Yes, go, my dear.'

"But a woman's voice cried out: 'Mélani!'

"The fat servant ran out and said: 'What do you want, Mademoiselle Claire?'

" 'The omelet, quickly.'

" 'In a minute, mademoiselle.' And coming back to us, she explained this summons.

" 'They ordered a cheese omelet at two o'clock as a slight collation.' And immediately she began to break eggs into a salad bowl and began to whip them vigorously, while I went out onto the landing and pulled the bell so as to announce my official arrival. Mélani opened the door to me and made me sit down in an anteroom while she went to tell my uncle that I had come. Then she came back and asked me to go in, while the abbé hid behind the door so that he might appear at the first sign.

"I was certainly very much surprised at seeing my uncle, for he was very handsome, very solemn and very elegant—the old rake.

"Sitting, almost lying, in a large armchair, his legs wrapped in blankets, with his hands, his long white hands, over the arms of the chair, he was waiting for death with biblical dignity. His white beard fell on his chest, and his hair which was also white mingled with it on his cheeks.

"Standing behind his armchair as if to defend him against me were two young women, two stout young women, who looked at me with the bold eyes of prostitutes. In their petticoats and morning wrappers, with bare arms, with coal-black hair twisted up onto the napes of their necks, with embroidered oriental slippers which showed their ankles and silk stockings, they looked like the immoral figures of some symbolical painting by the side of the dying man. Between the easy chair and the bed there was a table covered with a white cloth on which two plates, two glasses, two forks and two knives were waiting for the cheese omelet which had been ordered some time before of Mélani.

"My uncle said in a weak, almost breathless, but clear voice: 'Good morning, my child; it is rather late in the day to come to see me; our acquaintanceship will not last long.'

"I stammered out: 'It was not my fault, Uncle,' and he replied: 'No; I know that. It is your father's and mother's fault more than yours. How are they?'

" 'Pretty well, thank you. When they heard that you were ill they sent me to ask after you.'

" 'Ah! Why did they not come themselves?'

"I looked up at the two girls and said gently: 'It is not their fault if they could not come, Uncle. But it would be difficult for my father and impossible for my mother to come in here.' The old man did not reply but raised his hand toward mine, and I took the pale, cold hand and kept it in my own.

"The door opened; Mélani came in with the omelet and put it on the table, and the two girls immediately sat down in front of their plates and began to eat without taking their eyes off me.

"Then I said: 'Uncle, it would be a great pleasure for my mother to embrace you.'

" 'I also,' he murmured, 'should like——' He said no more, and I could think of nothing to propose to him, and nothing more was heard except the noise of the plates and the slight sound of eating mouths.

"Now the abbé, who was listening behind the door, seeing our embarrassment and thinking we had won the game, thought the time had come to interpose and showed himself. My uncle was so stupefied at that apparition that at first he remained motionless; then he opened his mouth as if he meant to swallow up the priest and cried out in a strong, deep, furious voice: 'What are you doing here?'

"The abbé, who was used to difficult situations, came forward, murmuring: 'I have come in your sister's name, Monsieur le Marquis; she has sent me—she would be so happy, monsieur——'

"But the marquis was not listening. Raising one hand, he pointed to the door with a proud and tragic gesture and said angrily and gasping for breath: 'Leave this room—go out—robber of souls. Go out from here, you violator of consciences! Go out from here, you picklock of dying men's doors!'

"The abbé went backward, and I, too, went to the door, beating a retreat with him, and the two little women who were avenged got up, leaving their omelet half eaten, and stood on either side of my uncle's armchair, putting their hands on his arms to calm him and to protect him against the criminal enterprises of the family and of religion.

"The abbé and I rejoined my mother in the kitchen, and Mélani again offered us chairs. 'I knew quite well that you would fail that way; we must try some other means, otherwise he will escape us.' And we began deliberating afresh, my mother being of one opinion and the abbé of another, while I held a third.

"We had been discussing the matter in a low voice for half an hour, perhaps, when a great noise of furniture being moved and of cries uttered by my uncle, more vehement and terrible even than the former had been, made us all jump up.

"Through the doors and walls we could hear him shouting: 'Go out—out—rascals—humbugs; get out, scoundrels—get out—get out!'

"Mélani rushed in but came back immediately to call me to help her, and I hastened in. Opposite to my uncle who was terribly excited by anger, almost standing up and vociferating, two men, one behind the other, seemed to be waiting till he should be dead with rage.

"By his long, ridiculous coat, his pointed English shoes, by his manners—like those of a tutor out of a situation—by his high collar, white necktie and straight hair, by his humble face, I immediately recognized the first as a Protestant minister.

"The second was the porter of the house who belonged to the Reformed religion and had followed us. Having known of our defeat, he had gone to fetch his own pastor in hope of a better fate. My uncle seemed mad with rage! If the sight of the Catholic priest, of the priest of his ancestors, had irritated the Marquis de Fumerol, who had become a freethinker, the sight of his porter's minister made him altogether beside himself. I therefore took the two men by the arm and threw them out of the room so violently that they fell up against each other twice between the two doors which led to the staircase; then I disappeared in my turn and returned to the kitchen, which was our headquarters, in order to take counsel with my mother and the abbé.

"But Mélani came back in terror, sobbing out: 'He is dying—he is dying. Come immediately—he is dying.'

"My mother rushed out. My uncle had fallen onto the carpet, full length along the floor, and did not move. I fancy he was already dead. My mother was superb at that moment! She went straight up to the two girls who were kneeling by the body and trying to raise it up and, pointing to the door with irresistible authority, dignity and majesty, she said: 'Now it is for you to go out.'

"And they went out without a protest and without saying a word. I must add that I was getting ready to turn them out as unceremoniously as I had done the parson and the porter.

"Then the Abbé Poivron administered extreme unction to my uncle with all the customary prayers and remitted all his sins, while my mother sobbed, kneeling near her brother. Suddenly, however, she exclaimed: 'He recognized me; he pressed my hand; I am sure he recognized me and thanked me! O God, what happiness!'

"Poor Mamma! If she had known or guessed to whom those thanks ought to have been addressed!

"They laid my uncle on his bed; he was certainly dead that time.

" 'Madame,' Mélani said, 'we have no sheets to bury him in; all the linen belongs to those two young ladies,' and when I looked at the omelet which they had not finished, I felt inclined to laugh and to cry at the same time. There are some strange moments and some strange sensations in life occasionally!"

"We gave my uncle a magnificent funeral with five speeches at the grave. Baron de Croiselles, the senator, showed in admirable terms that God always returns victorious into well-born souls which have gone astray for a moment. All the members of the Royalist and Catholic party followed the funeral procession with triumphant enthusiasm, speaking of that beautiful death after a somewhat restless life."

Viscount Roger ceased speaking, and those around him laughed. Then somebody said: "Bah! That is the story of all conversions *in extremis.*"

THE CASTAWAY

"Really, dear, I think you must be mad to go for a walk in the country in this weather. For the last two months you've had the oddest ideas. You drag me willynilly to the seaside, though you never thought of such a thing before in all the forty-five years of our married life. You make a point of choosing Fécamp, a melancholy hole, and now you've got such a passion for rushing about, you who could never be induced to stir out, that you want to walk about the fields on the hottest day in the year. Tell d'Apreval to go with you, since he falls in with all your whims. As for me, I'm going to have a rest."

Mme. de Cadour turned to her old friend:

"Are you coming with me, d'Apreval?"

He bowed and smiled with old-world gallantry.

"Where you go, I go," he said.

"Very well, go and get sunstroke," said M. de Cadour, and re-entered the Hôtel des Bains to lie down on his bed for an hour or two.

As soon as they were alone, the old woman and her aged companion started off. She clasped his hand and said very softly:

"At last! At last!"

"You are mad," he murmured. "I assure you you're mad. Think of the risk. If that man . . . ."

She started violently.

"Oh, Henry, don't call him 'that man.' "

"Well," he continued in a brusque voice, "if our son has any uneasy thoughts, if he suspects us, we're caught, both of us. You've done without seeing him for forty years. What's the matter with you now, then?"

They had followed the long road which leads from the sea to the town. They turned to the right to climb the hill of Etretat. The white road unwound itself before them under the blazing rain of sunlight. They walked slowly in the burning heat, taking short steps. She had taken her friend's arm and was walking straight ahead with a fixed, haunted stare.

"So you've never seen him again either?" she said.

"No, never."

"Is it possible?"

"My dear friend, don't let us begin this eternal discussion all over again. I have a wife and children, just as you have a husband; so that each of us has everything to fear from public opinion."

She did not answer. She was thinking of her lost youth, of old, unhappy, far-off things.

She had been married by her family, just as a young girl is married. She hardly knew her betrothed, a diplomat, and later she lived with him the life of any woman of fashion.

Then, however, a young man, M. d'Apreval, married like herself, fell passionately in love with her; and during a long absence of M. de Cadour on a political mission in India, she gave way to his desire.

Could she have resisted? Could she have denied herself? Would she have had the courage, the strength, not to yield?—for she loved him too. No, certainly no! It would have been too hard! She would have suffered too deeply! Life is very crafty and cruel! Can we avoid these temptations, or fly from the fate that marches upon us? How can a woman, alone, deserted, without love, without children, continue to run away from a passion surging in her? It is as though she fled from the light of the sun, to live to the end of her life in darkness.

And how plainly she remembered now the little things, his kisses, his smile, the way he stopped at the door to look at her, whenever he came to her house. What happy days, her only happy days, so soon over!

Then she discovered that she was with child; what agony!

Oh! the long terrible journey to the South, her misery, her incessant fear, her life hidden in the lonely little cottage on the shores of the Mediterranean, in the depths of the garden she dared not go beyond.

How well she remembered the long days she spent lying under an orange tree, her eyes lifted to the round flaming fruit in the green foliage! How she longed to go out, to go down to the sea, whose sweet scent came to her over the wall, whose little waves she heard upon the beach; and dreamed perpetually of its wide blue surface glittering in the sun, flecked with white sails, and rimmed by a mountain. But she dared not go through the gate. Supposing she were recognized, in this state, her altered figure crying her shame!

And the days of waiting, the last few tormenting days! The fears! The threatening pains! Then the awful night! What misery she had endured!

What a night it had been! How she had moaned and screamed! She could see even now the pale face of her lover, kissing her hand every minute, the doctor's smooth countenance, the nurse's white cap.

And what a convulsion she had felt in her heart at the child's shrill feeble cry, the first effort of a man's voice!

And the day after! The day after! The only day of her life on which she had seen and kissed her son, for never afterwards had she as much as set eyes on him!

Then, after that time, the long empty life, the thought of this child floating always in the void of her mind! She had never seen him again, not once, the little being who was her flesh and blood, her son! He had been seized, carried off, and hidden! She knew only that he was being brought up by Norman peasants, that he had himself become a peasant, that he had married, with a good dowry from the father whose name he did not know.

How many times, in the last forty years, she had longed to go away to see him, to kiss him! She did not think of him as grown up. She dreamed always of that scrap of humanity she had held for one day in her arms, clasped to her tortured body.

How many times she had said to her lover: "I can hold out no longer; I must see him; I am going!"

Always he had restrained her, held her back. She would not know how to contain herself, how to master her emotion. The man would guess, and would exploit the secret. She would be ruined.

"How is he?" she said.

"I don't know. I've never seen him again either."

"Is it possible? To have a son and not know him! To be afraid of him, to have cast him away as a disgrace!"

It was horrible.

They were still walking up the long road, oppressed by the blazing sun, still mounting the interminable hillside.

"It's like a judgment, isn't it?" she continued. "I've never had another child. I could not fight any longer my desire to see him; it's haunted me for forty years. A man couldn't understand these things. Remember that I am very near death. And I shall not have seen him again . . . never again; is it possible? How can I have waited so long? I've thought of him all my life, and what a terrible existence the thought has made it! Not once have I awakened, not once, do you hear, without my first thought being for him, for my child! How is he? Oh, how guilty I feel before him! Ought one to fear the world in such a case? I should have left all and followed him, brought him up, loved him. I should have been happier then, surely. But I did not dare. I was a coward. How I have suffered! Oh, those poor abandoned creatures, how they must hate their mothers!"

She stopped abruptly, choked with sobs. The whole valley was deserted and silent in the overpowering blaze of sunlight. Only the crickets uttered their harsh, ceaseless croak in the thin brown grass at the roadside.

"Sit down for a little," he said.

She let him lead her to the edge of the ditch, and sank down upon the grass, burying her face in her hands. Her white hair, falling in curls on each side of her face, became disheveled, and she wept, torn by her bitter grief.

He remained standing in front of her, uneasy, not knowing what to say to her.

"Come . . . be brave," he murmured.

"I will be," she said, rising to her feet. She dried her eyes and walked on with the shaky steps of an old woman.

A little further on the road ran under a group of trees which hid several houses. They could now hear the regular vibrant shock of a blacksmith's hammer on the anvil. Soon they saw, on the right, a cart halted before a kind of low house, and, in a shed, two men shoeing a horse.

M. d'Apreval went up to them.

"Pierre Benedict's farm?" he asked.

"Take the road on the left," answered one, "right by the little inn, and go straight on; it's the third after Poret's. You can't miss it."

They turned to the left. She was going very slowly now, her legs flagging, her heart thudding so violently that it snatched her breath away. At every step she muttered, as though it were a prayer:

"My God! Oh, my God!"

A violent access of emotion contracted her throat, making her totter on her feet as though she had been hamstrung.

M. d'Apreval, nervous and rather pale, said sharply:

"If you can't control yourself better, you'll betray us at once. Try to master your feelings."

"How can I?" she faltered. "My child! When I think that I'm about to see my child!"

They followed one of those little lanes that run between one farmyard and another, shut in between a double row of beeches along the roadside.

Suddenly they found themselves in front of a wooden gate shaded by a young pine tree.

"Here it is," he said.

She stopped short and looked round.

The yard, which was planted with apple trees, was large, stretching right up to the little thatched farmhouse. Facing it were the stables, the barn, the cow house, and the chicken run. Under a slate-roofed shed stood the farm vehicles, a two-wheeled cart, a wagon, and a gig. Four calves cropped the grass, beautifully green in the shade of the trees. The black hens wandered into every corner of the enclosure.

There was no sound to be heard; the door of the house was open, but no one was in view.

They entered the yard. At once a black dog leapt out of an old barrel at the foot of a large pear tree and began to bark furiously.

Against the wall of the house, on the way to the door, four beehives stood upon a plank, the straw domes in a neat line.

Halting in front of the house, M. d'Apreval shouted:

"Is anyone in?"

A child appeared, a little girl of about ten, dressed in a bodice and woollen petticoat, with bare and dirty legs. She looked timid and sullen and stood still in the doorway, as though to defend the entry.

"What d'you want?" she said.

"Is your father in?"

"No."

"Where is he?"

"I dunno."

"And your mother?"

"She's with the cows."

"Will she be back soon?"

"I dunno."

The old woman cried out abruptly in a hurried voice, as though fearing to be forcibly dragged away:

"I won't go without seeing him."

"We'll wait, my dear."

As they turned round, they caught sight of a peasant woman coming towards the house, carrying two heavy-looking tin pails on which the sun from time to time flashed a brilliant white flame.

She was lame in the right leg, and her chest was muffled in a rusty brown knitted garment, stained and bleached by rain and sun. She looked like some poor servant, dirty and wretched.

"There's Mother," said the child.

When she was near her dwelling she regarded the strangers with an evil, suspicious look; then went into the house as though she had not seen them.

She looked old; her face was hollowed, yellow, hard, the wooden face of rustics.
M. d'Apreval called her back.

"I say, we came in to ask you to sell us two glasses of milk."

Having set down her pails, she reappeared in the doorway and muttered:

"I don't sell milk."

"We're very thirsty. The lady is old and very tired. Can't we get something to
drink?"

The peasant woman stared at him with surly, uneasy eyes. At last she made up
her mind.

"Seeing you're here, I'll give you some all the same," she said, disappearing into
the house.

Then the child came out carrying two chairs, which she set under an apple tree;
and the mother came, in her turn, with two foaming cups of milk that she placed
in the visitors' hands.

She remained standing in front of them as though to keep watch on them and
guess their intentions.

"You're from Fécamp?" she said.

"Yes," replied M. d'Apreval, "we're there for the summer."

Then, after a pause, he added: "Could you sell us chickens every week?"

She hesitated, then replied:

"I might. Would you be wanting young birds?"

"Yes, young ones."

"What do you pay for them at market?"

D'Apreval, who did not know, turned to his companion: "What do you pay for
chickens, dear—young ones?"

"Four francs and four francs fifty," she faltered, her eyes full of tears.

The farmer's wife looked sideways at her, much surprised, and asked:

"Is the poor lady ill, that she's cryin'?"

He did not know what to answer, and stammered:

"No . . . No . . . She . . . she lost her watch on the way, a beautiful watch,
and it grieves her. If anyone picks it up, let us know."

Mme. Benedict thought this queer, and did not answer.

Suddenly she said:

"Here's himself."

She alone had seen him come in, for she was facing the gate. D'Apreval started
violently; Mme. de Cadour nearly fell as she turned frantically round in her chair.

A man was standing ten paces off, leading a cow at the end of a cord, bent
double, breathing hard.

"Damn the brute!" he muttered, taking no notice of the strangers.

He passed them, going towards the cowshed, in which he disappeared.

The old woman's tears were suddenly dried up; she was too bewildered for
speech or thought: her son, this was her son!

D'Apreval, stabbed by the same thought, said in a troubled voice:

"That is M. Benedict, is it not?"

"Who told you his name?" asked the farmer's wife, distrustful of them.

"The blacksmith at the corner of the highroad," he replied.

Then all were silent, their eyes fixed on the door of the cowshed, which made a sort of black hole in the wall of the building. They could see nothing inside, but vague sounds were to be heard, movements, steps muffled in the straw strewn on the ground.

He reappeared on the threshold, wiping his brow, and came back toward the house with a long slow step that jerked him up at every pace he took.

Again he passed in front of the strangers without appearing to notice them, and said to his wife:

"Go draw me a mug of cider; I be thirsty."

Then he entered his dwelling. His wife went off to the cellar leaving the two Parisians by themselves.

Mme. de Cadour was quite distracted.

"Let us go, Henry, let us go," she faltered.

D'Apreval took her arm, helped her to rise, and, supporting her with all his strength—for he felt certain that she would fall—he led her away, after throwing five francs on to one of the chairs.

As soon as they had passed through the gate, she began to sob, torn with grief, and stammering:

"Oh! Oh! Is this what you've made of him?"

He was very pale.

"I did what I could," he answered harshly. "His farm is worth eighty thousand francs. It isn't every middle-class child who has such a marriage portion."

They walked slowly back, without speaking another word. She was still sobbing; the tears ran unceasing from her eyes and rolled down her cheeks.

At last they stopped, and the pair reached Fécamp.

M. de Cadour was awaiting them for dinner. He began to laugh and cried out at sight of them:

"There you are, my wife's got a sunstroke. I'm delighted at it. Upon my word, I think she's been off her head for some time past."

Neither answered; and as the husband, rubbing his hands, inquired: "At all events, have you had a nice walk?" d'Apreval replied:

"Delightful, my dear fellow, perfectly delightful."

SAVED

The little Marquise de Rennedon came rushing in like a ball through the window. She began to laugh before she spoke, to laugh till she cried, like she had done a month previously, when she had told her friend that she had betrayed the marquis in order to have her revenge, but only once, just because he was really too stupid and too jealous.

The little Baroness de Grangerie had thrown the book which she was reading onto the sofa and looked at Annette curiously. She was already laughing herself, and at last she asked:

"What have you been doing now?"

"Oh, my dear!—my dear! It is too funny—too funny. Just fancy—I am saved!— saved!—saved!"

"How do you mean, saved?"

"Yes, saved!"

"From what?"

"From my husband, my dear, saved! Delivered! free! free! free!"

"How free? In what?"

"In what? Divorce! yes, a divorce! I have my divorce!"

"You are divorced?"

"No, not yet; how stupid you are! One does not get divorced in three hours! But I have my proofs that he has deceived me—caught in the very act—just think! —in the very act. I have got him tight."

"Oh, do tell me all about it! So he deceived you?"

"Yes, that is to say no—yes and no—I do not know. At any rate I have proofs, and that is the chief thing."

"How did you manage it?"

"How did I manage it? This is how! I have been energetic, very energetic. For the last three months he has been odious, altogether odious, brutal, coarse, a despot—in one word, vile. So I said to myself: This cannot last, I must have a divorce! But how?—for it is not very easy. I tried to make him beat me, but he would not. He vexed me from morning till night, made me go out when I did not wish to and to remain at home when I wanted to dine out; he made my life unbearable for me from one week's end to the other, but he never struck me.

"Then I tried to find out whether he had a mistress. Yes, he had one, but he took a thousand precautions in going to see her, and they could never be caught together. Guess what I did then?"

"I cannot guess."

"Oh! you could never guess. I asked my brother to procure me a photograph of the creature."

"Of your husband's mistress?"

"Yes. It cost Jacques fifteen louis, the price of an evening, from seven o'clock till midnight, including a dinner, at three louis an hour, and he obtained the photograph into the bargain."

"It appears to me that he might have obtained it anyhow by means of some artifice and without—without—without being obliged to take the original at the same time."

"Oh! she is pretty, and Jacques did not mind the least. And then I wanted some details about her, physical details about her figure, her breast, her complexion, a thousand things, in fact."

"I do not understand you."

"You shall see. When I had learned all that I wanted to know I went to a— how shall I put it?—to a man of business—you know—one of those men who transact business of all sorts—agents of—of—of publicity and complicity—one of those men—well, you understand what I mean."

"Pretty nearly, I think. And what did you say to him?"

"I said to him, showing the photograph of Clarisse (her name is Clarisse): 'Monsieur, I want a lady's maid who resembles this photograph. I require one who is pretty, elegant, neat and sharp. I will pay her whatever is necessary, and if it costs me ten thousand francs, so much the worse. I shall not require her for more than three months.'

"The man looked extremely astonished and said: 'Do you require a maid of an irreproachable character, madame?' I blushed and stammered: 'Yes, of course, for honesty.' He continued: 'And—then—as regards morals?' I did not venture to reply, so I only made a sign with my head which signified No. Then suddenly I comprehended that he had a horrible suspicion and, losing my presence of mind, I exclaimed: 'Oh! monsieur—it is for my husband, in order that I may surprise him.'

"Then the man began to laugh, and from his looks I gathered that I had regained his esteem. He even thought I was brave, and I would willingly have made a bet that at that moment he was longing to shake hands with me. However, he said to me: 'In a week, madame, I shall have what you require; I will answer for my success, and you shall not pay me until I have succeeded. So this is a photograph of your husband's mistress?'

" 'Yes, monsieur.'

" 'A handsome woman, and not too stout. And what scent?'

"I did not understand and repeated: 'What scent?'

"He smiled: 'Yes, madame, perfume is essential in tempting a man, for it unconsciously brings to his mind certain reminiscences which dispose him to action; the perfume creates an obscure confusion in his mind and disturbs and energizes him by recalling his pleasures to him. You must also try to find out what your husband is in the habit of eating when he dines with his lady, and you might give him the same dishes the day you catch him. Oh! we have got him, madame, we have got him.'

"I went away delighted, for here I had lighted on a very intelligent man.

"Three days later I saw a tall dark girl arrive at my house; she was very handsome, and her looks were modest and bold at the same time, the peculiar look of a female rake. She behaved very properly toward me, and as I did not exactly know what she was I called her mademoiselle, but she said immediately: 'Oh! pray, madame, only call me Rose.' And she began to talk.

" 'Well, Rose, you know why you have come here?'

" 'I can guess it, madame.'

" 'Very good, my girl—and that will not be too much bother for you?'

" 'Oh! madame, this will be the eighth divorce that I shall have caused; I am used to it.'

" 'Why, that is capital. Will it take you long to succeed?'

" 'Oh! madame, that depends entirely on Monsieur's temperament. When I have seen Monsieur for five minutes alone I shall be able to tell you exactly.'

" 'You will see him soon, my child, but I must tell you that he is not handsome.'

" 'That does not matter to me, madame. I have already separated some very ugly ones. But I must ask you, madame, whether you have discovered his favorite perfume?'

" 'Yes, Rose—verbena.'

" 'So much the better, madame, for I am also very fond of that scent! Can you also tell me, madame, whether Monsieur's mistress wears silk underclothing and nightdresses?'

" 'No, my child, cambric and lace.'

" 'Oh! then she is altogether of superior station, for silk underclothing is getting quite common.'

" 'What you say is quite true!'

" 'Well, madame, I will enter your service.' And so as a matter of fact she did immediately, and as if she had done nothing else all her life.

"An hour later my husband came home. Rose did not even raise her eyes to him, but he raised his eyes to her. She already smelled strongly of verbena. In five minutes she left the room, and he immediately asked me: 'Who is that girl?'

" 'Why—my new lady's maid.'

" 'Where did you pick her up?'

" 'Baroness de Grangerie got her for me with the best references.'

" 'Ah! she is rather pretty!'

" 'Do you think so?'

" 'Why, yes—for a lady's maid.'

"I was delighted, for I felt that he was already biting, and that same evening Rose said to me: 'I can now promise you that it will not take more than a fortnight. Monsieur is very easily caught!'

" 'Ah! you have tried already?'

" 'No, madame, he only asked what my name was, so that he might hear what my voice was like.'

" 'Very well, my dear Rose. Get on as quick as you can.'

" 'Do not be alarmed, madame; I shall only resist long enough not to make myself depreciated.'

"At the end of a week my husband scarcely ever went out; I saw him roaming about the house the whole afternoon, and what was most significant in the matter was that he no longer prevented me from going out. And I, I was out of doors nearly the whole day long—in order—in order to leave him at liberty.

"On the ninth day, while Rose was undressing me, she said to me with a timid air: 'It happened this morning, madame.'

"I was rather surprised, or rather overcome even, not at the part itself but at the way in which she told me, and I stammered out: 'And—and—it went off well?'

" 'Oh yes, very well, madame. For the last three days he has been pressing me, but I did not wish matters to proceed too quickly. You will tell me when you want us to be caught, madame.'

" 'Yes, certainly. Here! Let us say Thursday.'

" 'Very well, madame, I shall grant nothing more till then, so as to keep Monsieur on the alert.'

" 'You are sure not to fail?'

" 'Oh, quite sure, madame. I will excite him, so as to make him be there at the very moment which you may appoint.'

" 'Let us say five o'clock then.'

" 'Very well, madame, and where?'

" 'Well—in my bedroom.'

" 'Very good, madame, in your bedroom.'

"You will understand what I did then, my dear. I went and fetched Mamma and Papa first of all and then my uncle d'Orvelin, the president, and Monsieur Raplet, the judge, my husband's friend. I had not told them what I was going to show them, but I made them all go on tiptoe as far as the door of my room. I waited till five o'clock exactly, and oh, how my heart beat! I had made the porter come upstairs as well, so as to have an additional witness! And then—and then at the moment when the clock began to strike I opened the door wide. Ah! ah! ah! Here he was, evidently—it was quite evident, my dear. Oh, what a head! If you had only seen his head! And he turned round, the idiot! Oh, how funny he looked—I laughed, I laughed. And Papa was angry and wanted to give my husband a beating. And the porter, a good servant, helped him to dress himself before us—before us. He buttoned his braces for him—what a joke it was! As for Rose, she was perfect, absolutely perfect. She cried—oh! she cried very well. She is an invaluable girl. If you ever want her, don't forget!

"And here I am. I came immediately to tell you of the affair directly. I am free. Long live divorce!"

And she began to dance in the middle of the drawing room, while the little baroness, who was thoughtful and put out, said:

"Why did you not invite me to see it?"

THE CONFESSION

Marguerite de Thérelles was dying. Although she was only fifty-six, she looked at least seventy-five. She was gasping, paler than her sheets, shaken with frightful shudders, her face distorted, her eyes haggard, as though they saw some frightful thing.

Her elder sister, Suzanne, six years older, was sobbing on her knees at the bedside. A little table had been drawn up to the dying woman's couch, and on the tablecloth stood two lighted candles, for they were waiting for the priest, who was to administer extreme unction, the last sacrament.

The apartment wore the sinister aspect of all chambers of death, their air of despairing farewell. Medicine bottles stood on the tables, cloths lay about in corners, kicked or swept out of the way. The disordered chairs themselves looked frightened, as though they had run in every direction. For Death, the victor, was there, hidden, waiting.

The story of the two sisters was very touching. It had been told far and wide, and had filled many eyes with tears.

Suzanne, the elder, had once been deeply in love with a young man who loved her. They were betrothed and were only awaiting the day fixed for the wedding, when Henry de Sampierre died suddenly.

The young girl's despair was terrible, and she declared that she would never marry. She kept her word. She put on widow's clothes and never gave them up.

Then her sister, her little sister Marguerite, who was only twelve years old, came one morning and threw herself into her elder sister's arms, saying:

"Sister, I don't want you to be unhappy. I don't want you to cry all your life long. I will never leave you, never, never! I won't marry either. I will stay with you for ever and ever."

Suzanne kissed her, touched by her childish devotion, believing in it not at all.

But the little sister kept her word, and, despite her parents' prayers and her sister's entreaties, she never married. She was pretty, very pretty; she refused several young men who seemed to love her; she never left her sister.

They lived together all the days of their lives, without ever being parted. They lived side by side, inseparable. But Marguerite always seemed sad and depressed, more melancholy than the elder, as though crushed, perhaps, by her sublime self-sacrifice. She aged more rapidly, had white hair at the age of thirty, and, often ill, seemed the victim of some secret gnawing malady.

Now she was to be the first to die.

She had not spoken for twenty-four hours. She had only said, at the first glimmer of dawn:

"Go and fetch the priest; the time has come."

Since then she had lain still on her back, shaken with fits of shuddering, her lips trembling as though terrible words had risen from her heart and could not issue forth, her eyes wild with terror, a fearful sight.

Her sister, mad with grief, was crying brokenly, her forehead pressed against the edge of the bed, and repeating:

"Margot, my poor Margot, my little one!"

She had always called her "my little one," just as the younger had always called her "Sister."

Steps sounded on the staircase. The door opened. A choirboy appeared, followed by the old priest in his surplice. As soon as she saw him, the dying woman sat up with a convulsive movement, opened her lips, babbled two or three words, and fell to scraping her nails together as though she meant to make a hole in them.

The Abbé Simon went up to her, took her hand, kissed her on the brow, and said gently:

"God forgive you, my child; be brave, the time has come: speak."

Then Marguerite, shivering from head to foot, shaking the whole bed with her nervous movements, stammered:

"Sit down, Sister, and listen."

The priest bent down to Suzanne, still lying at the foot of the bed, raised her, placed her in an armchair, and, taking in each hand the hand of one of the sisters, murmured:

"O Lord God, give them strength, grant them thy pity!"

And Marguerite began to speak. The words came from her throat one by one, hoarse, deliberate, as though they were very weary.

"Mercy, mercy, Sister, forgive me! Oh, if you knew how all my life I have dreaded this moment! . . ."

"What have I to forgive you, little thing?" stammered Suzanne, her tears choking her. "You have given me everything, sacrificed everything for me; you are an angel."

But Marguerite interrupted her:

"Hush, hush! Let me speak . . . do not stop me . . . it is horrible . . . let me tell all . . . the whole story, without faltering. . . . Listen. . . . You remember . . . you remember . . . Henry. . . ."

Suzanne shuddered and looked at her. The younger sister continued:

"You must hear it all, if you are to understand. I was twelve, only twelve, you remember that, don't you? And I was spoiled, I did everything that came into my head! . . . Don't you remember how spoiled I was? . . . Listen. . . . The first time he came he wore high shining boots; he dismounted in front of the steps, and he apologized for his clothes, saying he had come with news for Father. You remember, don't you? . . . Don't speak . . . listen. When I saw him I was quite overcome, I thought him so handsome; and I remained standing in a corner of the drawing room all the time he was speaking. Children are strange . . . and terrible. . . . Oh, yes . . . I have dreamed of it!

"He came back . . . many times. . . . I gazed at him with all my eyes, with all my soul. . . . I was big for my age . . . and far more sophisticated than people supposed. He came again often. . . . I thought of nothing but him. I used to repeat very softly: 'Henry . . . Henry de Sampierre!'

"Then they said that he was going to marry you. It was a sore grief to me, Sister, oh, a sore, sore grief! I cried for three whole nights, without sleeping. He used to come every day, in the afternoon, after lunch, you remember, don't you? Don't speak . . . listen. You made him cakes, of which he was very fond . . . with flour, butter and milk. . . . Oh! I knew just how you made them. . . . I could make them this moment, if I had to. He would swallow them in a single mouthful, and then he would toss down a glass of wine . . . and then say: 'Delicious!' Do you remember how he used to say it?

"I was jealous, jealous. . . . The day of your wedding was drawing near. There was only a fortnight. I was going mad. I used to say to myself: 'He shall not marry Suzanne, no, I won't have it. . . . It is I who will marry him, when I am grown up. I shall never find a man I love so much! . . . And then one evening, ten days before the wedding, you went out with him to walk in front of the house, in the moonlight . . . and out there . . . under the pine tree, the big pine tree . . . he kissed you . . . held you . . . in his arms . . . for such a long time. . . . You haven't forgotten, have you? . . . It may have been the first time . . . yes . . . you were so pale when you came back into the drawing room!

"I saw you; I was there, in the copse. I grew wild with rage! If I could have done it, I would have killed you both!

"I said to myself: 'He shall not marry Suzanne, never! He shall not marry anyone. . . . I should be too unhappy. . . .' Suddenly I began to hate him terribly.

"Do you know what I did then? . . . Listen. I had seen the gardener make little balls with which to kill stray dogs. He crushed a bottle with a stone, and put the ground glass in a little ball of meat.

"I took a little medicine bottle from Mother's room, I smashed it up with a hammer, and hid the glass in my pocket. It was a glittering powder. . . . Next day, as soon as you had made the little cakes, I split them open with a knife and put the glass in. . . . He ate three of them . . . and I, too, ate one. . . . I threw the other six into the pond. . . . The two swans died three days later. . . . Don't speak . . . listen, listen. I was the only one who did not die. . . . But I have always been ill . . . listen. . . . He died . . . you know . . . listen . . . that was nothing. . . . It was afterwards, later . . . always . . . that it was most terrible . . . listen. . . .

"My life, my whole life . . . what torture! I said to myself: 'I will never leave my sister. And I will tell her all, in the hour of my death.' . . . There! And since then I have thought every moment of this hour, the hour when I shall have to tell you all. . . . Now it has come . . . it is terrible. . . . Oh! . . . Sister!

"Every moment the thought has been with me, morning and evening, day and night: 'I shall have to tell her, some day. . . .' I waited. . . . What torment! . . . It is done. . . . Do not say anything. . . . Now I am afraid. . . . I am afraid. . . . Oh, I am afraid! If I were to see him again, presently, when I am dead . . . see him again . . . do you dream of seeing him? . . . See him before you do! . . . I shall not dare. . . . I must . . . I am going to die. . . . I want you to forgive me. I want you to. . . . Without it, I cannot come into his presence. Oh, tell her to forgive me, Father, tell her. . . . I beg you. I cannot die without it. . . ."

She was silent, and lay panting, still clawing at the sheet with her shriveled fingers. . . .

Suzanne had hidden her face in her hands and did not stir. She was thinking of the man she might have loved so long! What a happy life they would have had! She saw him again, in the vanished long-ago, in the distant past forever blotted out. Oh, beloved dead, how you tear our hearts! Oh, that kiss, her only kiss! She had kept it in her soul. And then, nothing more, nothing more in all her life! . . .

Suddenly the priest stood up and cried out in a loud shaken voice:

"Mademoiselle Suzanne, your sister is dying!"

Then Suzanne let her hands fall apart and showed a face streaming with tears, and, falling upon her sister, she kissed her fiercely, stammering:

"I forgive you, I forgive you, little one. . . ."

THE DEVIL

The peasant was standing opposite the doctor, by the bedside of the dying old woman, and she, calmly resigned and quite lucid, looked at them and listened to their talking. She was going to die and she did not rebel at it, for her life was over —she was ninety-two.

The July sun streamed in at the window and through the open door and cast its hot flames onto the uneven brown clay floor which had been stamped down by four generations of clodhoppers. The smell of the fields came in also, driven by the brisk wind and parched by the noontide heat. The grasshoppers chirped themselves hoarse, filling the air with their shrill noise, like that of the wooden crickets which are sold to children at fair time.

The doctor raised his voice and said: "Honoré, you cannot leave your mother in this state; she may die at any moment." And the peasant, in great distress, replied: "But I must get in my wheat, for it has been lying on the ground a long time, and the weather is just right for it; what do you say about it, Mother?" And the dying woman, still possessed by her Norman avariciousness, replied yes with her eyes and her forehead and so urged her son to get in his wheat and to leave her to die alone. But the doctor got angry and, stamping his foot, he said: "You are no better than a brute; do you hear? And I will not allow you to do it. Do you understand? And if you must get in your wheat today, go and fetch Rapet's wife and make her look after your mother. I will have it. And if you do not obey me I will let you die like a dog when you are ill in your turn; do you hear me?"

The peasant, a tall thin fellow with slow movements who was tormented by indecision, by his fear of the doctor and his keen love for saving, hesitated, calculated and stammered out: "How much does La Rapet charge for attending sick people?"

"How should I know?" the doctor cried. "That depends upon how long she is wanted for. Settle it with her, by Jove! But I want her to be here within an hour; do you hear?"

So the man made up his mind. "I will go for her," he replied; "don't get angry, Doctor." And the latter left, calling out as he went: "Take care, you know, for I do not joke when I am angry!" And as soon as they were alone the peasant turned to his mother and said in a resigned voice: "I will go and fetch La Rapet, as the man will have it. Don't go off while I am away."

And he went out in his turn.

La Rapet, who was an old washerwoman, watched the dead and the dying of the neighborhood, and then as soon as she had sewn her customers into that linen cloth from which they would emerge no more, she went and took up her irons to smooth the linen of the living. Wrinkled like a last year's apple, spiteful, envious, avaricious with a phenomenal avarice, bent double, as if she had been broken in half across the loins by the constant movement of the iron over the linen, one might have said that she had a kind of monstrous and cynical affection for a death struggle. She never spoke of anything but of the people she had seen die, of the various kinds of deaths at which she had been present, and she related, with the greatest minuteness, details which were always the same, just like a sportsman talks of his shots.

When Honoré Bontemps entered her cottage he found her preparing the starch for the collars of the village women, and he said: "Good evening; I hope you are pretty well, Mother Rapet."

She turned her head round to look at him and said: "Fairly well, fairly well, and you?"

"Oh, as for me, I am as well as I could wish, but my mother is very sick."

"Your mother?"

"Yes, my mother!"

"What's the matter with her?"

"She is going to turn up her toes; that's what's the matter with her!"

The old woman took her hands out of the water and asked with sudden sympathy: "Is she as bad as all that?"

"The doctor says she will not last till morning."

"Then she certainly is very bad!" Honoré hesitated, for he wanted to make a few preliminary remarks before coming to his proposal, but as he could hit upon nothing, he made up his mind suddenly.

"How much are you going to ask to stop with her till the end? You know that I am not rich, and I cannot even afford to keep a servant girl. It is just that which has brought my poor mother to this state, too much work and fatigue! She used to work for ten, in spite of her ninety-two years. You don't find any made of that stuff nowadays!"

La Rapet answered gravely: "There are two prices: forty sous by day and three francs by night for the rich, and twenty sous by day and forty by night for the others. You shall pay me the twenty and forty." But the peasant reflected, for he knew his mother well. He knew how tenacious of life, how vigorous and unyielding she was. He knew, too, that she might last another week, in spite of the doctor's opinion, and so he said resolutely: "No, I would rather you would fix a price until the end. I will take my chance one way or the other. The doctor says she will die very soon. If that happens, so much the better for you and so much the worse for me, but if she holds out till tomorrow or longer, so much the better for me and so much the worse for you!"

The nurse looked at the man in astonishment, for she had never treated a death as a speculative job, and she hesitated, tempted by the idea of the possible gain. But almost immediately she suspected that he wanted to juggle her. "I can say nothing until I have seen your mother," she replied.

"Then come with me and see her."

She washed her hands and went with him immediately. They did not speak on the road; she walked with short, hasty steps, while he strode on with his long legs, as if he were crossing a brook at every step. The cows lying down in the fields, overcome by the heat, raised their heads heavily and lowed feebly at the two passers-by, as if to ask them for some green grass.

When they got near the house Honoré Bontemps murmured: "Suppose it is all over?" And the unconscious wish that it might be so showed itself in the sound of his voice.

But the old woman was not dead. She was lying on her back on her wretched bed, her hands covered with a pink cotton counterpane, horribly thin, knotty paws, like some strange animal's or like crabs' claws, hands closed by rheumatism, fatigue and the work of nearly a century which she had accomplished.

La Rapet went up to the bed and looked at the dying woman, felt her pulse, tapped her on the chest, listened to her breathing and asked her questions so as to hear her speak; then, having looked at her for some time longer, she went out of the room, followed by Honoré. His decided opinion was that the old woman would not last out the night, and he asked: "Well?" And the sick nurse replied: "Well, she may last two days, perhaps three. You will have to give me six francs, everything included."

"Six francs! Six francs!" he shouted. "Are you out of your mind? I tell you that she cannot last more than five or six hours!" And they disputed angrily for some time, but as the nurse said she would go home as the time was slipping away, and as his wheat would not come to the farmyard of its own accord, he agreed to her terms at last.

"Very well then, that is settled; six francs, including everything, until the corpse is taken out."

"That is settled, six francs."

And he went away with long strides to the wheat which was lying on the ground under the hot sun which ripens the grain, while the sick nurse returned to the house.

She had brought some work with her, for she worked without stopping by the side of the dead and dying, sometimes for herself, sometimes for the family who employed her as seamstress also, paying her rather more in that capacity. Suddenly she asked:

"Have you received the last sacrament, Mother Bontemps?"

The old peasant woman said no with her head, and La Rapet, who was very devout, got up quickly. "Good heavens, is it possible? I will go and fetch the curé," and she rushed off to the parsonage so quickly that the urchins in the street thought some accident had happened when they saw her trotting off like that.

The priest came immediately in his surplice, preceded by a choirboy, who rang a bell to announce the passage of the Host through the parched and quiet country. Some men, working at a distance, took off their large hats and remained motionless until the white vestment had disappeared behind some farm buildings; the women who were making up the sheaves stood up to make the sign of the cross;

the frightened black hens ran away along the ditch until they reached a well-known hole through which they suddenly disappeared, while a foal, which was tied up in a meadow, took fright at the sight of the surplice and began to gallop round at the length of its rope, kicking violently. The choirboy, in his red cassock, walked quickly, and the priest, the square biretta on his bowed head, followed him, muttering some prayers. Last of all came La Rapet, bent almost double, as if she wished to prostrate herself; she walked with folded hands, as if she were in church.

Honoré saw them pass in the distance, and he asked: "Where is our priest going to?" And his man, who was more acute, replied: "He is taking the sacrament to your mother, of course!"

The peasant was not surprised and said: "That is quite possible," and went on with his work.

Mother Bontemps confessed, received absolution and extreme unction, and the priest took his departure, leaving the two women alone in the suffocating cottage. La Rapet began to look at the dying woman and to ask herself whether it could last much longer.

The day was on the wane, and a cooler air came in stronger puffs, making a view of Epinal, which was fastened to the wall by two pins, flap up and down. The scanty window curtains, which had formerly been white but were now yellow and covered with flyspecks, looked as if they were going to fly off and seemed to struggle to get away, like the old woman's soul.

Lying motionless, with her eyes open, the old mother seemed to await the death which was so near and which yet delayed its coming, with perfect indifference. Her short breath whistled in her throat. It would stop altogether soon, and there would be one woman less in the world, one whom nobody would regret.

At nightfall Honoré returned, and when he went up to the bed and saw that his mother was still alive he asked: "How is she?" just as he had done formerly when she had been sick. Then he sent La Rapet away, saying to her: "Tomorrow morning at five o'clock without fail." And she replied: "Tomorrow at five o'clock."

She came at daybreak and found Honoré eating his soup, which he had made himself, before going to work.

"Well, is your mother dead?" asked the nurse.

"She is rather better, on the contrary," he replied with a malignant look out of the corners of his eyes. Then he went out.

La Rapet was seized with anxiety and went up to the dying woman, who was in the same state, lethargic and impassive, her eyes open and her hands clutching the counterpane. The nurse perceived that this might go on thus for two days, four nights, eight days, even, and her avaricious mind was seized with fear. She was excited to fury against the cunning fellow who had tricked her and against the woman who would not die.

Nevertheless, she began to sew and waited with her eyes fixed on the wrinkled face of Mother Bontemps. When Honoré returned to breakfast he seemed quite satisfied and even in a bantering humor, for he was carrying in his wheat under very favorable circumstances.

La Rapet was getting exasperated; every passing minute now seemed to her so much time and money stolen from her. She felt a mad inclination to choke this old ass, this headstrong old fool, this obstinate old wretch—to stop that short, rapid breath, which was robbing her of her time and money, by squeezing her throat a little. But then she reflected on the danger of doing so, and other thoughts came into her head, so she went up to the bed and said to her: "Have you ever seen the devil?"

Mother Bontemps whispered: "No."

Then the sick nurse began to talk and to tell her tales likely to terrify her weak and dying mind. "Some minutes before one dies the devil appears," she said, "to all. He has a broom in his hand, a saucepan on his head, and he utters loud cries. When anybody has seen him all is over, and that person has only a few moments longer to live"; and she enumerated all those to whom the devil had appeared that year: Josephine Loisel, Eulalie Ratier, Sophie Padagnau, Séraphine Grospied.

Mother Bontemps, who was at last most disturbed in mind, moved about, wrung her hands and tried to turn her head to look at the other end of the room. Suddenly La Rapet disappeared at the foot of the bed. She took a sheet out of the cupboard and wrapped herself up in it; then she put the iron pot onto her head so that its three short, bent feet rose up like horns, took a broom in her right hand and a tin pail in her left, which she threw up suddenly so that it might fall to the ground noisily.

Certainly when it came down it made a terrible noise. Then, climbing onto a chair, the nurse showed herself, gesticulating and uttering shrill cries into the pot which covered her face, while she menaced the old peasant woman, who was nearly dead, with her broom.

Terrified, with a mad look on her face, the dying woman made a superhuman effort to get up and escape; she even got her shoulders and chest out of bed; then she fell back with a deep sigh. All was over, and La Rapet calmly put everything back into its place; the broom into the corner by the cupboard, the sheet inside it, the pot onto the hearth, the pail onto the floor and the chair against the wall. Then with a professional air she closed the dead woman's enormous eyes, put a plate on the bed and poured some holy water into it, dipped the twig of boxwood into it and, kneeling down, she fervently repeated the prayers for the dead, which she knew by heart, as a matter of business.

When Honoré returned in the evening, he found her praying. He calculated immediately that she had made twenty sous out of him, for she had only spent three days and one night there, which made five francs altogether, instead of the six which he owed her.

THE MOTHER OF MONSTERS

I was reminded of this horrible story and this horrible woman on the sea front the other day, as I stood watching—at a watering place much frequented by the wealthy—a lady well known in Paris, a young, elegant, and charming girl, loved and respected by all who know her.

My story is now many years old, but it is impossible to forget such things.

I had been invited by a friend to make a long stay with him in a small country town. In order to do the honors of the district, he took me about all over the place; made me see the most celebrated views, the manor houses and castles, the local industries, the ruins; he showed me the monuments, the churches, the old carved doors, the trees of specially large size or uncommon shape, the oak of St. Andrew and the Roqueboise yew.

When, with exclamations of gratified enthusiasm, I had inspected all the curiosities in the district, my friend confessed, with every sign of acute distress, that there was nothing more to visit. I breathed again. I should be able, at last, to enjoy a little rest under the shade of the trees. But suddenly he exclaimed:

"Why, no, there is one more. There's the mother of monsters."

"And who," I asked, "is the mother of monsters?"

He answered: "She is a horrible woman, a perfect demon, a creature who every year deliberately produces deformed, hideous, frightful children, veritable monsters, and sells them to peepshow men.

"The men who follow this ghastly trade come from time to time to discover whether she has brought forth any fresh abortion, and if they like the look of the object, they pay the mother and take it away with them.

"She has eleven of these offspring. She is rich.

"You think I'm joking, making it all up, exaggerating. No, my friend, I'm only telling you the truth, the literal truth.

"Come and see this woman. I'll tell you afterwards how she became a monster-factory."

He took me off to the outskirts of the town.

She lived in a nice little house by the side of the road. It was pretty and well kept. The garden was full of flowers, and smelled delicious. Anyone would have taken it for the home of a retired lawyer.

A servant showed us into a little parlor, and the wretched creature appeared.

She was about forty, tall, hard-featured, but well built, vigorous, and wealthy, the true type of robust peasantry, half animal and half woman.

She was aware of the disapproval in which she was held, and seemed to receive us with malignant humility.

"What do the gentlemen want?" she inquired.

My friend replied: "We have been told that your last child is just like any other child, and not in the least like his brothers. I wanted to verify this. Is it true?"

She gave us a sly glance of anger and answered:

"Oh, no, sir, oh dear no! He's even uglier, mebbe, than the others. I've no luck, no luck at all, they're all that way, sir, all like that, it's something cruel; how can the good Lord be so hard on a poor woman left all alone in the world!"

She spoke rapidly, keeping her eyes lowered, with a hypocritical air, like a sacred wild beast. She softened the harsh tone of her voice, and it was amazing to hear these tearful high-pitched words issuing from that great bony body, with its coarse angular strength, made for violent gesture and wolfish howling.

"We should like to see your child," my friend asked.

She appeared to blush. Had I perhaps been mistaken? After some moments of silence she said, in a louder voice: "What would be the use of that?"

She had raised her head, and gave us a swift, burning glance.

"Why don't you wish to show him to us?" answered my friend. "There are many people to whom you show him. You know whom I mean."

She started up, letting loose the full fury of her voice.

"So that's what you've come for, is it? Just to insult me? Because my bairns are like animals, eh? Well, you'll not see them, no, no, no, you sha'n't. Get out of here. I know you all, the whole pack of you, bullying me about like this!"

She advanced towards us, her hands on her hips. At the brutal sound of her voice, a sort of moan, or rather a mew, a wretched lunatic screech, issued from the next room. I shivered to the marrow. We drew back before her.

In a severe tone my friend warned her:

"Have a care, She-devil"—the people all called her She-devil—"have a care, one of these days this will bring you bad luck."

She trembled with rage, waving her arms, mad with fury, and yelling:

"Get out of here, you! What'll bring me bad luck? Get out of here, you pack of unbelieving dogs, you!"

She almost flew at our throats; we fled, our hearts contracted with horror.

When we were outside the door, my friend asked:

"Well, you've seen her; what do you say to her?"

I answered: "Tell me the history of the brute."

And this is what he told me, as we walked slowly back along the white highroad, bordered on either side by the ripe corn that rippled like a quiet sea under the caress of a small gentle wind.

The girl had once been a servant on a farm, a splendid worker, well behaved and careful. She was not known to have a lover, and was not suspected of any weakness.

She fell, as they all do, one harvest night among the heaps of corn, under a stormy sky, when the still, heavy air is hot like a furnace, and the brown bodies of the lads and girls are drenched with sweat.

Feeling soon after that she was pregnant, she was tormented with shame and fear. Desirous at all costs of hiding her misfortune, she forcibly compressed her belly by a method she invented, a horrible corset made of wood and ropes. The more the growing child swelled her body, the more she tightened the instrument of torture, suffering agony, but bearing her pain with courage, always smiling and active, letting no one see or suspect anything.

She crippled the little creature inside her, held tightly in that terrible machine; she crushed him, deformed him, made a monster of him. The skull was squeezed almost flat and ran to a point, with the two great eyes jutting right out from the forehead. The limbs, crushed against the body, were twisted like the stem of a vine, and grew to an inordinate length, with the fingers and toes like spiders' legs.

The trunk remained quite small and round like a nut.

She gave birth to it in the open fields one spring morning.

When the women weeders, who had run to her help, saw the beast which was appearing, they fled shrieking. And the story ran round the neighborhood that she had brought a demon into the world. It was then that she got the name "She-devil."

She lost her place. She lived on charity, and perhaps on secret love, for she was a fine-looking girl, and not all men are afraid of hell.

She brought up her monster, which, by the way, she hated with a savage hatred, and which she would perhaps have strangled had not the curé, foreseeing the likelihood of such a crime, terrified her with threats of the law.

At last one day some passing showmen heard tell of the frightful abortion and asked to see it, intending to take it away if they liked it. They did like it, and paid the mother five hundred francs down for it. Ashamed at first, she did not want to let them see a beast of this sort; but when she discovered that it was worth money, that these people wanted it, she began to bargain, to dispute it penny by penny, inflaming them with the tale of her child's deformities, raising her prices with peasant tenacity.

In order not to be cheated, she made a contract with them. And they agreed to pay her four hundred francs a year as well, as though they had taken this beast into their service.

The unhoped-for good fortune crazed the mother, and after that she never lost the desire to give birth to another phenomenon, so that she would have a fixed income like the upper classes.

As she was very fertile, she succeeded in her ambition and apparently became expert at varying the shapes of her monsters according to the pressure they were made to undergo during the period of her pregnancy.

She had them long and short, some like crabs and others like lizards. Several died, whereat she was deeply distressed.

The law attempted to intervene, but nothing could be proved. So she was left to manufacture her marvels in peace.

She now has eleven of them alive, which bring her in from five to six thousand francs, year in and year out. One only is not yet placed, the one she would not show us. But she will not keep it long, for she is known now to all the circus proprietors in the world, who come from time to time to see whether she has anything new.

She even arranges auctions between them, when the creature in question is worth it.

My friend was silent. A profound disgust surged in my heart, a furious anger, and regret that I had not strangled the brute when I had her in my hands.

"Then who is the father?" I asked.

"Nobody knows," he replied. "He or they have a certain modesty. He, or they, remain concealed. Perhaps they share in the spoils."

I had thought no more of that far-off adventure until the other day, at a fashionable watering place, when I saw a charming elegant lady, the most skillful of coquettes, surrounded by several men who have the highest regard for her.

I walked along the front, arm in arm with my friend, the local doctor. Ten minutes later I noticed a nurse looking after three children who were rolling about on the sand.

A pathetic little pair of crutches lay on the ground. Then I saw that the three children were deformed, hunchbacked and lame; hideous little creatures.

The doctor said to me: "Those are the offspring of the charming lady you met just now."

I felt a profound pity for her and for them.

"The poor mother!" I cried. "How does she still manage to laugh?"

"Don't pity her, my dear fellow," replied my friend. "It's the poor children who are to be pitied. That's the result of keeping the figure graceful right up to the last day. Those monsters are manufactured by corsets. She knows perfectly well that she's risking her life at that game. What does she care, so long as she remains pretty and seductive?"

And I remembered the other, the peasant woman, the She-devil, who sold hers.

THE RABBIT

Old Lecacheur appeared at the door of his house at his usual hour, between five and a quarter past five in the morning, to look after his men who were going to work.

With a red face, only half awake, his right eye open and the left nearly closed, he was buttoning his braces over his fat stomach with some difficulty, all the time looking into every corner of the farmyard with a searching glance. The sun was darting his oblique rays through the beech trees by the side of the ditch and the apple trees outside, making the cocks crow on the dunghill and the pigeons coo on the roof. The smell of the cow stalls came through the open door, mingling in the fresh morning air with the pungent odor of the stable where the horses were neighing, with their heads turned toward the light.

As soon as his trousers were properly fastened Lecacheur came out and went first of all toward the hen house to count the morning's eggs, for he had been suspecting thefts for some time. But the servant girl ran up to him with lifted arms and cried:

"Master! Master! They have stolen a rabbit during the night."

"A rabbit?"

"Yes, master, the big gray rabbit, from the hutch on the left." Whereupon the farmer quite opened his left eye and said simply:

"I must see that."

And off he went to inspect it. The hutch had been broken open and the rabbit was gone. Then he became thoughtful, closed his left eye again, scratched his nose and after a little consideration said to the frightened girl who was standing stupidly before him:

"Go and fetch the gendarmes; say I expect them as soon as possible."

Lecacheur was mayor of the village, Pairgry-le-Gras, and ruled it like a tyrant on account of his money and position. As soon as the servant had disappeared in the direction of the village, which was only about five hundred yards off, he went into the house to have his morning coffee and to discuss the matter with his wife. He found her on her knees in front of the fire, trying to get it to burn up quickly. As soon as he got to the door he said:

"Somebody has stolen the gray rabbit."

She turned round so quickly that she found herself sitting on the floor and, looking at her husband with distressed eyes, she said:

"What is it, Cacheur! Somebody has stolen a rabbit?"

"The big gray one."

She sighed. "How sad! Who can have done it?"

She was a little, thin, active, neat woman, who knew all about farming. But Lecacheur had his own ideas about the matter.

"It must be that fellow Polyte."

His wife got up suddenly and said in a furious voice:

"He did it! He did it! You need not look for anyone else. He did it! You have said it, Cacheur!"

All her peasant's fury, all her avarice, all the rage of a saving woman against the man of whom she had always been suspicious and against the girl whom she had always suspected, could be seen in the contraction of her mouth, in the wrinkles in her cheeks and in the forehead of her thin, exasperated face.

"And what have you done?" she asked.

"I have sent for the gendarmes."

This Polyte was a laborer who had been employed on the farm for a few days and had been dismissed by Lecacheur for an insolent answer. He was an old soldier and was supposed to have retained his habits of marauding and debauchery from his campaigns in Africa. He did anything for a livelihood, but whether working as a mason, a navvy, a reaper, whether he broke stones or lopped trees, he was always lazy. So he remained in no position long and had, at times, to change his neighborhood to obtain work.

From the first day that he came to the farm Lecacheur's wife had detested him, and now she was sure that he had committed the robbery.

In about half an hour the two gendarmes arrived. Brigadier Sénateur was very tall and thin, and Gendarme Lenient, short and fat. Lecacheur made them sit down and told them the affair, and then they went and saw the scene of the theft, in order to verify the fact that the hutch had been broken open and to collect all the proofs they could. When they got back to the kitchen the mistress brought in some wine, filled their glasses and asked with a distrustful look:

"Shall you catch him?"

The brigadier, who had his sword between his legs, appeared thoughtful. Certainly he was sure of taking him if he was pointed out to him, but if not, he could not himself answer for being able to discover him. After reflecting for a long time he put this simple question:

"Do you know the thief?"

And Lecacheur replied with a look of Normandy slyness in his eyes:

"As for knowing him, I do not, as I did not see him commit the robbery. If I had seen him I should have made him eat it raw, skin and flesh, without a drop of cider to wash it down. As for saying who it is, I cannot, although I believe it is that good-for-nothing Polyte."

Then he related at length his troubles with Polyte, his leaving his service, his bad reputation, things which had been told him, accumulating insignificant and minute proofs. Then the brigadier, who had been listening very attentively while he emptied his glass and filled it again, turned to his gendarme with an indifferent air and said:

"We must go and look in the cottage of Severin's wife." At which the gendarme smiled and nodded three times.

Then Mme. Lecacheur came to them and very quietly, with all a peasant's cunning, questioned the brigadier in her turn. The shepherd Severin, a simpleton, a sort of brute who had been brought up from youth among his bleating flocks and who knew of scarcely anything besides them in the world, had nevertheless preserved the peasant's instinct for saving at the bottom of his heart. For years and years he had hidden in hollow trees and crevices in the rocks all that he earned, either as shepherd or by curing the fractures of animals (for the bonesetter's secret had been handed down to him by the old shepherd whose place he took) by touch or advice, for one day he bought a small property consisting of a cottage and a field for three thousand francs.

A few months later it became known that he was going to marry a servant notorious for her bad morals, the innkeeper's servant. The young fellows said that the girl, knowing that he was pretty well off, had been to his cottage every night and had taken him, bewitched him, led him on to matrimony little by little, night by night.

And then, having been to the mayor's office and to church, she lived in the house which her man had bought, while he continued to tend his flocks day and night on the plains.

And the brigadier added:

"Polyte has been sleeping with her for three weeks, for the thief has no place of his own to go to!"

The gendarme made a little joke:

"He takes the shepherd's blankets."

Mme. Lecacheur, seized by a fresh access of rage, of rage increased by a married woman's anger against debauchery, exclaimed:

"It is she, I am sure. Go there. Ah! The blackguard thieves!"

But the brigadier was quite unmoved.

"A minute," he said. "Let us wait until twelve o'clock; as Polyte goes and dines there every day, I shall catch them with it under their noses."

The gendarme smiled, pleased at his chief's idea, and Lecacheur also smiled now, for the affair of the shepherd struck him as very funny: deceived husbands are always amusing.

Twelve o'clock had just struck when the brigadier, followed by his man, knocked gently three times at the door of a small, lonely house situated at the corner of a wood, some five hundred yards from the village.

They stood close against the wall so as not to be seen from within and waited. As nobody answered, the brigadier knocked again in a minute or two. It was so quiet that the house seemed uninhabited, but Lenient, the gendarme, who had very quick ears, said that he heard somebody moving about inside. Sénateur got angry. He would not allow anyone to resist the authority of the law for a moment and, knocking at the door with the hilt of his sword, he cried out:

"Open the door in the name of the law."

As this order had no effect, he roared out:

"If you do not obey I shall smash the lock. I am the brigadier of the gendarmery, by God! Here, Lenient."

He had not finished speaking when the door opened and Sénateur saw before him a fat girl with a very red color, blowzy, with pendent breasts, big stomach and broad hips, a sort of sanguine and sensual female, the wife of the shepherd Severin. He entered the cottage.

"I have come to pay you a visit, as I want to make a little search," he said, and he looked about him. On the table there was a plate, a jug of cider and a glass half full, which proved that a meal had been going on. Two knives were lying side by side, and the shrewd gendarme winked at his superior officer.

"It smells good," the latter said.

"One might swear that it was stewed rabbit," Lenient added, much amused.

"Will you have a glass of brandy?" the peasant woman asked.

"No, thank you; I only want the skin of the rabbit that you are eating."

She pretended not to understand, but she was trembling.

"What rabbit?"

The brigadier had taken a seat and was calmly wiping his forehead.

"Come, come, you are not going to try and make us believe that you live on couch grass. What were you eating there all by yourself for your dinner?"

"I? Nothing whatever, I swear to you. A mite of butter on my bread."

"You are a novice, my good woman—a *mite of butter on your bread*. You are mistaken; you ought to have said: a mite of butter on the rabbit. By God, your butter smells good! It is special butter, extra-good butter, butter fit for a wedding, certainly not household butter!"

The gendarme was shaking with laughter and repeated:

"Not household butter, certainly."

As Brigadier Sénateur was a joker, all the gendarmes had grown facetious, and the officer continued:

"Where is your butter?"

"My butter?"

"Yes, your butter."

"In the jar."

"Then where is the butter jar?"

"Here it is."

She brought out an old cup, at the bottom of which there was a layer of rancid salt butter. The brigadier smelled it and said with a shake of his head:

"It is not the same. I want the butter that smells of the rabbit. Come, Lenient, open your eyes; look under the sideboard, my good fellow, and I will look under the bed."

Having shut the door, he went up to the bed and tried to move it, but it was fixed to the wall and had not been moved for more than half a century, apparently. Then the brigadier stooped and made his uniform crack. A button had flown off.

"Lenient," he said.

"Yes, Brigadier?"

"Come here, my lad, and look under the bed; I am too tall. I will look after the sideboard."

He got up and waited while his man executed his orders.

Lenient, who was short and stout, took off his kepi, laid himself on his stomach and, putting his face on the floor, looked at the black cavity under the bed. Then suddenly he exclaimed:

"All right, here we are!"

"What have you got? The rabbit?"

"No, the thief."

"The thief! Pull him out, pull him out!"

The gendarme had put his arms under the bed and laid hold of something. He pulled with all his might, and at last a foot shod in a thick boot appeared, which he was holding in his right hand. The brigadier grabbed it, crying:

"Pull, pull!"

And Lenient, who was on his knees by that time, was pulling at the other leg. But it was a hard job, for the prisoner kicked out hard and arched up his back across the bed.

"Courage! Courage! Pull! Pull!" Sénateur cried, and they pulled with all their strength—so hard that the wooden bar gave way and the victim came out as far as his head. At last they got that out also and saw the terrified and furious face of Polyte, whose arms remained stretched out under the bed.

"Pull away!" the brigadier kept on exclaiming. Then they heard a strange noise as the arms followed the shoulders and the hands the arms. In the hands was the handle of a saucepan and at the end of the handle the pan itself, which contained stewed rabbit.

"Good lord! Good lord!" the brigadier shouted in his delight, while Lenient took charge of the man. The rabbit's skin, an overwhelming proof, was discovered under the mattress, and the gendarmes returned in triumph to the village with their prisoner and their booty.

A week later, as the affair had made much stir, Lecacheur, on going into the *mairie* to consult the schoolmaster, was told that the shepherd Severin had been waiting for him for more than an hour. He found him sitting on a chair in a corner with his stick between his legs. When he saw the mayor he got up, took off his cap and said:

"Good morning, Maître Cacheur," and then he remained standing, timid and embarrassed.

"What do you want?" the former said.

"This is it, monsieur. Is it true that somebody stole one of your rabbits last week?"

"Yes, it is quite true, Severin."

"Who stole the rabbit?"

"Polyte Ancas, the laborer."

"Right! Right! And is it also true that it was found under my bed?"

"What do you mean, the rabbit?"

"The rabbit and then Polyte."

"Yes, my poor Severin, quite true, but who told you?"

"Pretty well everybody. I understand! And I suppose you know all about marriages,[1] as you marry people?"

"What about marriage?"

"With regard to one's rights."

"What rights?"

"The husband's rights and then the wife's rights."

"Of course I do."

"Oh! Then just tell me, M'sieu Cacheur, has my wife the right to go to bed with Polyte?"

"What do you mean by going to bed with Polyte?"

"Yes, has she any right before the law, and seeing that she is my wife, to go to bed with Polyte?"

"Why, of course not, of course not."

"If I catch him there again shall I have the right to thrash him and her also?"

"Why—why—why, yes."

"Very well, then; I will tell you why I want to know. One night last week, as I had my suspicions, I came in suddenly, and they were not behaving properly. I chucked Polyte out to go and sleep somewhere else, but that was all, as I did not

[1]In France the civil marriage is compulsory.

know what my rights were. This time I did not see them; I only heard of it from others. That is over, and we will not say any more about it; but if I catch them again—by God! if I catch them again—I will make them lose all taste for such nonsense, Maître Cacheur, as sure as my name is Severin."

THE KEEPER

After dinner we were recounting shooting adventures and accidents.

An old friend of ours, M. Boniface, a great slayer of beasts and drinker of wine, a strong and debonair fellow, full of wit, sense, and a philosophy at once ironical and resigned, which revealed itself in biting humor and never in melancholy, spoke abruptly:

"I know a shooting story, or rather a shooting drama, that's queer enough. It's not in the least like the usual tale of the kind, and I've never told it before; I didn't suppose that anyone would be interested in it.

"It's not very pleasant, if you know what I mean. I mean to say that it does not possess the kind of interest which affects, or charms, or agreeably excites.

"Anyhow, here it is."

"In those days I was about thirty-five, and mad on shooting. At that time I owned a very lovely piece of land on the outskirts of Jumièges, surrounded by forests and excellent for hares and rabbits. I used only to spend four or five days there a year, by myself, the limited accommodation not permitting of my bringing a friend.

"I had installed there as keeper an old retired policeman, a good man, hottempered and very conscientious in the performance of his duties, a terror to poachers and afraid of nothing. He lived by himself, some way out of the village, in a little house, or rather a hovel, consisting of two ground-floor rooms, a kitchen and a small storeroom, and of two more rooms on the first floor. One of these, a sort of box just large enough for a bed, a chest of drawers, and a chair, was reserved for me.

"Old Cavalier occupied the other. In saying that he was alone in this cottage, I expressed myself badly. He had taken with him his nephew, a hobbledehoy of fourteen, who fetched the provisions from the village, two miles off, and helped the old man in his daily duties.

"This youth was tall, thin, and somewhat stooping; his hair was so pale a yellow that it looked like the down on a plucked hen and so thin that he appeared to be bald. He had enormous feet and colossal hands, the hands of a giant.

"He squinted a little and never looked anyone straight in the face. He gave one the impression that he occupied in the human race the place that the musksecreting beasts hold in the animal kingdom. He was a polecat or a fox, was that boy.

"He slept in a sort of hole at the top of the little staircase which led to the two rooms. But during my short visits to the Pavilion—I called this hovel the Pavilion—Marius gave up his nest to an old woman from Ecorcheville named Céleste, who came in to cook for me, old Cavalier's concoctions being by no means good enough.

"Now you know the characters and the setting. Here is the story.

"It was in 1854, the fifteenth of October: I remember the date, and I shall never forget it.

"I left Rouen on horseback, followed by my dog, a big Dalmatian from Poitou, broad-chested and heavy-jowled, who rummaged about in the bushes like a Pont Audemer spaniel.

"My bag was slung on the saddle behind me, and I carried my gun by the sling. It was a cold day, with a high and mournful wind, and dark clouds rode in the sky.

"While ascending the slope of Canteleu I gazed at the broad valley of the Seine, through which the river meandered with serpentine twists as far as the horizon. On the left all the steeples of Rouen lifted to the sky, and on the right the view was blocked by the far-off tree-clad hills. I passed through the forest of Roumare, going now at a trot, now at a walking pace, and at about five o'clock I arrived at the Pavilion, where old Cavalier and Céleste were waiting for me.

"For the last ten years, at the same season, I had been presenting myself in the same way, and the same mouths welcomed me with the same words:

"'Good day, your honor. Your honor's health is good?'

"Cavalier had scarcely altered at all. He stood up to the passage of time like an old tree; but Céleste, especially in the last four years, was becoming almost unrecognizable.

"She was bent nearly double, and, although still active, she walked with the upper part of her body so bowed that it formed almost a right angle with her legs.

"The old woman was very devoted to me; she always seemed much affected at seeing me again, and whenever I left she used to say:

"'Think, this is maybe the last time, your honor.'

"And the poor servant's heartbroken, frightened farewell, her desperate resignation to inevitable death, so surely close upon her, stirred my heart strangely each year.

"I dismounted, and while Cavalier, with whom I had shaken hands, was leading my horse to the little shed which did duty for a stable, I entered the kitchen, which also served as the dining room, followed by Céleste.

"Then the keeper joined us again. Right from the first I saw that his face had not its customary expression. He seemed preoccupied, ill at ease, worried.

"'Well, Cavalier,' I said to him, 'is everything going all right?'

"'Yes and no,' he murmured. 'There's something that isn't at all all right.'

"'Well, what is it, man?' I asked. 'Tell me all about it.'

"But he shook his head.

"'No, monsieur, not yet. I don't want to pester you with my worries like this, when you've only just arrived.'

"I insisted, but he absolutely refused to tell me about it before dinner. His expression, however, told me that it was serious.

"Not knowing what to say to him, I asked:

"'And what about the game? Have we plenty?'

"'Oh, yes, there's plenty of game, plenty. I kept my eyes open, thanks be to God.'

"He said this with such desperate seriousness that it was positively comical. His large gray mustaches looked ready to fall off his lips.

"Suddenly I realized that I had not yet seen his nephew.

" 'And Marius, where has he gone to? Why hasn't he shown up?'

"The keeper started; he wheeled sharply and faced me.

" 'Well, monsieur, I'd sooner tell you the story straight out; yes, I'd sooner do that. It's about him that this thing's on my mind.'

" 'Ah. Well, where is he?'

" 'In the stable, monsieur; I'm expecting him to turn up any moment.'

" 'Well, what has he been doing?'

" 'This is the story, monsieur . . .'

"But the keeper hesitated none the less, his voice was changed and shook, his face was suddenly graven with deep wrinkles, the wrinkles of old age.

"Slowly he continued:

" 'Here it is. I noticed this winter that someone was laying snares in the wood of Roseraies, but I couldn't catch the man. I spent night after night there, monsieur; but no good. And during that time snares began to appear on the Ecorcheville side. I grew thin with rage. But as for catching the thief, impossible! You would have said the scoundrel was warned beforehand of my visits and my plans.

"But one day, while brushing Marius's breeches, his Sunday breeches, I found forty sous in his pocket. Now where had the boy got that from?

" 'I thought it over for a week, and I noticed that he was in the habit of going out; he used to go out just when I came back to bed, monsieur.

" 'Then I watched him, but I hadn't a doubt of the truth, oh, not a doubt of it. And one morning, when I had gone to bed just before he went off, I promptly got up again, and tracked him. And as for tracking, there's no one to touch me, monsieur.

" 'And I caught him, monsieur, setting snares on your land—Marius, my nephew, your keeper's nephew!

" 'My blood rushed through my body in one flood, and I nearly killed him on the spot. I gave him such a thrashing—— Oh, Lord! how I did beat him; and I promised him that when you came he would have another from me in your presence, for the sake of the lesson.

" 'That's all. I've gone thin with grief. You know what it means to be crossed like that. But what would you have done, now? He's got no father or mother. I'm the only one of his own blood the boy's got; I've brought him up; I couldn't turn him out, could I?

" 'But I've told him that if he does it again, it's the end, the end, more's the pity. There! Was I right, monsieur?'

"I held out my hand to him, and replied:

" 'You were right, Cavalier; you're a good fellow.'

"He rose.

" 'Thank you, monsieur. Now I'll go and fetch him; he must be punished, for the sake of the lesson.'

"I knew that it was useless to attempt to dissuade the old man from any plan he had already formed. So I let him have his own way.

"He went off to fetch the lad, and brought him back, holding him by the ear.

"I was seated on a cane chair, wearing the grave visage of a judge. Marius appeared to me to have grown; he was even uglier than the year before, with his evil, cunning expression. And his great hands looked monstrous.

"His uncle shoved him in front of me, and said in his military voice:

" 'Ask pardon from the master.'

"The boy did not utter a word.

"Then, seizing him under the arms, the ex-policeman lifted him off the ground and began to thrash him with such violence that I got up to stop the blows.

"The child was now bawling:

" 'Mercy!—mercy!—mercy! I promise . . .'

"Cavalier lowered him on to the ground and, forcing him on to his knees by pressing upon his shoulders, said:

" 'Ask pardon.' "

" 'I ask pardon,' murmured the young scamp, with downcast eyes.

"Thereupon his uncle lifted him to his feet and dismissed him with a blow which nearly knocked him down again.

"He made off, and I did not see him again that evening.

"But Cavalier seemed terribly distressed.

" 'He's a bad character,' he said, and throughout dinner he kept on saying:

" 'Oh! how it grieves me, monsieur; you don't know how it grieves me.'

"I tried to console him, but in vain. I went up to bed early, so as to be out shooting at break of day. My dog was already asleep upon the floor at the foot of my bed, when I blew out my candle.

"I was awakened in the middle of the night by the furious barking of Bock. I realized at once that my room was full of smoke. I leaped out of bed, lit the light, ran to the door, and opened it. A swirl of flames entered. The house was on fire.

"I promptly shut the strong oak door again, and, dragging on my breeches, I first of all lowered my dog from the window with a rope made of twisted sheets; then, throwing down my clothes, my game bag, and my gun, I made my escape in the same way.

"Then I began to shout with all my might:

" 'Cavalier! Cavalier! Cavalier!'

"But the keeper did not wake; the old policeman was a heavy sleeper.

"Through the lower windows I saw that the whole ground floor was nothing but a blazing furnace, and I saw too that it had been filled with straw to assist the fire.

"So it had been purposely fired!

"I resumed my furious shouts:

" 'Cavalier!'

"Then the thought came to me that the smoke was suffocating him. An idea leaped into my mind; slipping two cartridges into my gun, I fired straight at his window.

"The six panes crashed into the room in a welter of splintered glass. This time the old man had heard, and his terrified figure appeared at the window, clad in his nightshirt; he was terrified more than anything by the violent glare which lit up the whole front of his dwelling.

" 'Your house is on fire,' I shouted. 'Jump out of the window, quick, quick!'

"The flames suddenly darted through the lower windows, licked the wall, reached him, were on the point of surrounding him. He jumped and landed on his feet like a cat.

"It was high time. The thatched roof cracked in the middle, above the staircase, which formed a sort of chimney for the fire below; an immense red sheaf of flame rose in the air, widened, like the jet of a fountain, and sowed a shower of sparks round the cottage. In a few seconds it was nothing but a mass of flames.

" 'How did it catch fire?' asked Cavalier, bewildered.

" 'Someone set fire to the kitchen,' I replied.

" 'Who could have done it?' he murmured.

"Suddenly I guessed.

" 'Marius!' I said.

"The old man understood.

" 'Oh! Holy Mother of God!' he stammered; 'that's why he didn't come in again.'

"But a horrible thought ran through my brain. I cried:

" 'And Céleste? Céleste?'

"He did not answer, but the house collapsed before our eyes, forming nothing but a huge brazier, blinding, bleeding; a terrible pyre in which the poor woman could be no more than a glowing cinder, a cinder of human flesh.

"We had not heard a single cry.

"But, as the fire was reaching the neighboring shed, I suddenly thought of my horse, and Cavalier ran to set it free.

"He had scarcely opened the stable door when a swift, supple form passed between his legs, throwing him flat on his nose. It was Marius, running for all he was worth.

"In a second the man picked himself up. He wanted to run after the wretch, but, realizing that he could not hope to catch him, and maddened with an ungovernable rage, he yielded to one of those momentary, thoughtless impulses which can be neither foreseen nor restrained. He picked up my gun, which was lying upon the ground close by, set it to his shoulder, and before I could move, pulled the trigger, without even knowing whether the gun was loaded.

"One of the cartridges which I had put in to give warning of the fire had not gone off; the charge caught the fugitive full in the back, and flung him on his face, covered with blood. He began to scrabble at the ground with hands and knees, as though he was eager to go running upon all fours, like mortally wounded hares when they see the hunter come up.

"I dashed to him. The child was already in his death throes. He died before the flames were extinguished, without having uttered a word.

"Cavalier, still in his nightshirt, with bare legs, stood near us, motionless, bewildered.

"When the people arrived from the village, they took away my keeper, who was like a madman."

"I appeared at the trial as a witness and narrated the facts in detail, without altering a single incident. Cavalier was acquitted. But he left the district the same day, and disappeared.

"I have never seen him again.

"That's my shooting story, gentlemen."

THE MADWOMAN

"I can tell you a terrible story about the Franco-Prussian War," M. d'Endolin said to some friends assembled in the smoking room of Baron de Ravot's château. "You know my house in the Faubourg de Cormeilles. I was living there when the Prussians came, and I had for a neighbor a kind of madwoman who had lost her senses in consequence of a series of misfortunes. At the age of seven and twenty she had lost her father, her husband and her newly born child, all in the space of a month.

"When death has once entered into a house it almost invariably returns immediately, as if it knew the way, and the young woman, overwhelmed with grief, took to her bed and was delirious for six weeks. Then a species of calm lassitude succeeded that violent crisis, and she remained motionless, eating next to nothing and only moving her eyes. Every time they tried to make her get up she screamed as if they were about to kill her, and so they ended by leaving her continually in bed and only taking her out to wash her, to change her linen and to turn her mattress.

"An old servant remained with her to give her something to drink or a little cold meat from time to time. What passed in that despairing mind? No one ever knew, for she did not speak at all now. Was she thinking of the dead? Was she dreaming sadly, without any precise recollection of anything that had happened? Or was her memory as stagnant as water without any current? But however this may have been, for fifteen years she remained thus inert and secluded.

"The war broke out, and in the beginning of December the Germans came to Cormeilles. I can remember it as if it were but yesterday. It was freezing hard enough to split the stones, and I myself was lying back in an armchair, being unable to move on account of the gout, when I heard their heavy and regular tread and could see them pass from my window.

"They defiled past interminably, with that peculiar motion of a puppet on wires, which belongs to them. Then the officers billeted their men on the inhabitants, and I had seventeen of them. My neighbor, the crazy woman, had a dozen, one of whom was the commandant, a regular violent, surly swashbuckler.

"During the first few days everything went on as usual. The officers next door had been told that the lady was ill, and they did not trouble themselves about that in the least, but soon that woman whom they never saw irritated them. They asked what her illness was and were told that she had been in bed for fifteen years in consequence of terrible grief. No doubt they did not believe it and thought that the poor mad creature would not leave her bed out of pride, so that she might not come near the Prussians or speak to them or even see them.

"The commandant insisted upon her receiving him. He was shown into the room and said to her roughly: 'I must beg you to get up, madame, and come downstairs so that we may all see you.' But she merely turned her vague eyes on him without replying, and so he continued: 'I do not intend to tolerate any insolence, and if you do not get up of your own accord I can easily find means to make you walk without any assistance.'

"But she did not give any signs of having heard him and remained quite motionless. Then he got furious, taking that calm silence for a mark of supreme contempt, so he added: 'If you do not come downstairs tomorrow——' And then he left the room.

"The next day the terrified old servant wished to dress her, but the madwoman began to scream violently and resisted with all her might. The officer ran upstairs quickly, and the servant threw herself at his feet and cried: 'She will not come down, monsieur; she will not. Forgive her, for she is so unhappy.'

"The soldier was embarrassed, as in spite of his anger he did not venture to order his soldiers to drag her out. But suddenly he began to laugh and gave some orders in German, and soon a party of soldiers was seen coming out, supporting a mattress as if they were carrying a wounded man. On that bed, which had been unmade, the madwoman, who was still silent, was lying quite quietly, for she was quite indifferent to anything that went on, as long as they let her lie. Behind her a soldier was carrying a parcel of feminine attire, and the officer said, rubbing his hands: 'We will just see whether you cannot dress yourself alone and take a little walk.'

"And then the procession went off in the direction of the forest of Imauville; in two hours the soldiers came back alone, and nothing more was seen of the madwoman. What had they done with her? Where had they taken her to? No one knew.

"The snow was falling day and night and enveloped the plain and the woods in a shroud of frozen foam, and the wolves came and howled at our very doors.

"The thought of that poor lost woman haunted me, and I made several applications to the Prussian authorities in order to obtain some information and was nearly shot for doing so. When spring returned the army of occupation withdrew, but my neighbor's house remained closed, and the grass grew thick in the garden walks. The old servant had died during the winter, and nobody troubled any longer about the occurrence; I alone thought about it constantly. What had they done with the woman? Had she escaped through the forest? Had somebody found her and taken her to a hospital without being able to obtain any information from her? Nothing happened to relieve my doubts, but by degrees time assuaged my fears.

"Well, in the following autumn the woodcock were very plentiful, and as my gout had left me for a time, I dragged myself as far as the forest. I had already killed four or five of the long-billed birds, when I knocked over one which fell into a ditch full of branches, and I was obliged to get into it in order to pick it up, and I found that it had fallen close to a dead, human body. Immediately the recollection of the madwoman struck me like a blow in the chest. Many other people had perhaps died in the wood during that disastrous year, but though I do not know why, I was sure, sure, I tell you, that I should see the head of that wretched maniac.

"And suddenly I understood; I guessed everything. They had abandoned her on that mattress in the cold, deserted wood, and, faithful to her fixed idea, she had allowed herself to perish under that thick and light counterpane of snow without moving either arms or legs.

"Then the wolves had devoured her, and the birds had built their nests with the wool from her torn bed, and I took charge of her bones. I only pray that our sons may never see any wars again."

A BAD ERROR

I made Mme. Jadelle's acquaintance in Paris this winter. She pleased me infinitely at once. You know her as well as I—no—pardon me—nearly as well as I. You know that she is poetic and fantastic at one and the same time. You know she is free in her manner and of impressionable heart, impulsive, courageous, venturesome, audacious—above all, prejudiced and yet, in spite of that, sentimental, delicate, easily hurt, tender and modest.

She was a widow, and I adore widows, from sheer laziness. I was on the lookout for a wife, and I paid her my court. I knew her, and more than that, she pleased me. The moment came when I believed it would do to risk my proposal. I was in love with her and in danger of becoming too much so. When one marries he should not love his wife too much, or he is likely to make himself foolish; his vision is distorted, and he becomes silly and brutal at the same time. A man must assert himself. If he loses his head at first he risks being a nobody a year later.

So one day I presented myself at her house with light gloves on and I said to her: "Madame, I have the honor of loving you, and I have come to ask you if there is any hope of my pleasing you enough to warrant your placing your happiness in my care and taking my name."

She answered quietly: "What a question, sir! I am absolutely ignorant of whether you will please me sooner or later or whether you will not, but I ask nothing better than to make a trial of it. As a man, I do not find you bad. It remains to be seen how you are at heart and in character and habits. For the most part marriages are tempestuous or criminal because people are not careful enough in yoking themselves together. Sometimes a mere nothing is sufficient, a mania or tenacious opinion upon some moral or religious point, no matter what, a gesture which displeases or some little fault or disagreeable quality, to turn an affianced couple, however tender and affectionate, into a pair of irreconcilable enemies, incensed with, but chained to, each other until death. I will not marry, sir, without knowing the depths and corners and recesses of the soul of the man with whom I am to share my existence. I wish to study him at leisure, at least for some months.

"Here is what I propose. You will come and pass the summer in my house at De Lauville, my country place, and we shall see then if we are fitted to live side by side—I see you laugh! You have a bad thought. Oh, sir, if I were not sure of myself I would never make this proposition. I have for love, what you call love, you men, such a scorn, such a disgust, that a fall is impossible for me. Well, do you accept?"

I kissed her hand.

"When shall we start, madame?"

"The tenth of May."

"It is agreed."

A month later I was installed at her house. She was truly a singular woman. From morning until evening she was studying me. As she was fond of horses, we passed each day in riding through the wood, talking about everything, but she was always trying to probe my innermost thoughts, to which end she observed my slightest movement.

As for me, I became foolishly in love and did not trouble myself about the fitness of our characters. But I soon perceived that even my sleep was put under inspection. Someone slept in a little room adjoining mine, entering very late and with infinite precaution. This espionage for every instant finally made me impatient. I wished to hasten the conclusion and one evening thought of a way of bringing it about. She had received me in such a way that I had abstained from any new essay, but a violent desire invaded me to make her pay in some fashion for this restricted regime to which I had submitted, and I thought I knew a way.

You know Césarine, her chambermaid, a pretty girl from Granville, where all the women are pretty, and as blond as her mistress was brunette? Well, one afternoon I drew the little soubrette into my room and, putting a hundred francs in her hand, I said to her:

"My dear child, I do not wish you to do anything villainous, but I desire the same privilege toward your mistress that she takes toward me."

The little maid laughed with a sly look as I continued:

"I am watched day and night, I know. I am watched as I eat, drink, dress myself, shave and put on my socks, and I know it."

The little girl stammered: "Yes sir." Then she was silent. I continued:

"You sleep in the room next to mine to see if I snore or if I dream aloud; you cannot deny it!"

"Yes sir." Then she was silent again.

I became excited. "Oh well, my girl," I said, "you understand that it is not fair for everything to be known about me, while I know nothing of the person who is to be my wife. I love her with all my soul. She has the face, the heart and mind that I have dreamed of, and I am the happiest of men on this account; nevertheless, there are some things I would like to know better."

Césarine decided to put my bank note in her pocket. I understood that the bargain was concluded.

"Listen, my girl," I said. "We men—we care much for certain—certain details— physical details, which do not hinder a woman from being charming but which can change her price in our eyes. I do not ask you to say anything bad of your mistress or even to disclose to me her defects, if she has any. Only answer me frankly four or five questions, which I am going to put to you. You know Madame Jadelle as well as you do yourself, since you dress and undress her every day. Now then, tell me this: Is she as plump as she has the appearance of being?"

The little maid did not answer.

I continued: "You cannot, my child, be ignorant of the fact that women put cotton padding, you know—where—where—where they nourish their infants and also where they sit. Tell me, does she use padding?"

Césarine lowered her eyes. Finally she said timidly: "Ask whatever you want to, sir, I will answer all at one time."

"Well, my girl, there are some women whose knees meet, so much so that they touch with each step that they take, and there are others who have them far apart, which makes their limbs like the arches of a bridge, so that one might view the landscape between them. This is the prettier of the two fashions. Tell me, how are your mistress's limbs?"

Still the maid said nothing.

I continued: "There are some who have necks so beautiful that they form a great fold underneath. And there are some that have large arms with a thin figure. There are some that are very large before and nothing at all behind, and there are some large behind and nothing at all in front. All this is very pretty, very pretty, but I wish to know just how your mistress is made. Tell me frankly, and I will give you much more money."

Césarine looked at me out of the corner of her eye and, laughing with all her heart, answered: "Sir, aside from being dark, Mistress is made exactly like me."

Then she fled.

I had been made sport of. This was the time I found myself ridiculous, and I resolved to avenge myself at least upon this impertinent maid.

An hour later I entered the little room with precaution, where she listened to my sleeping, and unscrewed the bolts.

Toward midnight she arrived at her post of observation. I followed her immediately. On perceiving me she was going to cry out, but I put my hand over her mouth and, without too great effort, I convinced myself that if she had not lied Mme. Jadelle was very well made.

I even put much zest into this authentication which, though pushed a little far, did not seem to displease Césarine. She was, in very fact, a ravishing specimen of the Norman peasant race, strong and fine at the same time. She was wanting perhaps in certain delicate attentions that Henry VI would have scorned, but I revealed them to her quickly, and as I adore perfumes, I gave her a box the next evening with a flask of lavender water.

We were soon more closely bound to each other than I could have believed, almost friends. She became an exquisite mistress, naturally *spirituelle* and broken to pleasure. She had been a courtesan of great merit in Paris.

The delights which she brought me enabled me to await Mme. Jadelle's conclusion of proof without impatience. I became an incomparable character, supple, docile and complacent. My fiancée found me delightful beyond a doubt, and I judged from certain signs that I was soon to be accepted. I was certainly the happiest man in the world, awaiting tranquilly the legal kiss of the woman I loved, in the arms of a young and beautiful girl for whom I had much fondness.

It is here, madame, that I must ask your forbearance a little; I have arrived at a delicate point.

One evening as we were returning from a horseback ride, Mme. Jadelle complained sharply that her grooms had not taken certain measures prescribed by her for the horse she rode. She repeated many times: "Let them take care, I have a way of surprising them."

I passed a calm night in my bed. I awoke early, full of ardor and energy. Then I dressed myself.

I was in the habit of going up on the tower of the house each morning to smoke a cigarette. This was reached by a limestone staircase lighted by a large window at the top of the first story.

I advanced without noise, my feet encased in morocco slippers with wadded soles, and was climbing the first steps when I perceived Césarine bending out the window, looking down below.

Not that I saw Césarine entirely, but only a part of Césarine, and that the lower part. I loved this part just as much; of Mme. Jadelle I would have preferred, perhaps, the upper. She was thus so charming, so round, this part which offered itself to me, and only slightly clothed in a white skirt.

I approached so softly that the girl heard nothing. I put myself on my knees; with infinite precaution I took hold of the two sides of the skirt and, quickly, I raised it. I recognized there the full, fresh, plump, sweet ischial tuberosities of my mistress and threw there—your pardon, madame—I threw there a tender kiss, a kiss of a lover who dares anything.

I was surprised. It was verbena! But I had no time for reflection. I received a sudden blow, or rather a push in the face which seemed to break my nose. I uttered a cry that made my hair rise. The person had turned around—it was Mme. Jadelle!

She was fighting the air with her hands, like a woman who had lost consciousness. She gasped for some seconds, made a gesture of using a horsewhip and then fled.

Ten minutes later Césarine, stupefied, brought me in a letter. I read:

Mme. Jadelle hopes that M. de Brives will immediately rid her of his presence.

I departed. Well, I am not yet consoled. I have attempted every means and all explanations to obtain a pardon for my misunderstanding, but all proceedings have been nipped in the bud.

Since that moment, you see, I have in my—in my heart a scent of verbena which gives me an immoderate desire to smell the perfume again.

COCO

Throughout the neighborhood the Lucases' farm was known as "the Métairie," no one could say why. The peasants no doubt connected this word "Métairie" with an idea of wealth and size, for the farm was certainly the largest, most prosperous, and best-managed in the district.

The yard was very large, and was encircled by five rows of magnificent trees, planted to shelter the short delicate apple trees from the strong wind of the plain. It contained long tile-roofed buildings in which the hay and grain were stored, fine cow sheds built of flints, stabling for thirty horses, and a dwelling house of red brick that looked like a small country seat.

The manure heaps were well kept; the watchdogs lived in kennels, a crowd of chickens ran to and fro in the high grass.

Every day at noon fifteen persons, master, men, and maids, took their places at the long kitchen table on which the soup steamed in a great delft bowl with a pattern of blue flowers.

The animals—horses, cows, pigs, and sheep—were fat, clean, and well kept; and Lucas, a tall man beginning to acquire a paunch, made his rounds three times a day, watching over all and taking thought for all.

At the far end of the stable they kept, out of charity, a very old white horse that the mistress was anxious to have cared for until it died a natural death, because she had raised and always kept it, and because it stirred memories in her heart.

This old pensioner was looked after by a batman in the person of a fifteen-year-old lad named Isidore Duval, called Zidore for short, who, during the winter, gave him his ration of oats and his straw and, in the summer, was obliged to go four times a day and change the position where he was tied up, so that he might have plenty of fresh grass.

The animal, almost crippled, could hardly lift its heavy legs, thick at the knee and swollen above the hoofs. Its coat, which was no longer groomed, looked like white hair, and its long eyelashes gave its eyes a melancholy air.

When Zidore took it out to grass, he had to tug at the halter, so slowly did the animal walk; and the boy, stooping, panting, swore at it, exasperated at having the ancient nag to look after.

The farm hands, noticing the boy's anger towards Coco, laughed at it; they were always talking to Zidore about the horse, just to exasperate the lad. His friends chaffed him. In the village he was called Coco-Zidore.

The boy was furious and felt growing in himself a desire to be revenged on the horse. He was a thin child, long in the leg, very dirty, and with a mop of red, thick, coarse, bristling hair. He seemed stupid, spoke with a stammer, and with infinite labor, as though ideas were born with difficulty into his dull, brutish soul.

For a long time he felt surprised at the keeping of Coco, angry at seeing good stuff wasted on a useless beast. From the moment that it ceased working, it seemed to him wrong to feed it, revolting to waste good oats, so expensive as oats were, on this paralyzed jade. Often, in spite of the orders of Farmer Lucas, he econo- mized on the horse's food, supplying it with no more than half its ration, keeping back litter and hay. The hatred in his confused primitive mind grew sharper, the hatred of a grasping peasant, cunning, ferocious, brutal, and cowardly.

When summer came round again, he had to go and move the beast from place to place on its sloping meadow. It was a long way from the farm. More furious each morning, the lad plodded off across the cornfields. The men working in the fields shouted to him in jest:

"Hey! Zidore! Give my kind regards to Coco."

He never answered, but on the way he would break off a stick from a hedge, and as soon as he had tethered the old horse in a new place, he would allow it to resume its grazing and then, coming up treacherously, begin to thwack its hocks. The animal would try to escape, to rush away, to avoid the blows, and ran round at the end of its halter as though it were in a circus ring. The boy beat it savagely, running relentlessly after it, his teeth shut hard in anger.

Then he would go slowly away, without looking back, while the horse watched him go with its old eyes, its ribs projecting, and quite out of breath after so much trotting, and it would not lower its bony white head again until it had seen the young peasant's blue blouse vanish in the distance.

As the nights were warm, Coco was now left to sleep out of doors, away at the edge of the valley, beyond the wood. Zidore alone went to see the animal.

The boy had a further habit of amusing himself by throwing stones at it. He would sit down ten paces away on a bank and stay there for half an hour, from time to time flinging a jagged pebble at the old nag, which remained standing, chained up in front of its enemy and looking steadily at him, not daring to crop the grass until he was gone.

But one thought remained firmly planted in the lad's mind: Why feed this horse which did no work? It seemed to him as if this wretched jade were stealing another's victuals, the possessions of mankind, the property of the good God, were stealing even from himself, Zidore, who had to work for his food.

Little by little, every day, the boy lessened the circle of pasture which he gave it by moving the stake to which its halter was fixed.

The animal went without food, grew thin, pined away. Too weak to break the cord, it stretched out its head towards the broad expanse of green, shining grass so near at hand; the smell of it reached its nostrils but it could not touch it.

Then one morning Zidore had an idea: he decided not to go on moving Coco. He had had enough of walking so far for the sake of this miserable carcass.

But he came all the same, to enjoy his revenge. The anxious beast stared at him. He did not beat it that day. He walked round it, his hands in his pockets. He even pretended to change its position, but thrust the stake back into the same hole, and went away, delighted with his invention.

The horse, seeing him go, neighed to remind him; but the lad began to run, leaving it all alone in the valley, well tied up, and without a blade of grass within reach of its jaws.

Famished, it tried to reach the thick verdure that it could touch with the tip of its nostrils. It bent down on its knees, stretching its neck, thrusting forward its slobbering lips. All in vain. Throughout the day, the old beast wore itself out with useless, terrible struggles. Hunger ravaged it, a hunger rendered more frightful by the sight of all that good green food stretched out on every side.

The boy did not return that day. He roamed about the woods after birds' nests.

He reappeared the next day. Coco was lying down, exhausted. It rose at the sight of the boy, expecting that at last its position would be changed.

But the young peasant did not even touch the mallet lying in the ground. He came up, stared at the animal, flung a clod of earth at its muzzle, which splashed the white hair, and went away again, whistling.

The horse remained standing as long as it could still keep him in sight; then, feeling only too well that its attempts to reach the near-by grass would be useless, lay down once more upon its side and closed its eyes.

Next day Zidore did not come.

When, the following day, he drew near to Coco, who was still lying down, he saw that the horse was dead.

He remained standing, looking at it, pleased with his work, and at the same time surprised that it was already finished. He touched it with his foot, lifted one of its legs and then let it fall back again, sat down on the body and stayed there, his eyes fixed on the grass, without thinking of anything.

He returned to the farm, but did not mention the accident, for he wanted to go on playing truant at the times when he had been accustomed to go and change the horse's position.

He went to see it the next day. Crows took flight at his approach. Innumerable flies were crawling about the body and buzzing all round it.

On his return he announced the event. The beast was so old that no one was surprised. The master said to two hands:

"Get your spades and dig a hole where it lies."

The men buried the horse just at the spot where it had died of hunger.

The grass came up lush, verdant, and vigorous, nourished by the poor body.

EPIPHANY

"Ah!" said Captain the Count de Garens, "I should rather think that I do remember that Epiphany supper during the war!

"At the time I was quartermaster of cavalry, and for a fortnight I had been lurking about as a scout in front of the German advance guard. The evening before we had cut down a few uhlans and had lost three men, one of whom was that poor little Raudeville. You remember Joseph de Raudeville well, of course.

"Well, on that day my captain ordered me to take six troopers and occupy the village of Porterin, where there had been five fights in three weeks, and to hold it all night. There were not twenty houses left standing, nay, not a dozen, in that wasp's nest. So I took ten troopers and set out at about four o'clock; at five o'clock, while it was still pitch dark, we reached the first houses of Porterin. I halted and ordered Marchas—you know Pierre de Marchas who afterward married little Martel-Auvelin, the daughter of the Marquis de Martel-Auvelin—to go alone into the village and to report to me what he saw.

"I had chosen nothing but volunteers and all of good family. When on service it is pleasant not to be forced into intimacy with unpleasant fellows. This Marchas was as sharp as possible, as cunning as a fox and as supple as a serpent. He could scent the Prussians as well as a dog can scent a hare, could find victuals where we should have died of hunger without him and could obtain information from everybody—information which was always reliable—with incredible cleverness.

"In ten minutes he returned. 'All right,' he said; 'there have been no Prussians here for three days: It is a sinister place, is this village. I have been talking to a Sister of Mercy, who is attending to four or five wounded men in an abandoned convent.'

"I ordered them to ride on, and we penetrated into the principal street. On the right and left we could vaguely see roofless walls, hardly visible in the profound darkness. Here and there a light was burning in a room; some family had remained to keep its house standing as long as they were able, a family of brave, or of poor, people. The rain began to fall, a fine, icy-cold rain, which froze us before it wetted us through by merely touching our cloaks. The horses stumbled against stones, against beams, against furniture. Marchas guided us, going before us on foot and leading his horse by the bridle.

" 'Where are you taking us to?' I asked him. And he replied: 'I have a place for us to lodge in, and a rare good one.' And soon we stopped before a small house, evidently belonging to some person of the middle class, completely shut up, built onto the street with a garden in the rear.

"Marchas broke open the lock by means of a big stone which he picked up near the garden gate; then he mounted the steps, smashed in the front door with his feet and shoulders, lighted a bit of wax candle, which he was never without, and preceded us into the comfortable apartments of some rich, private individual, guiding us with admirable assurance, just as if he had lived in this house which he now saw for the first time.

"Two troopers remained outside to take care of our horses; then Marchas said to stout Ponderel, who followed him: 'The stables must be on the left; I saw that as we came in; go and put the animals up there, for we do not want them,' and then, turning to me, he said: 'Give your orders, confound it all!'

"Marchas always astonished me, and I replied with a laugh: 'I shall post my sentinels at the country approaches and I will return to you here.'

" 'How many men are you going to take?'

" 'Five. The others will relieve them at five o'clock in the evening.'

" 'Very well. Leave me four to look after provisions, to do the cooking and to set the table. I will go and find out where the wine is hidden away.'

"I went off to reconnoiter the deserted streets, until they ended in the open country, so as to post my sentries there.

"Half an hour later I was back and found Marchas lounging in a great arm-chair, the covering of which he had taken off, from love of luxury, as he said. He was warming his feet at the fire and smoking an excellent cigar, whose perfume filled the room. He was alone, his elbows resting on the arms of the chair, his cheeks flushed, his eyes bright, and looking delighted.

"I heard the noise of plates and dishes in the next room, and Marchas said to me, smiling in a beatific manner: 'This is famous; I found the champagne under the flight of steps outside, the brandy—fifty bottles of the very finest—in the kitchen garden under a pear tree which did not look to me to be quite straight when I looked at it by the light of my lantern. As for solids, we have two fowls, a goose, a duck and three pigeons. They are being cooked at this moment. It is a delightful part of the country.'

"I had sat down opposite to him, and the fire in the grate was burning my nose and cheeks.

" 'Where did you find this wood?' I asked.

" 'Splendid wood,' he replied. 'The owner's carriage. It is the paint which is causing all this flame, an essence of alcohol and varnish. A capital house!'

"I laughed for I found the creature was funny, and he went on: 'Fancy this being the Epiphany! I have had a bean put into the goose, but there is no queen; it is really very annoying!' And I repeated like an echo: 'It is annoying, but what do you want me to do in the matter?'

" 'To find some, of course.'

" 'Some women. Women? You must be mad!'

" 'I managed to find the brandy under the pear tree and the champagne under the steps, and yet there was nothing to guide me, while as for you, a petticoat is a sure sign. Go and look, old fellow.'

"He looked so grave, so convinced, that I could not tell whether he was joking or not. So I replied: 'Look here, Marchas, are you having a joke with me?'

" 'I never joke on duty.'

" 'But where the devil do you expect me to find any women?'

" 'Where you like; there must be two or three remaining in the neighborhood, so ferret them out and bring them here.'

"I got up, for it was too hot in front of the fire, and Marchas went on: 'Do you want an idea?'

" 'Yes.'

" 'Go and see the priest.'

" 'The priest? What for?'

" 'Ask him to supper and beg him to bring a woman with him.'

" 'The priest? A woman! Ha! ha! ha!'

"But Marchas continued with extraordinary gravity: 'I am not laughing; go and find the priest and tell him how we are situated, and, as he must be horribly dull, he will come. But tell him that we want one woman at least, a lady, of course, since we are all men of the world. He is sure to have the names of his female parishioners on the tips of his fingers, and if there is one to suit us and you manage it well he will indicate her to you.'

" 'Come, come, Marchas, what are you thinking of?'

" 'My dear Garens, you can do this quite well. It will be very funny. We are well bred, by Jove, and we will put on our most distinguished manners and our grandest style. Tell the abbé who we are, make him laugh, soften him, seduce him and persuade him!'

" 'No, it is impossible.'

"He drew his chair close to mine, and as he knew my weak side, the scamp continued: 'Just think what a swagger thing it will be to do and how amusing to tell about; the whole army will talk about it, and it will give you a famous reputation.'

"I hesitated, for the adventure rather tempted me. He persisted: 'Come, my little Garens. You are in command of this detachment and you alone can go and call on the head of the church in this neighborhood. I beg of you to go, and I promise you that after the war I will relate the whole affair in verse in the Revue des Deux Mondes. You owe this much to your men, for you have made them march enough during the last month.'

"I got up at last and asked: 'Where is the parsonage?'

" 'Take the second turning at the end of the street; you will then see an avenue, and at the end of the avenue you will find the church. The parsonage is beside it.' As I departed he called out: 'Tell him the bill of fare to make him hungry!'

"I discovered the ecclesiastic's little house without any difficulty; it was by the side of a large, ugly brick church. As there was neither bell nor knocker, I knocked at the door with my fist, and a loud voice from inside asked: 'Who is there?' to which I replied: 'A quartermaster of hussars.'

"I heard the noise of bolts and a key being turned. Then I found myself face to face with a tall priest with a large stomach, the chest of a prize fighter, formidable hands projecting from turned-up sleeves, a red face and the looks of a kind man. I gave him a military salute and said: 'Good day, monsieur l'abbé.'

"He had feared a surprise, some marauders' ambush, and he smiled as he replied: 'Good day, my friend; come in.' I followed him into a small room, with a red tiled floor, in which a small fire was burning, very different to Marchas' furnace. He gave me a chair and said: 'What can I do for you?'

" 'Monsieur, allow me first of all to introduce myself,' and I gave him my card, which he took and read half aloud: 'The Comte de Garens.'

"I continued: 'There are eleven of us here, monsieur l'abbé, five on grand guard and six installed at the house of an unknown inhabitant. The names of the six are Garens (that is I), Pierre de Marchas, Ludovic de Ponderel, Baron d'Etreillis, Karl Massouligny, the painter's son, and Joseph Herbon, a young musician. I have come to ask you, in their name and my own, to do us the honor of supping with us. It is an Epiphany supper, monsieur l'abbé, and we should like to make it a little cheerful.'

"The priest smiled and murmured: 'It seems to me to be hardly a suitable occasion for amusing oneself.'

"I replied: 'We are fighting every day, monsieur. Fourteen of our comrades have been killed in a month, and three fell as late as yesterday. That is war. We stake our life every moment; have we not, therefore, the right to amuse ourselves freely? We are Frenchmen; we like to laugh, and we can laugh everywhere. Our fathers laughed on the scaffold! This evening we should like to brighten ourselves up a little, like gentlemen, and not like soldiers; you understand me, I hope. Are we wrong?'

"He replied quickly: 'You are quite right, my friend, and I accept your invitation with great pleasure.' Then he called out: 'Hermance!'

"An old, bent, wrinkled, horrible peasant woman appeared and said: 'What do you want?'

" 'I shall not dine at home, my daughter.'

" 'Where are you going to dine then?'

" 'With some gentlemen, hussars.'

"I felt inclined to say: 'Bring your servant with you,' just to see Marchas' face, but I did not venture to and continued: 'Do you know anyone among your parishioners, male or female, whom I could invite as well?' He hesitated, reflected and then said: 'No, I do not know anybody!'

"I persisted: 'Nobody? Come, monsieur, think; it would be very nice to have some ladies, I mean to say, some married couples! I know nothing about your parishioners. The baker and his wife, the grocer, the—the—the—watchmaker—the —shoemaker—the—the chemist with his wife. We have a good spread and plenty of wine, and we should be enchanted to leave pleasant recollections of ourselves behind us with the people here.'

"The priest thought again for a long time and then said resolutely: 'No, there is nobody.'

"I began to laugh. 'By Jove, monsieur l'abbé, it is very vexing not to have an Epiphany queen, for we have the bean. Come, think. Is there not a married mayor, or a married deputy mayor, or a married municipal councilor or schoolmaster?'

" 'No, all the ladies have gone away.'

" 'What? Is there not in the whole place some good tradesman's wife, with her good tradesman, to whom we might give this pleasure, for it would be a pleasure to them, a great pleasure under present circumstances?'

"But suddenly the abbé began to laugh, and he laughed so violently that he fairly shook and exclaimed: 'Ha! ha! ha! I have got what you want, yes. I have got what you want! Ha! ha! ha! We will laugh and enjoy ourselves, my children; we will have some fun. How pleased the ladies will be, I say, how delighted they will be. Ha! ha! Where are you staying?'

"I described the house, and he understood where it was. 'Very good,' he said. 'It belongs to M. Bertin-Lavaille. I will be there in half an hour with four ladies. Ha! ha! ha! Four ladies!'

"He went out with me, still laughing, and left me, repeating: 'That is capital; in half an hour at Bertin-Lavaille's house.'

"I returned quickly, very much astonished and very much puzzled. 'Covers for how many?' Marchas asked as soon as he saw me.

" 'Eleven. There are six of us hussars besides the priest and four ladies.'

"He was thunderstruck, and I triumphant, and he repeated: 'Four ladies! Did you say four ladies?'

" 'I said four women.'

" 'Real women?'

" 'Real women.'

" 'Well, accept my compliments!'

" 'I will, for I deserve them.'

"He got out of his armchair, opened the door, and I saw a beautiful white table-cloth on a long table, round which three hussars in blue aprons were setting out the plates and glasses. 'There are some women coming!' Marchas cried. And the three men began to dance and to cheer with all their might.

"Everything was ready, and we were waiting. We waited for nearly an hour, while a delicious smell of roast poultry pervaded the whole house. At last, how-ever, a knock against the shutters made us all jump up at the same moment. Stout Ponderel ran to open the door, and in less than a minute a little Sister of Mercy appeared in the doorway. She was thin, wrinkled and timid and successively saluted the four bewildered hussars who saw her enter. Behind her the noise of sticks sounded on the tiled floor in the vestibule. As soon as she had come into the drawing room I saw three old heads in white caps following each other one by one, balancing themselves with different movements, one canting to the right, while the other canted to the left. Then three worthy women showed themselves, limping, dragging their legs behind them, crippled by illness and deformed through old age, three infirm old women, past service, the only three pensioners who were able to walk in the establishment which Sister Saint-Benedict managed.

"She had turned round to her invalids, full of anxiety for them, and then, seeing my quartermaster's stripes, she said to me: 'I am much obliged to you for thinking of these poor women. They have very little pleasure in life, and you are at the same time giving them a great treat and doing them a great honor.'

"I saw the priest, who had remained in the obscurity of the passage and who was laughing heartily, and I began to laugh in my turn, especially when I saw Marchas' face. Then, motioning the nun to the seats, I said: 'Sit down, Sister; we are very proud and very happy that you have accepted our unpretentious invitation.'

"She took three chairs which stood against the wall, set them before the fire, led her three old women to them, settled them on them, took their sticks and shawls which she put into a corner and then, pointing to the first, a thin woman with an enormous stomach who was evidently suffering from the dropsy, she said: 'This is Mother Paumelle, whose husband was killed by falling from a roof and whose son died in Africa; she is sixty years old.' Then she pointed to another, a tall woman, whose head shook unceasingly: 'This is Mother Jean-Jean, who is sixty-seven. She is nearly blind, for her face was terribly singed in a fire, and her right leg was half burned off.'

"Then she pointed to the third, a sort of dwarf, with protruding round, stupid eyes, which she rolled incessantly in all directions. 'This is La Putois, an idiot. She is only forty-four.'

"I bowed to the three women as if I were being presented to some Royal High-ness and, turning to the priest, I said: 'You are an excellent man, monsieur l'abbé, and we all owe you a debt of gratitude.'

"Everybody was laughing, in fact, except Marchas, who seemed furious, and just then Karl Massouligny cried: "Sister Saint-Benedict, supper is on the table!'

"I made her go first with the priest, then I helped up Mother Paumelle, whose arm I took, and dragged her into the next room, which was no easy task, for her swollen stomach seemed heavier than a lump of iron.

"Stout Ponderel gave his arm to Mother Jean-Jean, who bemoaned her crutch, and little Joseph Herbon took the idiot, La Putois, to the dining room, which was filled with the odor of the viands.

"As soon as we were opposite our plates the sister clapped her hands three times, and, with the precision of soldiers presenting arms, the women made a rapid sign of the cross, and then the priest slowly repeated the Benedictus in Latin. Then we sat down and the two fowls appeared, brought in by Marchas, who chose to wait rather than to sit down as a guest at this ridiculous repast.

"But I cried: 'Bring the champagne at once!' And a cork flew out with the noise of a pistol, and in spite of the resistance of the priest and the kind sister, the three hussars sitting by the side of the three invalids emptied their three full glasses down their throats by force.

"Massouligny, who possessed the faculty of making himself at home and of being on good terms with everyone wherever he was, made love to Mother Paumelle in the drollest manner. The dropsical woman who had retained her cheerfulness in spite of her misfortunes answered him banteringly in a high falsetto voice which seemed to be assumed, and she laughed so heartily at her neighbor's jokes that her large stomach looked as if it were going to rise up and get onto the table. Little Herbon had seriously undertaken the task of making the idiot drunk, and Baron d'Etreillis, whose wits were not always particularly sharp, was questioning old Jean-Jean about the life, the habits and the rules in the hospital.

"The nun said to Massouligny in consternation: 'Oh! oh! You will make her ill; pray do not make her laugh like that, monsieur. Oh, monsieur.' Then she got up and rushed at Herbon to take a full glass out of his hands which he was hastily emptying down La Putois's throat, while the priest shook with laughter, and said to the sister: 'Never mind, just this once it will not hurt her. Do leave them alone.'

"After the two fowls they ate the duck, which was flanked by the three pigeons and a blackbird, and then the goose appeared, smoking, golden-colored and diffusing a warm odor of hot, browned fat meat. La Paumelle, who was getting lively, clapped her hands; La Jean-Jean left off answering the baron's numerous questions, and La Putois uttered grunts of pleasure, half cries and half sighs, like little children do, when one shows them sweets. 'Allow me to carve this bird,' the abbé said. 'I understand these sorts of operations better than most people.'

" 'Certainly, monsieur l'abbé,' and the sister said: 'How would it be to open the window a little; they are too warm, and I am afraid they will be ill.'

"I turned to Marchas. 'Open the window for a minute.' He did so; the cold outer air as it came in made the candles flare and the smoke from the goose, which the abbé was scientifically carving, with a table napkin round his neck, whirl about. We watched him doing it without speaking now, for we were interested in his attractive handiwork and also seized with renewed appetite at the sight of that enormous golden-colored bird, whose limbs fell one after another into the brown gravy at the bottom of the dish. At that moment, in the midst of greedy silence which kept us all attentive, the distant report of a shot came in at the open window.

"I started to my feet so quickly that my chair fell down behind me, and I shouted: 'Mount, all of you! You, Marchas, will take two men and go and see what it is. I shall expect you back here in five minutes.' And while the three riders went off at full gallop through the night I got into the saddle with my three remaining hussars in front of the steps of the villa, while the abbé, the sister and the three old women showed their frightened faces at the window.

"We heard nothing more, except the barking of a dog in the distance. The rain had ceased, and it was cold, very cold. Soon I heard the gallop of a horse, of a single horse, coming back. It was Marchas, and I called out to him: 'Well?'

" 'It is nothing; François has wounded an old peasant who refused to answer his challenge and who continued to advance in spite of the order to keep off. They are bringing him here, and we shall see what is the matter.'

"I gave orders for the horses to be put back into the stable, and I sent my two soldiers to meet the others and returned to the house. Then the abbé, Marchas and I took a mattress into the room to put the wounded man on; the sister tore up a table napkin in order to make lint, while the three frightened women remained huddled up in a corner.

"Soon I heard the rattle of sabers on the road and I took a candle to show a light to the men who were returning. They soon appeared, carrying that inert, soft, long and sinister object which a human body becomes when life no longer sustains it.

"They put the wounded man on the mattress that had been prepared for him, and I saw at the first glance that he was dying. He had the death rattle and was spitting up blood which ran out of the corners of his mouth, forced out of his lungs by his gasps. The man was covered with it! His cheeks, his beard, his hair, his neck and his clothes seemed to have been rubbed, to have been dipped in a red tub; the blood had congealed on him and had become a dull color which was horrible to look at.

"The old man, wrapped up in a large shepherd's cloak, occasionally opened his dull, vacant eyes. They seemed stupid with astonishment, like the eyes of hunted animals which fall at the sportsman's feet, half dead before the shot, stupefied with fear and surprise.

"The abbé exclaimed: 'Ah! There is old Placide, the shepherd from Les Marlins. He is deaf, poor man, and heard nothing. Ah! O God! They have killed the unhappy man!' The sister had opened his blouse and shirt and was looking at a little blue hole in the middle of his chest which was not bleeding any more. 'There is nothing to be done,' she said.

"The shepherd was gasping terribly and bringing up blood with every breath. In his throat to the very depth of his lungs, they could hear an ominous and continued gurgling. The abbé, standing in front of him, raised his right hand, made the sign of the cross and in a slow and solemn voice pronounced the Latin words which purify men's souls. But before they were finished the old man was shaken by a rapid shudder, as if something had broken inside him; he no longer breathed. He was dead.

"When I turned round I saw a sight which was even more horrible than the death struggle of this unfortunate man. The three old women were standing up huddled close together, hideous and grimacing with fear and horror. I went up to them, and they began to utter shrill screams, while La Jean-Jean, whose leg had been burned and could no longer support her, fell to the ground at full length.

"Sister Saint-Benedict left the dead man, ran up to her infirm old women and without a word or a look for me wrapped their shawls round them, gave them their crutches, pushed them to the door, made them go out and disappeared with them into the dark night.

"I saw that I could not even let a hussar accompany them, for the mere rattle of a sword would have sent them mad with fear.

"The abbé was still looking at the dead man, but at last he turned to me and said:

" 'Oh! What a horrible thing.' "

HAPPINESS

It was teatime, just before the lamps were brought in. The villa overlooked the sea; the vanished sun had left the sky rose-tipped in its passing and powdered with golden dust; and the Mediterranean, without ripple or faintest movement, smooth, still gleaming with the light of the dying day, spread out a vast shield of burnished metal.

Far to the right, the jagged mountains lifted their black, sharp-cut bulk against the dim purple of the west.

They were speaking of love, retelling an ancient tale, saying over again things already said many, many times before. The soft melancholy dusk pressed upon their speech, so that a feeling of tenderness welled up in their hearts, and the word "love," constantly repeated, now in a man's strong voice, now in the high, clear tones of a woman, seemed to fill the little room, flitting about it like a bird, hovering like a spirit over them.

Can one love for years without end?

Yes, claimed some.

No, declared others.

They drew a distinction between various cases, made clear the qualities that divided them from others, quoted examples; and all, both men and women, filled with rushing, disquieting memories which they could not reveal and which hovered on their lips, seemed profoundly moved; they spoke of this commonplace yet supreme thing, this mysterious concord between two beings, with the deepest emotion and burning interest.

Suddenly one among them, whose eyes were fixed on the distant scene, exclaimed:

"Oh! Look! What's that, over there?"

Across the sea, on the rim of haze, rose a huge, gray, shapeless mass.

The women had risen and were staring uncomprehendingly at this amazing object, which none of them had ever seen before.

"It's Corsica," said someone. "It can be seen two or three times a year under exceptional atmospheric conditions, when the air is so perfectly clear as not to conceal it with those mists of water vapor in which distant prospects are always wrapped."

They could distinguish vaguely the mountain peaks, and fancied that they could see the snow on the summits. And everyone was surprised, disturbed, almost frightened at this abrupt appearance of a world, at this phantom risen from the sea. Such, perhaps, were the perilous visions of those who set out like Columbus across strange seas.

Then an old gentleman, who had not spoken, remarked:

"Oddly enough, in that island which has just swum into our sight—at the very moment when it would give force to what we have been saying and awaken one of my strangest memories—I came across a perfect instance of faithful love, miraculously happy love."

"Five years ago I made a tour in Corsica. That wild island is farther away from us, and less known to us, than America, although it is sometimes to be seen from the coasts of France, even as today.

"Imagine a world still in chaos, a maelstrom of mountains separated by narrow ravines down which rush foaming torrents; not a single level space, but only immense billows of granite and gigantic undulations in the ground covered with thickets or with lofty forests of chestnut and pine. It is virgin soil, uncultivated, deserted, although an occasional village may be descried, like a pile of rocks perched on the top of a mountain. There is no culture, no industry, no art. Never does one meet with a piece of carved wood, a block of sculptured stone, with any reminder of hereditary taste, rudimentary or refined, for gracious and beautiful things. That is the most striking thing in this superb, harsh country: its inherited indifference to that search for magical loveliness which is called art.

"Italy, where every palace, full of masterpieces, is itself a masterpiece, where marble, wood, bronze, iron, in fact all metals and stones, bear witness to the genius of man, where the tiniest heirlooms in old houses reveal a divine care for beauty, is to each one of us a sacred and beloved land, because she displays and proves to us the strong impulse, the grandeur, the power, and the triumph of the creative intelligence.

"Facing her, wild Corsica has remained just as she was in her earliest days. There man lives in his rude house, indifferent to all that does not affect his mere existence or his family quarrels. He has survived with the defects and qualities of all uncivilized races, violent, strong to hate, instinctively bloodthirsty, but also hospitable, generous, full of true piety, simple-hearted, opening his door to the passer-by and bestowing a loyal friendship in return for the smallest token of sympathy.

"For a month I had been wandering over this magnificent island, feeling as though I were at the end of the world. There are no inns, no taverns, no roads. Mule paths lead to the villages that cling to the flanks of the mountains and overlook the twisting gulfs from whose depths the heavy, muffled, deep roar of the torrent rises ceaselessly in the silence of evening. The traveler knocks at the house doors and asks for shelter for the night and food until next day. He sits down at the humble table and sleeps beneath the humble roof and in the morning shakes the outstretched hand of his host, who leads him to the edge of the village.

"One evening, after walking for ten hours, I came to a little house standing by itself in the depths of a narrow valley that fell into the sea a league farther on. The two steep slopes of the hillside, covered with thickets, boulders, and tall trees, were like two gloomy walls enclosing this unutterably mournful abyss.

"Round the hovel were a few vines, a small garden, and, further on, some large chestnut trees; enough, actually, for a bare existence, a fortune in that poor country.

"The woman who opened the door was old, hard-featured, and clean, which was unusual. The man, seated on a cane chair, got up to greet me and then sat down without saying a word.

" 'Please excuse him,' said his wife to me. 'He's deaf now. He's eighty-two.'

"She spoke perfect French. I was surprised.

" 'You are not Corsicans?' I asked her.

" 'No,' she replied, 'we come from the mainland. But we have lived here for fifty years.'

"A feeling of anguish and terror overwhelmed me at the thought of the fifty years that had rolled by in this dark hole, so far from towns and the life of men. An old shepherd came in, and we began to eat the only course of the dinner, a thick soup in which potatoes, bacon, and cabbage were all boiled together.

"When the short meal was over, I went out and sat before the door, my heart oppressed with the melancholy of that somber landscape, in the grip of that feeling of wretchedness which sometimes lays hold on the traveler, on sad evenings, in desolate places. It seems as though all things were coming to an end, life itself, and the universe. The dreadful misery of life is revealed in one blinding flash, and the isolation of all things, the nothingness of all things, and the black loneliness of our hearts, which soothe and deceive themselves with dreams until the coming of death itself.

"The old woman joined me, and, tormented by the curiosity which lives on in the hearts of even the most resigned of mortals, said to me:

" 'So you come from France?'

" 'Yes, I am traveling for pleasure.'

" 'You are from Paris, perhaps?'

" 'No, I come from Nancy.'

"At that it seemed to me that an extraordinary excitement was agitating her. How I saw this, or rather felt it, I do not know.

" 'You are from Nancy?' she repeated slowly.

"The husband appeared in the doorway, impassive, as are all deaf people.

" 'It does not matter,' she continued. 'He cannot hear.'

"Then, after a few seconds:

" 'Then you know people in Nancy?'

" 'Why, yes, almost everybody.'

" 'The Sainte-Allaize family?'

" 'Yes, very well; they were friends of my father's.'

" 'What is your name?'

"I told her. She stared intently at me, then said in that soft voice evoked by wakening memories:

" 'Yes, yes, I remember quite well. And the Brisenaves, what has become of them?'

" 'They are all dead.'

" 'Ah! And the Sirmonts, do you know them?'

" 'Yes, the youngest is a general.'

"At that she replied, shaking with excitement, with anguish, with I know not what confused powerful and intimate emotion, with I know not how pressing a need to confess, to tell everything, to speak of things she had until this moment kept locked in the secret places of her heart, and of the people whose name troubled the very depths of her soul:

" 'Yes, Henri de Sirmont. I know him well. He is my brother.'

"I lifted my eyes to her, quite dumbfounded with surprise. And suddenly I remembered.

"It had been a great scandal, long ago, in aristocratic Lorraine. As a young girl, beautiful, wealthy, Suzanne de Sirmont had run off with a non-commissioned officer in the hussar regiment of which her father was commander.

"He was a handsome lad; his parents were peasants, but he wore the blue dolman with a gallant air, this soldier who seduced his colonel's daughter. Doubtless she had seen him, noticed him, fallen in love with him as she watched the squadrons march past. But how had she spoken to him, how had they been able to meet and come to an understanding? How had she dared to make him realize that she loved him? This no one ever knew.

"Nothing had been guessed or foreseen. One evening, when the soldier had just completed his term of service, he disappeared with her. A search was made, but they were not found. No news of them was heard, and she was thought of as dead.

"And thus I had found her in this sinister valley.

"Then in my turn I answered:

" 'Yes, I remember well. You are Mademoiselle Suzanne.'

"She nodded 'yes.' Tears poured from her eyes. Then, glancing towards the old man, standing motionless on the threshold of his dwelling, she said to me:

" 'That is he.'

"And I realized that she still loved him, still saw him with eyes blinded by love.

" 'But at least you have been happy?' I asked.

"She answered, in a voice that came from her heart:

" 'Oh, yes, very happy. He has made me very happy. I have never had any regrets.'

"I gazed at her, a little sad, surprised, marveling at the power of love! This rich girl had followed this man, this peasant. She had stooped herself to a life without charm, luxury, or refinement of any sort, she had accustomed herself to an entirely simple existence. And she still loved him. She had become the wife of a country clodhopper, with a bonnet and a canvas skirt. She sat on a cane chair, she ate broth made of potatoes, cabbage, and bacon, out of an earthen platter set on a deal table. She slept on straw at his side.

"She had never a thought for anything but him. She had regretted neither jewels nor fine clothes nor fashion nor the comfort of armchairs nor the perfumed warmth of tapestry-hung rooms nor the softness of down whereon the body sinks to rest. She had never needed anything but him; so only that he was there, she wanted nothing.

"In early youth she had forsaken life and the world and those who had loved and nurtured her. She had come, alone with him, to this wild ravine. And he had been everything to her, all that a woman desires, all that she dreams of, all that she ceaselessly awaits, all for which she never ceases to hope. He had filled her existence with happiness from its beginning to its close.

"She could not have been happier.

"And all night long, as I listened to the hoarse breathing of the old soldier lying on his pallet beside the woman who had followed him so far, I thought of this strange and simple adventure, of her happiness, so complete, built of so little.

"I left next morning, after shaking hands with the old couple."

The teller of the tale was silent. A woman said:

"All the same, her ideal was too easy of attainment, her needs too primitive, her demands on life too simple. She must have been a stupid girl."

Another woman said slowly:

"What does it matter? She was happy."

In the distance, on the rim of the world, Corsica receded into the night, sinking slowly back into the sea, withdrawing the vast shadow that had appeared as though itself would tell the story of the two humble lovers sheltered by its shores.

THE UNKNOWN

We were talking of lucky adventures, and each of us had an odd happening to relate, delightful and unexpected encounters, in a railway carriage, in a hotel, abroad, on a seashore. Seashores, said Roger des Annettes, were uncommonly propitious for a love affair.

Gontran, who had said nothing, was appealed to.

"Paris is still the happiest hunting ground of all," said he. "With a woman, as with a book, we appreciate one more highly in a place where we never expected to find one; but the finest specimens are found only in Paris."

He was silent for some moments, then added:

"God, how adorable they are! Go out into our streets on any spring morning. They look as if they had come up like flowers, the little darlings pattering along beside the houses. What a charming, charming, charming sight! The scent of violets reaches us from the pavement; the bunches of violets that pass us in the slow-moving carts pushed on by the hawkers. The town is alive with spring, and we look at the women. Christ, how tempting they are in their light frocks, thin frocks, thin frocks through which their skin gleams! One strolls along, nose down to the scent and senses on fire; one strolls along and one sniffs them out and way-lays them. Such mornings are utterly divine.

"You notice her approaching in the distance, a hundred paces away you can find out and recognize the woman who will be delightful at close range. By a flower in her hat, a movement of her head, the swing of her body, you know her. She comes. You say to yourself: 'Attention, eyes front!' and walk past her with your eyes devouring her.

"Is she a slip of a girl running errands for a shop, a young woman coming from church or going to visit her lover? What's the odds! Her breast shows rounded under her transparent bodice. Oh, if only one might thrust a finger down beneath it—a finger, or one's lips! Does she look shy or bold, is her head dark or fair? What's the odds! The swift passage of this woman, as she flits past, sends a thrill down your spine. And how desire haunts us until evening for the woman we have met in such fashion! I'll swear I've treasured the memory of a round twenty of the dear creatures seen once or ten times like this, and I would have fallen madly in love with them if I had known them more intimately.

"But there you are, the women we cherish most fiercely are the ones we never know. Have you noticed it? It's very odd. Every now and then one catches a glimpse of women the mere sight of whom rouses in us the wildest desire. But one never more than glimpses them. For my part, when I think of all the adorable creatures whom I have jostled in the streets of Paris, I could hang myself for rage. Where are they? Who are they? Where could I find them again, see them again? There is a proverb which says that we are always rubbing elbows with happiness, and I'll take my oath that I've more than once walked past the woman who could have snared me like a linnet with the allure of her fragrant body."

Roger des Annettes had been listening with a smile, and answered:

"I know all that as well as you. Listen what happened to me, yes, to me. About five years ago I met for the first time, on the Pont de la Concorde, a tall and rather sturdy young woman who made on me an impression . . . oh, an altogether amazing impression! She was a brunette, a plump brunette, with gleaming hair growing low on her forehead and eyebrows that bracketed both eyes, under their high arch that stretched from temple to temple. The shadow of a mustache on her lip set one dreaming . . . dreaming . . . as the sight of a bunch of flowers on a table stirs dreams of a beloved wood. She had a shapely figure, firm rounded breasts held proudly like a challenge, offering themselves as a temptation. Her eyes were like inkstains on the gleaming white of her skin. This girl's eyes were not eyes but shadowed caverns, deep open caverns in her head, through which one saw right into her, entered into her. What a veiled empty gaze, untroubled by thought and utterly lovely!

"I imagined her to be a Jewess. I followed her. More than one man turned to look after her. She walked with a slightly swaggering gait, a little graceless but very disturbing. She took a cab in the Place de la Concorde. And I stood there like a stuck pig, beside the Obélisque; I stood transfixed by the fiercest passion of longing that had ever assailed me in my life.

"I remembered her for at least three weeks, then I forgot her.

"Six months later I saw her again in the Rue de la Paix, and at sight of her my heart leaped as if I had caught sight of some mistress whom I had loved to distraction. I halted the better to watch her approach. As she passed me, almost touching me, I seemed to be standing in the mouth of a furnace. Then, as she drew away, I felt as if a cool wind were blowing across my face. I did not follow her. I was afraid of committing some folly, afraid of myself.

"Again and again I saw her in my dreams. You know what such obsessions are.

"It was a year before I found her again; then, one evening at sunset, about the month of May, I recognized her in a woman who was walking in front of me up the Champs-Elysées.

"The Arc de l'Etoile lifted its somber outline against the flaming curtain of the sky. A golden dust, a mist of rosy light hung in the air; it was one of those glorious evenings which are the immortal glory of Paris.

"I followed her, wild with the longing to speak to her, to kneel at her feet, to tell her of the emotion which was choking me.

"Twice I walked past her in order to turn and meet her again. Twice, as I passed her, I experienced again that sensation of fiery heat which had come over me in the Rue de la Paix.

"She looked at me. Then I saw her enter a house in the Rue de Presbourg. I waited two hours in a doorway. She did not come out. At last I decided to question the concierge. He did not appear to understand me. 'She must have been a caller,' he said.

"And it was eight months before I saw her again.

"Then one January morning, during a spell of arctic cold, I was on my way down the Boulevard Malesherbes and running to warm myself, when at the corner of a street I collided so violently with a woman that she dropped a small parcel.

"I began apologies. It was she!

"For a moment I stood still, stunned by the suddenness of the shock; then, giving her back the parcel she had been carrying in her hand, I said abruptly:

" 'I am distressed and overjoyed, madame, to have rushed into you like this. Will you believe me that for more than two years I have noticed you, admired you, longed cruelly to make your acquaintance, and I could not manage to find out who you were nor where you lived? Pardon words like these, ascribe them to my passionate desire to be numbered among those who have the right to speak to you. Such a feeling could not wrong you, could it? You do not know me. I am Baron Roger des Annettes. Make your own inquiries: you will be told that I am a man you can admit to your house. If you refuse my request now, you will make me the most miserable wretch alive. I implore you, be kind, give me, allow me the chance to visit you.'

"She regarded me intently, out of her strange lusterless eyes, and answered smiling:

" 'Give me your address. I will come to your house.'

"I was so utterly dumbfounded that I must have shown it. But I am never long in recovering from such shocks and I hastened to give her a card, which she slipped into her pocket with a swift gesture, with a hand evidently used to manipulating clandestine letters.

"Becoming bold, I stammered:

" 'When shall I see you?'

"She hesitated, as if she had to make a complicated calculation, no doubt trying to recollect just what she had to do with each hour of her time; then she murmured:

" 'Sunday morning, is that right for you?'

" 'I am quite sure that it is all right.'

"Then she went away, after she had searched my face, judged me, summed me up, dissected me with that heavy insensible stare that seemed to leave something on one's skin, a kind of viscous fluid, as if her glance flung out on to human beings one of those dense liquids which devilfish use to cloud the water and lull their prey to sleep.

"All the time until Sunday, I gave myself up to the most desperate cudgeling of my wits, in the effort to make up my mind what she was and ascertain the correct attitude to adopt to her.

"Ought I to give her money? How much?

"I decided to buy a piece of jewelry, an uncommonly charming piece of jewelry too, and I placed it, in its case, on the mantelshelf.

"I waited for her, after a restless night.

"She arrived about ten o'clock, quite calm, quite placid, and gave me her hand as if we were old friends. I offered her a seat, I relieved her of her hat, her veil, her furs, her muff. Then, slightly embarrassed, I began to press her somewhat more hardily, for I had no time to lose.

"She asked for nothing better, and we had not exchanged twenty words before I began to undress her. She herself continued this ticklish business that I never succeed in finishing: I prick myself on pins, I twist strings into inextricable knots instead of undoing them; I mismanage and confuse everything, I delay it all and I lose my head.

"Do you know any moment in life, my dear, more marvelous than the moments when you are watching—standing just far enough away and using just enough discretion to avoid startling that ostrich modesty all women affect—a woman who is stripping herself for you of all the rustling garments that fall round her feet, one after another?

"And what is prettier, too, than the gestures with which they put off those adorable garments that slip to the ground, empty and stretched indolently out as if they had just been struck dead? How glorious and intoxicating is the revelation of her flesh, her naked arms and breasts after her bodice is off, and how disturbing the lines of her body glimpsed under the last veil of all!

"But all at once I saw an amazing thing, a black stain between her shoulders; for she had turned her back to me: a wide stain standing vividly out, black as night. I had promised, moreover, not to look at her.

"What was it? I had not the least doubt what it was, however, and the memory of that clearly visible mustache, the eyebrows joined above the eyes, of that mop of hair which covered her head like a helmet, ought to have prepared me for this shock.

"I was none the less dumbfounded and my mind was thronged suddenly with swift thoughts and strange remembered things. I imagined that I was looking at one of those enchantresses from the *Thousand and One Nights*, one of those fatal and faithless creatures who exist only to drag mortal men into unknown abysses. I thought of Solomon making the Queen of Sheba walk over a mirror to assure himself that she had not a cloven hoof.

"And . . . and when it came to the point of singing her my song of love, I discovered that I had no voice left, not even a trickle of sound, my dear. Or let's say I had a voice like a eunuch, which at first astonished and at last thoroughly displeased her, for she remarked, clothing herself with all dispatch:

"'There was not much point in putting me to this trouble, was there?'

"I wanted her to accept the ring bought for her, but she said deliberately and very stiffly: 'What do you take me for, monsieur?' so that I crimsoned to the ears under this accumulation of humiliations. And she departed without adding another word.

"And that is all there is to my adventure. But the worst of it is that, now, I am in love with her, and madly in love.

"I cannot see a woman without thinking of her. All others repel me, disgust me, in so far as they do not resemble her. I cannot press a kiss on another cheek without seeing her cheek beside the one that I am caressing, and without suffering agonies from the unappeased desire which torments me.

"She is present at all my rendezvous, at all the caresses that she spoils for me and renders hateful to me. She is always there, clothed or naked, my real mistress; she is there, pressed close to the other woman, standing or lying down, visible and unattainable. And I believe now that she was in very truth a woman under a spell, bearing between her shoulders a mysterious talisman.

"Who is she? Even now I do not know. I have met her twice again. I bowed to her. She made not the slightest return to my greeting, she pretended not to know me at all. Who is she? An Asiatic perhaps? Most likely an eastern Jewess.

Yes, a Jewess. I am convinced she is a Jewess. But why? Yes, why indeed? I do not know."

THE DOUBLE PINS

"Ah, my dear fellow, what jades women are!"

"What makes you say that?"

"Because they have played me an abominable trick."

"You?"

"Yes, me."

"Women or a woman?"

"Two women."

"Two women at once?"

"Yes."

"What was the trick?"

The two young men were sitting outside a café on the boulevard and drinking liqueurs mixed with water, those aperients which look like infusions of all the tints in a box of water colors. They were nearly the same age: twenty-five to thirty. One was dark and the other fair, and they had the same semi-elegant look of stock-jobbers, of men who go to the Stock Exchange and into drawing rooms, who are to be seen everywhere, who live everywhere and love everywhere. The dark one continued:

"I have told you of my connection with that little woman, a tradesman's wife, whom I met on the beach at Dieppe?"

"Yes."

"My dear fellow, you know how it is. I had a mistress in Paris whom I love dearly, an old friend, a good friend, who is virtually a habit, in fact, one I value very much."

"Your habit?"

"Yes, my habit and hers also. She is married to an excellent man, whom I also value very much, a very cordial fellow and a capital companion! I may say that my life is bound up with that house."

"Well?"

"Well! They could not manage to leave Paris, and I found myself a widower at Dieppe."

"Why did you go to Dieppe?"

"For a change of air. One cannot remain on the boulevards the whole time."

"And then?"

"Then I met the little woman I mentioned to you on the beach there."

"The wife of that head of a public office?"

"Yes, she was dreadfully dull; her husband only came every Sunday, and he is horrible! I understood her perfectly, and we laughed and danced together."

"And the rest?"

"Yes, but that came later. However, we met and we liked each other. I told her I liked her, and she made me repeat it so that she might understand it better, and she put no obstacles in my way."

"Did you love her?"

"Yes, a little! She is very nice."

"And what about the other?"

"The other was in Paris! Well, for six weeks it was very pleasant, and we returned here on the best of terms. Do you know how to break with a woman when that woman has not wronged you in any way?"

"Yes, perfectly well."

"How do you manage it?"

"I give her up."

"How do you do it?"

"I do not see her any longer."

"But supposing she comes to you?"

"I am not at home."

"And if she comes again?"

"I say I am not well."

"If she looks after you?"

"I play her some dirty trick."

"And if she puts up with it?"

"I write her husband anonymous letters so that he may look after her on the days that I expect her."

"That is serious! I cannot resist and do not know how to bring about a rupture, and so I have a collection of mistresses. There are some whom I do not see more than once a year, others every ten months, others on those days when they want to dine at a restaurant; those whom I have put at regular intervals do not worry me, but I often have great difficulty with the fresh ones so as to keep them at proper intervals."

"And then?"

"And then—then this little woman was all fire and flame, without any fault of mine, as I told you! As her husband spends all the whole day at the office, she began to come to me unexpectedly, and twice she nearly met my regular one on the stairs."

"The devil!"

"Yes; so I gave each of them her days, regular days, to avoid confusion. Saturday and Monday for the old one, Tuesday, Friday and Sunday for the new one."

"Why did you show her the preference?"

"Ah! My dear friend, she is younger."

"So that only gave you two days to yourself in a week."

"That is enough for one."

"Allow me to compliment you on that."

"Well, just fancy that the most ridiculous and most annoying thing in the world happened to me. For four months everything had been going on perfectly; I felt quite safe and I was really very happy, when suddenly, last Monday, the crash came.

"I was expecting my regular one at the usual time, a quarter past one, and was smoking a good cigar, dreaming, very well satisfied with myself, when I suddenly saw that it was past the time. I was much surprised, for she is very punctual, but I thought that something might have accidentally delayed her. However, half an hour passed, then an hour, an hour and a half, and then I knew that something must have detained her—a sick headache, perhaps, or some annoying visitor. That

sort of waiting is very vexatious, very annoying and enervating. At last I made up
my mind to go out and, not knowing what to do, I went to her and found her
reading a novel.

" 'Well,' I said to her. And she replied quite calmly:

" 'My dear, I could not come; I was hindered.'

" 'How?'

" 'By something else.'

" 'What was it?'

" 'A very annoying visit.'

"I saw she would not tell me the true reason, and as she was very calm, I did
not trouble myself any more about it, hoping to make up for lost time with the
other next day. On the Tuesday I was very excited and amorous in expectation
of the public official's little wife, and I was surprised that she did not come before
the appointed time. I looked at the clock every moment and watched the hands
impatiently, but the quarter passed, then the half-hour, then two o'clock. I could
not sit still any longer and walked up and down very soon in great strides, putting
my face against the window and my ears to the door, to listen whether she was
not coming upstairs.

"Half-past two, three o'clock! I seized my hat, rushed to her house. She was
reading a novel, my dear fellow! 'Well!' I said anxiously, and she replied as calmly
as usual:

" 'I was hindered and could not come.'

" 'By what?'

" 'An annoying visit.'

"Of course I immediately thought that they both knew everything, but she
seemed so calm and quiet that I set aside my suspicions and thought it was only
some strange coincidence, as I could not believe in such dissimulation on her
part. And so after half an hour's friendly talk, which was, however, interrupted a
dozen times by her little girl coming in and out of the room, I went away very
much annoyed. Just imagine the next day."

"The same thing happened?"

"Yes, and the next also. And that went on for three weeks without any explanation, without anything explaining such strange conduct to me, the secret of which
I suspected, however."

"They knew everything?"

"I should think so, by George. But how? Ah! I had a great deal of anxiety before I found it out."

"How did you manage it at last?"

"From their letters, for on the same day they both gave me their dismissal in
identical terms."

"Well?"

"This is how it was: You know that women always have an array of pins about
them. I know hairpins; I doubt them and look after them, but the others are much
more treacherous, those confounded little black-headed pins which look all alike
to us, great fools that we are, but which they can distinguish, just as we can distinguish a horse from a dog.

"Well, it appears that one day my official's little wife left one of those telltale
instruments pinned to the paper close to my looking glass. My usual one had
immediately seen this little black speck, no bigger than a flea, had taken it out

without saying a word and had left one of her pins, which was also black but of a different pattern, in the same place.

"The next day the official's wife wished to recover her property and immediately recognized the substitution. Then her suspicions were aroused, and she put in two and crossed them. My original one replied to this telegraphic signal by three black pellets, one on the top of the other, and as soon as this method had begun they continued to communicate with one another without saying a word, just to spy on each other. Then it appears that the regular one, being bolder, wrapped a tiny piece of paper round the little wire point and wrote upon it:

"*C. D., Poste Restante, Boulevard Malesherbes.*

"Then they wrote to each other. You understand that was not everything that passed between them. They set to work with precaution, with a thousand stratagems, with all the prudence that is necessary in such cases, but the regular one made a bold stroke and made an appointment with the other. I do not know what they said to each other; all that I know is that I had to pay the costs of their interview. There you have it all!"

"Is that all?"

"Yes."

"And you do not see them any more?"

"I beg your pardon, I see them as friends, for we have not quarreled altogether."

"And have they met again?"

"Yes, my dear fellow, they have become intimate friends."

"And has not that given you an idea?"

"No, what idea?"

"You great booby! The idea of making them put back the pins where they found them."

THE SIGNAL

The little Marchioness de Rennedon was still asleep in her dark and perfumed bedroom.

In her soft, low bed, between sheets of delicate cambric, fine as lace and caressing as a kiss, she was sleeping alone and tranquil, the happy and profound sleep of divorced women.

She was awakened by loud voices in the little blue drawing room, and she recognized her dear friend, the little Baroness de Grangerie, who was disputing with the lady's maid because the latter would not allow her to go into the marchioness's room. So the little marchioness got up, opened the door, drew back the door hangings and showed her head, nothing but her fair head, hidden under a cloud of hair.

"What is the matter with you that you have come so early?" she asked. "It is not nine o'clock yet."

The little baroness, who was very pale, nervous and feverish, replied: "I must speak to you. Something horrible has happened to me."

"Come in, my dear."

She went in; they kissed each other, and the little marchioness got back into her bed, while the lady's maid opened the windows to let in light and air. Then when she had left the room Madame de Rennedon went on: "Well, tell me what it is."

Baroness de Grangerie began to cry, shedding those pretty bright tears which make women more charming. She sobbed out without wiping her eyes, so as not to make them red: "Oh, my dear, what has happened to me is abominable, abominable. I have not slept all night, not a minute; do you hear? Not a minute. Here, just feel my heart how it is beating."

And, taking her friend's hand, she put it on her breast, on that firm, round covering of women's hearts which often suffices men and prevents them from seeking beneath. But her heart was really beating violently.

She continued: "It happened to me yesterday during the day at about four o'clock—or half-past four; I cannot say exactly. You know my apartments, and you know that my little drawing room, where I always sit, looks on to the Rue Saint-Lazare and that I have a mania for sitting at the window to look at the people passing. The neighborhood of the railway station is very gay, so full of motion and lively—just what I like! So yesterday I was sitting in the low chair which I have placed in my window recess; the window was open, and I was not thinking of anything, simply breathing the fresh air. You remember how fine it was yesterday!

"Suddenly I remarked a woman sitting at the window opposite—a woman in red. I was in mauve, you know, my pretty mauve costume. I did not know the woman, a new lodger, who had been there a month, and as it has been raining for a month, I had not yet seen her, but I saw immediately that she was a bad girl. At first I was very much shocked and disgusted that she should be at the window just as I was, and then by degrees it amused me to watch her. She was resting her elbows on the window ledge and looking at the men, and the men looked at her also, all or nearly all. One might have said that they knew of her presence by some means as they got near the house, that they scented her, as dogs scent game, for they suddenly raised their heads and exchanged a swift look with her, a sort of freemason's look. Hers said: 'Will you?' Theirs replied: 'I have no time,' or else: 'Another day,' or else: 'I have not got a sou,' or else: 'Hide yourself, you wretch!'

"You cannot imagine how funny it was to see her carrying on such a piece of work, though after all it is her regular business.

"Occasionally she shut the window suddenly, and I saw a gentleman go in. She had caught him like a fisherman hooks a gudgeon. Then I looked at my watch and I found that they never stopped longer than from twelve to twenty minutes. In the end she really infatuated me, the spider! And then the creature is so ugly.

"I asked myself: 'How does she manage to make herself understood so quickly, so well and so completely? Does she add a sign of the head or a motion of the hands to her looks?' And I took my opera glasses to watch her proceedings. Oh! They were very simple: first of all a glance, then a smile, then a slight sign with the head which meant: 'Are you coming up?' But it was so slight, so vague, so discreet, that it required a great deal of knack to succeed as she did. And I asked myself: 'I wonder if I could do that little movement from below upward, which was at the same time bold and pretty, as well as she does,' for her gesture was very pretty.

"I went and tried it before the looking glass and, my dear, I did it better than she, a great deal better! I was enchanted and resumed my place at the window.

"She caught nobody more then, poor girl, nobody. She certainly had no luck. It must really be very terrible to earn one's bread in that way, terrible and amusing occasionally, for really some of these men one meets in the street are rather nice.

"After that they all came on my side of the road and none on hers; the sun had turned. They came one after the other, young, old, dark, fair, gray, white. I saw some who looked very nice, really very nice, my dear, far better than my husband or than yours—I mean than your late husband, as you have got a divorce. Now you can choose.

"I said to myself: 'If I give them the sign will they understand me, who am a respectable woman?' And I was seized with a mad longing to make that sign to them. I had a longing, a terrible longing; you know, one of those longings which one cannot resist! I have some like that occasionally. How silly such things are, don't you think so? I believe that we women have the souls of monkeys. I have been told (and it was a physician who told me) that the brain of a monkey is very like ours. Of course we must imitate someone or other. We imitate our husbands when we love them during the first months after our marriage, and then our lovers, our female friends, our confessors when they are nice. We assume their ways of thought, their manners of speech, their words, their gestures, everything. It is very foolish.

"However, as for me, when I am much tempted to do a thing I always do it and so I said to myself: 'I will try it once, on one man only just to see. What can happen to me? Nothing whatever! We shall exchange a smile and that will be all, and I shall deny it most certainly.'

"So I began to make my choice. I wanted someone nice, very nice, and suddenly I saw a tall, very good-looking fellow coming alone. I like fair men, as you know. I looked at him; he looked at me. I smiled; he smiled. I made the movement, oh, so faintly; he replied yes with his head, and there he was, my dear! He came in at the large door of the house.

"You cannot imagine what passed through my mind then! I thought I should go mad. Oh, how frightened I was! Just think, he will speak to the servants! To Joseph, who is devoted to my husband! Joseph would certainly think that I had known that gentleman for a long time.

"What could I do, just tell me? And he would ring in a moment. What could I do, tell me? I thought I would go and meet him and tell him he had made a mistake and beg him to go away. He would have pity on a woman, on a poor woman. So I rushed to the door and opened it just at the moment when he was going to ring the bell, and I stammered out quite stupidly: 'Go away, monsieur, go away; you have made a mistake, a terrible mistake. I took you for one of my friends whom you are very like. Have pity on me, monsieur.'

"But he only began to laugh, my dear, and replied: 'Good morning, my dear, I know all about your little story; you may be sure. You are married and so you want forty francs instead of twenty, and you shall have them, so just show the way.'

"And he pushed me in, closed the door, and as I remained standing before him, horror-struck, he kissed me, put his arm round my waist and made me go back into the drawing room, the door of which had remained open. Then he began to look at everything, like an auctioneer, and continued: 'By Jove, it is very nice in your rooms, very nice. You must be very down on your luck just now to do the window business!'

"Then I began to beg him again. 'Oh, monsieur, go away, please go away! My husband will be coming in soon; it is just his time. I swear that you have made a mistake!' But he answered quite coolly: 'Come, my beauty, I have had enough of this nonsense, and if your husband comes in I will give him five francs to go and have a drink at the café opposite.' And then, seeing Raoul's photograph on the chimney piece, he asked me: 'Is that your—your husband?'

" 'Yes, that is he.'

" 'He looks like a nice, disagreeable sort of fellow. And who is this? One of your friends?'

"It was your photograph, my dear, you know, the one in ball dress. I did not know any longer what I was saying and I stammered: 'Yes, it is one of my friends.'

" 'She is very nice; you shall introduce me to her.'

"Just then the clock struck five, and Raoul comes home every day at half-past! Suppose he were to come home before the other had gone; just fancy what would have happened! Then—then I completely lost my head—altogether. I thought— I thought—that—that—the best thing would be—to get rid of—of this man—as quickly as possible. The sooner it was over—you understand."

The little Marchioness de Rennedon had begun to laugh, to laugh madly, with her head buried in her pillow, so that the whole bed shook, and when she was a little calmer she asked:

"And—and—was he good-looking?"

"Yes."

"And yet you complain?"

"But—but—don't you see, my dear, he said—he said—he should come again tomorrow—at the same time—and I—I am terribly frightened. You have no idea how tenacious he is and obstinate. What can I do—tell me—what can I do?"

The little marchioness sat up in bed to reflect, and then she suddenly said: "Have him arrested!"

The little baroness looked stupefied and stammered out: "What do you say? What are you thinking of? Have him arrested? Under what pretext?"

"That is very simple. Go to the commissary of police and say that a gentleman has been following you about for three months, that he had the insolence to go up to your apartments yesterday, that he has threatened you with another visit tomorrow and that you demand the protection of the law, and they will give you two police officers who will arrest him."

"But, my dear, suppose he tells——"

"They will not believe him, you silly thing, if you have told your tale cleverly to the commissary, but they will believe you, who are an irreproachable woman, and in society."

"Oh! I shall never dare to do it."

"You must dare, my dear, or you are lost."

"But think that he will—he will insult me if he is arrested."

"Very well, you will have witnesses, and he will be sentenced."

"Sentenced to what?"

"To pay damages. In such cases one must be pitiless!"

"Ah! Speaking of damages—there is one thing that worries me very much— very much indeed. He left me two twenty-franc pieces on the mantelpiece."

"Two twenty-franc pieces?"

"Yes."

"No more?"

"No."

"That is very little. It would have humiliated me. Well?"

"Well? What am I to do with that money?"

The little marchioness hesitated for a few seconds, and then she replied in a serious voice:

"My dear—you must make—you must make your husband a little present with it. That will be only fair!"

GRAVEYARD SIRENS

The five friends had finished their dinner; there were two bachelors and three married men, all middle-aged and wealthy. They assembled thus once a month in memory of old times and lingered to gossip over their coffee till late at night. Many a happy evening was spent in this way, for they were fond of one another's society and had remained closely united. Conversation among them was a sort of review of the daily papers, commenting on everything that interests and amuses Parisians. One of the cleverest, Joseph de Bardon, was a bachelor. He lived the life of a *boulevardier* most thoroughly and fantastically, without being debauched or depraved. It interested him, and as he was still young, being barely forty, he enjoyed it keenly. A man of the world in the broadest and best sense of the word, he possessed a great deal of wit without much depth, a general knowledge without real learning, quick perception without serious penetration; but his adventures and observations furnished him many amusing stories, which he told with so much philosophy and humor that society voted him very intellectual.

He was a favorite after-dinner speaker, always having some story to relate to which his friends looked forward. Presently he began to tell a story without being asked. Leaning on the table with a half-filled glass of brandy in front of his plate, in the smoky atmosphere filled with the fragrance of coffee, he seemed perfectly at ease, just as some beings are entirely at home in certain places and under certain conditions—as a goldfish in its aquarium, for instance, or a nun in her cloister.

Puffing at his cigar, he said:

"A rather curious thing happened to me a little while ago."

All exclaimed at once: "Tell us about it!"

Presently he continued:

"You all know how I love to roam around the city like a collector in search of antiquities. I enjoy watching people and things. About the middle of September, the weather being very fine, I went for a walk one afternoon without a definite purpose. Why do we men always have the vague impulse to call on some pretty woman? We review them in our mind, compare their respective charms, the interest they arouse in us, and finally decide in favor of the one that attracts us most.

"But when the sun shines brightly and the air is balmy sometimes we altogether lose the desire for calling.

"That day the sun was bright and the air balmy, so I simply lighted a cigar and started for the Boulevard Extérieur. As I was sauntering along I thought I would take a look around the cemetery at Montmartre. Now I have always liked cemeteries because they sadden and rest me, and I need that influence at times. Besides, many of my friends are laid to rest there, and I go to see them once in a while.

"As it happens, I once buried a romance in this particular cemetery—an old love of mine, a charming little woman whose memory awakens all kinds of regrets in me. I often dream beside her grave. All is over for her now!

"I like graveyards because they are such immense, densely populated cities. Just think of all the bodies buried in that small space, of the countless generations of Parisians laid there forever, eternally entombed in the little vaults of their little graves marked by a cross or a stone, while the living—fools that they are!—take up so much room and make such a fuss.

"Cemeteries have some monuments quite as interesting as those to be seen in the museums. Cavaignac's tomb I liken, without comparing it, to that masterpiece of Jean Goujon, the tombstone of Louis de Brézé in the subterranean chapel in the cathedral of Rouen. My friends, all so-called modern and realistic art originated there. That reproduction of Louis de Brézé is more lifelike and terrible, more convulsed with agony, than any one of the statues that decorate modern tombs.

"In Montmartre is Baudin's monument, and it is quite imposing; also the tombs of Gautier and Murger, where the other day I found a solitary wreath of yellow immortelles laid there—by whom do you suppose? Perhaps by the last *grisette*, grown old and possibly become a janitress in the neighborhood! It's a pretty little statue by Millet, but it is ruined by neglect and accumulated filth. Sing of youth, O Murger!

"Well, I entered the cemetery filled with a certain sadness, not too poignant, a feeling suggesting such thoughts as this: The place is not very cheerful, but I'm not to be put here yet.

"The impression of autumn, a warm dampness smelling of dead leaves, the pale, anemic rays of the sun, intensified and poetized the solitude of this place, which reminds one of death and of the end of all things.

"I walked slowly along the alleys of graves where neighbors no longer visit, no longer sleep together or read the papers. I began reading the epitaphs. There is nothing more amusing in the world. Labiche and Meilhac have never made me laugh as much as some of these tombstone inscriptions. I tell you these crosses and marble slabs on which the relatives of the dead have poured out their regrets and their wishes for the happiness of the departed, their hopes of reunion—the hypocrites!—make better reading than Balzac's funniest tales! But what I love in Montmartre are the abandoned plots filled with yew trees and cypress, the resting place of those departed long ago. However, the green trees nourished by the bodies will soon be felled to make room for those that have recently passed away, whose graves will be there under little marble slabs.

"After loitering awhile I felt tired and decided to pay my faithful tribute to my little friend's memory. When I reached the grave my heart was very sad. Poor child! She was so sweet and loving, so fair and white—and now—should her grave be reopened . . .

"Bending over the iron railing, I murmured a prayer which she probably never heard, and I turned to leave, when I caught sight of a woman in deep mourning kneeling beside a neighboring grave. Her crape veil was thrown back, disclosing her blonde hair which seemed illumined under the darkness of her hat. I forgot to leave.

"She seemed bowed with sorrow. She had buried her face in her hands, apparently lost in deep thought. With closed lids, as rigid as a statue, she was living over torturing memories and seemed herself a corpse mourning a corpse. Presently I saw that she was weeping, as there was a convulsive movement of her back and shoulders. Suddenly she uncovered her face. Her eyes, brimming with tears, were charming. For a moment she gazed around, as if awakening from a nightmare. She saw me looking at her and quickly hid her face again, greatly abashed. Now with convulsive sobs she bent her head slowly over the tombstone. She rested her forehead against it, and her veil, falling around her, covered the whiteness of the beloved sepulcher with a dark shroud. I heard her moan and then saw her fall to the ground in a faint.

"I rushed to her side and began slapping her hands and breathing on her temples, while reading this simple inscription on the tombstone:

"*Here lies Louis-Théodore Carrel, captain in the Marine Infantry, killed by the enemy in Tonkin. Pray for his soul.*

"This death was quite recent. I was moved almost to tears and renewed my efforts to revive the poor girl. At last she came to. I am not so very bad looking, and my face must have shown how upset I was, for her very first glance showed me that she was likely to be grateful for my care. Between sobs she told me of her marriage to the officer who had been killed in Tonkin within a year after their wedding. He had married her for love, she being an orphan and possessing nothing above the required dowry.

"I consoled her, comforted her and assisted her to her feet, saying:

" 'You must not stay here. Come away.'

" 'I am unable to walk,' she whispered.

" 'Let me help you,' I said.

" 'Thank you, you are very kind,' she murmured. 'Did you also come to mourn someone?'

" 'Yes, madame.'

" 'A woman?'

" 'Yes, madame.'

" 'Your wife?'

" 'A friend.'

" 'One may love a friend just as much as a wife, for passion knows no law,' said the lady.

" 'Yes, madame,' I replied.

"And so we left the spot together, she leaning on me and I almost carrying her through the alleys. As we came out she murmured:

" 'I'm afraid that I'm going to faint.'

" 'Wouldn't you like to take something, madame?' I inquired.

" 'Yes,' she said, 'I would.'

"I discovered a restaurant near at hand, where the friends of the dead gather to celebrate the end of their painful duty. We went in, and I made her drink a cup of hot tea, which appeared to give her renewed strength.

"A faint smile dawned on her lips, and she began telling me about herself: how terrible it was to go through life all alone, to be alone at home day and night, to have no one on whom to lavish love, confidence and intimacy.

"It all seemed sincere and sounded well coming from her. I was softened. She was very young, perhaps twenty. I paid her several compliments that appeared to please her, and as it was growing dark, I offered to take her home in a cab. She accepted. In the carriage we were so close to each other that we could feel the warmth of our bodies through our clothing, which really is the most intoxicating thing in the world.

"When the cab stopped in front of her home she said:

" 'I hardly feel able to walk upstairs, for I live on the fourth floor. You have already been so kind that I am going to ask you to assist me to my rooms.'

"I consented gladly. She walked up slowly, breathing heavily at each step. In front of her door she added:

" 'Do come in for a few minutes so that I can thank you again for your kindness.'

"And I, of course, followed her.

"Her apartment was modest, even a trifle poor, but well kept and in good taste.

"We sat down side by side on a small divan, and she again began to speak of her loneliness.

"Then she rang for the maid, so as to offer me some refreshments. But the girl failed to appear, and I joyfully concluded that this maid probably came only in the morning and was a sort of scrubwoman.

"She had taken off her hat. How pretty she was! Her clear eyes looked steadily at me, so clear and so steady that a great temptation came to me to which I promptly yielded. Clasping her in my arms, I kissed her again and again on her half-closed lids.

"She repelled me, struggling to free herself and repeating:

" 'Do stop—do end it.'

"What did she mean to imply by this word? Under such conditions, to 'end' could have at least two meanings. In order to silence her I passed from her eyes to her lips and gave to the word 'end' the conclusion I preferred. She did not resist very much, and as our eyes met after this insult to the memory of the departed captain, I saw that her expression was one of tender resignation, which quickly dispelled my misgivings.

"Then I grew attentive and gallant. After an hour's chat I asked her:

" 'Where do you dine?'

" 'In a small restaurant near by.'

" 'All alone?'

" 'Why, yes.'

" 'Will you take dinner with me?'

" 'Where?'

" 'In a good restaurant on the boulevard.'

"She hesitated a little but at last consented, consoling herself with the argument that she was so desperately lonely and adding, 'I must put on a lighter gown.'

"She retired to her room, and when she emerged she was dressed in a simple gray frock that made her look exquisitely slender. She apparently had different costumes for street and for cemetery wear!

"Our dinner was most pleasant and cordial. She drank some champagne, thereby becoming very animated and lively, and we returned to her apartment together.

"This liaison, begun among tombstones, lasted about three weeks. But man tires of everything and especially of women. So I pleaded an urgent trip and left her. Of course I managed to be generous, for which she was duly thankful, making me promise and even swear that I would come back, for she really seemed to care a little for me.

"In the meantime I found other attachments, and a month or so went by without the memory of this love being vivid enough to bring me back to her. Still, I had not forgotten her. She haunted me like a mystery, a psychological problem, an unsolved question.

"I can't tell why, but one day I imagined that I should find her in the cemetery. So I went back. I walked around a long time without meeting anyone but the usual visitors of the place, mourners who had not broken off all relations with their dead. The grave of the captain killed in Tonkin was deserted, without flowers or wreaths.

"As I was passing through another part of this great city of death I suddenly saw a couple in deep mourning coming toward me through one of the narrow paths hedged with crosses. When they drew near, oh, surprise! I recognized—her! She saw me and blushed. As I brushed past her she gave me a little wink that meant clearly: Don't recognize me, and also seemed to say: Do come back.

"The man who accompanied her was about fifty years old, fine looking and distinguished, an officer of the Legion of Honor. He was leading her just as I had, when we left the cemetery together.

"I was utterly nonplused, reluctant to believe what my eyes had just seen, and I wondered to what strange tribe of creatures this graveyard huntress belonged. Was she merely a clever courtesan, an inspired prostitute, who haunted cemeteries for men disconsolate at the loss of some woman, a mistress or a wife, and hungering for past caresses? Is it a profession? Are the cemeteries worked like the streets? Are there graveyard sirens? Or had she alone the idea—wonderful for its deep philosophy—to profit by the amorous regrets awakened in these awful places? I would have given a great deal to know whose widow she was that day!"

A MADMAN

He died a high-court judge, an upright magistrate whose irreproachable life was held up to honor in every court in France. Barristers, young puisne judges, judges, greeted with a low bow that marked their profound respect, his thin white impressive face lighted up by two fathomless gleaming eyes.

He had given up his life to the pursuit of crime and the protection of the weak. Swindlers and murderers had had no more formidable enemy, for he seemed to read, in the depths of their souls, their most secret thoughts, and penetrate at a glance the dark twistings of their motives.

He had died, in his eighty-second year, everywhere honored and followed by the regrets of a whole nation. Soldiers in scarlet trousers had escorted him to his grave, and men in white ties had delivered themselves round his coffin of grief-stricken speeches and tears that seemed sincere.

And then came the strange document that the startled solicitor discovered in the desk where he had been accustomed to keep the dossiers of famous criminals. It had for title:

"WHY?"

June 20, 1851. I have just left the court. I have condemned Blondel to death. Why did this man kill his five children? Why? Often, one comes across people to whose temperaments the taking of life affords a keen physical pleasure. Yes, yes, it must be a physical pleasure, perhaps the sharpest of all, for is not killing an act more like the act of creation than any other? To *make* and to *destroy*. In these two words is contained the history of the universe, the history of all worlds, of all that exists, all. Why is it so intoxicating to kill?

June 25. To think that there is a living being in there—loves, walks, runs! A living being. What is a living being? This thing possessed of life, bearing within itself the vital power of motion and a will that orders this motion. It is kin to nothing, this human being. Its feet do not belong to the ground. It is a germ of life wandering over the earth; and this germ of life, come I know not whence, can be destroyed at will. Then nothing, forever nothing. It decays, it is ended.

June 26. Then why is it a crime to kill? Yes, why? It is, on the contrary, a law of nature. The ordained purpose of every being is to kill: he kills to live, and he kills for the sake of killing. To kill is in our nature: we must kill. The beasts kill continually, every day, at every moment of their existence. Man kills continually to feed himself, but as he must also kill for sheer sensual satisfaction, he has invented sport. A child kills the insects that he finds, the little birds, all the little animals that come his way. But that does not satisfy the irresistible lust for wholesale killing which is in us. It is not enough to kill beasts; we must kill men too. In other days, we satisfied this need by human sacrifice. Today the necessities of living in a community have made murder a crime. We condemn it and punish the assassin. But since we cannot live without yielding to the innate and imperious instinct of death, we assuage it from time to time by wars in which one whole race butchers another. War is a debauch of blood, a debauch in which the armies sate themselves and on which not only plain citizens are drunken, but women and the children who every evening read under the lamp the hysterical recital of the massacres.

One would have imagined that scorn would be meted out to those destined to accomplish these slaughterings of men. No. They are heaped with honors. They are clad in gold and gorgeous raiment; they wear feathers on their heads, decorations on their breasts; and they are given crosses, rewards, honors of all kinds. They are haughty, respected, adored of women, acclaimed by the mob, and solely because their mission in life is to shed human blood. They drag through the streets their instruments of death, which the black-coated passer-by regards with envy. For killing is the glorious law thrust by nature into the profoundest impulse of our being. There is nothing more lovely and more honorable than to kill.

June 30. To kill is the law; because nature loves immortal youth. She seems to cry through all her unconscious acts: "Hasten! Hasten! Hasten!" As she destroys, so she renews.

July 2. Being—what is being? All and nothing. For thought, it is the reflection of all things. For memory and for science, it is an epitome of the world, the tale of which it bears within itself. Mirror of things, and mirror of deeds, each human being becomes a little universe within the universe.

But travel; look at the people swarming everywhere, and man is nothing now, nothing now, nothing! Get into a ship, put a wide space between yourself and the crowded shore, and you will soon see nothing but the coast. The infinitesimal speck of being disappears, so tiny it is, so insignificant. Traverse Europe in a swift train and look out through the window. Men, men, always men, innumerable, inglorious, swarming in the fields, swarming in the streets; dull-witted peasants able to do no more than turn up the earth; ugly women able to do no more than prepare food for their men, and to breed. Go to India, go to China, and you will see scurrying about more thousands of creatures, who are born, live, and die without leaving more trace than the ant crushed to death on the road. Go to the country of black men, herded in their mud huts; to the country of fair-skinned Arabs sheltered under a brown canvas that flaps in the wind, and you will understand that the solitary individual being is nothing, nothing. The race is all. What is the individual, the individual member of a wandering desert tribe? And men who are wise do not trouble themselves overmuch about death. Man counts for nothing with them. A man kills his enemy: it is war. That, in the old days, was the way of the world, in every great house, in every province.

Yes, journey over the world and watch the swarming of the innumerable and nameless human beings. Nameless? Aye, there's the rub! To kill is a crime because we have enumerated human beings. When they are born, they are registered, named, baptized. The law takes charge of them. Very well, then! The man who is not registered is of no account: kill him in the desert, kill him in the hills or in the plain, what does it matter! Nature loves death: she will not punish it.

What is verily sacred, is the social community. That's it! It is that which protects man. The individual is sacred because he is a member of the social community. Homage to the social state, the legal God. On your knees!

The state itself can kill because it has the right to alter the social community. When it has had two hundred thousand men butchered in a war, it erases them from the community, it suppresses them by the hands of its registrars. That is the end of it. But we who cannot alter the records of the town halls, we must respect life. Social community, glorious divinity who reigns in the temples of the municipalities, I salute you. You are stronger than nature. Ah! Ah!

July 3. To kill must be a strange pleasure and of infinite relish to a man. To have there, standing before him, a living, thinking being: to thrust in him a little hole, only a little hole, to see pouring out that red stuff which we call blood, which makes life, and then to have in front of one only a lump of nerveless flesh, cold, inert, emptied of thought.

August 5. I who have spent my life in judging, condemning, in killing by uttered words, in killing by the guillotine such as have killed by the knife, I, I, if I did as do all the assassins whom I have struck down, I, I, who would know it?

August 10. Who would ever know it? Who would suspect me, me—especially if I chose a creature in whose removal I have no interest?

August 15. The temptation. The temptation has entered into me like a worm that crawls. It crawls, it moves, it roves through my whole body, in my mind, which thinks only of one thing—to kill; in my eyes which lust to see blood, to see something die; in my ears, where there sounds continually something strange, monstrous, shattering, and stupefying, like the last cry of a human creature; in my legs, which tingle with desire to go, to go to the spot where the thing could come to pass; in my hands which tremble with lust to kill. What a glorious act it would be, a rare act, worthy of a free man, greater than other men, captain of his soul, and a seeker after exquisite sensations!

August 22. I could resist no longer. I have killed a small beast just to try, to begin with.

Jean, my man, had a goldfinch in a cage hung in a window of the servant's room. I sent him on an errand and I took the little bird in my hand—in my hand, where I felt the beating of his heart. He was warm. I went up to my room. From time to time, I clutched him harder, his heart beat faster; it was frightful and delicious. I all but choked him. But I should not have seen the blood.

Then I took the scissors, short nail scissors, and I cut his throat in three strokes, so cleverly. He opened his beak, he struggled to escape me, but I held him fast, oh, I held him; I would have held a mad bulldog, and I saw the blood run. How beautiful blood is, red, gleaming, clear! I longed to drink it. I wetted the end of my tongue with it. It was good. But he had so little of it, the poor little bird! I have not had time to enjoy the sight of it as I would have liked. It must be glorious to see a bull bleed to death.

And then I did all that assassins do, that real ones do. I washed the scissors, I washed my hands, I threw out the water, and I carried the body, the corpse, into the garden to bury it. I hid it in the strawberry bed. It will never be found. Every day I shall eat a strawberry from that plant. In very truth, how one can enjoy life when one knows how!

My man wept; he supposed that his bird had flown. How could he suspect me? Ah! Ah!

Aug. 25. I must kill a man. I must.

Aug. 30. It is done. What a simple thing it is!

I went to take a walk in the Bois de Vernes. I was thinking of nothing, no, of nothing. And there was a child on the road, a little boy eating a slice of bread and butter.

He stood still to let me pass and said:

"Good day, monsieur le président."

And the thought came into my head: "Suppose I were to kill him?"

I replied:

"Are you all alone, my boy?"

"Yes, sir."

"All alone in the wood?"

"Yes, sir."

The desire to kill intoxicated me like strong drink. I approached him stealthily, sure that he would run away. And then I seized him by the throat . . . I squeezed him, I squeezed him with all my strength. He looked at me with terrified eyes.

What eyes! Quite round, fathomless, clear, terrible. I have never experienced so savage an emotion . . . but so short. He clutched my wrists with his little hands, and his body writhed like a feather in the fire. Then he moved no more.

My heart thudded, ah! the bird's heart! I flung the body in a ditch, then grasses over him.

I went home again; I dined well. What an utterly simple affair!

That evening I was very gay, lighthearted, young again. I spent the rest of the evening at the prefect's house. They found me good company.

But I have not seen blood. I am calm.

Aug. 30. The corpse has been found. They are searching for the murderer. Ah! Ah!

Sept. 1. They have arrested two tramps. Proofs are lacking.

Sept 2. The parents have been to see me. They wept. Ah! Ah!

Oct. 6. They have discovered nothing. Some wandering vagabond must have struck the blow. Ah! Ah! If I had only seen the blood flow, I think I should now be quiet in my mind.

Oct. 10. The lust to kill possesses my every nerve. It is like the furious passions of love that torture us at twenty.

Oct. 20. Yet another. I was walking along the river, after breakfast. And I saw, under a willow, a fisherman fast asleep. It was high noon. A spade was stuck, it might have been for the purpose, in a near-by field of potatoes.

I took it, I came back; I lifted it like a club and, cutting through it with a single blow, I split the fisherman's head right open. Oh, how he bled! Crimson blood, full of brains. It trickled into the water, very gently. And I went on my way at a solemn pace. If anyone had seen me! Ah! Ah! I should have made an excellent assassin.

Oct. 25. The affair of the fisherman has roused a great outcry. His nephew, who used to fish with him, has been accused of the murder.

Oct. 26. The examining magistrate declares that the nephew is guilty. Everyone in the town believes it. Ah! Ah!

Oct. 27. The nephew has put up a poor defense. He declares that he had gone to the village to buy bread and cheese. He swears that his uncle was killed in his absence. Who believes him?

Oct. 28. The nephew is as good as condemned, so utterly have they made him lose his head. Ah! Ah! Justice!

Nov. 15. Crushing evidence accumulates against the nephew, who will inherit from his uncle. I shall preside at the assizes.

Jan. 25. To death! To death! To death! I have condemned him to death. Ah! Ah!

The solicitor-general spoke like an angel. Ah! Ah! Yet another. I shall go to see him executed.

March 20. It is done. He was guillotined this morning. He made a good end, very good. It gave me infinite pleasure. How sweet it is to see a man's head cut off! The blood spurted out like a wave, like a wave. Oh, if I could, I would have liked to bathe in it! What intoxicating ecstasy to crouch below it, to receive it in my hair and on my face, and rise up all crimson, all crimson! Ah, if people knew!

Now I shall wait, I can afford to wait. So little a thing might trip me up.

The manuscript contained several more papers, but without relating any fresh crime.

The alienists, to whom it was entrusted, declare that there exist in the world many undetected madmen, as cunning and as redoubtable as this monstrous maniac.

GROWING OLD

The two friends had finished dinner. From the window of the café they saw the boulevard full of people. They felt the warm zephyrs which prevail in Paris on sweet summer nights and make travelers raise their heads and desire to go out, to go down, one knows not where, under the leaves and dream of rivers lighted by the moon, of glowworms and of nightingales.

One of them, Henry Simon, sighed profoundly and said:

"Ah! I am getting old. It is sad. Formerly on evenings like this I felt the devil in my body. Now I feel only regrets. How quickly life goes!"

He was already a little stout and very bald; he was perhaps forty-five years old. The other, Peter Carnier, was older but thinner and more lively; he replied:

"As for me, my friend, I have grown old without perceiving it the least in the world. I was always gay, a jolly fellow, vigorous and all the rest. Now as one looks at himself each day in the mirror he does not perceive the work that age is accomplishing, because it is slow and regular and modifies his visage so gradually that the transition is unseen. Only for this we should die of chagrin after but two or three years' ravages. But we are not able to appreciate them. In order to take a reckoning it would be necessary to go six months without looking at ourselves; and then what a blow!

"And the women, my dear, how I pity them, the poor beings. All their happiness, all their power, all their life, is in their beauty, which lasts but ten years.

"I then grew old without suspecting it; I believed myself a young man, although I was nearly fifty years old. Never having felt an infirmity of any sort, I went along, happy and tranquil.

"The revelation of my decadence came to me in a simple but terrible fashion, which made me downcast for nearly six months. Since then I have accepted the part.

"I have often been in love, like all men, but once in particular. I met her at the seashore at Etretat about twelve years ago, a little after the war. There is nothing so pretty as this shore in the morning at the bathing hour. It is small, rounded like a horseshoe, incased in those high, white cliffs, pierced with those singular holes they call ports, one enormous one extending into the sea like a giant's leg, the other opposite, squat and round. A crowd of women assembles here on the right side of the shuffleboard, which they cover like a bright garden with their brilliant costumes—this box between the high rocks. The sun falls full upon the coast, upon umbrellas of all shades, upon the sea of a greenish blue. And all is gay, charming, smiling, to the eyes. You seat yourself near the water to watch the bathers. They descend in a bathrobe of flannel which they throw off with a pretty motion upon reaching the fringe of the foam from the short waves; they go into the sea with a little rapid step which is arrested sometimes by a delicious cold shiver or a slight suffocation.

"Few can stand this trial of the bath. It is there that one can judge them from the calf to the throat. The going out especially reveals the weak, although salt water may be a powerful help to flabby flesh.

"The first time that I saw this young woman thus I was delighted, ravished. She held good; she held firm. Then there are some faces whose charm enters into us suddenly, invades us at a single blow. It seemed to me that I had found the woman that I was born to love. I had that sensation, and it was like a shock.

"I had myself presented and was immediately captured as I never was before. She ravaged my heart. It is a frightful and delicious thing, the undergoing thus the domination of a woman. It is almost a punishment and, at the same time, an unbelievable happiness. Her look, her smile, her hair at the nape of the neck when the breeze moved it, all the little lines of her face, the least movement of her features delighted me and made me extremely fond of her. She took possession of me through all my being, by her gestures, her attitudes, even by the things she carried, which became bewitching to me. I would wait to see her veil thrown upon some piece of furniture, her gloves upon an armchair. Her costumes seemed to me inimitable. No one had hats like hers.

"She was married, and the husband came every Saturday to remain until Monday. He seemed to me very indifferent. I was not at all jealous of him; I know not why, but never a being seemed to have less importance in life or attract less of my attention than this man.

"How I loved her! And how beautiful she was, and gracious and young! She was youth, elegance and freshness even. Never before had I felt what a pretty being a woman is, so distinguished and delicate, so full of charm and grace! Never had I understood what a seducing beauty there is in the curve of her cheek, in the movement of her lips, in the round folds of her little ear, in the form of that simple organ which we call the nose.

"This lasted three months, and then I departed for America, my heart bruised and full of despair. But the thought of her remained in me persistent, triumphant. She possessed me at a distance as she had when I was near her.

"Some years passed. I had not forgotten her. Her charming image remained before my eyes and in my heart. My tenderness remained faithful to her, a tranquil tenderness now, something like a much-loved memory of the most beautiful, most attractive thing I had met in life.

"Twelve years are such a little thing in a man's existence! One scarcely feels them pass! They go one after another, these years, gently and quickly, slowly or hurriedly, each long but so soon finished! And they add so rapidly and leave so little trace behind them; they vanish so completely that in looking back over the time passed one cannot perceive anything and cannot comprehend how it is that they have made him old. It seemed to me truly that only a few months separated me from that charming season on the beach at Etretat.

"Last spring I went to dine at Maisons-Lafitte at the house of some friends. Just as the train was starting a large woman got into my car, followed by four little girls. I scarcely glanced at this large, round mother, with a face like a full moon incased in a beribboned hat.

"She breathed heavily, being out of breath from a quick walk. The children began to babble. I opened my newspaper and began to read.

"We were just passing Asnières when my neighbor said to me suddenly:

" 'Pardon me, sir, but are you not Monsieur Carnier?'

" 'Yes, madame.'

"Then she began to laugh, the laugh of a contented, brave woman, but a little sad, nevertheless.

" 'You do not recognize me?' she said.

"I hesitated. I fully believed that I had somewhere seen that face, but where? And when? I answered:

" 'Yes—and no—I certainly do recognize you but cannot recall your name.'

"She blushed a little as she said: 'Madame Julie Lefevre.'

"Never have I received such a blow. For a second it seemed to me that all was finished for me. I felt that a veil had been torn away from before my eyes and that I was about to discover something frightful and wounding.

"It was she! That great, gross, common woman, she? And she had borne these four girls since I had seen her. And these four beings astonished me as much as the mother herself. They had come from her; they were tall already, had taken her place in life. She no longer counted, she, that marvel of coquettish, refined grace. I had seen her yesterday, it seemed to me, and I found her again like this! Was it possible? A violent grief attacked my heart, and also a revolt against Nature even, an unreasonable indignation against her brutal work, so infamous and destructive.

"I looked at her, aghast. Then I took her by the hand, and the tears mounted to my eyes. I wept for her young; I wept for her dead. For I was not acquainted with this large lady.

"She, also affected, stammered:

" 'I am much changed, am I not? What can we expect after so long? You see, I have become a mother, nothing but a mother, a good mother. Adieu to all else; it is finished. Oh! I never thought that you would not recognize me if we met! And you, too, are changed; it took me some time to be sure that I was not deceived. You are quite gray. Think of it. Twelve years! Twelve years! My eldest daughter is already ten years old.'

"I looked at the child. I found in her something of the former charm of her mother, but something still undecisive, not yet formed, but near at hand. And life appeared as rapid to me as a train which passes.

"We arrived at Maisons-Lafitte. I kissed the hand of my old friend. I had found nothing to say to her but the most frightful commonplaces. I was too upset to talk.

"That evening, all alone in my room, I looked at myself for a long time in my glass. And I ended by recalling myself as I was, of looking back in thought to my brown mustache and my black hair and the physiognomy of my young face. Now I was old. Adieu!"

M. BELHOMME'S BEAST

The Havre stagecoach was just leaving Criquetot and all the passengers were waiting in the yard of the Commercial Hotel, kept by young Malandain, for their names to be called out.

The coach was yellow, on wheels that once were yellow too but now almost turned gray with accumulated layers of mud. The front wheels were quite small: those at the back, large and rickety, bore the well of the coach, which was unshapely and distended like the paunch of an animal.

Three white hacks harnessed in tandem, whose huge heads and large round knees were the most noticeable things about them, had to pull this conveyance, which had something monstrous in its build and appearance. Already the horses in front of this strange vehicle seemed to be asleep.

The driver, Césaire Horlaville, a corpulent little man but agile enough nevertheless by virtue of continually mounting the wheels and climbing on to the roof of his coach, with a face reddened by the open air of the countryside, by rain and storm and many brandies, and eyes always blinking as if still under the lash of wind and hail, appeared at the door of the hotel, wiping his mouth with the back of his hand. Large round hampers, full of scared poultry, stood in front of the solid countrywomen. Césaire Horlaville took these one by one and put them up on the roof of his vehicle; then, more carefully, he put up those which were filled with eggs: finally he tossed up from below a few little sacks of seed and small parcels wrapped in handkerchiefs, bits of cloth or paper. Then he opened the door at the back and, taking a list from his pocket, he called out from it:

"The reverend father from Gorgeville."

The priest came forward, a tall powerful man, broad, stout, purple in the face, and kindly. He lifted up his cassock to free his foot for stepping up, just as women lift up their skirts, and climbed into the rickety old coach.

"The schoolmaster from Rollebosc-les-Grinets."

The schoolmaster hurried forward, a tall and hesitating fellow, with a frock coat down to his knees; and disappeared in his turn through the open door.

"M. Poiret, two seats."

Poiret takes his place, tall and stooping, bent with drudgery, grown thin through lack of food, bony, and with a skin all withered from neglected ablutions. His wife followed him, small and wizened, looking very like a tired jade and clutching in both hands a huge green umbrella.

"M. Rabot, two seats."

Rabot, by nature irresolute, hesitated. He asked:

"Was it me you were calling?"

The driver, who had been nicknamed "Foxy," was going to make a joking reply, when Rabot took a header towards the door of the coach, thrust forward by a shove from his wife, a tall buxom wench with a belly as big and round as a barrel, and hands as large as a washerwoman's beetle.

And Rabot slipped into the coach like a rat into his hole.

"M. Caniveau."

A huge peasant, more beefy than a bull, summoned all his energy and was, in his turn, swallowed up inside the yellow well of the coach.

"M. Belhomme."

Belhomme, a tall skeleton of a man, drew near, his neck awry, his aspect dolorous, a handkerchief applied to his ear as if he suffered from very severe toothache.

All of them wore blue smocks over antique and peculiar jackets of black or green cloth, garments worn on special occasions which they would uncover in the streets of Havre; and their heads were covered with caps made of silk, as high as towers—the final elegance in that Norman countryside.

Césaire Horlaville shut the door of his coach, climbed on to his box, and cracked his whip.

The three horses seemed to wake up, and, shaking their necks, made audible a vague murmur of tiny bells.

Then the driver, bawling out "Gee up!" from the bottom of his lungs, lashed the animals with a sweep of the arm. They were roused, made an effort, and set off along the road at a slow and halting jog trot. And behind them the vehicle, jolting its loose panes and all the old iron of its springs, made an astounding jangle of tin and glassware, whilst each row of passengers, tossed and rocked by the jolts, surged up and down with every fall or rise of their uneven progress.

At first silence reigned, out of respect for the parish priest, whose presence put a restraint on their loquacity. He made the first remark, being of a garrulous and friendly disposition.

"Well, M. Caniveau," he said, "are you getting on all right?"

The big countryman, whose similarity of build, appearance, and paunch formed a bond between the priest and himself, replied, smiling:

"Much as usual, Father, much as usual, and how's yourself?"

"Oh, as for me, I can always get along!"

"And you, M. Poiret?" asked the reverend gentleman.

"I'd be all right, except for the colzas which have had nothing at all of a crop this year, and in business it is by the crops of colza that we make up our losses, as a rule."

"Well, well, times are hard!"

"Lord, yes, they're hard!" declared M. Rabot's hefty wife, in a voice like a policeman.

As she came from a neighboring village, the priest knew nothing of her but her name.

"Are you the Blondel girl?" he asked.

"Yes, that's me. I married Rabot."

Rabot, skinny, nervous, and complacent, saluted the priest with a smile; he saluted him by bowing his head deeply forward, as if to say: "Yes, this is really Rabot, whom the Blondel girl has married."

Abruptly, M. Belhomme, who kept his handkerchief over his ear, began to groan in a lamentable manner. He ground his teeth horribly, stamping his feet to express the most frightful suffering.

"Your toothache seems to be very bad?" demanded the priest.

The peasant stopped moaning for an instant to reply:

"Not a bit of it, Father. It's not my teeth, it's my ear, right down inside my ear."

"What's the matter with your ear then? An abscess?"

"I don't know whether it's an abscess, but I know it's a beast, a filthy beast, which got itself inside me when I was asleep on the hay in the loft."

"A beast! Are you sure?"

"Am I sure? As sure as heaven, Father, seeing it's gnawing away the inside of my ear. It'll eat out my head, for sure, it'll eat out my head. Oh, ger-ow, ger-ow, ger-ow!" . . . And he began stamping his feet again.

His audience was roused to the keenest interest. Each of them proffered different advice. Poiret would have it that it was a spider, the schoolmaster that it was a caterpillar. He had seen such a case before at Campemuret, in the Orne county, where he had lived for six years; though in this case the caterpillar had got into the head and come out through the nose. But the man had remained deaf in that ear, because the eardrum was split.

"It must have been a worm," declared the priest.

M. Belhomme, his head tilted on one side, and leaning it against the carriage door, for he had been the last to get in, went on groaning:

"Oh, ger-ow, ow, ow, I'm scared to death it's an ant, a big ant, it's gnawing so. There, Father, it's galloping and galloping . . . oh . . . ow . . . ow . . . it hurts like the devil!"

"Haven't you seen the doctor?" demanded Caniveau.

"Lord, no!"

"What for haven't you?"

Fear of doctors seemed to cure Belhomme.

He sat up, without however removing his handkerchief.

"What for haven't I? You've got money to waste on them, have you, for them good-for-nothings? You take yourself to them, once, twice, three times, four times, five times. And for that, a couple of crowns of a hundred sous apiece, two crowns at least. And you tell me what he'd have done for me, the good-for-nothing, you tell me what he'd have done! D'you know that?"

Caniveau laughed.

"Now how would I know? Where are you going anyway?"

"I'm off to Havre to see Chambrelan."

"What Chambrelan?"

"The healer, of course."

"What healer?"

"The healer who cured my dad."

"Your dad."

"Yes, my dad, in his time."

"What was the matter with your dad?"

"A great wind in his back, so as he could move nor foot nor leg."

"And what did your Chambrelan do for him?"

"He kneaded his back as if he was going to make bread of it, with both his hands. And it was all right again in a couple of hours."

Belhomme was quite sure in his mind that Chambrelan had also pronounced certain words over it, but he dared not say as much before the priest.

Laughing, Caniveau persisted.

"How d'you know it's not a rabbit you've got in your ear? It might have taken that earhole of yours for its burrow, seeing the undergrowth you've got growing outside. You wait. I'll make it run for its life."

And Caniveau, shaping his hands into a speaking trumpet, began to imitate the crying of hounds hot on the scent. He yelped, howled, whimpered, and bayed. Everybody in the coach began to laugh, even the schoolmaster who never laughed.

However, as Belhomme appeared irritated at being made fun of, the priest turned the conversation, and speaking to Rabot's lusty wife, said:

"I dare say you have a big family?"

"Yes, indeed, Father. And how hard it is to rear them!"

Rabot nodded his head, as if to say: "Oh, yes, it's hard to rear them."

"How many children have you?"

She stated magisterially, in a harsh deliberate voice:

"Sixteen children, Father. Fifteen of them by my good man."

And Rabot's smile broadened, as he knuckled his forehead. He managed fifteen children all by himself, he, Rabot. His wife said so. And there was no doubting her. He was proud of it, by George!

By whom was the sixteenth? She did not say. Probably it was the first. Perhaps everyone knew about it, for no one was surprised. Even Caniveau remained unmoved.

But Belhomme began to groan.

"Oh, ow . . . ow . . . ow . . . it fair tears me to bits. Hell!"

The coach drew up outside the Café Polyte. The priest said:

"If we were to drop a little water in your ear, it might bring the thing out with it. Would you like to try it?"

"For sure. I'm willing."

Everyone got down to assist at the operation.

The priest called for a basin, a napkin, and a glass of water; and he ordered the schoolmaster to hold the patient's head well over to one side, and then, as soon as the liquid should have penetrated into the passage, to swing it rapidly over the other way.

But Caniveau, who had straightway applied himself to Belhomme's ear to see whether he could not discover the beast with his naked eye, cried out:

"God bless my soul, what a sticky mess! You'll have to get that out, my boy. No rabbit could get out through that conglomeration of stuff. He'd stick fast with all four feet."

The priest examined the passage in his turn and realized that it was too narrow and too stuffed with wax to attempt the expulsion of the beast. It was the schoolmaster who cleared the path with a match and a bit of rag. Then, amid general anxiety, the priest poured down this scoured channel half a glass of water which ran over Belhomme's face and hair and down his neck. Then the schoolmaster turned the head abruptly back over the basin, as if he were trying to unscrew it. A few drops fell out into the white vessel. All the travelers flung themselves upon it. No beast had emerged.

However, Belhomme announcing: "I can't feel anything." the priest, triumphant, cried:

"It is certainly drowned!"

Everyone was pleased. They all got back into the coach.

But hardly had they got under way again when Belhomme burst out with the most terrible cries. The beast had wakened up and had become quite frantic. He even swore that it had now got into the head, that it was devouring his brain for him. He accompanied his howls with such contortions that Poiret's wife, believing him possessed of the devil, began to cry and make the sign of the cross. Then, the pain abating a little, the afflicted man related that it was now careering round his ear. He described with his finger the movements of the beast, seeming to see it, and follow it with a watchful eye.

"Look at it now, there it goes up again! . . . ow . . . ow . . . ow . . . oh, hell!" Caniveau lost patience.

"It's the water has sent it crazy, that beast of yours. Likely it's more used to wine."

His listeners burst out laughing. He added:

"As soon as you and me reach the Café Bourboux, give it a small brandy and I'll warrant it'll worry you no more."

But Belhomme could no longer endure his misery. He began to cry out as if his very inside was being torn out. The priest was obliged to support his head for him. His companions begged Césaire Horlaville to stop at the first house on the way.

It turned out to be a farm, lying near the roadside. Belhomme was carried to it; then they stretched him out on the kitchen table to begin the operation again. Caniveau persisted in advising Memboux brandy with the water, in order to make the beast either tipsy or drowsy, or perhaps kill it outright. But the priest preferred vinegar.

This time they poured in the liquid drop by drop, so that it would reach the farthest corner; then they left it for some minutes in the inhabited organ.

Another basin having been brought, Belhomme was turned bodily over by that lusty pair, the priest and Caniveau, while the schoolmaster banged with his finger on the healthy ear, the better to empty out the other.

Césaire Horlaville himself, whip in hand, had come in to watch.

All at once they saw in the bottom of the basin a small brown speck, no bigger than an onion seed. It was moving, however. It was a flea! Cries of surprise burst forth, then shouts of laughter. A flea! Oh, this was rich, this was very rich! Caniveau slapped his thigh, Césaire Horlaville cracked his whip, the priest burst into guffaws like the braying of an ass, the schoolmaster gave vent to a laugh like a sneeze, and the two women uttered little cries of merriment like nothing but the clucking of hens.

Belhomme was sitting on the table, and, resting the basin on his knees, he contemplated with grave intentness, and a gleam of angry joy in his eye, the vanquished beastie which turned and twisted in its drop of water.

He grunted: "So there you are, you swine," and spit at it.

The driver, beside himself with amusement, repeated:

"A flea, a flea! Oh, look at it, the little devil of a flea, the little devil of a flea!"

Then, his exuberance wearing off a little, he cried:

"Come now, let's be off. We've wasted enough time."

And the travelers, still laughing, made their way to the coach.

But Belhomme, last to come, declared:

"I'm off back to Criquetot. I've nothing to do at Havre."

The driver told him:

"Never mind that, pay your fare."

"I don't owe no more than half, seeing I've not done half the journey."

"You owe as much as if you'd done the lot."

And a dispute began which very soon became a furious quarrel. Belhomme swore that he would pay no more than twenty sous, Césaire Horlaville declared that he would have forty.

They shouted at each other, thrusting their faces close together and glaring into each other's eyes.

Caniveau clambered out of the coach.

"In the first place you owe forty sous to the priest, d'ye hear, and then drinks round to everyone, that makes it fifty-five, and out of that you'll have to give Césaire twenty. How's that, Foxy?"

The driver, delighted at the idea of Belhomme's having to screw out three francs seventy-five, replied:

"Right you are."

"Now then, pay up."

"I'll not pay. The priest's not a doctor, anyhow."

"If you don't pay, I'll put you back in the coach with Césaire and take you to Havre."

And seizing Belhomme round the waist, the giant lifted him up as if he had been a child.

The other realized that he would have to give in. He drew out his purse and paid.

Then the coach set off again for Havre, while Belhomme turned back towards Criquetot, and all the travelers, silent now, watched his blue peasant's smock, rolling along on his long legs down the white road.

A FRENCH ENOCH ARDEN

The sea lashes the shore with its short and monstrous waves. Little white clouds are scudding quickly across the great blue sky, swept by a rapid wind, like birds, and the village, in the fold of the valley which runs down to the ocean, lies broiling in the sun.

Quite at the entrance is the house of the Martin-Levesques, alone, at the side of the road. It is a little fisherman's cottage with clay walls and a thatched roof adorned with blue iris flowers. A garden as big as a handkerchief, where sprout some onions, a few cabbages, some parsley, some chervil, squares itself before the door. A hedge hems it in along the roadside.

The man has gone fishing, and the woman before the lodge is repairing the meshes of a big brown net hung on the wall like a great spider's web. A little girl of fourteen at the garden entrance, seated in a cane chair, leaning backward and resting her arm on the fence, is mending linen, the linen of the poor, already pieced and patched.

Another small girl, a year younger, is rocking in her arms a very little baby, yet without gestures or words, and the two youngsters of two or three years sitting on the ground are playing garden with their clumsy hands and throwing fistfuls of dust in each other's face.

No one speaks. Only the little rascal whom the girl is trying to put to sleep cries steadily with a sharp, weak little voice. A cat is sleeping at the window, and some blooming gillyflowers make, at the foot of the wall, a fine cushion of white blossoms, over which flies are buzzing.

The little girl who is sewing near the entrance calls suddenly: "Mamma."

"What is the matter with you?" replied the mother.

"There he is again."

She had been uneasy since morning because there was a man prowling about the house, an old man who seemed to be poor. They had observed him as they were going with their father to the boat to see him embark. He was seated on the edge of the ditch opposite their gate, and when they came back they found him still there, looking at the house.

He seemed ill and very wretched. He had not stirred for more than an hour; then, seeing he would be considered a malefactor, he had risen and departed, dragging one leg.

But soon they had seen him return with his slow and weary step, and again he had sat down, a little farther away this time, as if to watch them.

The mother and daughters were afraid. The mother especially, because she was of a timorous nature and because her husband Levesque was not expected to come from the sea until nightfall.

Her husband's name was Levesque; hers was Martin, and they were called the Martin-Levesques. This is why: She had married for her first husband a man named Martin, who went to Newfoundland every summer fishing for cod.

After two years of married life she had a little girl by him, and another, three months after the craft which carried her husband, the *Two Sisters*, a three-masted bark from Dieppe, disappeared.

No news was ever received from it; none of its crew ever came back; it was considered to be a total wreck.

The Martin woman waited for her second husband ten years, bringing up her children with great difficulty; then as she was a good, strong woman, a fisherman of the neighborhood, Levesque, a widower with a boy, asked her in marriage. She married him and had two children by him in three years.

They lived painfully, laboriously. Bread was dear and meat almost unknown in the household. They ran in debt at times with the baker, in winter, during the stormy months. The little ones were well, nevertheless. People said:

"They are brave folk, the Martin-Levesques. The wife is a hard worker, and Levesque has not his equal for fishing."

The little girl seated at the gate repeated: "You would think that he knew us. Perhaps it is some poor man from Epreville or from Auzebogo."

But the mother was not deceived. No, no, it wasn't anyone of the country, surely!

As he moved no more than a stake, and as he kept his eyes glued to the Martin-Levesques' cottage, the woman became furious and, fear making her brave, she seized a shovel and went out of the door.

"What are you doing there?" she called to the vagabond.

He answered in a gruff voice:

"I am taking the fresh air! Does that do you any harm?"

She replied:

"Why are you spying like this on my house?"

The man replied:

"I am not injuring anybody. Isn't it permitted to sit down by the roadside?"

Not finding an answer ready, she went back into the house.

The day passed slowly. Toward noon the man disappeared, but he came by again toward five o'clock. They did not see any more of him during the evening.

Levesque returned at dusk. They told him about it. He remarked:

"It is some skulker or good-for-nothing."

He went to bed, undisturbed, while his wife dreamed of this prowler who had looked at her so strangely.

When day came there was a great wind, and the sailor, seeing that he could not start out to sea, helped his wife at mending nets.

About nine o'clock the eldest daughter, a Martin, who had gone out to get some bread, came back running with a frightened air and cried:

"Ma, there he is again!"

The mother was startled and, very pale, said to her husband:

"Go and speak to him, Levesque, so that he won't watch us like this, because it worries me to death."

And Levesque, a big sailor with a complexion like a brick, a thickened beard, blue eyes, strong neck, always wearing woolen garments on account of the wind and rain at sea, walked out quietly and approached the straggler.

And they began to talk.

The mother and the children looked on from the distance, anxious and trembling.

Suddenly the unknown rose and came toward the house with Levesque.

The wife, terrified, drew back.

Her husband said to her:

"Give him a piece of bread and a glass of cider. He hasn't eaten anything since the day before yesterday."

They both entered the house, followed by the woman and the children. The vagabond sat down and began to eat, with his head lowered beneath the glances.

The mother, standing up, scrutinized him. The two big girls, the Martins, leaning against the door, one of them holding the latest baby, fixed their eager eyes upon him, and the two boys, seated in the ashes of the fireplace, had stopped playing with the black kettle to look at this stranger too.

Levesque, having taken a chair, asked him:

"Do you come from a distance?"

"I have come from Cette."

"On foot as far as that?"

"Yes, on foot. A man has to walk when he cannot afford to ride."

"And where are you going?"

"I was coming here."

"You know someone here?"

"That might be."

They were silent. He ate slowly, although he was famished, and he took a sip of cider after each mouthful of bread. He had a worn, wrinkled face and seemed to have suffered much.

Levesque brusquely asked him:

"What is your name?"

"My name is Martin."

A strange shudder shook the mother. She took a step forward, as if to scan the vagabond more closely, and stood opposite him with her arms hanging down and her mouth open. Nobody said anything further. Levesque finally resumed:

"Are you from here?"

He answered: "I am from here." And as he raised his head the woman's eyes and his met and remained fixed upon each other, as if their glances were fastened.

She suddenly said in a changed voice, low and trembling:

"It is you, my husband?"

He slowly replied:

"Yes, it is I."

He did not move, continuing to masticate the bread.

Levesque, more surprised than moved, stammered:

"It is you, Martin?"

The other man said simply:

"Yes, it is I."

And the second husband asked:

"Where have you come from?"

He first told his story.

"From the coast to Africa; I was wrecked on a reef. Three of us were saved, Picard, Vatinel and me. And then we were captured by savages who held us twelve years. Picard and Vatinel are dead. An English traveler passing that way took me and brought me to Cette, and here I am."

The woman began to weep, her face in her apron.

Levesque said:

"What shall we do now?"

Martin asked:

"You are her husband?"

Levesque replied:

"Yes, I am."

They looked at each other and were silent.

Then Martin, gazing at the children in a circle around him, nodded toward two girls.

"Those are mine."

Levesque said:

"They are yours."

He did not rise; he did not kiss them; he merely remarked:

"Good God! How tall they are."

Levesque repeated:

"What shall we do?"

Martin, perplexed, could not tell. Finally he decided:

"I will do as you wish. I don't want to injure you. It is vexing all the same, considering the house. I have two children; you have three, each his own. But the mother, is she yours or mine? I will consent to whatever you wish, but the house is mine, since my father left it to me, since I was born here and since there are papers for it at the notary's."

The woman still wept with little sobs stifled in the blue cloth of her apron. The two tall girls drew near and looked at their father with uneasiness.

He had finished eating. But Levesque had an idea:

"We must go to the priest; he will decide."

Martin rose, and as he approached his wife she threw herself sobbing upon his breast.

"My husband! You are here! Martin, my poor Martin, you are here!"

And she held him in her arms, suddenly pierced by a breath of olden times, by a great shock of memories which recalled to her the days when she was twenty and their first embraces.

Martin, himself moved, kissed her on the cap. The two children in the corner began to howl together, seeing their mother weep, and the last born, in the arms of the second Martin girl, shrieked with the sharp sound of a cracked fife.

Levesque, standing up, waited.

"Come," he said, "we must get this straightened out."

Martin released his wife, and as he looked at his two daughters their mother said to them:

"Kiss your father, at least."

They approached him together, astonished and a little afraid. And he kissed them one after the other on both cheeks with a big peasant's smack. And seeing this unknown approach, the little child uttered such piercing cries that it almost went into convulsions.

Then the two men went out together.

As they passed the Café du Commerce Levesque asked:

"Shall we have a little drop?"

"I would like it very much," said Martin.

They entered and sat down in a room which was vacant.

"Ho! Chicot, two bottles of wine, good wine. This is Martin who has come back, Martin of the *Two Sisters*, which was lost."

And the tavern keeper, three glasses in one hand and a carafe in the other, approached, large of paunch, ruddy, fat, and asked with a quiet air:

"What? You here, Martin?"

Martin replied: "I am here."

THE LITTLE ONE

M. Lemonnier had remained a widower with one child. He had loved his wife madly, with a noble and tender love, that never failed, throughout the whole of their life together. He was a good, honest fellow, simple, very simple in fact, free from diffidence and malice.

Having fallen in love with a poor neighbor, he asked for her hand and married her. He was in a fairly prosperous drapery business, was making quite a good amount of money, and did not for one moment imagine that the girl might not have accepted him for himself alone.

At all events she made him happy. He had no eyes for anybody or anything but her, thought only of her, and looked at her continually in an abandon of adoration. During meals he would commit a thousand blunders rather than look away from the beloved face; he would pour the wine into his plate and the water into the saltcellar, and then would burst out laughing like a child, declaring:

"There, you see I love you too much; it makes me do such a lot of silly things."

And she would smile, with an air of calm resignation, and then would turn away her eyes, as though embarrassed by her husband's worship, and would try to make him talk, to chat on any subject; but he would reach across the table and take her hand, and, holding it in his, would murmur:

"My little Jeanne, my dear little Jeanne."

She would end by growing vexed and exclaiming:

"Oh, do be reasonable; get on with your dinner, and let me get on with mine!"

He would utter a sigh and break off a mouthful of bread, which he would proceed slowly to munch.

For five years they had no children. Then suddenly she found herself with child. It was a delirious happiness for them. He would never leave her during the whole of her pregnancy; to such an extent, in fact, that her maid, an old nurse who had brought her up and was given to speaking her mind to them, would sometimes thrust him out of the house and lock the door, so as to force him to take the air.

He had formed an intimate friendship with a young man who had known his wife since her childhood, and who was second head clerk at the Prefecture. Monsieur Duretour dined three times a week at the Lemonniers', brought flowers for Madame and sometimes a box at the theater; and often, during dessert, the kind, affectionate Lemonnier would turn to his wife and exclaim:

"With a comrade like you and a friend like him, one is perfectly happy on earth."

She died in childbed. He nearly died too. But the sight of the child gave him courage: a little shriveled creature that moaned.

He loved the baby with a passionate and grief-stricken love, a morbid love, wherein remained the remembrance of death, but wherein survived something of his adoration of the dead woman. The boy was his wife's flesh, her continued being, a quintessence of her, as it were. He was her very life poured into another body; she had disappeared that he might exist. . . . And the father embraced him frantically. . . .

But also the child had killed her, had taken, stolen that adored existence, had fed upon it, had drunk up her share of life. . . . And M. Lemonnier replaced his son in the cradle and sat down beside him to contemplate him. He remained there for hours and hours, watching him, musing of a thousand sad or sweet things. Then, as the child was sleeping, he stooped over his face and wept into his coverings.

The child grew. The father could not forgo his presence for an hour; he would prowl about the nursery, take him out for walks, put on his clothes, wash him, give him his meals. His friend, M. Duretour, also seemed to cherish the baby, and would embrace him with rapture, with those frenzies of affection which are a parent's property. He would make him leap in his arms or ride a cockhorse for hours upon his leg, and suddenly, overturning him upon his knees, would raise his short frock and kiss the brat's fat thighs and round little calves.

"Isn't he a darling, isn't he a darling!" would murmur M. Lemonnier in delight, and M. Duretour would clasp the child in his arms, tickling his neck with his mustache.

Only Céleste, the old nurse, seemed to have no affection for the little one. She was vexed at his pranks and seemed exasperated by the cajolery of the two men.

"Is that any way to bring up a child?" she would exclaim. "You'll make a perfect monkey of him."

More years went by, and Jean attained the age of nine. He could scarcely read, he had been so spoiled, and he always did exactly as he liked. He had a stubborn will, a habit of obstinate resistance, and a violent temper. The father always gave way and granted him everything. M. Duretour was perpetually buying and bringing for the little one the toys he coveted, and fed him on cakes and sweets.

On these occasions Céleste would lose her temper, and exclaim:

"It's a shame, monsieur, a shame. You'll be the ruin of the child, the ruin of him, do you hear! But it's got to be stopped, and stopped it shall be, yes, I promise it shall, and before long, too."

"Well, what about it, my good woman?" M. Lemonnier would answer with a smile. "I'm too fond of him, I can't go against his will. It's up to you to take your share in his upbringing."

Jean was weak and somewhat ailing. The doctor declared him to be anemic, and ordered iron, red meat, and strong broth.

But the little one liked nothing but cakes and refused all other nourishment; and his father, in despair, stuffed him with cream tarts and chocolate éclairs.

One evening, as the two sat down to table alone together, Céleste brought in the soup tureen with an assurance and an air of authority unusual in her. She abruptly took off the lid, plunged the ladle into the middle of it, and announced:

"There's broth such as I've never made before; the little one really must have some, this time."

M. Lemonnier, terrified, lowered his head. He saw that this was not going down well.

Céleste took his plate, filled it herself, and placed it back in front of him.

He immediately tasted the soup and declared:

"Yes, it is excellent."

Then the servant took the little boy's plate and poured into it a whole ladleful of soup. She retired two paces and waited.

Jean sniffed it, pushed away the plate, and uttered a "pah" of disgust. Céleste, grown pale, went swiftly up to him and, seizing the spoon full of soup, thrust it forcibly into the child's half-open mouth.

He choked, coughed, sneezed, and spat, and, yelling, grasped his glass in his fist and flung it at his nurse. It caught her full in the stomach. At that, exasperated, she took the brat's head under her arm and began to ram spoonful after spoonful of soup down his gullet. He steadily vomited them back, stamping his feet with rage, writhing, choking, and beating the air with his hands, as red as though he were dying of suffocation.

At first the father remained in such stupefaction that he made no movement at all. Then suddenly he rushed forward with the wild rage of a madman, took the servant by the throat, and flung her against the wall.

"Get out! . . . out! . . . out! . . . brute!" he stammered.

But with a vigorous shake she repulsed him, and with disheveled hair, her cap hanging down her back, her eyes blazing, cried:

"What's come over you now? You want to beat me because I make the child eat his soup, when you'll kill him with your spoiling!"

"Out! . . . be off with you . . . off with you, brute!" he repeated, trembling from head to foot.

Then in a rage she turned upon him, and facing him eye to eye, said in a trembling voice:

"Ah! . . . You think . . . you think you're going to treat me like that, me, me? . . . No, never. . . . And for whose sake, for whose sake? . . . For that snotty brat who isn't even your own child! No . . . not yours! . . . No! not yours! . . . not yours! . . . not yours! Why everybody knows it, by God, except you. . . . Ask the grocer, the butcher, the baker, everyone, everyone. . . ."

She faltered, choked with anger, then was silent and looked at him.

He did not stir; livid, his arms waving wildly. At the end of several seconds he stammered in a feeble, tremulous voice, in which strong emotion still quivered:

"You say? . . . you say? . . . What do you say?"

Then she answered in a calmer voice:

"I say what I know, by God! What everyone knows."

He raised his two hands and, flinging himself upon her with the fury of a brute beast, tried to fell her to the ground. But she was strong, in spite of her age, and agile too. She slipped through his arms and, running round the table, once more in a violent rage, screeched:

"Look at him, look at him, you fool, and see if he isn't the living image of M. Duretour; look at his nose and eyes, are your eyes like that? Or your nose? Or your hair? And were hers like that? I tell you everybody knows it, everybody, except you! It's the laughingstock of the town! Look at him! Look at him! . . ."

She passed in front of the door, opened it, and disappeared.

Jean, terrified, remained motionless, staring at his soup plate.

At the end of an hour she returned, very softly, to see. The little one, after having devoured the cakes, a dish of custard, and a dish of pears in syrup, was now eating jam out of a pot with his soup spoon.

The father had gone out.

Céleste took the child, embraced him, and, with silent steps, carried him off to his room and put him to bed. And she returned to the dining room, cleared the table, and set everything in order, very uneasy in her mind.

No sound whatever was to be heard in the house. She went and set her ear to her master's door. He was not moving about the room. She set her eye to the keyhole. He was writing and seemed calm.

Then she went back to sit in her kitchen, so as to be ready for any circumstance, for she realized that something was in the air.

She fell asleep in her chair and did not wake until daybreak.

She did the household work, as was her custom every morning; she swept and dusted, and, at about eight o'clock, made M. Lemonnier's coffee.

But she dared not take it to her master, having very little idea how she would be received; and she waited for him to ring. He did not ring. Nine o'clock went by, then ten o'clock.

Céleste, alarmed, prepared the tray, and started off with a beating heart. In front of the door she stopped and listened. Nothing was stirring. She knocked, there was no answer. So, summoning up all her courage, she opened the door and went in; then, uttering a terrible shriek, she dropped the breakfast tray which she held in her hands.

M. Lemonnier was hanging right in the middle of his room, suspended by the neck from a ring in the ceiling. His tongue protruded in ghastly fashion. The slipper had fallen off his right foot and lay on the floor; the other slipper had remained upon the foot. An overturned chair had rolled to the bedside.

Céleste, at her wit's end, fled shrieking. All the neighbors ran up. The doctor discovered that death had taken place at midnight.

A letter, addressed to M. Duretour, was found upon the suicide's table. It contained this solitary line:

"*I leave and entrust the little one to you.*"

JULIE ROMAIN

In the springtime two years ago I was walking along the shores of the Mediterranean. What is more charming than to dream while walking over a lonely road? One enjoys the sunlight and the caressing wind when climbing the mountains or strolling by the seashore. And in his daydreams what illusions, what love poems, what adventures pass in two hours through the mind of one who idles along a road. Every possible hope, confused and joyous, penetrates him with the warm, light air; he inhales them with the breeze, and they give birth in his being to an appetite for happiness that increases like the hunger he acquires in walking. Sweet and fleeting thoughts sing in his soul as he comes closer to nature.

I followed the road that leads from Saint-Raphaël to Italy, or rather, I made my way through that superb and changing scenery which seems made to be celebrated in all the love poems of the earth. It seemed to me a pity to think that from Cannes to Monaco scarcely anyone comes into this part of country save to make trouble, to juggle with money or to display under this delicious sky and in this garden of roses and oranges base vanities, stupid pretensions and vile covetousness and to show the human mind as it is—servile, ignorant, arrogant and grasping.

Suddenly in one of the curves of the ravishing bays I saw a group of villas, four or five only, fronting on the sea at the foot of the mountain. Behind them was a wild forest of pines which covered two great valleys apparently without roads or outlet. Involuntarily I stopped in front of the gate of one of these chalets, so pretty was it, a little white cottage with brown decorations, covered with roses that climbed to the roof. The garden was filled with flowers of all colors and every size, coquettishly arranged in studied disorder. The lawn was dotted with flower beds; a vase with trailing vines stood on the step of the veranda, and over the windows hung clusters of purple grapes, while the stone balustrade that surrounded this charming dwelling was covered with enormous red morning-glories that looked like spots of blood. Behind the house stretched a long alley of orange trees in flower, which reached as far as the foot of the mountain.

On the door of the villa in small, gilt letters I read this name: "Villa d'Antan." I asked myself what poet or fairy inhabited the place, what inspired recluse had discovered it and created this dream of a dwelling that appeared to spring from masses of flowers.

A workman was breaking stones on the road at a short distance. I asked him the name of the proprietor of the chalet. He replied that it belonged to the famous Mme. Julie Romain.

Julie Romain! In my childhood I had often heard her spoken of, the great actress, the rival of Rachel! No woman had been more applauded or more loved—

more loved, above all! How many duels had been fought and how many suicides had been committed because of her, and how many wild adventures had been undertaken for her sake! What was her age now, that seductress? Sixty—no, seventy—seventy-five years. Julie Romain! Here, in this house! I recalled again the emotion created throughout France (I was twelve years old then) by her flight to Sicily with one lover, a poet, after her notorious quarrel with another adorer.

She fled with her new love one evening after a first-night representation during which the audience had applauded her for half an hour and called her out eleven times in succession. She went away with the poet in a post chaise, as was the custom then; they had crossed the sea in order to love in that antique island, daughter of Greece, under the immense grove of orange trees that surrounds Palermo, which is called the "Conque d'Ov."

Their ascent of Etna was gossiped about, and also how they hung over the immense crater, arm in arm, cheek against cheek, as if they desired to throw themselves into the gulf of fire.

He was dead now, the writer of affecting verses, of poems so brilliant that they dazzled a whole generation, and so subtle and mysterious that they opened a new world to other poets.

The other lover was dead also, the abandoned one, who created for her those musical expressions that remain in all hearts, expressions of triumph and despair that are at once intoxicating and heart-rending.

She lived here, in this house veiled with flowers!

I hesitated no longer. I rang the bell. A domestic came to open the door, a boy of eighteen years, awkward and shy, with hands that appeared to be in his way. I wrote on my card a gallant compliment to the old actress and an ardent prayer that she would receive me. Perhaps she might know my name and allow me to see her.

The young valet disappeared but soon returned and asked me to follow him. He showed me into a neat drawing room, correct in every detail in the style of Louis Philippe, with furniture of a cold and cumbersome fashion, the coverings of which were being removed in my honor by a little maid of about sixteen years, with a slender figure but not much beauty.

Then the servants left me alone. I looked around the room with interest. On the walls hung three portraits, one was of the actress in a celebrated role, another was of the poet-lover wearing a long frock coat, tight at the waist, and the ruffled shirt of those days, and the third was of the musician, seated before a clavichord. The lady was blond and charming in her portrait, but her pose was a little affected, as was the fashion of that day. Her charming mouth and blue eyes smiled graciously, and the technique of the painting was of a high degree of excellence. Those three remarkable faces seemed to be looking already at the next generation, and their surroundings had an air of a day that was past and of individualities that were no more.

A door opened, and a little woman entered. She was very old, very small, with eyebrows and bands of white hair. Somehow she reminded me of a white mouse, quick and furtive in her movements. She gave me her hand and, with a voice that was still fresh, vibrating and sonorous, she said graciously: "Thank you, monsieur. It is very kind of the men of today to remember the women of yesterday! Be seated!"

I told her that her house had attracted me, that I had tried to learn the name of the proprietor and, having learned it, I could not resist the desire to ring her bell.

"Your visit gives me the greater pleasure, monsieur," she said, "as it is the first time such an event has happened. When your card was handed to me with the gracious compliment it carried, I was as startled as if someone had announced an old friend who had been gone these twenty years. I am forgotten, truly forgotten; no one remembers me; no one will think of me until the day of my death; then all the papers will talk for three days of Julie Romain, telling anecdotes, giving details and souvenirs and scandals and, perhaps, pompous eulogies. Then that will be the end of me!"

She was silent a moment and then resumed: "And that will not be long now. In a few months, in a few days, perhaps, the little woman who is now alive will be nothing but a corpse!"

She raised her eyes to her portrait, which met her gaze as if smiling at that withered caricature of itself; then she looked at the two men, the scornful poet and the inspired musician, both of whom seemed to say: "What does that ruin ask of us?"

An indescribable, keen, irresistible sadness seized my heart, the sadness that overwhelms those whose lives are finished and who struggle still with memories, as a drowning man struggles in deep water.

From the place where I sat I could see brilliant and swiftly moving carriages passing along the road, going from Nice to Monte Carlo. And seated inside were beautiful young women, rich and happy, and men, smiling and satisfied. She followed my glance and, comprehending my thought, murmured with a resigned smile: "It is not possible to be and to have been at the same time."

"How beautiful life must have been for you!" I said.

She sighed deeply. "Yes, beautiful and sweet! It is for that reason that I regret it so much."

I saw that she was disposed to talk of herself, so softly and with delicate precautions, as one would touch a painful wound, I began to question her. She spoke of her success, of her intoxicating joys, of her friends, of her whole triumphant existence.

"Your greatest joy and your deepest happiness—did you owe them to the theater, madame?" I asked.

"Oh no!" she replied quickly.

I smiled and she added, raising her eyes with a sad look to the portraits of the two men:

"I owed my greatest happiness to them."

I could not refrain from asking her to which one she owed it.

"To both, monsieur! I even confuse them in my mind sometimes, and besides, I feel remorse toward one of them to this day."

"Then, madame, it is not to them but to the act of love itself that you owe your gratitude. They have merely been love's instruments."

"That is possible. But, ah, what wonderful instruments!"

"Are you certain that you have not been loved—that you would not have been loved as well, and perhaps better, by a simple man, one who was not great but who would have offered you his whole life, his whole heart, his whole being, every thought and every hour? With those two you had two formidable rivals—music and poetry."

She cried out with force, with that youthful voice which could still thrill the soul: "No, monsieur, no! A simpler man might have loved me better, perhaps, but he would not have loved me as those two did. Ah! But they knew how to sing the music of love as no other man in the world could have sung it.

"How they intoxicated me! Is it possible that any other man could have found that which they found in words and in sounds? Is it enough to love if one does not know how to put into love all the poetry and all the music of the sky and the earth? They knew, those two, how to make a woman ecstatic with joy, and with their songs and their words as well as with their deeds. Yes, there was perhaps more of illusion than reality in our passion, but those illusions lift you to the clouds, whereas realities alone always leave you on the earth. If others loved me more it was through them alone that I learned, felt and adored love!"

Suddenly she began to weep noiselessly tears of bitter sorrow. I appeared not to notice it and looked far away out of the window. After a few moments she went on:

"You see, monsieur, with most people the heart grows old with the body. With me that has not happened. My poor body is seventy-five years old, but my heart is only twenty. And that is the reason why I live all alone, with my flowers and my dreams."

Again a long silence fell between us. After a time she calmed herself and again spoke smilingly:

"How you would laugh at me, monsieur, if you knew how I pass my evenings when the weather is fine! I am ashamed of my folly and pity myself at the same time."

It was useless for me to beg her to tell me; she would not do so; then I rose to go, at which she cried, "What! so soon?"

I told her that I had intended to dine at Monte Carlo, and at once she asked a little timidly: "Would you not like to dine with me? It would give me very much pleasure."

I accepted her invitation immediately. She appeared delighted and rang the bell; then when she had given a few orders to the little maid, she said she would like to show me her house.

A kind of glass-covered veranda, full of plants, opened from the dining room and permitted one to see, from one end to the other, the long alley of orange trees, extending to the foot of the mountains. A low seat, hidden under the shrubbery, indicated that the aged actress often came to sit there.

Then we went into the garden to look at the flowers. Evening came on softly, one of those calm, warm evenings that brings forth all the perfumes of the earth. It was almost dark when we placed ourselves at the table. The dinner was excellent, and we sat long over it. We became quite intimate friends. A profound sympathy for her had sprung up in my heart. She drank a glass of wine and became more friendly and confidential.

"Let us go out and look at the moon," she said at last. "I adore the moon, the lovely moon! It has been the witness of my greatest joys. It seems to me that all my sweetest memories are treasured there and that I have only to look at it in order to have them come back to me. And sometimes, in the evening, I arrange for myself a pretty scene, so pretty—if you only knew! But no, you would laugh at me too much. I cannot tell you—I don't dare—no—no, I cannot tell you."

"Ah, madame, continue, I pray!" I begged of her. "What is your little secret? Tell me! I promise you not to laugh—I swear it!"

She hesitated; I took her hands, her poor little hands, so thin and cold, and kissed them one after the other many times, as her lovers were wont to do in former days. She was moved, though she still hesitated.

"You promise me not to laugh?" she said timidly.

"Yes, I swear it, madame!"

"Well then, come!" she said with a smile.

We rose from the table, and as the awkward youth in green livery drew back the chair behind her she spoke a few low, quick words in his ear.

He replied respectfully, "Yes, madame, immediately."

She took my arm and led me upon the veranda. The orange tree walk was a beautiful sight. The moon cast a slender line of silver among the trees, a long line of light that fell on the yellow sand between the dense and rounded branches. As the trees were in bloom, their delicious and penetrating perfume filled the air, and among the dark foliage were thousands of fireflies whose tiny flames looked like the seed of stars.

"Oh, what an ideal environment for a scene of love!" I cried.

She smiled. "Is it not? Is it not? You will see presently!"

She made me sit down beside her and murmured:

"The memory of such scenes is what makes me regret life. But you hardly dream of those things, you men of today. You are merely money-makers, businessmen. You don't know how to talk to us even. When I say 'us,' I mean women who are young. Love affairs have become merely liaisons, which originate often in an un-acknowledged bill of the dressmaker. If you find the bill more important than the woman, you disappear, but if you esteem the woman of greater value than the bill, you pay! Nice manners, and charming affections!"

She took my hand. "Look!" she said.

I was astonished and transported with pleasure at the charming picture that appeared. Below us, at the end of the alley and in the full moonlight, a youth and a maiden were coming toward us, clasping each other around the waist. They advanced, their arms entwined, walking slowly in the moon's rays, the soft effulgence of which bathed them completely.

They disappeared in the darkness for a moment, then reappeared farther down the avenue.

The youth was dressed in a white satin costume of the last century, with a broad hat over which hung an ostrich feather. The maiden wore a skirt with wide hoops, and her head was dressed with the high, powdered coiffure affected by beautiful dames in the days of the Regency.

At last they came to a halt about a hundred steps away from us and, standing in the middle of the alley, they embraced after saluting each other gracefully.

Suddenly I recognized the two little servants! Then I was seized with one of those irresistible desires to laugh that shake one all over. I did not laugh, however. I resisted the impulse and waited to see the next scene in this extraordinary comedy.

The lovers now returned toward the end of the alley, and distance again made them appear charming. They withdrew farther and farther away and at last disappeared like figures in a dream. The alley seemed lonely without them.

I took my departure also. I left immediately so that I should not see them again, for I thought it probable that the spectacle was made to last a long time, in order to recall all the past—that past of love and scenic effect, that fictitious past, deceiving and seductive, falsely yet truly charming—to cause the tender heart to

throb again in the romantic breast of the old actress and to use me as a final
instrument.

A MEMORY

How many memories of my youth came to me under the gentle caress of the
earliest summer sun! It is an age wherein all is good, glad, charming, and intoxicating. How exquisite are the memories of lost springs!

Do you recall, my old friends, my brothers, those years of gladness in which life
was but triumph and laughter? Do you recall the days when we roamed dis-
reputably about Paris, our radiant poverty, our walks in the woods newly clad in
green, our revels under the open sky outside the taverns on the banks of the Seine,
and our love adventures, so commonplace and so delicious?

I should like to relate one of those adventures. It dates from twelve years ago,
and already feels so old, so old, that it seems now at the other end of my life,
before the turning, the ugly turning whence suddenly I saw the end of the journey.

I was twenty-five in those days. I had just come to Paris; I worked in a government office, and Sundays seemed to me extraordinary festivals, full of exuberant
happiness, although nothing remarkable ever happened on them.

Every day is Sunday now. But I regret the times when I had only one a week.
How good it was! I had six francs to spend!

I awoke early, that particular morning, with that feeling of freedom well known
to clerks, the feeling of deliverance, rest, tranquillity, and independence.

I opened my window. The weather was glorious. The clear blue sky was spread
above the city, full of sunshine and swallows.

I dressed very quickly and went out, eager to spend the day in the woods, to
breathe the odor of the leaves; for I came of country stock and spent my childhood
on the grass and under the trees.

Paris was waking joyfully, in the warmth and the light. The fronts of the houses
shone, the concierges' canaries sang furiously in their cages, and gaiety ran down
the street, lighting up faces and stirring laughter everywhere, as though a mysterious happiness filled all animate and inanimate life in that radiant dawn.

I reached the Seine, to catch the *Swallow*, which was to take me to Saint-Cloud.

How I loved waiting for the boat upon the landing stage! I felt as though I
were off to the end of the world, to new and wonderful countries. I watched the
boat come into sight, away in the distance under the arch of the second bridge,
very small, with its plume of smoke, then larger, larger, always growing; and to my
mind it took on the airs and graces of a liner.

It came alongside the stage, and I embarked.

A crowd of people in their Sunday clothes were already on board, with gay
dresses, brilliantly colored ribbons, and fat scarlet faces. I placed myself right in
the bows and stood there watching quays, trees, houses, and bridges go by. And
suddenly I saw the great viaduct of Point-du-Jour barring the stream. It was the
end of Paris, the beginning of the country, and at once beyond the double line
of arches the Seine widened out, as though space and liberty had been granted to

it, becoming suddenly the lovely peaceful river that flows on across the plains, at the foot of the wooded hills, through the meadows, and along the edge of the forest.

After passing between two islands, the *Swallow* followed the curve of a slope whose green expanse was covered with white houses. A voice announced: "Bas-Meudon"; then, farther on: "Sèvres," and, still farther on: "Saint-Cloud."

I disembarked. And I hurried through the little town along the road to the woods. I had brought a map of the suburbs of Paris, lest I lose myself on the paths which run in every direction across the woods where the people of Paris go for their expeditions.

As soon as I was in the shade, I studied my route, which seemed perfectly simple. I was to turn to the right, then to the left, then to the left again, and I should arrive at Versailles by nightfall, for dinner.

And I began to walk slowly, beneath the fresh leaves, drinking in the fragrant air, perfumed with the odor of buds and sap. I walked with short steps, unmindful of the stacks of old paper, of the office, of my chief and my colleagues, and of files, and dreaming of the happy adventures that must assuredly be waiting for me in the stretches of that veiled, unknown future. I was filled with a thousand memories of childhood awakened in me by the scents of the country, and I went on, sunk in the fragrant, living, throbbing loveliness of the woods, warmed by the powerful June sun.

Sometimes I sat down by a bank and looked at the little flowers of every kind, whose names I had long known. I knew them all again, just as though they were the very ones I had once seen in my own country. They were yellow, red, and violet, delicate and dainty, lifted on high stalks or huddled close to the earth. Insects of every color and shape, short and squat or long and thin, extraordinary in their construction, frightful microscopic monsters, peacefully mounted the blades of grass, which bent under their weight.

Then I slept for some hours in a ditch, and went on again, rested and strengthened by my sleep.

In front of me opened a delightful alley, whose rather sparse leafage allowed drops of sunlight to shower everywhere upon the soil, and gleamed on the white daisies. It ran on endlessly, calm and empty. A solitary great hornet buzzed down it, pausing at times to sip a flower that stooped beneath it, and flying off again almost at once to come to rest again a little farther on. Its fat body looked like brown velvet striped with yellow, borne on wings that were transparent and inordinately small.

Suddenly I saw at the end of the path two people, a man and a woman, coming towards me. Annoyed at being disturbed in my quiet walk, I was on the point of plunging into the undergrowth when I fancied I heard them calling to me. The woman was actually waving her sunshade, and the man, in his shirt sleeves, his frock coat over one arm, was raising the other as a signal of distress.

I went towards them. They were walking hurriedly, both very red, she with little rapid steps, he with long strides. Ill-humor and weariness was visible on their faces.

The woman asked me at once:

"Monsieur, can you tell me where we are? My idiotic husband has lost us, after saying that he knew this district perfectly."

"Madame," I replied confidently, "you are going towards Saint-Cloud, and Versailles is behind you."

"What!" she continued, glancing with angry pity towards her husband. "Versailles is behind us? But that is precisely where we mean to have dinner!"

"So do I, madame; I am going there."

"Oh, dear, oh, dear, oh, dear!" she repeated, in the tone of overwhelming contempt with which women express their exasperation.

She was quite young, pretty, and dark, with a shadow of a mustache on her lip.

As for the man, he was perspiring and mopping his brow. Without doubt they were Parisian shopkeepers. The man looked overcome, tired out and miserable.

"But, my dear girl," he murmured, "it was you . . ."

She did not permit him to finish the sentence.

"It was I! . . . Ah! it is I now. Was it I who wanted to go off without inquiries, declaring that I could always find my way? Was it I who wanted to turn to the right at the top of the hill, declaring that I remembered the way? Was it I who undertook to look after Cachou . . ."

She had not finished speaking when her husband, as though he had suddenly gone out of his mind, uttered a piercing cry, a long, wild cry, which cannot be written in any language, but which was something like *teeeteeet*.

The young woman seemed neither surprised nor excited, and continued:

"No, upon my word, some people are too silly, always pretending to know everything. Was it I who took the Dieppe train last year instead of the Havre train? Tell me, was it I? Was it I who bet that M. Letournier lived in the Rue des Martyrs? . . . Was it I who wouldn't believe that Céleste was a thief? . . ."

And she continued furiously, with amazing rapidity of speech, piling up the most heterogeneous, unexpected, and grievous charges, furnished by all the intimate situations in their existence together, blaming her husband for all his actions, ideas, manners, experiments, and efforts, his whole life, in fact, from their wedding day up to the present moment.

He tried to stop her, to calm her, and faltered:

"But, my dear girl . . . it's no use . . . in front of the gentleman . . . we're making an exhibition of ourselves. It is of no interest to the gentleman."

And he turned his melancholy eyes upon the thickets, as though eager to explore their peaceful and mysterious depths, to rush into them, escape and hide from every eye. From time to time he again uttered his cry, a prolonged, very shrill *teeeteeet*. I imagined this habit was a nervous disorder.

The young woman abruptly turned to me and, changing her tone with remarkable rapidity, remarked:

"If monsieur will be good enough to permit us, we will go with him in order not to lose ourselves again and risk having to sleep in the wood."

I bowed; she took my arm and began to talk of a thousand things, of herself, her life, her family, and her business. They kept a glove shop in the Rue Saint-Lazare.

Her husband walked beside her, continually throwing wild glances into the thick of the trees, and every now and then shouting *teeeteeet*.

At last I asked him:

"Why do you shout like that?"

"It's my poor dog that I've lost," he replied with an air of consternation and despair.

"What? You have lost your dog?"

"Yes. He was barely a year old. He had never gone out of the shop. I wanted to take him for a walk in the woods. He had never seen grass or leaves before, and it pretty well sent him off his head. He began to run about, barking, and has disappeared in the forest. I should also tell you that he was very frightened of the railway; it may have made him lose his senses. I have called and called in vain; he has not come back. He will die of hunger in there."

Without turning towards her husband, the woman remarked:

"If you had kept him on the lead, it wouldn't have happened. People as silly as you have no business to have dogs."

"But, my dear girl, it was you . . ."

She stopped short; and looking into his eyes as though she were going to tear them out, she began once more her innumerable reproaches.

Night was falling. The veil of mist which covers the countryside at twilight was slowly unfolding; romance hovered around, born of the strange, delightful coolness that fills the woods at the approach of night.

Suddenly the young man stopped, and, feeling about himself frantically, exclaimed:

"Oh! I believe I have . . !"

"Well, what?" she asked, looking at him.

"I did not realize that I was carrying my frock coat on my arm."

"Well?"

"I have lost my letter case . . . my money is in it."

She quivered with rage and choked with indignation.

"That is the last straw. How idiotic you are, how perfectly idiotic! How can I have married such a fool? Well, go and look for it, and take care that you find it. I will go on to Versailles with this gentleman. I don't want to spend the night in the woods."

"Yes, dear," he replied meekly. "Where shall I find you?"

A restaurant had been recommended to me. I told him of it.

The husband turned back and, bending down towards the ground, scanning it with anxious eyes, he walked away, continually shouting *teeeteeet.*

It was a long time before he disappeared; the shades of evening, thicker now, obscured him at the far end of the path. Soon the outline of his body was seen no more, but for a long time we heard his melancholy *teeeteeet, teeeteeet,* becoming shriller as the night grew darker.

As for me, I walked on with lively, happy steps through the sweetness of the twilight, with the unknown woman leaning on my arm.

I racked my brain in vain for compliments. I remained silent, excited and enraptured.

But suddenly a highroad cut across our path. I saw that on the right, in a valley, there was quite a town.

What was this place?

A man was passing; I questioned him.

"Bougival," he replied.

I was thunderstruck.

"Bougival! Are you sure?"

"Damn it all, I live there!"

The little woman laughed uproariously.

I suggested taking a cab to Versailles.

"Certainly not!" she replied. "This is too funny, and I'm so hungry. I'm not a bit anxious; my husband will always find his way all right. It's a pleasure for me to be relieved of him for a few hours."

We accordingly entered a restaurant by the waterside, and I was bold enough to engage a private room.

She got thoroughly tipsy, I can assure you; sang, drank champagne, and did all sorts of crazy things . . . even the craziest of all.

That was my first adultery!

CONFESSING

The noon sun poured fiercely down upon the fields. They stretched in undulating folds between the clumps of trees that marked each farmhouse; the different crops, ripe rye and yellowing wheat, pale-green oats, dark-green clover, spread a vast striped cloak, soft and rippling, over the naked body of the earth.

In the distance, on the crest of a slope, was an endless line of cows, ranked like soldiers, some lying down, others standing, their large eyes blinking in the burning light, chewing the cud and grazing on a field of clover as broad as a lake.

Two women, mother and daughter, were walking with a swinging step, one behind the other, towards this regiment of cattle. Each carried two zinc pails, slung outwards from the body on a hoop from a cask; at each step the metal sent out a dazzling white flash under the sun that struck full upon it.

The women did not speak. They were on their way to milk the cows. When they arrive, they set down one of their pails and approach the first two cows, making them stand up with a kick in the ribs from wooden-shod feet. The beast rises slowly, first on its forelegs, then with more difficulty raises its large hind quarters, which seem to be weighted down by the enormous udder of livid pendulous flesh.

The two Malivoires, mother and daughter, kneeling beneath the animal's belly, tug with a swift movement of their hands at the swollen teat, which at each squeeze sends a slender jet of milk into the pail. The yellowish froth mounts to the brim, and the women go from cow to cow until they reach the end of the long line.

As soon as they finish milking a beast, they change its position, giving it a fresh patch of grass on which to graze.

Then they start on their way home, more slowly now, weighed down by the load of milk, the mother in front, the daughter behind.

Abruptly the latter halts, sets down her burden, sits down, and begins to cry.

Mme. Malivoire, missing the sound of steps behind her, turns round and is quite amazed.

"What's the matter with you?" she said.

Her daughter Céleste, a tall girl with flaming red hair and flaming cheeks, flecked with freckles as though sparks of fire had fallen upon her face one day as she worked in the sun, murmurs, moaning softly like a beaten child:

"I can't carry the milk any further."

Her mother looked at her suspiciously.

"What's the matter with you?" she repeated.

"It drags too heavy, I can't," replied Céleste, who had collapsed and was lying on the ground between the two pails, hiding her eyes in her apron.

"What's the matter with you, then?" said her mother for the third time. The girl moaned:

"I guess there's a baby on the way." And she broke into sobs.

The old woman now in her turn set down her load, so amazed that she could find nothing to say. At last she stammered:

"You . . . you . . . you're going to have a baby, you clod! How can that be?"

The Malivoires were prosperous farmers, wealthy and of a certain position, widely respected, good business folk, of some importance in the district.

"I guess I am, all the same," faltered Céleste.

The frightened mother looked at the weeping girl groveling at her feet. After a few seconds she cried:

"You're going to have a baby! A baby! Where did you get it, you slut?"

Céleste, shaken with emotion, murmured:

"I guess it was in Polyte's coach."

The old woman tried to understand, tried to imagine, to realize who could have brought this misfortune upon her daughter. If the lad was well off and of decent position, an arrangement might be come to. It wasn't so bad, yet. Céleste was not the first to be in the same way, but it was annoying all the same, seeing their position and the way people talked.

"And who was it, you slut?" she repeated.

Céleste, resolved to make a clean breast of it, stammered:

"I guess it was Polyte."

At that Mme. Malivoire, mad with rage, rushed upon her daughter and began to beat her with such fury that her hat fell off in the effort.

With great blows of the fist she struck her on the head, on the back, all over her body; Céleste, prostrate between the two pails, which afforded her some slight protection, shielded just her face with her hands.

All the cows, disturbed, had stopped grazing and turned round, staring with their great eyes. The last one mooed, stretching out its muzzle towards the women.

After beating her daughter till she was out of breath, Mme. Malivoire stopped, exhausted; her spirits reviving a little, she tried to get a thorough understanding of the situation.

"—— Polyte! Lord save us, it's not possible! How could you, with a carrier? You must have lost your wits. He must have played you a trick, the good-for-nothing!"

Céleste, still prostrate, murmured in the dust:

"I didn't pay my fare!"

And the old Norman woman understood.

Every week, on Wednesday and on Saturday, Céleste went to town with the farm produce, poultry, cream, and eggs.

She started at seven with her two huge baskets on her arm, the dairy produce in one, the chickens in the other, and went to the main road to wait for the coach to Yvetot.

She set down her wares and sat in the ditch, while the chickens with their short pointed beaks and the ducks with their broad flat bills thrust their heads between the wicker bars and looked about them with their round, stupid, surprised eyes.

Soon the bus, a sort of yellow box with a black leather cap on the top, came up, jerking and quivering with the trotting of the old white horse.

Polyte the coachman, a big jolly fellow, stout though still young, and so burned up by sun and wind, soaked by rain, and colored with brandy that his face and neck were brick-red, cracked his whip and shouted from the distance:

"Morning, Mam'selle Céleste. In good health, I hope?"

She gave him her baskets, one after the other, which he stowed in the boot; then she got in, lifting her leg high up to reach the step, and exposing a sturdy leg clad in a blue stocking.

Every time Polyte repeated the same joke: "Clumsy; it's not got any thinner." She laughed, thinking it funny.

Then he uttered a "Gee up, old girl!" which started off the thin horse. Then Céleste, reaching for her purse in the depths of her pocket, slowly took out five-pence, threepence for herself and twopence for the baskets, and handed them to Polyte over his shoulder.

He took them, saying:

"Aren't we going to have our little bit of sport today?"

And he laughed heartily, turning round towards her so as to stare at her at his ease.

She found it a big expense, the half franc for a journey of two miles. And when she had no coppers she felt it still more keenly; it was hard to make up her mind to part with a silver coin.

One day, as she was paying, she asked:

"From a good customer like me you oughtn't to take more than threepence."

He burst out laughing.

"Threepence, my beauty; why, you're worth more than that."

She insisted on the point.

"But you make a good two francs a month out of me."

He whipped up his horse and exclaimed:

"Look here, I'm an obliging fellow! We'll call it quits for a bit of sport."

"What do you mean?" she asked with an air of innocence.

He was so amused that he laughed till he coughed.

"A bit of sport is a bit of sport, damn it; a game for a lad and a lass, a dance for two without music."

She understood, blushed, and declared:

"I don't care for that sort of game, M. Polyte."

But he was in no way abashed, and repeated, with growing merriment:

"You'll come to it some day, my beauty, a bit of sport for a lad and a lass!"

And since that day he had taken to asking her, each time that she paid her fare:

"Aren't we going to have our bit of sport today?"

She, too, joked about it by this time, and replied:

"Not today, M. Polyte, but Saturday, for certain!"

And amid peals of laughter he answered:

"Saturday then, my beauty."

But inwardly she calculated that, during the two years the affair had been going on, she had paid Polyte forty-eight whole francs, and in the country forty-eight francs is not a sum which can be picked up on the roadside; she also calculated that in two more years she would have paid nearly a hundred francs.

To such purpose she meditated that, one spring day as they jogged on alone, when he made his customary inquiry: "Aren't we going to have our bit of sport yet?" she replied:

"Yes, if you like, M. Polyte."

He was not at all surprised, and clambered over the back of his seat, murmuring with a complacent air:

"Come along, then. I knew you'd come to it some day."

The old white horse trotted so gently that she seemed to be dancing upon the same spot, deaf to the voice which cried at intervals, from the depths of the vehicle: "Gee up, old girl! Gee up, then!"

Three months later Céleste discovered that she was going to have a child.

All this she had told her mother in a tearful voice. Pale with fury, the old woman asked:

"Well, what did it cost?"

"Four months; that makes eight francs, doesn't it?" replied Céleste.

At that the peasant woman's fury was utterly unleashed, and, falling once more upon her daughter, she beat her a second time until she was out of breath. Then she rose and said:

"Have you told him about the baby?"

"No, of course not."

"Why haven't you told him?"

"Because very likely he'd have made me pay for all the free rides!"

The old woman pondered awhile, then picked up her milk pails.

"Come on, get up, and try to walk home," she said, and, after a pause, continued:

"And don't tell him as long as he doesn't notice anything, and we'll make six or eight months' fares out of him."

And Céleste, who had risen, still crying, disheveled and swollen round the eyes, started off again with dragging steps, murmuring:

"Of course I won't say a word."

ROSALIE PRUDENT

There was a mystery in that affair about Rosalie Prudent, which neither the jury, nor the judge, nor the prosecuting attorney of the Republic himself could understand.

The girl Rosalie was a servant at the house of the Varambot family, of Mantes. She became enceinte and, unknown to her employers, had given birth to a child in the garret during the night and had then killed the child and buried it in the garden.

It was the ordinary story of most of the infanticides committed by servants. But one act remained inexplicable. The examination of the girl's room had resulted in the discovery of a complete layette for an infant, made by Rosalie herself, who had passed her nights during three months in cutting out the garments and sewing them. The grocer where she had bought her candles (paid for out of her wages), in order to perform this long task, came forward and testified to the fact of their purchase. In addition it was learned that the midwife of the town, informed by Rosalie of her condition, had given her all the advice and information necessary in case the child should be born at a time when aid was impossible to obtain. She had found a place, also, at Poissy for Rosalie Prudent, who foresaw her loss of situation, as the Varambots were severe on the subject of morality.

They appeared in court, the man and his wife, small provincials of moderate means, exasperated against the vulgar creature who had besmirched the immaculateness of their house. They would have liked to see her guillotined at once without trial, and they overwhelmed her with insults, which in their mouths became accusations.

The guilty one, a tall, handsome girl of lower Normandy, fairly well educated for her station, wept without ceasing and made no reply to them or to anyone. The court came to the conclusion that she had accomplished that act of barbarity in a moment of despair and insanity, since everything indicated that she had hoped to keep her infant and bring it up.

The judge tried once more to make her speak, to get her to acknowledge her crime and, having asked her with great kindness to do so, he made her understand at last that the jury sitting there to judge her did not wish her death but were ready to pity her.

The girl appeared to be making up her mind to speak at last.

"Tell us now at first who is the father of that child," said the judge.

Until that moment she had refused obstinately to divulge this fact. Now she replied suddenly, looking straight at her employers, who had come there in a rage to calumniate her.

"It is Monsieur Joseph, the nephew of Monsieur Varambot!"

Varambot and his wife started, and both cried at the same time:

"It is false! She lies! It is infamous!"

The judge bade them be silent and said:

"Continue, I beg of you, and tell us how it happened."

Then the girl began to speak hurriedly, seeming to find some comfort for her poor, solitary, bruised heart in giving vent to her sorrow before these severe-looking men, whom she had taken until then for enemies and inflexible judges.

"Yes, it was Monsieur Joseph Varambot—it happened when he came for his vacation last summer."

"What is the occupation of this Monsieur Joseph Varambot?"

"He is underofficer in the artillery, monsieur. He was two months at the house—two months of the summer. I wasn't thinking of anything when he began to look at me and then to say things to me and finally to make love to me the whole day long. I was easy, monsieur! He told me I was a handsome girl, that I pleased him, that I was to his taste. For myself, he pleased me, to be sure. What would you have done? Anyone listens to those things when one is alone—as I am. I am alone on the earth, monsieur. There is no one to whom I can talk—no one to whom I can tell my troubles. I have neither father, nor mother, nor brother nor sister—no one! He seemed like a brother who had come to me when he began to talk to me. And then he asked me to go down to the river one evening so that we might talk without making so much noise. And I went down there. Could I have known what would happen? He put his arms around my waist—of course I didn't want to—no, no! I couldn't help it. I wanted to cry; the air was so soft and warm—it was clear moonlight—I couldn't help it! No, I swear it to you, I couldn't help it—he did what he pleased. That lasted three weeks, as long as he remained. I would have followed him to the end of the world. But he went away, and I didn't know that I was *enceinte*—I didn't! I didn't know it until the month afterward."

She began to weep so violently that they were obliged to give her time to compose herself. Then the judge spoke in the tone of a father confessor: "Go on, my girl, go on."

She continued: "When I knew that I was *enceinte* I told Madame Boudin, the midwife, to whom one can tell these things, and I asked her what to do in case that happened without her. And then I made the clothes, night after night, until one o'clock in the morning; and then I looked for another place, for I knew very well I should be discharged, but I wished to remain in that house until the end, in order to economize the pennies, seeing that I had no money and that I would need it for the little one."

"Then you did not wish to kill him?"

"Oh! Surely not, monsieur."

"Why did you kill him then?"

"Here's how it happened. It came sooner than I thought it would. It took me in the kitchen as I was washing my dishes. Monsieur and Madame Varambot had retired already, so I went upstairs without trouble, holding to the banisters. I lay down on the floor in my room, so as not to soil the bed. That lasted perhaps one hour—but it may have been two or three—I can't tell, so much pain did I have— and then—and then it was over, and I took up my baby!

"Oh yes! I was happy, for sure! I did everything that Madame Boudin told me, everything! Then I laid him on the bed, and then another pain began, and it was a pain to kill anyone. If you knew what that was, you others, you wouldn't do as much I'm sure! I fell on my knees, and then on my back on the floor, and then it began all over again, and that, too, lasted one hour, or perhaps two, and there I was all alone. Finally there came another little one, yes, another, two of them, like that! I took it up as I took the first one, and I put it on the bed by the side of the other. One—two! Can it be possible, I said? Two babies! And I, who earn twenty francs a month! Say—was it possible for me to take care of them? To care for one—yes, I might do that by depriving myself, but not two!

"The thought of that turned my head. What do I know about it, I? Could I choose, say? Do I know? I saw myself come to my last day! I couldn't keep two, so I put the pillow on them without knowing what I was doing, and I threw myself on the bed and upon them too. And I stayed there, rolling and crying, until daylight, which I saw through the window. I looked at them—they were both dead under the pillow, quite dead. Then I took them under my arm. I went down the stairs and out in the garden; I took the gardener's spade and I buried them in the ground, as deep as I could, one here and the other there, not together, so that they could not talk of their mother, if they do talk, the little dead children. Do I know?

"And then I went back to my bed, and I was so sick that I could not get up. They made the doctor come, and he understood everything. That is the truth, Monsieur the Judge. Do what you want to me. I am ready."

During her speech half of the jurymen had been wiping their eyes over and over again, trying to hide their emotion. All the women in the courtroom were sobbing.

"At what spot in the garden did you bury the other infant?" asked the judge.

"Which one did you find?" Rosalie inquired.

"The one that was under the artichokes."

"Ah! The other is buried under the strawberries beside the well!" The poor girl began again to sob so loud that it was enough to break one's heart to hear her. The jury acquitted her.

A PARRICIDE

Counsel for the defense had pleaded insanity. How else was this strange crime to be accounted for?

One morning, in the reeds near Châton, two bodies had been found locked in each other's arms, those of a man and his wife. They were a couple well known in society, wealthy, no longer young, and only married the previous year, the woman having lost her first husband three years before.

They were not known to have any enemies, and they had not been robbed. They had apparently been thrown into the river from the bank, after having been struck, one after the other, with a long iron spike.

The inquest did not lead to any discovery. The watermen who were questioned knew nothing; the affair was on the point of being abandoned, when a young joiner from a neighboring village, named Georges-Louis, known as "the Gentleman," gave himself up.

To all interrogation he refused to make any other answer than:

"I had known the man for two years, the woman for six months. They often came to me to have old furniture mended, because I am good at the work."

And when he was asked: "Why did you kill them?" he would reply obstinately: "I killed them because I wanted to kill them."

Nothing more could be got out of him.

The man was doubtless an illegitimate child, formerly put out to nurse in the district and afterwards abandoned. He had no name except Georges-Louis, but since, as he grew up, he had shown himself unusually intelligent, with tastes and a natural delicacy quite foreign to his comrades, he had been nicknamed "the Gentleman," and was never called anything else. He was known to be remarkably clever as a joiner, the profession he had adopted. He even did a little carving in wood. He was also said to have ideas about his station, to be a follower of communistic doctrines, even of nihilism, a great reader of novels of adventure and bloodthirsty romances, an influential elector and a clever speaker at the working men's or peasants' debating club.

Counsel for the defense had pleaded insanity.

How, in truth, could it be supposed that this workman should have killed his best clients, clients who were both rich and generous (he admitted this), who in two years had given him work which had brought in three thousand francs (his books testified to it)? There was only one explanation: insanity, the obsession of a man who has slipped out of his class and avenges himself on society as a whole by the murder of two gentlefolk; and counsel made a neat allusion to his nickname of "the Gentleman," given to this outcast by the whole neighborhood.

"Consider the irony of the situation!" he exclaimed. "Was it not capable of

still more violently exciting this unhappy youth with no father nor mother? He is
an ardent republican; nay, he even belongs to that political party whose members
the state was once wont to shoot and deport, but which today she welcomes with
open arms, the party to whom arson is a first principle and murder a perfectly
simple expedient.

"These lamentable doctrines, nowadays acclaimed in debating societies, have
ruined this man. He has listened to men of the republican party, yes! and even
women too, demanding the blood of M. Gambetta, the blood of M. Grévy; his
diseased brain has succumbed: he has thirsted for blood, the blood of nobility!

"It is not this man, gentlemen, whom you should condemn, it is the Commune!"

Murmurs of approval ran to and fro. It was generally felt that counsel for the
defense had won his case. The public prosecutor did not reply.

Then the judge asked the prisoner the customary question:

"Prisoner at the bar, have you nothing to add in your defense?"

The man rose.

He was small in stature, with flaxen hair and gray eyes, steady and bright. A
strong, frank, sonorous voice came from the throat of this slender youth, and his
very first words altered at once the view that had been formed of him.

He spoke loudly, in a declamatory tone, but so clearly that his slightest words
carried to the ends of the large court:

"Your Worship, as I do not wish to go to a madhouse, and even prefer the
guillotine, I will tell you all.

"I killed the man and the woman because they were my parents.

"Now hear me and judge me.

"A woman, having given birth to a son, sent him out to nurse. It had been well
if she had known to what district her accomplice had carried the little creature,
innocent, but condemned to lasting misery, to the shame of illegitimate birth, to
worse than that: to death, since he was abandoned, since the nurse, no longer
receiving the monthly allowance, might well have left him, as such women often do,
to pine away, to suffer from hunger, to perish of neglect.

"The woman who suckled me was honest, more honest, more womanly, greater
of soul, a better mother, than my own mother. She brought me up. She was wrong
to do her duty. It is better to leave to their death the wretches who are flung out
into provincial villages, as rubbish is flung out at the roadside.

"I grew up with the vague impression that I was the bearer of some dishonor.
One day the other children called me 'bastard.' They did not know the meaning of
the word, which one of them had heard at home. Neither did I know its meaning,
but I sensed it.

"I was, I can honestly say, one of the most intelligent children in the school. I
should have been an honest man, Your Worship, perhaps a remarkable man, if
my parents had not committed the crime of abandoning me.

"And it was against me that this crime was committed. I was the victim, they
were the guilty ones. I was defenseless, they were pitiless. They ought to have
loved me: they cast me out.

"I owed my life to them—but is life a gift? Mine, at any rate, was nothing but
a misfortune. After their shameful desertion of me, I owed them nothing but revenge. They committed against me the most inhuman, the most shameful, the
most monstrous crime that can be committed against a human being.

"A man insulted strikes; a man robbed takes back his goods by force. A man deceived, tricked, tormented, kills; a man whose face is slapped kills; a man dishonored kills. I was more grievously robbed, deceived, tormented, morally slapped in the face, dishonored, than all the men whose anger you condone.

"I have avenged myself, I have killed. It was my lawful right. I took their happy lives in exchange for the horrible life which they imposed on me.

"You will call it parricide! Were they my parents, those people to whom I was an abominable burden, a terror, a mark of infamy; to whom my birth was a calamity and my life a threat of shame? They sought their selfish pleasure; they brought forth the child they had not counted on. They suppressed that child. My turn has come to repay them in kind.

"And yet, even at the eleventh hour, I was prepared to love them.

"It is now two years, as I have already told you, since the man, my father, came to my house for the first time. I suspected nothing. He ordered two articles of furniture. I learned later that he had obtained information from the village priest, under the seal of a secret compact.

"He often came; he gave me work and paid me well. Sometimes he even chatted with me on various subjects. I felt some affection for him.

"At the beginning of this year he brought his wife, my mother. When she came in she was trembling so violently that I thought she was the victim of a nervous disorder. Then she asked for a chair and a glass of water. She said nothing; she stared at my stock with the expression of a lunatic, and to all the questions he put to her she answered nothing but yes and no, quite at random! When she had gone, I thought her not quite right in the head.

"She came back the following month. She was calm, mistress of herself. They remained talking quite a long time that day, and gave me a big order. I saw her again three times without guessing anything; but one day, lo and behold! she began to talk to me about my life, my childhood, and my parents. I answered: 'My parents, madame, were wretches who abandoned me.' At that she set her hand to her heart and dropped senseless. I thought at once: 'This is my mother!' but was careful not to give myself away. I wanted her to go on coming.

"So I in my turn made inquiries. I learned that they had been married just the previous July, my mother having been only three years a widow. There had been rumors enough that they had been lovers during her first husband's lifetime, but no proof had been forthcoming. I was the proof, the proof they had first hidden, and hoped ultimately to destroy.

"I waited. She reappeared one evening, accompanied, as always, by my father. She seemed to be in a very agitated state that day, I do not know why. Then, just as she was going, she said to me:

" 'I wish you well, because I believe you are an honest lad and a good worker; doubtless you will be thinking of getting married some day; I have come to make it possible for you to choose freely any woman you prefer. I myself married the first time against the desires of my heart, and I know how much suffering it brings. Now I am rich, childless, free, mistress of my fortune. Here is your marriage portion.'

"She held out to me a large envelope.

"I stared fixedly at her, then said:

" 'Are you my mother?'

"She drew back three paces and hid her eyes in her hand, so that she could see me no more. He, the man, my father, supported her in his arms and shouted at me:

" 'You are mad!'

" 'Not at all,' I replied. 'I know very well that you are my parents. I am not to be deceived so easily. Admit it, and I will keep your secret; I will bear no malice, I will remain what I am now, a joiner.'

"He recoiled towards the door, still supporting his wife, who was beginning to sob. I ran and locked the door, put the key in my pocket, and continued:

" 'Look at her, then, and continue to deny that she is my mother!'

"At that he lost his self-control and turned very pale, terrified by the thought that the scandal hitherto avoided might suddenly come out; that their position, their good name, their honor would be lost at a blow.

" 'You're a scoundrel,' he stammered, 'trying to get money out of us. And yet they tell us to be good to the common people, the louts, to help them and succor them!'

"My mother, bewildered, was repeating over and over again:

" 'Let us go. Let us go.'

"Then, as the door was locked, he exclaimed:

" 'If you don't open the door immediately, I'll have you jailed for blackmail and assault!'

"I had kept my self-control; I opened the door, and saw them disappear in the darkness.

"At that I felt suddenly as though I had just been orphaned, abandoned, cast into the gutter. A dreadful sadness, mingled with rage, hatred, and disgust overwhelmed me. I felt a swollen rush of emotion through my whole being, a rising tide of justice, righteousness, honor, and spurned affection. I set off running in order to catch them up on the bank of the Seine, which they must follow in order to reach Châton station.

"I overtook them before long. The night became pitch-dark. I slunk along on the grass, so that they did not hear me. My mother was still crying. My father was saying:

" 'It is your own fault. Why did you insist on seeing him? It was madness, in our position. We might have done him kindness by stealth, without showing ourselves. Seeing that we could not hope to recognize him, what was the use of these perilous visits?'

"Then I threw myself in their path, a suppliant.

" 'Clearly you are my parents,' I stammered. 'You have already cast me off once; will you reject me a second time?'

"At that, Your Worship, he raised his hand to me, I swear it on my honor, on the law, on the State. He struck me, and as I seized him by his coat collar, he drew a revolver from his pocket.

"I saw red, I no longer knew what I did. I had my calipers in my pocket; I struck him, struck him with all my force.

"Then the woman began to cry: 'Help! Murder!' and tore at my beard. Apparently I killed her too. How can I know what I did at that moment?

"Then, when I saw them both lying on the ground, I threw them into the Seine, without thinking.

"That is all. Now judge me."

The prisoner sat down again. After this revelation the trial was postponed until the following session. It will soon come on again. If you and I were the jury, what should we do with this parricide?

THE OLIVE ORCHARD

I

When the shore-loafers of the small Provençal port of Garandou on the Bay of Pisca, between Marseilles and Toulon, caught sight of Abbé Vilbois' boat coming back from fishing, they went down to the beach to help him draw it in.

The abbé was alone in the boat, rowing like a seaman, with unusual energy, in spite of his fifty-eight years. His sleeves were turned up over his muscular arms, his cassock drawn up, gathered tightly between his knees, and unbuttoned at the top, his shovel hat on the seat beside him and a pith helmet covered with white linen on his head. He looked like one of those solidly built, fantastic priests from the tropics, more suited for adventure than for saying Mass.

Occasionally he looked behind to make sure of his landing, then pulled again with great energy, rhythmically and steadily, just to show the poor southern sailors how men from the North could row. The boat shot forward, touching the sand, over which it glided as if it were going to climb up the beach on its keel, then stopped dead, and the five men who were watching drew near; they were good-natured, cheerful, and on good terms with their priest.

"Well," said one of them with a strong Provençal accent, "had a good catch, your reverence?"

Abbé Vilbois shipped his oars, took off his helmet, put on his shovel hat, dropped his sleeves over his arms, buttoned up his cassock, and, resuming his priestly attitude—the bearing of the officiating priest of the village—he replied proudly:

"Yes, indeed, very good, three catfish, two eels, and a few rockfish."

Going up to the boat and leaning over the gunwale, the five fishermen examined the dead fish with an expert air: the fleshy catfish, the flat-headed eels—hideous sea serpents—and the violet rockfish with zigzag stripes and gold bands, the color of orange peel.

One of the men said: "I will carry them to the house, your reverence."

"Thanks, my good man."

Shaking hands, the priest started off followed by the one fisherman, the others staying behind to look after the boat.

The priest, robust and dignified, strode along with big, slow steps. As he still felt warm from his vigorous rowing, he took off his hat whenever he reached the slight shade of the olive trees, to expose his square-cut brow with its straight, white hair cut short—more the brow of an officer than of a priest—to the tepid night air now slightly freshened by a faint sea breeze. The village revealed itself up on the cliff in the middle of a wide valley that ran down like a plain towards the sea.

It was a night in July. The dazzling sun, nearing the crest of the distant hills, stretched out the priest's long shadow on the white road, buried under a shroud of dust; his exaggerated shovel hat, reflected in a broad, dark patch in the neighboring field, seemed to clamber up the tree trunks on the way, and drop quickly to the ground again, creeping about among the olives.

From under Abbé Vilbois' feet rose a cloud of that fine, floury dust that covers the roads of Provence in summer, curling around his cassock like a veil and coloring its hem with a faint wash of gray over the black. He strode along with the slow, measured gait of a mountaineer making an ascent. His unruffled eyes gazed upon the village of which he had been the curé for twenty years, the village he had picked out and obtained as a great favor, and where he hoped to die. The church— his church—crowned the wide circle of houses huddled together around it with its two uneven, square towers of brown stone whose profiles had stood out for centuries over the beautiful Southern valley, more like the donjons of a fortified castle than the steeples of a church.

The abbé was pleased because he had caught three catfish, two eels, and a few rockfish. This would be a new, minor triumph over his parishioners, who respected him chiefly because he was the strongest man in the country, in spite of his age. These little harmless vanities were his greatest pleasure. With a pistol he could cut off a flower from its stalk, sometimes he fenced with his neighbor, the tobacconist, who had been a regimental fencing master, and he rowed better than anyone on the coast.

In addition to which, Baron Vilbois, who at the age of thirty-two had become a priest after an unfortunate love affair, had been a man of the world, well known and a leader of fashion.

Descended from an old royalist family of Picardy, staunch churchmen, whose sons had been in the army, the church, and the law for several generations, his first intention was to enter holy orders on his mother's advice, but his father's objections prevailed, and he decided to go to Paris, study law, and then try for some important post at the law courts.

As he was finishing his course, his father died of pneumonia caught on a shooting expedition on the marshes, and his mother died shortly after of grief. Having thus suddenly inherited a large fortune, he gave up his plans of adopting any profession whatever and was content to live the life of a man of means. He was a handsome youth, whose intelligence was limited by the beliefs, traditions, and principles he had inherited from his family, together with the physical strength of a native of Picardy; everyone liked him, he was popular in the more serious circles of society and enjoyed life in the way that a wealthy, highly respected, conventional young man does.

Unfortunately, after a few meetings at a friend's house, he fell in love with a young actress, a student from the Conservatoire who had made a brilliant first appearance at the Odéon.

He fell in love with the violence and passion of a man destined to believe in absolute ideas. He fell in love, seeing her through the medium of the romantic part in which she had won great success the day she appeared in public for the first time.

She was pretty, naturally perverse, with the ways of a spoiled child that he called her "angel ways." She gained complete ascendancy over him, turning him into a raging maniac, a frenzied lunatic, one of those miserable beings whom the glance or the skirt of a woman consumes at the stake of a mortal passion. He made her his mistress, forced her to leave the stage, and loved her for four years with an ever growing passion. Indeed, he would have married her in spite of his name and the family tradition of honor had he not suddenly discovered that she was deceiving him with the friend who had introduced them to each other.

The blow fell with all the more force because she was *enceinte* and he was awaiting the child's birth to make up his mind to get married.

When he possessed all the proofs—letters accidentally found in a drawer—he accused her of infidelity, treachery, and double-dealing, with the brutality of a semisavage.

But this child of the Paris streets, impudent and vicious, feeling as sure of her second lover as she did of Vilbois, as bold as those viragoes of the revolution who climb the barricades out of sheer bravado, defied and insulted him, pointing to her condition when she saw him raise his hand.

He stopped and turned pale, remembering that a child of his was there within that polluted flesh, in that defiled body, that unclean creature: his child!

He threw himself at her to destroy them both, to blot out the double shame. Frightened at the ruin of her future, stumbling about under the force of his blows and seeing his foot ready to kick the swollen womb with its human embryo, she cried with hands outstretched to save herself:

"Don't kill me. It is not yours, it is his."

He started back, stupefied and overcome, his anger momentarily fading, while his foot hovered in mid-air, and he stammered:

"What . . . what are you saying?"

Wild with fright at the signal of death she had caught in his eyes and at the man's terrifying gesture, she repeated:

"It is not yours, it is his."

Quite overwrought, he muttered between clenched teeth:

"The child?"

"Yes."

"You are lying."

And again he lifted his foot for a crushing blow, while his mistress, now on her knees, tried to move away, murmuring all the time:

"But I tell you it is his. If it was yours, would not I have had it long ago?"

This argument struck him as being truth itself. In one of those flashes of thought when all the arguments on a question are seen together in a blinding clearness, precise, unanswerable, conclusive, irresistible, he was convinced, he knew that he was not the father of the wretched waif-child she was carrying; and relieved, freed, suddenly almost at rest, he gave up the idea of killing the jade.

He said more gently:

"Get up, go away, never let me see you again."

Quite subdued, she obeyed and went away.

He never saw her again.

He went away too, down to the south, to the sun, and stayed in a village in the middle of a valley on the Mediterranean. He was attracted by an inn facing the sea, took a room there, in which he stayed for eighteen months, lost in grief and despair, and living in complete isolation. He lived there obsessed by the memory of the woman who had betrayed him, of her charm, her physical appearance, her unbelievable witchery, and filled with longing for her presence, her caressings.

He wandered through the valleys of Provence, seeking relief for his aching head with its burden of memory in the sun that filtered gently through the dull gray leaves of the olive trees.

In this solitude of suffering the old piety, the steadied fervor of his early faith, revived in his heart. Religion, which had once seemed to him a refuge from the unknown, now appeared as a haven of escape from life's treachery and cruelty. He had never lost the habit of prayer, to prayer he therefore clung in his great sorrow, going regularly to the darkened church at dusk, where a solitary speck of light shone down the chancel from the lamp, the holy guardian of the sanctuary and symbol of the Divine Presence.

To him he confided his trouble, to his God, telling him all about his sorrow. He craved for advice, pity, help, protection, consolation, putting more and more feeling into his prayers, which grew in fervor from day to day.

His wounded heart, ravaged by carnal love, was bare and throbbing, longing for tenderness, and little by little, through prayer and piety, by giving himself up to that secret communion of the devout with the Saviour who brings consolation and is a sure refuge to those in distress, the love of God entered in him and drove out the intruder.

He went back to his early plans and decided that what remained of the life he had intended to devote to the Lord in its youth and purity should now be given to the Church.

He became a priest. Through family influence he was appointed priest of the Provençal village into which luck had thrown him, and having given a large part of his fortune to benevolent institutions, only retaining sufficient to enable him to be of use, and a help to the poor until he died, he settled down to a quiet life full of good works and of care for his fellow creatures.

He was a narrow-minded priest, but kind to his people, a religious leader with a soldier's temperament, a guide who forcibly led the sinner into the narrow way: the poor blind sinner lost in the forest of life where all our instincts, our desires, our tastes, are bypaths which lead us astray. But much of the man of old days remained. He still liked violent exercise, sport, and fencing, and he detested all women with the unreasoning fear of a child before some hidden danger.

II

The sailor who was with the priest felt the usual southern longing for a chat, but dared not begin, for the abbé exercised great authority over his flock. At last he ventured:

"So you are comfortable in your little house, your reverence?"

The bastide was one of those tiny houses frequented in summer by Provençals of town and country in search of fresh air. The abbé had rented this retreat in the middle of a field, five minutes' walk from the presbytery, which was too small and enclosed in the center of the parish, right up against the church.

Even in summer he did not live regularly at the cottage: he only went there occasionally for a few days to be amongst the fields and trees and to do some pistol practice.

"Yes, my friend," said the priest. "I am very comfortable there."

The low dwelling, looking as if it had grown like a Provençal mushroom, appeared among the trees. It was painted pink, its surface being speckled over with stripes and spots, split up into little bits by the olive leaves and branches from the trees in the open field.

At the same moment they saw a tall woman moving about in front of the door, getting the little dinner table ready as she went backwards and forwards, with methodical leisureliness setting the cloth for one, a plate, table napkin, piece of bread, and glass. She had on the little cap worn by the women of Arles: a pointed cone of black silk or velvet from which grows a white starched mushroom.

When the abbé was within hearing distance, he called out:

"Eh, Marguerite?"

She stopped to look round and, recognizing her master, said:

"Oh, it's you, your reverence?"

"Yes, I am bringing a good haul, you must grill me a catfish at once, cooked in butter, only butter, you hear?"

The servant, who had come to meet the two men, examined the fish the sailor was carrying, with an expert eye.

"But we have already got a chicken cooked with rice."

"Never mind that, tomorrow's fish is not as good as fish fresh from the sea. I am going to have a really choice meal, it does not often happen; moreover, it is not a great sin."

The servant picked out the fish and, as she was carrying it away, turned round:

"A man has been here three times to see you, your reverence."

Showing no interest, he asked:

"A man! What kind of man?"

"Well, the kind of man whose looks do not recommend him."

"What! a beggar?"

"Perhaps, I don't know. I rather think he is a maoufatan."

Abbé Vilbois laughed at the Provençal word meaning a bad lot, a tramp, for he knew how frightened Marguerite was, and that when she was at the cottage she was always thinking they were going to be murdered.

He gave the sailor a few sous, and was preparing to wash his face and hands, having kept his old habits of neatness and cleanliness, when Marguerite called out from the kitchen, where she was scraping the blood-flecked scales that came away from the fish like tiny pieces of silver:

"There he is!"

The abbé turned towards the road and saw a man, who seemed in the distance to be very badly dressed, walking towards the house with very small steps. He awaited him, still smiling at his servant's fright, thinking: "Upon my word, she must be right, he certainly looks a bad lot."

Without hurrying, the unknown individual drew near, hands in his pockets, and his eyes fixed upon the priest. He was young, with a fair, curly beard, and hair that fell in curls beneath his soft felt hat, a hat so dirty and crushed that no one could have guessed its original color and shape. He wore a brown overcoat, trousers that hung in a fringe over his ankles, and string sandals that gave him a slack, silent, disquieting walk—the hardly perceptible slouch of the tramp.

When a few steps away from the priest, he took off the ragged cap that covered his head with a flourish, exposing a withered, dissolute, but well-shaped head, bald on the top—a sign of fatigue or of early debauchery, for the man was certainly not over twenty-five.

The priest immediately took off his hat too, for he felt that this was no ordinary vagabond, or unemployed, neither was he the habitual jailbird wandering about between two prisons who had forgotten all speech except the mysterious language of the convict.

"Good day, your reverence," said the man. The priest replied simply: "Good day," not wishing to call this doubtful, ragged passer-by "sir." They stared at each other; the fixed steady look of the tramp made Abbé Vilbois feel uncomfortable, distressed as one feels when facing an unknown enemy, and overpowered by one of those strange feelings of uneasiness that send shivers through body and blood. At last the vagabond said:

"Well! do you recognize me?"

The priest replied, very astonished:

"Me? Not at all, I don't know you."

"Ah! You don't know me. Look at me again."

"What is the good of looking at you? I have never seen you before."

"That is true enough," said the other ironically, "but I will show you someone you do know."

He put on his hat and unbuttoned his coat, under which his chest was bare. A red sash wound round his thin waist held his trousers up over his hips.

He took an envelope from his pocket—an envelope marked with every possible kind of stain, the sort of envelope that tramps keep tucked away in the lining of their clothes and in which they put all kinds of identification papers, which may be genuine, faked, stolen, or legally correct, and which are the highly valued defenses of their individual liberty in case of any meeting with the police. From the envelope he drew a photograph about the size of a letter such as were formerly used. It was yellowish and crumpled with much handling, faded by the heat of the body against which it had been kept.

Holding it up to the abbé, he asked:

"And this, do you know it?"

The abbé took two steps forward to see better, then stopped; he turned pale, profoundly distressed, for this was a photograph of him taken for her in the bygone days of his love.

Still he did not understand and made no reply.

The vagabond repeated:

"Do you recognize this?"

The priest stammered:

"Well, yes."

"Who is it?"

"Me."

"It is really you?"

"Certainly."

"Right; now look at your photograph, then look at me."

The miserable priest had already seen that the two—the man in the photograph and the man standing at his side laughing, were as alike as two brothers, but still he did not understand and stammered:

"What do you want me to do?"

With a note of spite in his voice the beggar said:

"What do I want? Well, first of all I want you to recognize me."

"But who are you?"

"What am I? Ask the first comer on the road, ask the servant; if you like, let us go and ask the mayor of the village and show him the photograph; he will laugh about it, I can tell you that. Ah! you refuse to recognize me as your son, Papa Curé?"

The old man, lifting his arms with a biblical and despairing gesture, moaned:
"It can't be true."

The young man drew nearer and, facing him, said:

"Ah! It can't be true. Ah! you priest, you must stop telling lies, do you
hear?"

The expression on his face was threatening, his fists were doubled up, he spoke
with so much violence that the abbé, moving further away, asked himself which
of the two was making a mistake.

However, he insisted again:

"I have never had a child."

The other retorted:

"And you never had a mistress either?"

The old man with great determination uttered one word: making a dignified
assent:

"Yes."

"And this mistress was not with child when you turned her out?"

The old feeling of resentment, stifled twenty-five years ago—not really stifled
but confined deep down in the lover's heart—suddenly burst asunder the whole
fabric of his religious belief, of his resigned devotion to his God, as well as his
complete renunciation of worldly things: all that he had built up round it with so
much care; and, beside himself with rage, he shouted:

"I turned her out because she had deceived me and was with child by another,
otherwise I would have killed her, sir, and you too."

The young man hesitated, surprised at the sincerity of the curé's outburst; he
said in a gentler tone:

"And who told you the child was another's?"

"She did, she herself, while defying me."

Without questioning this statement, the vagabond said with the casual manner
of a street boy pronouncing judgment:

"Just so! Then Mamma made a mistake when she defied you, that is all there
is to be said."

Quickly regaining self-control after his sudden outburst, the abbé began to
question the boy:

"And who told you that you were my son?"

"She did when she was dying, your reverence. . . . Besides, what about this!"

And he held the little photograph up to the priest.

The old man took it, and with anguish in his heart he spent some time comparing the unknown passer-by with his old photograph—there could be no further
doubt that the youth was indeed his son.

He was seized with a feeling of distress, an intensely painful, indefinable feeling
like remorse for some old crime. He understood a little of what had happened,
and guessed the rest, and again he saw the brutal scene of their parting. To save
the life threatened by the man she had wronged, the woman—the deceitful, faithless female—had thrust this lie at him. . . . And the lie had succeeded. A son of
his had been born, grown up, and turned into this sordid road tramp stinking of
vice as a he-goat stinks of the beast.

He said in a low voice:

"Will you go for a short stroll with me so that we may clear the matter up?"

The other sneered:

"Will I? That is what I came for."

They went off together, side by side, through the orchard. The sun had gone down and the keen freshness of the southern twilight spread its invisible cooling cloak over the countryside. The abbé shivered; raising his eyes to heaven in the usual orthodox way, he saw all around him, trembling against the sky, the small gray leaves of the holy tree which had sheltered under its frail shadow the greatest of all suffering—the one and only moment of Christ's weakness. A short prayer of desperation burst from him, spoken with that inner voice that never passes the lips, with which believers call upon the Saviour: "O God, help me."

Then, turning towards his son:

"So then, your mother is dead?"

As he said the words: "Your mother is dead," a new wave of grief swept through him, making his heart sink, a curious torment of the flesh unable to forget a cruel echo of the torture he had suffered; as she was dead, the most painful feeling of all seemed to be the faint stirring within him of that delirious, shortlived happiness which had left nothing behind it but the scar of remembrance.

The young man replied:

"Yes, your reverence, my mother is dead."

"Long ago?"

"Three years ago."

Another doubt troubled the priest.

"Why did you not come sooner and look for me?"

The other hesitated.

"I could not. I was prevented. . . . But excuse me for interrupting the secrets which shall be revealed later on, with as many details as you please, to say that I have had nothing to eat since yesterday morning."

The old man was filled with pity, and quickly holding out his hands, he said: "Oh, my poor child."

The young man took the outstretched hands, which closed over his thin, moist, feverish fingers, and replied with his habitual flippancy:

"Good! Really, I begin to think we shall get on together in spite of what has happened."

The curé started walking again.

"Let us go and dine," he said.

Suddenly he remembered with a vague feeling of pleasure that was odd and confused, the beautiful fish he had caught, which with the chicken and rice would make a good meal for the wretched youngster.

The Arlésienne, anxious and beginning to grumble, was waiting for them at the door.

"Marguerite," cried the abbé, "take away the table and carry it into the room, quickly, quickly, and set the cloth for two, but quickly."

The servant did not move, scared at the thought that her master was going to dine with the criminal.

Then, Abbé Vilbois himself began to take the things away and remove what had been set for him into the only room on the ground floor.

Five minutes later he was seated opposite the vagabond before a tureen full of cabbage soup that sent up a faint cloud of boiling steam between their faces.

III

When the plates were full, the tramp started to swallow his soup greedily in quick following spoonfuls. The *abbé* was not hungry now, so he trifled with the delicious soup, leaving the bread at the bottom of the plate. He asked suddenly:

"What is your name?"

The man laughed, glad to be satisfying his hunger.

"Unknown Father," said he, "I have no surname except my mother's family name, which you have probably not forgotten. On the other hand, I have two Christian names, which, by the way, certainly do not suit me: Philippe-Auguste."

The *abbé* turned pale and asked with a strangled voice:

"Why were you given those Christian names?"

The vagabond shrugged his shoulders.

"Surely you can guess why. After leaving you, Mamma wanted to make your rival believe that I was his child, and he did believe it until about my fifteenth year. Then I grew too much like you. He repudiated me, the scoundrel! I had been given the two Christian names, Philippe-Auguste, and if I had had the luck not to be like anybody, or simply to have been the son of a third unknown ne'er-do-well, I should now be known as the Viscount Philippe-Auguste de Pravallon, the recently acknowledged son of the Count of that name, a senator. As for me, I christened myself 'No Luck.' "

"How do you know all this?"

"Because there were discussions in my presence, and violent they were, you may be sure. Ah! that is the sort of thing that teaches you life."

A still more painful and stricken feeling than he had yet suffered in the last half hour oppressed the priest. It was the beginning of a form of suffocation that would grow worse and worse until it killed him, caused not so much by the things he was told as by the way they were told, and by the brutish face of the outcast that gave emphasis to them. Between this man and himself, between his son and himself, he began to feel that swamp of moral filth that works as a deadly poison on certain beings. This was his son? He could not believe it. He wanted every proof, every possible proof; he must learn all, hear all, listen to all, and suffer all. Again he thought of the olive trees surrounding his little house, again he murmured: "O God, help me!"

Philippe-Auguste had finished his soup, and asked:

"Is there no more to eat, Abbé?"

The kitchen being outside the house in an annex, Marguerite could not hear the curé's voice, so he warned her of his needs by a few strokes on a Chinese gong that hung behind him on the wall.

He picked up a leather hammer and struck the round metal plaque several times. At first a faint sound escaped from it, which grew gradually and, gaining in weight, turned into the vibrating, sharp, violent, horrible, strident clamor of beaten copper.

The servant appeared. Her face was drawn, she glared at the scoundrel as if, with the instinct of a faithful dog, she felt a presentiment of the drama that was hanging over her master. In her hands she held the grilled fish, which sent out a delicious odor of melted butter. The *abbé* divided the fish from head to tail and offered the back fillet to the child of his youth.

"I caught it a short time ago," he said, a remnant of pride hovering in his distress.

Marguerite stayed in the room.

The priest continued:

"Bring some wine, good wine, some of the white wine of Cape Corsica."

She succeeded in hiding her disgust, but he was obliged to repeat sternly:

"Now then, two bottles." For when he offered wine to a guest—an unusual pleasure—he always offered himself a bottle too.

Philippe-Auguste said, beaming:

"A jolly good idea. I have not had a meal like this for a long time."

The servant came back in two minutes' time. Two minutes that had seemed as long as a twofold eternity to the abbé: the desire to know everything was scorching his blood and consuming it like hell-fire.

The bottles were uncorked, and still the servant lingered with eyes fixed on the young man.

"Leave us," said the curé.

She pretended not to hear.

He repeated, with a certain harshness:

"I ordered you to leave us alone."

Whereupon she left the room.

Philippe-Auguste ate the fish greedily, while his father, watching him, became more and more surprised and distressed at the degradation he saw in the face so like his own. The morsels that the Abbé Vilbois lifted to his lips refused to pass his contracted throat, and he chewed them slowly, casting about in his mind for the most urgent of the questions that crowded upon him.

He ended by saying:

"What did she die of?"

"Of lung trouble."

"Was she ill long?"

"About eighteen months."

"How did she get it?"

"No one knows."

A silence fell upon them. The abbé was lost in thought. He felt troubled by many things that he wanted to know, for since the day of his violent attack upon her, he had heard nothing. It was true that he had not wanted news; he had resolutely buried all memory of her and of his days of happiness. But now that she was dead, he felt a sudden violent desire to know everything, a jealous desire, almost a lover's desire.

He resumed:

"She was not alone, was she?"

"No, she was still living with him."

The old man shrank within himself.

"With him, with Pravallon?"

"Of course."

The man who had been betrayed calculated that the very woman who had deceived him had lived over thirty years with his rival.

Almost in spite of himself, he stammered:

"Were they happy together?"

The young man replied, grinning:

"Well, yes, though there were ups and downs. It would have been all right but for me. I have always spoiled everything."

"How's that, and why?" said the priest.

"I have already told you. Because he believed I was his son until I was about fifteen. But he was no fool, the old man, he himself discovered the likeness, and then there were rows. He accused Mamma of landing him in a mess. Mamma retorted: 'Am I to blame? When you took me, you knew quite well that I was the other's mistress.' The 'other' being you."

"Oh, so they talked about me sometimes?"

"Yes, but they never mentioned your name when I was present, except at the end, the very end. The last days when Mamma knew she was done for. They had no confidence in me."

"And you . . . did you soon learn that your mother was living an irregular life?"

"What do you think? I am not a fool, you bet; I never was. You guess these things directly, as soon as you know something of life."

Philippe-Auguste was pouring out one glass of wine after another. His eyes lighted up, intoxication quickly followed his long fast. The priest noticed this and was going to make him stop drinking, when he remembered that drink made men reckless and talkative, so he took the bottle and refilled the young man's glass.

Marguerite brought in the dish of chicken and rice. As she placed it on the table, she fixed her eyes on the tramp, then indignantly said to her master:

"Just look how drunk he is, your reverence."

"Leave us alone and go away," said the priest.

She went out slamming the door.

He asked:

"What did your mother say about me?"

"The usual thing that is said about the man you leave; that you were not easy to live with, a worry to a woman, and that you would have made her life very difficult with your ideas."

"Did she say that often?"

"Yes, sometimes in a roundabout way so that I should not understand, but I guessed what had happened."

"And you, how were you treated in the home?"

"Me? Very well at first, but very badly later on. When Mamma saw that I was a spoilsport, she chucked me out."

"How?"

"How! Quite easily. I played some pranks when I was about sixteen, so the idiots put me into a reformatory to get rid of me."

He put his elbows on the table, resting his cheeks on his hands, and quite drunk, his wits upside down in drink, he suddenly felt that irresistible wish to talk about himself that turns a drunkard into a driveling braggart. He was smiling prettily with all a woman's charm. The abbé recognized the perverse charm of the boy's smile, he not only recognized it, he also felt the spell of the charm— hateful but caressing—that had conquered and ruined him in the past. For the moment the child was more like his mother, not in feature, but in the alluring and insincere expression of his face, and more especially in the attraction of that misleading smile that seemed to open a door on all the incredible baseness of his nature.

Philippe-Auguste continued:

"Well, well! I have had a life, I have, ever since I left the reformatory, a curious life for which a novelist would pay a large sum. Really, old Dumas with his Monte Cristo never imagined stranger adventures than have happened to me."

He was silent, thinking things over with the philosophical seriousness of the meditative drunkard, then he said slowly:

"If you want a boy to turn out well, no matter what he has done he should never be sent to a reformatory, because of the people he has to mix with. I had a jolly good idea, but it failed. One night about nine o'clock I was wandering around with three pals, all four of us rather the worse for drink, on the main road near Folac ford, when what should I see but a carriage full of people asleep!—the man who was driving and his family; they lived at Martinon and were returning home after dining in town. I seized the horse by the reins and forced it on to the ferryboat, then pushed the boat into the middle of the river. That made a noise, and the driver woke up and, not able to see anything, whipped up his horse. Off it went and jumped into the stream with the carriage. They were all drowned! My pals informed against me. At first they laughed like anything as they watched me at work. We never thought it would turn out so badly. All we had hoped for was a bath, something to laugh about.

"Since that I have done worse out of revenge for the first joke, which, I must say, did not deserve punishment. However, there is nothing worth telling. I will only tell you about my last trick because I know that will please you. I paid him out for you."

The abbé looked at his son with terrified eyes and stopped eating.

Philippe-Auguste was going on with his story.

"No," the priest said, "not now, presently."

Turning round, he struck the strident Chinese cymbal and made it cry out.

Marguerite came at once.

Her master gave his orders so harshly that she bowed her head, afraid and docile:

"Bring us the lamp and all that is still to be put on the table; after that you must not come back unless I strike the gong."

She went out, came back again and put a white china lamp on the tablecloth, a big piece of cheese, some fruit, and then left the room.

The abbé said with determination:

"Now I am listening."

Quite undisturbed, Philippe-Auguste filled up his plate with dessert and filled his glass with wine. The second bottle was nearly empty although the curé had not touched it. The young man, his mouth sticky with food and drink, stammering, resumed:

"The last one, well, here you are. It is pretty bad. I had returned home . . . where I stayed in spite of them because they were afraid of me . . . afraid of me. . . . Ah! You must not annoy me. . . . You know . . . they were living together and yet not together. He had two homes, he had, one the senator's, the other the lover's. But he lived at Mamma's more than he did at his own home, because he could not do without her. Ah! . . . she was shrewd, she was knowing, Mamma . . . she knew how to hold a man, she did! She had taken him body and soul, and she kept him to the end. What fools men are! Well, I had returned and gained the mastery over them because they were afraid of me. I know my way about when necessary, and as for spite, cunning, and violence, I am anyone's match. Then Mamma fell ill and he settled her in a beautiful place near Meulan in the middle of a park as big as a forest. That lasted about eighteen months . . . as I have already told you. Then we felt the end approaching. He came from Paris every day, he was full of grief no doubt about it, real grief.

"Well, one morning they had been jabbering for nearly an hour, and I was wondering whatever they could be chattering about so long, when they called me; and Mamma said:

" 'I am on the point of death, and have something I want to tell you, in spite of the count's opinion'—she always called him 'the count' when she spoke about him—'it is the name of your father, who is still alive.'

"I had asked for it more than a hundred times . . . more than a hundred times . . . my father's name . . . more than a hundred times . . . and she had always refused to tell me. . . . I even think that I struck her one day to make her talk, but it was no use. And then, to get rid of me, she said that you had died penniless, that you were a good-for-nothing, an error of her youth, a maiden's slip, any old thing. She told the story so well that I swallowed it whole, the story of your death.

"As she was saying: 'It is your father's name,' the other, who was sitting in an armchair, repeated three times, just like this:

" 'You are wrong, you are wrong, you are wrong, Rosette.'

"Mamma sat up in bed. I can still see her with the red spots on her cheeks and her bright eyes, for she loved me in spite of all; she said to him:

" 'Then do something for him yourself, Philippe.'

"When talking to him she always called him 'Philippe' and me 'Auguste.'

"He started shouting out like a madman:

" 'For that blackguard, never, for that rogue, that jailbird, that . . . that . . . that . . .'

"He called me all kinds of names just as if he had done nothing else all his life except look for names for me. I nearly lost my temper, when Mamma bade me be quiet, and said to him:

" 'Then you want him to die of hunger, as I have nothing to give him.'

"He replied, not at all worried:

" 'Rosette, for thirty years I have given you thirty-five thousand francs a year, that makes over a million. Because of me you have led the life of a rich woman, a well-loved woman, and, I dare to add, a happy woman. I owe nothing to this blackguard who has spoiled our last years together, and he will get nothing from me. Useless to insist. Let him know the name of the other one, if you wish. I am sorry, but I wash my hands of the matter.'

"Then Mamma turned towards me. I said to myself: 'God . . . I am going to get my own father back . . . if he has any cash, I am a saved man . . .'

"She continued:

" 'Your father, the Baron of Vilbois, is now known as the Abbé Vilbois, curé of Girandou: near Toulon. He was my lover when I left him for this man.' She then told me everything except how she had tricked you about her pregnancy. But, there is it, women never tell the truth."

He sniggered, unconcerned, displaying all his vileness. He went on drinking and, with a still smiling face, continued:

"Mamma died two days . . . two days later. We followed her coffin to the grave, he and I . . . wasn't it comical! . . . eh! . . . he and I . . . and three servants . . . that was all. He was weeping like a cow . . . we were side by side . . . you would have said it was Papa and Papa's dear boy.

"Then we went home. Only the two of us. I said to myself: 'I must be off, without a halfpenny.' I had just fifty francs. What could I do to pay him out?

"He touched my arm and said:

" 'I want to speak to you.'

"I followed him to his study. He sat down before his table and plunged into tears, said that he would not treat me as badly as he had told Mamma he would; he begged me not to worry you. . . . As for that, that is our business, yours and mine. . . . He offered me a thousand-franc note . . . a thousand . . . a thousand . . . what could I do with a thousand francs . . . me . . . a man like me? I saw there were lots more in the drawer, a whole heap. At the sight of all that paper, I felt I wanted to do for someone. I held out my hand to take his gift, but instead of accepting his charity I sprang upon him, threw him down, strangling him until his eyes bulged out, then when I saw the end was near I gagged and trussed him, undressed him and turned him over, then . . . ah! . . . Ah! Ah! . . . I jolly well paid him out for you! . . ."

Philippe-Auguste coughed, choking with joy; the boy's lips curled with ferocious gaiety and reminded Abbé Vilbois of the smile of the woman for love of whom he had lost his head.

"After?" he said.

"After . . . Ah! Ah! Ah! . . . There was a big fire in the grate . . . it was December . . . in cold weather . . . she died . . . Mamma . . . a big coal fire . . . I took up the poker . . . made it all hot . . . you see . . . I made crosses on his back, eight, ten, I don't know how many, then I turned him over again and made the same number on his belly. Wasn't it funny, eh, Papa! That is how convicts were marked in the old days. He wriggled like an eel . . . but I had gagged him well, he could not make a noise. Then I took the notes—twelve of them—with my own that made thirteen . . . but they brought me no luck. Then I made off telling the servants not to disturb the Count until dinnertime as he was asleep.

"I was sure he would say nothing about it from dread of exposure, as he was a senator. But I was mistaken. Four days later I was pinched in a Paris restaurant. I got three years in jail. That is why I could not come and see you sooner."

He was still drinking and spluttering and could hardly pronounce one word clearly.

"Now . . . Papa . . . Papa curé! Isn't it funny to have a curé for a papa! . . . Ah! Ah! must be kind, very kind to the darling boy, because darling boy is out of the common . . . and he played a lovely trick . . . didn't he? . . . a lovely one . . . on the old man . . ."

The same feeling of rage that had maddened Abbé Vilbois in that final scene with the mistress who had betrayed him, seized him now towards this abominable wretch.

He who, in God's name, had dealt out forgiveness to many shameful secrets whispered in the privacy of the confessional was pitiless, merciless towards himself, he had ceased to call upon an all-merciful Father to help him, for he understood that no protection from heaven or earth could save anyone so afflicted with misfortune.

All the fire of his passionate heart and of his stirring blood, subdued by the discipline of his station in the Church, awoke in an irresistible revolt against this wretch—his own son—and against this likeness to himself, and more to that unworthy mother who had conceived the boy in her own likeness—and, more than all, against the fatality which had riveted this scoundrel to his paternal foot like the fetters of a galley slave.

He saw, he foresaw all this in a flash of clear-sightedness, shocked from his twenty-five years of pious tranquillity and rest into action.

Suddenly aware that he must take a high tone with this criminal and terrify him at the first words, he said through teeth clenched with anger, taking no account of the drunken state of the wretch:

"Now that you have told me all about it, listen. You must go away tomorrow morning. You must live in a place that I will choose and that you may not leave without my permission. I will make you a small allowance, just enough to live upon, for I have no money. If you disobey me once, this arrangement will come to an end and I will deal with you. . . ."

Although stupefied by wine, Philippe-Auguste understood the threat, and the criminal within him rose instantly to the surface. Hiccuping, he spat out some words:

"Ah! Papa, no use trying it on with me. . . . You are a curé. . . . I've got you in my power. . . . You will take it quietly, like the others."

The abbé started, the muscles of the old Hercules were aching to seize the bully, to bend him like a reed, and show him that he must submit to authority.

Pushing the table against the boy's chest, he shouted:

"Take care, take care. . . . I am afraid of nobody, not I."

Losing his balance, the drunkard rocked on his chair, then feeling that he was going to fall and that he was in the priest's power, with a villainous look on his face he stretched out his hand towards a knife that was lying on the cloth. Abbé Vilbois noticed the movement and gave the table a violent push that sent his son head over heels on to the floor, where he lay on his back. The lamp rolled along the ground and went out.

For a few seconds a thin tinkle of glasses jingling against each other sounded through the darkness, then the creeping of soft bodies over the stone floor, then silence.

With the crash of the fallen lamp, black night, swift and unexpected, had fallen upon the two, leaving them dazed as in the presence of some unspeakable horror.

The drunkard, crouching against the wall, never stirred; the priest remained on his chair, plunged in the blackness of the night that was gradually swallowing up his anger. The veil of darkness thrown over him stayed his anger and brought his furious outburst of temper to an end; other ideas took their place, black and sad as the darkness around him.

Silence reigned, a silence as dense as that of a closed tomb, in which nothing seemed to live or breathe. Not a sound came from without, no sound of wheels in the distance, no sound of a dog barking, not even the rustle of a slight breath of wind among the branches or the tapping of a twig against the walls.

The silence dragged on; it might have been an hour. Then suddenly the gong rang. It rang as if struck by a single hard stroke, sharp and loud, followed by a curious noise of something dropping and of an overturned chair.

On the alert, Marguerite rushed to the room, but on opening the door she drew back in terror of the impenetrable darkness. With pounding heart, and trembling all over, she called out in a low voice, panting for breath:

"Your reverence, your reverence."

There was no answer, not a sound.

"My God, my God, what have they done, what has happened?"

She dare not go in nor dare she go back to fetch a light: she was seized with a wild desire to run away, to escape, to scream, although her limbs shook so violently that she could hardly stand. She repeated:

"Your reverence, your reverence, it is I, Marguerite."

Suddenly, in spite of her fear, she felt she must save her master. One of those sudden fits of bravery that occasionally give women strength to perform heroic deeds filled her soul with the recklessness of terror, and running back to the kitchen, she fetched her lamp.

She stopped just inside the room. The first thing she saw was the vagabond lying against the wall, asleep or apparently asleep, then she saw the broken lamp, then under the table the black feet and black-stockinged legs of Abbé Vilbois, whose head must have knocked the gong as he fell over on to his back.

Breathless with fright, her hands trembling, she repeated:

"My God, my God, what is the matter?"

As she stepped forward slowly, taking small steps, she slipped on something greasy and nearly fell down.

Leaning forward, she saw a red liquid trickling over the red flags and spreading around her feet; quickly she ran towards the door, sure that what she had seen was blood.

Mad with terror, she fled from the place and, throwing aside the lamp so that she might see nothing more, she rushed out of doors in the direction of the village. She lurched along, knocking against the trees, with eyes fixed on the distant lights, screaming at the top of her voice.

Her shrill cries pierced the night like the sinister call of the common owl, and she screamed without ceasing: "The tramp . . . the tramp . . . the tramp . . ."

When she reached the nearest houses, scared men came out and gathered around her, but she was too excited to answer their questions; she had completely lost her head.

Finally they understood that some accident had happened at the curé's, and made up a party to go to his rescue.

The little pink-colored house in the middle of the olive orchard was invisible, black in the deep, silent night. Ever since the one light from the illuminated window had gone out like a closed eye, the house had been drowned in shadow, lost in the darkness, undiscoverable to those not familiar with the countryside.

Lights were soon moving about over the ground, through the trees, in the direction of the house, throwing long, yellow rays on the burned grass, and on the distorted trunks of the olives that looked like unreal monsters, like serpents of hell all twisted and misshapen. The beams projected in the distance suddenly showed up something whitish and vague in the darkness, then the low, square wall of the little house turned pink in the lanternlight. The lanterns were carried by the peasants, who accompanied two gendarmes with revolvers, the village constable, the mayor of the village, and Marguerite supported by some of the men, as she was in a state of collapse.

They hesitated for a minute in front of the still open, nightmarish doorway, but the inspector seized a lantern and entered, followed by the others.

The servant had not lied. The blood, now congealed, spread over the flags like a carpet. It had reached along as far as the vagabond, staining a leg and a hand.

Father and son were asleep. One, with cut throat, slept the everlasting sleep, the other slept the sleep of the drunkard. The two policemen threw themselves upon the latter and had handcuffed him before he awoke. He rubbed his eyes, stupefied, besotted with wine; when he saw the priest's corpse he had looked terrified, having no idea what had happened.

"Why ever did he not run away?" said the Mayor.

"He was too drunk," replied the inspector.

They all agreed with him: it never occurred to anyone that Abbé Vilbois might have caused his own death.

HIPPOLYTE'S CLAIM

The fat justice of the peace, with one eye closed and the other half-open, is listening with evident displeasure to the plaintiffs. Once in a while he gives a sort of grunt that foretells his opinion, and in a thin voice resembling that of a child, he interrupts them to ask questions. He has just rendered judgment in the case of M. Joly against M. Petitpas, the contestants having come to court on account of the boundary of a field which had been accidentally overstepped by M. Petitpas's farm hand, while the latter was plowing.

Now he calls the case of Hippolyte Lacour, vestryman and ironmonger, against Mme. Céleste Césarine Luneau, widow of Anthime Isidore Luneau.

Hippolyte Lacour is forty-five years old; he is tall and gaunt, with a clean-shaven face and long hair, and he speaks in a slow, singsong voice.

Mme. Luneau appears to be about forty years of age. She is built like a prize fighter, and her plain dress is stretched tightly over her portly form. Her enormous hips hold up her overflowing bosom in front, while in the back they support the great rolls of flesh that cover her shoulders. Her face, with strongly cut features, rests on a short, fat neck, and her strong voice is pitched at a key that makes the windows and the eardrums of her auditors vibrate. She is about to become a mother, and her huge form protrudes like a mountain.

The witnesses for the defense are waiting to be called.

His Honor begins: Hippolyte Lacour, state your complaint.

The plaintiff speaks: Your honor, it will be nine months on Saint Michael's Day that the defendant came to me one evening, after I had rung the Angelus, and began an explanation relating to her barrenness.

THE JUSTICE OF THE PEACE: Kindly be more explicit.

HIPPOLYTE: Very well, your honor. Well, she wanted to have a child and desired my participation. I didn't raise any objection, and she promised to give me one hundred francs. The thing was all cut and dried, and now she refuses to acknowledge my claim, which I renew before your honor.

THE JUSTICE: I don't understand in the least. You say that she wanted a child? What kind of child? Did she wish to adopt one?

HIPPOLYTE: No, your honor, she wanted a new one.

THE JUSTICE: What do you mean by a new one?

HIPPOLYTE: I mean a newborn child, one that we were to beget as if we were man and wife.

THE JUSTICE: You astonish me. To what end did she make this abnormal proposition?

HIPPOLYTE: Your honor, at first I could not make out her reasons and was taken a little aback. But as I don't do anything without thoroughly investigating beforehand, I called on her to explain matters to me, which she did. You see, her husband, Anthime Isidore, whom you knew as well as you know me, had died the week before, and his money reverted to his family. This greatly displeased her on account of the loss it meant, so she went to a lawyer who told her all about what might happen if a child should be born to her after ten months. I mean by this that if she gave birth to a child inside of the ten months following the death of Anthime Isidore, her offspring would be considered legitimate and would entitle her to the inheritance. She made up her mind at once to run the risk and came to me after church, as I have already had the honor of telling you, seeing that I am the father of eight living children, the eldest of whom is a grocer in Caen, department of Calvados, and legitimately married to Victoire-Elisabeth Rabou——

THE JUSTICE: These details are superfluous. Go back to the subject.

HIPPOLYTE: I am getting there, your honor. So she said to me: "If you succeed I'll give you one hundred francs as soon as I get the doctor's report." Well, your honor, I made ready to give entire satisfaction, and after eight weeks or so I learned with pleasure that I had succeeded. But when I asked her for the hundred francs she refused to pay me. I renewed my demands several times, never getting so much as a pin. She even called me a liar and a weakling, a libel which can be destroyed by glancing at her.

THE JUSTICE: Defendant, what have you to say?

MME. LUNEAU: Your honor, I say that this man is a liar.

THE JUSTICE: How can you prove this assertion?

MME. LUNEAU [red in the face, choking and stammering]: How can I prove it? What proofs have I? I haven't a single real proof that the child isn't his. But your honor, it isn't his; I swear it on the head of my dead husband.

THE JUSTICE: Well, whose is it then?

MME. LUNEAU [stammering with rage]: How do I know? How do—do I know? Everybody's, I suppose. Here are my witnesses, your honor. They're all here, the six of them. Now make them testify, make them testify. They'll tell——

THE JUSTICE: Collect yourself, Madame Luneau, collect yourself and reply calmly to my questions. What reason have you to doubt that this man is the father of the child you are carrying?

MME. LUNEAU: What reason? I have a hundred to one, a hundred? No, two hundred, five hundred, ten thousand, a million and more reasons to believe he isn't. After the proposal I made to him, with the promise of one hundred francs, didn't I learn he wasn't the father of his own children, your honor, not the father of one of 'em?

HIPPOLYTE [calmly]: That's a lie.

MME. LUNEAU [exasperated]: A lie! A lie, is it? I guess his wife has been seen by everybody around here. Call my witnesses, your honor, and make them testify.

HIPPOLYTE [calmly]: It's a lie.

MME. LUNEAU: It's a lie, is it? How about the red-haired ones then? I suppose they're yours too?

THE JUSTICE: Kindly refrain from personal attacks, or I shall be obliged to call you to order.

MME. LUNEAU: Well, your honor, I had my doubts about him, and said I to myself, two precautions are better than one, so I explained my position to Césaire Lepic, the witness who is present. Says he to me, "At your disposal, Madame Luneau," and he lent me his assistance in case Hippolyte should turn out to be unreliable. But as soon as the other witnesses heard that I wanted to make sure against any disappointment, I could have had more than a hundred, your honor, if I had wanted them. That tall one over there, Lucas Chandelier, swore at the time that I oughtn't to give Hippolyte Lacour a cent, for he hadn't more than the rest of them who had obliged me for nothing.

HIPPOLYTE: What did you promise for? I expected the money, your honor. No mistake with me—a promise given, a promise kept.

MME. LUNEAU [beside herself]: One hundred francs! One hundred francs! One hundred francs for that, you liar! The others there didn't ask a red cent! Look at 'em, all six of 'em! Make them testify, your honor; they'll tell, sure. [To Hippolyte.] Look at 'em, you liar! they're as good as you. They're only six, but I could have had one, two, three, five hundred of 'em for nothing, too, you robber!

HIPPOLYTE: Well, even if you'd had a hundred thousand——

MME. LUNEAU: I could, if I'd wanted 'em.

HIPPOLYTE: I did my duty, so it doesn't change matters.

MME. LUNEAU [slapping her protuberant form with both hands]: Then prove that it's you that did it; prove it, you robber! I defy you to prove it!

HIPPOLYTE [calmly]: Maybe I didn't do any more than anybody else. But you promised me a hundred francs for it. What did you ask the others for afterward? You had no right to. I guess I could have done it alone.

MME. LUNEAU: It is not true! Call my witnesses, your honor; they'll answer, sure.

The justice calls the witnesses in behalf of the defense. Six red, awkward individuals appear.

THE JUSTICE: Lucas Chandelier, have you any reason to suppose that you are the father of the child Madame Luneau is carrying?

LUCAS CHANDELIER: Yes sir.

THE JUSTICE: Célestin-Pierre Sidoine, have you any reason to suppose that you are the father of the child Madame Luneau is carrying?

CÉLESTIN-PIERRE SIDOINE: Yes sir.

The four other witnesses testify to the same effect.

The justice, after a pause, pronounces judgment: Whereas the plaintiff has reasons to believe himself the father of the child which Madame Luneau desired, Lucas Chandelier, Célestin-Pierre Sidoine and others have similar, if not conclusive, reasons to lay claim to the child.

But whereas Madame Luneau had previously asked the assistance of Hippolyte Lacour for a duly stated consideration:

And whereas one may not question the absolute good faith of Hippolyte Lacour, though it is questionable whether he had a perfect right to enter into such an agreement, seeing that the plaintiff is married and compelled by the law to remain faithful to his lawful spouse:

Therefore the court condemns Madame Luneau to pay an indemnity of twenty-five francs to Hippolyte Lacour for loss of time and unjustifiable abduction.

GUILLEMOT ROCK

This is the season for guillemots.

From April until the end of May, before the bathers arrive from Paris, one may observe, at the little watering place called Etretat, the sudden appearance of certain old gentlemen in top boots and tight shooting coats. They spend four or five days at the Hôtel Hauville, disappear, come again three weeks later; then, after a second stay, depart for good.

The following spring, they appear again.

They are the last hunters of the guillemot, the survivors of those of the old days; for thirty or forty years ago there were some twenty of these fanatics, but now they are but a few fanatical sportsmen.

The guillemot is a rare migrant whose habits are strange. For almost the whole of the year it lives in the neighborhood of Newfoundland and of the islands of Saint-Pierre and Miquelon; but at the nesting season a band of emigrants crosses the Atlantic and, every year, comes to lay its eggs and hatch them out on the same spot, the rock called Guillemot Rock, near Etretat. They are never to be found in any other spot than this. They have always come thither, they have always been shot, and they still keep coming back; they always will come back. As soon as the young birds have been raised, they go away again and disappear for a year.

Why do they never go elsewhere, choose some other point in the long white cliff, which runs unchanged from the Pas de Calais to Le Havre? What force, what unconquerable instinct, what age-long custom impels these birds to return to this spot? What was the manner of their first emigration, or the nature of the tempest which may long since have cast their sires upon this rock? And why have the children, the grandchildren, all the descendants of the first comers always returned thither?

They are not numerous; a hundred at the most, as though a solitary family possessed this tradition, performed this annual pilgrimage.

And every spring, as soon as the little wandering tribe is reinstalled upon its rock, the same hunters reappear in the village. Once, as young men, they were familiar to the inhabitants; today they are old, but still faithful to the regular meeting place that for the past thirty or forty years they have appointed for their gathering.

For nothing in the world would they fail to keep the appointment.

It was an April evening in one of the last years. Three of the old guillemot shooters had just arrived; one of them was missing, M. d'Arnelles.

He had written to no one, given no news! But he was not dead, like so many others; it would have been known. At last, weary of waiting, the firstcomers sat down to table; dinner was nearly over when a carriage rolled into the yard of the hostelry; and soon the late arrival entered.

He sat down, in excellent spirits, rubbing his hands, ate with a good appetite, and, as one of his companions expressed surprise at his wearing a frock coat, replied calmly:

"Yes, I had not time to change."

They went to bed as soon as they rose from the table, for, in order to surprise the birds, it is necessary to start well before daybreak.

Nothing is pleasanter than this sport, this early morning expedition.

At three in the morning the sailors wake the sportsmen by throwing gravel at their window panes. In a few minutes all are ready and down on the shingle beach. Although no twilight is yet visible, the stars have paled a little; the sea screams over the pebbles, the breeze is so cold that they shiver a little, despite their thick clothes.

Soon the two boats, pushed out by the men, rush down the slope of rounded pebbles, with a noise as of tearing canvas; then they are swaying upon the first waves. The brown sails are hoisted up the masts, swell slightly, tremble, hesitate, and, bulging once more, round-bellied, sweep the tarred hulls away towards the wide opening down the river, dimly visible in the gloom.

The sky grows clear; the darkness seems to melt away; the coast line appears, still veiled in mist, the long white coast line, straight as a wall. They pass the Manneporte, an enormous arch through which a ship could go, double the point of La Courtine, run past the vale of Antifer and the cape of the same name; and suddenly there rushes into sight a beach on which are hundreds of gulls. It is Guillemot Rock.

It is merely a small hump of cliff, and on the narrow ledges of rock the heads of birds are visible, watching the boats.

They are there, motionless, waiting, not daring as yet to fly away. Some, settled upon the extreme edges, look as though they are sitting on their hind parts, upright like bottles, for their legs are so short that, when they walk, they appear to be gliding on wheels, and, when they want to fly away, they are unable to start with a run and are obliged to let themselves fall like stones, almost on top of the men spying upon them.

They are aware of their weakness and the danger it entails and do not readily decide to fly.

But the sailors begin to shout and beat the gunwales with the wooden tholepins, and the birds, terrified, one by one launch out into the void and drop to the very level of the waves; then, their wings beating with swift strokes, they gather way, dart off, and reach the open spaces, unless a hail of shot casts them into the water.

For an hour they are slaughtered thus, one after another being forced to make off; and sometimes the females on their nests, utterly devoted to the business of hatching, refuse to leave, and ever and anon receive a volley which splashes their white plumage with spots of rosy blood, and the bird dies, still faithfully guarding her eggs.

On the first day, M. d'Arnelles shot with his customary enthusiasm; but, when they went off home at about ten o'clock, beneath the high and radiant sun which threw great triangles of light into the white clefts in the cliffs, he appeared somewhat distracted, and now and then he seemed lost in thought, unlike his usual self.

As soon as they were back on land, some sort of servant, clad in black, came and whispered with him. He appeared to reflect, to hesitate; then he replied:

"No, tomorrow."

And, next day, the shooting was resumed. This time M. d'Arnelles often missed his birds, though they let themselves fall almost on to the end of his gun barrel, and his friends, laughing, asked him if he was in love, if any secret trouble were tormenting his heart and brain. At last he admitted it.

"Yes, as a matter of fact I must be off directly, and I find it annoying."

"What, you're going away? Why?"

"Oh, urgent business. I can't stay any longer."

Then they began to talk of other things.

As soon as lunch was over, the servant in black reappeared. M. d'Arnelles ordered him to harness the horses, and the fellow was on the point of going out when the three other sportsmen intervened, insisting on an explanation, with many entreaties and demands that their friend should stay.

At last one of them said:

"But, look here, this business of yours can't be so very serious, if you've already waited two days."

The fourth, altogether perplexed, reflected, plainly a prey to conflicting ideas, torn between pleasure and duty, unhappy and ill at ease.

After a long period of meditation, he murmured with some hesitation:

"You see . . . you see, I am not alone here; I have my son-in-law with me."

There were cries and exclamations.

"Your son-in-law? . . . But where is he?"

At that he appeared suddenly confounded, and blushed.

"What? Didn't you know? Why . . . why . . . he is out in the barn. He's dead."

Stupefied silence reigned.

More and more distressed, M. d'Arnelles continued:

"I have had the misfortune to lose him; and, as I was taking the body to my home at Briseville, I made a slight detour just to keep our appointment here. But you will realize that I can delay no longer."

Then one of the sportsmen, bolder than the rest, suggested:

"But . . . since he is dead . . . it seems to me . . . that he might very well wait one more day."

The two others hesitated no longer.

"You can't deny that," they said.

M. d'Arnelles seemed relieved of a great weight, but, still somewhat uneasy, he inquired:

"You . . . you honestly think . . . ?"

As one man, the three others replied:

"Dash it all! dear boy, two days more or less won't make any difference to him in his condition."

Thereupon, perfectly at ease, the father-in-law turned round to the undertaker.

"Very well, my good man, let it be the day after tomorrow."

BENOIST

It all came over him one Sunday after Mass. He went out of church and followed the crossroad that led to his house, when he found himself behind the Martin girl who was also returning home.

BENOIST

The father walked beside his daughter with the important step of a rich farmer. Disdaining the blouse, he wore a kind of waistcoat of gray cloth and had on his head a melon-shaped hat with a wide brim. She, laced in a corset which she only wore once a week, walked very straight, her waist drawn in, her shoulders large, hips projecting, switching a little. Her hat was all flowers, the confection of an Yvetot milliner, and she showed her round, strong, supple neck, where little tendrils of hair were fluttering, moistened by the air and sun.

Benoist saw only her back, but he knew her face well, which was the reason he had noticed her still further. Suddenly he said to himself: "My, but she is pretty, just the same, that Martin girl!"

He looked at her as she walked along, admiring her crudely and feeling himself moved with desire. He had no need of seeing her face, none at all. He planted his eyes upon her figure, repeating to himself, as if he were speaking: "She is a pretty girl!"

The Martin girl turned to the right to enter Martinère, the farm of John Martin, her father. As she turned she looked back and saw Benoist, who looked queer to her. She cried out: "Good morning, Benoist." He answered: "Good morning, Mademoiselle Martin; good morning, Monsieur Martin," and passed on.

When he entered his house the soup was on the table. He seated himself opposite his mother, beside the hired man and boy, while the maidservant went to draw the cider. He ate a few spoonfuls then pushed his plate aside. His mother asked:

"What is the matter; don't you feel well?"

He answered: "No, I have something like a burning in my stomach and I have no appetite."

He watched the others eat, breaking off from time to time a mouthful of bread which he carried slowly to his lips and masticated a long time. He kept thinking of the Martin girl: "All the same, she is a pretty girl." And strange to say, he had never perceived it until this time, and now it had come to him so suddenly and so strongly that he was unable to eat any more. He scarcely touched the stew.

His mother said to him: "Come now, Benoist, do eat a little; it is a side of mutton and very good. When one has no appetite it is well to force oneself a little sometimes."

He swallowed a mouthful then pushed back his plate: "No, I cannot, decidedly."

Upon rising he made a tour of the farm and gave the boy a half holiday, promising to drive up the cattle in passing. The country was empty; it was a day of repose. From place to place in a field of clover the cows moved slowly, with bodies expanded, ruminating under the full sun. Some detached plows were standing in a corner of a plowed field, and the upturned earth, ready for the seed, displayed its large brown ridges in the midst of patches of yellow where bits of wheat and oat straw were left to decay after a late reaping.

An autumn wind, somewhat dry, was blowing over the plain, announcing a cool evening after sunset. Benoist sat down beside a ditch, put his hat on his knees as if he needed the air on his head and said aloud in the silence of the field: "When it comes to pretty girls, there is a pretty girl!"

He thought of her still in the evening in his bed and again on waking the next day. He was not sad; he was not discontented; he could not have told what was the trouble with him. But there was something which held him, something that fastened to his soul, an idea which would not leave him and which made a kind of tickling in his heart.

Sometimes we find a large fly shut up in a room. We hear it flying around and buzzing until the noise possesses us, irritates us. Suddenly it stops; we forget about it, but again it starts, forcing our attention. We can neither catch it nor kill it nor make it stay in place. Finally we resign ourselves to its humming. So the remembrance of the Martin girl agitated Benoist's mind; it was like an imprisoned fly.

Then a desire to see her again took possession of him, and he passed and repassed before the Martin farm. He saw her at last, hanging some linen upon a line between two apple trees.

It was warm, and she was protected only by a short skirt and a chemise, which showed to advantage the white arch made by her arms as she pinned up the napkins. He lay flat beside the ditch for more than an hour after she had gone. He returned to find himself more haunted than before.

For a month his mind was full of her, so that he trembled when her name was mentioned before him. He could not eat and had night sweats which hindered his sleeping. On Sunday at Mass he could not keep his eyes away from her. She perceived it and smiled at him, flattered at being appreciated.

Then one evening he suddenly met her in the road. She stopped on seeing him approach. He walked straight to her, suffocated by a fear that seized him, but resolved to speak to her. He commenced stammering:

"See here, Mademoiselle Martin, I can't endure this any longer."

And she answered him mockingly: "What is it that you cannot endure, Benoist?"

He replied: "That I think about you as long as there are hours in the day."

Placing her hands on her hips, she answered: "It is not I who force you to."

He murmured: "Yes, it is you, and I can neither sleep nor eat nor rest nor nothing."

Very low she said: "What do you think is necessary to cure you of it?"

He was struck dumb, his arms twitching, his eyes round, his mouth open. She struck him a sharp blow in the chest and ran away as fast as she could.

From this day they often met by the ditches or in the crossroad, generally at the close of day, when he was returning with his horses and she was driving the cows to the stable. He felt himself drawn, thrown toward her, by some great impulse of heart and body. He felt a desire to press her close, to strangle her, to eat her and make her a part of himself. And he had tremblings from powerlessness, from impatience and rage, from the fact that she was his complement, making together but one being.

There began to be gossip in the country. It was said they were promised to one another. Indeed, he had asked her if she would be his wife, and she had answered: "Yes." They were only waiting for an opportunity to speak of it to their parents.

Then suddenly she no longer came at certain hours to meet him. He could only get a glimpse of her at Mass on Sunday. And then one Sunday, after the sermon, the curate announced from the high pulpit that there was a promise of marriage between Victoire Adelaide Martin and Joseph Isidore Vallin.

Benoist felt as if he had raised blood. His ears buzzed; he could no longer hear anything, and he perceived after some time that he was weeping into his prayer book.

For a month he kept to his room. Then he began to work again. But he was not cured and still thought of her always. He shunned passing along the roads that surrounded her dwelling, not wishing to see even the trees of her yard, and this forced him to make a large circuit morning and evening.

She was now married to Vallin, the richest farmer in the district. Benoist no longer spoke to him, although they had been comrades since infancy.

Then one evening, as Benoist was passing across the common, he learned that she was enceinte. Instead of resenting this or its affecting him with a great grief, he found in it a kind of solace. It was finished now, well finished. They were more separated by this than by marriage. Truly, it was best so.

Some months passed, and still some months. He saw her sometimes, walking to the village with slow step. She blushed on seeing him, lowered her head and hastened her steps. And he turned out of his way in order not to cross her and look into his eyes.

But he thought, with the same terror as on that first morning, of finding himself face to face with her and obliged to speak to her. What could he say after all he had said to her in former times, holding her hands and kissing the locks about her cheeks? He still often thought of their meeting place by the side of the ditch. It was villainous to do as she did after so many promises.

However, little by little, anger left his heart; there was no longer anything but sadness. And one day he took his old way by the farm where she lived. He saw the roof of the house from afar. She was in there! Living there with another! The apple trees were in blossom; the fowls were singing about the barnyard. The whole place seemed empty, the folk having gone to the fields for the spring work. He stopped near the fence and looked into the yard. The dog lay sleeping before his kennel. Three calves were walking slowly, one behind the other, toward the pool. A large turkey cock was wheeling about before the door, parading before the poultry after the manner of a stage singer.

Benoist leaned against a post and suddenly felt himself seized with a desire to weep. But just then he heard a cry, a great, appealing cry, coming from the house. He stood lost in amazement, his hands clinched upon the bars, ever listening. Another cry, prolonged, piercing, came to his ears and entered his soul and his flesh. It was she who was in trouble! She!

Finally he started hurriedly across the inclosure, pushed open the door and saw her stretched out upon the floor in agony, her face livid, her eyes haggard, seized with the pains of childbirth.

He stood there, paler and trembling more than she, murmuring:
"I am here, my friend; here I am."

And she replied in gasps: "Oh, do not leave me, Benoist; do not leave me!"

He looked at her, not knowing what to say or what to do. She began to cry out again: "Oh! Oh! This tears me in two! Oh! Benoist!"

And she seemed frightfully tortured. Suddenly a furious desire to help her came over Benoist; he must appease her suffering, free her from this agony. He bent over and took her up and carried her to her bed. And although she groaned continually, he then undressed her, taking off her kerchief, her frock and her skirt. She began to bite her hands in order not to cry out. Then he did for he as he was accustomed to do for beasts, cows, sheep and mares: he aided her and received into his hands a large infant, which began to squall.

He wiped it and wrapped it in a cloth which was drying before the fire, then placed it on a pile of linen that lay on the table and returned to the mother. He put her on the floor again, changed the bed and put her in it. She whispered: "Thanks, Benoist, you have a brave heart." And she wept a little, as if some regret had seized her.

As for him, he loved her no longer, not at all. It was finished. Why? How? He could not have told. What had come to pass had cured him better than ten years of absence.

She asked, weak and trembling: "What is it?"

He answered in a calm voice: "It is a girl, and a handsome one."

They were again silent. At the end of a few seconds the mother, in a feeble voice, said: "Show her to me, Benoist."

He went and got the little one and was presenting it to her, as if it were bread that had been blessed, when the door opened and Isidore Vallin appeared. He could not understand at first, then suddenly he guessed it all.

Benoist, somewhat disconcerted, murmured: "I was passing; I was just passing when I heard a cry—and I came. Here is your child, Vallin!"

Then the husband, with tears in his eyes, took the frail little monkey that was held out to him, embraced it and stood for some seconds overcome; then he placed the child on the bed and extended both hands to Benoist, saying: "Done now, Benoist; you see, between us all is said. If you wish we shall from this time be friends; just that, a pair of friends."

And Benoist replied: "I am willing; certainly—I am willing."

A TRUE STORY

A gale was blowing out of doors; the autumn wind moaned and careered round the house, one of those winds which kill the last leaves and carry them off into the clouds.

The shooting party were finishing their dinner, still in their boots, flushed, animated, and inflamed. They were Normans, of a class between the nobles and the yeomen, half country squires, half peasants, rich and strong, capable of breaking the horns of the bulls when they catch hold of them at fairs.

All day long they had been shooting over the land of Maître Blondel, the mayor of Eparville, and were now at their meal round the large table, in the sort of half farmhouse, half countryseat owned by their host.

They spoke as ordinary men shout, laughed like wild beasts roaring, and drank like cisterns, their legs outstretched, their elbows on the tablecloth, their eyes shining beneath the flame of the lamps, warmed by a huge fire which cast blood-colored gleams over the ceiling; they were talking of shooting and of dogs. But they had reached the period when other ideas come into the heads of half-drunk men, and all eyes were turned on a sturdy, plump-cheeked girl who was carrying the great dishes of food in her red hands.

Suddenly a hefty fellow, named Séjour, who, after studying for the Church, had become a veterinary surgeon and looked after all the animals in the locality, exclaimed:

"By Gad, Blondel, there's no flies on that filly you've got there!"

There was a resounding laugh. Then an old nobleman, Monsieur de Varnetot, who had lost caste through taking to drink, lifted up his voice:

"Once upon a time I had a funny affair with a girl like that. I really must tell you the tale. Whenever I think of it, it reminds me of Mirza, the bitch I sold to the Comte d'Haussonnel: she returned every day as soon as she was unchained, she found it so hard to leave me. In the end I grew angry, and asked the comte to keep her chained up. Well, do you know what the poor beast did? She died of grief.

"But, to return to my maid, here's the story.

"I was twenty-five at the time, and was living a bachelor life on my Villebon estate. When a man's young, you know, and has money, and bores himself to tears every evening after dinner, he keeps his eyes open on every side.

"I soon discovered a young thing in service with Déboultot of Canville. You knew Déboultot, Blondel, didn't you? In short, the hussy took my fancy to such an extent that one day I went off to see her master, and suggested a bit of business to him. He was to let me have his servant, and I was to sell him my black mare, Cocote, which he'd been wanting for close on two years. He gave me his hand, with a 'Put it there, Monsieur de Varnetot.' The bargain was struck, the little girl came to my house, and I myself took my mare to Canville and let her go for three hundred crowns.

"At first everything went swimmingly. No one suspected anything; the only thing was that Tose loved me a little too much for my liking. She wasn't of the common stock, I tell you. There was no ordinary blood in her veins; it must have come from some other girl who went wrong with her master.

"In short, she adored me. It was all coaxing and billing and cooing, and calling me pet names as if I were her little dog; so many pretty loving ways that I began to think rather seriously.

"I said to myself: 'This mustn't go on, or I'll let myself be caught.' But I'm not easily caught, I'm not. I'm not the sort of fellow to be wheedled with a couple of kisses. In fact, my eyes were very much open, when she told me that she was in the family way.

"Crash! Bang! It was as though someone had fired a couple of shots into my chest. And she kissed me, kissed me and laughed and danced, fairly off her head with delight! I said nothing the first day, but I reasoned it out at night. 'Well, that's that,' I thought, 'but I must avoid the worst and cut her adrift; it's high time.' You see, my father and mother were at Barneville, and my sister, who was the wife of the Marquis d'Yspare, at Rollebec, two leagues from Villebon. I couldn't take any chances.

"But how was I to extricate myself? If she left the house, suspicions would be aroused, and people would talk. If I kept her, the cat would soon be out of the bag; and besides, I could not let her go like that.

"I spoke about it to my uncle, the Baron de Créteuil, an old buck who had had more than one such experience, and asked him for a word of advice. He replied calmly:

" 'You must get her married, my boy.'

"I jumped.

" 'Get her married, Uncle! But to whom?'

"He quietly shrugged his shoulders:

"'Anyone you like; that's your business, and not mine. If you're not a fool, you can always find someone.'

"I thought over this advice for a good week, and ended by saying to myself: 'My uncle's quite right.'

"So I began to rack my brains and search for a man; when one evening the justice of the peace, with whom I had been dining, told me:

"'Old Mother Paumelle's son has just been up to his larks again; he'll come to a bad end, will that boy. It's true enough that like father like son.'

"This Mother Paumelle was a sly old thing whose own youth had left something to be desired. For a crown she would assuredly have sold her soul, and her lout of a son into the bargain.

"I went to find her, and, very carefully, I made her understand the situation.

"As I was becoming embarrassed in my explanations, she suddenly asked me:

"'And what are you going to give the girl?'

"She was a cunning old thing, but I was no fool, and had made all my preparations.

"I had just three little bits of land away out near Sasseville, which were let out from my three Villebon farms. The farmers were always complaining that they were a long way off; to make a long story short, I had taken back these three fields, six acres in all, and, as my peasants were making an outcry about it, I let them all off their dues in poultry until the end of each lease. By this means I put the business through all right. Then I bought a strip of land from my neighbour, Monsieur d'Aumonté, and had a cottage built on it, all for fifteen hundred francs. In this way I made a little bit of property which did not cost me much, and I gave it to the girl as a dowry.

"The old woman protested: this was not enough; but I held to it, and we parted without settling anything.

"Early next morning the lad came to see me. I had almost forgotten what he looked like. When I saw him, I was reassured; he wasn't so bad for a peasant; but he looked a pretty dirty scoundrel.

"He took a detached view of the affair, as though he had come to buy a cow. When we had come to terms, he wanted to see the property, and off we went across the fields. The rascal kept me out there a good three hours; he surveyed the land, measured it, and took up sods and crushed them in his hands, as though he were afraid of being cheated over the goods. The cottage was not yet roofed, and he insisted on slate instead of thatch, because it required less upkeep!

"Then he said to me:

"'But what about the furniture? You're giving that!'

"'Certainly not,' I protested; 'it's very good of me to give you the farm.'

"'Not half,' he sniggered; 'a farm and a baby.'

"I blushed in spite of myself.

"'Come,' he continued, 'you'll give the bed, a table, the dresser, three chairs, and the crockery, or there's nothing doing.'

"I consented.

"And back we went. He had not yet said a word about the girl. But suddenly he asked, with a cunning, worried air:

"'But if she died, who would the stuff go to?'

"'Why, to you, of course,' I replied.

"That was all he had wanted to find out that morning. He promptly offered me his hand with a gesture of satisfaction. We were agreed.

"But, oh! I had some trouble to convince Rose, I can tell you. She grovelled at my feet, sobbed and repeated: 'It's you who suggest this, you! you!' She held out for more than a week, in spite of my reasoning and my entreaties. Women are silly things; once love gets into their heads, they can't understand anything. Common sense means nothing to them: love before all, all for love!

"At last I grew angry and threatened to turn her out. At that she gradually yielded, on condition that I allowed her to come and see me from time to time.

"I myself led her to the altar, paid for the ceremony, and gave the wedding breakfast. I did the thing in style. Then it was: 'Good-night, children!' I went and spent six months with my brother in Touraine.

"When I returned, I learnt that she had come to the house every week and asked for me. I hadn't been back an hour when I saw her coming with a brat in her arms. Believe me or not, as you like, but it meant something to me to see that little mite. I believe I even kissed it.

"As for the mother, she was a ruin, a skeleton, a shadow. Thin, and grown old. By God, marriage didn't suit her!

" 'Are you happy?' I inquired mechanically.

"At that she began to cry like a fountain, hiccuping and sobbing, and exclaimed:

" 'I can't, I can't do without you, now! I'd rather die! I can't!'

"She made the devil of a noise. I consoled her as best I could, and led her back to the gate.

"I found out that her husband beat her, and that the old harpy of a mother-in-law made life hard for her.

"Two days later she came back again; she took me in her arms and grovelled on the ground.

" 'Kill me, but I won't go back there any more,' she implored. Exactly what Mirza would have said if she had spoken!

"All this fuss was beginning to get on my nerves, and I cleared out for another six months. When I returned . . . when I returned, I learnt that she had died three weeks before, after having come back to the house every Sunday . . . still just like Mirza. The child too had died eight days later.

"As for the husband, the cunning rascal, he came into the inheritance. He's done well for himself since, so it seems; he's a town councillor now."

Then Monsieur de Varnetot added with a laugh:

"Anyhow, I made his fortune for him."

And Monsieur Séjour, the veterinary surgeon, raising a glass of brandy to his lips, gravely concluded the story with:

"Say what you like, but there's no place in this world for that sort of woman!"

FECUNDITY

They were walking, these two old friends, in the garden all in blossom, where the gay springtime stirred with life.

One was a senator and the other a member of the French Academy, grave, both of them, full of reason and logic, but solemn—people of mark and reputation.

They were speaking at first of politics, exchanging thoughts, not upon ideas but men, personalities, which in these matters always precede reason. Then they rose to reminiscences; then they were silent, continuing to walk side by side, both softened by the sweetness of the air.

A great basket of radishes sent forth their odor, fresh and delicate. A heap of flowers of every kind and color threw their sweetness to the breeze, while a radiant ebony tree full of yellow berries scattered to the wind its fine powder, a golden smoke which reminded one of honey and which carried, like the caressing powder of the perfumer, its embalmed seed across space.

The senator stopped, breathed in the fertile sweetness that was floating by him, looked at the blossoming tree, resplendent as a sun, from which the pollen was now escaping. And he said:

"When one thinks that these imperceptible atoms, which smell good, can bring into existence in a hundred places, miles from here, plants of their own kind, can start the sap and fiber of the female trees, creating from a germ, as we mortals do, they seem mortal and they will be replaced by other beings of the same essence forever, like us!"

Then, planted before the radiant ebony tree whose vivifying perfume permeated every breath of air, the senator added, as if addressing it:

"Ah! My jolly fellow, if you were to count your children you would be woefully embarrassed. And behold! Here is one that accomplishes them easily, who lets himself go without remorse and disturbs himself little about it afterward."

The academician replied: "We do as much, my friend."

The senator answered: "Yes, I do not deny that; we do forget ourselves sometimes, but we know it, at least, and that constitutes our superiority."

The other man shook his head: "No, that is not what I mean; you see, my dear, there is scarcely a man who does not possess some unknown children, those children labeled of unknown father, whom he has created, as this tree reproduces itself, almost unconsciously.

"If it became necessary to establish the count of the women we have had, we should be, should we not? as embarrassed as this ebony tree, which you call upon to enumerate his descendants.

"From eighteen to forty, perhaps, bringing into line all our passing encounters and contacts of an hour, it can easily be admitted that we have had intimate relations with two or three hundred women. Ah well, my friend, among this number are you sure that you have not made fruitful at least one and that you have not, upon the streets or in prison, some blackguard son who robs and assassinates honest people, that is to say, people like us? Or perhaps a daughter in some bad place? Or perhaps, if she chanced to be abandoned by her mother, a cook in somebody's kitchen?

"Think further that nearly all women that we call 'public' possess one or two children whose father they do not know, children caught in the hazard of their embraces at ten or twenty francs. In every trade there is profit and loss. These castaways constitute the 'loss' of their profession. Who were their generators? You—I—all of us, the men who are 'all right!' These are the results of our joyous dinners to friends, of our evenings of gaiety, of the hours when our flesh contents us and pushes us on to the completion of adventure.

"Robbers, rovers, all these miserable creatures, in short, are our children. And how much better that is for us than if we were theirs, for they reproduce also, these beggars!

"For my part I have a villainous story upon my conscience which I would like to tell you. It brings me incessant remorse, and more than that, continual doubt and an unappeasable uncertainty which at times tortures me horribly.

"At the age of twenty-five I had undertaken, with one of my friends, now counselor of state, a journey through Brittany on foot.

"After fifteen or twenty days of forced march, after having visited the coasts of the north and a part of Finistère, we arrived at Douarnenez; from there, in a day's march, we reached the wildest point of the Raz by the bay of Trepasses, where we slept in some village whose name ends in of. When the morning came a strange fatigue held my comrade in bed. I say bed from habit, since our bed was composed simply of two boxes of straw.

"It was impossible to remain in such a place. I forced him to get up, and we came into Audierne toward four or five o'clock in the evening. The next day he was a little better. We set out again, but on the way he was taken with intolerable weariness, and it was with great difficulty that we were able to reach Pont l'Abbé.

"There at least there was an inn. My friend went to bed, and the doctor, whom we called from Quimper, found a high fever without quite determining the nature of it.

"Do you know Pont l'Abbé? No? Well, it is the most characteristic Breton town from Point Raz to Morbihan—a region which contains the essence of Breton morals and legends and customs. Today, even, this corner of the country has scarcely changed at all. I say 'today, even,' because I return there now every year, alas!

"An old castle bathes the foot of its towers in a dismal pond, sad with the call of wild birds. A river, deep enough for coasters, comes up to the town. In the streets, narrowed by the old houses, the men wear great hats and embroidered waistcoats and the four coats, one above the other; the first, about the size of the hand, covers at least the shoulder blades, while the last stops just below the breeches.

"The girls, who are large, pretty and fresh-looking, wear a bodice of thick cloth which forms a breastplate and corset, constraining and leaving scarcely a suspicion of their swelling, martyrized busts. Their headdresses are also of strange fashion: over the temples two embroidered bands in color frame the face, binding the hair which falls in a sheet behind the head, and is mounted by a singular bonnet on the very summit, often of tissue of gold or silver.

"The servant at our inn was eighteen years old or more, with blue eyes, a pale blue, which were pierced with the two little black dots of the pupils, and with teeth short and white, which she showed always in laughing and which seemed made for biting granite.

"She did not know a word of French, speaking only the Breton patois, as do most of her compatriots.

"Well, my friend was no better, and although no malady declared itself, the doctor forbade his setting out, ordering complete rest. I spent the days near him, the little maid coming in frequently, bringing perhaps my dinner or some drink for him.

"I teased her a little, which seemed to amuse her, but we did not talk, naturally, since we could not understand each other.

"But one night, when I had remained near the sick man very late, I met, in going to my chamber, the girl entering hers. It was just opposite my open door. Then brusquely, without reflecting upon what I was doing and more in the way of a joke than anything, I seized her around the waist, and before she was over her astonishment I had taken her and shut her in my room. She looked at me, startled, excited, terrified, not daring to cry out for fear of scandal and of being driven out by her master at first and her father afterward.

"I had done this in laughter, but when I saw her there, the desire to possess her carried me away. There was a long and silent struggle, a struggle of body against body after the fashion of athletes, with arms drawn, contracted, twisted, respiration short, skin moist with perspiration. Oh! she fought valiantly, and sometimes we would hit a piece of furniture, a partition or a chair; then, always clutching each other, we would remain immovable for some seconds in the fear of some noise that would awaken someone; then we would commence again our exciting battle, I attacking, she resisting. Exhausted, finally, she fell, and I took her brutally upon the ground, upon the floor.

"As soon as she was released she ran to the door, drew the bolts and fled. I scarcely met her for some days following. She would not allow me to approach her. Then when my comrade was strong and we were to continue our journey, on the eve of our departure, she entered my apartment at midnight, barefooted, in her chemise, just as I was about to retire.

"She threw herself in my arms, drew me to her passionately and, until daylight, embraced me, caressed me, weeping and sobbing, giving me all the assurances of tenderness and despair that a woman can give when she does not know a word of our language.

"A week after this I had forgotten this adventure, so common and frequent when on a journey, the servants of the inns being generally destined to divert travelers thus.

"Thirty years passed without my thinking of, or returning to, Pont l'Abbé. Then in 1876, in the course of an excursion through Brittany, I happened to go there, as I was compiling a document which required statistics from the various parts of the country.

"Nothing seemed to have changed. The castle still soaked its gray walls in the pond at the entrance of the little town; the inn was there, too, although repaired, remodeled, with a modern air. On entering I was received by two young Bretons, of about eighteen, fresh and genteel, enlaced in their straight girdles of cloth and encapped with silver embroidery over their ears.

"It was about six o'clock in the evening. I had sat down to dine with the host, coming to serve me himself—fatality, without doubt—led me to ask him: 'Did you know the former master of this house? I passed a fortnight here once thirty years ago. I seem to be speaking to you from afar.'

"He answered: 'Those were my parents, sir.'

"Then I recounted the occasion of my stopping there, recalling my being detained by the illness of my comrade. He did not allow me to finish.

"'Oh! I remember that perfectly,' he said; 'I was fifteen or sixteen then. You slept in the room at the end of the hall and your friend in the one that is now mine, upon the street.'

"Then for the first time a lively remembrance of the pretty maid came back to me. I asked: 'You recall a genteel, pretty servant that your father had, who had, if I remember, sparkling eyes and fine teeth?'

"He replied: 'Yes sir; she died in childbed some time after.'

"And, pointing toward the courtyard where a thin, lame man was taking out some manure, he added: 'That is her son.'

"I began to laugh. 'He is not beautiful and does not resemble his mother at all. Takes after his father, no doubt.'

"The innkeeper replied: 'It may be, but they never knew who his father was. She died without telling, and no one here knew she had a lover. It was a famous surprise when we found it out. No one was willing to believe it.'

"A kind of disagreeable shiver went over me, one of those painful suggestions that touch the heart, like the approach of a heavy vexation. I looked at the man in the yard. He came now to draw some water for the horses and carried two pails, limping, making grievous effort with the limb that was shorter. He was ragged and hideously dirty, with long yellow hair, so matted that it hung in strings on his cheeks.

"The innkeeper added: 'He doesn't amount to anything but is taken care of by charity in the house. Perhaps he would have turned out better if he had been brought up like anybody. But you see how it is, sir? No father, no mother, no money! My parents took pity on him as a child, but after all—he was not theirs, you see.'

"I said nothing.

"I went to bed in my old room, and all night I could think of nothing but that frightful hostler, repeating to myself: 'What if that were my son? Could I have killed that girl and brought that creature into existence?'

"It was possible, surely. I resolved to speak to this man and to find out exactly the date of his birth. A difference of two months would arrest my doubts.

"I had him come to me the next day. But he could not speak French at all. He had the appearance of understanding nothing. Besides, he was absolutely ignorant of his age, which one of the maids asked him for me. And he held himself with the air of an idiot before me, rolling his cap in his knotty paws, laughing stupidly, with something of the old laugh of the mother in the corners of his mouth and eyes.

"But the host, becoming interested, went to look up his birth on the records. He entered into life eight months and twenty-six days after my departure from Pont l'Abbé, because I recalled perfectly arriving at Lorient on the fifteenth of August. The record said: 'Father unknown.' The mother was called Jeanne Karradec.

"Then my heart began to beat with pressing blows. I could not speak, so suffocated did I feel. And I looked at that brute, whose long yellow hair seemed dirty and more tangled than that of beasts. And the beggar, constrained by my look, ceased to laugh, turned his head and took himself off.

"Every day I would wander along the little river, sadly reflecting. But to what good? Nothing could help me. For hours and hours I would weigh all the reasons, good and bad, for and against the chances of my paternity, placing myself in inextricable positions, only to return again to the horrible suspicion, then to the conviction, more atrocious still, that this man was my son.

"I could not dine and I retired to my room. It was a long time before I could sleep. Then sleep came, a sleep haunted with insupportable visions. I could see this ninny laughing in my face and calling me 'Papa.' Then he would change into a dog and bite me in the calf of my leg; in vain I tried to free myself; he would follow me always and, in place of barking, he would speak, abusing me. Then he would go before my colleagues at the Academy called together for the purpose of deciding whether I was his father. And one of them cried: 'It is indubitable! See how he resembles him!'

"And in fact, I perceived that the monster did resemble me. And I awoke with this idea planted in my brain and with the foolish desire to see the man again and decide whether he did or did not have features in common with my own.

"I joined him as he was going to Mass (it was on Sunday) and gave him a hundred sous, scanning his face anxiously. He began to laugh in ignoble fashion, took the money; then, again constrained by my eye, he fled after having blurted out a word, almost inarticulate, which meant to say 'Thank you,' without doubt.

"That day passed for me in the same agony as the preceding. Toward evening I went to the proprietor and, with much caution, clothing of words, finesse and roundabout conversation, I told him that I had become interested in this poor being so abandoned by everybody and so deprived of everything and that I wished to do something for him.

"The man replied: 'Oh, don't worry about him, sir. He wants nothing; you will only make trouble for yourself. I employ him to clean the stable, and it is all that he can do. For that, I feed him, and he sleeps with the horses. He needs nothing more. If you have some old clothes give them to him, but they will be in pieces in a week.'

"I did not insist, reserving my opinion.

"The beggar returned that evening, horribly drunk, almost setting fire to the house, striking one of the horses a blow with a pickax and finally ended the score by going to sleep in the mud out in the rain, thanks to my generosity. They begged me the next day not to give him any more money. Liquor made him furious, and when he had two sous in his pocket he drank it. The innkeeper added: 'To give him money is the same as wishing to kill him.' This man had absolutely never had any money, save a few centimes thrown to him by travelers, and he knew no other destination for it but the alehouse.

"Then I passed some hours in my room with an open book which I made a semblance of reading, but without accomplishing anything except to look at this brute. My son! My son! I was trying to discover if he was anything like me. By force of searching I believed I recognized some similar lines in the brow and about the nose. And I was immediately convinced of a resemblance which only different clothing and the hideous mane of the man disguised.

"I could not stay there very long without becoming suspected, and I set out with breaking heart after having left with the innkeeper some money to sweeten the existence of his valet.

"For six years I lived with this thought, this horrible uncertainty, this abominable doubt. And each year I condemned myself to the punishment of seeing this brute wallow in his filth, imagining that he resembles me and of seeking, always in vain, to be helpful to him.

"And each year I come back more undecided, more tortured, more anxious. I have tried to have him instructed, but he is an idiot without resource. I have tried to render life less painful to him, but he is an irremediable drunkard and uses all the money that is given him for drink. And he knows very well how to sell his clothes and procure liquor.

"I have tried to arouse pity in his employer for him, that he might treat him more gently, offering him money always. The innkeeper, astonished, finally re- marked very sagely: 'All this that you would like to do for him only ruins him. He must be kept like a prisoner. As soon as he has time given him or favors shown, he becomes unmanageable. If you wish to do good to abandoned children, choose one that will respond to your trouble.'

"What could I say to that?

"And if I should disclose a suspicion of the doubts which torture me, this creature would certainly turn rogue and exploit me, compromise me, ruin me. He would cry out to me, 'Papa,' as in my dream.

"And I tell myself that I have killed the mother and ruined this atrophied being, larva of the stable, hatched and bred of vileness, this man who, treated as others are, might have been like others.

"And you will not understand the sensation, strange, confused and intolerable, the fear I have in his presence, from thinking that this has come from me, that he belongs to me by that intimate bond which binds father to son, that, thanks to the terrible laws of heredity, he is a part of me in a thousand things, by his blood and his hair and his flesh, and that he has the same germs of sickness and the same ferments of passion.

"And I have ever an unappeasable need of seeing him, and the sight of him makes me suffer horribly, and from my window down there I look at him as he works in the dunghill of the beasts, repeating to myself: 'That is my son!'

"And I feel, sometimes, an intolerable desire to embrace him. But I have never even touched his sordid hand."

The academician was silent. And his companion, the political man, murmured: "Yes indeed; we ought to occupy ourselves a little more with the children who have no fathers."

Then a breath of wind traversing the great tree shook its berries and enveloped with a fine, odorous cloud the two old men, who took long draughts of the sweet perfume.

And the senator added: "It is good to be twenty-five years old, and it is even good to have children like that."

ALEXANDER

As usual that day at four o'clock Alexander brought the three-wheeled invalid carriage in which by the doctor's orders he took his old, helpless mistress out until six o'clock every day, round to the front of Maramballe's little house.

When he had propped the light carriage against the step at the exact spot from which he could easily help the stout old lady he returned to the house and an angry voice was heard—the hoarse voice of a former soldier—using bad language: it was the voice of the master of the house, a retired infantry captain, Joseph Maramballe.

Then followed a noise of slammed doors, upset chairs and hasty footsteps, then nothing more; shortly after Alexander appeared in the doorway holding up Mme. Maramballe with all his strength, for the walk downstairs had quite exhausted the old lady. When, after a certain amount of trouble, she had been settled in a wheeled chair, Alexander took hold of the handle at the back and started off in the direction of the riverbank.

This was their usual way of crossing the small town, through which they passed amid respectful greetings that were certainly meant for the servant as well as for the old lady, for if she was loved and looked up to by everyone, he, the old trooper with his white, patriarchal beard, was considered the model servant.

The July sun shone down into the streets with cruel violence, bathing the low houses in a light made sad by its power and crudity. Dogs were asleep on the pavement in the line of shadow thrown by the walls, and Alexander, rather out of breath, hurried to reach the avenue that led to the bank of the river, as quickly as possible.

Mme. Maramballe dozed under her white parasol, the point of which swayed to and fro against the man's impassive face.

As they reached the avenue of limes, whose shade thoroughly woke her up, she said good-naturedly:

"Not so fast, my good fellow, you will kill yourself in this heat."

It never occurred to the kind-hearted woman, in her candid selfishness, that she now wanted to go slower because she had reached the shelter of the leaves.

Near the road over which the old limes formed an arch, the winding Navette flowed between two willow hedges. The wish-wash of the eddies, of water splashing over the rocks and of the sudden twists of the current, cast over the promenade a low song of moving water mingling with the freshness of the moisture-laden air.

After a rest, enjoying the green, cool charm of the place for some time, Mme. Maramballe said:

"Now I feel better. He certainly did not get out of the right side of the bed this morning."

Alexander replied:

"Oh, no, madame."

He had been in their service for thirty-five years, first as officer's orderly, then as an ordinary valet unwilling to leave his master; now for six years he had been wheeling his mistress through the narrow roads round the town.

This long, devoted service followed by daily companionship had established a certain familiarity between the old lady and the old servant, affectionate on her part and deferential on his.

They discussed household affairs as between equals. Their chief subject of conversation and of anxiety was the captain's bad temper, embittered by a long career that had opened brilliantly, run its course without promotion, and ended without glory.

Mme. Maramballe resumed the conversation:

"As for having bad manners, he certainly has. He forgets himself much too often since he left the army."

With a sigh Alexander completed his mistress's thought:

"Oh! Madame may say that he forgets himself every day and that he did even before he left the army."

"That is true. But he has had no luck, the poor man. He started by an act of bravery for which he was decorated when only twenty, then from the age of twenty to that of fifty he never rose higher than the rank of captain, although at the start he had counted on being at least a colonel when he retired."

"After all, Madame may say it is his own fault. Had he not always been about as gentle as a riding whip, his superiors would have liked him better and used their influence in his favor. It's no good being hard on others, you must please people if you want to get on."

"That he should treat us like that, well, that is our own fault because it suits us to stay with him, but it is a different matter for others."

Mme. Maramballe was thinking things over. Every day for years and years she had thought about the brutality of the man she married long ago because he was a fine-looking officer who had been decorated in his youth, and had a brilliant future, so everyone said. What mistakes one can make in life!

She said gently:

"Let us stop awhile, my poor Alexander, you must have a rest on your seat."

The seat was a small one, partly rotted away, placed at the turning of the avenue for the use of Sunday visitors. When they came this way Alexander always had a short rest on the seat.

He sat down, holding his fine, white, fan-shaped beard in his hands with a simple gesture full of pride; he grasped it tightly, then slid his closed fingers down to the bottom, which he held over the pit of his stomach for a few minutes, as if he wanted to fasten it there, and show off the great length of his growth.

Mme. Maramballe resumed:

"As for me, I married him: it is only just and natural that I should bear with his unkindness, but what I cannot understand is that you put up with it too, my good Alexander!"

He gave a slight shrug of his shoulders, saying:

"Oh, me . . . madame."

She added:

"It is a fact. I have often thought about it. You were his orderly when I married and could hardly do otherwise than put up with him. But since then, why have you stayed with us who pay so little and treat you so badly, when you might have done like others, settled down, married, had children, founded a family?"

He repeated:

"Oh, me, madame, that's another question." He stopped and began to pull his beard as if it were a bell ringing inside him, as if he wanted to pull it off; the scared look in his eyes showed his embarrassment.

Mme. Maramballe followed her own line of thought:

"You are not a peasant. You have been educated . . ."

He interrupted her with pride:

"I studied to be a land surveyor."

"Then why did you stay on with us, spoiling your life?"

He stammered:

"Why! Why! It is a natural weakness of mine."

"What do you mean, a natural weakness?"

"Yes, when I attach myself to anyone, I attach myself, that's the end of it."

She laughed.

"Come, you are not going to make me believe that Maramballe's kindness and gentleness have attached you to him for life."

Alexander moved restlessly about on the seat, visibly at a loss, and mumbled into his long mustache:

"It is not he, it is you!"

The old lady, whose sweet face was crowned by a snow-white ridge of curly hair that shone like swan's feathers, carefully put into curlpapers every day, gave a start and looked at her servant with surprise in her eyes.

"Me, my poor Alexander. But how?"

He looked up into the air first, then to one side, then into the distance, turning his head about as shy men do when forced to admit some shameful secret. Then with the courage of a soldier ordered into the firing line, he said:

"It's quite simple. The first time I took a letter from the lieutenant to Mademoiselle, and Mademoiselle with a smile gave me a franc, that settled the matter."

Not understanding, she insisted:

"Come, come, explain yourself."

Overcome by the terror of the criminal who knows that all is over when he confesses a crime, Alexander blurted out:

"I felt drawn towards Madame. There!"

She made no reply and did not look at him, while she turned this over in her mind. She was kind, straightforward, gentle, reasonable, and full of good feeling.

In a second she realized the great devotion of the unfortunate man who had given up everything to live near her, without saying a word. She wanted to cry.

"Let us go back," she said, looking serious, but with no feeling of anger.

He got up, walked round to the back of the wheeled chair and began to push it. As they approached the village they saw Captain Maramballe in the middle of the road, coming towards them.

As soon as he had joined them he said to his wife, obviously anxious to pick a quarrel:

"What is there for dinner?"

"A chicken and flageolets."

He shouted indignantly:

"Chicken, chicken again, always chicken, damn it! I have had enough, I have, of your chickens. Can't you think of anything else, must you always give me the same thing to eat every day?"

Resignedly, she replied:

"But, my darling, you know the doctor ordered it. It is the best thing for your digestion. There are lots of things I dare not give you that you should have if you did not suffer from indigestion."

Exasperated, he stood right in front of Alexander:

"If I am ill it is this brute's fault. For thirty-five years he has been poisoning me with his filthy cooking."

Mme. Maramballe turned her head round quickly to look at the old servant. Their eyes met in a glance which contained their mutual thanks.

A WAY TO WEALTH

"Do you know what has become of Lerémy?"

"He is captain of the Sixth Dragoons."

"And Pinson?"

"Subprefect."

"And Racollet?"

"Dead."

We hunted up other names which recalled to us young figures crowned with caps trimmed with gold braid. Later we found some of these comrades, bearded, bald, married, the fathers of many children; and these meetings, these changes, gave us some disagreeable shivers, as they showed us how short life is, how quickly everything changes and passes away.

My friend asked: "And Patience, the great Patience?"

I roared.

"Oh! If you want to hear about him, listen to me: Four or five weeks ago, as traveling inspector at Limoges, I was awaiting the dinner hour. Seated before the Grand Café in Theater Square, I closed my eyes wearily. The tradesmen were coming in in twos, or threes or fours, taking their absinthe or vermouth, talking in a loud voice of their business and that of others, laughing violently or lowering their voices when they communicated something important or delicate.

"I said to myself: 'What am I going to do after dinner?' And I thought of the long evening in this provincial town, of the slow, uninteresting walks through the unknown streets, of the overwhelming sadness which takes possession of the solitary traveler, of the people who pass, strangers in all things and through all things, the cut of their provincial coats, their hats, their trousers, their customs, local accent, their houses, shops and carriages of singular shape. And then the ordinary sounds to which one is not accustomed, the harassing sadness, which presses upon you little by little until you feel as if you were lost in a dangerous country, which oppresses you and makes you wish yourself back at the hotel, the hideous hotel, where your room preserves a thousand suspicious odors, where the bed makes one hesitate and the basin has a hair glued in the dirt at the bottom.

"I thought about all this as I watched them light the gas, feeling my isolated distress increase by the falling of the shadows. What was I going to do after dinner? I was alone, entirely alone, and lamentably lonesome.

"A big man came in, seated himself at a neighboring table and commanded in a formidable voice:

" 'Waiter, my bitters.'

"The 'my' in the phrase sounded like the report of a cannon. I understood immediately that everything in existence was his, belonged to him and not to any other, that he had his character and, by Jove! his appetite, his pantaloons, his no matter what, after his own fashion, absolute and more complete than important. He looked about him with a satisfied air. They brought him his bitters and he called:

" 'My paper.'

"I asked myself: 'Which is his paper, I wonder?' The name of that would certainly reveal to me his opinions, his theories, his hobbies and his nature.

"The waiter brought the *Times*. I was surprised. Why the *Times*, a grave, somber, doctrinal, heavy journal? I thought:

" 'He is then a wise man, of serious ways, regular habits, in short, a good commoner.'

"He placed on his nose some gold eyeglasses, turned around and, before commencing to read, cast another glance all around the room. He noticed me and immediately began to look at me in a persistent, uneasy fashion. I was on the point of asking him the reason for his attention, when he cried out from where he sat:

" 'By my pipe, if it is not Gontran Lardois!'

"I answered: 'Yes sir, you have not deceived yourself.'

"Then he got up brusquely and came toward me with outstretched hands.

" 'Ah, my old friend, how are you?' he asked.

"My greeting was constrained, not knowing him at all. Finally I stammered:

" 'Why—very well—and you?'

"He began to laugh: 'It appears that you do not know me.'

" 'No, not quite. It seems to me—however——'

"He tapped me on the shoulder.

" 'There, there! Not to bother you any longer, I am Patience, Robert Patience, your chum, your comrade.'

"I recognized him. Yes, Robert Patience, my comrade at college. It was no other. I pressed the hand he extended to me and said:

" 'Everything going well with you?'

" 'With me? Like a charm.'

"His laugh rang with triumph. He inquired:

" 'What has brought you here?'

"I explained to him that I was inspector of finances, making the rounds.

"He replied, observing my badge: 'Then you are successful?'

"I replied: 'Yes, rather; and you?'

" 'Oh! I? Very, very!'

" 'What are you doing now?'

" 'I am in business.'

" 'Then you are making money?'

" 'Lots of it. I am rich. But come to lunch with me tomorrow at noon, number 17 Coq-qui-chante Street; then you will see my place.'

"He appeared to hesitate a second then continued:

" 'You are still the good rounder of former times?'

" 'Yes, I hope so.'

" 'Not married?'

" 'No.'

" 'So much the better. And you are still as fond of fun and potatoes?'

"I commenced to find him deplorably commonplace. I answered, nevertheless: 'Yes.'

" 'And pretty girls?'

" 'As to that, yes.'

"He began to laugh with a good, hearty laugh.

" 'So much the better; so much the better,' he said. 'You recall our first farce at Bordeaux, when we had supper at the Roupie coffeehouse? Ha! What a night!'

"I recalled that night, surely, and the memory of it amused me. Other facts were brought to mind and still others. One would say:

" 'Do you remember the time we shut up the fawn in Father Latoque's cellar?'

"And he would laugh, striking his fist upon the table, repeating:

" 'Yes—yes—yes—and you remember the mouth of the professor in geography, Monsieur Marin, when we sent off a cracker on the map of the world just as he was orating on the principal volcanoes of the earth?'

"Then brusquely I asked him:

" 'And you, are you married?'

"He cried: 'For ten years, my dear fellow, and I have four children, most astonishing monkeys, but you will see them and their mother.'

"We were talking loud; the neighbors were looking around at us in astonishment. Suddenly my friend looked at his watch, a chronometer as large as a citron, and cried out:

" 'Thunder! It is rude, but I shall have to leave you; I am not free this evening.'

"He rose, took both my hands and shook them, as if he wished to break off my arms, and said:

" 'Tomorrow at noon, you remember?'

" 'I remember.'

"I passed the morning at work at the house of the general treasurer. He wished to keep me for luncheon, but I told him that I had an appointment with a friend. He accompanied me out. I asked him:

" 'Do you know where Coq-qui-chante Street is?'

"He answered: 'Yes, it is five minutes from here. As I have nothing to do, I will conduct you there.'

"And we set out on the way. Soon I noticed the street we sought. It was wide, pretty enough, at the border of the town and the country. I noticed the houses and perceived number 17. It was a kind of hotel with a garden at the back. The front, ornamented with frescoes in the Italian fashion, appeared to me in bad taste. There were goddesses hanging to urns and others whose secret beauties a cloud concealed. Two stone Cupids held up the number.

"I said to the treasurer: 'Here is where I am going.'

"And I extended my hand by way of leaving him. He made a brusque and singular gesture but said nothing, pressing the hand held out to him. I rang. A maid appeared. I said:

" 'Monsieur Patience, if you please. Is he at home?'

"She replied: 'He is here, sir. Do you wish to speak with him?'

" 'Yes.'

"The vestibule was ornamented with paintings from the brush of some local artist. Paul and Virginia were embracing under some palms drowned in a rosy light. A hideous oriental lantern hung from the ceiling. There were many doors, masked by showy hangings. But that which struck me particularly was the odor— a permeating, perfumed odor, recalling rice powder and the moldiness of cellars— an indefinable odor in a heavy atmosphere, as overwhelming as stifling, in which the human body becomes petrified. I ascended, behind the maid, a marble staircase which was covered by a carpet of some oriental kind and was led into a sumptuous drawing room.

"Left alone, I looked about me.

"The room was richly furnished, but with the pretension of an ill-bred parvenu. The engravings of the last century were pretty enough, representing women with high, powdered hair and very low-cut bodices surprised by gallant gentlemen in interesting postures. Another lady was lying on a great bed, toying with her foot with a little dog drowned in draperies. Another resisted her lover complacently, whose hand was in a suspicious place. One design showed four feet whose bodies could be divined, although concealed behind a curtain. The vast room, surrounded by soft divans, was entirely impregnated with this enervating odor which had already taken hold of me. There was something suspicious about these walls, these stuffs, this exaggerated luxury, in short, the whole place.

"I approached the window to look into the garden, of which I could see but the trees. It was large, shady, superb. A broad path was outlined on the turf, where a jet of water was playing in the air, brought in under some masonry some distance off. And suddenly three women appeared down there at the end of the garden, between two shapely shrubs. They were walking slowly, taking hold of each other's arms, clothed in long white dresses clouded with lace. Two of them were blonde and the other a brunette.

"They disappeared immediately among the trees. I remained transfixed, charmed, before this short but delightful apparition, which brought surging to my mind a whole poetic world. They were scarcely to be seen at all in that bower of leaves at the end of the park, so secluded and delicious. I must have dreamed, and these were the beautiful ladies of the last century wandering under the elm-tree hedge, the ladies whose light loves the clever gravures on the walls recalled. And I thought of those happy times, flowery, incorporeal, tender, when customs were so sweet and lips so easy.

"A great voice behind me made me leap back into the room. Patience had come in, radiant, extending both his hands.

"He looked at me out of the end of his eyes with the sly air of some amorous confidence and, with a large, comprehensive gesture, a Napoleonic gesture, pointed out his sumptuous drawing room, his park, with the three women passing again at the back, and in a triumphant voice that sang of pride said:

" 'And when you think that I commenced with nothing—my wife and my sisters-in-law!' "

THE PUTTER-TO-SLEEP

The Seine spread before my house without a wrinkle, varnished by the morning sun. It lay there, a lovely, wide, slow, long flood of silver, tarnished in places; and on the further side of the river a line of tall trees stretched along the bank a huge wall of verdure.

The feeling of life which begins again each morning, of life, fresh, gay, loving, shivered in the leaves, fluttered in the air, shimmered in the water.

They brought me my newspapers which the postman had just left, and I went out on to the bank with tranquil step to read them.

In the first I opened I caught the words "Suicide Statistics," and I was informed that this year more than eight thousand five hundred persons had killed themselves.

At that moment I saw them! I saw this hideous massacre of desperate creatures, tired of life. I saw people bleeding, their jaw shattered, their skull smashed, their chest pierced by a bullet, slowly dying, alone in a little hotel bedroom, and thinking nothing of their wound, always of their misery.

Others I saw, throat gaping or stomach ripped open, still holding in their hand the kitchen knife or the razor.

I saw others, seated before a glass in which matches were soaking, or sometimes before a little bottle with a red label. They would watch it with rigid eyes, motionless; then they would drink it, then wait; then a grimace would cross their faces, contract their lips; a fear crept into their eyes, for they did not know how much they would suffer before the end.

They would get up, stop, fall, and with hands clutching their stomachs, feel their organs burned and their entrails corroded by the liquid's flames, before their consciousness was overcast.

Others again I saw hanging from a nail in the wall, from the window fastening, from the ceiling bracket, from the beam of a barn, from the branch of a tree, beneath the evening drizzle. And I guessed all that they had done before they hung there, tongue lolling, motionless. I guessed the anguish of their hearts, their last hesitations, their movements in fixing the rope, trying whether it held firmly, passing it about their neck and letting themselves fall.

Others still I saw lying on their wretched beds, mothers with their little children, old men starving with hunger, girls torn with the agony of love, all rigid, stifled, suffocated, while in the center of the room still smoked the charcoal brazier.

And some I glimpsed walking to and fro by night on deserted bridges. These were the most sinister. The water eddied beneath the arches with a soft whisper. They did not see it . . . they guessed its presence, scenting its chilly odor! They desired it and feared it. They did not dare! However, they must. The hour was striking from some distant clock, and suddenly, in the wide silences of the darkness, there swept by me, quickly stifled, the splash of a body falling into the river, a few screams, the slapping of water beaten with hands. Sometimes there was nothing more than the plunge of their fall, when they had bound their arms or tied a stone to their feet.

Oh! poor folk, poor folk, poor folk, how I felt their anguish, how I died their deaths. I have passed through all their miseries; in one hour I have undergone all their tortures. I have known all the sorrows which led them to that place; for I feel degradation, deceiver of life, as no one more than I has felt it.

Yes, I have understood them, those feeble things, who—tormented by ill fortune, having lost their loved ones, awakened from their dreams of later reward, from the illusion of another existence, in which God would at last be just, after giving way to savage anger, and disabused of the mirage of happiness—have had enough of life, and would end this relentless tragedy or shameful comedy.

Suicide; it is the strength of them who have nothing left, the hope of them who believe no more, the sublime courage of the conquered! Yes, there is at least one door from this life; we can always open it and pass to the other side. Nature has made one gesture of pity; she has not imprisoned us. Mercy for the desperate!

While for the merely disabused, let them march forward free-souled and calm-hearted. They have nothing to fear, since they can depart; since behind them stands ever this door that the gods we dream of can never close.

So I meditated on this crowd of willing dead: more than eight thousand five hundred in a year. And it came to me that they had come together to hurl into the world a prayer, to cry their will, to demand something, to be later made real, when the world will understand better. It seemed to me that all these beings tortured, stabbed, poisoned, hung, suffocated, drowned, flocked, in one terrifying horde, like voters at the poll, to say to society: "Grant us at least a quiet death! Help us to die, you who will not help us to live! See, we are many, we have the right to speak in these days of liberty, of philosophic independence, and of democracy. Give those who renounce life the charity of a death neither repulsive nor fearful."

I let myself dream, leaving my thoughts to roam about this subject with bizarre, mysterious fancies.

I thought myself at one moment in a lovely city. It was Paris; but of what date? I wandered down the streets, looking at houses, theaters, public buildings, and then suddenly, in a square, I came on a huge edifice, graceful, alluring, handsome.

I was surprised when I read on the façade, in gilt letters: "Institute of Voluntary Death"!

The strangeness of those wakened dreams, where the spirit hovers in an unreal yet possible world! Nothing surprises; nothing shocks; and the unbridled fancy no longer distinguishes the comic or the doleful.

I went up to the building, and saw footmen in breeches seated in the hall before a cloakroom, as in the entrance to a club.

I went in to look round. One of them, rising, asked me:

"Do you want anything, sir?"

"I want to know what this place is."

"Nothing else?"

"No."

"Perhaps you would like me to take you to the secretary of the Institute, sir?"

I hesitated and then asked:

"I shall not be disturbing him?"

"Oh, not at all, sir. He is here to see people who want information."

"Very well. I will follow you."

He led me through some corridors in which a few old gentlemen were chatting; then I was conducted into a charming room, a little somber perhaps, furnished in black wood. A plump, potbellied young man was writing a letter and smoking a cigar the quality of which was evidenced by its excellent bouquet.

He rose. We bowed to each other, and when the footman had gone, he asked:

"How can I be of service to you?"

"You will forgive my indiscretion, sir," I replied. "I have never seen this establishment before. The few words inscribed on the façade surprised me, and I wanted to know what they betokened!"

He smiled before answering, then in a low voice with an air of satisfaction:

"Just, sir, that people who want to die, are killed here decently and quietly; I won't say agreeably."

I did not feel much moved, for this statement seemed to me on the whole very natural and just. But I was astonished that on this planet with its low, utilitarian, humanitarian ideas, egotistical and coercive of all real liberty, an enterprise of such a nature, worthy of an emancipated humanity, dare be undertaken.

I went on.

"How did this happen?"

"Sir," he replied, "the number of suicides grew so rapidly in the five years following the Exhibition of 1889, that immediate steps became necessary. People were killing themselves in the streets, at parties, in restaurants, at the theater, in railway carriages, at presidential banquets, everywhere. Not only was it a very ugly sight for those, such as myself, who are very fond of life, but, moreover, a bad example for the children. So it became necessary to centralize suicides."

"How did this rush of suicides arise?"

"I have no idea. In my heart, I think the world has grown old. We begin to see clearly and to accept our lot with an ill grace. Today it is the same with destiny as with the government, we know where we are: we decide that we are being cheated at all points, and so we depart. When we realize that Providence lies, cheats, robs and tricks human beings in the same way as a deputy his constituents, we are annoyed, and since we can't nominate another every quarter as we do our privileged representatives, we quit a place so definitely rotten!"

"Really."

"Oh, I don't complain."

"Will you tell me how the Institute works?"

"Willingly. You can always become a member when you want to. It is a club."

"A club?"

"Certainly, sir, and founded by the most eminent men of the country, by the best imaginations, and the clearest intelligences."

Laughing heartily, he added:

"And I swear people like it here."

"Here?"

"Yes, here."

"You astound me."

"Lord! they like it because the members of the club have no fear of death, which is the great spoiler of earthly pleasures!"

"But why, if they don't kill themselves, are they members of this club?"

"One can become a member without putting oneself under the obligation of committing suicide."

"Then?"

"Let me explain. Fired by the immeasurable growth of the number of suicides, and the hideous spectacle they offered, a society of pure benevolence was formed for the protection of the desperate to put at their disposal a calm and painless, if not unforeseen, death."

"Whoever gave authority for such a society?"

"General Boulanger during his short tenure of office. He could refuse nothing. Of course, he did no other good action. So a society was formed of farsighted, disabused, skeptical men who wished to build in the heart of Paris a kind of temple to the scorn of death. This building was at first a suspected place which no one would come near. Then the founders called a meeting and arranged a great reception of inauguration with Sarah Bernhardt, Judic, Théo, Granier and a score more. MM. de Rezke, Coquelin, Mounet-Sully, Paulus; then concerts, Dumas comedies, Meilhac, Halévy, Sardou. We only had one frost, one of Becque's plays, which seemed gloomy, but afterwards was very successful at the Comédie-Francaise. In the end, all Paris came. The club was launched!"

"In the midst of jubilations! What a ghastly jest!"

"Not at all. Why should death be gloomy? It should be indifferent. We have lightened death, we have made it blossom, we have perfumed it, we have made it easy. One learns to relieve suffering by example; one can see that it is nothing."

"I can quite understand people coming for the shows, but does anyone come for . . . it?"

"Not at once: they were distrustful."

"But later?"

"They came."

"Many?"

"In masses. We have more than forty a day. Practically no drowned are found in the Seine."

"Who was the first aspirant?"

"A member of the club."

"A God-fearer?"

"I don't think so. A sot, a ruined man, who had lost heavily at baccarat for three months."

"Really?"

"Our second was an Englishman, an eccentric. Then we had a lot of publicity in the newspapers; we told all about our methods; we made up deaths which we thought would attract. But the main impulse came from the lower classes."

"What are your methods?"

"Would you like to go round? I could explain as we went."

"Very much indeed."

He took his hat, opened the door, motioned me before him into a gambling room where men were playing as they play in all dives. He led me across several rooms. Everywhere was lively and gay chatter. I have rarely seen so vivacious a club, so animated, so mirthful.

As I seemed surprised, the secretary challenged me:

"Oh, the club has an unprecedented rage. The right people from all over the globe become members in order to have the air of mocking death. Once they are here, they think they have to be gay in order not to seem afraid. So they joke, laugh, play the buffoon; they have wit and learn to acquire it. Nowadays it is the most frequented and the most amusing place in Paris. The women even are getting busy to organize an annex for themselves."

"And in spite of all this, you have plenty of suicides in the house?"

"As I told you, between forty and fifty a day. The upper classes are rare, but there are plenty of poverty-stricken devils. And the middle classes too send a good many."

"And how . . . is it done?"

"Asphyxiation . . . very gently."

"Your apparatus?"

"A gas of our own invention. We hold the patent. On the other side of the building are the public entrances. Three little doors opening into side alleys. When a man or a woman knocks, we begin by interrogating them; then we offer them assistance, help, protection. If our client accepts, we make inquiries and often we succeed in saving them."

"Where do you find the money?"

"We possess a great deal. The membership subscription is very high. Then it is good form to make donations to the institute. The names of all donors are printed in the *Figaro*. Moreover, every wealthy man's suicide costs a thousand francs, a good pose to die in. The poor die gratis. . . ."

"How do you recognize the poor?"

"Oh, we guess, sir! And, too, they have to bring a certificate of indigence from the local police. If you knew how sinister their entry is! I have only visited that part of the establishment once; I shall never visit it again. As premises, they are nearly as good as this part, nearly as rich and comfortable, but the people . . . the people!!! If you could only see them arrive, old people in rags who are on the point of death, people starving of misery for months, fed at the corners like street dogs; tattered, gaunt women who are ill, paralyzed, incapable of making a living, and who say to us after having related their circumstances: 'You see, it can't go on, for I can do nothing and earn nothing.' I saw one old woman of eighty-seven who had lost all her children and all her grandchildren, and who had been sleeping out of doors for six weeks. I was sick with emotion at the sight. But then, we have so many different cases, without mentioning those who say nothing save to ask: 'Where is it?' Those we let in and it is all over at once."

I repeated, with constricted heart:

"And . . . where is it?"

"Here."

He opened a door, and went on:

"Come in. It is the room especially reserved for members, and the one that is used least. As yet we have had no more than eleven annihilations."

"Oh, you call it an . . . annihilation?"

"Yes, sir. After you."

I hesitated, but at last went in. It proved a delightful gallery, a kind of conservatory, which pale blue, soft rose, and light green glasses surrounded poetically in a kind of landscape tapestry. In this charming room there were divans, magnificent palms, sweet-scented flowers, particularly roses, books on the table, the *Revue des Deux Mondes*, boxes of duty-paid cigars, and, what surprised me, Vichy pastilles in a *bonbonnière*.

As I showed my astonishment my guide said: "Oh, people often come here for a chat," and went on:

"The public rooms are like this, though furnished more simply."

I asked a question.

He pointed with his finger to a chaise-longue upholstered in creamy crepe de Chine with white embroidery, beneath a tall shrub of species unknown to me, round the foot of which ran a flower bed of reseda.

The secretary added in a lower voice:

"The flower and the scent can be changed at will, for our gas, which is quite imperceptible, lends to death the scent of whatever flower the subject prefers. It is volatilized with essences. Would you like to smell it for a second?"

"No, thanks," I replied quickly, "not yet."

He began laughing.

"Oh, there's no danger, sir. I have made sure of that myself several times."

I was afraid to appear cowardly. I replied:

"Well, I'm quite agreeable."

"Sit down on the putter-to-sleep, then."

Slightly nervous, I seated myself on the low chair upholstered in crepe de Chine, and then lay full length. Almost at once I was enveloped by a delicious scent of reseda. I opened my mouth to receive it more easily, for my soul was already growing torpid, was forgetting, was savoring, in the first discomfort of asphyxiation, the bewitching intoxication of an enchanting and withering opium.

I was shaken by the arm.

"Ah, sir," said the secretary, laughing, "I see that you are letting yourself get caught."

But a voice, a real and not a dream voice, greeted me with a pleasant ring:

"Morning, sir, I trust you're well."

My dream fled. I saw the Seine beneath the sun, and, coming along the path, the local policeman, who touched his black kepi with its silver braid with his right hand.

I answered:

"Good morning, Marinel. Where are you off to?"

"I'm going to report on a drowned man they've fished up by Morillons. Another one who has chucked himself into the Seine. He'd taken off his trousers to tie his legs with."

AM I INSANE?

Am I insane or jealous? I know not which, but I suffer horribly. I committed a crime, it is true, but is not insane jealousy, betrayed love and the terrible pain I endure enough to make anyone commit a crime without actually being a criminal?

I have loved this woman to madness—and yet is it true? Did I love her? No, no! She owned me body and soul; I was her plaything; she ruled me by her smile, her look, the divine form of her body. It was all those things that I loved, but the woman contained in that body, I despise her, hate her. I always have hated her, for she is but an impure, perfidious creature in whom there was no soul; even less than that, she is but a mass of soft flesh in which dwells infamy!

The first few months of our union were deliciously strange. Her eyes were three different colors. No, I am not insane; I swear they were. They were gray at noon, shaded green at twilight and blue at sunrise. In moments of love they were blue, the pupils dilated and nervous. Her lips trembled, and often the tip of her pink tongue could be seen as that of a reptile ready to hiss. When she raised her heavy lids and I saw that ardent look, I shuddered, not only for the unceasing desire to possess her, but for the desire to kill this beast.

When she walked across the room each step resounded in my heart. When she disrobed and emerged infamous but radiant from the white mass of linen and lace, a sudden weakness seized me; my limbs gave way beneath me, and my chest heaved; I was faint, coward that I was!

Each morning when she awakened I waited for that first look; my heart filled with rage, hatred and disdain for this beast whose slave I was, but when she fixed those limpid blue eyes on me, that languishing look showing traces of lassitude, it was like a burning, unquenchable fire within me, inciting me to passion.

When she opened her eyes that day I saw a dull, indifferent look, a look devoid of desire, and I knew then she was tired of me. I saw it, knew it, felt right away that it was all over, and each hour and minute proved to me that I was right. When I beckoned her with my arms and lips she shrank from me.

"Leave me alone," she said. "You are horrid!"

Then I became suspicious, insanely jealous, but I am not insane, no indeed! I watched her slyly, not that she had betrayed me, but she was so cold that I knew another would soon take my place.

At times she would say:

"Men disgust me!" Alas! It was too true.

Then I became jealous of her indifference, of her thoughts, which I knew to be impure, and when she awakened sometimes with that same look of lassitude I suffocated with anger, and an irresistible desire to choke her and make her confess the shameful secrets of her heart took hold of me.

Am I insane? No.

One night I saw that she was happy. I felt, in fact I was convinced, that a new passion ruled her. As of old, her eyes shone; she was feverish, and her whole self fluttered with love.

I feigned ignorance, but I watched her closely. I discovered nothing, however. I waited a week, a month, almost a year. She was radiantly, ideally happy, as if soothed by some ephemeral caress.

At last I guessed. No, I am not insane; I swear I am not. How can I explain this inconceivable, horrible thing? How can I make myself understood? This is how I guessed.

She came in one night from a long ride on horseback and sank exhausted in a seat facing me. An unnatural flush tinted her cheeks, and her eyes—those eyes that I knew so well—had such a look in them. I was not mistaken; I had seen her look like that; she loved! But whom? What? I almost lost my head, and so as not to look at her I turned to the window. A valet was leading her horse to the stable, and she stood and watched him disappear; then she fell asleep almost immediately. I thought and thought all night. My mind wandered through mysteries too deep to conceive. Who can fathom the perversity and strange caprices of a sensual woman?

Every morning she rode madly through hills and dales and each time came back languid, exhausted. At last I understood. It was of the horse I was jealous—of the wind which caressed her face, of the drooping leaves and of the dewdrops, of the saddle which carried her! I resolved to be revenged. I became very attentive. Every time she came back from her ride I helped her down, and the horse made a vicious rush at me. She would pat him on the neck, kiss his quivering nostrils without even wiping her lips. I watched my chance.

One morning I got up before dawn and went to the path in the woods she loved so well. I carried a rope with me, and my pistols were hidden in my breast, as if I were going to fight a duel. I drew the rope across the path, tying it to a tree on each side, and hid myself in the grass. Presently I heard her horse's hoofs; then I saw her coming at a furious pace, her cheeks flushed, an insane look in her eyes. She seemed enraptured, transported into another sphere.

As the animal approached the rope he struck it with his fore feet and fell. Before she had struck the ground I caught her in my arms and helped her to her feet. I then approached the horse, put my pistol close to his ear and shot him—as I would a man.

She turned on me and dealt me two terrific blows across the face with her riding whip, which felled me, and as she rushed at me again I shot her!

Tell me, am I insane?

A WIFE'S CONFESSION

My friend, you have asked me to relate to you the liveliest recollections of my life. I am very old, without relatives, without children, so I am free to make a confession to you. Promise me one thing—never to reveal my name.

I have been much loved, as you know; I have often myself loved. I was very beautiful; I may say this today, when my beauty is gone. Love was for me the life of the soul, just as the air is the life of the body. I would have preferred to die rather than exist without affection, without having somebody always to care for me. Women often pretend to love only once with all the strength of their hearts; it has often happened to be so violent in one of my attachments that I thought it would be impossible for my transports ever to end. However, they always died out in a natural fashion, like a fire when it has no more fuel.

I will tell you today the first of my adventures, in which I was very innocent but which led to the others. The horrible vengeance of that dreadful chemist of Pecq recalls to me the shocking drama of which I was, in spite of myself, a spectator.

I had been a year married to a rich man, Comte Hervé de Ker—a Breton of ancient family, whom I did not love, you understand. True love needs, I believe, at any rate, freedom and impediments at the same time. The love which is imposed, sanctioned by law and blessed by the priest—can we really call that love? A legal kiss is never as good as a stolen kiss. My husband was tall in stature, elegant, and a really fine gentleman in his manners. But he lacked intelligence. He spoke in a downright fashion and uttered opinions that cut like the blade of a knife. He created the impression that his mind was full of ready-made views instilled into him by his father and mother, who had themselves got them from their ancestors. He never hesitated, but on every subject immediately made narrow-minded suggestions without showing any embarrassment and without realizing that there might be other ways of looking at things. One felt that his head was closed up, that no ideas circulated in it, none of those ideas which renew a man's mind and make it sound, like a breath of fresh air passing through an open window into a house.

The château in which we lived was situated in the midst of a desolate tract of country. It was a large, melancholy structure, surrounded by enormous trees, with tufts of moss on it, resembling old men's white beards. The park, a real forest, was inclosed in a deep trench called the ha-ha, and at its extremity, near the moorland, we had big ponds full of reeds and floating grass. Between the two, at the edge of a stream which connected them, my husband had got a little hut built for shooting wild ducks.

We had, in addition to our ordinary servants, a keeper, a sort of brute, devoted to my husband to the death, and a chambermaid, almost a friend, passionately attached to me. I had brought her back from Spain with me five years before. She was a deserted child. She might have been taken for a gypsy with her dusky skin, her dark eyes, her hair thick as a wood and always clustering around her forehead. She was at the time sixteen years old, but she looked twenty.

The autumn was beginning. We hunted much, sometimes on neighboring estates, sometimes on our own, and I noticed a young man, the Baron de C——, whose visits at the château became singularly frequent. Then he ceased to come; I thought no more about it, but I perceived that my husband changed in his demeanor toward me.

He seemed taciturn and preoccupied; he did not kiss me, and in spite of the fact that he did not come into my room, as I insisted on separate apartments in order to live a little alone, I often at night heard a furtive step drawing near my door and withdrawing a few minutes after.

As my window was on the ground floor, I thought I had also often heard some-one prowling in the shadow around the château. I told my husband about it, and, having looked at me intensely for some seconds, he answered:

"It is nothing—it is the keeper."

Now one evening, just after dinner, Hervé, who appeared to be extraordinarily gay, with a sly sort of gaiety, said to me:

"Would you like to spend three hours out with the guns, in order to shoot a fox who comes every evening to eat my hens?"

I was surprised. I hesitated, but as he kept staring at me with singular persistency, I ended by replying:

"Why, certainly, my friend." I must tell you that I hunted like a man the wolf and the wild boar. So it was quite natural that he should suggest this shooting expedition to me.

But my husband, all of a sudden, had a curiously nervous look, and all the evening he seemed agitated, rising up and sitting down feverishly.

About ten o'clock he suddenly said to me:

"Are you ready?"

I rose, and as he was bringing me my gun himself, I asked:

"Are we to load with bullets or with deer shot?"

He showed some astonishment; then he rejoined:

"Oh, only with deer shot; make your mind easy! That will be enough."

Then after some seconds he added in a peculiar tone:

"You may boast of having splendid coolness."

I burst out laughing.

"I? Why, pray? Coolness because I go to kill a fox? What are you thinking of, my friend?"

And we quietly made our way across the park. All the household slept. The full moon seemed to give a yellow tint to the old gloomy building, whose slate roof glittered brightly. The two turrets that flanked it had two plates of light on their summits, and no noise disturbed the silence of this clear, sad night, sweet and still, which seemed in a death trance. Not a breath of air, not a shriek from a toad, not a hoot from an owl; a melancholy numbness lay heavy on everything. When we were under the trees in the park a sense of freshness stole over me, together with the odor of fallen leaves. My husband said nothing, but he was listening; he was watching; he seemed to be smelling about in the shadows, possessed from head to foot by the passion for the chase.

We soon reached the edges of the ponds.

Their tufts of rushes remained motionless; not a breath of air caressed them, but movements which were scarcely perceptible ran through the water. Sometimes the surface was stirred by something, and light circles gathered around, like luminous wrinkles enlarging indefinitely.

When we reached the hut, where we were to lie in wait, my husband made me go in first; then he slowly loaded his gun, and the dry crackling of the powder produced a strange effect on me. He saw that I was shuddering and asked:

"Does this trial happen to be quite enough for you? If so, go back."

I was much surprised and I replied:

"Not at all. I did not come to go back without doing anything. You seem queer this evening."

He murmured:

"As you wish." And we remained there without moving.

At the end of about half an hour, as nothing broke the oppressive stillness of this bright autumn night, I said in a low tone:

"Are you quite sure he is passing this way?"

Hervé winced as if I had bitten him, and with his mouth close to my ear he said:

"Make no mistake about it! I am quite sure."

And once more there was silence.

I believe I was beginning to get drowsy when my husband pressed my arm, and his voice, changed to a hiss, said:

"Do you see him there under the trees?"

I looked in vain; I could distinguish nothing. And slowly Hervé now cocked his gun, all the time fixing his eyes on my face.

I was myself making ready to fire, and suddenly, thirty paces in front of us, appeared in the full light of the moon a man who was hurrying forward with rapid movements, his body bent, as if he were trying to escape.

I was so stupefied that I uttered a loud cry, but before I could turn round there was a flash before my eyes; I heard a deafening report, and I saw the man rolling on the ground, like a wolf hit by a bullet.

I burst into dreadful shrieks, terrified, almost going mad; then a furious hand—it was Hervé's—seized me by the throat. I was flung down on the ground then carried off by his strong arms. He ran, holding me up, till he reached the body lying on the grass, and he threw me on top of it violently, as if he wanted to break my head.

I thought I was lost; he was going to kill me, and he had just raised his heel up to my forehead when, in his turn, he was gripped, knocked down, before I could yet realize what had happened.

I rose up abruptly and I saw kneeling on top of him Porquita, my maid, clinging like a wildcat to him with desperate energy, tearing off his beard, his mustache and the skin of his face.

Then as if another idea had suddenly taken hold of her mind, she rose up and, flinging herself on the corpse, she threw her arms around the dead man, kissing his eyes and his mouth, opening the dead lips with her own lips, trying to find in them a breath and the long, long kiss of lovers.

My husband, picking himself up, gazed at me. He understood and, falling at my feet, said:

"Oh, forgive me, my darling. I suspected you, and I killed this girl's lover. It was my keeper that deceived me."

But I was watching the strange kisses of that dead man and that living woman, and her sobs and her writhings of sorrowing love, and at that moment I understood that I might be unfaithful to my husband.

A DIVORCE CASE

Mme. Chassel's counsel began his speech: My lord, gentlemen of the jury, the case which I am called on to defend before you would more suitably be treated by medicine than by justice and constitutes much more a pathological case than an ordinary case of law. At first sight the facts seem simple.

A young man, of considerable wealth, of a high-minded and ardent nature, a generous heart, falls in love with a supremely beautiful young girl, more than beautiful, adorable, as gracious, as charming, as good, and as tender as she is pretty, and he marries her.

For some time, he conducts himself towards her as a solicitous and affectionate husband; then he neglects her, bullies her, seems to feel for her an insurmountable aversion, an unconquerable dislike. One day even, he strikes her, not only without any right, but even without any excuse.

I will not labor to represent to you, gentlemen, his strange behavior, incomprehensible to everyone. I will not paint for you the unspeakable life of these two creatures and the frightful grief of this young woman.

To convince you I have only to read to you some fragments from a diary written each day by this poor man, this poor madman. For it is with a madman that we have to do, gentlemen, and the case is all the more curious, all the more interesting in that it recalls in many particulars the mania of the unfortunate prince who died recently, the fantastic king who reigned platonically in Bavaria. I will recall that case: the madness of a romantic.

You will remember all the tales told of that strange prince. He had built in the heart of the most magnificent scenery in his kingdom veritable fairy castles. Even the reality of the beauty of things and places were not enough for him, he imagined and created in these fantastic dwellings artificial horizons produced by means of theatrical devices, changes of scene, painted forests, fabled demesnes where the leaves of the trees were of precious stones. He had alps and glaciers, steppes, sandy deserts scorched by the sun; and at night, under the rays of the real moon, lakes illuminated below by fantastic electric lights. On these lakes swans floated and small boats glided, while an orchestra composed of the finest musicians in the world intoxicated the royal madman's senses with romance.

This man was chaste, this man was a virgin. He had never loved anything save a dream, his dream, his divine dream.

One evening he carried off in his boat a young woman, a great artiste, and begged her to sing. She sang, herself intoxicated by the beauty of the courtyards, by the warm, sweet air, by the fragrance of flowers and by the ecstasy of this young, handsome prince.

She sang, as women sing whom love has touched, then, distraught, trembling wildly, she fell on the king's heart and sought his lips.

But he threw her in the lake, and taking up his oars, gained the shore without troubling whether she were rescued or not.

Gentlemen of the jury, we have before us a case in all respects similar. I will do

no more than read to you now some passages from the diary which we discovered
in the drawer of a bureau.

How dull and ugly everything is, always the same, always hideous! How I dream
of a lovelier, nobler, more changeful world! How wretched would be the imagination of their God, if their God existed or if he had not created other things as
well.

Always woods, little woods, rivers that are like all other rivers, plains like all
other plains, all things are alike and monotonous. And man! . . . Man? . . .
What a horrible animal, wicked, proud and disgusting!

One should love, love madly, without seeing the object of one's love. For to see
is to understand, and to understand is to despise. One should love, intoxicating
oneself with the beloved as one gets drunk on wine, in such a way as to lose consciousness of what one is drinking. And drink, drink, drink, without drawing
breath, day and night.

I have found her, I think. She has in all her person something ideal that does
not seem of this world and lends wings to my dream. Oh, how far otherwise than
in reality do people seem to me in my dreams. She is fair, very fair, with hair full
of inexpressible delicate shades. Her eyes are blue. Blue eyes are the only ones that
ravish my soul. The whole being of a woman, the woman who exists in the depths
of my heart, shows itself to me in the eye, only in the eye.

Oh, a mystery! What mystery? The eye? . . . The whole universe lies therein,
because it sees it, because it reflects it. It contains the universe, things and beings,
forests and oceans, men and beasts, sunsets, stars, the arts, all, all, it sees, plucks,
and bears everything away; and it holds still more, it holds the soul, it holds the
thinking man, the man who loves, who laughs, who suffers. Oh, look into the blue
eyes of women; they are deep as the sea, changing as the sky, so sweet, so sweet,
sweet as gentle winds, sweet as music, sweet as kisses, transparent, so clear that one
sees behind, one sees the soul, the blue soul that colors them, that animates them,
that makes them divine.

Yes, the soul shares the colors of the glance. Only the blue soul bears the dream
in its depths, it has stolen its azure from sea and space.

The eye! Think of it! The eye! It drinks in the visible creation to feed thought.
It drinks in the world, color, movement, books, pictures, all beauty, all ugliness,
and creates ideas therefrom. And when it looks at me, it fills me with the sense of
a happiness not of this world. It foreshadows to us the things of which we are for
ever ignorant; it makes us realize that the realities of our thoughts are despicable
and filthy things.

I love her too for her manner of walking.
Même quand l'oiseau marche, on sent qu'il a des ailes, the poet said.
When she passes, one feels that she is not of the same race as ordinary women,
she is of a finer, more divine race.
I marry her to-morrow. . . . I am afraid . . . I am afraid of so many things.

Two beasts, two dogs, two wolves, two foxes, prowl through the woods and meet.
The one is male, the other female. They mate. They mate because of an animal in-

stinct which drives them to continue the race, their race, the race whose form, skin, stature, movements and habits they have.

All beasts do as much, without knowing why!

We too. . . .

All that I have done in marrying her is to obey this senseless urge that drives us towards the female.

She is my wife. So long as I desired her ideally, she was for me the unrealizable dream on the verge of being realized.

From the very second when I held her in my arms, she was no more than the being of whom nature has made use to bring to naught all my hopes.

Has she brought them to naught? No. Yet I am tired of her, tired of being unable to touch her, to brush her with my hand or my lips, without my heart swelling with an inexpressible disgust, not perhaps disgust with her, but a loftier, wider, more contemptuous disgust, disgust with the embrace of love, so vile as it has become for all refined beings, a shameful act which must be hidden, which is only spoken of in low tones, with blushes. . . .

I can no longer endure the sight of my wife approaching me, calling to me with smile and glance and arms. I can no longer endure it. I imagined once that her kiss would transport me to the heavens. One day she was suffering from a passing fever, and I caught in her breath the faint subtle almost imperceptible odor of human decay. I was utterly overcome!

Oh! flesh, seductive living dung, a mass of decay that walks, thinks, speaks, looks and smiles, full of fermenting food, rosy, pretty, tempting, full of deceit as is the soul . . .

Why is it only flowers that feel so good, great pale or brilliant flowers, whose tones and hues make my heart flutter and trouble my eyes? They are so beautiful, so delicate in structure, so varied and so sensual, half-open like mouths, more tempting than mouths, and hollow, with lips curled back, toothed, fleshy, powdered with a seed of life that engenders in each one of them a different perfume.

They reproduce themselves, they, only they, in all the world, without defilement of their inviolable race, giving off round themselves the divine incense of their love, the fragrant sweat of their caresses, the essence of their incomparable bodies, of their bodies that are adorned with all grace, all elegance, all form, and possess the fascination of all color forms; and the intoxicating charm of all scents . . .

Selected fragments, six months later.

. . . I love flowers, not as flowers but as delicate and material beings; I pass my days and my nights in the greenhouses where I hide them like women in harems.

Who, except myself, knows the sweetness, the maddening charm, the shuddering, sensual, ideal, superhuman ecstasy of these tender caresses; and these kisses on rosy flesh, on red flesh, on white flesh, the miraculously varied, delicate, rare, fine, unctuous flesh of these wonderful flowers?

I have greenhouses where no one enters but myself and the man who looks after them.

I enter them as if I were stepping into a place of secret delight. In the high glass gallery, I pass first between two throngs of corollas, shut, half open or spread wide, which slope from ground to roof. It is the first kiss they send me.

Those particular ones, those flowers, those that adorn this anteroom of my mysterious passions, are my servants and not my favorites.

They greet me, as I pass, with their changing brilliance and their fresh exhalations. They are darlings, coquettes, rising tier upon tier in eight rows on my right and eight rows on my left, and so crowded that they have the aspect of two gardens coming down to my feet.

My heart palpitates, my eye lights up at sight of them, the blood runs madly through my veins, my soul leaps within me, and my hands tremble already with the desire to touch them. I pass on. There are three closed doors at the end of this high gallery. I can make my choice. I have three harems.

But I turn oftenest to the orchids, my drowsy favorites. Their room is low, stifling. The damp, warm air makes my skin moist, my throat contract for want of air, and my fingers tremble. They come, these stranger women, from swampy, burning, unhealthy countries. They are as fascinating as sirens, deadly as poison, marvelously grotesque, soul-destroying, terrifying. See how like they are to butterflies with their enormous wings, their tiny paws, their eyes. For they have eyes. They look at me, they see me, prodigious, unbelievable beings, fairies, daughters of the holy earth, the impalpable air, and warm light, the mother of the world. Yes, they have wings and eyes and delicate shades that no painter can catch, all the charms, all the graces, all the shapes that one can dream of. Their sides are cleft, perfumed and transparent, open for love and more tempting than any woman's flesh. The unimaginable contours of their tiny bodies thrust the soul, drunk, into a paradise of visions and ideal delights. They quiver on their stems as if about to take flight. Will they fly, will they come to me? No, it is my heart which hovers above them like some mystic male creature, tortured with love.

No insect's wing can brush them. We are alone, they and I, in the translucent prison that I have built them. I watch them and I contemplate them, I admire them, I adore them, one after the other.

How sleek they are, how mysterious, rosy, with a rosiness that moistens the lips with desire. How I love them! The rim of their calyx is curled, paler than their throats, and the corolla hides itself there, mysterious seductive mouth, sweet to the tongue and displaying and concealing the delicate, wonderful and sacred organs of these divine little creatures which smell pleasant and do not talk.

Sometimes I am seized with a passion for one of them which endures as long as its existence, a few days, a few nights. Then it is taken from the common gallery and enclosed in a darling little glass retreat where a thread of water murmurs through a bed of tropic grass come from the islands of the great Pacific. And there I stay, at her side, ardent, feverish and tormented, knowing her death so close and watching her fade, while I possess her, while I breathe, drink, pluck her short life with one inexpressible caress.

When he had finished reading these fragments, counsel continued:

Decency, gentlemen of the jury, restrains me from continuing to lay before you the curious confessions of this shamefully idealistic madman. The few passages that I have just laid before you will be sufficient, I think, for you to understand this case of mental disease, less rare than one thinks in our age of hysterical dementia and corrupted decadence.

I feel therefore that my client is entitled more than any other woman to demand her divorce in the exceptional position in which she has been placed by the strange mental derangement of her husband.

MADAME PARISSE

I was seated on the mole of the little port of Obernon, near the hamlet of La Salis, watching Antibes in the setting sun. I have never seen anything so wonderfully beautiful. The little town, inclosed within its heavy fortifications of masonry (constructed by M. de Vauban), was situated in the middle of the Gulf of Nice. The great waves rolled in from afar to throw themselves at its feet, surrounding it with a garland of foam, and above the ramparts the houses could be seen, climbing one above another up to the two towers pointing to the sky like two horns on an ancient helmet and standing out against the milky whiteness of the Alps—an enormous, illimitable wall of snow that appeared to shut off the entire horizon. Between the white foam at the foot of the walls and the white snow on the border of the sky, the little city, sparkling and upright on the blue background of the nearest mountain, shone in the rays of the setting sun, looking like a pyramid of red-roofed houses, the façades of which were white, yet of such different shades of white that they seemed to be of many hues.

The sky above the Alps was of a pale blue that was almost white, as if the snow had given to it some of its own whiteness. A few silvery clouds floated near the pale summit, and on the other side of the gulf Nice lay on the edge of the water like a white ribbon between the sea and the mountains. Two great lateen sails, forced onward by a strong breeze, appeared to run before the waves. I gazed at the scene, enchanted with its beauty. It was one of those sights so charming, so rare, so exquisite, which seem to take possession of you and become one of those moments never to be forgotten, like certain happy memories. We think, we enjoy, we suffer, we are moved, from various causes, but we love by seeing! He that can feel deep emotion through the power of sight experiences the same keen joy, refined and profound, felt by the man with a sensitive and nervous ear when listening to music that stirs the heart.

I said to my companion, M. Martini, a pure-blooded southerner, "That is certainly one of the rarest spectacles that it ever has been my good fortune to admire. I have seen Mont-Saint-Michel, that enormous jewel of granite, spring forth from the sands at sunrise. I have seen in the Sahara Lake Raianecherqui, fifty kilometers in length, shine under a moon as brilliant as our sun and exhale toward the clouds a vapor as white as milk. I have seen in the Lipari Islands the fantastic sulphur crater of Volcanello, a giant flower, the center of which is a volcano that smokes and burns with a limitless yellow flame that spreads out over the ocean. But I have seen nothing more impressive than Antibes, standing before the Alps in the setting sun. And I cannot tell why, at this moment, souvenirs of olden days haunt me. Verses of Homer come into my mind. It is a city of the old Orient, Antibes; it is a city of the *Odyssey*, it is a western Troy—even though Troy was far from the sea."

M. Martini drew from his pocket a Sarty guide and read:

"'The city was originally a colony founded by the Phoenicians of Marseilles about the year 340 B.C. It received from them the Greek name of Antipolis, that is to say, "city over against," "city in front of another," because, in reality, it was situated opposite Nice, another colony of Marseilles. After the conquest of the Gauls, the Romans made of Antibes a municipal city, and her inhabitants enjoyed the privileges of a Roman city.

"'We know,'" he continued, "'by an epigram of Martial, that in his time——'"

I interrupted him, saying: "I don't care what it was! I tell you I have before my eyes a city of the *Odyssey*. Coast of Asia or coast of Europe—they are alike, and there is nothing on the other shore of the Mediterranean that awakens in me the memory of heroic days as does this."

The sound of an approaching step caused me to turn my head; a tall, dark woman was passing along the road that follows the sea in the direction of the cape.

M. Martini murmured, emphasizing the last words: "It is Madame Parisse— you know!"

No, I did not know, but this name thrown out, the name of the shepherd of Troy, confirmed me in my dream.

I said, however, "Who is this Madame Parisse?"

He appeared surprised that I did not know her story. I reaffirmed that I did not know it, and I looked at the woman, who went on without seeing us, dreaming, walking with a slow, stately step, like the dames of antiquity, without doubt. She was about thirty-five years old and beautiful yet, very beautiful, though perhaps a trifle too plump.

After she had passed out of sight M. Martini told me this story.

"Madame Parisse, a Mademoiselle Combelombe, had married, a year before the war of 1870, Monsieur Parisse, an employee of the government. She was then a beautiful young girl, as slender and gay as she has since become stout and sad. She had accepted Monsieur Parisse reluctantly; he was one of those little red-tape men with short legs, who make a great fuss in a pint measure, which is yet too large for them.

"After the war Antibes was occupied by a single battalion of line commanded by Monsieur Jean de Carmelin, a young officer who had been decorated during the campaign and had only recently received the four stripes. As he was greatly bored with the life in that fortress, in that suffocating molehill shut in by enormous double walls, the commander went quite often for a walk on the cape, a sort of park or forest, where there was a fine, fresh breeze.

"There he met Madame Parisse, who used also to come on summer evenings to breathe the fresh air under the trees. How was it that they loved? Can one tell? They met; they looked at each other, and when they could not meet they thought of each other, without doubt. The image of the young woman with the brown eyes, black hair and pale face, the image of that fresh and beautiful southern girl, who showed her pretty white teeth in smiling, remained floating before the eyes of the officer, who would continue his promenade, lost in thought, biting his cigar instead of smoking it. And the image of the commander in his close-fitting coat and red trousers, covered with gold lace, whose blond mustache curled on his lip, must have remained before the eyes of Madame Parisse when her husband, un-shaved, badly dressed, short of limb and with pursy stomach, returned home for supper.

"From meeting so often, they smiled at seeing each other, perhaps, and from that they came to think they knew each other. He bowed to her, certainly. She was surprised and inclined her head slightly, only just enough to escape being impolite. But at the end of two weeks she returned his salutations from afar before coming face to face.

"He talked to her! Of what? Of the setting sun, without any doubt! And they admired it together, looking deep into each other's eyes more often than at the horizon. And every day during two weeks there was some simple pretext for a little chat of several minutes. Then they dared to take a few steps together in talking of something or other, but their eyes spoke of a thousand things more intimate, of secret and charming things, the reflection of which in the softness and emotion of a look causes the heart to beat, because they reveal the soul better than words. Then he must have taken her hand and murmured those words which a woman divines without appearing to have heard them.

"It was admitted between them that they loved, without submitting their mutual knowledge to the proof of sensuality or passion. She would have been con-tent to remain indefinitely at the stage of romantic tenderness, but not he—he wished to go further. And he pressed her, every day more ardently, to give herself entirely to him. She resisted, did not wish it and even seemed resolved never to yield.

"One evening, however, she said to him, as if by chance: 'My husband has just gone to Marseilles and is going to remain there four days.'

"Jean de Carmelin threw himself at her feet, begging her to open her door that very evening near eleven o'clock. But she would not listen to him and returned home as if angry. The commandant was in a bad humor all the evening, and the next day, beginning at daybreak, he walked on the ramparts in a rage, going from the drum school to the platoon school and meting out reprimands to officers and men like one throwing stones into a crowd. But on returning for breakfast, he found under his napkin a note containing these four words: 'This evening, ten o'clock.' And he gave five francs, without any apparent reason, to the boy who served him.

"The day seemed long. He passed a part of it in prinking and perfuming him-self. At the moment when he placed himself at the table for dinner another envelope was handed to him. He found inside this telegram:

"*My darling, business terminated. I return this evening: train at nine.*

"Parisse.

"The commandant gave vent to an oath so violent that the boy let the soup tureen fall on the floor. What should he do? Certainly he wanted her, and that very night, too, let it cost what it might, and he would have her. He would have her by some means or another, if he had to arrest and imprison her husband. Suddenly an insane idea crossed his mind. He called for paper and wrote:

"Madame: *He will not return this evening. I swear it to you, and I will be at ten o'clock at the place you know. Fear nothing, I guarantee everything on my honor as an officer.*

"Jean de Carmelin.

"And, having sent this letter, he dined tranquilly. About eight o'clock he summoned Captain Gribois, who was next in command, and said to him, while rolling between his fingers the rumpled dispatch of Monsieur Parisse: 'Captain, I have received a telegram of a singular character, which it is impossible for me to communicate to you. You must go immediately and guard the gates of the city in such a way that no one—you understand, no one—either comes in or goes out before six o'clock tomorrow morning. You must place guards in the streets also and compel the inhabitants to go into their houses at nine o'clock. Anyone who is found outside after that hour will be conducted to his domicile *manu militari*. If your men meet me during the night they must retire at once with an air of not recognizing me. Do you understand me thoroughly?'

" 'Yes, Commandant.'

" 'I make you responsible for the execution of these orders, Captain.'

" 'Yes, Commandant.'

" 'Would you like a glass of chartreuse?'

" 'With pleasure, Commandant.'

"They touched glasses, drank the yellow liquor, and Captain Gribois departed.

"The train from Marseilles came into the station at exactly nine o'clock and left on the platform two travelers, then went on its way toward Nice.

"One of the travelers was tall and thin. He was a Monsieur Saribe, merchant in oils. The other passenger was short and stout—it was Monsieur Parisse. They started on their way together, their traveling bags in their hands, to reach the town, a kilometer distant. But on arriving at the gate the sentinels crossed their bayonets and ordered them off.

"Alarmed, amazed and filled with astonishment, they drew aside and deliberated; then, after taking counsel together, they returned with precaution to parley and to make known their names. But the soldiers must have received peremptory orders, for they threatened to shoot, and the two travelers, greatly frightened, took flight at the top of their speed, leaving behind them their bags which impeded their flight.

"The two unfortunate travelers made the circle of the ramparts and presented themselves at the Porte de Cannes. This also was closed and guarded as well by a menacing sentinel. Messieurs Saribe and Parisse, like prudent men, insisted no longer but returned to the station to find a shelter, for the road around the fortifications was not very safe after sunset.

"The employee at the station, surprised and sleepy, gave them permission to remain until daylight in the waiting room. They sat there without light, side by side on the green velvet-covered bench, too frightened to think of sleeping. The night was long for them.

"Toward half-past six they learned that the gates were open and that one could at last enter Antibes. They started for the town but did not find their bags along the way. When they had passed through the gates, still a little uneasy, the Commandant de Carmelin, with a sly look and his head in the air, came himself to meet and question them. He bowed to them politely and made excuses for having caused them to pass a bad night but said he had been obliged to execute orders.

"The people of Antibes were mystified. Some talked of a surprise meditated by the Italians, others of the landing of the imperial prince, and still others imagined an Orléanist plot. The truth was not guessed until later, when they learned that the battalion of the commandant had been sent far away and that Monsieur de Carmelin had been severely punished."

M. Martini ceased speaking, and soon after Mme. Parisse reappeared, her walk being finished. She passed sedately near me, her eyes on the Alps, the summits of which were ruddy with the last rays of the setting sun.

I desired to salute her, that poor, saddened woman who must think always of that one night of love, now so far in the past, and of the bold man who had dared, for a kiss from her, to put a whole city in a state of siege and compromise his future. Today he has probably forgotten her, unless sometimes, after drinking, he relates that audacious farce, so comic and so tender.

Had she ever seen him again? Did she love him still? And I thought: "Here, indeed, is a trait of modern love, grotesque and yet heroic. The Homer who will sing of this Helen and of the adventures of her Menelaus must have the soul of a Mérimée. And yet the captain, this lover of that deserted woman, was valiant, bold, beautiful, strong as Achilles and more cunning than Ulysses."

DUCHOUX

While descending the main staircase of the club, heated to such an extent that it felt like a hothouse, Baron Mordiane left his fur-lined overcoat open; but when the front door had closed after him, the intense cold suddenly pierced him to the marrow, making him feel thoroughly miserable. Besides that, he had been losing money, and for some time had suffered from indigestion and could no longer eat what he fancied.

He was about to return home, when the thought of his great bare room, his footman sleeping in the anteroom, the water singing on the gas stove in his dressing room, and the enormous bed, as old and gloomy as a deathbed, suddenly struck him with a chill even more acute than that of the frosty air.

For some years he had felt the burden of loneliness which sometimes overwhelms old bachelors. He had been strong, active and cheerful, spending his days in sport and his evenings at social functions. Now, he was growing dull, and no longer took interest in anything. All sport tired him, suppers and even dinners made him ill, while women bored him as much as they had once amused him.

The monotony of such evenings, of the same friends met in the same place— at the club—the same card parties with their run of good and bad luck evenly balanced, the same conversation on the same topics, the same wit from the same tongues, the same jokes on the same subjects, the same scandal about the same women, all sickened him so much that there were times when he thought seriously of suicide. He could no longer face this regular, aimless and commonplace life, both frivolous and dull, and, without knowing why, he longed for peace, rest and comfort.

He had certainly never thought of marrying, he lacked the courage to face a life of depression, conjugal slavery, and that hateful coexistence of two human beings who know each other so well that every word uttered by one is anticipated by the other and every thought, wish or opinion is immediately divined. He considered that a woman was only worth attention so long as one knew very little about her, while she was still mysterious and unfathomed, vague and perplexing. Therefore what he wanted was family life without the tryanny of family ties, although he was continually haunted by the memory of his son.

For the last year he had always been thinking about him, and felt an irritating longing to see him and make his acquaintance. The affair had taken place while he was a young man, in an atmosphere of romance and affection. The child was sent to the South of France and brought up near Marseille, without knowing his father's name. His father had paid for his upbringing, alike in his infancy, in his school days and in the activities that followed, ending up with a substantial settlement on a suitable marriage. A trustworthy lawyer had acted as intermediary without giving away the secret.

Baron Mordiane, then, only knew that a child of his was living somewhere near Marseille, that he had a reputation for being intelligent and well educated, and that he had married the daughter of an architect and surveyor, whom he succeeded in the business. He was also said to be making money.

Why should he not go and see this unknown son, without disclosing his identity, in order to study him at first hand and see whether, in case of need, he might find a welcome refuge in his home?

He had always treated him liberally, and had made a generous settlement, which had been gratefully received. He was therefore sure of not coming into conflict with an unreasonable pride, and the idea of leaving for the South had now become an oft-recurring desire which was making him restless. He was also urged by a curious feeling of self-pity, at the thought of that cheerful and comfortable home on the coast where he would find his charming young daughter-in-law, his grandchildren ready to welcome him, and his son; all this would remind him of that brief and happy love affair so many years ago. His only regret was his past generosity, which had assisted the young man on the road to prosperity and would prevent him from appearing amongst them as a benefactor. With these thoughts running through his mind he walked along, his head buried deep in his fur collar: his decision was quickly made. Hailing a passing cab, he drove home, and said to his valet, aroused from his sleep to open the door:

"Louis, we are leaving for Marseille tomorrow evening. We shall be there perhaps a fortnight. Make all preparations for the journey."

The train sped along the sandy banks of the Rhône, then over yellow plains and through village—a country with gaunt encircling mountains in the distance.

Baron Mordiane, awakened after a night in the sleeping car, gloomily contemplated his reflection in the little mirror in his dressing case. The crude light of the South showed up wrinkles he had never seen before and revealed a state of decrepitude that had passed unnoticed in the shaded light of Parisian flats. Looking at the corners of his eyes, the wrinkled eyelids, bald temples and forehead, he said to himself:

"Good heavens, I am worse than faded: I look worn out!"

His desire for peace suddenly increased, and for the first time in his life, he was conscious of a vague longing to take his grandchildren on his knee.

He hired a carriage in Marseille and about one o'clock in the afternoon he stopped before a dazzling white country house typical of the South of France, standing at the end of an avenue of plane trees. He beamed with pleasure as he went along the avenue and said to himself:

"It's damned nice."

Suddenly a youngster of about five or six rushed from behind the shrubs and stood motionless at the end of the drive, gazing round-eyed at the visitor.

Mordiane approached and said to him:

"Good afternoon, my boy!"

The youngster made no reply.

The baron then stooped and picked him up to kiss him, but so strong was the odor of garlic coming from the child that he quickly put him down again, murmuring: "Oh! he must be the gardener's son." And he went on toward the house.

On a line in front of the door, the washing was drying, shirts, napkins, towels, aprons, and sheets, while a display of socks hanging in rows on strings one above another filled the whole of a window, like the tiers of sausages in front of a pork butcher's shop.

The baron called out, and a servant appeared, truly southern in her dirty and unkempt state, with wisps of hair straggling across her face. Her well-stained skirt still retained some of its original gaudiness, suggesting a country fair or a mountebank's costume.

"Is M. Duchoux at home?"

In giving this name to the unwanted child many years ago, he had indulged his sense of humor at its expense.

"You want M. Duchoux?" the servant repeated.

"Yes."

"He is in the parlor, drawing plans."

"Tell him that M. Merlin wishes to see him."

She replied in surprise: "Oh! come in, if you wish him," and shouted:

"M. Duchoux, a visitor to see you!"

The baron entered a large room darkened by half-closed shutters and received a vague impression of dirt and disorder.

A short, bald-headed man, standing at an overcrowded table, was tracing lines on a large sheet of paper. He stopped his work and came forward.

His open waistcoat, slackened trousers, and rolled-up shirt sleeves showed how hot it was, and the muddy shoes that he was wearing pointed to recent rain.

"To whom have I the honor? . . ." he asked, with a strong southern accent.

"I am M. Merlin. I have come to consult you about some building land."

"Ah! yes. Certainly."

And turning towards his wife, who was knitting in the darkened room, Duchoux said:

"Clear one of the chairs, Josephine."

Mordiane saw a young woman, already showing signs of age, as do most provincial women of twenty-five for want of attention and regular cleanliness—in fact of all those precautions which form part of a woman's toilet, helping to preserve her youthful appearance, her charm and beauty up to the age of fifty. A neckerchief hung over her shoulders, and her hair, which was beautifully thick and black but twisted up in a slipshod fashion, looked as though it was seldom brushed. With her roughened hands she removed a child's dress, a knife, a piece of string, an empty flowerpot, and a greasy plate from a chair, and offered it to the visitor.

He sat down and then noticed that on the table at which Duchoux had been working, in addition to his books and papers, there were two freshly cut lettuces, a basin, a hairbrush, a napkin, a revolver, and several dirty cups.

The architect saw him glance at these and smilingly remarked: "I am sorry that the room is rather untidy; that is the children's fault," and he drew up his chair to talk to his client.

"You are looking for a piece of land in the neighborhood of Marseille?"

Although he was at some distance away, the baron smelt the odor of garlic which people of the South exhale as flowers do their perfume.

"Was that your son I met under the plane trees?" Mordiane inquired.

"Yes, the second."

"You have two sons, then?"

"Three, sir, one a year," replied Duchoux, evidently full of pride.

The baron thought that if they all had the same perfume, their nursery must be like a real conservatory. He resumed:

"Yes, I would like a nice piece of ground near the sea, on a secluded beach. . . ."

Then Duchoux began to explain. He had ten, twenty, fifty, a hundred and more plots of land of that kind, at all prices and to suit all tastes. The words came in a torrent as he smiled and wagged his round bald head in his satisfaction.

Meanwhile the baron remembered a little woman, slight, fair and rather sad, who used to say with such yearning: "My own beloved," that the memory alone made his blood run hot in his veins. She had loved him passionately, madly, for three months; then, becoming pregnant in the absence of her husband, who was governor of a colony, she had fled into hiding, distracted by fear and despair, until the birth of the child, whom Mordiane carried off one summer evening and whom they had never seen again.

She died of consumption three years later, in the colony where she had gone to rejoin her husband. It was her son who sat beside him now, who was saying with a metallic ring in his voice:

"As for this plot, sir, it is a unique opportunity . . ."

And Mordiane remembered the other voice, light as a zephyr, murmuring:

"My own beloved; we shall never part. . . ." The memory of the gentle, blue, devoted look in those eyes came back to him as he watched the round blue but vacant eyes of this ridiculous little man who was so like his mother, and yet. . . .

Yes, he looked more and more like her every minute; his intonation, his demeanor, his actions were the same; he resembled her as a monkey resembles a man; but he was of her blood, he had many of her little habits, though distorted, irritating and revolting. The baron was in an agony of fear, haunted suddenly by that terrible, still growing resemblance, which enraged, maddened, and tortured him like a nightmare, or like bitter remorse.

"When can we look at this land together?" he stammered.

"Why, tomorrow, if you like."

"Yes, tomorrow. What time?"

"At one o'clock."

"That will be all right."

The child he had met in the avenue appeared in the door and cried:

"Father!"

No one answered him.

Mordiane stood up trembling with an intense longing to escape. That word "father" had struck him like a bullet. He was sure that this cry of "father" that reeked of garlic, that was full of the South, was meant for him. Oh! how good had been the perfume of his sweetheart of bygone days!

As Duchoux was showing him out, the baron said to him:

"Is this house yours?"

"Yes, sir, I bought it recently, and I am proud of it. I am fortune's child, sir, and I make no secret of it; I am proud of it. I owe nothing to anyone; I am the child of my own efforts, and I owe everything to myself."

The child, who had stayed on the doorstep, again cried: "Father!" the voice coming from a greater distance.

Mordiane, shivering with fear, seized with panic, fled as one does from a great danger. "He will guess who I am," he thought to himself, "he will hug me in his arms and call me 'Father' and give me a kiss reeking of garlic."

"I shall see you tomorrow, sir."

"Tomorrow, at one o'clock."

The carriage rumbled along the white road.

"Driver, take me to the station," he shouted, while two voices seemed to ring in his ears. One of them, far away and sweet, the faint, sad voice of the dead, was saying: "My own beloved"; the other a metallic, shrill, repellent voice, crying: "Father!" much as one shouts: "Stop him!" when a thief is in flight.

As he came into the club the next evening, Count d'Etreillis said to him:

"We have not seen you for three days. Have you been ill?"

"Yes, I have not been very well. I suffer from headaches occasionally. . . ."

THE MOTHER SUPERIOR'S TWENTY-FIVE FRANCS

He really was comic, old Pavilly, with his great spider legs, his little body, his long arms, and his pointed beard, surmounted by a flame of red hair on the top of his skull.

He was a clown, a peasant clown, a born clown, born to play tricks, to raise laughter, to play parts, simple parts, since he was the son of a peasant, and a peasant himself, hardly able to read. Oh, yes, the good God had created him to amuse other people, the poor devils belonging to the countryside, who had no theaters and no feasts; and he amused them with all his might and main. In the café, they stood him drinks to keep him there, and he went on drinking without turning a hair, laughing and joking, playing tricks on everyone without annoying a single soul, while the onlookers rolled with laughter.

He was so comic that, ugly as he was, the girls themselves did not resist him, they were laughing so heartily. He carried them, with quips and jests, behind a wall, into a ditch, into a stable, then he tickled them and squeezed them, keeping up such an amusing patter, that they held their sides as they repulsed him. Then he leaped about, pretending he was going to hang himself, and they writhed, with tears in their eyes; he chose his moment and tumbled them over so handily that they surrendered all, even those who had defied him, to amuse themselves.

Well, towards the end of June, he undertook to help with the harvest, at Le Hariveau's, near Rouville. For three whole weeks he delighted the harvesters, men and women, by his pranks, from morning to night. In the daytime, he appeared in the fields, in the middle of the swaths of corn; he made his appearance in an old straw hat that hid his russet topknot, gathering up the yellow corn with his long skinny arms and binding it into sheaves, then stopping to sketch a comic gesture that evoked shouts of laughter down the length of the field from the workers, whose eyes never left him. At night, he glided like a crouching beast through the straw in the barns where the women slept, and his hands prowled about, rousing shouts and creating loud disturbances. They chased him off, using their sabots as weapons, and he fled on all fours, like a fantastic monkey, amid explosions of mirth from the entire room.

On the last day, as the wagonload of harvesters, adorned with ribbons and bagpipes, shouting and singing and joyously drunk, were going down the wide white road, drawn at the slow pace of six dappled horses, led by a youngster in a smock, with a cockade in his cap, Pavilly, in the middle of sprawling women, was dancing the dance of a drunken satyr, that kept the young rascals of boys openmouthed on the banksides of the farms, and the peasants lost in wonder at his incredible anatomy.

All at once, as they reached the fence of Le Hariveau's farm, he made a bound with upflung arms, but as he fell back he unluckily struck against the side of the long cart, went headlong over, fell on to the wheel, and bounced off on to the road.

His comrades flung themselves out. He moved no more, one eye shut, the other open, ghastly with fright, his great limbs stretched out in the dust.

When they touched his right leg, he began to cry out, and when they tried to stand him up, he fell down.

"I'll be bound he's broken his leg," cried a man.

He had indeed a broken leg.

Farmer Le Hariveau had him laid on a table; and a rider hurried to Rouville to find a doctor, who arrived an hour later.

The farmer was a very generous man, and he announced that he would pay for the man to be treated at the hospital.

So the doctor carried Pavilly off in his carriage, and deposited him in a whitewashed dormitory, where his fracture was set.

As soon as he realized that he would not die of it, and that he was going to be cared for, cured, pampered, and nourished, with nothing to do, lying on his back between two sheets, Pavilly was seized with an overwhelming merriment, and he began to laugh a silent perpetual laughter that revealed his decaying teeth.

As soon as a sister approached the bed, he grimaced contentedly at her, winking his eye, twisting his mouth, and moving his nose, which was very long and which he could move as he pleased. His neighbors in the dormitory, very ill as they were, could not refrain from laughing, and the sister in charge often came to his bedside to enjoy a quarter of an hour's amusement. He invented the most comic tricks for her, and quite new jests, and as he had in him the instinct for every sort of barnstorming, he turned devout to please her and spoke of the good God with the grave air of a man that knows that there are moments to which jests are inappropriate.

One day, he bethought himself of singing songs to her. She was delighted and came oftener; then, to turn his voice to good account, she brought him a book of hymns. Then he might be seen sitting up in his bed, for he was beginning to move himself about again, intoning in a falsetto voice the praises of the Eternal

Father, of Mary, and of the Holy Ghost, while the stout good sister, standing at his feet, beat time with one finger as she gave him the key. As soon as he could walk, the mother superior offered to keep him a little longer to sing the offices in the chapel, and serve at Mass, performing in this way the functions of a sacristan. He accepted. And for a whole month he could be seen, clad in a white surplice, limping slightly, intoning responses and psalms with such graceful bendings of the head that the number of the faithful grew and people deserted the parish church to attend vespers at the hospital.

But as everything comes to an end in this world, it became necessary to dismiss him when he was quite cured. The mother superior, by way of thanking him, made him a present of twenty-five francs.

As soon as Pavilly found himself in the street with this money in his pocket, he began to think what he should do. Return to the village? Certainly not before he had a drink, which had not happened to him for a long time, and he entered a café. He did not come to town more than once or twice a year, and he cherished, of one of those visits in particular, the confused and intoxicating remembrance of a debauch.

So he ordered a glass of cognac, which he swallowed at a gulp to lubricate his throat, then he poured down another to enjoy the taste of it.

As soon as the brandy, strong and fiery, had touched his palate and his tongue, reawakening the more sharply because of his long abstinence the well-loved and desired sensation of alcohol, caressing, stinging, spicing, and burning his mouth, he realized that he would drink the whole bottle, and he asked at once what it would cost, in order to save money on the separate glasses. They charged it to him at three francs, which he paid, then he set himself to get drunk with a contented mind.

He set about it with a certain method, however, being desirous of retaining enough sensibility to enjoy other pleasures. So as soon as he felt himself on the point of seeing the chimney pieces nod, he got up and went away, with faltering steps, his bottle under his arm, in search of a brothel.

He found it, not without difficulty, after having inquired of a wagoner who did not know it, a postman who directed him wrongly, a baker who began to curse and treated him as a filthy fellow, and, at last, a soldier who obligingly conducted him there, impressing on him to choose "the Queen."

Pavilly, although it was hardly noon, walked into this house of delights, where he was received by a servant who tried to turn him out. But he made her laugh by grimacing at her, showed her three francs, the ordinary price for the special entertainments of the place, and followed her with some difficulty up a very dark staircase which led to the first floor.

When he found himself in a room, he called for the Queen, and awaited her, swallowing another drink from the bottle itself.

The door opened, a girl appeared. She was tall, plump, red-faced, enormous. With an unerring glance, the glance of a connoisseur, she took the measure of the drunkard sprawling on a chair, and said to him:

"Aren't you ashamed to come at this time?"

He stammered:

"Why, princess?"

"Disturbing a lady before she's even had her meal."

He tried to laugh.

"There's no time to a brave man."

"There's no time for getting tipsy, neither, you old mug."

Pavilly lost his temper.

"I'm not a mug, to begin with, and I'm not tipsy neither."

"Not tipsy!"

"No, I'm not tipsy."

"Not tipsy, you couldn't stand on your feet even."

She regarded him with the savage anger of a woman whose companions are all dining.

He got himself up.

"Look at me, I'll dance a polka, I will."

And to prove his stability, he climbed on a chair, made a pirouette, and jumped on the bed, where his great muddy shoes plastered two frightful stains.

"Oh, you dirty beast," cried the girl.

Rushing at him, she drove her fist in his stomach, giving him such a blow that Pavilly lost his balance, seesawed over the foot of the couch, turned a complete caper, and fell back on the chest of drawers, dragging with him basin and water jug; then he rolled on the ground, uttering wild shouts.

The noise was so violent and his cries so piercing that the whole house came running, Monsieur, Madame, the servants, and all the members of the establishment.

Monsieur tried at first to pick the man up, but as soon as he had got him on his feet, the peasant lost his balance again, then began yelling that he had broken his leg, the other leg, the good one, the good one!

It was true. They ran to fetch a doctor. It was the very doctor who had attended Pavilly at Farmer Le Hariveau's.

"What, is it you again?" said he. "What's the matter with you?"

"It's the other leg that's got broken, too, Doctor."

"How did it happen, my man?"

"A wench."

Everyone was listening. The girls in their loose wrappers, their mouths still greasy from their interrupted meal, Madame furious, Monsieur uneasy.

"This is going to look bad," said the doctor. "You know that the town council regards you with small favor. You'll have to contrive to keep this business from getting about."

"What's to be done?" asked Monsieur.

"Well, the best thing to do would be to send this man to the hospital, which he's just left, by the way, and pay for his treatment."

Monsieur answered:

"I'd much rather pay than have a scandal."

So, half an hour later, Pavilly returned, drunk and moaning, to the dormitory he had left an hour earlier.

The mother superior flung up her arms, grieved because she was very fond of him, and smiling because she was not displeased to see him again.

"Well, my good man, what's the matter with you?"

"The other leg broken, Sister dear."

"Oh, so you've been climbing on loads of straw again, have you, you old mountebank?"

And Pavilly, confused and shy, stammered:

"No . . . no. . . . Not this time . . . not this time. . . . No . . . no . . . It's not my fault . . . not my fault. . . . It was a straw mattress did it."

She could not get any other explanation of the affair, and she never knew that her twenty-five francs was responsible for this relapse.

FORBIDDEN FRUIT

Before marriage they had loved each other chastely in the starlight. At first there was a charming meeting on the shore of the ocean. He found her delicious, the rosy young girl who passed him with her bright umbrellas and fresh costumes on the marine background. He loved this blonde, fragile creature in her setting of blue waves and immense skies. And he confounded the tenderness which this scarcely fledged woman caused to be born in him with the vague and powerful emotion awakened in his soul, in his heart and in his veins by the lovely salt air and the great seascape full of sun and waves.

She loved him because he paid her attention, because he was young and rich enough, genteel and delicate. She loved him because it is natural for young ladies to love young men who say tender words to them.

Then for three months they lived side by side, eye to eye and hand to hand. The greeting which they exchanged in the morning before the bath, in the freshness of the new day, and the adieu of the evening upon the sand under the stars, in the warmth of the calm night, murmured low and still lower, had already the taste of kisses, although their lips had never met.

They dreamed of each other as soon as they were asleep, thought of each other as soon as they awoke and, without saying so, called for and desired each other with their whole soul and body.

After marriage they adored each other above everything on earth. It was at first a kind of sensual, indefatigable rage, then an exalted tenderness made of palpable poesy, of caresses already refined and of inventions both genteel and ungenteel. All their looks signified something impure, and all their gestures recalled to them the ardent intimacy of the night.

Now, without confessing it, without realizing it, perhaps, they commenced to weary of one another. They loved each other, it is true, but there was nothing more to reveal, nothing more to do that had not often been done, nothing more to learn from each other, not even a new word of love, an unforeseen motion or an intonation, which sometimes is more expressive than a known word too often repeated.

They forced themselves, however, to relight the flame, enfeebled from the first embraces. They invented some new and tender artifice each day, some simple or complicated ruse, in the vain attempt to renew in their hearts the unappeasable ardor of the first days and in their veins the flame of the nuptial month.

From time to time, by dint of whipping their desire, they again found an hour of factitious excitement which was immediately followed by a disgusting lassitude.

They tried moonlight walks under the leaves in the sweetness of the night, the poesy of the cliffs bathed in mist, the excitement of public festivals.

Then one morning Henrietta said to Paul:

"Will you take me to dine at an inn?"

"Why, yes, my dearie."

"In a very well-known inn?"

"Yes."

He looked at her, questioning with his eye, understanding well that she had something in mind which she had not spoken.

She continued: "You know, an inn—how shall I explain it?—in a gallant inn, where people make appointments to meet each other?"

He smiled. "Yes. I understand, a private room in a large café?"

"That is it. But in a large café where you are known, where you have already taken supper—no, dinner—that is—I mean—I want—no, I do not dare say it!"

"Speak out, chérie; between us what can it matter? We are not like those who have little secrets from each other."

"No, I dare not."

"Oh! Come, now! Don't be so innocent. Say it."

"Well—oh! Well—I wish—I wish to be taken for your mistress—and that the waiters, who do not know that you are married, may look upon me as your mistress, and you, too—that for an hour you believe me your mistress in that very place where you have remembrances of—— That's all! And I myself will believe that I am your mistress. I want to commit a great sin—to deceive you—with yourself— there! It is very bad, but that is what I want to do. Do not make me blush—I feel that I am blushing—imagine—my wanting to take the trouble to dine with you in a place not quite the thing—in a private room where people devote them- selves to love every evening—every evening. It is very bad. I am as red as a peony! Don't look at me!"

He laughed, very much amused, and responded:

"Yes, we will go this evening to a very chic place where I am known."

Toward seven o'clock they mounted the staircase of a large café on the boulevard, he smiling, with the air of a conqueror, she timid, veiled, but delighted. When they were in a little room furnished with four armchairs and a large sofa covered with red velvet, the steward, in black clothes, entered and presented the bill of fare. Paul passed it to his wife.

"What do you wish to eat?" he said.

"I don't know; what do they have that is good here?"

Then he read off the list of dishes while taking off his overcoat, which he handed to a waiter. Then he said:

"Serve this menu: Bisque soup, deviled chicken, sides of hare, duck, American style, vegetable salad and dessert. We will drink champagne."

The steward smiled and looked at the young lady. He took the card, murmuring: "Will Monsieur Paul have a cordial or some champagne?"

"Champagne, very dry."

Henrietta was happy to find that this man knew her husband's name. They sat down side by side upon the sofa and began to eat.

Ten candles lighted the room, reflected in a great mirror, mutilated by the thousands of names traced on it with a diamond, making on the clear crystal a kind of huge cobweb.

Henrietta drank glass after glass to animate her, although she felt giddy from the first one. Paul, excited by certain memories, kissed his wife's hand repeatedly. Her eyes were brilliant.

She felt strangely moved by this suspicious situation; she was excited and happy, although she felt a little defiled. Two grave waiters, mute, accustomed to seeing everything and forgetting all, entered only when it was necessary and went out in the moments of overflow, going and coming quickly and softly.

Toward the middle of the dinner Henrietta was tipsy, completely tipsy, and Paul, in his gaiety, pressed her knee with all his force. She prattled now, boldly, her cheeks red, her look lively and dizzy.

"Oh, come, Paul," she said, "confess now, won't you? I want to know all."

"What do you mean, chérie?"

"I dare not say it."

"But you must always——"

"Have you had mistresses—many of them—before me?"

He hesitated, a little perplexed, not knowing whether he ought to conceal his good fortunes or boast of them.

She continued: "Oh! I beg you to tell me; have you had many?"

"Why, some."

"How many?"

"I don't know. How can one know such things?"

"You cannot count them?"

"Why, no!"

"Oh! Then you have had very many?"

"Yes."

"How many, do you suppose?—somewhere near——"

"I don't know at all, my dear. Some years I had many and some only a few."

"How many a year, should you say?"

"Sometimes twenty or thirty, sometimes four or five only."

"Oh! That makes more than a hundred women in all."

"Yes, somewhere near."

"Oh! How disgusting!"

"Why disgusting?"

"Because it is disgusting—when one thinks of all those women—bare—and always—always the same thing. Oh! It is disgusting all the same—more than a hundred women."

He was shocked that she thought it disgusting and responded with that superior air which men assume to make women understand that they have said something foolish:

"Well, that is curious! If it is disgusting to have a hundred women, it is equally disgusting to have one."

"Oh no, not at all!"

"Why not?"

"Because with one woman there is intrigue, there is a love that attaches you to her, while with a hundred women there is filthiness, misconduct. I cannot understand how a man can meddle with all those girls who are so foul."

"No, they are very neat."

"One cannot be neat, carrying on a trade like that."

"On the contrary, it is because of their trade that they are neat."

"Oh, pshaw! When one thinks of the nights they pass with others! It is ignoble!"

"It is no more ignoble than drinking from a glass from which I know not who drank this morning, and that has been less thoroughly washed—you may be certain of it."

"Oh, be still; you are revolting."

"But why ask me then if I have had mistresses?"

"Then tell me, were your mistresses all girls, all of them—the whole hundred?"

"Why, no—no. Some were actresses—some little working girls—and some women of the world."

"How many of them were women of the world?"

"Six."

"Only six?"

"Yes."

"Were they pretty?"

"Yes, of course."

"Prettier than the girls?"

"No."

"Which did you prefer, girls or women of the world?"

"Women of the world."

"Oh! How filthy! Why?"

"Because I do not care much for amateur talent."

"Oh! Horror! You are abominable, do you know it? But tell me, is it very amusing to pass from one to another like that?"

"Yes, rather."

"Very?"

"Very."

"What is there amusing about it? Is it because they do not resemble each other?"

"They do not."

"Ah! The women do not resemble each other?"

"Not at all."

"In nothing?"

"In nothing."

"That is strange! In what respect do they differ?"

"In every respect."

"In body?"

"Yes, in body."

"In the whole body?"

"Yes, in the whole body."

"And in what else?"

"Why, in the manner of—of embracing, of speaking, of saying the least thing."

"Ah! And it is very amusing, this changing?"

"Yes."

"And are men different too?"

"That I do not know."

"You do not know?"

"No."

"They must be different."

"Yes, without doubt."

She remained pensive, her glass of champagne in her hand. It was full, and she drank it at a draught; then placing the glass upon the table, she threw both arms around her husband's neck and murmured in his mouth:

"Oh, my dear, how I love you!" He seized her in a passionate embrace.

A waiter, who was entering, drew back, closing the door, and the service was interrupted for about five minutes.

When the steward again appeared, with a grave, dignified air, bringing in the fruits for the dessert, she was holding another glassful between her fingers and, looking to the bottom of the yellow, transparent liquid, as if to see there things unknown and dreamed of, she murmured with a thoughtful voice:

"Oh yes! It must be very amusing, all the same!"

THE PEDDLER

To our still young and inexperienced minds, how many fleeting associations, trifling things, chance meetings, humble dramas that we witness, guess at, or suspect, become as it were, guiding threads that lead gradually to a knowledge of the desolating truth about life.

As I dream idly of the past while roaming aimlessly about the country, my head in the clouds, little forgotten things, grave and gay, flash constantly through my mind and then take their flight like the hedge birds on my path.

This summer as I was wandering along a road in Savoy that overlooks the right bank of the Lake of Bourget, gazing upon the mass of shimmering blue water, water of a most unusual blue, pale and streaked with the slanting rays of the setting sun, my heart was stirred with the emotion I have always felt, since childhood, for the smooth surface of lake, river, and sea. On the other bank of the immense watery plain whose ends stretched away out of sight—one in the direction of the Rhône and the other towards Bourget—the high jagged mountain rose to the last peak of the Dent-du-Chat. On either side of the road the grapevines reached out from tree to tree, smothering the slender branches round which they twined under their leaves; spreading over the fields in green, yellow, and red garlands dotted with clusters of black grapes, which swung gaily between the tree trunks.

The road was dusty, white, and deserted. Suddenly a man bending under a heavy load stepped out from the grove of tall trees that encloses the village of St. Innocent, and came in my direction, leaning on a stick. As he approached I saw he was a hawker, one of those wandering peddlers who sell from door to door throughout the countryside, and suddenly a memory of bygone days, a trifle, flashed into my mind, simply a meeting at night between Argenteuil and Paris when I was twenty-five.

At that time boating was the pleasure of my life. I had a room at a cheap eating house in Argenteuil, and every evening I caught the civil-service train, that long slow train which deposits at station after station a crowd of fat, heavy men carrying small parcels, whose unattractive figures are due to lack of exercise and the shocking fit of their trousers to the chairs provided in government offices. The train, which smelled of offices, cardboard boxes, and official documents, landed me at Argenteuil, where my yawl awaited me, ready to skim over the water. With long strokes I set off for Bezons, Chatou, Epinay, or St. Ouen, where I dined. Then I went back, put away my boat, and, when there was a full moon, started off on foot for Paris.

Well, one night, on the white road, I saw a man walking in front of me. Oh, I was constantly meeting those night travelers of the Parisian suburbs so much dreaded by belated citizens. This man went slowly on before me, weighed down by a heavy load.

I soon overtook him, my footsteps echoing on the road. He stopped, turned round, then crossed the road as if to avoid me. As I was hurrying by he called out: "Hullo! Good evening, sir."

I replied: "Good evening, mate."

He went on: "Are you going far?"

"To Paris."

"You won't be long, you are going at a good pace. I can't walk quickly, my load is too heavy."

I slackened my pace. Why was the man talking to me? What was he carrying in that big bundle? Vague suspicions of crime darted through my mind and made me curious. Every morning the newspapers contain so many accounts of crimes committed in this very spot, at Gennevilliers, that some of them must be true. Such things are not invented merely to amuse readers—all this catalogue of arrests and varied misdeeds which fill up the columns.

However, this man's voice sounded rather scared, not at all bold, and up to the present his manner had been more courteous than aggressive.

In my turn I began to question him:

"And you, are you going far?"

"No farther than Asnières."

"Do you live at Asnières?"

"Yes, sir, I am a peddler by trade and I live at Asnières."

He had left the sidewalk where the foot passengers walk in the daytime under the shade of the trees and moved up towards the middle of the road. I did the same. We eyed each other suspiciously, holding our sticks in our hands. When I got near enough I felt quite reassured. He apparently felt the same, for he asked:

"Would you mind going a little slower?"

"Why?"

"Because I don't like this road by night. I am carrying goods on my back; and two are always better than one. Two men together are seldom attacked."

I knew that he was right and that he was afraid. So yielding to his wish, the stranger and I walked along side by side, at one o'clock in the morning on the road from Argenteuil to Asnières.

"Why, when it is so risky, are you going home so late?" I asked my companion.

He told me all about it. He had not intended to go back that evening, as he had set out that very morning with a big enough stock to last three or four days. But sales had been very good, so good that he was obliged to return home immediately in order to be able to deliver orders next day.

He explained with real satisfaction that he was an able salesman, having the gift of words, and that he managed to dispose of things that were awkward to carry by the display of trifles and a fund of amusing patter.

He added: "I have a shop at Asnières. My wife keeps it."

"Oh! so you are married?"

"Yes, sir, fifteen months ago. I have found a good little wife. She will be surprised when she sees me back tonight."

He told me about his marriage, how he had wanted the girl for over two years but she had not been able to make up her mind.

Since her childhood she had kept a small shop at the corner of the street where she sold all sorts of things: ribbons, flowers in summer, and chiefly very pretty shoe buckles, with other trifles of which she was able to make a specialty owing to the kindness of a manufacturer. She was well known in Asnières as Bluette, so called because she often wore blue. She earned good money because she was very capable in everything she did. She did not seem to be very well at present, and he thought she must be *enceinte*, but was not sure. Their business was thriving, and his special job was to travel about showing samples to the small shopkeepers in the neighboring districts; he was becoming a kind of traveling commission agent for certain manufacturers, and at the same time he worked for himself.

"And you—what do you do?" he said.

I started to bluff. I said that I had a sailing boat at Argenteuil and two racing yawls, that I came for a row every evening and, as I was fond of exercise, I sometimes returned to Paris, where I was engaged in professional work which, I led him to infer, paid me well.

He remarked: "Well! Well! if I had the tin you have, I would not amuse myself by trudging the roads at night. It isn't safe along here."

He cast a sidelong glance at me and I wondered whether, after all, he was not some cunning evildoer anxious to avoid useless risk.

I felt reassured when he murmured: "Not so fast, if you please. My pack is heavy."

As we saw the houses of Asnières in the distance he said: "I am near home now, for we don't sleep at the shop, which is guarded at night by a dog that is the equal of four men. Besides, rooms are far too dear in the center of the town. Now, listen sir; you have rendered me a great service, for I don't feel happy on the road with my pack. So now you must come in and drink a glass of warmed wine with my wife—if she wakes up, that is to say, for she sleeps soundly and does not like to be roused. Then without my pack I am not afraid, so, thick stick in hand, I'll see you to the gates of the city."

I declined the invitation; he insisted, and I persisted in my refusal; then he got so excited about it, was so genuinely distressed, and asked me with an air of wounded pride "whether I would not drink with a man like him," that I ended by giving in and followed him along a lonely road to one of those big dilapidated houses to be found on the outskirts of the suburbs.

I hesitated at the door. The big barracklike building must be a thieves' resort, a den of suburban robbers, but the peddler made me go first through the unlocked door and, with his hand on my shoulders, guided me through complete darkness while I groped towards a staircase, feeling that at any moment I might fall through some hole into a cellar.

When I had struck the first step he said: "Go up, we live on the sixth story."

I found a box of very large wax matches in my pocket and was able to light up the darkness. He followed me, panting under the weight of his pack as he repeated: "It's a long way up! It's a long way!"

When we were at the top of the house, he took out the key, fastened to his coat by a string, opened the door, and bade me enter.

The room was simply whitewashed; there was a table in the middle, six chairs, and a kitchen cupboard against the wall.

"I am going to call my wife," he said, "then I'll go to the cellar to fetch some wine; it won't keep up here."

He went over to one of the two doors opening out of the room, and called: "Bluette! Bluette!"

As Bluette made no reply he shouted louder: "Bluette! Bluette!"

Then, banging at the door with his fists, he muttered: "Confound you, won't you wake up?"

He waited and put his ear to the keyhole and said in a quieter tone:

"Well, never mind, if she is asleep, I must let her sleep. I am going to fetch the wine; I'll be back in two minutes."

He disappeared. I sat down and made the best of a bad job.

What had I come for? All of a sudden I gave a start, for I heard low voices, cautious, almost silent, movements in the wife's bedroom.

The devil! I must have fallen into a trap! Why had all the noise made by her husband, that banging on the door, not wakened this Bluette? It must have been a signal to his accomplices: "There is a mouse in the trap. I'll watch the exit, you do the rest." They were getting excited in the room, they were turning the key in the lock. My heart beat rapidly and I retreated to the far end of the room, murmuring: "Well, I must defend myself!" and, seizing a chair in both hands, I prepared for a lively struggle.

The door opened slightly and a hand appeared, holding it ajar; then a head, a man's head wearing a round felt hat, slid along between the door and the wall, and two eyes were staring at me. Then, so quickly that I had not time to think of defending myself, the man, the supposed criminal, a big chap with bare feet, evidently hurriedly dressed, without a tie, his shoes in his hand, a fine-looking specimen, indeed, who might be described as almost a gentleman, made one bound for the door and disappeared down the stairs.

I sat down again. This was beginning to be interesting. I waited for the husband, who was a long time getting the wine. At last I heard him coming upstairs and the sound of his steps made me laugh one of those forlorn laughs so difficult to suppress.

He came into the room bringing two bottles and asked: "Is my wife still asleep? You have not heard her moving about?"

I knew that she must be listening, and I said:

"No, I have heard nothing."

Then he called again: "Pauline!" but there was still no reply, no sound of anyone moving, so he explained to me: "You see, she doesn't like me to come home at night and have a drop with a friend."

"So you think she is not asleep?"

"Of course, she is not." He seemed annoyed but said: "Well, let us have a drink," and all at once he seemed to be quite determined to go on until both bottles were empty.

This time I was decided; I drank a glass and got up to go. He no longer suggested accompanying me, and, glancing at his wife's door with a sullen scowl, the scowl of anger peculiar to the lower classes, of a brute whose violence is held in check, he muttered: "She will have to open the door when you are gone."

I stared at the coward, now furious with a rage he could not explain, that was perhaps due to some obscure presentiment, the instinct of the betrayed male who dislikes closed doors. He had talked about her kindly, now he was certainly going to beat her.

He shouted as he shook the door again: "Pauline!"

A sleepy voice replied from the other side of the wall: "Eh! What?"

"Didn't you hear me come in?"

"No, I was asleep; go to hell."

"Open the door."

"When you are alone. I don't like you to bring men back with you at night for a drink."

Then I left, stumbling down the stairs, just as the other had done, whose accomplice I was. And as I started off for Paris, I thought that in that wretched home I had witnessed a scene of the eternal drama which is being played every day, in every form, in every country.

OLD OBJECTS

My dear Colette,

I don't know whether you still remember a line of verse by M. Sainte-Beuve which we read together and which I've never forgotten. For to me that line is full of meaning, frequently comforting my poor heart, and the more so recently.

To be born, to live and to die in the same house!

I am now all alone in this house where I was born, where I have lived, and in which I hope to die. Not that it is particularly gay every day, but it is pleasant, for here I am living with memories.

My son Henry is a lawyer; every year he comes to spend two months with me. Jeanne and her husband live at the other end of France, so it is I who visit her every fall. I am therefore alone here, all alone, but surrounded by familiar objects which constantly speak to me of my family, of the dead, and of the living who are far away.

I am old, and I do not read any longer; but I think all the time, or rather, I dream. Oh! I don't dream the way I used to when I was young. You remember our wild imaginations, the adventures we used to concoct in our twenty-year-old brains, and all the vistas of anticipated happiness!

None of that actually transpired: or rather, something else occurred, less charming, less romantic, but enough for those who can take courageously what life has brought them.

Do you know why we women are so often unhappy? It's because in our youth we had been taught to put too much faith in happiness! We are never brought up with the idea of fighting, struggling, suffering. So, at the first calamity our hearts are broken. We expect confidently a multitude of happy events; and all we get is an occasional approximation of happiness. And we immediately burst into tears.

Happiness, the true happiness of our dreams, I have never come to know it. It doesn't consist at all in terms of tremendous felicity, for that sort of felicity is rare and brief, but it is to be found rather in the unending expectation of a succession of joys which never materialize. Happiness is pleasant anticipation; it is the horizon of hope; it is, consequently, everlasting illusion. Yes, my dear, illusions are the only good things; and even in my old age I have them still and every day, the only difference being that their nature has changed, since my desires are also different. So, as I was telling you, I spend most of my time dreaming. What else would I do? I have two methods, which I will give you; they might be of some use to you.

The first is quite simple. It consists in sitting down before my fireplace in a low armchair which is easy on my old bones, and to turn toward my past.

How short life is, especially one spent entirely in the same place:

To be born, to live and to die in the same house!

Memories accumulate, are crammed together, and when you get old it sometimes seems that you were young only ten days ago. Yes, time has slipped by as if it were a matter of one day only—morning, noon, evening; finally night comes, night without a dawn.

As you look at the fire for hours on end, the past comes back as if it were only yesterday. You hardly know where you are; dreams carry you away and you live again your entire existence.

And frequently I have the illusion of being a girl again, I get to such an extent whiffs of the past, sensations and outbursts of youth, a quickening of the pulse, all the vitality of eighteen; and I have, clear as new realities, visions of things forgotten.

I relive most frequently my walks as a young girl. The other evening here in my armchair in front of the fire I recaptured vividly a sunset on Mont-Saint-Michel and immediately afterwards hunting on horseback in the forest of Urville, with the fragrance of wet sand and of dewy leaves, and the warmth of the sun plunging into the sea, and the moist mellowness of the first rays while I galloped in the thickets. Everything that went through my head at the time, my romantic exaltation before the infinite reaches of the sea, my happy and intense pleasure at the leaves brushing against my cheeks, my most trivial ideas, everything—the furtive reveries, desires, and feelings—everything, everything came back to me as if I were still there, as if fifty years had not intervened, fifty years which have cooled off my blood and substantially changed my hopes. But my other way of reliving the past is by far the better.

You may or may not know, my dear Colette, that nothing is destroyed in our house. Under the roof we have a storage room which we call "the room for old objects." Everything which is no longer used is thrown into it. I go up there and look around. And I find a lot of worthless objects which I had forgotten and which remind me of many things. Not at all those good friendly pieces of furniture that we have known since childhood and with which are associated recollections of events, joys or sorrows, red-letter days of our lives—pieces which because they have been a part of our lives, have assumed a sort of personality and physiognomy, which are the companions of our happy or somber hours, the only companions, alas, which we are certain not to lose, the only ones which will not die like the others, whose features, affectionate eyes, mouth, and voice have disappeared forever. Whereas I find in the mass of worn-out bric-a-brac these old, trivial, insignificant objects which for forty years had served us without being noticed and which, when you suddenly run across them again, seem as important and significant as faithful old friends. They produce on me the effect of people one has known for a long time without really knowing them and who suddenly of an evening, à propos of nothing, start to talk endlessly, to reveal their entire being and their innermost selves, which had hitherto remained unsuspected.

So I go from one to the other of these old objects with slight pangs of the heart. I say to myself, "Now *that* I broke on the evening Paul went to Lyons," or else, "Ah, here is Mother's little lantern that she used when she went to vespers on a winter evening."

There are even things in that attic which have no meaning for me, which come from my grandparents, things, consequently, which no one living today knew and whose history and adventures no one knows, whose owners even have been forgotten. No one has seen the hands which handled them or the eyes which looked on them. Those inspire me with long meditations. To me they are abandoned objects whose last friends are dead.

You, my dear Colette, must hardly understand all this, and you will smile at this nonsense, at my sentimental and childish idiosyncrasies. You are a Parisian, and Parisians don't know introspection, these inner musings. You lead your lives in public, with all your thoughts exteriorized. But I, living alone, can speak to you only of myself. In your answer please speak to me a little of yourself, so that I may be able to put myself in your place, as tomorrow you may be able to put yourself in mine.

But you will never completely understand M. Sainte-Beuve's line:

To be born, to live and to die in the same house!

Affectionate kisses, dear friend,

ADELAIDE

THE OLD MAN

A warm autumn sun fell on the barnyard over the tall beech trees bordering the ditches. Under the grass close-cropped by the cows the earth was moist, full of the recent rain. It gave way under foot with a sloshing sound. The heavy-laden apple trees scattered their pale green fruit over the deep green of the grass.

Four young heifers attached in a line were grazing, and they mooed once in a while toward the house. The fowl added color and motion to the manure heap in front of the stable and scratched, bustled about, and cackled, while the two roosters, crowing incessantly, hunted for worms and called their hens with a sharp cluck every time they found one.

The wooden gate opened. A man entered, probably no more than forty, but he looked sixty, wrinkled, gnarled, walking with wide slow steps, weighted by heavy wooden shoes full of straw. His outsized arms hung down along his body. As he approached the farm, a yellow mongrel tied to a large pear tree beside a barrel, which served as doghouse, wagged his tail, then began to bark joyously. The man cried out,

"Down, Finot!"

The dog obeyed.

A peasant woman came out of the house. Her bony figure, wide and flat, was revealed under a loose woolen jacket tied at the waist. A gray skirt, too short, reached the calves of her blue-stockinged legs, and she too wore straw-filled wooden shoes. A once white bonnet, now yellow, covered part of her hair, pulled tight over her head. Her dark face, thin, ugly, toothless, showed that wild animal-like expression peasant faces often have.

The man asked, "How is he?"

The woman replied, "The priest says it's the end. He won't last the night."

They both entered the house.

After crossing the kitchen they went into the bedroom, low, dark, with a single pane covered by a ragged piece of Norman calico barely admitting a bit of light. The big beams of the ceiling, darkened by the weather, black and smoked, crossed the room, supporting the thin attic floor, where legions of rats scurried about day and night.

The earthen floor, rough and damp, seemed soft, and in the rear of the room the bed showed dimly white. A regular, rough sound—hard breathing, gasping, whistling, with a gargling like a broken water pump—came from the shadowy bed on which an old man was dying, the peasant woman's father.

The man and the woman drew near and looked at the dying man with their placid, resigned expressions.

The son-in-law said, "This time it's the end. He won't even last till night."

The woman answered, "He's been gurgling like that since noon."

Then they were silent. The father's eyes were closed, his face was earth-colored, so dry it seemed wooden. Through his partly opened mouth came his hard choppy breath, and the gray linen sheet rose over his chest at each inhalation.

After a long silence the son-in-law said, "Nothing for it but to leave him be. I can't do nothing. All the same it's a shame for the plants, seeing it's good weather, 'cause they'll have to be transplanted tomorrow."

His wife seemed alarmed at this thought. She reflected a few moments, then declared,

"Since he's going to die, we won't bury him before Saturday. You'll have tomorrow for the planting."

The peasant cogitated, then said, "Yes, but tomorrow we've got to invite everybody to the funeral, and it'll take me five or six hours to go from Tourville to Manetot to tell the folks."

The woman after two or three minutes of silence declared, "It's not three o'clock yet so you can start out tonight and tell all the folks to Tourville. You can say he's passed away since he won't last the afternoon."

The man remained undecided for a few moments, weighing the advantages and the consequences of the idea. At last he said,

"All right. I'll go."

He started out, then turned around and said,

"You've got nothing to do, so pick some cooking apples and make four dozen turnovers for the folks that'll come to the funeral, seeing how we've got to have some cheer. You can light the oven with the sticks in the cider shed. They're dry."

And he left the bedroom, went into the kitchen, opened the buffet, took an enormous loaf of bread, carefully cut off a slice, gathered up in his hand all the crumbs that had fallen on the little table, and threw them into his mouth so as not to lose anything. Then he took a bit of salted butter on the tip of his knife from the bottom of a brown earthenware dish, spread it on his bread, and began to eat it, slowly, as he did everything.

And he walked back over the barnyard, quieted the dog, which had begun to bark again, went out to the road which skirted his ditch, and started out in the direction of Tourville.

Left alone, the woman set to work. She uncovered the flour bin, and prepared the dough. She kneaded it a long time, turning it over and over, patting it, crushing it, pounding it. Then she formed it into a large yellowish-white ball which she left on the corner of the table.

Next she went to get the apples, and, in order not to damage the tree with the pole, she climbed into it from a stool. She chose the apples with care, taking only the ripest, putting them into her apron.

A voice called to her from the road, "Hello there, Mme. Chicot!"

She turned around. It was a neighbor, Osime Favet, the mayor, who was on the way to fertilize his fields, sitting with his legs hanging on the pile of fertilizer.

"What can I do for you, Master Osime?"

"How's your father?"

She answered, "He's just about gone. The funeral's to be Saturday at seven o'clock, on account of the transplanting."

The neighbor replied, "All right. Good luck! Look after yourself."

She matched his good wishes with, "Thanks. You too." Then she continued picking apples.

As soon as she was back in the house she went to see her father, expecting to find him dead. But from the doorway she could hear his noisy monotonous rattle, and thinking it useless to approach the bed, so as not to lose time, she began to prepare the turnovers.

She wrapped the apples, one by one, in a thin layer of pastry and lined them up on the edge of the table. When she had made forty-eight balls, in rows of dozens, she thought of preparing supper, and she hung her kettle over the fire to cook the potatoes. For she had decided that it was useless to light the oven that day, having the entire day following to finish preparations.

Her husband returned about five o'clock. As soon as he had crossed the threshold, he asked,

"Is it over?"

She answered, "Not yet. He's still gurgling."

They went to see. The old man was in exactly the same state. His harsh breathing, regular as a clock movement, had neither accelerated nor diminished. It came and went every second, varying slightly in sound, according to whether the air entered or left his chest. His son-in-law looked at him, then said,

"He'll snuff out like a candle without you and me noticing."

They went back to the kitchen and, without speaking, sat down to supper. After the soup they ate bread and butter, then, as soon as the dishes were washed, they returned to the dying man's room.

The woman, holding a smoky little lamp, waved it in front of her father's face. But for the noisy breathing, one would have surely thought him dead.

The peasants' bed was hidden at the other end of the room, in a kind of alcove.

They went to bed without saying a word, put out the light, closed their eyes. And soon two uneven snores, one deeper, the other sharper, accompanied the continuous rattle of the dying man.

Rats ran in the attic.

The husband was awake with the first pale rays of day. His father-in-law was still alive. He shook his wife, uneasy at the resistance of the old man.

"Say, Phémie, he doesn't want to go. What would you do?" He valued his wife's good judgment. She answered,

"He'll not last the day for sure. There's nothing to fear. As long as the mayor doesn't mind us burying him tomorrow anyway, seeing they did it for old man Renard, who died just at sowing time."

He was convinced by the soundness of the reasoning, and he left for the fields.

His wife baked the turnovers, then did all the farm chores.

At noon the old man was not dead. The day helpers hired for the transplanting came in a body to look at the old man, who seemed reluctant to go. Each one had his say, then they went off to the fields.

At six o'clock when they returned the father was still breathing. His son-in-law was now frightened.

"What would you do now, Phémie?"

She did not know what to do either. They went to see the mayor, who was willing to be accommodating and would authorize the burial next day. The public health official they went to see gave his word also, to oblige Master Chicot, that he would predate the death certificate. The man and the woman went home easy.

They went to bed and to sleep as the night before, mingling their sonorous breathing with the feebler breathing of the old man.

When they awakened, he was not dead. This time they were thoroughly upset. They stood at the father's bedside considering him with distrust, as if he had wished to play a dirty trick on them, deceive them, frustrate them on purpose, but they were especially annoyed with him because of the time he was making them lose. The son-in-law asked,

"What the devil are we going to do?"

She did not know. She answered,

"Is it ever a nuisance, all the same!"

They could not now let all the guests know, who were going to arrive within the hour. They decided to wait, to explain the whole thing to them.

About ten minutes of seven the first ones appeared. The women in black, heads covered with a large veil, came with sad expressions. The men, uncomfortable in their broadcloth coats, approached more ponderously, by twos, discussing their crops.

Master Chicot and his wife, terrified, met them grieving, and suddenly at the very same moment, as they reached the first group, both began to cry. They explained the calamity, told of their embarrassment, offered chairs, moved about, excused themselves, tried to prove that everyone would have done as they did, spoke endlessly, suddenly so talkative that no one else had a chance to say anything. Going from one group to another, they said,

"I wouldn't have believed it. It's unbelievable he could have lasted so long!"

The guests, silent, a bit disappointed, like people who are missing an expected treat, did not know what to do, remained where they were, seated or standing. Some started to leave. Master Chicot would not let them.

"Let's have a bite anyway. We've made turnovers. Might as well eat them."

Faces lit up at this thought. People began talking in low voices. The yard was beginning to fill up. The early-comers spread the news to the new arrivals. They began to chat, the prospect of turnovers having cheered them up.

The women went inside to have a look at the dying man. They crossed themselves near the bed, stammered a prayer, went out. The men, less eager for this spectacle, merely glanced towards him from the window which was now open.

Madame Chicot explained the agony: "He's been like that for two days, no more or less, no better or worse. Doesn't he sound like a pump that's got no water?"

When everyone had seen the dying man, they remembered the food. But as there were too many to get them all into the kitchen, they took the table outside in front of the door. The four dozen turnovers placed on two large platters, golden brown and appetizing, drew all eyes. Each one reached out for one, fearing there might not be enough. But there were four left over.

Master Chicot, his mouth full, said,

"If the old man could see us now, it would break his heart. He was crazy about turnovers when he was alive."

A fat jolly peasant declared, "He won't eat any more now. Everybody's got to have his turn."

This reflection, instead of saddening the guests, seemed to amuse them. It was their turn to eat turnovers.

Madame Chicot, concerned by the expense, kept going to the cellar for cider. Pitchers came up and were emptied with the utmost speed. There was laughter now, the talk was louder, they were beginning to shout, as if they were at a banquet table.

All of a sudden an old peasant woman who had remained near the dying man, fascinated by this thing that would soon befall her, appeared at the window and cried out in a shrill voice,

"He's gone! He's gone!"

Everyone was silent. The women rushed to have a look.

He was indeed dead. He had stopped rattling. The men looked at each other, lowered their eyes, seemed ill at ease. Their mouths were still full of turnovers. The rascal had timed it very poorly.

The Chicots wept no more now. It was all over, and they were relieved. They kept saying, "We knew all along it couldn't last. If only he'd made up his mind last night, we wouldn't have had all this trouble."

What mattered was that it was over. He'd be buried Monday, that's all, and there would be more turnovers for the occasion.

The guests left talking it over, glad to have seen such a thing after all, and to have had refreshments.

And when the man and his wife were alone face to face, she said, her face twisted with anguish,

"Now I'll have to cook four dozen more! If only he'd made up his mind last night!"

The husband, more resigned, replied,

"Never mind. Won't have to do it every day."

THE COCONUT-DRINK VENDOR

I had heard the story of my uncle Oliver's death.

I knew that at the very moment when he was about to pass away gently, quietly, in the dimness of his large bedroom, whose shutters had been closed because of the fierce July sun, a little silver bell had broken the stifling silence of this burning summer afternoon. A clear voice had pierced the heavy heat,

"Fresh coconut! Have a cool drink, ladies! Coconut milk!"

My uncle moved a bit. Something akin to a smile appeared on his lips. A final look of whimsy lit up his eyes, which, soon after, became extinguished forever.

I was present at the reading of the will. My cousin Jacques naturally inherited most of his father's property. My father received some furniture as a token of brotherly affection. The last clause of the will concerned me. Here it is:

"To my nephew Pierre I leave a manuscript of several pages, which can be found in the left-hand drawer of my secretary; plus five hundred francs to buy a hunting gun, and 100 francs which he will please give for me to the first coconut-milk vendor he runs across!"

What a bombshell! The manuscript which was given me explained this astounding legacy. Here it is *in toto*:

"Man has always lived under the burden of superstition. It was once thought that a star came into being at the same moment as a child, that the star marked the vicissitudes of his life, indicating good fortune by its brilliance, misfortune by its dullness. People believed in the influence of comets, of leap years, of Fridays, of the number thirteen. Some imagine that certain people influence fate, cast an evil eye. They say, 'Whenever I meet so-and-so, it means ill luck.' All this is true. I believe in it. Let me explain: I do not believe in the occult influence of things or of persons; but I believe in a preordained chance. It is certain that chance brought about important events while comets appeared in our sky, that it put them there during leap years, that certain observed calamities fell on Friday or coincided with the number thirteen, that the sight of certain people coincided with the occurrence of certain events, etc. Out of all this superstitions are born. They are the result of partial, superficial observation, which sees the cause in the coincidence and does not seek beyond it.

"Now my star, my comet, my Friday, my number thirteen, my man of destiny is most certainly a coconut-milk vendor.

"I am told that on the day I was born a coconut-milk hawker had cried his wares under our windows all day long.

"At the age of eight as I was walking with my nursemaid on the Champs-Elysées, and as we were crossing the broad avenue, one of these merchants suddenly sounded his bell behind my back. My nurse was watching a regiment pass in the distance. I turned around to look at the coconut vendor. A shiny carriage drawn by two horses and moving like a flash of lightning was bearing down on us. The coachman shouted. My nurse did not hear, nor I. I felt myself knocked down, run over, mauled . . . and I found myself somehow in the arms of the coconut vendor, who, in order to comfort me, put my mouth under one of his spigots, opened it and doused me . . . which completely revived me.

"My nurse had her nose broken. And if she continued to look at regiments, they no longer looked at her.

"At sixteen I bought my first gun, and, the day before the opening of the hunting season I was going to the coach stop with my elderly mother, who held my arm and walked very slowly because of her rheumatism. All of a sudden I heard behind us the cry,

" 'Coconut! Coconut! Have a fresh coconut drink!'

"The voice drew nearer, followed us, pursued us. It seemed to be addressing me, as if it were an evil genius, an insult. I felt that people were looking at me, laughing at me. And the man continued to cry out, 'Fresh coconut!' as if he were jeering at my shiny gun, my new game bag, my *fresh* new hunting outfit of brown corduroy.

"I could hear him even inside the carriage.

"The next day I shot no game, but I did kill a dog, which I mistook for a hare; a chicken, which I thought was a partridge. A small bird alighted on a hedge. I fired. It flew away. But a terrible mooing startled me out of my wits. It lasted until nightfall . . . Alas! my poor father was obliged to compensate a farmer for the cow I had shot.

"One morning at the age of twenty-five I saw an old coconut-drink vendor, very wrinkled, very bent, who could scarcely walk, leaning on his stick and practically crushed by his tank. He seemed to me like a kind of god, like the patriarch, the ancestor, the grand mogul of all the coconut vendors in the universe. Whereupon I drank a glass of coconut milk and paid twenty sous for it. A deep voice, which seemed to come from the metal tank rather than from the man who was carrying it, rumbled,

" 'It will bring you good luck, monsieur.'

"That very day I met the woman who became my wife and made me eternally happy.

"Finally, here is how a coconut vendor prevented me from becoming a prefect.

"There had just been a revolution. A desire to serve the public suddenly possessed me. I was wealthy and respected. I knew a cabinet minister and asked for an appointment to discuss the matter with him. It was graciously arranged.

"On the appointed day—it was summer and frightfully hot—I put on light-colored trousers, matching gloves and shoes, the latter of cloth with patent-leather toes. The streets were burning. One was sucked into the melting sidewalks, and big sprinkling wagons made a cesspool of the streets. From square to square street cleaners were working in this warm and, so to speak, artificial mud, pushing it into the sewers. I was thinking only of my interview and was walking fast when I encountered one of these muddy waves. I was on the point of leaping over it, one, two . . . when a sharp, devastating cry pierced my ears,

" 'Coconut! Coconut! Have a fresh coconut drink!'

"This yell threw me off balance. I slipped. . . . It was an awful mess. . . . I was sitting in the mud. . . . My trousers had turned black. My white shirt was spattered with mud. My hat was swirling beside me. The insistent voice, hoarse with shouting, kept on:

" 'Coconut! Coconut! Have a fresh coconut drink!' And in front of me some twenty people, shaking with laughter, were grimacing at me.

"I ran home and changed at once, but the hour of my appointment had passed."

The manuscript closed thus:

"Be sure to have a coconut vendor for a friend, Pierre, my boy. As for me, I shall leave this world happy if I hear one on my deathbed."

The very next day on the Champs-Elysées I met an old, very old coconut-drink vendor, who looked really destitute. I gave him my uncle's hundred francs. My handsome gift made him tremble with amazement, and he said,

"Thank you kindly, young man. That will bring you luck."

THE CHARM DISPELLED

The boat was filled with people. As the passage promised to be good, many people of Havre were making a trip to Trouville.

They loosed the moorings; a last whistle announced the departure, and immediately the entire body of the vessel shook, while a sound of stirring water was heard all along the sides. The wheels turned for some seconds, stopped and then started gently. The captain upon his bridge having cried, "Go ahead!" through the tube which extends into the depths of the machinery, they now began to beat the waves with great rapidity.

We passed along the pier covered with people. Some that were on the boat waved their handkerchiefs, as if they were setting out for America, and the friends who remained behind responded in the same fashion.

The great July sun fell upon the red umbrellas, the bright costumes, the joyous faces and upon the ocean, scarcely moved by any undulations. As soon as they had left the port the little vessel made a sharp turn, pointing its nose directly for the far-off coast rising to meet the foam.

On our left was the mouth of the Seine, more than twelve miles wide. Here and there great buoys pointed out banks of sand, and one could see at a distance the fresh, muddy water of the river, which had not yet mingled with the salt brine, outlined in broad, yellow stripes upon the immense, pure green sheet of the open sea.

As soon as I boarded the boat I felt the need of walking up and down, like a sailor on his watch. Why? That I cannot say. But I began to circulate among the crowd of passengers on deck.

Suddenly someone called my name. I turned around. It was Henry Sidonie, whom I had not seen for ten years.

After we had shaken hands we resumed the walk of a bear in his cage, which I had been taking alone, while we talked of people and things. And we looked at the two lines of travelers seated on both sides of the boat, chatting all the while.

All at once Sidonie exclaimed with a veritable expression of rage: "It is crowded with English here! Nasty people!"

The boat was full of English, in fact. Men standing about scanned the horizon with an important air which seemed to say: "It is the English who are masters of the sea! Boom! Boom! Here we are!"

And the white veils upon their white hats had the air of flags in their self-sufficiency.

The thin young girls, whose boots recalled the naval construction of their country, wrapping their straight figures and thin arms in multicolored shawls, smiled vaguely at the radiant landscape. Their little heads, perched on the top of their long bodies, wearing the peculiarly shaped English hat, were finished at the back of the neck by their thin hair, coiled around to resemble sleeping adders.

And the old spinsters, still more lank, opening to the wind their national jaw, appeared to threaten space with their enormous yellow teeth. In passing near them one smells an odor of caoutchouc or some kind of dentifrice.

Sidonie repeated with an increasing anger:

"Nasty people! Why couldn't they be hindered from coming to France?"

I inquired laughingly: "Why, what do you care? As for me, I am perfectly indifferent to them."

He answered: "Yes, you are, indeed! But I—I married an Englishwoman. And there you have it!"

I stopped and laughed in his face. "The devil!" I said; "tell me about it. Has she made you so unhappy?"

He shrugged his shoulders as he replied: "No, not precisely."

"Then she—she has—deceived you?"

"Unfortunately, no. That would give me a cause for divorce, and I should be free."

"But I do not understand."

"You do not understand? That is not astonishing. Well, she simply learned the French language, nothing more! Listen:

"I had never had the least desire to marry when I went to pass the summer at Etretat two years ago. But there is nothing more dangerous than watering places. One cannot imagine to what an advantage young girls are seen there. Paris may be for women, but the country is for young girls.

"The idiotic promenades, the morning baths, lunches upon the grass, all are so many snares for marriage. And truly, there is nothing prettier than a girl of eighteen running across a field or picking flowers along the road.

"I made the acquaintance of an English family living at the same hotel as myself. The father resembled the men you see there, and the mother all other Englishwomen. They had two sons, boys all bones, who played at violent games with balls, sticks or rackets from morning until evening; then two girls, the elder a lean, well-preserved Englishwoman of maturity, the younger a wonder. She was a blonde, or rather a blondine, with a head that came from the skies. When they do undertake to be pretty, these wretches, they are divine. She had blue eyes, of the blue which seems to contain all the poetry, dreams, hopes and happiness of the world!

"What a horizon of infinite thought opens before you in the two eyes of a woman like that! How well she responds to the eternal, vague expectation of our hearts!

"It is only necessary to remember that Frenchmen always adore foreigners. As soon as we meet a Russian, an Italian, a Swede, a Spanish or an Englishwoman at all pretty, we fall in love with her immediately. Everything that comes from abroad fills us with enthusiasm, whether it be trouser cloth, hats, gloves, guns or—women. We are wrong, nevertheless.

"But I believe the most seductive thing about these exotics is their faulty pronunciation of our language. As soon as a woman speaks French badly she is charming. If she uses a wrong word she is exquisite, and if she jabbers in a manner quite unintelligible she becomes irresistible.

"You cannot imagine how pretty it is to hear a sweet, red mouth say: 'J'aime beaucoup la gigotte [I like mutton so much]'!

"My little English Kate spoke a most unlikely tongue. I could understand nothing of it in the first days; she invented so many unheard-of words. That was when I became absolutely in love with the comical, gay little monkey. All these crippled, strange, ridiculous terms took on a delicious charm upon her lips, and on the casino terrace in the evening, we had many long conversations, resembling spoken enigmas.

"I married her! I loved her foolishly, as one can love a dream. For the true lover adores nought but a dream which takes the shape of a woman. You recall Louis Bouilhet's admirable verse:

> "You only were, in those rarest days,
> A common instrument under my art;
> Like the bow, on the viol d'amour it plays,
> I dreamed my dream o'er your empty heart.

"Well, my dear, the greatest mistake I made was to give my wife a teacher of French. As long as she made a martyr of the dictionary and punished the grammar, I was fond of her. Our talks were very simple. She showed a surprising grace of mind, an incomparable elegance in her actions. She seemed to be a marvelous speaking jewel, a doll of flesh made to kiss, knowing how to make known or at least indicate the things she desired, uttering at times the strangest exclamations and expressing rather complicated sensations and emotions in a coquettish fashion, with a force as incomprehensible as it was unforeseen. She much resembled those pretty playthings which say 'papa' and 'mamma,' pronouncing them 'baba' and 'bamban.'

"Could I have believed that——

"She speaks now—she speaks—badly—very badly. She makes just as many mistakes, but I can understand her. Yes, I understand—I know—and I know her.

"I have opened my doll to see what was inside. I have seen. And one must talk, my dear!

"Ah! You don't know, you could never imagine the theories, the ideas, the opinions of a young Englishwoman, well brought up, in whom there is nothing to reproach, who repeats to me morning and evening all the phrases in the dictionary of conversation in use at the schools for young people.

"You have seen those favors for a cotillion, those pretty gilt-paper-covered execrable bonbons? I had one of them. I tore it open. I wished to taste what was inside and became so disgusted that now there is a rebellion in my feelings if I but see one of her compatriots.

"I have married a parakeet to whom an old-time instructress had taught French. Do you understand?"

The port of Trouville now showed its wooden piers covered with people. I said: "Where is your wife?"

He answered: "I have just taken her back to Etretat."

"And where are you going?"

"I? I am going to try and divert myself at Trouville."

Then after a silence he added: "You cannot imagine how irksome a wife can become sometimes."

MAKING A CONVERT

When Sabot entered the Martinville Inn they all laughed in advance. This rascal of a Sabot, how farcical he was! See how he disliked curates, for example! Ah yes, yes! He was ready to eat them, this merry fellow.

Théodule Sabot, master carpenter, represented the progressive party at Martinville. He was a tall, thin man, with gay, cunning eyes, hair glued to his temples, and thin lips. When he said: "Our holy father, the priest," in a certain fashion, everybody was convulsed. He made it a point to work on Sunday during Mass. Every year he would kill his pig on Monday of Holy Week in order to have blood pudding until Easter, and when he passed the curate he would always say in a way of a joke:

"Here's a man who finds his good God upon the roof."

The priest, a large man, very tall also, dreaded him because of his talk, which made partisans. Father Maritime was a politic man, a friend of ease. The struggle between them had gone on for ten years, a secret struggle, provoking and incessant. Sabot was municipal counselor. It was believed that he would be mayor, which would be decidedly bad for the church.

The elections were about to take place. The religious camp in Martinville trembled. Then one morning the curate set out for Rouen, announcing to his servant that he was going to see the archbishop.

Two days later he returned. He had a joyous, triumphant air. The next day everybody knew that the choir of the church was to be remodeled. A sum of six hundred francs had been given by Monsieur from his private cashbox.

All the old pine stalls were to be removed and be replaced by new ones of heart of oak. It was a considerable piece of carpenter work, and they were talking about it in every house that evening.

Théodule Sabot did not laugh. The next day when he went through the village his neighbors, friends and enemies said to him in a joking manner:

"Is it you who is to make over the choir of the church?"

He found nothing to answer, but he raged and raged silently. The rogues would add:

"It is a good job, not less than two or three hundred clear profit."

Two days later it was known that the repairs had been given to Célestin Chambrelan, the carpenter of Percheville. Then the news was contradicted; then it was said that all of the benches of the church were also to be renewed. This would be worth two thousand francs, as someone had found out from the administration. The excitement was great.

Théodule Sabot was not asleep. Never within the memory of man had a carpenter of the country executed a like piece of work. Then a rumor was heard that the curate was desolate at having to give this work to an out-of-town workman but that Sabot's opinions were so opposed to his that it was impossible to give it to him.

Sabot knew it. He betook himself to the priest's house at nightfall. The servant told him that the curate was in the church. He went there. Two Ladies of the Virgin, sourish old maids, were decorating the altar for the month of Mary under the direction of the priest. There he was, in the middle of the choir, swelling out his enormous front as he directed the work of the two women who, mounted on chairs, disposed of bouquets about the tabernacle.

Sabot felt under restraint in there, as if he were on the enemy's ground, but the desire of gain was ever pricking at his heart. He approached, cap in hand, without even noticing the Ladies of the Virgin, who remained standing, stupefied and immovable, upon the chairs. He stammered:

"Good evening, Monsieur Curate."

The priest responded without looking at him, all occupied with the altar:

"Good evening, Monsieur Carpenter."

Sabot, out of his element, could say nothing further. After a silence he said, however, "You are going to make some repairs?"

Father Maritime answered: "Yes, we are approaching the month of Mary."

Sabot repeated: "That's it, that's it," and then he was silent.

He felt now like withdrawing without saying anything more, but a glance of the eye around the choir restrained him. He perceived that there were sixteen stalls to be made, six to the right and eight to the left, the door of the sacristy occupying two places more. Sixteen stalls in oak would be worth three hundred francs, and in round numbers there ought to be two hundred francs' profit on the work if it was managed well. Then he stammered:

"I—I've come for the work."

The curate appeared surprised. He asked:

"What work?"

"The work of the repairs," murmured Sabot desperately.

Then the priest turned toward him and, looking him straight in the eye, said: "And you speak to me of working on the choir stalls of my church!"

The tone of Father Maritime's voice caused a cold chill to run down the back of Théodule Sabot and gave him a furious desire to scamper away. Nevertheless, he responded with humility:

"Why, yes, Monsieur Curate."

Then the priest folded his arms across his ample front and, as if powerless from surprise, replied:

"You—you—you—Sabot, come to ask that from me! You—the only impious soul in my parish! Why, it would be a scandal, a public scandal. The archbishop would reprimand me and send me to another place, perhaps."

He breathed hard for some seconds, then in a calmer tone he continued:

"I understand that it would be hard for you to see a work of so much importance go to a carpenter in a neighboring parish. But I could not do otherwise, at least not unless—no—it is impossible. You would never consent—and without that—never."

Sabot regarded critically the line of benches that came almost up to the door of the sacristy. Christopher! If one might be able to make this alteration! And he asked: "What is it you consider necessary? Say it."

The priest, in a firm tone, replied: "It would be necessary for me to have a statement of your good will."

Sabot murmured: "I should say nothing. I should say nothing—that would be understood."

The curate declared: "It would be necessary to take public communion at High Mass next Sunday."

The carpenter grew pale and without answering asked:

"And the church benches, are they going to be replaced with new ones too?"

The priest responded with assurance: "Yes, but that will come later."

Sabot repeated: "I would say nothing; I say nothing. In fact, I feel nothing derogatory to religion, and I believe in it, certainly; what ruffles me is the practice of it, but in this case, I should not show myself contrary."

The Ladies of the Virgin, having got down from their chairs, concealed themselves behind the altar; they were listening, pale with emotion.

The curate, seeing himself victorious, suddenly became friendly and familiar: "Well and good! Well and good!" he said. "You have spoken wisely instead of being foolish, you understand. We shall see. We shall see."

Sabot smiled in a constrained way as he asked: "Isn't there some way of giving this communion the slip?"

The priest, with severe countenance, replied:

"At the moment that this work is given to you I wish to be certain of your conversion." Then he continued more gently: "You will come to confess tomorrow, for it will be necessary for me to examine you at least twice."

Sabot repeated: "At least twice?"

"Yes."

The priest smiled. "You understand that it will be necessary to have a general clearing out, a complete cleansing. I shall expect you then tomorrow."

The carpenter, much moved, asked: "Where do you do this?"

"Why, in the confessional."

"In—that box there—in the corner? That is—scarcely—big enough for me, your box."

"Why so?"

"Seeing that—seeing that I am not accustomed to it. And seeing that I'm a little hard of hearing."

The curate showed himself lenient. "Ah well, you can come to my house, in my dining room. There we shall be all alone, face to face. How will that suit you?"

"That's it. That suits me, but your box, no."

"Well, tomorrow then, after the day's work, at six o'clock."

"It is understood, all plain and agreed upon; till tomorrow then, Monsieur Curate, and the rack for him who retracts."

And he extended his great, rude hand into which the priest let fall his own heartily. The smack of this handshake ran along under the arches and died away back in the organ pipes.

Théodule Sabot was not tranquil while he was at work the next day. The apprehension he felt was something like what one feels when he is going to have a tooth pulled. Every moment this thought would come to him: "I must go to confession this evening." And his troubled soul, the soul of an atheist not wholly convinced, became excited from the confused and powerful fear of some divine mystery.

He directed his steps toward the rectory when he had finished his day's work. The curate was waiting for him in the garden, reading his breviary as he walked up and down a narrow path. He seemed radiant and said with a great laugh:

"Ah well, here you are! Come in, come in, Monsieur Sabot, nobody is going to eat you."

And Sabot passed in first. He stammered:

"If you are not too busy I should be pleased to finish up our little business right away."

The curate answered: "At your service. I will get my surplice. One minute and I will listen to you."

The carpenter, so disturbed that he no longer had two ideas, watched him cover himself with the white garment with its pressed folds. The priest made a sign to him.

"Put your knees on this cushion."

Sabot remained standing, ashamed to have to kneel. He muttered:

"What's the use?"

But the priest became majestic. "One can only approach the tribunal of penitence on the knees."

And Sabot kneeled.

The priest said: "Recite the Confiteor."

Sabot asked: "What's that?"

"The Confiteor. If you do not know it repeat one by one, after me, the words I pronounce."

And the curate articulated the sacred prayer in a deliberate voice, scanning the words for the carpenter to repeat; then he said:

"Now, confess."

But Sabot said nothing more, not knowing how to commence.

Then Father Maritime came to his aid.

"My child, I will ask you some questions until you become a little more familiar with the customs. We will take up, one by one, the commandments of God. Listen to me and be not troubled. Speak very frankly, and never fear to say too much.

> *"One God alone you shall adore*
> *And you shall love him perfectly.*

Have you ever loved someone or something more than God? Do you love Him with all your soul, with all your heart and all the energy of your love?"

Sabot was sweating from the effort of his thought. Finally he said:

"No. Oh no, Monsieur Curate. I love the good God as much as I can. That is—yes—I love Him well. To say that I love Him better than my children, no, I cannot. To say that if it was necessary to choose between Him and my children I would choose the good God, that I could not. To say that I would be willing to lose a hundred francs for the love of the good God, no, I could not. But I love Him well, be sure; I love Him well, all the same."

The priest, very grave, declared: "It is necessary that you love Him before anything."

And Sabot, full of good will, answered: "I will do my best, Monsieur Curate."

Father Maritime continued: "God will not have you take His name in vain. Have you sometimes made use of an oath?"

"No. Oh no, indeed! I never swear. Sometimes in a moment of anger I speak the sacred name of God. That's all. I do not swear."

The priest cried: "But that is swearing." And then gravely: "Do it no more.

I will continue. You will remember the Sabbath to keep it holy. What do you do on Sunday?"

This time Sabot scratched his ear. Finally he said: "I serve the good God in my own way, Monsieur Curate. I serve Him—at home. I work on Sunday."

The curate was magnanimous in interrupting him. "I know you will be more proper in the future. I pass the Commandments following, sure that you have not failed in the first two. Let us see the sixth and the ninth. I repeat: 'The goods of another thou shalt not take, nor retain them knowingly.' Have you turned to your own use by any means the goods belonging to another?"

Théodule Sabot answered indignantly: "No! Ah no! I am an honest man, Monsieur Curate. I swear to that. Not to say that I have not sometimes counted more hours of work than I have done—I have sometimes done that. And I could not say that I have not put a few more centimes on notes, only a few sometimes. But as for robbing, no, no, indeed, no!"

The curate answered severely: "Take not a single centime, for that is robbery. Do it no more. 'False witness shalt thou not bear, nor lie about anything.' Have you lied?"

"No, not that. I am no liar. I am not that kind. If you ask if I have not told some stories for the sake of talking, I could not deny it. And to say that I have not made people believe what was not so, when it was for my interest to do so, I could not. But as for lies, I tell no lies."

The priest simply said: "Be a little more careful." Then he pronounced:

" 'Things of the flesh thou shalt not desire, except in marriage alone.'

"Have you desired or possessed another woman than your own?"

Sabot exclaimed with sincerity: "Oh no! As for that, no, Monsieur Curate. Deceive my poor wife? No! no! Not as much as the end of your finger. Not in thought, say nothing of action! That's true."

He was silent for some seconds, then, very low, as if some doubt had come over him, he said: "When I go to town, to say that I never go into a house, you know, one of the houses of license, for the sake of a bit of laughter and frolic and see another kind of skin, that I could not say—but I always pay, Monsieur Curate, I always pay, but I won't embarrass you with this that you have neither seen nor known."

The curate did not insist but gave the absolution.

Théodule Sabot executed the work of the choir stalls and received the sacrament in the months following.

THE CAKE

We will call her Mme. Anserre, though it was not her real name.

She was one of those Parisian comets who leave a sort of trail of fire behind them. She wrote poetry and short stories, was sentimental and ravishingly beautiful. Her circle was small and consisted only of exceptional people—those generally known as the kings of this, that, or the other. To be invited to her receptions stamped one as a person of intelligence; let us say that her invitations were appreciated for this reason. Her husband played the part of an obscure satellite: to be married to a star is no easy role. This husband had, however, a brilliant idea, that of creating a state within a state, of possessing some value in himself although only of secondary importance: he received on the same day as his wife did and had his special set who listened to him and appreciated his qualities, paying much more attention to him than they did to his brilliant companion.

He had devoted himself to agriculture, "armchair" agriculture, just as we have "armchair" generals—all those who are born, live, and die in the comfortable surroundings of the War Office—or "armchair" sailors—look at the Admiralty—or "armchair" colonizers, etc., etc. So he had studied agriculture seriously in its relation to the other sciences, with political economy and with the fine arts; we call everything art, even the horrible railway bridges are "works of art." He had finally reached the stage when he was known as a clever man, he was quoted in the technical reviews, and his wife had succeeded in getting him appointed a member of a commission at the Ministry of Agriculture.

He was satisfied with this modest glory. On the pretext of economy he invited his friends the same day his wife received hers, so that they all met each other, or rather they did not—they formed two groups. Madame's group of artists, academicians and Ministers gathered together in a kind of gallery which was furnished and decorated in Empire style. Monsieur generally retired with his "laborers" into a small room used as a smoking room which Mme. Anserre ironically described as "the salon of agriculture."

The two camps were quite distinct. Monsieur, without any feeling of jealousy, sometimes ventured into the academy, when cordial greetings were exchanged; but the academy disdained intercourse with the salon of agriculture; it was indeed rare that one of the kings of science, of philosophy, of this, that, or the other mingled with the "laborers."

These receptions were quite simple: nothing but tea and brioches were handed round. At first Monsieur had asked for two brioches, one for the Academy and one for the "laborers," but, Madame having quite rightly suggested that that would be a recognition of two different camps, two receptions, two groups, Monsieur did not press the matter, so there was only one brioche, which Mme. Anserre distributed first to the academy, after which it passed into the salon of agriculture.

Now the brioche became a subject of strange and unexpected proceedings in the academy. Mme. Anserre never cut it herself. That task always fell to the lot of one or other of the illustrious guests. This particular function, much sought after and considered a special honor, was a privilege that might last for some time or might soon be over: it might last three months, for instance, but scarcely ever longer, and it was noticed that the privilege of "cutting the brioche" carried with it other marks of superiority; it was a form of royalty, or, rather, very accentuated viceroyalty. The officiating cutter spoke with no uncertain voice, with a tone of marked command; and all the hostess's favors were bestowed upon him, all.

These happy beings were described in intimate circles as "the favorites of the brioche," and every change of favorite caused a sort of revolution in the academy. The knife was a scepter, the cake an emblem, and the elect received the congratulations of other members. The brioche was never cut by the "laborers," Monsieur himself being always excluded, although he ate his share.

The cake was cut in succession by poets, by painters, and by novelists. A great musician measured out the portions for some time and was succeeded by an ambassador. Occasionally a guest of minor importance but distinguished and much sought after, one of those who are called, in different epochs, "real gentleman," "perfect knight," or "dandy," and so forth, took his turn to cut the symbolic cake. Each one, during his short reign, showed the greatest consideration towards the lady's husband, then when came the hour of his dismissal he passed the knife on to another and mingled again with the crowd of followers and admirers of the "beautiful Mme. Anserre."

This lasted a very long time, but comets do not always shine with the same brilliance. Everything in the world grows old, and it gradually looked as if the eagerness of the cutters were growing weaker; they seemed to hesitate when the cake was held out to them; this office once so much coveted became less sought after; it was held a shorter time and was considered with less pride by the holder. Mme. Anserre was prodigal of smiles and amiability, but, alas! the cake was no longer willingly cut. Newcomers seemed to decline the honor, and old favorites reappeared one by one like dethroned kings temporarily replaced in power. Then the elected became very scarce indeed, and for a month, marvelous to relate, M. Anserre cut the cake, then he looked as if he were getting tired of it, and one evening Mme. Anserre, the beautiful Mme. Anserre, was seen cutting it herself. But she seemed bored, and the next day she insisted with such vehemence that the chosen guest dared not refuse.

However, the symbol was too well known; the guests stared at each other furtively with scared, anxious faces. To cut the brioche was nothing, but the privileges that accompanied this distinction now filled the chosen ones with terror, so that the minute the cake dish appeared, the academicians made a rush for the salon of agriculture as if to shelter behind the husband, who was always smiling, and when Mme. Anserre, in a state of anxiety, showed herself at the door, carrying the knife in one hand and the brioche in the other, they all gathered round her husband as if they were seeking his protection.

Some years passed and no one cut up the cake, but the old habit persisted and she who was still politely called "the beautiful Mme. Anserre" looked out each evening for some devotee to take the knife, and each time the same stampede took place: there was a general flight, cleverly arranged and full of combined and skillful maneuvers to avoid the offer that was rising to her lips.

But, one evening, a boy—ignorant of the ways of the world and quite unsophisticated—was introduced to the house. He knew nothing about the mystery of the brioche; therefore when it appeared and when the rest had all fled, and when Mme. Anserre took the cake from the footman, he remained quietly by her side.

She may have thought that he knew all about it; she smiled and said in a voice full of feeling: "Will you be so kind as to cut this brioche, dear monsieur?"

Flattered at the honor, he replied: "Certainly, madame, with the greatest pleasure."

In the distance—in the corners of the gallery, in the open doorway of the salon of agriculture—amazed faces were looking at him. Then, when the spectators saw the newcomer cutting the cake, they quickly came forward. An old poet jokingly slapped the neophyte on the shoulder and whispered: "Bravo, young man!"

The others gazed at him with curiosity and even Monsieur appeared surprised. As for the young man, he was astonished at the consideration he met with; above all, he failed to understand the marked attentions, the conspicuous favor, and the speechless gratitude of the mistress of the house.

Nevertheless, he eventually found out, though no one knew at what moment, in what place the revelation came to him, but when he appeared at the next reception he seemed preoccupied and half-ashamed, and looked anxiously round the room. When the bell rang for tea and the footman appeared, Mme. Anserre, with a smile, took the dish and looked round for her young friend, but he fled so precipitately that no trace of him could be found. Then she went off to look for him and discovered him at the end of the salon of "laborers" holding her husband's arm tightly and consulting him in an agonized manner as to the best method of destroying phylloxera.

"My dear monsieur, will you be so kind as to cup up this brioche?" she said.

He blushed to the roots of his hair, stammered, and completely lost his head. Thereupon M. Anserre took pity on him and, turning to his wife, said:

"My dear, it would be kind of you not to disturb us. We are discussing agriculture. Let Baptiste cut up the cake."

Since that day no one has ever cut Mme. Anserre's brioche.

A DEAD WOMAN'S SECRET

She had died painlessly, tranquilly, like a woman whose life was irreproachable; and she now lay on her back in bed, with closed eyes, calm features, her long white hair carefully arranged, as if she had again made her toilet ten minutes before her death. Her pale physiognomy was so composed now that she had passed away, so resigned, that one felt sure a sweet soul had dwelt in that body, that this serene grandmother had spent an untroubled existence, that this virtuous woman had ended her life without any shock, without any remorse.

On his knees beside the bed, her son, a magistrate of inflexible principles, and her daughter Marguerite—in religion, Sister Eulalie—were weeping distractedly. She had from the time of their infancy armed them with an inflexible code of morality, teaching them a religion without weakness and a sense of duty without any compromise. He, the son, had become a magistrate and, wielding the weapon of the law, struck down without pity the feeble and the erring. She, the daughter, quite penetrated with the virtue that had bathed her in this austere family, had become the spouse of God through disgust with men.

They had scarcely known their father; all they knew was that he had made their mother unhappy without learning any further details. The nun passionately kissed one hand of her dead mother, which hung down, a hand of ivory like that of Christ in the large crucifix which lay on the bed. At the opposite side of the prostrate body the other hand seemed still to grasp the rumpled sheet with that wondering movement which is called the fold of the dying, and the lines had retained little creases as a memento of those last motions which precede the eternal motionlessness. A few light taps at the door caused the two sobbing heads to look up, and the priest, who had just dined, entered the apartment. He was flushed, a little puffed from the effects of the process of digestion which had just commenced, for he had put a good dash of brandy into his coffee in order to counteract the

fatigue caused by the last nights he had remained up and that which he anticipated from the night that was still in store for him. He had put on a look of sadness, that simulated sadness of the priest to whom death is a means of livelihood.
He made the sign of the cross and, coming over to them with his professional
gestures, said:

"Well, my poor children, I have come to help you to pass these mournful hours."

But Sister Eulalie suddenly rose up.

"Thanks, Father, but my brother and I would like to be left alone with her.
These are the last moments that we now have for seeing her, so we want to feel
ourselves once more, the three of us, just as we were years ago when we—we—we
were only children and our poor—poor mother——" She was unable to finish with
the flood of tears that gushed from her eyes and the sobs that were choking her.

But the priest bowed with a more serene look on his face, for he was thinking
of his bed. "Just as you please, my children."

Then he kneeled down, again crossed himself, prayed, rose and softly stole away,
murmuring as he went: "She was a saint."

They were left alone, the dead woman and her children. A hidden timepiece
kept regularly ticking in its dark corner, and through the open window the soft
odors of hay and of woods penetrated with faint gleams of moonlight. No sound
in the fields outside, save the wandering croak of toads and now and then the
humming of some nocturnal insect darting in like a ball and knocking itself against
the wall.

An infinite peace, a divine melancholy, a silent serenity, surrounded this dead
woman, seemed to emanate from her, to evaporate from her into the atmosphere
outside and to calm Nature herself.

Then the magistrate, still on his knees, his head pressed against the bedclothes,
in a far-off, heartbroken voice that pierced through the sheets and the coverlet,
exclaimed:

"Mamma, Mamma, Mamma!" And the sister, sinking down on the floor, striking the wood with her forehead fanatically, twisting herself about and quivering
like a person in an epileptic fit, groaned: "Jesus, Jesus—Mamma—Jesus!"

And both of them, shaken by a hurricane of grief, panted with a rattling in
their throats.

Then the fit gradually subsided, and they now wept in a less violent fashion,
like the rainy calm that follows a squall on a storm-beaten sea. Then after some
time they rose and fixed their glances on the beloved corpse. And memories, those
memories of the past, so sweet, so torturing today, came back to their minds with
all those little forgotten details, those little details so intimate and familiar, which
make the being who is no more live over again. They recalled circumstances, words,
smiles, certain intonations of voice which belonged to one whom they should never
hear speaking to them again. They saw her once more happy and calm, and phrases
she used in ordinary conversation rose to their lips. They even remembered a little
movement of the hand, peculiar to her, as if she were keeping time when she was
saying something of importance.

And they loved her as they had never before loved her. And by the depth of
their despair they realized how strongly they had been attached to her and how
desolate they would find themselves now.

She had been their mainstay, their guide, the best part of their youth, of that
happy portion of their lives which had vanished; she had been the bond that

united them to existence, the mother, the mamma, the creative flesh, the tie that bound them to their ancestors. They would henceforth be solitary, isolated; they would have nothing on earth to look back upon.

The nun said to her brother:

"You know how Mamma used always to read over her old letters. They are all there in her desk. Suppose we read them in our turn and so revive all her life this night by her side. It would be like a kind of road of the cross, like making the acquaintance of her mother, of grandparents whom we never knew, whose letters are there and of whom she has so often talked to us; you remember?"

And they drew forth from the drawer a dozen little packets of yellow paper, carefully tied up and placed close to one another. They flung these relics on the bed and, selecting one of them on which the word "Father" was written, they opened and read what was in it.

It consisted of those very old letters which are to be found in old family writing desks, those letters which have the flavor of another century. The first said, "My darling"; another, "My beautiful little girl"; then others, "My dear child"; and then again, "My dear daughter." And suddenly the nun began reading aloud, reading for the dead her own history, all her tender souvenirs. And the magistrate listened, while he leaned on the bed with his eyes on his mother's face. And the motionless corpse seemed happy.

Sister Eulalie, interrupting herself said: "We ought to put them into the grave with her, to make a winding sheet of them and bury them with her."

And then she took up another packet on which the descriptive word did not appear.

And in a loud tone she began:

"My adored one, I love you to distraction. Since yesterday I have been suffering like a damned soul burned by the recollection of you. I feel your lips on mine, your eyes under my eyes, your flesh under my flesh. I love you! I love you! You have made me mad! My arms open! I pant with an immense desire to possess you again. My whole body calls out to you, wants you. I have kept in my mouth the taste of your kisses."

The magistrate rose up; the nun stopped reading. He snatched the letter from her and sought for the signature. There was none, save under the words, "He who adores you," the name "Henry." Their father's name was René. So then he was not the man.

Then the son, with rapid fingers, fumbled in the packet of letters, took another of them and read:

"I can do without your caresses no longer."

And standing up with the severity of a judge passing sentence, he gazed at the impassive face of the dead woman.

The nun, straight as a statue, with teardrops standing at each corner of her eyes, looked at her brother, waiting to see what he meant to do. Then he crossed the room, slowly reached the window and looked out thoughtfully into the night.

When he turned back Sister Eulalie, her eyes quite dry, still remained standing near the bed with a downcast look.

He went over to the drawer and flung in the letters which he had picked up from the floor. Then he drew the curtain round the bed.

And when the dawn made the candles on the table look pale the son rose from his armchair and, without even a parting glance at the mother whom he had separated from them and condemned, he said slowly:

"Now, my sister, let us leave the room."

LOVE'S AWAKENING

No one was surprised at the marriage of M. Simon Lebrument and Mlle. Jeanne Cordier. M. Lebrument came to buy out the office of M. Papillon; he needed, it was understood, money with which to pay for it, and Mlle. Jeanne Cordier had three hundred thousand francs clear in stocks and bonds.

M. Lebrument was a handsome bachelor, who had style, the style of a notary, a provincial style, but, after all, some style, which was a rare thing at Boutigny-le-Rebours.

Mlle. Cordier had grace and freshness, grace a little awkward and freshness a little fixed up, but she was, nevertheless, a pretty girl, desirable and entertaining.

The wedding ceremonies turned Boutigny topsy-turvy. The married couple was much admired when they returned to the conjugal domicile to conceal their happiness, having resolved to make a little simple journey to Paris after they had spent a few days together.

It was charming, these few days together, as M. Lebrument knew how to manage his early relations with his wife with a delicacy, a directness, and sense of fitness, that was remarkable. He took for his motto: "Everything comes to him who waits." He knew how to be patient and energetic at the same time. His success was rapid and complete.

At the end of four days Mme. Lebrument adored her husband. She could not bear to be a moment away from him. He must be near her all day long that she might caress his hands, his beard, his nose, etc. She would sit upon his knees and, taking him by the ears, would say: "Open your mouth and shut your eyes." He opened his mouth with confidence, shut his eyes halfway and then would receive a very long, sweet kiss that made great shivers in his back. And in his turn, he never had enough caresses, enough lips, enough hands, enough of anything with which to enjoy his wife from morning until evening and from evening until morning.

As soon as the first week had slipped away he said to his young companion:

"If you wish, we might leave for Paris Tuesday of next week. We shall be like two lovers who are not married, go about to the theaters, the restaurants, the concert cafés and everywhere, everywhere."

She jumped for joy. "Oh yes, yes!" she replied. "Let us go as soon as possible."

"And as we must not forget anything, you might ask your father to have your dowry ready; I will take it with me and at the same time pay Monsieur Papillon."

She answered: "I will speak to him about it tomorrow morning."

Then he seized her in his arms and began again the little tenderness she loved so much and had reveled in now for eight days.

The Tuesday following, the father-in-law and the mother-in-law accompanied their daughter and son-in-law to the station, whence they set out for the capital. The father-in-law remarked:

"I tell you it is imprudent to carry so much money in your pocketbook." And the young notary smiled.

"Do not be disturbed, Father-in-law," he answered. "I am accustomed to these things. You know that in my profession it often happens that I have nearly a million about me. By carrying it with me, we escape a lot of formalities and delays, to say the least. Do not give yourself any uneasiness."

Then the trainman cried out, "All aboard!" and they hurried into a compartment where they found themselves with two old ladies.

Lebrument murmured in his wife's ear: "How annoying! Now I cannot smoke."

She answered in a low tone: "I am sorry, too, but not on account of your cigar."

The engine puffed and started. The journey lasted an hour, during which they could not say anything of importance, because the two old ladies did not go to sleep.

When they were in the Saint-Lazare station in Paris M. Lebrument said to his wife:

"If you wish, my dear, we will first go and breakfast on the boulevard then return at our leisure to find our trunk and give it to the porter of some hotel."

She consented immediately. "Oh yes," she said, "let us breakfast in some restaurant. Is it far from here?"

"Yes, rather far, but we will take an omnibus."

She was astonished. "Why not a cab?" she asked.

He groaned as he said smilingly: "And you are economical! A cab for five minutes' ride at six sous per minute! You do not deprive yourself of anything!"

"That is true," she said, a little confused.

A large ominbus was passing, with three horses at a trot. Lebrument hailed it: "Conductor! Eh, conductor!"

The heavy carriage stopped. The young notary pushed his wife inside, saying hurriedly in a low voice:

"You get in while I climb up on the outside to smoke at least a cigarette before breakfast."

She had not time for any answer. The conductor, who had seized her by the arm to aid her in mounting the steps, pushed her into the bus, where she landed, half-frightened, upon a seat and in a sort of stupor watched the feet of her husband through the windows at the back as he climbed to the top of the imperial.

There she remained, immovable, between a large gentleman who smelled of a pipe and an old woman who smelled of a dog. All the other travelers, in two mute lines—a grocer's boy, a workman, a sergeant of infantry, a gentleman with gold-rimmed spectacles and a silk cap with enormous visors, like gutters, and two ladies with an important, mincing air, which seemed to say: "We are here, although we should be in a better place." Then there were two good sisters, a little girl in long hair and an undertaker. The assemblage had the appearance of a collection of caricatures in a freak museum, a series of expressions of the human countenance, like a row of grotesque puppets which one knocks down at a fair.

The jolts of the carriage made them toss their heads a little, and as they shook, the flesh of their cheeks trembled, and the disturbance of the rolling wheels gave them an idiotic or sleepy look.

The young woman remained inert. "Why did he not come with me?" she asked herself. A vague sadness oppressed her. He might, indeed, have deprived himself of his cigar!

The good sisters gave the signal to stop. They alighted, one after the other, leaving an odor of old and faded skirts.

Soon after they were gone another stopped the bus. A cook came in, red and out of breath. She sat down and placed her basket of provisions upon her knees. A strong odor of dishwater pervaded the omnibus.

"It is further than I thought," said the young woman to herself.

The undertaker got out and was replaced by a coachman who smelled of a stable. The girl in long hair was succeeded by an errand boy who exhaled the perfume of his walks.

The notary's wife perceived all these things, ill at ease and so disheartened that she was ready to weep without knowing why.

Some others got out; still others came in. The omnibus went on through the interminable streets, stopped at the station and began its route again.

"How far it is!" said Jeanne. "Especially when one has nothing for diversion and cannot sleep!" She had not been so much fatigued for many days.

Little by little all the travelers got out. She remained alone, all alone. The conductor shouted:

"Vaugirard!"

As she blushed he again repeated: "Vaugirard!"

She looked at him, not understanding that this must be addressed to her, as all her neighbors had gone. For the third time the man said: "Vaugirard!"

Then she asked: "Where are we?"

He answered in a gruff voice: "We are at Vaugirard, mademoiselle; I've told you twenty times already."

"Is it far from the boulevard?" she asked.

"What boulevard?"

"The Italian Boulevard."

"We passed that a long time ago."

"Ah! Will you be kind enough to tell my husband?"

"Your husband? Where is he?"

"On the outside."

"On the outside! It has been a long time since there was anybody there."

She made a terrified gesture. Then she said:

"How can it be? It is not possible. He got up there when I entered the omnibus. Look again; he must be there."

The conductor became rude. "Come, little one, this is talk enough. If there is one man lost there are ten to be found. Scamper out now! You will find another in the street."

The tears sprang to her eyes. She insisted: "But, sir, you are mistaken; I assure you that you are mistaken. He had a large pocketbook in his hand."

The employee began to laugh. "A large pocketbook? I remember. Yes, he got out at the Madeleine. That's right! He's left you behind! Ha! Ha!"

The carriage was standing still. She got down and looked up, in spite of herself, to the roof, with an instinctive movement of the eye. It was totally deserted.

Then she began to weep aloud, without thinking that anyone was looking at or listening to her. Finally she said:

"What is going to become of me?"

The inspector came up and inquired: "What's the matter?"

The conductor answered in a jocose fashion:

"This lady's husband has left her on the way."

The other replied: "Now, now, that is nothing. I am at your service." And he turned on his heels.

Then she began to walk ahead, too much frightened, too much excited to think even where she was going. Where was she going? What should she do? How could such an error have occurred? Such an act of carelessness, of disregard, of unheard-of distraction!

She had two francs in her pocket. To whom could she apply? Suddenly she remembered her cousin Barral, who was a clerk in the office of Naval Affairs.

She had just enough to hire a cab; she would go to him. And she met him just as he was starting for his office. Like Lebrument, he carried a large pocketbook under his arm.

She leaned out of the carriage and called: "Henry!"

He stopped, much surprised.

"Jeanne," he said, "here?—and alone? Where do you come from? What are you doing?"

She stammered, with her eyes full of tears: "My husband is lost somewhere."

"Lost? Where?"

"On the omnibus."

"On the omnibus! Oh!"

And she related to him the whole story, weeping much over the adventure.

He listened reflectively and then asked:

"This morning? And was his head perfectly clear?"

"Oh yes! And he had my dowry."

"Your dowry? The whole of it?"

"Yes, the whole of it—in order to pay for his office."

"Well, my dear cousin, your husband, whoever he is, is probably watching the wheel—this minute."

She did not yet comprehend. She stammered: "My husband—you say——"

"I say that he has run off with your—your capital—and that's all about it."

She remained standing there, suffocated with grief, murmuring:

"Then he is—he is—a wretch!"

Then overcome with emotion, she fell on her cousin's shoulder, sobbing violently.

As people were stopping to look at them, he guided her gently into the entrance of his house, supporting her body. They mounted the steps, and as the maid came to open the door he ordered her:

"Sophie, run to the restaurant and bring breakfast for two persons. I shall not go to the office this morning."

DREAMS

Five old friends had been dining together, an author, a doctor, and three wealthy bachelors of independent means.

All available topics of conversation had been exhausted, and that feeling of weariness which heralds the breaking up of such a gathering was already settling upon those present. One of the party, who for five minutes had been silently contemplating the lighted boulevard, with its noise and bustle, suddenly remarked:

"The days seem long when one has nothing to do from morning till night."

"And the nights also," added his neighbor. "I hardly sleep at all, amusements bore me and conversation is always the same. I never come across a new idea, and before talking to anybody I always have to struggle with a violent desire to remain quite silent and not listen to anyone. I don't know what to do in the evenings."

"I would give anything," the third idler said, "for some means of spending even two pleasant hours every day."

The author, who had just thrown his overcoat over his arm, came towards them and said:

"Anybody who could find a new vice and could pass it on to his fellow creatures, even though it might shorten life by half, would do a far greater service to humanity than anyone who might discover a means of securing perpetual health and youth."

The doctor began to laugh, and, biting off the end of his cigar, he said:

"Yes, but it is not found so easily as that. Ever since the beginning of the world the problem has been vigorously attacked. Primitive man instantly attained perfection in that line, but we can scarcely equal him."

One of the three idlers murmured:

"What a pity!"

A moment later he added:

"If only one could sleep, could sleep well, without feeling too warm or too cold, sleep with that exhaustion which comes from an evening of intense fatigue, sleep without dreaming!"

"Why without dreaming?" inquired his neighbor.

"Because dreams are not always pleasant," the other replied, "because they are always strange, improbable and incoherent, and while asleep we cannot even enjoy the best ones to the full. You must dream while awake."

"Who prevents you from doing so?" asked the author.

The doctor threw away his cigar.

"My dear fellow, daydreaming requires the exercise of great will power, and therefore leaves one very tired. Now one of the most delightful things in the world is a real dream—the mind wandering through pleasant visions—but it must come naturally, not under painful stimulation, and it should be accompanied by complete physical comfort. That kind of dream I can offer you, if you will promise not to abuse it."

The author shrugged his shoulders.

"Oh, yes," he said, "I know all about that; hashish, opium, green jain, the *paradis artificiels*. I have read Baudelaire's books and I have even tasted his famous drug, which made me very ill."

The doctor sat down again.

"No, I mean ether, simply ether; and I might add that you literary men ought to use it sometimes."

The three rich men came nearer, and one of them asked him to explain its effect.

"Let us come down to facts," the doctor replied; "I am leaving medicine and morality out of the question; I am only concerned at the moment with pleasure. You are indulging every day in excesses which are shortening your lives. I will bring a new sensation to your notice, possibly only for men of intelligence—that is to say, of considerable intelligence—dangerous, like everything which overexcites us, but none the less exquisite. I should add that a certain amount of preparation is required, that is to say, it is necessary to become accustomed to it, in order to experience to the full the singular effects of ether.

"They are different from the effects of hashish, opium and morphine, and they cease as soon as you stop inhaling it, while the other dream producers continue their action for hours.

"I will try to analyze as clearly as possible the feelings experienced by the use of ether, but so delicate and fleeting are those sensations that it is not an easy task.

"I first tried this remedy when I was suffering from violent neuralgia, and I have perhaps rather abused it since. I had sharp pains in the head and neck, and my skin became unbearably hot and feverish. I took a large flask of ether, and, lying down, I began slowly to inhale it. After a few minutes, I thought I heard a vague murmur, which soon became a kind of drone, and it seemed to me that the inside of my body was getting lighter—as light as air—and dissolving in vapor.

"Then came a sort of stupor, a drowsy feeling of comfort, in spite of the pains, which were still present but were no longer acute. They were pains such as one could endure with resignation, and no longer that terrible excruciating agony against which the whole tortured body protests.

"Soon that curious and delightful feeling of buoyancy spread from my body to my limbs, which in turn became light as a feather, as if the flesh and bones had disappeared and had left only the skin to enable me to feel the pleasure of living and resting in such comfort. I then realized that I was no longer in agony, the pain had vanished, melted away. I heard four voices, as if two conversations were going on at the same time, but I could not understand a single word; sometimes there was a confused jumble of sounds; sometimes I could distinguish words; but it was evident that what I heard was nothing but the intensified drumming in my ears. Far from being asleep, I was very much awake; my ideas, my sensations and my thoughts were marvelously clear and strong, aided by a feeling of exhilaration, a curious intoxication arising from a tenfold increase in my mental powers.

"It was not like the dreams produced by hashish, or the morbid illusions of opium; it was a wonderful clearness of thought, a new way of regarding and appreciating the important things in life, with the absolute certainty that this way was the right one.

"And I suddenly remembered the old Biblical idea. It seemed to me that I had eaten of the tree of knowledge and that all mysteries were solved, so powerful and irrefutable was this strange new logic. Arguments, reasons, and proofs crowded upon me, only to be upset by still stronger ones. My brain became a battlefield of ideas; I saw myself as a superior being, armed with an invincible intelligence, and I experienced a fierce joy in the discovery of my power.

"All this lasted a very long time, while I continued to inhale the ether in my flask. Suddenly I realized that it was empty, and felt most terribly grieved."

The four men spoke together:

"Doctor, give me a prescription for a pint of ether!"

But the doctor put on his hat and retorted:

"Certainly not! Go and be poisoned by somebody else!"

And he went out.

Ladies and gentlemen, if you feel inclined to try?——

BED NO. 29

When Captain Epivent passed in the street all the ladies turned to look at him.
He was the true type of a handsome officer of hussars. He was always on parade,
always strutted a little and seemed preoccupied and proud of his leg, his figure and
his mustache. He had superb ones, it is true, a superb leg, figure and mustache. The
last-named was blond, very heavy, falling martially from his lip in a beautiful sweep,
the color of ripe wheat, carefully turned at the ends and falling over both sides of
his mouth in two powerful sprigs of hair cut square across. His waist was thin, as
if he wore a corset, while a vigorous masculine chest, bulged and arched, spread
itself above his waist. His leg was admirable, a gymnastic leg, the leg of a dancer
whose muscular flesh outlined each movement under the clinging cloth of the red
pantaloon.

He walked with muscles taut, with feet and arms apart and with the slightly
balanced step of the cavalier who knows how to make the most of his limbs and his
carriage and who seems a conqueror in a uniform but looks commonplace in mufti.

Like many other officers, Captain Epivent carried a civil costume badly. He had
no air of elegance as soon as he was clothed in the gray or black of the shop clerk.
But in his proper setting he was a triumph. He had, besides, a handsome face, the
nose thin and curved, blue eyes and a good forehead. He was bald, without ever
being able to comprehend why his hair had fallen off. He consoled himself with
thinking that with a heavy mustache, a head a little bald was not so bad.

He scorned everybody in general, with a difference in the degrees of his scorn.

In the first place, for him the middle class did not exist. He looked at them as he
would look at animals, without according them more of his attention than he would
give to sparrows or chickens. Officers alone counted in his world, but he did not
have the same esteem for all officers. He only respected handsome men, an imposing
presence, the true, military quality being first. A soldier was a merry fellow, a devil,
created for love and war, a man of brawn, muscle and hair, nothing more. He classed
the generals of the French army according to their figure, their bearing and the
stern look of their faces. Bourbaki appeared to him the greatest warrior of modern
times.

He often laughed at the officers of the line who were short and fat and puffed
while marching. And he had a special scorn for the poor recruits from the poly-
technic schools, those thin little men with spectacles, awkward and unskillful, who
seemed as much made for a uniform as a wolf for saying Mass, as he often asserted.
He was indignant that they should be tolerated in the army, those abortions with
the lank limbs, who marched like crabs, did not drink, ate little and seemed to love
equations better than pretty girls.

Captain Epivent himself had constant successes and triumphs with the fair sex.

Every time he took supper in company with a woman he thought himself certain
of finishing the night with her upon the same mattress, and, if unsurmountable
obstacles hindered that evening, his victory was sure at least the following day.
His comrades did not like him to meet their mistresses, and the merchants in the
shops, who had their pretty wives at the counter, knew him, feared him and hated

him desperately. When he passed, the merchants' wives in spite of themselves exchanged a look with him through the glass of the front windows, one of those looks that avail more than tender words, which contain an appeal and a response, a desire and an avowal. And the husbands, who turned away with a sort of instinct, returned brusquely, casting a furious look at the proud, arched silhouette of the officer. And when the captain had passed, smiling and content with his impression, the merchants, handling with nervous hands the objects spread out before them, declared:

"There's a great dandy. When shall we stop feeding all these good-for-nothings who go dragging their tinware through the streets? For my part, I would rather be a butcher than a soldier. Then if there's blood on my table it is the blood of beasts, at least. And he is useful, is the butcher, and the knife he carries has not killed men. I do not understand how these murderers are tolerated, walking on the public streets, carrying with them their instruments of death. It is necessary to have them, I suppose, but at least let them conceal themselves and not dress up in masquerade, with their red breeches and blue coats. The executioner doesn't dress himself up, does he?"

The woman, without answering, would shrug her shoulders, while the husband, divining the gesture without seeing it, would cry:

"Anybody must be stupid to watch those fellows parade up and down."

Nevertheless, Captain Epivent's reputation for conquests was well established in the whole French army.

Now, in 1868, his regiment, the One Hundred and Second Hussars, came into garrison at Rouen.

He was soon known in the town. He appeared every evening toward five o'clock upon the Boïeldieu mall to take his absinthe and coffee at the Comedy, and before entering the establishment he would always take a turn upon the promenade to show his leg, his figure and his mustaches.

The merchants of Rouen who also promenaded there with their hands behind their backs, preoccupied with business affairs, speaking in high and low voices, would sometimes throw him a glance and murmur:

"Egad! That's a handsome fellow!"

But when they knew him they remarked:

"Look! Captain Epivent! But he's a rascal all the same!"

The women on meeting him had a very queer little movement of the head, a kind of shiver of modesty, as if they felt themselves grow weak or unclothed before him. They would lower their heads a little, with a smile upon their lips, as if they had a desire to be found charming and have a look from him. When he walked with a comrade the comrade never failed to murmur with jealous envy each time that he saw the sport:

"This rascal of an Epivent has the chances!"

Among the licensed girls of the town it was a struggle, a race, to see who would carry him off. They all came at five o'clock, the officers' hour, to the Boïeldieu mall and dragged their skirts up and down the length of the walk, two by two, while the lieutenants, captains and commanders, two by two, dragged their swords along the ground before entering the café.

One evening the beautiful Irma, the mistress, it was said, of M. Templier-Papon, the rich manufacturer, stopped her carriage in front of the Comedy and, getting out, made a pretense of buying some paper or some visiting cards of M. Paulard, the engraver, in order to pass before the officers' tables and cast a look at

Captain Epivent which seemed to say: "When you will," so clearly that Colonel Prune, who was drinking the green liquor with his lieutenant colonel, could not help muttering:

"Confound that fellow! He has the chances, that scamp!"

The remark of the colonel was repeated, and Captain Epivent, moved by this approbation of his superior, passed the next day and many times after that under the windows of the beauty in his most captivating attitude.

She saw him, showed herself and smiled.

That same evening he was her lover.

They attracted attention, made an exhibition of their attachment and mutually compromised themselves, both of them proud of their adventure.

Nothing was so much talked of in town as the beautiful Irma and the officer. M. Templier-Papon alone was ignorant of their relation.

Captain Epivent beamed with glory; every instant he would say:

"Irma happened to say to me," "Irma told me tonight," or, "Yesterday at dinner Irma said——"

For a whole year they walked with and displayed in Rouen this love like a flag taken from the enemy. He felt himself aggrandized by this conquest, envied, more sure of the future, surer of the decoration so much desired, for the eyes of all were upon him, and he was satisfied to find himself well in sight, instead of being forgotten.

But here war was declared, and the captain's regiment was one of the first to be sent to the front. The adieux were lamentable. They lasted the whole night long.

Sword, red breeches, cap and jacket were all overturned from the back of a chair upon the floor; robes, skirts, silk stockings, also fallen down, were spread around and mingled with the uniform in distress upon the carpet, the room upside down, as if there had been a battle; Irma, wild, her hair unbound, threw her despairing arms around the officer's neck, straining him to her, then, leaving him, rolled upon the floor, overturning the furniture, catching the fringes of the armchairs, biting their feet, while the captain, much moved but not skillful at consolation, repeated:

"Irma, my little Irma, do not cry so; it is necessary."

He occasionally wiped a tear from the corner of his eye with the end of his finger. They separated at daybreak. She followed her lover in her carriage as far as the first stopping place. Then she kissed him before the whole regiment at the moment of separation. They even found this very genteel, worthy and very romantic, and the comrades pressed the captain's hand and said to him:

"Confound you, rogue, she has a heart, all the same, the little one."

They seemed to see something patriotic in it.

The regiment was sorely proved during the campaign. The captain conducted himself heroically and finally received the Cross of Honor. Then the war ended; he returned to Rouen and the garrison.

Immediately upon his return he asked of news of Irma, but no one was able to give him anything exact. Some said she was married to a Prussian major. Others, that she had gone to her parents who were farmers in the suburbs of Yvetot.

He even sent his orderly to the mayor's office to consult the registry of deaths. The name of his mistress was not to be found.

He was very angry, which fact he paraded everywhere. He even took the enemy to task for his unhappiness, attributing to the Prussians, who had occupied Rouen, the disappearance of the young girl, declaring:

"In the next war they shall pay well for it, the beggars!"

Then one morning as he entered the messroom at the breakfast hour, an old porter, in a blouse and an oilcloth cap, gave him a letter, which he opened and read:

MY DEARIE: *I am in the hospital very ill, very ill. Will you not come and see me? It would give me so much pleasure!*   IRMA.

The captain grew pale and, moved with pity, declared:

"It's too bad! The poor girl! I will go there as soon as I breakfast."

And during the whole time at the table he told the officers that Irma was in the hospital and that he was going to see her that blessed morning. It must be the fault of those unspeakable Prussians. She had doubtless found herself alone without a sou, broken down with misery, for they must certainly have stolen her furniture.

"Ah, the dirty whelps!"

Everybody listened with great excitement. Scarcely had he slipped his napkin in his wooden ring, when he rose and, taking his sword from the peg and swelling out his chest to make him thin, hooked his belt and set out with hurried step to the city hospital.

But entrance to the hospital building, where he expected to enter immediately, was sharply refused him, and he was obliged to find his colonel and explain his case to him in order to get a word from him to the director.

This man, after having kept the handsome captain waiting some time in his anteroom, gave him an authorized pass and a cold and disapproving greeting.

Inside the door he felt himself constrained in this asylum of misery and suffering and death. A boy in the service showed him the way. He walked upon tiptoe, that he might make no noise, through the long corridors, where floated a slight, moist odor of illness and medicines. A murmur of voices alone disturbed the silence of the hospital.

At times through an open door the captain perceived a dormitory, with its rows of beds whose clothes were raised by the forms of the bodies.

Some convalescents were seated in chairs at the foot of their couches, sewing and clothed in the uniform gray cloth dress with white cap.

His guide suddenly stopped before one of these corridors filled with patients. He read on the door in large letters: "Syphilis." The captain started, then he felt that he was blushing. An attendant was preparing a medicine at a little wooden table at the door.

"I will show you," she said; "it is bed 29."

And she walked ahead of the officer. She indicated a bed: "There it is."

There was nothing to be seen but a bundle of bedclothes. Even the head was concealed under the coverlet. Everywhere faces were to be seen on the couches, pale faces, astonished at the sight of a uniform, the faces of women, young women and old women, but all seemingly plain and common in the humble, regulation garb.

The captain, very much disturbed, supporting his sword in one hand and carrying his cap in the other, murmured:

"Irma."

There was a sudden motion in the bed, and the face of his mistress appeared, but so changed, so tired, so thin, that he would scarcely have known it.

She gasped, overcome by emotion, and then said:

"Albert! Albert! It is you! Oh! I am so glad—so glad." And the tears ran down her cheeks.

The attendant brought a chair. "Be seated, sir," she said.

He sat down and looked at the pale, wretched countenance, so little like that of the beautiful, fresh girl he had left. Finally he said:

"What seems to be the matter with you?"

She replied, weeping: "You know well enough; it is written on the door." And she hid her eyes under the edge of the bedclothes.

Dismayed and ashamed, he continued: "How have you caught it, my poor girl?"

She answered: "It was those beasts of Prussians. They took me almost by force and then poisoned me."

He found nothing to add. He looked at her and kept turning his cap around on his knees.

The other patients gazed at him, and he believed that he detected an odor of putrefaction, of contaminated flesh, in this corridor full of girls tainted with this ignoble, terrible malady.

She murmured: "I do not believe that I shall recover. The doctor says it is very serious."

Then she perceived the cross upon the officer's breast and cried:

"Oh, you have been honored; now I am content. How contented I am! If I could only embrace you!"

A shiver of fear and disgust ran along the captain's skin at the thought of this kiss. He had a desire to make his escape, to be in the clear air and never see this woman again. He remained, however, not knowing how to make the adieux, and finally stammered:

"You took no care of yourself then."

A flame flashed in Irma's eyes: "No, the desire to avenge myself came to me when I should have broken away from it. And I poisoned them, too, all, all that I could. As long as there were any of them in Rouen, I had no thought for myself."

He declared in a constrained tone in which there was a little note of gaiety: "So far you have done some good."

Getting animated, and her cheekbones getting red, she answered:

"Oh yes, there will more than one of them die from my fault. I tell you, I had my vengeance."

Again he said: "So much the better." Then, rising, he added: "Well, I must leave you now, because I have only time to meet my appointment with the colonel."

She showed much emotion, crying out: "Already! You leave me already! And when you have scarcely arrived!"

But he wished to go at any cost and said:

"But you see that I came immediately, and it is absolutely necessary that I be at the colonel's at an appointed time."

She asked: "Is it still Colonel Prune?"

"Still Colonel Prune. He was twice wounded."

She continued: "And your comrades? Have some of them been killed?"

"Yes. Saint-Timon, Savagnat, Poli, Saprival, Robert, De Courson, Pasafil, Santal,

Caravan and Poivrin are dead. Sahel had an arm carried off and Courvoisin a leg amputated. Paquet lost his right eye."

She listened, much interested. Then suddenly she stammered:

"Will you kiss me, say, before you leave me? Madame Langlois is not there."

And in spite of the disgust which came to his lips, he placed them against the wan forehead, while she, throwing her arms around him, scattered random kisses over his blue jacket.

Then she said: "You will come again? Say that you will come again. Promise me that you will."

"Yes, I promise."

"When, now? Can you come Thursday?"

"Yes, Thursday."

"Thursday at two o'clock?"

"Yes, Thursday at two o'clock."

"You promise?"

"I promise."

"Adieu, my dearie."

"Adieu."

And he went away, confused by the staring glances of those in the dormitory, bending his tall form to make himself seem smaller. And when he was in the street he took a long breath.

That evening his comrades asked him: "Well, how is Irma?"

He answered in a constrained voice: "She has a trouble with the lungs; she is very ill."

But a little lieutenant, scenting something from his manner, went to head-quarters, and the next day when the captain went into mess he was welcomed by a volley of laughter and jokes. They had found vengeance at last.

It was learned further that Irma had made a spite marriage with the staff major of the Prussians, that she had gone through the country on horseback with the colonel of the Blue Hussars and many others, and that in Rouen she was no longer called anything but the "wife of the Prussians."

For eight days the captain was the victim of his regiment. He received by post and by messenger notes from those who can reveal the past and the future, circulars of specialists, and medicines, the nature of which was inscribed on the package.

And the colonel, catching the drift of it, said in a severe tone:

"Well, the captain had a pretty acquaintance! I send him my compliments."

At the end of twelve days he was appealed to by another letter from Irma. He tore it up with rage and made no reply to it.

A week later she wrote him again that she was very ill and wished to see him to say farewell.

He did not answer.

After some days more he received a note from a chaplain of the hospital:

The girl Irma Pavolin is on her deathbed and begs you to come.

He dared not refuse to oblige the chaplain, but he entered the hospital with a heart swelling with wicked anger, with wounded vanity and humiliation.

He found her scarcely changed at all and thought that she had deceived him.

"What do you wish of me?" he asked.

"I wish to say farewell. It appears that I am near the end."

He did not believe it.

"Listen," he said, "you have made me the laughingstock of the regiment, and I do not wish it to continue."

She asked: "What have I done?"

He was irritated at not knowing how to answer. But he said:

"Is it nothing that I return here to be joked by everybody on your account?"

She looked at him with languid eyes, where shone a pale light of anger, and answered:

"What can I have done? I have not been genteel with you, perhaps! Is it because I have sometimes asked for something? But for you, I would have remained with Monsieur Templier-Papon and would not have found myself here today. No, you see, if anyone has reproaches to make it is not you."

He answered in a clear tone: "I have not made reproaches, but I cannot continue to come to see you, because your conduct with the Prussians has been the shame of the town."

She sat up with a little shake in the bed as she replied:

"My conduct with the Prussians? But when I tell you that they took me, and when I tell you that if I took no thought of myself, it was because I wished to poison them! If I had wished to cure myself it would not have been so difficult, I can tell you! But I wished to kill them, and I have killed them, come now! I have killed them!"

He remained standing. "In any case," he said, "it was a shame."

She had a kind of suffocation and then replied:

"Why is it a shame for me to cause them to die and try to exterminate them, tell me? You did not talk that way when you used to come to my house in Jeanne-d'Arc Street. Ah! It is a shame! You have not done as much with your Cross of Honor! I deserve more merit than you, do you understand? More than you, for I have killed more Prussians than you!"

He stood, stupefied, before her, trembling with indignation. He stammered: "Be still—you must—be still—because those things—I cannot allow—anyone to touch upon——"

But she was not listening. "What harm have you done the Prussians? Would it ever have happened if you had kept them from coming to Rouen? Tell me! It is you who should stop and listen. And I have done more harm than you, I, yes, more harm to them than you, and I am going to die for it, while you are singing songs and making yourself fine to inveigle women."

Upon each bed a head was raised, and all eyes looked at this man in uniform who stammered again:

"You must be still—more quiet—you know——"

But she would not be quiet. She cried out:

"Ah, yes, you are a pretty poser! I know you well. I know you. And I tell you that I have done them more harm than you—I—and that I have killed more than all your regiment together. Come now, you coward."

He went away; in fact, he fled, stretching his long legs as he passed between the two rows of beds where the syphilitic patients were becoming excited. And he heard the gasping, stifled voice of Irma pursuing him:

"More than you—yes—I have killed more than you."

He tumbled down the staircase four steps at a time and ran until he was shut
fast in his room.

The next day he heard that she was dead.

MARROCA

You ask me, my dear friend, to send you my impressions of Africa and an account
of my adventures, especially of my love affairs, in this seductive land. You laughed
a great deal beforehand at my dusky sweethearts, as you called them, and declared
that you could see me, returning to France, followed by a tall ebony-colored
woman, with a yellow silk handkerchief round her head, and wearing voluminous
bright-colored trousers.

No doubt the Moorish dames will have their turn, for I have seen several who
made me feel very much inclined to fall in love with them. But by way of making
a beginning, I came across something better and very original.

In your last letter to me you say: "When I know how people love in a country
I know that country well enough to describe it, although I may never have seen
it." Let me tell you then that here they love furiously. From the very first moment one feels a sort of trembling ardor, of constant desire, to the very tips of
the fingers, which overexcites the powers and faculties of physical sensation, from
the simple contact of the hands down to the requirement which makes us commit so many follies.

Do not misunderstand me. I do not know whether you call love of the heart
a love of the soul, whether sentimental idealism, platonic love, in a word, can
exist on this earth; I doubt it myself. But that other love, sensual love, which has
something good, a great deal of good about it, is really terrible in this climate.
The heat, the burning atmosphere which makes you feverish, the suffocating blasts
of wind from the south, waves of fire from the desert which is so near us, that
oppressive sirocco which is more destructive and withering than fire, a perpetual
conflagration of an entire continent, burned even to its stones by a fierce and devouring sun, inflame the blood, excite the flesh and make brutes of us.

But to come to my story. I shall not dwell on the beginning of my stay in Africa.
After visiting Bona, Constantine, Biskra and Steif, I went to Bougie through the
defiles of Chabet, by an excellent road cut through a large forest, which follows
the sea at a height of six hundred feet above it and leads to that wonderful bay
of Bougie, which is as beautiful as that of Naples, of Ajaccio or of Douarnenez,
which are the most lovely that I know of.

Far away in the distance, before one rounds the large inlet where the water is
perfectly calm, one sees Bougie. It is built on the steep sides of a high hill covered
with trees, and forms a white spot on that green slope; it might almost be taken
for the foam of a cascade falling into the sea.

I had no sooner set foot in that small, delightful town, than I knew that I should
stay for a long time. In all directions the eye rests on rugged, strangely shaped
hilltops, so close together that you can hardly see the open sea, so that the gulf
looks like a lake. The blue water is wonderfully transparent, and the azure sky, a

deep azure, as if it had received two coats of color, expands its wonderful beauty above it. They seem to be looking at themselves in a glass, a veritable reflection of each other.

Bougie is a town of ruins, and on the quay is such magnificent ruin that you might imagine you were at the opera. It is the old Saracen Gate, overgrown with ivy, and there are ruins in all directions on the hills round the town, fragments of Roman walls, bits of Saracen monuments and remains of Arabic buildings.

I had taken a small Moorish house in the upper town. You know those dwellings, which have been described so often. They have no windows on the outside, but they are lighted from top to bottom by an inner court. On the first floor they have a large, cool room, in which one spends the days, and a terrace on the roof, on which one spends the nights.

I at once fell in with the custom of all hot countries, that is to say, of taking a siesta after lunch. That is the hottest time in Africa, the time when one can scarcely breathe, when the streets, the fields and the long, dazzling, white roads are deserted, when everyone is asleep or, at any rate, trying to sleep, attired as scantily as possible.

In my drawing room, which had columns of Arabic architecture, I had placed a large, soft couch, covered with a carpet from Djebel Amour. There, very nearly in the costume of Assan, I sought to rest, but I could not sleep, as I was tortured by continence. There are two forms of torture on this earth which I hope you will never know: the want of water and the want of women, and I do not know which is the worst. In the desert men would commit any infamy for the sake of a glass of clean, cold water, and what would one not do in some of the towns of the littoral for the companionship of a handsome woman? There is no lack of girls in Africa; on the contrary, they abound, but, to continue my comparison, they are as unwholesome as the muddy water in the pools of Sahara.

Well, one day when I was feeling more enervated than usual, I was trying in vain to close my eyes. My legs twitched as if they were being pricked, and I tossed about uneasily on my couch. At last, unable to bear it any longer, I got up and went out. It was a terribly hot day in the middle of July, and the pavement was hot enough to bake bread on. My shirt, which was soaked with perspiration, clung to my body; on the horizon there was a slight, white vapor, which seemed to be palpable heat.

I went down to the sea and, circling the port, walked along the shore of the pretty bay where the baths are. There was nobody about, and nothing was stirring; not a sound of bird or of beast was to be heard; the very waves did not lap, and the sea appeared to be asleep in the sun.

Suddenly, behind one of the rocks which were half covered by the silent water, I heard a slight movement. Turning round, I saw a tall, naked girl, sitting up to her bosom in the water, taking a bath; no doubt she reckoned on being alone at that hot period of the day. Her head was turned toward the sea, and she was moving gently up and down, without seeing me.

Nothing could be more surprising than that picture of a beautiful woman in the water, which was as clear as crystal, under a blaze of light. She was a statue. She turned round, uttered a cry and, half swimming, half walking, hid herself altogether behind her rock. I knew she must necessarily come out, so I sat down on the beach and waited. Presently she just showed her head, which was covered with thick black plaits of hair. She had a rather large mouth, with full lips, large, bold eyes, and her skin, which was tanned by the climate, looked like a piece of old, hard, polished ivory.

She called out to me: "Go away!" and her full voice, which corresponded to her strong build, had a guttural accent. As I did not move, she added: "It is not right of you to stop there, monsieur." I did not move, however, and her head disappeared. Ten minutes passed, and then her hair, then her forehead and then her eyes reappeared, but slowly and prudently, as if she were playing at hide-and-seek and were looking to see who was near. This time she was furious and called out: "You will make me catch a chill, for I shall not come out as long as you are there." Thereupon I got up and went away, but not without looking round several times. When she thought I was far enough off she came out of the water. Bending down and turning her back to me, she disappeared in a cavity of the rock behind a petticoat that was hanging up in front of it.

I went back the next day. She was bathing again, but she had a bathing costume and she began to laugh and showed her white teeth. A week later we were friends, and in another week we were eager lovers. Her name was Marroca, and she pronounced it as if there were a dozen rs in it. She was the daughter of Spanish colonists and had married a Frenchman, whose name was Pontabèze. He was in government employ, though I never exactly knew what his functions were. I found out that he was always very busy, and I did not care for anything else.

She then altered her time for having her bath and came to my house every day to take her siesta there. What a siesta! It could scarcely be called reposing! She was a splendid girl of a somewhat animal but superb type. Her eyes were always glowing with passion; her half-open mouth, her sharp teeth and even her smiles had something ferociously loving about them, and her curious long and conical breasts gave her whole body something of the animal, made her a sort of inferior yet magnificent being, a creature destined for unbridled love, and roused in me the idea of those ancient deities who gave expression to their tenderness on the grass and under the trees.

And then her mind was as simple as two and two are four, and a sonorous laugh served her instead of thought.

Instinctively proud of her beauty, she hated the slightest covering and ran and frisked about my house with daring and unconscious immodesty. When she was at last overcome and worn out by her cries and movements, she used to sleep soundly and peacefully, while the overwhelming heat brought out minute spots of perspiration on her brown skin.

Sometimes she returned in the evening, when her husband was on duty somewhere, and we used to lie on the terrace, scarcely covered by some fine, gauzy oriental fabric. When the full moon lit up the town and the gulf, with its surrounding frame of hills, we saw on all the other terraces a recumbent army of silent · phantoms who would occasionally get up, change their places and lie down again in the languorous warmth of the starry night.

In spite of the brightness of African nights, Marroca would insist upon stripping herself almost naked in the clear rays of the moon; she did not trouble herself much about anybody who might see us, and often, in spite of my fears and entreaties, she uttered long, resounding cries, which made the dogs in the distance howl.

One night, when I was sleeping under the starry sky, she came and kneeled down on my carpet and, putting her lips, which curled slightly, close to my face, she said:

"You must come and stay at my house."

I did not understand her and asked:

"What do you mean?"

"Yes, when my husband has gone away you must come and be with me."

I could not help laughing and said: "Why, as you come here?"

And when she went on, almost talking into my mouth, sending her hot breath into my throat and moistening my mustache with her lips:

"I want it as a remembrance."

Still I did not grasp her meaning. Then she put her arms around my neck and said: "When you are no longer here I shall think of it."

I was touched and amused at the same time and replied: "You must be mad. I would much rather stop here."

As a matter of fact, I have no liking for assignations under the conjugal roof; they are mousetraps in which the unwary are always caught. But she begged and prayed and even cried and at last said: "You shall see how I will love you there."

Her wish seemed so strange that I could not explain it to myself, but on thinking it over, I thought I could discern a profound hatred for her husband, the secret vengeance of a woman who takes a pleasure in deceiving him and who, moreover, wishes to deceive him in his own house.

"Is your husband very unkind to you?" I asked her. She looked vexed and said: "Oh no, he is very kind."

"But you are not fond of him?"

She looked at me with astonishment in her large eyes. "Indeed, I am very fond of him, very, but not so fond as I am of you."

I could not understand it all, and while I was trying to get at her meaning she pressed one of those kisses, whose power she knew so well, onto my lips and whispered: "But you will come, will you not?"

I resisted, however, and so she got up immediately and went away; nor did she come back for a week. On the eighth day she came back, stopped gravely at the door of my abode and said: "Are you coming to my house tonight? If you refuse I shall go away."

Eight days is a very long time, my friend, and in Africa those eight days are as good as a month. "Yes," I said and opened my arms, and she threw herself into them.

At night she waited for me in a neighboring street and took me to their house, which was very small and near the harbor. I first of all went through the kitchen, where they had their meals, and then into a very tidy, whitewashed room with photographs on the walls and paper flowers under a glass case. Marroca seemed beside herself with pleasure, and she jumped about and said: "There, you are at home now." And I certainly acted as though I were, though I felt rather embarrassed and somewhat uneasy.

Suddenly a loud knocking at the door made us start, and a man's voice called out: "Marroca, it is I."

She started: "My husband! Here, hide under the bed, quickly."

I was distractedly looking for my coat, but she gave me a push and panted out: "Come along, come along."

I lay down flat on my stomach and crept under the bed without a word, while she went into the kitchen. I heard her open a cupboard and then shut it again, and she came back into the room carrying some object which I could not see but which she quickly put down. Then as her husband was getting impatient, she said calmly: "I cannot find the matches." Suddenly she added: "Oh, here they are: I will come and let you in."

The man came in, and I could see nothing of him but his feet, which were enormous. If the rest of him was in proportion he must have been a giant.

I heard kisses, a little pat on her naked flesh and a laugh, and he said in a strong Marseille accent: "I forgot my purse, so I was obliged to come back; you were sound asleep, I suppose?"

He went to the cupboard and was a long time in finding what he wanted; and as Marroca had thrown herself onto the bed, as if she were tired out, he went up to her and no doubt tried to caress her, for she flung a volley of angry rs at him. His feet were so close to me that I felt a stupid, inexplicable longing to catch hold of them, but I restrained myself. When he saw that he could not succeed in his wish he got angry and said: "You are not at all nice tonight. Good-by."

I heard another kiss, then the big feet turned, and I saw the nails in his shoes as he went into the next room; the front door was shut, and I was saved!

I came slowly out of my retreat, feeling rather humiliated, and while Marroca danced a jig around me, shouting with laughter and clapping her hands, I threw myself heavily into a chair. But I jumped up with a bound, for I had sat down on something cold, and as I was no more dressed than my accomplice was, the contact made me start. I looked round. I had sat down on a small ax used for cutting wood and as sharp as a knife. How had it got there? I had certainly not seen it when I went in, but Marroca, seeing me jump up, nearly choked with laughter and coughed with both hands on her sides.

I thought her amusement rather out of place; we had risked our lives stupidly. I still felt a cold shiver down my back, and I was rather hurt at her foolish laughter.

"Supposing your husband had seen me?" I said.

"There was no danger of that," she replied.

"What do you mean? No danger? That is a good joke! If he had stooped down he must have seen me."

She did not laugh any more; she only looked at me with her large eyes, which were bright with merriment.

"He would not have stooped."

"Why?" I persisted. "Just suppose that he had let his hat fall, he would have been sure to pick it up, and then—I was well prepared to defend myself in this costume!"

She put her two strong, round arms about my neck and, lowering her voice, as she did when she said, "I adorre you," she whispered:

"Then he would never have got up again."

I did not understand her and said: "What do you mean?"

She gave me a cunning wink and put out her hand to the chair on which I had sat down, and her outstretched hands, her smile, her half-open lips, her white, sharp and ferocious teeth, all drew my attention to the little ax which was used for cutting wood, the sharp blade of which was glistening in the candlelight. While she put out her hand as if she were going to take it, she put her left arm round me and, drawing me to her and putting her lips against mine, with her right arm she made a motion as if she were cutting off the head of a kneeling man!

This, my friend, is the manner in which people here understand conjugal duties, love and hospitality!

OLD MILON

For the past month the great sun had been casting its broiling heat over the fields. Nature is unfolding radiantly beneath this shower of fire; as far as the eye can reach, the earth is green. To the ends of the horizon, the sky is blue. The Norman farms scattered over the plain look, from the distance, like little woods, enclosed in their girdle of slender beeches. From near at hand, when the worm-eaten gate is opened, it is as though one were looking at a giant garden, for all the aged apple trees, bony of limb like country folk, are in flower. The rows of black, crooked, twisted old trunks in the farmyard display their dazzling white and pink domes under the sky. The sweet perfume of their blossoming mingles with the rich stenches of the open cowshed and the steam of the fermenting dungheap overrun with hens.

It is noon. The family is at dinner in the shade of the pear tree by the door: the father, the mother, the four children, the two servants, and the three hired men. There is little speech. The soup is eaten, then the cover is taken off the dish, full of potatoes cooked in fat.

From time to time a maid rises and goes down to the cellar to refill the pitcher of cider.

The man, a big fellow of forty, gazes at a vine, still bare of leaves, which grows up the front of his house, and runs, writhing like a snake, under the shutters, the whole length of the wall.

"The old man's vine is budding early this year," he remarks at last. "Maybe it will bear."

The woman also turns round and looks at it, without speaking.

The vine is planted on the exact spot where the old man was shot.

It was during the war of 1870. The Prussians were occupying the entire district. General Faidherbe, with the northern army, was putting up a stout resistance.

The Prussian staff was quartered at this farm. The old peasant who owned it, old Milon, Pierre Milon, had taken them in and installed them as comfortably as he could.

For a month the German advance guard had remained in the village, reconnoitering. The French remained immovable ten leagues away; yet every night uhlans kept disappearing.

All the detachments of scouts, those who were sent out on picket duty, when only two or three men set out together, never returned.

They were found dead in the morning, in a field, beside a farmyard, or in a ditch. Their horses lay at the roadside, with their throats cut with a saber.

These murders all appeared to be committed by the same men, who could not be discovered.

The whole district was under a reign of terror. Peasants were shot on mere denunciation, and women imprisoned; an attempt was made to frighten the children into revealing the truth. Nothing was discovered.

But one morning old Milon was seen lying in his stable, with a slash cut across his face.

Two disemboweled uhlans were found three kilometers from the farm. One still held his blood-stained weapon in his hand. He had fought, had defended himself.

A council of war was immediately established in the open, in front of the farm, and the old man was brought in.

He was sixty-eight. He was small, thin, and slightly crooked, with big hands like the claws of a crab. His faded, thin hair, light as a duckling's down, concealed none of the flesh on his skull. The brown, creased skin on his neck showed veins which were lost under the jaws and reappeared at the temples. He was known throughout the neighborhood as a miser and a hard man in business.

He was made to stand, between four soldiers, in front of the kitchen table, which had been carried out of doors. Five officers and the colonel sat facing him.

The colonel began speaking, in French:

"Father Milon, since we have been here, we have had nothing but praise for you. You have always been obliging, and even zealous, in our service. But today a terrible charge rests upon you, and the matter must be cleared up. How did you get the wound in your face?"

The peasant did not reply.

"Your silence condemns you, Milon," continued the colonel. "But I will have an answer from you, do you hear? Do you know who killed the uhlans who were found this morning near the Calvary?"

"It was me," said the old man in a clear voice.

Amazed, the colonel remained silent for a second, staring fixedly at the prisoner. Old Milon remained impassive, with his besotted peasant expression, his eyes lowered as though he were talking to his priest. One thing only revealed his inner distress; again and again he kept swallowing his saliva, with a visible effort, as though his throat were tightly constricted.

The man's family, his son Jean, his daughter-in-law and two grandchildren, stood ten paces back, in frightened consternation.

"Do you also know who killed all the scouts in our army corps, who have been found every morning, in the district, for the past month?" went on the colonel.

"It was me," replied the old man, with the same brutish impassivity.

"You killed all of them?"

"Yes, all of them; it was me."

"You alone?"

"Me alone."

"Tell me how you set about it."

This time the man seemed affected; the necessity of speaking at some length visibly embarrassed him.

"How do I know?" he stammered. "I just did it like it happened."

"I warn you that you will have to tell me everything," said the colonel. "So you will do well to make up your mind to it at once. How did you begin?"

The man flung an uneasy glance to his anxious family behind him. He hesitated for another instant, then suddenly made up his mind.

"I was coming home one night, maybe ten o'clock, the day after you got here. You and your men, you'd taken more than fifty crowns' worth of my forage, with a cow and two sheep. I said to myself: 'So many times as they take twenty crowns' worth of stuff, so many times I'll pay them out for it.' And I'd other things on my mind, too; I'll tell you about them later. And then I saw one of your troopers smoking his pipe in my ditch, behind my barn. I went and got down my scythe, and came up very softly behind him; he never heard a sound. And I cut off his head with one blow, with a single blow, like an ear of corn; he never so much as said 'Oh!' You've only to look in the pond: you'll find him there in a coalsack, with a stone off the wall.

"I had my scheme. I took all his things, from boots to cap, and hid them in the cement kiln in Martin wood, behind the yard."

The old man was silent. The astounded officers gazed at one another. The questioning went on again; and this is what they learned:

Once the murder had been done, the man had lived this idea: "Kill Prussians!" He hated them with the cunning, desperate hatred of a peasant at once avaricious and patriotic. He had his scheme, as he said. He waited for a few days.

He was left free to come and go, enter and depart at his will, so humble, submissive, and obliging had he shown himself to the conquerors. Every night he saw the vedettes go out; and he went out himself, one night, having heard the name of the village for which the troopers were bound, and having learned, thanks to the constant presence of the soldiers, the few words of German he needed.

He walked out of his own farmyard, slipped into the wood, reached the cement kiln, walked to the far end of the long gallery, and, finding the dead man's clothes on the ground, he put them on.

Then he went prowling through the fields, crawling along, following the embankments so as to conceal himself, stopping to listen at the faintest sound, restless as a poacher.

When he judged that the time had come, he went near the road and hid in a hedge. He waited again. At last, at about midnight, he heard a horse's hoof ring out on the hard road. He set his ear to the ground to make sure that only one horseman was approaching; then made ready.

The uhlan came up at a fast trot, carrying dispatches. His eyes were on the lookout and his ears alert. When he was no more than ten paces distant, old Milon crawled across the road, groaning: "Hilfe! Hilfe! Help! help!" The horseman stopped, recognized a dismounted German, imagined that he was wounded, got off his horse, and went up to him without suspecting anything. As he bent over the stranger, he received the long curved blade of the saber clean through the stomach. He fell, without a death struggle, only quivering with a few final tremors.

Then the Norman, radiant with an old peasant's silent pleasure, rose, and, to please himself, cut the throat of the corpse. Then he dragged it to the ditch and threw it in.

The horse was quietly waiting for its master. Old Milon got into the saddle and galloped off across the plain.

An hour later he perceived two more uhlans side by side, returning to their camp. He went straight towards them, again shouting: "Hilfe! Hilfe!" The Prussians let him come on, recognizing the uniform, without any distrust. And the old man dashed between them like a cannon ball, felling both, one with his saber, the other with a revolver.

Then he cut the throats of the horses, German horses! Then he went quietly back to the cement kiln and hid a horse at the end of the dark gallery. He took off his uniform, put on his mean clothes again, and, getting into bed, slept till morning.

For the next four days he did not go out, as he was waiting for the end of the inquiry which had been opened; but on the fifth day he went out again and killed two more soldiers by the same stratagem.

Thenceforward he never stopped. Every night he wandered away, prowling about at random, killing Prussians first in one place, then elsewhere, galloping over the deserted fields, in the moonlight, a lost uhlan, a hunter of men. Then, his task over, leaving the bodies lying in the roads behind him, the old horseman returned to hide his horse and uniform in the cement kiln.

At about midday he would go out, with an unconcerned air, to take oats and water to his mount, which remained in the underground passage. He fed the beast without stint, for he demanded a great deal of work from it.

But, on the previous night, one of the men he had attacked had been on his guard and had slashed the old peasant's face with his saber.

Even so, he had killed both men! He had once more returned, hidden his horse, and put on his humble clothes again; but while walking home, he had been overtaken by faintness and had crawled to the stable, unable to reach the house.

He was found there, bleeding, in the straw.

When he had ended his tale, he suddenly raised his head and stared proudly at the Prussian officers.

"Have you nothing more to say?" asked the colonel, pulling his mustache.

"No, nothing more; the score is paid: I've killed sixteen of them, not one more and not one less."

"You know that you are going to die?"

"I never asked you for mercy."

"Have you been in the army?"

"Yes. I've been to the wars, in my time. And besides, it was you that killed my father, who was a soldier under the first emperor. Not counting that you killed my youngest son, François, last month, near Evreux. I owed you for that, and I've paid. We're quits."

The officers looked at one another.

The old man continued:

"Eight for my father, eight for my son, we're quits. I never sought a quarrel with you! I don't know you! I don't even know where you come from. And here you are at my house, ordering people about as though you were at home. I had my revenge on the others. I don't regret it."

And, drawing up his crippled body, the old man folded his arms in the attitude of a humble hero.

For a long time the Prussians whispered together. A captain, who had also lost his son, the month before, defended the greathearted old peasant.

Then the colonel rose and went up to old Milon, saying, in a low voice:

"Listen, gaffer, there may be a way of saving your life, if you . . ."

But the man was not listening. His eyes were fixed upon the conquering officer, and, while the wind stirred the wisps of hair on his head, he made a frightful grimace which distorted his thin face, all seamed as it was by the saber gash, and, swelling his chest, he spat, with all his might, full in the Prussian's face.

The furious colonel raised his hand, and for a second time the peasant spat in his face.

All the officers had risen and were shouting orders at the same time.

In less than a minute the old man, still quite impassive, was put against the wall and shot, smiling to Jean, his eldest son, his daughter-in-law, and the two little children, who stood watching, distracted with horror.

A PHILOSOPHER

Blérot had been my most intimate friend from childhood; we had no secrets from each other and were united heart and soul by a brotherly intimacy and a boundless confidence in each other. I had been intrusted with the secret of all his love affairs, as he had been with mine.

When he told me that he was going to get married I was hurt, just as if he had been guilty of a treacherous act with regard to me. I felt that it must interfere with that cordial and absolute affection which had united us hitherto. His wife would come between us. The intimacy of the marriage bed establishes a kind of complicity, a mysterious alliance between two persons, even when they have ceased to love each other. Man and wife are like two discreet partners who will not let anyone else into their secrets. But that close bond which the conjugal kiss fastens is widely loosened on the day on which the woman takes a lover.

I remember Blérot's wedding as if it were but yesterday. I would not be present at the signing of the marriage contract, as I have no particular liking for such ceremonies. I only went to the civil wedding and to the church.

His wife, whom I had never seen before, was a tall, slight girl with pale hair, pale cheeks, pale hands and eyes to match. She walked with a slightly undulating motion, as if she were on board a ship, and seemed to advance with the succession of long, graceful courtesies.

Blérot seemed very much in love with her. He looked at her constantly, and I felt a shiver of an immoderate desire for her pass through my frame.

I went to see him in a few days, and he said to me:

"You do not know how happy I am; I am madly in love with her, but then she is—she is——" He did not finish his sentence, but he put the tips of his fingers to his lips with a gesture which signified "divine! delicious! perfect!" and a good deal more besides.

I asked, laughing, "What? All that?"

"Everything that you can imagine," was his answer.

He introduced me to her. She was very pleasant, on easy terms with me, as was natural, and begged me to look upon their house as my own. I felt that he, Blérot, did not belong to me any longer. Our intimacy was altogether checked, and we hardly found a word to say to each other.

I soon took my leave and shortly afterward went to the East, returning by way of Russia, Germany, Sweden and Holland after an absence of eighteen months from Paris.

The morning after my arrival, as I was walking along the boulevards to breathe the air once more, I saw a pale man with sunken cheeks coming toward me, who was as much like Blérot as it was possible for a physical, emaciated man to resemble a strong, ruddy, rather stout man. I looked at him in surprise and asked myself:

"Can it possibly be he?" But he saw me and came toward me with outstretched arms, and we embraced in the middle of the boulevard.

After we had gone up and down once or twice from the Rue Drouot to the Vaudeville Theater, just as we were taking leave of each other—for he already seemed quite done up with walking—I said to him:

"You don't look at all well. Are you ill?"

"I do feel rather out of sorts," was all he said.

He looked like a man who was going to die, and I felt a flood of affection for my old friend, the only real one that I had ever had. I squeezed his hands.

"What is the matter with you? Are you in pain?"

"A little tired, but it is nothing."

"What does your doctor say?"

"He calls it anemia, and has ordered me to eat no white meat and to take tincture of iron."

A suspicion flashed across me.

"Are you happy?" I asked him.

"Yes, very happy; my wife is charming, and I love her more than ever."

But I noticed that he grew rather red and seemed embarrassed, as if he were afraid of any further questions, so I took him by the arm and pushed him into a café, which was nearly empty at that time of day. I forced him to sit down and, looking him straight in the face, I said:

"Look here, old fellow, just tell me the exact truth."

"I have nothing to tell you," he stammered.

"That is not true," I replied firmly. "You are ill, mentally, perhaps, and you dare not reveal your secret to anyone. Something or other is doing you harm, and I mean you to tell me what it is. Come, I am waiting for you to begin."

Again he got very red, stammered, and turning his head away, he said:

"It is very idiotic—but I—I am done for!"

As he did not go on, I said:

"Just tell me what it is."

"Well, I have got a wife who is killing me; that is all," he said abruptly, almost desperately.

I did not understand at first. "Does she make you unhappy? How? What is it?"

"No," he replied in a low voice, as if he were confessing some crime; "I love her too much; that is all."

I was thunderstruck at this singular avowal, and then I felt inclined to laugh, but at length I managed to reply:

"But surely, at least so it seems to me, you might manage to—to love her a little less."

He had got very pale again and at length made up his mind to speak to me openly, as he used to do formerly.

"No," he said, "that is impossible, and I am dying from it; I know; it is killing me, and I am really frightened. Some days, like today, I feel inclined to leave her, to go away altogether, to start for the other end of the world, so as to live for a long time; and then when the evening comes I return home in spite of myself, but slowly, and feeling uncomfortable. I go upstairs hesitatingly and ring, and when I go in I see her there, sitting in her easy chair, and she will say, 'How late you are.' I kiss her, and we sit down to dinner. During the meal I make this resolve: 'I will go directly it is over and take the train for somewhere, no matter where,' but when we get back to the drawing room I am so tired that I have not the courage to get up out of my chair, and so I remain and then—and then—and then—I succumb again."

I could not help smiling again. He saw it and said: "You may laugh, but I assure you it is very horrible."

"Why don't you tell your wife?" I asked him. "Unless she be a regular monster she would understand."

He shrugged his shoulders. "It is all very well for you to talk. I don't tell her because I know her nature. Have you ever heard it said of certain women, 'She has just married a third time?' Well, and that makes you laugh like you did just now, and yet it is true. What is to be done? It is neither her fault nor mine. She is so, because nature has made her so; I assure you, my dear old friend, she has the temperament of a Messalina. She does not know it, but I do; so much the worse for me. She is charming, gentle, tender, and thinks that our conjugal intercourse, which is wearing me out and killing me, is natural and quite moderate. She seems like an ignorant schoolgirl, and she really is ignorant, poor child.

"Every day I form energetic resolutions, for you must understand that I am dying. But one look of her eyes, one of those looks in which I can read the ardent desire of her lips, is enough for me, and I succumb at once, saying to myself: 'This is really the end; I will have no more of her death-giving kisses,' and then when I have yielded again, like I have today, I go out and walk and walk, thinking of death and saying to myself that I am lost, that all is over.

"I am mentally so ill that I went for a walk to Père Lachaise cemetery yesterday. I looked at all the graves, standing in a row like dominoes, and I thought to myself: 'I shall soon be there,' and then I returned home, quite determined to pretend to be ill and so escape, but I could not.

"Oh! You don't know what it is. Ask a smoker who is poisoning himself with nicotine whether he can give up his delicious and deadly habit. He will tell you that he has tried a hundred times without success, and he will, perhaps, add: 'So much the worse, but I would rather die than go without tobacco.' That is just the case with me. When once one is in the clutches of such a passion or such a habit, one must give oneself up to it entirely."

He got up and gave me his hand. I felt seized with a tumult of rage and with hatred for this woman, this careless, charming, terrible woman, and as he was buttoning up his coat to go out I said to him, brutally perhaps:

"But in God's name, why don't you let her have a lover, rather than kill yourself like that?"

He shrugged his shoulders without replying and went off.

For six months I did not see him. Every morning I expected a letter of invitation to his funeral, but I would not go to his house from a complicated feeling of contempt for him and for that woman, of anger, of indignation, of a thousand sensations.

One lovely spring morning I was in the Champs Elysées. It was one of those warm days which make our eyes bright and stir up in us a tumultuous feeling of happiness from the mere sense of existence. Someone tapped me on the shoulder and, turning round, I saw my old friend, looking well, stout and rosy.

He gave me both hands, beaming with pleasure, and exclaimed:

"Here you are, you erratic individual!"

I looked at him, utterly thunderstruck.

"Well, on my word—yes. By Jove! I congratulate you; you have indeed changed in the last six months!"

He flushed scarlet and said with an embarrassed laugh:

"One can but do one's best."

I looked at him so obstinately that he evidently felt uncomfortable, so I went on:

"So—now—you are—completely cured?"

He stammered hastily:

"Yes, perfectly, thank you." Then, changing his tone, "How lucky that I should have come across you, old fellow. I hope we shall often meet now."

But I would not give up my idea; I wanted to know how matters really stood, so I asked:

"Don't you remember what you told me six months ago? I suppose—I—eh—suppose you resist now?"

"Please don't talk any more about it," he replied uneasily; "forget that I mentioned it to you; leave me alone. But, you know, I have no intention of letting you go; you must come and dine at my house."

A sudden fancy took me to see for myself how matters stood, so that I might understand all about it, and I accepted.

His wife received me in a most charming manner, and she was, as a matter of fact, a most attractive woman. Her long hands, her neck and cheeks were beautifully white and delicate and marked her breeding, and her walk was undulating and delightful.

René gave her a brotherly kiss on the forehead and said:

"Has not Lucien come yet?"

"Not yet," she replied in a clear, soft voice; "you know he is almost always rather late."

At that moment the bell rang, and a tall man was shown in. He was dark, with a thick beard, and looked like a modern Hercules. We were introduced to each other; his name was Lucien Delabarre.

René and he shook hands in a most friendly manner, and then we went to dinner.

It was a most enjoyable meal, without the least constraint. My old friend spoke with me constantly in the old, familiar, cordial manner, just as he used to do. It was: "You know, old fellow!" "I say, old fellow!" "Just listen a moment, old fellow!" Suddenly he exclaimed:

"You don't know how glad I am to see you again; it takes me back to old times."

I looked at his wife and the other man. Their attitude was perfectly correct, though I fancied once or twice that they exchanged a rapid and furtive look.

As soon as dinner was over René turned to his wife and said:

"My dear, I have just met Pierre again, and I am going to carry him off for a walk and chat along the boulevards to remind us of old times. I am leaving you in very good company."

The young woman smiled and said to me as she shook hands with me:

"Don't keep him too long."

As we went along arm in arm I could not help saying to him, for I was determined to know how matters stood:

"What has happened? Do tell me!"

He, however, interrupted me roughly and answered like a man who has been disturbed without any reason.

"Just look here, old fellow; leave one alone with your questions."

Then he added, half aloud, as if talking to himself:

"After all, it would have been too stupid to have let oneself go to perdition like that."

I did not press him. We walked on quickly and began to talk. All of a sudden he whispered in my ear:

"I say, suppose we go and have a bottle of fizz with some girls! Eh?"

I could not prevent myself from laughing heartily.

"Just as you like; come along, let us go."

A MISTAKE

That day Boniface, the letter carrier, found in leaving the post office that his route would not be so long and therefore felt a lively delight.

He had charge of the country around Vireville and, when he returned in the evening, he often found he had covered over twenty miles in his long march.

Today the distribution would be easy; he could even stroll along a little and be home by three o'clock in the afternoon. What luck!

He went out along the Sennemare road and commenced his work. It was June, the month of verdure and flowers, the true month of the fields and meadows.

The man, in his blue blouse and black cap with red braid, crossed through bypaths, fields of millet, oats and wheat, buried to the shoulders in their depths; and his head, moving along above the feathery waves, seemed to float upon a calm and verdant sea, which a light breeze caused to undulate gently. He entered the farms through wooden gateways built on the slopes and shaded by two rows of beech trees, greeted the farmer by name: "Good morning, Monsieur Chicot," and passed him his newspaper, the *Little Norman*.

The farmer would wipe his hand on his trousers, receive the paper, and slide it into his pocket to read at his ease after the midday meal. The dogs, asleep in barrels under the drooping apple trees, yapped with fury, pulling at their chains, but the carrier, without turning, proceeded at his military gait, stretching his long limbs, the left arm over his bag, the right manipulating his cane, which marched like himself, in a continuous, hurried fashion.

He distributed his printed matter and his letters in the hamlet of Sennemare, then set out across the fields with a paper for the tax collector who lived in a little isolated house a quarter of a mile from the village.

He was a new collector, this M. Chapatis, arrived but the week before and lately married.

He took a Paris paper, and sometimes carrier Boniface, when he had time, would take a look at it before delivering it at its destination.

Now he opened his bag, took out the paper, slipped it out of its wrapper, unfolded it and began to read while walking. The first page did not interest him; politics did not arouse him; finance he always passed over, but the general facts of the day he read eagerly.

That day they were very exciting. He became so much interested in the story of a crime executed in a gamekeeper's lodge that he stopped in the middle of a clover field to read it more slowly. The details were frightful. A woodcutter, in passing the forester's house the morning after, had noticed a little blood upon the sill, as if someone had been bleeding from the nose. "The keeper must have killed a wolf last night," he thought, but coming nearer, he perceived that the door was left open and that the lock had been broken. Then, seized with fear, he ran to the village, notified the mayor, who took with him as a reinforcement the keeper of fields and the schoolmaster; these four men returned together. They found the forester with his throat cut before the chimney piece, his wife strangled on the bed and their little daughter, aged six years, stifled under two mattresses.

Carrier Boniface became so wrought up over the thought of this assassination whose horrible details had been revealed to him one by one that he felt a weakness in his limbs and said aloud:

"Christopher! But some of the people in this world are brutes!"

Then he replaced the journal in its wrapper and went on, his head full of visions of the crime. He arrived shortly at M. Chapatis's. He opened the gate of the little garden and approached the house. It was of low construction, containing only one story and a mansard roof. It was at least five hundred feet from its nearest neighbor.

The carrier mounted the two front steps, placed his hand upon the knob, trying to open the door, but found it locked. Then he perceived that the shutters had not been opened and that no one had come out that morning.

A feeling of alarm took possession of him, for M. Chapatis, since his arrival, had always been up rather early. It was then only ten minutes after seven, nearly an hour earlier than he usually got there. No matter. The tax collector ought to be up before that.

He made a tour around the house, walking with much precaution, as if he himself might be in some danger. He noticed nothing suspicious except a man's footprints on a strawberry bed.

But suddenly he remained motionless as he was passing a window, powerless from fright. A groan came from the house.

He approached nearer and, stepping over a border of thyme, glued his ear to the opening in order to hear better; assuredly someone was groaning. He could plainly hear long, dolorous sighs, a kind of rattle, a noise of struggle. Then the groans became louder and oft repeated, finally being accentuated and changing into cries.

Then Boniface, no longer doubtful that a crime was being committed, took to his legs, recrossed the little garden, flew across the field and the meadow, running until he was out of breath, his bag shaking and hitting against his hip, and arrived gasping and in dismay at the door of the police headquarters.

Brigadier Malautour was mending a broken chair by means of some brads and a hammer. Gendarme Rauter held the damaged piece of furniture between his knees and placed a nail at the edge of the crack; then the brigadier, chewing his mustache, his eyes round and moist with interest in his work, would pound—blows which fell on the fingers of his subordinate.

When the letter carrier perceived them he cried out:

"Come quick; someone is assassinating the tax collector. Quick! Quick!"

The two men ceased their work and raised their heads, the astonished heads of people surprised and perplexed.

Boniface, seeing more surprise than haste, repeated:

"Quick! Quick! The robbers are in the house. I heard the cries. There is no time to be lost."

The brigadier, placing his hammer on the ground, remarked: "How was it you found out about this?"

The carrier answered: "I went to carry the paper and two letters, when I noticed that the door was locked and that the collector had not been out. I walked around the house, trying to account for it, when suddenly I heard someone groan as if he were being strangled, as if his throat were being cut—and then I started as soon as I could to get you. There's no time to be lost."

"And you didn't try to help any?"

The carrier, much frightened, replied:

"I was afraid that one was too small a number."

Then the brigadier, convinced, said:

"Give me time to get into my uniform and I will follow you."

And he went into the building, followed by his subordinate, who carried the chair. They reappeared almost immediately, and all three started in quick, trained step for the scene of the crime.

Arriving near the house, they slackened their pace through precaution, and the brigadier drew his revolver; then they went softly into the garden and approached the walls of the dwelling. There was nothing to indicate that the malefactors had gone away. The door remained locked, the windows closed.

"Let us wait for them," murmured the brigadier.

But Boniface, palpitating with emotion, made them pass around to the other side and showed them an opening. "It is there," he said.

The brigadier advanced alone and fixed his ear against the board. The two others waited, ready for anything, watching him closely.

He remained a long time, motionless, listening. The better to bring his head near the wooden shutter, he had removed his three-cornered hat and held it in his right hand.

What did he hear? His face revealed nothing for some time, then suddenly his mustache rose at the corners; his cheeks took on folds as in a silent laugh and, stepping over the border of thyme, he came toward the two men who were looking at him in a kind of stupor.

Walking along on the tips of his toes, he made the sign for them to follow, and when they came to the gate he advised Boniface to slip the paper and the letters under the door.

The amazed carrier obeyed with perfect docility.

"And now, back again," said the brigadier.

When they had gone a little way he turned to the letter carrier with a jocose air, his eyes upturned and shining with fun, and said in a bantering tone:

"Well, you are a rogue, you are!"

The old fellow asked: "Why? I heard something. I swear to you I heard something."

Then the brigadier, no longer able to restrain himself, laughed aloud. He laughed to suffocation, his two hands holding his sides, doubling himself up, his eyes full of tears, and making frightful grimaces about the nose. Both of them were frightened to look at him.

As he could neither speak nor cease laughing nor make them understand, he made a gesture, a popular, meaning gesture. As they could not comprehend that either, he kept repeating it, motioning back always with his head.

Finally his subordinate caught the meaning suddenly and in his turn broke into formidable laughter. The old fellow remained stupefied between these two men who were twisting themselves into all shapes.

The brigadier finally became calm and, giving the old man a great tap on his waistcoat, like a jolly good fellow, he cried:

"What a farce! A holy farce! I shall record it as the Crime of Father Boniface!"

The carrier opened his enormous eyes and repeated:

"I swear to you that I heard something."

The brigadier began to laugh. His subordinate sat down on the grass beside the ditch and laughed at his ease.

"Ah! You heard something. And your wife, do you assassinate her that way, hey, you old joker?"

"My wife?"

And he stood reflecting a long time, then he continued:

"My wife. Yes, she bawls if I strike her—and bawls that are bawls, why? Was Monsieur Chapatis beating his wife?"

Then the brigadier, in a delirium of humor, turned him around by the shoulders as if he had been a puppet and whispered in his ear something that caused him to look besotted with astonishment.

Then the old man murmured pensively:

"No? Not that—not that. She said nothing—mine—I would never have believed—— Is it possible? One would swear that a murder——"

And confused, disconcerted and ashamed, he went on his way across the fields, while the two policemen, laughing continually and calling back to him from afar with barrack-room wit, watched his black cap as it disppeared in the tranquil sea of grain.

FLORENTINE

We were talking about girls, for what else is there to talk about among men? One of us said:

"Wait! A strange story occurs to me on this subject."

And he related it:

"One evening of last winter I was suddenly taken with one of those desolate lassitudes which are overwhelming in their attack upon soul and body from time to time. I was at home alone, and I knew well that if I remained there I should have a frightful fit of despondency, of the kind that leads to suicide when they return often.

"I put on my coat and went out without knowing at all what I was going to do. Having descended to the boulevard, I began to walk along past the cafés, nearly empty, for it was raining. One of those thin rains was falling that dampens the spirits as much as the clothes; not one of those good showers, striking one in a cascade and driving passers under the porte-cocheres, out of breath, but a rain that unceasingly deposits upon you imperceptible droplets and covers your clothing with a glistening, penetrating moisture.

"What should I do? I went up and returned, seeking some place to pass a couple of hours and discovering for the first time that there was not a place of diversion in all Paris in the evening. Finally I decided to enter the Folies-Bergères, that theater so amusing to street girls.

"There were very few in the great hall. The long, semicircular promenade contained but a few individuals, of a race usually known by their walk, their clothing, the cut of their hair and beard, their hats and their complexion. It is not often that one sees among them a man who seems clean, perfectly clean, and whose clothing has altogether the same air. As for the girls, they are always the same, as you know, plain, weary, drooping, walking with that quick step and that air of imbecile disdain which they assume, I know not why.

"I said to myself that truly not one of these flagging creatures, greasy rather than fat, either bloated or very thin, with the paunch of a prelate and their long legs bowed, was worth the louis that they obtained with much difficulty after having demanded five.

"But suddenly I perceived one of them, a little one that appeared genteel, not at all young, but fresh, droll and provoking. I stopped her and, in beastly fashion, without thinking, set my price for the night. I did not wish to return home alone, all alone; I preferred rather the company and embrace of this worthless woman.

"And so I followed her. She lived in a big, big house in Martyr Street. The gas was already extinguished on the staircase. I mounted slowly, constantly lighting taper matches, striking the steps with my feet, stumbling and ill at ease, following a petticoat, the rustle of which I heard before me.

"She stopped at the fourth story and, having shut again the inside door, she asked:

" 'And you wish to remain until tomorrow?'

" 'Yes. You know that was the agreement.'

" 'All right, my dear. I only wanted to know. Wait for me here a minute; I will return immediately.'

"And she left me in the darkness. I heard her close two doors, then it seemed to me she was speaking with somebody. I was surprised and disturbed. The idea of blackmail occurred to me. But I have fists and solid muscles. 'We shall see,' I thought.

"I listened with all attention, both of ear and mind. Someone was moving, walking about, but with great precaution. Then another door was opened, and it seemed to me that I still heard talking, but in a very low voice.

"She returned, bringing a lighted candle. 'You can enter now,' she said.

"She spoke familiarly, as a sign of possession. I entered, and after having crossed a dining room, where it was evident nobody ever dined, I entered a chamber like that of all these girls, a furnished room with rep curtains and eider-down silk quilt with suspicious poppy-red spots.

"She continued: 'Put yourself at ease, my dear.'

"I inspected the apartment with an eye of suspicion. There seemed nothing disquieting, however. She undressed herself so quickly that she was in bed before I had my overcoat off. Then she began to laugh:

" 'Well, what is the matter with you? Are you changed into a pillar of salt? Come! Make haste!'

"I imitated her and joined her. Five minutes later I had a foolish desire to dress again and go out. But the overwhelming lassitude which had seized me at my house returned to me, depriving me of all strength to move, and I remained, in spite of the disgust which I had for this public bed. The sensual charm which I believed I saw down there under the lights of the theater had disappeared in my arms, and I had with me, flesh to flesh, only a vulgar girl, like all the rest, whose indifferent and complaisant kiss had an aftertaste of garlic.

"I began to talk to her:

" 'Have you been here long?' I said.

" 'Six months the fifteenth of January.'

" 'Where were you before that?'

" 'I was in Clauzel Street. But the janitor made me so miserable that I left.'

"And she began to relate an interminable story of the concierge who had made some scandal about her.

"Suddenly I heard something moving near us. At first there was a sigh, then a light noise, but distinct, as if someone had fallen from a chair.

"I sat up quickly in bed and demanded: 'What was that noise?'

"She answered with assurance and composure: 'Don't disturb yourself, my dear; it is my neighbor. The partition is so thin that we hear all as if they were here. These are dirty boxes. They are made of pasteboard.'

"My indolence was so strong that I got down under the clothes again. We continued our talk. Incited by the curiosity which drives all men to question these creatures upon their first adventure, to wish to raise the veil from their first fault in order to find in them some far-off trace of innocence, that we may find something to love, perhaps, in the rapid recital evoked by their candor and the shame of long ago, I asked her about her first lover.

"I knew that she lied. What did it matter? Among all the lies I might discover, perhaps, some sincere or touching incident.

" 'Come,' I said, 'tell me who he was.'

" 'He was an oarsman.'

" 'Ah! Tell me about it. Where were you?'

" 'I was at Argenteuil.'

" 'What were you doing there?'

" 'I was maid in a restaurant.'

" 'What restaurant?'

" 'At the Freshwater Sailors; do you know it?'

" 'Well, yes; Bonafan's.'

" 'Yes, that's the one.'

" 'And how did he pay his court, this oarsman?'

" 'While I was making his bed. He forced me.'

"But suddenly I recalled the theory of a doctor of my acquaintance, an observing, philosophic doctor who, in his practice in a great hospital, had daily examples of these girl mothers and public girls and knew all the shame and misery of women, the poor women who become the hideous prey of the wandering male with money in his pocket.

" 'Invariably,' he told me, 'is a girl debauched by a man of her own class and station in life. I have made volumes of observations upon it. It is customary to accuse the rich of culling the flower of innocence from the children of the people. That is not true. The rich pay for the culled bouquet. They cull also, but at the second flowering; they never cut the first.'

"Then turning toward my companion, I began to laugh.

" 'You may as well know that I know all about your story. The oarsman was not the first, as you well know.'

" 'Oh yes, my dear, I swear it!'

" 'You are lying.'

" 'Oh no, I promise you I am not.'

" 'You lie. Come, tell me the truth.'

"She seemed to hesitate, astonished. I continued:

" 'I am a sorcerer, my good child, a hynotist. If you do not tell me the truth I shall put you to sleep, and then I can find it out.'

"She was afraid, being stupid like her kind. She murmured:

" 'How did you ever guess it?'

"I replied: 'Come, speak.'

" 'Oh! The first time, that amounted to nothing. It was at a festival in the country. They called in a chef for the occasion, M. Alexander. After he came he had it all his own way in the house. He ordered everybody, even to the master and mistress, as if he had been a king. He was a large, handsome man who would not stay in place before his stove. He was always crying out: "Here, some butter—some eggs—some Madeira!" And it was necessary to carry him everything on the run, or he would get angry and say things to you that would make you blush under the skirts.

" 'When the day was finished he would smoke his pipe before the door. And as I passed him with a pile of plates he said to me this: "Come, little goose, come down to the edge of the lake and show me the country." As for me, I went, like a fool, and scarcely had we arrived at the bank when he forced me so quickly that I did not even know that it was done. And then he went away by the nine o'clock train, and I never saw him again after that.'

"I asked: 'Is that all?'

"She stammered: 'Oh! I believe Florentine belongs to him.'

" 'Who is Florentine?'

" 'He is my little boy.'

" 'Ah! Very well. And you made the oarsman believe that he was the father, did you not?'

" 'Yes.'

" 'He had money, this oarsman?'

" 'Yes, he left me an income of three hundred francs for Florentine's support.'

"I commenced to be amused. I continued:

" 'Very well, my girl, very well. You are all less sensual than one would believe. And how old is Florentine now?'

"She answered: 'Twelve years old. He will take his first communion in the spring.'

" 'That is good, and since that you have made a trade with your conscience.'

"She sighed resignedly: 'One must do what she can.'

"But a great noise in another part of the room made me leap out of bed with a bound; it was the noise of one falling, then rising and groping with his hands upon the wall. I had seized the candle and was looking about, frightened and furious. She got up also and tried to hold me back, saying:

" 'It is nothing, my dear; I assure you it is nothing.'

"But I had discovered on which side of the wall this strange noise was. I went straight toward a concealed door at the head of the bed and opened it suddenly— and perceived there a poor little boy, trembling and staring at me with frightened eyes, a pale, thin little boy beside a large chair filled with straw, from which he had fallen.

"When he saw me he began to cry and, opening his arms to his mother:

" 'It was not my fault, Mamma; it was not my fault. I was asleep and I fell. You mustn't scold me, for it was not my fault.'

"I turned toward the woman and said:

" 'What does he mean?'

"She seemed confused and disheartened. But finally she said in a broken voice:

" 'What can you expect? I do not earn enough to put the child in school! I must take care of him somehow, and I cannot afford to hire another room. He sleeps with me when I have no one. When someone comes for an hour or two he can stay in the closet very well and keep quiet; he knows how. But when one remains all night, as you have, his muscles are fatigued from sleeping on the chair—and it is not the child's fault. I would like to see you—you—sleep all night on a chair. You would sing another song.'

"She was angry, wrought-up, and was crying.

"The child wept too. A poor child, pitiful and timid, a good child of the closet, of the cold, dark closet, a child who came from time to time to get a little warmth in the bed a moment empty.

"I, too, had a desire to weep.

"And I returned home to my own bed."

THE ORPHAN

Mlle. Source had adopted the boy under very sad circumstances. At the time, she was thirty-six years old, and her deformity (when a little girl she had slipped from her nurse's knee into the fire, and her face had been horribly burnt and was a terrible sight) had determined her not to marry, for she did not want to be married for her money.

A neighbor, who was with child when she became a widow, died in her confinement, leaving no money at all. Mlle. Source looked after the baby, put it out to nurse, brought it up, sent it to school, and then took the boy home when he was fourteen that she might have someone to love her in the empty house, someone to look after her and to sweeten her old age.

She lived on a little country estate four miles from Rennes, and had given up keeping a servant, because her expenses had more than doubled since she had adopted the orphan, her income of three thousand francs not being sufficient for three people.

She did her own cooking and housework and sent the youngster, who looked after the garden, to do the errands. He was gentle, shy, quiet, and affectionate, and she felt a deep joy—quite a new experience for her—when he kissed her without being astonished at or afraid of her ugliness. He called her Auntie and treated her like a mother.

In the evenings they both sat by the fireside while she prepared something nice for him: hot wine and toasted bread, which made an enjoyable light supper before going to bed. She often took him on her knee and fondled him, murmuring words of passionate tenderness. She used to call him "my little flower, my cherub, my darling angel, my precious jewel," to all of which he was gently submissive, laying his head on the old maid's shoulder.

Although nearly fifteen now, he was still little and frail, and looked rather unhealthy. Sometimes Mlle. Source would take him into town to see the only two relations she had left—distant cousins who were married and lived in one of the suburbs. The two women had a grievance against her for adopting the child, on account of her money, but they welcomed her nevertheless, still hoping for their share—in all probability one third—if the inheritance were equally divided.

She was very, very happy, her time being fully occupied with her child; she bought him books to develop his mind, and he became a great reader.

He no longer sat on her knee in the evenings to fondle her, but would rush to his chair by the fire and get his book. The light from the lamp, placed on the table just above his head, was reflected on his curly hair and part of his forehead; he never moved, never raised his eyes, but went on reading, entirely absorbed in the adventures in print.

Seated on the opposite side of the fire, she would gaze at him with a fixed, loving gaze, surprised at his concentration, feeling jealous, and often ready to cry about it. Every now and then she would say: "You will overtire yourself, my treasure!" hoping that he would raise his head and come and kiss her, but he never answered; he never heard her; he had not understood; he was oblivious of everything except the book he was reading.

For two years he simply devoured a great number of books, and there was a change in his character. He began to ask Mlle. Source for money, which she gave him, but as his demands kept growing she ended by refusing to give any more, for she was energetic and methodical, and could be sensible when necessary.

After much pleading he did obtain a considerable sum one evening, but when a few days later he begged for more, she was quite determined, and, indeed, she never yielded to his pleadings again.

He was apparently reconciled to do without and returned to his former ways, sitting quietly for hours with downcast eyes, lost in daydreaming. He never talked to Mlle. Source, and only replied to short, sharp sentences. However, he was charming and considerate to her, but never kissed her.

He occasionally made her feel frightened as they sat opposite each other by the fireside, silent and still. She wanted to rouse him, to say something, anything, to him, to break the silence which was as terrifying as the gloom of a forest. But he never seemed to hear her, and she trembled with terror—as poor weak women will —when she received no reply after speaking five or six times.

What was the matter? What was passing in that impenetrable mind? After some two or three hours spent in this way, she felt she must be going mad, she wanted to go away, to escape from the house, not only to avoid this everlasting dumb tête-à-tête, but to avoid, too, a vague unknown danger that she felt threatening her. She would often weep in her loneliness. What was the matter with him? She had only to express a wish and he carried it out without a murmur. If she wanted anything in town, he would go off and fetch it at once. She certainly had no ground for complaint! And yet——

A year passed by, and it struck her that there was another change in the young man. How had she noticed this, felt it, guessed it? No matter! She knew she was not mistaken, but she could not have put into words the change that had occurred in that strange youth's unknown thoughts. To her it seemed that where he had been beset with hesitation, he was now quite resolute; this idea struck her one evening when she caught him staring at her curiously, with an expression she had never seen before.

After that he watched her continually until she felt as if she must hide herself to avoid the cold glance always fixed upon her. For whole evenings he would stare at her, only turning away his eyes when, reduced to helplessness, she said: "Don't look at me like that, my child!" Then he would lower his head. But as soon as her back was turned she felt his eye upon her again. Wherever she went, he followed her with his tenacious gaze. Sometimes in the garden she would suddenly catch sight of him crouched among the shrubs as if he were hiding; or else when she was seated out of doors mending stockings, and he was digging in the vegetable garden, he would slyly and persistently watch her all the time he was at work. It was no use asking him: "What is the matter, my dear? You are so changed these last three years, I can't recognize you. I implore you to tell me what's wrong, what is filling your thoughts."

He invariably answered, in a quiet, tired voice: "But nothing's the matter, Auntie!" And when she insisted with: "Oh! my child, answer me, answer me when I speak to you. If you could know how you make me suffer, you would always answer, and you would not look at me in that way. Are you in trouble? Tell me, I will comfort you——" he would go off wearily, muttering: "But I assure you nothing's wrong with me."

He had not grown much, and still looked like a child though his features were those of a man. They were, however, hard and looked unfinished. He seemed somehow incomplete, unpleasant to the eye, only a sketch, so to speak, and as alarming as a mystery. He was quite closed to outer influences, impenetrable, a prey to some constant mental ferment, both active and dangerous.

Mlle. Source could not help feeling all this, and her anguish of mind prevented her from sleeping. She was assailed by appalling terror and horrible nightmares. She locked herself in her room and barricaded the door, tortured by a panic fear. Of what was she afraid?

She had no idea.

She was afraid of everything, the night, the walls, the shadows projected by the moon through the white curtains at the windows, and, above all, she was afraid of him.

Why?

What had she to fear? Did she know of anything?

She could not go on living like that. She knew she was menaced by some misfortune, some appalling misfortune.

One morning, secretly, she went to town to see her relatives and breathlessly told them what she felt. The two women thought she was going mad and tried to reassure her. She said to them: "If you only knew how he looks at me from morning till night! He never takes his eyes off me! Sometimes I want to shout for help, call in the neighbors, I am so afraid! But what could I say to them? He does nothing but stare at me."

The cousins said: "Does he ever treat you roughly, does he answer you rudely?"

She replied: "No, never; he does everything I wish, he works well and is very steady now; but I am beside myself with fright. He has some idea in his head, I know it, I know it. I won't stay any longer in the country alone with him."

The scared relatives told her that everyone would be surprised, that no one would understand, and advised her to put aside her fears and give up her plans, but they did not discourage her from coming to live in town, in the hope that the removal would secure all her property for the two of them. They even promised to help her sell her house and to find another one near them.

Mlle. Source went back home, but she was in such a state of nerves that she started at the least sound and her hands trembled at the merest trifle.

She visited her relatives again twice, now quite determined not to remain in her lonely country home, and at last she found a suitable little house in the suburb, which she secretly bought.

The contract was signed on a Tuesday morning, and the rest of the day was spent in arranging for the removal. Mlle. Source caught the eight P.M. coach, which passed about a mile and a half from the house, and stopped at the spot where the driver usually set her down. As he whipped up his horses he shouted: "Good night, Mlle. Source, good night!" and she replied as she was moving away: "Good night, Father Joseph."

At seven o'clock the next morning, the village postman noticed a big pool of fresh blood on the crossroad not far from the highway, and said to himself: "Halloa! Some drunken lout's nose has been bleeding." But a few steps farther on he picked up a fine cambric handkerchief stained with blood, and as he neared the ditch he thought he could see some strange object lying there.

Mlle. Source was lying at the bottom of the ditch with her throat cut. An hour later, the gendarmes, the magistrate and others in authority gathered round the corpse, all giving their opinion as to what had happened. The two relations, called as witnesses, came and told them of the old maid's fears and of the arrangements she had just made.

The orphan was arrested. Since his adopted mother's death he had done nothing but weep, plunged, at least to all appearances, in the deepest woe. He was able to prove that he had spent the evening up to eleven o'clock in a café; he had been seen by ten people who had been there until he left. As the coach driver declared that he had set the murdered woman down between half past nine and ten o'clock, the crime could only have been committed on the road leading from the highway to the house, not later than ten o'clock. The prisoner was acquitted.

By a will drawn up years before and left with a notary of Rennes, he was made sole legatee, and got all the property.

For a long time the country folk kept him at a distance, still suspecting him of the murder. His house, the dead woman's house, was looked upon as bearing a curse, and everybody avoided him in the street. But he was so companionable, so friendly, that the horrible suspicion about him was gradually forgotten. He was generous, considerate, and would chat at will with the humblest of his neighbors.

The notary, Maître Rameau, was one of the first to revise his opinions about him, being captivated by the young man's bright conversation. One evening when dining with the collector of taxes he declared that "a man with his gift of words— always good-humored—cannot have such a dreadful crime on his conscience." Impressed by the argument, the guests thought the matter over. They remembered the long conversations held by this man, who would stop them at the corner of the road and make them listen to him, who forced them into his house as they passed by, who made a better joke than the lieutenant of the armed police force himself, and was so infectiously cheerful that one could not help laughing when with him in spite of the repugnance he inspired.

Once more all doors were opened to him. He is now mayor of his commune.

CONSIDERATION

Simon Bombard often found life very bad! He was born with an unbelievable aptitude for doing nothing and with an immoderate desire to follow this vocation. All effort, whether moral or physical, each movement accomplished for a purpose, appeared to him beyond his strength. As soon as he heard anyone speak of anything serious he became confused, his mind being incapable of tension or even attention.

The son of a novelty merchant of Caen, he glided along smoothly, as they said in the family, until he was twenty-five years of age. But as his parents were always nearer bankruptcy than fortune, he suffered greatly for want of money.

He was a tall, large, pretty youth with red whiskers, worn Norman fashion, of florid complexion, blue eyes, sensual and gay, corpulence already apparent, and dressed with the swagger elegance of a provincial at a festival. He laughed, cried, and gesticulated at the same time, displaying a storm of good nature with all the assurance of the seasoned traveler. He considered that life was made principally for joys and pleasures, and as soon as it became necessary to curb his noisy enjoyment he fell into a kind of chronic somnolence, being incapable of sadness.

His need for money harassed him until he formed the habit of repeating a phrase now celebrated in his circle of acquaintance: "For ten thousand francs a year I would become an executioner."

Now he went each year to Trouville to pass two weeks. He called this "spending the season." He would install himself at the house of his cousins who gave him the use of a room, and from the day of his arrival to that of his departure he would promenade along the boardwalk which extends along the great stretch of seashore.

He walked with an air of confidence, his hands in his pockets or crossed behind his back, always clothed in ample garments, with light waistcoats and showy cravats, his hat somewhat over his ear and a cheap cigar in one corner of his mouth.

He went along, brushing by the elegantly dressed women and eying contemptuously the merry men who were ready to make a disturbance for the sake of it, and seeking—seeking—what he was seeking.

He was after a wife, counting entirely upon his face and his physique. He said to himself: "Why the devil, in all the crowd that comes here, should I not be able to find my fate?" And he hunted with the scent of a dog in the chase, with the Norman scent, sure that he should recognize her, the woman who would make him rich, the moment he perceived her.

It was one Monday morning that he murmured: "Wait, wait, wait!" The weather was superb, one of those yellow-and-blue days of the month of July, when one might say that the sky wept from the heat. The vast shore covered with people, costumes, colors, had the air of a garden of women, and the fishing boats with their brown sails, almost immovable upon the blue water which reflected them upside down, seemed asleep under the great sun at ten o'clock in the morning. There they remained opposite the wooden pier, some near, some farther off, some still farther, as if overcome by a summer-day idleness, too indifferent to seek the high sea or even to return to port. And down there one could vaguely perceive in the mist the coast of Havre, showing two white points on its summit, the light-houses of Sainte-Adresse.

He said to himself: "Wait, wait, wait!" For he had passed her now for the third time and perceived that she had noticed him, this mature woman, experienced and courageous, who was making a bid for his attention. He had noticed her before on the days preceding, because she seemed also in quest of someone. She was an Englishwoman, rather tall, a little thin, an audacious Englishwoman whom circumstances and much journeying had made a kind of man. Not bad, on the whole, walking along slowly with short steps, soberly and simply clothed, but wearing a queer sort of hat, as Englishwomen always do. She had rather pretty eyes, high cheekbones, a little red, teeth that were too long and always visible.

When he came to the pier he returned upon his steps to see if she would meet him again. He met her and she threw him a knowing glance, a glance which seemed to say: "Here I am!"

But how should he speak to her? He returned a fifth time, and when he was again face to face with her she dropped her umbrella. He threw himself forward, picked it up and presented it to her, saying:

"Permit me, madame."

She responded: "Oh, you are very kind!"

And then they looked at each other. They knew nothing more to say. But she blushed. Then, becoming courageous, he said:

"We are having beautiful weather here."

And she answered: "Oh, delicious!"

And then they remained opposite each other, embarrassed, neither thinking of going away. It was she who finally had the audacity to ask: "Have you been about here long?"

He answered, laughing: "Oh yes, about as long as I care about it." Then brusquely he proposed: "Would you like to go down to the pier? It is pretty there such days as this."

She simply said: "I should be much pleased."

And they walked along side by side, she with her harsh, direct allurement, he alluring her with his dandyism, which makes for rakishness later on.

Three months later the notables in the commercial world of Caen received one morning a square white card which said:

M. and Mme. Prosper Bombard have the honor to announce the marriage of their son, M. Simon Bombard, to Mrs. Kate Robertson.

and on the other side:

Mrs. Kate Robertson has the honor of announcing her marriage to M. Simon Bombard.

They went to live in Paris. The fortune of the wife amounted to fifteen thousand francs a year income, free and clear. Simon wished to have four hundred francs a month for his personal expenses. He had to prove that his tenderness merited this amount; he did prove it easily and obtained what he asked for.

At first everything went well. Young Mme. Bombard was no longer young, assuredly, and her freshness had undergone some wear, but she had a way of exacting things which made it impossible for anyone to refuse her. She would say with her grave, willful English accent: "Oh, Simon, now we must go to bed," which made Simon start toward the bed like a dog that had been ordered, "To your kennel." And she knew how to have her way by day and night in a manner there was no resisting.

She did not get angry; she made no scenes; she never cried; she never had the appearance of being irritated or hurt or even disturbed. She knew how to talk; that was all, and she spoke to the point and in a tone that admitted no contradiction.

More than once Simon was on the point of rebelling, but before the brief and imperious desires of this singular woman he found himself unable to stand out. Nevertheless, when the conjugal kisses began to be meager and monotonous and he had in his pocket what would bring him something greater, he paid for satiety, but with a thousand precautions.

Mme. Bombard perceived all this without his surmising it, and one evening she announced to him that she had rented a house at Mantes, where they would live in the future.

Then existence became harder. He tried various kinds of diversion which did not at all compensate for the conquests he had a taste for.

He fished with a line, learned how to tell the places which the gudgeon liked, which the roach and carp preferred, the favorite spots of the bream, and the kinds of bait that divers fishes will take.

But in watching his bob as it trembled on the surface of the water, other visions haunted his mind. Then he became the friend of the chief of the office of the subprefect and the captain of the police, and they played whist of evenings at the Commerce Café, but his sorrowful eye would disrobe the queen of clubs or the lady of the diamonds, while the problem of the absent legs on these two-headed figures would bring up images suddenly that confused his thoughts.

Then he conceived a plan, a true Norman plan of deceit. He would have his wife take a maid who would be a convenience to him, not a beautiful girl, a coquette, adorned and showy, but a gawky woman, rough and strong-backed, who would not arouse suspicions and whom he would acquaint beforehand with his plans.

She was recommended to them by the director of the city farm, his accomplice and obliging friend, who guaranteed her under all relations and conditions. And Mme. Bombard accepted with confidence the treasure they brought to her.

Simon was happy, happy with precaution, with fear and with unbelievable difficulties. He could never undress beyond the watchful eye of his wife, except for a few short moments from time to time, and then without tranquillity. He sought some plan, some stratagem, and he ended by finding one that suited him perfectly.

Mme. Bombard, who had nothing to do, retired early, while Bombard, who played whist at the Commerce Café, returned each evening at half past nine, exactly. He got Victorine to wait for him in the passageway of his house, under the vestibule steps in the darkness.

He only had five minutes or more, for he was always in fear of a surprise, but five minutes from time to time sufficed for his ardor, and he slid a louis into the servant's hand, for he was generous in his pleasures, and she would quickly remount to her garret.

And he laughed, he triumphed all alone and repeated aloud, like King Midas' barber fishing for the goldfish from the reeds on the riverbank: "The mistress is safe within."

And the happiness of having Mme. Bombard safely fixed within made up for him in great part for the imperfection and incompleteness of his conquest.

One evening he found Victorine waiting for him, as was her custom, but she appeared to him more lively, more animated than usual, and he remained perhaps ten minutes in the rendezvous in the corridor.

When he entered the conjugal chamber Mme. Bombard was not there. He felt a cold chill run down his back and sank into a chair, tortured with fear.

She appeared with a candlestick in her hand. He asked, trembling:

"You have been out?"

She answered quietly: "I went to the kitchen for a glass of water."

He forced himself to calm his suspicions of what she might have heard, but she seemed tranquil, happy, confident, and he was reassured.

When they entered the dining room for breakfast the next morning Victorine put the cutlets on the table. As she turned to go out Mme. Bombard handed her a louis which she held up delicately between her two fingers and said to her with her calm, serious accent:

"Wait, my girl, here are twenty francs which I deprived you of last night. I wish to give them to you."

And the girl, amazed, took the piece of gold which she looked at with a stupid air, while Bombard, frightened, opened his eyes wide at his wife.

WOMAN'S WILES

"Women?"

"Well, what do you say about women?"

"Well, there are no conjurers more subtle in taking us in at every available opportunity with or without reason, often for the sole pleasure of playing tricks on us. And they play these tricks with incredible simplicity, astonishing audacity, unparalleled ingenuity. They play tricks from morning till night, and they all do it—the most virtuous, the most upright, the most sensible of them. You may add that sometimes they are to some extent driven to do these things. Man has always idiotic fits of obstinacy and tyrannical desires. A husband is continually giving ridiculous orders in his own house. He is full of caprices; his wife plays on them even while she makes use of them for the purpose of deception. She persuades him that a thing costs so much because he would kick up a row if its price were higher. And she always extricates herself from the difficulty cunningly by means so simple and so sly that we gape with amazement when by chance we discover them. We say to ourselves in a stupefied state of mind, 'How is it we did not see this till now?'"

The man who uttered the words was an ex-minister of the Empire, the Comte de L——, thorough profligate, it was said, and a very accomplished gentleman. A group of young men were listening to him.

He went on:

"I was outwitted by an ordinary uneducated woman in a comic and thorough-going fashion. I will tell you about it for your instruction.

"I was at the time minister for foreign affairs, and I was in the habit of taking a long walk every morning in the Champs Elysées. It was the month of May; I walked along, sniffing in eagerly that sweet odor of budding leaves.

"Ere long I noticed that I used to meet every day a charming little woman, one of those marvelous, graceful creatures who bear the trade-mark of Paris. Pretty? Well, yes and no. Well made? No, better than that: her waist was too slight, her shoulders too narrow, her breast too full, no doubt, but I prefer those exquisite human dolls to that great statuesque corpse, the Venus of Milo.

"And then this sort of woman trots along in an incomparable fashion, and the very rustle of her skirt fills the marrow of your bones with desire. She seemed to give me a side glance as she passed me. But these women give you all sorts of looks —you never can tell.

"One morning I saw her sitting on a bench with an open book between her hands. I came across and sat down beside her. Five minutes later we were friends. Then each day, after the smiling salutation: 'Good day, madame,' 'Good day, monsieur,' we begin to chat. She told me that she was the wife of a government clerk, that her life was a sad one, that in it pleasures were few and cares numerous, and a thousand other things.

"I told her who I was, partly through thoughtlessness and partly, perhaps, through vanity. She pretended to be much astonished.

"Next day she called at the Ministry to see me, and she came again there so often that the ushers, having their attention drawn to her appearance, used to whisper to one another as soon as they saw her the name with which they had christened her: 'Madame Léon'—that is, my Christian name.

"For three months I saw her every morning without growing tired of her for a second, so well was she able incessantly to give variety and piquancy to her physical attractiveness. But one day I saw that her eyes were bloodshot and glowing with suppressed tears, that she could scarcely speak, so much was she preoccupied with secret troubles.

"I begged of her, I implored of her, to tell me what was the cause of her agitation.

"She faltered out at length with a shudder: 'I am—I am *enceinte!*'

"And she burst out sobbing. Oh! I made a dreadful grimace, and I have no doubt I turned pale, as men generally do at hearing such a piece of news. You cannot conceive what an unpleasant stab you feel in your breast at the announcement of an unexpected paternity of this kind. But you are sure to know it sooner or later. So in my turn I gasped: 'But—but—you are married, are you not?'

"She answered: 'Yes, but my husband has been away in Italy for the last two months, and he will not be back for some time.'

"I was determined at any cost to get out of my responsibility.

"I said: 'You must go and join him immediately.'

"She reddened to her very temples and with downcast eyes murmured: 'Yes— but——' She either dared not or would not finish the sentence.

"I understood and I prudently inclosed in an envelope the expenses of her journey."

"Eight days later, she sent me a letter from Genoa. The following week I received one from Florence. Then letters reached me from Leghorn, Rome and Naples.

"She said to me:

"*I am in good health, my dear love, but I am looking frightful. I would not care to have you see me till it is all over; you would not love me. My husband suspects nothing. As his business in this country will require him to stay there much longer, I will not return to France until after my confinement.*

"And at the end of about eight months I received from Venice these few words:

"*It is a boy.*

"Some time after she suddenly entered my study one morning, fresher and prettier than ever, and flung herself into my arms. And our former connection was renewed.

"I left the Ministry, and she came to live in my house in the Rue de Grenelle. She often spoke to me about the child, but I scarcely listened to what she said about it; it did not concern me. Now and then I placed a rather large sum of money in her hand, saying: 'Put that by for him.'

"Two more years glided by, and she was more and more eager to tell me some news about the youngster—'about Léon.'

"Sometimes she would say in the midst of tears: 'You don't care about him; you don't even wish to see him. If you could know what grief you cause me!'

"At last I was so much harassed by her that I promised one day to go next morning to the Champs Elysées when she took the child there for an airing.

"But at the moment when I was leaving the house I was stopped by a sudden apprehension. Man is weak and foolish. What if I were to get fond of this tiny being of whom I was the father—my son?

"I had my hat on my head, my gloves in my hands. I flung down the gloves on my desk and my hat on a chair.

" 'No, decidedly I will not go; it is wiser not to go.'

"My door flew open. My brother entered the room. He handed me an anonymous letter he had received that morning:

"*Warn the Comte de L——, your brother, that the little woman of the Rue Casette is impudently laughing at him. Let him make some inquiries about her.*

"I had never told anybody about this intrigue, and I now told my brother the history of it from the beginning to the end. I added:

" 'For my part, I don't want to trouble myself any further about the matter, but will you, like a good fellow, go and find out what you can about her?'

"When my brother had left me I said to myself: 'In what way can she have deceived me? She has other lovers? What does it matter to me? She is young, fresh and pretty; I ask nothing more from her. She seems to love me, and as a matter of fact, she does not cost me much. Really, I don't understand this business.'

"My brother speedily returned. He had learned from the police all that was to be known about her husband: A clerk in the Home Department, of regular habits and good repute and, moreover, a thinking man, but married to a very pretty woman, whose expenses seemed somewhat extravagant for her modest position. That was all.

"Now my brother, having sought for her at her residence and finding that she was gone out, succeeded, with the assistance of a little gold, in making the door-keeper chatter: 'Mme. D——, a very worthy woman, and her husband a very worthy man, not proud, not rich, but generous.'

"My brother asked for the sake of saying something:

" 'How old is her little boy now?'

" 'Why, she has not got any little boy, monsieur.'

" 'What? Little Léon?'

" 'No, monsieur, you are making a mistake.'

" 'I mean the child she had while she was in Italy two years ago.'

" 'She has never been in Italy, monsieur; she has not quitted the house she is living in for the last five years.'

"My brother, in astonishment, questioned the doorkeeper anew, and then he pushed his investigation of the matter further. No child, no journey.

"I was prodigiously astonished but without clearly understanding the final meaning of this comedy.

" 'I want,' I said to him, 'to have my mind perfectly clear about the affair. I will ask her to come here tomorrow. You shall receive her instead of me. If she has deceived me you will hand her these ten thousand francs, and I will never see her again. In fact, I am beginning to find I have had enough of her.'

"Would you believe it? I had been grieved the night before because I had a child by this woman, and I was now irritated, ashamed, wounded at having no more of her. I found myself free, released from all responsibility, from all anxiety, and yet I felt myself raging at the position in which I was placed.

"Next morning my brother awaited her in my study. She came in as quickly as usual, rushing toward him with outstretched arms, but when she saw who it was she at once drew back.

"He bowed and excused himself.

" 'I beg your pardon, madame, for being here instead of my brother, but he has authorized me to ask you for some explanations which he would find it painful to seek from you himself.'

"Then fixing on her face a searching glance, he said abruptly:

" 'We know you have not a child by him.'

"After the first moment of stupor she regained her composure, took a seat and gazed with a smile at this man who was sitting in judgment on her.

"She answered simply:

" 'No; I have no child.'

" 'We know also that you have never been in Italy.'

"This time she burst out laughing in earnest.

" 'No; I have never been in Italy.'

"My brother, quite stunned, went on:

" 'The comte has requested me to give you this money and to tell you that it is broken off.'

"She became serious again, calmly putting the money into her pocket and, in an ingenuous tone, asked:

"'And I am not, then, to see the comte any more?'

"'No, madame.'

"She appeared to be annoyed, and in a passionless voice she said:

"'So much the worse; I was very fond of him.'

"Seeing that she had made up her mind on the subject so resolutely, my brother, smiling in his turn, said to her:

"'Look here now, tell me why you invented all this long, tricky yarn, complicating it by bringing in the sham journey to Italy and the child?'

"She gazed at my brother in amazement, as if he had asked her a stupid question, and replied:

"'Well, I declare! How spiteful you are! Do you believe a poor little woman of the people such as I am—nothing at all—could have for three years kept on my hands the Comte de L——, minister, a great personage, a man of fashion, wealthy and seductive, if she had not taken a little trouble about it? Now it is all over. So much the worse. It couldn't last forever. Nonetheless, I succeeded in doing it for three years. You will say many things to him on my behalf.'

"She rose up. My brother continued questioning her:

"'But—the child? You had one to show him?'

"'Certainly—my sister's child. She lent it to me. I'd bet it was she gave you the information.'

"'Good! And all those letters from Italy?'

"She sat down again so as to laugh at her ease.

"'Oh! Those letters—well, they were a bit of poetry. The comte was not a minister of foreign affairs for nothing.'

"'But—another thing?'

"'Oh! The other thing is my secret. I don't want to compromise anyone.'

"And, bowing to him with a rather mocking smile, she left the room without any emotion, an actress who had played her part to the end."

And the Comte de L—— added by way of moral:

"So take care about putting your trust in that sort of turtledove!"

A CRY OF ALARM

I have received the following letter. Thinking that it may be of help to many of my readers, I hasten to make it known to them.

Paris, November 15, 1886.

SIR:

In short stories or newspaper articles you often write about subjects connected with what I shall call "current morality." I wish to submit some ideas which I think you could use for one of your articles.

I am not married. I am a bachelor, and apparently rather naïve, but I think most men are naïve in the same way. Being very trustful, it is difficult for me to recognize the natural astuteness of my neighbors. I go straight ahead, open-eyed, and don't look keenly enough behind either things or motives.

Most of us are in the habit of taking appearance for reality—of accepting people at their own valuation; very few possess the intelligence that enables them to detect the real secret character of others. The consequence of this particular and conventional way of looking at life is that we go through the world like moles; that we never believe what really is, but only what seems to be; that we exclaim: "How incredible!" when the truth is exposed, and that everything displeasing to our idealistic code of morality is classified as an exception, without realizing that nearly all the cases in point are due to these exceptions. A further consequence is that credulous fools, like myself, are the dupes of everybody—more especially of women who are clever at the game.

I have gone far afield before reaching the particular fact that is of interest to me.

I have a mistress, a married woman. Like many other men, I thought I had found the exception—a poor unhappy woman who was deceiving her husband for the first time. I had been—or rather I thought I had been—courting her for some time; I thought I had won her by my love and consideration, had triumphed by dint of my perseverance. I had indeed taken thousands of precautions, used thousands of tricks, and thousands of exquisite hesitations in order to overcome her resistance.

Well, this is what happened last week:

Her husband being away for some days, she asked if she could come and dine with me alone, asking me to wait upon her so that we could dispense with the servant. She had been obsessed for the last four or five months by the idea that she wanted to get drunk, completely drunk, without any cause for fear—without having to go home, speak to her maid, or walk in the presence of witnesses. She had often been what she called "cheerfully confused" without going any further, and had found it extremely pleasant, therefore she had promised herself to get thoroughly drunk, once, and only once. She told them at home that she was going to spend the night and following day with some friends near Paris, and arrived at my flat at dinnertime. Of course a woman can get drunk only on iced champagne! She drank a large glassful fasting, and had begun to ramble on before the oysters were served. I could reach the plates and dishes by stretching out my arm and I did the waiting with more or less success while listening to her chatter.

She drank glass after glass, obsessed by her one idea. She began to tell me interminable, wishy-washy accounts of her feelings as a girl. She went on and on, her eyes bright but vague, her tongue untied, her feather-headed ideas rolling on interminably like the telegraphic bands of blue paper to which there seems no end, and which run on to the tapping of the electric machine that covers them with unknown words. Occasionally she would ask me: "Am I drunk?" "No, not yet!" And she would start again. Soon she was drunk, not blind drunk but drunk enough, it seemed to me, to tell the truth. Her account of her girlhood's emotions was followed by more intimate confidences about her husband, which were very complete and uncomfortable to listen to, on the following pretext repeated over and over again: "I can say everything to you—to whom could I say everything if not to you?"

So I was made acquainted with her husband's habits and defects, all his little manias, and his most secret tastes.

She would say, asking for approbation: "Isn't he a bore? Say—isn't he a bore? You know how he has bored me to death—eh? So the very first time I saw you I said to myself: 'Halloa, I like that man. I'll have him as my lover.' After that you began to make love to me."

I must have looked rather queer, for she noticed my expression in spite of her drunkenness, and said, bursting with laughter: "Ah! booby, what precautions you did take—but when men make love to us, you dear old stupid, it is because we are willing—and then you must do it quickly or else you make us wait—you must be an idiot not to understand, not to see by our looks, that we are saying 'yes.' Ah! I had to wait for you, you softy! I didn't know how to make you understand that I was in a hurry—ah! yes, all right—flowers—poems—compliments—still more flowers—and then nothing more—I nearly gave you up, old man, you took so long to decide. And only to think that half the men in the world are like you, but the other half—ah!—ah!—ah!"

Her laugh made me shiver. I stammered: "The other half—well, the other half?"

She was still drinking, her eyes clouded by the wine, and her mind driven by the imperious desire to speak the truth peculiar to some drunkards.

She continued: "Ah! the other half move quickly—but all the same they're right, they are. There are days when they are unsuccessful, but there are others when they get what they want, in spite of everything. Dear old chap—if you only knew —how funny they are—the two kinds of men! You know, the shy ones like you can't imagine what the others are like—what they do—directly—when they are alone with us. They take risks. They get their faces slapped, it is true—but that makes no difference—they know quite well that we'll never tell. They know us, they do."

I was looking at her with the eyes of an inquisitor and with a wild desire to make her talk, to learn everything. How many times had I not asked myself the question: "How do other men behave to women, to our women?" I recognized, only by seeing in a drawing room, anywhere in public, two men speaking to the same woman, that if they, one after the other, were to be alone with her, they would approach her quite differently, even though they were on exactly the same footing with her. At the first glance one feels that certain men—endowed by nature with the gift of pleasing, or even only more disillusioned, bolder, than we are—will arrive in an hour's conversation with a woman they admire at a degree of intimacy which we could not reach in a year. Very well—these men, these pro-fessional, enterprising lovers, when the occasion presents itself, do they push the boldness of hands and lips to a point which would appear to us, the bashful sort, an odious outrage, but which women perhaps consider only a pardonable forward-ness, a rather unbecoming homage to their irresistible charms?

She threw herself back in her chair and burst into a fit of nervous, unnatural laughter, the laughter that leads to hysterics, and when she had calmed down a little, she said: "Ah! ah! old chap, improper?—that is to say, they stick at noth-ing—right away—at nothing—you understand—and still more——"

I felt as indignant as if she had unmasked some monstrous evil. "And you allow this, you women?"

"No—we don't allow it—we hit out—but we are amused, all the same. They are much more amusing than you others! Besides, one is always afraid, one is never sure—and it's delightful to be afraid—especially to be afraid of that. You have to watch them all the time—it is like fighting a duel. You look into their eyes to learn their thoughts, to see what they are going to do with their hands. You may say they are cads, but they love us better than you do!"

A curious, unexpected sensation came over me. Although I was a bachelor and determined to remain one, these impudent confidences suddenly made me feel like a husband. I felt I was the friend, the ally, the brother of all the trustful husbands who, if not actually robbed, are at least defrauded by these ready-fingered lovers of feminine underclothing. In obedience to that strange emotion—which still persists—I am writing to beg you to send a cry of alarm out to the army of unsuspecting husbands.

Nevertheless I had doubts, the woman was drunk and must be telling lies. I returned to the subject, saying: "How is it that you never tell anybody, you women?"

She looked at me with such profound, sincere pity that, for a moment, I thought astonishment had made her sober.

"My dear fellow, how stupid you are! Does one ever talk about such things— ah! ah! ah! Does a servant tell about his little perquisites, his discount on bills, etc.? Well, that, that's our discount. So long as we go no further, husbands should not complain. But how stupid you are! To talk about all that would be to give the alarm to every ninny! Besides, where's the harm so long as you do not yield?"

Quite confused, I asked another question: "So you have often been kissed?"

She replied with sovereign contempt for the man who could have a doubt on the subject: "Of course. Every woman has been kissed again and again. Try any one of them to see, you big idiot. Here, kiss Mme. de X —she is quite young and straight—kiss, my dear, kiss them and run your fingers over them, you'll see, you'll see. Ah! ah! ah!"

Suddenly she threw her full glass at the pendant cluster. The champagne, dripping down like drops of rain, put out three candles, stained the wallpaper, and wet the table, while the broken bits of crystal were scattered about the room. Then she tried to do the same thing with the bottle but I stopped her; then she began to shout at the top of her voice—the attack of hysterics had begun—just as I expected.

I had almost forgotten this drunken woman's confession when, a few days later, I found myself by chance at the same reception as that Mme. de X whom my mistress had advised me to kiss. We lived in the same district, so I offered to take her home, as she was alone that evening. She accepted the offer.

As soon as we were in the carriage I said to myself: "Now then, go ahead," but I dared not. I didn't know how to start, how to begin the attack. Suddenly, filled with the desperate courage of cowardice, I said: "How beautiful you were this evening."

Laughingly she replied: "So this evening was an exception, since you noticed it for the first time?"

I had no reply ready. It is quite clear that I am no good in the warfare of gallantry. However, after a few moments' reflection I hit upon the following remark: "No, but I never dared to tell you." She was astonished and said: "Why?" "Because it's—it's rather difficult." "Difficult to tell a woman she's pretty? Where do you come from? You must always say it—even if you don't mean it—because it is always a pleasure to hear."

Seized by a sudden fit of fantastic audacity, I caught her by the waist and tried to find her mouth with my lips. However, I must have been trembling and could not have appeared very terrible to her. I must also have made a mess of the attempt, for she only turned her head away and said:

"Oh! no! that's too bad, too bad. You go too quickly—take care of my hair. You can't kiss a woman who wears her hair as I do!"

Desperate and heartbroken at my failure, I had sunk back into my seat when the carriage stopped at her door. She got out, shook hands with me, and said most graciously: "Thanks for bringing me home, dear monsieur, and don't forget my advice."

Three days after, I met her again. She had forgotten all about it.

As for me, I am always thinking about those other men who know how to treat a woman's coiffure with consideration, and how to seize every opportunity.

I hand this letter, without any addition, over to the meditation of my men and women readers, married or single.

MOONLIGHT

Mme. Julie Roubère was awaiting her elder sister, Mme. Henriette Letore, who had just returned after a trip to Switzerland.

The Letore household had left nearly five weeks ago. Mme. Henriette had allowed her husband to return alone to their estate in Calvados, where some matters of business required his attention, and came to spend a few days in Paris with her sister. Night came on. In the quiet parlor darkened by twilight shadows Mme. Roubère was reading in an absent-minded fashion, raising her eyes whenever she heard a sound.

At last she heard a ring at the door, and presently her sister appeared, wrapped in a traveling cloak. And immediately, without any formal greeting, they clasped each other ardently, only desisting for a moment to begin embracing each other over again. Then they talked, asking questions about each other's health, about their respective families, and a thousand other things, gossiping, jerking out hurried, broken sentences, and rushing about while Mme. Henriette was removing her hat and veil.

It was now quite dark. Mme. Roubère rang for a lamp, and as soon as it was brought in she scanned her sister's face and was on the point of embracing her once more. But she held back, scared and astonished at the other's appearance. Around her temples Mme. Letore had two long locks of white hair. All the rest of her hair was of a glossy, raven-black hue, but there alone, at each side of her head, ran, as it were, two silvery streams which were immediately lost in the black mass surrounding them. She was, nevertheless, only twenty-four years old, and this change had come on suddenly since her departure for Switzerland.

Without moving, Mme. Roubère gazed at her in amazement, tears rising to her eyes, as she thought that some mysterious and terrible calamity must have fallen on her sister. She asked:

"What is the matter with you, Henriette?"

Smiling with a sad smile, the smile of one who is heartsick, the other replied:

"Why, nothing, I assure you. Were you noticing my white hair?"

But Mme. Roubère impetuously seized her by the shoulders and, with a searching glance at her, repeated:

"What is the matter with you? Tell me, what is the matter with you. And if you tell me a falsehood I'll soon find it out."

They remained face to face, and Mme. Henriette, who became so pale that she was near fainting, had two pearly tears at each corner of her drooping eyes.

Her sister went on asking:

"What has happened to you? What is the matter with you? Answer me!"

Then in a subdued voice the other murmured:

"I have—I have a lover."

And, hiding her forehead on the shoulder of her younger sister, she sobbed.

Then when she had grown a little calmer, when the heaving of her breast had subsided, she commenced to unbosom herself, as if to cast forth this secret from herself, to empty this sorrow of hers into a sympathetic heart.

Thereupon, holding each other's hands tightly grasped, the two women went over to a sofa in a dark corner of the room into which they sank, and the younger sister, passing her arm over the elder one's neck and drawing her close to her heart, listened.

"Oh! I recognize that there was no excuse for one; I do not understand myself, and since that day I feel as if I were mad. Be careful, my child, about yourself— be careful! If you only knew how weak we are, how quickly we yield, a moment of tenderness, one of those sudden fits of melancholy which steal into your soul, one of those longings to open your arms, to love, to embrace, which we all have at certain moments.

"You know my husband, and you know how fond of him I am, but he is mature and sensible and cannot even comprehend the tender vibrations of a woman's heart. He is always, always the same, always good, always smiling, always kind, always perfect. Oh! How I sometimes have wished that he would roughly clasp me in his arms, that he would embrace me with those slow, sweet kisses which make two beings intermingle, which are like mute confidences! How I wished that he was self-abandoned and even weak, so that he should have need of me, of my caresses, of my tears!

"This all seems very silly, but we women are made like that. How can we help it?

"And yet the thought of deceiving never came near me. Today it has happened, without love, without reason, without anything, simply because the moon shone one night on the Lake of Lucerne.

"During the month when we were traveling together my husband, with his calm indifference, paralyzed my enthusiasm, extinguished my poetic ardor. When we were descending the mountain paths at sunrise, when as the four horses galloped along with the diligence, we saw, in the transparent morning haze, valleys, woods, streams and villages. I clasped my hands with delight and said to him: 'What a beautiful scene, darling! Kiss me now!' He only answered, with a smile of chilling kindliness, 'There is no reason why we should kiss each other because you like the landscape.'

"And his words froze me to the heart. It seems to me that when people love each other they ought to feel more moved by love than ever in the presence of beautiful scenes.

"Indeed, he prevented the effervescent poetry that bubbled up within me from gushing out. How can I express it? I was almost like a boiler filled with steam and hermetically sealed.

"One evening (we had been for four days staying in the Hotel de Fluelen), Robert, having got one of his sick headaches, went to bed immediately after dinner, and I went to take a walk all alone along the edge of the lake.

"It was a night such as one might read of in a fairy tale. The full moon showed itself in the middle of the sky; the tall mountains, with their snowy crests, seemed to wear silver crowns; the waters of the lake glittered with tiny rippling motions. The air was mild, with that kind of penetrating freshness which softens us till we seem to be swooning, to be deeply affected without any apparent cause. But how sensitive, how vibrating, the heart is at such moments! How quickly it leaps up, and how intense are its emotions!

"I sat down on the grass and gazed at that vast lake, so melancholy and so fascinating, and a strange thing passed into me. I became possessed with an insatiable need of love, a revolt against the gloomy dullness of my life. What! would it never be my fate to be clasped in the arms of a man whom I loved on a bank like this under the glowing moonlight? Was I never, then, to feel on my lips those kisses so deep, delicious and intoxicating which lovers exchange on nights that seem to have been made by God for passionate embraces? Was I never to know such ardent, feverish love in the moonlit shadows of a summer's night?

"And I burst out weeping like a woman who has lost her reason. I heard some person stirring behind me. A man was intently gazing at me. When I turned my head round he recognized me and, advancing, said:

" 'You are weeping, madame?'

"It was a young barrister who was traveling with his mother and whom we had often met. His eyes had frequently followed me.

"I was so much confused that I did not know what answer to give or what to think of the situation. I told him I felt ill.

"He walked on by my side in a natural and respectful fashion and began talking to me about what we had seen during our trip. All that I had felt he translated into words; everything that made me thrill he understood perfectly, better even than I did myself. And all of a sudden he recited some verses of Alfred de Musset. I felt myself choking, seized with indescribable emotion. It seemed to me that the mountains themselves, the lake, the moonlight, were singing to me about things ineffably sweet.

"And it happened, I don't know how, I don't know why, in a sort of hallucination.

"As for him, I did not see him again till the morning of his departure.

"He gave me his card!"

And, sinking into her sister's arms, Mme. Letore broke into groans—almost into shrieks.

Then Mme. Roubère, with a self-contained and serious air, said very gently:

"You see, Sister, very often it is not a man that we love, but love. And your real lover that night was the moonlight."

DOUBTFUL HAPPINESS

I can tell you the name neither of the country nor of the man. It was far, far from here, upon a hot, fertile coast. We followed, since morning, the shore and the wheat fields and the sea covered with the sun. Flowers grew down very near the waves, the light waves, so sweet and sleepy. It was very warm, but a gentle heat, perfumed with the fat, humid, fruitful earth; one could believe that he was breathing germs.

I had been told that this evening I would find hospitality in the house of a Frenchman who lived at the end of the promontory in a grove of orange trees. Who was he? I do not know yet. He had arrived one morning, ten years before this, bought the land, planted his vines and sown his seed; he had worked, had this man, with passion and fury. Month after month and year after year he had added to his domains, making the fertile, virgin soil yield without ceasing and amassing a fortune by his indefatigable labor.

It was said that he worked constantly. Up with the dawn, going through his fields until night, superintending everything without rest, he seemed harassed by a fixed idea, tortured by an insatiable desire for money which nothing could distract or appease.

Now he seemed to be very rich.

The sun was setting when I reached his dwelling. This dwelling was at the end of a point in the midst of orange trees. It was a large, square house, very simple, overlooking the sea.

As I approached, a large, bearded man appeared in the doorway. Having saluted him, I asked for shelter for the night. He extended his hand and said, smiling:

"Enter, sir, you are at home."

He led me to a room, gave some orders to a servant with the perfect ease and good grace of a man of the world, then he left me, saying:

"We will dine when you are ready to come down."

We dined, tête-à-tête, upon a terrace opposite the sea. At first I spoke of his country, so rich, so far away, so little known! He smiled, answering in an abstracted way:

"Yes, this is a pretty country. But no country pleases one much when it is far from those they love."

"You regret France?"

"I—I long for Paris."

"Why not return there?"

"Oh! I am going to return there."

And gradually we began to talk of the French world, of the boulevards and of the many features of Paris. He asked me about men he had known, cities, names, all of them familiar names upon the vaudeville stage.

"Who does one see at Tortoni's these days?"

"The same ones, except the dead."

I looked at him with marked interest, pursued by some vague remembrance. Certainly I had seen that head somewhere! But where? And when? He seemed fatigued, although vigorous, sad, though resolute. His great blond beard fell upon his breast, and sometimes he would take it near his chin and draw it through his closed hand, slipping it along to the very end. He was a little bald but had thick eyebrows and a heavy mustache which mingled with the hair of his beard.

Behind us the sun was disappearing in the sea, throwing upon the coast a cloud of fire. The orange trees, in flower, exhaled a powerful, delicious fragrance on the evening air. Seeing nothing but me and fixing his look upon me, he seemed to discover in my eyes, to see at the depth of my soul, the well-known, much loved image of the broad walk, so far away, that extends from the Madeleine to the Rue Drouot.

"Do you know Bourtelle?" he asked.

"Yes, certainly."

"Is he much changed?"

"Yes, he is all white."

"And the Ridamie?"

"Always the same."

"And the women? Tell me about the women. Let us see. Did you know Suzanne Verner?"

"Yes, very well, to the end."

"Ah! And Sophie Astier?"

"Dead!"

"Poor girl! Can it be—— Did you know——"

He was suddenly silent. Then in a changed voice, his face growing pale, he continued:

"No, it is better not to speak of her; it disturbs me so."

Then as if to change the trend of his thought, he rose and said:

"Do you wish to go in?"

"I am willing to go." And I followed him into the house.

The rooms downstairs were enormous, bare, sad, and seemed abandoned. Some glass dishes were set upon the table by the tawny-skinned servants who constantly roamed around this dwelling. Two guns hung upon two nails on the wall, and in the corners were to be seen some spades, some fishlines, dried palm leaves and objects of every kind, placed there at random by those entering, that they might find them at hand should they chance to have need of them on going out.

My host smiled.

"This is a lodge, or rather the lodging place of an exile," he said, "but my chamber is more as it should be. Let us go in there."

I thought, on entering, that I was in a curiosity shop, so filled was the room with all kinds of things, things disconnected, strange and varied, that one felt to be souvenirs of something. Upon the walls were two pretty engravings of well-known paintings, some stuffs, some arms, swords, pistols; then, in the middle of the principal panel, a square of white satin in a gold frame.

Surprised, I approached to look at it, when I perceived a pin which held a hair in the middle of the shining silk.

My host placed his hand on my shoulder and said, smiling:

"That is the only thing that I see here and the only thing I have seen for ten years. M. Prudhomme exclaims: 'This sword is the most beautiful day in my life.' But I say: 'This pin is all of my life.'"

I sought for a commonplace phrase and ended by saying:

"You have suffered through some woman?"

He replied brusquely: "You may say I have suffered miserably, but come out on my balcony. A name has suddenly come to my lips that I have not dared to pronounce, because if you had answered 'dead' as you did when I spoke of Sophie Astier, my brain would be on fire, even today."

We were upon a large balcony where we could see two gulfs, one on the right and the other on the left, shut in by high, gray mountains. It was the hour of twilight, when the sun, entirely out of sight, no longer lights the earth, except by reflection from the sky.

He continued: "Do you know if Jeanne de Limours still lives?"

His eye, fixed on mine, was full of trembling anxiety. I smiled and answered:

"Yes indeed, and prettier than ever."

"You know her?"

"Yes."

He hesitated. Then asked: "Completely?"

"No."

He took my hand. "Tell me about her," he said.

"I have nothing to tell; she is one of the most charming women, or rather girls, in Paris, and the most courted. She leads an agreeable, princesslike existence; that is all."

He murmured: "I love her," as if he had said: "I am going to die." Then, brusquely: "Ah! For three years that was a frightful but delicious existence of ours. I was very near killing her five or six times, and she tried to put out my eyes with that pin you were just looking at. Wait! Do you see the little white point under my left eye? That shows how we loved each other! How can I explain this passion? You could never comprehend it.

"There should be such a thing as a simple love, born of the force of two hearts and two souls, and assuredly there is such a thing as an atrocious love, cruelly torturing, born of the invincible rapture of two beings totally unlike, who detest while they adore each other.

"This girl ruined me in three years. I possessed four millions which she squandered in her calm way, tranquilly, and destroyed with a sweet smile which seemed to fall from her eyes upon her lips.

"You know her? Then you know that there is something irresistible about her! What is it? I do not know. Is it those gray eyes, whose look enters into you and remains there like the barb of an arrow? Or is it rather that sweet smile, indifferent and seductive, which stays on her face like a mask? Her slow manner penetrates little by little and takes hold of you like a perfume, as does her tall figure, which seems to balance itself as she passes, for she glides instead of walking, and her sweet voice, which drags a little and is so pretty that it seems to be the music of her smile; her gestures, too, her always moderate gestures, always right, which intoxicate the eye, so harmonious are they.

"For three years I saw only her upon the earth! How I suffered! Because she deceived me as well as everybody else. Why? For no reason, only for the sake of deceiving. And when I found it out and accused her of being a street girl, a bad woman, she said tranquilly: 'Well, we are not married, are we?'

"Since I have come here I have thought much about her and have succeeded in understanding her; that girl is Manon Lescaut over again. Manon could never love without deceiving, and for her love, pleasure and money were all."

He was silent. Then after some minutes he added:

"When I had squandered my last sou for her she simply said to me: 'You understand, my dear, that I cannot live on air and weather. I love you very much; I love you more than anyone, but I must live. Misery and I can never dwell in the same house.'

"And if I could only tell you what an atrocious life I led by her side! Whenever I looked at her I had as much desire to kill her as I had to embrace her. Whenever I looked at her there came to me a furious desire to open my arms, press her to me until I strangled her. There was something about her, behind her eyes, something perfidious and unseizable which made me furious against her, and perhaps it was for that very reason that I loved her so much. In her the Feminine, the odious, frightful Feminine, was more prominent than in any other woman. She was charged and surcharged with it, as with a venomous fluid. She was Woman, more than anyone else has ever been.

"And whenever I went out with her she would cast her eyes over all men in such a fashion that she seemed to give herself to each one with only a look. This exasperated me but attached me more strongly to her, nevertheless. This creature belonged to everybody from merely passing through the street, in spite of me, in spite of herself, from her very nature, although the allurement was most modest and sweet. Do you understand?

"And what torment! At the theater, in a restaurant, it seemed to me that everyone possessed her before my eyes. And whenever I left her alone others did, in fact, possess her.

"It is ten years now since I saw her, and I love her now more than ever."

Night had spread over the earth. A powerful perfume of orange flowers was in the air.

I said to him: "Will you try to see her again?"

He answered: "Surely! I have here now, in money and land, seven or eight hundred thousand francs. When the million is completed I shall sell all and set out. With that I can have one year with her, one good, entire year. And then—adieu; my life will be finished."

I asked: "And after that?"

"After that," he answered, "I don't know. It will be finished. Perhaps I shall ask her to take me as a *valet de chambre*."

IN A RAILWAY CARRIAGE

The sun was vanishing behind the vast chains of hills whose loftiest peak is the Puy de Dôme, and the shadow of the crests filled the deep valley of Royat.

Several people were strolling in the park, round the bandstand. Others were still sitting together in groups, in spite of the sharp evening air.

In one of these groups an animated discussion was in progress, for a grave problem had arisen, and one which seriously perturbed Mmes. de Sarcagnes, de Vaulacelles, and de Bridoie. In a few days the holidays would begin, and the discussion

centered round the means of bringing home their sons, now at Jesuit and Domini-
can colleges.

Now, these ladies had not the least desire to undertake a journey to bring back
their offspring, and they did not know exactly who could be entrusted with this
delicate task. Paris was empty. They tried in vain to recall any name which offered
the necessary guarantees.

Their concern was the greater because an unsavory episode had occurred in a
railway carriage some few days before. And these ladies were firmly convinced that
all the women of the town spent their whole time in the express trains between
Auvergne and the Gare de Lyon in Paris. According to Mme. de Bridoie, the columns of personal gossip in *Gil Blas*, moreover, announced the presence at Vichy,
at Mont Dore, and La Bourboule of every known and unknown pretty lady. The
fact that they were there was proof that they must have come in a railway carriage;
and they would assuredly return in a railway carriage; they must indeed be compelled to go on returning in order to come back again every day. It was a continual
coming and going of damaged goods on this abominable line. The ladies lamented
that access to the stations was not forbidden to disreputable women.

Besides, Roger de Sarcagnes was fifteen years old, Gontran de Vaulacelles thirteen, and Roland de Bridoie eleven years. What was to be done? They could not,
under any circumstances, expose their darlings to the risk of meeting such creatures.
What might they hear, what might they see, and what might they find out if they
were to spend a whole day, or a night, in a compartment which held also one or
two of these vicious women with one or two of their companions!

There seemed no way out of the difficulty, and then Mme. de Martinsec happened to come past. She stopped to greet her friends, who poured their woes into
her ears.

"But what could be easier?" she cried. "I'll lend you the *abbé*. I can quite well
spare him for forty-eight hours. Rodolphe's education will not suffer during that
short time. He will go for your children and bring them home."

So it was arranged that Father Lecuir, a young and cultured priest and Rodolphe
de Martinsec's tutor, should go to Paris the following week to take charge of the
young people.

So the priest set out on Friday; and on Sunday morning he was at the Gare de
Lyon, ready, with his three youngsters, to take the eight o'clock express, the new
through express which had started to run only a few days before in response to the
unanimous demands of all the people taking the waters in Auvergne.

He walked down the platform, followed by his schoolboys, like a hen and her
chicks, in search of a compartment either empty or occupied by people whose
appearance was quite irreproachable, for his mind retained a lively sense of all the
meticulous commands laid upon him by Mmes. de Sarcagnes, de Vaulacelles, and
de Bridoie.

Suddenly he saw, standing outside the door of one compartment, an old gentleman and an old white-haired lady talking to another lady seated inside the carriage.
The old gentleman was an officer of the Legion of Honor, and they were all unmistakably gentlefolk. "This is the place for me," thought the *abbé*. He helped his
three pupils in and followed them.

The old lady was saying:

"Be sure to take the greatest care of yourself, my child."

The younger lady answered:

"Oh, yes, Mamma, don't be anxious."

"Call in the doctor as soon as ever you feel yourself in pain."

"Yes, yes, Mamma."

"Then good-by, my daughter."

"Good-by, Mamma."

They embraced each other warmly, then a porter shut the door and the train began to move.

They were alone. The abbé, in high delight, congratulated himself on his clever management, and began to talk to the young people entrusted to his care. The day he left, it had been arranged that Mme. de Martinsec should allow him to give the three boys lessons during the whole of the holidays, and he was anxious to test the abilities and dispositions of his new pupils.

The eldest, Roger de Sarcagnes, was one of those tall schoolboys who have shot up too rapidly, thin and pale, with joints that seemed to fit badly. He spoke slowly, with an air of simplicity.

Gontran de Vaulacelles, on the contrary, had remained short in stature, and squat; he was spiteful, sly, mischievous, and queer-tempered. He made fun of everyone, talked like a grown man, making equivocal answers that caused his parents some uneasiness.

The youngest, Roland de Bridoie, did not seem to have any aptitude for anything at all. He was a jolly little animal and resembled his father.

The abbé had warned them that they would be under his orders during the two summer months, and he read them a carefully worded lecture on their duty to him, on the way in which he intended to order their ways, and on the manner that he would adopt towards them.

He was an upright and simple-minded priest somewhat sententious and full of theories.

His conversation was interrupted by a loud sigh uttered by their fair neighbor. He turned his head towards her. She was sitting still in her corner, her eyes staring in front of her, her cheeks slightly pale. The abbé turned back to his disciples.

The train rushed on at full speed, running through plains and woods, passing under bridges and over bridges, and in its shuddering onrush shaking violently the long chain of travelers shut up in the carriages.

Meanwhile Gontran de Vaulacelles was questioning Father Lecuir about Royat and the amusements the place had to offer. Was there a river? Could you fish in it? Would he have a horse, as he had last year? And so on.

Abruptly, the young woman uttered something like a cry, an "Oh" of pain, quickly smothered.

Uneasy, the priest asked her:

"You are feeling unwell, madame?"

She answered:

"No, no, Father, it is nothing, a passing indisposition, nothing at all. I have been ailing for some time, and the motion of the train wearies me."

Her face had indeed become livid.

He insisted:

"Is there anything I can do for you, madame?"

"Oh, no, nothing at all, Father. Thank you so much."

The priest returned to his conversation with his pupils, accustoming them to his methods of teaching and discipline.

The hours went by. Now and then the train stopped and went on once more. The young woman seemed to be sleeping now, and she never moved, ensconced in her corner. Although the day was more than half gone, she had not yet eaten anything. The abbé thought: "This young lady must be very ill indeed."

The train was only two hours away from Clermont-Ferrand, when all at once the fair traveler began to moan. She looked as if she might fall from her seat, and, supporting herself on her hands, with wild eyes and distorted face, she repeated: "Oh, my God, oh, my God!"

The abbé rushed to her.

"Madame . . . madame . . . madame, what is the matter?"

She stammered:

"I . . . I . . . think that . . . that . . . that my baby is going to be born." And thereupon she began to cry out in the most terrifying fashion. From her lips issued a long-drawn and frantic sound which seemed to tear its way through her throat, a shrill frightful sound, with an ominous note in it that told her agony of mind and bodily torture.

The unfortunate priest, dazed, stood in front of her, and did not know what to do or what to say or what effort to make; he murmured: "My God, if I had only known! . . . my God, if I had only known!" He had crimsoned to the very whites of his eyes; and his three pupils stared in utter bewilderment at this outstretched moaning woman.

Suddenly, she writhed, lifting her arms over her head, and a strange shuddering seized her limbs, a convulsion that shook her from head to foot.

The abbé thought that she was going to die, to die there before him, deprived of help and care by his incompetence. So he said in a resolute voice:

"I will help you, madame. I don't know what to do . . . but I will help you as best I can. I owe aid to all suffering creatures."

Then, swinging round on the three youngsters, he cried:

"As for you, you are going to put your heads out of the windows, and if one of you turns round, he will copy out for me a thousand lines of Vergil."

He lowered the three windows himself, pushed the three heads into their places, drew the blue curtains round their necks, and repeated:

"If you stir as much as once, you shall not be allowed a single outing during the whole of the holidays. And don't forget that I never change my mind."

And he turned back to the young woman, rolling up the sleeves of his cassock.

Her moans came ceaselessly, with now and then a scream. The abbé, his face crimson, helped her, exhorted her, spoke words of comfort to her, and lifted his eyes every minute towards the three youngsters, who kept turning swift glances, quickly averted, towards the mysterious task performed by their new tutor.

"Monsieur de Vaulacelles, you will copy out for me the verb 'to disobey' twenty times!" he cried.

"Monsieur de Bridoie, you shall have no sweets for a month!"

Suddenly the young woman ceased her monotonous wailing, and almost in the same instant a strange thin cry, like a yelp or a miaow, brought the three school-boys round in one wild rush, sure that they had just heard a newly born puppy.

In his hands the abbé was holding a little naked babe. He regarded it with startled eyes; he seemed at once satisfied and abashed, near laughter and near tears;

he looked like a madman, so expressively distorted was his face by the rapid movement of his eyes, his lips, and his cheeks.

He observed, as if he were announcing an amazing piece of news to his pupils: "It's a boy."

Then he added immediately:

"Monsieur de Sarcagnes, pass me the bottle of water in the rack. That's right. Take out the stopper. That's quite right. Pour me out a few drops in my hand, only a few drops. . . . That's enough."

And he scattered the water on the bald forehead of the little creature he was holding, and announced:

"I baptize thee in the name of the Father, and of the Son, and of the Holy Ghost. Amen."

The train drew into the station of Clermont. The face of Madame de Bridoie appeared in the doorway. Then the abbé, quite losing his head, presented her with the tiny human animal that he had just acquired, and murmured:

"This lady has had a slight accident on the journey."

He conveyed the impression that he had picked the child up in a gutter; and, his hair wet with sweat, his bands round on his shoulder, his gown soiled, he repeated:

"They saw nothing . . . nothing at all—I'll answer for that. . . . All three of them looked out of the window. . . . I'll answer for that . . . they saw nothing."

And he descended from the compartment with four boys instead of the three he had gone to fetch, while Mmes. de Bridoie, de Vaulacelles, and de Sarcagnes, very pale, exchanged stupefied glances and found not a word to utter.

That evening, the three families dined together to celebrate the home-coming of the schoolboys. But no one had anything much to say; fathers, mothers, and children alike seemed preoccupied.

Suddenly the youngest, Roland de Bridoie, asked:

"Tell me, mamma, where did the abbé find that little boy?"

His mother evaded a direct answer:

"Come, get on with your dinner, and let us alone with your questions."

He was silent for some minutes, and then went on:

"There was no one there except the lady who had stomach-ache. The abbé must be a conjurer, like Robert Houdin who made a bowl full of fishes come under a cloth."

"Be quiet now. It was God who sent him."

"But where did God put him? I didn't see anything. Did he come in by the door? Tell me."

Madame de Bridoie, losing patience, replied:

"Come now, that's enough, be quiet. He came from under a cabbage, like all little babies. You know that quite well."

"But there wasn't a cabbage in the carriage."

Then Gontran de Vaulacelles, who was listening with a sly look on his face, smiled and said:

"Yes, there was a cabbage. But no one saw it except the abbé."

HUMILIATION

The two young women had the appearance of being buried in a bed of flowers. They were alone in an immense landau filled with bouquets like a giant basket. Upon the seat before them were two small hampers full of Nice violets, and upon the bearskin which covered their knees was a heap of roses, gillyflowers, marguerites, tuberoses and orange flowers, bound together with silk ribbons, which seemed to crush the two delicate bodies, only allowing to appear above the spread-out, perfumed bed the shoulders, arms and a little of their bodices, one of which was blue and the other lilac.

The coachman's whip bore a sheath of anemones; the horses' heads were decorated with wallflowers; the spokes of the wheels were clothed in mignonette, and in place of lanterns, there were two round, enormous bouquets, which seemed like the two eyes of this strange, rolling, flowery beast.

The landau went along Antibes Street at a brisk trot, preceded, followed and accompanied by a crowd of other garlanded carriages full of women concealed under a billow of violets. For it was the Flower Festival at Cannes.

They arrived at the Foncière Boulevard, where the battle took place. The whole length of the immense avenue, a double line of bedecked equipages was going and coming, like a ribbon without end. They threw flowers from one to the other. Flowers passed in the air like balls, hit the fair faces, hovered and fell in the dust where an army of street urchins gathered them.

A compact crowd, clamorous but orderly, looked on, standing in rows upon the sidewalks and held in place by policemen on horseback who passed along, pushing back the curious brutally with their feet, in order that the villains might not mingle with the rich.

Now the people in the carriages recognized each other, called to each other and bombarded one another with roses. A chariot full of pretty young women, clothed in red like devils, attracted and held all eyes. One gentleman, who resembled the portraits of Henry IV, threw repeatedly, with joyous ardor, a huge bouquet retained by an elastic. At the threat of the blow the women lowered their heads and hid their eyes, but the gracious projectile only described a curve and again returned to its master, who immediately threw it again to a new face.

The two young women emptied their arsenal with full hands and received a shower of bouquets; then after an hour of battle, a little wearied at the last, they ordered the coachman to take the road to the Juan Gulf, which skirts the sea.

The sun disappeared behind the Estérel, outlining in black upon a background of fire the lacy silhouette of the stretched-out mountain. The calm sea was spread out blue and clear as far as the horizon, where it mingled with the sky and with the squadron anchored in the middle of the gulf, having the appearance of a troop of monstrous beasts, immovable upon the water, apocalyptic animals, humpbacked and clothed in coats of mail, capped with thin masts like plumes and with eyes that lighted up when night came on.

The young women, stretched out under the fur robe, looked upon it languidly. Finally one of them said:

"How delicious these evenings are! Everything seems good. Is it not so, Margot?" The other replied: "Yes, it is good. But there is always something lacking."

"What is it? For my part, I am completely happy. I have need of nothing."

"Yes? You think so, perhaps. But whatever well-being surrounds our bodies, we always desire something more—for the heart."

Said the other, smiling: "A little love?"

"Yes."

They were silent, looking straight before them; then the one called Marguerite said: "Life does not seem supportable to me without that. I need to be loved, if only by a dog. And we are all so, whatever you may say, Simone."

"No, no, my dear. I prefer not to be loved at all than to be loved by no one of importance. Do you think, for example, that it would be agreeable to me to be loved by—by——"

She looked for someone by whom she could possibly be loved, casting her eyes over the neighboring country. Her eyes, after having made the tour of the whole horizon, fell upon the two metal buttons shining on the coachman's back, and she continued, laughing, "By my coachman?"

Mlle. Marguerite scarcely smiled as she replied:

"I can assure you it is very amusing to be loved by a domestic. This has happened to me two or three times. They roll their eyes so queerly that one is dying to laugh. Naturally, the more one is loved, the more severe she becomes, since otherwise, one puts herself in the way of being made ridiculous for some very slight cause, if anyone happened to observe it."

Mlle. Simone listened, her look fixed straight before her; then she declared:

"No, decidedly, the heart of my valet at my feet would not appear to me sufficient. But tell me how you perceived that you were loved."

"I perceived it in them as I do in other men; they become so stupid!"

"But others do not appear so stupid to me when they are in love."

"Idiots, my dear, incapable of chatting, of answering, of comprehending anything."

"And you? What effect did it have on you to be loved by a domestic? Were you moved—flattered?"

"Moved? No. Flattered? Yes, a little. One is always flattered by the love of a man, whoever he may be."

"Oh, now, Margot!"

"Yes, my dear. Wait! I will tell you a singular adventure that happened to me. You will see what curious things take place among us in such cases.

"It was four years ago in the autumn, when I found myself without a maid. I had tried five or six, one after the other, all of them incompetent, and almost despaired of finding one, when I read in the advertisements of a newspaper of a young girl knowing how to sew, embroider and dress hair, who was seeking a place and could furnish the best of references. She could also speak English.

"I wrote to the address given, and the next day the person in question presented herself. She was rather tall, thin, a little pale, with a very timid air. She had beautiful black eyes, a charming color, and she pleased me at once. I asked for her references; she gave me one written in English, because she had come, she said, from the house of Lady Ryswell, where she had been for ten years.

"The certificate attested that the girl was returning to France of her own will and that she had nothing to reproach her for during her long service with her, except a little of the *French coquettishness.*

"The modest turn of the English phrase made me smile a little, and I engaged the maid immediately. She came to my house the same day; she called herself Rose.

"At the end of a month I adored her. She was a treasure, a pearl, a phenomenon.

"She could dress my hair with exquisite taste; she could flute the lace of a cap better than the best of the professionals, and she could make frocks. I was amazed at her ability. Never had I been so well served.

"She dressed me rapidly with an astonishing lightness of hand. I never felt her fingers upon my skin, and nothing is more disagreeable to me than contact with a maid's hand. I immediately got into excessively idle habits, so pleasant was it to let her dress me from head to foot, from chemise to gloves—this tall, timid girl, always blushing a little and never speaking. After my bath she would rub me and massage me while I slept a little while on my divan; indeed, I came to look upon her more as a friend in poorer circumstances than a servant.

"One morning the concierge, with some show of mystery, said he wished to speak to me. I was surprised but let him enter. He was an old soldier, once orderly for my husband.

"He appeared to hesitate at what he was going to say. Finally he said stammeringly: 'Madame, the police captain for this district is downstairs.'

"I asked: 'What does he want?'

" 'He wants to search the house.'

"Certainly the police are necessary, but I do detest them. I never can make it seem a noble profession. And I answered, irritated as well as wounded:

" 'Why search here? For what purpose? There has been no burglary?'

"He answered:

" 'He thinks that a criminal is concealed somewhere here.'

"I began to be a little afraid and ordered the police captain to be brought that I might have some explanation. He was a man rather well brought up and decorated with the Legion of Honor. He excused himself, asked my pardon, then asserted that I had among my servants a convict!

"I was thunderstruck and answered that I could vouch for every one of them and that I would make a review of them for his satisfaction.

" 'There is Peter Courtin, an old soldier.'

"It was not he.

" 'The coachman, Francis Pingau, a peasant, son of my father's farmer.'

"It was not he.

" 'A stableboy, also from Champagne and also a son of peasants I had known, and no more except the footman, whom you have seen.'

"It was not any of them.

" 'Then, sir, you see that you have been deceived.'

" 'Pardon me, madame, but I am sure I am not deceived. As he has not at all the appearance of a criminal, will you have the goodness to have all your servants appear here before you and me, all of them?'

"I hesitated at first, then I yielded, summoning all my people, men and women.

"He looked at them all for an instant, then declared:

" 'This is not all.'

" 'Your pardon, sir,' I replied; 'this is all, except my own maid who could not possibly be confounded with a convict.'

"He asked: 'Could I see her too?'

" 'Certainly.'

"I rang, and Rose appeared immediately. Scarcely had she entered when he gave a signal, and two men, whom I had not seen, concealed behind the door, threw themselves upon her, seized her hands and bound them with cords.

"I uttered a cry of fury and was going to try and defend her. The captain stopped me:

" 'This girl, madame, is a man who calls himself John Nicholas Lecapet, condemned to death in 1879 for assassination preceded by violation. His sentence was changed to life imprisonment. He escaped four months ago. We have been on the search for him ever since.'

"I was dismayed, struck dumb. I could not believe it. The policeman continued, laughing:

" 'I can only give you one proof. His right arm is tattooed.'

"His sleeve was rolled up. It was true. The policeman added, certainly in bad taste:

" 'Doubtless you will be satisfied without the other proofs.'

"And he led away my maid!

"Well, if you will believe it, the feeling which was uppermost in me was that of anger at having been played with in this way, deceived and made ridiculous; it was not shame at having been dressed, undressed, handled and touched by this man, but—a—profound humiliation—the humiliation of a woman. Do you understand?"

"No, not exactly."

"Let us see. Think a minute. He had been condemned—for violation, this young man—and that—that humiliated me—there! Now do you understand?"

And Mlle. Simone did not reply. She looked straight before her, with her eyes singularly fixed upon the two shining buttons of the livery and with that sphinx's smile that women have sometimes.

THE WEDDING NIGHT

My dear Genevieve, you ask me to tell you about my wedding journey. How do you think I dare? Ah! Sly one, who had nothing to tell me, who even allowed me to guess at nothing—but there! Nothing from nothing!

Now you have been married eighteen months, yes, eighteen months, you, my best friend, who formerly said you could conceal nothing from me, and you had not the charity to warn me! If you had only given the hint! If you had only put me on my guard! If you had put one little simple suspicion in my soul, you might have hindered me from making the egregious blunder for which I still blush and which my husband will laugh at until his death. You alone are responsible for it! I have rendered myself frightfully ridiculous forever; I have committed one of those errors of which the memory is never effaced—and by your fault, wicked one! Oh! If I had known!

Wait! I take courage from writing and have decided to tell you all. But promise me not to laugh too much. And do not expect a comedy. It is a drama.

You recall my marriage. I was to start the same evening on my wedding journey. Certainly I did not at all resemble Paulette, whom Gyp tells us about in that droll account of her spiritual romance called *About Marriage*. And if my mother had said to me, as Mme. d'Hautretan did to her daughter: "Your husband will take you in his arms—and———" I should certainly not have responded as Paulette did, laughing: "Go no farther, Mamma, I know all that as well as you."

As for me, I knew nothing at all, and Mamma, my poor mamma, who is always frightened, dared not broach the delicate subject.

Well then, at five o'clock in the evening, after the collation, they told us that the carriage was waiting. The guests had gone; I was ready. I can still hear the noise of the trunks on the staircase and the blowing of Papa's nose, which seemed to indicate that he was weeping. In embracing me the poor man said: "Good courage!" as if I were going to have a tooth pulled. As for Mamma, she was a fountain. My husband urged me to hasten these painful adieux, and I was myself all in tears, although very happy. That is not easy to explain but is entirely true. All at once I felt something pulling at my dress. It was Bijou, wholly forgotten since morning. The poor beast was saying adieu to me after his fashion. This gave my heart a little blow, and I felt a great desire to embrace my dog. I seized him (you remember he is as large as a fist) and began to devour him with kisses. I love to caress animals. It gives me a sweet pleasure, causing a kind of delicious shiver.

As for him, he was like a mad creature; he waved his paws, licked me and nibbled, as he does when he is perfectly content. Suddenly he took my nose in his teeth, and I felt that he had really bitten me. I uttered a little cry and put the dog down. He had bitten, although only in play. Everybody was disturbed. They brought water, vinegar and some pieces of linen. My husband himself attended to it. It was nothing, after all, but three little holes which his teeth had made. At the end of five minutes the blood was stopped and we went away.

It had been decided that we should go on a journey through Normandy for about six weeks.

That evening we arrived at Dieppe. When I say evening, I mean midnight.

You know how I love the sea. I declared to my husband that I could not retire until I had seen it. He appeared very contrary. I asked him, laughing, if he was sleepy.

He answered: "No, my dear, but you must understand that I would like to be alone with you."

I was surprised. "Alone with me?" I replied. "But you have been alone with me all the way from Paris in the train."

He laughed. "Yes—but—in the train—that is not the same thing as being in our room."

I would not give up. "Oh well," I said, "we shall be alone on the beach, and that is all there is to it!"

Decidedly he was not pleased. He said: "Very well; as you wish."

The night was magnificent, one of those nights which brings grand, vague ideas to the soul—more sensations than thoughts, perhaps—that brings a desire to open the arms as if they were wings and embrace the heavens, but how can I express it? One always feels that these unknown things can be comprehended.

There was a dreaminess, a poesy in the air, a happiness of another kind than that of earth, a sort of infinite intoxication which comes from the stars, the moon, the silver, glistening water. These are the best moments of life. They are a glimpse of a different existence, an embellished, delicious existence; they are the revelation of what could be, of what will be, perhaps.

Nevertheless, my husband appeared impatient to return. I said to him: "Are you cold?"

"No."

"Then look at the little boat down there which seems alseep on the water. Could anything be better than this? I would willingly remain here until daybreak. Tell me, shall we wait and see aurora?"

He seemed to think that I was mocking him and very soon took me back to the hotel by force! If I had known! Oh, the poor creature!

When we were once alone I felt ashamed, constrained, without knowing why. I swear it. Finally I made him go into the bathroom while I got into bed.

Oh, my dear, how can I go further? Well, here it is! He took, without doubt, my extreme innocence for mischief, my extreme simplicity for profligacy, my confident, credulous abandon for some kind of tactics and paid no regard to the delicate management that is necessary in order to make a soul wholly unprepared comprehend and accept such mysteries.

All at once I believe he lost his head. Then fear seized me; I asked him if he wished to kill me. When terror invades, one does not reason or think further; one is mad. In one second I had imagined frightful things. I thought of various stories in the newspapers, of mysterious crimes, of all the whispered tales of young girls married to miserable men! I fought, repulsed him, was overcome with fright. I even pulled a wisp of hair from his mustache and, relieved by this effort, I arose, shouting: "Help! help!" I ran to the door, drew the bolts and hurried, nearly naked, downstairs.

Other doors opened. Men in night apparel appeared with lights in their hands. I fell into the arms of one of them, imploring his protection. He made an attack upon my husband.

I knew no more about it. They fought and they cried; then they laughed, but laughed in a way you could never imagine. The whole house laughed, from the cellar to the garret. I heard in the corridors and in the rooms about us explosions of gaiety. The kitchenmaids laughed under the roof, and the bellboy was in contortions on his bench in the vestibule.

Think of it! In a hotel!

Soon I found myself alone with my husband, who made me some summary explanations, as one explains a surgical operation before it is undertaken. He was not at all content. I wept until daylight, and we went away at the opening of the doors.

That is not all. The next day we arrived at Pourville, which is only an embryo station for baths. My husband overwhelmed me with little attentions and tender care. After a first misunderstanding he appeared enchanted. Ashamed and much cast down over my adventure of the evening before, I was also amiable as could be, and docile. But you cannot figure the horror, the disgust, almost the hatred that Henry inspired in me, when I knew the infamous secret that they conceal from young girls. I was in despair, as sad as death, mindful of everything and harassed by the need of being near my poor parents. The next day after we arrived at Etretat. All the bathers were in a flurry of excitement. A young woman had been bitten by a little dog and had just died of rabies. A great shiver ran down my back when I heard this story told at the hotel table. It seemed to me immediately that I was suffering in the nose, and I had strange feelings all along my limbs.

That night I could not sleep; I had completely forgotten my husband. What if I were going to die, too, from rabies? I asked for some details the next day from the proprietor of the hotel. He gave me some frightful ones. I passed the day in walking upon the shore. I thought I could no longer speak. Hydrophobia! What a horrible death!

Henry asked me: "What is the matter? You seem sad."

I answered: "Oh! Nothing! Nothing!"

My staring eyes were fixed upon the sea without seeing it, upon farms, upon the fields, without my ever being able to say what came under my gaze. For nothing in the world would I have confessed the thought that tortured me. Some pain, true pain was felt in my nose. I wished to return.

As soon as I was back in the hotel I shut myself up in order to examine the wound. There was nothing to be seen. Nevertheless, I could not doubt that it was working me great harm. I wrote immediately to my mother, a short letter which probably sounded strange. I asked an immediate reply to some insignificant questions. After having signed my name, I wrote: "Especially, do not forget to give me some news of Bijou."

The next day I could not eat, but I refused to see a physician. All day long I remained seated upon the beach, looking at the bathers in the water. They came, the thin and the stout, all hideous in their frightful costumes, but I never thought of laughing. I thought: "They are happy, these people! They have not been bitten! They are going to live! They have nothing to fear. They can amuse themselves at will because they are at peace!"

At that instant I carried my hand to my nose, touching it; was it not swollen? And soon I entered the hotel, shut myself in and looked at it in the glass. Oh, it had changed color. I should die now very soon.

That evening I felt all at once a sort of tenderness for my husband, a tenderness of despair. He appeared good to me; I leaned upon his arm. Twenty times I was on the point of telling him my distressing secret but ended in keeping silent.

He abused odiously my listlessness and the weakness of my soul. I had not the force to resist him, or even the will. I would bear all, suffer all!

The next day I received a letter from my mother. She replied to my questions but said not a word about Bijou. I immediately thought: "He is dead and they are concealing it from me." I wished to run to the telegraph office and send a dispatch. One thought stopped me: "If he really is dead they will not tell me." I then resigned myself to two more days of anguish. I wrote again. I asked them to send me the dog, for diversion, because I was a little lonesome.

A trembling fit took me in the afternoon. I could not raise a full glass without spilling half. The state of my soul was lamentable. I escaped from my husband at twilight and ran to the church. I prayed a long time. On returning I felt anew the pains in my nose and consulted a druggist whose shop was lighted. I spoke to him as if one of my friends had been bitten, asking his advice in the matter. He was an amiable man, very obliging. He advised me freely. But I forgot to notice what he said; my mind was so troubled. I only remember this: "Purging is often recommended." I bought many bottles of I know not what, under pretext of sending them to my friend.

The dogs that I met filled me with horror, creating in me a desire to flee at top of my speed. It seemed to me many times, also, that I had a desire to bite them. My night was horribly disturbed. My husband profited by it.

The next day I received a response from my mother. "Bijou," she said, "is very well, but it would expose him too much to send him alone on a railroad train." Then they would not send him to me. He was dead.

I could not yet sleep. As for Henry, he snored. He awoke many times. I was annihilated.

The next day I took a bath in the sea. I was almost overcome in entering the water; I was so frightfully cold. I was more than ever shocked by this frigid sensation. I trembled in every limb but felt no more pain in the nose.

By chance they presented me to the medical inspector of the baths, a charming man. I led up to my subject with extreme skill. I then said to him that my little dog had bitten me several days before and asked him what was necessary to be done if we discovered any inflammation. He laughed and answered: "In your situation, madame, I see only one remedy, which would be for you to make a new nose."

And as I did not comprehend, he added: "Your husband will see to that." And I was no better informed on leaving him than I was before.

Henry that evening seemed very gay, very happy. We went to the casino, but he did not wait for the end of the play before proposing to me to return. As there was nothing of interest to me, I followed him. But I could not remain in bed; all my nerves were unstrung and vibrating. Neither could he sleep. He embraced me, caressed me, became all sweetness and tenderness, as if he had finally guessed how much I was suffering. I accepted his caresses without even comprehending them or thinking about them.

But suddenly an extraordinary, fearful crisis seized me. I uttered a frightful cry, pushed back my husband, who took hold of me, ran into my room and began to beat my head and face against the door. It was rage! Horrible rage! I was lost!

Henry raised me up, himself frightened and trying to understand the trouble. I kept silent. I was resigned now. I awaited death. I knew that after some hours of respite another crisis would seize me, even to the last which would be mortal.

I allowed them to put me in the bed. At the point of day the irritating obsessions of my husband caused a new paroxysm, which was longer than the first. I had a desire to tear and bite and howl; it was terrible and, nevertheless, not so painful as I had believed.

Toward eight o'clock in the morning I slept for the first time in four nights. At eleven o'clock a beloved voice awoke me. It was Mamma, whom my letters had frightened and who had hastened to see me. She had in her hand a great basket, from whence came some little barks. I seized it, foolish in hope. I opened it, and Bijou jumped upon the bed, embraced me, gamboled about, rolled himself upon my pillow, frenzied with joy.

Ah well, my dearie, you may believe me if you will; I did not comprehend all until the next day! Oh, the imagination, how it works! And to think that I believed—— Tell me, was it not too foolish?

I have never confessed to anyone, you will understand why, the tortures of those four days. Think, if my husband had known! He has teased enough already about my adventures at Pourville. For my part, I cannot be too angry at his jests.

I am done. We have to accustom ourselves to everything in life.

THE NONCOMMISSIONED OFFICER

Quartermaster Varajou had obtained permission to pass eight days with his sister, Mme. Padoie. Varajou, who was in garrison at Rennes and led a jolly life there, finding himself high and dry with his family, had written to his sister that he would devote his week of liberty to her. Not that he loved Mme. Padoie so much, for she was a little moralist, devout and always irritating, but he was in need of money, in great need, and he remembered that of all his relatives, the Padoies were the only ones from whom he had never borrowed.

Father Varajou, an old horticulturist of Angers, now retired from business, had closed his purse to his rake of a son and had scarcely seen him for ten years. His daughter had married Padoie, a former employee of the Treasury who had since become collector at Vannes.

Varajou, then, on getting out of the train, took himself to the house of his brother-in-law. He found him in his office, in process of discussion with some Breton peasants of the neighborhood. Padoie raised himself from his chair, extended his hand across the table, which was covered with papers, and said: "Take a seat; I will be with you in a moment." Then he seated himself again and continued his discussion.

The peasants could not understand his explanations; the collector could not comprehend their reasoning; he spoke French; they spoke Breton, and the deputy who acted as interpreter seemed not to understand anyone.

It was long, very long. Varajou looked at his brother-in-law, thinking: "What an idiot!" Padoie must have been about fifty. He was tall, thin, bony, slow, hairy, with his eyebrows arching until they made spears of hair above his eyes. He wore on his head a velvet cap ornamented with gold braid, and his look had the tameness which his action showed. His words, his gestures, his thoughts, were all slow. Varajou kept repeating: "What an idiot!"

He was himself one of those noisy brawlers for whom life has no greater pleasures than those of the café and the public women. Outside these two poles of existence he understood nothing. Boasting, blustering, full of disdain for everybody, he despised the whole universe from the height of his ignorance. When he had said: "What a devil of a holiday!" he had expressed the highest degree of admiration of which his mind was capable.

Padoie, having finished with his peasants, turned to him and asked:

"You are well?"

"Not bad, as you see. And you?"

"Very well, thank you. It is amiable of you to think of coming to see us."

"Oh! I have thought of it for a long time, but you know in the military profession one doesn't have much liberty."

"Oh! I know, I know, and that is why it is very amiable of you."

"And Josephine is well?"

"Yes, yes, thank you; you shall see her very soon."

"Where is she?"

"She has gone to pay some visits; we have so many relatives here, and this is a very exacting, proper town."

"I have no doubt of it."

Then the door opened and Mme. Padoie appeared. She went toward her brother without eagerness, held up her cheek and asked:

"Have you been here long?"

"No, scarcely half an hour."

"Ah! I thought the train would be late. If you are ready, come into the parlor."

They passed into a neighboring room, leaving Padoie to his accounts and his collections. When they were alone she said:

"I have heard of some of your fine actions."

"What, for instance?"

"It appears that you have been conducting yourself like a blackguard, that you get tipsy and have been getting into debt."

He appeared very much astonished. "I?" he said. "Never in my life."

"Oh, you needn't deny it; I know all about it."

He still tried to defend himself, but she closed his mouth with so violent a lecture that he was forced to silence.

Then she said: "We dine at six o'clock; you are free until dinner. I cannot ask your company because I, not unfortunately, have some things to do." Left alone, he hesitated between sleeping and taking a walk. He looked for a door leading to his room and found one to the street. He decided in favor of the street.

He began to wander around slowly, his sword hitting against his legs, through the sad Breton town, so sleepy, so calm, so dead, that on the border of its inner sea they call it "The Morbihan." He looked at the little gray houses, the few passers, the empty shops, and said to himself: "Not gay, surely, or amusing, is Vannes. A sad idea, coming here!"

He sought the port, so dreary, returned by a solitary, desolate boulevard and was back before five o'clock. Then he threw himself upon his bed to sleep until dinner.

The maid woke him by knocking on the door and saying: "Dinner is served, sir!"

He descended. In the humid dining room, where the paper was nearly all unglued by the sun, a supper was waiting upon a round table without a cloth, for which three melancholy plates were set.

M. and Mme. Padoie entered at the same time as Varajou. They were seated, then the husband and wife made the sign of the cross upon the pit of their stomachs, after which Padoie served the soup, a thick soup. It was the day for potpie. After the soup came the beef, beef too much cooked, melted and fat, which had fallen apart in boiling. The noncommissioned officer masticated it slowly with disgust, with fatigue and rage.

Mme. Padoie said to her husband: "Are you going to the president's house this evening?"

"Yes, my dear."

"Do not stay late. You are all worn out every time you go out. You are not made for the world, with your bad health."

Then she spoke of the society of Vannes, of the excellent society where the Padoies were received with consideration, thanks to their religious sentiments.

Then they served a purée of potatoes with a dish of pork, in honor of the new arrival. Then some cheese, and it was finished. Not even coffee.

When Varajou understood that he was to pass the evening face to face with his sister, forced to undergo her reproaches, listen to her sermons, without even a solacing glass to cool his throat or to aid the remonstrances in slipping down, he concluded that the punishment was more than he could bear and declared that he must go to the armory to execute some commission under his leave of absence.

And he escaped at seven o'clock.

Scarcely was he in the street when he began to shake himself, like a dog just out of the water. He murmured: "What a blankety-blank-blank life of drudgery!" And he began to search for a café, the best café in town. He found it over a room, behind two gas jets. Inside, five or six men, some semigentlemen, a little noisy, were seated around some little tables drinking and chatting, while two billiard players were walking around the green cloth on which the ivory balls were hitting each other. They were counting: "Eighteen—nineteen. No luck. Oh! good shot! Well played! Eleven. You must play on the red. Twenty. Froze! Froze! Twelve. There! Was I right?"

Varajou ordered a demitasse and a small glass of brandy, of the best. Then he sat down and waited its coming.

He was accustomed to pass his evenings at liberty with his comrades in the clatter of glasses and the smoke of pipes. This silence, this calm, exasperated him. He began to drink, first his coffee then his brandy, and then he gave a second order. Now he had a desire to laugh, then to cry, then to sing and then of fighting someone.

He said to himself: "Jove! How this sets me up! I must make a feast of it." And the idea came to him of finding some girls to amuse himself with.

He called one of the employees: "Hey, waiter!"

"Yes sir!"

"Say, waiter, where can one go here to have a merry time?"

The man looked stupid at this question. Finally he answered: "I don't know, sir. Only here!"

"Here! And what do you call a merry time, I should like to know!"

"Oh! I don't know, sir, drinking beer or some good wine."

"Go on, you oyster! And the girls, where are they?"

"The girls! Ha! ha! ha!"

"Yes, the girls, where are they to be found here?"

"Girls?"

"Yes, yes, girls!"

The waiter came nearer to him and said in a low voice: "You want to know where there is a house?"

"Yes, of course!"

"You take the second street to the left and then the first to the right. It is number fifteen."

"Thanks, old man. Here is something for you."

"Thanks, sir."

And Varajou went out, repeating: "Second to the left, first to the right, fifteen." At the end of a few seconds he thought: "Second to the left—yes. But in coming out of the café, do I turn to the left or to the right? Bah! It doesn't make any difference. I shall soon find out."

And he walked on, turning into the second street at the left, then into the first at the right, and looked for number fifteen. It was a house of very good appearance, where he saw the windows of the first story lighted behind the closed shutters. The vestibule door was half open, and a lamp was burning in there.

"This is the place," thought the noncommissioned officer.

Then he entered and, as no one came, he called: "Hey there! Hey!"

A little maid appeared and was struck dumb on seeing a soldier. He said to her: "Good evening, my child. The ladies are upstairs?"

"Yes sir."

"In the salon?"

"Yes sir."

"And I can go right up?"

"Yes sir."

"The first door I come to?"

"Yes sir."

He went up and perceived in a room well lighted with two large lamps, a luster and two candelabra containing wax candles, four ladies in evening gowns, who seemed to be waiting for someone.

Three of them, the younger, were seated, with a somewhat starched appearance, upon a garnet velvet sofa, while the fourth, a woman about forty-five years of age, was arranging flowers in a vase; she was very large and wore a green silk frock which seemed like the envelope of a monstrous flower, her enormous arms and neck being like a rice-powdered rose.

The noncommissioned officer saluted: "Good evening, ladies."

The eldest one turned, appeared surprised, but bowed: "Good evening, sir."

He sat down. But seeing that he did not seem to be welcomed with any enthusiasm, he thought that without doubt only officers were admitted there, and the idea troubled him. Then he said to himself: "Bah! If one of them comes we shall see." And then he said: "Well, everything goes well?"

The large lady, the mistress of the house, doubtless, answered:

"Very well, thank you."

He found nothing more to say, and everybody was silent. Finally he began to be ashamed of his timidity and, laughing with a constrained laugh, said: "Oh well, there is nothing very merry about this—I'll pay for a bottle of wine——"

He had not finished his sentence when the door opened and Padoie, in evening clothes, appeared.

Varajou uttered a howl of joy and, jumping up, rushed at his brother-in-law, seized him in his arms and made him dance all around the room, crying: "Well, if here isn't Padoie! It is Padoie! It's Padoie!"

Then releasing the collector, who was lost in surprise, he said mockingly in his face: "Ah! Ah! Ah! Joker! Joker! You do break away then sometimes. Ah, what a joker. And my sister! You let her loose too—say!"

Realizing all the benefits from this unlooked-for situation, so impressed was he with the full force of it, that he threw himself upon a sofa and began to laugh so loud that the very furniture seemed to crack.

The three young ladies arose with one accord and escaped, while the elderly one repaired toward the door, ready to flee if it became necessary.

Then two gentlemen appeared, both in evening clothes and decorated. Padoie rushed toward them, saying: "Oh, Mr. President, he is mad—surely he is mad. They sent him to us to convalesce. You can see at once that he is mad."

Varajou seated himself, comprehending nothing about him but guessing that he had done something monstrously foolish. Finally he arose and, turning toward his brother-in-law, asked: "Where are we?"

And Padoie, seized suddenly with a foolish anger, stammered:

"Where are—where—where are we? Unfortunate—miserable—infamous fellow —where are we? In the house of the president—of the president of Mortemain— of Mortemain—of—of—of—Mortemain. Ah! Ah, you scamp—scamp—you scamp!"

IN THE COURTROOM

The hall of the justice of the peace of Gorgeville is full of peasants who, seated in rows along the walls, are awaiting the opening of the session.

There are tall and short, stout and thin, all with the trim appearance of a row of fruit trees. They have placed their baskets on the floor and remain silent, tranquil, preoccupied with their own affairs. They have brought with them the odor of the stable, of sweat, of sour milk and of the manure heap. Flies are buzzing under the white ceiling. Through the open door the crowing of cocks is heard.

Upon a sort of platform is a long table covered with green cloth. An old, wrinkled man sits there writing at the extreme left. A policeman, tipped back upon his chair, is gazing into the air at the extreme right. And upon the bare wall a great Christ in wood, twisted into a pitiable pose, seems to offer his eternal suffering for the cause of these brutes with the odor of beasts.

The justice of the peace enters finally. He is corpulent, high-colored, and rustles his magistrate's black robe as he walks with the rapid step of a large man in a hurry; he seats himself, places his cap upon the table and looks at the assemblage with an air of profound scorn.

He is a scholarly provincial, a bright mind of the district, one of those who translate Horace, relish the little verses of Voltaire, and know by heart Vert-Vert as well as the snuffy poetry of Parny.

He pronounces officially the words:

"Now, Monsieur Potel, call the cases." Then, smiling, he murmurs:

"Quidquid tentabam dicere versus erat."

Then the clerk of the court, in an unintelligible voice, jabbers:

"Mme. Victoire Bascule versus Isidore Paturon."

An enormous woman comes forward, a lady of the country town of the canton, with a much beribboned hat, a watch chain festooned upon her breast, rings on her fingers and earrings shining like lighted candles.

The justice greets her with a look of recognition, which savors of jest, and says:

"Mme. Bascule, state your troubles."

The opposing party stands on the other side. It is represented by three persons. Among them is a young peasant of twenty-five, as fat-cheeked as an apple and as red as a poppy. At his right is his wife, very young, thin, small, like a bantam chicken, with a narrow, flat head covered, as in Crete, with a pink bonnet. She has a round eye, astonished and angry, which looks sidewise, like that of poultry. At the left of the boy sits his father, an old, bent man, whose twisted body disappears in his starched blouse as if it were under a bell.

Mme. Bascule explains:

"Mr. Justice, for fifteen years I have treated this boy kindly. I brought him up and loved him like a mother; I have done everything for him; I have made a man of him. He promised me, he swore to me, that he would never leave me. He even took an oath, on account of which I gave him a little property, my land at Bec-de-Mortin, which is worth about six thousand. Then this little thing, little nothing, this brat——"

THE JUSTICE: Moderate your language, Mme. Bascule.

MME. BASCULE: A little—a little—I think I am understood—turns his head, does, I know not what, to him, neither do I know why, and he goes and marries her, this fool, this great beast, and gives her my property, my property at Bec-de-Mortin. Ah no; ah no. I have a paper—here it is—which gives me back my property now. We had a statement drawn up at the notary's for the property and a statement on paper for the sake of friendship. One is worth as much as the other. Each to his right, is it not so?

She holds toward the justice a stamped paper, wide-open.

ISIDORE PATURON: It is not true.

THE JUSTICE: Keep silent. You shall speak in your turn. [*He reads.*]

"I, the undersigned, Isidore Paturon, do, by this present, promise Madame Bascule, my benefactress, never to leave her while I live, and to serve her with devotion.
GORGEVILLE, August 5, 1883."

There is a cross here for the signature. Do you not know how to write?

ISIDORE: No. I don't.

THE JUSTICE: And is it you who made this cross?

ISIDORE: No, it was not I.

THE JUSTICE: Who did make it then?

ISIDORE: She did.

THE JUSTICE: You are ready to swear that you did not make this cross?

ISIDORE [*earnestly*]: Upon the head of my mother and my father, my grandmother and grandfather, and of the good God who hears me, I swear that it was not I. [*He raises his hand and strikes it against his side to emphasize his oath.*]

THE JUSTICE [*laughing*]: What have been your relations with Mme. Bascule, the lady here present?

ISIDORE: I have helped to amuse her. [*Grinning at the audience.*]

THE JUSTICE: Be careful of your expressions. Do you mean to say that your connections have not been as pure as she pretends?

FATHER PATURON [*taking up the narrative*]: He wasn't fifteen years old yet, not fifteen years old, M. Judge, when she debauched——

THE JUSTICE: Do you mean debauched?

THE FATHER: You understand me. He was not fifteen years old, I say. And for four years before that already, she had nursed him with the greatest care, feeding him like a chicken she was fattening, until he was ready to split, saving your respect. And then when the time had come that she thought was just right, then she depraved him.

THE JUSTICE: Depraved? And you allowed it?

THE FATHER: Her as well as another. It has to come.

THE JUSTICE: Then what have you to complain of?

THE FATHER: Nothing! Oh, I complain of nothing, of nothing, only that he cannot get free of her when he wants to. I ask the protection of the law.

MME. BASCULE: These people weary me with their lies, monsieur judge. I made a man of him.

THE JUSTICE: I see!

MME. BASCULE: And now he denies me, leaves me, robs me of my property.

ISIDORE: It is not true, monsieur judge. I wanted to leave her five years ago, seeing that she had fleshed up with excess, and that didn't suit me. It troubled me much. Why? I don't know. Then I told her I was going away. She wept like a gutter and promised me her property at Bec-de-Mortin to stay a few more years, if only four or five. As for me, I said yes, of course. And what would you have done? I stayed then five years day by day and hour by hour. I was free. Each to his own. I had paid well.

[Isidore's wife, quiet up to this time, cries out with a piercing, parrotlike voice]: Look at her, look at her, monsieur judge, the millstone, and see if it wasn't well paid for.

THE FATHER [raising his head with a convinced air]: Indeed, yes, well paid for. [Mme. Bascule sinks back upon her seat and begins to weep.]

THE JUSTICE [paternally]: What can you expect, dear madame? I can do nothing. You have given your land at Bec-de-Mortin away in a perfectly regular manner. It is his; it belongs to him. He had the incontestable right to do what he has done and to give it as a marriage gift to his wife. I have not entered into the question of—of—delicacy. I can only lay bare the facts from the point of view of the law. There is nothing more for me to do.

THE FATHER [in a fierce voice]: Then I can go home again?

THE JUSTICE: Certainly. [They go out under the sympathetic gaze of the peasants, as people do who win their case. Mme. Bascule sits in her seat, sobbing.]

THE JUSTICE [smiling]: Come, come, dear madame, go home now. And if I had any counsel to give you, I should say find another—another pupil.

MME. BASCULE [through her tears]: I cannot—cannot find one.

THE JUSTICE: I regret not being able to point one out to you. [She throws a despairing look toward Christ being tortured on the cross, then arises and walks away with little steps, hiccuping with chagrin and concealing her face in her handkerchief. The justice adds in a bantering voice]: Calypso would not be consoled at the departure of Ulysses. [Then in a grave tone, turning toward his clerk]: Call the next case.

THE CLERK [mumbling]: Célestin Polyte Lecacheur versus Prosper Magloire Dieulafait.

A PECULIAR CASE

When Captain Hector Marie de Fontenne married Mlle. Laurine d'Estelle the parents and friends feared it would be a bad match.

Mlle. Laurine, pretty, thin, blonde and confident, had at twelve the assurance of a woman of thirty. She was one of those precocious little Parisians who seems born with a full knowledge of life and of feminine tricks, with that audacity of thought, with that profound astuteness and suppleness of mind which make certain beings seem destined by fate to play with and deceive others, as they do. All their actions seem premeditated, their manner calculated, their words weighed with care, their whole existence a role which they are playing with people like themselves.

She was very charming and lively, with the liveliness that cannot restrain itself or be calm when something seems amusing or queer. She would laugh in the face of people in an almost impudent fashion but with so much grace that they were never angered. Then she was rich, very rich.

A priest served as intermediary when she married Captain de Fontenne. Brought up in a religious house, in a most austere fashion, this officer brought to his regiment the morals of the cloister and very strict, intolerant principles. He was one of those men who invariably becomes either a saint or a nihilist, in whom ideas install themselves as absolute mistresses, whose beliefs are inflexible, whose resolutions are not to be shaken.

He was a large, dark, young man, serious, severe, ingenuous, of simple mind, curt and obstinate, one of those men who pass through life without comprehending anything beneath them in variety or subtlety, who divine nothing, suspect nothing and admit what they think, what they judge and what they believe only when someone differs from them.

Mlle. Laurine saw him, understood him immediately and accepted him for her husband. They made an excellent pair. She was yielding, skillful and wise, knowing how to show herself to best advantage, always ready in good works and at festivals, assiduous at church and at the theater, at once worldly and religious, with a little air of irony and a twinkle in her eye when chatting gravely with her grave husband. She would relate to him all her charitable enterprises with all the priests of the parish and the vicinity, and she made use of these pious occupations in order to remain away from morning until night.

But sometimes, in the midst of the recital of some act of beneficence, a foolish laugh would seize her suddenly, a nervous laugh, impossible to check. The captain would look surprised, then disturbed, then a little shocked, as his wife would continue to laugh. When she became a little calm he would ask: "What is the matter, Laurine?" And she would answer: "Nothing. It is only the memory of such a funny thing that happened to me!" And she would relate some story.

Then during the summer of 1883 Captain Hector de Fontenne took part in the grand maneuvers of the thirty-second regiment of the army. One evening as they camped on the edge of a town, after ten days of tent and open field, ten days of fatigue and privation, the comrades of the captain resolved to have a good dinner.

At first Captain de Fontenne refused to accompany them; then as his refusal surprised them, he consented. His neighbor at table, the governor of Favré, talking continually of military operations, the only thing that interested the captain, turned to him to drink glass after glass with him. It had been very hot, a heavy, parching, thirst-inspiring heat, and the captain drank without thinking or perceiving that a new gaiety had entered into him, a certain lively, burning joy, a happiness of being, full of awakened desires, of unknown appetites and undefined hopes.

At the dessert he was tipsy. He talked and laughed and moved about, seized by a noisy drunkenness, the foolish drunkenness of a man ordinarily wise and tranquil.

Someone proposed to finish the evening at the theater. He accompanied his comrades. One of them recognized one of the actresses as someone he had formerly loved, and a supper was planned where a part of the feminine personnel of the troupe assisted.

The captain awoke the next day in an unknown room, in the arms of a pretty little blond woman who said to him on seeing him open his eyes: "Good morning, sweetheart!"

He could not comprehend at first; then little by little his memory returned, somewhat cloudy, however. Then he got up without saying a word, dressed himself and emptied his purse on the chimney piece. A shame seized him when he found himself standing up in position, his sword at his side, in this furnished room, where the rumpled curtains and sofa, marbleized with spots, had a suspicious appearance, and he dared not go out, since in descending the staircase he might meet someone; nor dared he pass before the concierge or go out in the street in the eyes of neighbors and passers-by.

The woman kept saying: "What has come over you? Have you lost your tongue? You had it fast enough last evening! Oh, what a muzzle!"

He bowed to her ceremoniously and, deciding upon flight, reached his abode with great steps, persuaded that one could guess from his manner and his bearing and his countenance that he had come out of the house of some girl.

And then remorse tortured him, the harassing remorse of a rigid, scrupulous man. He confessed and went to communion, but he still was ill at ease, followed ever by the memory of his fall and by a feeling of debt, a sacred debt contracted against his wife.

He did not see her again until the end of the month, because she went to visit her parents during the encampment of the troops. She came back to him with open arms and a smile upon her lips. He received her with an embarrassed attitude, the attitude of a guilty man, and until evening he scarcely talked with her.

When they found themselves alone she asked him: "What is the matter with you, my dear? I find you very much changed."

He answered in a constrained tone: "Oh, nothing, my dear, absolutely nothing."

"Pardon me, but I know you so well, and I feel sure there is something, some care, some angry feeling, something, I know not what!"

"Oh well, yes, there is something."

"And what is it?"

"It is impossible for me to tell you."

"To tell me? Why so? You disturb me."

"I have no reasons to give you. It is impossible for me to tell you."

She was seated upon a divan, and he walked up and down before her with his hands behind his back, avoiding the look of his wife.

Then she said: "Let us see. It is necessary for me to make you confess; it is my duty that I exact from you the truth; it is also my right. You should no more have a secret from me than I should from you."

His back was turned to her, framed in the high window, as he said:

"My dear, there are some things which are better not told. That which vexes me is one of them."

She got up, crossed the room, took him by the arm and, having forced him to turn around, placed her two hands upon his shoulders, then, smiling and cajoling, raised her eyes as she said:

"You see, Marie [she called him Marie in moments of tenderness], you could never conceal anything from me. I should believe you had done something bad."

He answered: "I have done something very bad."

She said gaily: "Oh, is it so bad as that? I am very much astonished at you!"

He responded quickly: "I shall say nothing further. It is useless to insist."

But she drew him to an armchair, forced him to sit down in it, then seated herself on his right knee and began kissing him with light, rapid kisses which just brushed the curled end of his mustache. Then she said:

"If you don't tell me we shall always be angry."

Pierced by remorse and tortured by his anguish, he answered: "If I should tell you what I have done you would never pardon me."

"On the contrary, my friend, I would pardon you immediately."

"No, it is impossible."

"I promise you."

"I tell you, it is impossible!"

"I swear that I will pardon you."

"No, my dear Laurine, you never could."

"How simple you are, my friend; you cannot deny it! In refusing to tell me what you have done, you allow me to think you have done something abominable, and I shall think constantly about it, regretting your silence as much as your unknown crime. While if you speak frankly, I shall forget it all by tomorrow."

"It is because——"

"What?"

He blushed up to the ears and said: "I shall confess to you as I would to a priest, Laurine."

On her lips was the sudden smile that she had sometimes in listening, and with a little mocking tone she said: "I am all ears."

He began: "You know, my dear, that I am a sober man. I drink only red wine and never liquors, as you know."

"Yes, I know."

"Well, imagine how I allowed myself to drink a little one evening toward the end of our encampment, when I was very thirsty, very much worn out with fatigue, weary and——"

"And you got tipsy? Oh, how hideous!"

"Yes, I was intoxicated," he replied with a severe air.

"And now were you wholly intoxicated so that you couldn't walk?"

"Oh no, not so much as that. But I lost my reason if not my equilibrium. I talked and laughed and made a fool of myself."

As he kept silent, she asked: "Is that all?"

"No."

"Ah, and after that?"

"After that I committed an infamous deed."

She looked at him, disturbed and troubled as well as somewhat excited.

"What then, my friend?"

"We had supped with—with some actresses—and I do not know how it was done, but—I have deceived you, Laurine!"

He made the statement in a grave, solemn tone. She gave a little toss to her head, and her eye brightened with a sudden gaiety, a profound, irresistible gaiety. Then she said:

"You—you—you have——"

And a little dry, nervous laugh broke forth and glided between her teeth two or three times and prevented her from speaking. She tried to take him seriously, but each time she tried to pronounce a word the laugh trembled at the bottom of her throat, leaped forth, was quickly stopped, but constantly reappeared, like gas in a bottle of champagne, pushing for escape, until the froth can no longer be retained. She put her hands on her lips to calm herself, that she might restrain this unfortunate gaiety. But the laugh ran through her fingers, shaking her chest and bursting forth in spite of her. She stammered: "You—you—have deceived me! Ha! ha! ha! ha! ha! ha! ha!"

And then she looked at him with a singular air, so mocking in spite of herself that he was speechless, stupefied. And suddenly, as if able to contain herself no longer, she burst forth again, laughing with the kind of laugh that seemed like an attack of nerves. Little jerking cries issued from her mouth, coming, it seemed, from the depths of her lungs. His two hands supported her bosom, and she was almost suffocated with long whoops like the cough in whooping cough.

With each effort that she made to calm herself a new paroxysm would begin, and each word that she tried to utter was only a greater contortion.

"My—my—my—poor friend. Ha! ha! ha! ha! ha! ha!"

He got up, leaving her alone upon the armchair and, becoming suddenly very pale, he said: "Laurine, this is more than unbecoming."

She stammered in a delirium of laughter:

"What—do you want? I—I—I cannot—— But—but you are so funny—ha! ha! ha! ha!"

He became livid and looked at her now with fixed eye, a strange thought awakening within him. Suddenly he opened his mouth as if to say something but said nothing; then, turning on his heel, he went out and shut the door.

Laurine, doubled up, weak and fainting, still laughed with a dying laugh, which occasionally took on new life, like the flame of a candle almost ready to go out.

A PRACTICAL JOKE

The jokes that are played nowadays are somewhat dismal. They are not like the inoffensive, laughable jokes of our forefathers; still, there is nothing more amusing than to play a good joke on someone, to force them to laugh at their own foolishness and, if they get angry, to punish them by playing a new joke on them.

I have played many a joke in my lifetime and I have had some played on me; some very good ones too. I have played some very laughable ones and some terrible ones. One of my victims died of the consequences, but it was no loss to anyone. I will tell about it someday, but it will not be an easy task, as the joke was not at all a nice one. It happened in the suburbs of Paris, and those who witnessed it are laughing yet at the recollection of it, though the victim died of it. May he rest in peace!

I will narrate two today. One in which I was the victim and another in which I was the instigator. I will begin with the former, as I do not find it so amusing, being the victim myself.

I had been invited by some friends in Picardy to come and spend a few weeks. They were fond of a joke like myself (I would not have known them had they been otherwise).

They gave me a rousing reception on my arrival. They fired guns, they kissed me and made such a fuss over me that I became suspicious.

"Be careful, old fox," I said to myself, "there is something up."

During dinner they all laughed immoderately. I thought to myself, "They are certainly projecting some good joke and intend to play it on me, for they laugh at nothing, apparently." I was on my guard all evening and looked at everybody suspiciously, even at the servants.

When bedtime came everybody escorted me to my room and bid me good night. I wondered why, and after shutting my door I stood in the middle of the room with the candle in my hand. I could hear them outside in the hall, whispering and laughing; they were watching me no doubt. I looked at the walls, inspected the furniture, the ceiling, the floor, but I found nothing suspicious. I heard footsteps close to my door; surely they were looking through the keyhole. Then it struck me that perhaps my light would go out suddenly and I would be left in the dark, so I lighted all the candles and looked around once more, but I discovered nothing. After having inspected the windows and the shutters, I closed the latter with care; then I drew the curtains and placed a chair against them. If someone should try to come in that way I would be sure to hear them, I thought. Then I sat down cautiously. I thought the chair would give way beneath me, but it was solid enough. I did not dare to go to bed, but as it was getting late I realized that I was ridiculous. If they were watching me, as I supposed they were, they certainly must have laughed heartily at my uneasiness, so I resolved to go to bed. Having made up my mind, I approached the alcove. The bed looked particularly suspicious to me, and I drew the heavy curtains back, pulled on them, but they held fast. "Perhaps a bucket of water is hidden on the top, all ready to fall on me, or else the bed may fall apart as soon as I lie on it," I thought. I racked my brain to try and remember all the different jokes I had played on others, so as to guess what might be in store for me; I was not going to be caught, not I!

Suddenly an idea struck me which I thought capital. I gently pulled the mattress off the bed, and it came toward me, along with the sheets and blankets. I dragged them in the middle of the room near the door and made my bed up again the best way I could, put out all the lights and felt my way into bed. I lay awake at least another hour, starting at every little sound, but everything seemed quiet, so I at last went to sleep.

I must have slept profoundly for some time, when suddenly I woke up with a start. Something heavy had fallen on me, and at the same time a hot liquid streamed all over my neck and chest, which made me scream with pain. A terrible noise filled my ears, as if a whole sideboard full of dishes had fallen in them. I was suffocating under the weight, so I reached out my hand to feel the object, and I felt a face, a nose and whiskers. I gave that face a terrible blow with my fist, but instantaneously I received a shower of blows which drove me out of bed in a hurry and out into the hall.

To my amazement I found it was broad daylight and everybody coming up the stairs to find out the cause of the noise. What we found was the valet, sprawled out on the bed, struggling among the broken dishes and tray. He had brought me some breakfast and, having encountered my improvised couch, had very unwillingly dropped the breakfast as well as himself on my face!

The precautions I had taken to close the shutters and curtains and to sleep in the middle of the room had been my undoing. The very thing I had so carefully avoided had happened.

They certainly had a good laugh on me that day!

The other joke I speak of dates back to my boyhood days. I was spending my vacation at home, as usual, in the old castle in Picardy.

I had just finished my second term at college and had been particularly interested in chemistry and especially in a compound called *phosphure de calcium* which, when thrown in water, would catch fire, explode, followed by fumes of an offensive odor. I had brought a few handfuls of this compound with me, so as to have fun with it during my vacation.

An old lady named Mme. Dufour often visited us. She was a cranky, vindictive, horrid old thing. I do not know why, but somehow she hated me. She misconstrued everything I did or said, and she never missed a chance to tattle about me, the old hag! She wore a wig of beautiful brown hair, although she was more than sixty, and the most ridiculous little caps adorned with pink ribbons. She was well thought of because she was rich, but I hated her to the bottom of my heart, and I resolved to revenge myself by playing a joke on her.

A cousin of mine, who was of the same age as I, was visiting us, and I communicated my plan to him, but my audacity frightened him.

One night when everybody was downstairs I sneaked into Mme. Dufour's room, secured a receptacle into which I deposited a handful of the calcium phosphate, having assured myself beforehand that it was perfectly dry, and ran to the garret to await developments.

Pretty soon I heard everybody coming upstairs to bed. I waited until everything was still, then I came downstairs barefooted, holding my breath, until I came to Mme. Dufour's door and looked at my enemy through the keyhole.

She was putting her things away and, having taken her dress off, she donned a white wrapper. She then filled a glass with water and, putting her whole hand in her mouth as if she were trying to tear her tongue out, she pulled out something pink and white which she deposited in the glass. I was horribly frightened but soon found it was only her false teeth she had taken out. She then took off her wig, and I perceived a few straggling white hairs on the top of her head. They looked so comical that I almost burst out laughing. She kneeled down to say her prayers, got up and approached my instrument of vengeance. I waited awhile, my heart beating with expectation.

Suddenly I heard a slight sound, then a series of explosions. I looked at Mme. Dufour; her face was a study. She opened her eyes wide, then shut them, then opened them again and looked. The white substance was crackling, exploding at the same time, while a thick, white smoke curled up mysteriously toward the ceiling.

Perhaps the poor woman thought it was some satanic fireworks, or perhaps that she had been suddenly afflicted with some horrible disease; at all events, she stood there, speechless with fright, her gaze riveted on the supernatural phenomenon. Suddenly she screamed and fell swooning to the floor. I ran to my room, jumped into bed and closed my eyes, trying to convince myself that I had not left my room and had seen nothing.

"She is dead," I said to myself; "I have killed her," and I listened anxiously to the sound of footsteps. I heard voices and laughter, and the next thing I knew my father was soundly boxing my ears.

Mme. Dufour was very pale when she came down the next day, and she drank glass after glass of water. Perhaps she was trying to extinguish the fire which she imagined was in her, although the doctor had assured her that there was no danger. Since then when anyone speaks of disease in front of her, she sighs and says:

"Oh, if you only knew! There are such strange diseases."

THE WRECK

It was yesterday, December the thirty-first.

I had just lunched with my old friend, Georges Garin. The servant brought him a letter covered with seals and foreign stamps.

"May I?" Georges asked.

"Certainly."

And he began to read eight pages written in a large English hand and crossed in all directions. He read it slowly with a grave intentness and the deep interest we take in the things that lie near our hearts.

Then he placed the letter on a corner of the chimney piece and said:

"Well, that's a queer story, and one I've never told you; a love story too, and it happened to me. A queer New Year's Day I had, that year. It's twenty years since. . . . I was thirty then, and now I'm fifty!

"In those days I was an inspector of the maritime insurance company that today I direct. I had arranged to spend New Year's Day on holiday in Paris, since it's usual to keep holiday that day, when I had a letter from the director ordering me to set out immediately for the island of Ré, where a three-master of St. Nazaire, insured by us, had run aground. It was then eight o'clock in the morning. I reached the company's offices at ten to receive my orders, and the same evening I took the express, which landed me at La Rochelle the following day, December the thirty-first.

"I had two hours to spare before going aboard the boat belonging to Ré, the Jean-Guiton. I took a walk round the town. La Rochelle really is a fantastic and strangely individual town, with its twisting labyrinthine streets, where the pavements run under endless galleries with covered arcades, like those of the Rue de Rivoli; but these stooping galleries and arcades are low and mysterious and look as if they had been built and left there as a setting for conspirators, the ancient and impressive setting of old wars, heroic, savage wars of religion. It is indeed the old Huguenot city, grave, discreet, not superbly built, and with none of those splendid monuments that make Rouen so magnificent, but remarkable by virtue of its whole air of austerity and a lurking cunning that it wears, this city of hard-fought battles, fated to hatch fantastic causes, this town which saw the rise of the Calvinist faith and gave birth to the conspiracy of the four sergeants.

"When I had wandered for some time through these odd streets, I went aboard a little steam tug, black and tubby, which was to take me to the island of Ré. She moved out, in an irritated sort of way, her whistle blowing off, slipped between the two old towers that guard the harbor, crossed the roadstead, got through the break-water built by Richelieu, with enormous stones that are visible at the surface of the water and shut in the town like a vast collar; then she veered to the right.

"It was one of those melancholy days that oppress and crush the mind, weigh on the heart, and deaden in us all strength and energy; a gray bitter day, darkened by a thick fog, as wet as rain, as cold as ice, and as unhealthy to breathe as a whiff from the sewers.

"Under this roof of low-hanging, sinister haze, the yellow sea, the shallow sandy sea of these endless beaches, lay without a ripple, motionless, lifeless, a sea of dis-colored, oily, stagnant water. The *Jean-Guiton* drove forward, rolling a little, as she always did; she cut through the sleek cloudy surface, leaving behind her a few waves, a brief heaving of the water, a slight rippling that shortly died away.

"I began to talk to the captain, a short, almost limbless man, as tubby as his ship and with just such a rolling gait. I wanted to gather some details of the loss that I was going to examine. A big square-built three-master of St. Nazaire, the *Marie-Joseph*, had run aground during a wild night, on the sandy shore of the island of Ré.

"The owner wrote that the storm had flung the vessel so high up that it had been impossible to refloat her, and that it would be necessary to get everything off her that could be got off. It was my duty to examine the situation of the wreck, to form an opinion as to what must have been her condition before the disaster, and to judge whether every effort had been made to get her off. I had come as the company's agent, to be a witness for the defense, if need be, in the legal inquiry.

"On receiving my report, the director had to take such measures as he judged necessary to protect our interests.

"The captain of the *Jean-Guiton* knew all the details of the affair, having been summoned to help, with his boat, in the attempts at salvage.

"He told me the story of the loss, a perfectly simple story. The *Marie-Joseph*, running before a furious gale, lost in the darkness, steering as best she could through a foaming sea—'a milk-soup sea,' the captain called it—had run aground on the vast sandbanks which at low tide turn the coasts of these parts into endless Saharas.

"As I talked, I looked round me and in front of me. Between the sea and the lowering sky was a clear space that gave a good view ahead. We were hugging a coast.

" 'Is this the island of Ré?' I asked.

" 'Yes, sir.'

"And all at once the captain stretched his right hand in front of us and showed me an almost indistinguishable object lying right out at sea.

" 'Look, there's your ship,' he said.

" 'The *Marie-Joseph*?'

" 'Yes, that's her.'

"I was astounded. This almost invisible object, which I had taken for a reef, seemed to me to lie at least three kilometers from land.

" 'But, Captain,' I answered, 'there must be a hundred fathoms of water at the place you're pointing out.'

"He burst out laughing.

" 'A hundred fathoms, my friend! . . . There aren't two, I tell you.'

"He was from Bordeaux. He went on:

" 'It will be high tide at twenty minutes to ten. You go out on the shore, your hands in your pockets, after you've lunched at the Dauphin, and I promise you that at ten to three, or three at the latest, you'll be able to walk dry-footed to the wreck, my friend, and you'll have an hour and three quarters to two hours to stay on board, not more, mind: you'd be caught by the tide. The farther out the sea goes, the faster it comes in. This coast is as flat as a louse. Mark my words and start back at ten to five; at half past seven you come on board the *Jean-Guiton*, which will land you this same evening on the quay at La Rochelle.'

"I thanked the captain, and I went and sat down in the bows of the tug to look at the little town of St. Martin with which we were rapidly coming up.

"It was like all the miniature ports that serve as chief towns to every barren little island lying off the coasts of continents. It was a large fishing village, one foot in the sea, one foot on land, living on fish and poultry, vegetables and cockles, turnips and mussels. The island is very low-lying, and sparsely cultivated; it seems to be thickly peopled none the less, but I did not penetrate inland.

"After lunch, I crossed a little headland; then, as the tide was rapidly going out, I walked across the sands to a sort of black rock which I could see above the water, far, far away.

"I walked quickly on this yellow plain, which had the resilience of living flesh and seemed to sweat under my feet. A moment ago the sea had been there; now I saw it slipping out of sight in the distance, and I could no longer distinguish the verge that separated sand and sea. I felt that I was watching a gigantic and supernatural transformation scene. One moment the Atlantic was in front of me, and then it had disappeared in the shore, as stage scenery disappears through trap doors, and now I was walking through a desert. Only the scent and the breath of the salt sea was still round me. I caught the smell of seaweed, the smell of salt water, the sharp healthy smell of the land. I walked quickly: I was no longer cold; I looked at the stranded wreck, which grew larger as I approached and now looked like a huge stranded whale.

"She seemed to spring from the ground, and in this vast flat yellow plain she assumed surprising proportions. She lay over on her side, split, broken, and through her sides, like the sides of a beast, showed her broken bones, bones of tarred wood pierced with great nails. The sand had already invaded her, entering by all the rents; it held her, possessed her, would never let her go again. She looked as if she had taken root in it. Her bows were deeply buried in this soft treacherous beach, while her stern, lifted clean off the ground, seemed to fling to heaven, like a desperate and appealing cry, the two white words on the black bulwarks: *Marie-Joseph*.

"I scrambled into this corpse of a ship over the lower side; then I reached the bridge and explored below. The daylight, coming in through the shattered hatches and the rents in the sides, flooded the long, somber, cavelike spaces, full of smashed woodwork, with a dim light. There was nothing left inside her but the sand that formed the flooring of this wooden-walled underworld.

"I began to make notes on the state of the vessel. I sat down on an empty broken barrel, and I wrote by the light of a large porthole through which I could see the boundless stretch of shore. Every now and again, I felt my skin contract with a strange shudder of cold and loneliness; and sometimes I stopped writing to listen to the vague mysterious sounds of the wreck: the sound of crabs scratching at the bulwarks with their hooked claws, the sound of a thousand small sea creatures already at work on the body of this death, and the gentle regular sound of the teredo worm ceaselessly gnawing, like the grinding of a gimlet, in every part of the old timbers, eating out their insides and devouring them all together.

"Suddenly I heard human voices quite near me. I leaped up as if I had seen a ghost. For a brief moment I verily thought I was going to see two drowned men rising from the bottom of this sinister shell to tell me the manner of their death. You may be sure it did not take me long to climb in all haste to the bridge, and I saw standing beside the ship a tall gentleman with three young girls, or rather a tall Englishman with three little English girls. They were certainly far more frightened than I had been when they saw a man rush violently up from the depths of the deserted three-master. The youngest of the girls ran away; the two others clutched their father with both arms; as for him, his mouth opened; he gave no other sign of surprise.

"Then, after a brief pause, he spoke:

"'Are you the owner of this vessel, sir?'

"'Yes, sir.'

"'Can I look over her?'

"'Yes, sir.'

"He then delivered himself of a long sentence in English, of which I could distinguish only the word 'gracious,' recurring several times.

"He looked round for a place to climb on board and I pointed him out the best place and offered him a hand. He got up; then we helped up the three little girls, now recovered from their fright. They were charming, especially the eldest, a fair-haired girl of eighteen, fresh as a flower, and so dainty, so adorably slender. Upon my word, a pretty English girl is like nothing so much as a frail sea flower. This one might just have sprung from the sand, and kept its gold in her hair. The exquisite freshness of these English girls makes one think of the faintly lovely colors of rosy shells, of mother-of-pearl, rare and mysterious, hidden in the fathomless depths of the seas.

"She spoke French a little better than the father, and interpreted between us. I had to tell the story of the wrecking in all its details, which I extemporized as if I had been present at the disaster. Then the whole family descended into the interior of the wreck. Little cries of astonishment broke from them as soon as they entered this dim shadowy gallery; and in a moment father and all three daughters were displaying sketching books which they had doubtless had concealed in their bulky waterproofs, and they all set themselves forthwith to make four pencil sketches of this strange and gloomy place.

"They sat side by side on a jutting beam, and the four sketching books supported on eight knees were covered with little black lines which evidently represented the gaping belly of the Marie-Joseph.

"The eldest girl talked to me as she worked, and I continued my inspection of the skeleton of the ship.

"I learned that they were spending the winter at Biarritz and that they had come to the island of Ré on purpose to look at this foundered three-master. These people had none of the English insolence; they were just jolly, kindhearted idiots, born wanderers such as England sends out over the whole world. The father, lank, lean, his red face encased in drooping white whiskers, for all the world like an animated sandwich, a slice of ham in the shape of a human head between two little hair cushions; the daughters, long-legged, like half-grown storks, as lean as their father, except the eldest, and all three of the girls charming, but especially the eldest.

"She had such a quaint way of speaking, of describing things, of understanding and failing to understand, of lifting to question me eyes as blue as the deep sea, of stopping the sketch to study the scene of her efforts, of setting to work again, and of saying 'Yes' or 'No,' that time went unheeded while I stood there watching and listening to her.

"Suddenly she murmured:

" 'I hear something moving lightly on this boat.'

"I listened carefully, and at once I heard a faint sound, a strange regular sound. What was it? I got up and went to look out of the porthole, and a wild shout broke from me. The sea had come up with us; it was on the point of surrounding us.

"We rushed to the bridge. It was too late. The sea was all round us, and running in towards the shore at a terrific speed. No, it didn't run, it slid, it glided over the ground, spread out like a monstrous stain. Only a few inches of water covered the sand, but the swiftly moving verge of the stealthy flood was already beyond our sight.

"The Englishman was in favor of plunging through it, but I restrained him; flight was impossible, on account of the deep pools that we had had to pick our way round as we came, and into which we should fall on the way back.

"We felt a sudden pang of mortal agony. Then the little English girl managed to smile and murmured:

" 'We're shipwrecked now.'

"I wanted to laugh; but I was paralyzed with fear, a frightful cowardly fear, as vile and treacherous as this advancing sea. In one moment of insight I saw all the dangers we were running. I wanted madly to cry: 'Help!' But who was there to hear me?

"The two smaller English girls huddled against their father, who was looking in consternation at the vast stretch of water round us.

"And night was falling, as swiftly as the sea was swelling, a heavy, damp, icy night.

" 'There's nothing for it but staying on the boat,' I said.

" 'Oh, yes,' the Englishman answered.

"We stayed up there a quarter of an hour, half an hour, I really don't know how long, watching the yellow water that deepened all round us, and swirled and seemed to boil and leap for joy over the wide recaptured shore.

"One of the little girls was cold, and we conceived the idea of going below to shelter from the small but icy wind that blew lightly in our faces and pricked our skin.

"I leaned over the hold. The ship was full of water, so we were forced to crouch against the aft bulwark, which afforded us a little shelter.

"Now the shadows of night were falling round us, and we pressed close together, surrounded by the darkness and the waters. I felt the English girl's shoulder trembling against my shoulder; her teeth chattered a little; but I felt too the gentle warmth of her body through her clothes, and this warmth thrilled me like a caress. We did not talk now; we stayed there motionless, mute, crouching as beasts in a ditch crouch against a storm.

"And yet, in spite of everything, in spite of the night, in spite of the terrible and growing damp, I began to feel glad to be there, glad of cold and danger, glad to be spending long hours of darkness and terror on this narrow hulk, close to this pretty and adorable young girl.

"I wondered why I was filled with so strange a sense of well-being and joy.

"Why? Who knows? Because she was there? And who was she? An unknown little English girl. I did not love her, I did not know her, and a passion of pity for her filled me, overwhelmed me. I longed to save her, to devote myself to her, to commit a thousand follies. A strange thing! How is it that the nearness of a woman bowls us over like this? Is it her grace that enslaves and enfolds us? The seductive charm of youth and beauty mounting to our heads like wine?

"Isn't it rather a fugitive touch of love, this mysterious love that never ceases to drive human beings into each other's arms, that tries its power the moment a man and a woman meet, piercing their hearts with a vague and deep and secret emotion, as the earth is given water that it may bear flowers?

"But the silence of the night and the sky grew terrifying, for we heard surging faintly round us the gentle swishing of wide waters, the hollow murmur of the rising sea, and the monotonous lapping of the tide against the boat.

"Suddenly I heard sobs. The smallest of the English girls was crying. Then the father tried to comfort her, and they began to talk in their own tongue, which I did not understand. I guessed that he was reassuring her, and that she was still afraid.

" 'You are not too cold?' I asked my neighbor.

" 'Oh, I'm dreadfully cold.'

"I wanted to give her my cloak; she declined it, but I had taken it off. I wrapped it round her in spite of her protests. In the brief struggle, I touched her hand and a marvelous thrill ran through my whole body.

"For some little time the air had been growing sharper and the water surging with more violence against the sides of the boat. I stood up; a great gust of wind blew in my face. The wind was rising.

"The Englishman noticed it at the same moment, and said simply:

" 'This is bad for us, this is.'

"It was bad indeed: it was certain death if a swell, even a light swell, got up to batter and shake the boat, already so broken and knocked about that the first fair-sized wave would carry it away in fragments.

"Our misery increased every moment as the gusts of wind grew more and more violent. The waves were breaking a little now, and through the shadows I saw white lines, lines of foam, rise and vanish, while each surge struck the hulk of the Marie-Joseph and sent through her a brief shudder that communicated itself to us.

"The English girl was trembling; I felt her shivering against me, and I felt a wild desire to seize her in my arms.

"In the distance, ahead of us, to left and right of us, and behind us, the lamps of lighthouses shone out down the coasts, white lights, yellow lights, red lights, revolving lights, like enormous eyes, like giant eyes watching us, spying on us, waiting hungrily to see us disappear. I found one of them particularly maddening. It went out and flashed on again every third second; it really was an eye, with an ever winking eyelid dropping over its fiery glance.

"Every now and then the Englishman struck a match to look at the time; then he replaced the watch in his pocket. All at once he spoke to me over his daughters' heads, with the utmost seriousness:

" 'Sir, I wish you a happy new year.'

"It was midnight. I held out my hand, and he shook it; then he spoke a few words of English, and suddenly he and his daughters began to sing 'God Save the King'; the sound rose in the darkness, in the silent air, and died in the vast gulf of space.

"For a moment I wanted to laugh; then a strange fierce emotion seized me.

"There was something at once menacing and superb in this song sung by these doomed and shipwrecked people; it was a prayer and it was magnificent, and worthy of that ancient glorious *Ave, Cæsar, morituri te salutamus.*

"When they had finished, I asked my neighbor to sing something alone, a song, a hymn, anything she liked, to help us forget our woes. She consented, and a moment later her clear young voice sounded out in the darkness. She sang what must have been a plaintive song, for the notes were long-drawn, fell slowly from her lips, and fluttered like wounded birds above the waves.

"The sea was rising: it was flinging itself against the wreck now. But I was conscious of nothing but this voice. I thought of the sirens too. If a boat had passed close by us, what would the sailors have said? My troubled mind lost itself in a dream. A siren. Was she not in very truth a siren, this sea maiden, who had kept me on this worm-eaten ship and in a little time would plunge with me into the waters? . . .

"The whole five of us were flung violently across the bridge, for the *Marie-Joseph* had rolled over on her right side. The English girl fell on top of me; I had seized her in my arms and I pressed passionate kisses on her cheek, the hollow of her temple, her hair, madly, not knowing or realizing what I was doing, thinking my last moment had come. The boat did not roll again; nor did we stir hand or foot.

" 'Kate,' said her father. The girl in my arms answered, 'Yes,' and made a movement to draw away. I swear that at that moment I could have wished the boat to break in two, so that she and I fell into the water together.

" 'A little seesaw,' the Englishman added. 'It's nothing. I have my three daughters safe.'

"Not seeing the eldest, he had at first believed her lost.

"I stood up slowly, and all at once I saw a light on the sea, quite near us. I shouted: there was an answering shout. It was a boat in search of us: the landlord of the hotel had foreseen our imprudence.

"We were saved. I was very sorry for it. They got us off our raft and took us back to St. Martin.

"The Englishman was rubbing his hands, and muttering:

" 'Now for a good supper! Now for a good supper!'

"We had supper. I was not happy. I was regretting the *Marie-Joseph.*

"Next day we had to go our separate ways, after many embraces and promises to write. They set off for Biarritz. For two pins I'd have followed them.

"I was a silly ass: I all but asked that young girl to marry me. I give you my word that if we had spent eight days together, I should have married her. How weak and incomprehensible man often is!

"Two years passed before I heard a word about them; then I received a letter from New York. She was married, and wrote to tell me so. And since then we have written every year, on the first of January. She tells me of her life, talks to me about her children, her sisters, never about her husband. Why? Ah, why? . . . As for me, I write to her of nothing but the *Marie-Joseph.* She is perhaps the only woman

that I have loved . . . no . . . that I would have loved. . . . Ah, well . . . who
knows? . . . Life hurries us on. . . . And then . . . and then . . . nothing is
left. . . . She must be old now. . . . I shouldn't recognize her. . . . Ah, the girl
of those days . . . the girl of the wreck . . . what a woman . . . divine! She
wrote to me that her hair is quite white. . . . My God . . . that hurts me in-
tolerably. . . . Her hair white. . . . No, the girl I knew no longer exists. . . .
How sad it is . . . all this! . . ."

A STRANGE FANCY

It was at the end of the dinner opening the hunting season at the house of Marquis
de Bertrans. Eleven hunters, eight young women, and the doctor of the neighborhood were seated around the great illuminated table covered with fruits and flowers.

They came to speak of love, and a great discussion arose, the eternal discussion
as to whether one could love truly but once or many times. They cited examples
of people who had never had but one serious love; they also cited other examples
of others who had loved often, violently. The men, generally, pretended that the
passion, like a malady, could strike the same person many times and strike to kill
if an obstacle appeared in his path. Although the point of view was not contestable,
the women, whose opinion depended upon poesy more than on observation,
affirmed that love, true love, the great love, could only fall once upon a mortal; that
it was like a thunderbolt, this love, and that a heart touched by it remained ever
after so vacant, ravaged and burned out that no other powerful sentiment, even a
dream, could again take root.

The marquis, having loved much, combated this belief in lively fashion:

"I will tell you that one can love many times with all his strength and all his
soul. You cite to me people who have killed themselves for love as proof of the
impossibility of a second passion. I answer that if they had not been guilty of this
foolishness of suicide, which removed them from all chance of another fall, they
would have been healed, and they would have recommenced again and again, until
their natural death. It is with lovers as it is with drunkards. He who has drunk will
drink—he who has loved will love. It is simply a matter of temperament."

They chose the doctor as arbitrator, an old Paris physician, retired to the country, and begged him to give his opinion.

To be exact, he had none. "As the marquis had said, it is an affair of temperament."

"As for myself," he continued, "I have known of one passion which lasted fifty-
five years without a day of respite and which was terminated only by death."

The marquis clapped his hands.

"This is beautiful," said a lady. "And what a dream to be so loved! What happiness to live fifty-five years enveloped in a deep, living affection! How happy and
benign must be the life of one who is adored like that!"

The doctor laughed.

"In fact, madame," he said, "you are deceived on that point, because the one
loved was a man. You know him; it is M. Chouquet, the village pharmacist. And
as for the woman, you knew her, too; it is the old woman who put cane seats in

chairs and came every year to this house. But how can I make you comprehend the matter?"

The enthusiasm of the women fell. On their faces a look of disgust said: "Pooh!" as if love could only strike those fine and distinguished creatures who were worthy of the interest of fashionable people.

The doctor continued:

"I was called three months ago to the bedside of this old woman. She was dying. She had come here in the old carriage that served her for a house, drawn by the nag that you have often seen and accompanied by her two great black dogs, her friends and guard. The curate was already there. She made us the executors of her will, and in order to unveil the meaning of her testament, she related the story of her life. I have never heard anything more singular or more affecting.

"Her father made chair seats and so did her mother. She had never known a home in any one place upon the earth. As a little girl she went around ragged and dirty. They would stop beside the road at the entrance to towns, unharness the horse and let him browse; the dog would go to sleep with his nose in his paws; the little one would play in the grass while the father and mother, under the shade of the elms bordering the roadside, would reseat all the old chairs in the neighborhood.

"No one ever talked in this ambulance dwelling. After the necessary words to decide who should make the tour of the houses and who should call out the well-known 'Chairs to mend!' they would sit down to plait the straw, face to face or side by side.

"When the child went too far away or struck up an acquaintance with some urchin in the village the angry voice of the father would call her: 'You come back here, you brat!' And these were the only words of tenderness she ever heard.

"When she grew larger they sent her around to collect the worn-out chairs to be rebottomed. Then she made some acquaintances from place to place among the street children. Then it would be the parents of her new friends who would call brutally to their children: 'Will you come here, you scamp! Let me catch you talking to that barefoot again!'

"Often the boys would throw stones at her. Sometimes ladies would give her a few pennies and look at her closely.

"One day—she was then eleven years old—as they were passing through this place, she met the little Chouquet behind the cemetery, weeping because some comrade had stolen two sous from him. The tears of this little well-to-do citizen, one of those fortunate ones from whom in her queer noddle she had imagined herself cut off, one of those beings always content and joyous, quite upset her. She went up to him, and when she learned the cause of his trouble, she poured into his hands all her savings, seven sous, which he took quite naturally, drying his tears. Then, mad with joy, she had the audacity to embrace him. As he was counting the money attentively, he allowed her to do it. Seeing that she was not repulsed or beaten, she did the same thing again. She embraced him with arms and heart. Then she ran away.

"What could have taken place in her miserable head after that? Did she attach herself to this booby because she had sacrificed for him her vagabond fortune or because she had given to him her first tender kiss? The mystery is the same for the small as for the great.

"For months she dreamed of this corner of the cemetery and of this boy. In the hope of seeing him again, she robbed her parents, keeping back a sou here and there, either from a chair seat or upon the provisions which she was sent to buy.

"When she returned here she had two francs in her pocket, but she only saw the little druggist very properly behind the big colored bottle of his father's shop, between a red decanter and a tapeworm. She loved him there still more, charmed, aroused to ecstasy by this glory of colored water, this apotheosis of shining crystal.

"This picture became an ineffaceable memory, and when she saw him the following year playing marbles near the school with his comrades, she threw herself upon him, seized him in her arms and kissed him with such violence that he began to howl with fear. Then in order to appease him, she gave him all her money—seventy cents, a real treasure which he looked at with bulging eyes.

"He took it and let her caress him as much as she wished.

"During the next four years she turned into his hand all her surplus, which he pocketed with a clear conscience, in exchange for permitted kisses. There was sometimes fifteen cents, sometimes forty and once only five and one half—and she wept with pain and humiliation at this, but it had been a bad year. The last time there was a five-franc piece, a great round piece that made him laugh with content.

"She thought of nothing but him, and he waited her return with a certain impatience, running to meet her, which made the heart of the girl leap with joy.

"Then he disappeared. They sent him away to college. She found it out by skillful questioning. Then she used her diplomacy to change her parents' itinerary and make them pass through there in vacation. She succeeded but for one year; then for two years she did not see him; then she scarcely recognized him, so much was he changed; he was so large and handsome in his coat with the brass buttons and so imposing. He feigned not to see her and passed proudly by near her.

"She wept over it for two days, and after that she suffered without ceasing.

"Every year she returned here, passing him without daring to bow and without his deigning to raise his eyes to her. She loved him passionately. She said to me: 'Doctor, he is the only man I have seen on earth; I have not known that there are others existing.'

"Her parents died. She continued their trade but took with her two dogs instead of one, two terrible dogs that no one would dare encounter.

"One day in entering this village, where her heart still remained, she perceived a young woman coming out of the Chouquet shop on the arm of her well-beloved. It was his wife. He was married.

"That evening she threw herself into the pond on the mayor's estate. A drunken man got her out and took her to the pharmacy. Chouquet, the son, came down in his dressing gown to care for her and, without appearing to recognize her, loosed her clothing and rubbed her, then said in a hard voice: 'My, but you are foolish! It is not necessary to make a beast of yourself like this!'

"That was sufficient to cure her. He had spoken to her! She was happy for a long time.

"He wanted no remuneration for his services, but she insisted upon paying him well. And all her life was spent like this. She made chair seats and thought of Chouquet. Every year she saw him behind his large windows. She had the habit of buying from him all her medical needs. In this way she could see him near to and speak to him and still give him a little money.

"As I told you in the beginning, she died this spring. After having related her sad history, she begged me to give to him whom she had so patiently loved all the savings of her life, because she had worked only for him, she said, fasting, even, in order to put aside and to be sure that he would think of her at least once after she was dead.

"She then gave me two thousand three hundred and twenty-seven francs. I allowed the curate twenty-seven for burial and carried off the rest when she had drawn her last breath.

"The next day I took myself to the house of the Chouquets. They had just finished breakfast, sitting opposite each other, large and red, smelling of their pharmaceutical products, important and satisfied.

"They made me be seated; they offered me a *kirsch*, which I accepted; then I commenced my discourse in an emotional voice, persuaded that they were going to weep.

"When they understood that he had been loved by this vagabond, this chair mender, this rover, Chouquet bounced with indignation, as if she had robbed him of his reputation, of the esteem of honest people, of his honor, of something of that delicacy that was dearer to him than life.

"His wife, also exasperated, kept repeating: 'The beggar! The beggar! The beggar!' without being able to find any other word.

"He got up and walked around the table with long strides, his Greek cap tipped over his ear. He muttered: 'Think of it, Doctor! This is a horrible thing to happen to a man! What is to be done? Oh, if I had known this while she was alive I would have had her arrested and shut up in prison. And she wouldn't have got out, I can tell you!'

"I was stupefied at the result of my pious proceedings. I neither knew what to say nor what to do. But I had to complete my mission. I said: 'She has charged me to give you all her savings, which amount to two thousand three hundred francs. As what I have told you seems to be so very disagreeable to you, perhaps it would be better to give this money to the poor.'

"They looked at me, the man and the woman, impotent from shock. I drew the money from my pocket, miserable money from all the country and of every mark, gold and sous mixed. Then I asked: 'What do you decide?'

"Mme. Chouquet spoke first. She said: 'But since it was the last wish of this woman—it seems to me that it would be difficult to refuse it.'

"The husband, somewhat confused, answered: 'We could always buy with that money something for our children.'

"I remarked dryly: 'As you wish.'

He continued: 'Yes, give it to us, since she has put it in your charge. We can always find means of using it in some good work.'

"I laid down the money, bowed and went out.

"The next day Chouquet came to me and said brusquely: 'She must have left a wagon here, that—that woman. What are you going to do with this wagon?'

" 'Nothing,' I said. 'Take it if you wish.'

" 'Exactly. Just what I want. I will make a lean-to of it for my kitchen stove.'

"He was going, but I recalled him. 'She also left an old horse and her two dogs. Do you want them?'

"He stopped, surprised: 'Ah no,' he answered, 'what could I do with them? Dispose of them as you wish.'

"Then he laughed and extended his hand, which I took. What else could I do? In our country a medical man and a druggist should not be enemies.

"I have kept the dogs at my house. The curate, who has a large yard, took the horse. The wagon serves Chouquet as a cabin, and he has bought five railroad bonds with the money.

"This is the only profound love that I have met in my life."

The doctor was silent. Then the marquis, with tears in his eyes, sighed. "Decidedly, it is only women who know how to love."

AFTER DEATH

All Véziers le Rethel had assisted at the funeral and interment of M. Badon-Leremince, and the last words of the discourse of the delegate of the district remained in the memory of all:

"He was an honest man, at least."

Honest man he had been in all the appreciable acts of his life: in his words, in his example, in his attitude, in his bearing, in his step, in the cut of his beard and the form of his hats. He had never said a word that did not contain an example, never gave alms without accompanying it with advice, never held a hand without having the air of giving it a kind of benediction.

He left two children, a son and a daughter. His son was general counselor, and his daughter, having married a notary, M. Poirel de la Voulte, held a high place in Véziers.

They were inconsolable at the death of their father, for they loved him sincerely.

As soon as the ceremonies were over they returned to the house of death, and all three together, the son, the daughter and the son-in-law, opened the will, whose seal was to be broken by them alone, and that only after the coffin had been placed in the earth. A direction upon the envelope expressed this wish.

It was M. Poirel de la Voulte who opened the paper, being accustomed to these things in the capacity of notary and, having adjusted his eyeglasses over his eyes, he read in a dull voice, made for particularizing contracts:

" 'My children, my dear children, I could not sleep tranquilly the eternal sleep if I did not make a confession to you from the other side of the tomb, the confession of a crime, remorse of which has rent my life. Yes, I have committed a crime, a frightful, abominable crime.

" 'I was twenty-six years old, had just been called to the Bar in Paris, and was living the life of young people from the provinces, stranded, without acquaintances, friends or parents in the city.

" 'I took a mistress. There are people who are indignant at this word, "mistress," but there are also beings who cannot live alone. I am one of these. Solitude fills me with a horrible agony, especially solitude in a lodging, before the fire in the evening. It seems to me then that I am alone upon earth, frightfully alone, surrounded by vague dangers and terrible, unknown things, and the partition which separates me from my neighbor, from my neighbor whom I do not know, makes him as far removed as the stars that I see from my window. A sort of fever invades me, a fever of impatience and fear, and the silence of the walls overpowers me. It is so profound, so sad, this silence of a room where one lives alone! It is a silence about the soul, and when the furniture cracks or starts, the courage wanes, for one expects no sound in this mournful dwelling place.

" 'How many times, unnerved, frightened by this mute immobility, have I begun to speak, to pronounce some words, without sequence, without reason, in order to make some noise. My voice then appeared to me so strange that I was afraid of that also. Is there anything more frightful than talking alone in an empty house? The voice seems like that of another, an unknown voice, speaking without cause to no one into the hollow air, with no ear to listen, for one knows, before the words are uttered into the space of the apartment, what the lips are about to say. And when they resound lugubriously in the silence they seem more like an echo, the echo of singular words pronounced low by the thoughts.

" 'I took a mistress, a young girl like all those young girls who live in Paris at some trade insufficient to support them. She was sweet, good and simple. Her parents lived at Poissy. She went to stay a few days with them from time to time.

" 'For a year I lived tranquilly enough with her, fully decided to leave her when I should see some young person with whom I was well enough pleased to want to marry. I would leave to this one a small income, since it is admitted in our society that the love of a woman ought to be paid for in money when she is poor, in jewels if she is rich.

" 'But behold, there came a day when she announced to me that she was enceinte. I was struck down and perceived in an instant the ruin of my whole existence. The chain was apparent that I must drag to my dying day, in the near future, in my old age, always, the chain of a woman bound to my life by a child, the chain of a child whom it would be necessary to bring up, watch over and protect, always concealing myself from him and him from the world. My mind was overturned by this news, and a confused desire, which I did not formulate but which I felt in my heart, took to showing itself, like people concealed behind portieres, waiting until someone tells them to appear, a criminal desire that roamed around at the bottom of my thoughts: If some accident could happen! There are so many of these little beings who die before birth!

" 'Oh! I did not desire the death of my mistress. Poor girl, I loved her well! But I wished, perhaps, the death of the other before I had seen it.

" 'It was born. I had a household in my bachelor's quarters, a false household with a child—a horrible thing. It resembled all infants. I could scarcely love it. Fathers, you see, do not love until later. They have not the instinctive, surpassing love and tenderness of mothers; their affection is awakened little by little, as their mind is drawn toward their children each day in the bonds which unite living beings together.

" 'A year passed away. I now fled from my too-small dwelling, where linen and blankets and stockings, the size of a pair of gloves, were dragging around, and a thousand things of this kind were left upon the furniture, especially upon the arm of the easy chair. I fled particularly to escape from hearing him cry, for he cried at all times, when he was changed, when he was washed, when one touched him, when he was put to bed, when he was taken up, without ceasing.

" 'I had made some acquaintances and had met her who was to become your mother. I came to love her, and a desire to marry her was awakened in me. I paid her my court; I asked her in marriage; she accepted me.

" 'And now I found myself in this predicament: To marry, having a child, this young girl whom I adored—or to tell the truth and renounce her and happiness, the future, everything, for her parents, rigid and scrupulous people, would never give her to me if they knew.

" 'I passed one month of horrible anguish, of moral torture, a month where a thousand thoughts frightened and haunted me, and I felt growing in me a hate against my son, against this little piece of living, crying flesh who barred my way, ruined my life and condemned me to an existence without hope, those vague hopes so charming to youth.

" 'At this time the mother of my companion fell ill, and I remained alone with the infant. It was in December. It was terribly cold. What a night! My mistress had gone. I had dined in my narrow dining room and then entered softly into the chamber where the little one slept.

" 'I seated myself in an armchair before the fire. The wind sighed, making the glass crack, a wind dry with frost, and I saw out of the window the stars scintillating with that bright light which they have on frosty nights.

" 'Then the besetting thought which had haunted me for a month entered my head again. Whenever I remained still it descended upon me, entered into me and roamed about. It gnawed me as fixed ideas gnaw, as a cancer gnaws into the flesh. It was there, in my head, in my heart, in my entire body, it seemed to me, and it devoured me as if it had been a beast. I tried to drive it, push it away, to open my thoughts to other things, to new hopes, as one opens a window to the fresh air of morning to drive out the vitiated air of night, but I could not, even for a second, get it out of my brain. I know not how to express this torture. It gnawed at my soul, and I felt with a frightful grief, a physical and moral grief, each succeeding pang.

" 'My existence was ended! How could I ever get out of the situation? How draw away or how confess?

" 'And I loved her who was to become your mother with a mad passion which this insurmountable obstacle further exaggerated.

" 'A terrible anger grew in me which tightened my throat, an anger which approached madness—mania! Surely I was mad that night!

" 'The child slept. I arose and went and looked at him sleeping. There he was, this abortion, this larva, this nothing, who condemned me to a life of unhappiness without appeal.

" 'He slept, his mouth open, buried in the bedclothes in a cradle near my bed, where I could not sleep myself!

" 'How did I accomplish what I did? Do I know? What force drove me; what power of malice possessed me? Oh! The temptation of the crime came to me without announcing itself. I only recall that my heart was beating furiously. It beat so strongly that I heard it as one hears the blows of a hammer behind a partition wall. I only recall that! My heart beating! In my head there was a strange confusion, a tumult, a derangement of reason, of complete cold-bloodedness. I was in one of those frightful hours of hallucination when a man is no longer conscious of his acts, either in direction or will.

" 'I gently raised the covers which concealed the body of my child; I threw them upon the foot of the cradle and looked at him all bare. He did not wake. Then I went toward the window very gently and opened it.

" 'A breath of cold air came in like an assassin, so cold that I drew back before it. The two candles flickered. And I remained there near the window for a long time, not daring to turn and see what was behind me and feeling ever upon my forehead, my cheeks, my hands, the fatal air that was constantly gliding in. This lasted a long time.

" 'I did not reflect. I was thinking of nothing. Suddenly a little cough made a frightful shiver pass through me from head to foot, a shiver which I can feel at this moment at the roots of my hair. With a startled movement I closed brusquely the two sides of the window and, turning, hastened to the cradle.

" 'He still slept, his mouth open, all bare. I touched his limbs; they were icy, and I covered him again. My heart seemed suddenly to break and to be filled with pity and tenderness for this poor little innocent being whom I had wished to kill. I kissed him over and over again upon his fine hair. Then I returned and seated myself before the fire.

" 'I thought with horror of what I had done and asked myself whence came these tempests of the soul when man loses all notion of things, all control of himself, and moves in a sort of fearful drunkenness, without knowing what he does, without knowing where he goes, like a ship in a hurricane.

" 'The child coughed once again, and I felt torn to the heart. If he should die! My God, my God! What would become of me?

" 'I got up and went to look at him; and with a candle in my hand I bent over him. Seeing him breathe tranquilly, I was reassured, even when he coughed for the third time. But I felt such a shock and made such a movement to arrest it (as one does at the sight of some frightful thing) that I let the candle fall.

" 'And, straightening myself after having picked it up, I perceived that my temples were moistened with sweat, with a sweat hot and cold at the same time, which produced an agony of the soul like that of some frightful, moral suffering or some unnamable torture, burning like fire and cold as ice, piercing the bones and the skin of my head.

" 'I remained bending over my son until daybreak, calming myself when he was quiet and transfixed by an abominable grief when a feeble cough came from his mouth.

" 'He awoke with red eyes, an inflamed throat and difficult breathing. When my mistress entered the house and saw him we sent immediately for a physician. He came in an hour and asked, after having examined him:

" ' "Has he taken cold?"

" 'I began to tremble, as very old people tremble, and stammered:

" ' "No, I think not." Then I asked:

" ' "What is the matter? Is it anything grave?"

" 'He answered:

" ' "I cannot say yet. I will return this evening."

" 'He returned in the evening. My son had passed nearly the whole day in an invincible sleepiness, coughing from time to time. A congestion of the lungs now showed itself.

" 'This lasted ten days. I cannot express what I suffered during those interminable hours which separate the morning from evening and the evening from the morning.

" 'He died. . . .

" 'And since—since that moment I have not passed an hour, no, not an hour, without that atrocious, cutting memory, a memory which gnaws, which tortures and rends the mind and stirs in me like a writhing beast chained up in the bottom of my soul.

" 'Oh! If I could have become mad!' "

M. Poirel de la Voulte put up his glasses, a movement which was usual with him when he had finished reading a contract, and the three heirs of the dead man looked at each other without saying a word, pale and immovable. At the end of a minute the notary said:

"This must be destroyed."

The two others lowered their heads in sign of assent. He lighted a candle, separated carefully the pages which contained the dangerous confession from the pages which contained the disposition of the money, then he presented them to the flame and threw them into the fireplace.

And they watched the white leaves as they were consumed. Soon they were nothing more than a lot of little black heaps. And as they still perceived some letters which were legible on the paper, the daughter crushed it with the end of her foot, mixing it with the old ashes.

Then they all three remained quiet for some time, looking at it as if they feared that the charred secret might fly away up the chimney.

ON CATS

Cape of Antibes.

Seated on a bench the other day at my door in the full sunlight, with a cluster of anemones in flower before me, I read a book recently published, an honest book, something uncommon and charming, *The Cooper*, by George Duval. A large white cat that belonged to the gardener jumped upon my lap and by the shock closed the book, which I placed at my side in order to caress the animal.

The weather was warm; a faint, suggestive odor of new flowers was in the air, and at times came little cool breezes from the great white summits that I could see in the distance. But the sun was hot and sharp, and the day was one of those that stir the earth, make it alive, break open the seed in order to animate the sleeping germs and cleave the buds so that the young leaves may spring forth. The cat rolled itself on my knees, lying on its back, its paws in the air, with claws protruding, then receding. The little creature showed its pointed teeth beneath its lips, and its green eyes gleamed in the half-closed slit of its eyelids. I caressed and rubbed the soft, nervous animal, supple as a piece of silk, smooth, warm, delicious, dangerous. She purred with satisfaction, yet was quite ready to scratch, for a cat loves to scratch as well as to be petted. She held out her neck and rolled again, and when I took my hand from her she raised herself and pushed her head against my lifted hand.

I made her nervous, and she made me nervous also, for although I like cats in a certain way, I detest them at the same time—those animals so charming and so treacherous. It gives me pleasure to fondle them, to rub under my hand their silky fur that sometimes crackles, to feel their warmth through this fine and exquisite covering. Nothing is softer, nothing gives to the skin a sensation more delicate, more refined, more rare, than the warm, living coat of a cat. But this living coat also communicates to me, through the ends of my fingers, a strange and ferocious desire to strangle the animal I am caressing. I feel in her the desire she has to bite and scratch me. I feel it, that same desire, as if it were an electric current communicated from her to me. I run my fingers through the soft fur, and the current passes through my nerves from my finger tips to my heart, even to my brain; it tingles throughout my being and causes me to shut my teeth hard.

And if the animal begins to bite and scratch me, I seize her by the neck; I give her a turn and throw her far from me, as I would throw a stone from a sling, so quickly and so brutally that she never has time to revenge herself.

I remember that when I was a child I loved cats, yet I had even then that strange desire to strangle them with my little hands, and one day at the end of the garden, at the beginning of the wood, I perceived suddenly something gray rolling in the high grass. I went to see what it was and found a cat caught in a snare, strangling, suffocating, dying. It rolled, tore up the ground with its claws, bounded, fell inert, then began again, and its hoarse, rapid breathing made a noise like a pump, a frightful noise which I hear yet. I could have taken a spade and cut the snare; I could have gone to find the servant or tell my father. No, I did not move, and with beating heart I watched it die with a trembling and cruel joy. It was a cat! If it had been a dog I would rather have cut the copper wire with my teeth then let it suffer a second more. When the cat was quite dead, but yet warm, I went to feel of it and pull its tail!

These little creatures are delicious, notwithstanding, delicious above all, because in caressing them while they are rubbing against our skin, purring and rolling on us, looking at us with their yellow eyes which seem never to see us, we realize the insecurity of their tenderness, the perfidious selfishness of their pleasure.

Some women also give us that sensation—women who are charming, tender, with clear yet false eyes, who have chosen us entirely for their gratification. Near them, when they open their arms and offer their lips, when a man folds them to his heart with bounding pulses, when he tastes the joy of their delicate caress, he realizes well that he holds a perfidious, tricky cat, with claws and fangs, an enemy in love who will bite him when she is tired of kisses.

Many of the poets have loved cats. Baudelaire has sung to them divinely.

I had one day the strange sensation of having inhabited the enchanted palace of the white cat, a magic castle where reigned one of those undulant, mysterious, troubling animals, the only one, perhaps, of all living creatures that one never hears walk.

This adventure occurred last year on this same shore of the Mediterranean. At Nice there was atrocious heat, and I asked myself as to whether there was not, somewhere in the mountains above us, a fresh valley where one might find a breath of fresh air.

Thorenc was recommended to me, and I wished to see it immediately. To get there I had first to go to Grasse, the town of perfumes, concerning which I shall write someday and tell how the essences and quintessences of flowers are manufactured there, costing up to two thousands francs the liter. I passed the night in an old hotel of the town, a poor kind of inn, where the quality of the food was as doubtful as the cleanliness of the rooms. I went on my way in the morning.

The road went straight up into the mountains, following the deep ravines, which were overshadowed by sterile peaks, pointed and savage. I thought that my advisers had recommended to me a very extraordinary kind of summer excursion, and I was almost on the point of returning to Nice the same day, when I saw suddenly before me, on a mountain which appeared to close the entrance to the entire valley, an immense and picturesque ruined castle, showing towers and broken walls, of a strange architecture, in profile against the sky. It proved to be an ancient castle that had belonged to the Templars, who in bygone days had governed this country of Thorenc.

I made a detour of this mountain and suddenly discovered a long, green valley, fresh and reposeful. Upon its level were meadows, running waters and willows, and on its sides grew tall pine trees. In front of the ruins, on the other side of the valley but standing lower, was an inhabited castle, called the Castle of the Four Towers, which was built about the year 1530. One could not see any trace of the Renaissance period, however. It was a strong and massive square structure, apparently possessing tremendous powers of resistance, and it was supported by four defensive towers, as its name would indicate.

I had a letter of introduction to the owner of this manor, who would not permit me to go to the hotel. The whole valley is one of the most charming spots in summer that one could dream of. I wandered about there until evening, and after dinner I went to the apartment that had been reserved for me. I first passed through a sort of sitting room, the walls of which were covered by old Cordova leather; then I went through another room, where by the light of my candle I noticed rapidly in passing several old portraits of ladies—those paintings of which Théophile Gautier has written.

I entered the room where my bed was and looked around me. The walls were hung with antique tapestries, where one saw rose-colored donjons in blue landscapes and great fantastic birds sitting under foliage of precious stones! My dressing room was in one of the towers. The windows, wide on the inside and narrowed to a mere slit on the outside, going through the entire thickness of the walls, were, in reality, nothing but loopholes through which one might kill an approaching enemy.

I shut my door, went to bed and slept. Presently I dreamed; usually one dreams a little of something that has passed during the day. I seemed to be traveling; I entered an inn, where I saw at a table before the fire a servant in complete livery and a mason—a strange association which did not astonish me. These people spoke of Victor Hugo, who had just died, and I took part in their conversation. At last I went to bed in a room, the door of which I could not shut, and suddenly I saw the servant and the mason, armed with sabers, coming softly toward my bed.

I awoke at once, and a few moments passed before I could recollect where I was. Then I recalled quickly my arrival of the day before at Thorenc, the occurrences of the evening and my pleasant reception by the owner. I was just about to close my eyes when I saw distinctly in the darkness in the middle of my room, at about the height of a man's head, two fiery eyes watching me.

I seized a match, and while striking it I heard a noise, a light, soft noise, like the sound of a wet rag thrown on the floor, but after I had lighted the candle I saw nothing but a tall table in the middle of the room. I rose, went through both apartments, looked under the bed and into the closets and found nothing. I thought then that perhaps I had continued dreaming after I was awake, and so I went to sleep again but not without trouble.

I dreamed again. This time I traveled once more, but in the Orient, in the country that I love. I arrived at the house of a Turk, who lived in the middle of a desert. He was a superb Turk—not an Arab, but a Turk, fat, friendly and charming. He was dressed in Turkish attire, with a turban on his head and a whole shopful of silk on his back—a real Turk of the Théâtre Français, who made me compliments while offering me sweetmeats, sitting on a voluptuous divan.

Then a little black boy took me to a room—all my dreams ended in this fashion in those days! It was a perfumed room decorated in sky blue, with skins of wild beasts on the floor, and before the fire—the idea of fire pursued me even in the desert—on a low chair, was a woman, lightly clothed, who was waiting on me. She was of the purest oriental type, with stars tattooed on her cheeks and forehead and chin; she had immense eyes, a beautiful form and slightly brown skin, a warm and exciting skin.

She looked at me, and I thought: "This is what I understand to be the true meaning of the word hospitality. In our stupid and prudish northern countries, with their hateful mawkishness of ideas and silly notions of morality, a man would never receive a stranger in this fashion."

I went up to the woman and spoke to her, but she replied only by signs, not knowing a word of my language, which the Turk, her master, understood so well. All the happier that she would be silent, I took her by the hand and led her toward my couch, where I placed myself by her side. . . .

But one always awakens at those moments! So I opened my eyes and was not greatly surprised to feel beneath my hand something soft and warm, which I caressed lovingly. Then, my mind clearing, I recognized that it was a cat, a big cat rolled up against my cheek, sleeping there with confidence. I left it there and composed myself to sleep once more. When daylight appeared he was gone, and I really thought I had dreamed he had been with me, for I could not understand how he could have come in and gone out, as my door was locked.

When I related my dream and my adventure to my agreeable host (not the whole of it!) he began to laugh and said: "He came in through his own door," and, raising a curtain, he showed me a little round hole in the wall. I learned then that the old habitations of this country have long narrow runways through the walls, which go from the cellar to the garret, from the servants' rooms to the rooms of the seigneur, and these passages render the cat king and master of the interior of the house. He goes where it pleases him, visits his domain at his pleasure, sleeps in all the beds, sees all, hears all, knows all the secrets, all the habits, all the shames of the house. Everywhere he is at home, the animal that moves without noise, the silent prowler, the nocturnal rover of the hollowed walls. And I thought of Baudelaire.

OLD AMABLE

The gray rainy sky seemed to press down on the vast brown plain. The scents of autumn, the melancholy scents of bare wet earth, fallen leaves and dead flowers, made the stagnant evening air duller and heavier. The peasants were still working, scattered through the fields, and waiting for the hour of Angelus: it would recall them to the farms whose thatched roofs showed here and there through the branches of the bare trees that sheltered the orchards from the wind.

At the edge of a road, a very small child sat on a heap of clothes, legs apart, playing with a potato that every now and then he let fall into his frock, while five women, bent double, with rumps in the air, were setting out colza seedlings in the near-by field. Moving slowly and methodically all down the big trench that the plow had just turned up, they thrust in a pointed wooden stick; the plant, already a little withered and lying limply over on its side, was thrust into the hole; then they covered up the root and went on with their work.

A man walking past, a whip in his hand, his feet thrust into sabots, stopped beside the child and lifted him up to be kissed. At that, one of the women straightened herself and came to him. She was a big red-faced girl, large of hip and waist and shoulder, a tall Norman female, with yellow hair and florid skin.

She spoke in a decided voice.

"Hullo, Césaire; well?"

The man, a slight sad-faced boy, murmured:

"There's nothing doing, as usual."

"He won't?"

"He won't."

"What you going to do?"

"How do I know?"

"Go and see the priest."

"All right."

"Go and see him right now."

"All right."

They stood looking at each other. He was still holding the child in his arms. He kissed it again and set it down once more on the women's clothes.

Across the sky line, between two farms, moved a horse plow driven by a man. Beast, machine and laborer passed with slow easy movements across the somber evening sky.

"What'd he say, your dad?"

"He said he wouldn't have it."

"Why wouldn't he have it?"

With a gesture the boy drew her attention to the child he had just set down on the ground, then with a glance he indicated the man behind the distant plow.

"Because your brat's his," he said slowly.

The girl shrugged her shoulders. "Lord, doesn't everyone know it's Victor's? And what o' that? I got myself into trouble. Am I the only one? My ma was in trouble before me, and yours too, before she married your dad. Who hasn't got themselves into trouble about here? I went wrong with Victor, but didn't he catch me in the barn when I was asleep? And then I went wrong again when I wasn't asleep. I'd ha' married him, I would, if he hadn't been a servant. Am I any the worse for that?"

The man said simply:

"I want you as you are, I do, with or without the brat. It's only my dad that's against it. But I'll get over that."

"Go and see the priest at once," she answered.

"I'm going."

And he lumbered off with his heavy countryman's gait; while the girl, her hands on her hips, went back to planting colza.

The fact was that the man now walking away, Césaire Houlbrèque, son of old deaf Amable Houlbrèque, wanted, against his father's will, to marry Céleste

Lévesque, who had had a child by Victor Lecoq, a mere servant lad employed at the time on her parents' farm, and dismissed for that very reason.

In the fields, moreover, caste divisions do not exist, and if the servant is thrifty, he can take a farm himself and become the equal of his old master.

So Césaire Houlbrèque went off, his whip under his arm, chewing the cud of his thoughts, and lifting one after another his heavy wooden shoes slimed with mud. He was sure he wanted to marry Céleste Lévesque, he wanted her with her child, because she was the woman he needed. He couldn't have said why, but he knew it, he was sure of it. He had only to look at her to be convinced of it and feel all strange and stirred up, and half-dazed with happiness. It even gave him pleasure to kiss the little boy, Victor's little boy, because he was born of her body.

And he stared without any resentment at the distant outline of the man driving the plow at the edge of the sky.

But old Amable would not have the marriage. He opposed it with the pigheaded obstinacy of a deaf man, a fury of obstinate rage.

In vain Césaire had shouted in his ear, the ear that could still hear a little.

"I'll look well after you, Dad. I tell you she's a good girl, a decent girl, and a good manager too."

"As long as I live," the old man repeated, "I'll not see it happen."

And nothing could persuade him, nothing could break down his savage determination. One hope only was left to Césaire. Old Amable feared the priest because he dreaded the death he felt approaching. He feared little enough the good God, or the devil, or hell, or purgatory, of which he had the haziest notions, but he feared the priest, who stood in his mind for the day of his burying, very much as a man might dread doctors through a horror of disease. For the past week Céleste, who knew this weakness of the old man, had been urging Césaire to see the priest; but Césaire had hesitated, because he was not himself very fond of black gowns; in his mind they stood for hands always outstretched for alms or for the holy bread.

He had made up his mind now, however, and he went towards the rectory, turning over in his mind how he would set forth his business.

Father Raffin, a small active priest, thin and always cleanshaven, was waiting for his dinner hour and warming his feet in front of his kitchen fire.

He merely turned his head as he saw the peasant come in, and demanded:

"Well, Césaire, what is it you want?"

"I want to talk to you, Father."

The man stood there, daunted, his cap in one hand and his whip in the other.

"Talk, then."

Césaire looked at the servant, an old woman dragging one foot after the other as she laid a place for her master on a corner of the table before the window.

"It's—it's, as you might say, a confession," he stammered.

At that, Father Raffin looked closely at his peasant; he noticed his confused face, uneasy bearing and wandering eye, and ordered:

"Marie, go to your room for five minutes while I talk to Césaire."

The servant flung an angry look at the man and went off muttering.

"Now," the priest added, "let's hear all about it."

The lad still hesitated, staring at his sabots, twisting his cap; he made up his mind abruptly:

"It's like this. I want to marry Céleste Lévesque."

"Well, my lad, what's to prevent you?"

"It's Dad won't have it."

"Your father?"

"Yes, my dad."

"What did your father say to you?"

"He said she's had a baby."

"She's not the first since our Mother Eve to have that happen to her."

"A baby by Victor, Victor Lecoq, the servant at Anthime Loisel."

"Ah, ah . . . so he won't have it?"

"He won't have it."

"Not at any price?"

"No more'n an ass that won't budge, saving your honor."

"What did you say to him, to persuade him?"

"I said to him she was a good girl, and decent, and a good manager."

"And that didn't persuade him. So you want me to speak to him?"

"That's just it. You talk to him."

"And how shall I talk to your father?"

"Well . . . as if you were preaching to make us give our pennies."

To the peasant mind the sole end of religion was to unloosen purses and empty men's pockets to fill the coffers of heaven. It was a sort of vast trading house where the priests were the salesmen, as cunning, shifty, and sharp as anyone, carrying on business for the good God at the expense of the country folk.

He knew quite well that the priests were of service, of great service to the poorest, the sick and the dying, helping, consoling, advising, sustaining, but all as a matter of money, in exchange for white coins, lovely shining silver paid out for sacraments and Masses, advice and protection, pardon for sins and indulgences, purgatory and paradise depending on the income and the generosity of the sinner.

Father Raffin, who knew his man and was by no means disturbed, began to laugh:

"Very well, I'll go and tell my little tale to your father, but as for you, my lad, you'll have to come to church."

Houlbrèque stretched out his hand and swore he would:

"If you fix this for me, I promise I will, on a poor man's word."

"That's a good lad. When do you want me to come and see your father?"

"The sooner the better, tonight if you can."

"In half an hour, then, after supper."

"In half an hour."

"That's settled, then. Good-by, my lad."

"Good-by, Father; thank you."

"None at all, my lad."

And Césaire Houlbrèque returned home, his heart eased of a great load.

He leased a small, a very small farm, for his father and he were not well off. They kept one servant, a fifteen-year-old girl who made their soup, looked after the poultry, milked the cows, and churned the butter, and they lived sparsely, although Césaire was a good husbandman. But they did not own enough land or enough stock to do more than make both ends meet.

The old man had given up working. Melancholy, as the deaf are, riddled with aches and pains, bent, twisted, he wandered through the fields, leaning on his stick, regarding man and beast with a harsh scornful stare. Sometimes he sat down on the edge of a ditch and remained there for hours, motionless, his thoughts drifting among the things that had been his whole life, the price of eggs and corn, the sun and the rain that spoiled or brought on the crops. And, racked with rheumatism, his old limbs still sucked up the dampness of the soil, as for seventy years they had sucked up the moisture exhaled from the walls of his low thatched cottage, roofed, too, with damp straw.

He returned home at dusk, took his place at the end of the table, in the kitchen, and when he had in front of him the earthenware bowl that held his soup, he grasped it in bent fingers that seemed to have taken on the curved shape of the bowl, and winter and summer he warmed his hands on it before beginning to eat, so as to lose nothing, not one particle of warmth that came from the fire which cost so much money, nor a drop of the soup that took fat and salt to make, nor a morsel of the bread that was made from the corn.

Then he climbed up a ladder to the attic where he had his mattress, while his son slept downstairs, in the depths of a sort of niche near the chimney place, and the servant shut herself in a kind of cell, a black hole which had once been used for storing potatoes.

Césaire and his father rarely spoke to each other. Only from time to time, when it was a question of selling a crop or buying a calf, the young man consulted the old one, making a speaking trumpet of his hands and shouting his reasons into his father's ear; and father Amable approved or disapproved in a slow hollow voice issuing from the pit of his stomach.

Césaire approached him after this fashion one evening as if it were a question of acquiring a horse or a young cow and conveyed to him, shouting in his ear at the top of his voice, his intention of marrying Céleste Lèvesque.

At that, the old man was angry. Why? On moral grounds? Probably not. A girl's virtue is lightly enough esteemed in the country. But his avarice, his deep-rooted savage instinct to thrift, revolted at the idea of his son bringing up a child who was not his own. His mind had leaped instantly to the thought of all the soup the child would swallow before he was old enough to make himself useful on the farm; he had reckoned up all the pounds of bread and all the pints of cider that the youngster would eat and drink until his fourteenth year; and he felt growing in him a crazy resentment against Césaire who had thought of none of these things.

He answered, in a voice of unwonted vigor:

"Have you taken leave of your senses?"

Then Césaire had set himself to enumerate his reasons, to relate Céleste's good points, and prove that she would save a hundred times the cost of the child. But the old man doubted the existence of these merits, while he could not doubt the existence of the child, and he reiterated stolidly, without offering any further reasons:

"I'll not have it! I'll not have it! You'll not do it as long as I'm alive."

And for three months they stuck at that deadlock, neither giving way an inch, and once a week, at least, they went over it all again, with the same arguments, the same words, the same gestures, and the same futile result.

It was after this that Céleste had advised Césaire to go and ask their priest's help.

When the young peasant got home he found his father already at the table, for his visit to the rectory had delayed him.

They dined in silence, sitting opposite each other, ate a little butter on their bread after the soup, and drank a glass of cider; then they sat motionless on their chairs, in the dim glimmer of the candle brought by the little servant to give her light to wash the bowls, dry the glasses and cut chunks of bread in preparation for the breakfast eaten at dawn.

There was a knock at the door: it opened immediately and the priest appeared. The old man lifted uneasy distrustful eyes, and with a foreboding of danger, started to climb his ladder, but Father Raffin put a hand on his shoulder and yelled in his ear:

"I have a word to say to you, old Amable."

Césaire had disappeared, profiting by the door left open by the priest. He did not want to listen, so much he dreaded the discussion; he did not want to feel his spirits gradually sinking with each obstinate refusal of his father; he preferred to learn the truth, good or bad, in one word afterwards; and he went out into the darkness. It was a moonless starless evening, one of those misty evenings when the air feels heavy with moisture. A faint smell of apples hung round the yard, for it was the time when the earliest apples were gathered, the *euribles*, as they say in the cider country. As Césaire walked past the walls of the cowsheds, the warm smell of living animals asleep in the straw floated through the narrow windows; and by the stable he heard the stamping of the horses and the sound of their jaws snatching and chewing the oats from the mangers.

He walked straight ahead, thinking about Céleste. In his simple mind, where ideas were hardly more than images born of direct contact with objects, thoughts of love took form only when he evoked the image of a big red-haired girl, standing in a sunken road, laughing, hands on hips.

It was thus he had seen her on the day when he first desired her. He had, however, known her since they were children, but never before this morning had he taken any particular notice of her. They had talked for some minutes; then he left her, and as he walked away, he kept on saying to himself: "Christ, that's a fine girl all the same. A pity she went wrong with Victor." He thought about it until evening, and all the next day as well.

When he saw her again, he felt a tickling sensation at the bottom of his throat, as if a feather had been pushed down his mouth into his chest; and after that, every time he found himself near her, he was surprised at the nervous tickling feeling that invariably attacked him.

Three weeks later he decided to marry her, so taken was he with her. He could not have said what had roused in him this overweening desire, but he expressed it by saying: "I'm possessed by her," as if the passion he bore within him for this girl was mastering him like an evil spirit. He did not mind at all that she had lost her virtue; it was only so much the worse; it did not spoil her; and he bore no ill will to Victor Lecoq for it.

But if the priest failed, what was he to do? He dared not think about that, so tortured was he by anxiety.

He had reached the rectory, and he sat down near the little wooden fence to wait for the priest's return.

He had been there perhaps an hour when he heard footsteps on the road, and despite the blackness of the night, he soon made out the still blacker shadow of a cassock.

He stood up, his legs trembling under him, afraid to speak, afraid to be told.

The priest saw him and said gaily:

"Well, my boy, it's all right."

Césaire stammered:

"All right . . . it can't be."

"Yes, my lad, but not without some trouble. What an obstinate old donkey your father is!"

"It can't be," the peasant repeated.

"But it is. Come and see me tomorrow noon, to arrange for the banns."

The man had seized the priest's hand. He gripped it, shook it, crushed it, babbling: "Indeed, indeed, indeed, Father . . . on the word of an honest man . . . you'll see me next Sunday in church."

II

The wedding took place towards the middle of December. It was a simple one, since the pair had not much money. Césaire, all in new clothes, was ready at eight in the morning to go and call for his betrothed and take her to the registrar; but as he was too early, he sat down by the kitchen table and waited for those of his relations and friends who were to accompany him.

It had been snowing for a week, and the brown earth, already made fruitful by the autumn sowing, had turned livid, and slept under a vast sheet of ice.

It was cold in the cottages, whose thatched roofs wore a white bonnet; and the round apple trees in the orchards looked as if they were in flower, powdered over as in the lovely month of their blossoming.

Today, the heavy clouds from the north, gray clouds swollen with fleecy showers, had vanished, and the blue sky opened on a white earth on which the rising sun flung silver rays.

Césaire sat staring in front of him through the window, thinking of nothing, quite happy.

The door opened; two women came in, peasants in their Sunday clothes, the aunt and cousin of the bridegroom; then three men cousins, then a woman neighbor. They found themselves chairs and sat silent and motionless, the women on one side of the kitchen and the men on the other, overwhelmed by a sudden timidity, the embarrassed melancholy that seizes people gathered together for a ceremony. Shortly one of the cousins asked:

"Isn't it time?"

"I'm sure 'tis," Césaire answered.

"Let's be off, then," cried another.

They rose to their feet. Césaire had been growing more and more uneasy: he stood up now and climbed the attic ladder to see if his father was ready. The old man, always up so early in the morning, had not yet put in an appearance. His son found him on his mattress, his eyes open and a malicious expression on his face.

He shouted right inside his ear:

"Come, Dad, get up. It's time to go to t'wedding."

The deaf man murmured in a dying voice:

"I can't. I've gotten such a chill it's stiffened my back. I can't move hand nor foot."

The young man stared at him in horror, seeing through the maneuver.

"Come, Dad, you must make yourself get up."

"I can't."

"Here, I'll help you."

And he bent over the old man, pushed back the quilt, took him by the arm and lifted him up. But father Amable began to groan:

"Hou, hou, hou! The pain! Hou, hou, I can't. My back's all knotted up."

Césaire realized that he could not do anything, and, furious with his father for the first time in his life, he cried:

"Very well, you won't get any dinner, for I'm having a meal at Polyte's inn. That'll teach you to behave like a mule."

And he scrambled down the ladder and set off, followed by his relatives and guests.

The men had turned up their trousers to keep the edges from getting sodden in the snow; the women held their petticoats well up, showing their thin ankles, their gray woolen stockings, and their bony shins, as stiff as broomsticks. The whole company rolled along in silence, one behind the other, picking their way with great caution, for fear of losing the road, which had quite vanished under the flat monotonous unbroken covering of snow.

As they approached each farm, they saw one or two people waiting to join them; and the procession grew longer and longer; it wound along, following the unseen line of the road, looking like a living rosary of black beads slithering over the white fields.

In front of the bride's door, a number of people were stamping their feet while they waited for the bridegroom. They hailed him when he appeared; and Céleste came out of her room at once, dressed in a blue gown, her shoulders covered with a little red shawl, and wearing a wreath of orange blossom on her head.

But everyone asked Césaire:

"Where's your dad?"

He made the embarrassed answer:

"He couldn't move with rheumatics."

The farmers shook their heads and looked at him with malicious incredulity.

They set off for the registrar's. A peasant woman carried Victor's child behind the future husband and wife, as if they were going to a christening; and the peasants, arm in arm now, in double file, made their way through the snow with the motion of a sloop on the sea.

After the mayor had married the betrothed in the little town hall, the priest proceeded to unite them in the modest house of God. He blessed their marriage and promised them a fruitful union; then he preached to them of wedded virtue, the simple healthy virtue of the country, work, peace, and faithfulness, while the child, feeling the cold, whimpered behind the bride's back.

The moment the couple reappeared on the threshold of the church, shots rang out in the cemetery moat. Nothing was visible but the barrels of the guns from which issued quick spurts of smoke; then a head emerged and looked at the procession; it was Victor Lecoq celebrating the marriage of his dear friend, congratulating her on her happiness and throwing her his vows with each flash of powder. He had recruited some of his friends, five or six hired men, to deliver these musketry salvos. Everyone agreed that he was behaving very well.

The meal took place at the inn kept by Polyte Cacheprune. Twenty places had been laid in the big dining room where the people dined on market day; and the great joint turning on the spit, the birds roasting in their juice, the black puddings crisping on the clear hot fire, filled the house with a pungent fragrance, the smoke of red-hot charcoal spattered with drops of grease, and the strong heavy smell of country food.

They sat down at the table at noon, and the soup was soon poured into the plates. Faces were already animated; mouths opened to utter broad jests, eyes wrinkled up in malicious mirth. They were going to enjoy themselves, by God.

The door opened, and old Amable appeared. He looked spiteful and furiously angry, and he dragged himself along on his sticks, groaning at every step to let them see how he was suffering.

Everyone fell silent at sight of him, but all at once old Malivoire, his neighbor and a fat jolly man who knew everyone's little ways, began to shout, as Césaire always did, making a speaking trumpet of his hands: "Hey, old fox, you've a good nose, you have, to smell Polyte's cooking from your house."

A great laugh burst from the throats of the guests. Malivoire, excited by his success, went on: "There's nothing like a plaster of black pudding for the rheumatics. It'll warm your inside, with a glass of brandy. . . ."

All the men shouted, hammering the table with their fists, rolling with laughter, bending and straightening their bodies as if they were working at a pump. The women clucked like hens, the servants writhed with amusement as they stood by the walls. Only old Amable did not laugh, and waited, without replying, while they laid a place for him.

They put him in the center of the table, facing his daughter-in-law, and he began to eat as soon as he was seated. It was his son who was paying, after all, and he must have his share of it. With each ladleful of soup that dropped into his stomach, with each mouthful of bread or meat chewed by his gums, with each glass of cider and wine that rolled down his gullet, he felt that he was getting back some of his property, taking back a little of his money that all these gluttons were devouring, saving a fragment of his possessions, in fact. And he ate in silence, with the obstinacy of a miser who hides halfpennies, with the gloomy tenacity that he used to bring to his persevering toil.

But all at once he saw Céleste's child at the foot of the table, sitting on a woman's knee, and his eyes never left it again. He continued to eat, his glance fixed on the little creature. The woman nursing him kept putting between his lips little bits of stew, which he nibbled, and the old man suffered more from the few mouthfuls sucked by this grub than from all that the rest of the guests swallowed.

The meal lasted till evening. Then everyone went home.

Césaire helped old Amable to his feet.

"Come, Dad, time to get home," he said. And he put his two sticks into his hands. Céleste took the child in her arms, and they went slowly through the somber night lit by the gleaming snow. The deaf old man, three parts drunk, and made all the more spiteful thereby, refused obstinately to get on. Several times he even sat down, with the idea that his daughter-in-law might take cold; and he groaned, without saying a word, delivering himself of a sort of long-drawn dolorous wail.

When they reached home, he climbed up to his attic at once, while Césaire made up a bed for the child near the wide nook where he and his wife were going to lie. But as the newly married pair did not go to sleep at once, they heard the old man tossing on his mattress for a long time, and several times he even spoke aloud, as if he were dreaming and giving away his thoughts despite himself, unable to keep them back, so obsessed he was by the one idea.

When he came down his ladder in the morning he saw his daughter-in-law hurrying round at work.

"Come, Dad!" she cried; "hurry up, here's some good soup."

And at the end of the table she set a round black earthen pot full of steaming liquid. He made no reply but sat down and took up the scalding bowl, and warmed his hands on it as he always did. It was such a cold day that he even pressed it against his chest and tried to get a little of the quick heat of the boiling water into his old body that so many winters had stiffened.

Then he sought his sticks and went out into the frozen fields until noon, until dinnertime, for he had seen Céleste's baby installed in a big soapbox, still asleep.

He kept altogether to himself. He went on living in the cottage as before, but he bore himself as if he were no longer part of it, no longer interested in anything, regarding these people, his son, the woman and the child, as strangers whom he did not know and to whom he never spoke.

The winter dragged on. It was long and hard. Then the first days of spring burst the seeds; and once more the peasants, like industrious ants, spent their days in the fields, working from dawn to dark, in the northeast wind, in rain, along the furrows of the brown earth that bore in its bosom the bread of man.

The year promised well for the newly married pair. The crops pushed up thick and hardy; there were no late frosts; and the blossoming apple trees scattered over the grass a pink and white snow that foretold a bumper harvest.

Césaire worked very hard, rising early and going to bed late, to save the cost of a hired man.

Sometimes his wife said to him:

"You'll make yourself ill in the long run."

"No, I'll not," he answered; "I'm used to it."

But one evening he came home so exhausted that he had to lie down without any supper. He rose at the usual hour in the morning; but he could not eat, in spite of his fast of the night before; and he had to come home in the middle of the afternoon to rest again. During the night, he began to cough; and he tossed on his mattress, feverish, with burning forehead, and dry tongue, consumed with a frightful thirst.

He did, however, go as far as his fields at daybreak; but the next day the doctor had to be called in, and pronounced him very ill, and down with inflammation of the lungs.

He never left now the nook which served him for bedroom. He could be heard coughing, panting and tossing in the depths of his hole. A candle had to be carried to the opening, in order to look at him, to give him his medicine or apply a cupping glass. Then his sunken face, disfigured by its growth of beard, became visible under a thick canopy of spider webs, which hung and floated, stirred by the draft. And the sick man's hands lay on the gray bedclothes as if they were dead.

Céleste cared for him with an anxious activity, made him drink remedies, applied blisters, came and went in the house; while old Amable remained on the edge of his attic, peering from that distance at the dark hollow where his son lay and suffered. He would not come any nearer, for his hatred of the woman, and he squatted there sulking like a jealous dog.

Six more days went by; then one morning when Céleste, who slept now on two wretched heaps of straw, went to see if her man was better, she could not hear his hurried breathing coming from his hidden bed. Terrified, she asked:

"Now, Césaire, how've you been tonight?"

He did not answer.

She put out her hand to touch him, and felt the cold flesh of his face. A long wail broke from her, the long wail of a woman in mortal fear. He was dead.

At her cry, the old deaf man appeared at the top of his ladder; and seeing Céleste rushing out to bring help, he hurried down and touched his son's face himself: the truth broke on him and he bent to fasten the door from the inside, to keep the woman from coming back to take possession of his home again, now that his son was no longer alive.

Then he sat down on a chair beside the dead man.

Neighbors arrived and shouted and knocked. He did not hear them. One of them broke a pane of the window and jumped into the room. Others followed; the door was opened again, and Céleste reappeared, weeping violently, with swollen cheeks and red eyes. Then old Amable, beaten, climbed back to his attic without saying a word.

The burial took place next day; then, after the ceremony, father-in-law and daughter-in-law found themselves alone in the farmhouse, with the child.

It was the usual hour for dinner. She lit the fire, prepared the soup, and set the plates on the table, while the old man sat in his chair and waited without appearing to notice her.

When the meal was ready, she shouted in his ear:

"Come, Dad, we must eat."

He rose, took his place at the end of the table, emptied his bowl, chewed his bread spread thin with butter, drank two glasses of cider and then went out.

It was one of those moist warm days, one of those beneficent days when life ferments, palpitating and blossoming, over the whole surface of the earth.

Old Amable followed a little path across the fields. He looked at the green shoots of corn and barley, and thought that his young lad was under the ground now, his poor young lad. He walked wearily along, dragging his legs and limping a little. And as he was alone in the fields, all alone under the blue sky, in the middle of growing crops, all alone with the larks he saw hovering over his head but whose airy song he could not hear, he began to weep as he walked.

Then he sat down near a pool and stayed there until evening, watching the little birds that came to drink; then, at nightfall, he went home, supped without saying a word and climbed to his attic.

And his life went on as in the past. Nothing was changed, except that his son Césaire slept in the cemetery.

What could the old man have done? He could not work now, he was only fit to eat the soup prepared by his daughter-in-law. And he swallowed it in silence, morning and night, glaring furiously at the child who sat facing him at the other side of the table and ate too. Then he went out, wandered over the country like a vagabond, went and hid himself behind barns to get an hour or two hours' sleep as if he was afraid of being seen, then as dusk fell he came home.

But weighty anxieties began to fill Céleste's thoughts. The fields needed a man to watch over them and work them. Someone ought to be there in the fields all the time, not just a hired man, but a real husbandman, a master, who knew his job and would have a real interest in the farm. A woman alone could not cultivate them, follow the prices of corn, direct the selling and buying of stock. Certain ideas came into her head, simple practical ideas, over which she pondered all night. She could not marry again before the year was up, and the immediate pressing needs must be attended to at once.

Only one man could help her in this quandary, Victor Lecoq, the father of her child. He was steady, and land-wise; with a little money in his pocket he would have made an excellent farmer. She knew that, having seen him working on her parents' farm.

So one morning, seeing him going along the road with a load of manure, she went out after him. When he saw her, he stopped his horses, and she spoke to him as if she had met him only the day before:

"Good day, Victor, how are you today?"

"I'm all right," he answered; "and how's yourself?"

"Oh, me, I'd be all right if I wasn't alone on the place, which worries me because of the land."

Then they talked on a long time, leaning against the wheel of the heavy wagon. Now and then the man scratched his forehead under his cap and reflected, while she, with crimson cheeks, talked earnestly, setting forth her reasons, all her affairs, her future plans; at last he murmured:

"Yes, it could be done."

She held out her hand like a peasant concluding a bargain, and asked:

"Is it settled?"

He gripped the outstretched hand:

"It's settled."

"On Sunday, then."

"On Sunday."

"All right; good-by, Victor."

"Good-by, Mme. Houlbrèque."

III

That Sunday was a feast day in the village, the yearly feast of their patron saint, called in Normandy the *assemblée.*

For a week, strange vehicles were seen coming by every road, dragged along by gray or roan hacks, and housing the traveling families of regular showmen, with gambling outfits, shooting galleries, and amusements of all kinds, and men showing curiosities, for whom the peasants had a curious name of their own.

Dirty caravans with flapping curtains, accompanied by a melancholy dog slinking with hanging head between the wheels, drew up one after the other in the village square. Then a tent was put up before each traveling house, and shining objects, glimpsed through holes in the canvas, roused to fever pitch the cupidity and curiosity of the village youngsters.

Early on the morning of the feast, all the booths were opened, displaying their glories of glass and porcelain; and the peasants on their way to Mass were already casting open, complacent glances on the unimposing stalls which were the same they saw year after year.

The square was crowded from early in the afternoon. Farmers with their wives and children came in from all the near-by villages, jolting along in two-wheeled carts that rattled like old iron and rocked like seesaws. They unharnessed at friends' houses; and the farmyards were filled with strange covered wagons, gray, lofty, narrow curving wagons, like long-legged deep-sea beasts.

And each family, infants in front, grownups behind, walked quickly to the assemblée, with smiling faces and hands hanging open, great red bony hands that were accustomed to toil and seemed embarrassed to have nothing to do.

A sleight-of-hand man blew his trumpet; the harmonium belonging to the wooden horses wafted its jerky wailing notes into the air, the wheel on the gaming table ground round with a noise like tearing cotton; rifle shots rang out in rapid succession. The slow-moving crowd ambled past the booths like a mass of slowly oozing paste, pushed about like a herd of beasts and moving clumsily round like lumbering animals accidentally let loose.

The girls, arms locked together in rows of five or six, twittered and sang; the lads followed them round, bandying jests, caps over one ear and blouses stiff with starch and puffed out like blue balloons.

The whole countryside was there, masters, laborers, and servants.

Old Amable himself, clad in an ancient and greenish frock coat, had come to see the assemblée, for he had never missed a single one.

He watched the gambling, halted in front of the shooting galleries to criticize the marksmanship, and took particular interest in a very simple game that consisted in throwing a big wooden ball into the open mouth of a fat man painted on a plank.

Suddenly someone tapped him on the shoulder. It was old Malivoire shouting: "Eh, Dad, come and have one with me."

And they sat down at a table in a drinking booth set up in the open air. They drank one brandy, then two brandies, then three brandies; and old Amable began to wander through the assemblée again. His thoughts were becoming a little confused, he smiled without knowing why he did, he stood smiling in front of the gaming table, and the wooden horses, and most of all in front of the coconut shy. He spent a long time at that, overcome with joy when a player knocked over the policeman or the priest, two authorities that he instinctively mistrusted. Then he went back and sat down in the drinking booth and took a glass of cider to refresh himself. It was late and night was falling. A neighbor said warningly:

"You'll get home too late for your supper stew, Dad."

Then he set out for the farm. A pleasant dusk, the warm dusk of spring evenings, stole slowly over the earth.

When he reached his door he thought he saw through the lighted window two people in the house. He halted, very surprised, then he went in and saw Victor Lecoq sitting at the table before a plateful of potatoes, eating supper in the very place where his son had always sat.

He turned abruptly round as if he meant to go out again. The night was quite dark now. Céleste stood up and shouted at him:

"Come here quick, Dad, we've got a good stew to celebrate the assemblée."

At that he obeyed her mechanically and sat down, looking slowly round at the man, the woman and the child. Then he began to eat placidly, as he did every day.

Victor Lecoq seemed to be quite at home, he kept talking to Céleste, and took the child on his knees and fondled it. And Céleste gave him another helping of food, filled his glass, seemed quite happy to be talking to him. Old Amable regarded both of them with a fixed stare, unable to hear anything they said. When he had finished his supper—and he had hardly eaten anything, so upset did he feel

—he got to his feet, and instead of climbing to his attic as he did every night, he opened the door and went out into the fields.

When he had gone, Céleste, a little uneasy, asked:

"Now what's to be done?"

Victor answered indifferently:

"Don't worry. He'll come back when he's tired."

Then she tidied the room, washed the plates and dried the table while the man calmly undressed. Then he slipped into the dark cavelike bedroom where she had slept with Césaire.

The yard door opened. Old Amable reappeared. As soon as he got inside, he looked all round the room, like an old dog with his nose on the scent. He was looking for Victor Lecoq. As he did not see him, he took the candle from the table and brought it near the dark nook where his son had died. In its dark recesses he saw the man stretched out under the clothes and already asleep. At that the deaf man turned softly away, put the candle down, and once more went out into the yard.

Céleste had finished her work; she had put her son to bed, made everything tidy, and sat waiting until her father-in-law came in, to lie down in her turn beside Victor.

She remained sitting in the chair, her hands idle in her lap, staring at nothing.

He did not come in, and she murmured, worried and annoyed:

"He'll make us burn a pennyworth of candle, the old good-for-nothing."

Victor answered from the depths of his bed:

"He's been out more than an hour. Better go and see if he's fallen asleep on the seat in front of the door."

"I'll go," she said, and, standing up, she took the light and went out, shading her eyes with her hand to help her to see in the darkness.

She saw nothing in front of the door, nothing on the seat, nothing on the dung-heap where the old man sometimes used to sit on warm days.

But just as she was turning back into the house, she happened to lift her eyes to the big apple tree that made a shade over the farm gate, and saw suddenly two feet, a man's two feet, dangling at the level of her face.

She screamed in terror: "Victor! Victor! Victor!"

He came running out in his shirt. She could not speak, and with her head turned aside so that she should not see it, she pointed to the tree with outstretched arm.

He did not understand, and he took the candle to see what was wrong. In the green thickness lit up by the light he was holding below it, he saw old Amable hung by the neck at a considerable height, in a halter from the stable.

A ladder was leaning against the trunk of the apple tree.

Victor ran for a hatchet, climbed the tree and cut the cord. But the old man was already cold; his tongue protruded horribly in a frightful grimace.

ONE PHASE OF LOVE

The walls of the cell were bare and whitewashed. A narrow, barred window, so high that it could not easily be reached, lighted this little room, the crazy man, seated on a straw chair, looked at us with a fixed eye, vague and haunting. He was thin, with wrinkled cheeks and almost white hair that one would think had grown white in a few months. His clothes seemed too large for his dried-up limbs, his shrunken chest and hollow body. One felt that this man had been ravaged by his thoughts, by a thought, as fruit is by a worm. His madness, his idea, was there in his head, obstinate, harassing, devouring. It was eating his body little by little. It, the Invisible, the Impalpable, the Unseizable, the Immaterial Idea, gnawed his flesh, drank his blood and extinguished his life.

What a mystery, that this man should be killed by a thought! He was an object of fear and pity, this madman! What strange dream, frightful and deadly, could dwell in his forehead to fold such profound and ever-changing wrinkles in it?

The doctor said to me: "He has terrible paroxysms of rage and is one of the most singularly demented people I have ever seen. His madness is of an amorous, erotic kind. He is a sort of necrophile. He has written a journal which shows as plainly as daylight the malady of his mind. His madness is visible, so to speak. If you are interested you may run through this document."

I followed the doctor into his office, and he gave me the journal of this miserable man.

"Read it," he said, "and give me your opinion about it."

Here is what the little book contained:

"Up to the age of thirty-two years I lived tranquilly without love. Life appeared to me very simple, very good and very easy. I was rich. I had a taste for some things but had never felt a passion for anything. It was good to live; I awoke happy each day to do things which it pleased me to do, and I went to bed, satisfied, with calm hope for the next day and a future without care.

"I had had some mistresses without ever having my heart torn by desire or my soul bruised by love after the possession. It is good so to live. It is better to love, but terrible. Still those who love, like everybody else, should find happiness, less than mine, perhaps, for love has come to me in an unbelievable manner.

"Being rich, I collected ancient furniture and antiques. Often I thought of the unknown hands which had touched these things, of the eyes that had admired them and the hearts that had loved them—for one does love such things! I often remained for hours and hours looking at a little watch of the last century. It was so dainty, so pretty with its enamel and gold embossing. And it still went, as on the day when some woman had bought it, delighted in the possession of so fine a jewel. It had not ceased to palpitate, to live its mechanical life, but had ever continued its regular ticktack, although a century had passed. Who then had first carried it upon her breast, in the warmth of the dress—the heart of the watch beating against the heart of the woman? What hand had held it at the ends of its warm fingers, then wiped the enameled shepherds, tarnished a little by the moisture of the skin? What eyes had looked upon this flowered dial, awaiting the hour, the dear hour, the divine hour?

"How I wished to see her, to know her, the woman who had chosen this rare and exquisite object. But she is dead! I am possessed by a desire for women of former times; I love all those who have loved long ago. The story of past tenderness fills my heart with regrets. Oh, beauty! The smiles, the caresses, of youth, the hopes! These things should be eternal!

"How I have wept during whole nights over the women of old, so beautiful, so tender, so sweet, whose lips have opened to the kiss and who are now dead! The kiss is immortal! It goes from lip to lip, from century to century, from age to age! Men take it and give it and die.

"The past attracts me; the present frightens me, because the future is death. I regret all that which is gone; I weep for those who have lived; I wish to stop the hour, to arrest time. But it goes, it goes; it passes away, and it takes me, from second to second, a little of me for the annihilation of tomorrow. And I shall never live again.

"Adieu, women of yesterday, I love you.

"And yet I have nothing to complain of. I have found her whom I awaited, and I have tasted through her of inconceivable pleasure.

"I was roaming around Paris on a sunny morning with joyous foot and happy soul, looking in the shops with the vague interest of a stroller. All at once I saw in a shop of antiquities an Italian piece of furniture of the seventeenth century. It was very beautiful, very rare. I attributed it to a Venetian artist named Vitelli, who belonged to that epoch. Then I passed along.

"Why did the remembrance of this piece of furniture follow me with so much force that I went back over my steps? I stopped again before the shop to look at it and felt that it tempted me.

"What a singular thing is temptation! One looks at an object, and little by little it seduces you, troubles you, takes possession of you like the face of a woman. Its charm enters into you, a strange charm which comes from its form, its color and its physiognomy. Already one loves it, wishes it, desires it. A need of possession takes you, a pleasant need at first, because timid, but increasing, becoming violent and irresistible. And the merchants seem to suspect, from the look in the eye, this secret, increasing desire. I bought that piece of furniture and had it carried to my house immediately. I placed it in my room.

"Oh! I pity those who do not know this sweet hobby of the collector with the trinket which he finally buys. He caresses it with his eye and hand as if it were flesh; he returns every moment to it, thinks of it continually, wherever he goes and whatever he may be doing. The thought of it follows him into the street, into the world, everywhere. And when he re-enters his house, before even removing his gloves or his hat, he goes to look at it with the tenderness of a lover.

"Truly, for eight days I adored that piece of furniture. I kept opening its doors and drawers; I handled it with delight and tasted all the intimate joys of possession.

"One evening, in feeling the thickness of a panel, I perceived that there might be a hiding place there. My heart began to beat, and I passed the night in searching out the secret, without being able to discover it.

"I came upon it the next day by forcing a piece of metal into a crevice in the paneling. A shelf slipped, and I saw, exposed upon a lining of black velvet, a marvelous head of hair that had belonged to some woman.

"Yes, a head of hair, an enormous twist of blonde hair, also red, which had been cut off near the skin and tied together with a golden cord.

"I stood there stupefied, trembling and disturbed! An almost insensible perfume, so old that it seemed like the soul of an odor, arose from this mysterious drawer and this most surprising relic.

"I took it gently, almost religiously, and lifted it from its resting place. Immediately it unwound, spreading out its golden billows upon the floor, where it fell, thick and light, supple and brilliant, like the fiery tail of a comet.

"A strange emotion seized me. To whom had this belonged? When? Under what circumstances? Why had it been shut up in this piece of furniture? What adventure, what drama, was connected with this souvenir? Who had cut it off? Some lover on a day of parting? Some husband on a day of vengeance? Or, perhaps, some woman herself, who bore on her brow the look of despair? Was it at the hour of entering the cloister that she had thrown there this fortune of love, as a token left to the world of the living? Was it the hour closing the tomb upon the young and beautiful dead that he who adored her took this diadem of her head, the only thing he could preserve of her, the only living part of her body that would not perish, the only thing that he could still love and caress and kiss in the transport of his grief?

"Was it not strange that this hair should remain there thus when there was no longer any vestige of the body with which she was born?

"It curled about my fingers and touched my skin with a singular caress, the caress of death. I felt myself affected, as if I were going to weep.

"I kept it a long time in my hands, then it seemed to me that it had some effect upon me, as if something of the soul still remained in it. And I laid it upon the velvet again, the velvet blemished by time, then pushed in the drawer, shut the doors of the closet and betook myself to the street to dream.

"I walked straight ahead, full of sadness and full of trouble, of the kind of trouble that remains in the heart after the kiss of love. It seemed to me I had lived in former times and that I had known this woman.

"And Villon's lines came to my lips, bringing with them a sob:

> "Tell me in what far-off land
> The Roman beauty, Flora, lives;
> Hipparchia, Thais' cousin, and
> All the beauty nature gives;
> Echo speak, thy voice awake
> Over river, stream, and lake.
> Where are beauty's smiles and tears?
> And where the snows of other years?

> "Blanche, as fair as lily's chalice,
> Singing sweet, with voice serene,
> Bertha Broadfoot, Beatrice, Alice,
> Ermengarde, Le Mayne's dear queen?
> Where is Joan, the good Lorraine,
> Whom th' English brought to death and fame?
> Where are all, O wisest seers,
> And where the snows of other years?

"When I returned to my house I had a strange desire to see my strange treasure again. I took it up and felt it, and in touching it a long shiver ran through my body.

"For some days, however, I remained in my ordinary state, although the thought of this hair never left me. Whenever I came in it was my first desire to look at it and handle it. I would turn the key of the secretary with the same trembling that one has in opening the door of his well-beloved, for I had in two hands and in my heart a confused, singular, continued, sensual need of burying my fingers in this charming rivulet of dead hair.

"Then when I had finished caressing it, when I had returned it to its resting place, I always felt that it was there, as if it were something alive, concealed, imprisoned; I felt it and I still desired it; again I had the imperious need of touching it, of feeling it, of enervating myself to the point of weariness from contact with this cold, glistening, irritating, exciting, delicious hair.

"I lived thus a month or two, I know not how long, with this thing possessing me, haunting me. I was happy and tortured, as in the expectation of love, as one is after the avowal which precedes the embrace.

"I would shut myself up alone with it in order to feel it upon my skin, to bury my lips in it, to kill it and bite it. I would roll it around my face, drink it in, drown my eyes in its golden waves and finally see the blonde life beyond it.

"I loved it! Yes, I loved it. I could no longer live away from it or be contented an hour without seeing it. I expected—I expected—what? I know not—her!

"One night I was suddenly awakened with a feeling that I was not alone in my room. I was alone, however. But I could not go to sleep again, and as I was tossing in the fever of insomnia, I rose and went to look at the twist of hair. It appeared to me sweeter than usual and more animated.

"Could the dead return? The kisses with which I had warmed it failed to give me happiness, and I carried it to my bed and lay down with it, pressing it to my lips, as one does a mistress he hopes to enjoy.

"The dead returned! She came! Yes, I saw her, touched her, possessed her as she was when alive in former times, large, blonde, plump, with cool breasts and with hips in form of a lyre. And I followed that divine, undulating line from the throat to the feet, in all the curves of the flesh, with my caresses.

"Yes, I possessed her every day and every night. She had returned, Death, Death the Beautiful, the Adorable, the Mysterious, the Unknown, and returned every night.

"My happiness was so great that I could not conceal it. I found near her a superhuman delight, and in possessing this Unseizable, Invisible Death, knew a profound, inexplicable joy. No lover ever tasted joys more ardent or more terrible.

"I knew not how to conceal my happiness. I loved this possession so much that I could not bear to leave it. I carried it with me always, everywhere. I walked with it through the city, as if it were my wife, conducting it to the theater and to restaurants as one would a mistress. But they saw it and guessed—they took me and threw me into prison, like a malefactor. They took it away. Oh, misery!"

The manuscript stopped there. And suddenly, as I raised my wondering eyes to the doctor, a frightful cry, a howl of fury and exasperated desire, filled the asylum.

"Listen," said the doctor, "it is necessary to douse that obscene maniac with water five times a day. It is only Sergeant Bertrand, the man who fell in love with the dead."

I stammered, moved with astonishment, horror and pity: "But that hair—did it really exist?"

The doctor got up, opened a closetful of vials and instruments and threw toward me, across his office, a long thick rope of blonde hair, which flew toward me like a bird of gold.

I trembled at feeling upon my hands its caressing, light touch. And I stood there, my heart beating with disgust and desire, the disgust we have in coming in contact with objects connected with crimes, and the desire like that which comes with the temptation to test some infamous and mysterious thing.

Shrugging his shoulders, the doctor added: "The mind of man is capable of any-thing."

GOOD REASONS

Solles Villa, July 30, 1883.

MY DEAR LUCY:

There is nothing new. We still live in the parlor, looking out to see the rain fall. One can scarcely go out at all in this frightful weather. We can only play comedies. And how stupid they are, my dear, these pieces in a drawing-room reper-toire. So forced, so heavy and gross! The jokes are like bullets from a cannon, always hitting someone. Nothing bright, nothing natural, good natured or elegant. These writers, truly, can know nothing of the world. They are entirely ignorant of how people think or speak among us. I could easily forgive them for scorning our customs or our manners, but I cannot forgive them for being ignorant of them. In order to be pointed they make a play upon words that a barracks would do well to deride; in order to be gay they serve us the wit they have culled outside the boule-vard, in the beer shops of so-called artists, where the same studied paradoxes have been repeated for fifty years.

Yes, we play a comedy. As there are only two women, my husband takes the part of a soubrette, shaving his face for it. You cannot imagine, my dear Lucy, how it changed him! I should not have known him—either by day or night. If he had not allowed his mustache to grow again immediately I believe that I should have become unfaithful, so much did I dislike it.

Truly, a man without a mustache is not a man. I do not care much for a beard, it always gives an appearance of neglect, but the mustache, oh, the mustache is indispensable to a manly physiognomy. No, one never could imagine how useful this little brush of hair upon the lip is to the eye and—to the relation of married people. There have come to me many reflections upon this subject, which I scarcely dare write to you. I could say them to you easily—in a low voice. But it is difficult to find words to express certain things, and some of these, which it would be hard to replace, cut a villainous figure upon paper, so that I can scarcely pen them. Then the subject is so delicate, so difficult, so awkward, that an infinite knowledge is necessary to approach it without danger.

Well, so much the worse if you do not understand. And now, my dear, try to read a little between the lines.

When my husband came to me shaved, I understood for the first time that I could never have a weakness for a strolling player or for a preacher, were he Father Didon himself, the most seductive of all! Then when I found myself alone with him (my husband), it was much worse.

Oh, my dear Lucy, never allow yourself to be embraced by a man without mus-taches; his lips have no taste, none whatever! There is no longer that charm, that softness and that—pepper, yes, that pepper of the true kiss. The mustache is the spice of it.

Imagine a piece of dry or even humid parchment applied to your lips. That is the caress of the shaven man. One wants very few of them, assuredly.

But whence comes the seduction of the mustache, you ask me? How do I know? At first it tickles in delicious fashion. One feels it before the mouth, and it makes a charming shiver pass through the whole body, even to the tips of the toes. It is that which caresses, which makes the flesh tremble and start, which gives the nerves that exquisite vibration and causes the utterance of that little "ah!" as if one had received a sudden chill.

And upon the neck! Yes, have you never felt a mustache upon your neck? It intoxicates and makes you shiver, runs down your back and to the ends of your fingers. You turn, shake your shoulders, twist your head; you wish to go and to stay; it is adorable yet irritating! But it is good!

And then again—truly, do I dare say more? A husband who loves you, yes, entirely, knows how to find spots and little corners for concealing kisses, little corners one would scarcely dream of alone. Well, without a mustache these kisses lose much of their zest, without saying that they are unbecoming! Explain that as you will! For my part, here is the reason I find for it. A lip without mustaches is bare, like a body without clothes, and it is necessary to have clothes, very few if you wish, but still some!

The Creator (I dare not use any other word in speaking of these things), the Creator saw the need of veiling the nooks of our flesh where love is concealed. A shaven mouth appears to me to resemble a forest, cut down, which sheltered a fountain where one came to drink and sleep.

This recalls to me the saying of a political man, which has been in my head for three months now. My husband, who reads the newspapers, read a very singular thing to me one evening by our minister of agriculture, who was then called M. Meline. Is there another one by this time? I am sure I do not know.

I was not listening, but this name, Meline, struck me. It recalled, I know not why, *Scenes of Bohemian Life*. I believed at once that he lived with a *grisette*. Only certain scraps of this piece entered my head. But M. Meline made to the inhabitants of Amiens, I believe, this statement, the meaning of which I have sought until now: "There is no patriotism without agriculture!" Well, this means, I have found out recently and now declare to you in my turn, that there is no love without a mustache. If one should tell him that it would seem strange, would it not?

There is no love without a mustache!

"There is no patriotism without agriculture," asserts M. Meline; he is right, this minister; I know it now!

From another point of view the mustache is essential. It determines the physiognomy. It gives it a sweet, tender, violent, foolish, rakish or enterprising air! The bearded man, really bearded, he who carries all his hair (oh! villainous word) upon his cheeks, never has any delicacy of expression because his features are concealed. And the form of the jaw and the chin show many things to him who can see.

In a mustache, a man preserves at the same time his attraction and his finesse.

And of what varied appearance they are, these mustaches! Some are curved, curled and coquettish. These seem to love women above all things!

Some are pointed, sharp as a needle, wicked. These have a preference for wine, horses and fights.

Some are enormous, drooping, frightful. These great ones generally conceal an excellent character, a goodness that approaches weakness and a gentleness that borders on timidity.

And then, above all else, why I adore a mustache is because it is French. It has descended to us from our fathers, the Gauls, and has continued as a sign of our national character.

It is romantic, gallant and brave. It dips itself dantily in wine and knows how to laugh with elegance, while large, bearded jaws are heavy in all that they do.

Wait! I recall something which made me weep bitter tears and which also made me love a mustache upon a man's lip, as I now plainly see.

It was during the war, when I was at home in Papa's house. I was a young girl then. One day there was a battle near the house. Since morning I had heard cannons and guns and, in the evening, a German colonel entered our house and installed himself there. He went away the next day. They came to tell my father that there had been many deaths on the field. He went to find them and bring them home, in order to bury them together. They laid them all along the avenue of pines on both sides from the stretcher on which they brought them. And as they commenced to smell badly, they threw some earth on the bodies to await the digging of the great ditch. In this way only their heads were to be seen, which seemed to come up out of the soil, yellow as the soil itself, with their eyes closed.

I wished to see them, but when I perceived these two lines of frightful faces I thought it would make me ill. I began to examine them, however, one by one, seeking to find out to what nation they belonged. Their uniforms were buried, concealed by the earth, but immediately, yes, immediately, my dear, I recognized them as Frenchmen by their mustaches!

Some had been shaved the day of the battle, as if wishing to be attractive to the last moment! Their beard, nevertheless, had grown a little, for you know it grows a little even after death. Others seemed to have gone a week without shaving, but all wore the French mustache, distinctly the proud mustache which seemed to say: "Do not confound me with my bearded friend, little one, I am your brother."

And I wept. Oh, I wept more than if I had not thus recognized them, the poor dead men!

I did wrong to tell you this story. Here I am now, sad and incapable of chatting any more. Adieu, then, my dear Lucy; I embrace you with all my heart. Long live the mustache!

JEANNE.

A FAIR EXCHANGE

M. Bontram, the celebrated Parisian advocate who for the last ten years had obtained many separations between badly matched husbands and wives, opened the door of his office and stood back to allow a new client to enter.

He was a large red man, with close blond whiskers, a corpulent man, full-blooded and vigorous. He bowed.

"Take a seat," said the advocate.

The client was seated and, after some hemming, said:

"I came to ask you, sir, to plead a divorce case for me."

"Speak, sir," said the advocate. "I am listening."

"I am, sir, an old notary."

"Already!"

"Yes, already. I am thirty-seven years of age."

"Continue."

"Sir, I have made an unfortunate marriage, very unfortunate."

"You are not the only one."

"I know it, and I pity the others. But my case is entirely different, and my complaint against my wife is of a very particular nature. I will commence at the marriage rite. I was married in strange fashion. Do you believe in dangerous ideas?"

"What do you mean by that?"

"Do you believe that certain ideas are as dangerous for the mind as poison is to the body?"

"Well, yes, perhaps."

"It is certain. There are ideas which enter into us, corrode us, and kill us or render us mad if we do not know how to resist them. They are a sort of poison to the soul. If we have the misfortune to allow one of these thoughts to glide in upon us, if we do not perceive at the beginning that it is an invader, a mistress, a tyrant, then it will extend itself hour by hour and day by day, will keep returning and finally install itself, driving out all ordinary occupation of our minds, absorbing our attention, changing our views and our judgment until we are lost.

"That is what happened to me, sir. As I have told you, I am a notary at Rouen, not poor but in straitened circumstances, full of care, forced to a constant economy, obliged to limit my tastes, yes, in everything! And it is hard, at my age.

"As a notary, I read with great care the advertisements on four pages of the newspapers, the wants, offers, little correspondence, etc., etc., and I had been enabled sometimes by this means to make advantageous marriages for my clients.

"One day, I fell upon this:

" 'A pretty girl, fashionable, well brought up, would marry honorable gentleman and bring him two million five hundred thousand francs, clear. No agencies.'

"On that very day I dined with two friends, one an attorney and the other the proprietor of a spinning mill. I don't know how the conversation turned to marriages, but I told them, laughing, about the pretty young lady with the two million five hundred thousand francs.

"The spinner said: 'What can these women be thinking of?'

"The attorney affirmed that he had several times seen excellent marriages made under these conditions and gave some details. Then he added, turning to me: 'Why the devil don't you look this up for yourself? Jove! That would drive away care, two million five hundred thousand francs.'

"We all three laughed over it and then spoke of other things. An hour later I returned home.

"It grew cold that night. Besides, I lived in an old house, one of those old houses of the provinces which resemble mushroom beds. In taking hold of the iron balustrade of the staircase a coldness penetrated my arm, and as I put out the other to find the wall, in coming in contact with it, a second shiver enveloped me, joining with the other in my lungs, filling me with pain, with sadness and weakness. And, seized by a sudden remembrance, I murmured: 'Gad! If I only had the two million five hundred thousand!'

"My room was dreary, the room of a bachelor in Rouen, which is taken care of by a maid who is also in charge of the kitchen. You know that kind of room! A great bed without curtains, a wardrobe, a commode and a dressing table, no fire.

Some coats were on the chairs, papers on the floor. I began to sing to the air of a concert-hall tune that I frequently heard about that time:

> "Two millions, two millions
> Are fine,
> With five hundred thousand
> And woman divine.

"In fact, I had not yet thought about the woman, but I thought of her then as I was sliding into my bed. I even thought of her so much that I was a long time getting to sleep.

"The next day, on opening my eyes, I remembered that I ought to be at Darnetal at eight o'clock on important business. To do this I must be up at six—and it was cold! Only think of two million five hundred thousand!

"I returned to my study about ten o'clock. In it was the odor of the red-hot stove, of old papers, with the papers of advance proceedings—nothing can equal these—and an odor of clerks—boots, overcoats, hair and skin, skin in winter, too little bathed, and all heated to seventy degrees.

"I breakfasted, as I do every day, on a cutlet and a piece of cheese. Then I put myself to work. For the first time I then began to think seriously of the pretty young lady with the two million five hundred thousand. Who was she? Why not write to her? Why not find out?

"Finally, sir, to abridge, for two weeks this idea haunted me, possessed me and tortured me. All my little cares and troubles, of which I had plenty but had thought little about before this time, began to sting me now like the sharp points of needles, and each of my sufferings made me think still more of the pretty young lady with the two millions.

"I ended by imagining all her history. When one desires a thing, sir, he is very apt to figure it as he hopes it to be. Certainly it was not natural that a young girl of good family, dowered in such a generous fashion, should be seeking a husband by means of the newspapers. Yet it might be that this girl was honorable but unhappy.

"Then at first this fortune of two million five hundred thousand had not struck me as anything fairylike. We are accustomed, we who read the offers of this nature, to propositions of marriage accompanied by six, eight, ten or even twelve millions. The figure of twelve millions is common enough. It pleases. I know well that we can scarcely believe the validity of these promises. They, however, make us enter into the spirit of fantastic numbers, render probable, up to a certain point in our listless credulity, the prodigious sums which they represent and dispose us to consider a dowry of two million five hundred thousand as very possible and right.

"Then a young girl, the natural child of a rich man and a chambermaid, having suddenly inherited from her father, could have learned at the same time of the stain upon her birth, and in order not to have to reveal it to some man whom she might have loved, she might make an appeal to the unknown by this means, which carries in itself a sort of avowal of defect.

"My supposition was stupid. I believed in it, nevertheless. We notaries ought never to read romances, but I read one in this, sir.

"Then I wrote, as a notary, in the name of a client, and I waited. Five days later, toward three o'clock in the afternoon, when I was hard at work in my office, the chief clerk announced:

" 'Mademoiselle Chantefrise.'

" 'Let her come in.'

"There appeared a woman about thirty, a little stout, dark and somewhat embarrassed.

" 'Be seated, mademoiselle.'

"She sat down and murmured: 'It is I, sir.'

" 'But I have not the honor of knowing you.'

" 'The person to whom you wrote.'

" 'About a marriage?'

" 'Yes sir.'

" 'Ah, very well!'

" 'I have come myself because I thought it better to attend to those things in person.'

" 'I am of your opinion, mademoiselle. And so you desire to marry?'

" 'Yes sir.'

" 'You have some family?'

"She hesitated, lowered her eyes and stammered: 'No sir. My mother and my father—are dead.'

"I started. Then I had guessed right—and a lively sympathy was suddenly awakened in my heart for this poor creature. I could not altogether spare her delicacy of feeling and I inquired:

" 'Your fortune is in your own right?'

"She responded this time without hesitating: 'Oh yes, sir!'

"I looked at her with close attention, and truly she did not displease me, only a little hard, harder than I would have liked. She was a beautiful person, a strong person, a masterly woman. And the idea came to me of playing with her a little comedy of sentiment, of becoming her lover, of supplanting my imaginary client, when I was once assured that the dowry was not illusory. I spoke to her of this client whom I depicted as a sad man, very honorable, but a little of an invalid.

"She said vivaciously: 'Oh, sir, I love people to be well.'

" 'But you will see him—only not for three or four days, because he left for England yesterday.'

" 'Oh, how annoying,' she replied.

" 'Well, yes and no. Are you in a hurry to return home?'

" 'Not at all.'

" 'Then stay here, and I will attempt to make the time pass pleasantly for you.'

" 'You are very amiable, sir.'

" 'You are at some hotel?'

"She named the best hotel in Rouen.

" 'Well then, Mademoiselle Chantefrise, will you permit your future—notary to offer to take you to dinner this evening?'

"She appeared to hesitate, seemed disturbed and undecided. Then she said: 'Yes sir.'

" 'I will be at your hotel at seven o'clock.'

" 'Yes sir.'

" 'Then until this evening, mademoiselle?'

" 'Yes sir.'

"And I conducted her as far as my door.

"At seven o'clock I was at her hotel. She had made a fresh toilet for me and received me in a very coquettish fashion. I took her to dine in a restaurant where I was known and ordered a troublesome menu. An hour later we were very friendly, and she had told me her story.

"She was the daughter of a great lady seduced by a gentleman, and she had been brought up among peasants. She was rich now, having inherited large sums from her father and from her mother, whose name she would never divulge, never. It was useless to ask it of her, useless to beg; she would never tell it. As I cared little to know these things, I asked about her fortune. She spoke about it like a practical woman, sure of herself, sure of her figures, of her titles, of her income, her interest and investments. Her understanding of these matters gave me great confidence in her, and I became gallant, with some reserve, nevertheless. But I showed her clearly that I had a liking for her.

"She affected an excessive refinement, not without grace. I offered her some champagne, and I drank some, which blurred my ideas. I then felt clearly that I was going to be entrapped, and I was afraid, afraid of myself and afraid of her, afraid that she was not moved and that she would not succumb. In order to calm myself I began again to speak to her of her fortune, saying that it would be necessary to precisely understand matters, since my client was a man of affairs.

"She answered with gaiety: 'Oh! I know. I have brought all the proofs.'

" 'Here to Rouen?'

" 'Yes, to Rouen.'

" 'You have them at the hotel?'

" 'Yes, I have them all there.'

" 'Could you show them to me?'

" 'Yes indeed.'

" 'This evening?'

" 'Yes indeed.'

"That pleased me in every way. I paid the score, and we went back to the hotel. She had, in fact, brought all her certificates. I could not doubt them, for I held them in my hands, felt them and read them. They put such a joy in my heart that I suddenly felt a violent desire to embrace her. I understood this as a chaste desire, the desire of a contented man. And I did embrace her, in fact, once, twice, ten times—so much that—with the aid of the champagne—I succumbed—or rather—no—she succumbed.

"Ah, sir, I had a head after that, and she! She wept like a fountain, begging me not to expose her or she should be lost. I promised all that she wished, and I myself got into a terrible state of mind.

"What was to be done? I had abused my client's confidence. That would not have been so bad if I had had a client for her, but I had none. I was the client, the simple client, the deceived client, and deceived by himself. What a situation! I could let her go, it is true. But the dowry, the handsome dowry, the good dowry, palpable and sure! And then, had I the right to let her go, the poor girl, after having thus surprised her? But what of the disquiet later on? How much security would one have with a woman who thus yielded?

"I passed a terrible night of indecision, tortured by remorse, ravaged by fears, buffeted by every scruple. But in the morning my reason cleared. I dressed myself with care and, as eleven o'clock struck, presented myself at the hotel where she was staying.

"On seeing me she blushed to the eyes. I said to her: 'Mademoiselle Chantefrise, there is only one thing to do to repair our wrong. I ask your hand in marriage.'

"She murmured: 'I give it to you.'

"I married her and all went well for six months. I had given up my office and lived as a stockholder, and truly I had not a reproach, not a single fault to find with my wife.

"Then I noticed that from time to time she made long visits. This happened on a certain day, one week Tuesday, the next week Wednesday. I began to believe myself deceived and I followed her. It was on a Tuesday. She went out on foot about one o'clock into Republic Street, turned to the right, by the street which follows the archiepiscopal palace, and took Great-Bridge Street to the Seine, followed the wharf up to Peter's bridge and crossed the water. From this moment she appeared disturbed, turning around often and looking sharply at all passers.

"As I was dressed like a coal driver, she did not know me. Finally she entered a dock on the left bank. I no longer doubted that her lover would arrive on the one forty-five train.

"I seated myself behind a dray and waited. A blow of the whistle—a crowd of passengers. She advanced, rushed forward, seized in her arms a little girl of three years, whom a large peasant accompanied, and embraced her with passion. Then she turned, perceived another child, younger, either girl or boy it might be, carried by another nurse, threw herself upon it, drew it to her with violence and went along escorted by the two monkeys and the two nurses toward the long, somber, deserted promenade of the Queen's Course.

"I returned home dismayed, distressed in mind, comprehending and still not comprehending, nor daring to guess. When she returned for dinner I threw these words at her:

" 'Whose children are those?'

" 'What children?' she asked.

" 'Those that you waited at the Saint-Sever train for.'

"She gave a great cry and fainted. When she returned to consciousness she confessed to me in a deluge of tears that she had four. Yes sir, two for Tuesday, two girls, and two for Wednesday, two boys.

"And this was—what shame! This was the origin of her fortune. The four fathers! She had amassed her dowry! Now, sir, what do advise me to do?"

The advocate replied with gravity: "Recognize your children, sir."

A TRAVELER'S NOTES

Seven o'clock. A whistle blows; we are off. The train passes over the turnplates with the noise of stage thunder, then it plunges into the night, panting, puffing up its steam, throwing gleams of red light on passing walls, hedges, woods, and fields.

We are six, three on each seat, under the light of the lamp. Opposite me is a stout lady with a stout gentleman, an old married couple. A hunchback sits in the left corner; beside me is a young married pair, or, at least, a young couple! Are they married? The young woman is pretty and seems modest, but she smells too strongly of perfume. What kind of perfume is it? I know it without being able to name it. Ah! now I've got it. *Peau d'Espagne?* That tells nothing. Let us wait and see.

The stout lady looks at the young woman with an air of hostility which sets me to thinking. The stout gentleman closes his eyes. Already! The hunchback has rolled himself up into a ball. I no longer see where his legs are. One sees nothing but his bright eye under a skullcap with a red tassel. Then he shrinks into his traveling shawl. He looks like a small parcel thrown down on the seat.

The old lady alone stays awake, suspicious, uneasy, like a watchman whose duty it is to guard the order and morality of the occupants of the carriage.

The young people do not move; their knees are under the same shawl, and their eyes are open, but they do not speak; are they married?

I also pretend to sleep, and watch.

Nine o'clock. The stout lady is about to give in; she closes her eyes spasmodically, and her head drops on her breast, but she lifts it up again by fits and starts. Then at last she goes to sleep.

O sleep! ridiculous mystery which makes faces appear so grotesque, you are the revealer of human ugliness. You uncover all shortcomings, all deformities and all defects. You turn every face touched by you into a caricature.

I rise and put the light blue shade over the lamp, and then I also go to sleep.

Every now and then the stopping of the train awakens me. An employee calls out the name of the town, and then we go on.

Here is the dawn. We are running alongside the Rhône, which is going down to the Mediterranean. Everybody is sleeping. The young people have their arms around each other. One of the feet of the young woman is peeping from under the shawl. She is wearing white stockings! That is commonplace: they are married! The air is not fresh in the compartment, and I open a window to change it. The cold coming in awakens everyone, except the hunchback, who is snoring under his cover.

The ugliness of the faces becomes more accentuated in the light of the new day.

The stout lady, with red face and untidy hair, looks awful. She glances around spitefully at her neighbors. The young woman looks smilingly at her companion. If she were not married she would have first looked at her mirror.

Here we are at Marseille. Twenty minutes' stop. I breakfast. We go on. The hunchback is missing, and we have, instead, two old gentlemen.

Then the two married couples, the old and the young, unpack their provisions. A chicken here, cold veal there, pepper and salt in paper, pickles in a handkerchief —everything to make you disgusted with food forever. I know nothing more common, more vulgar, more out of place, and more ill-bred than to eat in a carriage where there are other passengers.

If it is freezing, open the windows. If it is hot, close them and smoke your pipe, even if you detest tobacco; begin to sing, to bark, indulge in the most annoying eccentricities, take off your shoes and stockings and pare your toe-nails; in short, pay these ill-bred people in their own coin for their lack of good manners.

The far-sighted man will carry a bottle of benzine or petrol to sprinkle on the cushions when the people beside him begin to eat. Everything is permitted, anything is too good for the boors who poison you with the odor of their food.

Now we are running beside the blue sea. The sun beats down upon the coast dotted with charming towns.

Here is St. Raphaël. Yonder is St. Tropez, the little capital of that deserted, unknown, and delightful country called the Mountains of the Moors. A broad river not spanned by any bridge, the Argens, separates this wild peninsula from the continent, and one can walk there for a whole day without meeting a soul. Here the villages, perched upon the mountains, are the same as they were in former times, with their Oriental houses, their arcades, their low-vaulted doors ornamented with sculpture.

No railroad, no public conveyance penetrates into these splendid wooded valleys. Only an old mail boat carries the letters from Hyères and St. Tropez.

On we go. Here is Cannes, so pretty on the shore of its two gulfs, opposite the islands of Lérins, which would make two perfect paradises for the sick if they could be connected with the mainland.

Here is the Gulf of Juan; the armored squadron seems to lie asleep on the water.

Here is Nice. There is apparently an exhibition in the town. Let us go to see it.

Following a boulevard, which seems like a marsh, we reach a building on an elevation, in doubtful taste, which seems a miniature replica of the great palace of the Trocadéro.

Inside there are some people walking about in the midst of a chaos of boxes. The exhibition, which has been open for a long time, will doubtless be ready next year!

It would be attractive inside if it were finished. But it is far from that.

Two sections especially attract me: that of the comestibles and that of the fine arts. Alas! there really are preserved fruits of Grasse here, and a thousand other good things to eat. But—it is forbidden to sell them! One may only look at them! And that is so as not to injure the trade of the town! To exhibit sweetmeats for the mere pleasure of looking at them, and forbid anybody to taste them, really seems to be one of the finest inventions of the human mind.

The fine arts are—in preparation! Yet some halls are open, where one may see very fine landscapes by Harpignies, Guillemet, Le Poittevin, a superb portrait of Mademoiselle Alice Regnault by Courtois, a delightful Béraud, etc. As for the rest —when they are unpacked!

As one must see everything on visiting a place, I will treat myself to an air trip in the balloon of MM. Godard and Company.

The mistral is blowing. The balloon is swaying in an uneasy way. Suddenly there is an explosion; the cords of the net have broken. The public is forbidden to come within the enclosure, and I also am turned out.

I climb upon my carriage and survey the scene.

Every moment another rope snaps with a singular noise, and the brown skin of the balloon attempts to rise from the meshes that hold it. Then suddenly, under a more violent gust of wind, there is an immense tear from top to bottom of the great ball, which falls together like a limp cloth, torn and dead.

The next morning on awakening I call for the newspapers and read with astonishment: "The tempest now raging on our coast has compelled the management of the captive and free balloons of Nice to empty its great aerostat, in order to avoid accidents. The system of instantaneous emptying used by M. Godard is one of his inventions that redound most to his honor."

Oh! Oh! Oh! Oh, the dear public!

The entire coast of the Mediterranean is the El Dorado of the chemists. One must be ten times a millionaire to dare purchase even a simple box of cough drops from these haughty merchants, who ask the price of diamonds for their jujubes.

One can go from Nice to Monaco via La Corniche, along the seacoast. There is nothing more charming than this road cut in the rock, which skirts gulfs, passes under arches, and turns and twists along the mountain through wonderful country.

Here is Monaco on its rock, and behind it Monte Carlo. Hush! I can understand how those who like to gamble adore this pretty little town. But how somber and sad it is for those who do not gamble! There is no other pleasure, no other attraction.

Farther on is Mentone, the hottest place on the coast and the one most frequented by invalids. There oranges ripen and consumptives are cured.

I take the night train to return to Cannes. In my compartment there are two ladies and a man from Marseille who is determined to tell stories of railway accidents, murders, and thefts.

"I once knew a Corsican, madame, who came to Paris with his son. I speak of long ago, in the early days of the P. L. M. railway. I joined them, since we were friends, and off we went.

"The son, who was twenty years old, was utterly amazed at the running of the train, and stood leaning out of the window all the time to watch it. His father kept repeating to him: 'Heh! Take care, Matheo! Don't lean out too far, or you may hurt yourself.' But the boy did not even answer.

"I said to the father:

" 'Let him do it, if it amuses him.'

"But the father repeated:

" 'Come now, Matheo, don't lean out like that.'

"Then, as the son did not answer, he took him by the coat to make him come back into the carriage, and gave it a pull. And then the body fell back on our knees. He was minus his head, madame, for it had been cut off by a tunnel. And the neck was not even bleeding any longer; all the blood had flowed along the line."

One of the ladies heaved a sigh, closed her eyes, and sank upon her neighbor. She had fainted.

THE TOBACCO SHOP

I went down to Barviller alone because I saw in the guidebook (I do not remember which one): "A beautiful museum, two Rubens, one Tenier and a Ribera." I thought to myself: "I will see that. Then I will dine at the Hotel Europe, which the guidebook affirms excellent, and return tomorrow."

The museum was closed. They only opened it at the request of travelers. It was opened for my benefit, and I was able to look upon some daubs attributed by a whimsical collector to the first masters of painting.

After that I found myself alone with absolutely nothing to do. I was in a long street of a little unknown town, a kind of artery, through which I wandered, examining some of the poor little shops. I found it was only four o'clock, and I was

suddenly seized with that feeling of discouragement which makes simpletons of
the most energetic.

What could I do? Great heavens! What was there to do? I would have paid five
hundred francs for some distracting idea. Finding myself barren of invention, I
simply decided to smoke a good cigar and looked about for a tobacco shop. I soon
recognized one by its red lantern and entered it. The saleswoman held out several
boxes for me to choose from. Having looked carefully at the cigars, all of which
appeared detestable, I turned by chance and glanced at the proprietress.

She was a woman of about forty-five, strong and gray-haired. She had a fat, respectable face, in which I seemed to see something familiar. Could I have known
this woman somewhere? No, assuredly not. But it might be that I had seen her
somewhere. Yes, that was possible. The face before me must be an acquaintance
of my eyes, some old acquaintance lost to sight and, without doubt, changed by
being enormously fattened.

I murmured: "Excuse me, madame, for looking at you so closely, but it seems
to me that I have seen you before, long ago."

She responded, blushing a little: "It is strange—but I also——"

I exclaimed: "Ah, so it goes!"

She raised both hands in a comical despair, frightened by the sound of the old
name, and stammered: "Oh, oh! If anyone should hear you——" Then suddenly
she cried out in her turn: "Wait! It is you—George!" Then she looked around in
terror to see if anyone were listening. But we were alone, all alone!

"So-it-Goes!" How had I ever recognized her! "So-it-Goes," the poor "So-it-
Goes," the thin, the desolate "So-it-Goes," transformed into this fat, tranquil functionary of the government.

"So-it-Goes!" How many memories this name awakened in me: Bougival, "The
Frog," Chatou, the Fournaise restaurant, long journeys in a yawl along the steep
banks, in short, ten years of my life passed in that corner of the country, upon that
delicious part of the river.

There was a band of a dozen of us inhabiting the Galopois house at Chatou,
living a queer kind of life, half nude and half tipsy. The customs of canoeists have
changed since then. Now these gentlemen wear monocles.

Our band was composed of twenty canoeists, regular and irregular. On certain
Sundays there would only be four of them, on others, all. That is to say, some there
were there to stay; others came when they had nothing better to do. Five or six of
them lived together, after the fashion of men without wives, and among them
dwelt "So-it-Goes."

She was a poor, thin girl who limped. This gave her some of the attractions of
a grasshopper. She was timid, awkward and unskillful in all that she did. With fear
she attached herself to the humblest, the most unnoticed of us, anyone who would
keep her a day or a month, according to his means. How she ever came to be
among us, nobody knew. Someone had met her one evening at poker dice at a
riverside ball and had been led into one of those raffles for wives that were so
much the fashion. We invited her to lunch, seeing her seated alone at a little table
in the corner. No one could have asked her, but she made a part of our band.

We baptized her "So-it-Goes" (Ça Ira), because she was already complaining
of her destiny, of her misfortune and her sorrows. Each Sunday morning they
would say to her: "Well, 'So-it-Goes,' how goes it?" And she would always answer:
"Not so bad, but we must always hope that it will be better someday."

How this poor, ungraceful, awkward being came to adopt the trade which demands the most grace, tact, cleverness and beauty was a mystery. However, Paris is full of girls of love that are ugly enough to disgust a policeman.

What did she do the other six days of the week? She told us many times that she worked. At what? We were as ignorant of it as we were indifferent to her existence.

After that I nearly lost sight of her. Our group had dispersed little by little, leaving its place to another generation, to whom we also left "Ça Ira." I heard of her in going to breakfast at the Fournaise from time to time.

Our successors, not knowing why we had christened her as we did, believed her name to be oriental and called her Zaïra; then they bestowed her, with all their canoes and some of the canoeists, to the following generation. (A generation of canoeists generally lives three years upon the water, then leaves the Seine to enter the law, medicine or politics.)

Zaïra had now become Zara, and later Zara was modified into Sarah. Then they thought she was an Israelite.

The last ones, those with the monocles, called her simply "the Jewess." Then she simply disappeared. And behold! I had found her in Barviller, selling tobacco.

I said to her: "Well, how goes it now?"

She answered: "A little better."

I had a curiosity to know the life of this woman. At any other time I would not have cared; today I felt interested, puzzled, attracted. I asked her: "How did you come to get this place?"

"I don't know," she said. "It came to me when I was expecting the least."

"Was it at Chatou that you came upon it?"

"Oh no!"

"Then where?"

"At Paris, in a hotel where I lived."

"Ah, then you had a place in Paris?"

"Yes, I was with Madame Ravelet."

"Who is she, this Madame Ravelet?"

"And you don't know who Madame Ravelet is? Well!"

"No, I do not."

"The dressmaker, the great dressmaker of Rivoli Street."

And then she told me a thousand things of her former life, a thousand things of the secret life of the Parisian woman, the interior workings of a great dressmaking establishment, the life of the young ladies there, their adventures, their ideas, the whole story of the heart of a working girl, that sparrow hawk of the sidewalk who haunts the streets—in the morning in going to the shop, at midday strolling along bareheaded after her luncheon, and in the evening when she comes out to show herself.

Happy to speak of other days, she said: "You don't know what a mob it is, or what raids they make. We used to tell each other about them every day. Truly one can make a fool of a man, you know.

"The first tale I have to tell is on the subject of an umbrella. I had an old alpaca one, an umbrella to be ashamed of. As I was closing it upon my arrival one day there was the tall Louise before me, saying:

" 'What! You dare to go out with that?'

" 'But I have no other, and at this moment funds are low.'

"They were always low, funds were.

"She said to me: 'Go and get one at the Madeleine.'

"I was astonished. She continued: 'That is where we all get ours; one can get all one wants there.' And then she explained the thing to me. It was very simple.

"I went with Irma to the Madeleine. We found the sexton and explained to him how we had forgotten an umbrella the week before. He asked us to describe the handle, and I gave him a description of a handle with an agate apple on it. He took us into a room where there were more than fifty lost umbrellas; we looked them all over, but I did not find mine; I had, however, chosen a beauty, a perfect beauty with a carved ivory handle. A few days after Louise went and reclaimed it. She described it before seeing it, and he gave it to her without a suspicion.

"In order to do that sort of thing one has to dress very stylish."

And she laughed, opening the cover of a large box of tobacco and letting it fall again upon its hinges. She continued:

"Oh, we each had our turn at it and we did have some queer experiences. There were five of us living in the studio, four ordinaries and one very pretty, Irma, the beautiful Irma. She was very distinguished, as she had a lover in the Cabinet Council, but that did not hinder her from making him support her prettily. And one winter she said to us: 'You don't know what a way I have thought of to make a good thing.' And she told us her idea.

"You know, Irma had such a face to trouble the heads of all men, and such a figure! And hips that would make the water come in your mouth. So she thought of a way for each of us to make a hundred francs to buy some rings with, and she arranged the thing like this:

"You must know that I was not rich at that moment, any more than the others, and we were scarcely making a hundred francs in a month at the shop, certainly not more. We wished to know her plan. We each had two or three lovers who gave a little, but not much, and it sometimes happened that in the noonday walk we nabbed a gentleman who would come the next day; we would keep him for two weeks and then give him up. Such men as that never give very much. Those at Chatou—that was for pleasure. Oh, if you only knew some of the sly things we did; truly you would die from laughter. So when Irma proposed to us to make a hundred francs we were all on fire. It is very bad, what I am going to tell you, but that makes no difference; you know what life is, and when one has stayed four years at Chatou——

"Well, she said to us: 'At the Opera Ball we are going to get hold of some of the best men in Paris, the most distinguished and the richest. I know who they are.'

"We did not believe it at first, because such men are not made for dressmakers; for Irma, yes, but not for us. Oh, she was so stylish, that Irma! Do you know, we had the habit at the studio of saying that if the emperor had seen her he would certainly have married her.

"She made us dress ourselves in our best and said to us: 'You, none of you, will enter the ballroom but will stay outside in cabs in the neighboring streets. A gentleman will come and get into your carriage. When he has entered you will embrace him as prettily as you can, and then you will utter a great cry to show that you have made a mistake and that you expected someone else. This will excite the pigeon to take the place of another, and he will try to remain by force; you will resist; you will give him a hundred blows to drive him away—and then—you will go to supper with him—and you ought to get good damages.'

"You do not quite understand it yet, do you? Well, here is what she did, the rogue!

"She made all four of us get into carriages, four carriages of the circle, that were just as they should be, then she placed us in streets near the opera. She went to the ball alone. As she knew by name the most conspicuous men in Paris, because our establishment catered to their wives, she chose them for her intrigue. She could talk with them about anything, for she had a mind also. When she saw that one was half drunk she threw off her mask, and he was taken as in a net. He wished to take her away immediately, but she preferred to make an appointment with him in half an hour in a carriage opposite number 20 Taitbout Street. It was I who was in that carriage! I was well wrapped up and my face veiled. Suddenly a gentleman put his head in the door and asked: 'Is it you?'

"And I answered in a low tone: 'Yes, it is I; get in quickly.'

"He did so, and I seized him in my arms and embraced him, until his breath was almost gone; then I said:

"'Oh! I am so happy! I am so happy!'

"But suddenly I cried out: 'But it is not you! Oh dear! Oh dear!' And I began to weep.

"You can judge whether the man was embarrassed or not! He tried to console me; he excused himself and protested that he was also mistaken. As for me, I kept on weeping, but less and less, and I uttered great sighs. Then he said very sweet things to me.

"He was a man that was a man; and it pleased him to see me weeping less and less. To put a short thread in the needle, he proposed to take me to supper. I refused; I tried to leap from the carriage; he held me by taking me around the waist; then he embraced me, as I had him upon his entrance.

"And then—and then—we had supper—you understand—and he gave me— think of it—he gave me five hundred francs! Would you believe that there are such generous men?

"And the thing was a success for everybody. Louise, who received the least, got two hundred francs. But, you know, Louise—truly she was very thin!"

The woman of the tobacco shop went on thus, emptying her heart of all the memories amassed in the long time that she had been shut up with her official duties. The past, poor and queer though it was, moved her soul. She regretted this gallant, Bohemian life of the Parisian sidewalk, made up of privations and paid-for caresses, of laughter and misery and moments of stratagem and true love.

I said to her: "But how did you get into the tobacco business?"

She smiled, saying: "Oh! That is a story too. You must know that I had for a neighbor in my apartment, exactly opposite my door, a student—but one of those students who amounts to nothing. This one lived at the café from morning until evening; he loved billiards, as I have never seen anyone love the game.

"When I was alone we sometimes passed the evening together. It is by him that I had Roger."

"Who is Roger?"

"My son."

"Ah!"

"He—he gave me a little pension for the boy's education, but I did not think that man would ever amount to anything, as I had never seen a man so idle, never. At the end of ten years he was still in his first examinations. When his family saw that he would do nothing they called him home to the provinces, but we remained in correspondence on account of the child. And then, imagine, at the last elections, two years ago, I learned that he had been made a deputy in his county. And then he made some speeches in the Assembly. Truly, in a kingdom of blind men, as the saying is—— But, to finish, I went to find him, and immediately he obtained this tobacco business for me, as the daughter of an exile. It is true my father was exiled, but I never thought of this fact serving me in any way.

"Briefly—wait! Here is Roger."

A tall young man entered, grave, correct and proper.

He kissed his mother on the brow and she said: "This, sir, is my son, head clerk at the mayor's office. You know, he may be a future subprefect."

I saluted this functionary in a worthy manner and went back to my hotel, after having pressed with gravity the extended hand of "So-it-Goes."

A POOR GIRL

Yes, the memory of that evening can never be effaced. For half an hour I had the sinister sensation of invincible fatality; I had the same shivers that one has in descending the shaft of a mine. I touched the black depths of human misery; I seemed to comprehend fully how impossible an honest life is under some conditions.

It was just past midnight. I was going from the vaudeville to Drouot Street, following a crowd on the boulevard, all carrying umbrellas. A deluge of water poured rather than fell, veiling the gas jets and giving the street a sad appearance. The sidewalk glittered, more sticky than wet. The mass of people pressed on, seeing nothing.

Girls, with skirts raised, showed their ankles, allowing a white stocking to peep out in the dim nocturnal light, and waited in shadowed doorways. Some called to and some, bolder, jostled the passers, pronouncing in their ears two obscene, stupid words. They would follow a man some seconds and push against him, breathing in his face their putrid breath. Then, seeing their beguilements useless, they would leave him with an abrupt, discontented motion and start on again, swinging their hips.

I went along, spoken to by all, taken by the sleeve, harassed and moved with disgust. Suddenly I saw three of them running as if frightened, talking to each other in rapid fashion. Others also began to run, to flee, holding their robes with both hands in order to run more quickly. That day a blow had been given to the network of prostitution.

All at once I felt an arm under mine, while a terrified voice murmured in my ear: "Save me, sir, save me; do not leave me."

I looked at the girl. She was not twenty years old, yet faded already. I said to her: "Remain with me." And she murmured: "Oh, thank you!"

We arrived at the line of agents. She disclosed herself in order to let me pass. I met her farther on in Drouot Street.

My companion asked: "Will you come home with me?"

"No."

"Why not? You have rendered me a service that I shall not forget."

I answered, so not to embarrass her: "Because I am married."

"What difference does that make?"

"You see, my child, that is sufficient. I have helped you out of your difficulty, leave me quietly now."

The street was deserted and dark, truly unpleasant. And this woman, who held me by the arm, rendered more frightful still the sensation of sadness which enveloped me. She wished to embrace me. I recoiled with horror. And in a hard voice she said: "Once, for peace, won't you?"

And she made a movement of rage, then abruptly began to sob. I stood lost in wonder, not quite comprehending. Finally I said:

"Tell me, what is the matter with you?"

She murmured through her tears: "If you only knew it, it is not gay, this isn't."

"What is not gay?"

"This kind of life."

"Why have you chosen it then?"

"It was not my fault."

"Whose fault was it?"

"I know whose, I do."

A kind of interest in this abandoned creature took me and I said:

"Tell me your story."

And she told it to me.

"I was sixteen years old and in service at Yvetot at the house of Monsieur Lerable, a grain dealer. My parents were dead. I had no one. I saw, of course, that my master looked at me in a queer way and that he pinched my cheeks, and I had not long to ask myself what he meant. I knew things, certainly. In the country, one is sharpened. But Monsieur Lerable was old and devout, going to Mass every Sunday. I somehow never believed him capable! But the day came when he wished to take me in my kitchen. I resisted him, but it was done.

"There was opposite us a grocer, Monsieur Dunstan, who had a very pleasant boy in his shop, so much so that I allowed myself to be cajoled by him. That happens to everybody, does it not? I would leave the door open evenings that he might come in.

"But one night Monsieur Lerable heard some noise. He went up and found Antoine and tried to kill him. It was a battle with chairs, jugs of water and everything. As for me, I found my courage and fled into the street. That was how I started out.

"I was afraid, afraid of the world. But I dressed myself under a doorway and began to walk straight on. I believed of a truth that someone had been killed and that the policemen were after me already. I reached the highway to Rouen. I told myself that at Rouen I should be concealed well enough.

"It was so dark I could not see the ditches, and I heard the dogs barking on the farms. Do you know all the things one hears at night? There are birds that cry like a man being murdered, beasts that yap and beasts that whistle, and many other things that I do not understand. I was all goose flesh. Each step I made the sign of the cross. One cannot imagine how the heart can be helped by that. When the day appeared the idea of the policemen always took me by force, and I ran all that I could. Then I tried to calm myself.

"I felt hungry, all the same, in spite of my fear, but I had not anything, not one sou, for I had forgotten my money, all that I had on earth, which was eighteen francs. So I was obliged to walk with an empty stomach.

"It was hot. The sun burned. Midday was past, and I kept going on. Suddenly I heard some horses behind me. I turned to look. The mounted policemen! My blood gave a leap; I thought I should fall, but I went on. They would catch me. They were looking at me now. Then one of them, the elder, said:

" 'Good day, mademoiselle.'

" 'Good day, sir.'

" 'Where are you going to?'

" 'I am going to Rouen in service at a place that has been offered me.'

" 'Walking, like this?'

" 'Yes, walking.'

"My heart beat, sir, so that I could say no more. I kept thinking to myself: 'Now they will take me.' And I had such a desire to run that my legs danced. But they would have caught me immediately, you see.

"The old one began: 'We can journey together as far as Barantin, mademoiselle, since we are taking the same route.'

" 'With pleasure, sir,' I said.

"And we chatted a little. I made myself as pleasant as I could, you see, so much so that they believed what was not so. Then as we passed into a wood the old one said: 'Would you like to stop and rest a little on this moss?'

"And I, without thinking, said: 'As you wish, sir.'

"Then he dismounted and gave his horse to the other, and we two went away in the wood. There was nothing to be said. What could you have done in my place? He took what he wished and then said to me: 'It won't do to forget the comrade.'

"He returned to the horses, and the other rejoined me. I was so much ashamed that I could have wept, sir. But I dared not resist, you understand. Then we went on our way. I could speak no more; I had too much grief in my heart. And then I could no longer walk, I was so hungry. But in the village they gave me a glass of wine, which gave me new force for some time. And then they took to the trot so as not to go through Barantin in my company. And I seated myself by a ditch and wept until I had no more tears.

"I walked then for three hours more before reaching Rouen. It was seven o'clock in the evening when I arrived there. At first all the lights dazzled me. And then I did not know where I could sit down to rest. On the way there were the ditches and the grass where I could even lie down and sleep. But in the city, nothing.

"My limbs refused to hold my body, and I felt as if I were going to fall. And then it began to rain, a little fine rain, like this evening, which goes through you without your knowing it. I have no luck when it rains. I commenced to walk the streets. I looked at all the houses, saying to myself: 'There are beds and bread in there, but I cannot find as much as a crust or a bed of straw.'

"I went through some streets where women were speaking to men along the way. In such cases, sir, one must do what one can. I took my place with the others, inviting everybody. But no one answered me. I wished I was dead. This must have been near midnight. I no longer knew what I did. Finally a man listened to me.

He asked me: 'Where do you live?' Some kind of ruse was necessary, and I answered: 'I cannot take you to my house for I live with Mamma. But are there not
some houses where we could go?'

"He answered: 'It is not often that I spend twenty sous for a room.' Then he
added: 'Come along. I know a quiet spot where we shall not be interrupted.'

"He made me pass over a bridge then led me to the end of the town, into a
meadow near the river. I could do nothing but follow him. He made me sit down
and then began to ask why we had come there. As he was long in his affair, I
found myself so worn out with fatigue that I fell asleep. He went away without
giving me anything. I could not see a single step. Since that day I have had troubles
that I can never be cured of, because I slept all that night in the wet.

"I was awakened by two officers who took me to the station house and then to
prison, where I stayed eight days, while they tried to find out who I was and where
I had come from. I would not tell for fear of the consequences. They found out,
however, and released me after a verdict of innocence.

"Then it was necessary for me to make my living. I tried to find a place, but I
could not because I had come out of prison. Then I recalled the old judge who
had a turn to his eye, while he was judging me, like that of Father Lerable of
Yvetot. And I went to find him. I was not deceived. He gave me a hundred sous
when I left him, saying: 'You shall have as much every time, but don't come too
often, not more than twice a week.' I understood that well because of his age. But
it gave me a reflection. I said to myself: 'Young people make merry and amuse
themselves, but they are never fat, while with the old it is the other way.' And
since then I can always tell them, these old apes with their eyes in a groove and
a little ghost of a head.

"Do you know what I did, sir? I dressed up like a country girl who had come
to market and I walked the streets for my living. Oh! I could pinch them at the
first blow. I would say to myself: 'Here is one who will bite.' He would approach.
And then commence:

" 'Good day, mademoiselle.'

" 'Good day, sir.'

" 'Where are you going, like this?'

" 'I am returning home to Master's.'

" 'Do they live far, your people?'

" 'Rather far, but not so very.'

"Then he would not know what to say, and I would make my step a little
slower to allow him to explain. Then he would give me some compliments in a
low voice and then ask me to go home with him. I would refuse at first, you
understand, and then yield. I had two or three of that sort each morning, and all
my afternoons free. That was the good time of my life. I was not made of spleen.

"But it seems one can never be quiet for a long time. It was my misfortune to
make the acquaintance of a rich man of the world, an old president, who was all
of seventy-five years old. One evening he took me to dine in a restaurant of the
neighborhood. And then, you understand, he did not know how to be moderate.
He was dead at the dessert.

"I had three months in prison, because I was not under superintendence. Then
I came to Paris. And, oh, sir, it is hard here! Hard to live! One cannot expect to
eat every day; there are too many. But that is only so much the worse. Each to
his trouble, don't you say so?"

She was silent. I walked along by her side, my heart touched. Suddenly she began to be familiar with me, saying:

"So you will not go home with me, my dear?"

"No, I have told you so already."

"Oh well, good-by, and thanks all the same, without any hard feeling, but I assure you that you are wrong."

And she went away, plunging into the rain which was as fine as a veil. I watched her pass under a gas jet and then disappear in a shadow. Poor girl!

THE SUBSTITUTE

"Madame Bonderoi?"

"Yes, Madame Bonderoi."

"Impossible."

"I tell you it is."

"Madame Bonderoi, the old lady in a lace cap, the devout, the holy, the honorable Madame Bonderoi, whose little false curls look as if they were glued round her head?"

"That is the very woman."

"Oh, come, you must be mad."

"I swear to you that it is Madame Bonderoi."

"Then please give me the details."

"Here they are: During the life of Monsieur Bonderoi, the lawyer, people said that she utilized his clerks for her own particular service. She is one of these respectable middle-class women, with secret vices and inflexible principles, of whom there are so many. She liked good-looking young fellows, and I should like to know what is more natural than that? Do not we all like pretty girls?

"As soon as old Bonderoi was dead his widow began to live the peaceful and irreproachable life of a woman with a fair, fixed income. She went to church assiduously and spoke evil of her neighbors but gave no chance to anyone to speak ill of her, and when she grew old she became the little wizened, sour-faced, mischievous woman whom you know. Well, this adventure, which you would scarcely believe, happened last Friday.

"My friend, Jean d'Anglemare, is, as you know, a captain in a dragoon regiment which is quartered in the barracks in the Rue de la Rivette. When he got to his quarters the other morning he found that two men of his squadron had had a terrible quarrel. The duel took place between them. After the duel they became reconciled, and when their officer questioned them they told him what their quarrel had been about. They had fought on Madame Bonderoi's account."

"Oh!"

"Yes, my dear fellow, about Madame Bonderoi. But I will let Trooper Siballe speak.

" 'This is how it was, Captain. About a year and a half ago I was lounging about the barrack yard between six and seven o'clock in the evening, when a woman came up and spoke to me and said, just as if she had been asking her way: "Soldier, would you like to earn ten francs a week honestly?" Of course I told her that I should, and so she said: "Come and see me at twelve o'clock tomorrow morning. I am Madame Bonderoi, and my address is number 6, Rue de la Tranchée."

" ' "You may rely upon my being there, madame." And then she went away, looking very pleased, and added: "I am very much obliged to you, soldier."

" ' "I am obliged to you, madame," I replied. But I plagued my head about the matter until the time came, all the same.

" 'At twelve o'clock exactly I rang the bell, and she let me in herself. She had a lot of ribbons on her head.

" ' "We must make haste," she said, "as my servant might come in."

" ' "I am quite willing to make haste," I replied, "but what am I to do?"

" 'But she only laughed and replied: "Don't you understand, you great stupid?"

" 'I was no nearer her meaning, I give you my word of honor, Captain, but she came and sat down by me and said:

" ' "If you mention this to anyone I will have you put in prison, so swear that you will never open your lips about it."

" 'I swore whatever she liked, though I did not at all understand what she meant. My forehead was covered with perspiration, so I took my pocket handkerchief out of my helmet. She took it and wiped my brow with it; then she kissed me and whispered: "Then you will?"

" ' "I will do anything you like, madame," I replied, "as that is what I came for."

" 'Then she made herself clearly understood by her actions, and when I saw what it was, I put my helmet on a chair and showed her that in the dragoons a man never retires, Captain.

" 'Not that I cared much about it, for she was certainly not in her prime, but it is no good being too particular in such a matter, as francs are scarce, and then I have relations whom I like to help. I said to myself: "There will be five francs for my father, out of that."

" 'When I had finished my allotted task, Captain, I got ready to go, though she wanted me to stop longer, but I said to her:

" ' "To everyone their due, madame. A small glass of brandy costs two sous, and two glasses cost four."

" 'She understood my meaning and put a gold ten-franc piece into my hand. I do not like that coin. It is so small that if your pockets are not very well made and come at all unsewn one is apt to find it in one's boots or not to find it at all, and so, while I was looking at it, she was looking at me. She got red in the face, as she had misunderstood. my looks, and said: "Is not that enough?"

" ' "I did not mean that, madame," I replied, "but if it is all the same to you, I would rather have two five-franc pieces." And she gave them to me, and I took my leave.

" 'This has been going on for a year and a half, Captain. I go every Tuesday evening, when you give me leave to go out of barracks; she prefers that, as her servant has gone to bed then, but last week I was not well and I had to go into the infirmary. When Tuesday came I could not get out, and I was very vexed because of the ten francs which I had been receiving every week, and I said to myself:

" ' "If anybody goes there I shall be done for, and she will be sure to take an artilleryman," and that made me angry. So I sent for Paumelle, who comes from my part of the country, and I told him how matters stood:

" ' "There will be five francs for you and five for me," I said. He agreed and went, as I had given him full instructions. She opened the door as soon as he knocked and let him in, and as she did not look at his face, she did not perceive that it was not I, for you know, Captain, one dragoon is very like another with a helmet on.

" 'Suddenly, however, she noticed the change and she asked angrily: "Who are you? What do you want? I do not know you."

" 'Then Paumelle explained matters; he told her that I was not well and that I had sent him as my substitute, so she looked at him, made him also swear to keep the matter secret, and then she accepted him, as you may suppose, for Paumelle is not a bad-looking fellow either. But when he came back, Captain, he would not give me my five francs. If they had been for myself I should not have said a word, but they were for my father, and on that score I would stand no nonsense and said to him:

" ' "You are not particular in what you do, for a dragoon; you are a discredit to your uniform."

" 'He raised his fist, Captain, saying that fatigue duty like that was worth double. Of course everybody has his own ideas, and he ought not to have accepted it. You know the rest.'

"Captain d'Anglemare laughed until he cried as he told me the story, but he also made me promise to keep the matter a secret, just as he had promised the two soldiers. So above all do not betray me, but promise me to keep it to yourself."

"Oh! You may be quite easy about that. But how was it all arranged in the end?"

"How? It is a joke in a thousand! Mother Bonderoi keeps her two dragoons and reserves his own particular day for each of them, and in that way everybody is satisfied."

"Oh! That is capital! Really capital!"

"And he can send his old father and mother the money as usual, and thus morality is satisfied."

THE HERMIT

Together with some friends, we had been to see the old hermit living on an ancient tumulus, covered with great trees, in the midst of the vast plain that stretches from Cannes to La Napoule.

On the way back, we talked about these strange solitary laymen, once so numerous, whose kind have now almost disappeared from the earth. We sought for the moral motives, and made an effort to realize what could be the nature of the sorrows that formerly drove men into solitary places.

One of our companions said abruptly:

"I've known two recluses, a man and a woman. The woman must be still living. For five years she lived at the summit of an absolutely deserted hill on the Corsican coast, fifteen or twenty miles from any other house. She lived there with a nurse; I went to see her. She must undoubtedly have been a well-known woman of the world. She received us with courtesy, even with pleasure, but I knew nothing about her, and I discovered nothing.

"The man, now, well, I'll tell you his unfortunate fate.

"Turn around. Away over there, you see the peaked and wooded hill that stands out behind La Napoule, thrust up by itself in front of the peaks of the Estérel; its local name is the Hill of Serpents. That's where my recluse lived for about twelve years, within the walls of a small ancient temple.

"When I heard of him, I decided to make his acquaintance, and one March morning I set out for Cannes on horseback. I left my mount at the Napoule inn and began to climb this strange conical hill on foot; it is perhaps a hundred and fifty or two hundred yards high and covered with aromatic plants, mostly cytisus, whose scent is so strong and pungent that it is quite overpowering and makes you feel positively ill. The ground is stony and you often see long vipers slithering over the stones and disappearing in the grass. That's what gives the place its well-merited nickname of the Hill of Serpents. There are some days when the ground under your feet seems to give birth to these reptiles as you climb the bare, sun-scorched slope. They are so numberless that you daren't walk any farther; you are conscious of a strange uneasiness, not fear, for the creatures are harmless, but a kind of mystic terror. Several times I have had an odd sense that I was climbing a sacred hill of old, a fantastic hill, scented, mysterious, covered with and peopled by serpents and crowned with a temple.

"The temple is still there. At least, I am told that it was a temple. And I have refrained from trying to find out more about it, because I don't want to destroy the emotional appeal it has for me.

"Well, I climbed it that March morning, ostensibly to admire the scenery. As I approached the top I did indeed see walls, and, sitting on a stone, a man. He was hardly more than forty-five years old, although his hair was quite white; but his beard was still almost black. He was stroking a cat that curled on his knees, and he appeared to take no interest in me. I explored the ruins; a corner of them, roofed over, enclosed behind a construction of branches, straw, grass, and stones, formed his dwelling place; then I returned and stood beside him.

"The view from the hill is splendid. On the right the Estérel hills lift their strange truncated peaks; beyond them the rimless sea stretches to the far-off Italian coast with its innumerable headlands, and over against Cannes the flat green islands of Lérins seem to float on the water, the father of them thrusting into the open sea a massive great castle, ancient and battlemented, its walls rising from the waves.

"Then the Alps, their heads still hooded in the snows, rear their great bulk and dominate the green coast with its string of villas and white, tree-fast towns that at this distance look like innumerable eggs laid on the edge of the shore.

"I murmured: 'Gad, what a view!'

"The man lifted his head and said: 'Yes, but when you see it every day and all day, it gets monotonous.'

"So he could speak, my recluse, he could talk and he was bored. I had him.

"I did not stay very long that day, and I did not try to do more than find out the form his misanthropy took. The impression he made on me was that of a man utterly weary of his fellow creatures, tired of everything, hopelessly disillusioned, and disgusted with himself and with the rest of mankind.

"I left him after half an hour's conversation. But I came back a week later, and once again the following week, and then every week; so that long before the end of two months we were friends.

"Then, one evening in late May, I decided that the moment had come, and I carried up some food to have dinner with him on the Hill of Serpents.

"It was one of those southern evenings heavy with the mingled perfume of flowers that this countryside grows as the north grows corn, to make almost all the scents that women use for their bodies and their clothes: an evening when old men's senses stir and swoon in dreams of love born of the fragrance of innumerable orange trees filling the gardens and all the folds of the valley.

"My recluse greeted me with obvious pleasure, and willingly consented to share my dinner.

"I made him drink a little wine, to which he had long been unused; it exhilarated him, and he began to talk of his past life. I got the impression that he had always lived in Paris, and the life of a gay bachelor.

"I asked him abruptly: 'What mad impulse made you come and perch on this hilltop?'

"He answered readily: 'Oh, because I had the severest blow a man could have. But why should I hide my unhappy fate from you? It might make you pity me, perhaps. And besides . . . I have never told anyone . . . never . . . and I should like to know . . . just once . . . how it struck another person . . . what he thought of it.

" 'I was born in Paris, educated in Paris, and I grew up and lived in that city. My parents had left me a few thousand francs' income, and I had enough influence to get a quiet subordinate post which made me well off, for a bachelor.

" 'Since early youth I had led the life of a bachelor. You know what that's like. Free, with no family ties, determined never to burden myself with a wife, I spent now three months with one woman, now six months with another, then a companionless year, sipping honey among the multitude of girls on offer or on sale.

" 'This easy-going manner of life, call it commonplace if you like, suited me well enough, and satisfied my natural love of change and novelty. I lived on the boulevard, in theaters and cafés, always out, almost homeless, although I had a comfortable house. I was one of the thousands of people who let themselves drift through life, like corks, for whom the walls of Paris are the walls of the world, who trouble themselves for nothing, since there is nothing they ardently desire. I was what you call a good sort, with no outstanding virtues and no vices. There you have me. And I've a quite accurate knowledge of myself.

" 'So, from the time I was twenty to my fortieth year, my life ran on, slow or fast, with nothing to disturb its even flow. They go so quickly, those uneventful Parisian years when nothing ever happens that the mind remembers as a turning point, those long crowded years, gay trivial years when you eat and drink and laugh without knowing why, and, desiring nothing, yet touch your lips to all the savor of life and every kiss that offers. You were young; and then you are old without having done any of the things that other men do, without any ties, any roots, any place in life, almost without friends, without parents, without wives, without children.

" 'Well, I reached the fortieth year of my easy pleasant life; and to celebrate this anniversary I invited myself to a good dinner in one of the best restaurants. I was alone in the world; it pleased my sense of what was fitting to celebrate the day alone.

" 'Dinner over, I could not decide what to do next. I rather wanted to go to a theater; and then I was struck with the idea of making a pilgrimage to the Quartier Latin, where I studied law. So I made my way across Paris and wandered unthinkingly into one of those cafés where you are served by girls.

" 'The one who looked after my table was very young, pretty, and bubbling over with laughter. I offered her a drink, which she readily accepted. She sat down opposite me and looked me over with an expert eye, unable to make out what kind of masculine creature she had to deal with. She was fair-haired, fair altogether; she was a clear-skinned, healthy girl, and I guessed her to be plump and rosy under the swelling folds of her bodice. I murmured all the meaningless gallantries that one always says to these girls, and as she was really very charming, the whim suddenly seized me to take her out . . . just to celebrate my fortieth birthday. It was neither long nor difficult to arrange. She was unattached . . . had been for a fortnight, she told me . . . and she at once agreed to come and have supper with me at the Halles when her work was over.

" 'As I was afraid that she wouldn't stick to me—you never know what will happen, nor who'll come into these beer shops, nor what a woman will take into her head to do—I stayed there the whole evening, waiting for her.

" 'I had been unattached myself for a month or two, and as I watched this adorable neophyte of love flitting from table to table, I wondered if I shouldn't do as well to take her on for a time. What I'm describing to you is one of the daily commonplace adventures in a Parisian's life.

" 'Forgive these crude details; men who have never known an ideal love take and choose their women as they choose a chop at the butcher's, without bothering about anything but the quality of their flesh.

" 'Well, I went with her to her house—for I've too much respect for my own sheets. It was a workgirl's tiny room, on the fifth floor, clean and bare; I spent two delightful hours there. She had an uncommonly graceful and charming way with her, that little girl.

" 'When I was ready to go, I walked towards her mantelshelf to deposit thereon the usual present. I had arranged a day for a second interview with the little wench, who was still lying in bed. I saw dimly a clock under a glass case, two vases of flowers, and two photographs, one of which was very old, one of those negatives on glass called daguerreotypes. I bent casually to look at this portrait, and I stood there paralyzed, too surprised to understand. . . . It was myself, my first portrait, one that I had had made long ago when I was a student living in the Quartier Latin.

" 'I snatched it up to examine it more closely. I'd made no mistake . . . and I felt like laughing, it struck me as so queer and unexpected.

" ' "Who is this gentleman?" I demanded.

" ' "That's my father, whom I never knew," she answered. "Mamma left it to me and told me to keep it, because it would be useful to me some day. . . ."

" 'She hesitated, burst out laughing, and added: "I don't know what for, upon my word. It's not likely he'll come and recognize me."

" 'My heart leaped madly, like the galloping of a runaway horse. I laid the picture on its face on the mantelshelf, put two hundred-franc notes that I had in my pocket on top of it, without at all thinking what I was doing, and hurried out crying: "See you again soon! . . . Good-by, my dear . . . good-by!"

" 'I heard her answer: "On Wednesday." I was on the darkened stairs and groping my way down them.

" 'When I got outside, I saw that it was raining, and I set off with great strides, taking the first road.

" 'I walked straight on, dazed, bewildered, raking my memory. Was it possible? Yes, I suddenly remembered a girl who had written to me, about a month after we had broken off relations, that she was with child by me. I had torn up or burned the letter, and forgotten the whole thing. I ought to have looked at the photograph of the woman on the little girl's mantelshelf. But should I have recognized her? I had a vague memory of it as the photograph of an old woman.

" 'I reached the quay. I saw a bench and sat down. It was raining. Now and then people hurried past under umbrellas. Life had become for me hateful and revolting, full of miserable shameful things, infamies willed or predestined. My daughter . . . perhaps I had just possessed my own daughter. And Paris, vast somber Paris, gloomy, dirty, sad, black, with all its shuttered houses, was full of suchlike things, adulteries, incests, violated children. I remembered all I'd been told of bridges haunted by vicious and degraded wretches.

" 'Without wishing or knowing it, I had sunk lower than those vile creatures. I had climbed into my daughter's bed.

" 'I could have thrown myself in the water. I was mad. I wandered about until daybreak, then I went back to my house to think things out.

" 'I decided on what seemed to me the most prudent course. I would have a solicitor send for the girl and ask her under what circumstances her mother had given her the portrait of the man she believed to be her father: I would tell him that I was acting on behalf of a friend.

" 'The solicitor carried out my instructions. It was on her deathbed that the woman had made a statement about the father of her child, and before a priest whose name I was given.

" 'Then, always in the name of this unknown friend, I made half my fortune over to this child, about a hundred and forty thousand francs, arranging it so that she could only touch the interest of it; then I sent in my resignation, and here I am.

" 'I was wandering along this coast, and I found this hill and stopped here . . . since . . . I have forgotten how long since that was.

" 'What do you think of me? . . . and of what I did?'

"I gave him my hand and answered:

" 'You did the right thing. There are plenty of men who would have attached less importance to such a vile accident.'

" 'I know that,' he replied, 'but I almost went mad. I must have had a tender conscience without ever guessing it. And I'm afraid of Paris now, as believers must be afraid of hell. I've had a blow on the head, that's all, a blow like a tile falling on you as you walk down the street. Time is making it more bearable.'

"I left my recluse. His story disturbed me profoundly.

"I saw him again twice, then I went away, because I never stay in the south after the end of May.

"When I came back the following year, the man was no longer living on the Hill of Serpents, and I have never heard a word about him since.

"That's the story of my hermit."

A PASSION

The sea was brilliant and unruffled, scarcely stirred, and on the pier the entire town of Havre watched the ships as they came on.

They could be seen at a distance in great numbers, some of them, the steamers, with plumes of smoke; the others, the sailing vessels, drawn by almost invisible tugs, lifting toward the sky their bare masts, like leafless trees.

They hurried from every end of the horizon toward the narrow mouth of the jetty which devoured these monsters, and they groaned, they shrieked, they hissed while they spat out puffs of steam like animals panting for breath.

Two young officers were walking on the landing stage, where a number of people were waiting, saluting or returning salutes and sometimes stopping to chat.

Suddenly one of them, the taller, Paul d'Henricol, pressed the arm of his comrade, Jean Renoldi, then, in a whisper, he said:

"Hallo, here's Madame Poincot; give a good look at her. I assure you that she's making eyes at you."

She was moving along on the arm of her husband. She was a woman of about forty, very handsome still, slightly stout, but, owing to her graceful fullness of figure, as fresh as she was at twenty. Among her friends she was known as the Goddess, on account of her proud gait, her large black eyes and the air of nobility attached to her person. She remained irreproachable; never had the least suspicion cast a breath on her life's purity. She was regarded as the very type of a virtuous, uncorrupted woman—so upright that no man had ever dared to think of her.

And yet for the last month Paul d'Henricol had been assuring his friend Renoldi that Mme Poincot was in love with him, and he maintained that there was no doubt of it.

"Be sure I don't deceive myself. I see it clearly. She loves you—she loves you passionately, like a chaste woman who has never loved. Forty years is a terrible age for virtuous women when they possess senses; they become foolish and commit utter follies. She is hit, my dear fellow; she is falling like a wounded bird and is ready to drop into your arms. I say—just look at her!"

The tall woman, preceded by her two daughters, aged twelve and fifteen years, suddenly turned pale on her approach as her eyes lighted on the officer's face. She gave him an ardent glance, concentrating her gaze upon him, and no longer seemed to have any eyes for her children, her husband or any other person around her. She returned the salutation of the two young men without lowering her eyes, glowing with such a flame that a doubt at last forced its way into Lieutenant Renoldi's mind.

His friend said in the same hushed voice: "I was sure of it. Did you not notice her this time? By Jove, she is a nice woman!"

But Jean Renoldi had no desire for a society intrigue. Caring little for love, he longed, above all, for a quiet life and contented himself with occasional amours such as a young man can always have. All the sentimentality, the attentions and the tenderness which a well-bred woman exacts bored him. The chain, however slight it might be, which is always formed by an adventure of this sort, filled him with fear. He said: "At the end of a month I'll have had enough of it, and I'll be forced to wait patiently for six months through politeness."

Then a rupture would exasperate him, with the senses, the illusions, the clinging attachment, of the abandoned woman.

He avoided meeting Mme Poincot.

But one evening he found himself by her side at a dinner party, and he felt on his skin, in his eyes and even in his heart the burning glance of his fair neighbor. Their hands met and almost involuntarily were pressed together in a warm clasp. Already the intrigue was almost begun.

He saw her again, always in spite of himself. He realized that he was loved. He felt himself moved by a kind of pitying vanity when he saw what a violent passion for him swayed this woman's breast. So he allowed himself to be adored and merely displayed gallantry, hoping that the affair would be only sentimental.

But one day she made an appointment with him for the ostensible purpose of seeing him and talking freely to him. She fell, swooning, into his arms, and he had no alternative but to be her lover.

And this lasted six months. She loved him with an unbridled, panting love. Absorbed in this frenzied passion, she no longer bestowed a thought on anything else. She surrendered herself to it utterly; her body, her soul, her reputation, her position, her happiness—she had cast all into that fire of her heart as one casts, as a sacrifice, every precious object into a funeral pyre.

He had for some time grown tired of her and deeply regretted his easy conquest as a fascinating officer, but he was bound, held prisoner. At every moment she said to him: "I have given you everything. What more would you have?" He felt a desire to answer:

"But I have asked nothing from you, and I beg of you to take back what you gave me."

Without caring about being seen, compromised, ruined, she came to see him every evening, her passion becoming more inflamed each time they met. She flung herself into his arms, strained him in a fierce embrace, fainted under the force of rapturous kisses which to him were now terribly wearisome.

He said in a languid tone: "Look here! Be reasonable!"

She replied:

"I love you," and sank on her knees, gazing at him for a long time in an attitude of admiration. At length, exasperated by her persistent gaze, he tried to make her rise.

"Sit down. Let us talk," he said.

She murmured: "No, leave me," and remained there, her soul in a state of ecstasy.

He said to his friend D'Henricol:

"You know, 'twill end by my beating her. I won't have any more of it! It must end, and that without further delay!" Then he went on: "What do you advise me to do?"

The other replied: "Break it off."

And Renoldi added, shrugging his shoulders:

"You speak indifferently about the matter; you believe that it is easy to break with a woman who tortures you with attention, who annoys you with kindness, who persecutes you with her affection, whose only care is to please you and whose only wrong is that she gave herself to you in spite of you."

But suddenly one morning the news came that the regiment was about to be removed from the garrison. Renoldi began to dance with joy. He was saved! Saved without scenes, without cries! Saved! All he had to do now was to wait patiently for two months more. Saved!

In the evening she came to him more excited than she had ever been before. She had heard the dreadful news, and without taking off her hat she caught his hands and pressed them nervously, with her eyes fixed on his and her voice vibrating and resolute.

"You are leaving," she said; "I know it. At first I felt heartbroken; then I under-stood what I had to do. I don't hesitate about doing it. I have come to give you the greatest proof of love that a woman can offer. I'll follow you. For you I am abandoning my husband, my children, my family. I am ruining myself, but I am happy. It seems to me that I am giving myself to you over again. It is the last and the greatest sacrifice. I am yours forever!"

He felt a cold sweat down his back and was seized with a dull and violent rage, the anger of weakness. However, he became calm and, in a disinterested tone, with a show of kindness, he refused to accept her sacrifice, tried to appease her, to bring her to reason, to make her see her own folly! She listened to him, staring at him with her great black eyes and with a smile of disdain on her lips, and said not a word in reply. He went on talking to her, and when at length he stopped, she said merely:

"Can you really be a coward? Can you be one of those who seduce a woman and then throw her over through sheer caprice?"

He became pale and renewed his arguments; he pointed out to her the inev-itable consequences of such an action to both of them as long as they lived—how their lives would be shattered and how the world would shut its doors against them. She replied obstinately: "What does it matter when we love each other?" Then all of a sudden he burst out furiously:

"Well then, I will not. No—do you understand? I will not do it, and I forbid you to do it." Then, carried away by the rancorous feeling which had seethed within him so long, he relieved his heart:

"Ah, damn it all, you have now been sticking onto me for a long time in spite of myself, and the best thing for you now is to take yourself off. I'll be much obliged if you do so, upon my honor!"

She did not answer him, but her livid countenance began to look shriveled up, as if all her nerves and muscles had been twisted out of shape. And she went away without saying good-by.

The same night she poisoned herself.

For a week she was believed to be in a hopeless condition. And in the city people gossiped about the case and pitied her, excusing her sin on account of the violence of her passion, for overstrained emotions, becoming heroic through their intensity, always obtain forgiveness for whatever is blameworthy in them. A woman who kills herself is, so to speak, not an adulteress. And ere long there was a feeling of general reprobation against Lieutenant Renoldi for refusing to see her again—a unanimous sentiment of blame.

It was a matter of common talk that he had deserted her, betrayed her, ill treated her. The colonel, overcome by compassion, brought his officer to book in a quiet way. Paul d'Henricol called on his friend: "Deuce take it, Renoldi, it's a damnable shame to let a woman die; it's not the right thing, anyhow."

The other, enraged, told him to hold his tongue, whereupon D'Henricol made use of the word "infamy." The result was a duel; Renoldi was wounded, to the satisfaction of everybody, and was for some time confined to his bed.

She heard about it and only loved him the more for it, believing that it was on her account he had fought the duel, but, as she was too ill to move, she was unable to see him again before the departure of the regiment.

He had been three months in Lille when he received one morning a visit from the sister of his former mistress.

After long suffering and a feeling of dejection, which she could not conquer, Mme Poincot's life was now despaired of, and she merely asked to see him for a minute, only a minute, before closing her eyes forever.

Absence and time had appeased the young man's satiety and anger; he was touched, moved to tears, and he started at once for Havre.

She seemed to be in the agonies of death. They were left alone together, and by the bedside of this woman whom he now believed to be dying and whom he blamed himself for killing, though it was not by his own hand, he was fairly crushed with grief. He burst out sobbing, embraced her with tender, passionate kisses, more lovingly than he had ever done in the past. He murmured in a broken voice:

"No, no, you shall not die! You shall get better! We shall love each other forever—forever!"

She said in faint tones:

"Then it is true. You do love me, after all?"

And he, in his sorrow for her misfortunes, swore, promised to wait till she had recovered and, full of loving pity, kissed again and again the emaciated hands of the poor woman whose heart was panting with feverish, irregular pulsations.

The next day he returned to the garrison.

Six weeks later she went to meet him, quite old looking, unrecognizable and more enamored than ever.

In his condition of mental prostration, he consented to live with her. Then when they remained together as if they had been legally united, the same colonel who had displayed indignation with him for abandoning her objected to this irregular connection as being incompatible with the good example officers ought to give in a regiment. He warned the lieutenant on the subject and then furiously denounced his conduct, so Renoldi retired from the army.

He went to live in a village on the shore of the Mediterranean, the classic sea of lovers.

And three years passed. Renoldi, bent under the yoke, was vanquished and became accustomed to the woman's unchanging devotion. His hair had now turned white.

He looked upon himself as a man done for, gone under. Henceforth, he had no hope, no ambition, no satisfaction in life, and he looked forward to no pleasure in existence.

But one morning a card was placed in his hand with the name "Joseph Poincot, Shipowner, Havre."

The husband! The husband, who had said nothing, realizing that there was no use in struggling against the desperate obstinacy of women. What did he want?

He was waiting in the garden, having refused to come into the house. He bowed politely but would not sit down, even on a bench in a gravel path, and he commenced talking clearly and slowly.

"Monsieur, I did not come here to address reproaches to you. I know too well how things happened. I have been the victim of—we have been the victims of—a kind of fatality. I would never have disturbed you in your retreat if the situation had not changed. I have two daughters, monsieur. One of them, the elder, loves a young man and is loved by him. But the family of this young man is opposed to the marriage, basing their objection on the situation of—my daughter's mother. I have no feeling of either anger or spite, but I love my children, monsieur. I have, therefore, come to ask my wife to return home. I hope that today she will consent to go back to my house—to her own house. As for me, I will make a show of having forgotten, for—for the sake of my daughters."

Renoldi felt a wild movement in his heart, and he was inundated with a delirium of joy, like a condemned man who receives a pardon.

He stammered: "Why, yes—certainly, monsieur. I myself—— Be assured of it. No doubt—it is right; it is only quite right."

This time M. Poincot no longer declined to sit down.

Renoldi then rushed up the stairs and, pausing at the door of his mistress's room to collect his senses, entered gravely.

"There is somebody below waiting to see you," he said. " 'Tis to tell you something about your daughters."

She rose. "My daughters? What about them? They are not dead?"

He replied: "No, but a serious situation has arisen which you alone can settle."

She did not wait to hear more but rapidly descended the stairs.

Then he sank down on a chair, greatly moved, and waited.

He waited a long, long time. Then he heard angry voices belowstairs and made up his mind to go down.

Mme Poincot was standing up, exasperated, just on the point of going away, while her husband had seized hold of her dress, exclaiming: "But remember that you are destroying our daughters, your daughters, our children!"

She answered stubbornly:

"I will not go back to you!"

Renoldi understood everything, came over to them in a state of great agitation and gasped:

"What, does she refuse to go?"

She turned toward him and, with a kind of shamefacedness, addressing him without any familiarity of tone in the presence of her legitimate husband, said:

"Do you know what he asks me to do? He wants me to go back and live under one roof with him!"

And she tittered with a profound disdain for this man, who was appealing to her almost on his knees.

Then Renoldi, with the determination of a desperate man playing his last card, began talking to her in his turn and pleaded the cause of the poor girls, the cause of the husband, his own cause. And when he stopped, trying to find some fresh argument, M. Poincot, at his wit's end, murmured in the affectionate style in which he used to speak to her in days gone by:

"Look here, Delphine! Think of your daughters!"

Then she turned on both of them a glance of sovereign contempt, and after that, flying with a bound toward the staircase, she flung at them these scornful words: "You are a pair of wretches!"

Left alone, they gazed at each other for a moment, both equally crestfallen, equally crushed. M. Poincot picked up his hat, which had fallen down near where he sat, dusted off his knees the signs of kneeling on the floor, then, raising both hands sorrowfully, while Renoldi was seeing him to the door, remarked with a parting bow:

"We are very unfortunate, monsieur."

Then he walked away from the house with a heavy step.

THE ORDERLY

The cemetery, filled with officers, looked like a field covered with flowers. The kepis and the red trousers, the stripes and the gold buttons, the shoulder knots of the staff, the braid of the chasseurs and the hussars, passed through the midst of the tombs, whose crosses, white or black, opened their mournful arms—their arms of iron, marble or wood—over the vanished race of the dead.

Colonel Limousin's wife had just been buried. She had been drowned two days before while taking a bath. It was over. The clergy had left, but the colonel, supported by two brother officers, remained standing in front of the pit, at the bottom of which he saw still the oaken coffin wherein lay, already decomposed, the body of his young wife.

He was almost an old man, tall and thin, with white mustaches, and three years ago he had married the daughter of a comrade, left an orphan on the death of her father, Colonel Sortis.

The captain and the lieutenant, on whom their commanding officer was leaning, attempted to lead him away. He resisted, his eyes full of tears which he heroically held back and murmuring, "No, no, a little while longer!" He persisted in remaining there, his legs bending under him, at the side of that pit, which seemed to him bottomless, an abyss into which had fallen his heart and his life, all that he held dear on earth.

Suddenly General Ormont came up, seized the colonel by the arm and, dragging him from the spot almost by force, said: "Come, come, my old comrade! You must not remain here."

The colonel thereupon obeyed and went back to his quarters. As he opened the door of his study, he saw a letter on the table. He took it in his hands and was near falling with surprise and emotion: he recognized his wife's handwriting. And the letter bore the postmark and the date of the same day. He tore open the envelope and read:

"Father: Permit me to call you still father as in days gone by. When you receive this letter I shall be dead and under the clay. Therefore, perhaps, you may forgive me.

"I do not want to excite your pity or to extenuate my sin. I only want to tell the entire and complete truth, with all the sincerity of a woman who, in an hour's time, is going to kill herself.

"When you married me through generosity I gave myself to you through gratitude, and I loved you with all my girlish heart. I loved you as I loved my own father—almost as much, and one day while I sat on your knee and you were kissing me, I called you 'Father' in spite of myself. It was a cry of the heart, instinctive, spontaneous. Indeed, you were to me a father, nothing but a father. You laughed and said to me, 'Address me always in that way, my child; it gives me pleasure.'

"We came to the city, and—forgive me, Father—I fell in love. Ah! I resisted long, well, nearly two years—and then I yielded, I sinned, I became a fallen woman.

"And as to him? You will never guess who he is. I am easy enough about that matter, since there were a dozen officers always around me and with me, whom you called my twelve constellations.

"Father, do not seek to know him and do not hate him. He only did what any man, no matter who, would have done in his place, and then I am sure that he loved me, too, with all his heart.

"But listen! One day we had an appointment in the isle of Bécasses—you know, the little isle close to the mill. I had to get there by swimming, and he had to wait for me in a thicket and then to remain there till nightfall so that nobody should see him going away. I had just met him when the branches opened, and we saw Philippe, your orderly, who had surprised us. I felt that we were lost, and I uttered a great cry. Thereupon he said to me—he, my lover—'Go, swim back quietly, my darling, and leave me here with this man.'

"I went away so excited that I was near drowning myself, and I came back to you expecting that something dreadful was about to happen.

"An hour later Philippe said to me in a low tone in the lobby outside the drawing room, where I met him: 'I am at Madame's orders, if she has any letters to give me.' Then I knew that he had sold himself and that my lover had bought him.

"I gave him some letters, in fact—all my letters—he took them away and brought me back the answers.

"This lasted about two months. We had confidence in him, as you had confidence in him yourself.

"Now, Father, here is what happened. One day, in the same isle which I had to reach by swimming, but this time alone, I found your orderly. This man had been waiting for me, and he informed me that he was going to reveal everything about us to you and deliver to you letters he had kept, stolen, if I did not yield to his desires.

"Oh, Father, Father, I was filled with fear—a cowardly fear, an unworthy fear, a fear above all of you, who had been so good to me and whom I had deceived—fear on his account, too—you would have killed him—for myself also perhaps! I cannot tell; I was mad, desperate; I thought of once more buying this wretch who loved me, too—how shameful!

"We are so weak, we women; we lose our heads more easily than you do. And then when a woman once falls, she always falls lower and lower. Did I know what I was doing? I understood only that one of you two and I were going to die, and I gave myself to this brute.

"You see, Father, that I do not seek to excuse myself. Then, then—then what I should have foreseen happened—he had the better of me again and again, when he wished, by terrifying me. He, too, has been my lover, like the other, every day. Is not this abominable? And what punishment, Father!

"So then it is all over with me. I must die. While I lived I could not confess such a crime to you. Dead, I dare everything. I could not do otherwise than die—nothing could have washed me clean—I was too polluted. I could no longer love or be loved. It seemed to me that I stained everyone by merely allowing my hand to be touched.

"Presently I am going to take my bath, and I will never come back. This letter for you will go to my lover. It will reach him when I am dead, and without anyone knowing anything about it, he will forward it to you, accomplishing my last wishes. And you shall read it on your return from the cemetery.

"Adieu, Father! I have no more to tell you. Do whatever you wish and forgive me."

The colonel wiped his forehead, which was covered with perspiration. His coolness, the coolness of days when he had stood on the field of battle, suddenly came back to him. He rang.

A manservant made his appearance. "Send in Philippe to me," said the colonel. Then he opened the drawer of his table.

The man entered almost immediately—a big soldier with red mustaches, a malignant look and a cunning eye.

The colonel looked him straight in the face.

"You are going to tell me the name of my wife's lover."

"But, my colonel——"

The officer snatched his revolver out of the half-open drawer.

"Come! Quick! You know I do not jest!"

"Well—my colonel—it is Captain Saint-Albert."

Scarcely had he pronounced this name when a flame flashed between his eyes and he fell on his face, his forehead pierced by a ball.

FEMININE MEN

How often we hear people say, "That man is charming, but he is a woman, a regular girl." They are alluding to the feminine men, the bane of our country.

For all we men in France are feminine, that is, fickle, fanciful, innocently treacherous, without consistency in our convictions or our will, violent and weak, as women are.

But the most irritating of the species is assuredly the Parisian and the *boulevardier*, in whom the appearance of intelligence is more marked, and who combines in himself all the attractions and all the faults of charming harlots to an exaggerated degree in virtue of his masculine temperament.

Our Chamber of Deputies is full of feminine men. They form the greater number of the amiable opportunists whom one might call "the charmers." It is they who control by soft words and deceitful promises, who know how to shake hands in such a manner as to win hearts, how to say "my dear friend" in a certain tactful way to the people they know the least, to change their minds without suspecting it, to be carried away by each new idea, to be sincere in their weathercock convictions, to let themselves be deceived as they deceive others, to forget the next morning what they affirmed the day before.

The newspapers are full of male prostitutes. That is probably where one finds them most, but it is also where they are most needed. Certain papers, like the *Journal des Débats* and the *Gazette de France*, are exceptions.

Assuredly, every good journalist must be something of a prostitute—that is, at the command of the public, supple in following unconsciously the shades of public opinion, wavering and varying, sceptical and credulous, wicked and devout, a braggart and a true man, enthusiastic and ironical, and always convinced while believing in nothing.

Foreigners, our anti-types, as Mme. Abel called them, the stubborn English and the heavy Germans, regard us with a certain amazement mingled with contempt, and will continue so to regard us till the end of time. They consider us frivolous. It is not that, we are feminine. And that is why people love us in spite of our faults, why they come back to us despite the evil spoken of us; these are lovers' quarrels!

The effeminate man, as one meets him in this world, is so charming that he captivates you after five minutes' chat. His smile seems made for you; you cannot believe that his voice does not assume specially tender intonations on your account. When he leaves you it seems as if you had known him for twenty years. One is quite ready to lend him money if he asks for it. He has enchanted you, like a woman.

If he does not act quite straight with you, you cannot bear any malice, he is so nice when you next meet him. If he asks your pardon you long to ask pardon of him. Does he tell lies? You cannot believe it. Does he put you off indefinitely with promises that he does not keep? You lay as much store by his promises as though he had moved heaven and earth to render you a service.

When he admires anything he goes into such raptures that he convinces you. He once adored Victor Hugo, whom he now treats as a back number. He pretends that he fought for Zola, whom he has abandoned for Barbey d'Aurevilly. And when he admires, he permits no qualifications; he would slap your face for a word. But when he becomes scornful, his contempt is unbounded and allows of no protest.

In short, he understands nothing.

Listen to two girls talking.

"Then you are angry with Julia?" "I should say so. I slapped her face." "What had she done?" "She told Pauline that I was broke thirteen months out of twelve, and Pauline told Gontran—you understand." "You were living together in the Rue Clauzel?" "We lived together four years in the Place Bréda; we quarreled about a pair of stockings that she said I had worn—it wasn't true—silk stockings that she had bought at Mother Martin's. Then I gave her a pounding and she left me at once. I met her six months ago and she asked me to come and live with her, as she has rented a flat that is twice too large."

One goes on one's way and hears no more. But on the following Sunday as one is on the way to Saint Germain two young women get into the same railway carriage. One recognizes one of them at once, it is Julia's enemy. The other is—Julia!

And there are endearments, caresses, plans. "Tell me, Julia—listen, Julia," etc.

The man of the species has his friendships of this kind. For three months he cannot bear to leave his old Jack, his dear Jack. There is no one but Jack in the world. He is the only one who has any intelligence, any sense, any talent. He alone is somebody in Paris. One meets them everywhere together, they dine together, walk about in company, and every evening see each other home, walking back and forth without being able to part.

Three months later, if Jack is mentioned:

"There is a cad, a bounder, a scoundrel for you. I know him well, you may be sure. And he is not even honest, and ill-bred," etc., etc.

Three months later, and they are living together.

But one morning one hears that they have fought a duel, then embraced each other, amid tears, on the dueling ground.

For the rest, they are the dearest friends in the world, furious with each other half the year, abusing and loving each other by turns, squeezing each other's hands till they almost crush the bones, and ready to run each other through the body for a misunderstanding.

For the relations of these feminine men are uncertain. Their temper is governed by fits and starts, their enthusiasms unexpected, their affection subject to sudden revulsions, their excitement is liable to eclipse. One day they love you, the next day they will hardly look at you, for they have, in fact, a harlot's nature, a harlot's charm, a harlot's temperament, and all their sentiments are like the affections of harlots.

They treat their friends as kept women treat their pet dogs.

Their friends are like the little doggie which they hug, feed with sugar, and allow to sleep on the pillow, but which they would throw out of a window in a moment of impatience; which they swing round, holding it by the tail, squeeze in their arms till they almost strangle it, and plunge, without any reason, in a pail of cold water.

Then, what a strange thing it is when a feminine man falls in love with a real harlot! He beats her, she scratches him, they execrate each other, cannot bear the sight of each other, and yet cannot part, linked together by no one knows what mysterious bonds of the heart. She deceives him, he knows it, sobs, and forgives her. He sleeps in the bed which another man is paying for, and firmly believes his conduct is irreproachable. He despises and adores her without seeing that she would be justified in despising him. They are both atrociously unhappy and yet cannot separate. They cast invectives, reproaches and abominable accusations at each other from morning till night, and when they have reached the climax and are vibrating with rage and hatred, they fall into each other's arms and kiss each other ardently, their souls and bodies of strumpets united.

The feminine man is brave and a coward at the same time. He has, more than another, the exalted sentiment of honor, but is lacking in the sense of simple honesty, and, circumstances favoring him, he would defalcate and commit infamies which do not trouble his conscience, for he obeys without questioning the oscillations of his ideas, which are always impulsive.

To him it seems permissible and almost right to cheat a shopkeeper. He considers it honorable not to pay his debts, unless they are gambling debts—that is, somewhat shady. He dupes people whenever the laws of society admit of his doing so. When he is short of money he borrows in all ways, not always being scrupulous as to tricking the lenders, but he would, with sincere indignation, run his sword through anyone who would even suspect him of lacking in delicacy.

J O S E P H

They were both of them drunk, quite drunk, tiny Baroness Andrée de la Fraisières and little Countess Noemi de Gardens. They had dined alone together in the large room facing the sea. The soft breeze of a summer evening blew in at the open window, soft and fresh at the same time, a breeze that smelled of the sea. The two young women, stretched at length in their lounging chairs, sipped their chartreuse as they smoked their cigarettes, talking most confidentially, telling each other details which nothing but this charming intoxication could have permitted their pretty lips to utter.

Their husbands had returned to Paris that afternoon, leaving them alone in that little watering place which they had chosen so as to avoid those gallant marauders who are constantly encountered at fashionable seaside resorts. As they were absent for five days in the week, they objected to country excursions, luncheons on the grass, swimming lessons and those sudden familiarities which spring up in the idle life of similar resorts. To them Dieppe, Etretat, Trouville, seemed places to be avoided, and they had rented a house which had been built and abandoned by an eccentric individual in the valley of Roqueville, near Fécamp, and there they buried their wives for the whole summer.

The two ladies were drunk. Not knowing what to hit upon to amuse themselves, the little baroness had suggested a good dinner and champagne. To begin with, they had found great amusement in cooking this dinner themselves; then they had eaten it merrily and had imbibed freely, in order to allay the thirst excited by the heat of the fire. Now they were chattering and talking nonsense, from time to time gently moistening their throats with chartreuse. In fact they did not in the least know any longer what they were saying.

The countess, with her feet in the air on the back of a chair, was farther gone than her friend.

"To complete an evening like this," she said, "we ought to have a gallant apiece. Had I foreseen this some time ago, I would have sent to Paris for two men I know and would have let you have one."

"I can always find one," the other replied; "I could have one this very evening if I wished."

"What nonsense! At Roqueville, my dear? It would have to be some peasant then."

"No, not altogether."

"Well, tell me all about it."

"What do you want me to tell you?"

"About your lover."

"My dear, I do not want to live without being loved, for I should fancy I was dead if I were not loved."

"So should I."

"Is not that so?"

"Yes. Men cannot understand it! And especially our husbands!"

"No, not in the least. How can you expect it to be different? The love which we want is made up of being spoiled, of gallantries and of pretty words and actions. That is the nourishment of our hearts; it is indispensable to our life, indispensable, indispensable."

"True, dear."

"I must feel that somebody is thinking of me always, everywhere. When I go to sleep and when I wake up I must know that somebody loves me somewhere, that I am being dreamed of, longed for. Without that I should be wretched, wretched! Oh yes, unhappy enough to do nothing but cry."

"I am just the same."

"You must remember that anything else is impossible. After a husband has been nice for six months, or a year or two years, he usually degenerates into a brute, yes, a regular brute. He won't put himself out for anything but shows his real self; he makes a scene on the slightest provocation and sometimes without any provocation whatever. One cannot love a man with whom one lives constantly."

"That is quite true."

"Isn't it? What was I saying? I cannot in the least remember."

"You were saying that all husbands are brutes!"

"Yes, brutes. All of them."

"That is true."

"And then?"

"What do you mean?"

"What was I saying just then?"

"I don't know, because you did not say it!"

"But I had something to tell you."

"Oh yes; well, go on."

"Oh! I have got it."

"Well, I am listening."

"I was telling you that I can find lovers everywhere."

"How do you manage it?"

"Like this. Now follow me carefully. When I get to some fresh place I take notes and make my choice."

"You make your choice?"

"Yes, of course I do. First of all, I take notes. I ask questions. Above all, a man must be discreet, rich and generous; is not that so?"

"Quite true!"

"And then he must please me, as a man."

"Of course."

"Then I bait the hook for him."

"Bait the hook?"

"Yes, just as one does to catch fish. Have you never fished with a hook and line?"

"No, never."

"You've lost some fun then; it is very amusing, and besides that, instructive. Well then, I bait the hook."

"How do you do it?"

"How dense you are. Don't we catch the men we want to catch without their having any choice? And they really think that they choose—the fools—but it is we who choose—always. Just think, when one is not ugly or stupid, as is the case with us, all men run after us, all—without exception. We look them over from morning till night, and when we have selected one we fish for him."

"But that does not tell me how you do it."

"How I do it! Why, I do nothing; I allow myself to be looked at; that is all."

"Only allow yourself to be looked at?"

"Why, yes; that is quite enough. When you have allowed yourself to be looked at several times a man immediately thinks you the most lovely, the most seductive of women, and then he begins to make love to you. You give him to understand that he is not bad looking, without actually saying anything to him, of course, and he falls in love like a log. You have him fast, and it lasts a longer or a shorter time, according to his qualities."

"And do you catch all whom you please like that?"

"Nearly all."

"Oh! So there are some who resist?"

"Sometimes."

"Why?"

"Oh! A man is a Joseph for three reasons: First, because he is in love with another woman; secondly, because he is excessively timid, or thirdly, because he is —how shall I say it?—incapable of carrying out the conquest of a woman to the end."

"Oh, my dear! Do you really believe——"

"I am sure of it. There are many of this latter class, many, many, many more than people think. Oh, they look just like everybody else—they strut like peacocks. No, when I said peacocks I made a mistake, for they have not a peacock's virility."

"Oh, my dear!"

"As to the timid, they are sometimes unspeakably stupid. They are the sort of men who ought not to undress themselves, even when they are going to bed alone, where there is a looking glass in the room. With them one must be energetic, make use of looks and squeeze their hands, and even that is useless sometimes. They never know how or where to begin. When one faints in their presence—as a last resource—they try to bring you round, and if you do not recover your senses immediately they go and get assistance.

"For myself, I confess to a preference for other women's lovers. I carry them by assault at the point of the bayonet, my dear!"

"That is all very well, but when there are no men, as in this place, for instance?"

"I find them!"

"You find them. But where?"

"Everywhere. But that reminds me of my story.

"Now listen. Just two years ago my husband made me pass the summer on his estate at Bougrolles. There was nothing there—you know what I mean, nothing, nothing, nothing whatever! In the neighboring country houses there were a few disgusting boors, men who cared for nothing but shooting and lived in country houses which had not even a bathroom. They were the sort of men who go to bed covered with perspiration, men you can't improve, because their daily lives are dirty. Now just guess what I did!"

"I cannot possibly."

"Ha! ha! ha! I had just been reading a number of George Sand's novels which exalt the man of the people, novels in which the workmen are sublime and the men of the world are criminals. In addition to this I had seen *Ruy Blas* the winter before, and it had impressed me very much. Well, one of our farmers had a son, a good-looking young fellow of two and twenty who had studied for the priesthood but had left the seminary in disgust. Well, I took him as footman!"

"Oh! And then? What afterward?"

"Then—then, my dear, I treated him very haughtily but let him see a good deal of my person. I did not entice this rustic on; I simply inflamed him!"

"Oh, Andrée!"

"Yes, and I enjoyed the fun very much. People say that servants count for nothing! Well, he did not count for much. I used to give him his orders every morning while my maid was dressing me and every evening as well while she was undressing me."

"Oh, Andrée!"

"My dear, he caught fire like a thatched roof. Then at meals I used continually to talk about cleanliness, about taking care of one's person, about baths and shower baths, until at the end of a fortnight he bathed in the river morning and night and used so much scent as to poison the whole château. I had to forbid him to use perfume, telling him, with furious looks, that men ought never to use any scent but eau de cologne."

"Oh, Andrée!"

"Then I took it into my head to get together a library suitable to the country. I sent for a few hundred moral novels which I lent to all our peasants and all my servants. A few books—a few poetical books, such as excite the minds of schoolboys and schoolgirls, had found their way into my collection. These I gave to my footman. That taught him life—a funny sort of life."

"Oh, Andrée!"

"Then I grew familiar with him and used to 'thou'[1] him. I had given him the name Joseph. My dear, he was in a terrible state. He got as thin as a barn-door cock and rolled his eyes like an idiot. I was extremely amused; it was one of the most delightful summers I ever spent."

"And then?"

"Then? Oh yes, one day when my husband was away from home I told him to order the basket carriage and to drive me into the wood. It was warm, very warm. There!"

"Oh, Andrée, do tell me all about it. It is so amusing."

"Here, have a glass of chartreuse, otherwise I shall empty the decanter myself. Well, I felt ill on the road."

"How?"

"You are dense. I told him that I was not feeling well and that he must lay me on the grass, and when I was lying there I told him I was choking and that he must unlace me. And then when I was unlaced I fainted."

"Did you go right off?"

"Oh, dear, no, not the least."

"Well?"

"Well, I was obliged to remain unconscious for nearly an hour, as he could find no means of bringing me round. But I was very patient and did not open my eyes."

"Oh, Andrée!"

"And what did you say to him?"

[1]The second person singular is used in French—as in German—among relations and intimate friends, and to servants.

"I? Nothing at all! How was I to know anything, as I was unconscious? I thanked him and told him to help me into the carriage, and he drove me back to the château, but he nearly upset us in turning into the gate!"

"Oh, Andrée! And is that all?"

"That is all."

"You did not faint more than that once?"

"Only once, of course! I did not want to take such a fellow for my lover."

"Did you keep him long after that?"

"Yes, of course. I have him still. Why should I have sent him away? I had nothing to complain of."

"Oh, Andrée! And is he in love with you still?"

"Of course he is."

"Where is he?"

The little baroness put out her hand to the wall and touched the electric bell. The door opened almost immediately, and a tall footman came in who diffused a scent of eau de cologne all round him.

"Joseph," said the baroness to him, "I am afraid I am going to faint; send my lady's maid to me."

The man stood motionless, like a soldier before his officer, looking ardently at his mistress who continued: "Be quick, you great idiot, we are not in the wood today, and Rosalie will attend to me better than you can." He turned on his heels and went, and the countess asked nervously: "What shall you say to your maid?"

"I shall tell her what we have been doing! No, I shall merely get her to unlace me; it will relieve my chest, for I can scarcely breathe. I am drunk, my dear—so drunk that I should fall if I were to get up from my chair."

REGRET

M. Savel, who was called in Mantes "Father Savel," had just risen from bed. He wept. It was a dull autumn day; the leaves were falling. They fell slowly in the rain, resembling another rain, but heavier and slower. M. Savel was not in good spirits. He walked from the fireplace to the window and from the window to the fireplace. Life has its somber days. It will no longer have any but somber days of sixty-two. He is alone, an old bachelor, with nobody about him. How sad it is to die alone, all alone, without the disinterested affection of anyone!

He pondered over his life, so barren, so void. He recalled the days gone by, the days of his infancy, the house, the house of his parents, his college days, his follies, the time of his probation in Paris, the illness of his father, his death. He then returned to live with his mother. They lived together, the young man and the old woman, very quietly, and desired nothing more. At last the mother died. How sad a thing is life! He had lived always alone, and now in his turn he, too, would soon be dead. He would disappear, and that would be the finish. There would be no more of Savel upon the earth. What a frightful thing! Other people would live, they would live, they would laugh. Yes, people would go on amusing themselves, and he would no longer exist! Is it not strange that people can laugh, amuse themselves, be joyful under that eternal certainty of death! If this death were only probable, one could then have hope; but no, it is inevitable, as inevitable as that night follows the day.

If, however, his life had been complete! If he had done something; if he had had adventures, grand pleasures, successes, satisfaction of some kind or another. But now, nothing. He had done nothing, never anything but rise from bed, eat at the same hours and go to bed again. And he had gone on like that to the age of sixty-two. He had not even taken unto himself a wife, as other men do. Why? Yes, why was it that he was not married? He might have been, for he possessed considerable means. Was it an opportunity which had failed him? Perhaps! But one can create opportunities. He was indifferent; that was all. Indifference had been his greatest drawback, his defect, his vice. How some men miss their lives through indifference! To certain natures it is so difficult to get out of bed, to move about, to take long walks, to speak, to study any question.

He had not even been in love. No woman had reposed on his bosom in a complete abandon of love. He knew nothing of this delicious anguish of expectation, of the divine quivering of the pressed hand, of the ecstasy of triumphant passion.

What superhuman happiness must inundate your heart when lips encounter lips for the first time, when the grasp of four arms makes one being of you, a being unutterably happy, two beings infatuated with each other.

M. Savel was sitting down, his feet on the fender, in his dressing gown. Assuredly his life had been spoiled, completely spoiled. He had, however, loved. He had loved secretly, dolorously and indifferently, just as was characteristic of him in everything. Yes, he had loved his old friend, Mme Saudres, the wife of his old companion, Saudres. Ah, if he had known her as a young girl! But he had encountered her too late; she was already married. Unquestionably he would have asked her hand; that he would! How he had loved her, nevertheless, without respite, since the first day he had set eyes on her!

He recalled without emotion all the times he had seen her, his grief on leaving her, the many nights that he could not sleep because of his thinking of her.

In the mornings he always got up somewhat less amorous than in the evening.

Why? Seeing that she was formerly pretty and plump, blonde and joyous. Saudres was not the man she would have selected. She was now fifty-two years of age. She seemed happy. Ah, if she had only loved him in days gone by! Yes, if she had only loved him! And why should she not have loved him, he, Savel, seeing that he loved her so much, yes, her, Mme Saudres?

If only she could have divined something! Had she not divined anything; had she not seen anything, never comprehended anything? But then, what would she have thought? If he had spoken what would she have answered?

And Savel asked himself a thousand other things. He reviewed his whole life, seeking to grasp again a multitude of details.

He recalled all the long evenings spent at the house of Saudres, when the latter's wife was young and so charming.

He recalled many things that she had said to him, the sweet intonations of her voice, the little significant smiles that meant so much.

He recalled the walks that the three of them had had, along the banks of the Seine, their lunches on the grass on the Sundays, for Saudres was employed at the subprefecture. And all at once the distinct recollection came to him of an afternoon spent with her in a little plantation on the banks of the river.

They had set out in the morning, carrying their provisions in baskets. It was a bright spring morning, one of those days which inebriate one. Everything smelled fresh; everything seemed happy. The voices of the birds sounded more joyous, and the flapping of their wings more rapid. They had lunch on the grass under the willow trees, quite close to the water, which glittered in the sun's rays. The air was balmy, charged with odors of fresh vegetation; they had drunk the most delicious wines. How pleasant everything was on that day!

After lunch Saudres went to sleep on the broad of his back. "The best nap he had in his life," he said when he woke up.

Mme Saudres had taken the arm of Savel, and they had started to walk along the river's bank.

She leaned tenderly on his arm. She laughed and said to him: "I am intoxicated, my friend, I am quite intoxicated." He looked at her, his heart beating rapidly. He felt himself grow pale, hoping that he had not looked too boldly at her and that the trembling of his hands had not revealed his passion.

She had decked her head with wild flowers and water lilies, and she had asked him: "Do you not like to see me appear thus?"

As he did not answer—for he could find nothing to say; he should rather have gone down on his knees—she burst out laughing, a sort of discontented laughter which she threw straight in his face, saying: "Great goose, what ails you? You might at least speak!"

He felt like crying and could not even yet find a word to say.

All these things came back to him now as vividly as on the day when they took place. Why had she said this to him, "Great goose, what ails you? You might at least speak!"

And he recalled how tenderly she had leaned on his arm. And in passing under a shady tree he had felt her ear leaning against his cheek, and he had tilted his head abruptly, for fear that she had not meant to bring their flesh into contact.

When he had said to her: "Is it not time to return?" she darted at him a singular look. "Certainly," she said, "certainly," regarding him at the same time in a curious manner. He had not thought of anything then, and now the whole thing appeared to him quite plain.

"Just as you like, my friend. If you are tired let us go back."

And he answered:

"It is not that I am fatigued, but Saudres has perhaps waked up now."

And she had said: "If you are afraid of my husband's being awake, that is another thing. Let us return."

In returning she remained silent and leaned no longer on his arm. Why?

At this time it had never occurred to him to ask himself, "Why?" Now he seemed to apprehend something that he had not then understood.

What was it?

M. Savel felt himself blush, and he got up at a bound, feeling thirty years younger, believing that he now understood Mme Saudres then to say, "I love you."

Was it possible? That suspicion which had just entered into his soul tortured him. Was it possible that he could not have seen, not have dreamed?

Oh, if that could be true, if he had rubbed against such good fortune without laying hold of it!

He said to himself: "I wish to know. I cannot remain in this state of doubt. I wish to know!" He put on his clothes quickly, dressed in hot haste. He thought: "I am sixty-two years of age; she is fifty-two; I may ask her that now without giving offense."

He started out.

The Saudres' house was situated on the other side of the street, almost directly opposite his own. He went up to it, knocked, and a little servant came to open the door.

"You there at this hour, Monsieur Savel? Has some accident happened to you?"

M. Savel responded:

"No, my girl, but go and tell your mistress that I want to speak to her at once."

"The fact is, Madame is preparing her stock of pear jams for the winter, and she is standing in front of the fire. She is not dressed, as you may well understand."

"Yes, but go and tell her that I wish to see her on an important matter."

The little servant went away, and Savel began to walk with long, nervous strides up and down the drawing room. He did not feel himself the least embarrassed, however. Oh, he was merely going to ask her something, as he would have asked her about some cooking recipe, and that was: "Do you know that I am sixty-two years of age?"

The door opened and Madame appeared. She was now a gross woman, fat and round, with full cheeks and a sonorous laugh. She walked with her arms away from her body and her sleeves tucked up to the shoulders, her bare arms all smeared with sugar juice. She asked anxiously:

"What is the matter with you, my friend; you are not ill, are you?"

"No, my dear friend, but I wish to ask you one thing which to me is of the first importance, something which is torturing my heart, and I want you to promise that you will answer me candidly."

She laughed. "I am always candid. Say on."

"Well then. I have loved you from the first day I ever saw you. Can you have any doubt of this?"

She responded, laughing, with something of her former tone of voice:

"Great goose! What ails you? I knew it well from the very first day!"

Savel began to tremble. He stammered out: "You knew it? Then——"

He stopped.

She asked:

"Then what?"

He answered:

"Then—what would you think?—what—what—what would you have answered?"

She broke forth into a peal of laughter, which made the sugar juice run off the tips of her fingers onto the carpet.

"I? But you did not ask me anything. It was not for me to make a declaration."

He then advanced a step toward her.

"Tell me—tell me—— You remember the day when Saudres went to sleep on the grass after lunch—when we had walked together as far as the bend of the river, below——"

He waited expectantly. She had ceased to laugh and looked at him straight in the eyes.

"Yes, certainly. I remember it."

He answered, shivering all over.

"Well, that day—if I had been—if I had been—enterprising—what would you have done?"

She began to laugh as only a happy woman can laugh who has nothing to regret and responded frankly in a voice tinged with irony:

"I would have yielded, my friend."

She then turned on her heels and went back to her jam making.

Savel rushed into the street, cast down, as though he had encountered some great disaster. He walked with giant strides through the rain, straight on, until he reached the river, without thinking where he was going. When he reached the bank he turned to the right and followed it. He walked a long time, as if urged on by some instinct. His clothes were running with water; his hat was crushed in, as soft as a piece of rag and dripping like a thatched roof. He walked on, straight in front of him. At last he came to the place where they had lunched so long, long ago, the recollection of which had tortured his heart. He sat down under the leafless trees and wept.

THE DEAF-MUTE

My dear friend, you ask me why I do not return to Paris; you will be astonished and almost angry, I suppose, when I give you the reason, which will, without doubt, be revolting to you: "Why should a hunter return to Paris at the height of the woodcock season?"

Certainly I understand and like life in the city very well, that life which leads from the chamber to the sidewalk, but I prefer a freer life, the rude life of the hunter in autumn.

In Paris it seems to me that I am never out of doors; for, in fact, the streets are only great, common apartments without a ceiling. Is one in the air between two walls, his feet upon stone or wooden pavement, his view shut in everywhere by buildings, without any horizon of verdure, fields or wood? Thousands of neighbors jostle you, push you, salute you and talk with you, but the fact of receiving water upon an umbrella when it rains is not sufficient to give me the impression or the sensation of space.

Here I perceive clearly and deliciously the difference between indoors and out. But it was not of that that I wish to speak to you.

Well then, the woodcocks are flying.

And it is necessary to tell you that I live in a great Norman house, in a valley, near a little river, and that I hunt nearly every day.

Other days I read; I even read things that men in Paris have not the time to become acquainted with, very serious things, very profound, very curious, written by a brave, scholarly genius, a foreigner who has spent his life studying the subject and observing the facts relative to the influence of the functions of our organs upon our intelligence.

But I was speaking to you of woodcocks.

My two friends, the D'Orgemol brothers, and myself remain here during the hunting season, awaiting the first frost. Then when it freezes we set out for their farm in Cannetot, near Fécamp, because there is a delicious little wood there, a divine wood, where every woodcock that flies comes to lodge.

You know the D'Orgemols, those two giants, those Normans of ancient times, those two males of the old, powerful conquering race which invaded France, took England and kept it, established itself on every coast of the world, made towns everywhere, passed like a flood over Sicily, creating there an admirable art, struck down kings, pillaged the proudest cities, matched popes in their priestly tricks and ridiculed them, more sly than the Italian pontiffs themselves, and above all, left children in all the beds of the world. These D'Orgemols are two Normans of the best stamp and are all Norman—voice, accent, mind, blond hair and eyes, which are the color of the sea.

When we are together we talk the patois; we live, think and act in Norman; we become Norman landowners, more peasants than farmers.

For two weeks now we have been waiting for woodcocks. Every morning Simon, the elder, will say: "Hey! Here's the wind coming round to the east, and it's going to freeze. In two days they will be here."

The younger, Gaspard, more exact, waits for the frost to come before he announces it.

But last Thursday he entered my room at dawn, crying out:

"It has come! The earth is all white. Two days more and we shall go to Cannetot."

Two days later, in fact, we do set out for Cannetot. Certainly you would have laughed to see us. We take our places in a strange sort of hunting wagon that my father had constructed long ago. Constructed is the only word that I can use in speaking of this monstrous carriage, or rather this earthquake on wheels. There was room for everything inside: a place for provisions, a place for the guns, place for the trunks and places of clear space for the dogs. Everything is sheltered except the men, perched on seats as high as a third story, and all this supported by four gigantic wheels. One mounted as best he could, making his feet, hands and even his teeth serve him for the occasion, for there was no step to give access to the edifice.

Now the two D'Orgemols and myself scaled this mountain, clothed like Laplanders. We have on sheepskins, wear enormous, woolen stockings outside our pantaloons and gaiters outside our woolen stockings; we also have some black fur caps and white fur gloves. When we are installed, John, my servant, throws us our three terriers, Pif, Paf and Mustache. Pif belongs to Simon, Paf to Gaspard and Mustache to me. They look like three crocodiles covered with hair. They are long, low, and crooked, with bent legs and so hairy that they have the look of a yellow thicket. Their eyes can scarcely be seen under their eyebrows, or their teeth through their beards. One could never shut them into the rolling kennels of the carriage. Each one puts his own dog under his feet to keep him warm.

And now we are off, shivering abominably. It is cold and freezing hard. We are contented. Toward five o'clock we arrive. The farmer, Master Picot, is expecting us, waiting before the door. He is also a jolly fellow, not tall, but round, squat, vigorous as a bulldog, sly as a fox, always laughing, always contented, knowing how to make money out of all of us.

It is a great festival for him when the woodcock arrives. The farm is large, and on it an old building set in an apple orchard, surrounded by four rows of beech trees, which battle against the winds from the sea all the year.

We enter the kitchen where a bright fire is burning in our honor. Our table is set against the high chimney, where a large chicken is turning and roasting before the clear flame, and whose gravy is running into an earthen dish beneath.

The farmer's wife salutes us, a tall, quiet woman, wholly occupied with the cares of her house, her head full of accounts, the price of grain, of poultry, of mutton and beef. She is an orderly woman, set and severe, known for her worth in the neighborhood.

At the end of the kitchen is set the long table where all the farm hands, drivers, laborers, stableboys, shepherds and women servants sit down. They eat in silence under the active eye of the mistress, watching us dine with Master Picot, who says witty things to make us laugh. Then, when all her servants are fed, Mme Picot takes her repast alone at one corner of the table, a rapid and frugal repast, watching the serving maid meanwhile. On ordinary days she dines with all the rest.

We all three sleep, the D'Orgemols and myself, in a bare, white room, white-washed with lime, containing only our three beds, three chairs and three basins.

Gaspard always wakes first and sounds the echoing watchword. In half an hour everybody is ready, and we set out with Master Picot who hunts with us.

M. Picot prefers me to his masters. Why? Without doubt because I am not his master. So we two reach the woods by the right, while the two brothers come to the attack by the left. Simon has the care of the dogs, all three attached to the end of a rope.

For we are not hunting woodcock but the wolf. We are convinced that it is better to find the woodcock than to seek it. If one falls upon one and kills it, there you are! But when one specially wishes to meet one, he can never quite bring him down. It is truly a beautiful and curious thing, hearing the loud report of a gun in the fresh morning air and then the formidable voice of Gaspard filling the space as he howls:

"Woodcock! There it is."

As for me, I am sly. When I have killed a woodcock I cry out: "Wolf!" And then I triumph in my success when we go to a clear place for the midday lunch.

Here we are then, Master Picot and I, in the little woods, where the leaves fall with a sweet and continued murmur, with a dry murmur, a little sad, for they are dead. It is cold, a light cold which stings the eyes, the nose and the ears and powders with a fine, white moss the limbs of the trees and the brown, plowed earth. But there is warmth through all our limbs under the great sheepskin. The sun is gay in the blue air which it warms scarcely at all, but it is gay. It is good to hunt in the woods on fresh mornings in winter.

Down below a dog is loudly baying. It is Pif. I know his thin voice, but it ceases. Then there is another cry and then another, and Paf in his turn begins to bark. And what has become of Mustache? Ah, there is a little cry like that of a chicken being strangled! They have stirred up a wolf. Attention, Master Picot!

They separate, then approach each other, scatter again and then return; we follow their unforeseen windings, coming out into little roads, the mind on the alert, finger on the trigger of the gun.

They turn toward the fields again, and we turn also. Suddenly there is a gray spot, a shadow, crossing the bypath. I aim and fire. The light smoke rises in the blue air, and I perceive under a bush a bit of white hair which moves. Then I shout with all my force, "Wolf, wolf! There he is!" And I show him to the three dogs, the three hairy crocodiles, who thank me by wagging their tails. Then they go off in search of another.

Master Picot joins me. Mustache begins to yap. The farmer says: "There must be a hare there at the edge of the field."

The moment that I came out of the wood I perceived, not ten steps from me, enveloped in his immense, yellowish mantle and wearing his knitted, woolen cap such as shepherds wear at home, Master Picot's herdsman Gargan, the deaf-mute. I said, "Good morning," to him, according to our custom, and he raised his hand to salute me. He had not heard my voice, but had seen the motion of my lips.

For fifteen years I had known this shepherd. For fifteen years I had seen him each autumn on the border or in the middle of the field, his body motionless and always knitting in his hands. His flock followed him like a pack of hounds, seeming to obey his eye.

Master Picot now took me by the arm, saying:

"Did you know that the shepherd killed his wife?"

I was stupefied. "What, Gargan—the deaf-mute?"

"Yes, this winter, and his case was tried at Rouen. I will tell you about it."

And he led me into the underbrush, for the shepherd knew how to catch words from his master's lips, as if he heard them spoken. He could understand only him; but, watching his face closely, he was no longer deaf, and the master, on the other hand, seemed to divine, like a sorcerer, the meaning of all the mute's pantomime, the gestures of his fingers, the expression of his face and the motion of his eyes.

Here is his simple story, the various, somber facts as they came to pass:

Gargan was the son of a marl digger, one of those men who go down into the marlpit to extract that kind of soft, dissolving stone, sown under the soil. A deaf-mute by birth, he had been brought up to watch the cows along the ditches by the side of the roads.

Then, picked up by Picot's father, he had become the shepherd on his farm. He was an excellent shepherd, devout, upright, knowing how to find the lost members of his flock, although nobody had taught him anything.

When Picot took the farm in his turn, Gargan was thirty years old and looked forty. He was tall, thin and bearded—bearded like a patriarch.

About this time a good woman of the country, Mme Martel, died very poor, leaving a girl fifteen years old who was called "Drops," because of her immoderate love for brandy.

Picot took in this ragged waif, employed her in light duties, giving her a home without pay in return for her work. She slept under the barn, in the stable or the cow house, upon straw or on the manure heap, anywhere, it mattered not where, for they could not give a bed to this barefoot. She slept, then, no matter where, with no matter whom, perhaps with the plowman or the stableboy. But it happened soon that she gave her attention to the deaf-mute and coupled herself with him in a continued fashion. What united these two miserable beings? How had they understood each other? Had he ever known a woman before this barn rover, he who had never talked with anyone? Was it she who found him in his wheeled hut and seduced him, like an Eve of the rut, at the edge of the road? No one knows. They only know that one day they were living together as husband and wife.

No one was astonished by it, and Picot found it a very natural coupling. But the curate heard of this union without a Mass and was angry. He reproached Mme

Picot, disturbed her conscience and threatened her with mysterious punishments. What was to be done? It was very simple. They must go and be married at the church and at the mayor's. They had nothing, either of them: he, not a whole pair of pantaloons, she, not a petticoat of a single kind of cloth. So there was nothing to oppose what the law and religion required. They were united in an hour before the mayor and the curate and believed that all was regulated for the best.

Now it soon became a joke in the country (pardon the villainous word) to make a deceived husband of this poor Gargan. Before she was married, no one thought of sleeping with "Drops," but now each one wished his turn, for the sake of a laughable story. Everybody went there for a little glass behind the husband's back. The affair made so much noise that even some of the Goderville gentlemen came to see her.

For a half pint "Drops" would finish the spectacle with no matter whom, in a ditch, behind a wall, anywhere, while the silhouette of the motionless Gargan could be seen knitting a stocking not a hundred feet from there, surrounded by his bleating flock. And they laughed about it enough to make themselves ill in all the cafés of the country. It was the only thing talked of in the evening before the fire, and upon the road the first thing one would ask: "Have you paid your drop to 'Drops'?" Everyone knew what that meant.

The shepherd never seemed to see anything. But one day the Poirot boy, of Sasseville, called to Gargan's wife from behind the mill, showing her a full bottle. She understood and ran to him, laughing. Now scarcely were they engaged in their criminal deed when the herdsman fell upon them as if he had come out of a cloud. Poirot fled at full speed, his breeches about his heels, while the deaf-mute, with a cry of a beast, sprang at his wife's throat.

The people working in the fields ran toward them. It was too late; her tongue was black; her eyes were coming out of her head; the blood was flowing from her nose. She was dead.

The shepherd was tried by the judge at Rouen. As he was a mute, Picot served as interpreter. The details of the affair amused the audience very much. But the farmer had but one idea: his herdsman must be acquitted. And he went about it in earnest.

At first he related the deaf-mute's whole story, including that of his marriage; then when he came to the crime, he himself questioned the assassin.

The assemblage was very quiet.

Picot pronounced the words slowly: "Did you know that she had deceived you?" And at the same time he asked the question with his eyes in pantomime.

The other answered "No" with his head.

"Were you asleep in the mill when you surprised her?" And he made a gesture of a man seeing some disgusting thing.

The other answered "Yes" with his head.

Then the farmer, imitating the signs of the mayor who married them and of the priest who united them in the name of God, asked his servant if he had killed his wife because she was bound to him before men and before heaven.

The shepherd answered "Yes" with his head.

Picot then said to him: "Come, tell us how it happened."

Then the deaf-mute reproduced the whole scene in pantomime. He showed how he was asleep in the mill, that he was awakened by feeling the straw move, that he had watched quietly and had seen the whole thing.

He rose between the two policemen and brusquely imitated the obscene movement of the criminal couple entangled before him.

A tumultuous laugh went through the hall then stopped short, for the herdsman, with haggard eyes, moving his jaw and his great beard as if he had bitten something, with arms extended and head thrown forward, repeated the terrible action of a murderer who strangles a being.

And he howled frightfully, so excited with anger that one would think he believed he still held her in his grasp, and the policemen were obliged to seize him and seat him by force in order to calm him.

A great shiver of agony ran through the assembly. Then Master Picot, placing his hand upon his servant's shoulder, said simply: "He knows what honor is, this man does."

And the shepherd was acquitted.

As for me, my dear friend, I listened to this adventure to its close, much moved, and have related it to you in gross terms in order not to change the farmer's story. But now there is a report of a gun from the woods, and the formidable voice of Gaspard is heard growling in the wind, like the sound of a cannon:

"Woodcock! There is one."

And this is how I employ my time, watching for the woodcock to pass, while you are also going to the Bois to see the first winter costumes.

AT THE CHURCH DOOR

He used to live in a little house near the main road at the entrance to a village. After he married the daughter of a farmer in the district he set up as a wheelwright, and as they both worked hard, they amassed a small fortune. But one thing caused them great sorrow; they had no children. At last a child was born to them, and they called him Jean. They showered kisses upon him, wrapped him up in their affection, and became so fond of him that they could not let an hour pass without seeing him. When he was five years old a circus passed through the village and pitched its tent on the square in front of the town hall.

Jean had seen them and had slipped out of the house. After a long search his father discovered him in the midst of the trained goats and dogs. He was sitting on the knee of an old clown and was shouting with laughter.

Three days later, at dinnertime, just as they were sitting down to table, the wheelwright and his wife discovered that their son was not in the house. They looked in the garden, and as they did not find him there, the father went to the roadside and shouted with all his might: "Jean!"

Night was falling, and a brownish mist filled the horizon, and everything retreated into the dark and gloomy distance. Three tall fir trees close by seemed to be weeping. No voice replied, but the air was full of vague moaning. The father listened for a long time, believing that he could hear something, now on his right, now on his left, and he plunged wildly into the night, calling incessantly: "Jean! Jean!"

He ran on until daybreak, filling the shadows with his cries, frightening the prowling animals, his heart torn by a terrible anguish, so that at times he thought he was going mad. His wife remained seated at the door and wept until morning. Their son was never found.

From that time they aged rapidly in their sorrow, which nothing could console. Finally they sold their house and set out to look for their son themselves. They questioned the shepherds on the hills, the passing tradesmen, the peasants in the villages and the authorities in the towns. But it was a long time since their son had been lost. Nobody knew anything, and probably he himself had now forgotten his name and his birthplace. They wept and lost all hope. Very soon their money was exhausted, and they hired themselves out by the day to the farmers and innkeepers, discharging the most humble tasks, living on the leavings of others, sleeping out of doors, and suffering from cold. But as they became feeble from overwork, nobody would employ them, and they were compelled to beg along the roads. They accosted travelers with sad faces and supplicating voices, imploring a piece of bread from the harvesters eating their dinner beneath a tree, at midday in the fields. They devoured it in silence, seated on the edge of the ditches. An innkeeper to whom they related their misfortunes, said to them one day:

"I also knew someone who lost a daughter; it was in Paris he found her."

Immediately they set out for Paris.

When they reached the great city they were frightened by its size and by the crowds in the streets. But they realized that he must be amongst all these people, without knowing how to set about finding him. Then they were afraid they would not recognize him, for they had not seen him for fifteen years. They visited every street and square, stopping wherever they saw a crowd gathered, in the hope of a chance meeting, some prodigious stroke of luck, an act of pity on the part of Fate. They would often wander blindly ahead, clinging to each other, and looking so sad and so poor that people gave them alms without being asked. Every Sunday they spent the day in front of the churches, watching the crowds going in and out, and scanning each face for a distant resemblance. Several times they fancied they recognized him, but they were always mistaken.

At the door of one of the churches to which they returned most frequently there was an old man who sprinkled holy water, and who had become their friend. His own story was also very sad, and their commiseration for him led to a great friendship between them. They finally lived together in a wretched garret at the top of a big house, a great distance out, near the open fields, and sometimes the wheelwright took his new friend's place at the church, when the old man was ill. One very harsh winter came, the old sprinkler of holy water died, and the parish priest appointed in his place the wheelwright, of whose misfortunes he had heard.

Then he came every morning and seated himself in the same place, on the same chair, wearing out the old stone column against which he leaned with the continual rubbing of his back. He gazed fixedly at every man who entered, and he looked forward to Sunday with the impatience of a schoolboy, because that was the day when the church was constantly full of people.

He grew very old, getting weaker and weaker under the damp arches, and every day his hope crumbled away. By this time he knew everyone who came to mass, their hours, their habits, and he could recognize their steps on the tiled floor. His life had become so narrowed that it was a great event for him when a stranger entered the church. One day two ladies came; one old and the other young. Probably a mother and daughter, he thought. Behind them a young man appeared, who followed them, and when they went out he saluted them. After having offered them holy water he took the arm of the older lady.

"That must be the young lady's intended," thought the wheelwright.

For the rest of the day he racked his memory to discover where he once had seen a young man like that. But the one he was thinking of must now be an old man, for he seemed to have known him away back in his youth.

The same man came back frequently to escort the two ladies, and this vague resemblance, remote yet familiar, which he could not identify, obsessed the old man so much that he made his wife come to aid his feeble memory.

One evening, as it was getting dark, the strangers entered together. When they had passed, the husband said:

"Well, do you know who he is?"

His wife was troubled and tried, in turn, to remember. Suddenly she whispered:

"Yes . . . yes . . . but he is darker, taller, stronger, and dressed like a gentleman, yet, father, he has the same face, you know, as you had when you were young."

The old man gave a start.

It was true, the young man resembled him, and he resembled his brother who was dead, and his father, whom he remembered while he was still young. They were so deeply stirred that they could not speak. The three people were coming down the aisle and going out. The man touched the sprinkler with his finger, and the old man who was holding it shook so much that the holy water rained upon the ground.

"Jean?" he cried.

The man stopped and looked at him.

"Jean?" he repeated softly.

The two ladies looked at him in astonishment.

Then for the third time he said, sobbing: "Jean?"

The man stooped and looked closely into his face, then a recollection of childhood flashed in his mind, and he replied:

"Father Pierre and Mother Jeanne!"

He had forgotten everything, his father's other name, and that of his own birthplace, but he still remembered these two words, so often repeated: "Father Pierre; Mother Jeanne!"

He knelt down with his head on the knees of the old man and wept. Then he kissed his father and mother by turns, while their voices were choked by joy unlimited. The two ladies also cried, for they realized that great happiness had come. They all went home with the young man, who told them his story.

The circus people had kidnaped him, and for three years he had traveled with them through many countries. Then the company broke up, and one day an old lady in a château gave a sum of money to adopt him, because she liked him. As he was intelligent, they sent him to school and college, and, as the old lady had no children, she left her fortune to him. He also had searched for his parents, but as the only thing he could remember was the two names, "Father Pierre and Mother Jeanne," he could not discover them. Now he was going to be married, and he introduced his fiancée, who was as good as she was pretty.

When the two old people, in their turn, had related their sorrows and sufferings, they embraced him again, and that night they stayed awake very late, for they were afraid to go to bed lest happiness, which had evaded them so long, should abandon them once more, when they were asleep. But they had exhausted the endurance of misfortune, and lived happily till the end.

MAGNETISM

It was at the close of a dinner party of men, at the hour of endless cigars and incessant sips of brandy, amid the smoke and the torpid warmth of digestion and the slight confusion of heads generated by such a quantity of eatables and by the absorption of so many different liquors.

Those present were talking about magnetism, about Donato's tricks and about Dr Charcot's experiences. All of a sudden those men, so skeptical, so happy go lucky, so indifferent to religion of every sort, began telling stories about strange occurrences, incredible things which nevertheless had really happened, they contended, falling back into superstitions, beliefs, clinging to these last remnants of the marvelous, becoming devotees to this mystery of magnetism, defending it in the name of science. There was only one person who smiled, a vigorous young fellow, a great pursuer of girls of light behavior and a hunter also of frisky matrons, in whose mind there was so much incredulity about everything that he would not even enter upon a discussion of such matters.

He repeated with a sneer:

"Humbug! Humbug! Humbug! We need not discuss Donato, who is merely a very smart juggler. As for Monsieur Charcot, who is said to be a remarkable man of science, he produces on me the effect of those storytellers of the school of Edgar Allan Poe who go mad through constantly reflecting on queer cases of insanity. He has set forth some nervous phenomena, which are unexplained and inexplicable; he makes his way into that unknown region which men explore every day and, not being able to comprehend what he sees, he remembers perhaps too well the explanations of certain mysteries given by priests. Besides, I would like to hear him speak on these subjects; that would be quite a different thing from your repetition of what he says."

The words of the unbeliever were listened to with a kind of pity, as if he had blasphemed in the midst of an assembly of monks.

One of these gentlemen exclaimed:

"And yet miracles were performed in former days."

But the other replied: "I deny it. Why cannot they be performed any longer?"

Thereupon each man referred to some fact, or some fantastic presentiment, or some instance of souls communicating with each other across space or some use of secret influences produced by one being or another. And they asserted, they maintained, that these things had actually occurred, while the skeptic went on repeating energetically: "Humbug! Humbug! Humbug!"

At last he rose up, threw away his cigar and with his hands in his pockets said: "Well, I, too, am going to relate to you two stories, and then I will explain them to you. Here they are:

"In the little village of Etretat the men, who are all seafaring folk, go every year to Newfoundland to fish for cod. Now one night the little son of one of these fishermen woke up with a start, crying out that his father was dead. The child was quieted, and again he woke up, exclaiming that his father was drowned. A month later the news came that his father had, in fact, been swept off the deck of his smack by a billow. The widow then remembered how her son had awaked and spoken of his father's death. Everyone said it was a miracle, and the affair caused a great sensation. The dates were compared, and it was found that the accident and the dream had very nearly coincided, whence they drew the conclusion that they had happened on the same night and at the same hour. And there is the mystery of magnetism."

The storyteller stopped suddenly.

Thereupon one of those who had heard him, much affected by the narrative, asked:

"And can you explain this?"

"Perfectly, monsieur. I have discovered the secret. The circumstance surprised me and even embarrassed me very much, but I, you see, do not believe on principle. Just as others begin by believing, I begin by doubting, and when I don't at all understand, I continue to deny that there can be any telepathic communication between souls, certain that my own sagacity will be enough to explain it. Well, I have gone on inquiring into the matter, and I have ended, by dint of questioning all the wives of the absent seamen, in convincing myself that not a week passes without one of themselves or their children dreaming and declaring when they wake that the father was drowned. The horrible and continual fear of this accident makes them always talk about it. Now if one of these frequent predictions coincides, by a very simple chance, with the death of the person referred to, people at once declare it to be a miracle, for they suddenly lose sight of all the other predictions of misfortune that have remained unconfirmed. I have myself known fifty cases where the persons who made the prediction forgot all about it in a week afterward. But if, in fact, the man was dead, then the recollection of the thing immediately revived, and people will be ready to believe in the intervention of God, according to some, and in magnetism, according to others."

One of the smokers remarked:

"What you say is right enough, but what about your second story?"

"Oh, my second story is a very delicate matter to relate. It is to myself it happened, and so I don't place any great value on my own view of the matter. One is never a good judge in a case where he is one of the parties concerned. At any rate, here it is:

"Among my acquaintances in society there was a young woman on whom I had never bestowed a thought, whom I had never even looked at attentively, never taken any notice of, as the saying is.

"I classed her among the women of no importance, though she was not quite bad looking; in fact, she appeared to me to possess eyes, a nose, a mouth, some sort of hair—just a colorless type of countenance. She was one of those beings on whom one only thinks by accident, without taking any particular interest in the individual, and who never excites desire.

"Well, one night as I was writing some letters by my own fireside before going to bed, I was conscious, in the midst of that train of sensual images that sometimes float before one's brain in moments of idle reverie, while I held the pen in my hand, of a kind of light breath passing into my soul, a little shudder of the heart and immediately, without reason, without any logical connection of thought, I saw distinctly, saw as if I had touched her, saw from head to foot, uncovered, this young woman for whom I had never cared save in the most superficial manner when her name happened to recur to my mind. And all of a sudden I discovered in her a heap of qualities which I had never before observed, a sweet charm, a fascination that made me languish; she awakened in me that sort of amorous uneasiness which sends you in pursuit of a woman. But I did not remain thinking of her long. I went to bed and was soon asleep. And I dreamed.

"You have all had these strange dreams which render you masters of the impossible, which open to you doors that cannot be passed through, unexpected joys, impenetrable arms!

"Which of us in these agitated, exciting, palpitating slumbers has not held, clasped, embraced, possessed with an extraordinary acuteness of sensation the woman with whom our minds were occupied? And have you ever noticed what superhuman delight these good fortunes of dreams bestow upon us? Into what mad intoxication they cast you! With what passionate spasms they shake you! With what infinite, caressing, penetrating tenderness they fill your heart for her whom you hold fainting and hot in that adorable and sensual illusion which seems so like reality!

"All this I felt with unforgettable violence. This woman was mine, so much mine that the pleasant warmth of her skin remained between my fingers; the odor of her skin remained in my brain; the taste of her kisses remained on my lips; the sound of her voice lingered in my ears; the touch of her clasp still clung to my side, and the burning charm of her tenderness still gratified my senses long after my exquisite but disappointing awakening.

"And three times the same night I had a renewal of my dream.

"When the day dawned she beset me, possessed me, haunted my brain and my flesh to such an extent that I no longer remained one second without thinking of her.

"At last, not knowing what to do, I dressed myself and went to see her. As I went up the stairs to her apartment I was so much overcome by emotion that I trembled and my heart panted; I was seized with vehement desire from head to foot.

"I entered the apartment. She rose up the moment she heard my name pronounced, and suddenly our eyes met in a fixed look of astonishment.

"I sat down.

"I uttered in a faltering tone some commonplaces which she seemed not to hear. I did not know what to say or to do. Then abruptly I flung myself upon her, seizing her with both arms, and my entire dream was accomplished so quickly, so easily, so madly, that I suddenly began to doubt whether I was really awake. She was, after this, my mistress for two years."

"What conclusion do you draw from it?" said a voice.

The storyteller seemed to hesitate.

"The conclusion I draw from it—well, by Jove, the conclusion is that it was just a coincidence! And in the next place, who can tell? Perhaps it was some glance of hers which I had not noticed and which came back that night to me—one of those mysterious and unconscious evocations of memory which often brings before us things ignored by our own consciousness, unperceived by our minds!"

"Let that be just as you wish it," said one of his table companions when the story was finished, "but if you don't believe in magnetism after that, you are an ungrateful fellow, my dear boy!"

THE FALSE GEMS

M. Lantin had met the young woman at a soiree at the home of the assistant chief of his bureau and at first sight had fallen madly in love with her.

She was the daughter of a country physician who had died some months previously. She had come to live in Paris with her mother, who visited much among her acquaintances, in the hope of making a favorable marriage for her daughter. They were poor and honest, quiet and unaffected.

The young girl was a perfect type of the virtuous woman whom every sensible young man dreams of one day winning for life. Her simple beauty had the charm of angelic modesty, and the imperceptible smile which constantly hovered about her lips seemed to be the reflection of a pure and lovely soul. Her praises resounded on every side. People were never tired of saying: "Happy the man who wins her love! He could not find a better wife."

Now M. Lantin enjoyed a snug little income of seven hundred dollars and, thinking he could safely assume the responsibilities of matrimony, proposed to this model young girl and was accepted.

He was unspeakably happy with her; she governed his household so cleverly and economically that they seemed to live in luxury. She lavished the most delicate attentions on her husband, coaxed and fondled him, and the charm of her presence was so great that six years after their marriage M. Lantin discovered that he loved his wife even more than during the first days of their honeymoon.

He only felt inclined to blame her for two things: her love of the theater and a taste for false jewelry. Her friends (she was acquainted with some officers' wives) frequently procured for her a box at the theater, often for the first representations of the new plays, and her husband was obliged to accompany her, whether he willed or not, to these amusements, though they bored him excessively after a day's labor at the office.

After a time M. Lantin begged his wife to get some lady of her acquaintance to accompany her. She was at first opposed to such an arrangement, but, after much persuasion on his part, she finally consented—to the infinite delight of her husband.

Now with her love for the theater came also the desire to adorn her person. True, her costumes remained as before, simple and in the most correct taste, but she soon began to ornament her ears with huge rhinestones which glittered and sparkled like real diamonds. Around her neck she wore strings of false pearls, and on her arms bracelets of imitation gold.

Her husband frequently remonstrated with her, saying:

"My dear, as you cannot afford to buy real diamonds, you ought to appear adorned with your beauty and modesty alone, which are the rarest ornaments of your sex."

But she would smile sweetly and say:

"What can I do? I am so fond of jewelry. It is my only weakness. We cannot change our natures."

Then she would roll the pearl necklaces around her fingers and hold up the bright gems for her husband's admiration, gently coaxing him.

"Look! Are they not lovely? One would swear they were real."

M. Lantin would then answer smilingly:

"You have Bohemian tastes, my dear."

Often of an evening, when they were enjoying a tête-à-tête by the fireside, she would place on the tea table the leather box containing the "trash," as M. Lantin called it. She would examine the false gems with a passionate attention, as though they were in some way connected with a deep and secret joy, and she often insisted on passing a necklace around her husband's neck and, laughing heartily, would exclaim: "How droll you look!" Then she would throw herself into his arms and kiss him affectionately.

One evening in winter she attended the opera and on her return was chilled through and through. The next morning she coughed, and eight days later she died of inflammation of the lungs.

M. Lantin's despair was so great that his hair became white in one month. He wept unceasingly; his heart was torn with grief, and his mind was haunted by the remembrance, the smile, the voice—by every charm of his beautiful dead wife.

Time, the healer, did not assuage his grief. Often during office hours, while his colleagues were discussing the topics of the day, his eyes would suddenly fill with tears, and he would give vent to his grief in heart-rending sobs. Everything in his wife's room remained as before her decease, and here he was wont to seclude himself daily and think of her who had been his treasure—the joy of his existence.

But life soon became a struggle. His income, which in the hands of his wife had covered all household expenses, was now no longer sufficient for his own immediate wants, and he wondered how she could have managed to buy such excellent wines and such rare delicacies, things which he could no longer procure with his modest resources.

He incurred some debts and was soon reduced to absolute poverty. One morning, finding himself without a cent in his pocket, he resolved to sell something, and immediately the thought occurred to him of disposing of his wife's paste jewels. He cherished in his heart a sort of rancor against the false gems. They had always irritated him in the past, and the very sight of them spoiled somewhat the memory of his lost darling.

To the last days of her life she had continued to make purchases, bringing home new gems almost every evening. He decided to sell the heavy necklace which she seemed to prefer and which, he thought, ought to be worth about six or seven francs, for although paste it was, nevertheless, of very fine workmanship.

He put it in his pocket and started out in search of a jeweler's shop. He entered the first one he saw, feeling a little ashamed to expose his misery and also to offer such a worthless article for sale.

"Sir," he said to the merchant, "I would like to know what this is worth."

The man took his necklace, examined it, called his clerk and made some remarks in an undertone; then he put the ornament back on the counter and looked at it from a distance to judge of the effect.

M. Lantin was annoyed by all this detail and was on the point of saying: "Oh! I know well enough it is not worth anything," when the jeweler said: "Sir, that necklace is worth from twelve to fifteen thousand francs, but I could not buy it unless you tell me now whence it comes."

The widower opened his eyes wide and remained gaping, not comprehending the merchant's meaning. Finally he stammered: "You say—are you sure?" The other replied dryly: "You can search elsewhere and see if anyone will offer you more. I consider it worth fifteen thousand at the most. Come back here if you cannot do better."

M. Lantin, beside himself with astonishment, took up the necklace and left the store. He wished time for reflection.

Once outside, he felt inclined to laugh and said to himself: "The fool! Had I only taken him at his word! That jeweler cannot distinguish real diamonds from paste."

A few minutes after, he entered another store in the Rue de la Paix. As soon as the proprietor glanced at the necklace he cried out:

"Ah, *parbleu!* I know it well; it was bought here."

M. Lantin was disturbed and asked:

"How much is it worth?"

"Well, I sold it for twenty thousand francs. I am willing to take it back for eighteen thousand when you inform me, according to our legal formality, how it comes to be in your possession."

This time M. Lantin was dumfounded. He replied:

"But—but—examine it well. Until this moment I was under the impression that it was paste."

Said the jeweler:

"What is your name, sir?"

"Lantin—I am in the employ of the minister of the interior. I live at Number 16 Rue des Martyrs."

The merchant looked through his books, found the entry and said: "That necklace was sent to Madame Lantin's address, 16 Rue des Martyrs, July 20, 1876."

The two men looked into each other's eyes—the widower speechless with astonishment, the jeweler scenting a thief. The latter broke the silence by saying:

"Will you leave this necklace here for twenty-four hours? I will give you a receipt."

"Certainly," answered M. Lantin hastily. Then, putting the ticket in his pocket, he left the store.

He wandered aimlessly through the streets, his mind in a state of dreadful confusion. He tried to reason, to understand. He could not afford to purchase such a costly ornament. Certainly not. But then it must have been a present!—a present! —a present from whom? Why was it given her?

He stopped and remained standing in the middle of the street. A horrible doubt entered his mind—she? Then all the other gems must have been presents too! The earth seemed to tremble beneath him; the tree before him was falling; throwing up his arms, he fell to the ground, unconscious. He recovered his senses in a pharmacy into which the passers-by had taken him and was then taken to his home. When he arrived he shut himself up in his room and wept until nightfall. Finally, overcome with fatigue, he threw himself on the bed, where he passed an uneasy, restless night.

The following morning he arose and prepared to go to the office. It was hard to work after such a shock. He sent a letter to his employer, requesting to be excused. Then he remembered that he had to return to the jeweler's. He did not like the idea, but he could not leave the necklace with that man. So he dressed and went out.

It was a lovely day; a clear blue sky smiled on the busy city below, and men of leisure were strolling about with their hands in their pockets.

Observing them, M. Lantin said to himself: "The rich, indeed, are happy. With money it is possible to forget even the deepest sorrow. One can go where one pleases and in travel find that distraction which is the surest cure for grief. Oh, if I were only rich!"

He began to feel hungry, but his pocket was empty. He again remembered the necklace. Eighteen thousand francs! Eighteen thousand francs! What a sum!

He soon arrived in the Rue de la Paix, opposite the jeweler's. Eighteen thousand francs! Twenty times he resolved to go in, but shame kept him back. He was hungry, however, very hungry, and had not a cent in his pocket. He decided quickly, ran across the street in order not to have time for reflection and entered the store.

The proprietor immediately came forward and politely offered him a chair; the clerks glanced at him knowingly.

"I have made inquiries, Monsieur Lantin," said the jeweler, "and if you are still resolved to dispose of the gems I am ready to pay you the price I offered."

"Certainly, sir," stammered M. Lantin.

Whereupon the proprietor took from a drawer eighteen large bills, counted and handed them to M. Lantin, who signed a receipt and with a trembling hand put the money into his pocket.

As he was about to leave the store he turned toward the merchant, who still wore the same knowing smile, and, lowering his eyes, said:

"I have—I have other gems which I have received from the same source. Will you buy them also?"

The merchant bowed: "Certainly, sir."

M. Lantin said gravely: "I will bring them to you." An hour later he returned with the gems.

The large diamond earrings were worth twenty thousand francs; the bracelets, thirty-five thousand; the rings, sixteen thousand; a set of emeralds and sapphires, fourteen thousand; a gold chain with solitaire pendant, forty thousand—making the sum of one hundred and forty-three thousand francs.

The jeweler remarked jokingly:

"There was a person who invested all her earnings in precious stones."

M. Lantin replied seriously:

"It is only another way of investing one's money."

That day he lunched at Voisin's and drank wine worth twenty francs a bottle. Then he hired a carriage and made a tour of the Bois, and as he scanned the various turnouts with a contemptuous air he could hardly refrain from crying out to the occupants:

"I, too, am rich! I am worth two hundred thousand francs."

Suddenly he thought of his employer. He drove up to the office and entered gaily, saying:

"Sir, I have come to resign my position. I have just inherited three hundred thousand francs."

He shook hands with his former colleagues and confided to them some of his projects for the future; then he went off to dine at the Café Anglais.

fell on the ground with a deep sigh. We all came round her, and as for me, I stamped on the ground, not knowing what to do, quite unable to make up my mind to abandon that man and girl like that. Suddenly one of the soldiers, a Parisian whom they had nicknamed Pratique, said:

" 'Come, comrades, we must carry the young lady, otherwise we shall not show ourselves Frenchmen, confound it!'

"I really believe that I swore with pleasure and said: 'That is very good of you, my children; I will take my share of the burden.'

"We could indistinctly see the trees of a little wood on the left through the darkness. Several men went into it and soon came back with a bundle of branches twisted into a litter.

" 'Who will lend us his cloak? It is for a pretty girl, comrades,' Pratique said, and ten cloaks were thrown to him. In a moment the girl was lying, warm and comfortable, among them and was raised upon six shoulders. I placed myself at their head, on the right, and very pleased I was with my charge.

"We started off much more briskly, as if we had been having a drink of wine, and I even heard a few jokes. A woman is quite enough to electrify Frenchmen, you see. The soldiers, who were reanimated and warm, had almost reformed their ranks, and an old *franctireur*[2] who was following the litter, waiting for his turn to replace the first of his comrades who might give in, said to one of his neighbors, loud enough for me to hear:

" 'I am not a young man now, but, by Jove, there is nothing like a woman to make you feel queer from head to foot!'

"We went on, almost without stopping, until three o'clock in the morning, when suddenly our scouts fell back again. Soon the whole detachment showed nothing but a vague shadow on the ground, as the men lay on the snow, and I gave my orders in a low voice and heard the harsh, metallic sound of the cocking of rifles. There in the middle of the plain some strange object was moving about. It might have been taken for some enormous animal running about, which uncoiled itself like a serpent or came together into a coil, then suddenly went quickly to the right or left, stopped and then went on again. But presently the wandering shape came near, and I saw a dozen lancers, one behind the other, who were trying to find their way, which they had lost.

"By this time they were so near that I could hear the panting of the horses, the clink of the swords and the creaking of the saddles and so cried: 'Fire!'

"Fifty rifleshots broke the stillness of the night; then there were four or five reports, and at last one single shot was heard. When the smoke had cleared away we saw that the twelve men and nine horses had fallen. Three of the animals were galloping away at a furious pace. One of them was dragging the body of its rider behind it. His foot had caught in the stirrup, and his body rebounded from the ground in a horrible way.

"One of the soldiers behind me gave a harsh laugh and said: 'There are a few more widows now!'

"Perhaps he was married. And another added: 'It did not take long!'

"A head was put out of the litter.

" 'What is the matter?' she asked. 'You are fighting?'

" 'It is nothing, mademoiselle,' I replied; 'we have got rid of a dozen Prussians!'

[2]Volunteers in the Franco-German war of 1870–71, of whom the Germans often made short work when caught.

" 'Poor fellows!' she said. But as she was cold, she quickly disappeared beneath the cloaks again, and we started off once more. We marched on for a long time, and at last the sky began to grow pale. The snow became quite clear, luminous and bright, and a rosy tint appeared in the east. Suddenly a voice in the distance cried:

" 'Who goes there?'

"The whole detachment halted, and I advanced to say who we were. We had reached the French lines, and as my men defiled before the outpost, a commandant on horseback, whom I had informed of what had taken place, asked in a sonorous voice as he saw the litter pass him:

" 'What have you there?'

"And immediately a small head covered with light hair appeared, disheveled and smiling, and replied:

" 'It is I, monsieur.'

"At this the men raised a hearty laugh, and we felt quite lighthearted, while Pratique, who was walking by the side of the litter, waved his kepi and shouted:

" 'Vive la France!' And I felt really moved. I do not know why, except that I thought it a pretty and gallant thing to say.

"It seemed to me as if we had just saved the whole of France and had done something that other men could not have done, something simple and really patriotic. I shall never forget that little face, you may be sure, and if I had to give my opinion about abolishing drums, trumpets and bugles, I should propose to replace them in every regiment by a pretty girl, and that would be even better than playing the *Marseillaise*. By Jove! it would put some spirit into a trooper to have a Madonna like that, a living Madonna, by the colonel's side."

He was silent for a few moments and then, with an air of conviction and jerking his head, continued:

"You see, we are very fond of women, we Frenchmen!"

WAS IT A DREAM?

I had loved her madly!

Why does one love? Why does one love? How queer it is to see only one being in the world, to have only one thought in one's mind, only one desire in the heart and only one name on the lips—a name which comes up continually, rising, like the water in a spring, from the depths of the soul to the lips, a name which one repeats over and over again, which one whispers ceaselessly, everywhere, like a prayer.

I am going to tell you our story, for love only has one, which is always the same. I met her and lived on her tenderness, on her caresses, in her arms, in her dresses, on her words, so completely wrapped up, bound and absorbed in everything which came from her that I no longer cared whether it was day or night, or whether I was dead or alive, on this old earth of ours.

And then she died. How? I do not know; I no longer know anything. But one evening she came home wet, for it was raining heavily, and the next day she coughed, and she coughed for about a week and took to her bed. What happened I do not remember now, but doctors came, wrote and went away. Medicines were brought, and some women made her drink them. Her hands were hot, her forehead was burning, and her eyes bright and sad. When I spoke to her she answered me, but I do not remember what we said. I have forgotten everything, everything, everything! She died, and I very well remember her slight, feeble sigh. The nurse said: "Ah!" and I understood; I understood!

I knew nothing more, nothing. I saw a priest who said: "Your mistress?" And it seemed to me as if he were insulting her. As she was dead, nobody had the right to say that any longer, and I turned him out. Another came who was very kind and tender, and I shed tears when he spoke to me about her.

They consulted me about the funeral, but I do not remember anything that they said, though I recollected the coffin and the sound of the hammer when they nailed her down in it. Oh! God, God!

She was buried! Buried! She! In that hole! Some people came—female friends. I made my escape and ran away. I ran and then walked through the streets, went home and the next day started on a journey.

Yesterday I returned to Paris, and when I saw my room again—our room, our bed, our furniture, everything that remains of the life of a human being after death —I was seized by such a violent attack of fresh grief that I felt like opening the window and throwing myself out into the street. I could not remain any longer among these things, between these walls which had inclosed and sheltered her, which retained a thousand atoms of her, of her skin and of her breath, in their imperceptible crevices. I took up my hat to make my escape, and just as I reached the door I passed the large glass in the hall, which she had put there so that she might look at herself every day from head to foot as she went out, to see if her toilet looked well and was correct and pretty from her little boots to her bonnet.

I stopped short in front of that looking glass in which she had so often been reflected—so often, so often, that it must have retained her reflection. I was standing there trembling with my eyes fixed on the glass—on that flat, profound, empty glass—which had contained her entirely and had possessed her as much as I, as my passionate looks had. I felt as if I loved that glass. I touched it; it was cold. Oh, the recollection! Sorrowful mirror, burning mirror, horrible mirror, to make men suffer such torments! Happy is the man whose heart forgets everything that it has contained, everything that has passed before it, everything that has looked at itself in it or has been reflected in its affection, in its love! How I suffer!

I went out without knowing it, without wishing it, and toward the cemetery. I found her simple grave, a white marble cross, with these few words:

She loved, was loved and died.

She is there below, decayed! How horrible! I sobbed with my forehead on the ground, and I stopped there for a long time, a long time. Then I saw that it was getting dark and a strange, mad wish, the wish of a despairing lover, seized me. I wished to pass the night, the last night, in weeping on her grave. But I should be seen and driven out. How was I to manage? I was cunning and got up and began to roam about in that city of the dead. I walked and walked. How small this city is in comparison with the other, the city in which we live. And yet how much more numerous the dead are than the living. We want high houses, wide streets and much room for the four generations who see the daylight at the same time, drink water from the spring and wine from the vines and eat bread from the plains.

And for all the generations of the dead, for all that ladder of humanity that has descended down to us, there is scarcely anything, scarcely anything! The earth takes them back, and oblivion effaces them. Adieu!

At the end of the cemetery I suddenly perceived that I was in its oldest part, where those who had been dead a long time are mingling with the soil, where the crosses themselves are decayed, where possibly newcomers will be put tomorrow. It is full of untended roses, of strong and dark cypress trees, a sad and beautiful garden, nourished on human flesh.

I was alone, perfectly alone. So I crouched in a green tree and hid myself there completely amid the thick and somber branches. I waited, clinging to the stem like a shipwrecked man does to a plank.

When it was quite dark I left my refuge and began to walk softly, slowly, inaudibly, through that ground full of dead people. I wandered about for a long time but could not find her tomb again. I went on with extended arms, knocking against the tombs with my hands, my feet, my knees, my chest, even with my head, without being able to find her. I groped about like a blind man finding his way; I felt the stones, the crosses, the iron railings, the metal wreaths and the wreaths of faded flowers! I read the names with my fingers, by passing them over the letters. What a night! What a night! I could not find her again!

There was no moon. What a night! I was frightened, horribly frightened in these narrow paths between two rows of graves. Graves! Graves! Graves! Nothing but graves! On my right, on my left, in front of me, around me, everywhere there were graves! I sat down on one of them, for I could not walk any longer; my knees were so weak. I could hear my heart beat! And I heard something else as well. What? A confused, nameless noise. Was the noise in my head, in the impenetrable night or beneath the mysterious earth, the earth sown with human corpses? I looked all around me, but I cannot say how long I remained there; I was paralyzed with terror, cold with fright, ready to shout out, ready to die.

Suddenly it seemed to me that the slab of marble on which I was sitting was moving. Certainly it was moving, as if it were being raised. With a bound I sprang onto the neighboring tomb, and I saw, yes, I distinctly saw the stone which I had just quitted rise upright. Then the dead person appeared, a naked skeleton, pushing the stone back with its bent back. I saw it quite clearly, although the night was so dark. On the cross I could read:

Here lies Jacques Olivant, who died at the age of fifty-one. He loved his family, was kind and honorable and died in the grace of the Lord.

The dead man also read what was inscribed on the tombstone; then he picked up a stone off the path, a little, pointed stone, and began to scrape the letters carefully. He slowly effaced them, and with the hollows of his eyes he looked at the places where they had been engraved. Then with the tip of the bone that had been his forefinger he wrote in luminous letters, like those lines which boys trace on walls with the tip of a lucifer match:

Here reposes Jacques Olivant, who died at the age of fifty-one. He hastened his father's death by his unkindness, as he wished to inherit his fortune; he tortured his wife, tormented his children, deceived his neighbors, robbed everyone he could and died wretched.

When he had finished writing, the dead man stood motionless, looking at his
work. On turning around I saw that all the graves were open, that all the dead
bodies had emerged from them and that all had effaced the lines inscribed on the
gravestones by their relations substituting the truth instead. And I saw that all had
been the tormentors of their neighbors—malicious, dishonest, hypocrites, liars,
rogues, calumniators, envious; that they had stolen, deceived, performed every disgraceful, every abominable action, these good fathers, these faithful wives, these
devoted sons, these chaste daughters, these honest tradesmen, these men and
women who were called irreproachable. They were all writing at the same time,
on the threshold of their eternal abode, the truth, the terrible and the holy truth
of which everybody was ignorant, or pretended to be ignorant, while they were
alive.

I thought that she also must have written something on her tombstone and
now, running without any fear among the half-open coffins, among the corpses
and skeletons, I went toward her, sure that I should find her immediately. I recognized her at once without seeing her face, which was covered by the winding sheet,
and on the marble cross where shortly before I had read:

She loved, was loved and died.

I now saw:

*Having gone out in the rain one day in order to deceive her lover, she caught
cold and died.*

It appears that they found me at daybreak, lying on the grave, unconscious.

MADEMOISELLE PEARL

It really was an odd notion of mine to choose Mlle. Pearl for queen that particular
evening.

Every year I went to eat my Twelfth-night dinner at the house of my old friend
Chantal. My father, whose most intimate friend he was, had taken me there when
I was a child. I had continued the custom, and I shall doubtless continue it as
long as I live, and as long as there is a Chantal left in the world.

The Chantals, moreover, lead a strange life; they live in Paris as if they were
living in Grasse, Yvetot, or Pont-à-Mousson.

They owned a small house with a garden, near the Observatory. There they lived
in true provincial fashion. Of Paris, of the real Paris, they knew nothing and suspected nothing; they were far, very far away. Sometimes, however, they made a
journey, a long journey. Mme. Chantal went to the big stores, as they called it
among themselves. And this is the manner of an expedition to the big stores.

Mlle. Pearl, who keeps the keys of the kitchen cupboards—for the linen cupboards are in the mistress's own charge—Mlle. Pearl perceives that the sugar is
coming to an end, that the preserves are quite finished, and that there's nothing
worth talking about left in the coffee bag.

Then, put on her guard against famine, Mme. Chantal passes the rest of the stores in review and makes notes in her memorandum book. Then, when she has written down a quantity of figures, she first devotes herself to lengthy calculations, followed by lengthy discussions with Mlle. Pearl. They do at last come to an agreement and decide what amount of each article must be laid in for a three months' supply: sugar, rice, prunes, coffee, preserves, tins of peas, beans, crab, salt, and smoked fish, and so on and so forth.

After which they appoint a day for making the purchases, and set out together in a cab, a cab with a luggage rack on top, to a big grocery store over the river in the new quarters, with an air of great mystery, and return at dinner time, worn out but still excited, jolting along in the carriage, its roof covered with packages and sacks like a removal van.

For the Chantals, all that part of Paris situated at the other side of the Seine constituted the new quarter, quarters inhabited by a strange noisy people, with the shakiest notions of honesty, who spent their days in dissipation, their nights feasting, and threw money out of the windows. From time to time, however, the young girls were taken to the theater to the Opéra Comique or the Française, when the play was recommended by the paper M. Chantal read.

The young girls are nineteen and seventeen years old today; they are two beautiful girls, tall and clear-skinned, very well trained, too well trained, so well trained that they attract no more attention than two pretty dolls. The idea never occurred to me to take any notice of them or to court the Chantal girls; I hardly dared speak to them, they seemed so unspotted from the world; I was almost afraid of offending against the proprieties in merely raising my hat.

The father himself is a charming man, very cultured, very frank, very friendly, but desirous of nothing so much as repose, quiet, and tranquillity, and mainly instrumental in mummifying his family into mere symbols of his will, living and having their being in a stagnant peacefulness. He read a good deal, from choice, and his emotions were easily stirred. His avoidance of all contact with life, common jostlings and violence had made his skin, his moral skin, very sensitive and delicate. The least thing moved and disturbed him, hurt him.

The Chantals had some friends, however, but friends admitted to their circle with many reserves, and chosen carefully from neighboring families. They also exchanged two or three visits a year with relatives living at a distance.

As for me, I dine at their house on the fifteenth of August and on Twelfth-night. That is as sacred a duty to me as Easter communion to a Catholic.

On the fifteenth of August a few friends were asked, but on Twelfth-night I was the only guest and the only outsider.

II

Well, this year, as in every other year, I had gone to dine at the Chantals' to celebrate Epiphany.

I embraced M. Chantal, as I always did, Mme. Chantal, and Mlle. Pearl, and I bowed deeply to Mlles. Louise and Pauline. They questioned me about a thousand things, boulevard happenings, politics, our representatives, and what the public thought of affairs in Tonkin. Mme. Chantal, a stout lady whose thoughts always impressed me as being square blocks of stone, was wont to enunciate the following phrase at the end of every political discussion: "All this will produce a crop of misfortunes in the future." Why do I always think that Mme. Chantal's thoughts are square? I don't really know why; but my mind sees everything she says in this fashion: a square, a solid square with four symmetrical angles. There are other people whose thoughts always seems to me round and rolling like circles. As soon as they begin a phrase about something, out it rolls, running along, issuing in the shape of ten, twenty, fifty round thoughts, big ones and little ones, and I see them running behind each other out of sight over the edge of the sky. Other persons have pointed thoughts. . . . But this is somewhat irrelevant. We sat down to table in the usual order, and dinner passed without anyone uttering a single memorable word. With the sweets, they brought in the Twelfth-night cake. Now, each year, M. Chantal was king. Whether this was a series of chances or a domestic convention I don't know, but invariably he found the lucky bean in his piece of cake, and he proclaimed Mme. Chantal queen. So I was amazed to find in a mouthful of pastry something very hard that almost broke one of my teeth. I removed the object carefully from my mouth and I saw a tiny china doll no larger than a bean. Surprise made me exclaim: "Oh!" They all looked at me and Chantal clapped his hands and shouted: "Gaston's got it. Gaston's got it. Long live the king! Long live the king!"

The others caught up the chorus: "Long live the king!" And I blushed to my ears, as one often does for no reason whatever in slightly ridiculous situations. I sat looking at my boots, holding the fragment of china between two fingers, forcing myself to laugh, and not knowing what to do or what to say, when Chantal went on: "Now he must choose a queen."

I was overwhelmed. A thousand thoughts and speculations rushed across my mind in a second of time. Did they want me to choose out one of the Chantal girls? Was this a way of making me say which one I liked the better? Was it a gentle, delicate, almost unconscious feeler that the parents were putting out towards a possible marriage? The thought of marriage stalks all day and every day in families that possess marriageable daughters; it takes innumerable shapes and guises and adopts every possible means. I was suddenly dreadfully afraid of compromising myself, and extremely timid too, before the obstinately correct and rigid bearing of Mlles. Louise and Pauline. To select one of them over the head of the other seemed to me as difficult as to choose between two drops of water; and I was horribly disturbed at the thought of committing myself to a path which would lead me to the altar willy-nilly, by gentle stages and incidents as discreet, as insignificant, and as easy as this meaningless kingship.

But all at once I had an inspiration, and I proffered the symbolic little doll to Mlle. Pearl. At first everyone was surprised, then they must have appreciated my delicacy and discretion, for they applauded furiously, shouting: "Long live the queen! Long live the queen!"

As for the poor old maid, she was covered with confusion; she trembled and lifted a terrified face. "No . . . no . . . no . . ." she stammered; "not me . . . I implore you . . . not me . . . I implore you."

At that, I looked at Mlle. Pearl for the first time in my life, and wondered what sort of a woman she was.

I was used to seeing her about this house, but only as you see old tapestried chairs in which you have been sitting since you were a child, without ever really noticing them. One day, you couldn't say just why, because a ray of sunlight falls across the seat, you exclaim: "Why, this is a remarkable piece of furniture!" and you discover that the wood has been carved by an artist and that the tapestry is very uncommon. I had never noticed Mlle. Pearl.

She was part of the Chantal family, that was all; but what? What was her standing? She was a tall, thin woman who kept herself very much in the background, but she wasn't insignificant. They treated her in a friendly fashion, more intimately than a housekeeper, less so than a relation. I suddenly became aware now of various subtle shades of manner that I had never troubled about until this moment. Mme. Chantal said: "Pearl." The young girls: "Mlle. Pearl," and Chantal never called her anything but "mademoiselle," with a slightly more respectable air perhaps.

I set myself to consider her. How old was she? Forty? Yes, forty. She was not old, this maiden lady, she made herself look old. I was suddenly struck by this obvious fact. She did her hair, dressed herself, and got herself up to look absurd, and in spite of it all she was not at all absurd. So innately graceful she was, simply and naturally graceful, though she did her best to obscure it and conceal it. What an odd creature she was, after all! Why hadn't I paid more attention to her? She did her hair in the most grotesque way in ridiculous little gray curls; under this crowning glory of a middle-aged Madonna, she had a broad placid forehead, graven with two deep wrinkles, the wrinkles of some enduring sorrow, then two blue eyes, wide and gentle, so timid, so fearful, so humble, two blue eyes that were still simple, filled with girlish wonder and youthful emotions, and griefs endured in secret, softening her eyes and leaving them untroubled.

Her whole face was clear-cut and reserved, one of those faces grown worn without being ravaged or faded by the weariness and the fevered emotions of life.

What a pretty mouth, and what pretty teeth! But she seemed as if she dared not smile.

Abruptly, I began to compare her with Mme. Chantal. Mlle. Pearl was undoubtedly the better of the two, a hundred times better, nobler, more dignified.

I was astounded by my discoveries. Champagne was poured out. I lifted my glass to the queen and drank her health with a pretty compliment. I could see that she wanted to hide her face in her napkin; then, when she dipped her lips in the translucent wine, everyone cried: "The queen's drinking, the queen's drinking!" At that she turned crimson and choked. They laughed; but I saw clearly that she was well liked in the house.

III

As soon as dinner was over, Chantal took me by the arm. It was the hour for his cigar, a sacred hour. When he was alone, he went out into the street to smoke; when he had someone to dinner, he took them to the billiard room, and he played as he smoked. This evening they had lit a fire in the billiard room, since it was Twelfth-night; and my old friend took his cue, a very slender cue which he chalked with great care; then he said:

"Now, sonny."

He always spoke to me as if I were a little boy: I was twenty-five years old but he had known me since I was four.

I began to play; I made several caroms; I missed several more; but my head was filled with drifting thoughts of Mlle. Pearl, and I asked abruptly:

"Tell me, M. Chantal, is Mlle. Pearl a relation of yours?"

He stopped playing, in astonishment, and stared at me.

"What, don't you know? Didn't you know Mlle. Pearl's story?"

"Of course not."

"Hasn't your father ever told you?"

"Of course not."

"Well, well, that's queer, upon my word, it's queer. Oh, it's quite an adventure."

He was silent, and went on:

"And if you only knew how strange it is that you should ask me about it today, on Twelfth-night!"

"Why?"

"Why, indeed! Listen. It's forty-one years ago, forty-one years this very day, the day of Epiphany. We were living then at Roüy-le-Tors, on the ramparts; but I must first tell you about the house, if you're to understand the story properly. Roüy is built on a slope, or rather on a mound which thrusts out of a wide stretch of meadow land. We had there a house with a beautiful hanging garden, supported on the old ramparts. So that the house was in the town, on the street, while the garden hung over the plain. There was also a door opening from this garden on to the fields, at the bottom of a secret staircase which went down inside the thick masonry of the walls, just like a secret staircase in a romance. A road ran past this door, where a great bell hung, and the country people brought their stuff in this way, to save themselves going all the way round.

"Can you see it all? Well, this year, at Epiphany, it had been snowing for a week. It was like the end of the world. When we went out onto the ramparts to look out over the plain, the cold of that vast white countryside struck through to our very bones; it was white everywhere, icy cold, and gleaming like varnish. It really looked as if the good God had wrapped up the earth to carry it away to the lumber room of old worlds. It was rare and melancholy, I can tell you.

"We had all our family at home then, and we were a large family, a very large family: my father, my mother, my uncle and my aunt; my two brothers and my four cousins; they were pretty girls; I married the youngest. Of all that company, there are only three left alive: my wife, myself, and my sister-in-law at Marseille. God, how a family dwindles away: it makes me shiver to think of it. I was fifteen years old then, and now I'm fifty-six.

"Well, we were going to eat our Twelfth-night dinner and we were very gay, very gay. Everybody was in the drawing room waiting for dinner, when my eldest brother, Jacques, took it into his head to say: 'A dog's been howling out in the fields for the last ten minutes; it must be some poor beast that's got lost.'

"The words were hardly out of his mouth when the garden bell rang. It had a heavy clang like a church bell and reminded you of funerals. A shiver ran through the assembled company. My father called a servant and told him to go and see who was there. We waited in complete silence, we thought of the snow that lay over the whole countryside. When the man came back, he declared he had seen nothing. The dog was still howling: the howls never stopped, and came always from the same direction.

"We went in to dinner, but we were a little uneasy, especially the young ones. All went well until the joint was on the table, and then the bell began to ring again; it rang three times, three loud long clangs that sent a thrill to our very finger tips and stopped the breath in our throats. We sat staring at each other, our forks in the air, straining our ears, seized by fear of some supernatural horror.

"At last my mother said: 'It's very queer that they've been so long coming back; don't go alone, Baptiste: one of the gentlemen will go with you.'

"My uncle François got up. He was as strong as Hercules, very proud of his great strength and afraid of nothing on earth. 'Take a gun,' my father advised him. 'You don't know what it might be.'

"But my uncle took nothing but a walking stick and went out at once with the servant.

"The rest of us waited there, shaking with terror and fright, neither eating nor speaking. My father tried to comfort us. 'You'll see,' he said, 'it'll be some beggar or some passer-by lost in the snow. He rang once, and when the door wasn't opened immediately, he made another attempt to find his road: he didn't succeed and he's come back to our door.'

"My uncle's absence seemed to us to last an hour. He came back at last, furiously angry, and cursing:

" 'Not a thing, by God, it's someone playing a trick. Nothing but that cursed dog howling a hundred yards beyond the walls. If I'd taken a gun, I'd have killed him to keep him quiet.'

"We went on with our dinner, but we were still very anxious; we were quite sure that we hadn't heard the last of it; something was going to happen, the bell would ring again in a minute.

"It did ring, at the very moment when we were cutting the Epiphany cake. The men leaped to their feet as one man. My uncle François, who had been drinking champagne, swore that he was going to murder IT, in such a wild rage that my mother and my aunt flung themselves on him to hold him back. My father was quite calm about it; he was slightly lame too (he dragged one leg since he had broken it in a fall from his horse), but now he declared that he must know what it was, and that he was going out. My brothers, who were eighteen and twenty years old, ran in search of their guns, and as no one was paying any attention to me, I grabbed a rook rifle and got ready to accompany the expedition myself.

"It set off at once. My father and my uncle led off, with Baptiste, who was carrying a lantern. My brothers Jacques and Paul followed, and I brought up the rear, in spite of the entreaties of my mother, who stayed behind in the doorway, with her sister and my cousins.

"Snow had been falling again during the last hour and it lay thick on the trees. The pines bent under the heavy ghostly covering, like white pyramids or enormous sugar loaves; the slighter shrubs, palely glimmering in the shadows, were only dimly visible through the gray curtain of small hurrying flakes. The snow was falling so thickly that you couldn't see more than ten paces ahead. But the lantern threw a wide beam of light in front of us. When we began to descend the twisting staircase hollowed out of the wall, I was afraid, I can tell you. I thought someone was walking behind me and I'd be grabbed by the shoulder and carried off; I wanted to run home again, but as I'd have had to go back the whole length of the garden, I didn't dare.

"I heard them opening the door on to the fields; then my uncle began to swear: 'Blast him, he's gone. If I'd only seen his shadow, I wouldn't have missed him, the b———!'

"The look of the plain struck me with a sense of foreboding, or rather the feel of it in front of us, for we couldn't see it; nothing was visible but a veil of snow hung from edge to edge of the world, above, below, in front of us, to left of us and right of us, everywhere.

"'There, that's the dog howling,' added my uncle. 'I'll show him what I can do with a gun, I will. And that'll be something done, at any rate.'

"But my father, who was a kindly man, answered: 'We'd do better to go and look for the poor animal: he's whining with hunger. The wretched beast is barking for help; he's like a man shouting in distress. Come on.'

"We started off through the curtain, through the heavy ceaseless fall, through the foam that was filling the night and the air, moving, floating, falling; as it melted, it froze the flesh on our bones, froze it with a burning cold that sent a sharp swift stab of pain through the skin with each prick of the little white flakes.

"We sank to our knees in the soft, cold, feathery mass, and we had to lift our legs right up to get over the ground. The farther we advanced, the louder and clearer grew the howling of the dog. 'There he is!' cried my uncle. We stopped to observe him, like prudent campaigners coming upon the enemy at night.

"I couldn't see anything; then I came up with the others and I saw him; he was a terrifying and fantastic object, that dog, a great black dog, a shaggy sheep dog with a head like a wolf, standing erect on his four feet at the far end of the long track of light that the lantern flung out across the snow. He didn't move; he stared at us with never a sound.

"'It's queer he doesn't rush at us or away from us,' said my uncle. 'I've the greatest mind to stretch him out with a shot.'

"'No,' my father said decidedly, 'we must catch him.'

"'But he's not alone,' my brother Jacques added. 'He has something beside him.'

"He actually had something behind him, something gray and indistinguishable. We began to walk cautiously towards him.

"Seeing us draw near, the dog sat down on his haunches. He didn't look vicious. He seemed, on the contrary, pleased that he had succeeded in attracting someone's attention.

"My father went right up to him and patted him. The dog licked his hands; and we saw that he was fastened to the wheel of a small carriage, a sort of toy carriage wrapped all round in three or four woolen coverings. We lifted the wrappings carefully; Baptiste held his lantern against the opening of the carriage—which was like a kennel on wheels—and we saw inside a tiny sleeping child.

"We were so astonished that we couldn't get out a single word. My father was the first to recover: he was warmhearted and somewhat emotional; he placed his hand on the top of the carriage and said: 'Poor deserted thing, you shall belong to us.' And he ordered my brother Jacques to wheel our find in front of us.

"'A love child,' my father added, 'whose poor mother came and knocked at my door on Epiphany night, in memory of the Christ child.'

"He stood still again and shouted into the darkness four times, at the top of his voice, to all the four corners of the heavens: 'We have got him safe.' Then he rested his hand on his brother's shoulder and murmured: 'Suppose you'd fired at the dog, François?'

"My uncle said nothing, but crossed himself earnestly in the darkness; he was very devout, for all his swaggering ways.

"We had loosed the dog, who followed us.

"Upon my word, our return to the house was a pretty sight. At first we had great difficulty in getting the carriage up the rampart staircase; we succeeded at last, however, and wheeled it right into the hall.

"How comically surprised and delighted and bewildered Mamma was! And my poor little cousins (the youngest was six) were like four hens round a nest. At last we lifted the child, still sleeping, from its carriage. It was a girl about six weeks old. And in her clothes we found ten thousand francs in gold, yes, ten thousand francs, which Papa invested to bring her in a dowry. So she wasn't the child of poor parents . . . she may have been the child of a gentleman by a respectable young girl belonging to the town, or even . . . we made innumerable speculations, and we never knew anything . . . except that . . . never a thing . . . never a thing. . . . Even the dog wasn't known to anyone. He didn't belong to the district. In any event, the man or woman who had rung three times at our door knew very well what sort of people my parents were when they chose them for their child.

"And that's how Mlle. Pearl found her way into the Chantal house when she was six weeks old.

"It was later that she got the name of Mlle. Pearl. She was first christened Marie Simone Claire, Claire serving as her surname.

"We certainly made a quaint entry into the dining room with the tiny wide-awake creature, looking round her at the people and the lights, with wondering troubled blue eyes.

"We sat down at the table again, and the cake was cut. I was king and I chose Mlle. Pearl for queen, as you did just now. She hadn't any idea that day what a compliment we were paying her.

"Well, the child was adopted, and brought up as one of the family. She grew up: years passed. She was a charming, gentle, obedient girl. Everyone loved her, and she would have been shamefully spoiled if my mother had not seen to it that she wasn't.

"My mother had a lively sense of what was fitting and a proper reverence for caste. She consented to treat little Claire as she did her own children, but she was none the less insistent that the distance between us should be definitely marked and the position clearly laid down.

"So as soon as the child was old enough to understand, she told her how she had been found, and very gently, tenderly even, she made the little girl realize that she was only an adopted member of the Chantal family, belonging to them but really no kin at all.

"Claire realized the state of affairs with an intelligence beyond her years and an instinctive wisdom that surprised us all; and she was quick to take and keep the place allotted to her, with so much tact, grace, and courtesy that she brought tears to my father's eyes.

"My mother herself was so touched by the passionate gratitude and timid devotion of this adorable and tender-hearted little thing that she began to call her 'my daughter.' Sometimes, when the young girl had shown herself more than commonly sweet-natured and delicate, my mother pushed her glasses onto her forehead, as she always did when much moved, and repeated: 'The child's a pearl, a real pearl.' The name stuck to little Claire: she became Mlle. Pearl for all of us from that time and for always."

IV

Monsieur Chantal was silent. He was sitting on the billiard table, swinging his feet; his left hand fiddled with a ball and in his right hand he crumpled the woolen rag we called "the chalk rag" and used for rubbing out the score on the slate. A little flushed, his voice muffled, he was speaking to himself now, lost in his memories, dreaming happily through early scenes and old happenings stirring in his thoughts, as a man dreams when he walks through old gardens where he grew up, and where each tree, each path, each plant, the prickly holly whose plump red berries crumble between his fingers, evoke at every step some little incident of his past life, the little insignificant delicious incidents that are the very heart, the very stuff of life.

I stood facing him, propped against the wall, leaning my hands on my useless billiard cue.

After a moment's pause he went on: "God, how pretty she was at eighteen— and graceful—and perfect! Oh, what a pretty—pretty—pretty—sweet—gay—and charming girl! She had such eyes . . . blue eyes . . . limpid . . . clear . . . I've never seen any like them . . . never."

Again he was silent. "Why didn't she marry?" I asked.

He didn't answer me: he answered the careless word "marry."

"Why? why? She didn't want to . . . didn't want to. She had a dowry of ninety thousand francs too, and she had several offers . . . she didn't want to marry. She seemed sad during those years. It was just at the time I married my cousin, little Charlotte, my wife, to whom I'd been engaged for six years."

I looked at M. Chantal and thought that I could see into his mind, and that I'd come suddenly upon the humble cruel tragedy of a heart at once honorable, upright, and pure, that I'd seen into the secret unknown depths of a heart that no one had really understood, not even the resigned and silent victims of its dictates.

Pricked by a sudden savage curiosity, I said deliberately:

"Surely you ought to have married her, M. Chantal?"

He started, stared at me, and said:

"Me? Marry whom?"

"Mlle. Pearl."

"But why?"

"Because you loved her more than you loved your cousin."

He stared at me with strange, wide, bewildered eyes, then stammered:

"I loved her? . . . I? . . . how? What are you talking about?"

"It's obvious, surely? Moreover, it was on her account that you delayed so long before marrying the cousin who waited six years for you."

The cue fell from his left hand, and he seized the chalk rag in both hands and, covering his face with it, began to sob into its folds. He wept in a despairing and ridiculous fashion, dripping water from eyes and nose and mouth all at once like a squeezed sponge. He coughed, spat, and blew his nose on the chalk rag, dried his eyes, choked, and overflowed again from every opening in his face, making a noise in his throat like a man gargling.

Terrified and ashamed, I wanted to run away, and I did not know what to say, or do, or try to do.

And suddenly Mme. Chantal's voice floated up the staircase: "Have you nearly finished your smoke?"

I opened the door and called: "Yes, madame, we're coming down."

Then I flung myself on her husband, seized him by the elbows, and said: "M. Chantal, Chantal my friend, listen to me; your wife is calling you, pull yourself together, pull yourself together, we must go downstairs; pull yourself together."

"Yes . . . yes . . ." he babbled. "I'm coming . . . poor girl . . . I'm coming . . . tell her I'm just coming."

And he began carefully drying his face on the rag that had been used to rub the score off the slate for two or three years; then he emerged, white and red in streaks, his forehead, nose, cheeks, and chin dabbled with chalk, his eyes swollen and still full of tears.

I took his hands and led him towards his bedroom, murmuring: "I beg your pardon, I humbly beg your pardon, M. Chantal, for hurting you like this . . . but . . . I didn't know . . . you . . . you see."

He shook my hand. "Yes . . . yes . . . we all have our awkward moments."

Then he plunged his face in his basin. When he emerged, he was still hardly presentable, but I thought of a little ruse. He was disturbed when he looked at himself in the glass, so I said "You need only tell her you've got a speck of dust in your eye, and you can cry in front of everyone as long as you like."

He did at last go down, rubbing his eyes with his handkerchief. They were all very concerned; everyone wanted to look for the speck of dust, which no one could find, and they related similar cases when it had become necessary to call in a doctor.

I had betaken myself to Mlle. Pearl's side and I looked at her, tormented by a burning curiosity, a curiosity that became positively painful. She really must have been pretty, with her quiet eyes, so big, so untroubled, so wide that you'd have thought they were never closed as ordinary eyes are. Her dress was a little absurd, a real old maid's dress, that hid her real charm but could not make her look graceless.

I thought that I could see into her mind as I had just seen into the mind of M. Chantal, that I could see every hidden corner of this simple humble life, spent in the service of others; but I felt a sudden impulse to speak, an aching persistent impulse to question her, to find out if she too had loved, if she had loved him; if like him she had endured the same long bitter secret sorrow, unseen, unknown, unguessed of all, indulged only at night in the solitude and darkness of her room. I looked at her, I saw her heart beating under her high-necked frock, and I wondered if night after night this gentle wide-eyed creature had stifled her moans in the depths of a pillow wet with her tears, sobbing, her body torn with long shudders, lying there in the fevered solitude of a burning bed.

And like a child breaking a plaything to see inside it, I whispered to her: "If you had seen M. Chantal crying just now, you would have been sorry for him."

She trembled: "What, has he been crying?"

"Yes, he's been crying."

"Why?"

She was very agitated. I answered:

"About you."

"About me?"

"Yes. He told me how he loved you years ago, and what it had cost him to marry his wife instead of you."

Her pale face seemed to grow a little longer; her wide eyes shut suddenly, so swiftly that they seemed closed never to open again. She slipped from her chair to the floor and sank slowly, softly, across it, like a falling scarf.

"Help, quick, quick, help!" I cried. "Mlle. Pearl is ill."

Mme. Chantal and her daughters rushed to help her, and while they were bringing water, a napkin, vinegar, I sought my hat and hurried away.

I walked away with great strides, sick at heart and my mind full of remorse and regret. And at the same time I was almost happy; it seemed to me that I had done a praiseworthy and necessary action.

Was I wrong or right? I asked myself. They had hidden their secret knowledge in their hearts like a bullet in a healed wound. Wouldn't they be happier now? It was too late for their grief to torture them again, and soon enough for them to recall it with a tender pitying emotion.

And perhaps some evening in the coming spring, stirred by moonlight falling through the branches across the grass under their feet, they will draw close to one another and clasp each other's hands, remembering all their cruel hidden suffering. And perhaps, too, the brief embrace will wake in their blood a faint thrill of the ecstasy they have never known, and in the hearts of these two dead that for one moment are alive, it will stir the swift divine madness, the wild joy that turns the least trembling of true lovers into a deeper happiness than other men can ever know in all their life.

TWO LITTLE SOLDIERS

Every Sunday, the moment they were dismissed, the two little soldiers made off. Once outside the barracks, they struck out to the right through Courbevoie, walking with long, rapid strides, as though they were on a march.

When they were beyond the last of the houses they slackened pace along the bare, dusty roadway which goes toward Bezons.

They were both small and thin and looked quite lost in their coats, which were too big and too long. Their sleeves hung down over their hands, and they found their enormous red breeches, which compelled them to waddle, very much in the way. Under their stiff, high helmets their faces had little character—two poor, sallow Breton faces, simple with an almost animal simplicity and with gentle and quiet blue eyes.

They never conversed during these walks but went straight on, each with the same thought in his head. This thought atoned for the lack of conversation; it was this, that just inside the little wood near Les Champioux they had found a place which reminded them of their own country, where they could feel happy again.

When they arrived under the trees where the roads from Colombes and from Châtou cross, they would take off their heavy helmets and wipe their foreheads. They always halted on the Bezons bridge to look at the Seine and would remain there two or three minutes, bent double, leaning on the parapet.

Sometimes they would gaze out over the great basin of Argenteuil, where the skiffs might be seen scudding, with their white, careening sails, recalling perhaps the look of the Breton waters, the harbor of Vanne, near which they lived, and the fishing boats standing out across the Morbihan to the open sea.

Just beyond the Seine they bought their provisions from a sausage merchant, a baker and a wine seller. A piece of blood pudding, four sous' worth of bread and a liter of "petit bleu" constituted the provisions which they carried off in their handkerchiefs. After they had left Bezons they traveled slowly and began to talk.

In front of them a barren plain studded with clumps of trees led to the wood, to the little wood which had seemed to them to resemble the one at Kermarivan. Grainfields and hayfields bordered the narrow path, which lost itself in the young greenness of the crops, and Jean Kerderen would always say to Luc le Ganidec:

"It looks like it does near Plounivon."

"Yes; exactly."

Side by side they strolled, their souls filled with vague memories of their own country, with awakened images as naïve as the pictures on the colored broadsheets which you buy for a penny. They kept on recognizing, as it were, now a corner of a field, a hedge, a bit of moorland, now a crossroad, now a granite cross. Then, too, they would always stop beside a certain landmark, a great stone, because it looked something like the cromlech at Locneuven.

Every Sunday on arriving at the first clump of trees Luc le Ganidec would cut a switch, a hazel switch, and begin gently to peel off the bark, thinking meanwhile of the folk at home. Jean Kerderen carried the provisions.

From time to time Luc would mention a name or recall some deed of their childhood in a few brief words, which caused long thoughts. And their own country, their dear, distant country, recaptured them little by little, seizing on their imaginations and sending to them from afar her shapes, her sounds, her well-known prospects, her odors—odors of the green lands where the salt sea air was blowing.

No longer conscious of the exhalations of the Parisian stables, on which the earth of the banlieue fattens, they scented the perfume of the flowering broom, which the salt breeze of the open sea plucks and bears away. And the sails of the boats from the riverbanks seemed like the white wings of the coasting vessels seen beyond the great plain which extended from their homes to the very margin of the sea.

They walked with short steps, Luc le Ganidec and Jean Kerderen, content and sad, haunted by a sweet melancholy, by the lingering, ever-present sorrow of a caged animal who remembers his liberty.

By the time that Luc had stripped the slender wand of its bark they reached the corner of the wood where every Sunday they took breakfast. They found the two bricks which they kept hidden in the thicket and kindled a little fire of twigs, over which to roast the blood pudding at the end of a bayonet.

When they had breakfasted, eaten their bread to the last crumb and drunk their wine to the last drop, they remained seated side by side upon the grass, saying nothing, their eyes on the distance, their eyelids drooping, their fingers crossed as at Mass, their red legs stretched out beside the poppies of the field. And the leather of their helmets and the brass of their buttons glittered in the ardent sun, making the larks, which sang and hovered above their heads, cease in mid-song.

Toward noon they began to turn their eyes from time to time in the direction of the village of Bezons, because the girl with the cow was coming. She passed by them every Sunday on her way to milk and change the pasture of her cow—the only cow in this district which ever went out of the stable to grass. It was pastured in a narrow field along the edge of the wood a little farther on.

They soon perceived the girl, the only human being within vision, and were gladdened by the brilliant reflections thrown off by the tin milk pail under the rays of the sun. They never talked about her. They were simply glad to see her without understanding why.

She was a big strong wench with red hair, burned by the heat of sunny days, a sturdy product of the environs of Paris.

Once, finding them seated in the same place, she said:

"Good morning. You two are always here, aren't you?"

Luc le Ganidec, the bolder, stammered:

"Yes, we come to rest."

That was all. But the next Sunday she laughed on seeing them, laughed with a protecting benevolence and a feminine keenness which knew well enough that they were bashful. And she asked:

"What are you doing there? Are you trying to see the grass grow?"

Luc was cheered up by this and smiled likewise. "Maybe we are."

"That's pretty slow work," she said.

He answered, still laughing: "Well, yes, it is."

She went on. But coming back with a milk pail full of milk, she stopped again before them and said:

"Would you like a little? It will taste like home."

With the instinctive feeling that they were of the same peasant race as she, being herself perhaps also far away from home, she had divined and touched the spot.

They were both touched. Then with some difficulty she managed to make a little milk run into the neck of the glass bottle in which they carried their wine. And Luc drank first, with little swallows, stopping every minute to see whether he had drunk more than his half. Then he handed the bottle to Jean.

She stood upright before them, her hands on her hips, her pail on the ground at her feet, glad at the pleasure which she had given.

Then she departed, shouting: "*Allons*, adieu! Till next Sunday!"

And as long as they could see her at all they followed with their eyes her tall silhouette, which faded, growing smaller and smaller, seeming to sink into the verdure of the fields.

When they were leaving the barracks the week after Jean said to Luc:

"Oughtn't we to buy her something good?"

They were in great embarrassment before the problem of the choice of a delicacy for the girl with the cow. Luc was of the opinion that a little tripe would be the best, but Jean preferred some *berlingots* because he was fond of sweets. His choice fairly made him enthusiastic, and they bought at a grocer's two sous' worth of white and red candies.

They ate their breakfast more rapidly than usual, being nervous with expectation.

Jean saw her first. "There she is!" he cried. Luc added: "Yes, there she is."

While yet some distance off she laughed at seeing them. Then she cried:

"Is everything going as you like it?"

And in unison they asked:

"Are you getting on all right?"

Then she conversed, talked to them of simple things in which they felt an interest—of the weather, of the crops and of her master.

They were afraid to offer the candies, which were slowly melting away in Jean's pocket.

At last Luc grew bold and murmured:

"We have brought you something."

She demanded, "What is it? Tell me!"

Then Jean, blushing up to his ears, managed to get at the little paper cornucopia and held it out.

She began to eat the little bonbons, rolling them from one cheek to the other, where they made little round lumps. The two soldiers, seated before her, gazed at her with emotion and delight.

Then she went to milk her cow and once more gave them some milk on coming back.

They thought of her all the week; several times they even spoke of her. The next Sunday she sat down with them for a little longer talk, and all three, seated side by side, their eyes lost in the distance, clasping their knees with their hands, told the small doings, the minute details of life in the villages where they had been born, while over there the cow, seeing that the milkmaid had stopped on her way, stretched out toward her its heavy head with its dripping nostrils and gave a long low to call her.

Soon the girl consented to eat a bit of bread with them and drink a mouthful of wine. She often brought them plums in her pocket, for the season of plums had come. Her presence sharpened the wits of the two little Breton soldiers, and they chattered like two birds.

But one Tuesday Luc le Ganidec asked for leave—a thing which had never happened before—and he did not return until ten o'clock at night. Jean racked his brains uneasily for a reason for his comrade's going out in this way.

The next Thursday Luc, having borrowed ten sous from his bedfellow, again asked and obtained permission to leave the barracks for several hours. When he set off with Jean on their Sunday walk his manner was very queer, quite restless and quite changed. Kerderen did not understand, but he vaguely suspected something without divining what it could be.

They did not say a word to one another until they reached their usual halting place, where from their constant sitting in the same spot the grass was quite worn away. They ate their breakfast slowly. Neither of them felt hungry.

Before long the girl appeared. As on every Sunday, they watched her coming. When she was quite near Luc rose and made two steps forward. She put her milk pail on the ground and kissed him. She kissed him passionately, throwing her arms about his neck without noticing Jean, without remembering that he was there, without even seeing him.

And he sat there desperate, poor Jean, so desperate that he did not understand, his soul quite overwhelmed, his heart bursting, but not yet understanding himself. Then the girl seated herself beside Luc, and they began to chatter.

Jean did not look at them. He now divined why his comrade had gone out twice during the week, and he felt within him a burning grief, a kind of wound, that sense of rending which is caused by treason.

Luc and the girl went off together to change the position of the cow. Jean followed them with his eyes. He saw them departing side by side. The red breeches of his comrade made a bright spot on the road. It was Luc who picked up the mallet and hammered down the stake to which they tied the beast.

The girl stooped to milk her, while he stroked the cow's sharp spine with a careless hand. Then they left the milk pail on the grass and went deep into the wood.

Jean saw nothing but the wall of leaves where they had entered, and he felt himself so troubled that if he had tried to rise he would certainly have fallen. He sat motionless, stupefied by astonishment and suffering, with an agony which was simple but deep. He wanted to cry, to run away, to hide himself, never to see anybody any more.

Soon he saw them issuing from the thicket. They returned slowly, holding each other's hands as in the villages do those who are promised. It was Luc who carried the pail.

They kissed one another again before they separated, and the girl went off after having thrown Jean a friendly "Good evening" and a smile which was full of meaning. Today she no longer thought of offering him any milk.

The two little soldiers sat side by side, motionless as usual, silent and calm, their placid faces betraying nothing of all which troubled their hearts. The sun fell on them. Sometimes the cow lowed, looking at them from afar.

At their usual hour they rose to go back. Luc cut a switch. Jean carried the empty bottle to return it to the wine seller at Bezons. Then they sallied out upon the bridge and, as they did every Sunday, stopped several minutes in the middle to watch the water flowing.

Jean leaned, leaned more and more, over the iron railing, as though he saw in the current something which attracted him. Luc said: "Are you trying to drink?" Just as he uttered the last word Jean's head overbalanced his body, his legs described a circle in the air and the little blue-and-red soldier fell in a heap, struck the water and disappeared.

Luc, his tongue paralyzed with anguish, tried in vain to shout. Farther down he saw something stir; then the head of his comrade rose to the surface of the river and sank immediately. Farther still he again perceived a hand, a single hand, which issued from the stream and then disappeared. That was all.

The bargemen who dragged the river did not find the body that day.

Luc set out alone for the barracks, going at a run, his soul filled with despair. He told of the accident with tears in his eyes and a husky voice, blowing his nose again and again: "He leaned over. He—he leaned over—so far—so far that his head turned a somersault, and—and—so he fell—he fell——"

Choked with emotion, he could say no more. If he had only known!

THE WILL

I knew that tall young fellow, René de Bourneval. He was an agreeable man, though of a rather melancholy turn of mind and prejudiced against everything, very skeptical and fond of tearing worldly hypocrisies to pieces. He often used to say:

"There are no honorable men or, at any rate, they only appear so when compared to low people."

He had two brothers whom he shunned, the Messrs de Courcils. I thought they were by another father, on account of the difference in the name. I had frequently heard that something strange had happened in the family, but I did not know the details.

As I took a great liking to him, we soon became intimate, and one evening, when I had been dining with him alone, I asked him by chance: "Are you by your mother's first or second marriage?" He grew rather pale; then he flushed and did not speak for a few moments; he was visibly embarrassed. Then he smiled in that melancholy and gentle manner peculiar to him and said:

"My dear friend, if it will not weary you I can give you some very strange particulars about my life. I know you to be a sensible man, so I do not fear that our friendship will suffer by my revelations, and should it suffer, I should not care about having you for my friend any longer.

"My mother, Madame de Courcils, was a poor, little, timid woman, whom her husband had married for the sake of her fortune. Her whole life was a continual martyrdom. Of a loving, delicate mind, she was constantly ill treated by the man who ought to have been my father, one of those boors called country gentlemen. A month after their marriage he was living with a servant, and besides that, the wives and daughters of his tenants were his mistresses, which did not prevent him from having three children by his wife, that is, if you count me in. My mother said nothing and lived in that noisy house like a little mouse. Set aside, disparaged, nervous, she looked at people with bright, uneasy, restless eyes, the eyes of some terrified creature which can never shake off its fear. And yet she was pretty, very pretty and fair, a gray blonde, as if her hair had lost its color through her constant fears.

"Among Monsieur de Courcil's friends who constantly came to the château there was an ex-cavalry officer, a widower, a man to be feared, a man at the same time tender and violent and capable of the most energetic resolution, Monsieur de Bourneval, whose name I bear. He was a tall thin man with a heavy black mustache, and I am very like him. He was a man who had read a great deal and whose ideas were not like those of most of his class. His great-grandmother had been a friend of J. J. Rousseau, and you might have said that he had inherited something of this ancestral connection. He knew the *Contrat Social* and the *Nouvelle Héloïse* by heart, and, indeed, all those philosophical books which led the way to the overthrow of our old usages, prejudices, superannuated laws and imbecile morality.

"It seems that he loved my mother, and she loved him, but their intrigue was carried on so secretly that no one guessed it. The poor, neglected, unhappy woman must have clung to him in a despairing manner and in her intimacy with him must have imbibed all his ways of thinking, theories of free thought, audacious ideas of independent love. But as she was so timid that she never ventured to speak aloud, it was all driven back, condensed and expressed in her heart, which never opened itself.

"My two brothers were very cruel to her, like their father, and never gave her a caress. Used to seeing her count for nothing in the house, they treated her rather like a servant, and so I was the only one of her sons who really loved her and whom she loved.

"When she died I was seventeen, and I must add, in order that you may understand what follows, that there had been a lawsuit between my father and my mother. Their property had been separated to my mother's advantage, as, thanks to the workings of the law and the intelligent devotion of a lawyer to her interests, she had preserved the right to make her will in favor of anyone she pleased.

"We were told that there was a will lying at the lawyer's and were invited to be present at the reading of it. I can remember it as if it were yesterday. It was a grand, dramatic, yet burlesque and surprising scene, brought about by the post-humous revolt of a dead woman, by a cry for liberty from the depths of her tomb, on the part of a martyred woman who had been crushed by a man's habits during her life and who, from her grave, uttered a despairing appeal for independence.

"The man who thought that he was my father, a stout, ruddy-faced man who gave you the idea of a butcher, and my brothers, two great fellows of twenty and twenty-two, were waiting quietly in their chairs. Monsieur de Bourneval, who had been invited to be present, came in and stood behind me. He was very pale and bit his mustache, which was turning gray. No doubt he was prepared for what was going to happen. The lawyer, after opening the envelope in our presence, double-locked the door and began to read the will, which was sealed with red wax and the contents of which he knew not."

My friend stopped suddenly and got up, and from his writing table took an old paper, unfolded it, kissed it and then continued:

"This is the will of my beloved mother:

" 'I, the undersigned, Anne-Catherine-Geneviève-Mathilde de Croixluce, the legitimate wife of Léopold-Joseph Gontran de Courcils, sound in body and mind, here express my last wishes:

" 'I first of all ask God and then my dear son René to pardon me for the act I am about to commit. I believe that my child's heart is great enough to under-stand me and to forgive me. I have suffered my whole life long. I was married out of calculation, then despised, misunderstood, oppressed and constantly deceived by my husband.

" 'I forgive him, but I owe him nothing.

" 'My eldest sons never loved me, never caressed me, scarcely treated me as a mother, but during my whole life I was everything that I ought to have been, and I owe them nothing more after my death. The ties of blood cannot exist without daily and constant affection. An ungrateful son is less than a stranger; he is a culprit, for he has no right to be indifferent toward his mother.

" 'I have always trembled before men, before their unjust laws, their inhuman customs, their shameful prejudices. Before God, I have no longer any fear. Dead, I fling aside disgraceful hypocrisy; I dare to speak my thoughts, and to avow and to sign the secret of my heart.

" 'I therefore leave that part of my fortune of which the law allows me to dispose, as a deposit with my dear lover Pierre-Gennes-Simon de Bourneval, to revert after-ward to our dear son René.

" '(This wish is, moreover, formulated more precisely in a notarial deed.)

" 'And I declare before the Supreme Judge who hears me that I should have cursed heaven and my own existence if I had not met my lover's deep, devoted, tender, unshaken affection, if I had not felt in his arms that the Creator made His creatures to love, sustain and console each other and to weep together in the hours of sadness.

" 'Monsieur de Courcils is the father of my two elder sons; René alone owes his life to Monsier de Bourneval. I pray to the Master of men and of their destinies to place father and son above social prejudices, to make them love each other until they die and to love me also in my coffin.

" 'These are my last thoughts and my last wish.

'MATHILDE DE CROIXLUCE.'

"Monsieur de Courcils had risen, and he cried:

" 'It is the will of a mad woman.'

"Then Monsieur de Bourneval stepped forward and said in a loud and penetrating voice: 'I, Simon de Bourneval, solemnly declare that this writing contains nothing but the strict truth, and I am ready to prove it by letters which I possess.'

"On hearing that Monsieur de Courcils went up to him, and I thought that they were going to collar each other. There they stood, both of them, tall, one stout and the other thin, both trembling. My mother's husband stammered out:

" 'You are a worthless wretch!'

"And the other replied in a loud, dry voice:

" 'We will meet somewhere else, monsieur. I should have already slapped your ugly face and challenged you a long time ago if I had not, before all else, thought of the peace of mind of that poor woman whom you made to suffer so much during her lifetime.'

"Then, turning to me, he said:

" 'You are my son; will you come with me? I have no right to take you away, but I shall assume it if you will allow me.' I shook his hand without replying, and we went out together; I was certainly three parts mad.

"Two days later Monsieur de Bourneval killed Monsieur de Courcils in a duel. My brothers, fearing some terrible scandal, held their tongues. I offered them, and they accepted, half the fortune which my mother had left me. I took my real father's name, renouncing that which the law gave me but which was not really mine. Monsieur de Bourneval died three years afterward, and I have not consoled myself yet."

He rose from his chair, walked up and down the room and, standing in front of me, said:

"I maintain that my mother's will was one of the most beautiful and loyal as well as one of the grandest acts that a woman could perform. Do you not think so?"

I gave him both my hands.

"Most certainly I do, my friend."

A COUNTRY EXCURSION

For five months they had been talking of going to lunch at some country restaurant in the neighborhood of Paris, on Mme Dufour's birthday, and as they were looking forward very impatiently to the outing, they had risen very early that morning. M. Dufour had borrowed the milkman's tilted cart and drove himself. It was a very neat, two-wheeled conveyance with a hood, and in it Mme Dufour, resplendent in a wonderful sherry-colored silk dress, sat by the side of her husband.

The old grandmother and the daughter were accompanied with two chairs, and a yellow-haired youth of whom, however, nothing was to be seen except his head lay at the bottom of the trap.

When they got to the bridge of Neuilly, M. Dufour said: "Here we are in the country at last!" At that warning his wife grew sentimental about the beauties of nature. When they got to the crossroads at Courbevoie they were seized with admiration for the tremendous view down there: on the right was the spire of Argenteuil Church; above it rose the hills of Sannois and the mill of Orgemont, while on the left the aqueduct of Marly stood out against the clear morning sky. In the distance they could see the terrace of Saint-Germain, and opposite to them, at the end of a low chain of hills, the new fort of Cormeilles. Afar—a very long way off, beyond the plains and villages—one could see the somber green of the forests.

The sun was beginning to shine in their faces; the dust got into their eyes, and on either side of the road there stretched an interminable tract of bare, ugly country, which smelled unpleasantly. You would have thought that it had been ravaged by a pestilence which had even attacked the buildings, for skeletons of dilapidated and deserted houses or small cottages left in an unfinished state, as if the contractors had not been paid, reared their four roofless walls on each side.

Here and there tall factory chimneys rose up from the barren soil, the only vegetation on that putrid land, where the spring breezes wafted an odor of petroleum and soot, mingled with another smell that was even still less agreeable. At last, however, they crossed the Seine a second time. It was delightful on the bridge; the river sparkled in the sun, and they had a feeling of quiet satisfaction and enjoyment in drinking in purer air, not impregnated by the black smoke of factories or by the miasma from the deposits of night soil. A man whom they met told them that the name of the place was Bezons, so M. Dufour pulled up and read the attractive announcement outside an eating house:

"Restaurant Poulin, stews and fried fish, private rooms, arbors and swings."

"Well! Madame Dufour, will this suit you? Will you make up your mind at last?"

She read the announcement in her turn and then looked at the house for a time.

It was a white country inn, built by the roadside, and through the open door she could see the bright zinc of the counter at which two workmen out for the day were sitting. At last she made up her mind and said:

"Yes, this will do; and, besides, there is a view."

So they drove into a large yard studded with trees behind the inn, which was only separated from the river by the towing path, and got out. The husband sprang out first and held out his arms for his wife. As the step was very high, Mme Dufour, in order to reach him, had to show the lower part of her limbs, whose former slenderness had disappeared in fat. M. Dufour, who was already getting excited by the country air, pinched her calf and then, taking her in his arms, set her onto the ground as if she had been some enormous bundle. She shook the dust out of the silk dress and then looked round to see in what sort of place she was.

She was a stout woman of about thirty-six, full-blown and delightful to look at. She could hardly breathe, as she was laced too tightly, which forced the heaving mass of her superabundant bosom up to her double chin. Next the girl put her hand onto her father's shoulder and jumped lightly down. The youth with the yellow hair had got down by stepping on the wheel, and he helped M. Dufour to get the grandmother out. Then they unharnessed the horse, which they tied up to a tree, and the carriage fell back with both shafts in the air. The man and boy took off their coats, washed their hands in a pail of water and then joined the ladies, who had already taken possession of the swings.

Mlle Dufour was trying to swing herself standing up, but she could not succeed in getting a start. She was a pretty girl of about eighteen, one of those women who suddenly excite your desire when you meet them in the street and who leave you with a vague feeling of uneasiness and of excited senses. She was tall, had a small waist and large hips, with a dark skin, very large eyes and very black hair. Her dress clearly marked the outlines of her firm, full figure which was accentuated by the motion of her hips as she tried to swing herself higher. Her arms were stretched over her head to hold the rope, so that her bosom rose at every movement she made. Her hat, which a gust of wind had blown off, was hanging behind her, and as the swing gradually rose higher and higher she showed her delicate limbs up to the knees each time, and the wind from the perfumed petticoats, more heady than the fumes of wine, blew into the faces of her father and friend who were looking at her in admiration.

Sitting in the other swing, Mme Dufour kept saying in a monotonous voice:

"Cyprian, come and swing me; do come and swing me, Cyprian!"

At last he complied and, turning up his shirt sleeves as if he intended to work very hard, with much difficulty he set his wife in motion. She clutched the two ropes and held her legs out straight so as not to touch the ground. She enjoyed feeling giddy from the motion of the swing, and her whole figure shook like a jelly on a dish, but as she went higher and higher she grew too giddy and got frightened. Every time she was coming back she uttered a shriek which made all the little urchins come round, and down below, beneath the garden hedge, she vaguely saw a row of mischievous heads, making various grimaces as they laughed.

When a servant girl came out they ordered lunch.

"Some fried fish, a stewed rabbit, salad and dessert," Mme Dufour said with an important air.

"Bring two quarts of beer and a bottle of claret," her husband said.

"We will have lunch on the grass," the girl added.

The grandmother, who had an affection for cats, had been petting one that belonged to the house and had been bestowing the most affectionate words on it for the last ten minutes. The animal, no doubt secretly pleased by her attentions, kept close to the good woman but just out of reach of her hand and quietly walked round the trees against which she rubbed herself, with her tail up, purring with pleasure.

"Hallo!" exclaimed the youth with the yellow hair who was ferreting about. "Here are two swell boats!" They all went to look at them and saw two beautiful skiffs in a wooden boathouse which were as beautifully finished as if they had been objects of luxury. They were moored side by side, like two tall, slender girls, in their narrow, shining length and aroused in one a wish to float in them on warm summer mornings and evenings along flower-covered banks of the river, where the trees dip their branches into the water, where the rushes are continually rustling in the breeze and where the swift kingfishers dart about like flashes of blue lightning.

The whole family looked at them with great respect.

"They are indeed two swell boats," M. Dufour repeated gravely, and he examined them closely, commenting on them like a connoisseur. He had been in the habit of rowing in his younger days, he said, and when he had that in his hands —and he went through the action of pulling the oars—he did not care a fig for anybody. He had beaten more than one Englishman formerly at the Joinville regattas. He grew quite excited at last and offered to make a bet that in a boat like that he could row six miles an hour without exerting himself.

"Lunch is ready," said the waitress, appearing at the entrance to the boathouse. They all hurried off, but two young men were already lunching at the best place, which Mme Dufour had chosen in her mind as her seat. No doubt they were the owners of the skiffs, for they were dressed in boating costume. They were stretched out, almost lying, on chairs and were sunburned and had on flannel trousers and thin cotton jerseys with short sleeves which showed their bare arms, which were as strong as blacksmiths'. They were two strong young fellows, who thought a great deal of their vigor and who showed in all their movements that elasticity and grace of limb which can only be acquired by exercise and which is so different to the awkwardness with which the same continual work stamps the mechanic.

They exchanged a rapid smile when they saw the mother and then a look on seeing the daughter.

"Let us give up our place," one of them said; "it will make us acquainted with them."

The other got up immediately and holding his black-and-red boating cap in his hand, he politely offered the ladies the only shady place in the garden. With many excuses they accepted, and so that it might be more rural, they sat on the grass, without either tables or chairs.

The two young men took their plates, knives, forks, etc., to a table a little way off and began to eat again. Their bare arms, which they showed continually, rather embarrassed the young girl, who even pretended to turn her head aside and not to see them. But Mme Dufour, who was rather bolder, tempted by feminine curiosity, looked at them every moment and no doubt compared them with the secret unsightliness of her husband. She had squatted herself on the ground with her legs tucked under her, after the manner of tailors, and kept wriggling about continually under the pretext that ants were crawling about her somewhere. M. Dufour, whom the politeness of the strangers had put into rather a bad temper, was trying to find a comfortable position, which he did not, however, succeed in doing, while the youth with the yellow hair was eating as silently as an ogre.

"It is lovely weather, monsieur," the stout lady said to one of the boating men. She wished to be friendly, because they had given up their place.

"It is, indeed, madame," he replied; "do you often go into the country?"

"Oh! Only once or twice a year, to get a little fresh air, and you, monsieur?"

"I come and sleep here every night."

"Oh! That must be very nice."

"Certainly it is, madame." And he gave them such a practical account of his daily life that in the hearts of these shopkeepers, who were deprived of the meadows and who longed for country walks, it roused that innate love of nature which they all felt so strongly the whole year round behind the counter in their shop.

The girl raised her eyes and looked at the oarsmen with emotion, and M. Dufour spoke for the first time.

"It is indeed a happy life," he said. And then he added: "A little more rabbit, my dear?"

"No, thank you," she replied and, turning to the young men again and pointing to their arms, asked: "Do you never feel cold like that?"

They both laughed and amazed the family by telling of the enormous fatigue they could endure, of bathing while in a state of tremendous perspiration, of rowing in the fog at night, and they struck their chests violently to show how they sounded.

"Ah! You look very strong," the husband said, and he did not talk any more of the time when he used to beat the English. The girl was looking at them askance now, and the young fellow with the yellow hair, as he had swallowed some wine the wrong way, and was coughing violently, bespattered Mme Dufour's sherry-colored silk dress. Madame got angry and sent for some water to wash the spots.

Meanwhile it had grown unbearably hot; the sparkling river looked like a blaze of fire, and the fumes of the wine were getting into their heads. M. Dufour, who had a violent hiccup, had unbuttoned his waistcoat and the top of his trousers, while his wife, who felt choking, was gradually unfastening her dress. The youth was shaking his yellow wig in a happy frame of mind and kept helping himself to wine, and as the old grandmother felt drunk, she endeavored to be very stiff and dignified. As for the girl, she showed nothing except a peculiar brightness in her eyes, while the brown skin on the cheeks became more rosy.

The coffee finished them off; they spoke of singing, and each of them sang or repeated a couplet, which the others repeated enthusiastically. Then they got up with some difficulty, and while the two women, who were rather dizzy, were getting some fresh air the two males, who were altogether drunk, were performing gymnastic tricks. Heavy, limp and with scarlet faces, they hung awkwardly onto the iron rings without being able to raise themselves, while their shirts were continually threatening to part company with their trousers and to flap in the wind like flags.

Meanwhile the two boating men had got their skiffs into the water. They came back and politely asked the ladies whether they would like a row.

"Would you like one, Monsieur Dufour?" his wife exclaimed. "Please come!"

He merely gave her a drunken look without understanding what she said. Then one of the rowers came up with two fishing rods in his hand, and the hope of catching a gudgeon, that great aim of the Parisian shopkeeper, made Dufour's dull eyes gleam. He politely allowed them to do whatever they liked while he sat in the shade under the bridge, with his feet dangling over the river, by the side of the young man with the yellow hair who was sleeping soundly close to him.

One of the boating men made a martyr of himself and took the mother.

"Let us go to the little wood on the Ile aux Anglais!" he called out as he rowed off. The other skiff went slower, for the rower was looking at his companion so intently that he thought of nothing else. His emotion paralyzed his strength, while the girl, who was sitting on the steerer's seat, gave herself up to the enjoyment of being on the water. She felt disinclined to think, felt a lassitude in her limbs, a complete self-relaxation, as if she were intoxicated. She had become very flushed and breathed pantingly. The effect of the wine, increased by the extreme heat, made all the trees on the bank seem to bow as she passed. A vague wish for enjoyment, a fermentation of her blood, seemed to pervade her whole body, and she was also a little agitated by this tête-à-tête on the water, in a place which seemed depopulated by the heat, with this young man who thought her so pretty, whose looks seemed to caress her skin and whose eyes were as penetrating and exciting as the sun's rays.

Their inability to speak increased their emotion, and they looked about them. At last he made an effort and asked her name.

"Henriette," she said.

"Why! My name is Henri," he replied. The sound of their voices calmed them, and they looked at the banks. The other skiff had gone ahead of them and seemed to be waiting for them. The rower called out:

"We will meet you in the wood; we are going as far as Robinson's,[1] because

[1] A well-known restaurant on the banks of the Seine, much frequented by the bourgeoisie.

Madame Dufour is thirsty." Then he bent over his oars again and rowed off so quickly that he was soon out of sight.

Meanwhile a continual roar which they had heard for some time came nearer, and the river itself seemed to shiver, as if the dull noise were rising from its depths.

"What is that noise?" she asked. It was the noise of the weir, which cut the river in two, at the island. He was explaining it to her, when above the noise of the waterfall they heard the song of a bird, which seemed a long way off.

"Listen!" he said. "The nightingales are singing during the day, so the females must be sitting."

A nightingale! She had never heard one before, and the idea of listening to one roused visions of poetic tenderness in her heart. A nightingale! That is to say, the invisible witness of the lover's interview which Juliet invoked on her balcony,[2] that celestial music which is attuned to human kisses, that eternal inspirer of all those languorous romances which open idealized visions to the poor, tender little hearts of sensitive girls!

She wanted to hear a nightingale.

"We must not make a noise," her companion said, "and then we can go into the wood and sit down close to it."

The skiff seemed to glide. They saw the trees on the island, the banks of which were so low that they could look into the depths of the thickets. They stopped; he made the boat fast; Henriette took hold of Henri's arm, and they went beneath the trees.

"Stoop," he said, so she bent down, and they went into an inextricable thicket of creepers, leaves and reed grass, which formed an impenetrable retreat and which the young man laughingly called "his private room."

Just above their heads, perched in one of the trees which hid them, the bird was still singing. He uttered shakes and roulades and then long, vibrating sounds that filled the air and seemed to lose themselves in the distance, across the level country, through that burning silence which hung low upon the whole country round. They did not speak for fear of frightening the bird away. They were sitting close together, and slowly Henri's arm stole round the girl's waist and squeezed it gently. She took that daring hand, but without anger, and kept removing it whenever he put it round her, not, however, feeling at all embarrassed by this caress, just as if it had been something quite natural which she was resisting just as naturally.

She was listening to the bird in ecstasy. She felt an infinite longing for happiness, for some sudden demonstration of tenderness, for a revelation of divine poesy. She felt such a softening at her heart and such a relaxation of her nerves that she began to cry without knowing why. The young man was now straining her close to him, and she did not remove his arm; she did not think of it. Suddenly the nightingale stopped, and a voice called out in the distance:

"Henriette!"

"Do not reply," he said in a low voice; "you will drive the bird away."

But she had no idea of doing so, and they remained in the same position for some time. Mme Dufour had sat down somewhere or other, for from time to time they heard the stout lady break out into little bursts of laughter.

The girl was still crying; she was filled with strange sensations. Henri's head

[2] Romeo and Juliet, Act III, Scene V.

was on her shoulder, and suddenly he kissed her on the lips. She was surprised and angry and, to avoid him, she stood up.

They were both very pale when they quitted their grassy retreat. The blue sky looked dull to them; the ardent sun was clouded over to their eyes; they perceived not the solitude and the silence. They walked quickly side by side without speaking or touching each other, appearing to be irreconcilable enemies, as if disgust had sprung up between them and hatred between their souls. From time to time Henriette called out: "Mamma!"

By and by they heard a noise in a thicket, and Mme Dufour appeared, looking rather confused, and her companion's face was wrinkled with smiles that he could not check.

Mme Dufour took his arm, and they returned to the boats. Henri went on first, still without speaking, by the girl's side, and at last they got back to Bezons. M. Dufour, who had sobered up, was waiting for them very impatiently, while the youth with the yellow hair was having a mouthful of something to eat before leaving the inn. The carriage was in the yard, with the horse in, and the grandmother, who had already gotten in, was frightened at the thought of being overtaken by night before they got back to Paris, the outskirts not being safe.

The young men shook hands with them, and the Dufour family drove off.

"Good-by, until we meet again!" the oarsmen cried, and the answers they got were a sigh and a tear.

Two months later, as Henri was going along the Rue des Martyrs, he saw "Dufour, Ironmonger," over a door. So he went in and saw the stout lady sitting at the counter. They recognized each other immediately, and after an interchange of polite greetings he inquired after them all.

"And how is Mademoiselle Henriette?" he inquired specially.

"Very well, thank you; she is married."

"Ah!" Mastering his feelings, he added: "To whom was she married?"

"To that young man who went with us, you know; he has joined us in business."

"I remember him perfectly."

He was going out, feeling unhappy though scarcely knowing why, when Madame called him back.

"And how is your friend?" she asked rather shyly.

"He is very well, thank you."

BERTHA

My old friend—one has friends occasionally who are much older than oneself— my old friend Dr Bonnet had often invited me to spend some time with him at Riom, and as I did not know Auvergne, I made up my mind to go there in the summer of 1876.

I got there by the morning train, and the first person I saw on the platform was the doctor. He was dressed in a gray suit and wore a soft, black, wide-brimmed, high-crowned felt hat, which was narrow at the top like a chimney pot, a hat which hardly anyone except an Auvergnant would wear and which smacked of the charcoal burner. Dressed like that, the doctor had the appearance of an old young man with a spare body under a thin coat and a large head covered with white hair.

He embraced me with the evident pleasure which country people feel when they meet long-expected friends and, stretching out his arm, said proudly: "This is Auvergne!"

I saw nothing before me, except a range of mountains whose summits, which resembled truncated cones, must have been extinct volcanoes.

Then, pointing to the name of the station, he said:

"Riom, the fatherland of magistrates, the pride of the magistracy, ought rather to be the fatherland of doctors."

"Why?" I asked.

"Why?" he replied with a laugh. "If you transpose the letters you have the Latin word *mori*, to die. That is the reason why I settled here, my young friend."

And delighted at his own joke, he carried me off, rubbing his hands.

As soon as I had swallowed a cup of coffee he made me go and see the town. I admired the chemist's house and the other celebrated houses, which were all black, but as pretty as knickknacks, with their façades of sculptured stone. I admired the statue of the Virgin, the patroness of butchers, and he told me an amusing story about this, which I will relate some other time. Then Dr Bonnet said to me:

"I must beg you to excuse me for a few minutes while I go and see a patient, and then I will take you to Chatel-Guyon, so as to show you the general aspect of the town and all the mountain chain of the Puy-de-Dôme before lunch. You can wait for me outside; I shall only go upstairs and come down immediately."

He left me outside one of those old, gloomy, silent, melancholy houses which one sees in the provinces. This one appeared to look particularly sinister, and I soon discovered the reason. All the large windows on the first floor were half boarded up with wooden shutters. The upper part of them alone could be opened, as if one had wished to prevent the people who were locked up in that huge stone trunk from looking into the street.

When the doctor came down again I told him how it had struck me, and he replied:

"You are quite right; the poor creature who is living there must never see what is going on outside. She is a madwoman, or rather an idiot, what you Normans would call a *Niente*.[1] It is a miserable story, but a very singular pathological case at the same time. Shall I tell you of it?"

I begged him to do so, and he continued:

"Twenty years ago the owners of this house, who were my patients, had a daughter who was seemingly like all other girls. But I soon discovered that while her body became admirably developed her intellect remained stationary.

"She began to walk very early but could not talk. At first I thought she was deaf but discovered that although she heard perfectly, she did not understand anything that was said to her. Violent noises made her start and frightened her, without her understanding how they were caused.

"She grew up into a superb woman, but she was dumb, from an absolute want of intellect. I tried all means to introduce a gleam of sense into her head, but nothing succeeded. I thought that I noticed that she knew her nurse, though as soon as she was weaned she failed to recognize her mother. She could never pro-

[1] A Nothing, i.e., an idiot.

nounce that word, which is the first that children utter and the last which men murmur when dying on the field of battle. She sometimes tried to talk but produced nothing but incoherent sounds.

"When the weather was fine she laughed continually, emitting low cries which might be compared to the twittering of birds. When it rained she cried and moaned in a mournful, terrifying manner, like the howling of a dog when death occurs in a house.

"She was fond of rolling on the grass, like young animals do, and of running about madly. She used to clap her hands every morning when the sun shone into her room and would jump out of bed and insist, by signs, on being dressed as quickly as possible so that she might get out.

"She did not appear to distinguish between people, between her mother and her nurse, or between her father and me or between the coachman and the cook. I liked her parents, who were very unhappy on her account, very much, and went to see them nearly every day. I dined with them tolerably frequently, which enabled me to remark that Bertha (they had called her Bertha) seemed to recognize the various dishes and to prefer some to others. At that time she was twelve years old but as fully formed in figure as a girl of eighteen and taller than I was. Then the idea struck me of developing her greediness and by such means to try and produce some slight power of discernment into her mind—to force her, by the diversity of flavors, if not by reason, to arrive at instinctive distinctions, which would of themselves constitute a species of analysis akin to thought. Later on, by appealing to her senses and by carefully making use of those which could serve us, we might hope to obtain a kind of reaction on her intellect and by degrees increase the involuntary action of her brain.

"One day I put two plates before her, one of soup and the other of very sweet vanilla cream. I made her taste each of them successively, then I let her choose for herself, and she ate the plate of cream. In a short time I made her very greedy, so greedy that it appeared as if the only idea she had in her head was the desire for eating. She recognized the various dishes perfectly, stretched out her hands toward those that she liked and took hold of them eagerly, crying when they were taken from her. Then I thought I would try and teach her to come to the dining room when the dinner bell rang. It took a long time, but I succeeded in the end. In her vacant intellect there was a fixed correlation between the sound and her taste, a correspondence between two senses, an appeal from one to the other and, consequently, a sort of connection of ideas—if one can term an instinctive hyphen between two organic functions an idea—and so I carried my experiments further and taught her, with much difficulty, to recognize mealtimes on the face of the clock.

"It was impossible for me for a long time to attract her attention to the hands, but I succeeded in making her remark the clockwork and the striking apparatus. The means I employed were very simple. I asked them not to have the bell rung for lunch but that everybody should get up and go into the dining room when the little brass hammer struck twelve o'clock, but I found great difficulty in making her learn to count the strokes. She ran to the door each time she heard the clock strike, but by degrees she learned that all the strokes had not the same value as regards meals, and she frequently fixed her eyes, guided by her ears, on the dial of the clock.

"When I noticed that I took care, every day at twelve and at six o'clock, to place my fingers on the figures twelve and six as soon as the moment she was waiting for had arrived. I soon noticed that she attentively followed the motion of the small brass hands, which I had often turned in her presence.

"She had understood! Perhaps I should rather say that she had seized the idea. I had succeeded in getting the knowledge, or rather the sensation, of the time into her, just as is the case with carp, who certainly have no clocks but know that they are fed every day at a certain time.

"When once I had obtained that result, all the clocks and watches in the house occupied her attention almost exclusively. She spent her time in looking at them, in listening to them and in waiting for mealtimes, and once something very funny happened. The striking apparatus of a pretty little Louis XVI clock that hung at the head of her bed had got out of order, and she noticed it. She sat for twenty minutes with her eyes on the hands, waiting for it to strike ten, but when the hand passed the figure she was astonished at not hearing anything. So stupefied was she, indeed, that she sat down, no doubt overwhelmed by a feeling of violent emotion, such as attacks us in the face of some terrible catastrophe. She had the wonderful patience to wait until eleven o'clock, in order to see what would happen, but, as she naturally heard nothing, she was suddenly either seized with a wild fit of rage at having been deceived and imposed upon by appearances, or else was overcome by the fear which a frightened creature feels at some terrible mystery or by the furious impatience of a passionate individual who meets with some obstacle. She took up the tongs from the fireplace and struck the clock so violently that she broke it to pieces in a moment.

"It is evident, therefore, that her brain did act and calculate, obscurely it is true, and within very restricted limits, for I could never succeed in making her distinguish persons as she distinguished the time. To stir her intellect it was necessary to appeal to her passions in the material sense of the word, and we soon had another and, alas, a very terrible proof of this!

"She had grown up into a splendid girl, a perfect type of a race, a sort of lovely and stupid Venus. She was sixteen, and I have rarely seen such perfection of form, such suppleness and such regular features. I said she was a Venus; yes, a fair, stout, vigorous Venus, with large, bright, vacant eyes, blue as the flowers of the flax plant. She had a large mouth with full lips, the mouth of a glutton, of a sensualist, a mouth made for kisses. Well, one morning her father came into my consulting room with a strange look on his face and, sitting down, without even replying to my greeting, he said:

"'I want to speak to you about a very serious matter. Would it be possible—would it be possible for Bertha to marry?'

"'Bertha to marry! Why, it is quite impossible!'

"'Yes, I know, I know,' he replied. 'But reflect, Doctor—don't you think—perhaps—we hoped—if she had children—it would be a great shock to her, but a great happiness, and who knows whether maternity might not rouse her intellect?'

"I was in a state of great perplexity. He was right, and it was possible that such a new situation and that wonderful instinct of maternity which beats in the hearts of the lower animals as it does in the heart of a woman, which makes a hen fly at a dog's jaws to defend her chickens, might bring about a revolution, an utter change in her vacant mind, and set the motionless mechanism of her thoughts into movement. And then, moreover, I immediately remembered a personal instance. Some years previously I had possessed a spaniel bitch which was so stupid that I could do nothing with her, but when she had had pups she became, if not exactly clever, yet as intelligent as many other dogs who have not been thoroughly broken.

"As soon as I foresaw the possibility of this the wish to get Bertha married grew on me, not so much out of friendship for her and her poor parents, as from scientific curiosity. What would happen? It was a singular problem, and I said to her father:

" 'Perhaps you are right. You might make the attempt—but—but you will never find a man to consent to marry her.'

" 'I have found somebody,' he said in a low voice.

"I was dumfounded and said: 'Somebody really suitable? Someone of your own rank and position in society?'

" 'Decidedly,' he replied.

" 'Oh! And may I ask his name?'

" 'I came on purpose to tell you and to consult you. It is Monsieur Gaston du Boys de Lucelles.'

"I felt inclined to exclaim: 'What a wretch,' but I held my tongue, and after a few moments' silence I said:

" 'Oh! Very good. I see nothing against it.'

"The poor man shook me heartily by the hand and said:

" 'She is to be married next month.'

"Monsieur Gaston du Boys de Lucelles was a scapegrace of good family, who, after having spent all that he had inherited from his father and having incurred debts by all kinds of doubtful means, had been trying to discover some other way of obtaining money. Hence this method. He was a good-looking young fellow and in capital health, but fast—one of that odious tribe of provincial fast men—and appeared to me to be the sort of a husband who could be got rid of later, by making him an allowance. He came to the house to pay his addresses and to strut about before the idiot girl who, however, seemed to please him. He brought her flowers, kissed her hands, sat at her feet and looked at her with affectionate eyes, but she took no notice of any of his attentions and made no distinction between him and the other persons about her.

"However, the marriage took place, and you may guess how excited my curiosity was. I went to see Bertha the next day, to try and discover from her looks whether any feeling had been roused in her, but I found her just the same as she was every day, wholly taken up with the clock and dinner, while he, on the contrary, appeared really in love and tried to rouse his wife's spirits and affection by little endearments and such caresses as one bestows on a kitten. He could think of nothing better.

"I called upon the married couple pretty frequently, and I soon perceived that the young woman knew her husband and gave him those eager looks which she had hitherto only bestowed on sweet dishes.

"She followed his movements, knew his step on the stairs or in the neighboring rooms and clapped her hands when he came in. Her face was changed and brightened by the flames of profound happiness and of desire. She loved him with her whole body and with all her being, to the very depths of her poor, weak soul, and with all her heart, the poor heart of some grateful animal. It was really a delightful and innocent picture of simple passion, of carnal yet modest passion, such as nature planted in mankind before man complicated and disfigured it by all the various shades of sentiment. But he soon grew tired of this ardent, beautiful, dumb creature and did not spend more than an hour a day with her, thinking it sufficient to devote his nights to her, and she began to suffer in consequence. She used to wait for him from morning till night with her eyes on the clock. She did not even look after the meals now, for he took all his away from home, Clermont, Chatel-Guyon, Royat, no matter where, as long as he was not obliged to come home.

"She began to grow thin; every other thought, every other wish, every other expectation and every other confused hope disappeared from her mind, and the hours during which she did not see him became hours of terrible suffering to her. Soon he used frequently not to come home at night; he spent them with women at the casino at Royat and did not come home until daybreak. But she never went to bed before he returned. She would remain sitting motionless in an easy chair, with her eyes fixed on the clock, which turned so slowly and regularly round the china face on which the hours were painted.

"When she heard the trot of his horse in the distance she would sit up with a start. When he came into the room she would get up with the movements of a phantom and point to the clock, as if to say to him: 'Look how late it is!'

"He began to be afraid of this amorous and jealous half-witted woman and flew into a rage, like brutes do, and one night he even went so far as to strike her, so they sent for me. When I arrived she was writhing and screaming in a terrible crisis of pain, anger, passion; how do I know what? Can anyone tell what goes on in such undeveloped brains?

"I calmed her by subcutaneous injections of morphine and forbade her to see that man again, for I saw clearly that marriage would infallibly kill her by degrees.

"Then she went mad! Yes, my dear friend, that idiot has gone mad. She is always thinking of him and waiting for him; she waits for him all day and night, awake or asleep, at this very moment, ceaselessly. When I saw her getting thinner and thinner, never taking her eyes off the clocks, I had them removed from the house. I thus make it impossible for her to count the hours or to remember from her indistinct reminiscences at what time he used to come home. I hope to destroy the recollection of it in time and to extinguish that ray of thought which I had kindled with so much difficulty.

"The other day I tried an experiment. I offered her my watch. She took it and looked at it for some time; then she began to scream terribly, as if the sight of that little object had suddenly aroused her recollection, which was beginning to grow indistinct. She is pitiably thin now, with hollow and brilliant eyes, and she walks up and down ceaselessly, like a wild beast does in its cage. I have had bars put to the windows and have had the seats fixed to the floor, so as to prevent her from looking to see whether he is coming.

"Oh, her poor parents! What a life they must lead!"

We had got to the top of the hill, and the doctor turned round and said to me: "Look at Riom from here."

The gloomy town looked like some ancient city. Behind it, a green, wooded plain studded with towns and villages and bathed in a soft blue haze extended until it was lost in the distance. Far away on my right there was a range of lofty mountains with round summits or truncated cones, and the doctor began to enumerate the villages, towns and hills and to give me the history of all of them. But I did not listen to him; I was thinking of nothing but the mad woman and only saw her. She seemed to be hovering over that vast extent of country like a mournful ghost, and I asked him abruptly:

"What has become of the husband?"

My friend seemed rather surprised, but after a few moments' hesitation he replied:

"He is living at Royat on an allowance that they make him and is quite happy; he leads a very fast life."

As we were going slowly back, both of us silent and rather low-spirited, an English dogcart, drawn by a thoroughbred horse, came up behind us and passed us rapidly. The doctor took me by the arm.

"There he is," he said.

I saw nothing except a gray felt hat, cocked over one ear, above a pair of broad shoulders, driving off in a cloud of dust.

WALTER SCHNAFFS' ADVENTURE

Since his entrance into France, with the army of the invasion, Walter Schnaffs judged himself the most unfortunate of men. He was stout, walked with difficulty, puffed much, and suffered frightfully with his feet, which were very broad and fat. Outwardly, he seemed peaceful and benevolent, neither brave nor bloodthirsty, the father of four children whom he adored, and married to a young, blond woman whose caresses and cares and tenderness he desperately regretted every evening. He loved to rise late and go to bed early, to eat slowly of good things and drink beer in cafés. He felt that all that was sweet in existence disappeared with this life; and he had at heart a terrible fear and hatred, both instinctive and reasonable, of cannons, guns, revolvers, and swords, and especially of bayonets, feeling himself incapable of maneuvering rapidly enough to defend his great body with such a weapon.

And, when night had come and he had lain down to sleep upon the earth, wrapped in his blanket by the side of his comrades, who were snoring, he thought long of his home, left behind him in Germany, and of the dangers sown all along the route. "If I should be killed what would become of the little ones?" he thought. "Who would feed them and bring them up?" At that very moment they were not rich, in spite of the debts he had contracted before he started, in order to leave them a little money. And sometimes Walter Schnaffs wept.

At the beginning of a battle he felt his knees growing so weak that he would have fallen had he not known that the whole army would pass over his body. The whistling of the bullets made his hair stand on end. For some months he lived thus, in terror and in anguish.

His army corps was advancing toward Normandy. One day he was sent out to reconnoiter with a small detachment which was simply to explore a part of the country and report immediately. All seemed calm in the country; nothing indicated a prepared resistance.

The Prussians were descending quietly into a little valley divided by deep ravines when a violent fusillade stopped them short, laying low one in twenty of their men; and a company of sharpshooters, coming out suddenly from a little wood, plunged forward with their bayonets fixed.

Walter Schnaffs remained motionless at first, so surprised and dismayed that he did not even think of fleeing. Then a foolish desire to run away seized him; but he thought immediately that he could run only like a tortoise in comparison with the thin Frenchmen, who were coming on in leaps and bounds, like a troop of goats. Then, perceiving but six steps before him a large ditch full of brushwood covered with dead leaves, he jumped in with both feet, without even thinking how deep it was, as one might jump from a bridge into a river. He went like a dart, through a thick layer of creepers and sharp twigs, which tore his face and hands as he fell, and found himself seated heavily on a bed of stones. Raising his eyes, he could see the sky through the hole that he had made. This hole might lead to his discovery, and he dragged himself along cautiously, on all fours, at the bottom of this ditch, under a roof of enlaced branches, going with all speed possible as far as he could from the combat. Then he stopped and seated himself, crouching like a hare in the midst of the tall dry grass.

For some time longer he heard the reports of the guns and the cries of the wounded, then the clamor of the struggle grew feebler and finally ceased. All became still and calm.

Suddenly something moved near him. He had a fearful shock. It was a little bird, which, standing upon a branch, had shaken the dry leaves. For nearly an hour, the man's heart beat with heavy, rapid strokes.

Night came on, filling the ravine with shadows. The soldier began to think. What was he going to do? What would become of him? Should he rejoin his regiment? But how? And where? Was it necessary to begin over again the life of anguish, of fear, of fatigue and suffering that he had led since the beginning of the war? No! He would never have the courage. He would never have the energy necessary to support the marches and confront the dangers of each minute.

But what was to be done? He could not remain in this ravine and conceal himself there until the end of hostilities. Certainly not. If he were not obliged to eat, this prospect might not have deterred him; but he must eat, and eat every day.

Thus he found himself alone, under arms, in uniform, in the enemy's territory, far from those able to defend him. Cold shivers ran through his body. Suddenly he thought: "If only I were a prisoner!" And his heart trembled with the desire, a violent, immoderate desire to be made prisoner by the French. He would be safely lodged and fed, under shelter from bullets and swords, without possible apprehension, in a good prison well guarded. A prisoner! What a dream!

His resolution was made immediately: "I will go and give myself up as a prisoner." He got up resolved to execute his project without a minute's delay. But he remained there, suddenly assailed by cowardly reflections and new fears.

Where should he go to give himself up? And how? On which side? And frightful images of death invaded his soul. He might run some terrible dangers in venturing out alone through the country in his metal-pointed helmet. If he should meet some country people? These peasants, seeing a Prussian soldier lost, a de-

fenseless Prussian, would kill him like a stray dog! They would murder him, with
their forks, their pickaxes, their scythes, their shovels! They would reduce him to
pulp and make mincemeat of him with the savagery of exasperated conquerors.

And if he should meet some sharpshooters? These madmen, without law or
discipline, would shoot him to amuse themselves, to pass away an hour, for the
fun of seeing his face. And he could already imagine himself against a wall, facing
a dozen gun barrels, whose little round, black holes seemed to be looking at him.

And if he should meet the French army? The advance guard would take him
for a spy, for some brave and hardy rogue of a trooper sent out alone to reconnoiter,
and would shoot him down at once. And he could already hear the irregular reports
of the guns of soldiers concealed in the woods, while he, standing in the middle
of a field, would be riddled with bullets like a strainer, and he could feel them
entering his flesh. He sat down again in despair. His situation appeared to be
hopeless.

Night had now come, night still and dark. He no longer moved, and started at
every unknown and slight noise which passed in the shadows. A rabbit, bobbing
up and down on the edge of his burrow, almost put Walter Schnaffs to flight. The
cries of the screech owl tore his soul, rending it with sudden fear, as painful as
wounds. He stared with his big eyes, trying to penetrate the shadows; and he imagined every moment that he heard some one walking near him.

After interminable hours and the anguish of the damned, he perceived through
his ceiling of branches that the sky was becoming bright. Then immense relief
came to him; his members relaxed in sudden repose; his heart was easy; his eyes
closed. He fell asleep.

When he awoke, the sun seemed to him to be nearly in the middle of the sky;
it should, therefore, be midday. No noise troubled the dull peace of the fields;
and Walter Schnaffs perceived that he was seized with acute hunger. He yawned,
his mouth watering at the thought of sausage, the good military sausage, and he
got a pain in his stomach.

He stood up, took some steps, felt that his legs were feeble, and sat down again
to think. For three or four hours more he argued for and against, changing his
mind every moment, unhappy, drawn this way and that by the most contradictory
arguments.

One idea seemed to him logical and practical: that was to watch until some
villager passed, alone, without arms or dangerous tools, to run up to him and
deliver himself into his hands, making him understand that he was giving himself
up. Then he removed his helmet, the point of which might betray him, and put his
head out of his hole with infinite precautions.

No single human being was in sight. Down there, to the right, a little village
sent to the sky the smoke from its roofs, the smoke from its kitchens! To the left,
he perceived at the end of an avenue of trees, a great castle flanked with turrets.
He waited until evening, suffering frightfully, seeing nothing but flocks of crows
and hearing nothing but the dull rumbling of his stomach.

Again the night fell upon him. He stretched himself out at the bottom of his
retreat and fell into a feverish sleep, haunted by nightmares, the sleep of a famished
man. The dawn again rose upon him. He again set himself to watch, but the
countryside was as empty as the day before. And a new fear entered the mind of
Walter Schnaffs—the fear of dying of hunger. He saw himself stretched at the
bottom of that hole, on his back, his eyes closed. Then some animals, small ani-

mals of every sort, would come and begin to eat his dead body, attacking him everywhere simultaneously, slipping in under his garments to bite his cold flesh. And a great raven would pick his eyes out with its sharp beak.

Then he became mad, imagining that he was swooning from weakness and could no longer walk. And he prepared to start toward the village, resolved to dare all, to defy all; but he perceived three peasants going to the fields with their forks on their shoulders, and he plunged back into his hiding place.

When evening darkened the plain again, he got out slowly from the ditch and started on the way, crouching, fearful, his heart beating, towards the far-off castle, preferring to enter that rather than the village, which seemed to him as dangerous as a den of tigers.

The lower windows were brilliantly lighted, one of them being open; and a strong odor of food, cooked food, came from it, entering Walter Schnaffs' nostrils and penetrating to the depths of his body, causing his body to become tense and his breath to come in gasps. It drew him irresistibly, inspiring his heart with desperate audacity. And suddenly, without thinking, he appeared at the window with his helmet on his head.

Eight servants were dining around a big table. Suddenly a maid sat still with her mouth open, letting her glass fall, her eyes staring. Then, every glance followed hers.

They perceived the enemy! My God! The Prussians are attacking the castle!

At first this was a single cry, made up of eight cries in eight different tones, a cry of horrible fear, then there was a tumultuous moving, a hustling, a melee, a general flight for the farthest door. Chairs fell, men knocked over the women to get ahead of them. In two seconds the room was empty, abandoned, with a table covered with eatables in front of Walter Schnaffs, who stood still in amazement outside the window.

After some moments of hesitation, he jumped over the window sill and advanced towards the plates. His keen hunger made him tremble like one in a fever; but terror still held him and paralyzed him. He listened. The whole house seemed to tremble; doors opened and shut, and rapid steps sounded on the floor above. The uneasy Prussian strained his ears to catch these confused noises; then he heard heavy sounds as if bodies were falling in the soft earth at the foot of the walls, human bodies jumping from the first story.

Then all movement, all agitation ceased, and the great castle became silent as a tomb.

Walter Schnaffs seated himself before a plate still intact, and began to eat. He ate with great mouthfuls as if he feared being interrupted too soon, before he had devoured enough. He threw the pieces with both hands into his mouth, opened like a trap; huge pieces of food descended into his stomach, one after the other, straining his throat in passing. Sometimes he interrupted himself, feeling ready to burst, like an overfilled pipe. He took the cider pitcher and poured its contents down his throat, as one washes out a stopped-up conduit.

He emptied all the plates, all the dishes, and all the bottles; then, full of liquid and eatables, besotted, red, shaking with hiccups, his mouth greasy, his mind troubled, he unbuttoned his uniform in order to breathe, incapable of taking another step. His eyes closed, his ideas became vague; he dropped his heavy head in his crossed arms on the table and sweetly lost all consciousness of his surroundings.

The waning crescent lighted the horizon vaguely through the trees of the park. It was the cold hour which precedes the day. Sometimes a ray of the moon glittered like a point of steel among the shadows of the thicket.

The quiet castle appeared like a great, black silhouette against the clear sky. Two windows alone on the ground floor were still brilliantly lighted. Suddenly, a voice of thunder cried:

"Forward! To the assault! Come on, boys!"

Then, in an instant, the doors, shutters, even the windows, were broken down by the rush of men who dashed forward, breaking and overturning all in their way, invading the house. In an instant fifty men, armed to the teeth, bounded into the kitchen where Walter Schnaffs was peacefully sleeping; and, presenting to his breast their loaded guns, they seized him, rolled him over, threw him down, and bound him hand and foot.

He was breathless with astonishment, too dazed to understand, beaten, battered and mad with terror. Suddenly a fat military-looking man, covered with gold lace, planted his foot upon his body, calling out vociferously:

"You are my prisoner! Surrender!"

The Prussian understood only the single word "prisoner," and groaned: "Ja, ja, ja!"

He was taken up, bound to a chair, and examined with a lively curiosity by his conquerors, who were puffing like porpoises. Many of them sat down, overcome by emotion and fatigue.

He smiled; he could smile now, sure at last of being a prisoner!

An officer entered and announced:

"Colonel, the enemy is put to flight. Many of them appear to have been wounded. We are now masters of the place."

The fat officer, wiping his brow, shouted: "Victory!" And, drawing a little notebook from his pocket, he wrote:

"After a desperate struggle, the Prussians had to beat a retreat, taking their dead and wounded with them, estimated at about fifty men. Several remain in our hands."

The young officer inquired: "Colonel, what measures are to be taken?"

The colonel replied: "We shall fall back in order to avoid a resumption of the offensive with artillery and superior forces." And he gave the order to depart.

The column re-formed in the shadow under the wall of the castle, and set off, surrounding, with great care, Walter Schnaffs, bound and guarded by six warriors with revolvers in hand. Scouts were sent out to reconnoiter the route. They advanced with great care, halting from time to time. At daybreak they arrived at the subprefect's, in La Roche-Oysel, whose National Guard had accomplished this feat of arms.

The people of the town, anxious and excited, awaited them. When they saw the prisoner's helmet, fearful shouts arose. Women lifted up their hands, old people wept, a grandfather threw his crutch at the Prussian and wounded the nose of one of his guards. The colonel shouted: "Look out for the safety of the prisoner!"

Finally, they came to the town hall. The prison was opened, and Walter Schnaffs was thrown in, freed from his fetters. Two hundred men, in arms, mounted guard on the building.

Then, in spite of the symptoms of indigestion which had been troubling him for some time, the Prussian, mad with joy, began to dance, to dance madly, raising his arms and legs and uttering frenzied cries, until he fell exhausted against the wall. He was a prisoner! He was saved.

And thus it was that the castle of Champignet was retaken from the enemy after only six hours of occupation.

Colonel Ratier, cloth merchant, who accomplished this feat at the head of the National Guards of La Roche-Oysel, was decorated for it.

THE LOG

It was a small drawing room with thick hangings and with a faint aromatic smell of flowers and scent in the air. A large fire was burning in the grate, and one lamp, covered with a shade of old lace, on the corner of the mantelpiece threw a soft light onto the two persons who were talking.

She, the mistress of the house, was an old lady with white hair, one of those adorable old ladies whose unwrinkled skin is as smooth as the finest paper and is scented, impregnated with perfume, the delicate essences used in the bath for so many years having penetrated through the epidermis.

He was a very old friend, who had never married, a constant friend, a companion in the journey of life, but nothing else.

They had not spoken for about a minute and were both looking at the fire, dreaming of nothing in particular. It was one of those moments of sympathetic silence between people who have no need to be constantly talking in order to be happy together. Suddenly a large log, a stump covered with burning roots, fell out. It fell over the firedogs onto the drawing-room floor, scattering great sparks all round. The old lady sprang up with a scream, as if to run away, but he kicked the log back onto the hearth and trod out the burning sparks with his boots.

When the disaster was repaired there was a strong smell of burning. Sitting down opposite to his friend, the man looked at her with a smile and said as he pointed to the log:

"That accident recalls the reason I never married."

She looked at him in astonishment, with the inquisitive gaze of women who wish to know everything, eying him as women do who are no longer young, with intense and malicious curiosity. Then she asked:

"How so?"

"Oh, it is a long story," he replied; "a rather sad and unpleasant story.

"My old friends were often surprised at the coldness which suddenly sprang up between one of my best friends, whose Christian name was Julien, and myself. They could not understand how two such intimate and inseparable friends as we had been could suddenly become almost strangers to one another. I will tell you the reason of it.

"He and I used to live together at one time. We were never apart, and the friendship that united us seemed so strong that nothing could break it.

"One evening when he came home he told me that he was going to be married, and it gave me a shock, just as if he had robbed me or betrayed me. When a man's friend marries all is over between them. The jealous affection of a woman, a suspicious, uneasy and carnal affection, will not tolerate that sturdy and frank attachment, that attachment of the mind and of the heart, and the mutual confidence which exists between two men.

"However great the love may be that unites them, a man and a woman are always strangers in mind and intellect; they remain belligerents; they belong to different races. There must always be a conqueror and a conquered, a master and a slave; now the one, now the other—they are never equal. They press each other's hands, hands trembling with amorous passion, but they never press them with a long, strong, loyal pressure, a pressure which seems to open hearts and to lay them bare in a burst of sincere, strong, manly affection. Ancient philosophers, as a consolation for old age, sought for a good reliable friend and grew old with him in that communion of thought which exists between men. They did not marry and procreate children who would, when grown, abandon them.

"Well, my friend Julien married. His wife was pretty, charming, a light, curly-haired, plump, bright little woman, who seemed to worship him. At first I went but rarely to their house, as I was afraid of interfering with their affection and averse to being in their way. But somehow they attracted me to their house; they were constantly inviting me and seemed very fond of me. Consequently, by degrees I allowed myself to be allured by the charm of their life. I often dined with them, and frequently, when I returned home at night, thought that I would do as he had done and get married, as I found my empty house very dull. They seemed very much in love with one another and were never apart.

"Well, one evening Julien wrote and asked me to go to dinner, and naturally I went.

" 'My dear fellow,' he said, 'I must go out directly afterward on business, and I shall not be back until eleven o'clock, but I shall not be later. Can I depend on you to keep Bertha company?'

"The young woman smiled.

" 'It was my idea,' she said, 'to send for you.'

"I held out my hand to her.

" 'You are as nice as ever,' I said, and I felt a long, friendly pressure of my fingers, but I paid no attention to it. We sat down to dinner, and at eight o'clock Julien went out.

"As soon as he had gone a kind of strange embarrassment immediately seemed to come over his wife and me. We had never been alone together yet, and in spite of our daily increasing intimacy this tête-à-tête placed us in a new position. At first I spoke vaguely of those indifferent matters with which one fills up an embarrassing silence, but she did not reply and remained opposite to me, looking down in an undecided manner, as if thinking over some difficult subject. As I was at a loss for commonplace ideas I held my tongue. It is surprising how hard it is at times to find anything to say.

"And then again I felt in the air, in my bones, so to speak, something which it is impossible for me to express, that mysterious premonition which tells you beforehand of the secret intentions, be they good or evil, of another person with respect to yourself.

"The painful silence lasted some time, and then Bertha said to me:

" 'Will you kindly put a log on the fire, for it is going out.'

"So I opened the box where the wood was kept, which was placed just where yours is, took out the largest log and put it on top of the others, which were three parts burned, and then silence reigned in the room again.

"In a few minutes the log was burning so brightly that it scorched our faces, and the young woman raised her eyes to me—eyes that had a strange look to me.

" 'It is too hot now,' she said; 'let us go and sit on the sofa over there.'

"So we went and sat on the sofa, and then she said suddenly, looking me full in the face:

" 'What should you do if a woman were to tell you that she was in love with you?'

" 'Upon my word,' I replied, very much at a loss for an answer, 'I cannot imagine such a case, but it would very much depend upon the woman.'

"She gave a hard, nervous, vibrating laugh, one of those false laughs which seem as if they would break thin glasses, and then she added: 'Men are never venturesome or acute.' And after a moment's silence she continued: 'Have you ever been in love, Monsieur Paul?' I was obliged to acknowledge that I certainly had been, and she asked me to tell her all about it, whereupon I made up some story or other. She listened to me attentively with frequent signs of approbation or contempt, and then suddenly she said:

" 'No, you understand nothing about the subject. It seems to me that real love must unsettle the mind, upset the nerves and distract the head; that it must—how shall I express it?—be dangerous, even terrible, almost criminal and sacrilegious; that it must be a kind of treason; I mean to say that it is almost bound to break laws, fraternal bonds, sacred obstacles; when love is tranquil, easy, lawful and without danger is it really love?'

"I did not know what answer to give her, and this philosophical reflection occurred to me: 'Oh, female brain, here indeed you show yourself!'

"While speaking she had assumed a demure, saintly air, and, resting on the cushions, she stretched herself out at full length, with her head on my shoulders and her dress pulled up a little, so as to show her red silk stockings, which looked still brighter in the firelight. In a minute or two she continued:

" 'I suppose I have frightened you?' I protested against such a notion, and she leaned against my breast altogether, and without looking at me she said: 'If I were to tell you that I love you what would you do?'

"And before I could think of an answer she had thrown her arms round my neck, had quickly drawn my head down and put her lips to mine.

"My dear friend, I can tell you that I did not feel at all happy! What, deceive Julien? Become the lover of this little, silly, wrongheaded, cunning woman, who was no doubt terribly sensual and for whom her husband was already not sufficient! To betray him continually, to deceive him, to play at being in love merely because I was attracted by forbidden fruit, danger incurred and friendship betrayed? No, that did not suit me, but what was I to do? To imitate Joseph would be acting a very stupid and, moreover, difficult part, for this woman was maddening in her perfidy, inflamed by audacity, palpitating and excited. Let the man who has never felt on his lips the warm kiss of a woman who is ready to give herself to him throw the first stone at me!

"Well, a minute more—you understand what I mean? A minute more and— I should have been—no, she would have been—when a loud noise made us both jump up. The log had fallen into the room, knocking over the fire irons and the fender, and was scorching the carpet, having rolled under an armchair.

"I jumped up like a madman, and as I was replacing the log on the fire the door opened hastily, and Julien came in.

" 'I have done,' he said in evident pleasure. 'The business was over two hours sooner than I expected!'

"Yes, my dear friend, without that log I should have been caught in the very act, and you know what the consequences would have been!

"You may be sure that I took good care never to be overtaken in a similar situation again, never, never. Soon afterward I saw Julien was giving me the 'cold shoulder,' as they say. His wife was evidently undermining our friendship; by degrees he got rid of me, and we have altogether ceased to meet.

"That is why I have not got married; it ought not to surprise you, I think."

BRIC-A-BRAC

"If you would like to see the interesting bric-a-brac there, come with me," said my friend Boisrené.

He then led me to the first story of a beautiful house in a great street in Paris. We were received by a very strong man of perfect manners who took us from piece to piece, showing us rare objects of which he mentioned the price carelessly. Great sums, ten, twenty, thirty, fifty thousand francs, came from his lips with so much grace and facility that one could not doubt that millions were shut up in the strongboxes of this merchantman of the world.

I had known him by name for a long time. Very clever, very tactful, very intelligent, he served as intermediary for all sorts of transactions. In touch with all the richest amateurs of Paris and even of Europe and America, knowing their tastes, their preferences for the moment, he brought them by a word or a dispatch, if they lived in some far-off town, when he knew that some object was to be sold that would please them.

Men in the best of society had had recourse to him in times of embarrassment, perhaps to get money for play, perhaps to pay a debt, perhaps to sell a picture, a family jewel or a tapestry or even to sell a horse, where the owner was in close straits.

It was said that he never refused his services when he could foresee any chance of gain.

Boisrené seemed intimate with this curiosity merchant. They had managed more than one affair together. I myself looked at the man with much interest.

He was tall, thin, bald and very elegant. His sweet, insinuating voice had a particular charm, a tentative charm, which gives to things a special value. When he held an article in his fingers, he turned it, re-turned it and looked at it with so much directness, tactfulness, elegance and sympathy that the object was at once embellished, transformed by his touch and his look. And one would immediately estimate it at a higher cost than before it passed from the show-case to his hand.

"And your Christ, the beautiful Christ of the Renaissance," said Boisrené, "that you showed me last year?"

The man smiled and replied:

"It is sold, and in rather a strange fashion. In fact, the whole story of a Parisian woman is in the sale. Would you like me to tell it to you?"

"Yes indeed."

"Do you know the Baroness Samoris?"

"Yes and no. I have only seen her once, but I know who she is!"

"You know fully?"

"Yes."

"Are you willing to tell me, that I may see whether you are deceived or not?"

"Very willing. Madame Samoris is a woman of the world who has a daughter without ever having had a husband, as the saying goes. But if she has not had a husband she has lovers, after a discreet fashion, so that they are received into certain society which is tolerant or blind. She is constant at church, receives the sacrament with reflection, after the fashion of one who knows and never will compromise herself. She hopes her daughter will make a good marriage. Is it not so?"

"Yes, but I will complete your information; she is a kept woman who makes herself respected by her lovers more than if she did not live with them. That is rare merit, for in this way one obtains whatever is desired of a man. The one whom she chooses, without which a man would have doubts, pays court a long time, desires her with fear, solicits with shame, obtains with astonishment and possesses with consideration. He does not perceive that he pays, so much tact does she use in taking, and she maintains their relation with such a tone of reserve, of dignity, of propriety, that in going away from her he would slap the face of a man capable of suspecting the virtue of his mistress. And that with the best faith in the world.

"I have rendered some services to this woman in many of her undertakings. She has no secrets from me.

"Somewhere in the first days of January she came to me to borrow thirty thousand francs. I had not the amount at hand, you understand, but as I desired to oblige her I begged her to tell me her situation fully, that I might see if there was anything I could do for her.

"She told me things in such precautionary language as she might use in relating a most delicate story for her daughter's first communion. I finally understood that times were hard and that she found herself without a sou. The commercial crisis, political disturbances which the government actually seemed to entertain with pleasure, rumors of war and the general constraint had made money hesitate, even in the hands of lovers. And then she could not, this honest woman, give herself to the first comer.

"A man of the world, of the best world, was necessary for her, one who would preserve her reputation while furnishing the daily needs. A rake would compromise her forever, even though he were very rich, and make the marriage of her daughter problematical. She could not think of business arrangements, of dishonoring intermediaries who might be able to relieve her of her embarrassment for a time. She must maintain the standard of her house, continue to receive with open doors, in order not to lose the hope of finding among her visitors the discreet and distinguished friend whom she was waiting to choose.

"For my part, I observed to her that there seemed little chance of my thirty thousand francs returning to me since, when they were eaten up, she would have to obtain sixty thousand at a single blow in order to give me half.

"She was disconsolate while listening to me, and I could think of nothing to be done, when an idea, a truly genial idea, crossed my mind. I had just bought the Christ of the Renaissance which I showed you, an admirable piece, the most beautiful in that style that I have ever seen.

" 'My dear friend,' I said to her, 'I am going to make you take this little ivory home with you. You can invent an ingenious story, touching, poetic, whatever you wish, which will explain your desire of parting with it. It can be understood that it is an heirloom of the family, inherited from your father.

" 'I will see some amateurs for you and take them there myself. The rest you will attend to. I will let you understand their situation by a word, a watchword. This piece is worth fifty thousand francs, but I let you have it for thirty thousand. The difference will be yours.'

"She reflected some moments with a profound air and then replied:

" 'Yes, perhaps it is a good idea. I thank you very much.'

"The next day I sent the Christ of the Renaissance to her house, and that evening I sent to her the Baron Saint-Hospital. For three months I addressed clients to her, clients of the best, who were confident of my judgment in business. But I heard no one speak of her.

"Then, having received a foreign customer who spoke very bad French, I decided to present him myself at the house of Madame Samoris, in order to let him see the piece.

"A footman all in black received us and showed us into a pretty drawing room furnished with taste, where we waited some minutes. She appeared, charming, extending her hand to me, making us be seated. When I explained the motive of my visit she rang.

"The footman reappeared.

" 'See if Mademoiselle Isabelle can let us enter her chapel,' she said to him.

"The young girl herself brought the response. She was about fifteen, with a good, modest appearance and all the freshness of youth. She wished to guide us herself into her chapel.

"It was a sort of pious boudoir, where a silver lamp was burning before the Christ of the Renaissance, my property, couched on a bed of black velvet. The setting of the scene was charming and very clever. The child made the sign of the cross and then said: 'Look, gentlemen, is it not beautiful?'

"I took the object, examined it and declared it remarkable. The stranger also considered it, but he seemed much more occupied with the women than with the Christ.

"One felt good in their home, felt the incense, the flowers, the perfume. One found complete repose there. It was truly a comfortable dwelling, inviting to rest.

"When we had re-entered the drawing room I broached, with reserve and delicacy, the question of price. Madame Samoris asked, lowering her eyes, fifty thousand francs. Then she added:

" 'If you wish to see it again, sir, I scarcely ever go out before three o'clock, and you will find me here any day.'

"In the street the stranger asked me some details about the baroness, whom he found charming. But I did not undertake to say much for her or of her.

"Three months more passed.

"One morning, not more than five days ago, she came to my house at the breakfast hour and, placing a pocketbook in my hand, said: 'My dear, you are an angel.

Here are fifty thousand francs! *I* have bought your Christ of the Renaissance, and I pay twenty thousand francs more than the price agreed upon, on the condition that you will always—always send me clients—because the piece is still for sale.' "

THE TOMB

On the seventeenth of July, 1883, at half past two o'clock in the morning, the caretaker of Béziers cemetery, who lived in a little house at the end of the burying ground, was awakened by the yelping of his dog, which was locked in the kitchen.

He immediately went downstairs and saw that the animal was scenting something under the door and barking furiously, as though some tramp had been prowling about the house. Vincent, the caretaker, took up his gun and went out cautiously.

His dog ran off in the direction of General Bonnet's Avenue and stopped short in front of Mme. Tomoiseau's monument.

The caretaker, advancing cautiously, soon noticed a dim light in the direction of Malenvers Avenue. He slipped in amongst the tombstones and witnessed a most horrible deed of desecration.

A young man had disinterred the corpse of a young woman, buried the day before, and he was dragging it out of the grave.

A small dark lantern, placed on a pile of earth, lit up this hideous scene.

Vincent, the caretaker, pounced upon the criminal, felled him to the ground, bound his hands, and took him to the police station.

He was a young lawyer from the city, rich and well thought of. His name was Courbataille.

He was tried. The public prosecutor recalled the monstrous deeds committed by Sergeant Bertrand, and aroused the audience.

The crowd was thrilled with indignation. As soon as the magistrate sat down the cry arose: "Put him to death! Put him to death!" The president had great difficulty in restoring silence.

Then he said, in a serious tone of voice:

"Accused, what have you to say in your defense?"

Courbataille, who had refused counsel, arose. He was a handsome youth, large, dark, with an open countenance, strong features, and a fearless eye.

The crowd began to hiss.

He was not disconcerted, but commenced speaking with a slightly husky voice, a little low in the beginning, but gradually gaining in strength:

"Your honor,

"Gentlemen of the jury,

"I have very little to say. The woman whose tomb I violated was my mistress. I loved her.

"I loved her, not with a sensual love, not simply from kindness of soul and heart, but with an absolute, perfect love, with mad passion.

"Listen to what I have to say:

"When I first met her, I felt a strange sensation on seeing her. It was not astonishment, nor admiration, for it was not what is called love at first sight, but it was a delightful sensation, as though I had been plunged in a tepid bath. Her movements captivated me, her voice enchanted me, it gave me infinite pleasure to watch everything about her. It also seemed to me that I had known her for a long time, that I had seen her before. She seemed to have some of my spirit within her.

"She seemed to me like an answer to an appeal from my soul, to this vague and continuous appeal which forces us toward Hope throughout the whole course of our lives.

"When I became a little better acquainted with her, the mere thought of seeing her again filled me with a deep and exquisite agitation; the touch of her hand in mine was such a joy to me that I had never imagined the like before; her smile made my eyes shine with joy, and made me feel like running about, dancing, rolling on the ground.

"Then she became my mistress.

"She was more than that to me, she was my life itself. I hoped for nothing more on earth, I wished for nothing more, I longed for nothing more.

"Well, one evening, as we were taking a rather long walk by the bank of the stream, we were caught by the rain. She felt cold.

"The next day she had inflammation of the lungs. Eight days later she died.

"During those dying hours, astonishment and fear prevented me from understanding or thinking.

"When she was dead, I was so stunned by brutal despair that I was unable to think. I wept.

"During all the horrible phases of interment my wild, excessive grief was the sorrow of a man beside himself, a sort of sensual physical grief.

"Then when she was gone, when she was under the ground, my mind suddenly became clear, and I passed through a train of mental suffering so terrible that even the love she had given me was dear at such a price.

"Then I was seized with an obsession.

"I shall never see her again.

"After reflecting on that for a whole day, it maddens you.

"Think of it! A being is there, one whom you adore, a unique being, for in the whole wide world there is no one who resembles her. This being has given herself to you, with you she creates this mysterious union called love. Her glance seems to you vaster than space, more charming than the world, her bright glance full of tender smiles. This being loves you. When she speaks to you her voice overwhelms you with happiness.

"And suddenly she disappears! Think of it! She disappears not only from your sight, but from everybody's. She is dead. Do you understand what that word means? Never, never, never more, nowhere, will this being exist. Those eyes will never see again. Never will this voice, never will any voice like this, among human voices, pronounce one word in the same way that she pronounced it.

"There will never be another face born like hers. Never, never! The cast of statues is kept; the stamp that reproduces objects with the same outlines and the same colors is preserved. But this body and this face will never be seen again on this earth. And still there will be born thousands of beings, millions, thousands of millions, and even more, and among all these women there will never be found one like her. Can that be possible? It makes one mad to think of it!

"She lived twenty years, no more, and she has disappeared forever, forever, forever! She thought, she smiled, she loved me. Now there is nothing more. The flies which die in the autumn are of as much importance as we in creation. Nothing more! And I thought how her body, her fresh, warm body, so soft, so white, so beautiful, was rotting away in the depths of a box under the ground. And her soul, her mind, her love—where were they?

"Never to see her again! Never again! My mind was haunted by the thought of that decomposing body, which I, however, might still recognize!

"I set out with a shovel, a lantern, and a hammer. I climbed over the cemetery wall. I found the hole where her grave was. It had not yet been entirely filled up. I uncovered the coffin and raised one of the planks. An awful odor, the abominable breath of putrefaction, arose in my face. Oh, her bed, perfumed with iris!

"However, I opened the coffin and thrust in my lighted lantern, and saw her. Her face was blue, swollen, horrible! Black liquid had flowed from her mouth.

"She! It was she! I was seized with horror. But I put out my arm and caught her hair to pull this monstrous face towards me! It was at that moment I was arrested.

"All night I carried with me, as one retains the perfume of a woman after a sexual embrace, the filthy smell of this putrefaction, the odor of my beloved!

"Do what you like with me."

A strange silence seemed to hang over the hall. People appeared to be awaiting something more. The jury withdrew to deliberate. When they returned after a few minutes, the accused did not seem to have any fears, nor even any thoughts. In the traditional formula the judge informed him that his peers had found him not guilty.

He did not make a movement, but the public applauded.

THE ARTIST'S WIFE

Curved like a crescent moon, the little town of Etretat, with its white cliffs and its blue sea, was reposing under the sun of a grand July day. At the two points of the crescents were the two gates, the little one at the right and the large one at the left, as if it were gradually advancing to the water—on one side a dwarfed foot, on the other, a leg of giant proportions; and the spire, nearly as high as the cliff, large at the base and fine at the summit, pointed its slim head toward the heavens.

Along the beach, upon the float, a crowd was seated, watching the bathers. Upon the terrace of the casino another crowd, seated or walking, paraded under the full light of day, a garden of pretty costumes, shaded by red and blue umbrellas embroidered in great flowers of silk. At the end of the promenade, on the terrace, there were other people, calm, quiet, walking slowly along up and down, as far as possible from the elegant multitude.

A young man, well known and celebrated as a painter, John Summer, was walking along with a listless air beside an invalid chair in which reposed a young woman, his wife. A domestic rolled the little carriage along gently, while the crippled woman looked with sad eyes upon the joy of the heavens, the joy of the day and the joy of other people.

They were not talking; they were not looking at each other. The woman said: "Let us stop a little."

They stopped, and the painter seated himself upon a folding chair arranged for him by the valet. Those who passed behind the couple, sitting there mute and motionless, regarded him with pitying looks. A complete legend of devotion had found its way about. He had married her in spite of her infirmity, moved by his love, they said.

Not far from there two young men were seated on a capstan, chatting and looking off toward the horizon.

"So it is not true," one of them said. "I tell you I know much of John Summer's life."

"Then why did he marry her? For she was really an invalid at the time, was she not?"

"Just as you see her now. He married her—he married her—as one marries—well, because he was a fool!"

"How is that?"

"How is that? That is how, my friend. That is the whole of it. One is a goose because he is a goose. And then, you know, painters make a specialty of ridiculous marriages; they nearly always marry their models, or some old mistress or some one of the women among the varied assortment they run up against. Why is it? Does anyone know? It would seem, on the contrary, that constant association with this race that we call models would be enough to disgust them forever with that kind of female. Not at all. After having made them pose they marry them. Read that little book of Alphonse Daudet, Artists' Wives, so true, so cruel and so beautiful.

"As for the couple you see there, the accident that brought about that marriage was of a unique and terrible kind. The little woman played a comedy, or rather a frightful drama. In fact, she risked all for all. Was she sincere? Does she really love John? Can one ever know that? Who can determine with any precision the real from the make-believe in the acts of women? They are always sincere in an eternal change of impressions. They are passionate, criminal, devoted, admirable and ignoble, ready to obey unseizable emotions. They lie without ceasing, without wishing to, without knowing it, without comprehension, and they have this, in spite of this, an absolute freedom from sensation and sentiment, which they evince in violent resolutions, unexpected, incomprehensible folly, putting to rout all our reason, all our custom of deliberation and all our combination of egotism. The unforeseen bluntness of their determination makes them, to us, indecipherable enigmas. We are always asking: 'Are they sincere? Are they false?'

"But, my friend, they are sincere and false at the same time, because it is in their nature to be the two extremes and neither the one nor the other. Look at the means the most honest employ for obtaining what they wish. They are both complicated and simple, these means are. So complicated that we never guess them in advance, so simple that after we have been the victims of them we cannot help being astonished and saying to ourselves: 'My! Did she play me as easily as that?' And they succeed always, my good friend, especially when it is a question of making us marry them.

"But here is John Summer's story:

"The little wife was a model, as the term is usually understood. She posed for him. She was pretty, particularly elegant and possessed, it appears, a divine figure. He became her lover, as one becomes the lover of any seductive woman he sees often. He imagines he loves her with his whole soul. It is a singular phenomenon. As soon as one desires a woman he believes sincerely that he can no longer live without her. They know very well that their time has arrived. They know that disgust always follows possession; that in order to pass one's existence by the side of another being, not brutal, physical appetite, so quickly extinguished, is the need, but an accordance of soul, of temperament, of humor. In a seduction that one undertakes in bodily form it is necessary to mingle a certain sensual intoxication with a charming depth of mind.

"Well, he believed that he loved her; he made her a heap of promises of fidelity and lived completely with her. She was gentle and endowed with that undeniable elegance which the Parisian woman acquires so easily. She tippled and babbled and said silly things, which seemed *spirituelle*, from the droll way in which she put them. She had each moment some little trick or pretty gesture to charm the eye of the painter. When she raised an arm or stooped down her movements were always perfect, exactly as they should be.

"For three months John did not perceive that, in reality, she was like all models. They rented for the summer a little house at Andressy. I was there one evening when the first disquiet germinated in the mind of my friend.

"As the night was radiant, we wished to take a turn along the bank of the river. The moon threw in the water a glittering shower of light, crumbling its yellow reflections in the eddy, in the current, in the whole of the large river, flowing slowly along.

"We were going along the bank, a little quiet from the vague exaltation which the dreaminess of the evening threw about us. We were wishing we might accomplish superhuman things, might love some unknown beings, deliciously poetic. Strange ecstasies, desires and aspirations were trembling in us.

"And we kept silent, penetrated by the serene and living freshness of the charming night, by that freshness of the moon which seems to go through the body, penetrate it, bathe the mind, perfume it and steep it in happiness.

"Suddenly Josephine (she called herself Josephine) cried out:

" 'Oh! did you see the great fish that jumped down there?'

"He replied without looking or knowing: 'Yes, dearie.'

"She was angry. 'No, you have not seen it since your back was turned to it.'

"He laughed. 'Yes, it is true. It is so fine here that I was thinking of nothing.'

"She was silent, but at the end of a minute the need of speaking seized her and she asked:

" 'Are you going to Paris tomorrow?'

"He answered: 'I don't know.'

"Again she was irritated.

" 'Perhaps you think it is amusing to walk out without saying anything,' she said; 'one usually talks if he is not too stupid.'

"He said nothing. Then, knowing well, thanks to her wicked, womanly instinct, that he would be exasperated, she began to sing that irritating air with which our ears and minds had been wearied for the past two years:

" *'I was looking in the air.'*

"He murmured: 'I beg you be quiet.'

"She answered furiously: 'Why should I keep quiet?'

"He replied: 'You will arouse the neighborhood.'

"Then the scene took place, the odious scene, with unexpected reproaches, tempestuous recriminations, then tears. All was over. They went back to the house. He allowed her to go on without reply, calmed by the divine evening and overwhelmed by the whirlwind of foolishness.

"Three months later he was struggling desperately in the invincible, invisible bonds with which habit enlaces our life. She held him, oppressed him, martyrized him. They quarreled from morning until evening, insulting and combating each other.

"Finally he wished to end it, to break, at any price. He sold all his work, realizing some twenty thousand francs (he was then little known) and, borrowing some money from friends, he left it all on the chimney piece with a letter of adieu.

"He came to my house as a refuge. Toward three o'clock in the afternoon the bell rang. I opened the door. A woman jumped into my face, brushed me aside and rushed into my studio; it was she.

"He stood up on seeing her enter. She threw at his feet the envelope containing the bank notes with a truly noble gesture and said with short breath:

" 'Here is your money. I do not care for it.'

"She was very pale and trembling, ready, apparently, for any folly. He, too, grew pale, pale from anger and vexation, ready, perhaps, for any violence.

"He asked: 'What do you want, then?'

"She replied: 'I do not wish to be treated like a child. You have implored me and taken me. I ask you for nothing—only protect me.'

"He stamped his foot, saying: 'No, it is too much! And if you believe that you are going——'

"I took hold of his arm. 'Wait, John,' I said, 'let me attend to it.'

"I went toward her and gently, little by little, I reasoned with her, emptying the sack of arguments that are usually employed in such cases. She listened to me motionless, with eyes fixed, obstinate and dumb. Finally, thinking of nothing more to say and seeing that the affair would not end pleasantly, I struck one more last note. I said:

" 'He will always love you, little one, but his family wishes him to marry, and you know——'

"This was a surprise for her! 'Ah! Ah! Now I comprehend,' she began.

"And, turning toward him, she continued: 'And so—you are going to marry!'

"He answered carelessly: 'Yes.'

"Then she took a step forward. 'If you marry I will kill myself—you understand?'

" 'Well then, kill yourself,' he hissed over his shoulder.

"She choked two or three times, her throat seeming bound by a frightful anguish. 'You say—you say—— Repeat it!'

"He repeated: 'Well, kill yourself, if that pleases you!'

"She replied, very pale with fright: 'It is not necessary to dare me. I will throw myself from that window.'

"He began to laugh, advanced to the window, opened it, bowed like a person allowing someone to precede him, saying:

" 'Here is the way; after you!'

"She looked at him a second with fixed eyes, terribly excited; then, taking a leap, as one does in jumping a hedge in the field, she passed before him, before me, leaped over the sill and disappeared.

"I shall never forget the effect that this open window made upon me after having seen it traversed by that falling body; it appeared to me in a second great as the sky and as empty as space. And I recoiled instinctively, not daring to look, as if I had fallen myself.

"John, dismayed, made no motion.

"They took up the poor girl with both legs broken. She could never walk again.

"Her lover, foolish with remorse and perhaps touched by remembrance, took her and married her. There you have it, my dear."

The evening was come. The young woman, being cold, wished to go in, and the domestic began to roll the invalid's little carriage toward the village. The painter walked along beside his wife without having exchanged a word with her for an hour.

IN THE SPRING

When the first fine spring days come and the earth awakes and assumes its gar-ment of verdure, when the perfumed warmth of the air caresses your face and fills your lungs and even seems to reach your heart, you feel vague longings for an undefined happiness, a wish to run, to walk anywhere and everywhere, to inhale the soul of the spring. As the winter had been very severe the year before, this longing assumed an intoxicating feeling in May; it was like a superabundance of sap.

Well, one morning on waking I saw from my window the blue sky glowing in the sun above the neighboring houses. The canaries hanging in the windows were singing loudly, and so were the servants on every floor; a cheerful noise rose up from the streets, and I went out, with my spirits as bright as the day, to go—I did not exactly know where. Everybody I met seemed to be smiling; an air of happiness appeared to pervade everything in the warm light of returning spring. One might almost have said that a breeze of love was blowing through the city, and the young women whom I saw in the streets in morning toilets, in the depths of whose eyes there lurked a hidden tenderness and who walked with languid grace, filled my heart with agitation.

Without knowing how or why, I found myself on the banks of the Seine. Steamboats were starting for Suresnes, and suddenly I was seized by an uncon-querable wish for a walk through the wood. The deck of the mouche[1] was crowded with passengers, for the sun in early spring draws you out of the house in spite of yourself, and everyone was active, visiting and gossiping with the people sitting near.

I had a female neighbor, a little workgirl, no doubt, who possessed the true Parisian charm. Her little head had light curly hair like frizzed light, which came down to her ears and to the nape of her neck, danced in the wind and then became such fine, such light-colored down that you could scarcely see it but on which you felt an irresistible desire to impress a shower of kisses.

Under the magnetism of my looks she turned her head toward me and then immediately looked down, while a slight dimpling of the flesh, the forerunner of a smile, also showed that fine, pale down which the sun was gilding a little.

The calm river grew wider; the atmosphere was warm and perfectly still, but a murmur of life seemed to fill all space.

My neighbor raised her eyes again, and this time, as I was still looking at her,

[1]Fly. A name given to the small steamboats on the Seine.

she smiled, decidedly. She was charming, and in her passing glance I saw a thousand things of which I had hitherto been ignorant. I saw in it unknown depths, all the charm of tenderness, all the poetry which we dream of, all the happiness which we are continually in search of. I felt an insane longing to open my arms and to carry her off somewhere so as to whisper the sweet music of words of love into her ears.

I was just going to speak to her when somebody touched me on the shoulder. Turning round in some surprise, I saw an ordinary-looking man, who was neither young nor old who gazed at me sadly.

"I should like to speak to you," he said.

I made a grimace, which he no doubt saw, for he added:

"It is a matter of importance."

I got up, therefore, and followed him to the other end of the boat, and then he said:

"Monsieur, when winter comes, with its cold, wet and snowy weather, your doctor says to you constantly: 'Keep your feet warm, guard against chills, colds, bronchitis, rheumatism and pleurisy.'

"Then you are very careful; you wear flannel, a heavy greatcoat and thick shoes, but all this does not prevent you from passing two months in bed. But when spring returns, with its leaves and flowers, its warm, soft breezes and its smell of the fields, causing you vague disquiet and causeless emotion, nobody says to you:

"'Monsieur, beware of love! It is lying in ambush everywhere; it is watching for you at every corner; all its snares are laid; all its weapons are sharpened; all its guiles are prepared! Beware of love. Beware of love. It is more dangerous than brandy, bronchitis or pleurisy! It never forgives and makes everybody commit irreparable follies.'

"Yes, monsieur, I say that the French government ought to put large public notices on the walls with these words: 'Return of spring. French citizens, beware of love'; just as they put: 'Beware of paint.'

"However, as the government will not do this I must supply its place, and I say to you: 'Beware of love,' for it is just going to seize you, and it is my duty to inform you of it, just as in Russia they inform anyone that his nose is frozen."

I was much astonished at this individual and, assuming a dignified manner, I said:

"Really, monsieur, you appear to me to be interfering in a matter which is no business of yours."

He made an abrupt movement and replied:

"Ah, monsieur, monsieur! If I see that a man is in danger of being drowned at a dangerous spot, ought I to let him perish? So just listen to my story, and you will see why I ventured to speak to you like this.

"It was about this time last year that it occurred. But, first of all, I must tell you that I am a clerk in the Admiralty, where our chiefs, the commissioners, take their gold lace as quill-driving officers seriously and treat us like foretop men on board a ship. Well, from my office I could see a small bit of blue sky and the swallows, and I felt inclined to dance among my portfolios.

"My yearning for freedom grew so intense that in spite of my repugnance I went to see my chief, who was a short, bad-tempered man, who was always cross. When I told him that I was not well he looked at me and said: 'I do not believe it, monsieur, but be off with you! Do you think that any office can go on with clerks like you?' I started at once and went down the Seine. It was a day like this, and I took the *mouche* to go as far as Saint-Cloud. Ah! What a good thing it would have been if my chief had refused me permission to leave the office for the day.

"I seemed to expand in the sun. I loved it all: the steamer, the river, the trees, the houses, my fellow passengers, everything. I felt inclined to kiss something, no matter what; it was love laying its snare. Presently, at the Trocadéro, a girl with a small parcel in her hand came on board and sat down opposite to me. She was certainly pretty, but it is surprising, monsieur, how much prettier women seem to us when it is fine, at the beginning of the spring. Then they have an intoxicating charm, something quite peculiar about them. It is just like drinking wine after the cheese.

"I looked at her, and she also looked at me, but only occasionally, like that girl did at you just now, but at last, by dint of looking at each other constantly, it seemed to me that we knew each other well enough to enter into conversation, and I spoke to her, and she replied. She was decidedly pretty and nice, and she intoxicated me, monsieur!

"She got out at Saint-Cloud, and I followed her. She went and delivered her parcel, but when she returned the boat had just started. I walked by her side, and the warmth of the air made us both sigh.

" 'It would be very nice in the wood,' I said.

" 'Indeed, it would!' she replied.

" 'Shall we go there for a walk, mademoiselle?'

"She gave me a quick, upward look, as if to see exactly what I was like, and then after a little hesitation, she accepted my proposal, and soon we were there, walking side by side. Under the foliage, which was still rather thin, the tall, thick, bright green grass was inundated by the sun and full of small insects making love to one another, and birds were singing in all directions. My companion began to jump and to run, intoxicated by the air and the smell of the country, and I ran and jumped behind her. How stupid we are at times, monsieur!

"Then she wildly sang a thousand things; opera airs and the song of Musette! The song of Musette! How poetical it seemed to me then! I almost cried over it. Ah! Those silly songs make us lose our heads; take my advice, never marry a woman who sings in the country, especially if she sings the song of Musette!

"She soon grew tired and sat down on a grassy slope, and I sat down at her feet. I took her hands, her little hands, so marked with the needle, and they moved me. I said to myself: 'These are the sacred marks of toil.' Oh, monsieur, do you know what those sacred marks of labor mean? They mean all the gossip of the workroom, the whispered blackguardism, the mind soiled by all the filth that is talked; they mean lost chastity, foolish chatter, all the wretchedness of daily bad habits, all the narrowness of ideas which belongs to women of the lower orders, united in the girl whose sacred fingers bear the sacred marks of toil.

"Then we looked into each other's eyes for a long while. What power a woman's eye has! How it agitates us; how it invades our very being, takes possession of us and dominates us. How profound it seems, how full of infinite promise! People call that looking into each other's souls! Oh, monsieur, what humbug! If we could see into each other's souls we should be more careful of what we did. However, I was caught and crazy after her and tried to take her into my arms, but she said: 'Hands off!' Then I threw myself down and opened my heart to her and poured out all the affection that was suffocating me, my head on her knees. She seemed surprised at my manner and gave me a sidelong glance, as if to say: 'Ah! So that is the way women make a fool of you, old fellow! Very well, we will see.' In love, monsieur, men are the artists, and women are the dealers.

"No doubt I could have won her, and I saw my own stupidity later, but what I wanted was not a woman's person; it was love; it was the ideal. I was sentimental, when I ought to have been using my time to a better purpose.

"As soon as she had had enough of my declarations of affection she got up, and we returned to Saint-Cloud, but I did not leave her until we got to Paris. But she looked so sad as we were returning that at last I asked her what was the matter.

" 'I am thinking,' she replied, 'that this has been one of those days of which we have but few in life.'

"And my heart beat as if it would break my ribs.

"I saw her on the following Sunday, and the next Sunday and every Sunday. I took her to Bougival, Saint-Germain, Maisons-Lafitte, Poissy, to every suburban resort of lovers.

"The little jade, in turn, pretended to love me until, at last, I altogether lost my head, and three months later I married her.

"What can you expect, monsieur, when a man is a clerk, living alone, without any relations or anyone to advise him? You say to yourself: 'How sweet life would be with a wife!'

"And so you get married, and she calls you names from morning till night, understands nothing, knows nothing, chatters continually, sings the song of Musette at the top of her voice (oh! that song of Musette, how tired one gets of it!), quarrels with the charcoal dealer, tells the porter all her domestic details, confides all the secrets of her bedroom to the neighbor's servant, discusses her husband with the tradespeople and has her head so stuffed with stupid stories, with idiotic superstitions, with extraordinary ideas and monstrous prejudices that I—for what I have said applies particularly to myself—shed tears of discouragement every time I talk to her."

He stopped, as he was rather out of breath and very much moved. I looked at him, for I felt pity for this poor, artless devil, and I was just going to give him some sort of answer when the boat stopped. We were at Saint-Cloud.

The little woman who had so taken my fancy got up in order to land. She passed close to me and gave me a side glance and a furtive smile—one of those smiles that drive you wild; then she jumped on the landing stage. I sprang forward to follow her, but my neighbor laid hold of my arm. I shook myself loose, however, whereupon he seized the skirt of my coat and pulled me back, exclaiming:

"You shall not go! You shall not go!" in such a loud voice that everybody turned round and laughed. I remained standing motionless and furious, but without venturing to face scandal and ridicule, and the steamboat started.

The little woman on the landing stage looked at me as I went off with an air of disappointment, while my persecutor rubbed his hands and whispered to me:

"You must admit that I have done you a great service."

NIGHT: A NIGHTMARE

I love night passionately. I love it as one loves one's country or one's mistress. I love it with all my senses, with my eyes, which see it; with my sense of smell, which inhales it; with my ears, which listen to its silence; with my whole body, which is caressed by its shadows. The larks sing in the sunlight, in the blue heavens, in the warm air, in the light air of clear mornings. The owl flies at night, a somber patch passing through black space, and, rejoicing in the black immensity that intoxicates him, he utters a vibrant and sinister cry.

In the daytime I am tired and bored. The day is brutal and noisy. I rarely get up, I dress myself languidly, and I go out regretfully. Every movement, every gesture, every word, every thought, tires me as though I were raising a crushing load.

But when the sun goes down a confused joy invades my whole being. I awaken and become animated. As the shadows lengthen I feel quite different, younger, stronger, more lively, happier. I watch the great soft shadows falling from the sky and growing deeper. They envelop the city like an impenetrable and impalpable wave; they hide, efface and destroy colors and forms; they embrace houses, people and buildings in their imperceptible grasp. Then I would like to cry out with joy like the screech owls, to run upon the roofs like the cats, and an impetuous, invincible desire to love burns in my veins. I go, I walk, sometimes in the darkened outskirts of Paris, sometimes in the neighboring woods, where I hear my sisters, the beasts, and my brothers, the poachers, prowling.

One is finally killed by what one violently loves. But how shall I explain what happens to me? How can I ever make people understand that I am able to tell it? I do not know, I cannot tell. I only know that this is—that is all.

Well, yesterday—was it yesterday?—yes, no doubt, unless it was earlier, a day, a month, a year earlier . . . I do not know, but it must have been yesterday, because since then no day has risen, no sun has dawned. But how long has it been night? How long? Who can tell? Who will ever know?

Yesterday, then, I went out after dinner, as I do every evening. It was very fine, very mild, very warm. As I went down towards the boulevards I looked above my head at the black streams full of stars, outlined in the sky between the roofs of the houses, which were turning round and causing this rolling stream of stars to undulate like a real river.

Everything was distinct in the clear air, from the planets to the gaslight. So many lights were burning above, in the city, that the shadows seemed luminous. Bright nights are more joyful than days of bright sunshine. The cafés on the boulevard were flaring; people were laughing, passing up and down, drinking. I went into a theater for a few moments. Into what theater, I cannot tell. There was so much light in there that I was depressed, and I came out again with my heart saddened by the clash of brutal light on the gold of the balcony, by the factitious glitter of the great crystal chandelier, by the glaring footlights, by the melancholy of this artificial and crude light. I arrived at the Champs-Elysées, where the openair concerts look like conflagrations in the branches. The chestnut trees, touched with yellow light, look as if they were painted, like phosphorescent trees. The electric bulbs, like pale dazzling moons, like eggs from the moon, fallen from heaven, like monstrous, living pearls, caused the streaks of gaslight, filthy, ugly gaslight and the garlands of colored, lighted glasses to grow pale beneath their pearly, mysterious and regal light.

I stopped beneath the Arc de Triomphe to look at the avenue, the long and wonderful, starry avenue, leading to Paris between two rows of fire and the stars! The stars above, the unknown stars, thrown haphazard through infinity, where they form those strange shapes which make us dream and think so much.

I entered the Bois de Boulogne, where I remained for a long, long time. I was seized by a strange thrill, a powerful and unforeseen emotion, and exaltation of mind which bordered on frenzy. I walked on and on, and then I returned. What time was it when I passed again beneath the Arc de Triomphe? I do not know. The city was sleeping, and clouds, great black clouds, were slowly spreading over the sky.

For the first time I felt that something strange was going to happen, something new.

It seemed to be getting cold, that the air was becoming thicker, that night, my beloved night, was weighing heavily upon my heart. The avenue was deserted now. Two solitary policemen were walking near the cabstand, and a string of vegetable carts was going to the Halles along the roadway, scarcely lit by the gas jets, which seemed to be dying out. They moved along slowly, laden with carrots, turnips, and cabbages. The invisible drivers were asleep, the horses were walking with an even step, following the carts in front of them and making no noise on the wooden pavement. As they passed each lamp on the footpath, the carrots showed up red in the light; the turnips white, the cabbages green, and they passed one after another, these carts which were as red as fire, as white as silver, and as green as emeralds. I followed them, then I turned into the Rue Royale and returned to the boulevards. There was nobody to be seen; none of the cafés was open and only a few belated pedestrians in a hurry. I had never seen Paris so dead and so deserted. I looked at my watch. It was two o'clock.

Some force was driving me, the desire to walk. So I went as far as the Bastille. There I became aware that I had never seen so dark a night, for I could not even see the Colonne de Juillet, whose Genius in gold was lost in the impenetrable obscurity. A curtain of clouds as dense as the ether had buried the stars and seemed to be descending upon the world to blot it out.

I retraced my steps. There was nobody about me. However, at the Place du Château d'Eau, a drunken man almost bumped into me, then disappeared. For some time I could hear his sonorous and uneven steps. I went on. At the top of the Faubourg Montmartre a cab passed, going in the direction of the Seine. I hailed it but the driver did not reply. Near the Rue Drouot a woman was loitering: "Listen, dearie——" I hastened my steps to avoid her outstretched hand. Then there was nothing more. In front of the Vaudeville Theater a ragpicker was searching in the gutter. His little lantern was moving just above the ground. I said to him: "What time is it, my good man?"

"How do I know?" he grumbled. "I have no watch."

Then I suddenly perceived that the lamps had all been extinguished. I know that at this time of year they are put out early, before dawn, for the sake of economy. But daylight was still far off, very far off indeed!

"Let us go to the Halles," I said to myself; "there at least I shall find life."

I set off, but it was too dark even to see the way. I advanced slowly, as one does in a forest, recognizing the streets by counting them. In front of the Crédit Lyonnais a dog growled. I turned up the Rue de Grammont and lost my way. I wandered about, and then I recognized the Bourse by the iron railings around it. The whole of Paris was sleeping, a deep, terrifying sleep. In the distance a cab rumbled, one solitary cab, perhaps it was the one which had passed me a while back. I tried to reach it, going in the direction of the noise, through streets that were lonely and dark, dark and somber as death. Again I lost my way. Where was I? What nonsense to put out the lights so soon! Not one person passing by. Not one late reveler, not one thief, not even the mewing of an amorous cat? Nothing.

Where on earth were the police? I said to myself: "I will shout and they will come." I shouted. There was no answer. I called more loudly. My voice vanished without an echo, weak, muffled, stifled by the night, the impenetrable night. I yelled: "Help! Help! Help!" My desperate cry remained unanswered. What time was it? I pulled out my watch, but I had no matches. I listened to the gentle ticktick of the little mechanism with a strange and unfamiliar pleasure. It seemed to be a living thing. I felt less lonely. What a mystery! I resumed my walk like a blind man, feeling my way along the wall with my stick, and every moment I raised my eyes to the heavens, hoping that day would dawn at last. But the sky was dark, all dark, more profoundly dark than the city.

What could the time be? It seemed to me I had been walking an infinite length of time, for my legs were giving way beneath me, my breast was heaving and I was suffering horribly from hunger. I decided to ring at the first street door. I pulled the copper bell and it rang sonorously through the house. It sounded strangely, as if that vibrating noise were alone in the house. I waited. There was no answer. The door did not open. I rang again. I waited again—nothing! I got frightened! I ran to the next house, and, twenty times in succession, I rang the bells in the dark corridors where the concierge was supposed to sleep, but he did not awake. I went on further, pulling the bells and the knockers with all my strength, kicking and knocking with my hand and stick on the doors, which remained obstinately closed.

Suddenly I perceived that I had reached the Halles. The market was deserted, not a sound, not a movement, not a cart, not a man, not a bundle of flowers or vegetables—it was empty, motionless, abandoned, dead. I was seized with a horrible terror. What was happening? Oh, my God, what was happening?

I set off again. But the time? The time? Who would tell me the time? Not a clock struck in the churches or the public buildings. I thought: "I will open the glass of my watch and feel the hands with my fingers." I pulled out my watch. . . . It was not going. . . . It had stopped. Nothing more, nothing more, not a ripple in the city, not a light, not the slightest suspicion of a sound in the air. Nothing! Nothing more! not even the distant rumbling of a cab! Nothing more. I had reached the quays, and a cold chill rose from the river. Was the Seine still flowing? I wanted to know, I found the steps and went down. I could not hear the current rushing under the bridge. . . . A few more steps. . . .

Then sand. . . . Mud . . . then water. I dipped my hand into it. It was flowing . . . flowing . . . cold . . . cold . . . cold . . . almost frozen . . . almost
dried up . . . almost dead.

I fully realized that I should never have the strength to come up, and that I
was going to die there . . . in my turn, of hunger, fatigue and cold.

THE RENDEZVOUS

Although she had her bonnet and jacket on, with a black veil over her face and
another in her pocket, which would be put on over the other as soon as she had
got into a cab, she was tapping the top of her little boot with the point of her
parasol and remained sitting in her room, unable to make up her mind to keep
this appointment.

And yet how many times within the last two years had she dressed herself
thus, when she knew that her husband would be on the Stock Exchange, in order
to go to the bachelor chambers of handsome Viscount de Martelet.

The clock behind her was ticking loudly; a book which she had half read was
lying open on a little rosewood writing table between the windows, and a strong,
sweet smell of violets from two bunches in Dresden china vases mingled with
a vague smell of verbena which came through the half-open door of her dressing
room.

The clock struck three; she rose up from her chair, turned round to look at
herself in the glass and smiled. "He is already waiting for me and will be getting
tired."

Then she left the room, told her footman that she would be back in an hour,
at the latest—which was a lie—went downstairs and ventured into the street on
foot.

It was toward the end of May, that delightful time of the year when spring
seems to be besieging Paris, flowing over its roofs, invading its houses through
their walls and making the city look gay, shedding brightness over its granite
façades, the asphalt of its pavements, the stones on its streets, bathing and intoxicating it with new life, like a forest putting on its spring vesture.

Mme Haggan went a few steps to the right, intending, as usual, to go along
the Parade Provence, where she would hail a cab. But the soft air, that feeling of
summer which penetrates our breasts on some days, now took possession of her
so suddenly that she changed her mind and went down the Rue de la Chaussée
d'Antin, without knowing why, but vaguely attracted by a desire to see the trees
in the Place de la Trinité.

"He may just wait ten minutes longer for me," she said to herself. And the
idea pleased her as she walked slowly through the crowd. She fancied that she
saw him growing impatient, looking at the clock, opening the window, listening
at the door, sitting down for a few moments, getting up again, not daring to
smoke, as she had forbidden him to do so when she was coming to him, and
throwing despairing looks at his box of cigarettes.

She walked slowly, interested in what she saw, the shops and the people she
met, walking slower and slower and so little eager to get to her destination that

she only sought for some pretext for stopping. At the end of the street, in the little square, the green lawns attracted her so much that she went in, took a chair and, sitting down, watched the hands of the clock as they moved.

Just then the half-hour struck, and her heart beat with pleasure when she heard the chimes. She had gained half an hour; then it would take her a quarter of an hour to reach the Rue de Miromesnil and a few minutes more in strolling along—an hour! A whole hour saved from her rendezvous! She would not stop three quarters of an hour, and that business would be finished once more.

She disliked going there as a patient dislikes going to the dentist. She had an intolerable recollection of all their past meetings, one a week on an average, for the last two years, and the thought that another was to take place immediately made her shiver with misery from head to foot. Not that it was exactly painful, like a visit to the dentist, but it was wearisome, so wearisome, so complicated, so long, so unpleasant, that anything, even a visit to the dentist, would have seemed preferable to her.

She went on, however, but very slowly, stopping, sitting down, going hither and thither, but she went. Oh, how she would have liked to miss this meeting, but she had left the unhappy viscount in the lurch twice running during the last month, and she did not dare to do it again so soon. Why did she go to see him? Oh, why? Because she had acquired the habit of doing it and had no reason to give poor Martelet when he wanted to know the why! Why had she begun it? Why? She did not know herself any longer. Had she been in love with him? Very possibly! Not very much, but a little, a long time ago! He was very nice, much sought after, perfectly dressed, most courteous, and after the first glance he was a perfect lover for a fashionable woman.

He had courted her for three months—the normal period, an honorable strife and sufficient resistance—and then she had consented. What emotion, what nervousness, what terrible, delightful fear attended that first meeting in his small, ground-floor bachelor rooms in the Rue de Miromesnil. Her heart? What did her little heart of a woman who had been seduced, vanquished, conquered, feel when she for the first time entered the door of the house which was her nightmare? She really did not know! She had quite forgotten. One remembers a fact, a date, a thing, but one hardly remembers after the lapse of two years what an emotion, which soon vanished because it was very slight, was like. But she had certainly not forgotten the others, that rosary of meetings, that road to the cross of love and its stations, which were so monotonous, so fatiguing, so similar to each other that she felt nauseated.

The very cabs were not like the other cabs which you use for ordinary purposes! Certainly the cabmen guessed. She felt sure of it by the very way they looked at her, and the eyes of these Paris cabmen are terrible! When you realize that these jehus constantly identify in the courts of justice, after a lapse of several years, the faces of criminals whom they have only driven once, in the middle of the night, from some street or other to a railway station and that they carry daily almost as many passengers as there are hours in the day and that their memory is good enough for them to declare: "That is the man whom I took up in the Rue des Martyrs and put down at the Lyons Railways Station at twelve o'clock at night on July tenth last year!" Is it not terrible to risk what a young woman risks when she is going to meet her lover and has to trust her reputation to the first cabman she meets? In two years she had employed at least one hundred or more of them in that drive to the Rue de Miromesnil, reckoning only one a week. They were so many witnesses who might appear against her at a critical moment.

As soon as she was in the cab she took another veil, as thick and dark as a domino mask, out of her pocket and put it on. That hid her face, but what about the rest, her dress, her bonnet and her parasol? They might be remarked—they might, in fact, have been seen already. Oh, what misery she endured in this Rue de Miromesnil! She thought she recognized the foot passengers, the servants, everybody, and almost, before the cab had stopped, she jumped out and ran past the porter who was standing outside his lodge. He must know everything, everything—her address, her name, her husband's profession—everything, for those porters are the most cunning of policemen! For two years she had intended to bribe him, to give him (to throw at him one day as she passed him) a hundred-franc banknote, but she had never dared to do it. She was frightened. What of? She did not know! Of his calling her back if he did not understand? Of a scandal? Of a crowd on the stairs? Of being arrested, perhaps? To reach the viscount's door she had only to ascend half a flight of stairs, but it seemed to her as high as the tower of St Jacques's Church.

As soon as she had reached the vestibule she felt as if she were caught in a trap. The slightest noise before or behind her nearly made her faint. It was impossible for her to go back because of that porter who barred her retreat, and if anyone came down at that moment she would not dare to ring at Martelet's door but would pass it as if she had been going elsewhere! She would have gone up and up and up! She would have mounted forty flights of stairs! Then when everything seemed quiet again down below she would run down, feeling terribly frightened, lest she should not recognize the apartment.

He would be there in a velvet coat lined with silk, very stylish, but rather ridiculous, and for two years he had never altered his manner of receiving her, not in a single movement! As soon as he had shut the door he used to say: "Let me kiss your hands, my dear, dear friend!" Then he would follow her into the room, where with closed shutters and lighted candles, out of refinement, no doubt, he would kneel down before her and look at her from head to foot with an air of adoration. On the first occasion that had been very nice and very successful, but now it seemed to her as if she saw M. Delaunay acting the last scene of a successful piece for the hundred and twentieth time. He might really change his manner of acting. But, no, he never altered his manner of acting, poor fellow. What a good fellow he was, but so commonplace!

And how difficult it was to undress and dress without a lady's maid! Perhaps that was the moment when she began to take a dislike to him. When he said: "Do you want me to help you?" she could have killed him. Certainly there were not many men as awkward as he was or as uninteresting. Certainly little Baron de Isombal would never have asked her in such a manner: "Do you want me to help you?" He would have helped her; he was so witty, so funny, so active. But there! He was a diplomatist; he had been about in the world and had roamed everywhere and, no doubt, had dressed and undressed women arrayed in every possible fashion!

The church clock struck the three quarters. She looked at the dial and said: "Oh, how anxious he will be!" And then she quickly left the square. But she had not taken a dozen steps outside when she found herself face to face with a gentle-man who bowed profoundly to her.

"Why! Is that you, Baron?" she said in surprise. She had just been thinking of him.

"Yes, madame." And then after asking how she was he continued: "Do you know that you are the only one—you will allow me to say of my lady friends, I hope—who has not yet seen my Japanese collection?"

"But, my dear baron, a lady cannot go to a bachelor's room like this."

"What do you mean? That is a great mistake when it is a question of seeing a rare collection!"

"At any rate, she cannot go alone."

"And why not? I have received a number of ladies alone, only for the sake of seeing my collection! They come every day. Shall I tell you their names? No—I will not do that; one must be discreet, even when one is not guilty. As a matter of fact, there is nothing improper in going to the house of a well-known seriously minded man who holds a certain position, unless one goes for an improper reason!"

"Well, what you have said is certainly correct at bottom."

"So you will come and see my collection?"

"When?"

"Well, now, immediately."

"Impossible, I am in a hurry."

"Nonsense, you have been sitting in the square for this last half-hour."

"You were watching me?"

"I was looking at you."

"But I am sadly in a hurry."

"I am sure you are not. Confess that you are in no particular hurry."

Mme Haggan began to laugh and said: "Well, no—not very."

A cab passed close by them, and the little baron called out: "Cabman!" The vehicle stopped and, opening the door, he said: "Get in, madame."

"But, Baron! No, it is impossible today; I really cannot."

"Madame, you are acting very imprudently. Get in! People are beginning to look at us, and you will collect a crowd; they will think I am trying to carry you off, and we shall both be arrested; please get in!"

She got in, frightened and bewildered, and he sat down by her side, saying to the cabman: "Rue de Provence."

But suddenly she exclaimed: "Good heavens! I have forgotten a very important telegram; please drive to the nearest telegraph office first of all."

The cab stopped a little farther on in the Rue de Châteaudun, and she said to the baron: "Would you kindly get me a fifty-centimes telegraph form? I promised my husband to invite Martelet to dinner tomorrow and had quite forgotten it."

When the baron returned and gave her the blue telegraph form she wrote in a pencil:

My dear friend, I am not at all well. I am suffering terribly from neuralgia, which keeps me in bed. Impossible to go out. Come and dine tomorrow night so that I may obtain my pardon.

JEANNE,

She wetted the gum, fastened it carefully and addressed it to Viscount de Martelet, 240 Rue de Miromesnil, and then, giving it back to the baron, she said: "Now, will you be kind enough to throw this in the telegram box?"

AN ARTIFICE

The old doctor and his young patient were talking by the side of the fire. There was nothing really the matter with her, except that she had one of those little feminine ailments from which pretty women frequently suffer—slight anemia, nervous attack and a suspicion of fatigue, probably of that fatigue from which newly married people often suffer at the end of the first month of their married life, when they have made a love match.

She was lying on the couch and talking. "No, Doctor," she said; "I shall never be able to understand a woman deceiving her husband. Even allowing that she does not love him, that she pays no heed to her vows and promises, how can she give herself to another man? How can she conceal the intrigue from other people's eyes? How can it be possible to love amid lies and treason?"

The doctor smiled and replied: "It is perfectly easy, and I can assure you that a woman does not think of all those little subtle details when she has made up her mind to go astray. I even feel certain that no woman is ripe for true love until she has passed through all the promiscuousness and all the irksomeness of married life, which, according to an illustrious man, is nothing but an exchange of ill-tempered words by day and perfunctory caresses at night. Nothing is more true, for no woman can love passionately until after she has married.

"As for dissimulation, all women have plenty of it on hand on such occasions. The simplest of them are wonderful tacticians and extricate themselves from the greatest dilemmas in an extraordinary way."

The young woman, however, seemed incredulous. "No, Doctor," she said; "one never thinks until after it has happened of what one ought to have done in a dangerous affair, and women are certainly more liable than men to lose their heads on such occasions."

The doctor raised his hands. "After it has happened, you say! Now I will tell you something that happened to one of my female patients whom I always considered an immaculate woman.

"It happened in a provincial town. One night when I was sleeping profoundly, in that deep, first sleep from which it is so difficult to rouse yourself, it seemed to me in my dreams as if the bells in the town were sounding a fire alarm, and I woke up with a start. It was my own bell which was ringing wildly, and as my footman did not seem to be answering the door, I in turn pulled the bell at the head of my bed. Soon I heard banging and steps in the silent house, and then Jean came into my room and handed me a letter which said: 'Madame Lelièvre begs Doctor Siméon to come to her immediately.'

"I thought for a few moments, and then I said to myself: 'A nervous attack, vapors, nonsense; I am too tired.' And so I replied: 'As Doctor Siméon is not at all well, he must beg Madame Lelièvre to be kind enough to call in his colleague, Monsieur Bonnet.'

"I put the note into an envelope and went to sleep again, but about half an hour later the street bell rang again, and Jean came to me and said: 'There is somebody downstairs—I do not quite know whether it is a man or a woman, as the individual is so wrapped up—who wishes to speak to you immediately. He says it is a matter of life and death for two people.' Whereupon I sat up in bed and told him to show the person in.

"A kind of black phantom appeared who raised her veil as soon as Jean had left the room. It was Madame Bertha Lelièvre, quite a young woman, who had been married for three years to a large shopkeeper in the town and was said to have been the prettiest girl in the neighborhood.

"She was terribly pale; her face was contracted like the faces of mad people are occasionally, and her hands trembled violently. Twice she tried to speak without being able to utter a sound, but at last she stammered out:

" 'Come—quick—quick, Doctor. Come—my—my lover has just died in my bedroom.' She stopped, half suffocated with emotion, and then went on: 'My husband will—be coming home from the club very soon.'

"I jumped out of bed without even considering that I was only in my night-shirt and dressed myself in a few moments. Then I said: 'Did you come a short time ago?'

" 'No,' she said, standing like a statue petrified with horror. 'It was my servant—she knows.' And then after a short silence she went on: 'I was there—by his side.' And she uttered a sort of cry of horror, and after a fit of choking, which made her gasp, she wept violently, shaking with spasmodic sobs for a minute or two. Then her tears suddenly ceased, as if dried by an internal fire, and with an air of tragic calmness she said: 'Let us make haste.'

"I was ready, but I exclaimed: 'I quite forgot to order my carriage.'

" 'I have one,' she said; 'it is his, which was waiting for him!' She wrapped herself up so as to completely conceal her face, and we started.

"When she was by my side in the darkness of the carriage she suddenly seized my hand and, crushing it in her delicate fingers, she said with a shaking voice that proceeded from a distracted heart: 'Oh! If you only knew, if you only knew what I am suffering! I loved him; I have loved him distractedly, like a madwoman, for the last six months.'

" 'Is anyone up in your house?' I asked.

" 'No, nobody except Rose, who knows everything.'

"We stopped at the door. Evidently everybody was asleep, and we went in without making any noise by means of her latchkey and walked upstairs on tiptoe. The frightened servant was sitting on the top of the stairs with a lighted candle by her side, as she was afraid to stop by the dead man. I went into the room, which was turned upside down, as if there had been a struggle in it. The bed, which was tumbled and open, seemed to be waiting for somebody; one of the sheets was thrown onto the floor, and wet napkins with which they had bathed the young man's temples were lying by the side of a wash hand basin and a glass, while a strong smell of vinegar pervaded the room.

"The dead man's body was lying at full length in the middle of the room, and I went up to it, looked at it and touched it. I opened the eyes and felt the hands, and then, turning to the two women who were shaking as if they were frozen, I said to them: 'Help me to lift him onto the bed.' When we had laid him gently onto it I listened to his heart, put a looking glass to his lips and then said: 'It is all over; let us make haste and dress him.' It was a terrible sight!

"I took his limbs one by one, as if they had belonged to some enormous doll, and held them out to the clothes which the women brought, and they put on his socks, drawers, trousers, waistcoat and lastly the coat, but it was a difficult matter to get the arms into the sleeves.

"When it came to buttoning his boots the two women kneeled down, while I held the light. As his feet were rather swollen it was very difficult, and as they could not find a buttonhook they had to use their hairpins. When the terrible toilet was over I looked at our work and said: 'You ought to arrange his hair a little.' The girl went and brought her mistress's large-toothed comb and brush, but as she was trembling and pulling out his long, tangled hair in doing it, Mme Lelièvre took the comb out of her hand and arranged his hair as if she were caressing him. She parted it, brushed his beard, rolled his mustaches gently round her fingers, as she had no doubt been in the habit of doing in the familiarities of their intrigue.

"Suddenly, however, letting go of his hair, she took her dead lover's inert head in her hands and looked for a long time in despair at the dead face, which no longer could smile at her. Then, throwing herself onto him, she took him into her arms and kissed him ardently. Her kisses fell like blows onto his closed mouth and eyes, onto his forehead and temples, and then, putting her lips to his ear, as if he could still hear her and as if she were about to whisper something to him, to make their embraces still more ardent, she said several times in a heart-rending voice: 'Adieu, my darling!'

"Just then the clock struck twelve, and I started up. 'Twelve o'clock!' I exclaimed. 'That is the time when the club closes. Come, madame, we have not a moment to lose!'

"She started up, and I said: 'We must carry him into the drawing room.' When we had done this I placed him on a sofa and lit the chandeliers, and just then the front door was opened and shut noisily. The husband had come back, and I said: 'Rose, bring me the basin and the towels and make the room look tidy. Make haste, for heaven's sake! Monsieur Lelièvre is coming in.'

"I heard his steps on the stairs and then his hands feeling along the walls. 'Come here, my dear fellow,' I said; 'we have had an accident.'

"And the astonished husband appeared in the door with a cigar in his mouth and said: 'What is the matter? What is the meaning of this?'

" 'My dear friend,' I said, going up to him, 'you find us in great embarrassment. I had remained late, chatting with your wife and our friend, who had brought me in his carriage, when he suddenly fainted, and in spite of all we have done he has remained unconscious for two hours. I did not like to call in strangers, and if you will now help me downstairs with him I shall be able to attend to him better at his own house.'

"The husband, who was surprised but quite unsuspicious, took off his hat. Then he took his rival, who would be quite inoffensive for the future, under the arms. I got between his two legs as if I had been a horse between the shafts, and we went downstairs while his wife lighted us. When we got outside I held the body up so as to deceive the coachman and said: 'Come, my friend; it is nothing; you feel better already, I expect. Pluck up your courage and make an attempt. It will soon be over.' But as I felt that he was slipping out of my hands I gave him a slap on the shoulder which sent him forward and made him fall into the carriage; then I got in after him.

"Monsieur Lelièvre, who was rather alarmed, said to me: 'Do you think it is anything serious?' To which I replied, 'No,' with a smile, as I looked at his wife, who had put her arm into that of her legitimate husband and was trying to see into the carriage.

"I shook hands with them and told my coachman to start, and during the whole drive the dead man kept falling against me. When we got to his house I said that he had become unconscious on the way home and helped to carry him upstairs, where I certified that he was dead and acted another comedy to his distracted family. At last I got back to bed, not without swearing at lovers."

The doctor ceased, though he was still smiling, and the young woman, who was in a very nervous state, said: "Why have you told me that terrible story?"

He gave her a gallant bow and replied:

"So that I may offer you my services if necessary."

SOLITUDE

We had been dining at the house of a friend, and the dinner had been very gay. After it broke up, one of the party, an old friend, said to me:

"Let us take a stroll in the Champs Elysées."

I agreed, and we went out, slowly walking up the long promenade under trees hardly yet covered with leaves. There was hardly a sound, save that confused and constant murmur which Paris makes. A fresh breeze fanned our faces, and a legion of stars were scattered over the black sky like a golden powder.

My companion said to me:

"I do not know why, but I breathe better here at night than anywhere else. It seems to me that my thoughts are enlarged. I have at times a sort of glimmering in my soul that makes me believe, for a second, that the divine secret of things is about to be discovered. Then the window is closed, and my vision is ended."

From time to time we saw two shadows glide along the length of the thickets; then we passed a bench where two people, seated side by side, made but one black spot.

My friend murmured:

"Poor things! They do not inspire me with disgust but with an immense pity. Among all the mysteries of human life there is one which I have penetrated; our great torment in this existence comes from the fact that we are eternally alone— all our efforts and all our actions are directed toward escaping this solitude. Those two lovers there on the benches in the open air are seeking, as we—as all creatures are seeking—to make their isolation cease, if only for a minute or less. They are living and always will live alone, and we also.

"This is more or less apparent to all of us. For some time I have endured this abominable pain of having understood, of having discovered the frightful solitude in which I live, and I know that nothing can make it cease—nothing. Do you hear? Whatever we may attempt, whatever we may do, whatever may be the misery of our hearts, the appeal of our lips, the clasp of our arms, we are always alone. I have asked you to walk tonight so that I shall not have to enter my own house, because now I suffer horribly from the solitude of my home. What good does it do me? I speak to you; you listen to me, yet we are both alone, side by side but alone. You understand?

" 'Blessed are the poor in spirit,' say the Scriptures. They have the illusion of happiness. They do not feel our solitary misery; they do not wander, as I do, through life, without contact save of elbows, without joy save the egotistic satisfaction of understanding, of seeing, of divining and of suffering eternally from the knowledge of our never-ending isolation.

"You think me slightly deranged—do you not? Listen to me. Since I have felt the solitude of my being it seems to me that I am daily sinking more deeply into a dark vault, whose sides I cannot find, whose end I do not know and which, perhaps, has no end. I sink without anyone with me or around me, without any living person making this same gloomy journey. This vault is life. Sometimes I hear noises, voices, cries. I timidly advance toward these confused sounds. But I never know exactly from whom they come; I never meet anybody; I never find another hand in this darkness that surrounds me. Do you understand?

"Some men have occasionally divined this frightful suffering. De Musset has written:

"Who comes? Who calls me? No one.
I am alone. One o'clock strikes.
O Solitude! O Misery!

But with him there is only a passing doubt and not a definite certainty as with me. He was a poet; he peopled life with fantasies, with dreams. He was never really alone. I—I am alone.

"Gustave Flaubert, one of the great unfortunates of this world, because he was one of the great lights, wrote to a friend this despairing phrase: 'We are all in a desert. Nobody understands anybody.'

"No, nobody understands anybody—whatever one thinks, whatever one says, whatever one attempts. Does the earth know what passes in those stars that are hurled like a spark of fire across the firmament—so far that we perceive only the splendor of some? Think of the innumerable army of others lost in infinitude—so near to each other that they form perhaps a whole, as the molecules of a body!

"Well, man does not know what passes in another man any more. We are farther from one another than the stars, and far more isolated, because thought is unfathomable.

"Do you know anything more frightful than this constant contact with beings that we cannot penetrate? We love one another as if we were fettered, very close, with extended arms, without succeeding in reaching one another. A torturing need of union hampers us, but all our efforts remain barren, our abandonment useless, our confidences unfruitful, our embraces powerless, our caresses vain. When we wish to join each other our sudden emotions make us only clash against each other.

"I never feel myself more alone than when I open my heart to some friend, because I then better understand the insuperable obstacle. He is there, my friend; I see his clear eyes above me, but the soul behind them I do not see. He listens to me. What is he thinking? Yes, what is he thinking? You do not understand this torment! He hates me, perhaps, or scorns me or mocks me! He reflects upon what

I have said; he judges me; he rails at me; he condemns me and considers me either very mediocre or a fool.

"How am I to know what he thinks? How am I to know whether he loves me as I love him and what is at work in that little round head? What a mystery is the unknown thought of a being, the hidden and independent thought that we can neither know nor control, neither command nor conquer!

"And I! I have wished in vain to give myself up entirely, to open all the doors of my soul, and I do not succeed in giving myself up. I still remain in the depth, the very depth, the secret abode of me, where no one can penetrate. No one can discover it or enter there, because no one resembles me, because no one understands anyone.

"You, at least, understand me at this moment; no, you think I am mad! You examine me; you shrink from me! You ask yourself: 'What's the matter with him tonight?' But if you succeed in seizing, in divining, one day my horrible and subtle suffering, come to me and say only: 'I have understood you!' and you will make me happy, for a second, perhaps.

"Women make me still more conscious of my solitude. Misery! Misery! How I have suffered through women, because they, more than men, have often given me the illusion of not being alone!

"When one falls in love it seems as though one expands. A superhuman felicity envelops you! Do you know why? Do you know why you feel then this sensation of exceeding happiness? It is simply because one imagines himself no longer alone. Isolation, the abandonment of the human being, seems to cease. What an error!

"More tormented even than we by this eternal need of love which gnaws at our solitary heart are women, the great delusion and the dream.

"You know those delicious hours passed face to face with a being with long hair, charming features and a look that excited us to love. What delirium misleads our mind! What illusion carries us away! Does it not seem that presently our souls shall form but one? But this 'presently' never comes, and after weeks of waiting, of hope and of deceptive joy you find yourself again, one day, more alone than you have ever been before.

"After each kiss, after each embrace, the isolation is increased. And how frightfully one suffers!

"Has not Sully Prudhomme written:

> "Caresses are only restless transports,
> Fruitless attempts of poor love which essay
> The impossible union of souls by the bodies.

"And then—good-by. It is over. One hardly recognizes the woman who has been everything to us for a moment of life and whose thoughts, intimate and commonplace, undoubtedly, we have never known.

"At the very hour when it would seem in that mysterious accord of beings, in the complete intermingling of ideas and of aspirations, that you were sounding the very depth of her soul, one word—one word only, sometimes—will reveal your error, will show you, like a flash of lightning in the night, the black abyss between you.

"And still, that which is best in the world is to pass a night near a woman you love without speaking, completely happy in the sole sensation of her presence. Ask no more, for two beings have never yet been united.

"As to myself, now I have closed my soul. I tell no more to anybody what I believe, what I think or what I love. Knowing myself condemned to this horrible solitude, I look upon things without expressing my opinion. What matter to me opinions, quarrels, pleasures or beliefs! Being unable to participate with anyone, I have withdrawn myself from all. My invisible self lives unexplored. I have common phrases for answers to the questions of each day and a smile which says yes when I do not even wish to take the trouble of speaking. Do you understand?"

We had traversed the long avenue to the Arc de Triomphe and had then walked back to the Place de la Concorde, for he had said all this slowly, adding many other things which I no longer remember.

He stopped and, stretching his arm toward the great granite obelisk standing on the pavement of Paris, losing its long Egyptian profile in the night of the stars— an exiled monument, bearing on its side the history of its country written in strange signs—said brusquely: "Look—we are all like that stone."

Then he left me without adding a word. Was he intoxicated? Was he mad? Was he wise? I do not yet know. Sometimes it seems to me that he was right; sometimes it seems to me that he had lost his mind.

A NORMAN

We had just left Rouen, and were going along the road to Jumièges at a brisk trot. The light carriage spun along between the fields, then the horse slowed down to climb the hill of Canteleu.

At that point there is one of the most magnificent views in the world. Behind us Rouen, the town of churches, of Gothic belfries, carved like ornaments of ivory; in front, St. Sever, the suburb of factories, which raises its thousand smoking chimneys to the great sky, opposite the thousand sacred spires of the old city.

Here is the steeple of the cathedral, the highest of the human monuments; and down there the "fire pump" of "la foudre," its rival, almost as tall, which overtops by a meter the highest pyramid of Egypt.

Before us the undulating Seine winds along, sown with islands, bordered on the right by white cliffs, crowned by a forest, and on the left by immense level fields, with another forest on their edge, far away in the distance.

From place to place, great ships were anchored along the banks of the wide river. Three enormous steamers were going out, one after another, toward Havre; and a string of boats consisting of a three-master, two schooners, and a brig, were coming up to Rouen, towed by a little tug, which vomited a cloud of black smoke.

My companion, born in the country, did not see this surprising landscape from the same point of view as I. But he smiled continually; he seemed to be laughing to himself. Suddenly he exclaimed: "Ah! you are about to see something funny— the chapel of Father Matthew. That is something really good, my boy."

I looked at him in astonishment. He continued:

"I am going to give you a flavor of Normandy that will remain in your nose. Father Matthew is the handsomest Norman in the province, and his chapel is one of the wonders of the world, no more no less. But I will give you first a few words of explanation. Father Matthew, or 'Father Booze' as they also call him, is an old sergeant major, returned to his native village. He unites, in admirable proportions, the perfect humbug of the old soldier and the sly malice of the Norman. On his return to these parts, thanks to innumerable protectors and incredible trickeries, he was made the guardian of a miraculous chapel, a chapel protected by the Virgin and frequented principally by pregnant girls. He baptized the marvelous statue there as: 'Notre Dame du Gros-Ventre,' and he treats it with a certain mocking familiarity which does not exclude respect. He has himself composed and had printed a special prayer for his GOOD VIRGIN. This prayer is a masterpiece of unintentional irony, of Norman wit, where ridicule is mixed with fear of the saint, a superstitious fear of secret influence of some kind. He does not believe much in his patron saint; nevertheless, he believes in her a little and treats her gently as a matter of policy.

"Here is the beginning of this extraordinary prayer:

" 'Our good Lady, the Virgin Mary, natural patroness of girl mothers, in this country and in all the earth, protect your servant who has sinned in a moment of forgetfulness.'

"The supplication terminates thus:

" 'Especially, do not forget to speak for me to your sainted husband, and intercede with God the Father that he may accord me a good husband like your own.'

"This prayer, forbidden by the clergy of the country, is sold by him privately, and is regarded as helpful by those who repeat it with unction. In fact, he speaks of the good Virgin as a valet might of his master, some redoubtable prince, knowing all his little intimate secrets. He knows a host of amusing stories about her which he whispers amongst friends after he has been drinking.

"But you must see for yourself.

"As the revenue furnished by the patroness did not seem sufficient, he has added to his chief asset, the Virgin, a little trade in saints. He keeps them all, or nearly all. And, as room was lacking in the chapel, he stocked them in the woodshed, from which he gets them whenever the faithful ask for them. He has carved these wonderfully comical statuettes himself, out of wood, and painted them all green, a solid color, one year when they painted his house. You know the saints heal maladies; but each has his specialty, and one must not run into error or confusion in these things. They are jealous one of the other, like play actors.

"So that they may not make any mistake, the poor old women come and consult Matthew.

" 'For bad ears, what saint is best?' they say.

" 'Well, there is Saint Osymus, who is good; and there is also Saint Pamphilus, who is not bad,' he tells them.

"That is not all. When Matthew has time on his hands, he drinks. But he drinks like an artist, one that is sure of himself, so much so that he is tipsy regularly every evening. He is tipsy, but he knows it; he knows it so well that he notes each day the exact degree of his drunkenness. It is his principal occupation. The chapel comes afterward.

"And he has invented—listen to this and prepare for a surprise—he has invented the boozometer. The instrument does not yet exist, but Matthew's observations are as precise as those of a mathematician. You will hear him say continually:

" 'Since Monday, I have not gone above forty-five.' Or, 'I was between fifty-two and fifty-eight,' or 'I had sixty-six to seventy,' or, perhaps, 'Ah! confound it, I believed I was in the fifties, when here I find I was at seventy-five!'

"He never makes a mistake. He says that he has not yet reached the hundredth degree, but, as he admits that his observations cease to be precise after he has passed ninety, one cannot absolutely rely upon this statement.

"When Matthew recognizes that he has passed ninety, you may be sure that he is really tipsy. On these occasions, his wife, Mélie, another marvel, works herself into great anger. She waits for him at the door when he enters, and shrieks: 'Here you are, you nasty pig, you drunken good-for-nothing.'

"Then Matthew, no longer laughing, plants himself before her, and in severe tone says: 'Be still, Mélie, this is no time to talk. Wait till tomorrow.'

"If she continues to vociferate, he approaches her, and with trembling voice says: 'Shut your jaw; I am in the nineties; I can no longer measure; I am going to hurt some one; take care!'

"Then Mélie beats a retreat.

"If she tries the next day to return to the subject, he laughs in her face and answers: 'Come, come! enough of that; that is all over. So long as I have not reached the hundredth degree, there is no harm done. But if I pass that, I will allow you to correct me, I give you my word!' "

We had reached the summit of the hill. The road lay through the wonderful forest of Roumare. The autumn, the marvelous autumn, mixed her gold and purple with the last green leaves, still vivid, as if some drops of sunlight had rained down from the sky into the thickest of the wood.

We crossed Duclair; then, instead of continuing toward Jumièges, my friend turned to the left, and, taking a short cut, struck into the wood. And soon, from the summit of a green hill, we discovered anew the magnificent valley of the Seine and the tortuous river itself, winding along at our feet.

Upon the right, a little building, with a slate roof and a clock tower as high as an umbrella, leaned against a pretty house with green shutters, all clothed in honeysuckle and roses.

A loud voice cried out: "Here are some friends!" And Matthew appeared upon the threshold. He was a man of sixty, thin, wearing a pointed beard and long, white mustaches. My companion shook hands with him and introduced me. Matthew made us enter a cool, clean kitchen, which also served as a living room.

"I, sir," said Matthew, "have no distinguished apartment. I like better not to get too far from the eatables. The pots and pans, you see, are company." Then, turning toward my friend, he added:

"Why have you come on Thursday? You know well that it is My Lady's consultation day. I cannot go out this afternoon."

Then, running to the door, he uttered a terrible call: "Mé-li-ee!" which must have made the sailors raise their heads in the ships going up and down the river, at the bottom of the valley.

Mélie did not answer.

Then Matthew winked maliciously: "She is not pleased with me, you see, because yesterday I was up to ninety."

My neighbor began to laugh. "Ninety, Matthew! How was that?"

Matthew answered: "I will tell you. I found last year only twenty rasières of cider apples. There were no more, but in order to make good cider these are the best. I made a barrelful, and yesterday I tapped it. As for nectar, that is nectar;

you will say so, too. I had Polyte here. We took a drink and then another drink without quenching our thirst, for one could drink it till tomorrow. I drank so much, one drink after another, that I felt a coolness in my stomach. I said to Polyte: 'If we should take a glass of brandy, now, it would heat us up.' He consented. But brandy—that put a fire in my body, so hot that it was necessary to return to the cider. So there it was! From coolness to heat and from heat to coolness, I perceived that I was in the nineties. Polyte was far beyond a hundred.''

The door opened. Mélie appeared, and immediately, before she said "Good day" to us, exclaimed: "Pigs! You were far beyond the hundred mark, both of you!"

Matthew was angry, but answered: "Say not so, Mélie, say not so; I have never been beyond a hundred."

They gave us an exquisite breakfast, before the door under two lime trees, at the side of the little chapel of "Notre Dame du Gros-Ventre," with the beautiful landscape before us. And Matthew related to us, with raillery mingled with credulity, some unlikely stories of miracles.

We had drunk much of the adorable cider, pungent and sweet, cool and powerful, which he preferred to all liquids, and were smoking our pipes, sitting astride our chairs, when two good women presented themselves.

They were old, dried, and bent. After bowing, they asked for Saint Blanc. Matthew winked his eye toward us, and said:

"I will go and get him for you." And he disappeared into his woodshed.

He remained there five minutes, then returned with face filled with consternation. Raising his arms, he declared:

"I don't know at all where he is. I cannot find him. I am sure that I had him!" Then, making a horn of his hands, he called: "Mélie!"

From the foot of the garden his wife answered: "What is it?"

"Where is Saint Blanc? I can't find him in the shed!"

Then Mélie threw back this explanation:

"Wasn't it him you took to stop the hole in the rabbit hutch last week?"

Matthew started. "Good God. Maybe that's so."

Then he said to the two women: "Follow me."

They followed. We almost suffocated with laughter. In fact, Saint Blanc, stuck in the earth like a common stake, stained with mud and filth, was being used to make one corner of the rabbit hutch.

When they perceived him, the two good women fell on their knees, crossed themselves, and began to murmur their oremus. Matthew hurried to them. "Wait," said he, "you are kneeling in the dirt; I will bring you some straw."

And he went to find some straw and made them a prayer cushion. Then, seeing that his saint was muddy, and believing without doubt that it would be bad for the trade, he added: "I am going to clean him up a bit."

He took a pail of water and a brush and began to wash the wooden figure vigorously. Meantime the two old women continued to pray.

When he had finished, he said: "Now it is all right." And then he brought us back for another drink.

As he raised the glass to his lips, he stopped and said, with an air of embarrassment: "Well, indeed, when I put Saint Blanc in the rabbit hutch, I was sure he would never earn me another penny. For two years there had been no demand for him. But the saints, you see, never die."

He drank and continued:

"Come, let us have another. Amongst friends you must never go less than fifty, and we're only at thirty-eight."

THE SPECTER

In speaking of a recent lawsuit our conversation had turned on sequestration, and each of us thereupon had a story to tell—a story affirmed to be true. We were a party of intimate friends who had passed a pleasant evening, now drawing to a close, in an old family residence in the Rue de Grenelle. The aged Marquis de la Tour-Samuel, bowed 'neath the weight of eighty-two winters, at last rose and, leaning on the mantelpiece, said in somewhat trembling tones:

"I also know something strange, so strange that it has been a haunting memory all my life. It is now fifty-six years since the incident occurred, and yet not a month has passed in which I have not seen it again in a dream, so great was and is the impression of fear it left on my mind. For ten minutes I experienced such horrible fright that, ever since, a sort of constant terror has made me tremble at unexpected noises, and objects half-seen in the gloom of night inspire me with a mad desire to take flight. In short, I am afraid of the dark!

"Ah no! I would not have avowed that before having reached my present age! Now I can say anything. I have never receded before real danger. So at eighty-two years of age I do not feel compelled to be brave over an imaginary danger.

"The affair upset me so completely and caused me such lasting and mysterious uneasiness that I never spoke of it to anyone. I will now tell it to you exactly as it happened, without any attempt at explanation.

"In July 1827 I was in garrison at Rouen. One day as I was walking on the quay I met a man whom I thought I recognized without being able to recall exactly who he was. Instinctively I made a movement to stop; the stranger perceived it and at once extended his hand.

"He was a friend to whom I had been deeply attached as a youth. For five years I had not seen him, and he seemed to have aged half a century. His hair was quite white, and he walked with a stoop as though completely worn out. He apparently comprehended my surprise, for he told me of the misfortune which had shattered his life.

"Having fallen madly in love with a young girl, he married her, but after a year of more than earthly happiness she died suddenly of heart failure. He had left his château on the very day of her burial and had come to live at Rouen. There he still dwelt, more dead than alive, desperate and solitary, exhausted by grief and so miserable that he thought constantly of suicide.

" 'Now that I have found you again,' he said, 'I will ask you to render me an important service. It is to go to my old home and get for me, from the desk of my bedroom—our bedroom—some papers which I greatly need. I cannot send a servant or an agent, as discretion and absolute silence are necessary. As for myself, nothing on earth would induce me to re-enter that house. I will give you the key of the room, which I myself locked on leaving, and the key of my desk—also a note to my gardener, telling him to open the château for you. But come and breakfast with me tomorrow, and we will arrange all that.'

"I promised to do him the slight favor he asked. For that matter, it was nothing of a trip, his property being but a few miles distant from Rouen and easily reached in an hour on horseback.

"At ten o'clock the following day, I breakfasted tête-à-tête with my friend, but he scarcely spoke.

"He begged me to pardon him; the thought of the visit I was about to make to that room, the scene of his dead happiness, overwhelmed him, he said. He, indeed, seemed singularly agitated and preoccupied, as though undergoing some mysterious mental combat.

"At length he explained to me exactly what I had to do. It was very simple. I must take two packages of letters and a roll of papers from the first drawer on the right of the desk of which I had the key. He added, 'I need not beg you to refrain from glancing at them.'

"I was wounded at that remark and told him so somewhat sharply. He stammered, 'Forgive me, I suffer so,' and tears came to his eyes.

"At about one o'clock I took leave of him to accomplish my mission.

"The weather was glorious, and I cantered over the turf, listening to the songs of the larks and the rhythmical striking of my sword against my boot. Then I entered the forest and walked my horse. Branches of the trees caressed my face as I passed, and now and then I caught a leaf with my teeth, from sheer gladness of heart at being alive and strong on such a radiant day.

"As I approached the château I took from my pocket the letter I had for the gardener and was astonished at finding it sealed. I was so irritated that I was about to turn back without having fulfilled my promise but reflected that I should thereby display undue susceptibility. My friend's state of mind might easily have caused him to close the envelope without noticing that he did so.

"The manor seemed to have been abandoned for twenty years. The open gate was dropping from its hinges; the walks were overgrown with grass, and the flower beds were no longer distinguishable.

"The noise I made by tapping loudly on a shutter brought an old man from out a door near by, who seemed stunned with astonishment at seeing me. On receiving my letter he read it, reread it, turned it over and over, looked me up and down, put the paper in his pocket and finally asked:

" 'Well! What is it you wish?'

"I replied shortly: 'You ought to know, since you have just read your master's orders. I wish to enter the château.'

"He seemed overcome. 'Then you are going in—in her room?'

"I began to lose patience and said sharply: 'Of course, but is that your affair?'

"He stammered in confusion: 'No sir, but it is because—that is, it has not been opened since—since the—death. If you will be kind enough to wait five minutes I will go to—to see if——'

"I interrupted him angrily: 'Look here, what do you mean with your tricks? You know very well you cannot enter the room, since I have the key!'

"He no longer objected. 'Then, sir, I will show you the way.'

" 'Show me the staircase and leave me. I'll find my way without you.'

" 'But—sir—indeed——'

"This time I silenced him effectually, pushed him aside and went into the house.

"I first traversed the kitchen, then two rooms occupied by the servant and his wife; next, by a wide hall, I reached the stairs, which I mounted, and recognized the door indicated by my friend.

"I easily opened it and entered. The apartment was so dark that at first I could distinguish nothing. I stopped short, my nostrils penetrated by the disagreeable, moldy odor of long-unoccupied rooms. Then as my eyes slowly became accustomed to the darkness I saw plainly enough a large and disordered bedroom, the bed without sheets but still retaining its mattresses and pillows on one of which was a deep impression, as though an elbow or a head had recently rested there.

"The chairs all seemed out of place. I noticed that a door, doubtless that of a closet, had remained half open.

"I first went to the window, which I opened to let in the light, but the fastenings of the shutters had grown so rusty that I could not move them. I even tried to break them with my sword but without success. As I was growing irritated over my useless efforts and could now see fairly well in the semi-obscurity, I renounced the idea of getting more light and went over to the writing table.

"Seating myself in an armchair and letting down the lid of the desk, I opened the designated drawer. It was full to the top. I needed but three packages, which I knew how to recognize, and began searching for them.

"I was straining my eyes in the effort to read the superscriptions, when I seemed to hear, or rather feel, something rustle back of me. I paid no attention, believing that a draught from the window was moving some drapery. But in a minute or so another movement, almost imperceptible, sent a strangely disagreeable little shiver over my skin. It was so stupid to be affected, even slightly, that self-respect prevented my turning around. I had then found the second packet I needed and was about to lay my hand on the third when a long and painful sigh, uttered just over my shoulder, made me bound like a madman from my seat and land several feet away. As I jumped I had turned about, my hand on the hilt of my sword and, truly, had I not felt it at my side I should have taken to my heels like a coward.

"A tall woman, dressed in white, stood gazing at me from the back of the chair where I had been sitting an instant before.

"Such a shudder ran through all my limbs that I nearly fell backward. No one can understand unless he has felt it that frightful, unreasoning terror! The mind becomes vague; the heart ceases to beat; the entire body grows as limp as a sponge.

"I do not believe in ghosts; nevertheless, I completely gave way to a hideous fear of the dead, and I suffered more in those few moments than in all the rest of my life from the irresistible anguish of supernatural fright. If she had not spoken I should have died, perhaps! But she spoke; she spoke in a sweet, sad voice that set my nerves vibrating. I dare not say that I became master of myself and recovered my reason. No! I was so frightened that I scarcely knew what I was doing, but a certain innate pride, a remnant of soldierly instinct, made me, almost in spite of myself, maintain a creditable countenance.

"She said: 'Oh, sir, you can render me a great service.'

"I wanted to reply, but it was impossible for me to pronounce a word. Only a vague sound came from my throat.

"She continued: 'Will you? You can save me, cure me. I suffer frightfully. I suffer, oh, how I suffer!' And she slowly seated herself in the armchair, still looking at me.

"'Will you?' she said.

"I replied, 'Yes' by a nod, my voice still being paralyzed.

"Then she held out to me a tortoise-shell comb and murmured:

" 'Comb my hair; oh, comb my hair; that will cure me; it must be combed. Look at my head—how I suffer, and my hairs pulls so!'

"Her hair, unbound, very long and very black, it seemed to me, hung over the back of the chair and touched the floor.

"Why did I receive that comb with a shudder, and why did I take in my hands the long, black hair which gave to my skin a gruesomely cold sensation, as though I were handling snakes? I cannot tell.

"That sensation has remained in my fingers, and I still tremble when I think of it.

"I combed her hair. I handled, I know not how, those icy locks. I twisted, knotted and plaited and braided them. She sighed and bowed her head, seeming to be happy. Suddenly she said: 'Thank you!' snatched the comb from my hands and fled by the door that I had noticed ajar.

"Left alone, I experienced for several seconds the horrible agitation of one who awakens from a nightmare. At length I regained my full senses; I ran to the window and with a mighty effort burst open the shutters, letting a flood of light into the room. Immediately I sprang to the door by which she had departed. I found it closed and immovable!

"Then a mad desire to flee came on me like a panic, the panic which soldiers know in battle. I seized the three packets of letters on the open secretary, ran from the room, dashed down the stairs, found myself outside, I know not how, and, seeing my horse a few steps off, leaped into the saddle and galloped away.

"I stopped only when I reached Rouen and my lodgings. There I shut myself into my room to reflect. For an hour I anxiously strove to convince myself that I had been the victim of a hallucination. I was about ready to believe that all I had seen was a vision, an error of my senses, when, as I approached the window, my eyes fell by chance upon my chest. Around the buttons of my uniform were entwined a quantity of long black hairs! One by one, with trembling fingers, I plucked them off and threw them away.

"I then called my orderly, feeling unable to see my friend that day, wishing, also, to reflect more fully upon what I ought to tell him. I had his letters carried to him, for which he gave the messenger a receipt. He asked after me most particularly and on being told I was ill—had had a sunstroke—appeared exceedingly anxious. Next morning I went to him, determined to tell him the truth. He had gone out the evening before and not yet returned. I called again during the day; my friend was still absent. After waiting a week longer without news of him I advised the authorities, and a judicial search was instituted. Not the slightest trace of his whereabouts or manner of disappearance was discovered.

"A minute inspection of the abandoned château revealed nothing of a suspicious character. There was no indication that a woman had been concealed there.

"After these fruitless researches all further efforts were abandoned, and in the fifty-six years that have elapsed since then I have heard nothing more."

THE RELIC

To the Abbé Louis d'Ennemare at Soissons:

My Dear Abbé,

My marriage with your cousin is broken off in the stupidest manner on account of a foolish trick which I involuntarily played my intended in a fit of embarrassment, and I turn to you, my old schoolfellow, to help me out of the difficulty. If you can I shall be grateful to you until I die.

You know Gilberte, or rather you think you know her, for do we ever understand women? All their opinions, their ideas, their creeds, are a surprise to us. They are all full of twists and turns, of the unforeseen or unintelligible arguments, of defective logic and of obstinate ideas, which seem final but which they alter because a little bird comes and perches on the window ledge.

I need not tell you that your cousin is very religious, as she was brought up by the White (or was it the Black?) Ladies at Nancy. You know that better than I do, but what you perhaps do not know is that she is just as excitable about other matters as she is about religion. She is as unstable as a leaf whirled away by the wind, and she is more of a girl than a woman, for she is moved or irritated in a moment, loves in a moment, hates in a moment and changes in a moment. She is pretty, as you know, and more charming than I can say or you can guess.

Well, we became engaged, and I adored her, as I adore her still, and she appeared to love me.

One evening I received a telegram summoning me to Cologne for a consultation which might be followed by a serious and difficult operation. As I had to start the next morning I went to wish Gilberte good-by and tell her that I should not dine with them on Wednesday, but on Friday, the day of my return. Ah! Take care of Fridays, for I assure you they are unlucky!

When I told her that I had to go to Germany I saw that her eyes filled with tears, but when I said I should be back very soon she clapped her hands and said:

"I am very glad you are going then! You must bring me back something, a mere trifle, just a souvenir, but a souvenir that you have chosen for me. You must find out what I should like best, do you hear? And then I shall see whether you have any imagination."

She thought for a few moments and then added:

"I forbid you to spend more than twenty francs on it. I want it for the intention and for the remembrance of your penetration and not for its intrinsic value."

And then after another moment's silence she said in a low voice and with downcast eyes:

"If it costs you nothing in money and if it is something very ingenious and pretty I will—I will kiss you."

The next day I was in Cologne. It was a case of a terrible accident, which had thrown a whole family into despair, and a difficult amputation was necessary. They put me up—I might almost say they locked me up—and I saw nobody but people in tears, who almost deafened me with their lamentations. I operated on a man who appeared to be in a moribund state and nearly died under my hands. I remained with him two nights, and then when I saw that there was a chance of his recovery I drove to the station. I had, however, made a mistake in the trains and had an hour to wait, and so I wandered about the streets, still thinking of my poor patient, when a man accosted me. I do not know German, and he was totally ignorant of French, but at last I made out that he was offering me some relics. I thought of Gilberte, for I knew her fanatical devotion, and here was my present ready to hand, so I followed the man into a shop where religious objects were for sale and I bought a small piece of a bone of one of the Eleven Thousand Virgins.

The pretended relic was inclosed in a charming old silver box, and that determined my choice. Putting my purchase into my pocket, I went to the railway station and so to Paris.

As soon as I got home I wished to examine my purchase again, and on taking hold of it I found that the box was open and the relic lost! It was no good to hunt in my pocket and to turn it inside out; the small bit of bone, which was no bigger than half a pin, had disappeared.

You know, my dear little abbé, that my faith is not very great, but, as my friend, you are magnanimous enough to put up with my coldness, to leave me alone and wait for the future, as you say. But I absolutely disbelieve in the relics of second-hand dealers in piety, and you share my doubts in that respect. Therefore the loss of that bit of sheep's carcass did not grieve me, and I easily procured a similar fragment, which I carefully fastened inside my casket, and then I went to see my intended.

As soon as she saw me she ran up to me, smiling and anxious, and said to me:

"What have you brought?"

I pretended to have forgotten, but she did not believe me, and I made her beg me and beseech me, even. But when I saw that she was devoured by curiosity I gave her the sacred silver box. She appeared overjoyed.

"A relic? Oh! A relic!"

And she kissed the box passionately, so that I was ashamed of my deception. She was not quite satisfied, however, and her uneasiness soon turned to terrible fear, and, looking straight into my eyes she said:

"Are you sure that it is authentic?"

"Absolutely certain."

"How can you be so certain?"

I was caught, for to say that I had bought it through a man in the streets would be my destruction. What was I to say? A wild idea struck me, and I said in a low, mysterious voice:

"I stole it for you."

She looked at me with astonishment and delight in her large eyes.

"Oh! You stole it? Where?"

"In the cathedral, in the very shrine of the Eleven Thousand Virgins."

Her heart beat with pleasure, and she murmured:

"Oh! Did you really do that for me? Tell me all about it!"

There was no end of it, and I could not go back. I made up a fanciful story with precise details. I had given the custodian of the building a hundred francs to be allowed to go about the building by myself; the shrine was being repaired, but I happened to be there at the breakfast time of the workmen and clergy;

by removing a small panel I had been enabled to seize a small piece of bone (oh! so small) among a quantity of others (I said a quantity, as I thought of the amount that the remains of the skeletons of eleven thousand virgins must produce). Then I went to a goldsmith's and bought a casket worthy of the relic, and I was not sorry to let her know that the silver box cost me five hundred francs.

But she did not think of that; she listened to me, trembling, in an ecstasy, and, whispering: "How I love you!" she threw herself into my arms.

Just note this: I had committed sacrilege for her sake; I had committed a theft; I had violated a shrine, violated and stolen holy relics, and for that she adored me, thought me loving, tender, divine. Such is woman, my dear abbé, every woman.

For two months I was the best of lovers. In her room she made a kind of magnificent chapel in which to keep this bit of mutton chop which, as she thought, had made me commit that love crime, and she worked up her religious enthusiasm in front of it every morning and evening. I had asked her to keep the matter secret, for fear, as I said, that I might be arrested, condemned and given over to Germany, and she kept her promise.

Well, at the beginning of the summer she was seized by an irresistible wish to see the scene of my exploit, and she begged her father so persistently (without telling him her secret reason) that he took her to Cologne, but without telling me of their trip, according to his daughter's wish.

I need not tell you that I had not seen the interior of the cathedral. I do not know where the tomb (if there be a tomb) of the Eleven Thousand Virgins is, and then it appears that it is unapproachable, alas!

A week afterward I received ten lines, breaking off our engagement, and then an explanatory letter from her father, whom she had, somewhat late, taken into her confidence.

At the sight of the shrine she had suddenly seen through my trickery and my lie and had also found out that I was innocent of any other crime. Having asked the keeper of the relics whether any robbery had been committed, the man began to laugh and pointed out to them how impossible such a crime was, but from the moment I had plunged my profane hand into venerable relics I was no longer worthy of my fair-haired and delicate betrothed.

I was forbidden the house! I begged and prayed in vain; nothing could move the fair devotee, and I grew ill from grief. Well, last week her cousin, Mme d'Arville, who is also your relative, sent word that she should like to see me, and when I called she told me on what conditions I might obtain my pardon, and here they are. I must bring Gilberte a relic, a real, authentic relic, certified to be such by our Holy Father, the Pope, of some virgin and martyr, and I am going mad from embarrassment and anxiety.

I will go to Rome, if needful, but I cannot call on the Pope unexpectedly and tell him my stupid adventure; and, besides, I doubt whether they let private individuals have relics. Could not you give me an introduction to some cardinal, or only to some French prelate, who possesses some remains of a female saint? Or perhaps you may have the precious object she wants in your collection.

Help me out of my difficulty, my dear abbé, and I promise you that I will be converted ten years sooner than I otherwise should be!

Mme d'Arville, who takes the matter seriously, said to me the other day: "Poor Gilberte will never marry."

My dear old schoolfellow, will you allow your cousin to die the victim of a stupid piece of business on my part? Pray prevent her from being the eleventh thousand and one virgin.

Pardon me, I am unworthy, but I embrace you and love you with all my heart.

Your old friend,
HENRI FONTAL.

IN THE COUNTRY

The two cottages stood side by side at the foot of a hill near a little seaside resort. The two peasants labored hard on the fertile soil to rear their little ones, of whom each family had four.

Before the adjoining doors a whole troop of brats swarmed from morning till night. The two eldest were six years old, and the youngest were about fifteen months; the marriages, and afterwards the births, having taken place nearly simultaneously in both families.

The two mothers could hardly distinguish their own offspring among the lot, and as for the fathers, they mixed them up completely. The eight names danced in their heads; they were always getting them mixed up; and when they wished to call one child, the men often called three names before getting the right one.

The first of the two cottages, as you came up from the watering place, Rolleport, was occupied by the Tuvaches, who had three girls and one boy; the other house sheltered the Vallins, who had one girl and three boys.

They all subsisted frugally on soup, potatoes, and fresh air. At seven o'clock in the morning, then at noon, then at six o'clock in the evening, the housewives got their broods together to give them their food, as the gooseherds collect their flocks. The children were seated, according to age, before the wooden table polished by fifty years of use, the mouths of the youngest hardly reaching the level of the table. Before them was placed a bowl filled with bread, soaked in the water in which the potatoes had been boiled, half a cabbage, and three onions; and the whole line ate until their hunger was appeased. The mother herself fed the smallest.

A little meat in the pot on Sundays was a feast for all; and the father on this day sat longer over the meal, repeating: "I wish we could have this every day."

One afternoon, in the month of August, a phaeton unexpectedly stopped in front of the cottages, and a young woman, who was driving the horses, said to the gentleman sitting at her side:

"Oh, look at all those children, Henri! How pretty they are, tumbling about in the dust, like that!"

The man did not answer, accustomed to these outbursts of admiration, which were a pain and almost a reproach to him. The young woman continued:

"I must hug them! Oh, how I should like to have one of them—that one there —the little tiny one!"

Springing down from the carriage, she ran toward the children, took one of the two youngest—a Tuvache child—and lifting him up in her arms, she kissed him

(Copyright, 1923, by Alfred A. Knopf, Inc.)

passionately on his dirty cheeks, on his tousled hair daubed with earth, and on his little hands, with which he fought vigorously to get away from the caresses, which displeased him.

Then she got into the carriage again, and drove off at a lively trot. But she returned the following week, and, seating herself on the ground, took the youngster in her arms, stuffed him with cakes, gave sweets to all the others, and played with them like a young girl, while the husband waited patiently in the carriage.

She returned again; made the acquaintance of the parents, and reappeared every day with her pockets full of dainties and pennies.

Her name was Mme. Henri d'Hubières.

One morning, on arriving, her husband alighted with her, and without stopping to talk to the children, who now knew her well, she entered the farmer's cottage.

They were busy chopping wood for the fire. They rose to their feet in surprise, brought forward chairs, and waited expectantly.

Then the woman, in a broken, trembling voice, began:

"My good people, I have come to see you, because I should like—I should like to take—your little boy with me——"

The country people, too bewildered to think, did not answer.

She recovered her breath, and continued: "We are alone, my husband and I. We would keep it. Are you willing?"

The peasant woman began to understand. She asked:

"You want to take Charlot from us? Oh, no, indeed!"

Then M. d'Hubières intervened:

"My wife has not made her meaning clear. We wish to adopt him, but he will come back to see you. If he turns out well, as there is every reason to expect, he will be our heir. If we, by any chance, should have children, he will share equally with them; but if he should not reward our care, we should give him, when he comes of age, a sum of twenty thousand francs, which will be deposited immediately in his name, with a lawyer. As we have thought also of you, we will pay you, until your death, a pension of one hundred francs a month. Do you understand me?"

The woman had risen to her feet, furious.

"You want me to sell you Charlot? Oh, no, that's not the sort of thing to ask of a mother! Oh, no! That would be an abomination!"

The man, grave and deliberate, said nothing; but approved of what his wife said by a continued nodding of his head.

Madame d'Hubières, in dismay, began to weep; turning to her husband with a voice full of tears, the voice of a child used to having all its wishes gratified, she stammered:

"They will not do it, Henri, they will not do it."

Then he made a last attempt: "But, my friends, think of the child's future, of his happiness, of——"

The peasant woman, however, exasperated, cut him short:

"We know all about that! We've heard all that before! Get out of here, and don't let me see you again—the idea of wanting to take away a child like that!"

Madame d'Hubières remembered that there were two quite young children, and she asked, through her tears, with the tenacity of a willful and spoiled woman:

"But is the other little one not yours?"

Father Tuvache answered: "No, it is our neighbors'. You can go to them if you wish." And he went back into his house, whence could be heard the indignant voice of his wife.

The Vallins were at table, slowly eating slices of bread which they parsimoniously spread with a little rancid butter on a plate between the two.

M. d'Hubières recommenced his proposals, but with more insinuations, more oratorical precautions, more shrewdness.

The two country people shook their heads, in sign of refusal, but when they learned that they were to have a hundred francs a month, they considered the matter, consulting one another by glances, much disturbed. They kept silent for a long time, tortured, hesitating. At last the woman asked: "What do you say to it, father?" In a weighty tone he said: "I say that it's not to be despised."

Madame d'Hubières, trembling with anguish, spoke of the future of their child, of his happiness, and of the money which he could give them later.

The peasant asked: "This pension of twelve hundred francs, will it be promised before a lawyer?"

M. d'Hubières responded: "Why, certainly, beginning with tomorrow."

The woman, who was thinking it over, continued:

"A hundred francs a month is not enough to pay for depriving us of the child. That child would be working in a few years; we must have a hundred and twenty francs."

Tapping her foot with impatience, Mme. d'Hubières granted it at once, and, as she wished to carry off the child with her, she gave a hundred francs extra, as a present, while her husband drew up a paper. And the young woman, radiant, carried off the howling brat, as one carries away a wished-for knickknack from a shop.

The Tuvaches, from their door, watched her departure, silent, serious, perhaps regretting their refusal.

Nothing more was heard of little Jean Vallin. The parents went to the lawyer every month to collect their hundred and twenty francs. They had quarreled with their neighbors, because Mother Tuvache grossly insulted them, continually, repeating from door to door that one must be unnatural to sell one's child; that it was horrible, disgusting bribery. Sometimes she would take her Charlot in her arms, ostentatiously exclaiming, as if he understood:

"I didn't sell you, I didn't! I didn't sell you, my little one! I'm not rich, but I don't sell my children!"

And this went on for years and years. Every day coarse jeers were shouted outside the door so that they could be heard in the neighboring house. Mother Tuvache finally believed herself superior to the whole countryside because she had not sold Charlot. Those who spoke of her used to say:

"I know, of course, that it was a tempting offer; yet she behaved like a real mother."

She was cited as a model, and Charlot, who was nearly eighteen—brought up with this idea, which was constantly repeated—thought himself superior to his comrades because he had not been sold.

The Vallins lived comfortably, thanks to the pension. That was the cause of the unappeasable fury of the Tuvaches, who had remained miserably poor. Their eldest went away to serve his time in the army; Charlot alone remained to labor with his old father, to support the mother and two younger sisters.

He had reached twenty-one years when, one morning, a brilliant carriage stopped before the two cottages. A young gentleman, with a gold watch chain, got out, giving his hand to an aged, white-haired lady. The old lady said to him: "It is there, my child, at the second house." And he entered the house of the Vallins as if he were at home.

The old mother was washing her aprons; the infirm father was asleep in the chimney corner. Both raised their heads, and the young man said:

"Good morning, Papa; good morning, Mamma!"

They both stood up, frightened! In a flutter, the peasant woman dropped her soap into the water, and stammered:

"Is it you, my child? Is it you, my child?"

He took her in his arms and hugged her, repeating: "Good morning, Mamma," while the old man, all trembling, said, in the calm tone which he never lost: "Here you are, back again, Jean," as if he had just seen him a month ago.

When they had recognized each other again, the parents wished to take their boy out in the neighborhood, and show him. They took him to the mayor, to the deputy, to the priest, and to the schoolmaster.

Charlot, standing on the threshold of his cottage, watched him pass.

In the evening, at supper, he said to the old people: "You must have been stupid to let the Vallins' boy be taken."

The mother answered, obstinately: "I wouldn't sell my child."

The father remained silent. The son continued:

"It is unfortunate to be sacrificed like that."

Then Father Tuvache, in an angry tone, said:

"Are you going to reproach us for having kept you?" And the young man said, brutally:

"Yes, I reproach you for having been such fools. Parents like you cause the misfortune of children. You deserve that I should leave you."

The old woman wept over her plate. She moaned, as she swallowed the spoonfuls of soup, half of which she spilled: "One may kill oneself to bring up children!"

Then the boy said, roughly: "I'd rather not have been born than be what I am. When I saw the other fellow, my heart stood still. I said to myself: 'See what I should have been now!'" He got up: "See here, I feel that I would do better not to stay here, because I would throw it in your faces from morning till night, and I would make your life miserable. I'll never forgive you for that!"

The two old people were silent, downcast, in tears.

He continued: "No, the thought of that would be too much. I'd rather look for a living somewhere else."

He opened the door. The sound of voices entered. The Vallins were celebrating the return of their child.

Then Charlot stamped with rage, and, turning to his parents, he shouted:

"You silly yokels!"

And he disappeared into the night.

THE BED

On a hot afternoon during last summer the large auction rooms seemed asleep, and the auctioneers were knocking down the various lots in a listless manner. In a back room on the first floor two or three lots of old silk ecclesiastical vestments were lying in a corner.

They were copes for solemn occasions and graceful chasubles on which embroidered flowers surrounded symbolic letters on a yellowish ground, which had originally been white. Some secondhand dealers were there, two or three men with dirty beards and a fat woman with a big stomach, one of those women who deal in secondhand finery and manage illicit love affairs, women who are brokers in old and young human flesh, just as much as they are in new and old clothes.

Presently a beautiful Louis XV chasuble was put up for sale, which was as pretty as the dress of a marchioness of that period. It had retained all its colors and was embroidered with lilies of the valley round the cross and long blue irises, which came up to the foot of the sacred emblem, and with wreaths of roses in the corners. When I had bought it I noticed that there was a faint scent about it, as if it were permeated with the remains of incense or still pervaded by delicate, sweet scents by bygone years, by the memory of a perfume, the soul of an evaporated essence.

When I got home I wished to have a small chair of the same period covered with it, and as I was handling it in order to take the necessary measures I felt some paper beneath my fingers. When I cut the lining some letters fell at my feet. They were yellow with age, and the faint ink was the color of rust; outside the sheets, which were folded in the fashion of years long past, it was addressed in a delicate hand to "M. l'Abbé d'Argence."

The first three letters merely settled places of meeting, but here is the third:

"MY FRIEND, I am very unwell, ill, in fact, and I cannot leave my bed. The rain is beating against my windows, and I lie dreaming comfortably and warmly under my eider-down coverlet. I have a book of which I am very fond and which seems as if it really applied to me. Shall I tell you what it is? No, for you would only scold me. Then when I have read a little, I think and will tell you what about.

"Having been in bed for three days, I think about my bed and even in my sleep I meditate on it still. I have come to the conclusion that the bed comprehends our whole life, for we were born in it, we live in it, and we shall die in it. If, therefore, I had M. de Crébillon's pen, I should write the history of a bed, and what exciting and terrible, as well as delightful and moving, occurrences would not such a book contain! What lessons and what subjects for moralizing could one not draw from it for everyone?

"You know my bed, my friend, but you will never guess how many things I have discovered in it within the last three days and how much more I love it in consequence. It seems to me to be inhabited, haunted, if I may say so, by a number of people I never thought of who, nevertheless, have left something of themselves in that couch.

"Ah! I cannot undrstand people who buy new beds, beds to which no memories or cares are attached. Mine, ours, which is so shabby and so spacious, must have held many existences in it from birth to the grave. Think of that, my friend; think of it all; review all those lives, a great part of which was spent between these four posts, surrounded by these hangings embroidered by human figures, which have seen so many things. What have they seen during the three centuries since they were first put up?

"Here is a young woman lying in this bed.

"From time to time she sighs, and then she groans and cries out; her mother is with her, and presently a little creature that makes a noise like a cat mewing and which is all shriveled and wrinkled appears. It is a male child to which she has given birth, and the young mother feels happy in spite of her pain; she is nearly suffocated with joy at that first cry and stretches out her arms, and those around her shed tears of pleasure. For that little morsel of humanity which has come from her means perpetuation of the blood, of the heart and of the soul of the old people, who are looking on, trembling with excitement.

"And then here are two lovers who for the first time are together in that tabernacle of life. They tremble, but, transported with delight, they have the delicious sensation of being close together, and by degrees their lips meet. That divine kiss makes them one, that kiss which is the gate of a terrestrial heaven, that kiss which speaks of human delights, which continually promises them, announces them and precedes them. And their bed is agitated like the tempestuous sea; it bends and murmurs and itself seems to become animated and joyous, for the maddening mystery of love is being accomplished on it. What is there sweeter, what more perfect in this world, than those embraces which make one single being out of two and which give to both of them at the same moment the same thought, the same expectation and the same maddening pleasure, a joy which descends upon them like a celestial and devouring fire?

"Do you remember those lines from some old poet which you read to me last year? I should like to have them embroidered on the top of my bed, where Pyramus and Thisbe are continually looking at me out of their tapestried eyes.

"And think of death, my friend, of all those who have breathed out their last sigh to God in this bed. For it is also the tomb of hopes ended, the door which closes everything after having been the entrance to the world. What cries, what anguish, what sufferings, what groans, how many arms stretched out toward the past, what appeals to a happiness that has vanished forever, what convulsions, what death rattles, what gaping lips and distorted eyes have there not been in this bed from which I am writing to you, during the three centuries that it has sheltered human beings!

"The bed, you must remember, is the symbol of life; I have discovered this within the last three days. There is nothing good except the bed, and are not some of our best moments spent in sleep?

"But then again, we suffer in bed! It is the refuge of those who are ill and suffering, a place of repose and comfort for worn-out bodies, in one word, a part and parcel of humanity.

"Many other thoughts have struck me, but I have not time to note them down for you, and then, should I remember them all? Besides that, I am so tired that I mean to shake up my pillows, stretch myself out at full length and sleep a little. But be sure and come to see me at three o'clock tomorrow; perhaps I may be better and able to prove it to you.

"Good-by, my friend; here are my hands for you to kiss, and I also offer you my lips."

THE AWAKENING

During the three years that she had been married she had not left the Val de Ciré, where her husband possessed two cotton mills. She led a quiet life and, although without children, she was quite happy in her house among the trees, which the workpeople called the "château."

Although M. Vasseur was considerably older than she was he was very kind. She loved him, and no guilty thought had ever entered her mind.

Her mother came and spent every summer at Ciré and then returned to Paris for the winter as soon as the leaves began to fall.

Jeanne coughed a little every autumn, for the narrow valley through which the river wound was very foggy for five months in the year. First of all, slight mists hung over the meadows, making all the low-lying ground look like a large pond out of which the roofs of the houses rose. Then a white vapor, which rose like a tide, enveloped everything, turning the valley into a phantom land through which men moved like ghosts, without recognizing each other ten yards off, and the trees, wreathed in mist and dripping with moisture, rose up through it.

But the people who went along the neighboring hills and looked down upon the deep, white depression of the valley, saw the two huge chimneys of M. Vasseur's factories rising above the mist below. Day and night they vomited forth two long trails of black smoke, the sole indication that people were living in the hollow, which looked as if it were filled with a cloud of cotton.

That year, when October came, the medical men advised the young woman to go and spend the winter in Paris with her mother, as the air of the valley was dangerous for her weak chest, and she went. For a month or so she thought continually of the house which she had left, the home to which she seemed rooted, the well-known furniture and quiet ways which she loved so much. But by degrees she grew accustomed to her new life and got to like entertainments, dinner and evening parties and balls.

Till then she had retained her girlish manners, had been undecided and rather sluggish, walked languidly and had a tired smile, but now she became animated and merry and was always ready for pleasure. Men paid her marked attentions, and she was amused at their talk and made fun of their gallantries, as she felt sure that she could resist them, for she was rather disgusted with love from what she had learned of it in marriage.

The idea of giving up her body to the coarse caresses of such bearded creatures made her laugh with pity and shudder a little with ignorance.

She asked herself how women could consent to degrading contacts with strangers, the more so as they were already obliged to endure them with their legitimate husbands. She would have loved her husband much more if they had lived together like two friends and had restricted themselves to chaste kisses, which are the caresses of the soul.

But she was much amused by their compliments, by the desire which showed itself in their eyes, a desire she did not share, by declarations of love whispered into her ear as they were returning to the drawing room after some grand dinner, by words murmured so low that she almost had to guess them, words which left her blood quite cool and her heart untouched while gratifying her unconscious coquetry, kindling a flame of pleasure within her, making her lips open, her eyes grow bright, and her woman's heart, to which homage was due, quiver with delight.

She was fond of those tête-à-têtes in the dusk, when a man grows pressing, hesitates, trembles, and falls on his knees. It was a delicious and new pleasure to her to know that they felt a passion which left her quite unmoved, able to say no by a shake of the head and by pursing her lips, able to withdraw her hands, to get up and calmly ring for lights and to see the man who had been trembling at her feet get up, confused and furious when he heard the footman coming.

She often uttered a hard laugh, which froze the most burning words, and said harsh things, which fell like a jet of icy water on the most ardent protestations, while the intonations of her voice were enough to make any man who really loved her kill himself. There were two especially who made obstinate love to her, although they did not at all resemble one another.

One of them, Paul Péronel, was a tall man of the world, gallant and enterprising, a man who was accustomed to successful love affairs, one who knew how to wait and when to seize his opportunity.

The other, M. d'Avancelle, quivered when he came near her, scarcely ventured to express his love but followed her like a shadow and gave utterance to his hopeless desire by distracted looks and the assiduity of his attentions to her. She made him a kind of servant and treated him as if he were her slave.

She would have been much amused if anybody had told her that she would love him, and yet she did love him after a singular fashion. As she saw him continually, she had grown accustomed to his voice, to his gestures, and to his manner, just as one grows accustomed to those with whom one meets continually. Often his face haunted her in her dreams, and she saw him as he really was: gentle, delicate in all his actions, humble, but passionately in love. She would awake full of these dreams, fancying that she still heard him and felt him near her, until one night (most likely she was feverish) she saw herself alone with him in a small wood, where they were both sitting on the grass. He was saying charming things to her, while he pressed and kissed her hands. She could feel the warmth of his skin and of his breath, and she was stroking his hair in a very natural manner.

We are quite different in our dreams from what we are in real life. She felt full of love for him, full of calm and deep love, and was happy in stroking his forehead and in holding him against her. Gradually he put his arms around her, kissed her eyes and her cheeks without her attempting to get away from him; their lips met, and she yielded.

When she saw him again, unconscious of the agitation that he had caused her, she felt that she grew red, and while he was telling her of his love she was continually recalling to mind their previous meeting, without being able to get rid of the recollection.

She loved him, loved him with refined tenderness, chiefly from the remembrance of her dream, although she dreaded the accomplishment of the desires which had arisen in her mind.

At last he perceived it, and then she told him everything, even to the dread of his kisses, and she made him swear that he would respect her, and he did so. They spent long hours of transcendental love together, during which their souls alone embraced, and when they separated they were enervated, weak and feverish.

Sometimes their lips met, and with closed eyes they reveled in that long, yet chaste caress. She felt, however, that he could not resist much longer, and as she did not wish to yield, she wrote and told her husband that she wanted to come to him and to return to her tranquil, solitary life. But in reply he wrote her a very kind letter and strongly advised her not to return in the middle of the winter and so expose herself to the sudden change of climate and to the icy mists of the valley, and she was thunderstruck and angry with that confiding man, who did not guess, who did not understand, the struggles of her heart.

February was a warm, bright month, and although she now avoided being alone with M. d'Avancelle, she sometimes accepted his invitation to drive round the lake in the Bois de Boulogne with him when it was dusk.

On one of those evenings, it was so warm that it seemed as if the sap in every tree and plant were rising. Their cab was going at a walk; it was growing dusk, and they were sitting close together, holding each other's hands, and she said to herself:

"It is all over; I am lost!" For she felt her desires rising in her again, the imperious demand for that supreme embrace which she had undergone in her dream. Every moment their lips sought each other, clung together and separated, only to meet again immediately.

He did not venture to go into the house with her but left her at her door, more in love with him than ever and half fainting.

M. Paul Péronel was waiting for her in the little drawing room without a light, and when he shook hands with her he felt how feverish she was. He began to talk in a low, tender voice, lulling her tired mind with the charm of amorous words.

She listened to him without replying, for she was thinking of the other; she thought she was listening to the other and thought she felt him leaning against her in a kind of hallucination. She saw only him and did not remember that any other man existed on earth, and when her ears trembled at those three syllables: "I love you," it was he, the other man, who uttered them, who kissed her hands, who strained her to his breast like the other had done shortly before in the cab. It was he who pressed victorious kisses on her lips; it was he whom she held in her arms and embraced, to whom she was calling with all the longings of her heart, with all the overwrought ardor of her body.

When she awoke from her dream she uttered a terrible cry. Paul Péronel was kneeling by her and was thanking her passionately, while he covered her disheveled hair with kisses, and she almost screamed out: "Go away! Go away! Go away!"

And as he did not understand what she meant and tried to put his arm round her waist again, she writhed as she stammered out:

"You are a wretch, and I hate you! Go away! Go away!" And he got up in great surprise, took up his hat and went.

The next day she returned to Val de Ciré, and her husband, who had not expected her for some time, blamed her for her freak.

"I could not live away from you any longer," she said.

He found her altered in character and sadder than formerly, but when he said to her: "What is the matter with you? You seem unhappy. What do you want?" she replied:

"Nothing. Happiness exists only in our dreams in this world."

Avancelle came to see her the next summer, and she received him without any emotion and without regret, for she suddenly perceived that she had never loved him, except in a dream from which Paul Péronel had brutally roused her.

But the young man, who still adored her, thought as he returned to Paris:

"Women are really very strange, complicated and inexplicable beings."

WORDS OF LOVE

Sunday, ——

You do not write to me; I never see you; you never come, so I must suppose that you have ceased to love me. But why? What have I done? Pray tell me, my own dear love. I love you so much, so dearly! I should like always to have you near me, to kiss you all day while I call you every tender name that I could think of. I adore you; I adore you; I adore you, my beautiful cock. Your affectionate hen.

SOPHIE.

Monday, ——

MY DEAR FRIEND:

You will understand absolutely nothing of what I am going to say to you, but that does not matter, and if my letter happens to be read by another woman it may be profitable to her.

Had you been deaf and dumb, I should no doubt have loved you for a very long time, and the cause of what has happened is that you can talk; that is all.

In love, you see, dreams are always made to sing, but in order that they may do so, they must not be interrupted, and when one talks between two kisses one always interrupts that frenzied dream which our souls indulge in, that is, unless they utter sublime words, and sublime words do not come out of the little mouths of pretty girls.

You do not understand me at all, do you? So much the better; I will go on. You are certainly one of the most charming and adorable women I have ever seen.

Are there any eyes on earth that contain more dreams than yours, more unknown promises, greater depths of love? I do not think so. And when that mouth of yours, with its curved lips, smiles and shows the ivory gates within, one is tempted to say that from this ravishing mouth comes ineffable music, something inexpressibly delicate, a sweetness which extorts sighs.

It is then that you speak to me, and that is what troubles me—don't you see—troubles me more than tongue can tell. I would prefer never to see you at all.

You go on pretending not to understand anything, do you not? But I calculated on that.

Do you remember the first time you came to see me at my residence? How gaily you stepped inside, an odor of violets, which clung to your skirts, heralding your entrance; how we looked at each other for ever so long, without uttering a word, after which we embraced like two fools. Then from that time to the end we never exchanged a word.

But when we separated, did not our trembling hands and our eyes say many things, things which cannot be expressed in any language. At least, I thought so, and when you went away you murmured:

"We shall meet again soon!"

That was all you said, and you will never guess what delightful dreams you left me, all that I, as it were, caught a glimpse of, all that I fancied I could guess in your thoughts.

You see, my poor child, for men who are not stupid, who are rather refined and somewhat superior, love is such a complicated instrument that the merest trifle puts it out of order. You women never perceive the ridiculous side of certain things when you love, and you fail to see the grotesqueness of some expressions.

Why does a word which sounds quite right in the mouth of a small, dark woman seem quite wrong and funny in the mouth of a fat, light-haired woman? Why are the wheedling ways of the one altogether out of place in the other?

Why is it that certain caresses which are delightful from the one should be wearisome from the other? Why? Because in everything, and especially in love, perfect harmony—absolute agreement in motion, voice, words and in demonstrations of tenderness—is necessary in the person who moves, speaks and manifests affection; harmony is necessary in age, in height, in the color of the hair and in the style of beauty.

If a woman of thirty-five, who has arrived at the age of violent, tempestuous passion, were to preserve the slightest traces of the caressing archness of her love affairs at twenty, were not to understand that she ought to express herself differently, look at her lover differently and kiss him differently, were not to see that she ought to be a Dido and not a Juliet, she would infallibly disgust nine lovers out of ten, even if they could not account to themselves for their estrangement. Do you understand me? No? I hoped so.

From the time that you gave rein to your tenderness it was all over for me, my dear friend. Sometimes we would embrace for five minutes in one interminable kiss, one of those kisses which makes lovers close their eyes, lest part of it should escape through their clouded soul which it is ravaging. And then when our lips separated, you would say to me:

"That was nice, you fat old dog."

At such moments I could have beaten you, for you gave me successively all the names of animals and vegetables which you doubtless found in some cookery book or gardener's manual. But that is nothing.

The caresses of love are brutal, bestial and, if one comes to think of it, grotesque! Oh! My poor child, what joking elf, what perverse sprite could have prompted the concluding words of your letter to me? I have made a collection of them, but out of love for you I will not show them to you.

And sometimes you really said things which were quite inopportune. For instance, you managed now and then to let out an exalted "I love you!" on such singular occasions that I was obliged to restrain a strong desire to laugh. There are times when the words "I love you!" are so out of place that they become indecorous; let me tell you that.

But you do not understand me, and many other women also will not understand me but think me stupid, though that matters very little to me. Hungry men eat like gluttons, but people of refinement are disgusted at it and often feel an invincible dislike for a dish on account of a mere trifle. It is the same with love as with cookery.

What I cannot comprehend, for example, is that certain women who fully understand the irresistible attraction of fine, embroidered stockings, the exquisite charm of shades, the witchery of valuable lace concealed in the depths of their underclothing, the exciting zest of hidden luxury and all the subtle delicacies of female elegance never understand the invincible disgust with which words that are out of place or foolishly tender inspire us.

At times coarse and brutal expressions work wonders, as they excite the senses and make the heart beat, and they are allowable at the hours of combat. Is not that sentence of Cambronne's sublime?[1]

Nothing shocks us that comes at the right time, but then, we must also know when to hold our tongue and to avoid phrases à la Paul de Kock at certain moments.

And I embrace you passionately, on the condition that you say nothing.

RENÉ.

THE LEGEND OF MONT-SAINT-MICHEL

I had first seen it from Cancale, this fairy castle planted in the sea. I had seen it dimly, like a gray shadow rising in the foggy sky. I saw it again from Avranches at sunset. The immense stretch of sand was red, the horizon was red, the whole boundless bay was red; alone, the abbey, growing out there in the distance like a fantastic manor, like a dream palace, incredibly strange and beautiful—this alone remained almost black in the purple of the dying day.

The following morning at dawn I went towards it across the sands. My eyes fastened on this gigantic jewel, as big as a mountain, cut like a cameo, and as dainty as lace. The nearer I approached the greater my admiration grew, for perhaps nothing in the world is more wonderful or more perfect.

As surprised as if I had discovered the habitation of a god, I wandered through those halls supported by frail or massive columns, through those corridors open to the sky, raising my eyes in wonder to those spires which looked like rockets starting for the sky, and to that incredible crowd of towers, of gargoyles, of slender and charming ornaments, fireworks of stone, granite lace, a masterpiece of colossal and delicate architecture.

As I was looking up in ecstasy, a Lower Normandy peasant came up to me and told me the story of the great quarrel between Saint Michel and the devil.

A skeptical genius has said: "God made man in his image; man has returned the compliment."

This saying is an eternal truth, and it would be very curious to write the history of the local divinity on every continent, as well as the history of the patron saints in each one of our provinces. The Negro has his ferocious man-eating idols; the polygamous Mohammedan fills his paradise with women; the Greeks, like a practical people, have deified all the passions.

Every village in France is under the influence of some protecting saint, modified according to the characteristics of the inhabitants.

Saint Michel watches over Lower Normandy—Saint Michel, the radiant and

[1]At Waterloo, General Cambronne is reported to have said, when called on to surrender: "The guard dies but does not surrender." But according to Victor Hugo, in Les Misérables, he used the expression "Merde!" which cannot be put into English fit for polite ears.

victorious angel, the sword carrier, the hero of heaven, the victorious, the conqueror of Satan.

But this is how the Lower Normandy peasant, cunning, underhand, and tricky, understands and tells of the struggle between the great saint and the devil:

To escape from the malice of his neighbor the demon, Saint Michel built himself, in the open ocean, this habitation worthy of an archangel; and only such a saint could build a residence of such magnificence.

But, as he still feared the approaches of the Evil One, he surrounded his domain with quicksands, more treacherous even than the sea.

The devil lived in a humble cottage on the hill; but he owned all the pastures surrounded by the sea, the rich lands where grow the finest crops, the prosperous valleys, and all the fertile hills of the country; but the saint ruled only over the sands. So Satan was rich, whereas Saint Michel was as poor as a beggar.

After a few years of fasting the saint grew tired of this state of affairs, and began to think of some compromise with the devil; but the matter was by no means easy, as Satan kept a good hold on his crops.

He thought the thing over for about six months; then one morning he set out for land. The demon was eating his soup in front of his door when he saw the saint; he immediately rushed toward him, kissed the hem of his sleeve, invited him in, and offered him refreshments.

Saint Michel drank a bowl of milk and then began: "I have come here to propose to you a good bargain."

The devil, candid and trustful, answered: "Very well."

"Here it is. Give me all your lands."

Satan, growing alarmed, tried to speak: "But——"

The saint continued: "Listen first. Give me all your lands. I will take care of all the work, the plowing, the sowing, the fertilizing, everything, and we will share the crops equally. Do you agree?"

The devil, who was naturally lazy, accepted. He only asked in addition for a few of those delicious red mullet which are caught around the lonely hill. Saint Michel promised the fish.

They shook hands and spat on one side to show that it was a bargain, and the saint continued: "Here, so that you will have nothing to complain of, choose whatever you prefer: that part of the harvest which will be above ground, or in the ground." Satan cried out: "I choose all that will be above ground."

"It's a bargain!" said the saint. And he went away.

Six months later, all over the immense domain of the devil, one could see nothing but carrots, turnips, onions, salsify, all the plants whose juicy roots are good and savory, and whose leaves are useless, good for nothing but for feeding animals.

Satan got nothing and wished to break the contract, calling Saint Michel a swindler.

But the saint, who had developed quite a taste for agriculture, went back to see the devil, and said: "Really, I hadn't thought of that at all; it was just an accident; no fault of mine. And to make things fair with you, this year I'll let you take everything that is under the ground."

"Very well," answered Satan.

The following spring, all the Evil Spirit's lands were covered with heavy corn,

oats as big as beans, linseed, magnificent colzas, red clover, peas, cabbage, artichokes, everything that blossoms into grains or fruit in the sunlight.

Once more Satan received nothing, and this time he completely lost his temper.
He took back his fields and remained deaf to all the new overtures of his neighbor.

A whole year rolled by. From the top of his lonely manor, Saint Michel looked
at the distant and fertile lands, and watched the devil direct the work, take in
his crops, and thresh the corn. And he grew angry, exasperated at his powerlessness.
As he was no longer able to deceive Satan, he decided to wreak vengeance on him,
and he went out to invite him to dinner for the following Monday.

"You have been very unfortunate in your dealings with me," he said; "I know
it; but I don't want any ill feeling between us, and I expect you to dine with me.
I'll give you some good things to eat."

Satan, who was as greedy as he was lazy, accepted eagerly. On the day which
had been decided on, he donned his finest clothes and set out for the mount.

Saint Michel sat him down to a magnificent meal. First there was a *vol-au-vent*,
full of cocks' crests and kidneys, with meatballs, then two big red mullet with
cream sauce, a turkey stuffed with chestnuts soaked in wine, some salt-marsh lamb
as tender as possible, vegetables which melted in the mouth, and nice warm
galette which was brought on smoking and gave out a delicious odor of butter.

They drank pure cider, sparkling and sweet, and powerful red wine, and after
each course more room was made with some old apple brandy.

The devil drank and ate to his heart's content; in fact, he took so much that
he found himself uncomfortable.

Then Saint Michel arose in anger, and cried, in a voice like thunder: "What!
before me, rascal! you dare—before me——"

Satan, terrified, ran away, and the saint, seizing a stick, pursued him. They ran
around through the halls, turning around the pillars, running up the staircases,
galloping along the cornices, jumping from gargoyle to gargoyle. The poor demon,
who was terribly ill, was running about madly and soiling the saint's home. At last
he found himself at the top of the last terrace, from which could be seen the immense bay, with its distant cities, sands, and pastures. He could no longer escape,
and the saint came up behind him and gave him a furious kick, which shot him
through space like a cannonball.

He shot through the air like a javelin and fell down heavily in front of the
town of Mortain. His horns and claws stuck deep into the rock, which keeps
through eternity the traces of this fall of Satan's.

He stood up again, limping, crippled until the end of time, and as he looked
at the fatal abbey in the distance, standing out against the setting sun, he understood well that he would always be vanquished in this unequal struggle; and he
went away limping, heading for distant countries, leaving to his enemy his fields,
his hills, his valleys, and his pastures.

And this is how Saint Michel, the patron saint of Normandy, vanquished the
devil.

Another people would have dreamed of this battle in an entirely different
manner.

CHRISTMAS EVE

"The Christmas Eve supper![1] Oh no, I shall never go in for that again!" Stout Henri Templier said that in a furious voice, as if someone had proposed some crime to him, while the others laughed and said:

"What are you flying into a rage about?"

"Because a Christmas Eve supper played me the dirtiest trick in the world, and ever since I have felt an insurmountable horror for that night of imbecile gaiety."

"Tell us about it."

"You want to know what it was? Very well then, just listen.

"You remember how cold it was two years ago at Christmas; cold enough to kill poor people in the streets. The Seine was covered with ice; the pavements froze one's feet through the soles of one's boots, and the whole world seemed to be at the point of congealing.

"I had a big piece of work on and refused every invitation to supper, as I preferred to spend the night at my writing table. I dined alone and then began to work. But about ten o'clock I grew restless at the thought of the gay and busy life all over Paris, at the noise in the streets which reached me in spite of everything, at my neighbors' preparations for supper which I heard through the walls. I hardly knew any longer what I was doing; I wrote nonsense, and at last I came to the conclusion that I had better give up all hope of producing any good work that night.

"I walked up and down my room; I sat down and got up again. I was certainly under the mysterious influence of the enjoyment outside, and I resigned myself to it. So I rang for my servant and said to her:

" 'Angela, go and get a good supper for two: some oysters, a cold partridge, some crayfish, ham and some cakes. Put out two bottles of champagne, lay the cloth and go to bed.'

"She obeyed in some surprise, and when all was ready I put on my greatcoat and went out. The great question remained: 'Whom was I going to bring in to supper?' My female friends had all been invited elsewhere, and if I had wished to have one I ought to have seen about it beforehand. So I thought that I would do a good action at the same time and said to myself:

" 'Paris is full of poor and pretty girls who will have nothing on the table tonight and who are on the lookout for some generous fellow. I will act the part of Providence to one of them this evening, and I will find one if I have to go to every pleasure resort, and I will hunt till I find one to my choice.' So I started off on my search.

"I certainly found many poor girls who were on the lookout for some adventure, but they were ugly enough to give a man a fit of indigestion, or thin enough to freeze in their tracks if they stopped, and you all know that I have a weakness for stout women. The more flesh they have, the better I like them, and a female colossus would be my ideal.

[1] A great institution in France, and especially in Paris, at which black puddings are an indispensable dish.

"Suddenly, opposite the Théâtre des Variétés, I saw a figure to my liking. I trembled with pleasure and said:

" 'By Jove! What a fine girl!'

"It only remained for me to see her face, for a woman's face is the dessert.

"I hastened on, overtook her and turned round suddenly under a gas lamp. She was charming, quite young, dark, with large, black eyes, and I immediately made my proposition which she accepted without any hesitation, and a quarter of an hour later we were sitting at supper in my lodgings. 'Oh, how comfortable it is here,' she said as she came in and looked about her with evident satisfaction at having found a supper and a bed on that bitter night. She was superb, so beautiful that she astonished me, and so stout that she fairly captivated me.

"She took off her cloak and hat, sat down and began to eat, but she seemed in low spirits, and sometimes her pale face twitched as if she were suffering from hidden sorrow.

" 'Have you anything troubling you?' I asked her.

" 'Bah! Don't let us think of troubles!'

"And she began to drink. She emptied her champagne glass at a draught, filled it again and emptied it again without stopping, and soon a little color came into her cheeks and she began to laugh.

"I adored her already, kissed her continually and discovered that she was neither stupid, nor common nor coarse as ordinary streetwalkers are. I asked her for some details about her life, but she replied:

" 'My little fellow, that is no business of yours!' Alas, an hour later!

"At last it was time to retire, and while I was clearing the table, which had been laid in front of the fire, she undressed herself quickly and got in. My neighbors were making a terrible din, singing and laughing like lunatics, and so I said to myself:

" 'I was quite right to go out and bring in this girl; I should never have been able to do any work.'

"At this moment, however, a deep groan made me look around, and I said:

" 'What is the matter with you, my dear?'

"She did not reply but continued to utter painful sighs, as if she were suffering horribly, and I continued:

" 'Do you feel ill?' And suddenly she uttered a cry, a heart-rending cry, and I rushed up to the bed with a candle in my hand.

"Her face was distorted with pain, and she was wringing her hands, panting and uttering long, deep groans which sounded like a rattle in the throat and were painful to hear. I asked her in consternation:

" 'What is the matter with you? Do tell me what is the matter.'

" 'Oh, the pain! The pain!' she said. I pulled up the bedclothes and I saw, my friends, that she was in labor.

"Then I lost my head and ran and knocked at the wall with my fists, shouting: 'Help! Help!'

"My door was opened almost immediately, and a crowd of people came in, men in evening clothes, women in full dress, harlequins, Turks, musketeers, and the inroad startled me so that I could not explain myself, while they who had thought that some accident had happened or that a crime had been committed could not understand what was the matter. At last, however, I managed to say:

" 'This—this—woman—is being confined.'

"Then they looked at her and gave opinion. A friar, especially, declared that he knew all about it and wished to assist nature, but as they were all as drunk as pigs I was afraid that they would kill her. So I rushed downstairs without my hat to fetch an old doctor who lived in the next street. When I came back with him the whole house was up; the gas on the stairs had been relighted; the lodgers from every floor were in my room, while four boatmen were finishing my champagne and crayfish.

"As soon as they saw me they raised a loud shout. A milkmaid presented me with a horrible little wrinkled specimen of humanity that was mewing like a cat and said to me:

" 'It is a girl.'

"The doctor examined the woman, declared that she was in a dangerous state, as the event had occurred immediately after supper, and took his leave, saying he would immediately send a sick nurse and a wet nurse. An hour later the two women came, bringing all that was requisite with them.

"I spent the night in my armchair, too distracted to be able to think of the consequences, and almost as soon as it was light the doctor came again. He found his patient very ill and said to me:

" 'Your wife, monsieur——'

" 'She is not my wife,' I interrupted him.

" 'Very well then, your mistress; it does not matter to me.'

"He told me what must be done for her, what her diet must be, and then wrote a prescription.

"What was I to do? Could I send the poor creature to the hospital? I should have been looked upon as a brute in the house and in all the neighborhood. So I kept her in my rooms, and she had my bed for six weeks.

"I sent the child to some peasants at Poissy to be taken care of, and she still costs me fifty francs a month, for as I had paid at first, I shall be obliged to go on paying as long as I live. Later on she will believe that I am her father. But to crown my misfortunes, when the girl had recovered I found that she was in love with me, madly in love with me, the baggage!"

"Well?"

"Well, she had grown as thin as a homeless cat, and I turned the skeleton out of doors. But she watches for me in the streets, hides herself, so that she may see me pass, stops me in the evening when I go out in order to kiss my hand and, in fact, worries me enough to drive me mad. That is why I never keep Christmas Eve now."

MADAME BAPTISTE

When I went into the waiting room at the station at Loubain the first thing I did was to look at the clock, and I found that I had two hours and ten minutes to wait for the Paris express.

I felt suddenly tired, as if I had walked twenty miles. Then I looked about me, as if I could find some means of killing the time on the station walls. At last I went out again and halted outside the gates of the station, racking my brains to find something to do. The street, which was a kind of boulevard planted with acacias, between two rows of houses of unequal shape and different styles of architecture, houses such as one only sees in a small town, ascended a slight hill, and at the extreme end of it there were some trees, as if it ended in a park.

From time to time a cat crossed the street and jumped over the gutters carefully. A cur sniffed at every tree and hunted for fragments from the kitchens, but I did not see a single human being. I felt listless and disheartened. What could I do with myself? I was already thinking of the inevitable and interminable visit to the small café at the railway station where I should have to sit over a glass of un-drinkable beer and an illegible newspaper, when I saw a funeral procession coming out of a side street into the one in which I was, and the sight of the hearse was a relief to me. It would, at any rate, give me something to do for ten minutes.

Suddenly, however, my curiosity was aroused. The corpse was followed by eight gentlemen, one of whom was weeping, while the others were chatting together. But there was no priest, and I thought to myself: "This is a nonreligious funeral," but then I reflected that a town like Loubain must contain at least a hundred freethinkers who would have made a point of making a manifestation. What could it be then? The rapid pace of the procession clearly proved that the body was to be buried without ceremony and, consequently, without the intervention of re-ligion.

My idle curiosity framed the most complicated suppositions, and as the hearse passed a strange idea struck me, which was to follow it with the eight gentlemen. That would take up my time for an hour at least, and I, accordingly, walked with the others with a sad look on my face, and on seeing this the two last turned round in surprise and then spoke to each other in a low voice.

No doubt they were asking each other whether I belonged to the town, and then they consulted the two in front of them, who stared at me in turn. The close attention they paid me annoyed me, and to put an end to it I went up to them and, after bowing, said:

"I beg your pardon, gentlemen, for interrupting your conversation, but seeing a civil funeral, I have followed it although I did not know the deceased gentleman whom you are accompanying."

"It is a woman," one of them said.

I was much surprised at hearing this and asked:

"But it is a civil funeral, is it not?"

The other gentleman, who evidently wished to tell me all about it, then said: "Yes and no. The clergy have refused to allow us the use of the church."

On hearing that I uttered a prolonged "A-h!" of astonishment. I could not un-derstand it at all, but my obliging neighbor continued:

"It is rather a long story. This young woman committed suicide, and that is the reason why she cannot be buried with any religious ceremony. The gentleman who is walking first and who is crying is her husband."

I replied with some hesitation:

"You surprise and interest me very much, monsieur. Shall I be indiscreet if I ask you to tell me the facts of the case? If I am troubling you think that I have said nothing about the matter."

The gentleman took my arm familiarly.

"Not at all, not at all. Let us stop a little behind the others, and I will tell it to you, although it is a very sad story. We have plenty of time before getting to the cemetery, whose trees you see up yonder, for it is a stiff pull up this hill."

And he began:

"This young woman, Madame Paul Hamot, was the daughter of a wealthy merchant in the neighborhood, Monsieur Fontanelle. When she was a mere child of eleven she had a terrible adventure: a footman violated her. She nearly died in consequence, and the wretch's brutality betrayed him. A terrible criminal case was the result, and as it was proved that for three months the poor young martyr had been the victim of that brute's disgraceful practices, he was sentenced to penal servitude for life.

"The little girl grew up, stigmatized by her disgrace, isolated, without any companions, and grown-up people would scarcely kiss her, for they thought they would soil their lips if they touched her forehead. She became a sort of monster, a phenomenon to all the town. People said to each other in a whisper: 'You know little Fontanelle,' and everybody turned away in the streets when she passed. Her parents could not even get a nurse to take her out for a walk, and the other servants held aloof from her, as if contact with her would poison everybody who came near her.

"It was pitiable to see the poor child when the brats played every afternoon. She remained quite by herself, standing by her maid and looking at the other children amusing themselves. Sometimes, yielding to an irresistible desire to mix with the other children, she advanced timidly, with nervous gestures, and mingled with a group with furtive steps, as if conscious of her own infamy. And immediately the mothers, aunts and nurses used to come running from every seat, taking the children intrusted to their care by the hand and dragging them brutally away.

"Little Fontanelle would remain isolated, wretched, without understanding what it meant, and then would begin to cry, heartbroken with grief, and to run and hide her head in her nurse's lap, sobbing.

"As she grew up it was worse still. They kept the girls from her, as if she were stricken with the plague. Remember that she had nothing to learn, nothing; that she no longer had the right to the symbolical wreath of orange flowers; that almost before she could read she had penetrated that redoubtable mystery which mothers scarcely allow their daughters to guess, trembling as they enlighten them on the night of their marriage.

"When she went through the streets, always accompanied by a governess—as if her parents feared some fresh, terrible adventure—with her eyes cast down under the load of that mysterious disgrace which she felt was always weighing upon her, the other girls, who were not nearly so innocent as people thought, whispered and giggled as they looked at her knowingly and immediately turned their heads absently if she happened to look at them. People scarcely greeted her; only a few men bowed to her, and the mothers pretended not to see her, while some young blackguards called her 'Madame Baptiste,' after the name of the footman who had outraged and ruined her.

"Nobody knew the secret torture of her mind, for she hardly ever spoke and never laughed; her parents themselves appeared uncomfortable in her presence, as if they bore her a constant grudge for some irreparable fault.

"An honest man would not willingly give his hand to a liberated convict, would he, even if that convict were his own son? And Monsieur and Madame Fontanelle looked on their daughter as they would have done on a son who had just been

released from the hulks. She was pretty and pale, tall, slender, distinguished looking, and she would have pleased me very much, monsieur, but for that unfortunate
affair.

"Well, when a new subprefect was appointed here eighteen months ago he
brought his private secretary with him. He was a queer sort of fellow who had
lived in the Latin Quarter,[1] it appears. He saw Mademoiselle Fontanelle and fell
in love with her, and when told of what occurred he merely said: 'Bah! That is
just a guarantee for the future, and I would rather it should have happened before
I married her than afterward. I shall sleep tranquilly with that woman.'

"He paid his addresses to her, asked for her hand and married her, and then,
not being deficient in boldness, he paid wedding calls,[2] as if nothing had happened.
Some people returned them; others did not, but at last the affair began to be forgotten and she took her proper place in society.

"She adored her husband as if he had been a god, for you must remember that
he had restored her to honor and to social life, that he had braved public opinion,
faced insults and, in a word, performed a courageous act, such as few men would
accomplish, and she felt the most exalted and unceasing love for him.

"When she became pregnant and it was known, the most particular people
and the greatest sticklers opened their doors to her, as if she had been definitely
purified by maternity.

"It is funny but true, and thus everything was going on as well as possible, when
the other day the feast of the patron saint of our town occurred. The subprefect,
surrounded by his staff and the authorities, presided at the musical competition,
and when he had finished his speech the distribution of medals began, which Paul
Hamot, his private secretary, handed to those who were entitled to them.

"As you know, there are always jealousies and rivalries which make people forget
all propriety. All the ladies of the town were there on the platform, and, in his
proper turn, the bandmaster from the village of Mourmillon came up. This band
was only to receive a second-class medal, for you cannot give first-class medals to
everybody, can you? But when the private secretary handed him his badge the man
threw it in his face and exclaimed:

" 'You may keep your medal for Baptiste. You owe him a first-class one, also,
just as you do me.'

"There were a number of people there who began to laugh. The common herd
are neither charitable nor refined, and every eye was turned toward that poor lady.
Have you ever seen a woman going mad, monsieur? Well, we were present at the
sight! She got up and fell back on her chair three times in succession, as if she
wished to make her escape but saw that she could not make her way through the
crowd. Then another voice in the crowd exclaimed:

" 'Oh! Oh! Madame Baptiste!'

"And a great uproar, partly laughter and partly indignation, arose. The word
was repeated over and over again; people stood on tiptoe to see the unhappy
woman's face; husbands lifted their wives up in their arms so that they might see
her, and people asked:

" 'Which is she? The one in blue?'

"The boys crowed like cocks, and laughter was heard all over the place.

[1] The students' quarter in Paris.
[2] In France and Germany the newly married couple pay the wedding calls, the reverse of our
custom.

"She did not move now on her state chair, just as if she had been put there for the crowd to look at. She could not move or disappear or hide her face. Her eyelids blinked quickly, as if a vivid light were shining in her face, and she panted like a horse that is going up a steep hill, so that it almost broke one's heart to see it. Meanwhile, however, Monsieur Hamot had seized the ruffian by the throat, and they were rolling on the ground together amid a scene of indescribable confusion, and the ceremony was interrupted.

"An hour later, as the Hamots were returning home, the young woman, who had not uttered a word since the insult but who was trembling as if all her nerves had been set in motion by springs, suddenly sprang on the parapet of the bridge and threw herself into the river before her husband could prevent it. The water is very deep under the arches, and it was two hours before her body was recovered. Of course she was dead."

The narrator stopped and then added:

"It was, perhaps, the best thing she could do in her position. There are some things which cannot be wiped out, and now you understand why the clergy refused to have her taken into church. Ah! If it had been a religious funeral the whole town would have been present, but you can understand that her suicide, added to the other affair, made families abstain from attending her funeral. And then it is not an easy matter here to attend a funeral which is performed without religious rites."

We passed through the cemetery gates, and I waited, much moved by what I had heard, until the coffin had been lowered into the grave before I went up to the poor husband, who was sobbing violently, to press his hand vigorously. He looked at me in surprise through his tears and said:

"Thank you, monsieur."

I was not sorry that I had followed the funeral.

REVENGE

As they were still speaking of Pranzini, M. Maloureau, who had been attorney general under the empire, said:

"I knew another case like that, a very curious affair, curious from many points, as you shall see.

"I was at that time imperial attorney in the province and stood very well at court, thanks to my father, who was first president at Paris. I had charge of a still-celebrated case called 'The Affair of Schoolmaster Moiron.'

"Monsieur Moiron, a schoolmaster in the north of France, bore an excellent reputation in all the country thereabout. He was an intelligent, reflective, very religious man and had married in the district of Boislinot, where he practiced his profession. He had had three children who all died in succession from weak lungs. After the loss of his own little ones he seemed to lavish upon the urchins confided to his care all the tenderness concealed in his heart. He bought with his own pennies playthings for his best pupils, the diligent and good. He allowed them to have play dinners and gorged them with dainties of candies and cakes. Everybody loved and praised this brave man, this brave heart, and it was like a blow when five of his pupils died of the same disease that had carried off his children. It was believed that an epidemic prevailed, caused by the water being made impure from drought. They looked for the cause without discovering it more than they did at the symptoms, which were very strange. The children appeared to be taken with a languor, could eat nothing, complained of pains in the stomach and finally died in most terrible agony.

"An autopsy was made of the last to die, but nothing was discovered. The entrails were sent to Paris and analyzed but showed no sign of any toxic substance.

"For one year no further deaths occurred; then two little boys, the best pupils in the class, favorites of Father Moiron, expired in four days' time. An examination was ordered, and in each body fragments of pounded glass were found imbedded in the organs. They concluded that the two children had eaten imprudently of something carelessly prepared. Sufficient broken glass remained in the bottom of a bowl of milk to have caused this frightful accident, and the matter would have rested there had not Moiron's servant been taken ill in the interval. The physician found the same morbid signs that he observed in the preceding attacks of the children and, upon questioning her, finally obtained the confession that she had stolen and eaten some bonbons brought by the master for his pupils.

"Upon order of the court the schoolhouse was searched, and a closet was found full of sweetmeats and dainties for the children. Nearly all these edibles contained fragments of glass or broken needles.

"Moiron was immediately arrested. He was so indignant and stupefied at the weight of suspicion upon him that he was nearly overcome. Nevertheless, the indications of his guilt were so apparent that they fought hard in my mind against my first conviction, which was based upon his good reputation, his entire life of truthfulness and the absolute absence of any motive for such a crime.

"Why should this good, simple, religious man kill children, and the children whom he seemed to love best? Why should he select those he had feasted with dainties, for whom he had spent in playthings and bonbons half his stipend?

"To admit this it must be concluded that he was insane. But Moiron seemed so reasonable, so calm, so full of judgment and good sense! It was impossible to prove insanity in him.

"Proofs accumulated, nevertheless! Bonbons, cakes, pâtés of marshmallow and other things seized at the shops where the schoolmaster got his supplies were found to contain no suspected fragment.

"He pretended that some unknown enemy had opened his closet with a false key and placed the glass and needles in the eatables. And he implied a story of heritage dependent on the death of a child, sought out and discovered by a peasant and so worked up as to make the suspicion fall upon the schoolmaster. This brute, he said, was not interested in the other poor children who had to die also.

"This theory was plausible. The man appeared so sure of himself and so pitiful that we should have acquitted him without doubt if two overwhelming discoveries had not been made at one blow. The first was a snuffbox full of ground glass! It was his own snuffbox in a secret drawer of his secretary, where he kept his money.

"He explained this in a manner not acceptable, by saying that it was the last ruse of an unknown guilty one. But a merchant of Saint-Marlouf presented himself at the house of the judge, telling him that Moiron had bought needles of him many times, the finest needles he could find, breaking them to see whether they suited him.

"The merchant brought as witnesses a dozen persons who recognized Moiron at first glance. And the inquest revealed the fact that the schoolmaster was at Saint-Marlouf on the days designated by the merchant.

"I pass over the terrible depositions of the children upon the master's choice of dainties and his care in making the little ones eat in his presence and destroying all traces of the feast.

"Public opinion, exasperated, recalled capital punishment and took on a new force from terror which permitted no delays or resistance.

"Moiron was condemned to death. His appeal was rejected. No recourse remained to him for pardon. I knew from my father that the emperor would not grant it.

"One morning, as I was at work in my office, the chaplain of the prison was announced. He was an old priest who had a great knowledge of men and a large acquaintance among criminals. He appeared troubled and constrained. After talking a few moments of other things he said abruptly on rising:

" 'If Moiron is decapitated, Monsieur Attorney General, you will have allowed the execution of an innocent man.'

"Then without bowing he went on, leaving me under the profound effect of his words. He had pronounced them in a solemn, affecting fashion, opening lips, closed and sealed by confession, in order to save a life.

"An hour later I was on my way to Paris, and my father, at my request, asked an immediate audience with the emperor.

"I was received the next day. Napoleon III was at work in a little room when we were introduced. I exposed the whole affair, even to the visit of the priest, and in the midst of the story the door opened behind the chair of the emperor, and the empress, who believed him alone, entered. His Majesty consulted her. When she had run over the facts she exclaimed:

" 'This man must be pardoned! He must, because he is innocent.'

"Why should this sudden conviction of a woman so pious throw into my mind a terrible doubt?

"Up to that time I had ardently desired a commutation of the sentence. And now I felt myself the puppet, the dupe of a criminal ruse, which had employed a priest and the confession as a means of defense.

"I showed some hesitation to their majesties. The emperor remained undecided, solicited on one hand by his natural goodness and on the other held back by the fear of allowing himself to play a miserable part, but the empress, convinced that the priest had obeyed a divine call, repeated: 'What does it matter? It is better to spare a guilty man than to kill an innocent one.' Her advice prevailed. The penalty of death was commuted, and that of hard labor was substituted.

"Some years after I heard that Moiron, whose exemplary conduct at Toulon had been made known again to the emperor, was employed as a domestic by the director of the penitentiary. And then I heard no word of this man for a long time.

"About two years after this, when I was passing the summer at the house of my cousin De Larielle, a young priest came to me one evening as we were sitting down to dinner and wished to speak to me.

"I told them to let him come in, and he begged me to go with him to a dying man who desired, before all else, to see me. This had happened often during my long career as judge, and although I had been put aside by the republic I was still called upon from time to time in like circumstances.

"I followed the ecclesiastic, who made me mount into a little miserable lodging under the roof of a high house. There upon a pallet of straw I found a dying man, seated with his back against the wall in order to breathe. He was a sort of grimacing skeleton with deep, shining eyes.

"When he saw me he murmured: 'You do not know me?'

" 'No.'

" 'I am Moiron.'

"I shivered but said: 'The schoolmaster?'

" 'Yes.'

" 'How is it you are here?'

" 'That would be too long—I haven't time—I am going to die. They brought me this curate—and as I knew you were here, I sent him for you. It is to you that I wish to confess—since you saved my life before—the other time——'

"He seized with his dry hands the straw of his bed and continued in a rasping, bass voice:

" 'Here it is—I owe you the truth—to you, because it is necessary to tell it to someone before leaving the earth.

" 'It was I who killed the children—all. It was I—for vengeance!

" 'Listen. I was an honest man, very honest—very honest—very pure—adoring God—the good God—the God that they teach us to love and not the false God, the executioner, the robber, the murderer, who governs the earth. I had never done wrong, never committed a villainous act. I was pure as one unborn.

" 'After I was married I had some children, and I began to love them as never father or mother loved their own. I lived only for them. I was foolish. They died, all three of them! Why? Why? What had I done? I? I had a change of heart, a furious change. Suddenly I opened my eyes as of one awakening, and I learned that God is wicked. Why had He killed my children? I opened my eyes and I saw that He loved to kill. He loves only that, monsieur. He exists only to destroy! God is a murderer! Some death is necessary to Him every day. He causes them in all fashions, the better to amuse Himself. He has invented sickness and accident in order to divert Himself through all the long months and years. And when He is weary He has epidemics, pests, the cholera, quinsy, smallpox.

" 'How do I know all that this monster has imagined? All these evils are not enough to suffice. From time to time He sends war in order to see two hundred thousand soldiers laid low, bruised in blood and mire, with arms and legs torn off, heads broken by bullets, like eggs that fall along the road.

" 'That is not all. He has made men who eat one another. And then, as men become better than He, He has made beasts to see the men chase them, slaughter and nourish themselves with them. That is not all. He has made all the little animals that live for a day, flies which increase by myriads in an hour, ants that one crushes and others, many, so many that we cannot even imagine them. And all kill one another, chase one another, devour one another, murdering without ceasing. And the good God looks on and is amused, because He sees all for Himself, the largest as well as the smallest, those which are in drops of water as well as those in the stars. He looks at them all and is amused! Ugh! Beast!

" 'So I, monsieur, I also have killed some children. I acted the part for Him. It was not He who had them. It was not He; it was I. And I would have killed still more, but you took me away. That's all!

" 'I was going to die, guillotined. I! How He would have laughed, the reptile! Then I asked for a priest and lied to him. I confessed. I lied and I lived.

" 'Now it is finished. I can no longer escape Him. But I have no fear of Him, monsieur. I understand Him too well.'

"It was frightful to see this miserable creature, hardly able to breathe, talking in hiccups, opening an enormous mouth to eject some words scarcely heard, pulling up the cloth of his straw bed and, under a cover nearly black, moving his meager limbs as if to save himself.

"Oh! Frightful being and frightful remembrance!

"I asked him: 'You have nothing more to say?'

" 'No, monsieur.'

" 'Then farewell.'

" 'Farewell, sir, one day or the other.'

"I turned toward the priest whose somber silhouette was on the wall.

" 'You will remain, Monsieur l'Abbé?'

" 'I will remain.'

"Then the dying man sneered: 'Yes, yes, He sends crows to dead bodies.'

"As for me, I had seen enough. I opened the door and went away in self-protection."

QUEEN HORTENSE

They called her Queen Hortense in Argenteuil. No one ever knew why. Perhaps because she spoke firmly, like an officer giving orders. Perhaps because she was large, bony, and imperious. Perhaps because she governed a multitude of domestic animals, hens, dogs, cats, canaries, and parrots—those animals so dear to old maids. But she neither spoiled these familiar subjects, nor addressed them with loving words, those tender puerilities which seem to slip from the lips of a woman to the velvety coat of a purring cat. She governed her beasts with authority. She ruled.

She was an old maid, one of those old maids with harsh voice and awkward gesture, whose soul seems hard. She had always had young servants, because youth more easily adapts itself to strong wills. She never allowed contradiction from any person, nor argument, nor would she tolerate hesitation, or indifference, or idleness, or fatigue. No one ever heard her complain, or regret what was, or envy others. "To each one his share," she would say, with fatalistic conviction. She never went to church, cared nothing for the priests, scarcely believed in God, and called all religious things "stuff for mourners."

For thirty years she had lived in her little house, with its tiny garden in front, extending along the street, never modifying her way of living, changing only her maids, and that mercilessly, when they became twenty-one years old.

She replaced, without tears and without regrets, her dogs or cats or birds when they died of old age or by accident, and she buried the dead animals in a flower bed, heaping the earth above them with a small spade and treading it down with perfect indifference.

She had in the town a few acquaintances, the families of clerks, whose men traveled to Paris every day. From time to time, they would invite her to spend the evening and drink a cup of tea with them. She inevitably fell asleep on these occasions, and they were obliged to wake her up so that she could go home. She never allowed any one to accompany her, having no fear by night or day. She seemed to have no love for children.

She occupied her time with a thousand masculine cares, carpentry, gardening, cutting or sawing wood, repairing her old house, even doing mason's work when it was necessary.

She had some relatives who came to see her twice a year. Her two sisters, Mme. Cimme and Mme. Columbel, were married, one to an herbalist, the other to a man with small private means. Mme. Cimme had no children; Mme. Columbel had three: Henri, Pauline, and Joseph. Henri was twenty-one, Pauline seventeen, and Joseph only three, having come when one would have thought the mother past the age. No tenderness united this old maid to her kinsfolk.

In the spring of 1882, Queen Hortense became suddenly ill. The neighbors went for a doctor, whom she drove away. When the priest presented himself she got out of bed, half-naked, and put him out. The little maid, weeping, made herb tea for her.

After three days in bed, the situation became so grave that the carpenter living next door, on the advice of the doctor, who had returned to the house on his own authority, took it upon himself to summon the two families.

They arrived by the same train, about ten o'clock in the morning; the Columbels having brought their little Joseph.

When they arrived at the garden gate, they saw the maid seated on a chair against the wall, weeping. The dog lay asleep on the mat before the front door, under a broiling sun; two cats that looked dead lay stretched out on the window sills, with eyes closed and paws and tails extended at full length. A great clucking hen was promenading before the door, at the head of a flock of chicks covered with yellow down, and in a large cage hung against the wall, covered with chickweed, were several birds, singing themselves hoarse in the light of this hot spring morning.

Two others, inseparable, in a little cage in the form of a cottage, remained quiet, side by side on their perch.

M. Cimme, a large, wheezy personage, who always entered a room first, pushing aside men and women when it was necessary, remarked to the maid: "Well, Céleste! Is it so bad as that?"

The little maid sobbed through her tears:

"She doesn't know me any more. The doctor says it is the end."

They all looked at one another.

Mme. Cimme and Mme. Columbel embraced each other instantly, without saying a word.

They resembled each other very much, always having their hair parted in the middle and wearing shawls of red cashmere, as bright as hot coals.

Cimme turned toward his brother-in-law, a pale man, yellow and thin, tormented by indigestion, who limped badly, and said to him in a serious tone:

"Gad! It was time!"

But no one dared to go into the room of the dying woman, situated on the ground floor. Cimme himself let the others go before him. Columbel was the first to make up his mind; he entered, balancing himself like the mast of a ship, making a noise on the floor with the ferrule of his walking stick.

The two women ventured to follow, and M. Cimme brought up the line.

Little Joseph remained outside, drawn by the sight of the dog.

A ray of sunlight fell on the bed, just lighting up the hands which moved nervously, opening and shutting without ceasing. The fingers moved as if a thought animated them, as if they would signify something, indicate some idea, obey some intelligence. The rest of the body remained motionless under the sheet. The angular figure gave no start. The eyes remained closed.

The relatives arranged themselves in a semicircle and, without saying a word, watched the heaving breast and the short breathing. The little maid had followed them, still shedding tears.

Finally, Cimme asked: "What did the doctor say exactly?"

The servant stammered: "He said we must leave her alone, that nothing more could be done."

Suddenly the lips of the old maid began to move. She seemed to pronounce some silent words, concealed in her dying brain, and her hands quickened their singular movement.

Then she spoke in a little, thin voice, quite unlike her own, a voice that seemed to come from far off, perhaps from the bottom of that heart always closed.

Cimme walked upon tiptoe, finding this spectacle painful. Columbel, whose lame leg was growing tired, sat down.

The two women remained standing.

Queen Hortense muttered something quickly, which they were unable to understand. She pronounced some names, called tenderly some imaginary persons:

"Come here, my little Philippe, kiss your mother. You love Mamma, don't you, my child? You, Rose, you will watch your little sister while I am out. Above all, don't leave her alone, do you hear? And I forbid you to touch matches."

She was silent some seconds; then, in a loud tone, as if she was calling, she said: "Henriette!" She waited a little and continued: "Tell your father to come and speak to me before going to his office." Then suddenly: "I am not very well today, dear; promise me you will not return late; you will tell your chief that I am ill. You know it is dangerous to leave the children alone when I am in bed. I am going to make you a dish of rice and sugar for dinner. The little ones like it so much. Claire will be so pleased!"

She began to laugh, a youthful and noisy laugh, as she had never laughed before. "Look at Jean," she said, "how funny he looks. He has smeared himself with jam, the dirty little thing! Look! my dear, how funny he looks!"

Columbel, who kept changing the position of his lame leg every moment, murmured: "She is dreaming that she has children and a husband; the end is near."

The two sisters did not move, but seemed surprised and stunned.

The little maid said: "Will you take off your hats and your shawls, and go into the other room?"

They went out without having said a word. And Columbel followed them limping, leaving the dying woman alone again.

When they were relieved of their outer garments, the women seated themselves. Then one of the cats left the window, stretched herself, jumped into the room, then upon the knees of Mme. Cimme, who began to caress her.

They heard from the next room the voice of the dying woman, living, without doubt, in this last hour, the life she had wished for, pouring out her dreams at the very moment when all would be finished for her.

Cimme, in the garden, played with little Joseph and the dog, enjoying himself, with all the gaiety of a fat man in the country, without a thought for the dying woman.

But suddenly he entered, and addressed the maid: "I say, my girl, are you going to give us some lunch? What are you going to eat, ladies?"

They decided upon an omelet of fine herbs, a piece of fillet with new potatoes, cheese, and a cup of coffee.

And as Mme. Columbel was fumbling in her pocket for her purse Cimme stopped her, and turning to the maid said, "You must have some money?" and she answered: "Yes, sir."

"How much?"

"Fifteen francs."

"That's enough. Make haste, now, my girl, because I am getting hungry."

Mme. Cimme, looking out at the climbing flowers bathed in the sunlight, and at two pigeons making love on the roof opposite, said, with a heartbroken air: "It is unfortunate to have come for so sad an event. It would be nice in the country, today."

Her sister sighed without answering, and Columbel murmured, moved perhaps by the thought of a walk:

"My leg plagues me awfully."

Little Joseph and the dog made a terrible noise, one shouting with joy and the other barking violently. They played at hide-and-seek around the three flower beds, running after each other like mad.

The dying woman continued to call her children, chatting with each, imagining that she was dressing them, that she caressed them, that she was teaching them to read: "Come, Simon, repeat, A, B, C, D. You do not say it well; see, D, D, D, do you hear? Repeat, now . . ."

Cimme declared: "It is extraordinary the things one talks about at such times."

Then said Mme. Columbel: "It would be better, perhaps, to go in there."

But Cimme dissuaded her from it:

"Why go in, since we are not able to do anything for her? Besides we are as well off here."

No one insisted. Madame observed the two green birds called inseparable. She remarked pleasantly upon this singular fidelity, and blamed men for not imitating these little creatures. Cimme looked at his wife and laughed, singing with a bantering air, "Tra-la-la, Tra-la-la," as if to say he could tell some things about his own fidelity.

Columbel, taken with cramps in his stomach, struck the floor with his cane. The other cat entered, its tail in the air. They did not sit down at table until one o'clock.

When he had tasted the wine, Columbel, who could drink only choice Bordeaux, called the servant:

"I say, is there nothing better than this in the cellar?"

"Yes, sir; there is some of the wine that was served when you used to come here."

"Oh, well, go and bring three bottles."

They tasted this wine, which seemed excellent. Not that it was of a remarkable vintage, but it had been fifteen years in the cellar. Cimme declared it was real wine for invalids.

Columbel, seized with a desire to possess this Bordeaux, asked of the maid: "How much is left of it, my girl?"

"Oh, nearly all, sir; Mademoiselle never drank any of it. It is at the bottom of the cellar."

Then Columbel turned toward his brother-in-law: "If you wish, Cimme, I will take this wine in exchange for something else; it agrees with my stomach wonderfully."

The hen, in her turn, had entered with her troop of chicks; the two women amused themselves by throwing crumbs to them. Joseph and the dog were sent back into the garden, as they had eaten enough.

Queen Hortense spoke continually, but in a whisper now, so that it was no longer possible to distinguish the words.

When they had finished the coffee, they all went in to learn the condition of the sick woman. She seemed calm.

They went out and seated themselves in a circle in the garden, to digest their food.

Presently the dog began to run around the chairs with all speed, carrying something in his mouth. The child ran wildly after him. Both disappeared into the house. Cimme fell asleep, with his stomach in the sun.

The dying woman began to speak loudly again. Then suddenly she shouted.

The two women and Columbel hastened in to see what had happened. Cimme awakened but did not move, as he did not care for such things.

The dying woman was sitting up, staring with haggard eyes. Her dog, to escape the pursuit of little Joseph, had jumped upon the bed, and across the dying woman. Entrenched behind the pillow, he was peeping at his comrade with eyes glistening, ready to jump again at the least movement. He held in his mouth one of the slippers of his mistress, all torn by his teeth, as he had been playing with it for an hour.

The child, intimidated by the woman rising so suddenly before him, stood motionless before the bed.

The hen, which had also entered, had jumped upon a chair, frightened by the noise, and was desperately calling to her chicks, which were peeping, frightened, from under the four legs of the chair.

Queen Hortense cried out in piercing tones: "No, no, I do not wish to die! I don't want to! Who will bring up my children? Who will care for them? Who will love them? No I won't! . . . I am not . . ."

She fell back. All was over.

The dog, much excited, jumped into the room and skipped about.

Columbel ran to the window and called his brother-in-law: "Come quickly! come quickly! I believe she is gone."

Then Cimme got up and resolutely went into the room, muttering: "It did not take so long as I thought it would."

COMPLICATION

After swearing for a long time that he would never marry, Jack Boudillère suddenly changed his mind. It happened one summer at the seashore quite unexpectedly.

One morning, as he was extended on the sand, watching the women come out of the water, a little foot caught his attention because of its slimness and delicacy. Raising his eyes higher, the entire person seemed attractive. Of this entire person he had, however, seen only the ankles and the head, emerging from a white flannel bathing suit fastened with care. He may be called sensuous and impressionable, but it was by grace of form alone that he was captured. Afterward he was held by the charm and sweet spirit of the young girl, who was simple and good and fresh, like her cheeks and her lips.

Presented to the family, he was pleased and straightway became love mad. When he saw Bertha Lannis at a distance, on the long stretch of yellow sand, he trembled from head to foot. Near her he was dumb, incapable of saying anything or even of thinking, with a kind of bubbling in his heart, a humming in his ears and a frightened feeling in his mind. Was this love?

He did not know; he understood nothing of it, but the fact remained that he was fully decided to make this child his wife.

Her parents hesitated a long time, deterred by the bad reputation of the young man. He had a mistress, it was said, an old mistress, an old and strong entanglement, one of those chains that is believed to be broken but which continues to hold, nevertheless. Beyond this he had loved, for a longer or shorter period, every woman who had come within reach of his lips.

But he withdrew from the woman with whom he had lived, not even consenting to see her again. A friend arranged her pension, assuring her a subsistence. Jack paid, but he did not wish to speak to her, pretending henceforth that he did not know her name. She wrote letters which he would not open. Each week brought him a new disguise in the handwriting of the abandoned one. Each week a greater anger developed in him against her, and he would tear the envelope in two without opening it, without reading a line, knowing beforehand the reproaches and complaints of the contents.

One could scarcely credit her perseverance, which lasted the whole winter long, and it was not until spring that her demand was satisfied.

The marriage took place in Paris during the early part of May. It was decided that they should not take the regular wedding journey. After a little ball, composed of a company of young cousins who would not stay past eleven o'clock and would not prolong forever the care of the day of ceremony, the young couple intended to pass their first night at the family home and to set out the next morning for the seaside where they had met and loved.

The night came, and they were dancing in the great drawing room. The newly married pair had withdrawn from the rest into a little Japanese boudoir shut off by silk hangings and scarcely lighted this evening except by the dim rays from a colored lantern in the shape of an enormous egg, which hung from the ceiling. The long window was open, allowing at times a fresh breath of air from without to blow upon their faces, for the evening was soft and warm, full of the odor of spring-time.

They said nothing but held each other's hands, pressing them from time to time with all their force. She was a little dismayed by this great change in her life but smiling, emotional, ready to weep, often ready to swoon from joy, believing the entire world changed because of what had come to her, a little disturbed with-out knowing the reason why and feeling all her body, all her soul, enveloped in an indefinable, delicious lassitude.

Her husband she watched persistently, smiling at him with a fixed smile. He wished to talk but found nothing to say and remained quiet, putting all his ardor into the pressure of the hand. From time to time he murmured, "Bertha!" and each time she raised her eyes to his with a sweet and tender look. They would look at each other a moment, then his eyes, fascinated by hers, would fall.

They discovered no thought to exchange. But they were alone, except as a danc-ing couple would sometimes cast a glance at them in passing, a furtive glance, as if it were the discreet and confidential witness of a mystery.

A door at the side opened; a domestic entered, bearing upon a tray an urgent letter which a messenger had brought. Jack trembled as he took it, seized with a vague and sudden fear, the mysterious, abrupt fear of misfortune.

He looked long at the envelope, not knowing the handwriting, not daring to open it, wishing not to read, not to know the contents, desiring to put it in his pocket and to say to himself: "Tomorrow, tomorrow I shall be far away and it will not matter!" But upon the corner were two words underlined, very urgent, which frightened him. "You will permit me, my dear," he said, and he tore off the wrap-per. He read the letter, growing frightfully pale, running over it at a glance and then seeming to spell it out.

When he raised his head his whole countenance was changed. He stammered: "My dear little one, a great misfortune has happened to my best friend. He needs me immediately in a matter of—of life and death. Allow me to go for twenty minutes. I will return immediately."

She, trembling and affrighted, murmured: "Go, my friend!" not yet being enough of a wife to dare to ask or demand to know anything. And he disappeared. She remained alone, listening to the dance music in the next room.

He had taken a hat, the first he could find, and descended the staircase upon the run. As soon as he was mingled with the people on the street he stopped under a gaslight in a vestibule and reread the letter. It said:

SIR: *The Ravet girl, your old mistress, has given birth to a child which she asserts is yours. The mother is dying and implores you to visit her. I take the liberty of writing to you to ask whether you will grant the last wish of this woman, who seems to be very unhappy and worthy of pity.*

Your servant,

D. BONNARD.

When he entered the chamber of death she was already in the last agony. He would not have known her. The physician and the two nurses were caring for her, dragging across the room some buckets full of ice and linen.

Water covered the floor; two tapers were burning on a table; behind the bed, in a little wicker cradle, a child was crying, and with each of its cries the mother would try to move, shivering under the icy compresses.

She was bleeding, wounded to death, killed by this birth. Her life was slipping away, and in spite of the ice, in spite of all care, the hemorrhage continued, hastening her last hour.

She recognized Jack and tried to raise her hand. She was too weak for that, but the warm tears began to glide down her cheeks.

He fell on his knees beside the bed, seized one of her hands and kissed it frantically; then little by little he approached nearer to the wan face which strained to meet him. One of the nurses, standing with a taper in her hand, observed them, and the doctor looked at them from the remote corner of the room.

With a far-off voice, breathing hard, she said: "I am going to die, my dear; promise me you will remain till the end. Oh, do not leave me now, not at the last moment!"

He kissed her brow, her hair, with a groan. "Be tranquil!" he murmured. "I will stay."

It was some minutes before she was able to speak again; she was so weak and overcome. Then she continued: "It is yours, the little one. I swear it before God; I swear it to you upon my soul; I swear it at the moment of death. I have never loved any man but you—promise me not to abandon it." He tried to take in his arms the poor, weak body, emptied of its lifeblood. He stammered, excited by remorse and chagrin: "I swear to you I will bring it up and love it. It shall never be separated from me." Then she held Jack in an embrace. Powerless to raise her head, she held up her blanched lips in an appeal for a kiss. He bent his mouth to receive this poor, suppliant caress.

Calmed a little, she murmured in a low tone: "Take it, that I may see that you love it."

He placed it gently on the bed between them. The little creature ceased to cry. She whispered: "Do not stir!" And he remained motionless. There he stayed, holding in his burning palms a hand that shook with the shiver of death, as he had held, an hour before, another hand that had trembled with the shiver of love. From time to time he looked at the hour with a furtive glance of the eye, watching the hand as it passed midnight, then one o'clock, then two.

The doctor retired. The two nurses, after roaming around for some time with light steps, slept now in their chairs. The child slept, and the mother, whose eyes were closed, seemed to be resting also.

Suddenly, as the pale daylight began to filter through the torn curtains, she extended her arms with so startling and violent a motion that she almost threw the child upon the floor. There was a rattling in her throat; then she turned over motionless, dead.

The nurses hastened to her side, declaring: "It is over."

He looked once at this woman he had loved, then at the hand that marked four o'clock and, forgetting his overcoat, fled in his evening clothes with the child in his arms.

After she had been left alone his young bride had waited calmly at first in the Japanese boudoir. Then, seeing that he did not return, she went back to the drawing room, indifferent and tranquil in appearance, but frightfully disturbed. Her mother, perceiving her alone, asked where her husband was. She replied: "In his room; he will return presently."

At the end of an hour, as everybody asked about him, she told of the letter, of the change in Jack's face and her fears of some misfortune.

They still waited. The guests had gone; only the parents and her relatives remained. At midnight they put the bride in her bed, shaking with sobs. Her mother and two aunts were seated on the bed listening to her weeping. Her father had gone to the police headquarters to make inquiries. At five o'clock a light sound was heard in the corridor. The door opened and closed softly. Then suddenly a cry, like the mewing of a cat, went through the house, breaking the silence.

All the women of the house were out with one bound, and Bertha was the first to spring forward, in spite of her mother and her aunt, clothed only in her night robe.

Jack, standing in the middle of the room, livid, breathing hard, held the child in his arms.

The four women looked at him, frightened, but Bertha suddenly became rash, her heart wrung with anguish, and ran to him, saying: "What is it? What have you there?"

He had a foolish air and answered in a husky voice: "It is—it is—I have here a child whose mother has just died." And he put into her arms the howling little marmot.

Bertha, without saying a word, seized the child and embraced it, straining it to her heart. Then, turning toward her husband with her eyes full of tears, she said: "The mother is dead, you say?" He answered: "Yes, just died—in my arms. I had broken with her since last summer—I knew nothing about it—only the doctor sent for me and——"

Then Bertha murmured: "Well, we will bring up this little one."

FORGIVENESS

She had been brought up in one of those families who live shut up within themselves, entirely apart from the rest of the world. They pay no attention to political events, except to chat about them at the table, and changes in government seem so far, so very far away that they are spoken of only as a matter of history—like the death of Louis XVI or the advent of Napoleon.

Customs change; fashions succeed each other, but changes are never perceptible in this family where old traditions are always followed. And if some impossible story arises in the neighborhood the scandal of it dies at the threshold of this house.

The father and mother, alone in the evening, sometimes exchange a few words on such a subject, but in an undertone, as if the walls had ears.

With great discretion the father says: "Do you know about this terrible affair in the Rivoil family?"

And the mother replies: "Who would have believed it? It is frightful!"

The children doubt nothing but come to the age of living, in their turn, with a bandage over their eyes and minds, without knowing that one does not always think as he speaks or speaks as he acts, without knowing that it is necessary to live at war with the world or, at least, in armed peace, without surmising that the ingenuous are frequently deceived, the sincere trifled with and the good wronged.

Some live until death in this blindness of probity, loyalty and honor, so upright that nothing can open their eyes. Others, undeceived, without knowing much, are weighted down with despair and die, believing that they are the puppets of an exceptional fatality, the miserable victims of unlucky circumstances or, particularly, bad men.

The Savignols arranged a marriage for their daughter when she eighteen. She married a young man from Paris, George Barton, whose business was on the Exchange. He was an attractive youth with a smooth tongue, and he observed all the outward proprieties necessary. But at the bottom of his heart he sneered at his guileless parents-in-law, calling them, among his friends, "My dear fossils."

He belonged to a good family, and the young girl was rich. He took her to live in Paris.

She became one of the provincials of Paris of whom there are many. She remained ignorant of the great city, of its elegant people, of its pleasures and its customs, as she had always been ignorant of the perfidy and mystery of life.

Shut up in her own household, she scarcely knew the street she lived in, and when she ventured into another quarter it seemed to her that she had journeyed far into an unknown, strange city. She would say in the evening:

"I crossed the boulevards today."

Two or three times a year her husband took her to the theater. These were feast days not to be forgotten, which she recalled continually.

Sometimes at table, three months afterward, she would suddenly burst out laughing and exclaim:

"Do you remember that ridiculous actor who imitated the cock's crowing?"

All her interests were within the boundaries of the two allied families, who represented the whole of humanity to her. She designated them by the distinguishing prefix "the," calling them respectively "the Martinets" or "the Michelins."

Her husband lived according to his fancy, returning whenever he wished, sometimes at daybreak, pretending business and feeling in no way constrained, so sure was he that no suspicion would ruffle this candid soul.

But one morning she received an anonymous letter. She was too much astonished and dismayed to scorn this letter, whose author declared himself to be moved by interest in her happiness, by hatred of all evil and love of truth. Her heart was too pure to understand fully the meaning of the accusations.

But it revealed to her that her husband had had a mistress for two years, a young widow, Mme Rosset, at whose house he passed his evenings.

She knew neither how to pretend nor to spy nor to plan any sort of ruse. When he returned for luncheon she threw him the letter, sobbing, and then fled to her room.

He had time to comprehend the matter and prepare his response before he rapped at his wife's door. She opened it immediately without looking at him. He smiled, sat down and drew her to his knee. In a sweet voice and a little jocosely he said:

"My dear little one, Mme Rosset is a friend of mine. I have known her for ten years and like her very much. I may add that I know twenty other families of whom I have not spoken to you, knowing that you care nothing for the world or for forming new friendships. But in order to finish once for all these infamous lies, I will ask to dress yourself after luncheon, and we will go to pay a visit to this young lady, who will become your friend at once, I am sure." She embraced her husband eagerly, and, from feminine curiosity, which no sooner sleeps than wakes again, she did not refuse to go to see this unknown woman of whom, in spite of all, she was still suspicious. She felt by instinct that a known danger is sooner overcome.

They were ushered into a little apartment on the fourth floor of a handsome house. It was a coquettish little place, full of bric-a-brac and ornamented with works of art. After about five minutes' waiting in a drawing room where the light was dimmed by its generous window draperies and portieres, a door opened and a young woman appeared. She was very dark, small, rather plump and looked astonished, although she smiled. George presented them: "My wife, Madame Julie Rosset."

The young widow uttered a little cry of astonishment and joy and came forward with both hands extended. She had not hoped for this happiness, she said, knowing that Mme Barton saw no one. But she was so happy! She was so fond of George! (She said George quite naturally, with sisterly familiarity.) And she had had great desire to know his young wife and to love her too.

At the end of a month these two friends were never apart from each other. They met every day, often twice a day, and nearly always dined together, either at one house or at the other. George scarcely even went out now, no longer pretended delay on account of business, but said he loved his own chimney corner.

Finally an apartment was left vacant in the house where Mme Rosset resided. Mme Barton hastened to take it in order to be nearer her new friend.

During two whole years there was a friendship between them without a cloud, a friendship of heart and soul, tender, devoted and delightful. Bertha could not speak without mentioning Julie's name, for to her Julie represented perfection. She was happy with a perfect happiness, calm and secure.

But Mme Rosset felt ill. Bertha never left her. She passed nights of despair; her husband, too, was brokenhearted.

One morning, in going out from his visit, the doctor took George and his wife aside and announced that he found the condition of their friend very grave.

When he had gone out the young people, stricken down, looked at each other and then began to weep.

They both watched that night near the bed. Bertha would embrace the sick one tenderly, while George, standing silently at the foot of her couch, would look at them with dogged persistence. The next day she was worse.

Finally, toward evening, she declared herself better and persuaded her friends to go home to dinner.

They were sitting sadly at table, scarcely eating anything, when the maid brought George an envelope. He opened it, turned pale and, rising, said to his wife in a constrained way: "Excuse me, I must leave you for a moment. I will return in ten minutes. Please don't go out." And he ran into his room for his hat.

Bertha waited, tortured by a new fear. But, yielding in all things, she would not go up to her friend's room again until he had returned.

As he did not reappear, the thought came to her to look in his room to see whether he had taken his gloves, which would show whether he had really gone somewhere.

She saw them there at first glance. Near them lay a rumpled paper.

She recognized it immediately; it was the one that had called George away.

And a burning temptation took possession of her, the first of her life, to read—

to know. Her conscience struggled in revolt, but curiosity lashed her on, and grief directed her hand. She seized the paper, opened it, recognized the trembling handwriting as that of Julie and read:

Come alone and embrace me, my poor friend; I am going to die.

She could not understand it all at once, but stood stupefied, struck especially by the thought of death. Then suddenly the familiarity of it seized upon her mind. This came like a great light, illuminating her whole life, showing her the infamous truth, all their treachery, all their perfidy. She saw now their cunning, their sly looks, her good faith played with, her confidence turned to account. She saw them looking into each other's faces under the shade of her lamp at evening, reading from the same book, exchanging glances at the end of certain pages.

And her heart, stirred with indignation, bruised with suffering, sank into an abyss of despair that had no boundaries.

When she heard steps she fled and shut herself in her room.

Her husband called her: "Come quickly; Madame Rosset is dying!"

Bertha appeared at her door and said with trembling lips:

"Go alone to her; she had no need of me."

He looked at her sheepishly, careless from anger, and repeated:

"Quick, quick! She is dying!"

Bertha answered: "You would prefer it to be I."

Then he understood, probably, and left her to herself, going up again to the dying one.

There he wept without fear or shame, indifferent to the grief of his wife, who would no longer speak to him or look at him, but who lived shut in with her disgust and angry revolt, praying to God morning and evening.

They lived together, nevertheless, eating together face to face, mute and hopeless.

After a time he tried to appease her a little. But she would not forget. And so their life continued, hard for them both.

For a whole year they lived thus, strangers one to the other. Bertha almost became mad.

Then one morning, having set out at dawn, she returned toward eight o'clock carrying in both hands an enormous bouquet of roses, of white roses, all white.

She sent word to her husband that she would like to speak to him. He came in disturbed, troubled.

"Let us go out together," she said to him. "Take these flowers, they are too heavy for me."

He took the bouquet and followed his wife. A carriage awaited them, which started as soon as they were seated.

It stopped before the gate of a cemetery. Then Bertha, her eyes full of tears, said to George: "Take me to her grave."

He trembled, without knowing why, but walked on before, holding the flowers in his arms. Finally he stopped before a shaft of white marble and pointed to it without a word.

She took the bouquet from him and, kneeling, placed it at the foot of the grave. Then her heart was raised in suppliant, silent prayer.

Her husband stood behind her, weeping, haunted by memories.

She arose and put out her hands to him.

"If you wish we will be friends," she said.

THE WHITE WOLF

This is the story the old Marquis d'Arville told us after a dinner in honor of Saint Hubert at the house of Baron des Ravels. They had run down a stag that day. The marquis was the only one of the guests who had not taken part in the chase. He never hunted.

During the whole of the long repast they had talked of scarcely anything but the massacre of animals. Even the ladies interested themselves in the sanguinary and often unlikely stories, while the orators mimicked the attacks and combats between man and beast, raising their arms and speaking in thunderous tones.

M. d'Arville talked much with a certain poesy, a little flourish, but full of effect. He must have repeated this story often—it ran so smoothly—never halting at a choice of words in which to clothe an image.

"Gentlemen, I never hunt, nor did my father or my grandfather or my great-great-grandfather. The last named was the son of a man who hunted more than all of you. He died in 1764. I will tell you how. He was named John and was married and became the father of the man who was my great-great-grandfather. He lived with his younger brother Francis d'Arville in our castle in the midst of a deep forest in Lorraine.

"Francis d'Arville always remained a boy through his love for hunting. They both hunted from one end of the year to the other without cessation or weariness. They loved nothing else, understood nothing else, talked only of this and lived for this alone.

They were possessed by this terrible, inexorable passion. It consumed them, having taken entire control of them, leaving no place for anything else. They had agreed not to put off the chase for any reason whatsoever. My great-great-grand-father was born while his father was following a fox, but John d'Arville did not interrupt his sport and swore that the little beggar might have waited until after the death cry! His brother Francis showed himself still more hotheaded than he. The first thing on rising he would go to see the dogs, then the horses; then he would shoot some birds about the place, even when about to set out hunting big game.

"They were called in the country Monsieur the Marquis and Monsieur the Cadet, noblemen then not acting as do those of our time who wish to establish in their titles a descending scale of rank, for the son of a marquis is no more a count, or the son of a viscount a baron, than the son of a general is a colonel by birth. But the niggardly vanity of the day finds profit in this arrangement. To return to my ancestors:

"They were, it appears, immoderately large, bony, hairy, violent and vigorous. The younger one was taller than the elder and had such a voice that, according to a legend he was very proud of, all the leaves of the forest moved when he shouted.

"And when mounted, ready for the chase, it must have been a superb sight to see these two giants astride their great horses.

"Toward the middle of the winter of that year, 1764, the cold was excessive and the wolves became ferocious.

"They even attacked belated peasants, roamed around houses at night, howled from sunset to sunrise and ravaged the stables.

"At one time a rumor was circulated. It was said that a colossal wolf of grayish-white color, which had eaten two children, devoured the arm of a woman, strangled all the watchdogs of the country, was now coming without fear into the house inclosures and smelling around the doors. Many inhabitants affirmed that they had felt his breath, which made the lights flicker. Shortly a panic ran through all the province. No one dared to go out after nightfall. The very shadows seemed haunted by the image of this beast.

"The brothers D'Arville resolved to find and slay him. So they called together for a grand chase all the gentlemen of the country.

"It was in vain. They had beaten the forests and scoured the thickets but had seen nothing of him. They killed wolves, but not that one. And each night after such a chase the beast, as if to avenge himself, attacked some traveler or devoured some cattle, always far from the place where they had sought him.

"Finally one night he found a way into the swine house of the castle D'Arville and ate two beauties of the best breed.

"The two brothers were furious, interpreting the attack as one of bravado on the part of the monster—a direct injury, a defiance. Therefore, taking all their best-trained hounds, they set out to run down the beast with courage, excited by anger.

"From dawn until the sun descended behind the great nut trees they beat about forests with no result.

"At last both of them, angry and disheartened, turned their horses' steps into a bypath bordered by rushwood. They were marveling at the baffling power of this wolf, when suddenly they were seized with a mysterious fear.

"The elder said:

"'This can be no ordinary beast. One might say he can think like a man.'

"The younger replied:

"'Perhaps we should get our cousin, the bishop, to bless a bullet for him, or ask a priest to pronounce some words to help us.'

"Then they were silent.

"John continued: 'Look at the sun, how red it is. The great wolf will do mischief tonight.'

"He had scarcely finished speaking when his horse reared. Francis' horse started to run at the same time. A large bush covered with dead leaves rose before them, and a colossal beast, grayish white, sprang out, scampering away through the wood.

"Both gave a grunt of satisfaction and, bending to the necks of their heavy horses, they urged them on with the weight of their bodies, exciting them, hastening with voice and spur, until these strong riders seemed to carry the weight of their beasts between their knees, carrying them by force as if they were flying.

"Thus they rode, crashing through forests, crossing ravines, climbing up the sides of steep gorges and sounding the horn at frequent intervals to arouse the people and the dogs of the neighborhood.

"But suddenly, in the course of this breakneck ride, my ancestor struck his forehead against a large branch and fractured his skull. He fell to the ground as if dead, while his frightened horse disappeared in the surrounding thicket.

"The younger D'Arville stopped short, sprang to the ground, seized his brother in his arms and saw that he had lost consciousness.

"He sat down beside him, took his disfigured head upon his knees, looking earnestly at the lifeless face. Little by little a fear crept over him, a strange fear that he had never before felt, fear of the shadows, of the solitude, of the lonely woods and also of the chimerical wolf, which had now come to be the death of his brother.

"The shadows deepened; the branches of the trees crackled in the sharp cold. Francis arose shivering, incapable of remaining there longer and already feeling his strength fail. There was nothing to be heard, neither the voice of dogs nor the sound of a horn; all within this invisible horizon was mute. And in this gloomy silence and the chill of evening there was something strange and frightful.

"With his powerful hands he seized John's body and laid it across the saddle to take it home, then mounted gently behind it, his mind troubled by horrible, supernatural images, as if he were possessed.

"Suddenly in the midst of these fears a great form passed. It was the wolf. A violent fit of terror seized upon the hunter; something cold, like a stream of ice water, seemed to glide through his veins, and he made the sign of the cross, like a monk haunted with devils, so dismayed was he by the reappearance of the frightful wanderer. Then, his eyes falling upon the inert body before him, his fear was quickly changed to anger, and he trembled with inordinate rage.

"He pricked his horse and darted after him.

"He followed him through copses, over ravines and around great forest trees, traversing wood that he no longer recognized, his eye fixed upon a white spot, which was ever flying from him as night covered the earth.

"His horse also seemed moved by an unknown force. He galloped on with neck extended, crashing over small trees and rocks, with the body of the dead stretched across him on the saddle. Brambles caught in his mane; his head, where it had struck the trunks of trees, was spattered with blood; the marks of the spurs were over his flanks.

"Suddenly the animal and its rider came out of the forest, rushing through a valley as the moon appeared above the hills. This valley was stony and shut in by enormous rocks, over which it was impossible to pass; there was no other way for the wolf but to turn on his steps.

"Francis gave such a shout of joy and revenge that the echo of it was like the roll of thunder. He leaped from his horse, knife in hand.

"The bristling beast, with rounded back, was awaiting him, his eyes shining like two stars. But before joining in battle, the strong hunter, grasping his brother, seated him upon a rock, supporting his head, which was now but a mass of blood, with stones, and cried aloud to him, as to one deaf: 'Look, John! Look here!'

"Then he threw himself upon the monster. He felt himself strong enough to overthrow a mountain, to crush the very rocks in his hands. The beast meant to kill him by sinking his claws in his vitals, but the man had seized him by the throat without even making use of his weapon and strangled him gently, waiting until his breath stopped and he could hear the death rattle at his heart. And he laughed with the joy of dismay, clutching more and more with a terrible hold and crying out in his delirium: 'Look, John! Look!' All resistance ceased. The body of the wolf was limp. He was dead.

"Then Francis, taking him in his arms, threw him down at the feet of his elder brother, crying out in an expectant voice: 'Here, here, my little John; here he is!'

"Then he placed upon the saddle the two bodies, the one above the other, and started on his way.

"He returned to the castle laughing and weeping, like Gargantua at the birth of Pantagruel, shouting in triumph and stamping with delight in relating the death of the beast, and moaning and tearing at his beard in calling the name of his brother.

"Often later, when he recalled this day, he would declare with tears in his eyes: 'If only poor John had seen me strangle the beast he would have died content, I am sure!'

"The widow of my ancestor inspired in her son a horror of the chase, which was transmitted from father to son down to myself."

The Marquis d'Arville was silent. Someone asked: "Is the story a legend or not?"

And the narrator replied:

"I swear to you it is true from beginning to end."

Then a lady in a sweet little voice declared:

"It is beautiful to have passions like that."

THE FATHER

Jean de Valnoix is a friend of mine whom I visit from time to time. He lives in a little house in the woods at the edge of a river. He retired from Paris after leading a wild life for fifteen years. Suddenly he had enough of pleasures, dinners, men, women, cards, everything; and he came to live in this little place where he had been born.

There are two or three of us who go, from time to time, to spend a fortnight or three weeks with him. He is certainly delighted to see us when we arrive, and pleased to be alone again when we leave. So I went to see him last week, and he received me with open arms. We would spend the time, sometimes together, sometimes alone. Usually he reads and I work during the daytime, and every evening we talk until midnight.

Well, last Tuesday, after a scorching day, towards nine o'clock in the evening we were both of us sitting and watching the water flow at our feet; we were exchanging very vague ideas about the stars which were bathing in the current and which seemed to swim along ahead of us. Our ideas were very vague, confused, and brief, for our minds are very limited, weak, and powerless. I was growing sentimental about the sun, which dies in the Great Bear. One can only see it on very clear nights, it is so pale. When the sky is the least bit clouded it disappears. We were thinking of the creatures which people these worlds, of their possible forms, of their unthinkable faculties and unknown organs, of the animals and plants of every kind, of all the kingdoms and forms of matter, of all the things which man's dreams can barely touch.

Suddenly a voice called from the distance: "Monsieur, monsieur!"

Jean answered: "Here I am, Baptiste!"

When the servant had found us he announced: "It's Monsieur's gipsy."

My friend burst out laughing, a thing which he rarely did, then he asked: "Is today the nineteenth of July?"

"Yes, monsieur."

"Very well. Tell her to wait for me. Give her some supper. I'll see her in ten minutes."

When the man had disappeared my friend took me by the arm saying: "Let us walk along slowly, while I tell you this story.

"Seven years ago, when I arrived here, I went out one evening to take a walk in the forest. It was a beautiful day, like today, and I was walking along slowly under the great trees, looking at the stars through the leaves, drinking in the quiet restfulness of night and the forest.

"I had just left Paris forever. I was tired out, more disgusted than I can say by all the foolish, low, and nasty things which I had seen and in which I had participated for fifteen years.

"I walked along for a great distance in this deep forest, following a path which leads to the village of Crouzilles, about ten miles from here.

"Suddenly my dog, Bock, a great St. Germain, which never left me, stopped short and began to growl. I thought that perhaps a fox, a wolf or a boar might be in the neighborhood; I advanced gently on tiptoe, in order to make no noise, but suddenly I heard mournful human cries, plaintive, muffled and moving.

"Surely some murder was being committed. I rushed forward, taking a tight grip on my heavy oak cane, a regular club.

"I was coming nearer to the moans, which now became more distinct, but strangely muffled. They seemed to be coming from some house, perhaps from the hut of some charcoal burner. Three feet ahead of me Bock was running, stopping, barking, starting again, very excited, and growling all the time. Suddenly another dog, a big black one with burning eyes, barred our progress. I could clearly see his white fangs, which seemed to be shining in his mouth.

"I ran towards him with uplifted stick, but Bock had already jumped, and the two beasts were rolling on the ground with their teeth buried in each other. I went past them and almost bumped into a horse lying in the road. As I stopped, in surprise, to examine the animal, I saw in front of me a wagon, or, rather, a caravan, such as are inhabited by circus people and the itinerant merchants who go from fair to fair.

"The cries were coming from there, frightful and continuous. As the door opened on the other side I turned around this vehicle and rushed up the three wooden steps, ready to jump on the malefactor.

"What I saw seemed so strange to me that I could not understand it at first. A man was kneeling, and seemed to be praying, while in the only bed something impossible to recognize, a half-naked creature, whose face I could not see, was moving, twisting about, and howling. It was a woman in labor.

"As soon as I understood the kind of accident which was the cause of these screams, I made my presence known, and the man, wild with grief, and apparently from the neighborhood of Marseille, begged me to save him, to save her, promising me with many words an incredible gratitude. I had never seen a birth; I had never helped a female creature, woman, dog, or cat, in such a circumstance, and I naïvely said so, as I stupidly watched this thing which was screaming so in the bed.

"Then when I had gathered my wits again, I asked the grief-stricken man why he did not go to the next village. His horse must have caught in a rut and had broken his leg.

" 'Well, my man,' I exclaimed, 'there are two of us now, and we will drag your wife to my house.'

"But the howling dogs forced us to go outside, and we had to separate them by beating them with our sticks, at the risk of killing them. Then the idea struck me to harness them with us, one to the right and the other to the left, in order to help us. In ten minutes everything was ready, and the wagon started forward slowly, shaking the poor, suffering woman each time it bumped over the deep ruts.

"Such a road, my friend! We were going along, panting, groaning, perspiring, slipping, and falling, while our poor dogs puffed along beside us.

"It took three hours to reach the cottage. When we arrived before the door the cries from the wagon had ceased. Mother and child were doing well.

"They were put to bed, and then I had a horse harnessed up in order to go for a physician, while the man, an inhabitant of Marseille, reassured, consoled, and triumphant, was stuffing himself with food and getting dead drunk in order to celebrate this happy birth.

"It was a girl.

"I kept these people with me for a week. The mother, Mlle. Elmire, was an extraordinary lucid fortuneteller, who promised me an interminable life and countless joys.

"The following year, on exactly the same day, towards nightfall, the servant who has just called me came to me in the smoking room after dinner and said: 'It's the gipsy of last year who has come to thank Monsieur.'

"I had her come into the house, and I was dumfounded when I saw beside her a tall blond fellow, a man from the North, who bowed and spoke to me as chief of the community. He had heard of my kindness to Mlle. Elmire, and he had not wished to let this anniversary go by without bringing to me their thanks and a testimony of their gratitude.

"I gave them supper in the kitchen, and offered them my hospitality for the night. They left the following day.

"The woman returns every year at the same date with the child, a fine little girl, and a new . . . lord and master each time. One man only, a fellow from Auvergne, who thanked me in his strange accent, came back two years in succession. The little girl calls them all 'Papa,' just as one says 'monsieur' with us."

We were arriving at the house, and we could barely distinguish three shadows standing on the steps, waiting for us. The tallest one took a few steps forward, made a great bow, and said: "Monsieur le Comte, we have come today in recognition of our gratefulness. . . ."

He was a Belgian!

After him, the little one spoke in the shrill, singing voice which children use when they recite a compliment.

I appeared to know nothing, and I took Mlle. Elmire to one side, and, and after a few questions, I asked her: "Is that the father of your child?"

"Oh! no, monsieur."

"Is the father dead?"

"Oh! no, monsieur. We still see each other from time to time. He is a gendarme."

"What! then it wasn't the fellow from Marseille who was there at the birth?"

"Oh! no, monsieur. That was a rascal who stole all my savings."

"And the gendarme, the real father, does he know his child?"

"Oh! yes, monsieur, and he loves her very much; but he can't take care of her because he has others by his wife."

TOINE

Everybody for ten leagues round knew Toine, fat Toine, "Toine-my-Fine," Antoine Mâcheblé, the landlord of Tournevent.

He had made famous this village, buried in the depths of the valley which descended to the sea. It was a poor peasant hamlet, composed of a dozen Norman houses surrounded by ditches and encircled by trees. The houses were huddled together in this shrub-covered ravine behind the curve of the hill, which had caused the village to be called Tournevent. As birds conceal themselves in the furrows during a storm, they seemed to have sought a shelter in this hollow, a shelter against the fierce salt winds of the sea, which gnawed and burned like fire and withered and destroyed like the blasts of winter.

The whole hamlet seemed to be the property of Antoine Mâcheblé, who was, besides, often called Toine and Toine-my-Fine, on account of a matter of speech of which he constantly availed himself. "My Fine is the best in France," he would say. His "Fine" was his cognac, be it understood. For twenty years he had watered the country with his cognac, and in serving his customers he was in the habit of saying: "It warms the stomach and clears the head; there is nothing better for your health, my son." He called everybody "my son," although he had never had a son of his own.

Ah yes, everyone knew old Toine, the biggest man in the canton or even in the arrondissement. His little house seemed too ridiculously small to contain him, and when he was seen standing in his doorway, where he spent the greater part of every day, one wondered how he could enter his dwelling. But he did enter each time a customer presented himself, for Toine-my-Fine was invited by right to levy a little glass on all who drank in his house.

His café bore on its sign the legend "The Rendezvous of Friends," and old Toine was truly the friend of all the country round. People came from Fécamp and Montivilliers to see him and tipple with him and to hear his stories, for this great, good-natured man could make a tombstone laugh. He could joke without giving offense, wink an eye to express what he dare not utter and punch one's ribs in a fit of gaiety, so as to force a laugh in spite of oneself. And then it was a curiosity just to see him drink. He drank all that was offered him by everybody with a joy in his wicked eye, a joy which came from a double pleasure: the pleasure of regaling himself first and the pleasure of heaping up money at the expense of his friends afterward. The blackguards of the community wondered why Toine had no children and one day asked him as much. With a wicked wink he replied: "My wife is not attractive enough for such a fine fellow as I am."

The quarrels of Toine and his homely wife were as much enjoyed by the tipplers as was their favorite cognac, for they had squabbled through the whole thirty years of their married life. Only Toine was good natured over it, while his wife was furious. She was a tall peasant woman who walked with long, stiltlike strides and carried on her thin, flat body the head of an ugly screech owl. She spent her whole time in rearing poultry in the little yard behind the public house and was renowned for the success with which she fattened her fowls.

When any of the great ladies of Fécamp gave a feast to the people of quality it was necessary to the success of the repast that it should be garnished with the celebrated fowl from Mother Toine's poultry yard.

But she was born with a vile temper and had continued to be dissatisfied with everything. Angry with everybody, she was particularly so with her husband. She jeered at his gaiety, his popularity, his good health and his embonpoint; she treated him with the utmost contempt because he got his money without working for it and because, as she said, he ate and drank as much as ten ordinary men. She declared every day that he was only fit to be littered in the stable with the naked swine, whom he resembled, and that he was only a mass of fat that made her sick at her stomach. "Wait a little, wait a little," she would shriek in his face; "we shall soon see what is going to happen! This great windbag will burst like a sack of grain!"

Toine laughed till he shook like a bowl of jelly and, tapping his enormous belly, replied: "Ah, my old hen, let us see you try to make your chickens as fat as this."

And, rolling up his sleeve, he showed his brawny arm. "Do you not see the feathers growing already?" he cried. And the customers would strike their fists on the table and fairly writhe with joy and would stamp their feet and spit upon the floor in a delirium of delight.

The old woman grew more furious than ever and shouted at the top of her lungs: "Just wait a bit; we shall see what will happen. Your Toine-my-Fine will burst like a sack of grain."

And she rushed out, maddened with rage at the laughter of the crowd of drinkers.

Toine, in fact, was a wonder to see, so fat and red and short of breath had he grown. He was one of those enormous creatures with whom Death seems to amuse himself by tricks, gaieties and fatal buffooneries, making irresistibly comic the slow work of destruction. Instead of showing himself, as toward others, in white hairs, shrunken limbs, wrinkles and general feebleness which made one say with a shiver: "Heavens, how he has changed!" he took pleasure in fattening Toine, in making a droll monster of him, in reddening his face and giving him the appearance of superhuman health, and the deformities which he inflicted on other beings became in Toine's case laughable and diverting instead of sinister and pitiable.

"Wait a little, wait a little," muttered Mother Toine as she scattered the grain about her poultry yard; "we are going to see what will happen."

II

It happened that Toine had a seizure and fell smitten with a paralytic stroke. They carried the giant to the little chamber partitioned off at the rear of the café in order that he might hear what was going on on the other side of the wall and converse with his friends, for his brain remained clear while his enormous body was prone and helpless. They hoped for a time that his mighty limbs would recover some of their energy, but this hope disappeared very soon, and Toine-my-Fine was forced to pass his days and nights in his bed, which was made up but once a week with the help of four friends who lifted him by his four limbs while his mattress was turned. He continued cheerful but with a different kind of gaiety, more timid, more humble and with the pathetic fear of a little child in the presence of his wife, who scolded and raged all the day long. "There he lies, the great glutton, the good-for-nothing idler, the nasty thing!" she cried. Toine replied nothing, only winking his eye behind the old woman's back, and turned over in the bed, the only movement he was able to make. He called this change "making a move to the north" or "a move to the south." His only entertainment now was to listen to the conversation in the café and to join in the talk across the wall, and when he recognized the voice of a friend he would cry: "Hello, my son; is it thou, Célestin?"

And Célestin Maloisel would reply: "It is me, Father Toine. How do you gallop today, my great rabbit?"

"I cannot gallop yet, Célestin," Toine would answer, "but I am not growing thin either. The shell is good." Soon he invited his intimates into his chamber for company, because it pained him to see them drinking without him. He told them it grieved him not to be able to take his cognac with them. "I can stand everything else," he said, "but not to drink with you makes me sad, my sons."

Then the screech owl's head of Mother Toine would appear at the window, and she would say: "Look, look at him, this great hulking idler, who must be fed and washed and scoured like a pig!"

And when she disappeared a red-plumaged rooster sometimes perched on the window sill and, looking about with his round and curious eye, gave forth a shrill crow. And sometimes two or three hens flew in and scratched and pecked about the floor, attracted by the crumbs which fell from Father Toine's plate.

The friends of Toine-my-Fine very soon deserted the café for his chamber, and every afternoon they gossiped around the bed of the big man. Bedridden as he was, this rascal of a Toine still amused them; he would have made the devil himself laugh, the jolly fellow! There were three friends who came every day: Célestin Maloisel, a tall, spare man with a body twisted like the trunk of an apple tree; Prosper Horslaville, a little dried-up old man with a nose like a ferret, malicious and sly as a fox, and Césaire Paumelle, who never uttered a word but who enjoyed himself all the same. These men brought in a board from the yard, which they placed across the bed and on which they played dominoes from two o'clock in the afternoon until six. But Mother Toine soon interfered; she could not endure that her husband should amuse himself by playing dominoes in his bed, and each time she saw the play she bounded into the room in a rage, overturned the board, seized the dominoes and carried them into the café, declaring that it was enough to feed this great lump of tallow without seeing him divert himself at the expense of hard-working people. Célestin Maloisel bent his head before the storm, but Prosper Horslaville tried to further excite the old woman whose rages amused him. Seeing her one day more exasperated than usual, he said: Hello, Mother Toine! Do you know what I would do if I were in your place?"

She waited for an explanation, fixing her owllike eyes upon him. He continued:

"Your husband, who never leaves his bed, is as hot as an oven. I should set him to hatching out eggs."

She remained stupefied, thinking he was jesting, watching the meager and sly face of the peasant, who continued:

"I would put five eggs under each arm the same day that I set the yellow hen; they would all hatch out at the same time, and when they were out of their shells

I would put your husband's chicks under the hen for her to bring up. That would bring you some poultry, Mother Toine."

The old woman was amazed. "Can that be?" she asked.

Prosper continued: "Why can't it? Since they put eggs in a warm box to hatch, one might as well put them in a warm bed."

She was greatly impressed with this reasoning and went out, composed and thoughtful.

Eight days later she came into Toine's chamber with her apronful of eggs and said: "I have just put the yellow hen to set with ten eggs under her; here are ten for you! Be careful not to break them!"

Toine was astonished. "What do you mean?" he cried.

"I mean that you shall hatch them, good-for-nothing."

Toine laughed at first, then as she insisted he grew angry; he resisted and obstinately refused to allow her to put the eggs under his great arms that his warmth might hatch them. But the baffled old woman grew furious and declared: "You shall have not a bite to eat so long as you refuse to take them—there, we'll see what will happen!"

Toine was uneasy, but he said nothing till he heard the clock strike twelve, then he called to his wife, who bawled from the kitchen: "There is no dinner for you today, you great idler!"

He thought at first she was joking, but when he found she was in earnest he begged and prayed and swore by fits, turned himself to the north and the south and, growing desperate under the pangs of hunger and the smell of the viands, he pounded on the wall with his great fists until at last, worn out and almost famished, he allowed his wife to introduce the eggs into his bed and place them under his arms. After that he had his soup.

When his friends arrived as usual, they believed Toine to be very ill; he seemed constrained and in pain.

Then they began to play dominoes as formerly, but Toine appeared to take no pleasure in the game and put forth his hand so gingerly and with such evident precaution that they suspected at once something was wrong.

"Hast thou thy arm tied?" demanded Horslaville.

Toine feebly responded: "I have a feeling of heaviness in my shoulder."

Suddenly someone entered the café, and the players paused to listen. It was the mayor and his assistant, who called for two glasses of cognac and then began to talk of the affairs of the country. As they spoke in low tones, Toine tried to press his ear against the wall, and, forgetting his eggs, he gave a sudden lunge to the north, which made an omelet of them in short order. At the oath he uttered Mother Toine came running in and, divining the disaster, she uncovered him with a jerk. She stood a moment too enraged and breathless to speak at the sight of the yellow poultice pasted on the flank of her husband. Then, trembling with fury, she flung herself on the paralytic and began to pound him with great force on the body, as though she were pounding her dirty linen on the banks of the river. She showered her blows upon him with the force and rapidity of a drummer beating his drum.

The friends of Toine were choking with laughter, coughing, sneezing, uttering exclamations, while the frightened man parried the attacks of his wife with due precaution in order not to break the five eggs he still had on the other side.

III

Toine was conquered. He was compelled to hatch eggs. He had to renounce the innocent pleasure of dominoes, to give up any effort to move to the north or south, for his wife deprived him of all nourishment every time he boke an egg. He lay on his back, with his eyes fixed on the ceiling, his arms extended like wings, warming against his immense body the incipient chicks in their white shells. He spoke only in low tones, as if he feared a noise as much as a movement, and he asked often about the yellow hen in the poultry yard who was engaged in the same task as himself. The old woman went from the hen to her husband, and from her husband to the hen, possessed and preoccupied with the little broods which were maturing in the bed and in the nest. The country-people, who soon learned the story, came in, curious and serious, to get the news of Toine. They entered on tiptoe as one enters a sickchamber and inquired with concern:

"How goes it, Toine?"

"It has to go," he answered, "but it is so long, I am tired of waiting. I get excited and feel cold shivers galloping all over my skin."

One morning his wife came in very much elated and exclaimed: "The yellow hen has hatched seven chicks; there were but three bad eggs!"

Toine felt his heart beat. How many would he have?

"Will it be soon?" he asked with the anguish of a woman who is about to become a mother.

The old woman, who was tortured by the fear of failure, answered angrily:

"It is to be hoped so!"

They waited.

The friends, seeing that Toine's time was approaching, became very uneasy themselves. They gossiped about it in the house and kept all the neighbors informed of the progress of affairs. Toward three o'clock Toine grew drowsy. He slept now half the time. He was suddenly awakened by an unusual tickling under his left arm. He put his hand carefully to the place and seized a little beast covered with yellow down, which struggled between his fingers. His emotion was so great that he cried out and let go the chick, which ran across his breast. The café was full of people. The customers rushed into the room and circled around the bed, while Mother Toine, who had arrived at the first sound, carefully caught the fledgling as it nestled in her husband's beard. No one uttered a word. It was a warm April day; one could hear through the open window the clucking of the yellow hen calling to her newborn. Toine, who perspired with emotion and agony, murmured: "I feel another one under my left arm."

His wife plunged her great, gaunt hand under the bedclothes and drew forth a second chick with all the precautions of a midwife.

The neighbors wished to see it and passed it from hand to hand, regarding it with awe, as though it were a phenomenon. For the space of twenty minutes no more were hatched, then four chicks came out of their shells at the same time. This caused a great excitement among the watchers.

Toine smiled, happy at his success, and began to feel proud of this singular paternity. Such a sight had never been seen before. This was a droll man, truly! "That makes six," cried Toine. "Sacré bleu, what a christening there will be!"

And a great laugh rang out from the public. Other people now crowded into the café and filled the doorway, with outstretched necks and curious eyes.

"How many has he?" they inquired.

"There are six."

Mother Toine ran with the new fledglings to the hen, who, clucking distractedly, erected her feathers and spread wide her wings to shelter her increasing flock of little ones.

"Here comes another one!" cried Toine. He was mistaken—there were three of them. This was a triumph! The last one chipped its shell at seven o'clock in the evening. All Toine's eggs were good! He was delivered and, delirious with joy, he seized and kissed the frail little creature on the back. He could have smothered it with caresses. He wished to keep this little one in his bed until the next day, moved by the tenderness of a mother for this being to whom he had given life, but the old woman carried it away as she had done the others, without listening to the supplications of her husband.

The friends of Toine went home delighted, conversing of the event by the way.

Horslaville remained after the others had gone and, approaching the ear of Toine, whispered: "You will invite me to the first fricassee, will you not?"

At the idea of a fricassee the visage of Toine brightened, and he answered:

"Certainly I will invite thee, my son."

AN ENTHUSIAST

We were just passing through Gisors, when I was awakened by hearing a trainman call the name of the town. I was falling off to sleep again when a frightful jolt threw me across to a large lady opposite me.

A wheel had broken on the locomotive, which was now lying across the track. The tender and baggage car were also derailed and were lodged by the side of the great, dying machine, which moaned and groaned and sputtered and puffed, like a fallen horse in the street whose breast heaves and nostrils smoke, wheezing and shivering in its whole body, yet incapable of any effort toward getting up and continuing on the way.

Our engine proved to be neither dead nor wounded; there was only some derangement, but the train could not go on, and we stood looking at the maimed iron beast that could no longer draw us but lay barring the track. It would be necessary, without doubt, to have a relief train sent out from Paris.

It was ten o'clock in the morning, and I decided immediately to go back to Gisors for breakfast. In walking along upon the track I said to myself: "Gisors, Gisors, I certainly know someone here. Who is it? Gisors? Let me see. I have some friend in this town." The name immediately sprang into my mind: "Albert Marambot."

He was an old comrade in college whom I had not seen for a dozen years or so and who was a practitioner of the medical profession at Gisors. Often he had written inviting me to visit him; I had always promised to go but had never gone. Now I would certainly take advantage of the opportunity.

I asked the first passer-by if he knew where Dr. Marambot lived. He replied without hesitation, with the drawling accent of the Norman:

"Dauphine Street."

Soon I found on the door of the house indicated a large copperplate on which was engraved the name of my old comrade. I rang; the servant who opened the door, a girl with yellow hair and slow motion, kept repeating in a stupid fashion: "He's gone out; he's gone out."

I heard a sound of forks and glasses inside and called out: "Hey, there! Marambot!" A door opened and a large, well-favored man appeared, looking disturbed and holding a napkin in his hand.

I never should have known him. One would say he was forty-five at least, and in a second his whole provincial life appeared before me, dulling, stupefying and aging him. In a single bound of thought, more rapid than the gesture of extending my hand to him, I knew his whole existence, his manner of life, his bent of mind and his theories of living. I suspected the long repasts which had rounded his body, the little naps after dinner in the torpor of a heavy digestion sprinkled with brandy, and the vague contemplation of the sick, with thoughts of roast fowl waiting before the fire. His conversation on cooking, cider, brandy and wine, upon certain dishes and well-made sauces appropriate for them, revealed to me nothing more than I perceived in the red puffiness of his cheeks, the heaviness of his lips and the dullness of his eyes.

I said to him: "You do not know me. I am Raoul Aubertin."

He opened his arms and almost stifled me. His first word was:

"You certainly haven't breakfasted?"

"No."

"What luck! I am just sitting down at the table, and I have an excellent trout."

Five minutes later I was seated at the table opposite him. I said to him: "You are still a bachelor?"

"Surely!" he answered.

"And you manage to amuse yourself here?"

"I never find it tedious; I am too much occupied. I have my patients and my friends, eat well, sleep well and love to laugh and to hunt. That is the way it goes."

"Then life does not get monotonous in this little town?"

"No, my dear fellow, not when one is busy. A little town, when you come to sum it up, is like a large one. Events and pleasures are less varied, but they take on more importance. Relatives and friends are less numerous, but we meet them oftener. When we know every window in sight each one interests us, and we are more curious about them than we should be about a whole street in Paris. It is very amusing, a little town, you know, very amusing, very amusing. Now this Gisors, I have it on the end of my fingers from its origin up to today. You have no idea how comical its history is."

"You are a native of Gisors?"

"I? No, I come from Gournay, its neighbor and rival. Gournay is to Gisors what Lucullus was to Cicero. Here all is for glory; they are called 'the proud people of Gisors.' At Gournay all is for the stomach; they are spoken of as 'the eaters of Gournay.' It is very funny, this country is."

I noticed that I was eating something truly exquisite, some fish roe enveloped in a case of jelly, the viand aromatic with herbs, and the jelly delicately seasoned.

Smacking my lips for the sake of flattering Marambot, I said: "This is good!"

He smiled. "Two things are necessary for this," he said, "and difficult to obtain, good jelly and good eggs. Oh, good eggs, how rare they are, with the yellow of a reddish tinge and well flavored! I myself have a preference for two things, eggs and poultry. I keep my egg layers in a special way. I have my own ideas. In the egg, as in the flesh of the chicken, or of mutton or beef, we find and ought to taste the substance, the quintessence, of the nourishment of the animal. How much better one can eat if he pays attention to these things."

I laughed. "You are an epicure then?"

"Surely! It is only imbeciles who are not epicures. One is an epicure as he is artistic, as he is well informed, as he is poetical. Taste is a delicate organ, as respectable and as capable of being perfected as the eye or the ear. To lack taste is to be deprived of an exquisite faculty—that of discerning the quality of food, as one discerns the qualities of a book or a work of art; it is to be deprived of an essential sense, of an attribute of human superiority; it is to belong to one of the innumerable classes of the infirm or disgraced or simpletons that compose our race; it is to have the mouth of a beast and, in a word, the mind of a beast. A man who cannot distinguish between a crayfish and a lobster, a herring and this admirable fish that carries in it all the savors and aromas of the sea, between a mackerel and a whitefish, a winter pear and a *Duchesse*, is capable of confounding Balzac with Eugene Sue, a symphony of Beethoven with a military march by the leader of a regiment band and the Apollo Belvedere with the statue of General Blanmont!"

"Who is this General Blanmont?" I asked.

"Ah, it is true, you do not know him! That shows, indeed, that you do not know Gisors! My dear friend, I said a moment ago that we call the people of this town 'the proud people of Gisors.' Never was epithet more merited. But—we will breakfast first, and then I shall tell you about our town and take you around to visit it."

He ceased speaking from time to time to drink slowly a little glass of wine which he looked at tenderly before setting on the table. With napkin fastened about his neck, with cheekbones reddening and whiskers blossoming about his mouth as it worked, he was amusing to look at.

He made me eat to suffocation. Then when I wished to go back to the railway station he seized me in his arms and drew me away in another street. The town, of a pretty, provincial character, was overlooked by its fortress, the most curious monument of military architecture of the eighth century that there is in France. The rear of the fortress overlooked, in its turn, a long, green valley, where the heavy cows of Normandy browsed and chewed their cuds in the pastures.

The doctor said to me: "Gisors, town of four thousand inhabitants, on the borders of the Eure, was mentioned in the *Commentaries* of Caesar: Caesaris ostium, then Caesartium, Caesortium, Gisortium, Gisors. I could take you to the encampment of the Roman army, of which there are traces quite visible still."

I laughed and replied: "My dear friend, it seems to me that you are threatened with a special malady that you ought to study—you, a medical man—something that might be called the spirit of rivalry."

He stopped short. "The spirit of rivalry, my friend," he said, "is nothing else than natural patriotism. I love my house, my town and my province throughout its whole extent, because I find there the customs of my village, but if I love the frontier, if I defend it, if I am angry when the stranger sets his foot there, it is because I already feel my own house menaced, because the frontier, which I do not know, is the road to my province. Thus I am a Norman, a true Norman, and in spite of my rancor against Germany and my desire for vengeance, I do not detest it; I do not hate it by instinct as I hate the English, the veritable enemy, the hereditary enemy, the natural enemy of the Norman, because the English have passed over the soil settled by my ancestors and pillaged and ravaged it twenty times, and the aversion to this perfidious people has been transmitted to me with life itself from my father. Wait, here is the statue of the general."

"What general?"

"General Blanmont. We thought we ought to have a statue. We are not 'the proud people of Gisors' for nothing! Then we discovered General Blanmont. Just look through the glass door in this library."

I turned toward the front of a bookcase where a small collection of volumes, yellow, red and blue, met my eye. In reading the titles a desire to laugh seized me; they were: Gisors, Its Origin and Future, by M. X——, Member of Many Learned Societies, History of Gisors, by Abbé ——, Gisors, from Caesar to Our Time, by Dr. C. D——, The Glories of Gisors, by an Inquirer.

"My dear boy," began Marambot, "not a year passes, not one year, you understand, without at least one new history of Gisors appearing. We have twenty-three of them."

"And who are the celebrities of Gisors?" I asked.

"Oh! I cannot tell you all of them; I shall only tell you the principal ones. First we have General Blanmont, then Baron Davillier, the celebrated ceramist who explored Spain and the Balearic Islands and revealed to collectors some admirable Spanish-Arabian porcelains. In letters we have a journalist of great merit, now dead, Charles Brainne, and among the living, the very eminent director of the Rouen Gazetteer, Charles Lapierre, and many more, still many more."

We were going along rapidly through a steep street beaten upon by a June sun so hot that it had driven the inhabitants within doors. Suddenly at the other end of this road a man appeared, a drunken man, reeling. He came on, with head down, arms hanging at his sides and tottering limbs, at a jerky gait of six or eight rapid steps, followed by a rest. Then an energetic bound would take him to the middle of the street, where he would stop short and balance himself upon his feet, hesitating between a fall and a new attack of energy. Then he would repeat the operation in another direction. Finally he ran against a house, where he seemed to stick fast, as if he would enter it through the wall. Then he turned and looked before him, his mouth open, his eyes blinking in the sun, and with a wrench of his back he detached himself from the wall and started again.

A little yellow dog, a famished cur, followed him, barking, stopping when he stopped and starting when he started.

"Wait," said Marambot, "there is one of Madame Huisson's rose winners."

I was much astonished and replied: "Madame Huisson's rose winners? What do you mean?"

The doctor laughed. "Oh! It is a way we have here of calling a man a drunkard. It comes from an old story now passed into legend, which was true, nevertheless, in all points."

"Is it amusing, this story?"

"Very amusing."

"Then tell it, will you?"

"Very willingly. There was once in this town an old lady, very virtuous herself and the protector of virtue, who was called Madame Huisson. And you must know I am telling you true names and not fictitious ones. Madame Huisson occupied herself with good works, helping the poor and encouraging those that merited it. She was little, walking with quick, short steps, and wore a black silk wig. She was very polite and ceremonious, on excellent terms with the good God, as represented by Abbé Malou, and she had a profound, inborn horror of the vice the Church calls luxury. Pregnancies before marriage made her lose her temper, exasperating her to the point of making her beside herself.

"It was the epoch when they were crowning virtue with roses in the suburbs of Paris, and the idea came to Madame Huisson to have the same kind of festival in Gisors. She discussed it with Abbé Malou, who immediately made out a list of candidates for her.

"But Madame Huisson had in her service as maid an old woman named Frances, as strict as her mistress. When the priest had gone the mistress called her servant and said to her: 'Frances, here are the names of some girls that the curate proposes for the prize of virtue; make it your business to find out what people think of them around here.'

"And Frances began to go about the country. She culled all the deceptions, stories, suspicions and tattle, and, for fear of forgetting some of the details, she wrote them down with her expenses in her kitchen book, and every morning she took the book to Madame Huisson who read it carefully after adjusting her spectacles over her thin nose:

"*Bread, four sous. Milk, two sous. Butter, eight sous.*

"*Malvina Levesque went wild last year with Matthew Poilu. One leg of mutton, twenty-five sous. Salt, one sou.*

"*Rosalie Vatinel was met in the wood with Caesar Pienoir at dusk by Madame Onesime, ironer, the twentieth of July. Radishes, one sou. Vinegar, two sous. Sorrel, two sous. Josephine Durdent, that nobody had believed had any fault, is found to have a correspondence with the son of Oportun, who is in service at Rouen and who sent her a bonnet by the diligence for a present.*

"Not a girl escaped intact in this scrupulous inquisition. Frances asked questions of everybody—the neighbors, the traders, the schoolmaster, the sisters of the school—and summed up the reports.

"As there is not a girl in the universe upon whom comments have not been passed at one time or another, not a single young woman beyond slander was found in the whole countryside.

"Now Madame Huisson wished her rose winner to be like Caesar's wife, above suspicion, and she stood amazed, desolate and in despair before the kitchen book of her maidservant.

"They enlarged the circle of inquiry even to the neighboring villages but found no favorable result. The mayor was consulted. All his protégées were judged unsatisfactory. Those of Doctor Barbesol had no greater success, in spite of the precision of scientific guaranties.

"One morning Frances came in from one of her tours and said to her mistress:

"'It seems, madame, that if you wish to crown somebody there is nobody but Isidore in all the vicinity that is worthy of it.'

"Madame Huisson remained quiet and thoughtful.

"She knew Isidore well, the son of Virginia, the fruit seller. His proverbial chastity had been the delight of Gisors for many years, serving as a pleasant theme of conversation and amusement for the girls, who made themselves very merry at his expense. Over twenty-one in age, large, awkward, slow and timid, he helped his mother at her trade, passing his days in picking over fruits and vegetables, seated on a chair before the door.

"He had an abnormal fear of petticoats that caused him to lower his eyes when a fair customer looked at him and smiled, and this timidity, being well known, rendered him the sport of all the wags of the place. Bold words, impure allusions, expressions of doubtful meaning, made him blush so quickly that Doctor Barbesol nicknamed him the thermometer of modesty. Did he know anything or did he not? his rogues of neighbors would ask one another. Was it simply a presentiment of unknown mysteries or honest indignation for vile relations, intended for love alone, which seemed to move so strongly the son of Virginia, the fruit seller? The imps of the neighborhood would run up before his shop and throw pieces of filth in his face just to see him lower his eyes. The girls amused themselves passing and repassing his door, calling out bewitchingly to him, until he would go into the house. Some of the boldest would provoke him openly for the sake of laughing at him, asking him to meet them and proposing abominable things.

"And so Madame Huisson kept thinking.

"Certainly Isidore was a case of exceptional virtue, notorious and unassailable. No one, even the most skeptical, the most incredulous, could or would have dared to have a suspicion that Isidore was guilty of the slightest infraction of the moral law. No one had ever seen him in a café or met him in the streets in the evening. He went to bed at eight o'clock and arose at four. He was perfection, a pearl.

"Nevertheless, Madame Huisson hesitated. The idea of substituting a masculine rose winner for a feminine troubled her, disturbing her not a little, and she resolved to consult Abbé Malou.

"The abbé replied: 'What do you wish to recompense, madame? It is virtue, is it not, and nothing but virtue? What matters it then whether it be male or female? Virtue is eternal; it has neither country nor sex; it is simply virtue!'

"Thus encouraged, Madame Huisson went to find the mayor. He approved of it at once. 'Let us make it a beautiful ceremony,' he said, 'and in one year, if we find a young woman as worthy as Isidore, we will then crown her. In this way we shall set a beautiful example to Nantes. Let us not be exclusive but welcome merit wherever we find it.'

"Isidore, engaged for the occasion, blushed very red but seemed content. The ceremony was fixed for the fifteenth of August, the feast day of the Virgin Mary and also that of the Emperor Napoleon.

"The municipality decided to give a grand demonstration in honor of this solemnity and ordered as a stage for the crowners an enlargement of the charming ramparts of the old fortress, which I shall soon take you to see.

"By a natural revolution of public spirit Isidore's virtue, scoffed at until that day, had suddenly become respectable, since it would bring him five hundred francs, besides a little expense book, which was a mountain of consideration and glory to spare. The girls now regretted their frivolity, their laughter and their freedom of manner, and Isidore, although as modest and timid as ever, had taken on a little air of satisfaction which bespoke an inward joy.

"On the eve of the fifteenth of August the whole of Dauphine Street was hung with draperies. Ah! I have forgotten to tell you from what event the street received its name. It appears that years ago the princess—some princess, I don't know her name—had been detained so long by the authorities in some public demonstration that, in the midst of a triumphal march across the town, she stopped the procession before one of the houses of this street and exclaimed: 'Oh, what a pretty house! How I wish I might visit it! To whom does it belong?' They gave her the name of the owner, who was sought out and led, proud but confused, before the princess. She got out of her carriage, entered the house, inspected it from top to bottom, even remaining in one particular room for some minutes. When she had gone the people, flattered by the honor received by a citizen of Gisors, cried: 'Long live the princess!' But a little song was composed by a joker, and the street received a royal name because of the lines, which run thus:

> "The princess, in a hurry,
> Without priest, as she ought to,
> Had, with a little water,
> Baptized it.

"But to return to Isidore. They threw flowers all along the course of the procession, as they do for processions on the church feast days. The National Guard was on foot under orders from its chief, Commander Desbarres, an old soldier of the Grand Army who displayed with pride the Cross of Honor given to him by Napoleon himself for the beard of a Cossack culled with a single blow of the saber by the commander from the chin of its owner in the retreat from Russia.

"The company he commanded, besides being a corps composed of the elite, celebrated in all the province, was the company of Gisors grenadiers, who were in demand at every celebration of note within a radius of fifteen or twenty miles. They tell how King Louis Philippe, passing in review the militia of Eure, once stopped in astonishment before the Gisors company and exclaimed: 'Oh, who are these handsome grenadiers?'

" 'From Gisors,' replied the general.

" 'I can scarcely believe it,' murmured the king.

"Now Commander Desbarres came with these men, music at the head, to take Isidore from his mother's shop. After a little air had been played under his windows the rose winner himself appeared on the threshold. He was clothed in white duck from head to foot and wore on his head a straw cap which had on it, like a cockade, a bouquet of orange flowers.

"This question of costume had much disturbed Madame Huisson, who hesitated a long time between the black coat of the first communicant and the complete suit of white. But Frances, her counselor, decided in favor of the white, as it would tend to give the rose winner the air of a great poet.

"Behind him appeared his protector, his godmother, Madame Huisson, triumphant. She took his arm upon going out, and the mayor walked at the other side of the hero. The drums beat. Commander Desbarres shouted: 'Present arms!' And the procession started on its march to the church amid a large concourse of people assembled from all the neighboring towns and villages.

"After a short Mass and a touching address by Abbé Malou they repaired to the coronation grounds, where the banquet was served under a tent. Before sitting down at the table the mayor had a word to say. Here is his discourse verbatim. I learned it by heart because it was so beautiful:

" 'Young man, a good woman, loved by the poor and respected by the rich, Madame Huisson, whom the entire country thanks here through my voice, had the thought, the happy, beneficent thought, of founding in this town a prize of virtue, which would be a precious encouragement offered to the inhabitants of this beautiful country.

" 'You, young man, are the first one crowned in the dynasty of chastity and of this wise woman. Your name will remain at the head of this list of the deserving ones, and it will be necessary that your life, you understand, your whole life, shall be in accord with this beginning. Today, face to face with this noble woman who recompenses your virtuous conduct, face to face with these soldier-citizens who have taken up arms in your honor and with these sympathetic people, reunited to cheer you, or rather, to cheer in your virtue, may you contract the solemn engagement toward this town, toward all of us to set, until the day of your death, the excellent example of your youth. Do not forget, young man, that you are the first grain sown in the field of hope; give us the fruits that we expect from you.'

"The mayor took three steps, opened his arms and pressed the sobbing Isidore to his heart.

"The rose winner was sobbing, but without knowing why, from a confusion of emotion, pride and a tenderness, vague and joyous.

"Then the mayor put in his hand a silk purse which rang with gold, five hundred francs in gold! And in the other hand he put the little expense book. Then in a solemn voice he pronounced these words: 'Homage, glory and riches to virtue!' "

"Commander Desbarres shouted: 'Bravo!' The grenadiers followed his example, and the people applauded. Madame Huisson was drying her eyes.

"Then they took their places around the table where the banquet was served. It was magnificent and prolonged. Dish followed dish; yellow cider and red wine fraternized in neighboring glasses and mingled in the same stomachs. The rattle of dishes and of voices and the music, which played softly, made a continuous, profound rumble that lost itself in the clear sky where the swallows were flying. Madame Huisson readjusted her black silk wig from time to time, as it became tipped over one ear in her chat with Abbé Malou. The mayor, excited, talked politics with Commander Desbarres, and Isidore ate, Isidore drank, as he never had eaten or drunk before! He took and retook of everything, perceiving for the first time that it was sweet to feel himself filled with good things which first gave pleasure to his palate. He had adroitly loosened the buckle of his trousers, which bound him under the pressure of growing corpulence, and silent, a little disturbed by the knowledge that a drop of wine had fallen on his white coat, he ceased to eat in order to carry his glass to his mouth and keep it there as long as possible, that he might taste the wine slowly.

"The hour of the toasts struck. They were numerous and well applauded. The evening came; they had been at the table since midday. Already vapors soft and

milky-white were floating in the valley, clothing lightly with the shadow of night
the brooks and the fields; the sun touched the horizon; the cows bellowed from
afar in the brown haze of the pastures. The feast was ended. They were going
back to Gisors. The procession, broken now, was marching helter-skelter. Madame
Huisson had taken Isidore's arm and was giving him numerous injunctions,
hurried but excellent.

"They arrived at the door of the fruit seller, and the rose winner was left
at his mother's house. She had not yet returned. Invited by her family to celebrate the triumph of her son, she had taken luncheon with her sister after following the procession as far as the banquet tent. So Isidore was alone in the
shop, which was almost dark.

"He seated himself upon a chair, agitated by wine and by pride, and looked
about him. Carrots, cabbages and onions diffused through the closed room the
strong odor of vegetables, mingling their rude garden aroma with a sweet, penetrating fragrance, the fresh and light perfume escaping from a basket of peaches.

"The rose winner took a peach and ate it, although he was already as round
as a pumpkin. Then suddenly excited with joy, he began to dance, and something
rattled in his coat. He was surprised, thrust his hand in his pocket and brought
out the purse with the five hundred francs which he had forgotten in his
drunkenness. Five hundred francs! What a fortune! He turned the money out
upon the counter and dropped it slowly through his fingers so as to see them
all at the same time. There were twenty-five of them, twenty-five round pieces of
gold! All gold! They shone upon the wood in the thick shadows, and he counted
them and recounted them, placing his finger upon each one, murmuring: 'One,
two, three, four, five—one hundred; six, seven, eight, nine, ten—two hundred.'
Then he put them in his purse again and concealed it in his pocket.

"Who can know and who can say what sort of combat took place in the soul
of this rose winner between the evil and the good, the tumultuous attack of
Satan, his snares and deceits, the temptations that he threw into this timid, virgin
heart? What suggestions, what images, what covetous desires, had the rogue of all
rogues invented for moving and ruining this chosen soul? He seized his cap,
chosen by Madame Huisson, his cap which still bore the bouquet of orange
flowers, and, going out by the street back of the house, he disappeared into the
night.

"Virginia, the fruit seller, having been told that her son had returned, came
back almost immediately and found the house empty. She waited without being astonished at first; then at the end of a quarter of an hour she began to inquire. The neighbors in Dauphine Street had seen Isidore enter the house and
had not seen him go out again. Then they searched for him but could not find
him. The fruit seller, much disturbed, ran to the mayor. The mayor knew nothing about the youth, except that he had left him at his mother's door. Madame
Huisson left her bed when she heard that her protégé had disappeared. She immediately put on her wig and went to Virginia's house. Virginia, who had a soul
easily moved, wept tears among her cabbages, carrots and onions.

"They feared some accident. What? Commander Desbarres called out the
mounted police, who made a tour around the whole town; he found, on the
road from Pontoise, the little bouquet of orange flowers. It was placed upon a
table around which the authorities sat in deliberation. The rose winner had

been the victim of some stratagem on account of jealousy; but how? What means had they employed to carry off this innocent one, and to what end?

"Weary of searching without finding, the authorities retired. Virginia, alone, watched in her tears.

"The next evening, when the diligence from Paris was passing through the village on its return, the people of Gisors learned with surprise that their rose winner had stopped the coach two hundred meters from their town, had mounted, paid for his place with a louis of the money they had given him and that he had alighted calmly in the heart of the great city.

"The excitement in the country was considerable. Letters were exchanged between the mayor and the chief of police at Paris, but they led to no discovery. Day followed day, until a week had passed.

"Then one morning Doctor Barbesol, going out at an early hour, saw a man sitting in a doorway, clothed in grimy white, sleeping with his head against the wall. He approached him and recognized Isidore. Trying to awaken him, he found it impossible. The ex-rose winner slept with a sleep so profound, unconquerable and unusual that the doctor, much surprised, sought aid in carrying the young man to Boncheval's pharmacy. When they lifted him a bottle, apparently empty, was lying under him and, having smelled of it, the doctor declared it had contained brandy. It was an indication that served their purpose. They understood. Isidore was drunk, had been drunk and besotted for eight days and was too disgusting to be touched by a ragpicker. His beautiful costume of white duck had become a grimy rag, yellow, greasy, muddy, slashed and wholly debased, and his person exhaled all sorts of nauseating odors from the brook of vice.

"He was washed, preached to, shut up and for four days did not go out. He seemed honest and repentant. They had not found upon him either the purse with the five hundred francs or the expense book or his gold watch, a sacred inheritance from his father, the fruiterer.

"On the fifth day he risked himself in Dauphine Street. Curious looks followed him, and he went along by the houses with lowered head and shifty eyes. They lost sight of him on the way from the town through the valley. But two hours later he reappeared, giggling and hitting himself against walls. He was drunk again, hopelessly drunk.

"Nothing could cure him. Driven out by his mother, he became a driver of coal wagons for the business house of Pougrisel, which exists today. His reputation as a drunkard became so great and extended so far that even at Evreux they spoke of the rose winner of Madame Huisson, and the legends of the country have preserved this nickname.

"A good deed is never lost."

Dr. Marambot rubbed his hands in finishing his history.

"Did you know this rose winner yourself?" I inquired.

"Yes," he said, "I had the honor of shutting his eyes."

"How did he die?"

"In a crisis of delirium tremens, naturally."

We had come to the old fortress heaped with ruined walls overlooking the tower of Saint Thomas of Canterbury, and the tower called the Prisoner. Marambot told me the history of this prisoner, who, with the end of a nail, covered the walls of his dungeon with sculpture, following the movements of the sun across the narrow slit in a murderer's cell.

Then I learned that Clotaire II had given Gisors to his cousin Saint Romain, Bishop of Rouen, that Gisors ceased to be the capital of Vexin after the treaty of Saint Clair on the Epte, that the town is the first strategic point of that part of France and that it has been, on account of this advantage, taken and retaken an infinite number of times. Upon the order of William the Red, the celebrated engineer, Robert de Bellesme, constructed there a powerful fortress, attacked later by Louis the Great, then by the Norman barons; it was defended by Robert de Candos, ceded finally by Louis the Great to Geoffrey Plantagenet and was retaken from the English, following the treaty of the Templars. It was disputed between Philip Augustus and Richard the Lionhearted, burned by Edward III of England, who could not take the castle, rebuilt by the English again in 1419, surrendered later to Charles VII by Richard de Marbury, taken by the Duke of Calabre, occupied by the League, inhabited by Henry IV, etc.

And Marambot, convinced, almost eloquent, repeated: "What scoundrels those English are! And what drinkers, my dear friend, and all rose winners, are those hypocrites, every one of them!"

After that there was a silence, and he held out his arms to the thin little river that glistened through the level fields. Then he said:

"You know that Henry Monnier was one of the most assiduous of fishermen on the banks of the Epte?"

"No, I did not know it."

"And Bouffé, my dear fellow, Bouffé was here as painter and glazier."

"Oh, come now!"

"Yes, truly. How can you be so ignorant of these things?"

THE TRAVELER'S STORY

We went up on the bridge again after dinner. The Mediterranean before us had not a ripple on its whole surface in which a great, calm moon was reflected. The huge steamer sped along, throwing to the heavens sown with stars a great serpent of black smoke. And behind us the whitened water, agitated by the rapid passing of the heavy ship, seemed to be in torture, beaten into froth by the screw and changed from its smooth splendor where it lay quiet under the rays of the brilliant moon.

We were there, several of us, silent, admiring, our eyes turned toward Africa, whither we were bound. The commander, smoking a cigar as he stood among us, suddenly took up the conversation of the dinner table:

"Yes, I did have some fears that day. My ship had been six hours with that rocking in the hold, beaten by the sea. Happily we were picked up toward evening by an English collier that had spied us."

Then a great man of burly figure and grave aspect, one of those men who seem to have come from some unknown and distant country, from the midst of incessant dangers, whose tranquil eye, in its profundity, appears to hold in some way the foreign landscapes he has seen—one of those men who give the impression of possessing great courage—spoke for the first time:

"You say, Commander, that you were afraid? I cannot believe that. You deceive yourself in the word and in the sensation you experienced. An energetic man is never afraid in the face of pressing danger. He is moved, excited, anxious, but fear is another thing."

The commander, laughing, replied: "Nonsense! I tell you frankly that I was afraid."

Then the man with the bronze tint said in a slow manner:

"Allow me to explain myself! Fear (and the hardiest men can experience fear) is something frightful, an atrocious sensation, like the decomposition of the soul, a frightful spasm of thought and of the heart, of which the mere remembrance sends a shiver of agony through the frame. But this is not felt when one is brave, or before an attack, or before inevitable death or before any of all the known forms of peril; it is felt in abnormal circumstances, under certain mysterious influences, in the face of vague dangers. True fear is something like a reminiscence of fantastic terrors of other times. A man who believes in spirits and who imagines that he sees a specter in the night should understand fear in all its horror.

"As for me, I have understood what fear is in broad day. It was about ten years ago. I also felt it again last winter, one night in December.

"Yet I have taken many chances, had many adventures that seemed mortal. I have often fought. I have been left for dead by robbers. I have been condemned as an insurgent in America, doomed to be hanged and thrown into the sea from the bridge of a ship in China. Each time I believed myself lost but undertook to make the best of it immediately, without grief or even regret.

"But fear—that is something else.

"I had a presentiment in Africa—although presentiment is a daughter of the north—the sun dissipates it like a fog. Notice that well, gentlemen. Among the Orientals life counts for nothing. They are always resigned to meet death. Nights are clear and free from the disquieting shadows which haunt the brains of the people of cold countries. In the Orient they understand panic, but they are ignorant of fear.

"Well! Here is what happened to me on African soil:

"I had crossed the great dunes in the south of Ouargla. That is one of the strangest countries in the world. You are familiar with level sand, the true sand of the interminable shore of the sea. Well, figure to yourselves the ocean itself sand, and in the midst of a hurricane; imagine a silent tempest of motionless waves in yellow dust. They are as high as mountains, these unequal waves, different from each other and raised suddenly, like unchained billows, but greater still and streaked like water waves. Upon this furious sea, mute, immovable, the sun of the south turns its implacable and direct flame, devouring it. It is necessary to climb these waves of golden ashes, to redescend, to climb again, to climb incessantly without repose and without shade. Horses puff, sinking to their knees, and, slipping in, they go down the other side of these surprising little hills.

"We were two friends, followed by eight spahis and four camels with their drivers. We could no longer speak, as we were suffocated with heat and fatigue and parched with thirst, like this burning desert. Suddenly one of our men uttered a kind of cry. All stopped, and we remained motionless, surprised by an inexplicable phenomenon, known only to travelers in these lost countries.

"Somewhere near us, in an indeterminate direction, a drum was beating, the mysterious drum of the dunes. It was heard distinctly, at first vibrating loudly, then more feebly, stopping, then taking up its fantastic rolling again.

"The Arabs, much frightened, looked at one another, and one said in his own language: 'Death is upon us.'

"Just then, suddenly, my companion, my friend, almost my brother, fell on his head from his horse, overcome with sunstroke. And for the next two hours, during which I tried in vain to save him, that unseizable drum filled my ears with its monotonous noise, intermittent and incomprehensible.

"I felt slipping into my bones a fear, true fear, hideous fear, in the face of my dead friend, well beloved, in this hole, burning up in the sun, between four mountains of sand, where an unknown echo brought to us the rapid beating of a drum, two hundred miles from any French village.

"That day I understood what it was to have fear, and I understood it still better on one other occasion."

The commander interrupted the speaker: "Pardon, sir, but this drum? What was it?"

The traveler answered: "That I do not know. No one knew. The officers, often surprised by this singular noise, attributed it generally to a great echo, multiplied, swelled immeasurably by the little valleys of the dunes, caused by particles of sand being carried in the wind and hurled against a bunch of dried herbs, because they always noticed that the phenomenon was produced in the neighborhood of plants dried in the sun and hard as parchment. This drum then was a kind of mirage of sound. That is all. But I learned that later.

"Now I come to my second emotion.

"This came to me last winter in a forest in the northeast of France. The night fell two hours earlier than usual, the sky was so cloudy. I had for a guide a peasant who walked at my side through a little road under an arch of pines through which the unchained wind howled dismally. Between the hilltops I could see clouds scurrying away in line, lost clouds, which seemed to be fleeing before some fright. Sometimes under a powerful whirlwind, the whole forest bowed in the same breath with a groan of suffering. And the cold took me by force in spite of my rapid walk and heavy clothing.

"We were going to take supper and sleep at the house of a forest guide whose house was not far from the place where we were. I was going there to hunt.

"My guide would sometimes raise his eyes and mutter: 'Bad weather!' Then he spoke of the people to whose house we were going. The father had killed a poacher two years before, and since then he had seemed somber, as if haunted by a memory. His two sons were married and lived with him.

"The shadows were profound. I could see nothing before me or about me, and the branches of the trees, clashing against each other, filled the night with confusion. Finally I perceived a light, and soon my companion knocked on a door. The sharp cries of women responded. Then the voice of a man, a strangled voice, asked: 'Who is there?' My guide gave our names. We entered. It was a picture never to be forgotten.

"An old man with white hair and a mad expression of the eye awaited us in the middle of the kitchen with a loaded gun in his hand, while two great fellows, armed with hatchets, guarded the door. I distinguished in the dark corner two women on their knees, their faces turned against the wall.

"They explained it. The old man put up his gun and ordered them to prepare my room; then as the women did not budge he said brusquely:

" 'You see, sir, I killed a man here two years ago tonight. Last year he came back to me. I am expecting him this evening.'

"Then he added in a tone that made me laugh:

" 'So we are not quite easy.'

"I reassured him as best I could, happy to have come just at this time to assist at the spectacle of this superstitious terror. I told stories and succeeded in calming them all somewhat.

"Near the entrance was an old dog, whiskered and nearly blind, one of those dogs that resemble people we know, asleep, with his nose in his paws.

"Outside the raging tempest was beating against the little house, and through a small hole, a kind of Judas place, near the door I suddenly saw, by a sharp flash of lightning, a clump of great trees overturned by the wind.

"In spite of my efforts I felt sure that a profound terror held these people, and each time that I ceased to speak all ears seemed to be listening to something in the distance. Weary of trying to dispel these imbecile fears, I asked permission to go to bed, when the old guard suddenly made a bound from his chair, seized his gun again and stuttered in a faraway voice:

" 'Here he is! Here he is! I'm waiting for him!'

"The two women fell upon their knees in their corners, concealing their faces, and the sons took up their hatchets. I was trying to appease them again when the sleeping dog awoke suddenly and, raising his head, stretching his neck and looking toward the fire with eyes almost closed, began to utter the most lugubrious howls, of the sort that give a start to travelers in the country at night. All eyes were turned toward him; he remained motionless, resting upon his paws, as if haunted by a vision.

"He was howling at something invisible, unknown, frightful, no doubt, because his hair was bristling. The guide, now livid, cried out:

" 'He feels him! He feels him! He was there when I killed him!'

"And the two excited women began to howl with the dog.

"In spite of myself a great shiver ran down between my shoulders. The sight of the terrified animal in that place, at that hour, in the midst of those benighted people, was frightful.

"For an hour the dog howled without ceasing; his wails sounded as if he were in agony from a dream. And fear, ungovernable fear, entered my being. Fear of what? Did I know what? It was fear, and that was all.

"We remained motionless, livid, in expectation of some frightful event, with listening ear and beating heart, starting at the least noise. And the dog began to go about the room, touching the walls and growling. That beast nearly made us mad!

"The peasant who had brought me threw himself upon the animal in a kind of paroxysm of furious terror and, opening the door, with a little push threw it outside.

"He was then silent, and all of us remained plunged in a silence more terrifying still. Suddenly we all started with surprise. A form glittered on the wall, the outside wall toward the forest; then it passed against the door, which it seemed to touch with hesitating hand; then we heard nothing for two minutes, which almost drove us out of our senses; then it returned, always rubbing against the wall, and it scratched lightly, as a child does with his nail; then suddenly a head appeared against the glass, a white head with luminous eyes like those of a deer. And there came from his mouth an indistinct sound, a plaintive murmur.

"Then a fearful noise resounded through the kitchen. The old guide had shot. And immediately the sons hurried to block up the door, putting against it the great table and bringing the side table to its assistance.

"And I swear to you that from the fracas of that gunshot, which I had not expected, I had such an agony of heart and soul and body that I felt myself swooning, ready to die of fear.

"We remained there until light, incapable of moving, not saying a word, stiff with indescribable fright.

"They did not dare take down the barricade until, through a crevice in the door, they saw a ray of daylight.

"At the foot of the wall, opposite the door, the old dog lay, his mouth pierced with a ball.

"He had gone out of the yard, crossing through a hole under the fence."

The man with the bronzed visage was silent, but he added soon:

"That night I ran into no danger, but I would rather encounter all the hours that have brought me the greatest peril than that one minute of the shooting at the shaggy head of the old dog."

A JOLLY FELLOW

They called him Saint Anthony because his name was Anthony, and also, perhaps, because he was a joyous good lover, fond of joking, powerful at eating and drinking and had a vigorous hand with servants, although he was more than sixty years old. He was a tall peasant of the country of Caux, of high color, great in chest and girth and was perched upon long legs that seemed too thin for the weight of his body.

A widower, he lived alone with his maid and his two menservants on his farm, which he directed in sly, jovial fashion, careful of his interests, attending to business affairs, the breeding of the cattle and the cultivation of the land. His two sons and three daughters, married to advantage, lived in the neighborhood and came once a month to dine with their father. His vigor was known in all the country about; people said, as if it were a proverb: "He is as strong as Saint Anthony."

When the Prussian invasion occurred Saint Anthony, at the inn, promised to eat an army, for, like a true Norman, he was a romancer and a little of a coward and a blusterer. He brought his heavy fist down on the wooden table, making it jump, while the cups and glasses danced, and he cried out with red face and cunning eye in the false anger of the jovial fellow: "In heaven's name! Will it be necessary to eat some of them?" He counted on the Prussians not coming any farther than Tanneville, but when he learned that they were at Rautot, he would not go out of his house, and he watched without ceasing through the little window of his kitchen, expecting every moment to see the glint of bayonets.

One morning, as he was eating soup with his servants, the door opened and the mayor of the commune, Master Chicot, appeared, followed by a soldier,

wearing on his head a black cap set off with a point of copper. Saint Anthony arose
with a bound; everybody looked at him, expecting to see him cut the Prussian
in pieces, but he contented himself with shaking hands with the mayor, who said
to him: "Here's one of 'em for you to take care of, Saint Anthony. They came
in the night. I haven't been surly with them, seeing they talk of shooting and
burning if the least thing happens. You are warned. Give him something to eat.
He seems a good lad. I am going to the other houses to seek quarters for the rest
of them. There is enough for everybody." And he went out.

Father Anthony looked at his Prussian and grew pale. He was a great boy, fat
and white, with blue eyes and blond hair, bearded up to the cheekbones, and he
seemed stupid and timid, like a good child. The Norman rogue comprehended him
immediately, as he thought, and, reassured, made him a sign to sit down. Then
he asked: "Will you have some soup?"

The stranger did not understand. Anthony then made an audacious move and,
pushing a full plate under the nose of his unexpected guest, he said: "There, eat
that, you big pig!"

The soldier responded: "Ja," and began to eat ravenously, while the farmer, triumphant, feeling his power recognized, winked his eye at his servants, who made
strange faces and had a great desire to laugh but were restrained by fear.

When the Prussian had cleared his plate Saint Anthony served him another,
the contents of which disappeared like the first, but he recoiled before the third
helping, which the farmer tried by force to make him eat, repeating: "Come, now,
put that inside of you. You shall grow fat, or I'll know the reason why, my pig!"

And the soldier, comprehending nothing except that he was urged to eat all he
wanted, laughed with a contented air, making a sign that he was full.

Then Saint Anthony, suddenly becoming familiar, tapped him on the front,
saying: "He has enough in his paunch, has my pig!" But upon this he doubled
himself with laughter, growing red enough for an attack of apoplexy, and was
unable to speak for a moment. An idea had seized him which suffocated him with
laughter: "That's it! That's it!" he cried. "Saint Anthony and his pig! I am Saint
Anthony, and this is my pig!" And the three servants laughed loudly in their turn.

The old man was so pleased with his jest that he ordered the maid to bring
some brandy of the ten-year-old brand with which he regaled everybody. They
drank with the Prussian, who smacked his lips as a bit of delicate flattery, in order
to indicate that he found it delicious. And Saint Anthony cried out in his face:
"Yes! This is something fine! You don't find anything like it at home, my pig!"

After this Father Anthony never went out without his Prussian. He had found
his opportunity. It was vengeance to him, the vengeance of a great rogue. And all
the people of the countryside, who were trembling with fear, laughed until in
torture behind the backs of their conquerors at the farce of Saint Anthony and his
pig. Indeed, as a joke, they thought it had not its equal. He had only to say a few
things like this: "Go along, pig! Go!" in order to provoke convulsions of merriment.

He would go among his neighbors every afternoon with his German, their arms
around each other, and would present him with a gay air, tapping him on the
shoulder and saying: "See! Here is my pig! Look at him and tell me if you think
he is getting fat, this here animal!"

And the peasants fairly bubbled with laughter—he was such a wag, this rogue
of an Anthony!

"I'll sell him to you, Caesar," he would say, "for three pistoles."

"I take him, Anthony, and invite you to come and have some of the pudding."

"Me," said Anthony, "what I want is some of the feet."

"Punch his body and see how fat he is!" said Caesar.

And everybody would wink slyly, not laughing too much, however, for fear the Prussian might surmise finally that they were mocking him. Anthony alone, growing bolder every day, would pinch the calves of his legs, crying out: "Nothing but fat!" or strike him on the back and shout: "There's some good bacon!" Then the old man, capable of lifting an anvil, would seize him in his arms and raise him up in the air, declaring: "He weighs six hundred and not a bit of waste!"

He got into the habit of offering his pig something to eat wherever they went. It was the great pleasure, the great diversion of every day. "Give him whatever you like," he would say; "he will swallow it." And when they would inquire if the man wished some bread and butter, potatoes, cold mutton or venison, Anthony would say to him: "Here you are now; it's your choice!"

The soldier, stupid and gentle, ate for politeness, enchanted with so much attention; he would make himself sick rather than refuse, and he was growing fat, truly, too stout for his uniform, which fairly delighted Saint Anthony, who kept telling him: "You know, my pig, it's pretty soon going to be necessary for you to have a new cage."

They became apparently the best friends in the world. And when the old man went on business into the surrounding country the Prussian accompanied him of his own accord, for the sole pleasure of being with him.

The weather was very rigorous; it had frozen hard; the terrible winter of 1870 seemed to throw all plagues together upon France.

Father Anthony, who looked out for things ahead and took advantage of opportunities, foreseeing that he would need manure for his spring work, bought some of a neighbor who found himself in straits; he arranged to go each evening with his cart and bring it home, a load at a time. And so toward evening of each day he was to be seen on the way to Haules' farm, half a mile distant, always accompanied by his pig. And everybody ran along with them, as they go on Sunday to a grand Mass, for each day was a feast day for feeding the animal.

But the time came when the soldier began to be suspicious. And, when they laughed too much he rolled his eyes as if disturbed, and sometimes they sent forth a spark of anger.

One evening when he had eaten to the extent of his capacity, he refused to swallow another morsel and undertook to start up and go away. But Saint Anthony stopped him with a blow on the wrist and, placing his two hands on the Prussian's shoulders, he sat him down again so hard that the chair cracked under him.

A perfect tempest of gaiety followed, and Anthony, radiant, picked up his pig, rubbing the wounded spot with the semblance of healing it. Then he declared: "Since you won't eat you shall drink, by Jimminy!" And somebody went to the alehouse for brandy.

The soldier rolled his eyes in wicked fashion, but he drank, nevertheless, as much as they wished, and Saint Anthony held his head, to the great amusement of his assistants.

The Norman, red as a tomato, with fiery eye, filled the glasses, drinking and guying him with: "To your sweetheart!" And the Prussian, without a word, encompassed glass after glass of these bumpers of cognac.

It was a struggle, a battle, a defense. In heaven's name, who could drink the most? They could take no more, either of them, when the bottle was drained, but neither was conquered. They were neck and neck, and that was all. It would be necessary to start over the next day.

They went out stumbling and started homeward beside the cart filled with manure, which two horses dragged slowly along. The snow began to fall, and the night, without a moon, seemed to shed a sad light over this death of the plains. The cold took hold of the two men, increasing their drunkenness, and Saint Anthony, discontented at not having triumphed, amused himself with pushing his pig by the shoulder, trying to make him fall over into the ditch. The man evaded the attacks by retreat, and each time he would mutter some German words in an irritated tone, which made the farmer laugh heartily. Finally the Prussian became angry, and just at the moment when Anthony gave him another push he responded with a terrible blow of the fist which made the old colossus totter.

Then, inflamed with brandy, the old fellow seized the man by the arms and shook him for some seconds, as if he had been a child, and then threw him with all his might to the other side of the road. Content with his execution, he folded his arms and laughed in good earnest.

But the soldier got up quickly, bareheaded, his cap having rolled off, and, drawing his sword, made a plunge for Father Anthony. When the farmer saw this he seized his great fork of yellow holly, strong and supple as a beef tendon.

The Prussian came on with his head lowered, weapon in front of him, sure of killing his foe. But the old man, grasping with firm hand the blade whose point was aimed to pierce his body, turned it aside and struck his enemy such a sharp blow upon the temple with the point of the fork that he fell at his feet. Then the peasant looked at his fallen foe, frightened, stupefied with astonishment, seeing the body shake with spasms at first and then lying motionless upon its face. He stooped, turned him over and looked at him a long time. The man's eyes were closed, and a little stream of blood was running from a hole in the forehead. In spite of the darkness Father Anthony could distinguish the brown spot of blood on the snow.

He remained there, bewildered, while his cart went on at the horses' regular step. What was to be done? He would shoot him! Then the Prussians would burn his place and work ruin throughout the country! But what should he do? What should he do? How conceal the body, conceal the death, deceive the Prussians? He could hear voices in the distance, in the silence of the snowstorm. Then he became excited and, seizing the cap, he put it on the man's head again and, taking him by the back, he raised him up, ran, overtook his team and threw the body on the manure. Once at home, he could think what to do.

He went along with short steps, racking his brain but unable to decide anything. He understood the matter and felt sure that he was lost. Finally he came to his house. A bright light shone through a dormer window; his servant was not yet asleep. Then he made his wagon back quickly to the edge of a hole in the field. He thought by overturning the load the body would fall underneath in the ditch, and he tipped the cart over. As he had thought, the man was buried under the manure. Anthony evened off the heap with his fork and stuck it in the ground at the side. He called his manservant, ordered him to put the horses in the stable and went to his chamber.

He went to bed, reflecting continually upon what he had done, but no helpful idea came to him, and his fear increased when he was quiet in bed. The Prussians would shoot him! The sweat of fear started out upon him; his teeth chattered; he got up, shivering so that he could scarcely hold his clothes to get into them. He went down into the kitchen, took a bottle of liquor from the sideboard and went back to his chamber. He drank two large glasses of liquor in succession, adding a new drunkenness to the old one, without calming the agony of his soul. He felt that he had made a pretty mess of it this time!

He walked the floor to and fro, seeking a ruse or explanation for his wickedness. And from time to time he would rinse his mouth with a draught of the ten-year-old cognac to put some heart into his body. But he could think of nothing, nothing. Toward midnight his watchdog, a kind of half wolf, which he called Devour, began the howl of death. Father Anthony trembled to the marrow. And each time that the beast began his long, mournful wail again a shiver of fear would run along the skin of the old man.

He had fallen upon a chair with weak knees; he was besotted, unable to do more, expecting that Devour would continue his wailing, and his nerves were played upon by every form of fear that could set them vibrating. The clock downstairs struck five. The dog was still howling, and the farmer was becoming mad. He got up and started to unchain the animal so that he might no longer listen to it. He went downstairs, opened the door and went out into the night.

The snow was falling still. All was white. The farm buildings were great black spots. As he approached the kennel the dog pulled on his chain. He loosed him. Then Devour made a bound, stopped short, with hair bristling, paws trembling, smelling the air, his nose turned toward the manure heap.

Saint Anthony trembled from head to foot, muttering: "What's the matter with you, dirty beast?" And he advanced some steps, casting a penetrating eye through the uncertain shadows, the undefined shadows of the courtyard. Then he saw the form of a man seated on his manure heap!

He looked at the figure and gasped with horror, motionless. But suddenly he perceived near him the handle of his fork stuck in the earth. He pulled it from the soil and, in one of those transports of fear which make cowardly men more bold, he rushed on with it to see who the man was.

It was he, the Prussian, soiled from his bed of manure, the warmth of which had revived him and partly brought him back to his senses. He had seated himself mechanically and was resting there upon the snow which had powdered him well, over the filth and blood, still besotted by drunkenness, stunned by the blow and exhausted from his wounds.

He perceived Anthony and, too much stupefied to understand anything, he made a movement as if to rise. The old man, as soon as he recognized him, fumed like a wild beast. He sputtered: "Ah, pig, pig! You are not dead! You have come to denounce me right away—— Wait—wait!" And, throwing himself upon the German, he raised his four-pointed fork like a lance and brought it down with all the force of his two arms in the man's breast, even to the handle. The soldier turned over on his back with a long death sigh, while the old farmer drew the weapon from the wound and replunged it in the body, blow upon blow, striking like a madman, stamping with his feet upon the head and the rest of the body, which was still palpitating and from which the blood spouted in great jets.

Then he stopped, overcome with the violence of his effort, breathing the air in great draughts, appeased by the accomplishment of his deed.

As the cocks began to crow in the poultry yard and the day was dawning, he set himself to work to bury the man. He dug into the manure heap until he came to earth, then dug still deeper, working in a disorderly fashion, with furious force in his arms and his whole body. When the trench was long enough he rolled the dead body into it with the fork, replaced the earth, kicking it about until it was level, put the manure over it again and smiled to see the snow thicken and complete his work, wholly covering all traces with its white veil.

Then he stuck his fork into the manure and returned to the house. His bottle was still half full upon the table. He emptied it with a gulp, threw himself upon the bed and slept profoundly.

He awoke sobered, his mind calm and active, capable of judging the case and foreseeing results. At the end of an hour he was scouring the country, asking everybody the whereabouts of the soldier. He went to the officers to find out, he said, why they had taken his man away.

As the Prussians knew nothing of the peculiar situation between the two men they were not suspicious, and Anthony even directed the search, affirming that the Prussian had gone running after some petticoat nearly every evening.

An old refugee policeman, who kept an inn in a neighboring village and who had a pretty daughter, was arrested on suspicion of being the murderer and was shot.

ROOM NO. 11

"What! You do not know why President Amandon was removed?"

"No, not at all."

"As far as he is concerned, it would never have been known. But it is a story of the strangest sort."

"Relate it to me."

"You remember Madame Amandon, that pretty brunette, thin, and so distinguished and pretty that she was called Madame Marguerite in all Perthuis-le-Long?"

"Yes, perfectly."

"Very well, then. You recall also how much she was respected and considered and better loved than anyone in the town; she knew how to receive, how to organize a festival or a charity fair, how to find money for the poor and how to please the young people in a thousand ways.

"She was very elegant and very coquettish, nevertheless, but in a Platonic fashion, and with the charming elegance of the provinces, for she was a provincial, this pretty little woman, an exquisite provincial.

"The poets and writers who are all Parisian sing to us of the Parisian woman and of her charm because they know only her, but I declare here that the provincial is worth a hundred times more when she is of superior quality.

"The provincial has an attraction all her own; she is more discreet than the Parisian, more humble, promising nothing and giving much, while the Parisian, for the most part, promises much and gives nothing but deshabille.

"The Parisian is a triumph in the elegant effrontery of falseness; the provincial, an example of the modesty of truth.

"Yet the provincial, with her air of homely alertness, her deceitful, schoolgirl candor, her smile which means nothing and her good little passions, direct and tenacious, is capable of a thousand times more deceit, artifice and feminine invention than all the Parisians together for gratifying her own tastes or vices, and that without awakening suspicion or scandal or gossip in the little town which watches her with all its eyes from all its windows.

"Madame Amandon was a type of this rare race, but charming. Never had anyone suspected her; never had anyone thought that her life was not as limpid as her look, a sly look, transparent and warm, but seemingly so honest—you should have seen it!

"Then she had admirable tact, a marvelous ingenuity and power of invention and unbelievable simplicity.

"She picked all her lovers from the army and kept them three years, the time of their sojourn in the garrison. In short, she not only had love; she had sense.

"When some new regiment arrived at Perthuis-le-Long she carefully observed all the officers between thirty and forty years of age—for before thirty one is not discreet, and after forty one is often feeble.

"Oh! She knew the list of officers as well as the colonel. She knew all, all the habits, manners, instruction, education, physical qualities, the power of resistance to fatigue, the character, whether patient or violent, the fortune and the tendency to closeness or prodigality of each of them. Then she made her choice. She gave the preference to men of calm allurement, like herself, but they must be handsome. She also wished them to have had no previous entanglements, any passion having the power to leave traces, or that had made any trouble. Because the man whose loves are mentioned is never a very discreet man.

"After having decided upon the one she would love for the three years of his regulation sojourn, it only remained to throw down the gauntlet.

"While some women would find themselves embarrassed, would have taken ordinary means, following the way of others, having court paid them in marked-off stages of conquest and resistance, allowing her fingers to be kissed one day, her wrist the next, her cheek the following, then the lips, then the rest, she had a method more prompt, more discreet and more sure. She gave a ball.

"The chosen officer was invited to dance with the mistress of the house. Then in waltzing, led on by the rapid movement, bewildered by the intoxication of the dance, she would throw herself against him, as if giving herself, and hold his hand with a nervous, continued pressure.

"If he did not comprehend he was only a fool, and she passed on to the next, classed as number two, on the list of her desires.

"If he comprehended the thing was done, without fuss, without compromising gallantries, without numerous visits.

"What could be more simple or more practical?

"How women might make use of a process similar to this to make us understand their pleasure! How much it would suppress difficulties, hesitations and trouble from misunderstanding! How often we pass by, without knowing it, a possible happiness, without suspecting it, because we are unable to penetrate the mystery of thought, the secret abandon of the will, the mute appeal of the flesh, the unknown soul of a woman whose mouth preserves silence, whose eye is impenetrable and clear.

"When the chosen one comprehended he asked for a rendezvous. But she always

made him wait a month or six weeks in order to watch and be sure that he had
no dangerous faults.

"During this time he was racking his brain to think of some place where they
could meet without peril and imagining combinations difficult and unsafe.

"Then at some official feast she would say to him in a low voice:

" 'Come Tuesday evening at nine o'clock to the Golden Horse Hotel near the
ramparts, on the Vouziers road, and ask for Mademoiselle Clarisse. I shall be
waiting for you. And be sure to be in civil dress.'

"For eight years she had, in fact, rented this furnished room by the year in this
obscure inn. It was an idea of her first lover which she found practical, and after
the man departed she kept the nest.

"Oh, it was a mediocre nest: four walls covered with gray paper adorned with
blue flowers, a pine bedstead under muslin curtains, an armchair bought at her
order by the innkeeper's wife, two chairs and some necessary articles for the toilet
—what more was needed?

"Upon the walls were three large photographs. Three colonels on horseback,
the colonels of her lovers! Why not? It would not do to preserve the true likeness,
the exact likeness, but she could perhaps keep some souvenirs by proxy.

"And she had never been recognized by anyone in all these visits to the Golden
Horse, you ask?

"Never, by anyone!

"The means she employed were admirable and simple. She had thought out
and organized some charity reunions and religious meetings, some of which she
attended, others she did not. Her husband, knowing her good works, which cost
him dear, lived without suspicions. Then when a rendezvous had been agreed
upon, she would say at dinner before the servants:

" 'I am going this evening to the association for making flannel bandages for
old paralytics.'

"And she went out about eight o'clock, went straight to the association, came
out again very soon, passed through divers streets and, finding herself alone in
some little street, in some somber corner without a light, she would take off her
hat, replace it by a maid's cap which she carried under her mantle, fold a kerchief
after the same fashion and tie it over her shoulders, carrying her hat and the
garment she had worn in a napkin; she would go trotting along, full of courage,
the hips uncovered, like a good little maid that had been sent upon some errand,
and sometimes she would even run, as if she were in a great hurry.

"Who could have recognized in this trim servant the lively wife of President
Amandon?

"She would arrive at the Golden Horse, go up to her room, of which she had
the key, and the big proprietor, Master Trouveau, seeing her pass his desk, would
murmur:

" 'There is Mademoiselle Clarisse coming to meet some lover.'

"He had indeed guessed something, the rogue, but did not try to learn more,
and he would certainly have been much surprised to find that his client was
Madame Amandon, or Madame Marguerite, as she was called in Perthuis-le-Long.
And this is how the horrible discovery took place.

"Never had Mademoiselle Clarisse come to her meeting place two evenings in
succcession, never, being too nice and too prudent for that. And Master Trouveau
knew this well, since not once in eight years had he seen her come the next day

after a visit. Often, therefore, in days of need he had disposed of her room for a night.

"Now sometime last summer Monsieur Amandon, the trustful president, absented himself from home for a week. It was in July. Madame was ardently in love, and as there was no fear of being surprised, she asked her lover, the handsome Commander Varangelles, one Tuesday evening on leaving him if he wished her to return the next day.

"He replied: 'With all my heart!'

"And it was agreed that they should return at the usual hour on Wednesday. She said to him in a low tone:

" 'If you arrive first, my dear, you can wait for me in bed.'

"Then they embraced and separated. The next day, as Master Trouveau sat reading the Perthuis *Tablet*, the Republican organ of the town, he cried out to his wife who was plucking a fowl in the courtyard:

" 'Here! The cholera has broken out in the country. There was a man died yesterday of it in Vauvigny.' But he thought no more about it, his inn being full of people and business very good.

"Toward noon a traveler presented himself on foot, a kind of tourist, who ordered a good breakfast, after having drunk two absinthes. And as he was very warm, he absorbed a bottle of wine and two bottles of water at least. Then he took his coffee and his little glass, or rather three little glasses. And feeling a little heavy, he asked for a room where he might sleep for an hour or two. There was no longer a vacant room, and the proprietor, after consulting his wife, gave him Mademoiselle Clarisse's.

"The man went in there, and toward five o'clock, as he had not been seen to come out, the landlord went to wake him. What was his astonishment to find him dead!

"The innkeeper descended to find his wife: 'Say," he whispered to her, 'the tourist I put in number 11, I believe is dead.'

"She raised her arms, crying: 'It's not possible! Lord God! It is the cholera!'

Master Trouveau shook his head:

" 'I should sooner believe that it was a cerebral congestion, seeing that he is as black as the dregs of wine.'

"But the mistress was frightened and kept repeating:

" 'It is not necessary to say; it is not necessary to say that we think it is cholera. Go and make the report and say nothing. They will take him away in the night, and no one will know about it. What is neither seen nor heard perplexes nobody.'

"The man murmured: "Mademoiselle Clarisse was here yesterday; the room will be free this evening.'

"And he found the doctor who made out the certificate, 'From congestion after a copious repast.' Then he made an agreement with the commissioner of police to remove the dead body toward midnight, that there might be no suspicion about the hotel.

"It was scarcely nine o'clock when Madame Amandon went secretly up the staircase of the Golden Horse without being seen by anyone. She reached her room, opened the door and entered. A candle was burning upon the chimney piece. She turned toward the bed. The commander, she thought, was already there and had closed the curtains.

"She said to him: 'One minute, dearie, and I will be there.'

"And she disrobed with a feverish haste, throwing her boots upon the floor and her corset upon the armchair. Then, her black dress and skirts having fallen in a circle around her, she stood in her red silk chemise like a flower that is ready to blossom.

"As the commander said not a word, she asked:

" 'Are you asleep, my big fellow?'

"He did not answer, and she began to laugh, murmuring:

" 'Wait! He is asleep. It is too funny!'

"She kept on her black silk stockings and, running to the bed, glided in quickly, seizing him full in the arms and kissing him on the lips in order to wake him suddenly. It was the cold dead body of the traveler.

"For one second she remained immovable, too frightened to comprehend anything. But the cold of this inert flesh penetrated her own, giving her an atrocious fright before her mind had time to reflect.

"She made a bound out of the bed, trembling from head to foot; then running to the chimney piece, she seized the candle, returned, and looked! And she perceived a frightful visage that she had never before seen, black, swollen, with eyes closed and a horrible grimace of the jaw.

"She uttered a cry, one of those piercing, interminable cries which women utter in their fright, and, letting the candle fall, she opened the door and fled, unclothed, down the passage, continuing to scream in frightful fashion. A commercial traveler in his socks, who occupied room number 4, came out immediately and received her in his arms.

"He asked, much startled: 'What is the matter, pretty child?'

"She stammered out, terrified: 'Someone has been killed—in—my room!'

"Other guests appeared. The landlord himself ran out.

"And suddenly the commander showed his tall figure at the end of the corridor. When she saw him she threw herself toward him, crying:

" 'Save me, save me, Gontran. Someone has been killed in our room.'

"Explanations were difficult. Master Trouveau, however, told the truth and demanded that they release Mademoiselle Clarisse, for whom he vouched with his own head. But the commercial traveler in socks, having examined the dead body, declared that a crime had been committed, and he convinced the other strangers that Mademoiselle Clarisse and her lover should not be allowed to depart.

"They were obliged to await the arrival of the police commissioner, who gave them their liberty, but was not discreet.

"The following month President Amandon received promotion with a new place of residence."

A LIVELY FRIEND

They had been constantly in each other's society for a whole winter in Paris. After having lost sight of each other, as generally happens in such cases, after leaving college, the two friends met again one night, long years after, already old and white-haired, the one a bachelor, the other married.

M. de Meroul lived six months in Paris and six months in his little château at Tourbeville. Having married the daughter of a gentleman in the district, he had lived a peaceful, happy life with the indolence of a man who has nothing to do. With a calm temperament and a sedate mind, without any intellectual audacity or tendency toward revolutionary independence of thought, he passed his time in mildly regretting the past, in deploring the morals and the institutions of today and in repeating every moment to his wife, who raised her eyes to heaven and sometimes her hands also, in token of energetic assent:

"Under what a government do we live, great God!"

Mme de Meroul mentally resembled her husband, just as if they had been brother and sister. She knew by tradition that one ought, first of all, to reverence the Pope and the king!

And she loved them and respected them from the bottom of her heart, without knowing them, with a poetic exaltation, with a hereditary devotion, with all the sensibility of a well-born woman. She was kindly in every feeling of her soul. She had no child and was incessantly regretting it.

When M. de Meroul came across his old schoolfellow Joseph Mouradour at a ball he experienced from this meeting a profound and genuine delight, for they had been very fond of one another in their youth.

After exclamations of astonishment over the changes caused by age in their bodies and their faces they had asked one another a number of questions as to their respective careers.

Joseph Mouradour, a native of the south of France, had become a councilor general in his own neighborhood. Frank in his manners, he spoke briskly and without any circumspection, telling all his thoughts with sheer indifference to prudential considerations. He was a Republican, of that race of good-natured Republicans who make their own ease the law of their existence and who carry freedom of speech to the verge of brutality.

He called at his friend's address in Paris and was immediately a favorite on account of his easy cordiality, in spite of his advanced opinions. Mme de Meroul exclaimed:

"What a pity! Such a charming man!"

M. de Meroul said to his friend in a sincere and confidential tone: "You cannot imagine what a wrong you do to our country." He was attached to his friend, nevertheless, for no bonds are more solid than those of childhood renewed in later life. Joseph Mouradour chaffed the husband and wife, called them "my loving turtles" and occasionally gave vent to loud declarations against people who were behind the age, against all sorts of prejudices and traditions.

When he thus directed the flood of his democratic eloquence the married pair, feeling ill at ease, kept silent through a sense of propriety and good breeding; then the husband tried to turn off the conversation in order to avoid any friction. Joseph Mouradour did not want to know anyone unless he was free to say what he liked.

Summer came round. The Merouls knew no greater pleasure than to receive their old friends in their country house at Tourbeville. It was an intimate and healthy pleasure, the pleasure of homely gentlefolk who had spent most of their lives in the country. They used to go to the nearest railway station to meet some of their guests and drove them to the house in their carriage, watching for compliments on their district, on the rapid vegetation, on the condition of the roads in the department, on the cleanliness of the peasants' houses, on the bigness of the cattle they saw in the fields, on everything that met the eye as far as the edge of the horizon.

They liked to have it noticed that their horses trotted in a wonderful manner for animals employed a part of the year in field work, and they awaited with anxiety the newcomer's opinion on their family estate, sensitive to the slightest word, grateful for the slightest gracious attention.

Joseph Mouradour was invited, and he announced his arrival. The wife and the husband came to meet the train, delighted to have the opportunity of doing the honors of their house.

As soon as he perceived them Joseph Mouradour jumped out of his carriage with a vivacity which increased their satisfaction. He grasped their hands warmly, congratulated them and intoxicated them with compliments.

He was quite charming in his manner as they drove along the road to the house; he expressed astonishment at the height of the trees, the excellence of the crops and the quickness of the horse.

When he placed his foot on the steps in front of the château M. de Meroul said to him with a certain friendly solemnity:

"Now you are at home."

Joseph Mouradour answered: "Thanks, old fellow; I counted on that. For my part, besides, I never put myself out with my friends. That's the only hospitality I understand.

Then he went up to his own room, where he put on the costume of a peasant, as he was pleased to describe it, and he came down again not very long after, attired in blue linen, with yellow boots, in the careless rig-out of a Parisian out for a holiday. He seemed, too, to have become more common, more jolly, more familiar, having assumed along with his would-be rustic garb a free-and-easy swagger which he thought suited the style of dress. His new apparel somewhat shocked M. and Mme de Meroul, who even at home on their estate always remained serious and respectable, as the particle "de" before their name exacted a certain amount of ceremonial, even with their intimate friends.

After lunch they went to visit the farms, and the Parisian stupefied the respectable peasants by talking to them as if they were a comrade of theirs.

In the evening the curé dined at the house—a fat old priest, wearing his Sunday suit, who had been specially asked that day in order to meet the newcomer.

When Joseph saw him he made a grimace, then he stared at the priest in astonishment as if he belonged to some peculiar race of beings, the like of which he had never seen before at such close quarters. He told a few stories allowable enough with a friend after dinner but apparently somewhat out of place in the presence of an ecclesiastic. He did not say, "Monsieur l'Abbé" but merely "Monsieur," and he embarrassed the priest with philosophical views as to the various superstitions that prevailed on the surface of the globe.

He remarked:

"Your God, monsieur, is one of those persons whom we must respect, but also one of those who must be discussed. Mine is called Reason; he has from time immemorial been the enemy of yours."

The Merouls, greatly put out, attempted to divert his thoughts. The curé left very early.

Then the husband gently remarked:

"You went a little too far with that priest."

But Joseph immediately replied:

"That's a very good joke too! Am I to bother my brains about a devil dodger? At any rate, do me the favor of not ever again having such an old fogy to dinner. Confound his impudence!"

"But, my friend, remember his sacred character."

Joseph Mouradour interrupted him:

"Yes, I know. We must treat them like girls who get roses for being well behaved! That's all right, my boy! When these people respect my convictions I will respect theirs!"

This was all that happened that day.

Next morning Mme de Meroul, on entering her drawing room, saw lying on the table three newspapers which made her draw back in horror, Le Voltaire, La République Française and La Justice.

Presently Joseph Mouradour, still in his blue blouse, appeared on the threshold reading L'Intransigéant attentively. He exclaimed:

"Here is a splendid article by Rochefort. That fellow is marvelous."

He read the article in a loud voice, laying so much stress on its most striking passages that he did not notice the entrance of his friend.

M. de Meroul had a paper in each hand: Le Gaulois for himself and Le Clarion for his wife.

The ardent prose of the master writer who overthrew the empire, violently declaimed, recited in the accent of the south, rang through the peaceful drawing room, shook the old curtains with their rigid folds, seemed to splash the walls, the large upholstered chairs, the solemn furniture fixed in the same position for the past century, with a hail of words, rebounding, impudent, ironical and crushing.

The husband and the wife, the one standing, the other seated, listened in a state of stupor, so scandalized that they no longer even ventured to make a gesture. Mouradour flung out the concluding passage in the article as one sets off a stream of fireworks; then in an emphatic tone he remarked:

"That's a stinger, eh?"

But suddenly he perceived the two prints belonging to his friend, and he seemed himself for a moment overcome with astonishment. Then he came across to his host with great strides, demanding in an angry tone:

"What do you want to do with these papers?"

M. de Meroul replied in a hesitating voice:

"Why, these—these are my—my newspapers."

"Your newspapers! Look here now, you are only laughing at me! You will do me the favor to read mine to stir you up with a few new ideas, and, as for yours— this is what I do with them——"

And before his host, filled with confusion, could prevent him, he seized the two newspapers and flung them out through the window. Then he gravely placed La Justice in the hands of Mme de Meroul and Le Voltaire in those of her husband, himself sinking into an armchair to finish L'Intransigéant.

The husband and the wife, through feelings of delicacy, made a show of reading a little, then they handed back the Republican newspapers which they touched with their finger tips as if they had been poisoned.

Then Mouradour burst out laughing and said:

"A week of this sort of nourishment, and I'll have you converted to my ideas."

At the end of a week, in fact, he ruled the house. He had shut the door on the curé, whom Mme de Meroul went to see in secret. He gave orders that neither the *Gaulois* nor the *Clarion* were to be admitted into the house, which a manservant went to get in a mysterious fashion at the post office and which, on his entrance, were hidden away under the sofa cushions. He regulated everything just as he liked, always charming, always good natured, a jovial and all-powerful tyrant.

Other friends were about to come on a visit, religious people with Legitimist opinions. The master and mistress of the château considered it would be impossible to let them meet their lively guest and, not knowing what to do, announced to Joseph Mouradour one evening that they were obliged to go away from home for a few days about a little matter of business, and they begged of him to remain in the house alone.

He showed no trace of emotion and replied:

"Very well, 'tis all the same to me; I'll wait here for you as long as you like. What I say is this—there need be no ceremony between friends. You're quite right to look after your own affairs—why the devil shouldn't you? I'll not take offense at your doing that, quite the contrary. It only makes me feel quite at my ease with you. Go, my friends—I'll wait for you."

M. and Mme de Meroul started next morning.

He is waiting for them.

THE PATRON

He would never have dared to hope that such good fortune would be his! The son of a provincial sheriff, Jean Marin had come to Paris, like so many others, to study law in the Latin Quarter. In the various cafés which he had successively patronized, he had made friends with a number of talkative students, who chattered about politics as they drank their beer. He developed great admiration for them and became their follower, even paying for their drinks when he happened to have any money.

Afterwards, he practiced law and handled some suits, which he lost, when, one morning, he read in the papers that a friend of his student days had become a deputy. Again he became his faithful servant, the friend who discharges all the troublesome errands, whom one sends for when he is wanted, and with whom one stands on no ceremony.

But it so happened, by the chance of politics, that the deputy became a minister, and six months afterwards, Jean Marin was appointed state councilor.

At first, he was so puffed up with pride that he almost lost his head. He would take walks just to show himself off, as if the people he met in the street could guess his position just by looking at him. He always managed to say to the various tradespeople he dealt with, as well as to the news dealers and even the cabmen:

"I, who am a state councilor . . ."

He naturally experienced, as the direct result of his profession and his newly acquired dignity, an imperative desire to patronize. He would offer his influence to everyone he met, at all times, and with inexhaustible generosity.

When he ran up against a man he knew on the boulevard, he would rush up to him in a delighted manner, shake hands, inquire after his health and then, without waiting for any inquiry, would blurt out:

"You know I am state councilor, and I am absolutely at your service. If there is anything I can do for you, I hope you will call on me unhesitatingly. In my position, a man can do a lot for his friends."

Then he would go into some café with this friend and ask for some writing paper and a pen and ink—"just one sheet, waiter, I want to write a letter of introduction."

He wrote quantities of these letters, sometimes twenty, thirty, and fifty a day. He wrote them at the Café Américain, at Bignono's, at Tortoni's, at the Maison-Dorée, at the Café Riche, at the Helder, at the Café Anglais, at the Napolitain, everywhere. He addressed them to every official in the Republic, from magistrates to ministers. And he was happy, thoroughly happy.

One morning, as he was leaving his rooms to go to the State Council it began to rain. He was inclined to take a cab, but did not, finally deciding that he would walk.

The shower became very heavy, soaking the pavements, and inundating the streets. M. Marin was compelled to seek shelter in a doorway. An old priest had already taken refuge there, an old, white-haired priest. Before he had been appointed state councilor, M. Marin did not care much for the clergy. But now, ever since a cardinal had consulted him regarding some delicate matter, he treated the clergy with consideration. The downpour was so heavy that the two men were forced to take refuge in the concierge's box, to avoid getting splashed. M. Marin, who was constantly impelled to brag about himself, declared:

"A very bad day, monsieur l'abbé."

The old priest bowed:

"Ah! yes, monsieur, and it is all the more disagreeable when one is in Paris for a few days only."

"Ah! so you live in the provinces?"

"Yes, monsieur, I am only passing through Paris."

"Indeed, it is most annoying to have rain when one is spending a day or so in the capital. We officials, who live here all the year round, do not mind it."

The abbé made no reply and looked into the street, where the rain was beginning to stop a little. And suddenly clutching his gown in both hands, he resolved to brave the elements.

M. Marin, seeing him depart, shouted:

"You will get drenched, monsieur l'abbé. Wait a few minutes more, the rain will stop."

The old man wavered and then said:

"Well, I'm in a great hurry. I have a very urgent engagement."

M. Marin appeared very much concerned.

"But you will certainly be wet through. May I ask where you are going?"

The priest seemed to hesitate a moment, but then he said:

"I am going in the direction of the Palais Royal."

"Well then, if you will allow me, monsieur l'abbé, I will offer you the shelter of my umbrella. I am going to the State Council. I am a state councilor."

The old priest raised his eyes, looked at the speaker and exclaimed:

"I am greatly obliged to you, monsieur, and accept your offer with pleasure."

Then M. Marin took him by the arm, and they set out. He led him along, watching over him and giving advice:

"Be careful of this gutter, monsieur l'abbé. Look out for the carriage wheels, they throw mud all over one. Mind the umbrellas! Nothing is more of a danger to the eyes than the sharp ends of an umbrella! The women, especially, are so careless; they never mind anything and thrust their sunshades and their umbrellas right under people's noses. And they never go out of anyone's way, either. They seem to think that they own the whole city. I think myself that their education has been sadly neglected."

And M. Marin chuckled gleefully.

The priest made no reply. He picked his way carefully along the streets, slightly bent, choosing with discrimination the dry spots on the pavement so as not to bespatter his shoes and gown.

M. Marin went on:

"I suppose you are in Paris for a little rest?"

The old man retorted:

"No, I have come on business."

"Oh! anything important? Might I inquire what it is? If I can be of service to you, I would only be too glad."

The abbé looked embarrassed. He mumbled:

"Oh! it's a little personal matter. A little difficulty with—with my bishop. It could hardly interest you. It is something about the adjustment—the adjustment of some ecclesiastical matter."

M. Marin became eager.

"Why, these matters are always referred to the State Council. In this case I wish you would make use of me."

"Yes, it is to the State Council I am going. You are most kind. I have an appointment with M. Lerepère and M. Savon, and maybe I will interview M. Petitpas also.

M. Marin came to a stop.

"Why, they are my friends, monsieur l'abbé, my dearest friends, fine fellows, all of them. I shall warmly recommend you to them. Rely on me."

The priest thanked him and protested his undying gratitude.

M. Marin was delighted.

"Oh! you can thank your stars, monsieur l'abbé, that you met me. You will see how smoothly everything will go now."

They finally reached the State Council. M. Marin conducted the priest to his office, installed him before the open fire and then sat down at his desk and wrote:

"*My dear colleague, allow me to recommend most heartily to you a very worthy priest, M. l'Abbé . . .*"

He paused and inquired:

"Your name, please?"

"Abbé Ceinture."

M. Marin wrote:

"*M. l'Abbé Ceinture, who needs your intercession in a little matter which he will lay before you.*

"*I am glad of this opportunity which allows me, my dear colleague . . . .*"

And he concluded with the customary compliments.

After he had written the three letters, he handed them to his protégé, who departed amid renewed protestations of gratitude.

M. Marin attended to his official duties, went home, spent a quiet day and slept peacefully that night. The next morning he woke up happy, dressed and sat down to read the papers.

The first one he opened was a radical organ. He read:

"Our Clergy and our Officials.

"There seems to be no end to the misdeeds of the clergy. A certain priest named Ceinture, convicted of having conspired against the existing government, accused of infamous acts that we will not even mention, suspected besides of being a former Jesuit transformed into an ordinary priest, revoked by his bishop for reasons which are said to be unprintable, and summoned to Paris to explain his conduct, has found a warm partisan in the State Councilor Marin, who did not hesitate to give this cassocked rascal the most enthusiastic letters of recommendation to all his Republican colleagues.

"We wish to call the minister's attention to the unqualifiable attitude of this state councilor . . ."

M. Marin sprang to his feet, slammed down the paper and rushed off to see his colleague Petitpas, who exclaimed:

"Well you must have gone crazy to recommend that old conspirator to me."

Thoroughly bewildered, M. Marin retorted:

"No . . . no . . . you see, I was deceived myself. He looked like such a good man. . . . He tricked me . . . he tricked me most shamefully. I beg of you to condemn him severely, most severely. I shall go myself to the Attorney General and the Archbishop of Paris, yes, to the Archbishop. . . ."

And he sat down abruptly at M. Petitpas's desk and wrote:

"My Lord: I have the honor to inform Your Grace that I have been made a victim of the intrigues and lies of a certain Abbé Ceinture, who shamefully took advantage of my good faith.

"Misled by the protestations of this priest, I was induced . . ."

Then, after he had signed his name to the letter and sealed it, he turned to his colleague and remarked:

"Look here, my dear friend, I hope this will be a lesson to you never to recommend anyone."

THE IMPOLITE SEX

MADAME DE X. TO MADAME DE L.

Etretat, Friday.

MY DEAR AUNT, I am going to pay you a visit without making much fuss about it. I shall be at Les Fresnes on the second of September, the day before the hunting season opens; I do not want to miss it so that I may tease these gentlemen. You are very obliging, Aunt, and I would like you to allow them to dine with you, as you usually do when there are no strange guests, without dressing or shaving for the occasion, on the ground that they are fatigued.

They are delighted, of course, when I am not present. But I shall be there, and I shall hold a review, like a general, at the dinner hour, and if I find a single one of them at all careless in dress, no matter how little, I mean to send him down to the kitchen to the servant maids.

The men of today have so little consideration for others and so little good manners that one must be always severe with them. We live indeed in an age of vulgarity. When they quarrel with one another they attack one another with insults worthy of street porters, and in our presence they do not conduct themselves even as well as our servants. It is at the seaside that you see this most clearly. They are to be found there in battalion, and you can judge them in the lump. Oh, what coarse beings they are!

Just imagine, in a train one of them, a gentleman who looked well, as I thought, at first sight, thanks to his tailor, was dainty enough to take off his boots in order to put on a pair of old shoes! Another, an old man who was probably some wealthy upstart (these are the most ill bred), while sitting opposite to me, had the delicacy to place his two feet on the seat quite close to me. This is a positive fact.

At the watering places there is an unrestrained outpouring of unmannerliness. I must here make one admission—that my indignation is perhaps due to the fact that I am not accustomed to associate as a rule with the sort of people one comes across here, for I should be less shocked by their manners if I had the opportunity of observing them oftener. In the inquiry office of the hotel I was nearly thrown down by a young man who snatched the key over my head. Another knocked against me so violently without begging my pardon or lifting his hat, coming away from a ball at the casino, that he gave me a pain in the chest. It is the same way with all of them. Watch them addressing ladies on the terrace; they scarcely ever bow. They merely raise their hands to their headgear. But, indeed, as they are all more or less bald, it is the best plan.

But what exasperates and disgusts me especially is the liberty they take of talking publicly, without any precaution whatsoever, about the most revolting adventures. When two men are together they relate to each other in the broadest language and with the most abominable comments really horrible stories, without caring in the slightest degree whether a woman's ear is within reach of their voices. Yesterday on the beach I was forced to go away from the place where I sat in order not to be any longer the involuntary confidante of an obscene anecdote told in such immodest language that I felt as much humiliated as I was indignant at having heard it. Would not the most elementary good breeding have taught them to speak in a lower tone about such matters when we are near at hand? Etretat is, moreover, the country of gossip and scandal. From five to seven o'clock you can see people wandering about in quest of nasty stories about others, which they retail from group to group. As you remarked to me, my dear aunt, tittle-tattle is the mark of petty individuals and petty minds. It is also the consolation of women who are no longer loved or sought after. It is enough for me to observe the women who are fondest of gossiping to be persuaded that you are quite right.

The other day I was present at a musical evening at the casino, given by a remarkable artist, Mme Masson, who sings in a truly delightful manner. I took the opportunity of applauding the admirable Coquelin, as well as two charming boarders of the vaudeville, M——— and Meillet. I was able, on the occasion, to see all the bathers collected together this year on the beach. There were not many persons of distinction among them.

One day I went to lunch at Yport. I noticed a tall man with a beard who was coming out of a large house like a castle. It was the painter, Jean Paul Laurens. He is not satisfied apparently with imprisoning the subjects of his pictures, he insists on imprisoning himself.

Then I found myself seated on the shingle close to a man still young of gentle and refined appearance, who was reading some verses. But he read them with such concentration, with such passion, I may say, that he did not even raise his eyes toward me. I was somewhat astonished, and I asked the conductor of the baths, without appearing to be much concerned, the name of this gentleman. I laughed inwardly a little at this reader of rhymes; he seemed behind the age for a man. This person, I thought, must be a simpleton. Well, Aunt, I am now infatuated about this stranger. Just fancy, his name is Sully Prudhomme! I turned round to look at him at my ease, just where I sat. His face possesses the two qualities of calmness and elegance. As somebody came to look for him, I was able to hear his voice, which is sweet and almost timid. He would certainly not tell obscene stories aloud in public or knock against ladies without apologizing. He is sure to be a man of refinement, but his refinement is of an almost morbid, vibrating character. I will try this winter to get an introduction to him.

I have no more news to tell you, my dear aunt, and I must interrupt this letter in haste, as the post hour is near. I kiss your hands and your cheeks.

Your devoted niece,
BERTHE DE X.

P.S.—I should add, however, by way of justification of French politeness, that our fellow countrymen are, when traveling, models of good manners in comparison with the abominable English, who seem to have been brought up by stableboys, so much do they take care not to incommode themselves in any way, while they always incommode their neighbors.

MADAME DE L. TO MADAME DE X.

Les Fresnes, Saturday.

MY DEAR CHILD, Many of the things you have said to me are very reasonable, but that does not prevent you from being wrong. Like you, I used formerly to feel very indignant at the impoliteness of men, who, as I supposed, constantly treated me with neglect; but as I grew older and reflected on everything, putting aside coquetry and observing things without taking any part in them myself, I perceived this much—that if men are not always polite, women are always indescribably rude.

We imagine that we should be permitted to do anything, my darling, and at the same time we consider that we have a right to the utmost respect, and in the most flagrant manner we commit actions devoid of that elementary good breeding of which you speak with passion.

I find, on the contrary, that men have, for us, much consideration, as compared with our bearing toward them. Besides, darling, men must needs be and are what we make them. In a state of society where women are all true gentlewomen all men would become gentlemen.

Mark my words; just observe and reflect.

Look at two women meeting in the street. What an attitude each assumes toward the other! What disparaging looks! What contempt they throw into each glance! How they toss their heads while they inspect each other to find something to condemn! And if the footpath is narrow do you think one woman will make room for another or will beg pardon as she sweeps by? When two men jostle each other by accident in some narrow lane, each of them bows and at the same time gets out of the other's way, while we women press against each other, stomach to stomach, face to face, insolently staring each other out of countenance.

Look at two women who are acquaintances meeting on a staircase before the drawing-room door of a friend of theirs to whom one has just paid a visit and to whom the other is about to pay a visit. They begin to talk to each other and block up the passage. If anyone happens to be coming up behind them, man or woman, do you imagine that they will put themselves half an inch out of their way? Never! Never!

I was waiting myself, with my watch in my hands, one day last winter at a certain drawing-room door. Behind me two gentlemen were also waiting without showing any readiness to lose their temper, like me. The reason was that they had long grown accustomed to our unconscionable insolence.

The other day, before leaving Paris, I went to dine with no less a person than your husband in the Champs Elysées, in order to enjoy the open air. Every table was occupied. The waiter asked us not to go and there would soon be a vacant table.

At that moment I noticed an elderly lady of noble figure, who, having paid the amount of her check, seemed on the point of going away. She saw me, scanned me from head to foot and did not budge. For more than a full quarter of an hour she sat there, immovable, putting on her gloves and calmly staring at those who were waiting like myself. Now two young men who were just finishing their dinner, having seen me in their turn, quickly summoned the waiter in order to pay whatever they owed and at once offered me their seats, even insisting on standing while waiting for their change. And, bear in mind, my fair niece, that I am no longer pretty, like you, but old and white-haired.

It is we (do you see?) who should be taught politeness, and the task would be such a difficult one that Hercules himself would not be equal to it. You speak to me about Etretat and about the people who indulge in tittle-tattle along the beach of that delightful watering place. It is a spot now lost to me, a thing of the past, but I found much amusement there in days gone by.

There were only a few of us, people in good society, really good society, and a few artists, and we all fraternized. We paid little attention to gossip in those days.

Well, as we had no insipid casino, where people only gather for show, where they talk in whispers, where they dance stupidly, where they succeed in thoroughly boring one another, we sought some other way of passing our evenings pleasantly. Now just guess what came into the head of one of our husbandry? Nothing else than to go and dance each night in one of the farmhouses in the neighborhood.

We started out in a group with a street organ, generally played by Le Poittevin, the painter, with a cotton nightcap on his head. Two men carried lanterns. We followed in procession, laughing and chattering like a pack of fools.

We woke up the farmer and his servant maids and laboring men. We got them to make onion soup (horror), and we danced under the apple trees to the sound of the barrel organ. The cocks waking up began to crow in the darkness of the outhouses; the horses began prancing on the straw of their stables. The cool air of the country caressed our cheeks with the smell of grass and of new-mown hay.

How long ago it is! How long ago it is. It is thirty years since then!

I do not want you, my darling, to come for the opening of the hunting season. Why spoil the pleasure of our friends by inflicting on them fashionable toilets after a day of vigorous exercise in the country? This is the way, child, that men are spoiled. I embrace you.

Your old aunt,
GENEVIEVE DE L.

THE BLIND MAN

How is it that the sunlight gives us such joy? Why does this radiance when it falls on the earth fill us so much with the delight of living? The sky is all blue; the fields are all green, the houses all white, and our ravished eyes drink in those bright colors which bring mirthfulness to our souls. And then there springs up in our hearts a desire to dance, a desire to run, a desire to sing, a happy lightness of thought, a sort of enlarged tenderness; we feel a longing to embrace the sun.

The blind, as they sit in the doorways, impassive in their eternal darkness, remain as calm as ever in the midst of this fresh gaiety, and, not comprehending what is taking place around them, they continue every moment to stop their dogs from gamboling.

When, at the close of the day, they are returning home on the arm of a young brother or a little sister, if the child says: "It was a very fine day!" the other answers: "I could notice that 'twas fine. Lulu wouldn't keep quiet."

I have known one of these men whose life was one of the most cruel martyrdoms that could possibly be conceived.

He was a peasant, the son of a Norman farmer. As long as his father and mother lived he was more or less taken care of; he suffered little save from his horrible infirmity, but as soon as the old people were gone a life of atrocious misery commenced for him. A dependent on a sister of his, everybody in the farmhouse treated him as a beggar who was eating the bread of others. At every meal the very food he swallowed was made a subject of reproach against him; he was called a drone, a clown, and although his brother-in-law had taken possession of his portion of the inheritance, the soup was given to him grudgingly—just enough to save him from dying.

His face was very pale, and his two big white eyes were like wafers. He remained unmoved in spite of the insults inflicted upon him, so shut up in himself that one could not tell whether he felt them at all.

Moreover, he had never known any tenderness; his mother had always treated him very unkindly, caring scarcely at all for him, for in country places the useless are obnoxious, and the peasants would be glad, like hens, to kill the infirm of their species.

As soon as the soup had been gulped down he went to the door in summertime and sat down, to the chimney corner in wintertime and, after that, never stirred till night. He made no gesture, no movement; only his eyelids, quivering from some nervous affection, fell down sometimes over his white, sightless orbs. Had he any intellect, any thinking faculty, any consciousness of his own existence? Nobody cared to inquire as to whether he had or no.

For some years things went on in this fashion. But his incapacity for doing anything as well as his impassiveness eventually exasperated his relatives, and he became a laughingstock, a sort of martyred buffoon, a prey given over to native ferocity, to the savage gaiety of the brutes who surrounded him.

It is easy to imagine all the cruel practical jokes inspired by his blindness. And in order to have some fun in return for feeding him they now converted his meals into hours of pleasure for the neighbors and of punishment for the helpless creature himself.

The peasants from the nearest houses came to this entertainment; it was talked about from door to door, and every day the kitchen of the farmhouse was full of people. For instance, they put on the table in front of his plate, when he was beginning to take the soup, a cat or a dog. The animal instinctively scented out the man's infirmity and, softly approaching, commenced eating noiselessly, lapping up the soup daintily, and when a rather loud licking of the tongue awakened the poor fellow's attention, it would prudently scamper away to avoid the blow of the spoon directed at it by the blind man at random!

Then the spectators, huddled against the walls, burst out laughing, nudged each other and stamped their feet on the floor. And he, without ever uttering a word, would continue eating with the aid of his right hand, while stretching out his left to protect and defend his plate.

At another time they made him chew corks, bits of wood, leaves or even filth, which he was unable to distinguish.

After this they got tired even of these practical jokes, and the brother-in-law, mad at having to support him always, struck him, cuffed him incessantly, laughing at the useless efforts of the other to ward off or return the blows. Then came a new pleasure—the pleasure of smacking his face. And the plowmen, the servant girls and even every passing vagabond were every moment giving him cuffs, which caused his eyelashes to twitch spasmodically. He did not know where to hide himself and remained with his arms always held out to guard against people coming too close to him.

At last he was forced to beg.

He was placed somewhere on the highroad on market days, and as soon as he heard the sound of footsteps or the rolling of a vehicle he reached out his hat, stammering:

"Charity, if you please!"

But the peasant is not lavish, and for whole weeks he did not bring back a sou.

Then he became the victim of furious, pitiless hatred. And this is how he died.

One winter the ground was covered with snow, and it froze horribly. Now his brother-in-law led him one morning at this season a great distance along the highroad in order that he might solicit alms. The blind man was left there all day, and when night came on the brother-in-law told the people of his house that he could find no trace of the mendicant. Then he added:

"Pooh! Best not bother about him! He was cold and got someone to take him away. Never fear! He's not lost. He'll turn up soon enough tomorrow to eat the soup."

Next day he did not come back.

After long hours of waiting, stiffened with the cold, feeling that he was dying, the blind man began to walk. Being unable to find his way along the road, owing to its thick coating of ice, he went on at random, falling into dikes, getting up again without uttering a sound, his sole object being to find some house where he could take shelter.

But by degrees the descending snow made a numbness steal over him, and his feeble limbs being incapable of carrying him farther, he had to sit down in the middle of an open field. He did not get up again.

The white flakes which kept continually falling buried him so that his body, quite stiff and stark, disappeared under the incessant accumulation of their rapidly thickening mass, and nothing any longer indicated the place where the corpse was lying.

His relatives made pretense of inquiring about him and searching for him for about a week. They even made a show of weeping.

The winter was severe, and the thaw did not set in quickly. Now one Sunday, on their way to Mass, the farmers noticed a great flight of crows, who were whirling endlessly above the open field and then, like a shower of black rain, descended in a heap at the same spot, ever going and coming.

The following week these gloomy birds were still there. There was a crowd of them up in the air, as if they had gathered from all corners of the horizon, and they swooped down with a great cawing into the shining snow, which they filled curiously with patches of black and in which they kept rummaging obstinately. A young fellow went to see what they were doing and discovered the body of the blind man, already half devoured, mangled. His wan eyes had disappeared, pecked out by the long voracious beaks.

And I can never feel the glad radiance of sunlit days without sadly remembering and gloomily pondering over the fate of the beggar so deprived of joy in life that his horrible death was a relief for all those who had known him.

THE CORSICAN BANDIT

The road, with a gentle winding, reached the middle of the forest. The huge pine trees spread above our heads a mournful-looking vault and gave forth a kind of long, sad wail, while at either side their straight, slender trunks formed, as it were, an army of organ pipes from which seemed to issue the low, monotonous music of the wind through the treetops.

After three hours' walking there was an opening in this row of tangled branches. Here and there an enormous pine parasol, separated from the others, opening like an immense umbrella, displayed its dome of dark green; then all of a sudden we gained the boundary of the forest, some hundreds of meters below the defile which leads into the wild valley of Niolo.

On the two projecting heights which commanded a view of this pass, some old trees, grotesquely twisted, seemed to have mounted with painful efforts, like scouts who had started in advance of the multitude heaped together in the rear. When we turned round we saw the entire forest stretched beneath our feet, like a gigantic basin of verdure, whose edges, which seemed to reach the sky, were composed of bare racks shutting in on every side.

We resumed our walk, and ten minutes later we found ourselves in the defile.

Then I beheld an astonishing landscape. Beyond another forest, a valley, but a valley such as I had never seen before, a solitude of stone ten leagues long, hollowed out between two high mountains, without a field or tree to be seen. This was the Niolo Valley, the fatherland of Corsican liberty, the inaccessible citadel, from which the invaders had never been able to drive out the mountaineers.

My companion said to me: "It is here that all our bandits have taken refuge."

Ere long we were at the farther end of this chasm, so wild, so inconceivably beautiful.

Not a blade of grass, not a plant—nothing but granite. As far as our eyes could reach we saw in front of us a desert of glittering stone, heated like an oven by a burning sun which seemed to hang for that very purpose right above the gorge. When we raised our eyes toward the crests we stood dazzled and stupefied by what we saw. They looked red and notched like festoons of coral, for all the summits are made of porphyry, and the sky overhead seemed violet, lilac, discolored by the vicinity of these strange mountains. Lower down the granite was of scintillating gray, and under our feet it seemed rasped, pounded; we were walking over shining powder. At our right, along a long and irregular course, a tumultuous torrent ran with a continuous roar. And we staggered along under this heat, in this light, in this burning, arid, desolate valley cut by this ravine of turbulent water which seemed to be ever hurrying onward without being able to fertilize these rocks, lost in this furnace which greedily drank it up without being penetrated or refreshed by it.

But suddenly there was visible at our right a little wooden cross sunk in a little heap of stones. A man had been killed there, and I said to my companion:

"Tell me about your bandits."

He replied:

"I knew the most celebrated of them, the terrible Saint Lucia. I will tell you his history.

"His father was killed in a quarrel by a young man of the same district, it is said, and Saint Lucia was left alone with his sister. He was a weak and timid youth, small, often ill, without any energy. He did not proclaim the vendetta against the assassin of his father. All his relatives came to see him and implored of him to take vengeance; he remained deaf to their menaces and their supplications.

"Then, following the old Corsican custom, his sister, in her indignation, carried away his black clothes in order that he might not wear mourning for a dead man who had not been avenged. He was insensible to even this outrage, and rather than take down from the rack his father's gun, which was still loaded, he shut himself up, not daring to brave the looks of the young men of the district.

"He seemed to have even forgotten the crime, and he lived with his sister in the obscurity of their dwelling.

"But one day the man who was suspected of having committed the murder was about to get married. Saint Lucia did not appear to be moved by this news; but, no doubt out of sheer bravado, the bridegroom, on his way to the church, passed before the two orphans' house.

"The brother and the sister, at their window, were eating little fried cakes when the young man saw the bridal procession moving past the house. Suddenly he began to tremble, rose up without uttering a word, made the sign of the cross, took the gun which was hanging over the fireplace and went out.

"When he spoke of this later on he said: 'I don't know what was the matter with me; it was like fire in my blood; I felt that I should do it, that in spite of everything I could not resist. I concealed the gun in a cave on the road to Corte.'

"An hour later he came back with nothing in his hand and with his habitual sad air of weariness. His sister believed that there was nothing further in his thoughts.

"But when night fell he disappeared.

"His enemy had, the same evening, to repair to Corte on foot, accompanied by his two bridesmen.

"He was pursuing his way, singing as he went, when Saint Lucia stood before him and, looking straight in the murderer's face, exclaimed: 'Now is the time!' and shot him point-blank in the chest.

"One of the bridesmen fled; the other stared at the young man, saying:

"'What have you done, Saint Lucia?'

"Then he was going to hasten to Corte for help, but Saint Lucia said in a stern tone:

"'If you move another step I'll shoot you through the legs.'

"The other, aware that till now he had always appeared timid, said to him: 'You would not dare to do it!' and he was hurrying off when he fell instantaneously, his thigh shattered by a bullet.

"And Saint Lucia, coming over to where he lay, said:

"'I am going to look at your wound; if it is not serious I'll leave you there; if it is mortal I'll finish you off.'

"He inspected the wound, considered it mortal and, slowly reloading his gun, told the wounded man to say a prayer and shot him through the head.

"Next day he was in the mountains.

"And do you know what this Saint Lucia did after this?

"All his family were arrested by the gendarmes. His uncle, the curé, who was suspected of having incited him to this deed of vengeance, was himself put into prison and accused by the dead man's relatives. But he escaped, took a gun in his turn and went to join his nephew in the cave.

"Next Saint Lucia killed, one after the other, his uncle's accusers and tore out their eyes to teach the others never to state what they had seen with their eyes.

"He killed all the relatives, all the connections of his enemy's family. He massacred during his life fourteen gendarmes, burned down the houses of his adversaries and was up to the day of his death the most terrible of the bandits whose memory we have preserved."

The sun disappeared behind Monte Cinto, and the tall shadow of the granite mountain went to sleep on the granite of the valley. We quickened our pace in order to reach before night the little village of Albertaccio, nothing better than a heap of stones welded beside the stone flanks of a wild gorge. And I said as I thought of the bandit:

"What a terrible custom your vendetta is!"

My companion answered with an air of resignation:

"What would you have? A man must do his duty!"

THE DUEL

In society they called him "the handsome Signoles." He called himself Viscount
Gontram Joseph de Signoles.

An orphan and master of a sufficient fortune, he cut something of a figure, as
the saying is. He had an attractive form, enough readiness of speech to make some
attempt at wit, a certain natural grace of manner, an air of nobility and pride
and a mustache which was both formidable and pleasant to the eye—a thing
that pleases the ladies.

He was in demand in drawing rooms, sought for by waltzers, and he inspired
in men that smiling enmity which one has for people of energetic physique. He
was suspected of some love affairs which showed him capable of much discretion
for a young man. He lived happily, tranquil, in a state of moral well-being most
complete. It was well known that he was good at handling a sword and still better
with a pistol.

"'If I were to fight," he said, "I should choose a pistol. With that weapon I am
sure of killing my man."

Now one evening, having escorted two young women, friends of his, to the
theater, being also accompanied by their husbands, he offered them, after the
play, an ice at Tortoni's. They had been there about ten minutes when he perceived that a gentleman seated at a neighboring table gazed persistently at one
of the ladies of his party. She seemed troubled and disturbed, lowering her eyes.
Finally she said to her husband:

"That man is staring me out of countenance. I do not know him; do you?"

The husband, who had seen nothing, raised his eyes but declared:

"No, not at all."

The young woman replied, half laughing, half angry: "It is very annoying; that
individual is spoiling my ice."

The husband shrugged his shoulders, replying:

"Pshaw! Pay no attention to him. If we were to notice all the insolent people
we meet there would be no end to it."

But the viscount arose brusquely. He could not allow this unknown man to spoil
an ice he had offered. It was to him that the injury was addressed, as it was through
him and for him that his friends had entered this café. The affair then concerned
him only. He advanced toward the man and said to him:

"You have, sir, a manner of looking at these ladies that is not to be tolerated.
I beg to ask you to cease this attention."

The other replied: "So you command me to keep the peace, do you?"

With set teeth the viscount answered: "Take care, sir, or you will force me to
forget myself!"

The gentleman replied with a single word, an obscene word which resounded
from one end of the café to the other, and made each guest start with a sudden
movement, as if they were all on springs. Those that were in front turned around;
all the others raised their heads; three waiters turned about on their heels as if
on pivots; the two ladies at the counter bounded forward then entirely turned

their backs upon the scene, as if they had been two automatons obeying the same manipulation.

There was a great silence. Then suddenly a sharp noise rent the air. The viscount had struck his adversary. Everybody got up to interpose. Cards were exchanged.

After the viscount had returned home he walked up and down his room at a lively pace for some minutes. He was too much agitated to reflect upon anything. One idea only hovered over his mind: a duel, and yet this idea awoke in him as yet no emotion whatever. He had done what he ought to do; he had shown himself what he ought to be. People would talk of it, approve of it and congratulate him. He said aloud in a high voice, as one speaks when he is much troubled in thought:

"What a beast that man is."

Then he sat down and began to reflect. He would have to find some seconds in the morning. Whom should he choose? He thought over the people of his acquaintance who were the most celebrated and in the best positions. He took finally Marquis de la Tour-Noire and Colonel Bourdin, a great lord and a soldier who was very strong. Their names would carry in the journals. He perceived that he was thirsty and he drank, one after the other, three glasses of water; then he began to walk again. He felt himself full of energy. By showing himself hot-brained, resolute in all things, by exacting rigorous, dangerous conditions and by claiming a serious duel, a very serious one, his adversary would doubtless withdraw and make some excuses.

He took up the card which he had drawn from his pocket and thrown upon the table and reread it as he had in the café by a glance of the eye, and again in the cab, on returning home, by the light of a gas jet: "George Lamil, 51 Moncey Street." That was all.

He examined these assembled letters which appeared so mysterious to him, his senses all confused: George Lamil? Who was this man? What had he done? Why had he looked at that woman in such a way? Was it not revolting that a stranger, an unknown, should come to trouble his life thus at a blow, because he had been pleased to fix his insolent gaze upon a woman? And the viscount repeated again in a loud voice:

"What a brute."

Then he remained motionless, standing, thinking, his look ever fixed upon the card. A certain anger against this piece of paper was awakened in him, a hateful anger which was mingled with a strange sentiment of malice. It was stupid, this whole story! He took a penknife which lay open at his hand and pricked the card through the middle of the printed name, as if he were using a poniard upon someone.

So he must fight! Should he choose the sword or pistol? For he considered himself the insulted one. With the sword he risked less, but with the pistol there was a chance of his adversary withdrawing. It is rarely that a duel with the sword is mortal, a reciprocal prudence hindering the combatants from keeping near enough to each other for the point to strike very deep; with the pistol he risked his life very seriously, but he could also meet the affair with all the honors of the situation and without arriving at a meeting. He said aloud:

"It is necessary to be firm. He will be afraid."

The sound of his own voice made him tremble, and he began to look about him. He felt very nervous. He drank still another glass of water, then commenced to undress, preparatory to retiring.

When he was ready he put out his light and closed his eyes. Then he thought:

"I have all day tomorrow to busy myself with my affairs. I must sleep first in order to be calm."

He was very warm under the clothes, but he could not succeed in falling asleep. He turned and turned again, remained for five minutes upon his back, then placed himself upon his left side, then rolled over to the right.

He was still thirsty. He got up and drank. Then a kind of disquiet seized him: "Can it be that I am afraid?" he said.

Why should his heart begin to beat so foolishly at each of the customary noises about his room?—when the clock was going to strike and the spring made that little grinding noise as it raised itself to make the turn? And he found it was necessary for him to open his mouth in order to breathe for some seconds following this start, so great was his feeling of oppression. He began to reason with himself upon the possibilities of the thing:

"What have I to fear?"

No, certainly, he should not fear, since he was resolved to follow it out to the end and since he had fully made up his mind to fight without a qualm. But he felt himself so profoundly troubled that he asked himself:

"Can it be that I am afraid in spite of myself?"

And this doubt invaded him, this disquiet, this fear; if a force more powerful than his will, dominating, irresistible, should conquer him, what would happen to him? Yes, what would happen? Certainly he could walk upon the earth if he wished to go there. But if he should tremble? And if he should lose consciousness? And he thought of his situation, of his reputation, of his name.

And a singular desire took possession of him to get up and look at himself in the glass. He relighted his candle. When he perceived his face reflected in the polished glass he scarcely knew himself, and it seemed to him that he had never seen himself before. His eyes appeared enormous; he was pale, certainly; he was pale, very pale.

He remained standing there before the mirror. He put out his tongue as if to examine the state of his health, and suddenly this thought entered his brain after the fashion of a bullet:

"After tomorrow at this time I shall perhaps be dead."

And his heart began to beat furiously.

"After tomorrow at this time I shall perhaps be dead. This person opposite me, this being I have so often seen in this glass, will be no more. How can it be? I am here; I see myself; I feel that I am alive, and in twenty-four hours, I shall be stretched upon that bed, dead, my eyes closed, cold, inanimate, departed."

He turned around to the bed and distinctly saw himself stretched on his back in the same clothes he had worn on going out. In his face were the lines of death, and a rigidity in the hands that would never stir again.

Then a fear of his bed came over him, and in order to see it no more he passed into his smoking room. Mechanically he took a cigar, lighted it and began to walk about. He was cold. He went toward the bell to waken his valet, but he stopped with his hand on the cord.

"This man would perceive at once that I am afraid."

He did not ring but made a fire. His hands trembled a little from a nervous shiver when they came in contact with any object. His mind wandered; his thoughts from trouble became frightened, hasty and sorrowful; an intoxication seemed to invade his mind as if he were drunk. And without ceasing he asked:

"What am I going to do? What is going to become of me?"

His whole body was vibrating, traversed by a jerking and a trembling; he got up and approached the window, opening the curtains.

The day had dawned, a summer day. A rose-colored sky made the city rosy on roof and wall. A great fall of spread-out light, like a caress from the rising sun, enveloped the waking world, and with this light a gay, rapid, brutal hope invaded the heart of the viscount. He was a fool to allow himself to be thus cast down by fear even before anything was decided, before his witnesses had seen those of this George Lamil, before he yet knew whether he was going to fight a duel.

He made his toilet, dressed himself and walked out with firm step.

He repeated constantly in walking:

"It will be necessary for me to be energetic, very energetic. I must prove that I am not afraid."

His witnesses, the marquis and the colonel, placed themselves at his disposal and, after having shaken hands with him energetically, discussed the conditions. The colonel asked:

"Do you wish it to be a serious duel?"

The viscount responded: "Very serious."

The marquis continued: "Will you use a pistol?"

"Yes."

"We leave you free to regulate the rest."

The viscount enunciated in a dry, jerky voice:

"Twenty steps at the order and on raising the arm instead of lowering it. Exchange of bullets until one is grievously wounded."

The colonel declared in a satisfied tone:

"These are excellent conditions. You shoot well; all the chances are in your favor."

They separated. The viscount returned home to wait for them. His agitation, appeased for a moment, grew now from minute to minute. He felt along his arms, his legs and in his breast a kind of trembling, of continued vibration; he could not keep still, either sitting or standing. There was no longer an appearance of saliva in his mouth, and each instant he made a noisy movement with his tongue, as if to unglue it from the roof of his mouth.

He wished to breakfast but he could not eat. Then the idea came to him of drinking to give himself courage, and he brought out a small bottle of rum, which he swallowed in six glasses, one after the other.

A heat, like that of a burning fire, invaded him, followed almost immediately by a numbness of the soul. He thought:

"I have found the remedy. Now all goes well."

But at the end of an hour he had emptied the bottle and his state of agitation became intolerable. He felt a foolish impulse to roll on the ground, to cry out and bite. Then night fell.

A stroke of the bell gave him such a shock that he had not sufficient strength left to rise and receive his witnesses. He dared not even speak to them to say,

"Good evening," to pronounce a single word, for fear that they would discover a change in his voice.

The colonel announced:

"All is arranged according to the conditions that you have fixed upon. Your adversary claimed the privileges of the offended, but he soon yielded and accepted all. His witnesses are two military men."

The viscount pronounced the word:

"Thanks."

The marquis continued:

"Excuse us if we only come in and go out, for we have still a thousand things to occupy our attention. A good doctor will be necessary, since the combat is only to cease after a severe wound, and you know that bullets are no trifles. Then a place must be found in some proximity to a house, where we may carry the wounded if necessary, etc., etc.; finally we have but two or three hours for it."

The viscount, for the second time, articulated:

"Thanks."

The colonel asked:

"How is it with you? Are you calm?"

"Yes, very calm, thank you."

The two men then retired.

When he again found himself alone it seemed to him that he was mad. His domestic having lighted the lamps, he seated himself before his table to write some letters. After having traced at the top of a page: "This is my testament," he arose with a shake and put it away from him, feeling himself incapable of forming two ideas or of sufficient resolution to decide what was to be done.

So he was going to fight a duel! There was no way to avoid it. How could he ever go through it? He wished to fight; it was his intention and firm resolution so to do, and yet he felt that in spite of all his effort of mind and all the tension of his will he would not be able to preserve even the necessary force to go to the place of meeting. He tried to imagine the combat, his own attitude and the position of his adversary.

From time to time his teeth chattered in his mouth with a little hard noise. He tried to read and took down the Châteauvillard code of dueling. Then he asked himself:

"Has my opponent frequently fought? Is he known? Is he classed? How am I to know?"

He remembered Baron de Vaux's book of experts with the pistol, and he ran through it from one end to the other. George Lamil was not mentioned. Nevertheless, if this man were not an expert he would not so readily have accepted this dangerous weapon and these mortal conditions.

He opened, in passing, a box of Gastinne Renettes which stood on a little stand, took out one of the pistols, held it in a position to fire and raised his arm. But he trembled from head to foot, and the gun worked upon all his senses.

Then he said: "It is impossible. I cannot fight in this condition."

He looked at the end of the barrel, at that little black deep hole that spits out death; he thought of the dishonor, of the whisperings in his circle, of the laughs in the drawing rooms, of the scorn of the ladies, of the allusions of the journals, of all the insults that cowards would throw at him.

He continued to examine the weapon and, raising the cock, he suddenly saw a priming glittering underneath like a little red flame. The pistol was loaded then, through a chance forgetfulness. And he found in this discovery a confused, inexplicable joy.

If in the presence of the other man he did not have that calm, noble bearing that he should have, he would be lost forever. He would be spotted, branded, with the sign of infamy, hunted from the world! And this calm, heroic bearing he would not have; he knew it; he felt it. However, he was brave, since he did wish to fight! He was brave, since . . . The thought that budded never took form, even in his own mind, for, opening his mouth wide, he brusquely thrust the barrel of his pistol into his throat and pulled the trigger. . . .

When his valet, hearing the report, hastened to him, he found him dead upon his back. A jet of blood had splashed upon the white paper on the table and made a great red spot upon these four words:

"This is my testament."

MOTHER SAVAGE

I had not returned to Virelogne for fifteen years. I went back there to hunt in the autumn, staying with my friend Serval, who had finally rebuilt his château, which had been destroyed by the Prussians.

I was infinitely fond of that country. There are delicious corners in this world which have a sensual charm for the eyes. One loves them with a physical love. We folk whom nature attracts, keep certain tender recollections, often keen, for certain springs, certain woods, certain ponds, certain hills, which have touched us like happy events. Sometimes even memory returns toward a forest nook, or a bit of a river bank, or a blossoming orchard, seen only once, on some happy day, which has remained in our heart like those pictures of women seen in the street, on a spring morning, with a white, transparent costume, and which leave in our soul and flesh an unappeased, unforgettable desire, the sensation of having just missed happiness.

At Virelogne, I loved the whole region, sowed with little woods and traversed by brooks which ran through the soil like veins bringing blood to the earth.

We fished in them for crayfish, trout, and eels! Divine happiness! We could bathe in certain places and often found woodcock in the tall grass which grew on the banks of those little narrow streams.

I went, light as a goat, watching my two dogs forage in front of me. Serval, a hundreds yards away, on my right, was beating up a field of lucerne. I went around the thickets which formed the boundaries of the Sandres forest, and I perceived a hut in ruins.

Suddenly I recollected that I had seen it for the last time in 1869, neat, vine-clad, with chickens before the door. What is sadder than a dead house with its skeleton standing, dilapidated and sinister?

I recalled also that a woman had given me a glass of wine there, on a day when I was very tired, and that Serval had then told me the story of the inhabitants. The father, an old poacher, had been killed by the gendarmes. The son, whom I had seen before, was a tall, wizened lad who was likewise considered a ferocious killer of game. People called them the Savage family.

Was it a name or a nickname? I hailed Serval. He came with his long stride, as if he were walking on stilts.

I asked him: "What has become of those people?" And he told me this adventure.

II

"When war was declared, the younger Savage, who was then about thirty-three years old, enlisted, leaving his mother alone in the house. People did not pity the old woman very much, because they knew that she had money.

"So she stayed all alone in this isolated house, so far from the village, on the edge of the woods. She was not afraid, however, being of the same race as her men, a strong, tall, thin, old woman, who seldom laughed, and with whom no one joked. The women of the fields do not laugh much, anyway. That is the men's business! They have a sad and narrow soul, leading a life which is gloomy and without bright spots.

"The peasant learns a little of the noisy gaiety of the pothouse, but his wife remains serious, with a constantly severe expression of countenance. The muscles of her face never learn the motions of laughter.

"Mother Savage continued her usual existence in her hut, which was soon covered with snow. She came to the village once a week to get bread and a little meat: then she returned to her cottage. As people spoke of wolves, she carried a gun on her shoulder, her son's gun, rusty, with the stock worn by the rubbing of the hand. She was a curious sight, this tall Savage woman, a little bent, walking with slow strides through the snow, the barrel of the weapon extending beyond the black headdress, which imprisoned the white hair that no one had ever seen.

"One day the Prussians arrived. They were distributed among the inhabitants according to the means and resources of each. The old woman, who was known to be rich, had four soldiers billeted upon her.

"They were four big young men with fair flesh, fair beard, and blue eyes, who had remained stout in spite of the fatigues they had endured, and good fellows even if they were in a conquered territory. Alone with this old woman, they showed themselves full of consideration for her, sparing her fatigue and expense as far as they could do so. All four might have been seen making their toilette at the well in the morning, in their shirt sleeves, splashing their pink-and-white flesh, the flesh of the men of the North, in the water, on cold snowy days, while Mother Savage came and went preparing their soup. Then they might have been observed cleaning the kitchen, polishing the floor, chopping wood, peeling potatoes, washing the clothes, doing all the household duties, like four good sons around their mother.

"But she thought continually of her own son, the old mother, of her tall, thin boy with his crooked nose, brown eyes, and stiff mustache which made a cushion of black hair on his upper lip. She asked each of the soldiers installed at her hearth:

"'Do you know where the French regiment has gone, the Twenty-third Infantry? My boy is in it.'

"They answered: 'No, we don't know anything at all about it.'

"And understanding her grief and worry they, who had mothers at home, rendered her a thousand little services.

"She liked them very well, moreover, her four enemies: for peasants seldom have patriotic hatreds: that is the business of the superior classes. The humble, those who pay the most because they are poor, and because every new burden rests upon them, those who are killed in masses, who form the true cannon fodder because they are numerous, those who, in a word, suffer most cruelly the atrocious miseries of the poor, because they are the weakest and the most unresisting, understand little of those bellicose ardors, the excitable points of honor and those pretended political combinations which exhaust two nations in six months, the victorious as well as the vanquished.

"They said in the country, speaking of Mother Savage's Germans: 'There are four who have found a snug berth.'

"Now, one morning, as the old woman was alone in the house, she perceived afar off on the plain a man coming toward her home. Soon she recognized him: it was the postman, charged with distributing letters. He handed her a folded paper, and she drew from their case her spectacles which she used for sewing, and read:

" 'Madame Savage, this is to give you sad news. Your son Victor was killed by a cannon ball yesterday, which virtually cut him in two. I was very near, as we were side by side in the company and he had asked me to tell you the same day if anything happened to him.

" 'I took his watch from his pocket to bring it to you when the war is finished.

" 'I remain your friend,

" 'CÉSAIRE RIVOT.

" 'Soldier of the 2d class, in the 23d Infantry.'

"The letter was dated three weeks back.

"She did not weep. She stood motionless, so astounded that she did not yet suffer.

"She thought: 'Victor is killed!'

"Then little by little the tears came to her eyes and grief overwhelmed her heart. Ideas came to her one by one, frightful, torturing ideas. She would never kiss him again, her big boy, never again. The gendarmes had killed the father, the Prussians had killed the son. He had been cut in two by a cannon ball. And it seemed to her that she saw the thing, the horrible thing: the head falling, the eyes open, while he gnawed the end of his big mustache, as he did in moments of anger.

"What had they done with his body afterwards? If they had only sent her boy back to her, as they had her husband, with a bullet in his forehead.

"But she heard a sound of voices. It was the Prussians, who were returning from the village. She quickly hid the letter in her pocket, and received them tranquilly, with her ordinary expression on her face, having had time to wipe her eyes.

"They were all four laughing, delighted, for they were bringing back a fine rabbit, stolen no doubt, and they made a sign to the old woman that they were going to have something good to eat.

"She applied herself at once to the duties of preparing the breakfast, but when it came to killing the rabbit, her heart failed her. And yet it was not the first. One of the soldiers killed it with a blow behind the ears.

"Once the animal was dead, she took the red body out of the skin; but the sight of the blood which she touched, which covered her hands, of the warm blood which she felt getting cold and coagulating, made her tremble from head to foot; and she kept seeing her tall boy cut in two and all bleeding, like this still palpitating animal.

"She sat at the table with her Prussians, but she could not eat, not even a mouthful. They devoured the rabbit without troubling about her. She looked at them aside without speaking, nursing an idea, with her countenance so impassive that they perceived nothing.

"Suddenly she said: 'I don't even know your names, and it is a month since we have been together.' They understood, not without difficulty, what she wished and gave her their names. That was not enough, she made them write them for her on a piece of paper, with the address of their families, and resting her spectacles on her large nose she scanned this unknown handwriting, then she folded the sheet and put it in her pocket, with the letter which told of the death of her son.

"When the meal was finished, she said to the men:

"'I am going to work for you.'

"And she began to carry straw to the garret in which they slept.

"They were astonished at this act. She explained to them that they would be less cold; and they assisted her. They piled the bundles of straw up to the roof, and thus they made for themselves a sort of big room with four walls of forage, warm and sweet-smelling, where they would sleep wonderfully.

"At dinner one of them was disturbed to see that Mother Savage did not eat anything. She asserted that she had cramps. Then she lighted a good fire to warm herself, and the four Germans climbed to their lodging by the ladder which they used every evening.

"As soon as the trap door was closed, the old woman took away the ladder, then she noiselessly opened the outside door and returned to get more bundles of straw, with which she filled the kitchen. She went out barefooted in the snow, so softly that the men heard nothing. From time to time she listened to the deep and uneven snores of the four sleeping soldiers. When she thought her preparations were sufficient, she threw into the fire one of the bundles of straw, and when it had ignited she piled it on the others, and then went out again and looked.

"A brilliant light illuminated in a few seconds all the interior of the cottage; then it became a frightful brazier, a gigantic, glowing furnace, whose gleams shone through the narrow window and cast a dazzling light upon the snow.

"Then a great cry came from the top of the house; there was a clamor of human shrieks, of heart-rending appeals of anguish and terror. Then, the trap door having sunk down into the interior, a whirlwind of fire leaped through the attic, pierced the thatched roof, and ascended to the sky like the flame of a great torch; and the whole cottage was burning.

"Nothing more was heard inside but the crackling of the flames, the crumbling of the walls, and the crashing of the beams. The roof suddenly fell in, and the glowing remnant of the house shot up into the air, amid a cloud of smoke, a great fountain of sparks.

"The white field, lighted up by the fire, glistened like a cloth of silver tinted with red.

"A bell in the distance began to ring. The old Savage woman stood erect before her ruined home, armed with a gun, her son's, for fear one of the men should escape.

"When she saw that her work was finished, she threw the weapon in the fire. A report rang out.

"The people arrived, peasants and Prussians.

"They found the woman sitting on the trunk of a tree, tranquil and satisfied.

"A German officer who could speak French like a Frenchman asked her:

" 'Where are the soldiers?'

"She stretched her thin arm toward the red mass of flames, which were now dying down, and answered in a strong voice:

" 'They are in there!'

"All pressed around her. The Prussian asked:

" 'How did the fire start?'

"She replied:

" 'I set the house on fire.'

"They did not believe her, thinking that the sudden disaster had made her mad. Then, as everybody gathered around and listened, she related the whole thing from beginning to end, the arrival of the letter to the last cry of the men, burning up with the house. She did not forget a single detail of what she had felt nor what she had done.

"When she had finished she drew two papers from her pocket, and, to distinguish them in the last gleams of the fire, she again put on her spectacles. Then she said, showing one of them: 'This is the death of Victor.' Showing the other, she added, nodding her head toward the red ruins: 'And this is the list of their names, so that some one may write the news home about them.'

"She quietly handed the white sheet to the officer, who took her by the shoulders, and she resumed:

" 'You will write how it happened, and you will tell their relatives that it was I who did it, Victoire Simon, the Savage; don't forget.'

"The officer shouted some orders in German, to the soldiers; they seized her and threw her against the still heated walls of the house. Then a squad of twelve men drew up in a rank opposite her, at a distance of twenty yards. She did not stir. She had understood. She waited.

"An order resounded, which was followed by a long report of muskets. One delayed shot went off all alone, after the others.

"The old woman did not fall. She sank down as if some one had mowed off her legs.

"The Prussian officer aproached. She was cut almost in two, and in her shriveled hand she held her letter, bathed in blood."

My friend Serval added:

"It was by way of reprisal that the Germans destroyed the château of the district, which belonged to me."

I thought of the mothers of the poor gentle young fellows burned there: and of the atrocious heroism of that other mother, shot against the wall.

And I picked up a little pebble, still blackened by the fire.

THE LOVE OF LONG AGO

The old-fashioned château was built on a wooded height. Tall trees surrounded it with dark greenery, and the vast park extended its vistas here over a deep forest and there over an open plain. Some little distance from the front of the mansion stood a huge stone basin in which marble nymphs were bathing. Other basins arranged in order succeeded each other down as far as the foot of the slope, and a hidden fountain sent cascades dancing from one to the other.

From the manor house, which preserved the grace of a superannuated coquette, down to the grottos incrusted with shellwork, where slumbered the loves of a bygone age, everything in this antique demesne had retained the physiognomy of former days. Everything seemed to speak still of ancient customs, of the manners of long ago, of faded gallantries and of the elegant trivialities so dear to our grand-mothers.

In a parlor in the style of Louis XV, the walls of which were covered with shepherds courting shepherdesses, beautiful ladies in hoop petticoats and gallant gentlemen in wigs, a very old woman, who seemed dead as soon as she ceased to move, was almost lying down in a large easy chair while her thin, mummylike hands hung down, one at each side of her.

Her eyes were gazing languidly toward the distant horizon, as if they sought to follow the park visions of her youth. Through the open window every now and then came a breath of air laden with the scent of grass and the perfume of flowers. It made her white locks flutter around her wrinkled forehead and old memories sweep through her brain.

Beside her on a tapestried stool a young girl, with long, fair hair hanging in plaits over her neck, was embroidering an altar cloth. There was a pensive expression in her eyes, and it was easy to see that while her agile fingers worked her brain was busy with thoughts.

But the old lady suddenly turned her head.

"Berthe," she said, "read something out of the newspapers for me so that I may still know sometimes what is happening in the world."

The young girl took up the newspaper and cast a rapid glance over it.

"There is a great deal about politics, Grandmamma; am I to pass it by?"

"Yes, yes, darling. Are there no accounts of love affairs? Is gallantry then dead in France that they no longer talk about abductions or adventures as they did formerly?"

The girl made a long search through the columns of the newspaper.

"Here is one," she said. "It is entitled, 'A Love Drama.'"

The old woman smiled through her wrinkles. "Read that for me," she said.

And Berthe commenced. It was a case of vitriol throwing. A wife, in order to avenge herself on her husband's mistress, had burned her face and eyes. She had left the Assize Court acquitted, declared to be innocent, amid the applause of the crowd.

The grandmother moved about excitedly in her chair and exclaimed:

"This is horrible—why, it is perfectly horrible! See whether you can find anything else to read for me, darling."

Berthe again made a search, and further down in the reports of criminal cases at which her attention was still directed she read:

"*Gloomy Drama.*—*A shopgirl, no longer young, allowed herself to yield to the embraces of a young man. Then to avenge herself on her lover, whose heart proved fickle, she shot him with a revolver. The unhappy man is maimed for life. The jury consisted of men of moral character and took the part of the murderess—regarding her as the victim of illicit love. They honorably acquitted her.*"

This time the old grandmother appeared quite shocked and in a trembling voice said:

"Why, you are mad then nowadays. You are mad! The good God has given you love, the only allurement in life. Man has added to this gallantry, the only distraction of our dull hours, and here you are mixing up with vitriol and revolvers, as if one were to put mud into a flagon of Spanish wine."

Berthe did not seem to understand her grandmother's indignation.

"But, Grandmamma, this woman avenged herself. Remember, she was married, and her husband deceived her."

The grandmother gave a start.

"What ideas have they been putting into the heads of you young girls of today?"

Berthe replied:

"But marriage is sacred, Grandmamma."

The grandmother's heart, which had its birth in the great age of gallantry, gave a sudden leap.

"It is love that is sacred," she said. "Listen, child, to an old woman who has seen three generations and who has had a long, long experience of men and women. Marriage and love have nothing in common. We marry to found a family, and we cannot dispense with marriage. If society is a chain, each family is a link in that chain. In order to weld those links we always seek for metals of the same kind. When we marry we must bring together suitable conditions; we must combine fortunes, unite similar races and aim at the common interests, which are riches and children. We marry only once, my child, because the world requires us to do so, but we may love twenty times in one lifetime because nature has made us able to do this. Marriage, you see, is law, and love is an instinct which impels us sometimes along a straight and sometimes along a crooked path. The world has made laws to combat our instincts—it was necessary to make them—but our instincts are always stronger, and we ought not to resist them too much because they come from God, while the laws only come from men. If we did not perfume life with love, as much love as possible, darling, as we put sugar into drugs for children, nobody would care to take it just as it is."

Berthe opened her eyes widely in astonishment. She murmured:

"Oh, Grandmamma, we can only love once."

The grandmother raised her trembling hands toward heaven, as if again to invoke the defunct god of gallantries. She exclaimed indignantly:

"You have become a race of serfs, a race of common people. Since the revolution it is impossible any longer to recognize society. You have attached big words to every action and wearisome duties to every corner of existence; you believe in equality and eternal passion. People have written verses telling you that people have died of love. In my time verses were written to teach men to love every woman. And we!—when we liked a gentleman, my child, we sent him a page. And when a fresh caprice came into our hearts we were not slow in getting rid of the last lover—unless we kept both of them."

The old woman smiled with a keen smile, and a gleam of roguery twinkled in her gray eye, the sprightly, skeptical roguery of those people who did not believe that they were made of the same clay as the others and who lived as rulers for whom common restrictions were not made.

The young girl, turning very pale, faltered out:

"So then women have no honor."

The grandmother ceased to smile. If she had kept in her soul some of Voltaire's irony she had also a little of Rousseau's glowing philosophy. "No honor because we loved and dared to say so and even boasted of it? But, my child, if one of us among the greatest ladies in France were to live without a lover, she would have the entire court laughing at her. Those who wished to live differently had only to enter a convent. And you imagine perhaps that your husbands will love you alone all their lives. As if, indeed, this could be the case. I tell you that marriage is a thing necessary in order that society should exist, but it is not in the nature of our race, do you understand? There is only one good thing in life, and that is love. And how you misunderstand it! How you spoil it! You treat it as something solemn, like a sacrament, or something to be bought, like a dress."

The young girl caught the old woman's trembling hands in her own.

"Hold your tongue, I beg of you, Grandmamma!"

And on her knees, with tears in her eyes, she prayed to heaven to bestow on her a great passion, one eternal passion alone, in accordance with the dream of modern poets, while her grandmother, kissing her on the forehead, still penetrated by that charming, healthy logic by which philosophers of gallantry sprinkled salt upon the life of the eighteenth century, murmured:

"Take care, my poor darling! If you believe in such follies as this you will be very unhappy."

THE FARMER'S WIFE

One day Baron René du Treilles said to me:

"Will you come and open the hunting season with me in my farmhouse at Marinville? By doing so, my dear fellow, you will give me the greatest pleasure. Besides, I am all alone. This will be a hard hunting bout, to start with, and the house where I sleep is so primitive that I can only bring my most intimate friends there."

I accepted his invitation. So on Saturday we started by the railway line running into Normandy and alighted at the station of Alvimare. Baron René, pointing out to me a country jaunting car drawn by a restive horse, driven by a big peasant with white hair, said to me:

"Here is our equipage, my dear boy."

The man extended his hand to his landlord, and the baron pressed it warmly, asking:

"Well, Maître Lebrument, how are you?"

"Always the same, M'sieu l' Baron."

We jumped into this hen coop suspended and shaken on two immense wheels. The young horse, after a violent swerve, started into a gallop, flinging us into the air like balls. Every fall backward onto the wooden bench gave me the most dreadful pain.

The peasant kept repeating in his calm, monotonous voice:

"There, there! It's all right, all right, Moutard, all right!"

But Moutard scarcely heard and kept scampering along like a goat.

Our two dogs behind us, in the empty part of the hen coop, stood erect and sniffed the air of the plains as if they could smell the game.

The baron gazed into the distance with a sad eye. The vast Norman landscape, undulating and melancholy as an immense English park, with farmyards surrounded by two or four rows of trees and full of dwarfed apple trees which rendered the houses invisible, gave a vista, as far as the eye could see, of old forest trees, tufts of wood and hedgerows, which artistic gardeners provide for when they are tracing the lines of princely estates.

And René de Treilles suddenly exclaimed:

"I love this soil; I have my very roots in it."

A pure Norman, tall and strong, with the more or less projecting paunch of the old race of adventurers who went to found kingdoms on the shores of every ocean, he was about fifty years of age, ten years less perhaps than the farmer who was driving us. The latter was a lean peasant, all skin and bone, one of those men who live a hundred years.

After two hours' traveling over stony roads, across that green and monotonous plain, the vehicle entered one of those fruit gardens which adorn the fronts of farmhouses and drew up before an old structure falling into decay, where an old maidservant stood waiting at the side of a young fellow who seized the horse's bridle.

We entered the farmhouse. The smoky kitchen was high and spacious. The copper utensils and the earthenware glistened under the reflection of the big fire. A cat lay asleep under the table. Within you inhaled the odor of milk, of apples, of smoke, that indescribable smell peculiar to old houses where peasants have lived—the odor of the soil, of the walls, of furniture, of stale soup, of washing and of the old inhabitants, the smell of animals and human beings intermingled, of things and of persons, the odor of time and of things that have passed away.

I went out to have a look at the farmyard. It was big, full of old apple trees, dwarfed and crooked, and laden with fruit which fell on the grass around them. In this farmyard the smell of apples was as strong as that of the orange trees which blossom on the banks of southern rivers.

Four rows of beeches surrounded this inclosure. They were so tall that they seemed to touch the clouds at this hour of nightfall, and their summits, through which the night winds passed, shook and sang a sad, interminable song.

I re-entered the house. The baron was warming his feet at the fire and was listening to the farmer's talk about country matters. He talked about marriages, births and deaths, then about the fall in the price of corn and the latest news about the selling value of cattle. The "Veularde" (as he called a cow that had been bought at the fair of Veules) had calved in the middle of June. The cider

had not been first class last year. The apricot apples were almost disappearing
from the country.

Then we had dinner. It was a good rustic meal, simple and abundant, long and
tranquil. And while we were dining I noticed the special kind of friendly familiarity
between the baron and the peasant which had struck me from the start.

Without, the beeches continued sobbing in the night wind, and our two dogs
shut up in a shed were whining and howling in uncanny fashion. The fire was
dying out in the big grate. The maidservant had gone to bed. Maître Lebrument
said in his turn:

"If you don't mind, M'sieu l' Baron, I'm going to bed. I am not used to staying
up late."

The baron extended his hand toward him and said: "Go, my friend," in so
cordial a tone that I said as soon as the man had disappeared:

"He is devoted to you, this farmer?"

"Better than that, my dear fellow! It is a drama, an old drama, simple and very
sad, that attaches him to me. Here is the story:

"You know my father was a colonel in a cavalry regiment. His orderly was this
young fellow, now an old man, the son of a farmer. Then when my father retired
from the army he took this retired soldier, then about forty, as his servant. I was
at that time about thirty. We lived then in our old château of Valrenne near
Caudebec-in-Caux.

"At this period my mother's chambermaid was one of the prettiest girls you
could see, fair-haired, slender and sprightly in manner, a genuine specimen of the
fascinating Abigail, such as we scarcely ever find nowadays. Today these creatures
spring up into hussies before their time. Paris, with the aid of the railways, attracts
them, calls them, takes hold of them as soon as they are bursting into womanhood
—these little wenches who, in old times, remained simple maidservants. Every
man passing by, as long ago recruiting sergeants did with conscripts, entices and
debauches them—foolish lassies—till now we have only the scum of the female
sex for servant maids, all that is dull, nasty, common and ill formed, too ugly even
for gallantry.

"Well, this girl was charming, and I often gave her a kiss in dark corners—
nothing more, I swear to you! She was virtuous, besides, and I had some respect
for my mother's house, which is more than can be said of the blackguards of the
present day.

"Now it happened that my father's manservant, the ex-soldier, the old farmer
you have just seen, fell in love with this girl but in an unusual sort of way. The
first thing we noticed was that his memory was affected; he did not pay attention
to anything.

"My father was incessantly saying: 'Look here, Jean! What's the matter with
you? Are you well?'

" 'No, no, M'sieu l' Baron. There's nothing the matter with me.'

"Jean got thin. Then when serving at table he broke glasses and let plates fall.
We thought he must have been attacked by some nervous malady, and we sent
for the doctor, who thought he could detect symptoms of spinal disease. Then
my father, full of anxiety about his faithful manservant, decided to place him in a
private hospital. When the poor fellow heard of my father's intentions he made
a clean breast of it.

" 'M'sieu l' Baron——'

" 'Well, my boy?'

" 'You see, the thing I want is not physic.'

" 'Ha! What is it then?'

" 'It's marriage!'

"My father turned round and stared at him in astonishment.

" 'What's that you say—eh?'

" 'It's marriage.'

" 'Marriage? So then, you donkey, you're in love.'

" 'That's how it is, M'sieu l' Baron.'

"And my father began to laugh in such an immoderate fashion that my mother called through the wall of the next room:

" 'What in the name of goodness is the matter with you, Gontran?'

"My father replied:

" 'Come here, Catherine.'

"And when she came in he told, with tears in his eyes from sheer laughter, that his idiot of a servant man was lovesick.

"But my mother, instead of laughing, was deeply affected.

" 'Who is it that you have fallen in love with, my poor fellow?' she asked.

"He answered without hesitation:

" 'With Louise, Madame la Baronne.'

"My mother said with the utmost gravity: 'We must try to arrange the matter the best way we can.'

"So Louise was sent for and questioned by my mother. She said in reply that she knew all about Jean's liking her, that in fact Jean had spoken to her about it several times but that she did not want him. She refused to say why.

"And two months elapsed during which my father and mother never ceased to urge this girl to marry Jean. As she declared she was not in love with any other man, she could not give any serious reason for her refusal. My father at last overcame her resistance by means of a big present of money and started the pair of them on a farm on the estate—this very farm. At the end of three years I learned that Louise had died of consumption. But my father and my mother died, too, in their turn, and it was two years more before I found myself face to face with Jean.

"At last one autumn day, about the end of October, the idea came into my head to go hunting on this part of my estate, which my tenant had told me was full of game.

"So one evening, one wet evening, I arrived at this house. I was shocked to find the old soldier who had been my father's servant perfectly white-haired, though he was not more than forty-five or forty-six years of age. I made him dine with me at the very table where we're now sitting. It was raining hard. We could hear the rain battering at the roof, the walls and the windows, flowing in a perfect deluge into the farmyard, and my dog was howling in the shed where the other dogs are howling tonight.

"All of a sudden, when the servant maid had gone to bed, the man said in a timid voice:

" 'M'sieu l' Baron.'

" 'What is it, my dear Jean?'

" 'I have something to tell you.'

" 'Tell it, my dear Jean.'

" 'You remember Louise, my wife?'

" 'Certainly I do remember her.'

" 'Well, she left me a message for you.'

" 'What was it?'

" 'A—a—well, it was what you might call a confession.'

" 'Ha! And what was it about?'

" 'It was—it was—I'd rather, all the same, tell you nothing about it, but I must —I must. Well, it's this—it wasn't consumption she died of at all. It was grief— well, that's the long and the short of it. As soon as she came to live here, after we were married, she grew thin; she changed so that you wouldn't know her at the end of six months—no, you wouldn't know her, M'sieu l' Baron. It was all just as before I married her, but it was different, too, quite another sort of thing.

" 'I sent for the doctor. He said it was her liver that was affected—he said it was what he called a "hepatic" complaint—I don't know these big words, M'sieu l' Baron. Then I bought medicine for her, heaps on heaps of bottles that cost about three hundred francs. But she'd take none of them; she wouldn't have them; she said: "It's no use, my poor Jean; it wouldn't do me any good." I saw well that she had some hidden trouble, and then I found her one time crying and I didn't know what to do—no, I didn't know what to do. I bought caps and dresses and hair oil and earrings for her. No good! And I saw that she was going to die. And so one night in the end of November, one snowy night, after remaining the whole day without stirring out of the bed, she told me to send for the curé. So I went for him. As soon as he had come she saw him. Then she asked him to let me come into the room and she said to me: "Jean, I'm going to make a confession to you. I owe it to you, Jean. I have never been false to you, never!— never, before or after you married me. M'sieu le Curé is there and can tell it is so, and he knows my soul. Well, listen, Jean. If I am dying it is because I was not able to console myself for leaving the château—because—I was too—too fond of the young baron, Monsieur René—too fond of him, mind you, Jean; there was no harm in it! This is the thing that's killing me. When I could see him no more I felt that I should die. If I could only have seen him I might have lived, only seen him, nothing more. I wish you'd tell it to him someday by and by, when I am no longer here. You will tell him—swear you will, Jean—swear it in the presence of M'sieu le Curé! It will console me to know that he will know it one day—that this was the cause of my death! Swear it!"

" 'Well, I gave her my promise, M'sieu l' Baron, and on the faith of an honest man I have kept my word.'

"And then he ceased speaking, his eyes filling with tears.

"Upon my soul, my dear boy, you can't form any idea of the emotion that filled me when I heard this poor devil, whose wife I had caused the death of without knowing it, telling me this story on that wet night in this very kitchen.

"I exclaimed: 'Ah, my poor Jean! My poor Jean!'

"He murmured: 'Well, that's all, M'sieu l' Baron. I could do nothing one way or another—and now it's all over!'

"I caught his hand across the table, and I began to cry.

"He asked: 'Will you come and see her grave?' I nodded by way of assent, for I couldn't speak. He rose up, lighted a lantern, and we walked through the blinding rain which, in the light of the lamp, looked like falling arrows.

"He opened a gate, and I saw some crosses of blackwood.

"Suddenly he said: 'There it is, in front of a marble slab,' and he flashed the lantern close to it so that I could read the inscription:

"To Louise-Hortense Marinet,
Wife of Jean-François Lebrument, farmer.
She was a faithful wife! God rest her soul!

"We fell on our knees in the damp grass, he and I, with the lantern between us, and I saw the rain beating on the white marble slab. And I thought of the heart of her sleeping there in her grave. Ah, poor heart! Poor heart!

"Since then I have been coming here every year. And I don't know why, but I feel as if I were guilty of some crime in the presence of this man who always shows that he forgives me!"

BESIDE A DEAD MAN

He was slowly dying, as consumptives die. I saw him sitting down every day at two o'clock under the windows of the hotel, facing the tranquil sea, on an open-air bench. He remained for some time without moving in the heat of the sun, gazing mournfully at the Mediterranean. Every now and then he cast a glance at the lofty mountain with vaporous summits which shuts in Mentone; then with a very slow movement he crossed his long legs, so thin that they seemed two bones, around which fluttered the cloth of his trousers, and opened a book, which was always the same. And then he did not stir any more but read on, read on with his eye and with his mind; all his poor expiring body seemed to read; all his soul plunged, lost itself, disappeared, in this book up to the hour when the cool air made him cough a little. Then he got up and re-entered the hotel.

He was a tall German with a fair beard, who breakfasted and dined in his own room and spoke to nobody.

A vague curiosity attracted me to him. One day I sat down by his side, having taken up a book, too, to keep up appearances, a volume of Musset's poems.

And I began to run through *Rolla*.

Suddenly my neighbor said to me in good French:

"Do you know German, monsieur?"

"Not at all, monsieur."

"I am sorry for that. Since chance has thrown us side by side, I could have lent you, I could have shown you, an inestimable thing—this book which I hold in my hand."

"What is it, pray?"

"It is a copy of my master, Schopenhauer, annotated with his own hand. All the margins, as you may see, are covered with his handwriting."

I took the book from him reverently, and I gazed at those forms incomprehensible to me, but which revealed the immortal thoughts of the greatest shatterer of dreams who had ever dwelt on earth.

And Musset's verses arose in my memory:

Hast thou found out, Voltaire, that it is bliss to die,
Or does thy hideous smile over thy bleached bones fly?

And involuntarily I compared the childish sarcasm, the religious sarcasm, of Voltaire with the irresistible irony of the German philosopher whose influence is henceforth ineffaceable.

Let us protest and let us be angry; let us be indignant or let us be enthusiastic. Schopenhauer has marked humanity with the seal of his disdain and of his disenchantment. A disabused pleasure seeker, he overthrew beliefs, hopes, poetic ideals and chimeras, destroyed the aspirations, ravaged the confidence of souls, killed love, dragged down the chivalrous worship of women, crushed the illusions of hearts and accomplished the most gigantic task ever attempted by skepticism. He passed over everything with his mocking spirit and left everything empty. And even today those who execrate him seem to carry portions of his thought, in spite of themselves, in their own souls.

"So then you were intimately acquainted with Schopenhauer?" I said to the German.

He smiled sadly.

"Up to the time of his death, monsieur."

And he spoke to me about the philosopher and told me about the almost supernatural impression which this strange being made on all who came near him.

He gave me an account of the interview of the old iconoclast with a French politician, a doctrinaire Republican, who wanted to get a glimpse of this man and found him in a noisy tavern, seated in the midst of his disciples, dry, wrinkled, laughing with an unforgettable laugh, eating and tearing ideas and beliefs with a single word, as a dog tears with one bite of his teeth the tissues with which he plays.

He repeated for me the comment of this Frenchman as he went away, scared and terrified: "I thought that I had spent an hour with the devil."

Then he added:

"He had, indeed, monsieur, a frightful smile, which terrified us even after his death. I can tell you an anecdote about it not generally known, if it has any interest for you."

And he began in a tired voice, interrupted by frequent fits of coughing:

"Schopenhauer had just died, and it was arranged that we should watch in turn, two by two, till morning.

"He was lying in a large apartment, very simple, vast and gloomy. Two wax candles were burning on the bedside stand.

"It was midnight when I took up my task of watching along with one of our comrades. The two friends whom we replaced had left the apartment, and we came and sat down at the foot of the bed.

"The face was not changed. It was laughing. That pucker which we knew so well lingered still around the corners of the lips, and it seemed to us that he was about to open his eyes, to move and to speak. His thought, or rather his thoughts, enveloped us. We felt ourselves more than ever in the atmosphere of his genius, absorbed, possessed, by him. His domination seemed to us even more sovereign now that he was dead. A sense of mystery was blended with the power of this incomparable spirit.

"The bodies of these men disappear, but they remain themselves, and in the night which follows the stoppage of their heart's beating I assure you, monsieur, they are terrifying.

"And in hushed tones we talked about him, recalling to mind certain sayings, certain formulas of his, those startling maxims which are like jets of flame flung, by means of some words, into the darkness of the unknown life.

" 'It seems to me that he is going to speak,' said my comrade. And we stared with uneasiness bordering on fear at the motionless face with its eternal laugh. Gradually we began to feel ill at ease, oppressed, on the point of fainting. I faltered:

" 'I don't know what is the matter with me, but, I assure you, I am not well.'

"And at that moment we noticed that there was an unpleasant odor from the corpse.

"Then my comrade suggested that we should go into the adjoining room and leave the door open, and I assented to this proposal.

"I took one of the wax candles which burned on the bedside stand, and I left the second behind. Then we went and sat down at the other end of the adjoining apartment so as to be able to see from where we were the bed and the corpse clearly revealed by the light.

"But he still held possession of us. One would have said that his immaterial essence, liberated, free, all-powerful and dominating, was flitting around us. And sometimes, too, the dreadful smell of the decomposing body came toward us and penetrated us, sickening and indefinable.

"Suddenly a shiver passed through our bones; a sound, a slight sound, came from the death chamber. Immediately we fixed our glances on him, and we saw, yes, monsieur, we saw distinctly, both of us, something white flying over the bed, falling on the carpet and vanishing under the armchair.

"We were on our feet before we had time to think of anything, distracted by stupefying terror, ready to run away. Then we stared at each other. We were horribly pale. Our hearts throbbed so fiercely that our clothes swelled over our chests. I was the first to speak.

" 'You saw?'

" 'Yes, I saw.'

" 'Can it be that he is not dead?'

" 'Why not, when the body is putrefying?'

" 'What are we to do?'

"My companion said in a hesitating tone:

" 'We must go and look.'

"I took our wax candle and I entered first, searching with my eye through all the large apartment with its dark corners. There was not the least movement now, and I approached the bed. But I stood transfixed with stupor and fright: Schopenhauer was no longer laughing! He was grinning in a horrible fashion, with his lips pressed together and deep hollows in his cheeks. I stammered out:

" 'He is not dead!'

"But the terrible odor rose up to my nose and stifled me. And I no longer moved but kept staring fixedly at him, scared as if in the presence of an apparition. Then my companion, having seized the other wax candle, bent forward. Then he touched my arm without uttering a word. I followed his glance, and I saw on the floor, under the armchair by the side of the bed, all white on the dark carpet, open as if to bite, Schopenhauer's set of artificial teeth.

"The work of decomposition, loosening the jaws, had made it jump out of the mouth.

"I was really frightened that day, monsieur."

And as the sun was sinking toward the glittering sea the consumptive German rose from his seat, gave me a parting bow and retired into the hotel.

THE LOCK

The four glasses which were standing in front of the diners were still nearly half full, which is a sign, as a general rule, that the guests are quite so. They were beginning to speak without waiting for an answer; no one took any notice of anything except what was going on inside him; voices grew louder, gestures more animated, eyes brighter.

It was a bachelors' dinner of confirmed old celibates. They had instituted this regular banquet twenty years before, christening it "the Celibate," and at the time there were fourteen of them, all fully determined never to marry. Now there were only four of them left; three were dead and the other seven were married.

These four stuck firmly to it, and, as far as lay in their power, they scrupulously observed the rules which had been laid down at the beginning of their curious association. They had sworn, hand in hand, to turn aside every woman they could from the right path, and their friends' wives for choice, and more especially those of their most intimate friends. For this reason, as soon as any of them left the society, in order to set up in domestic life for himself, he took care to quarrel definitely with all his former companions.

Besides this, they were pledged at every dinner to relate most minutely their last adventures, which had given rise to this familiar phrase among them: "To lie like an old bachelor."

They professed, moreover, the most profound contempt for woman, whom they talked of as an animal made solely for their pleasure. Every moment they quoted Schopenhauer, who was their god, and his well-known essay "On Women"; they wished that harems and towers might be reintroduced, and had the ancient maxim: "Mulier, perpetuus infans," woven into their table linen, and below it, the line of Alfred de Vigny: "La femme, enfant malade et douze fois impure." So that by dint of despising women they lived only for them, while all their efforts and all their desires were directed toward them. Those of them who had married called them old fops, made fun of them, and—feared them.

When they began to feel the exhilarating effects of the champagne, the tales of their old bachelor experiences began.

On the day in question, these old fellows, for they were old by this time, and the older they grew the more extraordinary strokes of luck in the way of love affairs they had to relate, were quite talkative. For the last month, according to their own accounts, each of them had seduced at least one woman a day. And what women! the youngest, the noblest, the richest, and the most beautiful!

After they had finished their stories, one of them, he who had spoken first and had therefore been obliged to listen to all the others, rose and said:

"Now that we have finished drawing the longbow, I should like to tell you, not my last, but my first adventure—I mean the first adventure of my life, my

first fall—for it is a moral fall after all, in the arms of Venus. Oh! I am not going
to tell you my first—what shall I call it?—my first appearance; certainly not. The
leap over the first ditch (I am speaking figuratively) has nothing interesting about
it. It is generally rather a muddy one, and one picks oneself up rather abashed,
with one charming illusion the less, with a vague feeling of disappointment and
sadness. That realization of love the first time one experiences it is rather repugnant; we had dreamed of it as being so different, so delicate, so refined. It leaves
a physical and moral sense of disgust behind it, just as when one has happened
to put one's hand on a toad. You may rub your hand as hard as you like, but the
moral feeling remains.

"Yes! one very soon gets quite used to it; there is no doubt about that. For my
part, however, I am very sorry it was not in my power to give the Creator the
benefit of my advice when he was arranging these little matters. I wonder what I
should have done? I am not quite sure, but I think, with the English savant, John
Stuart Mill, I should have managed differently; I should have found some more
convenient and more poetical combination, yes—more poetical.

"I really think that the Creator showed himself to be too naturalistic—too—
what shall I say? His invention lacks poetry.

"However, what I am going to tell you is about my first woman of the world,
the first woman in society I ever made love to. I beg your pardon, I ought to say
the first woman of the world that ever triumphed over me. For at first it is we who
allow ourselves to be taken, while, later on—it is the . . . same thing!

"She was a friend of my mother, a charming woman in every way. When such
women are chaste, it is generally from sheer stupidity, and when they are in love
they are furiously so. And then—we are accused of corrupting them! Yes, yes of
course! With them it is always the rabbit that begins and never the sportsman.
I know all about it; they don't seem to lure us, but they do it all the same, and
do what they like with us, without its being noticed, and then they actually accuse us of having ruined them, dishonored them, degraded them, and all the rest
of it.

"The woman in question certainly had a great desire to be 'degraded' by me.
She may have been about thirty-five, while I was scarcely two-and-twenty. I no
more thought of seducing her than I did of turning Trappist. Well, one day when
I was calling on her, and while I was looking at her dress with considerable astonishment, for she had on a morning wrapper which was open as wide as a
church door when the bells are ringing for Mass, she took my hand and squeezed
it—squeezed it, you know, as they will do at such moments—and said, with a
deep sigh, one of those sighs, you know, which come right from the bottom of
the chest: 'Oh! don't look at me like that, child!' I got as red as a tomato, and
felt more nervous than usual, naturally. I was very much inclined to bolt, but she
held my hand tightly, and putting it on her well-developed bust, she said: 'Just
feel how my heart beats!' Of course it was beating, and I began to understand
what was the matter, but I did not know what to do. I have changed considerably
since then.

"As I remained standing there, with one hand on the soft covering of her
heart, while I held my hat in the other, and continued to look at her with a confused, silly smile—a timid frightened smile—she suddenly drew back, and said
in an irritated voice:

" 'Young man, what are you doing? You are indecent and badly brought up.'

"You may be sure I took my hand away quickly, stopped smiling, and stammering out some excuse, got up and took my leave as if I had lost my head.

"But I was caught, and dreamed of her. I thought her charming, adorable; I fancied that I loved her, that I had always loved her, and I determined to see her again. I decided to be enterprising, to be more than that even.

"When I saw her again she gave me a shy smile. Oh, how that little smile upset me! And she shook hands with a long, significant pressure.

"From that day it seems that I made love to her; at least, she declared afterward that I had ruined her, captured her, dishonored her, with rare Machiavellism, with consummate cleverness, with the calculations of a mathematician and the cunning of an Apache Indian.

"But one thing troubled me strangely: where was my triumph to be accomplished? I lived with my family, and on this point my family was most particular. I was not bold enough to venture into a hotel in broad daylight with a woman on my arm, and I did not know whom to ask for advice.

"Now, my fair friend had often said in joke that every young man ought to have a room for himself somewhere or other from home. We lived in Paris, and this was a sort of inspiration. I took a room, and she came. She came one day in November; I should have liked to put off her visit because I had no fire, and I had no fire because the chimney smoked. The very evening before I had spoken to my landlord, a retired shopkeeper, about it, and he had promised that he would come himself with the chimney expert in a day or two to see what could be done.

"As soon as she came in, I said:

" 'There is no fire because my chimney smokes.'

"She did not even appear to hear me, but stammered: 'That does not matter, I have plenty of fire'; and when I looked surprised, she stopped short in confusion, and went on: 'I don't know what I am saying; I am mad. I have lost my head. Oh! what am I doing? Why did I come? How unhappy I am! What a disgrace, what a disgrace!' And she threw herself sobbing into my arms.

"I thought that she really felt remorse, and swore that I would respect her. Then, however, she sank down at my knees, sighing: 'But don't you see that I love you, that you have overcome me, that it seems as though you had thrown a charm over me?'

"Then I thought it was about time to show myself a man. But she trembled, got up, ran, and hid behind a wardrobe, crying out: 'Oh! Don't look at me; no! no! If only you did not see me, if we were only in the dark! I am ashamed in the light. Cannot you imagine it? What a dreadful dream! Oh! this light, this light!'

"I rushed to the window; I closed the outside shutters, drew the curtains, and hung a coat over a ray of light that peeped in, and then, stretching out my hands so as not to fall over the chairs, with my heart beating, I groped for her, and found her.

"This was a fresh journey for the two of us then, feeling our way, with our hands united, toward the other corner where the alcove was. I don't suppose we went straight, for first of all I knocked against the mantelpiece and then against a chest of drawers before finding what we wanted. Then I forgot everything in a frantic ecstasy. It was an hour of folly, madness, superhuman joy, followed by a delicious lassitude, in which we slept in each other's arms.

"I was half dreaming; but in my dream I fancied that some one was calling me and crying for help; then I received a violent blow, and opened my eyes.

" 'Oh———h!' The setting sun, magnificent and red, shone full into the room through the door, which was wide open. It seemed to look at us from the verge of the horizon, illuminating us both, especially my companion, who was screaming, struggling, and twisting, and trying with hands and feet to get hold of a corner of a sheet, a curtain or anything else, while in the middle of the room stood my landlord in a morning coat with the concierage by his side, and a chimney sweep, as black as the devil, who were looking at us with stupid eyes.

"I sprang up in a rage, ready to jump at his throat, and shouted:

" 'What the deuce are you doing in my room?'

"The chimney sweep laughed so that he let his brush fall onto the floor. The concierge seemed to have gone mad, and the landlord stammered:

" 'But, monsieur, it was—it was—about the chimney—the chimney, the chimney which——'

" 'Go to the devil!' I roared. So he took off his hat, which he had kept on in his confusion, and said, in a confused but very civil manner:

" 'I beg your pardon, monsieur; if I had known, I should not have disturbed you; I should not have come. The concierge told me you had gone out. Pray excuse me.' And they all went out.

"Ever since that time I never draw the curtains, but I am always very careful to lock the door first."

A QUEER NIGHT IN PARIS

Maître Saval, notary at Vernon, was passionately fond of music. Still young, though already bald, always carefully shaved, a little corpulent, as was fitting, wearing a gold pince-nez instead of old-fashioned spectacles, active, gallant and joyous, he passed in Vernon for an artist. He thrummed on the piano and played on the violin and gave musical evenings where interpretations were given of new operas.

He had even what is called a bit of a voice, nothing but a bit, a very little bit of a voice, but he managed it with so much taste that cries of "Bravo!" "Exquisite!" "Surprising!" "Adorable!" issued from every throat as soon as he had murmured the last note.

He was a subscriber to a music publisher in Paris who sent all new pieces to him. From time to time to the high society of the town he sent little notes something in this style:

"You are invited to be present on Monday evening at the house of M. Saval, notary, Vernon, at the first production of *Sais*."

A few officers, gifted with good voices, formed the chorus. Two or three of the vine dressers' families also sang. The notary filled the part of leader of the orchestra with so much skill that the bandmaster of the 190th Regiment of the line said one day at the Café de l'Europe:

"Oh, Monsieur Saval is a master. It is a great pity that he did not adopt the career of an artist."

When his name was mentioned in a drawing room there was always found somebody to declare: "He is not an amateur; he is an artist, a genuine artist." And two or three persons would repeat in a tone of profound conviction: "Oh yes, a genuine artist," laying particular stress on the word "genuine."

Every time that a new work was interpreted at a big Parisian theater, M. Saval paid a visit to the capital. Last year, according to his custom, he went to hear *Henry VIII*. He then took the express which arrives in Paris at 4:30 P.M., intending to return by the 12:35 A.M. train so as not to have to sleep at a hotel. He had put on evening dress, a black coat and white tie, which he concealed under his overcoat with the collar turned up.

As soon as he had planted his foot on the Rue d'Amsterdam he felt in quite a jovial mood and said to himself:

"Decidedly the air of Paris does not resemble any other air. It has in it something indescribably stimulating, exciting, intoxicating, which fills you with a strange longing to gambol and to do many other things. As soon as I arrive here it seems to me, all of a sudden, that I have taken a bottle of champagne. What a life one can lead in this city in the midst of artists! Happy are the elect, the great men who enjoy renown in such a city! What an existence is theirs!"

And he made plans; he would have liked to know some of those celebrated men, to talk about them in Vernon and to spend an evening with them from time to time in Paris.

But suddenly an idea struck him. He had heard allusions to little cafés in the outer boulevards at which well-known painters, men of letters and even musicians gathered, and he proceeded to go toward Montmartre at a slow pace.

He had two hours before him. He wanted to have a look round. He passed in front of taverns frequented by belated Bohemians, gazing at the different faces, seeking to discover the artists. Finally, he came to the sign of The Dead Rat and, allured by the name, he entered.

Five or six women, with their elbows resting on the marble tables, were talking in low tones about their love affairs, the quarrels of Lucie with Hortense and the scoundrelism of Octave. They were no longer young but were fat or thin, tired out, used up. You could see that they were almost bald, and they drank bocks like men.

M. Saval sat down at some distance from them and waited, for the hour for taking absinthe was at hand.

A tall young man soon came in and took a seat beside him. The landlady called him "Monsieur Romantin." The notary quivered. Was this the Romantin who had taken a medal at the last Salon?

The young man made a sign to the waiter:

"You will bring up my dinner at once and then carry to my new studio, 15 Boulevard de Clichy, thirty bottles of beer and the ham I ordered this morning. We are going to have a housewarming."

M. Saval immediately ordered dinner. Then he took off his overcoat so that his dress coat and his white tie could be seen. His neighbor did not seem to notice him. M. Saval glanced sideways at him, burning with the desire to speak to him.

Two young men entered in red velvet and peaked beards in the fashion of Henry III. They sat down opposite Romantin.

The first of the pair said:

"It is for this evening?"

Romantin pressed his hand.

"I believe you, old chap, and everyone will be there. I have Bonnat, Guillemet, Gervex, Béraud, Hébert, Duez, Clairin and Jean-Paul Laurens. It will be a glorious blowout! And women too! Wait till you see! Every actress without exception—of course, I mean, you know all those who have nothing to do this evening."

The landlord of the establishment came across.

"Do you often have this housewarming?"

The painter replied:

"Certainly—every three months, each quarter."

M. Saval could not restrain himself any longer and in a hesitating voice said:

"I beg your pardon for intruding on you, monsieur, but I heard your name pronounced, and I would be very glad to know if you really are Monsieur Romantin whose work in the last Salon I have so much admired."

The painter answered:

"I am the person, monsieur."

The notary then paid the artist a very well-turned compliment, showing that he was a man of culture. The painter, gratified, thanked him politely in reply. Then they chatted. Romantin returned to the subject of his housewarming, going into details as to the magnificence of the forthcoming entertainment.

M. Saval questioned him as to all the men he was going to receive, adding:

"It would be an extraordinary piece of good fortune for a stranger to meet at one time so many celebrities assembled in the studio of an artist of your rank."

Romantin, overcome, answered: "If it would be agreeable to you, come."

M. Saval accepted the invitation with enthusiasm, reflecting:

"I'll always have time enough to see *Henry VIII.*"

Both of them had finished their meal. The notary insisted on paying the two bills, wishing to repay his neighbor's civilities. He also paid for the drinks of the young fellows in red velvet; then he left the establishment with the painter.

They stopped in front of a very long house, by no means high, the first story of which had the appearance of an interminable conservatory. Six studios stood in a row with their fronts facing the boulevards.

Romantin was the first to enter. Ascending the stairs, he opened a door and lighted a match and then a candle.

They found themselves in an immense apartment, the furniture of which consisted of three chairs, two easels and a few sketches lying on the floor along the walls. M. Saval remained standing at the door in a stupefied state of mind.

The painter remarked:

"Here you are! We've got to the spot, but everything has yet to be done."

Then, examining the high, bare apartment, whose ceiling was veiled in shadows, he said:

"We might make a great deal out of this studio."

He walked around it, surveying it with the utmost attention, then went on:

"I have a mistress who might easily give us a helping hand. Women are incomparable for hanging drapery. But I sent her to the country today in order to get her off my hands this evening. It is not that she bores me, but she is too much lacking in the ways of good society. It would be embarrassing to my guests."

He reflected for a few seconds and then added:

"She is a good girl but not easy to deal with. If she knew that I was holding a reception she would tear out my eyes."

M. Saval had not even moved; he did not understand.

The artist came over to him.

"Since I have invited you, you are going to give me some help."

The notary said emphatically:

"Make any use of me you please. I am at your disposal."

Romantin took off his jacket.

"Well, citizen, to work! We are first going to clean up."

He went to the back of the easel on which there was a canvas representing a cat and seized a very worn-out broom.

"I say! Just brush up while I look after the lighting."

M. Saval took the broom, inspected it and then began to sweep the floor very awkwardly, raising a whirlwind of dust.

Romantin, disgusted, stopped him: "Deuce take it! You don't know how to sweep the floor! Look at me!"

And he began to roll before him a heap of grayish sweepings, as if he had done nothing else all his life. Then he gave back the broom to the notary, who imitated him.

In five minutes such a cloud of dust filled the studio that Romantin asked:

"Where are you? I can't see you any longer."

M. Saval, who was coughing, came nearer to him. The painter said to him:

"How are you going to manage to get up a chandelier."

The other, stunned, asked:

"What chandelier?"

"Why, a chandelier to light—a chandelier with wax candles."

The notary did not understand.

He answered: "I don't know."

The painter began to jump about, cracking his fingers.

"Well, monseigneur, I have found out a way."

Then he went more calmly:

"Have you got five francs about you?"

M. Saval replied:

"Why, yes."

The artist said:

"Well, you'll go and buy for me five francs' worth of wax candles while I go and see the cooper."

And he pushed the notary in his evening coat into the street. At the end of five minutes they had returned, one of them with the wax candles and the other with the hoop of a cask. Then Romantin plunged his hand into a cupboard and drew forth twenty empty bottles, which he fixed in the form of a crown around the hoop. He then came down and went to borrow a ladder from the doorkeeper after having explained that he obtained the favors of the old woman by painting the portrait of her cat exhibited on the easel.

When he mounted the ladder he said to M. Saval:

"Are you active?"

The other, without understanding, answered:

"Why, yes."

"Well, you just climb up there and fasten this chandelier for me to the ring of the ceiling. Then you must put a wax candle in each bottle and light it. I tell you, I have a genius for lighting up. But off with your coat, damn it! You are just like a Jeames."

The door was opened violently. A woman appeared with her eyes flashing and remained standing on the threshold. Romantin gazed at her with a look of terror. She waited some seconds, crossed her arms over her breast and then in a shrill, vibrating, exasperated voice said:

"Ha, you villain, is this the way you leave me?"

Romantin made no reply. She went on:

"Ha, you scoundrel! You are again doing the swell, while you pack me off to the country. You'll soon see the way I'll settle your jollification. Yes, I'm going to receive your friends."

She grew warmer.

"I'm going to slap their faces with the bottles and the wax candles."

Romantin uttered one soft word:

"Mathilde."

But she did not pay any attention to him; she went on:

"Wait a little, my fine fellow! Wait a little!"

Romantin went over to her and tried to take her by the hands.

"Mathilde."

But she was now fairly under way, and on she went, emptying the vials of her wrath with strong words and reproaches. They flowed out of her mouth like a stream sweeping a heap of filth along with it. The words hurled out seemed struggling for exit. She stuttered, stammered, yelled, suddenly recovering her voice to cast forth an insult or a curse.

He seized her hands without her having even noticed it. She did not seem to see anything, so much occupied was she in holding forth and relieving her heart. And suddenly she began to weep. The tears flowed from her eyes without making her stem the tide of her complaints. But her words had taken a howling, shrieking tone; they were a continuous cry interrupted by sobbings. She commenced afresh twice or three times till she stopped, as if something were choking her, and at last she ceased with a regular flood of tears.

Then he clasped her in his arms and kissed her hair, himself affected.

"Mathilde, my little Mathilde, listen. You must be reasonable. You know, if I give a supper party to my friends it is to thank these gentlemen for the medal I got at the Salon. I cannot receive women. You ought to understand that. It is not the same with artists as with other people."

She stammered in the midst of her tears:

"Why didn't you tell me this?"

He replied:

"It was in order not to annoy you, not to give you pain. Listen, I'm going to see you home. You will be very sensible, very nice; you will remain quietly waiting for me in bed, and I'll come back as soon as it's over."

She murmured:

"Yes, but you will not begin over again?"

"No, I swear to you!"

He turned toward M. Saval, who had at last hooked on the chandelier.

"My dear friend, I am coming back in five minutes. If anyone arrives in my absence do the honors for me, will you not?"

And he carried off Mathilde, who kept drying her eyes with her handkerchief as she went along.

Left to himself, M. Saval succeeded in putting everything around him in order. Then he lighted the wax candles and waited.

He waited for a quarter of an hour, half an hour, an hour. Romantin did not return. Then suddenly there was a dreadful noise on the stairs, a song shouted out in chorus by twenty mouths and a regular march like that of a Prussian regiment. The whole house was shaken by the steady tramp of feet. The door flew open, and a motley throng appeared—men and women in a row, holding one another arm in arm, in pairs, and kicking their heels on the floor in proper time—advancing into the studio like a snake uncoiling itself. They howled:

> "Come, let us all be merry,
> Pretty maids and soldiers gay!"

M. Saval, thunderstruck, remained standing in evening dress under the chandelier. The procession of revelers caught sight of him and uttered a shout:
"A Jeames! A Jeames!"
And they began whirling round him, surrounding him with a circle of vociferation. Then they took each other by the hand and went dancing about madly

He attempted to explain:
"Messieurs—Messieurs—Mesdames——"
But they did not listen to him. They whirled about, they jumped, they brawled.
At last the dancing ceased. M. Saval uttered the word:
"Messieurs——"
A tall young fellow, fair-haired and bearded to the nose, interrupted him:
"What's your name, my friend?"
The notary, quite scared, said:
"I am Monsieur Saval."
A voice exclaimed:
"You mean Baptiste."
A woman said:
"Let the poor waiter alone! You'll end by making him get angry. He's paid to attend on us and not to be laughed at by us."
Then M. Saval noticed that each guest had brought his own provisions. One held a bottle of wine, another a pie. This one had a loaf of bread, that one a ham.
The tall, fair young fellow placed in his hands an enormous sausage and gave him orders:
"Go and settle up the sideboard in the corner over there. You are to put the bottles at the left and the provisions at the right."
Saval, getting quite distracted, exclaimed:
"But, messieurs, I am a notary!"
There was a moment's silence and then a wild outburst of laughter. One suspicious gentleman asked:
"How are you here?"
He explained, telling about his project of going to the opera, his departure from Vernon, his arrival in Paris and the way in which he had spent the evening.
They sat around him to listen to him; they greeted him with words of applause and called him Scheherazade.
Romantin did not come back. Other guests arrived. M. Saval was presented to them so that he might begin his story over again. He declined; they forced him to relate it. They fixed him on one of three chairs between two women who kept

constantly filling his glass. He drank; he laughed; he talked; he sang too. He tried to waltz with his chair and fell on the floor.

From that moment he forgot everything. It seemed to him, however, that they undressed him, put him to bed and that his stomach got sick.

When he awoke it was broad daylight, and he lay stretched with his feet against a cupboard in a strange bed.

An old woman with a broom in her hand was glaring angrily at him. At last she said:

"Clear out, you blackguard! Clear out! What right has anyone to get drunk like this?"

He sat up in his bed, feeling very ill at ease. He asked:

"Where am I?"

"Where are you, you dirty scamp? You are drunk. Take your rotten carcass out of here as quick as you can—and lose no time about it!"

He wanted to get up. He found that he was naked in the bed. His clothes had disappeared. He blurted out:

"Madame, I——"

Then he remembered. What was he to do? He asked:

"Did Monsieur Romantin come back?"

The doorkeeper shouted:

"Will you take your dirty carcass out of this so that he at any rate may not catch you here?"

M. Saval said in a state of confusion:

"I haven't got my clothes; they have been taken away from me."

He had to wait, to explain his situation, give notice to his friends and borrow some money to buy clothes. He did not leave Paris till evening.

And when people talk about music to him in his beautiful drawing room in Vernon, he declares with an air of authority that painting is a very inferior art.

A DUEL

The war was over. The Germans occupied France. The country was panting like a wrestler lying under the knee of his successful opponent.

The first trains from Paris, after the city's long agony of famine and despair, were making their way to the new frontiers, slowly passing through the country districts and the villages. The passengers gazed through the windows at the ravaged fields and burned hamlets. Prussian soldiers, in their black helmets with brass spikes, were smoking their pipes on horseback or sitting on chairs in front of the houses which were still left standing. Others were working or talking just as if they were members of the families. As you passed through the different towns you saw entire regiments drilling in the squares, and in spite of the rumble of the carriage wheels you could, every moment, hear the hoarse words of command.

M. Dubuis, who during the entire siege had served as one of the National Guard in Paris, was going to join his wife and daughter, whom he had prudently sent away to Switzerland before the invasion.

Famine and hardship had not diminished the big paunch so characteristic of the rich, peace-loving merchant. He had gone through the terrible events of the past year with sorrowful resignation and bitter complaints at the savagery of men. Now that he was journeying to the frontier at the close of the war he saw the Prussians for the first time, although he had done duty at the ramparts and stanchly mounted guard on cold nights.

He stared with mingled fear and anger at those bearded armed men installed all over French soil as if in their own homes, and he felt in his soul a kind of fever of impotent patriotism even while he yielded to that other instinct of discretion and self-preservation which never leaves us. In the same compartment two Englishmen, who had come to the country as sight-seers, were gazing around with looks of stolid curiosity. They were both stout also and kept chattering in their own language, sometimes referring to their guidebook and reading in loud tones the names of the places indicated.

Suddenly the train stopped at a little village station, and a Prussian officer jumped up with a great clatter of his saber on the double footboard of the railway carriage. He was tall, wore a tight-fitting uniform, and his face had a very shaggy aspect. His red hair seemed to be on fire, and his long mustache and beard, of a paler color, was stuck out on both sides of his face, which it seemed to cut in two.

The Englishmen at once began staring at him with smiles of newly awakened interest, while M. Dubuis made a show of reading a newspaper. He sat crouched in a corner, like a thief in the presence of a gendarme.

The train started again. The Englishmen went on chatting and looking out for the exact scene of different battles, and all of a sudden, as one of them stretched out his arm toward the horizon to indicate a village, the Prussian officer remarked in French, extending his long legs and lolling backward:

"We killed a dozen Frenchmen in that village and took more than a hundred prisoners."

The Englishmen, quite interested, immediately asked:

"Ha! And what is the name of this village?"

The Prussian replied:

"Pharsbourg."

He added: "We caught these French blackguards by the ears."

And he glanced toward M. Dubuis, laughing into his mustache in an insulting fashion.

The train rolled on, always passing through hamlets occupied by the victorious army. German soldiers could be seen along the roads, on the edges of fields, standing in front of gates or chatting outside cafés. They covered the soil like African locusts.

The officer said with a wave of his hand:

"If I were in command I'd take Paris, burn everything and kill everybody. No more France!"

The Englishmen, through politeness, replied simply:

"Ah yes."

He went on:

"In twenty years all Europe, all of it, will belong to us. Prussia is more than a match for all of them."

The Englishmen, getting uneasy, said nothing in answer to this. Their faces, which had become impassive, seemed made of wax behind their long whiskers.

Then the Prussian officer began to laugh. And then, lolling back, he began to
sneer. He sneered at the downfall of France, insulted the prostrate enemy; he
sneered at Austria which had been recently conquered; he sneered at the furious
but fruitless defense of the departments; he sneered at the Garde Mobile and
at the useless artillery. He announced that Bismarck was going to build a city of
iron with the captured cannons. And suddenly he pushed his boots against the
thigh of M. Dubuis, who turned his eyes away, reddening to the roots of his hair.

The Englishmen seemed to have assumed an air of complete indifference, as if
they had found themselves all at once shut up in their own island, far from the
din of the world.

The officer took out his pipe and, looking fixedly at the Frenchman, said:
"You haven't got any tobacco—have you?"

M. Dubuis replied:
"No, monsieur."

The German said:
"You might go and buy some for me when the train stops next."

And he began laughing afresh as he added:
"I'll let you have the price of a drink."

The train whistled and slackened its pace. They had reached a station which
had been burned down, and here there was a regular stop.

The German opened the carriage door and, catching M. Dubuis by the arm,
said:
"Go and do what I told you—quick, quick!"

A Prussian detachment occupied the station. Other soldiers were looking on
from behind wooden gratings. The engine was already getting up steam in order
to start off again. Then M. Dubuis hurriedly jumped on the platform and, in
spite of the warnings of the stationmaster, dashed into the adjoining compartment.

He was alone! He tore open his waistcoat, so rapidly did his heart beat, and,
panting for breath, he wiped the perspiration off his forehead.

The train drew up at another station. And suddenly the officer appeared at
the carriage door and jumped in, followed close behind by the two Englishmen, who were impelled by curiosity. The German sat facing the Frenchman
and, laughing still, said:
"You did not want to do what I asked you."

M. Dubuis replied: "No, monsieur."

The train had just left the station when the officer said:
"I'll cut off your mustache to fill my pipe with." And he put out his hand
toward the Frenchman's face.

The Englishmen kept staring in the same impassive fashion with fixed glances.
Already the German had caught hold of the mustache and was tugging at it,
when M. Dubuis, with a backstroke of his hand, threw back the officer's arm
and, seizing him by the collar, flung him down on the seat. Then, excited to a
pitch of fury, with his temples swollen and his eyes glaring he kept throttling the
officer with one hand while with the other, clenched, he began to strike him
violent blows in the face. The Prussian struggled, tried to draw his saber and to
get a grip, while lying back, on his adversary. But M. Dubuis crushed him with
the enormous weight of his stomach and kept hitting him without taking
breath or knowing where his blows fell. Blood flowed down the face of the Ger-

man, who, choking and with a rattling in his throat, spat forth his broken teeth and vainly strove to shake off this infuriated man who was killing him.

The Englishmen had got on their feet and came closer to see better. They remained standing, full of mirth and curiosity, ready to bet for or against each of the combatants.

And suddenly M. Dubuis, exhausted by his violent efforts, went and resumed his seat without uttering a word.

The Prussian did not attack him, for the savage assault had scared and terrified the officer. When he was able to breathe freely he said.

"Unless you give me satisfaction with pistols I will kill you."

M. Dubuis replied:

"Whenever you like. I'm quite ready."

The German said:

"Here is the town of Strasbourg. I'll get two officers to be my seconds, and there will be time before the train leaves the station."

M. Dubuis, who was puffing as much as the engine, said to the Englishmen:

"Will you be my seconds?" They both answered together:

"Oh yes."

And the train stopped.

In a minute the Prussian had found two comrades who carried pistols, and they made their way toward the ramparts.

The Englishmen were continually looking at their watches, shuffling their feet and hurrying on with the preparations, uneasy lest they should be too late for the train.

M. Dubuis had never fired a pistol in his life. They made him stand twenty paces away from his enemy. He was asked:

"Are you ready?"

While he was answering "Yes, monsieur," he noticed that one of the Englishmen had opened his umbrella in order to keep off the rays of the sun.

A voice gave the word of command.

"Fire!"

M. Dubuis fired at random without minding what he was doing, and he was amazed to see the Prussian staggering in front of him, lifting up his arms and, immediately afterward, falling straight on his face. He had killed the officer.

One of the Englishmen ejaculated: "Ah!" quivering with delight, satisfied curiosity and joyous impatience. The other, who still kept his watch in his hand, hurried him in double-quick time toward the station, his fellow countryman counting their steps with his arms pressed close to his sides: "One, two! One, two!"

And all three marching abreast, they rapidly made their way to the station like three grotesque figures in a comic newspaper.

The train was on the point of starting. They sprang into their carriage. Then the Englishmen, taking off their traveling caps, waved them three times over their heads, exclaiming:

"Hip! hip! hip! hurrah!"

Then gravely, one after the other, they stretched out their right hands to M. Dubuis and then went back and sat in their own corner.

THE KISS

My little darling: so you are crying from morning until night and from night until morning, because your husband leaves you; you do not know what to do and so you ask your old aunt for advice; you must consider her quite an expert. I don't know as much as you think I do, and yet I am not entirely ignorant of the art of loving, or, rather, of making one's self loved, in which you are a little lacking. I can admit that at my age.

You say that you are all attention, love, kisses and caresses for him. Perhaps that is the very trouble; I think you kiss him too much.

My dear, we have in our hands the most terrible power in the world: love.

Man is gifted with physical strength, and he exercises force. Woman is gifted with charm, and she rules with caresses. It is our weapon, formidable and invincible, but we should know how to use it.

We are the mistresses of the world you know. To tell the history of Love from the beginning of the world would be to tell the history of man himself. Everything springs from it, the arts, great events, customs, wars, the overthrow of empires.

In the Bible you find Delilah, Judith; in fables we find Omphale, Helen; in history the Sabines, Cleopatra, and many others.

Therefore we reign supreme, all-powerful. But, like kings, we must make use of delicate diplomacy.

Love, my dear, is made up of imperceptible sensations. We know that it is as strong as death, but also as frail as glass. The slightest shock breaks it, our power crumbles, and we are never able to build it up again.

We have the power of making ourselves adored, but we lack one tiny thing, understanding of the various shades of caresses, the subtle feeling for what is excessive in the manifestations of our tender feelings. When we are embraced we lose the sentiment of delicacy, while the man over whom we rule remains master of himself, capable of judging the foolishness of certain words. Take care, my dear; that is the defect in our armor. It is our Achilles' heel.

Do you know whence comes our real power? From the kiss, the kiss alone! When we know how to offer and give up our lips we can become queens.

The kiss is only a preface, however, but a charming preface. More charming than the realization itself. A preface which can always be read over again, whereas one cannot always read over the book.

Yes, the meeting of lips is the most perfect, the most divine sensation given to human beings, the supreme limit of happiness. It is in the kiss alone that one sometimes seems to feel this union of souls after which we strive, the intermingling of swooning hearts, as it were.

Do you remember the verses of Sully-Prudhomme:

> Les caresses ne sont que d'inquiets transports,
> Infructueux essais du pauvre Amour qui tente
> L'impossible union des âmes par le corps.

One caress alone gives this deep sensation of two beings welded into one—it is the kiss. No violent delirium of complete possession equals this trembling approach of the lips, this first moist and fresh contact, and then the long, lingering, motionless rapture.

Therefore, my dear, the kiss is our strongest weapon, but we must take care not to dull it. Do not forget that its value is only relative, purely conventional. It continually changes according to circumstances, the state of expectancy and the ecstasy of the mind. I will call attention to one example.

Another poet, François Coppée, has written a line which we all remember, a line which we find delightful, which moves our very hearts.

After describing the expectancy of a lover, waiting in a room one winter's evening, his anxiety, his nervous impatience, the terrible fear of not seeing her, he described the arrival of the beloved woman, who at last enters hurriedly, out of breath, bringing with her a breath of winter, and he exclaims:

Oh! les premiers baisers à travers la voilette!

Is that not a line of exquisite sentiment, a delicate and charming observation, a perfect truth? All those who have hastened to a clandestine meeting, whom passion has thrown into the arms of a man, well do they know these first delicious kisses through the veil; and they tremble at the memory of them. And yet their sole charm lies in the circumstances, from being late, from the anxious expectancy; but from the purely—or, rather, impurely, if you prefer—sensual point of view, they are detestable.

Think! Outside it is cold. The young woman has walked quickly; the veil is moist from her cold breath. Little drops of water shine in the lace. The lover seizes her and presses his burning lips to her liquid breath. The moist veil, which discolors and carries the dreadful odor of chemical dye, penetrates into the young man's mouth, moistens his mustache. He does not taste the lips of his beloved, he tastes the dye of this lace moistened with cold breath. And yet, like the poet, we would all exclaim:

Oh! les premiers baisers à travers la voilette!

Therefore, the value of this caress being entirely a matter of convention, we must be careful not to abuse it.

Well, my dear, I have several times noticed that you are very clumsy. However, you are not alone in that fault; the majority of women lose their authority by abusing the kiss with untimely kisses. When they feel that their husband or their lover is a little tired, at those times when the heart as well as the body needs rest, instead of understanding what is going on within him, they persist in giving inopportune caresses, tire him by the obstinacy of begging lips and give caresses lavished with neither rhyme nor reason.

Trust my experience. First, never kiss your husband in public, in the train, at the restaurant. It is bad taste; do not give in to your desires. He would feel ridiculous and would never forgive you.

Beware of useless kisses lavished in intimacy. I am sure that you abuse them. For instance, I remember one day that you did something quite shocking. Probably you do not remember it.

All three of us were together in the drawing room, and, as you did not stand on ceremony before me, your husband was holding you on his knees and kissing you at great length on the neck, the lips and throat. Suddenly you exclaimed: "Oh! the fire!" You had been paying no attention to it, and it was almost out. A few lingering embers were glowing on the hearth. Then he rose, ran to the woodbox, from which he dragged two enormous logs with great difficulty, when you came to him with begging lips, murmuring:

"Kiss me!" He turned his head with difficulty and tried to hold up the logs at the same time. Then you gently and slowly placed your mouth on that of the poor fellow, who remained with his neck out of joint, his sides twisted, his arms almost dropping off, trembling with fatigue and tired from his desperate effort. And you kept drawing out this torturing kiss, without seeing or understanding. Then when you freed him, you began to grumble: "How badly you kiss!" No wonder!

Oh, take care of that! We all have this foolish habit, this stupid and inconsiderate impulse to choose the most inconvenient moments. When he is carrying a glass of water, when he is putting on his shoes, when he is tying his cravat—in short, when he finds himself in any uncomfortable position—then is the time which we choose for a caress which makes him stop for a whole minute in the middle of what he is doing, with the sole desire of getting rid of us!

Do not think that this criticism is insignificant. Love, my dear, is a delicate thing. The least little thing offends it: everything depends on the tact of our caresses. An ill-placed kiss may do any amount of harm.

Try following my advice.

Your old aunt,
COLLETTE.

OLD MONGILET

In the office old Mongilet was looked upon as an eccentric. He was an old employee, a good-natured creature, who had never been outside Paris but once in his life.

It was the end of July, and each of us, every Sunday, went to roll in the grass, or bathe in the river in the country near by. Asnières, Argenteuil, Chatou, Bougival, Maisons, Poissy, had their habitués and their ardent admirers. We argued about the merits and advantages of all these places, celebrated and delightful to all employees in Paris.

Old Mongilet would say:

"You are like a lot of sheep! A nice place, this country you talk of!"

And we would ask:

"Well, how about you, Mongilet? Don't you ever go on an excursion?"

"Yes, indeed. I go in an omnibus. When I have had a good luncheon, without any hurry, at the wineshop below, I look up my route with a plan of Paris, and the timetable of the lines and connections. And then I climb up on top of the bus, open my umbrella and off we go. Oh, I see lots of things, more than you, I bet! I change my surroundings. It is as though I were taking a journey across the world, the people are so different in one street and another. I know my Paris better than anyone. And then, there is nothing more amusing than the entresols. You would not believe what one sees in there at a glance. One can guess a domestic scene simply at the sight of the face of a man who is roaring; one is amused on passing by a barber's shop, to see the barber leave his customer whose face is covered with lather to look out in the street. One exchanges heartfelt glances with the milliners just for fun, as one has no time to alight. Ah, how many things one sees!

"It is the drama, the real, the true, the drama of nature, seen as the horses trot by. Heavens! I would not not give my excursions in the omnibus for all your stupid excursions in the woods."

"Come and try it, Mongilet, come to the country once just to see."

"I was there once," he replied, "twenty years ago, and you will never catch me there again."

"Tell us about it, Mongilet."

"If you wish to hear it. This is how it was: You knew Boivin, the old clerk, whom we called Boileau?"

"Yes, perfectly."

"He was my office chum. The rascal had a house at Colombes and always invited me to spend Sunday with him. He would say:

"'Come along, Maculotte (he called me Maculotte for fun). You will see what a nice walk we shall take.'

"I let myself be entrapped like an animal and set out, one morning, by the eight o'clock train. I arrived at a kind of town, a country town where there is nothing to see, and I at length found my way to an old wooden door with an iron bell, at the end of an alley between two walls.

"I rang, and waited a long time, and at last the door was opened. What was it that opened it? I could not tell at the first glance. A woman or an ape? The creature was old, ugly, covered with old clothes that looked dirty and wicked. It had chickens' feathers in its hair and looked as though it would devour me.

" 'What do you want?' she said.

" 'M. Boivin.'

" 'What do you want of him, of M. Boivin?'

"I felt ill at ease on being questioned by this fury. I stammered: 'Why—he expects me.'

" 'Ah, it is you who are coming to lunch?'

" 'Yes,' I stammered, trembling.

"Then, turning toward the house, she cried in an angry tone:

" 'Boivin, here is your man!'

"It was my friend's wife. Little Boivin appeared immediately on the threshold of a sort of barrack of plaster covered with zinc that looked like a foot warmer. He wore white duck trousers covered with stains and a dirty Panama hat.

"After shaking my hands warmly, he took me into what he called his garden. It was at the end of another alleyway enclosed by high walls and was a little square the size of a pocket handkerchief, surrounded by houses that were so high that the sun could reach it only two or three hours in the day. Pansies, pinks, wallflowers and a few rose bushes were languishing in this well without air and hot as an oven from the refraction of heat from the roofs.

" 'I have no trees,' said Boivin, 'but the neighbors' walls take their place. I have as much shade as in a wood.'

"Then he took hold of a button of my coat and said in a low tone.

" 'You can do me a service. You saw the wife. She is not agreeable, eh? Today, as I had invited you, she gave me clean clothes; but if I spot them all is lost. I counted on you to water my plants.'

"I agreed. I took off my coat, rolled up my sleeves, and began to work the handle of a kind of pump that wheezed, puffed and rattled like a consumptive as it emitted a thread of water like a Wallace drinking fountain. It took me ten minutes to fill the watering pot, and I was in a bath of perspiration. Boivin directed me:

" 'Here—this plant—a little more; enough—now this one.'

"The watering pot leaked, and my feet got more water than the flowers. The bottoms of my trousers were soaking and covered with mud. And twenty times running I kept it up, soaking my feet afresh each time and perspiring anew as I worked the handle of the pump. And when I was tired out and wanted to stop, Boivin, in a tone of entreaty, said as he put his hand on my arm:

" 'Just one more watering pot full—just one, and that will be all.'

"To thank me he gave me a rose, a big rose, but hardly had it touched my buttonhole than it fell to pieces, leaving only a hard little green knot as a decoration. I was surprised, but said nothing.

"Mme. Boivin's voice was heard in the distance: 'Are you ever coming? When I tell you lunch is ready——!'

"We went towards the foot warmer. If the garden was in the shade, the house, on the other hand, was in the blazing sun, and the sweating room in the Turkish bath is not so hot as was my friend's dining room.

"Three plates, at the side of which were some half-washed forks, were placed on a table of yellow wood in the middle of which stood an earthenware dish containing warmed-up boiled beef and potatoes. We began to eat.

"A large water bottle full of water lightly colored with wine attracted my attention. Boivin, embarrassed, said to his wife:

" 'See here, my dear, just on a special occasion, are you not going to give us some plain wine?'

"She looked at him furiously.

" 'So that you may both get tipsy, is that it, and stay here gabbing all day? Thanks for the special occasion!'

"He said no more. After the stew she brought in another dish of potatoes cooked with bacon. When this dish was finished, still in silence, she announced:

"That is all! Now get out!'

"Boivin looked at her in astonishment.

" 'But the pigeon—the pigeon you plucked this morning?'

"She put her hands on her hips:

" 'Perhaps you have not had enough? Because you bring people here is no reason why we should devour all that there is in the house. What is there for me to eat this evening?'

"We rose. Boivin whispered:

" 'Wait for me a second, and we will skip.'

"He went into the kitchen where his wife had gone, and I overheard him say:

" 'Give me twenty sous, my dear.'

" 'What do you want with twenty sous?'

" 'Why, one does not know what may happen. It is always better to have some money.'

"She yelled so that I should hear:

" 'No, I will not give it to you! As the man has had luncheon here, the least he can do is to pay your expenses for the day.'

"Boivin came back to fetch me. As I wished to be polite I bowed to the mistress of the house, stammering:

" 'Madame—many thanks—kind welcome.'

" 'That's all right,' she replied. 'But do not bring him back drunk, for you will have to answer to me, you know!'

"We set out. We had to cross a perfectly bare plain under the burning sun. I attempted to gather a flower along the road and gave a cry of pain. It had hurt my hand frightfully. They call these plants nettles. And, everywhere, there was a smell of manure, enough to turn your stomach.

"Boivin said, 'Have a little patience and we will reach the riverbank.'

"We reached the river. Here there was an odor of mud and dirty water, and the sun blazed down on the water so that it burned my eyes. I begged Boivin to go under cover somewhere. He took me into a kind of shanty filled with men, a riverboat men's tavern.

"He said:

" 'This does not look very grand, but it is very comfortable.'

"I was hungry. I ordered an omelet. But lo and behold, at the second glass of wine, that beggar Boivin, lost his head, and I understood why his wife gave him water diluted.

"He got up, declaimed, wanted to show his strength, interfered in a quarrel between two drunken men who were fighting, and, but for the landlord, who came to the rescue, we should both have been killed.

"I dragged him away, holding him up until we reached the first bush, where I deposited him. I lay down beside him and, it seems, I fell asleep. We must certainly have slept a long time, for it was dark when I awoke. Boivin was snoring at my side. I shook him; he rose but he was still drunk, though a little less so.

"We set out through the darkness across the plain. Boivin said he knew the way. He made me turn to the left, then to the right, then to the left. We could see neither sky nor earth, and found ourselves lost in the midst of a kind of forest of wooden stakes that came as high as our noses. It was a vineyard, and these were the supports. There was not a single light on the horizon. We wandered about in this vineyard for about an hour or two, hesitating, reaching out our arms without coming to the end, for we kept retracing our steps.

"At length Boivin fell against a stake, which tore his cheek, and he remained in a sitting posture on the ground, uttering with all his might long and resounding halloos, while I screamed 'Help! Help!' as loud as I could, lighting wax matches to show the way to our rescuers and also to keep up my courage.

"At last a peasant, out late, heard us and put us on our right road. I took Boivin to his home, but as I was leaving him on the threshold of his garden, the door opened suddenly and his wife appeared, a candle in her hand. She frightened me horribly.

"As soon as she saw her husband, whom she must have been waiting for since dark, she screamed, as she darted toward me:

" 'Ah, scoundrel, I knew you would bring him back drunk!'

"My, how I made my escape, running all the way to the station, and as I thought the fury was pursuing me I shut myself in an inner room as the train was not due for half an hour.

"That is why I never married, and why I never go out of Paris."

THE UMBRELLA

Mme Oreille was a very economical woman; she thoroughly knew the value of a halfpenny and possessed a whole storehouse of strict principles with regard to the multiplication of money, so that her cook found the greatest difficulty in making what the servants call their "market penny," while her husband was hardly allowed any pocket money at all. They were, however, very comfortably off and had no children. It really pained Mme Oreille to see any money spent; it was like tearing at her heartstrings when she had to take any of those nice crown pieces out of her pocket, and whenever she had to spend anything, no matter how necessary it was, she slept badly the next night.

Oreille was continually saying to his wife:

"You really might be more liberal, as we have no children and never spend our income."

"You don't know what may happen," she used to reply. "It is better to have too much than too little."

She was a little woman of about forty, very active, rather hasty, wrinkled, very neat and tidy and with a very short temper. Her husband very often used to complain of all the privations she made him endure; some of them were particularly painful to him, as they touched his vanity.

He was one of the upper clerks in the War Office and only stayed there in obedience to his wife's wish, so as to increase their income, which they did not nearly spend.

For two years he had always come to the office with the same old patched umbrella, to the great amusement of his fellow clerks. At last he got tired of their jokes and insisted upon his wife buying him a new one. She bought one for eight francs and a half, one of those cheap things which large houses sell as an advertisement. When the others in the office saw the article, which was being sold in Paris by the thousand, they began their jokes again, and Oreille had a dreadful time of it with them. They even made a song about it, which he heard from morning till night all over the immense building.

Oreille was very angry and peremptorily told his wife to get him a new one, a good silk one, for twenty francs and to bring him the bill, so that he might see that it was all right.

She bought him one for eighteen francs and said, getting red with anger as she gave it to her husband:

"This will last you for five years at least."

Oreille felt quite triumphant and obtained a small ovation at the office with his new acquisition. When he went home in the evening his wife said to him, looking at the umbrella uneasily:

"You should not leave it fastened up with the elastic; it will very likely cut the silk. You must take care of it, for I shall not buy you a new one in a hurry."

She took it, unfastened it and then remained dumfounded with astonishment and rage. In the middle of the silk there was a hole as big as a sixpenny piece, as if made with the end of a cigar.

"What is that?" she screamed.

Her husband replied quietly without looking at it:

"What is it? What do you mean?"

She was choking with rage and could hardly get out a word.

"You—you—have burned—your umbrella! Why—you must be—mad! Do you wish to ruin us outright?"

He turned round hastily, as if frightened.

"What are you talking about?"

"I say that you have burned your umbrella. Just look here."

And rushing at him, as if she were going to beat him, she violently thrust the little circular burned hole under his nose.

He was so utterly struck dumb at the sight of it that he could only stammer out:

"What—what is it? How should I know? I have done nothing, I will swear. I don't know what is the matter with the umbrella."

"You have been playing tricks with it at the office; you have been playing the fool and opening it, to show it off!" she screamed.

"I only opened it once to let them see what a nice one it was; that is all, I declare."

But she shook with rage and got up one of those conjugal scenes which make a peaceable man dread the domestic hearth more than a battlefield where bullets are raining.

She mended it with a piece of silk cut out of the old umbrella, which was of a different color, and the next day Oreille went off very humbly with the mended article in his hand. He put it into a cupboard and thought no more of it than of some unpleasant recollection.

But he had scarcely got home that evening when his wife took the umbrella from him, opened it and nearly had a fit when she saw what had befallen it, for the disaster was now irreparable. It was covered with small holes which, evidently, proceeded from burns, just as if someone had emptied the ashes from a lighted pipe onto it. It was done for utterly, irreparably.

She looked at it without a word, in too great a passion to be able to say anything. He also, when he saw the damage, remained almost dumb, in a state of frightened consternation.

They looked at each other; then he looked onto the floor. The next moment she threw the useless article at his head, screaming out in a transport of the most violent rage, for she had now recovered her voice:

"Oh, you brute! You brute! You did it on purpose, but I will pay you out for it. You shall not have another.

And then the scene began again. After the storm had raged for an hour he at last was enabled to explain himself. He declared that he could not understand it at all and that it could only proceed from malice or from vengeance.

A ring at the bell saved him; it was a friend whom they were expecting to dinner.

Mme Oreille submitted the case to him. As for buying a new umbrella, that was out of the question; her husband should not have another. The friend very sensibly said that in that case his clothes would be spoiled, and they were certainly worth more than the umbrella. But the little woman, who was still in a rage, replied:

"Very well then, when it rains he may have the kitchen umbrella, for I will not give him a new silk one."

Oreille utterly rebelled at such an idea.

"All right," he said; "then I shall resign my post. I am not going to the office with the kitchen umbrella."

The friend interposed:

"Have this one recovered; it will not cost much."

But Mme Oreille, being in the temper that she was, said:

"It will cost at least eight francs to recover it. Eight and eighteen are twenty-six. Just fancy, twenty-six francs for an umbrella! It is utter madness!"

The friend, who was only a poor man of the middle classes, had an inspiration:

"Make your fire insurance pay for it. The companies pay for all articles that are burned, as long as the damage has been done in your own house."

On hearing this advice the little woman calmed down immediately, and then after a moment's reflection she said to her husband:

"Tomorrow, before going to your office, you will go to the Maternelle Insurance Company, show them the state your umbrella is in and make them pay for the damage."

M. Oreille fairly jumped, he was so startled at the proposal.

"I would not do it for my life! It is eighteen francs lost; that is all. It will not ruin us."

The next morning he took a walking stick when he went out, for luckily it was a fine day.

Left at home alone, Mme Oreille could not get over the loss of her eighteen francs by any means. She had put the umbrella on the dining-room table, and she looked at it without being able to come to any determination.

Every moment she thought of the insurance company, but she did not dare to encounter the quizzical looks of the gentlemen who might receive her, for she was very timid before people and grew red at a mere nothing, feeling embarrassed when she had to speak to strangers.

But regret at the loss of the eighteen francs pained her as if she had been wounded. She tried not to think of it any more, and yet every moment the recollection of the loss struck her painfully. What was she to do, however? Time went on, and she could not decide; but suddenly, like all cowards, she made up her mind.

"I will go, and we will see what will happen."

But first of all she was obliged to prepare the umbrella so that the disaster might be complete and the reason of it quite evident. She took a match from the mantelpiece, and between the ribs she burned a hole as big as the palm of her hand. Then she rolled it up carefully, fastened it with the elastic band, put on her bonnet and shawl and went quickly toward the Rue de Rivoli, where the insurance office was.

But the nearer she got the slower she walked. What was she going to say, and what reply would she get?

She looked at the numbers of the houses; there were still twenty-eight. That was all right; she had time to consider, and she walked slower and slower. Suddenly she saw a door on which was a large brass plate with "La Maternelle Insurance Office" engraved on it. Already! She waited for a moment, for she felt nervous and almost ashamed; then she went past, came back, went past again and came back again.

At last she said to herself:

"I must go in, however, so I may as well do it now as later."

She could not help noticing, however, how her heart beat as she entered. She went into an enormous room with grated wicket openings all round and a man behind each of them, and as a gentleman carrying a number of papers passed her, she stopped him and said timidly:

"I beg your pardon, monsieur, but can you tell me where I must apply for payment for anything that has been accidentally burned?"

He replied in a sonorous voice:

"The first door on the left; that is the department you want."

This frightened her still more, and she felt inclined to run away, to make no claim, to sacrifice her eighteen francs. But the idea of that sum revived her courage, and she went upstairs, out of breath, stopping at almost every other step.

She knocked at a door which she saw on the first landing, and a clear voice said in answer:

"Come in!"

She obeyed mechanically and found herself in a large room where three solemn gentlemen, each with a decoration in his buttonhole, were standing talking.

One of them asked her: "What do you want, madame?"

She could hardly get out her words but stammered: "I have come—I have come on account of an accident, something——"

He very politely pointed out a seat to her.

"If you will kindly sit down I will attend to you in a moment."

And, returning to the other two, he went on with the conversation.

"The company, gentlemen, does not consider that it is under any obligation to you for more than four hundred thousand francs, and we can pay no attention to your claim to the further sum of a hundred thousand, which you wish to make us pay. Besides that, the surveyor's valuation——"

One of the other interrupted him:

"That is quite enough, monsieur; the law courts will decide between us, and we have nothing further to do than to take our leave." And they went out after mutual ceremonious bows.

Oh, if she could only have gone away with them, how gladly she would have done it; she would have run away and given up everything. But it was too late, for the gentleman came back and said, bowing:

"What can I do for you, madame?"

She could scarcely speak, but at last she managed to say:

"I have come—for this."

The manager looked at the object which she held out to him in mute astonishment. With trembling fingers she tried to undo the elastic and succeeded, after several attempts, and hastily opened the damaged remains of the umbrella.

"It looks to me to be in a very bad state of health," he said compassionately.

"It cost me twenty francs," she said with some hesitation.

He seemed astonished. "Really! As much as that?"

"Yes, it was a capital article, and I wanted you to see the state it is in."

"Very well, I see; very well. But I really do not understand what it can have to do with me."

She began to feel uncomfortable; perhaps this company did not pay for such small articles, and she said:

"But—it is burned."

He could not deny it.

"I see that very well," he replied.

She remained openmouthed, not knowing what to say next; then, suddenly forgetting that she had left out the main thing, she said hastily:

"I am Madame Oreille; we are assured in La Maternelle, and I have come to claim the value of this damage. I only wanted you to have it recovered," she added quickly, fearing a positive refusal.

The manager was rather embarrassed and said:

"But really, madame, we do not sell umbrellas; we cannot undertake such kinds of repairs."

The little woman felt her courage reviving; she was not going to give up without a struggle; she was not even afraid now, so she said:

"I only want you to pay me the cost of repairing it; I can quite well get it done myself."

The gentleman seemed rather confused.

"Really, madame, it is such a very small matter! We are never asked to give compensation for such trivial losses. You must allow that we cannot make good pocket handkerchiefs, gloves, brooms, slippers, all the small articles which are every day exposed to the chances of being burned."

She got red and felt inclined to fly into a rage.

"But, monsieur, last December one of our chimneys caught fire and caused at least five hundred francs' damage. Monsieur Oreille made no claim on the company, and so it is only just that it should pay for my umbrella now."

The manager, guessing that she was telling a lie, said with a smile:

"You must acknowledge, madame, that it is very surprising that Monsieur Oreille should have asked no compensation for damages amounting to five hundred francs and should now claim five or six francs for mending an umbrella."

She was not the least put out and replied:

"I beg your pardon, monsieur, the five hundred francs affected Monsieur Oreille's pocket, whereas this damage, amounting to eighteen francs, concerns Madame Oreille's pocket only, which is a totally different matter."

As he saw that he had no chance of getting rid of her and that he would only be wasting his time, he said resignedly:

"Will you kindly tell me how the damage was done?"

She felt that she had won the victory and said:

"This is how it happened, monsieur: In our hall there is a bronze stick-and-umbrella stand, and the other day when I came in, I put my umbrella into it. I must tell you that just above there is a shelf for the candlesticks and matches. I put out my hand, took three or four matches and struck one, but it missed fire, so I struck another, which ignited but went out immediately, and a third did the same."

The manager interrupted her to make a joke:

"I suppose they were government matches then?"

She did not understand him and went on:

"Very likely. At any rate, the fourth caught fire, and I lit my candle and went into my room to go to bed, but in a quarter of an hour I fancied that I smelled something burning, and I have always been terribly afraid of fire. If ever we have an accident it will not be my fault, I assure you. I am terribly nervous since our chimney was on fire, as I told you, so I got up and hunted about everywhere, sniffing like a dog after game, and at last I noticed that my umbrella was burning. Most likely a match had fallen between the folds and burned it. You can see how it has damaged it."

The manager had taken his cue and asked her:

"What do you estimate the damage at?"

She did not know what to say, as she was not certain what amount to put on it, but at last she replied:

"Perhaps you had better get it done yourself. I will leave it to you."

He, however, naturally refused.

"No, madame, I cannot do that. Tell me the amount of your claim; that is all I want to know."

"Well—I think that—— Look here, monsieur, I do not want to make any money out of you, so I will tell you what we will do. I will take my umbrella to the maker, who will recover it in good, durable silk, and I will bring the bill to you. Will that suit you, monsieur?"

"Perfectly, madame; we will settle it on that basis. Here is a note for the cashier, who will repay you whatever it costs you."

He gave Mme Oreille a slip of paper. She took it, got up and went out, thanking him, for she was in a hurry to escape lest he should change his mind.

She went briskly through the streets, looking out for a really good umbrella maker, and when she found a shop which appeared to be a first-class one she went in and said confidently:

"I want this umbrella recovered in silk, good silk. Use the very best and strongest you have; I don't mind what it costs."

DENIS

M. Marambot opened the letter which his servant Denis gave him and smiled.

For twenty years Denis had been a servant in this house. He was a short, stout, jovial man, who was known throughout the countryside as a model servant. He asked:

"Is Monsieur pleased? Has Monsieur received good news?"

M. Marambot was not rich. He was an old village chemist, a bachelor, who lived on an income acquired with difficulty by sellings drugs to the farmers. He answered:

"Yes, my boy. Old man Malois is afraid of the lawsuit with which I am threatening him. I shall get my money tomorrow. Five thousand francs will not hurt the account of an old bachelor."

M. Marambot rubbed his hands with satisfaction. He was a man of quiet temperament, more sad than gay, incapable of any prolonged effort, careless in business.

He could undoubtedly have amassed a greater income had he taken advantage of the deaths of colleagues established in more important centers, by taking their places and carrying on their business. But the trouble of moving and the thought of all the preparations had always stopped him. After thinking the matter over for a few days, he would just say:

"Bah! I'll wait until the next time. I'll not lose anything by the delay. I may even find something better."

Denis, on the contrary, was always urging his master to new enterprises. Of an energetic temperament, he would continually repeat:

"Oh! If I had only had the capital to start out with, I could have made a fortune! One thousand francs would do me."

M. Marambot would smile without answering and would go out in his little garden, where, his hands behind his back, he would walk about dreaming.

All day long, Denis sang the joyful refrains of the folksongs of the district. He even showed an unusual activity, for he cleaned all the windows of the house, energetically rubbing the glass, and singing at the top of his voice.

M. Marambot, surprised at his zeal, said to him several times, smiling:

"My boy, if you work like that there will be nothing left for you to do tomorrow."

The following day, at about nine o'clock in the morning, the postman gave Denis four letters for his master, one of them very heavy. M. Marambot immediately shut himself up in his room until late in the afternoon. He then handed his servant four letters for the mail. One of them was addressed to M. Malois; it was undoubtedly a receipt for the money.

Denis asked his master no questions; he appeared to be as sad and gloomy that day as he had seemed joyful the day before.

Night came. M. Marambot went to bed as usual and slept.

He was awakened by a strange noise. He sat up in his bed and listened. Suddenly the door opened and Denis appeared, holding in one hand a candle and in the other a carving knife, his eyes staring, his face contracted as though moved by some deep emotion; he was as pale as a ghost.

In his astonishment M. Marambot thought that he was sleepwalking, and he was going to get out of bed and assist him when the servant blew out the light and rushed for the bed. His master stretched out his hands to receive the shock, which knocked him over on his back; he was trying to seize the hands of his servant, whom he now thought to be crazy, in order to avoid the blows which the latter was aiming at him.

He was struck by the knife; once in the shoulder, once in the forehead and the third time in the chest. He fought wildly, waving his arms around in the darkness, kicking and crying:

"Denis! Denis! Are you mad? Listen, Denis!"

But the latter, gasping for breath, kept up his furious attack: always striking, always repulsed, sometimes with a kick, sometimes with a punch, and rushing forward again furiously.

M. Marambot was wounded twice more, once in the leg and once in the stomach. But, suddenly, a thought flashed across his mind, and he began to shriek:

"Stop, stop, Denis, I have not yet received my money!"

The man immediately ceased, and his master could hear his labored breathing in the darkness.

M. Marambot then went on:

"I have received nothing. M. Malois takes back what he said, the lawsuit will take place; that is why you carried the letters to the mail. Just read those on my desk."

With a final effort, he reached for his matches and lit the candle.

He was covered with blood. His sheets, his curtains, and even the walls, were spattered with red. Denis, standing in the middle of the room, was also bloody from head to foot.

When he saw the blood M. Marambot thought himself dead, and fell unconscious.

At break of day he revived. It was some time, however, before he regained his senses, and was able to understand or remember. But, suddenly, the memory of the attack and of his wounds returned to him, and he was filled with such terror that he closed his eyes in order not to see anything. After a few minutes he grew calmer and began to think. He had not died immediately, therefore he might still recover. He felt weak, very weak; but he had no real pain, although he noticed an uncomfortable smarting sensation in several parts of his body. He also felt icy cold, and all wet, and as though wrapped up in bandages. He thought that this dampness came from the blood which he had lost; and he shivered at the dreadful thought of this red liquid which had come from his veins and covered his bed. The idea of seeing this terrible spectacle again so upset him that he kept his eyes closed with all his strength, as though they might open in spite of himself.

What had become of Denis? He had probably escaped.

But what could he, Marambot, do now? Get up? Call for help? But if he should make the slightest motions, his wounds would undoubtedly open up again and he would die from loss of blood.

Suddenly he heard the door of his room open. His heart almost stopped. It was certainly Denis who was coming, to finish him up. He held his breath in order to make the murderer think that he had been successful.

He felt his sheet being lifted up, and then someone feeling his stomach. A sharp pain near his hip made him start. He was being very gently washed with cold water. Therefore, someone must have discovered the misdeed and he was being cared for. A wild joy seized him; but, prudently, he did not wish to show that he was conscious. He opened one eye, just one, with the greatest precaution.

He recognized Denis standing beside him, Denis himself! Mercy! He hastily closed his eye again.

Denis. What could he be doing? What did he want? What awful scheme could he now be carrying out?

What was he doing? Well, he was washing him in order to hide the traces of his crime! And he would now bury him in the garden, under ten feet of earth, so that no one could discover him! Or perhaps in the wine cellar under the bottles of old wine! And M. Marambot began to tremble like a leaf. He kept saying to himself: "I am lost, lost!" He closed his eyes in order not to see the knife as it descended for the final stroke. It did not come. Denis was now lifting him up and bandaging him. Then he began carefully to dress the wound on his leg, as his master had taught him to do when he was a pharmacist.

There was no longer any doubt. His servant, after wishing to kill him, was trying to save him.

Then M. Marambot, in a dying voice, gave him the practical piece of advice:

"Wash the wounds in a diluted solution of carbolic acid!"

Denis answered:

"This is what I am doing, monsieur."

M. Marambot opened both his eyes. There was no sign of blood either on the bed, on the walls, or on the murderer. The wounded man was stretched out on clean white sheets.

The two men looked at each other.

Finally M. Marambot said calmly:

"You have been guilty of a great crime."

Denis answered:

"I am trying to make up for it, monsieur. If you will not tell on me, I will serve you as faithfully as in the past."

This was no time to anger his servant. M. Marambot murmured as he closed his eyes:

"I swear not to tell on you."

Denis saved his master. He spent days and nights without sleep, never leaving the sickroom, preparing drugs, broths, potions, feeling his pulse, anxiously counting the beats, attending him with the skill of a trained nurse and the devotion of a son.

He continually asked:

"Well, monsieur, how do you feel?"

M. Marambot would answer in a weak voice:

"A little better, my boy, thank you."

And when the sick man would wake up at night, he would often see his servant seated in an armchair weeping silently.

Never had the old chemist been so cared for, so fondled, so spoiled. At first he had said to himself:

"As soon as I am well I shall get rid of this rascal."

He was now convalescing, and from day to day he would put off dismissing his murderer. He thought that no one would ever show him such care and attention, for he held this man through fear; and he warned him that he had left a document with a lawyer denouncing him to the law if any new accident should occur.

This precaution seemed to guarantee him against any future attack; and he then asked himself if it would not be wiser to keep this man near him, in order to watch him closely.

Just as formerly, when he would hesitate about taking some larger place of business, he could not make up his mind to any decision.

"There is plenty of time," he would say to himself.

Denis continued to show himself an admirable servant. M. Marambot was well. He kept him.

One morning, just as he was finishing breakfast, he suddenly heard a great noise in the kitchen. He hastened in there. Denis was struggling with two gendarmes. An officer was taking notes on his pad.

As soon as he saw his master, the servant began to sob, exclaiming:

"You told on me, monsieur, that's not right, after what you promised me. You have broken your word of honor, M. Marambot; that's not right, that's not right!"

M. Marambot, bewildered and distressed at being suspected, lifted his hand.

"I swear to you before God, my boy, that I did not tell on you. I haven't the slightest idea how the police could have found out about your attack on me."

The officer started:

"You say that he attacked you, M. Marambot?"

The bewildered chemist answered:

"Yes—but I did not tell on him—I haven't said a word—I swear it—he has served me excellently from that time on—"

The officer pronounced severely:

"I will take down your testimony. The law will take notice of this new action, of which it was ignorant, M. Marambot. I was commissioned to arrest your servant for the theft of two ducks surreptitiously taken by him from M. Duhamel of which act there are witnesses. I shall make a note of your information."

Then, turning toward his men, he ordered:

"Come on, let us start!"

The two gendarmes dragged Denis out.

The lawyer used the plea of insanity, contrasting the two misdeeds in order to strengthen his argument. He had clearly proved that the theft of the two ducks came from the same mental condition as the eight knife wounds in the body of Marambot. He had cunningly analyzed all the phases of this transitory condition of mental aberration, which could, doubtless, be cured by a few months' treatment in a reputable sanatorium. He had spoken in enthusiastic terms of the continued devotion of this faithful servant, of the care with which he had surrounded his master, wounded by him in a moment of alienation.

Touched by this memory, M. Marambot felt the tears rising to his eyes.

The lawyer noticed it, opened his arms with a broad gesture, spreading out the long black sleeves of his robe like the wings of a bat, and exclaimed:

"Look, look, gentlemen of the jury, look at those tears. What more can I say for my client? What speech, what argument, what reasoning would be worth these tears of his master? They speak louder than I do, louder than the law; they cry: 'Mercy, for the poor wandering mind of a while ago!' They implore, they pardon, they bless!"

He was silent and sat down.

Then the judge, turning to Marambot, whose testimony had been excellent for his servant, asked him:

"But, monsieur, even admitting that you consider this man insane, that does not explain why you should have kept him. He was none the less dangerous."

Marambot, wiping his eyes, answered:

"Well, your honor, what can you expect? Nowadays it's so hard to find good servants—I could never have found a better one."

Denis was acquitted and put in a sanatorium at his master's expense.

THE DONKEY

There was not a breath of air stirring; a heavy mist was lying over the river. It was like a layer of dull white cotton placed on the water. The banks themselves were indistinct, hidden behind strange fogs. But day was breaking and the hill was

becoming visible. At its foot, in the dawning light of day, the plaster houses began
to appear like white spots. Cocks were crowing in the barnyard.

On the other side of the river, hidden behind the fogs just opposite Frette, a
slight noise from time to time broke the dead silence of the quiet morning. At
times it was an indistinct plashing, like the cautious advance of a boat, then again
a sharp noise like the rattle of an oar, and then the sound of something dropping
in the water. Then silence.

Sometimes whispered words, coming perhaps from a distance, perhaps from
quite near, pierced through these opaque mists. They passed by like wild birds
which have slept in the rushes and which fly away at the first light of day, crossing
the mist and uttering a low and timid sound which wakes their brothers along the
shores.

Suddenly along the bank, near the village, a barely perceptible shadow appeared
on the water. Then it grew, became more distinct, and, coming out of the foggy
curtain which hung over the river, a flat boat, manned by two men, pushed up on
the grass.

The one who was rowing rose and took a pailful of fish from the bottom of the
boat, then he threw the dripping net over his shoulder. His companion, who had
not made a motion, exclaimed: "Say, Mailloche, get your gun and see if we can't
land some rabbit along the shore."

The other one answered: "All right. I'll be with you in a minute." Then he disappeared, in order to hide their catch.

The man who had stayed in the boat slowly filled his pipe and lighted it. His
name was Labouise, but he was called Chicot, and was in partnership with Maillochon, commonly called Mailloche, practicing the doubtful and undefined profession of junk gatherers along the shore.

They were a low order of sailors, and they navigated regularly only in the months
of famine. The rest of the time they acted as junk gatherers. Rowing about on the
river day and night, watching for any prey, dead or alive, poachers on the water
and nocturnal hunters, sometimes hunting deer in the St. Germain forests, sometimes looking for drowned people and searching their clothes, picking up floating
rags and empty bottles; thus did Labouise and Maillochon live easily.

At times they would set out on foot about noon and stroll along straight ahead.
They would dine in some inn on the shore and leave again side by side. They
would remain away for a couple of days; then one morning they would be seen
rowing about in the tub which they called their boat.

At Joinville or at Nogent some boatman would be looking for his boat, which
had disappeared one night, probably stolen, while twenty or thirty miles from
there, on the Oise, some shopkeeper would be rubbing his hands, congratulating
himself on the bargain he had made when he bought a boat the day before for
fifty francs, which two men offered him as they were passing.

Maillochon reappeared with his gun wrapped up in rags. He was a man of forty
or fifty, tall and thin, with the restless eye of people who are worried by legitimate
troubles, the eyes of hunted animals. His open shirt showed his hairy chest, but
he seemed never to have had any more hair on his face than a short brush of a
mustache and a few stiff hairs under his lower lip. He was bald around the temples. When he took off the dirty cap that he wore his scalp seemed to be covered
with a fluffy down, like the body of a plucked chicken, ready for the spit.

Chicot, on the contrary, was red, fat, short, and hairy. He looked like a raw beefsteak hidden in a fireman's cap. He continually kept his left eye closed, as if he were aiming at something or at somebody, and when people jokingly cried to him: "Open your eye, Labouise!" he would answer quietly: "Never fear, kid, I open it when there's cause to."

He had a habit of calling every one "kid," even his scavenger companion.

He took up the oars again, and once more the boat disappeared in the heavy mist, which was now turned snowy white in the pink-tinted sky.

"What kind of lead did you take, Maillochon?" Labouise asked.

"Very small, number nine; that's the best for rabbits."

They were approaching the other shore so slowly, so quietly that no noise betrayed them. This bank belongs to the St. Germain forest and is the boundary line for rabbit hunting. It is covered with burrows hidden under the roots of trees, and the creatures at daybreak frisk about, running in and out of the holes.

Maillochon was kneeling in the bow, watching, his gun hidden on the floor. Suddenly he seized it, aimed, and the report echoed for some time throughout the quiet country.

Labouise, in a few strokes, touched the beach, and his companion, jumping to the ground, picked up a little gray rabbit, not yet dead.

Then the boat once more disappeared into the fog in order to get to the other side, where it could keep away from the gamekeepers.

The two men seemed to be riding easily on the water. The weapon had disappeared under the board which served as a hiding place, and the rabbit was stuffed into Chicot's loose shirt.

After about a quarter of an hour Labouise asked: "Well, kid, shall we get one more?"

"That will suit me," Maillochon answered.

The boat started swiftly down the current. The mist, which was hiding both shores, was beginning to rise. The trees could be barely perceived, as through a veil, and the little clouds of fog were floating up from the water. When they drew near the island, the end of which is opposite Herblay, the two men slackened their pace and began to watch. Soon a second rabbit was killed.

Then they went down until they were halfway to Conflans. Here they stopped their boat, tied it to a tree, and went to sleep in the bottom of it.

From time to time Labouise would sit up and look over the horizon with his open eye. The last of the morning mist had disappeared, and the large summer sun was climbing in the blue sky.

On the other side of the river the vineyard-covered hill stretched out in a semicircle. One house stood out alone at the summit. Everything was silent.

Something was moving slowly along the towpath, advancing with difficulty. It was a woman dragging a donkey. The stubborn, stiff-jointed beast occasionally stretched out a leg in answer to its companion's efforts, and it proceeded thus, with outstretched neck and ears lying flat, so slowly that one could not tell when it would ever be out of sight.

The woman, bent double, was pulling, turning round occasionally to strike the donkey with a stick.

As soon as he saw her, Labouise exclaimed: "Hey, Mailloche!"

Maillochon answered: "What's the matter?"

"Want to have some fun?"

"Of course!"

"Then hurry, kid; we're going to have a laugh."

Chicot took the oars. When he had crossed the river he stopped opposite the woman and called: "Hey, sister!"

The woman stopped dragging her donkey and looked.

Labouise continued: "What are you doing—going to the locomotive show?"

The woman made no reply. Chicot continued: "That nag must have won a prize at the races. Where are you taking him at that speed?"

At last the woman answered. "I'm going to Macquart, at Champioux, to have him killed. He's worthless."

Labouise answered: "You're right. How much do you think Macquart will give you for him?"

The woman wiped her forehead on the back of her hand and hesitated, saying: "How do I know? Perhaps three francs, perhaps four."

Chicot exclaimed: "I'll give you five francs and your errand's done! How's that?"

The woman considered the matter for a second and then exclaimed: "Done!"

The two men landed. Labouise grasped the animal by the bridle. Maillochon asked in surprise: "What do you expect to do with that carcass?"

Chicot this time opened his other eye in order to express his gaiety. His whole red face was grinning with joy. He chuckled: "Don't worry, kid. I've got my idea."

He gave five francs to the woman, who then sat down by the road to see what was going to happen. Then Labouise, in great humor, got the gun and held it out to Maillochon, saying: "Each one in turn, we're going after big game, kid. Don't get so near or you'll kill it right off! You must make the pleasure last a little."

He placed his companion about forty paces from the victim. The ass, feeling itself free, was trying to get a little of the tall grass, but it was so exhausted that it swayed on its legs as if it were about to fall.

Maillochon aimed slowly and said: "A little pepper for the ears; watch, Chicot!" And he fired.

The tiny shot struck the donkey's long ears, and he began to shake them in order to get rid of the stinging sensation. The two men were doubled up with laughter and stamped their feet with joy. The woman, indignant, rushed forward; she did not want her donkey to be tortured, and she offered to return the five francs. Labouise threatened her with a thrashing and pretended to roll up his sleeves. He had paid, hadn't he? Well, then, he would take a shot at her skirts, just to show that it didn't hurt. She went away, threatening to call the police. They could hear her protesting indignantly and cursing as she went her way.

Maillochon held out the gun to his comrade, saying: "It's your turn, Chicot."

Labouise aimed and fired. The donkey received the charge in his thighs, but the shot was so small and came from such a distance that he thought he was being stung by flies, for he began to thrash himself with his tail.

Labouise sat down to laugh more comfortably, while Maillochon reloaded the weapon, so happy that he seemed to sneeze into the barrel. He stepped forward a few paces, and, aiming at the same place that his friend had shot at, he fired again. This time the beast started, tried to kick, and turned its head. At last a little blood was running. It had been wounded and felt a sharp pain, for it tried to run away with a slow, limping, jerky gallop.

Both men darted after the beast, Maillochon with a long stride, Labouise with the short breathless trot of a little man. But the donkey, tired out, had stopped, and, with a bewildered look, was watching his two murderers approach. Suddenly he stretched his neck and began to bray.

Labouise, out of breath, had taken the gun. This time he walked right up close, as he did not wish to begin the chase over again.

When the poor beast had finished its mournful cry, like a last call for help, the man called: "Hey, Mailloche! Come here, kid; I'm going to give him some medicine." And while the other man was forcing the animal's mouth open, Chicot stuck the barrel of his gun down its throat, as if he were trying to make it drink a potion. Then he said: "Look out, kid, here she goes!"

He pressed the trigger. The donkey stumbled back a few steps, fell down, tried to get up again, and finally lay on its side and closed its eyes. The whole body was trembling, its legs were kicking as if it were trying to run. A stream of blood was oozing through its teeth. Soon it stopped moving. It was dead.

The two men stopped laughing. It was over too quickly; they had not had their money's worth. Maillochon asked: "Well, what are we going to do now?"

Labouise answered: "Don't worry, kid. Get the thing on the boat; we're going to have some fun when night comes."

They went and got the boat. The animal's body was placed on the bottom, covered with fresh grass, and the two men stretched out on it and went to sleep.

Toward noon Labouise drew a bottle of wine, some bread and butter and raw onions from a hiding place in their muddy, worm-eaten boat, and they began to eat.

When the meal was over they once more stretched out on the dead donkey and slept. At nightfall Labouise awoke and shook his comrade, who was snoring like a buzz saw. "Come on, kid," he ordered.

Maillochon began to row. As they had plenty of time they went up the Seine slowly. They coasted along the reaches covered with water lilies, and the heavy, mud-covered boat slipped over the lily pads and bent the flowers, which stood up again as soon as they had passed.

When they reached the wall of the Eperon, which separates the St. Germain forest from the Maisons-Laffitte Park, Labouise stopped his companion and explained his idea to him. Maillochon was moved by a prolonged, silent laugh.

They threw into the water the grass which had covered the body, took the animal by the feet, and hid it behind some bushes. Then they got into their boat again and went to Maisons-Laffitte.

The night was perfectly black when they reached the wineshop of old man Jules. As soon as the dealer saw them he came up, shook hands with them, and sat down at their table. They began to talk of one thing and another. By eleven o'clock the last customer had left and old man Jules winked at Labouise and asked: "Well, have you got any?"

Labouise made a motion with his head and answered: "Perhaps so, perhaps not!"

The dealer insisted: "Perhaps you've got nothing but gray ones?"

Chicot dug his hands into his flannel shirt, drew out the ears of a rabbit and declared: "Three francs a pair!"

Then began a long discussion about the price. Two francs sixty-five, and the two rabbits were delivered. As the two men were getting up to go, old man Jules, who had been watching them, exclaimed: "You have something else, but you won't say what."

Labouise answered: "Possibly, but it is not for you; you're too stingy."

The man, growing eager, kept asking: "What is it? Something big? Perhaps we might make a deal."

Labouise, who seemed perplexed, pretended to consult Maillochon with a glance. Then he answered in a slow voice: "This is how it is. We were in the bushes at Eperon when something passed right near us, to the left, at the end of the wall. Mailloche takes a shot and it drops. We skipped on account of the game people. I can't tell you what it is, because I don't know. But it's big enough. But what is it? If I told you I'd be lying, and you know, kid, between us everything's above-board."

Anxiously the man asked: "Think it's a deer?"

Labouise answered: "Might be and then again it might not! Deer?—unh-unh—might be a little big for that! Mind you, I don't say it's a doe, because I don't know, but it might be."

Still the dealer insisted: "Perhaps it's a buck?"

Labouise stretched out his hand, exclaiming: "No, it's not that! It's not a buck. I should have seen the horns. No, it's not a buck!"

"Why didn't you bring it with you?" asked the man.

"Because, kid, from now on I sell on the spot. Plenty of people will buy. All you have to do is to take a walk over there, find the thing and take it. No risk for me."

The innkeeper, growing suspicious, exclaimed: "Supposing he wasn't there!"

Labouise once more raised his hand and said: "He's there, I swear—first bush to the left. What it is, I don't know. But it's not a buck, I'm positive. It's for you to find out what it is. Twenty francs, cash down!"

Still the man hesitated: "Couldn't you bring it?"

Maillochon then became spokesman:

"Then there is no bargain. If it is a buck, it will be fifty francs, if it is a doe, twenty-five; that's our price."

The dealer decided: "It's a bargain for twenty francs."

And they shook hands over the deal.

Then he took out four big five-franc pieces from the cash drawer, and the two friends pocketed the money. Labouise arose, emptied his glass and left. As he was disappearing in the shadows he turned round to explain: "It isn't a buck. I don't know what it is!—but it's there. I'll give you back your money if you find nothing!"

And he disappeared in the darkness. Maillochon, who was following him, kept punching him in the back to express his delight.

THE QUESTION OF LATIN

This question of Latin, with which we were so much bothered some time since, recalls to my mind a story—a story of my youth.

I was finishing my studies with a teacher in a big central town, at the Institution Robineau, celebrated through the entire province, owing to the special attention paid there to Latin studies.

For the past ten years the Institution Robineau beat at every competitive examination the imperial lycée of the town and all the colleges of the subprefecture, and these constant successes were due, they said, to an usher, a simple usher, M. Piquedent, or rather Père Piquedent.

He was one of those middle-aged men, quite gray, whose real age it is impossible to know and whose history we can guess at first glance. Having entered as an usher at twenty into the first institution that presented itself so that he could proceed to take out his degree of doctor of laws, he found himself so much enmeshed in his sinister life that he remained as usher all his life. But his love for Latin did not leave him but harassed him like an unhealthy passion. He continued to read the poets, the prose writers, the historians, to interpret them, to study their meaning, to comment on them, with a perseverance bordering on madness.

One day the idea came into his head to force all the students of his class to answer him in Latin only, and he persisted in this resolution until at last they were capable of sustaining an entire conversation with him just as they would in their mother tongue. He listened to them as a leader of an orchestra listens to his musicians rehearsing and, striking his desk every moment with his ruler, he exclaimed:

"Monsieur Lefrère, Monsieur Lefrère, you are committing a solecism! You are not recalling the rule to mind."

"Monsieur Plantel, your turn of phrase is altogether French and in no way Latin. You must understand the genius of a language. Look here, listen to me."

Now it came to pass that the pupils of the Institution Robineau carried off at the end of the year all the prizes for composition, translation and Latin conversation.

Next year the principal, a little man, as cunning as an ape and with the same grinning and grotesque physique, had printed on his programs, on his advertisements and painted on the door of his institution:

"Latin studies a specialty. Five first prizes carried off in the five classes of the lycée.

"Two prizes of honor at the general competitive examinations with all the lycées and colleges of France."

For ten years the Institution Robineau triumphed in the same fashion. Now my father, allured by these successes, sent me as a day pupil to Robineau's—or, as we called it, Robinetto or Robinettino—and made me take special private lessons from Père Piquedent at the rate of five francs per hour, out of which the usher got two francs and the principal three francs. I was at the time in my eighteenth year and was in the philosophy class.

These private lessons were given in a little room looking out on the street. It so happened that Père Piquedent, instead of talking Latin to me, as he did when teaching publicly in the institution, kept telling about his troubles in French. Without relations, without friends, the poor man conceived an attachment for me and poured out into my heart his own misery.

He had never for the last ten or fifteen years chatted confidentially with anyone.

"I am like an oak in a desert," he said: "Sicut quercus in solitudine."

The other ushers disgusted him. He knew nobody in the town, since he had no liberty for the purpose of making acquaintances.

"Not even the nights, my friend, and that is the hardest thing on me. The dream of my life is to have a room of my own with furniture, my own books, little things that belonged to myself and which others could not touch. And I have nothing of my own, nothing except my shirt and my frock coat, nothing, not even my mattress and my pillows! I have not four walls to shut myself up in, except when I come to give a lesson in this room. Do you see what this means—a man forced to spend his life without ever having the right, without ever finding the time, to shut himself up all alone, no matter where, to think, to reflect, to work, to dream? Ah, my dear boy, a key, the key of a door which one can open—this is happiness, mark you, the only happiness!

"Here all day long the study with all those dirty brats jumping about in it, and during the night the dormitory with the same dirty brats snoring. And I have to sleep in the public bed at the end of two rows of beds occupied by these brats whom I must look after. I can never be alone, never! If I go out I find the street full of people, and when I am tired of walking I go into some café crowded with smokers and billiard players. I tell you that it is a regular prison."

I asked him:

"Why did you not take up some other line, Monsieur Piquedent?"

He exclaimed:

"What, my little friend? I am not a bootmaker or a joiner or a hatter or a baker or a hairdresser. I only know Latin, and I have not the diploma which would enable me to sell my knowledge at a high price. If I were a doctor I would sell for a hundred francs what I now sell for a hundred sous, and I would supply it probably of an inferior quality, for my academic rank would be enough to sustain my reputation."

Sometimes he would say to me:

"I have no rest in life except in the hours spent with you. Don't be afraid! You'll lose nothing by that. I'll make it up to you in the study by teaching you to speak twice as much Latin as the others."

One day I grew bolder and offered him a cigarette. He stared at me with astonishment at first, then he gave a glance toward the door:

"If anyone were to come in, my dear boy!"

"Well, let us smoke at the window," I said.

And we went and leaned with our elbows on the window sill facing the street, keeping our hands over the little rolls of tobacco wrapped up in tissue paper so that they concealed them from view like a shell. Just opposite to us was a laundry. Four women in white bodices were passing over the linen spread out before them the heavy hot irons, letting a damp fume escape from them.

Suddenly another, a fifth carrying on her arm a large basket which made her back stoop, came out to bring the customers their shirts and chemises, their handkerchiefs and their sheets. She stopped on the threshold as if she were already fatigued; then she raised her eyes, smiled when she saw us smoking, flung at us with her left hand, which was free, the sly kiss characteristic of a free-and-easy working-woman, and she went away at a slow pace, dragging her shoes after her.

She was a damsel of about twenty, small, rather thin, pale, rather pretty, with the manners of a street wench and eyes laughing under her ill-combed fair hair.

Père Piquedent, affected, began murmuring:

"What an occupation for a woman. Really a trade only fit for a horse."

And he spoke with emotion about the misery of the people. He had a heart which swelled with lofty democratic sentiment, and he referred to the fatiguing pursuits of the working class with phrases borrowed from Jean Jacques Rousseau and with sobs in his throat.

Next day, as we were resting our elbows at the same window, the same workwoman perceived us and cried out to us: "Good day, my scholars!" in a comical sort of tone, while she made a contemptuous gesture with her hands.

I flung her a cigarette, which she immediately began to smoke. And the four other ironers rushed out to the door with outstretched hands to get cigarettes also.

And each day a friendly relationship was being formed between the working-women of the pavement and the idlers of the boarding school.

Père Piquedent was really a comic sight to look at. He trembled at being noticed, for he might have lost his place, and he made timid and ridiculous gestures, quite a theatrical display of amorousness, to which the women responded with a regular fusillade of kisses.

A perfidious idea sprang up in my head. One day, on entering our room, I said to the old usher in a low tone:

"You would not believe it, Monsieur Piquedent, I met the little washerwoman! You know the one—the woman who had the basket—and I spoke to her!"

He asked, rather excited by the tone I had taken:

"What did she say to you?"

"She said to me—goodness gracious!—she said she thought you were very nice. The fact of the matter is, I believe, that she is a little in love with you." I saw that he was growing pale. He exclaimed:

"She is laughing at me, of course. These things don't happen at my age."

I said gravely:

"How is that? You are very nice."

As I felt that my trick had produced its effect on him, I did not press the matter

But every day I pretended that I had met the little laundress and that I had spoken to her about him, so that in the end he believed me and sent her ardent and earnest kisses.

Now it happened that one morning on my way to the boarding school I really came across her. I accosted her without hesitation, as if I had known her for the last ten years.

"Good day, mademoiselle. Are you quite well?"

"Very well, monsieur, thank you."

"Will you have a cigarette?"

"Oh, not in the street."

"You may smoke it at home."

"In that case, I will."

"Let me tell you, mademoiselle, there's something you don't know."

"What is that, monsieur?"

"The old gentleman—my old professor, I mean——"

"Père Piquedent."

"Yes, Père Piquedent. So you know his name?"

"Faith, I do! What of that?"

"Well, he is in love with you!"

She burst out laughing like a crazy woman and exclaimed:

"This is only humbug!"

"Oh no, 'tis no humbug! He keeps talking of you all the time he is giving lessons. I bet that he'll marry you!"

She ceased laughing. The idea of marriage makes every girl serious. Then she repeated with an incredulous air:

"This is humbug!"

"I swear to you 'tis true."

She picked up her basket which she had laid down at her feet.

"Well, we'll see," she said. And she went away.

Presently, when I had reached the boarding school, I took Père Piquedent aside and said:

"You must write to her; she is mad about you."

And he wrote a long letter of a soft and affectionate character, full of phrases and circumlocutions, metaphors and similes, philosophy and academic gallantry, and I took on myself the responsibility of delivering it to the young woman.

She read it with gravity, with emotion; then she murmured:

"How well he writes! It is easy to see he has got education! Does he really mean to marry me?"

I replied intrepidly: "Faith, he has lost his head about you!"

"Then he must invite me to dinner on Sunday at the Ile des Fleurs."

I promised that she would be invited.

Père Piquedent was much touched by everything I told him about her.

I added:

"She loves you, Monsieur Piquedent, and I believe her to be a decent girl. It is not right to seduce her and then abandon her."

He replied in a firm tone:

"I hope I, too, am a decent man, my friend."

I confess I had at the time no plan. I was playing a practical joke, a school boy's practical joke, nothing more. I had been aware of the simplicity of the old usher, his innocence and his weakness. I amused myself without asking myself how it would turn out. I was eighteen and had been for a long time looked upon at the lycée as a knowing practical joker.

So it was agreed that Père Piquedent and I should set out in a hackney coach for the ferry of Queue de Vache, that we should there pick up Angèle and that I should get them to come into my boat, for at this time I was fond of boating. I would then bring them to the Ile des Fleurs, where the three of us would dine. I had made it my business to be present, in order the better to enjoy my triumph, and the usher, consenting to my arrangement, proved clearly, in fact, that he had lost his head by thus risking his post.

When we arrived at the ferry where my boat had been moored since morning, I saw in the grass, or rather above the tall weeds of the bank, an enormous red parasol resembling a monstrous wild poppy. Under the parasol waited the little laundress in her Sunday clothes. I was surprised. She was really nice looking, though pale and graceful with a suburban gracefulness.

Père Piquedent raised his hat and bowed. She put out her hand toward him, and they stared at one another without uttering a word. Then they stepped into my boat; and I took the oars.

They were seated side by side on the seat near the stern. The usher was the first to speak:

"This is nice weather for a row in a boat."

She murmured: "Oh yes."

She drew her hand through the current, skimming the water with her fingers, which raised up a thin, transparent little stream like a sheet of glass. It made a light sound, a gentle ripple, as the boat moved along.

When they were in the restaurant she took it on herself to speak and order dinner—fried fish, a chicken and salad; then she led us on toward the isle which she knew perfectly.

After this she was gay, romping and even rather mocking.

Up to the dessert no question of love arose. I had treated them to champagne, and Père Piquedent was tipsy. Herself slightly elevated, she called out to him:

"Monsieur Piquenez."

He said all of a sudden:

"Mademoiselle, Monsieur Raoul has communicated my sentiments to you."

She became as serious as a judge.

"Yes, monsieur."

"Are you going to give any answer?"

"We never reply to these questions!"

He panted with emotion and went on:

"After all, a day will come when I may make you like me."

She smiled: "You big fool! You are very nice."

"In short, mademoiselle, do you think that later on we might——"

She hesitated a second, then in a trembling voice she said:

"Is it in order to marry me you say that? For never otherwise, you know."

"Yes, mademoiselle!"

"Well, that's all right, Monsieur Piquedent!"

It is thus that these two silly creatures promised marriage to each other through the wiles of a reckless schoolboy. But I did not believe that it was serious, nor indeed did they themselves, perhaps.

On her part there was a certain feeling of hesitation.

"You know, I have nothing—not four sous."

He stammered, for he was as drunk as Silenus:

"I have saved five thousand francs."

She exclaimed triumphantly:

"Then we can set up in business?"

He became restless. "In what business?"

"What do I know about that? We shall see. With five thousand francs we could do many things. You don't want me to go and live in your boarding school, do you?"

He had not looked forward so far as this, and he stammered in great perplexity:

"What business could we set up in? It is not convenient, for all I know is Latin!"

She reflected in her turn, passing in review all the professions which she had longed for.

"You could not be a doctor?"

"No, I have not the diploma."

"Or a chemist?"

"No more than the other."

She uttered a cry, a cry of joy. She had discovered it.

"Then we'll buy a grocer's shop! Oh, what luck! We'll buy a grocer's shop! Not on a big scale, all the same; with five thousand francs one cannot go far."

He was shocked at the suggestion.

"No, I can't be a grocer. I am—I am—too well known. I only know Latin— that's all I know."

But she poured a glass of champagne down his throat. He drank it and was silent.

We got back into the boat. The night was dark, very dark. I saw clearly, however, that he had caught her by the waist and that they were hugging each other again and again.

It was a frightful catastrophe. Our escapade was discovered with the result that Père Piquedent was dismissed. And my father, in a fit of anger, sent me to finish my course of philosophy at Ribaudet's School.

Six months later I passed for my degree of bachelor of arts. Then I went to study law in Paris, and I did not return to my native town till ten years after.

At the corner of the Rue de Serpent a shop caught my eye. Over the door were the words: "Colonial products—Piquedent," then underneath, so as to enlighten the most ignorant: "Grocery."

I exclaimed: "Quantum mutatus ab illo!"

He raised his head, left his female customer and rushed toward me with outstretched hands.

"Ah, my young friend, my young friend, here you are! What luck! What luck!"

A beautiful woman, very plump, abruptly left the counter and flung herself on my breast. I had some difficulty in recognizing her, so fat had she grown.

I asked: "So then you're going on well?"

Piquedent had gone back to weigh the groceries:

"Oh, very well, very well, very well. I have made three thousand francs clear this year!"

"And what about the Latin, Monsieur Piquedent?"

"Oh, goodness gracious! the Latin—the Latin—the Latin. Well, you see, it does not keep the pot boiling!"

MOTHER AND SON!!!

We were chatting in the smoking room after a dinner at which only men were present. We talked about unexpected legacies, strange inheritances. Then M. le Brument, who was sometimes called the "illustrious master" and at other times the "illustrious advocate," came and stood with his back to the fire.

"I have," he said, "just now to search for an heir who disappeared under peculiarly terrible circumstances. It is one of those simple and ferocious dramas of ordinary life, a thing which possibly happens every day and which is, nevertheless, one of the most dreadful things I know. Here are the facts:

"Nearly six months ago I got a message to come to the side of a dying woman. She said to me:

" 'Monsieur, I want to intrust to you the most delicate, the most difficult and the most wearisome mission that can be conceived. Be good enough to take cognizance of my will, which is there on the table. A sum of five thousand francs is left to you as a fee if you do not succeed and of a hundred thousand francs if you do succeed. I want to have my son found after my death.'

"She asked me to assist her to sit up in the bed in order that she might be able to speak with greater ease, for her voice, broken and gasping, was gurgling in her throat.

"I saw that I was in the house of a very rich person. The luxurious apartment.

with a certain simplicity in its luxury, was upholstered with materials solid as the walls, and their soft surfaces imparted a caressing sensation, so that every word uttered seemed to penetrate their silent depths and to disappear and die there.

"The dying woman went on:

" 'You are the first to hear my horrible story. I will try to have strength enough to go on to the end of it. You must know everything so that you, whom I know to be a kindhearted man as well as a man of the world, should have a sincere desire to aid me with all your power.

" 'Listen to me.

" 'Before my marriage I loved a young man, whose suit was rejected by my family because he was not rich enough. Not long afterward I married a man of great wealth. I married him through ignorance, through obedience, through indifference, as young girls do marry.

" 'I had a child, a boy. My husband died in the course of a few years.

" 'He whom I had loved had got married in his turn. When he saw that I was a widow he was crushed by horrible grief at knowing that he was not free. He came to see me; he wept and sobbed so bitterly before my eyes that it was enough to break my heart. He at first came to see me as a friend. Perhaps I ought not to have seen him. What could I do? I was alone, so sad, so solitary, so hopeless! And I loved him still. What sufferings we women have sometimes to endure!

" 'I had only him in the world, my parents also being dead. He came frequently; he spent whole evenings with me. I should not have let him come so often, seeing that he was married. But I had not enough will power to prevent him from coming.

" 'How am I to tell you what next happened? He became my lover. How did this come about? Can I explain it? Can anyone explain such things? Do you think it could be otherwise when two human beings are drawn toward each other by the irresistible force of a passion by which each of them is possessed? Do you believe, monsieur, that it is always in our power to resist, that we can keep up the struggle forever and refuse to yield to the prayers, the supplications, the tears, the frenzied words, the appeals on bended knees, the transports of passion, with which we are pursued by the man we adore, whom we want to gratify in his slightest wishes, whom we desire to crowd with every possible happiness and whom, if we are to be guided by a worldly code of honor, we must drive to despair? What strength would it not require? What a renunciation of happiness? What self-denial? And even what virtuous selfishness?

" 'In short, monsieur, I was his mistress, and I was happy. For twelve years I was happy. I became—and this was my greatest weakness and my greatest piece of cowardice—I became his wife's friend.

" 'We brought up my son together; we made a man of him, a thorough man, intelligent, full of sense and resolution, of large and generous ideas. The boy reached the age of seventeen.

" 'He, the young man, was fond of my—my lover, almost as fond of him as I was myself, for he had been equally cherished and cared for by both of us. He used to call him his "dear friend" and respected him immensely, having never received from him anything but wise counsels and a good example of rectitude, honor and probity. He looked upon him as an old, loyal and devoted comrade of his mother, as a sort of moral father, tutor, protector—how am I to describe it?

" 'Perhaps the reason why he never asked any questions was that he had been accustomed from his earliest years to see this man in the house by his side and by my side, always concerned about us both.

" 'One evening the three of us were to dine together (these were my principal festive occasions), and I waited for the two of them, asking myself which of them would be the first to arrive. The door opened; it was my old friend. I went toward him with outstretched arms, and he drew his lips toward mine in a long, delicious kiss.

" 'All of a sudden a sound, a rustling which was barely audible, that mysterious sensation which indicated the presence of another person, made us start and turn round with a quick movement. Jean, my son, stood there, livid, staring at us.

" 'There was a moment of atrocious confusion. I drew back, holding out my hands toward my son as if in supplication, but I could see him no longer. He had gone.

" 'We remained facing each other—my lover and I—crushed, unable to utter a word. I sank down on an armchair, and felt a desire, a vague, powerful desire to fly, to go out into the night and to disappear forever. Then convulsive sobs rose up in my throat, and I wept, shaken with spasms, with my heart torn asunder, all my nerves writhing with the horrible sensation of an irremediable misfortune and with that dreadful sense of shame which, in such moments as this, falls on a mother's heart.

" 'He looked at me in a scared fashion, not venturing to approach me or to speak to me or to touch me, for fear of the boy's return. At last he said:

" ' "I am going to follow him—to talk to him—to explain matters to him. In short, I must see him and let him know——"

" 'And he hurried away.

" 'I waited—I waited in a distracted frame of mind, trembling at the least sound, convulsed with terror and filled with some unutterably strange and intolerable emotion by every slight crackling of the fire in the grate.

" 'I waited for an hour, for two hours, feeling my heart swell with a dread I had never before experienced, with such an anguish as I would not wish the greatest of criminals to experience. Where was my son? What was he doing?

" 'About midnight a messenger brought me a note from my lover. I still know it contents by heart:

" '*Has your son returned? I did not find him. I am down here. I do not want to go up at this hour.*

" 'I wrote in pencil on the same slip of paper:

" '*Jean has not returned. You must go and find him.*

" 'And I remained all night in the armchair, waiting for him.

" 'I felt as if I were going mad. I longed to run wildly about, to roll myself on the floor. And yet I did not even stir but kept waiting hour after hour. What was going to happen? I tried to imagine, to guess. But I could form no conception in spite of my efforts, in spite of the tortures of my soul!

" 'And now my apprehension was lest they might meet. What would they do in that case? What would my son do? My mind was lacerated by fearful doubts, by terrible suppositions.

" 'You understand what I mean, do you not, monsieur?

" 'My chambermaid, who knew nothing, who understood nothing, was coming in every moment, believing, naturally, that I had lost my reason. I had sent her away with a word or a movement of the hand. She went for the doctor, who found me in the throes of a nervous fit.

" 'I was put to bed. Then came an attack of brain fever. When I regained consciousness after a long illness I saw beside my bed my—lover—alone. I exclaimed:

" ' "My son? Where is my son?'

" 'He replied:

" ' "I assure you every effort has been made by me to find him, but I have failed!"

" 'Then, becoming suddenly exasperated and even indignant—for women are subject to such outbursts of unaccountable and unreasoning anger—I said:

" ' "I forbid you to come near me or to see me again unless you find him. Go away!"

" 'He did go away.

" 'I have never seen one or the other of them since, monsieur, and thus I have lived for the last twenty years.

" 'Can you imagine what all this meant to me? Can you understand this monstrous punishment, this slow, perpetual laceration of a mother's heart, this abominable, endless waiting? Endless, did I say? No; it is about to end, for I am dying. I am dying without ever again seeing either of them—either one or the other!

" 'He—the man I loved—has written to me every day for the last twenty years, and I—I have never consented to see him, even for one second, for I had a strange feeling that if he came back here it would be at that very moment my son would again make his appearance! Ah, my son, my son! Is he dead? Is he living? Where is he hiding? Over there perhaps, at the other side of the ocean, in some country so far away that even its very name is unknown to me! Does he ever think of me? Ah, if he only knew! How cruel children are! Did he understand to what frightful suffering he condemned me, into what depths of despair, into what tortures, he cast me while I was still in the prime of life, leaving me to suffer like this even to this moment when I am going to die—me, his mother, who loved him with all the violence of a mother's love! Oh, isn't it cruel, cruel?

" 'You will tell him all this, monsieur—will you not? You will repeat for him my last words:

" ' "My child, my dear, dear child, be less harsh toward poor women! Life is already brutal and savage enough in its dealing with them. My dear son, think of what the existence of your poor mother has been ever since the day when you left her. My dear child, forgive her and love her, now that she is dead, for she has had to endure the most frightful penance ever inflicted on a woman." '

"She gasped for breath, shuddering, as if she had addressed her last words to her son and as if he stood by her bedside.

"Then she added:

" 'You will tell him also, monsieur, that I never again saw—the other.'

"Once more she ceased speaking, then in a broken voice she said:

" 'Leave me now, I beg of you. I want to die all alone, since they are not with me.' "

Maître le Brument added:

"I left the house, messieurs, crying like a fool, so vehemently, indeed, that my coachman turned round to stare at me.

"And to think that every day heaps of dramas like this are being enacted all around us!

"I have not found the son—that son—well, say what you like about him, but I call him that criminal son!"

HE?[1]

My dear friend, you cannot understand it by any possible means, you say, and I perfectly believe you. You think I am going mad? It may be so, but not for the reasons which you suppose.

Yes, I am going to get married, and I will tell you what has led me to take that step.

My ideas and my convictions have not changed at all. I look upon all legalized cohabitation as utterly stupid, for I am certain that nine husbands out of ten are cuckolds, and they get no more than their deserts for having been idiotic enough to fetter their lives and renounce their freedom in love, the only happy and good thing in the world, for having clipped the wings of fancy which continually drive us on toward all women. You know what I mean. More than ever I feel that I am incapable of loving one woman alone, because I shall always adore all the others too much. I should like to have a thousand arms, a thousand mouths and a thousand —*temperaments*, to be able to strain an army of these charming creatures in my embrace at the same moment.

And yet I am going to get married!

I may add that I know very little of the girl who is going to become my wife tomorrow; I have only seen her four or five times. I know that there is nothing unpleasant about her, and that is enough for my purpose. She is small, fair and stout, so of course the day after tomorrow I shall ardently wish for a tall, dark, thin woman.

She is not rich and belongs to the middle classes. She is a girl such as you may find by the gross, well adapted for matrimony, without any apparent faults and with no particularly striking qualities. People say of her: "Mademoiselle Lajolle is a very nice girl," and tomorrow they will say: "What a very nice woman Madame Raymon is." She belongs, in a word, to that immense number of girls who make very good wives for us till the moment comes when we discover that we happen to prefer all other women to that particular woman we married.

"Well," you will say to me, "what on earth do you get married for?"

I hardly like to tell you the strange and seemingly improbable reason that urged me on to this senseless act; the fact, however, is that I am frightened of being alone!

I don't know how to tell you or to make you understand me, but my state of mind is so wretched that you will pity and despise me.

I do not want to be alone any longer at night; I want to feel that there is some-one close to me, touching me, a being who can speak and say something, no matter what it be.

I wish to be able to awaken somebody by my side, so that I may be able to ask some sudden question even, if I feel inclined, so that I may hear a human voice

[1]It was in this story that the first gleams of De Maupassant's approaching madness became apparent. Thenceforward he began to revel in the strange and terrible, until his malady had seized him wholly. "A Madman" is in a similar vein.

and feel that there is some waking soul close to me, someone whose reason is at work, so that when I hastily light the candle I may see some human face by my side—because—because—I am ashamed to confess it—because I am afraid of being alone.

Oh, you don't understand me yet.

I am not afraid of any danger; if a man were to come into the room I should kill him without trembling. I am not afraid of ghosts, nor do I believe in the supernatural. I am not afraid of dead people, for I believe in the total annihilation of every being that disappears from the face of this earth.

Well, yes, well, it must be told; I am afraid of myself, afraid of that horrible sensation of incomprehensible fear.

You may laugh if you like. It is terrible, and I cannot get over it. I am afraid of the walls, of the furniture, of the familiar objects, which are animated, as far as I am concerned, by a kind of animal life. Above all, I am afraid of my own dreadful thoughts, of my reason, which seems as if it were about to leave me, driven away by a mysterious and invisible agony.

At first I feel a vague uneasiness in my mind which causes a cold shiver to run all over me. I look round, and of course nothing is to be seen, and I wish there were something there, no matter what, as long as it were something tangible; I am frightened, merely because I cannot understand my own terror.

If I speak I am afraid of my own voice. If I walk I am afraid of I know not what, behind the door, behind the curtains, in the cupboard or under my bed, and yet all the time I know there is nothing anywhere, and I turn round suddenly because I am afraid of what is behind me, although there is nothing there and I know it.

I get agitated; I feel that my fear increases, and so I shut myself up in my own room, get into bed and hide under the clothes, and there, cowering down, rolled into a ball, I close my eyes in despair and remain thus for an indefinite time, remembering that my candle is alight on the table by my bedside and that I ought to put it out, and yet—I dare not do it!

It is very terrible, is it not, to be like that?

Formerly I felt nothing of all that; I came home quite comfortably and went up and down in my rooms without anything disturbing my calmness of mind. Had anyone told me that I should be attacked by a malady—for I can call it nothing else —of most improbable fear, such a stupid and terrible malady as it is, I should have laughed outright. I was certainly never afraid of opening the door in the dark; I used to go to bed slowly without locking it and never got up in the middle of the night to make sure that everything was firmly closed.

It began last year in a very strange manner, on a damp autumn evening. When my servant had left the room after I had dined I asked myself what I was going to do. I walked up and down my room for some time, feeling tired without any reason for it, unable to work and without enough energy to read. A fine rain was falling, and I felt unhappy, a prey to one of those fits of casual despondency which makes us feel inclined to cry or to talk, no matter to whom, so as to shake off our depressing thoughts.

I felt that I was alone and that my rooms seemed to me to be more empty than they had ever been before. I was surrounded by a sensation of infinite and overwhelming solitude. What was I to do? I sat down, but then a kind of nervous impatience agitated my legs so that I got up and began to walk about again. I was feverish, for my hands, which I had clasped behind me, as one often does when walking slowly, almost seemed to burn one another. Then suddenly a cold shiver ran down my back, and I thought the damp air might have penetrated into my room, so I lit the fire for the first time that year and sat down again and looked at the flames. But soon I felt that I could not possibly remain quiet. So I got up again and determined to go out, to pull myself together and to seek a friend to bear me company.

I could not find anyone, so I went on to the boulevards to try and meet some acquaintance or other there.

I was wretched everywhere, and the wet pavement glistened in the gaslight, while the oppressive mist of the almost impalpable rain lay heavily over the streets and seemed to obscure the light from the lamps.

I went on slowly, saying to myself, "I shall not find a soul to talk to."

I glanced into several cafés, from the Madeleine as far as the Faubourg Poissonière, and saw many unhappy-looking individuals sitting at the tables, who did not seem even to have enough energy left to finish the refreshments they had ordered.

For a long time I wandered aimlessly up and down, and about midnight I started off for home; I was very calm and very tired. My concierge opened the door at once, which was quite unusual for him, and I thought that another lodger had no doubt just come in.

When I go out I always double-lock the door of my room. Now I found it merely closed, which surprised me, but I supposed that some letters had been brought up for me in the course of the evening.

I went in and found my fire still burning, so that it lighted up the room a little. In the act of taking up a candle I noticed somebody sitting in my armchair by the fire, warming his feet, with his neck toward me.

I was not in the slightest degree frightened. I thought very naturally that some friend or other had come to see me. No doubt the porter, whom I had told when I went out, had lent him his own key. In a moment I remembered all the circumstances of my return, how the street door had been opened immediately and that my own door was only latched and not locked.

I could see nothing of my friend but his head. He had evidently gone to sleep while waiting for me, so I went up to him to rouse him. I saw him quite clearly; his right arm was hanging down and his legs were crossed, while his head, which was somewhat inclined to the left of the armchair, seemed to indicate that he was asleep. "Who can it be?" I asked myself. I could not see clearly, as the room was rather dark, so I put out my hand to touch him on the shoulder, and it came in contact with the back of the chair. There was nobody there; the seat was empty.

I fairly jumped with fright. For a moment I drew back as if some terrible danger had suddenly appeared in my way; then I turned round again, impelled by some imperious desire to look at the armchair again. I remained standing upright, panting with fear, so upset that I could not collect my thoughts, and ready to drop.

But I am naturally a cool man and soon recovered myself. I thought: "It is a mere hallucination; that is all," and I immediately began to reflect about this phenomenon. Thoughts fly very quickly at such moments.

I had been suffering from a hallucination; that was an incontestable fact. My mind had been perfectly lucid and had acted regularly and logically, so there was nothing the matter with the brain. It was only my eyes that had been deceived;

they had had a vision, one of those visions which lead simple folk to believe in miracles. It was a nervous accident to the optical apparatus, nothing more; the eyes were rather overwrought, perhaps.

I lit my candle, and when I stooped down to the fire in so doing I noticed that I was trembling, and I raised myself up with a jump, as if somebody had touched me from behind.

I was certainly not by any means reassured.

I walked up and down a little and hummed a tune or two. Then I double-locked my door and felt rather reassured; now, at any rate, nobody could come in.

I sat down again and thought over my adventure for a long time; then I went to bed and put out my light.

For some minutes all went well; I lay quietly on my back. Then an irresistible desire seized me to look round the room, and I turned onto my side.

My fire was nearly out, and the few glowing embers threw a faint light on to the floor by the chair, where I fancied I saw the man sitting again.

I quickly struck a match, but I had been mistaken, for there was nothing there; I got up, however, and hid the chair behind my bed and tried to get to sleep as the room was now dark. But I had not forgotten myself for more than five minutes when in my dream I saw all the scene which I had witnessed as clearly as if it were reality. I woke up with a start and, having lit the candle, sat up in bed without venturing even to try and go to sleep again.

Twice, however, sleep overcame me for a few moments in spite of myself, and twice I saw the same thing again, till I fancied I was going mad. When day broke, however, I thought that I was cured and slept peacefully till noon.

It was all past and over. I had been feverish, had had the nightmare; I don't know what. I had been ill, in a word, but yet I thought that I was a great fool.

I enjoyed myself thoroughly that evening; I went and dined at a restaurant; afterward I went to the theater and then started home. But as I got near the house I was seized by a strange feeling of uneasiness once more; I was afraid of *seeing* him again. I was not afraid of him, not afraid of his presence, in which I did not believe, but I was afraid of being deceived again; I was afraid of some fresh hallucination, afraid lest fear should take possession of me.

For more than an hour I wandered up and down the pavement; then I thought that I was really too foolish and returned home. I panted so that I could scarcely get upstairs and remained standing outside my door for more than ten minutes; then suddenly I took courage and pulled myself together. I inserted my key into the lock and went in with a candle in my hand. I kicked open my half-open bedroom door and gave a frightened look toward the fireplace; there was nothing there. Ah!

What a relief and what a delight! What a deliverance; I walked up and down briskly and boldly, but I was not altogether reassured and kept turning round with a jump; the very shadows in the corners disquieted me.

I slept badly and was constantly disturbed by imaginary noises, but I did not see *him*; no, that was all over.

Since that time I have been afraid of being alone at night. I feel that the specter is there close to me, around me, but it has not appeared to me again. And supposing it did, what would it matter, since I do not believe in it and know that is is nothing?

It still worries me, however, because I am constantly thinking of it: *his right* arm hanging down and his head inclined to the left like a man who was asleep. Enough of that, in heaven's name! I don't want to think about it!

Why, however, am I so persistently possessed with this idea? His feet were close to the fire!

He haunts me; it is very stupid, but so it is. Who and what is HE? I know that he does not exist except in my cowardly imagination, in my fears and in my agony! There—enough of that!

Yes, it is all very well for me to reason with myself, to stiffen myself, so to say, but I cannot remain at home because I know he is there. I know I shall not see him again; he will not show himself again; that is all over. But he is there all the same in my thoughts. He remains invisible, but that does not prevent his being there. He is behind the doors, in the closed cupboards, in the wardrobe, under the bed, in every dark corner. If I open the door or the cupboard, if I take the candle to look under the bed and throw a light onto the dark places, he is there no longer, but I feel that he is behind me. I turn round, certain that I shall not see him, that I shall never see him again, but he is, nonetheless, behind me.

It is very stupid; it is dreadful, but what am I to do? I cannot help it.

But if there were two of us in the place I feel certain that he would not be there any longer, for he is there just because I am alone, simply and solely because I am alone!

MONSIEUR JOCASTE

Madame, do you recollect our great quarrel one evening in the little Japanese drawing room, about the father who committed incest? Do you recollect how indignant you were, the violent words you flung at me, and how angry you became, and do you also remember all I said in defense of that man? You blamed me. I appeal against you.

No one in the world, you declared, no one could uphold the infamous deed which I defended. Today I am going to tell this tale to the public.

Perhaps someone might be found who, although not excusing the brutal deed, would understand that one cannot struggle against certain fatalities that seem to be horrible fantasies of all-powerful Nature.

When sixteen years old she had been married to a hardhearted old man, a businessman who married her for her money. She was a darling blond creature, gay and dreamy at the same time, and yearning for an ideal happiness. Disillusion fell on her heart and broke it. Suddenly she understood life—no future, the destruction of her hopes, and one wish alone took possession of her soul, and that was to have a child to claim her love.

But she did not have one. Two years passed. She fell in love with a young man twenty-three years old, who was wildly in love with her. For some time she firmly resisted his advances. He was called Pierre Martel.

But one winter's evening they found themselves alone, at her house. He had come to drink a cup of tea. Then they sat down near the fire, on a low seat. They scarcely spoke. They were passionately in love with each other, stung with desire their lips thirsted wildly for other lips, their arms trembled with a desire to open and embrace someone.

The lamp, draped with lace, shed a cosy light in the silent drawing room.

Although they were both embarrassed, they occasionally exchanged a few words, but when their eyes met their hearts trembled.

How can acquired sentiments withstand the violence of instinct? How can the appearance of reserve withstand the irresistible desires of nature?

It happened that their fingers touched. And that was enough. They were overcome by passion. They embraced, and she yielded.

She became pregnant. By her husband, or by her lover. How did she know? Doubtless by her lover.

Then she became very much frightened and felt sure that she would die in her confinement, and she insisted that the man who was the cause of her being in this condition should swear over and over again to watch over the child during its whole life, to refuse it nothing, to be everything to it, yes, everything, and, if necessary, even to commit a crime in order to insure its happiness.

She carried this to an absurd extent. She became more and more worked up as her confinement drew near.

She died giving birth to a girl.

The young man was in the depths of despair, in fact his despair was so great that he could not hide it; perhaps the husband suspected something; perhaps he knew that he could not have been the father of the girl! He forbade the house to the man who thought himself the real father, hid the child from him, and had it brought up in seclusion.

Many years passed.

Pierre Martel forgot all about it, as one forgets everything. He became rich, but he could not love anyone now, and he had not married. His life was ordinary; that of a happy, quiet man. He had never heard a word about the husband he had deceived, nor about the young girl he thought was his.

Well, one morning he received a letter from a comparative stranger, who happened to mention the death of his old rival, and he was somewhat disturbed and filled with remorse. What had become of this child, his child? Could he do nothing for her? He inquired about her. She had been brought up by an aunt, and she was poor, miserably poor.

He wanted to see her and to help her. He called on the only relation of the orphan.

Even his name awoke no memory. He was forty years old and still looked like a young man. He was received, but he did not dare to say that he had known her mother, fearing it would give rise to suspicion later on.

Well, as soon as she entered the little sitting room where he anxiously awaited her coming, he trembled for he was all but overcome by surprise. It was she, the other woman! the woman who was dead!

She was the same age, had the same eyes, the same hair, the same figure, the same smile, the same voice. The illusion was so real that it maddened him; all the tumultuous love of days gone by sprang up from the depths of his heart. She likewise was both gay and unaffected. At once they became friends and shook hands.

On returning home he found that the old wound had been opened again, and he wept desperately; he held his head in his hands and wept for the woman who had died, haunted by memories and by the familiar words she used to say; he was plunged in despair from which there was no escape.

He visited the house in which the young girl resided. He could no longer live without her, without her merry talk, the rustle of her gown, the intonation of her voice. And now in his thoughts and in his heart he confounded the two women, the one gone before and the living one, forgetting distance, the time that had elapsed, and death; always loving that one in this one, and this one in memory of the other, not trying to understand why, to know why, never even asking himself if she could be his daughter.

Occasionally, when he noticed the discomfort in which the woman lived, whom he adored with this double passion, which he, himself, could not understand, he felt terribly about it.

What could he do? Could he offer money? How could he do it? What right had he? Could he play the role of guardian? He seemed scarcely older than she; everyone would take him for her lover. Should he get a husband for her? This thought suddenly surged up in his soul and frightened him. Then he became calmer. Who would ask her hand in marriage? She had nothing, not a cent.

Her aunt noticed how often he came and saw quite plainly that he was in love with this child. And what was he waiting for? Did he know?

One evening they were alone. They were talking softly side by side on the sofa in the little sitting room. Suddenly he took her hand in a paternal manner. He held it, and his heart and senses were awakened against his will, he did not dare to reject the hand which she had given him, and yet he felt himself growing weaker as he held it. Suddenly she threw herself in his arms. For she loved him ardently as her mother had done, just as though she had inherited this fatal passion.

Completely beside himself, he put his lips to her blond hair, and, as she raised her head to escape, their mouths met.

People become mad at times. They were so now.

When he reached the street he walked straight ahead, not knowing what he would do.

I recollect, madame, your indignant exclamation: "He had no choice but to commit suicide!"

I answered you: "And as for her? Should he have killed her also?"

The child loved him to distraction, madly, with the fatal and hereditary passion which had thrown her, a virgin, ignorant and distracted, on the breast of this man. She had acted in this manner owing to the irresistible intoxication of her entire being, which made her lose control of herself, which made her give herself, carried away by tumultuous instinct, and throw herself into the arms of her lover.

If he were to kill himself what would become of her? . . . She would die! . . . She would die dishonored, in despair, suffering terrible tortures.

What should he do?

Leave her, give her a marriage portion, marry her to someone else? . . . In that case she would die; she would die from grief, without accepting his money or another husband, for she had given herself to him. He had ruined her life, destroyed every possibility of happiness for her; he had condemned her to everlasting misery, to everlasting despair, to everlasting fire, to everlasting solitude, or to death.

Besides he loved her himself also! He revolted at the thought that he loved her extravagantly. She was his own daughter, be it so. The hazard of impregnation, a contact of a second had made—of that being allied to him by no legal bond—his daughter, whom he cherished as he had her mother, and even more, as though he were possessed of two passions.

Besides was she really his daughter? What did that matter anyhow? Who would know it?

Ardent memories brought back the vow made to the dying woman. He had promised to give his entire life to the child, "to commit a crime if necessary to insure her happiness."

And he loved her so that he plunged headlong into this abominable and pleasing crime, tortured by pain and ravaged by desire.

Who will know about it, the other man, the father, being dead?

"So be it!" said he; "this secret sin may break my heart. As she does not suspect it, I alone will carry its weight."

He asked for her hand, and he married her.

I don't know if they were happy, but I should have done as he did, madame.

THE AVENGER

When M. Antoine Leuillet married the Widow Mathilde Souris he had been in love with her for nearly ten years.

M. Souris had been his friend, his old college chum. Leuillet was very fond of him but found him rather a muff. He often used to say: "That poor Souris will never set the Seine on fire."

When Souris married Mlle Mathilde Duval, Leuillet was surprised and somewhat vexed, for he had a slight weakness for her. She was the daughter of a neighbor of his, a retired haberdasher with a good deal of money. She was pretty, well mannered and intelligent. She accepted Souris on account of his money.

Then Leuillet cherished hopes of his friend's wife. He was a handsome man, not at all stupid and also well off. He was confident that he would succeed; he failed. Then he fell in love with her, and he was the sort of lover who is rendered timid, prudent and embarrassed by intimacy with the husband. Mme Souris fancied that he no longer meant anything serious by his attentions to her, and she became simply his friend. This state of affairs lasted nine years.

Now one morning Leuillet received a startling communication from the poor woman. Souris had died suddenly of aneurysm of the heart.

He got a terrible shock, for they were of the same age; but the very next moment a sensation of profound joy, of infinite relief, of deliverance, penetrated his body and soul. Mme Souris was free.

He had the tact, however, to make such a display of grief as the occasion required; he waited for the proper time to elapse and attended to all the conventional usages. At the end of fifteen months he married the widow.

His conduct was regarded as not only natural but generous. He had acted like a good friend and an honest man. In short, he was happy, quite happy.

They lived on terms of the closest confidence, having from the first understood and appreciated each other. One kept nothing secret from the other, and they told each other their inmost thoughts. Leuillet now loved his wife with a calm, trustful affection; he loved her as a tender, devoted partner, who is an equal and confidant. But there still lingered in his soul a singular and unaccountable grudge against the deceased Souris, who had been the first to possess this woman, who had even robbed her of her youth and her soul and who had even robbed her of her poetic attributes. The memory of the dead husband spoiled the happiness of the living husband, and this posthumous jealousy now began to torment Leuillet's heart day and night.

The result was that he was incessantly talking about Souris, asking a thousand minute and intimate questions about him and seeking information as to all his habits and personal characteristics. And he pursued him with railleries even into the depths of the tomb, recalling with self-satisfaction his oddities, emphasizing his absurdities and pointing out his defects.

Constantly he would call out to his wife from one end to the other of the house:

"Hello, Mathilde!"

"Here I am, dear."

"Come and let us have a chat."

She always came over to him, smiling, well aware that Souris was to be the subject of the chat and anxious to gratify her second husband's harmless fad.

"I say, do you remember how Souris wanted one day to prove to me that small men are always better loved than big men?"

And he launched out into reflections unfavorable to the defunct husband, who was small, and discreetly complimentary to himself, as he happened to be tall.

And Mme Leuillet let him think that he was quite right, and she laughed very heartily, turned the first husband into ridicule in a playful fashion for the amusement of his successor, who always ended by remarking:

"Never mind! Souris was a muff!"

They were happy, quite happy. And Leuillet never ceased to testify his unabated attachment to his wife by all the usual manifestations.

Now one night, when they happened to both be kept awake by a renewal of youthful ardor, Leuillet, who held his wife clasped tightly in his arms and had his lips glued to hers, said:

"Tell me this, darling."

"What?"

"Souris—'tisn't easy to put the question—was he very—very loving?"

She gave him a warm kiss as she murmured:

"Not as much as you, my sweet."

His male vanity was flattered and he went on:

"He must have been—rather a flat—eh?"

She did not answer. There was merely a sly little laugh on her face, which she pressed close to her husband's neck.

He persisted in his questions:

"Come now! Don't deny that he was a flat—well, I mean, rather an awkward sort of fellow."

She nodded slightly.

"Well, yes, rather awkward."

He went on:

"I'm sure he used to weary you many a night—isn't that so?"

This time she had an access of frankness, and she replied:

"Oh yes."

He embraced her once more when she made this acknowledgment and murmured:

"What an ass he was! You were not happy with him?"

"No. He was not always jolly."

Leuillet felt quite delighted, making a comparison in his own mind between his wife's former situation and her present one.

He remained silent for some time; then with a fresh outburst of curiosity he said:

"Tell me this!"

"What?"

"Will you be quite candid—quite candid with me?"

"Certainly, dear."

"Well, look here! Were you ever tempted to—to deceive this imbecile Souris?"

Mme Leuillet uttered a little "Oh!" in a shamefaced way and again cuddled her face closer to her husband's chest. But he could see that she was laughing.

"Come now, confess it! He had a head just suited for a cuckold, this blockhead! It would be so funny! The good Souris! Oh, I say, darling, you might tell it to me—only to me!"

He emphasized the words, "to me," feeling certain that if she wanted to show any taste when she deceived her husband, he, Leuillet, would have been the man; and he quivered with joy at the expectation of this avowal, sure that if she had not been the virtuous woman she was he could not have won her then.

But she did not reply, laughing incessantly as if at the recollection of something infinitely comic.

Leuillet, in his turn, burst out laughing at the notion that he might have made a cuckold of Souris. What a good joke! What a capital lot of fun, to be sure!

He exclaimed in a voice broken by convulsions of laughter:

"Oh, poor Souris! Poor Souris! Ah yes, he had that sort of head—oh, certainly he had!"

And Mme Leuillet now twisted herself under the sheets, laughing till the tears almost came into her eyes.

And Leuillet repeated: "Come, confess it! Confess it! Be candid. You must know that it cannot be unpleasant to me to hear such a thing."

Then she stammered, still choking with laughter:

"Yes, yes."

Her husband pressed her for an answer:

"Yes what? Look here! Tell me everything."

She was now laughing in a more subdued fashion and, raising her mouth up to Leuillet's ear, which was held toward her in anticipation of some pleasant piece of confidence, she whispered: "Yes—I did deceive him!"

He felt a cold shiver down his back and, utterly dumfounded, he gasped:

"You—you—did—really—deceive him?"

She was still under the impression that he thought the thing infinitely pleasant and replied:

"Yes—really—really."

He was obliged to sit up in bed, so great was the shock he received, holding his breath, just as overwhelmed as if he had just been told that he was a cuckold himself. At first he was unable to articulate properly; then after the lapse of a minute or so he merely ejaculated:

"Ah!"

She, too, had stopped laughing now, realizing her mistake too late.

Leuillet at length asked:

"And with whom?"

She kept silent, cudgeling her brain to find some excuse.

He repeated his question:

"With whom?"

At last she said:

"With a young man."

He turned toward her abruptly and in a dry tone said:

"Well, I suppose it wasn't with some kitchen slut. I ask you, who was the young man—do you understand?"

She did not answer. He tore away the sheet which she had drawn over her head and pushed her into the middle of the bed, repeating:

"I want to know with what young man—do you understand?"

Then she replied, having some difficulty in uttering the words:

"I only wanted to laugh." But he fairly shook with rage.

"What? How is that? You only wanted to laugh? So then you were making game of me? I'm not going to be satisfied with these evasions, let me tell you! I ask you what was the young man's name?"

She did not reply but lay motionless on her back.

He caught hold of her arm and pressed it tightly:

"Do you hear me, I say? I want you to give me an answer when I speak to you."

Then she said in nervous tones:

"I think you must be going mad! Let me alone!"

He trembled with fury, so exasperated that he scarcely knew what he was saying, and, shaking her with all his strength, he repeated:

"Do you hear me? Do you hear me?"

She wrenched herself out of his grasp with a sudden movement and with the tips of her fingers slapped her husband on the nose. He entirely lost his temper, feeling that he had been struck, and angrily pounced down on her.

He now held her under him, boxing her ears in a most violent manner and exclaiming:

"Take that—and that—and that. There you are, you trollop, you strumpet—you strumpet!"

Then when he was out of breath, exhausted from beating her, he got up and went over to the bureau to get himself a glass of sugared orange water, almost ready to faint after his exertion.

And she lay huddled up in bed, crying and heaving great sobs, feeling that there was an end of her happiness and that it was all her own fault.

Then in the midst of her tears she faltered:

"Listen, Antoine, come here! I told you a lie—listen! I'll explain it to you."

And now, prepared to defend herself, armed with excuses and subterfuges, she slightly raised her head, all disheveled under her crumpled nightcap.

And he, turning toward her, drew close to her, ashamed of having whacked her but feeling still in his heart's core as a husband an inexhaustible hatred against the woman who had deceived his predecessor, Souris.

THE CONSERVATORY

M. and Mme Lerebour were about the same age, but Monsieur looked younger, although he was the weaker of the two. They lived near Mantes in a pretty estate which they had bought after having made a fortune by selling printed cottons.

The house was surrounded by a beautiful garden, containing a poultry yard, Chinese kiosk and a little conservatory at the end of the avenue. M. Lerebour was short, round and jovial, with the joviality of a shopkeeper of epicurean tastes. His wife, lean, self-willed and always discontented, had not succeeded in overcoming her husband's good humor. She dyed her hair and sometimes read novels which made dreams pass through her soul, although she affected to despise writings of this kind. People said she was a woman of strong passions without her having ever done anything to sustain that opinion. But her husband sometimes said: "My wife is a gay woman," with a certain knowing air which awakened suppositions.

For some years past, however, she had shown herself aggressive toward M. Lerebour, always irritated and hard, as if a secret and unavoidable grief tormented her. A sort of misunderstanding was the result. They scarcely spoke to each other, and Madame, whose name was Palmyre, was incessantly heaping unkind compliments, wounding allusions, bitter words, without any apparent reason, on Monsieur, whose name was Gustave.

He bent his back, bored though gay, all the same, endowed with such a fund of contentment that he endured her domestic bickerings. He asked himself, nevertheless, what unknown cause could have thus embittered his spouse, for he had a strong feeling that her irritation had a hidden reason, but so difficult to penetrate that his efforts to do so were in vain.

He often said to her: "Look here, my dear, tell me what you have against me. I feel that you are concealing something."

She invariably replied: "But there is nothing the matter with me, absolutely nothing. Besides, if I had some cause for discontent it would be for you to guess at it. I don't like men who understand nothing, who are so soft and incapable that one must come to their assistance to make them grasp the slightest thing."

He murmured dejectedly: "I see clearly that you don't want to say anything."

And he went away, still striving to unravel the mystery.

The nights especially became painful to him, for they always shared the same bed, as one does in good and simple households. It was not, therefore, mere ordinary ill temper that she displayed toward him. She chose the moment when they were lying side by side to load him with the liveliest raillery. She reproached him principally for his corpulence: "You take up all the room; you are becoming so fat."

And she forced him to get up on the slightest pretext, sending him downstairs to look for a newspaper she had forgotten or a bottle of orange water, which he failed to find, as she had herself hidden it away. And she exclaimed in a furious and sarcastic tone: "You might, however, know where to find it, you big booby!" When he had been wandering about the sleeping house for a whole hour and returned to the room empty handed, the only thanks she gave him was to say:

"Come, get back to bed; it will make you thin to take a little walking; you are becoming as flabby as a sponge."

She kept waking him every moment by declaring that she was suffering from cramps in her stomach and insisting on his rubbing her with flannel soaked in eau de cologne. He would make efforts to cure her, grieved at seeing her ill, and would propose to go and rouse up Céleste, their maid. Then she would get angry, crying: "You must be a fool. Well, it is over; I am better now, so go back to bed, you big lout."

To his question: "Are you quite sure you have got better?" she would fling this harsh answer in his face:

"Yes, hold your tongue! Let me sleep! Don't worry me any more about it! You are incapable of doing anything, even of rubbing a woman."

He got into a state of deep dejection. "But, my darling——"

She became exasperated: "I want no 'buts.' Enough, isn't it? Give me some rest now." And she turned her face to the wall.

Now one night she shook him so abruptly that he started up in terror and found himself in a sitting posture with a rapidity which was not habitual with him. He stammered:

"What? What's the matter?"

She caught him by the arm and pinched him till he cried out. Then she gave him a box on the ear. "I hear some noise in the house."

Accustomed to the frequent alarms of Mme Lerebour, he did not disturb himself very much and quietly asked:

"What sort of noise, my darling?"

She trembled as if she were in a state of terror and replied: "Noise—why noise —the noise of footsteps. There is someone."

He remained incredulous. "Someone? You think so? But, no, you must be mistaken. Besides, whom do you think it can be?"

She shuddered.

"Who? Who? Why, thieves, of course, you imbecile!"

He plunged softly under the sheets.

"Ah no, my darling! There is nobody. I dare say you dreamed it."

Then she flung off the coverlet and, jumping out of bed in a rage: "Why, then you are just as cowardly as you are incapable! In any case, I shall not let myself be massacred owing to your pusillanimity." And, snatching up the tongs from the fireplace, she placed herself in a fighting attitude in front of the bolted door.

Moved by his wife's display of valor, perhaps ashamed, he rose up in his turn sulkily and without taking off his nightcap he seized the shovel and placed himself face to face with his better half.

They waited for twenty minutes in the deepest silence. No fresh noise disturbed the repose of the house. Then Madame, becoming furious, got back into bed, saying: "Nevertheless, I'm sure there is someone."

In order to avoid anything like a quarrel he did not make an allusion during the next day to this panic. But next night Mme Lerebour woke up her husband with more violence still than the night before and, panting, she stammered: "Gustave, Gustave, somebody has just opened the garden gate!"

Astonished at this persistence, he fancied that his wife must have had an attack of somnambulism and was about to make an effort to shake off this dangerous state when he thought he heard, in fact, a slight sound under the walls of the house. He rose up, rushed to the window, and he saw—yes, he saw—a white figure quickly passing along one of the garden walks.

He murmured, as if he were on the point of fainting: "There is someone." Then he recovered his self-possession, felt more resolute and suddenly, carried away by the formidable anger of a proprietor whose territory has been encroached upon, he said: "Wait, wait and you shall see!"

He rushed toward the writing desk, opened it, took out the revolver and dashed out into the stairs. His wife, filled with consternation, followed him, exclaiming: "Gustave, Gustave, don't abandon me; don't leave me alone! Gustave! Gustave!"

But he scarcely heard her; he had by this time laid his hand on the garden gate.

Then she went back rapidly and barricaded herself in the conjugal chamber.

She waited five minutes, ten minutes, a quarter of an hour. Wild terror took possession of her. Without doubt they had killed him; they had seized, garroted, strangled him. She would have preferred to hear the report of the six barrels of the revolver, to know that he was fighting, that he was defending himself. But this great silence, this terrifying silence of the country overwhelmed her.

She rang for Céleste. Céleste did not come in answer to the bell. She rang again, on the point of swooning, of sinking into unconsciousness. The entire house remained without a sound. She pressed her burning forehead to the window, seeking to peer through the darkness without. She distinguished nothing but the blacker shadows of a row of trees beside the gray ruts on the roads.

It struck half-past twelve. Her husband had been absent for forty-five minutes. She would never see him again. No! She would never see him again. And she fell on her knees, sobbing.

Two light knocks at the door of the apartment called out to her: "Open, pray, Palmyre—'tis I." She rushed forward, opened the door and, standing in front of him with her arms akimbo and her eyes full of tears, exclaimed: "Where have you been, you dirty brute? Ah, you left me here by myself, nearly dead of fright. You care no more about me than if I never existed."

He closed the bedroom door; then he laughed and laughed like a madman, grinning from ear to ear, with his hands on his sides, till the tears came into his eyes.

Mme Lerebour, stupefied, remained silent.

He stammered: "It was—it was—Céleste who had an appointment in the conservatory. If you knew what—what I have seen——"

She had turned pale, choking with indignation.

"Eh? Do you tell me so? Céleste? In my house? In—my—house—in my—my—in my conservatory? And you have not killed the man who was her accomplice? You had a revolver and did not kill him? In my house—in my house!"

She sat down, not feeling able to do anything.

He danced a caper, snapped his fingers, smacked his tongue and, still laughing: "If you knew—if you knew——" He suddenly gave her a kiss.

She tore herself away from him and in a voice broken with rage she said: "I will not let this girl remain one day longer in my house, do you hear? Not one day —not one hour. When she returns to the house we will throw her out."

M. Lerebour had seized his wife by the waist, and he planted rows of kisses on her neck, loud kisses, as in bygone days. She became silent once more, petrified with astonishment. But he, holding her clasped in his arms, drew her softly toward the bed.

Toward half-past nine in the morning Céleste, astonished at not having yet seen her master and mistress, who always rose early, came and knocked softly at their door.

They were in bed and were gaily chatting side by side. She stood there astonished and said: "Madame, it is the coffee."

Mme Lerebour said in a very soft voice: "Bring it here to me, my girl. We are a little tired; we have slept very badly."

Scarcely had the servant maid gone than M. Lerebour began to laugh again, tickling his wife under the chin and repeating: "If you knew. Oh, if you knew."

But she caught his hands. "Look here! Keep quiet, my darling; if you laugh like this you will make yourself ill."

And she kissed him softly on the eyes.

Mme Lerebour has no more fits of sourness. Sometimes on bright nights the husband and wife come with furtive steps along the clumps of trees and flower beds as far as the little conservatory at the end of the garden. And they remain there planted side by side, with their faces pressed against the glass as if they were looking at something strange and full of interest going on within.

They have increased Céleste's wages.

But M. Lerebour has got thin.

MY WIFE

It was at the close of a dinner party consisting of men, married men, old friends, who sometimes met together without their wives, like bachelors, as in former days. They had eaten for a long while, and had drunk a great deal, talked on every subject and renewed happy memories of days gone by, those glowing memories that cause the lips to smile and the heart to tremble in spite of oneself.

Someone said:

"Do you remember, George, our excursion to St. Germain with those two young girls from Montmartre?"

"Certainly! Of course I do."

And they brought up details, this and that, a thousand little things, the thoughts of which gave them pleasure even now.

They happened to speak about marriage, and everyone said in a serious voice: "Oh! if I had it to do over again! . . ." George Duportin added: "It is strange how easily you drop into it. You make up your mind never to take a wife, and then in the spring you go away into the country; the weather is warm; the summer promises well; everything is in bloom; you meet a young girl at a friend's house . . . presto! it is done. You come home married."

Pierre Létoile cried out: "Just so! that's my story, only in my case the circumstances were peculiar . . ."

His friend interrupted him: "As for you, you have nothing to complain of. You surely have the most charming wife in the world, she is pretty, amiable, in fact, perfect; certainly you are the happiest of us all."

The former replied:

"I'm not responsible for that."

"Why not?"

"It is true that I have a perfect wife, but I married her in spite of myself."

"Nonsense."

"Yes—this is the story: I was thirty years old, and I thought no more of marrying than of hanging myself. Young girls always seemed to me insipid, and I was exceedingly fond of pleasure.

"In the month of May I was invited to the wedding of my cousin Simon d'Erabel, in Normandy. It was a real Norman wedding. The people sat down at table at five o'clock in the afternoon, and at eleven o'clock they were still eating. On this occasion my partner was a Mlle. Dumoulin, the daughter of a retired colonel, a blonde young woman with a military air, well-built, fearless and loquacious. She monopolized me completely all day long, took me walking in the park, made me dance whether I wanted to or not, and bored me.

"I said to myself: 'I'll bear it today, but tomorrow I'll escape. I've had enough.'

"About eleven o'clock at night the women retired to their rooms and the men remained to smoke while drinking, or to drink while smoking if you prefer.

"Through the open window could be seen the rustic ball. Country lads and lasses skipped in a circle while they sang in a loud voice the tune of a wild dance feebly accompanied by two violinists and a clarinetist who used the top of a large kitchen table as a platform. The tumultuous song of the country people sometimes completely drowned the sound of the instruments; and the feeble music, torn to pieces by their uncontrolled voices, seemed to fall from the sky in shreds, in small fragments of scattered notes. From two huge casks surrounded by flaming torches there poured drink for the crowd. Two men were busy rinsing the glasses, or bowls, in a tub so as to have them ready as quickly as possible to place under the faucets from which ran the red thread of wine or the golden thread of pure cider; and the thirsty dancers, the sedate elderly people, the perspiring girls, came there extending their arms to take, in their turn, whatever kind of cup they could find and, throwing back their heads, took copious draughts of whichever drink they preferred. On one table was bread, butter, cheeses, and sausages. Everybody swallowed a mouthful from time to time; and on the starlit field this healthy and energetic fete was a pleasure to behold and made me want to drink to the health of those huge casks and eat hard bread with butter and a raw onion.

"A foolish desire took possession of me to take part in their festivities, and I left my companions.

"I must acknowledge that I was then somewhat tipsy, and soon became quite drunk.

"I seized the hand of a strong peasant girl who was out of breath, and I made her skip around wildly until I was breathless. After drinking some more wine I seized another jolly girl and, to refresh myself, I swallowed a full bowl of cider, and I began to jump about like one possessed.

"I was supple; the lads were delighted and watched me as they tried to imitate me; all the girls wanted to dance with me, and they skipped about heavily, with cowlike grace.

"At last, after many dances and glass after glass of wine and cider I became so tipsy, about two o'clock in the morning, that I could hardly stand up.

"I was conscious of my condition, and I wanted to go to my bedroom. The château was asleep, silent, and somber.

"I had no matches, and everyone had gone to bed. As soon as I was inside the vestibule I was seized with dizziness: I had great difficulty in finding the banister; at last I came across it by chance, as I was groping about, and I sat down on the first step of the staircase trying to collect my ideas.

"My bedroom was on the second floor, the third door to the left. Happily I had not forgotten that. Confident that I remembered correctly, I got up again, but not without difficulty, and I began to go upstairs, step by step, my hands glued to the iron railing to prevent myself from falling, and trying my best not to make any noise.

"Three or four times my foot missed the following step, and I fell on my knees, but thanks to the strength of my arms and my great determination I avoided rolling downstairs.

"At last I reached the second story and ventured down the corridor, groping along the walls. Here was one door: I counted 'One'; but a sudden dizziness made me let go the wall and turn round in an erratic circle that threw me against the other partition. I tried to return in a straight line. The passage was long and difficult, but at last I came up against the side wall and I once more carefully felt my way along it until I came to another door. To make certain that I was not mistaken, I again counted aloud: 'Two'; and I continued walking. After some time I found the third, and I said: 'Three, that's mine,' and as I turned the key in the lock the door opened. In spite of my confusion, I thought, 'as the door opens, it must be my room,' and I advanced in the darkness after closing the door softly.

"I came up against something soft, my couch, and I stretched myself out on it.

"In my condition I did not try to find my night table, my candlestick, or my matches. It would have taken me two hours or so. It would have taken me as long again to undress, and perhaps even then I would not have succeeded, so I did not attempt it.

"I took off my shoes, unbuttoned my vest, which felt uncomfortably tight, and, loosening my trousers, slept most soundly.

"I must have been sleeping a long while, when I was suddenly awakened by a penetrating voice calling out quite near me: 'What, you lazy girl, still asleep? Do you know that it is ten o'clock?'

"A woman's voice replied: 'Already! I was so tired yesterday.'

"Half-asleep, I asked myself what this conversation meant.

"Where was I? What had I done?

"My mind wandered, as it was still wrapped in a thick cloud. The first voice replied: 'I will open your curtains.'

"And I heard steps approaching. I sat up completely bewildered. Then a hand was placed upon my head. I made a quick movement. The voice demanded emphatically: 'Who's there?' I took good care not to answer. Two angry hands caught hold of me. In my turn I seized someone, and a terrible struggle began. We fought, overturning the furniture and striking against the walls.

"The woman's voice cried out in a frightened tone: 'Help, help!'

"The servants, the neighbors, and the frightened ladies all hurried to the scene. They opened the shutters, and drew back the curtains. I was grappling with Colonel Dumoulin!

"I had slept beside his daughter's bed.

"As soon as we had been separated, I fled to my room, stupefied with fright. I locked myself in and sat down, placing my feet on a chair, for my shoes were in the young woman's room.

"I heard a great commotion throughout the château, doors opening and shutting, whispering, and rapid steps.

"After half an hour someone knocked at my door. I cried, 'Who's there?' It was my uncle, the father of the young man who had been married the previous evening, and I let him in.

"He was pale and furiously angry, and he was very severe with me. 'You have conducted yourself in my house like a cad, do you hear?' Then in a softer tone he added: 'What a damned idiot you are to let them catch you there at ten o'clock in the morning! You slept like a log in that room instead of going as soon after as possible.'

"I exclaimed: 'But uncle, I assure you that there was nothing amiss, I mistook my door because I was tipsy.'

"He shrugged his shoulders: 'Go along, don't tell me any such nonsense.' I raised my hand. 'I swear to you on my honor.' My uncle continued: 'Yes, that's all right, you are in duty bound to say that.'

"I became angry in my turn, and I told him all about my mishap. He gazed at me in astonishment, not knowing what he ought to believe.

"Then he went out to confer with the colonel. I also learned that a kind of court composed of mothers had been formed, and that the different phases of the situation had been submitted to them.

"An hour later he returned, sat down with the air of a judge, and began: 'Whichever way it is, I see only one way out of it for you and that is to marry Mlle. Dumoulin.'

"I was so frightened that I jumped up.

" 'Do that! never in the world!'

"He gravely asked: 'What do you intend to do then?'

"I artlessly replied: 'Well—I shall leave as soon as my boots are returned.' My uncle replied: 'No joking if you please. The colonel has resolved to blow out your brains as soon as he sees you, and you may be sure it is not a vain threat. I suggested a duel, but he replied: "No, I tell you I will blow his brains out."

" 'Let us now look at this question from another standpoint.

" 'Either you ruined this child—so much the worse for you, my boy, young girls should not be treated thus—or else you made a mistake because you were tipsy, as you say. Then so much the worse for you. You should not have placed yourself in such a foolish position. Whichever way it is, the young girl has lost her reputation, for the explanations of a drunkard are never believed. In this case she is the real victim, the only victim. Think it over.'

"And he departed while I cried after him: 'Say what you like, I won't marry her.'

"After this I remained alone for an hour.

"Then my aunt came in her turn. She was weeping. She tried every way of reasoning with me. No one believed in my mistake. No one could believe that this young girl had forgotten to lock her door in a house full of people. The colonel had struck her, and she had been sobbing all the morning. It was a terrible scandal that could not be effaced.

"And my good aunt added: 'All the same, ask her hand in marriage; perhaps you may find means of escape while discussing the marriage contract.' This view confronted me. And I consented to write my offer. An hour later I left for Paris.

"The next day I was advised that my suit had been accepted. So, in three weeks' time, as I could not find an excuse or evade it in any way, the banns were published, the invitations sent out, the contract signed, and one Monday morning I found myself in the chancel of a lighted church, by the side of a weeping young girl, having previously sworn to the mayor that I consented to take her as my companion—until the death of one of us.

"I had not seen her since, and I glanced sideways at her with a certain hostile astonishment. Well, she was not ugly; no, not in the least ugly. I said to myself, 'There's a woman who will not be very amusing every day.'

"She did not look at me once until evening, and never addressed a word to me.

"Toward the middle of the night I entered the nuptial chamber intending to tell her what I had decided to do, for I was master now.

"I found her seated in an armchair, dressed in her day clothes, her eyes red, and face pale. She arose as soon as I entered and came toward me with a serious air.

" 'Sir,' said she to me, 'I am willing to do what you order me. I will kill myself if you wish.'

"She looked so pretty in this heroic part, the daughter of the colonel, that I embraced her as I had a right to, and soon saw that I had not been cheated.

"I have been married five years, and I have never regretted it in the least."

Pierre Létoile stopped speaking. His companions laughed. One of them said: "Marriage is a lottery; one should never choose numbers, those drawn at haphazard are the best."

And the other added in conclusion: "Yes, but do not forget that it was the Providence that watches over drunkards, who chose for Pierre."

LETTER FOUND ON A CORPSE

You ask me, madame, whether I am laughing at you? You cannot believe that a man has never been smitten with love? Well, no, I have never loved, never!

What is the cause of this? I really cannot tell. Never have I been under the influence of that sort of intoxication of the heart which we call love! Never have I lived in that dream, in that exaltation, in that state of madness, into which the image of a woman casts us. I have never been pursued, haunted, roused to fever heat, lifted up to Paradise, by the thought of meeting, or by the possession of, a being who had suddenly become for me more desirable than any good fortune, more beautiful than any other creature, more important than the whole world! I have never wept; I have never suffered on account of any of you. I have not passed my nights thinking of one woman without closing my eyes. I have no experience of waking up with the thought and the memory of her shedding her illumination on me. I have never known the wild desperation of hope when she was about to come or the divine sadness of regret when she parted with me, leaving behind her in the room a delicate odor of violet powder.

I have never been in love.

I, too, have often asked myself why this is. And truly I can scarcely tell. Nevertheless, I have found some reasons for it, but they are of a metaphysical character, and perhaps you will not be able to appreciate them.

I suppose I sit too much in judgment on women to submit much to their fascination. I ask you to forgive me for this remark. I am going to explain what I mean. In every creature there is a moral being and a physical being. In order to love it would be necessary for me to find a harmony between these two beings which I have never found. One has always too great a predominance over the other, sometimes the physical.

The intellect which we have a right to require in a woman, in order to love her, is not the same as virile intellect. It is more and it is less. A woman must have a mind open, delicate, sensitive, refined, impressionable. She has no need of either power or initiative in thought, but she must have kindness, elegance, tenderness, coquetry and that faculty of assimilation which, in a little while, raises her to an equality with him who shares her life. Her greatest quality must be tact, that subtle sense which is to the mind what touch is to the body. It reveals to her a thousand little things, contours, angles and forms in the intellectual life.

Very frequently pretty women have not intellect to correspond with their personal charms. Now the slightest lack of harmony strikes me and pains me at the first glance. In friendship this is not of importance. Friendship is a compact in which one fairly divides defects and merits. We may judge of friends, whether man or woman, take into account the good they possess, neglect the evil that is in them, appreciate their value exactly, while giving ourselves up to an intimate sympathy of a deep and fascinating character.

In order to love one must be blind, surrender oneself absolutely, see nothing, reason from nothing, understand nothing. One must adore the weakness as well as the beauty of the beloved object, renounce all judgment, all reflection, all perspicacity.

I am incapable of such blindness and rebel against a seductiveness not founded on reason. This is not all. I have such a high and subtle idea of harmony that nothing can ever realize my ideal. But you will call me a madman. Listen to me. A woman, in my opinion, may have an exquisite soul and a charming body without that body and that soul being in perfect accord with one another. I mean that persons who have noses made in a certain shape are not to be expected to think in a certain fashion. The fat have no right to make use of the same words and phrases as the thin. You who have blue eyes, madame, cannot look at life and judge of things and events as if you had black eyes. The shades of your eyes should correspond, by a sort of fatality, with the shades of your thought. In perceiving these things I have the scent of a bloodhound. Laugh if you like, but it is so.

And yet I imagined that I was in love for an hour, for a day. I had foolishly yielded to the influence of surrounding circumstances. I allowed myself to be beguiled by the mirage of an aurora. Would you like to hear this short history?

I met one evening a pretty, enthusiastic woman who wanted, for the purpose of humoring a poetic fancy, to spend a night with me in a boat on a river. I would have preferred—but, no matter, I consented.

It was in the month of June. My fair companion chose a moonlight night in order to excite her imagination all the better.

We had dined at a riverside inn, and then we set out in the boat about ten o'clock. I thought it a rather foolish kind of adventure, but as my companion pleased me I did not bother myself too much about this. I sat down on the seat facing her, seized the oars, and off we started.

I could not deny that the scene was picturesque. We glided past a wooded isle full of nightingales, and the current carried us rapidly over the river covered with silvery ripples. The grasshoppers uttered their shrill, monotonous cry; the frogs croaked in the grass by the river's bank, and the lapping of the water as it flowed on made around us a kind of confused, almost imperceptible murmur, disquieting, which gave us a vague sensation of mysterious fear.

The sweet charm of warm nights and of streams glittering in the moonlight penetrated us. It seemed bliss to live and to float thus, to dream and to feel by one's side a young woman sympathetic and beautiful.

I was somewhat affected, somewhat agitated, somewhat intoxicated by the pale brightness of the night and the consciousness of my proximity to a lovely woman.

"Come and sit beside me," she said.

I obeyed. She went on:

"Recite some verses for me."

This appeared to me rather too much. I declined; she persisted. She certainly wanted to have the utmost pleasure, the whole orchestra of sentiment, from the moon to the rhymes of poets. In the end I had to yield, and, as if in mockery, I recited for her a charming little poem by Louis Bouilhet, of which the following are a few strophes:

> I hate the poet who with tearful eye
>   Murmurs some name while gazing tow'rds a star,
> Who sees no magic in the earth or sky,
>   Unless Lizette or Ninon be not far.
>
> The bard who in all Nature nothing sees
>   Divine, unless a petticoat he ties
> Amorously to the branches of the trees,
>   Or nightcap to the grass, is scarcely wise.
>
> He has not heard the eternal's thunder-tone,
>   The voice of Nature in her various moods,
> He cannot tread the dim ravines alone,
>   And of no woman dream 'mid whispering woods.

I expected some reproaches. Nothing of the sort. She murmured: "How true it is!"

I remained stupefied. Had she understood?

Our boat was gradually drawing nearer to the bank and got entangled under a willow which impeded its progress. I drew my arm around my companion's waist and very gently moved my lips toward her neck. But she repulsed me with an abrupt, angry movement:

"Have done, pray! You are rude!"

I tried to draw her toward me. She resisted, caught hold of the tree and nearly upset us both into the water. I deemed it the prudent course to cease my importunities.

She went on:

"I would rather have you capsized. I feel so happy. I want to dream—that is so nice." Then in a slightly malicious tone she added:

"Have you then already forgotten the verses you recited for me just now?"

She was right. I became silent.

She went on:

"Come, row!"

And I plied at the oars once more. I began to find the night long and to see the absurdity of my conduct. My companion said to me:

"Will you make me a promise?"

"Yes. What is it?"

"To remain quiet, well behaved and discreet if I permit you——" ·

"What? Say what you mean!"

"Here is what I mean! I want to lie down on my back in the bottom of the boat with you by my side. I forbid you to touch me, to embrace me—in short to —caress me. If you move I'll capsize the boat."

And then we lay down side by side, our eyes turned toward the sky, while the boat glided slowly through the water. We were rocked by the gentle movement of the shallop. The light sounds of the night came to us more distinctly in the bottom of the boat, sometimes causing us to start. And I felt springing up within me a strange, poignant emotion, an infinite tenderness, something like an irresistible impulse to open my arms in order to embrace, to open my heart in order to love, to give myself, to give my thoughts, my body, my life, my entire being to someone.

My companion murmured like one in a dream:

"Where are we? Where are we going? It seems to me that I am quitting the earth. How sweet it is! Ah, if you loved me—a little!"

My heart began to throb. I had no answer to give. It seemed to me that I loved her. I had not longer any violent desire. I felt happy there by her side, and that was enough for me.

And thus we remained for a long, long time without stirring. We caught each other's hands; some delightful force rendered us motionless, an unknown force stronger than ourselves, an alliance, chaste, intimate, absolute, of our persons lying there touching each other. What was this? How do I know? Love, perhaps.

Little by little the dawn appeared. It was three o'clock in the morning. Slowly a great brightness spread over the sky. The boat knocked against something. I rose up. We had come close to a tiny islet.

But I remained ravished, in a state of ecstasy. In front of us stretched the shining firmament, red, rosy, violet, spotted with fiery clouds resembling golden vapors. The river was glowing with purple, and three houses on one side of it seemed to be burning.

I bent toward my companion. I was going to say: "Oh, look!" But I held my tongue, quite dazed, and I could no longer see anything except her. She, too, was rosy, with the rosy flesh tints with which must have mingled a little the hue of the sky. Her tresses were rosy; her eyes were rosy; her teeth were rosy; her dress, her laces, her smile, all were rosy. And in truth I believed, so overpowering was the illusion, that the aurora was there before me.

She rose softly to her feet, holding out her lips to me, and I moved toward her, trembling, delirious, feeling indeed that I was going to kiss heaven, to kiss happiness, to kiss a dream which had become a woman, to kiss an ideal which had descended into human flesh.

She said to me: "You have a caterpillar in your hair." And suddenly I felt myself becoming as sad as if I had lost all hope in life.

That is all, madame. It is puerile, stupid. But I am sure that since that day it would be impossible for me to love. And yet—who can tell?"

[The young man upon whom this letter was found was yesterday taken out of the Seine between Bougival and Marly. An obliging bargeman, who had searched the pockets in order to ascertain the name of the deceased, brought this paper to the author.]

THE LITTLE CASK

Jules Chicot, the innkeeper who lived at Epreville, pulled up his tilbury in front of Mother Magloire's farmhouse. He was a tall man of about forty, fat and with a red face and was generally said to be a very knowing customer.

He hitched his horse up to the gatepost and went in. He owned some land adjoining that of the old woman. He had been coveting her plot for a long while, and had tried in vain to buy it a score of times, but she had always obstinately refused to part with it.

"I was born here, and here I mean to die," was all she said.

He found her peeling potatoes outside the farmhouse door. She was a woman of about seventy-two, very thin, shriveled and wrinkled, almost dried up, in fact, and much bent, but as active and untiring as a girl. Chicot patted her on the back in a very friendly fashion and then sat down by her on a stool.

"Well, Mother, you are always pretty well and hearty, I am glad to see."

"Nothing to complain of, considering, thank you. And how are you, Monsieur Chicot?"

"Oh, pretty well, thank you, except a few rheumatic pains occasionally; otherwise I should have nothing to complain of."

"That's all the better!"

And she said no more, while Chicot watched her going on with her work. Her crooked, knotty fingers, hard as a lobster's claws, seized the tubers which were lying in a pail, as if they had been a pair of pincers, and peeled them rapidly, cutting off long strips of skin with an old knife which she held in the other hand, throwing the potatoes into the water as they were done. Three daring fowl jumped one after another into her lap, seized a bit of peel and then ran away as fast as their legs would carry them with it in their beaks.

Chicot seemed embarrassed, anxious, with something on the tip of his tongue which he could not get out. At last he said hurriedly:

"I say, Mother Magloire——"

"Well, what is it?"

"You are quite sure that you do not want to sell your farm?"

"Certainly not; you may make up your mind to that. What I have said I have said, so don't refer to it again."

"Very well, only I fancy I have thought of an arrangement that might suit us both very well."

"What is it?"

"Here you are: You shall sell it to me and keep it all the same. You don't understand? Very well, so just follow me in what I am going to say."

The old woman left off peeling her potatoes and looked at the innkeeper attentively from under her bushy eyebrows and the innkeeper went on:

"Let me explain myself: Every month I will give you a hundred and fifty francs. You understand me, I suppose? Every month I will come and bring you thirty crowns,[1] and it will not make the slightest difference in your life—not the very slightest. You will have your own home just as you have now, will not trouble yourself about me and will owe me nothing; all you will have to do will be to take my money. Will that arrangement suit you?"

He looked at her good-humoredly, one might have said benevolently, and the old woman returned his looks distrustfully, as if she suspected a trap, and said:

"It seems all right as far as I am concerned, but it will not give you the farm."

"Never mind about that," he said; "you will remain here as long as it pleases God Almighty to let you live; it will be your home. Only you will sign a deed before a lawyer making it over to me after your death. You have no children, only nephews and nieces for whom you don't care a straw. Will that suit you? You will keep everything during your life, and I will give the thirty crowns a month. It is a pure gain as far as you are concerned."

The old woman was surprised, rather uneasy, but, nevertheless, very much tempted to agree and answered:

"I don't say that I will not agree to it, but I must think about it. Come back in a week and we will talk it over again, and I will then give you my definite answer."

And Chicot went off as happy as a king who had conquered an empire.

Mother Magloire was thoughtful and did not sleep at all that night; in fact, for four days she was in a fever of hesitation. She smelled, so to say, that there was something underneath the offer which was not to her advantage, but then the thought of thirty crowns a month, of all those coins chinking in her apron, falling to her, as it were, from the skies without her doing anything for it filled her with covetousness.

She went to the notary and told him about it. He advised her to accept Chicot's offer but said she ought to ask for a monthly payment of fifty crowns instead of thirty, as her farm was worth sixty thousand francs at the lowest calculation.

"If you live fifteen years longer," he said, "even then he will only have paid forty-five thousand francs for it."

The old woman trembled with joy at this prospect of getting fifty crowns a month, but she was still suspicious, fearing some trick, and she remained a long time with the lawyer, asking questions without being able to make up her mind to go. At last she gave him instructions to draw up the deed and returned home with her head in a whirl, just as if she had just drunk four jugs of new cider.

[1]The old name for a five-franc piece.

When Chicot came again to receive her answer she took a lot of persuading and declared that she could not make up her mind to agree to his proposal, though she was all the time on tenterhooks lest he should not consent to give the fifty crowns. At last when he grew urgent she told him what she expected for her farm.

He looked surprised and disappointed and refused.

Then in order to convince him she began to talk about the probable duration of her life.

"I am certainly not likely to live more than five or six years longer. I am nearly seventy-three and far from strong, even considering my age. The other evening I thought I was going to die and could hardly manage to crawl into bed."

But Chicot was not going to be taken in.

"Come, come, old lady, you are as strong as the church tower and will live till you are a hundred at least; you will be sure to see me put underground first."

The whole day was spent in discussing the money, and as the old woman would not give way, the landlord consented to give the fifty crowns, and she insisted upon having ten crowns over and above to strike the bargain.

Three years passed by, and the old dame did not seem to have grown a day older. Chicot was in despair. It seemed to him as if he had been paying that annuity for fifty years, that he had been taken in, outwitted and ruined. From time to time he went to see his annuitant, just as one goes in July to see when the harvest is likely to begin. She always met him with a cunning look, and one would have felt inclined to think that she was congratulating herself on the trick she had played on him. Seeing how well and hearty she seemed, he very soon got into his tilbury again, growling to himself:

"Will you never die, you old brute?"

He did not know what to do and felt inclined to strangle her when he saw her. He hated her with a ferocious, cunning hatred, the hatred of a peasant who has been robbed, and began to cast about for means of getting rid of her.

One day he came to see her again, rubbing his hands like he did the first time when he proposed the bargain, and after having chatted for a few minutes he said:

"Why do you never come and have a bit of dinner at my place when you are in Epreville? The people are talking about it and saying that we are not on friendly terms, and that pains me. You know it will cost you nothing if you come, for I don't look at the price of a dinner. Come whenever you feel inclined; I shall be very glad to see you."

Old Mother Magloire did not need to be told twice, and the next day but one —she was going to the town in any case, it being market day, in her gig driven by her man—she, without any demur, put her trap up in Chicot's stable and went in search of her promised dinner.

The publican was delighted and treated her like a princess, giving her roast fowl, black pudding, leg of mutton and bacon and cabbage. But she ate next to nothing. She had always been a small eater and had generally lived on a little soup and a crust of bread and butter.

Chicot was disappointed and pressed her to eat more, but she refused. She would drink next to nothing either and declined any coffee, so he asked her:

"But surely you will take a little drop of brandy or liquor?"

"Well, as to that, I don't know that I will refuse." Whereupon he shouted out:

"Rosalie, bring the superfine brandy—*the special*—you know."

The servant appeared, carrying a long bottle ornamented with a paper vine leaf, and he filled two liquor glasses.

"Just try that; you will find it first-rate."

The good woman drank it slowly in sips, so as to make the pleasure last all the longer, and when she had finished her glass, draining the last drops so as to make sure of all, she said:

"Yes, that is first-rate!"

Almost before she had said it Chicot had poured her out another glassful. She wished to refuse, but it was too late, and she drank it very slowly, as she had done the first, and he asked her to have a third. She objected, but he persisted.

"It is as mild as milk, you know. I can drink ten or a dozen without any ill effect; it goes down like sugar and leaves no headache behind; one would think that it evaporated on the tongue. It is the most wholesome thing you can drink."

She took it, for she really wished to have it, but she left half the glass.

Then Chicot, in an excess of generosity, said:

"Look here, as it is so much to your taste, I will give you a small keg of it, just to show that you and I are still excellent friends." Then she took her leave, feeling slightly overcome by the effects of what she had drunk.

The next day the innkeeper drove into her yard and took a little iron-hooped keg out of his gig. He insisted on her tasting the contents to make sure it was the same delicious article, and when they had each of them drunk three more glasses he said as he was going away:

"Well, you know, when it is all gone there is more left; don't be modest, for I shall not mind. The sooner it is finished the better pleased I shall be."

Four days later he came again. The old woman was outside her door cutting up the bread for her soup.

He went up to her and put his face close to hers so that he might smell her breath, and when he smelled the alcohol he felt pleased.

"I suppose you will give me a glass of *the special?*" he said. And they had three glasses each.

Soon, however, it began to be whispered abroad that Mother Magloire was in the habit of getting drunk all by herself. She was picked up in her kitchen, then in her yard, then in the roads in the neighborhood and was often brought home like a log.

Chicot did not go near her any more, and when people spoke to him about her he used to say, putting on a distressed look:

"It is a real pity that she should have taken to drink at her age, but when people get old there is no remedy. It will be the death of her in the long run."

And it certainly was the death of her. She died the next winter. About Christmas time she fell down unconscious in the snow and was found dead the next morning.

And when Chicot came in for the farm he said:

"It was very stupid of her; if she had not taken to drink she might very well have lived for ten years longer."

RUST

During his whole life, he had had only one insatiable passion, love of sport. He went out every day, from morning till night, with the greatest ardor, in summer and winter, spring and autumn, on the marshes, when it was close time on the plains and in the woods. He shot, he hunted, he coursed, he ferreted and trapped both birds and animals; he spoke of nothing but shooting and hunting, he dreamed of it, and continually repeated:

"How miserable any man must be who does not care for sport!"

And now that he was past fifty, he was well, robust, stout, and vigorous, though rather bald, and he kept his mustache cut quite short, so that it might not cover his lips and interfere with his blowing the horn.

He was never called by anything but his first Christian name, M. Hector, but his full name was Baron Hector Gontran de Coutelier, and he lived in a small manor house which he had inherited, in the middle of the woods; and though he knew all the nobility of the department and met its male representatives out shooting and hunting, he regularly visited only one family, the Courvilles, who were very pleasant neighbors and had been allied to his race for centuries. In their house he was liked and taken the greatest care of, and he used to say: "If I were not a sportsman, I should like to be here always."

M. de Courville had been his friend and comrade from childhood, and lived quietly as a gentleman farmer with his wife, daughter, and son-in-law, M. de Darnetot, who did nothing, under the pretext of being absorbed in historical research.

Baron de Coutelier often went and dined with his friends, as much with the object of telling them of the shots he had made as of anything else. He had long stories about dogs and ferrets, of which he spoke as if they were persons of note whom he knew very well. He analyzed them and explained their thoughts and intentions:

"When Médor saw that the corn crake was leading him such a dance, he said to himself: 'Wait a bit, my friend, we will have a joke.' And then, with a jerk of the head to me, to make me go into the corner of the clover field, he began to quarter the sloping ground, noisily brushing through the clover to drive the bird into a corner from which it could not escape.

"Everything happened as he had foreseen. Suddenly, the corn crake found itself on the edge of the wood, and it could not go any farther without showing itself; the corn crake thought to himself, 'Caught, by Jove,' and crouched down. Médor stood and pointed, looking round at me, but at a sign from me, he drew up to it, flushed the corn crake; bang! down it came, and Médor, as he brought it to me, wagged his tail, as much as to say: 'How about that, M. Hector?'"

Courville, Darnetot, and the two ladies laughed very heartily at those picturesque descriptions into which the baron threw his whole heart. He grew animated, moved his arms about, and gesticulated with his whole body; and when he de-

scribed the death of anything he had killed, he gave a formidable laugh, and said:
"Isn't that a good one?"

As soon as they began to speak about anything else, he stopped listening, and sat by himself, humming a few notes to imitate a hunting horn. And when there was a pause between two sentences on those moments of sudden calm which come between the war of words, a hunting tune was heard, "Ta, ta, ta, ra, ra," which the baron sang, puffing his cheek as if he were blowing his horn.

He had lived only for field sports and was growing old, without thinking about it, or guessing it, when he had a severe attack of rheumatism, and was confined to his bed for two months and nearly died of grief and boredom.

As he kept no female servant, for an old footman did all the cooking, he could not get any hot poultices, nor could he have any of those little attentions, nor anything that an invalid requires. His gamekeeper was his sick nurse, and, as the servant found the time hang just as heavily on his hands as it did on his master's, he slept nearly all day and all night in an easy chair while the baron was swearing and flying into a rage between the sheets.

The ladies of the De Courville family came to see him occasionally, and those were hours of calm and comfort for him. They prepared his herb tea, attended to the fire, served him his breakfast daintily, by the side of his bed, and when they were going again he used to say:

"By Jove! You ought to come here altogether," which made them laugh heartily.

When he was getting better and was beginning to go out shooting again, he went to dine with his friends one evening; but he was not at all in his usual spirits. He was tormented by one continual fear—that he might have another attack before shooting began, and when he was taking his leave at night, when the women were wrapping him up in a shawl and tying a silk handkerchief round his neck, which he allowed to be done for the first time in his life, he said in a disconsolate voice:

"If it begins all over again, I shall be done for."

As soon as he had gone, Mme. Darnetot said to her mother:

"We ought to try and get the baron married."

They all raised their hands at the proposal. How was it that they had never thought of it before? And during all the rest of the evening they discussed the widows whom they knew, and their choice fell on a woman of forty, who was still pretty, fairly rich, very good-tempered, and in excellent health, whose name was Mme. Berthe Vilers, and, accordingly, she was invited to spend a month at the château. She was very bored at home and was very glad to come; she was lively and active, and M. de Coutelier took her fancy immediately. She amused herself with him as if he had been a living toy, and spent hours in asking him slyly about the sentiments of rabbits and the machinations of foxes, and he gravely distinguished between the various ways of looking at things which different animals had, and ascribed plans and subtle arguments to them just as he did to men of his acquaintance.

The attention she paid him delighted him, and one evening, to show his esteem for her, he asked her to go out shooting with him, which he had never done to any woman before, and the invitation appeared so funny to her that she accepted it.

It was quite an amusement for them to fit her out; everybody offered her something, and she came out in a sort of short riding habit, with boots and men's breeches, a short petticoat, a velvet jacket, which was too tight for her across the chest, and a huntsman's black velvet cap.

The baron seemed as excited as if he were going to fire his first shot. He minutely explained to her the direction of the wind, and how different dogs worked. Then he took her into a field, and followed her as anxiously as a nurse does when her charge is trying to walk for the first time.

Médor soon made a point, and stopped with his tail out stiff and one paw up, and the baron, standing behind his pupil, was trembling like a leaf, and whispered:

"Look out, they are par . . . par . . . partridges." And almost before he had finished, there was a loud whir-whir, and a covey of large birds flew up in the air with a tremendous noise.

Mme. Vilers was startled, shut her eyes, fired off both barrels, and staggered at the recoil of the gun; but when she had recovered her self-possession, she saw that the baron was dancing about like a madman and that Médor was bringing back the two partridges which she had killed.

From that day, M. de Coutelier was in love with her, and he used to say, raising his eyes: "What a woman!" And he used to come every evening now to talk about shooting.

One day, M. de Courville, who was walking part of the way with him, asked him, suddenly:

"Why don't you marry her?"

The baron was altogether taken by surprise, and said:

"What? I? Marry her? . . . Well . . . really . . ."

And he said no more for a while, but then, suddenly shaking hands with his companion, he said:

"Good-by, my friend," and quickly disappeared in the darkness.

He did not go again for three days, but when he reappeared, he was pale from thinking the matter over, and graver than usual. Taking M. de Courville aside, he said:

"That was a capital idea of yours; try and persuade her to accept me. By Jove, a woman like that, you might say, was made for me. We shall be able to have some sort of sport together, all the year round."

As M. de Courville felt certain that his friend would not meet with a refusal, he replied:

"Propose to her immediately, my dear fellow, or would you rather that I did it for you?"

But the baron grew suddenly nervous, and said, with some hesitation:

"No . . . no. . . . I must go to Paris for . . . for a few days. As soon as I come back, I will give you a definite answer." No other explanation was forthcoming, and he started the next morning.

He made a long stay. One, two, three weeks passed, but M. de Coutelier did not return, and the Courvilles, who were surprised and uneasy, did not know what to say to their friend, whom they had informed of the baron's wishes. Every other day they sent to his house for news of him, but none of his servants had a line.

But one evening, while Mme. Vilers was singing and accompanying herself on the piano, a servant came with a mysterious air and told M. de Courville that a gentleman wanted to see him. It was the baron, in a traveling suit, who looked much altered and older, and as soon as he saw his old friend, he seized both his hands, and said in a somewhat tired voice: "I have just returned, my dear friend, and I have come to you immediately; I am thoroughly knocked up."

Then he hesitated in visible embarrassment, and presently said:

"I wished to tell you . . . immediately . . . that . . . that affair . . . you know what I mean . . . must come to nothing."

M. de Courville looked at him in stupefaction. "Must come to nothing? . . . Why?"

"Oh! Do not ask me, please; it would be too painful for me to tell you; but you may rest assured that I am acting like an honorable man. I can not . . . I have no right . . . no right, you understand, to marry this lady, and I will wait until she has gone, to come here again; it would be too painful for me to see her. Good-by." And he absolutely ran away.

The whole family deliberated and discussed the matter, surmising a thousand things. The conclusion they came to was that the baron's past life concealed some great mystery, that, perhaps, he had natural children, or some love affair of long standing. At any rate, the matter seemed serious, and, so as to avoid any difficult complications, they tactfully informed Mme. Vilers of the state of affairs, and she returned home just as much of a widow as she had come.

Three months more passed. One evening, when he had dined rather too well, and was rather unsteady on his legs, M. de Coutelier, while he was smoking his pipe with M. de Courville, said to him:

"You would really pity me, if you only knew how continually I am thinking about your friend."

But the other, who had been rather vexed at the baron's behavior in the circumstances, told him exactly what he thought of him:

"By Jove, my good friend, when a man has any secrets in his existence, as you have, he does not make advances to a woman, immediately, as you did, for you must surely have foreseen the reason why you had to draw back."

The baron left off smoking in some confusion.

"Yes, and no; at any rate, I could not have believed what actually happened."

Whereupon, M. de Courville lost his patience, and replied:

"One ought to foresee everything."

But M. de Coutelier replied in a low voice, in case anybody should be listening: "I see that I have hurt your feelings, and will tell you everything, so that you may forgive me. You know that for twenty years I have lived only for sport; I care for nothing else and think about nothing else. Consequently, when I was on the point of undertaking certain obligations with regard to this lady, I felt some scruples of conscience. Since I have given up the habit of . . . of love, there! I have not known whether I was still capable of . . . of . . . you know what I mean. . . . Just think! It is exactly sixteen years since . . . I for the last time . . . you understand what I mean. In this neighborhood, it is not easy to . . . you know. And then, I had other things to do. I prefer to use my gun, and so before entering into an engagement before the mayor and the priest to . . . well, I was frightened. I said to myself: 'Confound it; suppose I missed fire!' An honorable man always keeps his engagements, and in this case I was undertaking sacred duties with regard to this lady, and so, to make sure, I decided to go and spend a week in Paris.

"At the end of that time, nothing, absolutely nothing occurred. And it was not for want of trying. I went to the best there was, and they did everything they could. Yes . . . they certainly did their best! . . . And yet . . . they went away with nothing to show . . . nothing . . . nothing. . . . I waited . . . I waited for a fortnight, three weeks, continually hoping. In the restaurants, I ate a number of highly seasoned dishes, which upset my stomach, and . . . and it was still the same thing . . . or rather, nothing. You will, therefore, understand, that, in such circumstances, and having assured myself of the fact, the only thing I could do was . . . was . . . to withdraw; and I did so."

M. de Courville had to struggle very hard not to laugh, and he shook hands with the baron, saying:

"I am very sorry for you," and accompanied him halfway home.

When he got back and was alone with his wife, he told her everything, nearly choking with laughter; she, however, did not laugh, but listened very attentively, and when her husband had finished, she said, very seriously:

"The baron is a fool, my dear; he was frightened, that is all. I will write and ask Berthe to come back here as soon as possible."

And when M. de Courville observed that their friend had made such long and useless attempts, she merely said:

"Nonsense! When a man loves his wife, you know . . . that sort of thing always comes right in the end."

And M. de Courville made no reply, as he felt rather embarrassed himself.

POOR ANDREW

The lawyer's house looked on to the square. Behind it there was a nice well-kept garden, with a back entrance into a narrow street which was almost always deserted and from which it was separated by a wall.

At the bottom of that garden Maître Moreau's wife had promised, for the first time, to meet Captain Sommerive, who had been making love to her for a long time.

Her husband had gone to Paris for a week, so she was quite free for the time being. The captain had begged so hard, and he loved her so ardently, and she felt so isolated, so misunderstood, so neglected amid all the law business which seemed to be her husband's sole pleasure, that she had given away her heart without even asking herself whether he would give her anything else at some future time.

Then after some months of platonic love, of pressing of hands, of kisses rapidly stolen behind a door, the captain had declared that he would ask permission to exchange and leave town immediately if she would not grant him a meeting, a real meeting, during her husband's absence. So at length she yielded to his importunity.

Just then she was waiting, close against the wall, with a beating heart; when at length she heard somebody climbing up the wall she nearly ran away.

Suppose it were not he but a thief? But no; someone called out softly, "Matilda!" And when she replied, "Etienne!" a man jumped onto the path with a crash.

It was he—and what a kiss!

For a long time they remained in each other's arms with united lips. But suddenly a fine rain began to fall, and the drops from the leaves fell onto her neck and made her start. Whereupon he said:

"Matilda, my adored one, my darling, my angel, let us go indoors. It is twelve o'clock; we can have nothing to fear; please let us go in."

"No, dearest; I am too frightened."

But he held her in his arms and whispered in her ear:

"Your servants sleep on the third floor, looking on to the square, and your room, on the first, looks on to the garden, so nobody can hear us. I love you so that I wish to love you entirely from head to foot." And he embraced her vehemently.

She resisted still, frightened and even ashamed. But he put his arms round her, lifted her up and carried her off through the rain, which was by this time descending in torrents.

The door was open; they groped their way upstairs, and when they were in the room he bolted the door while she lit a candle.

Then she fell, half fainting, into a chair, while he kneeled down beside her.

At last she said, panting:

"No! No! Etienne, please let me remain a virtuous woman; I should be too angry with you afterward, and after all, it is so horrid, so common. Cannot we love each other with a spiritual love only? Oh, Etienne!"

But he was inexorable, and then she tried to get up and escape from his attacks. In her fright she ran to the bed in order to hide herself behind the curtains, but it was a dangerous place of refuge, and he followed her. But in haste he took off his sword too quickly, and it fell onto the floor with a crash. And then a prolonged, shrill child's cry came from the next room, the door of which had remained open.

"You have awakened the child," she whispered, "and perhaps he will not go to sleep again."

He was only fifteen months old and slept in a room adjoining hers, so that she might be able to hear him.

The captain exclaimed ardently:

"What does it matter, Matilda? How I love you; you must come to me, Matilda."

But she struggled and resisted in her fright.

"No! No! Just listen how he is crying; he will wake up the nurse, and what should we do if she were to come? We should be lost. Just listen to me, Etienne. When he screams at night his father always takes him into our bed, and he is quiet immediately; it is the only means of keeping him still. Do let me take him."

The child roared, uttering shrill screams, which pierced the thickest walls and could be heard by passers-by in the streets.

In his consternation the captain got up, and Matilda jumped out and took the child into her bed, when he was quiet at once.

Etienne sat astride on a chair and made a cigarette, and in about five minutes Andrew went to sleep again.

"I will take him back," his mother said, and she took him back very carefully to his bed.

When she returned the captain was waiting for her with open arms and put his arms round her in a transport of love, while she, embracing him more closely, said, stammering:

"Oh, Etienne, my darling, if you only knew how I love you; how——"

Andrew began to cry again, and he, in a rage, exclaimed:

"Confound it all, won't the little brute be quiet?"

No, the little brute would not be quiet but howled all the louder, on the contrary.

She thought she heard a noise downstairs; no doubt the nurse was coming, so she jumped up and took the child into bed, and he grew quiet directly.

Three times she put him back, and three times she had to fetch him again, and an hour before daybreak the captain had to go, swearing like a proverbial trooper, and to calm his impatience Matilda promised to receive him again the next night. Of course he came, more impatient and ardent than ever, excited by the delay.

He took care to put his sword carefully into a corner; he took off his boots like a thief and spoke so low that Matilda could hardly hear him. At last he was just going to be really happy when the floor, or some piece of furniture or perhaps the bed itself creaked; it sounded as if something had broken, and in a moment a cry, feeble at first, but which grew louder every moment, made itself heard. Andrew was awake again.

He yapped like a fox, and there was not the slightest doubt that if he went on like that the whole house would awake, so his mother, not knowing what to do, got up and brought him. The captain was more furious than ever, but did not move, and very carefully he put out his hand, took a small piece of the child's skin between his two fingers, no matter where it was, the thighs or elsewhere, and pinched it. The little one struggled and screamed in a deafening manner, but his tormentor pinched everywhere, furiously and more vigorously. He took a morsel of flesh and twisted and turned it and then let go in order to take hold of another piece and then another and another.

The child screamed like a chicken having its throat cut or a dog being mercilessly beaten. His mother caressed him, kissed him and tried to stifle his cries by her tenderness, but Andrew grew purple, as if he were going into convulsions, and kicked and struggled with his little arms and legs in an alarming manner.

The captain said softly:

"Try and take him back to his cradle; perhaps he will be quiet."

And Matilda went into the other room with the child in her arms. As soon as he was out of his mother's bed he cried less loudly, and when he was in his own he was quiet, with the exception of a few broken sobs. The rest of the night was tranquil.

The next night the captain came again. As he happened to speak rather loudly, Andrew awoke again and began to scream. His mother went and fetched him immediately, but the captain pinched so hard and long that the child was nearly suffocated by its cries; its eyes turned in its head, and it foamed at the mouth. As soon as it was back in its cradle it was quiet, and in four days Andrew did not cry any more to come into his mother's bed.

On Saturday evening the lawyer returned and took his place again at the domestic hearth and in the conjugal chamber. As he was tired with his journey he went to bed early, but he had not long lain down when he said to his wife:

"Why, how is it that Andrew is not crying? Just go and fetch him, Matilda; I like to feel that he is between us."

She got up and brought the child, but as soon as he saw that he was in that bed in which he had been so fond of sleeping a few days previous he wriggled and screamed so violently in his fright that she had to take him back to his cradle.

M. Moreau could not get over his surprise. "What a very funny thing! What is the matter with him this evening? I suppose he is sleepy?"

"He has been like that all the time that you were away; I have never been able to have him in bed with me once."

In the morning the child woke up and began to laugh and play with his toys.

The lawyer, who was an affectionate man, got up, kissed his offspring and took him into his arms to carry him to their bed. Andrew laughed with that vacant laugh of little creatures whose ideas are still vague. He suddenly saw the bed and his mother in it, and his happy little face puckered up, till suddenly he began to scream furiously and struggled as if he were going to be put to the torture.

In his astonishment his father said:

"There must be something the matter with the child," and mechanically he lifted up his little nightshirt.

He uttered a prolonged "O—o—h!" of astonishment. The child's calves, thighs and buttocks were covered with blue spots as big as halfpennies.

"Just look, Matilda!" the father exclaimed; "this is horrible!" And the mother rushed forward in a fright. It was horrible, no doubt the beginning of some sort of leprosy, of one of those strange affections of the skin which doctors are often at a loss to account for. The parents looked at one another in consternation.

"We must send for the doctor," the father said.

But Matilda, pale as death, was looking at her child who was spotted like a leopard. Then suddenly, uttering a violent cry as if she had seen something that filled her with horror, she exclaimed:

"Oh, the wretch!"

In his astonishment M. Moreau asked: "What are you talking about? What wretch?"

She got red up to the roots of her hair and stammered:

"Oh, nothing, but I think I can guess—it must be—we ought to send for the doctor. It must be that wretch of a nurse who has been pinching the poor child to make him keep quiet when he cries."

In his rage the lawyer sent for the nurse and very nearly beat her. She denied it most impudently but was instantly dismissed, and the municipality having been informed of her conduct, she will find it a hard matter to get another situation.

A FISHING EXCURSION

Paris was blockaded, desolate, famished. The sparrows were few, and anything that was to be had was good to eat.

On a bright morning in January, M. Morissot, a watchmaker by trade but idler through circumstances, was walking along the boulevard, sad, hungry, with his hands in the pockets of his uniform trousers, when he came face to face with a brother-in-arms whom he recognized as an old-time friend.

Before the war Morissot could be seen at daybreak every Sunday, trudging along with a cane in one hand and a tin box on his back. He would take the train to Colombes and walk from there to the Isle of Marante where he would fish until dark.

It was there he had met M. Sauvage, who kept a little notion store in the Rue Notre Dame de Lorette, a jovial fellow and passionately fond of fishing like himself. A warm friendship had sprung up between these two, and they would fish side by side all day, very often without saying a word. Some days, when everything looked fresh and new and the beautiful spring sun gladdened every heart, M. Morissot would exclaim:

"How delightful!" and M. Sauvage would answer:

"There is nothing to equal it."

Then again on a fall evening, when the glorious setting sun, spreading its golden mantle on the already tinted leaves, would throw strange shadows around the two friends, Sauvage would say:

"What a grand picture!"

"It beats the boulevard!" would answer Morissot. But they understood each other quite as well without speaking.

The two friends had greeted each other warmly and had resumed their walk side by side, both thinking deeply of the past and present events. They entered a café, and when a glass of absinthe had been placed before each Sauvage sighed:

"What terrible events, my friend!"

"And what weather!" said Morissot sadly; "this is the first nice day we have had this year. Do you remember our fishing excursions?"

"Do I! Alas, when shall we go again!"

After a second absinthe they emerged from the café, feeling rather dizzy— that lightheaded effect which alcohol has on an empty stomach. The balmy air had made Sauvage exuberant, and he exclaimed:

"Suppose we go!"

"Where?"

"Fishing."

"Fishing! Where?"

"To our old spot, to Colombes. The French soldiers are stationed near there, and I know Colonel Dumoulin will give us a pass."

"It's a go; I am with you."

An hour after, having supplied themselves with their fishing tackle, they arrived at the colonel's villa. He had smiled at their request and had given them a pass in due form.

At about eleven o'clock they reached the advance guard and, after presenting their pass, walked through Colombes and found themselves very near their destination. Argenteuil, across the way, and the great plains toward Nanterre were all deserted. Solitary, the hill of Orgemont and Sannois rose clearly above the plains, a splendid point of observation.

"See," said Sauvage, pointing to the hills, "the Prussians are there."

Prussians! They had never seen one, but they knew that they were all around Paris, invisible and powerful, plundering, devastating and slaughtering. To their superstitious terror they added a deep hatred for this unknown and victorious people.

"What if we should meet some?" said Morissot.

"We would ask them to join us," said Sauvage in true Parisian style.

Still they hesitated to advance. The silence frightened them. Finally Sauvage picked up courage.

"Come, let us go on cautiously."

They proceeded slowly, hiding behind bushes, looking anxiously on every side, listening to every sound. A bare strip of land had to be crossed before reaching the river. They started to run. At last they reached the bank and sank into the bushes, breathless, but relieved.

Morissot thought he heard someone walking. He listened attentively, but no, he heard no sound. They were indeed alone! The little island shielded them from view. The house where the restaurant used to be seemed deserted; feeling reassured, they settled themselves for a good day's sport.

Sauvage caught the first fish, Morissot the second, and every minute they would bring one out which they would place in a net at their feet. It was indeed miraculous! They felt that supreme joy which one feels after having been deprived for months of a pleasant pastime. They had forgotten everything, even the war!

Suddenly they heard a rumbling sound, and the earth shook beneath them. It was the cannon on Mont Valérien. Morissot looked up and saw a trail of smoke, which was instantly followed by another explosion. Then they followed in quick succession.

"They are at it again," said Sauvage, shrugging his shoulders. Morissot, who was naturally peaceful, felt a sudden, uncontrollable anger.

"Stupid fools! What pleasure can they find in killing each other?"

"They are worse than brutes!"

"It will always be thus as long as we have governments."

"Well, such is life!"

"You mean death!" said Morissot, laughing.

They continued to discuss the different political problems, while the cannon on Mont Valérien sent death and desolation among the French.

Suddenly they started. They had heard a step behind them. They turned and beheld four big men in dark uniforms, with guns pointed right at them. Their fishing lines dropped out of their hands and floated away with the current.

In a few minutes the Prussian soldiers had bound them, cast them into a boat and rowed across the river to the island which our friends had thought deserted. They soon found out their mistake when they reached the house, behind which stood a score or more of soldiers. A big burly officer, seated astride a chair, smoking an immense pipe, addressed them in excellent French:

"Well, gentlemen, have you made a good haul?"

Just then a soldier deposited at his feet the netful of fish which he had taken care to take along with him. The officer smiled and said:

"I see you have done pretty well, but let us change the subject. You are evidently sent to spy upon me. You pretended to fish so as to put me off the scent, but I am not so simple. I have caught you and shall have you shot. I am sorry, but war is war. As you passed the advance guard you certainly must have the password; give it to me, and I will set you free."

The two friends stood side by side, pale and slightly trembling, but they answered nothing.

"No one will ever know. You will go back home quietly, and the secret will disappear with you. If you refuse, it is instant death! Choose!"

They remained motionless, silent. The Prussian officer calmly pointed to the river.

"In five minutes you will be at the bottom of this river! Surely you have a family, friends, waiting for you?"

Still they kept silent. The cannon rumbled incessantly. The officer gave orders in his own tongue then moved his chair away from the prisoners. A squad of men advanced within twenty feet of them, ready for command.

"I give you one minute, not a second more!"

Suddenly approaching the two Frenchmen, he took Morissot aside and whispered:

"Quick, the password. Your friend will not know; he will think I changed my mind." Morissot said nothing.

Then, taking Sauvage aside, he asked him the same thing, but he also was silent. The officer gave further orders, and the men leveled their guns. At that moment Morissot's eyes rested on the netful of fish lying in the grass a few feet away. The sight made him faint and, though he struggled against it, his eyes filled with tears. Then, turning to his friend:

"Farewell, Monsieur Sauvage!"

"Farewell, Monsieur Morissot!"

They stood for a minute hand in hand, trembling with emotion which they were unable to control.

"Fire!" commanded the officer.

The squad of men fired as one. Sauvage fell straight on his face. Morissot, who was taller, swayed, pivoted and fell across his friend's body, his face to the sky, while blood flowed freely from the wound in the breast. The officer gave further orders, and his men disappeared. They came back presently with ropes and stones, which they tied to the feet of the two friends, and four of them carried them to the edge of the river. They swung them and threw them in as far as they could. The bodies, weighted by stones, sank immediately. A splash, a few ripples and the water resumed its usual calmness. The only thing to be seen was a little blood floating on the surface. The officer calmly retraced his steps toward the house, muttering:

"The fish will get even now."

He perceived the netful of fish, picked it up, smiled and called:

"Wilhelm!"

A soldier in a white uniform approached. The officer handed him the fish, saying:

"Fry these little things while they are still alive; they will make a delicious meal."

And, having resumed his position on the chair, he puffed away at his pipe.

AFTER

"My darlings," said the comtesse, "you must go to bed."

The three children, two girls and a boy, rose up to kiss their grandmother.

Then they said good night to M. le Curé, who had dined at the château, as he did every Thursday.

The Abbé Mauduit sat two of the young ones on his knees, passing his long arms clad in black behind the children's necks and, drawing their heads toward him with a paternal movement, he kissed each of them on the forehead with a long, tender kiss.

Then he again set them down on the floor, and the little beings went off, the boy in front and the girls behind.

"You are fond of children, Monsieur le Curé," said the comtesse.

"Very fond, madame."

The old woman raised her bright eyes toward the priest.

"And—has your solitude never weighed too heavily on you?"

"Yes, sometimes."

He became silent, hesitated and then added: "But I was never made for ordinary life."

"What do you know about it?"

"Oh, I know very well. I was made to be a priest; I followed my own path."

The comtesse kept staring at him:

"Look here, Monsieur le Curé, tell me this—tell me how it was that you resolved to renounce forever what makes us love life—the rest of us—all that consoles and sustains us? What is it that drove you, impelled you, to separate yourself from the great natural path of marriage and the family. You are neither an enthusiast nor a fanatic, neither a gloomy person nor a sad person. Was it some strange occurrence, some sorrow, that led you to take lifelong vows?"

The Abbé Mauduit rose up and drew near to the fire, stretching out to the flames the big shoes that country priests generally wear. He seemed still hesitating as to what reply he should make.

He was a tall old man with white hair, and for the last twenty years had been the pastor of the parish of Sainte-Antoine-du-Rocher. The peasants said of him, "There's a good man for you!" And indeed he was a good man, benevolent, friendly to all, gentle and, to crown all, generous. Like Saint Martin, he had cut his cloak in two. He freely laughed and wept, too, for very little, just like a woman —a thing that prejudiced him more or less in the hard minds of the country people.

The old Comtesse de Saville, living in retirement in her château of Rocher in order to bring up her grandchildren, after successive deaths of her son and her daughter-in-law, was very much attached to the curé and used to say of him: "He has a kind heart!"

The abbé came every Thursday to spend the evening at the château, and they were close friends, with the open and honest friendship of old people.

She persisted:

"Look here, Monsieur le Curé, 'tis your turn now to make a confession!"

He repeated: "I was not made for a life like everybody else. I saw it myself, fortunately, in time and have had many proofs since that I made no mistake on that point.

"My parents, who were mercers in Verdiers and rather rich, had much ambition on my account. They sent me to a boarding school while I was very young. You cannot conceive what a boy may suffer at college by the mere fact of separation, of isolation. This monotonous life without affection is good for some and detestable for others. Young people often have hearts more sensitive than one supposes, and by shutting them up thus too soon, far from those they love, we may develop to an excessive extent a sensibility which is of an overstrung kind and which becomes sickly and dangerous.

"I scarcely ever played; I never had companions; I passed my hours in looking back to my home with regret; I spent the whole night weeping in my bed. I sought to bring up before my mind recollections of my own home, trifling recollections of little things, little events. I thought incessantly of all I had left behind there. I became almost imperceptibly an oversensitive youth to whom the slightest annoyances were dreadful griefs.

"Together with this, I remained taciturn, self-absorbed, without expansion, without confidants. This work of mental exaltation was brought about obscurely but surely. The nerves of children are quickly excited; one ought to realize the fact that they live in a state of deep quiescence up to the time of almost complete development. But does anyone reflect that for certain students an unjust imposition can be as great a pang as the death of a friend afterward? Does anyone realize the fact that certain young souls have, with very little cause, terrible emotions and are in a very short time diseased and incurable souls?

"This was my case. This faculty of regret developed itself in me in such a fashion that my existence became a martyrdom.

"I did not speak about it; I said nothing about it, but gradually I acquired a sensibility, or rather a sensitivity, so lively that my soul resembled a living wound. Everything that touched it produced in it twitchings of pain, frightful vibrations and veritable ravages. Happy are the men whom nature has buttressed with indifference and cased in stoicism.

"I reached my sixteenth year. An excessive timidity had come to me from this aptitude to suffer on account of everything. Feeling myself unprotected against all the attacks of chance or fate, I feared every contact, every approach, every event. I lived on the watch, as if under the constant threat of an unknown and always expected misfortune. I was afraid either to speak or to act publicly. I had, indeed, the sensation that life is a battle, a dreadful conflict in which one receives terrible blows, grievous, mortal wounds. In place of cherishing, like all men, the hope of good fortune on the morrow, I only kept a confused fear of it, and I felt in my own mind a desire to conceal myself—to avoid combat in which I should be vanquished and slain.

"As soon as my studies were finished they gave me six months' time to choose a career. Suddenly a very simple event made me see clearly into myself, showed me the diseased condition of my mind, made me understand the danger and caused me to make up my mind to fly from it.

"Verdiers is a little town surrounded with plains and wood. In the central street stands my parents' house. I now passed my days far from this dwelling which I had so much regretted, so much desired. Dreams were awakened in me, and I walked all alone in the fields in order to let them escape and fly away. My father and my mother, quite occupied with business and anxious about my future, talked to me only about their profits or about my possible plans. They were fond of me in the way that hardheaded, practical people are; they had more reasons than heart in their affection for me. I lived imprisoned in my thoughts and trembling with eternal uneasiness.

"Now one evening after a long walk, as I was making my way home with quick strides so as not to be late, I met a dog trotting toward me. He was a species of red spaniel, very lean, with long curly ears.

"When he was ten paces away from me he stopped. I did the same. Then he began wagging his tail and came over to me with short steps and nervous movements of his whole body, going down on his paws as if appealing to me and softly shaking his head. He then made a show of crawling with an air so humble, so sad, so suppliant, that I felt the tears coming into my eyes. I came near him; he ran away; then he came back again, and I bent down, trying to coax him to approach me with soft words. At last he was within reach, and I gently caressed him with the most careful hands.

"He grew bold, rose up bit by bit, laid his paws on my shoulders and began to lick my face. He followed me into the house.

"This was really the first being I had passionately loved, because he returned my affection. My attachment to this animal was certainly exaggerated and ridiculous. It seemed to me in a confused sort of way that we were brothers, lost on this earth, and therefore isolated and without defense, one as well as the other. He never quitted my side. He slept at the foot of my bed, ate at my table in spite of the objections of my parents and followed me in my solitary walks.

"I often stopped at the side of a ditch, and I sat down in the grass. Sam would lie on my knees and lift up my hand with the end of his nose so that I might caress him.

"One day toward the end of June, as we were on the road from Saint-Pierre-de-Chavrol, I saw the diligence from Pavereau coming along. Its four horses were going at a gallop. It had a yellow box seat and imperial crowned with black leather. The coachman cracked his whip; a cloud of dust rose up under the wheels of the heavy vehicle then floated behind, just as a cloud would do.

"And all of a sudden, as the vehicle came close to me, Sam, perhaps frightened by the noise and wishing to join me, jumped in front of it. A horse's foot knocked him down. I saw him rolling over, turning round, falling back again on all fours, and then the entire coach gave two big jolts, and behind it I saw something quivering in the dust on the road. He was nearly cut in two; all his intestines were hanging through his stomach, which had been ripped open, and spurts of blood fell to the ground. He tried to get up, to walk, but he could only move his two front paws and scratch the ground with them, as if to make a hole. The two others were already dead. And he howled dreadfully, mad with pain.

"He died in a few minutes. I cannot describe how much I felt and suffered. I was confined to my own room for a month.

"Now one night my father, enraged at seeing me in such a state for so little, exclaimed:

"'How then will it be when you have real griefs if you lose your wife or children?'

"And I began to see clearly into myself. I understood why all the small miseries of each day assumed in my eyes the importance of a catastrophe; I saw that I was organized in such a way that I suffered dreadfully from everything, that every painful impression was multiplied by my diseased sensibility, and an atrocious fear of life took possession of me. I was without passions, without ambitions; I resolved to sacrifice possible joys in order to avoid sorrows. Existence is short, but I made up my mind to spend it in the service of others, in relieving their troubles and enjoying their happiness. By having no direct experience of either one or the other I would only be conscious of passionless emotions.

"And if you only knew how, in spite of this, misery tortures me, ravages me. But what would be for me an intolerable affliction has become commiseration, pity.

"The sorrows which I have every day to concern myself about I could not endure if they fell on my own heart. I could not have seen one of my children die without dying myself. And I have, in spite of everything, preserved such a deep and penetrating fear of circumstances that the sight of the postman entering my house makes a shiver pass every day through my veins, and yet I have nothing to be afraid of now."

The Abbé Mauduit ceased speaking. He stared into the fire in the huge grate, as if he saw there mysterious things, all the unknown portions of existence which he would have been able to live if he had been more fearless in the face of suffering.

He added then in a subdued tone:

"I was right. I was not made for this world."

The comtesse said nothing at first, but at length, after a long silence, she remarked:

"For my part, if I had not my grandchildren I believe I would not have the courage to live."

And the curé rose up without saying another word.

As the servants were asleep in the kitchen, she conducted him herself to the door which looked out on the garden, and she saw his tall shadow, revealed by the reflection of the lamp, disappearing through the gloom of night.

Then she came back, sat down before the fire and pondered over many things on which we never think when we are young.

AN ADVENTURE IN PARIS

Is there any stronger feeling than curiosity in a woman? Fancy seeing, knowing, touching what one has dreamed about! What would a woman not do for that? Once a woman's eager curiosity is roused, she will be guilty of any folly, commit any imprudence, venture upon anything, and recoil from nothing. I am speaking of women who are really women, who are endowed with that triple-bottomed disposition, which appears to be reasonable and cool on the surface but whose three secret compartments are filled as follows: the first with female uneasiness, which is always in a state of fluttering; the next with sly tricks which are colored with an imitation of good faith, with the sophistical and formidable wiles of apparently devout women; and the last with all those charming, improper acts, with that delightful deceit, exquisite perfidy, and all those wayward qualities which drive lovers who are stupidly credulous to suicide but delight others.

The woman whose adventure I am about to relate was a little person from the provinces who had been insipidly respectable till then. Her life, which was apparently so calm, was spent at home, with a busy husband and two children, whom she brought up like an irreproachable woman. But her heart beat with unsatisfied curiosity and unknown longing. She was continually thinking of Paris, and she read the fashionable papers eagerly. The accounts of parties, of the dresses and various entertainments, excited her longing; but, above all, she was strangely agitated by those paragraphs which were full of double meaning, by those veils which were half-raised by clever phrases, and which gave her a glimpse of culpable and ravishing delights, and from her home in the provinces she saw Paris in an apotheosis of magnificent and corrupt luxury.

During the long nights, when she dreamed, lulled by the regular snores of a husband, sleeping on his back by her side, with a silk handkerchief tied round his head, she saw in her sleep those well-known men whose names appeared regularly on the first page of the newspapers like stars in the dark sky. She pictured to herself their lives—continual excitement, constant debauches, orgies such as they practiced in ancient Rome, which were horribly voluptuous, with refinements of sensuality so complicated that she could not even imagine them.

The boulevards seemed to her to be a kind of abyss of human passions, and there could be no doubt that the houses there concealed mysteries of prodigious love. But she felt that she was growing old, without having known life, except in those regular, horribly monotonous, everyday occupations which constitute the happiness of the home. She was still pretty, for she was well preserved by a tranquil existence, like winter fruit in a closed cupboard; but she was consumed, agitated and upset by her secret desires. She used to ask herself whether she should die without having experienced any of those damning, intoxicating joys, without having plunged once, just once, into that flood of Parisian voluptuousness.

By dint of much perseverance, she paved the way for a journey to Paris, found a pretext, got some relatives to invite her, and, as her husband could not go with her, she went alone. As soon as she arrived, she invented a reason for remaining for some days, or rather for some nights, if necessary, as she told him that she had met some friends who lived a little way out of town.

And then she set out on a voyage of discovery. She went up and down the boulevards, without seeing anything except roving and licensed vice. She looked into the large cafés, and read the agony column of the *Figaro*, which every morning seemed to her like a tocsin, a summons to love. But nothing put her on the track of those orgies of actors and actresses; nothing revealed to her those temples of debauchery which opened, she imagined, at some magic word, like the cave in the *Arabian Nights* or the catacombs in Rome, where the mysteries of a persecuted religion were secretely celebrated.

Her relatives, who were quite middle-class people, could not introduce her to any of those well-known men, of whose names her head was full; and in despair she was thinking of returning, when chance came to her aid. One day, as she was going along the Rue de la Chaussée d'Antin, she stopped to look into a shop full of those colored Japanese knickknacks, which attract the eye by their color. She was looking at the grotesque little ivories, the tall vases of flaming enamel, and the curious bronzes, when she heard the shopkeeper inside dilating, with many bows, on the value of an enormous, potbellied, comical figure—which was quite unique, he said—to a little, bald-headed, gray-bearded man.

Every moment the shopkeeper repeated his customer's name, which was a celebrated one, in a voice like a trumpet. The other customers, young women and well-dressed gentlemen, gave a swift and furtive but respectful glance at the celebrated writer, who was looking admiringly at the china figure. They were both equally ugly, as ugly as two brothers who had sprung from the same mother.

"To you the price will be a thousand francs, M. Varin, and that is exactly what it cost me. I should ask anybody else fifteen hundred, but I think a great deal of literary and artistic customers, and have special prices for them. They all come to me, M. Varin. Yesterday, M. Busnach bought a large, antique goblet from me, and the other day I sold two candelabra like this (aren't they beautiful?) to M. Alexandre Dumas. If M. Zola were to see that Japanese figure he would buy it immediately, M. Varin."

The author hesitated in perplexity, as he wanted to have the figure, but the price was above him, and he thought no more about being stared at than if he had been alone in the desert. She came in trembling, with her eyes fixed shamelessly upon him, and she did not even ask herself whether he were good-looking, elegant, or young. It was Jean Varin himself, Jean Varin. After a long struggle and painful hesitation, he put the figure down onto the table.

"No, it is too expensive," he said.

The shopkeeper's eloquence redoubled. "Oh! M. Varin, too expensive? It is worth two thousand francs if it is worth a sou."

But the man of letters replied sadly, still looking at the figure with the enameled eyes: "I do not say it is not; but it is too expensive for me."

And thereupon, she, seized by a kind of mad audacity, came forward and said: "What will you charge me for the figure?"

The shopkeeper, in surprise, replied: "Fifteen hundred francs, madame."

"I will take it."

The writer, who had not even noticed her till that moment, turned round suddenly. He looked at her from head to foot, with half-closed eyes, observantly, and then he took in the details, like a connoisseur. She was charming, suddenly animated by the flame which had hitherto been dormant in her. And then, a woman who gives fifteen hundred francs for a knickknack is not to be met with every day.

But she was overcome by a feeling of delightful delicacy, and turning to him, she said in a trembling voice:

"Excuse me, monsieur; no doubt I have been rather hasty, as perhaps you had not finally made up your mind."

He, however, only bowed, and said: "Indeed I had, madame."

And she, filled with emotion, continued: "Well, monsieur, if either today, or at any other time, you change your mind, you can have this Japanese figure. I only bought it because you seemed to like it."

He was visibly flattered, and smiled. "I should much like to find out how you know who I am?" he said.

Then she told him how she admired him, and became quite eloquent as she quoted his works, and while they were talking, he rested his arms on a table and fixed his bright eyes upon her, trying to make out who and what she really was. But the shopkeeper, who was pleased to have that living puff of his goods, called out, from the other end of the shop: "Just look at this, M. Varin; is it not beautiful?"

And then everyone looked round, and she almost trembled with pleasure at being seen talking so intimately with such a well-known man.

At last, however, intoxicated, as it were, by her feelings, she grew bold, like a general who is about to order an assault.

"Monsieur," she said, "will you do me a great, a very great pleasure? Allow me to offer you this funny Japanese figure, as a souvenir from a woman who admires you passionately, and whom you have seen for ten minutes."

He refused. She persisted, but still he resisted her offer, very much amused and laughing heartily. But that only made her more obstinate, and she said: "Very well, then, I shall take it to your house immediately; where do you live?"

He refused to give her his address, but she got it from the shopkeeper, and when she had paid for her purchase she ran out to take a cab. The writer went after her, as he did not wish to accept a present from a person whom he did not know. He reached her just as she was jumping into a vehicle, and, getting in after her, he almost fell on top of her as the cab gave a jolt. Then he sat down by her side, feeling very much annoyed.

It was no good for him to argue and to beg her; she showed herself intractable, and when they got to the door, she stated her conditions: "I will undertake not to leave this with you," she said, "if you will promise to do all I want today." And the whole affair seemed so funny to him that he agreed.

"What do you generally do at this time?" she asked him; and after hesitating for a few moments, he replied: "I generally go for a walk."

"Very well, then, we will go to the Bois de Boulogne!" she said, in a resolute voice, and they started.

He was obliged to tell her the names of all the well-known women, pure or impure, with every detail about them—their mode of life, their habits, their homes, and their vices; and when it was getting dusk, she said to him: "What do you do every day at this time?"

"I have some absinthe," he replied, with a laugh.

"Very well, then, monsieur," she went on seriously; "let us go and have some absinthe."

They went into a large café on the boulevard which he frequented, where he met some of his colleagues, whom he introduced to her. She was half beside herself with pleasure, and kept saying to herself: "At last! At last!"

But time went on, and she asked: "Is it your dinnertime?" To which he replied: "Yes."

"Then, let us go and have dinner."

When they left Bignon's after dinner, she wanted to know what he did in the evening, and, looking at her fixedly, he replied: "That depends; sometimes I go to the theater."

"Very well, then, let us go to the theater."

They went to the Vaudeville with a pass, thanks to him, and, to her great pride, the whole house saw her sitting by his side in the balcony stalls.

When the play was over, he gallantly kissed her hand, and said: "It only remains for me to thank you for this delightful day."

But she interrupted him: "What do you do at this time, every night?"

"Why—why—I go home."

She began to laugh, a little tremulous laugh: "Very well, monsieur, let us go to your rooms."

They did not say anything more. She shivered occasionally, from head to foot, feeling inclined to stay and inclined to run away, but with a fixed determination, after all, to see it out to the end. She was so excited that she had to hold on to the banister as she went upstairs, and he went on ahead of her, with a wax match in his hand.

As soon as they were in the room, she undressed herself quickly, and retired without saying a word, and then she waited for him, cowering against the wall. But she was as simple as it was possible for a provincial lawyer's wife to be, and he was more exacting than a pasha with three tails, and so they did not at all understand each other.

At last, however, he went to sleep. The night passed, and the silence was only disturbed by the ticktock of the clock, while she, lying motionless, thought of her conjugal nights, and by the light of the Chinese lantern she looked, nearly heart-broken, at the little fat man lying on his back, whose round stomach raised up the bedclothes, like a balloon filled with gas. He snored with the noise of a wheezy organ pipe, with prolonged snorts and comic chokings. His few hairs profited by his sleep to stand up in a very strange way, as if they were tired of having been fastened for so long to that pate, whose bareness they were trying to cover. And a thin stream of saliva ran from the corner of his half-opened mouth.

At last daylight appeared through the drawn blinds. She got up and dressed herself without making any noise, and had already half opened the door, when she made the lock creak, and he woke up and rubbed his eyes. He was some moments before he quite came to himself, and then, when he remembered all that had happened, he said:

"What! Are you going already?"

She remained standing, in some confusion, and then said, in a hesitating voice: "Yes, of course; it is morning."

Then he sat up, and said: "Look here, I have something to ask you, in my turn." And as she did not reply, he went on: "You have surprised me most confoundedly since yesterday. Be open, and tell me why you did it all, for upon my word I cannot understand it in the least."

She went close up to him, blushing as if she had been a virgin, and said: "I wanted to know—what—what vice—really was, and—well—well, it is not at all funny."

And she ran out of the room and downstairs into the street.

A number of sweepers were busy in the streets, brushing the pavements, the roadway, and sweeping everything on one side. With the same regular motion, the motion of mowers in a meadow, they pushed the mud in front of them in a semi-circle. She met them in every street, like dancing puppets, walking automatically with a swaying motion, and it seemed to her as if something had been swept out of her; as if her overexcited dreams had been pushed into the gutter, or into the drain. So she went home, out of breath and very cold, and all that she could remember was the sensation of the motion of those brooms sweeping the streets of Paris in the early morning.

When she got into her room, she threw herself onto her bed and cried.

THE SPASM

The hotel guests slowly entered the dining room and sat down in their places. The waiters began to attend on them in a leisurely fashion so as to enable those who were late to arrive and to avoid bringing back the dishes. The old bathers, the habitués, those whose season was advancing, looked with interest toward the door whenever it opened, with a desire to see new faces appearing.

This is the principal distraction of health resorts. People look forward to the dinner hour in order to inspect each day's new arrivals, to find out who they are, what they do and what they think. A vague longing springs up in the mind, a longing for agreeable meetings, for pleasant acquaintances, perhaps for love adventures. In this life of elbowings, strangers, as well as those with whom we have come into daily contact, assume an extreme importance. Curiosity is aroused; sympathy is ready to exhibit itself, and sociability is the order of the day.

We cherish antipathies for a week and friendships for a month; we see other people with different eyes when we view them through the medium of the acquaintanceship that is brought about at health resorts. We discover in men suddenly, after an hour's chat in the evening after dinner, or under the trees in the park where the generous spring bubbles up, a high intelligence and astonishing merits, and a month afterward we have completely forgotten these new friends, so fascinating when we first met them.

There also are formed lasting and serious ties more quickly than anywhere else. People see each other every day; they become acquainted very quickly, and with the affection thus originated is mingled something of the sweetness and self-abandonment of long-standing intimacies. We cherish in after years the dear and tender memories of those first hours of friendship, the memory of those first conversations through which we have been able to unveil a soul, of those first glances which interrogate and respond to the questions and secret thoughts which the mouth has not as yet uttered, the memory of that first cordial confidence, the memory of that delightful sensation of opening our hearts to those who are willing to open theirs to us.

And the melancholy of health resorts, the monotony of days that are alike, help from hour to hour in this rapid development of affection.

Well, this evening, as on every other evening, we awaited the appearance of strange faces.

Only two appeared, but they were very remarkable looking, a man and a woman —father and daughter. They immediately produced the same effect on my mind as some of Edgar Poe's characters, and yet there was about them a charm, the charm associated with misfortune. I looked upon them as the victims of fatality. The man was very tall and thin, rather stooped, with hair perfectly white, too white for his comparatively youthful physiognomy, and there was in his bearing and in his person that austerity peculiar to Protestants. The daughter, who was probably twenty-four or twenty-five, was small in stature and was also very thin, very pale and had the air of one worn out with utter lassitude. We meet people like this from time to time, people who seem too weak for the tasks and the needs of daily life, too weak to move about, to walk, to do all that we do every day. This young girl was very pretty, with the diaphanous beauty of a phantom, and she ate with extreme slowness, as if she were almost incapable of moving her arms. It must have been she assuredly who had come to take the waters.

They found themselves facing me at the opposite side of the table, and I at once noticed that the father had a very singular nervous spasm. Every time he wanted to reach an object his hand made a hooklike movement, a sort of irregular zigzag, before it succeeded in touching what it was in search of, and after a little while this action was so wearisome to me that I turned aside my head in order not to see it. I noticed, too, that the young girl, during meals, wore a glove on her left hand.

After dinner I went for a stroll in the park of the thermal establishment. This led toward the little Auvergnese station of Châtel Guyon, hidden in a gorge at the foot of the high mountain, of that mountain from which flow so many boiling springs, rising from the deep bed of extinct volcanoes. Over there, above us, the domes, which had once been craters, raised their mutilated heads on the summit of the long chain. For Châtel Guyon is situated at the spot where the region of domes begins. Beyond it stretches out the region of peaks and, farther on again, the region of precipices.

The Puy de Dôme is the highest of the domes; the Peak of Sancy is the loftiest of the peaks, and Cantal is the most precipitous of these mountain heights.

This evening it was very warm. I walked up and down a shady path on the side of the mountain overlooking the park, listening to the opening strains of the casino band. I saw the father and the daughter advancing slowly in my direction. I saluted them, as we are accustomed to salute our hotel companions at health resorts, and the man, coming to a sudden halt, said to me:

"Could you not, monsieur, point out to us a short walk, nice and easy, if that is possible, and excuse my intrusion on you?"

I offered to show them the way toward the valley through which the little river flowed, a deep valley forming a gorge between two tall, craggy, wooded slopes. They gladly accepted my offer, and we talked naturally about the virtues of the waters.

"Oh," he said, "my daughter has a strange malady, the seat of which is unknown. She suffers from incomprehensible nervous disorders. At one time the doctors think she has an attack of heart disease; at another time they imagine it is some affection of the liver, and at another time they declare it to be a disease of the spine. Today her condition is attributed to the stomach, which is the great caldron and regulator of the body, the protean source of diseases with a thousand forms and a thousand susceptibilities to attack. This is why we have come here. For my part, I am rather inclined to think it is the nerves; in any case, it is very sad."

Immediately the remembrance of the violent spasmodic movement of his hand came back to my mind, and I asked him:

"But is this not the result of heredity? Are not your own nerves somewhat affected?"

"Mine? Oh no—my nerves have always been very steady."

Then suddenly, after a pause, he went on:

"Ah! You are alluding to the spasm in my hand every time I want to reach for anything? This arises from a terrible experience which I had. Just imagine, this daughter of mine was actually buried alive!"

I could only give utterance to the word "Ah!" so great were my astonishment and emotion.

He continued:

"Here is the story. It is simple. Juliette had been subject for some time to serious attacks of the heart. We believed that she had a disease of that organ and we were prepared for the worst.

"One day she was carried into the house cold, lifeless, dead. She had fallen down unconscious in the garden. The doctor certified that life was extinct. I watched by her side for a day and two nights. I laid her with my own hands in the coffin, which I accompanied to the cemetery where she was deposited in the family vault. It is situated in the very heart of Lorraine.

"I wished to have her interred with her jewels, bracelets, necklaces, rings, all presents which she had got from me and with her first ball dress on.

"You may easily imagine the state of mind in which I was when I returned home.

She was the only companion I had, for my wife has been dead for many years. I found my way to my own apartment in a half-distracted condition, utterly exhausted, and I sank into my easy chair without the capacity to think or the strength to move. I was nothing better now than a suffering, vibrating machine, a human being who had, as it were, been flayed alive; my soul was like a living wound.

"My old valet Prosper, who had assisted me in placing Juliette in her coffin and preparing her for her last sleep, entered the room noiselessly and asked:

" 'Does Monsieur want anything?'

"I merely shook my head by way of answering no.

"He urged: 'Monsieur is wrong. He will bring some illness on himself. Would Monsieur like me to put him to bed?'

"I answered: 'No! Let me alone!' And he left the room.

"I know not how many hours slipped away. Oh, what a night, what a night! It was cold. My fire had died out in the huge grate, and the wind, the winter wind, an icy wind, a hurricane accompanied by frost and snow, kept blowing against the window with a sinister and regular noise.

"How many hours slipped away? There I was without sleeping, powerless, crushed, my eyes wide open, my legs stretched out, my body limp, inanimate, and my mind torpid with despair. Suddenly the great bell of the entrance gate, the bell of the vestibule, rang out.

"I got such a shock that my chair cracked under me. The solemn, ponderous sound vibrated through the empty château as if through a vault. I turned round to see what the hour was by my clock. It was just two in the morning. Who could be coming at such an hour?

"And abruptly the bell again rang twice. The servants, without doubt, were afraid to get up. I took a wax candle and descended the stairs. I was on the point of asking: 'Who is there?'

"Then I felt ashamed of my weakness, and I slowly opened the huge door. My heart was throbbing wildly; I was frightened; I hurriedly drew back the door, and in the darkness I distinguished a white figure standing erect, something that resembled an apparition.

"I recoiled, petrified with horror, faltering:

" 'Who—who—who are you?'

"A voice replied:

" 'It is I, Father.'

"It was my daughter. I really thought I must be mad, and I retreated backward before this advancing specter. I kept moving away, making a sign with my hand, as if to drive the phantom away, that gesture which you have noticed—that gesture of which since then I have never got rid.

"The apparition spoke again:

" 'Do not be afraid, Papa; I was not dead. Somebody tried to steal my rings and cut one of my fingers; the blood began to flow, and this reanimated me.'

"And, in fact, I could see that her hand was covered with blood.

"I fell on my knees, choking with sobs and with a rattling in my throat.

"Then when I had somewhat collected my thoughts, though I was still so much dismayed that I scarcely realized the gruesome good fortune that had fallen to my lot, I made her go up to my room and sit down in my easy chair; then I rang excitedly for Prosper to get him to light up the fire again and to get her some wine and summon the rest of the servants to her assistance.

"The man entered, stared at my daughter, opened his mouth with a gasp of alarm and stupefaction and then fell back, insensible.

"It was he who had opened the vault and who had mutilated and then abandoned my daughter, for he could not efface the traces of the theft. He had not even taken the trouble to put back the coffin into its place, feeling sure, besides, that he would not be suspected by me, as I completely trusted him.

"You see, monsieur, that we are very unhappy people."

He stopped.

The night had fallen, casting its shadows over the desolate, mournful vale, and a sort of mysterious fear possessed me at finding myself by the side of those strange beings, of this young girl who had come back from the tomb and this father with his uncanny spasm.

I found it impossible to make any comment on this dreadful story. I only murmured:

"What a horrible thing!"

Then after a minute's silence I added:

"Suppose we go back; I think it is getting cold."

And we made our way back to the hotel.

A MEETING

It was all an accident, a pure accident. Tired of standing, Baron d'Etraille went—as all the princess's rooms were open on that particular evening—into an empty bedroom, which appeared almost dark after coming out of the brilliantly lighted drawing rooms.

He looked round for a chair in which to have a doze, as he was sure his wife would not go away before daylight. As soon as he got inside the door he saw the big bed with its azure-and-gold hangings in the middle of the great room, looking like a catafalque in which love was buried, for the princess was no longer young. Behind it a large bright spot looked like a lake seen at a distance from a window. It was a big looking glass which, discreetly covered with dark drapery very rarely let down, seemed to look at the bed, which was its accomplice. One might almost fancy that it felt regrets and that one was going to see in it charming shapes of nude women and the gentle movement of arms about to embrace them.

The baron stood still for a moment, smiling and rather moved, on the threshold of this chamber dedicated to love. But suddenly something appeared in the looking glass, as if the phantoms which he had evoked had come up before him. A man and a woman who had been sitting on a low couch hidden in the shade had risen, and the polished surface, reflecting their figures, showed that they were kissing each other before separating.

The baron recognized his wife and the Marquis de Cervigné. He turned and went away, like a man fully master of himself, and waited till it was day before taking away the baroness. But he had no longer any thoughts of sleeping.

As soon as they were alone he said:

"Madame, I saw you just now in the Princess de Raynes's room. I need say no more, for I am not fond either of reproaches, acts of violence or of ridicule. As I wish to avoid all such things, we shall separate without any scandal. Our lawyers will settle your position according to my orders. You will be free to live as you please when you are no longer under my roof, but as you will continue to bear my name, I must warn you that should any scandal arise I shall show myself inflexible."

She tried to speak, but he stopped her, bowed and left the room.

He was more astonished and sad than unhappy. He had loved her dearly during the first period of their married life, but his ardor had cooled, and now he often had a caprice, either in a theater or in society, though he always preserved a certain liking for the baroness.

She was very young, hardly four and twenty, small, slight—too slight—and very fair. She was a true Parisian doll: clever, spoiled, elegant, coquettish, witty, with more charm than real beauty. He used to say familiarly to his brother when speaking of her:

"My wife is charming, attractive, but—there is nothing to lay hold of. She is like a glass of champagne that is all froth—when you have got to the wine it is very good, but there is too little of it unfortunately."

He walked up and down the room in great agitation, thinking of a thousand things. At one moment he felt in a great rage and felt inclined to give the marquis a good thrashing, to horsewhip him publicly in the club. But he thought that would not do; it would not be the thing; he would be laughed at and not the other, and he felt that his anger proceeded more from wounded vanity than from a broken heart. So he went to bed but could not get to sleep.

A few days afterward it was known in Paris that the Baron and Baroness d'Etraille had agreed to an amicable separation on account of incompatibility of temper. Nobody suspected anything; nobody laughed, and nobody was astonished.

The baron, however, to avoid meeting her, traveled for a year; then he spent the summer at the seaside and the autumn in shooting, returning to Paris for the winter. He did not meet his wife once.

He did not even know what people said about her. At any rate, she took care to save appearances, and that was all he asked for.

He got dreadfully bored, traveled again, restored his old castle of Villebosc, which took him two years; then for over a year he received relays of friends there, till at last, tired of all these commonplace, so-called pleasures, he returned to his mansion in the Rue de Lills, just six years after their separation.

He was then forty-five, with a good crop of gray hair, rather stout and with that melancholy look of people who have been handsome, sought after, much liked and are deteriorating daily.

A month after his return to Paris he took cold on coming out of his club and had a bad cough, so his medical man ordered him to Nice for the rest of the winter.

He started by the express on Monday evening. He was late, got to the station only a very short time before the departure of the train and had barely time to get into a carriage, with only one other occupant, who was sitting in a corner so wrapped in furs and cloaks that he could not even make out whether it was a man or a woman, as nothing of the figure could be seen. When he perceived that he could not find out he put on his traveling cap, rolled himself up in his rugs and stretched himself out comfortably to sleep.

He did not wake up till the day was breaking and looked immediately at his fellow traveler. He had not stirred all night and seemed still to be sound asleep.

Baron d'Etraille made use of the opportunity to brush his hair and his beard and to try and freshen himself up a little generally, for a night's traveling changes one's looks very much when one has attained a certain age.

A great poet has said:

When we are young our mornings are triumphant!

Then we wake up with a cool skin, a bright eye and glossy hair. When one grows old one wakes up in a different state. Dull eyes, red, swollen cheeks, dry lips, the hair and beard all disarranged, impart an old, fatigued, worn-out look to the face.

The baron opened his traveling dressing case, made himself as tidy as he could and then waited.

The engine whistled and the train stopped, and his neighbor moved. No doubt he was awake. They started off again, and then an oblique ray of the sun shone into the carriage, just onto the sleeper, who moved again, shook himself and then calmly showed his face.

It was a young, fair, pretty, stout woman, and the baron looked at her in amazement. He did not know what to believe. He could have sworn that it was his wife —but wonderfully changed for the better: stouter—why, she had grown as stout as he was, only it suited her much better than it did him.

She looked at him quietly, did not seem to recognize him and then slowly laid aside her wraps. She had that calm assurance of a woman who is sure of herself, the insolent audacity of a first awaking, knowing and feeling that she was in her full beauty and freshness.

The baron really lost his head. Was it his wife or somebody else who was as like her as any sister could be? As he had not seen her for six years he might be mistaken.

She yawned, and he knew her by the gesture. She turned and looked at him again, calmly, indifferently, as if she scarcely saw him, and then looked out at the country again.

He was upset and dreadfully perplexed and waited, looking at her sideways, steadfastly.

Yes; it was certainly his wife. How could he possibly have doubted? There could certainly not be two noses like that, and a thousand recollections flashed through him, slight details of her body, a beauty spot on one of her limbs and another on her back. How often he had kissed them! He felt the old feeling of the intoxication of love stealing over him, and he called to mind the sweet odor of her skin, her smile when she put her arms onto his shoulders, the soft intonations of her voice, all her graceful, coaxing ways.

But how she had changed and improved! It was she and yet not she. He thought her riper, more developed, more of a woman, more seductive, more desirable, adorably desirable.

And this strange, unknown woman, whom he had accidentally met in a railway carriage belonged to him; he had only to say to her:

"I insist upon it."

He had formerly slept in her arms, existed only in her love, and now he had found her again certainly, but so changed that he scarcely knew her. It was another and yet she at the same time. It was another who had been born, formed and grown since he had left her. It was she, indeed; she whom he had possessed but who was now altered, with a more assured smile and greater self-possession. There were two women in one, mingling a great deal of what was new and unknown with many sweet recollections of the past. There was something singular, disturbing, exciting about it—a kind of mystery of love in which there floated a delicious confusion. It was his wife in a new body and in a new flesh which his lips had never pressed.

And he remembered that in six or seven years everything changes in us; only outlines can be recognized, and sometimes even they disappear.

The blood, the hair, the skin, all change and are reconstituted, and when people have not seen each other for a long time they find when they meet another totally different being, although it be the same and bear the same name.

And the heart also can change. Ideas may be modified and renewed, so that in forty years of life we may, by gradual and constant transformations, become four or five totally new and different beings.

He dwelt on this thought till it troubled him; it had first taken possession of him when he surprised her in the princess's room. He was not the least angry; it was not the same woman that he was looking at—that thin, excitable doll of those days.

What was he to do? How should he address her? And what could he say to her? Had she recognized him?

The train stopped again. He got up, bowed and said: "Bertha, do you want anything I can bring you?"

She looked at him from head to foot and answered, without showing the slightest surprise or confusion or anger, but with the most perfect indifference:

"I do not want anything—thank you."

He got out and walked up and down the platform in order to think and, as it were, to recover his senses after a fall. What should he do now? If he got into another carriage it would look as if he were running away. Should he be polite or importunate? That would look as if he were asking for forgiveness. Should he speak as if he were her master? He would look like a fool, and besides, he really had no right to do so.

He got in again and took his place.

During his absence she had hastily arranged her dress and hair and was now lying stretched out on the seat, radiant, but without showing any emotion.

He turned to her and said: "My dear Bertha, since this singular chance has brought us together after a separation of six years—a quite friendly separation— are we to continue to look upon each other as irreconcilable enemies? We are shut up together, tête-à-tête, which is so much the better or so much the worse. I am not going to get into another carriage, so don't you think it is preferable to talk as friends till the end of our journey?"

She answered quite calmly again: "Just as you please."

Then he suddenly stopped, really not knowing what to say, but as he had plenty of assurance he sat down on the middle seat and said:

"Well, I see I must pay my court to you; so much the better. It is, however, really a pleasure, for you are charming. You cannot imagine how you have improved in the last six years. I do not know any woman who could give me that delightful sensation which I experienced just now when you emerged from your wraps. I should really have thought such a change impossible."

Without moving her head or looking at him she said: "I cannot say the same with regard to you; you have certainly deteriorated a great deal."

He got red and confused, and then with a smile of resignation he said:

"You are rather hard."

"Why?" was the reply. "I am only stating facts. I don't suppose you intend to offer me your love? It must, therefore, be a matter of perfect indifference to you what I think about you. But I see it is a painful subject, so let us talk of something else. What have you been doing since I last saw you?"

He felt rather out of countenance and stammered:

"I? I have traveled, shot and grown old, as you see. And you?"

She said quite calmly: "I have taken care of appearances as you ordered me."

He was very nearly saying something brutal, but he checked himself and kissed his wife's hand.

"And I thank you," he said.

She was surprised. He was indeed strong and always master of himself.

He went on: "As you have acceded to my first request, shall we now talk without any bitterness?"

She made a little movement of surprise.

"Bitterness! I don't feel any; you are a complete stranger to me. I am only trying to keep up a difficult conversation."

He was still looking at her, carried away in spite of her harshness, and he felt seized with a brutal desire, the desire of the master.

Perceiving that she had hurt his feelings, she said:

"How old are you now? I thought you were younger than you look."

He grew pale.

"I am forty-five," and then he added: "I forgot to ask after Princess de Raynes. Are you still intimate with her?"

She looked at him as if she hated him:

"Yes, certainly I am. She is very well, thank you."

They remained sitting side by side, agitated and irritated. Suddenly he said:

"My dear Bertha, I have changed my mind. You are my wife, and I expect you to come with me today. You have, I think, improved both morally and physically, and I am going to take you back again. I am your husband, and it is my right to do so."

She was stupefied and looked at him, trying to divine his thoughts, but his face was resolute and impenetrable.

"I am very sorry," she said, "but I have made other engagements."

"So much the worse for you," was his reply. "The law gives me the power, and I mean to use it."

They were getting to Marseilles, and the train whistled and slackened speed. The baroness got up, carefully rolled up her wraps, and then turning to her husband, she said:

"My dear Raymond, do not make a bad use of the tête-à-tête which I had carefully prepared. I wished to take precautions, according to your advice, so that I might have nothing to fear from you or from other people, whatever might happen. You are going to Nice, are you not?"

"I shall go wherever you go."

"Not at all; just listen to me, and I am sure that you will leave me in peace. In a few moments, when we get to the station, you will see the Princess de Raynes and Countess Hermit waiting for me with their husbands. I wished them to see us and to know that we spent the night together in the railway carriage. Don't be alarmed; they will tell it everywhere as a most surprising fact.

"I told you just now that I had carefully followed your advice and saved appearances. Anything else does not matter, does it? Well, in order to do so, I wished to be seen with you. You told me carefully to avoid any scandal, and I am avoiding it, for I am afraid——I am afraid——"

She waited till the train had quite stopped, and as her friends ran up to open the carriage door, she said:

"I am afraid that I am *enceinte*."

The princess stretched out her arms to embrace her, and the baroness said, pointing to the baron, who was dumb with astonishment and trying to get at the truth:

"You do not recognize Raymond? He has certainly changed a good deal and he agreed to come with me so that I might not travel alone. We take little trips like this occasionally, like good friends who cannot live together. We are going to separate here; he has had enough of me already."

She put out her hand, which he took mechanically, and then she jumped out onto the platform among her friends who were waiting for her.

The baron hastily shut the carriage door, for he was too much disturbed to say a word or come to any determination. He heard his wife's voice and their merry laughter as they went away.

He never saw her again, nor did he ever discover whether she had told him a lie or was speaking the truth.

A NEW YEAR'S GIFT

Jacques de Randal, having dined at home alone, told his valet he might go and then sat down at a table to write his letters.

He finished out every year by writing and dreaming, making for himself a sort of review of things that had happened since last New Year's Day, things that were now all over and dead; and in proportion as the faces of his friends rose up before his eyes, he wrote them a few lines, a cordial "Good morning" on the first of January.

So he sat down, opened a drawer, took out of it a woman's photograph, gazed at it a few moments and kissed it. Then, having laid it beside a sheet of note paper, he began:

My Dear Irène: You must have by this time the little souvenir which I sent you. I have shut myself up this evening in order to tell you——

The pen here ceased to move, Jacques rose up and began walking up and down the room.

For the last six months he had a mistress, not a mistress like the others, a woman with whom one engages in a passing intrigue, of the theatrical world or the demimonde, but a woman whom he loved and won. He was no longer a young man although still comparatively young, and he looked on life seriously in a positive and practical spirit.

Accordingly he drew up the balance sheet of his passion, as he drew up every year the balance sheet of friendships that were ended or freshly contracted, of circumstances and persons that had entered his life. His first ardor of love having grown calmer, he asked himself with the precision of a merchant making a calculation what was the state of his heart with regard to her, and he tried to form an idea of what it would be in the future. He found there a great and deep affection, made up of tenderness, gratitude and the thousand subtleties which give birth to long and powerful attachments.

A ring of the bell made him start. He hesitated. Should he open? But he deemed it was his duty to open on this New Year's night to the unknown who knocks while passing, no matter who it may be.

So he took a wax candle, passed through the antechamber, removed the bolts, turned the key, drew the door back and saw his mistress standing pale as a corpse, leaning against the wall.

He stammered: "What is the matter with you?"

She replied: "Are you alone?"

"Yes."

"Without servants?"

"Yes."

"You are not going out?"

"No."

She entered with the air of a woman who knew the house. As soon as she was in the drawing room she sank into the sofa and, covering her face with her hands, began to weep dreadfully.

He kneeled down at her feet, seized hold of her hands to remove them from her eyes, so that he might look at them, and exclaimed:

"Irène, Irène, what is the matter with you? I implore of you to tell me what is the matter with you."

Then in the midst of her sobs she murmured: "I can no longer live like this."

He did not understand.

"Like this? What do you mean?"

"Yes. I can no longer live like this. I have endured so much. He struck me this afternoon."

"Who—your husband?"

"Yes—my husband."

"Ha!"

He was astonished, having never suspected that her husband could be brutal. He was a man of the world, of the better class, a clubman, a lover of horses, a theatergoer and an expert swordsman; he was known, talked about, appreciated everywhere, having very courteous manners but a very mediocre intellect, an absence of education and of the real culture needed in order to think like all well-bred people and, finally, a respect for all conventional prejudices.

He appeared to devote himself to his wife, as a man ought to do in the case of wealthy and well-bred people. He displayed enough anxiety about her wishes, her health, her dresses and, beyond that, left her perfectly free.

Randal, having become Irène's friend, had a right to the affectionate hand-

clasp which every husband endowed with good manners owes to his wife's intimate
acquaintances. Then when Jacques, after having been for some time the friend,
became the lover, his relations with the husband were more cordial.

Jacques had never dreamed that there were storms in this household, and he
was scared at this unexpected revelation.

He asked:

"How did it happen? Tell me."

Thereupon she related a long history, the entire history of her life, since the
day of her marriage—the first discussion arising out of a mere nothing, then accentuating itself in the estrangement which grows up each day between two
opposite types of character.

Then came quarrels, a complete separation, not apparent, but real; next her
husband showed himself aggressive, suspicious, violent. Now he was jealous, jealous of Jacques, and this day even, after a scene, he had struck her.

She added with decision: "I will not go back to him. Do with me what you
like."

Jacques sat down opposite to her, their knees touching each other. He caught
hold of her hands:

"My dear love, you are going to commit a gross, an irreparable, folly. If you
want to quit your husband put wrongs on one side, so that your situation as a
woman of the world may be saved."

She asked as she cast at him a restless glance:

"Then what do you advise me?"

"To go back home and to put up with your life there till the day when you
can obtain either a separation or a divorce with the honors of war."

"Is not this thing which you advise me to do a little cowardly?"

"No, it is wise and reasonable. You have a high position, a reputation, to safeguard, friends to preserve and relations to deal with. You must not lose all these
through a mere caprice."

She rose up and said with violence:

"Well, no! I cannot have any more of it! It is at an end! It is at an end!"

Then, placing her two hands on her lover's shoulders and looking at him
straight in the face, she asked:

"Do you love me?"

"Yes."

"Really and truly?"

"Yes."

"Then keep me!"

He exclaimed:

"Keep you? In my own house? Here? Why, you are mad. It would mean losing
you forever, losing you beyond hope of recall! You are mad!"

She replied slowly and seriously, like a woman who feels the weight of her
words:

"Listen, Jacques. He has forbidden me to see you again, and I will not play this
comedy of coming secretly to your house. You must either lose me or take me."

"My dear Irène, in that case, obtain your divorce, and I will marry you."

"Yes, you will marry me in—two years at the soonest. Yours is a patient love."

"Look here! Reflect! If you remain here he'll come tomorrow to take you away,
seeing that he is your husband, seeing that he has right and law on his side."

"I did not ask you to keep me in your own house, Jacques, but to take me anywhere you like. I thought you loved me enough to do that. I have made a mistake. Good-by!"

She turned round and went toward the door so quickly that he was only able to catch hold of her when she was outside the room.

"Listen, Irène."

She struggled and did not want to listen to him any longer, her eyes full of tears and with these words only on her lips:

"Leave me alone! Leave me alone! Leave me alone!"

He made her sit down by force and, falling once more on his knees at her feet, he now brought forward a number of arguments and counsels to make her understand the folly and terrible risk of her project. He omitted nothing which he deemed it necessary to say to convince her, finding in his very affection for her strong motives of persuasion.

As she remained silent and cold he begged of her, implored of her, to listen to him, to trust him, to follow his advice.

When he had finished speaking she only replied:

"Are you disposed to let me go away now? Take away your hands so that I may rise up."

"Look here, Irène."

"Will you let go?"

"Irène—is your resolution irrevocable?"

"Do let me go."

"Tell me only whether this resolution, this foolish resolution of yours, which you will bitterly regret, is irrevocable."

"Yes; let me go!"

"Then stay. You know well that you are at home here. We shall go away to-morrow morning."

She rose up, in spite of him, and said in a hard tone:

"No. It is too late. I do not want sacrifice; I want devotion."

"Stay! I have done what I ought to do; I have said what I ought to say. I have no further responsibility on your behalf. My conscience is at peace. Tell me what you want me to do and I will obey."

She resumed her seat, looked at him for a long time and then asked in a very calm voice:

"Explain, then."

"How is that? What do you wish me to explain?"

"Everything—everything that you have thought about before coming to this resolution. Then I will see what I ought to do."

"But I have thought about nothing at all. I ought to warn you that you are going to accomplish an act of folly. You persist; then I ask to share in this act of folly, and I even insist on it."

"It is not natural to change one's opinion so quickly."

"Listen, my dear love. It is not a question here of sacrifice or devotion. On the day when I realized that I loved you I said this to myself, which every lover ought to say to himself in the same case: 'The man who loves a woman, who makes an effort to win her, who gets her and who takes her, contracts, so far as he is himself and so far as she is concerned, a sacred engagement.' It is, mark you,

a question of dealing with a woman like you and not with a woman of an impulsive and yielding disposition.

"Marriage, which has a great social value, a great legal value, possesses in my
eyes only a very slight moral value, taking into account the conditions under
which it generally takes place.

"Therefore, when a woman, united by this lawful bond but having no attachment to a husband whom she cannot love, a woman whose heart is free, meets a
man for whom she cares and gives herself to him, when a man who has no other
tie takes a woman in this way, I say that they pledge themselves toward each
other by this mutual and free agreement much more than by the 'Yes' uttered in
the presence of the mayor.

"I say that if they are both honorable persons their union must be more intimate, more real, more healthy, than if all the sacraments had consecrated it.

"This woman risks everything. And it is exactly because she knows it, because
she gives everything, her heart, her body, her soul, her honor, her life, because she
has foreseen all miseries, all dangers, all catastrophes, because she dares to do a
bold act, an intrepid act, because she is prepared, determined to brave everything—her husband, who might kill her, and society, which may cast her out.
This is why she is heroic in her conjugal infidelity; this is why her lover in taking
her must also have foreseen everything and preferred her to everything, whatever
might happen. I have nothing more to say. I spoke in the beginning like a man
of sense whose duty it was to warn you, and now there is left in me only one
man—the man who loves you. Say then what I am to do!"

Radiant, she closed his mouth with her lips and said to him in a low tone:

"It is not true, darling! There is nothing the matter! My husband does not
suspect anything. But I wanted to see, I wanted to know, what you would do.
I wished for a New Year's gift—the gift of your heart—another gift besides the
necklace you have just sent me. You have given it to me. Thanks! Thanks! God
be thanked for the happiness you have given me!"

A FAMILY AFFAIR

The Neuilly steam tram had just passed the Porte Maillot and was going along
the broad avenue that terminates at the Seine. The small engine that was attached
to the car whistled, to warn any obstacle to get out of its way, let off steam,
panted like a person out of breath from running; and it pistons made a rapid noise,
like iron legs running. The oppressive heat of the end of a summer day lay over
the whole city, and from the road, although there was not a breath of wind stirring, there arose a white, chalky, opaque, suffocating, and warm dust which stuck
to the moist skin, filled the eyes, and got into the lungs. People were standing in
the doors of their houses in search of a little air.

The windows of the steam tram were down, and the curtains fluttered in the
wind. There were very few passengers inside, because on such warm days people
preferred the top or the platforms. The few inside consisted of stout women in
strange toilettes, shopkeepers' wives from the suburbs, who made up for the dis-

tinguished looks which they did not possess by ill-assumed dignity; of gentlemen
tired of their office, with yellow faces, who stooped with one shoulder higher
than the other in consequence of long hours of work bending over the desk. Their
uneasy and melancholy faces also spoke of domestic troubles, of constant want
of money, of former hopes that had been finally disappointed. They all belonged
to that army of poor, threadbare devils who vegetate economically in mean,
plastered houses, with a tiny grass border for a garden, in the midst of the district
where rubbish is deposited, on the outskirts of Paris.

Near the door a short, fat man, with a puffy face and a big stomach, dressed
in black and wearing a decoration in his buttonhole, was talking to a tall, thin
man, attired in a dirty, white linen suit all unbuttoned, and wearing a white
Panama hat. The former spoke so slowly and hesitatingly that occasionally it
almost seemed as if he stammered; it was M. Caravan, chief clerk in the Admiralty. The other, who had formerly been surgeon on board a merchant ship,
had set up a practice in Courbevoie, where he applied the vague remnants of
medical knowledge which he had retained after an adventurous life to healing
the wretched population of that district. His name was Chenet, and he had made
the people call him Doctor, and strange rumors were current as to his morality.

M. Caravan had always led the normal life of a man in a government office.
Every morning for the last thirty years he had invariably gone the same way to
his office, had met the same men going to business at the same time and nearly
on the same spot, returned home every evening the same way, and again met the
same faces, which he had seen growing old. Every morning, after buying his halfpenny paper at the corner of the Fauborg St. Honoré, he bought his two rolls
and then rushed to his office, like a culprit giving himself up to justice. He got
to his desk as quickly as possible, always feeling uneasy, as if expecting a rebuke
for some neglect of duty of which he might have been guilty.

Nothing had ever occurred to change the monotonous order of his existence;
no event affected him except the work of his office, gratuities, and promotion. He
never spoke of anything but of his duties, either at the Admiralty or at home, for
he had married the portionless daughter of one of his colleagues. His mind, which
was in a state of atrophy from his depressing daily work, had no other thoughts,
hopes, or dreams than such as related to the office, and there was a constant source
of bitterness that spoiled every pleasure that he might have had, and that was the
employment of so many commissioners of the Navy, "tinmen," as they were
called, because of their silver lace, as first-class clerks and heads of departments.
Every evening at dinner he discussed the matter hotly with his wife, who shared
his angry feelings, and proved to their own satisfaction that it was in every way
unjust to give jobs in Paris to men who ought properly to have been employed
in the Navy.

He was old now, and had scarcely noticed how his life was passing, for school
had merely been exchanged, without any transition, for the office, and the ushers
at whom he had formerly trembled were replaced by his chiefs, of whom he was
terribly afraid. When he had to go into the rooms of these official despots, it made
him tremble from head to foot, and that constant fear had given him a very awkward manner in their presence, a humble demeanor, and a kind of nervous stammering.

He knew nothing more about Paris than a blind man could know, who was
led to the same spot by his dog every day. If he read the account of any uncom-

mon events, or of scandals, in his halfpenny paper, they appeared to him like
fantastic tales, which some pressman had made up out of his own head in order
to amuse minor clerks. He did not read the political news, which his paper frequently altered as the cause which subsidized them might require, for he was not
fond of innovations, and when he went through the Avenue of the Champs-
Elysées every evening, he looked at the surging crowd of pedestrians and at the
stream of carriages, like a traveler who has lost his way in a strange country.

As he had completed his thirty years of obligatory service that year, on the first
of January, he had had the cross of the Legion of Honor bestowed upon him,
which, in the semimilitary public offices, is a recompense for the long and miserable slavery—the official phrase is "loyal services"—of unfortunate convicts who
are riveted to their desks. That unexpected dignity gave him a high and new idea
of his own capacities and altogether altered him. He immediately left off wearing
light trousers and fancy waistcoats and wore black trousers and long coats, on
which his "ribbon," which was very broad, showed off better. He got shaved every
morning, trimmed his nails more carefully, changed his linen every two days, from
a legitimate sense of what was proper and out of respect for the national order of
which he formed a part. In fact, from that day he was another Caravan, scrupulously clean, majestic, and condescending.

At home, he said "my cross" at every moment, and he had become so proud of
it that he could not bear to see other men wearing any other ribbon in their
buttonholes. He got angry when he saw strange orders, which "nobody ought to
be allowed to wear in France," and he bore Chenet a particular grudge, as he met
him on a tramcar every evening, wearing a decoration of some sort or another,
white, blue, orange, or green.

The conversation of the two men, from the Arc de Triomphe to Neuilly, was
always the same. That day as usual they discussed, first of all, various local abuses,
which disgusted them both, and the mayor of Neuilly received his full share of
the blame. Then, as invariably happens in the company of a medical man, Caravan began to enlarge on the subject of illness, as, in that manner, he hoped to
obtain a little gratuitous advice or even a consultation if he were careful enough
not to give himself away. His mother had been causing him no little anxiety for
some time; she had frequent and prolonged fainting fits, and, although she was
ninety, she would not take care of herself.

Caravan grew quite tenderhearted when he mentioned her great age, and more
than once asked Doctor Chenet, emphasizing the word "doctor," whether he had
often met anyone as old as that. And he rubbed his hands with pleasure; not,
perhaps, that he cared very much about seeing the good woman last forever here
on earth, but because the long duration of his mother's life was, as it were, an
earnest of old age for himself. Then he continued:

"In my family, we last long, and I am sure that, unless I meet with an accident,
I shall not die until I am very old."

The officer of health looked at him with pity, glancing for a moment at his
neighbor's red face, his short, thick neck, his "corporation," as Chenet called it,
which hung down between two flaccid, fat legs, and the apoplectic rotundity of
the old, flabby official. Lifting the dirty Panama hat that he wore from his head,
he said, with a snigger:

"I am not so sure of that, old fellow; your mother is as tough as nails, and I
should say that your life is not a very good one."

This rather upset Caravan, who did not speak again until the tram put them down at their destination. The two friends got out, and Chenet asked his friend to have a glass of vermouth at the Café du Globe, opposite, a place which both of them were in the habit of frequenting. The proprietor, who was a friend of theirs, held out two fingers to them, which they shook across the bottles on the counter, and then they joined three of their friends, who were playing at dominoes and had been there since midday. They exchanged cordial greetings, with the usual inquiry: "Anything fresh?" Then the three players continued their game and held out their hands without looking up when the others wished them "Good night" and went home to dinner.

Caravan lived in a small, two-storied house in Courbevoie, near the meeting of the roads; the ground floor was occupied by a hairdresser. Two bedrooms, a dining room, and a kitchen, where mended chairs wandered from room to room, as they were wanted, formed the whole of their apartments, and Mme. Caravan spent nearly her whole time in cleaning them up, while her daughter, Marie-Louise, who was twelve, and her son, Philippe-Auguste, were running about with all the little, dirty, mischievous brats of the neighborhood and playing in the gutters.

Caravan had installed his mother, whose avarice was notorious in the neighborhood, and who was terribly thin, in the room above them. She was always in a bad temper and never passed a day without quarreling and flying into furies. She used to apostrophize the neighbors standing at their own doors, the vegetable vendors, the street sweepers, and the street boys in the most violent language. The latter, to have their revenge, used to follow her at a distance when she went out and call out rude things after her.

A little servant from Normandy, who was incredibly giddy and thoughtless, performed the household work and slept on the second floor in the same room as the old woman for fear of anything happening to her in the night.

When Caravan got in, his wife, who suffered from a chronic passion for cleaning, was polishing up the mahogany chairs, which were scattered about the room, with a piece of flannel. She always wore cotton gloves and adorned her head with a cap, ornamented with many colored ribbons, which was always tilted on one ear, and whenever anyone caught her polishing, sweeping, or washing she used to say:

"I am not rich; everything is very simple in my house, but cleanliness is my luxury, and that is worth quite as much as any other."

As she was gifted with sound, obstinate, practical common sense, she swayed her husband in everything. Every evening during dinner, and afterward, when they were in bed, they talked over the business in the office, and although she was twenty years younger, he confided everything to her as if she had had the direction, and followed her advice in every matter.

She had never been pretty, and now had grown ugly; in addition to that she was short and thin, while her careless and tasteless way of dressing herself hid the few, small feminine attributes which might have been brought out if she had possessed any skill in dress. Her petticoats were always awry, and she frequently scratched herself, no matter on what place, totally indifferent as to who might be there, out of a sort of habit which had become almost an unconscious movement. The only ornaments that she allowed herself were silk ribbons, which she had in great profusion and of various colors mixed together, in the pretentious caps which she wore at home.

As soon as she saw her husband she got up and said, as she kissed him:

"Did you remember Potin, my dear?"

He fell into a chair, in consternation, for that was the fourth time he had forgotten a commission that he had promised to do for her.

"It is a fatality," he said; "in spite of my thinking of it all day long, I am sure to forget it in the evening."

But as he seemed really so very sorry, she merely said, quietly:

"You will think of it tomorrow, I daresay. Anything fresh at the office?"

"Yes, a great piece of news: another tinman has been appointed senior chief clerk." She became angry.

"To what department?"

"The department of foreign supplies."

"So he succeeds Ramon. That was the very post that I wanted you to have. And what about Ramon?"

"He retires on his pension."

She grew furious, her cap slid down on her shoulder, and she continued:

"There is nothing more to be done in that hole now. And what is the name of the new commissioner?"

"Bonassot."

She took up the *Naval Year Book*, which she always kept close at hand, and looked him up:

" 'Bonassot — Toulon. Born in 1851. Student-Commissioner in 1871. Sub-Commissioner in 1875.' Has he been to sea?" she continued, and at that question Caravan's looks cleared up, and he laughed until his sides shook.

"Just like Balin—just like Balin, his chief." Then he added an old office joke and laughed more than ever:

"It would not even do to send them by water to inspect the Point-du-Jour, for they would be sick on the Seine steamboats."

But she remained as serious as if she had not heard him, and then she said in a low voice, while she scratched her chin:

"If only we had a deupty to fall back upon. When the Chamber hears all that is going on at the Admiralty, the minister will be turned out——"

She was interrupted by a terrible noise on the stairs. Marie-Louise and Philippe-Auguste, who had just come in from the gutter, were giving each other slaps all the way upstairs. Their mother rushed at them furiously, and, taking each of them by an arm, she dragged them into the room, shaking them vigorously. But as soon as they saw their father they rushed up to him. He kissed them affectionately, and taking one of them on each knee, he began to talk to them.

Philippe-Auguste was an ugly, ill-kempt little brat, dirty from head to foot, with the face of an idiot, and Marie-Louise was already like her mother—spoke like her, repeated her words, and even imitated her movements. She also asked him whether there was anything fresh at the office, and he replied merrily:

"Your friend, Ramon, who comes and dines here every Sunday, is going to leave us, little one. There is a new senior head clerk."

She looked at her father, and with a precocious child's pity, she said:

"So somebody has been put over your head again!"

He stopped laughing and did not reply. Then, in order to create a diversion, he said, addressing his wife, who was cleaning the windows:

"How is Mamma, up there?"

Madame Caravan left off rubbing, turned round, pulled her cap up, as it had fallen quite onto her back, and said, with trembling lips:

"Ah! yes; let us talk about your mother. She has created a pretty scene. Just think that a short time ago Mme. Lebaudin, the hairdresser's wife, came upstairs to borrow a packet of starch from me, and, as I was not at home, your mother called her a beggarwoman and turned her out; but I gave it to the old woman. She pretended not to hear, as she always does when one tells her unpleasant truths, but she is no more deaf than I am, as you know. It is all a sham, and the proof of it is that she went up to her own room immediately without saying a word."

Caravan, taken aback, did not utter a word, and at that moment the little servant came in to announce dinner. In order to let his mother know, he took a broom handle, which always stood hidden in a corner, and rapped loudly on the ceiling three times, and then they went into the dining room. Mme. Caravan, Junior, helped the soup and waited for the old woman. But she did not come, and the soup was getting cold, so they began to eat slowly, and when their plates were empty they waited again. Then Mme. Caravan, who was furious, attacked her husband:

"She does it on purpose, you know that as well as I do. But you always uphold her."

In great perplexity between the two, he sent up Marie-Louise to fetch her grandmother and sat motionless, with his eyes down, while his wife tapped her glass angrily with her knife. In about a minute the door flew open suddenly, and the child came in again, out of breath and very pale, and said quickly:

"Grandmamma has fallen down on the ground."

Caravan jumped up, threw his table napkin down, and rushed upstairs, while his wife, who thought it was some trick of her mother-in-law, followed more slowly, shrugging her shoulders as if to express her doubt. When they got upstairs, however, they found the old woman lying at full length in the middle of the room, and when they turned her over they saw that she was insensible and motionless. Her skin looked more wrinkled and yellow than usual, her eyes were closed, her teeth clenched, and her thin body was stiff.

Caravan kneeled down by her and began to moan:

"My poor mother! my poor mother!" he said. But the other Mme. Caravan said:

"Bah! She has only fainted again, that is all, and she has done it to prevent us from dining comfortably, you may be sure of that."

They put her on the bed, undressed her completely, and Caravan, his wife, and the servant began to rub her, but in spite of their efforts, she did not recover consciousness, so they sent Rosalie, the servant, to fetch "Doctor" Chenet. He lived a long way off, on the quay going toward Suresnes, and so it was a considerable time before he arrived. He came at last, however, and, after having looked at the old woman, felt her pulse, and auscultated her, he said:

"It is all over."

Caravan threw himself on the body, sobbing violently. He kissed his mother's rigid face and wept so that great tears fell on the dead woman's face, like drops of water. Naturally, Mme. Caravan, Junior, showed a decorous amount of grief, uttered feeble moans as she stood behind her husband, and she rubbed her eyes vigorously.

But, suddenly, Caravan raised himself up, with his thin hair in disorder, and, looking very ugly in his grief, said:

"But, are you sure, doctor? Are you quite sure?"

The medical man stooped over the body, and, handling it with professional dexterity, as a shopkeeper might do, when showing off his goods, he said: "See, my dear friend, look at her eye."

He raised the eyelid, and the old woman's look reappeared under his finger, altogether unaltered, unless, perhaps, the pupil was rather larger, and Caravan felt a severe shock at the sight. Then M. Chenet took her thin arm, forced the fingers open, and said, angrily, as if he had been contradicted:

"Just look at her hand; I never make a mistake, you may be quite sure of that."

Caravan fell on the bed, and almost bellowed, while his wife, still whimpering, did what was necessary.

She brought the night table, on which she spread a table napkin. Then she placed four wax candles on it, which she lighted; then took a sprig of box, which was hanging over the chimney glass, and put it between the candles, into the plate, which she filled with clean water as she had no holy water. After a moment's rapid reflection, she threw a pinch of salt into the water, no doubt thinking she was performing some sort of act of consecration by doing that. When she had finished the setting which is supposed to be appropriate to death, she remained standing motionless, and the medical man, who had been helping her, whispered to her:

"We must take Caravan away."

She nodded assent, and, going up to her husband, who was still on his knees, sobbing, she raised him up by one arm while Chenet took him by the other.

They put him into a chair, and his wife kissed his forehead and then began to lecture him. Chenet enforced her words, and preached firmness, courage, and resignation—the very things which are always wanting in such overwhelming misfortune—and then both of them took him by the arms again and led him out.

He was crying like a big child, with convulsive sobs; his arms were hanging down and his legs seemed useless; he went downstairs without knowing what he was doing, and moved his legs mechanically. They put him into the chair which he always occupied at dinner, in front of his empty soup plate. And there he sat, without moving, with his eyes fixed on his glass, so stupefied with grief that he could not even think.

In a corner, Mme. Caravan was talking with the doctor and asking what the necessary formalities were, as she wanted to obtain practical information. At last, M. Chenet, who appeared to be waiting for something, took up his hat and prepared to go, saying that he had not dined yet; whereupon she exclaimed:

"What! You have not dined? But stop here, doctor; don't go. You shall have whatever we can give you, for, of course, you will understand that we won't eat much." However, he made excuses and refused, but she persisted, and said:

"You really must stop; at times like this people like to have friends near them, and, besides that, perhaps you will be able to persuade my husband to take some nourishment; he must keep up his strength."

The doctor bowed, and, putting down his hat, said:

"In that case, I will accept your invitation, madame."

She gave Rosalie, who seemed to have lost her head, some orders, and then sat down, "to pretend to eat," as she said, "to keep the doctor company."

The soup was brought in again, and M. Chenet took two helpings. Then there came a dish of tripe, which exhaled a smell of onions, and which Mme. Caravan made up her mind to taste.

"It is excellent," the doctor said, at which she smiled, and, turning to her husband, she said:

"Do take a little, my poor Alfred, only just to get something into your stomach. Remember that you have got to pass the night watching by her!"

He held out his plate, docilely, just as he would have gone to bed if he had been told to, obeying her in everything without resistance and without reflection, and, therefore, he ate. The doctor helped himself three times, while Mme. Caravan, from time to time, fished out a large piece on the end of her fork and swallowed it with a sort of studied inattention.

When a salad bowl full of macaroni was brought in, the doctor said:

"By Jove! That is what I am very fond of." And this time Mme. Caravan helped everybody. She even filled the children's saucers, which they had scraped clean, and who, being left to themselves, had been drinking wine without any water, and were now kicking each other under the table.

Chenet remembered that Rossini, the composer, had been very fond of that Italian dish, and suddenly he exclaimed:

"Why! that rhymes, and one could begin some lines like this:

> "The Maestro Rossini
> Was fond of macaroni."

Nobody listened to him, however. Mme. Caravan, who had suddenly grown thoughtful, was thinking of all the probable consequences of the event, while her husband made bread pellets, which he put on the tablecloth and looked at with a fixed, idiotic stare. As he was devoured by thirst, he was continually raising his glass to his lips, and the consequence was that his senses, already rather upset by the shock and grief, seemed to dance about vaguely in his head, which was heavy from the laborious process of digestion which had begun.

Meanwhile, the doctor, who had been drinking away steadily, was getting visibly drunk, and Mme. Caravan herself felt the reaction which follows all nervous shocks. She was agitated and excited, and although she had been drinking nothing but water, she felt her head rather confused.

By and by, Chenet began to relate stories of deaths that appeared funny to him. In the suburbs of Paris, which are full of people from the provinces, one meets with the indifference toward death, even of a father or a mother, which all peasants show; a want of respect, an unconscious callousness which is common in the country and rare in Paris. Said he:

"Why, I was sent for last week to the Rue de Puteaux, and when I went, I found the sick person (and there was the whole family calmly sitting near the bed) finishing a bottle of liqueur of aniseed, which had been bought the night before to satisfy the dying man's fancy."

But Mme. Caravan was not listening; she was continually thinking of the inheritance, and Caravan was incapable of understanding anything.

Soon Rosalie served coffee, which had been made very strong, to keep up their courage, and, as every cup was well dosed with cognac, it made all their faces red and confused their ideas still more. To make matters still worse, Chenet suddenly seized the brandy bottle and poured out "a drop just to wash their mouths out with," as he termed it, for each of them. Then, without speaking any more, overcome, in spite of themselves, by that feeling of animal comfort which alcohol affords after dinner, they slowly sipped the sweet cognac, which formed a yellowish syrup at the bottom of their cups.

The children had gone to sleep, and Rosalie carried them off to bed. Then, Caravan, mechanically obeying that wish to forget oneself which possesses all unhappy persons, helped himself to brandy again several times, and his dull eyes grew bright. At last the doctor rose to go, and, seizing his friend's arm, he said:

"Come with me; a little fresh air will do you good. When you are in trouble, you must not stick to one spot."

The other obeyed mechanically, put on his hat, took his stick, and went out, and both of them went arm in arm toward the Seine, in the starlight night.

The air was warm and sweet, for all the gardens in the neighborhood are full of flowers at that season of the year, and their scent, which is scarcely perceptible during the day, seems to awaken at the approach of night, and mingles with the light breezes which blow upon them in the darkness.

The broad avenue, with its two rows of gas lamps, which extend as far as the Arc de Triomphe, was deserted and silent, but there was the distant roar of Paris, which seemed to have a reddish vapor hanging over it. It was a kind of continual rumbling, which was at times answered by the whistle of a train at full speed, in the distance, traveling to the ocean through the provinces.

The fresh air on the faces of the two men rather overcame them at first, made the doctor lose his equilibrium a little and increased Caravan's giddiness, from which he had suffered since dinner. He walked as if he were in a dream; his thoughts were paralyzed, although he felt no great grief, for he was in a state of mental torpor that prevented him from suffering, and he even felt a sense of relief which was increased by the warm scent of the night.

When they reached the bridge, they turned to the right and faced the fresh breeze from the river, which rolled along, calm and melancholy, bordered by tall poplar trees. The stars looked as if they were floating on the water and were moving with the current. A slight, white mist that floated over the opposite banks filled their lungs with a sensation of cold, and Caravan stopped suddenly, for he was struck by that smell from the water, which brought back old memories to his mind. For suddenly, in his mind, he saw his mother again, in Picardy, as he had seen her years before, kneeling in front of their door and washing the heaps of linen by her side in the little stream that ran through their garden. He almost fancied that he could hear the sound of the wooden beetle with which she beat the linen, in the calm silence of the country, and her voice, as she called out to him: "Alfred, bring me some soap." And he smelled the odor of the trickling water, of the mist rising from the wet ground, of the heap of wet linen which he should never forget, the less that it came back to him on the very evening on which his mother died.

He stopped, paralyzed by a sudden feeling of anguish. It was like a beam of light illuminating all at once the whole extent of his misfortune, and this meeting with vagrant thoughts plunged him into a black abyss of irremediable despair. He felt heartbroken at that eternal separation. His life seemed cut in half, all his youth gone, swallowed up by that death. All the former life was over and done with, all the recollections of his youthful days would vanish; for the future, there would be nobody to talk to him of what had happened in days gone by, of the people he had known of old, of his own part of the country, and of his past life; that was a part of his existence which was gone forever, and the other might as well end now.

Then the procession of memories came. He saw his mother as she was when younger, wearing well-worn dresses, which he remembered for such a long time that they seemed inseparable from her. He recollected her in various forgotten circumstances, her suppressed appearance, the different tones of her voice, her habits, her manias, her fits of anger, the wrinkles on her face, the movements of her thin fingers, and all her well-known attitudes, which she would never have again, and, clutching hold of the doctor, he began to moan and weep. His flabby legs began to tremble, his whole stout body was shaken by his sobs, all he could say was:

"My mother, my poor mother, my poor mother!"

But his companion, who was still drunk, and who intended to finish the evening in certain places of bad repute that he frequented secretly, made him sit down on the grass by the riverside and left him almost immediately, under the pretext that he had to see a patient.

Caravan went on crying for a long time, and then, when he had got to the end of his tears—when his grief had, so to speak, run out of him—he again felt relief, repose, and sudden tranquillity.

The moon had risen and bathed the horizon in its soft light. The tall poplar trees had a silvery sheen on them, and the mist on the plain looked like floating snow. The river, in which the stars were no longer reflected, and which looked as if it were covered with mother-of-pearl, flowed on, rippled by the wind. The air was soft and sweet, and Caravan inhaled it almost greedily, thinking that he could perceive a feeling of freshness, of calm and of superhuman consolation pervading him.

He really tried to resist that feeling of comfort and relief, and he kept on saying to himself: "My mother, my poor mother!" He tried to make himself cry, from a kind of conscientious feeling, but he could not succeed in doing so any longer, and the sad thought which had made him sob so bitterly a short time before had almost passed away. In a few moments he rose to go home, and returned slowly, under the influence of that serene night, with a heart soothed in spite of himself.

When he reached the bridge, he saw the last tramcar, ready to start, and the lights through the windows of the Café du Globe, and felt a longing to tell somebody of the catastrophe that had happened, to excite pity, to make himself interesting. He put on a woeful face, pushed open the door, and went up to the counter, where the landlord always stood. He had counted on creating an effect, and had hoped that everybody would get up and come to him with outstretched hands, and say: "Why, what is the matter with you?" But nobody noticed his disconsolate face, so he rested his two elbows on the counter, and, burying his face in his hands, he murmured: "Good heavens! Good heavens!"

The landlord looked at him and said: "Are you ill, M. Caravan?"

"No, my friend," he replied, "but my mother has just died."

"Ah!" the other exclaimed, and, as a customer at the other end of the establishment asked for a glass of beer, he replied: "All right, I'm coming," and he went to attend to him, leaving Caravan almost stupefied at his want of sympathy.

The three domino players were sitting at the same table which they had occupied before dinner, totally absorbed in their game, and Caravan went up to them, in search of pity, but as none of them appeared to notice him, he made up his mind to speak.

"A great misfortune has happened to me since I was here," he said.

All three raised their heads slightly at the same instant, but kept their eyes fixed on the pieces which they held in their hands.

"What do you say?"

"My mother has just died."

Whereupon one of them said: "Oh! By Jove!" with that false air of sorrow which indifferent people assume. Another, who could not find anything to say, emitted a sort of sympathetic whistle, shaking his head at the same time, and the third turned to the game again, as if he were saying to himself: "Is that all!"

Caravan had expected some of those expressions that are said to "come from the heart," and when he saw how his news was received he left the table, indignant at their calmness before a friend's sorrow, although at that moment he was so dazed with grief that he hardly felt it, and went home.

His wife was waiting for him in her nightgown, sitting in a low chair by the open window, still thinking of the inheritance.

"Undress yourself," she said; "we will talk when we are in bed."

He raised his head, and, looking at the ceiling, he said:

"But there is nobody up there."

"I beg your pardon, Rosalie is with her, and you can go and take her place at three o'clock in the morning, when you have had some sleep."

He only partially undressed, however, so as to be ready for anything that might happen, and after tying a silk handkerchief round his head, he joined his wife, who had just got in between the sheets. For some time they remained side by side, and neither of them spoke. She was thinking.

Even in bed, her nightcap was adorned with a pink bow, and was pushed rather over one ear, as was the way with all the caps that she wore. Presently, she turned toward him and said:

"Do you know whether your mother made a will?"

He hesitated for a moment, and then replied:

"I—I do not think so. No, I am sure that she did not."

His wife looked at him, and she said, in a low, furious voice:

"I call that infamous; here we have been wearing ourselves out for ten years in looking after her, and have boarded and lodged her! Your sister would not have done so much for her, nor I either, if I had known how I was to be rewarded! Yes, it is a disgrace to her memory! I daresay that you will tell me that she paid us, but one cannot pay one's children in ready money for what they do; that obligation is recognized after death; at any rate, that is how honorable people act. So I have had all my worry and trouble for nothing! Oh, that is nice! that is very nice!"

Poor Caravan, who felt nearly distracted, kept on saying:

"My dear, my dear, please, please be quiet."

She grew calmer by degrees, and, resuming her usual voice and manner, she continued:

"We must let your sister know tomorrow."

He started, and said:

"Of course we must; I had forgotten all about it; I will send her a telegram the first thing in the morning."

"No," she replied, like a woman who has foreseen everything; "no, do not send it before ten or eleven o'clock, so that we may have time to turn round before she comes. It does not take more than two hours to get here from Charenton, and we can say that you lost your head from grief. If we let her know in the course of the day, that will be soon enough and will give us time to look round."

But Caravan put his hand to his forehead, and in the same timid voice in which he always spoke of his chief, the very thought of whom made him tremble, he said:

"I must let them know at the office."

"Why?" she replied. "On such occasions like this, it is always excusable to forget. Take my advice, and don't let him know; your chief will not be able to say anything to you, and you will put him into a nice fix."

"Oh! yes, I shall, indeed, and he will be in a terrible rage, too, when he notices my absence. Yes, you are right; it is a capital idea, and when I tell him that my mother is dead, he will be obliged to hold his tongue."

And he rubbed his hands in delight at the joke, when he thought of his chief's face; while the body of the dead old woman lay upstairs, beside the sleeping servant.

But Mme. Caravan grew thoughtful, as if she were preoccupied by something which she did not care to mention. But at last she said:

"Your mother had given you her clock, had she not; the girl playing at cup and ball?"

He thought for a moment, and then replied:

"Yes, yes; she said to me a long time ago, when she first came here: 'I shall leave the clock to you, if you look after me well.' "

Mme. Caravan was reassured, and regained her serenity and said:

"Well, then, you must go and fetch it out of her room, for if we get your sister here, she will prevent us from having it."

He hesitated: "Do you think so?" That made her angry.

"I certainly think so; as soon as it is in our possession, she will know nothing at all about where it came from; it belongs to us. It is just the same with the chest of drawers with the marble top that is in her room; she gave it to me one day when she was in a good temper. We will bring it down at the same time."

Caravan, however, seemed incredulous, and said:

"But, my dear, it is a great responsibility!"

She turned on him furiously.

"Oh! Indeed! Will you never alter? You would let your children die of hunger, rather than make a move. Does not that chest of drawers belong to us, since she gave it to me? And if your sister is not satisfied, let her tell me so, me! I don't care a straw for your sister. Come, get up, and we will bring down what your mother gave us, immediately."

Trembling and vanquished, he got out of bed, and began to put on his trousers, but she stopped him:

"It is not worth while to dress yourself; your underclothes are quite enough; I mean to go as I am."

They both left the room in their nightclothes, went upstairs quite noiselessly, opened the door, and went into the room where the four lighted tapers and the plate with the sprig of box alone seemed to be watching the old woman in her rigid repose; for Rosalie, who was lying back in the easy chair with her legs stretched out, her hands folded in her lap, and her head on one side, was also quite motionless, and snoring with her mouth wide open.

Caravan took the clock, which was one of those grotesque objects that were produced so plentifully under the Empire. A girl in gilt bronze was holding a cup and ball, and the ball formed the pendulum.

"Give that to me," his wife said, "and take the marble top off the chest of drawers."

He put the marble on his shoulder with a considerable effort, and they left the room. Caravan had to stoop in the doorway, and he trembled as he went downstairs, while his wife walked backward, so as to light him, holding the candlestick in one hand and the clock under her other arm.

When they were in their own room, she heaved a sigh.

"We have got over the worst part of the job," she said; "so now let us go and fetch the other things."

But the drawers were full of the old woman's wearing apparel, which they must manage to hide somewhere, and Mme. Caravan soon thought of a plan.

"Go and get that wooden box in the passage; it is hardly worth anything and we may just as well put it here."

And when he had brought it upstairs, the change began. One by one, she took out all the collars, cuffs, chemises, caps, all the well-worn things that had belonged to the poor woman lying there behind them, and arranged them methodically in the wooden box, in such a manner as to deceive Mme. Braux, the deceased woman's other child, who would be coming the next day.

When they had finished, they first of all carried the drawers downstairs, and the remaining portion afterward, each of them holding an end. It was some time before they could make up their minds where it would stand best; but at last they settled upon their own room, opposite the bed, between the two windows. As soon as it was in its place, Mme. Caravan filled it with her own things. The clock was placed on the chimney piece in the dining room. They looked to see what the effect was, and were both delighted with it, agreeing that nothing could be better. Then they got into bed, she blew out the candle, and soon everybody in the house was asleep.

It was broad daylight when Caravan opened his eyes again. His mind was rather confused when he woke up, and he did not clearly remember what had happened for a few minutes; when he did, he felt it painfully, and he jumped out of bed, almost ready to cry again.

He very soon went to the room overhead, where Rosalie was still sleeping in the same position as the night before, for she did not wake up once during the whole time. He sent her to do her work, put fresh tapers in the place of those that had burned out, and then he looked at his mother, revolving in his mind those apparently profound thoughts, those religious and philosophical commonplaces, which trouble people of mediocre minds in the face of death.

But he went downstairs as soon as his wife called him. She had written out a list of what had to be done during the morning, which rather frightened him when he saw it.

1. Lodge a declaration of death at the town hall.
2. See the coroner.
3. Order the coffin.

4. Give notice to the church.
5. Go to the undertaker.
6. Order the notices of her death at the printer's.
7. Go to the lawyer.
8. Telegraph the news to all the family.

Besides all this, there were a number of small commissions; so he took his hat and went out. As the news had got abroad, Mme. Caravan's female friends and neighbors soon began to come in, and begged to be allowed to see the body. There had been a scene at the hairdresser's, on the ground floor, about the matter between husband and wife while he was shaving a customer. While busily knitting the woman had said: "Well, there is one less, and one as great a miser as one ever meets with. I certainly was not very fond of her; but, nevertheless, I must go and have a look at her."

The husband, while lathering his customer's chin, said:

"That is another queer fancy! Nobody but a woman would think of such a thing. It is not enough for them to worry you during life, but they cannot even leave you in peace when you are dead."

But his wife, not put out in the least, replied: "I can't help it; I must go. It has been on me since the morning. If I were not to see her, I should think about it all my life, but when I have had a good look at her, I shall be satisfied."

The knight of the razor shrugged his shoulders and remarked in a low voice to the gentleman whose cheek he was scraping:

"Now, what sort of ideas do you think these confounded females have? I should not amuse myself by inspecting a corpse!"

But his wife heard him, and replied very quietly:

"But I do, I do." And then, putting her knitting down on the counter, she went upstairs, to the first floor, where she met two other neighbors. These had just come, and were discussing the event with Mme. Caravan, who was giving them the details. Then the four went together to the mortuary chamber. The women went in softly, and, one after the other, sprinkled the bedclothes with the salted water, knelt down, made the sign of the cross while they mumbled a prayer, then got up, and, openmouthed, regarded the corpse for a long time, while the daughter-in-law of the dead woman, with her handkerchief to her face, pretended to be sobbing piteously.

When she turned to walk away, whom should she perceive standing close to the door but Marie-Louise and Philippe-Auguste, who were curiously taking stock of things. Then, forgetting to control her temper, she threw herself upon them with uplifted hand, crying out in a furious voice: "Will you get out of this, you brats."

Ten minutes later, going upstairs again with another contingent of neighbors, she prayed, wept profusely, performed all her duties, and again caught the children following her upstairs. She boxed their ears soundly, but the next time she paid no heed to them, and at each fresh influx of visitors the two urchins followed in the wake, crowded themselves up in a corner, slavishly imitating everything they saw their mother do.

When afternoon came round the crowds of curious people began to diminish, and soon there were no more visitors. Mme. Caravan, returning to her own apartments, began to make the necessary preparations for the funeral ceremony, and the deceased was left by herself.

The window of the room was open. A torrid heat entered along with clouds of dust; the flames of the four candles were flickering in the direction of the corpse, and upon the cloth which covered the face, the closed eyes, the two hands stretched out, small flies alighted, came, went, and buzzed up and down incessantly, being the only companions of the old woman during the next hour.

Marie-Louise and Philippe-Auguste, however, had now left the house and were running up and down the street. They were soon surrounded by their playmates, and by little girls, especially, who were older, and who were interested in the mysteries of life and asked questions in the manner of persons of great importance.

"Then your grandmother is dead?"

"Yes, she died yesterday evening."

"What does a dead person look like?"

Then Marie began to explain, telling all about the candles, the sprig of box and the cadaverous face. It was not long before great curiosity was aroused in the breasts of all the children, and they asked to be allowed to go upstairs to look at the departed.

Then Marie-Louise arranged a party for the first visit, consisting of five girls and two boys—the biggest and the most courageous. She made them take off their shoes so that they might not be discovered. The troop filed into the house and mounted the stairs as stealthily as an army of mice.

Once in the chamber, the little girl, imitating her mother, regulated the ceremony. She solemnly walked in advance of her comrades, went down on her knees, made the sign of the cross, moistened the lips of the corpse with a few drops of water, stood up again, sprinkled the bed, and while the children all crowded together were approaching—frightened and curious, and eager to look at the face and hands of the deceased—she began suddenly to simulate sobbing, and to bury her eyes in her little handkerchief. Then, instantly consoled on thinking of the other children downstairs waiting at the door, she withdrew in haste, returning in a minute with another group, and then a third; for all the little ruffians of the neighborhood, even to the little beggars in rags, had congregated in order to participate in this new pleasure. Each time she repeated her mother's grimaces with absolute perfection.

At length, however, she tired of it. Some game or another attracted the children away from the house, and the old grandmother was left alone, forgotten suddenly by everybody.

A dismal gloom pervaded the chamber, and upon the dry and rigid features of the corpse the dying flames of the candles cast occasional gleams of light.

Toward eight o'clock, Caravan ascended to the chamber of death, closed the windows, and renewed the candles. On entering now he was quite composed, evidently accustomed to regard the corpse as though it had been there for a month. He even went the length of declaring that, as yet, there were no signs of decomposition, making this remark just at the moment when he and his wife were about to sit down at table. "Pshaw!" she responded, "she is made of wood; she will keep for a year."

The soup was eaten without a word being uttered by anyone. The children, who had been free all day, were now worn out by fatigue and were sleeping soundly in their chairs, and nobody ventured to break the silence.

Suddenly the flame of the lamp went down. Mme. Caravan immediately turned up the wick, a prolonged, gurgling noise ensued, and the light went out. She had forgotten to buy oil during the day. To send for it now to the grocer's would keep back the dinner, and everybody began to look for candles. But none were to be found except the night lights which had been placed upon the table upstairs, in the death chamber.

Mme. Caravan, always prompt in her decisions, quickly dispatched Marie-Louise to fetch two, and her return was awaited in total darkness.

The footsteps of the girl who had ascended the stairs were distinctly heard. Then followed silence for a few seconds, and then the child descended precipitately. She threw open the door affrighted, and in a choked voice murmured: "Oh! Papa, Grandmamma is dressing herself!"

Caravan bounded to his feet with such precipitation that his chair rolled over against another chair. He stammered out: "What! What do you say?"

But Marie-Louise, gasping with emotion, repeated: "Grand—Grand—Grand-mamma is putting on her clothes, and is coming downstairs."

Caravan rushed boldly up the staircase, followed by his wife, dumfounded; but he came to a standstill before the door of the room, overcome with terror, not daring to enter. What was he going to see? Mme. Caravan, more courageous, turned the handle of the door and stepped forward into the room.

The room seemed to be darker, and in the middle of it, a tall emaciated figure moved about. The old woman stood upright, and in awakening from her lethargic sleep, before even full consciousness had returned to her, in turning upon her side and raising herself on her elbow, she had extinguished three of the candles which burned near the mortuary bed. Then, recovering her strength, she got out of bed and began to look for her things. The absence of her chest of drawers had at first given her some trouble, but, after a little, she had succeeded in finding her things at the bottom of the wooden trunk, and was now quietly dressing. She emptied the dishful of salted water, replaced the box which contained the latter behind the looking glass, arranged the chairs in their places, and was ready to go downstairs when her son and daughter-in-law appeared.

Caravan rushed forward, seized her by the hands, and embraced her with tears in his eyes, while his wife, who was behind him, repeated in a hypocritical tone of voice: "Oh, what a blessing! Oh, what a blessing!"

But the old woman, not at all moved, without even appearing to understand, as rigid as a statue, and with glazed eyes, simply asked: "Will dinner soon be ready?"

He stammered out, not knowing what he said:

"Oh, yes, Mother, we have been waiting for you."

And with an alacrity unusual in him he took her arm, while Mme. Caravan the younger seized the candle and lighted them downstairs, walking backward in front of them, step by step, just as she had done the previous night, in front of her husband, when he was carrying the marble.

On reaching the first floor, she ran against people who were ascending. It was the family from Charenton, Mme. Braux, followed by her husband.

The wife, tall and fleshy, with the stomach of a victim of dropsy, opened wide her astonished eyes, ready to take flight. The husband, a shoemaker and socialist, a little hairy man, the perfect image of a monkey, murmured, quite unconcerned: "Well, what next? Is she resurrected?"

As soon as Mme. Caravan recognized them, she made despairing signs to them; then speaking aloud, she said: "Mercy! How do you mean! Look there! What a happy surprise!"

But Mme. Braux, dumfounded, understood nothing. She responded in a low voice: "It was your telegram which made us come; we believed it was all over."

Her husband, who was behind her, pinched her to make her keep silent. He added with a malignant laugh, which his thick beard concealed: "It was very kind of you to invite us here. We set out in posthaste"—a remark which showed clearly the hostility that for a long time had reigned between the households. Then, just as the old woman had arrived at the last steps, he pushed forward quickly and rubbed against her cheeks the hair which covered his face, bawling out in her ear, on account of her deafness: "How well you look, Mother; sturdy as usual, hey?"

Mme. Braux, in her amazement at seeing the old woman alive whom they all believed to be dead, dared not even embrace her; and her enormous bulk blocked up the passage and hindered the others from advancing. The old woman, uneasy and suspicious, but without speaking, looked at everyone around her. Her little gray eyes, piercing and hard, fixed themselves now on the one and now on the other, full of thoughts which could be read by her embarrassed children.

Caravan, to explain matters, said: "She has been somewhat ill, but she is better now—quite well, indeed, are you not, Mother?"

Then the good woman, stopping in her walk, responded in a husky voice, as though it came from a distance: "It was catalepsy. I heard you all the while."

An embarrassing silence followed. They entered the dining room, and in a few minutes sat down to an improvised dinner.

Only M. Braux had retained his self-possession; his gorilla features grinned wickedly, while he let fall some words of double meaning which painfully disconcerted everyone.

But the bell in the hall kept on ringing every second; and Rosalie, who had lost her head, came looking for Caravan, who dashed out, throwing down his napkin. His brother-in-law even asked him whether it was not one of his visiting days, to which he stammered out, "No, a few messages; nothing of importance."

Next, a packet was brought in, which he began to open without thinking, and the death announcements, with black borders, appeared. Reddening up to the very eyes, Caravan closed the envelope, and pushed it into his waistcoat pocket.

His mother had not seen it! She was looking intently at her clock, which stood on the mantelpiece, and the embarrassment increased in the midst of a glacial silence. Turning her wrinkled old witch's face toward her daughter, the old woman, from whose eyes flashed fierce malice, said:

"On Monday bring me your little girl. I want so much to see her."

Mme. Braux, her features illuminated, exclaimed: "Yes, Mother, I will," while Mme. Caravan the younger became pale and seemed to be enduring the most excruciating agony. The two men, however, gradually drifted into conversation, and soon became embroiled in a political discussion. Braux maintained the most revolutionary and communistic doctrines, gesticulating and throwing about his arms, his eyes gleaming in his hairy countenance.

"Property, sir," he said, "is a robbery perpetrated on the working classes; the land is the common property of every man; hereditary rights are an infamy and a disgrace." But, hereupon, he suddenly stopped, having all the appearance of a man who has just said something foolish: then, resuming, after a pause, he said in softer tones: "But, I can see quite well that this is not the proper moment to discuss things."

The door was opened, and "Doctor" Chenet appeared. For a moment he seemed bewildered, but, regaining his composure, he approached the old woman, and said:

"Ah, ha! Mamma, you are better today. Oh! I never had any doubt but you would come round again; in fact, I said to myself as I was mounting the staircase: 'I have an idea that I shall find the old woman on her feet once more.' " Then he tapped her gently on the back: "Ah! she is as solid as the Pont Neuf, she will bury us all out: you will see if she does not."

He sat down, accepted the coffee that was offered him, and soon began to join in the conversation of the two men, backing up Braux, for he himself had been mixed up in the Commune.

Now the old woman, feeling herself fatigued, wished to leave the room, at which Caravan rushed forward. She thereupon looked him in the eyes and said to him:

"You must carry my clock and chest of drawers upstairs again without a moment's delay."

"Yes, Mamma," he replied, stammering; "yes, I will do so."

The old woman then took the arm of her daughter and withdrew from the room. The two Caravans remained rooted to the floor, silent, plunged in the deepest despair, while Braux rubbed his hands and sipped his coffee, gleefully.

Suddenly Mme. Caravan, consumed with rage, attacked him, exclaiming: "You are a thief, a scoundrel, a cur. I would spit in your face, if—— I would—I—would——" She could find nothing further to say, suffocating as she was with rage, while Braux still sipped his coffee, laughing.

His wife, returning just then, rushed at her sister-in-law, and both—the one with her enormous bulk, the other, epileptic and spare—with angry voices and hands trembling, hurled wild insults at each other.

Chenet and Braux now interposed, and the latter, taking his better half by the shoulders, pushed her out of the door in front of him, shouting:

"Get out, you ass: you make too much noise." Then the two were heard in the street quarreling with each other, until they had disappeared in the distance.

M. Chenet also took his departure, leaving the Caravans alone, face to face. The husband fell back in his chair, and with the cold sweat standing out in beads on his temples murmured: "What on earth shall I say at the office?"

MY UNCLE SOSTHENES

My uncle Sosthenes was a freethinker, like many others are, from pure stupidity; people are very often religious in the same way. The mere sight of a priest threw him into a violent rage; he would shake his fist and grimace at him and touch a piece of iron when the priest's back was turned, forgetting that the latter action showed a belief after all, the belief in the evil eye.

Now when beliefs are unreasonable one should have all or none at all. I myself am a freethinker; I revolt at all the dogmas which have invented the fear of death, but I feel no anger toward places of worship, be they Catholic, Apostolic, Roman, Protestant, Greek, Russian, Buddhist, Jewish or Mohammedan. I have a peculiar manner of looking at them and explaining them. A place of worship represents the homage paid by man to "The Unknown." The more extended our thoughts and our views become, the more The Unknown diminishes and the more places of worship will decay. I, however, in the place of church furniture, in the place of pulpits, reading desks, altars, and so on, would fit them up with telescopes, microscopes and electrical machines; that is all.

My uncle and I differed on nearly every point. He was a patriot, while I was not—for after all, patriotism is a kind of religion; it is the egg from which wars are hatched.

My uncle was a Freemason, and I used to declare that they are stupider than old women devotees. That is my opinion, and I maintain it; if we must have any religion at all the old one is good enough for me.

What is their object? Mutual help to be obtained by tickling the palms of each other's hands. I see no harm in it, for they put into practice the Christian precept: "Do unto others as ye would they should do unto you." The only difference consists in the tickling, but it does not seem worth while to make such a fuss about lending a poor devil half-a-crown.

To all my arguments my uncle's reply used to be:

"We are raising up a religion against a religion; free thought will kill clericalism. Freemasonry is the headquarters of those who are demolishing all deities."

"Very well, my dear uncle," I would reply (in my heart I felt inclined to say, "You old idiot!"); "it is just that which I am blaming you for. Instead of destroying, you are organizing competition; it is only a case of lowering the prices. And then if you only admitted freethinkers among you I could understand it, but you admit anybody. You have a number of Catholics among you, even the leaders of the party. Pius IX is said to have been one of you before he became Pope. If you call a society with such an organization a bulwark against clericalism, I think it is an extremely weak one."

"My dear boy," my uncle would reply with a wink, "our most formidable actions are political; slowly and surely we are everywhere undermining the monarchical spirit."

Then I broke out: "Yes, you are very clever! If you tell me that Freemasonry is an election machine I will grant it you. I will never deny that it is used as a machine to control candidates of all shades; if you say that it is only used to hoodwink people, to drill them to go to the voting urn as soldiers are sent under fire, I agree with you; if you declare that it is indispensable to all political ambitions because it changes all its members into electoral agents, I should say to you, 'That is as clear as the sun.' But when you tell me that it serves to undermine the monarchical spirit I can only laugh in your face.

"Just consider that vast and democratic association which had Prince Napoleon for its grand master under the empire, which has the crown prince for its grand master in Germany, the Czar's brother in Russia and to which the Prince of Wales and King Humbert and nearly all the royalists of the globe belong."

"You are quite right," my uncle said; "but all these persons are serving our projects without guessing it."

I felt inclined to tell him he was talking a pack of nonsense.

It was, however, indeed a sight to see my uncle when he had a Freemason to dinner.

On meeting they shook hands in a manner that was irresistibly funny; one could see that they were going through a series of secret, mysterious pressures. When I wished to put my uncle in a rage I had only to tell him that dogs also have a manner which savors very much of Freemasonry when they greet one another on meeting.

Then my uncle would take his friend into a corner to tell him something important, and at dinner they had a peculiar way of looking at each other and of drinking to each other, in a manner as if to say: "We know all about it, don't we?"

And to think that there are millions on the face of the globe who are amused at such monkey tricks! I would sooner be a Jesuit.

Now in our town there really was an old Jesuit who was my uncle's detestation. Every time he met him, or if he only saw him at a distance, he used to say: "Go on, you toad!" And then, taking my arm, he would whisper to me:

"Look here, that fellow will play me a trick someday or other; I feel sure of it."

My uncle spoke quite truly, and this was how it happened, through my fault also.

It was close on Holy Week, and my uncle made up his mind to give a dinner on Good Friday, a real dinner with his favorite chitterlings and black puddings. I resisted as much as I could and said:

"I shall eat meat on that day, but at home, quite by myself. Your *manifestation*, as you call it, is an idiotic idea. Why should you manifest? What does it matter to you if people do not eat any meat?"

But my uncle would not be persuaded. He asked three of his friends to dine with him at one of the best restaurants in the town, and as he was going to pay the bill, I had certainly, after all, no scruples about *manifesting*.

At four o'clock we took a conspicuous place in the most frequented restaurant in the town, and my uncle ordered dinner in a loud voice for six o'clock.

We sat down punctually, and at ten o'clock we had not finished. Five of us had drunk eighteen bottles of fine still wines and four of champagne. Then my uncle proposed what he was in the habit of calling: "the archbishop's feat." Each man put six small glasses in front of him, each of them filled with a different liqueur, and then they had all to be emptied at one gulp, one after another, while one of the waiters counted twenty. It was very stupid, but my uncle thought it was very suitable to the occasion.

At eleven o'clock he was dead drunk. So we had to take him home in a cab and put him to bed, and one could easily foresee that his anticlerical demonstration would end in a terrible fit of indigestion.

As I was going back to my lodgings, being rather drunk myself, with a cheerful machiavellian drunkenness which quite satisfied all my instincts of skepticism, an idea struck me.

I arranged my necktie, put on a look of great distress and went and rang loudly at the old Jesuit's door. As he was deaf he made me wait a longish while, but at length he appeared at his window in a cotton nightcap and asked what I wanted.

I shouted out at the top of my voice:

"Make haste, reverend sir, and open the door; a poor, despairing, sick man is in need of your spiritual ministrations."

The good, kind man put on his trousers as quickly as he could and came down without his cassock. I told him in a breathless voice that my uncle, the freethinker, had been taken suddenly ill. Fearing it was going to be something serious, he had been seized with a sudden fear of death and wished to see a priest and talk to him, to have his advice and comfort, to make up with the Church and to confess, so as to be able to cross the dreaded threshold at peace with himself, and I added in a mocking tone:

"At any rate, he wishes it, and if it does him no good it can do him no harm."

The old Jesuit, who was startled, delighted and almost trembling, said to me:

"Wait a moment, my son, I will come with you."

But I replied: "Pardon me, Reverend Father, if I do not go with you, but my convictions will not allow me to do so. I even refused to come and fetch you, so I beg you not to say that you have seen me but to declare that you had a presentiment—a sort of revelation of his illness."

The priest consented and went off quickly, knocked at my uncle's door, was soon let in, and I saw the black cassock disappear within that stronghold of Freethought.

I hid under a neighboring gateway to wait for events. Had he been well, my uncle would have half murdered the Jesuit, but I knew that he would scarcely be able to move an arm, and I asked myself gleefully what sort of scene would take place between these antagonists, what explanation would be given and what would be the issue of this situation, which my uncle's indignation would render more tragic still?

I laughed till I had to hold my sides and said to myself, half aloud: "Oh! what a joke, what a joke!"

Meanwhile it was getting very cold. I noticed that the Jesuit stayed a long time and thought: "They are having an explanation, I suppose."

One, two, three hours passed, and still the Reverend Father did not come out. What had happened? Had my uncle died in a fit when he saw him, or had he killed the cassocked gentleman? Perhaps they had mutually devoured each other. This last supposition appeared very unlikely, for I fancied that my uncle was quite incapable of swallowing a grain more nourishment at that moment.

At last the day broke. I was very uneasy, and not venturing to go into the house myself, I went to one of my friends who lived opposite. I roused him, explained matters to him, much to his amusement and astonishment, and took possession of his window.

At nine o'clock he relieved me, and I got a little sleep. At two o'clock I, in my turn, replaced him. We were utterly astonished.

At six o'clock the Jesuit left with a very happy and satisfied look on his face, and we saw him go away with a quiet step.

Then, timid and ashamed, I went and knocked at my uncle's door. When the servant opened it I did not dare to ask her any questions but went upstairs without saying a word.

My uncle was lying pale, exhausted, with weary, sorrowful eyes and heavy arms, on his bed. A little religious picture was fastened to one of the bed curtains with a pin.

"Why, Uncle," I said, "you in bed still? Are you not well?"

He replied in a feeble voice:

"Oh, my dear boy, I have been very ill; nearly dead."

"How was that, Uncle?"

"I don't know; it was most surprising. But what is stranger still is that the Jesuit priest who has just left—you know, that excellent man whom I have made such fun of—had a divine revelation of my state and came to see me."

I was seized with an almost uncontrollable desire to laugh and with difficulty said: "Oh, really!"

"Yes, he came. He heard a Voice telling him to get up and come to me, because I was going to die. It was a revelation."

I pretended to sneeze so as not to burst out laughing; I felt inclined to roll on the ground with amusement.

In about a minute I managed to say indignantly: "And you received him, Uncle, you? You, a freethinker, a Freemason? You did not have him thrown out of doors?"

He seemed confused and stammered:

"Listen a moment, it is so astonishing—so astonishing and providential! He also spoke to me about my father; it seems he knew him formerly."

"Your father, Uncle? But that is no reason for receiving a Jesuit."

"I know that, but I was very ill, and he looked after me most devotedly all night long. He was perfect; no doubt he saved my life; those men are all more or less doctors."

"Oh, he looked after you all night? But you said just now that he had only been gone a very short time."

"That is quite true; I kept him to breakfast after all his kindness. He had it at a table by my bedside while I drank a cup of tea."

"And he ate meat?"

My uncle looked vexed, as if I had said something very much out of place, and then added:

"Don't joke, Gaston; such things are out of place at times. He has shown me more devotion than many a relation would have done, and I expect to have his convictions respected."

This rather upset me, but I answered, nevertheless: "Very well, Uncle, and what did you do after breakfast?"

"We played a game of bezique, and then he repeated his breviary while I read a little book which he happened to have in his pocket and which was not by any means badly written."

"A religious book, Uncle?"

"Yes and no, or rather—no. It is the history of their missions in Central Africa and is rather a book of travels and adventures. What these men have done is very grand."

I began to feel that matters were going badly, so I got up. "Well, good-by, Uncle," I said, "I see you are going to leave Freemasonry for religion; you are a renegade."

He was still rather confused and stammered:

"Well, but religion is a sort of Freemasonry."

"When is your Jesuit coming back?" I asked.

"I don't—I don't know exactly; tomorrow, perhaps, but it is not certain."

I went out, altogether overwhelmed.

My joke turned out very badly for me! My uncle became radically converted, and if that had been all I should not have cared so much. Clerical or Freemason, to me it is all the same—six of one and half a dozen of the other—but the worst of it is that he has just made his will—yes, made his will—and has disinherited me in favor of that rascally Jesuit!

ALL OVER

The Comte de Lormerin had just finished dressing himself. He cast a parting glance at the large glass which occupied an entire panel of his dressing room and smiled.

He was really a fine-looking man still, though he was quite gray. Tall, slight, elegant, with no projecting paunch, with a scanty mustache of doubtful shade on his thin face which seemed fair rather than white, he had presence, that chic, in short, that indescribable something which establishes between two men more difference than millions of dollars.

He murmured: "Lormerin is still alive!"

And he made his way into the drawing room, where his correspondence awaited him.

On his table, where everything had its place, the worktable of the gentleman who never works, there were a dozen letters lying beside three newspapers of different opinions. With a single touch of the finger he exposed to view all these letters, like a gambler giving the choice of a card, and he scanned the handwriting —a thing he did each morning before tearing open the envelopes.

It was for him a moment of delightful expectancy, of inquiry and vague anxiety. What did these sealed, mysterious papers bring him? What did they contain of pleasure, of happiness or of grief? He surveyed them with a rapid sweep of the eye, recognizing in each case the hand that wrote them, selecting them, making two or three lots, according to what he expected from them. Here, friends; there, persons to whom he was indifferent; farther on, strangers. The last kind always gave him a little uneasiness. What did they want from him? What hand had traced those curious characters full of thoughts, promises or threats?

This day one letter in particular caught his eye. It was simple, nevertheless, without seeming to reveal anything, but he regarded it with disquietude, with a sort of internal shiver.

He thought: "From whom can it be? I certainly know this writing and yet I can't identify it."

He raised it to a level with his face, holding it delicately between two fingers, striving to read through the envelope without making up his mind to open it.

Then he smelled it and snatched up from the table a little magnifying glass which he used in studying all the niceties of handwriting. He suddenly felt unnerved. "Whom is it from? This hand is familiar to me, very familiar. I must have often read its prosings, yes, very often. But this must have been a long, long time ago. Who the deuce can it be from? Pooh! 'Tis only from somebody asking for money."

And he tore open the letter. Then he read:

MY DEAR FRIEND: You have, without doubt, forgotten me, for it is now twenty-five years since we saw each other. I was young; I am old. When I bade you farewell I quitted Paris in order to follow into the provinces my husband, my old husband whom you used to call "my hospital." Do you remember him? He died five years ago, and now I am returning to Paris to get my daughter married, for I have a daughter, a beautiful girl of eighteen, whom you have never seen. I informed you about her entrance into the world, but you certainly did not pay much attention to so trifling an event.

You, you are always the handsome Lormerin, so I have been told. Well, if you still recollect Lise, whom you used to call "Lison," come and dine this evening with her, with the elderly Baronne de Vance, your ever faithful friend, who, with some emotion, stretches out to you, without complaining at her lot, a devoted hand which you must clasp but no longer kiss, my poor "Jaquelet."

LISE DE VANCE

Lormerin's heart began to throb. He remained sunk in his armchair, with the letter on his knees, staring straight before him, overcome by poignant feelings that made the tears mount up to his eyes!

If he had ever loved a woman in his life it was this one, little Lise, Lise de Vance, whom he called "Cinder-Flower" on account of the strange odor of her hair and the pale gray of her eyes. Oh, what a fine, pretty, charming creature she was, this frail baronne, the wife of that old, gouty, pimply baron who had abruptly carried her off to the provinces, shut her up, kept her apart through jealousy, through jealousy of the handsome Lormerin.

Yes, he had loved her and he believed that he, too, had been truly loved. She gave him the name of "Jaquelet" and used to pronounce the word in an exquisite fashion.

A thousand memories that had been effaced came back to him, far off and sweet and melancholy now. One evening she called on him on her way home from a ball, and they went out for a stroll in the Bois de Boulogne, she in evening dress, he in his dressing jacket. It was springtime; the weather was beautiful. The odor of her bodice embalmed the warm air—the odor of her bodice, and also a little, the odor of her skin. What a divine night! When they reached the lake, as the moon's rays fell across the branches into the water, she began to weep. A little surprised, he asked her why.

She replied:

"I don't know. 'Tis the moon and the water that have affected me. Every time I see poetic things they seize hold of my heart and I have to cry."

He smiled, moved himself, considering her feminine emotion charming—the emotion of a poor little woman whom every sensation overwhelms. And he embraced her passionately, stammering:

"My little Lise, you are exquisite."

What a charming love affair, short-lived and dainty it had been, and all over, too, so quickly, cut short in the midst of its ardor by this old brute of a baron who had carried off his wife and never shown her afterward to anyone!

Lormerin had forgotten, in good sooth, at the end of two or three months. One woman drives out the other so quickly in Paris when one is a bachelor! No matter! He had kept a litle chapel for her in his heart, for he had loved her alone! He assured himself now that this was so.

He rose up and said aloud: "Certainly I will go and dine with her this evening!"

And instinctively he turned round toward the glass in order to inspect himself from head to foot. He reflected: "She must have grown old unpleasantly, more than I have!" And he felt gratified at the thought of showing himself to her still handsome, still fresh, of astonishing her, perhaps of filling her with emotion and making her regret those bygone days so far, far distant!

He turned his attention to the other letters. They were not of importance.

The whole day he kept thinking of this phantom. What was she like now? How funny it was to meet in this way after twenty-five years! Would he alone recognize her?

He made his toilet with feminine coquetry, put on a white waistcoat, which suited him better, with the coat, sent for the hairdresser to give him a finishing touch with the curling iron, for he had preserved his hair, and started very early in order to show his eagerness to see her.

The first thing he saw on entering a pretty drawing room, freshly furnished, was his own portrait, an old, faded photograph, dating from the days of his good fortune, hanging on the wall in an antique silk frame.

He sat down and waited. A door opened behind him. He rose up abruptly and, turning round, beheld an old woman with white hair who extended both hands toward him.

He seized them, kissed them one after the other with long, long kisses, then, lifting up his head, he gazed at the woman he had loved.

Yes, it was an old lady, an old lady whom he did not recognize and who, while she smiled, seemed ready to weep.

He could not abstain from murmuring:

"It is you, Lise?"

She replied:

"Yes, it is I; it is I, indeed. You would not have known me, isn't that so? I have had so much sorrow—so much sorrow. Sorrow has consumed my life. Look at me now—or rather don't look at me! But how handsome you have kept—and young! If I had by chance met you in the street I would have cried, 'Jaquelet!' Now sit down and let us, first of all, have a chat. And then I'll show you my daughter, my grown-up daughter. You'll see how she resembles me—or rather how I resembled her—no, it is not quite that; she is just like the 'me' of former days —you shall see! But I wanted to be alone with you first. I feared that there would be some emotion on my side at the first moment. Now it is all over—it is past. Pray be seated, my friend."

He sat down beside her, holding her hand, but he did not know what to say; he did not know this woman—it semed to him that he had never seen her before. What had he come to do in this house? Of what could he speak? Of the long ago? What was there in common between him and her? He could no longer recall anything to mind in the presence of this grandmotherly face. He could no longer recall to mind all the nice, tender things, so sweet, so bitter, that had assailed his heart some time since when he thought of the other, of little Lise, of the dainty Cinder-Flower. What then had become of her, the former one, the one he had loved—that woman of far-off dreams, the blonde with gray eyes, the young one who used to call him Jaquelet so prettily?

They remained side by side, motionless, both constrained, troubled, profoundly ill at ease.

As they only talked in commonplace phrases, broken and slow, she rose up and pressed the button of the bell.

"I am going to call Renée," she said.

There was a tap at the door, then the rustle of a dress; next a young voice exclaimed:

"Here I am, Mamma!"

Lormerin remained scared, as if at the sight of an apparition.

He stammered:

"Good day, mademoiselle."

Then, turning toward the mother:

"Oh, it is you!"

In fact, it was she, she whom he had known in bygone days, the Lise who had vanished and came back! In her he found the woman he had won twenty-five years before. This one was even younger still, fresher, more childlike.

He felt a wild desire to open his arms, to clasp her to his heart again, murmuring in her ear:

"Good day, Lison!"

A manservant announced: "Dinner is ready, madame." And they proceeded toward the dining room.

What passed at this dinner? What did they say to him and what could he say in reply? He found himself plunged in one of those strange dreams which border on insanity. He gazed at the two women with a fixed idea in his mind, a morbid, self-contradictory idea: "Which is the real one?"

The mother smiled, repeating over and over again: "Do you remember?" And it was in the bright eye of the young girl that he found again his memories of the past. Twenty times he opened his mouth to say to her: "Do you remember, Lison?" forgetting this white-haired lady who was regarding him with looks of tenderness.

And yet there were moments when he no longer felt sure, when he lost his head. He could see that the woman of today was not exactly the woman of long ago. The other one, the former one, had in her voice, in her glance, in her entire being, something which he did not find again in the mother. And he made efforts to recall his ladylove, to seize again what had escaped from her, what this resuscitated one did not possess.

The baronne said:

"You have lost your old sprightliness, my poor friend."

He murmured: "There are many other things that I have lost!"

But in his heart, touched with emotion, he felt his old love springing to life once more like an awakened wild beast ready to bite him.

The young girl went on chattering, and every now and then some familiar phrase of her mother which she had borrowed, a certain style of speaking and thinking, that resemblance of mind and manner which people acquire by living together, shook Lormerin from head to foot. All these things penetrated him, making the reopened wound of his passion bleed anew.

He got away early and took a turn along the boulevard. But the image of this young girl pursued him, haunted him, quickened his heart, inflamed his blood. Instead of two women, he now saw only one, a young one, the one of former days returned, and he loved her as he had loved her prototype in bygone years. He loved her with greater ardor after an interval of twenty-five years.

He went home to reflect on this strange and terrible thing and to think on what he should do.

But as he was passing, with a wax candle in his hand, before the glass, the large glass in which he had contemplated himself and admired himself before he started, he saw reflected there an elderly, gray-haired man, and suddenly he recollected what he had been in olden days, in the days of little Lise. He saw himself charming and handsome, as he had been when he was loved! Then, drawing the light nearer, he looked at himself more closely, as one inspects a strange thing with a magnifying glass, tracing the wrinkles, discovering those frightful ravages which he had not perceived till now.

And he sat down, crushed at the sight of himself, at the sight of his lamentable image, murmuring:

"All over, Lormerin!"

MY LANDLADY

"At that time," said George Kervelen, "I was living in furnished lodgings in the Rue des Saintes-Pères.

"When my father had made up his mind that I should go to Paris to continue my law studies there had been a long discussion about settling everything. My allowance had been fixed at first at two thousand five hundred francs, but my poor mother was so anxious that she said to my father that if I spent my money badly I might not take enough to eat, and then my health would suffer, and so it was settled that a comfortable boardinghouse should be found for me and that the amount should be paid to the proprietor himself, or herself, every month.

"Some of our neighbors told us of a certain Madame Kergaran, a native of Brittany, who took in boarders, and so my father arranged matters by letter with this respectable person at whose house I and my luggage arrived one evening.

"Madame Kergaran was a woman of about forty. She was very stout, had a voice like a drill sergeant and decided everything in a very abrupt manner. Her house was narrow, with only one window opening on to the street on each story, which rather gave it the appearance of a ladder of windows, or better, perhaps, of a slice of a house sandwiched in between two others.

"The landlady lived on the first floor with her servant; the kitchen and dining room were on the second, and four boarders from Brittany lived on the third and fourth, and I had two rooms on the fifth.

"A little dark corkscrew staircase led up to these attics. All day long Madame Kergaran was up and down these stairs like a captain on board ship. Ten times a day she would go into each room, noisily superintending everything, seeing that the beds were properly made, the clothes well brushed, that the attendance was all that it should be; in a word, she looked after her boarders like a mother, and better than a mother.

"I soon made the acquaintance of my four fellow countrymen. Two were medical and two were law students, but all impartially endured the landlady's despotic yoke. They were as frightened of her as a boy robbing an orchard is of a rural policeman.

"I, however, immediately felt that I wished to be independent; it is my nature to rebel. I declared at once that I meant to come in at whatever time I liked, for

Madame Kergaran had fixed twelve o'clock at night as the limit. On hearing this she looked at me for a few moments and then said:

"'It is quite impossible; I cannot have Annette called up at any hour of the night. You can have nothing to do out of doors at such a time.'

"I replied firmly that according to the law she was obliged to open the door for me at any time.

"'If you refuse,' I said, 'I shall get a policeman to witness the fact and go and get a bed at some hotel, at your expense, in which I shall be fully justified. You will, therefore, be obliged either to open the door for me or to get rid of me. Do which you please.'

"I laughed in her face as I told her my conditions. She could not speak for a moment for surprise, then she tried to negotiate, but I was firm, and she was obliged to yield. It was agreed that I should have a latchkey, on my solemn undertaking that no one else should know it.

"My energy made such a wholesome impression on her that from that time she treated me with marked favor; she was most attentive and even showed me a sort of rough tenderness which was not at all unpleasing. Sometimes when I was in a jovial mood I would kiss her by surprise, if only for the sake of getting the box on the ears which she gave me immediately afterward. When I managed to duck my head quickly enough her hand would pass over me as swiftly as a ball, and I would run away, laughing, while she would call after me:

"'Oh, you wretch, I will pay you out for that.'

"However, we soon became real friends.

"It was not long before I made the acquaintance of a girl who was employed in a shop and whom I constantly met. You know what such sort of love affairs are in Paris. One fine day, going to a lecture, you meet a girl going to work arm in arm with a friend. You look at her and feel that pleasant little shock which the eyes of some women give you. The next day at the same time, going through the same street, you meet her again, and the next and the succeeding days. At last you speak, and the love affair follows its course just like an illness.

"Well, by the end of three weeks I was on that footing with Emma which precedes intimacy. The fall would indeed have taken place much sooner, had I known where to bring it about. The girl lived at home and utterly refused to go to a hotel. I did not know how to manage, but at last I made the desperate resolve to take her to my room some night at about eleven o'clock, under the pretense of giving her a cup of tea. Madame Kergaran always went to bed at ten, so that we could get in by means of my latchkey without exciting any attention and go down again in an hour or two in the same way.

"After a good deal of entreaty on my part Emma accepted my invitation.

"I did not spend a very pleasant day, for I was by no means easy in my mind. I was afraid of complications, of a catastrophe, of some scandal. At night I went into a café and drank two cups of coffee and three or four glasses of cognac, to give me courage, and when I heard the clock strike half-past ten I went slowly to the place of meeting, where she was already waiting for me. She took my arm in a coaxing manner, and we set off slowly toward my lodgings. The nearer we got to the door the more nervous I got, and I thought to myself: 'If only Madame Kergaran is in bed already.'

"I said to Emma two or three times:

" 'Above all things, don't make any noise on the stairs,' to which she replied, laughing:

" 'Are you afraid of being heard?'

" 'No,' I said, 'but I am afraid of waking the man who sleeps in the room next to me, who is not at all well.'

"When I got near the house I felt as frightened as a man does who is going to the dentist's. All the windows were dark, so no doubt everybody was asleep, and I breathed again. I opened the door as carefully as a thief, let my fair companion in, shut it behind me and went upstairs on tiptoe, holding my breath and striking wax matches, lest the girl should make a false step.

"As we passed the landlady's door I felt my heart beating very quickly. But we reached the second floor, then the third and at last the fifth and got into my room. Victory!

"However, I only dared to speak in a whisper and took off my boots so as not to make any noise. The tea, which I made over a spirit lamp, was soon drunk, and then I became pressing, till little by little, as if in play, I, one by one, took off my companion's garments. She yielded while resisting, blushing, confused.

"She had absolutely nothing on except a short white petticoat when my door suddenly opened and Madame Kergaran appeared with a candle in her hand, in exactly the same costume as Emma.

"I jumped away from her and remained standing up, looking at the two women, who were looking at each other. What was going to happen?

"My landlady said in a lofty voice which I had never heard from her before:

" 'Monsieur Kervelen, I will not have prostitutes in my house.'

" 'But, Madame Kergaran,' I stammered, 'the young lady is a friend of mine. She just came in to have a cup of tea.'

" 'People don't take tea in their chemises. You will please make this person go directly.'

"Emma, in a natural state of consternation, began to cry and hid her face in her petticoat, and I lost my head, not knowing what to do or say. My landlady added with irresistible authority:

" 'Help her to dress and take her out at once.'

"It was certainly the only thing I could do, so I picked up her dress from the floor, put it over her head and began to fasten it as best I could. She helped me, crying all the time, hurrying and making all sorts of mistakes and unable to find either buttonholes or laces, while Madame Kergaran stood by, motionless, with the candle in her hand, looking at us with the severity of a judge.

"As soon as Emma was dressed, without even stopping to button her boots, she rushed past the landlady and ran downstairs. I followed her in my slippers and half undressed and kept repeating: 'Mademoiselle! Mademoiselle!'

"I felt that I ought to say something to her, but I could not find anything. I overtook her just by the street door and tried to take her into my arms, but she pushed me violently away, saying in a low, nervous voice: 'Leave me alone, leave me alone!' and so ran out into the street, closing the door behind her.

"When I went upstairs again I found that Madame Kergaran was waiting on the first landing. I went up slowly, expecting and ready for anything.

"Her door was open, and she called me in, saying in a severe voice:

" 'I want to speak to you, Monsieur Kervelen.'

"I went in with my head bent. She put her candle on the mantelpiece, and then, folding her arms over her expansive bosom, which a fine white dressing jacket hardly covered, she said:

" 'So, Monsieur Kervelen, you think my house is a house of ill fame?'

"I was not at all proud. I murmured:

" 'Oh dear, no! But, Madame Kergaran, you must not be angry; you know what young men are.'

" 'I know,' was her answer, 'that I will not have such creatures here, so you will understand that. I expect to have my house respected, and I will not have it lose its reputation; you understand me? I know——'

"She went on thus for at least twenty minutes, overwhelming me with the good name of her house, with reasons for her indignation, and loading me with severe reproofs. I went to bed crestfallen and resolved never again to try such an experiment, so long, at least, as I continued to be a lodger of Madame Kergaran."

PAUL'S MISTRESS

The Restaurant Grillon, a small commonwealth of boatmen, was slowly emptying. In front of the door all was tumult—cries and calls—and huge fellows in white jerseys gesticulated with oars on their shoulders.

The ladies in bright spring toilettes stepped aboard the skiffs with care, and, seating themselves astern, arranged their dresses, while the landlord of the establishment, a mighty, red-bearded, self-possessed individual of renowned strength, offered his hand to the pretty creatures and kept the frail crafts steady.

The rowers, bare-armed, with bulging chests, took their places in their turn, playing to the gallery as they did so—a gallery consisting of middle-class people dressed in their Sunday clothes, of workmen and soldiers leaning upon their elbows on the parapet of the bridge, all taking a great interest in the sight.

One by one the boats cast off from the landing stage. The oarsmen bent forward and then threw themselves backward with even swing, and under the impetus of the long curved oars the swift skiffs glided along the river, grew smaller in the distance, and finally disappeared under the railway bridge as they descended the stream toward La Grenouillère. One couple only remained behind. The young man, still almost beardless, slender, with a pale countenance, held his mistress, a thin little brunette with the air of a grasshopper, by the waist; and occasionally they gazed into each other's eyes. The landlord shouted:

"Come, M. Paul, make haste," and they drew near.

Of all the guests of the house, M. Paul was the most liked and most respected. He paid well and punctually, while the others hung back for a long time if indeed they did not vanish without paying. Besides which he was a sort of walking advertisement for the establishment, inasmuch as his father was a senator. When a stranger would inquire: "Who on earth is that little chap who thinks so much of his girl?" some habitué would reply, half aloud, with a mysterious and important air: "Don't you know? That is Paul Baron, a senator's son."

And invariably the other would exclaim:

"Poor devil! He has got it badly."

Mother Grillon, a good and worthy business woman, described the young man and his companion as "her two turtledoves," and appeared quite touched by this passion, which was profitable for her business.

The couple advanced at a slow pace. The skiff *Madeleine* was ready, and at the moment of embarking they kissed each other, which caused the public collected on the bridge to laugh. M. Paul took the oars and rowed away for La Grenouillère.

When they arrived it was just upon three o'clock, and the large floating café overflowed with people.

The immense raft, sheltered by a tarpaulin roof, is joined to the charming island of Croissy by two narrow footbridges, one of which leads into the center of the aquatic establishment while the other unites with a tiny islet, planted with a tree and called "the Flower Pot," and thence leads to land near the bath office.

M. Paul made fast his boat alongside the establishment, climbed over the railing of the café, and then, grasping his mistress's hands, assisted her out of the boat. They both seated themselves at the end of a table opposite each other.

On the opposite side of the river along the towpath, a long string of vehicles was drawn up. Cabs alternated with the fine carriages of the swells; the first, clumsy, with enormous bodies crushing the springs, drawn by broken-down hacks with hanging heads and broken knees; the second, slightly built on light wheels, with horses slender and straight, their heads well up, their bits snowy with foam, and with solemn coachmen in livery, heads erect in high collars, waiting bolt upright, with whips resting on their knees.

The bank was covered with people who came off in families, in parties, in couples, or alone. They plucked at the blades of grass, went down to the water, ascended the path, and, having reached the spot, stood still awaiting the ferryman. The clumsy punt plied incessantly from bank to bank, discharging its passengers upon the island. The arm of the river (called the dead arm) upon which this refreshment wharf lay seemed asleep, so feeble was the current. Fleets of yawls, of skiffs, of canoes, of podoscaphs, of gigs, of craft of all forms and of all kinds, crept about upon the motionless stream, crossing each other, intermingling, running foul of one another, stopping abruptly under a jerk of the arms only to shoot off afresh under a sudden strain of the muscles and gliding swiftly along like great yellow or red fishes.

Others arrived continually; some from Chatou up the stream; others from Bougival down it; laughter crossed the water from one boat to another, calls, admonitions, or imprecations. The boatmen exposed the bronzed and knotted muscles of their biceps to the heat of the day; and, like strange floating flowers, the silk parasols, red, green, blue, or yellow, of the ladies bloomed in the sterns of the boats.

A July sun flamed high in the heavens; the atmosphere seemed full of burning merriment; not a breath of air stirred the leaves of the willows or poplars.

In front, away in the distance, the inevitable Mont Valérien reared its fortified ramparts, tier above tier, in the intense light; while on the right the divine slopes of Louveciennes, following the bend of the river, disposed themselves in a semicircle, displaying in turn across the rich and shady lawns of large gardens the white walls of country seats.

Upon the outskirts of La Grenouillère a crowd of pedestrians moved about beneath the giant trees which make this corner of the island one of the most delightful parks in the world.

Women and girls with yellow hair and breasts developed beyond all measurement, with exaggerated hips, their complexions plastered with rouge, their eyes daubed with charcoal, their lips blood-red, laced up, rigged out in outrageous dresses, trailed the crying bad taste of their toilettes over the fresh greensward; while beside them young men posed in their fashion-plate garments with light gloves, patent-leather boots, canes the size of a thread, and single eyeglasses emphasizing the insipidity of their smiles.

Opposite La Grenouillère the island is narrow, and on its other side, where also a ferry boat plies, bringing people unceasingly across from Croissy, the rapid branch of the river, full of whirlpools and eddies and foam, rushes along with the strength of a torrent. A detachment of pontoon builders, in the uniform of artillerymen, was encamped upon this bank, and the soldiers seated in a row on a long beam watched the water flowing.

In the floating establishment there was a boisterous and uproarious crowd. The wooden tables upon which the spilled refreshments made little sticky streams were covered with half-empty glasses and surrounded by half-tipsy individuals. The crowd shouted, sang, and brawled. The men, their hats at the backs of their heads, their faces red, with the shining eyes of drunkards, moved about vociferating and evidently looking for the quarrels natural to brutes. The women, seeking their prey for the night, sought for free liquor in the meantime; and the unoccupied space between the tables was dominated by the customary local public, a whole regiment of rowdy boatmen, with their female companions in short flannel skirts.

One of them performed on the piano and appeared to play with his feet as well as his hands; four couples glided through a quadrille, and some young men watched them, polished and correct, men who would have looked respectable did not their innate viciousness show in spite of everything.

For there you see all the scum of society, all its well-bred debauchery, all the seamy side of Parisian society—a mixture of counterjumpers, of strolling players, of low journalists, of gentlemen in tutelage, of rotten stockjobbers, of ill-famed debauchees, of old, used-up, fast men; a doubtful crowd of suspicious characters, half-known, half-sunk, half-recognized, half-criminal, pickpockets, rogues, procurers of women, sharpers with dignified manners and a bragging air which seems to say: "I shall kill the first man who treats me as a scoundrel."

The place reeks of folly and stinks of vulgarity and cheap gallantry. Male and female are just as bad one as the other. There dwells an odor of so-called love, and there one fights for a "yes," or for a "no," in order to sustain a worm-eaten reputation, which a thrust of the sword or a pistol bullet only destroys further.

Some of the neighboring inhabitants looked in out of curiosity every Sunday; some young men, very young, appeared there every year to learn how to live, some promenaders lounging about showed themselves there; some greenhorns wandered thither. With good reason is it named La Grenouillère.[1] At the side of the covered wharf where drink was served, and quite close to the Flower Pot, people bathed. Those among the women who possessed the requisite roundness of form came there to display their wares and to get clients. The rest, scornful, although well filled out with wadding, supported by springs, corrected here and altered there, watched their dabbling sisters with disdain.

The swimmers crowded onto a little platform to dive. Straight like vine poles

[1] A frog swamp.

or round like pumpkins, gnarled like olive branches, bowed over in front, or thrown backward by the size of their stomachs, and invariably ugly, they leaped into the water, splashing it over the drinkers in the café.

Notwithstanding the great trees which overhang the floating house, and notwithstanding the vicinity of the water, a suffocating heat filled the place. The fumes of the spilled liquors mingled with the effluvia of the bodies and with the strong perfumes with which the skin of the trader in love is saturated and which evaporate in this furnace. But beneath all these diverse scents a slight aroma of *poudre de riz* lingered, disappearing and reappearing, and perpetually encountered as though some concealed hand had shaken an invisible powder puff in the air. The show was on the river, where the perpetual coming and going of the boats attracted the eyes. The girls in the boats sprawled upon their seats opposite their strong-wristed males and scornfully contemplated the dinner-hunting females prowling about the island.

Sometimes when a crew in full swing passed at top speed, the friends who had gone ashore gave vent to shouts, and all the people, as if suddenly seized with madness, commenced to yell.

At the bend of the river toward Chatou fresh boats continually appeared. They came nearer and grew larger, and as faces became recognizable the vociferations broke out anew.

A canoe covered with an awning and manned by four women came slowly down the current. She who rowed was petite, thin, faded, in a cabin boy's costume, her hair drawn up under an oilskin hat. Opposite her, a lusty blonde, dressed as a man, with a white flannel jacket, lay upon her back at the bottom of the boat, her legs in the air, resting on the seat at each side of the rower. She smoked a cigarette, while at each stroke of the oars, her chest and her stomach quivered, shaken by the stroke. At the back, under the awning, two handsome girls, tall and slender, one dark and the other fair, held each other by the waist as they watched their companions.

A cry arose from La Grenouillère, "There's Lesbos," and all at once a furious clamor, a terrifying scramble took place; the glasses were knocked down; people clambered onto the tables; all in a frenzy of noise bawled: "Lesbos! Lesbos! Lesbos!" The shout rolled along, became indistinct, was no longer more than a kind of deafening howl, and then suddenly it seemed to start anew, to rise into space, to cover the plain to fill the foliage of the great trees, to extend to the distant slopes, and reach even to the sun.

The rower, in the face of this ovation, had quietly stopped. The handsome blonde, stretched out upon the bottom of the boat, turned her head with a careless air, as she raised herself upon her elbows; and the two girls at the back commenced laughing as they saluted the crowd.

Then the hullabaloo redoubled, making the floating establishment tremble. The men took off their hats, the women waved their handkerchiefs, and all voices, shrill or deep, together cried:

"Lesbos."

It was as if these people, this collection of the corrupt, saluted their chiefs like the warships which fire guns when an admiral passes along the line.

The numerous fleet of boats also saluted the women's boat, which pushed along more quickly to land farther off.

M. Paul, contrary to the others, had drawn a key from his pocket and whistled with all his might. His nervous mistress grew paler, caught him by the arm to make him be quiet; and upon this occasion she looked at him with fury in her eyes. But he appeared exasperated, as though borne away by jealousy of some man or by deep anger, instinctive and ungovernable. He stammered, his lips quivering with indignation:

"It is shameful! They ought to be drowned like puppies with a stone about the neck."

But Madeleine instantly flew into a rage; her small and shrill voice became a hiss, and she spoke volubly, as though pleading her own cause:

"And what has it to do with you—you indeed? Are they not at liberty to do what they wish, since they owe nobody anything? You shut up and mind your own business."

But he cut her speech short:

"It is the police whom it concerns, and I will have them marched off to St. Lazare; indeed I will."

She gave a start.

"You?"

"Yes, I! And in the meantime I forbid you to speak to them—you understand, I forbid you to do so."

Then she shrugged her shoulders and grew calm in a moment:

"My dear, I shall do as I please; if you are not satisfied, be off, and instantly. I am not your wife, am I? Very well then, hold your tongue."

He made no reply, and they stood face to face, their lips tightly closed, breathing quickly.

At the other end of the great wooden café the four women made their entry. The two in men's costumes marched in front: the one thin like an oldish tomboy, with a yellow tinge on her temples; the other filling out her white flannel garments with her fat, swelling out her wide trousers with her buttocks and swaying about like a fat goose with enormous legs and yielding knees. Their two friends followed them, and the crowd of boatmen thronged about to shake their hands.

The four had hired a small cottage close to the water's edge and lived there as two households would have lived.

Their vice was public, recognized, patent to all. People talked of it as a natural thing, which almost excited their sympathy, and whispered in very low tones strange stories of dramas begotten of furious feminine jealousies, of the stealthy visit of well-known women and of actresses to the little house close to the water's edge.

A neighbor, horrified by these scandalous rumors, notified the police, and the inspector, accompanied by a man, had come to make inquiry. The mission was a delicate one; it was impossible, in short, to accuse these women, who did not abandon themselves to prostitution, of any tangible crime. The inspector, very much puzzled, and, indeed, ignorant of the nature of the offenses suspected, had asked questions at random, and made a lofty report conclusive of their innocence.

The joke spread as far as St. Germain. They walked about Grenouillère establishment with mincing steps like queens and seemed to glory in their fame, rejoicing in the gaze that was fixed on them, so superior to this crowd, to this mob, to these plebeians.

Madeleine and her lover watched them approach, and the girl's eyes lit up.

When the first two had reached the end of the table, Madeleine cried:

"Pauline!"

The large woman turned and stopped, continuing all the time to hold the arm of her feminine cabin boy:

"Good gracious, Madeleine! Do come and talk to me, my dear."

Paul squeezed his fingers upon his mistress's wrist, but she said to him, with such an air: "You know, my dear, you can clear out, if you like," that he said nothing and remained alone.

Then they chatted in low voices, all three of them standing. Many pleasant jests passed their lips, they spoke quickly; and Pauline now and then looked at Paul, by stealth, with a shrewd and malicious smile.

At last, unable to put up with it any longer, he suddenly rose and in a single bound was at their side, trembling in every limb. He seized Madeleine by the shoulders.

"Come, I wish it," said he; "I have forbidden you to speak to these sluts."

Whereupon Pauline raised her voice and set to work blackguarding him with her Billingsgate vocabulary. All the bystanders laughed; they drew near him; they raised themselves on tiptoe in order the better to see him. He remained dumb under this downpour of filthy abuse. It appeared to him that the words which came from that mouth and fell upon him defiled him like dirt, and, in presence of the row which was beginning, he fell back, retraced his steps, and rested his elbows on the railing toward the river, turning his back upon the victorious women.

There he stayed watching the water, and sometimes with rapid gesture, as though he could pluck it out, he removed with his nervous fingers the tear which stood in his eye.

The fact was that he was hopelessly in love, without knowing why, notwithstanding his refined instincts, in spite of his reason, in spite, indeed, of his will. He had fallen into this love as one falls into a muddy hole. Of a tender and delicate disposition, he had dreamed of liaisons, exquisite, ideal, and impassioned, and there that little bit of a woman, stupid like all prostitutes, with an exasperating stupidity, not even pretty, but thin and a spitfire, had taken him prisoner, possessing him from head to foot, body and soul. He had submitted to this feminine witchery, mysterious and all-powerful, this unknown power, this prodigious domination—arising no one knows whence, but from the demon of the flesh—which casts the most sensible man at the feet of some harlot or other without there being anything in her to explain her fatal and sovereign power.

And there at his back he felt that some infamous thing was brewing. Shouts of laughter cut him to the heart. What should he do? He knew well, but he could not do it.

He steadily watched an angler upon the bank opposite him, and his motionless line.

Suddenly, the worthy man jerked a little silver fish, which wriggled at the end of his line, out of the river. Then he endeavored to extract his hook, pulled and turned it, but in vain. At last, losing patience, he commenced to tear it out, and all the bleeding gullet of the fish, with a portion of its intestines came out. Paul shuddered, rent to his heartstrings. It seemed to him that the hook was his love, and that if he should pluck it out, all that he had in his breast would come out in the same way, at the end of a curved iron, fixed in the depths of his being, to which Madeleine held the line.

A hand was placed upon his shoulder; he started and turned; his mistress was at his side. They did not speak to each other; and like him she rested her elbows upon the railing, and fixed her eyes upon the river.

He tried to speak to her and could find nothing. He could not even disentangle his own emotions; all that he was sensible of was joy at feeling her there close to him, come back again, as well as shameful cowardice, a craving to pardon everything, to allow everything, provided she never left him.

At last, after a few minutes, he asked her in a very gentle voice:

"Would you like to go? It will be nicer in the boat."

She answered: "Yes, darling."

And he assisted her into the skiff, pressing her hands, all softened, with some tears still in his eyes. Then she looked at him with a smile and they kissed each other again.

They reascended the river very slowly, skirting the willow-bordered, grass-covered bank, bathed and still in the afternoon warmth. When they had returned to the Restaurant Grillon, it was barely six o'clock. Then, leaving their boat, they set off on foot towards Bezons, across the fields and along the high poplars which bordered the river. The long grass ready to be mowed was full of flowers. The sinking sun glowed from beneath a sheet of red light, and in the tempered heat of the closing day the floating exhalations from the grass, mingled with the damp scents from the river, filled the air with a soft languor, with a happy light, with an atmosphere of blessing.

A soft weakness overtook his heart, a species of communion with this splended calm of evening, with this vague and mysterious throb of teeming life, with the keen and melancholy poetry which seems to arise from flowers and things and reveals itself to the senses at this sweet and pensive time.

Paul felt all that; but for her part she did not understand anything of it. They walked side by side; and, suddenly, tired of being silent, she sang. She sang in her shrill, unmusical voice some street song, some catchy air, which jarred upon the profound and serene harmony of the evening.

Then he looked at her and felt an impassable abyss between them. She beat the grass with her parasol, her head slightly inclined, admiring her feet and singing, dwelling on the notes, attempting trills and venturing on shakes. Her smooth little brow, of which he was so fond, was at that time absolutely empty! empty! There was nothing therein but this canary music; and the ideas which formed there by chance were like this music. She did not understand anything of him; they were now as separated as if they did not live together. Did his kisses never go any farther than her lips?

Then she raised her eyes to him and laughed again. He was moved to the quick and, extending his arms in a paroxysm of love, he embraced her passionately.

As he was rumpling her dress she finally broke away from him, murmuring by way of compensation as she did so:

"That's enough. You know I love you, my darling."

But he clasped her around the waist and, seized by madness, he started to run with her. He kissed her on the cheek, on the temple, on the neck, all the while dancing with joy. They threw themselves down panting at the edge of a thicket, lit up by the rays of the setting sun, and before they had recovered breath they were in one another's arms without her understanding his transport.

They returned, holding each other by the hand, when, suddenly, through the trees, they perceived on the river the skiff manned by the four women. Fat Pauline also saw them, for she drew herself up and blew kisses to Madeleine. And then she cried:

"Until tonight!"

Madeleine replied: "Until tonight!"

Paul felt as if his heart had suddenly been frozen.

They re-entered the house for dinner and installed themselves in one of the arbors, close to the water. They began to eat in silence. When night arrived, the waiter brought a candle enclosed in a glass globe, which gave a feeble and glimmering light; and they heard every moment the bursts of shouting from the boatmen in the large room on the first floor.

Toward dessert, Paul, taking Madeleine's hand, tenderly said to her:

"I feel very tired, my darling; unless you have any objection, we will go to bed early."

She, however, understood the ruse, and shot an enigmatical glance at him—that glance of treachery which so readily appears in the depths of a woman's eyes. Having reflected she answered:

"You can go to bed if you wish, but I have promised to go to the ball at La Grenouillère."

He smiled in a piteous manner, one of those smiles with which one veils the most horrible suffering, and replied in a coaxing but agonized tone:

"If you were really nice, we should remain here, both of us."

She indicated "no" with her head, without opening her mouth.

He insisted:

"I beg of you, my darling."

Then she roughly broke out:

"You know what I said to you. If you are not satisfied, the door is open. No one wishes to keep you. As for myself, I have promised; I shall go."

He placed his two elbows upon the table, covered his face with his hands, and remained there pondering sorrowfully.

The boat people came down again, shouting as usual, and set off in their vessels for the ball at La Grenouillère.

Madeleine said to Paul:

"If you are not coming, say so, and I will ask one of these gentlemen to take me."

Paul rose.

"Let us go!" murmured he.

And they left.

The night was black, the sky full of stars, but the air was heat-laden by oppressive breaths of wind, burdened with emanation and with living germs, which destroyed the freshness of the night. It offered a heated caress, made one breathe more quickly, gasp a little, so thick and heavy did it seem. The boats started on their way, bearing Venetian lanterns at the prow. It was not possible to distinguish the craft, but only the little colored lights, swift and dancing up and down like frenzied glowworms, while voices sounded from all sides in the shadows. The young people's skiff glided gently along. Now and then, when a fast boat passed near them, they could, for a moment, see the white back of the rower, lit up by his lantern.

When they turned the elbow of the river, La Grenouillère appeared to them in the distance. The establishment, *en fête*, was decorated with flags and garlands of colored lights, in grapelike clusters. On the Seine some great barges moved about slowly, representing domes, pyramids, and elaborate monuments in fires of all colors. Illuminated festoons hung right down to the water, and sometimes a red or blue lantern, at the end of an immense invisible fishing rod, seemed like a great swinging star.

All this illumination spread a light around the café, lit up the great trees on the bank, from top to bottom, the trunks standing out in pale gray and the leaves in milky green upon the deep black of the fields and the heavens. The orchestra, composed of five suburban artists, flung far its public-house dance music, poor of its kind and jerky, inciting Madeleine to sing anew.

She wanted to go in at once. Paul wanted first to take a stroll on the island, but he was obliged to give way. The attendance was now more select. The boatmen, almost alone, remained, with here and there some better-class people, and young men escorted by girls. The director and organizer of this spree, looking majestic in a jaded black suit, walked about in every direction, bald-headed and worn by his old trade of purveyor of cheap public amusements.

Fat Pauline and her companions were not there; and Paul breathed again.

They danced; couples opposite each other capered in the maddest fashion, throwing their legs in the air until they were upon a level with the noses of their partners.

The women, whose thighs seemed disjointed, pranced around with flying skirts which revealed their underclothing, wriggling their stomachs and hips, causing their breasts to shake, and spreading the powerful odor of perspiring female bodies.

The men squatted like toads, some making obscene gestures; some twisted and distorted themselves, grimacing and hideous; some turned cartwheels on their hands, or, perhaps, trying to be funny, posed with exaggerated gracefulness.

A fat servant maid and two waiters served refreshments.

The café boat being only covered with a roof, and having no wall whatever to shut it in, this harebrained dance flaunted in the face of the peaceful night and of the firmament powdered with stars.

Suddenly, Mont Valérien, opposite, appeared, illumined as if some conflagration had arisen behind it. The radiance spread and deepened upon the sky, describing a large luminous circle of white, wan light. Then something or other red appeared, grew greater, shining with a burning crimson, like that of hot metal upon the anvil. It gradually developed into a round body rising from the earth; and the moon, freeing itself from the horizon, rose slowly into space. As it ascended, the purple tint faded and became yellow, a shining bright yellow, and the satellite grew smaller in proportion as its distance increased.

Paul watched the moon for some time, lost in contemplation, forgetting his mistress; when he returned to himself the latter had vanished.

He sought her, but could not find her. He threw his anxious eye over table after table, going to and fro unceasingly, inquiring for her from one person and then another. No one had seen her. He was tormented with uneasiness, when one of the waiters said to him:

"You are looking for Mme. Madeleine, are you not? She left a few moments ago, with Mme. Pauline." And at the same instant, Paul perceived the cabin boy and the two pretty girls standing at the other end of the café, all three holding each other's waists and lying in wait for him, whispering to one another. He understood, and, like a madman, dashed off into the island.

He first ran toward Chatou, but, having reached the plain, retraced his steps. Then he began to search the dense coppices, occasionally roaming about distractedly, or halting to listen.

The toads all about him poured out their short metallic notes.

From the direction of Bougival, some unknown bird warbled a song which reached him faintly from the distance.

Over the broad fields the moon shed a soft light, resembling powdered wool; it penetrated the foliage, silvered the bark of the poplars, and riddled with its brilliant rays the waving tops of the great trees. The entrancing poetry of this summer night had, in spite of himself, entered into Paul, athwart his infatuated anguish, stirring his heart with ferocious irony and increasing even to madness his craving for an ideal tenderness, for passionate outpourings on the breast of an adored and faithful woman. He was compelled to stop, choked by hurried and rending sobs.

The convulsion over, he went on.

Suddenly, he received what resembled the stab of a dagger. There, behind that bush, some people were kissing. He ran thither; and found an amorous couple whose faces were united in an endless kiss.

He dared not call, knowing well that she would not respond, and he had a frightful dread of coming upon them suddenly.

The flourishes of the quadrilles, with the earsplitting solos of the cornet, the false shriek of the flute, the shrill squeaking of the violin, irritated his feelings, and increased his suffering. Wild and limping music was floating under the trees, now feeble, now stronger, wafted hither and thither by the breeze.

Suddenly he thought that possibly she had returned. Yes, she had returned! Why not? He had stupidly lost his head, without cause, carried away by his fears, by the inordinate suspicions which had for some time overwhelmed him. Seized by one of those singular calms which will sometimes occur in cases of the greatest despair, he returned toward the ballroom.

With a single glance of the eye, he took in the whole room. He made the round of the tables and abruptly again found himself face to face with the three women. He must have had a doleful and queer expression of countenance, for all three burst into laughter.

He made off, returned to the island, and threw himself into the coppice panting. He listened again, listened a long time, for his ears were singing. At last, however, he believed he heard farther off a little, sharp laugh, which he recognized at once; and he advanced very quietly, on his knees, removing the branches from his path, his heart beating so rapidly, that he could no longer breathe.

Two voices murmured some words, the meaning of which he did not understand, and then they were silent.

Then, he was possessed by a frightful longing to fly, to save himself, forever, from this furious passion which threatened his existence. He was about to return to Chatou and take the train, resolved never to come back again, never again to see her. But her likeness suddenly rushed in upon him, and he mentally pictured the moment in the morning when she would awake in their warm bed, and would press coaxingly against him, throwing her arms around his neck, her hair disheveled, and a little entangled on the forehead, her eyes still shut and her lips apart ready to receive the first kiss. The sudden remembrance of this morning caress filled him with frantic recollections and the maddest desire.

The couple began to speak again; and he approached, stooping low. Then a faint cry rose from under the branches quite close to him. He advanced again, in spite of himself, irresistibly attracted, without being conscious of anything—and he saw them.

If her companion had only been a man! But that! *that!* He felt as though he were spellbound by the very infamy of it. And he stood there astounded and overwhelmed, as if he had discovered the mutilated corpse of one dear to him, a crime against nature, a monstrous, disgusting profanation. Then, in an involuntary flash of thought, he remembered the little fish whose entrails he had felt being torn out! But Madeleine murmured: "Pauline!" in the same tone in which she had often called him by name, and he was seized by such a fit of anguish that he turned and fled.

He struck against two trees, fell over a root, set off again, and suddenly found himself near the rapid branch of the river, which was lit up by the moon. The torrentlike current made great eddies where the light played upon it. The high bank dominated the stream like a cliff, leaving a wide obscure zone at its foot where the eddies could be heard swirling in the darkness.

On the other bank, the country seats of Croissy could be plainly seen.

Paul saw all this as though in a dream; he thought of nothing, understood nothing, and all things, even his very existence, appeared vague, far-off, forgotten, and closed.

The river was there. Did he know what he was doing? Did he wish to die? He was mad. He turned, however, toward the island, toward *her*, and in the still air of the night, in which the faint and persistent burden of the music was borne up and down, he uttered, in a voice frantic with despair, bitter beyond measure, and superhumanly low, a frightful cry:

"Madeleine!"

His heart-rending call shot across the great silence of the sky, and sped over the horizon. Then with a tremendous leap, with the bound of a wild animal, he jumped into the river. The water rushed on, closed over him, and from the place where he had disappeared a series of great circles started, enlarging their brilliant undulations, until they finally reached the other bank. The two women had heard the noise of the plunge. Madeleine drew herself up and exclaimed:

"It is Paul"—a suspicion having arisen in her soul—"he has drowned himself"; and she rushed toward the bank, where Pauline rejoined her.

A clumsy punt, propelled by two men, turned round and round on the spot. One of the men rowed, the other plunged into the water a great pole and appeared to be looking for something. Pauline cried:

"What are you doing? What is the matter?"

An unknown voice answered:

"It is a man who has just drowned himself."

The two haggard women, huddling close to each other, followed the maneuvers of the boat. The music of La Grenouillère continued to sound in the distance, seeming with its cadences to accompany the movements of the somber fishermen; and the river, which now concealed a corpse, whirled round and round, illuminated. The search was prolonged. The horrible suspense made Madeleine shiver all over. At last, after at least half an hour, one of the men announced:

"I have got him."

And he pulled up his long pole very gently, very gently. Then something large appeared upon the surface. The other boatman left his oars, and, by uniting their strength and hauling upon the inert weight, they succeeded in getting it into their boat.

Then they made for land, seeking a place well lighted and low. At the moment they landed, the women also arrived. The moment she saw him, Madeleine fell back with horror. In the moonlight he already appeared green, with his mouth, his eyes, his nose, his clothes full of slime. His fingers, closed and stiff, were hideous. A kind of black and liquid plaster covered his whole body. The face appeared swollen, and from his hair, plastered down by the ooze, there ran a stream of dirty water.

The two men examined him.

"Do you know him?" asked one.

The other, the Croissy ferryman, hesitated:

"Yes, it certainly seems to me that I have seen that head; but you know when a body is in that state one cannot recognize it easily." And then, suddenly:

"Why, it's M. Paul!"

"Who is M. Paul?" inquired his comrade.

The first answered:

"Why, M. Paul Baron, the son of the senator, the little chap who was so much in love."

The other added, philosophically:

"Well, his fun is ended now; it is a pity, all the same, when one is rich!"

Madeleine had fallen on the ground sobbing. Pauline approached the body and asked:

"Is he really quite dead?"

The men shrugged their shoulders.

"Oh! after that length of time, certainly."

Then one of them asked:

"Was it not at Grillon's that he lodged?"

"Yes," answered the other; "we had better take him back there, there will be something to be made out of it."

They embarked again in their boat and set out, moving off slowly on account of the rapid current. For a long time after they were out of sight of the place where the women remained, the regular splash of the oars in the water could be heard.

Then Pauline took the poor weeping Madeleine in her arms, petted her, embraced her for a long while, and consoled her.

"How can you help it? it is not your fault, is it? It is impossible to prevent men from doing silly things. He did it of his own free will; so much the worse for him, after all!"

And then lifting her up:

"Come, my dear, come and sleep at the house; it is impossible for you to go back to Grillon's tonight."

And she embraced her again, saying: "Come, we will cure you."

Madeleine arose, and, weeping all the while, but with fainter sobs, laid her head upon Pauline's shoulder, as though she had found a refuge in a closer and more certain affection, more familiar and more confiding, and she went off slowly.

THE HORRIBLE

The shadows of a balmy night were slowly falling. The women remained in the drawing room of the villa. The men, seated or astride on garden chairs, were smoking in front of the door, forming a circle round a table laden with cups and wineglasses.

Their cigars shone like eyes in the darkness which, minute by minute, was growing thicker. They had been talking about a frightful accident which had occurred the night before—two men and three women drowned before the eyes of the guests in the river opposite.

General de G—— remarked:

"Yes, these things are affecting, but they are not horrible.

"The horrible, that well-known word, means much more than the terrible. A frightful accident like this moves, upsets, scares; it does not horrify. In order that we should experience horror, something more is needed than the mere excitation of the soul, something more than the spectacle of the dreadful death; there must be a shuddering sense of mystery or a sensation of abnormal terror beyond the limits of nature. A man who dies, even in the most dramatic conditions, does not excite horror; a field of battle is not horrible; blood is not horrible; the vilest crimes are rarely horrible.

"Now here are two personal examples, which have shown me what is the meaning of horror:

"It was during the war of 1870. We were retreating toward Pont-Audemer, after having passed through Rouen. The army, consisting of about twenty thousand men, twenty thousand men in disorder, disbanded, demoralized, exhausted, was going to re-form at Havre.

"The earth was covered with snow. The night was falling. They had not eaten anything since the day before and were flying rapidly, the Prussians not far off. The Norman country, livid, dotted with the shadows of the trees surrounding the farms, stretched away under a heavy and sinister black sky.

"Nothing else could be heard in the wan twilight save the confused sound, soft and undefined, of a marching throng, an endless tramping, mingled with the vague clink of canteens or sabers. The men, bent, round-shouldered, dirty, in many cases even in rags, dragged themselves along, hurrying through the snow with a long, broken-backed stride.

The skin of their hands stuck to the steel of their muskets' butt ends, for it was freezing dreadfully that night. I frequently saw a little soldier take off his shoes in order to walk barefooted, so much did his footgear bruise him; and with every step he left a track of blood. Then after some time he sat down in a field for a few minutes' rest and never got up again. Every man who sat down died.

"Should we have left behind us those poor, exhausted soldiers who fondly counted on being able to start afresh as soon as they had somewhat refreshed their stiffened legs? Now scarcely had they ceased to move and to make their almost frozen blood circulate in their veins, than an unconquerable torpor congealed them, nailed them to the ground, closed their eyes, and in one second the overworked human mechanism collapsed. They gradually sank down, their heads falling toward their knees, without, however, quite tumbling over, for their loins and their limbs lost the capacity for moving and became as hard as wood, impossible to bend or straighten.

"The rest of us, more robust, kept still straggling on, chilled to the marrow of our bones, advancing by dint of forced movement through the night, through that snow, through that cold and deadly country, crushed by pain, by defeat, by despair, above all, overcome by the abominable sensation of abandonment, of death, of nothingness.

"I saw two gendarmes holding by the arm a curious-looking little man, old, beardless, of truly surprising aspect.

"They were looking out for an officer, believing that they had caught a spy. The word 'spy' at once spread through the midst of the stragglers, and they gathered in a group round the prisoner. A voice exclaimed: 'He must be shot!' And all these soldiers who were falling from utter prostration, only holding themselves on their feet by leaning on their guns, felt of a sudden that thrill of furious and bestial anger which urges on a mob to massacre.

"I wanted to speak! I was at that time in command of a battalion, but they no longer recognized the authority of their commanding officers; they would have shot me.

"One of the gendarmes said: 'He has been following us for the last three days. He has been asking information from everyone about the artillery.'

"I took it on myself to question this person:

"'What are you doing? What do you want? Why are you accompanying the army?'

"He stammered out some words in some unintelligible dialect. He was, indeed, a strange being, with narrow shoulders, a sly look and such an agitated air in my presence that I had no longer any real doubt that he was a spy. He seemed very aged and feeble. He kept staring at me from under his eyes with a humble, stupid and crafty air.

"The men all round us exclaimed:

"'To the wall! To the wall!'

"I said to the gendarmes:

"'Do you answer for the prisoner?'

"I had not ceased speaking when a terrible push threw me on my back, and in a second I saw the man seized by the furious soldiers, thrown down, struck, dragged along the side of the road and flung against a tree. He fell in the snow, nearly dead already.

"And immediately they shot him. The soldiers fired at him, reloaded their guns, fired again with the desperate energy of brutes. They fought with each other to have a shot at him, filed off in front of the corpse and kept firing at him, just as people at a funeral keep sprinkling holy water in front of a coffin.

"But suddenly a cry arose of 'The Prussians! The Prussians!' And all along the horizon I heard the great noise of this panic-stricken army in full flight.

"The panic, generated by these shots fired at this vagabond, had filled his very executioners with terror, and without realizing that they were themselves the originators of the scare they rushed away and disappeared in the darkness.

"I remained alone in front of the corpse with the two gendarmes whom duty had compelled to stay with me.

"They lifted up this riddled piece of flesh, bruised and bleeding.

" 'He must be examined,' I said to them.

"And I handed them a box of vestas which I had in my pocket. One of the soldiers had another box. I was standing between the two.

"The gendarme, who was feeling the body, called out:

" 'Clothed in a blue blouse, trousers and a pair of shoes.'

"The first match went out; we lighted a second. The man went on as he turned out the pockets:

" 'A horn knife, check handkerchief, a snuffbox, a bit of pack thread, a piece of bread.'

"The second match went out; we lighted a third. The gendarme, after having handled the corpse for a long time, said:

" 'That is all.'

"I said:

" 'Strip him. We shall perhaps find something near the skin.'

"And in order that the two soldiers might help each other in this task, I stood between-them to give them light. I saw them, by the rapid and speedily extinguished flash of the match, take off the garments one by one and expose to view that bleeding bundle of flesh, still warm, though lifeless.

"And suddenly one of them exclaimed:

" 'Good God, Colonel, it is a woman!'

"I cannot describe to you the strange and poignant sensation of pain that moved my heart. I could not believe it, and I kneeled down in the snow before this shapeless pulp of flesh to see for myself: it was a woman.

"The two gendarmes, speechless and stunned, waited for me to give my opinion on the matter. But I did not know what to think, what theory to adopt.

"Then the brigadier slowly drawled out:

" 'Perhaps she came to look for a son of hers in the artillery whom she had not heard from.'

"And the other chimed in:

" 'Perhaps, indeed, that is so.'

"And I, who had seen some terrible things in my time, began to weep. I felt, in the presence of this corpse, in that icy-cold night, in the midst of that gloomy plain, at the sight of this mystery, at the sight of this murdered stranger, the meaning of that word 'horror.'

"Now I had the same sensation last year while interrogating one of the survivors of the Flatters' Mission, an Algerian sharpshooter.

"You probably know some of the details of this atrocious drama. It is possible, however, that you are unacquainted with all.

"The colonel traveled through the desert into the Sudan and passed through the immense territory of the Tuaregs who are, in that great ocean of sand which stretches from the Atlantic to Egypt and from the Sudan to Algeria, a sort of pirate, resembling those who ravaged the seas in former days.

"The guides who accompanied the column belonged to the tribe of Chambaa, of Ouargla.

"One day they pitched their camp in the middle of the desert, and the Arabs declared that as the spring was a little farther away, they would go with all their camels to look for water.

"Only one man warned the colonel that he had been betrayed. Flatters did not believe this and accompanied the convoy with the engineers, the doctors and nearly all his officers.

"They were massacred round the spring and all the camels captured.

"The captain of the Arab Intelligence Department at Ouargla, who had remained in the camp, took command of the survivors, spahis and sharpshooters, and commenced the retreat, leaving behind the baggage and the provisions for want of camels to carry them.

"Then they started on their journey through this solitude without shade and without limit, under a devouring sun, which parched them from morning till night.

"One tribe came to tender its submission and brought dates as a tribute. They were poisoned. Nearly all the French died, and among them, the last officer.

"There now only remained a few spahis, with their quartermaster Pobéguin and some native sharpshooters of the Chambaa tribe. They had still two camels left. These disappeared one night along with two Arabs.

"Then the survivors feared that they would have to eat each other up. As soon as they discovered the flight of the two men with the two beasts, those who remained separated and proceeded to march one by one through the soft sun, at a distance of more than a gunshot from each other.

"So they went on all day, and when they reached a spring each of them came up to drink at it in turn as soon as each solitary marcher had moved forward the number of yards arranged upon. And thus they continued marching the whole day, raising, everywhere they passed in that level, burned-up expanse, those little columns of dust which, at a distance, indicate those who are trudging through the desert.

"But one morning one of the travelers made a sudden turn and drew nearer to his neighbor. And they all stopped to look.

"The man toward whom the famished soldier drew near did not fly but lay flat on the ground and took aim at the one who was coming on. When he believed he was within gunshot he fired. The other was not hit and continued to advance and, cocking his gun in turn, killed his comrade.

"Then from the entire horizon the others rushed to seek their share. And he who had killed the fallen man, cutting the corpse into pieces, distributed it.

"Then they once more placed themselves at fixed distances, these irreconcilable allies, preparing for the next murder which would bring them together.

"For two days they lived on this human flesh, which they divided among each other. Then the famine came back, and he who had killed the first man began killing afresh. And again, like a butcher, he cut up the corpse and offered it to his comrades, keeping only his own portion of it. The retreat of cannibals continued. The last Frenchman Pobéguin was massacred at the side of a well the very night before the supplies arrived.

"Do you understand now what I mean by the horrible?"

This was the story told us a few nights ago by General de G———.

THE FIRST SNOWFALL

The long promenade of La Croisette runs in a curve up to the edge of the blue water. Over there, at the right, the Esterel advances far into the sea. It obstructs the view, shutting in the horizon with the pretty southern aspect of its peaked, numerous and fantastic summits.

At the left, the isles of Sainte-Marguerite and Saint-Honorat, lying in the water, present long aisles of fir trees.

And all along the great gulf, all along the tall mountains that encircle Cannes, the white villa residences seem to be sleeping in the sunlight. You can see them from a distance, the bright houses, scattered from the top to the bottom of the mountains, dotting the dark greenery with specks of snow.

Those near the water open their gates on the vast promenade which is lashed by the quiet waves. The air is soft and balmy. It is one of those days when in this southern climate the chill of winter is not felt. Above the walls of the gardens may be seen orange trees and citron trees full of golden fruit. Ladies advance with slow steps over the sand of the avenue, followed by children rolling hoops or chatting with gentlemen.

A young lady has just passed out through the door of her coquettish little house facing La Croisette. She stops for a moment to gaze at the promenaders, smiles and, with the gait of one utterly enfeebled, makes her way toward an empty bench right in front of the sea. Fatigued after having gone twenty paces, she sits down, out of breath. Her pale face seems that of a dead woman. She coughs and raises to her lips her transparent fingers, as if to stop those shakings that exhaust her.

She gazes at the sky full of sunshine and at the swallows, at the zigzag summits of the Esterel over there and at the sea, quite close to her, so blue, so calm, so beautiful.

She smiles still and murmurs:

"Oh, how happy I am!"

She knows, however, that she is going to die, that she will never see the spring-time, that in a year, along the same promenade, these same people who pass before her now will come again to breathe the warm air of this charming spot, with their children a little bigger, with their hearts all filled with hopes, with tenderness, with happiness, while at the bottom of an oak coffin the poor flesh which is left to her still today will have fallen into a condition of rottenness, leaving only her bones lying in the silk robe which she has selected for a winding sheet.

She will be no more. Everything in life will go on as before for others. For her life will be over—over forever. She will be no more. She smiles and inhales as well as she can with her diseased lungs, the perfumed air of the gardens.

And she sinks into a reverie.

She recalls the past. She had been married four years ago to a Norman gentle-man. He was a strong young man, bearded, healthy looking, with wide shoulders, narrow mind and joyous disposition.

They had been united through worldly motives which she did not quite understand. She would willingly have said "Yes." She did say "Yes" with a movement of the head in order not to thwart her father and mother. She was a Parisian, gay and full of the joy of living.

Her husband brought her home to his Norman château. It was a huge stone building surrounded by tall trees of great age. A high clump of fir trees shut out the view in front. On the right an opening in the trees presented a view of the plain which stretched out, quite flat, up to the distant farmsteads. A crossroad passed before the boundary line leading to the highroad three kilometers away.

Oh, she could remember everything—her arrival, her first day in her new abode and her isolated fate afterward.

When she stepped out of the carriage she glanced at the old building and laughingly exclaimed:

"It does not look gay!"

Her husband began to laugh in his turn and replied:

"Pooh! We get used to it! You'll see. I never feel bored in it, for my part."

That day they passed their time in embracing each other, and she did not find it too long. This lasted for the best part of three months. The days passed one after the other in insignificant yet absorbing occupations. She learned the value and the importance of the little things of life. She knew that people can interest themselves in the price of eggs which cost a few centimes more or less, according to the seasons.

It was summer. She went to the fields to see the harvest cut. The gaiety of the sunshine kept up the gaiety of her heart.

The autumn came. Her husband went hunting. He started in the morning with his two dogs, Medor and Mirza. Then she remained alone without grieving herself, moreover, at Henry's absence. She was, however, very fond of him, but he was not missed by her. When he returned home her affection was especially absorbed by the dogs. She took care of them every evening with a mother's affection, caressed them incessantly, gave them a thousand charming little names which she had no idea of applying to her husband.

He invariably told her all about his hunting. He pointed out the places where he found partridges, expressed his astonishment at not having caught any hares in Joseph Ledentu's clover, or else appeared indignant at the conduct of M. Lechapelier, of Havre, who always followed the border of his estates to shoot game that had been started by him, Henry de Parville.

She replied: "Yes indeed; it is not right," thinking of something else all the while.

The winter came, the Norman winter, cold and rainy. The endless rainstorms came down on the slates of the great many-angled roof, rising like a blade toward the sky. The road seemed like streams of mud, the country a plain of mud, and no noise could be heard save that of water falling; no movement could be seen save the whirling flight of crows rolling themselves out like a cloud, alighting on a field and then hurrying away again.

About four o'clock the army of dark, flying creatures came and perched in the tall beeches at the left of the château, emitting deafening cries. During nearly an hour they fluttered from treetop to treetop, seemed to be fighting, croaked and made the gray branches move with their black wings. She gazed at them each evening with a pressure of the heart, so deeply was she penetrated by the lugubrious melancholy of the night falling on the desolate grounds.

Then she rang for the lamp, and she drew near the fire. She burned heaps of wood without succeeding in warming the spacious apartments invaded by the humidity. She felt cold every day, everywhere, in the drawing room, at meals, in her own apartment. It seemed to her she was cold even in the marrow of her bones. He only came in to dinner; he was always hunting or else occupied with sowing seed, tilling the soil and all the work of the country.

He used to come back jolly and covered with mud, rubbing his hands while he exclaimed:

"What wretched weather!" Or else: "It is a good thing to have a fire." Or sometimes: "Well, how are you today? Do you feel in good spirits?"

He was happy, in good health, without desires, thinking of nothing else save this simple, sound and quiet life.

About December, when the snow had come, she suffered so much from the icy-cold air of the château which seemed to have acquired a chill with the centuries it had passed through, as human beings do with years, that she asked her husband one evening:

"Look here, Henry! You ought to have a hot-air plant put into the house; it would dry the walls. I assure you, I cannot warm myself from morning till night."

At first he was stunned at this extravagant idea of introducing a hot-air plant into his manor house. It would have seemed more natural to him to have his dogs fed out of his silver plate. Then he gave a tremendous laugh which made his chest heave, while he exclaimed:

"A hot-air plant here! A hot-air plant here! Ha! ha! ha! What a good joke!"

She persisted:

"I assure you, dear, I feel frozen; you don't feel it because you are always moving about, but all the same, I feel frozen."

He replied, still laughing:

"Pooh! You will get used to it, and besides, it is excellent for the health. You will only be all the better for it. We are not Parisians, damn it, to live in hothouses! And besides, the spring is quite near."

About the beginning of January a great misfortune befell her. Her father and her mother died of a carriage accident. She came to Paris for the funeral. And her mind was entirely plunged in grief on account of it for about six months.

The softness of fine days at length awakened her, and she lived a sad, drifting life of languor until autumn.

When the cold weather came back she was brought face to face for the first time with the gloomy future. What was she to do? Nothing. What was going to happen to her henceforth? Nothing. What expectation, what hope, could revive her heart? None. A doctor who was consulted declared that she would never have children.

Sharper, more penetrating still than the year before, the cold made her suffer continually.

She stretched out her shivering hands to the big flames. The glaring fire burned her face, but icy puffs seemed to slip down her back and to penetrate between the flesh and her underclothing. And she shook from head to foot. Innumerable currents of air appeared to have taken up their abode in the apartment, living, crafty currents of air, as cruel as enemies. She encountered them every moment; they were incessantly buffeting her, sometimes on the face, sometimes on the hands, sometimes on the neck, with their treacherous, frozen breath.

Once more she spoke of a hot-air plant, but her husband heard her request as if she were asking for the moon. The introduction of such an apparatus at Parville appeared to him as impossible as the discovery of the Philosopher's Stone.

Having been at Rouen on business one day, he brought back to his wife a dainty foot warmer made of copper, which he laughingly called a "portable hot-water heater," and he considered that this would prevent her henceforth from ever being cold.

Toward the end of December she understood that she could not live thus always, and she said timidly one evening at dinner:

"Listen, dear. Are we not going to spend a week or two in Paris before spring?"

He was stupefied.

"In Paris? In Paris? But what are we to do there? No, by Jove! We are better off here. What odd ideas come into your head sometimes."

She faltered:

"It might distract us a little."

He did not understand.

"What is it you want to distract you? Theaters, evening parties, dinners in town? You know well, however, that in coming here you ought not to expect any distractions of that kind!"

She saw a reproach in these words and in the tone in which they were uttered. She relapsed into silence. She was timid and gentle, without resisting power and without strength of will.

In January the cold weather returned with violence. Then the snow covered the earth.

One evening, as she watched the great whirling cloud of crows winding round the trees, she began to weep in spite of herself.

Her husband came in. He asked in great surprise:

"What is the matter with you?"

He was happy, quite happy, never having dreamed of another life or other pleasures. He had been born and had grown up in this melancholy district. He felt well in his own house, at his ease in body and mind.

He did not realize that we may desire events, have a thirst for changing pleasures; he did not understand that it does not seem natural to certain beings to remain in the same places during the four seasons; he seemed not to know that spring, summer, autumn and winter have for multitudes of persons new pleasures in new countries.

She could not say anything in reply, and she quickly dried her eyes. At last she murmured in a distracted sort of way:

"I am—I—I am a little sad—I am a little bored."

But she was seized with terror for having even said so much, and she added very quickly:

"And besides—I am—I am a little cold."

At this statement he got angry.

"Ah yes, still your idea of the hot-air plant. But look here, deuce take it, you have only had one cold since you came here."

The night came. She went up to her room, for she had insisted on having a separate apartment. She went to bed. Even in the bed she felt cold. She thought: "Is it to be like this always, always till death?"

And she thought of her husband. How could he have said this: "You have only had one cold since you came here"?

Then she must get ill; she must cough in order that he might understand what she suffered!

And she was filled with indignation, the angry indignation of a weak, a timid being.

She must cough. Then without doubt he would take pity on her. Well, she would cough; he would hear her coughing; the doctor should be called in; he would see that her husband would see.

She got up with her legs and her feet naked, and a childish idea made her smile. "I want a hot-air plant, and I must have it. I shall cough so much that he'll have to put one into the house."

And she sat down almost naked in a chair. She waited an hour, two hours. She shivered, but she did not catch cold. Then she resolved to make use of a bold expedient.

She noiselessly left her room, descended the stairs and opened the garden gate.

The earth, covered with snow, seemed dead. She abruptly thrust forward her naked foot and plunged it into the light and icy froth. A sensation of cold, painful as a wound mounted up to her heart. However, she stretched out the other leg and began to descend the steps slowly.

Then she advanced through the grass, saying to herself:

"I'll go as far as the fir trees."

She walked with quick steps, out of breath, choking every time she drove her foot through the snow.

She touched the first fir tree with her hand, as if to convince herself that she carried out her plan to the end; then she went back into the house. She believed two or three times that she was going to fall, so torpid and weak did she feel. Before going in, meanwhile, she sat in that icy snow, and she even gathered some in order to rub on her breast.

Then she went in and got into bed. It seemed to her at the end of an hour that she had a swarm of ants in her throat and that other ants were running all over her limbs. She slept, however.

Next day she was coughing, and she could not get up.

She got inflammation of the lungs. She became delirious, and in her delirium she asked for a hot-air plant. The doctor insisted on having one put in. Henry yielded, but with an irritated repugnance.

She could not be cured. The lungs, severely attacked, made those who attended on her uneasy about her life.

"If she remains here she will not last as long as the next cold weather," said the doctor.

She was sent to the south. She came to Cannes, recognized the sun, loved the sea and breathed the air of orange blossoms. Then in the spring she returned north. But she lived with the fear of being cured, with the fear of the long winters of Normandy, and as soon as she was better she opened her window by night while thinking of the sweet banks of the Mediterranean. And now she was going to die. She knew it and yet she was contented.

She unfolds a newspaper which she had not already opened and reads this heading:

The First Snow in Paris

After this she shivers and yet smiles. She looks across the Esterel which is turning rose colored under the setting sun. She looks at the vast blue sea, so very blue also, and rises up and returns to the house with slow steps, only stopping to cough, for she had remained out too long, and she has caught cold, a slight cold.

She finds a letter from her husband. She opens it, still smiling, and she reads:

MY DEAR LOVE: *I hope you are going on well and that you do not regret too much our beautiful district. We have had for some days past a good frost which announces snow. For my part, I adore this weather, and you understand that I am keeping that cursed hot-air plant of yours going——*

She ceases reading, quite happy at the thought that she has had her hot-air plant. Her right hand, which holds the letter, falls down slowly over her knees, while she raises her left hand to her mouth, as if to calm the obstinate cough which is tearing her chest.

THE LEGACY

Although it was not yet ten o'clock, the employees were pouring in like waves through the great doorway of the Ministry of Marine, having come in haste from every corner of Paris, for the first of the year was approaching, the time for renewed zeal—and for promotions. A noise of hurrying footsteps filled the vast building, which was as tortuous as a labyrinth and honeycombed with inextricable passages pierced by innumerable doors opening into the various offices.

Each one entered his particular room, pressed the hands of his colleagues who had already arrived, threw off his coat, put on his office jacket, and seated himself before the table, where a pile of papers awaited him. Then they went for news into the neighboring offices. They asked whether their chief had arrived, if he was in an agreeable humor, and if the day's mail was a heavy one.

The clerk in charge of "general matter," M. César Cachelin, an old noncommissioned officer of the marine infantry, who had become chief clerk by priority of office, registered in a big book all the documents as they were brought in by the messenger. Opposite him the copying clerk, old Father Savon, a stupid old fellow, celebrated throughout the whole ministry for his conjugal misfortunes, copied in a slow hand a dispatch from the chief, sitting with his body held sidewise and his eyes askew, in the attitude of the careful copyist.

M. Cachelin, a big man, whose short, white hair stood up like a brush on his head, talked all the time while performing his daily work: "Thirty-two dispatches from Toulon. That port gives us as much as any four others put together."

(Copyright, 1923, by Alfred A. Knopf, Inc.)

Then he asked the old man Savon the question he put to him every morning: "Well, Father Savon, how is Madame?"

The old man, without stopping his work, replied: "You know very well, M. Cachelin, that subject is a most painful one to me."

Then the chief clerk laughed as he laughed every day at hearing the same phrase.

The door opened and M. Maze entered. He was a handsome, dark young fellow dressed with an exaggerated elegance, who thought his position beneath his dignity and his person and manners above his position. He wore large rings, a heavy gold watch chain, a monocle (which he discarded while at work), and he made a frequent movement of his wrists in order to bring into view his cuffs, ornamented with great shining buttons.

At the door he asked: "Much work today?" M. Cachelin replied: "It is always Toulon which keeps sending in. One can easily see that the first of the year is at hand, from the way they are hustling down there."

But another employee, a great joker, always in high spirits, appeared in his turn and said, laughing:

"We are not hustling at all, are we?" Then taking out his watch he added: "Seven minutes to ten and every man at his post! By George, what do you think of that? and I'll wager anything that His Dignity, M. Lesable, arrived at nine o'clock—at the same hour as our illustrious chief."

The chief clerk ceased writing, put his pen behind his ear, and, leaning his elbow on the desk, said: "Oh! there is a man for you! If he does not succeed, it will not be for want of trying."

M. Pitolet, seating himself on the corner of the table and swinging his leg, replied:

"But he will succeed, Papa Cachelin; he will succeed, you may be sure. I will bet you twenty francs to a sou that he will be chief within ten years."

M. Maze, who rolled a cigarette while warming his calves before the fire, said:

"Pshaw! for my part I would rather remain all my life on a salary of twenty-four hundred francs than wear myself to a skeleton the way he is doing."

Pitolet turned on his heels and said in a bantering tone: "But that does not prevent you, my dear fellow, from being here on this twentieth of December before ten o'clock."

The other shrugged his shoulders with an air of indifference. "Hang it all! I do not want everybody to walk over my head, either! Since you come here to see the sun rise, I am going to do it, too, however much I may deplore your officiousness. From doing that to calling the chief 'dear master,' as Lesable does, and staying until half past six and then carrying work home with you is a long way. Besides, I am in society and I have other demands upon my time."

M. Cachelin had ceased his registering and begun to dream, his eyes fixed on vacancy. At last he asked: "Do you believe that he will get an increase again this year?"

Pitolet cried: "I will bet you ten to one he gets it. He is not wearing himself out for nothing."

And so they talked of the eternal question of promotion, which for a month had excited the whole hive of clerks from the ground floor to the roof.

They calculated chances, computed figures, compared their various claims to promotion, and waxed indignant over former injustices. These discussions lasted from morning until evening, and the next day were begun all over again, with the same reasons, the same arguments, the same words.

A new clerk entered, a little, pale, sick-looking man, M. Boissel, who lived as in a romance of Alexandre Dumas père. Everything with him was an extraordinary adventure, and he recounted every morning to his friend Pitolet his strange encounters of the previous evening, imaginary scenes enacted in his house, strange cries uttered in the street which caused him to open his window at half past three in the morning. Every day he had separated combatants, stopped runaway horses, rescued women from danger; and, although of a deplorably weak constitution he talked unceasingly, in a slow and satisfied tone, of exploits accomplished by his strong arm.

As soon as he understood that they were talking of Lesable he declared: "Some day I will give that little pup his deserts; and if he ever walks over my head, I'll give him something that will prevent him from trying again."

Maze, continuing to smoke, sneered: "You would do well, then, to begin at once, for I hear on good authority that you are to be set aside this year for Lesable."

Boissel raised his hand. "I swear that if——"

The door opened once more, and a dapper little man wearing the side whiskers of an officer of marine or lawyer, and a high, stiff collar, who spoke his words rapidly as though he could not take the time to finish what he had to say, entered quickly with a preoccupied manner. He shook hands all around with the air of a man who had no leisure for dallying, and, approaching the chief clerk said: "My dear Cachelin, will you give me the Chapelou papers, rope yarn, Toulon A.T.V., 1875?"

The clerk rose, reached for a portfolio above his head, took out a package of sealed documents wrapped in blue linen, and presenting them said: "There, M. Lesable; you remember the chief took three dispatches from their package yesterday."

"Yes, I have them. Thanks," and the young man went out hurriedly.

Hardly had he gone when Maze ejaculated:

"Well! what an air! One would swear he was already chief."

And Pitolet replied: "Patience, patience; he will be before any of us."

M. Cachelin had not resumed his writing. A fixed thought seemed to have taken possession of him. At last he said: "He has a fine future, that boy!"

But Maze murmured in a disdainful tone: "For those who think the ministry is a career—yes. For the others it is a little——"

Pitolet interrupted him: "Perhaps you intend to become ambassador?"

The other made an impatient gesture. "It is not a question of me. I can take care of myself. That has nothing to do with the fact that the position of the head of a department will never be anything very much."

Father Savon, the copyist, had never ceased his work. But for some little time he had been dipping his pen in the inkstand, then wiping it vigorously on the sponge which stood in a little glass of water on his desk, without being able to trace a letter. The black liquid slipped along the point of the metal and fell in round spots on the paper. The good man, driven to despair as sheet after sheet of paper was thus spoiled, said in a deep and sorrowful voice:

"Here is more adulterated ink!"

A shout of laughter came from every mouth. Cachelin shook the table with his stomach. Maze bent double, as though he were going up the chimney backward.

Pitolet stamped and roared and waved his hands in the air, and even Boissel was almost suffocated, although he generally looked at these things on the tragic rather than the comic side.

But Father Savon, wiping his pen on the tail of his overcoat, said: "There is nothing to laugh at. I have to go over my whole work two or three times."

He took from his box another sheet of paper, laid his wax sheet over it, and commenced again at the beginning: "Monsieur le Ministre and dear colleague—" The pen now held the ink and traced the letters neatly. The old man settled down into his oblique posture and continued his copy.

The others had not stopped laughing. They were fairly choking. For six months they had played the same game on the poor old fellow, who had never detected it. It consisted in pouring several drops of oil on the damp sponge used for wiping pens. The metal, thus becoming coated with liquid grease, would not take the ink, and the perplexed copying clerk would pass hours in using boxes of pens and bottles of ink, and finally declare that the supplies of the department were becoming perfectly worthless.

Then the jokers would torment the old man in other ways. They put gunpowder in his tobacco, poured drugs into his drinking water, and made him believe that, since the Commune, the majority of articles for general use had been adulterated by the Socialists to put the government in the wrong and bring about a revolution. He had conceived a terrible hatred against anarchists, whom he believed to be concealed everywhere, and had a mysterious fear of an unknown woman, veiled and formidable.

A sharp ring of the bell sounded in the corridor. They well knew the emphatic ring of their chief, M. Torchebeuf, and each one sprang toward the door that he might regain his own compartment.

Cachelin returned to his work. Then he laid down his pen again and took his head in his hands and began to think.

He turned over in his mind an idea which had tormented him for some time. An old noncommissioned officer of the marine infantry, retired after receiving three wounds, one at Senegal and two at Cochin China, who had been given a position in the ministry as an exceptional favor, he had had to endure many miseries, many hardships, and many griefs in his long career as an insignificant subordinate. He considered authority, official authority, as the finest thing in the world. The head of a department seemed to him an exceptional being, living in a higher sphere; and the employee of whom he heard it said: "He is a sharp one; he will get there yet," appeared to him of another race, another nature, than himself.

He had therefore for his colleague Lesable a high respect which approached veneration, and he cherished the secret desire, which was never absent from his mind, to have him marry his daughter.

She would be rich one day, very rich. This was known throughout the entire ministry, for his sister, Mlle. Cachelin, possessed a million, a clear, cool million, acquired through love, they said, but purified by belated piety.

This ancient spinster, who had led a gay life in her youth, had retired with five hundred thousand francs, which she had more than doubled in eighteen years, thanks to her ferocious economy and more than frugal habits. She had lived for a long time with her brother, who was a widower with one daughter, Coralie; but she did not contribute in the slightest degree to the expenses of the house, guarding and accumulating her gold, and always repeating to Cachelin: "It makes no difference, since it is all for your daughter; but marry her quickly, for I want to see my little nephews around me. It is she who will give me the joy of embracing a child of our blood."

This was well understood at the office, and suitors were not lacking for Coralie's hand. It was said that Maze himself, the handsome Maze, the lion of the bureau, hovered around Father Cachelin with a palpable intent. But the former sergeant, who had roamed through all latitudes, wanted a young man with a future, a young man who would be chief, and who would be able to make some return to him, the old clerk. Lesable suited him to a nicety, and he cast about in his mind for a means of attaching him to himself.

All of a sudden he sat upright, striking his hands together. He had found it. He well understood the weakness of each one of his colleagues. Lesable could be approached only through his vanity, his professional vanity. He would go to him and demand his protection as one goes to a senator or a deputy—as one goes to a high personage.

Not having had any promotion for five years, Cachelin considered himself as certain to obtain one this year. He would make it appear then that he owed it to Lesable, and would invite him to dinner as a means of thanking him.

As soon as his project was conceived he began to put it into execution. He took off his office jacket, put on his coat, and, gathering up all the registered papers which concerned the services of his colleague, he betook himself to the office which Lesable occupied all alone, by special favor, because of his zeal and the importance of his functions.

The young man was writing at a great table, covered with bundles of documents and loose papers numbered with red or blue figures.

As soon as he saw the chief clerk enter, he said in a familiar tone which also betokened consideration: "Well, my dear fellow, do you bring me a lot of business?"

"Yes, a good deal. And then I want to speak to you."

"Sit down, my friend; I am listening."

Cachelin seated himself, coughed, put on a troubled look, and finally said in a despondent tone:

"This is what brings me here, M. Lesable. I will not beat about the bush. I will be frank like an old soldier. I have come to demand a service of you."

"What is it?"

"In a few words, I wish very much to be promoted this year. I have nobody to help me, and I have thought of you."

Lesable reddened somewhat. He was surprised, flattered, and filled with a pleased confusion. However, he replied:

"But I am nobody here, my friend. I am much less than you, who are going to be principal clerk. I can do nothing. Believe me that if——"

Cachelin cut him short with respectful brusqueness: "Oh, nonsense. You have the ear of the chief, and if you speak a word for me I shall get it. Remember that in eighteen months I shall have the right to retire, and I shall be just five hundred francs to the bad if I obtain nothing on the first of January. I know very well that they say: 'Cachelin is all right; his sister has a million.' It is true enough that my sister has a million, but she doesn't give any of it away. It is also true that her fortune is for my daughter, but my daughter and I are two different persons. I shall be in a nice fix if, when my daughter and my son-in-law are rolling in their carriage, I have nothing to eat. You see my position, do you not?"

Lesable agreed. "It is true—what you say is very true. Your son-in-law may not be well disposed toward you. Besides, one is always more at ease when owing nothing to anybody. Well, I promise you I shall do my best; I shall speak to the chief, place the case before him, and shall insist if it be necessary. Count on me!"

Cachelin rose, took the hands of his colleague, and, pressing them hard while he shook them in military fashion, stammered: "Thank you, thank you; believe me, if ever I have the opportunity—if I can ever——" He stopped, not being able to finish what he had begun, and went away making the corridor resound with the rhythmical tread of an old trooper.

But he heard from afar the sharp ring of a bell and he began to run. He knew that ring. It was the chief, M. Torchebeuf, who wanted him.

Eight days later Cachelin found one morning on his desk a sealed letter, which contained the following:

"MY DEAR COLLEAGUE: *I am happy to announce to you that the minister, at the instance of our director and our chief, yesterday signed your nomination to the position of principal clerk. You will receive tomorrow your official notification. Until then you know nothing, you understand?*

> Yours ever,
> LESABLE."

César ran at once to the office of his young colleague, thanked him, excused himself, offered his everlasting devotion, overwhelmed him with his gratitude.

It was known on the morrow that M. Lesable and Cachelin had each been promoted. The other employees must wait another year, receiving by way of compensation a gratuity which varied from one hundred and fifty to three hundred francs.

M. Boissel declared that he would lie in wait for Lesable at the corner of the street at midnight some night and give him a drubbing which would leave its mark. The other clerks kept silent.

The following Monday, on his arrival, Cachelin went to the office of his protector, entered with solemnity, and in a ceremonious tone said: "I hope that you will do me the honor to dine with us during the New Year holidays. You may choose the day yourself."

The young man, somewhat surprised, raised his head and looked his colleague full in the face. Then he replied without removing his eyes, that he might read the thoughts of the other: "But, my dear fellow, you see—all my evenings are promised here for some time to come."

Cachelin insisted in a good-humored tone: "Oh, but, I say, you will not disappoint us by refusing, after the service that you have rendered me. I beg you in the name of my family and in mine."

Lesable hesitated, perplexed. He had understood well enough, but he did not know what to reply, not having had time to reflect and to weigh the pros and the cons. At last he thought: "I commit myself to nothing by going to dinner," and he accepted with a satisfied air, choosing the Saturday following. He added, smiling: "So that I shall not have to get up too soon the next morning."

II

M. Cachelin lived in a small apartment on the fifth floor of a house at the upper end of the Rue Rochechouart. There was a balcony from which one could see all Paris, and three rooms, one for his sister, one for his daughter, and one for himself. The dining room served also for a parlor.

He occupied himself during the whole week in preparing for this dinner. The menu was discussed at great length, in order that they might have a repast which should be at the same time homelike and elegant. The following was finally decided upon: A consommé with eggs, shrimps and sausage for hors d'œuvre, a lobster, a fine chicken, preserved peas, a *pâté de foie gras*, a salad, an ice, and dessert.

The *foie gras* was ordered from a neighboring pork butcher with the injunction to furnish the best quality. The pot alone cost three francs and a half.

For the wine, Cachelin applied to the wine merchant at the corner who supplied him with the red beverage with which he ordinarily quenched his thirst. He did not want to go to a big dealer, reasoning thus: "The small dealers find few occasions to sell their best brands. On this account they keep them a long time in their cellars, and they are therefore better."

He came home at the earliest possible hour on Saturday to assure himself that all was ready. The maid who opened the door for him was red as a tomato, for she had lighted her fire at midday through fear of not being ready in time, and had roasted her face at it all day. Emotion also excited her. He entered the dining room to inspect everything. In the middle of the little room the round table made a great white spot under the bright light of a lamp covered with a green shade.

The four plates were almost concealed by napkins folded in the form of an archbishop's miter by Mlle. Cachelin, the aunt, and were flanked by knives and forks of white metal. In front of each stood two glasses, one large and one small. César found this insufficient at a glance, and he called: "Charlotte!"

The door at the left opened and a little old woman appeared. Older than her brother by ten years, she had a narrow face framed with white ringlets. She did these up in papers every night.

Her thin voice seemed too weak for her little bent body, and she moved with a slightly dragging step and tired gestures.

They had said of her when she was young: "What a dear little creature!"

She was now a shriveled-up old woman, very clean because of her early training, headstrong, spoiled, narrow-minded, fastidious, and easily irritated. Having become very devout, she seemed to have totally forgotten the adventures of her past.

She asked: "What do you want?"

He replied: "I find that two glasses do not make much of a show. If we could have champagne—it would not cost me more than three or four francs; we have the glasses already, and it would entirely change the aspect of the table."

Mlle. Charlotte replied: "I do not see the use of going to that expense. But you are paying; it does not concern me."

He hesitated, seeking to convince himself:

"I assure you it would be much better. And then, with the cake it would make things more lively." This decided him. He took his hat and went downstairs, returning in five minutes with a bottle under his arm which bore a large white label, ornamented with an enormous coat of arms, the words: "Grand vin mousseux de Champagne du Comte de Chatel-Rénovau."

Cachelin declared: "It cost only three francs, and the man says it is delicious."

He took the champagne glasses from the cupboard and placed them before each place.

The door at the right opened. His daughter entered. She was a tall girl with firm, rosy flesh—a handsome daughter of a strong race. She had chestnut hair and blue eyes. A simple gown outlined her round and supple figure; her voice was strong, almost the voice of a man, with those deep notes which make the nerves vibrate. She cried: "Heavens! Champagne! What luck!" clapping her hands like a child.

Her father said to her: "I wish you to be particularly nice to this gentleman; he has done such a lot for me."

She began to laugh—a sonorous laugh, which said: "I know."

The bell in the vestibule rang. The doors opened and closed and Lesable appeared.

He wore a black coat, a white cravat, and white gloves. He created a stir. Cachelin sprang forward, embarrassed and delighted: "But, my dear fellow, this is among ourselves. See me—I am in ordinary dress."

The young man replied: "I know, you told me so; but I never go out in the evening without my dress coat." He saluted, his opera hat under his arm, a flower in his buttonhole. César presented him: "My sister, Mlle. Charlotte; my daughter Coralie, whom at home we call Cora."

Everybody bowed. Cachelin continued: "We have no salon. It is rather troublesome, but one gets used to it."

Lesable replied: "It is charming."

Then he was relieved of his hat, which he wished to hang up, and he began immediately to draw off his gloves.

They sat down and looked at one another across the table, and no one said anything more until Cachelin asked: "Did the chief remain late tonight? I left very early to help the ladies."

Lesable replied in a careless tone: "No, we went away together, because we were obliged to discuss the matter of the payment for the canvases at Brest. It is a very complicated affair, which will give us a great deal of trouble."

Cachelin believed he ought to bring his sister into the conversation, and turning to her said: "It is M. Lesable who decides all the difficult questions at the office. One might say that he was the deputy chief."

The old spinster bowed politely, saying: "Oh, I know that Monsieur has great capabilities."

The maid entered, pushing open the door with her knee, and holding aloft with both hands a great soup tureen. Then the master of the house cried: "Come— dinner! Sit there, M. Lesable, between my sister and my daughter. I hope you are not afraid of the ladies," and the dinner began.

Lesable made himself agreeable, with a little air of self-sufficiency, almost of condescension, and he glanced now and then at the young girl, astonished at her freshness, at her beautiful, appetizing health. Mlle. Charlotte showed her best side, knowing the intentions of her brother, and she took part in the conversation so long as it was confined to commonplace topics. Cachelin was radiant; he talked and joked in a loud voice while he poured out the wine bought an hour previous at the store on the corner: "A glass of this little Burgundy, M. Lesable. I do not say that it is anything remarkable, but it is good; it is from the cellar and it is pure—I can say that much. We get it from some friends down there."

The young girl said nothing; a little red, a little shy, she was awed by the presence of this man, whose thoughts she suspected.

When the lobster appeared, César declared: "Here comes a personage whose acquaintance I shall be glad to make."

Lesable, smiling, told a story of a writer who had called the lobster "the cardinal of the seas," not knowing that before being cooked the animal was a dark greenish black. Cachelin laughed with all his might, repeating: "Ha, ha, ha! that is first rate!" But Mlle. Charlotte, becoming serious, said sharply:

"I do not see anything amusing in that. That gentleman was an improper person. I understand all kinds of pleasantries, but I am opposed to anything which casts ridicule on the clergy in my presence."

The young man, who wished to please the old maid, profited by this occasion to make a profession of the Catholic faith. He spoke of the bad taste of those who treated great truths with lightness. And in conclusion he said: "For myself I respect and venerate the religion of my fathers; I have been brought up in it, and I will remain in it till my death."

Cachelin laughed no longer. He rolled little crumbs of bread between his finger and thumb while he murmured: "That's right, that's right." Then he changed the conversation, and, with an impulse natural to those who follow the same routine every day, he said: "Our handsome Maze—must have been furious at not having been promoted?"

Lesable smiled. "Well, why not? To everyone according to his deserts." And they continued talking about the ministry, which interested everybody, for the two women knew the employees almost as well as Cachelin himself, through hearing them spoken of every day.

Mlle. Charlotte was particularly pleased to hear about Boissel, on account of his romantic spirit and the adventures he was always telling about, while Cora was secretly interested in the handsome Maze. They had never seen either of the men, however.

Lesable talked about them with a superior air, as a minister might have done in speaking of his staff.

"Maze is not lacking in a certain kind of merit, but when one wishes to accomplish anything it is necessary to work harder than he does. He is fond of society and of pleasure. All that distracts the mind; he will never advance much on this account. He will be an assistant secretary, perhaps, thanks to the influence he commands, but nothing more. As for Pitolet, he is a good clerk, I must say. He has a superficial elegance which cannot be gainsaid, but nothing deep. There is a young man whom one could never put at the head of an important bureau, but who can always be utilized by an intelligent chief who would lay out his work for him."

"And M. Boissel?" asked Mlle. Charlotte.

Lesable shrugged his shoulders: "A poor chap, a poor chap. He can see nothing in its proper proportions, and is continually imagining wonderful stories while half-asleep. To us he is of no earthly use."

Cachelin began to laugh. "But the best of all," he declared, "is old Father Savon."

Then everybody laughed.

After that they talked of the theaters and the different plays of the year. Lesable judged the dramatic literature of the day with the same authority, concisely classifying the authors, determining the strength and weakness of each, with the assurance of a man who believes himself to be infallible and universal.

They had finished the roast. César now uncovered the pot of foie gras with the most delicate precautions, which made one imagine the contents to be something wonderful. He said: "I do not know if this one will be a success, but generally they are perfect. We get them from a cousin who lives in Strasbourg."

With respectful deliberation each one ate the butcher's pâté in its little yellow pot.

But disaster came with the ice. It was a sauce, a soup, a clear liquid which floated in the dish. The little maid had begged the pastry cook's boy, who brought the ice at seven o'clock, to take it out of the mold himself, fearing that she would not know how.

Cachelin, in despair, wished to make her carry it back again; then he calmed himself at the thought of the Twelfth-night cake, which he divided with great mystery as though it contained a prime secret. All fixed their gaze on the symbolic cake, then Mlle. Charlotte directed that each one close his eyes while taking a piece.

Who would be the king? A childish, expectant smile was on the lips of everyone. M. Lesable uttered a little "ah" of astonishment, and showed between his thumb and forefinger a great white bean still covered with pastry. Cachelin began to applaud, then cried: "Choose the queen! choose the queen!"

The king hesitated an instant only. Would it not be a politic act to choose Mlle. Charlotte? She would be flattered, brought over, his friend ever after! Then he reflected that it was really Mlle. Cora for whom he had been invited, and that he would seem like a ninny in choosing the aunt. He turned toward his youthful neighbor, and, handing her the royal bean said: "Mademoiselle, will you permit me to offer it to you?" And they looked one another in the face for the first time.

She replied: "Thank you, monsieur," and received the gage of sovereignty.

He thought: "She is enormously pretty, this girl. Her eyes are superb. She is gay, too, if I am not mistaken!"

A sharp detonation made the two women jump. Cachelin had just opened the champagne, which escaped from the bottle and ran over the tablecloth. Then the glasses were filled with the frothy stuff and the host declared: "It is of good quality, one can see that." But as Lesable was about to drink to prevent his glass from running over, César cried: "The king drinks! the king drinks! the king drinks!" And Mlle. Charlotte, also excited, squeaked in her thin voice: "The king drinks! the king drinks!"

Lesable emptied his glass with composure, and replacing it on the table said: "You see I am not lacking in assurance." Then turning toward Mlle. Cora he said: "It is yours, mademoiselle!"

She wished to drink, but everybody having cried: "The queen drinks! the queen drinks!" she blushed, began to laugh, and put the glass down again.

The end of the dinner was full of gaiety; the king showed himself most attentive and gallant toward the queen. Then when they had finished the liqueurs, Cachelin announced:

"We will have the table cleared away now to give us more room. If it is not raining, we can go to the balcony for a few minutes." He wanted Lesable to see the view, although it was night.

The glass door was thrown open. A moist, warm breeze entered. It was mild outdoors as in the month of April. They all mounted the step which separated the dining room from the large balcony. They could see nothing but a vague glimmer hovering over the great city, like the gilt halos which they put on the heads of the saints. In some spots this light seemed more brilliant, and Cachelin began to explain:

"See, that is the Eden blazing down there. Look at the line of the boulevards. Isn't it wonderful, how you can distinguish them! In the daytime it is splendid, this view. You would have to travel a long way before you saw anything finer!"

Lesable was leaning on the iron balustrade, by the side of Cora, who gazed into the void, silent, distraught, seized of a sudden with one of those melancholy languors which sometimes oppress the soul. Mlle. Charlotte returned to the room, fearing the damp. Cachelin continued to speak, his outstretched hand indicating the places where they would find the Invalides, the Trocadéro, the Arc de Triomphe.

Lesable in a low voice asked: "And you, Mlle. Cora, do you like to look at Paris from this height?"

She gave a little shiver, as though she had been dreaming and answered: "I? Yes, especially at night. I think of all the things which are happening there in front of us. How many happy people and how many who are unhappy in all these houses! If one could see everything, how many things one might learn!"

He came a little nearer, until their elbows and their shoulders touched:

"By moonlight this should be like fairyland."

She murmured: "Ah, yes, indeed. One would say it was an engraving by Gustave Doré. What a pleasure it would be to take a long walk on these roofs."

Then he questioned her regarding her tastes, her dreams, her pleasures. And she replied without embarrassment, after the manner of an intelligent, sensible girl—one who was not more imaginative than was necessary.

He found her full of good sense, and he said to himself that it would be wonderfully sweet to put his arm about that firm, round figure and to press a score of little slow kisses, as one drinks in little sips of excellent brandy, on that fresh cheek, near the ear, just where a ray from the lamp fell upon it. He felt himself attracted, moved by the sensation of the proximity of a beautiful woman, by the thirst for her ripe and virginal flesh, and by that delicate seductive influence a young girl possesses. It seemed to him he could remain there for hours, nights, weeks, forever, leaning towards her, feeling her near to him, thrilled by the charm of that contact. And something like a poetic sentiment stirred his heart in the face of that great Paris, spread out before him, brilliant in her nocturnal life, her life of pleasure and debauchery. It seemed to him that he dominated the enormous city, that he hovered over it; and he thought how delicious it would be to recline every evening on such a balcony beside a woman, to love her and be loved by her, to press her to his breast, far above the vast city, and all the earthly loves it contained, above all the vulgar satisfactions, and common desires, near to the stars.

There are nights when even the least exalted souls begin to dream, and Lesable felt as though he was spreading his wings for the first time. Perhaps he was a little tipsy.

Cachelin went inside to get his pipe and came back lighting it. "I know," he said, "that you do not smoke or I would offer you a cigarette. There is nothing more delightful than to smoke here. If I had to live on the ground floor I should die. We could do it if we wanted to, for the house belongs to my sister, as well as the two neighboring ones—the one on the right and the one on the left. She has a nice little revenue from these alone. They did not cost a great deal, either, when she bought them." And turning toward the window he cried: "How much did you pay for the ground here, Charlotte?"

Then the thin voice of the old spinster was heard speaking. Lesable could only hear broken fragments of the sentences: "In 1863—thirty-five francs—built afterward—the three houses—a banker—sold for at least five hundred thousand francs——"

She talked of her fortune with the complacency of an old soldier who reels off stories of his campaigns. She enumerated her purchases, the high offers she had since had, the rise in values, etc.

Lesable, immediately interested, turned about, resting now his back against the balustrade of the balcony. But as he still caught only tantalizing scraps of what the old woman said, he brusquely left his young companion and went within where he might hear everything; and seating himself beside Mlle. Charlotte conversed with her for a long time on the probable increase in rents and what income should accrue from money well placed in stocks and bonds. He left toward midnight, promising to return.

A month later there was nothing talked about in the whole office but the marriage of Jacques Léopold Lesable with Mlle. Céleste Coralie Cachelin.

III

The young people began housekeeping on the same floor with Cachelin and Mlle. Charlotte, in an apartment similar to theirs from which the tenant was expelled.

A certain uneasiness, however, disturbed the mind of Lesable: the aunt had not wished to assure her heritage to Cora by any definitive act. She had, however, consented to swear "before God" that her will was made and deposited with Maître Belhomme, the notary. She had promised, moreover, that her entire fortune should revert to her niece on one sole condition. Being pressed to reveal this condition she refused to explain herself, but averred with a little amiable smile that it was very easy of fulfillment.

Notwithstanding these explanations and the stubbornness of the pious old woman, Lesable thought he ought to have further assurance; but, as the young woman pleased him greatly, his desire triumphed over his incertitude, and he yielded to the determined efforts of Cachelin.

Now he was happy, notwithstanding that he was always tormented by a doubt, and he loved his wife, who had in no wise disappointed his expectations. His life flowed along, tranquil and monotonous. He became, in several weeks, perfectly inured to his new position of married man, and he continued to be the same faithful and accomplished employee as formerly.

A year rolled away. The first of the year came round again. He did not receive, to his great surprise, the promotion on which he had counted. Maze and Pitolet alone passed to the grade above, and Boissel declared confidentially to Cachelin that he had promised himself to give his two fellow clerks a good thrashing at the main entrance before everybody. But he did nothing.

For a whole week Lesable did not sleep a wink because of the anguish he felt at not having been promoted, despite his zeal. He had been working like a dog; he had filled the place of the assistant chief, M. Rabut, who had been in the hospital of Val-de-Grâce for nine months; he had been coming to the office at half past eight every morning, remaining until half past six in the evening. What more could they ask? If they could not appreciate such faithful service he would do like the others, that was all. To everyone according to his deserts. How could M. Torchebeuf, who had always treated him like a son, have sacrificed him thus? He wanted to get at the bottom of the thing. He would go to the chief and have an explanation with him.

On Monday morning, therefore, before the arrival of his comrades, he knocked at the door of that potentate.

A sharp voice cried: "Come in!" He entered.

Seated before a great table strewn with papers, his little body bent over a writing pad which his big head almost touched, M. Torchebeuf was busily writing. On seeing his favorite employee he said cheerfully: "Good morning, Lesable; you are well?"

The young man replied: "Good morning, dear master, I am very well; and you?"

The chief ceased writing and turned about in his revolving chair. His frail, slender body, clad in a black surtout of severe cut, seemed ridiculously disproportioned to the great leather-covered chair. The brilliant rosette of an officer of the Legion of Honor, a hundred times too large for the small body which it decorated, burned like a live coal upon his narrow chest. His skull was of considerable size, as though the entire development of the individual had been at the top, after the manner of mushrooms.

His chin was pointed, his cheeks hollow, his eyes protruding, and his great bulging forehead was surmounted with white hair which he wore thrown backward.

M. Torchebeuf said: "Sit down, my friend, and tell me what brings you here."

Toward all the other clerks he displayed a military brusqueness, considering himself to be their captain, for the ministry was to him as a great vessel, the flagship of all the French fleet.

Lesable, somewhat moved, a little pale, stammered: "Dear master, I come to ask you if I have been lacking in any way."

"Certainly not, my dear fellow; why do you ask me such a question?"

"Because I was a little surprised at not receiving my promotion this year, as in former years. Allow me to finish my explanation, dear master, and pardon my audacity. I know that I have obtained from you exceptional favors and unlooked-for advantages. I know that promotions are only made, as a general thing, every two or three years; but permit me to remind you that I furnish the bureau with nearly four times the amount of work of an ordinary employee, and at least twice as much time. If, then, you put in the balance the result of labor and the remuneration, you will certainly find the one far outweighs the other."

He had carefully prepared this speech, which he judged to be excellent.

M. Torchebeuf, surprised, hesitated before replying. At length he said in a rather cool tone: "Although it is not admissible, on principle, that these subjects should be discussed between chief and employee, I am willing to reply for this once to your question regarding your very meritorious services.

"I proposed your name for promotion as in preceding years. The chief, however, crossed out your name on the ground that by your marriage your fortune was assured. You are to come into an inheritance such as your modest colleagues can never hope to possess. Is it not, therefore, just to take into consideration the condition of each one? You will be rich, very rich. Three hundred francs more per year will be as nothing to you, whereas this little increase will count for a great deal in the pockets of the others. There, my friend, you have the reason why you remain stationary this year."

Lesable, irritated and covered with confusion, retired.

That evening at dinner he was disagreeable to his wife. She, however, was gay and pleasant as usual. Although she was of an even temper, she was headstrong, and when she desired anything greatly she never yielded her point. She possessed no longer for him the sensual charm of the early days, and although he still looked upon her with the eye of desire, for she was fresh and charming, he experienced at times that disillusion so near to estrangement which soon comes to two beings who live a common life. The thousand trivial or grotesque details of existence, the loose toilettes of the morning, the common linen robe-de-chambre, the faded peignoir, for they were not rich, and all the necessary home duties which are seen too near at hand in a poor household—all these things took the glamour from marriage and withered the flower of poetry which, from a distance, is so attractive to lovers.

Aunt Charlotte also rendered herself as disagreeable as possible. She never went out, but stayed indoors and busied herself in everything which concerned the two young people. She wished everything conducted in accordance with her notions, made observations on everything, and as they had a horrible fear of offending her, they bore it all with resignation, but also with a suppressed and ever increasing exasperation.

She went through their apartment with her slow, dragging step, constantly saying in her sharp, nasal voice: "You ought to do this; you certainly ought to do that."

When the husband and wife found themselves alone together, Lesable, who was a perfect bundle of nerves, would cry out: "Your aunt is growing intolerable. I won't stand her here any longer, do you hear? I won't stand it!" And Cora would reply tranquilly: "What do you want me to do?"

Then flying into a passion he would say: "It is dreadful to have such a family!"

And she, still calm, would reply: "Yes, the family is dreadful, but the inheritance is good, isn't it? Now don't be an imbecile. You have as much interest as I in managing Aunt Charlotte."

Then he would be silent, not knowing what to say.

The aunt now harried them unceasingly on the subject of a child. She pushed Lesable into corners and hissed in his face: "My nephew, I intend that you shall be a father before I die. I want to see my little heir. You cannot make me believe that Cora was not made to be a mother. It is only necessary to look at her. When one gets married, my nephew, it is to have a family—to send out little branches. Our Holy Mother, the Church, forbids sterile marriages. I know very well that you are not rich, and that a child causes extra expense. But after me you will want for nothing. I want a little Lesable, do you understand? I want him."

When, after fifteen months of marriage, her desire was not yet realized, she began to have doubts and became very urgent; and she gave Cora in private advice

—practical advice, that of a woman who has known many things in her time, and who has still the recollection of them on occasion.

But one morning she was not able to rise from her bed, feeling very unwell. As she had never been ill before, Cachelin ran in great agitation to the door of his son-in-law: "Run quickly for Dr. Barbette," he said, "and you will tell the chief, won't you, that I shall not be at the office today."

Lesable passed an agonizing day, incapable of working himself, or of giving directions to the other clerks. M. Torchebeuf, surprised, remarked: "You are somewhat distraught today, M. Lesable." And Lesable answered nervously: "I am greatly fatigued, dear master; I have passed the entire night at the bedside of our aunt, whose condition is very serious."

The chief replied coldly: "As M. Cachelin is with her I think that should suffice. I cannot allow my bureau to be disorganized for the personal reasons of my employees."

Lesable had placed his watch on the table before him, and he waited for five o'clock with feverish impatience. As soon as the big clock in the grand court struck he hurried away, quitting the office, for the first time, at the regular hour.

He even took a cab to return home, so great was his anxiety, and he mounted the staircase at a run. The nurse opened the door; he stammered: "How is she?"

"The doctor says that she is very low."

His heart began to beat rapidly. He was greatly agitated. "Ah, indeed!"

Could she, by any chance, be going to die?

He did not dare to go into the sick woman's chamber now, and he asked that Cachelin, who was watching by her side, be called.

His father-in-law appeared immediately, opening the door with precaution. He had on his dressing gown and skullcap, as on the pleasant evenings which he passed in the corner by the fire, and he murmured in a low voice: "It's very bad, very bad. She has been unconscious since four o'clock. She even received the viaticum this afternoon."

Then Lesable felt a weakness descending into his legs, and he sat down.

"Where is my wife?"

"She is at the bedside."

"What is it the doctor says? Tell me exactly."

"He says it is a stroke. She may come out of it, but she may also die tonight."

"Do you need me? If not, I would rather not go in. It would be very painful to me to see her in this state."

"No, go to your own apartment. If there is anything new I will call you at once."

Lesable went to his own quarters. The apartment seemed to him changed—it was larger, clearer. But, as he could not keep still, he went out onto the balcony.

They were then in the last days of July, and the great sun, on the point of disappearing behind the two towers of the Trocadéro, rained fire on the immense conglomeration of roofs.

The sky, a brilliant shining red at the horizon, took on, higher up, tints of pale gold, then of yellow, then of green—a delicate green flecked with light; then it became blue—a pure and fresh blue overhead.

The swallows passed like flashes, scarcely visible, painting against the vermilion sky the curved and flying profile of their wings. And above the infinite number of houses, above the far-off country, floated a rose-tinted cloud, a vapor of fire toward which ascended, as in an apotheosis, the points of the church steeples and all the slender pinnacles of the monuments. The Arc de Triomphe appeared enormous and black against the conflagration on the horizon, and the dome of the Invalides seemed another sun fallen from the firmament upon the roof of a building.

Lesable held with his two hands to the iron railing, drinking in the air as one drinks of wine, feeling a desire to leap, to cry out, to make violent gestures, so completely was he given over to a profound and triumphant joy. Life seemed to him radiant, the future full of richness! What would he do? And he began to dream.

A noise behind him made him tremble. It was his wife. Her eyes were red, her cheeks slightly swollen: she looked tired. She bent down her forehead for him to kiss; then she said: "We are going to dine with papa so that we may be near her. The nurse will not leave her while we are eating."

He followed her into the next apartment.

Cachelin was already at table awaiting his daughter and his son-in-law. A cold chicken, a potato salad, and a compote of strawberries were on the buffet, and the soup was smoking in the plates.

They sat down at table. Cachelin said: "These are the days that I wouldn't like to see often. They are not gay." He said this with a tone of indifference and a sort of satisfaction in his face. He set himself to eat with the appetite of a hungry man, finding the chicken excellent and the potato salad most refreshing.

But Lesable felt his stomach oppressed and his mind ill at ease. He hardly ate at all, keeping his ear strained toward the next room, which was as still as though no one was within it. Nor was Cora hungry, but silent and tearful she wiped her eyes from time to time with the corner of her napkin. Cachelin asked: "What did the chief say?" and Lesable gave the details, which his father-in-law insisted on having to the last particular, making him repeat everything as though he had been absent from the ministry for a year.

"It must have made a sensation there when it became known that she was sick." And he began to dream of his glorious re-entry when she should be dead, at the head of all the other clerks. He said, however, as though in reply to a secret remorse: "It is not that I desire any evil to the dear woman. God knows I would have her preserved for many years yet, but it will have that effect all the same. Father Savon will even forget the Commune on account of it."

They were commencing to eat their strawberries, when the door of the sick-room opened. The commotion among the diners was such that with a common impulse all three of them sprang to their feet, terrified. The little nurse appeared, still preserving her calm, stupid manner, and said tranquilly:

"She has stopped breathing."

Cachelin, throwing his napkin among the dishes, sprang forward like a madman; Cora followed him, her heart beating; but Lesable remained standing near the door, spying from a distance the white spot of the bed, scarcely visible by the light of the dying day. He saw the back of his father-in-law as he stooped over the couch, examining but disturbing nothing; and suddenly he heard his voice, which seemed to him to come from afar—from very far off—the other end of the world, one of those voices which pass through our dreams and which tell us astonishing things. Cachelin said: "It is all over. She is dead." He saw his wife fall upon her knees and bury her face in the bedclothes, sobbing. Then he decided to go in, and, as Cachelin straightened himself up, the young man saw on the whiteness of the pillow the face of Aunt Charlotte, so hollow, so rigid, so pale, that with its closed eyes it looked like the face of a waxen figure.

He asked in a tone of anguish: "Is it over?"

Cachelin, who was gazing at his sister, too, turned towards Lesable, and the two men looked at each other.

"Yes," replied the elder, wishing to force his face into an expression of sorrow, but the two understood one another at a glance, and without knowing why, instinctively, they shook hands, as though each would thank the other for a service rendered.

Then, without losing any time, they quickly occupied themselves with the offices required by the dead.

Lesable undertook to fetch the doctor, and to discharge as quickly as possible the most urgent errands.

He took his hat and ran down the staircase, in haste to be in the street, to be alone, to breathe, to think, to rejoice in solitude over his good fortune.

When he had attended to his errands, instead of returning he went across to the boulevard, possessed with a desire to see the crowds, to mingle in the movement of the happy life of the evening. He felt like crying out to the passers-by: "I have fifty thousand francs a year," and he walked along, his hands in his pockets, stopping before the show windows, examining the rich stuffs, the jewels, the artistic furniture, with this joyous thought: "I can buy these for myself now."

Suddenly he stopped in front of a mourning store, and the startling thought came into his mind: "What if she is not dead? What if they are mistaken?"

And he quickly turned homeward with this doubt troubling his mind.

On entering he demanded: "Has the doctor come?"

Cachelin replied: "Yes, he has confirmed the death, and is now writing the certificate."

They re-entered the death chamber. Cora was still weeping, seated in an armchair. She wept very gently, without noise, almost without grief now, with that facility for tears which women have.

As soon as they were all three alone in the room Cachelin said in a low voice: "Now that the nurse has gone to bed, we might look around to see if anything is concealed in the furniture."

The two men set about the work. They emptied the drawers, rummaged through the pockets, unfolded every scrap of paper. By midnight they had found nothing of interest. Cora had fallen asleep, and she snored a little, in a regular fashion. César said: "Are we going to stay here until daybreak?" Lesable, perplexed, thought it was the proper thing. Then the father-in-law said: "In that case let us bring in armchairs"; and they went out to get the two big, soft easy chairs which furnished the room of the young married couple.

An hour later the three relatives slept, with uneven snorings, before the corpse, icy in its eternal immobility.

They awakened when, at daybreak, the little nurse entered the chamber. Cachelin immediately said, rubbing his eyes: "I have been a little drowsy for the last half hour."

Lesable, who was not sitting very upright, declared: "Yes, I noticed it very plainly. As for me I have not lost consciousness for a second; I just closed my eyes to rest them."

Cora went to her own room.

Then Lesable asked with apparent indifference:

"When do you think we should go to the notary's to find out about the will?"

"Why—this morning if you wish."

"Is it necessary that Cora should accompany us?"

"That would be better, perhaps, since she is in fact the heir."

"In that case I shall go and tell her to get ready."

Lesable went out with a quick step.

The office of Maître Belhomme was just opening its doors when Cachelin, Lesable, and his wife presented themselves in deep mourning, with faces full of woe.

The notary at once appeared and, greeting them, bade them sit down. Cachelin spoke up: "Monsieur, you remember me: I am the brother of Mlle. Charlotte Cachelin. These are my daughter and my son-in-law. My poor sister died yesterday; we will bury her tomorrow. As you are the depositary of her will, we come to ask you if she has not formulated some request relative to her inhumation, or if you have not some communcation to make to us."

The notary opened a drawer, took out an envelope from which he drew a paper, and said:

"Here, monsieur, is a duplicate of the will, the contents of which I will make you acquainted with immediately. The other document, exactly similar to this, is to remain in my hands." And he read:

"I, the undersigned, Victorine Charlotte Cachelin, here express my last wishes:

"I leave my entire fortune, amounting to about one million one hundred and twenty thousand francs, to the children who will be born of the marriage of my niece Céleste Coralie Cachelin, the possession of the income to go to the parents until the majority of the eldest of their descendants.

"The provisions which follow regulate the share which shall fall to each child, and the share remaining to the parents until their death.

"In the event of my death before my niece has an heir, all my fortune is to remain in the hands of my notary, for the term of three years, for my wish above expressed to be complied with if a child is born during that time.

"But in the case of Coralie's not obtaining from Heaven a descendant during the three years following my death, my fortune is to be distributed, by the hands of my notary, among the poor and the benevolent institutions contained in the following list."

There followed an interminable series of names of communities, of societies, of orders, and of instructions.

Then Maître Belhomme politely placed the paper in the hands of Cachelin, who stood speechless with astonishment.

The notary thought he ought to add something by way of explanation to his visitors.

"Mlle. Cachelin," said he, "when she did me the honor to speak to me for the first time of her project of making her will according to this plan, expressed to me the great desire which she had to see an heir of her race. She replied to all my reasoning by a more and more positive expression of her wishes, which were based, moreover, on a religious sentiment, she holding every sterile union to be the sign of divine malediction. I have not been able to modify her intentions in the least. Believe me, I regret this fact exceedingly." Then he added, smiling at Coralie: "But I do not doubt that the desideratum of the deceased will be quickly realized."

And the three relatives went away, too bewildered to think of anything.

Side by side they walked home, without speaking, ashamed and furious, as though they had robbed each other. All of Cora's grief, even, had suddenly disappeared, the ingratitude of her aunt driving away all disposition to weep.

At last Lesable, whose pale lips were drawn with rage, said to his father-in-law:

"Pass me that paper, that I may read it with my own eyes." Cachelin handed him the document and the young man began to read. He had stopped on the footpath and, jostled by the passers-by, he stood there scanning the words with his piercing and practical eye. The two others waited a few steps in front, still silent.

Then he handed back the paper, saying:

"There is nothing to be done. She has tricked us beautifully."

Cachelin, who was irritated by the failure of his hopes, replied:

"It was for you to have a child, damn it! You knew well enough that she wanted it long ago."

Lesable shrugged his shoulders without answering.

On entering they found a crowd of people awaiting them, those whose calling brings them where a corpse is. Lesable went to his room, not wishing to be bothered, and César spoke roughly to all of them, crying out to them to leave him in peace, demanding that they get through with it as quickly as possible, thinking that they were very long in relieving him of the dead.

Cora, shut up in her room, made no sound, but after an hour Cachelin came and rapped on the door of his son-in-law.

"I come, my dear Léopold," said he, "to submit some reflections to you, for it is necessary to come to some understanding. My opinion is that we should give her a befitting funeral in order to give no hint at the Ministry of what has happened. We will arrange about the expense. Besides, nothing is lost. You have not been married very long, and it would be too great a misfortune if you had no children. You must set about it, that's all. And now to business. Will you drop in at the Ministry after a while? I am going to address the envelopes for the death announcements."

Lesable grudgingly agreed that his father-in-law was right, and they sat down face to face, each at an end of a long table, to fill in the black-bordered cards.

Then they lunched. Cora reappeared, indifferent as though nothing of what had passed concerned her, and she ate a good deal, having fasted the evening before.

As soon as the meal was finished she returned to her room. Lesable left to go to the Ministry, and Cachelin installed himself on the balcony, his chair tilted back, in order to enjoy a pipe.

The broad sun of a summer day fell perpendicularly upon the multitude of roofs, some of which were pierced with windows which blazed as with fire and threw back the dazzling rays which the sight could not sustain.

And Cachelin, in his shirt sleeves, looked, with his eyes blinking under this stream of light, upon the green hillocks far, far away beyond the great city, beyond the dusty suburbs. He thought of how the Seine flowed there, broad, calm, and fresh, at the foot of hills which had trees on their slopes, and how much

better it would be to be lying on one's stomach in that greenery on the bank
of the river, gazing into the water, than to be sitting on the burning lead of his
balcony. And an uneasiness oppressed him, the tormenting thought, the grievous
sensation of their disaster, of that unfortunate, unexpected thing, so much more
bitter and brutal because the hope had been so ardent and so long-lived; and he
said aloud, as people do in time of great trouble of mind, in the uprooting of a
fixed idea: "Damned old witch!"

Behind him in the bedroom he heard the movements of those who were busying themselves with the preparations for the funeral, and the continuous noise
of the hammer which nailed up the coffin. He had not looked at his sister since
his visit to the lawyer.

But little by little the warmth, the gaiety, the clear charm of this beautiful day
penetrated to his mind and his soul, and he thought that things were not so
desperate. Why should his daughter not have a child? She had not been married
two years yet! His son-in-law appeared vigorous, well built, and in good health,
although small. They would have a child, and then besides, by Jupiter, they
had to!

Lesable furtively entered the Ministry and slunk to his room. He found on the
table a paper bearing these words: "The chief wants you." He made a gesture
of impatience. He felt a revolt against this yoke which had again fallen on his
back; then a sudden and violent desire to succeed seized him. He would be chief
in his turn, and soon; he would then go higher still. Without removing his frock
coat he went at once to M. Torchebeuf. He presented himself with one of those
solemn faces which one assumes on sad occasions. But there was something more
—an expression of sincere and profound sorrow, that involuntary dejection which
a deep disappointment leaves upon the features.

The head of the chief was bent over his papers. He raised it suddenly, and said
in a sharp tone: "I have needed you all morning. Why have you not come?"

Lesable replied: "Dear master, we have had the misfortune to lose my aunt,
Mlle. Cachelin, and I have just come to ask you to attend the funeral, which will
take place tomorrow."

The frown on the brow of M. Torchebeuf immediately disappeared, and he
replied with a touch of consideration: "That alters the case, my dear friend. I
thank you and give you the day, for you must have a great deal to attend to."

But Lesable, desiring to show his zeal, said: "Thanks, dear master, everything
is finished, and I expected to remain here until the regular hour for closing."

And he returned to his desk.

The news soon spread, and his fellows came from all the departments to bring
him their congratulations rather than their condolences, and also to see how he
bore himself. He endured their speeches and their looks with the resigned appearance of an actor, and also with a tact which astonished them.

"He conducts himself very well," said some.

"Well he may," added others; "he ought to be content—lucky dog!"

Maze, more audacious than any of them, asked with the careless air of a man
of the world: "Do you know exactly the amount of the fortune?"

Lesable replied in a perfectly disinterested tone: "No, not precisely. The will
says about twelve hundred thousand francs. I know that, as the notary was obliged
to make us acquainted immediately with certain clauses relative to the funeral."

It was the general opinion that Lesable would not remain in the Ministry.

With an income of sixty thousand francs one does not remain a quill driver. One is somebody and can be something according to one's inclination.

Some thought that he was aiming at the Cabinet; others believed that he thought of the Chamber of Deputies. The chief was expecting to receive his resignation to transmit to the head of the department.

The entire Ministry came to the funeral, which was thought to be very meager. But the word was around: "It is Mlle. Cachelin herself who wished it so. It was in the will."

On the very next day Cachelin was at his post, and Lesable, after a week of indisposition, also returned, a little pale but assiduous and zealous as formerly. One would have said that nothing unlooked-for had happened to them. It was only remarked that they ostentatiously smoked very large cigars, that they talked of consols, railways, of stocks and shares, like men who have scrip in their pockets, and it became known, in a short time, that they had rented a country house in the neighborhood of Paris, in which to spend the summer season.

"They are miserly like the old woman," they said. "It runs in the family. Birds of a feather flock together. But it doesn't look well to retain a clerkship with such a fortune."

In a short time the matter was forgotten. They were rated and judged.

IV

After the burial of Aunt Charlotte, Lesable thought again of the million, and, tormented by a rage all the more violent because it must be kept secret, he hated all the world on account of his deplorable ill luck. "Why, having been married two years, have I not had a child?" he asked himself, and the fear of seeing his household remain sterile made his heart sink. Then, as an urchin who sees from afar the shining prize at the end of the goal, and swears to himself to attain it, and exerts all the vigor and tenacity necessary to reach it, so Lesable took the desperate resolution to become a parent. So many others had, why might not he also? Perhaps he had been negligent, careless, ignorant of something, the consequence of complete indifference. Never having felt a violent desire for an heir, he had never directed all his energies to obtaining this result. He determined to concentrate all his efforts; he would neglect nothing, and he must succeed because he so much desired to. But when he returned home, he felt ill enough to take to his bed. The disappointment had been too bitter and he bowed himself to the blow.

This nervous strain brought him to such a state that the physician judged his condition serious enough to prescribe absolute rest as well as an interminable course of treatment. They feared brain fever. In eight days, however, he was about again and resumed his work at the office. But he dare not yet, he believed, approach the conjugal bed. He hesitated and trembled as a general who is going to give battle, a battle on which depends his future. Each evening he awaited the next day, hoping for an access of virility and energy, a happy moment in which he might accomplish his desire. He felt his pulse every minute, and if it was too feeble or too rapid, he took a tonic, ate raw meat, and strengthened himself in every possible way. As his improvement was not very rapid, Lesable determined to pass the hot months in the country. He persuaded himself that the country air would be a sovereign balm for his weakness, and he assured himself of the accomplishment of the hoped-for-success. He said to his father-in-law, in a confidential tone: "When we are once in the country my health will improve, and all will go well." That one word "country" seemed to carry for him a mysterious significance.

They rented a small house in the village of Bezons, and the whole family took up their residence there. The two men started out on foot every morning for the station of Colombes, returning in the evening.

Cora, enchanted at living thus on the banks of the peaceful river, would seat herself on the sward, gather flowers, and bring home great bunches of delicate, trembling ferns.

Every evening they all three walked along the river as far as the tollgate of Morue, and, entering, drank a bottle of beer at the Restaurant des Tilleuls. The river, retarded by the long file of stakes, poured between them and leaped, bubbled, and foamed for the distance of a hundred feet. The roaring of the falls made the ground tremble, while a fine mist of vapor floated in the air, rising from the cascade like a light smoke, throwing on the surroundings a delightful odor of spray and a savor of wet earth. As night fell, a great light below and in front indicated Paris, and Cachelin exclaimed every evening: "What a city, after all!"

From time to time, a train, passing on the iron bridge which crossed the end of the island, made a rolling as of thunder and suddenly disappeared, sometimes to the left, sometimes to the right, toward Paris or toward the sea. They returned home slowly, seating themselves on the bank, watching the moon rise and pour on the river her soft and yellow light, which seemed to fuse with the water, and the wrinkles of the current moved like waves of fire. The toads uttered their short and metallic cries. The calls of the night birds rang out on the air, and sometimes a large, mute shadow glided on the river, troubling her calm and luminous course. It was a band of freebooters who, throwing in suddenly their net, drew it back without noise into their boat, dragging in its vast and somber mesh a shoal of shining and trembling gudgeons, like a treasure drawn from the bottom of the sea, a living treasure of silver fish.

Cora, deeply moved, leaned tenderly upon the arm of her husband, whose design she suspected, although nothing of it had been spoken between them. It was for them like a new betrothal, a second expectation of the kiss of love. Sometimes he would bestow a furtive caress behind her ear, on that charming spot of tender flesh where curls the first hair. She responded by a pressure of the hand, and they attracted while refusing each other, incited and held back by a will more energetic, by the phantom of the million. Cachelin, appeased by the hope which he felt around him, was happy. He drank deeply and ate much, feeling, born in him at twilight, the hour of poetry, that foolish tenderness which comes to the dullest persons in certain aspects of nature: a rain of light through the branches, a sunset behind the distant hills, with purple reflections on the water. He declared: "As for me, in the presence of such things I believe in God. It touches me here," and he indicated the pit of his stomach. "I feel myself turned upside down. I feel queer. It seems to me I have been steeped in a bath which makes me want to cry."

As for Lesable, his health rapidly improved. He was seized with sudden ardors, which he did not understand, and he felt a desire to run like a young colt, to roll in the grass and neigh with delight.

He thought the favored time was approaching. It was a true wedding night.

Then they had a new honeymoon full of caresses and hopes. Later they perceived that their experiments were fruitless and their confidence was in vain.

But in the midst of despair Lesable did not lose courage; he continued to make the most superhuman efforts. His wife, moved by the same desire and trembling with the same fear, more robust too than he, encouraged him in his attempts and stimulated his flagging ardor. They returned to Paris in the early days of October.

Life became hard for them again. Unkind words fell from their lips, and Cachelin, who scented the situation, harassed them with the coarse and venomous epigrams of an old trooper.

And one incessant thought pursued them, tortured them, and sharpened their mutual rancor—that of the unattainable legacy. Cora now carried a sharp tongue and lashed her husband. She treated him like a little boy, a mere brat, a man of no importance. Cachelin at every meal repeated: "If I were rich, I should have children in plenty; when one is poor it is necessary to be reasonable." Then turning to his daughter he added: "You must be like me; but there——" and he looked at his son-in-law significantly, accompanying the look with a movement of the shoulders full of contempt.

Lesable made no reply. He felt himself to be a superior man allied to a family of boors.

At the Ministry they noticed the alteration in his manner, and even the chief one day asked him: "Are you not ill? You appear to me to be somewhat changed."

Lesable replied: "Not at all, my dear sir. I am a little tired, perhaps, having worked very constantly, as you may have seen."

He counted very surely on his promotion at the end of the year, and he had resumed, in his hope, the laborious life of a model employee. But among the meager bonuses that were distributed Lesable's was the smallest of all, and Cachelin received nothing. Struck to the heart, Lesable sought the chief, whom, for the first time, he addressed as "monsieur."

"Of what use is it, monsieur, to work as I do, if I do not reap any reward?"

The head of M. Torchebeuf appeared to bristle.

"I have already told you, M. Lesable, that I will admit of no discussion of this nature between us. I repeat to you again that your claim is unreasonable, your actual fortune being so great as compared to the poverty of your colleagues——"

Lesable could not contain himself. "But I have nothing, monsieur. Our aunt has left her fortune to the first child which shall be born of our marriage. We live, my father-in-law and I, on our salaries."

The chief was greatly surprised. "If you have no fortune today, you will be rich, in any case, at some future day. It amounts to the same thing."

Lesable withdrew, more cast down by his failure than by the uncertainty of Aunt Charlotte's million.

As Cachelin came to his desk some days later the handsome Maze entered with a smile on his lips; next Pitolet appeared, his eyes shining; then Boissel opened the door and advanced with an excited air, tittering and exchanging meaning looks with the others. Old Savon continued his copying, his clay pipe in the corner of his mouth, seated on his high chair, his feet twisted about the rounds after the fashion of little boys. Nobody spoke. They seemed to be waiting for something, and Cachelin continued to register his papers, announcing in a loud voice according to his custom: "Toulon: furniture for the officers of the Richelieu.

Lorient: diving apparatus for the Desaix. Brest: samples of sails of English manufacture."

Lesable entered. He came now every morning for information in regard to the
affairs which concerned him, his father-in-law no longer taking the trouble to send
him instructions by the office boy.

While he was looking amongst the papers spread out on the table of the chief
clerk, Maze watched him from his corner, rubbing his hands, and Pitolet, who was
rolling a cigarette, seemed full of mirth he could not control. He turned toward
the copying clerk:

"Say now, Papa Savon, you have learned many things in your time, haven't
you?"

The old man, knowing they meant to tease him and to speak to him of his
wife, did not reply.

Pitolet began: "You must have discovered the secret of begetting children, since
you have had several."

The old clerk raised his head. "You know, M. Pitolet, that I do not like any joking on this subject. I have had the misfortune to marry an unworthy woman, and
when I became convinced of her faithlessness I separated from her."

Maze asked in an indifferent tone: "You have had several proofs of her infidelity, have you not?"

And the old man gravely replied: "I have."

Pitolet put in again: "That has not prevented you from becoming the father
of three or four children, I am told."

The poor old man, growing very red, stammered: "You are trying to wound
me, M. Pitolet; but you will not succeed. My wife has had, in fact, three children.
I have reason to believe that the first-born is mine, but I deny the two others."

Pitolet continued: "Everybody says, in truth, that the first one is yours. That
is sufficient. It is very gratifying to have a child, very gratifying and very delightful.
I wager Lesable there would be enchanted to have one—only one, like you."

Cachelin had stopped writing. He did not laugh, although old Savon was his
butt ordinarily, and he had poured out his stock of cruel jokes on the subject of
the old clerk's conjugal sorrows.

Lesable had collected his papers; but feeling himself attacked he wished to
remain, held back by pride, confused and irritated and wishing to know who had
betrayed his secret.

Then the recollection of the confidence he had made to his chief came back to
him, and he at once understood it was necessary to express his indignation if he
did not wish to become the butt of the whole Ministry.

Boissel marched up and down the room, all the time tittering. He imitated the
hoarse voices of the street criers, and bellowed: "The secret of begetting children,
for ten centimes—two sous! Buy the secret of begetting children—revealed by
M. Savon, with many horrible details." Everybody began to laugh except Lesable
and his father-in-law, and Pitolet, turning toward the order clerk said: "What is
the matter with you, Cachelin? You seem to have lost your habitual gaiety. One
would think that you do not find it amusing to believe that old Savon could have
had a child by his wife. I think it very funny. Everybody cannot do as much."

Lesable pretended to be deeply absorbed in his papers and to hear nothing of
what was going on about him, but he was as white as a ghost.

Boissel took up the strain in the same mocking voice: "The utility of heirs for getting an inheritance, ten centimes, two sous; who will buy?"

Then Maze, who thought this was very poor sort of wit, and who personally was enraged at Lesable having robbed him of the hope of a fortune which he had secretly cherished, said pointedly: "What is the matter with you, Lesable? You are very pale."

Lesable raised his head and looked his colleague full in the face. He hesitated a second, while his lip trembled as he tried to formulate a bitter reply, but, unable to find the phrase he sought, he responded: "There is nothing the matter with me. I am only astonished that you display so much delicacy."

Maze, who stood with his back to the fire and his hands under his coattails, replied, laughing: "One does the best one can, old man. We are like you, we do not always succeed——"

An explosion of laughter interrupted his words. Old Savon, who now vaguely comprehended that the clerks no longer addressed their railleries to him, looked around with his mouth gaping and his pen suspended in the air. And Cachelin waited, ready to come to blows with the first person who came in his way.

Lesable stammered: "I do not understand. In what have I not succeeded?"

The handsome Maze dropped the tails of his coat, and began to stroke his mustache. "I know that you ordinarily succeed in all that you undertake. I have done wrong to speak of you. Besides, we were speaking of old Savon's children, and not of yours, as you haven't any. Now since you succeed in all your enterprises, it is evident that, if you do not have children, it is because you do not want them."

"What business is it of yours?" demanded Lesable sharply.

At this provoking tone Maze in his turn raised his voice: "Hold on! what do you take me for? Try to be polite, or I'll settle you!"

Lesable trembled with anger, and losing all self-control, replied: "M. Maze, I am not, like you, a great booby, or a great coxcomb. And I forbid you ever to speak to me again. I care neither for you nor for your kind." And he threw a look of defiance at Pitolet and Boissel.

Maze suddenly understood that true force is in calmness and irony, but wounded in his most vulnerable part—his vanity—he wished to strike his enemy to the very heart, and replied in the protecting tone of a benevolent well-wisher, but with rage in his eyes: "My dear Lesable, you pass all bounds. But I understand your vexation. It is pitiful to lose a fortune, and to lose it for so little, for a thing so easy, so simple. If you wish, I will do you this service myself, for nothing, out of pure friendship. It is only an affair of five minutes——"

He was still speaking when Lesable hurled the inkstand of old Savon full at his head.

A flood of ink covered his face and metamorphosed him into a Negro with surprising rapidity. He sprang forward, rolling the whites of his eyes, with his hands raised ready to strike. But Cachelin covered his son-in-law, and grasping Maze by the arms pushed him aside, and, after pounding him well, dashed him against the wall. Maze disengaged himself with a violent effort and rushed through the door, crying to the two men: "You shall soon hear from me!" Pitolet and Boissel followed him.

Boissel explained his moderation by declaring he should have killed some one if he had taken part in the struggle.

As soon as he entered his room Maze endeavored to remove the stain, but without success. The ink was violet and was indelible and ineffaceable. He stood before his glass, furious and disconsolate, rubbing savagely at his face with a napkin rolled in a knot. He obtained only a richer black, mixed with red, the blood coming to the surface with the friction.

Boissel and Pitolet strove to advise and console him. One suggested the application of pure olive oil, the other prescribed a bath of ammonia. The office boy was sent to ask the advice of a chemist. He brought back a yellow liquid and pumice stone, which was used with no result.

Maze, disheartened, sank into a chair and declared: "Now it only remains to settle the question of honor. Will you act as seconds for me, and demand of M. Lesable a sufficient apology, or the reparation by arms?"

They both at once consented and began to discuss the steps to be taken. They had no idea about affairs of this kind, but, not wishing to betray their ignorance, and desiring to appear correct, their advice was timorous and conflicting. It was finally decided that they should consult a sea captain who was attached to the Ministry to look after the coal distribution. But he was as ignorant as they were. After some moments of reflection, however, he advised them to go and see Lesable and ask to be put in touch with two of his friends.

As they proceeded to the office of their colleague, Boissel suddenly stopped. "Is it not imperative that we should have gloves?" he asked.

Pitolet hesitated an instant. "Perhaps it is," he replied seriously. But in order to procure the gloves it would have been necessary to go out, and the chief was rather severe.

They sent the office boy to bring an assortment from the nearest glove store. To decide upon the color was a question of time. Boissel preferred black. Pitolet thought that shade out of place in the circumstances. At last they chose violet.

Seeing the two men enter gloved and solemn, Lesable raised his head and brusquely demanded: "What do you want?"

Pitolet replied: "Monsieur, we are charged by our friend, M. Maze, to ask of you an apology, or a reparation by arms for the insult you have inflicted on him."

Lesable, still greatly exasperated, cried: "What, he insults me, and sends you to provoke me? Tell him that I despise him—that I despise all he can say or do."

Boissel advanced with a tragic air. "You will force us, monsieur, to publish in the papers an official report, which will be very disagreeable to you."

Pitolet maliciously added: "And which will gravely injure your honor and your future advancement."

Lesable, overwhelmed, looked at them. What should he do? He sought to gain time. "Will you wait a moment in the office of M. Pitolet? You shall have my answer in ten minutes."

When at last alone he looked around him, seeking for some counsel, some protection.

A duel! He was going to fight a duel!

He sat terrified, with a beating heart. He, a peaceful man, who had never dreamed of such a possibility, who was not prepared for the risk, whose courage was not equal to such a formidable event. He rose from his chair and sat down again, his heart wildly beating, his legs sinking under him. His anger and his strength had totally deserted him.

But the thought of the opinion of the Ministry, the gossip the story would make among his acquaintances, aroused his failing pride, and, not knowing what to decide, he sought his chief to ask his advice. M. Torchebeuf was surprised and perplexed. An armed encounter seemed to him unnecessary, and he thought a duel would demoralize the service. He replied: "I can give you no advice. It is a question of honor, which does not concern me. Do you wish that I should give you a note to Commandant Bouc? He is a competent man in such matters and will be able to advise you."

Lesable accepted the offer, and saw the commandant, who even consented to be his second; he took an under chief for another.

Boissel and Pitolet waited with their gloves on. They had borrowed two chairs from another office, in order to have four seats.

They saluted gravely and took their places, while Pitolet explained the situation. The commandant, having listened attentively, replied: "The case is serious, but it does not appear to me to be irreparable. Everything depends on the intention." He was a sly old sailor who was enjoying himself.

A long discussion began regarding the reciprocal apologies the principals should make. M. Maze acknowledging not to have had the intention to offend, M. Lesable should hasten to avow himself in the wrong in throwing the inkstand at the head of M. Maze, and pray to be excused for his inconsiderate violence.

The four proxies returned to their clients.

Maze, seated before his table, was agitated by the dread of the possible duel, although expecting to see his adversary retreat, and regarded his face attentively in one of those little, round tin mirrors which the employees concealed in a drawer for the purpose of adjusting their hair and ties before leaving in the evening. He read the letter of apology which had been prepared by the seconds of both parties, and declared with evident satisfaction: "That appears to me to be very honorable; I am willing to sign it."

Lesable, for his part, accepted without discussion the arrangement of his seconds, and declared: "As this is the result of your mutual consultation, I can but acquiesce."

The four plenipotentiaries assembled. The letters were exchanged, they saluted gravely, and so the affair terminated. An extraordinary excitement reigned in the Ministry. The employees, carrying the news, passed from one door to the other and lingered to gossip about in the lobbies. When they heard how the affair had ended, there was general disappointment. Some one said: "Still, that will not get Lesable a baby." And the saying took. One employee made a rhyme upon it.

But at the moment when everything seemed adjusted, a difficulty suggested itself to Boissel: "What would be the attitude of the two adversaries when they found themselves face to face? Would they speak, or would they ignore each other?" It was decided that they should meet, as if by chance, in the office of the chief, and exchange, in the presence of M. Torchebeuf, some words of politeness.

This ceremony was accordingly accomplished, and Maze, having sent for a carriage, returned home to try to remove the stain from his face.

Lesable and Cachelin drove home together without speaking, mutually exasperated, each blaming the other for the disgraceful affair.

The moment he entered the house, Lesable threw his hat violently on the table and cried out to his wife: "I have had enough of it! I have a duel on your account now!" She looked at him in angry surprise.

"A duel? How is that?"

"Because Maze has insulted me on your account."

She approached him. "On my account? How?"

He threw himself passionately into an armchair and exclaimed: "He has insulted me—no need to say any more about it."

But she would know. "You must repeat to me the words he used about me."

Lesable blushed, and then stammered: "He told me—he told me—it was in regard to your sterility."

She gave a start; then recoiling in fury, the paternal rudeness showing through the woman's nature, she burst out:

"I! I am sterile, am I? What does that clown know about it? Sterile with you, yes; because you are not a man. But if I had married another, no matter who, do you hear? I should have had children. Ah, you had better talk! It has cost me dear to have married a softy like you! And what did you reply to this good-for-nothing?"

Lesable, frightened before this storm, stuttered: "I—I slapped his face."

She looked at him in astonishment.

"And what did he do?"

"He sent me a challenge; that was all."

She was instantly interested, attracted, like all women, by the dramatic element, and she asked, immediately softened, and suddenly seized with a sort of esteem for this man who was going to risk his life for her sake:

"When are you going to fight him?"

He replied tranquilly: "We are not going to fight: the matter has been arranged by our seconds. Maze has sent me an apology."

Transported with rage, she boxed his ears. "Ah, he insults me in your presence, and you permit it, and refuse to fight him! It needed but this to make you a coward."

Enraged at this he cried: "I command you to hold your tongue. I know better than you do how to protect my honor. To convince you, here is the letter of M. Maze; take it and read it, and see for yourself."

She took the letter, ran her eye over it, and divining the whole truth, sneered: "You wrote him a letter also? You are afraid of each other. What cowards men are! If we were in your place, we women—after all, it is I who have been insulted, your wife, and you are willing to let it pass. That need not astonish me, for you are not man enough to beget a child. That explains everything. You are as impotent before women as you are cowardly among men. Ah, I have married a nice worm!"

She had suddenly assumed the voice and gestures of her father, the coarse and vulgar manners of an old trooper and the intonations of a man.

Standing before him, her hands on her hips, tall, strong, vigorous, her chest protruding, her cheeks flushed, her voice deep and vibrant, she looked at this little man seated in front of her, a trifle bald, clean shaven except for the short side whiskers of the lawyer, and she felt a desire to crush, to strangle him.

She continued: "You are capable of nothing—of nothing whatever! You allow everybody at the Ministry, even, to be promoted over your head!"

The door opened, and Cachelin entered, attracted by the sound of their voices, and demanded to know what was the matter. "I told the truth to that worm!" answered Cora.

Lesable raised his eyes, and for the first time noticed the resemblance between father and daughter. It seemed to him that a veil was lifted and the pair were revealed in their true colors—the same coarse nature was common to both; and he, a ruined man, was condemned to live between the two forever.

Cachelin exclaimed: "If you only could get a divorce! It is not very satisfactory to have married a capon."

At that word, trembling and blazing with fury, Lesable sprang up with a bound. He rushed at his father-in-law shouting: "Get out of here! Begone! You are in my house—do you understand?—and I order you to leave it." He seized from the table a bottle of sedative water and brandished it like a club.

Cachelin, intimidated, backed out of the room, muttering: "What will he do next, I wonder?"

But Lesable was too angry to be easily appeased. He turned upon his wife, who regarded this outburst in astonishment, and placing the bottle on the table cried: "As for you—as for you——" But as words failed him to express his rage, he was choked into silence, and stood glaring at her with a distorted visage.

She began to laugh.

This mocking laughter put him beside himself, and, springing upon her he seized her by the throat with his left hand, while he boxed her ears furiously with the right. She recoiled, terrified and suffocating, and fell backward on the bed, while he continued to strike her. Suddenly he raised himself, out of breath, exhausted and heartily ashamed of his brutality; he stammered: "There—there—there—that will do!"

But she did not move; it seemed as if he had killed her. She lay on her back, on the side of the bed, her face concealed by her hands.

He approached her in alarm, wondering what had happened, and expecting her to uncover her face and look at him. She made no sign, and suspense becoming intolerable he murmured: "Cora, Cora, speak!" But she did not move or reply.

What was the matter with her? What was she going to do?

His rage had passed—fallen as suddenly as it had been aroused. He felt that his conduct was odious, almost criminal. He had beaten his wife, his own wife—he who was circumspect, cold, and courteous. And in the softness his remorse awakened, he would ask her forgiveness. He threw himself on his knees at her side and covered with kisses the cheek he had just smitten. He softly touched the end of a finger of the hand that covered her face. She seemed to feel nothing. He coaxed her, caressing her as one caresses a beaten dog. She took no notice of him. "Cora, listen: I have done wrong! Cora, hear me!" She seemed as one dead. Then he tried to take her hand from her face. It obeyed his effort passively, and he saw an open eye, which stared at him with a fixed and alarming gaze.

He continued: "Listen, Cora, I was transported with fury. It was your father who drove me to do this shameful thing. A man cannot take such an insult as that." She made no reply, as if she heard nothing. He did not know what to say, or what to do. He kissed her under the ear, and raising himself he saw a tear in the corner of her eye, a great tear which rolled slowly down her cheek, and her eyelids fluttered and closed convulsively. He was seized with shame, deeply moved, and opening his arms he threw himself on his wife; he removed the other hand from her face and covered it with kisses, crying: "My poor Cora, forgive me! forgive me!"

Still she wept, without a sound, without a sob, as one weeps from the deepest grief. He held her pressed closely against him, caressing her and whispering in her ear all the tender words he could command. But she remained insensible. However, she ceased to weep. They continued thus a long time locked in each other's arms.

The night fell, folding in its somber shadow the little room; and when it was entirely dark he was emboldened to solicit her pardon in a manner that was calculated to revive their hopes.

When they had risen he resumed his ordinary voice and manner, as if nothing had happened. She appeared, on the contrary, softened, and spoke in a gentler tone than usual, regarding her husband with submissive, almost caressing eyes, as if this unexpected correction had relaxed her nerves and softened her heart.

Lesable said quietly: "Your father must be tired of being alone so long. It will soon be dinnertime; go and fetch him."

She obeyed him.

It was seven o'clock indeed, and the little maid announced dinner, as Cachelin, serene and smiling, appeared with his daughter. They seated themselves at table and talked on this evening with more cordiality than they had done for a long time, as if something agreeable had happened to everybody.

V

But their hopes, always sustained, always renewed, ended in nothing. From month to month their expectations declined, in spite of the persistence of Lesable and the co-operation of his wife. They were consumed with anxiety. Each without ceasing reproached the other for their want of success, and the husband in despair, emaciated, fatigued, had to suffer all the vulgarity of Cachelin, who in their domestic warfare called him "M. Lecoq," in remembrance, no doubt, of the day that he missed receiving a bottle in his face for having called his son-in-law a capon.

He and his daughter, whose interests were in league, enraged by the constant thought of this great fortune so near, and yet impossible to seize, racked their invention to humiliate and torture this impotent man, who was the cause of all their misfortune.

As they sat at table, Cora repeated each day: "There is very little for dinner. If we were rich, it would be otherwise. It is not my fault."

When Lesable set out for his office, she called from her room: "Do not forget your umbrella or you will come back as muddy as an omnibus wheel. It's not my fault that you are still obliged to follow the trade of a quill driver."

When she went out herself, she never failed to cry: "If I had married another man, I should have a carriage of my own."

Every hour and on every occasion she harped on this subject. She pricked her husband with reproaches, lashed him with insult, held him alone guilty, and made him responsible for the loss of the fortune that should have been hers.

At last, one evening, losing all patience, Lesable exclaimed: "In the dog's name, can't you hold your tongue? From first to last it is your fault, and yours alone, do you hear, if we have not a child, because I have already had one."

He lied, preferring anything to this eternal reproach, to this shame of appearing impotent. She looked at him, astonished at first, seeking the truth in his eyes; at last comprehending, and full of disdain, she cried: "You have a child, have you?"

He replied with effrontery: "Yes, an illegitimate child, that I am bringing up at Asnières."

She answered quietly: "We will go and see it tomorrow, so that I may find out what he is like."

He only blushed to the ears and stammered: "Just as you please."

She rose the next morning at seven o'clock, very much to her husband's astonishment.

"Are we not going to see your child? You promised me yesterday evening. Perhaps you haven't got it any more today."

He sprang from the bed hastily. "It is not my child we are going to see, but a physician who will give us his opinion on your case."

She replied in the tone of a woman who was sure of herself: "I shall ask nothing better."

Cachelin was instructed to inform the chief that his son-in-law was ill, and Lesable and his wife, advised by a neighboring chemist, rang at one o'clock exactly the office bell of Dr. Lefilleul, author of several works on the hygiene of generation.

They were shown into a salon decorated in white and gold, but scantily furnished in spite of the number of chairs and sofas. They seated themselves and waited. Lesable was excited, trembling, and also ashamed. Their turn came at last, and they were shown into a sort of office, where they were received by a short, stout man of dignified and ceremonious demeanor.

He waited till they should explain their case, but Lesable had not courage to utter a word and blushed up to the roots of his hair. It therefore devolved on his wife to speak, and with a resolute manner and in a tranquil voice, she made known their errand.

"Monsieur, we have come to discover the reason why we cannot have children. A large fortune depends upon this for us."

The consultation was long, minute, and painful. Cora alone seemed unembarrassed, and submitted to the critical examination of the medical expert, sustained by the great interest she had at stake.

After having studied for nearly two hours the constitutions of the married pair, the practitioner said: "I discover nothing either abnormal or special. Your case is by no means an uncommon one. There is as much divergence in constitutions as in characters. When we see so many households out of joint through incompatibility of temper, it is not astonishing to see others sterile through incompatibility of physique. Madame appears to be particularly well fitted for the offices of motherhood. Monsieur, on his side, although presenting no conformation outside of the general rule, seems to me enfeebled, perhaps the consequence of his ardent desire to become a parent. Will you permit me to make an auscultation?"

Lesable, greatly disturbed, removed his waistcoat, and the doctor glued his ear to the thorax, and then to the back of his patient, tapping him continuously from the throat to the stomach, and from the loins to the nape of his neck. He discovered a slight irregularity in the action of his heart, and even a menace to the right lung. "—It is necessary for you to be very careful, monsieur, very careful. This is anemia, and comes from exhaustion—nothing else. These conditions, although now insignificant, may in a short time become incurable."

Lesable turned pale with anguish and begged for a prescription.

The doctor ordered a complicated regime consisting of iron, raw meat and soup, combined with exercise, rest, and a sojourn in the country during the hot weather. He indicated, moreover, the symptoms that proclaimed the desired fecundity, and initiated them into the secrets which were usually practiced with success in such cases.

The consultation cost forty francs.

When they were in the street, Cora burst out full of wrath:

"I have discovered what my fate is to be!"

Lesable made no reply. He was tormented by anxiety, he was recalling and weighing each word of the physician. Had the doctor made a mistake, or had he judged truly? He thought no more of the inheritance now, or the desired offspring; it was a question of life or death. He seemed to hear a whistling in his lungs, and his heart sounded as though it were beating in his ears. In crossing the garden of the Tuileries he was overcome with faintness and had to sit down to recover himself. His wife, as though to humiliate him by her superior strength, remained standing in front of him, regarding him from head to foot with pitying contempt. He breathed heavily, exaggerating the effort by his fears, and with the fingers of his left hand on his right wrist he counted the pulsations of the artery.

Cora, who was stamping with impatience, cried: "When will you be ready? It's time to stop this nonsense!" He arose with the air of a martyr and went on his way without uttering a word.

When Cachelin was informed of the result of the consultation, his fury knew no bounds. He bawled out: "We know now whose fault it is to a certainty. Ah, well!" And he looked at his son-in-law with his ferocious eyes as though he would devour him.

Lesable neither listened nor heard, being totally absorbed in thoughts of his health and the menace to his existence. Father and daughter might say what they pleased. They were not in his skin, and as for him he meant to preserve his skin at all hazards. He had the various prescriptions of the physician filled, and at each meal he produced an array of bottles with the contents of which he dosed himself regardless of the sneers of his wife and her father. He looked at himself in the glass every instant, placed his hand on his heart each moment to study its action, and removed his bed to a dark room which was used as a clothes closet to put himself beyond the reach of carnal temptation.

He conceived for his wife a hatred mingled with contempt and disgust. All women, moreover, appeared to him to be monsters, dangerous beasts, whose mission it was to destroy men; and he thought no more of the will of Aunt Charlotte except as one recalls a past accident which might have been fatal.

Some months passed. There remained but one year before the fatal term.

Cachelin had suspended in the dining room an enormous calendar, from which he effaced a day each morning, raging at the impotence of his son-in-law, who was allowing this great fortune to escape week by week. And the thought that he would have to drudge at the office all his life, and limit his expenses to the pitiful sum of two thousand francs a year, filled him with a passion of anger that found vent in the most violent abuse. He could not look at Lesable without shaking with rage, with a brutal desire to beat, to crush, to trample on him. He hated him with an inordinate hatred. Every time he saw him open the door and enter the room, it seemed to him that a robber had broken into the house and robbed him of a sacred inheritance. He hated him more than his most mortal enemy, and despised him at the same time for his weakness, and above all for the baseness which caused him to sacrifice their common hope of posterity to the fear of his health. Lesable, in fact, lived as completely apart from his wife as if no tie united them. He never approached or touched her; he avoided even looking at her, as much through shame as through fear.

Cachelin, every morning asked his daughter: "Well, how about your husband? Has he made up his mind?"

And she would reply: "No, Papa."

Each evening saw the most painful scenes take place at table. Cachelin continually reiterated: "When a man is not a man, he had better get out and yield his place to another."

And Cora added: "The fact is, there are some men who are both useless and wearisome. I do not know why they are permitted to live only to become a burden to everyone."

Lesable dosed himself and made no reply. At last one day his father-in-law cried: "Say, you, if you do not change your manners now that your health is improving, do you know what my daughter means to do?

The son-in-law raised his eyes, foreseeing a new outrage. Cachelin continued: "She will take somebody else, confound you! You may consider yourself lucky if she hasn't done so already. When a girl has married a weakling like you, she is entitled to do anything."

Lesable, turning livid with wrath, replied: "It is not I who prevents her from following your good counsel."

Cora lowered her eyes, and Cachelin, knowing that he had said an outrageous thing, remained silent and confused.

VI

At the office the two men seemed to live on good enough terms. A sort of tacit pact was entered into between them to conceal from their colleagues their internal warfare. They addressed each other as "my dear Cachelin," "my dear Lesable"; they even feigned to laugh and talk together as men who were satisfied and happy in their domestic relations.

Lesable and Maze, for their part, comported themselves in the presence of each other with the ceremonious politeness of adversaries who had met in battle.

The duel they had escaped, but whose shadow had chilled them, exacted of them an exaggerated courtesy, a more marked consideration, and perhaps a secret desire for reconciliation, born of the vague fear of a new complication. Their attitude was recognized and approved as that of men of the world, who had had an affair of honor. They saluted each other from a distance with severe gravity, and with a flourish of hats that was graceful and dignified. They did not speak, their pride preventing either from making the first advances. But one day, Lesable, whom the chief demanded to see immediately, to show his zeal, started with a great rush through the lobby and ran right into the stomach of an employee. It was Maze. They recoiled before each other, and Lesable exclaimed with eager politeness: "I hope I have not hurt you, monsieur?"

Maze responded: "Not at all, sir."

From this moment they thought it expedient to exchange some phrases when they met. Then, in the interchange of courtesies, there were little attentions they paid each other from which arose in a short time certain familiarities, then an intimacy tempered with reserve and restrained by a certain hesitation; then on the strength of their increasing good will and visits made to the room of each other, a comradeship was established. They often gossiped together now of the news that found its way into the bureau. Lesable laid aside his air of superiority, and Maze no longer paraded his social successes. Cachelin often joined in the conversation and watched with interest their growing friendship. Sometimes as the handsome Maze left the apartment with head erect and square shoulders, he turned to his son-in-law and hissed: "There goes a fine man!" One morning when they were all four together, for old Savan never left his copying, the chair of the old clerk, having been tampered with no doubt by some practical joker, collapsed under him, and the good man rolled on the floor uttering cries of affright. The three others flew to his assistance. The order clerk attributed this machination to the Communists, and Maze earnestly desired to see the wounded part. Cachelin and he even essayed to take off the poor old fellow's clothes to dress the injury, they said, but he resisted desperately, crying that he was not hurt.

When the fun was over, Cachelin suddenly exclaimed: "I say, M. Maze, now that we are all together, can you not do us the honor of dining with us next Sunday? It will give pleasure to all three of us, myself, my son-in-law, and my daughter, who has often heard your name when we speak of the office. Shall it be yes?"

Lesable added his entreaty, but more coldly than his father-in-law: "Pray come," he said; "it will give us great pleasure."

Maze hesitated, embarrassed and smiling at the remembrance of past events. Cachelin urged him: "Come, say we may expect you!"

"Very well, then, I accept."

Cachelin said on entering the house: "Cora, do you know that M. Maze is coming here to dinner next Sunday?"

Cora, surprised at first, stammered: "M. Maze? Really!" She blushed up to her hair without knowing why. She had so often heard him spoken of, his manners, his successes, for he was looked upon at the office as a man who was irresistible with women, that she had long felt a desire to know him.

Cachelin continued rubbing his hands: "You will see that he is a real man, and a fine fellow. He is as tall as a carabineer; he does not resemble your husband there."

She did not reply, confused as if they had divined her dreams of him.

They prepared this dinner with as much solicitude as the one to which Lesable had been formerly invited. Cachelin discussed the dishes, wishing to have everything served in perfection; and, as though a confidence unavowed and still undetermined had risen up in his heart, he seemed more gay, tranquilized by some secret and sure prevision.

Through all that Sunday he watched the preparations with the utmost solicitude, while Lesable was doing some urgent work, brought the evening before from the office.

It was the first week of November, and the new year was at hand.

At seven o'clock Maze arrived, in high good humor. He entered as though he felt very much at home, with a compliment and a great bouquet of roses for Cora. He added, as he presented them, in the familiar tone of a man of the world: "It seems to me, madame, I know you already, and that I have known you from your childhood, for many years your father has spoken to me of you."

Cachelin, seeing the flowers, cried: "Ah, they are charming!" and his daughter recalled that Lesable had not brought her a bouquet the day he was introduced.

The handsome clerk seemed enchanted, laughing and bestowing on Cora the most delicate flatteries, which brought the color to her cheeks.

He found her very attractive. She thought him charming and seductive. When he had gone, Cachelin exclaimed: "Isn't he a fine fellow? What havoc he creates! They say he can wheedle any woman!"

Cora, less demonstrative, avowed, however, that she thought him very agreeable, and not so much of a poseur as she had believed.

Lesable, who semed less sad and weary than usual, acknowledged that he had underrated Maze on his first acquaintance.

Maze returned at intervals, which gradually grew shorter. He delighted everybody. They petted and coddled him. Cora prepared for him the dishes he liked, and the intimacy of the three men soon became so great that they were seldom seen apart.

The new friend took the whole family to the theater in boxes procured through the press. They returned on foot, through the streets thronged with people, to the door of Lesable's apartments, Maze and Cora walking before, keeping step, hip to hip, swinging with the same movement, the same rhythm, like two beings created to walk side by side through life. They spoke to each other in a low tone, laughing softly together, and seemed to understand each other instinctively: sometimes the young woman would turn her head and throw behind her a glance at her husband and father.

Cachelin followed them with a look of benevolent regard, and often, forgetting that he spoke to his son-in-law, he declared: "They have the same physique exactly. It is a pleasure to see them together."

Lesable replied quietly: "Yes, they are about the same figure." He was happy now in the consciousness that his heart was beating more vigorously, that his lungs acted more freely, and that his health had improved in every respect; his rancor against his father-in-law, whose cruel taunts had now entirely ceased, vanished little by little.

The first day of January he was promoted to the chief clerkship. His joy was so excessive over his happy event that on returning home he embraced his wife for the first time in six months. She appeared embarrassed, as if he had done something improper, and she looked at Maze, who had called to present to her his devotion and respect on the first day of the year. He also had an embarrassed air and turned toward the window like a man who does not wish to see.

But Cachelin very soon resumed his brutalities, and began to harass his son-in-law with his coarse jests.

Sometimes he even attacked Maze, as though he blamed him also for the catastrophe suspended over them—the inevitable date of which approached nearer every minute.

Cora alone appeared composed, entirely happy and radiant. She had forgotten, it seemed, the threatening nearness of the term.

March had come. All hope seemed lost, for it would be three years on the twentieth of July since Aunt Charlotte's death.

An early spring had advanced the vegetation, and Maze proposed to his friends one Sunday to make an excursion to the banks of the Seine, to gather the violets in the shady places. They set out by a morning train and got off at Maisons-Laffitte. A breath of winter still lingered among the bare branches, but the turf was green and lustrous, flecked with flowers of white and blue, and the fruit trees on the hillsides seemed garlanded with roses as their bare branches showed through the clustering blossoms. The Seine, thick and muddy from the late rains, flowed slowly between its banks gnawed by the frosts of winter; and all the country, steeped in vapor, exhaled a savor of sweet humidity under the warmth of the first days of spring.

They wandered in the park. Cachelin, more glum than usual, tapped his cane on the graveled walk, thinking bitterly of their misfortune, so soon to be irremediable. Lesable, morose also, feared to wet his feet in the grass, while his wife and Maze were gathering flowers to make a bouquet. Cora for several days had seemed suffering, and looked weary and pale. She was soon tired and wished to return for luncheon. They came upon a little restaurant near an old ruined mill, and the traditional repast of a Parisian picnic party was soon served under a green arbor, on a little table covered with two napkins, and quite near the banks of the river. They had fried gudgeons and roast beef cooked with potatoes, and they had come to the salad of fresh green lettuce, when Cora rose brusquely and ran toward the river, pressing her napkin with both hands to her mouth.

Lesable, uneasy, wondered what could be the matter. Maze disconcerted, blushed, and stammered, "I do not know—she was well a moment since."

Cachelin appeared frightened, and remained seated, with his fork in the air, a leaf of salad suspended at the end. Then he rose, trying to see his daughter. Bending forward, he perceived her leaning against a tree and seeming very ill. A swift suspicion flashed through his mind, and he fell back into his seat and regarded with an embarrassed air the two men, both of whom seemed now equally confused. He looked at them with anxious eyes, no longer daring to speak, wild with anguish and hope.

A quarter of an hour passed in utter silence. Then Cora reappeared, a little pale and walking slowly. No one questioned her; each seemed to divine a happy event, difficult to speak of. They burned to know, but feared also to hear, the truth. Cachelin alone had the courage to ask: "You are better now?" And she replied: "Yes, thank you; there is not much the matter; but we will return early, as I have a light headache." When they set out she took the arm of her husband as if to signify something mysterious she had not yet dared to avow.

They separated at the station of St. Lazare. Maze, making a pretext of some business affair which he had just remembered, bade them adieu, after having shaken hands with all of them. As soon as Cachelin was alone with his daughter and his son-in-law, he asked: "What was the matter with you at breakfast?"

But Cora did not reply at first; after hesitating for a moment she said: "It was nothing much; a little sickness of the stomach was all." She walked with a languid step, but with a smile on her lips.

Lesable was ill at ease, his mind distracted; haunted with confused and contradictory ideas, angry, feeling an unavowable shame, cherishing a cowardly jealousy, he was like those sleepers who close their eyes in the morning that they may not see the ray of light which glides between the curtains and strikes the bed like a brilliant shaft.

As soon as he entered the house, he shut himself in his own room, pretending to be occupied with some unfinished work. Then Cachelin, placing his hands on his daughter's shoulders, exclaimed: "You are pregnant, aren't you?"

She stammered: "Yes, I think so. Two months."

Before she had finished speaking, he bounded with joy, then began to dance the cancan around her, an old recollection of his garrison days. He lifted his leg and leaped like a young kid in spite of his great paunch and made the whole apartment shake with his gambols. The furniture jostled, the glasses on the buffet rattled, and the chandelier oscillated like the lamp of a ship.

He took his beloved daughter in his arms and embraced her frantically. Then tapping her lightly on the shoulder he cried: "Ah, it is done, then, at last! Have you told your husband?"

She murmured, suddenly intimidated: "No—not yet—I—I—was waiting——"

But Cachelin exclaimed: "Good, very good. You find it awkward. I will run and tell him myself." And he rushed to the apartment of his son-in-law. On seeing him enter, Lesable, who was doing nothing, rose and looked inquiringly at Cachelin, who left him no time for conjecture but cried: "Do you know your wife is in the family way?"

The husband was stricken speechless, his countenance changed, and the blood surged to the roots of his hair: "What? How? Cora? you say——" He faltered when he recovered his voice.

"I say that she is pregnant; do you understand? Now is our chance!"

In his joy he took Lesable's hands and pressed and shook them, as if to felicitate him, to thank him, and cried: "Ah, at last it is true, it is true! it is true! Think of the fortune we shall have!" and unable to contain himself longer, he caught his son-in-law in his arms and embraced him, crying: "More than a million! think of it! more than a million!" and he began to dance more violently than ever.

"But come, she is waiting for you, come and embrace her, at least," and taking him by the shoulders he pushed Lesable before him, and threw him like a ball into the apartment were Cora stood anxiously waiting and listening.

The moment she saw her husband, she recoiled, stifled with a sudden emotion. He stood before her, pale and severe. He had the air of a judge, and she of a culprit. At last he said: "It seems that you are pregnant."

She stammered in a trembling voice: "Yes, that seems to be the case."

But Cachelin seized each of them by the neck, and, bringing them face to face, cried: "Now kiss each other, by George! It is a fitting occasion."

And after releasing them, he capered about like a schoolboy, shouting: "Victory, victory, we have won our case! I say, Léopold, we must purchase a country house; there, at least, you will certainly recover your health." At this idea Lesable trembled. His father-in-law continued: "We will invite M. Torchebeuf and his wife to visit us, and as the under chief is at the end of his term you may take his place. That is the way to bring it about."

Lesable was now beginning to regard things from Cachelin's standpoint, and he saw himself receiving his chief at a beautiful country place on the banks of the river, dressed in coat of white twill, with a Panama hat on his head.

Something sweet entered into his heart with this hope, something warm and good seemed to melt within him, rendering him light of heart and healthier in feeling. He smiled, still without speaking.

Cachelin, intoxicated with joy, transported at the thought of his fine prospects, continued:

"Who knows, we may gain some political influence. Perhaps you will be deputy. At all events, we can see the society of the neighborhood and enjoy some luxuries. And you shall have a little pony to convey you every morning to the station."

These images of luxury, of elegance and prosperity aroused the drooping spirits of Lesable. The thought that he could be driven in his own carriage, like the rich people he had so often envied, filled him with satisfaction, and he could not refrain from exclaiming: "Ah, that will be delightful indeed."

Cora, seeing him won over, smiled tenderly and gratefully, and Cachelin, who saw no obstacles now in the way of indulgence, declared: "We will dine at the restaurant, to celebrate the happy event."

When they reached home, the two men were a little tipsy, and Lesable, who saw double and whose ideas were all topsy-turvy, could not find his bedroom. He made his way by mistake, or forgetfulness, into the long vacant bed of his wife. And all night long it seemed to him that the bed oscillated like a boat, rolling and pitching as though it would upset. He was even a little seasick.

He was surprised on awaking to find Cora in his arms. She opened her eyes with a smile and kissed him with a sudden effusion of gratitude and affection. Then she said to him, in that caressing voice which women employ in their cajoleries: "If you wish to be very nice, you will not go to your office today. There is no need to be so punctual now that we are going to be rich, and we will make a little visit to the country, all by ourselves."

Lesable was content to remain quiet, with the feeling for self-indulgence which follows an evening of excess, and the warmth of the bed was grateful. He felt the drowsy wish to lie a long time, to do nothing more but to live in tranquil idleness. An unusual sloth paralyzed his soul and subdued his body, and one vague, happy, and continuous thought never left him—he was going to be rich, independent.

But suddenly a fear seized him, and he whispered softly, as if he thought the walls might hear him: "Are you very sure you are pregnant, after all?"

She reassured him at once. "Oh, yes! I am certain of it. I could not be mistaken."

And, as if still doubting, he traced the outline of her figure with his hand, and feeling convinced declared: "Yes, it is true—but you will not be brought to bed before the date. They will contest our right on that account, perhaps."

At this supposition she grew angry.

"Oh, no indeed, they are not going to trick us now after so much misery, so much trouble, and so many efforts. Oh, no, indeed!" She was overwhelmed with indignation. "Let us go at once to the notary," she said.

But his advice was to get a physician's certificate first, and they presented themselves again to Dr. Lefilleul.

He recognized them immediately, and exclaimed: "Ah well, have you succeeded?"

They both blushed up to their ears, and Cora a little shamefacedly stammered: "I believe we have, doctor."

The doctor rubbed his hands, crying: "I expected it, I expected it. The means I recommended to you never fail; at least, only from some radical incapacity of one of the parties."

When he had made an examination of the young wife, he declared: "It is true, bravo!" and he wrote on a sheet of paper:

"I, the undersigned, doctor of medicine, of the Faculty of Paris, certify that Mme. Léopold Lesable, nee Cachelin, presents all the symptoms of pregnancy, dating from over three months."

Then, turning toward Lesable: "And you," he said, "how is that chest and that heart?" and having made an auscultation, he declared that the patient was entirely cured. They set out happy and joyous, arm in arm, with elastic steps. But on the route Léopold had an idea. "We had better go home, before we see the lawyer, and rearrange your dress; you'll put two or three towels under your belt. It will draw attention to it and that will be better; he will not believe then that we are trying to gain time."

They returned home, and he himself undressed his wife in order to adjust the deception. Ten consecutive times Lesable changed the position of the towels, and stepped back some paces to get the proper effect, wishing to obtain an absolutely perfect resemblance. Satisfied with the result at last, they set out again and walked proudly through the streets, Lesable carrying himself with the air of one whose virility was established and patent to all the world.

The notary received them kindly. Then he listened to their explanation, ran his eye over the certificate, and, as Lesable insisted, "For the rest, monsieur, it is only necessary to glance for a second," he threw a convinced look on the telltale figure of the young woman.

There was a moment of anxious suspense, when the man of law declared: "Assuredly, whether the infant is born or to be born, it exists, it lives; so we will suspend the execution of the testament till the confinement of Madame."

After leaving the office of the notary, they embraced each other on the stairway, so exuberant was their joy.

VII

From the moment of this happy discovery, the three relatives lived in the most perfect accord. They were good-humored, reasonable, and kind. Cachelin had recovered all his old gaiety, and Cora loaded her husband with attentions. Lesable also seemed like another man, and more gay than he had ever been in his life. Maze came less often, and seemed ill at ease in the family circle; they received him kindly, but with less warmth than formerly, for happiness is egotistical and excludes strangers.

Cachelin himself seemed to feel a certain secret hostility against the handsome clerk whom some months before he had introduced so eagerly into his household. It was he who announced to this friend the pregnancy of Cora. He said to him brusquely: "You know my daughter is pregnant!"

Maze, feigning surprise, replied: "Ah, indeed! you ought to be very happy."

Cachelin responded with a "Humph!" for he perceived that his colleague, on the contrary, did not appear to be delighted. Men care but little to see in this state (whether or not the cause lies with them) women in whom they are interested.

Every Sunday, however, Maze continued to dine with the family, but it was no longer pleasant to spend the evenings with them, albeit no serious difference had arisen; and this strange embarrassment increased from week to week. One evening, just after Maze had gone, Cachelin cried with an air of annoyance: "That fellow is beginning to weary me to death!"

Lesable replied: "The fact is, he does not improve on acquaintance." Cora lowered her eyes. She did not give her opinion. She always seemed embarrassed in the presence of the handsome Maze, who, on his side, appeared almost ashamed when he found himself near her. He no longer smiled on looking at her as formerly, no longer asked her and her husband to accompany him to the theater, and the intimacy, which till lately had been so cordial, seemed to have become but an irksome burden.

One Thursday, when her husband came home to dinner, Cora kissed him with more coquetry than usual and whispered in his ear:

"Perhaps you are going to scold me now?"

"Why should I?" he inquired.

"Well, because—M. Maze came to see me a little while ago, and, as I do not wish to be gossiped about on his account, I begged him never to come when you were not at home. He seemed a little hurt."

Lesable, very much surprised, demanded:

"Very well, what did he say to that?"

"Oh! he did not say much, but it did not please me all the same, and then I asked him to cease his visits entirely. You know very well that it is you and Papa who brought him here—I was not consulted at all about it—and I feared you would be displeased because I had dismissed him."

A grateful joy beamed from the face of her husband.

"You did right, perfectly right, and I even thank you for it."

She went on, in order to establish the understanding between the two men, which she had arranged in advance: "At the office you must conduct yourself as though nothing had happened, and speak to him as you have been in the habit of doing; but he is not to come here any more."

Taking his wife tenderly in his arms, Lesable impressed long kisses on her eyelids and on her cheeks. "You are an angel! You are an angel!" he repeated, and he felt pressing against his stomach the already lusty child.

VIII

Nothing of importance happened up to the date of Cora's confinement, which occurred on the last day of September. The child, being a daughter, was called Désirée. As they wished to make the christening an imposing event, it was decided to postpone the ceremony until they were settled in the new country house which they were going to buy.

They chose a beautiful estate at Asnières, on the hills that overlook the Seine. Great changes had taken place during the winter. As soon as the legacy was secured, Cachelin asked for his pension, which was granted, and he left the office. He employed his leisure moments in cutting, with the aid of a little scroll saw, the covers of cigar boxes. He made clocks, caskets, jardinieres, and all sorts of odd little pieces of furniture. He had a passion for this work, the taste for which had come to him on seeing a peripatetic merchant working thus with sheets of wood on the Avenue de l'Opéra; and each day he obliged everybody to admire some new design both complicated and puerile. He was amazed at his own work and kept on saying: "It is astonishing what one can accomplish!"

The assistant chief, M. Rabot, being dead at last, Lesable fulfilled the duties of his place, although he did not receive the title, for sufficient time had not elapsed since his last promotion.

Cora had become a wholly different woman, more refined, more elegant, instinctively divining all the transformations that wealth imposes. On New Year's Day she made a visit to the wife of her husband's chief, a commonplace person who remained a provincial notwithstanding a residence of thirty-five years in Paris, and she put so much grace and seductiveness into her prayer that Mme. Torchebeuf should stand godmother to her child that the good woman consented. Grandpapa Cachelin was the godfather.

The ceremony took place on a brilliant Sunday in June. All the employees of the office were invited to witness it, except the handsome Maze, who was seen no more in the Cachelin circle.

At nine o'clock Lesable waited at the railway station for the train from Paris, while a groom, in livery covered with great gilt buttons, held by the bridle a plump pony hitched to a brand-new phaeton.

The engine whistled, then appeared, dragging its train of cars, which soon discharged their freight of passengers.

M. Torchebeuf descended from a first-class carriage with his wife, in a magnificent toilette, while Pitolet and Boissel got out of a second-class carriage. They had not dared to invite old Savon, but it was understood that they were to meet him by chance in the afternoon and bring him to dinner with the consent of the chief.

Lesable hurried to meet his superior, who advanced slowly, the lapel of his frock coat ornamented with a decoration that resembled a full-blown red rose. His enormous head, surmounted by a large hat that seemed to crush his small body, gave him the appearance of a phenomenon, and his wife, if she had stood on tiptoe, could have looked over his head without any trouble.

Léopold, radiant, bowed and thanked his guests. He seated them in the phaeton, then, running toward his two colleagues, who were walking modestly behind, he pressed their hands, regretting that his phaeton was too small to accommodate them also. "Follow the quay," he directed, "and you will reach my door—'Villa Désirée,' the fourth one after the turn. Make haste!"

And mounting the phaeton, he took the reins and drove off, while the groom leaped lightly to the little seat behind.

The ceremony was very brilliant, and afterwards they returned for luncheon. Each one found under his napkin a present proportioned to his station. The godmother received a bracelet of solid gold, her husband a scarfpin of rubies, Boissel a pocket book of Russian leather, and Pitolet a superb meerschaum pipe. "It was Désirée," they said, "who offered these presents to her new friends."

Mme. Torchebeuf, blushing with confusion and pleasure, placed on her fat arm the brilliant circle, and, as the chief wore a narrow black cravat which would not receive the pin, he stuck the jewel in the lapel of his frock coat, under the Legion of Honor, as if it had been another decoration of an inferior order.

Outside the window the shining band of the river was seen, curving toward Suresnes, its banks shaded with trees. The sun fell in a rain on the water, making it seem a river of fire. The beginning of the repast was rather solemn, being made formal by the presence of M. and Mme. Torchebeuf. After a while, however, things began to go better. Cachelin threw out some heavy jokes, which he felt would be permitted him since he was rich, and everyone laughed at them. If Pitolet or Boissel had uttered them, the guests would certainly have been shocked.

At dessert, the infant was brought in and received a kiss from each of the company. Smothered in a cloud of snowy lace, the baby looked at the guests with its blue eyes void of intelligence or expression, and rolled its bald head from side to side with an air of newly awakened interest.

Pitolet, amid the confusion of voices, whispered in the ear of Boissel: "It looks like a little Mazette."

The joke went round the Ministry next day.

At two o'clock the health of the newly christened baby was drunk, and Cachelin proposed to show his guests over the property and then to take them for a walk on the banks of the Seine.

They moved in a slow procession from room to room, from the cellar to the garret; then they examined the garden tree by tree, plant by plant; after which, separating into two parties, they set out for a walk.

Cachelin, who did not feel at home in the company of ladies, drew Boissel and Pitolet into a café on the bank of the river, while Mmes. Torchebeuf and Lesable, with their husbands, walked in the opposite direction, these refined ladies not being able to mingle with the common Sunday herd.

They walked slowly along the path, followed by the two men, who talked gravely of the affairs of the office. On the river the boats were continually passing, propelled by long strokes of the oars in the hands of jolly fellows, the muscles of whose bare arms rolled under the sunburned skin. Women, reclining on black or white fur rugs, managed the tillers, drowsing under the hot sun, holding open over their heads, like enormous flowers floating on the surface of the water, umbrellas of red, yellow, and blue silk. Cries from one boat to the other, calls, and shouts, and a remote murmur of human voices lower down, confused and continuous, indicated where the swarming crowds were enjoying a holiday.

Long files of fishermen stood motionless all along the river, while the swimmers, almost naked, standing in heavy fishing boats, plunged in head foremost, climbed back upon the boats, and leaped into the water again.

Mme. Torchebeuf looked on in surprise.

Cora said to her: "It is like this every Sunday; it spoils this charming country for me."

A canoe moved softly by. Two women rowed, while two men were stretched in the bottom of the boat. One of the women, turning her head towards the shore, cried:

"Hello! hello! you respectable women! I have a man for sale, very cheap! Do you want him?"

Cora turned away contemptuously and, taking the arm of her companion, said: "We cannot remain here; let us go. What infamous creatures!"

They moved away as M. Torchebeuf was saying to Lesable: "It is settled for the first of January. The head of the department has positively promised me."

"I don't know how to thank you, dear master," Lesable replied.

When they reached home they found Cachelin, Pitolet, and Boissel laughing immoderately and almost carrying old Savon, whom they jokingly declared they had found on the beach in the company of a girl.

The frightened old man was crying: "It is not true, no, it is not true. It is not right to say that, M. Cachelin, it is not kind."

And Cachelin, choking with laughter, cried: "Ah, you old rogue, did you not call her your 'sweet goose quill'? We caught you, you rascal!"

Then the ladies, too, began to laugh at the dismay of the poor old man.

Cachelin continued: "With M. Torchebeuf's permission, we will keep him prisoner as a punishment and make him dine with us."

The chief good-humoredly consented, and they continued to laugh about the lady abandoned by the old man, who protested all the time, annoyed at this mischievous farce.

The subject was the occasion of inexhaustible wit throughout the evening, which sometimes even bordered on the obscene.

Cora and Mme. Torchebeuf, seated under a tent on the lawn, watched the reflections of the setting sun, which threw upon the leaves a purple glow.

Not a breath stirred the branches, a serene and infinite peace fell from the calm and flaming heavens.

Some boats still passed, more slowly, drifting with the tide.

Cora remarked: "It appears that poor M. Savon married a bad woman."

Mme. Torchebeuf, who was familiar with everything of the office, replied:

"Yes, she was an orphan, very much too young for him, and deceived him with a worthless fellow, and she ended in running away with him."

Then the fat lady added: "I say he was a worthless fellow, but I know nothing about it. It is reported that they loved one another very much. In any case, old Savon is not very seductive."

Mme. Lesable replied gravely:

"That is no excuse; the poor man is much to be pitied. Our next door neighbor, M. Barbou, has had the same experience. His wife fell in love with a sort of painter who passed his summers here, and she has gone abroad with him. I do not understand how women can fall so low. To my mind it seems a special chastisement should be meted out to those wicked creatures who bring shame upon their families."

At the end of the alley the nurse appeared, carrying the little Désirée wrapped in her laces. The child, all rosy in the red gold of the evening light, was coming towards the two women. She stared at the fiery sky with the same pale and astonished eyes with which she regarded their faces.

All the men who were talking at a distance drew near, and Cachelin, seizing his little granddaughter, tossed her aloft in his arms as if he would carry her to the skies. Her figure was outlined against the brilliant line of the horizon, while her long white robe almost touched the ground; and the grandfather cried: "Look! isn't this the best thing in the world, after all, Father Savon?"

But the old man made no reply, having nothing to say, or perhaps thinking too many things.

A servant opened the door and announced: "Madame is served!"

THE WOODEN SHOES

The old priest was sputtering out the last words of his sermon over the white caps of the peasant women and the rough or greasy heads of the men. The large baskets of the farmers' wives who had come from a distance to attend Mass were on the ground beside them, and the heavy heat of a July day caused them all to exhale a smell like that of cattle or of a flock of sheep, and the cocks could be heard crowing through the large west door, which was wide open, as well as the lowing of the cows in a neighboring field.

"As God wishes. Amen!" the priest said. Then he ceased, opened a book and, as he did every week, began to give notice of all the small parish events for the following week. He was an old man with white hair who had been in the parish for over forty years and from the pulpit was in the habit of discoursing familiarly to them all, so he went on: "I will recommend Désiré Vallin, who is very ill, to your prayers, and also La Paumelle, who is not recovering from her confinement satisfactorily."

He had forgotten the rest, and so he looked for the slips of paper which were put away in a breviary. At last he found two and continued: "I will not have the lads and girls come into the churchyard in the evening, as they do; otherwise I shall inform the rural policeman. Monsieur Césaire Omont would like to find a respectable girl as servant." He reflected for a few moments and then added: "That is all, my brethren, and I wish that all of you may find the Divine mercy." And he came down from the pulpit to finish Mass.

When the Malandains had returned to their cottage, which was the last in the village of La Sablière, on the road to Fourville, the father, a thin, wrinkled old peasant, sat down at the table, while his wife took the saucepan off the fire, and Adelaide, the daughter, took the glasses and plates out of the sideboard. Then the father said: "I think that place at Maître Omont's ought to be a good one, as he is a widower and his daughter-in-law does not like him. He is all alone and has money. I think it would be a good thing to send Adelaide there."

His wife put the black saucepan on to the table, took the lid off, and while the steam, which smelled strongly of cabbage, rose into the air she pondered on the suggestion. Presently the old man continued: "He has got some money, that is certain, but anyone going there ought to be very sharp, and Adelaide is not that at all."

His wife replied: "I might go and see, all the same," and, turning to her daughter, a strapping, silly-looking girl with yellow hair and fat red cheeks, like apples, she said: "Do you hear, you great silly? You are to go to Maître Omont's and offer yourself as his servant, and you will do whatever he tells you."

The girl began to laugh in a foolish manner, without replying, and then the three began their dinner. In a few minutes the father continued: "Listen to me, girl, and try not to make a mistake about what I am going to say to you." And slowly and minutely he laid down for her her line of conduct, anticipating the minutest details and preparing her for the conquest of an old widower who was on unfriendly terms with his family. The mother ceased eating to listen to him, and she sat there, with her fork in her hand, looking at her husband and her daughter by turns and following every word with concentrated and silent attention, while Adelaide remained listless, docile and stupid, with vague and wandering eyes.

As soon as their meal was over her mother made her put her cap on, and they both started off to see M. Césaire Omont. He lived in a small brick house adjoining his tenants' cottages, for he had retired and was living by subdividing and letting his land.

He was about fifty-five years old and was stout, jovial and rough mannered, as rich men often are. He laughed and shouted loud enough to make the walls fall down, drank brandy and cider by the glassful and was said to be still of an amorous disposition, in spite of his age. He liked to walk about his fields with his hands behind his back, digging his wooden shoes into the fat soil, looking at the sprouting corn or the flowering colza with the eye of a retired farmer, at his ease, who likes to see the crops but does not trouble himself about them any longer. People used to say of him: "There is a Mr Merry-man, who does not get up in a good temper every day."

He received the two women as he was finishing his coffee, with his fat stomach against the table and, turning round, said: "What do you want?"

The mother was spokeswoman. "This is our girl Adelaide, and I have come to ask you to take her as servant, as Monsieur le Curé told us you wanted one."

Maître Omont looked at the girl, and then he said roughly: "How old is the great she-goat?"

"Twenty last Michaelmas Day, Monsieur Omont."

"That is settled; she will have fifteen francs a month and her food. I shall expect her tomorrow to make my soup in the morning." And he dismissed the two women.

The next day Adelaide entered upon her duties and began to work hard, without saying a word, as she was in the habit of doing at home. About nine o'clock, as she was scrubbing the kitchen floor, Monsieur Omont called her: "Adelaide!"

She came immediately, saying: "Here I am, master." As soon as she was opposite him, with her red and neglected hands and her troubled looks, he said: "Now just listen to me, so that there may be no mistake between us. You are my servant, but nothing else; you understand what I mean. We shall keep our shoes apart."

"Yes, master."

"Each in our own place, my girl, you in your kitchen, I in my dining room, and with that exception everything will be for you just as it is for me. Is that settled?"

"Yes, master."

"Very well; that is all right, and now go to your work."

And she went out to attend to her duties, and at midday she served up her master's dinner in the little dining room with the flowered paper on the walls, and then when the soup was on the table she went to tell him. "Dinner is ready, master."

He went in and sat down, looked round, unfolded his table napkin, hesitated for a moment, and then in a voice of thunder he shouted: "Adelaide!"

She rushed in, terribly frightened, for he had shouted as if he meant to murder her.

"Well, in heaven's name, where is your place?"

"But, master!"

"I do not like to eat alone," he roared; "you will sit there or go to the devil, if you don't choose to do so. Go and get your plate and glass."

She brought them in, feeling very frightened, and stammered: "Here I am, master," and then sat down opposite to him. He grew jovial, clinked glasses with her, rapped the table and told her stories to which she listened with downcast eyes, without daring to say a word, and from time to time she got up to fetch some bread, cider or plates. When she brought in the coffee she only put one cup before him, and then he grew angry again and growled:

"Well, what about yourself?"

"I never take any, master."

"Why not?"

"Because I do not like it."

Then he burst out afresh: "I am not fond of having my coffee by myself, confound it! If you will not take it here you can go to the devil. Go and get a cup and make haste about it."

So she went and fetched a cup, sat down again, tasted the black liquor and made faces over it but swallowed it to the last drop, under her master's furious looks. Then he made her also drink her first glass of brandy as an extra drop, the second as a livener and the third as a kick behind, and then he told her to go and wash up her plates and dishes, adding that she was "a good sort of girl."

It was the same at supper, after which she had to play dominoes with him. Then he sent her to bed, saying that he would come upstairs soon. So she went to her room, a garret under the roof, and after saying her prayers, undressed and got into bed. But very soon she sprang up in a fright, for a furious shout had shaken the house. "Adelaide!" She opened her door and replied from her attic: "Here I am, master."

"Where are you?"

"In bed, of course, master."

Then he roared out: "Will you come downstairs, in heaven's name? I do not like to sleep alone, and, by Jove, if you object you can just go at once."

Then in her terror she replied from upstairs: "I will come, master." She looked for her candle, and he soon heard her small clogs pattering down the stairs. When she had got to the bottom steps he seized her by the arm, and as soon as she had left her light wooden shoes by the side of her master's heavy boots he pushed her into his room, growling out: "Quicker than that, confound it!"

And without knowing what she was saying she answered: "Here I am, here I am, master."

Six months later, when she went to see her parents one Sunday, her father looked at her curiously and then said: "Are you not *enceinte?*"

She remained thunderstruck and looked at her waist and then said: "No, I do not think so."

Then he asked her, for he wanted to know everything: "Just tell me, didn't you mix your clogs together one night?"

"Yes, I mixed them the first night and then every other night."

"Well, then you are *enceinte*, you great fool!"

On hearing that she began to sob and stammered: "How could I know? How was I to know?" Old Malandain looked at her knowingly and appeared very pleased, and then he asked: "What did you not know?" And amid tears she replied: "How was I to know how children were made?" And when her mother came back the man said, without any anger: "There, she is *enceinte* now."

But the woman was furious; her finer instinct revolted, and she called her daughter, who was in tears, every name she could think of—a "trollop" and a "strumpet." Then, however, the old man made her hold her tongue, and as he took up his cap to go and talk the matter over with Master Césaire Omont, he remarked: "She is actually more stupid than I thought she was; she did not even know what he was doing, the fool!"

On the next Sunday, after the sermon, the old curé published the banns between Monsieur Onufre-Césaire Omont and Céleste-Adelaide Malandain.

BOITELLE

Père Boitelle (Antoine) had the reputation through the whole country of a specialist in dirty jobs. Every time a pit, a dunghill or a cesspool required to be cleared away, or a dirt hole to be cleansed out, he was the person employed to do it.

He would come there with his nightman's tools and his wooden shoes covered with dirt and would set to work, whining incessantly about the nature of his occupation. When people asked him why he did this loathsome work he would reply resignedly:

"Faith, 'tis for my children whom I must support. This brings in more than anything else."

He had, indeed, fourteen children. If anyone asked him what had become of them he would say with an air of indifference:

"There are only eight of them left in the house. One is out at service, and five are married."

When the questioner wanted to know whether they were well married he replied vivaciously:

"I did not cross them. I crossed them in nothing. They married just as they pleased. We shouldn't go against people's likings—it turns out badly. I am a night cartman because my parents went against my likings. But for that I would have become a workman like the others."

Here is the way his parents had thwarted him in his likings:

He was at that time a soldier stationed at Harve, not more stupid than another or sharper either, a rather simple fellow, in truth. During his hours of freedom his greatest pleasure was to walk along the quay where the bird dealers congregate. Sometimes alone, sometimes with a soldier from his own part of the country, he would slowly saunter along by cages where parrots with green backs and yellow heads from the banks of the Amazon, parrots with gray backs and red heads from Senegal, enormous macaws, which looked like birds brought up in conservatories, with their flowerlike feathers, plumes and tufts, parakeets of every shape, painted with minute care by that excellent miniaturist, God Almighty, with the little young birds hopping about, yellow, blue and variegated, mingling their cries with the noise of the quay, added to the din caused by the unloading of the vessels, as well as by passengers and vehicles—a violent clamor, loud, shrill and deafening, as if from some distant, monstrous forest.

Boitelle would stop with strained eyes, wide-open mouth, laughing and enraptured, showing his teeth to the captive cockatoos who kept nodding their white or yellow topknots toward the glaring red of his breeches and the copper buckle of his belt. When he found a bird that could talk he put questions to it, and if it happened at the time to be disposed to reply and to hold a conversation with him, he would remain there till nightfall, filled with gaiety and contentment. He also found heaps of fun in looking at the monkeys and could conceive no greater luxury for a rich man than to possess these animals, just like cats and dogs. This taste for the exotic he had in his blood, as people have a taste for the chase or for medicine or for the priesthood. He could not refrain, every time the gates of the barracks

opened, from going back to the quay, as if drawn toward it by an irresistible longing.

Now on one occasion, having stopped almost in ecstasy before an enormous
ararauna, which was swelling out its plumes, bending forward and bridling up again,
as if making the court curtsies of parrot land, he saw the door of a little tavern
adjoining the bird dealer's shop opening, and his attention was attracted by a young
Negress with a silk kerchief tied round her head, sweeping into the street the rubbish and the sand of the establishment.

Boitelle's attention was soon divided between the bird and the woman, and he
really could not tell which of these two beings he contemplated with the greater
astonishment and delight.

The Negress, having got rid of the sweepings of the tavern, raised her eyes and,
in her turn, was dazzled by the soldier's uniform. There she stood, facing him, with
her broom in her hands as if she were presenting arms for him, while the ararauna
continued making curtsies. Now at the end of a few seconds the soldier began to get
embarrassed by this attention, and he walked away gingerly so as not to present the
appearance of beating a retreat.

But he came back. Almost every day he passed in front of the Colonial Tavern,
and often he could distinguish through the windowpanes the figure of the little
black-skinned maid filling out bocks or glasses of brandy for the sailors of the port.
Frequently, too, she would come out to the door on seeing him. Soon, without even
having exchanged a word, they smiled at one another like old acquaintances, and
Boitelle felt his heart moved when he saw suddenly glittering between the dark
lips of the girl her shining row of white teeth. At length he ventured one day to
enter and was quite surprised to find that she could speak French like everyone else.
The bottle of lemonade, of which she was good enough to accept a glassful, remained in the soldier's recollection memorably delicious, and it became habitual
with him to come and absorb in this little tavern on the quay all the agreeable
drinks which he could afford.

For him it was a treat, a happiness, on which his thoughts were constantly dwelling, to watch the black hand of the little maid pouring out something into his glass
while her teeth, brighter than her eyes, showed themselves as she laughed. When
they had kept company in this way for two months they became fast friends, and
Boitelle, after his first astonishment at discovering that this Negress was in principle
as good as the best girls in the country, that she exhibited a regard for economy,
industry, religion and good conduct, loved her more on that account and became so
much smitten with her that he wanted to marry her.

He told her about his intentions, which made her dance with joy. Besides, she
had a little money, left her by a female oyster dealer who had picked her up when
she had been left on the quay at Havre by an American captain. This captain had
found her, when she was only about six years old, lying on bales of cotton in the
hold of his ship, some hours after his departure from New York. On his arrival in
Havre he there abandoned to the care of this compassionate oyster dealer the little
black creature who had been hidden on board his vessel; he could not tell how or
why.

The oyster woman having died, the young Negress became a servant at the
Colonial Tavern.

Antoine Boitelle added: "This will be all right if my parents don't go against it.

I will never go against them, you understand—never! I'm going to say a word or two to them the first time I go back to the country."

On the following week, in fact, having obtained twenty-four hours' leave, he went to see his family, who cultivated a little farm at Tourteville near Yvetot.

He waited till the meal was finished, the hour when the coffee baptized with brandy makes people more openhearted, before informing his parents that he had found a girl answering so well to his likings in every way that there could not exist any other in all the world so perfectly suited to him.

The old people, at this observation, immediately assumed a circumspect air and wanted explanations. At first he concealed nothing from them except the color of her skin.

She was a servant, without much means but strong, thrifty, clean, well conducted and sensible. All these were better than money would be in the hands of a bad housewife. Moreover, she had a few sous, left her by a woman who had reared her —a good number of sous, almost a little dowry—fifteen hundred francs in the savings' bank. The old people, overcome by his talk and relying, too, on their own judgment, were gradually giving way when he came to the delicate point. Laughing in rather a constrained fashion, he said:

"There's only one thing you may not like. She is not white."

They did not understand, and he had to explain at some length and very cautiously, to avoid shocking them, that she belonged to the dusky race of which they had only seen samples among figures exhibited at Epinal. Then they became restless, perplexed, alarmed, as if he had proposed a union with the devil.

The mother said: "Black? How much of her is black? Is it the whole of her?"
He replied: "Certainly. Everywhere, just as you are white everywhere."
The father interposed: "Black? Is it as black as the pot?"
The son answered: "Perhaps a little less than that. She is black, but not disgustingly black. The curé's cassock is black, but it is not uglier than a surplice; white is white."
The father said: "Are there more black people besides her in her country?"
And the son, with an air of conviction, exclaimed: "Certainly!"
But the old man shook his head: "This must be disagreeable!"
Said the son: "It isn't more disagreeable than anything else, seeing that you get used to it in no time."
The mother asked: "It doesn't soil linen more than other skins, this black skin?"
"Not more than your own, as it is her proper color."
Then after many other questions it was agreed that the parents should see this girl before coming to any decision and that the young fellow, whose period of service was coming to an end in the course of a month, should bring her to the house in order that they might examine her and decide by talking the matter over whether or not she was too dark to enter the Boitelle family.

Antoine accordingly announced that on Sunday, the twenty-second of May, the day of his discharge, he would start for Tourteville with his sweetheart.

She had put on, for this journey to the house of her lover's parents, her most beautiful and most gaudy clothes, in which yellow, red and blue were the prevailing colors, so that she had the appearance of one adorned for a national fete.

At the terminus, as they were leaving Havre, people stared at her very much, and Boitelle was proud of giving his arm to a person who commanded so much atten-

tion. Then in the third-class carriage in which she took a seat by his side she excited
so much astonishment among the peasants that the people in the adjoining compartments got up on their benches to get a look at her over the wooden partition
which divided the different portions of the carriage from one another. A child, at
sight of her, began to cry with terror; another concealed his face in his mother's
apron. Everything went off well, however, up to their arrival at their destination.
But when the train slackened its rate of motion as they drew near Yvetot, Antoine
felt ill at ease, as he would have done at an inspection when he did not know his
drill practice. Then as he put his head out through the carriage door he recognized,
some distance away, his father, who was holding the bridle of the horse yoked to a
carriage, and his mother, who had made her way to the railed portion of the platform where a number of spectators had gathered.

He stepped out first, gave his hand to his sweetheart and, holding himself erect,
as if he were escorting a general, he advanced toward his family.

The mother, on seeing this black lady in variegated costume in her son's company, remained so stupefied that she could not open her mouth, and the father
found it hard to hold the horse, which the engine or the Negress caused to rear
for some time without stopping. But Antoine, suddenly seized with the unmingled
joy of seeing once more the old people, rushed forward with open arms, embraced
his mother, embraced his father, in spite of the nag's fright, and then, turning
toward his companion, at whom the passengers on the platform stopped to stare
with amazement, he proceeded to explain:

"Here she is! I told you that at first sight she seems odd, but as soon as you
know her, in very truth, there's not a better sort in the whole world. Say good morrow to her without making any bother about it."

Thereupon Mère Boitelle, herself nearly frightened out of her wits, made a sort
of curtsy, while the father took off his cap, murmuring: "I wish you good luck!"

Then without further delay they climbed up on the car, the two women at the
lower end on seats, which made them jump up and down as the vehicle went
jolting along the road, and the two men outside on the front seat.

Nobody spoke. Antoine, ill at ease, whistled a barrack-room air; his father lashed
the nag, and his mother, from where she sat in the corner, kept casting sly glances
at the Negress, whose forehead and cheekbones shone in the sunlight like well-
blacked shoes.

Wishing to break the ice, Antoine turned round.

"Well," he said, "we don't seem inclined to talk."

"We must get time," replied the old woman.

He went on:

"Come, tell us the little story about that hen of yours that laid eight eggs."

It was a funny anecdote of long standing in the family. But as his mother still
remained silent, paralyzed by emotion, he started the talking himself and narrated,
with much laughter on his own part, this memorable adventure. The father, who
knew it by heart, brightened up at the opening words of the narrative; his wife soon
followed his example, and the Negress herself, when he had reached the drollest
part of it, suddenly gave vent to a laugh, so noisy, rolling, and torrentlike, that the
horse, becoming excited, broke into a gallop for a little while.

This served as the introduction to their acquaintanceship. The company at
length began to chat.

On reaching the house they all alighted, and he conducted his sweetheart to a room so that she might take off her dress, to avoid staining it while preparing a good dish intended to win the old people's affections by appealing to their stomachs. Then he drew his parents aside near the door and with beating heart asked:

"Well, what do you say now?"

The father said nothing. The mother, less timid, exclaimed:

"She is too black. No indeed, this is too much for me. It turns my blood."

"That may be, but it is only for the moment."

They then made their way into the interior of the house where the good woman was somewhat affected at the spectacle of the Negress engaged in cooking. She at once proceeded to assist her, with petticoats tucked up, active in spite of her age.

The meal was an excellent one—very long, very enjoyable. When they had afterward taken a turn together Antoine said to his father:

"Well, Dad, what do you say to this?"

The peasant took care never to compromise himself.

"I have no opinion about it. Ask your mother."

So Antoine went back to his mother and, leading her to the end of the room, said:

"Well, Mother, what do you think of her?"

"My poor lad, she is really too black. If she were only a little less black I would not go against you, but this is too much. One would think it was Satan!"

He did not press her, knowing how obstinate the old woman had always been, but he felt a tempest of disappointment sweeping over his heart. He was turning over in his mind what he ought to do, what plan he could devise, surprised, moreover, that she had not conquered them already as she had captivated himself. And they all four set out with slow steps through the cornfields, having again relapsed into silence. Whenever they passed a fence they saw a countryman sitting on the stile and a group of brats climbing up to stare at them. People rushed out into the road to see the "black" whom young Boitelle had brought home with him. At a distance they noticed people scampering across the fields as they do when the drum beats to draw public attention to some living phenomenon. Père and Mère Boitelle, scared by this curiosity which was exhibited everywhere through the country at their approach, quickened their pace, walking side by side, leaving far behind their son, whose dark companion asked what his parents thought of her.

He hesitatingly replied that they had not yet made up their minds.

But on the village green people rushed out of all the houses in a flutter of excitement, and at the sight of the gathering rabble old Boitelle took to his heels and regained his abode, while Antoine, swelling with rage, his sweetheart on his arm, advanced majestically under the battery of staring eyes opened wide in amazement.

He understood that it was at an end, that there was no hope for him, that he could not marry his Negress. She also understood it, and as they drew near the farmhouse they both began to weep. As soon as they had got back to the house she once more took off her dress to aid the mother in her household duties and followed her everywhere, to the dairy, to the stable, to the hen house, taking on herself the hardest part of the work, repeating always, "Let me do it, Madame Boitelle," so that when night came on the old woman, touched but inexorable, said to her son: "She is a good girl, all the same. 'Tis a pity she is so black, but indeed she is too much so. I couldn't get used to it. She must go back again. She is too black!"

And young Boitelle said to his sweetheart:

"She will not consent. She thinks you are too black. You must go back again. I will go with you to the train. No matter—don't fret. I am going to talk to them after you have started."

He then conducted her to the railway station, still cheering her up with hope, and when he had kissed her he put her into the train, which he watched as it passed out of sight, his eyes swollen with tears. In vain did he appeal to the old people. They would not give their consent.

And when he had told this story, which was known all over the country, Antoine Boitelle would always add:

"From that time forward I have had no heart for anything—for anything at all. No trade suited me any longer, and so I became what I am—a night cartman."

People would say to him: "Yet you got married."

"Yes, and I can't say that my wife didn't please me, seeing that I've got fourteen children, but she is not the other one, oh no—certainly not! The other one, mark you, my Negress, she had only to give me one glance and I felt as if I were in heaven!"

SELFISHNESS

We read lately in the journals the following lines:

Boulogne-Sur-Mer, January 22.

A frightful disaster has occurred which throws into consternation our maritime population, so grievously afflicted two years since. The fishing boat, commanded by Shipmaster Javel, entering into port, was carried to the west and broken upon the rocks of the breakwater near the pier. In spite of the efforts of the salvage boat and of life lines shot out to them, four men and a cabin boy perished. The bad weather continues. We fear new calamities.

Who is this Shipmaster Javel? Is he the brother of the one-armed Javel? If this poor man, tossed by the waves and dead, perhaps, under the debris of his boat cut in pieces, is the one I think he is, he assisted eighteen years ago at another drama, terrible and simple as are all the formidable dramas of the billows.

Javel the elder was then master of a smack. The smack is the fishing boat par excellence. Solid, fearing no kind of weather, with round body, rolled incessantly by the waves, like a cork, always lashed by the hard, foul winds of the Channel, it travels the sea indefatigably, with sail filled, making in its wake a path which reaches the bottom of the ocean, detaching all the sleeping creatures from the rocks, the flat fishes glued to the sand, the heavy crabs with their hooked claws and the lobster with his pointed mustaches.

When the breeze is fresh and the waves choppy the boat puts about to fish. A rope is fastened to the end of a great wooden shank tipped with iron, which is let down by means of two cables slipping over two spools at the extreme end of the craft. And the boat, driving under wind and current, drags after her this apparatus, which ravages and devastates the bottom of the sea.

Javel had on board his younger brother, four men and a cabin boy. He had set out from Boulogne in fair weather to cast the nets. Then suddenly the wind arose, and an unlooked-for squall forced the boat along over the waters. It gained the coast of England, but a tremendous sea beat so against the cliffs and the shore that it was impossible to enter port. The little boat put to sea again and returned to the coast of France. The tempest continued to make the piers unapproachable, enveloping them with foam and shutting off all places of refuge by noise and danger.

The fishing boat set out again, running under the billows, tossed about, shaken up, suffocated in mountains of water, but merry in spite of all, accustomed to heavy weather, which sometimes held it for five or six hours between the two countries, unable to land in the one or the other.

Finally the hurricane ceased when they came out into open sea, and although the sea was still high, the commander ordered them to cast the net. Then the great fishing tackle was thrown overboard, and two men at one side and two at the other began to unwind from rollers the cable which held it. Suddenly it touched the bottom, but a high wave tipped the boat. Javel the younger, who was in the prow directing the casting of the net, tottered and found his arm caught between the cable, stopped an instant by the motion, and the wood on which it slipped. He made a desperate effort with his other hand to lift the cable, but the net already dragged and the rapidly slipping cable would not yield.

Faint from pain, he called. All ran to him. His brother left the helm. They threw their full force upon the rope, forcing it away from the arm it was grinding. It was in vain. "We must cut it," said a sailor, and he drew from his pocket a large knife which could, in two blows, save young Javel's arm. But to cut was to lose the net, and the net meant money, much money—five hundred francs; it belonged to the elder Javel, who held to his property.

With tortured heart he cried out: "No, don't cut; I'll luff the ship." And he ran to the wheel, putting the helm about. The boat scarcely obeyed, paralyzed by the net which counteracted its power and dragged, besides, from the force of the leeway and the wind.

Young Javel fell to his knees with set teeth and haggard eyes. He said nothing. His brother returned, fearing the sailor's cutting.

"Wait! Wait!" he said. "Don't cut; we must cast anchor."

The anchor was thrown overboard, all the chain payed out, and they then tried to take a turn around the capstan with the cables in order to loosen the strain from the weight of the net. They were successful finally and released the arm which hung inert under a sleeve of bloody woolen cloth.

Young Javel was nearly beside himself. They removed the covering from his arm and then saw something horrible, bruised flesh, from which the blood spurted in waves, as if it were forced by a pump. The man himself looked at his arm and murmured: "Fool!"

Then as the hemorrhage made a river on the deck of the boat, the sailors cried: "He'll lose all his blood. We must bind the vein!"

They then took a rope, a great, black, tarred rope and, twisting it around the member above the wound, bound it with all their strength. Little by little the jets of blood stopped and finally ceased altogether.

Young Javel arose, his arm hanging by his side. He took it by the other hand, raised it, turned it, shook it. Everything was broken; the bones were crushed completely; only the muscles held it to his body. He looked at it with sad eyes, as if reflecting. Then he seated himself on a folded sail, and his comrades came around him, advising him to soak it continually to prevent its turning black.

They put a bucket near him, and from minute to minute he would pour water from a glass upon the horrible wound, leaving a thread of color in the clear water.

"You would be better down below," said his brother. He went down but at the end of an hour came up again, feeling better not to be alone. And then, he preferred the open air. He sat down again upon the sail and continued bathing his arm.

The fishing was good. Large fishes with white bodies were lying beside him, shaken by the spasms of death. He looked at them without ceasing to sprinkle his mangled flesh.

When they started to return to Boulogne another gale of wind prevented. The little boat began again its mad course, bounding, tumbling, shaking sadly the wounded man.

The night came. The weather was heavy until daybreak. At sunrise they could see England again, but as the sea was a little less rough, they turned toward France, beating in the wind.

Toward evening young Javel called his comrades and showed them black traces and a villainous look of decay around that part of his arm which was no longer joined to his body.

The sailors looked at it, giving advice. "That must be gangrene," said one.

"It must have salt water on it," said another.

Then they brought salt water and poured it on the wound. The wounded man became livid, grinding his teeth and twisting with pain, but he uttered no cry.

When the burning grew less he said to his brother: "Give me your knife." The brother gave it to him.

"Hold this arm up for me, drawn out straight."

His brother did as he was asked.

Then he began to cut. He cut gently, with caution, severing the last tendons with the sharp blade as one would a thread with a razor. Soon he had only a stump. He fetched a deep sigh and said: "That had to be done. Fool!"

He seemed relieved and breathed with force. He continued to pour water on the part of his arm remaining to him.

The night was still bad, and they could not land. When the day appeared young Javel took his detached arm and examined it carefully. Putrefaction had begun. The comrades came also and examined it, passing it from hand to hand, touching it, turning it over and smelling it.

His brother said: "It's about time to throw that into the sea."

Young Javel was angry; he replied: "No; oh no! I will not. It is mine, isn't it? Worse still, it is my arm." He took it and held it between his legs.

"It won't grow any less putrid," said the elder.

Then an idea came to the wounded man. In order to keep the fish which they kept out a long time, they had with them barrels of salt. "Couldn't I put it in there in the brine?" he asked.

"That's so," declared the others.

Then they emptied one of the barrels, already full of fish from the last few days, and at the bottom they deposited the arm. Then they turned salt upon it and replaced the fishes, one by one.

One of the sailors made a little joke: "Perhaps I could sell it if I cried it around town."

And everybody laughed except the Javel brothers.

The wind still blew. They beat about in sight of Boulogne until the next day at ten o'clock. The wounded man still poured water on his arm. From time to time he would get up and walk from one end of the boat to the other. His brother, who was at the wheel, shook his head and followed him with his eye.

Finally they came into port.

The doctor examined the wound and declared it in good shape. He dressed it perfectly and ordered rest. But Javel could not go to bed without seeing his arm again and went quickly back to the dock to find the barrel which he had marked with a cross.

They emptied it before him, and he found his arm refreshed, well preserved in the salt. He wrapped it in a napkin brought for this purpose and took it home.

His wife and children examined carefully this fragment of their father, touching the fingers, taking up the grains of salt that had lodged under the nails. Then they went to the joiner for a little coffin.

The next day a complete procession of the crew of the fishing smack followed the detached arm to its interment. The two brothers, side by side, conducted the ceremony. The parish priest held the coffin under his arm.

Javel the younger gave up going to sea. He obtained a small position in port, and later, whenever he spoke of the accident, he would say to his auditor in a low tone: "If my brother had been willing to cut the cable I should still have my arm, be sure. But he was looking to his own pocket."

OF DOCTOR HERACLIUS GLOSS

I

The Intellectual Qualities of Doctor Heraclius Gloss

Doctor Heraclius Gloss was a very learned man. Although no book whatever bearing his name had ever been sold in the local bookshops, all the inhabitants of the erudite city of Balançon looked upon Doctor Heraclius Gloss as a very learned man.

How was he then a doctor? And of what? No one could say. What was certain was that his father and his grandfather had been called "Doctor" by their fellow citizens. He had inherited their title at the same time that he had inherited their name and their goods. In his family one became "doctor" from father to son, just as, from father to son, one was named Heraclius Gloss.

Moreover, though he possessed no diploma signed and countersigned by every member of some illustrious faculty, Doctor Heraclius was, none the less, a very worthy and a very learned man. One had only to see the forty shelves loaded with books, which covered the four walls of his enormous study, to be quite convinced that no more learned doctor had ever honored the city of Balançon. And finally, each time his name was mentioned in the presence of either the dean or the president, they would smile enigmatically. It was even rumored that one day the president had delivered a long eulogy of him in Latin before the archbishop. The wit-

ness who told the story actually cited besides, as undeniable proof, the following
words which had been pronounced:

Parturiunt montes, nascitur ridiculus mus.

What is more, the dean and the president dined at his home every Sunday. And
thus no one would have dared to dispute that Doctor Heraclius Gloss was a very
learned man.

II

The Physical Appearance of Doctor Heraclius Gloss

If it is true, as certain philosophers claim, that there is perfect harmony between
the moral and the physical natures of a man and that one can read in the lines
of the face the chief characteristics of a man, then Doctor Heraclius was certainly
not meant to give the lie to such an assertion. He was small, alert, and energetic.
There was in him something of the rat, the ant, and the terrier; that is to say, he
belonged to the species of investigators, of cogitators, of hunters, and of the indefatigable. Looking at him, one could not understand how all the doctrines which
he had studied could ever be contained in so small a head. It was more easily
conceivable, on the other hand, that he himself could have burrowed his way
into science and lived there, nibbling like a rat in a thick book.

What was most peculiar about him was the extraordinary thinness of his figure.
His friend the dean claimed, perhaps not without reason, that he must have been
forgotten for several centuries and pressed together with a rose and a violet in
the leaves of a folio volume—for he was always very fastidious and scented. His
face especially was so like a razor blade that the stems of his gold spectacles, extending far beyond his temples, had the effect of a great yardarm on the mast
of a ship.

"If he had not been the learned Doctor Heraclius," the president of the faculty
of Balançon would occasionally declare, "he would certainly have made an excellent
paper knife."

He wore a wig, dressed with care, was never ill, loved animals, did not detest
his fellow men, and adored quails on the spit.

III

How Doctor Heraclius Spent His Days

As soon as the doctor was up, washed, and shaved, and had breakfasted on a roll
and butter dipped in a cup of chocolate flavored with vanilla, he would go down
into his garden. Like all town gardens it was not very big, but it was pleasant,
shady, full of flowers, quiet, and, I would almost say, in meditation. In short, if
one tried to picture the ideal garden for a philosopher in search of Truth, one
would get some notion of the one round which Doctor Heraclius Gloss took three
or four brisk turns before settling down to his daily lunch of quails on the spit.
This mild exercise, he used to say, was excellent the first thing in the morning.
It quickened one's circulation, numbed by sleep, cleared one's mind, and kept
the digestive tract in fine shape.

After that, the doctor had his lunch. Then, as soon as he had had his coffee—
which he took at one gulp, for he never succumbed to the sleepiness provoked

by the digestive process begun at table—he put on his big overcoat and went out. And each day, after having passed the faculty and compared the time of his clumsy Louis XV watch with that of the haughty dial of the university clock, he disappeared into the Ruelle des Vieux Pigeons, whence he emerged only to return to his dinner.

What would Doctor Heraclius Gloss do in the Ruelle des Vieux Pigeons? What did he do, good heavens? Why, that is where he sought philosophic truth, and here is how:

All the bookdealers in Balançon had their shops in this obscure and dirty little street, and it would have taken years to read the titles alone of all the obscure works which lay piled from cellar to attic in each of the fifty-odd shacks which comprised the Ruelle des Vieux Pigeons. Doctor Heraclius Gloss considered the alley, its houses, its bookdealers, and its books as his own private property.

It often happened that as some bric-a-brac merchant was on his way to bed, he would hear a noise in his attic and would creep stealthily up, armed with an enormous ancient torch, only to find Doctor Heraclius Gloss, waist-high in a pile of books, holding with one hand the remains of a candle which was melting, while with the other he was turning the pages of some old manuscript in which he hoped to discover the Truth. And the poor doctor would be quite surprised to hear that the belfry clock had long since struck nine and that he would have to eat an execrable dinner.

It is clear that Doctor Heraclius took his research seriously.

He had plumbed the depths of all philosophies, ancient and modern. He had studied the sects of India and the religions of the Negroes of Africa. There was no tribe, however insignificant, among the barbarians of the North or the savages of the South whose religions he had not explored. But alas! the more he studied, searched, investigated, meditated, the more uncertain he became.

"My friend," he said to the president one evening, "how much happier than we are men like Columbus who go forth across the seas in search of a new world! All they have to do is to go straight ahead. The difficulties they have to face are no more than material obstacles which a resolute man always surmounts, while we, tossed incessantly on an ocean of uncertainty, suddenly carried away by a hypothesis like a ship by the north wind, encounter, as though it were a head wind, an opposing doctrine, which forces us back without hope to the port from which we started."

One night when he was philosophizing with the dean he said to him, "How right we are, my friend, to claim that truth resides in a well. We thrust down buckets for fish but bring up only clear water. You can imagine how I spell the word bucket."[1]

It was the only pun he was ever heard to make.

IV

How Doctor Heraclius Spent His Nights

When Doctor Heraclius returned home he was generally much fatter than when he went out, for each of his pockets—and he had eighteen of them—was stuffed with old philosophy books, which he had just bought in the Ruelle des Vieux

[1] In the French a pun on the two words sceaux (buckets) and sots (fools).—*Translator's note.*

Pigeons; and the facetious president claimed that if a chemist had analyzed him at that moment, he would have discovered that two thirds of the doctor was made up of old paper.

At seven o'clock Heraclius Gloss would have his dinner, and while eating he would peruse the musty tomes which he had just acquired.

At half past eight the doctor would leave his table with great dignity. He was no longer the alert and lively little man that he had been all day, but a serious thinker whose head was bent by the gravity of deep meditation, the way a porter is doubled up under the weight of the burden he is carrying. After a solemn injunction: "I am at home to no one," to his housekeeper, he would disappear into his study, sit down before a desk heaped with books, and meditate. What a curious spectacle for any one who could have looked into the doctor's mind at that moment—this monstrous procession of contradictory divinities and disparate beliefs, this fantastic interlacing of doctrines and hypotheses. His mind was like an arena in which the champions of all philosophies tilted against each other in a gigantic tournament. The doctor amalgamated, combined, and mixed the old oriental spiritualism with German materialism, the ethics of the Apostles with those of Epicurus. He tried combinations of doctrine as one experiments in a laboratory with chemical compounds. But the truth he sought so avidly never came to the surface, and his good friend the president maintained that this philosophic truth, eternally sought, was much like a philosopher's stone—a stumbling block.

At midnight the doctor would go to bed, and his dreams when asleep were the same as those of his waking hours.

V

How the Dean Placed His Hopes in Eclecticism, the Doctor in Revelation, and the President in Digestion

One evening when the dean, the president, and the doctor were together in the latter's vast study, they had a most interesting discussion.

"My friend," said the dean, "one ought to be an eclectic and an epicurean. Choose that which is good and reject that which is evil. Philosophy is a huge garden which extends all over the world. Pluck the brilliant flowers of the East, the pale blossoms of the North, the wild violets and cultivated roses, make a bouquet of them and inhale its perfume. If its fragrance is not the most exquisite imaginable, it will at least be very pleasant and a thousand times more fragrant than that of a single flower—be its scent the strongest in the world."

"More varied," replied the doctor, "but more fragrant, no—not at least if one could but find the flower which combines and concentrates in itself the scents of all the others. For in your bouquet you could not prevent certain smells from destroying each other, and, in philosophy, certain beliefs from contradicting each other. The truth is one, so with your eclecticism you will never obtain other than a truth composed of fragments. I too was an eclectic in my day, but now I am an absolutist. What I desire is not a chance approximation, but the absolute truth. I believe that every intelligent man feels this, and on the day when he meets it on his path he will exclaim: 'That's it!' The same is true of beauty. In my own case, I did not know what love was until the age of twenty-five. I had seen pretty women, but was indifferent to them. It would have been necessary to take something from each of them to form the ideal being I had in mind, and, even then, as with the bouquet of which you spoke just now, I should not have obtained perfect beauty, which is indissoluble, like gold and the truth. But one day I at last met that woman. I knew that it was she, and I loved her."

The doctor was so stirred by his recollections that he stopped, and the president looked towards the dean with a meaningful smile. After a moment Heraclius Gloss went on:

"We must place all our hopes in revelation. It was revelation which lit the way for the Apostle Paul on the road to Damascus, and brought him to the Christian faith . . ."

"Which is not the true faith," interrupted the president with a laugh, "since you do not believe in it. So revelation is no more sure than eclecticism."

"Pardon me, my friend," countered the doctor. "Paul was not a philosopher. He had only a partial revelation. His mind could not grasp the absolute truth, which is abstract. But philosophy has advanced since then, and on the day when some circumstance or other—perhaps a book or a word—reveals the truth to a man enlightened enough to understand it, it will suddenly make everything clear, and all superstition will vanish before it as the stars vanish at sunrise."

"Amen!" said the president, "but the next day a second man will be enlightened and a third on the day after. Then they will hurl their revelations at each other's heads. Fortunately, however, revelations are not very dangerous weapons."

"But don't you believe in anything?" exclaimed the doctor, who was beginning to get angry.

"I believe in digestion," replied the president solemnly. "I swallow with indifference every creed, dogma, morality, superstition, hypothesis, and illusion, just as at a good dinner I eat with equal pleasure some hors d'oeuvre, roasts, vegetables, dessert, and fruit, after which I stretch out philosophically on my bed, assured that my undisturbed digestion will bring me pleasant sleep during the night and life and health on the morrow."

"Take my advice," the dean hastened to interpose, "and let us not push the comparison any farther."

An hour later as they were leaving the house of the learned Heraclius, the president suddenly began to laugh and said,

"Poor doctor, if the truth is revealed to him in the form of the loved one, he will be the most deceived man that the world has ever known."

At that point a drunkard who was making his way home with difficulty fell down from sheer fright when he heard the dean's boisterous laugh mingling its deep bass with the president's piercing falsetto.

VI

How for the Doctor the Road to Damascus Turned Out to Be the Ruelle des Vieux Pigeons, and How the Truth Was Revealed to Him in the Form of a Metempsychosic Manuscript

On the 17th of March in the year of grace 17—, the doctor woke up with a high fever. Several times during the night he had dreamed of a tall white man, dressed in classic attire, who touched him on the forehead with his finger and spoke unintelligible words. To the learned Heraclius this dream seemed to be a very significant warning. But why was it a warning, and in what sense was it significant? The doctor did not know precisely, but he anticipated something, nevertheless.

After his lunch he went as usual to the Ruelle des Vieux Pigeons and just as it was striking noon entered number 31, the shop belonging to Nicolas Bricolet, dealer in costumes, antique furniture, secondhand books, and, in his spare time, cobbler as well. The doctor, on an inspired impulse, went up directly to the attic, put his hand up to the third shelf of a Louis XIII bookcase, and pulled out a bulky parchment manuscript entitled,

MY EIGHTEEN METEMPSYCHOSES. AN ACCOUNT OF MY LIVES SINCE THE YEAR 184
OF THE SO-CALLED CHRISTIAN ERA.

Immediately following this strange title was the following introduction, which Heraclius Gloss deciphered without delay.

"This manuscript, which contains the true story of my transmigrations, was begun by me in the city of Rome in the year CLXXXIV of the Christian era, as stated above. This explanation, destined to enlighten mankind on the alternations of reappearances of the soul, is composed by me, this 16th day of April, 1748, in the town of Balançon, where fate has cast me.

"Any enlightened man, interested in philosophical problems, needs merely to scan these pages, and light will be revealed to him in the most startling way.

"For this reason I am going to summarize in a few lines the essence of my story, which can be examined below, however little the reader may know of Latin, Greek, German, Italian, Spanish, and French. For in the different periods when I have reappeared as a human being, I have lived among divers peoples. Next I will explain by what association of ideas, what psychological precautions and what mnemonic devices I inevitably reached metempsychosic conclusions.

"In the year 184 I was a philosopher living in Rome. As I was strolling one day along the Appian Way the idea occurred to me that Pythagoras might well have been like the still faint dawn of a great day on the point of breaking. From that moment I had but one desire, one aim, one obsession—to recapture my past. But alas! all my efforts were fruitless. There came back to me no memory of a previous existence.

"Then one day I saw by chance on the pedestal of a statue of Jupiter, which stood in my entrance hall, certain marks which I had carved there in my youth and which suddenly reminded me of an event long since forgotten. This was like a flash of light to me. I realized that if a few years, even a single night, were sufficient to efface a memory, how much more certainly things accomplished in previous existences and over which had passed the great sleep of intervening animal lives would disappear from our consciousness.

"So I carved my own story on stone tablets in the hope that fate would one day bring them before my eyes again and that for me they would act like the writing on the pedestal of the statue.

"Things turned out as I wished. A century later I was commissioned to demolish an old house on the site of which a palace was to be built.

"One day my workmen brought me a broken stone covered with writing, which they had uncovered while preparing the foundations. I began to decipher it, and as I read the life of the author of those lines, I had sudden flashes from a forgotten past. Little by little I saw light. I began to understand. I remembered. It was I who had engraved that stone.

"But during the interval of a century, what had I done? What had I been? What tribulations had I undergone? I was unable to fathom the mystery.

"One day, however, I had a clue, but it was so faint and nebulous that I would not dare to mention it. An old man, a neighbor of mine, told me that fifty years previously (just nine months before I was born) much amusement was caused in Rome by an adventure which befell Senator Marcus Antonius Cornelius Lipa. His wife, who was pretty and considered perverse, had purchased from some Phoenician merchants a large monkey, which she became extremely fond of. Senator Cornelius Lipa was jealous of the affection which his better half showed for this quadruped with the face of a man, and killed him. Upon hearing this story I had a very vague notion that the monkey was myself and that in that form I had long suffered as a penalty for a mortal sin, but I could remember nothing clear or precise. However, I was led to establish the following hypothesis, which at least has the merit of being plausible.

"Animal form is a penance imposed on souls for crimes committed as human beings. The memory of a superior existence is given to the beast in order to punish him by the consciousness of his fall.

"Only a soul which has been purified by suffering may subsequently regain human form. It then forgets the animal periods through which it has passed, since it is regenerated and since such knowledge would constitute needless suffering. Consequently, man should preserve and respect the beast, just as one respects a sinner who is repentant, and also in order that he may himself be protected when he, in his turn, reappears in animal form. This, in effect, is analogous to the Christian ethic: 'Do not unto others what you would not have done unto you.'

"The account of my transmigrations will show how I had the good fortune to recapture my memories in each of my lives; how I retranscribed the story, first on brass tablets, then on Egyptian papyrus, and finally, long afterwards, on German parchment, such as I am using today.

"It remains for me to deduce from this doctrine its philosophic conclusion.

"All philosophies have been baffled by the insoluble problem of the destiny of the soul. The Christian doctrines which prevail nowadays assert that God will bring together the righteous in paradise and will send the wicked to hell where they will burn with the devil. But modern common sense no longer believes in a God with the countenance of a patriarch sheltering the souls of the good under his wings as a hen shelters her chickens. Moreover, Christian doctrines are refuted by reason, for paradise and hell cannot actually be anywhere.

"Since space, which is infinite, is filled with worlds similar to our own, since by multiplying the generations which have succeeded each other since the beginning of this world, by those which have teemed in the innumerable worlds inhabited like ours, the number of souls would attain such grotesque and impossible proportions—the multiplication thereof being infinite—that God would inevitably lose his head, however levelheaded he may be. The devil would be in a similar fix, all of which would produce one hell of a situation.

"Since the number of righteous and wicked souls is infinite, since space is infinite too, it would lead us to the following conclusion: that paradise and hell would both be everywhere, which would actually mean nowhere.

"Reason, on the other hand, does not contradict the metempsychosic faith.

"The soul, passing from the snake to the pig, from the pig to the bird, from the bird to the dog, finally reaches the monkey and man. The soul always starts afresh

when each new fault is committed, up till the moment when it achieves the fulfillment of terrestrial purification, which permits it to pass on to a superior world.
Thus it progresses ceaselessly from beast to beast and from sphere to sphere, proceeding from the most imperfect state to the most perfect, in order to arrive at
last in the planet of supreme happiness, whence a fresh fault will again precipitate
it into the regions of supreme suffering to recommence its transmigrations.

"The circle, that universal and fatal sign, embodies thus the vicissitudes of our
lives just as it governs the evolution of worlds."

VII

How a Line of Verse by Corneille May Be Interpreted in Two Ways

By the time the doctor had finished reading this strange document, he was transfixed with stupefaction. Then, without any bargaining, he acquired it for the sum
of twelve livres and eleven sous, the bookdealer having passed it off on him as a
Hebrew manuscript discovered in the ruins of Pompeii.

For four days and nights the doctor remained in his study, and by dint of
patience and with the help of dictionaries managed to decipher, more or less suc-
cessfully, the German and Spanish sections of the manuscript, for, though he knew
Greek, Latin, and a little Italian, he was almost entirely ignorant of German and
Spanish. At length, fearing that he might have grossly misinterpreted their meaning, he begged his friend, the president, who was fully versed in these two languages, to check his translation. This the latter did with pleasure, but it was three
whole days before he could set himself seriously to the task, because every time
he glanced through the doctor's translation he was overcome by a fit of laughter
so prolonged and so violent that twice he almost had convulsions. When he was
asked the reason for this extraordinary hilarity, he replied:

"The reason? Well, there are three: first, the ludicrous countenance of my
worthy colleague Heraclius; second, his equally ludicrous translation, which is as
much like the text as a guitar is like a windmill; and finally, the text itself, which
is the most ludicrous thing conceivable."

Oh, obdurate president! Nothing could convince him. Had the sun itself come
in person to burn his beard and his hair, he would have taken it for a candle.

As for Doctor Heraclius Gloss, I need hardly say that he was in a state of beati-
tude, radiant, transformed. Like Pauline, he said to everyone he encountered:

"I see, I feel, I believe, I am disabused."

And each time the president would interrupt him with the remark that it was
not so much *disabused* as abused.[2]

VIII

How, Just as One Can Be More Royalist than the King and More Catholic than the Pope, One Can Likewise Be More of a Metempsychosist than Pythagoras

Great as may be the joy of a shipwrecked man who has drifted for long days
and nights, lost on the ocean on a fragile raft, without mast or sail or compass and

[2]In the original version Maupassant has a play on words which cannot be conveyed
in English, the pun revolving around the words *désabusé* (disabused) and *des abusés*
(among the abused).—*Translator's note.*

without hope, when he suddenly catches sight of land which he has so long desired, such joy was as nothing compared with that which filled Doctor Heraclius Gloss when, after being for so long tossed by the surge of the philosophies on the raft of uncertainty, he entered at length, triumphant and emancipated, the haven of metempsychosis.

The truth of this doctrine had struck him so forcibly that he embraced it immediately down to its most extreme conclusions. For him nothing in the doctrine was obscure, and in a few days, by means of meditation and calculations, he reached the point of being able to fix the exact date on which a man who died in any particular year would reappear on earth. He knew approximately the time of all the transmigrations of a soul through the series of inferior beings, and according to the presumed total of good or evil accomplished in the last period of its life as a human being, he could calculate the very moment when this soul would enter into the body of a snake, a pig, a work horse, an ox, a dog, an elephant or a monkey. The reappearances of a given soul in its superior form succeeded each other at regular intervals regardless of its previous sins.

Thus the degree of punishment, always in proportion to the degree of culpability, consisted not in the duration of exile under animal forms, but in the sojourn, more or less long, which the soul had to make within the body of an impure beast. The scale of beasts began in the lowest stages with the snake or the pig and ended with the monkey, "which is man deprived of speech," said the doctor, to which his worthy friend, the president, always replied that by the same process of reasoning Heraclius Gloss was nothing else but a monkey endowed with speech.

IX

Obverse and Reverse

Doctor Heraclius was very happy during the days following his surprising discovery. He lived in a state of downright jubilation. He was full of great elation over surmounted difficulties, unveiled mysteries, and great hopes realized. Metempsychosis encompassed him like the sky. It seemed to him that a curtain had been suddenly pulled aside and that his eyes had been opened to things hitherto unknown.

He made his dog sit at table beside him, and in solemn tête-à-têtes before the fire sought to fathom in the eye of the simple animal the mystery of previous existences.

There were, however, two dark blots on his happiness—the dean and the president. The dean shrugged his shoulders vehemently every time Heraclius tried to convert him to the metempsychotic doctrine, and the president made his life miserable with the most uncalled-for jests. That was particularly intolerable. Whenever the doctor began to expound his doctrine, the diabolical president would agree with him. He would assume the air of a disciple drinking in the words of a great apostle, and he would invent the most incredible animal genealogies for all their mutual friends. He would say, for example, that Labonde, the cathedral bellringer, from the time of his first transmigration could have been nothing but a melon, and that since then he had scarcely changed at all, being content to ring morning and evening the bell under which he had grown. He claimed that the Abbé Rosencroix, senior curate at St. Eulalia, had undoubtedly been a pest of a crow, for he had preserved both its dress and its traits. Then, inverting the roles in the most deplorable manner, he would declare that M. Bocaille, the druggist, was only a degenerate ibis, since he was obliged to use an instrument to administer a remedy so simple that, according to Herodotus, the sacred bird used to give it to himself with no other help than that of his long beak.

X

How a Mountebank Can Be More Cunning than a Learned Doctor

Nevertheless, Doctor Heraclius continued his series of discoveries without becoming discouraged. Henceforth every animal had a mysterious significance in his eyes. He ceased to see the animal itself in contemplating the man who was purifying himself in its form, and the mere sight of this expiatory outer form would make it possible for him to reconstruct the past sins of the soul therein.

One day as he was strolling in the main square of Balançon he saw a large wooden shack from which came the sound of terrible howling, while on the platform just outside a disjointed clown urged the crowd to come and see the terrible Tomahawk, or Rumbling Thunder, the mighty tamer of Apaches. Strangely stirred, Heraclius paid the fee of ten centimes and went in. O Fortune, that watches over great minds! No sooner had he entered the shack than he saw an enormous cage on which were inscribed these four words which suddenly burst forth upon his dazzled eyes: "Creature of the Woods." The doctor immediately experienced that nervous trembling which results from great mental shocks, and shaking with emotion, went close to the cage. He saw an enormous monkey sitting quietly on its posterior with its legs crossed like a tailor or a Turk. Before this superb specimen of man in his last transmigration Heraclius Gloss, pale with joy, plunged into profound meditation. At the end of a few minutes the creature of the woods, divining without doubt the irresistible sympathy suddenly produced in the heart of the man of cities who was staring fixedly at him, began to make such a frightful grimace at his regenerate brother that the doctor felt the hairs of his head stand on end. Then, having executed a fantastic somersault absolutely incompatible with the dignity of a man, even totally depraved, the quadruped gave way to the most unseemly hilarity right under the doctor's nose. The doctor, however, found nothing shocking in the gaiety of this victim of ancient sins. On the contrary, he saw in it one similarity the more with mankind, a still greater probability of relationship, and his scientific curiosity became so intense that he resolved to buy this master of grimaces regardless of the cost, in order to study him at leisure. What an honor for himself, what a triumph for the great doctrine, if he should succeed at last in getting into communication with the animal aspect of humanity, in understanding this poor monkey and making the monkey understand him!

Naturally enough, the proprietor of the menagerie was loud in praise of his charge. He was the most intelligent, gentle, well-behaved, lovable animal that he had even seen in all his long career as a showman of wild beasts. And to prove his word he went close to the bars of the cage and put his hand inside. The monkey promptly bit it as a little joke. Naturally, too, the proprietor demanded a fabulous price, which Heraclius paid without argument. Then, preceded by two porters bent double under the enormous cage, the doctor left triumphantly for home.

XI

In Which It Is Shown that Heraclius Gloss Was in No Way Exempt from All the Weaknesses of the Strong Sex

But the nearer he got to his house, the slower he walked, for a problem far more difficult than that of philosophic truth was disturbing his mind, a problem which the unfortunate doctor formulated thus:

"What device can I use to conceal from my servant Honorine the presence of this human being in the raw under my roof?"

Ah! The simple truth is that poor Heraclius, who could face undaunted the formidable shrugs of the dean's shoulders and the terrible jests of the president, was far from being so brave before the outbursts of his servant Honorine. But why should the doctor have been so afraid of this fresh-faced, pleasant little woman who seemed so lively and do devoted to her master's interests? Why? Ask rather why Hercules dallied at the feet of Omphale, and why Samson allowed Delilah to rob him of his strength and his courage, which, as the Bible tells us, were in his hair.

One day, alas! when the doctor was walking in the fields, nursing his despair over a great passion wherein he had been betrayed (for it was not without cause that the dean and the president had so much fun at Heraclius' expense on their way home on a certain evening), he met at the corner of a hedge a little girl tending sheep. The learned man, who had not always and exclusively been searching for philosophic truth and who, besides, did not at that time suspect the great mystery of metempsychosis, instead of paying attention to the sheep, as he certainly would have done if he had known facts of which he was then ignorant, began, alas! to chat with the girl who was tending them. Soon afterwards he took her into his service, and this first act of weakness led to others. In a short time he was himself as one of the sheep in her hands, and it was whispered that if this rustic Delilah, like the one in the Bible, had cut off the hair of the poor unsuspecting man, she had, nevertheless, not shorn his forehead of all ornament.

Alas! What he had feared came to pass and even exceeded his apprehensions. At the very sight of the creature of the woods in his wire cage, Honorine abandoned herself to an outburst of unbecoming fury, and having overwhelmed her master with a shower of most ill-sounding epithets, turned to let her anger fall upon her unexpected guest. But the animal, doubtless because he did not have the same reasons as the doctor to humor such an ill-mannered housekeeper, began to cry and howl and stamp and gnash his teeth. He clung to the bars of his cage in such a furious manner and accompanied his action with such indiscreet gestures obviously meant for her that she was obliged to take refuge, like a defeated warrior, in her kitchen.

And so, master of the field and delighted by the unexpected help with which his intelligent companion had furnished him, Heraclius had the monkey taken into his study and installed the cage and its occupant in front of his desk in a corner by the fire.

XII

Wherein It Is Seen that Tamer and Doctor Are Not Synonymous

Then began an exchange of the most significant kind of glances between the two individuals who were thus face to face, and each day for a whole week the

doctor passed long hours in conversing ocularly (or so, at least, he thought) with
the interesting subject which he had acquired. But that was not enough. What
Heraclius wanted was to study the animal at liberty, to surprise its secrets, its desires, its thoughts, to allow it to come and go at will, and, by being on constant
intimate terms with it, to watch it recover forgotten habits and thus to identify
by unmistakable signs the memory of a former life. But for this his guest would
have to be free, that is to say, the cage would have to be opened. Now the prospect
of this undertaking was anything but reassuring. In vain the doctor tried the influence of personal magnetism, as well as the influence of cakes and nuts. The
animal's reaction was quite disturbing to Heraclius whenever he approached the
cage too closely. But one day, unable to resist the desire which was tormenting
him, he stepped forward, briskly turned the key in its lock, opened the door wide,
and, trembling with emotion, retreated a few steps and awaited the consequences,
which were not long in materializing.

The astonished monkey hesitated at first, and then in one bound was outside
his cage and in another on the table. In the twinkling of an eye he had swept aside
the papers and books. Then a third leap brought him into the arms of the doctor,
and the manifestation of his affection was so violent that if Heraclius had not been
wearing a wig, his few remaining hairs would undoubtedly have been snatched
away by the fingers of his formidable brother. But if the monkey was agile, the
doctor was no less so. He sprang first to the right, then to the left, slipped like
an eel under the table, sailed over the sofa like a hare, and, with the monkey hot
on his heels, reached the door and managed to slam it behind him. Then, panting
like a horse at the finish of a race, he leaned against the wall to save himself from
collapsing.

Heraclius Gloss was prostrate for the rest of the day. He felt thoroughly upset,
but what principally concerned him was that he had absolutely no idea how he
and his inconsiderate guest would be enabled to get out of their respective positions. He brought a chair up to the protective door, and peeked through the keyhole. He saw—wonder of wonders! unexpected joy!—the happy conqueror comfortably ensconced in an armchair warming his feet at the fire. In his first transport
of joy the doctor almost went back into the room, but on reflection decided
otherwise, and the idea came to him as by revelation that starvation would no
doubt succeed where kindness had failed. For once events proved him right, for
the famished monkey capitulated. Moreover, since he was a good sort of a monkey
at heart, the reconciliation was complete, and from that day forward the doctor
and his companion lived like two old friends.

XIII

*How Doctor Heraclius Gloss Found Himself in Exactly the Same Position as
Good King Henry IV Who, Having Heard Two Master Lawyers Present Their
Arguments, Decided that Both Were Right*

Some time after this memorable day heavy rain prevented Doctor Heraclius
from going down to his garden as was his custom. He spent the entire morning in
his study observing his monkey in a philosophic spirit. The monkey, perched on
a secretary, was amusing himself by throwing paper balls at the dog Pythagoras,
who was stretched out in front of the fireplace. The doctor was studying the

gradations and the evolution of mind of these fallen men, comparing the degree
of subtlety displayed by the two animals he was observing.

"In the dog," he reflected, "instinct still dominates, while in the monkey reason
prevails. The former smells, hears, and sees with those marvelous organs which
for him are a good half of his intelligence, the latter deduces and thinks."

At that moment the monkey, irritated by the indifference and immobility of
his enemy who, with his head between his paws, was content to lift his eyes occasionally toward the aggressor dominating him from above, decided to come down
and reconnoiter. He jumped ever so lightly from the table and crept forward so
quietly that the only sounds that could be heard were the crackling of the fire
and the ticking of the clock, which seemed to make a tremendous noise in the
dead silence of the study. Then with an abrupt and unexpected movement he
seized in both hands the fluffy tail of poor Pythagoras. But the dog, perfectly
motionless, had followed every movement of the monkey. His stillness was but a
trap to lure his hitherto unassailable adversary within reach. The moment the
clever monkey, pleased with his strategem, grabbed Pythagoras' tail, the latter
jumped up and before the other could escape had plunged his powerful teeth into
his rival's thigh. Heaven knows how the struggle would have ended if Heraclius
had not intervened, but when he had re-established peace, he wondered, as he sat
down again quite out of breath, whether, everything considered, his dog had not
on this occasion been more crafty than the animal commonly referred to as "craft
personified." Heraclius remained plunged in deep perplexity.

XIV

In Which Heraclius Almost Consumed Beautiful Ladies of the Past on a Spit

At noon that day the doctor went into the dining room, sat down at the table,
tucked his napkin into his collar, and placed the precious manuscript open beside
him. But as he was about to lift to his mouth a little wing of quail, plump and
fragrant, he glanced at the holy book, and the few lines on which his eyes fell
blazed more terribly before him than did those famous words suddenly written
on the wall by an unknown hand in the banquet hall of the celebrated King
Belshazzar.

This is what the doctor saw:

". . . Abstain from all food which once had life, for when you eat flesh you are
eating your own kind, and whoever, imbued with the great metempsychotic truth,
kills and devours animals that are nought else but men in their inferior forms, is
as culpable as the ferocious cannibal who feasts upon his vanquished foe."

And on the table, fresh and plump, held together by a little silver skewer and
giving forth an appetizing smell, were half a dozen quails.

The struggle between mind and stomach was formidable, but be it said to the
glory of Heraclius, it was short. The poor man, quite overcome and afraid lest he
might not for long be able to resist such fearful temptation, called his servant and
in a broken voice enjoined her to remove the abominable dish at once and to
serve henceforth only eggs, milk, and vegetables. Honorine almost collapsed on
hearing this startling request. She was about to protest, but before the inflexible
gaze of her master she hurried off with the condemned birds, consoling herself,
however, with the pleasant thought that, generally speaking, what is one person's
loss is another's gain.

"Quails, quails, what could quails have been in a previous life?" poor Heraclius wondered as he sadly ate a superb cauliflower à la crème, which on that day struck him as disastrously tasteless. What sort of human being could have been elegant, delicate, and refined enough to pass into the bodies of these pretty little creatures, so charming and so exquisite? Ah! That was it! It could only be the adorable little mistresses of old times . . . and the doctor grew pale again at the thought of having eaten for his lunch every day for more than thirty years half a dozen beautiful ladies of a past age.

XV

How the President Interpreted God's Commandments

On the evening of this unlucky day the dean and the president came to talk for an hour or two with Heraclius in his study. The doctor immediately told them of his embarrassing predicament and explained to them how quails and other edible animals were out of the question for him, just as ham is to a Jew. Whereupon the dean, who no doubt had had a poor dinner, lost all control and blasphemed in such a terrible way that the poor doctor, although respecting the dean while deploring his blindness, was thoroughly embarrassed. As for the president, he entirely approved of Heraclius' scruples, reminding him that a disciple of Pythagoras who fed on the flesh of animals could expose himself to the risk of eating his father's ribs garnished with mushrooms or the truffled feet of an ancestor, and he quoted in support of his theory the fourth commandment of the Christian God:

Honor thy father and thy mother that thy days may be long upon the land . . .

"It is true," he added, "that I, who am no believer, rather than let myself die of hunger, would prefer to change the divine precept slightly, or even to replace it by this one:

"Devour thy father and thy mother that thy days may be long in the land."

XVI

How the Forty-second Reading of the Manuscript Shed New Light into the Doctor's Mind

Just as a rich man can derive new pleasures and new satisfactions from his great fortune, so Doctor Heraclius, in possession of the priceless manuscript, made astonishing discoveries therein each time that he reread it.

One evening when he had finished reading it for the forty-second time, a sudden inspiration struck him like lightning. As we have already seen, the Doctor could tell approximately at what date a man who had disappeared would complete his transmigrations and reappear in his original form. He was thus suddenly thunderstruck by the thought that the author of the manuscript might have regained his place in humanity. Then, as feverishly excited as an alchemist who thinks himself on the point of discovering the philosopher's stone, he set to work on the most minute calculations to establish the probability of this assumption, and after several hours of persistent work on erudite metempsychotic deductions, he convinced himself that this man must be his contemporary or, at any rate, be on the point of being reborn to the life of reason.

However, since Heraclius owned no document which indicated the precise date of the great metempsychosist's death, he could not establish with certainty the moment of his reappearance.

No sooner had he envisaged identifying this being who, in his eyes, was more than man, more than philosopher, almost more than a god, when he was seized by one of those powerful emotions one feels when one suddenly learns that one's father, whom for years one had thought dead, is living and near at hand.

The holy anchorite whose entire life has been nourished by the love and the meditation of Christ, and who realizes suddenly that his God was about to appear before him, would not have been more overcome than was Doctor Heraclius Gloss when he was certain that he would one day meet the author of his manuscript.

XVII

How Doctor Heraclius Gloss Went About Finding the Author of the Manuscript

A few days later readers of the *Balançon Star* noted with astonishment on the fourth page of the paper the following announcement:

> *Pythagoras—Rome in the year 184—document found on the pedestal of a statue of Jupiter—philosopher, architect, soldier, laborer, monk, mathematician, doctor, poet, sailor—think and remember—the story of your life is in my hands.—Write H. G. c/o General Delivery, Balançon.*

The doctor was certain that if the man whom he so eagerly desired to find happened to read this notice, incomprehensible to anyone else, he would at once grasp its hidden meaning and would come to him. So every day before sitting down to his breakfast he went to the post office to inquire if there were any letters addressed to H.G., and each time he pushed open the door on which was written "Letters, Inquiries, Stamps" he was actually more excited than a lover about to open his first letter from his beloved.

But alas! Day after day went by despairingly alike. The clerk gave the doctor the same answer each morning, and each morning Heraclius returned home more gloomy and more discouraged. Now the inhabitants of Balançon, like everybody else in the world, eager for news, indiscreet, slanderous, and inquisitive, soon connected the strange announcement appearing in the *Star* with the daily visits of the doctor to the post office. And naturally they wondered what the mystery was all about and began to speculate.

XVIII

In Which Doctor Heraclius Recognizes with Astonishment the Author of the Manuscript

Unable to sleep one night, the doctor got up between one and two in the morning to reread a passage that he thought he had not understood too well. He put on his slippers and opened the door of his room as quietly as possible so as not to awaken all the human animals expiating their sins under his roof. Now whatever had been the previous states of these lucky creatures, they had certainly never

before enjoyed such perfect peace and happiness, for the excellent man was so
kindhearted that he provided them with good food, good beds, and everything
else they needed. Without making the slightest sound, the doctor reached his
study door and went in. Now Heraclius was unquestionably a courageous man. He
was not afraid of specters or ghosts, but however fearless a man may be, certain
terrors, like cannon balls, will shake the most intrepid courage. The doctor stopped
paralyzed, livid, horrified, his eyes haggard and his hair on end, his teeth chattering and his whole body shaken by the awful shock of the incredible spectacle
which confronted him.

His work lamp was burning on his table, and under its light, with his back
turned to the door through which he himself had entered he saw . . . Doctor
Heraclius Gloss intently reading his manuscript. There was no possible doubt. It
was clearly himself. Over his shoulders was his own antique silk dressing gown
embroidered with large red flowers, and on his head was his Greek cap made of
black velvet with gold trim. The doctor realized that if his other self were to turn
around, if the two Heracliuses were to look upon each other face to face, the one
who was shaking in his boots at that very moment would fall dead before his
double. Just then, however, shaken by another wave of jitters, he relaxed his hold
on the candlestick he was carrying, and it fell noisily to the floor. This clatter sent
him into a frenzied leap forward. His other self whirled sharply around, and the
petrified doctor recognized . . . his monkey. For some seconds his thoughts swirled
in his head like dead leaves carried away with the storm. Then he was suddenly
overcome with a feeling of joy more potent than he had ever before experienced,
for he now realized that the author whom he had sought, whom he had longed
for as the Jews long for the Messiah, stood before him. It was his monkey. Nearly
beside himself with ecstasy, he dashed forward, seized the adored creature in his
arms, and embraced him with such frenzy as no beloved was ever embraced by
her lover. Then he sat down across from him on the other side of the fireplace
and remained gazing at him in blissful contemplation until dawn.

XIX

How the Doctor Found Himself in a Terrible Dilemma

But just as the most beautiful summer days are sometimes abruptly spoiled by
a dreadful storm, so the doctor's happiness was suddenly marred by a most frightening thought. He had found the author for whom he had been searching, certainly.
But alas! it was only a monkey. There was no question that they could understand
each other, but they could never converse. The doctor came down to earth with
a crash. Gone were those long interviews from which he had hoped to learn so
much, gone that wonderful crusade which they were to have undertaken together
against superstition. For by himself the doctor did not possess weapons adequate
to overthrow the hydra of ignorance. He needed a man, an apostle, a confessor, a
martyr, a role which could scarcely be filled by a monkey. What was he to do? An
imperious voice sounded in his ears:

"Kill him!"

Heraclius trembled. In a trice he saw that if he killed the monkey the soul thus
freed would immediately enter the body of an infant about to be born, and that
it would then be necessary to wait at least twenty years before that infant reached

maturity. By that time the doctor would be seventy. It was possible, certainly. But would he be able to relocate the man? Moreover, his religion forbade him to do away with any living being under penalty of committing a murder; if he did this, his own soul would pass after death into the body of a wild animal, as was decreed for murderers. But what did it matter? He would be a martyr to science and to faith. He seized an enormous Turkish scimitar which was hanging from a suit of armor, and, like Abraham on the mountain, was about to strike when a thought interrupted the impulse. What if this man's sins were not yet expiated? Suppose his soul, instead of entering into that of a child, were to return for a second time into the body of a monkey? This was possible, probable even, nearly certain. In thus committing a futile crime, the doctor would condemn himself to a terrible punishment without benefiting his fellow men. He fell back lifeless into his chair. These prolonged intense emotions having exhausted him, he fainted.

XX

In Which the Doctor Has a Little Talk with His Maid

It was seven in the morning when Heraclius opened his eyes, and Honorine was bathing his temples with vinegar. The doctor's first thought was for his monkey. But the animal had disappeared.

"My monkey! Where is my monkey?" he exclaimed.

"You said it! It's about time we talked about him," retorted the short-tempered maid, who frequently behaved as if she were the mistress. "Wouldn't it be a great pity if he were lost! A fine animal, upon my word! He mimics everything he sees you do. Didn't I find him trying on your boots? And then this morning when I picked you up here—heavens knows what mad ideas you've got into your head lately, to the point of preventing you from sleeping in your own bed—that nasty animal, which is actually a devil in the guise of a monkey, had put on your skullcap and your bathrobe. He was looking at you and laughing, as though it were a huge joke to see a man who had fainted. Then when I tried to come to you, the brute jumped at me as though he wanted to eat me, but, thank heaven, I'm not easily frightened and can still swing hard. So I grabbed the shovel and let him have it so hard that he ran away into your bedroom where he's probably up to more mischief now."

"You hit my monkey!" roared the exasperated doctor. "Get this into your head, woman, from now on he is to be respected and waited on like a master of the house."

"I should say so! Not only is he a master of the house, but for some time he has been lording it over the master of the house too," grumbled Honorine, as she went off to her kitchen, convinced that Doctor Heraclius Gloss was quite mad.

XXI

In Which It Is Shown that a Good Friend Can Lighten the Heaviest Sorrow

As the doctor had said, from that day on the monkey became the real master of the house, and Heraclius became the humble servant of the noble beast. He observed him with infinite tenderness for hours at a time, treated him with the gentleness of a lover, lavished on him a whole dictionary of tender phrases, clasped his hand as one does to a friend, talked to him earnestly, explaining anything that might seem obscure, filling the animal's life with gentle care and infinite solicitude. And the monkey accepted it all as calmly as a god receiving the worship of the faithful.

Heraclius, like all great minds living in solitude, isolated by their superiority over the common level of foolishness of ordinary people, had up till then felt himself alone. Alone in his work, alone in his aspirations, in his struggles and his failures, alone even in his discovery and his triumph. He had not yet imposed his doctrine on the masses. He had not even managed to convince his two most intimate friends, the dean and the president. But from the day on which he discovered his monkey to be the great philosopher of his dreams, the doctor felt less isolated.

As he was convinced that all animals were deprived of speech only because of past misdeeds, and that as part of the same punishment they were endowed with the remembrance of previous existences, Heraclius became passionately devoted to his companion, and in doing this consoled himself for all the trials he had to endure. For, in fact, the doctor's life had for some time become sadder. The dean and the president came to see him less frequently, and this left a large void in his existence. They had even ceased coming to dinner on Sundays since the day he had decreed that no food which had once had life should be served at his table. This change of habit was a great sacrifice, even for him, and now and again it assumed the proportions of a genuine grief, for he who had heretofore been so impatient for his pleasant lunch hour now practically dreaded it. He would go sadly into his dining room knowing full well that there was nothing to look forward to, and he was continuously haunted by visions of quails on the spit, which gave him quite a complex. But alas! his feeling of guilt was not so much over the many quails eaten but rather over the bleak prospect of a quail-less future.

XXII

In Which the Doctor Discovers that His Monkey Resembles Him Even More than He Imagined

One morning the Doctor was awakened by a strange noise. He jumped out of bed, dressed hurriedly, and rushed into the kitchen, whence came extraordinary sounds of stamping and kicking.

For some time Honorine had been harboring in her mind black schemes of vengeance against the intruder who had stolen her master's affection. Now the treacherous woman, knowing the tastes and the appetites of these animals, had somehow managed to tie the poor monkey firmly to a leg of her kitchen table. Then when she was certain that he was securely attached she went to the other end of the room and amused herself by tempting him with a feast best calculated to excite his greed, and thus inflicted on him the tortures of Tantalus, tortures such as are reserved in hell for the worst possible sinners. And the perverse housekeeper roared with laughter and invented further refinements of torture such as would occur only to a woman. The man-monkey writhed in fury at the sight of the savory dishes beyond his reach, and in his rage at finding himself tied to the leg of the heavy table, made horrible faces, thereby adding to the enjoyment of his tormentor.

At last, just as the solicitous master appeared in the doorway, the victim of this nasty trick made a supreme effort and succeeded in breaking the cords which held him, and, had it not been for the determined intervention of the indignant Heraclius, heaven knows the beast would surely have eaten his master out of house and home.

XXIII

How the Doctor Realized that His Monkey Had Shamelessly Deceived Him

This time anger got the better of affection, and the doctor, seizing the monkey-philosopher by the throat, dragged him howling into the study, where he administered the most spine-splitting thrashing ever received by a metempsychosist.

When Heraclius' tired arm relaxed its hold on the throat of the poor beast, who after all was guilty only of the same appetites as those of his superior brother, the monkey freed himself from the grasp of his outraged master, jumped onto the table, took the doctor's enormous snuff box, and flung it, wide open, at its owner's head. Heraclius barely had time to close his eyes to avoid the whirlwind of snuff which would certainly have blinded him. When he opened them the criminal had disappeared, taking with him the manuscript of which he was presumed to be the author.

Heraclius' consternation was boundless. He dashed like a madman in pursuit of the fugitive, determined to recover the precious manuscript regardless of the sacrifice. He explored the house from cellar to attic, opened all his closets and looked under all the furniture, but his search was utterly fruitless. At last he went to sit in despair under a tree in his garden.

Feeling several strange little taps on his head, caused, as he thought at first, by dead leaves brought down by the wind, he was surprised to notice a little ball of paper roll in front of him on the path. He picked it up and opened it. Horrors! It was a page of his manuscript. Panic-stricken, Heraclius looked up in consternation and saw the abominable beast calmly preparing fresh missiles of the same kind with an expression of joyous satisfaction on his face that Satan himself could not have exceeded when he saw Adam accept the fatal apple, which, from Eve to Honorine, women have ever tempted us with. At this spectacle a terrible thought suddenly flashed through the doctor's mind, and he realized that he had been deceived, tricked, and duped in the most outrageous way by this hairy impostor, who was no more the author of the manuscript than he was the Pope or the Grand Turk. The precious document would have disappeared altogether had not Heraclius caught sight of a garden hose near at hand, one of those used by gardeners to reach the outermost flower beds. He snatched it up and, manipulating it with almost superhuman strength, gave the wretch such a totally unexpected bath that he began to hop from branch to branch with shrill cries. But the monkey, dodging cleverly to obtain a moment's respite, suddenly flung the torn parchment straight in his adversary's face, jumped down from the tree, and fled toward the house.

But before the manuscript had touched the doctor, the poor man had fallen on his back with his arms and his legs in the air, completely overcome with emotion. When he rose, he had not the strength to avenge this new outrage. So he made his way painfully back to his study, where he discovered to his joy that only three pages were missing.

XXIV

Eureka!

A visit from the dean and the president restored him. All three talked for an hour or two without the slightest allusion to metempsychosis. But as his two friends were about to leave Heraclius could not contain himself any longer. While the dean was struggling into his bearskin coat, he drew aside the president, of whom he was less afraid, and poured out his tale of woe. He told him how he thought he had found the author of the manuscript, how he had been mistaken, how the wretched monkey had duped him in the most outrageous way, and how utterly in despair he felt. Indeed, he was so shaken by the total collapse of his illusions that he broke down and wept. The president, much moved, took his hands and was about to speak when the dean's solemn voice called out from the hall, "Aren't you ever coming, Mr. President?"

"Well, now," said the president, throwing his arms around the grieving doctor, and smiling tenderly as one does to console a naughty child, "cheer up, my friend. Perhaps you yourself are the author of the manuscript."

Then he went out into the dark street, leaving Heraclius speechless at the door.

The doctor went slowly back to his study, muttering as he went along, "Perhaps I am the author of the manuscript." He made another careful study of the way in which the document had been recovered at each appearance of its author, and then he recalled how he himself had discovered it. The dream which had preceded the happy day like a providential warning, the emotion he had felt on entering the Ruelle des vieux Pigeons, all this came back to him, clearly, distinctly, brilliantly. Then he stood straight up, spreading out his arms as though he had seen a vision, and cried in a resounding voice, "It is I! It is I!" The whole house seemed to shake. Pythagoras barked violently. The disturbed animals suddenly woke up and became so excited that it seemed as though each one was bent on celebrating in his own tongue the marvelous resurrection of the prophet of metempsychosis. At length, in the grip of an overwhelming emotion, Heraclius sat down, opened the last page of this new Bible, and reverently added to it the entire history of his life.

XXV

Ego Sum Qui Sum

From that day on Heraclius was filled with overweening pride. In the same way that the Messiah sprang from God the Father, so he had sprung from Pythagoras, or, rather, he himself was Pythagoras, for in the past he had lived in the body of that philosopher. Thus his genealogy could challenge that of the most aristocratic families. He looked upon all the great men in the history of the race with supreme contempt, and their highest achievements seemed insignificant beside his. He stood in sublime isolation in the universe of man and beast. He was metempsychosis itself, and his house was its temple.

He had forbidden both his servant and his gardener to kill animals considered noxious. Caterpillars and slugs multiplied in his garden, and, in the guise of enormous spiders with hairy legs, one-time mortals paraded their loathsome transformation on the walls of his study—which made that rascal of a president say that if all ex-vandals duly metamorphosed were to swoop down onto the too sensitive-minded doctor's skull, even so, he would not wage war on the poor ostracised parasites. Only one thing troubled Heraclius in this superb period of fulfillment. This was the continual spectacle of animals devouring each other—spiders lying in wait for flies, birds carrying off the spiders, cats swallowing the birds, and his own dog Pythagoras joyfully strangling any cat which passed within reach of his teeth.

From morning till night he followed the slow progressive evolution of metempsychosis at every degree in the animal scale. He had sudden revelations as he watched sparrows pecking in drainpipes, and ants, those industrious and foresighted workers, moved him particularly. In them he saw all lazy and unproductive people who, as an expiation for their past idleness and irresponsibility, had been condemned to this endless labor. For hours at a time he lay with his nose in the grass watching them, and he marveled at his own insight.

Then, like Nebuchadnezzar, he would crawl on all fours, rolling in the dust with his dog, sharing the life of his animals, groveling with them. For him, man gradually disappeared from creation, and soon he was conscious only of animals. When he thought of them he felt that he was their brother. He spoke only to them, and when, by chance, he was obliged to talk to men, he seemed as helpless as if among foreigners and was shocked at the stupidity of his fellow creatures.

XVI

What Went on at Mme. Labotte's, the Fruiterer's, 26 Rue de la Maraîcherie

Mlle. Victoire, first-class cook to the dean of the faculty of Balançon, Mlle. Gertrude, servant of the president of the same faculty, and Mlle. Anastasie, housekeeper to the Abbé Beaufleury, curate of St. Eulalia: such was the worthy group which happened to meet at the store of Mme. Labotte, fruiterer, 26 Rue de la Maraîcherie, one Thursday morning.

These ladies, with their shopping baskets on their left arms and little white lace caps set coquettishly on their heads so that the ribbons hung down their backs, were listening breathlessly to Mlle. Anastasie, who was telling them how the Abbé Beaufleury had exorcised a poor woman possessed of five devils on the preceding day.

Suddenly Mlle. Honorine, Doctor Heraclius' housekeeper, rushed in like a whirlwind and sank into a chair, overcome by emotion. Then, when she saw that they were all thoroughly intrigued, she burst out:

"No, it's really too much! I don't care what people say. I'm not staying with him any longer."

And then she hid her face in her hands and began to sob.

A moment later, when she was a little calmer, she went on:

"After all, it's not the poor man's fault if he's mad."

"Who is mad?" asked Mme. Labotte.

"My master, of course, Doctor Heraclius," Honorine replied.

"So what the dean said is true then—your master has lost his mind?" inquired Mlle. Victoire.

"I should say so!" exclaimed Mlle. Anastasie. "The curé was telling Abbé Rosencroix the other day that Doctor Heraclius was a real reprobate, that he worshiped animals, like a certain Mr. Pythagoras, who, it seems, is as abominable as Luther."

"What's the trouble now?" interrupted Mlle. Gertrude. "What's happened to you?"

"Well, just think," said Honorine, drying her eyes on the corner of her apron, "for nearly six months now my poor master has gone batty over animals. He thinks he was created to serve them. He speaks to them as though they were rational human beings, and you'd think that he could hear a voice answering him. Anyway, since mice have gotten into my pantry, I set a trap last night. This morning I found I'd caught one. I called the cat and was just going to give him the little beast when the master rushed in like a madman. He snatched the trap out of my hands and let the brute loose. And when I got angry he turned on me and up-braided me in the vilest language."

There was a tense silence for some minutes, and then Mlle. Honorine added:

"After all, I can't really blame the poor man too much. He's mad."

Two hours later the story of the doctor and the mouse had gone the rounds of every kitchen in Balançon. All the bourgeois were telling it to each other at lunch-time. During coffee after dinner that evening M. le Premier related the tale to six solemnly attentive magistrates who had dined with him. At eleven o'clock the prefect, who was giving a party, was conveying his apprehension to six administra-tive yes-men, and when he asked the president for his opinion, the latter, who was parading his white tie and his propensity for gossip from group to group, answered as follows:

"After all, what does this prove, my dear Prefect? Only that if La Fontaine were still living, he could write a new fable entitled 'The Philosopher's Mouse,' which would end up 'The sillier of the two is not the one you think.' "

XXVII

How Doctor Heraclius did not Agree with the Dauphin, who, Having Saved a Monkey from Drowning, Dived back in again and went on Looking for a Man to Save

When Heraclius went out the following morning he noticed that everyone looked at him with curiosity as he passed, and that people turned back to look at him again. At first all this attention astonished him. He wondered why, and thought that perhaps his doctrine had spread without his knowledge and that he was on the point of being appreciated by his fellow citizens. He was suddenly filled with a great tenderness towards these people, whom he already saw as his enthusiastic disciples, and he began to bow right and left, like a prince among his people. The whisperings that followed him he interpreted as murmurs of praise, and he beamed with joy at the thought of the imminent consternation of the dean and the presi-dent.

He was still in that state when he reached the Quai de la Brille. A few steps away, a group of excited children, roaring with laughter, were throwing stones into the water, while some sailors, puffing at their pipes, seemed interested in the children's game. Heraclius approached and then suddenly drew back as though he had received a powerful blow in the chest. Ten yards from the riverbank, sinking and coming up again by turns, a kitten was drowning. The poor little animal was making desperate efforts to reach the bank, but each time she showed her head above water a stone thrown by one of the urchins, who were enjoying her agony, made her go under again. The cruel brats were vying with each other and urging each other on, and when a particularly good shot hit the poor creature there were shouts of laughter and cries of joy. Suddenly a sharp stone hit the kitten on the middle of the forehead, and a trickle of blood appeared on its white fur. The torturers burst into shouts of joy and applause, which, however, turned suddenly into a terrible panic. Livid, trembling with rage, upsetting everything before him, and striking out with fists and feet, the doctor hurled himself among the brats like a wolf in a flock of sheep. Their terror was such and their flight so rapid that one of them, beside himself, jumped into the river and disappeared. Heraclius removed his coat at once, kicked off his shoes, and dived in. He was seen to swim vigorously for a moment or two, catch hold of the kitten just as she was sinking, and swim back to shore. Then he sat down on a stone and dried and caressed the little creature which he had snatched from death. He took it lovingly into his arms like a baby, ignoring the child, whom two sailors had just saved, and, indifferent to the din around him, he strode off toward his house, forgetting his shoes and coat on the riverbank.

XXVIII

This Story will Prove That, if you Want to Save a fellow Creature from Harm and Believe that it is Better to Rescue a Cat than a Man, you will Arouse the Anger of your Neighbors. All Roads Lead to Rome, but Metempsychosis Leads to the Insane Asylum. (Balançon Star)

Two hours later a huge crowd of shouting people was jostling and pushing in front of the doctor's windows. Presently a shower of stones shattered the panes, and the crowd was about to break down the doors, when the police appeared at the end of the street. Things gradually calmed down, and the mob finally dispersed, but two policemen remained outside the doctor's house until the following day. That night the doctor was in a state of extreme agitation. He told himself that the letting loose of the crowd on him was due to the underhand machinations of the priests and to the explosion of hatred which a new religion always arouses among the followers of an old one. It was not long before he had reached the state of mind of a martyr and was ready to confess his faith before his tormentors. He brought into his study as many animals as the room would hold, and dawn found him sleeping with his dog, a goat, a sheep, and clasping to his heart the kitten which he had saved.

A loud knock at his door awakened him, and Honorine led in a solemn-looking individual followed by two detectives, with the public health officer in the background. The solemn individual identified himself as the chief of police and courteously requested Heraclius to follow him. Very much upset, the latter did so and was made to get into a carriage waiting at the door. Then, sitting next to the chief of police, with the health officer and one detective facing him and the other detective on the seat beside the driver, Heraclius soon noticed that they were driving down the Rue des Juifs, through the Place de l'Hôtel de Ville and the Boulevard de la Pucelle. At last they stopped outside a grim-looking building on the door of which was written "Home for the Mentally Defective." The doctor suddenly realized the terrible trap into which he had fallen and the diabolic craft of his enemies. Summoning all his strength, he tried to dash into the street, but two powerful hands forced him back into his seat. Then began an awful fight between him and the three men. Heraclius struggled and twisted, swung and bit,

screaming with rage all the time. But at last he was overpowered, tied up firmly
and carried into the somber building. Its heavy door closed behind him with an
ominous sound.

He was taken into a narrow, sinister-looking cell. The fireplace, the window,
and the mirror were solidly barred, the bed and the one chair were securely attached to the floor by iron chains, and there was no piece of furniture which could
be picked up and handled by the occupant of this prison. As it turned out, events
proved that these precautions were by no means unnecessary, for as soon as the
doctor found himself in these new quarters, he gave way to the rage that was
suffocating him. He tried to smash the furniture, to tear out the bars, and to break
the windowpanes. Failing in this, he rolled on the floor and let out such blood-
curdling yells that two uniformed guards rushed in, followed by a tall bald-headed
man in black. At a sign from him, the two men seized Heraclius and in an instant
had him in a straightjacket. Then they seemed to wait for instructions. The man
in black considered Heraclius for a moment and then said:

"Take him to the shower room."

Heraclius was led into a large cold room in the middle of which was an empty
tub. Still yelling, he was undressed and placed in this tub. Before he knew what
was happening, he was literally paralyzed by the most awful avalanche of icy
water that ever struck the back of any human being—even in extreme Arctic
regions. Heraclius was unable to utter a sound. The man in black, who had been
watching him all the time, felt his pulse and said:

"Let him have another one."

A second torrent descended from the ceiling, and the doctor collapsed, shaking,
choking, gasping, as he slid to the bottom of the icy tub. He was then picked up,
wrapped in warm blankets and put to bed in his cell, where he slept dead to the
world for thirty-five hours.

He awakened the following morning with his pulse normal and his head clear.
For some minutes he considered his plight, and then he began to read his manuscript, which he had taken care not to leave behind. The man in black presently
appeared, and when lunch was brought, they had it together. The doctor, who
had not forgotten his cold shower of the other day, was very quiet and polite and
made no mention of the incident which had culminated in such a misadventure
but conversed for a long time most entertainingly, in an endeavor to prove to his
host that he was as sane as the Seven Sages of Greece.

The man in black, as he was leaving, gave the doctor permission to take a
walk in the large garden of the institution. Some fifty persons were strolling there.
Some were laughing, shouting, and haranguing each other. Others were sober and
melancholy.

One of the first persons the doctor noticed was a tall man with a long beard
and white hair, who was walking alone, deep in thought. Somehow the doctor felt
interested in the fate of this unknown man, and at the same time the stranger
raised his eyes and stared fixedly at Heraclius. Whereupon they advanced toward
each other, bowed ceremoniously, and began to talk. The doctor discovered that
his companion was Dagobert Félorme, and that he was a professor of modern
languages at the college of Balançon. Heraclius could see nothing wrong with the
man's mind and was wondering what could have brought him to such a place,
when suddenly the other man stopped, clasped Heraclius' hand firmly, and asked:

"Do you believe in metempsychosis?"

The doctor felt faint, unable to speak. Their glances met, and for some time they remained gazing at each other. At last Heraclius was overcome by his emotion, and tears welled up in his eyes. He opened his arms and they embraced. Then, one confidence leading to another, it was soon obvious that they were inspired by the same faith and were apostles of the same doctrine. There was no essential point on which they disagreed. But as the doctor came to see for himself this astounding similarity of thought, a curious feeling of uneasiness came over him, for it seemed to him that the more the stranger grew in his esteem, the more he himself lost in his own. Jealousy was eating into his heart.

Suddenly his companion exclaimed:

"I am metempsychosis. I am the discoverer of the evolution of souls, and I am the one who fathomed the destinies of men. I was Pythagoras."

The doctor stopped dead, pale as a mortuary sheet.

"I beg your pardon," he said, "I am Pythagoras."

Once again they stared at each other, and then the man continued,

"I have been philosopher, architect, soldier, laborer, monk, mathematician, doctor, poet, and sailor."

"So have I," said Heraclius.

"I have written my life history in Latin, Greek, German, Italian, Spanish, and French," shouted the stranger.

"So have I," answered Heraclius.

Both stopped speaking and looked daggers at each other.

"In the year 184," screamed the other, "I was a philosopher in Rome."

Then the doctor, shaking like a leaf in a gust of wind, drew his precious document from his pocket and brandished it like a weapon under his adversary's nose. The stranger sprang back.

"That's my manuscript," he yelled and attempted to grab it.

"It's mine," roared Heraclius, and with surprising agility he raised the disputed article above his head, changed it to his other hand behind his back, and manipulated it in the most extraordinary fashion so as to keep it away from his frenzied rival. The stranger gnashed his teeth, stamped his feet, and bellowed:

"Thief! Thief! Thief!"

Then with a swift and diabolical lunge he managed to get hold of a corner of the paper which Heraclius was trying to keep from him. For some seconds they pulled with equal anger and force in opposite directions, and then, as neither would give way, the manuscript, which constituted a sort of physical link between the two men, put an end to the contest with the wisdom of King Solomon by tearing into two equal parts. This naturally permitted the two belligerents to sit down with a jolt ten paces apart, each clutching his half of the spoils of victory in clenched fists.

They remained sitting, but continued to stare at each other like rival forces which, having tested each other's strength, are loath to come to grips again.

Dagobert Félorme was the first to reopen hostilities.

"The proof that I am the author of this manuscript," he said, "is that I knew of it before you."

Heraclius did not answer, and the other went on:

"The proof that I am the author of the manuscript is that I can repeat it from end to end in the seven languages in which it is written."

Heraclius did not answer, for he was in deep thought. A revolution was taking place in him. There was no possible doubt—the victory belonged to his rival. But this author, whom at one time he had invoked with all his prayers, now disgusted him as a false god. For, like a dethroned god, he was now himself revolting against divinity. So long as he had not considered himself as the author of the manuscript, he had longed to meet its author, but from the day when he began to say, "It was I who wrote this. *I* am metempsychosis," he could not henceforth permit another to take his place. Like a man who would burn his house down rather than see it occupied by someone else, he was setting fire to both temple and god, even to see metempsychosis go up in smoke, as soon as a stranger ascended the altar which he had erected for himself. Thus, after a long silence, he said slowly and solemnly:

"You are mad."

At this, his enemy sprang at him like a lunatic, and a new struggle more terrible than the first would have begun, had not the guards dashed up and returned these instigators of religious wars to their respective cells.

For a month the doctor did not leave his cell. He spent his days alone, with his head between his hands in profound meditation. From time to time the dean and the president came to see him, and by means of clever comparisons and delicate allusions gradually contributed to the transformation that was taking place in his mind. Thus they told him how a certain Dagobert Félorme, professor of languages at the college of Balançon, had lost his mind while writing a philosophical treatise on the doctrines of Pythagoras, Aristotle, and Plato, a dissertation which he imagined he had begun under the Emperor Commodus.

At last, one beautiful sunny morning the doctor came to himself. Once more he was the Heraclius of the good old days. Warmly shaking hands with his two friends, he told them that he had renounced forever metempsychosis, expiations in animal form, and transmigrations, and he beat himself on the breast in admission of his errors.

A week later the doors of the asylum were opened to let him out into the world of free men.

XXIX

From the Frying Pan into the Fire

Heraclius paused for a moment on the doorstep of the fatal building and took a deep breath of the invigorating air of liberty. Then, with the brisk gait that had been his formerly, he set off toward his house. After he had been walking for about five minutes, a street urchin saw him and at once gave a long whistle, which was promptly answered from a neighboring street. A second urchin appeared on the run, and the first one pointed to Heraclius and shouted with all his might:

"Here's the animal man out of the nut house."

Keeping close behind the doctor, they both began to imitate with remarkable skill the cries of every known animal. Presently a dozen or more joined them, forming a noisy and an annoying escort to the ex-metempsychosist. One of them walked ten paces in front of the doctor, carrying like a banner a broom handle to which was attached a rabbit skin, no doubt fished out of a garbage can. Three others directly behind him made an ear-splitting drum escort. Then came the hapless doctor, whose tightly buttoned coat and cap pulled over his eyes made him look like a general at the head of his troops. After him ran a horde of urchins doing somersaults, jumping up and down, squealing, roaring, barking, miaouing, neighing, mooing, crowing, and performing tricks, to the great amusement of the townsfolk standing at their doors. Heraclius, beside himself, walked faster and faster. Suddenly, a stray dog got in his way, and in a fit of rage the doctor let fly such a savage kick at the creature, which only recently he would have protected, that the poor thing ran off yelping with pain. This action was greeted by such noisy acclaim that Heraclius lost his head and began to run with all his might, with the army at his heels.

The mob swept like a whirlwind through the main streets and came to a sudden stop outside the doctor's house. Finding the door ajar, he burst in and slammed the door behind him. Still on the run, he reached his study. There he was greeted by the monkey, who stuck out his tongue at him by way of welcome. This made Heraclius recoil, as though a ghost had appeared. For his monkey was the living souvenir of all his misfortunes, the chief cause of his madness and of all the humiliations and outrages to which he had been subjected. He seized an oak stool within reach and with one blow split the miserable creature's skull. The monkey dropped dead at his feet. Then, appeased at last, Heraclius sank into an armchair and unbuttoned his coat.

When Honorine appeared, she almost fainted with joy at the sight of her master. In her delight she threw her arms around him and kissed him on both cheeks, forgetting the distance which traditionally exists between the master and his servant, in which the doctor had himself always set the example.

Meanwhile, the gang had not dispersed, but was still making such a din outside the door that Heraclius, vexed, went down into his garden.

A horrible sight met his eyes.

Honorine, who really loved her master, while deploring his madness, had wanted to give him a pleasant surprise for his homecoming. She had looked after all the animals in the house like a mother, so that, as a natural consequence of animal fecundity, the garden looked like the interior of Noah's ark at the end of the forty days' flood. It was a veritable bedlam of animals, under which trees, shrubs, grass, and earth had entirely disappeared. The branches touched the ground under the weight of swarms of birds, while under them dogs, cats, goats, sheep, chickens, ducks, and turkeys rolled in the dust. The air resounded with a cacophony much like the one produced by the wild brats on the other side of the house.

Heraclius could restrain himself no longer. He grabbed a spade leaning against the wall, and, like the renowned warriors whose exploits are related by Homer, leaping this way and that, swinging wildly right and left, by the time his rage had abated he had exterminated every one of his harmless friends. Terrified chickens flew over the walls, and cats climbed into the trees. But nothing within reach escaped him. The mess was beyond description. On the ground covered with corpses he collapsed from sheer exhaustion and fell asleep on the field of carnage like a victorious general.

Next day, feeling like his normal self, he thought of taking a walk around the town, but as soon as he left the house the street urchins, who had been lying in wait for him, started chasing him once more, shouting:

"Oho! the animal man! Oho! the animal lover!" And they began to make the same noises as on the previous day, only with infinite variations.

The doctor made a hasty retreat. He was choking with rage, and, unable to vent it on his fellow men, he vowed eternal enmity and relentless war against all animals. From then on, he had only one desire, one aim, one ceaseless preoccupation—to kill animals. He lay in wait for them from morning till night. He set nets in the garden to catch birds and traps in the gutters to catch the neighbors' cats. Tidbits of succulent meat placed near the half-open door attracted passing dogs, upon which the door would slam forever. It was not long before complaints poured in from all quarters. The chief of police came several times in person to order him to stop his relentless warfare. His existence became a succession of lawsuits, but nothing could arrest his vengeance. At last the indignation became general, and this time it was so violent that he undoubtedly would have been lynched by the mob but for the intervention of armed force. All the doctors in Balançon were summoned to the county seat, and they declared unanimously that Doctor Heraclius Gloss was mad. For the second time he was led through the town between two policemen, and the massive door of the Home for the Mentally Defective closed once again behind him.

XXX

How the Proverb, "The More the Merrier," Is Not Always Quite True

When Heraclius went down to the courtyard the next day, the first person he encountered was the author of the manuscript on metempsychosis. The two enemies advanced toward each other cautiously but resolutely. A circle was immediately formed around them. Dagobert Félorme shouted:

"Here's the man who wanted to steal my life's work, who wanted to appropriate the glory of my discovery."

A murmur swept through the crowd. Heraclius answered:

"This is the man who claims that animals are men and men animals."

Then they both began to talk at once, and becoming more and more excited, as on the first occasion, presently came to blows. The other inmates separated them.

From that day on each spent his days in enlisting recruits for his cause, and in no time the whole community was divided into two rival factions, both so zealous, resolute, and intransigent that whenever a metempsychosist happened to run across an adversary, a violent battle would ensue. To avoid these sanguinary encounters the superintendent was obliged to arrange separate recreation hours for each faction, for there had never been such bitter hatred between two rival sects since the quarrel between the Guelphs and the Ghibellines. Thanks to this prudent arrangement, however, the leaders of the hostile clans lived happily, beloved and listened to by their disciples, obeyed and venerated.

Sometimes during the night the sound of a dog howling and barking outside the walls would make Heraclius and Dagobert tremble in their beds. It was the faithful Pythagoras, who, having escaped his master's vengeance by a miracle, had followed him to the threshold of his new home and was trying to enter it, oblivious of the fact that it was a place into which man alone has the right to enter.

THE WATCHDOG

Mme Lefevre was a country woman, a widow, one of those half peasants with ribbons and furbelows on her cap, a person who spoke with some care, taking on grandiose airs in public and concealing a pretentious, brute soul under an exterior comically glossed over, as she concealed her great red hands under gloves of ecru silk.

She had for a servant a simple rustic, named Rose. The two women lived in a little house with green shutters on a highway in Normandy, in the center of the country of Caux. As there was a garden spot in front of the house, they cultivated some vegetables.

One night someone robbed them of a dozen onions. When Rose perceived the larceny she ran to tell Madame, who came down in a wool petticoat. Here was a sorrow and a terror, besides! Someone had robbed, robbed Mme Lefevre! And when a robber visits one in the country he may come again.

And the two frightened women studied the footprints, prattled and supposed certain things.

"Here," they would say, "they must have passed here. They must have put their foot on the wall and then leaped into the flower bed."

And they trembled for the future. How could they sleep peacefully now?

The news of the robbery spread. The neighbors arrived to prove and discuss the matter, each in his turn. To each newcomer the two women explained their observations and their ideas. A farmer on the other side of them said:

"You ought to keep a dog."

That was true, that was; they ought to keep a dog, even if it were good for nothing but to give an alarm. Not a big dog, monsieur! What would they do with a big dog? It would ruin them to feed it! But a little dog, a little puppy that could yap.

When everybody was gone Mme Lefevre discussed this idea of having a dog for a long time. After reflection she made a thousand objections, terrified at the thought of a bowlful of porridge. Because she was of that race of parsimonious country dames who always carry pennies in their pockets, in order to give alms ostensibly along the street and to the contributions on Sunday.

Rose, who loved animals, brought forward her reasons and defended them with astuteness. And finally it was decided that they should have a dog, but a little dog.

They began to look for one but could only find big ones, swallowers of food enough to make one tremble. The Rolleville grocer had one, very small, but he asked two francs for him, to cover the expense of bringing him up. Mme Lefevre declared that she was willing to feed a dog, but she never would buy one.

Then the baker, who knew the circumstances, brought them one morning a little yellow animal, nearly all paws, with the body of a crocodile, the head of a fox, a tail, trumpet-shaped, a regular plume, large like the rest of his person. Mme Lefevre found this cur that cost nothing very beautiful. Rose embraced it and then asked its name. The baker said it was Pierrot.

He was installed in an old soapbox, and he was given first a drink of water. He drank. Then they gave him a piece of bread. He ate.

Mme Lefevre, somewhat disturbed, had one idea:

"When he gets accustomed to the house we can let him run loose. He will find something to eat in roaming around the country."

In fact, they did let him run, but it did not prevent him from being famished. Besides, he only barked to ask for his pittance, in which case he did indeed bark with fury.

Anybody could enter the garden. Pierrot would go and caress each newcomer, remaining absolutely mute. Nevertheless, Mme Lefevre became accustomed to the beast. She even came to love it and to give it from her hand, sometimes, pieces of bread dipped in the sauce from her meat.

But she had never dreamed of a tax, and when they came to her for eight francs—eight francs, madame!—for this little cur of a dog that would not even bark, she almost fainted from shock. It was immediately decided that they must get rid of Pierrot. No one wanted him. All the inhabitants for ten miles around refused him. Then it was resolved that by some means they must make him acquainted with the little house. Now to be acquainted with the little house is to eat of the chalk pit. They make all dogs acquainted with the little house when they wish to get rid of them.

In the midst of a vast plain there appeared a kind of hut, or rather, the little roof of a cottage, rising above the sod. It is the entrance to the marlpit. One great shaft went down about twenty meters, where it was met by a series of long galleries, penetrating the mine.

Once a year they descended in a sort of carriage and marled the clay. All the rest of the time the pit serves as a cemetery for condemned dogs, and often, when one passes near the mouth, there comes to his ears plaintive howls, furious barking and lamentable appeals.

Hunting and shepherd dogs flee with fright at the first sound of these noises, and when one stoops down above this opening he finds an abominable odor of putrefaction. Frightful dramas have taken place within the bounds of this shadow.

When a beast suffers from hunger at the bottom of the pit for ten or twelve days, nourished only on the remains of his predecessors, sometimes a new animal, larger and more vigorous, is suddenly thrown in. There they are, alone, famished, their eyes glittering. They watch each other, follow each other, hesitate anxiously. But hunger presses; they attack each other, struggling a long time, infuriated, and the strong eats the weak, devouring him alive.

When it was decided that they would get rid of Pierrot they looked about them for an executioner. The laborer who was digging in the road demanded six sous for the trouble. This appeared exaggerated folly to Mme Lefevre. A neighbor's boy would be content with five sous; that was still too much. Then Rose observed that it would be better for them to take him themselves, because he would not then be tortured on the way and warned of his lot, and so it was decided that they go together at nightfall.

They gave him this evening a good soup with a bit of butter in it. He swallowed it to the last drop. And when he wagged his tail with contentment Rose took him in her apron.

They went at a great pace, like marauders, across the plain. As soon as they reached the pit Mme Lefevre stooped to listen; she wanted to know if any other beast was howling in there. No, there was no sound. Pierrot would be alone. And Rose, who was weeping, embraced him then threw him in the hole. And they stooped, both of them, and listened.

They heard first a heavy thud, then the sharp, broken cry of a wounded beast, then a succession of imploring supplications, the head raised to the opening.

He yapped; oh, how he yapped!

They were seized with remorse, with a foolish, inexplicable fear. They jumped up and ran away. And as Rose ran more quickly, Mme Lefevre would cry: "Wait, Rose, wait for me!"

Their night was filled with frightful nightmares. Mme Lefevre dreamed that she seated herself at the table to eat soup, and when she uncovered the tureen Pierrot was in it. He darted out and bit her on the nose. She awoke and thought she heard the barking still; she listened; she was deceived. Again she slept and found herself upon a great road, an interminable road, that she must follow. Suddenly, in the middle of the road, she perceived a basket, a great farmer's basket, a basket that brought her fear. Nevertheless, she finished by opening it, and Pierrot, hidden within, seized her hand, not loosing it again: And she knew that she was lost, carrying about forever suspended upon her arm a dog with open mouth.

At the dawn of day she arose, almost insane, and ran to the pit.

He was barking, barking still; he had barked all night. She began to sob and called him with a thousand caressing names. He responded with all the tender inflections a dog's voice is capable of. Then she wished to see him again, promising herself to make him happy to the day of her death. She ran to the house of the man in charge of the mine and told him her story. The man listened without laughing. When she had finished he said: "You want your dog? That will be four francs."

It was a shock. All her grief vanished at a blow.

"Four francs!" she said. "Four francs? Would you make a murderer of yourself?"

He replied: "You believe that I am going to bring my ropes and tackle and set them up and go down there with my boy and get bitten, perhaps, by your mad dog, for the pleasure of giving him back to you? You shouldn't have thrown him in there!"

She went away, indignant. "Four francs!"

As soon as she entered she called Rose and told her the demands of the miner. Rose, always resigned, answered: "Four francs! It is considerable money, madame." Then she added that they might throw the poor dog something to eat so that it might not die there.

Mme Lefevre approved gladly, and again they set out with a big piece of bread and butter. They broke off morsels which they threw in one after the other, calling in turn to Pierrot. And as soon as the dog had got one piece he barked for the next.

They returned that evening, then the next day, every day. But never more than one journey.

One morning, at the moment they dropped the first morsel, they heard suddenly a formidable barking in the shaft. There were two of them! Another dog had been thrown in, a big dog!

Rose cried: "Pierrot!" And Pierrot answered: "Yap, yap!" Then they began to feed him, but each time they threw down a bit they heard a terrible tussle, then the plaintive cries of Pierrot, bitten by his companion, who ate all, being the stronger.

Then they specified: "This is for you, Pierrot!" Pierrot evidently got nothing.

The two women, amazed, looked at each other. And Mme Lefevre declared in a sharp voice:

"I certainly can't feed all the dogs they throw in there. We must give it up."

Overcome with the idea of all those dogs living at her expense, she went away, carrying even the bread that she had begun to feed to poor Pierrot.

Rose followed, wiping her eyes on the corner of her blue apron.

CHRISTENING

"Come, doctor, a little more cognac." "With pleasure." The old navy doctor watched the golden liquid flow into his glass, held it up to the light, took a sip and kept it in his mouth a long while before swallowing it and said:

"What a delicious poison! I should say, what a captivating destroyer of humanity! You do not know it as I know it. You may have read that remarkable book called *L'Assommoir*, but you have not seen a whole tribe of savages exterminated by this same poison. I have seen with my own eyes a strange and terrible drama which was the result of too much alcohol. It happened not very far from here, in a little village near Pont-l'Abbé in Brittany. I was on a vacation and was living in the little country house which my father had left me. You all know that wild country surrounded by the sea—that wicked sea, always lying in wait for some new victim! The poor fishermen go out day and night in their little boats, and the wicked sea upsets their boats and swallows them! Fearlessly they go out, yet feeling uneasy as to their safety, but half of the time they are intoxicated. 'When the bottle is full we feel safe, but when it is empty we feel lost,' they say. If you got into their huts you will never find the father and if you ask the woman what has become of her man, she will answer, pointing to the raging sea: 'He stayed there one night when he had too much drink, and my eldest son too.' She has still four strong boys; it will be their turn soon!

"Well, as I have said, I was living at my little country house with one servant, an old sailor and the Breton family who took care of the place during my absence, which consisted of two sisters and the husband of one of them, who was also my gardener.

"Toward Christmas of that year the gardener's wife gave birth to a boy, and he asked me to be godfather. I could not very well refuse, and on the strength of it he borrowed ten francs from me, for the 'church expenses,' he said.

"The christening was to take place on the second of January. For the past week the ground had been covered with snow and it was bitter cold. At nine o'clock of the morning designated Kerandec and his sister-in-law arrived in front of my door with a nurse carrying the baby wrapped up in a blanket, and we started for the church. The cold was terrific, and I wondered how the poor little child could stand such cold. These Bretons must be made of iron, I thought, if they can stand going out in such weather at their birth!

"When we arrived at the church the door was closed. The priest had not come yet. The nurse sat on the steps and began to undress the child. I thought at first that she only wanted to arrange his clothes, but to my horror I saw that she was taking every stitch of clothing off his back! I was horrified at such imprudence and I went toward her, saying:

" 'What in the world are you doing? Are you crazy? Do you want to kill him?'

" 'Oh no, master,' she answered placidly, 'but he must present himself before God naked.' His father and aunt looked on calmly. It was the custom in Brittany, and if they had not done this, they said, something would happen to the child.

"I got furiously angry. I called the father all kinds of names; I threatened to leave them and tried to cover the child by force, but in vain. The nurse ran away from me with the poor little naked body, which was fast becoming blue with the biting cold. I had made up my mind to leave these brutes to their ignorance, when I saw the priest coming along, followed by the sexton and an altar boy. I ran toward him and told him in a few words what these brutes had done, but he was not a bit surprised; nor did he hurry.

" 'What can I do, my dear sir? It is the custom; they all do it.'

" 'But for goodness' sake, hurry up,' I cried impatiently.

" 'I cannot go any faster,' he answered, and at last he entered the vestry. We waited outside the church door, and I suffered terribly at hearing that poor little wretch crying with pain. At last the door opened and we went in, but the child had to remain naked during the whole ceremony. It seemed to me as if it would never come to an end. The priest crawled along like a turtle, muttered his Latin words slowly, as if he took pleasure in torturing the poor little baby. At last the torture came to an end, and the nurse wrapped the child in his blanket again. By that time the poor little thing was chilled through and was crying piteously.

" 'Will you come in and sign your name to the register?' asked the priest.

"I turned to the gardener and urged him to go home immediately and warm the child up, so as to avoid pneumonia if there was still time. He promised to follow my advice and left with his sister-in-law and the nurse. I followed the priest into the vestry, and when I had signed the register he demanded five francs. As I had given ten francs to the father, I refused. The priest threatened to tear up the certificate and to annul the ceremony, and I, in my turn, threatened to prosecute him. We quarreled for a long time, but at last I paid the five francs.

"As soon as I got home I ran to Kerandec's house, but neither he nor his sister-in-law nor the nurse had come home. The mother was in bed shivering with cold, and she was hungry, not having eaten anything since the day before.

" 'Where on earth did they go?' I asked. She did not seem the least bit surprised and answered calmly:

" 'They went to have a drink in honor of the christening.' That also was the custom, and I thought of my ten francs which I had given the father and which would pay for the drinks, no doubt. I sent some beef tea to the mother and had a good fire made in her room. I was so angry at those brutes that I made up my mind to discharge them when they came back, but what worried me most was the poor little baby. What would become of him?

"At six o'clock they had not come back. I ordered my servant to wait for them and I went to bed.

"I slept soundly, as a sailor will sleep, until daybreak and did not wake until my servant brought me some hot water. As soon as I opened my eyes I asked him about Kerandec. The old sailor hesitated then finally answered:

" 'He came home past midnight as drunk as a fool; the Kermagan woman and the nurse too. I think they slept in a ditch, and the poor little baby died without their even noticing it.'

" 'Dead!' I cried, jumping to my feet.

" 'Yes sir, they brought it to the mother, and when she saw it she cried terribly, but they made her drink to forget her sorrow.'

" 'What do you mean by "they made her drink"?'

" 'This, sir. I only found out this morning. Kerandec had no more liquor and no more money to buy any, so he took the wood alcohol that you gave him for the lamp, and they drank that until they had finished the bottle, and now the Kerandec woman is very sick.'

"I dressed in haste, seized a cane with the firm intention of chastising those human brutes and ran to the gardener's house. The mother lay helpless, dying from the effects of the alcohol, with the discolored corpse of her baby lying near her, while Kerandec and the Kermagan woman lay snoring on the floor.

"I did everything in my power to save the woman, but she died at noon."

The old doctor, having concluded his narrative, took the bottle of cognac, poured out a glass for himself and, having held it up to the light, swallowed the golden liquid and smacked his lips.

A COSTLY OUTING

Hector de Gribelin, descendant of an old provincial family, had spent his early years in his ancestral home and had finished his studies under the guidance of an old abbé. The family was far from rich, but they kept up appearances the best way they could. At the age of twenty a position was procured for him at the navy administration, at one thousand five hundred francs a year, but like a great many, not being prepared for the battle, his first three years of office life had been exceedingly hard.

He had renewed acquaintance with a few old friends of his family, poor like himself, but living in the secluded Faubourg Saint-Germain, keeping up appearances at any cost, sacrificing everything in order to hold their rank.

It was there he had met and married a young girl, titled but penniless. Two children had blessed their union. Hector and his wife struggled constantly to make both ends meet, and for the past four years they had known no other distractions than a walk on Sunday to the Champs Elysées and a few evenings at the theater, a friend giving them tickets.

His chief had just intrusted him with some extra work, and he received the extra compensation of three hundred francs. Coming home that night, he said to his wife:

"My dear Henriette, we ought to do something with this money, a little outing in the country for the children, for instance."

They had a lengthy discussion and finally decided on a family picnic.

"We have had so very few outings," said Hector, "that we may as well do things right. We will hire a rig for you and the little ones, and I will hire a horse; it will do me good."

They talked of nothing else all week. Each night he would dance his elder son up and down on his foot and say:

"This is the way Papa will ride next Sunday." And the boy would ride chairs all day, screaming:

"This is Papa on horseback." Even the servant marveled when she heard Hector tell of his feats on horseback when he was home and how he would ride at the side of the carriage.

"When once on a horse I am afraid of nothing," he would say. "If they could give me a frisky animal I would like it all the better. You will see how I ride, and if you like, we can come back by the Champs Elysées when everybody is coming home. We shall cut quite a figure, and I should not be sorry to meet some-one from the office; there is nothing like it to inspire respect."

At last Sunday came. The carriage and the horse were at the door, and Hector came down immediately, holding a newly bought riding whip, to look the horse over. He examined him from head to foot, opened his mouth, told his age, and as the family was coming out at that moment, he discoursed on horses in general and that one in particular, which he declared to be an excellent animal.

When everyone was comfortably placed in the carriage Hector examined the saddle and, mounting with a spring, dropped on the horse with such force that he immediately set up a dance which almost threw his rider. Hector became flus-tered and tried to calm him, saying: "Come, old fellow, be quiet." And, having succeeded in calming him a little, he asked:

"Is everybody ready?"

Everybody said they were, and the party proceeded. All eyes were turned on Hector, who affected the English seat and leaped up and down on his saddle in an exaggerated manner. He looked straight before him, contracting his brow and looking very pale. His wife and the servant each held one of the boys on their laps, and every minute they would say:

"Look at Papa!" And the boys, overcome with joy, uttered piercing screams.

The horse, frightened at so much noise, started off at a gallop, and while Hector tried to stop him his hat fell off. The driver had to come down and pick it up, and, having recovered it, Hector shouted to his wife:

"Make the children stop screaming, will you? They will make the horse run away."

They arrived at last. The baskets having been opened, they lunched on the grass. Although the driver looked after the horses Hector went every minute to see if his horse wanted anything. He patted him and fed him bread, cake and sugar.

"He is a great trotter," he said to his wife. "He shook me at first, but you saw how quickly I subdued him. He knows his master now."

They came back by the Champs Elysées as agreed. The weather being beautiful, the avenue was crowded with carriages and the sidewalks lined with pedestrians. The horse, scenting the stable, suddenly took to his heels. He dashed between carriages like a whirlwind, and Hector's efforts to stop him were unavailing. The carriage containing his family was far behind. In front of the Palais de l'Industrie the horse turned to the right at a gallop. An old woman was at that moment leisurely crossing the street, and Hector, who was unable to stop the horse, shouted: "Hey there, hey!" But the old woman was deaf, perhaps, for she slowly kept on until the horse struck her with such force that she turned a triple somersault and landed ten feet away. Several people shouted: "Stop him."

Hector was distracted and held on desperately to the horse's mane, crying: "Help, help!" A terrible shock sent him over the horse's head like a bomb, and he landed in the arms of a policeman who was running toward him. An angry crowd gathered. An old gentleman wearing a decoration was especially angry.

"Confound it, sir!" he said, "if you cannot ride a horse why do you not stay at home instead of running over people!"

Four men were carrying the old woman, who to all appearances was dead.

"Take this woman to a drugstore," said the old gentleman, "and let us go to the station house."

A crowd followed Hector, who walked between two policemen, while a third led his horse. At that moment the carriage appeared, and his wife, taking in the situation at a glance, ran toward him; the servant and the children came behind, crying. He explained that his horse had knocked a woman down, but it was nothing; he would be home very soon.

Arrived at the station house, he gave his name, his place of employment and awaited news of the injured woman. A policeman came back with the information that the woman's name was Mme Simon and that she was a charwoman, sixty-five years old. She had regained consciousness, but she suffered internally, she claimed. When Hector found that she was not dead he recovered his spirits and promised to defray the expenses of her illness. He went to the drugstore where they had taken the old woman. An immense crowd blocked the doorway. The old woman was whining and groaning pitifully. Two doctors were examining her.

"There are no bones broken," they said, "but we are afraid she is hurt internally."

"Do you suffer much?" asked Hector.

"Oh yes."

"Where?"

"I feel as if my inside was on fire."

"Then you are the cause of the accident?" said a doctor, approaching.

"Yes sir," said Hector.

"This woman must go to a sanitarium. I know one where they will take her for six francs a day; shall I fix it for you?"

Hector thanked him gratefully and went home relieved. He found his wife in tears, and he comforted her, saying:

"Don't worry; she is much better already. I sent her to a sanitarium, and in three days she will be all right."

After his work the next day he went to see Mme Simon. She was eating some beef soup which she seemed to relish.

"Well," said Hector, "how do you feel?"

"No better, my poor man," she answered. "I feel as good as dead!"

The doctor advised waiting; complications might arise. He waited three days then went to see the old woman again. Her skin was clear, her eyes bright, but as soon as she saw Hector she commenced to whine:

"I can't move any more, my poor man; I'll be like this for the rest of my days!"

Hector felt a shiver running up and down his back. He asked for the doctor and inquired about the patient.

"I am puzzled," the doctor said. "Every time we try to lift her up or change her position she utters heart-rending screams; still, I am bound to believe her. I cannot say that she shams until I have seen her walk."

The old woman listened attentively, a sly look on her face. A week, two, then a month passed, and still Mme Simon did not leave her chair. Her appetite was excellent; she gained flesh and joked with the other patients. She seemed to accept her lot as a well-earned rest after fifty years of labor as a charwoman.

Hector came every day and found her the same, always repeating:

"I can't move, my poor man; I can't!"

When Hector came home his wife would ask with anxiety:

"How is Madame Simon?"

"Just the same; absolutely no change," answered Hector dejectedly.

They dismissed the servant and economized more than ever. The money received from his chief had been spent. Hector was desperate, and one day he called four doctors to hold a consultation. They examined Mme Simon thoroughly, while she watched them slyly.

"We must make her walk," said one of the doctors.

"I can't, gentlemen; I can't!"

They took hold of her and dragged her a few steps, but she freed herself and sank to the floor emitting such piercing screams that they carried her back to her chair very gently.

They reserved their opinion but concluded, however, that she was incapacited for work.

When Hector brought the news to his wife she collapsed.

"We had much better take her here; it would cost us less."

"In our own house! What are you thinking of?"

"What else can we do, dear? I am sure it is no fault of mine!"

A KING'S SON

The boulevard, that river of life, was rushing along under the golden light of the setting sun. All the sky was red, dazzling red, and behind the Madeleine an immense, brilliant cloud threw into the long avenue an oblique shower of fire, vibrating like the rays from live coals.

The gay crowd moved along in this ruddy mist as if they were in an apotheosis. Their faces were golden; their black hats and coats were reflected in shades of purple; the varnish of their shoes threw red lights upon the asphalt of the sidewalks.

Before the cafés men were drinking brilliantly colored drinks, which one might take for precious stones melted in the crystal.

In the midst of the consumers two officers in very rich uniforms caused all eyes to turn in their direction on account of their gold braid and grand bearing. They were chatting pleasantly, without motive, rejoicing in this glory of life, in the radiant beauty of the evening. And they looked at the crowd—at the slow men and the hurrying women who left behind them an attractive, disturbing odor.

All at once an enormous Negro, clothed in black, corpulent, decorated with trinkets all over his duck waistcoat, his face shining as if it had been oiled, passed before them with an air of triumph. He smiled at the passers-by; he smiled at the vendors of the newspapers; he smiled at the shining heavens and the whole of Paris. He was so large that he towered above all their heads, and all the loungers that he left behind him turned to contemplate his back.

Suddenly he perceived the officers and, pushing aside the drinkers, he rushed toward them. When he was before their table he planted upon them his shining, delighted eyes and, raising the corners of his mouth to his ears, showed his white teeth, shining like a crescent moon in a black sky. The two men, stupefied, looked at this ebony giant without understanding his merriment.

Then he cried out in a voice that made everybody at all the tables laugh:

"Good evenin', my lieutenant."

One of the officers was chief of a battalion; the other was a colonel. The first said:

"I do not know you, sir, and cannot think what you can want of me."

The Negro replied:

"Me like you much, Lieutenant Védie, siege of Bézi, much grapes, hunt me up."

The officer, much astonished, looked closely at the man, seeking to place him in his memory. Suddenly he cried:

"Timbuctoo?"

The Negro, radiant, struck himself on his leg, uttered a most strident laugh and bellowed:

"Yes, ya, ya, my lieutenant, remember Timbuctoo, ya, good evenin'."

The officer extended his hand, laughing now himself with all his heart. Then Timbuctoo became grave. He seized the officer's hand and kissed it as the custom is in Arabia, so quickly that it could not be stopped. In a confused manner the military man said to him, his voice rather severe:

"Come, Timbuctoo, we are not in Africa. Be seated and tell me how you came to be here."

Timbuctoo swelled out his ample front and stammered, from trying to talk too quickly:

"Got much money, much, great rest'rant, good eat; Prussians come, much steal, much; French cooking; Timbuctoo chef to emperor, two hundred thousand francs for me. Ah! ah! ah! ah!"

And he laughed, twisting himself and howling, with a perfect madness of joy in his eye.

When the officer who comprehended this strange language had asked him questions for some time he said to him:

"Well, good-by now, Timbuctoo; I will see you again."

The Negro immediately arose, shook the hand that was extended to him, properly this time, and, continuing to laugh, cried:

"Good evenin', good evenin', my lieutenant."

He went away so content that he gesticulated as he walked until he was taken for a crazy man.

The colonel asked: "Who was that brute?"

The commander responded: "A brave boy and a brave soldier. I will tell you what I know of him; it is funny enough.

"You know that at the commencement of the war of 1870 I was shut up in

Bézières, which the Negro calls Bézi. We were not besieged but blockaded. The Prussian lines surrounded us everywhere, beyond the reach of cannon, no longer shooting at us but starving us little by little.

"I was then a lieutenant. Our garrison was composed of troops of every nature, the debris of cut-up regiments, fugitives and marauders separated from the body of the army. We even had eleven Turcos arrive finally one evening from no one knew where. They presented themselves at the gates of the town, harassed, hungry, drunk and in tatters. They were given to me.

"I soon recognized the fact that they were averse to all discipline, that they were always absent and always tipsy. I tried the police station, even the prison, without effect. My men disappeared for whole days, as if they had sunk into the earth, then reappeared, intoxicated enough to fall. They had no money. Where did they get their drink? How and by what means?

"This began to puzzle me much, especially as these savages interested me with their eternal laugh and their character, which was that of a great, roguish child.

"I then perceived that they blindly obeyed the biggest one of them all, the one you have just seen. He governed them by his will, planned their mysterious enterprises and was chief, all-powerful and incontestable. I made him come to my house and I questioned him. Our conversation lasted a good three hours, so great was my difficulty in penetrating his surprising mixture of tongues. As for him, poor devil, he made the most unheard-of efforts to be understood, invented words, gesticulated, fairly sweated from his difficulty, wiped his brow, puffed, stopped and then began suddenly again when he thought he had found a new means of explaining himself.

"I finally divined that he was the son of a great chief, a sort of Negro king in the neighborhood of Timbuctoo. I asked him his name. He responded something like 'Chavaharibouhalikhranafotapolara.' It appeared simpler to me to call him by the name of his country: 'Timbuctoo.' And eight days later all the garrison was calling him that and nothing else.

"A foolish desire seized me of finding out where this ex-African prince found his drink. And I discovered it in a singular way.

"One morning I was on the ramparts studying the horizon, when I perceived something moving in a vine near by. It was at the time of the vintage; the grapes were ripe, but I scarcely gave this a thought. My idea was that some spy was approaching the town, and I organized an expedition complete enough to seize the prowlers. I myself took the command, having obtained the general's authorization.

"Three small troops were to set out through three different gates and join near the suspected vine to watch. In order to cut off the retreat of any spy one detachment had to make a march of an hour at least. One man remained upon the wall for observation, to indicate to me by a sign that the person sought had not left the field. We preserved a deep silence, crawling, almost lying in the wheel ruts. Finally we reached the designated point; I suddenly deployed my soldiers, charging them quickly upon the vine and found Timbuctoo traveling along among the vine stocks on four paws, eating grapes, or rather, snapping them up as a dog eats his soup, his mouth full of leaves even, snatching the bunches off with a blow of his teeth.

"I wished to make him get up; there was no longer any mystery, and I comprehended why he dragged himself along upon his hands and knees.

"When he was planted upon his feet he swayed back and forth for some seconds, extending his arms and striking his nose. He was as tipsy as any tipsy man I have ever seen.

"They brought him away on two poles. He never ceased to laugh all along the route, gesticulating with his arms and legs.

"That was the whole of it. My merry fellows had drunk of the grape itself. Then when they could no longer drink and could not budge, they went to sleep on the spot.

"As for Timbuctoo, his love for the vine passed all belief and all measure. He lived down there after the fashion of the thrushes, which he hated with the hatred of a jealous rival. He repeated without ceasing:

" 'The th'ushes eat all g'apes, the d'unkards.'

"One evening someone came to find me. Off over the plain something seemed to be moving toward us. I did not have my glass with me and could not distinguish what it was. It looked like a great serpent rolling itself along, or a funeral procession; how could I tell?

"I sent some men to meet this strange caravan, which soon appeared in triumphal march. Timbuctoo and nine of his companions were carrying a sort of altar, made of campaign chairs, upon which were eight cut-off heads, bloody and grimacing. The tenth Turco dragged a horse by the tail to which another was attached, and six other beasts still followed, held in the same fashion.

"This is what I learned. Having set out for the vine, my Africans had suddenly perceived a detachment of Prussian soldiers approaching a neighboring village. Instead of fleeing they concealed themselves; then when the officers put foot to the ground at an inn to refresh themselves, the eleven merry ones threw themselves upon them, put to flight the uhlans who believed themselves attacked, killed the two sentinels, then the colonel and the five officers comprising his escort.

"That day I embraced Timbuctoo. But I also perceived that he walked with difficulty; I believed that he was wounded. He began to laugh and said to me:

" 'Me get p'ovisions for country.'

"It seems that Timbuctoo had not made war for the sake of honor but for gain. All that he found, all that appeared to him to have any value whatever, everything that glistened, especially, he plunged into his pocket. And what a pocket! An abyss that begun at the hip and extended to the heels. Having learned the word of a trooper, he called it his 'profound.' It was, in fact, his profound! He had detached the gold from the Prussian uniforms, the copper from their helmets, the buttons, etc., and thrown them all into his profound, which was full to the brim.

"Each day he cast in there every glistening object that fell under his eye—pieces of tin or pieces of money—which sometimes gave him an infinitely droll figure.

"He counted on bringing things back like an ostrich, which he resembled like a brother—this son of a king, tortured by a desire to devour these shining bodies. If he had not had his profound what would he have done? Doubtless he would have swallowed them.

"Each morning his pocket was empty. He had a kind of general store where he heaped up his riches. Where? No one could ever discover.

"The general, foreseeing the uproar that Timbuctoo had created, had the bodies quickly interred in a neighboring village before it was discovered that they had been decapitated. The Prussians came the next day. The mayor and seven distinguished inhabitants were shot immediately, as it had been learned through informers that they had denounced the Germans.

"The winter had come. We were harassed and desperate. There was fighting now every day. The starved men could no longer walk. The eight Turks alone (three had been killed) were fat and shining, vigorous and always ready for battle. Timbuctoo even grew stout. He said to me one day:

" 'You much hungry, me good food.'

"In fact, he brought me an excellent fillet. Of what? We had neither beeves, sheep, goats, asses nor pigs. It was impossible for him to procure a horse. I reflected upon all this after having devoured my viand. Then a terrible thought came to me. These Negroes were born near a country where they ate men! And every day soldiers were falling all about them! I questioned Timbuctoo. He did not wish to say anything. I did not insist, but henceforth I ate no more of his presents.

"He adored me. One night the snow overtook us at the outposts. We were seated on the ground. I looked with pity upon the poor Negroes shivering under this white, freezing powder. As I was very cold, I began to cough. Immediately I felt something close around me like a great warm cover. It was Timbuctoo's mantle, which he had thrown around my shoulders.

"I arose and returned the garment to him, saying:

" 'Keep it, my boy, you have more need of it than I.'

"He answered: 'No, no, my lieutenant, for you, me not need, me hot, hot!'

"And he looked at me with suppliant eyes. I replied:

" 'Come, obey, keep your mantle; I wish it.'

"The Negro arose, drew his saber which he knew how to make cut like a scythe, held in the other the large cloak that I had refused and said:

" 'So you not take mantle, me cut; no mantle.'

"He would have done it. I yielded.

"Eight days later we had capitulated. Some among us had been able to get away. The others were going out of the town and giving themselves up to the conquerors.

"I directed my steps toward the armory, where we were to reunite, when I met face to face a Negro giant clothed in white duck and wearing a straw cap. It was Timbuctoo. He seemed radiant and walked along, his hands in his pockets, until we came to a little shop where in the window there were two plates and two glasses.

"I asked him: 'What are you doing here?'

"He responded:

" 'Me not suffer, me good cook; me make Colonel Algeie to eat; me feed Prussians, steal much, much.'

"The mercury stood at ten degrees. I shivered before this Negro in white duck. Then he took me by the arm and made me enter. There I perceived a huge sign that he was going to hang up before his door as soon as I had gone out, for he had some modesty. I read, traced by the hand of some accomplice, these words:

"MILITARY-CUISINE OF M. TIMBUCTOO.

Formerly caterer to H. M. the Emperor.

Paris Artist. Prices Moderate.

"In spite of the despair which was gnawing at my heart I could not help laughing, and I left my Negro to his new business. It would have availed nothing to have him taken prisoner.

"You see how he has succeeded, the rascal; Bézières today belongs to Germany. Timbuctoo's restaurant was the beginning of revenge."

WAITER, A BOCK!

Why, on this particular evening, did I enter a certain beer shop? I cannot explain it. It was bitterly cold. A fine rain, a watery mist, floated about, veiling the gas jets in a transparent fog, making the pavements under the shadow of the shop fronts glitter, which revealed the soft slush and the soiled feet of the passers-by.

I was going nowhere in particular; was simply having a short walk after dinner. I had passed the Crédit Lyonnais, the Rue Vivienne and several other streets. Suddenly I descried a large café, which was more than half full. I walked inside with no object in mind. I was not the least thirsty.

By a searching glance I detected a place where I would not be too much crowded. So I went and sat down by the side of a man who seemed to me to be old and who smoked a halfpenny clay pipe, which had become as black as coal. From six to eight beer saucers were piled up on the table in front of him, indicating the number of bocks he had already absorbed. With that same glance I had recognized in him a "regular toper," one of those frequenters of beer houses who come in the morning as soon as the place is open and only go away in the evening when it is about to close. He was dirty, bald to about the middle of the cranium, while his long gray hair fell over the neck of his frock coat. His clothes, much too large for him, appeared to have been made for him at a time when he was very stout. One could guess that his pantaloons were not held up by braces and that this man could not take ten paces without having to pull them up and readjust them. Did he wear a vest? The mere thought of his boots and the feet they enveloped filled me with horror. The frayed cuffs were as black at the edges as were his nails.

As soon as I had sat down near him this queer creature said to me in a tranquil tone of voice:

"How goes it with you?"

I turned sharply round to him and closely scanned his features, whereupon he continued:

"I see you do not recognize me."

"No, I do not."

"Des Barrets."

I was stupefied. It was Count Jean des Barrets, my old college chum.

I seized him by the hand, so dumfounded that I could find nothing to say. I at length managed to stammer out:

"And you, how goes it with you?"

He responded placidly:

"With me? Just as I like."

He became silent. I wanted to be friendly, and I selected this phrase:

"What are you doing now?"

"You see what I am doing," he answered, quite resignedly.

I felt my face getting red. I insisted:

"But every day?"

"Every day is alike to me," was his response, accompanied with a thick puff of tobacco smoke.

He then tapped on the top of the marble table with a sou to attract the attention of the waiter and called out:

"Waiter, two bocks."

A voice in the distance repeated:

"Two bocks instead of four."

Another voice, more distant still, shouted out:

"Here they are, sir, here they are."

Immediately there appeared a man with a white apron carrying two bocks, which he set down foaming on the table, the foam running over the edge onto the sandy floor.

Des Barrets emptied his glass at a single draught and replaced it on the table, sucking in the drops of beer that had been left on his mustache. He next asked:

"What is there new?"

"I know of nothing new, worth mentioning, really," I stammered. "But nothing has grown old for me; I am a commercial man."

In an equable tone of voice he said:

"Indeed—does that amuse you?"

"No, but what do you mean by that? Surely you must do something!"

"What do you mean by that?"

"I only mean, how do you pass your time?"

"What's the use of occupying myself with anything? For my part, I do nothing at all, as you see, never anything. When one has not got a sou one can understand why one has to go to work. What is the good of working? Do you work for yourself or for others? If you work for yourself you do it for your own amusement, which is all right; if you work for others you reap nothing but ingratitude."

Then, sticking his pipe into his mouth, he called out anew:

"Waiter, a bock! It makes me thirsty to keep calling so. I am not accustomed to that sort of thing. Yes, I do nothing; I let things slide and I am growing old. In dying I shall have nothing to regret. If so, I should remember nothing outside this public house. I have no wife, no children, no cares, no sorrows, nothing. That is the very best thing that could happen to one."

He then emptied the glass which had been brought him, passed his tongue over his lips and resumed his pipe.

I looked at him, stupefied, and asked him:

"But you have not always been like that?"

"Pardon me, sir; ever since I left college."

"It is not a proper life to lead, my dear sir; it is simply horrible. Come, you must indeed have done something; you must have loved something; you must have friends."

"No, I get up at noon; I come here; I have my breakfast; I drink my bock; I remain until evening; I have my dinner; I drink bock. Then about one in the morning I return to my couch, because the place closes up. And it is this latter that embitters me more than anything. For the last ten years I have passed six tenths of my time on this bench in my corner and the other four tenths in my bed, never changing. I talk sometimes with the habitués."

"But on arriving in Paris what did you do at first?"

"I paid my devoirs to the Café de Medicis."

"What next?"

"Next? I crossed the water and came here."

"Why did you take even that trouble?"

"What do you mean? One cannot remain all one's life in the Latin Quarter. The students make too much noise. But I do not move about any longer. Waiter, a bock."

I now began to think that he was making fun of me, and I continued:

"Come now, be frank. You have been the victim of some great sorrow; despair in love, no doubt! It is easy to see that you are a man whom misfortune has hit hard. What age are you?"

"I am thirty years of age, but I look to be forty-five at least."

I looked him straight in the face. His shrunken figure, badly cared for, gave one the impression that he was an old man. On the summit of his cranium a few long hairs shot straight up from a skin of doubtful cleanness. He had enormous eyelashes, a large mustache and a thick beard. Suddenly I had a kind of vision—I know not why—the vision of a basin filled with noisome water, the water which should have been applied to that poll. I said to him:

"Verily, you look to be more than that age. Of a certainty you must have experienced some great disappointment."

He replied:

"I tell you that I have not. I am old because I never take air. There is nothing that vitiates the life of a man more than the atmosphere of a café."

I could not believe him.

"You must surely have been married as well? One could not get bald-headed as you are without having been much in love."

He shook his head, sending down his back little hairs from the scalp.

"No, I have always been virtuous."

And, raising his eyes toward the luster which beat down on our heads, he said:

"If I am bald-headed it is the fault of the gas. It is the enemy of hair. Waiter, a bock. You must be thirsty also?"

"No, thank you. But you certainly interest me. When did you have your first discouragement? Your life is not normal; is not natural. There is something under it all."

"Yes, and it dates from my infancy. I received a heavy blow when I was very young. It turned my life into darkness, which will last to the end."

"How did it come about?"

"You wish to know about it? Well then, listen. You recall, of course, the castle in which I was brought up, seeing that you used to visit it for five or six months during the vacations. You remember that large gray building in the middle of a great park and the long avenues of oaks, which opened toward the four cardinal points? You remember my father and my mother, both of whom were ceremonious, solemn, and severe?

"I worshiped my mother; I was suspicious of my father, but I respected both, accustomed always as I was to see everyone bow before them. In the country they were *monsieur le comte* and *madame la comtesse*, and our neighbors, the Tannemares, the Ravelets, the Brennevilles, showed the utmost consideration for them.

"I was then thirteen years old, happy, satisfied with everything, as one is at that age, and full of joy and vivacity.

"Now toward the end of September, a few days before entering the *lycée*, while I was enjoying myself in the mazes of the park, climbing the trees and swinging on the branches, I saw crossing an avenue my father and mother, who were walking together.

"I recall the thing as though it were yesterday. It was a very windy day. The whole line of trees bent under the pressure of the wind, moaned, and seemed to utter cries—cries dull, yet deep—so that the whole forest groaned under the gale.

"Evening had come on, and it was dark in the thickets. The agitation of the wind and the branches excited me, made me skip about like an idiot and howl in imitation of the wolves.

"As soon as I perceived my parents I crept furtively toward them under the branches, in order to surprise them, as though I had been a veritable wolf. But suddenly seized with fear, I stopped a few paces from them. My father, a prey to the most violent passion, cried:

" 'Your mother is a fool; moreover, it is not your mother that is the question; it is you. I tell you that I want money, and I will make you sign this.'

"My mother responded in a firm voice:

" 'I will not sign it. It is Jean's fortune; I shall guard it for him and I will not allow you to devour it with strange women, as you have your own heritage.'

"Then my father, full of rage, wheeled round and seized his wife by the throat and began to slap her full in the face with the disengaged hand.

"My mother's hat fell off; her hair became disheveled and fell down her back; she essayed to parry the blows but could not escape from them. And my father, like a madman, banged and banged at her. My mother rolled over on the ground, covering her face in both her hands. Then he turned her over on her back in order to batter her still more, pulling away the hands which were covering her face.

"As for me, my friend, it seemed as though the world had come to an end, that the eternal laws had changed. I experienced the overwhelming dread that one has in presence of things supernatural, in presence of irreparable disaster. My boyish head whirled round and soared. I began to cry with all my might without knowing why, a prey to terror, to grief, to a dreadful bewilderment. My father heard me. I believed that he wanted to kill me, and I fled like a hunted animal, running straight in front of me through the woods.

"I ran perhaps for an hour, perhaps for two; I know not. Darkness had set in; I tumbled over some thick herbs, exhausted, and I lay there lost, devoured by terror, eaten up by a sorrow capable of breaking forever the heart of a child. I became cold; I became hungry. At length day broke. I dared neither get up, walk, return home, or save myself, fearing to encounter my father, whom I did not wish to see again.

"I should probably have died of misery and of hunger at the foot of a tree if the guard had not discovered me and led me by force.

"I found my parents wearing their ordinary aspect. My mother alone spoke to me:

" 'How you have frightened me, you naughty boy; I have been the whole night sleepless.'

"I did not answer but began to weep. My father did not utter a single word.

"Eight days later I entered the *lycée.*

"Well, my friend, it was all over with me. I had witnessed the other side of things, the bad side; I have not been able to perceive the good side since that day. What things have passed in my mind, what strange phenomena have warped my ideas, I do not know. But I no longer have a taste for anything, a wish for anything, a love for anybody, a desire for anything whatever, no ambition, no hope. And I always see my poor mother lying on the ground in the avenue while my father was maltreating her. My mother died a few years after; my father lives still. I have not seen him since. Waiter, a bock."

A waiter brought him his bock, which he swallowed at a gulp. But in taking his pipe again, trembling as he was, he broke it. Then he made a violent gesture:

"Zounds! This is indeed a grief, a real grief. I have had it for a month, and it was coloring so beautifully!"

Then he went off through the vast saloon, which was now full of smoke and of people drinking, calling out:

"Waiter, a bock—and a new pipe."

MOHAMMED FRIPOULI

"Shall we have our coffee on the roof?" asked the captain.

I answered:

"Yes, certainly."

He rose. It was already dark in the room which was lighted only by the interior court, after the fashion of Moorish houses. Before the high, ogive windows, convolvulus vines hung from the gnat terrace where they passed the hot summer evenings. There only remained upon the table some grapes, big as plums, some fresh figs of a violet hue, some yellow pears, some long, plump bananas and some Tougourt dates in a basket of alfa.

The Moor who waited on them opened the door, and I went upstairs to the azure walls which received from above the soft light of the dying day.

And soon I gave a deep sigh of happiness on reaching the terrace. It overlooked Algiers, the harbor, the roadstead and the distant shores.

The house, bought by the captain, was a former Arab residence, situated in the midst of the old city, among those labyrinthine little streets where swarm the strange population of the African coasts.

Beneath us the flat, square roofs descended, like steps of giants, to the pointed roofs of the European quarter of the city. Behind these might be perceived the flags of the boats at anchor, then the sea, the open sea, blue and calm under the blue and calm sky.

We stretched ourselves upon the mats, our heads resting upon cushions, and while leisurely sipping the savory coffee of the locality, I gazed at the first stars in the dark azure. They were hardly perceptible, so far away, so pale, as yet giving scarcely any light.

A light heat, a winged heat, caressed our skins. And at times the warm, heavy air in which there was a vague odor, the odor of Africa, seemed the hot breath of the desert, coming over the peaks of Atlas. The captain, lying on his back, said:

"What a country, my dear boy! How soft life is here! How peculiar and delicious repose is in this land! How the nights seem to be made for dreams."

I looked at the stars coming out with a lazy, yet active curiosity, with a drowsy happiness.

I murmured:

"You might tell me something of your life in the south."

Captain Marret was one of the oldest officers in the army of Africa, an officer of fortune, a former spahi, who had cut his way to his present rank.

Thanks to him, to his relations and friendships, I had been able to accomplish a superb trip to the desert, and I had come that evening to thank him before going to France.

He said: "What kind of a story do you want? I have had so many adventures during twelve years of sand that I can't think of a single one." And I replied: "Well, tell me of the Arabian women." He did not reply. He remained stretched out with his arms bent and his hands under his head, and I noticed at times the odor of his cigar, the smoke of which went straight up into the sky, so breezeless was the night.

And all of a sudden he began to laugh.

"Ah yes, I'll tell you about a queer affair which occurred in my first days in Algeria.

"We had then in the army of Africa some extraordinary types, such as have not been seen since, types which would have amused you so much, in fact, that you would have wanted to spend all your life in this country.

"I was a simple spahi, a little spahi, twenty years old, light-haired, swaggering, supple and strong. I was attached to a military command at Boghar. You know Boghar, which they call the balcony of the south. You have seen from the top of the fort the beginning of this land of fire, devoured, naked, tormented, stony and red. It is really the antechamber to the desert, the broiling and superb frontier of the immense region of yellow solitudes.

"Well, there were forty of us spahis at Boghar, a company of *joyeux* and a squadron of *Chasseurs d'Afrique*, when it was learned that the tribe of the Ouled-Berghi had assassinated an English traveler, come, no man knows how, into the country, for the English have the devil in their bodies.

"Punishment had to be given for the crime against a European, but the commanding officer hesitated at sending a column, thinking, in truth, that one Englishman wasn't worth so much of a movement.

"Now as he was talking of this affair with the captain and the lieutenant, a quartermaster of spahis, who was waiting for orders, proposed all at once to go and punish the tribe if they would give him only six men. You know that in the south they are more free than in the city garrisons, and there exists between officer and soldier a sort of comradeship which is not found elsewhere.

"The captain began to laugh:

" 'You, my good man?'

" 'Yes, Captain, and if you desire it I will bring you back the whole tribe as prisoners.'

"The commandant, who had fantastic ideas, took him at his word.

" 'You will start tomorrow morning with six men of your own selection, and if you don't accomplish your purpose look out for yourself.'

"The subofficer smiled in his mustache.

" 'Fear nothing, Commandant. My prisoners shall be here Wednesday noon at latest.'

"The quartermaster, Mohammed Fripouli, as he was called, was a Turk, a true Turk, who had entered the service of France after a life which had been very much knocked about and not altogether too clean. He had traveled in many places, in Greece, in Asia Minor, in Egypt, in Palestine, and he had been forced to pay a good many forfeits on the way. He was an ex-Bashi-Bazouk, bold, ferocious and gay, with the calm gaiety of the Oriental. He was stout, very stout, but supple as a monkey, and he rode a horse marvelously well. His mustache, incredibly thick and long, always aroused in me a confused idea of the crescent moon and a scimitar. He hated the Arabs with a deadly hatred, and he pursued them with frightful cruelty, continually inventing new tricks, calculated and terrible perfidies. He was possessed, too, of incredible strength and inconceivable audacity.

"The commandant said to him: 'Choose your men, my blade.'

"Mohammed took me. He had confidence in me, the brave man, and I was grateful to him, body and soul, for this choice, which gave me as much pleasure as the Cross of Honor later.

"So we started the next morning at dawn, all seven of us, and nobody else. My comrades were composed of those bandits, those plunderers, who, after marauding and playing the vagabond in all possible countries, finish by taking service in some foreign legion. Our army in Africa was then full of these rascals, excellent soldiers but not at all scrupulous.

"Mohammed had given to each to carry ten pieces of rope about a meter in length. I was charged, besides as being the youngest and the least heavy, with a piece about a hundred meters long. When he was asked what he was going to do with all that rope he answered with his sly and placid air:

" 'It is to fish for the Arabs.'

"And he winked his eye mischievously, an action which he had learned from an old *Chasseur d'Afrique* from Paris.

"He marched in front of our squad, his head wrapped in a red turban, which he always wore in a campaign, and he smiled with cunning chuckles in his enormous mustache.

"He was truly handsome, this big Turk, with his powerful paunch, his shoulders of a colossus and his tranquil air. He rode a white horse of medium height, but strong, and the rider seemed ten times too big for his mount.

"We were passing through a long, dry ravine, bare and yellow, in the valley of the Chelif, and we talked of our expedition. My companions had all possible accents, there being among them a Spaniard, a Greek, an American and two Frenchmen. As for Mohammed Fripouli, he spoke with an incredibly thick tongue.

"The sun, the terrible sun, the sun of the south, which no one knows anything about on the other side of the Mediterranean, fell upon our shoulders, and we advanced at a walk, as they always do in that country.

"All day we marched without meeting a tree or an Arab.

"Toward one o'clock in the afternoon we had eaten, near a little spring which flowed between the rocks, the bread and dried mutton which we had brought in our knapsacks, then, after twenty minutes' rest, went out again on our way.

"Toward six o'clock in the evening, finally, after a long detour which our leader had forced us to make, we discovered behind a knob a tribe encamped. The brown, low tents made dark spots on the yellow earth, looking like great mushrooms growing at the foot of this red hill which was burned by the sun.

"They were our game. A little farther away, on the edge of a meadow of alfa of a dark green color, the tied horses were pasturing.

" 'Gallop!' ordered Mohammed, and we arrived like a whirlwind in the midst of the camp. The women, terrified, covered with white rags which hung floating upon them, ran quickly to their canvas huts, cringing and crouching and crying like hunted beasts. The men, on the contrary, came from all sides to defend themselves. We struck right for the tallest tent, that of the aga.

"We kept our sabers in the scabbards, after the example of Mohammed, who galloped in a singular fashion. He sat absolutely motionless, erect upon his small horse, which strove under him madly to carry such a weight. And the tranquillity of the rider with his long mustache contrasted strangely with the liveliness of the animal.

"The native chief came out of his tent as we arrived before it. He was a tall thin man, dark, with a gleaming eye, full forehead and arched eyebrows.

"He cried in Arabic:

" 'What do you want?'

"Mohammed, stopping his horse short, replied in his language: 'Was it you who killed the English traveler?'

"The aga said in a strong voice:

" 'I am not going to be examined by you!'

"There was around us, as it were, a rumbling tempest. The Arabs ran up from all sides, pressing and surrounding us, all the time vociferating loudly.

"They had the air of ferocious birds of prey, with their big curved noses, their thin faces with high cheekbones, their flowing garments, agitated by their gestures.

"Mohammed smiled, his turban crooked, his eye excited, and I saw shivers of pleasure on his cheeks which were pendulous, fleshy and wrinkled.

"He replied in a thunderous voice:

" 'Death to him who has given death!'

"And he pointed his revolver at the brown face of the aga. I saw a little smoke leap from the muzzle; then a red foam of blood and brains spurted from the forehead of the chief. He fell like a block on his back, spreading out his arms, which lifted like wings the folds of his burnous.

"Truly, I thought my last day had come; such a terrible tumult rose about us.

"Mohammed had drawn his saber. We unsheathed ours, like him. He cried, whirling away the men, who were pressing him the closest:

" 'Life to those who submit. Death to all others.'

"And seizing the nearest in his herculean grasp, he dragged him to his saddle, tied his hands, yelling to us:

" 'Do as I, and saber those who resist.'

"In five minutes we had captured twenty Arabs, whose wrists we securely bound. Then we pursued the fleeing ones, for there had been a perfect rout around us at the sight of the naked sabers. We captured about twenty more men.

"Over all the plains might be seen white objects which were running. The women were dragging along their children and uttering piercing cries. The yellow dogs, like jackals, barked around us and showed us their white fangs.

"Mohammed, who seemed mad with joy, leaped from his horse at a bound and, seizing the cord which I had brought:

" 'Attention!' he cried, 'two men to the ground.'

"Then he made a terrible and peculiar thing—a string of prisoners, or rather a string of hanged men. He had firmly tied the two wrists of the first captive, then he made a running knot around his neck with the same cord, which bound his neck. Our fifty prisoners soon found themselves fastened in such a way that the slightest movement of one to flee would strangle him as well as his two neighbors. Every gesture they made pulled on the noose around their necks, and they had to march with the same step with but a pace separating one from another, under the penalty of falling immediately, like a hare in a snare.

"When this strange deed was done Mohammed began to laugh with his silent laughter, which shook his stomach without a sound leaving his mouth.

" 'That's an Arabian chain,' he said.

"We began to twist and turn before the terrified and piteous faces of the prisoners.

" 'Now,' cried our chief, 'at each end fix me that.'

"A stake was fastened at each end of this ribbon of white-clad captives, like phantoms, who stood motionless, as if they had been changed into stones.

" 'Now let us dine!' said the Turk. A fire was made and a sheep was cooked, which we ate with our fingers. Then we had some dates which we found in the trees, drank some milk obtained in the Arab tents, and we picked up a few silver trinkets forgotten by the fugitives. We were tranquilly finishing our repast when I perceived, on the hill opposite, a singular gathering. It was the women who had just now fled, nothing but women. They came running toward us. I pointed them out to Mohammed Fripouli.

"He smiled.

" 'It is the dessert!' he said.

" 'Ah yes, the dessert.'

"They approached, running like mad women, and soon we were peppered with stones which they hurled at us without stopping their pace; then we saw that they were armed with knives, tent stakes and old utensils.

" 'To horse!' cried Mohammed. It was time. The attack was terrible. They came to free the prisoners and tried to cut the rope. The Turk, understanding the danger, became furious and shouted: 'Saber them! Saber them! Saber them!" And as we stood motionless, disturbed by this new kind of charge, hesitating at killing women, he threw himself upon the advancing band.

"He charged all alone this battalion of women in tatters, and he began to saber them, the wretch, like a madman, with such rage and fury that a white body might be seen to fall at every stroke of his arm.

"He was so terrible that the women, terrified, fled as quickly as they had come, leaving on the ground a dozen dead and wounded, whose crimson blood stained their white garments.

"And Mohammed, frowning, turned toward us, exclaiming:

" 'Start, start, my sons! They will come back.'

"And we beat a retreat, conducting at a slow step our prisoners, who were paralyzed by fear of strangulation.

"The next day noon struck as we arrived at Boghar with our chain of hanged men. Only six died on the way. But it had often been necessary to loosen the knots from one end of the convoy to the other, for every shock half strangled ten captives at once."

The captain was silent. I did not say anything in reply. I thought of the strange country where such things could be seen and I gazed at the innumerable and shining flock of stars in the dark sky.

"BELL"

He had known better days in spite of his misery and infirmity. At the age of fifteen he had had both legs cut off by a carriage on the highway near Varville. Since that time he had begged, dragging himself along the roads, across farmyards, balanced upon his crutches which brought his shoulders to the height of his ears. His head seemed sunk between two mountains.

Found as an infant in a ditch by the curate of Billettes on the morning of All Souls' Day, he was, for this reason, baptized Nicholas Toussaint (All Saints); brought up by charity, he was a stranger to all instruction, crippled from having drunk several glasses of brandy offered him by the village baker for the sake of a laughable story, and since then a vagabond, knowing how to do nothing but hold out his hand.

Formerly Baroness d'Avary gave him a kind of kennel full of straw beside her poultry house to sleep in, on the farm adjoining her castle, and he was sure, in days of great hunger, of always finding a piece of bread and a glass of cider in the kitchen. He often received a few sous, also, thrown by the old lady from her steps or her chamber window. Now she was dead.

In the villages they gave him scarcely anything. They knew him too well. They were tired of him, having seen his little, deformed body on the two wooden legs going from house to house for the last forty years. And he went there because it was the only corner of the country that he knew on the face of the earth—these three or four hamlets where he dragged out his miserable life. He had tried the frontier for his begging but had never passed the boundaries, for he was not accustomed to anything new.

He did not even know whether the world extended beyond the trees which had always limited his vision. He had never asked. And when the peasants, tired of meeting him in their fields or along their ditches, cried out to him: "Why do you not go to some other villages in place of always stumping about here?" he did not answer but took himself off, seized by a vague and unknown fear, that fear of the poor who dread a thousand things, confusedly—new faces, injuries, suspicious looks from people whom they do not know, the police who patrol the roads in twos and make a plunge at them, by instinct, in the bushes or behind a heap of stones.

When he saw them from afar, shining in the sun, he suddenly developed a singular agility, the agility of a wild animal to reach his lair. He tumbled along on his crutches, letting himself fall like a bundle of rags and rolling along like a ball, becoming so small as to be almost invisible, keeping close as a hare running for covert, mingling his brown tatters with the earth. He had, however, never had any trouble with them. But this fear and this slyness were in his blood, as if he had received them from his parents whom he had never seen.

He had no refuge, no roof, no hut, no shelter. He slept anywhere in summer, and in winter he slipped under the barns or into the stables with a remarkable adroitness. He always got out before anyone was aware of his presence. He knew all the holes in the buildings that could be penetrated; and, manipulating his crutches with a surprising vigor, using them as arms, he would sometimes crawl by the sole strength of his wrists into the hay barns, where he would remain four or five days without budging when he had gathered together sufficient provisions for his needs.

He lived like the animals in the wood, in the midst of men without knowing anyone, without loving anyone and exciting in the peasants only a kind of indifferent scorn and resigned hostility. They nicknamed him "Bell," because he balanced himself between his two wooden pegs like a bell between its two standards.

For two days he had had nothing to eat. No one would give him anything. They would now have nothing more to do with him. The peasants in their doors, seeing him coming, would cry out to him from afar:

"You want to get away from here now. 'Twas only three days ago that I gave you a piece of bread!"

And he would turn about on his props and go on to a neighboring house, where he would be received in the same fashion.

The women declared from one door to another:

"One cannot feed that vagabond the year round."

Nevertheless, the vagabond had need of food every day. He had been through Saint-Hilaire, Varville and Billettes without receiving a centime or a crust of bread. Tournolles remained as his only hope, but to reach it he must walk two leagues upon the highway, and he felt too weary to drag himself along, his stomach being as empty as his pocket.

He set out on the way, nevertheless.

It was December, and a cold wind blew over the fields, whistling among the bare branches. The clouds galloped across the low, somber sky, hastening one knew not where. The cripple went slowly, placing one support before the other with wearisome effort, balancing himself upon the part of a leg that remained to him, which terminated in a wooden foot bound about with rags.

From time to time he sat down by a ditch and rested for some minutes. Hunger gave him a distress of soul, confused and heavy. He had but one idea: to eat. But he knew not by what means.

For three hours he toiled along the road; then when he perceived the trees of the village he hastened his movements.

The first peasant he met, of whom he asked alms, responded to him:

"You here yet, you old customer? I wonder if we are ever going to get rid of you!"

And Bell took himself away. From door to door he was treated harshly and sent away without receiving anything. He continued his journey, however, patient and obstinate. He received not one sou.

Then he visited the farms, picking his way across ground made moist by the rains, so spent that he could scarcely raise his crutches. They chased him away, everywhere. It was one of those cold, sad days when the heart shrivels, the mind is irritated, the soul is somber and the hand does not open to give or to aid.

When he had finished the rounds of all the houses he knew he went and threw himself down by a ditch which ran along by M. Chiquet's yard. He unhooked himself, as one might say to express how he let himself fall from between his two high crutches, letting them slip along his arms. And he remained motionless for a long time, tortured by hunger but too stupid to well understand his unfathomable misery.

He awaited he knew not what, with that vague expectation which ever dwells in us. He awaited in the corner of that yard, under a freezing wind, for that mysterious aid which one always hopes will come from heaven or mankind, without asking how or why or through whom it can arrive.

A flock of black hens passed him, seeking their living from the earth which nourishes all beings. Every moment they picked up a grain or an invisible insect then continued their search slowly, but surely.

Bell looked at them without thinking of anything; then there came to him— to his stomach rather than to his mind—the idea, or rather the sensation, that these animals were good to eat when roasted over a fire of dry wood.

The suspicion that he would be committing a robbery only touched him slightly. He took a stone which lay at his hand and, as he had skill in this way, killed neatly the one nearest him that was approaching. The bird fell on its side, moving its wings. The others fled, half balanced upon their thin legs, and Bell, climbing again upon his crutches, began to run after them, his movements much like that of the hens.

When he came to the little black body, touched with red on the head, he received a terrible push in the back, which threw him loose from his supports and sent him rolling ten steps ahead of them. And M. Chiquet, exasperated, threw himself upon the marauder, rained blows upon him, striking him like a madman, as a robbed peasant strikes with his fist and his knee, upon all the infirm body which could not defend itself.

The people of the farm soon arrived and began to help their master beat the beggar. Then when they were tired of beating they picked him up, carried him and shut him up in the woodhouse while they went to get a policeman.

Bell, half dead, bloody and dying of hunger, lay still upon the ground. The evening came, then the night and then the dawn. He had had nothing to eat.

Toward noon the policemen appeared, opening the door with precaution as if expecting resistance, for M. Chiquet pretended that he had been attacked by robbers against whom he had defended himself with great difficulty.

The policeman cried out:

"Come there now! Stand up!"

But Bell could no longer move, although he did try to hoist himself upon his sticks. They believed this a feint, a sly ruse for the purpose of doing some mischief, and the two men handled him roughly, standing him up and planting him by force upon his crutches.

And fear had seized him, that native fear of the yellow long belt, that fear of the Newgate bird before the detective, of the mouse before the cat. And by superhuman effort he succeeded in standing.

"March!" said the policeman. And he marched. All the employees of the farm watched him as he went. The women shook their fists at him; the men sneered at and threatened him. They had got him finally! Good riddance.

He went away between the two guardians of the peace. He found energy enough in his desperation to enable him to drag himself along until evening, when he was completely stupefied, no longer knowing what had happened, too bewildered to comprehend anything.

The people that he met stopped to look at him in passing, and the peasants murmured:

"So that is the robber!"

They came toward nightfall to the chief town in the district. He had never been seen there. He did not exactly understand what was taking place or what was likely to take place. All these frightful, unheard-of things, these faces and these new houses, filled him with consternation.

He did not say a word, having nothing to say, because he comprehended nothing. Besides, he had not talked to anybody for so many years that he had almost lost the use of his tongue, and his thoughts were always too confused to formulate into words.

They shut him up in the town prison. The policeman did not think he needed anything to eat, and they left him until the next day.

When they went to question him in the early morning they found him dead upon the ground. Surprise seized them!

HAUTOT AND HIS SON

I

In front of the building, half farmhouse, half manor house—one of those semi-feudal country dwellings of mixed character now occupied by wealthy farmers—the dogs chained to the apple trees in the courtyard were barking and howling at the sight of the bags carried by the gamekeepers, and at the mischievous boys. In the large dining room-kitchen, Hautot and his son and M. Bermont, the tax collector, and M. Mondarn, the notary, were having a bite and a mouthful of wine before they went out shooting, for it was the first day of the season.

The elder Hautot, proud of his possessions, was boasting of the game that his guests would find in his shoot. He was a big Norman, one of those powerful, ruddy, big-boned men who can lift a cartload of apples onto their shoulders. Half peasant, half gentleman, rich, respected, influential, autocratic, he had first insisted that his son César should work up to the third form so that he might be well informed, and then he had stopped his education for fear of his becoming a fine gentleman without any interest in the farm.

Nearly as tall as his father, but thinner, César Hautot was a good son, docile, contented, full of admiration and respect and regard for the wishes and opinions of the elder Hautot.

M. Bermont, the tax collector, a short stout man whose red cheeks showed a thin network of violet veins like the tributaries and winding streams of a river on a map, asked:

"And hares—are there any hares?"

The elder Hautot replied:

"As many as you please, especially in the hollows of Puysatier."

"Where shall we begin?" asked the good-natured notary: he was pale and fat, his flesh bulging out in his tight-fitting, brand-new shooting kit recently bought at Rouen.

"In that direction, through the bottoms. We will drive the partridges into the open and fall upon them."

Hautot got up. The others followed his example, took their guns from the corner, examined the locks, stamped their feet to ease them in their boots, not yet softened by the warmth within. Then they went out, and the dogs straining at the leash barked and beat the air with their paws.

They set out towards the hollows, which were in a little glen, or rather in a long undulating stretch of poor land unfit for cultivation, furrowed with ditches and covered with ferns—an excellent preserve for game.

The sportsmen took their places, Hautot senior to the right, Hautot junior to the left, with the two guests in the center. The keepers and gamebag carriers followed. The solemn moment had come when sportsmen are waiting for the first shot, their hearts beating more rapidly, and their nervous fingers unable to leave the trigger alone.

Suddenly there was a shot. Hautot had fired. They all stopped and saw a partridge, one of a covey flying as swiftly as possible, drop into a ditch covered with thick shrubs. The excited sportsman started to run, taking big strides, dragging aside the briers in his path, and disappeared into the thicket to look for the bird.

Almost immediately a second shot was heard.

"Ha! Ha! the rascal," exclaimed M. Bermont, "he must have started a hare from the undergrowth."

They all waited, with eyes fixed on the mass of dense underwood. The notary, making a trumpet of his hands, shouted: "Have you got them?"

As there was no reply from the elder Hautot, César, turning towards the gamekeeper, said: "Go and help him, Joseph. We must keep in line. We'll wait."

And Joseph, a man with an old, lean body and swollen joints, set off at an easy pace down to the ditch, searching for a suitable opening with the caution of a fox. Then, suddenly, he shouted: "Oh, hurry up! Hurry up! There has been an accident!"

They all hurried along and plunged through the briers. Hautot had fallen on his side in a faint with both hands pressed on his abdomen, from which long trickles of blood flowed onto the grass through his linen jacket, torn by a bullet. In letting go of his gun to pick up the dead partridge that lay within reach, he had dropped it and the second discharge going off in the fall had torn open his bowels. They drew him out of the ditch, undressed him and saw a frightful wound through which the intestines protruded. Then after binding him up as well as they could they carried him home and waited for the doctor who had been sent for, as well as the priest.

When the doctor arrived, he shook his head gravely, and turning towards young Hautot, who was sobbing on a chair, he said:

"My poor boy, this looks bad."

But when the wound was dressed, the patient moved his fingers, first opened his mouth, then his eyes, cast around him a troubled, haggard glance, then appeared to be trying to recall, to understand, and he murmured:

"Good God, I am done for."

The doctor held his hand.

"No, no; a question of a few days' rest, it will be all right."

Hautot resumed:

"I am done for! I am torn to bits! I know!"

Then, suddenly:

"I want to talk to my son, if there is time."

In spite of himself, César was weeping, and repeated like a little boy:

"Papa, Papa, poor Papa!"

But the father said in a more determined tone:

"Come, stop crying, this is no time for tears. I have something to say to you. Sit down there, close to me, it will soon be over, and I shall be easier in my mind. You others, please leave us alone for a minute."

As soon as they were alone:

"Listen, my boy. You are twenty-four, one can talk to you. After all there is not such a mystery about these matters as we attach to them. You know that your mother has been dead seven years and that I am only forty-five, seeing that I married when I was nineteen. Is that not true?"

The son stammered:

"Yes, quite true."

"So then your mother has been dead for seven years, and I am still a widower. Well! a man like me cannot remain a widower at thirty-seven, you agree?"

The son replied:

"That's quite true."

Gasping for breath, very pale and his face drawn with pain, the father continued:

"God! how I suffer! Well, you understand. Man is not made to live alone, but I did not want to give your mother a successor, since I had promised I would not do so. Well . . . you understand?"

"Yes, Father."

"Well, I kept a girl at Rouen, number 18 Rue de l'Eperlan, the second door on the third floor—I am telling you all this, don't forget—this young girl has been as nice as nice to me, loving, devoted, a real wife. You understand, my lad?"

"Yes, Father."

"Well, if I am taken, I owe her something, something substantial that will place her out of the reach of want. You understand?"

"Yes, Father."

"I tell you she is good, really good, and but for you and the memory of your mother and also because we three lived here together in this house, I would have brought her here, and then married her, sure enough. . . . Listen . . . listen . . . my lad, I might have made a will. . . . I have not done so! I did not want to. . . . You must never write things down . . . not things of that sort . . . it is bad for the rightful heirs . . . then it muddles up everything . . . it ruins everyone. . . . Look you, never go in for legal documents, never have anything to do with them. If I am rich it is because I have avoided them all my life. You understand, my boy!"

"Yes, Father."

"Now listen. . . . Listen attentively. . . . So I have made no will. . . . I did not want to. . . . Besides, I know you, you are kindhearted, you are not greedy, not stingy. I said to myself that when I saw the end within sight, I would tell you all about it and would beg you not to forget my darling: Caroline Donet, 18 Rue de l'Eperlan, the second door on the right, don't forget. Further, go there directly I am gone—and make such arrangements that she will have no reason to complain. You have plenty. . . . You can spare it—I am leaving you well provided for. Listen! You won't find her at home on weekdays. She works at Mme. Moreau's in the Rue Beauvoisine. Go on a Thursday. She always expects me on Thursdays. It has been my day for six years. Poor thing, how she will cry! I tell you all this, my boy, because I know you so well. You cannot tell these things to everybody, either to the notary or to the priest. These things happen, everyone knows that, but no one talks about them except when they are obliged. Then again there must be no outsider in the secret, nobody except the family, because a family is the same as an individual! You understand?"

"Yes, Father."

"You promise?"

"Yes, Father."

"You swear to this?"

"Yes, Father."

"I beg, I pray, do not forget, my boy. It means so much to me."

"No, Father."

"You will go yourself. I want you to make sure of everything."

"Yes, Father."

"And then, you will see . . . you will see what she says. I can't tell you more about it. You swear?"

"Yes, Father."

"That's right, my boy. Embrace me. *Adieu*, I am done for, I know it. Tell the others they may come in."

The son embraced his father, sobbing as he did so, then, obedient as usual, he opened the door, and the priest appeared in a white surplice carrying the holy oils.

But the dying man had closed his eyes and refused to open them again, he would not make any response nor would he make any sign to show that he understood.

The man had talked enough, he could not continue. Besides, he now felt quiet in his mind and wanted to die in peace. He felt no need to confess to the priest when he had just made his confession to his son, who at all events belonged to the family.

Surrounded by his friends and servants on their bended knees, he received the last rites, was purified, and was given absolution, no change of expression on his face showing that he still lived.

He died towards midnight after four hours of convulsive movements indicating terrible suffering.

II

He was buried on Tuesday, the shooting season having opened on Sunday. On returning home from the cemetery César Hautot spent the rest of the day weeping. He scarcely slept that night and felt so sad when he awoke that he wondered how he could manage to go on living.

However, until evening he kept on thinking that in accordance with his father's dying wish he must go to Rouen the following day, and see this girl, Caroline Donet, who lived at 18 Rue de l'Eperlan, the second door on the third story. He went on repeating the name and address under his breath—just as a prayer is repeated—so as not to forget, and he ended by stammering them unceasingly, without thinking about anything, to such a point had his mind become obsessed by the set phrase.

Accordingly, about eight o'clock next day he ordered Graindorge to be harnessed to the tilbury and set out at the long, swinging pace of the heavy Norman horse along the high road from Ainville to Rouen. He was wearing a black frock coat, a silk hat, and trousers strapped under his shoes. Owing to the circumstances he had not put on his flowing blue blouse, so easily taken off at the journey's end, over his black clothes to protect them from dust and dirt.

He got to Rouen just as it was striking ten, put up as usual at the Hôtel des Bons Enfants, in the Rue des Trois Mariés, submitted to being embraced by the landlord, his wife and their five sons, for they had heard the sad news; later on he had to tell them all about the accident, which made him shed tears, repel their offers of service thrust upon him on account of his wealth, and even refuse luncheon, which hurt their feelings.

Having wiped the dust off his hat, brushed his coat and cleaned his boots, he started to seek the Rue de l'Eperlan without daring to make any inquiries, for fear of being recognized and of arousing suspicion.

At last, unable to find the place, he caught sight of a priest, and trusting to the professional discretion of the priesthood, he asked for help.

It was only about one hundred steps farther on—the second street to the right.

Then he hesitated. Up to the present he had blindly obeyed the will of his dead father. But now he felt agitated, confused, humiliated at the idea of finding himself—he, the son—in the presence of the woman who had been his father's mistress.

All our better feelings developed by centuries of family training, all that he had been taught since early childhood about women of loose character, the instinctive distrust that all men feel of these women even when they marry them, all his narrow-minded peasant virtue; all combined to disturb him, to make him hesitate, and fill him with shame.

But he said to himself: "I promised my father. I must not fail." So he pushed the partly opened door of number 18, discovered a dark staircase, went up three flights, saw first one door, then a second, then found a bell rope, which he pulled.

The dingdong that sounded in the next room sent a shiver through his body. The door opened and he found himself face to face with a well-dressed young lady, a brunette with rosy cheeks, who gazed at him with eyes full of astonishment.

He did not know what to say, and she, who suspected nothing and was expecting the father, did not invite him in. They looked at each other about thirty seconds until, at last, she said:

"What do you want, sir?"

He muttered:

"I am the young Hautot."

She started, turned pale, and stammered as if she had known him for a long time:

"M. César?"

"Yes."

"Well?"

"I have a message for you from my father."

She exclaimed: "My God!" and moved away so that he might enter. He closed the door and followed her.

Then he caught sight of a little boy of four or five years playing with a cat, seated on the ground in front of a stove from which rose the odor of food being kept hot.

"Sit down," she said.

He sat down. She said: "Well?"

He dare not say anything, he fixed his eyes on the table standing in the middle of the room that was laid for two grownups and a child. He looked at the chair with its back to the fire, the plate, the table napkin and glasses, the bottle of red wine already opened, and the bottle of white wine still uncorked. That was his father's chair, with its back to the fire. They were expecting him. That was his bread near the fork, he knew that because the crust had been removed on account of Hautot's bad teeth. Then, raising his eyes, he noticed his father's portrait hanging on the wall, the large photograph taken at Paris the year of the Exhibition, the same one that hung above the bed in the room at Ainville.

The young woman asked again:

"Well, M. César?"

She stared at him. Her face was deathly white with anxiety, and she waited, her hands trembling with fear.

Then he picked up courage:

"Well, mademoiselle, Papa died on Sunday, the first day of the season."

She was too overcome to make any movement. After a silence of a few seconds, she faltered almost inaudibly:

"Oh, it's not possible?"

Then the tears came to her eyes, and covering her face with her hands, she burst out sobbing.

Seeing his mother cry, the little boy turned round and began to roar at the top of his voice. Then, understanding that the sudden grief was caused by the unknown visitor, he threw himself upon César, caught hold of his trousers with one hand and hit his shins as hard as he could with the other. César felt bewildered, deeply affected, thus placed between the woman mourning for his father and the child who was defending his mother. Their emotion communicated itself to him and his eyes filled with tears, so, to regain his self-control, he began to talk.

"Yes," he said, "the accident occurred on Sunday morning, at eight o'clock." And he told the story in detail, as if she were listening to him, mentioning the most trivial matters with the characteristic thoroughness of the peasant. The child, who had kept on beating César, was now kicking his ankles.

When he reached the point of Hautot's anxiety for her, she heard her name mentioned and, taking her hands from her face, asked:

"Excuse me! I was not following you. I would like to know—would it be a bother to you to begin all over again?"

He began the story in the same words: "The accident occurred Sunday morning at eight o'clock."

He repeated everything, at great length, with pauses and occasional reflections of his own. She listened eagerly, feeling with a woman's keen sensitiveness the

events as they were unfolded, and, trembling with horror, exclaimed at intervals:
"My God!" The boy, thinking that she was all right again, took hold of his
mother's hand instead of beating César, and listened attentively as if he understood what was happening.

When the story was finished, young Hautot continued:

"Now, we'll settle matters together according to his wishes. Listen! I am well
off, he has left me plenty. I don't want you to have anything to complain about."

She interrupted quickly:

"Oh! M. César, not today. My heart is . . . Another time . . . another day.
. . . No, not today. . . . If I accept, listen. . . . It is not for myself . . . no, no,
no, I swear. It is for the child. Besides, what you give will be placed to his account."

Whereupon César, feeling troubled, guessed the truth and stammered:

"So then . . . it is his . . . the little one?"

"Why, yes," she said.

The young Hautot looked at his brother with confused feelings both intense
and painful.

After a long silence, for she was crying again, César, very embarrassed, went on:

"Well, Mam'selle Donet, I am going. When would you like to talk this over?"

She exclaimed:

"Oh! no, don't go! don't go! Don't leave me all alone with Emile. I would die
of grief. I have nobody in the world, nobody but my little one. Oh, what misery,
what misery, M. César. Do sit down. Tell me some more. Tell me how he spent
his time at home."

César, accustomed to obey, sat down again.

She drew another chair near to his, in front of the stove on which the food
prepared for lunch was bubbling, took Emile on her lap and asked César hundreds
of questions about his father—such simple questions about his ordinary everyday
life that without reasoning on the subject he felt that she had loved Hautot
with all the strength of her aching heart.

And by the natural association of his scanty thoughts he returned to the
accident and began to tell her all about it again giving the same details as before.

When he said: "He had a hole in the stomach into which you could put your
two fists," she uttered a faint cry and her eyes again filled with tears. Infected by
her grief, César began to weep too, and, as tears always soften the heart, he bent
over Emile, whose forehead was close to his own mouth, and kissed him.

Recovering her breath, the mother murmured:

"Poor boy, he is an orphan now."

"And so am I," said César.

They said no more.

But suddenly the housewife's practical instinct, accustomed to think of everything, reawakened.

"I expect you have had nothing to eat this morning, M. César?"

"No, mam'selle."

"Oh! You must be hungry. You will have a bite?"

"Thank you," he said, "I am not hungry; I have been too worried."

She replied:

"In spite of grief one must go on living, you are surely not going to refuse.

Then that will keep you here a little longer. When you are gone, I don't know what I shall do."

He yielded after a little hesitation, and sitting down with his back to the fire, facing her, he ate some of the tripe that was crackling in the oven and drank a glass of red wine. But he would not allow her to uncork the white wine. Several times he wiped the mouth of the small boy, who had smeared his chin all over with gravy.

As he got up to go, he asked:

"When would you like me to come back to talk the matter over, Mam'selle Donet?"

"If it is all the same to you, next Thursday, M. César. I shall not waste any time that way, as I am always free on Thursdays."

"That will suit me—next Thursday."

"You will come to lunch, won't you?"

"Oh! as for that, I can't promise."

"Well, you know, it is easier to talk when eating. Besides, there is more time."

"Well, all right. At twelve o'clock then."

And off he went after having kissed little Emile and shaken hands with Mlle. Donet.

III

The week seemed long to César Hautot. He had never felt so lonely, and the solitude seemed unbearable. Hitherto he had lived with his father, just like his shadow, following him to the fields and superintending the execution of his orders; and when he did leave him for a short time it was only to meet again at dinner. They spent their evenings sitting opposite each other, smoking their pipes and talking about horses, cows or sheep; and the handshake they exchanged every morning was the symbol of deep family affection.

Now César was alone. He strolled about looking on while the harvesters worked, expecting at any moment to see his father's tall gesticulating form at the far end of a field. To kill time he visited his neighbors, telling all about the accident to those who had not already heard it and telling it over again to those who had. Then having reached the end of all that interested him, he would sit down at the side of the road and wonder whether this kind of life would last very long.

He often thought of Mlle. Donet. He remembered her with pleasure. He had found her ladylike, gentle, and good, exactly as his father had described her. Undoubtedly, so far as goodness was concerned, she was good. He was determined to do the thing handsomely and give her two thousand francs a year, settling the capital on the child. He even felt a certain pleasure at the prospect of seeing her again on the following Thursday and making all the arrangements for her future. Then, although the idea of the brother, the little chap of five—his father's son—did worry and annoy him, it also filled him with a friendly feeling. This illegitimate youngster, though he would never bear the name of Hautot, was, in a sense a member of the family life, whom he might adopt or abandon as he pleased but who would always remind him of his father.

So that when, on Thursday morning, he was trotting along the road to Rouen on Graindorge's back, he felt lighter-hearted, more at peace than he had done since his bereavement.

On entering Mlle. Donet's apartment, he saw the table laid as on the previous Thursday, the only difference being that the crust had been left on the bread.

He shook hands with the young woman, kissed Emile on both cheeks and sat down feeling more or less at home in spite of his heart being heavy. Mlle. Donet seemed to him to have grown thinner and paler. She must have wept bitterly. She appeared rather awkward in his presence, as if she now understood what she had not felt the previous week when under the first impression of her loss. She treated him with exaggerated respect, showing stricken humility and waiting upon him with solicitude as if to repay by her attentions and devotion the kindness he had shown her. The lunch dragged on as they discussed the business that had brought him to the house. She did not want so much money. It was too much, far too much. She earned enough to keep herself and she only wanted Emile to find a small sum awaiting him when he was grown up. César was firm, and even added a present of one thousand francs for her mourning.

When he had finished his coffee, she asked:

"Do you smoke?"

"Yes . . . I have my pipe."

He felt his pocket. Good heavens! he had forgotten it. He was quite miserable until she brought out his father's pipe, which had been put away in a cupboard. He accepted her offer of the pipe, took hold of it, recognized it and smelled it, said what a good one it was, in a voice choked with feeling, filled it with tobacco and lighted it. Then he set Emile astride on his knee and let him play at horses while the mother removed the tablecloth and put the dirty dishes aside in the bottom of the cupboard, intending to wash up as soon as he had gone.

About three o'clock he got up reluctantly, very depressed at the idea of leaving.

"Well, Mlle. Donet," he said, "I wish you good afternoon. It has been a pleasure to make your further acquaintance."

She stood before him, blushing, deeply moved, and gazed at him while she thought of the father.

"Shall we never see each other again?"

He replied simply:

"Why, yes, mademoiselle, if it gives you any pleasure."

"Indeed it will, M. César. So till next Thursday, if that suits you?"

"Yes, Mlle. Donet."

"You will come to lunch, without fail?"

"Well—as you are so kind, I won't refuse."

"It's settled then, next Thursday, at twelve, the same as today."

"Thursday at twelve, Mlle. Donet!"

THE VICTIM

The north wind whistled in a tempest, carrying through the sky the enormous winter clouds, heavy and black, which threw, in passing, furious rainbursts over the earth.

A heavy sea moaned and shook the coast, hurrying upon the shore enormous waves, slow and dribbling, which rolled with the noise of artillery. They come in slowly, one after the other, as high as mountains, scattering from their heads in the wind the white foam that seems like the sweat of monsters.

The tempest rushed into the little valley of Yport, whistling and groaning, whirling the slates from the roofs, breaking down fortifications, knocking over chimneys, darting through the streets in such gusts that one could not walk there without keeping close to the walls, and lifting up children like leaves and throwing them into the fields beyond the houses.

They had brought the fishing boats to land, for fear of the sea which would sweep the whole coast at full tide, and some sailors, concealed behind the round wall of the breakwater, lay on their sides watching the anger of the heavens and the sea.

Then they went away little by little, because night fell upon the tempest, enveloping in shadow the excited ocean and all the disturbance of the elements in fury.

Two men still remained, their hands in their pockets, with backs rounded under a sudden squall, woolen caps drawn down to the eyes, two great Norman fishermen with rough beards for collars, with skin browned by the salt winds of the open sea, with blue eyes pricked out in the middle in a black dot, the piercing eyes of mariners who see to the end of the horizon like birds of prey.

One of them said:

"Come, let us go, Jeremy. We will pass the time at dominoes. I will pay."

The other still hesitated, tempted by the game and the drink, knowing well that he would get drunk if he went into Paumelle's and held back by the thought of his wife at home alone in their hovel.

He remarked: "It looks as if you had made a bet to get me tipsy every night. Tell me, what's the object, since you always pay?"

And he laughed at all the brandy he had drunk at the expense of the other, laughed with the contented laugh of a Norman who has the best of it.

Mathurin, his comrade, kept pulling him by the arm. "Come," he would say, "come, Jeremy. It is not the evening to go home without anything warm on the inside. What are you afraid of? Your wife will warm the bed for you!"

Jeremy responded: "Only the other evening I couldn't find the door—they almost had to go fishing for me in the brook in front of our house!"

And he laughed still at the memory of this vagary and went patiently toward Paumelle's café, where the illuminated glass shone brilliantly. He went, drawn along by Mathurin and pushed by the wind, incapable of resisting these two forces.

The low hall was filled with sailors, smoke and noise. All the men, clothed in wool, their elbows on the table, were talking in loud voices to make themselves heard. The more drinkers that entered, the more was it necessary to howl into the uproar of voices and of dominoes hitting against the marble, with an attempt to make more noise still.

Jeremy and Mathurin seated themselves in a corner and commenced a game, and little glasses disappeared, one after another, into the depth of their throats.

Then they played other games and drank more glasses. Mathurin always turned and winked an eye to the proprietor, a large man as red as fire and who laughed as if he knew about some good farce, and Jeremy guzzled the alcohol, balanced his head, uttered roars of laughter, looking at his companion with a stupid, contented air.

Finally all the clients were going. And each time that one of them opened the door to go out a blast entered the café, driving in a whirlwind the smoke of the pipes, swinging the lamps to the end of their chains and making their flames dance. And they could hear suddenly the profound shock of an inrolling wave and the moaning of the squall.

Jeremy, his clothing loosened at the neck, took the pose of a tipsy man, one leg extended, one arm falling, while in the other hand he held his dominoes.

They were alone now with the proprietor, who approached them full of interest. He asked:

"Well, Jeremy, how goes it in the interior? Are you refreshed with all this sprinkling?"

And Jeremy muttered. "Since it slipped down—makes it dry in there."

The café keeper looked at Mathurin with a sly air. Then he asked:

"And your brother, Mathurin, where is he at this hour?"

The sailor answered with a quiet laugh:

"Where it is warm; don't you worry."

And the two looked at Jeremy who triumphantly put down the double six, announcing:

"There! the Syndic."

When they had finished the game the proprietor declared:

"You know, my lads, I must put up the shutters. But I will leave you a lamp and bottle. There's twenty sous left for it. You will shut the outside door, Mathurin, and slip the key under the step as you did the other night."

Mathurin answered: "Don't worry. I understand."

Paumelle shook hands with both his tardy clients and mounted heavily his wooden staircase. For some minutes his heavy step resounded in the little house; then a loud creaking announced that he had put himself in bed.

The two men continued to play; from time to time a more violent rage of the tempest shook the door, making the walls tremble, and the two men would raise their heads as if someone was about to enter. Then Mathurin took the bottle and filled Jeremy's glass.

Suddenly the clock suspended over the counter sounded midnight. Its hoarse ring resembled a crash of pans, and the blows vibrated a long time with the resonance of old iron.

Mathurin immediately rose, like a sailor whose quart is finished. He said:

"Come, Jeremy, we must break off."

The other put himself in motion with more difficulty, got his equilibrium by leaning against the table; then he reached the door and opened it, while his companion extinguished the light.

When they were in the street and Mathurin had locked the door he said:

"Well, good night, till tomorrow."

And he disappeared into the shadows.

Jeremy took three steps, extended his hands, met a wall which held him up and then began to walk along stumblingly. Sometimes a gust rushing through the straight street threw him forward, making him run for some steps; then when the violence of the wind ceased he would stop short and, having lost his poise, begin to vacillate upon the capricious legs of a drunken man.

He went by instinct toward his dwelling, as birds fly to their nest. Finally he recognized his door and began to fumble to find the keyhole to place his key in it.

He could not find it and swore in an undertone. Then he struck upon it with his fist, calling his wife to come and aid him:

"Melina! Eh, Melina!"

As he leaned against the door in order not to fall, it yielded, flew open, and Jeremy, losing his balance, entered his house in a tumble, then rolled upon his nose into the room; he felt that something heavy had passed over his body and then fled into the night.

He did not move, perplexed with fright, astonished, in the devil of a fright, from the spirits of all the mysterious and shadowy things, and he waited a long time without daring to make a sound. But as he saw that nothing more moved, a little reason came back to him, the troubled reason of vagary.

And he slowly sat up. Then he waited still a long time and finally said:

"Melina!"

His wife did not answer.

Then suddenly a doubt went through his obscure brain, a wavering doubt, a vague suspicion. He did not move; he remained there, seated on the floor in the dark, gathering his ideas, clutching his reflections as incomplete and uncertain as his legs.

He called again:

"Tell me who it was, Melina; tell me who it was. I will do nothing to you."

He waited. No voice came out of the shadow. He reasoned out loud now:

"I am drunk—all same! I am drunk! He made me drink like this now! He kept me from coming back home. I am drunk!"

Then he repeated: "Tell me who it was, Melina, or I'm going to do harm."

After having waited again he continued with the slow and obstinate logic of an intoxicated man:

"It was him kept me at that lazy Paumelle's, and other evenings, too, so I couldn't come home. He's some 'complice. Ah, carrion!"

Slowly he got up on his knees. A sudden anger helped him, mingling with the fermentation of the drink. He repeated:

"Tell me who it was, Melina, or I'm going to beat you; I give you warning."

He was standing now, trembling with anger, as if the alcohol which he had in his body was inflamed in his veins. He took a step, hit against a chair, seized it, walked to the bed, touched it and felt there the warm body of his wife.

Then, excited with rage, he cried:

"Ah, there you are, filth, and you wouldn't answer."

And, raising the chair which he held in his robust sailor's fist, he brought it down before him with exasperated fury. A scream arose from the bed, a terrified, piercing cry. Then he began to beat like a thrasher in a barn. Nothing moved now. The chair was broken in pieces. One leg remained in his hand, and he hit with it until he gasped.

Then suddenly he stopped and asked:

"Will you tell me who it was now?"

Melina did not answer.

Then, worn out with fatigue and stupid from his violence, he sat down again upon the floor, fell over and was asleep.

When the day appeared, a neighbor, seeing the door open, entered. He perceived Jeremy snoring upon the floor, where lay the debris of a chair, and on the bed a pulp of flesh and blood.

THE ENGLISHMAN

They made a circle around Judge Bermutier, who was giving his opinion of the mysterious affair that had happened at Saint-Cloud. For a month Paris had doted on this inexplicable crime. No one could understand it at all.

M. Bermutier, standing with his back to the chimney, talked about it, discussed the divers opinions but came to no conclusions.

Many women had risen and come nearer, remaining standing, with eyes fixed upon the shaven mouth of the magistrate whence issued these grave words. They shivered and vibrated, crisp through their curious fear, through that eager, insatiable need of terror which haunts their soul, torturing them like a hunger.

One of them, paler than the others, after a silence, said:

"It is frightful. It touches the supernatural. We shall never know anything about it."

The magistrate turned toward her, saying:

"Yes, madame, it is probable that we never shall know anything about it. As for the word 'supernatural,' when you come to use that, it has no place here. We are in the presence of a crime skillfully conceived, very skillfully executed and so well enveloped in mystery that we cannot separate the impenetrable circumstances which surround it. But once in my life I had to follow an affair which seemed truly to be mixed up with something very unusual. However, it was necessary to give it up, as there was no means of explaining it."

Many of the ladies called out at the same time, so quickly that their voices sounded as one:

"Oh, tell us about it."

M. Bermutier smiled gravely, as judges should, and replied:

"You must not suppose, for an instant, that I, at least, believed there was anything superhuman in the adventure. I believe only in normal causes. And if in place of using the word 'supernatural' to express what we cannot comprehend we should simply use the word 'inexplicable,' it would be much better. In any case, the surrounding circumstances in the affair I am going to relate to you, as well as the preparatory circumstances, have affected me much. Here are the facts:

"I was then judge of instruction at Ajaccio, a little white town lying on the border of an admirable gulf that was surrounded on all sides by high mountains.

"What I particularly had to look after there were the affairs of vendetta. Some of them were superb, as dramatic as possible, ferocious and heroic. We find there the most beautiful subjects of vengeance that one could dream of, hatred a century old, appeased for a moment but never extinguished, abominable plots, assassinations becoming massacres and almost glorious battles. For two years I heard of nothing but the price of blood, of the terribly prejudiced Corsican who is bound to avenge all injury upon the person of him who is the cause of it or upon his nearest descendants. I saw old men and infants, cousins, with their throats cut, and my head was full of these stories.

"One day we learned that an Englishman had rented for some years a little villa at the end of the gulf. He had brought with him a French domestic, picked up at Marseilles on the way.

"Soon everybody was occupied with this singular person who lived alone in his house, only going out to hunt and fish. He spoke to no one, never came to the town and every morning practiced shooting with a pistol and a rifle for an hour or two.

"Some legends about him were abroad. They pretended that he was a high personage fled from his own country for political reasons; then they affirmed that he was concealing himself after having committed a frightful crime. They even cited some of the particularly horrible details.

"In my capacity of judge I wished to get some information about this man. But it was impossible to learn anything. He called himself Sir John Rowell.

"I contented myself with watching him closely, although in reality there seemed nothing to suspect regarding him.

"Nevertheless, as rumors on his account continued, grew and became general, I resolved to try and see this stranger myself and for this purpose began to hunt regularly in the neighborhood of his property.

"I waited long for an occasion. It finally came in the form of a partridge which I shot and killed before the very nose of the Englishman. My dog brought it to me, but, immediately taking it, I went and begged Sir John Rowell to accept the dead bird, excusing myself for intrusion.

"He was a tall man with red hair and red beard, very large, a sort of placid, polite Hercules. He had none of the so-called British haughtiness and heartily thanked me for the delicacy in French, with a beyond-the-Channel accent. At the end of a month we had chatted together five or six times.

"Finally one evening, as I was passing by his door, I perceived him astride a chair in the garden, smoking his pipe. I saluted him and he asked me in to have a glass of beer. It was not necessary for him to repeat before I accepted.

"He received me with the fastidious courtesy of the English, spoke in praise of France and of Corsica and declared that he loved that country and that shore.

"Then with great precaution in the form of a lively interest, I put some questions to him about his life and his projects. He responded without embarrassment, told me that he had traveled much, in Africa, in the Indies and in America. He added, laughing:

" 'I have had many adventures, oh yes!'

"I began to talk about hunting, and he gave me many curious details of hunting the hippopotamus, the tiger, the elephant and even of hunting the gorilla.

"I said: 'All these animals are very formidable.'

"He laughed. 'Oh no! The worst animal is man.' Then he began to laugh with the hearty laugh of a big, contented Englishman. He continued:

" 'I have often hunted man also.'

"He spoke of weapons and asked me to go into his house to see his guns of various makes and kinds.

"His drawing room was hung in black, in black silk embroidered with gold. There were great yellow flowers running over the somber stuff, shining like fire.

" 'It is Japanese cloth,' he said.

"But in the middle of a large panel a strange thing attracted my eye. Upon a square of red velvet a black object was attached. I approached and found it was a hand, the hand of a man. Not a skeleton hand, white and characteristic, but a black, desiccated hand with yellow joints, with the muscles bare and on them traces of old blood, of blood that seemed like a scale, over the bones sharply cut off at about the middle of the forearm, as with a blow of a hatchet. About the wrist was an enormous iron chain, riveted, soldered to this unclean member, attaching it to the wall by a ring sufficiently strong to hold an elephant.

"I asked: 'What is that?'

"The Englishman responded tranquilly:

" 'It belonged to my worst enemy. It came from America. It was broken with a saber, cut off with a sharp stone and dried in the sun for eight days. Oh, very good for me, that was!'

"I touched the human relic which must have belonged to a colossus. The fingers were immoderately long and attached by enormous tendons that held the straps of skin in place. This dried hand was frightful to see, making one think, naturally, of the vengeance of a savage.

"I said: 'This man must have been very strong.'

"With gentleness the Englishman answered:

"Oh yes, but I was stronger than he. I put this chain on him to hold him.'

"I thought he spoke in jest and replied:

" 'The chain is useless now that the hand cannot escape.'

"Sir John Rowell replied gravely: 'It always wishes to escape. The chain is necessary.'

"With a rapid, questioning glance I asked myself: 'Is he mad or is that an unpleasant joke?'

"But the face remained impenetrable, tranquil and friendly. I spoke of other things and admired the guns.

"Nevertheless, I noticed three loaded revolvers on the pieces of furniture, as if this man lived in constant fear of attack.

"I went there many times after that; then for some time I did not go. We had become accustomed to his presence; he had become indifferent to us.

"A whole year slipped away. Then one morning toward the end of November my domestic awoke me with the announcement that Sir John Rowell had been assassinated in the night.

"A half-hour later I entered the Englishman's house with the central commissary and the captain of police. The servant, lost in despair, was weeping at the door. I suspected him at first but afterward found that he was innocent.

"The guilty one could never be found.

"Upon entering Sir John's drawing room I perceived his dead body stretched out upon its back in the middle of the room. His waistcoat was torn; a sleeve was hanging, and it was evident that a terrible struggle had taken place.

"The Englishman had been strangled! His frightfully black and swollen face seemed to express an abominable fear; he held something between his set teeth, and his neck, pierced with five holes apparently done with a pointed iron, was covered with blood.

"A doctor joined us. He examined closely the prints of fingers in the flesh and pronounced these strange words:

" 'One would think he had been strangled by a skeleton.'

"A shiver ran down my back, and I cast my eyes to the place on the wall where I had seen the horrible, torn-off hand. It was no longer there. The chain was broken and hanging.

"Then I bent over the dead man and found in his mouth a piece of one of the fingers of the missing hand, cut off, or rather sawed off, by the teeth exactly at the second joint.

"Then they tried to collect evidence. They could find nothing. No door had been forced, no window opened or piece of furniture moved. The two watchdogs on the premises had not been aroused.

"Here, in a few words, is the deposition of the servant:

"For a month his master had seemed agitated. He had received many letters which he had burned immediately. Often, taking a whip in anger which seemed like dementia, he had struck in fury this dried hand fastened to the wall and taken, one knew not how, at the moment of a crime.

"He had retired late and shut himself in with care. He always carried arms. Often in the night he talked out loud, as if he were quarreling with someone. On that night, however, there had been no noise, and it was only on coming to open the windows that the servant had found Sir John assassinated. He suspected no one.

"I communicated what I knew of the death to the magistrates and public officers, and they made minute inquiries upon the whole island. They discovered nothing.

"One night, three months after the crime, I had a frightful nightmare. It seemed to me that I saw that hand, that horrible hand, running like a scorpion or a spider along my curtains and my walls. Three times I awoke; three times I fell asleep and again saw that hideous relic galloping about my room, moving its fingers like paws.

"The next day they brought it to me, found in the cemetery upon the tomb where Sir John Rowell was interred—for they had not been able to find his family. The index finger was missing.

"This, ladies, is my story. I know no more about it."

The ladies were terrified, pale and shivering. One of them cried:

"But that is not the end, for there was no explanation! We cannot sleep if you do not tell us what was your idea of the reason of it all."

The magistrate smiled with severity and answered:

"Oh, certainly, ladies, but it will spoil all your terrible dreams. I simply think that the legitimate proprietor of the hand was not dead and that he came for it with the one that remained to him. But I was never able to find out how he did it. It was one kind of revenge."

One of the women murmured:

"No, it could not be thus."

And the judge of information, smiling still, concluded:

"I told you in the beginning that my explanation would not satisfy you."

ONE EVENING

The steamer *Kleber* had stopped, and I looked with pleasure at the beautiful gulf of Bougie, which spread out ahead of us. The Kabylian forests covered the high mountains; in the distance the yellow sand edged the blue sea with powdered gold, while the sun fell in torrents of fire over the white houses of the small town.

The warm African breeze wafted the delightful odor of the desert to my nostrils, the odor of that great mysterious continent into which men from the north rarely penetrate. For three months I had been wandering on the borders of that great unknown world, on the outskirts of that strange land of the ostrich, camel, gazelle, hippopotamus, gorilla, elephant and Negro. I had seen the Arab galloping in the wind, like a waving standard. I had slept under the brown tents, in the shifting homes of these white birds of the desert. I was drunk with light, with magic, and with wide horizons.

But now after this final excursion I had to leave, go back to France, to Paris, that city of futile gossip, of commonplace preoccupations, and of continual handshaking. I must reluctantly say farewell to the things I loved, to things so new to me and of which I had barely caught a glimpse.

A fleet of small boats surrounded the steamer. I jumped into one belonging to a young Negro, and was soon on the quay near the old Saracen gate, whose gray ruins at the entrance of the Kabylian town looked like an old family coat of arms.

As I was standing beside my suitcase, looking at the big vessel at anchor in the roads and filled with admiration at the beauty of the coast, the circle of mountains bathed by blue waters more exquisite than those of Naples, as beautiful as those of Ajaccio and Porto in Corsica, I felt a heavy hand on my shoulder.

I turned to find a tall man with a long beard, a straw hat on his head and wearing flannels, by my side, staring at me with blue eyes.

"Are you not my old schoolmate?" he said.

"Possibly. What is your name?"

"Tremoulin."

"By Jove! You were in my class."

"Ah! Old chap, I recognized you at once."

And his long beard was rubbed against my cheeks.

He seemed so glad, so jolly, so happy to see me that in an outburst of friendliness I squeezed both hands of my former schoolfellow and felt very pleased to meet him again.

For four years Tremoulin had been my greatest friend at school. In those days his tall, thin body seemed to carry an overheavy head, a large, round head that bent his neck first to the right, then to the left, and crushed the narrow chest of the long-legged schoolboy.

Tremoulin was the great prize winner of our class: he was very intelligent, gifted with marvelous facility, a rare suppleness of mind, and an instinctive leaning towards literature. We were quite convinced at college that he would turn out a celebrated man, a poet no doubt, for he wrote poetry and was full of ingeniously sentimental ideas. His father, who was a chemist in the Panthéon district, was not considered well off.

As soon as he had taken his bachelor's degree I lost sight of him.

"What are you doing here?" I exclaimed.

He replied, smiling: "I am a settler."

"Bah! You are busy growing things?"

"I gather in the crops, too."

"Of what?"

"Of grapes, from which I make wine."

"You are successful?"

"Very."

"So much the better, old chap."

"Were you going to a hotel?"

"Of course."

"Well, then, you must come home with me instead."

"But . . ."

"That's settled."

And he said to the young Negro who was watching us: "Home, Ali."

Ali replied: "Yes, sir," and started running with my suitcase on his shoulder, raising the dust with his black feet.

Tremoulin caught hold of my arm and led me off. First he asked questions about my journey, my impressions, and seemed to like me better than ever for my enthusiastic reply. His home was an old Moorish house with an inner courtyard having no windows on the street and dominated by a terrace which, in its turn, dominated those of the neighboring houses, the gulf, the forests, the mountains, and the sea.

I exclaimed: "Ah! That's the real thing; the East casts its spell over me in this spot. What a lucky dog you are to live here! What nights you must spend on the terrace! Do you sleep there?"

"Yes, in summer. We will go up this evening. Do you like fishing?"

"What kind?"

"Fishing by torchlight."

"Yes. I love it."

"Well, we'll go after dinner, then come back and have cool drinks on the roof."

After I had had a bath, he took me to see the captivating Kabylian town, a real cascade of white houses tottering down towards the sea, then we returned home as night was falling, and after a good dinner set off for the quay.

We could see nothing but the lights of the streets and the stars, the big twinkling, shining stars of the African heavens.

A boat was waiting in a corner of the harbor. As soon as we got in, a man whose face I could not distinguish began to row, while my friend got the brazier ready for lighting. He said to me: "You know, I do the spearing. No one is better at it."

"My congratulations."

We had rounded a kind of mole and were now in a little bay full of high rocks whose shadows looked like towers built in the water, and I suddenly realized that the sea was phosphorescent. The oars which beat it gently and rhythmically kindled, as they fell, a weird, moving flame that followed in our wake and then died out. Bending over, I watched the flow of pale light scattered by the oars—the indescribable fire of the sea, that chilly fire kindled by a movement, that dies as soon as the waters return to rest. The three of us glided over the stream of light through the darkness.

Where were we going? I could not see my companions, I could see nothing but the luminous ripple and the sparks of water thrown up by the oars. The heat was intense. The darkness seemed as if it had been heated in an oven, and I felt uneasy in my mind about this mysterious voyage with the two men in the silently moving boat.

Dogs—those thin Arabian dogs with red coats, pointed muzzles and bright eyes —were barking in the distance as they bark every night in every quarter of the world, from the shore of the sea to the depth of the desert where wandering tribes pitch their tents. Foxes, jackals, hyenas answered back; and doubtless, not very far away, a solitary lion was growling in some pass of the Atlas Mountains.

Suddenly the boatman stopped. Where could we be? I heard a faint scratching noise close to me and by the light of a match I saw a hand—only a hand—carrying the fragile light towards the iron grating piled up with wood like a floating funeral pyre that hung from the bow.

I gazed, full of surprise, at this novel, disquieting scene, and excitedly watched the slender flame reach out towards a handful of dried heather that began to crackle.

Then in the stillness of the night a sheet of flame shot up, illuminating under the dark pall that hung over us, the boat and two men—an old, thin, pale, wrinkled sailor with knotted kerchief on his head, and Tremoulin, whose fair beard shone in the sudden glare of light.

"Forward," he shouted, and the old man began to row, surrounded by the blaze of fire, under the dome of mobile dusk that accompanied us. Tremoulin kept throwing wood on the brazier, now burning brightly.

I bent over the side again and saw the bottom of the sea. A few feet below the boat that strange kingdom of the waters unfolded itself—waters which like the air above give life to beast and plant. The brazier cast its brilliant light as far as the rocks and we glided over amazing forests of red, pink, green, and yellow weeds. Between them and us there lay a crystal-clear medium that made them look fairy-like, turning them into a dream—a dream springing from the depths of the ocean. This clear, limpid water that one knew was there without seeing it caused a strange feeling of unreality to come between us and this weird vegetation, making it as mysterious as the land of dreams.

At times the weeds came up to the surface, like floating hair, hardly stirred by the slow passage of the boat.

Among the seaweed, thin silver fish darted about, visible for a second, then lost to sight. Others, still asleep, floated about in the watery undergrowth, gleaming, graceful, and impossible to catch. A crab would run off to hide itself in a hole, or a bluish, transparent jellyfish, hardly visible—a pale azure-colored flower, a real flower of the sea—allowed its liquid mass to be dragged along in the slight ripple made by the boat. Then, suddenly, the ground at the bottom disappeared under a fog of thickened glass, and I saw huge rocks and gloomy-colored seaweed, vaguely illuminated by the light from the brazier.

Tremoulin, who was standing in the bows with his body bent forward, holding the sharp pointed trident called a spearing hook in his hands, closely watched ricks, weeds, and water, with the intensity of a beast in pursuit of its prey. Suddenly, with a quick, gentle movement, he darted the forked head of his weapon into the sea so swiftly that it speared a large fish swimming away from us.

I had seen nothing but Tremoulin's sudden movement, but I heard him grunt with joy and as he raised his hook in the light of the brazier I saw a wriggling conger eel, pierced by the iron teeth. After looking at it and showing it to me while he held it over the fire, my friend threw it into the bottom of the boat. The sea serpent, with its body pierced by seven wounds, slid and crawled about and grazed my feet in its search for a hole to escape by; then, having found a pool of brackish water between the ribs of the boat, it crouched there almost dead, twisting itself round and round.

Every minute Tremoulin was gathering up, with remarkable skill and amazing rapidity, all the strange inhabitants of the salt waters. In turn I saw held over the fire, convulsed with agony, silver catfish, eels spotted with blood, prickly scorpions, and dry, weird-looking fish that spat out into and turned the sea black.

I thought I heard the cry of birds in the night and raised my head in an attempt to see from whence came the sharp whistling sounds, now short, now long, now near, now far away. There were so many different sounds that a cloud of wings seemed to be hovering over us, attracted doubtless by the fire. At times the noise seemed to deceive the ear and come from the sea.

I asked: "Whatever is that whistling?"

"The falling cinders."

It was indeed caused by the brazier dropping a shower of burning twigs into the sea. They fell down red-hot or in flames, and went out with a soft, penetrating, queer protest, sometimes like a chuckle and sometimes like the short greeting of a passing emigrant. Drops of resin droned like cannon balls or hornets and suddenly expired in their plunge into the water. The noise was certainly like human voices: an indescribable, faint murmur of life straying about in the shadow near us.

Suddenly Tremoulin shouted: "Ah—the beggar!"

He threw his spear, and when he pulled it up I saw what looked like a big lump of throbbing red flesh wrapped round the teeth of the fork and sticking to the wood. It was an octopus that was twining and untwining long, soft tentacles covered with suckers around the handle.

He held up his victim and I saw the sea monster's two huge eyes look at me; they were bulging, terrible eyes that emerged from a kind of pocket like a tumor. The beast, thinking it was free, slowly stretched out one of its feelers in my direction. The end was as fine as a piece of thread, and as soon as the greedy arm had hooked itself onto the seat, another was uncurled and raised itself to follow the first.

There was a feeling of irresistible force about that soft, sinewy mass. Tremoulin opened his knife and plunged it swiftly between the beast's eyes. We heard a sigh, a sound of escaping air, and the octopus ceased to move. It was not dead, however, but its power was destroyed, its splendor gone, it would never again drink blood or suck a crab dry.

Tremoulin unwound the now useless tentacles from the sides of the boat and suddenly filled with anger, shouted: "Wait a bit, I'll make it hot for you."

With a stroke of the spear he picked up the beast, raised it in the air, held it to the fire, rubbing the thin fleshy ends of its arms against the red-hot bars of the brazier. They crackled as the heat of the fire twisted and contracted them and I ached all over at the idea of how the hideous beast must be suffering.

"Don't do that," I cried.

He replied quite calmly: "Bah! Anything's good enough for that thing," and threw the burst, lacerated body of the octopus into the boat, where it dragged itself between my legs to the hole of brackish water and lay down to die amongst the dead fish.

And so our fishing continued until the wood began to run short. When there was not enough to keep the fire going, Tremoulin thrust the brazier into the water, and night, which the brilliant flames had kept at a distance, fell upon us, wrapping us once more in its gloom.

The old sailor began to row slowly and regularly. I had no idea what was port or what land, nor what was sea or what the entrance to the gulf. The octopus still moved about close to my feet, and my nails hurt as if they too had been burned. Suddenly I saw the lights: we were entering the port.

"Are you sleepy?" my friend asked.

"No, not in the least."

"Then let us go and have a talk on the roof."

"With pleasure."

Just as we reached the terrace I saw the crescent moon rising behind the mountains. The warm breath of the wind slipped slowly by, full of faint, almost imperceptible, odors, as if it were sweeping up the scents of all the gardens and towns of every sun-scorched country on its way.

Around us the white houses with their square roofs descended towards the sea, we could see human forms lying down or standing up on the roofs, either asleep or dreaming in the starlight; whole families wrapped in long, flannel garments resting in the hush of the night from the heat of the day.

Suddenly it seemed as if the soul of the East was taking possession of me, that poetic, legendary soul of a simple and fanciful people. My mind was full of the Bible and the *Arabian Nights*: I heard prophets telling of miracles and saw princesses in silk Turkish trousers sauntering about on palace terraces, while incense whose smoke curled up in the shape of genii, burned in silver lamps.

I said to Tremoulin: "You are lucky to live here."

He replied: "Chance brought me here."

"Chance?"

"Yes, chance and misfortune."

"You have been miserable?"

"Very."

He was standing up in front of me, wrapped in his burnoose, and the tone of his voice made me shiver, it was so full of misery.

After a moment's silence he continued:

"I can tell you my grief. It may do me good to talk about it."

"Tell me about it."

"Do you really mean it?"

"Yes."

"Very well, then. You remember what I was like at college: more or less a poet brought up in a chemist's shop. My dream was to write books, and I tried after I had taken my degree but did not succeed. I published a volume of verse, then a novel, without selling more of one than of the other, then I wrote a play which was never acted.

"Then I fell in love, but I am not going to tell you all about that.

"Next door to my father's shop there lived a tailor who had a daughter; it was she I loved. She was intelligent and had passed high-school examinations; she was mentally alert, her mind being in keeping with her body. She looked fifteen although she was really twenty-two. She was very small, with refined features, slim figure, delicate complexion, in every way like a dainty water color. Her nose, mouth, her blue eyes and fair hair, her smile, figure, hands, indeed her whole being, seemed more fit for a glass case than for an open-air life. Nevertheless she was vivacious, supple in her movements and incredibly active, and I was very much in love with her. Two or three walks in the Luxembourg Gardens, near the Médicis fountain, I remember as the happiest time of my life. You must know all about that queer phase of love's folly when every thought is centered on worship of the loved one. You are nothing but a maniac haunted by a woman; nothing exists in the world but her.

"We were soon engaged, and I told her of my plans for the future, of which she disapproved. She did not believe in me as a poet, novelist, or dramatic author, and thought that trade, if successful, could procure perfect happiness. So I gave up the idea of writing books, I resigned myself to selling them and bought a book shop —the Universal Library—at Marseille, its former owner being dead.

"I had three good years. We had made our shop into a kind of literary *salon* where all the cultured men in the town met for conversation. They came to the shop as they would have gone to a club and discussed books, poets, and more especially politics. My wife, who was the head of the sales department, was very popular in the town; as for me, while they were all talking downstairs I was at work in my study on the first floor, which communicated with the shop by a winding staircase. I heard voices, laughter, discussions, and sometimes stopped writing to listen to what was going on. I was secretly writing a novel—which I never finished.

"The most regular frequenters were M. Montina, a man of private means, a tall, handsome type of man, often met with in the South, with black hair and eyes full of flattery; M. Barbet, a magistrate; two businessmen, MM. Faucil and Labarrègue; and General the Marquis de Flèche, head of the royalist party, the most important man in the province, aged sixty-six.

"Business was good, and I was happy, very happy. However, one day about three o'clock I was obliged to go out, and when I was in the Rue St. Ferreol I saw a woman come out of a house whose figure was so like my wife's that I would have said to myself 'It is she' had I not left her ill at home.

"She was walking ahead of me very quickly, and never looking back; in spite of myself I started to follow her with a feeling of surprise and uneasiness. I said to myself:

" 'It is not she. No. That's impossible, as she had a headache. Besides, what would she be doing in that house?

"Still I wanted to clear the matter up, so I hurried after her. Whether she felt or guessed I was behind her or whether she recognized my step, I can't say, but she turned round suddenly. It was she! When she saw me she blushed and stopped, then said with a smile: 'Hello, is it you?'

"I felt sick at heart and said: 'Yes. So you did go out? And your headache?'

" 'It was better. I have been on an errand.'

" 'Where to?'

" 'To Laussade's, in the Rue Cassinelli, to order some pencils.'

"She looked me full in the face. She was not blushing now, on the contrary, she was rather pale. Her clear, limpid eyes—ah! a woman's eyes!—seemed full of truth, but I had a vague, painful feeling that they were full of lies. I was more worried, more uncomfortable than she was, I dared not suspect her, and yet I felt sure she was telling me a lie. Why was she doing it? I had no idea, so I merely said: 'You were quite right to go out if you felt better.'

" 'Yes. I felt much better.'

" 'Are you going home?'

" 'Of course I am.'

"I left her and wandered about the streets alone. What was going on? While I was talking to her I knew instinctively that she was lying, but now I could not believe it, and when I went home to dinner I was angry with myself for having suspected her, even for a moment.

"Have you ever been jealous? Whether you have or not makes no difference. The first hot breath of jealousy had touched my heart. I could think of no explanation, I could not believe anything. I only knew that she had lied. You must remember that every evening when we were alone together, after all the customers and the clerks had left, either when strolling down towards the port in fine weather or else in my study when the weather was bad, I opened my heart to her without reserve, for I loved her. She was part of my life, the greater part, and all my happiness, and in her little hands she held captive my poor trusting, faithful heart.

"In the early days of doubt and distress before suspicion grew into a certainty I was depressed and cold to the marrow, just as you feel before a serious illness. I was always cold, really cold, and could neither eat nor sleep.

"Why had she lied to me? What was she doing in that house? I had been there to try and find out, but without success. The man who lived on the first floor, an upholsterer, told me all about his neighbors but without giving me any clue. A midwife lived on the second floor, a dressmaker and a manicure on the third, and two cabmen with their families in the attics.

"Why had she lied to me? It would have been so easy to say that she was coming from the dressmaker's or the manicure's. Oh! how I longed to ask them questions, too. I did not, for fear she might be warned and guess my suspicions.

"One thing was certain, she had been to the house and was concealing the fact from me, so that there was some mystery. But what? At times I thought there must be a good reason, some hidden charitable deed, some information she wanted, and I accused myself for suspecting her. Have we not all the right to our little, innocent secrets, to that second, inner life for which we are not obliged to account to anybody? Because he has been given a young girl as companion, has a man the right to expect that she shall never have a thought, can never do anything, without telling him about it? Does marriage mean the renunciation of all liberty, all independence? Might she not have gone to the dressmaker's without telling me, and might she not be helping the wife of one of the cabmen? Perhaps she thought that, without blaming her, I might criticize the reason she had for going to the house, although there was no harm in it. She knew me through and through, all my slightest peculiarities, and probably was afraid, if not of being reproached, at least of a discussion. She had very pretty hands, and I ended by thinking that she was having them secretly manicured in the suspected house, and that she would not confess to it so as to avoid any appearance of extravagance. She was very methodical and thrifty and looked after the household expenses most carefully. Doubtless she would have felt herself lowered in my eyes had she admitted to this slight piece of feminine extravagance. Women's souls are full of subtlety and natural trickery.

"But all my reasoning failed to reassure me. I was jealous. My suspicions tormented me, torturing and preying upon my mind. As yet it was not a suspicion but simply suspicion. I endured misery and frightful anguish. An obscure thought possessed me—a thought covered with a veil, and a veil I dared not raise, for beneath it lay a terrible doubt. . . . A lover! . . . Had she a lover? . . . Think of it! think of it! It was unlikely, impossible . . . and yet? . . .

"Montina's face was always before my eyes. I saw the tall insipid beauty, with shiny hair, smiling into her face, and I said to myself: 'It is he.' I made up a story of their intrigue. They had been talking of a book, discussing some amorous adventure, finding an incident similar to their own, and from this had followed the rest. I kept a lookout, a prey to the most abominable torture that man can endure. I bought shoes with rubber soles so that I could move about silently, and I spent my life going up and down the little winding staircase so as to catch them. Often I crept down the stairs on my hands, head first, to see what they were doing. Then I had to go up again backwards, with great difficulty, after finding that the clerk was always there with them. I lived in a state of continual suffering. I could think of nothing, I could not work, nor could I look after the business. As soon as I had left the house, as soon as I had walked a hundred yards along the street, I said to myself: 'He is there,' and back I went. He was not, so I went out again! But I had hardly left the house when I thought: 'He has come now,' and returned again.

"This went on every day.

"The night was worse still, for I felt her by my side, in my bed. There she was asleep or pretending to be asleep! Was she asleep? Of course not. Then that was another lie?

"I lay motionless on my back, on fire from the warmth of her body, panting and in agony. I was filled with a vile but steady desire to get up, take a candle and hammer, and with a single stroke split her head open to see what was inside! I knew that I would find nothing but a nasty mess of brains and blood, nothing else. I would have learned nothing. Impossible to find anything out! And her eyes! When she looked at me, I was seized with a wild fit of fury. You may look at her—she looks back at you! Her eyes are clear, candid—and false, false, false! and no one can guess what lies behind them. I longed to stick needles into them, to burst open the mirrors of deceit.

"How well I understand the Inquisition! I could have twisted her wrists in the iron bracelets: Speak. . . . Confess! . . . You won't? Just wait! . . . I could have strangled her by degrees. . . . Speak, confess! . . . You won't? . . . And I would have squeezed, squeezed, until her throat began to rattle, until she choked to death. . . . Or else I would have burned her fingers over the fire. . . . Oh, that I would have done with great pleasure! . . . Speak . . . speak then. . . . You won't? I would have held them on the red-hot coal, they would have been roasted at the tips . . . then she would have spoken . . . surely! . . . she would have spoken. . . ."

Tremoulin, standing erect with clenched fists, shouted his story. On the neighboring roofs, around us, the ghostly shadows awoke and sat up, they listened, disturbed in their sleep. As for me, I was deeply moved, and completely gripped by the tale I was listening to.

In the darkness I saw before me the little woman, the little, fair, vivacious, artful woman, as if I had known her. I saw her selling her books, talking to the men who found her childlike manner disturbing, and in her delicate doll-like head I could see petty, crafty ideas, stupid, exaggerated ideas, the dreams of musk-scented milliners attracted by the heroes of romantic novels. I suspected her just as he did. I hated and detested her, and would also willingly have burned her fingers to make her confess.

He continued more calmly: "I don't know why I am telling you all this. I have never yet spoken about it. Never—but I have seen nobody for two years. I have not talked to a single person, and the whole thing was seething within me like fermenting wine. I am emptying my heart of its pain, unluckily for you!

"Well, I had made a mistake, it was worse than I thought, much worse. Just listen. I fell back on the usual trick, I pretended to go away. Every time I left the house my wife lunched out. I need not tell you how I bribed a waiter at the restaurant so that I might catch them.

"The door of the private room was to be opened for me, and I arrived at the appointed time determined to kill them both. I coud imagine the whole scene as clearly as if it had already occurred. I could see myself going in. A small table covered with glasses, bottles, and plates separated her from Montina, and they would be so surprised when they saw me that they would not attempt to move. Without saying a word I would bring down the loaded stick I was carrying on the man's head; killed by one blow, he would crumple up with his face on the table. Then, turning towards her—I would give her time—a few seconds—to understand what was happening and to stretch her arms out to me, mad with terror, before dying in her turn. Oh I was quite ready. Strong, determined, and happy, happy to the point of intoxication. The idea of her terrified look at the raised stick, of her hands stretched out imploringly, of her strangled cry, of her face, suddenly livid and convulsed, avenged me beforehand. I had no intention of killing her at one blow! You must think me fierce, don't you? But you don't know what a man suffers. To think that a woman—wife or mistress—one loves is giving herself to another, surrenders herself to him as she had done to you, and accepts his kisses as she has done yours. It is terrible, appalling. Anyone who has suffered that agony is capable of anything. I am surprised there are not more murders, for all who have been betrayed—every one of them—want to kill, have gloated over the idea of death: in the solicitude of their own room or on a lonely road, haunted by the hallucination of satisfied vengeance, they have in imagination either strangled the betrayer or beaten him to death.

"I arrived at the restaurant and asked whether they were there. The bribed waiter replied: 'Yes, sir,' and, taking me upstairs, showed me a door, saying: 'In here.' I grasped my stick as if my fingers were made of iron, and went in.

"The moment was well chosen. They were kissing each other, but it was not Montina. It was the General de Flèche, aged sixty-six!

"I was so sure I was going to find the other one there that I was rigid with surprise.

"Besides . . . besides . . . I don't yet know exactly how it all happened. If I had found the other I would have been wild with rage! But this one! This old pot-bellied man with his hanging cheeks made me choke with disgust. She, who looked about fifteen, had given herself to this fat old man almost in his dotage, because he was a marquis, a general, the friend and representative of dethroned kings. No, I can't say what I felt, nor what I thought about it. I could not raise my hand against the old man. That would have been disgraceful! No, I no longer wanted to kill my own wife, but all women capable of such behavior. I was not jealous now, I felt as full of despair as if I had seen the horror of horrors!

"You may say what you like about men, they are not so vile as that! If you do meet one he is held up to universal derision. The husband or lover of an old woman is more despised than a thief. We men are a decent lot, as a rule, but they, they are prostitutes with hearts full of filth. They give themselves to all men, young or old, for the most contemptible reasons, because it is their profession, their vocation, their function in life. They are the eternal, unconscious, placid prostitutes who give their bodies without disgust because it is the merchandise of love, whether they sell them to the old man with money in his pocket who hangs about the streets or whether they give them, for the glory of it, to a lewd old monarch, or to a celebrated and repulsive old man! . . ."

He cried aloud like a prophet of old, in a tone of wrath, under the starry sky. With the fury of desperation he told about the exalted shame of all the mistresses of kings: the shame, considered worthy of respect of all young girls who marry old men; and the tolerance showed to all young wives who smilingly accept old men's kisses.

As he called them up I could see them all from the beginning of time, surging around us in the Eastern night: girls, beautiful girls with vile souls like beasts who, ignoring the age of the male, are docile to senile desire. They rose up before me, the handmaids of the patriarchs praised in the Bible, Hagar, Ruth, Lot's daughters, the dark Abigail, the virgin of Shunem whose caresses restored David to life, and all those others, young, fat, white patricians or plebeians, irresponsible females belonging to a master, the unclean flesh of submissive slaves, whether paid for in money or bought by the glamour of greatness.

I asked: "What did you do?"

"I went away," he replied, simply. "And here I am."

For a long time we stayed together without saying a word, just dreaming! . . .

I have retained an unforgettable impression of that evening. All that I had seen, felt, heard, guessed; the fishing excursion, perhaps the octopus too, and that harrowing story amid white phantoms on the neighboring roofs, all combined to produce a unique sensation. Certain chance meetings, certain inexplicable combinations of events, contain—without any outward appearance of the unusual—a greater amount of the secret quintessence of life than is spread over whole days of ordinary happenings.

SENTIMENT

It was during the hunting season at the country seat of the De Bannevilles. The autumn was rainy and dull. The red leaves, instead of crackling under foot, rotted in the hollows after the heavy showers.

The forest, almost leafless, was as humid as a bathroom. There was a moldy odor under the great trees, stripped of their fruits, which enveloped one on entering, as if a lye had been made from the steeped herbs, the soaked earth and the continuous rainfall. The hunters' ardor was dampened; the dogs were sullen, their tails lowered and their hair matted against their sides, while the young huntresses, their habits drenched with rain, returned each evening, depressed in body and spirit.

In the great drawing room after dinner they played lotto, but without enthusiasm, as the wind made a clattering noise upon the shutters and forced the old weather vanes into a spinning-top tournament. Someone suggested telling stories as they are told in books, but no one could think of anything very amusing. The hunters narrated some of their adventures with the gun, the slaughter of wolves, for example, and the ladies racked their brains without finding anywhere the imagination of Scheherazade.

They were about to abandon this form of diversion, when a young lady, carelessly playing with the hand of her old, unmarried aunt, noticed a little ring made of blond hair, which she had often seen before but thought nothing about.

Moving it gently about the finger, she said suddenly: "Tell us the history of this ring, Auntie; it looks like the hair of a child——"

The old maiden reddened and then grew pale, then in a trembling voice she replied: "It is sad, so sad that I never care to speak about it. All the unhappiness of my life is centered in it. I was young then, but the memory of it remains so painful that I weep whenever I think of it."

They wished very much to hear the story, but the aunt refused to tell it; finally they urged so much that she at length consented.

"You have often heard me speak of the Santèze family, now extinct. I knew the last three men of this family. They all died within three months in the same manner. This hair belonged to the last one. He was thirteen years old when he killed himself for me. That appears very strange to you, doesn't it?

"It was a singular race, a race of fools, if you will, but of charming fools, of fools for love. All, from father to son, had these violent passions, waves of emotion, which drove them to deeds most exalted, to fanatical devotion and even to crime. Devotion was to them what it is to certain religious souls. Those who become monks are not of the same nature as drawing-room favorites. One might almost say, as a proverb, 'He loved like a Santèze.'

"To see them was to divine this characteristic. They all had curly hair, growing low upon the brow, beard crinkly, eyes large, very large, whose rays seemed to penetrate and disturb you, without your knowing just why.

"The grandfather of the one of whom this is the souvenir, after many adventures and some duels on account of entanglements with women, when toward sixty became passionately taken with the daughter of his farmer. I knew them both. She was blonde, pale, distinguished looking, with a soft voice and a sweet look, so sweet that she reminded one of a Madonna. The old lord took her home with him and immediately became so captivated that he was unable to pass a minute away from her. His daughter and his daughter-in-law, who lived in the house, found this perfectly natural, so much was love a tradition of the family. When one was moved by a great passion nothing surprised them, and if anyone expressed a different notion before them, of disunited lovers or revenge after some treachery, they would both say in the same desolate voice: 'Oh, how he (or she) must have suffered before coming to that!' Nothing more. They were moved with pity by all dramas of the heart and never spoke slightingly of them, even when they were unworthy.

"One autumn a young man, Monsieur de Gradelle, invited for the hunting, eloped with the young woman.

"Monsieur de Santèze remained calm, as if nothing had happened. But one morning they found him in the kennel in the midst of the dogs.

"His son died in the same fashion in a hotel in Paris, while on a journey in 1841, after having been deceived by an opera singer.

"He left a child of eleven years and a widow, the sister of my mother. She came with the little one to live at my father's house on the De Bertillon estate. I was then seventeen.

"You could not imagine what an astonishing, precocious child this little Santèze was. One would have said that all the powers of tenderness, all the exaltation of his race, had fallen upon this one, the last. He was always dreaming and walking alone in a great avenue of elms that led from the house to the woods. I often watched this sentimental youngster from my window as he walked up and down with his hands behind his back, with bowed head, sometimes stopping to look up, as if he saw and comprehended things beyond his age and experience.

"Often after dinner, on clear nights, he would say to me: 'Let us go and dream, Cousin.' And we would go together into the park. He would stop abruptly in the clear spaces where the white vapor floats, that soft light with which the moon lights up the clearings in the woods, and say to me, seizing my hands: 'Look! Look there! But you do not understand; I feel it. If you comprehended you would be happy. One must know how to love.' I would laugh and embrace him, this boy, who loved me until his dying day.

"Often, too, after dinner he would seat himself upon my mother's knee. 'Come, Aunt,' he would say to her, 'tell us some love story.' And my mother, for his pleasure, would tell him all the family legends, the passionate adventures of his fathers, as they had been told a thousand times, true and false. It is these stories that have ruined these men; they never concealed anything and prided themselves upon not allowing a descendant of their house to lie.

"He would be uplifted, this little one, by these terrible or affecting tales, and sometimes he would clap his hands and cry out: 'I, too; I, too, know how to love, better than any of them.'

"Then he began to pay me his court, a timid, profoundly tender devotion, so droll that one could but laugh at it. Each morning I had flowers picked by him, and each evening, before going to his room, he would kiss my hand, murmuring: 'I love you!'

"I was guilty, very guilty, and I have wept since, unceasingly, doing penance all my life by remaining an old maid—or rather an affianced widow, his widow. I amused myself with this childish devotion, even inciting him. I was coquettish, enticing as if he were a man, caressing and deceiving. I excited this child. It was a joke to me and a pleasing diversion to his mother and mine. He was eleven years old! Think of it! Who would have taken seriously this passion of a midget! I kissed him as much as he wished. I even wrote sweet letters to him that our mothers read. And he responded with letters of fire that I still have. He had a belief all his own in our intimacy and love, judging himself a man. We had forgotten that he was a Santèze!

"This lasted nearly a year. One evening in the park he threw himself down at my knees, kissing the hem of my dress with furious earnestness, repeating: 'I love you! I love you! I love you and shall even to death. If you ever deceive me, understand, if you ever leave me for another, I shall do as my father did.' And he added in a low voice that gave one the shivers: 'You know what I shall do!'

"Then as I remained amazed and dumfounded, he got up and, stretching himself on tiptoe, for I was much taller than he, he repeated in my ear my name, my first name, 'Genevieve!' in a voice so sweet, so pretty, so tender, that I trembled to my very feet.

"I muttered: 'Let us return to the house!' He said nothing further but followed me. As we were ascending the steps he stopped me and said: 'You know if you abandon me I shall kill myself.'

"I understood now that I had gone too far and immediately became more reserved. When he reproached me for it one day I answered him: 'You are now too large for this kind of joking and too young for serious love. I will wait.'

"I believed myself freed from him.

"He was sent away to school in the autumn. When he returned the following summer I had become engaged. He understood at once and for over a week preserved so calm an appearance that I was much disturbed.

"The ninth day, in the morning, I perceived on rising a little paper slipped under my door. I seized it and read: 'You have abandoned me, and you know what I said. You have ordered my death. As I do not wish to be found by anyone but you, come into the park at the place where last year I said that I loved you, and look up.'

"I felt myself becoming mad. I dressed quickly and ran quickly, so quickly that I fell exhausted at the designated spot. His little school cap was on the ground in the mud. It had rained all night. I raised my eyes and saw something concealed by the leaves, for there was a wind blowing, a strong wind.

"After that I knew nothing of what I did. I shouted, fainted, perhaps, and fell, then got up and ran to the house. I recovered my reason in my bed, with my mother for my pillow.

"I at first believed that I had dreamed all this in a frightful delirium. I muttered: 'And he, he—Gontran, where is he——'

"Then they told me it was all true. I dared not look at him again, but I asked for a lock of his blond hair. Here—it—is." And the old lady held out her hand in a gesture of despair.

Then after much use of her handkerchief and drying of her eyes she continued: "I broke off my engagement without saying why—and I—have remained always the—widow of this child thirteen years old."

Then her head fell upon her breast, and she wept pensively for a long time.

And as they dispersed to their rooms for the night, a great hunter, whose quiet she had disturbed somewhat, whispered in the ear of his neighbor:

"What a misfortune to be so sentimental! Don't you think so?"

TRAVELING

Ste. Agnès, May 6.

MY DEAR FRIEND,

You asked me to write to you often, and particularly to tell you what I had seen. You also asked me to search through my memories of travel and find some of those short anecdotes which one hears from a peasant met by the way, from some hotelkeeper, or some passing stranger, and which remain in the memory like the key to a country. You believe that a landscape sketched in a few lines, or a short story told in a few words, reveals the true character of a country, makes it live, visibly and dramatically. I shall try to do as you wish. From time to time I will send you letters, in which I shall not mention ourselves, but only the horizon and the people who move on it. Now I begin.

Spring, it seems to me, is a season when one should eat and drink landscapes. It is the season for sensations, as the autumn is the season for thought. In spring the country stirs the body; in autumn it penetrates the mind.

This year I wanted to inhale orange blossoms, and I set out for the South at the time when everybody comes back from there. I passed through Monaco, the town of pilgrims, the rival of Mecca and Jerusalem, without leaving my money in anybody else's pocket, and I ascended the high hills beneath a canopy of lemon, orange, and olive trees.

Did you ever sleep in a field of orange trees in bloom? The air which one inhales deliciously is a quintessence of perfumes. This powerful and sweet smell, as savory as a sweetmeat, seems to penetrate one, to impregnate, to intoxicate, to induce languor, to bring about a dreamy and somnolent torpor. It is like opium prepared by fairy hands and not by chemists.

This is a country of gorges. The sides of the mountains are seamed and slashed all over, and in these winding crevices grow veritable forests of lemon trees. At intervals, where the abrupt ravine stops at a sort of ledge, man has fashioned reservoirs which catch the water from the rain storms. They are great holes with smooth walls, which offer no projection to catch the hand of those who fall.

I was walking slowly through one of these rising valleys, looking through the leaves at the bright fruit still remaining on the branches. The narrow gorge made the heavy perfumes of the flowers more penetrating; in there the air seemed dense because of them. I felt tired and wanted to sit down. A few drops of water rolled on the grass, I thought a spring must be near, and I climbed higher to find it. But I reached the edge of one of these huge, deep reservoirs. I sat down cross-legged and remained dreaming in front of the hole, which seemed to be full of ink, so black and stagnant was the water in it. Down below, through the branches, I could see, like splashes, bits of the Mediterranean, blindingly dazzling. But my glance constantly returned to this vast and somber hole which seemed uninhabited by any form of water life, its surface was so still.

Suddenly a voice made me start. An old gentleman, looking for flowers (for this country is the richest in Europe for botanists), asked me:

"Are you a relative of those poor children?"

I looked at him in astonishment.

"What children?"

Then he seemed embarrassed and answered with a bow:

"I beg your pardon. Seeing you so absorbed in that reservoir I imagined you were thinking of the awful drama which took place there."

I wanted to know all about it, and I asked him to tell me the story.

It is a very gloomy and heartbreaking story, my dear, and very commonplace, at the same time. It is simply like an incident from the daily papers. I do not know whether my emotion is to be attributed to the dramatic way in which it was told to me, to the mountain background, or to the contrast between the joyous flowers and sunshine and this dark, murderous hole. My heart was torn and my nerves shaken by this story, which may not seem so terribly poignant to you, perhaps, as you read it in your room, without seeing the scene in which the drama is laid.

It was in the spring a few years back. Two little boys often used to play on the edge of this cistern while their tutor read a book, lying under a tree. Now, one hot afternoon, a piercing cry aroused the man, who was dozing, and the noise of water splashing after a fall caused him to get up immediately. The younger of the two children, aged eleven years, was yelling, standing near the reservoir, whose troubled, rippling surface had closed over the elder, who had just fallen in while running along the stone ledge.

The distracted tutor, without waiting, without thinking, jumped into the depths, and did not appear again, having struck his head against the bottom. At the same moment, the little boy, who had come to the surface, was waving his arms to his brother. The child who was on dry land lay down and stretched out, while the other tried to swim, to reach the wall, and soon four little hands seized and held each other, clutching in a convulsive grip. Both felt the keen joy of being restored to life, the thrill of a peril that has passed. The elder tried to climb up, but could not, the wall being steep, and the younger, being too weak, was slowly slipping towards the hole. Then they remained motionless, seized again with terror, and waited.

The smaller boy grasped the hand of the older with all his might, and wept nervously, saying: "I can't pull you up. I can't pull you up." Then, suddenly he began to shout: "Help! Help!" But his piping voice hardly pierced the dome of foliage above their heads. They remained there for a long time, for hours and hours, face to face, these two children, with the same thought, the same fear, the awful dread lest one of them, becoming exhausted, should loosen his weakened grip. And they kept on calling in vain. At length, the elder, who was shaking with cold, said to the younger: "I can't go on. I am going to fall. Good-by, little brother." And the other repeated, with heaving breath: "Not yet, not yet; wait!" Evening came on, quiet evening, its stars reflected in the water. The elder boy, who was fainting, said: "Let go one hand, I want to give you my watch." He had received it as a present a few days before, and since then it had been the chief care of his heart. He succeeded in getting it, handed it up, and the younger, who was sobbing, placed it on the grass beside him.

It was now completely dark. The two unfortunate creatures were overcome and could scarcely hold out much longer. The bigger boy, feeling that his hour had come, murmured again: "Good-by, little brother. Kiss Papa and Mamma." His paralyzed fingers relaxed. He sank and did not come up again. . . .

The younger, who was left alone, began to cry madly: "Paul! Paul!" but his brother never returned. Then he dashed away, falling over stones, shaken by the most terrible anguish that can wring the heart of a child, and arrived in the drawing room where his parents were waiting. He lost his way again when taking them to the reservoir. He could not find the way. Finally he recognized the place. "It is there; yes, it is there." The cistern had to be emptied, and the owner would not allow this, as he needed the water for his lemon trees. In the end the two bodies were recovered, but not until the next day.

You see, my dear, that this is just a common newspaper story. But if you had seen the hole, you would have been moved to the bottom of your heart at the thought of this child's agony, hanging onto his brother's arm, of this interminable struggle on the part of two children accustomed only to laugh and play, and by that simple little detail: the giving over of the watch. I said to myself: "Fate preserve me from ever receiving such a relic!" I do not know of anything more terrible than the memory that clings to a familiar object that one cannot get rid of. Think that every time he touches this sacred watch, the survivor will see the horrible scene again, the cistern, the wall, the calm water, and the distorted face of his brother, still alive but as surely lost as though he were already dead. During his whole life, at every moment that vision will be there, evoked the moment the tip of his finger touches his watch pocket.

I felt sad until evening. I went off, still going higher, leaving the region of orange trees for the regions of olive trees only, and the latter for the pine-tree region. Then I entered a valley of stones, reaching the ruins of an old castle, built, they say, in the tenth century, by a Saracen chief, a wise man, who got baptized for love of a girl.

Mountains everywhere around me, and in front of me the sea, the sea on which there is a scarcely visible patch: Corsica, or, rather, the shadow of Corsica.

But on the mountaintops reddened by the setting sun, in the vast heavens, and on the sea, on the whole superb horizon I had come to admire, I saw only two poor children, one lying along the edge of a hole filled with black water, the other sunk up to his neck, held together by their hands, weeping face to face, distracted. And all the time I seemed to hear a feeble voice saying: "Good-by, little brother. I give you my watch."

This letter will seem very lugubrious to you, my dear friend. Another time I shall try to be more cheerful.

FRANCIS

We were going out of the asylum when I perceived in one corner of the courtyard a tall thin man who was forever calling an imaginary dog. He would call out with a sweet and tender voice: "Cocotte, my little Cocotte; come here, Cocotte; come here, my beauty," striking his leg, as one does to attract the attention of an animal. I asked the doctor what the matter was with the man.

"Oh, that is an interesting case," he said; "he is a coachman named Francis, and he became insane from drowning his dog."

I insisted upon his telling me the story. The most simple and humble things sometimes strike most to our hearts.

And here is the adventure of this man which was known solely to a groom, his comrade.

In the suburbs of Paris lived a rich, middle-class family. Their villa was in the midst of a park, on the bank of the Seine. Their coachman was this Francis, a country boy, a little awkward, but of good heart, simple and easily duped.

When he was returning one evening to his master's house a dog began to follow him. At first he took no notice of it, but the persistence of the beast in walking on his heels caused him finally to turn around. He looked to see if he knew this dog. No, he had never seen it before.

The dog was frightfully thin and had great hanging dugs. She trotted behind the man with a woeful, famished look, her tail between her legs, her ears close to her head, and stopped when he stopped, starting again when he started.

He tried to drive away this skeleton of a beast. "Get out! If you want to save yourself—— Go, now! Hou! Hou!" She would run away a few steps and then sit down, waiting; then when the coachman started on again, she followed behind him.

He made believe to pick up stones. The animal fled a little way with a great shaking of the flabby mammillae, but followed again as soon as the man turned his back.

Then the coachman Francis took pity and called her. The dog approached timidly, her back bent in a circle and all the ribs showing under the skin. The man smoothed these projecting bones and, moved by pity for the misery of the beast, said: "Come along then!" Immediately the tail began to move; she felt the welcome, the adoption, and instead of staying at her new master's heels she began to run ahead of him.

He installed her on some straw in his stable, then ran to the kitchen in search of bread. When she had eaten her fill she went to sleep, curled up, ringlike.

The next day the coachman told his master who allowed him to keep the animal. She was a good beast, intelligent and faithful, affectionate and gentle.

But immediately they discovered in her a terrible fault. She was inflamed with love from one end of the year to the other. In a short time she had made the acquaintance of every dog about the country, and they roamed about the place day and night. With the indifference of a girl, she shared her favors with them, feigning to like each one best, dragging behind her a veritable mob composed of many different models of the barking race, some as large as a fist, others as tall as an ass. She took them to walk through routes with interminable courses, and when she stopped to rest in the shade they made a circle about her and looked at her with tongues hanging out.

The people of the country considered her a phenomenon; they had never seen anything like it. The veterinary could not understand it.

When she returned to the stable in the evening the crowd of dogs made seige for proprietorship. They wormed their way through every crevice in the hedge which inclosed the park, devastated the flower beds, broke down the flowers, dug holes in the urns, exasperating the gardener. They would howl the whole night about the building where their friend lodged, and nothing could persuade them to go away.

In the daytime they even entered the house. It was an invasion, a plague, a calamity. The people of the house met at any moment on the staircase, and even in the rooms, little yellow pug dogs with tails decorated, hunting dogs, bulldogs, wolfhounds with filthy skin, vagabonds without life or home, besides some new-world enormities which frightened the children.

All the unknown dogs for ten miles around came, from one knew not where, and lived, no one knew how, disappearing all together.

Nevertheless, Francis adored Cocotte. He had named her Cocotte, "without malice, sure that she merited her name." And he repeated over and over again: "This beast is a person. It only lacks speech."

He had a magnificent collar in red leather made for her, which bore these words, engraved on a copperplate: "Mlle Cocotte, from Francis, the coachman."

She became enormous. She was as fat as she had been thin, her body puffed out, under which hung always the long, swaying mammillae. She had fattened suddenly and walked with difficulty, the paws wide apart, after the fashion of people that are too large, the mouth open for breath, wide open as soon as she tried to run.

She showed a phenomenal fecundity, producing, four times a year, a litter of little animals, belonging to all varieties of the canine race. Francis, after having chosen the one he would leave her "to take the milk," would pick up the others in his stable apron and pitilessly throw them into the river.

Soon the cook joined her complaints to those of the gardener. She found dogs under her kitchen range, in the cupboards and in the coalbin, always fleeing whenever she encountered them.

The master, becoming impatient, ordered Francis to get rid of Cocotte. The man, inconsolable, tried to place her somewhere. No one wanted her. Then he resolved to lose her and put her in charge of a wagoner who was to leave her in the country the other side of Paris, beyond De Joinville-le-Pont.

That same evening Cocotte was back.

It became necessary to take measures. For the sum of five francs they persuaded a cook on the train to Havre to take her. He was to let her loose when they arrived.

At the end of three days she appeared again in her stable, harassed, emaciated, exhausted.

The master was merciful and insisted on nothing further.

But the dogs soon returned in greater numbers than ever and were more provoking. And as they were giving a great dinner one evening a stuffed chicken was carried off by a dog under the nose of the cook, who dared not dispute the right to it.

This time the master was angry and, calling Francis to him, said hotly: "If you don't kick this beast into the water tomorrow morning I shall put you out, do you understand?"

The man was undone, but he went up to his room to pack his trunk, preferring to leave the place. Then he reflected that he would not be likely to get in anywhere else, dragging this unwelcome beast behind him; he remembered that he was in a good house, well paid and well fed, and he said to himself that it was not worth while giving up all this for a dog. He enumerated his own interests and finished by resolving to get rid of Cocotte at dawn the next day.

However, he slept badly. At daybreak he was up and, preparing a strong cord, he went in search of the dog. She arose slowly, shook herself, stretched her limbs and came to greet her master. Then his courage failed and he began to stroke her tenderly, smoothing her long ears, kissing her on the muzzle, lavishing upon her all the loving names that he knew.

A neighboring clock struck; he could no longer hesitate. He opened the door. "Come," he said. The beast wagged her tail, understanding only that she was to go out.

They reached the bank and chose a place where the water seemed deepest. Then he tied one end of the cord to the beautiful leather collar and, taking a great stone, attached it to the other end. Then he seized Cocotte in his arms and kissed her furiously, as one does when he is taking leave of a person. Then he held her right around the neck, fondling her and calling her "My pretty Cocotte, my little Cocotte," and she responded as best she could, growling with pleasure.

Ten times he tried to throw her in, and each time his heart failed him.

Then abruptly he decided to do it and, with all his force, hurled her as far as possible. She tried at first to swim, as she did when taking a bath, but her head, dragged by the stone, went under again and again. She threw her master a look of despair, a human look, battling, as a person does when drowning. Then before the whole body sank, the hind paws moved swiftly in the water; then they disappeared also.

For five minutes bubbles of air came to the surface as if the river had begun to boil. And Francis, haggard, excited, with heart palpitating, believed he saw Cocotte writhing in the slime. And he said to himself with the simplicity of a peasant: "What does she think of me by this time, that beast?"

He almost became idiotic. He was sick for a month and each night saw the dog again. He felt her licking his hands; he heard her bark.

It was necessary to call a physician. Finally he grew better, and his master and mistress took him to their estate near Rouen.

There he was still on the bank of the Seine. He began to take baths. Every morning he went down with the groom to swim across the river.

One day, as they were amusing themselves splashing in the water, Francis suddenly cried out to his companion:

"Look at what is coming toward us. I am going to make you taste a cutlet."

It was an enormous carcass, swelled and stripped of its hair, its paws moving forward in the air, following the current.

Francis approached it, making his jokes:

"What a prize, my boy! My! But it is not fresh! It is not thin; that is sure!"

And he turned about, keeping at a distance from the great putrefying body.

Then suddenly he kept still and looked at it in strange fashion. He approached it again, this time near enough to touch. He examined carefully the collar, took hold of the leg, seized the neck, made it turn over, drew it toward him and read upon the green copper that still adhered to the discolored leather: "Mlle Cocotte, from Francis, the coachman."

The dead dog had found her master sixty miles from their home!

He uttered a fearful cry and began to swim with all his might toward the bank, shouting all the way. And when he reached the land he ran, all bare, through the country. He was mad!

THE ASSASSIN

The guilty man was defended by a very young lawyer, a beginner, who spoke thus:

"The facts are undeniable, gentlemen of the jury. My client, an honest man, an irreproachable employee, gentle and timid, assassinated his employer in a moment of anger, which seems to me incomprehensible. If you will allow me I would like to look into the psychology of the crime, so to speak, without wasting any time or attempting to excuse anything. We shall then be able to judge better.

"John Nicholas Lougère is the son of very honorable people who made of him a simple, respectful man.

"That is his crime: respect! It is a sentiment, gentlemen, which we of today no longer know, of which the name alone seems to exist while its power has disappeared. It is necessary to enter certain old, modest families to find this severe tradition, this religion of a thing or of a man, this sentiment where belief takes on a sacred character, this faith which doubts not, or smiles or entertains a suspicion.

"One cannot be an honest man, a truly honest man in the full force of the term, and be respectful. The man who respects has his eyes closed. He believes. We others, whose eyes are wide open upon the world, who live here in this hall of justice, this purger of society, where all infamy runs aground, we others who are the confidants of shame, the devoted defenders of all human meanness, the support, not to say the supporters, of male and female sharpers, from a prince to a tramp, we who welcome with indulgence, with complacence, with a smiling benevolence, all the guilty and defend them before you, we who, if we truly love our profession, measure our legal sympathy by the size of the crime, we could never have a respectful soul. We see too much of this river of corruption, which catches the chiefs of power as well as the lowest scamp; we know too much of how it gives and takes and sells itself. Places, offices, honors brutally exchanged for a little money or skillfully exchanged for titles and interests in industrial enterprises, or sometimes, simply for the kiss of a woman.

"Our duty and our profession force us to be ignorant of nothing, to suspect everybody, because everybody is doubtful, and we are taken by surprise when we find ourselves face to face with a man, like the assassin seated before you, who possesses the religion of respect to such a degree that he will become a martyr for it.

"We others, gentlemen, have a sense of honor, a certain need of propriety, from a disgust of baseness, from a sentiment of personal dignity and pride, but we do not carry at the bottom of our hearts the blind, inborn, brutal faith of this man.

"Let me tell you the story of his life:

"He was brought up, like many another child, to separate all human acts into two parts: the good and the bad. He was shown the good with an irresistible authority which made him only distinguish the bad, as we distinguish day and night. His father did not belong to the superior race of minds who, looking from a height, see the sources of belief and recognize the social necessities born of these distinctions.

"He grew up, religious and confident, enthusiastic and limited. At twenty-two he married. His wife was a cousin, brought up as he was, simple and pure as he was. His was the inestimable privilege of having for a companion an honest woman with a true heart, the rarest and most respectable thing in the world. He had for his mother that veneration which surrounds mothers in patriarchal families, that profound respect which is reserved for divinities. This religion he reflected somewhat upon his wife, and it became scarcely less as conjugal familiarity increased. He lived in absolute ignorance of double dealing, in a state of constant uprightness and tranquil happiness which made him a being apart from the world. Deceiving no one, he had never a suspicion than anyone would deceive him.

"Some time before his marriage he had become cashier in the office of Monsieur Langlais, the man who was lately assassinated by him.

"We know, gentlemen of the jury, by the testimony of Madame Langlais and of her brother Monsieur Perthuis, a partner of her husband, of all the family and of all the higher employees of the bank, that Lougère was a model employee, upright, submissive, gentle, prompt and deferential toward his superiors. They treated him with the consideration due to his exemplary conduct. He was accustomed to this homage and to a kind of respect shown to Madame Lougère, whose worthiness was upon all lips.

"But she died of typhoid fever in a few days' time. He assuredly felt a profound grief, but the cold, calm grief of a methodical heart. Only from his pallor and from a change in his looks was one able to judge how deeply he had been wounded.

"Then, gentlemen, the most natural thing in the world happened.

"This man had been married ten years. For ten years he had been accustomed to feel the presence of a woman near him always. He was habituated to her care, her familiar voice upon his return, the good night at evening, the cheerful greeting of the morning, the gentle rustle of the dress so dear to the feminine heart, to that caress, at once loverlike and maternal, which renders life pleasant, to that loved presence that made the hours move less slowly. He was also accustomed to being spoiled at table, perhaps, and to all those attentions which become little by little so indispensable.

"He could no longer live alone. Then to pass the interminable evenings he got into the habit of spending an hour or two in a neighboring wineshop. He would drink a glass and sit there motionless, following with heedless eye the billiard balls running after one another under the smoke of the pipes, listening to, without hearing, the discussion of the players, the disputes of his neighbors over politics and the sound of laughter that sometimes went up from the other end of the room from some unusual joke. He often ended by going to sleep from sheer lassitude and weariness. But at the bottom of his heart and of his flesh there was the irresistible need of a woman's heart and flesh, and without thinking he approached each evening a little nearer to the desk where the cashier, a pretty blonde, sat, attracted to her unconquerably because she was a woman.

"At first they chatted, and he got into the habit, so pleasant for him, of passing the evening by her side. She was gracious and kind, as one learns in this occupation to smile, and she amused herself by making him renew his order as often as possible, which makes business good.

"But each day Lougère was becoming more and more attached to this woman whom he did not know, whose whole existence he was ignorant of and whom he loved only because he was in the way of seeing nobody else.

"The little creature was crafty and soon perceived that she could reap some benefit from this guileless man; she then sought out the best means of exploiting him. The most effective, surely, was to marry him.

"This she accomplished without difficulty.

"Need I tell you, gentlemen of the jury, that the conduct of this girl had been most irregular and that marriage, far from putting a check to her flight, seemed on the contrary to render it more shameless?

"From the natural sport of feminine astuteness, she seemed to take pleasure in deceiving this honest man with all the employees of his office. I said with all. We have letters, gentlemen. There was soon a public scandal, of which the husband alone, as usual, was the only one ignorant.

"Finally this wretch, with an interest easy to understand, seduced the son of the proprietor, a young man nineteen years old, upon whose mind and judgment she had a deplorable influence. Monsieur Langlais, whose eyes had been closed up to that time through friendship for his employee, resented having his son in the hands, I should say in the arms, of this dangerous woman and was legitimately angry.

"He made the mistake of calling Lougère to him on the spot and of speaking to him of his paternal indignation.

"There remains nothing more for me to say, gentlemen, except to read to you the recital of the crime, made by the lips of the dying man and submitted as evidence. It says:

"*I learned that my son had given to this woman, that same night, ten thousand francs, and my anger was stronger on that account. Certainly I never suspected the* honorableness of Lougère, but a certain kind of blindness is more dangerous than positive faults. And so I had him come to me and told him that I should be obliged to deprive myself of his services.

"He remained standing before me, terrified and not comprehending. He ended by demanding, rather excitedly, some explanation. I refused to give him any, affirming that my reasons were wholly personal. He believed then that I suspected him of indelicacy and, very pale, besought, implored me to explain. Held by this idea, he was strong and began to talk loud. As I kept silent he abused and insulted me, until he arrived at such a degree of exasperation that I was fearful of results.

"Then suddenly, upon a wounding word that struck upon a full heart, I threw the whole truth in his face.

"He stood still some seconds, looking at me with haggard eyes. Then I saw him take from my desk the long shears, which I use for making margins to certain registers; I saw him fall upon me with uplifted arm and I felt something enter my throat just above the breast, without noticing any pain.

"This, gentlemen of the jury, is the simple recital of this murder. What more can be said for his defense? He respected his second wife with blindness because he respected his first with reason."

After a short deliberation the prisoner was acquitted.

OUR LETTERS

Night hours in the train induce sleep in some and insomnia in others. With me, any journey prevents my sleeping on the following night.

I had arrived, about five o'clock, at the estate of Abelle, which belongs to my friends, the Murets d'Artus, to spend three weeks there. It is a pretty house, built by one of their grandfathers in the latter half of the last century, and it has remained in the family. Therefore it has that intimate character of dwellings that have always been inhabited, furnished, animated, and enlivened by the same people. Nothing changes; none of the soul evaporates from the dwelling, in which the furniture has never been moved; the tapestries, never taken down, have become worn out, faded, discolored, on the same walls. None of the old furniture leaves the place; only from time to time it is moved a little to make room for a new piece, which enters there like a newborn infant in the midst of brothers and sisters.

The house is on a hill in the center of a park which slopes down to the river, where there is a little stone bridge. Beyond the water the fields stretch out in the distance, where cows wander slowly, pasturing on the moist grass; their humid eyes seem full of the dew, mist, and freshness of the pasture. I love this dwelling, just as one loves a thing which one ardently desires to possess. I return here every autumn with infinite delight; I leave with regret.

After I had dined with this friendly family, by whom I was received like a relative, I asked my chum, Paul Muret: "Which room did you give me this year?"

"Aunt Rose's room."

An hour later, followed by her three children, two tall little girls and a great lump of a boy, Mme. Muret d'Artus installed me in Aunt Rose's room, where I had not yet slept.

When I was alone I examined the walls, the furniture, the general aspect of the room, in order to attune my mind to it. I knew it, but not very well, as I had entered it only once or twice, and I looked indifferently at a pastel portrait of Aunt Rose, who gave her name to the room.

This old Aunt Rose, with her hair in curls, looking at me from behind the glass, made very little impression on my mind. She looked to me like a woman of former days, with principles and precepts, as strong on the maxims of morality as on cooking recipes, one of these old aunts who are a wet blanket on gaiety and the stern and wrinkled angel of provincial families.

I never had heard her spoken of; I knew nothing of her life or of her death. Did she belong to this century or to the preceding one? Had she left this earth after a calm or a stormy existence? Had she given up to heaven the pure soul of an old maid, the calm soul of a spouse, the tender one of a mother, or one moved by love? What difference did it make? The name alone, "Aunt Rose," seemed ridiculous, common, ugly.

I picked up a candle and looked at her severe face, hanging far up in an old gilt frame. Then, as I found it insignificant, disagreeable, even unsympathetic, I began to examine the furniture. It dated from the period of Louis XVI, the Revolution, and the Directoire. Not a chair, not a curtain had entered this room since then, and it gave out the subtle odor of memories, which is the combined odor of wood, cloth, chairs, hangings, peculiar to places wherein have lived hearts that have loved and suffered.

I retired but did not sleep. After I had tossed about for an hour or two, I decided to get up and write some letters.

I opened a little mahogany desk with brass trimmings, which was placed between the two windows, in hope of finding some ink and paper; but all I found was a quill pen, very much worn, made of a porcupine's quill and chewed at the end. I was about to close this piece of furniture when a shining spot attracted my attention: it looked like the yellow head of a nail, and it formed a little round lump at the corner of a tray. I scratched it with my finger, and it seemed to move. I seized it between two fingernails, and pulled as hard as I could. It came toward me gently. It was a long gold pin which had been slipped into a hole in the wood and remained hidden there.

Why? I immediately thought that it must have served to work some spring which hid a secret, and I looked. It took a long time. After at least two hours of investigation, I discovered another hole opposite the first one, but at the bottom of a groove. Into this I stuck my pin: a little shelf sprang up in my face, and I saw two packages of yellow letters, tied with a blue ribbon.

I read them. Here are two of them:

So you wish me to return to you your letters, my dearest. Here they are, but it pains me to obey. Of what are you afraid? That I might lose them? But they are under lock and key. Do you fear that they might be stolen? I guard against that, for they are my dearest treasure.

Yes, it pains me deeply. I wondered whether, perhaps, you might not be feeling some regret at the bottom of your heart? Not regret at having loved me, for I know that you still do, but regret at having expressed on white paper this living love in hours when your heart did not confide in me, but in the pen you held in your hand. When we love, we have need of confession, need of talking or writing, and we either talk or write. Words fly away, those sweet words made of music, air, and tenderness, warm and light, which escape as soon as they are uttered, which remain in the memory alone, but which one can neither see, touch nor kiss, like the words written by your hand. Your letters? Yes, I am returning them to you! But with what sorrow!

Undoubtedly, you must have had an afterthought of delicate shame at expressions that are ineffaceable. In your sensitive and timid soul, which can be hurt by an impalpable shade, you must have regretted having written to a man that you loved him. You remembered sentences that called up recollections, and you said to yourself: "I will make ashes of those words."

Be satisfied, be calm. Here are your letters. I love you.

MY FRIEND:

No, you have not understood me, you have not guessed. I do not regret, and I never shall, that I told you of my affection. I will always write to you, but you must return my letters to me as soon as you have read them.

I shall shock you, dear, when I tell you the reason for this demand. It is not poetic, as you imagined, but practical. I am afraid, not of you, but of some mischance. I am guilty. I do not wish my fault to affect others than myself.

Understand me well. You and I may both die. You might fall off your horse, since you ride every day; you might die from a sudden attack, from a duel, from heart disease, from a carriage accident, in a thousand ways. For, if there is only one death, there are more ways of its reaching us than there are days for us to live.

Then your sisters, your brother, or your sister-in-law might find my letters! Do you think that they love me? I doubt it. And then, even if they adored me, is it possible for two women and one man to know a secret—such a secret!—and not to tell of it?

I seem to be saying something very dreadful by speaking first of your death and then suspecting the discreetness of your relatives.

But don't all of us die sooner or later? And it is almost certain that one of us will precede the other under the ground. We must therefore foresee all dangers, even that one.

As for me, I will keep your letters beside mine, in the secret of my little desk. I will show them to you there, sleeping side by side in their silken hiding place, full of our love, like lovers in a tomb.

You will say to me: "But if you should die first, my dear, your husband will find these letters."

Oh! I fear nothing. First of all, he does not know the secret of my desk, and he will not look for it. And even if he finds it after my death, I fear nothing.

Did you ever stop to think of all the love letters that have been found in the drawers of dead women? I have been thinking of this for a long time, and that is the reason I decided to ask you for my letters.

Think that never, do you understand, never, does a woman burn, tear or destroy the letters in which she is told that she is loved. That is our whole life, our whole hope, expectation and dream. These little pieces of paper which bear our name in caressing terms are relics, and we women have chapels, especially chapels in which we are the saints. Our love letters are our titles to beauty, grace, seduction, the intimate vanity of our womanhood; they are the treasures of our heart. No, a woman never destroys these secret and delicious archives of her life.

But, like everybody else, we die, and then—then these letters are found! Who finds them? The husband. Then what does he do? Nothing. He burns them.

Oh, I have thought a great deal about that! Just think that every day women are dying who have been loved; every day the traces and proofs of their fault fall into the hands of their husbands, and that there is never a scandal, never a duel.

Think, my dear, of what a man's heart is. He avenges himself on a living woman; he fights with the man who has dishonored her, kills him while she lives, because—well, why? I do not know exactly why. But if, after her death, he finds similar proofs, he burns them, and no one is the wiser, and he continues to shake hands with the friend of the dead woman, and feels quite at ease that these letters should not have fallen into strange hands, and that they are destroyed.

Oh, how many men I know among my friends who must have burned such proofs, and who pretend to know nothing, and yet who would have fought madly had they found them when she was still alive! But she is dead. Honor has changed. The grave gives absolution for conjugal sins.

Therefore, I can safely keep our letters, which, in your hands, would be a menace to both of us. Do you dare to say that I am not right?

I love you and kiss you.

                                                        ROSE.

I raised my eyes to the portrait of Aunt Rose, and as I looked at her severe, wrinkled face, I thought of all those women's souls which we do not know, and which we suppose to be so different from what they really are, whose inborn and ingenuous craftiness we never can penetrate, their quiet duplicity; and a verse of Vigny returned to my memory:

"Toujours ce compagnon dont le cœur n'est pas sûr."

THE CRIPPLE

This adventure happened to me about 1882.

I had just settled myself in the corner of an empty carriage, and I had shut the door, in the hope of being left undisturbed, when it was abruptly reopened and I heard a voice say:

"Take care, sir, we are just at the crossing of the lines: the footboard is very high."

Another voice answered:

"Don't worry, Laurent, I'll hold fast."

Then a head appeared, covered with a round cap, and two hands, clinging to the leather straps that hung from both sides of the carriage door, slowly hoisted up a fat body whose feet on the footboard produced the sound of a stick striking the ground.

But when the man had got the upper part of his body into the compartment,

(Copyright, 1926, by Alfred A. Knopf, Inc.)

I saw the black-painted end of a wooden leg appearing in the limp-hanging leg of his trousers, followed shortly by a similar stump.

A head came into view behind this traveler and asked:

"Are you all right, sir?"

"Yes, my boy."

"Then here are your parcels and your crutches."

And a manservant, who had the appearance of an old soldier, climbed up too, carrying in his arms a quantity of things wrapped in black and yellow papers, carefully tied with strings, and placed them one after another on the rack above his master's head. Then he said:

"There you are, sir, that's the lot. There are five of them: the sweets, the doll, the drum, the gun, and the *pâté de foie gras*."

"That's right, my boy."

"I hope you'll have a comfortable journey, sir."

"Thanks, Laurent; keep yourself fit."

The man went away, reclosing the door, and I looked at my neighbor.

He must have been about thirty-five years old, although his hair was almost white; he wore various decorations, he was mustached and very stout, a victim to the short-winded obesity that falls on strong, active men whom some infirmity deprives of exercise.

He mopped his forehead, panted, and giving me a direct glance, said:

"Does the smoke annoy you, sir?"

"No, sir."

That eye, that voice, that face, I knew them well. But where, where did I get my knowledge? I had certainly met the fellow, I had talked to him, I had shaken his hand. It went a long way back, a very long way, it was lost in those mists where the mind seems to grope after memories and pursue them, like flying phantoms, without grasping them.

He too was now scrutinizing my face in the fixed and tenacious manner of a man who has some dim remembrance but cannot quite place it.

Our eyes, embarrassed by this unwinking exchange of glances, turned away; then, a few minutes later, drawn back once more by the secret obstinate will of the laboring memory, they met again, and I said:

"God bless my soul, sir, instead of looking at one another out of the corner of our eyes for an hour, wouldn't it be more sensible to join forces in discovering where we knew each other?"

My neighbor answered pleasantly:

"You're quite right, sir."

I told him my name.

"My name is Henry Bouclair. I'm a magistrate."

He hesitated a moment; then with that uncertainty of glance, and voice produced by severe mental tension, he said:

"Oh, just so. I met you at the Poincels', a long time ago, before the war, it must be twelve years since."

"Yes, sir . . . ah . . . you're Lieutenant Revalière?"

"Yes, I was even Captain Revalière until the day when I lost my feet, both at one stroke, from a passing ball."

And we looked at one another again, now that we knew each other.

I recalled perfectly having seen this handsome, slender youth who led cotillions with an agile, graceful energy, and who had been nicknamed, I believe, "La Trombe."[1] But behind this vision, sharply evoked, hovered yet another one I could not grasp, some story that I had known and forgotten, one of those stories to which one lends a friendly and short-lived interest, and which leave in one's mind only an almost imperceptible trace.

There had been a love affair in those days. I recaptured just that particular emotional impression in the depths of my memory, but nothing more, an emotional impression comparable to the scent which—to a dog's nose—the foot of an animal deposits on the ground.

Little by little, however, the shadows lifted and the face of a young girl rose before my eyes. Then her name burst in my head like an exploding cracker: Mlle. de Mandal. I recalled the whole affair now. It was indeed a love story, but a commonplace one. That young girl loved that young man, when I met him, and people talked of their approaching marriage. He himself seemed very much in love, very happy.

I lifted my eyes towards the rack where all the parcels carried by my neighbor's servant were shaking with the jolts of the train, and the man's voice sounded again in my ears as if he had hardly finished speaking.

He had said:

"There you are, sir, that's the lot. There are five of them: the sweets, the doll, the drum, the gun, and the *pâté de foie gras*."

Thereupon, in a flash, a romance developed and unfolded itself in my head. It was, moreover, exactly like all the romances I had read, in which sometimes the young man, sometimes the young girl, marries his or her betrothed after the catastrophe, bodily or financial. So this officer who had been maimed in the war, had after the campaign come back to find the girl who had promised to marry him, and she had kept her word and given herself to him.

I considered it very beautiful but quite simple, as one considers simple all the self-sacrifices and all the denouements of books and plays. It always seems to us, as we read or as we listen, in these schools of magnanimity, that we should have sacrificed ourselves with enthusiastic pleasure, with superb impulsiveness. But we are put sorely out of temper, next day, when some luckless friend comes to borrow a little money from us.

Then, suddenly, another supposition, less romantic and more realistic, took the place of the first. Perhaps he had married before the war, before the frightful accident when his legs were shot away, and she, desolate and resigned, had been forced to take back, care for, console and sustain this husband, who had left her strong and handsome and returned with feet mowed off, a dreadful wreckage condemned to immobility, to impotent rages and an inevitable obesity.

Was he happy or in torment? A desire, at first vague, then increasing, at last irresistible, came upon me, to learn his story, to know at least the principal points of it, which would allow me to guess what he could not or would not say.

I talked to him, my thoughts busy all the time. We had exchanged a few commonplace words; and, my eye turned towards the rack, I kept thinking: "So, he has three children. The sweets are for his wife, the doll for his little girl, the drum and the gun for his boys, the *pâté de foie gras* for himself."

I asked him abruptly:

"You are a father, sir?"

[1] Waterspout.

He answered:

"No, sir."

I felt suddenly confused, as if I had committed a gross breach of taste, and I added:

"I beg your pardon. I had imagined that you were, from hearing your man speak of the toys. One hears things without listening, and draws conclusions in spite of oneself."

He smiled, then murmured:

"No, I am not even married. I never got any farther than the preliminaries."

I had the air of suddenly remembering.

"Oh . . . that's so, you were engaged when I knew you, engaged to Mlle. de Mandal, I think."

"Yes, sir, you have an excellent memory."

I became outrageously audacious, and added:

"Yes, I think I remember also having heard that Mlle. de Mandal had married Monsieur . . . Monsieur . . ."

He uttered the name placidly:

"M. de Fleurel."

"Yes, that's it. Yes . . . I even remember having heard your wound spoken of in this connection."

I looked him full in the face; and he blushed.

His full, swollen face, which the constant accession of blood had already made purple, took on a still deeper hue.

He replied eagerly, with the abrupt earnestness of a man who is pleading a cause lost beforehand, lost in his mind and in his heart, but which he wishes to carry in the eyes of the world.

"People are wrong, sir, to couple my name with Mme. de Fleurel's. When I returned from the war, without my feet, alas, I would never, never have allowed her to become my wife. Was such a thing possible? One does not marry to make a parade of generosity, sir: one marries to live every day, every hour, every minute, every second with one man; and if this man is deformed, as I am, to marry him is to be condemned to a suffering which will last until death. Oh, I understand, I admire all sacrifices, all devotions when they have a limit, but I do not countenance a woman's renunciation of the whole of a life in which she hopes for happiness, of all joys, of all dreams, just to satisfy the admiration of the gallery. When I hear, on the floor of my room, the clatter of my stumps and my crutches, the noise like a mill wheel that I make with every step I take, I feel exasperated to the verge of strangling my servant. Do you think one could allow a woman to bear what one cannot endure oneself? And then, do you suppose they're pretty, my stumps of legs? . . ."

He was silent. What could I say to him? I felt that he was right. Could I blame her, despise her, even give judgment against him, or against her? No. And yet? This denouement, conforming as it did to convention, the golden rule, truth, and appearances, did not satisfy my appetite for romance. Those heroic stumps called for a splendid sacrifice of which I had been deprived, and I felt cheated thereby.

I asked him abruptly:

"Mme. de Fleurel has children?"

"Yes, a girl and two boys. I am taking these toys to them. Her husband and she have been very good to me."

The train was climbing the hills of St. Germain. It ran through the tunnels, entered the station, came to a standstill.

I was going to offer my arm to help the mutilated officer to descend when two hands were stretched out to him through the open door.

"How do you do, my dear Revalière?"

"Ah, how do you do, Fleurel?"

Behind the man, his wife stood smiling, radiant, still pretty, waving greetings with her gloved fingers. Beside her, a little girl was jumping for joy, and two small boys were staring with greedy eyes at the drum and the gun emerging from the carriage rack in their father's hands.

When the cripple reached the platform, all the children embraced him. Then they set off, and the small girl lovingly held the polished crossbar of one crutch in her tiny hands, as she would have been able to hold her big friend's thumb when she walked beside him.

SEMILLANTE

The widow of Paolo Saverini lived alone with her son in a poor little house on the ramparts of Bonifacio. The town, built upon the side of the mountain, suspended in spots above the sea, overlooks, through a defile bristling with rocks, the lowest part of Sardinia. At its foot, on the other side, and almost entirely surrounding it, is a cut in the cliff, which resembles a gigantic corridor and serves as a port; it leads up to the first houses (after a long circuit between the two abrupt walls), the little Italian or Sardinian fishing boats, and every two weeks the old, broken-winded steamer that plies between there and Ajaccio.

Upon the white mountains the bunch of houses makes a spot whiter still. They have the appearance of nests of wild birds, fastened thus upon this rock, overlooking this terrible passageway where ships scarcely dare venture. The wind, without repose, harasses the sea, harasses the bare coast, which is nibbled by it until it has but little vegetation; it rushes into the defile, whose two sides it strips bare. The track of pale foam, fastened to black points on the innumerable rocks which pierce the waves, has the look of bits of cloth floating and palpitating upon the surface of the water.

The house of the widow Saverini, soldered to the edge of the cliff, had three windows opening upon this wild and desolated horizon.

She lived there alone with her son Antoine and their dog Semillante, a great, thin beast with long, coarse hair, of a race that watches the herds. This dog served the young man for hunting.

One evening after a dispute, Antoine Saverini was killed traitorously with a blow of a knife by Nicholas Ravolati who, the same night, went over to Sardinia.

When the old woman received the body of her child, which some passers-by brought to her, she did not weep but remained a long time motionless, looking at him. Then, extending her wrinkled hand upon the dead body, she promised revenge. She did not wish anyone to remain with her, and she shut herself up with the body and the dog.

The dog howled. She howled, this beast, in a continuous fashion at the foot of the bed, her head extended toward her master, her tail held fast between her legs. She no more stirred than did the mother, who, hanging now upon the body, her eyes fixed, was weeping great tears while gazing at him.

The young man, upon his back, clothed in his coat of gray cloth, torn and bloody about the breast, seemed to be asleep. And there was blood everywhere: on his shirt, drawn up in the first moments, on his waistcoat, his trousers, upon his face and his hands. Little clots of blood had coagulated in his beard and in his hair.

The old mother began to speak to him. At the sound of her voice the dog was silent.

"Come, come," she said; "you shall be avenged, my little one, my boy, my poor child. Sleep, sleep; you shall be avenged, do you hear? It is your mother who promises! And she always keeps her word, does your mother, as you know well."

And gently she bent over him, gluing her cold lips to his dead mouth. Then Semillante began to groan again. She uttered a long, plaintive monotone, harrowing and terrible.

There they remained, the corpse, the woman and the beast, until morning.

Antoine Saverini was buried the next day, and soon no one spoke of him more in Bonifacio.

He had left no brother, no near relatives. There was no man to follow up the revenge. Alone, the mother thought of it, the old woman.

On the other side of the defile she saw each morning and evening a white spot on the coast. It was the little Sardinian village, Longosardo, where Corsican bandits took refuge when too closely pursued. They almost peopled this hamlet opposite the shore of their own country and awaited there the moment of returning, of going back again to the brakes. It was in this village, she knew, that Nicholas Ravolati had taken refuge.

All alone the whole day long, seated before her window, she would look down there and think of vengeance. How could she do it without anyone to help, infirm as she was and so near death? But she had promised; she had sworn it upon his dead body. She could not forget; she must not delay. How should she accomplish it? She could not sleep at night; she had no repose, no ease; she sought obstinately. The dog slept at her feet and, sometimes raising her head, howled to the distance. Since her master was no longer there, she often howled thus, as if she were calling him, as if her soul, that of an inconsolable beast, had preserved a remembrance of him that nothing could efface.

One night, as Semillante began to howl in this way, the mother suddenly had an idea, a savage, vindictive, ferocious idea. She meditated upon it until morning; then, rising at the approach of day, she betook herself to the church. She prayed, prostrate upon the floor, humbled before God, supplicating him to aid her, to sustain her, to give to her poor, spent body force that would be sufficient to avenge the death of her son.

Then she returned. She had in her yard an old barrel with the head knocked in, which caught the rain from the gutters. She emptied it and turned it over, making it fast to the soil by means of some stakes and stones; then she chained Semillante in this niche and went into her house.

Now she walked about constantly in her room without repose, her eye fixed upon the coast of Sardinia. He was down there, was that assassin.

The dog howled all day and all night. The old woman carried her some water in the morning in a bowl. But nothing more; no soup, no bread.

The day slipped away. Semillante, weakened from want of food, slept. The next day she had shining eyes and bristling hair; she pulled desperately at her chain.

Still the old woman gave her nothing to eat. The beast became furious, baying with raucous voice. The night passed away thus. Then at the break of day Mother Saverini went to the house of a neighbor and begged him to give her two bundles of straw. She took some old clothes that her husband had formerly worn and filled them full of the fodder to simulate a human body.

Having stuck a stick in the ground before Semillante's niche, she bound the manikin to it, giving him the appearance of standing. Then she formed a head by means of a package of old linen.

The dog, surprised, looked at the straw man and was silent, although devoured with hunger.

Then the old woman went to the butcher's and bought a long piece of black pudding. She returned home, lighted a wood fire in her yard and cooked this pudding. Semillante, excited, bounded about and frothed at the mouth, her eyes fixed upon the meat, the fumes of which entered her stomach.

Next the woman made a cravat for the straw man of this smoking sausage. She wound it many times about his neck, as if to make it penetrate him. When this was done she unchained the dog.

With a formidable leap the beast reached the manikin's throat and, her paws upon his shoulders, began to tear him to pieces. She fell back, a piece of her prey in her mouth, then leaped upon him again, sinking her teeth in the cords, snatching some particles of nourishment, fell back again and rebounded, enraged. She tore away the face with great blows of the teeth, tearing into shreds the whole neck.

The old woman, mute and motionless, looked on, her eyes lighting up. She rechained the beast, made her fast two days again and repeated this strange operation.

For three months she accustomed the dog to this kind of struggle, to a repast conquered by tooth and claw. She did not chain her now but set her upon the manikin with a gesture.

She taught her to tear him, to devour him, even without anything eatable hung around his throat. She would give her afterward, as a recompense, the pudding she had cooked for her.

Whenever she perceived the manikin Semillante growled and turned her eyes toward her mistress who would cry: "Go!" in a whistling tone, at the same time raising her finger.

When she thought the right time had come, Mother Saverini went to confession and to communion one morning in ecstatic fervor; then, having clothed herself in male attire so that she looked like a feeble old man, she went with a Sardinian fisherman, who took her and her dog to the other side of the defile.

She had, in a sack of cloth, a large piece of pudding. Semillante had fasted for two days. Every few moments the old woman made her smell of the pleasant food and endeavored to excite her.

They entered into Longosardo. The Corsican went into a wineshop. She presented herself at a baker's and asked where Nicholas Ravolati lived. He had taken his old trade, that of a carpenter. He was working alone at the back of his shop.

The old woman opened the door and called:

"Hey, Nicholas!"

He turned around; then, loosing the dog, she cried out:

"Go! Go! Devour him! Devour him!"

The animal, excited, threw herself upon him and seized him by the throat. The man extended his arms, clinched her and rolled upon the floor. For some minutes he twisted himself, beating the soil with his feet; then he remained motionless, while Semillante dug at his neck until it was in shreds.

Two neighbors, seated before their doors, recalled perfectly having seen an old man go out of the shop with a black dog at his side, which was eating, as he went along, something brown that his master gave him.

That evening the old woman returned to her house. She slept well that night.

IN PORT

I

Having left Havre on May 3, 1882, for a voyage in Chinese waters, the three-masted sailing ship *Notre Dame des Vents* re-entered Marseille harbor on August 8, 1886, after a four years' voyage. She had discharged her original cargo in the Chinese port to which she had been chartered, and had there and then picked up a new freight for Buenos Aires, and from thence had shipped cargo for Brazil.

Various other voyages, not to speak of damages, repairs, several months spent becalmed, storms that blew her out of her course, and all the accidents, adventures and misadventures of the sea, had detained far from her land this three-masted Norman boat now returned to Marseille with a hold full of tin boxes containing American preserved foods.

At the beginning of the voyage she had on board, besides the captain and the mate, fourteen sailors, eight Normans and six Bretons. At the end only five Bretons and four Normans remained; the Breton had died at sea; the four Normans, who had disappeared in various circumstances, had been replaced by two Americans, a Negro and a Norwegian shanghaied one evening in a Singapore den.

The great ship, sails furled, yards forming a cross with mast stem, drawn by a Marseille tug that panted along before her, rolled in a slight swell that died gently away in the calm waters behind her; she passed in front of the Château d'If, then under all the gray rocks of the roadstead over which the setting sun flung a reek of gold, and entered the old harbor where, lying by each other alongside the quays, were gathered ships from all corners of the globe, huddled together, large and small, of all shapes and riggings, like a fish soup of boats in this too confined basin, full of foul water, where the hulls grazed and rubbed against each other, for all the world as if they were pickled in salt-water liquor.

Notre Dame des Vents took her place between an Italian brig and an English schooner which drew apart to make way for their comrade; then, when all the formalities of customs and harbor had been complied with, the captain gave two thirds of his crew shore leave for the evening.

It was already night. The lights of Marseille were lit. In the warmth of the summer evening, an odor of garlic-flavored cooking hung over the noisy city, alive with the sound of voices, rumblings, clatterings, all the gaiety of the South.

As soon as they felt land under them, the ten men who had been tossed for months on the sea began to walk very carefully, with hesitant steps like creatures strayed out of their element, unaccustomed to cities, two by two in a procession.

They rolled along, taking their bearings, following the scent down the bystreets that opened on to the harbor, their blood on fire with a hunger for love that had grown stronger and stronger in their bodies throughout their last sixty-six days at sea. The Normans marched ahead, led by Célestin Duclos, a tall, shrewd, sturdy young fellow who captained the others whenever they set foot on shore. He found out the best places, devised ways and means to his liking, and refrained from risking himself too readily in the brawls so common between sailors on shore. But when he did get involved in one, he was absolutely fearless.

After hesitating some little time between the obscure streets that ran down to the sea like sewers, from which rose a heavy smell, as it were the very breath of hovels, Célestin decided on a sort of winding passage where lighted lamps, bearing enormous numbers on their frosted colored glass, were hung out above the doors. Under the narrow arch of the doorways, women in aprons, looking like servant girls and seated on rush-bottomed chairs, got up at their approach, made three steps to the edge of the stream that ran down the middle of the street, and stood right across the path of the line of men that advanced slowly, singing and chuckling, excited already by the neighborhood of these prostitutes' cells.

Sometimes in the depths of a lobby a second door padded with brown leather opened abruptly, and behind it appeared a stout half-naked woman, whose heavy thighs and plump arms were sharply outlined under a coarse, tight-fitting shift of white cotton. Her short petticoat looked like a hooped girdle, and the soft flesh of her bosom, arms, and shoulders made a rosy patch against a bodice of black velvet edged with gold lace. She called to them from far off: "Are you coming in, dearies?" and sometimes came out herself to clutch one of them, pulling him towards her doorway with all her might, clinging to him like a spider dragging in a body bigger than itself. The man, excited by her touch, resisted feebly, and the others halted to watch him, hesitating between their desire to go in without further delay and their desire to make this appetizing stroll last a little longer. Then, when after the most exhausting effort the woman had dragged the sailor to the threshold of her abode, into which the whole company were about to plunge after him, Célestin Duclos, who was a judge of such houses, would suddenly cry: "Don't go in there, Marchand, it's not the right one."

Whereupon, obedient to this command, the man disengaged himself with brutal violence, and the friends fell again into line, pursued by the obscene abuse of the exasperated women while other women, all the way down the passage ahead of them, came out of their doors, attracted by the noise, and poured out hoarse-voiced enticing appeals. They went on their way, growing more and more excited, between the cajoling cries and seductive charms offered by the chorus of love's doorkeepers down the length of the street before them, and the vile curses flung after them by the chorus behind, the despised chorus of disappointed women. Now and then they met other companies of men, soldiers marching along with swords clattering against their legs, more sailors, a solitary citizen or so, a few shop assistants. Everywhere opened other narrow streets, starred with evil beacon lights. They walked steadily through this labyrinth of hovels on the greasy cobbled streets, oozing streams of foul water, between houses full of women's flesh.

At last Duclos made up his mind and, halting in front of a fairly decent-looking house, marshaled his company into it.

II

The entertainment lacked nothing! For four hours the ten sailors took their fill of love and wine. Six months' pay vanished on it.

They were installed, lords of all they surveyed, in the big saloon, regarding with unfriendly eyes the ordinary clients who installed themselves at little tables in corners, where one of the women who were still disengaged, dressed like over-grown babies or music-hall singers, ran to attend on them, and then sat down beside them.

Each man had on arrival selected his companion whom he retained through-out the evening, for the lower orders are not promiscuous. Three tables had been dragged together, and after the first round of drinks, the procession, fallen into two ranks and increased by as many women as there were sailors, re-formed on the staircase. The noise made by the four feet of each couple was heard for some time on the wooden steps, while this long file of lovers plunged through the narrow door that led to the bedrooms.

Then they came down again for more drinks; went up again, came down again.

Now, very nearly drunk, they began to bawl. Each man, with reddened eyes, his fancy on his knee, sang or shouted, hammering on the table with doubled fists, rolled the wine round his throat, giving full play to the beast in man. In the midst of them, Célestin Duclos, holding tight a tall red-cheeked wench, seated astride on his knee, regarded her ardently. Not so drunk as the others—not that he had drunk any less—he could still think of more than the one thing, and more human than the rest, he tried to talk to her. His thoughts were a little elusive, slipping from his grasp, returning and disappearing before he could remember just what he had wanted to say.

He laughed, repeating:

"Then, then . . . you've been here a long time."

"Six months," replied the girl.

He appeared pleased with her, as if that were a proof of good conduct, and went on:

"Do you like this life?"

She hesitated, then spoke resignedly:

"One gets through with it. It's no worse than anything else. Being a servant or walking the streets, they're both dirty jobs."

He seemed to approve this truth too.

"You're not from these parts?" said he.

She shook her head without speaking.

"Do you come from far?"

She nodded, still silent.

"Where from?"

She seemed to search her mind, trying to collect her memories, then she mur-mured:

"From Perpignan."

Again he showed great satisfaction, and said:

"Oh, yes."

In her turn she asked him:

"You're a sailor, aren't you?"

"Yes, my sweet."

"Have you come a long way?"

"Oh, yes! I've seen countries, ports, and all that."

"I suppose you sailed round the world?"

"I dare say, more like twice than once."

Again she seemed to hesitate, searching in her mind for something forgotten, then, in a rather altered, grave voice, she said:

"You have come across a good many ships in your voyages?"

"I have that, my sweet."

"Perhaps you've even come across *Notre Dame des Vents?*"

He chuckled.

"No later than a week ago."

She turned pale, all the blood ebbing from her cheeks, and asked:

"Is that true, really true?"

"As true as I'm telling you."

"You're not telling me a lie?"

He lifted his hand.

"God's truth I'm not," said he.

"Then do you know whether Célestin Duclos is still with her?"

He was surprised, uneasy, and wanted to know more before replying.

"Do you know him?"

She became suspicious too.

"No, not me, it's some woman who knows him."

"One of the women here?"

"No, outside."

"In the street?"

"No, another."

"What woman?"

"Oh, just a woman, a woman like me."

"What's this woman want with him?"

"How should I know, what d'you think?"

They stared into each other's eyes, trying to read the thoughts behind, guessing that something serious was going to come of this.

He went on:

"Can I see this woman?"

"What would you say to her?"

"I'd say . . . I'd say . . . that I have seen Célestin Duclos."

"Is he all right?"

"As right as you or me, he's a lad."

She was silent again, collecting her thoughts, then, very slowly, asked:

"Where was she bound for, the *Notre Dame des Vents?*"

"Well, to Marseille."

She could not repress a start.

"Really?"

"Yes, really."

"Do you know Duclos?"

"Yes. I know him."

She hesitated again, then said softly:

"Good. That's a good thing."

"What d'you want with him?"

"Listen, you can tell him . . . nothing!"

He continued to stare at her, more and more uneasy. He must know the whole now.

"Do you know him then?"

"No," said she.

"Then what d'you want with him?"

She came to a sudden decision, got up, ran to the bar where the proprietress sat enthroned, seized a lemon, cut it open, pouring the juice into a glass, then filled up the glass with plain water and, bringing it to him, said:

"Drink this."

"Why?"

"To sober you up. After that I'll talk to you."

He drank obediently, wiped his lips with the back of his hand, and declared:

"That's all right, I'm listening to you."

"You must promise me not to tell him that you have seen me, nor who told you what I am just going to tell you. Swear it."

He lifted his hand, with a knowing air.

"I swear it."

"On the good God himself?"

"Yes, on the good God."

"Well, you're to tell him that his father is dead, that his mother is dead, that his brother is dead, all three of them in the same month, of typhoid fever, in January, 1883, three and a half years ago."

And now it was he who felt the blood rush through his body, and for some moments he sat there, so overcome that he could find nothing to say in reply, then he began to have doubts and asked:

"Are you sure?"

"I'm quite sure."

"Who told it to you?"

She put her hands on his shoulders and, peering into his eyes, said:

"You swear you won't give me away?"

"I swear it."

"I'm his sister."

Her name broke involuntarily from his mouth:

"Françoise?"

She regarded him again fixedly, then, overwhelmed by a crazy fear, by a profound feeling of horror, murmured under her breath, against his mouth:

"Oh, oh, is it you, Célestin?"

They sat rigid, eyes staring into eyes.

Round them, the sailors went on shouting. The noise of glasses, fists, and heels beating in tune to the choruses, and the shrill cries of the women, mingled with the uproarious songs.

He felt her against him, held close to him, warm and terrified, his sister! Then, in a mere whisper, afraid lest someone overhear him, so low that she herself could hardly hear:

"My God, I've done a fine thing!"

Her eyes filled with tears in an instant, and she stammered:

"It's not my fault, is it?"

But he said abruptly:

"So they're dead?"

"Yes, they're dead."

"Dad, and mother, and my brother?"

"All three in the same month, as I've just told you. I was left alone, with nothing but what I stood up in, seeing that I owed money to the chemist and the doctor and for burying the three bodies, which I paid off with the furniture.

"After that I went as servant to old Cacheux, you know him, the cripple. I was just exactly fifteen then, seeing that you went away when I was not quite fourteen. I got into trouble with him. You're a fool when you're young. Then I went as housemaid to a solicitor; he seduced me too and set me up in a room in Havre. It wasn't long before he stopped coming; I spent three days without food and then, since I couldn't get any work, I went into a house, like many another. I've seen the world too, I have, and a dirty world at that! Rouen, Evreux, Lille, Bordeaux, Perpignan, Nice, and now here I am at Marseille!"

Tears poured out of her eyes and her nose, wetting her cheeks, and ran down into her mouth.

She went on:

"I thought you were dead too, my poor Célestin."

He said:

"I would never have known you again, you were so little then, and now you're so big, but how was it you didn't recognize me?"

She made a despairing gesture.

"I see so many men that they all look alike to me."

He was still staring into her eyes in the grip of a confused emotion, an emotion so overwhelming that he wanted to cry like a beaten child. He still held her in his arms, sitting astride his legs, his hands spread out on the girl's back, and now by dint of staring at her, he recognized her at last, the little sister left in the country with the three she had watched die while he tossed at sea.

All at once he took her new-found face in his great sailor's paws and began to embrace her as a man embraces his flesh and blood. Then sobs, a man's terrible sobs, long-drawn surging cries, rose in his throat like the hiccups of a drunken man.

He stammered:

"To see you, to see you again, Françoise, my little Françoise . . ."

Suddenly he leaped to his feet and began to swear in a dreadful voice, bringing his fist down on the table with such violence that the overturned glasses broke to atoms. Then he took three steps, staggered, flung out his arms and fell face downwards. He rolled on the floor, shouting, beating the ground with arms and legs, and utterings such groans that they were like the death rattle of a man in agony.

All the sailors looked at him and laughed.

"He isn't half drunk," said one.

"Put him to bed," said another; "if he goes out they'll stick him in jail."

Then, as he had money in his pockets, the proprietress offered a bed, and the other sailors, themselves so drunk that they couldn't stand, hoisted him up the narrow staircase to the bedroom of the woman who had lately received him, and who remained sitting on a chair, at the foot of that guilty couch, weeping over him, until morning.

SUICIDES

Scarcely a day goes by without the newspapers containing an account like this:

Tenants of No. 40 B—— Street were startled Wednesday night by the report of two shots that proceeded from the apartment occupied by M. X. The door was burst open and he was found on the floor in a pool of blood, his hand still grasping the revolver with which he committed suicide. M. X was fifty-seven years old and prosperous. He had everything to live for, and no reason can be ascribed for his tragic act.

What grief and secret despair, what burning sorrows, lead these people, who are supposed to be happy, to end their lives? Financial troubles and love tragedies are hinted at, but as nothing really precise ever becomes known, these deaths are pronounced "mysterious."

A letter that was found on the table of one of these suicides who wrote it during his last night on earth, with the loaded pistol within his reach, has come into our possession. We deem it interesting, though it reveals no great tragedy such as one usually expects to find at the bottom of these rash acts. It only tells of the slow succession of the little ills of life, of the inevitable disorganization of a solitary existence weaned from its illusions; it makes clear those tragic endings which no others but people of high-strung, supersensitive temperaments can understand.

This is the letter:

"It is midnight. When I finish this letter I intend to destroy myself. Why? I will endeavor to explain, not for those who read this, but for myself, in order to strengthen my failing courage and to convince myself of the now-fatal necessity of my determination which, if not carried out tonight, could only be deferred.

"I was brought up by parents who believed in everything, and so I, too, believed. My dream lasted a long time. But now its last illusions have fled.

"The past few years have wrought a great change in me. The things that used to seem most alluring and desirable have lost their attraction. The true meaning of life has dawned upon me in all its brutal reality; the true reason of love disgusts me even with poetical sentiment.

"We are nothing but the eternal toys of illusions, as foolish as they are charming, which reblossom as soon as they fade.

"Getting on in years, I became resigned to the utter shallowness of life, to the uselessness of any effort, to the vanity of any hope, when suddenly tonight after dinner I viewed the futility of everything in a different light.

"Formerly I was happy. Everything charmed me; the women I met in the streets, the streets themselves, my own home, even the shape of my clothes, was a subject of interest to me. But finally the repetition of these visions bored and annoyed me; I feel like a theatergoer seeing the same play night after night.

"During the last thirty years I have arisen at the same hour, have dined at the same place, eating the same things, served at the same times by different waiters.

"I have tried to travel! But the sensation of forlornness that came over me in strange places deterred me. I felt so isolated and small on this immense earth that I hastened to return home.

"But the furnishings of my apartment that have not been changed in thirty-odd years, the worn places on the chairs which I recollect when they were new, even the odor of the place (for after a while each home acquires a distinctive atmosphere) gave me every night an awful, nauseating sense of melancholy.

"Does not everything repeat itself in an eternal, heart-rending fashion? The way in which I put my key into the latch hole, the spot where I find the match-box, the first glance I give the room after striking a light, all these little things make me desire to fling myself out of the window, so as to end for good and all the series of monotonous incidents which fill life and from which there is no escape.

"Every day when shaving in front of my little mirror I feel like cutting my throat; the same face with soap on its cheeks that stares at me has driven me many a time to cry out from sheer despondency.

"Today I hardly care to meet the people whose society I used to enjoy, because I know too well what they are going to say and what I shall reply; the trend of their thoughts is as familiar as the drift of their arguments. Each brain is like a circus ring around which gallops a poor, imprisoned horse. No matter what our efforts or dodges may be, we cannot escape from the circular ring, which has no unexpected turns, no door opening on the unknown. We must go around forever through the same joys, the same jokes, the same beliefs, habits, disgusts.

"The fog was dreadful tonight. It covered the boulevard, dimming the gaslights that shone like so many smoky candles. A heavier weight than usual oppressed me. My digestion was probably in bad shape. A good digestion is a great blessing. It gives to artists inspiration, to thinkers clear ideas, to young men amorous desires and to everyone happiness.

"It lets us eat our fill and, after all, this is the greatest satisfaction. A weak stomach predisposes one to skepticism and unbelief and incites bad dreams and morbidity. I have noticed it very, very often. Perhaps I would not care to die to-night if my digestion were perfect.

"When I seated myself in the chair in which I have sat every night the past thirty years, I glanced around and felt so depressed that I thought I should become distracted.

"I wondered how I could escape from myself? To be occupied appeared to me even more intolerable than to remain inactive. I had the idea of putting my old papers in order. I have intended to arrange them for a long time. For thirty years I have flung letters and bills together in the same drawer, and the confusion resulting therefrom has often caused me a great deal of trouble. But the mere idea of straightening out anything gives me such mental and physical distress that I never have had sufficient courage to undertake the odious task.

"So I sat down at my desk and opened it, intending to look over my old papers and to destroy some. At first I felt quite helpless before the heaps of yellowed leaves, but finally I extricated one of them.

"Never, if you value your life, dare touch the desk or the tomb that contains old letters! And if by chance you should open it, close your eyes so as to shut out the letters, lest a long-forgotten but suddenly recognized handwriting awaken a world of recollections; take the fatal pages and throw them into the fire, and when they are ashes stamp them into invisible dust or else you will be lost—as I have been—for the last hour.

"The first letters I picked out did not interest me. They were from men I meet once in a while and for whom I feel no great interest. But all at once an envelope attracted my eyes. It bore my name written in a broad, firm hand; tears filled my eyes. Here was a letter from my dearest friend, the one in whom I used to confide in my youth and who knew my hopes; he arose before me so clearly with his outstretched hand and good-natured smile that a shudder ran through my frame. Yes, the dead come back, for I saw him! Our memory is a world far more perfect than the real universe, for it brings to life those who have gone forever.

"With misty eyes and trembling hands I read over all the letters, while my poor crushed heart throbbed with a pain so acute that I groaned aloud like a man whose limbs are being tortured.

"I went over my whole life, and it was like floating along a familiar river. I recognized people whose names long ago had been blotted from my mind. Only their faces had stamped themselves upon my memory. My mother's letters revived recollections of the old servants of our household, brought back all the little insignificant details that impress themselves on a child's brain.

"Yes, I even saw my mother as she looked in the gowns of years ago, with the changed appearance she would assume with each new style of hairdressing she successively adopted. She haunted me most in a silk gown of some gorgeous pattern, and I remembered what she said to me one day, wearing that robe: 'Robert, my child, if you fail to hold yourself erect you will be round-shouldered all your life.'

"On opening another drawer I suddenly gazed on my love trinkets—a satin slipper, a torn handkerchief, several locks of hair, some pressed flowers, even a garter.

"My romances, whose heroines, if still living, must have white hair, arose before me with all the bitterness of loved things forever gone. Oh, the young brows shaded by golden hair, the clasped hands, the speaking glances, the throbbing hearts, the smile that promises the lips and the lips that promise all—then the first kiss—long, unending, with no thought but of the immense ecstasy to come!

"I grasped with both hands the cherished tokens and I kissed them passionately. My harassed soul beheld each one of my loves at the moment of sweet surrender—and I suffered worse torments than those imagined in the descriptions of hell.

"A single letter remained. It had been written by me and was dictated fifty years ago by my teacher.

"It ran:

"MY DEAR MAMMA:

"*I am seven years old today. As it is the age of reason, I want to thank you for having brought me into this world.*

"*Your loving little son,*
"ROBERT.

"This was the last. I had arrived at the very beginning of my life and I turned to face the prospect of the remaining years. I see nothing but a hideous and lonely old age with all its accompanying disablements—all is over, over, over! Nobody to care for me.

"The revolver lies here on the table. I am loading it. Never read over your old letters."

And this is the reason why so many men kill themselves, while one searches their lives in vain for the discovery of some hidden tragedy.

A PORTRAIT

"Look, there's Milial," said someone near me. I looked at the man they were pointing out, for I had long wanted to make the acquaintance of this Don Juan.

He was no longer young. His gray hair, a shaggy gray, was a little like one of those skin caps that certain northern races wear on their heads, and his fine, rather long beard, falling to his chest, also bore a resemblance to fur. He was talking to a woman, leaning towards her, speaking in a low voice, while he looked at her with a tender gaze, eloquent of homage and affection.

I knew his manner of life, or at least such of it as was known to people. He had been loved madly, many times, and his name had been mixed up in various dramas that had taken place. He was spoken of as a very fascinating, almost irresistible man. When, in order to discover whence came these powers he had, I questioned the women who were loudest in his praise, they invariably replied, after having thought about it for a while:

"I don't know . . . it's a question of charm."

Certainly, he was not handsome. He had none of the elegances which we imagine to be attributes of the conquerors of feminine hearts. I used to wonder, with much interest, in what lay his fascination. In his wit? . . . No one had ever quoted his sayings to me, nor even celebrated his intelligence. . . . In his glance? . . . Perhaps. . . . Or in his voice? . . . Some people's voices have sensuous and irresistible attractions, the savor of exquisite foods. One hungers to hear them, and the sound of their words penetrates our sensibilities, like an epicurean dish.

A friend was passing; I asked him:

"Do you know M. Milial?"

"Yes."

"Please introduce us."

A minute later we were exchanging handshakes and conversing between two doors. What he said was just, pleasant to listen to, but in no way superlative. He had indeed a beautiful voice, soft, caressing, musical; but I have heard voices more taking, more moving. One listened to it with pleasure, as one watches the flowing of a pleasant stream. No great effort of thought was necessary to follow it, no hidden meaning roused one's curiosity, no anticipation kept one's interest on the alert. His conversation was actually tranquilizing, and awoke in us neither a lively desire to respond and contradict, nor a delighted approbation.

It was, moreover, as easy to make a reply to him as to listen. The reply rose to one's lips of its own accord, as soon as he had finished talking, and the phrases ran towards him as if what he had said made them issue quite naturally from one's mouth.

I was shortly struck by a reflection. I had known him for a quarter of an hour, and it seemed to me that he was an old friend of mine, that everything about him had been familiar to me for a long time: his face, his gestures, his voice, his ideas.

Abruptly, after a few moments of talk, he seemed to me to have established himself on an intimate footing. All doors between us were open, and perhaps, of my own volition, I would—had he solicited them—have made confidences which ordinarily are given only to one's oldest friends.

There was certainly a mystery about it. The barriers that separate all creatures, and which time removes one by one, when sympathy, like tastes, an identical intellectual culture, and constant relationship have little by little unpadlocked them, seemed not to exist between him and me, nor, doubtless, between him and all people, men and women, whom chance threw in his path.

At the end of half an hour, we separated, agreeing to see each other again often, and he gave me his address after having invited me to dine with him the next day but one.

I forgot the hour and arrived too early: he had not come in. A correct and silent servant showed me into a beautiful drawing room, a rather dim, intimate, studied room. I felt at home there, as in my own house. How often I have remarked the effect of the place in which one lives on one's mind and disposition. There are rooms where one always feels stupid: there are others, on the contrary, where one always feels alert. Some rooms sadden us, although they are light, white and gilded: others make for gaiety, although they are hung in quiet colors. Our eye, like our heart, has its hates and its likings, which often it does not openly declare to us, imposing them secretly and stealthily on our imaginations. The harmony of furniture and walls, the style of our whole surroundings, act instantly on our intellectual nature as the air of forest, sea, or mountain modifies our physical nature.

I was seated on a divan completely covered with cushions, and I felt suddenly sustained, borne up, held in place by these small silk-covered sacks of feathers, as if the form and place of my body had been impressed beforehand on this furniture.

Then I looked round. There was nothing startling in the room; it was filled with lovely unobtrusive things, furniture at once rare and simple, oriental curtains that did not seem to have come from the Louvre but from the interior of a harem, and, facing me, the portrait of a woman. It was a portrait of medium size, showing the head and upper part of the body, and the hands holding a book. She was young, bareheaded, her hair arranged in smooth folds, and she was smiling with a faint sadness. It may have been because she was bareheaded, or it may well have been due to the effect of her very artless charm, but never had a woman's portrait seemed to me so much at home as did this portrait in this place. Almost all those I know are definitely on show, whether the lady is in elaborate dress, with her hair becomingly arranged and an air of being fully conscious that she is posing before the painter in the first place, and ultimately before all the people who will look at her, or whether she has adopted an attitude of abandon, and attired herself with careful informality.

Some are standing, majestic creatures, in all their beauty, with an air of hauteur which they cannot have sustained for long in the ordinary course of their lives; others languish in the immobility of the painted canvas; and all of them have some trifle, a flower or a jewel, a fold of their gown or their lips, which one feels to have been arranged by the painter, for the sake of an effect. Whether they wear a hat, a lace scarf on their head, or simply their hair, they convey the impression of something just a little unnatural. Why? One doesn't know, since one does not know them at all, but the impression is there. They have the air of paying a visit somewhere, among people whom they wish to please: before whom they wish to appear to their best advantage: and they have studied their attitude, sometimes a modest one, sometimes arrogant.

What shall I say of this portrait? She was in her own home and alone. Yes, she was alone, for she was smiling as people smile when they think in solitude on something at once sad and sweet, and not as they smile when they are being looked at. She was so much alone and so much in her own place, that she created solitude in this huge room, absolute solitude. She dwelt in it, filled it, she alone gave it life: a crowd of people might enter there, and all of them speak, laugh, even sing: she would be there, forever alone, smiling a solitary smile, and alone she would bring it alive with her pictured gaze.

Her gaze was unique, too. It was turned directly to me, caressing and steady, but it did not see me. All portraits know that they are being contemplated, and they answer with their eyes, with eyes that see and think, that follow us unwinkingly from the moment we enter the room where they inhabit until the moment we leave it.

This portrait did not see me, did not see anything, although its glance was bent directly on me. I recalled Baudelaire's amazing line:

Et tes yeux attirants comme ceux d'un portrait.

They did indeed attract me in an irresistible fashion, they disturbed me in some strange, powerful, novel way, these painted eyes that had lived, that perhaps were still living. Oh, what infinite soothing charm—like a passing breeze, seductive as the fading sky of a rose and blue and lilac twilight, and faintly melancholy like the night that follows on its heels—came from that somber frame and those impenetrable eyes. Those eyes, those eyes created by a few strokes of the brush, held in their depths the mystery of that which seems to be and is not, of that which a woman's look can express, of that which wakes in our hearts the first stirring of love.

The door opened. M. Milial came in. He apologized for being late. I apologized for being early. Then I said to him:

"Is it indiscreet to ask you who this woman is?"

He answered:

"It is my mother, who died very young."

And at that I understand whence came this man's inexplicable charm.

A MIRACLE

Dr. Bonenfant was searching his memory, saying, half aloud: "A Christmas story—some remembrance of Christmas?"

Suddenly he cried: "Yes, I have one, and a strange one, too: it is a fantastic story. I have seen a miracle! Yes, ladies, a miracle, and on Christmas night."

It astonishes you to hear me speak thus, a man who believes scarcely anything. Nevertheless, I have seen a miracle! I have seen it, I tell you, seen, with my own eyes; that is what I call seeing.

Was I very much surprised, you ask? Not at all, because if I do not believe from your viewpoint I believe in faith, and I know that it can remove mountains. I could cite many examples, but I might make you indignant, and I should risk diminishing the effect of my story.

In the first place, I must confess that if I had not been convinced and converted by what I have seen, I have at least been strongly moved, and I am going to strive to tell it to you naïvely, as if I had the credulity of an Auvergnat.

I was then a country doctor, living in the town of Rolleville, on the plains of Normandy. The winter that year was terrible. By the end of November the snow came after a week of heavy frosts. One could see from afar the great snow clouds coming from the north, and then the descent of the white flakes commenced. In one night the whole plain was in its winding sheet. Farms, isolated in their square inclosures behind their curtains of great trees powdered with hoarfrost, seemed to sleep under the accumulation of this thick, light covering.

No noise could reach this dead country. The crows alone in large flocks outlined long festoons in the sky, living their lives to no purpose, swooping down upon the livid fields and picking at the snow with their great beaks. There was nothing to be heard but the vague, continued whisper of this white powder as it persistently fell. This lasted for eight days and then stopped. The earth had on its back a mantle five feet in thickness. And during the next three weeks a sky spread itself out over this smooth, white mass, hard and glistening with frost, which was clear blue crystal by day and at night all studded with stars, as if the hoarfrost grew by their light.

The plain, the hedges, the elms of the inclosures, all seemed dead, killed by the cold. Neither man nor beast went out. Only the chimneys of the cottages, clothed in white linen, revealed concealed life by the fine threads of smoke which mounted straight into the frosty air. From time to time one heard the trees crack, as if their wooden limbs were breaking under the bark. And sometimes a great branch would detach itself and fall, the resistless cold petrifying the sap and breaking the fibers. Dwellings set here and there in fields seemed a hundred miles away from one another. One lived as he could. I alone endeavored to go to my nearest clients, constantly exposing myself to the danger of remaining in some hole in the winding sheet of snow.

I soon perceived that a mysterious terror had spread over the country. Such a plague, they thought, was not natural. They pretended that they heard voices at night and sharp whistling and cries, as of someone passing. These cries and the whistles came, without doubt, from emigrant birds which traveled at twilight and flew in flocks toward the south. But it was impossible to make this frightened people listen to reason. Fear had taken possession of their minds, and they listened to every extraordinary event.

The forge of Father Vatinel was situated at the end of the hamlet of Epivent, on the highway, now invisible and deserted. As the people needed bread, the black-smith resolved to go to the village. He remained some hours chattering with the inhabitants of the six houses which formed the center of the country, took his bread and his news and a little of the fear which had spread over the region and set out before night.

Suddenly, in skirting a hedge, he believed he saw an egg on the snow; yes, an egg was lying there, all white like the rest of the world. He bent over it, and in fact it was an egg. Where did it come from? What hen could have gone out there and laid an egg in that spot? The smith was astonished; he could not comprehend it, but he picked it up and took it to his wife.

"See, wife, here is an egg that I found on the way."

The woman tossed her head, replying:

"An egg on the way? And this kind of weather! You must be drunk, surely."

"No, no, my lady, it surely was at the foot of the hedge, and not frozen but still warm. Take it; I put it in my bosom so that it wouldn't cool off. You shall have it for your dinner."

The egg was soon shining in the saucepan where the soup was simmering, and the smith began to relate what he had heard around the country. The woman listened, pale with excitement.

"Surely I have heard some whistling," she said, "but it seemed to come from the chimney."

They sat down to table, ate their soup first and then, while the husband was spreading the butter on his bread, the woman took the egg and examined it with suspicious eye.

"And if there should be something in this egg?" she said.

"What, think you, would you like to have in it?"

"I know very well."

"Go ahead and eat it. Don't be a fool."

She opened the egg. It was like all eggs, and very fresh. She started to eat it but hesitated, tasting, then leaving, then tasting it again. The husband said:

"Well, how does it taste, that egg?"

She did not answer but finished swallowing it. Then suddenly she set her eyes on her husband, fixed, haggard and excited, raised her arms, turned and twisted them, convulsed from head to foot, and rolled on the floor, sending forth horrible shrieks. All night she struggled in these frightful spasms, trembling with fright, deformed by hideous convulsions. The smith, unable to restrain her, was obliged to bind her. And she screamed without ceasing, with voice indefatigable:

"I have it in my body! I have it in my body!"

I was called the next day. I ordered all the sedatives known, but without effect. She was mad. Then with incredible swiftness, in spite of the obstacle of deep snow, the news, the strange news, ran from farm to farm: "The smith's wife is possessed!" And they came from all about, not daring to go into the house, to listen to the cries of the frightened woman, whose voice was so strong that one could scarcely believe it belonged to a human creature.

The curate of the village was sent for. He was a simple old priest. He came in surplice, as if to administer comfort to the dying, and pronounced with extended hands some formulas of exorcism, while four men held the foaming, writhing woman on the bed. But the spirit was not driven out.

Christmas came without any change in the weather. In the early morning the priest came for me.

"I wish," he said, "to ask you to assist me tonight at a service for this unfortunate woman. Perhaps God will work a miracle in her favor at the same hour that he was born of a woman."

I replied: "I approve heartily, Monsieur l'Abbé, but if the spell is to be broken by ceremony (and there could be no more propitious time to start it) she can be saved without remedies."

The old priest murmured: "You are not a believer, doctor, but aid me, will you not?" I promised him my aid.

The evening came, and then the night. The clock of the church was striking, throwing its plaintive voice across the extent of white, glistening snow. Some black figures were wending their way slowly in groups, drawn by the bronze call from the bell. The full moon shone with a dull, wan light at the edge of the horizon, rendering more visible the desolation of the fields. I had taken four robust men with me and with them repaired to the forge.

The possessed one shouted continually, although bound to her bed. They had clothed her properly, in spite of her resistance, and now they brought her out. The church was full of people, illuminated but cold; the choir chanted their monotonous notes; the serpent hummed; the little bell of the acolyte tinkled, regulating the movements of the faithful.

I had shut the woman and her guards into the kitchen of the parish house and awaited the moment that I believed favorable.

I chose the time immediately following communion. All the peasants, men and women, had received their God, resolving to submit to the severity of His will. A great silence prevailed while the priest finished the divine mystery. Upon my order, the door opened and the four men brought in the mad woman.

When she saw the lights, the crowd on their knees, the choir illuminated and the gilded tabernacle she struggled with such vigor that she almost escaped from us, and she gave forth cries so piercing that a shiver of fright ran through the church. All bowed their heads; some fled. She had no longer the form of a woman, her hands being distorted, her countenance drawn, her eyes protruding. They held her up until after the march of the choir and then allowed her to squat on the floor.

Finally the priest arose; he waited. When there was a moment of quiet he took in his hands a silver vessel with bands of gold, upon which was the consecrated white wafer and, advancing some steps, extended both arms above his head and presented it to the frightened stare of the maniac. She continued to shout, but with eyes fixed upon the shining object. And the priest remained thus, motionless, as if he had been a statue.

This lasted a long, long time. The woman seemed seized with fear, fascinated; she looked fixedly at the bright vessel, trembled violently, but at intervals, and cried out incessantly, but with a less piercing voice.

It happened that she could not longer lower her eyes, that they were riveted on the Host, that she could no longer groan, that her body became pliable and that she sank down, exhausted. The crowd was prostrate, brows to earth.

The possessed one now lowered her eyelids quickly, then raised them again, as if powerless to endure the sight of her God. She was silent. And then I myself perceived that her eyes were closed. She slept the sleep of the somnambulist, the hypnotist—pardon, conquered by the contemplation of the silver vessel with the bands of gold, overcome by the Christ victorious.

They carried her out, inert, while the priest returned to the altar. The assistants, thrown into wonderment, intoned a "Te Deum."

The smith's wife slept for the next four hours; then she awoke without any remembrance either of the possession or of the deliverance. This, ladies, is the miracle that I saw.

Dr. Bonenfant remained silent for a moment, then he added in rather disagreeable voice:

"And I could never refuse to swear to it in writing."

MY TWENTY-FIVE DAYS

I had just taken possession of my room in the hotel, a narrow apartment between two papered partitions, so that I could hear all the sounds made by my neighbors. I was beginning to arrange in the glass cupboard my clothes and my linen; when I opened the drawer which was in the middle of this piece of furniture, I immediately noticed a manuscript of rolled paper. Having unrolled it, I spread it open before me and read this title:

MY TWENTY-FIVE DAYS

It was the diary of a bather, of the last occupant of my room, and had been left behind there in forgetfulness at the hour of departure.

These notes may be of some interest to sensible and healthy persons who never leave their own homes. It is for their benefit that I here transcribe them without altering a letter.

"Châtel-Guyon, July 15.

"At the first glance it is not gay, this country. So I am going to spend twenty-five days here to have my liver and my stomach treated and to get rid of flesh. The twenty-five days of a bather are very like the twenty-eight days of a reserviste; they are all devoted to fatigue duty, severe fatigue duty. Today, nothing as yet; I am installed; I have made the acquaintance of locality and the doctors. Châtel-Guyon is composed of a stream in which flows yellow water, in the midst of several mountain peaks, where are erected a casino, houses and stone crosses. At the side of the stream, in the depths of the valley, may be seen a square building surrounded by a little garden; this is the establishment of the baths. Sad people wander around this building—the invalids. A great silence reigns in these walks shaded by trees; this is not a pleasure station but a true health station; you take care of your health here through conviction, but you cannot get cured, it seems.

"Competent people declare that the mineral springs perform true miracles here. However, no votive offering is hung around the cashier's office.

"From time to time a gentleman or a lady comes over to a kiosk with a slate roof, which shelters a woman of smiling and gentle aspect and a spring boiling in a basin of cement. Not a word is exchanged between the invalid and the female custodian of the healing water. She hands to the newcomer a little glass in which air bubbles quiver in the transparent liquid. The other drinks and goes off with a grave step in order to resume his interrupted walk under the trees.

"No noise in the little park, no breath of air in the leaves, no voice breaks through this silence. Inscribed over the entrance to this district should be: 'Here you no longer laugh; you nurse yourself.'

"The people who chat resemble mutes who open their mouths in order to simulate sounds, so much are they afraid of letting their voices escape.

"In the hotel the same silence. It is a big hotel where you dine solemnly with people of good position, who have nothing to say to each other. Their manners bespeak good breeding, and their faces reflect the conviction of a superiority of which it would be difficult to give actual proof.

"At two o'clock I make my way up to the casino, a little wooden hut perched on a hillock, to which one climbs by paths frequented by goats. But the view from that height is admirable. Châtel-Guyon is situated in a very narrow valley, exactly between the plain and the mountains. At the left I see the first great waves of the mountains of Auvergne covered with wood, exhibiting here and there big gray spots, their hard lava bones, for we are at the foot of the extinct volcanoes. At the right, through the narrow slope of the valley, I discover a plain infinite as the sea, steeped in a bluish fog which lets one only dimly discern the villages, the towns, the yellow fields of ripe corn and the green square of meadowland shaded with apple trees. It is the Limagne, immense and flat, always enveloped in a light veil of vapor.

"The night has come. And now, after having dined alone, I write these lines beside my open window. I hear over there in front of me the little orchestra of the casino, which plays airs just as a wild bird sings all alone in the desert.

"From time to time a dog barks. This great calm does me good. Good night.

"July 16. Nothing. I have taken a bath, or rather a douche. I have swallowed three glasses of water and I have walked in the pathways of the park for a quarter of an hour between each glass, then half an hour after the last. I have begun my twenty-five days.

"July 17. Remarked two mysterious, pretty women who are taking their baths and their meals after everyone else.

"July 18. Nothing.

"July 19. Saw the two pretty women again. They have style and a little indescribable air which I like very much.

"July 20. Long walk in a charming wooded valley as far as the Hermitage of Sans-Souci. This country is delightful though sad; it is so calm, so sweet, so green. Along the mountain roads you meet the long wagons loaded with hay drawn by two cows at a slow pace or held back in descending the slopes by their straining heads, which are tied together. A man with a big black hat on his head is driving them with a slight switch, tipping them on the side or on the forehead, and often with an ample gesture, a gesture energetic and grave, he suddenly draws them up when the excessive load hastens their journey down the rougher descents.

"The air is good in these valleys. And if it is very warm the dust bears with it a light odor of vanilla and of the stable, for so many cows pass over these routes that they leave a little scent everywhere. And the odor is a perfume, whereas it would be a stench if it came from other animals.

"July 21. Excursion to the valley of the Enval. It is a narrow gorge inclosed in superb rocks at the very foot of the mountain. A stream flows through the space between the heaped-up boulders.

"As I reached the bottom of this ravine I heard women's voices, and I soon perceived the two mysterious ladies of my hotel, who were chatting, seated on a stone.

"The occasion appeared to me a good one, and without hesitation I presented myself. My overtures were received without embarrassment. We walked back together to the hotel. And we talked about Paris. They knew, it seemed, many people whom I knew too. Who can they be?

"I shall see them tomorrow. There is nothing more amusing than such meetings as this.

"*July 22.* Day almost entirely passed with the two unknown ladies. They are very pretty, by Jove, one a brunette and the other a blonde. They say they are widows. Hum!

"I offered to accompany them in a visit to Royat tomorrow, and they accepted my offer.

"Châtel-Guyon is less sad than I thought on my arrival.

"*July 23.* Day spent at Royat. Royat is a little cluster of hotels at the bottom of a valley, at the gate of Clermont-Ferrand. A great deal of society there. A great park full of movement. Superb view of the Puy-de-Dôme seen at the end of a perspective of vales.

"I am greatly occupied with my fair companions, which is flattering to myself. The man who escorts a pretty woman always believes himself crowned with an aureole, with much more reason, therefore, the man who goes along with one on each side of him. Nothing is so pleasant as to dine in a restaurant well frequented, with a female companion at whom everybody stares, and besides, there is nothing better calculated to set a man up in the estimation of his neighbors.

"To go to the Bois in a trap drawn by a sorry nag or to go out into the boulevard escorted by a plain woman are the two most humiliating accidents which could strike a delicate heart preoccupied with the opinions of others. Of all luxuries woman is the rarest and the most distinguished; she is the one that costs most and which we desire most; she is, therefore, the one that we like best to exhibit under the jealous eyes of the public.

"To show the world a pretty woman leaning on your arm is to excite, all at once, every kind of jealousy. It is as much as to say: 'Look here! I am rich, since I possess this rare and costly object; I have taste, since I have known how to discover this pearl; perhaps, even, I am loved, unless I am deceived by her, which would still prove that others, too, consider her charming.'

"But what a disgraceful thing it is to bring an ugly woman with you through the city! And how many humiliating things this gives people to understand!

"In the first place, they assume she must be your wife, for how could it be supposed that you would have an unattractive mistress? A real wife might be ungraceful, but then her ugliness suggests a thousand things disagreeable to you. One supposes you must be a notary or a magistrate, as those two professions have a monopoly of grotesque and well-dowered spouses. Now is this not painful for a man? And then it seems to proclaim to the public that you have the odious courage and are even under a legal obligation to caress that ridiculous face and that ill-shaped body, and that you will, without doubt, be shameless enough to make a mother of this by no means desirable being, which is the very height of ridicule.

"*July 24.* I never leave the side of the two unknown widows whom I am beginning to know well. This country is delightful and our hotel is excellent. Good season. The treatment has done me an immense amount of good.

"*July 25.* Drive in a landau to the lake of Tazenat. An exquisite and unexpected party, decided on at lunch. Abrupt departure after getting up from the table. After a long journey through the mountains we suddenly perceived an admirable little lake, quite round, quite blue, clear as glass and situated at the bottom of a dead crater. One edge of this immense basin is barren; the other is wooded. In the midst of the trees is a small house, where sleeps a good-natured, intellectual man, a sage who passes his days in this Virgilian region. He opens his dwelling for us. An idea comes into my head. I exclaim: 'Suppose we bathe?'

" 'Yes,' they said, 'but—costumes?'

" 'Bah! We are in the desert.'

"And we did bathe!

"If I were a poet, how I would describe this unforgettable vision of bodies young and naked in the transparency of the water! The sloping high sides shut in the lake, motionless, glittering and round, like a piece of silver; the sun pours into it its warm light in a flood, and along the rocks the fair flesh slips into the almost invisible wave in which the swimmers seemed suspended. On the sand at the bottom of the lake we saw the shadows of the light movements passing and repassing!

"*July 26.* Some persons seemed to look with shocked and disapproving eyes at my rapid intimacy with the two fair widows! Persons so constituted imagine that life is made for worrying oneself. Everything that appears to be amusing becomes immediately a breach of good breeding or morality. For them duty has inflexible and mortally sad rules.

"I would draw their attention with all respect to the fact that duty is not the same for Mormons, Arabs, Zulus, Turks, Englishmen and Frenchmen and that one will find very virtuous people among all those nations. As for me, I take a little off each people's notion of duty, and of the whole I make a result comparable to the morality of holy King Solomon.

"*July 27.* Good news. I have grown 620 grams thinner. Excellent, this water of Châtel-Guyon! I am bringing the widows to dine at Riom. Sad town! Its anagram constitutes an offense in the vicinity of healing springs: Riom, Mori.

"*July 28.* Hoity-toity! My two widows have been visited by two gentlemen who came to look for them. Two widows, without doubt. They are leaving this evening. They have written to me on fancy note paper.

"*July 29.* Alone! Long excursion on foot to the extinct crater of Nackère. Splendid view.

"*July 30.* Nothing. I am taking the treatment.

"*July 31.* Ditto. Ditto. This pretty country is full of polluted streams. I am drawing the notice of the municipality to the abominable sink which poisons the road in front of the hotel. All the remains of the kitchen of the establishment are thrown into it. This is a good way to breed cholera.

"*August 1.* Nothing. The treatment.

"*August 2.* Admirable walk to Châteauneuf, a station for rheumatic patients where everybody is lame. Nothing can be queerer than this population of cripples!

"*August 3.* Nothing. The treatment.

"*August 4.* Ditto. Ditto.

"*August 5.* Ditto. Ditto.

"*August 6.* Despair! I have just weighed myself. I have got fatter by 310 grams. But what then?

"*August 7.* Sixty-six kilometers in a carriage in the mountain. I will not mention the name of the country through respect for its women.

"This excursion had been pointed out to me as a beautiful one and one that was rarely made. After four hours on the road I arrived at a rather pretty village on the border of a river in the midst of an admirable wood of walnut trees. I had not yet seen a forest of walnut trees of such dimensions in Auvergne. It constitutes, moreover, all the wealth of the district, for it is planted on the common. This common was formerly only a hillside covered with brushwood. The authorities had tried in vain to get it cultivated. It was scarcely enough to feed a few sheep.

"Today it is a superb wood, thanks to the women, and it has a curious name: it is called—'the Sins of the Curé.'

"Now it is right to say that the women of the mountain district have the reputation of being light, lighter than in the plain. A bachelor who meets them owes them at least a kiss, and if he does not take more he is only a blockhead. If we think rightly on it, this way of looking at the matter is the only one that is logical and reasonable. As woman, whether she be of the town or the country, has for her natural mission to please man, man should always prove that she pleases him. If he abstains from every sort of demonstration this means that he has found her ugly; it is almost an insult to her. If I were a woman I would not receive a second time a man who failed to show me respect at our first meeting, for I would consider that he had failed to appreciate my beauty, my charm and my feminine qualities.

"So the bachelors of the village X—— often proved to the women of the district that they found them to their taste, and, as the curé was unable to prevent these demonstrations as gallant as they were natural, he resolved to utilize them for the profit of the natural prosperity. So he imposed as a penance on every woman who had gone wrong a walnut to be planted on the common. And every night lanterns were seen moving about like will-o'-the-wisps on the hillock, for the erring ones scarcely liked to perform their penances in broad daylight.

"In two years there was no room any longer on the lands belonging to the village, and today they calculate that there are more than three thousand trees around the belfry which rings for the offices through their foliage. These are 'the Sins of the Curé.'

"Since we have been seeking for so many plans for rewooding in France the Administration of Forests might surely enter into some arrangement with the clergy to employ a method so simple as that employed by this humble curé.

"*August 8.* Treatment.

"*August 9.* I am packing up my trunks and saying good-by to the charming little district, so calm and silent, to the green mountain, to the quiet valleys, to the deserted casino from which you can see, almost veiled by its light, bluish mist, the immense plain of the Limagne.

"I shall leave tomorrow."

Here the manuscript stopped. I wish to add nothing to it, my impressions of the country not having been exactly the same as those of my predecessor. For I did not find the two widows!

ALLOUMA

One of my friends had told me that if, during my travels in Algeria, I happened to be in the neighborhood of Bordj-Ebbaba, I was to be sure to visit his old friend Auballe, who had settled down there.

These names had passed from my mind, and the settler was far from my thoughts, when by pure chance I came across him.

For a month I had been roaming afoot over that magnificent country which stretches from Algiers to Cherchel, Orléansville, and Tiaret, a region both barren and wooded, its scenery both imposing and friendly. Between the mountains, dense forests of pines clothe the narrow valleys through which the winter torrents rush. Enormous trees fallen across the ravine serve as bridges for the Arabs, and support a mass of creepers which twine around their dead trunks and deck them anew with life. In the secluded folds of the mountains there are dells awe-inspiring in their beauty and streamlets whose level banks, covered with rosebay, delight the eye with their inconceivable charm.

But my sweetest memories of the journey are those of my afternoon walks along the shady roads over those undulating hills, from which one overlooks a vast russet-brown expanse of rolling country, stretching from the bluish sea to the mountain range of the Ouarsenis, crowned by the cedar forests of Téniet-el-Haâd.

On the day I was speaking of, I had lost my way. I had just surmounted a crest from the top of which I could see, above a line of hills, the extensive plain of the Mitidja, and far in the background, on the summit of another range of mountains, almost invisible in the distance, that strange monument called the Christians' Tomb, the burying place, so they say, of a family of Mauretanian kings. I went down the other side, towards the south, while before me, stretching as far as the peaks upreared against the clear sky on the edge of the desert, there appeared a broken rocky country, tawny in color as if all the hills were covered with lion skins sewn together. Here and there, higher than the rest, rose a yellowish, pointed hummock, like the hairy back of a camel.

I walked rapidly, lighthearted, as one feels when following the intricate windings of a mountain path. Life has no burdens during these vigorous tramps in the keen mountain air; body and soul, thoughts and cares alike, all cease to trouble. That day I was oblivious of all the cares that oppress and torture our lives, oblivious of everything but the joy of that descent. In the distance I discerned Arab encampments, brown pointed tents, clinging to the ground like shellfish to the rocks, or little cabins, mere huts made of branches, from which a gray smoke issued. White forms, men or women, wandered slowly about, and the bells of the herds sounded thinly in the evening air.

The strawberry trees along my path drooped under their curious load and spattered the road with their purple fruit. They looked like martyred trees from which a bloody sweat dripped, for at the end of each branch hung a red spot like a drop of blood.

The soil around them was covered with this scarlet rain, and the fruit trodden underfoot left gory stains on the ground. Now and again, springing upwards as I went along, I gathered some of the ripest and ate them.

Now all the valleys were filling with a white mist which rose slowly like the steam from a bull's flanks, and above the mountains which rose on the horizon, bordering the Sahara, flamed a sunset like an illuminated missal. Long streaks of gold alternating with streaks of blood red (more blood; the whole story of man is blood and gold!), while here and there, between the streaks, a narrow opening yielded a glimpse of a greenish-blue sky, far off as a dream.

Oh! how far I was from everything and everybody connected with a town dweller's life, even far from myself, a kind of wandering being, without consciousness or thought, merely seeing things as I went along and liking what I saw; far also from the road I had planned to follow and which I had forgotten about, for with the approach of night I realized that I was lost.

Darkness fell upon the land like a pall, and I could see nothing in front of me but the mountain looming in the distance. Seeing tents in a valley, I went down to them, and endeavored to make the first Arab I met understand where I wanted to go. I cannot tell whether he guessed my meaning, but he replied at great length in a tongue of which I understood not a word. In despair, I had made up my mind to spend the night near the camp, wrapped in a rug, when amongst the strange words which came from his mouth, I thought I recognized the name of Bordj-Ebbaba.

"Bordj-Ebbaba?" I repeated, and he replied: "Yes, yes!"

I showed him two francs, a fortune to him, and he started off, I following him. Oh, for a long time in the darkness of the night, I followed this pale phantom who hurried barefooted before me over stony paths on which I continually stumbled.

Suddenly a light appeared. We came to the door of a white house, a kind of small fort, straight-walled and with no windows on the outside. I knocked, and the howling of dogs came from within. A Frenchman's voice inquired: "Who is there?"

"Does M. Auballe live here?" I replied.

"Yes."

The door opened, and I was face to face with M. Auballe himself, a tall, fair-haired fellow, down at heel, a pipe in his mouth, looking like a good-natured Hercules.

I introduced myself, and he held out both hands to me, saying: "Make yourself at home, sir."

A quarter of an hour later I was dining exceedingly well opposite my host, who continued to smoke.

I knew his story. After having wasted a lot of money on women, he had invested all he had left in an Algerian estate, and had planted a vineyard. The vines were doing well; he was happy, and had the serene air of a contented man. I could not understand how this gay Parisian had been able to get used to this monotonous, solitary life, and I questioned him about it.

"How long have you been here?" I asked.

"Nine years."

"Don't you get terrible fits of depression?"

"No, one gets reconciled to this country, and then ends by liking it. You would scarcely believe how it grips people by means of a host of trivial animal instincts that we are unconscious of in ourselves. At first we become attached to it by the subtle, inexplicable satisfaction of our senses. The air and the climate conquer our bodies, in spite of ourselves, and the cheerful sunlight which floods the country keeps the mind clear and peaceful without any trouble. Through our eyes it pours into us continuously, and you might truly say that it purges the darkest recesses of the soul."

"And women?" I asked.

"Ah! one misses them a little."

"Only a little?"

"My God! Yes—a little. For even amongst the tribes, one always finds accommodating natives who wish to copy European ways."

He turned to the Arab who was waiting on me, a tall dark fellow with black eyes gleaming under his turban, and said:

"Leave us, Mohammed; I will call you when I want you."

Then, turning to me, he explained:

"He understands French, and I am going to tell you a story in which he plays a great part."

On Mohammed's departure, he began:

"I had been here about four years, still very little at home in this country whose language I was only just beginning to stammer, and compelled from time to time to spend several days in Algiers to avoid breaking right away from the pleasures that had in the past caused my downfall.

"I had bought this farmhouse, a *bordj*, as they call it, an old fortified guard-house, some hundreds of yards from the native encampment whose men I employ in my fields. From this tribe—a branch of the tribe of Ulad Taadja—I had chosen for my personal servant a strapping fellow, Mohammed ben Lam'har, whom you have just seen, and he soon became extremely devoted to me. As he did not like sleeping in a house that he was not accustomed to, he pitched his tent a few steps from the door, so that I could call him from my window.

"My life, well, you can guess it. All day I supervised the clearing and planting, I hunted a little, and dined with the officers of the neighboring stations, or they came to dine with me.

"As for . . . amusements—you have heard about those. Algiers supplied all the very best; and now and again an accommodating and sympathetic Arab would stop me in the middle of a walk, to suggest that he should bring me home a native woman in the evening. Sometimes I accepted his offer, but more often I refused, thinking of the trouble that might follow.

"One evening in early summer, on returning from a tour of inspection around the fields, I wanted Mohammed, and entered his tent without calling, a thing I often did.

"On a big, red, woolen rug—one of those made in Jebel Amour—thick and soft as a mattress, a woman was sleeping, a girl in fact, almost nude, with her arms crossed over her eyes. Her white body, gleaming in the light admitted through the raised flap, seemed to me to be one of the most perfect specimens I had ever seen. Round here women are very beautiful, tall and uncommonly graceful in form and features.

"Somewhat confused, I dropped the flap of the tent and returned to the house.

"I am very fond of women. That lightning vision had pierced me through and through, kindling again in my blood the old, formidable ardor which had obliged me to leave France. It was a warm evening in July, and I spent nearly the whole night at the window, my eyes fixed on the dark shadow on the ground which was Mohammed's tent.

"When he came into my room the next day, I looked him full in the face, and he lowered his head like a man who feels ashamed and guilty. Did he guess what I knew?

"I asked him bluntly: 'So you are married, Mohammed?'

"I saw him blush, and he stammered:

" 'No, sir.'

"I made him speak French, and, as he had given me lessons in Arabic, the result was one of the most incoherent jumbles imaginable.

" 'Then why is there a woman under your roof?' I retorted.

" 'She is from the South,' he murmured.

" 'Ah! she is from the South. That does not tell me how she comes to be in your tent.'

"Without answering my question, he continued:

" 'She is very pretty.'

" 'Yes, indeed! Well, the next time you have a very pretty woman from the South to stay with you, please show her into my cabin and not into yours. Do you understand, Mohammed?'

"He replied very earnestly: 'Yes, sir.'

"I must confess that during the whole day my feelings were dominated by the memory of that Arab girl lying on the red rug, and on my way back to dinner, I wanted to go into Mohammed's tent again. In the evening he waited on me as usual, coming and going with impassive face, and I was often on the point of asking whether he was going to keep this very pretty southern maiden for long under his camel-skin roof.

"About nine o'clock, still haunted by the lure of the female, which is as tenacious as the hunting instinct of dogs, I went out for a breath of air, taking a short walk in the direction of the brown canvas tent, through which I could see the bright flame of a lamp. Then I wandered further away, lest Mohammed should find me near his quarters.

"On returning an hour later, I saw clearly his characteristic profile in silhouette on the tent. Then, taking my key from my pocket, I made my way into the bordj where there slept, as I did, my steward, two French laborers, and an old cook brought from Algiers.

"I went upstairs and was surprised to notice a streak of light under my door. I opened it, and saw facing me, seated on a wicker chair beside the table on which a candle was burning, a girl with the face of a statue, quietly waiting for me, and wearing all the silver trinkets which the women of the South wear on legs and arms, on the throat and even on the stomach. Her eyes, dilated by the use of kohl, were looking at me; her forehead, her cheeks and her chin were studded with four little blue marks delicately tattooed on the skin. Her arms, loaded with bangles, rested on her thighs, which were covered by a kind of red silk jibbah which hung from her shoulders.

"Seeing me come in, she stood upright before me, covered with her barbarous jewelry, in an attitude of proud submission.

" 'What are you doing here?' I said to her in Arabic.

" 'I am here because I was told to come.'

" 'Who told you to come?'

" 'Mohammed.'

" 'All right. Sit down.'

"She sat down and lowered her eyes, while I stood looking at her.

"She had an unusual face: with regular, refined features with a slightly animal expression, but mystical like that of a Buddha. Her thick lips, colored with a kind of reddish bloom which was also apparent elsewhere on her skin, pointed to a slight mixture of Negro blood, although her hands and arms were irreproachably white.

"Perplexed, tempted and embarrassed, I felt doubtful as to what I ought to do. In order to gain time, and to give myself an opportunity to consider the problem, I asked further questions about her origin, her arrival in this country and her connection with Mohammed. But she only answered those which least interested me, and I found it impossible to ascertain why or when she had come, with what object, on whose orders, or what had taken place between her and my servant.

"Just as I was going to tell her to return to Mohammed's tent, she apparently anticipated my words, suddenly drew herself up, and raising her bare arms, while the tinkling bracelets slid in a mass towards her shoulders, she clasped her hands behind my neck and drew me towards her with an air of entreaty and irresistible willfulness.

"Her eyes, burning with the desire to bewitch, with that need of conquest that imparts a feline fascination to the immodest gaze of a woman, appealed to me, captivated me, robbed me of all power of resistance, and roused me to an impetuous passion. It was a short, silent and violent struggle carried on through the medium of the eyes alone, the eternal struggle between the primitive man and woman, in which man is always conquered.

"Her hands behind my head drew me, with slow, increasing, irresistible pressure, towards her smiling red lips, to which I suddenly pressed mine, holding her close to me, while the silver bangles, from her throat to her feet, jingled under the pressure.

"She was as wiry, supple, and healthy as an animal, with the tricks and movements, the grace, and even the scent of a gazelle, which gave her kisses a rare indescribable flavor, as foreign to my senses as a taste of some tropical fruit.

"After a while . . . I say after a while, it was perhaps as dawn was breaking, I decided to send her away, thinking that she would go just as she had come. I had not yet considered what I would do with her, what she would do with me. But as soon as she understood my intention, she murmured:

" 'If you send me away, where would you have me go? I will have to sleep out of doors, in the dark. Let me sleep on the carpet at the foot of your bed.'

"What could I say? What could I do? I reflected that Mohammed, in his turn, was doubtless watching the lighted window of my room, and all kinds of problems, which had not occurred to me in the embarrassment of the first few moments, now confronted me.

" 'Stay here,' I said; 'we must talk it over.'

"My decision was made almost immediately. Since this girl had been thrown into my arms, I would keep her as a kind of slave mistress, hidden in my house, like the women of the harems. When she no longer pleased me, it would always be easy to get rid of her somehow, for in Africa these creatures belong to us almost body and soul.

" 'I will be kind to you,' I said, 'I will treat you well, but I want to know who you are, and where you come from.'

"She understood that she had to tell me something, and related her story to me, or rather a story, for she was probably lying from beginning to end, as Arabs invariably do, with or without a motive.

"The habit of lying is one of the most surprising and incomprehensible features of the native character. These people who are so steeped in Islamism that it forms a part of them, governs their instincts, modifies their racial characteristics, and differentiates them from others in mental outlook as much as the color of the skin differentiates the Negro from the white man, are liars to the backbone, to such an extent that one can never believe what they say. Do they owe it to their religion? I cannot say. One must have lived among them to understand to what a degree falsehood forms a part of their whole existence and becomes a kind of second nature, a necessity of life.

"She told me, then, that she was a daughter of a caid of Ouled-Sidi-Cheik and of a woman captured by him in a raid on the Tuaregs. This woman must have been a black slave, or at least the offspring of an earlier mixture of Arab and Negro blood. It is well known that Negresses are highly prized in harems, where they play the part of aphrodisiacs.

"Nothing of this origin was evident except in the purplish color of her lips and the dark flush on her long supple breasts. The rest belonged to the beautiful southern race, white and slender, her features as simple and regular as the head of an Indian image, a likeness which was enhanced by her wide-set eyes.

"Of her real life I could get no real information. She described it to me in disconnected trifles which seemed to pour haphazard from a confused memory, mingled with delightfully childish remarks. It was like a picture of nomadic life from the brain of a squirrel leaping from tent to tent, from camp to camp and from tribe to tribe.

"All this was narrated with the serious air which this strange race always preserves, with the expression of an idol descending to gossip, and with a rather comical gravity.

"When she had finished, I realized that I had absorbed nothing of her long story, full of trifling incidents stored up in her nimble brain, and I wondered whether she had not been merely playing with me in this meaningless and serious gossip, which left me no wiser than before about her or any event in her life.

"I reflected on this conquered race in the midst of whom we settle, or rather who settle in the midst of us, whose language we are beginning to speak, whose everyday life we see going on under the flimsy canvas of their tents, on whom we impose our laws, our regulations and our customs, and of whom we know nothing. All this, mark you, goes on as though we were not there, as though we had not been watching little else for nearly sixty years. We no more know what happens under that hut made of branches or under that little cone of cloth anchored to the ground with stakes than we know what the so-called civilized Arabs in the Moorish houses in Algiers are doing or thinking. Behind the whitewashed walls of their dwellings in the city, behind the leafy screens of their huts, or behind the brown curtain of camel skin flapping in the wind, they live on our thresholds unknown, mysterious, sly, and untrustworthy, smiling and impenetrable in their submission. Believe me, when I look at the neighboring encampment from a distance through my field glasses, I find that they have superstitions, ceremonies, and innumerable customs still unknown and not even suspected by us! Never, perhaps, has a race conquered by force been able to escape so completely from any effective domination, moral influence or persistent but useless inquiry on the part of their conquerors.

"I suddenly felt, as never before, that secret and impassable barrier which nature has mysteriously erected between the races, raised between me and that Arab girl who had just offered herself to me.

"Thinking of it for the first time, I asked her:

" 'What is your name?'

"She had been silent for some minutes, and I saw her start involuntarily as if she had forgotten that I was there. Then I saw in her eyes that the short interval had been sufficient for sleep to claim her, a sudden irresistible slumber, almost overwhelming, like everything that seizes the changing fancies of women.

"She replied dully, stifling a yawn: 'Allouma.'

" 'You want to go to sleep?' I continued.

" 'Yes,' she replied.

" 'Very well, then, sleep,' I said.

"She quietly stretched herself by my side, lying face down, her forehead resting on her crossed arms, and I felt almost at once that her primitive, fugitive thoughts had vanished in sleep.

"As for me, lying near her, I began to wonder why Mohammed had given her to me. Had he played the part of the generous and self-sacrificing servant who gives up the woman he had taken for himself, or had he acted on an idea more complex and practical in thus giving up to me this girl who had taken my fancy? An Arab, where women are concerned, has the most rigorous standards coupled with the most inexplicable tolerance, and one can understand his stern yet easy-going morality no better than his other feelings. Perhaps in my chance entry into his tent I had forestalled the kindly intentions of this thoughtful servant who had intended for me this woman—his friend, perhaps even his mistress.

"Tormented by all these possibilities, I became so tired that, in my turn, I gradually fell into a deep slumber.

"The creaking of my door aroused me; Mohammed was coming in to wake me as he did every morning. He opened the window, through which poured a flood of daylight, lighting up the figure of Allouma still asleep on the bed; then he gathered up my trousers, waistcoat, and jacket from the floor in order to brush them. He did not look at the woman lying by my side, he did not even appear to notice that she was there, and his gravity, his demeanor and his expression were the same as usual. But the light and movement, the slight patter of the man's bare feet, and the feeling of the fresh air on her skin and in her lungs roused Allouma from her torpor. She stretched her arms, turned over and opened her eyes, looked at me and at Mohammed with the same indifference, and sat up. Then she murmured:

" 'I am hungry now.'

" 'What will you have to eat?' I inquired.

" 'Kahoua.'[1]

" 'Coffee with bread and butter?'

" 'Yes.'

"Mohammed, standing near our bed, my clothes over his arm, waited for orders.

[1]An Arab dish.

" 'Bring something to eat for Allouma and myself,' I told him, and he went out without the least trace of astonishment or annoyance on his face.

"When he had gone, I asked the young Arab girl:

" 'Do you wish to live in my house?'

" 'Yes, I am willing.'

" 'I will give you a room for yourself, and a woman to wait on you.'

" 'You are generous, and I am grateful for it.'

" 'But if you do not behave yourself, I will send you away from here.'

" 'I will do anything you want of me.'

"She took my hand and kissed it, in token of submission.

"Mohammed returned, bringing a tray with breakfast.

" 'Allouma is going to live in the house,' I told him. 'Spread some rugs in the room at the end of the passage, and send for the wife of Abd-el-Kader-el-Hadara to come and wait on her.'

" 'Yes, sir.'

"That was all he said.

"An hour later, my beautiful Arab girl was installed in a large, well-lighted room; and when I came to see that everything was right, she entreated me to give her a wardrobe with a mirror on the door. I promised and left her squatting on a rug made in Jebel Amour, a cigarette in her mouth, and gossiping with the old Arab woman whom I had engaged, as if they had known each other all their lives."

II

"For a month I was very happy with her, and in a queer fashion I became attached to this creature of another race, who seemed to me to be almost of another species, born on a neighboring planet.

"I did not love her; no, one does not love the young women of this primitive continent. Between them and ourselves, even between them and their own men-folk, the Arabs, love as we understand it does not exist. They are too primitive, their feelings are insufficiently refined to arouse in our souls that sentimental exaltation which is the poetry of love. There is no mental or moral intoxication blended with the physical intoxication which these charming and worthless creatures stimulate in us.

"Yet they grip us and take possession of us just as other women do, but in a different way, less tenacious, less painful and sorrowful.

"My feelings in that way I cannot yet describe with any accuracy. I told you a little while ago that Africa, this bare artless country, devoid of all intellectual attraction, gradually overcomes us by an indefinable and unfailing charm, by the breath of its atmosphere, by the constant mildness of the early mornings and the evenings, by its delightful sunlight and by the feeling of well-being that it instills in us. Well, Allouma attracted me in the same way by numberless hidden and fascinating enticements, by the keen allurements, not of her caresses, for she was typically oriental in her nonchalance, but of her charming unconstraint.

"I left her absolutely free to come and go as she pleased, and she passed at least one afternoon out of every two in the neighboring camp, amongst my native laborers' womenfolk. Often, too, she would spend a whole day admiring herself in the glazed mahogany wardrobe that I had obtained from Miliana. She admired herself in all conscience, standing before the great glass door in which she followed her movements with deep and serious attention. She would walk with her head thrown back in order to pass judgment on her hips and her back, turn, move away and come back again, until, tired of moving about, she would sit on a hassock and contemplate her reflection face to face, her mind absorbed in this occupation.

"After a little while, I noticed that she went out nearly every day after breakfast and disappeared completely until the evening.

"Feeling somewhat anxious, I asked Mohammed whether he knew what she might be doing during this lengthy absence.

" 'Don't let it trouble you,' he replied, unconcernedly, 'the feast of Ramadan will soon be here. She has to carry out her devotions.'

"He also seemed delighted with the presence of Allouma in the house, but not once did I detect the least sign of anything suspicious between them, nor did they even seem to be in collusion or to hide anything from me.

"I therefore accepted the situation, though without understanding it, leaving the solution to the workings of time and chance.

"Often, after inspecting my fields, the vines and the clearings, I would go for a long walk. You know the magnificent forests of this part of Algeria, those almost impenetrable ravines where the fallen pine trees dam the torrents and those little dells full of rosebay which from the mountain tops look like Oriental carpets spread out along the watercourses. You know that frequently in these woods and on these slopes, where never a soul seems to have penetrated, you may suddenly come across the snow-white dome of a *koubba* containing the bones of a lonely, humble Marabout, visited at infrequent intervals by a few determined followers, who come from the neighboring village with candles in their pockets to light them on the tomb of the holy man.

"One evening, as I was returning, I passed close to one of these Mohammedan chapels, and, glancing through the ever open door, I saw that a woman was praying before the shrine. It made a charming picture, this Arab girl bowed on the floor in the ruined building, where the wind entered at will and piled up into yellowish heaps in the corners the withered, delicate pine needles. I approached, in order to see better, and recognized Allouma. Absorbed in her devotions, she neither saw nor heard me, and continued to address the saint in a low voice, thinking herself alone with him and pouring out to God's servant all her troubles. Sometimes she stopped awhile to meditate, to remember what she had still to say, to make sure of forgetting none of her store of confidences; at other times she grew excited as if he had answered her, or as if he had advised her to do something against her will, against which she was arguing.

"I stole away noiselessly, as I had come, and returned to dinner.

"In the evening I sent for her, and as she came in I saw on her face a thoughtful look that was not usually there.

" 'Sit down there,' I said to her, indicating a seat on the couch by my side.

"She sat down, and as I leaned towards her to kiss her, she drew her head back quickly.

"I was astonished, and asked her what was the matter.

" 'It is Ramadan,' she said.

"I began to laugh.

" 'And the Marabout has forbidden you to allow yourself to be kissed during Ramadan?'

" 'Oh, yes! I am an Arab, and you are an infidel.'

" 'That would be a great sin?'

" 'Oh, yes!'

" 'Then you have eaten nothing all day, until sunset?'

" 'No, nothing.'

" 'But after sunset you had something to eat?'

" 'Yes.'

" 'Well, then, as it is quite dark now, you cannot be less strict on food than on anything else.'

"She looked ruffled and hurt, and retorted with a haughtiness that I had not known in her before:

" 'If an Arab girl let herself be touched by an infidel during Ramadan, she would be accursed forever.'

" 'And this will last for the whole of the month?'

"She replied with a definite air:

" 'Yes, the whole month of Ramadan.'

"I adopted a tone of annoyance, and said to her:

" 'Very well, you may go and spend Ramadan with your family.'

"She seized my hands and clasped them to her, crying:

" 'Oh! I beg of you, don't be cruel; you shall see how good I will be. Let us keep Ramadan together, if you will. I will look after you, I will do anything you fancy, but don't be cruel.'

"I could not help smiling at her quaint air of grief, and sent her away to bed.

"An hour later, as I was going to bed, there were two light taps on my door, so light that I scarcely heard them.

" 'Come in,' I cried, and Allouma entered, carrying a large tray loaded with Arab delicacies, sweet fried croquettes, and a strange collection of native pastry.

"She laughed, showing her fine teeth, and repeated:

" 'We are going to keep Ramadan together.'

"You know that the fasting which begins at dawn and ends at dusk, at the moment when the eye cannot distinguish between a white and a black thread, is followed every evening by private little feasts in which eating goes on until dawn. It follows that for a native not overburdened by his conscience, Ramadan merely consists in transposing day and night. Allouma, however, was more conscientious about it. She placed her tray between us on the couch, and taking in her long slender fingers a little powdered ball, she put it in my mouth, murmuring:

" 'Eat this, it is good.'

"I munched the light cake, which was indeed excellent, and asked her:

" 'Did you make that?'

" 'Yes, I did.'

" 'For me?'

" 'Yes, for you.'

" 'To enable me to tolerate Ramadan?'

" 'Yes, don't be unkind! I will bring you some every day.'

"What a terrible month I spent there! a sugary, insipid, maddening month, full of little indulgences, temptations, fits of anger and vain struggles against an invincible resistance.

"Then, when the three days of Beiram arrived, I celebrated them in my own way, and Ramadan was forgotten.

"A very hot summer passed, and towards the early days of autumn, Allouma seemed to be preoccupied and abstracted and took no interest in anything.

"One evening, when I sent for her, she was not in her room, and, thinking that she was somewhere about the house, I sent someone to look for her. She had not come back, so I opened the window and called for Mohammed.

"His answer came from within the tent:

" 'Yes, sir?'

" 'Do you know where Allouma is?'

" 'No, sir. She is not lost, is she?'

"A few seconds later, he entered my room, so agitated that he could not suppress his anxiety.

" 'Allouma lost?' he asked.

" 'Yes, she has disappeared.'

" 'Surely not.'

" 'Go and look for her,' I told him.

"He remained standing there, lost in thought and trying to grasp the situation. Then he entered Allouma's room, where her clothes were scattered in truly oriental disorder. He examined everything like a policeman, or rather he snuffed around like a dog, and then, incapable of further effort, he murmured with an air of resignation:

" 'Gone! she is gone!'

"For my part, I feared some accident, a fall down a ravine, a sprained joint, and I sent out all the men in the camp with orders to search until they had found her.

"They searched for her all night, the whole of the next day, and for a week, but could discover no clue that would put us on the right track. I suffered badly, for I missed her; the house seemed empty and life seemed a desert. Then disturbing thoughts began to pass through my mind: I thought that she might have been kidnaped, or even killed. But every time I attempted to question Mohammed or to tell him my fears, he replied steadfastly:

" 'No, she has gone away.'

"Then he added the Arab word 'r'ezale,' meaning a gazelle, as if to say that she ran quickly and was far away.

"Three weeks passed, and I had given up hope of ever seeing my Arab mistress again, when one morning Mohammed, his face beaming with joy, came into my room and said:

" 'Allouma has returned, sir!'

"I jumped out of bed and asked him where she was.

" 'She does not dare to come in! Look, under the tree over there!'

"And with outstretched arm he pointed through the window to a whitish shadow at the foot of an olive tree.

"I got up and went out. As I approached that bundle of cloth which seemed to have been thrown against the twisted trunk, I recognized the large dark eyes and the tattooed stars on the long well-formed face of the native girl who had bewitched me. As I advanced, I was seized by a fit of anger, a longing to strike her, to make her suffer in revenge.   .

"I called to her from a distance:

" 'Where have you been?'

"She did not reply, and remained motionless, as if she scarcely lived, resigned to the expected blows.

"I was now standing right above her, gazing with astonishment at the rags she wore, tatters of silk and wool, gray with dust, and torn and filthy.

"With my hand raised as if to a dog, I repeated:

" 'Where have you been?'

" 'From over there,' she murmured.

" 'From where?'

" 'From the tribe.'

" 'From what tribe?'

" 'From my own.'

" 'Why did you go away?'

"Seeing that I was not going to strike her, she plucked up a little courage, and said in a low voice:

" 'I wanted . . . I wanted . . . I could not live in the house any longer.'

"I saw tears in her eyes, and I immediately felt a foolish sort of pity. I stooped towards her, and on turning round to sit down I perceived Mohammed watching in the distance.

"Very gently I continued:

" 'Come, will you tell me why you went away?'

"Then she told me that she had for a long time felt in her heart the nomad's irresistible desire to get back to a tent, to sleep, run and roll on the sand, to wander from plain to plain with the herds, to feel nothing over her head, or between the yellow stars of heaven and the blue stars on her face, but the thin curtain of worn and patched cloth through which one can see, awakening in the night, the gleam of countless spots of light.

"She pictured this to me so simply, so forcibly and so reasonably that I was convinced of the truth of it, and, feeling sorry for her, I asked:

" 'Why didn't you tell me that you wanted to go away for a while?'

" 'Because you would not have liked . . .'

" 'If you had promised to come back, I would have given you permission.'

" 'You would not have believed me.'

"Seeing that I was not angry, she laughed, and added:

" 'You see, it is all over. I have come back and here I am. I had to spend a few days over there. Now I have had enough: it is all over and done with. I have come back and I am no longer unhappy. I am very pleased. You are not cruel to me.'

" 'Come to the house,' I said to her.

"She stood up, and I took her hand, held her slender fingers; and triumphant in her rags, with a jingling of bracelets, necklaces and ornaments, she walked solemnly towards my house, where Mohammed was waiting for us.

"Before going in, I repeated:

" 'Allouma, if at any time you want to go home, tell me so and I will let you go.'

" 'You promise?' she asked cautiously.

" 'Yes, I promise.'

" 'I promise also. When I feel homesick,' and she placed her hands on her forehead with a magnificent gesture, 'I will tell you that I must go yonder, and you will let me go.'

"I accompanied her to her room, followed by Mohammed bringing water, for we had not yet been able to warn the wife of Abd-el-Kader-el-Hadara of the return of her mistress.

"She entered, perceived the mirror, and with joy in her face ran towards it as if to welcome a long-lost mother. She looked at herself for a few seconds, then pouted and said to the mirror, with a shade of annoyance:

" 'Wait a minute, I have silk dresses in the wardrobe. I will be beautiful very soon.'

"I left her to flirt with her reflection in the glass.

"Our life together went on as before, and I fell more and more under the strange spell, the physical allurement of this girl, for whom at the same time I felt a kind of paternal superiority.

"All went well for six months, and then I felt that she was again becoming nervous, restless and rather sad. One day I said to her:

" 'Do you want to go home?'

" 'Yes, I should like to.'

" 'You did not dare to tell me?'

" 'No, I did not dare.'

" 'Very well, then: you may go.'

"She seized my hands and kissed them as she did in all her outbursts of gratitude, and the next day she had disappeared.

"As before, she returned after about three weeks, again in tatters, black with dust and sunburn, and satiated with the nomad's life, with sand and with freedom. During two years she went home in that way four times.

"I used to take her back cheerfully and without jealousy, for I felt that jealousy could not exist without love as we understand love in our own country. Certainly, I might very well have killed her if I had caught her deceiving me, but it would have been rather as I would have thrashed a disobedient dog, from pure anger. I would not have felt that torture, that consuming fire, that terrible suffering that constitute jealousy in the North. I said just now that I might have killed her as I would have thrashed a disobedient dog. I loved her, in fact, rather as one might love a very rare animal, a dog or a horse that one could not replace. She was a wonderful, a delightful animal, but no more, in the form of a woman.

"I can hardly describe what a gulf separated our souls, although no doubt our hearts came into contact at times and responded to the touch. She was a pleasant object in my house and in my life, one to which I had become accustomed and which appealed only to my physical senses.

"One morning Mohammed came into my room with a strange expression on his face, an anxious look sometimes seen in an Arab's eyes, which suggests a cat, apprehensive and ready to run, when faced by a dog.

"Seeing his face, I asked:

" 'Hullo! what is the matter?'

" 'Allouma has gone away.'

"I began to laugh.

" 'Gone? where to?'

" 'Gone right away, sir.'

" 'What, gone right away?'

" 'Yes, sir.'

" 'You must be mad, my lad!'

" 'No, sir.'

" 'Why has she gone away? How? Come, explain yourself!'

"He stood still, unwilling to speak; and then, all of a sudden, he gave vent to one of those typical outbursts of rage which occasionally confront us in the streets between two fanatical Arabs, in which oriental silence and gravity give place to the wildest gestures and the most ferocious threats.

"Then in the midst of his ravings I gathered that Allouma had fled with my shepherd.

"I had to calm Mohammed and drag from him, one by one, the full details.

"It was a long story. I understood at last that for a week he had been keeping watch on Allouma, who had been meeting, behind the nearby clumps of cactus or in the ravine where the rosebay grew, a tramp who had been engaged as a shepherd by my superintendent about the end of the month before.

"Mohammed had seen her go out the night before, and he had not seen her come back, and he repeated, with an incensed air:

" 'Gone, sir: she has gone for good.'

"I cannot tell why, but his conviction that she had eloped with this vagabond instantly came home to me also, absolutely and irresistibly. It seemed absurd and improbable, yet all the more certain when one considered the irrational logic typical of women.

"With aching heart, and fuming with rage, I strove to recall this man's features, and I suddenly recollected seeing him, a week or two before, standing on a hillock in the midst of his flock and looking at me. He was a big Bedouin whose bare limbs matched the color of his rags, a typical savage brute with prominent cheekbones, a crooked nose, a receding chin and thin legs, like a tall skeleton clothed in tatters, with the treacherous eyes of a jackal.

"I was quite certain that she had fled with this scoundrel. Why? Because she was Allouma, a child of the desert. Another girl in Paris, a streetwalker, would have run away with my coachman or with a frequenter of the slums.

" 'It is all right,' I said to Mohammed. 'If she has gone, so much the worse for her. Leave me alone; I have some letters to write.'

"He went away, surprised at my calm. I got up and opened the window and began to draw in deep breaths of the stifling air which the sirocco was bringing from the South. Then I thought to myself:

" 'Good heavens, she is a . . . woman, like many others. Can anyone tell why they do these things, what makes them love and follow a man, or leave him?'

"Yes, occasionally we know: generally we do not. At times, we are doubtful.

"Why had she disappeared with that repulsive brute? Why, indeed? It may have been because for practically a whole month the wind had been blowing from the South.

"A breath of wind! That was reason enough! Did she know, do any of them, even the most introspective of them, know in most cases why they do certain things? No more than a weathercock swinging in the wind. The slightest breeze sways the light vane of copper, iron, or wood, in the same way that some imperceptible influence, some fleeting impression, stirs and guides the fickle fancy of a woman, whether she be from town or country, from a suburb or from the desert.

"They may realize, afterwards, if they consider it and understand, why they have done one thing rather than another; but, at the time, they have no idea, for they are the playthings of their susceptibilities, the feather-brained slaves of events and environment, of chance and caprice, and of all their lightest whims."

M. Auballe had risen to his feet. He took a few steps, looked at me and laughingly said:

"There you have a desert love affair!"

"What if she comes back?" I inquired.

"The wicked girl!" he murmured. "Yet I should be very glad all the same."

"And you would forgive the shepherd?"

"Good heavens, yes. Where women are concerned, one must either forgive . . . or ignore."

A LUCKY BURGLAR

They were seated in the dining room of a hotel in Barbizon.

"I tell you, you will not believe it."

"Well, tell it anyhow."

"All right, here goes. But first I must tell you that my story is absolutely true in every respect, even if it does sound improbable." And the old artist commenced:

"We had dined at Soriel's that night. When I say dined, that means that we were all pretty well tipsy. We were three young madcaps. Soriel (poor fellow, he is dead now), Le Poittevin, the marine painter, and myself. Le Poittevin is dead also.

"We had stretched ourselves on the floor of the little room adjoining the studio, and the only one in the crowd who was rational was Le Poittevin. Soriel, who was always the maddest, lay flat on his back, with his feet propped up on a chair, discussing war and the uniforms of the empire, when suddenly he got up, took out of the big wardrobe where he kept his accessories a complete hussar's uniform and put it on. He then took a grenadier's uniform and told Le Poittevin to put it on, but he objected, so we forced him into it. It was so big for him that he was completely lost in it. I arrayed myself as a cuirassier. After we were ready Soriel made us go through a complicated drill. Then he exclaimed: 'As long we are troopers let us drink like troopers.'

"The punch bowl had been brought out and filled for the second time. We were bawling some old camp songs at the top of our voices, when Le Poittevin, who in spite of all the punch had retained his self-control, held up his hand and said: 'Hush! I am sure I heard someone walking in the studio.'

"'A burglar!' said Soriel, staggering to his feet. 'Good luck!' And he began the Marseillaise:

"'To arms, citizens!'

"Then he seized several weapons from the wall and equipped us according to our uniforms. I received a musket and a saber. Le Poittevin was handed an enormous gun with a bayonet attached. Soriel, not finding just what he wanted, seized a pistol, stuck it in his belt and, brandishing a battle-ax in one hand, he opened the studio door cautiously. The army advanced. Having reached the middle of the room, Soriel said:

"'I am general. You (pointing to me), the cuirassiers, will keep the enemy from retreating—that is, lock the door. You (pointing to Le Poittevin), the grenadiers, will be my escort.'

"I executed my orders and rejoined the troops, who were behind a large screen reconnoitering. Just as I reached it I heard a terrible noise. I rushed up with the candle to investigate the cause of it, and this is what I saw. Le Poittevin was piercing the dummy's breast with his bayonet, and Soriel was splitting his head open with his ax! When the mistake had been discovered the general commanded: 'Be cautious!'

"We had explored every nook and corner of the studio for the past twenty minutes without success, when Le Poittevin thought he would look in the cupboard. As it was quite deep and very dark, I advanced with the candle and looked in. I drew back, stupefied. A man, a real, live man this time, stood there looking at me! I quickly recovered myself, however, and locked the cupboard door. We then retired a few paces to hold a council.

"Opinions were divided. Soriel wanted to smoke the burglar out; Le Poittevin suggested starvation, and I proposed to blow him up with dynamite. Le Poittevin's idea being finally accepted as the best, we proceeded to bring the punch and pipes into the studio, while Le Poittevin kept guard with his big gun on his shoulder, and, settling ourselves in front of the cupboard, we drank the prisoner's health. We had done this repeatedly, when Soriel suggested that we bring out the prisoner and take a look at him.

"'Hooray!' I cried. We picked up our weapons and made a mad rush for the cupboard door. It was finally opened, and Soriel, cocking his pistol which was not loaded, rushed in first. Le Poittevin and I followed, yelling like lunatics, and after a mad scramble in the dark we at last brought out the burglar. He was a haggard-looking, white-haired old bandit, with shabby, ragged clothes. We bound him hand and foot and dropped him in an armchair. He said nothing.

"'We will try this wretch,' said Soriel, whom the punch had made very solemn. I was so far gone that it seemed to me quite a natural thing. Le Poittevin was named for the defense and I for the prosecution. The prisoner was condemned to death by all except his counsel.

"'We will now execute him,' said Soriel. 'Still, this man cannot die without repenting,' he added, feeling somewhat scrupulous. 'Let us send for a priest.'

"I objected that it was too late, so he proposed that I officiate and forthwith told the prisoner to confess his sins to me. The old man was terrified. He wondered what kind of wretches we were, and for the first time he spoke. His voice was hollow and cracked:

"'Say, you don't mean it, do you?'

"Soriel forced him to his knees and, for fear he had not been baptized, poured a glass of rum over his head, saying: 'Confess your sins; your last hour has come!'

"'Help! Help!' screamed the old man, rolling himself on the floor and kicking everything that came his way. For fear he should wake the neighbors we gagged him.

"'Come, let us end this,' said Soriel impatiently. He pointed his pistol at the old man and pressed the trigger. I followed his example, but as neither of our guns was loaded we made very little noise. Le Poittevin, who had been looking on, said:

" 'Have we really the right to kill this man?'

" 'We have condemned him to death!' said Soriel.

" 'Yes, but we have no right to shoot a civilian. Let us take him to the station house.'

"We agreed with him, and as the old man could not walk we tied him to a board, and Le Poittevin and I carried him, while Soriel kept guard in the rear. We arrived at the station house. The chief, who knew us and was well acquainted with our manner of joking, thought it was a great lark and laughingly refused to take our prisoner in. Soriel insisted, but the chief told us very sternly to quit our fooling and go home and be quiet. There was nothing else to do but to take him back to Soriel's.

" 'What are we going to do with him?' I asked.

" 'The poor man must be awfully tired!' said Le Poittevin sympathizingly.

"He did look half head, and in my turn I felt a sudden pity for him (the punch, no doubt), and I relieved him of his gag.

" 'How do you feel, old man?' I asked.

" 'By Jingo! I have enough of this,' he groaned.

"Then Soriel softened. He unbound him and treated him as a long-lost friend. The three of us immediately brewed a fresh bowl of punch. As soon as it was ready we handed a glass to the prisoner, who quaffed it without flinching. Toast followed toast. The old man could drink more than the three of us put together, but as daylight appeared, he got up and calmly said: 'I shall be obliged to leave you; I must get home now.'

"We begged him not to go, but he positively refused to stay any longer. We were awfully sorry and took him to the door, while Soriel held the candle above his head, saying: 'Look out for the last step.' "

AN ODD FEAST

It was in the winter of—I do not remember what year—that I went to Normandy to visit my bachelor cousin, Jules de Baneville, who lived alone in the old manor, with a cook, a valet and a keeper. I had the hunting fever and for a month did nothing else from morning until night.

The castle, an old gray building surrounded with pines and avenues of tall oak trees, looked as if it had been deserted for centuries. The antique furniture and the portraits of Jules's ancestors were the only inhabitants of the spacious rooms and halls now closed.

We had taken shelter in the only habitable room, an immense kitchen, which had been plastered all over to keep the rats out. The big, white walls were covered with whips, guns, horns, etc., and in the huge fireplace a brushwood fire was burning, throwing strange lights around the corners of the dismal room. We would sit in front of the fire every night, our hounds stretched in every available space between our feet, dreaming and barking in their sleep, until, getting drowsy, we would climb to our rooms and slip into our beds, shivering.

It had been freezing hard that day, and we were sitting as usual in front of the fire, watching a hare and two partridges being roasted for dinner, and the savory smell sharpened our appetites.

"It will be awfully cold going to bed tonight," said Jules.

"Yes, but there will be plenty of ducks tomorrow morning," I replied indifferently.

The servant had set our plates at one end of the table and those of the servants at the other.

"Gentlemen, do you know it is Christmas Eve?" she asked.

We certainly did not; we never looked at the calendar.

"That accounts for the bells ringing all day," said Jules. "There is midnight service tonight."

"Yes sir, but they also rang because old Fournel is dead."

Fournel was an old shepherd, well known in the country. He was ninety-six years old and had never known a day's sickness until a month ago, when he had taken cold by falling into a pool on a dark night and had died of the consequences.

"If you like," said Jules, "we will go and see these poor people after dinner."

The old man's family consisted of his grandson, fifty-eight years old, and the latter's wife, one year younger. His children had died years ago. They lived in a miserable hut at the entrance of the village.

Perhaps Christmas Eve in a lonely castle was an incentive, at all events we were very talkative that night. Our dinner had lasted way into the night, and long after the servant had left us we sat there smoking pipe after pipe, narrating old experiences, telling of past revels and the surprises of the morrow which followed our adventures. Our solitude had brought us closer together, and we exchanged those confidences which only intimate friends can.

"I am going to church, sir," said the servant, reappearing.

"What, so soon!" exclaimed Jules.

"It lacks only a quarter of twelve, sir."

"Let us go to church too," said Jules. "The midnight service is very attractive in the country."

I assented and, having wrapped ourselves up, we started for the village. It was bitterly cold, but a clear, beautiful night. We could hear the peasants' wooden shoes on the crisp, frozen earth and the church bell ringing in the distance. The road was dotted here and there with dancing lights. It was the peasants carrying lanterns, lighting the way for their wives and children. As we approached the village Jules said:

"Here is where the Fournels live; let us go in."

We knocked repeatedly, but in vain. A neighboring peasant informed us that they had gone to church to pray for their grandfather.

"We will see them on our way back," said Jules.

The service had begun when we entered the church. It was profusely decorated with small candles, and to the left, in a small chapel, the birth of Christ was represented by wax figures, pine brush forming a background. The men stood with bowed heads, and the women, kneeling, clasped their hands in deep devotion. After a few minutes Jules said:

"It is stifling in here; let us go outside."

We left the shivering peasants to their devotions and, regaining the deserted road, we resumed our conversation. We had talked so long that the service was over when we came back to the village. A small ray of light filtered through the Fournels' door.

"They are watching their dead," said Jules. "They will be pleased to see us."

We went in. The low, dark room was lighted only by a smoking candle, placed in the middle of the large, coarse table, under which a bread bin had been built, taking up the whole length of it. A suffocating odor of roasted blood pudding pervaded every corner of the room. Seated face to face were Fournel and his wife, a gloomy and brutish expression on their faces. Between the two was a single plate of the pudding, the popular dish on Christmas Eve, out of which they would take turns in cutting a piece off, spread it on their bread and munch in silence. When the man's glass was empty the woman would fill it out of an earthen jar containing cider.

They asked us to be seated and to "join them," but at our refusal they continued to munch. After a few minutes' silence Jules said:

"Well, Anthime, so your grandfather is dead!"

"Yes sir, he died this afternoon."

The woman snuffed the candle in silence and I, for the want of something to say, added:

"He was quite old, was he not?"

"Oh, his time was up," she answered; "he was no earthly use here."

An invincible desire to see the old man took possession of me, and I asked to see him. The two peasants suddenly became agitated and exchanged questioning glances. Jules noticed this and insisted. Then the man with a sly, suspicious look asked:

"What good would it do you?"

"No good," said Jules, "but why will you not let us see him?"

"I am willing," said the man, shrugging his shoulders, "but it is kind of unhandy just now."

We conjectured all sorts of things. Neither of them stirred. They sat there with eyes lowered, a sullen expression on their faces seeming to say: "Go away."

"Come, Anthime, take us to his room," said Jules with authority.

"It's no use, my good sir; he isn't there any more," said the man resolutely.

"Where is he?" said Jules.

The woman interrupted, saying:

"You see, sir, we had no other place to put him so we put him in the bin until morning." And, having taken the top of the table off, she held the candle near the opening. We looked in, and sure enough, there he was, a shriveled, gray mass, his gray hair matted about his face, barefooted and rolled up in his shepherd's cloak, sleeping his last sleep among crusts of bread as ancient as himself.

His grandchildren had used as a table the bin which held his body!

Jules was indignant and, pale with anger, said:

"You villains! Why did you not leave him in his bed?"

The woman burst into tears and spoke rapidly:

"You see, my good gentlemen, it's just this way. We have but one bed, and being only three, we slept together; but since he's been so sick we slept on the floor. The floor is awful hard and cold these days, my good gentlemen, so when he died this afternoon we said to ourselves: "As long as he is dead he doesn't feel anything, and what's the use of leaving him in bed? He'll be just as comfortable in the bin.' We can't sleep with a dead man, my good gentlemen—now can we?"

Jules was exasperated and went out, banging the door, and I after him, laughing myself sick.

WHO KNOWS?

My God! My God! So at last I am going to write down what has happened to me. But shall I be able to? Shall I dare?—so fantastic, so inexplicable, so incomprehensible, so crazy is it.

If I were not certain of what I had seen, certain that there has been in my reasoning no faulty link, no error in my investigations, no lacuna in the relentless sequence of my observations, I would have believed myself to be merely the victim of a hallucination, the sport of a strange vision. After all, who knows?

I am today in a private asylum; but I entered it voluntarily, urged thereto by prudence, and fear. Only one living creature knows my story. The doctor here. I am going to write it. I hardly know why. To rid myself of it, for it fills my thoughts like an unendurable nightmare.

Here it is:

I have always been a recluse, a dreamer, a sort of detached philosopher, full of kindly feeling, content with little, with no bitterness against men or resentment against heaven. I lived alone, all my life, because of a sort of uneasiness that the presence of other people induces in me! How can I explain it? I could not explain it. I don't refuse to see people, to talk to them, to dine with friends, but when I have endured their nearness for some time, even those with whom I am most intimate, they weary me, exhaust me, get on my nerves, and I suffer an increasing exasperating longing to see them go or to go myself, to be alone.

This longing is more than a desire, it is an irresistible necessity. And if I had to endure the continued presence of the people in whose company I was, if I were compelled, not to listen but to go on for any length of time hearing their conversation, some accident would certainly befall me. What? Ah, who knows? Perhaps merely a fainting fit? Yes, probably that!

I have such a passion for solitude that I cannot even endure the nearness of other people sleeping under my roof: I cannot live in Paris because of the indefinable distress I feel there. I die spiritually, and I am as tortured in my body and my nerves by the vast crowd that swarms and lives round me, even when it sleeps. Oh, the slumber of other people is more unendurable than their speech! And I can never rest when at the other side of the wall I am aware of lives held in suspense by these regular eclipses of consciousness.

Why am I so made? Who knows? The cause is perhaps quite simple. I am quickly wearied of all that exists outside myself. And there are many people similarly constituted.

There are two races dwelling on earth. Those who need other people, who are distracted, occupied, and refreshed by other people, and who are worried, exhausted, and unnerved by solitude as by the ascension of a terrible glacier or the crossing of a desert; and those, on the other hand, who are wearied, bored, embarrassed, utterly fatigued by other people, while isolation calms them and the detachment and imaginative activity of their minds bathes them in peace.

In effect, this is a usual psychical phenomenon. Some people are made to live an outward life, others to live within themselves. I myself have a short and quickly exhausted power of attention to the outside world, and as soon as it has reached its limit I suffer in my whole body and my whole mind an intolerable distress.

The result is that I attach myself, that I attached myself strongly to inanimate things that assume for me the importance of living creatures, and that my house has become, had become a world where I lived a solitary and active life, surrounded by things, furniture, intimate trifles, as sympathetic to my eyes as faces. I had filled it with them little by little. I had decorated it so, and I felt myself housed, content, satisfied, as happy as in the arms of a loving woman whose familiar caress was become a calm and pleasant need.

I had had this house built in a beautiful garden which shut it off from the roads, and at the gate of a town where I could, when occasion arose, find the social resources to which, at odd moments, I felt impelled. All my servants slept in a distant building at the end of the kitchen garden, which was surrounded by a great wall. The somber folding down of the nights, in the silence of my habitation, lost, hidden, drowned under the leaves of great trees, was so tranquilizing, so pleasant to me, that every evening I delayed going to bed for several hours, to enjoy it the longer.

That particular day, *Sigurd* had been played at the local theater. It was the first time I had heard this beautiful fairylike musical drama, and it had given me the greatest pleasure.

I walked home, at a brisk pace, my head full of sounding rhythms, my eyes filled with visions of loveliness. It was dark, dark, so unfathomably dark that I could hardly make out the high road and several times almost went headlong into the ditch. From the toll gate to my house is about two thirds of a mile, perhaps a little more, maybe about twenty minutes' slow walking. It was one o'clock in the morning, one or half past; the sky was growing faintly light in front of me, and a slip of a moon rose, the wan slip of the moon's last quarter. The crescent moon of the first quarter, that rises at four or five o'clock in the evening, is brilliant, gay, gleaming like silver, but the moon that rises after midnight is tawny, sad and sinister: it is a real Witches' Sabbath of a moon. Every walker by night must have made this observation. The moon of the first quarter, be it thin as a thread, sends out a small joyous light that fills the heart with gladness and flings clear shadows over the earth; the moon of the last quarter scarcely spreads a dying light, so wan that it hardly casts any shadow at all.

I saw from some way off the somber mass of my garden, and, sprung from I know not where, there came to me a certain uneasiness at the idea of entering it. I slackened my step. It was very mild. The heavy weight of trees wore the aspect of a tomb where my house was buried.

I opened my gateway and made my way down the long avenue of sycamore trees, which led to the house, arched and vaulted overhead like a high tunnel, crossing shadowy groves and winding round lawns where under the paling shadows clumps of flowers jeweled the ground with oval stains of indeterminate hues.

As I approached the house, a strange uneasiness took possession of me. I halted. There was no sound. There was not a breath of air in the leaves. "What's the matter with me?" I thought. For ten years I had entered in like manner without feeling the faintest shadow of disquietude. I was not afraid. I have never been afraid at night. The sight of a man, a marauder, a thief, would have filled me with fury, and I would have leaped on him without a moment's hesitation. I was armed, moreover. I had my revolver. But I did not touch it, for I wished to master this sense of terror that was stirring in me.

What was it? A presentiment? The mysterious presentiment that takes possession of one's senses when they are on the verge of seeing the inexplicable? Perhaps? Who knows?

With every step I advanced, I felt my skin creep, and when I was standing under the wall of my vast house, with its closed shutters, I felt the need of waiting a few moments before opening the door and going inside. So I sat down on a bench under the windows of my drawing room. I remained there, a little shaken, my head leaning against the wall, my eyes open on the shadows of the trees. During these first instants, I noticed nothing unusual round me. I felt a sort of droning sound in my ears, but that often happened to me. It sometimes seems to me that I hear trains passing, that I hear clocks striking, that I hear the footsteps of a crowd.

Then shortly, these droning sounds became more distinct, more differentiated, more recognizable. I had been mistaken. It was not the usual throbbing sound of my pulse that filled my ears with these clamorings, but a very peculiar, though very confused noise that came, no doubt about it, from the interior of my house.

I made it out through the wall, this continuous noise, which was rather a disturbance than a noise, a confused movement of a crowd of things, as if all my furniture was being pushed, moved out of its place and gently dragged about.

Oh, for an appreciable time longer I doubted the evidence of my ears. But when I had pressed myself against a shutter the better to make out this strange disturbance of my house, I became convinced, certain, that something abnormal and incomprehensible was taking place in my house. I was not afraid, but I was— how shall I say it?—stunned with astonishment. I did not draw my revolver— having a strong suspicion that I should not need it. I waited.

I waited a long time, unable to come to any decision, my mind quite lucid, but wildly anxious. I waited, standing there, listening the whole time to the noise that went on increasing: at times it rose to a violent pitch, and seemed to become a muttering of impatience, of anger, of a mysterious tumult.

Then, suddenly ashamed of my cowardice, I seized my bunch of keys, I chose the one I wanted, I thrust it in the lock, I turned it twice, and pushing the door with all my force, I sent the door clattering against the inner wall.

The crash rang out like a pistol shot, and, amazingly, from top to bottom of my house, a formidable uproar broke out in answer to this explosive sound. It was so sudden, so terrible, so deafening, that I recoiled some steps and, although I still felt it to be useless, I drew my revolver from its holster.

I went on waiting, oh, some little time. I could distinguish, now, an extraordinary tap-tapping on the steps of my staircase, on the floors, on the carpets, a tap-tapping, not of shoes, of slippers worn by human beings, but of crutches, wooden crutches, and iron crutches that rang out like cymbals. And then all at once I saw, on the threshold of my door, an armchair, my big reading chair, come swaggering out. It set off through the garden. Others followed it, the chairs out of my drawing room, then the low couches dragging themselves along like crocodiles on their short legs, then all my chairs, leaping like goats, and the little stools trotting along like hares.

Imagine the tumult of my mind! I slipped into a grove of trees, where I stayed, crouched, watching the whole time this march-past of my furniture, for they were all taking their departure, one after the other, quickly or slowly, according to their shapes and weight. My piano, my large grand, passed, galloping like a runaway horse, with a murmur of music in its depths; the smallest objects gliding over the gravel like ants, brushes, glass dishes, goblets, where the moonlight hung glowworm lamps. The hangings slithered past in whorls, like octopuses. I saw my writing table appear, a rare piece of the last century, which contained all the letters I have received, the whole story of my heart, an old story which caused me so much suffering. And it held photographs too.

Suddenly, I was no longer afraid. I flung myself on it and seized it as one seizes a thief, as one seizes a flying woman; but it pursued its irresistible course, and in spite of my efforts, in spite of my anger, I could not retard its progress. As I was making a desperate resistance to this terrible force I fell on the ground, struggling with it. Thereupon it tumbled me over, and dragged me over the gravel, and the pieces of furniture that were following it were already beginning to walk over me, trampling over my legs and bruising them; then, when I had loosed my hold of it, the others passed over my body like a cavalry charge over a dismounted soldier.

Mad with fear at last, I managed to drag myself out of the main avenue and to hide myself again among the trees, to watch the disappearance of the meanest, smallest, most overlooked by me, most insignificant objects that had belonged to me.

Then far away, in my house, now as full of echoing sounds as empty houses are, I heard the dreadful sound of shutting doors. They clashed shut from top to bottom of the building, until the hall door that I myself, in my mad folly, had opened for their flight, had finally shut itself, last of all.

I fled too, running towards the town, and I did not recover my self-control until I was in the streets and meeting belated wayfarers. I went and rang at the door of a hotel where I was known. I had beaten my clothes with my hands to remove the dust, and I explained that I had lost my bunch of keys which contained also the key of the kitchen garden, where my servants were sleeping in a house isolated behind the enclosing wall that preserved my fruit and my vegetables from marauding visitors.

I buried myself up to my eyes in the bed they gave me. But I could not sleep, and I waited for daybreak, listening to the beating of my heart. I had given orders that my people were to be warned at dawn, and my man knocked on my door at seven o'clock in the morning.

His face seemed convulsed with emotion.

"A terrible thing happened last night, sir," he said.

"What's that?"

"The whole furniture of the house has been stolen, sir, everything, everything, down to the very smallest articles."

This news pleased me. Why? Who knows? I had myself absolutely in hand, absolutely determined to dissimulate, to say nothing to anyone about what I had seen, to hide it: bury it in my conscience like a frightful secret. I answered:

"They must be the same people who stole my keys. We must warn the police at once. I will get up and be with you in a few moments."

The investigations lasted five months. They discovered nothing, they did not find the smallest of my possessions, not the faintest trace of the thieves. Lord! if I had told what I knew. If I had told . . . they would have shut me up: me— not the robbers, but the man who had been able to see such a thing.

Oh, I know enough to hold my tongue. But I did not refurnish my house. It was quite useless. The thing would have happened again and gone on happening. I did not want to enter the house again. I did not enter it. I never saw it again.

I went to Paris, to a hotel, and I consulted doctors on my nervous state, which had been giving me much uneasiness since that deplorable night.

They ordered me to travel. I followed their advice.

II

I began by traveling in Italy. The sun did me good. For six months, I wandered from Genoa to Venice, Venice to Florence, Florence to Rome, Rome to Naples. Then I went over Sicily, a country alike notable for its climate and its monuments, relics of the Greek and Norman occupation. I turned to Africa, I peacefully crossed the huge calm yellow desert over which camels, gazelles, and vagabond Arabs wander, and almost nothing haunts the light, crystalline air, neither by night nor day.

I returned to France by Marseille, and, despite the gaiety of the province, the dimmer light of the sky saddened me. Once more I felt, on returning to the Continent, the curious fancy of a sick man who believed himself cured and whom a dull pain warns that the flame of his malady is not quite extinguished.

Then I came back to Paris. A month later, I was bored with it. It was autumn, and before winter came on, I wanted to make an expedition across Normandy, with which I had no acquaintance.

I began at Rouen, of course, and for eight days I wandered ecstatically, enthusiastically, through this medieval city, in this amazing mirror of extraordinary Gothic monuments.

Then about four o'clock one afternoon, as I was attempting some unreal street in which a stream, black as the ink they call Robec Water, flows, my attention, wholly fixed on the bizarre and antiquated character of the houses, was suddenly distracted by a glimpse of a line of secondhand dealers' shops which succeeded each other from door to door. How well they had chosen, these obscene traffickers in rubbish, their pitch in this fantastic alley, perched above the evil watercourse, beneath the roofs bristling with tiles and slates on which still creaked the weathercocks of bygone days!

In the depths of those dark stairs, all higgledy-piggledy could be seen carved presses, Rouen, Neders, Moustiers, pottery, painted statues, or some in oak, Christs, Virgins, saints, church ornaments, chasubles, copes, even chalices, and even painted shrines from which the Almighty has been dismantled. Curious, are they not? these caverns in these tall houses, in these huge towns, filled from cellar to attic with every kind of article whose existence seemed ended, but which outlived their natural owners, their century, their period, their fashion, to be bought by new generations as curiosities.

My weakness for trinkets reawakened in this city of antiquaries. I went from stall to stall, crossing in two strides the bridges made of four rotten planks thrown across the nauseous Robec Water.

Heavens! What a shock! One of my most handsome wardrobes met my eyes

at the end of a vault crowded with articles, looking like the entrance to the catacombs of a cemetery for old furniture. I drew nearer, trembling in every limb,
trembling so much that I dared not touch it. I put out my hand, I hesitated. It
was really it, after all: a unique Louis XIII wardrobe, easily recognizable by anyone who had ever seen it. Suddenly casting my eyes a little further, into the
deeper shadows of the shop, I caught sight of three of my armchairs, covered with
petit point tapestry; then, still further back, my two Henri II tables, so rare that
people came to Paris to look at them.

Think! Think of my state of mind!

But I went on, incapable, tortured with emotion. But I went forward, for I am
a brave man, as a knight of the Dark Ages thrust his way into a nest of sorcery.
Step by step, I found everything which had belonged to me, my chandeliers, my
books, my pictures, my hangings, my armors, everything except the desk full of
my letters, which I could see nowhere.

I went on, climbing down dim galleries, climbing up to higher floors. I was
alone. I shouted; no one answered. I was alone; there was no one in this vast house,
tortuous as a maze.

Night fell, and I had to sit down in the shadows of my own chairs, for I would
not go away. From time to time I called: "Hallo! Hallo! Is anyone there?"

I must have been there for certainly more than an hour when I heard steps,
light footsteps and slow, I don't know where. I was on the point of fleeing, but
taking heart, I called once more and saw a light in an adjoining room.

"Who is there?" said a voice.

I replied: "A customer."

The answer came:

"It is very late to come into shops like this."

"I have been waiting for more than an hour," I returned.

"You could come back tomorrow!"

"Tomorrow, I shall have left Rouen."

I did not dare go forward, and he did not come. All the time, I was watching
the reflection of his light illuminating a tapestry on which two angels hovered
above the bodies on a battlefield. It, too, belonged to me. I said:

"Well! Are you coming?"

He answered:

"I am waiting for you."

I rose and went towards him.

In the middle of a large room stood a tiny man, tiny and very fat, the fatness
of a freak, a hideous freak.

He had an extraordinary beard of straggling hair, thin-grown and yellowish,
and not a hair on his head. Not a hair! As he held his candle at arm's length to
see me the better, his skull looked to me like a little moon in this vast room clut-
tered with old furniture. His face was wrinkled and swollen, his eyes scarcely
visible.

I bargained for three chairs, which were mine, and paid for them on the spot
an enormous sum, giving only the number of my room at the hotel. They were
to be delivered before nine o'clock on the following morning.

Then I departed. He accompanied me to the door with many polite expressions.

I at once betook me to the head police station, where I related the story of the theft of my furniture and of the discovery I had just made.

They immediately asked for information by telegram from the department which had had charge of the burglary, asking me to wait for the reply. An hour later a quite satisfactory answer arrived.

"I shall have this man arrested and questioned at once," the chief told me, "for he may possibly have been suspicious and made away with your belongings. If you dine and come back in a couple of hours, I will have him here and make him undergo a fresh examination in your presence."

"Most certainly, sir. My warmest thanks. . . ."

I went to my hotel and dined with a better appetite than I could have believed possible. Still I was contented enough. They had him. Two hours later I went back to the chief inspector, who was waiting for me.

"Well, sir," he said, as soon as he saw me, "they haven't found your man. My fellows haven't been able to put their hands on him!"

"Ah!" I felt that I should faint. "But . . . you have found his house all right?" I asked.

"Quite. It will be watched and held until he comes back. But as for himself, vanished!"

"Vanished?"

"Vanished. Usually he spends the evenings with his neighbor, herself a dealer, a queer old witch, Widow Bidoin. She has not seen him this evening and can give no information about him. We must wait till tomorrow."

I departed. How sinister, how disturbing, how haunted the streets of Rouen seemed to me.

I slept badly enough, with nightmares to drag me out of each bout of sleep. As I did not want to appear either too worried or in too much haste, I waited on the following day until ten o'clock before going to the police station.

The dealer had not appeared. His shop remained closed.

The inspector said to me:

"I have taken all the necessary steps. The department has charge of the affair; we will go off together to this shop and have it opened, and you shall point out your belongings to me."

We were driven there in a carriage. Some policemen with a locksmith were posted in front of the shop door, which stood open.

When I entered, I found neither my wardrobe, my armchairs, nor my tables, nor anything—nothing of what had furnished my house—absolutely nothing, even though on the previous evening I could not move a step without meeting one of my pieces.

The inspector, surprised, at first looked at me with distrust.

"Good God, sir!" I said, "the disappearance of this furniture coincides amazingly with the disappearance of the dealer."

He smiled:

"True enough. You were wrong to buy and pay for those things of yours yesterday. It put him on his guard!"

I replied:

"What seems incomprehensible to me is that all the places where my furniture stood are now occupied by other pieces!"

"Oh," answered the inspector, "he had the whole night, and accomplices too, no doubt. This house probably communicates with its neighbors. Never mind, sir, I am going to move very quickly in this matter. This rogue won't keep out of our hands very long, now we hold his retreat!"

Ah, my heart, my poor heart, how it was beating.

I stayed in Rouen for a fortnight. The man did not return. My God! My God! Is there any man alive who could confound, could overreach him? Then on the morning of the sixteenth day, I received from my gardener, the caretaker of my pillaged and still empty house, the following strange letter:

SIR:

I beg to inform you that last night there occurred something which no one can fathom, the police no more than ourselves. All the furniture has come back, everything without exception, down to the very smallest objects. The house is now exactly the same as it was on the night of the burglary. It is enough to drive one off one's head. It happened during the night of Friday–Saturday. The drive is cut up as if they had dragged everything from the gate to the door—exactly as it was on the day of the disappearance.

We await you, sir, while remaining,

Your obedient servant,
PHILIPPE RAUDIN.

Ah, no, no, no, no! I will never go back there!

I took the letter to the police inspector.

"This restitution has been made very skillfully," he said. "Let's pretend to do nothing now. We'll catch our man one of these days."

But he is not caught. No. They haven't got him, and I am as afraid of him now as if he was a wild beast lurking behind me.

Not to be found! He is not to be found, this moon-headed monster. Never will he be caught. He will never again come back to his house. What does that matter to him! I am the only person who could confront him, and I will not.

I will not! I will not! I will not!

And if he returns, if he comes back to his shop, who could prove that my furniture was in his place? Mine is the only evidence against him; and I am well aware that it is regarded with suspicion.

Oh, no, such a life was no longer bearable. And I could not keep the secret of what I had seen. I could not go on living like anyone else with the dread that such happenings would begin again.

I went to see the doctor in charge of this private asylum, and told him the whole story.

After questioning me for a long time, he said:

"Would you be willing to remain here for some time?"

"Very willing."

"You have means?"

"Yes."

"You would like separate quarters?"

"Yes."

"Would you care to see friends?"

"No, not a soul. The man from Rouen might dare, for vengeance' sake, to follow me here."

And I have been alone, alone, quite alone, for three months. I am almost at peace. I have only one fear. . . . Suppose the antique dealer went mad . . . and suppose they brought him to this retreat. . . . The prisoners themselves are not safe. . . .

A TRAVELER'S TALE

The car was full as we left Cannes. We were conversing; everybody was acquainted. As we passed Tarascon someone remarked: "Here's the place where they assassinate people."

And we began to talk of the mysterious and untraceable murderer, who for the last two years had taken, from time to time, the life of a traveler. Everyone made his guess; everyone gave his opinion; the women shudderingly gazed at the dark night through the car windows, fearing suddenly to see a man's head at the door. We all began telling frightful stories of terrible encounters, meetings with madmen in a flying express, of hours passed opposite a suspected individual.

Each man knew an anecdote to his credit; each one had intimidated, overpowered and throttled some evildoer in most surprising circumstances, with an admirable presence of mind and audacity.

A physician, who spent every winter in the south, desired, in his turn, to tell an adventure:

"I," he said, "never have had the luck to test my courage in an affair of this kind, but I knew a woman, now dead, one of my patients, to whom the most singular thing in the world happened, and also the most mysterious and pathetic.

"She was Russian, the Countess Marie Baranow, a very great lady, of an exquisite beauty. You know how beautiful the Russian women are, or at least how beautiful they seem to us, with their fine noses, their delicate mouths, their eyes of an indescribable color, a blue-gray, and their cold grace, a little hard! They have something about them, mischievous and seductive, haughty and sweet, tender and severe, altogether charming to a Frenchman. At the bottom it is, perhaps, the difference of race and of type which makes me see so much in them.

"Her physician had seen for many years that she was threatened with a disease of the lungs and had tried to persuade her to come to the south of France, but she obstinately refused to leave St Petersburg. Finally, the last autumn, deeming her lost, the doctor warned her husband, who directed his wife to start at once for Mentone.

"She took the train, alone in her car, her servants occupying another compartment. She sat by the door, a little sad, seeing the fields and villages pass, feeling very lonely, very desolate in life, without children, almost without relatives, with a husband whose love was dead and who cast her thus to the end of the world without coming with her, as they send a sick valet to the hospital.

"At each station her servant Ivan came to see if his mistress wanted anything. He was an old domestic, blindly devoted, ready to accomplish all the orders which she should give him.

"Night fell, and the train rolled along at full speed. She could not sleep, being wearied and nervous.

"Suddenly the thought struck her to count the money which her husband had given her at the last minute in French gold. She opened her little bag and emptied the shining flood of metal on her lap.

"But all at once a breath of cold air struck her face. Surprised, she raised her head. The door had just opened. The Countess Marie, bewildered, hastily threw a shawl over the money spread upon her lap and waited. Some seconds passed, then a man in evening dress appeared, bareheaded, wounded on the hand and panting. He closed the door, sat down, looked at his neighbor with gleaming eyes and then wrapped a handkerchief around his wrist, which was bleeding.

"The young woman felt herself fainting with fear. This man, surely, had seen her counting her money and had come to rob and kill her.

"He kept gazing at her, breathless, his features convulsed, doubtless ready to spring upon her.

"He suddenly said:

"'Madame, don't be afraid!'

"She made no response, being incapable of opening her mouth, hearing her heartbeats and a buzzing in her ears.

"He continued:

"'I am not a malefactor, madame.'

"She continued to be silent, but by a sudden movement which she made, her knees meeting, the gold coins began to run to the floor as water runs from a spout.

"The man, surprised, looked at this stream of metal, and he suddenly stooped to pick it up.

"She, terrified, rose, casting her whole fortune on the carpet, and ran to the door to leap out upon the track.

"But he understood what she was going to do and, springing forward, seized her in his arms, seated her by force and held her by the wrists.

"'Listen to me, madame,' he said, 'I am not a malefactor; the proof of it is that I am going to gather up this gold and return it to you. But I am a lost man, a dead man, if you do not assist me to pass the frontier. I cannot tell you more. In an hour we shall be at the last Russian station; in an hour and twenty minutes we shall cross the boundary of the empire. If you do not help me I am lost. And yet I have neither killed anyone, nor robbed nor done anything contrary to honor. This I swear to you. I cannot tell you more.'

"And kneeling down, he picked up the gold, even hunting under the seats for the last coins, which had rolled to a distance. Then when the little leather bag was full again he gave it to his neighbor without saying a word and returned to seat himself at the other corner of the compartment. Neither of them moved. She kept motionless and mute, still faint from terror, but recovering little by little. As for him, he did not make a gesture or a motion, remained sitting erect, his eyes staring in front of him, very pale, as if he were dead. From time to time she threw a quick look at him and as quickly turned her glance away. He appeared to be about thirty years of age and was very handsome, with the mien of a gentleman.

"The train ran through the darkness, giving at intervals its shrill signals, now slowing up in its progress and again starting off at full speed. But presently its progress slackened, and after several sharp whistles it came to a full stop.

"Ivan appeared at the door for his orders.

"The Countess Marie, her voice trembling, gave one last look at her companion; then she said to her servant in a quick tone:

" 'Ivan, you will return to the count; I do not need you any longer.'

"The man, bewildered, opened his enormous eyes. He stammered:

" 'But, my lady——'

"She replied:

" 'No, you will not come with me; I have changed my mind. I wish you to stay in Russia. Here is some money for your return home. Give me your cap and cloak.'

"The old servant, frightened, took off his cap and cloak, obeying without question, accustomed to the sudden whims and caprices of his masters. And he went away with tears in his eyes.

"The train started again, rushing toward the frontier.

"Then the Countess Marie said to her neighbor:

" 'These things are for you, monsieur—you are Ivan, my servant. I make only one condition to what I am doing: that is that you shall not speak a word to me, either to thank me or for anything whatsoever.'

"The unknown bowed without uttering a syllable.

"Soon the train stopped again, and officers in uniform visited the train.

"The countess handed them her papers and, pointing to the man seated at the end of the compartment, said:

" 'That is my servant Ivan, whose passport is here.'

"The train again started.

"During the night they sat opposite each other, both mute.

"When morning came, as they stopped at a German station, the unknown got out; then, standing at the door, he said:

" 'Pardon me, madame, for breaking my promise, but as I have deprived you of a servant it is proper that I should replace him. Have you need of anything?'

"She replied coldly:

" 'Go and find my maid.'

"He went to summon her. Then he disappeared.

"When she alighted at some station for luncheon she saw him at a distance looking at her. They finally arrived at Mentone."

II

The doctor was silent for a second and then resumed:

"One day while I was receiving patients in my office, a tall young man entered. He said to me:

" 'Doctor, I have come to ask you news of the Countess Marie Baranow. I am a friend of her husband, although she does not know me.'

"I answered:

" 'She is lost. She will never return to Russia.'

"And suddenly this man began to sob, then he rose and went out, staggering like a drunken man.

"I told the countess that evening that a stranger had come to make inquiries about her health. She seemed moved and told me the story which I have just related to you. She added:

" 'That man, whom I do not know at all, follows me now like my shadow. I meet him every time I go out. He looks at me in a strange way, but he has never spoken to me!'

"She pondered a moment then added:

" 'Come, I'll wager that he is under the window now.'

"She left her reclining chair, went to the window and drew back the curtain and actually showed me the man who had come to see me, seated on a bench at the edge of the side wall with his eyes raised toward the house. He perceived us, rose and went away without once turning around.

"Then I understood a sad and surprising thing, the mute love of these two beings who were not acquainted with each other.

"He loved her with the devotion of a rescued animal, grateful and devoted to the death. He came every day to ask me, 'How is she?' understanding that I had guessed his feelings. And he wept frightfully when he saw her pass, weaker and paler every day.

"She said to me:

" 'I have never spoken but once to that singular man, and yet it seems as if I had known him for twenty years.'

"And when they met she returned his bow with a serious and charming smile. I felt that although she was given up and knew herself lost she was happy to be loved thus, with this respect and constancy, with this exaggerated poetry, with this devotion, ready for anything.

"Nevertheless, faithful to her superexcited obstinacy, she absolutely refused to learn his name, to speak to him. She said:

" 'No, no, that would spoil this strange friendship. We must remain strangers to each other.'

"As for him, he was certainly a kind of Don Quixote, for he did nothing to bring himself closer to her. He intended to keep to the end the absurd promise never to speak to her which he had made in the car.

"Often during her long hours of weakness she rose from her reclining chair and partly opened the curtain to see whether he were there beneath the window. And when she had seen him, ever motionless upon his bench, she came back to lie down again with a smile upon her lips.

"She died one morning about ten o'clock.

"As I left the house he came to me, his countenance showing that he had already learned the news.

" 'I would like to see her for a second in your presence,' he said.

"I took him by the arm, and we entered the house together.

"When he was beside the bed of the dead woman he seized her hand and gave it a long and passionate kiss; then he went away like a man bereft of his senses."

The doctor again was silent. Then he resumed:

"There you have, certainly, the most singular railroad adventure that I know. It must also be said that men are queer lunatics."

A woman murmured in a low tone:

"Those two people were less crazy than you think. They were—they were——"

But she could speak no longer because she was weeping. As the conversation was changed to calm her, no one ever knew what she had intended to say.

LITTLE LOUISE ROQUE

Mederic Rompel, the postman, familiarly called by the country people "Mederi," started at his usual hour from the posthouse at Rouy-le-Tors. Having passed through the little town, striding like an old trooper, he cut across the meadows of Villaumes in order to reach the bank of the Brindelle, which led him along the water's edge to the village of Carvelin, where his distribution commenced. He traveled quickly, following the course of the narrow river, which frothed, murmured and boiled along its bed of grass under the arching willow trees. The big stones, impeding the flow of water, created around them a sort of aqueous necktie ending in a knot of foam. In some places there were cascades a foot wide, often invisible, which made under the leaves, under the tendrils, under a roof of verdure, a noise at once angry and gentle. Farther on the banks widened out, and you saw a small, placid lake where trout were swimming in the midst of all that green vegetation which keeps undulating in the depths of tranquil streams.

Mederic went on without a halt, seeing nothing and with only one thought in his mind: "My first letter is for the Poivron family; then I have one for Monsieur Renardet, so I must cross the wood."

His blue blouse, fastened round his waist by a black leathern belt, moved in quick, regular fashion above the green hedge of willow trees, and his stick of stout holly kept time with the steady march of his feet.

He crossed the Brindelle over a bridge formed of a single tree thrown lengthwise, with a rope attached to two stakes driven into the riverbanks as its only balustrade.

The wood, which belonged to M. Renardet, the mayor of Carvelin and the largest landowner in the district, consisted of a number of huge old trees, straight as pillars, and extended for about half a league along the left bank of the stream which served as a boundary for this immense arch of foliage. Alongside the water there were large shrubs warmed by the sun, but under the trees you found nothing but moss, thick, soft, plastic moss, which exhaled into the stagnant air a light odor of loam and withered branches.

Mederic slackened his pace, took off his black cap trimmed with red lace and wiped his forehead, for it was by this time hot in the meadows, though not yet eight o'clock in the morning.

He had just recovered from the effects of the heat and had accelerated his pace when he noticed at the foot of a tree a knife, a child's small knife. As he picked it up he discovered a thimble and then a needlecase not far away.

Having found these objects, he thought: "I'll intrust them to the mayor," and resumed this journey. But now he kept his eyes open, expecting to find something else.

"All of a sudden he drew up stiffly, as if he had run up against a wooden bar. Ten paces in front of him on the moss lay stretched on her back a little girl, quite naked. She was about twelve years old. Her arms were hanging down, her legs parted and her face covered with a handkerchief. There were little spots of blood on her thighs.

Mederic now advanced on tiptoe, as if afraid to make a noise; he apprehended some danger and glanced toward the spot uneasily.

What was this? No doubt she was asleep. Then he reflected that a person does not go to sleep thus, naked, at half-past seven in the morning under cool trees. Then she must be dead, and he must be face to face with a crime. At this thought a cold shiver ran through his frame, although he was an old soldier. And then a murder was such a rare thing in the country—and above all the murder of a child —that he could not believe his eyes. But she had no wound—nothing save these blood drops on her legs. How then had she been killed?

He stopped when quite near her and stared at her while leaning on his stick. Certainly he knew her, as he knew all the inhabitants of the district, but not being able to get a look at her face, he could not guess her name. He stooped forward in order to take off the handkerchief which covered her face then paused with outstretched hand, restrained by an idea that occurred to him.

Had he the right to disarrange anything in the condition of the corpse before the magisterial investigation? He pictured justice to himself as a general whom nothing escapes, who attaches as much importance to a lost button as to a stab of a knife in the stomach. Perhaps under this handkerchief evidence to support a capital charge could be found; in fact, if there were sufficient proof there to secure a conviction it might lose its value if touched by an awkward hand.

Then he straightened up with the intention of hastening toward the mayor's residence, but again another thought held him back. If the little girl was still alive, by any chance, he could not leave her lying there in this way. He sank on his knees very gently, a yard away from her, through precaution, and stretched his hand toward her feet. The flesh was icy cold, with that terrible coldness which makes dead flesh frightful and leaves us no longer in doubt. The letter carrier, as he touched her, felt his heart leap to his mouth, as he said himself afterward, and his lips were parched with dry saliva. Rising up abruptly, he rushed off through the trees to M. Renardet's house.

He hurried on in double-quick time, with his stick under his arm, his hands clenched and his head thrust forward and his leathern bag, filled with letters and newspapers, flapping regularly at his side.

The mayor's residence was at the end of the wood, which he used as a park, and one side of it was washed by a little lagoon formed at this spot by the Brindelle.

It was a big square house of gray stone, very old. It had stood many a siege in former days, and at the end of it was a huge tower, twenty meters high, built in the water. From the top of this fortress the entire country around could be seen in olden times. It was called the Fox's Tower, without anyone knowing exactly why; and from the appellation, no doubt, had come the name Renardet, borne by the owners of this fief, which had remained in the same family, it was said, for more than two hundred years. For the Renardets formed part of that upper middle class which is all but noble and was met with so often in the provinces before the Revolution.

The postman dashed into the kitchen where the servants were taking breakfast and exclaimed:

"Is the mayor up? I want to speak to him at once."

Mederic was recognized as a man of weight and authority, and it was soon understood that something serious had happened.

As soon as word was brought to M. Renardet he ordered the postman to be
sent up to him. Pale and out of breath, with his cap in his hand, Mederic found
the mayor seated in front of a long table covered with scattered papers.

He was a big, tall man, heavy and red-faced, strong as an ox and greatly liked
in the district, though of an excessively violent disposition. Very nearly forty years
old and a widower for the past six months, he lived on his estate like a country
gentleman. His choleric temperament had often brought him into trouble, from
which the magistrates of Rouy-le-Tors, like indulgent and prudent friends, had
extricated him. Had he not one day thrown the conductor of the diligence from
the top of his seat because the latter had nearly crushed his retriever Micmac?
Had he not broken the ribs of a gamekeeper who had abused him for having
passed through a neighbor's property with a gun in his hand? Had he not even
caught by the collar the subprefect, who stopped in the village in the course of
an administrative round described by M. Renardet as an electioneering tour, for
he was against the government, according to his family tradition?

The mayor asked:

"What's the matter now, Mederic?"

"I have found a little girl dead in your wood."

Renardet rose up, with his face the color of brick.

"A little girl, do you say?"

"Yes, m'sieu, a little girl, quite naked, on her back, with blood on her, dead—
quite dead!"

The mayor gave vent to an oath:

"By God, I'd make a bet 'tis little Louise Roque! I have just learned that she
did not go home to her mother last night. Where did you find her?"

The postman pointed out where the place was, gave full details and offered to
conduct the mayor to the spot.

But Renardet became brusque:

"No. I don't need you. Send the steward, the mayor's secretary and the doctor
immediately to me and resume your rounds. Quick, go quick and tell them to
meet me in the wood."

The letter carrier, a man used to discipline, obeyed and withdrew, angry and
grieved at not being able to be present at the investigation.

The mayor, in his turn, prepared to go out. He took his hat, a big soft hat,
and paused for a few seconds on the threshold of his abode. In front of him
stretched a wide lawn in which three large patches were conspicuous—three large
beds of flowers in full bloom, one facing the house and the others at either side
of it. Farther on rose skyward the principal trees in the wood, while at the left,
above the spot where the Brindelle widened into a pool, could be seen long
meadows, an entirely flat green sweep of country, cut by dikes and monsterlike
willows, twisted dwarf trees, always cut short, having on their thick squat trunks
a quivering tuft of branches.

To the right, behind the stables, the outhouses and the buildings connected
with the property, might be seen the village, which was prosperous, being mainly
inhabited by raisers of oxen.

Renardet slowly descended the steps in front of his house and, turning to the
left, gained the water's edge, which he followed at a slow pace, his hands behind
his back. He went on with bent head, and from time to time he glanced round in
search of the persons for whom he had sent.

When he stood beneath the trees he stopped, took off his hat and wiped his forehead as Mederic had done, for the burning sun was shedding its fiery rain upon the ground. Then the mayor resumed his journey, stopped once more and retraced his steps. Suddenly stooping down, he sopped his handkerchief in the stream that glided at his feet and stretched it round his head, under his hat. Drops of water flowed along his temples, over his purple ears, over his strong red neck, and trickled one after the other under his white shirt collar.

As yet nobody had appeared; he began tapping with his foot, then he called out: "Hallo! Hallo!"

A voice at his right answered: "Hallo! Hallo!" and the doctor appeared under the trees. He was a thin little man, an ex-military surgeon, who passed in the neighborhood for a very skillful practitioner. He limped, having been wounded while in the service, and had to use a stick to assist him in walking.

Next came the steward and the mayor's secretary, who, having been sent for at the same time, arrived together. They seemed scared as they hurried forward, out of breath, walking and trotting in turn in order to hasten and moving their arms up and down so vigorously that they seemed to do more work with them than with their legs.

Renardet said to the doctor:

"You know what the trouble is about?"

"Yes, a child found dead in the wood by Mederic."

"That's quite correct. Come on."

They walked on side by side, followed by the two men.

Their steps made no noise on the moss; their eyes were gazing downward right in front of them.

The doctor hastened his steps, interested by the discovery. As soon as they were near the corpse he bent down to examine it without touching it. He had put on a pair of glasses, as you do when you are looking at some curious object; then he turned round very quietly and said without rising up:

"Violated and assassinated, as we shall prove presently. The little girl, moreover, is almost a woman—look at her throat."

Her two breasts, already nearly full-developed, fell over her chest, relaxed by death. The doctor lightly drew away the handkerchief which covered her face. It was almost black, frightful to look at, the tongue protruding, the eyes bloodshot. He went on:

"Faith, she was strangled the moment the deed was done."

He felt her neck:

"Strangled with the hands without leaving any special trace, neither the mark of the nails nor the imprint of the fingers. Quite right. It is little Louise Roque, sure enough!"

He delicately replaced the handkerchief.

"There's nothing for me to do. She's been dead for the last hour at least. We must give notice of the matter to the authorities."

Renardet, standing up with his hands behind his back, kept staring with a stony look at the little body exposed to view on the grass. He murmured:

"What a wretch! We must find the clothes."

The doctor felt the hands, the arms, the legs. He said:

"She must have been bathing, no doubt. They ought to be at the water's edge."

The mayor thereupon gave directions:

"Do you, Princèpe [this was his secretary], go and look for those clothes for me along the river. Do you, Maxime [this was the steward], hurry on toward Rouy-le-Tors and bring on here to me the examining magistrate with the gendarmes. They must be here within an hour. You understand."

The two men quickly departed, and Renardet said to the doctor:

"What miscreant has been able to do such a deed in this part of the country?"

The doctor murmured:

"Who knows? Everyone is capable of that! Everyone in particular and nobody in general. However, it must be some prowler, some workman out of employment. As we live under a republic, we must expect to meet this sort of miscreant along the roads."

Both of them were Bonapartists. The mayor went on:

"Yes, it could only be a stranger, a passer-by, a vagabond without heart or home."

The doctor added with the shadow of a smile on his face:

"And without a wife. Having neither a good supper nor a good bed, he procured the rest for himself. You can't tell how many men there may be in the world capable of a crime at a given moment. Did you know that this little girl had disappeared?"

And with the end of his stick he touched one after the other the stiffened fingers of the corpse, resting on them as on the keys of a piano.

"Yes, the mother came last night to look for me about nine o'clock, the child not having come home for supper up to seven. We went to try and find her along the roads up to midnight, but we did not think of the wood. However, we needed daylight to carry out a search with a practical result."

"Will you have a cigar?" said the doctor.

"Thanks, I don't care to smoke. It gives me a turn to look at this."

They remained standing in front of the young girl's body, pale and still, on the dark background of moss. A big fly was walking along one of the thighs; it stopped at the bloodstains, went on again, always rising higher, ran along the side with his lively, jerky movements, climbed up one of the breasts, then came back again to explore the other. The two men silently watched this wandering black speck. The doctor said:

"How tantalizing it is, a fly on the skin! The ladies of the last century had good reason to paste them on their faces. Why has the fashion gone out?"

But the mayor seemed not to hear, plunged as he was in deep thought.

All of a sudden he turned around, surprised by a shrill noise. A woman in a cap and a blue apron rushed up through the trees. It was the mother, La Roque. As soon as she saw Renardet she began to shriek:

"My little girl, where's my little girl?" in such a distracted manner that she did not glance down at the ground. Suddenly she saw the corpse, stopped short, clasped her hands and raised both her arms while she uttered a sharp, heart-rending cry—the cry of a mutilated animal. Then she rushed toward the body, fell on her knees and snatched the handkerchief that covered the face. When she saw that frightful countenance, black and convulsed, she recoiled with a shudder, then pressed her face against the ground, giving vent to terrible and continuous choking screams, her mouth close to the thick moss.

Her tall thin frame, to which her clothes clung tightly, was palpitating, shaken with convulsions. They could see her bony ankles and withered limbs, covered with thick blue stockings, shivering horribly. Unconsciously she dug at the soil with her crooked fingers as if to make a grave in which to hide herself.

The doctor pityingly said in a low tone:

"Poor old woman!"

Renardet felt a strange rumbling in his stomach; then he gave vent to a sort of loud sneeze that issued at the same time through nose and mouth and, drawing his handkerchief from his pocket, began to weep copiously, coughing, sobbing noisily, wiping his face and stammering:

"Damn—damn—damned pig to do this! I would like to see him guillotined!"

But Princèpe reappeared with his hands empty. He murmured:

"I have found nothing, M'sieu le Maire, nothing at all anywhere."

The mayor, scared, replied in a thick voice, drowned in tears:

"What is it you could not find?"

"The little girl's clothes."

"Well—well—look again and find them—or you'll have to answer to me."

The man, knowing that the mayor would not brook opposition, set forth again with hesitating steps, casting on the corpse horrified and timid glances.

Distant voices arose under the trees, a confused sound, the noise of an approaching crowd, for Mederic had, in the course of his rounds, carried the news from door to door. The people of the neighborhood, stupefied at first, had gone gossiping from their own firesides into the street and from one threshold to another. Then they gathered together. They talked over, discussed and commented on the event for some minutes, and they had now come to see it for themselves.

They arrived in groups, a little faltering and uneasy through fear of the first impression of such a scene on their minds. When they saw the body they stopped, not daring to advance and speaking low. Then they grew bold, went on a few steps, stopped again, advanced once more and soon formed around the dead girl, her mother, the doctor and Renardet a thick circle, agitated and noisy, which swayed forward under the sudden pushes of the last comers. And now they touched the corpse. Some of them even bent down to feel it with their fingers. The doctor kept them back. But the mayor, waking abruptly out of his torpor, broke into a rage and, seizing Dr Labarbe's stick, flung himself on his townspeople, stammering:

"Clear out—clear out—you pack of brutes—clear out!"

And in a second the crowd of sight-seers had fallen back two hundred meters.

La Roque was lifted up, turned round and placed in a sitting posture; she remained weeping with her hands clasped over her face.

The occurrence was discussed among the crowd, and young lads, with eager eyes, curiously scrutinized the nude body of the girl. Renardet perceived this and, abruptly taking off his vest, flung it over the little girl, who was entirely lost to view under the wide garment.

The spectators drew quietly nearer. The wood was filled with people, and a continuous hum of voices rose up under the tangled foliage of the tall trees.

The mayor, in his shirt sleeves, remained standing, with his stick in his hands, in a fighting attitude. He seemed exasperated by this curiosity on the part of the people and kept repeating:

"If one of you comes nearer I'll break his head just as I would a dog's."

The peasants were greatly afraid of him. They held back. Dr Labarbe, who was smoking, sat down beside La Roque and spoke to her in order to distract her attention. The old woman soon removed her hands from her face and replied with a flood of tearful words, pouring forth her grief in rapid sentences. She told the whole story of her life, her marriage, the death of her man—a bullsticker who had been gored to death—the infancy of her daughter, her wretched existence as a widow without resources and with a child to support. She had only this one, her little Louise, and the child had been killed—killed in this wood. All of a sudden she felt anxious to see it again and, dragging herself on her knees toward the corpse, she raised up one corner of the garment that covered it; then she let it fall again and began wailing once more. The crowd remained silent, eagerly watching the mother's gestures.

But all of a sudden there was a swaying of the crowd and a cry of "The gendarmes! The gendarmes!"

Two gendarmes appeared in the distance, coming on at a rapid trot, escorting their captain and a little gentleman with red whiskers, who was bobbing up and down like a monkey on a big white mare.

The steward had found M. Putoin, the examining magistrate, just at the moment when he was mounting to take his daily ride, for he posed as a good horseman, to the great amusement of the officers.

He dismounted along with the captain and pressed the hands of the mayor and the doctor, casting a ferretlike glance on the linen vest which swelled above the body lying underneath.

When he was thoroughly acquainted with the facts he first gave orders to get rid of the public, whom the gendarmes drove out of the wood but who soon reappeared in the meadow and formed a line, a long line of excited and moving heads all along the Brindelle, on the other side of the stream.

The doctor in his turn gave explanations of which Renardet took a note in his memorandum book. All the evidence was given, taken down and commented on without leading to any discovery. Maxime, too, came back without having found any trace of the clothes.

This surprised everybody; no one could explain it on the theory of theft, since these rags were not worth twenty sous, so this theory was inadmissible.

The examining magistrate, the mayor, the captain and the doctor set to work by searching in pairs, putting aside the smallest branches along the water.

Renardet said to the judge:

"How does it happen that this wretch should conceal or carry away the clothes and should then leave the body exposed in the open air and visible to everyone?"

The other, sly and knowing, answered:

"Perhaps a dodge. This crime has been committed either by a brute or by a crafty blackguard. In any case, we'll easily succeed in finding him."

The rolling of a vehicle made them turn their heads. It was the deputy magistrate, another doctor and the registrar of the court who had arrived in their turn. They resumed their searches, all chatting in an animated fashion.

Renardet said suddenly:

"Do you know that I am expecting you to lunch with me?"

Everyone smilingly accepted the invitation, and the examining magistrate, finding that the case of little Louise Roque was quite enough to bother about for one day, turned toward the mayor.

"I can have the body brought to your house, can I not? You have a room in which you can keep it for me till this evening."

The other got confused and stammered:

"Yes—no—no. To tell the truth, I prefer that it should not come into my house on account of—on account of my servants who are already talking about ghosts in—in my tower, in the Fox's Tower. You know—I could no longer keep a single one. No—I prefer not to have it in my house."

The magistrate began to smile:

"Good! I am going to get it carried off at once to Rouy for the legal examination."

Turning toward the doctor:

"I can make use of your trap, can I not?"

"Yes, certainly."

Everybody came back to the place where the corpse lay. La Roque, now seated beside her daughter, had caught hold of her hand and was staring right before her, with a wandering, listless eye.

The two doctors endeavored to lead her away so that she might not witness the dead girl's removal, but she understood at once what they wanted to do and, flinging herself on the body, she seized it in both arms. Lying on top of the corpse, she exclaimed:

"You shall not have it—'tis mine—'tis mine now. They have killed her for me, and I want to keep her—you shall not have her!"

All the men, affected and not knowing how to act, remained standing around her. Renardet fell on his knees and said to her:

"Listen, La Roque, it is necessary—in order to find out who killed her. Without this it could not be found out. We must make a search for him in order to punish him. When we have found him we'll give her up to you. I promise you this."

This explanation shook the woman's mind, and a feeling of hatred manifested in her distracted glance.

"So then they'll take him?"

"Yes, I promise you that."

She rose up, deciding to let them do as they liked, but when the captain remarked: "'Tis surprising that her clothes cannot be found," a new idea which she had not previously thought of abruptly found an entrance into her brain, and she asked:

"Where are her clothes? They're mine. I want them. Where have they been put?"

They explained to her that they had not been found; then she called out for them with desperate obstinacy and with repeated moans:

"They're mine—I want them. Where are they? I want them!"

The more they tried to calm her, the more she sobbed and persisted in her demands. She no longer wanted the body; she insisted on having the clothes, as much, perhaps, through the unconscious cupidity of a wretched being to whom a piece of silver represents a fortune as through maternal tenderness.

And when the little body, rolled up in blankets which had been brought out from Renardet's house, had disappeared in the vehicle, the old woman, standing under the trees, held up by the mayor and the captain, exclaimed:

"I have nothing, nothing, nothing in the world, not even her little cap—her little cap."

The curé had just arrived, a young priest already growing stout. He took it on himself to carry off La Roque, and they went away together toward the village. The mother's grief was modified under the sugary words of the clergyman, who promised her a thousand compensations. But she incessantly kept repeating: "If I had only her little cap."

This idea now dominated every other.

Before they were out of hearing Renardet exclaimed:

"You will lunch with us, Monsieur l'Abbé—in an hour's time?"

The priest turned his head round and replied:

"With pleasure, Monsieur le Maire. I'll be with you at twelve."

And they all directed their steps toward the house whose gray front and large tower, built on the edge of the Brindelle, could be seen through the branches.

The meal lasted a long time. They talked about the crime, and everybody was of the same opinion. It had been committed by some tramp passing there by chance while the little girl was bathing.

Then the magistrates returned to Rouy, announcing that they would return next day at an early hour. The doctor and the curé went to their respective homes, while Renardet, after a long walk through the meadows, returned to the wood, where he remained walking till nightfall with slow steps, his hands behind his back.

He went to bed early and was still asleep next morning when the examining magistrate entered his room. He rubbed his hands together with a self-satisfied air. He said:

"Ha! ha! Still sleeping? Well, my dear fellow, we have news this morning."

The mayor sat up on his bed.

"What, pray?"

"Oh! Something strange. You remember well how the mother yesterday clamored for some memento of her daughter, especially her little cap? Well, on opening her door this morning, she found on the threshold her child's two little wooden shoes. This proves that the crime was perpetrated by someone from the district, someone who felt pity for her. Besides, the postman Mederic found and brought me the thimble, the scissors and the needlecase of the dead girl. So then the man in carrying off the clothes in order to hide them, must have let fall the articles which were in the pocket. As for me, I attach special importance to the wooden shoes, as they indicate a certain moral culture and a faculty for tenderness on the part of the assassin. We will therefore, if you have no objection, pass in review together the principal inhabitants of your district."

The mayor got up. He rang for hot water to shave with and said:

"With pleasure, but it will take rather a long time, so let us begin at once."

M. Putoin sat astride on a chair, thus pursuing even in a room his mania for horsemanship. Renardet now covered his chin with a white lather while he looked at himself in the glass; then he sharpened his razor on the strop and went on:

"The principal inhabitant of Carvelin bears the name of Joseph Renardet, mayor, a rich landowner, a rough man who beats guards and coachmen——"

The examining magistrate burst out laughing.

"That's enough; let us pass on to the next."

"The second in importance is ill, Pelledent, his deputy, a rearer of oxen, an equally rich landowner, a crafty peasant, very sly, very closefisted on every question of money, but incapable in my opinion of having perpetrated such a crime."

M. Putoin said:

"Let us pass on."

Then while continuing to shave and wash himself, Renardet went on with the moral inspection of all the inhabitants of Carvelin. After two hours' discussion their suspicions were fixed on three individuals who had hitherto borne a shady reputation—a poacher named Cavalle, a fisher for club and crayfish named Paquet and a bullsticker named Clovis.

II

The search for the perpetrator of the crime lasted all the summer, but he was not discovered. Those who were suspected and those who were arrested easily proved their innocence, and the authorities were compelled to abandon the attempt to capture the criminal.

But the murder seemed to have moved the entire country in a singular fashion. It left a disquietude, a vague fear, a sensation of mysterious terror, springing not merely from the impossibility of discovering any trace of the assassin, but above all from that strange finding of the wooden shoes in front of La Roque's door on the day after the crime. The certainty that the murderer had assisted at the investigation and that he was doubtless still living in the village left a gloomy impression on every mind and hung over the neighborhood like a constant menace.

The wood, besides, had become a dreaded spot, a place to be avoided and supposed to be haunted.

Formerly the inhabitants used to come and lounge there every Sunday afternoon. They used to sit down on the moss at the foot of the huge trees or walk along the water's edge, watching the trout gliding under the green undergrowth. The boys used to play bowls, hide-and-seek and other games in certain places where they had upturned, smoothed out and leveled the soil, and the girls, in rows of four or five, used to trip along, holding one another by the arms and screaming out with their shrill voices ballads which grated on the ear, disturbed the tranquil air with discord and set the teeth on edge like vinegar. Now nobody ventured into and under the towering trees, as if afraid of finding there some corpse lying on the ground.

Autumn arrived; the leaves began to fall. They fell day and night from the tall trees, whirling round and round to the ground, and the sky could be seen through the bare branches. Sometimes when a gust of wind swept over the treetops the slow, continuous rain suddenly grew heavier and became a hoarsely growling storm, which drenched the moss with thick yellow water that made the ground swampy and yielding. And the almost imperceptible murmur, the floating, ceaseless whisper, gentle and sad, of this rainfall seemed like a low wail, and the continually falling leaves, like tears, big tears shed by the tall mournful trees which were weeping, as it were, day and night over the close of the year, over the ending of warm dawns and soft twilights, over the ending of hot breezes and bright suns and also, perhaps, over the crime which they had seen committed under the shade of their branches, over the girl violated and killed at their feet. They wept in the silence of the desolate empty wood, the abandoned, dreaded wood, where the soul, the childish soul of the dead little girl, must have been wandering all alone.

The Brindelle, swollen by the storms, rushed on more quickly, yellow and angry, between its dry banks lined with thin, bare willow hedges.

Renardet suddenly resumed his walks under the trees. Every day at sunset he came out of his house, descended the front steps slowly and entered the wood in a dreamy fashion, with his hands in his pockets. For a long time he would pace over the damp, soft moss, while a legion of rooks, rushing to the spot from all the neighboring haunts in order to rest in the tall summits, spread themselves through space like an immense mourning veil floating in the wind, uttering violent and sinister screams. Sometimes they would perch on the tangled branches, dotting with black spots the red sky, the sky crimsoned with autumn twilight. Then all of a sudden they would set off again, croaking frightfully and trailing once more above the wood the long darkness of their flight. Then they would swoop down at last on the highest treetops, and gradually their cawings would die away, while advancing night merged their black plumes into the blackness of space.

Renardet was still strolling slowly under the trees; then, when the darkness prevented him from walking any longer, he went back to the house, sank all of a heap into his armchair in front of the glowing hearth and dried his feet at the fire.

Now one morning an important bit of news was circulated around the district: the mayor was getting his wood cut down.

Twenty woodcutters were already at work. They had commenced at the corner nearest to the house, and they worked rapidly in the master's presence.

At first the loppers climbed up the trunk. Tied to it by a rope collar, they clung round it in the beginning with both arms, then, lifting one leg, struck the tree hard with the edge of a steel instrument attached to each foot. The edge penetrated the wood and remained stuck in it, and the man rose up as if on a step in order to strike with the steel attached to the other foot, and then once more supported himself till he could lift his first foot again.

With every upward movement was slipped higher the rope collar which fastened him to the tree. Over his loins hung and glittered the steel hatchet. He kept continually climbing in easy fashion, like some parasite attacking a giant, mounting slowly up the immense trunk, embracing it and spurring it in order to decapitate it.

As soon as he reached the lowest branches he stopped, detached from his side the sharp ax and struck. Slowly, methodically, he chopped at the limb close to the trunk. Suddenly the branch cracked, gave way, bent, tore itself off and fell, grazing the neighboring trees in its fall. Then it crashed down on the ground with a great sound of broken wood, and its lighter branches quivered for a long time.

The soil was covered with fragments which other men cut in their turn, bound in bundles and piled in heaps, while the trees which were still left standing looked like enormous posts, gigantic forms amputated and shorn by the keen steel axes of the cutters.

When the lopper had finished his task he left at the top of the straight slender shaft of the tree the rope collar which he had brought up with him, descending again with spurlike prods along the discrowned trunk which the woodcutters below attacked at the base, striking it with heavy blows which resounded through all the rest of the wood.

When the base of the tree seemed pierced deeply enough some men commenced dragging, to the accompaniment of a signal cry in which all joined harmoniously, at the rope attached to the top. All of a sudden the immense column cracked and tumbled to the earth with the dull sound and shock of a distant cannon shot. Each day the wood grew thinner, losing its trees one by one, as an army loses its soldiers.

Renardet no longer walked up and down. He remained from morning till night contemplating, motionless, with his hands behind his back, the slow death of his wood. When a tree fell he placed his foot on it as if it were a corpse. Then he raised his eyes to the next with a kind of secret, calm impatience, as if he expected or hoped for something at the end of this massacre.

Meanwhile they were approaching the place where little Louise Roque had been found. A length they came to it—one evening at the hour of twilight.

As it was dark, the sky being overcast, the woodcutters wanted to stop their work, putting off till next day the fall of an enormous beech tree. But Renardet objected to this, insisting that even at this late hour they should lop and cut down this giant, which had overshadowed and seen the crime.

When the lopper had laid it bare, had finished its toilet for the guillotine, and the woodcutters had sapped its base, five men commenced hauling at the rope attached to the top.

The tree resisted; its powerful trunk, although cut halfway through, was as rigid as iron. The workmen, altogether, with a sort of regular jump, strained at the rope, stooping down to the ground, and they gave vent to a cry with lungs out of breath, so as to indicate and direct their efforts.

Two woodcutters stood close to the giant with axes in their grip, like two executioners ready to strike once more, and Renardet, motionless, with his hand on the bark, awaited the fall with an uneasy, nervous feeling.

One of the men said to him:

"You're too near, Monsieur le Maire. When it falls it may hurt you."

He did not reply and did not recoil. He seemed ready to catch the beech tree in his open arms in order to cast it on the ground like a wrestler.

All at once at the foot of the tall column of wood there was a shudder which seemed to run to the top, like a painful shiver; it bent slightly, ready to fall, but still resisted. The men, in a state of excitement, stiffened their arms, renewed their efforts with greater vigor, and, just as the tree, breaking, came crashing down, Renardet suddenly made a forward step, then stopped, his shoulders raised to receive the irresistible shock, the mortal blow which would crush him to the earth.

But the beech tree, having deviated a little, only grazed against his loins, throwing him on his face five meters away.

The workmen rushed forward to lift him up. He had already risen to his knees, stupefied, with wandering eyes, and passing his hand across his forehead, as if he were awaking out of an attack of madness.

When he had got to his feet once more the men, astonished, questioned him, not being able to understand what he had done. He replied in faltering tones that he had had for a moment a fit of abstraction, or rather a return to the days of his childhood, that he imagined he had to pass under that tree, just as street boys rush in front of vehicles driving rapidly past, that he had played at danger, that for the past eight days he felt this desire growing stronger within him, asking himself whether every time a tree was cracking, was on the point of falling, he could pass beneath it without being touched. It was a piece of stupidity, he confessed, but everyone has these moments of insanity, these temptations to boyish folly.

He made this explanation in a slow tone, searching for his words and speaking in a stupefied fashion.

Then he went off saying:

"Till tomorrow, my friends—till tomorrow."

As soon as he had reached his study he sat down before his table, which his lamp, covered with a shade, lighted up brightly, and, clasping his hands over his forehead, began to cry.

He remained crying for a long time, then wiped his eyes, raised his head and looked at the clock. It was not yet six o'clock.

"I have time before dinner."

And he went to the door and locked it. He then came back and sat down before his table. He pulled out a drawer in the middle of it and, taking from it a revolver, laid it down over his papers, under the glare of the lamp. The barrel of the fire-arm glittered and cast reflections which resembled flames.

Renardet gazed at it for some time with the uneasy glance of a drunken man; then he rose and began to pace up and down the room.

He walked from one end of the apartment to the other, stopped from time to time and started to pace up and down again a moment afterward. Suddenly he opened the door of his dressing room, steeped a towel in the water jug and mois-tened his forehead, as he had done on the morning of the crime.

Then he began to walk up and down once more. Each time he passed the table the gleaming revolver attracted his glance and tempted his hand, but he kept watching the clock, thinking:

"I have still time."

It struck half-past six. Then he took up the revolver, opened his mouth wide with a frightful grimace and stuck the barrel into it, as if he wanted to swallow it. He remained in this position for some seconds without moving, his finger on the lock; then suddenly seized with a shudder of horror, he dropped the pistol on the carpet and fell back on his armchair, sobbing:

"I can't. I dare not! My God! My God! My God! How can I have the courage to kill myself?"

There was a knock at the door. He rose up in a stupefied condition. A servant said:

"Monsieur's dinner is ready."

He replied: "All right. I'm going down."

He picked up the revolver, locked it up again in the drawer, then looked at him-self in the glass over the mantelpiece to see whether his face did not look too much troubled. It was as red as usual, a little redder perhaps. That was all. He went down and seated himself before the table.

He ate slowly, like a man who wants to drag on the meal, who does not want to be alone with himself.

Then he smoked several pipes in the dining room while the plates were being removed. After that he went back to his room.

As soon as he was alone he looked under his bed, opened all his cupboards, explored every corner, rummaged through all the furniture. Then he lighted the tapers over the mantelpiece and, turning round several times, ran his eye all over the apartment in an anguish of terror that made his face lose its color, for he knew well that he was going to see her as he did every night—little Louise Roque, the little girl he had violated and afterward strangled.

Every night the odious vision came back again. First it sounded in his ears like the snorting that is made by a threshing machine or the distant passage of a train

over a bridge. Then he commenced to pant, to feel suffocated, and had to unbutton his shirt collar and loosen his belt. He moved about to make his blood circulate; he tried to read; he attempted to sing. It was in vain. His thoughts, in spite
of himself, went back to the day of the murder, made him go through it again in
all its most secret details, with all the violent emotions he had experienced from
first to last.

He had felt on rising up that morning, the morning of the horrible day, a little
vertigo and dizziness which he attributed to the heat, so that he remained in his
room till the time came for lunch.

After the meal he had taken a siesta, then toward the close of the afternoon
he had gone out to breathe the fresh, soothing breeze under the trees in the wood.

But as soon as he was outside the heavy scorching air of the plain oppressed
him more. The sun, still high in the heavens, poured out on the parched, dry and
thirst soil floods of ardent light. Not a breath of wind stirred the leaves. Beasts
and birds, even the grasshoppers, were silent. Renardet reached the tall trees and
began to walk over the moss where the Brindelle sent forth a slight, cool vapor
under the immense roof of trees. But he felt ill at ease. It seemed to him that an
unknown, invisible hand was squeezing his neck, and he could scarcely think
rationally, having usually few ideas in his head. For the last three months, only
one thought haunted him, the thought of marrying again. He suffered from living
alone, suffered from it morally and physically. Accustomed for ten years past to
feeling a woman near him, habituated to her presence every moment, to her
embrace each successive day, he had need, an imperious and perplexing need, of
incessant contact with her and the regular touch of her lips. Since Mme Renardet's
death he had suffered continually without knowing why, had suffered from not
feeling her dress brush against his legs every day and, above all, from no longer
being able to grow calm and languid in her arms. He had been scarcely six months
a widower, and he had already been looking out through the district for some
young girl or some widow he might marry when his period of mourning was at
an end.

He had a chaste soul, but it was lodged in a vigorous Herculean body, and
carnal images began to disturb his sleep and his vigils. He drove them away; they
came back again, and he murmured from time to time, smiling at himself:

"Here I am, like Saint Antony."

Having had this morning several besetting visions, the desire suddenly came
into his breast to bathe in the Brindelle in order to refresh himself and reduce
his feverishness.

He knew, a little farther on, of a large deep spot where the people of the neighborhood came sometimes to take a dip in the summer. He went there.

Thick willow trees hid this clear pool of water where the current rested and
went to sleep for a little while before starting on its way again. Renardet, as he
appeared, thought he heard a light sound, a faint splash which was not that of
the stream or the banks. He softly put aside the leaves and looked. A little girl,
quite naked in the transparent water, was beating the waves with both hands,
dancing about in them a little and dipping herself with pretty movements. She
was not a child, nor was she yet a woman. She was plump and well formed, yet
had an air of youthful precocity, as of one who had grown rapidly and who was
now almost ripe. He no longer moved, overcome with surprise, with a pang of
desire, holding his breath with a strange, poignant emotion. He remained there,

his heart beating as if one of his sensual dreams had just been realized, as if an impure fairy had conjured up before him this young creature, this little rustic Venus born of the river foam, who was making his heart beat faster.

Suddenly the little girl came out of the water and without seeing him came over to where he stood, looking for her clothes in order to dress herself. While she was gradually approaching him with little hesitating steps, through fear of the sharp pointed stones, he felt himself pushed toward her by an irresistible force, by a bestial transport of passion, which stirred up all his carnality, stupefied his soul and made him tremble from head to foot.

She remained standing some seconds behind the willow tree which concealed him from view. Then, losing his reason entirely, he opened the branches, rushed on her and seized her in his arms. She fell, too scared to offer any resistance, too much terror-stricken to cry out, and he possessed her without understanding what he was doing.

He woke up from his crime as one wakes out of a nightmare. The child burst out weeping.

He said:

"Hold your tongue! Hold your tongue! I'll give you money."

But she did not hear him; she went on sobbing.

He went on:

"Come now, hold your tongue! Do hold your tongue. Keep quiet."

She still kept shrieking, writhing in the effort to get away from him. He suddenly realized that he was ruined, and he caught her by the neck to stop her from uttering these heart-rending, dreadful screams. As she continued to struggle with the desperate strength of a being who is flying from death, he pressed his enormous hands on that little throat, swollen with cries. In a few seconds he had strangled her, so furiously did he grip her, yet not intending to kill but only to silence her.

Then he rose up, overwhelmed with horror.

She lay before him with her face bleeding and blackened. He was going to rush away when there sprang up in his agitated soul the mysterious and undefined instinct that guides all beings in the hour of danger.

It was necessary to throw the body into the water, but he did not; another impulse drove him toward the clothes, of which he made a thin parcel. Then as he had a piece of twine, he tied it up and hid it in a deep portion of the stream, under the trunk of a tree, the foot of which was immersed in the Brindelle.

Then he went off at a rapid pace, reached the meadows, took a wide turn in order to show himself to peasants who dwelt some distance away on the opposite side of the district and came back to dine at the usual hour, telling his servants all that was supposed to have happened during his walk.

He slept, however, that night—slept with a heavy, brutish sleep, such as the sleep of persons condemned to death must occasionally be. He opened his eyes at the first glimmer of dawn and waited, tortured by the fear of having his crime discovered, for his usual waking hour.

Then he would have to be present at all the stages of the inquiry as to the cause of death. He did so after the fashion of a somnambulist, in a hallucination which showed him things and human beings in a sort of dream, in a cloud of intoxication, with that dubious sense of unreality which perplexes the mind at times of the greatest catastrophes.

The only thing that pierced his heart was La Roque's cry of anguish. At that

moment he felt inclined to cast himself at the old woman's feet and to exclaim:
" 'Tis I."

But he restrained himself. He went back, however, during the night to fish up
the dead girl's wooden shoes, in order to carry them to her mother's threshold.

As long as the inquiry lasted, so long as it was necessary to guide and aid justice,
he was calm, master of himself, sly and smiling. He discussed quietly with the
magistrates all the suppositions that passed through their minds, combated their
opinions and demolished their arguments. He even took a keen and mournful
pleasure in disturbing their investigations, in confuting their ideas, in showing the
innocence of those whom they suspected.

But from the day when the investigation came to a close he became gradually
nervous, more excitable than he had been before, although he mastered his irri-
tability. Sudden noises made him jump up with fear; he shuddered at the slightest
thing, trembled sometimes from head to foot when a fly alighted on his forehead.
Then he was seized with an imperious desire for motion which compelled him
to keep continually on foot and made him remain up whole nights walking to and
fro in his own room.

It was not that he was goaded by remorse. His brutal mind did not lend itself
to any shade of sentiment or of moral terror. A man of energy and even of violence, born to make war, to ravage conquered countries and to massacre the
vanquished, full of the savage instincts of the hunter and the fighter, he scarcely
took count of human life. Though he respected the Church through policy, he
believed neither in God nor in the devil, expecting consequently in another life
neither chastisement nor recompense for his acts. As his sole creed, he retained a
vague philosophy composed of all the ideas of the encyclopedists of the last century. He regarded religion as a moral sanction of the law, both one and the other
having been invented by men to regulate social relations.

To kill anyone in a duel, or in a battle, or in a quarrel, or by accident, or for
the sake of revenge or even through bravado would have seemed to him an amusing and clever thing and would not have left more impression on his mind than
a shot fired at a hare, but he had experienced a profound emotion at the murder
of this child. He had, in the first place, perpetrated it in the distraction of an
irresistible gust of passion, in a sort of sensual tempest that had overpowered his
reason. And he had cherished in his heart, cherished in his flesh, cherished on his
lips, cherished even to the very tips of his murderous fingers, a kind of bestial
love, as well as a feeling of horror and grief, toward this little girl he had surprised
and basely killed. Every moment his thoughts returned to that horrible scene, and
though he endeavored to drive away the picture from his mind, though he put
it aside with terror, with disgust, he felt it surging through his soul, moving about
in him, waiting incessantly for the moment to reappear.

Then in the night he was afraid, afraid of the shadows falling around him. He
did not yet know why the darkness seemed frightful to him, but he instinctively
feared it, felt that it was peopled with terrors. The bright daylight did not lend
itself to fears. Things and beings were seen there; there only natural things and
beings which could exhibit themselves in the light of day could be met. But the
night, the impenetrable night, thicker than walls and empty, the infinite night,
so black, so vast, in which one might brush against frightful things, the night
when one feels that mysterious terror is wandering, prowling about, appeared to
him to conceal an unknown danger, close and menacing.

What was it?

He knew it ere long. As he sat in his armchair rather late one evening when he could not sleep, he thought he saw the curtain of his window move. He waited in an uneasy state of mind, with beating heart. The drapery did not stir, then all of a sudden it moved once more. He did not venture to rise up; he no longer ventured to breathe, and yet he was brave. He had often fought, and he would have liked to catch thieves in his house.

Was it true that this curtain did move? he asked himself, fearing that his eyes had deceived him. It was, moreover, such a slight thing, a gentle flutter of lace, a kind of trembling in its folds, less than such an undulation as is caused by the wind.

Renardet sat still with staring eyes and outstretched neck. Then he sprang to his feet abruptly, ashamed of his fear, took four steps, seized the drapery with both hands and pulled it wide apart. At first he saw nothing but darkened glass, resembling plates of glittering ink. The night, the vast, impenetrable night, stretched out before him as far as the invisible horizon. He remained standing in front of the illimitable shadow and suddenly perceived a light, a moving light, which seemed some distance away.

Then he put his face close to the windowpane, thinking that a person looking for crayfish might be poaching in the Brindelle, for it was past midnight. The light rose up at the edge of the stream under the trees. As he was not yet able to see clearly, Renardet placed his hands over his eyes. Suddenly this light became an illumination, and he beheld little Louise Roque naked and bleeding on the moss. He recoiled, frozen with horror, sank into his chair and fell backward. He remained there some minutes, his soul in distress; then he sat up and began to reflect. He had had a hallucination—that was all: a hallucination due to the fact that a marauder of the night was walking with a lantern in his hand near the water's edge. What was there astonishing, besides, in the circumstance that the recollection of his crime should sometimes bring before him the vision of the dead girl?

He rose up, swallowed a glass of wine and sat down again. He thought:

"What am I to do if this came back?"

And it did come back; he felt it; he was sure of it. Already his glance was drawn toward the window; it called him; it attracted him. In order to avoid looking at it he turned aside his chair. Then he took a book and tried to read, but it seemed to him that he presently heard something stirring behind him, and he swung round his armchair on one foot.

The curtain still moved—unquestionably it did move this time; he could no longer have any doubt about it.

He rushed forward and seized it in his grasp so violently that he knocked it down with its fastener. Then he eagerly pressed his face against the glass. He saw nothing. All was black without, and he breathed with the delight of a man whose life has just been saved.

Then he went back to his chair and sat down again, but almost immediately he felt a longing to look out through the window once more. Since the curtain had fallen the space in front of him made a sort of dark patch, fascinating and terrible, on the obscure landscape. In order not to yield to this dangerous temptation he took off his clothes, extinguished the lamp and lay down, shutting his eyes.

Lying on his back, motionless, his skin hot and moist, he awaited sleep. Suddenly a great gleam of light flashed across his eyelids. He opened them, believing that his dwelling was on fire. All was black as before, and he leaned on his elbow in order to try to distinguish his window, which had still for him an unconquerable attraction. By dint of straining his eyes he could perceive some stars, and he arose, groped his way across the room, discovered the panes with his outstretched hands and placed his forehead close to them. There below, under the trees, the body of the little girl glittered like phosphorus, lighting up the surrounding darkness.

Renardet uttered a cry and rushed toward his bed, where he lay till morning, his head hidden under the pillow.

From that moment his life became intolerable. He passed his days in apprehension of each succeeding night, and each night the vision came back again. As soon as he had locked himself up in his room he strove to struggle, but in vain. An irresistible force lifted him up and pushed him against the glass, as if to call the phantom, and ere long he saw it lying in the spot where the crime was committed, lying with arms and legs outspread, just in the way the body had been found.

Then the dead girl rose up and came toward him with little steps, just as the child had done when she came out of the river. She advanced quietly, passing straight across the grass and over the border of withered flowers. Then she rose up into the air toward Renardet's window. She came toward him, as she had come on the day of the crime. And the man recoiled before the apparition—he retreated to his bed and sank down upon it, knowing well that the little one had entered the room and that she now was standing behind the curtain, which presently moved. And until daybreak he kept staring at this curtain with a fixed glance, ever waiting to see his victim depart.

But she did not show herself any more; she remained there behind the curtain which quivered tremulously now and then.

And Renardet, his fingers clinging to the bedclothes, squeezed them as he had squeezed the throat of little Louise Roque.

He heard the clock striking the hours, and in the stillness the pendulum kept time with the loud beating of his heart. And he suffered, the wretched man, more than any man had ever suffered before.

Then as soon as a white streak of light on the ceiling announced the approaching day, he felt himself free, alone at last, alone in his room, and then he went to sleep. He slept some hours—a restless, feverish sleep in which he retraced in dreams the horrible vision of the night just past.

When later on he went down to breakfast he felt exhausted, as if after prodigious fatigue, and he scarcely ate anything, haunted as he was by the fear of what he had seen the night before.

He knew, however, that it was not an apparition, that the dead do not come back and that his sick soul, possessed by one thought alone, by an indelible remembrance, was the only cause of his punishment, was the only evoker of that awful image, brought back by it to life, called up by it and raised by it before his eyes, in which the ineffaceable resemblance remained imprinted. But he knew, too, that he could not cure it, that he could never escape from the savage persecution of his memory, and he resolved to die rather than endure these tortures any longer.

Then he pondered how he would kill himself. He wished for some simple and

natural death which would preclude the idea of suicide. For he clung to his reputation, to the name bequeathed to him by his ancestors, and if there was any
suspicion as to the cause of his death people's thoughts might be perhaps directed
toward the mysterious crime, toward the murderer who could not be found, and
they would not hesitate to accuse him.

A strange idea came into his head, that of letting himself be crushed by the tree
at the foot of which he had assassinated little Louise Roque. So he determined to
have the wood cut down and to simulate an accident. But the beech tree refused
to smash his ribs.

Returning to his house, a prey to utter despair, he had snatched up his revolver,
and then he did not dare to fire it.

The dinner bell summoned him. He could eat nothing and went upstairs again.
But he did not know what he was going to do. Now that he had escaped the first
time he felt himself a coward. Presently he would be ready, fortified, decided,
master of his courage and of his resolution; just now he was weak and feared death
as much as he did the dead girl.

He faltered out to himself:

"I will not venture it again—I will not venture it."

Then he glanced with terror, first at the revolver on the table and next at the
curtain which hid his window. It seemed to him, moreover, that something horrible
would occur as soon as his life was ended. Something? What? A meeting with
her, perhaps! She was watching for him; she was waiting for him; she was calling
him, and her object was to seize him in her turn, to exhibit herself to him every
night so that she might draw him toward the doom that would avenge her and
lead him to death.

He began to cry like a child, repeating:

"I will not venture it again—I will not venture it."

Then he fell on his knees and murmured: "My God! My God!" without believing, nevertheless, in God. He no longer dared, in fact, to look out through his
window where he knew the apparition was visible or at the table where his revolver
gleamed.

When he had risen up he said:

"This cannot last; there must be an end of it."

The sound of his voice in the silent room made a shiver of fear pass through his
limbs, but as he could not come to a decision, as he felt certain that his finger
would always refuse to pull the trigger of his revolver, he turned round to hide his
head under the bedclothes and to plunge into reflection.

He would have to find some way in which he could force himself to die, to
invent some device against himself which would not permit of any hesitation on
his part, any delay, any possible regrets. He began to envy condemned criminals
who are led to the scaffold surrounded by soldiers. Oh, if he could only beg of
someone to shoot him; if he could, confessing the state of his soul, confessing his
crime to a sure friend who would never divulge it, obtain from him death.

But from whom could he ask this terrible service? From whom? He cast about
for one among his friends whom he knew intimately. The doctor? No, he would
talk about it afterward, most certainly. And suddenly a fantastic idea entered his
mind. He would write to the examining magistrate who was on terms of close
friendship with him and would denounce himself as the perpetrator of the crime.
He would in this letter confess everything, revealing how his soul had been tor-

tured, how he resolved to die, how he had hesitated about carrying out his resolution and what means he had employed to strengthen his failing courage. And in the name of their old friendship he would implore of the other to destroy the letter as soon as he had ascertained that the culprit had inflicted justice on himself. Renardet could rely on this magistrate; he knew him to be sure, discreet, incapable of even an idle word. He was one of those men who have an inflexible conscience, governed, directed, regulated by their reason alone.

Scarcely had he formed this project when a strange feeling of joy took possession of his heart. He was calm now. He would write his letter slowly; then at daybreak he would deposit it in the box nailed to the wall in his office; then he would ascend his tower to watch for the postman's arrival, and when the man in the blue blouse came in sight he would cast himself headlong onto the rocks on which the foundations rested. First he would take care to be seen by the workmen who were cutting down his wood. He would then climb to the parapet some distance up which bore the flagstaff displayed on fete days. He would smash this pole with a shake and precipitate it along with him.

Who would suspect that it was not an accident? And he would be dashed to pieces, having regard to his weight and the height of the tower.

Presently he got out of bed, went over to the table and began to write. He omitted nothing, not a single detail of the crime, not a single detail of the torments of his heart, and he ended by announcing that he had passed sentence on himself—that he was going to execute the criminal—and begged of his friend, his old friend, to be careful that there should never be any stain on his memory.

When he had finished his letter he saw that the day had dawned.

He closed it, sealed it and wrote the address; then he descended with light steps, hurried toward the little white box fastened to the wall in the corner of the farmhouse, and when he had thrown into it the fatal paper which made his hand tremble he came back quickly, shot the bolts of the great door and climbed up to his tower to wait for the passing of the postman, who would convey his death sentence.

He felt self-possessed now. Liberated! Saved!

A cold dry wind, an icy wind, passed across his face. He inhaled it eagerly, with open mouth, drinking in its chilling kiss. The sky was red, with a burning red, the red of winter, and all the plain whitened with frost glistened under the first rays of the sun, as if it had been powdered with bruised glass.

Renardet, standing up with his head bare, gazed at the vast tract of country before him, the meadow to the left, and to the right the village whose chimneys were beginning to smoke with the preparations for the morning meal. At his feet he saw the Brindelle flowing toward the rocks where he would soon be crushed to death. He felt himself reborn on that beautiful frosty morning, full of strength, full of life. The light bathed him and penetrated him like a newborn hope. A thousand recollections assailed him, recollections of similar mornings, of rapid walks, the hard earth which rang under his footsteps, of happy chases on the edges of pools where wild ducks sleep. At the good things that he loved, the good things of existence rushed into memory, penetrated him with fresh desires, awakened all the vigorous appetites of his active, powerful body.

And he was about to die? Why? He was going to kill himself stupidly because he was afraid of a shadow—afraid of nothing. He was still rich and in the prime of life! What folly! All he wanted was distraction, absence, a voyage in order to forget.

This night even he had not seen the little girl because his mind was preoccupied and so had wandered toward some other subject. Perhaps he would not see her any more. And even if she still haunted him in his house, certainly she would not follow him elsewhere! The earth was wide; the future was long.

Why die?

His glance traveled across the meadows, and he perceived a blue spot in the path which wound alongside of the Brindelle. It was Mederic coming to bring letters from the town and to carry away those of the village.

Renardet got a start; a sensation of pain shot through his breast, and he rushed toward the winding staircase to get back his letter, to demand it back from the postman. Little did it matter to him now whether he was seen. He hurried across the grass moistened by the light frost of the previous night, and he arrived in front of the box in the corner of the farmhouse exactly at the same time as the letter carrier.

The latter had opened the little wooden door and drew forth the papers deposited there by the inhabitants of the locality.

Renardet said to him:

"Good morrow, Mederic."

"Good morrow, M'sieu le Maire."

"I say, Mederic, I threw a letter into the box that I want back again. I came to ask you to give it back to me."

"That's all right, M'sieu le Maire—you'll get it."

And the postman raised his eyes. He stood petrified at the sight of Renardet's face. The mayor's cheeks were purple; his eyes were glaring with black circles round them as if they were sunk in his head; his hair was all tangled, his beard untrimmed, his necktie unfastened. It was evident that he had not gone to bed.

The postman asked:

"Are you ill, M'sieu le Maire?"

The other, suddenly comprehending that his appearance must be unusual, lost countenance and faltered:

"Oh no—oh no. Only I jumped out of bed to ask you for this letter. I was asleep. You understand?"

Said Mederic: "What letter?"

"The one you are going to give back to me."

Mederic now began to hesitate. The mayor's attitude did not strike him as natural. There was perhaps a secret in that letter, a political secret. He knew Renardet was not a Republican, and he knew all the tricks and chicaneries employed at elections.

He asked:

"To whom is it addressed, this letter of yours?"

"To Monsieur Putoin, the examining magistrate—you know my friend, Monsieur Putoin, well!"

The postman searched through the papers and found the one asked for. Then he began looking at it, turning it round and round between his fingers, much perplexed, much troubled by the fear of committing a grave offense or of making an enemy for himself of the mayor.

Seeing his hesitation, Renardet made a movement for the purpose of seizing the letter and snatching it away from him. This abrupt action convinced Mederic that some important secret was at stake and made him resolve to do his duty, cost what it might.

So he flung the letter into his bag and fastened it up with the reply:

"No, I can't, M'sieu le Maire. From the moment it is addressed and sent to the magistrate I can't."

A dreadful pang wrung Renardet's heart, and he murmured:

"Why, you know me well. You are even able to recognize my handwriting. I tell you I want that paper."

"I can't."

"Look here, Mederic, you know that I'm incapable of deceiving you—I tell you I want it."

"No, I can't."

A tremor of rage passed through Renardet's soul.

"Damn it all, take care! You know that I don't go in for chaffing and that I could get you out of your job, my good fellow, and without much delay either. And then I am the mayor of the district after all, and I now order you to give me back that paper."

The postman answered firmly:

"No, I can't, M'sieu le Maire."

Thereupon, Renardet, losing his head, caught hold of the postman's arms in order to take away his bag, but, freeing himself by a strong effort and springing backward, the letter carrier raised his holly stick. Without losing his temper he said emphatically:

"Don't touch me, M'sieu le Maire, or I'll strike. Take care, I'm only doing my duty!"

Feeling that he was lost, Renardet suddenly became humble, gentle, appealing to him like a crying child:

"Look here, look here, my friend, give me back that letter and I'll give you money. Stop! Stop! I'll give you a hundred francs; you understand?—a hundred francs!"

The postman turned on his heel and started on his journey.

Renardet followed him, out of breath, faltering:

"Mederic, Mederic, listen! I'll give you a thousand francs; you understand?—a thousand francs."

The postman still went on without giving any answer.

Renardet went on:

"I'll make your fortune; you understand?—whatever you wish—fifty thousand francs—fifty thousand francs—fifty thousand francs for that letter! What does it matter to you? You won't? Well, a hundred thousand—I say—a hundred thousand francs—a hundred thousand francs."

The postman turned back, his face hard, his eye severe.

"Enough of this, or else I'll repeat to the magistrate everything you have just said to me."

Renardet stopped abruptly. It was all over. He turned back and rushed toward his house, running like a hunted animal.

Then in his turn Mederic stopped and watched this flight with stupefaction. He saw the mayor re-entering his own house and he waited still, as if something astonishing was about to happen.

Presently the tall form of Renardet appeared on the summit of the Fox's Tower. He ran round the platform like a madman. Then he seized the flagstaff and shook it furiously without succeeding in breaking it; then all of a sudden, like a swimmer taking a plunge, he dived into the air with his two hands in front of him.

Mederic rushed forward to give succor. As he crossed the park he saw the woodcutters going to work. He called out to them, telling them an accident had occurred, and at the foot of the walls they found a bleeding body, the head of which was crushed on a rock. The Brindelle surrounded this rock, and over its clear, calm waters, swollen at this point, could be seen a long, thin red stream of mingled brains and blood.

THE ORIENT

Autumn is here! When I feel the first touch of winter I always think of my friend who lives down yonder on the Asiatic frontier.

The last time I entered his house I knew that I should not see him again. It was towards the end of September, three years ago. I found him stretched out on his divan, dreaming under the influence of opium. Holding out his hand to me without moving, he said:

"Stay here. Talk and I will answer you, but I shall not move, for you know that when once the drug has been swallowed you must stay on your back."

I sat down and began to tell him a thousand things about Paris and the boulevards.

But he interruped me.

"What you are saying does not interest me in the least, for I am thinking only of countries under other skies. Oh, how poor Gautier must have suffered, always haunted by the longing for the Orient! You don't know what that means, how that country takes hold of you, how it captivates you, penetrates you to your inmost being and will not let you go. It enters into you through the eye, through the skin, all its invisible seductions, and it holds you by an invisible thread, which is unceasingly pulling you, in whatever spot on earth chance may have flung you. I take the drug in order to muse on that land in the delicious torpor of opium."

He stopped and closed his eyes.

"What makes it so pleasant to you to take this poison?" I asked. "What physical joy does it give, that people take it until it kills them?"

"It is not a physical joy," he replied; "it is better than that, it is more. I am often sad; I detest life, which wounds me every day on all sides, with all its angles, its hardships. Opium consoles for everything, makes one resigned to everything. Do you know that state of mind that I might call gnawing irritation? I ordinarily live in that state. And there are two things that can cure me of it: opium or the Orient. As soon as I have taken opium I lie down and wait, perhaps one hour, and sometimes two. Then, when it begins to take effect I feel first a slight trembling in the hands and feet, not a cramp, but a vibrant numbness; then little by little I have the strange and delicious sensation of feeling my limbs disappear. It seems to me as if they were taken off, and this feeling grows upon me until it fills me completely. I have no longer a body; I retain merely a kind of pleasant memory of it. Only my head is there, and it works. I dream. I think with an infinite, material joy, with unequaled lucidity, with a surprising penetration. I reason, I deduce, I understand everything. I discover ideas that never before have come to me; I descend to new depths and mount to marvelous heights; I float in an ocean of thought, and I taste the incomparable happiness, the ideal enjoyment of the chaste and serene intoxication of pure intelligence."

Again he stopped and closed his eyes. I said: "Your longing for the Orient is due only to this constant intoxication. You are living in a state of hallucination. How can one long for that barbarous country, where the mind is dead, where the sterile imagination does not go beyond the narrow limits of life and makes no effort to take flight, to expand and conquer?"

"What does practical thought matter?" he replied. "What I love is dreaming. That only is good, and that only is sweet. Implacable reality would lead me to suicide, if dreaming did not permit me to wait.

"You say that the Orient is the land of barbarians. Stop, wretched man! It is the country of the sages, the hot country where one lets life flow by, where angles are rounded.

"We are the barbarians, we men of the West who call ourselves civilized; we are hateful barbarians who live a painful life, like brutes.

"Look at our cities built of stone and our furniture made of hard and knotty wood. We mount, panting, a high, narrow stairway, to go into stuffy apartments into which the cold wind comes whistling, only to escape immediately again through a chimney which creates deadly currents of air that are strong enough to turn a windmill. Our chairs are hard, our walls cold and covered with ugly paper; everywhere we are wounded by angles—angles on our tables, on our mantels, on our doors and on our beds. We live standing up or sitting in our chairs, but we never lie down except to sleep, which is ridiculous, for in sleeping you are not conscious of the happiness there is in being stretched out flat.

"And then to think of our intellectual life! It is filled with incessant struggle and strife. Worry hovers over us and preoccupations pester us; we no longer have time to seek and pursue the two or three good things within our reach.

"It is war to the finish. And our character, even more than our furniture, is full of angles—angles everywhere.

"We are hardly out of bed when we hasten to our work, in rain or snow. We fight against rivals, competition, hostility. Every man is an enemy whom we must fear and overcome and with whom we must resort to ruse. Even love has with us its aspects of victory and defeat: that also is a struggle."

He reflected for some moments and then continued:

"I know the house that I am going to buy. It is square, with a flat roof and wooden trimmings, in the oriental fashion. From the terrace you can see the sea, where white sails like pointed wings are passing, and Greek or Turkish vessels. There are hardly any openings on the outside walls. A large garden, where the air is heavy under the shadow of palms, is in the center of this abode. A jet of water rises from under the trees and falls in spray into a large marble basin, the bottom of which is covered with golden sand. I shall bathe there at any hour of the day, between two pipes, two dreams, two kisses.

"I will not have any servant, any hideous maid with greasy apron who kicks up the dirty bottom of her skirt with her worn shoes. Oh, that kick of the heel which shows the yellow ankle! It fills my heart with disgust, and yet I cannot avoid it. Those wretches all do it.

"I shall no longer hear the tramping of shoes on the floor, the loud slamming of doors, the crash of breaking dishes.

"I will have beautiful black slaves, draped in white veils, who run barefoot over heavy carpets.

"My walls shall be soft and rounded, like a woman's breasts; and my divans, ranged in a circle around each apartment, shall be heaped with cushions of all shapes, so that I may lie down in all possible postures.

"Then, when I am tired of this delicious repose, tired of enjoying immobility and my eternal dream, tired of the calm pleasure of well-being, I shall have a swift black or white horse brought to my door.

"And I shall ride away on it, drinking in the air which stings and intoxicates, the air that whistles when one is galloping furiously.

"And I shall fly like an arrow over this colored earth, which intoxicates the eye with the effect of the flavor of wine.

"In the calm of the evening I shall ride madly toward the wide horizon, which is tinged rose color by the setting sun. Everything is rosy down there in the twilight, the scorched mountains, the sand, the clothing of the Arabs, the white coat of the horses.

"Pink flamingos rise out of the marshes under the pink sky, and I shall shout deliriously, bathed in the illimitable rosiness of the world.

"I shall no longer see men dressed in black, sitting on uncomfortable chairs and drinking absinth while talking of business or walking along the pavements in the midst of the deafening noise of cabs in the street.

"I shall know nothing of the state of the Bourse, the fluctuations of stocks and shares, all the useless stupidities in which we waste our short, miserable and treacherous existence. Why all this trouble, all this suffering, all these struggles? I shall rest, sheltered from the wind, in my bright, sumptuous home.

"And I shall have four or five wives in luxurious apartments—five wives who have come from the five continents of the world and who will bring to me a taste of feminine beauty as it flowers in all races."

Again he stopped, and then he said softly:

"Leave me."

I went, and I never saw him again.

Two months later he sent me these three words only: "I am happy."

His letter smelled of incense and other sweet perfumes.

HOW HE GOT THE LEGION OF HONOR

Some people are born with a predominant instinct, with some vocation or some desire which demands recognition as soon as they begin to speak or to think.

Ever since he was a child M. Caillard had only had one idea in his head—to be decorated. When he was still quite a small boy he used to wear a zinc Cross of the Legion of Honor in his tunic, just like other children wear a soldier's cap, and he took his mother's hand in the street with a proud look, sticking out his little chest with its red ribbon and metal star so that it might show to advantage.

His studies were not a success, and he failed in his examination for bachelor of arts; so not knowing what to do, he married a pretty girl, for he had plenty of money of his own.

They lived in Paris, like many rich middle-class people do, mixing with their own particular set without going among other people, proud of knowing a deputy, who might perhaps be a minister someday, while two chiefs of division were among their friends.

But M. Caillard could not get rid of his one absorbing idea, and he felt constantly unhappy because he had not the right to wear a little bit of colored ribbon in his buttonhole.

When he met any men who were decorated on the boulevards, he looked at them askance, with intense jealousy. Sometimes, when he had nothing to do in the afternoon, he would count them and say to himself: "Just let me see how many I shall meet between the Madeleine and the Rue Drouot."

Then he would walk slowly, looking at every coat with a practiced eye for the little bit of red ribbon, and when he had got to the end of his walk he always said the numbers out loud. "Eight officers and seventeen knights. As many as that! It is stupid to sow the cross broadcast in that fashion. I wonder how many I shall meet going back?"

And he returned slowly, unhappy when the crowd of passers-by interfered with his seeing them.

He knew the places where most of them were to be found. They swarmed in the Palais Royal. Fewer were seen in the Avenue de l'Opera than in the Rue de la Paix, while the right side of the boulevard was more frequented by them than the left.

They also seemed to prefer certain cafés and theaters. Whenever he saw a group of white-haired old gentlemen standing together in the middle of the pavement, interfering with the traffic, he used to say to himself: "They are officers of the Legion of Honor," and he felt inclined to take off his hat to them.

He had often remarked that the officers had a different bearing from mere knights. They carried their heads higher, and you felt that they enjoyed greater official consideration and a more widely extended importance.

Sometimes again the worthy man would be seized with a furious hatred for everyone who was decorated; he felt like a Socialist toward them. Then, when he got home, excited at meeting so many crosses—just like a poor, hungry wretch is on passing some dainty provision shop—he used to ask in a loud voice:

"When shall we get rid of this wretched government?" And his wife would be surprised and ask:

"What is the matter with you today?"

"I am indignant," he would reply, "at the injustice I see going on around us. Oh! The Communards were certainly right!"

After dinner he would go out again and look at the shops where all the decorations were sold and examine all the emblems of various shapes and colors. He would have liked to possess them all and to have walked gravely at the head of a procession with his crush hat under his arm and his breast covered with decorations, radiant as a star, amid a buzz of admiring whispers and a hum of respect. But alas! He had no right to wear any decoration whatever.

He used to say to himself: "It is really too difficult for any man to obtain the

Legion of Honor unless he is some public functionary. Suppose I try to get appointed an officer of the Academy!"

But he did not know how to set about it and spoke to his wife on the subject, who was stupefied.

"Officer of the Academy! What have you done to deserve it?"

He got angry. "I know what I am talking about; I only want to know how to set about it. You are quite stupid at times."

She smiled. "You are quite right; I don't understand anything about it."

An idea struck him: "Suppose you were to speak to Monsieur Rosselin, the deputy, he might be able to advise me. You understand I cannot broach the subject to him directly. It is rather difficult and delicate but, coming from you, it might seem quite natural."

Mme Caillard did what he asked her, and M. Rosselin promised to speak to the minister about it. Then Caillard began to worry him till the deputy told him he must make a formal application and put forward his claims.

"What were his claims?" he said. "He was not even a bachelor of arts."

However, he set to work and produced a pamphlet with the title, *The People's Right to Instruction*, but he could not finish it for want of ideas.

He sought for easier subjects and began several in succession. The first was, *The Instruction of Children by Means of the Eye.* He wanted gratuitous theaters to be established in every poor quarter of Paris for little children. Their parents were to take them there when they were quite young, and by means of a magic lantern all the notions of human knowledge were to be imparted to them. There were to be regular courses. The sight would educate the mind, while the pictures would remain impressed on the brain, and thus science would, so to say, be made visible. What could be more simple than to teach universal history, natural history, geography, botany, zoology, anatomy, etc., etc., thus?

He had his ideas printed in tract form and sent a copy to each deputy, ten to each minister, fifty to the president of the Republic, ten to each Parisian and five to each provincial newspaper.

Then he wrote on *Street Lending Libraries.* His idea was to have little carts full of books drawn about the streets, like orange carts are. Every householder or lodger would have a right to ten volumes a month by means of a halfpenny subscription.

"The people," M. Caillard said, "will only disturb itself for the sake of its pleasures, and since it will not go to instruction, instruction must come to it," etc., etc.

His essays attracted no attention, but he sent in his application and he got the usual formal official reply. He thought himself sure of success, but nothing came of it.

Then he made up his mind to apply personally. He begged for an interview with the minister of public instruction, and he was received by a young subordinate, already very grave and important, who kept touching the buttons of electric bells to summon ushers and footmen and officials inferior to himself. He declared to M. Caillard that his matter was going on quite favorably and advised him to continue his remarkable labors. So M. Caillard set at it again.

M. Rosselin, the deputy, seemed now to take a great interest in his success and gave him a lot of excellent, practical advice. Rosselin was decorated, although nobody knew exactly what he had done to deserve such a distinction.

He told Caillard what new studies he ought to undertake; he introduced him to learned societies which took up particularly obscure points of science, in the hope of gaining credit and honors thereby, and he even took him under his wing at the Ministry.

One day when he came to lunch with his friend (for several months past he had constantly taken his meals there), he said to him in a whisper as he shook hands: "I have just obtained a great favor for you. The Committee on Historical Works is going to intrust you with a commission. There are some researches to be made in various libraries in France."

Caillard was so delighted that he could scarcely eat or drink, and a week later he set out. He went from town to town, studying catalogues, rummaging in lofts full of dusty volumes, and was a bore to all the librarians.

One day, happening to be at Rouen, he thought he should like to embrace his wife, whom he had not seen for more than a week, so he took the nine o'clock train, which would land him at home by twelve at night.

He had his latchkey, so he went in without making any noise, delighted at the idea of the surprise he was going to give her. She had locked herself in. How tiresome! However, he cried out through the door:

"Jeanne, it is I."

She must have been very frightened, for he heard her jump out of bed and speak to herself, as if she were in a dream. Then she went to her dressing room, opened and closed the door and went quickly up and down her room, barefoot, two or three times, shaking the furniture till the vases and glasses sounded. Then at last she asked:

"Is it you, Alexander?"

"Yes, yes," he replied; "make haste and open the door."

As soon as she had done so she threw herself into his arms, exclaiming:

"Oh! What a fright! What a surprise! What a pleasure!"

He began to undress himself methodically, like he did everything, and from a chair he took his overcoat, which he was in the habit of hanging up in the hall. But suddenly he remained motionless, struck dumb with astonishment—there was a red ribbon in the buttonhole!

"Why," he stammered, "this—this—this overcoat has got the rosette in it!"

In a second his wife threw herself on him and, taking it from his hands, she said:

"No! You have made a mistake—give it to me."

But he still held it by one of the sleeves without letting it go, repeating in a half-dazed manner:

"Oh! Why? Just explain. Whose overcoat is it? It is not mine, as it has the Legion of Honor on it."

She tried to take it from him, terrified, and hardly able to say:

"Listen—listen—give it me. I must not tell you—it is a secret—listen to me."

But he grew angry and turned pale:

"I want to know how this overcoat comes to be here. It does not belong to me."

Then she almost screamed at him:

"Yes, it does; listen—swear to me—well—you are decorated."

She did not intend to joke at his expense.

He was so overcome that he let the overcoat fall and dropped into an armchair.

"I am—you say I am—decorated?"

"Yes, but it is a secret, a great secret."

She had put the glorious garment into a cupboard and came to her husband, pale and trembling.

"Yes," she continued, "it is a new overcoat that I have had made for you. But I swore that I would not tell you anything about it, as it will not be officially announced for a month or six weeks, and you were not to have known till your return from your business journey. Monsieur Rosselin managed it for you."

"Rosselin!" he contrived to utter in his joy. "He has obtained the decoration for me? He—— Oh!"

And he was obliged to drink a glass of water.

A little piece of white paper had fallen to the floor out of the pocket of the overcoat. Caillard picked it up; it was a visiting card, and he read out:

"Rosselin—deputy."

"You see how it is?" said his wife.

He almost cried with joy, and a week later it was announced in the *Journal Officiel* that M. Caillard had been awarded the Legion of Honor on account of his exceptional services.

MY UNCLE JULES

A poor old man with white hair begged us for alms. My companion, Joseph Davranche, gave him five francs. Noticing my surprised look, he said:

"That poor unfortunate reminds me of a story which I shall tell you, the memory of which continually pursues me. Here it is:

"My family, which came originally from Havre, was not rich. We just managed to make both ends meet. My father worked hard, came home late from the office, and earned very little. I had two sisters.

"My mother suffered a good deal from our reduced circumstances, and she often had harsh words for her husband, veiled and sly reproaches. The poor man then made a gesture which used to distress me. He would pass his open hand over his forehead, as if to wipe away perspiration which did not exist, and he would answer nothing. I felt his helpless suffering. We economized on everything and never would accept an invitation to dinner, so as not to have to return the courtesy. All our provisions were bought at reduced prices, whatever was left over in the shops. My sisters made their own gowns, and long discussions would arise on the price of a piece of braid worth fifteen centimes a yard. Our meals usually consisted of soup and beef prepared with every kind of sauce. They say it is wholesome and nourishing, but I should have preferred a change.

"I used to go through terrible scenes on account of lost buttons and torn trousers.

"Every Sunday, dressed in our best, we would take our walk along the pier. My father, in a frock coat, high hat and kid gloves, would offer his arm to my mother, decked out and beribboned like a ship on a holiday. My sisters, who were always ready first, would await the signal for leaving; but at the last minute someone always found a spot on my father's frock coat, and it had to be wiped away quickly with a rag moistened with benzine.

"My father, in his shirt sleeves, his silk hat on his head, would await the completion of the operation, while my mother would make haste, putting on her spectacles and taking off her gloves in order not to spoil them.

"Then we set out ceremoniously. My sisters marched on ahead, arm in arm. They were of marriageable age and had to be shown off. I walked on the left of my mother and my father on her right. I remember the pompous air of my poor parents in these Sunday walks, their stern expression, their stiff walk. They moved slowly, with a serious expression, their bodies straight, their legs stiff, as if something of extreme importance depended upon their appearance.

"Every Sunday, when the big steamers were returning from unknown and distant countries, my father would invariably utter the same words:

" 'What a surprise it would be if Jules were on that one! Eh?'

"My uncle Jules, my father's brother, was the only hope of the family, after being its only fear. I had heard about him since childhood, and it seemed to me that I should recognize him immediately, knowing as much about him as I did. I knew every detail of his life up to the day of his departure for America, although this period of his life was spoken of only in hushed tones.

"It seems that he had led a bad life, that is to say, he had squandered a little money, which action, in a poor family, is one of the greatest crimes. With rich people a man who amuses himself only sows his wild oats. He is what is generally called 'a sport.' But among needy families a boy who forces his parents to break into the capital becomes a good-for-nothing, a rascal, a scamp. And this distinction is just, although the action be the same, for consequences alone determine the seriousness of the act.

"Well, Uncle Jules had visibly diminished the inheritance on which my father had counted, after he had swallowed his own to the last penny. Then, according to the custom of the times, he had been shipped off to America on a freighter going from Havre to New York.

"Once there, my uncle began to sell something or other, and he soon wrote that he was making a little money and that he shortly hoped to be able to indemnify my father for the harm he had done him. This letter caused a profound emotion in the family. Jules, who up to that time had not been worth his salt, suddenly became a good man, a kindhearted fellow, true and honest like all the Davranches.

"One of the captains told us that he had rented a large shop and was doing an important business.

"Two years later a second letter came, saying: 'My dear Philippe, I am writing to tell you not to worry about my health, which is excellent. Business is good. I leave tomorrow for a long trip to South America. I may be away for several years without sending you any news. If I shouldn't write, don't worry. When my fortune is made I shall return to Havre. I hope that it will not be too long, and that we shall all live happily together. . . .'

"This letter became the gospel of the family. It was read on the slightest provocation, and it was shown to everybody.

"For ten years nothing was heard from Uncle Jules; but as time went on my father's hope grew, and my mother, also, often said:

" 'When that good Jules is here, our position will be different. There is one who knew how to get along!'

"And every Sunday, while watching the big steamers approaching from the horizon, pouring out a stream of smoke, my father would repeat his eternal question:

" 'What a surprise it would be if Jules were on that one! Eh?'

"We almost expected to see him waving his handkerchief and crying:

" 'Hey! Philippe!'

"Thousands of schemes had been planned on the strength of this expected return; we were even to buy a little house with my uncle's money—a little place in the country near Ingouville. In fact, I wouldn't swear that my father had not already begun negotiations.

"The elder of my sisters was then twenty-eight, the other twenty-six. They were not yet married, and that was a great grief to everyone.

"At last a suitor presented himself for the younger one. He was a clerk, not rich, but honorable. I have always been morally certain that Uncle Jules' letter, which was shown him one evening, had swept away the young man's hesitation and definitely decided him.

"He was eagerly accepted, and it was decided that after the wedding the whole family should take a trip to Jersey.

"Jersey is the ideal trip for poor people. It is not far; one crosses a strip of sea in a steamer and lands on foreign soil, as this little island belongs to England. Thus, a Frenchman, in a two hours' sail, can observe a neighboring people at home and study their customs.

"This trip to Jersey completely absorbed our ideas, was our sole anticipation, the constant thought of our minds.

. "At last we left. I see it as plainly as if it had happened yesterday. The boat was getting up steam against the quay at Granville; my father, bewildered, was superintending the loading of our three pieces of baggage; my mother, nervous, had taken the arm of my unmarried sister, who seemed lost since the departure of the other one, like the last chicken of a brood; behind us came the bride and groom, who always stayed behind, a thing that often made me turn around.

"The whistle sounded. We got on board, and the vessel, leaving the pier, forged ahead through a sea as flat as a marble table. We watched the coast disappear in the distance, happy and proud, like all who do not travel much.

"My father was swelling out his chest in the breeze, beneath his frock coat, which had that morning been very carefully cleaned; and he spread around him that odor of benzine which always made me recognize Sunday. Suddenly he noticed two elegantly dressed ladies to whom two gentlemen were offering oysters. An old, ragged sailor was opening them with his knife and passing them to the gentlemen, who would then offer them to the ladies. They ate them in a dainty manner, holding the shell on a fine handkerchief and advancing their mouths a little in order not to spot their dresses. Then they would drink the liquid with a rapid little motion and throw the shell overboard.

"My father was probably pleased with this delicate manner of eating oysters on a moving ship. He considered it good form, refined, and, going up to my mother and sisters, he asked:

" 'Would you like me to offer you some oysters?'

"My mother hesitated on account of the expense, but my two sisters immediately accepted. My mother said in a provoked manner:

" 'I am afraid that they will hurt my stomach. Offer the children some, but not too much, it would make them sick.' Then, turning toward me, she added:

" 'As for Joseph, he doesn't need any. Boys shouldn't be spoiled.'

"However, I remained beside my mother, finding this discrimination unjust. I watched my father as he pompously conducted my two sisters and his son-in-law toward the ragged old sailor.

"The two ladies had just left, and my father showed my sisters how to eat them without spilling the liquor. He even tried to give them an example, and seized an oyster. He attempted to imitate the ladies, and immediately spilled all the liquid over his coat. I heard my mother mutter:

" 'He would do far better to keep quiet.'

"But, suddenly, my father appeared to be worried; he retreated a few steps, stared at his family gathered around the old shell opener, and quickly came toward us. He seemed very pale, with a peculiar look. In a low voice he said to my mother:

" 'It's extraordinary how that man opening the oysters looks like Jules.'

"Astonished, my mother asked:

" 'What Jules?'

"My father continued:

" 'Why, my brother. If I did not know that he was well off in America, I should think it was he.'

"Bewildered, my mother stammered:

" 'You are mad! As long as you know that it is not he, why do you say such foolish things?'

"But my father insisted:

"Go on over and see, Clarisse! I would rather have you see with your own eyes.'

"She arose and walked to her daughters. I, too, was watching the man. He was old, dirty, wrinkled, and did not lift his eyes from his work.

"My mother returned. I noticed that she was trembling. She exclaimed quickly:

" 'I believe that it is he. Why don't you ask the captain? But be very careful that we don't have this rogue on our hands again!'

"My father walked away, but I followed him. I felt strangely moved.

"The captain, a tall, thin man with blond whiskers, was walking along the bridge with an important air as if he were commanding the Indian mail steamer.

"My father addressed him ceremoniously, and questioned him about his' profession, adding many compliments.

" 'What might be the importance of Jersey? What did it produce? What was the population? The customs? The nature of the soil?' etc., etc.

" 'You have there an old shell opener who seems quite interesting. Do you know anything about him?'

"The captain, whom this conversation began to weary, answered dryly:

" 'He is some old French tramp whom I found last year in America, and I brought him back. It seems that he has some relatives in Havre, but that he doesn't wish to return to them because he owes them money. His name is Jules—Jules Darmanche or Darvanche or something like that. It seems that he was once rich over there, but you can see what's left of him now.'

"My father turned ashy pale and muttered, his throat contracted, his eyes haggard:

" 'Ah! ah! very well, very well. I'm not in the least surprised. Thank you very much, captain.'

"He went away, and the astonished sailor watched him disappear. He returned to my mother so upset that she said to him:

" 'Sit down; someone will notice that something is the matter.'

"He sank down on a bench and stammered:

" 'It's he! It's he!'

"Then he asked:

" 'What are we going to do?'

"She answered quickly:

" 'We must get the children out of the way. Since Joseph knows everything, he can go and get them. We must take good care that our son-in-law doesn't find out.'

"My father seemed absolutely bewildered. He murmured:

" 'What a catastrophe!'

"Suddenly growing furious, my mother exclaimed:

" 'I always thought that that thief never would do anything, and that he would drop down on us again! As if one could expect anything from a Davranche!'

"My father passed his hand over his forehead, as he always did when his wife reproached him. She added:

" 'Give Joseph some money so that he can pay for the oysters. All that is needed to cap the climax would be to be recognized by that beggar. That would be very pleasant! Let's go down to the other end of the boat, and take care that that man doesn't come near us!'

"They gave me five francs and walked away.

"Astonished, my sisters were awaiting their father. I said that Mamma had felt a sudden attack of seasickness, and I asked the shell opener:

" 'How much do we owe you, monsieur?'

"I felt like laughing: he was my uncle! He answered:

" 'Two francs fifty.'

"I held out my five francs and he returned the change. I looked at his hand; it was a poor, wrinkled, sailor's hand, and I looked at his face, an unhappy old face. I said to myself:

" 'That is my uncle, the brother of my father, my uncle!'

"I gave him a tip of one franc. He thanked me:

" 'God bless you, my young sir!'

"He spoke like a poor man receiving alms. I couldn't help thinking that he must have begged over there! My sisters looked at me, surprised at my generosity. When I returned the two francs to my father, my mother asked me in surprise:

" 'Was there three francs' worth? That is impossible.'

"I answered in a firm voice:

" 'I gave ten sous as a tip.'

"My mother started, and, staring at me, she exclaimed:

" 'You must be crazy! Give ten sous to that man, to that vagabond——'

"She stopped at a look from my father, who was pointing at his son-in-law. Then everybody was silent.

"Before us, on the distant horizon, a purple shadow seemed to rise out of the sea. It was Jersey.

"As we approached the breakwater a violent desire seized me once more to see my uncle Jules, to be near him, to say to him something consoling, something tender. But as no one was eating any more oysters, he had disappeared, having probably gone below to the dirty hold which was the home of the poor wretch."

THE HORLA

May 8. What a glorious day! I have spent the whole morning lying on the grass in front of my house, under the enormous plane tree that forms a complete covering, shelter and shade for it. I love this country, and I love living here because it is here I have my roots, those deep-down slender roots that hold a man to the place where his forefathers were born and died, hold him to ways of thought and habits of eating, to customs as to particular foods, to local fashions of speech, to the intonations of country voices, to the scent of the soil, the villages, and the very air itself.

I love this house of mine where I grew up. From my windows I see the Seine flowing alongside my garden, beyond the high road, almost at my door, the great wide Seine, running from Rouen to Havre, covered with passing boats.

Away to the left, Rouen, the widespread town, with its blue roofs lying under the bristling host of Gothic belfries. They are beyond number, frail or sturdy, dominated by the leaden steeples of the cathedral and filled with bells that ring out in the limpid air of fine mornings, sending me the sweet and far-off murmur of their iron tongues, a brazen song borne to me on the breeze, now louder, now softer, as it swells or dies away.

How beautiful this morning has been!

Towards eleven o'clock a long convoy of boats followed each other past my gate, behind a squat tug looking like a fly, and wheezing painfully as it vomited thick clouds of smoke.

After two English yachts whose crimson awnings rose and fell against the sky, came a splendid three-masted Brazilian, all white, gloriously clean and glittering. The sight of this ship filled me with such joy that I saluted her, I don't know why.

May 11. I have had a slight fever for the last few days; I feel ill or rather unhappy.

Whence come these mysterious influences that change our happiness to dejection and our self-confidence to discouragement? It is as if the air, the unseen air, were full of unknowable powers whose mysterious nearness we endure. I wake full of joy, my throat swelling with a longing to sing. Why? I go down to the waterside; and suddenly, after a short walk, I come back home wretched, as if some misfortune were waiting me there. Why? Has a chill shudder, passing lightly over my skin, shaken my nerves and darkened my spirit? Have the shapes of the clouds, or the color of the day, the ever-changing color of the visible world, troubled my mind as they slipped past my eyes? Does anyone know? Everything that surrounds us, everything that we see unseeing, everything that we brush past unknowing, everything that we touch impalpably, everything that we meet unnoticing, has on us, on the organs of our bodies, and through them on our thoughts, on our very hearts, swift, surprising and inexplicable effects.

How deep it is, this mystery of the Invisible! We cannot fathom it with our miserable senses, with our eyes that perceive neither the too small, nor the too great, nor the too near, nor the too distant, nor the inhabitants of a star, nor the inhabitants of a drop of water . . . with our ears that deceive us, transmitting the vibrations of the air to us as sonorous sounds. They are fairies who by a miracle transmute movement into sound, from which metamorphosis music is born, and make audible in song the mute quivering of nature . . . with our smell, feebler than a dog's . . . with our taste, that can only just detect the age of a wine.

If only we had other organs to work other miracles on our behalf, what things we could discover round us!

May 16. I am certainly ill, I have been so well since last month. I have a fever, a rotten fever, or rather a feverish weakness that oppresses my mind as wearily as my body. All day and every day I suffer this frightful sense of threatened danger, this apprehension of coming ill or approaching death, this presentiment which is doubtless the warning signal of a lurking disease germinating in my blood and my flesh.

May 18. I have just consulted my doctor, for I was not getting any sleep. He found that my pulse is rapid, my eyes dilated, my nerves on edge, but no alarming symptom of any kind. I am to take douches and drink bromide of potassium.

May 25. No change. My case is truly strange. As night falls, an incomprehensible uneasiness fills me, as if the night concealed a frightful menace directed at me. I dine in haste, then I try to read; but I don't understand the words: I can hardly make out the letters. So I walk backwards and forwards in my drawing room, oppressed by a vague fear that I cannot throw off, fear of sleeping and fear of my bed.

About ten o'clock I go up to my room. The instant I am inside the room I double-lock the door and shut the windows; I am afraid . . . of what? I never dreaded anything before . . . I open my cupboards, I look under my bed; I listen . . . listen . . . to what? It's a queer thing that a mere physical ailment, some disorder in the blood perhaps, the jangling of a nerve thread, a slight congestion, the least disturbance in the functioning of this living machine of ours, so imperfect and so frail, can make a melancholic of the happiest of men and a coward of the bravest. Then I lie down and wait for sleep as if I were waiting to be executed. I wait for it, dreading its approach; my heart beats, my legs tremble; my whole body shivers in the warmth of the bedclothes, until the moment I fall suddenly on sleep, like a man falling into deep and stagnant waters, there to drown. Nowadays I never feel the approach of this perfidious sleep, which lurks near me, spying on me, ready to take me by the hand, shut my eyes, steal my strength.

I sleep—for a long time—two or three hours—then a dream—no—a nightmare seizes me. I feel that I am lying down and that I am asleep . . . I feel it and I know it . . . and I feel too that someone approaches me, looks at me, touches me, climbs on my bed, kneels on my chest, takes my neck between his hands and squeezes . . . squeezes . . . with all his might, strangling me.

I struggle madly, in the grip of the frightful impotence that paralyzes us in dreams; I try to cry out—I can't; I try to move—I can't; panting, with the most frightful efforts, I try to turn round, to fling off this creature who is crushing and choking me—I can't do it.

And suddenly I wake up, terrified, covered with sweat. I light a candle. I am alone.

The crisis over—a crisis that happens every night—I fall at last into a quiet sleep, until daybreak.

June 2. My case has grown worse. What can be the matter with me? Bromide is useless, douches are useless. Lately, by way of wearying a body already quite exhausted, I went for a tramp in the forest of Roumare. At first I thought that the fresh air, the clear sweet air, full of the scents of grass and trees, was pouring a new blood into my veins and a new strength into my heart. I followed a broad glade, then I turned towards Boville, by a narrow walk between two ranks of immensely tall trees that flung a thick green roof, almost a black roof, between the sky and me.

A sudden shudder ran through me, not a shudder of cold but a strange shudder of anguish.

I quickened my pace, uneasy at being alone in this wood, unreasonably, stupidly terrified by the profound solitude. Abruptly I felt that I was being followed, that someone was on my heels, as near as near, touching me.

I swung round. I was alone. I saw behind me only the straight open walk, empty, high, terrifyingly empty; it stretched out in front of me too, as far as the eye could see, as empty, and frightening.

I shut my eyes. Why? And I began to turn round on my heel at a great rate like a top. I almost fell; I opened my eyes again; the trees were dancing; the earth was swaying; I was forced to sit down. Then, ah! I didn't know now which way I had been walking. Strange thought! Strange! Strange thought! I didn't know anything at all now. I took the right-hand way, and found myself back in the avenue that had led me into the middle of the forest.

June 3. The night has been terrible. I am going to go away for several weeks. A short journey will surely put me right.

July 2. Home again. I am cured. I have had, moreover, a delightful holiday. I visited Mont-Saint-Michel, which I didn't know.

What a vision one gets, arriving at Avranches as I did, towards dusk! The town lies on a slope, and I was taken into the public garden, at the end of the city. A cry of astonishment broke from me. A shoreless bay stretched before me, as far as eye could see: it lay between opposing coasts that vanished in distant mist; and in the midst of this vast tawny bay, under a gleaming golden sky, a strange hill, somber and peaked, thrust up from the sands at its feet. The sun had just sunk, and on a horizon still riotous with color was etched the outline of this fantastic rock that bore on its summit a fantastic monument.

At daybreak I went out to it. The tide was low, as on the evening before, and as I drew near it, the miraculous abbey grew in height before my eyes. After several hours' walking I reached the monstrous pile of stones that supports the little city dominated by the great church. I clambered up the steep narrow street. I entered the most wonderful Gothic dwelling made for God on this earth, as vast as a town, with innumerable low rooms hollowed out under the vaults and high galleries slung over slender columns. I entered this gigantic granite jewel, as delicate as a piece of lace, pierced everywhere by towers and airy belfries where twisting stairways climb, towers and belfries that by day against a blue sky and by night against a dark sky lift strange heads, bristling with chimeras, devils, fantastic beasts and monstrous flowers, and are linked together by slender carved arches.

When I stood on the top I said to the monk who accompanied me: "What a glorious place you have here, Father!"

"We get strong winds," he answered, and we fell into talk as we watched the incoming sea run over the sand and cover it with a steel cuirass.

The monk told me stories, all the old stories of this place, legends, always legends.

One of them particularly impressed me. The people of the district, those who lived on the mount, declared that at night they heard voices on the sands, followed by the bleating of two she-goats, one that called loudly and one calling softly. Unbelievers insisted that it was the crying of sea birds which at one and the same time resembled bleatings and the wailing of human voices: but benighted fishermen swore that they had met an old shepherd wandering on the dunes, between two tides, round the little town flung so far out of the world. No one ever saw the head hidden in his cloak: he led, walking in front of them, a goat with the face of a man and a she-goat with the face of a woman; both of them had long white hair and talked incessantly, disputing in an unknown tongue, then abruptly ceased crying to begin a loud bleating.

"Do you believe it?" I asked the monk.

He murmured: "I don't know."

"If," I went on, "there existed on the earth beings other than ourselves, why have we not long ago learned to know them; why have you yourself not seen them? Why have I not seen them myself?"

He answered: "Do we see the hundred-thousandth part of all that exists? Think, there's the wind, the greatest force in nature, which throws down men, shatters buildings, uproots trees, stirs up the sea into watery mountains, destroys cliffs, and tosses the tall ships against the shore, the wind that kills, whistles, groans, roars—have you seen it, can you see it? Nevertheless, it exists."

Before his simple reasoning I fell silent. This man was either a seer or a fool. I should not have cared to say which; but I held my peace. What he had just said, I had often thought.

July 3. I slept badly; I am sure there is a feverish influence at work here, for my coachman suffers from the same trouble as myself. When I came home yesterday, I noticed his strange pallor.

"What's the matter with you, Jean?" I demanded.

"I can't rest these days, sir; I'm burning the candle at both ends. Since you went away, sir, I haven't been able to throw it off."

The other servants are all right, however, but I am terrified of getting caught by it again.

July 4. It has surely caught me again. My old nightmares have come back. Last night I felt crouching on me someone who presses his mouth on mine and drinks my life between my lips. Yes, he sucked it from my throat like a leech. Then he rose from me, replete, and I awoke, so mangled, bruised, enfeebled, that I could not move. If this goes on for many days more, I shall certainly go away again.

July 5. Have I lost my reason? What has just happened, what I saw last night, is so strange that my head reels when I think of it.

Following my invariable custom in the evenings, I had locked my door; then, feeling thirsty, I drank half a glass of water and I happened to notice that my carafe was filled up right to its crystal stopper.

I lay down after this and fell into one of my dreadful slumbers, from which I was jerked about two hours later by a shock more frightful than any of the others.

Imagine a sleeping man, who has been assassinated and who wakes with a knife through his lung, with the death rattle in his throat, covered with blood, unable to breathe, and on the point of death, understanding nothing—and there you have it.

When I finally recovered my sanity, I was thirsty again; I lit a candle and went towards the table where I had placed my carafe. I lifted it and held it over my glass; not a drop ran out. It was empty! It was completely empty. At first, I simply didn't understand; then all at once a frightful rush of emotion so overwhelmed me that I was forced to sit down, or say rather that I fell into a chair! Then I leaped up again and looked round me! Then I sat down again, lost in surprise and fear, in front of the transparent crystal. I gazed at it with a fixed stare, seeking an answer to the riddle. My hands were trembling. Had someone drunk the water? Who? I? It must have been me. Who could it have been but me? So I was a somnambulist, all unaware I was living the mysterious double life that raises the doubt whether there be not two selves in us, or whether, in moments when the spirit lies uncon- scious, an alien self, unknowable and unseen, inhabits the captive body that obeys this other self as it obeys us, obeys it more readily than it obeys us.

Oh, can anyone understand my frightful agony? Can anyone understand the feelings of a sane-minded, educated, thoroughly rational man, staring in abject terror through the glass of his carafe, where the water has disappeared while he slept? I remained there until daylight, not daring to go back to bed.

July 6. I am going mad. My carafe was emptied again last night—or, rather, I emptied it.

But is it I? Is it I? Who can it be? Who? Oh, my God! Am I going mad? Who will save me?

July 10. I have just made some astonishing experiments. Listen!

On the 6th of July, before lying down in bed, I placed on my table wine, milk, water, bread, and strawberries.

Someone drank—I drank—all the water, and a little of the milk. Neither the wine nor the bread nor the strawberries were touched.

On the 7th of July, I made the same experiment and got the same result.

On the 8th of July, I left out the water and the milk. Nothing was touched.

Finally, on the 9th of July, I placed only the water and milk on my table, taking care to wrap the carafes in white muslin cloths and to tie down the stoppers. Then I rubbed my lips, my beard, and my hands with a charcoal pencil and lay down.

The usual overpowering sleep seized me, followed shortly by the frightful waken- ing. I had not moved, my bedclothes themselves bore no marks. I rushed towards my table. The cloths wrapped round the bottles remained spotless. I untied the cords, shaking with fear. All the water had been drunk! All the milk had been drunk! Oh, my God! . . .

I am leaving for Paris at once.

July 13. Paris. I suppose I lost my head during the last few days! I must have been the sport of my disordered imagination, unless I really am a somnambulist or have fallen under one of those indubitable but hitherto inexplicable influences that we call suggestions. However that may be, my disorder came very near to lunacy, and twenty-four hours in Paris have been enough to restore my balance.

Yesterday I went to the races and made various calls. I felt myself endowed with new vital strength, and I ended my evening at the Théâtre Français. They were presenting a play by the younger Dumas; and his alert, forceful intelligence com- pleted my cure. There can be no doubt that loneliness is dangerous to active minds. We need round us men who think and talk. When we live alone for long periods, we people the void with phantoms.

I returned to the hotel in high spirits, walking along the boulevards. Amid the jostling of the crowd, I thought ironically on my terrors, on my hallucinations of a week ago, when I had believed, yes, believed that an invisible being dwelt in my body. How weak and shaken and speedily unbalanced our brains are immediately they are confronted by a tiny incomprehensible fact!

Instead of coming to a conclusion in these simple words: "I do not understand because the cause eludes me," at once we imagine frightening mysteries and super-natural powers.

July 14. Fête de la République. I walked through the streets. The rockets and the flags filled me with a childish joy. At the same time, it is vastly silly to be joyous on a set day by order of the government. The mob is an imbecile herd, as stupid in its patience as it is savage when roused. You say to it: "Enjoy yourself," and it enjoys itself. You say to it: "Go and fight your neighbor." It goes to fight. You say to it: "Vote for the Emperor." It votes for the Emperor. Then you say to it: "Vote for the Republic." And it votes for the Republic.

Its rulers are as besotted; but instead of obeying men they obey principles, which can only be half-baked, sterile, and false in so much as they are principles, that is to say, ideas reputed certain and immutable, in this world where nothing is sure, since light and sound are both illusions.

July 16. Yesterday I saw some things that have profoundly disturbed me.

I dined with my cousin, Mme. Sablé, whose husband commands the 76th Light Horse at Limoges. At her house I met two young women, one of whom has married a doctor, Dr. Parent, who devotes himself largely to nervous illnesses and the extraordinary discoveries that are the outcome of the recent experiments in hyp-notism and suggestion.

He told us at length about the amazing results obtained by English scientists and by the doctors of the Nancy school.

The facts that he put forward struck me as so fantastic that I confessed myself utterly incredulous.

"We are," he declared, "on the point of discovering one of the most important secrets of nature, I mean one of the most important secrets on this earth; for there are certainly others as important, away yonder, in the stars. Since man began to think, since he learned to express and record his thoughts, he has felt the almost impalpable touch of a mystery impenetrable by his clumsy and imperfect senses, and he has tried to supplement the impotence of his organic powers by the force of his intelligence. While this intelligence was still in a rudimentary stage, this haunting sense of invisible phenomena clothed itself in terrors such as occur to simple minds. Thus are born popular theories of the supernatural, the legends of wandering spirits, fairies, gnomes, ghosts. I'll add the God myth itself, since our conceptions of the artificer-creator, to whatever religion they belong, are really the most uninspired, the most unintelligent, the most inacceptable products of the fear-clouded brain of human beings. Nothing is truer than that saying of Voltaire's: 'God has made man in His image, but man has retorted upon Him in kind.'

"But for a little over a century we have had glimpse of a new knowledge. Mesmer and others have set our feet on a fresh path, and, more specially during the last four or five years, we have actually reached surprising results."

My cousin, as incredulous as I, smiled. Dr. Parent said to her: "Shall I try to put you to sleep, madame?"

"Yes, do."

She seated herself in an armchair, and he looked fixedly into her eyes, as if he were trying to fascinate her. As for me, I felt suddenly uneasy: my heart thumped, my throat contracted. I saw Mme. Sablé's eyes grow heavy, her mouth twitch, her bosom rise and fall with her quick breathing.

Within ten minutes she was asleep.

"Go behind her," said the doctor.

I seated myself behind her. He put a visiting card in her hands and said to her: "Here is a looking glass: what can you see in it?"

"I see my cousin," she answered.

"What is he doing?"

"He is twisting his mustache."

"And now?"

"He is drawing a photograph from his pocket."

"Whose photograph is it?"

"His."

She was right! And this photograph had been sent me at my hotel only that very evening.

"What is he doing in the photograph?"

"He is standing, with his hat in his hand."

Evidently she saw, in this card, this piece of white pasteboard, as she would have seen in a glass.

The young women, terrified, cried: "That's enough, that's quite enough."

But the doctor said authoritatively: "You will get up tomorrow at eight o'clock; then you will call on your cousin at his hotel and you will beg him to lend you five thousand francs that your husband has asked you to get and will exact on his next leave."

Then he woke her up.

On my way back to the hotel, I thought about this curious séance, and I was assailed by doubts, not of the absolutely unimpeachable good faith of my cousin, whom since our childhood I had looked upon as my sister, but of the possibility of trickery on the doctor's part. Had he concealed a looking glass in his hand and held it before the slumbering young woman when he was holding before her his visiting card? Professional conjurers do things as strange.

I had reached the hotel by now and I went to bed.

Then in the morning, towards half-past eight, I was roused by my man, who said to me:

"Mme. Sablé wishes to speak to you at once, sir."

I got hurriedly into my clothes and had her shown in.

She seated herself, very agitated, her eyes downcast, and, without lifting her veil, said:

"I have a great favor to ask you, my dear cousin."

"What is it, my dear?"

"I hate to ask it of you, and yet I must. I need, desperately, five thousand francs."

"You? You need it?"

"Yes, I, or rather my husband, who has laid it on me to get it."

I was so astounded that I stammered as I answered her. I wondered whether she and Dr. Parent were not actually making fun of me, whether it weren't a little comedy they had prepared beforehand and were acting very well.

But as I watched her closely my doubts vanished entirely. The whole affair was so distasteful to her that she was shaking with anguish, and I saw that her throat was quivering with sobs.

I knew that she was very rich and I added:

"What! do you mean to say that your husband can't call on five thousand francs! Come, think. Are you sure he told you to ask me for it?"

She hesitated for a few moments as if she were making a tremendous effort to search her memory, then she answered:

"Yes . . . yes. . . . I'm quite sure."

"Has he written to you?"

She hesitated again, reflecting. I guessed at the tortured striving of her mind. She didn't know. She knew nothing except that she had to borrow five thousand francs from me for her husband. Then she plucked up courage to lie.

"Yes, he has written to me."

"But when? You didn't speak to me about it yesterday."

"I got his letter this morning."

"Can you let me see it?"

"No . . . no . . . no . . . it is very intimate . . . too personal. . . . I've . . . I've burned it."

"Your husband must be in debt, then."

Again she hesitated, then answered:

"I don't know."

I told her abruptly:

"The fact is I can't lay my hands on five thousand francs at the moment, my dear."

A kind of agonized wail broke from her.

"Oh, I implore you, I implore you, get it for me."

She grew dreadfully excited, clasping her hands as if she were praying to me. The tone of her voice changed as I listened: she wept, stammering, torn with grief, goaded by the irresistible command that had been laid on her.

"Oh, I implore you to get it. . . . If you knew how unhappy I am! . . . I must have it today."

I took pity on her.

"You shall have it at once, I promise you."

"Thank you, thank you," she cried. "How kind you are!"

"Do you remember," I went on, "what happened at your house yesterday evening?"

"Yes."

"Do you remember that Dr. Parent put you to sleep?"

"Yes."

"Very well, he ordered you to come this morning and borrow five thousand francs from me, and you are now obeying the suggestion."

She considered this for a moment and answered:

"Because my husband wants it."

I spent an hour trying to convince her, but I did not succeed in doing so.

When she left, I ran to the doctor's house. He was just going out, and he listened to me with a smile. Then he said:

"Now do you believe?"

"I must."

"Let's go call on your cousin."

She was already asleep on a day bed, overwhelmed with weariness. The doctor felt her pulse and looked at her for some time, one hand lifted towards her eyes that slowly closed under the irresistible compulsion of his magnetic force.

When she was asleep:

"Your husband has no further need for five thousand francs. You will forget that you begged your cousin to lend it to you, and if he speaks to you about it, you will not understand."

Then he woke her up. I drew a notecase from my pocket.

"Here is what you asked me for this morning, my dear."

She was so dumfounded that I dared not press the matter. I did, however, try to rouse her memory, but she denied it fiercely, thought I was making fun of her, and at last was ready to be angry with me.

Back at the hotel. The experience has disturbed me so profoundly that I could not bring myself to take lunch.

July 19. I have told several people about this adventure and been laughed at for my pains. I don't know what to think now. The wise man says: Perhaps?

July 21. I dined at Bougival, then I spent the evening at the rowing-club dance. There's no doubt that everything is a question of places and persons. To believe in the supernatural in the island of Grenouillère would be the height of folly . . . . but at the top of Mont-Saint-Michel? . . . in the Indies? We are terrified under the influence of our surroundings. I am going home next week.

July 30. I have been home since yesterday. All is well.

August 2. Nothing fresh. The weather has been glorious. I spend my days watching the Seine run past.

August 4. The servants are quarreling among themselves. They declare that someone breaks the glasses in the cupboard at night. My man blames the cook, who blames the housemaid, who blames the other two. Who is the culprit? It would take a mighty clever man to find out.

August 6. This time, I am not mad. I've seen something. . . . I've seen something. . . . I've seen something. . . . I have no more doubts. . . . I've seen it. . . . I'm still cold to my finger tips. . . . My nerves are still racked with terror. . . . I've seen it.

At two o'clock, in broad daylight, I was walking in my rose garden . . . between the autumn roses that are just coming out.

As I paused to look at a Géant des Batailles, which bore three superb flowers, I saw, I distinctly saw, right under my eye, the stem of one of these roses bend as if an invisible hand had twisted it, then break as if the hand had plucked it. Then the flower rose, describing in the air the curve that an arm would have made carrying it towards a mouth, and it hung suspended in the clear air, quite alone, motionless, a terrifying scarlet splash three paces from my eyes.

I lost my head and flung myself on it, grasping at it. My fingers closed on nothing: it had disappeared. Then I was filled with a savage rage against myself; a rational serious-minded man simply does not have such hallucinations.

But was it really an hallucination? I turned round to look for the flower, and my eyes fell on it immediately: it had just been broken off and was lying between the two roses that still remained on the branch.

Then I went back to the house, my senses reeling: now I was sure as sure as I am that day follows night that there lived at my side an invisible being who fed on milk and water, who could touch things, take them, move them from one place to another, endowed therefore with a material nature, imperceptible to our senses though it was, and living beside me, under my roof. . . .

August 7. I slept quietly. He has drunk the water from my carafe, but he did not disturb my sleep.

I wonder if I am mad. Sometimes as I walk in the blazing sunshine along the riverbank, I am filled with doubts of my sanity, not the vague doubts I have been feeling, but precise and uncompromising doubts. I have seen madmen; I have known men who were intelligent, lucid, even exceptionally clearheaded in everything in life but on one point. They talked quite clearly, easily, and profoundly about everything, until suddenly their mind ran onto the rocks of their madness and was there rent in pieces, strewn to the winds and foundered in the fearful raging sea, filled with surging waves, fogs, squalls, that we call "insanity."

I should certainly have thought myself mad, absolutely mad, if I were not conscious, if I were not perfectly aware of my state of mind, if I did not get to the bottom of it and analyze it with such complete clearness. I must be, in fact, no worse than a sane man troubled with hallucinations. There must be some unknown disturbance in my brain, one of those disturbances that modern physiologists are trying to observe and elucidate; and this disturbance has opened a deep gulf in my mind, in the orderly and logical working of my thoughts. Similar phenomena take place in a dream that drags us through the most unreal phantasmagoria without sowing the least surprise in our minds because the mechanism of judgment, the controlling censor, is asleep, while the imaginative faculty wakes and works. Can one of the invisible strings that control my mental keyboard have become muted?

Sometimes, after an accident, a man loses his power to remember proper names or verbs or figures or only dates. The localization of all the different faculties of the mind is now proved. Is there anything surprising, therefore, in the idea that my power of examining the unreality of certain hallucinations has ceased to function in my brain just now?

I thought of all this as I walked by the side of the water. The sunlight flung a mantle of light across the river, clothing the earth with beauty, filling my thoughts with love of life, of the swallows whose swift flight is a joy to my eyes, of the riverside grasses whose shuddering whisper contents my ears.

Little by little, however, I fell prey to an inexplicable uneasiness. I felt as though some force, an occult force, were paralyzing my movements, halting me, hindering me from going on any further, calling me back. I was oppressed by just such an unhappy impulse to turn back as one feels when a beloved person has been left at home ill and one is possessed by a foreboding that the illness has taken a turn for the worse.

So, in spite of myself, I turned back, sure that I should find bad news waiting in my house, a letter or a telegram. There was nothing; and I was left more surprised and uneasy than if I had had yet another fantastic vision.

August 8. Yesterday I spent a frightful night. He did not manifest himself again, but I felt him near me, spying on me, watching me, taking possession of me, dominating me, and more to be feared when he hid himself in this way than if he gave notice of his constant invisible presence by supernatural phenomena.

However, I slept.

August 9. Nothing, but I am afraid.

August 10. Nothing; what will happen tomorrow?

August 11. Still nothing: I can't remain in my home any longer, with this fear and these thoughts in my mind: I shall go away.

August 12. Ten o'clock in the evening. I have been wanting to go away all day. I can't. I have been wanting to carry out the easy simple act that will set me free —go out—get into my carriage to go to Rouen—I can't. Why?

August 13. Under the affliction of certain maladies, all the resources of one's physical being seem crushed, all one's energy exhausted, one's muscles relaxed, one's bones grown as soft as flesh, and one's flesh turned to water. In a strange and wretched fashion I suffer all these pains in my spiritual being. I have no strength, no courage, no control over myself, no power even to summon up my will. I can will nothing; but someone wills for me—and I obey.

August 14. I am lost. Someone has taken possession of my soul and is master of it; someone orders all my acts, all my movements, all my thoughts. I am no longer anything, I am only a spectator, enslaved, and terrified by all the things I do. I wish to go out. I cannot. He does not wish it; and I remain, dazed, trembling, in the armchair where he keeps me seated. I desire no more than to get up, to raise myself again. I can't do it. I am riveted to my seat; and my seat is fast to the ground, in such fashion that no force could lift us.

Then, all at once, I must, must, must go to the bottom of my garden and pick strawberries and eat them. Oh, my God! my God! my God! Is there a God? If there is one, deliver me, save me, help me! Pardon me! Pity me! Have mercy on me! How I suffer! How I am tortured! How terrible this is!

August 15. Well, think how my poor cousin was possessed and overmastered when she came to borrow five thousand francs from me. She submitted to an alien will that had entered into her, as if it were another soul, a parasitic, tyrannical soul. Is the world coming to an end?

But what is this being, this invisible being who is ruling me? This unknowable creature, this wanderer from a supernatural race.

So Unseen Ones exist? Then why is it that since the world began they have never manifested themselves in so unmistakable a fashion as they are now manifesting themselves to me? I have never read of anything like the things that are happening under my roof. If I could only leave it, if I could only go away, fly far away and return no more, I should be saved, but I can't.

August 16. Today I was able to escape for two hours, like a prisoner who finds the door of his cell accidentally left open. I felt that I was suddenly set free, that he had withdrawn himself. I ordered the horses to be put in the carriage as quickly as possible and I reached Rouen. Oh, what a joy it was to find myself able to tell a man: "Go to Rouen," and be obeyed!

I stopped at the library and asked them to lend me the long treatise of Dr. Hermann Herestauss on the unseen inhabitants of the antique and modern worlds.

Then, just as I was getting back into my carriage, with the words, "To the station," on my lips, I shouted—I didn't speak, I shouted—in a voice so loud that the passers-by turned round: "Home," and I fell, overwhelmed with misery, onto the cushions of my carriage. He had found me again and taken possession once more.

August 17. What a night! what a night! Nevertheless it seems to me that I ought to congratulate myself. I read until one o'clock in the morning. Hermann Herestauss, a doctor of philosophy and theogony, has written an account of all the invisible beings who wander among men or have been imagined by men's minds. He describes their origins, their domains, their power. But none of them is the least like the being who haunts me. It is as if man, the thinker, has had a foreboding vision of some new being, mightier than himself, who shall succeed him in this world; and, in his terror, feeling him draw near and unable to guess at the nature of this master, he has created all the fantastic crowd of occult beings, dim phantoms born of fear.

Well, I read until one o'clock and then I seated myself near my open window to cool my head and my thoughts in the gentle air of night.

It was fine and warm. In other days how I should have loved such a night!

No moon. The stars wavered and glittered in the black depths of the sky. Who dwells in these worlds? What forms of life, what living creatures, what animals or plants do they hold? What more than we do the thinkers in those far-off universes know? What more can they do than we? What do they see that we do not know of? Perhaps one of them, some day or other, will cross the gulf of space and appear on our earth as a conqueror, just as in olden days the Normans crossed the sea to subdue wealthy nations.

We others are so infirm, so defenseless, so ignorant, so small, on this grain of dust that revolves and crumbles in a drop of water.

So dreaming, I fell asleep, in the fresh evening air.

I slept for about forty minutes and opened my eyes again without moving, roused by I know not what vague and strange emotions. At first I saw nothing, then all at once I thought that the page of a book lying open on my table had turned over of itself. Not a breath of air came in at the window. I was surprised and I sat waiting. About four minutes later, I saw, I saw, yes, I saw with my own eyes another page come up and turn back on the preceding one, as if a finger had folded it back. My armchair was empty, seemed empty; but I realized that he was there, *he*, sitting in my place and reading. In one wild spring, like the spring of a maddened beast resolved to eviscerate his trainer, I crossed the room to seize him and crush him and kill him. But before I had reached it my seat turned right over as if he had fled before me . . . my table rocked, my lamp fell and was extinguished, and my window slammed shut as if I had surprised a malefactor who had flung himself out into the darkness, tugging at the sashes with all his force.

So he had run away; he had been afraid, afraid of me, me!

Then . . . then . . . tomorrow . . . or the day after . . . or some day . . . I should be able to get him between my fingers, and crush him against the ground. Don't dogs sometimes bite and fly at their masters' throats?

August 18. I've been thinking things over all day. Oh, yes, I'll obey him, satisfy his impulses, do his will, make myself humble, submissive, servile. He is the stronger. But an hour will come. . . .

August 19. I know now. . . . I know. . . . I know everything! I have just read the following in the *Revue du Monde Scientifique:* "A strange piece of news reaches us from Rio de Janeiro. Madness, an epidemic of madness, comparable to the contagious outbursts of dementia that attacked the peoples of Europe in the Middle Ages, is raging at this day in the district of São Paulo. The distracted inhabitants are quitting their houses, deserting their villages, abandoning their fields, declaring themselves to be pursued, possessed, and ordered about like a human herd by certain invisible but tangible beings, vampires of some kind, who feed on their vitality while they sleep, in addition to drinking milk and water without, apparently, touching any other form of food.

"Professor Dom Pedro Henriquez, accompanied by several learned doctors, has set out for the district of São Paulo, to study on the spot the origins and the forms taken by this surprising madness, and to suggest to the Emperor such measures as appear to him most likely to restore the delirious inhabitants to sanity."

Ah! I remember, I remember the lovely three-masted Brazilian that sailed past my windows on the eighth of last May, on her way up the Seine. I thought her such a bonny, white, gay boat. The Being was on board her, come from over the sea, where his race is born. He saw me. He saw my house, white like the ship, and he jumped from the vessel to the bank. Oh, my God!

Now I know, I understand. The reign of man is at an end.

He is here, whom the dawning fears of primitive peoples taught them to dread. He who was exorcised by troubled priests, evoked in the darkness of night by wizards who yet never saw him materialize, to whom the foreboding vision of the masters who have passed through this world lent all the monstrous or gracious forms of gnomes, spirits, jinns, fairies, and hobgoblins. Primitive terror visualized him in the crudest forms; later, wiser men have seen him more clearly. Mesmer foresaw him, and it is ten years since doctors made the most exact inquiries into the nature of his power, even before he exercised it himself. They have been making a plaything of this weapon of the new God, this imposition of a mysterious will on the enslaved soul of man. They called it magnetism, hypnotism, suggestion . . . anything you like. I have seen them amusing themselves with this horrible power like foolish children. Woe to us! Cursed is man! He is here . . . the . . . the . . . what is his name? . . . the . . . it seems as if he were shouting his name in my ear and I cannot hear it . . . the . . . yes . . . he is shouting it. . . . I am listening. . . . I can't hear. . . . Again, tell me again . . . the . . . Horla. . . . I heard . . . the Horla . . . it is he . . . the Horla . . . he is here!

Oh, the vulture has been used to eat the dove, the wolf to eat the sheep; the lion to devour the sharp-horned buffalo; the man to kill the lion with arrow, spear and gun; but the Horla is going to make of man what we have made of the horse and the cow: his thing, his servant, and his food, by the mere force of his will. Woe to us!

But sometimes the beast rebels and kills his tamer . . . I too want . . . I could . . . but I must know him, touch him, see him. Scientists say that the eye of the beast is not like ours and does not see as ours does. . . . And my eye fails to show me this newcomer who is oppressing me.

Why? Oh, the words of the monk of Mont-Saint-Michel come to my mind: "Do we see the hundred-thousandth part of all that exists? Think, there's the wind, the greatest force in nature, which throws down men, shatters buildings, uproots trees, stirs up the sea into watery mountains, destroys cliffs, and tosses the tall ships against the shore, the wind that kills, whistles, groans, roars—have you seen it, can you see it? Nevertheless, it exists."

And I considered further: my eye is so weak, so imperfect, that it does not distinguish even solid bodies that have the transparency of glass. If a looking glass that has no foil backing bars my path, I hurl myself against it as a bird that has got into a room breaks its head on the windowpane. How many other things deceive and mislead my eye? Then what is there to be surprised at in its failure to see a new body that offers no resistance to the passage of light?

A new being! why not? He must assuredly come! why should we be the last? Why is he not seen of our eyes as are all the beings created before us? Because his form is nearer perfection, his body finer and completer than ours—ours, which is so weak, so clumsily conceived, encumbered by organs always tired, always breaking down like a too complex mechanism, which lives like a vegetable or a beast, drawing its substance with difficulty from the air, the herbs of the field, and meat, a living machine subject to sickness, deformity and corruption, drawing its breath in pain, ill-regulated, simple and fantastic, ingeniously ill-made, clumsily and delicately erected, the mere rough sketch of a being who could become intelligent and noble.

There have been so few kinds created in the world, from the bivalve to man. Why not one more, when we reach the end of the period of time that separates each successive appearance of a species from that which appeared before it?

Why not one more? Why not also new kinds of trees bearing monstrous flowers, blazing with color and filling all the countryside with their perfume? Why not other elements than fire, air, earth, and water? There are four, only four sources of our being! What a pity! Why not forty, four hundred, four thousand? How poor, niggardly and brutish is life! grudgingly given, meanly conceived, stupidly executed. Consider the grace of the elephant, the hippopotamus! The elegance of the camel!

You bid me consider the butterfly! a winged flower! I can imagine one vast as a hundred worlds, with wings for whose shape, beauty, color, and sweep I cannot find any words. But I see it . . . it goes from star to star, refreshing and perfuming them with the soft, gracious wind of its passing. And the people of the upper air watch it pass, in an ecstasy of joy!

What is the matter with me? It is he, he, the Horla, who is haunting me, filling my head with these absurdities! He is in me; he has become my soul; I will kill him.

August 19. I will kill him. I have seen him! I was sitting at my table yesterday evening, making a great show of being very absorbed in writing. I knew quite well that he would come and prowl round me, very close to me, so close that I might be able to touch him, seize him, perhaps? And then! . . . then, I should be filled with the strength of desperation; I should have hands, knees, chest, face, teeth to strangle him, crush him, tear him, rend him.

With every sense quiveringly alert, I watched for him.

I had lit both my lamps and the eight candles on my chimney piece, as if I thought I should be more likely to discover him by this bright light.

In front of me was my bed, an old oak four-poster; on my right, the fireplace; on my left, my door carefully shut, after I had left it open for a long time to attract him; behind me, a very tall cupboard with a mirror front, which I used every day to shave and dress by, and in which I always regarded myself from head to foot whenever I passed in front of it.

Well, I pretended to write to deceive him, because he was spying on me too; and, all at once, I felt, I was certain, that he was reading over my shoulder, that he was there, his breath on my ear.

I stood up, my hand outstretched, and turned round, so quickly that I almost fell. What do you think? . . . the room was as light as day, and I could not see myself in my looking glass! It was empty, transparent, deep, filled with light! I was not reflected in it . . . and I was standing in front of it. I could see the wide limpid expanse of glass from top to bottom. And I stared at it with a distraught gaze: I daren't move another step, I daren't make another movement; nevertheless I felt that he was there, whose immaterial body had swallowed up my reflection, but that he would elude me still.

How frightened I was! A moment later my reflection began to appear in the depths of the looking glass, in a sort of mist, as if I were looking at it through water; this water seemed to flow from left to right, slowly, so that moment by moment my reflection emerged more distinctly. It was like the passing of an eclipse. The thing that was concealing me appeared to possess no sharply defined outlines, but a kind of transparent opacity that gradually cleared.

At last I could see myself from head to foot, just as I saw myself every day when I looked in the glass.

I had seen him! The horror of it is still on me, making me shudder.

August 20. How can I kill him? Since I can't touch him? Poison? But he would see me put it in the water; and besides, would our poisons affect an immaterial body? No . . . No, they certainly would not. . . . Then how? . . . how?

August 21. I have sent for a locksmith from Rouen, and ordered him to fit my room with iron shutters, such as they have in certain hotels in Paris, to keep out robbers. He is to make me, also, a similar sort of door. Everyone thinks me a coward, but much I care for that!

September 10. Rouen, Hôtel Continental. It is done . . . it is done . . . but is he dead? My brain reels with what I have seen.

Yesterday the locksmith put up my iron shutters and my iron door, and I left everything open until midnight, although it began to get cold.

All at once I felt his presence, and I was filled with joy, a mad joy. I rose slowly to my feet, and walked about the room for a long time, so that he should suspect nothing; then I took off my boots and carelessly drew on my slippers; then I closed my iron shutters, and, sauntering back towards the door, I double-locked it too. Then I walked back to the window and secured it with a padlock, putting the key in my pocket.

Suddenly I realized that he was prowling anxiously round me, he was afraid now, and commanding me to open them for him. I almost yielded: I did not yield, but, leaning on the door, I set it ajar, just wide enough for me to slip out backwards; and as I am very tall my head touched the lintel. I was sure that he could not have got out and I shut him in, alone, all alone. Thank God! I had him! Then I ran downstairs; in the drawing room which is under my room, I took both my lamps and emptied the oil all over the carpet and the furniture, everything; then I set it on fire, and I fled after having double-locked the main door.

And I went and hid myself at the bottom of my garden, in a grove of laurels. How long it took, how long! Everything was dark, silent, still, not a breath of air, not a star, mountains of unseen clouds that lay so heavily, so heavily, on my spirit.

I kept my gaze fixed on my house, and waited. How long it took! I was beginning to think that the fire had died out of itself, or that he, He, had put it out, when one of the lower windows fell in under the fierce breath of the fire and a flame, a great red and yellow flame, a long, curling, caressing flame, leaped up the white wall and pressed its kiss on the roof itself. A flood of light poured over trees, branches, leaves, and with that a shudder, a shudder of fear, ran through them. The birds woke; a dog howled: I thought the dawn was at hand. In a moment two more windows burst into flame and I saw that the lower half of my house was now one frightful furnace. But a cry, a frightful piercing agonized cry, a woman's cry, stabbed the night, and two skylights opened. I had forgotten my servants. I saw their distraught faces and their widely waving arms. . . .

Then, frantic with horror, I began to run towards the village, shouting: "Help! help! fire! fire!" I met people already on their way to the house and I turned back with them to look at it.

By now the house was no more than a horrible and magnificent funeral pyre, a monstrous pyre lighting up the whole earth, a pyre that was consuming men, Him, Him, my prisoner, the new Being, the new Master, the Horla!

The whole roof fell in with a sudden crash, and a volcano of flames leaped to the sky. Through all the windows open on the furnace, I saw the fiery vat, and I reflected that he was there, in this oven, dead. . . .

Dead? Perhaps? . . . His body? Perhaps that body through which light fell could not be destroyed by the methods that kill our bodies?

Suppose he is not dead? . . . Perhaps only time has power over the Invisible and Dreadful One. Why should this transparent, unknowable body, this body of the spirit, fear sickness, wounds, infirmity, premature destruction?

Premature destruction? The source of all human dread! After man, the Horla. After him who can die any day, any hour, any moment, by accidents of all kinds, comes he who can only die in his appointed day, hour and moment, when he has attained the limit of his existence.

No . . . no . . . I know, I know . . . he is not dead . . . so . . . so . . . I must kill myself, now.

USELESS BEAUTY

A very elegant victoria with two beautiful black horses was drawn up in front of the mansion. It was a day in the latter end of June, about half-past five in the afternoon, and the sun shone warm and bright into the large courtyard.

The Countess de Mascaret came down just as her husband, who was coming home, appeared in the carriage entrance. He stopped for a few moments to look at his wife and grew rather pale. She was very beautiful, graceful and distinguished-looking with her long oval face, her complexion like gilt ivory, her large gray eyes and her black hair, and she got into her carriage without looking at him, without even seeming to have noticed him, with such a particularly highbred air that the furious jealousy by which he had been devoured for so long again gnawed at his heart. He went up to her and said: "You are going for a drive?"

She merely replied disdainfully: "You see I am!"

"In the Bois de Boulogne?"

"Most probably."

"May I come with you?"

"The carriage belongs to you."

Without being surprised at the tone of voice in which she answered him, he got in and sat down by his wife's side and said: "Bois de Boulogne." The footman jumped up by the coachman's side, and the horses, as usual, pawed the ground and shook their heads until they were in the street. Husband and wife sat side by side without speaking. He was thinking how to begin a conversation, but she maintained such an obstinately hard look that he did not venture to make the attempt. At last, however, he cunningly, accidentally as it were, touched the countess's gloved hand with his own, but she drew her arm away with a movement which was so expressive of disgust that he remained thoughtful in spite of his usual authoritative and despotic character. "Gabrielle!" he said at last.

"What do you want?"

"I think you are looking adorable."

She did not reply but remained lying back in the carriage looking like an irritated queen. By that time they were driving up the Champs Elysées, toward the Arc de Triomphe. That immense monument at the end of the long avenue raised its colossal arch against the red sky, and the sun seemed to be sinking onto it, showering fiery dust on it from the sky.

The stream of carriages, with the sun reflecting from the bright, plated harness and the shining lamps, was like a double current flowing, one toward the town and one toward the wood, and the Count de Mascaret continued: "My dear Gabrielle!"

Then, unable to bear it any longer, she replied in an exasperated voice:

"Oh, do leave me in peace, pray! I am not even at liberty to have my carriage to myself now." He, however, pretended not to hear her and continued: "You have never looked so pretty as you do today."

Her patience was decidedly at an end, and she replied with irrepressible anger: "You are wrong to notice it, for I swear to you that I will never have anything to do with you in that way again." He was stupefied and agitated and, his violent nature gaining the upper hand, he exclaimed: "What do you mean by that?" in such a manner as revealed rather the brutal master than the amorous man. But she replied in a low voice so that the servants might not hear amid the deafening noise of the wheels:

"Ah! What do I mean by that? What do I mean by that? Now I recognize you again! Do you want me to tell everything?"

"Yes."

"Everything that has been on my heart since I have been the victim of your terrible selfishness?"

He had grown red with surprise and anger, and he growled between his closed teeth: "Yes, tell me everything."

He was a tall, broad-shouldered man, with a big red beard, a handsome man, a nobleman, a man of the world, who passed as a perfect husband and an excellent father, and now for the first time since they had started she turned toward him and looked him full in the face. "Ah! You will hear some disagreeable things, but you must know that I am prepared for everything, that I fear nothing, and you less than anyone today."

He also was looking into her eyes and already was shaking with passion; then he said in a low voice: "You are mad."

"No, but I will no longer be the victim of the hateful penalty of maternity, which you have inflicted on me for eleven years! I wish to live like a woman of the world, as I have the right to do, as all women have the right to do."

He suddenly grew pale again and stammered: "I do not understand you."

"Oh yes; you understand me well enough. It is now three months since I had my last child, and as I am still very beautiful, and as, in spite of all your efforts, you cannot spoil my figure, as you just now perceived when you saw me on the outside flight of steps, you think it is time that I should become *enceinte* again."

"But you are talking nonsense!"

"No, I am not; I am thirty and I have had seven children, and we have been married eleven years, and you hope that this will go on for ten years longer, after which you will leave off being jealous."

He seized her arm and squeezed it, saying: "I will not allow you to talk to me like that for long."

"And I shall talk to you till the end, until I have finished all I have to say to you, and if you try to prevent me I shall raise my voice so that the two servants who are on the box may hear. I only allowed you to come with me for that object, for I have these witnesses, who will oblige you to listen to me and to contain yourself; so now pay attention to what I say. I have always felt an antipathy for you and I have always let you see it, for I have never lied, monsieur. You married me in spite of myself; you forced my parents, who were in embarrassed circumstances, to give me to you because you were rich, and they obliged me to marry you, in spite of my tears.

"So you bought me, and as soon as I was in your power, as soon as I had become your companion, ready to attach myself to you, to forget your coercive and threatening proceedings, in order that I might only remember that I ought to be a devoted wife and to love you as much as it might be possible for me to love you, you became jealous—you—as no man has ever been before, with the base, ignoble jealousy of a spy, which was as degrading for you as it was for me. I had not been married eight months when you suspected me of every perfidiousness, and you even told me so. What a disgrace! And as you could not prevent me from being beautiful and from pleasing people, from being called in drawing rooms and also in the newspapers one of the most beautiful women in Paris; you tried everything you could think of to keep admirers from me, and you hit upon the abominable idea of making me spend my life in a constant state of motherhood, until the time when I should disgust every man. Oh, do not deny it! I did not understand it for some time, but then I guessed it. You even boasted about it to your sister, who told me of it, for she is fond of me and was disgusted at your boorish coarseness.

"Ah! Remember our struggles, doors smashed in and locks forced! For eleven years you have condemned me to the existence of a brood mare. Then as soon as I was pregnant you grew disgusted with me, and I saw nothing of you for months and I was sent into the country to the family mansion, among fields and meadows, to bring forth my child. And when I reappeared, fresh, pretty and indestructible, still seductive and constantly surrounded by admirers, hoping that at last I should live a little like a young rich woman who belongs to society, you were seized by jealousy again, and you recommenced to persecute me with that infamous and hateful desire from which you are suffering at this moment by my side. And it is not the desire of possessing me—for I should never have refused myself to you—but it is the wish to make me unsightly.

"Besides this, that abominable and mysterious circumstance took place which I was a long time in penetrating (but I grew acute by dint of watching your thoughts and actions). You attached yourself to your children with all the security which they gave you while I bore them in my womb. You felt affection for them with all your aversion for me and in spite of your ignoble fears, which were momentarily allayed by your pleasure in seeing me a mother.

"Oh! How often have I noticed that joy in you! I have seen it in your eyes and guessed it. You loved your children as victories and not because they were of your own blood. They were victories over me, over my youth, over my beauty, over my charms, over the compliments which were paid me and over those who whispered round me, without paying them to me. And you are proud of them; you make a parade of them; you take them out for drives in your coach in the Bois de Boulogne, and you give them donkey rides at Montmorency. You take them to theatrical matinees so that you may be seen in the midst of them and that people may say: 'What a kind father!' and that it may be repeated."

He had seized her wrist with savage brutality and squeezed it so violently that she was quiet, though she nearly cried out with the pain. Then he said to her in a whisper:

"I love my children; do you hear? What you have just told me is disgraceful in a mother. But you belong to me; I am master—your master. I can exact from you what I like and when I like—and I have the law on my side."

He was trying to crush her fingers in the strong grip of his large, muscular hand, and she, livid with pain, tried in vain to free them from that vise which was crushing them; the agony made her pant, and the tears came into her eyes. "You see that I am the master and the stronger," he said. And when he somewhat loosened his grip she asked him: "Do you think that I am a religious woman?"

He was surprised and stammered: "Yes."

"Do you think that I could lie if I swore to the truth of anything to you before an altar on which Christ's body is?"

"No."

"Will you go with me to some church?"

"What for?"

"You shall see. Will you?"

"If you absolutely wish it, yes."

She raised her voice and said: "Philip!" And the coachman, bending down a little, without taking his eyes from his horses, seemed to turn his ear alone toward his mistress, who said: "Drive to St Philip-du-Roule's." And the victoria, which had reached the entrance of the Bois de Boulogne, returned to Paris.

Husband and wife did not exchange a word during the drive. When the carriage stopped before the church Countess de Mascaret jumped out and entered it, followed by the count a few yards behind her. She went without stopping as far as the choir screen and, falling on her knees at a chair, she buried her face in her hands. She prayed for a long time, and he, standing behind her, could see that she was crying. She wept noiselessly, like women do weep when they are in great and poignant grief. There was a kind of undulation in her body, which ended in a little sob, hidden and stifled by her fingers.

But Count de Mascaret thought that the situation was long drawn out, and he touched her on the shoulder. That contact recalled her to herself, as if she had been burned, and, getting up, she looked straight into his eyes.

"This is what I have to say to you. I am afraid of nothing, whatever you may do to me. You may kill me if you like. One of your children is not yours, and one only; that I swear to you before God who hears me here. That is the only revenge which was possible for me in return for all your abominable male tyrannies, in return for the penal servitude of childbearing to which you have condemned me. Who was my lover? That you will never know! You may suspect everyone, but you will never find out. I gave myself up to him without love and without pleasure, only for the sake of betraying you, and he made me a mother. Which is his child? That also you will never know. I have seven; try and find out! I intended to tell you this later, for one cannot completely avenge oneself on a man by deceiving him, unless he knows it. You have driven me to confess it today; now I have finished."

She hurried through the church toward the open door, expecting to hear behind her the quick steps of her husband whom she had defied and to be knocked to the ground by a blow of his fist, but she heard nothing and reached her carriage. She jumped into it at a bound, overwhelmed with anguish and breathless with fear; she called out to the coachman, "Home!" and the horses set off at a quick trot.

II

The Countess de Mascaret was waiting in her room for dinnertime, like a criminal sentenced to death awaits the hour of his execution. What was he going to do? Had he come home? Despotic, passionate, ready for any violence as he was, what was he meditating; what had he made up his mind to do? There was no sound in the house, and every moment she looked at the clock. Her maid had come and dressed her for the evening and had then left the room again. Eight o'clock struck; almost at the same moment there was two knocks at the door, and the butler came in and told her that dinner was ready.

"Has the count come in?"

"Yes, Madame la Comtesse; he is in the dining room."

For a moment she felt inclined to arm herself with a small revolver which she had bought some weeks before, foreseeing the tragedy which was being rehearsed in her heart. But she remembered that all the children would be there, and she took nothing except a smelling bottle. He rose somewhat ceremoniously from his chair. They exchanged a slight bow and sat down. The three boys with their tutor, Abbé Martin, were on her right, and the three girls with Miss Smith, their English governess, were on her left. The youngest child, who was only three months old, remained upstairs with his nurse.

The abbé said grace, as was usual when there was no company, for the children did not come down to dinner when there were guests present; then they began dinner. The countess, suffering from emotion which she had not at all calculated upon, remained with her eyes cast down, while the count scrutinized now the three boys and now the three girls with uncertain, unhappy looks, which traveled from one to the other. Suddenly, pushing his wineglass from him, it broke, and the wine was spilled on the tablecloth, and at the slight noise caused by this little accident the countess started up from her chair, and for the first time they looked at each other. Then almost every moment, in spite of themselves, in spite of the irritation of their nerves caused by every glance, they did not cease to exchange looks, rapid as pistol shots.

The abbé, who felt that there was some cause for embarrassment which he could not divine, tried to get up a conversation and started various subjects, but his useless efforts gave rise to no ideas and did not bring out a word. The countess, with feminine tact and obeying the instincts of a woman of the world, tried to answer him two or three times, but in vain. She could not find words in the perplexity of her mind, and her own voice almost frightened her in the silence of the large room, where nothing else was heard except the slight sound of plates and knives and forks.

Suddenly her husband said to her, bending forward: "Here, amid your children, will you swear to me that what you told me just now is true?"

The hatred which was fermenting in her veins suddenly roused her, and replying to that question with the same firmness with which she had replied to his looks, she raised both her hands, the right pointing toward the boys and the left toward the girls, and said in a firm, resolute voice and without any hesitation: "On the heads of my children, I swear that I have told you the truth."

He got up and, throwing his table napkin onto the table with an exasperated movement, turned round and flung his chair against the wall. Then he went out without another word, while she, uttering a deep sigh, as if after a first victory, went on in a calm voice: "You must not pay any attention to what your father has just said, my darlings; he was very much upset a short time ago, but he will be all right again in a few days."

Then she talked with the abbé and with Miss Smith and had tender, pretty words for all her children, those sweet, spoiling mother's ways which unlock little hearts.

When dinner was over she went into the drawing room with all her little following. She made the elder ones chatter, and when their bedtime came she kissed them for a long time and then went alone into her room.

She waited for she had no doubt that he would come, and she made up her mind then, as her children were not with her, to defend her human flesh, as she defended her life as a woman of the world; and in the pocket of her dress she put the little loaded revolver which she had bought a few weeks before. The hours went by; the hours struck, and every sound was hushed in the house. Only cabs continued to rumble through the streets, but their noise was only heard vaguely through the shuttered and curtained windows.

She waited, energetic and nervous, without any fear of him now, ready for anything and almost triumphant, for she had found means of torturing him continually during every moment of his life.

But the first gleams of dawn came in through the fringe at the bottom of her curtains without his having come into her room, and then she awoke to the fact, much to her surprise, that he was not coming. Having locked and bolted her door for greater security, she went to bed at last and remained there with her eyes open, thinking and barely understanding it all, without being able to guess what he was going to do.

When her maid brought her tea she at the same time gave her a letter from her husband. He told her that he was going to undertake a longish journey, and in a postscript he added that his lawyer would provide her with such money as she might require for her expenses.

III

It was at the opera, between two of the acts in *Robert the Devil*. In the stalls the men were standing up with their hats on, their waistcoats cut very low so as to show a large amount of white shirt front in which the gold and precious stones of their studs glistened. They were looking at the boxes crowded with ladies in low dresses, covered with diamonds and pearls, women who seemed to expand like flowers in that illuminated hothouse, where the beauty of their faces and the whiteness of their shoulders seemed to bloom for inspection in the midst of the music and of human voices.

Two friends with their backs to the orchestra were scanning those parterres of elegance, that exhibition of real or false charms, of jewels, of luxury and of pretension which showed itself off all round the Grand Theater. One of them, Roger de Salnis, said to his companion, Bernard Grandin: "Just look how beautiful Countess de Mascaret still is."

Then the elder, in turn, looked through his opera glasses at a tall lady in a box opposite, who appeared to be still very young and whose striking beauty seemed to appeal to men's eyes in every corner of the house. Her pale complexion, of an ivory tint, gave her the appearance of a statue, while a small diamond coronet glistened on her black hair like a cluster of stars.

When he had looked at her for some time Bernard Grandin replied with a jocular accent of sincere conviction: "You may well call her beautiful!"

"How old do you think she is?"

"Wait a moment. I can tell you exactly, for I have known her since she was a child, and I saw her make her debut into society when she was quite a girl. She is —she is—thirty—thirty-six."

"Impossible!"

"I am sure of it."

"She looks twenty-five."

"She has had seven children."

"It is incredible."

"And what is more, they are all seven alive, as she is a very good mother. I go to the house, which is a very quiet and pleasant one, occasionally, and she presents the phenomenon of the family in the midst of the world."

"How very strange! And have there never been any reports about her?"

"Never."

"But what about her husband? He is peculiar, is he not?"

"Yes and no. Very likely there has been a little drama between them, one of those little domestic dramas which one suspects, which one never finds out exactly, but which one guesses pretty nearly."

"What is it?"

"I do not know anything about it. Mascaret leads a very fast life now, after having been a model husband. As long as he remained a good spouse he had a shocking temper and was crabbed and easily took offense, but since he has been leading his present rackety life he has become quite indifferent, but one would guess that he has some trouble, a worm gnawing somewhere, for he has aged very much."

Thereupon the two friends talked philosophically for some minutes about the secret, unknowable troubles which differences of character or perhaps physical antipathies, which were not perceived at first, give rise to in families. Then Roger de Salnis, who was still looking at Mme de Mascaret through his opera glasses, said:

"It is almost incredible that that woman has had seven children!"

"Yes, in eleven years, after which, when she was thirty, she put a stop to her period of production in order to enter into the brilliant period of entertaining, which does not seem near coming to an end."

"Poor women!"

"Why do you pity them?"

"Why? Ah! my dear fellow, just consider! Eleven years of maternity for such a woman! What a hell! All her youth, all her beauty, every hope of success, every poetical ideal of a bright life, sacrificed to that abominable law of reproduction which turns the normal woman into a mere machine for maternity."

"What would you have? It is only nature!"

"Yes, but I say that nature is our enemy, that we must always fight against nature, for she is continually bringing us back to an animal state. You may be sure that God has not put anything on this earth that is clean, pretty, elegant or accessory to our ideal, but the human brain has done it. It is we who have introduced a little grace, beauty, unknown charm and mystery into creation by singing about it, interpreting it, by admiring it as poets, idealizing it as artists and by explaining it as learned men who make mistakes, who find ingenious reasons, some grace and beauty, some unknown charm and mystery, in the various phenomena of nature.

"God only created coarse beings, full of germs of disease, and who, after a few years of bestial enjoyment, grow old and infirm, with all the ugliness and all the want of power of human decrepitude. He only seems to have made them in order that they may reproduce their species in a repulsive manner and then die like ephemeral insects. I said, *reproduce their species in a repulsive manner*, and I adhere to that expression. What is there, as a matter of fact, more ignoble and more repugnant than that ridiculous act of the reproduction of living beings, against which all delicate minds always have revolted and always will revolt? Since all the organs which have been invented by this economical and malicious Creator serve two purposes, why did he not choose those that were unsullied, in order to intrust them with that sacred mission, which is the noblest and the most exalted of all human functions? The mouth which nourishes the body by means of material food also diffuses abroad speech and thought. Our flesh revives itself by means of itself, and at the same time ideas are communicated by it. The sense of smell which gives the vital air to the lungs imparts all the perfumes of the world to the brain: the smell of flowers, of woods, of trees, of the sea. The ear which enables us to communicate with our fellow men, has also allowed us to invent music, to create dreams, happiness, the infinite and even physical pleasure by means of sounds!

"But one might say that the Creator wished to prohibit man from ever ennobling and idealizing his commerce with women. Nevertheless, man has found love, which is not a bad reply to that sly Deity, and he has ornamented it so much with literary poetry that woman often forgets the contact she is obliged to submit to. Those among us who are powerless to deceive themselves have invented vice and refined debauchery, which is another way of laughing at God and of paying homage, immodest homage, to beauty.

"But the normal man makes children, just as a beast that is coupled with another by law.

"Look at that woman! Is it not abominable to think that such a jewel, such a pearl, born to be beautiful, admired, feted and adored, has spent eleven years of her life in providing heirs for the Count de Mascaret?"

Bernard Grandin replied with a laugh: "There is a great deal of truth in all that, but very few people would understand you."

Salnis got more and more animated. "Do you know how I picture God myself?"

he said. "As an enormous creative organ unknown to us, who scatters millions of worlds into space, just as one single fish would deposit its spawn in the sea. He creates, because it is His function as God to do so, but He does not know what He is doing and is stupidly prolific in His work and is ignorant of the combinations of all kinds which are produced by His scattered germs. Human thought is a lucky little local, passing accident, which was totally unforeseen and is condemned to disappear with this earth and to recommence perhaps here or elsewhere, the same or different, with fresh combinations of eternally new beginnings. We owe it to this slight accident which has happened to His intellect that we are very uncomfortable in this world which was not made for us, which had not been prepared to receive us, to lodge and feed us or to satisfy reflecting beings, and we owe it to Him also that we have to struggle without ceasing against what are still called the designs of Providence, when we are really refined and civilized beings."

Grandin, who was listening to him attentively, as he had long known the surprising outbursts of his fancy, asked him: "Then you believe that human thought is the spontaneous product of blind, divine parturition?"

"Naturally. A fortuitous function of the nerve centers of our brain, like some unforeseen chemical action which is due to new mixtures and which also resembles a product of electricity, caused by friction or the unexpected proximity of some substance, and which, lastly, resembles the phenomena caused by the infinite and fruitful fermentations of living matter.

"But, my dear fellow, the truth of this must be evident to anyone who looks about him. If human thought, ordained by an omniscient Creator, had been intended to be what it has become, altogether different from mechanical thoughts and resignation, so exacting, inquiring, agitated, tormented, would the world which was created to receive the beings which we now are have been this unpleasant little dwelling place for poor fools, this salad plot, this rocky, wooded and spherical kitchen garden where your improvident Providence has destined us to live naked in caves or under trees, nourished on the flesh of slaughtered animals, our brethren, or on raw vegetables nourished by the sun and the rain?

"But it is sufficient to reflect for a moment, in order to understand that this world was not made for such creatures as we are. Thought, which is developed by a miracle in the nerves of the cells and our brain, powerless, ignorant and confused as it is, and as it will always remain, makes all of us who are intellectual beings eternal and wretched exiles on earth.

"Look at this earth, as God has given it to those who inhabit it. Is it not visibly and solely made, planted and covered with forests, for the sake of animals? What is there for us? Nothing. And for them? Everything. They have nothing to do but to eat or go hunting and eat each other, according to their instincts, for God never foresaw gentleness and peaceable manners; He only foresaw the death of creatures which were bent on destroying and devouring each other. Are not the quail, the pigeon and the partridge the natural prey of the hawk? The sheep, the stag and the ox that of the great flesh-eating animals, rather than meat that has been fattened to be served up to us with truffles, which have been unearthed by pigs for our special benefit?

"As to ourselves, the more civilized, intellectual and refined we are, the more we ought to conquer and subdue that animal instinct, which represents the will of God in us. And so in order to mitigate our lot as brutes, we have discovered and made everything, beginning with houses, then exquisite food, sauces, sweetmeats, pastry, drink, stuffs, clothes, ornaments, beds, mattresses, carriages, railways and innumerable machines, besides arts and sciences, writing and poetry. Every ideal comes from us as well as the amenities of life, in order to make our existence as simple reproducers, for which divine Providence solely intended us, less monotonous and less hard.

"Look at this theater. Is there not here a human world created by us, unforeseen and unknown by eternal destinies, comprehensible by our minds alone, a sensual and intellectual distraction, which has been invented solely by and for that discontented and restless little animal that we are.

"Look at that woman, Madame de Mascaret. God intended her to live in a cave naked or wrapped up in the skins of wild animals, but is she not better as she is? But speaking of her, does anyone know why and how her brute of a husband, having such a companion by his side and especially after having been boorish enough to make her a mother seven times, has suddenly left her to run after bad women?"

Grandin replied: "Oh, my dear fellow, this is probably the only reason. He found that always living with her was becoming too expensive in the end, and from reasons of domestic economy he has arrived at the same principles which you lay down as a philosopher."

Just then the curtain rose for the third act, and they turned round, took off their hats and sat down.

IV

The Count and Countess Mascaret were sitting side by side in the carriage which was taking them home from the opera, without speaking. But suddenly the husband said to his wife: "Gabrielle!"

"What do you want?"

"Don't you think that this has lasted long enough?"

"What?"

"The horrible punishment to which you have condemned me for the last six years."

"What do you want? I cannot help it."

"Then tell me which of them it is."

"Never."

"Think that I can no longer see my children or feel them round me without having my heart burdened with this doubt. Tell me which of them it is, and I swear that I will forgive you and treat it like the others."

"I have not the right to."

"You do not see that I can no longer endure this life, this thought which is wearing me out or this question which I am constantly asking myself, this question which tortures me each time I look at them. It is driving me mad."

"Then you have suffered a great deal?" she said.

"Terribly. Should I, without that, have accepted the horror of living by your side and the still greater horror of feeling and knowing that there is one among them whom I cannot recognize and who prevents me from loving the others?"

She repeated: "Then you have really suffered very much?" And he replied in a constrained and sorrowful voice:

"Yes, for do I not tell you every day that it is intolerable torture to me? Should I have remained in that house near you and them if I did not love them? Oh! You have behaved abominably toward me. All the affection of my heart I have bestowed upon my children, and that you know. I am for them a father of the olden time, as I was for you a husband of one of the families of old, for by instinct I have remained a natural man, a man of former days. Yes, I will confess it, you have made me terribly jealous, because you are a woman of another race, of another soul, with other requirements. Oh! I shall never forget the things that you told me, but from that day I troubled myself no more about you. I did not kill you because then I should have had no means on earth of ever discovering which of our—of your—children is not mine. I have waited but I have suffered more than you would believe, for I can no longer venture to love them, except, perhaps, the two eldest; I no longer venture to look at them, to call them to me, to kiss them; I cannot take them onto my knee without asking myself: 'Can it be this one?' I have been correct in my behavior toward you for six years, and even kind and complaisant; tell me the truth, and I swear that I will do nothing unkind."

He thought, in spite of the darkness of the carriage, that he could perceive that she was moved and, feeling certain that she was going to speak at last, he said: "I beg you, I beseech you, to tell me."

"I have been more guilty than you think perhaps," she replied, "but I could no longer endure that life of continual pregnancy, and I had only one means of driving you from my bed. I lied before God, and I lied with my hand raised to my children's heads, for I have never wronged you."

He seized her arm in the darkness and, squeezing it as he had done on that terrible day of their drive in the Bois de Boulogne, he stammered: "Is that true?"

"It is true."

But he in terrible grief said with a groan: "I shall have fresh doubts that will never end! When did you lie, the last time or now? How am I to believe you at present? How can one believe a woman after that? I shall never again know what I am to think. I would rather you had said to me: 'It is Jacques,' or, 'It is Jeanne.'"

The carriage drove them into the courtyard of their mansion, and when it had drawn up in front of the steps the count got down first, as usual, and offered his wife his arm to help her up. And then as soon as they had reached the first floor he said: "May I speak to you for a few moments longer?"

And she replied: "I am quite willing."

They went into a small drawing room, while a footman in some surprise lit the wax candles. As soon as he had left the room and they were alone he continued: "How am I to know the truth? I have begged you a thousand times to speak, but you have remained dumb, impenetrable, inflexible, inexorable, and now today you tell me that you have been lying. For six years you have actually allowed me to believe such a thing! No, you are lying now; I do not know why, but out of pity for me perhaps?"

She replied in a sincere and convincing manner: "If I had not done so I should have had four more children in the last six years!"

And he exclaimed: "Can a mother speak like that?"

"Oh!" she replied. "I do not at all feel that I am the mother of children who have never been born; it is enough for me to be the mother of those that I have and to love them with all my heart. I am—we are—women who belong to the civilzed world, monsieur, and we are no longer, and we refuse to be, mere females who restock the earth."

She got up, but he seized her hands. "Only one word, Gabrielle. Tell me the truth!"

"I have just told you. I have never dishonored you."

He looked her full in the face, and how beautiful she was, with her gray eyes, like the cold sky. In her dark hairdress, on that opaque night of black hair, there shone the diamond coronet, like a cluster of stars. Then he suddenly felt, felt by a kind of intuition, that this grand creature was not merely a being destined to perpetuate his race, but the strange and mysterious product of all the complicated desires which have been accumulating in us for centuries but which have been turned aside from their primitive and divine object and which have wandered after a mystic, imperfectly seen and intangible beauty. There are some women like that, women who blossom only for our dreams, adorned with every poetical attribute of civilization, with that ideal luxury, coquetry and esthetic charm which should surround the living statue who brightens our life.

Her husband remained standing before her, stupefied at the tardy and obscure discovery, confusedly hitting on the cause of his former jealousy and understanding it all very imperfectly. At last he said: "I believe you, for I feel at this moment that you are not lying, and formerly I really thought that you were."

She put out her hand to him: "We are friends then?"

He took her hand and kissed it and replied: "We are friends. Thank you, Gabrielle."

Then he went out, still looking at her and surprised that she was still so beautiful and feeling a strange emotion arising in him which was, perhaps, more formidable than antique and simple love.

END